Praise for Brandon Sanderson and *The Hero of Ages:*

'This adventure brings the Mistborn epic fantasy trilogy to a dramatic and surprising climax . . . Sanderson's saga of consequences offers complex characters and a compelling plot, asking hard questions about loyalty, faith and responsibility' *Publishers Weekly*

'Transcendent . . . the characterization is stellar, the world-building solid, and the plot intricate and compelling – if you havn't read the first two books, go and do so immediately, then buy this one. You won't regret it' *Romantic Times*

'A great epic fantasy . . . Fans of Terry Goodkind and Terry Brooks will find *The Well of Ascension* fulfilling, satisfying, and incredibly exciting' *SFRevu.com*

'Brandon Sanderson is the real thing – an exciting storyteller with a unique and powerful vision' *David Farland*

'Sanderson is astonishingly wise' *Orson Scott Card*

Also by Brandon Sanderson from Gollancz:

The Final Empire
The Well of Ascension

THE HERO OF AGES

Mistborn Book Three

BRANDON SANDERSON

An Orion paperback

First published in Great Britain in 2010 by
Gollancz
An imprint of The Orion Publishing Group
Orion House, 5 Upper St Martin's Lane,
London WC2H 9EA
An Hachette UK Company

31 33 35 37 39 38 36 34 32

A CIP catalogue record for this book
is available from the British Library

ISBN 978 0 575 08994 5

Printed and bound in Great Britain by Clays Ltd, Elcograf S.p.A.

The Orion Publishing Group's policy is to use papers that are natural, renewable and recyclable products and made from wood grown in sustainable forests. The logging and manufacturing processes are expected to conform to the environmental regulations of the country of origin.

www.brandonsanderson.com
www.orionbooks.co.uk

FOR JORDAN SANDERSON,

Who can explain to any who ask
What it's like to have a brother
Who spends most of his time dreaming.

(Thanks for putting up with me.)

CONTENTS

ACKNOWLEDGMENTS

As always, I owe a whole lot of people a whole lot of thanks for helping make this book what it is today. First and foremost, my editor and my agent—Moshe Feder and Joshua Bilmes—are to be noted for their exceptional ability to help a project reach its fullest potential. Also, my wonderful wife, Emily, has been a great support and aid to the writing process.

As before, Isaac Stewart (Nethermore.com) did the fine map work, chapter symbols, and circle of Allomantic metals. I truly appreciate Christian McGrath's artwork as well; this time it's resulted in my personal favorite of the three Mistborn covers. Thanks to Larry Yoder for being awesome, and Dot Lin for her publicity work for me at Tor. Denis Wong and Stacy Hague-Hill for their assistance to my editor, and the—as always—marvelous Irene Gallo and Seth Lerner for their art direction.

Alpha readers for this book include Paris Elliott, Emily Sanderson, Krista Olsen, Ethan Skarstedt, Eric J. Ehlers, Eric "More Snooty" James Stone, Jillena O'Brien, C. Lee Player, Bryce Cundick/Moore, Janci Patterson, Heather Kirby, Sally Taylor, Bradley Reneer, Steve "Not Bookstore Guy Anymore" Diamond, General Micah Demoux, Zachary "Spook" J. Kaveney, Alan Layton, Janette Layton, Kaylynn ZoBell, Nate Hatfield, Matthew Chambers, Kristina Kugler, Daniel A. Wells, The Indivisible Peter Ahlstrom, Marianne Pease, Nicole Westenskow, Nathan Wood, John David Payne, Tom Gregory, Rebecca Dorff, Michelle Crowley, Emily Nelson, Natalia Judd, Chelise Fox, Nathan Crenshaw, Madison VanDen-Berghe, Rachel Dunn, and Ben OleSoon.

In addition I'm thankful to Jordan Sanderson—to whom this book is dedicated—for his tireless work on the Web site. Jeff Creer, also, did a great job with the art for Brandon Sanderson.com. Stop by and check it out!

Terris Dominance
Farmost Dominance
Western Dominance
Northern Dominance
Central Dominance
Crescent Dominance
Southern Dominance
Southern Islands
Eastern Dominance
Remote Dominance
16. Lake Tyrian
17. Lake Luthadel
18. The Black Lake
19. River Searan
20. North Seran
21. South Seran
22. The River Channerel
The Final Empire
1. Luthadel
2. Pits of Hathsin
3. Urteau 4. Fadrex City
5. Tremredare 6. Tathingdwen
7. Conventical of Seran
8. Mount Derytatith, historic location of The Well of Ascension
The Ashmounts: 9. Tyrian
10. Zerinah 11. Faleast 12. Doriel
13. Morag 14. Kalling 15. Torinost
2007

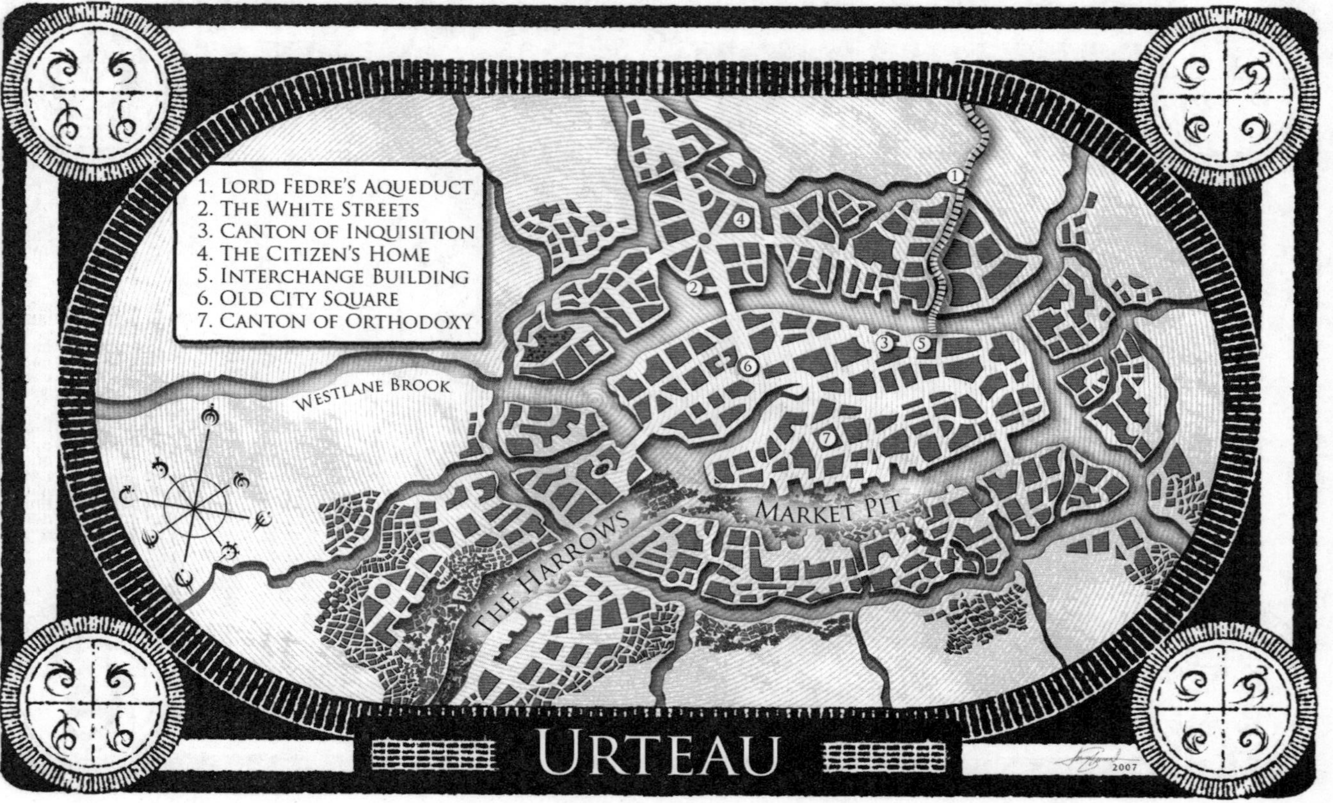
URTEAU
1. Lord Fedre's Aqueduct
2. The White Streets
3. Canton of Inquisition
4. The Citizen's Home
5. Interchange Building
6. Old City Square
7. Canton of Orthodoxy
Westlane Brook
The Harrows
Market Pit
2007

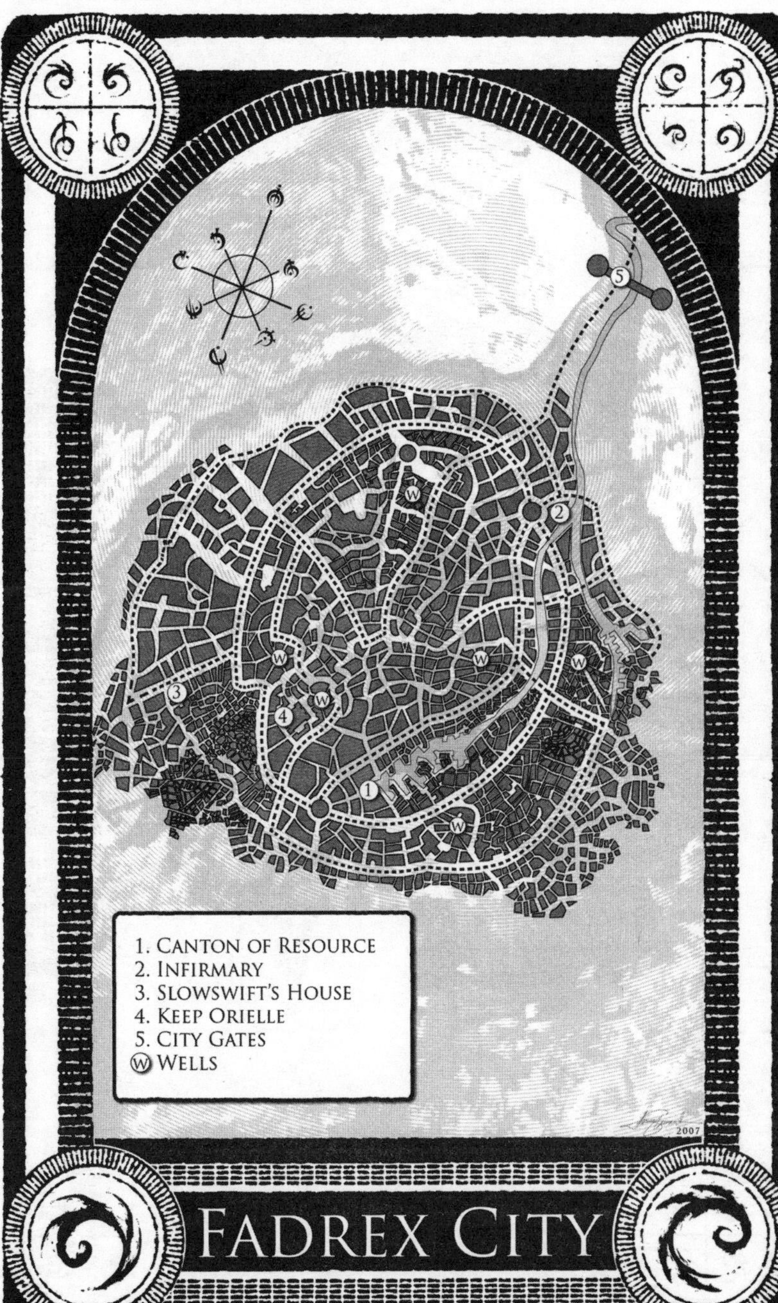
1. Canton of Resource
2. Infirmary
3. Slowswift's House
4. Keep Orielle
5. City Gates
W Wells
2007

Fadrex City

PROLOGUE

MARSH STRUGGLED TO KILL HIMSELF.

His hand trembled as he tried to summon the strength to make himself reach up and pull the spike free from his back and end his monstrous life. He had given up on trying to break free. Three years. Three years as an Inquisitor, three years imprisoned in his own thoughts. Those years had proven that there was no escape. Even now, his mind clouded.

And then *It* took control. The world seemed to vibrate around him; then suddenly he could see clearly. Why had he struggled? Why had he worried? All was as it should be.

He stepped forward. Though he could no longer see as normal men did—after all, he had large steel spikes driven point-first through his eyes—he could sense the room around him. The spikes protruded from the back of his skull; if he reached up to touch the back of his head, he could feel the sharp points. There was no blood.

The spikes gave him power. Everything was outlined in fine blue Allomantic lines, highlighting the world. The room was of modest size, and several companions—also outlined in blue, the Allomantic lines pointing at the metals contained in their very blood—stood with Marsh. Each one had spikes through his eyes.

Each one, that is, except for the man tied to the table in front of him. Marsh smiled, taking a spike off of the table beside him, then hefting it. His prisoner wore no gag. That would have stopped the screams.

"Please," the prisoner whispered, trembling. Even a Terrisman steward would break down when confronted by his own violent death. The man struggled weakly. He was in a very awkward position, as he had been tied to the table on top of another person. The table had been designed that way, with depressions to allow for the body underneath.

"What is it you want?" the Terrisman asked. "I can tell you no more about the Synod!"

Marsh fingered the brass spike, feeling its tip. There was work to do, but he hesitated, relishing the pain and terror in the man's voice. Hesitated so that he could . . .

Marsh grabbed control of his own mind. The room's scents lost their sweetness, and instead reeked with the stench of blood and death. His joy turned to horror. His prisoner was a Keeper of Terris—a man who had worked his entire life for the good of others. Killing him would be not only a crime, but a tragedy. Marsh tried to take command, tried to force his arm up and around to grab the linchpin spike from his back—its removal would kill him.

Yet, *It* was too strong. The force. Somehow, it had control over Marsh—and it needed him and the other Inquisitors to be its hands. It was free—Marsh could still feel it exulting in that—but something kept it from affecting the world too much by itself. An opposition. A force that lay over the land like a shield.

It was not yet complete. It needed more. Something else . . . something hidden. And Marsh would find that something, bring it to his master. The master that Vin had freed. The entity that had been imprisoned within the Well of Ascension.

It called itself Ruin.

Marsh smiled as his prisoner began to cry; then he stepped forward, raising the spike in his hand. He placed it against the whimpering man's chest. The spike would need to pierce the man's body, passing through the heart, then be driven into the body of. the Inquisitor tied below. Hemalurgy was a messy art.

That was why it was so much fun. Marsh picked up a mallet and began to pound.

PART ONE

LEGACY OF THE SURVIVOR

I am, unfortunately, the Hero of Ages.

1

FATREN SQUINTED UP AT THE red sun, which hid behind its perpetual screen of dark haze. Black ash fell lightly from the sky, as it did most days lately. The thick flakes fell straight, the air stagnant and hot, without even a hint of a breeze to lighten Fatren's mood. He sighed, leaning back against the earthen bulwark, looking over Vetitan. His town.

"How long?" he asked.

Druffel scratched his nose. His face was stained black with ash. He hadn't given much thought to hygiene lately. Of course, considering the stress of the last few months, Fatren knew that he himself wasn't much to look at either.

"An hour, maybe," Druffel said, spitting into the dirt of the bulwark.

Fatren sighed, staring up at the falling ash. "Do you think it's true, Druffel? What people are saying?"

"What?" Druffel asked. "That the world is ending?"

Fatren nodded.

"Don't know," Druffel said. "Don't really care."

"How can you say that?"

Druffel shrugged, scratching himself. "Soon as those koloss arrive, I'll be dead. That's pretty much the end of the world for me."

Fatren fell silent. He didn't like to voice his doubts; he was supposed to be the strong one. When the lords had left the town—a farming community, slightly more urban than a northern plantation—Fatren had been the one who had convinced the skaa to go ahead with their planting. Fatren had been the one to keep the press gangs away. In a time when most villages and plantations had lost every able-bodied man to one army or another, Vetitan still had a working population. It had cost much of their crops in bribes, but Fatren had kept the people safe.

Mostly.

"The mists didn't leave until noon today," Fatren said quietly. "They're staying later and later. You've seen the crops, Druff. They're not doing well—not enough sunlight, I'd guess. We won't have food to eat this winter."

"We won't last 'til winter," Druffel said. "Won't last 'til nightfall."

The sad thing—the thing that was really disheartening—was that Druffel had once been the optimist. Fatren hadn't heard his brother laugh in months. That laughter had been Fatren's favorite sound.

Even the Lord Ruler's mills weren't able to grind Druff's laughter out of him, Fatren thought. *But these last two years have.*

"Fats!" a voice called. "Fats!"

Fatren looked up as a young boy scrambled along the side of the bulwark. They'd barely finished the fortification—it had been Druffel's idea, back before he'd really given up. Their town contained some seven thousand people, which made it fairly large. It had taken a great deal of work to surround the entire thing with a defensive mound.

Fatren had barely a thousand real soldiers—it had been very hard to gather that many from such a small population—with maybe another thousand men who were too young, too old, or too unskilled to fight well. He didn't really know how big the koloss army was, but it was bound to be larger than two thousand. A bulwark was going to be of very little use.

The boy—Sev—finally puffed up to Fatren. "Fats!" Sev said. "Someone's coming!"

"Already?" Fatren asked. "Druff said the koloss were still a while away!"

"Not a koloss, Fats," the boy said. "A man. Come see!"

Fatren turned to Druff, who wiped his nose and shrugged. They followed Sev around the inside of the bulwark, toward the front gate. Ash and dust swirled on the packed earth, piling in corners, drifting. There hadn't been much time for cleaning lately. The women had to work the fields while the men trained and made war preparations.

War preparations. Fatren told himself that he had a force of two thousand "soldiers," but what he really had were a thousand skaa peasants with swords. They'd had two years of training, true, but they had very little real fighting experience.

A group of men clustered around the front gates, standing on the bulwark or leaning against its side. *Maybe I was wrong to spend so much of our resources training soldiers,* Fatren thought. *If those thousand men had worked the mines instead, we'd have some ore for bribes.*

Except, koloss didn't take bribes. They just killed. Fatren shuddered, thinking of Garthwood. That city had been bigger than his own, but fewer than a hundred survivors had made their way to Vetitan. That had been three months ago. He'd hoped, irrationally, that the koloss would be satisfied with destroying that city.

He should have known better. Koloss were never satisfied.

Fatren climbed up to the top of the bulwark, and soldiers in patched clothing and bits of leather made way for him. He peered through the falling ash across a dark landscape that looked as if it were blanketed in deep black snow.

A lone rider approached, wearing a dark, hooded cloak.

"What do you think, Fats?" one of the soldiers asked. "Koloss scout?"

Fatren snorted. "Koloss wouldn't send a scout, especially not a human one."

"He has a horse," Druffel said with a grunt. "We could use

another of those." The city only had five. All were suffering from malnutrition.

"Merchant," one of the soldiers said.

"No wares," Fatren said. "And it would take a brave merchant to travel these parts alone."

"I've never seen a refugee with a horse," one of the men said. He raised a bow, looking at Fatren.

Fatren shook his head. Nobody fired as the stranger rode up, moving at an unhurried pace. He stopped his mount directly before the city gates. Fatren was proud of those. Real, true wooden gates mounted in the earthen bulwark. He'd gotten both wood and fine stone from the lord's manor at the city center.

Very little of the stranger was visible beneath the thick, dark cloak he wore to protect himself from the ash. Fatren looked over the top of the bulwark, studying the stranger, and then he glanced up at his brother, shrugging. The ash fell silently.

The stranger leaped from his horse.

He shot straight upward, as if propelled from beneath, cloak whipping free as he soared. Underneath it, he wore a uniform of brilliant white.

Fatren cursed, jumping backward as the stranger crested the top of the bulwark and landed on the top of the wooden gate itself. The man was an Allomancer. A nobleman. Fatren had hoped those would all stick to their squabbles in the North and leave his people in peace.

Or, at least, their peaceful deaths.

The newcomer turned. He wore a short beard, and had his dark hair shorn close. "All right, men," he said, striding across the top of the gate with an unnatural sense of balance, "we don't have much time. Let's get to work." He stepped off the gate onto the bulwark. Immediately, Druffel pulled his sword on the newcomer.

The sword jerked from Druffel's hand, yanked into the air by an unseen force. The stranger snatched the weapon as it passed his head. He flipped the sword around, inspecting it. "Good steel," he said, nodding. "I'm impressed. How many of your soldiers are this well equipped?" He flipped the weapon in his hand, handing it back toward Druffel hilt-first.

Druffel glanced at Fatren, confused.

"Who *are* you, stranger?" Fatren demanded with as much courage as he could muster. He didn't know a lot about Allomancy, but he was pretty certain this man was Mistborn. The stranger could probably kill everyone atop the bulwark with barely a thought.

The stranger ignored the question, turning to scan the city. "This bulwark goes around the entire perimeter of the city?" he asked, turning toward one of the soldiers.

"Um . . . yes, my lord," the man said.

"How many gates are there?"

"Just the one, my lord."

"Open the gate and bring my horse in," the newcomer said. "I assume you have stables?"

"Yes, my lord," the soldier said.

Well, Fatren thought with dissatisfaction as the soldier ran off, *this newcomer certainly knows how to command people.* Fatren's soldier didn't even pause to think that he was obeying a stranger without asking for permission. Fatren could already see the other soldiers straightening a bit, losing their wariness. This newcomer talked like he expected to be obeyed, and the soldiers were responding. This wasn't a nobleman like the ones Fatren had known back when he was a household servant at the lord's manor. This man was different.

The stranger continued his contemplation of the city. Ash fell on his beautiful white uniform, and Fatren thought it a shame to see the garment being dirtied. The newcomer nodded to himself, then began to walk down the side of the bulwark.

"Wait," Fatren said, causing the stranger to pause. "*Who are you?*"

The newcomer turned, meeting Fatren's eyes. "My name is Elend Venture. I'm your emperor."

With that, the man turned and continued down the embankment. The soldiers made way for him; then many of them followed behind.

Fatren glanced at his brother.

"Emperor?" Druffel muttered, then spat.

Fatren agreed with the sentiment. What to do? He'd never fought an Allomancer before; he wasn't even certain how to begin. The "emperor" had certainly disarmed Druffel easily enough.

"Organize the people of the city," the stranger—Elend Venture—said from ahead. "The koloss will come from the north—they'll ignore the gate, climbing over the bulwark. I want the children and the elderly concentrated in the southernmost part of the city. Pack them together in as few buildings as possible."

"What good will that do?" Fatren demanded. He hurried after the "emperor"—he didn't really see any other option.

"The koloss are most dangerous when they're in a blood frenzy," Venture said, continuing to walk. "If they do take the city, then you want them to spend as long as possible searching for your people. If the koloss frenzy wears off while they search, they'll grow frustrated and turn to looting. Then your people might be able to sneak away without being chased."

Venture paused, then turned to meet Fatren's eyes. The stranger's expression was grim. "It's a slim hope. But, it's something." With that, he resumed his pace, walking down the city's main thoroughfare.

From behind, Fatren could hear the soldiers whispering. They'd all heard of a man named Elend Venture. He was the one who had seized power in Luthadel after the Lord Ruler's death over two years before. News from up north was scarce and unreliable, but most of it mentioned Venture. He had fought off all rivals to the throne, even killing his own father. He'd hidden his nature as a Mistborn, and was supposedly married to the very woman who had slain the Lord Ruler. Fatren doubted that such an important man—one who was likely more legend than fact—had made his way to such a humble city in the Southern Dominance, especially unaccompanied. Even the mines weren't worth much anymore. The stranger had to be lying.

But . . . he *was* obviously an Allomancer . . .

Fatren hurried to keep up with the stranger. Venture—or whoever he was—paused in front of a large structure near the center of the city. The old offices of the Steel Ministry. Fatren had ordered the doors and windows boarded up.

"You found the weapons in there?" Venture asked, turning toward Fatren.

Fatren stood for a moment. Then, finally, shook his head. "From the lord's mansion."

"He left weapons behind?" Venture asked with surprise.

"We think he intended to come back for them," Fatren said. "The soldiers he left eventually deserted, joining a passing army. They took what they could carry. We scavenged the rest."

Venture nodded to himself, rubbing his bearded chin in thought as he stared at the old Ministry building. It was tall and ominous, despite—or perhaps because of—its disuse. "Your men look well trained. I didn't expect that. Do any of them have battle experience?"

Druffel snorted quietly, indicating that he thought this stranger had no business being so nosy.

"Our men have fought enough to be dangerous, stranger," Fatren said. "Some bandits thought to take rule of the city from us. They assumed we were weak, and would be easily cowed."

If the stranger saw the words as a threat, he didn't show it. He simply nodded. "Have any of you fought koloss?"

Fatren shared a look with Druffel. "Men who fight koloss don't live, stranger," he finally said.

"If that were true," Venture said, "I'd be dead a dozen times over." He turned to face the growing crowd of soldiers and townspeople. "I'll teach you what I can about fighting koloss, but we don't have much time. I want captains and squad leaders organized at the city gate in ten minutes. Regular soldiers are to form up in ranks along the bulwark—I'll teach the squad leaders and captains a few tricks, then they can carry the tips to their men."

Some of the soldiers moved, but—to their credit—most

of them stayed where they were. The newcomer didn't seem offended that his orders weren't obeyed. He stood quietly, staring down the armed crowd. He didn't seem frightened, nor did he seem angry or disapproving. He just seemed . . . regal.

"My lord," one of the soldier captains finally asked. "Did you . . . bring an army with you to help us?"

"I brought two, actually," Venture said. "But we don't have time to wait for them." He met Fatren's eyes. "You wrote and asked for my help. And, as your liege, I've come to give it. Do you still want it?"

Fatren frowned. He'd never asked this man—or any lord—for help. He opened his mouth to object, but paused. *He'll let me pretend that I sent for him,* Fatren thought. *Act like this was part of the plan all along. I could give up rule here without looking like a failure.*

We're going to die. But, looking into this man's eyes, I can almost believe that we have a chance.

"I . . . didn't expect you to come alone, my lord," Fatren found himself saying. "I was surprised to see you."

Venture nodded. "That is understandable. Come, let's talk tactics while your soldiers gather."

"Very well," Fatren said. As he stepped forward, however, Druffel caught his arm.

"What are you doing?" his brother hissed. "You *sent* for this man? I don't believe it."

"Gather the soldiers, Druff," Fatren said.

Druffel stood for a moment, then swore quietly and stalked away. He didn't look like he had any intention of gathering the soldiers, so Fatren waved for two of his captains to do it. That done, he joined Venture, and the two walked back toward the gates, Venture ordering a few soldiers to walk ahead of them and keep people back so that he and Fatren could speak more privately. Ash continued to fall from the sky, dusting the street black, clustering atop the city's stooped, one-story buildings.

"Who are you?" Fatren asked quietly.

"I am who I said," Venture said.

"I don't believe you."

"But you trust me," Venture said.

"No. I just don't want to argue with an Allomancer."

"That's good enough, for now," Venture said. "Look, friend, you have *ten thousand* koloss marching on your city. You need whatever help you can get."

Ten thousand? Fatren thought, feeling stupefied.

"You're in charge of this city, I assume?" Venture asked.

Fatren shook out of his stupor. "Yes," he said. "My name is Fatren."

"All right, Lord Fatren, we—"

"I'm no lord," Fatren said.

"Well, you just became one," Venture said. "You can choose a surname later. Now, before we continue, you need to know my conditions for helping you."

"What kind of conditions?"

"The nonnegotiable kind," Venture said. "If we win, you'll swear fealty to me."

Fatren frowned, stopping in the street. Ash fell around him. "So that's it? You saunter in before a fight, claiming to be some high lord, so you can take credit for our victory? Why should I swear fealty to a man I only met a few minutes before?"

"Because if you don't," Venture said quietly, "I'll just take command anyway." Then he continued to walk.

Fatren stood for a moment; then he rushed forward and caught up to Venture. "Oh, I see. Even if we survive this battle, we'll end up ruled by a tyrant."

"Yes," Venture said.

Fatren frowned. He hadn't expected the man to be so blunt.

Venture shook his head, regarding the city through the falling ash. "I used to think that I could do things differently. And, I still believe that I'll be able to, someday. But, for now, I don't have a choice. I need your soldiers and I need your city."

"My city?" Fatren asked, frowning. "Why?"

Venture held up a finger. "We have to survive this battle first," he said. "We'll get to other things later."

Fatren paused, and was surprised to realize that he *did* trust the stranger. He couldn't have explained exactly why he felt that way. This was simply a man to follow—a leader such as Fatren had always wanted to be.

Venture didn't wait for Fatren to agree to the "conditions." It wasn't an offer, but an ultimatum. Fatren hurried to catch up again as Venture entered the small square in front of the city gates. Soldiers bustled about. None of them wore uniforms—their only method of distinguishing a captain from a regular soldier was a red band tied around the arm. Venture hadn't given them much time to gather—but, then, they all knew the city was about to be attacked. They had been gathered anyway.

"Time is short," Venture repeated in a loud voice. "I can teach you only a few things, but they will make a difference.

"Koloss range in size from small ones that are about five feet tall to the huge ones, which are about twelve feet tall. However, even the little ones are going to be stronger than you are. Expect that. Fortunately, the creatures fight without coordination between individuals. If a koloss's comrade is in trouble, he won't bother to help.

"They attack directly, without guile, and try to use blunt force to overwhelm. Don't let them! Tell your men to gang up on individual koloss—two men for the small ones, three or four for the big ones. We won't be able to maintain a very large front, but that will keep us alive the longest.

"Don't worry about creatures that get around our line and enter the city—we'll have the civilians hidden at the very back of your town, and the koloss who bypass our line might turn to pillaging, leaving others to fight alone. That's what we want! Don't chase them down into the city. Your families will be safe.

"If you're fighting a big koloss, attack the legs, bring it down before you go for the kill. If you're fighting a small one, make certain your sword or spear doesn't get caught in their loose skin. Understand that koloss aren't stupid—they're just unsophisticated. Predictable. They'll come at you the easiest way possible, and attack only in the most direct manner.

"The most important thing for you to understand is that they *can* be beaten. We'll do it today. Don't let yourselves become intimidated! Fight with coordination, keep your heads, and I promise you that we *will survive*."

The soldier captains stood in a small cluster, looking at Venture. They didn't cheer at the speech, but they did seem a little more confident. They moved off to pass on Venture's instructions to their men.

Fatren approached the emperor quietly. "If your count is correct, they outnumber us five to one."

Venture nodded.

"They're bigger, stronger, and better trained than we are."

Venture nodded again.

"We're doomed, then."

Venture finally looked at Fatren, frowning, black ash dusting his shoulders. "You're not doomed. You have something they don't—something very important."

"What's that?"

Venture met his eyes. "You have me."

"My lord emperor!" a voice called from atop the bulwark. "Koloss sighted!"

They already call to him first, Fatren thought. Fatren wasn't certain whether to be insulted or impressed.

Venture immediately jumped up to the top of the bulwark, using his Allomancy to cross the distance in a quick bound. Most of the soldiers stooped or hid behind the top of the fortification, keeping a low profile despite the distance of their enemies. Venture, however, stood proud in his white cape and uniform, shading his eyes, squinting toward the horizon.

"They're setting up camp," he said, smiling. "Good. Lord Fatren, prepare the men for an assault."

"An *assault*?" Fatren asked, scrambling up behind Venture.

The emperor nodded. "The koloss will be tired from marching, and will be distracted by making camp. We'll never have a better opportunity to attack them."

"But, we're on the defensive!"

Venture shook his head. "If we wait, they'll eventually whip themselves into a blood frenzy, then come against us. We need to attack, rather than just wait to be slaughtered."

"And abandon the bulwark?"

"The fortification is impressive, Lord Fatren, but ultimately useless. You don't have the numbers to defend the entire perimeter, and the koloss are generally taller and more stable than men. They'll just take the bulwark from you, then hold the high ground as they push down into the city."

"But—"

Venture looked at him. His eyes were calm, but his gaze was firm and expectant. The message was simple. *I am in charge now.* There would be no more arguing.

"Yes, my lord," Fatren said, calling over messengers to pass the orders.

Venture stood watching as the messenger boys dashed off. There seemed to be some confusion among the men—they weren't expecting to attack. More and more eyes turned toward Venture, standing tall atop the bulwark.

He really does look like an emperor, Fatren thought despite himself.

The orders moved down the line. Time passed. Finally, the entire army was watching. Venture pulled out his sword and held it high in the ash-scattered sky. Then, he took off down the bulwark in an inhumanly quick dash, charging toward the koloss camp.

For a moment, he ran alone. Then, surprising himself, Fatren gritted his teeth against shaking nerves and followed.

The bulwark exploded with motion, the soldiers charging with a collective yell, running toward death with their weapons held high.

Holding the power did strange things to my mind. In just a few moments, I became familiar with the power itself, with its history, and with the ways it might be used.

Yet, this knowledge was different from experience, or even ability to use that power. For instance, I knew how to move a planet in the sky. Yet, I didn't know where to place it so that it wouldn't be too close, or too far, from the sun.

2

AS ALWAYS, TENSOON'S DAY BEGAN in darkness. Part of that was due, of course, to the fact that he didn't have any eyes. He could have created a set—he was of the Third Generation, which was old, even for a kandra. He had digested enough corpses that he had learned how to create sensory organs intuitively without a model to copy.

Unfortunately, eyes would have done him little good. He didn't have a skull, and he had found that most organs didn't function well without a full body—and skeleton—to support them. His own mass would crush eyes if he moved the wrong way, and it would be very difficult to turn them about to see.

Not that there would be anything to look at. TenSoon moved his bulk slightly, shifting inside his prison chamber. His body was little more than a grouping of translucent muscles—like a mass of large snails or slugs, all connected, somewhat more malleable than the body of a mollusk. With concentration, he could dissolve one of the muscles and either meld it with another one, or make something new. Yet, without a skeleton to use, he was all but impotent.

He shifted in his cell again. His very skin had a sense of its own—a kind of taste. Right now, it tasted the stench of his own excrement on the sides of the chamber, but he didn't dare turn off this sense. It was one of his only connections to the world around him.

The "cell" was actually nothing more than a grate-covered stone pit. It was barely large enough to hold his mass. His captors dumped food in from the top, then periodically poured water in to hydrate him and wash his excrement out through a small drainage hole at the bottom. Both this hole and those in the locked grate above were too small for him to slide through—a kandra's body was supple, but even a pile of muscles could be squeezed only so small.

Most people would have gone mad from the stress of being so confined for . . . he didn't even *know* how long it had been. Months? But TenSoon had the Blessing of Presence. His mind would not give in easily.

Sometimes he cursed the Blessing for keeping him from the blissful relief of madness.

Focus, he told himself. He had no brain, not as humans did, but he was able to think. He didn't understand this. He wasn't certain if any kandra did. Perhaps those of the First Generation knew more—but if so, they didn't enlighten everyone else.

They can't keep you here forever, he told himself. *The First Contract says . . .*

But he was beginning to doubt the First Contract—or, rather, that the First Generation paid any attention to it. But, could he blame them? TenSoon was a Contract-breaker. By his own admission, he had gone against the will of his master, helping another instead. This betrayal had ended with his master's death.

Yet, even such a shameful act was the least of his crimes. The punishment for Contract-breaking was death, and if TenSoon's crimes had stopped there, the others would have killed him and been done with it. Unfortunately, there was much more at stake. TenSoon's testimony—given to the Second Generation in a closed conference—had revealed a much more dangerous, much more important, lapse.

TenSoon had betrayed his people's secret.

They can't execute me, he thought, using the idea to keep him focused. *Not until they find out who I told.*

The secret. The precious, precious secret.

I've doomed us all. My entire people. We'll be slaves again. No, we're already slaves. We'll become something else—automatons, our minds controlled by others. Captured and used, our bodies no longer our own.

This was what he had done—what he had potentially set in motion. The reason he deserved imprisonment and death. And yet, he wished to live. He should despise himself. But, for some reason, he still felt he had done the right thing.

He shifted again, masses of slick muscle rotating around one another. Midshift, however, he froze. Vibrations. Someone was coming.

He arranged himself, pushing his muscles to the sides of the pit, forming a depression in the middle of his body. He needed to catch all of the food that he could—they fed him precious little. However, no slop came pouring down through the grate. He waited, expectant, until the grate unlocked. Though he had no ears, he could feel the coarse vibrations as the grate was dragged back, its rough iron finally dropped against the floor above.

What?

Hooks came next. They looped around his muscles, grabbing him and ripping his flesh as they pulled him out of the pit. It hurt. Not just the hooks, but the sudden freedom as his body was spilled across the floor of the prison. He unwillingly tasted dirt and dried slop. His muscles quivered, the unfettered motion of being outside the cell felt strange, and he strained, moving his bulk in ways that he had nearly forgotten.

Then it came. He could taste it in the air. Acid, thick and pungent, presumably in a gold-lined bucket brought by the prison keepers. They were going to kill him after all.

But, they can't! he thought. *The First Contract, the law of our people, it—*

Something fell on him. Not acid, but something hard. He touched it eagerly, muscles moving against one another, tasting it, testing it, feeling it. It was round, with holes, and several sharp edges . . . a skull.

The acid stink grew sharper. Were they stirring it? TenSoon moved quickly, forming around the skull, filling it. He already had some dissolved flesh stored inside of an organ-like pouch. He brought this out, oozing it around the skull, quickly making skin. He left the eyes alone, working on lungs, forming a tongue, ignoring lips for the moment. He worked with a sense of desperation as the taste of acid grew strong, and then . . .

It hit him. It seared the muscles on one side of his body, washing over his bulk, dissolving it. Apparently, the Second Generation had given up on getting his secrets from him. However, before killing him, they knew they had to give him an opportunity to speak. The First Contract required it—hence the skull. However, the guards obviously had orders to kill him before he could actually say anything in his defense. They followed the form of the law, yet at the very same time they ignored its intent.

They didn't realize, however, how quickly TenSoon could work. Few kandra had spent as much time on Contracts as he had—all of the Second Generation, and most of the Third, had long ago retired from service. They led easy lives here in the Homeland.

An easy life taught one very little.

Most kandra took hours to form a body—some younger ones needed days. In seconds, however, TenSoon had a rudimentary tongue. As the acid moved up his body, he forced out a trachea, inflated a lung, and croaked out a single word:

"Judgment!"

The pouring stopped. His body continued to burn. He worked through the pain, forming primitive hearing organs inside the skull cavity.

A voice whispered nearby. "Fool."

"Judgment!" TenSoon said again.

"Accept death," the voice hissed quietly. "Do not put yourself in a position to cause further harm to our people. The First Generation has granted you this chance to die because of your years of extra service!"

TenSoon paused. A trial would be public. So far, only a select few knew the extent of his betrayal. He could die, cursed as a Contract-breaker but retaining some measure of respect for his prior career. Somewhere—likely in a pit in this very room—there were some who suffered endless captivity, a torture that would eventually break even the minds of those endowed with the Blessing of Presence.

Did he want to become one of those? By revealing his actions in an open forum, he would earn himself an eternity of pain. Forcing a trial would be foolish, for there was no hope of vindication. His confessions had already damned him.

If he spoke, it would not be to defend himself. It would be for other reasons entirely.

"Judgment," he repeated, this time barely whispering.

In some ways, having such power was too overwhelming, I think. This was a power that would take millennia to understand. Remaking the world would have been easy, had one been familiar with the power. Yet, I realized the danger inherent in my ignorance. Like a child suddenly given awesome strength, I could have pushed too hard, and left the world a broken toy I could never repair.

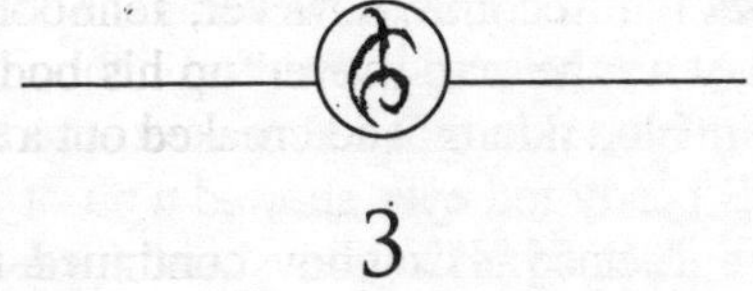

3

ELEND VENTURE, SECOND EMPEROR OF the Final Empire, had not been born a warrior. He'd been born a nobleman—which, in the Lord Ruler's day, had essentially made Elend a professional socialite. He'd spent his youth learning to play the frivolous games of the Great Houses, living the pampered lifestyle of the imperial elite.

It wasn't odd for him to have ended up a politician. He'd

always been interested in political theory, and while he'd been more a scholar than a true statesman, he'd known that someday he'd rule his house. Yet, he hadn't made a very good king at first. He hadn't understood that there was more to leadership than good ideas and honest intentions. Far more.

I doubt you will ever be the type of leader who can lead a charge against the enemy, Elend Venture. The words had been spoken by Tindwyl—the woman who'd trained him in practical politics. Remembering those words made Elend smile as his soldiers crashed into the koloss camp.

Elend flared pewter. A warm sensation—now familiar to him—burst to life in his chest, and his muscles became taut with extra strength and energy. He'd swallowed the metal earlier, so that he could draw upon its powers for the battle. He was an Allomancer. That still awed him sometimes.

As he'd predicted, the koloss were surprised by the attack. They stood motionless for a few moments, shocked—even though they must have seen Elend's newly recruited army as it charged. Koloss had trouble dealing with the unexpected. They found it hard to comprehend a group of weak, outnumbered humans attacking their camp. So, it took them time to adjust.

Elend's army made good use of that time. Elend himself struck first, flaring his pewter to give himself yet more power as he cut down the first koloss. It was a smaller beast. Like all of its kind, it was human-like in form, though it had oversized, drooping blue skin that seemed detached from the rest of its body. Its beady red eyes showed a bit of inhuman surprise as it died, Elend yanking his sword from its chest.

"Strike quickly!" he yelled as more koloss turned from their firepits. "Kill as many as you can before they frenzy!"

His soldiers—terrified, but committed—charged in around him, overrunning the first few groups of koloss. The "camp" was little more than a place where the koloss had tromped down ash and the plants beneath, then dug firepits. Elend could see his men growing more confident at their initial success, and he encouraged them by Pulling on their emotions with Allomancy, making them braver. He was more comfortable with this form of Allomancy—he still hadn't quite gotten the hang of leaping about with metals the way Vin did. Emotions, however—those he understood.

Fatren, the city's burly leader, stuck near Elend as he led a group of soldiers toward a large pack of koloss. Elend kept an eye on the man. Fatren was the ruler of this small city; if he died, it would be a blow to morale. Together, they rushed a small group of surprised koloss. The largest beast in that group was some eleven feet tall. Like that of all large koloss, this creature's skin—once loose—was now pulled tight around its oversized body. Koloss never stopped growing, but their skin always remained the same size. On the younger creatures, it hung loose and folded. On the big ones, it stretched and ripped.

Elend burned steel, then threw a handful of coins into the air in front of him. He Pushed on the coins, throwing his weight against them, spraying them at the koloss. The beasts were too tough to fall to simple coins with any reliability, but the bits of metal would injure and weaken them.

As the coins flew, Elend charged the large koloss. The beast pulled a huge sword off its back, and it seemed elated at the prospect of a fight.

The koloss swung first, and it had an awesome reach. Elend had to jump backward—pewter making him more nimble. Koloss swords were massive, brutish things, so blunt they were almost clubs. The force of the blow shook the air; Elend wouldn't have had a chance to turn the blade aside, even with pewter helping him. In addition, the sword—or, more accurately, the koloss holding it—weighed so much that Elend wouldn't be able to use Allomancy to Push it out of the creature's hands. Pushing with steel was all about weight and force. If Elend Pushed on something heavier than himself, he'd be thrown backward.

So, Elend had to rely on the extra speed and dexterity of pewter. He threw himself out of his dodge, dashing to the side, watching for a backhand. The creature turned, silent, eyeing Elend, but didn't strike. It hadn't quite frenzied yet.

Elend stared down his oversized enemy. *How did I get here?* he thought, not for the first time. *I'm a scholar, not a warrior.* Half the time he thought he had no business leading men at all.

The other half the time, he figured that he thought too much. He ducked forward, striking. The koloss anticipated the move, and tried to bring its weapon down on Elend's head. Elend, however, reached out and Pulled on the sword of another koloss—throwing that creature off balance and allowing two of Elend's men to slay it, and also Pulling Elend himself to the side. He just barely evaded his opponent's weapon. Then, as he spun in the air, he flared pewter and struck from the side.

He sheared completely through the beast's leg at the knee, toppling it to the ground. Vin always said that Elend's Allomantic power was unusually strong. Elend wasn't certain about that—he didn't have much experience with Allomancy—but the force of his own swing did send him stumbling. He managed to regain his footing, however, and then took off the creature's head.

Several of the soldiers were staring at him. His white uniform was now sprayed with bright red koloss blood. It wasn't the first time. Elend took a deep breath as he heard inhuman screams sounding through the camp. The frenzy was beginning.

"Form up!" Elend shouted. "Make lines, stay together, prepare for the assault!"

The soldiers responded slowly. They were far less disciplined than the troops Elend was accustomed to, but they did an admirable job of bunching up at his command. Elend glanced across the ground before them. They'd managed to take down several hundred koloss—an amazing feat.

The easy part, however, was over.

"Stay firm!" Elend yelled, running down in front of the soldier line. "But keep fighting! We need to kill as many of them as quickly as possible! *Everything* depends on this! Give them your fury, men!"

He burned brass and Pushed on their emotions, Soothing

away their fear. An Allomancer couldn't control minds—not human minds, at least—but he *could* encourage some emotions while discouraging others. Again, Vin said that Elend was able to affect far more people than should have been possible. Elend had gained his powers recently, directly from a place he now suspected was the original source of Allomancy.

Under the influence of the Soothing, his soldiers stood up straight. Again, Elend felt a healthy respect for these simple skaa. He was giving them bravery and taking away some of their fear, but the determination was their own. These were good people.

With luck, he'd be able to save some of them.

The koloss attacked. As he'd hoped, a large group of the creatures broke away from the main camp and charged toward the village. Some of the soldiers cried out, but they were too busy defending themselves to follow. Elend threw himself into the fray whenever the line wobbled, shoring up the weak point. As he did so, he burned brass and tried to Push on the emotions of a nearby koloss.

Nothing happened. The creatures were resistant to emotional Allomancy, particularly when they were already being manipulated by someone else. However, when he *did* break through, he could take complete control of them. That, required time, luck, and a determination to fight tirelessly.

And so, he did. He fought alongside the men, watching them die, killing koloss as his line bent at the edges, forming a half circle to keep his troops from being surrounded. Even so, the fighting was grim. As more and more koloss frenzied and charged, the odds quickly turned against Elend's group. Still, the koloss resisted his emotional manipulation. But they were getting closer . . .

"We're doomed!" Fatren screamed.

Elend turned, a bit surprised to see the beefy lord beside him and still alive. The men continued to fight. Only about fifteen minutes had passed since the start of the frenzy, but the line was already beginning to buckle.

A speck appeared in the sky.

"You've led us to die!" Fatren yelled. He was covered in koloss blood, though a patch on his shoulder looked to be his own. "Why?" Fatren demanded.

Elend simply pointed as the speck grew larger.

"What is it?" Fatren asked over the chaos of battle.

Elend smiled. "The first of those armies I promised you."

Vin fell from the sky in a tempest of horseshoes, landing directly at the center of the koloss army.

Without hesitating, she used Allomancy to Push a pair of horseshoes toward a turning koloss. One took the creature in the forehead, throwing it backward, and the other shot over its head, hitting another koloss. Vin spun, flipping out another shoe, shooting it past a particularly large beast and taking down a smaller koloss behind him.

She flared iron, Pulling that horseshoe back, catching it around the larger koloss's wrist. Immediately, her Pull yanked her toward the beast—but it also threw the creature off balance. Its massive iron sword dropped to the ground as Vin hit the creature in the chest. Then, she Pushed off the fallen sword, throwing herself upward in a backward flip as another koloss swung at her.

She shot some fifteen feet into the air. The sword missed, cutting off the head of the koloss beneath her. The koloss who had swung didn't seem to mind that it had killed a comrade; it just looked up at her, bloodred eyes hateful.

Vin Pulled on the fallen sword. It lurched up at her, but also pulled her down with its weight. She caught it as she fell—the sword was nearly as tall as she was, but flared pewter let her handle it with ease—and she sheared free the attacking koloss's arm as she landed.

She took its legs off at the knees, then left it to die as she spun toward other opponents. As always, the koloss seemed fascinated—in an enraged, baffled way—with Vin. They associated large size with danger and had difficulty understanding how a small woman like Vin—twenty years old, barely over five feet in height and slight as a willow—could pose a threat. Yet, they saw her kill, and this drew them to her.

Vin was just fine with that.

She screamed as she attacked, if only to add some sound to the too-silent battlefield. Koloss tended to stop yelling as they entered their frenzy, growing focused only on killing. She threw out a handful of coins, Pushing them toward the group behind her, then jumped forward, Pulling on a sword.

A koloss in front of her stumbled. She landed on its back, attacking a creature beside it. This one fell, and Vin rammed her sword down into the back of the one below her. She Pushed herself to the side, Pulling on the sword of the dying koloss. She caught this weapon, cut down a third beast, then threw the sword, Pushing it like a giant arrow into the chest of a fourth monster. That same Push threw her backward out of the way of an attack. She grabbed the sword from the back of the one she'd stabbed before, ripping the weapon free even as the creature died. And, in one fluid stroke, she slammed it down through the collarbone and chest of a fifth beast.

She landed. Koloss fell dead around her.

Vin was not fury. She was not terror. She had grown beyond those things. She had seen Elend die—had held him in her arms as he did—and had known that she had let it happen. Intentionally.

And yet, he still lived. Every breath was unexpected, perhaps undeserved. Once, she'd been terrified that she would fail him. But, she had found peace—somehow—in understanding that she couldn't keep him from risking his life. In understanding that she didn't *want* to keep him from risking his life.

So, she no longer fought out of fear for the man she loved. Instead, she fought with an understanding. She was a knife—Elend's knife, the Final Empire's knife. She didn't fight to protect one man, but to protect the way of life he had created, and the people he struggled so hard to defend.

Peace gave her strength.

Koloss died around her, and scarlet blood—too bright to be human—stained the air. There were ten thousand in this army—far too many for her to kill. However, she didn't need to slaughter every koloss in the army.

She just had to make them afraid.

Because, despite what she'd once assumed, koloss *could* feel fear. She saw it building in the creatures around her, hidden beneath frustration and rage. A koloss attacked her, and she dodged to the side, moving with pewter's enhanced speed. She slammed a sword into its back as she moved, and spun, noticing a massive creature pushing its way through the army toward her.

Perfect, she thought. It was big—perhaps the biggest one she had ever seen. It had to be almost thirteen feet tall. Heart failure should have killed it long ago, and its skin was ripped half free, hanging in wide flaps.

It bellowed, the sound echoing across the oddly quiet battlefield. Vin smiled, then burned duralumin. Immediately, the pewter already burning inside of her exploded to give her a massive, instantaneous burst of strength. Duralumin, when used with another metal, amplified that second metal and made it burn out in a single burst, giving up all of its power at once.

Vin burned steel, then Pushed outward in all directions. Her duralumin-enhanced Push crashed like a wave into the swords of the creatures running at her. Weapons ripped free, koloss were thrown backward, and massive bodies scattered like mere flakes of ash beneath the bloodred sun. Duralumin-enhanced pewter kept her from being crushed as she did this.

Her pewter and steel both disappeared, burned away in single flash of power. She pulled out a small vial of liquid—an alcohol solution with metal flakes—and downed it in a single gulp, restoring her metals. Then, she burned pewter and leaped over fallen, disoriented koloss toward the massive creature she had seen earlier. A smaller koloss tried to stop her, but she caught its arm by the wrist, then twisted, breaking the joint. She took the creature's sword, ducking beneath another koloss's attack, and spun, felling three different koloss in one sweep by cutting at their knees.

As she completed her spin, she rammed her sword into the earth point-first. As expected, the large, thirteen-foot-tall beast attacked a second later, swinging a sword that was so large that it made the air roar. Vin planted her sword just in time, for—even with pewter—she never would have been able to parry this enormous creature's weapon. That weapon, however, slammed into the blade of her sword, which was stabilized by the earth below. The metal quivered beneath her hands, but she held against the blow.

Fingers still stinging from the shock of such a powerful block, Vin let go of the sword and jumped. She didn't Push—she didn't need to—but landed on the cross guard of her sword and leaped off it. The koloss showed that same, characteristic surprise as it saw her leap thirteen feet into the air, leg drawn back, tasseled mistcloak flapping.

She kicked the koloss directly in the side of the head. The skull cracked. Koloss were inhumanly tough, but her flared pewter was enough. The creature's beady eyes rolled back in its head, and it collapsed. Vin Pushed slightly on the sword, keeping herself up long enough so that when she fell, she landed directly on the felled koloss's chest.

The koloss around her froze. Even in the midst of the blood fury, they were shocked to see her drop such an enormous beast with only a kick. Perhaps their minds were too slow to process what they had just seen. Or, perhaps in addition to fear, they really could feel a measure of wariness. Vin didn't know enough about them to tell. She did understand that in a regular koloss army, what she'd just done would have earned her the obedience of every creature that had watched her.

Unfortunately, this army was being controlled by an external force. Vin stood up straight, could see Elend's small, desperate army in the distance. Under Elend's guidance, they held. The fighting humans would have an effect on the koloss similar to Vin's mysterious strength—the creatures wouldn't understand how such a small force could hold against them. They wouldn't see the attrition, or the dire situation of Elend's group; they would simply see a smaller, inferior army standing and fighting.

Vin turned to resume combat. The koloss approached her with more trepidation, but they still came. That was the oddity about koloss. They never retreated. They felt fear, they just couldn't act on it. It did, however, weaken them. She could see it in the way they approached her, the way they looked. They were close to breaking.

And so, she burned brass and Pushed on the emotions of one of the smaller creatures. At first, it resisted. She shoved harder. And, finally, something broke within the creature and he became hers. The one who had been controlling him was too far away, and was focused on too many koloss at once. This creature—its mind confused because of the frenzy, emotions in a turmoil because of its shock, fear, and frustration—came completely under Vin's mental control.

Immediately, she ordered the creature to attack his companions. He was cut down a moment later, but not before he killed two other koloss. As Vin fought, she snatched up another koloss, then another. She struck randomly, fighting with her sword to keep the koloss distracted as she plucked members from their group and turned them. Soon, the area around her was in chaos, and she had a small line of koloss fighting for her. Every time one fell, she replaced it with two more.

As she fought, she spared a glance for Elend's group again, and was relieved to find a large segment of koloss fighting alongside the group of humans. Elend himself moved among them, no longer fighting, focused on snatching koloss after koloss to his side. It had been a gamble for Elend to come to this city on his own, one she wasn't sure she approved of. For the moment, she was just glad she'd managed to catch up in time.

Taking Elend's cue, she stopped fighting, and instead concentrated on commanding her small force of koloss, snatching up new members one at a time. Soon, she had a group of almost a hundred fighting for her.

Won't be long now, she thought. And, sure enough, she soon caught sight of a speck in the air, shooting toward her through the falling ash. The speck resolved into a figure in dark robes, bounding over the army by Pushing down on koloss swords. The tall figure was bald, its face tattooed. In the ash-darkened light of midday, Vin could make out the two thick spikes that had been driven point-first through its eyes. A Steel Inquisitor, one she didn't recognize.

The Inquisitor hit hard, cutting down one of Vin's stolen koloss with a pair of obsidian axes. It focused its sightless gaze on Vin, and despite herself she felt a stirring of panic. A succession of distinct memories flashed in her mind. A dark night, rainy and shadowed. Spires and towers. A pain in her side. A long night spent captive in the Lord Ruler's palace.

Kelsier, the Survivor of Hathsin, dying on the streets of Luthadel.

Vin burned electrum. This created a cloud of images around her, shadows of possible things she could do in the future. Electrum, the Allomantic complement of gold. Elend had started calling it "poor man's atium." It wouldn't affect the battle much, other than to make her immune to atium, should the Inquisitor have any.

Vin gritted her teeth, dashing forward as the koloss army overwhelmed her few remaining stolen creatures. She jumped, Pushing slightly on a fallen sword and letting her momentum carry her toward the Inquisitor. The specter lifted its axes, swinging, but at the last moment Vin Pulled herself to the side. Her Pull wrenched a sword from the hands of a surprised koloss, and she caught this while spinning in the air, then Pushed it at the Inquisitor.

He Pushed the massive wedge of a weapon aside with barely a glance. Kelsier had managed to defeat an Inquisitor, but only after a great deal of effort. He himself had died moments later, struck dead by the Lord Ruler.

No more memories! Vin told herself forcefully. *Focus on the moment.*

Ash whipped past her as she spun in the air, still flying from her Push against the sword. She landed, foot slipping in koloss blood, then dashed at the Inquisitor. She'd deliberately lured him out, killing and controlling his koloss, forcing him to reveal himself. Now she had to deal with him.

She whipped out a glass dagger—the Inquisitor would be able to Push away a koloss sword—and flared her pewter. Speed, strength, and poise flooded her body. Unfortunately, the Inquisitor would have pewter as well, making them equal.

Except for one thing. The Inquisitor had a weakness. Vin ducked an axe swipe, Pulling on a koloss sword to give herself the speed to get out of the way. Then, she Pushed on the same weapon, throwing herself forward as she jabbed for the Inquisitor's neck. He fended her off with a swipe of the hand, blocking her dagger arm. But, with her other hand, she grabbed the side of his robe.

Then she flared iron and *Pulled* behind her, yanking on a dozen different koloss swords at once. The sudden Pull propelled her backward. Steelpushes and Ironpulls were jolting, blunt things that had far more power than subtlety. With pewter flared, Vin hung on to the robe, and the Inquisitor obviously stabilized himself by Pulling on koloss weapons in front of him.

The robe gave, ripping down the side, leaving Vin holding a wide section of cloth. The Inquisitor's back lay exposed, and she should have been able to see a single spike—similar to those in the eyes—protruding from the creature's back However, that spike was hidden by a metal shield that covered the Inquisitor's back and ran underneath his arms and around his front. Like a formfitting breastplate, it covered his back, something like a sleek turtle's shell.

The Inquisitor turned, smiling, and Vin cursed. That dorsal spike—driven directly between every Inquisitor's shoulder blades—was their weakest point. Pulling it free would kill the creature. That, obviously, was the reason for the plate—something Vin suspected the Lord Ruler would have forbidden. He had *wanted* his servants to have weaknesses, so that he could control them.

Vin didn't have much time for thought, for the koloss

were still attacking. Even as she landed, tossing aside the ripped fabric, a large, blue-skinned monster swung at her. Vin jumped, cresting the sword as it swung beneath her, then Pushed against it to give herself some height.

The Inquisitor followed, now on the attack. Ash spun in the air currents around Vin as she bounded across the battlefield, trying to think. The only other way she knew to kill an Inquisitor was to behead it—an act more easily contemplated than completed, considering that the fiend would be toughened by pewter.

She let herself land on a deserted hill on the outskirts of the battlefield. The Inquisitor thumped to the ashen earth behind her. Vin dodged an axe blade, trying to get in close enough to slash. But the Inquisitor swung with his other blade, and Vin took a gash in the arm as she turned the weapon aside with her dagger.

Warm blood dribbled down her wrist. Blood the color of the red sun. She growled, facing down her inhuman opponent. Inquisitor smiles disturbed her. She threw herself forward, to strike again.

Something flashed in the air.

Blue lines, moving quickly—the Allomantic indication of nearby bits of metal. Vin barely had time to twist herself out of her attack as a handful of coins surprised the Inquisitor from behind, cutting into his body in a dozen different places.

The creature screamed, spinning, throwing out drops of blood as Elend hit the ground atop the hill. His brilliant white uniform was soiled with ash and blood, but his face was clean, his eyes bright. He carried a dueling cane in one hand, the other rested against the earth, steadying him from his Steeljump. His physical Allomancy still lacked polish.

Yet, he was Mistborn, like Vin. And now the Inquisitor was wounded. Koloss were crowding around the hill, clawing their way toward the top, but Vin and Elend still had a few moments. She dashed forward, raising her knife, and Elend attacked as well. The Inquisitor tried to watch both of them at once, its smile finally fading. It moved to jump away.

Elend flipped a coin into the air. A single, sparkling bit of copper spun through the flakes of ash. The Inquisitor saw this, and smiled again, obviously anticipating Elend's Push. It assumed that its weight would transfer through the coin, then hit Elend's weight, since Elend would be Pushing as well. Two Allomancers of near-similar weight, shoving against each other. They would both be thrown back—the Inquisitor to attack Vin, Elend into a pile of koloss.

Except, the Inquisitor didn't anticipate Elend's Allomantic strength. How could it? Elend did stumble, but the Inquisitor was thrown away with a sudden, violent Push.

He's so powerful! Vin thought, watching the surprised Inquisitor fall. Elend was no ordinary Allomancer—he might not have learned perfect control yet, but when he flared his metals and Pushed, he could really *Push.*

Vin dashed forward to attack as the Inquisitor tried to reorient himself. He managed to catch her arm as her knife fell, his powerful grip throwing a shock of pain up her already wounded arm. She cried out as he threw her to the side.

Vin hit the ground and rolled, throwing herself back up to her feet. The world spun, and she could see Elend swinging his dueling cane at the Inquisitor. The creature blocked the swing with an arm, shattering the wood, then ducked forward and rammed an elbow into Elend's chest. The emperor grunted.

Vin Pushed against the koloss who were now only a few feet away, shooting herself toward the Inquisitor again. She'd dropped her knife—but, then, he'd also lost his axes. She could see him glancing to the side, toward where the weapons had fallen, but she didn't give him a chance to go for them. She tackled him, trying to throw him back to the ground. Unfortunately, he was much larger—and much stronger—than she was. He tossed her down in front of him, knocking the breath from her.

The koloss were upon them. But Elend had grabbed one of the fallen axes, and he struck for the Inquisitor.

The Inquisitor moved with a sudden jolt of speed. Its form

became a blur, and Elend swung only at empty air. Elend spun, shock showing on his face as the Inquisitor came up, wielding not an axe, but—oddly—a metal spike, like the ones in his own body but sleeker and longer. The creature raised the spike, moving inhumanly fast—faster even than any Allomancer should have managed.

That was no pewter run, Vin thought. *That wasn't even duralumin.* She scrambled to her feet, watching the Inquisitor. The creature's strange speed faded, but it was still in a position to hit Elend directly in the back with the spike. Vin was too far away to help.

But the koloss weren't. They were cresting the hill, mere feet from Elend and his opponent. Desperate, Vin flared brass and grabbed the emotions of the koloss closest to the Inquisitor. Even as the Inquisitor moved to attack Elend, her koloss spun, swinging its wedge-like sword, hitting the Inquisitor directly in the face.

It didn't separate the head from the body. It just crushed the head completely. Apparently, that was sufficient, for the Inquisitor dropped without a sound, falling motionless.

A shock ran through the koloss army.

"Elend!" Vin said. "Now!"

The emperor turned away from the dying Inquisitor, and she could see the look of concentration on his face. Once, Vin had seen the Lord Ruler affect an entire city square full of people with his emotional Allomancy. He had been stronger than she was; far stronger—even—than Kelsier.

She couldn't see Elend burn duralumin, then brass, but she could feel it. Feel him pressing on her emotions as he sent out a general wave of power, Soothing thousands of koloss at once. They all stopped fighting. In the distance, Vin could make out the haggard remnants of Elend's peasant army, standing in an exhausted circle of bodies. Ash continued to fall. It rarely stopped, these days.

The koloss lowered their weapons. Elend had won.

This is actually what happened to Rashek, I believe. He pushed too hard. He tried to burn away the mists by moving the planet closer to the sun, but he moved it too far, making the world far too hot for the people who inhabited it.

The ashmounts were his solution to this. He had learned that shoving a planet around required too much precision, so instead he caused the mountains to erupt, spewing ash and smoke into the air. The thicker atmosphere made the world cooler, and turned the sun red.

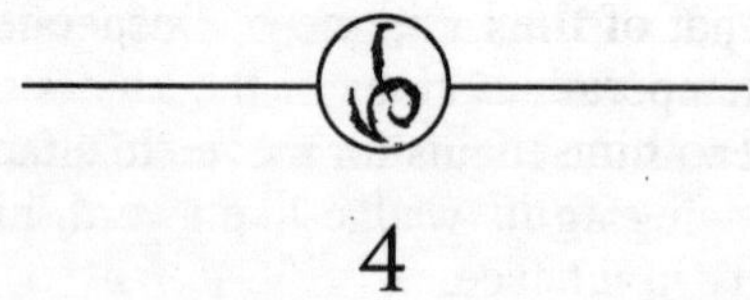

4

SAZED, CHIEF AMBASSADOR OF THE New Empire, studied the sheet of paper in front of him. *The tenets of the Canzi people,* it read. *On the beauty of mortality, the importance of death, and the vital function of the human body as a partaker of the divine whole.*

The words were written in his own hand, copied out of one of his Feruchemical metalminds—where he had storages containing literally thousands of books. Beneath the heading, filling most of the sheet in cramped writing, he had listed the basic beliefs of the Canzi and their religion.

Sazed settled back in his chair, holding up the paper and going over his notes one more time. He'd been focusing on this one religion for a good day now, and he wanted to make a decision about it. Even before the day's study, he'd known much about the Canzi faith, for he'd studied it—along with all of the other pre-Ascension religions—for most of his life. Those religions had been his passion, the focus of all of his research.

And then the day had come where he'd realized that all of his learning had been meaningless.

The Canzi religion contradicts itself, he decided, making a notation with his pen at the side of the paper. *It explains that all creatures are part of the "divine whole" and implies that each body is a work of art created by a spirit who decides to live in this world.*

However, one of its other tenets is that the evil are punished with bodies that do not function correctly. A distasteful doctrine, in Sazed's mind. Those who were born with mental or physical deficiencies deserved compassion, perhaps pity, but not disdain. Besides, which of the religion's ideals were true? That spirits chose and designed their bodies as they wished, or that they were punished by the body chosen for them? And what of the influence of lineage upon a child's features and temperament?

He nodded to himself, made a note at the bottom of the sheet of paper. *Logically inconsistent. Obviously untrue.*

"What is that you have there?" Breeze asked.

Sazed looked up. Breeze sat beside a small table, sipping his wine and eating grapes. He wore one of his customary nobleman's suits, complete with a dark jacket, a bright red vest, and a dueling cane—with which he liked to gesture as he spoke. He'd gained back most of the weight he'd lost during Luthadel's siege and its aftermath, and could reasonably be described as "portly" once again.

Sazed looked down. He carefully placed the sheet alongside some hundred others inside his portfolio, then closed the cloth-wrapped board cover and did up the ties. "It is nothing of consequence, Lord Breeze," he said.

Breeze sipped quietly at his wine. "Nothing of consequence? You seem to always be puttering around with those sheets of yours. Whenever you have a free moment, you pull one of them out."

Sazed set the portfolio beside his chair. How to explain? Each of the sheets in the thick portfolio outlined one of the over three hundred different religions the Keepers had collected. Each and every one of those religions was now effectively "dead," as the Lord Ruler had stamped them out very early in his reign, some thousand years before.

One year ago, the woman Sazed loved had died. Now, he wanted to know . . . no, he *had* to know . . . if the religions of the world had answers for him. He would find the truth, or he would eliminate each and every faith.

Breeze was still looking at him.

"I would rather not talk about it, Lord Breeze," Sazed said.

"As you wish," Breeze said, raising his cup. "Perhaps you could use your Feruchemist's powers to listen in on the conversation happening in the next room . . ."

"I do not think it would be polite to do so."

Breeze smiled. "My dear Terrisman—only you would come to conquer a city, then worry about being 'polite' to the dictator you're threatening."

Sazed glanced down, feeling slightly abashed. But, he could not deny Breeze's remarks. Though the two of them had brought no army with them to Lekal City, they had indeed come to conquer. They simply intended to do it with a piece of paper rather than a sword.

It all hinged on what was happening in the next room. Would the king sign the treaty or not? All Breeze and Sazed could do was wait. He itched to get his portfolio out, to look over the next religion in the stack. He'd been considering the Canzi for over a day, and now that he'd made a decision about it, he wished to move on to the next sheet. During the last year, he'd gotten through about two-thirds of the religions. Barely a hundred remained, though the number was closer to two hundred if he took into account all of the subsects and denominations.

He was close. Over the next few months, he'd be able to get through the rest of the religions. He wanted to give each one fair consideration. Surely, one of the remaining ones would strike him as containing the essence of truth he was searching for. Surely one of them would tell him what had happened to Tindwyl's spirit without contradicting itself on a half-dozen different points.

But, for the moment, he felt self-conscious reading in front of Breeze. So, Sazed forced himself to sit and wait patiently.

The room around him was ornate, after the fashion of the old imperial nobility. Sazed wasn't used to such finery, not anymore. Elend had sold or burned most of his lavish trappings—his people had needed food and warmth during the winter. King Lekal hadn't done the same, it appeared, though perhaps that was because the winters were less harsh here in the South.

Sazed glanced out the window beside his chair. Lekal City didn't have a true palace—it had been just a country estate until about two years ago. The manor house, however, did have a nice view over the growing town—which was more of a large shantytown than it was a true city.

Still, that shantytown controlled lands that were dangerously inside Elend's defensive perimeter. They needed the security of King Lekal's allegiance. And so, Elend had sent a contingent—including Sazed, who was his chief ambassador—to secure the loyalty of the Lekal king. That man deliberated in the next room with his aides, trying to decide whether or not to accept the treaty—which would make them subjects of Elend Venture.

Chief Ambassador of the New Empire . . .

Sazed was not very fond of his title, for it implied that he was actually a citizen of the empire. His people, the Terris people, had sworn to call no man master again. They had spent a thousand years being oppressed, being bred like animals and turned into perfect, docile servants. Only with the fall of the Final Empire had the Terris become free to rule themselves.

So far, the Terris people hadn't done a very good job of that. Of course, it didn't help that the Steel Inquisitors had slaughtered the entire Terris ruling council, leaving Sazed's people without direction or leadership.

In a way, we're hypocrites anyway, he thought. *The Lord Ruler was secretly a Terrisman. One of our own did those horrible things to us. What right do we have to insist on calling no foreigner master? It wasn't a foreigner that destroyed our people, our culture, and our religion.*

And so, Sazed served as Elend Venture's chief ambassador.

Elend was a friend—a man Sazed respected like few others. To Sazed's mind, even the Survivor himself hadn't possessed Elend Venture's strength of character. The emperor hadn't tried to assume authority over the Terris people, even after he had accepted the refugees into his lands. Sazed wasn't sure if his people were free or not, but they owed Elend Venture a large debt. Sazed would gladly serve as the man's ambassador.

Even if there were other things Sazed felt he should be doing. Such as leading his people.

No, Sazed thought, glancing at his portfolio. *No. A man with no faith cannot lead them. I must find the truth for myself first. If such a thing exists.*

"It certainly is taking them long enough," Breeze said, eating a grape. "One would think that after all the talking we did to get to this point, they'd know by now whether they intended to sign the thing or not."

Sazed glanced toward the elaborately carved door on the other side of the room. What would King Lekal decide? Did he really have a choice? "Did we do the right thing here, do you think, Lord Breeze?" Sazed found himself asking.

Breeze snorted. "Right and wrong don't come into it. If *we* hadn't come to bully King Lekal, someone else would have. It comes down to basic strategic necessity. Or, that's how I see it—perhaps I'm just more calculating than others."

Sazed eyed the stocky man. Breeze was a Soother—in fact, he was the most brazen, flagrant Soother Sazed had ever known. Most Soothers used their powers with discrimination and subtlety, nudging emotions only at the most opportune times. Breeze, however, played with *everyone's* emotions. Sazed could feel the man's touch on his own feelings at that moment, in fact—though only because he knew what to look for.

"If you will excuse the observation, Lord Breeze," Sazed said, "you do not fool me as easily as you believe you do."

Breeze raised an eyebrow.

"I know you are a good man," Sazed said. "You work very hard to hide it. You make a great show of being callous and selfish. Yet, to those watching what you do and not just what you say, you become far more transparent."

Breeze frowned, and Sazed got a little stab of pleasure at surprising the Soother. He obviously hadn't expected Sazed to be so blunt.

"My dear man," Breeze said, sipping his wine, "I'm disappointed in you. Weren't you just speaking about being polite? Well, it's not *at all* polite to point out a crusty old pessimist's dark inner secret."

"Dark inner secret?" Sazed asked. "That you're kind-hearted?"

"It's an attribute in myself that I've worked very hard to discourage," Breeze said lightly. "Unfortunately, I prove too weak. Now, to completely divert us from this subject—which I find *far* too discomforting—I shall return to your earlier question. You ask if we are doing the right thing? Right thing how? By forcing King Lekal to become a vassal to Elend?"

Sazed nodded.

"Well then," Breeze said, "I'd have to say that yes, we did the right thing. Our treaty will give Lekal the protection of Elend's armies."

"At the cost of his own freedom to govern."

"Bah," Breeze said with a wave of his hand. "We both know that Elend is a far better ruler than Lekal could ever hope to be. Most of his people are living in half-finished shacks, for the Lord Ruler's sake!"

"Yes, but you must admit that we bullied him."

Breeze frowned. "That's how all politics is. Sazed, this man's nephew sent an army of koloss to destroy Luthadel! He's lucky Elend didn't just come down and wipe out the entire city in retribution. We have bigger armies, more resources, and better Allomancers. This people will be far better off once Lekal signs that treaty. What is wrong with you, my dear man? You argued all these same points not two days ago at the negotiating table."

"I apologize, Lord Breeze," Sazed said. "I . . . seem to find myself feeling contrary of late."

Breeze didn't respond at first. "It still hurts, does it?" he asked.

That man is far too good at understanding the emotions of others, Sazed thought. "Yes," he finally whispered.

"It will stop," Breeze said. "Eventually."

Will it? Sazed thought, looking away. It had been a year. It still felt . . . as if nothing would ever be right again. Sometimes, he wondered if his immersion in the religions was simply a way of hiding from his pain.

If that were so, then he'd chosen a poor way to cope, for the pain was always there waiting for him. He had failed. No, his *faith* had failed *him.* Nothing was left to him.

It was all. Just. Gone.

"Look," Breeze said, drawing his attention, "sitting here and waiting for Lekal to make up his mind is obviously making us anxious. Why don't we talk about something else? How about telling me about one of those religions you have memorized. You haven't tried to convert me in months!"

"I stopped wearing my copperminds nearly a year ago, Breeze."

"But surely you remember a bit," Breeze said. "Why don't you try to convert me? You know, for old times' sake and all that."

"I don't think so, Breeze."

It felt like a betrayal. As a Keeper—a Terris Feruchemist—he could store memories inside of pieces of copper, then withdraw them later. During the time of the Final Empire, Sazed's kind had suffered much to gather their vast stores of information—and not just about religions. They had gathered every shred of information they could find about the time before the Lord Ruler. They'd memorized it, passed it on to others, depending on their Feruchemy to maintain accuracy.

Yet they'd never found the one thing they sought most urgently, the thing that had begun their quest: the religion of the Terris people. It had been erased by the Lord Ruler during the first century of his reign.

Still, so many had died, worked, and bled so that Sazed

could have the vast storages he'd inherited. And he had taken them off. After retrieving his notes about each religion, writing them down on the pages he now carried in his portfolio, he'd removed each and every one of his metalminds and stored them away.

They just . . . didn't seem to matter anymore. At times, nothing did. He tried not to dwell too much on that. But the thought lurked in his mind, terrible and impossible to banish. He felt tainted, unworthy. As far as Sazed knew, he was the last living Feruchemist. They didn't have the resources to search right now, but in a year's time, no Keeper refugees had made their way to Elend's domain. Sazed was it. And, like all Terris stewards, he'd been castrated as a child. The hereditary power of Feruchemy might very well die with him. There would be some small trace of it left in the Terris people, but given the Lord Ruler's efforts to breed it away and the deaths of the Synod . . . things did not look good.

The metalminds remained packed away, carried along wherever he went, but never used. He doubted he would ever draw upon them again.

"Well?" Breeze asked, rising and walking over to lean against the window beside Sazed. "Aren't you going to tell me about a religion? Which is it going to be? That religion where people made maps, maybe? The one that worshipped plants? Surely you've got one in there that worships wine. That might fit me."

"Please, Lord Breeze," Sazed said, looking out over the city. Ash was falling. It always did these days. "I do not wish to speak of these things."

"What?" Breeze asked. "How can that be?"

"If there were a God, Breeze," Sazed said, "do you think he'd have let so many people be killed by the Lord Ruler? Do you think he'd have let the world become what it is now? I will not teach you—or anyone—a religion that cannot answer my questions. Never again."

Breeze fell silent.

Sazed reached down, touching his stomach. Breeze's comments pained him. They brought his mind back to that terrible time a year before, when Tindwyl had been killed. When Sazed had fought Marsh at the Well of Ascension, and had nearly been killed himself. Even through his clothing, he could feel the scars on his abdomen, where Marsh had hit him with a collection of metal rings, piercing Sazed's skin and nearly killing him.

He'd drawn upon the Feruchemical power of those very rings to save his life, healing his body, engulfing them within him. Soon after, however, he'd stored up some health and then had a surgeon remove the rings from his body. Despite Vin's protests that having them inside him would be an advantage, Sazed was worried that it was unhealthy to keep them embedded in his own flesh. Besides, he had just wanted them gone.

Breeze turned to look out the window. "You were always the best of us, Sazed," he said quietly. "Because you believed in something."

"I am sorry, Lord Breeze," Sazed said. "I do not mean to disappoint you."

"Oh, you don't disappoint me," Breeze said. "Because I don't believe what you've said. You're not meant to be an atheist, Sazed. I have a feeling you'll be no good at it—doesn't suit you at all. You'll come around eventually."

Sazed looked back out the window. He was brash for a Terrisman, but he did not wish to argue further.

"I never did thank you," Breeze said.

"For what, Lord Breeze?"

"For pulling me out of myself," Breeze said. "For forcing me to get up, a year ago, and keep going. If you hadn't helped me, I don't know that I would ever have gotten over . . . what happened."

Sazed nodded. On the inside, however, his thoughts were more bitter. *Yes, you saw destruction and death, my friend. But the woman* you *love is still alive. I could have come back too, if I hadn't lost her. I could have recovered, as you did.*

The door opened.

Sazed and Breeze both turned. A solitary aide entered,

bearing an ornate sheet of parchment. King Lekal had signed the treaty at the bottom. His signature was small, almost cramped, in the large space allotted. He knew he was beaten.

The aide set the treaty on the table, then retreated.

Each time Rashek tried to fix things, he made them worse. He had to change the world's plants to make them able to survive in the new, harsh environment. Yet, that change left the plants less nutritious to mankind. Indeed, the falling ash would make men sick, causing them to cough like those who spent too long mining beneath the earth. And so Rashek changed mankind itself as well, altering them so that they could survive.

5

ELEND KNELT BESIDE THE FALLEN Inquisitor, trying to ignore the mess that was left of the thing's head. Vin approached, and he noted the wound on her forearm. As usual, she all but ignored the injury.

The koloss army stood quietly on the battlefield around them. Elend still wasn't comfortable with the idea of controlling the creatures. He felt . . . tainted by even associating with them. Yet, it was the only way.

"Something's wrong, Elend," Vin said.

He looked up from the body. "What? You think there might be another one around?"

She shook her head. "Not that. That Inquisitor moved too quickly at the end. I've never seen a person—Allomancer or not—with that kind of speed."

"He must have had duralumin," Elend said, looking down.

For a time, he and Vin had held an edge, since they'd had access to an Allomantic metal the Inquisitors hadn't known about. Reports now indicated that edge was gone.

Fortunately, they still had electrum. The Lord Ruler was to be thanked for that, actually. Poor man's atium. Normally, an Allomancer who was burning atium was virtually invincible—only another Allomancer burning the metal could fight him. Unless, of course, one had electrum. Electrum didn't grant the same invincibility as atium—which allowed an Allomancer to see slightly into the future—but it *did* make one immune to atium.

"Elend," Vin said, kneeling, "it wasn't duralumin. The Inquisitor was moving too quickly even for that."

Elend frowned. He had seen the Inquisitor move only out of the corner of his eye, but surely it hadn't been *that* fast. Vin had a tendency to be paranoid and assume the worst.

Of course, she also had a habit of being right.

She reached out and grabbed the front of the corpse's robe, ripping it free. Elend turned away. "Vin! Have respect for the dead!"

"I have no respect for these things," she said, "nor will I ever. Did you see how that thing tried to use one of its spikes to kill you?"

"That *was* odd. Perhaps he felt he couldn't get to the axes in time."

"Here, look."

Elend glanced back. The Inquisitor had the standard spikes—three pounded between the ribs on each side of the chest. But . . . there was another one—one Elend hadn't seen in any other Inquisitor corpse—pounded directly through the front of this creature's chest.

Lord Ruler! Elend thought. *That one would have gone right through its heart. How did it survive?* Of course, if two spikes through the brain didn't kill it, then one through the heart probably wouldn't either.

Vin reached down and yanked the spike free. Elend winced. She held it up, frowning. "Pewter," she said.

"Really?" Elend asked.

She nodded. "That makes ten spikes. Two through the eyes and one through the shoulders: all steel. Six through the ribs: two steel, four bronze. Now this, a pewter one—not to mention the one he tried to use on you, which appears to be steel."

Elend studied the spike in her hand. In Allomancy and Feruchemy, different metals did different things—he could only guess that for Inquisitors, the type of metal used in the various spikes was important as well. "Perhaps they don't use Allomancy at all, but some . . . third power."

"Maybe," Vin said, gripping the spike, standing up. "We'll need to cut open the stomach and see if it had atium."

"Maybe this one will finally have some." They always burned electrum as a precaution; so far, none of the Inquisitors they'd met had actually possessed any atium.

Vin shook her head, staring out over the ash-covered battlefield. "We're missing something, Elend. We're like children, playing a game we've watched our parents play, but not really knowing any of the rules. And . . . our opponent created the game in the first place."

Elend stepped around the corpse, moving over to her. "Vin, we don't even known that it's out there. The thing we saw a year ago at the Well . . . perhaps it's gone. Perhaps it left, now that it's free. That could be all it wanted."

Vin looked at him. He could read in her eyes that she didn't believe that. Perhaps she saw that he didn't really believe it either.

"It's out there, Elend," she whispered. "It's directing the Inquisitors; it knows what we're doing. That's why the koloss always move against the same cities we do. It has power over the world—it can change text that has been written, create miscommunications and confusion. It knows our plans."

Elend put a hand on her shoulder. "But today we beat it—and, it sent us this handy koloss army."

"And how many humans did we lose trying to capture this force?"

Elend didn't need to speak the answer. *Too many.* Their

numbers were dwindling. The mists—the Deepness—were growing more powerful, choking the life from random people, killing the crops of the rest. The Outer Dominances were wastelands—only those closest to the capital, Luthadel, still got enough daylight to grow food. And even that area of livability was shrinking.

Hope, Elend thought forcefully. *She needs that from me; she's always needed that from me.* He tightened his grip on her shoulder, then pulled her into an embrace. "We'll beat it, Vin. We'll find a way."

She didn't contradict him, but she obviously wasn't convinced. Still, she let him hold her, closing her eyes and resting her head against his chest. They stood on the battlefield before their fallen foe, but even Elend had to admit that it didn't feel like much of a victory. Not with the world collapsing around them.

Hope! he thought again. *I belong to the Church of the Survivor, now. It has only one prime commandment.*

Survive.

"Give me one of the koloss," Vin finally said, pulling out of the embrace.

Elend released one of the medium-large creatures, letting Vin take control of it. He still didn't quite understand how they controlled the creatures. Once he had control of a koloss, he could control it indefinitely—whether sleeping or awake, burning metals or not. There were many things he didn't understand about Allomancy. He'd had only a year to use his powers, and he had been distracted by ruling an empire and trying to feed his people, not to mention the wars. He'd had little time for practice.

Of course, Vin had less time than that to practice before she killed the Lord Ruler himself. Vin, however, was a special case. She used Allomancy as easily as other people breathed; it was less a skill to her than an extension of who she was. Elend might be more powerful—as she always insisted—but she was the true master.

Vin's lone koloss wandered over and picked up the fallen Inquisitor and the spike. Then, Elend and Vin walked down the hill—Vin's koloss servant following—toward the human army. The koloss troops split and made a passage at Elend's command. He suppressed a shiver even as he controlled them.

Fatren, the dirty man who ruled the city, had thought to set up a triage unit—though Elend wasn't very confident in the abilities of a group of skaa surgeons.

"Why'd they stop?" Fatren asked, standing in front of his men as Vin and Elend approached across the ash-stained ground

"I promised you a second army, Lord Fatren," Elend said. "Well, here it is."

"The koloss?" he asked.

Elend nodded.

"But they're the army that came to destroy us."

"And now they're ours," Elend said. "Your men did very well. Make certain they understand that this victory was theirs. We had to force that Inquisitor out into the open, and the only way to do that was to turn his army against itself. Koloss become afraid when they see something small defeating something large. Your men fought bravely; because of them, these koloss are ours."

Fatren scratched his chin. "So," he said slowly, "they got afraid of us, so they switched sides?"

"Something like that," Elend said, looking over the soldiers. He mentally commanded some koloss to step forward. "These creatures will obey orders from the men in this group. Have them carry your wounded back to the city. However, make certain not to let your men attack or punish the koloss. They are our servants now, understand?"

Fatren nodded.

"Let's go," Vin said, eagerness sounding in her voice as she looked over at the small city.

"Lord Fatren, do you want to come with us, or do you want to supervise your men?" Elend asked.

Fatren's eyes narrowed. "What are you going to do?"

"There is something in your city we need to claim."

Fatren paused. "I'll come, then." He gave some orders to

his men while Vin waited impatiently. Elend gave her a smile, then finally Fatren joined them, and the three walked back toward the Vetitan gate.

"Lord Fatren," Elend said as they walked, "you should address me as 'my lord' from now on."

Fatren looked up from his nervous study of the koloss standing around them.

"Do you understand?" Elend said, meeting the man's eyes.

"Um . . . yes. My lord."

Elend nodded, and Fatren fell a little behind him and Vin, as if showing an unconscious deference. He didn't seem rebellious—for now, he was probably happy to be alive. Perhaps he would eventually resent Elend for taking command of his city, but by then, there would be little he could do. Fatren's people would be accustomed to the security of being part of a larger empire, and the stories of Elend's mysterious command of the koloss—and therefore salvation of the city—would be too strong. Fatren would never rule again.

So easily I command, Elend thought. *Just two years ago, I made even more mistakes than this man. At least he managed to keep his city's people together in a time of crisis. I lost my throne, until Vin conquered it back for me.*

"I worry about you," Vin asked. "Did you have to start the battle without me?"

Elend glanced to the side. There was no reproach in her voice. Just concern.

"I wasn't sure when—or even *if*—you'd arrive," he said. "The opportunity was just too good. The koloss had just marched an entire day. We probably killed five hundred before they even decided to start attacking."

"And the Inquisitor?" Vin asked. "Did you really think you could take him on your own?"

"Did you?" Elend asked. "You fought him for a good five minutes before I was able to get there and help."

Vin didn't use the obvious argument—that she was by far the more accomplished Mistborn. Instead, she just walked silently. She still worried about him, even though she no longer tried to protect him from all danger. Both her worry and her willingness to let him take risks were part of her love for him. And he sincerely appreciated both.

The two of them tried to stay together as much as possible, but that wasn't always feasible—such as when Elend had discovered a koloss army marching on an indefensible city while Vin was away delivering orders to Penrod in Luthadel. Elend had hoped she would return to his army camp in time to find out where he had gone, then come help, but he hadn't been able to wait. Not with thousands of lives at stake.

Thousands of lives . . . and more.

They eventually reached the gates. A crowd of soldiers who had either arrived late to the battle or been too afraid to charge stood atop the bulwark, looking down with awe. Several thousand koloss had gotten past Elend's men and tried to attack the city. These now stood motionless—by his silent command—waiting outside the bulwark.

The soldiers opened the gates, letting in Vin, Elend, Fatren, and Vin's single koloss servant. Most of them eyed Vin's koloss with distrust—as well they should. She ordered it to put down the dead Inquisitor, then made it follow as the three of them walked down the ash-piled city street. Vin had a philosophy: the more people who saw koloss and grew accustomed to the creatures, the better. It made the people less frightened of the beasts, and made it easier to fight should they have to face koloss in battle.

They soon approached the Ministry building that Elend had first inspected upon entering the city. Vin's koloss walked forward and began to rip the boards off of its doors.

"The Ministry building?" Fatren said. "What good is it? We already searched it."

Elend eyed him.

"My lord," Fatren said belatedly.

"The Steel Ministry was linked directly to the Lord Ruler," Elend said. "Its obligators were his eyes across the empire, and through them he controlled the nobility, watched over commerce, and made certain that orthodoxy was maintained."

The koloss yanked the door open. Moving inside, Elend burned tin, enhancing his eyesight so that he could see in the dim light. Vin, obviously doing the same, had little trouble picking her way across the broken boards and furniture littering the floor. Apparently, Fatren's people hadn't just "searched" the place—they'd ransacked it.

"Yeah, I know about obligators," Fatren said. "There aren't any of them here, my lord. They left with the nobility."

"The obligators saw to some very important projects, Fatren," Elend said. "Things like trying to discover how to use new Allomantic metals, or like searching for lines of Terris blood that were breeding true. One of their projects is of particular interest to us."

"Here," Vin said, calling out from beside something set in the floor. A hidden trapdoor.

Fatren glanced back toward the sunlight, perhaps wishing that he'd decided to bring a few soldiers with him. Beside the trapdoor, Vin lit a lantern she'd salvaged from somewhere. In the blackness of a basement, even tin wouldn't provide sight. Vin opened the trapdoor, and they made their way down the ladder. It eventually ended in a wine cellar.

Elend walked to the center of the small cellar, surveying it as Vin began to check the walls. "I found it," she said a second later, rapping her fist on a certain portion of the stone block wall. Elend walked forward, joining her. Sure enough, there was a thin slit in the stones, barely visible. Burning steel, Elend could see two faint blue lines pointing to metal plates hidden behind the stone. Two stronger lines pointed behind him, toward a large metal plate set into the wall, affixed very securely with enormous bolts bored into the stone.

"Ready?" Vin asked.

Elend nodded, flaring his iron. They both Pulled on the plate buried in the stone wall, steadying themselves by Pulling back against the plates on the back wall.

Not for the first time, the foresight of the Ministry impressed Elend. How could they have known that someday, a group of skaa would take control of this city? And yet, this door had not only been hidden—it had been crafted so that only someone with Allomancy could open it. Elend continued to Pull in both directions at once, feeling as if his body were being stretched between two horses. But, fortunately, he had the power of pewter to strengthen his body and keep it from ripping apart. Vin grunted in effort beside him, and soon a section of the wall began to slide open toward them. No amount of prying would have been able to wedge the thick stone open, and only a lengthy, arduous effort would have been enough to break through. Yet, with Allomancy, they opened the door in a matter of moments.

Finally, they let go. Vin exhaled in exhaustion, and Elend could tell that it had been more difficult for her than it was for him. Sometimes, he didn't feel justified in having more power than she—after all, he'd been an Allomancer for far less time.

Vin picked up her lantern, and they moved into the now-open room. Like the other two Elend had seen, this cavern was enormous. It extended into the distance, their lantern's light making only a faint dent in the blackness. Fatren gasped in wonder as he joined them in the doorway. The room was filled with shelves. Hundreds of them. Thousands of them.

"What is it?" Fatren asked.

"Food," Elend said. "And basic supplies. Medicines, cloth, water."

"So much," Fatren said. "Here, all along . . ."

"Go get more men," Elend said. "Soldiers. We'll need them to guard the entrance, to keep people from breaking in and stealing the contents."

Fatren's face hardened. "This place belongs to my people."

"*My* people, Fatren," Elend said, watching Vin walk into the room, bearing the light with her. "This city is mine, now, as are its contents."

"You came to rob us," Fatren accused. "Just like the bandits who tried to take the city last year."

"No," Elend said, turning toward the soot-stained man. "I came to conquer you. There's a difference."

"I don't see one."

Elend gritted his teeth to keep himself from snapping at the man—the fatigue, the draining effect of leading an empire that seemed doomed—put him on edge so often lately. *No,* he told himself. *Men like Fatren need more than another tyrant. They need someone to look up to.*

Elend approached the man, and intentionally didn't use emotional Allomancy on him. Soothing was effective in many situations, but it wore off quickly. It was not a method to make permanent allies.

"Lord Fatren," Elend said. "I want you to think carefully about what you're arguing for. What would happen if I *did* leave you? With this much food, this much wealth down here? Can you trust your people not to break in, your soldiers not to try selling some of this to other cities? What happens when the secret of your food supply gets out? Will you welcome the thousands of refugees who will come? Will you protect them, and this cavern, against the raiders and bandits who will follow?"

Fatren fell silent.

Elend laid a hand on the man's shoulder. "I meant what I said above, Lord Fatren. Your people fought well—I was very impressed. They owe their survival today to you—your foresight, your training. Mere hours ago, they assumed they would be slaughtered by koloss. Now, they are not only safe, but under the protection of a much larger army.

"Don't fight this. You've struggled well, but it is time to have allies. I won't lie to you—I'm going to take the contents of this cavern, whether you resist me or not. However, I intend to give you the protection of my armies, the stability of my food supplies, and my word of honor that you can continue to rule your people under me. We need to work together, Lord Fatren. That's the only way any of us are going to survive the next few years."

Fatren looked up. "You're right, of course," he said. "I'll go get those men you asked for, my lord."

"Thank you," Elend said. "And, if you have anyone who can write, send them to me. We'll need to catalogue what we have down here."

Fatren nodded, then left.

"Once, you couldn't do things like that," Vin said from a short distance away, her voice echoing in the large cavern.

"Like what?"

"Give a man such forceful commands," she said. "Take control away from him. You'd have wanted to give these people a vote on whether or not they should join your empire."

Elend looked back at the doorway. He stood silently for a moment. He hadn't used emotional Allomancy, and yet he felt as if he'd bullied Fatren anyway. "Sometimes, I feel like a failure, Vin. There should be another way."

"Not right now, there isn't," Vin said, walking up to him, putting a hand on his arm. "They need you, Elend. You know that they do."

He nodded. "I know it. I just can't help thinking that a better man would have found a way to make the will of the people work along with his rule."

"You did," she said. "Your parliamentary assembly still rules in Luthadel, and the kingdoms you reign over maintain basic rights and privileges for the skaa."

"Compromises," Elend said. "They only get to do what they want as long as *I* don't disagree with them."

"It's enough. You have to be realistic, Elend."

"When my friends and I met together, I was the one who spoke of the perfect dreams, of the great things we'd accomplish. I was always the idealist."

"Emperors don't have that luxury," Vin said quietly.

Elend looked at her, then sighed, turning away.

Vin stood, watching Elend in the cold lantern-light of the cavern. She hated seeing such regret, such . . . disillusionment in him. In a way, his current problems seemed even worse than the self-doubt he had once struggled with. He seemed to see himself as a failure despite what he had accomplished.

And yet, he didn't let himself wallow in that failure. He moved on, working despite his regret. He was a harder man than he had once been. That wasn't necessarily a bad thing. The old Elend had been a man who was easily dismissed by many—a genius who had wonderful ideas, but little ability to lead. Still, she missed some of what was gone. The simple idealism. Elend was still an optimist, and he was still a scholar, but both attributes seemed tempered by what he had been forced to endure.

She watched him move along one of the storage shelves, trailing a finger in the dust. He brought the finger up, looking at it for a moment, then snapped it, throwing a small burst of dust into the air. The beard made him look more rugged—like the wartime commander he had become. A year of solid training with Allomancy and the sword had strengthened his body, and he'd needed to get his uniforms retailored to fit properly. The one he wore now was still stained from battle.

"This place is amazing, isn't it?" Elend asked.

Vin turned, glancing into the darkness of the storage cavern. "I suppose."

"He knew, Vin," Elend said. "The Lord Ruler. He suspected that this day would come—a day when the mists returned and food would be scarce. So, he prepared these supply depots."

Vin joined Elend beside a shelf. She knew from previous caverns that the food would still be good, much of it processed in one of the Lord Ruler's canneries, and would remain so for years in storage. The amount in this cavern could feed the town above for years. Unfortunately, Vin and Elend had more to worry about than a single town.

"Imagine the effort this must have taken," Elend said, turning over a can of stewed beef in his hand. "He would have had to rotate this food every few years, constantly packing and storing new supplies. And he did it for centuries, without anyone knowing what he was doing."

Vin shrugged. "It's not so hard to keep secrets when you're a god-emperor with a fanatical priesthood."

"Yes, but the effort . . . the sheer scope of it all . . ." Elend paused, looking at Vin. "You know what this means?"

"What?"

"The Lord Ruler thought it could be beaten. The Deepness, the thing that we released. The Lord Ruler thought he could eventually win."

Vin snorted. "It doesn't have to mean that, Elend."

"Then why go through all of this? He must have thought that fighting wasn't hopeless."

"People struggle, Elend. Even a dying beast will still keep fighting, will do anything to stay alive."

"You have to admit that these caverns are a good sign, though," Elend said.

"A good sign?" Vin asked quietly, stepping closer. "Elend, I know you're just trying to find hope in all this, but I have trouble seeing 'good signs' anywhere lately. You have to admit now that the sun is getting darker. Redder. It's even worse down here, in the South."

"Actually," Elend said, "I doubt that the sun has changed at all. It must be all the smoke and ash in the air."

"Which is another problem," Vin said. "The ash falls almost perpetually now. People are having trouble keeping it out of their streets. It blots out the light, making everything darker. Even if the mists *don't* kill off next year's crops, the ash will. Two winters ago—when we fought the koloss at Luthadel—was the first I'd seen snow in the Central Dominance, and this last winter was even worse. These aren't things we can fight, Elend, no matter how big our army!"

"What do you expect me to do, Vin?" Elend asked, slamming his can of stew down on the shelf. "The koloss are gathering in the Outer Dominances. If we don't build our defenses, our people won't *last* long enough to starve."

Vin shook her head. "Armies are short-term. This," she said, sweeping her hand across the cavern. "*This* is short-term. What are we doing here?"

"We're surviving. Kelsier said—"

"Kelsier is *dead,* Elend!" Vin snapped. "Am I the only one who sees the irony in that? We call him the Survivor, but he is the one who didn't survive! He *let* himself become a martyr. He committed suicide. How is that surviving?"

She stood for a moment, looking at Elend, breathing deeply. He stared back, apparently undaunted by her outburst.

What am I doing? Vin thought. *I was just thinking about how much I admired Elend's hope. Why argue with him now?*

They were stretched so thin. Both of them.

"I don't have answers for you, Vin," Elend said in the dark cavern. "I can't even begin to understand how to fight something like the mist. Armies, however, I can deal with. Or, at least, I'm learning how."

"I'm sorry," Vin said, turning away. "I didn't mean to argue again. It's just so frustrating."

"We're making progress," Elend said. "We'll find a way, Vin. We'll survive."

"Do you really think we can do it?" Vin asked, turning to look him in the eyes.

"Yes," Elend said.

And she believed him. He had hope, and always would. That was a big part of why she loved him so much.

"Come on," Elend said, laying a hand on her shoulder. "Let's find what we came for."

Vin joined him, leaving her koloss behind, walking into the depths of the cavern as they heard footsteps outside. There was more than one reason they had come to this place. The food and the supplies—of which they passed seemingly endless shelves—were important. However, there was more.

A large metal plate was set into the back wall of the rough-hewn cavern. Vin read the words inscribed on it out loud.

" 'This is the last metal I will tell you about,' " she read. " 'I have trouble deciding the purpose of it. It allows you to see the past, in a way. What a person could have been, and who they might have become, had they made different choices. Much like gold, but for others.

" 'By now, the mists have likely come again. Such a foul, hateful thing. Scorn it. Don't go out in it. It seeks to destroy us all. If there is trouble, know that you can control the koloss and the kandra by use of several people Pushing on their emotions at once. I built this weakness into them. Keep the secret wisely.' "

Beneath that was listed an Allomantic compound of metals, one with which Vin was already familiar. It was the alloy of atium they called malatium—Kelsier's Eleventh Metal. So the Lord Ruler *had* known about it. He'd simply been as baffled as the rest of them as to its purpose.

The plate had been written by the Lord Ruler, of course. Or, at least, he'd ordered it written as it was. Each previous cache had also contained information, written in steel. In Urteau, for instance, she had learned about electrum. In the one to the east, they'd found a description of aluminum—though they'd already known about that metal.

"Not much new there," Elend said, sounding disappointed. "We already knew about malatium and about controlling koloss. Though, I'd never thought to have several Soothers Push at the same time. That might be helpful." Before, they'd thought it took a Mistborn burning duralumin to get control of koloss.

"It doesn't matter," Vin said, pointing at the other side of the plate. "We have *that.*"

The other half of the plate contained a map, carved into steel, just like the maps they had found in the other three storage caverns. It depicted the Final Empire, divided into dominances. Luthadel was a square at the center. An "X" to the east marked the main thing they'd come looking for: the location of the final cavern.

There were five, they thought. They'd found the first one beneath Luthadel, near the Well of Ascension. It had given the location of the second, to the east. The third had been in Urteau—Vin had been able to sneak into that one, but they hadn't managed to recover the food yet. That one had led them here, to the south.

Each map had two numbers on it—a five and a lower number. Luthadel had been number one. This one was number four.

"That's it," Vin said, running her fingers along the carved inscriptions on the plate. "In the Western Dominance, as you guessed. Somewhere near Chardees?"

"Fadrex City," Elend said.

"Cett's home?"

Elend nodded. He knew far more about geography than she.

"That's the place, then," Vin said. "The one where *it* is."

Elend met her eyes, and she knew he understood her. The caches had grown progressively larger and more valuable. Each one had a specialized aspect to it as well—the first had contained weapons in addition to its other supplies, while the second had contained large amounts of lumber. As they'd investigated each successive cache, they'd grown more and more excited about what the last one might contain. Something spectacular, surely. Perhaps even *it*.

The Lord Ruler's atium cache.

It was the most valuable treasure in the Final Empire. Despite years of searching, nobody had ever located it. Some said it didn't even exist. But, Vin felt that it had to. Despite a thousand years of controlling the sole mine that produced the extremely rare metal, he had allowed only a small portion of atium to enter the economy. Nobody knew what the Lord Ruler had done with the greater portion he had kept to himself for all those centuries.

"Now, don't get too excited," Elend said. "We have no proof that we'll find the atium in that final cavern."

"It has to be there," Vin said. "It makes sense. Where else would the Lord Ruler store his atium?"

"If I could answer that, we'd have found it."

Vin shook her head. "He put it somewhere safe, but somewhere where it would eventually be found. He left these maps as clues to his followers, should he—somehow—be defeated. He didn't want an enemy who captured one of the caverns to be able to find them all instantly."

A trail of clues that led to one, final cache. The most important one. It made sense. It *had* to. Elend didn't look convinced. He rubbed his bearded chin, studying the reflective plate in their lantern light. "Even if we find it," he said, "I don't know that it will help that much. What good is money to us now?"

"It's more than money," she said. "It's power. A weapon we can use to fight."

"Fight the mists?" he asked.

Vin fell silent. "Perhaps not," she finally said. "But the koloss, and the other armies. With that atium, your empire becomes secure. . . . Plus, atium is part of all this, Elend. It's only valuable because of Allomancy—but Allomancy didn't exist until the Ascension."

"Another unanswered question," Elend said. "Why did that nugget of metal I ingested make me Mistborn? Where did it come from? Why was it placed at the Well of Ascension, and by whom? Why was there only one left, and what happened to the others?"

"Maybe we'll find the answer once we take Fadrex," Vin said.

Elend nodded. She could tell he considered the information contained in the caches the most important reason to track them down, followed closely by the supplies. To him, the possibility of finding atium was relatively unimportant. Vin couldn't explain why she felt he was so wrong in this regard. The atium *was* important. She just knew it. Her earlier despair lightened as she looked over the map. They had to go to Fadrex. She knew it.

The answers would be there.

"Taking Fadrex won't be easy," Elend noted. "Cett's enemies have entrenched themselves quite solidly there. I hear a former Ministry obligator is in charge."

"The atium will be worth it," Vin said.

"If it's there," Elend said.

She gave him a flat stare.

He held up a hand. "I'm just trying to do what you told me, Vin—I'm trying to be realistic. However, I agree that

Fadrex will be worth the effort. Even if the atium isn't there, we need the supplies in that store. We need to know what the Lord Ruler left us."

Vin nodded. She herself no longer had any atium. She'd burned up their last bit a year and a half ago, and she'd never gotten used to how exposed she felt without it. Electrum softened that fear somewhat, but not completely.

Voices sounded from the other end of the cavern, and Elend turned. "I should go speak to them," he said. "We're going to have to organize things in here quickly."

"Have you told them yet that we're going to have to move them back to Luthadel?"

Elend shook his head. "They won't like it," he said. "They're becoming independent, as I always hoped they would."

"It has to be done, Elend," Vin said. "This city is well outside our defensive perimeter. Plus, they can't have more than a few hours of mistless daylight left this far out. Their crops are already doomed."

Elend nodded, but he continued to stare out into the darkness. "I come, I seize control of their city, take their treasure, then force them to abandon their homes. And from here we go to Fadrex to conquer another."

"Elend—"

He held up a hand. "I know, Vin. It must be done." He turned, leaving the lantern and walking toward the doorway. As he did, his posture straightened, and his face became more firm.

Vin turned back to the plate, rereading the Lord Ruler's words. On a different plate, much like this one, Sazed had found the words of Kwaan, the long-dead Terrisman who had changed the world by claiming to have found the Hero of Ages. Kwaan had left his words as a confession of his errors, warning that some kind of force was working to change the histories and religions of mankind. He'd worried that the force was suborning the Terris religion in order to cause a "Hero" to come to the North and release it.

That was exactly what Vin had done. She'd called herself

hero, and had released the enemy—all the while thinking that she was sacrificing her own needs for the good of the world.

She ran her fingers across the large plate.

We have to do more than just fight wars! she thought, angry at the Lord Ruler. *If you knew so much, why didn't you leave us more than this? A few maps in scattered halls filled with supplies? A couple of paragraphs, telling us about metals that are of barely any use? What good is a cave full of food when we have an entire empire to feed!*

Vin stopped. Her fingers—made far more sensitive by the tin she was burning to help her eyesight in the dark cavern—brushed against grooves in the plate's surface. She knelt, leaning close, to find a short inscription carved in the metal, at the bottom, the letters much smaller than the ones up above.

Be careful what you speak, it read. *It can hear what you say. It can read what you write. Only your thoughts are safe.*

Vin shivered.

Only your thoughts are safe.

What had the Lord Ruler learned in his moments of transcendence? What things had he kept in his mind forever, never writing them down for fear of revealing his knowledge, always expecting that he would eventually be the one who took the power when it came again? Had he, perhaps, planned to use that power to destroy the thing that Vin had released?

You have doomed yourselves. . . . The Lord Ruler's last words, spoken right before Vin had thrust the spear through his heart. He'd known. Even then—before the mists had started coming during the day, before she'd begun hearing the strange thumpings that led her to the Well of Ascension—even then, she'd worried.

Be careful what you speak . . . only your thoughts are safe.

I have to figure this out. I have to connect what we have, find the way to defeat—or outwit—this thing that I've loosed.

And I can't talk this over with anyone, or it will know what I'm planning.

Rashek soon found a balance in the changes he made to the world—which was fortunate, for his power burned away quite quickly. Though the power he held seemed immense to him, it was truly only a tiny fraction of something much greater.

Of course, he did end up naming himself the "Sliver of Infinity" in his religion. Perhaps he understood more than I give him credit for.

Either way, we had him to thank for a world without flowers, where plants grew brown rather than green, and where people could survive in an environment where ash fell from the sky on a regular basis.

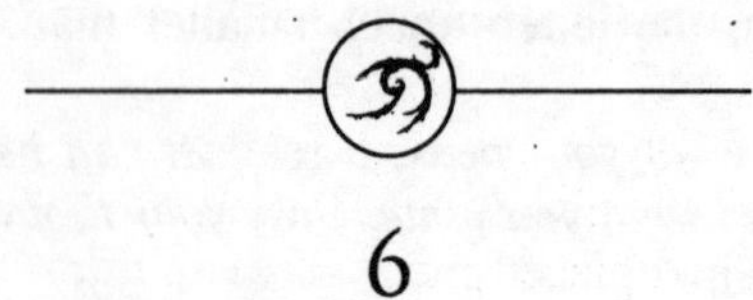

6

I'M TOO WEAK, MARSH THOUGHT.

Lucidity came upon him suddenly, as it often did when Ruin wasn't watching him closely. It was like waking from a nightmare, fully aware of what had been going on in the dream, yet confused as to the reasoning behind his actions.

He continued to walk through the koloss camp. Ruin still controlled him, as it always did. Yet, when it didn't press hard enough against Marsh's mind—when it didn't focus on him—sometimes, Marsh's own thoughts returned.

I can't fight it, he thought. Ruin couldn't read his thoughts, of that he was fairly confident. And yet, Marsh couldn't fight or struggle in any way. When he did, Ruin immediately asserted control once again. This had been proven to Marsh a dozen times over. Sometimes he managed to quiver a finger, perhaps halt a step, but that was the best he could do.

It was depressing. However, Marsh had always considered himself to be a practical man, and he forced himself to acknowledge the truth. He was never going to gain enough control over his body to kill himself.

Ash fell as he walked through the camp. Did it ever stop these days? He almost wished that Ruin wouldn't ever let go of his mind. When his mind was his own, Marsh saw only pain and destruction. When Ruin controlled him, however, the falling ash was a thing of beauty, the red sun a marvelous triumph, the world a place of sweetness in its death.

Madness, Marsh thought, approaching the center of camp. *I need to go mad. Then I won't have to deal with all of this.*

Other Inquisitors joined him at the center of the camp, walking with quiet swishes of their robes. They didn't speak. They never spoke—Ruin controlled them all, so why bother with conversation? Marsh's brethren had the normal spikes in their heads, driven into the skull. Yet, he could also see telltale signs of the new spikes, jutting from their chests and backs. Marsh had placed many of them himself, killing the Terrismen that had either been captured in the north or tracked down across the land.

Marsh himself had a new set of spikes, some driven between the ribs, others driven down through the chest. They were a beautiful thing. He didn't understand why, but they excited him. The spikes had come through death, and that was pleasant enough—but there was more. He knew, somehow, that the Inquisitors had been incomplete—the Lord Ruler had withheld some abilities to make the Inquisitors more dependent upon him. To make certain they couldn't threaten him. But now, what he'd kept back had been provided.

What a beautiful world, Marsh thought, looking up into the falling ash, feeling the light, comforting flakes upon his skin.

I speak of us as "we." The group. Those of us who were trying to discover and defeat Ruin. Perhaps my thoughts are now tainted, but I like to look back and see the sum of what we were doing as a single, united assault, though we were all involved in different processes and plans.

We were one. That didn't stop the world from ending, but that's not necessarily a bad thing.

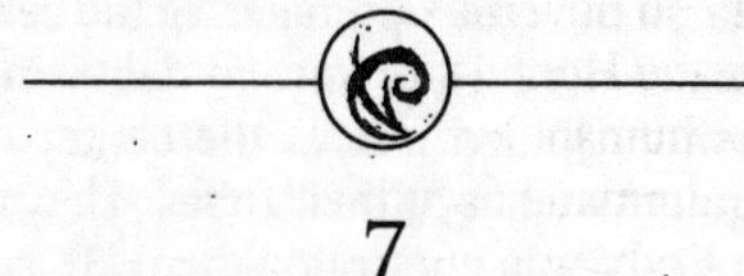

7

THEY GAVE HIM BONES.

TenSoon flowed around them, dissolving muscles, then reforming them into organs, sinew, and skin. He built a body around the bones, using skills gained over centuries spent eating and digesting humans. Corpses only, of course—he had never killed a man. The Contract forbade such things.

After a year in his pit of a prison, he felt as if he had forgotten how to use a body. What was it like to touch the world with rigid digits, rather than a body that flowed against the confines of stone? What was it like to taste and smell with only tongue and nostrils, rather than with every bit of skin exposed to the air. What was it like to . . .

To see. He opened his eyes and gasped, drawing first breath into remade, full-sized lungs. The world was a thing of wonder and of . . . light. He had forgotten that, during the months of near madness. He pushed himself to his knees, looking down at his arms. Then, he reached up, feeling his face with a tentative hand.

His body wasn't that of any specific person—he would have needed a model to produce such a replica. Instead, he had covered the bones with muscles and skin as best he could. He was old enough that he knew how to create a reasonable approximation of a human. The features wouldn't be handsome; they might even be a little grotesque. That, however, was more than good enough for the moment. He felt . . . real again.

Still on hands and knees, he looked up at his captor. The cavern was lit only by a glowstone—a large, porous rock set atop a thick column base. The bluish fungus that grew on the rock made enough of a glow to see by—especially if one had specifically grown eyes that were good at seeing in dim blue light.

TenSoon knew his captor. He knew most kandra, at least up to the Sixth and Seventh Generations. This kandra's name was VarSell. In the Homeland, VarSell didn't wear the bones of an animal or human, but instead used a True Body—a set of false bones, human-shaped, crafted by a kandra artisan. VarSell's True Body was quartz, and he left his skin translucent, allowing the stone to sparkle faintly in the fungal light as he studied TenSoon.

I made my body opaque, TenSoon realized. *Like that of a human, with tan skin to obscure the muscles beneath.* Why had that come so naturally to him? Once, he had cursed the years he spent among the humans, using their bones instead of a True Body. Perhaps he had fallen to that same old default because his captors hadn't given him a True Body. Human bones. An insult, of sorts.

TenSoon stood. "What?" he asked at the look in VarSell's eyes.

"I just picked a random set of bones from the storeroom," VarSell said. "It's ironic that I would give you a set of bones that you'd originally contributed."

TenSoon frowned. *What?*

And then he made the connection. The body that TenSoon had created around the bones must look convincing—as if it were the original one that these bones had belonged to. VarSell assumed that TenSoon had been able to create such a realistic approximation because he'd originally digested the human's corpse, and therefore knew how to create the right body around the bones.

TenSoon smiled. "I've never worn these bones before."

VarSell eyed him. He was of the Fifth Generation—two centuries younger than TenSoon. Indeed, even among those of the Third Generation, few kandra had as much experience with the outside world as TenSoon.

"I see," VarSell finally said.

TenSoon turned, looking over the small chamber. Three more Fifth Generationers stood near the door, watching him. Like VarSell, few of them wore clothing—and those who did wore only open-fronted robes. Kandra tended to wear little while in the Homeland, as that allowed them to better display their True Bodies.

TenSoon saw two sparkling rods of metal embedded in the clear muscles of each Fifth's shoulders—all three had the Blessing of Potency. The Second Generation was taking no risk of his escaping. It was, of course, another insult. TenSoon had come to his fate willingly.

"Well?" TenSoon asked, turning back to VarSell. "Are we to go?"

VarSell glanced at one of his companions. "Forming the body was expected to take you longer."

TenSoon snorted. "The Second Generation is unpracticed. They assume that because it still takes them many hours to create a body, the rest of us require the same amount of time."

"They are your elder generation," VarSell said. "You should show them respect."

"The Second Generation has been sequestered in these caves for centuries," TenSoon said, "sending the rest of us to serve Contracts while they remain lazy. I passed them in skill long ago."

VarSell hissed, and for a moment TenSoon thought the younger kandra might slap him. VarSell restrained himself, barely—to TenSoon's amusement. After all, as a member of the Third Generation, TenSoon was senior to VarSell—much in the same way that the Seconds were supposedly senior to TenSoon.

Yet, the Thirds were a special case. They always had been. That's why the Seconds kept them out on Contracts so much—it wouldn't do to have their immediate underlings around all the time, upsetting their perfect little kandra utopia.

"Let's go, then," VarSell finally decided, nodding for two of his guards to lead the way. The other one joined VarSell, walking behind TenSoon. Like VarSell, these three had True Bodies formed of stone. Those were popular among the Fifth Generation, who had time to commission—and use—lavish True Bodies. They were the favored pups of the Seconds, and tended to spend more time than most in the Homeland.

They had given TenSoon no clothing. So, as they walked, he dissolved his genitals, and re-formed a smooth crotch, as was common among the kandra. He tried to walk with pride and confidence, but he knew this body wouldn't look very intimidating. It was emaciated—he'd lost much mass during his imprisonment and more to the acid, and he hadn't been able to form very large muscles.

The smooth, rock tunnel had probably once been a natural formation, but over the centuries, the younger generations had been used during their infancy to smooth out the stone with their digestive juices. TenSoon didn't see many other kandra. VarSell kept to back corridors, obviously not wanting to make too much of a show.

I've been away so long, TenSoon thought. *The Eleventh Generation must have been chosen by now. I still don't know most of the Eighth, let alone the Ninth or Tenth.*

He was beginning to suspect that there wouldn't be a Twelfth Generation. Even if there were, things could not continue as they had. The Father was dead. What, then, of the First Contract? His people had spent ten centuries enslaved to humankind, serving the Contracts in an effort to keep themselves safe. Most of the kandra hated men for their situation. Up until recently, TenSoon had been one of those.

It's ironic, TenSoon thought. *But, even when we wear True Bodies, we wear them in the form of humans. Two arms, two legs, even faces formed after the fashion of mankind.*

Sometimes he wondered if the unbirthed—the creatures that the humans called mistwraiths—were more honest than their brothers the kandra. The mistwraiths would form a body however they wished, connecting bones in odd arrangements, making almost artistic designs from both human and animal bones. The kandra, though—they created bodies that looked human. Even while they cursed humankind for keeping them enslaved.

Such a strange people they were. But they were his. Even if he had betrayed them.

And now I have to convince the First Generation that I was right in that betrayal. Not for me. For them. For all of us.

They passed through corridors and chambers, eventually arriving at sections of the Homeland that were more familiar to TenSoon. He soon realized that their destination must be the Trustwarren. He would argue his defense in his people's most sacred place. He should have guessed.

A year of torturous imprisonment had earned him a trial before the First Generation. He'd had a year to think about what to say. And if he failed, he'd have an eternity to think about what he'd done wrong.

It is too easy for people to characterize Ruin as simply a force of destruction. Think rather of Ruin as intelligent decay. Not simply chaos, but a force that sought in a rational—and dangerous—way to break everything down to its most basic forms.

Ruin could plan and carefully plot, knowing if he built one thing up, he could use it to knock down two others. The nature of the world is that when we create something, we often destroy something else in the process.

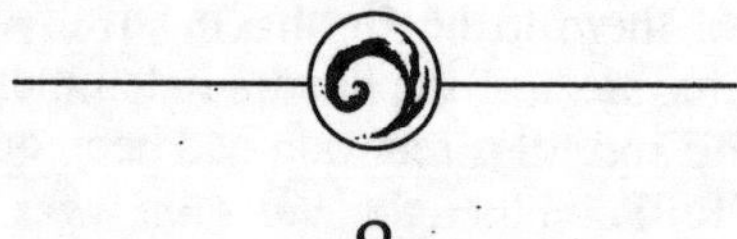

8

ON THE FIRST DAY OUT of Vetitan, Vin and Elend murdered a hundred of the villagers. Or, at least, that was how Vin felt.

She sat on a rotting stump at the center of camp, watching

the sun approach the distant horizon, knowing what was about to happen. Ash fell silently around her. And the mists appeared.

Once—not so long ago—the mists had come only at night. During the year following the Lord Ruler's death, however, that had changed. As if a thousand years of being confined to the darkness had made the mists restless.

And so, they had begun to come during the day. Sometimes, they came in great rolling waves, appearing out of nowhere, disappearing as quickly. Most commonly, however, they just appeared in the air like a thousand phantoms, twisting and growing together. Tendrils of mist that sprouted, vine-like tentacles creeping across the sky. Each day, they retreated a little bit later in the day, and each day they appeared a little earlier in the evening. Soon—perhaps before the year ended—they would smother the land permanently. And this presented a problem, for ever since that night when Vin had taken the power of the Well of Ascension, the mists killed.

Elend had had trouble believing Sazed's stories two years before, when the Terrisman had come to Luthadel with horrific reports of terrified villagers and mists that killed. Vin too had assumed that Sazed was mistaken. A part of her wished she could continue in that delusion as she watched the waiting townspeople, huddled together on the broad open plain, surrounded by soldiers and koloss.

The deaths began as soon as the mists appeared. Though the mists left most of the people alone, they chose some at random, causing them to begin shaking. These fell to the ground, having a seizure, while their friends and family watched in shock and horror.

Horror was still Vin's reaction. That, and frustration. Kelsier had promised her that the mists were an ally—that they would protect her and give her power. She'd believed that to be true until the mists started to feel alien to her, hiding shadowed ghosts and murderous intent.

"I hate you," she whispered as the mists continued their grisly work. It was like watching a beloved old relative pick strangers out of a crowd and, one at a time, slit their throats. And there was nothing at all she could do. Elend's scholars had tried everything—hoods to keep the mists from being breathed in, waiting to go outside until the mists had already established themselves, rushing people inside the moment they started shaking. Animals were immune for some reason, but every human was potentially susceptible. If one went outside in the mists, one risked death, and nothing could prevent it.

It was over soon. The mists gave the fits to fewer than one in six, and only a small fraction of those died. Plus, one only needed to risk these new mists once—one gamble, and then you were immune. Most who fell sick would recover. That was no comfort to the families of those who died.

She sat on her stump, staring out into the mists, which were still lit by the setting sun. Ironically, it was more difficult for her to see than it would have been if it were dark. She couldn't burn much tin, lest the sunlight blind her—but without it, she couldn't pierce the mists.

The result was a scene that reminded her why she had once feared the mists. Her visibility reduced to barely ten feet, she could see little more than shadows. Amorphous figures ran this way and that, calling out. Silhouettes knelt or stood terrified. Sound was a traitorous thing, echoing against unseen objects, cries coming from phantom sources.

Vin sat among them, ash raining around her like burnt tears, and bowed her head.

"Lord Fatren!" Elend's voice called, causing Vin to look up. Once, his voice hadn't carried nearly as much authority. That seemed like so long ago. He appeared from the mists, dressed in his second white uniform—the one that was still clean—his face hardened against the mortalities. She could feel his Allomantic touch on those around him as he approached—his Soothing would make the people's pain less acute, but he didn't Push as hard as he could have. She knew from talking to him that he didn't feel it was right to remove all of a person's grief at the death of one they loved.

"My lord!" she heard Fatren say, and saw him approaching. "This is a disaster!"

"It looks far worse than it is, Lord Fatren," Elend said. "As I explained, most of those who have fallen will recover."

Fatren stopped beside Vin's stump. Then, he turned and stared into the mists, listening to the weeping and the pain of his people. "I can't believe we did this. I can't . . . I can't believe you talked me into making them stand in the mists."

"Your people needed to be inoculated, Fatren," Elend said.

It was true. They didn't have tents for all of the townsfolk, and that left only two options. Leave them behind in their dying village, or force them north—make them go out in the mists, and see who died. It was terrible, and it was brutal, but it would have happened eventually. Still, even though she knew the logic of what they had done, Vin felt terrible for being part of it.

"What kind of monsters are we?" Fatren asked in a hushed tone.

"The kind we have to be," Elend said. "Go make a count. Find out how many are dead. Calm the living and promise them that no further harm will come from the mists."

"Yes, my lord," Fatren said, moving away.

Vin watched him go. "We murdered them, Elend," she whispered. "We told them it would be all right. We forced them to leave their village and come out here, to die."

"It will be all right," Elend said, laying a hand on her shoulder. "Better than a slow death in that village."

"We could have given them a choice."

Elend shook his head. "There was no choice. Within a few months, their city will be covered in mists permanently. They would have had to stay inside their homes and starve, or go out into the mists. Better that we take them to the Central Dominance, where there is still enough mistless daylight to grow crops."

"The truth doesn't make it any easier."

Elend stood in the mists, ash falling around him. "No," he said. "It doesn't. I'll go gather the koloss so they can bury the dead."

"And the wounded?" Those the mists attacked, but didn't kill, would be sick and cramped for several days, perhaps longer. If the usual percentages held, then nearly a thousand of the villagers would fall into that category.

"When we leave tomorrow, we'll have the koloss carry them. If we can get to the canal, then we can probably fit most of them on the barges."

Vin didn't like feeling exposed. She'd spent her childhood hiding in corners, her adolescence playing the silent nighttime assassin. So it was incredibly difficult *not* to feel exposed while traveling with five thousand tired villagers along one of the Southern Dominance's most obvious routes.

She walked a short distance away from the townspeople—she never rode—and tried to find something to distract herself from thinking about the deaths the evening before. Unfortunately, Elend was riding with Fatren and the other town leaders, busy trying to smooth relations. That left her alone.

Except for her single koloss.

The massive beast lumbered beside her. She kept it close partially out of convenience; she knew it would make the villagers keep their distance from her. As willing as she was to be distracted, she didn't want to deal with those betrayed, frightened eyes. Not right now.

Nobody understood the koloss, least of all Vin. She'd discovered how to control them, using the hidden Allomantic trigger. Yet, during the thousand years of the Lord Ruler's reign, he had kept the koloss separated from mankind, letting very little be known about them beyond their brutal prowess in battle and their simple bestial nature.

Even now, Vin could feel her koloss tugging at her, trying to break free. It didn't like being controlled—it wanted to attack her. It could not, fortunately; she controlled it, and would continue to do so whether awake or asleep, burning metals or not, unless someone stole the beast from her.

Even linked as they were, there was so much Vin didn't understand about the creatures. She looked up, and found the koloss staring at her with its bloodred eyes. Its skin was stretched tight across its face, the nose pulled completely flat.

The skin was torn near the right eye, and a jagged rip ran down to the corner of its mouth, letting a flap of blue skin hang free, exposing the red muscles and bloodied teeth below.

"Don't look at me," the creature said, speaking in a sluggish voice. Its words were slurred, partially from the way its lips were pulled.

"What?" Vin asked.

"You don't think I'm human," the koloss said, speaking slowly, deliberately—like the others she had heard. It was like they had to think hard between each word.

"You *aren't* human," Vin said. "You're something else."

"I will be human," the koloss said. "We will kill you. Take your cities. Then we will be human."

Vin shivered. It was a common theme among koloss. She'd heard others make similar remarks. There was something very chilling about the flat, emotionless way the koloss spoke of slaughtering people.

They were created by the Lord Ruler, she thought. *Of course they're twisted. As twisted as he was.*

"What is your name?" she asked the koloss.

It continued to lumber beside her. Finally, it looked at her. "Human."

"I know you want to be human," Vin said. "What is your name?"

"That is my name. Human. You call me Human."

Vin frowned as they walked. *That almost seemed . . . clever.* She'd never taken the opportunity to talk to koloss before. She'd always assumed that they were of a homogeneous mentality—just the same stupid beast repeated over and over.

"All right, Human," she said, curious. "How long have you been alive?"

He walked for a moment, so long that Vin thought he had forgotten the question. Finally, however, he spoke. "Don't you see my bigness?"

"Your bigness? Your size?"

Human just kept walking.

"So you all grow at the same rate?"

He didn't answer. Vin shook her head, suspecting that the question was too abstract for the beast.

"I'm bigger than some," Human said. "Smaller than some—but not very many. That means I'm old."

Another sign of intelligence, she thought, raising an eyebrow. From what Vin had seen of other koloss, Human's logic was impressive.

"I hate you," Human said after a short time spent walking. "I want to kill you. But I can't kill you."

"No," Vin said. "I won't let you."

"You're big inside. Very big."

"Yes," Vin said. "Human, where are the girl koloss?"

The creature walked several moments. "Girl?"

"Like me," Vin said.

"We're not like you," he said. "We're big on the outside only."

"No," Vin said. "Not my size. My . . ." How did one describe gender? Short of stripping, she couldn't think of any methods. So, she decided to try a different tactic. "Are there baby koloss?"

"Baby?"

"Small ones," Vin said.

The koloss pointed toward the marching koloss army. "Small ones," he said, referring to some of the five-foot-tall koloss.

"Smaller," Vin said.

"None smaller."

Koloss reproduction was a mystery that, to her knowledge, nobody had ever cracked. Even after a year spent fighting with the beasts, she'd never found out where new ones came from. Whenever Elend's koloss armies grew too small, she and he stole new ones from the Inquisitors.

Yet, it was ridiculous to assume that the koloss didn't reproduce. She'd seen koloss camps that weren't controlled by an Allomancer, and the creatures killed each other with fearful regularity. At that rate, they would have killed themselves off after a few years. Yet, they had lasted for ten centuries.

That implied a very quick rise from child to adult, or so

Sazed and Elend seemed to think. They hadn't been able to confirm their theories, and she knew their ignorance frustrated Elend greatly—especially since his duties as emperor left him little time for the studies he'd once enjoyed so much.

"If there are none smaller," Vin asked, "then where do new koloss come from?"

"New koloss come from us," Human finally said.

"From you?" Vin asked, frowning as she walked. "That doesn't tell me much."

Human didn't say anything further. His talkative mood had apparently passed.

From us, Vin thought. *They bud off of each other, perhaps?* She'd heard of some creatures that, if you cut them the right way, each half would grow into a new animal. But, that couldn't be the case with koloss—she'd seen battlefields filled with their dead, and no pieces rose to form new koloss. But she'd also never seen a female koloss. Though most of the beasts wore crude loincloths, they were—as far as she knew—all male.

Further speculation was cut off as she noticed the line ahead bunching up; the crowd was slowing. Curious, she dropped a coin and left Human behind, shooting herself over the people. The mists had retreated hours ago, and though night was again approaching, for the moment it was both light and mistless.

Therefore, as she shot through the falling ash, she easily picked out the canal up ahead. It cut unnaturally through the ground, far straighter than any river. Elend speculated that the constant ashfall would soon put an end to most of the canal systems. Without skaa laborers to dredge them on a regular basis, they would fill up with ashen sediment, eventually clogging to uselessness.

Vin soared through the air, completing her arc, heading toward a large mass of tents stationed beside the canal. Thousands of fires spit smoke into the afternoon air, and men milled about, training, working, or preparing. Nearly fifty thousand soldiers bivouacked here, using the canal route as a supply line back to Luthadel.

Vin dropped another coin, bounding through the air again.

She quickly caught up to the small group of horses that had broken off from Elend's line of tired, marching skaa. She landed—dropping a coin and Pushing against it slightly to slow her descent, throwing up a spray of ash as she hit.

Elend reined in his horse, smiling as he surveyed the camp. The expression was rare enough on his lips these days that Vin found herself smiling as well. Ahead, a group of men waited for them—their scouts would have long since noticed the townspeople's approach.

"Lord Elend!" said a man sitting at the head of the army contingent. "You're ahead of schedule!"

"I assume you're ready anyway, General," Elend said, dismounting.

"Well, you know me," Demoux said, smiling as he approached. The general wore well-used armor of leather and steel, his face bearing a scar on one cheek, the left side of his scalp missing a large patch of hair where a koloss blade had nearly taken his head. Ever formal, the grizzled man bowed to Elend, who just slapped him on the shoulder affectionately.

Vin's smile lingered. *I remember when that man was little more than a fresh recruit standing frightened in a tunnel.* Demoux wasn't actually that much older than she was, even though his tanned face and callused hands gave that impression.

"We've held position, my lord," Demoux said as Fatren and his brother dismounted and joined the group. "Not that there was much to hold it against. Still, it was good for my men to practice fortifying a camp."

Indeed, the army's camp beside the canal was surrounded by heaped earth and spikes—a considerable feat, considering the army's size.

"You did well, Demoux," Elend said, turning back to look over the townspeople. "Our mission was a success."

"I can see that, my lord," Demoux said, smiling. "That's a fair pack of koloss you picked up. I hope the Inquisitor leading them wasn't *too* sad to see them go."

"Couldn't have bothered him too much," Elend said. "Since he was dead at the time. We found the storage cavern as well."

"Praise the Survivor!" Demoux said.

Vin frowned. At his neck, hanging outside his clothing, Demoux wore a necklace that bore a small silver spear: the increasingly popular symbol of the Church of the Survivor. It seemed odd to her that the weapon that had killed Kelsier would become the symbol of his followers.

Of course, she didn't like to think about the other possibility—that the spear might not represent the one that had killed Kelsier. It might very well represent the one that she herself had used to kill the Lord Ruler. She'd never asked Demoux which it was. Despite three years of growing Church power, Vin had never become comfortable with her own part in its doctrine.

"Praise the Survivor indeed," Elend said, looking over the army's supply barges. "How did your project go?"

"Dredging the southern bend?" Demoux asked. "It went well—there was blessed little else to do while we waited. You should be able to get barges through there now."

"Good," Elend said. "Form two task forces of five hundred men. Send one with barges back to Vetitan for the supplies we had to leave down in that cavern. They will transfer the supplies to the barges and send them up to Luthadel."

"Yes, my lord," Demoux said.

"Send the second group of soldiers north to Luthadel with these refugees," Elend said, nodding to Fatren. "This is Lord Fatren. He's in command of the townspeople. Have your men respect his wishes, as long as they are reasonable, and introduce him to Lord Penrod."

Once—not long ago—Fatren would probably have complained about being handed off. However, his time with Elend had transformed him surprisingly quickly. The dirty leader nodded gratefully at the escort. "You . . . aren't coming with us then, my lord?"

Elend shook his head. "I have other work to do, and your people need to get to Luthadel, where they can begin farming. Though, if any of your men wish to join my army, they are welcome. I'm always in need of good troops, and against the odds, you succeeded in training a useful force."

"My lord . . . why not just compel them? Pardon me, but that's what you've done so far."

"I compelled your people to safety, Fatren," Elend said. "Sometimes even a drowning man will fight the one who tries to save him and must be compelled. My army is a different matter. Men who don't want to fight are men you can't depend on in battle, and I won't have any of those in my army. You yourself need to go to Luthadel—your people need you—but please let your soldiers know that I will gladly welcome any of them into our ranks."

Fatren nodded. "All right. And . . . thank you, my lord."

"You are welcome. Now, General Demoux, are Sazed and Breeze back yet?"

"They should arrive sometime this evening, my lord," Demoux said. "One of their men rode ahead to let us know."

"Good," Elend said. "I assume my tent is ready?"

"Yes, my lord," Demoux said.

Elend nodded, suddenly looking very tired to Vin.

"My lord?" Demoux asked eagerly. "Did you find the . . . other item? The location of the final cache?"

Elend nodded. "It's in Fadrex."

"Cett's city?" Demoux asked, laughing. "Well, he'll be happy to hear that. He's been complaining for over a year that we haven't ever gotten around to conquering it back for him."

Elend smiled wanly. "I've been half convinced that if we did, Cett would decide that he—and his soldiers—didn't need us anymore."

"He'll stay, my lord," Demoux said. "After the scare Lady Vin gave him last year . . ."

Demoux glanced at Vin, trying to smile, but she saw it in his eyes. Respect, far too much of it. He didn't joke with her the way he did with Elend. She still couldn't believe that Elend had joined that silly religion of theirs. Elend's intentions had been political—by joining the skaa faith, Elend had forged a link between himself and the common people. Even so, the move made her uncomfortable.

A year of marriage had taught her, however, that there

were some things one just had to ignore. She could love Elend for his desire to do the right thing, even when she thought he'd done the opposite.

"Call a meeting this evening, Demoux," Elend said. "We have much to discuss—and let me know when Sazed arrives."

"Should I inform Lord Hammond and the others of the meeting's agenda, my lord?"

Elend paused, glancing toward the ashen sky. "Conquering the world, Demoux," he finally said. "Or, at least, what's left of it."

Allomancy was, indeed, born with the mists. Or, at least, Allomancy began at the same time as the mists' first appearances. When Rashek took the power at the Well of Ascension, he became aware of certain things. Some were whispered to him by Ruin; others were granted to him as an instinctive part of the power.

One of these was an understanding of the Three Metallic Arts. He knew, for instance, that the nuggets of metal in the Chamber of Ascension would make those who ingested them into Mistborn. These were, after all, fractions of the very power in the Well itself.

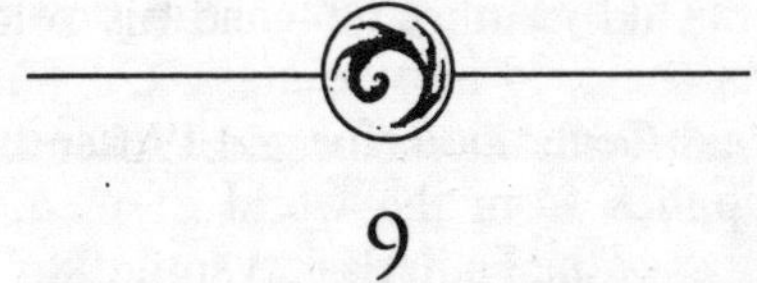

9

TENSOON HAD VISITED THE TRUSTWARREN before; he was of the Third Generation. He had been born seven centuries ago, when the kandra were still new—though by that time, the First Generation had already given over the raising of new kandra to the Second Generation.

The Seconds hadn't done very well with TenSoon's

generation—or, at least, that was how the Seconds felt. They'd wanted to form a society of individuals who followed strict rules of respect and seniority. A "perfect" people who lived to serve their Contracts—and, of course, the members of the Second Generation.

Up until his return, TenSoon had generally been considered one of the least troublesome of the Thirds. He'd been known as a kandra who cared little for Homeland politics; one who served out his Contracts, content to keep himself as far away from the Seconds and their machinations as possible. It was ironic indeed that TenSoon would end up on trial for the most heinous of kandra crimes.

His guards marched him right into the center of the Trustwarren—onto the platform itself. TenSoon wasn't certain whether to be honored or ashamed. Even as a member of the Third Generation, he hadn't often been allowed so near the Trust.

The room was large and circular, with metal walls. The platform was a massive steel disk set into the rock floor. It wasn't very high—perhaps a foot tall—but it was ten feet in diameter. TenSoon's feet felt cold hitting its slick surface, and he was reminded again of his nudity. They didn't bind his hands; that would have been too much of an insult even for him. Kandra obeyed the Contract, even those of the Third Generation. He would not run, and he would not strike down one of his own. He was better than that.

The room was lit by lamps, rather than glowstone, though each lamp was enclosed in blue glass. Oil was difficult to get—the Second Generation, for good reason, didn't want to rely on supplies from the world of men. The people above, even most of the Father's servants, didn't know there was a centralized kandra government. It was much better that way.

In the blue light, TenSoon could easily see the members of the Second Generation—all twenty of them, standing behind their lecterns, arranged in tiers on the far side of the room. They were close enough to see, study, and speak to—yet far enough away that TenSoon felt isolated, standing alone in the center of the platform. His feet were cold. He looked down, and noticed the small hole in the floor near his toes. It was cut into the steel disk of the platform.

The Trust, he thought. It was directly underneath him.

"TenSoon of the Third Generation," a voice said.

TenSoon looked up. It was KanPaar, of course. He was a tall kandra—or, rather, he preferred to use a tall True Body. Like all of the Seconds, his bones were constructed of the purest crystal—his with a deep red tint. It was an impractical body in many ways. Those bones wouldn't stand up to much punishment. Yet, for the life of an administrator in the Homeland, the weakness of the bones was apparently an acceptable trade-off for their sparkling beauty.

"I am here," TenSoon said.

"You insist on forcing this trial?" KanPaar said, keeping his voice lofty, reinforcing his thick accent. By staying away from humans for so long, his language hadn't been corrupted by their dialects. The Seconds' accents were similar to that of the Father, supposedly.

"Yes," TenSoon said.

KanPaar sighed audibly, standing behind his fine stone lectern. Finally, he bowed his head toward the upper reaches of the room. The First Generation watched from above. They sat in their individual alcoves running around the perimeter of the upper room, shadowed to the point where they were little more than humanoid lumps. They did not speak. That was for the Seconds.

The doors behind TenSoon opened, and hushed voices sounded, feet rustling. He turned, smiling to himself as he watched them enter. Kandra of various sizes and ages. The very youngest ones wouldn't be allowed to attend an event this important, but those of the adult generations—everyone up through the Ninth Generation—could not be denied. This was his victory, perhaps the only one he would have in the entire trial.

If he was to be condemned to endless imprisonment, then he wanted his people to know the truth. More important, he wanted them to hear this trial, to hear what he had to say. He would not convince the Second Generation, and who knew what the Firsts would silently think, sitting in their shadowed alcoves? The younger kandra, however . . . perhaps they would listen. Perhaps they would do something, once TenSoon was gone. He watched them file in, filling the stone benches. There were hundreds of kandra now. The elder generations—Firsts, Seconds, Thirds—were small in number, since many had been killed in the early days, when the humans had feared them. However, later generations were well populated—the Tenth Generation had over a hundred individuals in it. The Trustwarren's benches had been constructed to hold the entire kandra population, but they were now filled just by those who happened to be free from both duty and Contract.

He had hoped that MeLaan wouldn't be in that group. Yet, she was virtually the first in the doors. For a moment, he worried that she'd rush across the chamber—stepping on the platform, where only the most blessed or cursed were allowed. Instead, she froze just inside the doorway, forcing others to push around her in annoyance as they found seats.

He shouldn't have recognized her. She had a new True Body—an eccentric one, with bones made of wood. They were thin and willowy in an exaggerated, unnatural way: her wooden skull long with a pointed triangular chin, her eyes too large, twisted bits of cloth sticking from her head like hair. The younger generations were pushing the boundaries of propriety, annoying the Seconds. Once, TenSoon would probably have agreed with them—even now, he was something of a traditionalist. Yet, this day, her rebellious body simply made him smile.

That seemed to give her comfort, and she found a seat, near the front, with a group of other Seventh Generationers. They all had deformed True Bodies—one too much like a block, another actually sporting four arms.

"TenSoon of the Third Generation," KanPaar said formally, quieting the crowd of watching kandra. "You have obstinately demanded judgment before the First Generation. By the First Contract, we cannot condemn you without first allowing you the opportunity to plead before the Firsts. Should they see fit to stay your punishment, you will be freed. Otherwise, you must accept the fate the Council of Seconds assigns you."

"I understand," TenSoon said.

"Then," KanPaar said, leaning forward on his lectern. "Let us begin."

He's not worried at all, TenSoon realized. *He actually sounds like he's going to enjoy this.*

And why not? After centuries of preaching that the Third Generation is filled with miscreants? They've tried all this time to overcome their mistakes with us—mistakes like giving us too much freedom, letting us think that we were as good as they were. By proving that I—the most "temperate" of the Thirds—am a danger, KanPaar will win a struggle he's been fighting for most of his life.

TenSoon had always found it strange how threatened the Seconds felt by the Thirds. It had taken them only one generation to understand their mistakes—the Fourths were nearly as loyal as the Fifths, with only a few deviant members.

And yet, with some of the younger generations—MeLaan and her friends providing an example—acting as they did . . . well, perhaps the Seconds had a right to feel threatened. And TenSoon was to be their sacrifice. Their way of restoring order and orthodoxy.

They were certainly in for a surprise.

Nuggets of pure Allomancy, the power of Preservation itself. Why Rashek left one of those nuggets at the Well of Ascension, I do not know. Perhaps he didn't see it, or perhaps he intended to save it to bestow upon a fortunate servant.

Perhaps he feared that someday, he would lose his powers,

and would need that nugget to grant him Allomancy. Either way, I bless Rashek for his oversight, for without that nugget, Elend would have died that day at the Well.

10

LARSTAISM WAS A DIFFICULT ONE for Sazed to measure. The religion seemed innocent enough. They knew much about it; a Keeper during the fourth century had managed to uncover an entire trove of prayer materials, scriptures, notes, and writings which had once belonged to a high-ranking member of the religion.

And yet, the religion itself didn't seem very . . . well, religious. It had focused on art, not the sacred in the usual sense, and had centered around donating money to support monks so that they could compose poetry and paint and sculpt works of art. That, actually, blocked Sazed's attempts to dismiss it, as he couldn't find any contradictions in its doctrines. It just didn't have enough of those for them to conflict with one another.

He held the paper in front of him, shaking his head, reading over the sheet again. It was strapped to the front of the portfolio to keep it from being caught in the wind, and a parasol strapped to his saddle kept most of the ash from smearing the page. He had heard Vin complain that she didn't know how people could possibly read while riding a horse, but this method made it rather easy.

He didn't have to turn pages. He simply read the same words over and over, turning them in his mind, playing with them. Trying to decide. Did this one have the truth? It was the one that Mare, Kelsier's wife, had believed. She'd been one of the few people Sazed had ever met who had chosen to believe in one of the old religions he had preached.

The Larsta believed that life was about seeking the divine, he read. *They taught that art draws us closer to understanding divinity. Since not all men can spend their time in art, it is to the benefit of society as a whole to support a group of dedicated artists to create great works, which then elevate those who experience them.*

That was all well and good, in Sazed's estimation, but what about questions of life and death? What about the spirit? What *was* the divine, and how could such terrible things happen to the world if divinity did exist?

"You know," Breeze said from the saddle of his horse, "there's something amazing about all of this."

The comment broke Sazed's concentration. He sighed, looking up from his research. The horse continued to clop along beneath him. "Amazing about what, Lord Breeze?"

"The ash," Breeze said. "I mean, look at it. Covering everything, making the land look so black. It's simply astounding how *dreary* the landscape has become. Back in the Lord Ruler's reign, everything was brown, and most plants grown outdoors looked as if they were on the very edge of sickly death. I thought *that* was depressing. But ash falling every day, burying the entire land . . ." The Soother shook his head, smiling. "I wouldn't have thought it possible for things to actually be worse without the Lord Ruler. But, well, we've certainly made a mess! Destroying the world. That's no mean feat, if you think about it. I wonder if we should be impressed with ourselves."

Sazed frowned. Occasional flakes drifted from the sky, the upper atmosphere darkened by its usual dark haze. The ashfall was light, if persistent, falling steadily for nearly two months now. Their horses moved through a good half-foot of the stuff as they moved southward, accompanied by a hundred of Elend's soldiers. How long would it be before the ash grew so deep that travel was impossible? It already drifted several feet high in some places.

Everything was black—the hills, the road, the entire countryside. Trees drooped with the weight of ash on their leaves and branches. Most of the ground foliage was likely dead—bringing even two horses with them on the trip to Lekal City had been difficult, for there was nothing for them to graze on. The soldiers had been forced to carry feed.

"I do have to say, however," Breeze continued, chatting along in his normal way, protected from the ash by a parasol attached to the back of his saddle, "the ash *is* a tad unimaginative."

"Unimaginative?"

"Why, yes," Breeze said. "While I do happen to like black as a color for suits, I otherwise find it a somewhat uninspired hue."

"What else would the ash be?"

Breeze shrugged. "Well, Vin says that there's something behind all this, right? Some evil force of doom or whatever? Well, if *I* were said force of doom, then I certainly wouldn't have used my powers to turn the land black. It just lacks flair. Red. Now, *that* would be an interesting color. Think of the possibilities—if the ash were red, the rivers would run like blood. Black is so monotonous that you can forget about it, but red—you'd always be thinking, 'Why, look at that. That hill is red. That evil force of doom trying to destroy me certainly has style.' "

"I'm not convinced there is any 'evil force of doom,' Breeze," Sazed said.

"Oh?"

Sazed shook his head. "The ashmounts have *always* spewed out ash. Is it really that much of a stretch to assume that they have become more active than before? Perhaps this is all the result of natural processes."

"And the mists?"

"Weather patterns change, Lord Breeze," Sazed said. "Perhaps it was simply too warm during the day for them to come out before. Now that the ashmounts are emitting more ash, it would make sense that the days are growing colder, and so the mists stay longer."

"Oh? And if that were the case, my dear man, then why haven't the mists stayed out during the day in the winters? It was colder then than the summer, but the mists always left when day arrived."

Sazed grew silent. Breeze made a good point. Yet, as Sazed checked each new religion off of his list, he wondered more and more if they were simply *creating* an enemy in this "force" Vin had felt. He didn't know anymore. He didn't believe for a moment that she would have fabricated her stories. Yet, if there were no truth in the religions, was it too much of a stretch to infer that the world was simply ending because it was time?

"Green," Breeze finally said.

Sazed turned.

"Now, that would be a color with style," Breeze said. "Different. You can't see green and forget about it—not like you can black or brown. Wasn't Kelsier always talking about plants being green, once? Before the Ascension of the Lord Ruler, before the first time the Deepness came upon the land?"

"That's what the histories claim."

Breeze nodded thoughtfully. "Style indeed," he said. "It would be pretty, I think."

"Oh?" Sazed asked, genuinely surprised. "Most people with whom I have spoken seem to find the concept of green plants rather odd."

"I thought that once, but now, after seeing black all day, every day . . . Well, I think a little variety would be nice. Fields of green . . . little specks of color . . . what did Kelsier call those?"

"Flowers," Sazed said. The Larsta had written poems about them.

"Yes," Breeze said. "It will be nice when those return."

"Return?"

Breeze shrugged. "Well, the Church of the Survivor teaches that Vin will someday cleanse the sky of ash and the air of mists. I figure while she's at it, she might as well bring back the plants and the flowers. Seems like a suitably feminine thing to do, for some reason."

Sazed sighed, shaking his head. "Lord Breeze," he said, "I realize that you are simply trying to encourage me. However, I have serious trouble believing that *you* accept the teachings of the Church of the Survivor."

Breeze hesitated. Then, he smiled. "So I overdid it a bit, did I?"

"A tad."

"It's difficult to tell with you, my dear man. You're so aware of my touch on your emotions that I can't use much Allomancy, and you've been so . . . well, different lately." Breeze's voice grew wistful. "Still, it would be nice to see those green plants our Kelsier always spoke of. After six months of ash . . . well, it makes a man at least *want* to believe. Perhaps that's enough for an old hypocrite like me."

The sense of despair inside Sazed wanted to snap that simply *believing* wasn't enough. Wishing and believing hadn't gotten him anywhere. It wouldn't change the fact that the plants were dying and the world was ending.

It wasn't worth fighting, because nothing meant anything.

Sazed forced himself to stop that line of thought, but it was difficult. He worried, sometimes, about his melancholy. Unfortunately, much of the time, he had trouble summoning even the effort to care about his own pessimistic bent.

The Larsta, he told himself. *Focus on that religion. You need to make a decision.*

Breeze's comments had set Sazed thinking. The Larsta focused so much on beauty and art as being "divine." Well, if divinity was in any way related to art, then a god *couldn't* in any way be involved in what was happening to the world. The ash, the dismal, depressing landscape . . . it was more than just "unimaginative," as Breeze had put it. It was completely insipid. Dull. Monotonous.

Religion not true, Sazed wrote at the bottom of the paper. *Teachings are directly contradicted by observed events.*

He undid the straps on his portfolio and slipped the sheet in, one step closer to having gone through all of them. Sazed could see Breeze watching out of the corner of his eye; the Soother loved secrets. Sazed doubted the man would be all that impressed if he discovered what the work was really about. Either way, Sazed just wished that Breeze would leave him alone when it came to these studies.

I shouldn't be curt with him, though, Sazed thought. He

knew the Soother was, in his own way, just trying to help. Breeze had changed since they'd first met. Early on—despite glimmers of compassion—Breeze really had been the selfish, callous manipulator that he now only pretended to be. Sazed suspected that Breeze had joined Kelsier's team not out of a desire to help the skaa, but because of the challenge the scheme had presented, not to mention the rich reward Kelsier had promised.

That reward—the Lord Ruler's atium cache—had proven to be a myth. Breeze had found other rewards instead.

Up ahead, Sazed noticed someone moving through the ash. The figure wore black, but against the field of ash, it was easy to pick out even a hint of flesh tone. It appeared to be one of their scouts. Captain Goradel called the line to a halt, then sent a man forward to meet the scout. Sazed and Breeze waited patiently.

"Scout report, Lord Ambassador," Captain Goradel said, walking up to Sazed's horse a short time later. "The emperor's army is just a few hills away—less than an hour."

"Good," Sazed said, relishing the thought of seeing something other than the dreary hills of black.

"They've apparently seen us, Lord Ambassador," Goradel said. "Riders are approaching. In fact, they are—"

"Here," Sazed said, nodding into the near distance, where he saw a rider crest the hill. This one was very easy to pick out against the black. Not only was it moving very quickly—actually galloping its poor horse along the road—but it was also pink.

"Oh, dear," Breeze said with a sigh.

The bobbing figure resolved into a young woman with golden hair, wearing a bright pink dress—one that made her look younger than her twenty-something years. Allrianne had a fondness for lace and frills, and she tended to wear colors that made her stand out. Sazed might have expected someone like her to be a poor equestrian. Allrianne, however, rode with easy mastery, something one would need in order to remain on the back of a galloping horse while wearing such a frivolous dress.

The young woman reared her horse up in front of Sazed's soldiers, spinning the animal in a flurry of ruffled fabric and golden hair. About to dismount, she hesitated, eyeing the half-foot-deep layer of ash on the ground.

"Allrianne?" Breeze asked after a moment of silence.

"Hush," she said. "I'm trying to decide if it's worth getting my dress dirty to scamper over and hug you."

"We could wait until we get back to the camp . . ."

"I couldn't embarrass you in front of your soldiers that way," she said.

"Technically, my dear," Breeze said, "they're not *my* soldiers at all, but Sazed's."

Reminded of Sazed's presence, Allrianne looked up. She smiled prettily toward Sazed, then bent herself in a horseback version of a curtsy. "Lord Ambassador," she said, and Sazed felt a sudden—and unnatural—fondness for the young lady. She was Rioting him. If there was anyone more brazen with their Allomantic powers than Breeze, it was Allrianne.

"Princess," Sazed said, nodding his head to her.

Finally, Allrianne made her decision and slipped off the horse. She didn't quite "scamper"—instead, she held up her dress in a rather unladylike fashion. It would have been immodest if she hadn't been wearing what appeared to be several layers of lace petticoats underneath.

Eventually, Captain Goradel came over and helped her up onto Breeze's horse so that she was sitting in the saddle in front of him. The two had never been officially married—partially, perhaps, because Breeze felt embarrassed to be in a relationship with a woman so much younger than himself. When pressed on the issue, Breeze had explained that he didn't want to leave her as a widow when he died—something he seemed to assume would happen immediately, though he was only in his mid-forties.

We'll all die soon, the way things are going, Sazed thought. *Our ages do not matter.*

Perhaps that was part of why Breeze had finally accepted having a relationship with Allrianne. Either way, it was obvious from the way he looked at her—from the way he held her with a delicate, almost reverent touch—that he loved her very much.

Our social structure is breaking down, Sazed thought as the column began to march again. *Once, the official stamp of a marriage would have been essential, especially in a relationship involving a young woman of her rank.*

And yet, who was there to be "official" for now? The obligators were all but extinct. Elend and Vin's government was a thing of wartime necessity—a utilitarian, martially organized alliance of cities. And looming over it all was the growing awareness that something was seriously wrong with the world.

Why bother to get married if you expected the world would end before the year was out?

Sazed shook his head. This was a time when people needed structure—needed *faith*—to keep them going. He should have been the one to give it to them. The Church of the Survivor tried, but it was too new, and its adherents were too inexperienced with religion. Already there were arguments about doctrine and methodology, and each city of the New Empire was developing its own mutant variant of the religion.

In the past, Sazed had taught religions without feeling a need to believe in each one. He'd accepted each as being special in its own way, and offered them up, as a waiter might serve an appetizer he himself didn't feel like eating.

Doing so now seemed hypocritical to Sazed. If this people needed faith, then he should not be the one to give it to them. He would not teach lies, not anymore.

Sazed splashed his face with the basin's cold water, enjoying the pleasurable shock. The water dribbled down his cheeks and chin, carrying with it stains of ash. He dried his face with a clean towel, then took out his razor and mirror so that he could shave his head properly.

"Why do you keep doing that?" asked an unexpected voice.

Sazed spun. His tent in the camp had been empty just moments before. Now, however, someone stood behind him. Sazed smiled. "Lady Vin."

She folded her arms, raising an eyebrow. She had always moved stealthily, but she was getting so good that it amazed even him. She'd barely rustled the tent flap with her entrance. She wore her standard shirt and trousers, after male fashion, though during the last two years she had grown her raven hair to a feminine shoulder length. There had been a time when Vin had seemed to crouch wherever she went, always trying to hide, rarely looking others in the eye. That had changed. She was still easy to miss, with her quiet ways, thin figure, and small stature. She now always looked people in the eye, however.

And that made a big difference.

"General Demoux said that you were resting, Lady Vin," Sazed noted.

"Demoux knows better than to let me sleep through your arrival."

Sazed smiled to himself, then gestured toward a chair so that she could sit.

"You can keep shaving," she said. "It's all right."

"Please," he said, gesturing again.

Vin sighed, taking the seat. "You never answered my question, Saze," she said. "Why do you keep wearing those steward's robes? Why do you keep your head shaved, after the fashion of a Terris servant? Why worry about showing disrespect by shaving while I'm here? You're not a servant anymore."

He sighed, carefully seating himself in the chair across from Vin. "I'm not exactly sure *what* I am anymore, Lady Vin."

The tent walls flapped in a gentle breeze, a bit of ash blowing in through the door, which Vin hadn't tied closed behind herself. She frowned at his comment. "You're Sazed."

"Emperor Venture's chief ambassador."

"No," Vin said. "That might be what you *do,* but that's not what you *are.*"

"And what am I, then?"

"Sazed," she repeated. "Keeper of Terris."

"A Keeper who no longer wears his copperminds?"

Vin glanced toward the corner, toward the trunk where he kept them. His copperminds, the Feruchemical storages that contained the religions, histories, stories, and legends of peoples long dead. It all sat waiting to be taught, waiting to be added to. "I fear that I have become a very selfish man, Lady Vin," Sazed said quietly.

"That's silly," Vin said. "You've spent your entire life serving others. I know of nobody more selfless than you."

"I do appreciate that sentiment," he said. "But I fear that I must disagree. Lady Vin, we are not a people new to sorrow. You know better than anyone here, I think, the hardships of life in the Final Empire. We have all lost people dear to us. And yet, I seem to be the only one unable to get over my loss. I feel childish. Yes, Tindwyl is dead. In all honesty, I did not have much time with her before she did pass. I have no reason to feel as I do.

"Still, I cannot wake up in the morning and not see darkness ahead of me. When I place the metalminds upon my arms, my skin feels cold, and I remember time spent with her. Life lacks all hope. I should be able to move on, but I cannot. I am weak of will, I think."

"That just isn't true, Sazed," Vin said.

"I must disagree."

"Oh?" Vin asked. "And if you really were weak of will, would you be able to disagree with me?"

Sazed paused, then smiled. "When did you get so good at logic?"

"Living with Elend," Vin said with a sigh. "If you prefer irrational arguments, don't marry a scholar."

I almost did. The thought came to Sazed unbidden, but it quieted his smile nonetheless. Vin must have noticed, for she cringed slightly.

"Sorry," she said, looking away.

"It is all right, Lady Vin," Sazed said. "I just . . . I feel so weak. I cannot be the man my people wish me to be. I am, perhaps, the very last of the Keepers. It has been a year since the Inquisitors attacked my homeland, killing even the child Feruchemists, and we have seen no evidence that others of my sect survived. Others were out of the city, certainly and inevitably, but either Inquisitors found them or other tragedy did. There has certainly been enough of that lately, I think."

Vin sat with her hands in her lap, looking uncharacteristically weak in the dim light. Sazed frowned at the pained expression on her face. "Lady Vin?"

"I'm sorry," she said. "It's just that . . . you've always been the one who gives advice, Sazed. But, now what I need advice about is you."

"There is no advice to give, I fear."

They sat in silence for a few moments.

"We found the stockpile," Vin said. "The next-to-last cavern. I made a copy for you of the words we found, etched in a thin sheet of steel so they'll be safe."

"Thank you."

Vin sat, looking uncertain. "You're not going to look at it, are you?"

Sazed paused, then shook his head. "I do not know."

"I can't do this alone, Sazed," Vin whispered. "I can't fight it by myself. I *need* you."

The tent grew quiet. "I . . . am doing what I can, Lady Vin," Sazed finally said. "In my own way. I must find answers for myself before I can provide them to anyone else. Still, have the etching delivered to my tent. I promise that I will at least look at it."

She nodded, then stood. "Elend's having a meeting tonight. To plan our next moves. He wants you there." She trailed a faint perfume as she moved to leave. She paused beside his chair. "There was a time," she said, "after I'd taken the power at the Well of Ascension, when I thought Elend would die."

"But he did not," Sazed said. "He lives still."

"It doesn't matter," Vin said. "I thought him dead. I knew he was dying—I held that power, Sazed, power *you can't imagine*. Power you'll never be able to imagine. The power to destroy worlds and remake them anew. The power to see and to understand. I saw him, and I knew he would die. And knew I held the power in my hands to save him."

Sazed looked up.

"But I didn't," Vin said. "I let him bleed, and released the power instead. I consigned him to death."

"How?" Sazed asked. "How could you do such a thing?"

"Because I looked into his eyes," Vin said, "and knew it was what he wanted me to do. You gave me that, Sazed. You taught me to love him enough to let him die."

She left him alone in the tent. A few moments later, he returned to his shaving, and found something sitting beside his basin. A small, folded piece of paper.

It contained an aged, fading drawing of a strange plant. A flower. The picture had once belonged to Mare. It had gone from her to Kelsier, and from him to Vin.

Sazed picked it up, wondering what Vin intended to say by leaving him the picture. Finally, he folded it up and slipped it into his sleeve, then returned to his shaving.

The First Contract, oft spoken of by the kandra, was originally just a series of promises made by the First Generation to the Lord Ruler. They wrote these promises down, and in doing so codified the first kandra laws. They were worried about governing themselves, independently of the Lord Ruler and his empire. So, they took what they had written to him, asking for his approval.

He commanded it cast into steel, then personally scratched a signature into the bottom. This code was the first thing that a kandra learned upon awakening from his or her life as a mistwraith. It contained commands to revere earlier generations, simple legal rights granted to each kandra, provisions for creating new kandra, and a demand for ultimate dedication to the Lord Ruler.

Most disturbingly, the First Contract contained a provision which, if invoked, would require the mass suicide of the entire kandra people.

11

KANPAAR LEANED FORWARD ON HIS lectern, red crystalline bones sparkling in the lamplight. "All right, then, TenSoon, traitor to the kandra people. You have demanded this judgment. Make your plea."

TenSoon took a deep breath—it felt so good to be able to do that again—and opened his mouth to speak.

"Tell them," KanPaar continued, sneering, "explain, if you can, why you killed one of our own. A fellow kandra."

TenSoon froze. The Trustwarren was quiet—the generations of kandra were far too well behaved to rustle and make noise like a crowd of humans. They sat with their bones of rock, wood, or even metal, waiting for TenSoon's answer.

KanPaar's question wasn't the one TenSoon had expected.

"Yes, I killed a kandra," TenSoon said, standing cold and naked on the platform. "That is not forbidden."

"Need it be forbidden?" KanPaar accused, pointing. "Humans kill each other. Koloss kill each other. But they are both of Ruin. *We* are of Preservation, the chosen of the Father himself. We don't kill one another!"

TenSoon frowned. This was a strange line of questioning. *Why ask this?* he thought. *My betrayal of all our people is surely a greater sin than the murder of one.*

"I was compelled by my Contract," TenSoon said frankly. "You must know, KanPaar. *You* are the one who assigned me to the man Straff Venture. We all know what kind of person he was."

"No different from any other *man,*" spat one of the Seconds.

Once, TenSoon would have agreed. Yet, he knew that there were some humans, at least, who *were* different. He had betrayed Vin, and yet she hadn't hated him for it. She had understood, and had felt mercy. Even if they hadn't already become friends, even if he hadn't grown to respect her greatly, that one moment would have earned her his devoted loyalty.

She was counting on him, even if she didn't know it. He stood a little straighter, looking KanPaar in the eyes. "I was assigned to the man Straff Venture by paid Contract," TenSoon said. "He gave me over to the whims of his twisted son, Zane. It was Zane who commanded that I kill the kandra OreSeur and take his place, so that I could spy on the woman Vin."

There were a few hushed whispers at her name. *Yes, you've heard of her. The one who slew the Father.*

"And so you did what this Zane commanded?" KanPaar asked loudly. "You killed another kandra. You murdered a *member of your own generation*!"

"You think I enjoyed it?" TenSoon demanded. "OreSeur was my generation brother—a kandra I had known for seven hundred years! But . . . the Contract . . ."

"Forbids killing," KanPaar said.

"It forbids the killing of men."

"And is not a kandra life worth more than that of a man?"

"The words are specific, KanPaar," TenSoon snapped. "I know them well—I helped write them! We were both there when these service Contracts were created using the First Contract itself as a model! They forbid us from killing humans, but not each other."

KanPaar leaned forward again. "Did you argue with this Zane? Suggest perhaps that he should perform the murder himself? Did you even try to get out of killing one of our people?"

"I do not argue with my masters," TenSoon said. "And I certainly didn't want to tell the man Zane how to kill a kandra. His instability was well known."

"So, you didn't argue," KanPaar said. "You simply killed OreSeur. And then you took his place, pretending to be him."

"That is what we do," TenSoon said with frustration. "We take the place of others, acting as spies. That is the entire *point* of the Contract!"

"We do these things to *humans,*" snapped another Second. "This is the first case where a kandra has been used to imitate another kandra. It is a disturbing precedent you set."

It was brilliant, TenSoon thought. *I hate Zane for making me do it, but I can still see the genius in it. Vin never even suspected me. Who would?*

"You should have refused to do this act," KanPaar said. "You should have pled the need for clarification of your Contract. If others were to begin using us in this way, to kill one another, then we could be wiped out in a matter of years!"

"You betrayed us all with your rashness," said another.

Ah, TenSoon thought. *So that is their plan. They establish me as a traitor first, so that what I say later lacks credibility.* He smiled. He was of the Third Generation; it was time he started acting like it.

"I betrayed us with my rashness?" TenSoon asked. "What of you, glorious Seconds? Who was it who allowed a Contract to be assigned to Kelsier himself? You gave a kandra servant *to the very man who was planning to kill the Father*!"

KanPaar stiffened, as if he'd been slapped, translucent face angry in the blue lamplight. "It is not your place to make accusations, Third!"

"I have no place anymore, it seems," TenSoon said. "None of us do, now that the Father is dead. We have no right to complain, for we helped it happen."

"How were we to know this man would succeed when others hadn't," a Second sputtered. "He paid so well that—"

KanPaar cut the other off with a sharp wave of the hand. It wasn't good for those of the Second Generation to defend themselves. However, HunFoor—the kandra who had spoken—hadn't ever really fit in with the others of his generation. He was a little more . . . dense.

"You shall speak no more of this, Third," KanPaar said, pointing at TenSoon.

"How can I defend myself if I cannot—"

"You aren't *here* to defend yourself," KanPaar said. "This is not a trial—you have already admitted your guilt. This is a judgment. Explain your actions, then let the First Generation pronounce your fate!"

TenSoon fell silent. It was not time to push. Not yet.

"Now," KanPaar said, "this thing you did in taking the place of one of your own brothers is bad enough. Need we speak on, or would you accept judgment now?"

"We both know that OreSeur's death has little to do with why I am here," TenSoon said.

"Very well," said KanPaar. "Let us move on, then. Why don't you tell the First Generation why—if you are such a Contract-abiding kandra—you *broke* Contract with your master, disobeying his interests and helping his enemy instead?"

KanPaar's accusation echoed in the room. TenSoon closed his eyes, thinking back to that day over a year ago. He remembered sitting quietly on the floor of Keep Venture, watching as Zane and Vin fought.

No. It hadn't been a fight. Zane had been burning atium, which had made him all but invincible. Zane had played with Vin, toying with and mocking her.

Vin hadn't been TenSoon's master—TenSoon had killed her kandra and taken his place, spying on Vin at Zane's order. Zane. *He* had been TenSoon's master. *He* had held TenSoon's Contract.

But against all of his training, TenSoon had helped Vin. And, in doing so, he had revealed to her the great Secret of the kandra. Their weakness: that an Allomancer could use their powers to take complete control of a kandra's body. The kandra served their Contracts to keep this Secret hidden—they became servants, lest they end up as slaves. TenSoon opened his eyes to the quiet chamber. This was the moment he had been planning for.

"I didn't break my Contract," he announced.

KanPaar snorted. "You said otherwise when you came to us a year ago, Third."

"I told you what happened," TenSoon said, standing tall. "What I said was not a lie. I helped Vin instead of Zane. Partially because of my actions, my master ended up dead at Vin's feet. But I did not break my Contract."

"You imply that Zane *wanted* you to help his enemy?" KanPaar said.

"No," TenSoon said. "I did not break my Contract because I decided to serve a greater Contract. The First Contract!"

"The Father is dead!" one of the Seconds snapped. "How could you serve our Contract with him?"

"He is dead," TenSoon said. "That is true. But the First Contract did not die with him! Vin, the Heir of the Survivor, was the one who killed the Lord Ruler. *She* is our Mother now. Our First Contract is with her!"

He had expected outcries of blasphemy and condemnation. Instead, he got shocked silence. KanPaar stood, stupefied, behind his stone lectern. The members of the First Generation were silent, as usual, sitting in their shadowed alcoves.

Well, TenSoon thought, *I suppose that means I should continue.* "I *had* to help the woman Vin," he said. "I could not let Zane kill her, for I had a duty to her—a duty that began the moment she took the Father's place."

KanPaar finally found his voice. "*She*? Our Mother? She killed the Lord Ruler!"

"And took his place," TenSoon said. "She is one of us, in a way."

"Nonsense!" KanPaar said. "I had expected rationalizations, TenSoon—perhaps even lies. But these fantasies? These blasphemies?"

"Have you been outside recently, KanPaar?" TenSoon asked. "Have you left the Homeland in the last century at all? Do you understand what is happening? The Father is *dead.* The land is in upheaval. While returning to the Homeland a year ago, I saw the changes in the mists. They no longer behave as they always have. We cannot continue as we have. The Second Generation may not yet realize it, but Ruin has come! Life will end. The time that the World-bringers spoke of—perhaps the time for the Resolution—is here!"

"You are delusional, TenSoon. You've been amongst the humans too—"

"Tell them what this is all really about, KanPaar," Ten-Soon interrupted, voice rising. "Don't you want my *real* sin known? Don't you want the others to hear?"

"Don't force this, TenSoon," KanPaar said, pointing again. "What you've done is bad enough. Don't make it—"

"I told her," TenSoon said, cutting him off again. "I told her our *Secret.* At the end, she used me. Like the Allomancers of old. She took control of my body, using the Flaw, and she made me fight against Zane! *This* is what I've done. I've be-trayed us all. She knows—and I'm certain that she has told others. Soon they'll all know how to control us. And, do you know *why* I did it? Is it not the point of this judgment for me to speak of my purposes?"

He kept talking, despite the fact that KanPaar tried to speak over him. "I did it because she has the *right* to know our Secret," TenSoon shouted. "She is the Mother! She in-herited everything the Lord Ruler had. Without her, we have nothing. We cannot create new Blessings, or new kandra, on our own! The Trust is hers, now! We should go to her. If this truly is the end of all things, then the Resolution will soon come. She will—"

"Enough!" KanPaar bellowed.

The chamber fell silent again.

TenSoon stood, breathing deeply. For a year, trapped in his pit, he'd planned how to proclaim that information. His people had spent a thousand years, ten generations, follow-ing the teachings of the First Contract. They deserved to hear what had happened to him.

And yet, it felt so . . . inadequate to just scream it out like some raving human. Would any of his people really believe? Would he change anything at all?

"You have, by your own admission, betrayed us," KanPaar said. "You've broken Contract, you've murdered one of your own generation, and you've told a human how to dominate us. You demanded judgment. Let it come."

TenSoon turned quietly, looking up toward the alcoves where the members of the First Generation watched.

Perhaps . . . perhaps they'll see that what I say is true. Perhaps my words will shock them, and they'll realize that we need to offer service to Vin, rather than just sit in these caves and wait while the world ends around us.

But, nothing happened. No motion, no sound. At times, TenSoon wondered if anyone still lived up there. He hadn't spoken with a member of the First Generation for centuries—they limited their communications strictly to the Seconds.

If they did still live, none of them took the opportunity to offer TenSoon clemency. KanPaar smiled. "The First Generation has ignored your plea, Third," he said. "Therefore, as their servants, we of the Second Generation will offer judgment on their behalf. Your sentencing will occur in one month's time."

TenSoon frowned. *A month? Why wait?*

Either way, it was over. He bowed his head, sighing. He'd had his say. The kandra now knew that their Secret was out—the Seconds could no longer hide that fact. Perhaps his words would inspire his people to action.

TenSoon would probably never know.

Rashek moved the Well of Ascension, obviously.

It was very clever of him—perhaps the cleverest thing he did. He knew that the power would one day return to the Well, for power such as this—the fundamental power by which the world itself was formed—does not simply run out. It can be used, and therefore diffused, but it will always be renewed.

So, knowing that rumors and tales would persist, Rashek changed the very landscape of the world. He put mountains in what became the North, and named that location Terris. Then he flattened his true homeland, and built his capital there.

He constructed his palace around that room at its heart, the room where he would meditate, the room that was a replica of his old hovel in Terris. A refuge created during the last moments before his power ran out.

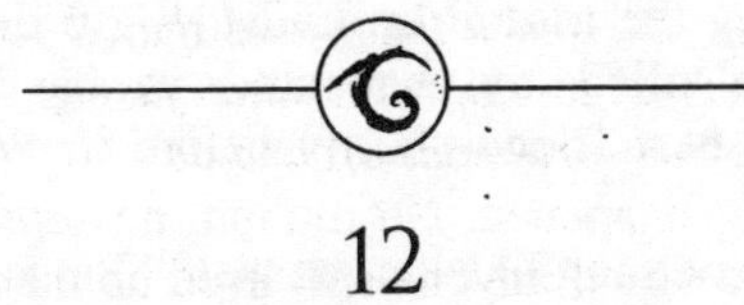

12

"I'M WORRIED ABOUT HIM, ELEND," Vin said, sitting on their bedroll.

"Who?" Elend asked, looking away from the mirror. "Sazed?"

Vin nodded. When Elend awoke from their nap, she was already up, bathed, and dressed. He worried about *her* sometimes, working herself as hard as she did. He worried even more now that he too was Mistborn, and understood the limitations of pewter. The metal strengthened the body, letting one postpone fatigue—but at a price. When the pewter ran out or was turned off, the fatigue returned, crashing down on you like a collapsing wall.

Yet Vin kept going. Elend was burning pewter too, pushing himself, but she seemed to sleep half as much as he did. She was harder than he was—strong in ways he would never know.

"Sazed will deal with his problems," Elend said, turning back to his dressing. "He must have lost people before."

"This is different," Vin said. He could see her in the reflection, sitting cross-legged behind him in her simple clothing. Elend's stark white uniform was just the opposite. It shone with its gold-painted wooden buttons, intentionally crafted with too little metal in them to be affected by Allomancy. The clothing itself had been made with a special cloth that was easier to scrub clean of ash. Sometimes, he felt guilty at all the work it took to make him look regal. Yet it was necessary. Not for his vanity, but for his image. The image for which his men marched to war. In a land of black, Elend wore white—and became a symbol.

"Different?" Elend asked, doing up the buttons on his jacket sleeves. "What is different about Tindwyl's death? She fell during the assault on Luthadel. So did Clubs and Dockson. You killed my own father in that battle, and I beheaded my best friend shortly before it. We've all lost people."

"He said something like that himself," Vin said. "But, it's more than just one death to him. I think he sees a kind of betrayal in Tindwyl's death—he always was the only one of us who had faith. He lost that when she died, somehow."

"The only one of us who had faith?" Elend asked, plucking a wooden, silver-painted pin off his desk and affixing it to his jacket. "What about this?"

"You belong to the Church of the Survivor, Elend," Vin said. "But you don't have faith. Not like Sazed did. It was like . . . he *knew* everything would turn out all right. He trusted that something was watching over the world."

"He'll deal with it."

"It's not just him, Elend," Vin said. "Breeze tries too hard."

"What does that mean?" Elend asked with amusement.

"He Pushes on everyone's emotions," Vin said. "He Pushes too hard, trying to make others happy, and he laughs too hard. He's afraid, worried. He shows it by overcompensating."

Elend smiled. "You're getting as bad as he is, reading everybody's emotions and telling them how they're feeling."

"They're my friends, Elend," Vin said. "I *know* them. And, I'm telling you—they're giving up. One by one, they're beginning to think we can't win this one."

Elend fastened the final button, then looked at himself in the mirror. Sometimes, he still wondered if he fit the ornate suit, with its crisp whiteness and implied regality. He looked into his own eyes, looking past the short beard, warrior's body, and scarred skin. He looked into those eyes, searching for the king behind them. As always, he wasn't completely impressed with what he saw.

He carried on anyway, for he was the best they had. Tindwyl had taught him that. "Very well," he said. "I trust that you're right about the others—I'll do something to fix it."

That, after all, was his job. The title of emperor carried with it only a single duty.

To make everything better.

"All right," Elend said, pointing to a map of the empire hanging on the wall of the conference tent. "We timed the arrival and disappearance of the mists each day, then Noorden and his scribes analyzed them. They've given us these perimeters as a guide."

The group leaned in, studying the map. Vin sat at the back of the tent, as was still her preference. Closer to the shadows. Closer to the exit. She'd grown more confident, true—but that didn't make her careless. She liked to be able to keep an eye on everyone in the room, even if she did trust them.

And she did. Except maybe Cett. The obstinate man sat at the front of the group, his quiet teenage son at his side, as always. Cett—or, *King* Cett, one of the monarchs who had sworn allegiance to Elend—had an unfashionable beard, an even more unfashionable mouth, and two legs that didn't work. That hadn't kept him from nearly conquering Luthadel over a year before.

"Hell," Cett said. "You expect us to be able to read that thing?"

Elend tapped the map with his finger. It was a rough sketch of the empire, similar to the one they'd found in the cavern, only more up to date. It had several large concentric circles inscribed on it.

"The outermost circle is the place where the mists have completely taken the land, and no longer leave at all during the daylight." Elend moved his finger inward to another circle. "This circle passes through the village we just visited, where we found the cache. This marks four hours of daylight. Everything inside the circle gets more than four hours. Everything outside of it gets less."

"And the final circle?" Breeze asked. He sat with Allrianne as far away from Cett as the tent would allow. Cett still had a habit of throwing things at Breeze: insults, for the most part, and occasionally knives.

Elend eyed the map. "Assuming the mists keep creeping toward Luthadel at the same rate, that circle represents the area that the scribes feel will get enough sunlight this summer to support crops."

The room fell silent.

Hope is for the foolish, Reen's voice seemed to whisper in the back of Vin's mind. She shook her head. Her brother, Reen, had trained her in the ways of the street and the underground, teaching her to be mistrustful and paranoid. In doing so, he'd also taught her to survive. It had taken Kelsier to show her that it was possible to both trust and survive—and it had been a hard lesson. Even so, she still often heard Reen's phantom voice in the back of her mind—more a memory than anything else—whispering her insecurities, bringing back the brutal things he had taught her.

"That's a fairly small circle, El," Ham said, still studying the map. The large-muscled man sat with General Demoux between Cett and Breeze. Sazed sat quietly to the side. Vin glanced at him, trying to judge if their previous conversation had lifted his depression any, but she couldn't tell.

They were a small group: only nine, if one counted Cett's son, Gneorndin. But, it included pretty much all that was left of Kelsier's crew. Only Spook, doing reconnaissance in the North, was missing. Everyone was focused on the map. The final circle was, indeed, very small—not even as big as the Central Dominance, which held the imperial capital of Luthadel. What the map said, and Elend implied, was that over ninety percent of the empire wouldn't be able to support crops this summer.

"Even this small bubble will be gone by next winter," Elend said.

Vin watched the others contemplate, and realize—if they hadn't already—the horror of what was upon them. *It's like Alendi's logbook said,* she thought. *They couldn't fight the Deepness with armies. It destroyed cities, bringing a slow, terrible death. They were helpless.*

The Deepness. That was what they'd called the mists—or, at least, that was what the surviving records called them. Perhaps the thing they fought, the primal force Vin had released, was behind the obfuscation. There was really no way of knowing for sure what had once been, for the entity had the power to change records.

"All right, people," Elend said, folding his arms. "We need options. Kelsier recruited you because you could do the impossible. Well, our predicament is pretty impossible."

"He didn't recruit me," Cett pointed out. "I got pulled by my balls into this little fiasco."

"I wish I cared enough to apologize," Elend said, staring at them. "Come on. I know you have thoughts."

"Well, my dear man," Breeze said, "the most obvious option appears to be the Well of Ascension. It seems the power there was built to fight the mists."

"Or to free the thing hiding in them," Cett said.

"That doesn't matter," Vin said, causing heads to turn. "There's no power at the Well. It's gone. Used up. If it ever returns, it will be in another thousand years, I suspect."

"That's a little bit long to stretch the supplies in those storage caches," Elend said.

"What if we grew plants that need very little light?" Ham asked. As always, he wore simple trousers and a vest. He was a Thug, and could burn pewter—which made him resistant to heat and cold. He'd cheerfully walk around sleeveless on a day that would send most men running for shelter.

Well, maybe not cheerfully. Ham hadn't changed overnight, as Sazed had. Ham, however, *had* lost some of his joviality. He tended to sit around a lot, looks of consternation on his face, as if he were considering things very, very carefully—and not much liking the answers he came up with.

"There are plants that don't need light?" Allrianne asked, cocking her head.

"Mushrooms and the like," Ham said.

"I doubt we could feed an entire empire on mushrooms," Elend said. "Though it's a good thought."

"There have to be other plants, too," Ham said. "Even if the mists come all day, there will be some light that gets through. Some plants have to be able to live on that."

"Plants we can't eat, my dear man," Breeze pointed out.

"Yes, but maybe animals can," Ham said.

Elend nodded thoughtfully.

"Blasted little time left for horticulture," Cett noted. "We should have been working on this sort of thing years ago."

"We didn't know most of this until a few months ago," Ham said.

"True," Elend said. "But the Lord Ruler had a thousand years to prepare. That's why he made the storage caverns—and we still don't know what the last one contains."

"I don't like relying on the Lord Ruler, Elend," Breeze said with a shake of his head. "He must have prepared those caches knowing that he'd be dead if anyone ever had to use them."

Cett nodded. "The idiot Soother has a point. If I were the Lord Ruler, I'd have stuffed those caches with poisoned food and pissed-in water. If I were dead, then everyone else ought to be as well."

"Fortunately, Cett," Elend said with a raised eyebrow, "the Lord Ruler has proven more altruistic than we might have expected."

"Not something I ever thought I'd hear," Ham noted.

"He was emperor," Elend said. "We may not have liked his rule, but I can understand him somewhat. He wasn't spiteful—he wasn't even evil, exactly. He just . . . got carried away. Besides, he resisted this thing that we're fighting."

"This thing?" Cett asked. "The mists?"

"No," Elend said. "The thing that was trapped in the Well of Ascension."

It is called Ruin, Vin thought suddenly. *It will destroy everything.*

"This is why I've decided we need to secure that last cache," Elend said. "The Lord Ruler lived through this once—he knew how to prepare. Perhaps we'll find plants that can grow without sunlight. Each of the caches so far has had repeats—food stores, water—but each one has held something new as well. In Vetitan, we found large stores of the first eight Allomantic metals. The thing in that last cache might be just what we need in order to survive."

"That's it, then!" Cett said, smiling broadly through his beard. "We *are* marching on Fadrex, aren't we?"

Elend nodded curtly. "Yes. The main force of the army will march for the Western Dominance once we break camp here."

"Ha!" Cett said. "Penrod and Janarle can suck on *that* for a few days."

Vin smiled faintly. Penrod and Janarle were the two other most important kings under Elend's imperial rule. Penrod governed Luthadel, which was why he wasn't with them currently, and Janarle ruled the Northern Dominance—the kingdom that included House Venture's hereditary lands.

The largest city in the north, however, had been seized in a revolt while Janarle—with Elend's father, Straff Venture—had been away laying siege to Luthadel. So far, Elend hadn't been able to spare the troops necessary to take Urteau back from its dissidents, so Janarle ruled in exile, his smaller force of troops used to maintain order in the cities he *did* control.

Both Janarle and Penrod had made a point of finding reasons to keep the main army from marching on Cett's homeland.

"Those bastards won't be at all happy when they hear about this," Cett said.

Elend shook his head. "Does everything you say have to contain one vulgarity or another?"

Cett shrugged. "What's the point of speaking if you can't say something interesting?"

"Swearing isn't interesting," Elend said.

"That's your own damned opinion," Cett said, smiling.

"And, you really shouldn't be complaining, Emperor. If you think the things *I* say are vulgar, you've been living in Luthadel far too long. Where I come from, people are embarrassed to use pretty words like 'damn.' "

Elend sighed. "Anyway, I—".

He was cut off as the ground began to shake. Vin was on her feet in seconds, looking for danger as the others cursed and reached for stability. She threw back the tent flap, peering through the mists. Yet, the shaking subsided quickly, and it caused very little chaos in the camp, all things considered. Patrols moved about, checking for problems—officers and Allomancers under Elend's command. Most of the soldiers, however, just remained in their tents.

Vin turned back toward the tent's room. A few of the chairs had fallen over, travel furniture disturbed by the earthquake. The others slowly returned to their seats. "Sure have been a lot of those lately," Ham said. Vin met Elend's eyes, and could see concern in them.

We can fight armies, we can capture cities, but what of ash, mists, and earthquakes? What about the world falling apart around us?

"Anyway," Elend said, voice firm despite the concerns Vin knew he must feel, "Fadrex has to be our next goal. We can't risk missing the cache, and the things it might contain."

Like the atium, Reen whispered in Vin's head as she sat back down. "Atium," she said out loud.

Cett perked up. "You think it'll be there?"

"There are theories," Elend said, eyeing Vin. "But we have no proof."

"It will be there," she said. *It has to be. I don't know why, but we* have *to have it.*

"I hope it isn't," Cett said. "I marched halfway across the blasted empire to try and steal that atium—if it turns out I left it beneath my own city . . ."

"I think we're missing something important, El," Ham said. "Are you talking about *conquering* Fadrex City?"

The room fell still. Up until this point, Elend's armies had been used defensively, attacking koloss garrisons or the camps of small warlords and bandits. They had bullied a few cities into joining with him, but they had never actually assaulted a city and taken it by force.

Elend turned, looking back toward the map. Even from the side, Vin could see his eyes—the eyes of a man hardened by two years of near-perpetual war.

"Our primary goal will be to take the city by diplomacy," Elend said.

"Diplomacy?" Cett said. "Fadrex is *mine*. That damn obligator stole it from me! There's no need to worry your conscience about attacking him, Elend."

"No need?" Elend asked, turning. "Cett, those are your people—your soldiers—we'd have to kill to get into that city."

"People die in war," Cett said. "Feeling bad about it doesn't remove the blood from your hands, so why bother? Those soldiers turned against me; they deserve what they'll get."

"It's not that simple," Ham said. "If there was no way for the soldiers to fight this usurper, then why expect them to give up their lives?"

"Especially for a man who was, himself, a usurper," Elend said.

"Either way," Ham said, "reports describe that city as being very well defended. It will be a tough stone to break, El."

Elend stood quietly for a moment, then eyed Cett, who still looked inordinately pleased with himself. The two seemed to share something—an understanding. Elend was a master of theory, and had probably read as much on war as anyone. Cett seemed to have a sixth sense for warfare and tactics, and had replaced Clubs as the empire's prime military strategist.

"Siege," Cett said.

Elend nodded. "If King Yomen won't respond to diplomacy, then the only way we'll get in that city—short of killing half our men breaking in—is by besieging it and making him desperate."

"Do we have time for that?" Ham asked, frowning.

"Besides Urteau," Elend said, "Fadrex City and the surrounding areas are the only major sections of the Inner Dominances that maintain a strong enough force to be threatening. That, plus the cache, means we can't afford to simply leave them alone."

"Time is on our side, in a way," Cett said, scratching his beard. "You don't just attack a city like Fadrex, Ham. It has fortifications, one of the few cities besides Luthadel that could repel an army. But, since it's outside of the Central Dominance, it's probably already hurting for food."

Elend nodded. "While we have all of the supplies we found in the storage caches. If we block off the highway, then hold the canal, they'll *have* to surrender the city eventually. Even if they've found the cache—which I doubt—we will be able to outlast them."

Ham frowned. "I guess. . . ."

"Besides," Elend added, "if things get tough, we do have about twenty thousand koloss we can draw upon."

Ham raised an eyebrow, though said nothing. The implication was clear. *You'd turn koloss against other people?*

"There is another element to this," Sazed said softly. "Something we have, as of yet, not discussed." Several people turned, as if they'd forgotten he was there.

"The mists," Sazed said. "Fadrex City lies well beyond the mist perimeter, Emperor Venture. Will you subject your army to fifteen percent casualties before you even arrive at the city?"

Elend fell quiet. So far, he'd managed to keep most of his soldiers out of the mists. It seemed wrong to Vin that their army had been protected from the sickness, while the villagers had been forced to go out in the mists. And yet, where they camped, there was still a significant amount of mistless daylight, and they also had enough tents to hold all of the soldiers, something they'd lacked when moving the villagers.

Mists rarely went into buildings, even cloth ones. There had been no reason to risk killing some of the soldiers, since they'd been able to avoid it. It seemed hypocritical to Vin, but so far, it still made sense.

Elend met Sazed's eyes. "You make a good point," he said. "We can't protect the soldiers from this forever. I forced the villagers of Vetitan to immunize themselves; I suspect that I will have to make the army do the same, for the same reasons."

Vin sat back quietly. She often wished for the days when she'd had nothing to do with such decisions—or, better yet, when Elend hadn't been forced to make them.

"We march for Fadrex," Elend said again, turning from the group. He pointed at the map. "If we're going to pull through this—and by 'we,' I mean all the people of the New Empire—we're going to need to band together and concentrate our populations near the Central Dominance. It will be the only place that can grow food this summer, and we'll need every bit of manpower we can muster to clear ash and prepare the fields. That means bringing the people of Fadrex under our protection.

"That also means," he said, pointing toward the northeastern section of the map, "that we'll need to suppress the rebellion in Urteau. Not only does the city there contain a storage cache—with grain we desperately need for a second planting down in the Central Dominance—but the city's new rulers are gathering strength and an army. Urteau is well within staging distance of Luthadel, as we discovered back when my father marched on us. I will *not* have a repeat of that event."

"We don't have enough troops to march on both fronts at once, El," Ham said.

Elend nodded. "I know. In fact, I'd rather avoid marching on Urteau. That was my father's seat—the people there had good reason to rebel against him. Demoux, report?"

Demoux stood. "We had a steel-inscribed message from Spook while Your Majesty was away," he said. "The lad says that the faction controlling Urteau is made up of skaa rebels."

"That sounds promising," Breeze noted. "Our kind of people."

"They're . . . quite harsh with noblemen, Lord Breeze,"

Demoux said. "And they include anyone with noble parents in that group."

"A little extreme, I'd think," Ham said.

"A lot of people thought Kelsier was extreme too," Breeze said. "I'm certain we can talk reason into these rebels."

"Good," Elend said, "because I'm counting on you and Sazed to bring Urteau under our control without the use of force. There are only five of these caches, and we can't afford to lose one. Who knows what we'll eventually discover in Fadrex—it might require us to return to the other caches to find something we missed." He turned, looking at Breeze, then Sazed.

"We can't just sneak the food out of Urteau," he said. "If the rebellion in that city spreads, it could cause the entire empire to fracture back into splinters. We *have* to bring the men there to our side."

The members of the room nodded, as did Vin. They knew from personal experience how much power a small rebellion could exert on an empire.

"The Fadrex siege could take some time," Elend said. "Long before summer arrives, I want you to have secured that northern cache and subdued the rebellion. Send the seed stock down to the Central Dominance for planting."

"Don't worry," Breeze said. "I've seen the kinds of governments skaa set up—by the time we get there, the city will probably be on the edge of collapse anyway. Why, they'll likely be relieved to get an offer to join the New Empire!"

"Be wary," Elend said. "Spook's reports have been sparse, but it sounds as if tensions in the city are extreme. We'll send a few hundred soldiers with you as protection." He looked back at the map, eyes narrowing slightly. "Five caches, five cities. Urteau is part of this all, somehow. We can't afford to let it slip away."

"Your Majesty," Sazed said. "Is my presence required on that trip?"

Elend frowned, glancing back at Sazed. "You have something else you need to be doing, Sazed?"

"I have research I would do," the Keeper said.

"I respect your wishes, as always," Elend said. "If you think this research is important . . ."

"It's of a personal nature, Your Majesty," Sazed said.

"Could you do it while helping in Urteau?" Elend asked. "You're a Terrisman, which lends you a credibility none of us can claim. Beyond that, people respect and trust you, Sazed—with good reason. Breeze, on the other hand, has something of a . . . reputation."

"I worked hard for it, you know," Breeze said.

"I'd really like to have you lead that team, Sazed," Elend said. "I can't think of a better ambassador than the Holy Witness himself."

Sazed's expression was unreadable. "Very well," he finally said. "I shall do my best."

"Good," Elend said, turning to regard the rest of the group. "Then there's one last thing I need to ask of you all."

"And what is that?" Cett asked.

Elend stood for a few moments, looking over their heads, appearing thoughtful. "I want you to tell me about the Survivor," he finally said.

"He was lord of the mists," Demoux said immediately.

"Not the rhetoric," Elend said. "Someone tell me about the man, Kelsier. I never met him, you know. I saw him once, right before he died, but I never knew him."

"What's the point?" Cett asked. "We've all heard the stories. He's practically a god, if you listen to the skaa."

"Just do as I ask," Elend said.

The tent was still for a few moments. Finally, Ham spoke. "Kell was . . . grand. He wasn't just a man, he was bigger than that. Everything he did was large—his dreams, the way he spoke, the way he thought. . . ."

"And it wasn't false," Breeze added. "I can tell when a man is being a fake. That's why I started my first job with Kelsier, actually. Amidst all the pretenders and posturers, he was genuine. Everyone wanted to be the best. Kelsier really was."

"He was a man," Vin said quietly. "Just a man. Yet, you

always knew he'd succeed. He made you be what he wanted you to be."

"So he could use you," Breeze said.

"But you were better when he was done with you," Ham added.

Elend nodded slowly. "I wish I could have known him. Early in my career, I always compared myself to him. By the time I heard of Kelsier, he was already becoming a legend. It was unfair to force myself to try and be him, but I worried regardless. Anyway, those of you who knew him, maybe you can answer another question for me. What do you think he'd say, if he saw us now?"

"He'd be proud," Ham said immediately. "I mean, we defeated the Lord Ruler, and we built a skaa government."

"What if he saw us at this conference?" Elend said.

The tent fell still again. When someone spoke what they were all thinking, it came from a source Vin hadn't expected.

"He'd tell us to laugh more," Sazed whispered.

Breeze chuckled. "He was completely insane, you know. The worse things got, the more he'd joke. I remember how chipper he was the very day after one of our worst defeats, when we lost most of our skaa army to that fool Yeden. Kell walked in, a spring in his step, making one of his inane jokes."

"Sounds insensitive," Allrianne said.

Ham shook his head. "No. He was just determined. He always said that laughter was something the Lord Ruler couldn't take from him. He planned and executed the overthrow of a thousand-year empire—and he did it as a kind of . . . penance for letting his wife die thinking that he hated her. But, he did it all with a smirk on his lips. Like every joke was his way of slapping fate in the face."

"We need what he had," Elend said.

The room's eyes turned back toward him.

"We can't keep doing this," Elend said. "We bicker amongst ourselves, we mope about, watching the ash fall, convinced that we're doomed."

Breeze chuckled. "I don't know if you noticed the earthquake a few minutes ago, my dear man, but the world appears to be ending. That is an indisputably depressing event."

Elend shook his head. "We can survive this. But, the only way that will happen is if our people don't give up. They need leaders who laugh, leaders who feel that this fight *can* be won. So, this is what I ask of you. I don't care if you're an optimist or a pessimist—I don't care if secretly, you think we'll all be dead before the month ends. On the outside, I want to see you smiling. Do it in defiance, if you have to. If the end does come, I want this group to meet that end smiling. As the Survivor taught us."

Slowly, the members of the former crew nodded—even Sazed, though his face seemed troubled.

Cett just shook his head. "You people are all insane. How I ended up with you, I'll never know."

Breeze laughed. "Now, that's a lie, Cett. You know *exactly* how you ended up joining with us. We threatened to kill you if you didn't!"

Elend was looking at Vin. She met his eyes, and nodded. It had been a good speech. She wasn't certain if his words would change anything—the crew could never again be the way it had been at the beginning, laughing freely around Clubs's table in the evening hours. However, maybe if they kept Kelsier's smile in mind, they'd be less likely to forget just why it was they kept struggling on.

"All right, people," Elend finally said. "Let's start preparations. Breeze, Sazed, Allrianne—I'll need you to talk with the scribes about supply estimates for your trip. Ham, send word to Luthadel and tell Penrod to have our scholars work on culturing plants that can grow in very little sunlight. Demoux, pass the word to the men. We march tomorrow."

Hemalurgy, it is called, because of the connection to blood. It is not a coincidence, I believe, that death is always involved in the transfer of powers via Hemalurgy. Marsh once described it as a "messy" process. Not the adjective I would have chosen. It's not disturbing enough.

13

I'M MISSING SOMETHING, MARSH THOUGHT.

He sat in the koloss camp. Just sitting. He hadn't moved in hours. Ash dusted him like a statue. Ruin's attention had been focused elsewhere lately, and Marsh had been left with more and more time to himself.

He still didn't struggle. Struggle just brought Ruin's attention.

Isn't that what I want? he thought. *To be controlled?* When Ruin forced him to see things its way, the dying world seemed wonderful. That bliss was far superior to the dread he felt while sitting on the stump, slowly being buried in ash.

No. No, that's not what I want! It was bliss, true, but it was false. As he had once struggled against Ruin, he now struggled against his own sense of inevitability.

What am I missing? he thought again, distracting himself. The koloss army—three hundred thousand strong—hadn't moved in weeks. Its members were slowly, yet relentlessly, killing each other. It seemed a waste of resources to let the army stagnate, even if the creatures could apparently eat even the dead plants beneath the ash to survive.

They can't possibly live on that for long, can they? He didn't know much about the koloss, despite spending the better part of a year with them. They appeared to be able to eat almost anything, as if just filling their stomachs were more important than actual nutrition.

What was Ruin waiting for? Why not take his army in and attack? Marsh was familiar enough with Final Empire geography to recognize that he was stationed in the North, near Terris. Why not move down and strike Luthadel?

There were no other Inquisitors in the camp. Ruin had called them to other tasks, leaving Marsh alone. Of all the Inquisitors, Marsh had been given the largest number of new spikes—he had ten new ones planted at various places in his body. That ostensibly made him the most powerful of the Inquisitors. Why leave him behind?

Yet . . . what does it matter? he wondered. *The end has come. There is no way to beat Ruin. The world will end.*

He felt guilty for the thought. If he could have turned his eyes downward in shame, he would have. There had been a time when he'd run the entire skaa rebellion. Thousands had looked to him for leadership. And then . . . Kelsier had been captured. As had Mare, the woman both Kelsier and Marsh had loved.

When Kelsier and Mare had been cast into the Pits of Hathsin, Marsh had left the rebellion. His rationale had been simple. If the Lord Ruler could catch Kelsier—the most brilliant thief of his time—then he would catch Marsh eventually too. It hadn't been fear that had driven Marsh's retirement, but simple realism. Marsh had always been practical. Fighting had proven useless. So why do it?

And then Kelsier had returned and done what a thousand years of rebellious skaa hadn't been able to: He'd overthrown the empire, facilitating the death of the Lord Ruler himself.

That should have been me, Marsh thought. *I served the rebellion all my life, then gave up just before they finally won.*

It was a tragedy, and it was made worse by the fact that Marsh was doing it again. He was giving up.

Damn you, Kelsier! he thought with frustration. *Can't you leave me be even in death?*

And yet, one harrowing, undeniable fact remained. Mare

had been right. She had chosen Kelsier over Marsh. And then, when both men had been forced to deal with her death, one had given up.

The other had made her dreams come true.

Marsh knew why Kelsier had decided to overthrow the Final Empire. It hadn't been for the money, the fame, or even—as most suspected—for revenge. Kelsier knew Mare's heart. He'd known that she dreamed of days when plants flourished and the sky was not red. She'd always carried with her that little picture of a flower, a copied copy of a copy—a depiction of something that had been lost to the Final Empire long ago.

But, Marsh thought bitterly, *you didn't make her dreams a reality, Kelsier. You failed. You killed the Lord Ruler, but that didn't fix anything. It made things worse!*

The ash continued to fall, blowing around Marsh in a lazy breeze. Koloss grunted, and in the near distance one screamed as his companion killed him.

Kelsier was dead now. But, he had died for her dream. Mare had been right to pick him, but she was dead too. Marsh wasn't. Not yet. *I can fight still,* he told himself. *But how?* Even moving his finger would draw Ruin's attention.

Although, during the last few weeks, he hadn't struggled at all. Perhaps that was why Ruin decided it could leave Marsh alone for so long. The creature—or the force, or whatever it was—wasn't omnipotent. Marsh suspected, however, that it could move about freely, watching the world and seeing what was happening in various parts of it. No walls could block its view—it seemed to be able to watch anything.

Except a man's mind.

Perhaps . . . perhaps if I stop struggling long enough, I'll be able to surprise it when I finally do decide to strike.

It seemed as good a plan as any. And, Marsh knew exactly what he would do, when the time came. He'd remove Ruin's most useful tool. He'd pull the spike from his back and kill himself. Not out of frustration, and not out of despair. He knew that he had some important part to play in Ruin's plans. If he removed himself at the right time, it could give the others the chance they needed.

It was all he could give. Yet, it seemed fitting, and his new confidence made him wish he could stand and face the world with pride. Kelsier had killed himself to secure freedom for the skaa. Marsh would do the same—and in doing so, hope to help save the world itself from destruction.

PART TWO

CLOTH AND GLASS

Ruin's consciousness was trapped by the Well of Ascension, kept mostly impotent. That night, when we discovered the Well for the first time, we found something we didn't understand. A black smoke, clogging one of the rooms.

Though we discussed it after the fact, we couldn't decide what that was. How could we possibly have known?

The body of a god—or, rather, the power of a god, since the two are really the same thing. Ruin and Preservation inhabited power and energy in the same way a person inhabits flesh and blood.

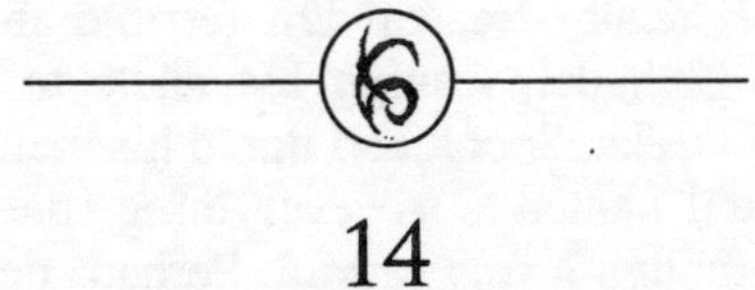

14

SPOOK FLARED TIN.

He let it burn within him—burn brightly, burn powerfully. He never turned it off anymore. He just left it on, letting it roar, a fire within him. Tin was one of the slowest-burning of metals, and it wasn't difficult to obtain in the amounts necessary for Allomancy.

He moved down the silent street. Even with Kelsier's now-famous proclamations that the skaa need not fear the mists, few people went out at night. For, at night, the mists came. Deep and mysterious, dark and omnipresent, the mists were one of the great constants of the Final Empire. They came every night. Thicker than a simple fog, they swirled in definite patterns—almost as if the different banks, streams, and fronts of mist were living things. Almost playful, yet enigmatic.

To Spook, however, they were barely an obstruction anymore. He'd always been told not to flare his tin too much; he'd been warned not to become dependent upon it. It would do dangerous things to his body, people said. And, the truth was, they were right. He had flared his tin nonstop for a year straight—never letting up, keeping his body in a constant state of super-heightened senses—and it *had* changed him. He worried that the changes would, indeed, be dangerous.

But he needed them, for the people of Urteau needed him.

Stars blazed in the sky above him like a million tiny suns. They shone through the mists, which had—during the last year—become diaphanous and weak. At first, Spook had thought the world itself was changing. Then he had realized that it was just his perception. Somehow, by flaring tin for so long, he had permanently enhanced his senses to a point far beyond what other Allomancers could attain.

He'd almost stopped. The flared tin had begun as a reaction to Clubs's death. He still felt terrible about the way he'd escaped Luthadel, leaving his uncle to die. During those first few weeks, Spook had flared his metals as almost a penance—he'd wanted to *feel* everything around him, take it all in, even though it was painful. Perhaps because it was painful.

But then he'd started to change, and that had worried him. But, the crew always talked about how hard Vin pushed herself. She rarely slept, using pewter to keep herself awake and alert. Spook didn't know how that worked—he was no Mistborn, and could only burn one metal—but he figured that if burning his one metal could give him an advantage, he'd better take it. Because they were going to need every advantage they could get.

The starlight was like daylight to him. During the actual day, he had to wear a cloth tied across his eyes to protect them, and even then going outside was sometimes blinding. His skin had become so sensitive that each pebble in the ground—each crack, each flake of stone—felt like a knife jabbing him through the soles of his shoes. The chill spring air seemed freezing, and he wore a thick cloak.

However, he had concluded that these nuisances were small prices to pay for the opportunity to become . . . whatever it was he had become. As he moved down the street, he could hear people shuffling and turning in their beds, even through their walls. He could sense a footstep from yards away. He could see on a dark night as no other human ever had.

Perhaps he'd find a way to become useful to the others. Always before, he'd been the least important member of the crew. The dismissible boy who ran errands or kept watch while the others made plans. He didn't resent them for that—they'd been right to give him such simple duties. Because of his street dialect, he'd been difficult to understand, and while all the other members of the crew had been handpicked by Kelsier, Spook had joined by default since he was Clubs's nephew.

Spook sighed, shoving his hands in his trouser pockets as he walked down the too-bright street. He could feel each and every thread in the fabric.

Dangerous things were happening, he knew that: the way the mists lingered during the day, the way the ground shook as if it were a sleeping man, periodically suffering a terrible dream. Spook worried he wouldn't be of much help in the critical days to come. A little over a year before, his uncle had died after Spook fled the city. Spook had run out of fear, but also out of a knowledge of his own impotence. He wouldn't have been able to help during the siege.

He didn't want to be in that position again. He wanted to be able to help, somehow. He wouldn't run into the woods, hiding while the world ended around him. Elend and Vin had sent him to Urteau to gather as much information as he could about the Citizen and his government there, and so Spook intended to do his best. If that meant pushing his body beyond what was safe, so be it.

He approached a large intersection. He looked both ways down the intersecting streets—the view clear as day to his eyes. *I may not be Mistborn, and I may not be emperor,* he thought. *But I'm something. Something new. Something Kelsier would be proud of.*

Maybe this time I can help.

He saw no motion in either direction, so he slipped onto the street and moved to the north. It felt strange, sometimes, slinking quietly along a street that seemed brightly lit. Yet, he knew that to others it would be dark, with only starlight to see by, the mist blocking and obscuring as ever. Tin helped an Allomancer pierce the mists, and Spook's increasingly sensitive eyes were even better at this. He brushed through the mists, barely noticing them.

He heard the patrol long before he saw it. How could someone *not* hear that clanking of armor, not feel that clatter of feet on the cobblestones? He froze, standing with his back to the earthen wall bordering the street, watching for the patrol.

They bore a torch—to Spook's enhanced eyes, it looked like a blazing beacon of near-blinding brilliance. The torch marked them as fools. Its light wouldn't help—just the reverse. The light reflected off the mists, enveloping the guards in a little bubble of light that ruined their night vision.

Spook stayed where he was, motionless. The patrol clanked forward, moving down the street. They passed within a few feet of him, but didn't notice him standing there. There was something . . . invigorating about being able to watch, feeling at once completely exposed and perfectly unseen. It made him wonder why the new Urteau government even bothered with patrols. Of course, the government's skaa officials would have very little experience with the mists.

As the guard patrol disappeared around a corner—bearing their glaring torch with them—Spook turned back to his task. The Citizen would be meeting with his aides this night, if his schedule held. Spook intended to listen in on that conversation. He moved carefully down the street.

No city could compare with Luthadel in sheer size, but

Urteau made a respectable effort. As the hereditary home of the Venture line, it had once been a much more important—and well-maintained—city than it was now. That decline had begun even before the death of the Lord Ruler. The most obvious sign of that was the roadway Spook now walked on. Once, the city had been crisscrossed with canals that had functioned as watery streets. Those canals had gone dry some time ago, leaving the city crossed by deep, dusty troughs that grew muddy when it rained. Rather than filling them in, the people had simply begun to use the empty bottoms as roads.

The street Spook now used had once been a wide waterway capable of accommodating even large barges. Ten-foot-high walls rose on either side of the sunken street, and buildings loomed above, built up against the lip of the canal. Nobody had been able to give Spook a definite, or consistent, answer as to why the canals had emptied—some blamed earthquakes, others blamed droughts. The fact remained, however, that in the hundred years since the canals had lost their water, nobody had found an economical way to refill them.

And so, Spook continued down the "street," feeling like he was walking in a deep slot. Numerous ladders—and the occasional ramp or flight of stairs—led up to the sidewalks and the buildings above, but few people ever walked up there. The streetslots—as the city's residents called them—had simply become normal.

Spook caught a scent of smoke as he walked. He glanced up, and noted a gap in the horizon of buildings. Recently, a building on this street had been burned to the ground. The house of a nobleman. His sense of smell, like his other senses, was incredibly sensitive. So it was possible that he was smelling smoke from long ago, when buildings had burned during the initial rampages following Straff Venture's death. And yet, the scent seemed too strong for that. Too recent.

Spook hurried on. Urteau was dying slowly, decaying, and a lot of the blame could be placed on its ruler, the Citizen. Long ago, Elend had given a speech to the people of

Luthadel. It had been the night when the Lord Ruler had died, the night of Kelsier's rebellion. Spook remembered Elend's words well, for the man had spoken of hatred, rebellion, and the dangers associated with them. He'd warned that if the people founded their new government on hatred and bloodshed, it would consume itself with fear, jealousy, and chaos.

Spook had been in that audience, listening. He now saw that Elend was right. The skaa of Urteau had overthrown their noble rulers, and—in a way—Spook was proud of them for doing so. He felt a growing fondness for the city, partially because of how devoutly they tried to follow what the Survivor had taught. Yet, their rebellion hadn't stopped with the ousting of the nobility. As Elend had predicted, the city had become a place of fear and death.

The question was not *why* it had happened, but how to stop it.

For now, that wasn't Spook's job. He was just supposed to gather information. Only familiarity—gained during weeks spent investigating the city—let him know when he was getting close, for it was frustratingly difficult to keep track of where one was down in the streetslots. At first, he had tried to stay out of them, slipping through smaller alleyways above. Unfortunately, the slots networked the entire city, and he'd wasted so much time going up and down that he'd eventually realized that the slots really were the only viable way of getting around.

Unless one were Mistborn, of course. Unfortunately, Spook couldn't hop from building to building on lines of Allomantic power. He was stuck in the slots. He made the best of it.

He picked a ladder and swung onto it, climbing up. Though he wore leather gloves, he could feel the grain of the wood. Up top, there was a small sidewalk running along the streetslot. An alleyway extended ahead of him, leading into a cluster of houses. A building at the end of the small street was his goal, but he did not move toward it. Instead, he waited quietly, searching for the signs he knew were there.

Sure enough, he caught a rustling motion in a window a few buildings down. His ears caught the sound of footsteps in another building. The street ahead of him was being watched.

Spook turned aside. While the sentries were very careful to watch the alleyway, they unintentionally left another avenue open: their own buildings. Spook crept to the right, moving on feet that could feel each pebble beneath them, listening with ears that could hear a man's increased breathing as he spotted something unusual. He rounded the outside of a building, turning away from the watchful eyes, and entering a dead-end alleyway on the other side. There, he lay a hand against the wall of the building.

There were vibrations inside the room; it was occupied, so he moved on. The next room alerted him immediately, as he heard whispered voices inside. The third room, however, gave him nothing. No vibrations of motion. No whispers. Not even the muted thudding of a heartbeat—something he could sometimes hear, if the air were still enough. Taking a deep breath, Spook quietly worked open the window lock and slipped inside.

It was a sleeping chamber, empty as he'd anticipated. He'd never come through this particular room before. His heart thumped as he closed the shutters, then slipped across the floor. Despite the near-total darkness, he had no trouble seeing in the room. It barely seemed dim to him.

Outside the room, he found a more familiar hallway. He easily snuck past two guard rooms, where men watched the street outside. There was a thrill in doing these infiltrations. Spook was in one of the Citizen's own guardhouses, steps away from large numbers of armed soldiers. They should have taken care to guard their own building better.

He crept up the stairs, making his way to a small, rarely used room on the third floor. He checked for vibrations, then slipped inside. The austere chamber was piled with a mound of extra bedrolls and a dusty stack of uniforms. Spook smiled as he moved across the floor, stepping carefully and quietly, his highly sensitive toes able to feel loose, squeaky, or warped boards. He sat down on the windowsill itself, confident that nobody outside would be able to see well enough to spot him.

The Citizen's house lay a few yards away. Quellion decried ostentation, and had chosen for his headquarters a structure of modest size. It had probably once been a minor nobleman's home, and had only a small yard, which Spook could easily see into from his vantage. The building itself glowed, light streaking from every crack and window. It was as if the building were filled with some awesome power, and on the verge of bursting.

But, then, that was just the way that Spook's overflared tin made him see any building that had lights on inside.

Spook leaned back, legs up on the windowsill, back against the frame. The window contained neither glass nor shutters, though there were nail holes on the side of the wood, indicating that there had once been something there. The reason the shutters had been removed didn't matter to Spook—the lack of them meant that this room was unlikely to be entered at night. Mists had already claimed the room, though they were so faint to Spook's eyes that he had had trouble seeing them.

For a while, nothing happened. The building and grounds below remained silent and still in the night air. Eventually, however, she appeared.

Spook perked up, watching the young woman leave the house and enter the garden. She had on a light brown skaa's dress—a garment she somehow wore with striking elegance. Her hair was darker than the dress, but not by much. Spook had seen very few people with her shade of deep auburn hair—at least, few people who had been able to keep it clean of ash and soot.

Everyone in the city knew of Beldre, the Citizen's sister, though few had ever seen her. She was said to be beautiful—and in this case, the rumors were true. However, nobody had ever mentioned her sadness. With his tin flared so high, Spook felt like he was standing next to her. He could see her deep, sorrowful eyes, reflecting light from the shining building behind her.

There was a bench in the yard. It sat before a small shrub. It was the only plant left in the garden; the rest had been torn up and plowed under, leaving behind blackish brown earth. From what Spook had heard, the Citizen had declared that ornamental gardens were of the nobility. He claimed that such places had only been possible through the sweat of skaa slaves—just another way the nobility had achieved high levels of luxury by creating equally high levels of work for their servants.

When the people of Urteau had whitewashed the city's murals and shattered its stained-glass windows, they had also torn up all the ornamental gardens.

Beldre sat down on her bench, hands held motionless in her lap, looking down at the sad shrub. Spook tried to convince himself that *she* wasn't the reason why he made certain to always sneak in and listen to the Citizen's evening conferences, and he was mostly successful. These were some of the best spying opportunities Spook got. Being able to see Beldre was simply a bonus. Not that he cared *that* much, of course. He didn't even know her.

He thought that even as he sat there, staring down at her, wishing he had some way to talk to her.

But, this wasn't the time for that. Beldre's exile to the garden meant that her brother's meeting was about to start. He always kept her near, but apparently didn't want her hearing state secrets. Unfortunately for him, his window opened toward Spook's vantage point. No normal man—not even an ordinary Tineye or Mistborn—could have heard what was being said inside. But Spook wasn't, by any stretched definition of the word, normal.

I won't be useless anymore, he thought with determination as he listened for words spoken in confidence. They passed through the walls, across the short space, and arrived at his ears.

"All right, Olid," said a voice. "What news?" The voice was, by now, familiar to Spook. Quellion, the Citizen of Urteau.

"Elend Venture has conquered another city," said a second voice—Olid, the foreign minister.

"Where?" Quellion demanded. "What city?"

"An unimportant one," Olid said. "To the south. Barely five thousand people."

"It makes no sense," said a third voice. "He immediately abandoned the city, taking its populace with him."

"But he got another koloss army, somehow," Olid added.

Good, Spook thought. The fourth storage cavern was theirs. Luthadel wouldn't starve for a while yet. That only left two to secure—the one here in Urteau, and the last one, wherever that turned out to be.

"A tyrant needs no real reason for what he does," Quellion said. He was a young man, but not foolish. At times, he sounded like other men Spook had known. Wise men. The difference, then, was one of extremity.

Or, perhaps, timing?

"A tyrant simply conquers for the thrill of control," Quellion continued. "Venture isn't satisfied with the lands he's taken—he never will be. He'll just keep on conquering. Until he comes for us."

The room fell silent.

"He's reportedly sending an ambassador to Urteau," the third voice said. "A member of the Survivor's own crew."

Spook perked up.

Quellion snorted. "One of the liars? Coming here?"

"To offer us a treaty, the rumors say," Olid said.

"So?" Quellion asked. "Why do you mention this, Olid? Do you think we should make a pact with the tyrant?"

"We can't fight him, Quellion," Olid said.

"The Survivor couldn't fight the Lord Ruler," Quellion said. "But he did anyway. He died, but still won, giving the skaa courage to rebel and overthrow the nobility."

"Until that bastard Venture took control," the third voice said.

The room fell silent again.

"We can't give in to Venture," Quellion finally said. "I will not hand this city to a nobleman, not after what the Survivor did for us. Of all the Final Empire, only Urteau achieved

Kelsier's goal of a skaa-ruled nation. Only we burned the homes of the nobility. Only we cleansed our town of them and their society. Only we obeyed. The Survivor will watch over us."

Spook shivered quietly. It felt very strange to be hearing men he didn't know speak of Kelsier in such tones. Spook had walked with Kelsier, learned from Kelsier. What right did these men have to speak as if they had known the man who had become their Survivor?

The conversation turned to matters more mundane. They discussed new laws that would forbid certain kinds of clothing once favored by the nobility, and then made a decision to give more funding to the genealogical survey committee. They needed to root out any in the city who were hiding noble parentage. Spook took notes so he could pass them on to the others. However, he had trouble keeping his eyes from trailing back down to the young woman in the garden.

What brings her such sorrow? he wondered. A part of him wanted to ask—to be brash, as the Survivor would have been, and hop down to demand of this solemn, solitary girl why she stared at that plant with such melancholy. In fact, he found himself moving to stand before he caught himself.

He might be unique, he might be powerful, but—as he had to remind himself again—he was no Mistborn. His was the way of silence and stealth.

So, he settled back. Content, for the moment, to lean down and watch her, feeling that somehow—despite their distance, despite his ignorance—he understood that feeling in her eyes.

The ash.

I don't think the people really understood how fortunate they were. During the thousand years before the Collapse, they pushed the ash into rivers, piled it up outside of cities, and generally just let it be. They never understood that without the microbes and plants Rashek had developed to break down the ash particles, the land would quickly have been buried.

Though, of course, that did eventually happen anyway.

15

THE MISTS BURNED. BRIGHT, FLARING, lit by the red sunlight, they seemed a fire that enveloped her.

Mist during the day was unnatural. But even the nightmists didn't seem to be Vin's anymore. Once, they had shadowed and protected her. Now she found them increasingly alien. When she used Allomancy it seemed that the mists pulled away from her slightly—like a wild beast shying away from a bright light.

She stood alone before the camp, which was silent despite the fact that the sun had risen hours ago. So far, Elend continued to keep his army protected from the mists by ordering them to remain in their tents. Ham argued that exposing them wasn't necessary, but Vin's instinct said that Elend would stick to his plan to order his soldiers into the mist. They needed to be immune.

Why? Vin thought, looking up through the sunlit mists. *Why have you changed? What is different?* The mists danced around her, moving in their usual, strange pattern of shifting streams and swirls. It seemed to Vin that they began to move more rapidly. Quivering. Vibrating.

The sun seemed to grow hotter, and the mists finally retreated, vanishing like water evaporating on a warming pan. The sunlight hit her like a wave, and Vin turned, watching the mists go, their death like an echoing scream.

They're not natural, Vin thought as guards called the all clear. The camp immediately began to shift and move, men striding from tents, going about the morning's activity with a flare of urgency. Vin stood at the head of the camp, dirt road beneath her feet, motionless canal to her right. Both seemed more *real* now that the mists were gone.

She had asked Sazed and Elend their opinions of the mists—whether they were natural or . . . something else. And both men, like the scholars they were, had quoted theories to support *both* sides of the argument. Sazed, at least, had eventually made a decision—he'd come down on the side of the mists being natural.

Even the way that the mists choke some people, leaving others alive, could be explained, Lady Vin, he had explained. *After all, insect stings kill some people, while barely bothering others.*

Vin wasn't that interested in theories and arguments. She had spent most of her life thinking of the mists like any other weather pattern. Reen and the other thieves had mostly scoffed at tales that made the mists out to be supernatural. Yet, as Vin had become an Allomancer, she had grown to know the mists. She *felt* them, a sense that seemed to have grown even more potent on the day she'd touched the power of the Well of Ascension.

They disappeared too quickly. When they burned away in the sunlight, they withdrew like a person fleeing for safety. Like . . . a man who used all of his strength fighting, then finally gave up to retreat. In addition, the mists didn't appear indoors. A simple tent was enough to protect the men inside. It was as if the mists somehow understood that they were excluded, unwelcome.

Vin glanced back toward the sun, glowing like a scarlet ember behind the dark haze of the upper atmosphere. She wished TenSoon were there, so she could talk to him about her worries. She missed the kandra a great deal, more than she'd ever assumed that she would. His simple frankness had been a good match to her own. She still didn't know what had happened to him after he'd returned to his people; she'd tried to find another kandra to deliver a message for her, but the creatures had become very scarce lately.

She sighed and turned, walking quietly back into camp.

It was impressive how quickly the men managed to get

the army moving. They spent the mornings sequestered inside their tents, caring for armor and weapons, the cooks preparing what they could. By the time Vin had crossed a short distance, cooking fires had burst alight, and tents began to collapse, soldiers working quickly to prepare for departure.

As she passed, some of the men saluted. Others bowed their heads in reverence. Still others glanced away, looking uncertain. Vin didn't blame them. Even *she* wasn't sure what her place was in the army. As Elend's wife, she was technically their empress, though she wore no royal garb. To many, she was a religious figure, the Heir of the Survivor. She didn't really want that title either.

She found Elend and Ham conversing outside of the imperial tent, which was in an early stage of disassembly. Though they stood out in the open, their mannerisms completely nonchalant, Vin was immediately struck by how far the two men were standing from the workers, as if Elend and Ham didn't want the men to hear. Burning tin, she could make out what they were saying long before she reached them.

"Ham," Elend said quietly, "you know I'm right. We can't keep doing this. The further we penetrate into the Western Dominance, the more daylight we'll lose to the mists."

Ham shook his head. "You'd really stand by and watch your own soldiers die, El?"

Elend's face grew hard, and he met Vin's eyes as she joined them. "We can't afford to wait out the mists every morning."

"Even if it saves lives?" Ham asked.

"Slowing down *costs* lives," Elend said. "Each hour we spend out here brings the mists closer to the Central Dominance. We're planning to be at siege for some time, Ham—and that means we need to get to Fadrex as soon as possible."

Ham glanced at Vin, looking for support. She shook her head. "I'm sorry, Ham. Elend is right. We can't have our entire army dependent upon the whims of the mists. We'd be exposed—if someone attacked us in the morning, our men would either have to respond and get struck down by the mists, or hide in their tents and wait."

Ham frowned, then excused himself, tromping through the fallen ash to help a group of soldiers pack away their tents. Vin stepped up beside Elend, watching the large soldier go.

"Kelsier was wrong about him," she finally said.

"Who?" Elend asked. "Ham?"

Vin nodded. "At the end—after Kelsier died—we found a last note from him. He said that he'd chosen the members of the crew to be leaders in his new government. Breeze to be an ambassador, Dockson to be a bureaucrat, and Ham to be a general. The other two fit their roles perfectly, but Ham . . ."

"He gets too involved," Elend said. "He has to know each man he commands personally or it makes him uncomfortable. And, when he knows them all that well, he grows attached."

Vin nodded quietly, watching Ham begin to laugh and work with the soldiers.

"Listen to us," Elend said, "callously talking about the lives of those who follow us. Perhaps it would be better to grow attached, like Ham. Maybe then I wouldn't be so quick to order people to their deaths."

Vin glanced at Elend, concerned at the bitterness in his voice. He smiled, trying to cover it up, then glanced away. "You need to do something with that koloss of yours. He's been poking around the camp, scaring the men."

Vin frowned. As soon as she thought of the creature, she became aware of where it was—near the edge of the camp. It was always under her command, but she could only take direct, full control of it when she concentrated. Otherwise, it would follow her general orders—staying in the area, not killing anything.

"I should go make sure the barges are ready to move,"

Elend said. He glanced at her, and when she didn't indicate that she'd go with him, he gave her a quick kiss, then departed.

Vin moved through the camp again. Most of the tents were down and stowed, and the soldiers were making quick work of their food. She passed out of the perimeter, and found Human sitting quietly, ash drifting slightly against his legs. He watched the camp with red eyes, his face broken by the ripped skin which hung from his right eye down to the corner of his mouth.

"Human," she said, folding her arms.

He looked over at her, then stood, ash falling from his eleven-foot, overly muscled blue figure. Even with the number of creatures she'd killed, even knowing she controlled this one completely, Vin had a moment of reflexive fear as she stood before the massive beast with its tightly stretched skin and bleeding rips.

"Why did you come to camp?" she said, shaking off her panic.

"I am human," he said with his slow, deliberate tone.

"You're koloss," she said. "You know that."

"I should have a house," Human said. "Like those."

"Those are tents, not houses," Vin said. "You can't come to camp like this. You have to stay with the other koloss."

Human turned, glancing toward the south, where the koloss army waited, separate from the humans. They remained under Elend's control, twenty thousand in number, now that they'd picked up the ten thousand that had been waiting with the main bulk of the army. It made more sense to leave them under Elend's control, since—in terms of raw power—he was a much stronger Allomancer than Vin.

Human looked back at Vin. "Why?"

"Why do you have to stay with the others?" Vin asked. "Because you make the people in the camp uncomfortable."

"Then they should attack me," Human said.

"That's why you're not a human," Vin said. "We don't attack people just because they make us uncomfortable."

"No," Human said. "You make *us* kill them instead."

Vin paused, cocking her head. Human, however, just looked away, staring at the human camp again. His beady red eyes made his face hard to read, but Vin almost sensed a . . . longing in his expression.

"You're one of us," Human said.

Vin looked up. "Me?"

"You're like us," he said. "Not like them."

"Why do you say that?" Vin asked.

Human looked down at her. "Mist," he said.

Vin felt a momentary chill, though she had no real idea why. "What do you mean?"

Human didn't respond.

"Human," she said, trying another tactic. "What do you think of the mists?"

"They come at night."

Vin nodded. "Yes, but what do you think of them. Your people. Do they fear the mists? Does it ever kill them?"

"Swords kill," Human said. "Rain doesn't kill. Ash doesn't kill. Mist doesn't kill."

Fairly good logic, Vin thought. *A year ago, I would have agreed with it.* She was about to give up on the line of reasoning, but Human continued.

"I hate it," he said.

Vin paused.

"I hate it because it hates me," Human said. He looked at her. "*You* feel it."

"Yes," Vin said, surprising herself. "I do."

Human regarded her, a line of blood trailing out of the ripped skin near his eye, running stark down his blue skin, mixing with flakes of ash. Finally, he nodded, as if giving approval to her honest reply.

Vin shivered. *The mist isn't alive,* she thought. *It can't hate me. I'm imagining things.*

But . . . once, years ago, she had drawn upon the mists. When fighting the Lord Ruler, she had somehow gained a power over them. It had been as if she'd used the mist itself to fuel her Allomancy instead of metals. It was only with that power that she'd been able to defeat the Lord Ruler.

That had been a long time ago, and she'd never been able to replicate the event. She'd tried time and again over the years, and after so many failures, she was beginning to think that she must have been mistaken. Certainly, in more recent times, the mists had been unfriendly. She tried to keep telling herself that there was nothing supernatural about it, but she knew that wasn't true. What of the mist spirit, the thing that had tried to kill Elend—and then had saved him by showing her how to make him into an Allomancer? It was real, of that she was certain, even if she hadn't seen it in over a year.

What of the hesitance she felt toward the mists, the way they pulled away from her? The way they stayed out of buildings, and the way they killed. It all seemed to point to what Human had said. The mists—the Deepness—hated her. And, finally, she acknowledged what she had been resisting for so long.

The mists were her enemy.

They are called Allomantic savants. Men or women who flare their metals so long, and so hard, that the constant influx of Allomantic power transforms their very physiology.

In most cases, with most metals, the effects of this are very slight. Bronze burners, for instance, often become bronze savants without knowing it. Their range is expanded from burning the metal so long. Becoming a pewter savant is dangerous, as it requires pushing the body so hard in a state where one cannot feel exhaustion or pain. Most accidentally kill themselves before the process is complete, and in my opinion, the benefit isn't worth the effort.

Tin savants, however . . . now, they are something special. Endowed with senses beyond what any normal Allomancer would need—or even want—they become slaves to what they touch, hear, see, smell, and taste. Yet, the abnormal power of these senses gives them a distinct, and interesting, advantage.

One could argue that, like an Inquisitor who has been transformed by a Hemalurgic spike, the Allomantic savant is no longer even human.

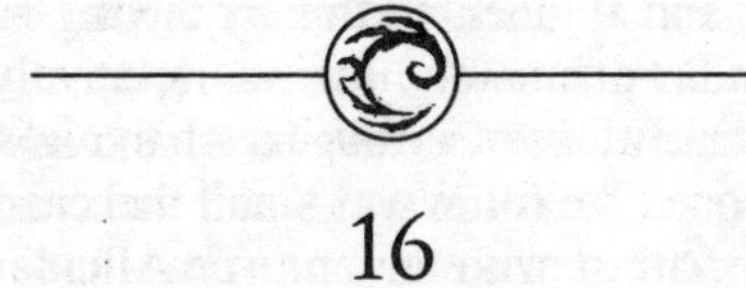

16

SPOOK AWOKE TO DARKNESS.

That was happening less and less frequently lately. He could feel the blindfold on his face, tied tightly across his eyes and over his ears. It dug into his overly sensitive skin, but it was far better than the alternative. Starlight was as bright as the sun to his eyes, and footsteps in the hallway outside his room could sound like thunderclaps. Even with the thick cloth, even with his ears plugged with wax, even with the shutters drawn tight and hung with a cloth, it was sometimes hard for him to sleep.

The muffling was dangerous. It left him vulnerable. And yet, lack of sleep would be even more dangerous. Perhaps the things he'd done to his body by burning tin would kill him. Yet, the more time he spent among the people of Urteau, the more he felt they were going to need his help to survive the dangers that were coming. He needed an edge. He worried that he'd made the wrong decision, but at least he'd made a decision. He would continue as he had, and hope that it was enough.

He groaned quietly, sitting up, taking off the cloth and pulling the wax from his ears. The room was dark, but even the faint light creeping through the shutters—their gaps stuffed with cloth—was enough for him to see by.

Tin flared comfortably in his stomach. His reserve was nearly gone, burned away during the night. His body now used it as instinctively as it drew breath or blinked. He had heard that Thugs could burn pewter to heal their bodies even if they were unconscious from their wounds. The body understood what it needed.

He reached into a small pail beside his bed, pulling out a small handful of tin dust. He'd brought a lot with him from Luthadel, and augmented this by buying more through the underground. Fortunately, tin was relatively cheap. He dumped his handful into a mug on his nightstand, then moved to the door. The room was small and cramped, but he didn't have to share it with anyone. That made it lavish by skaa standards.

He squeezed his eyes shut, then pulled open the door. The luminosity of a sunlit hallway crashed against him. He gritted his teeth against the light, intense despite his shut eyelids, and felt about on the ground. He found the jug of fresh water—drawn from the well for him by the inn's servants—and pulled it inside, then shut the door.

He blinked, walking across the room to fill his mug. He drank it, washing down the tin. It would be enough for the entire day. He took an extra handful and stuffed it into a pouch, just in case.

A few minutes later he was dressed and ready. He sat down on the bed, closing his eyes, preparing for the day. If the Citizen's spies were to be believed, other members of Elend's team were on their way to Urteau. They were probably under orders to secure the storage cache and quell the rebellion; Spook would need to learn as much as he could before they arrived.

He sat, going over plans, thinking to himself. He could feel feet thumping in the rooms around him—the wooden structure seemed to shake and tremble like some enormous hive filled with bustling workers. Outside, he could hear voices calling, yelling, speaking. Bells rang faintly. It was early yet, barely past noon, but the mists would be gone—Urteau got about six or seven hours of mistless daylight, making it a place where crops could still grow and man could still thrive.

Normally, Spook would have slept through the hours of daylight. However, there were things he needed to do. He opened his eyes, then reached to his nightstand, picking up a pair of spectacles. They had been specially crafted, at his request, to hold lenses that made no corrections to his vision. They were just filled with regular glass.

He put these on, then retied the cloth around his head, covering the front and sides of the lenses. Even with his heightened senses, he couldn't see through his own eyelids. However, with the spectacles on, he could open his eyes and wear the cloth at the same time. He felt his way to the window, then he pulled off the blanket and threw open the shutters.

Hot—nearly scalding—sunlight bathed him. The cloth bit into the skin of his head. But he could see. The cloth blocked just enough light to keep him from being blinded, yet was translucent enough to allow vision. It was like the mists, actually—the cloth was nearly invisible to him, for his eyes were enhanced beyond the point of reason. His mind just filtered out the cloth's interference.

Spook nodded to himself, then picked up his dueling cane and made his way from the room.

"I know you're a quiet one," Durn said, rapping softly on the ground in front of him with a pair of sticks. "But even you have to admit that this is better than living under the lords."

Spook sat in a streetslot, back to the stone wall that had sustained the canal, head bowed slightly. Marketpit was the widest of the streetslots of Urteau. Once, it had been a waterway so broad that three boats abreast could moor in its center while leaving room on both sides for the passage of others in either direction. Now it had become a central boulevard for the city, which also made it a prime location for tradesmen and beggars.

Beggars like Spook and Durn. They sat at the very side of the slot, buildings looming like fortress walls above. Few of the passers paid any attention to the ragged men. Nobody paused to notice that one of them seemed to be watching the crowd carefully, despite the dark cloth over his eyes, while the other spoke far too articulately to have been educated in the gutter.

Spook didn't respond to Durn's question. In his youth, the way he spoke—with a thick accent, language littered with slang—had marked him, made people dismiss him. Even now, he didn't have a glib tongue or charming manner like Kelsier's. So, instead, Spook just tried to say as little as possible. Less chance of getting himself into trouble that way.

Oddly, instead of finding him *easier* to dismiss when he didn't talk, it seemed that people paid more attention to him. Durn continued to pound out his rhythm, like a street performer with no audience. It was too soft against the earthen floor for anyone to hear—unless one were Spook.

Durn's rhythm was perfect. Any minstrel would have envied him.

"I mean, look at the market," Durn continued. "Under the Lord Ruler, most skaa could never engage openly in commerce. We have something beautiful here. Skaa ruling skaa. We're happy."

Spook could see the market. It seemed to him that if the people were truly happy, they'd wear smiles, rather than downcast looks. They'd be shopping and browsing, rather than quickly picking out what they wanted, then moving on. Plus, if the city were the happy utopia it was supposed to be, there wouldn't be a need for the dozens of soldiers who watched the crowd. Spook shook his head. Everybody wore nearly the exact same clothing—colors and styles dictated by the Citizen's orders. Even begging was heavily regulated. Men would soon arrive to count Spook's offerings, tally how much he had earned, then take the Citizen's cut.

"Look," Durn said, "do you see anyone being beaten or killed on the street? Surely that's worth a few strictures."

"The deaths happen in quiet alleys now," Spook said softly. "At least the Lord Ruler killed us openly."

Durn frowned, sitting back, thumping the ground with his sticks. It was a complex pattern. Spook could feel the vibrations through the ground, and found them soothing. Did the people know the talent they passed, quietly beating the ground they walked upon? Durn could have been a master musician. Unfortunately, under the Lord Ruler, skaa didn't play music. And under the Citizen . . . well, it generally wasn't good to draw attention to yourself, no matter what the method.

"There it is," Durn said suddenly. "As promised."

Spook glanced up. Through the mutters, the sounds, the flashes of color and the powerful scents of refuse, people, and goods for sale, Spook saw a group of prisoners, being escorted by soldiers in brown. Sometimes, the flood of sensation was almost overwhelming to him. However, as he'd once told Vin, burning tin wasn't about what one could sense, but about what one could ignore. And he had learned very well to focus on the senses he needed, shunting aside that which would distract.

The market goers made way for the group of soldiers and their prisoners. The people bowed their heads, watching solemnly.

"You still want to follow?" Durn asked.

Spook stood.

Durn nodded, then stood and grabbed Spook by the shoulder. He knew that Spook could really see—or, at least, Spook assumed that Durn was observant enough to have noticed that fact. They both maintained the act, however. It was common among beggars to adopt a guise of being afflicted in an attempt to elicit more coins. Durn himself walked with a masterful false limp, and had his hair pulled out in sickly patches. Yet, Spook could smell soap on the man's skin and fine wine on his breath. He was a thief lord; there were few more powerful in the city. Yet, he was clever enough with his disguises that he could walk about on the streets unnoticed.

They weren't the only ones following the soldiers and their prisoners. Skaa wearing the approved gray trailed the group like ghosts—a quiet, shuffling mass in the falling ash. The soldiers walked to a ramp leading out of the streetslots, guiding the people into a wealthier section of the town, where some of the canals had been filled in and cobbled.

Soon, the dead spots began to appear. Charred scars—ruins

that had once been homes. The smell of smoke was almost overpowering to Spook, and he had to start breathing through his mouth. They didn't have to walk very far before arriving at their destination. The Citizen himself was in attendance. He rode no horse—those had all been shipped to the farms, for only crass noblemen were too good to walk the ground on their own feet. He did, however, wear red.

"What's that he's wearing?" Spook whispered as Durn led him around the side of the crowd. The Citizen and his retinue stood on the steps of a particularly grand mansion, and the skaa were clustering around. Durn led Spook to a place where a group of toughs had muscled themselves an exclusive piece of the street with a good vantage of the Citizen. They nodded to Durn, letting him pass without comment.

"What do you mean?" Durn asked. "The Citizen is wearing what he always does—skaa trousers and a work shirt."

"They're red," Spook whispered. "That's not an approved color."

"As of this morning it is. Government officers can wear it. That way, they stand out, and people in need can find them. Or, at least, that's the official explanation."

Spook frowned. However, something else caught his attention.

She was there.

It was natural, of course—she accompanied her brother wherever he went. He was particularly worried for her safety, and seldom let her out of his sight. She wore the same look as always, eyes sorrowful within a frame of auburn hair.

"Sad group today," Durn said, and at first Spook thought he was referring to Beldre. However, Durn was nodding toward the group of prisoners. They looked just like the rest of the people in the city—gray clothing, ash-stained faces, subservient postures. The Citizen, however, stepped forward to explain the differences.

"One of the first proclamations this government made," he announced, "was one of solidarity. We are a skaa people. The 'noblemen' chosen by the Lord Ruler oppressed us for ten centuries. Urteau, we decided, would become a place of freedom. A place like the Survivor himself prophesied would come."

"You've got the count?" Durn whispered to Spook.

Spook nodded. "Ten," he said, counting the prisoners. "The ones we expected. You're not earning your coin, Durn."

"Watch."

"These," the Citizen said, bald scalp shining in the red sunlight as he pointed at the prisoners. "These didn't heed our warning. They knew, as all of you know, that any nobleman who stayed in this city would forfeit his life! This is our will—*all* of our will.

"But, like all of their kind, these were too arrogant to listen. They tried to hide. But, they think themselves above us. They always will. That exposes them."

He paused, then spoke again. "And that is why we do what we must."

He waved his soldiers forward. They shoved the prisoners up the steps. Spook could smell the oil on the air as the soldiers opened the house's doors and pushed the people in. Then, the soldiers barred the door from the outside and took up a perimeter. Each soldier lit a torch and threw it on the building. It didn't take superhuman senses to feel the heat that soon blazed to life, and the crowd shied back—revolted and frightened, but fascinated.

The windows had been boarded shut. Spook could see fingers trying to pry the wood free, could hear people screaming. He could hear them thumping against the locked door, trying to break their way out, crying in terror.

He longed to do something. Yet, even with tin, he couldn't fight an entire squad of soldiers on his own. Elend and Vin had sent him to gather information, not play their hand. Still, he cringed, calling himself a coward as he turned away from the burning building.

"This should not be," Spook whispered harshly.

"They were noblemen," Durn said.

"No they weren't! Their parents might have been, but these were skaa. Normal people, Durn."

"They have noble blood."

"So do we all, if you look back far enough," Spook said.

Durn shook his head. "This is the way it has to be. This is the Survivor—"

"Do *not* speak his name in association with this barbarity," Spook hissed.

Durn was quiet for a moment, the only sounds that of the flames and those dying inside them. Finally, he spoke. "I know it's hard to see, and perhaps the Citizen is too eager. But . . . I heard *him* speak once. The Survivor. This is the sort of thing he taught. Death to the noblemen; rule by the skaa. If you'd heard him, you'd understand. Sometimes, you have to destroy something in order to build something better."

Spook closed his eyes. Heat from the fire seemed to be searing his skin. He *had* heard Kelsier speak to crowds of skaa. And, Kelsier had said the things that Durn now referred to. Then, the Survivor had been a voice of hope, of spirit. His same words repeated now, however, became words of hatred and destruction. Spook felt sick.

"Again, Durn," he said, looking up, feeling particularly harsh, "I don't pay you to spout Citizen propaganda at me. Tell me why I'm here, or you'll get no further coin from me."

The large beggar turned, meeting Spook's eyes behind the cloth. "Count the skulls," he said quietly. With that, Durn took his hand off Spook's shoulder and retreated into the crowd.

Spook didn't follow. The scents of smoke and burning flesh were growing too powerful for him. He turned, pushing his way through the crowd, seeking fresh air. He stumbled up against a building, breathing deeply, feeling the rough grain of its wood press against his side. It seemed to him that the falling flakes of ash were a part of the pyre behind, bits of death cast upon the wind.

He heard voices. Spook turned, noting that the Citizen and his guards had moved away from the fire. Quellion was addressing the crowd, encouraging them to be vigilant. Spook watched for a time, and finally the crowd began to leave, trailing the Citizen as he moved back toward the market pit.

He's punished them, now he needs to bless them. Often, especially after executions, the Citizen visited the people personally, moving between stalls in the market, shaking hands and giving encouragement.

Spook took off down a side street. He soon passed out of the wealthier section of town, arriving at a place where the street fell away before him. He chose a place where the retaining wall had collapsed, forming a slope down into the dry canal, then hopped down, skidding his way to the bottom. He pulled up the hood of his cloak, obscuring his covered eyes, and made his way through the busy street with the dexterity of one who had grown up a street urchin.

Even taking a more roundabout route, he arrived at Marketpit before the Citizen and his retinue. Spook watched through the raining ash as the man moved down a broad ramp of earth, trailed by a following that numbered in the hundreds.

You want to be him, Spook thought, crouching beside a merchant's stall. *Kelsier died to bring this people hope, and now you think to steal his legacy.*

This man was no Kelsier. This man wasn't even worthy to utter the Survivor's name.

The Citizen moved about, maintaining a paternal air, speaking to the people of the market. He touched them on the shoulders, shook hands, and smiled benevolently. "The Survivor would be proud of you." Spook could hear his voice even over the noise of the crowd. "The ash that falls is a sign from him—it represents the fall of the empire, the ashes of tyranny. From those ashes we will make a new nation! One ruled by skaa."

Spook edged forward, putting down the top of his hood and feeling before himself with his hands, as if he were blind. He carried his dueling cane across his back, in a strap obscured by the folds of his baggy gray shirt. He was more than capable when it came to moving through crowds. While Vin had always worked hard to remain obscure and unseen,

Spook had managed to achieve both things without ever trying. In fact, he'd often tried the opposite. He'd dreamed of being a man like Kelsier—for even before he'd met the Survivor, Spook had heard stories of the man. The greatest skaa thief of their time—a man bold enough to try to rob the Lord Ruler himself.

And yet, try as he might, Spook had never been able to distinguish himself. It was just too easy to ignore yet another ash-faced boy, especially if you couldn't understand his thick Eastern slang. It had taken actually meeting Kelsier—seeing how he could move people by talking—to finally convince Spook to abandon his dialect. That was when Spook had begun to understand that there was a power in words.

Spook subtly moved his way toward the front of the crowd watching the Citizen. He got jostled and shoved, but nobody cried out against him. A blind man who had gotten caught up in the press of people was easy to ignore—and what was ignored could get where it wasn't supposed to. With some careful positioning, Spook soon placed himself at the front of the group, barely an arm's length from the Citizen.

The man smelled of smoke.

"I understand, good woman," the Citizen was saying as he held an elderly woman's hands. "But your grandson is needed where he is, working the fields. Without him and his kind, we would not be able to eat! A nation ruled by skaa also has to be one *worked* by skaa."

"But . . . can't he come back, even for a bit?" the woman asked.

"In time, good woman," the Citizen said. "In time." His crimson uniform made him the only splash of color on the street, and Spook found himself staring. He tore his eyes away and continued to maneuver, for the Citizen was not his goal.

Beldre stood to the side, as usual. Always watching, but never interacting. The Citizen was so dynamic that his sister was easily forgotten. Spook understood that feeling quite well. He let a soldier jostle him, pushing him out of the Citizen's way. That jostle placed Spook right next to Beldre. She smelt just faintly of perfume.

I thought that was supposed to be forbidden.

What would Kelsier have done? He'd have attacked, perhaps, killing the Citizen. Or, he'd have moved against the man in another way. Kelsier wouldn't have let such terrible things happen—he'd have acted.

Perhaps he would have tried to make an ally out of someone trusted by the Citizen?

Spook felt his heart—always so much louder to him now—beat faster. The crowd began to move again, and he let himself get shoved up against Beldre. The guards weren't watching—they were focused on the Citizen, keeping him safe with so many random elements around.

"Your brother," Spook whispered in her ear, "you approve of his murders?"

She spun, and he noticed for the first time that her eyes were green. He stood in the crowd, letting it shove him away as she searched, trying to figure out who had spoken. The crowd, following her brother, carried her from Spook.

Spook waited, being jostled in the sea of elbows, for a short time. Then he began to maneuver again, pushing through the people with subtle care until he was again beside Beldre.

"You think this is any different from what the Lord Ruler did?" he whispered. "I once saw him gather up random people and execute them in the Luthadel city square."

She spun again, finally identifying Spook among the moving crowd. He stood still, meeting her eyes despite the blindfold. People moved between them, and she was carried away.

Her mouth moved. Only someone with the enhanced senses of tin could have seen with enough detail to make out the words on her lips.

"Who are you?"

He pushed his way through the crowd one more time. The Citizen was apparently planning to make a big speech up ahead, capitalizing on the increasingly large crowd. People were bunching up around the podium that lay in the middle of the market; it was getting more difficult to move through them.

Spook reached her, but felt the crowd pulling him away again. So, he reached between a pair of bodies and grabbed her hand, pulling her wrist as he moved with the surgings of the crowd's motion. She spun, of course, but she didn't cry out. The crowd moved around them, and she turned to meet his blindfolded eyes through the throng.

"Who are you?" Beldre asked again. Though he was close enough to have heard her had she spoken, no sound escaped her lips. She just mouthed the words. Behind her, on the podium, her brother began to preach.

"I'm the man who will kill your brother," Spook said softly.

Again, he had expected a reaction from her—a scream, perhaps. An accusation. His actions here had been impulsive, born from his frustration at not being able to help the people who were executed. If she *did* scream, he realized, it could bring his death.

Yet she remained silent, flakes of ash falling between them.

"Others have said that same thing," she mouthed.

"Others were not me."

"And who are you?" she asked a third time.

"The companion of a god. A man who can see whispers and feel screams."

"A man who thinks he knows better for this people than their own chosen ruler?" she mouthed. "There will always be dissenters who balk at what must be done."

He still had her hand. He gripped it tightly, pulling her close. The crowd crowded the podium, leaving her and Spook at their rear, like shells left on a beach by the retreating waves.

"I *knew* the Survivor, Beldre," he whispered harshly. "He named me, called me friend. What you've done in this city would horrify him—and I'm *not* going to let your brother continue to pervert Kelsier's legacy. Bring him warning, if you must. Tell Quellion that I'm coming for him."

The Citizen had stopped speaking. Spook glanced up, looking toward the lectern. Quellion stood upon it, looking out over his crowd of followers. Looking at Spook and Beldre, standing together at the back of the crowd. Spook hadn't realized how exposed they had become.

"You there!" the Citizen cried. "What are you doing with my sister!"

Damn! Spook thought, releasing the girl and dashing away. However, one major inconvenience of the streetslots was their high, steep walls. There were very few ways to get out of the market, and those were all being watched by members of Quellion's security forces. At the Citizen's shouted command, soldiers began to dash forward from their posts, wearing leather and carrying steel.

Fine, Spook thought, charging the nearest group of soldiers. If he could get through them, he could reach a ramp up, perhaps disappear into the alleys between buildings above.

Swords scraped from scabbards. Behind Spook, people cried out in shock. He reached into the ragged tears of his cloak and whipped forth his dueling cane.

And then, he was among them.

Spook wasn't a warrior, not really. He'd trained with Ham, of course—Clubs had insisted that his nephew know how to defend himself. However, the crew's true warriors had always been their Mistborn, Vin and Kelsier, with Ham—as a Pewterarm—providing brute force, if necessary.

Yet, Spook had spent a lot of time training, lately, and while doing so he had discovered something interesting. He had something that Vin and Kelsier could never have had: a blurring array of sensory knowledge that his body could instinctively use. He could feel disturbances in the air, sense tremors in the floor, and could know where people were simply by how close their heartbeats sounded.

He was no Mistborn, but he was still very dangerous. He

felt a soft wind, and knew a sword was swinging for him. He ducked. He felt a footstep on the ground, and knew someone was attacking from the side. He stepped away. It was almost like having atium.

Sweat flew from his brow as he spun, and he cracked his dueling cane into the back of one soldier's head. The man fell—Spook's weapon was crafted of the finest hardwood. But, just to be certain, he brought the butt of the weapon down on the fallen man's temple, knocking him out of the battle for good.

He heard someone grunt beside him—soft, yet telling. Spook whipped his weapon to the side and smacked it against the attacking soldier's forearm. The bones broke, and the soldier cried out, dropping his weapon. Spook rapped him on the head. Then, Spook spun, lifting his cane to block the third soldier's strike.

Steel met wood, and the steel won, Spook's weapon breaking. However, it stopped the sword strike long enough for Spook to duck away and grab a fallen warrior's sword. It was different from the swords he'd practiced with—the men of Urteau preferred long, thin blades. Still, Spook only had one soldier left—if he could cut the man down, he'd be free.

Spook's opponent seemed to realize that he had the advantage. If Spook ran, it would expose his back to attack. However, if Spook stayed, he'd soon be overwhelmed. The soldier circled warily, trying to stall for time.

So, Spook attacked. He raised his blade, trusting in his enhanced senses to compensate for the difference in training. The soldier raised his weapon to parry as Spook swung.

Spook's sword froze in the air.

Spook stumbled, trying to force the weapon forward, but it was strangely held in place—as if he were trying to push it through something solid, rather than air. It was as if . . .

Someone was Pushing against it. Allomancy. Spook glanced desperately around him, and immediately found the source of the power. The person Pushing had to be directly opposite Spook, for Allomancers could only Push away from themselves.

Quellion, the Citizen, had joined his sister. The Citizen met Spook's gaze, and Spook could see effort in the man's eyes as he clutched his sister, using her weight for support as he Pushed against Spook's sword, interfering in the battle as Kelsier himself once had, long ago when visiting the caverns where his army trained.

Spook dropped the weapon, letting it fly backward out of his hands, then threw himself to the ground. He felt the draft of an enemy sword swinging overhead, narrowly missing him. His own weapon clanged to the ground a short distance from him, its ringing loud in his ears.

He didn't have time to gather his breath; he could only push himself up to dodge the soldier's follow-up blow. Fortunately, Spook wasn't wearing any metal that Quellion could Push against to influence the fight any further. That was a habit that Spook was glad he'd never lost.

The only choice was to run. He couldn't fight, not with an Allomancer interfering. He turned while the soldier prepared another swing. Then, Spook threw himself forward, getting inside the soldier's guard. He ducked under the man's arm and dashed to the side, hoping to run past and leave the soldier confused.

Something caught his foot.

Spook spun. At first, he assumed that Quellion was Pulling on him somehow. Then, he saw that the soldier on the ground—the first one he'd dropped—had grabbed his foot.

I hit that man in the head twice! Spook thought with frustration. *There's no way he's still conscious!*

The hand squeezed his foot, yanking Spook backward with an inhuman strength. With strength like that, the man had to be a Thug—a pewter burner, like Ham.

Spook was in serious trouble.

Spook kicked, managing to break free, then stumbled to his feet. But a Thug would have the power of pewter—he'd be able to run faster, and farther, than Spook.

Two Allomancers, counting the Citizen himself, Spook thought. *Somebody isn't as disdainful of noble blood as he claims!*

The two soldiers advanced on him. Yelling in frustration—hearing his own heart thump like a pounding drum—Spook threw himself at the Thug and grappled the man, taking him by surprise. In that moment of confusion, Spook spun him around, using the Thug's body like a shield to protect himself from the third soldier.

He hadn't counted on the Citizen's brutal training. Quellion always spoke of sacrifice and necessity. Apparently, this philosophy extended to his soldiers, for the man with the sword rammed his weapon straight through his friend's back, piercing his heart and driving the weapon directly into Spook's chest. It was a move only a man with the strength and precision of a Thug could have performed.

Three Allomancers, Spook thought, dazed, as the soldier tried to pull his sword free from two bodies. The body of the dead man was a weight that finally snapped the blade.

How did I even survive this long? They must have been trying not to reveal their powers. Trying to remain hidden from the population. . . .

Spook stumbled backward, feeling blood on his chest. Oddly, he didn't feel pain. His heightened senses should have made the pain so powerful that—

It hit. Everything went black.

The subtlety displayed in the ash-eating microbes and enhanced plants shows that Rashek got better and better at using the power. It burned out in a matter of minutes—but to a god, minutes can pass like hours. During that time, Rashek began as an ignorant child who shoved a planet too close to the sun, grew into an adult who could create ashmounts to cool the air, then finally became a mature artisan who could develop plants and creatures for specific purposes.

It also shows his mind-set during his time with Preservation's power. Under its influence he was obviously in a protective mode. Instead of leveling the ashmounts and trying to push the planet back into place, he was reactive, working furiously to fix problems that he himself had caused.

17

ELEND RODE AT THE FRONT of his men, astride a brilliant white stallion that had been scrubbed clean of ash. He turned his mount, looking over the ranks of nervous soldiers. They waited in the evening light, and Elend could see their terror. They had heard rumors, then had those rumors confirmed by Elend the day before. Today, his army would become immunized to the mists.

Elend rode through their ranks, General Demoux riding a roan stallion beside him. Both horses were big destriers, brought on the trip to impress more than for usefulness. Elend and the other officers would spend most of the trip riding in canal boats, rather than on horseback.

He didn't worry about the morality of his decision to expose his forces to the mists—at least, he didn't worry about it at that moment. Elend had learned something very important about himself: He was honest. Perhaps too honest. If he was uncertain, it would show in his face. The soldiers would sense his hesitation. So he'd learned to confine his worries and concerns to times when he was only with those closest to him. That meant Vin saw too much of his brooding. However, it left him free at other times to project confidence.

He moved quickly, letting his horse's hooves beat a thunder for the men to hear. Occasionally, he heard captains call out for their men to be firm. Even so, Elend saw the anxiety in his soldiers' eyes. And could he blame them? This day, the men would face an enemy that they could not fight, and could not resist. Within the hour, seven hundred of them would lay dead. About one in fifty. Not bad odds, on a grand scale—but that meant little to a man standing and feeling the mist creep around him.

The men stood their ground. Elend was proud of them. He had given those who wished it the opportunity to return to Luthadel instead of facing the mists. He still needed troops in the capital, and he'd rather not march with men unwilling to go into the mists. Almost none had gone. The vast majority had instead lined up in full ranks without having to be ordered, wearing full battle gear, armor polished and oiled, uniforms looking as clean as possible in the ash-stained wilderness. It seemed right to Elend for them to be in their armor. It made them seem as if they were going to battle—and, in a way, they were.

They trusted him. They knew that the mists were advancing toward Luthadel, and understood the importance of capturing the cities with storage caverns. They believed in Elend's ability to do something to save their families.

Their trust made him even more determined. He reined in his horse, turning the massive beast beside a rank of soldiers. He flared pewter, making his body stronger, giving more power to his lungs, then Rioted the emotions of the men to make them braver.

"Be strong!" he shouted.

Heads turned toward him, and the clanking of armor hushed. His own voice was so loud in his ears that he had to dampen his tin. "These mists will strike down some of us. However, most of us will be untouched—and most who fall will recover! Then, none of us need fear the mists again. We *cannot* arrive at Fadrex City without having inoculated ourselves! If we did so, we would risk being attacked in the morning, when we are hiding in our tents. Our enemies would force us out into the mists anyway, and we would have to fight with a sixth of our men shaking on the ground from sickness!"

He turned his horse, Demoux following behind, and moved along the ranks. "I do not know why the mists kill. But I trust in the Survivor! He named himself Lord of the Mists. If some of us die, then it is his will. Stay strong!"

His reminders seemed to have some effect. The soldiers stood a little straighter, facing west, toward where the sun would soon set. Elend reined in again, sitting tall and letting himself be seen.

"They look strong, my lord," Demoux said quietly, moving his horse up beside Elend's. "It was a good speech."

Elend nodded.

"My lord . . ." Demoux said, "did you mean what you said about the Survivor?"

"Of course I did."

"I'm sorry, my lord," Demoux said. "I didn't mean to question your faith, it's just that . . . well, you don't have to keep up the charade of belief, if you don't want to."

"I gave my word, Demoux," Elend said, frowning and glancing at the scarred general. "I do what I say."

"I believe you, my lord," Demoux said. "You are an honorable man."

"But?"

Demoux paused. "But . . . if you don't really believe in the Survivor, I don't think he would want you speaking in his name."

Elend opened his mouth to reprimand Demoux for his lack of respect, but stopped himself. The man spoke with honesty, from his heart. That wasn't the kind of thing to punish.

Besides, he might have had a point. "I don't know what I believe, Demoux," Elend said, looking back at the field of soldiers. "Certainly not in the Lord Ruler. Sazed's religions have been dead for centuries, and even he has stopped talking about them. It seems to me that leaves the Church of the Survivor as the only real option."

"With all due respect, my lord," Demoux said. "That's not a very strong profession of faith."

"I'm having trouble with faith lately, Demoux," Elend said, looking up, watching flakes of ash drift through the air. "My last god was killed by the woman I eventually married—a woman you claim as a religious figure, but who spurns your devotion."

Demoux nodded quietly.

"I don't reject your god, Demoux," Elend said. "I meant what I said—I think having faith in Kelsier is better than the alternatives. And, considering what's going to be coming at us in the next few months, I'd rather believe that something—anything—is out there helping us."

They were quiet for a few moments.

"I know that the Lady Heir objects to our worship of the Survivor, my lord," Demoux finally said. "She knew him, as did I. What she doesn't understand is that the Survivor has become so much more than just the man Kelsier."

Elend frowned. "That sounds like you calculatedly made him a god, Demoux—that you believe in him as a symbol only."

Demoux shook his head. "I'm saying that Kelsier was a man, but a man who gained something—a mantle, a portion of something eternal and immortal. When he died, he wasn't just Kelsier, the crewleader. Don't you think it odd that he was never Mistborn before he went to the Pits?"

"That's the way Allomancy works, Demoux," Elend said. "You don't gain your powers until you Snap—until you face something traumatic, something that nearly kills you."

"And you don't think that Kelsier experienced those kinds of events before the Pits?" Demoux asked. "My lord, he was a thief who robbed from obligators and noblemen. He lived a very dangerous life. You think he could have avoided beatings, near-deaths, and emotional anguish?"

Elend paused.

"He gained his powers at the Pits," Elend said quietly, "because something else came upon him. People who knew him speak of how he was a changed man when he came back. He had purpose—he was driven to accomplish something the rest of the world thought impossible."

Demoux shook his head. "No, my lord. Kelsier the man died in those Pits, and Kelsier the Survivor was born. He was granted great power, and great wisdom, by a force that is above us all. *That* is why he accomplished what he did. *That* is why we worship him. He still had the follies of a man, but he had the hopes of a divinity."

Elend turned away. The rational, scholarly side of him understood exactly what was happening. Kelsier was gradually being deified, his life made more and more mystical by those who followed him. Kelsier had to be invested with heavenly power, for the Church couldn't continue to revere a mere man.

And yet, another part of Elend was glad for the rationalization, if only because it made the story that much more believable. After all, Demoux was right. How *did* a man living on the streets last so long before Snapping?

Someone screamed.

Elend looked up, scanning the ranks. Men began to shuffle as the mists appeared, sprouting in the air like growing plants. He couldn't see the soldier who had fallen. Soon, the point was moot, for others began to scream.

The sun began to be obscured, blazing red as it approached the horizon. Elend's horse shuffled nervously. The captains ordered the men to remain steady, but Elend could still see motion. In the group before him, pockets appeared in the ranks as men randomly collapsed to the ground, like marionettes whose strings had been cut. They shook on the ground, other soldiers backing away in horror, mist moving all around.

They need me, Elend thought, grabbing his reins, Pulling on the emotions of those around him. "Demoux, let's ride."

He turned his horse. Demoux did not follow.

Elend spun. "Demoux? What—"

He choked off immediately. Demoux sat in the mists, shaking horribly. Even as Elend watched, the balding soldier slipped from his saddle, collapsing to the ankle-deep ash below.

"Demoux!" Elend yelled, hopping down, feeling like a fool. He'd never thought to wonder if Demoux was susceptible—he'd just assumed that he, like Vin and the others, was already immune. Elend knelt beside Demoux, his legs in the ash, listening to soldiers scream and captains yell for order. His friend shook and twisted, gasping in pain.

And the ash continued to fall.

Rashek didn't solve all the world's problems. In fact, with each thing he did fix, he created new issues. However, he was clever enough that each subsequent problem was smaller than the ones before it. So, instead of plants that died from the distorted sun and ashy ground, we got plants that didn't provide quite enough nutrition.

He did save the world. True, the near-destruction was his fault in the first place—but he did an admirable job, all things considered. At least he didn't release Ruin to the world as we did.

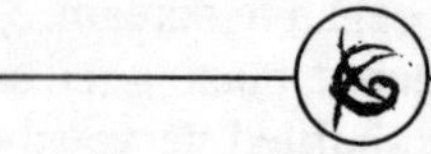

18

SAZED SLAPPED HIS HORSE ON the rump, sending it galloping away. The beast's hooves kicked up chunks of packed ash as it ran. Its coat had once been a keen white; now it was a rough gray. Its ribs were beginning to show—it was malnourished to the point that it was no longer reasonable to expect it to carry a rider, and they could no longer afford to spare food for it.

"Now, that's a sad sight," Breeze noted, standing beside Sazed on the ash-covered road. Their guard of two hundred soldiers waited quietly, watching the beast run. Sazed couldn't help feeling that the release of their final horse was a symbol.

"You think it will be able to survive?" Breeze asked.

"I suspect that it will still be able to poke beneath the ash and find nourishment for a time," Sazed said. "It will be difficult, however."

Breeze grunted. "Living's difficult work for all of us, these days. Well, I wish the creature the best of luck. Are you going to join Allrianne and me in the carriage?"

Sazed glanced over his shoulder, toward the vehicle, which had been lightened, then rigged to be pulled by soldiers. They had removed the doors and hung curtains instead, and had removed sections of the back as well. With the decreased weight and two hundred men to take turns, the vehicle wouldn't be too much of a burden. Still, Sazed knew he would feel guilty being pulled by others. His old servant's instincts were too strong.

"No," Sazed said. "I shall walk for a bit. Thank you."

Breeze nodded, walking to the carriage to sit with Allrianne, a soldier holding a parasol over his head until he was inside. Now exposed to the ash, Sazed put up the hood of his travel robe, hefted his portfolio in his arm, then strode across the black ground to the front of the line.

"Captain Goradel," he said. "You may continue your march."

They did so. It was a rough hike—the ash was growing thick, and it was slick and tiring to walk on. It moved and shifted beneath the feet, almost as difficult as walking on sand. As hard as the hike was, however, it wasn't enough to distract Sazed from his troubled feelings. He had hoped that visiting the army—meeting with Elend and Vin—would give him a respite. The two were dear friends, and their affection for one another tended to bolster him. He had, after all, been the one to perform their marriage.

Yet, this meeting had left him even more troubled. *Vin allowed Elend to die,* he thought. *And she did it because of things I taught her.*

He carried the picture of a flower in his sleeve pocket, trying to make sense of his conversation with Vin. How had Sazed become the one that people came to with their problems? Couldn't they sense that he was simply a hypocrite, capable of formulating answers that sounded good, yet incapable of following his own advice? He felt lost. He felt a weight, squeezing him, telling him to simply give up.

How easily Elend spoke of hope and humor, as if being happy were simply a decision one made. Some people assumed that it was. Once, Sazed might have agreed with them. Now, his stomach simply twisted, and he felt sick at the thought of taking pretty much any action. His thoughts were constantly invaded by doubts.

This is what religion is for, Sazed thought as he tromped through the ash at the head of the column, carrying his pack on his shoulders. *It helps people through times like these.*

He looked down at his portfolio. Then, he opened it and leafed through the pages as he walked. Hundreds finished, and not a single one of the religions had provided the answers he sought. Perhaps he simply knew them too well. Most of the crew had trouble worshipping Kelsier as the other skaa did, for they knew of his faults and his quirks. They knew him as a man first, and as a god second. Perhaps the religions were the same to Sazed. He knew them so well that he could see their flaws too easily.

He did not disparage the people who had followed the religions, but Sazed—so far—had found only contradiction and hypocrisy in each religion he studied. Divinity was supposed to be perfect. Divinity didn't let its followers get slaughtered, and certainly didn't allow the world to be destroyed by good men who were just trying to save it.

One of the remaining ones would provide an answer. There *had* to be truth he could discover. As his feelings of dark suffocation threatened to overwhelm him, he fell to his studies, taking out the next sheet in line and strapping it to the outside of the portfolio. He would study it as he walked, carrying the portfolio with the sheet on the bottom when he wasn't reading, thereby keeping the ash off of it.

He'd find the answers. He dared not think what he would do if there weren't any.

They eventually passed into the Central Dominance, entering lands where men could still struggle for food and life.

Breeze and Allrianne stayed in the carriage, but Sazed was glad to walk, even if it made his religions difficult to study.

He wasn't certain what to make of the cultivated fields. They passed scores of them—Elend had packed as many people as possible into the Central Dominance, then had ordered all of them to grow food for the coming winter. Even those skaa who had lived in the cities were well accustomed to hard work, and they quickly did as Elend ordered. Sazed wasn't certain if the people understood just how dire their situation was, or if they were simply happy to have someone tell them what to do.

The roadside grew heaped with tall piles of ash. Each day, the skaa workers had to clear away the ash that had fallen during the night. This unending task—along with the need to carry water to most of the new, unirrigated fields—created a very labor-intensive system of agriculture.

The plants did grow, however. Sazed's troop passed field after field, each one budding with brown plants. The sight should have brought him hope. Yet, it was difficult to look upon the sprouting stalks and not feel an even greater despair. They looked so weak and small beside the massive piles of ash. Even forgetting the mists, how was Elend going to feed an empire in these conditions? How long would it be before there was simply too much ash to move? Skaa worked the fields, their postures much as they had been during the days of the Lord Ruler. What had really changed for them?

"Look at them," a voice said. Sazed turned to see Captain Goradel walking up beside him. Bald and rugged, the man had a good-natured disposition—a trait common in the soldiers whom Ham promoted.

"I know," Sazed said quietly.

"Even with the ash and the mist, seeing them gives me hope."

Sazed looked up sharply. "Really?"

"Sure," Goradel said. "My family were farmers, Master Terrisman. We lived in Luthadel, but worked the outer fields."

"But, you were a soldier," Sazed said. "Weren't you the one who led Lady Vin into the palace the night she killed the Lord Ruler?"

Goradel nodded. "Actually, I led Lord Elend into the palace to rescue Lady Vin, though she turned out to not need much help from us. Anyway, you're right. I was a soldier in the Lord Ruler's palace—my parents disowned me when I joined up. But, I just couldn't face working in the fields my whole life."

"It is arduous work."

"No, it wasn't that," Goradel said. "It wasn't the labor, it was the . . . hopelessness. I couldn't stand to work all day to grow something I knew would belong to someone else. That's why I left the fields to become a soldier, and that's why seeing these farms gives me hope."

Goradel nodded toward a passing field. Some of the skaa looked up, then waved as they saw Elend's banner. "These people," Goradel said, "they work because they want to."

"They work because if they don't, they will starve."

"Sure," Goradel said. "I guess you're right. But they're not working because someone will beat them if they don't—they're working so that their families and their friends won't die. There's a difference in that, to a farmer. You can see it in the way they stand."

Sazed frowned as they walked, but said nothing further.

"Anyway, Master Terrisman," Goradel said, "I came to suggest that we make a stop at Luthadel for supplies."

Sazed nodded. "I suspected that we would do so. I, however, will need to leave you for a few days as you go to Luthadel. Lord Breeze can take command. I shall meet up with you on the northern highway."

Goradel nodded, moving back to make the arrangements. He didn't ask why Sazed wanted to leave the group, or what his destination was.

Several days later, Sazed arrived—alone—at the Pits of Hathsin. There was little to distinguish the area, now that the ash covered everything. Sazed's feet kicked up clumps of it as he moved to the top of a hill. He looked down on the valley that contained the Pits—the place where Kelsier's wife had been murdered. The place where the Survivor had been born.

It was now the home of the Terris people.

There were few of them remaining. They had never been a very large population, and the coming of the mists and the difficult trek down to the Central Dominance had claimed many lives. There were, perhaps, forty thousand of them left. And a good many of the men were eunuchs, like Sazed.

Sazed moved down the slope toward the valley. It had been a natural place to settle the Terris people. During the days of the Lord Ruler, hundreds of slaves had worked here, watched over by hundreds more soldiers. That had ended when Kelsier had returned to the Pits and destroyed their ability to produce atium. However, the Pits still had the buildings and infrastructure that had supported them during their working days. There was plenty of fresh water, and some shelter. The Terris people had improved on this, building other structures across the valley, making what was once the most terrifying of prison camps into a pastoral group of villages.

Even as Sazed walked down the hillside, he could see people brushing away the ash from the ground, letting the natural plant life poke through to provide grazing for the animals. The scrub that formed the dominant foliage in the Central Dominance was a resilient, hardy group of plants, and they were adapted to ash, and didn't need as much water as farm crops. That meant that the Terris people actually had easier lives than most. They were herdsman, as they had been even during the centuries before the Lord Ruler's Ascension. A hearty, short-legged breed of sheep mulled about on the hills, chewing down the uncovered stalks of scrub.

The Terris people, Sazed thought, *living lives easier than most. What a strange world it has become.*

His approach soon attracted attention. Children ran for their parents, and heads poked from shacks. Sheep began to gather around Sazed as he walked, as if hoping that he had come bearing treats of some sort.

Several aged men rushed up the hillside, moving as quickly as their gnarled limbs would allow. They—like Sazed—still wore their steward's robes. And, like Sazed, they kept them cleaned of ash, showing the colorful V-shaped patterns that ran down the fronts. Those patterns had once indicated the noble house that the steward served.

"Lord Sazed!" one of the men said eagerly.

"Your Majesty!" said another.

Your Majesty. "Please," Sazed said, raising his hands. "Do not call me that."

The two aged stewards glanced at each other. "Please, Master Keeper. Let us get you something warm to eat."

Yes, the ash was black. No, it should not have been. Most common ash has a dark component, but is just as much gray or white as it is black.

Ash from the ashmounts . . . it was different. Like the mists themselves, the ash covering our land was not truly a natural thing. Perhaps it was the influence of Ruin's power—as black as Preservation was white. Or, perhaps it was simply the nature of the ashmounts, which were designed and created specifically to blast ash and smoke into the sky.

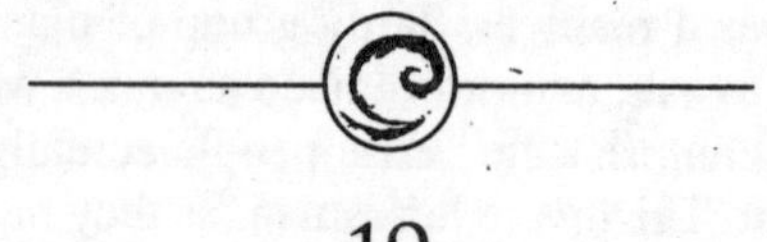

19

"GET UP!"

Everything was dark.

"*Get up!*"

Spook opened his eyes. Everything seemed so dull, so

muted. He could barely see. The world was a dark blur. And . . . he felt numb. Dead. Why couldn't he feel?

"Spook, you need to get up!"

The voice, at least, was clear. Yet, everything else felt muddy. He couldn't quite manage to think. He blinked, groaning quietly. What was wrong with him? His spectacles and cloth were gone. That should have left him free to see, but everything was so dark.

He was out of tin.

There was nothing burning in his stomach. The familiar flame, a comforting candle within, was no longer there. It had been his companion for over a year, always there. He'd feared what he was doing, but had never let it die. And now it was gone.

That was why everything seemed so dull. Was this really how other people lived? How he used to live? He could barely see—the sharp, rich detail he'd grown accustomed to was gone. The vibrant colors and crisp lines. Instead, everything was bland and vague.

His ears felt clogged. His nose . . . he couldn't smell the boards beneath him, couldn't tell the species of wood by scent. He couldn't smell the bodies that had passed. He couldn't feel the thumpings of people moving about in other rooms.

And . . . he *was* in a room. He shook his head, sitting up, trying to think. Immediately, a pain in his shoulder made him gasp. The wound had not been cared for. He remembered the sword piercing him near the shoulder. That was not a wound one recovered from easily—indeed, his left arm didn't seem to work right, one of the reasons he was having so much trouble rising.

"You've lost a lot of blood," the voice said. "You'll die soon, even if the flames don't take you. Don't bother to look for the pouch of tin at your belt—they took that."

"Flames?" Spook croaked, blinking. How did people survive in a world that was this dark?

"Can't you feel them, Spook? They're near."

There *was* a light nearby, down a hallway. Spook shook his head, trying to clear his mind. *I'm in a house,* he thought. *A nice one. A nobleman's house.*

And they're burning it down.

This, finally, gave him motivation to stand, though he immediately dropped again, his body too weak—his mind too fuzzy—to keep him on his feet.

"Don't walk," the voice said. Where had he heard that voice before? He trusted it. "Crawl," it said.

Spook did as commanded, crawling forward.

"No, not *toward* the flames! You have to get out, so you can punish those who did this to you. Think, Spook!"

"Window," Spook croaked, turning to the side, crawling toward one of them.

"Boarded shut," the voice said. "You saw this before, from the outside. There's only one way to survive. You have to listen to me."

Spook nodded dully.

"Go out the room's other door. Crawl toward the stairs leading to the second floor."

Spook did so, forcing himself to keep moving. His arms were so numb they felt like weights tied to his shoulders. He'd been flaring tin so long that normal senses just didn't seem to work for him anymore. He found the stairs, though he was coughing by the time he got there. That would be because of the smoke, a part of his mind told him. It was probably a good thing he was crawling.

He could feel the heat as he climbed. The flames seemed to be chasing him, claiming the room behind him as he moved up the stairs, still dizzy. He reached the top, then slipped on his own blood, slumping against the side of the wall, groaning.

"Get up!" the voice said.

Where have I heard that voice before? he thought again. *Why do I want to do what it says?* It was so close. He'd have it, if his mind weren't so muddled. Yet, he obeyed, forcing himself to his hands and knees again.

"Second room on the left," the voice commanded.

Spook crawled without thinking. Flames crept up the

stairs, flickering across the walls. His nose was weak, like his other senses, but he suspected that the house had been soaked with oil. It made for a faster, more dramatic burn that way.

"Stop. This is the room."

Spook turned left, crawling into the room. It was a study, well furnished. The thieves in the city complained that ransacking places like this one wasn't worth the effort. The Citizen forbade ostentation, and so expensive furniture couldn't be sold, even on the black market. Nobody wanted to be caught owning luxuries, lest they end up burning to death in one of the Citizen's executions.

"Spook!"

Spook had heard of those executions. He'd never seen one. He'd paid Durn to keep an eye out for the next one. Spook's coin would get him advance warning, as well as a good position to watch the building burn down. Plus, Durn promised he had another tidbit, something Spook would be interested in. Something worth the coin he'd paid.

Count the skulls.

"Spook!"

Spook opened his eyes. He'd fallen to the floor and begun to drift off. Flames were already burning the ceiling. The building was dying. There was no way Spook would get out, not in his current condition.

"Go to the desk," the voice commanded.

"I'm dead," Spook whispered.

"No you're not. Go to the desk."

Spook turned his head, looking at the flames. A figure stood in them, a dark silhouette. The walls dripped, bubbled, and hissed, their plaster and paints blackening. Yet, this shadow of a person didn't seem to mind the fire. That figure seemed familiar. Tall. Commanding.

"You . . . ?" Spook whispered.

"Go to the desk!"

Spook rolled to his knees. He crawled, dragging his useless arm, moving to the side of the desk.

"Right drawer."

Spook pulled it open, then leaned against the side, slumping. Something was inside.

Vials?

He reached for them eagerly. They were the kinds of vials used by Allomancers to store metal shavings. With trembling fingers, Spook picked one up, then it slipped free of his numb fingers. It shattered. He stared at the liquid that had been inside—an alcohol solution that would keep the metal flakes from corroding, as well as help the Allomancer drink them down.

"Spook!" the voice said.

Dully, Spook took another vial. He worked off the stopper with his teeth, feeling the fires blaze around him. The far wall was nearly gone. The fires crept toward him.

He drank the contents of the vial, then searched inside of himself, seeking tin. But there was none. Spook cried out in despair, dropping the vial. It had contained no tin. How would that have saved him anyway? It would have made him feel the flames, and his wound, more acutely.

"Spook!" the voice commanded. "Burn it!"

"There is no tin!" Spook yelled.

"Not tin! The man who owned this house was no Tineye!"

Not tin. Spook blinked. Then—reaching within himself—he found something completely unexpected. Something he'd never thought to ever see, something that shouldn't have existed.

A new metal reserve. He burned it.

His body flared with strength. His trembling arms became steady. His weakness seemed to flee, cast aside like darkness before the rising sun. He felt tension and power, and his muscles grew taut with anticipation.

"Stand!"

His head snapped up. He leaped to his feet, and this time the dizziness was gone. His mind still felt numb, but something was clear to him. Only one metal could have changed his body, making it strong enough to work despite his terrible wound and blood loss.

Spook was burning pewter.

The figure stood in the flames, dark, hard to make out. "I've given you the blessing of pewter, Spook," the voice said. "Use it to escape this place. You can break through the boards on the far side of that hallway, escape out onto the roof of the building nearby. The soldiers won't be watching for you—they're too busy controlling the fire so it doesn't spread."

Spook nodded. The heat didn't bother him anymore. "Thank you."

The figure stepped forward, becoming more than just a silhouette. Flames played against the man's firm face, and Spook's suspicions were confirmed. There was a reason he'd trusted that voice, a reason why he'd done what it had said.

He'd do whatever this man commanded.

"I didn't give you pewter just so you could live, Spook," Kelsier said, pointing. "I gave it to you so you could get revenge. Now, go!"

More than one person reported feeling a sentient hatred in the mists. This is not necessarily related to the mists killing people, however. For most—even those it struck down—the mists seemed merely a weather phenomenon, no more sentient or vengeful than a terrible disease.

For some few, however, there was more. Those it favored, it swirled around. Those it was hostile to, it pulled away from. Some felt peace within it, others felt hatred. It all came down to Ruin's subtle touch, and how much one responded to his promptings.

20

TENSOON SAT IN HIS CAGE.

The cage's very existence was an insult. Kandra were not like men—even if he were not imprisoned, TenSoon would not have run or tried to escape. He had come willingly to his fate.

And yet, they locked him up. He wasn't certain where they had gotten the cage—it certainly wasn't something kandra normally would need. Still, the Seconds had found it and erected it in one of the main caverns of the Homeland. It was made of iron plates and hard steel bars with a strong wire mesh stretched across all four faces to keep him from reducing his body to base muscles and wriggling through. It was another insult.

TenSoon sat inside, naked on the cold iron floor. Had he accomplished anything other than his own condemnation? Had his words in the Trustwarren been of any value at all?

Outside his cage, the caverns glowed with the light of cultivated mosses, and kandra went about their duties. Many stopped, studying him. This was the purpose of the long delay between his judgment and sentencing. The Second Generationers didn't need weeks to ponder what they were going to do to him. However, TenSoon had forced them to let him speak his mind, and the Seconds wanted to make certain he was properly punished. They put him on display, like some human in the stocks. In all the history of the kandra people, no other had ever been treated in such a way. His name would be a byword of shame for centuries.

But we won't last centuries, he thought angrily. *That was what my speech was all about.*

But, he hadn't given it very well. How could he explain to the people what he felt? That their traditions were coming to a focus, that their lives—which had been stable for so long—were in drastic need of change?

What happened above? Did Vin go to the Well of Ascension? What of Ruin, and Preservation? The gods of the kandra people were at war again, and the only ones who knew of them were pretending that nothing was happening.

Outside his cage, the other kandra lived their lives. Some trained the members of the newer generations—he could see Elevenths moving along, little more than blobs with some glistening bones. The transformation from mistwraith to kandra was a difficult one. Once given a Blessing, the mistwraith would lose most of its instincts as it gained sentience, and would have to relearn how to form muscles and bodies. It was a process that took many, many years.

Other adult kandra went about food preparation. They would stew a mixture of algae and fungi inside stone pits, not unlike the one in which TenSoon would spend eternity. Despite his former hatred of mankind, TenSoon had always found the opportunity to enjoy outside food—particularly aged meat—a very tempting consolation for going out on a Contract.

Now, he barely had enough to drink, let alone enough to eat. He sighed, looking through the bars at the vast cavern. The caves of the Homeland were enormous, far too large for the kandra to fill. But, that was what many of his people liked about them. After spending years in a Contract—serving a master's whims, often for decades at a time—a place that offered the option of solitude was quite precious.

Solitude, TenSoon thought. *I'll have plenty of that, soon enough.* Contemplating an eternity in prison made him a little less annoyed with the people who came to gawk at him. They would be the last of his people he ever saw. He recognized many of them. The Fourths and Fifths came to spit at the ground before him, showing their devotion to the Seconds. The Sixths and the Sevenths—who made up the bulk of the Contract fillers—came to pity him and shake their heads for a friend fallen. The Eighths and Ninths came out of curiosity, amazed that one so aged could have fallen so far.

And then he saw a particularly familiar face amidst the watching groups. TenSoon turned aside, ashamed, as MeLaan approached, pain showing in those overly large eyes of hers.

"TenSoon?" a whisper soon came.

"Go away, MeLaan," he said quietly, his back to the bars, which only let him look out at another group of kandra, watching him from the other side.

"TenSoon . . ." she repeated.

"You need not see me like this, MeLaan. Please go."

"They shouldn't be able to do this to you," she said, and he could hear the anger in her voice. "You're nearly as old as they, and far more wise."

"They are the Second Generation," TenSoon said. "They are chosen by those of the First. They lead us."

"They don't *have* to lead us."

"MeLaan!" he said, finally turning toward her. Most of the gawkers stayed back, as if TenSoon's crime were a disease they could catch. MeLaan crouched alone beside his cage, her True Body of spindly wooden bones making her look unnaturally slim.

"You could challenge them," MeLaan said quietly.

"What do you think we are?" TenSoon asked. "Humans, with their rebellions and upheavals? We are kandra. We are of Preservation. We follow order."

"You still bow before them?" MeLaan hissed, pressing her thin face up against the bars. "After what you said—with what is happening above?"

TenSoon paused. "Above?"

"You were right, TenSoon," she said. "Ash cloaks the land in a mantle of black. The mists come during the day, killing both crops and people. Men march to war. Ruin has returned."

TenSoon closed his eyes. "They will do something," he finally said. "The First Generation."

"They are old," MeLaan said. "Old, forgetful, impotent."

TenSoon opened his eyes. "You have changed much."

She smiled. "They should never have given children of a new generation to be raised by a Third. There are many of us, the younger ones, who would fight. The Seconds can't rule forever. What can we do, TenSoon? How can we help you?"

Oh, child, he thought. *You don't think that they know about you?*

Those of the Second Generation were not fools. They might be lazy, but they were old and crafty—TenSoon understood this, for he knew each of them quite well. They would have kandra listening, waiting to see what was said at his cage. A kandra of the Fourth or Fifth Generation who had the Blessing of Awareness could stand a distance away, and still hear every word being spoken at his cage.

TenSoon was kandra. He had returned to receive his punishment because that was right. It was more than honor, more than Contract. It was who he was.

And yet, if the things MeLaan had said were true . . .

Ruin has returned.

"How can you just sit here?" MeLaan said. "You're stronger than they are, TenSoon."

TenSoon shook his head. "I broke Contract, MeLaan."

"For a higher good."

At least I convinced her.

"Is it true, TenSoon?" she asked very quietly.

"What?"

"OreSeur. He had the Blessing of Potency. You must have inherited it, when you killed him. Yet, they didn't find it on your body when they took you. So, what did you do with it? Can I fetch it for you? Bring it, so that you can fight?"

"I will not fight my own people, MeLaan," TenSoon said. "I am kandra."

"Someone must lead us!" she hissed.

That statement, at least, was true. But, it wasn't TenSoon's right. Nor, really, was it the right of the Second Generation—or even the First Generation. It was the right of the one who had created them. That one was dead. But, another had taken his place.

MeLaan was silent for a time, still kneeling beside his cage. Perhaps she waited for him to offer encouragement, or perhaps to become the leader she sought. He didn't speak.

"So, you just came to die," she finally said.

"To explain what I've discovered. What I've felt."

"And then what? You come, proclaim dread news, then leave us to solve the problems on our own?"

"That's not fair, MeLaan," he said. "I came to be the best kandra I know how."

"Then fight!"

He shook his head.

"It's true then," she said. "The others of my generation, they said that you were broken by that last master of yours. The man Zane."

"He did not break me," TenSoon said.

"Oh?" MeLaan said. "And why did you return to the Homeland in that . . . body you were using?"

"The dog's bones?" TenSoon said. "Those weren't given to me by Zane, but by Vin."

"So *she* broke you."

TenSoon exhaled quietly. How could he explain? On one hand, it seemed ironic to him that MeLaan—who intentionally wore a True Body that was inhuman—would find his use of a dog's body so distasteful. Yet, he could understand. It had taken him quite some time to appreciate the advantages of those bones.

He paused.

But, no. He had not come to bring revolution. He had come to explain, to serve the interests of his people. He would do that by accepting his punishment, as a kandra should.

And yet . . .

There was a chance. A slim one. He wasn't even certain he wanted to escape, but if there was an opportunity . . . "Those bones I wore," TenSoon found himself saying. "You know where they are?"

MeLaan frowned. "No. Why would you want them?"

TenSoon shook his head. "I don't," he said, choosing his words carefully. "They were disgraceful! I was made to wear them for over a year, forced into the humiliating role of a dog. I would have discarded them, but I had no corpse to ingest and take, so I had to return here wearing that horrid body."

"You're avoiding the real issue, TenSoon."

"There is no real issue, MeLaan," he said, turning away from her. Whether or not his plan worked, he didn't want the Seconds punishing her for associating with him. "I will not rebel against my people. Please, if you truly wish to help me, just let me be."

MeLaan hissed quietly, and he heard her stand. "You were once the greatest of us."

TenSoon sighed as she left. *No, MeLaan. I was never great. Up until recently, I was the most orthodox of my generation, a conservative distinguished only by his hatred of humans. Now, I've become the greatest criminal in the history of our people, but I did it mostly by accident.*

That isn't greatness. That's just foolishness.

It should be no surprise that Elend became such a powerful Allomancer. It is a well-documented fact—though that documentation wasn't available to most—that Allomancers were much stronger during the early days of the Final Empire.

In those days, an Allomancer didn't need duralumin to take control of a kandra or koloss. A simple Push or Pull on the emotions was enough. In fact, this ability was one of the main reasons that the kandra devised their Contracts with the humans—for, at that time, not only Mistborn, but Soothers and Rioters could take control of them at the merest of whims.

21

DEMOUX SURVIVED.

He was one of the larger group, the fifteen percent who grew sick, but did not die. Vin sat atop the cabin of her narrowboat, arm resting on a wooden ledge, idly fingering her mother's earring—which, as always, she wore in her ear. Koloss brutes trudged along the towpath, dragging the barges and boats down the canal. Many of the barges still carried supplies—tents, foodstuffs, pure water. Several had been emptied, however, their contents carried on the backs of the surviving soldiers, making room for the wounded.

Vin turned away from the barges, looking toward the front of the narrowboat. Elend stood at the prow, as usual, staring west. He did not brood. He looked like a king, standing straight-backed, staring determinedly toward his goal. He looked so different now from the man he had once been, with his full beard, his longer hair, his uniforms that had been scrubbed white. They were growing worn. Not ragged . . . they were still clean and sharp, as white as things could get in the current state of the world. They were just no longer new. They were the uniforms of a man who had been at war for two years straight.

Vin knew him well enough to sense that all was not well. However, she also knew him well enough to sense that he didn't want to talk about it for the moment.

She stood and stepped down, burning pewter unconsciously to heighten her balance. She slid a book off a bench beside the boat's edge, and settled down quietly. Elend would talk to her eventually—he always did. For the moment, she had something else to engage her.

She opened the book to the marked page and reread a particular paragraph. *The Deepness must be destroyed,* the words said. *I have seen it, and I have felt it. This name we give it is too weak a word, I think. Yes, it is deep and unfathomable, but it is also terrible. Many do not realize that it is sentient, but I have sensed its mind, such as it is, the few times I have confronted it directly.*

She eyed the page for a moment, sitting back on her bench. Beside her, the canal waters passed, covered with a froth of floating ash.

The book was Alendi's logbook. It had been written a thousand years before by a man who had thought himself to be the Hero of Ages. Alendi hadn't completed his quest; he had been killed by one of his servants—Rashek—who had then taken the power at the Well of Ascension and become the Lord Ruler.

Alendi's story was frighteningly close to Vin's own. She

had also assumed herself to be the Hero of Ages. She had traveled to the Well, and had been betrayed. She, however, hadn't been betrayed by one of her servants—but instead by the force imprisoned within the Well. That force was, she assumed, behind the prophecies about the Hero of Ages in the first place.

Why do I keep coming back to this paragraph? she thought, eyeing it again. Perhaps it was because of what Human had said to her—that the mists hated her. She had felt that hatred herself, and it appeared that Alendi had felt the same thing.

But, could she even trust the logbook's words? The force she had released, the thing she called Ruin, had proven that it could change things in the world. Small things, yet important ones. Like the text of a book, which was why Elend's officers were now instructed to send all messages via memorized words or letters etched into metal.

Regardless, if there had been any clues to be gained by reading the logbook, Ruin would have removed them long ago. Vin felt as if she'd been led by the nose for the last three years, pulled by invisible strings. She had thought she was having revelations and making great discoveries, but all she'd really been doing was following Ruin's bidding.

Yet, Ruin is not omnipotent, Vin thought. *If it were, there would have been no fight. It wouldn't have needed to trick me into releasing it.*

It cannot know my thoughts. . . .

Even that knowledge was frustrating. What good were her thoughts? Always before, she'd had Sazed, Elend, or TenSoon to talk with about problems like this. This wasn't a task for Vin; she was no scholar. Yet, Sazed had turned his back on his studies, TenSoon had returned to his people, and Elend was far too busy lately to worry about anything but his army and its politics. That left Vin. And she still found reading and scholarship to be stuffy and boring.

Yet, she was also becoming more and more comfortable with the idea of doing what was necessary, even if she found it distasteful. She was no longer just her own person. She belonged to the New Empire. She had been its knife—now it was time to try a different role.

I have to do it, she thought, sitting in the red sunlight. *There is a puzzle here—something to be solved. What was it Kelsier liked to say?*

There's always another secret.

She remembered Kelsier, standing boldly before a small group of thieves, proclaiming that they would overthrow the Lord Ruler and free the empire. *We're thieves,* he'd said. *And we're extraordinarily good ones. We can rob the unrobbable and fool the unfoolable. We know how to take an incredibly large task and break it down to manageable pieces, then deal with each of those pieces.*

That day, when he'd written up the team's goals and plans on a small board, Vin had been amazed by how possible he had made an impossible task seem. That day, a little bit of her had begun to believe that Kelsier could overthrow the Final Empire.

All right, Vin thought. *I'll begin like Kelsier did, by listing the things that I know for certain.*

There *had* been a power at the Well of Ascension, so that much about the stories was true. There had also been something alive, imprisoned in or near the Well. It had tricked Vin into using the power to destroy its bonds. Maybe she could have used that power to destroy Ruin instead, but she'd given it up.

She sat thoughtfully, tapping her finger against the back of the logbook. She could still remember wisps of what it had felt like to hold that power. It had awed her, yet at the same time felt natural and right. In fact, while she held it, *everything* had felt natural. The workings of the world, the ways of men . . . it was like the power had been more than simple capability. It had been understanding as well.

That was a tangent. She needed to focus on what she knew before she could philosophize on what she needed to do. The power was real, and Ruin was real. Ruin had retained some ability to change the world while confined—Sazed had confirmed that his texts had been altered to suit Ruin's purpose.

Now Ruin was free, and Vin assumed that it was behind the violent mist killings and the falling ash.

Though, she reminded herself, *I don't know either of those things for certain.* What did she know about Ruin? She had touched it, felt it, in that moment she had released it. It had a need to destroy, yet it was not a force of simple chaos. It didn't act randomly. It planned and thought. And, it didn't seem able to do anything it wanted. Almost as if it followed specific rules . . .

She paused. "Elend?" she called.

The emperor turned from his place beside the prow.

"What is the first rule of Allomancy?" Vin asked. "The first thing I taught you?"

"Consequence," Elend said. "Every action has consequences. When you Push on something heavy, it will push you back. If you Push on something light, it will fly away."

It was the first lesson that Kelsier had taught Vin, as well as—she assumed—the first lesson his master had taught him.

"It's a good rule," Elend said, turning back to his contemplation of the horizon. "It works for all things in life. If you throw something into the air, it will come back down. If you bring an army into a man's kingdom, he will react . . ."

Consequence, she thought, frowning. *Like things falling back when thrown into the sky. That's what Ruin's actions feel like to me. Consequences.* Perhaps it was a remnant of touching the power, or perhaps just some rationalization her unconscious mind was giving her. Yet, she felt a logic to Ruin. She didn't understand that logic, but she could recognize it.

Elend turned back toward her. "That's why I like Allomancy, actually. Or, at least, the theory of it. The skaa whisper about it, call it mystical, but it's really quite rational. You can tell what an Allomantic Push is going to do as certainly as you can tell what will happen when you drop a rock off the side of the boat. For every Push, there is a Pull. There are no exceptions. It makes simple, logical sense—unlike the ways of men, which are filled with flaws, irregularities, and double meanings. Allomancy is a thing of nature."

A thing of nature.

For every Push, there is a Pull. A consequence.

"That's important," Vin whispered.

"What?"

A consequence.

The thing she had felt at the Well of Ascension had been a thing of destruction, like Alendi described in his logbook. But, it hadn't been a creature, not like a person. It had been a force—a thinking force, but a force nonetheless. And forces had rules. Allomancy, weather, even the pull of the ground. The world was a place that made sense. A place of logic. Every Push had a Pull. Every force had a consequence.

She had to discover, then, the laws relating to the thing she was fighting. That would tell her how to beat it.

"Vin?" Elend asked, studying her face.

Vin looked away. "It's nothing, Elend. Nothing I can speak of, at least."

He watched her for a moment. *He thinks that you're plotting against him,* Reen whispered from the back of her mind. Fortunately, the days when she had listened to Reen's words were long past. Indeed, as she watched Elend, she saw him nod slowly, and accept her explanation. He turned back to his own contemplations.

Vin rose, walking forward, laying a hand on his arm. He sighed, raising the arm and wrapping it around her shoulders, pulling her close. That arm, once the weak arm of a scholar, was now muscular and firm.

"What are you thinking about?" Vin asked.

"You know," Elend said.

"It was necessary, Elend. The soldiers had to get exposed to the mists eventually."

"Yes," Elend said. "But there's something more, Vin. I fear I'm becoming like *him.*"

"Who?"

"The Lord Ruler."

Vin snorted quietly, pulling closer to him.

"This is something he would have done," Elend said. "Sacrificing his own men for a tactical advantage."

"You explained this to Ham," Vin said. "We can't afford to waste time."

"It's still ruthless," Elend said. "The problem isn't that those men died, it's that I was so willing to make it happen. I feel . . . *brutal,* Vin. How far will I go to see my goals achieved? I'm marching on another man's kingdom to take it from him."

"For the greater good."

"That has been the excuse of tyrants throughout all time. I know it. Yet, I press on. *This* is why I didn't want to be emperor. This is why I let Penrod take my throne from me back during the siege. I didn't want to be the kind of leader who had to do things like this. I want to protect, not besiege and kill! But, is there any other way? Everything I do seems like it *must* be done. Like exposing my own men in the mists. Like marching on Fadrex City. We have to get to that storehouse—it's the only lead we have that could even possibly give us some clue as to what we're supposed to do! It all makes such sense. Ruthless, brutal sense."

Ruthlessness is the most practical of emotions, Reen's voice whispered. She ignored it. "You've been listening to Cett too much."

"Perhaps," Elend said. "Yet, his is a logic I find difficult to ignore. I grew up as an idealist, Vin—we both know that's true. Cett provides a kind of balance. The things he says are much like what Tindwyl used to say."

He paused, shaking his head. "Just a short time ago, I was talking with Cett about Allomantic Snapping. Do you know what the noble houses did to ensure that they found the Allomancers among their children?"

"They had them beaten," Vin whispered. A person's Allomantic powers were always latent until something traumatic brought them out. A person had to be brought to the brink of death and survive—only then would their powers be awakened. It was called Snapping.

Elend nodded. "It was one of the great, dirty secrets of so-called noble life. Families often lost children to the beatings—those beatings had to be brutal for them to evoke

Allomantic abilities. Each house was different, but they generally specified an age before adolescence. When a boy or girl hit that age, they were taken and beaten near to death."

Vin shivered slightly.

"I vividly remember mine," Elend said. "Father didn't beat me himself, but he did watch. The saddest thing about the beatings was that most of them were pointless. Only a handful of children, even noble children, became Allomancers. I didn't. I was beaten for nothing."

"You stopped those beatings, Elend," Vin said softly. He had drafted a bill soon after becoming king. A person could choose to undergo a supervised beating when they came of age, but Elend had stopped it from happening to children.

"And I was wrong," Elend said softly.

Vin looked up.

"Allomancers are our most powerful resource, Vin," Elend said, looking out over the marching soldiers. "Cett lost his kingdom, nearly his life, because he couldn't marshal enough Allomancers to protect him. And I made it illegal to search out Allomancers in my population."

"Elend, you stopped the *beating of children.*"

"And if those beatings could save lives?" Elend asked. "Like exposing my soldiers could save lives? What about Kelsier? He only gained his powers as a Mistborn *after* he was trapped in the Pits of Hathsin. What would have happened if he'd been beaten properly as a child? He would always have been Mistborn. He could have saved his wife."

"And then wouldn't have had the courage or motivation to overthrow the Final Empire."

"And is what we have any better?" Elend asked. "The longer I've held this throne, Vin, the more I've come to realize that some of the things the Lord Ruler did weren't evil, but simply effective. Right or wrong, he maintained order in his kingdom."

Vin looked up, catching his eyes, forcing him to look down at her. "I don't like this hardness in you, Elend."

He looked out over the blackened canal waters. "It doesn't control me, Vin. I don't agree with most of the things the

Lord Ruler did. I'm just coming to understand him—and that understanding worries me." She saw questions in his eyes, but also strengths. He looked down and met her eyes. "I can hold this throne only because I know that at one point, I was willing to give it up in the name of what was right. If I ever lose that, Vin, you need to tell me. All right?"

Vin nodded.

Elend looked back at the horizon again. *What is it he hopes to see?* Vin thought.

"There has to be a balance, Vin," he said. "Somehow, we'll find it. The balance between whom we wish to be and whom we need to be." He sighed. "But for now," he said, nodding to the side, "we simply have to be satisfied with who we are."

Vin glanced to the side as a small courier skiff from one of the other narrowboats pulled up alongside theirs. A man in simple brown robes stood upon it. He wore large spectacles, as if attempting to obscure the intricate Ministry tattoos around his eyes, and he was smiling happily.

Vin smiled herself. Once, she had thought that a happy obligator was *always* a bad sign. That was before she'd known Noorden. Even during the days of the Lord Ruler, the contented scholar had probably lived most of his life in his own little world. He provided a strange proof that even in the confines of what had once been—in her opinion—the most evil organization in the empire, one could find good men.

"Your Excellency," Noorden said, stepping off of the skiff and bowing. A couple of assistant scribes joined him on the deck, lugging books and ledgers.

"Noorden," Elend said, joining the man on the foredeck. Vin followed. "You have done the counts I asked?"

"Yes, Your Excellency," Noorden said as an aide opened up a ledger on a pile of boxes. "I must say, this was a difficult task, what with the army moving about and the like."

"I'm certain you were thorough as always, Noorden," Elend said. He glanced at the ledger, which seemed to make sense to him, though all Vin saw was a bunch of random numbers.

"What's it say?" she asked.

"It lists the number of sick and dead," Elend said. "Of our thirty-eight thousand, nearly six thousand were taken by the sickness. We lost about five hundred and fifty."

"Including one of my own scribes," Noorden said, shaking his head.

Vin frowned. Not at the death, at something else, something itching at her mind . . .

"Fewer dead than expected," Elend said, pulling thoughtfully at his beard.

"Yes, Your Excellency," Noorden said. "I guess these soldier types are more rugged than the average skaa population. The sickness, whatever it is, didn't strike them as hard."

"How do you know?" Vin asked, looking up. "How do you know how many *should* have died?"

"Previous experience, my lady," Noorden said in his chatty way. "We've been tracking these deaths with some interest. Since the disease is new, we're trying to determine exactly what causes it. Perhaps that will lead us to a way to treat it. I've had my scribes reading what we can, trying to find clues of other diseases like this. It seems a little like the shakewelts, though that's usually brought on by—"

"Noorden," Vin said, frowning. "You have figures then? Exact numbers?"

"That's what His Excellency asked for, my lady."

"How many fell sick to the disease?" Vin asked. "Exactly?"

"Well, let me see . . ." Noorden said, shooing his scribe away and checking the ledger. "Five thousand two hundred and forty-three."

"What percentage of the soldiers is that?" Vin asked.

Noorden paused, then waved over a scribe and did some calculations. "About thirteen and a half percent, my lady," he finally said, adjusting his spectacles.

Vin frowned. "Did you include the men who died in your calculations?"

"Actually, no," Noorden said.

"And which total did you use?" Vin asked. "The total number of men in the army, or the total number who hadn't been in the mists before?"

"The first."

"Do you have a count for the second number?" Vin asked.

"Yes, my lady," Noorden said. "The emperor wanted an accurate count of which soldiers would be affected."

"Use that number instead," Vin said, glancing at Elend. He seemed interested.

"What is this about, Vin?" he asked as Noorden and his men worked.

"I'm . . . not sure," Vin said.

"Numbers are important for generalizations," Elend said. "But I don't see how . . ." He trailed off as Noorden looked up from his calculations, then cocked his head, saying something softly to himself.

"What?" Vin asked.

"I'm sorry, my lady," Noorden said. "I was just a bit surprised. The calculation came out to be exact—precisely sixteen percent of the soldiers fell sick. To the man."

"A coincidence, Noorden," Elend said. "It isn't *that* remarkable for calculations to come out exact."

Ash blew across the deck. "No," Noorden said, "no, you are right, Your Excellency. A simple coincidence."

"Check your ledgers," Vin said. "Find percentages based on other groups of people who have caught this disease."

"Vin," Elend said, "I'm no statistician, but I have worked with numbers in my research. Sometimes, natural phenomena produce seemingly odd results, but the chaos of statistics actually results in normalization. It might appear strange that our numbers broke down to an exact percentage, but that's just the way that statistics work."

"Sixteen," Noorden said. He looked up. "Another exact percentage."

Elend frowned, stepping over to the ledger.

"This third one here isn't exact," Noorden said, "but that's only because the base number isn't a multiple of twenty-five.

A fraction of a person can't really become sick, after all. Yet, the sickness in this population here is within a single person of being exactly sixteen percent."

Elend knelt down, heedless of the ash that had dusted the deck since it had last been swept. Vin looked over his shoulder, scanning the numbers.

"It doesn't matter how old the average member of the population is," Noorden said, scribbling. "Nor does it matter where they live. Each one shows the *exact* same percentage of people falling sick."

"How could we have not noticed this before?" Elend asked.

"Well, we did, after a fashion," Noorden said. "We knew that *about* four in twenty-five caught the sickness. However, I hadn't realized how exact the numbers were. This is indeed odd, Your Excellency. I know of no other disease that works this way. Look, here's an entry where a hundred scouts were sent into the mists, and *precisely* sixteen of them fell sick!"

Elend looked troubled.

"What?" Vin asked.

"This is wrong, Vin," Elend said. "Very wrong."

"It's like the chaos of normal random statistics has broken down," Noorden said. "A population should never react *this* precisely—there should be a curve of probability, with smaller populations reflecting the expected percentages least accurately."

"At the very least," Elend said, "the sickness should affect the elderly in different ratios from the healthy."

"In a way, it does," Noorden said as one of his assistants handed him a paper with further calculations. "The *deaths* respond that way, as we would expect. But, the total number who fall sick is always sixteen percent! We've been paying so much attention to how many died, we didn't notice how unnatural the percentages of those stricken were."

Elend stood. "Check on this, Noorden," he said, gesturing toward the ledger. "Do interviews, make certain the data hasn't been changed by Ruin, and find out if this trend holds.

We can't jump to conclusions with only four or five examples. It could all just be a large coincidence."

"Yes, Your Excellency," Noorden said, looking a bit shaken. "But . . . what if it's not a coincidence? What does it mean?"

"I don't know," Elend said.

It means consequence, Vin thought. *It means that there are laws, even if we don't understand them.*

Sixteen. Why sixteen percent?

The beads of metal found at the Well—beads that made men into Mistborn—were the reason why Allomancers used to be more powerful. Those first Mistborn were as Elend Venture became—possessing a primal power, which was then passed down through the lines of the nobility, weakening a bit with each generation.

The Lord Ruler was one of these ancient Allomancers, his power pure and unadulterated by time and breeding. That is part of why he was so mighty compared to other Mistborn—though, admittedly, his ability to mix Feruchemy and Allomancy was what produced many of his most spectacular abilities. Still, it is interesting to me that one of his "divine" powers—his essential Allomantic strength—was something every one of the original nine Allomancers possessed.

22

SAZED SAT IN ONE OF the nicer buildings at the Pits of Hathsin—a former guardhouse—holding a mug of hot tea. The Terris elders sat in chairs before him, a small stove providing warmth. On the next day, Sazed would have to leave to catch up with Goradel and Breeze, who would be well on their way to Urteau by now.

The sunlight was dimming. The mists had already come, and they hung just outside the glass window. Sazed could just barely make out depressions in the dark ground outside—cracks, in the earth. There were dozens of the cracks; the Terris people had built fences to mark them. Only a few years ago, before Kelsier had destroyed the atium crystals, men had been forced to crawl down into those cracks, seeking small geodes which had beads of atium at their centers.

Each slave who hadn't been able to find at least one geode a week had been executed. There were likely still hundreds, perhaps thousands, of corpses pinned beneath the ground, lost in deep caverns, dead without anyone knowing or caring.

What a terrible place this was, Sazed thought, turning away from the window as a young Terriswoman closed the shutters. Before him on the table were several ledgers which showed the resources, expenditures, and needs of the Terris people.

"I believe I suggested keeping these figures in metal," Sazed said.

"Yes, Master Keeper," said one of the elderly stewards. "We copy the important figures into a sheet of metal each evening, then check them weekly against the ledgers to make certain nothing has changed."

"That is well," Sazed said, picking through one of the ledgers, sitting in his lap. "And sanitation? Have you addressed those issues since my last visit?"

"Yes, Master Keeper," said another man. "We have prepared many more latrines, as you commanded—though we do not need them."

"There may be refugees," Sazed said. "I wish for you to be able to care for a larger population, should it become necessary. But, please. These are only suggestions, not commands. I claim no authority over you."

The group of stewards shared glances. Sazed had been busy during his time with them, which had kept him from dwelling on his melancholy thoughts. He'd made sure they had enough supplies, that they kept a good communication with Penrod in Luthadel, and that they had a system in place for settling disputes among themselves.

"Master Keeper," one of the elders finally said. "How long will you be staying?"

"I must leave in the morning, I fear," Sazed said. "I came simply to check on your needs. This is a difficult time to live, and you could be easily forgotten by those in Luthadel, I think."

"We are well, Master Keeper," said one of the others. He was the youngest of the elders, and he was only a few years younger than Sazed. Most of the men here were far older—and far wiser—than he. That they should look to him seemed wrong.

"Will you not reconsider your place with us, Master Keeper?" asked another. "We want not for food or for land. Yet, what we do lack is a leader."

"The Terris people were oppressed long enough, I think," Sazed said. "You have no need for another tyrant king."

"Not a tyrant," one said. "One of our own."

"The Lord Ruler was one of our own," Sazed said quietly.

The group of men looked down. That the Lord Ruler had proven to be Terris was a shame to all of their people.

"We need someone to guide us," one of the men said. "Even during the days of the Lord Ruler, he was not our leader. We looked to the Keeper Synod."

The Keeper Synod—the clandestine leaders of Sazed's sect. They had led the Terris people for centuries, secretly working to make certain that Feruchemy continued, despite the Lord Ruler's attempts to breed the power out of the people.

"Master Keeper," said Master Vedlew, senior of the elders.

"Yes, Master Vedlew?"

"You do not wear your copperminds."

Sazed looked down. He hadn't realized it was noticeable that, beneath his robes, he wasn't wearing the metal bracers. "They are in my pack."

"It seems odd, to me," Vedlew said, "that you should work

so hard during the Lord Ruler's time, always wearing your metalminds in secret, despite the danger. Yet, now that you are free to do as you wish, you carry them in your pack."

Sazed shook his head. "I cannot be the man you wish me to be. Not right now."

"You are a Keeper."

"I was the lowest of them," Sazed said. "A rebel and a reject. They cast me from their presence. The last time I left Tathingdwen, I did so in disgrace. The common people cursed me in the quiet of their homes."

"Now they bless you, Master Sazed," said one of the men.

"I do not deserve those blessings."

"Deserve them or not, you are all we have left."

"Then we are a sorrier people than we may appear."

The room fell silent.

"There was another reason why I came here, Master Vedlew," Sazed said, looking up. "Tell me, have any of your people died recently in . . . odd circumstances?"

"Of what do you speak?" the aged Terrisman asked.

"Mist deaths," Sazed said. "Men who are killed by simply going out into the mists during the day."

"That is a tale of the skaa," one of the other men scoffed. "The mists are not dangerous."

"Indeed," Sazed said carefully. "Do you send your people out to work in them during the daylight hours, when the mists have not yet retreated for the day?"

"Of course we do," said the younger Terrisman. "Why, it would be foolish to let those hours of work pass."

Sazed found it difficult not to let his curiosity work on that fact. Terrismen weren't killed by the daymists.

What was the connection?

He tried to summon the mental energy to think on the issue, but he felt traitorously apathetic. He just wanted to hide somewhere where nobody would expect anything of him. Where he wouldn't have to solve the problems of the world, or even deal with his own religious crisis.

He almost did just that. And yet, a little part of him—a spark from before—refused to simply give up. He would at least continue his research, and would do what Elend and Vin asked of him. It wasn't *all* he could do, and it wouldn't satisfy the Terrismen who sat here, looking at him with needful expressions.

But, for the moment, it was all Sazed could offer. To stay at the Pits would be to surrender, he knew. He needed to keep moving, keep working.

"I'm sorry," he said to the men, setting aside the ledger. "But this is how it must be."

During the early days of Kelsier's original plan, I remember how much he confused us all with his mysterious "Eleventh Metal." He claimed that there were legends of a mystical metal that would let one slay the Lord Ruler—and that Kelsier himself had located that metal through intense research.

Nobody really knew what Kelsier did in the years between his escape from the Pits of Hathsin and his return to Luthadel. When pressed, he simply said that he had been in "the West." Somehow in his wanderings he discovered stories that no Keeper had ever heard. Most of the crew didn't know what to make of the legends he spoke of. This might have been the first seed that made even his oldest friends begin to question his leadership.

23

IN THE EASTERN LANDS, NEAR the wastelands of grit and sand, a young boy fell to the ground inside a skaa shack. It was many years before the Collapse, and the Lord Ruler still lived. Not that the boy knew of such things. He was a dirty, ragged thing—like most other skaa children in the Final Empire. Too young to be put to work in the mines, he spent his days ducking away from his mother's care and running about with the packs of children who foraged in the dry, dusty streets.

Spook hadn't been that boy for some ten years. In a way, he was aware that he was delusional—that the fever of his wounds was causing him to come in and out of consciousness, dreams of the past filling his mind. He let them run. Staying focused required too much energy.

And so, he remembered what it felt like as he hit the ground. A large man—all men were large compared with Spook—stood over him, skin dirtied with the dust and grime of a miner. The man spat on the dirty floor beside Spook, then turned to the other skaa in the room. There were many. One was crying, the tears leaving lines of cleanliness on her cheeks, washing away the dust.

"All right," the large man said. "We have him. Now what?"

The people glanced at each other. One quietly closed the shack's door, shutting out the red sunlight.

"There's only one thing to be done," another man said. "We turn him in."

Spook looked up. He met the eyes of the crying woman. She looked away. "Wasing the where of what?" Spook demanded.

The large man spat again, setting a boot against Spook's neck, pushing him back down against the rough wood. "You shouldn't have let him run around with those street gangs, Margel. Damn boy is barely coherent now."

"What happens if we give him up?" asked one of the other men. "I mean, what if they decide that we're like him? They could have *us* executed! I've seen it before. You turn someone in, and those . . . things come searching for everyone that knew him."

"Problems like his run in the family, they do," another man said.

The room grew quiet. They all knew about Spook's family.

"They'll kill us," said the frightened man. "You know they

will! I've seen them, seen them with those spikes in their eyes. Spirits of death, they are."

"We can't just let him run about," another man said. "They'll discover what he is."

"There's only one thing to be done," the large man said, pressing down on Spook's neck even harder.

The room's occupants—the ones Spook could see—nodded solemnly. They couldn't turn him in. They couldn't let him go. But, nobody would miss a skaa urchin. No Inquisitor or obligator would ask twice about a dead child found in the streets. Skaa died all the time.

That was the way of the Final Empire.

"Father," Spook whispered.

The heel came down harder. "You're not my son! My son went into the mists and never came out. You must be a mistwraith."

Spook tried to object, but his neck was pressed down too tight. He couldn't breathe, let alone speak. The room started to grow black. And yet, his ears—supernaturally sensitive, enhanced by powers he barely understood—heard something.

Coins.

The pressure on his neck grew weaker. He was able to gasp for breath, his vision returning. And there, spilled on the ground before him, was a scattering of beautiful copper coins. Skaa weren't paid for their work—the miners were given goods instead, barely enough to survive on. Yet, Spook had seen coins occasionally passing between noble hands. He'd once known a boy who had found a coin, lost in the dusty grime of the street.

A larger boy had killed him for it. Then, a nobleman had killed that boy when he'd tried to spend it. It seemed to Spook that no skaa would want coins—they were far too valuable, and far too dangerous. And yet, every eye in the room stared at that spilled bag of wealth.

"The bag in exchange for the boy," a voice said. Bodies parted to where a man sat at a table at the back of the room. He wasn't looking at Spook. He just sat, quietly spooning gruel into his mouth. His face was gnarled and twisted, like leather that had been sitting in the sun for far too long. "Well?" the gnarled man said between bites.

"Where did you get money like this?" Spook's father demanded.

"None of your business."

"We can't let the boy go," one of the skaa said. "He'll betray us! Once they catch him, he'll tell them that we knew!"

"They won't catch him," the gnarled man said, taking another bite of food. "He'll be with me, in Luthadel. Besides, if you *don't* let him go, I'll just go ahead and tell the obligators about you all." He paused, lowering his spoon, glancing at the crowd with a crusty look. "Unless you're going to kill me too."

Spook's father finally took his heel off Spook's neck as he stepped toward the gnarled stranger. However, Spook's mother grabbed her husband's arm. "Don't, Jedal," she said softly—but not too softly for Spook's enhanced ears. "He'll kill you."

"He's a traitor," Spook's father spat. "Servant in the Lord Ruler's army."

"He brought us coins. Surely taking his money is better than simply killing the boy."

Spook's father looked down at the woman. "*You* did this! You sent for your brother. You knew he'd want to take the boy!"

Spook's mother turned away.

The gnarled man finally set down his spoon, then stood. People backed away from his chair in apprehension. He walked with a pronounced limp as he crossed the room.

"Come on, boy," he said, not looking at Spook as he opened the door.

Spook rose slowly, tentatively. He glanced at his mother and father as he backed away. Jedal stooped down, finally gathering up the coins. Margel met Spook's eyes, then turned away. *This is all I can give you,* her posture seemed to say.

Spook turned, rubbing his neck, and rushed into the hot red sunlight after the stranger. The older man hobbled along, walking with a cane. He glanced at Spook as he walked.

"You have a name, boy?"

Spook opened his mouth, then stopped. His old name didn't seem like it would do any more. "Lestibournes," he finally said.

The old man didn't bat an eye. Later, Kelsier would decide that Lestibournes was too difficult to say, and name him "Spook" instead. Spook never did figure out whether or not Clubs knew how to speak Eastern street slang. Even if he did, Spook doubted that he'd understand the reference.

Lestibournes. Lefting I'm born.

Street slang for "I've been abandoned."

I now believe that Kelsier's stories, legends, and prophecies about the "Eleventh Metal" were fabricated by Ruin. Kelsier was looking for a way to kill the Lord Ruler, and Ruin—ever subtle—provided a way.

That secret was indeed crucial. Kelsier's Eleventh Metal provided the very clue we needed to defeat the Lord Ruler. However, even in this, we were manipulated. The Lord Ruler knew Ruin's goals, and would never have released him from the Well of Ascension. So, Ruin needed other pawns—and for that to happen, the Lord Ruler needed to die. Even our greatest victory was shaped by Ruin's subtle fingers.

24

DAYS LATER, MELAAN'S WORDS STILL pricked TenSoon's conscience.

You come, proclaim dread news, then leave us to solve the problems on our own? During his year of imprisonment, it had seemed simple. He would make his accusations, deliver his information, then accept the punishment he deserved.

But now, strangely, an eternity of imprisonment seemed

like the easy way out. If he let himself be taken in such a manner, how was he better than the First Generation? He would be avoiding the issues, content to be locked away, knowing that the outside world was no longer his problem.

Fool, he thought. *You'll be imprisoned for eternity—or, at least, until the kandra themselves are destroyed, and you die of starvation. That's not the easy way out! By accepting your punishment, you're doing the honorable, orderly thing.*

And by so doing, he would leave MeLaan and the others to be destroyed as their leaders refused to take action. What's more, he would leave Vin without the information she needed. Even from within the Homeland, he could feel the occasional rumbles in the rock. The earthquakes were still remote, and the others likely ignored them. But TenSoon worried.

The end could be nearing. If it was, then Vin needed to know the truths about the kandra. Their origins, their beliefs. Perhaps she could use the Trust itself. Yet, if he told Vin anything more, it would mean an even greater betrayal of his people. Perhaps a human would have found it ridiculous that he would hesitate now. However, so far, his true sins had been impulsive, and he'd only later rationalized what he'd done. If he fought his way free of prison, it would be different. Willful and deliberate.

He closed his eyes, feeling the chill of his cage, which still sat alone in the large cavern—the place was mostly abandoned during the sleeping hours. What was the point? Even with the Blessing of Presence—which let TenSoon focus, despite his uncomfortable confines—he could think of no way to escape the meshed cage and its Fifth Generation guards, who all bore the Blessing of Potency. Even if he did get out of the cage, TenSoon would have to pass through dozens of small caverns. With his body mass as low as it was, he didn't have the muscles to fight, and he couldn't outrun kandra who had the Blessing of Potency. He was trapped.

In a way, this was comforting. Escape was not something he preferred to contemplate—it simply wasn't the kandra way. He had broken Contract, and deserved punishment. There was honor in facing the consequences of one's actions.

Wasn't there?

He shifted positions in his cell. Unlike that of a real human, the skin of his naked body did not become sore or chapped from the extended exposure, for he could re-form his flesh to remove wounds. However, there was little to do about the cramped feeling he got from being forced to sit in the small cage for so long.

Motion caught his attention. TenSoon turned, surprised to see VarSell and several other large Fifths approaching his cage, their quartzite stone True Bodies ominous in size and coloring.

Time already? TenSoon thought. With the Blessing of Presence, he was able to mentally recount the days of his imprisonment. It was nowhere near time. He frowned, noting that one of the Fifths carried a large sack. For a moment, TenSoon had a flash of panic as he pictured them towing him away inside the sack.

It looked filled already, however.

Dared he hope? Days had passed since his conversation with MeLaan, and while she had returned several times to look at him, they had not spoken. He'd almost forgotten his words to her, said in the hope that they would be overheard by the minions of the Second Generation. VarSell opened the cage and tossed the sack in. It clinked with a familiar sound. Bones.

"You are to wear those to the trial," VarSell said, leaning down and putting a translucent face up next to TenSoon's bars. "Orders of the Second Generation."

"What is wrong with the bones I now wear?" TenSoon asked carefully, pulling over the sack, uncertain whether to be excited or ashamed.

"They intend to break your bones as part of your punishment," VarSell said, smiling. "Something like a public execution—but where the prisoner lives through the process. It's a simple thing, I know—but the display ought to leave . . . an impression on some of the younger generations."

TenSoon's stomach twisted. Kandra could re-form their bodies, true, but they felt pain just as acutely as any human. It would take quite a severe beating to break his bones, and with the Blessing of Presence, there would be no release of unconsciousness for him.

"I still don't see the need for another body," TenSoon said, pulling out one of the bones.

"No need to waste a perfectly good set of human bones, Third," VarSell said, slamming the cage door closed. "I'll be back for your current bones in a few hours."

The leg bone he pulled out was not that of a human, but a dog. A large wolfhound. It was the very body TenSoon had been wearing when he'd returned to the Homeland over a year before. He closed his eyes, holding the smooth bone in his fingers.

A week ago, he'd spoken of how much he despised these bones, hoping that the Second Generation's spies would carry the news back to their masters. The Second Generation was far more traditional than MeLaan, and even she had found the thought of wearing a dog's body distasteful. To the Seconds, forcing TenSoon to wear an animal's body would be supremely degrading.

That was exactly what TenSoon had been counting on.

"You'll look good, wearing that," VarSell said, standing to leave. "When your punishment comes, everyone will be able to see you for what you really are. No *kandra* would break his Contract."

TenSoon rubbed the thighbone with a reverent finger, listening to VarSell's laughter. The Fifth had no way of knowing that he'd just given TenSoon the means he needed to escape.

The Balance. Is it real?

We've almost forgotten this little bit of lore. Skaa used to talk about it, before the Collapse. Philosophers discussed it a great deal in the third and fourth centuries, but by Kelsier's time, it was mostly a forgotten topic.

But it was real. There was a physiological difference between skaa and nobility. When the Lord Ruler altered mankind to make them more capable of dealing with ash, he changed other things as well. Some groups of people—the noblemen—were created to be less fertile, but taller, stronger, and more intelligent. Others—the skaa—were made to be shorter, hardier, and to have many children.

The changes were slight, however, and after a thousand years of interbreeding, the differences had largely been erased.

25

"FADREX CITY," ELEND SAID, STANDING in his customary place near the narrowboat's prow. Ahead, the broad Conway Canal—the primary canal route to the west—continued into the distance, turning to the northwest. To Elend's left, the ground rose in a broken incline, forming a set of steep rock formations. He could see them rising much higher in the distance.

Closer to the canal, however, a broad city was nestled in the very center of a large group of rock formations. The deep red and orange rocks were the type left behind when wind and rain wore away weaker sections of stone, and many of them reached high, like spires. Others formed jagged, hedge-like barriers—like stacks of enormous blocks that had been fused together, reaching some thirty and forty feet into the air.

Elend could barely see the tips of the city's buildings over the stone formations. Fadrex had no formal city wall, of course—only Luthadel had been allowed one of those—but the rising rocks around the city formed a set of terrace-like natural fortifications.

Elend had been to the city before. His father had made certain to introduce him in all of the Final Empire's main cultural centers. Fadrex hadn't been one of those, but it had been on the way to Tremredare, once known as the capital of the West. In forging his new kingdom, however, Cett had ignored Tremredare, instead establishing his capital in Fadrex. A clever move, in Elend's estimation—Fadrex was smaller, more defensible, and had been a major supply station for numerous canal routes.

"The city looks different from the last time I was here," Elend said.

"Trees," Ham said, standing beside him. "Fadrex used to have trees growing on the rocky shelves and plateaus." Ham glanced at him. "They're ready for us. They cut down the trees to provide a better killing field and to keep us from sneaking up close."

Elend nodded. "Look down there."

Ham squinted, though it obviously took him a moment to pick out what Elend's tin-enhanced eyes had noticed. On the northern side of the city—the one closest to the main canal route—the rock terraces and shelves fell down into a natural canyon. Perhaps twenty feet across, it was the only way into the city, and the defenders had cut several troughs into the floor. They were bridged at the moment, of course, but getting through that narrow entryway, with pits in front of the army and archers presumably firing from the rocky shelves above, with a gate at the end . . .

"Not bad," Ham said. "I'm just glad they decided not to drain the canal on us."

As they'd moved west, the land had risen—requiring the convoy to pass through several massive lock mechanisms. The last four had been jammed intentionally, requiring hours of effort to get them working.

"They rely on it too much," Elend said. "If they survive our siege, they'll need to ship in supplies. Assuming any can be had."

Ham fell silent. Finally, he turned, looking back up the dark canal behind them. "El," he said. "I don't think that much more will be traveling this canal. The boats barely made it this far—there's too much ash clogging it. If we go home, we'll do so on foot."

"'If' we go home?"

Ham shrugged. Despite the colder western weather, he still wore only a vest. Now that Elend was an Allomancer, he could finally understand the habit. While burning pewter, Elend barely felt the chill, though several of the soldiers had complained about it in the mornings.

"I don't know, El," Ham finally said. "It just seems portentous to me. Our canal closing behind us as we travel. Kind of like fate is trying to strand us here."

"Ham," Elend said, "*everything* seems portentous to you. We'll be fine."

Ham shrugged.

"Organize our forces," Elend said, pointing. "Dock us in that inlet over there, and set up camp on the mesa."

Ham nodded. He was still looking backward, however. Toward Luthadel, which they had left behind.

They don't fear the mists, Elend thought, staring up through the darkness at the rocky formations that marked the entrance into Fadrex City. Bonfires blazed up there, lighting the night. Often, such lights were futile—signifying man's fear of the mists. These fires were different, somehow. They seemed a warning; a bold declaration of confidence. They burned brightly, high, as if floating in the sky.

Elend turned, walking into his illuminated commander's tent, where a small group of people sat waiting for him. Ham, Cett, and Vin. Demoux was absent, still recovering from mistsickness.

We're spread thin, Elend thought. *Spook and Breeze in the North, Penrod back at Luthadel, Felt watching the storage cache in the East . . .*

"All right," Elend said, letting the tent flaps close behind him. "Looks like they're holed up in there pretty well."

"Initial scout reports are in, El," Ham said. "We're guessing about twenty-five thousand defenders."

"Not as many as I expected," Elend said.

"That bastard Yomen has to keep control of the rest of my kingdom," Cett said. "If he pulled all of his troops into the capital, the other cities would overthrow him."

"What?" Vin asked, sounding amused. "You think they'd rebel and switch back to your side?"

"No," Cett said, "they'd rebel and try to take over the kingdom themselves! That's the way this works. Now that the Lord Ruler is gone, every little lord or petty obligator with half a taste of power thinks he can run a kingdom. Hell, I tried it—so did you."

"We were successful," Ham pointed out.

"And so was Lord Yomen," Elend said, folding his arms. "He's held this kingdom since Cett marched on Luthadel."

"He all but forced me out," Cett admitted. "He had half the nobility turned against me before I even struck toward Luthadel. I said I was leaving him in charge, but we both knew the truth. He's a clever one—clever enough to know he can hold that city against a larger force, letting him spread his troops out to maintain the kingdom, and to endure a longer siege without running out of supplies."

"Unfortunately, Cett's probably right," Ham said. "Our initial reports placed Yomen's forces at somewhere around eighty thousand men. He'd be a fool to not have a few units within striking distance of our camp. We'll have to be wary of raids."

"Double the guards and triple scout patrols," Elend said, "particularly during the early morning hours, when the daymist is out to obscure, but the sun is up to provide light."

Ham nodded.

"Also," Elend said thoughtfully, "order the men to stay in their tents during the mists—but tell them to be ready for a raid. If Yomen thinks that we're afraid to come out, perhaps we can bait one of his 'surprise' attacks against us."

"Clever," Ham said.

"That won't get us past those natural walls, though,"

Elend said, folding his arms. "Cett, what do you say?"

"Hold the canal," Cett said. "Post sentries up around those upper rock formations to make certain that Yomen doesn't resupply the city via secret means. Then, move on."

"What?" Ham asked with surprise.

Elend eyed Cett, trying to decide what the man meant. "Attack surrounding cities? Leave a force here that's large enough to stymie a siege-break, then capture other parts of his territory?"

Cett nodded. "Most of the cities around here aren't fortified at all. They'd cave in without a fight."

"A good suggestion," Elend said. "But we won't do it."

"Why not?" Cett asked.

"This isn't just about conquering your homeland back, Cett," Elend said. "Our primary reason for coming here is to secure that storage cache—and I hope to do that without resorting to pillaging the countryside."

Cett snorted. "What do you expect to find in there? Some magical way to stop the ash? Even atium wouldn't do that."

"Something's in there," Elend said. "It's the only hope we have."

Cett shook his head. "You've been chasing a puzzle left by the Lord Ruler for the better part of a year, Elend. Hasn't it ever occurred to you that the man was a sadist? There's no secret. No magical way out of this. If we're going to survive the next few years, we're going to have to do it on our own—and that means securing the Western Dominance. The plateaus in this area represent some of the most elevated farmland in the empire—and higher altitude means closer to the sun. If you're going to find plants that survive despite the daymists, you'll have to grow them here."

They were good arguments. *But I can't give up,* Elend thought. *Not yet.* Elend had read the reports of supplies back in Luthadel, and had seen the projections. Ash was killing crops as much or more than the mists were. More land wouldn't save his people—they needed something else. Something that, he hoped, the Lord Ruler left for them.

The Lord Ruler didn't hate his people, and he wouldn't

want them to die out, even if he were defeated. He left food, water, supplies. And, if he knew secrets, he would have hidden them in the caches. There will be something here.

There has to be.

"The cache remains our primary target," Elend said. To the side, he could see Vin smiling.

"Fine," Cett said, sighing. "Then you know what we have to do. This siege could take a while."

Elend nodded. "Ham, send our engineers in under cover of mist. See if they can find a way for our troops to cross those troughs. Have the scouts search out streams that might run into the city—Cett, presumably you can help us locate some of these. And, once we get spies into the city, have them search out food stores that we can ruin."

"A good start," Cett said. "Of course, there's one easy way to sow chaos in that city, to perhaps make them surrender without a fight . . ."

"We're not going to assassinate King Yomen," Elend said.

"Why not?" Cett demanded. "We've got *two* Mistborn. We'll have no difficulty killing off the Fadrex leadership."

"We don't work that way," Ham said, face growing dark.

"Oh?" Cett asked. "That didn't stop Vin from tearing a hole through my army and attacking *me* back before we teamed up."

"That was different," Ham said.

"No," Elend said, interrupting. "It wasn't. The reason we're not going to assassinate Yomen, Cett, is because I want to try diplomacy first."

"Diplomacy?" Cett asked. "Didn't we just march an army of forty thousand soldiers on his city? That's not a diplomatic move."

"True," Elend said, nodding. "But we haven't attacked, not yet. Now that I'm here in person, I might as well try talking before sending out knives in the night. We might be able to persuade Lord Yomen that an alliance will benefit him more than a war."

"If we make an alliance," Cett said, leaning forward in his chair, "I don't get my city back."

"I know," Elend said.

Cett frowned.

"You seem to be forgetting yourself, Cett," Elend said. "You did not 'team up' with me. You knelt before me, offering up oaths of service in exchange for not getting executed. Now, I appreciate your allegiance, and I *will* see you rewarded with a kingdom to rule under me. However, you don't get to choose where that kingdom is, nor when I will grant it."

Cett paused, sitting in his chair, one arm resting on his useless, paralyzed legs. Finally, he smiled. "Damn, boy. You've changed a lot in the year I've known you."

"So everyone is fond of telling me," Elend said. "Vin. You think you can get into the city?"

She raised an eyebrow. "I hope that was meant to be rhetorical."

"It was meant to be polite," Elend said. "I need you to do some scouting. We know next to nothing about what's been going on in this dominance lately—we've focused all of our efforts on Urteau and the South."

Vin shrugged. "I can go poke around a bit. I don't know what you expect me to find."

"Cett," Elend said, turning, "I need names. Informants, or perhaps some noblemen that might still be loyal to you."

"Noblemen?" Cett asked, amused. "Loyal?"

Elend rolled his eyes. "How about some that could be bribed to pass on a little information."

"Sure," Cett said. "I'll write up some names and locations. Assuming they still live in the city. Hell, assuming they're even still alive. Can't count on much these days."

Elend nodded. "We won't take any further action until we have more information. Ham, make certain the soldiers dig in well—use the field fortifications that Demoux taught them. Cett, see that those guard patrols get set up, and make certain our Tineyes remain alert and on watch. Vin will scout and see if she can sneak into the cache like she did in Urteau. If we know what's in there, then we can better judge whether to gamble on trying to conquer the city or not."

The various members of the group nodded, understanding that the meeting was over. As they left, Elend stepped back out into the mists, looking up at the distant bonfires burning on the rocky heights.

Quiet as a sigh, Vin stepped up to his side, following his gaze. She stood for a few moments. Then she glanced to the side, where a pair of soldiers were entering the tent to carry Cett away. Her eyes narrowed in displeasure.

"I know," Elend said quietly, knowing that she was thinking of Cett again and his influence over Elend.

"You didn't deny that you might turn to assassination," Vin said softly.

"Hopefully it won't come to that."

"And if it does?"

"Then I'll make the decision that is best for the empire."

Vin was silent for a moment. Then, she glanced at the fires up above.

"I could come with you," Elend offered.

She smiled, then kissed him. "Sorry," she said. "But you're noisy."

"Come now. I'm not *that* bad."

"Yes you are," Vin said. "Plus, you smell."

"Oh?" he asked, amused. "What do I smell like?"

"An emperor. A Tineye would pick you out in seconds."

Elend raised his eyebrows. "I see. And, don't you possess an imperial scent as well?"

"Of course I do," Vin said, wrinkling her nose. "But I know how to get rid of it. Either way, you're not good enough to go with me, Elend. I'm sorry."

Elend smiled. *Dear, blunt Vin.*

Behind him, the soldiers left the tent, carrying Cett. An aide walked up, delivering to Elend a short list of informants and noblemen who might be willing to talk. Elend passed it to Vin. "Have fun," he said.

She dropped a coin between them, kissed him again, then shot up into the night.

I am only just beginning to understand the brilliance of the Lord Ruler's cultural synthesis. One of the benefits afforded him by being both immortal and—for all relevant purposes—omnipotent was a direct and effective influence on the evolution of the Final Empire.

He was able to take elements from a dozen different cultures and apply them to his new, "perfect" society. For instance, the architectural brilliance of the Khlenni builders is manifest in the keeps that the high nobility construct. Khlenni fashion sense—suits for gentlemen, gowns for ladies—is another thing the Lord Ruler decided to appropriate.

I suspect that despite his hatred of the Khlenni people—of whom Alendi was one—Rashek had a deep-seated envy of them as well. The Terris of the time were pastoral herdsmen, the Khlenni cultured cosmopolitans. However ironic, it is logical that Rashek's new empire would mimic the high culture of the people he hated.

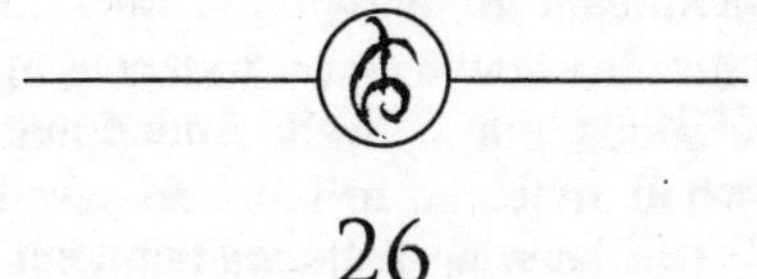

26

SPOOK STOOD IN HIS LITTLE one-room lair, a room that was—of course—illegal. The Citizen forbade such places, places where a man could live unaccounted, unwatched. Fortunately, forbidding such places didn't eliminate them.

It only made them more expensive.

Spook was lucky. He barely remembered leaping from the burning building, clutching six Allomantic vials, coughing and bleeding. He didn't at all remember making it back to his lair. He should probably be dead. Even surviving the fires, he should have been sold out—if the proprietor of his little illegal inn had realized who Spook was and what he'd escaped, the promise of reward would undoubtedly have been irresistible.

But, Spook had survived. Perhaps the other thieves in the lair thought he had been on the wrong side of a robbery. Or, perhaps they simply didn't care. Either way, he was able to stand in front of the room's small mirror, shirt off, looking in wonder at his wound.

I'm alive, he thought. *And . . . I feel pretty good.*

He stretched, rolling his arm in its socket. The wound hurt far less than it should have. In the very dim light, he was able to see the cut, scabbed over and healing. Pewter burned in his stomach—a beautiful complement to the familiar flame of tin.

He was something that shouldn't exist. In Allomancy, people either had just one of the eight basic powers, or they had all fourteen powers. One or all. Never two. Yet, Spook had tried to burn other metals without success. Somehow, he had been given pewter alone to complement his tin. Amazing as that was, it was overshadowed by a greater wonder.

He had seen Kelsier's spirit. The Survivor had returned and had shown himself to Spook.

Spook had no idea how to react to that event. He wasn't particularly religious, but . . . well, a dead man—one some called a god—had appeared to him and saved his life. He worried that it had been an hallucination. But, if that were so, how had he gained the power of pewter?

He shook his head, reaching for his bandages, but paused as something twinkled in the mirror's reflection. He stepped closer, relying—as always—upon starlight from outside to provide illumination. With his extreme tin senses, it was easy to see the bit of metal sticking from the skin in his shoulder, even though it only protruded a tiny fraction of an inch.

The tip of that man's sword, Spook realized, *the one that stabbed me. It broke—the end must have gotten embedded in my skin.* He gritted his teeth, reaching to pull it free.

"No," Kelsier said. "Leave it. It, like the wound you bear, is a sign of your survival."

Spook started. He glanced about, but there was no apparition this time. Just the voice. Yet, he was certain he'd heard it.

"Kelsier?" he hesitantly asked.

There was no response.

Am I going mad? Spook wondered. *Or . . . is it like the Church of the Survivor teaches?* Could it be that Kelsier had become something greater, something that watched over his followers? And, if so, did Kelsier *always* watch him? That felt a little bit . . . unsettling. However, if it brought him the power of pewter, then who was he to complain?

Spook turned and put his shirt on, stretching his arm again. He needed more information. How long had he been delirious? What was Quellion doing? Had the others from the crew arrived yet?

Taking his mind off of his strange visions for the moment, he slipped out of his room and onto the dark street. As lairs went, his wasn't all that impressive—a room behind the hidden door in a slum alleyway wall. Still, it was better than living in one of the crowded shanties he passed as he made his way through the dark, mist-covered city.

The Citizen liked to pretend that everything was perfect in his little utopia, but Spook had not been surprised to find that it had slums, just like every other city he'd ever visited. There were many people in Urteau who, for one reason or another, weren't fond of living in the parts of town where the Citizen could keep watch on them. These had aggregated in a place known as the Harrows, a particularly cramped canal far from the main trenches.

The Harrows was clogged with a disorderly mash of wood and cloth and bodies. Shacks leaned against shacks, buildings leaned precariously against earth and rock, and the entire mess piled on top of itself, creeping up the canal walls toward the dark sky above. Here and there, people slept under only a dirty sheet stretched between two bits of urban flotsam—their millennium-old fear of the mists giving way before simple necessity.

Spook shuffled down the crowded canal. Some of the piles of half-buildings reached so high and wide that the sky narrowed to a mere crack far above, shining down its midnight light, too dim to be of use to any eyes but Spook's.

Perhaps the chaos was why the Citizen chose not to visit the Harrows. Or, perhaps he was simply waiting to clean them out until he had a better grip on his kingdom. Either way, his strict society, mixed with the poverty it was creating, made for a curiously open nighttime culture. The Lord Ruler had patrolled the streets. The Citizen, however, preached that the mists were of Kelsier—and so could hardly forbid people to go out in them. Urteau was the first place in Spook's experience where a person could walk down a street at midnight and find a small tavern open and serving drinks. He moved inside, cloak pulled tight. There was no proper bar, just a group of dirty men sitting around a dug-out firepit in the ground. Others sat on stools or boxes in the corners. Spook found an empty box, and sat down.

Then he closed his eyes and listened, filtering through the conversations. He could hear them all, of course—even with his earplugs in. So much about being a Tineye wasn't about what you could hear, but what you could ignore.

Footsteps thumped near him, and he opened his eyes. A man wearing trousers sewn with a dozen different buckles and chains stopped in front of Spook; then thumped a bottle on the ground. "Everyone drinks," the man said. "I have to pay to keep this place warm. Nobody just sits for free."

"What have you got?" Spook asked.

The bartender kicked the bottle. "House Venture special vintage. Aged fifty years. Used to go for six hundred boxings a bottle."

Spook smiled, fishing out a pek—a coin minted by the Citizen to be worth a fraction of a copper clip. A combination of economic collapse and the Citizen's disapproval of luxury meant that a bottle of wine that had once been worth hundreds of boxings was now practically worthless.

"Three for the bottle," the bartender said, holding out his hand.

Spook brought out two more coins. The bartender left the

bottle on the floor, and so Spook picked it up. He had been offered no corkscrew or cup—both likely cost extra, though this vintage of wine did have a cork that stuck up a few inches above the bottle's lip. Spook eyed it.

I wonder. . . .

He had his pewter on a low burn—not flared like his tin. Just there enough to help with the fatigue and the pain. In fact, it did its job so well that he'd nearly forgotten about his wound during the walk to the bar. He stoked the pewter a bit, and the rest of the wound's pain vanished. Then, Spook grabbed the cork, pulling it with a quick jerk. It came free of the bottle with barely a hint of resistance.

Spook tossed the cork aside. *I think I'm going to like this,* he thought with a smile.

He took a drink of the wine straight from the bottle, listening for interesting conversations. He had been sent to Urteau to gather information, and he wouldn't be much use to Elend or the others if he stayed lying in bed. Dozens of muffled conversations echoed in the room, most of them harsh. This wasn't the kind of place where one found men loyal to the local government—which was precisely why Spook had found his way to the Harrows in the first place.

"They say he's going to get rid of coins," a man whispered at the main firepit. "He's making plans to gather them all up, keep them in his treasury."

"That's foolish," another voice replied. "He minted his own coins—why take them now?"

"It's true," the first voice said. "I seen him speak on it myself. He says that men shouldn't have to rely on coins—that we should have everything together, not having to buy and sell."

"The Lord Ruler never let skaa have coins either," another voice grumbled. "Seems that the longer old Quellion is in charge, the more he looks like that rat the Survivor killed."

Spook raised an eyebrow, taking another chug of wine. Vin, not Kelsier, was the one who had killed the Lord Ruler. Urteau, however, was a significant distance from Luthadel. They probably hadn't even known about the Lord Ruler's fall until weeks after it happened. Spook moved on to another conversation, searching for those who spoke in furtive whispers. He found exactly what he was listening for in a couple of men sharing a bottle of fine wine as they sat on the floor in the corner.

"He has most everyone catalogued now," the man whispered. "But he's not done yet. He has those scribes of his, the genealogists. They're asking questions, interrogating neighbors and friends, trying to trace everyone back five generations, looking for noble blood."

"But, he only kills those who have noblemen back two generations."

"There's going to be a division," the other voice whispered. "Every man who is pure back five generations will be allowed to serve in the government. Everyone else will be forbidden. It's a time when a man could make a great deal of coin if he could help people hide certain events in their past."

Hum, Spook thought, taking a swig of wine. Oddly, the alcohol didn't seem to be affecting him very much. *The pewter,* he realized. *It strengthens the body, makes it more resistant to pains and wounds. And, perhaps, helps it avoid intoxication?*

He smiled. The ability to drink and not grow drunk—an advantage of pewter that nobody had told him about. There had to be a way to use such a skill.

He turned his attention to other bar patrons, searching for useful tidbits. Another conversation spoke of work in the mines. Spook felt a chill and a flicker of remembrance. The men spoke of a coal mine, not a gold mine, but the grumbles were the same. Cave-ins. Dangerous gas. Stuffy air and uncaring taskmasters.

That would have been my life, Spook thought. *If Clubs hadn't come for me.*

To this day, he still didn't understand. Why had Clubs traveled so far—visiting the distant eastern reaches of the Final Empire—to rescue a nephew he'd never met? Surely there had been young Allomancers in Luthadel who had been equally deserving of his protection.

Clubs had spent a fortune, traveled a long distance in

an empire where skaa were forbidden to leave their home cities, and had risked betrayal by Spook's father. For that, Clubs had earned the loyalty of a wild street boy who—before that time—had run from any authority figure who tried to control him.

What would it be like? Spook thought. *If Clubs hadn't come for me, I would never have been in Kelsier's crew. I might have hidden my Allomancy and refused to use it. I might have simply gone to the mines, living my life like any other skaa.*

The men commiserated about the deaths of several who had fallen to a cave-in. It seemed that for them, little had changed since the days of the Lord Ruler. Spook's life would have been like theirs, he suspected. He'd be out in those Eastern wastes, living in sweltering dust when outside, working in cramped confines the rest of the time.

Most of his life, it seemed that he had been a flake of ash, pushed around by whatever strong wind came his way. He'd gone where people told him to go, done what they'd wanted him to. Even as an Allomancer, Spook had lived his life as a nobody. The others had been great men. Kelsier had organized an impossible revolution. Vin had struck down the Lord Ruler himself. Clubs had led the armies of revolution, becoming Elend's foremost general. Sazed was a Keeper, and had carried the knowledge of centuries. Breeze had moved waves of people with his clever tongue and powerful Soothing, and Ham was a powerful soldier. But Spook, he had simply watched, not really doing anything.

Until the day he ran away, leaving Clubs to die.

Spook sighed, looking up. "I just want to be able to help," he whispered.

"You can," Kelsier's voice said. "You can be great. Like I was."

Spook started, glancing about. But, nobody else appeared to have heard the voice. Spook sat back uncomfortably. However, the words made sense. Why did he always berate himself so much? True, Kelsier hadn't picked him to be on the crew, but now the Survivor himself had appeared to Spook and granted him the power of pewter.

I could help the people of this city, he thought. *Like Kelsier helped those of Luthadel. I could do something important: bring Urteau into Elend's empire, deliver the storage cache as well as the loyalty of the people.*

I ran away once. I don't ever have to do that again. I won't *ever do that again!*

Smells of wine, bodies, ash, and mold hung in the air. Spook could feel the very grain in the stool beneath him despite his clothing, the movements of people throughout the building shuffling and vibrating the ground beneath his feet. And, with all of this, pewter burned inside of him. He flared it, made it strong alongside his tin. The bottle cracked in his hand, his fingers pressing too hard, though he released it quickly enough to keep it from shattering. It fell toward the floor, and he snatched it from the air with his other hand, the arm moving with blurring quickness.

Spook blinked, awed at the speed of his own motions. Then, he smiled. *I'm going to need more pewter,* he thought.

"That's him."

Spook froze. Several of the conversations in the room had stopped, and to his ears—accustomed to a cacophony—the growing silence was eerie. He glanced to the side. The men who had been speaking of the mines were looking at Spook, speaking softly enough that they probably assumed he couldn't hear them.

"I'm telling you I saw him get *run through* by the guards. Everyone thought he was dead even before they burned him."

Not good, Spook thought. He hadn't thought himself memorable enough for people to notice. But . . . then again, he had attacked a group of soldiers in the middle of the city's busiest market.

"Durn's been talking about him," the voice continued. "Said he was of the Survivor's own crew . . ."

Durn, Spook thought. *So he* does *know who I really am. Why has he been telling people my secrets? I thought he was more careful than that.*

Spook stood up as nonchalantly as he could, then fled into the night.

Yes, Rashek made good use of his enemy's culture in developing the Final Empire. Yet, other elements of imperial culture were a complete contrast to Khlennium and its society. The lives of the skaa were modeled after the slave peoples of the Canzi. The Terris stewards resembled the servant class of Urtan, which Rashek conquered relatively late in his first century of life.

The imperial religion, with its obligators, actually appears to have arisen from the bureaucratic mercantile system of the Hallant, a people who were very focused on weights, measures, and permissions. The fact that the Lord Ruler would base his Church on a financial institution shows—in my opinion—that he worried less about true faith in his followers, and more about stability, loyalty, and quantifiable measures of devotion.

27

VIN SHOT THROUGH THE DARK night air. Mist swirled about her, a spinning, seething storm of white upon black. It darted close to her body, as if snapping at her, but never came closer than a few inches away—as if blown back by some current of air. She remembered a time when the mist had skimmed close to her skin, rather than being repelled. The transition had been gradual; it had taken months before she had realized the change.

She wore no mistcloak. It felt odd to be leaping about in the mists without one of the garments, but in truth, she was quieter this way. Once, the mistcloak had been useful in making guards or thieves turn away at her passing. However, like the era of friendly mists, that time had passed. So, instead, she wore only a black shirt and trousers, both closely fitted to her body to keep the sounds of flapping fabric to a minimum. As always, she wore no metal save for the coins in her pouch and an extra vial of metals in her sash. She pulled out a coin now—its familiar weight wrapped in a layer of cloth—and threw it beneath her. A Push against the metal sent it slamming into the rocks below, but the cloth dampened the sound of its striking. She used the Push to slow her descent, popping her up slightly into the air.

She landed carefully on a rock ledge, then Pulled the coin back into her hand. She crept across the rocky shelf, fluffy ash beneath her toes. A short distance away, a small group of guards sat in the darkness, whispering quietly, watching Elend's army camp—which was now little more than a haze of campfire light in the mists. The guards spoke of the spring chill, commenting that it seemed colder this year than it had in previous ones. Though Vin was barefoot, she rarely noticed the cold. A gift of pewter.

Vin burned bronze, and heard no pulsings. None of the men were burning metals. One of the reasons Cett had come to Luthadel in the first place was because he'd been unable to raise enough Allomancers to protect him from Mistborn assassins. No doubt Lord Yomen had experienced similar trouble recruiting Allomancers, and he probably wouldn't have sent those he did have out into the cold to watch an enemy camp.

Vin crept past the guard post. She didn't need Allomancy to keep her quiet—she and her brother, Reen, had sometimes been burglars, sneaking into homes. She had a lifetime of training that Elend would never know or understand. He could practice with pewter all he liked—and he really was getting better—but he'd never be able to replicate instincts honed by a childhood spent sneaking to stay alive.

As soon as she was past the guard post, she jumped into the mists again, using her sound-deadened coins as anchors. She gave the fires at the front of the city a wide berth, instead rounding to the rear of Fadrex. Most of the patrols would be at the front of the city, for the back was protected by the steep walls of the rising rock formations. Of course, that barely inconvenienced Vin, and she soon found herself dropping several hundred feet through the air along a rock wall before landing in an alley at the very back of the city.

She took to the roofs and did a quick survey, jumping from street to street in wide Allomantic leaps. She was quickly impressed with Fadrex's size. Elend had called the city "provincial," and Vin had imagined a town barely larger than a village. Once they'd arrived, she'd instead begun to imagine a barricaded, austere city—more like a fort. Fadrex was neither.

She should have realized that Elend—who had been raised in the sprawling metropolis of Luthadel—would have a skewed concept of what constituted a large city. Fadrex was plenty big. Vin counted several skaa slums, a smattering of noble mansions, and even two Luthadel-style keeps. The grand stone structures sported the typical arrangement of stained-glass windows and soaring, buttressed walls. These were undoubtedly the homes of the most important nobles in the city.

She landed on a rooftop near one of the keeps. Most of the buildings in the city were only a single story or two, which was quite a change from the high tenements of Luthadel. They were spaced out a bit more, and tended to be flat and squat, rather than tall and peaked. That only made the massive keep seem so much larger by comparison. The building was rectangular, with a row of three peaked towers rising from each end. Ornamented white stonework ran around the entire perimeter at the top.

And the walls, of course, were lined with beautiful stained-glass windows, lit from inside. Vin crouched on a low rooftop, looking at the colored beauty of the swirling mists. For a moment, she was taken back to a time three years before, when she had attended balls in keeps like this one in Luthadel as part of Kelsier's plan to overthrow the Final Empire. She had been an uncertain, nervous thing back then, worried that her newfound world of a trustworthy crew and beautiful parties would collapse around her. And, in a way, it had—for that world was gone. She had helped to destroy it.

Yet, during those months, she had been content. Perhaps more content than any other time in her life. She loved Elend, and was glad life had progressed to the point where she could call him husband, but there had been a delicious innocence about her early days with the crew. Dances spent with Elend reading at her table, pretending to ignore her. Nights spent learning the secrets of Allomancy. Evenings spent sitting around the table at Clubs's shop, sharing laughter with the crew. They'd faced the challenge of planning something as large as the fall of an empire, yet felt no burden of leadership or weight of responsibility for the future.

Somehow, she had grown into a woman in between the fall of kings and collapse of worlds. Once she had been terrified of change. Then she had been terrified of losing Elend. Now her fears were more nebulous—worries of what would come after she was gone, worries of what would happen to the people of the empire if she failed to divine the secrets she sought.

She turned from her contemplation of the large, castle-like keep, Pushing herself off of a chimney brace and into the night. Attending those balls in Luthadel had changed her dramatically, leaving a residual effect that she'd never been able to shake. Something within her had responded instantly to the dancing and the parties. For the longest time, she'd struggled to understand how that part of her fit into the rest of her life. She still wasn't certain she knew the answer. Was Valette Renoux—the girl she had pretended to be at the balls—really a part of Vin, or just a fabrication devised to serve Kelsier's plot?

Vin bounded across the city, making cursory notes of fortifications and troop placements. Ham and Demoux would probably find a way to get true military spies into the city eventually, but they'd want to hear preliminary information from Vin. She also made note of living conditions. Elend had hoped that the city would be struggling, a factor that his siege would exacerbate, making Lord Yomen more likely to capitulate.

She found no obvious signs of mass starvation or disrepair—though it was difficult to tell much at night. Still, the city streets were kept swept of ash, and a remarkable number of the noble homes appeared occupied. She would have expected the noble population to be the first to bolt at news of an approaching army.

Frowning to herself, Vin completed her loop of the city, landing in a particular square that Cett had suggested. The mansions here were separated from each other by large grounds and cultivated trees; she walked along the street, counting them off. At the fourth mansion, she leaped up and over the gate, then moved up the hill to the house.

She wasn't certain what she expected to find—Cett had been absent from the city for two years, after all. Yet, he'd indicated that this informant was the most likely to be of help. True to Cett's instructions, the rear balcony of the mansion was lit. Vin waited in the darkness suspiciously, the mist cold and unfriendly, yet providing cover. She didn't trust Cett—she worried that he still bore her a grudge for her attack on his keep in Luthadel a year before. Wary, she dropped a coin and launched herself into the air.

A lone figure sat on the balcony, fitting the description in Cett's instructions. Those same instructions gave this informant the nickname Slowswift. The old man appeared to be reading by the light of a lamp. Vin frowned, but as instructed, she landed on the balcony railing, crouching beside a ladder that would have allowed a more mundane visitor to approach.

The old man did not look up from his book. He puffed quietly on a pipe, a thick woolen blanket across his knees. Vin wasn't certain if he noticed her or not. She cleared her throat.

"Yes, yes," the old man said calmly. "I shall be with you in a moment."

Vin cocked her head, looking at the strange man with his bushy eyebrows and frosty white hair. He was dressed in a nobleman's suit, with a scarf and an overcoat that bore an oversized fur collar. He appeared to be completely unconcerned by the Mistborn crouching on his railing. Eventually, the elderly man closed his book, then turned toward her. "Do you enjoy stories, young lady?"

"What kind of stories?"

"The best kind, of course," Slowswift said, tapping his book. "The kind about monsters and myths. Longtales, some call them—stories told by skaa around the fires, whispering of mistwraiths, sprites, and brollins and such."

"I don't have much time for stories," Vin said.

"Seems that fewer and fewer people do, these days." A canopy kept off the ash, but he seemed unconcerned about the mists. "It makes me wonder what is so alluring about the real world that gives them all such a fetish for it. It's not a very nice place these days."

Vin did a quick check with bronze, but the man burned nothing. What was his game? "I was told that you could give me information," she said carefully.

"That I can certainly do," the man said. Then he smiled, glancing at her. "I have a wealth of information—though somehow I suspect that you might find most of it useless."

"I'll listen to a story, if that's what it will cost."

The man chuckled. "There's no surer way to kill a story than to make it a 'cost,' young lady. What is your name, and who sent you?"

"Vin Venture," Vin said. "Cett gave me your name."

"Ah," the man said. "That scoundrel still alive?"

"Yes."

"Well, I suppose I could chat with someone sent by an old writing friend. Come down off that railing—you're giving me vertigo."

Vin climbed down, wary. "Writing friend?"

"Cett is one of the finest poets I know, child," said Slowswift, waving her toward a chair. "We shared our work with one another for a good decade or so before politics stole him away. He didn't like stories either. To him, everything had to be gritty and 'real,' even his poetry. Seems like an attitude with which you'd agree."

Vin shrugged, sitting in the indicated chair. "I suppose."

"I find that ironic in a way you shall never understand," the old man said, smiling. "Now, what is it you wish of me?"

"I need to know about Yomen, the obligator king."

"He's a good man."

Vin frowned.

"Oh," Slowswift said. "You didn't expect that? Everyone who is your enemy must also be an evil person?"

"No," Vin said, thinking back to the days before the fall of the Final Empire. "I ended up marrying someone my friends would have named an enemy."

"Ah. Well then, Yomen is a fine man, and a decent king. A fair bit better a king than Cett ever was, I'd say. My old friend tries too hard, and that makes him brutal. He doesn't have the subtle touch that a leader needs."

"What has Yomen done that is so good, then?" Vin asked.

"He kept the city from falling apart," Slowswift said, puffing on his pipe. The smoke mixed with the swirling mists. "Plus, he gave both nobility and skaa what they wanted."

"Which was?"

"Stability, child. For a time, the world was in turmoil—neither skaa nor nobleman knew his place. Society was collapsing, and people were starving. Cett did little to stop that—he fought constantly to keep what he'd killed to obtain. Then Yomen stepped in. People saw authority in him. Before the Collapse, the Lord Ruler's Ministry had ruled, and the people were ready to accept an obligator as a leader. Yomen immediately took control of the plantations and brought food to his people, then he returned the factories to operation, started work in the Fadrex mines again, and gave the nobility a semblance of normalcy."

Vin sat quietly. Before, it might have seemed incredible to her that—after a thousand years of oppression—the people would willingly return to slavery. Yet, something similar had happened in Luthadel. They had ousted Elend, who had granted them great freedoms, and had put Penrod in charge—all because he promised them a return to what they had lost.

"Yomen is an obligator," she said.

"People like what is familiar, child."

"They're oppressed."

"Someone must lead," the old man said. "And, someone must follow. That is the way of things. Yomen has given the people something they've been crying for since the Collapse—identity. The skaa may work, they may be beaten, they may be enslaved, but they know their place. The nobility may spend their time going to balls, but there is an order to life again."

"Balls?" Vin asked. "The world is ending, and Yomen is throwing *balls*?"

"Of course," Slowswift said, taking a long, slow puff on his pipe. "Yomen rules by maintaining the familiar. He gives the people what they had before—and balls were a large part of life before the Collapse, even in a smaller city like Fadrex. Why, there is one happening tonight, at Keep Orielle."

"On the very day an army arrived to besiege the city?"

"You just pointed out that the world seems very close to disaster," the old man said, pointing at her with his pipe. "In the face of that, an army doesn't mean much. Plus, Yomen understands something even the Lord Ruler didn't—Yomen always personally attends the balls thrown by his subjects. In doing so, he comforts and reassures them. That makes a day like this, when an army arrived, a perfect day for a ball."

Vin sat back, uncertain what to think. Of all the things she had expected to find in the city, courtly balls were very low on the list. "So," she said. "What's Yomen's weakness? Is there something in his past that we can use? What quirks of personality make him vulnerable? Where should we strike?"

Slowswift puffed quietly on his pipe, a breeze blowing mist and ash across his elderly figure.

"Well?" Vin asked.

The old man let out a breath of mist and smoke. "I just told you that I like the man, child. What would possess me to give you information to use against him?"

"You're an informant," Vin said. "That's what you do—sell information."

"I'm a storyteller," Slowswift corrected. "And not every story is meant for every set of ears. Why should I talk to those who would attack my city and overthrow my liege?"

"We'd give you a powerful position in the city once it is ours."

Slowswift snorted quietly. "If you think such things would interest me, then Cett obviously told you little regarding my temperament."

"We could pay you well."

"I sell information, child. Not my soul."

"You're not being very helpful," Vin noted.

"And tell me, dear child," he said, smiling slightly. "Why exactly should I care?"

Vin frowned. *This is,* she thought, *undoubtedly the strangest informant meeting I've ever been to.*

Slowswift puffed on his pipe. He didn't appear to be waiting for her to say anything. In fact, he seemed to think the conversation was over.

He's a nobleman, Vin thought. *He likes the way that the world used to be. It was comfortable. Even skaa fear change.*

Vin stood. "I'll tell you why you should care, old man. Because the ash is falling, and soon it will cover up your pretty little city. The mists kill. Earthquakes shake the landscape, and the ashmounts burn hotter and hotter. Change is looming. Eventually, even Yomen won't be able to ignore it. You hate change. I hate it too. But things can't stay the same—and that's well, for when nothing changes in your life, it's as good as being dead." She turned to leave.

"They say you'll stop the ash," the old man said quietly from behind. "Turn the sun yellow again. They call you Heir of the Survivor. Hero of Ages."

Vin paused, turning to look through the traitorous mist toward the man with his pipe and closed book. "Yes," she said.

"Seems like quite the destiny to live up to."

"It's either that or give up."

Slowswift sat silently for a moment. "Sit down, child," the old man finally said, gesturing toward the seat again.

Vin reseated herself.

"Yomen is a good man," Slowswift said, "but only a mediocre leader. He's a bureaucrat, a member of the Canton of Resource. He can make things happen—get supplies to the right places, organize construction projects. Ordinarily, that would have made him a good enough ruler. However . . ."

"Not when the world is ending," Vin said softly.

"Precisely. If what I've heard is true, then your husband is a man of vision and action. If our little city is going to survive, then we'll need to be part of what you are offering."

"What do we do, then?"

"Yomen has few weaknesses," Slowswift said. "He's a calm man, and an honorable one. However, he has an unfailing belief in the Lord Ruler and his organization."

"Even now?" Vin asked. "The Lord Ruler died!"

"Yes, so?" Slowswift asked, amused. "And your Survivor? Last I checked, he was somewhat dead as well. Didn't seem to hinder his revolution much, now did it?"

"Good point."

"Yomen is a believer," Slowswift said. "That may be a weakness; it may be a strength. Believers are often willing to attempt the seemingly impossible, then count on providence to see them through." He paused, glancing at Vin. "That sort of behavior can be a weakness *if* the belief is misplaced."

Vin said nothing. Belief in the Lord Ruler *was* misplaced. If he'd been a god, then she wouldn't have been able to kill him. In her mind, it was a rather simple matter.

"If Yomen has another weakness," Slowswift said, "it is his wealth."

"Hardly a weakness."

"It is if you can't account for its source. He got money somewhere—a suspiciously vast amount of it, far more than even local Ministry coffers should have been able to provide. Nobody knows where it came from."

The cache, Vin thought, perking up. *He really does have the atium!*

"You reacted a little too strongly to that one," Slowswift said, taking a puff on his pipe. "You should try to give less away when speaking with an informant."

Vin flushed.

"Anyway," the old man said, turning back to his book, "if that is all, I should like to return to my reading. Give my regards to Ashweather."

Vin nodded, rising and moving over toward the banister. As she did, however, Slowswift cleared his throat. "Usually," he noted, "there is compensation for acts such as mine."

Vin raised an eyebrow. "I thought you said that stories shouldn't cost."

"Actually," Slowswift noted, "I said that a story itself shouldn't be a cost. That is very different from the story itself costing something. And, while some will argue, I believe that a story without cost is one considered worthless."

"I'm sure that's the only reason," Vin said, smiling slightly as she tossed her bag of coins—minus a few cloth-covered ones to use for jumping—to the old man. "Gold imperials. Still good here, I assume?"

"Good enough," the old man said, tucking them away. "Good enough . . ."

Vin jumped out into the night, leaping a few houses away, burning bronze to see if she felt any Allomantic pulses from behind. She knew that her nature made her irrationally suspicious of people who appeared weak. For the longest time, she'd been convinced that Cett was Mistborn, simply because he was paraplegic. Still, she checked on Slowswift. This was one old habit that she didn't feel much need to extinguish.

No pulses came from behind. Soon, she moved on, pulling out Cett's instructions, searching out a second informant. She trusted Slowswift's words well enough, but she would like confirmation. She picked an informant on the other side of the spectrum—a beggar named Hoid whom Cett claimed could be found in a particular square late at night.

A few quick jumps brought her to the location. She landed atop a roof and looked down, scanning the area. The ash had been allowed to drift here, piling in corners, making a general mess of things. A group of lumps huddled in an alley beside the square. Beggars, without home or job. Vin had lived like that at times, sleeping in alleys, coughing up ash, hoping it wouldn't rain. She soon located a figure that wasn't sleeping like the others, but sitting quietly in the light ashfall. Her ears picked out a faint sound. The man was humming to himself, as the instructions said that he might be doing.

Vin hesitated.

She couldn't decide what it was, but something bothered her about the situation. It wasn't right. She didn't stop to think, she simply turned and jumped away. That was one of the big differences between her and Elend—she didn't always need a reason. A feeling was enough. He always wanted to tease things out and find a *why,* and she loved him for his logic. However, he would have been very frustrated about her decision to turn away from the square as she had.

Perhaps nothing bad would have happened if she'd gone into the square. Perhaps something terrible would have occurred. She would never know, nor did she need to know. As she had countless other times in her life, Vin simply accepted her instincts and moved on.

Her flight took her along a street that Cett had noted in his instructions. Curious, Vin didn't search out another informant, but instead followed the road, bounding from anchor to anchor in the pervasive mists. She landed on a cobbled street a short distance from a building with lit windows.

Blocky and utilitarian, the building was nonetheless daunting—if only because of its size. Cett had written that the Canton of Resource was the largest of the Steel Ministry buildings in the city. Fadrex had acted as a kind of way station between Luthadel and more important cities to the west. Near several main canal routes and well fortified against banditry, the city was the perfect place for a Canton of Resource regional headquarters. Yet, Fadrex hadn't been important enough to attract the Cantons of Orthodoxy or Inquisition—traditionally the most powerful of the Ministry departments.

That meant that Yomen, as head obligator at the Resource building, had been the area's top religious authority. From what Slowswift said, Vin assumed that Yomen was pretty much a standard Resource obligator: dry, boring, but terribly efficient. And so, of course, he'd chosen to make his old Canton building into his palace. It was what Cett had suspected, and Vin could easily see that it was true. The building bustled with activity despite the late hour, and was guarded by platoons of soldiers. Yomen had probably chosen the building in order to remind everyone where his authority originated.

Unfortunately, it was also where the Lord Ruler's supply cache would be located. Vin sighed, turning from her contemplation of the building. Part of her wanted to sneak in and try to find her way down to the cavern beneath. Instead, she dropped a coin and shot herself into the air. Even Kelsier wouldn't have tried breaking into the place on his first night of scouting. She'd gotten into the one in Urteau, but it had been abandoned. She had to confer with Elend and study the city for a few days before she did something as bold as sneak into a fortified palace.

Using starlight and tin, Vin read off the name of the third and final informant. It was another nobleman, which wasn't surprising, considering Cett's own station. She began moving in the direction indicated. However, as she moved, she noticed something.

She was being followed.

She only caught hints of him behind her, obscured by the patterns of swirling mist. Tentatively, Vin burned bronze, and was rewarded with a very faint thumping from behind. An obscured Allomantic pulse. Usually, when an Allomancer burned copper—as the one behind her was doing—it made him invisible to the Allomantic bronze sense. Yet, for some reason Vin had never been able to explain, she could see through this obfuscation. The Lord Ruler had been able to do likewise, as had his Inquisitors.

Vin continued to move. The Allomancer following her obviously believed himself—or herself—invisible to Vin's senses. He moved with quick, easy bounds, following at a safe distance. He was good without being excellent, and he was obviously Mistborn, for only a Mistborn could have burned both copper and steel at the same time.

Vin wasn't surprised. She'd assumed that if there were any Mistborn in the city, her leaping would draw their attention.

Just in case, she hadn't bothered burning any copper herself, leaving her pulses open to be heard by anyone—Mistborn or Seeker—who was listening. Better an enemy drawn out than one hiding in the shadows.

She increased her pace, though not suspiciously so, and the person following had to move quickly to keep up. Vin kept going toward the front of the city, as if planning to leave. As she got closer, her Allomantic senses produced twin blue lines pointing at the massive iron brackets holding the city gates to the rock at their sides. The brackets were large, substantial sources of metal, and the lines they gave off were bright and thick.

Which meant they would make excellent anchors. Flaring her pewter to keep from being crushed, Vin *Pushed* on the brackets, throwing herself backward.

Immediately, the Allomantic pulses behind her disappeared.

Vin shot through ash and mist, even her tight clothing flapping slightly from the wind. She quickly Pulled herself down to a rooftop and crouched, tense. The other Allomancer must have stopped burning his metals. But why would he do that? Did he know that she could pierce copperclouds? If he did, then why had he followed her so recklessly?

Vin felt a chill. There was something else that gave off Allomantic pulses in the night. The mist spirit. She hadn't seen it in over a year. In fact, during her last encounter with it, it had nearly killed Elend—only to then restore him by making him Mistborn.

She still didn't know how the spirit fit into all of this. It wasn't Ruin—she had felt Ruin's presence when she'd freed him at the Well of Ascension. They were different.

I don't even know if this was *the spirit tonight,* Vin told herself. Yet, the one tailing her had vanished so abruptly. . . .

Confused, and chilled, she Pushed herself out of the city and quickly made her way back to Elend's camp.

One final aspect of the Lord Ruler's cultural manipulation is quite interesting: that of technology.

I have already mentioned that Rashek chose to use Khlenni architecture, which allowed him to construct large structures and gave him the civil engineering necessary to build a city as large as Luthadel. In other areas, however, he suppressed technological advancements. Gunpowder, for instance, was so frowned upon by Rashek that knowledge of its use disappeared almost as quickly as knowledge of the Terris religion.

Apparently, Rashek found it alarming that armed with gunpowder weapons, even the most common of men could be nearly as effective as archers with years of training. And so, he favored archers. The more training-dependent military technology was, the less likely it was that the peasant population would be able to rise up and resist him. Indeed, skaa revolts always failed in part for this very reason.

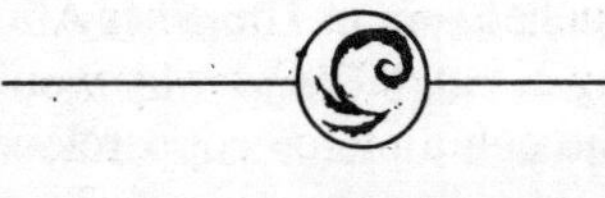

28

"ARE YOU SURE IT WAS the mist spirit?" Elend asked, frowning, a half-finished letter—scribed into a steel foil sheet—sitting on his desk before him. He'd decided to sleep in his cabin aboard the narrowboat, rather than in a tent. Not only was it more comfortable, he felt more secure with walls around him, as opposed to canvas.

Vin sighed, sitting down on their bed, pulling her legs up and setting her chin on her knees. "I don't know. I kind of got spooked, so I fled."

"Good thing," Elend said, shivering as he remembered what the mist spirit had done to him.

"Sazed was convinced that the mist spirit wasn't evil," Vin said.

"So was I," Elend said. "If you'll remember, I'm the one who walked right up to it, telling you that I felt it was friendly. That was right about the time it stabbed me."

Vin shook her head. "It was trying to keep me from releasing Ruin. It thought that if you were dying, I would take the power for myself and heal you, rather than giving it up."

"You don't know its intentions for certain, Vin. You could be connecting coincidences in your mind."

"Perhaps. However, it led Sazed to discover that Ruin was altering text."

That much, at least, was true—if, indeed, Sazed's account of the matter could be trusted. The Terrisman had been a little bit . . . inconsistent since Tindwyl had died. *No,* Elend told himself, feeling an instant stab of guilt. *No, Sazed is trustworthy. He might be struggling with his faith, but he is still twice as reliable as the rest of us.*

"Oh, Elend," Vin said softly. "There's so much we don't know. Lately, I feel like my life is a book written in a language I don't know how to read. The mist spirit is related to all this, but I can't even begin to fathom how."

"It's probably on our side," Elend said, though it was hard not to keep flashing back to memories of how it had felt to be stabbed, to feel his life fading away. To die, knowing what it would do to Vin.

He forced himself back to the conversation at hand. "You think the mist spirit tried to keep you from releasing Ruin, and Sazed says it gave him important information. That makes it the enemy of our enemy."

"For the moment," Vin said. "But, the mist spirit is much weaker than Ruin. I've felt them both. Ruin was . . . vast. Powerful. It can hear whatever we say—can see all places at once. The mist spirit is far fainter. More like a memory than a real force or power."

"Do you still think it hates you?"

Vin shrugged. "I haven't seen it in over a year. Yet, I'm pretty sure that it isn't the sort of thing that changes, and I always felt hatred and animosity from it." She paused, frowning. "That was the beginning. That night when I first saw the mist spirit was when I began to sense that the mists were no longer my home."

"Are you sure the spirit isn't what kills people and makes them sick?"

Vin nodded. "Yes, I'm sure." She was adamant about this, though Elend felt she was a bit quick to judge. Something ghost-like, moving about in the mists? It seemed like just the kind of thing that would be related to people dying suddenly in those same mists.

Of course, the people who died in the mists didn't die of stabbings, but of a shaking disease. Elend sighed, rubbing his eyes. His unfinished letter to Lord Yomen sat on his desk—he'd have to get back to it in the morning.

"Elend," Vin said. "Tonight, I told someone that I'd stop the ash from falling and turn the sun yellow."

Elend raised an eyebrow. "That informant you spoke of?"

Vin nodded. The two sat in silence.

"I never expected you to admit something like that," he finally said.

"I'm the Hero of Ages, aren't I? Even Sazed said so, before he started to go strange. It's my destiny."

"The same 'destiny' that said you would take up the power of the Well of Ascension, then release it for the greater good of mankind?"

Vin nodded.

"Vin," Elend said with a smile, "I really don't think 'destiny' is the sort of thing we need to worry about right now. I mean, we have proof that the prophecies were twisted by Ruin in order to trick people into freeing him."

"Someone has to worry about the ash," Vin said.

There wasn't much he could say to that. The logical side of him wanted to argue, claiming that they should focus on the things they could do—making a stable government, uncovering the secrets left by the Lord Ruler, securing the supplies in the caches. Yet, the constant ashfall seemed to be growing even denser. If that continued, it wouldn't be long before the sky was nothing more than a solid black storm of ash.

It just seemed so difficult to think that Vin—his wife—could do anything about the color of the sun or the falling ash. *Demoux is right,* he thought, tapping his fingers across the metallic letter to Lord Yomen. *I'm really not a very good member of the Church of the Survivor.*

He looked across the cabin at her, sitting on the bed, expression distant as she thought about things that shouldn't have to be her burden. Even after leaping about all night, even after their days spent traveling, even with her face dirtied by ash, she was beautiful.

At that moment, Elend realized something. Vin didn't need another person worshipping her. She didn't need another faithful believer like Demoux, especially not in Elend. He didn't need to be a good member of the Church of the Survivor. He needed to be a good husband.

"Well, then," he said. "Let's do it."

"What?" Vin asked.

"Save the world," Elend said. "Stop the ash."

Vin snorted quietly. "You make it sound like a joke."

"No, I'm serious," he said, standing. "If this is what you feel you must do—what you feel that you are—then let's do it. I'll help however I can."

"What about your speech before?" Vin said. "In the last storage cavern—you talked about division of labor. Me working on the mists, you working on uniting the empire."

"I was wrong."

Vin smiled, and suddenly Elend felt as if the world had been put back together just a bit.

"So," Elend said, sitting on the bed beside her. "What have you got? Any thoughts?"

Vin paused. "Yes," she said. "But I can't tell you."

Elend frowned.

"It's not that I don't trust you," Vin said. "It's Ruin. In the last storage cavern, I found a second inscription on the plate, down near the bottom. It warned me that anything I speak—

or that I write—will be known by our enemy. So, if we talk too much, *he* will know our plans."

"That makes it a bit difficult to work on the problem together."

Vin took his hands. "Elend, do you know why I finally agreed to marry you?"

Elend shook his head.

"Because I realized that you trusted me," Vin said. "Trusted me as nobody ever has before. On that night, when I fought Zane, I decided that I had to give my trust to you. This force that's destroying the world, we have something that it can never understand. I don't necessarily need your help; I need your trust. Your hope. It's something I've never had of myself, and I rely on yours."

Elend nodded slowly. "You have it."

"Thank you."

"You know," Elend added, "during those days when you refused to marry me, I constantly thought about how strange you were."

She raised an eyebrow. "Well, that's romantic."

Elend smiled. "Oh, come on. You have to admit that you're unusual, Vin. You're like some strange mixture of a noblewoman, a street urchin, and a cat. Plus, you've managed—in our short three years together—to kill not only my god, but my father, my brother, *and* my fiancée. That's kind of like a homicidal hat trick. It's a strange foundation for a relationship, wouldn't you say?"

Vin just rolled her eyes.

"I'm just glad I don't have any other close relatives," Elend said. Then, he eyed her. "Except for you, of course."

"I'm not about to drown myself, if that's what you're getting at."

"No," Elend said. "I'm sorry. I'm just . . . well, you know. Anyway, I was explaining something. In the end, I stopped worrying about how strange you seemed. I realized that it didn't really *matter* if I understood you, because I trusted you. Does that make sense? Either way, I guess I'm saying that I agree. I don't really know what you're doing, and I don't have any clue how you're going to achieve it. But, well, I trust that you'll do it."

Vin pulled close to him.

"I just wish there were something I could do to help," Elend said.

"Then take the whole numbers part," Vin said, frowning distastefully. Though she'd been the one to think something was odd about the percentages of those who fell to the mists, Elend knew that she found numbers troublesome. She didn't have the training, or the practice, to deal with them.

"You're sure that's even related?" Elend asked.

"You were the one who thought that the percentages were so strange."

"Good point. All right, I'll work on it."

"Just don't tell me what you discover," Vin said.

"Well, how is *that* going to help anything?"

"Trust," Vin said. "You can tell me what to do, just don't tell me why. Maybe we can stay ahead of this thing."

Stay ahead of it? Elend thought. *It has the power to bury the entire empire in ash, and can apparently hear every single word we say. How do we "stay ahead" of something like that?* But, he had just promised to trust Vin, so he did so.

Vin pointed at the table. "Is that your letter to Yomen?"

Elend nodded. "I'm hoping that he'll talk to me, now that I'm actually here."

"Slowswift does seem to think that Yomen is a good man. Maybe he'll listen."

"Somehow, I doubt it," Elend said. He sat softly for a moment, then made a fist, gritting his teeth in frustration. "I told the others that I want to try diplomacy, but I *know* that Yomen is going to reject my message. That's why I brought my army in the first place—I could have just sent you to sneak in, like you did in Urteau. However, sneaking in didn't help us much there; we still have to secure the city if we want the supplies.

"We *need* this city. Even if you hadn't felt so driven to discover what was in the cache, I would have come here. The threat Yomen poses to our kingdom is too strong, and the possibility that the Lord Ruler left important information in that cache can't be ignored. Yomen has grain in that storage, but the land here won't get enough sunlight to grow it. So, he'll probably feed it to the people—a waste, when we don't have enough to plant and fill the Central Dominance. We have to take this city, or at least make an ally out of it.

"But, what do I do if Yomen won't talk? Send armies to attack nearby villages? Poison the city's supplies? If you're right, then he's found the cache, which means he'll have more food than we hoped. Unless we destroy that, he might outlast our siege. But, if I do destroy it, his people will starve . . ." Elend shook his head. "Do you remember when I executed Jastes?"

"That was well within your right," Vin said quickly.

"I believe it was," Elend said. "But I killed him because he led a group of koloss to my city, then let them ravage my people. I've nearly done the same thing here. There are twenty thousand of the beasts outside."

"You can control them."

"Jastes thought he could control them too," Elend said. "I don't want to turn those creatures loose, Vin. But what if the siege fails, and I have to try and break Yomen's fortifications? I won't be able to do that without the koloss." He shook his head. "If only I could *talk* to Yomen. Perhaps I could make him see reason, or at least convince myself that he needs to fall."

Vin paused. "There . . . might be a way."

Elend glanced over, catching her eyes.

"They're still staging balls inside the city," Vin said. "And King Yomen attends every one."

Elend blinked. At first, he assumed that he must have misunderstood her. However, the look in her eyes—that wild determination—persuaded him otherwise. Sometimes, he saw a touch of the Survivor in her; or, at least, of the man the stories claimed Kelsier had been. Bold to the point of recklessness. Brave and brash. He'd rubbed off on Vin more than she liked to admit.

"Vin," he said flatly, "did you just suggest that we attend a *ball* being held in the middle of a city we're besieging?"

Vin shrugged. "Sure. Why not? We're both Mistborn—we can get into that city without much trouble at all."

"Yes, but . . ." He trailed off.

I'd have a room filled with the very nobility I'm hoping to intimidate—not to mention have access to the man who refuses to meet with me, in a situation where he'd have trouble running away without looking like a coward.

"You think it's a good idea," Vin said, smiling impishly.

"It's a *crazy* idea," Elend said. "I'm emperor—I shouldn't be sneaking into the enemy city so I can go to a party."

Vin narrowed her eyes, staring at him.

"I will admit, however," Elend said, "that the concept *does* have considerable charm."

"Yomen won't come meet us," Vin said, "so we go in and crash his party."

"It's been a while since I've been to a ball," Elend said speculatively. "I'll have to dig up some good reading material for old time's sake."

Suddenly, Vin grew pale. Elend paused, glancing at her, sensing that something was wrong. Not with what he'd said, something else. *What is it? Assassins? Mist spirits? Koloss?*

"I just realized something," Vin said, looking at him with those intense eyes of hers. "I can't go to a ball—I didn't bring a gown!"

The Lord Ruler didn't just forbid certain technologies, he suppressed technological advancement completely. It seems odd now that during the entirety of his thousand-year reign, very little progress was made. Farming techniques, architectural methods—even fashion remained remarkably stable during the Lord Ruler's reign.

He constructed his perfect empire, then tried to make it stay that way. For the most part, he was successful. Pocket watches—another Khlenni appropriation—that were made in the tenth century of the empire were nearly identical to those made during the first. Everything stayed the same.

Until it all collapsed, of course.

29

LIKE MOST CITIES IN THE Final Empire, Urteau had been forbidden a city wall. In the early days of Sazed's life, before he'd rebelled, the fact that cities couldn't build fortifications had always seemed a subtle indication to him of the Lord Ruler's vulnerability. After all, if the Lord Ruler was worried about rebellions and cities that could stand against him, then perhaps he knew something that nobody else did: that he *could* be defeated.

Thoughts like those had led Sazed to Mare, and finally to Kelsier. And now, they led him to the city of Urteau—a city that finally *had* rebelled against noble leadership. Unfortunately, it lumped Elend Venture in with all the other nobles.

"I don't like this, Master Keeper," Captain Goradel said, walking beside Sazed, who—for the sake of his image—now rode in the carriage with Breeze and Allrianne. After leaving the Terris people behind, Sazed had hurriedly caught up with Breeze and the others, and they were finally entering the city that was their destination.

"Things are supposed to be kind of brutal in there," Goradel continued. "I don't think you'll be safe."

"I doubt it's as bad as you think," Sazed said.

"What if they take you captive?" Goradel asked.

"My dear man," Breeze said, leaning forward to look out at Goradel. "That's why kings *send* ambassadors. This way, if someone gets captured, the king is still safe. We, my friend, are something Elend can never be: expendable."

Goradel frowned at that. "*I* don't feel very expendable."

Sazed peered out of the carriage, looking at the city through the falling ash. It was large, and was one of the oldest cities in the empire. He noted with interest that as they approached, the road sloped downward, entering an empty canal trough.

"What's this?" Allrianne asked, sticking her blond head out of the other side of the carriage. "Why'd they build their roads in ditches?"

"Canals, my dear," Breeze said. "The city used to be filled with them. Now they're empty—an earthquake or something diverted a river."

"It's creepy," she said, bringing her head back in. "It makes the buildings look twice as tall."

As they entered the city proper—their two hundred soldiers marching around them in formation—they were met by a delegation of Urteau soldiers in brown uniforms. Sazed had sent word ahead of their coming, of course, and the king—the Citizen, they called him—had given Sazed leave to bring his small contingent of troops into the city.

"They say that their king wants to meet with you immediately, Master Terrisman," Goradel said, walking back to the carriage.

"The man doesn't waste time, does he?" Breeze asked.

"We'll go, then," Sazed said, nodding to Goradel.

"You aren't wanted here."

Quellion, the Citizen, was a short-haired man with rough skin and an almost military bearing. Sazed wondered where the man—apparently a simple farmer before the Collapse—had gained such leadership skills.

"I realize that you have no desire to see foreign soldiers in your city," Sazed said carefully. "However, you must have realized that we do not come to conquer. Two hundred men is hardly an invading force."

Quellion stood at his desk, arms clasped behind his back. He wore what appeared to be regular skaa trousers and shirt, though both had been dyed a deep red verging on maroon. His "audience chamber" was a large conference room in what had once been a nobleman's house. The walls had been whitewashed and the chandelier removed. Stripped of its furniture and finery, the room felt like a box.

Sazed, Breeze, and Allrianne sat on hard wooden stools, the only comfort the Citizen had offered them. Goradel stood at the back with ten of his soldiers as a guard.

"It isn't about the soldiers, Terrisman," Quellion said. "It's about the man who sent you."

"Emperor Venture is a good and reasonable monarch," Sazed said.

Quellion snorted, turning to one of his companions. He had many of these—perhaps twenty—and Sazed assumed they were members of his government. Most wore red, like Quellion, though their clothing hadn't been dyed as deeply.

"Elend Venture," Quellion said, raising a finger, turning back to Sazed, "is a liar and a tyrant."

"That isn't true."

"Oh?" Quellion asked. "And how did he gain his throne? By defeating Straff Venture and Ashweather Cett in war?"

"War was—"

"War is often the excuse of tyrants, Terrisman," Quellion said. "My reports said that his Mistborn wife forced the kings to kneel before him that day—forced them to swear their loyalty to him or be slaughtered by his koloss brutes. Does that sound like the actions of a 'good and reasonable' man?"

Sazed didn't respond.

Quellion stepped forward, laying both hands palm-down on the top of his desk. "Do you know what we've done to the noblemen in this city, Terrisman?"

"You've killed them," Sazed said quietly.

"Just as the Survivor ordered," Quellion said. "You claim to have been his companion, before the fall. Yet, you serve one of the very noble houses he sought to overthrow. Doesn't that strike you as inconsistent, Terrisman?"

"Lord Kelsier accomplished his purpose in the death of the Lord Ruler," Sazed said. "Once that was achieved, peace—"

"Peace?" Quellion asked. "Tell me, Terrisman. Did you ever hear the Survivor speak of peace?"

Sazed hesitated. "No," he admitted.

Quellion snorted. "At least you're honest. The only reason I'm talking to you is because Venture was clever enough to send a Terrisman. If he'd sent a nobleman, I would have killed the cur and sent his blackened skull back as an answer."

The room fell silent. Tense. After a few moments of waiting, Quellion turned his back on Sazed, facing his companions. "You sense that?" he asked his men. "Can you feel yourselves begin to feel ashamed? Look at your emotions—do you suddenly feel a fellowship with these servants of a liar?"

He turned back, glancing at Breeze. "I've warned you all of Allomancy, the black tool of the nobility. Well, now you get to feel it. That man—sitting beside our *distinguished* Terrisman—is known as Breeze. He's one of the world's most vile men. A Soother of no small skill."

Quellion turned to address Breeze. "Tell me, Soother. How many friends have your magics made for you? How many enemies have you forced to kill themselves? That pretty girl beside you—did you use your arts to hex her into your bed?"

Breeze smiled, raising his cup of wine. "My dear man, you have, of course, found me out. However, instead of congratulating yourself for noticing my touch, perhaps you should ask yourself why I manipulated you into saying what you just did."

Quellion paused—though, of course, Breeze was bluffing. Sazed sighed. An indignant reaction would have been far more appropriate—but, then, that wasn't Breeze's way. Now the Citizen would spend the rest of the meeting wondering if his words were being guided by Breeze.

"Master Quellion," Sazed said, "these are dangerous times. Surely you have noticed that."

"We can protect ourselves well enough," Quellion said.

"I'm not speaking of armies or bandits, Citizen. I'm speaking of mists and ash. Have you noticed that the mists are lingering longer and longer during the daylight hours? Have you noticed them doing strange things to your people, causing the deaths of some who go out?"

Quellion did not contradict him or call his words foolish. That told Sazed enough. People had died in this city.

"The ash falls perpetually, Citizen," Sazed said. "The mists are deadly, and the koloss run free. This would be a very good time to have powerful alliances. In the Central Dominance, we can grow better crops, for we get more sunlight. Emperor Venture has discovered a method of controlling the koloss. Whatever is to come in the next few years, it would be very advantageous to be Emperor Venture's friend."

Quellion shook his head, as if in resignation. He turned to his companions again. "You see—just as I told you. First, he tells us he comes in peace, then he moves on to threats. Venture controls the koloss. Venture controls the food. Next he'll be saying that Venture controls the mists!" Quellion turned back to Sazed. "We don't have any use for threats here, Terrisman. We aren't worried about our future."

Sazed raised an eyebrow. "And why is that?"

"Because *we* follow the Survivor," Quellion said. "Be gone from my sight."

Sazed stood. "I would like to stay in the city and perhaps meet with you again."

"That meeting will not happen."

"Regardless," Sazed said. "I would prefer to stay. You have my promise that my men will not cause trouble. Might I have your leave?" He bowed his head in deference.

Quellion muttered something under his breath before waving a hand at him. "If I forbid you, then you'll just sneak in. Stay if you must, Terrisman, but I warn you—follow our laws and do not make trouble."

Sazed bowed further, then retreated with his people.

"Well," Breeze said, settling back into the carriage, "murderous revolutionaries, everybody wearing the same gray clothing, ditch-like streets where every tenth building has been burned to the ground. This is a lovely place Elend chose for us to visit—remind me to thank him upon our return."

Sazed smiled, though he felt little humor.

"Oh, don't look so grim, old man," Breeze said, waving with his cane as the carriage began to roll, their soldiers surrounding it. "Something tells me that Quellion there isn't half as threatening as his bearing implies. We'll convince him eventually."

"I'm not certain, Lord Breeze. This place . . . it's different from the other cities we've visited. The leaders aren't as desperate, and the people are more subservient. We won't have an easy time of it here, I think."

Allrianne poked Breeze's arm. "Breezy, do you see that, over there?"

Breeze squinted against the light, and Sazed leaned forward, glancing out the side of the carriage. A group of people had created a bonfire in the courtyard. The massive blaze sent a twisting line of smoke into the air. Sazed reflexively looked for a tinmind to draw upon and enhance his vision. He shoved the impulse aside, instead squinting against the afternoon light.

"It looks like . . ."

"Tapestries," said one of their soldiers, marching at the side of the carriage. "And furniture—rich things that are signs of the nobility, according to the Citizen. The burning was staged for your benefit, of course. Quellion probably keeps storehouses of the stuff so that he can order them burned at dramatically appropriate times."

Sazed froze. The soldier was remarkably well informed.

Sazed looked closely, suspicious. Like all of their men, this one wore his cloak hood up against the falling ash. As the man turned his head, Sazed could see that—oddly—he wore a thick bandage tied across his eyes, as if he were blind. Despite that, Sazed recognized the face.

"Spook, my dear boy!" Breeze exclaimed. "I knew you'd turn up eventually. Why the blindfold?"

Spook didn't answer the question. Instead, he turned, glancing back at the burning flames of the bonfire. There seemed a . . . tension to his posture.

The cloth must be thin enough to see through, Sazed thought. That was the only explanation for the way Spook moved with ease and grace, despite the cloth. Though, it certainly seemed thick enough to be obscuring. . . .

Spook turned back to Sazed. "You're going to need a base of operations in the city. Have you chosen one yet?"

Breeze shook his head. "We were thinking of using an inn."

"There aren't any true inns in the city," Spook said. "Quellion says that citizens should care for one another, letting visitors stay in each other's homes."

"Hmm," Breeze said. "Perhaps we'll need to camp outside."

Spook shook his head. "No. Follow me."

"The Ministry Canton of Inquisition?" Sazed asked, frowning as he climbed out of the carriage.

Spook stood ahead of them, on the steps leading into the grand building. He turned, nodding his strange, cloth-wrapped head. "Quellion hasn't touched any of the Ministry buildings. He ordered them boarded up, but he didn't ransack or burn them. I think he's afraid of Inquisitors."

"A healthy and rational fear, my boy," Breeze said, still sitting inside the carriage.

Spook snorted. "The Inquisitors aren't going to bother us, Breeze. They're far too busy trying to kill Vin. Come on."

He walked up the steps, and Sazed followed. Behind, he

could hear Breeze sigh with an exaggerated sound, then call for one of the soldiers to bring a parasol against the ash.

The building was broad and imposing, like most Ministry offices. During the days of the Lord Ruler, these buildings had stood as reminders of imperial might in every city across the Final Empire. The priests who had filled them had mostly been bureaucrats and clerks—but, then, that had been the real power of the Final Empire. Its control of resources and management of people.

Spook stood beside the building's broad, boarded-up doors. Like most structures in Urteau, it was built of wood, rather than stone. He stared up, as if watching the falling ash, as he waited for Sazed and Breeze. He had always been a quiet one, even more so since his uncle's death during the assault on Luthadel. As Sazed arrived, Spook began to rip boards free from the front of the building. "I'm glad you're here, Sazed," he said.

Sazed moved to help pull off boards. He heaved, trying to get the nails undone—yet, he must have chosen one of the more stubborn boards, for though the ones Spook grabbed came free with ease, Sazed's refused to even budge. "And why is it you're glad I am here, Lord Spook?"

Spook snorted. "I'm no lord, Saze. Never did get Elend to give me a title."

Sazed smiled. "He said that you only wanted one to impress women."

"Of course I did," Spook said, smiling as he ripped free another board. "What other reason would there be to have a title? Anyway, please just call me Spook. It's a good name."

"Very well."

Spook reached over, using a single, casual hand to pull off the board Sazed had tried to budge. *What?* Sazed thought with shock. Sazed was by no means muscular—but, then, he hadn't thought that Spook was either. The lad must have been practicing with weights.

"Anyway," Spook said, turning, "I'm glad you're here, because I have things to discuss with you. Things that others might not understand."

Sazed frowned. "Things of what nature?"

Spook smiled, then threw his shoulder against the door, opening it into a dark, cavernous chamber. "Things of gods and men, Sazed. Come on."

The boy disappeared into the darkness. Sazed waited outside, but Spook never lit a lantern. He could hear the young man moving around inside.

"Spook?" he finally called out. "I can't see in there. Do you have a lantern?"

There was a pause. "Oh," Spook's voice said. "Right." A moment later, a light sparked, and a lantern began to glow.

Breeze sauntered up behind Sazed. "Tell me, Sazed," he said quietly, "is it me, or has that boy changed since we last saw him?"

"He seems far more self-confident," Sazed said, nodding to himself. "More capable as well. But, what do you suppose is the purpose of that blindfold?"

Breeze shrugged, taking Allrianne's arm. "He always was an odd one. Perhaps he thinks it will disguise him and help keep him from being recognized as a member of Kelsier's crew. Considering the improvement in the boy's disposition—and diction—I'm willing to deal with a quirk or two."

Breeze and Allrianne entered the building, and Sazed waved to Captain Goradel, indicating that he should make a perimeter outside. The man nodded, sending a squad of soldiers up to follow Sazed and the others. Finally, Sazed frowned to himself and entered the building.

He wasn't certain what he had been expecting. The building had been part of the Canton of Inquisition—the most infamous of the Ministry's arms. It wasn't a place Sazed relished entering. The last building like this he'd entered had been the Conventical of Seran, and it had been decidedly eerie. This building, however, proved to be nothing like the Conventical—it was just another bureaucratic office. It was furnished a little more austerely than most Ministry buildings, true, but it still had tapestries on the wooden walls and broad red rugs on the floor. The trim was of metal, and there were hearths in every room.

As Sazed followed Breeze and Spook through the building, he was able to imagine what the building had been like during the days of the Lord Ruler. There would have been no dust, then, but instead an air of crisp efficiency. Administrators would have sat at those desks, collecting and filing information about noble houses, skaa rebels, and even other Ministry Cantons. There had been a longstanding feud between the Canton of Orthodoxy, which had administered the Lord Ruler's empire, and the Canton of Inquisition, which had policed it.

This was not a place of fear at all, but rather a place of ledgers and files. The Inquisitors had probably visited this building only rarely. Spook led them through several cluttered rooms toward a smaller storage chamber at the back. Here, Sazed could see that the dust on the floor had been disturbed.

"You've been here before?" he asked, entering the room after Spook, Breeze, and Allrianne.

Spook nodded. "As has Vin. Don't you remember the report?" With that, he felt about on the floor, eventually finding a hidden latch and opening a trapdoor. Sazed peered down into the dark cavern below.

"What's he talking about?" Allrianne whispered to Breeze. "Vin's been here?"

"She did reconnaissance in this city, dear," Breeze said. "To find . . ."

"The cache," Sazed said as Spook began to climb down a ladder into the darkness. He left the lantern behind. "The supply cache left behind by the Lord Ruler. All of them are underneath Ministry buildings."

"Well, that's what we're here to recover, isn't it?" Allrianne asked. "So, we've got it. Why bother with that Citizen fellow and his crazy peasants?"

"There's no way we could get these supplies out of the city with the Citizen in control." Spook's voice drifted up, echoing slightly. "There's too much down here."

"Besides, my dear," Breeze said. "Elend didn't just send us to get these supplies—he sent us to quell a rebellion. We can't have one of our major cities in revolt, and we *particularly* can't afford to let the rebellion spread. I must say, though, it does feel odd to be on this side of the problem—stopping a rebellion, rather than starting one."

"We may have to organize a rebellion *against* the rebellion, Breeze," Spook's voice echoed from below. "If that makes you feel any more comfortable. Anyway, are you three coming down or not?"

Sazed and Breeze shared a look, then Breeze gestured toward the dark pit. "After you."

Sazed picked up the lantern and climbed down the ladder. At the bottom, he found a small stone chamber, one wall of which had been pulled back to reveal a cavern. He stepped inside, Breeze reaching the ground behind him, then helping Allrianne down.

Sazed raised the lantern, staring quietly.

"Lord Ruler!" Breeze said, stepping up beside him. "It's enormous!"

"The Lord Ruler prepared these caches in case of a disaster," Spook said, standing ahead of them in the cavern. "They were meant to help the empire through what we're now facing. They wouldn't be much good if they weren't created on a grand scale."

"Grand" was correct. They stood on a ledge near the ceiling of the cavern, and a vast chamber extended out below. Sazed could see row upon row of shelves lining the cavern floor.

"I think we should set up our base here, Sazed," Spook said, moving toward stairs that led down to the cavern floor. "It's the only defensible place in the city. If we move our troops into the building above, we can use this cavern for supplies—and can even fall back in here in an emergency. We could defend this even against a determined assault."

Sazed turned, regarding the stone doorway into the chamber. It was small enough that only one man could pass through at a time—which meant that it would be very easy to guard. And, there was probably a way to shut it again.

"Suddenly I feel a whole lot safer in this city," Breeze noted.

Sazed nodded. He turned, regarding the cavern again. In the distance, he could hear something. "Is that water?"

Spook was moving down steps. Again, his voice echoed

hauntingly in the chamber. "Each cache has a specialty—something it contains more of than all the others."

Sazed moved down the steps as Goradel's soldiers entered the chamber behind Breeze. Though the soldiers had brought more lanterns, Breeze and Allrianne stuck close to Sazed as they descended.

Soon, Sazed realized he could see something sparkling in the distance. He held the lantern high, pausing on the steps as he saw that some of the darkness in the distance was too flat to be part of the cavern floor.

Breeze whistled quietly as they studied the enormous underground lake. "Well," he noted, "I guess now we know where all the water from those canals went."

Originally, men assumed that Rashek's persecution of the Terris religion came from hatred. Yet, now that we know that Rashek was himself a Terrisman, his destruction of that religion seems odd. I suspect it had something to do with the prophecies about the Hero of Ages. Rashek knew that Preservation's power would eventually return to the Well of Ascension. If the Terris religion had been allowed to survive, then perhaps—someday—a person would find their way to the Well and take up the power, then use it to defeat Rashek and overthrow his empire. So, he obscured knowledge of the Hero and what he was supposed to do, hoping to keep the secret of the Well to himself.

30

"YOU'RE NOT GOING TO TRY and talk me out of this?" Elend asked, amused.

Ham and Cett shared a look.

"Why would we do that, El?" Ham asked, standing at the

front of the boat. In the distance, the sun was setting, and the mists had already begun to gather. The boat rocked quietly, and soldiers milled about on the shore, preparing for night. One week had passed since Vin's initial scouting of Fadrex, and she still hadn't managed to sneak into the storage cache.

The night of the next ball had arrived, and Elend and Vin were planning to attend.

"Well, I can think of a couple of reasons why you might object," Elend said, counting them off on his fingers. "First, it isn't wise to expose me to potential capture. Second, by revealing myself at the party, I'll show that I'm Mistborn, confirming rumors that Yomen may not believe. Third, I'll be putting both of our Mistborn in the same place, where they can be easily attacked—that can't be a good idea. Finally, there's the fact that going to a ball in the middle of a war is just *plain crazy.*"

Ham shrugged, leaning with one elbow against the deck railing. "This isn't so different from when you entered your father's camp during the siege of Luthadel. Except you weren't Mistborn then, and you weren't in such a position of political power. Yomen would be crazy to make a move against you—he has to know that if you're in the same room with him, he's in mortal danger himself."

"He'll run," Cett said from his seat. "This party will end the moment you arrive."

"No," Elend said, "I don't think it will." He glanced back toward their cabin. Vin was still getting ready—she'd had the camp tailors modify one of the cooking girls' dresses. Elend was worried. No matter how good the dress turned out to be, it would look out of place compared to the lavish ball gowns.

He turned back to Cett and Ham. "I don't think Yomen will run. He has to know that if Vin wanted to kill him, she'd attack his palace in secret. He's trying very hard to pretend that nothing has changed since the Lord Ruler disappeared. When we show up at the ball, it will make him think that we're willing to pretend with him. He'll stay and see if he can gain some advantage by meeting with us on his terms."

"The man's a fool," Cett said. "I can't believe he'd want to go back to the way things were."

"At least he's trying to give his subjects what they want. That's where you went wrong, Cett. You lost your kingdom the moment you left because you didn't care to try pleasing anyone."

"A king doesn't have to please anyone," Cett snapped. "He's the one with the army—that means other people have to please *him*."

"Actually," Ham said, rubbing his chin, "that theory can't be true. A king has to please somebody—after all, even if he intended to *force* everyone to do what he said, he'd still have to at least please his army. But then, I guess if the army is pleased simply by being allowed to push people around, you might have an argument . . ."

Ham trailed off, looking thoughtful, and Cett scowled. "Does everything have to be some damn logic puzzle to you?" he demanded. Ham just continued to rub his chin.

Elend smiled, glancing at his cabin again. It was good to hear Ham acting like himself. Cett protested Ham's comments almost as much as Breeze did. In fact . . . *Maybe that's why Ham hasn't been quite so prone to his little logic puzzles lately,* Elend thought. *There hasn't been anyone around to complain about them.*

"So, Elend . . ." Cett said. "If you die, I'm in charge, right?"

"Vin will take command if something happens to me," Elend said. "You know that."

"Right," Cett said. "And if both of you die?"

"Sazed is next in the imperial succession after Vin, Cett. We've discussed that."

"Yes, but what about this army?" Cett said. "Sazed is off in Urteau. Who leads these men until we meet up with him?"

Elend sighed. "If, somehow, Yomen manages to kill both Vin and myself, then I suggest that you run—because yes, you'd be in charge here, and the Mistborn who killed us is likely to come for you next."

Cett smiled in satisfaction, though Ham frowned at this.

"You've never wanted titles, Ham," Elend pointed out. "And you've chafed at every leadership position I've given you."

"I know," he said. "But what about Demoux?"

"Cett has more experience," Elend said. "He's a better man than he pretends, Ham. I trust him. That will have to be enough for you. Cett, if things turn bad, I charge you with returning to Luthadel and searching out Sazed to tell him that he's emperor. Now, I think that—"

Elend paused as the door to his cabin opened. He turned, putting on his best consoling smile, then froze.

Vin stood in the doorway wearing a stunning black gown with silver trim, cut after a modern fashion. Somehow, it managed to look sleek despite the bell-shaped skirt, which fanned out with petticoats. Her pure black hair, which she often wore pulled back in a tail, was down, and it now reached to her collarbone, neatly trimmed and curling just slightly. The only jewelry she wore was her simple earring, the one she'd gotten from her mother when she was just a child.

He always thought she was beautiful. And yet . . . how long had it been since he'd seen her in a gown, with her hair and makeup done? He tried to say something, give her a compliment, but his voice just kind of trailed off.

She walked over on light feet, kissing him briefly. "I'll take that as an indication that I managed to put this thing on right. I'd forgotten what a *pain* gowns could be. And the makeup! Honestly, Elend, you're never allowed to complain about those suits of yours again."

Beside them, Ham was chuckling. Vin turned. "What?"

"Ah, Vin," Ham said, leaning back and folding his muscular arms, "when did you go and grow up on me? It seems like just last week you were scrambling about, hiding in corners, wearing the haircut of a boy and the attitude of a mouse."

Vin smiled fondly. "Do you remember when we first met? You thought I was a twixt."

Ham nodded. "Breeze nearly fainted dead away when he

found we'd been talking with a Mistborn all that time! Honestly, Vin. Sometimes I can't believe that you were that same frightened girl Kelsier brought into the crew."

"It *has* been five years, Ham. I'm twenty-one now."

"I know," Ham said, sighing. "You're like my own children, adults before I had time to know them as kids. In fact, I probably know you and El better than I know any of them . . ."

"You'll get back to them, Ham," Vin said, reaching over and laying a hand on his shoulder. "Once this is all over."

"Oh, I know that," he said, smiling, ever the optimist. "But, you can never have back what you've missed. I hope all this turns out to be worth it."

Elend shook his head, finally finding his voice. "I have only one thing to say. If that dress is what the cooking girls are wearing, I'm paying them *far* too much."

Vin laughed.

"Seriously, Vin," Elend said. "The army's tailors are good, but there's no way that dress came from materials we had in camp. Where did you get it?"

"It's a mystery," Vin said, narrowing her eyes and smiling. "We Mistborn are incredibly mysterious."

Elend paused. "Um . . . I'm Mistborn too, Vin. That doesn't make any sense."

"We Mistborn need not make sense," Vin said. "It's beneath us. Come on—the sun's already down. We need to get moving."

"Have fun dancing with our enemies," Ham said as Vin hopped from the boat, then Pushed herself up through the mists. Elend waved farewell, Pushing himself into the air as well. As he shot away, his tin-enhanced ears heard Ham's voice talking to Cett.

"So . . . you can't go anywhere unless someone carries you, right?" the Thug asked.

Cett grunted.

"Well then," Ham said, sounding very pleased. "I've got quite a number of philosophical puzzles you might enjoy. . . ."

* * *

Allomantic jumping was *not* easy when one was wearing a ball gown. Every time Vin started to descend, the bottom of the dress flared up around her, ruffling and flapping like a flock of startled birds.

Vin wasn't particularly worried about showing off what was under the dress. Not only was it too dark for most people to see, but she wore leggings beneath the petticoats. Unfortunately, flapping dresses—and the drag they created in the air—made steering a jump much more difficult. They also made a lot of noise. She wondered what the guards thought as she passed over the rocky shelves that were the natural city walls. To her ear, she sounded like a dozen waving flags, beating against themselves in the middle of a windstorm.

She finally slowed, aiming for a rooftop that had been cleared of ash. She hit lightly, bouncing up and spinning, dress flaring, before landing and waiting for Elend. He followed, landing less smoothly with a hard thump and a grunt. It wasn't that he was bad at Pushing and Pulling—he just hadn't had as much practice as Vin. She'd probably been much like him during her first years as an Allomancer.

Well . . . maybe not like him, she thought fondly as Elend dusted himself off. *But, I'm sure a lot of other Allomancers were about at Elend's level after only a year of practice.*

"That was quite the series of jumps, Vin," Elend said, puffing slightly as he glanced back toward the cliff-like rock formations, their fires burning high in the night. Elend wore his standard white military uniform, one of the same ones that Tindwyl had designed for him. He'd had this one scrubbed free of ash, and he'd gotten his beard trimmed.

"I couldn't land often," Vin explained. "These white petticoats will stain with ash easily. Come on—we need to get inside."

Elend turned, smiling in the darkness. He actually looked excited. "The dress. You paid a dressmaker inside the city to make it for you?"

"Actually, I paid a friend inside the city to have it made for me, and to get me the makeup." She jumped away, heading toward Keep Orielle—which, according to Slowswift, was the site of the evening's ball. She kept to the air, never landing. Elend followed behind, using the same coins.

Soon, they approached a burst of color in the mists, like an aurora from one of Sazed's stories. The bubble of light turned into the massive keep she had seen during her previous infiltration, its stained-glass windows shining from the inside. Vin angled herself downward, streaking through the mists. She briefly considered dropping to the ground out in the courtyard—away from watchful eyes—so that she and Elend could approach the doors subtly. Then she decided against it.

This wasn't an evening for subtlety.

So, instead she dropped directly down onto the carpeted steps leading up to the main entrance of the castle-like building. Her landing blew away flakes of ash, creating a little pocket of cleanliness. Elend landed beside her a second later, then stood up straight, his brilliant white cape flapping around him. At the top of the steps, a pair of uniformed servants had been greeting guests and ushering them into the building. Both men froze, stunned expressions on their faces.

Elend held out his arm to Vin. "Shall we?"

Vin took the arm. "Yes," she said. "Preferably before those men can get the guards."

They strode up the steps, sounds of surprise coming from behind, where a small group of noblemen had been exiting their carriage. Ahead, one of the servants moved forward and cut off Vin and Elend. Elend carefully placed a hand against the man's chest, then shoved him aside with a pewter-fueled push. The man stumbled backward into the wall. The other one went running for the guards.

Inside the antechamber, waiting nobility began to whisper and question. Vin heard them asking if anyone recognized these strange newcomers, one in black, the other in white. Elend strode forward firmly, Vin at his side, causing people to stumble over themselves and move out of the way. Elend and Vin passed quickly through the small room, and Elend handed a name card to a servant who waited to announce arrivals into the ballroom proper.

They waited on the servant, and Vin realized that she'd begun holding her breath. It seemed as if she were reliving a dream—or was it a fond memory? For a moment, she was that same young girl of over four years before, arriving at Keep Venture for her very first ball, nervous and worried that she wouldn't be able to play her part.

Yet, she felt none of that same insecurity. She didn't worry if she'd find acceptance or belief. She'd slain the Lord Ruler. She'd married Elend Venture. And—more remarkable than either accomplishment—somehow in the chaos and mess she'd discovered who she was. Not a girl of the streets, though that was where she'd been raised. Not a woman of the court, though she appreciated the beauty and grace of the balls. Someone else.

Someone she liked.

The servant reread Elend's card, growing pale. He looked up. Elend met the man's eyes, then gave a small nod, as if to say, "Yes, I'm afraid that it's true."

The servant cleared his throat, and Elend led Vin into the ballroom.

"High Emperor, Lord Elend Venture," the servant announced in a clear voice. "And the Empress Vin Venture, Heir of the Survivor, Hero of Ages."

The entire ballroom grew suddenly—and unnaturally—quiet. Vin and Elend paused at the front of the room, giving the gathered nobility a chance to see them. It appeared that Keep Orielle's grand main hall, like Keep Venture's, was also its ballroom. However, instead of being tall with a broad, arched roof, this room had a relatively low ceiling and small, intricate designs in the stonework. It was as if the architect had tried for beauty on a delicate scale, rather than an imposing one.

The entire chamber was crafted from white marble of various shades. While it was large enough to hold hundreds of people—plus a dance floor and tables—it still felt intimate. The room was divided by rows of ornamental marble pillars, and it was further partitioned with large stained-glass panels that ran from floor to ceiling. Vin was impressed—most keeps in Luthadel left their stained glass to the perimeter walls, so they could be lit from outside. While this keep did have some of those, she quickly realized that the true masterpieces had been placed here, freestanding inside the ballroom, where they could be admired from both sides.

"By the Lord Ruler," Elend whispered, scanning the gathered people. "They really *do* think they can just ignore the rest of the world, don't they?"

Gold, silver, bronze, and brass sparkled upon figures in brilliant ball gowns and sharp gentlemen's suits. The men generally wore dark clothing, and the women generally wore colors. A group of musicians played strings in a far corner, their music unimpeded by the shocked atmosphere. Servants waited, uncertain, bearing drinks and foods.

"Yes," Vin whispered. "We should move out of the doorway. When the guards come, we'll want to be mingled in the crowd to make the soldiers uncertain if they want to attack."

Elend smiled, and she knew he was remarking to himself about her tendency to keep her back from being exposed. However, she also knew that he realized she was right. They walked down the short set of marble steps, joining the party.

Skaa might have shied away from such a dangerous couple, but Vin and Elend wore the costume of noble propriety. The aristocracy of the Final Empire were quite adept at playing pretend—and when they were uncertain how to behave, they fell back on the old standard: proper manners.

Lords and ladies bowed and curtsied, acting as if the emperor and empress's attendance had been completely expected. Vin let Elend take the lead, as he had far more experience than she with matters of court. He nodded to those they passed, displaying just the right amount of self-assurance. Behind, guards finally arrived at the doors. They stopped, however, obviously wary about disturbing the party.

"There," Vin said, nodding to their left. Through a

stained-glass partition, she could make out a figure sitting at an elevated table.

"I see him," Elend said, leading her around the glass, and giving Vin her first sight of Aradan Yomen, king of the Western Dominance.

He was younger than she'd expected—perhaps as young as Elend. Roundfaced with serious eyes, Yomen had his head shaved bald, after the manner of obligators. His dark gray robes were a mark of his station, as were the complicated patterns of tattoos around his eyes, which proclaimed him a very high-ranking member of the Canton of Resource.

Yomen stood up as Vin and Elend approached. He looked utterly dumbfounded. Behind, the soldiers had begun to carefully work their way into the room. Elend paused a distance from the high table, with its white cloth and pure crystal place settings. He met Yomen's gaze, the other guests so quiet that Vin guessed most were holding their breaths.

Vin checked her metal reserves, turning slightly, keeping an eye on the guards. Then, from the corner of her eye, she saw Yomen raise his hand and subtly wave the guards back.

Chatter began in the room almost immediately. Yomen sat back down, looking troubled, and did not return to his meal.

Vin looked up at Elend. "Well," she whispered, "we're in. What now?"

"I need to talk to Yomen," Elend said. "But I'd like to wait a little bit first; give him a chance to get used to our presence."

"Then we should mingle."

"Split up? We can cover more nobility that way."

Vin hesitated.

"I can protect myself, Vin," Elend said, smiling. "I promise."

"All right." Vin nodded, though that wasn't the only reason she'd paused.

"Talk to as many people as you can," Elend said. "We're here to shatter this people's image of safety. After all, we just proved that Yomen can't keep us out of Fadrex—and we're showing that we're so unthreatened by him that we'll waltz into a ball that he's attending. Once we've made a bit of a stir, I'll talk to their king, and they'll all be certain to listen in."

Vin nodded. "When you mingle, watch for people who look like they might be willing to support us against the current government. Slowswift implied that there are some in the city who aren't pleased with the way their king is handling things."

Elend nodded, kissed her cheek, and then she was alone. Vin stood in her beautiful gown, feeling a moment of shock. Over the last two years, she'd explicitly worked to keep herself out of situations where she would wear gowns and mingle with nobility. She'd determinedly worn trousers and shirts, making it her self-appointed duty to sow discomfort in those she found too full of themselves.

Yet, she had been the one to suggest this infiltration to Elend. Why? Why put herself back in this position? She wasn't displeased with who she was—she didn't need to prove anything by putting on another silly gown and making courtly conversation with a bunch of nobility she didn't know.

Did she?

No use fidgeting about it now, Vin thought, scanning the crowd. Noble balls in Luthadel—and she could only assume here—were very polite affairs, designed to encourage mingling, and therefore facilitate political give and take. Balls had once been the main form of sport for the nobility, who had lived privileged lives under the Lord Ruler because their ancestors had been his friends back before his Ascension.

And so, the party was made up of small groups—some mixed couples, but many clusters of just women or just men. A pair was not expected to stay together the entire time. There were side rooms where gentlemen could retire and drink with their allies, leaving the women to converse in the ballroom.

Vin walked forward, slipping a cup of wine off the tray of a passing servant. By splitting up, Elend and she had indicated that they were open to conversation with others. Unfortunately, it had been a long, long time since Vin had to be alone at a party like this. She felt awkward, uncertain whether to approach one of the groups, or wait to see if anyone came to her. She felt somewhat as she had that first night, when she'd gone to Keep Venture posing as a lone noblewoman, Sazed her only guide.

That day, she'd played a part, hiding in her role as Valette Renoux. She couldn't do that anymore. Everyone knew who she really was. That would have bothered her, once, but it didn't anymore. Still, she couldn't just do what she'd done then—stand around and wait for others to come to her. The entire room seemed to be staring at her.

She strode through the beautiful white room, aware of how much her black dress stood out against the women in their colors. She moved around the slices of colored glass that hung from the ceiling like crystalline curtains. She'd learned from her earlier balls that there was one thing she could always count on: Whenever noblewomen gathered, one always set herself up as the most important.

Vin found her with ease. The woman had dark hair and tan skin, and she sat at a table surrounded by sycophants. Vin recognized that arrogant look, that way the woman's voice was just loud enough to be imperious, but just soft enough to make everyone hang on her words.

Vin approached with determination. Years ago, she'd been forced to start at the bottom. She didn't have time for that. She didn't know the subtle political intricacies of the city—the allegiances and rivalries. However, there was one thing of which she was fairly confident.

Whichever side this woman was on, Vin wanted to be on the opposite one.

Several of the sycophants looked up as Vin approached, and they grew pale. Their leader had the poise to remain aloof. *She'll try to ignore me,* Vin thought. *I can't leave her that option.* Vin sat at the table directly across from the woman. Then, Vin turned and addressed several of the younger sycophants.

"She's planning to betray you," Vin said.

The women glanced at each other.

"She has plans to get out of the city," Vin said. "When the army attacks, she won't be here. And she's going to leave you all to die. Make an ally of me, however, and I will see that you are protected."

"Excuse me?" the lead woman said, her voice indignant. "Did I invite you to sit here?"

Vin smiled. *That was easy.* A thieving crewleader's basis of power was money—take that away, and he'd fall. For a woman like this, her power was in the people who listened to her. To make her react, one simply had to threaten to take her minions.

Vin turned to confront the woman. "No, you didn't invite me. I invited myself. Someone needs to warn the women here."

The woman sniffed. "You spread lies. You know nothing of my supposed plans."

"Don't I? You're not the type to let a man like Yomen determine your future, and if the others here think about it, they'll realized that there's no way you would let yourself get caught in Fadrex City without plans to escape. I'm surprised you're even still here."

"Your threats do not frighten me," the lady said.

"I haven't threatened you yet," Vin noted, sipping her wine. She gave a careful Push on the emotions of the women at the table, making them more worried. "We could get to that, if you wish—though, technically, I've got your entire city under threat already."

The woman narrowed her eyes at Vin. "Don't listen to her, ladies."

"Yes, Lady Patresen," one of the women said, speaking a little too quickly.

Patresen, Vin thought, relieved that someone had finally mentioned the woman's name. *Do I know that name?* "House Patresen," Vin said idly. "Isn't that a cousin family of House Elariel?"

Lady Patresen remained quiet.

"I killed an Elariel once," Vin said. "It was a good fight. Shan was a very clever woman, and a skilled Mistborn." She leaned in. "You may think that the stories about me are exaggerations. You may assume that I didn't really kill the Lord Ruler, and that the talk is simply propaganda crafted to help stabilize my husband's rule.

"Think as you wish, Lady Patresen. However, there is one thing you *must* understand. You are not my adversary. I don't have *time* for people like you. You're a petty woman in an insignificant city, part of a doomed culture of nobility. I'm not talking to you because I want to be part of your schemes; you can't even understand how unimportant they are to me. I'm just here to voice a warning. We're going to take this city—and when we do, there will be little room for people who were against us."

Patresen paled just slightly. However, her voice was calm when she spoke. "I doubt that's true. If you could take the city as easily as you claim, then you would have already."

"My husband is a man of honor," Vin said, "and decided that he wished to speak with Yomen before attacking. I, however, am not quite so temperate."

"Well, *I* think that—"

"You don't understand, do you?" Vin asked. "It doesn't matter what you think. Look, I know you're the type with powerful connections. Those connections will have told you by now the numbers we bring. Forty thousand men, twenty thousand koloss, and a full contingent of Allomancers. Plus two Mistborn. My husband and I did not come to this conference to make allies, or even to make enemies. We came to give warning. I suggest you take it."

She punctuated her last comment with a powerful Soothing. She wanted it to be obvious to the women, to let them know that they were—indeed—under her power. Then, she stood, trailing away from the table.

What she had said to Patresen wasn't really that important—the important thing was that Vin had been seen confronting the woman. Hopefully, that would put Vin on a side in the local politics, making her less threatening to some factions in the room. That, in turn, would make her more accessible, and—

The sound of chairs scooting back from the table came from behind her. Vin turned, suspicious, and saw most of Lady Patresen's clique approaching in a hurry, leaving their leader sitting virtually alone at her table, a scowl on her face.

Vin tensed.

"Lady Venture," one of the women said. "Perhaps you would let some of us . . . introduce you at the party?"

Vin frowned.

"Please," the woman said very quietly.

Vin blinked in surprise. She'd expected the women to resent her, not *listen* to her. She glanced about. Most of the women looked so intimidated that Vin thought they might wilt away, like leaves in the sun. Feeling a little bemused, Vin nodded her head and let herself be led into the party for introductions.

Rashek wore both black and white. I think he wanted to show that he was a duality, Preservation and Ruin.

This, of course, was a lie. After all, he had only touched one of the powers—and only in a very small way at that.

31

"LORD BREEZE GUESSED CORRECTLY," SAZED said, standing at the front of their small group. "As far as I can tell, the diversion of waters into this underground reservoir was intentional. The project must have taken decades. It required widening natural passageways so that the water—which once fed the river and canals above—instead flowed into this cavern."

"Yes, but what's the point?" Breeze asked. "Why waste so much effort to move a river?"

Three days in Urteau had allowed them to do as Spook had suggested, moving their troops into the Ministry building, ostensibly taking up residence inside of it. The Citizen couldn't know about the cache, otherwise he would have ransacked it. That meant Sazed and his team held a distinct advantage should events in the city turn ugly.

They had pulled some of the furniture from the building above and arranged it—with sheets and tapestries to create "rooms"—amid the shelves in the cavern. Logic dictated that the cavern was the best place to spend their time, for should someone attack the Ministry building, the cavern was where they wanted to be. True, they'd be trapped—but with the supplies they had, they'd be able to survive indefinitely and work out a plan of escape.

Sazed, Breeze, Spook, and Allrianne sat in one of these partitioned-off areas among the shelves of food. "The reason that the Lord Ruler made this lake is simple, I think." Sazed turned, glancing over his shoulder at the lake. "That water comes via an underground river, filtered—in all likelihood—through layers of rock. It is pure water, the likes of which you rarely see in the Final Empire. No ash, no sediment. The purpose of that water is to sustain a population should a disaster occur. If it were still flowing into the canals above, it would quickly get soiled and polluted by the population living in the city."

"The Lord Ruler was looking to the future," Spook said, still wearing his strange eye bandage. He'd turned aside all questions and promptings regarding why he wore it, though Sazed was beginning to suspect it had to do with burning tin.

Sazed nodded at the young man's comment. "The Lord Ruler wasn't worried about causing financial ruin in Urteau—he just wanted to make certain this cavern had access to a constant, flowing source of fresh water."

"Isn't this all beside the point?" Allrianne asked. "So we have water. What about that maniac running the city?"

Sazed paused, and the others turned to look to him. *I am, unfortunately, in charge.* "Well," he said, "we should speak of this. Emperor Venture has asked us to secure the city. As the Citizen has proven unwilling to meet with us again, we shall need to discuss other options."

"That man needs to go," Spook said. "We need assassins."

"I fear that wouldn't work very well, my dear boy," Breeze said.

"Why not?" Spook asked. "We killed the Lord Ruler, and that worked pretty well."

"Ah," Breeze said, raising a finger, "but the Lord Ruler was irreplaceable. He was a god, and so killing him created a psychological impact on his populace."

Allrianne nodded. "This Citizen's not a force of nature, but a man—and men can be replaced. If we assassinate Quellion, one of his lackeys will simply take his place."

"And we will be branded as murderers," Breeze added.

"What, then?" Spook asked. "We leave him alone?"

"Of course not," Breeze said. "If we want to take this city, we need to undermine him, *then* remove him. We prove that his entire system is faulty—that his government is, in essence, silly. If we manage that, we won't just stop him, we'll stop everyone who has worked with him and supported him. That is the only way we're going to take Urteau short of marching an army in here and seizing it by force."

"And, since His Majesty kindly left us *without* any troops to speak of . . ." Allrianne said.

"I am not convinced that such rash action is required," Sazed said. "Perhaps, given more time, we'll be able to work with this man."

"Work with *him*?" Spook asked. "You've been here three days—isn't that enough for you to see what Quellion is like?"

"I have seen," Sazed said. "And, to be perfectly honest, I do not know that I can fault the Citizen's views."

The cavern fell silent.

"Perhaps you should explain yourself, my dear man," Breeze said, sipping at a cup of wine.

"The things that the Citizen says are not false," Sazed

said. "We cannot blame him for teaching the very same things that Kelsier did. The Survivor spoke of killing the nobility—goodness knows, we all saw him engaging in *that* activity often enough. He spoke of revolution and of skaa ruling themselves."

"He spoke of extreme actions during extreme times," Breeze said. "That's what you do when you need to motivate people. Even Kelsier wouldn't have taken it this far."

"Perhaps," Sazed said. "But can we really be surprised that people who heard Kelsier speak have created this society? And, what right have we to take it from them? In a way, they've been truer to Kelsier than we have. Can you really say that you think he'd be pleased to find out that we put a nobleman on the throne not one day after he died?"

Breeze and Spook glanced at each other, and neither contradicted him.

"It's just not right," Spook finally said. "These people claim to know Kelsier, but they don't. He didn't want people to be grim and bullied—he wanted them to be free and happy."

"Indeed," Breeze said. "Besides, we *did* choose to follow Elend Venture—and he's given us an order. Our empire needs these supplies, and we can't afford to let an organized rebellion seize and control one of the most important cities in the empire. We need to secure this cache and protect the people of Urteau. It's for the greater good, and all that!"

Allrianne nodded her agreement—and, as always, Sazed felt her touch on his emotions.

For the greater good . . . Sazed thought. He knew that Spook was right. Kelsier wouldn't want this warped society being perpetuated in his name. Something needed to be done. "Very well," he said. "What should our course of action be?"

"Nothing, for now," Breeze said. "We need time to feel out the city's climate. How close are the people to rebelling against dear Quellion? How active is the local criminal element? How corruptible are the men who serve the new government? Give me some time to discover answers to these questions, and then we can decide what to do."

"I still say we do it as Kelsier did," Spook said. "Why can't we just topple the Citizen like he did the Lord Ruler?"

"I doubt that would work," Breeze said, sipping his wine.

"Why not?" Spook asked.

"For a very simple reason, my dear boy," Breeze said. "We don't have Kelsier anymore."

Sazed nodded. That much was true—though he did wonder if they would ever be rid of the Survivor's legacy. In a way, the battle in this town had been inevitable. If Kelsier had possessed one flaw, it had been his extreme hatred of the nobility. It was a passion that had driven him, had helped him accomplish the impossible. However, Sazed feared it would destroy those whom it had infected.

"Take the time you need, Breeze," Sazed said. "Let me know when you think we are ready to take the next step."

Breeze nodded, and the meeting broke up. Sazed stood, sighing quietly. As he did, he met Breeze's eyes, and the man winked at him with a smile that seemed to say, "This won't be half as difficult as you think." Sazed smiled back, and he felt Breeze's touch on his emotions, trying to encourage him.

Yet, the Soother's hand was too light. Breeze couldn't have known the conflict that still twisted inside of Sazed. A conflict about much more than Kelsier and the problems in Urteau. He was glad for a little bit of time to wait in the city, for he still had much work to do with the religions listed, one per sheet, in his portfolio.

Even that work was difficult for him to get to recently. He did his best to give the others leadership, as Elend had asked. However, the pernicious darkness Sazed felt inside of him refused to be shaken away. It was more dangerous to him, he knew, than anything else he had faced while serving with the crew, because it made him feel as if he didn't care.

I must *keep working,* he decided, walking away from the meeting place, carefully sliding his portfolio off of a nearby shelf. *I have to keep searching. I must not give up.*

It was far more difficult than that, however. In the past, logic and thought had always been his refuge. However, his emotions didn't respond to logic. No amount of thinking about what he *should* be doing could help him.

He ground his teeth, walking, hoping that the motion would help him work out the knots within himself. A part of him wanted to go out and study the new form of the Church of the Survivor that had sprung up here in Urteau. However, that seemed like a waste of time. The world was ending, why study one more religion? He already knew this one was false; he'd dismissed the Church of the Survivor early in his studies. It was filled with more contradictions than almost any in his portfolio.

More filled with passion as well.

All the religions in his collection were alike in one respect; they had failed. The people who'd followed them had died, been conquered, their religions stamped out. Was that not proof enough for him? He'd tried preaching them, but he'd very, very rarely had any success.

It was all meaningless. Everything was ending anyway.

No! Sazed thought. *I will find the answers. The religions didn't disappear completely—the Keepers preserved them. There must be answers in one of them. Somewhere.*

Eventually, he found his way to the wall of the cavern, which held the steel plate inscribed by the Lord Ruler. They already had a record of what it said, of course, but Sazed wanted to see it and read it for himself. He looked up at the metal, which reflected the light of a nearby lantern, reading the words of the very man who had destroyed so many religions.

The plan, the words said, *is simple. When the power returns to the Well, I will take it and make certain the thing remains trapped.*

And still I worry. It has proven far more clever than I had assumed, infecting my thoughts, making me see and feel things I do not wish to. It is so subtle, so careful. I cannot see how it could cause my death, but still I worry.

If I am dead, then these caches will provide some measure

of protection for my people. I fear what is coming. What might be. If you read this now, and I am gone, then I fear for you. Still, I will try to leave what help I can.

There are metals of Allomancy which I have shared with none. If you are a priest of mine, working this cavern and reading these words, know that you will incur my wrath if you share this knowledge. However, if it is true that the force has returned and I am unable to deal with it, then perhaps knowledge of electrum will give you some aid. My researchers have discovered that mixing an alloy of forty-five percent gold and fifty-five percent silver creates a new Allomantic metal. Burning it will not give you the power of atium, but will provide some help against those who themselves burn it.

And that was it. Beside the words was a map, indicating the location of the next cache—the one in the small southern mining village that Vin and Elend had secured a short time back. Sazed read over the words again, but they only served to enhance his sense of despair. Even the Lord Ruler seemed to feel helpless in the face of their current predicament. He'd planned to be alive, he'd planned for none of this to happen. But he'd known that his plans might not work.

Sazed turned, leaving the plate behind, walking to the bank of the underground lake. The water lay like black glass, undisturbed by wind or ash, though it did ripple slightly from the current. A pair of lanterns sat by the edge of the water, burning quietly, marking the bank. Behind him, a short distance away, some of the soldiers had made camp—though a good two-thirds of them kept to the upstairs to make certain the building had the look of being lived in. Others searched the cavern walls in hopes of finding a secret exit. They would all be a lot more comfortable within the cavern if they knew they had a means of escaping it, should they get attacked.

"Sazed."

Sazed turned, then nodded to Spook as the young man walked up to join him on the bank of the black still water. They stood together quietly, contemplative.

This one has troubles of his own, Sazed thought, noting the way that Spook watched the waters. Then, surprisingly, Spook reached up and untied the cloth from his eyes. He pulled it free, revealing a pair of spectacles underneath, perhaps used to keep the cloth from pressing his eyes closed. Spook removed the spectacles and blinked, squinting. His eyes began to water, then he reached down and put out one of the two lanterns, leaving Sazed standing in very dim light. Spook sighed, standing and wiping his eyes.

So it is *his tin,* Sazed thought. As Sazed considered the thought, he realized that he had often seen the young man wearing gloves—as if to protect his skin. Sazed suspected that if he watched closely, he'd see the boy put in earplugs as well. *Curious.*

"Sazed," Spook said, "I wanted to talk to you about something."

"Please, speak as you wish."

"I . . ." Spook trailed off, then glanced at Sazed. "I think Kelsier is still with us."

Sazed frowned.

"Not alive, of course," Spook said quickly. "But, I think he's watching over us. Protecting us . . . that sort of thing."

"That's a pleasant sentiment, I think," Sazed said. *Completely false, of course.*

"It's not just a sentiment," Spook replied. "He's here. I was just wondering if there was anything in any of those religions you studied that talked about things like that."

"Of course," Sazed said. "Many of them spoke of the dead remaining as spirits to help, or curse, the living."

They fell silent, Spook obviously waiting for something.

"Well?" Spook asked. "Aren't you going to preach a religion to me?"

"I don't do that anymore," Sazed said quietly.

"Oh," Spook said. "Um, why not?"

Sazed shook his head. "I find it hard to preach to others that which has offered me no solace, Spook. I am looking through them, trying to discover which—if any of them—are right and true. Once I have that knowledge, I will be happy to share with you any that seem most likely to contain truth. For now, however, I believe none of them, and therefore will preach none of them."

Surprisingly, Spook didn't argue with him. Sazed had found it frustrating that his friends—people who were, for the most part, determined atheists—would grow so offended when he threatened to join them in their lack of belief. And yet, Spook didn't offer arguments.

"It makes sense," the young man finally said. "Those religions *aren't* true. After all, Kelsier is the one who watches over us, not those other gods."

Sazed closed his eyes. "How can you say that, Spook? You lived with him—you knew him. We both know that Kelsier was no god."

"The people of this city think he is."

"And where has it gotten them?" Sazed asked. "Their belief has brought oppression and violence. What is the good of faith if *this* is the result? A city full of people misinterpreting their god's commands? A world of ash and pain and death and sorrow?" Sazed shook his head. "That is why I no longer wear my metalminds. Religions which cannot offer more than this do not deserve to be taught."

"Oh," Spook said. He knelt down, dipping a hand in the water, then shivered. "That makes sense too, I guess—though I'd have guessed it was because of *her*."

"What do you mean?"

"Your woman," Spook said. "The other Keeper—Tindwyl. I heard her talk about religion. She didn't think very much of it. I'd have thought that maybe you wouldn't talk about religion anymore because that might be what she'd have wanted."

Sazed felt a chill.

"Anyway," Spook said, standing, wiping off his hand, "the people of this city know more than you think they do. Kelsier *is* watching over us."

With that, the boy trailed away. Sazed, however, wasn't listening. He stood, staring at the ebony waters.

Because that might be what she'd have wanted. . . .

Tindwyl had thought religion to be foolish. She had said that people who looked toward ancient prophecies or unseen forces were seeking excuses. During her last few weeks with Sazed, this had often been a topic of conversation—even slight contention—between the two of them, for their research had dealt with the prophecies regarding the Hero of Ages.

That research had turned out to be useless. At best, the prophecies were the vain hopes of men who wished for a better world. At worst, they had been cleverly placed to further the goals of a malignant force. Either way, he had believed strongly in his work at that time. And Tindwyl had helped him. They had searched through their metalminds, sifting through centuries of information, history, and mythology, seeking references to the Deepness, the Hero of Ages, and the Well of Ascension. She had worked with him, claiming that her interest was academic, not religious. Sazed suspected that she'd had a different motivation.

She'd wanted to be with him. She had suppressed her dislike of religion out of a desire to be involved with what he found important. And, now that she was dead, Sazed found himself doing what *she'd* found important. Tindwyl had studied politics and leadership. She'd loved to read the biographies of great statesmen and generals. Had he unconsciously agreed to become Elend's ambassador so that he could involve himself in Tindwyl's studies, just as she—before her death—had given herself over to his?

He wasn't certain. In truth, he thought his problems were deeper than that. However, the fact that *Spook* had been the one to make such an astute observation gave Sazed pause. It was a very clever way of looking at things. Instead of contradicting him, Spook had offered a possible explanation.

Sazed was impressed. He turned out, looking across the waters for a time and contemplating what Spook had said. Then, he pulled out the next religion in his portfolio and began to consider it. The sooner he got through them, the sooner he could—hopefully—find the truth.

Allomancy, obviously, is of Preservation. The rational mind will see this. For, in the case of Allomancy, net power is gained. It is provided by an external source—Preservation's own body.

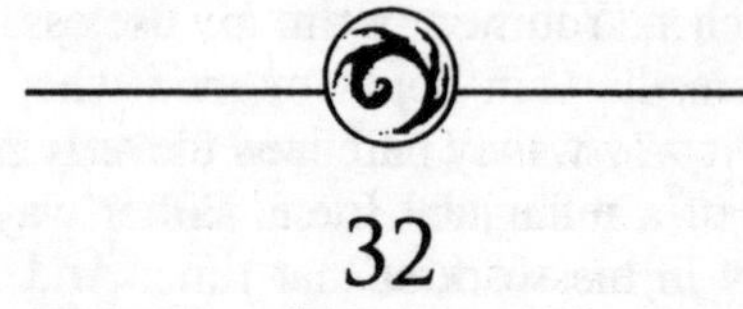

32

"ELEND, IS THAT REALLY YOU?"

Elend turned with shock. He'd been mingling at the ball, talking with a group of men who had turned out to be distant cousins of his. The voice from behind, however, seemed far more familiar. "Telden?" Elend asked. "What are you doing here!"

"I live here, El," Telden said, clasping hands with Elend.

Elend was dumbfounded. He hadn't seen Telden since his house had escaped Luthadel in the days of chaos following the death of the Lord Ruler. Once, this man had been one of Elend's best friends. To the side, Elend's cousins made a graceful withdrawal. "I thought you were in BasMardin, Tell," Elend said.

"No," Telden said. "That's where my house settled, but I thought that the area was too dangerous, what with the koloss rampages. I moved inward to Fadrex once Lord Yomen came to power—he quickly gained a reputation for being able to provide stability."

Elend smiled. The years had changed his friend. Telden had once been the model of a debonair ladies' man, his hair and expensive suits intended to draw attention. It wasn't that the older Telden had grown sloppy, but he obviously didn't take as much care to appear stylish. He'd always been a large man—tall and kind of rectangular—and the extra weight he'd gained made him look far more . . . ordinary than he once had.

"Elend," Telden said, shaking his head. "You know, for

the longest time, I refused to believe that you'd really managed to seize power in Luthadel."

"You were there at my coronation!"

"I thought that they had picked you as a puppet, El," Telden said, rubbing his wide chin. "I thought . . . well, I'm sorry. I guess I just didn't have much faith in you."

Elend laughed. "You were right, my friend. I turned out to be a terrible king."

Telden obviously wasn't sure how to reply to that.

"I did get better at the job," Elend said. "I just had to stumble through a few messes first."

Partygoers shuffled through the divided ballroom. Though those watching did their best to appear uninterested and aloof, Elend could tell that they were doing the noble equivalent of gawking. He glanced to the side, where Vin stood in her gorgeous black dress, surrounded by a group of women. She seemed to be doing well—she took to the courtly scene far better than she liked to let herself think or admit. She was graceful, poised, and the center of attention.

She was also alert—Elend could tell by the way she managed to keep her back to a wall or glass partition. She'd be burning iron or steel, watching for sudden movements of metal that might indicate an attacking Coinshot. Elend began burning iron as well, and he made certain to keep burning brass to Soothe the emotions of those in the room, keeping them from feeling too angry or threatened by his intrusion. Other Allomancers—Breeze, or even Vin—would have had trouble Soothing an entire room at once. For Elend, with his inordinate power, it barely took any attention.

Telden still stood nearby, looking troubled. Elend tried to say something to start their conversation again, but he struggled to come up with anything that wouldn't sound awkward. It had been nearly four years since Telden had left Luthadel. Before that, he had been one of the friends with whom Elend had discussed political theory, planning with the idealism of youth for the day when they would lead their houses. Yet, the days of youth—and their idealistic theories—were gone.

"So . . ." Telden said. "This is where we end up, is it?"

Elend nodded.

"You're not . . . really going to attack the city, are you?" Telden asked. "You're just here to intimidate Yomen, right?"

"No," Elend said softly. "I will conquer the city if I have to, Telden."

Telden flushed. "What happened to you, Elend? Where is the man who talked about rights and legality?"

"The world caught up with me, Telden," Elend said. "I can't be the man I was."

"So you become the Lord Ruler instead?"

Elend hesitated. It felt odd to have another confront him with his own questions and arguments. Part of him felt a stab of fear—if Telden asked these things, then Elend had been right to worry about them. Perhaps they were true.

Yet, a stronger impulse flared within him. An impulse nurtured by Tindwyl, then refined by a year of struggling to bring order to the shattered remains of the Final Empire.

An impulse to trust himself.

"No, Telden," Elend said firmly. "I'm not the Lord Ruler. A parliamentary council rules in Luthadel, and there are others like it in every city I've brought into my empire. This is the first time that I've marched on a city with my armies out of a need to conquer, rather than protect—and that is only because Yomen himself took this city from an ally of mine."

Telden snorted. "You set yourself up as emperor."

"Because that's what the people *need,* Telden," Elend said. "They don't want to return to the days of the Lord Ruler—but they would rather do that than live in chaos. Yomen's success here proves that much. The people want to know that someone is watching over them. They had a god-emperor for a thousand years—now is not the time to leave them without a leader."

"You mean to tell me that you're just a figurehead?" Telden asked, folding his arms.

"Hardly," Elend said. "But, eventually, I hope to be. We both know I'm a scholar and not a king."

Telden frowned. He didn't believe Elend. And yet, Elend

found that fact didn't bother him. Something about saying those words, about confronting the skepticism, made him recognize the validity of his own confidence. Telden didn't understand—he hadn't lived through what Elend had. The young Elend himself wouldn't have agreed with what he was now doing. A part of that youth still had a voice inside of Elend's soul—and he would never quiet it. However, it was time to stop letting it undermine him.

Elend put a hand on his friend's shoulder. "It's all right, Tell. It took me years to convince you that the Lord Ruler was a terrible emperor. I fully expect it to take the same amount of time to convince you that I'll be a good one."

Telden smiled wanly.

"Going to tell me that I've changed?" Elend asked. "Seems all the rage lately."

Telden laughed. "I thought that was obvious. No need to point it out."

"What, then?" Elend asked.

"Well . . ." Telden said. "I was actually going to chide you for not inviting me to your wedding! I'm hurt, El. Truly. I spent the better part of my youth giving you relationship advice, then when you finally pick a girl, you don't even let me know about the marriage!"

Elend laughed, turning to follow Telden's gaze toward Vin. Confident and powerful, yet somehow delicate and graceful. Elend smiled with pride. Even during the glory days of the Luthadel ball scene, he couldn't remember a woman commanding as much attention as Vin now did. And, unlike Elend, she'd stepped into this ball without knowing a single person.

"I feel a little like a proud parent," Telden said, laying a hand on Elend's shoulder. "There were days I was convinced that you were hopeless, El! I figured you'd someday wander into a library and just disappear completely. We'd find you twenty years later covered with dust, picking through some philosophy text for the seven hundredth time. Yet, here you are, married—and to a woman like that!"

"Sometimes, I don't understand either," Elend said. "I

can't ever come up with any logical reason why she would want to be with me. I just . . . have to trust her judgment."

"Either way, you did well."

Elend raised an eyebrow. "I seem to remember that *you* once tried to talk me out of spending time with her."

Telden flushed. "You have to admit, she *was* acting very suspiciously when she came to those parties."

"Yes," Elend said. "She seemed too much like a real person to be a noblewoman." He looked over at Telden, smiling. "However, if you'll excuse me, I have something I need to do."

"Of course, El," Telden said, bowing slightly as Elend withdrew. The move felt a little odd coming from Telden. They didn't really know each other anymore. However, they did have memories of friendship.

I didn't tell him that I killed Jastes, Elend thought as he made his way through the room, its members parting easily for him. *I wonder if he knows.*

Elend's enhanced hearing picked out a general rise in excitement among the whispered conversations as people realized what he was doing. He'd given Yomen time enough to deal with his surprise; it was time to confront the man. Though part of Elend's purpose in visiting the ball was to intimidate the local nobility, the main reason was still to speak with their king.

Yomen watched Elend approach the high table—and, to his credit, the obligator did not look frightened at the prospect of a meeting. His meal still remained uneaten, however. Elend didn't wait for permission to come to the table, but he did pause and wait as Yomen waved for servants to clear space and set Elend a place directly across the high table from him.

Elend sat, trusting in Vin—mixed with his own burning steel and tin—to warn him of attacks from behind. He was the only one on this side of the table, and Yomen's dining companions all retired as Elend seated himself, leaving the two rulers alone. In another situation, the image might have looked ridiculous: two men seated across from each other with empty table wings extending a great distance to either side. The white tablecloth and crystalline dinnerware were pristine, just as it would have been during the Lord Ruler's day.

Elend had sold all such finery he owned, struggling to feed his people during the last few winters.

Yomen laced his fingers on the table in front of him—his meal taken away by silent servants—and studied Elend, his cautious eyes framed by intricate tattoos. Yomen wore no crown, but he *did* wear a single bead of metal tied so that it hung in the center of his forehead.

Atium.

"There is a saying in the Steel Ministry," Yomen finally said. " 'Sit down to dine with evil, and you will ingest it with your meal.' "

"It's a good thing we're not eating, then," Elend said, smiling slightly.

Yomen did not smile back.

"Yomen," Elend said, growing more serious. "I come to you now, not as an emperor seeking for new lands to control, but as a desperate king seeking allies. The world has become a dangerous place—the land itself seems to be fighting us, or at least falling apart beneath us. Accept my hand of friendship, and let us be done with wars."

Yomen didn't reply. He just sat, fingers laced, studying Elend.

"You doubt my sincerity," Elend said. "I can't say that I blame you, since I marched my army up to your doorstep. Is there a way that I can persuade you? Would you be willing to enter into talks or parley?"

Again, no answer. So, this time, Elend just waited. The room around them felt still.

Yomen finally spoke. "You are a flagrant and garish man, Elend Venture."

Elend bristled at that. Perhaps it was the ball setting, perhaps it was the way Yomen so flippantly ignored his offer. However, Elend found himself responding to the comment in a way he might have years before, when he hadn't been a king at war. "It's a bad habit I've always had," Elend said. "I'm afraid that the years of rule—and of being trained in propriety—haven't changed one fact: I'm a terribly rude man. Bad breeding would be my guess."

"You find this a game," the obligator said, eyes hard. "You come to my city to slaughter my people, then you dance into my ball hoping to frighten the nobility to the point of hysteria."

"No," Elend said. "No, Yomen, this is no game. The world seems near to ending, and I'm just doing my best to help as many people survive as possible."

"And doing your best includes conquering my city?"

Elend shook his head. "I'm not good at lying, Yomen. So, I'll be truthful with you. I don't want to kill anyone—as I said, I'd rather we simply made a truce and were done with it. Give me the information I seek, pool your resources with mine, and I will not force you to give up your city. Deny me, and things will grow more difficult."

Yomen sat quietly for a moment, music still being played softly in the background, vibrating over the hum of a hundred polite conversations.

"Do you know why I dislike men like you, Venture?" Yomen finally asked.

"My insufferable charm and wit?" Elend asked. "I doubt it's my good looks—but, compared to that of an obligator, I suppose even my face could be enviable."

Yomen's expression darkened. "How did a man like you ever end up at a table of negotiation?"

"I was trained by a surly Mistborn, a sarcastic Terrisman, and a group of disrespectful thieves," Elend said, sighing. "Plus, on top of that, I was a fairly insufferable person to begin with. But, kindly continue with your insult—I didn't mean to interrupt."

"I don't like you," Yomen continued, "because you have the gall to believe that you *deserve* to take this city."

"I do," Elend said. "It belonged to Cett; half the soldiers I brought with me on this march once served him, and this is their homeland. We've come to liberate, not conquer."

"Do these people look to you like they need liberation?" Yomen said, nodding to the dancing couples.

"Yes, actually," Elend said. "Yomen, you're the upstart here—not me. You have no right to this city, and you know it."

"I have the right given me by the Lord Ruler."

"We don't accept the Lord Ruler's right to rule," Elend said. "That's why we killed him. Instead, we look to the *people's* right to rule."

"Is that so?" Yomen said, hands still laced before him. "Because, as I recall, the people of *your* city chose Ferson Penrod to be their king."

Good point, that one, Elend had to admit.

Yomen leaned forward. "This is the reason I don't like you, Venture. You're a hypocrite of the worst kind. You pretended to let the people be in charge—but when they ousted you and picked another, you had your Mistborn conquer the city back for you. You rule by force, not by common consent, so don't talk to me about *rights.*"

"There were . . . circumstances in Luthadel, Yomen. Penrod was working with our enemies, and he bought himself the throne through manipulating the assembly."

"That sounds like a flaw in the system," Yomen said. "A system that *you* set up—a system replacing the one of order that existed before it. A people depend on stability in their government; they need someone to look to. A leader that they can trust, a leader with true authority. Only a man chosen by the Lord Ruler has that claim on authority."

Elend studied the obligator. The frustrating thing was, he almost agreed with the man. Yomen said things that Elend himself had said, even if they were twisted a bit by his perspective as an obligator.

"Only a man chosen by the Lord Ruler has that claim on authority . . ." Elend said, frowning. The phrase sounded familiar. "That's from Durton, isn't it? *Calling of Trust*?"

Yomen paused. "Yes."

"I prefer Gallingskaw, when it comes to divine right."

Yomen made a curt gesture. "Gallingskaw was a heretic."

"That makes his theories invalid?" Elend asked.

"No," Yomen said. "It shows that he lacked the ability to reason soundly—otherwise he wouldn't have gotten himself executed. *That* affects the validity of his theories. Besides, there is no divine mandate in the common man, as he proposed."

"The Lord Ruler was a common man before he took his throne," Elend said.

"Yes," Yomen said, "but the Lord Ruler touched divinity at the Well of Ascension. That imprinted the Sliver of Infinity upon him, and gave him the Right of Inference."

"Vin, my wife, touched that same divinity."

"I don't accept that story," Yomen said. "As it has been said, the Sliver of Infinity was unique, unplanned, uncreated."

"Don't bring Urdree into this," Elend said, raising a finger. "We both know he was more a poet than a real philosopher—he ignored convention, and never gave proper attributions. At least give me the benefit of the doubt and quote Hardren. He'd give you a much better foundation."

Yomen opened his mouth, then stopped, frowning. "This is pointless," he said. "Arguing philosophy will not remove the fact that you have an army camped outside my city, nor change the fact that I find you a hypocrite, Elend Venture."

Elend sighed. For a moment, he'd thought that they might be able to respect one another as scholars. There was one problem, however. Elend saw true loathing in Yomen's eyes. And, Elend suspected that there was a deeper reason for it than Elend's alleged hypocrisy. After all, Elend *had* married the woman who had killed Yomen's god.

"Yomen," Elend said, leaning in. "I realize we have differences. However, one thing seems clear—we both care about the people of this empire. We both took the time to study political theory, and we both apparently focused on the texts that held the good of the people up as the prime reason for rule. We should be able to make this work.

"I want to offer you a deal. Accept kingship under me—you'd be able to stay in control, with very few changes in your government. I will need access to the city and its resources, and we will need to discuss setting up a parliamentary council. Other than that, you may continue as you wish—you can even keep throwing your parties and teaching about the Lord Ruler. I will trust your judgment."

Yomen did not scoff at the offer, but Elend could tell that he also didn't give it much weight. He had likely already known what Elend would say.

"You mistake one thing, Elend Venture," Yomen said.

"And that is?"

"That I can be intimidated, bribed, or influenced."

"You're no fool, Yomen," Elend said. "Sometimes, fighting isn't worth its cost. We both know that you can't beat me."

"That is debatable," Yomen said. "Regardless, I do not respond well to threats. Perhaps if you didn't have an army camped on my doorstep, I could see my way to an alliance."

"We both know that without an army on your doorstep, you wouldn't even have listened to me," Elend said. "You refused every messenger I sent, even before I marched here."

Yomen just shook his head. "You seem more reasonable than I would have thought, Elend Venture, but that doesn't change facts. You already have a large empire of your own. In coming here, you betray your arrogance. Why did you need my dominance? Wasn't what you already had enough?"

"Firstly," Elend said, raising a finger, "I feel that I need to remind you again that you stole this kingdom from an ally of mine. I had to come here eventually, if only to make good on promises I gave Cett. However, there's something much larger at play here." Elend hesitated, then made a gamble. "I need to know what is in your storage cavern."

Elend was rewarded with a slight look of surprise on Yomen's face, and that was all the confirmation Elend needed. Yomen did know about the cavern. Vin was right. And considering that atium displayed so prominently on his forehead, perhaps she was right about what was contained in the cavern.

"Look, Yomen," Elend said, speaking quickly. "I don't care about the atium—it's barely of any value anymore. I need to know what instructions the Lord Ruler left in that cavern. What information is there for us? What supplies did he find necessary for our survival?"

"I don't know what you are talking about," Yomen said flatly. He wasn't a particularly good liar.

"You asked me why I came here," Elend said. "Yomen, it's not about conquering or taking this land from you. I realize you may find that hard to believe, but it's the truth. The Final Empire is dying. Surely you've seen that. Mankind needs to band together, pool its resources—and you have vital clues we need. Don't force me to break down your gates to get them. Work with me."

Yomen shook his head. "There is your mistake again, Venture. You see, I don't care if you attack me." He met Elend's eyes. "It would be better for my people to fight and to *die* than to be ruled by the man who overthrew our god and destroyed our religion."

Elend held those eyes, and saw determination in them.

"That's how it has to be?" Elend said.

"It is," Yomen said. "I can expect an attack in the morning, then?"

"Of course not," Elend said, standing. "Your soldiers aren't starved yet. I'll get back to you in a few months." *Maybe then you'll be more willing to deal.*

Elend turned to go, then hesitated. "Nice party, by the way," he said, glancing back at Yomen. "Regardless of what I believe, I do think that your god would be pleased with what you've done here. I think you should reconsider your prejudices. The Lord Ruler probably isn't fond of Vin and me, but I'd say that he'd rather that your people live than get themselves killed."

Elend nodded in respect, then left the high table, feeling more frustrated than he showed. It felt like Yomen and he had been so close, and yet at the same time, an alliance seemed impossible. Not while the obligator had such hatred of Elend and Vin.

He forced himself to relax, walking. There was little he could do about the situation at the moment—it would take the siege to make Yomen rethink his position. *I'm at a ball,* Elend thought, wandering. *I should enjoy what I can of it, letting myself be seen by the nobility here, intimidating them and making them think about helping us instead of Yomen. . . .*

A thought occurred to him. He glanced at Vin, then waved a servant over to him.

"My lord?" the man asked.

"I need you to fetch something for me," Elend said.

Vin was the center of attention. Women pandered to her, hung on her words, and looked to her as a model. They wanted to know news from Luthadel, to hear about fashion, politics, and events from the great city. They didn't reject her, or even seem to resent her.

The instant acceptance was the strangest thing Vin had ever experienced. She stood amid the women in their gowns and finery, and was foremost among them. She knew that it was just because of her power—yet, the women of this city seemed almost desperate to have someone to look to. An empress.

And Vin found herself enjoying it. There was a part of her that had craved this acceptance since the first day she'd attended a ball. She'd spent that year being mistreated by most of the women of court—some had let her join with their company, but she'd always been an insignificant country noblewoman with no connections or significance. It was a shallow thing, this acceptance, but sometimes even shallow things feel important. Plus, there was something else about it. As she smiled toward a newcomer—a young niece that one of the women wanted to meet Vin—Vin realized what it was.

This is part of me, she thought. *I didn't want it to be—perhaps because I didn't believe that I deserved it. I found this life too different, too full of beauty and confidence. Yet, I* am *a noblewoman. I* do *fit in here.*

I was born to the streets by one parent, but I was born to this by another.

She'd spent the first year of Elend's reign trying so hard to protect him. She'd forced herself to focus only on her street side, the side that had been trained to be ruthless, for that, she thought, would give her the power to defend what she loved. Yet, Kelsier had shown her another way to be powerful. And, that power was connected with the nobility—with their intrigue, their beauty, and their clever schemes. Vin had taken almost immediately to life at court, and that had frightened her.

That's it, she thought, smiling at another curtsying young girl. *That's why I always felt that this was wrong. I didn't have to work for it, so I couldn't believe that I deserved it.*

She'd spent sixteen years on the streets—she'd earned that side of her. Yet, it had taken her barely a month to adapt to noble life. It had seemed impossible to her that something that came so easily could be as important a part of herself as the years spent on the streets.

But it was.

I had to confront this, she realized. *Tindwyl tried to make me do it, two years ago, but I wasn't ready.*

She needed to prove to herself not only that she could move among the nobility, but that she belonged with them. Because that proved something much more important: that the love she'd earned from Elend during those few early months wasn't based on a falsehood.

It's . . . true, Vin thought. *I can be both. Why did it take me so long to figure it out?*

"Excuse me, ladies," a voice said.

Vin smiled, turning as the women parted to make way for Elend. Several of the younger ones got dreamy expressions on their faces as they regarded Elend with his warrior's body, his rugged beard, and his white imperial uniform. Vin suppressed a huff of annoyance. *She'd* loved him long before he'd become dreamy.

"Ladies," Elend said to the women, "as Lady Vin herself will be quick to tell you, I'm rather ill-mannered. That, in itself, would be a very small sin. Unfortunately, I'm also quite unconcerned about my own disregard for propriety. So, therefore, I'm going to steal my wife away from you all and selfishly monopolize her time. I'd apologize, but that's not the sort of thing we barbarians do."

With that, and with a smile, he held out his elbow to her. Vin smiled back, taking the arm and allowing him to lead her away from the pack of women.

"Thought you might want some room to breathe," Elend said. "I can only imagine how it must make you feel to be surrounded by a virtual army of puffballs."

"I appreciate the rescue," Vin said, though it wasn't actually true. How was Elend to know that she'd suddenly discovered that she fit in with those puffballs? Besides, just because they wore frills and makeup didn't mean they weren't dangerous—she'd learned that much easily her first few months. The thought distracted her such that she didn't notice where Elend was leading her until they were almost there.

When she did realize it, she stopped immediately, jerking Elend back. "The dance floor?" she asked.

"Indeed," he said.

"But, I haven't danced in almost four years!"

"Neither have I," Elend said. He stepped closer. "But, it would be terrible to miss the opportunity. After all, we never did get to dance."

It was true. Luthadel had gone into revolt before they'd gotten an opportunity to dance together, and after that, there hadn't been time for balls or frivolity. She knew Elend understood how much she missed not having had the chance. He'd asked her to dance on the first night when they'd met, and she'd turned him down. She still felt as if she'd given up some unique opportunity on that first evening.

And so, she let him lead her up onto the slightly raised dance floor. Couples whispered, and as the song ended, everyone else furtively departed the dance floor, leaving Vin and Elend alone—a figure in lines of white, and another in curves of black. Elend put an arm at her waist, turning her toward him, and Vin found herself traitorously nervous.

This is it, she thought, flaring pewter to keep from shaking. *It's finally happening. I finally get to dance with him!*

At that moment—as the music began—Elend reached into his pocket and pulled out a book. He raised it with one hand, the other on her waist, and began to read.

Vin's jaw dropped, then she whacked him on the arm. "What do you think you're doing?" she demanded as he shuffled through the dance steps, still holding his book. "Elend! I'm trying to have a special moment here!"

He turned toward her, smiling with a terribly mischievous grin. "Well, I want to make that special moment as authentic as possible. I mean, you are dancing with *me,* after all."

"For the first time!"

"All the more important to be certain that I make the right impression, Miss Valette!"

"Oh, for . . . Will you please just put the book away?"

Elend smiled more deeply, but slid the book back into his pocket, taking her hand and dancing with her in a more proper manner. Vin flushed as she saw the confused crowd standing around the dance floor. They obviously had no idea what to make of Elend's behavior.

"You *are* a barbarian," Vin told him.

"A barbarian because I read books?" Elend said lightly. "That's one that Ham will have a great time with."

"Honestly," Vin said, "where did you even get a book here?"

"I had one of Yomen's servants fetch it for me," Elend said. "From the keep library. I knew they'd have it—*Trials of Monument* is a rather famous work."

Vin frowned. "Do I recognize that title?"

"It was the book that I was reading that night on the Venture balcony," Elend said. "The time we first met."

"Why, Elend! That's almost romantic—in a twisted 'I'm going to make my wife want to kill me' sort of way."

"I thought you'd appreciate it," he said, turning lightly.

"You're in rare form tonight. I haven't seen you like this for quite some time."

"I know," he said, sighing. "To be honest, Vin, I feel a bit guilty. I'm worried that I was too informal during my conversation with Yomen. He's so stiff that my old instincts—the ones that always made me respond to people like him with mockery—came out."

Vin let him lead the dance, looking up at him. "You're just acting like yourself. That's a good thing."

"My old self didn't make a good king," Elend said.

"The things you learned about kingship didn't have to do with your personality, Elend," Vin said. "They had to do with other things—about confidence, and about decisiveness. You can have those things and still be yourself."

Elend shook his head. "I'm not sure I can. Certainly, tonight, I should have been more formal. I allowed the setting to make me lax."

"No," Vin said firmly. "No, I'm *right* about this, Elend. You've been doing the exact thing I have. You've been so determined to be a good king that you've let it squish who you really are. Our responsibilities shouldn't have to destroy us."

"They haven't destroyed you," he said, smiling behind his short beard.

"They nearly did," Vin said. "Elend, I had to realize that I could be both people—the Mistborn of the streets and the woman of the court. I had to acknowledge that the new person I'm becoming is a valid extension of who I am. But for you, it's opposite! You have to realize that who you were is still a valid part of you. That person makes silly comments, and does things just to provoke a reaction. But, he's also lovable and kindhearted. You can't lose those things just because you're emperor."

He got that look in his face, the thoughtful one, the one that meant he was going to argue. Then, however, he hesitated.

"Coming to this place," he said, looking at the beautiful windows and watching the nobility, "it's reminded me of what I spent most of my life doing. Before I had to be a king. Even then, I was trying to do things my way—I went off and read during balls. But, I didn't do it away in the library, I did it in the ballroom. I didn't want to hide, I wanted to express discontent with my father, and reading was my way."

"You were a good man, Elend," Vin said. "Not an idiot, as you now seem to think that you were. You were a little undirected, but still a good leader. You took control of Luthadel and stopped the skaa from committing a slaughter in their rebellion."

"But then, the whole Penrod fiasco . . ."

"You had things to learn," Vin said. "Like I did. But, please don't become someone else, Elend. You can be both Elend the emperor and Elend the man."

He smiled deeply, then pulled her close, pausing their dance. "Thank you," he said, then kissed her. She could tell that he hadn't made his decision yet—he still thought that he needed to be more of a hard warrior than a kind scholar. However, he was thinking. That was enough, at the moment.

Vin looked up into his eyes, and they returned to the dance. Neither spoke; they simply let the wonder of the moment hold them. It was a surreal experience for Vin. Their army was outside, the ash was falling perpetually, and the mists were killing people. Yet, inside this room of white marble and sparkling colors, she danced with the man she loved for the first time.

They both spun with the grace of Allomancy, stepping as if on the wind, moving as if made of mist. The room grew hushed, the nobility like a theater audience, watching some grand performance, not two people who hadn't danced in years. And yet, Vin knew it was wonderful, something that had rarely been seen. Most noble Mistborn couldn't afford to appear too graceful, lest they give away their secret powers.

Vin and Elend had no such inhibitions. They danced as if to make up for the four years lost, as if to throw their joy in the face of an apocalyptic world and a hostile city. The song began to wind down. Elend pulled her against him, and her tin let her feel his heartbeat so close. It was beating far more swiftly than a simple dance could account for.

"I'm glad we did this," he said.

"There's another ball soon," she said. "In a few weeks."

"I know," he said. "As I understand it, that ball is going to be held at the Canton of Resource."

Vin nodded. "Thrown by Yomen himself."

"And, if the supply cache is hidden anywhere in the city, it will most likely be beneath that building."

"We'd have an excuse—and a precedent—to get in."

"Yomen has some atium," Elend said. "He's wearing a bead of it on his forehead. Though, just because he has one bead doesn't mean he has a wealth of it."

Vin nodded. "I wonder if he's found the storage cavern."

"He has," Elend said, "I'm sure of it. I got a reaction out of him when I mentioned it."

"That still shouldn't stop us," Vin said, smiling. "We go to his ball, sneak into the cavern, find out what the Lord Ruler left there, then decide what to do about the siege—and the city—based on that?"

"Seems like a good plan," Elend said. "Assuming I can't get him to listen to reason. I was *close,* Vin. I can't help but think that there might be a chance to bring him to our side."

She nodded.

"All right, then," he said. "Ready to make a grand exit?"

Vin smiled, then nodded. As the music ended, Elend spun and threw her to the side, and she Pushed off of the metal dance floor rim. She shot out over the crowd, guiding herself toward the exit, dress flapping.

Behind, Elend addressed the crowd. "Thank you so much for letting us join you. Anyone who wants to escape the city will be allowed passage through my army."

Vin landed and saw the crowd turn as Elend jumped over their heads, fortunately managing to guide himself through the relatively low room without crashing into any windows or hitting the ceiling. He joined her at the doors, and they escaped through the antechamber and into the night.

Hemalurgy is of Ruin. It destroys. By taking abilities from one person and giving them to another—in reduced amounts—power is actually lost. In line with Ruin's own appointed purpose—breaking down the universe into smaller and smaller pieces—Hemalurgy gives great gifts, but at a high cost.

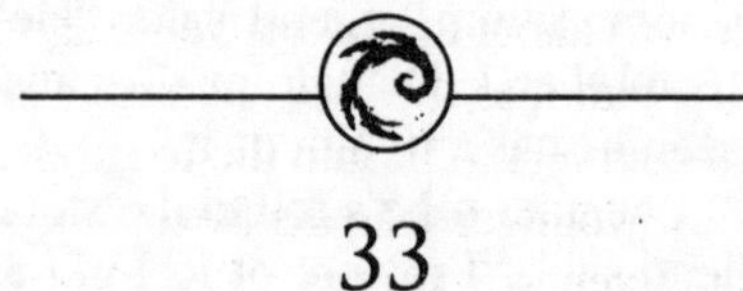

33

HUMANS MIGHT HAVE SCORNED TENSOON, perhaps throwing things at him or yelling curses as he passed. Kandra were too orderly for that kind of display, but TenSoon could feel their disdain. They watched as he was taken from his cage, then led back to the Trustwarren for judgment. Hundreds of eyes regarded him, set in bodies with bones of steel, glass, rock, and wood. The younger kandra were more extreme in form, the older were more orthodox.

All were accusatory.

Before, at the trial, the crowd had been curious—perhaps horrified. That had changed; TenSoon's time spent in the display cage had worked as intended. The Second Generation had been able to promote his infamy, and kandra who had once, perhaps, been sympathetic to him now watched with disgust. In a thousand years of history, the kandra had never had a criminal such as TenSoon.

He bore the stares and the scorn with a raised head, padding through the corridor in a dog's body. It was strange to him, how natural the bones felt. He'd only spent a year's time wearing them, but putting them on again—discarding the scrawny, naked human body—felt more like returning home than coming back to the Homeland had a year before.

And so, what was supposed to be a humiliation for him became, instead, something of a triumph. It had been a wild hope, but he'd manipulated the Second Generation into giving him back the dog's body. The sack had even contained the body's hair and nails—likely, they had simply collected the entire mess after forcing TenSoon to abandon it and enter his prison a year ago.

The comfortable bones gave him strength. This was the body that Vin had given him. She was the Hero of Ages. He had to believe that.

Otherwise he was about to make a very big mistake.

His guards led him into the Trustwarren. This time, there were too many observers to fit into the room, so the Seconds declared that those younger than the Seventh Generation had to wait outside. Even so, kandra filled the rows of stone seats. They sat silently as TenSoon was led to the slightly raised metallic disk set into the center of the stone floor. The broad doors were left open, and younger kandra crowded outside, listening.

TenSoon looked up as he stepped onto his platform. The lump-like shadows of the First Generation waited above, each one in his separate alcove, backlit faintly in blue.

KanPaar approached his lectern. TenSoon could see the satisfaction in the way KanPaar slid across the floor. The Second felt that his triumph was complete—what happened to those who ignored the directives of the Second Generation would not soon be forgotten. TenSoon settled back on his haunches, guarded by two kandra with the Blessing of Potency twinkling in each shoulder. They carried large mallets.

"TenSoon of the Third Generation," KanPaar said loudly. "Are you ready to bear the sentence of your judgment?"

"There will be no judgment," TenSoon said. His words slurred, coming from the dog's mouth, but they were clear enough to understand.

"No judgment?" KanPaar asked, amused. "You now seek to back out of what you yourself demanded?"

"I came to give information, not to be judged."

"I—"

"I'm not speaking to you, KanPaar," TenSoon said, turning from the Second to look up. "I'm talking to them."

"They heard your words, Third," KanPaar snapped. "Control yourself! I will not let you turn this judgment into a circus, as you did before."

TenSoon smiled. Only a kandra would consider a mild argument to be a 'circus.' TenSoon didn't turn away from the First Generation's alcoves, however.

"Now," KanPaar said. "We—"

"You!" TenSoon bellowed, causing KanPaar to sputter again. "First Generation! How long will you sit in your comfortable home, pretending that the world above doesn't exist? You think that if you ignore the problems, they won't affect you? Or, is it that you've stopped believing in your own teachings?

"The days of mist have come! The endless ash now falls! The earth shakes and trembles. You can condemn me, but you must not ignore me! The world will soon die! If you want people—in all of their forms—to survive, you must act! You must be ready! For you may soon need to command our people to accept the Resolution!"

The room fell silent. Several of the shadows above shuffled, as if discomfited—though kandra generally didn't react in such a way. It was too disorderly.

Then a voice—soft, scratchy, and very tired—spoke from above. "Proceed, KanPaar."

The comment was so unexpected that several members of the audience actually gasped. The First Generation never spoke in the presence of lessers. TenSoon wasn't awed—he'd seen them, and talked with them, before they'd grown too superior to deal with anyone but the Seconds. No, he wasn't awed. He was just disappointed.

"My faith in you was misplaced," he said, mostly to himself. "I should not have returned."

"TenSoon of the Third Generation!" KanPaar said, standing up straight, crystalline True Body sparkling as he pointed. "You have been sentenced to the ritual imprisonment of ChanGaar! You will be beaten to the point of fracture, then bricked into a pit, with only one hole for your daily slop. You will remain there for ten generations! Only after that will you be executed by starvation! Know that your greatest sin was that of rebellion. If you had not strayed from the advice and wisdom of this council, you would never have thought it right to break the First Contract. Because of you, the Trust has been endangered, as has every kandra of every generation!"

KanPaar let the pronouncement ring in the chamber. TenSoon sat quietly on his haunches. KanPaar had obviously expected some kind of response from him, but TenSoon gave none. Finally, KanPaar gestured to the guards beside TenSoon, who hefted their fearsome hammers.

"You know, KanPaar," TenSoon said, "I learned a few important things while wearing these bones a year ago."

KanPaar gestured again. The guards raised their weapons.

"It's something I had never paused to consider," TenSoon said. "Humans, if you think about it, just aren't built for speed. Dogs, however, *are*."

The hammers fell.

TenSoon leaped forward.

The powerful dog's haunches launched him into motion. TenSoon was a member of the Third Generation. Nobody had been eating and emulating bodies as long as he had, and he knew how to pack muscles into a body. In addition, he had spent a year wearing the bones of a wolfhound, being forced to try to keep up with his Mistborn master. He had undergone what had effectively been a year of training by one of the most talented Allomancers the world had ever known.

On top of that, a body mass that had translated from a scrawny human made quite a substantial wolfhound. This, combined with his skill in crafting bodies, meant that when TenSoon jumped, he *jumped*. His guards cried out in shock as TenSoon sprang away, his leap taking him at least ten feet across the room. He hit the ground running, but didn't head for the door. They'd be expecting that.

Instead he sprang directly toward KanPaar. The foremost of Seconds cried out, throwing up ineffectual hands as a hundred pounds of wolfhound crashed into him, throwing him to the stone floor. TenSoon heard sharp cracks as KanPaar's delicate bones shattered, and KanPaar screamed in a very un-kandra-like way.

That seems appropriate, TenSoon thought, shoving his way through the ranks of the Seconds, shattering bones. *Honestly, what kind of vain fool wears a True Body made of crystal?*

Many of the kandra didn't know how to react. Others—especially the younger ones—had spent a lot of time around humans on Contracts, and they were more accustomed to chaos. These scattered, leaving their elder companions sitting on the benches in shock. TenSoon darted between bodies, heading toward the doors. The guards beside the podium—the ones who would have shattered his bones—rushed to KanPaar's side, their filial sense of duty overriding their desire to prevent his escape. Besides, they must have seen the crowd clogging the doorway, and assumed that TenSoon would be slowed.

As soon as he reached the crowd, TenSoon jumped again. Vin had required him to be able to leap incredible heights, and he'd practiced with many different muscle structures. This jump wouldn't have impressed Vin—TenSoon no longer had the Blessing of Potency he'd stolen from OreSeur—but it was more than enough to let him clear the watching kandra. Some cried out, and he landed in a pocket of open space, then leaped again toward the open cavern beyond.

"No!" he heard echoing from the Trustwarren. "Go after him!"

TenSoon took off in a loping dash down one of the corridors. He ran quickly—far more quickly than anything bipedal could have managed. With his canine body, he hoped he'd be able to outrun even kandra bearing the Blessing of Potency.

Farewell, my home, TenSoon thought, leaving the main cavern behind. *And farewell to what little honor I had left.*

PART THREE

THE BROKEN SKIES

Feruchemy, it should be noted, is the power of balance. Of the three powers, only it was known to men before the conflict between Preservation and Ruin came to a head. In Feruchemy, power is stored up, then later drawn upon. There is no loss of energy—just a changing of the time and rate of its use.

34

MARSH STRODE INTO THE SMALL town. Workers atop the makeshift gate—which looked flimsy enough that a determined knock would send it toppling—froze in place. Ash sweepers noticed him pass with shock, then horror. It was odd, how they watched, too terrified to flee. Or, at least, too terrified to be the first one to flee.

Marsh ignored them. The earth trembled beneath him in a beautiful song—quakes were common, here, in the shadow of Mount Tyrian. It was the ashmount closest to Luthadel. Marsh walked through Elend Venture's own territory. But, of course, the emperor had abandoned it. That seemed an invitation to Marsh, and to the one who controlled him. They were really the same. Marsh smiled as he walked.

A small piece of him was still free. He let it sleep, however. Ruin needed to think he had given up. That was the point. And so, Marsh held back only a tiny bit, and he did not fight. He let the ashen sky become a thing of bespeckled beauty, and treated the death of the world as a blessed event.

Biding his time. Waiting.

The village was an inspiring sight. The people were starving here, even though they were within the Central Dominance: Elend Venture's "protected" area. They had the wonderful, haunted expressions of those who were close to giving up hope. The streets were barely maintained, the homes—which had once been the dwellings of noblemen, but were now filled with hungry skaa—covered in ash, their gardens stripped and their structures cannibalized to feed fires during the winter.

The gorgeous sight made Marsh smile with satisfaction. Behind him, people finally started to move, fleeing, doors slamming. There were probably some six or seven thousand people living in the town. They were not Marsh's concern. Not at the moment.

He was interested only in a single, specific building. It looked little different from the others, a mansion in a fine row. The town had once been a stopping place for travelers, and had grown to be a favored place for nobility to construct second homes. A few noble families had lived here permanently, overseeing the many skaa who had worked the plantations and fields on the plains outside.

The building Marsh chose was slightly better maintained than those around it. The garden was, of course, more weeds than cultivation, and the outer mansion walls hadn't seen a good scrubbing in years. However, fewer sections of it looked to have been broken apart for firewood, and a guard actually stood watch at the front gate.

Marsh killed him with one of the razor-sharp metal triangles that had once been used in the Lord Ruler's ceremonies. Marsh Pushed it through the guard's chest even as the man opened his mouth in challenge. The air was oddly still and quiet as the guard's voice cut off, and he toppled to the side in the road. The skaa who watched from nearby homes knew better than to react, and didn't stir.

Marsh hummed to himself as he strolled up the front walk to the mansion, startling a small flock of ravens who had come to roost. Once this path would have been a calming stroll through gardens, the way marked by flagstones. Now it was simply a hike through a weed-filled field. The man who owned the place obviously couldn't afford more than the lone gate guard, and nobody raised an alarm at Marsh's approach. He was actually able to walk right up to the front doors. Smiling to himself, he knocked.

A maidservant opened the doors. She froze when she saw Marsh, taking in his spiked eyes, his unnaturally tall figure, his dark robes. Then she began to tremble.

Marsh held out a hand, palm up, with another of the triangles. Then he Pushed it straight into her face. It snapped out the back of the skull, and the woman toppled. He stepped over her body and entered the house.

It was far nicer inside than the exterior had led him to expect. Rich furnishings, freshly painted walls, intricate ceramics. Marsh raised an eyebrow, scanning the room with his spiked eyes. The way his sight worked, it was hard for him to distinguish colors, but he was familiar enough with his powers now that he could pick them out if he wanted. The Allomantic lines from the metals inside of most things were really quite expressive.

To Marsh, the mansion was a place of pristine whiteness and bright blobs of expensive color. Marsh searched through it, burning pewter to enhance his physical abilities, allowing him to walk much more lightly than would otherwise have been possible. He killed two more servants in the course of his exploration, and eventually moved up to the second floor.

He found the man he wanted sitting at a desk in a top-floor room. Balding, wearing a rich suit. He had a petite mustache set in a round face, and was slumped, eyes closed, a bottle of hard liquor empty at his feet. Marsh saw this with displeasure.

"I come all this way to get you," Marsh said. "And when I finally find you, I discover that you have intoxicated yourself into a stupor?"

The man had never met Marsh, of course. That didn't stop Marsh from feeling annoyed that he wouldn't be able to see the look of terror and surprise in the man's eyes when he found an Inquisitor in his home. Marsh would miss out on the fear, the anticipation of death. Briefly, Marsh was tempted to wait until the man sobered up so that the killing could be performed properly.

But, Ruin would have none of that. Marsh sighed at the injustice of it, then slammed the unconscious man down against the floor and drove a small bronze spike through his heart. It wasn't as large or thick as an Inquisitor spike, but it killed just as well. Marsh ripped it out of the man's heart, leaving the former nobleman dead, blood pooling on the floor.

Then, Marsh walked out, leaving the building. The nobleman—Marsh didn't even know his name—had used Allomancy recently. The man was a Smoker, a Misting who could create copperclouds, and the use of his ability had drawn Ruin's attention. Ruin had been wanting an Allomancer to drain.

And so, Marsh had come to harvest the man's power and draw it into the spike. It seemed something of a waste to him. Hemalurgy—particularly Allomantic imbues—was much more potent when one could drive the spike through the victim's heart and directly into a waiting host. That way, very little of the Allomantic ability was lost. Doing it this way—killing the Allomancer to make a spike, then traveling somewhere else to place it—would grant the new host far less power.

But, there was no getting around it in this case. Marsh shook his head as he stepped over the maidservant's body again, moving out into the unkempt gardens. No one accosted, or even looked at, him as he made his way to the front gates. There, however, he was surprised to find a couple of skaa men kneeling on the ground.

"Please, Your Grace," one said as Marsh passed. "Please, send the obligators back to us. We will serve better this time."

"You have lost that opportunity," Marsh said, staring at them with his spikeheads.

"We will believe in the Lord Ruler again," another said. "He fed us. Please. Our families have no food."

"Well," Marsh said. "You needn't worry about that for long."

The men knelt, confused, as Marsh left. He didn't kill them, though part of him wished to. Unfortunately, Ruin wanted to claim that privilege for himself.

Marsh walked across the plain outside the town. After about an hour's time he stopped, turning to look back at the community and the towering ashmount behind it.

At that moment, the top left half of the mountain exploded, spewing a deluge of dust, ash, and rock. The earth shook, and a booming sound washed over Marsh. Then, flaming hot and red, a large gout of lava began to flow down the side of the ashmount toward the edge of the shallow lake and the town on its shore.

Marsh shook his head. Yes. Food was *hardly* this town's biggest problem. They really needed to get their priorities straight.

Hemalurgy is a power about which I wish I knew far less. To Ruin, power must have an inordinately high cost—using it must be attractive, yet must sow chaos and destruction in its very implementation.

In concept, it is a very simple art. A parasitic one. Without other people to steal from, Hemalurgy would be useless.

35

"YOU'LL BE ALL RIGHT HERE?" Spook asked.

Breeze turned away from the brightened tavern, raising an eyebrow. Spook had brought him—along with several of Goradel's soldiers in street clothing—to one of the larger, more reputable locations. Voices rang within.

"Yes, this should be fine," Breeze said, eyeing the tavern.

"Skaa out at night. Never thought I'd see that. Perhaps the world really *is* ending. . . ."

"I'm going to go to one of the poorer sections of town," Spook said quietly. "There are some things I want to check on."

"Poorer sections," Breeze said musingly. "Perhaps I should accompany you. I've found that the poorer people are, the more likely they are to let their tongues wag."

Spook raised an eyebrow. "No offense, Breeze, but I kind of think you'd stand out."

"What?" Breeze asked, nodding toward his utilitarian brown worker's outfit—quite a change from his usual suit and vest. "I'm wearing these dreadful clothes, aren't I?"

"Clothing isn't everything, Breeze. You've kind of got a . . . bearing about you. Plus, you don't have much ash on you."

"I was infiltrating the lower ranks before you were born, child," Breeze said, wagging a finger at him.

"All right," Spook said. He reached to the ground, scooping up a pile of ash. "Let's just rub this into your clothing and on your face. . . ."

Breeze froze. "I'll meet you back at the lair," he finally said.

Spook smiled, dropping the ash as he disappeared into the mists.

"I never did like him," Kelsier whispered.

Spook left the richer section of town, moving at a brisk pace. When he hit the streetslot, he didn't stop, but simply leaped off the side of the road and plummeted twenty feet.

His cloak flapped behind him as he fell. He landed easily and continued his quick pace. Without pewter, he would certainly have broken some limbs. Now he moved with the same dexterity he'd once envied in Vin and Kelsier. He felt exhilarated. With pewter flaring inside of him, he never felt tired—never even felt fatigued. Even simple acts, like walking down the street, made him feel full of grace and power.

He moved quickly to the Harrows, leaving behind the streets of better men, entering the cluttered, overpacked alley-like streetslot, knowing exactly where he'd find his quarry. Durn was one of the leading figures in the Urteau underworld. Part informant, part beggar lord, the unfulfilled musician had become a sort of mayor of the Harrows. Men like that had to be where people could find—and pay—them.

Spook still remembered that first night after waking from his fevers a few weeks back, the night when he'd visited a tavern and heard men talking about him. Over the next few days, he'd visited several other taverns, and had heard others mention rumors that spoke of Spook. Sazed and Breeze's arrival had kept Spook from confronting Durn—the apparent source of the rumors—about what he'd been telling people. It was time to correct that oversight.

Spook picked up his pace, leaping heaps of discarded boards, dashing around piles of ash, until he reached the hole that Durn called home. It was a section of canal wall that had been hollowed out to form a kind of cave. Though the wooden framing around the door looked as rotted and splintered as everything else in the Harrows, Spook knew it to be reinforced on the back with a thick oaken bar.

Two brutes sat watch outside. They eyed Spook as he stopped in front of the door, cloak whipping around him. It was the same one he'd been wearing when he'd been tossed into the fire, and it was still spotted with burn marks and holes.

"The boss isn't seeing anyone right now, kid," said one of the big men, not rising from his seat. "Come back later."

Spook kicked the door. It broke free, its hinges snapping, the bar shattering its mountings and tumbling backward.

Spook stood for a moment, shocked. He had too little experience with pewter to gauge its use accurately. If he was shocked, however, the two brutes were stunned. They sat, staring at the broken door.

"You may need to kill them," Kelsier whispered.

No, Spook thought. *I just have to move quickly.* He dashed into the open hallway, needing no torch or lantern by which to see. He whipped spectacles and a cloth out of his pocket as he approached the door at the end of the hallway, fixing them in place even as the guards called out behind him.

He threw his shoulder against the door with a bit more care, slamming it open but not breaking it. He moved into a well-lit room where four men sat playing chips at a table. Durn was winning.

Spook pointed at the men as he skidded to a stop. "You three. Out. Durn and I have business."

Durn sat at the table, looking genuinely surprised. The brutes rushed up behind Spook, and he turned, falling to a crouch, reaching under his cloak for his dueling cane.

"It's all right," Durn said, standing. "Leave us."

The guards hesitated, obviously angry at being passed so easily. Finally, however, they withdrew, Durn's gambling partners going with them. The door closed.

"That was quite the entrance," Durn noted, sitting back down at his table.

"You've been talking about me, Durn," Spook said, turning. "I've heard people discussing me in taverns, mentioning your name. You've been spreading rumors about my death, telling people that I was on the Survivor's crew. How did you know who I was, and why have you been using my name?"

"Oh, come now," Durn said, scowling. "How anonymous did you think you were? You're the Survivor's friend, and you spend a good half of your time living in the emperor's own palace."

"Luthadel's a long way from here."

"Not so far that news doesn't travel," Durn said. "A Tineye comes to town, spying about, flaunting seemingly endless funds? It wasn't really that hard to figure out who you were. Besides, there's your eyes."

"What about them?" Spook asked.

The ugly man shrugged. "Everyone knows that strange things happen around the Survivor's crew."

Spook wasn't certain what to make of that. He walked forward, looking over the cards on the table. He picked one up, feeling its paper. His heightened senses let him feel the bumps on the back.

"Marked cards?" he asked.

"Of course," Durn said. "Practice game, to see if my men could read the patterns right."

Spook tossed the card onto the table. "You still haven't told me why you've been spreading rumors about me."

"No offense, kid," Durn said. "But . . . well, you're supposed to be dead."

"If you believed that, then why bother talking about me?"

"Why do you think?" Durn said. "The people love the Survivor—and anything related to him. That's why Quellion uses his name so often. But, if I could show that Quellion killed one of Kelsier's own crew . . . well, there are a lot of people in this city who wouldn't like that."

"So, you're just trying to help," Spook said flatly. "Out of the goodness of your heart."

"You're not the only one who thinks that Quellion is killing this city. If you're really of the Survivor's crew, you'll know that sometimes, people fight."

"I find it difficult to think of you as an altruist, Durn. You're a thief."

"So are you."

"We didn't know what we were getting into," Spook said. "Kelsier promised us riches. How do you gain from all this?"

Durn snorted. "The Citizen is very bad for business. Venture red wine being sold for a fraction of a clip? Our smuggling has been choked to a trickle because everyone fears buying our goods. Things were *never* this bad under the Lord Ruler." He leaned in. "If your friends staying in the old Ministry building think they can do something about that lunatic running this city, then tell them they'll have my support. There isn't a large underground left in this city, but Quellion will be surprised at the damage it can do if manipulated the right way."

Spook stood quietly for a moment. "There's a man milking for information in the tavern on Westbrook Lane. Send someone to contact him. He's a Soother—the best one you'll ever meet—but he stands out a bit. Make your offer to him."

Durn nodded.

Spook turned to go, then glanced back at Durn. "Don't mention my name to him, or what happened to me."

With that, he left through the hallway, passing the guards and the displaced crooks from the card game. Spook pulled off his blindfold as he stepped into the daylight-like brightness of the starlit night.

He strolled through the Harrows, trying to decide what he thought of the meeting. Durn hadn't revealed anything all *that* important. Yet, Spook felt as if something were happening around him, something he hadn't planned on, something he couldn't quite decipher. He was becoming more comfortable with Kelsier's voice, and with his pewter, but he was still worried that he wouldn't be able to live up to the position he'd fallen into.

"If you don't get to Quellion soon," Kelsier said, "he's going to find your friends. He's already preparing assassins."

"He won't send them," Spook said quietly. "Especially if he's heard Durn's rumors about me. Everyone knows that Sazed and Breeze were on your crew. Quellion won't take them out unless they prove to be such a threat that he has no other choice."

"Quellion is an unstable man," Kelsier said. "Don't wait too long. You don't want to find out how irrational he can be."

Spook fell silent. Then, he heard footsteps, approaching quickly. He felt the vibrations in the ground. He spun and loosened his cloak, reaching for his weapon.

"You're not in danger," Kelsier said quietly.

Spook relaxed as someone rushed around the alley corner. It was one of the men from Durn's chips game. The man was puffing, his face flushed with exhaustion. "My lord!" he said.

"I'm no lord," Spook said. "What happened? Is Durn in danger?"

"No, sir," the man said. "I just . . . I . . ."

Spook raised an eyebrow.

"I need your help," the man said between breaths. "When we realized who you were, you were already gone. I just . . ."

"Help with what?" Spook said tersely.

"My sister, sir," the man said. "She got taken by the Citizen. Our . . . father was a nobleman. Durn hid me, but Mailey, she got sold by the woman I'd left her with. Sir, she's only seven. He's going to burn her in a few days!"

Spook frowned. *What does he expect me to do?* He opened his mouth to ask that very question, but then stopped. He wasn't the same man anymore. He wasn't limited as the old Spook would have been. He could do something else.

What Kelsier would have done.

"Can you gather ten men?" Spook asked. "Friends of yours, willing to take part in some late-night work?"

"Sure. I guess. Does this have to do with saving Mailey?"

"No," Spook said. "It has to do with your payment for saving Mailey. Get me those workers, and I'll do what I can to help your sister."

The man nodded eagerly.

"Do it now," Spook said, pointing. "We start tonight."

In Hemalurgy, the type of metal used in a spike is important, as is the positioning of that spike on the body. For instance, steel spikes take physical Allomantic powers—the ability to burn pewter, tin, steel, or iron—and bestow them upon the person receiving the spike. Which of these four is granted, however, depends on where the spike is placed.

Spikes made from other metals steal Feruchemical abilities. For example, all of the original Inquisitors were given a pewter spike, which—after first being pounded through the body of a Feruchemist—gave the Inquisitor the ability to store up healing power. (Though they couldn't do so as quickly as a real Feruchemist, as per the law of Hemalurgic decay.) This, obviously, is where the Inquisitors got their infamous ability to recover from wounds quickly, and was also why they needed to rest so much.

36

"YOU SHOULDN'T HAVE GONE IN," Cett said flatly.

Elend raised an eyebrow, riding his stallion through the center of his camp. Tindwyl had taught him that it was good to be seen by one's people, especially in situations where he could control the way he was perceived. He happened to agree with this particular lesson, and so he rode, wearing a black cloak to mask the ash's smudges, making certain his soldiers knew that he was among them. Cett rode with him, tied into his specially made saddle.

"You think I put myself in too much danger by entering the city?" Elend asked, nodding to a group of soldiers who had paused in their morning labors to salute him.

"No," Cett said, "we both know that I don't give a damn whether you live or die, boy. Besides, you're Mistborn. You could have gotten out if things turned dangerous."

"Why, then?" Elend asked. "Why was it a mistake?"

"Because," Cett said. "You met the people inside. You talked with them, danced among them. Hell, boy. Can't you see why that's such a problem? When the time comes to attack, you'll worry about people you're going to hurt."

Elend rode in silence for a moment. The morning mists were a normal thing to him now. They obscured the camp, masking its size. Even to his tin-enhanced eyes, distant tents became silhouetted lumps. It was as if he rode through some mythical world, a place of muffled shadows and distant noises.

Had it been a mistake for him to enter the city? Perhaps. Elend knew the theories Cett spoke of—he understood how important it was for a general to view his enemies not as individuals, but as numbers. Obstacles.

"I'm glad for my choice," Elend said.

"I know," Cett said, scratching at his thick beard. "That's what frustrates me, to be honest. You're a compassionate man. That's a weakness, but it isn't the real problem. The *problem* is your inability to deal with your own compassion."

Elend raised an eyebrow.

"You should know better than to let yourself grow attached to your enemy, Elend," Cett said. "You should have known how you would react, and planned so that you could avoid this very situation! Hell, boy, every leader has weaknesses—the ones who win are the ones who learn how to smother those weaknesses, not give them fuel!" When Elend didn't respond to that, Cett simply sighed. "All right, then, let's talk about the siege. The engineers have blocked off several streams that lead into the city, but they don't think those were the primary sources of water."

"They weren't," Elend said. "Vin has located six main wells within the city itself."

"We should poison them," Cett said.

Elend fell silent. The two halves of him still warred inside. The man he had been just wanted to protect as many people as possible. The man he was becoming, however, was more realistic. It knew that sometimes he had to kill—or at least discomfort—in order to save.

"Very well," Elend said. "I'll have Vin do it tonight—and I'll have her leave a message written on the wells saying what we've done."

"What good will that do?" Cett asked, frowning.

"I don't want to kill the people, Cett," Elend said, "I want to worry them. This way, they'll go to Yomen for water. With the entire city making demands, he should go through the water supply in his storage cache pretty quickly."

Cett grunted. He seemed pleased, however, that Elend had taken his suggestion. "And the surrounding villages?"

"Feel free to bully them," Elend said. "Organize a force of ten thousand, and send them out to harass—but not kill. I want Yomen's spies in the area to send him worried notes about his kingdom collapsing."

"You're trying to play this halfway, lad," Cett said. "Eventually, you'll have to choose. If Yomen doesn't surrender, you'll have to attack."

Elend reined in his horse outside the command tent. "I know," he said softly.

Cett snorted, but he fell silent as servants came out of the tent to unstrap him from the saddle. As they started, however, the earth began to tremble. Elend cursed, struggling to maintain control of his horse as it grew skittish. The shaking rattled tents, knocking poles free and collapsing a couple of them, and Elend heard the clang of metal as cups, swords, and other items were knocked to the ground. Eventually, the rumbling subsided, and he glanced to the side, checking on Cett. The man had managed to keep control of his mount, though one of his useless legs swung free from the saddle, and he looked as if he was about to fall off. His servants rushed to his side to help.

"Damn things are growing more and more frequent," Cett said.

Elend calmed his horse, which stood puffing in the mists. Around the camp, men cursed and yelled, dealing with the aftermath of the earthquake. They were indeed growing more frequent; the last one had only been a few weeks before. Earthquakes weren't supposed to be common in the Final Empire—during his youth, he'd never heard of one happening in the inner dominances.

He sighed, climbing from his horse and handing the beast off to an aide, then followed Cett into the command tent. The servants sat Cett in a chair, then retreated, leaving the two of them alone. Cett glanced up at Elend, looking troubled. "Did that fool Ham tell you about the news from Luthadel?"

"Or the lack of it?" Elend asked, sighing. "Yes." Not a peep had come from the capital city, let alone the supplies Elend had ordered brought down the canal.

"We don't have *that* much time, Elend," Cett said quietly. "A few months, at most. Time enough to weaken Yomen's resolve, perhaps make his people get so thirsty that they begin to look forward to invasion. But, if we don't get resupplied, there's no way we'll be able to maintain this siege."

Elend glanced at the older man. Cett sat in his chair with an arrogant expression, looking back at Elend, meeting his eyes. So much about what the crippled man did was about posturing—Cett had lost the use of his legs to disease long ago, and he couldn't intimidate people physically. So, he had to find other ways to make himself threatening.

Cett knew how to hit where it hurt. He could pick at the very faults that bothered people and exploit their virtues in ways that Elend had rarely seen even accomplished Soothers manage. And he did all this while covering up a heart that Elend suspected was far softer than Cett would ever admit.

He seemed particularly on edge this day. As if worried about something. Something important to him—something he'd been forced to leave behind, perhaps?

"She'll be all right, Cett," Elend said. "Nothing will happen to Allrianne while she's with Sazed and Breeze."

Cett snorted, waving an indifferent hand—though he did look away. "I'm better off without the damn fool of a girl around. Let that Soother have her, I say! Anyway, we're not talking about me, we're talking about you and this siege!"

"Your points have been noted, Cett," Elend said. "We will attack if I deem it necessary." As he spoke, the tent flaps parted, and Ham sauntered in, accompanied by a figure Elend hadn't seen in several weeks—at least not out of bed.

"Demoux!" Elend said, approaching the general. "You're up and about!"

"Barely, Your Majesty," Demoux said. He did still look pale. "However, I have recovered enough strength to move around a bit."

"The others?" Elend asked.

Ham nodded. "Mostly up and about as well. Demoux is among the last batch. A few more days, and the army will be back to full strength."

Minus those who died, Elend thought.

Cett eyed Demoux. "Most of the men recovered weeks

ago. A bit weaker in the constitution than one might expect, eh, Demoux? That's what I've been hearing, at least."

Demoux blushed.

Elend frowned at this. "What?"

"It is nothing, Your Majesty," Demoux said.

"It's never 'nothing' in my camp, Demoux," Elend said. "What am I missing?"

Ham sighed, pulling over a chair. He sat on it backward, resting his muscular arms across its back. "It's just a rumor moving through the camp, El."

"Soldiers," Cett said. "They're all the same—superstitious as housewives."

Ham nodded. "Some of them have gotten it into their heads that the men who got sick from the mists were being punished."

"Punished?" Elend asked. "For what?"

"Lack of faith, Your Majesty," Demoux said.

"Nonsense," Elend said. "We all know that the mists struck randomly."

The others shared looks, and Elend had to pause and reconsider. *No. The strikes weren't random—at least, the statistics surrounding them weren't.* "Regardless," he said, deciding to change the subject, "what are your daily reports?"

The three men took turns talking about their various duties in the bivouac. Ham saw to morale and training, Demoux to supplies and camp duties, Cett to tactics and patrols. Elend stood with hands clasped behind his back, listening to the reports, but only with half an ear. They weren't much different from the previous day, though it was good to see Demoux back at his duties. He was far more efficient than his assistants.

As they talked, Elend's mind wandered. The siege was going fairly well, but a part of him—the part trained by Cett and Tindwyl—chafed at the waiting game. He might just be able to take the city straight out. He had koloss, and all accounts said that his troops were far more experienced than those inside of Fadrex. The rock formations would provide cover for the defenders, but Elend wasn't in so bad a position that he couldn't win.

But doing so would cost many, many lives.

That was the step he balked at—the last step that would take him from defender to aggressor. From protector to conqueror. And he was frustrated at his own hesitation.

There was another reason going into the city had been bad for Elend. It had been better for Elend to think of Yomen as an evil tyrant, a corrupt obligator loyal to the Lord Ruler. Now, unfortunately, he knew Yomen to be a reasonable man. And one with very good arguments. In a way, his indictment of Elend was true. Elend *was* a hypocrite. He spoke of democracy, yet he had taken his throne by force.

It was what the people had needed from him, he believed. But it did make him a hypocrite. Still, by that same logic, he knew he should send Vin to assassinate Yomen. But, could Elend order the death of a man who had done nothing wrong besides getting in his way?

Assassinating the obligator seemed as twisted an action as sending his koloss to attack the city. *Cett is right,* Elend thought. *I'm trying to play both sides on this one.* For a moment, while talking to Telden during the ball, he had felt so sure of himself. And, in truth, he still believed what he'd claimed. Elend *wasn't* the Lord Ruler. He *did* give his people more freedom and more justice.

However, he realized that this siege could tip the balance between who he was and who he feared he would become. Could he really justify invading Fadrex, slaughtering its armies and pillaging its resources, all ostensibly in the name of protecting the people of the empire? Could he dare do the opposite: back away from Fadrex, and leave the secrets in that cavern—the secrets that could potentially save the entire empire—to a man who still thought the Lord Ruler would return to save his people?

He wasn't ready to decide. For now, he was determined to exhaust every other option. Anything that would keep him from needing to invade the city. That included besieging the city to make Yomen more pliant. That also included sneaking

Vin into the storage cavern. Her reports indicated that the building was very heavily guarded. She wasn't certain if she could get into it on an ordinary night. However, during a ball, defenses might be more porous. It would be the perfect time to try to get a glimpse at what was hidden in that cavern.

Assuming Yomen hasn't simply removed the Lord Ruler's last inscription, Elend thought. *Or that there was even something there in the first place.*

Yet, there was a chance. The Lord Ruler's final message, the last bit of help he had left for his people. If Elend could find a way to get that help without breaking his way into the city, killing thousands, he would take it.

Eventually, the men finished with their reports, and Elend dismissed them. Ham went quickly, wanting to get in on a morning sparring session. Cett was gone a few moments later, carried back to his own tent. Demoux, however, lingered. It was sometimes hard to remember just how young Demoux was—barely older than Elend himself. The balding scalp and numerous scars made the man look much older than he was, as did the still-visible effects of his extended illness.

Demoux was hesitant about something. Elend waited, and finally the man dropped his eyes, looking embarrassed. "Your Majesty," he said, "I feel that I must ask to be released from my post as general."

"And why do you say that?" Elend asked carefully.

"I don't think I'm worthy of the position anymore."

Elend frowned.

"Only a man trusted by the Survivor should command in this army, my lord," Demoux said.

"I'm sure that he does trust you, Demoux."

Demoux shook his head. "Then why did he give me the sickness? Why pick me, of all the men in the army?"

"I've told you, it was random luck, Demoux."

"My lord," Demoux said, "I hate to disagree, but we both know that isn't true. After all, you were the one who pointed out that those who fell sick did so at Kelsier's will."

Elend paused. "I did?"

Demoux nodded. "On that morning when we exposed our army to the mists, you shouted out for them to remember that Kelsier is the Lord of the Mists, and that the sickness must—therefore—be his will. I think you were right. The Survivor *is* Lord of the Mists. He proclaimed it so himself, during the nights before he died. He's behind the sickness, my lord. I know he is. He saw those who lacked faith, and he cursed them."

"That isn't what I meant, Demoux," Elend said. "I was implying that Kelsier wanted us to suffer this setback, but not that he was targeting specific individuals."

"Either way, my lord, you said the words."

Elend waved his hand dismissively.

"Then how do you explain the strange numbers, my lord?" Demoux asked.

"I'm not sure," Elend said. "I'll admit that the number of people who fell sick does produce an odd statistic, but that doesn't say anything about you specifically, Demoux."

"I don't mean that number, my lord," Demoux said, still looking down. "I mean the number who remained sick while the others recovered."

Elend paused. "Wait. What is this?"

"Haven't you heard, my lord?" Demoux asked in the quiet tent. "The scribes have been talking about it, and it's gotten around to the army. I don't think that most of them understand the numbers and such, but they understand that *something* strange is happening."

"What numbers?" Elend asked.

"Five thousand people got taken by the sickness, my lord," Demoux said.

Exactly sixteen percent of the army, Elend thought.

"Of those, some five hundred died," Demoux said. "Of those remaining, almost everyone recovered in one day."

"But some didn't," Elend said. "Like you."

"Like me," Demoux said softly. "Three hundred and twenty-seven of us remained sick when the others got better."

"So?" Elend asked.

"That's exactly one-sixteenth of those who fell to the sickness, my lord," Demoux said. "And we stayed sick *exactly* sixteen days. To the hour."

The tent flap rustled quietly in the breeze. Elend fell quiet, and couldn't completely suppress a shiver. "Coincidence," he finally said. "Statisticians looking for connections can *always* find odd coincidences and statistical anomalies, if they try hard enough."

"This doesn't seem like a simple anomaly, my lord," Demoux said. "It's precise. The same number keeps showing up, over and over. Sixteen."

Elend shook his head. "Even if it does, Demoux, it doesn't *mean* anything. It's just a number."

"It's the number of months the Survivor spent in the Pits of Hathsin," Demoux said.

"Coincidence."

"It's how old Lady Vin was when she became Mistborn."

"Again, coincidence," Elend said.

"There seem to be an awful lot of coincidences related to this, my lord," Demoux said.

Elend frowned, folding his arms. Demoux was right on that point. *My denials are getting us nowhere. I need to know what people are thinking, not just contradict them.*

"All right, Demoux," Elend said. "Let's say that none of these things are coincidences. You seem to have a theory of what they mean."

"It's what I said earlier, my lord," Demoux said. "The mists are of the Survivor. They take certain people and kill them, others of us they make sick—leaving the number sixteen as a proof that he really was behind the event. So, therefore, the people who grow the most sick are the ones who have displeased him the most."

"Well, except for the ones who *died* from the sickness," Elend noted.

"True," Demoux said, looking up. "So . . . maybe there's hope for me."

"That wasn't supposed to be a comforting comment, Demoux. I still don't accept all of this. Perhaps there *are* oddities, but your interpretation is based on speculation. Why would the Survivor be displeased with you? You're one of his most faithful priests."

"I took the position for myself, my lord," Demoux said. "He didn't choose me. I just . . . started teaching what I'd seen, and people listened to me. That must be what I did to offend him. If he'd wanted that from me, he'd have chosen me when he was alive, don't you think?"

I don't think the Survivor cared much about this when he was alive, Elend thought. *He just wanted to stir up enough anger in the skaa that they would rebel.*

"Demoux," Elend said, "you know that the Survivor didn't organize this religion when he was alive. Only men and women like you—those who looked toward his teachings *after* he died—have been able to build up a community of the faithful."

"True," Demoux. "But he *did* appear to some people after his death. I wasn't one of those people."

"He didn't appear to anyone," Elend said. "That was OreSeur the kandra wearing his body. You know that, Demoux."

"Yes," Demoux said. "But, that kandra acted at the Survivor's request. And, I wasn't on the list to get visited."

Elend laid a hand on Demoux's shoulder, looking in the man's eyes. He had seen the general, worn and grizzled beyond his age, determinedly stare down a savage koloss a full five feet taller than he was. Demoux was not a weak man, either in body or in faith.

"Demoux," Elend said, "I mean this in the kindest way, but your self-pity is getting in the way. If these mists took *you,* then we need to use that as proof that their effects have *nothing* to do with Kelsier's displeasure. We don't have time for you to question yourself right now—we both know you're twice as devoted as any other man in this army."

Demoux flushed.

"Think about it," Elend said, giving Demoux a little extra Allomantic shove in the emotions, "in you, we have obvious proof that a person's faithfulness has nothing to do with whether or not they're taken by the mists. So, rather than letting you mope, we need to move on and find the *real* reason the mists are behaving as they are."

Demoux stood for a moment, then finally nodded. "Perhaps you're right, my lord. Maybe I'm jumping to conclusions."

Elend smiled. Then, he paused, thinking about his own words. *Obvious proof that a person's faithfulness has nothing to do with whether they're taken by the mists. . . .*

It wasn't exactly true. Demoux was one of the strongest believers in the camp. What of the others who had been sick as long as he? Had they been, perhaps, men of extreme faith as well? Elend opened his mouth to ask the question of Demoux. That was when the shouting started.

Hemalurgic decay was less obvious in Inquisitors that had been created from Mistborn. Since they already had Allomantic powers, the addition of other abilities made them awesomely strong.

In most cases, however, Inquisitors were created from Mistings. It appears that Seekers, like Marsh, were the favored recruits. For, when a Mistborn wasn't available, an Inquisitor with enhanced bronze abilities was a powerful tool for searching out skaa Mistings.

37

SCREAMS ROSE IN THE DISTANCE. Vin started upright in her cabin. She hadn't been sleeping, though she'd been close. Another night of scouting Fadrex City had left her tired.

All fatigue was forgotten, however, as the sounds of battle clanged from the north. *Finally!* she thought, throwing off her blankets and dashing from the cabin. She wore her standard trousers and shirt, and—as always—carried several vials of metals. She downed one of these as she scrambled across the deck of the narrowboat.

"Lady Vin!" one of the bargemen called through the day-mists. "The camp has been attacked!"

"And about time, too," Vin said as she Pushed herself off the boat's cleats, hurling herself into the air. She shot through the morning mists, curls and wisps of white making her feel as a bird might flying through a cloud.

With tin, she soon found the battle. Several groups of men on horseback had ridden into the north section of camp, and were apparently trying to make their way toward the supply barges, which floated in a well-protected bend in the canal. A group of Elend's Allomancers had set up a perimeter at one side, Thugs in the front, Coinshots picking off the riders from behind. The regular soldiers held the middle, fighting well, since the horsemen were slowed by the camp's barricades and fortifications.

Elend was right, Vin thought with pride, descending through the air. *If we hadn't exposed our men to the mists, we'd be in trouble right now.*

The king's planning had saved their supplies and baited out one of Yomen's harrying forces. The riders had probably expected to run easily through the camp—catching the soldiers unaware and trapped by mist—then set fire to the supply barges. Instead, Elend's scouts and patrols had provided enough warning, and the enemy cavalry was bogged down in a head-on fight.

Yomen's soldiers were punching through into the camp on the south side. Though Elend's soldiers fought well, their enemies were mounted. Vin plunged down through the sky, flaring pewter and strengthening her body. She tossed a coin, Pushing on it to slow herself, and hit the dark ground, throwing up a huge spray of ash. The southern bank of riders had penetrated as far as the third line of tents. Vin chose to land right in the middle of them.

No horseshoes, Vin thought as soldiers began to turn toward her. *And spears—stone-tipped—instead of swords. Yomen certainly is careful.*

It almost felt like a challenge. Vin smiled, the adrenaline feeling good after so many days spent waiting. Yomen's captains began to call out, turning their attack toward Vin. In seconds, they had a force of some thirty riders galloping straight at her.

Vin stared them down. Then she jumped. She didn't need steel to get herself high—her pewter-enhanced muscles were enough for that. She crested the lead soldier's spear, feeling it pass through the air beneath her. Ash swirled in the morning mists as Vin's foot took the soldier in the face, throwing him backward from the saddle. She landed beside his rolling body, then dropped a coin and Pushed herself to the side, out of the way of galloping hooves. The unfortunate rider she'd unhorsed cried out as his friends inadvertently trampled him.

Vin's Push carried her through the open flaps of a large canvas sleeping tent. She rolled to her feet, and then—still in motion—Pushed against the tent's metal stakes, ripping them from the ground.

The walls shook, and there was a snap of canvas as the tent shot upward into the air, spread taut as its stakes all went different directions. Ash blew outward from the burst of air, and soldiers on both sides of the conflict turned toward Vin. She allowed the tent to fall down in front of her, then Pushed. The canvas caught the air, puffing out, and the stakes ripped free from the tent, shooting forward to spear horses and riders.

Men and beasts fell. Canvas fluttered to the ground before Vin. She smiled, then jumped over the discarded tangle as the riders tried to organize another assault. She didn't give them time. Elend's soldiers in the area had pulled back, shoring up the center of the defensive line, leaving Vin free to attack without fear of harming her own men.

She dashed between the horsemen, their massive mounts hindering them as they tried to keep track of her. Men and horses spun, and Vin Pulled, tearing tents out of the ground and using their metal stakes like arrows. Dozens fell before her.

The sound of galloping came from behind, and Vin spun to see that one of the enemy officers had managed to organize another charge. Ten men came straight at her, some with spears leveled, others drawing bows.

Vin didn't like killing. But she loved Allomancy—loved the challenge of using her skills, the strength and thrill of the Pushes and Pulls, the electric sense of power that came only from a body flared with pewter. When men such as these gave her an excuse to fight, she didn't restrain herself.

The arrows didn't have a chance against her. Pewter gave her speed and balance as she spun out of the way, Pulling on a metal source behind her. She jumped into the air as a rippling tent passed beneath her, carried forward by her Pull a moment before. She landed, then Pushed on several of its stakes—a couple on each of two tent corners. The tent folded upon itself, looking a bit like a napkin with someone pulling tightly on opposite corners.

And this hit the legs of the horses like a tripwire. Vin burned duralumin, then Pushed. The horses in front screamed, the improvised weapon scattering them to the ground. The canvas ripped, and the stakes pulled free, but the damage was done—those in front tripped those behind, and men tumbled beside their beasts.

Vin downed another vial to replenish her steel. Then she Pulled, whipping another tent toward her. As it grew close, she jumped, then spun and Pushed the tent toward another group of mounted men behind. The tent's stakes struck one of the soldiers in the chest, throwing him backward. He crashed through the other soldiers, causing chaos.

The man hit the ground, slumping lifeless into the ash. Still tied to him by the stakes in his chest, the canvas tent fluttered down, covering his body like a funeral shroud. Vin spun, seeking more enemies. The riders, however, were beginning to withdraw. She stepped forward, intending to chase them down, but stopped. Someone was watching her—she could see his shadow in the mist. She burned bronze.

The figure thumped with the power of metals. Allomancer. Mistborn. He was far too short to be Elend, but she couldn't tell much more than that through the shadow of mist and ash.

Vin didn't pause to think. She dropped a coin and shot herself toward the stranger.

He leaped backward, Pushing himself into the air as well. Vin followed, quickly leaving the camp behind, bounding after the Allomancer. He quickly made his way to the city, and she followed, moving in vast leaps over an ashen landscape. Her quarry crested the rock formations at the front of the city, and Vin followed, landing just a few feet from a surprised guard patrol, then launching herself over crags and windswept rocks into Fadrex proper.

The other Allomancer stayed ahead of her. There was no playfulness to his motions, as there had been with Zane. This man was really trying to escape. Vin followed, now leaping over rooftops and streets. She gritted her teeth, frustrated at her inability to catch up. She timed each jump perfectly, barely pausing as she chose new anchors and Pushed herself from arc to arc.

Yet, he was good. He rounded the city, forcing her to push herself to keep up. *Fine*! she finally thought, then prepared her duralumin. She'd gotten close enough to the figure that he was no longer shadowed in mist, and she could see that he was real and corporeal, not some phantom spirit. She was increasingly certain that this was the man she'd sensed watching her when she'd first come into Fadrex. Yomen had a Mistborn.

However, to fight the man, she'd first need to catch him. She waited for the right moment, just when he was beginning to crest one of his arcing jumps, then extinguished her metals and burned duralumin. Then she Pushed.

A crash sounded behind her as her unnatural Push shattered the door she'd used as an anchor. She was thrown forward with a terrible burst of speed, like an arrow released from a bow. She approached her opponent with awesome speed.

And found nothing. Vin cursed, turning her tin back on. She couldn't leave it on while burning duralumin—otherwise, her tin would burn away in a single flash, leaving her blinded. But, she'd effectively done the same thing by turning it off. She Pulled herself down from her duralumin Push to land maladroitly atop a nearby roof. She crouched as she scanned the misty air.

Where did you go? she thought, burning bronze, trusting in her innate—yet still unexplained—ability to pierce copperclouds to reveal her opponent. No Allomancer could hide from Vin unless he completely turned off his metals.

Which, apparently this man had done. Again. This was the second time he'd eluded her.

It bespoke a disquieting possibility. Vin had tried very hard to keep her ability to pierce copperclouds a secret, but it had been nearly four years since her discovery of it. Zane had known about it, and she couldn't know who else had guessed, based on things she could do. Her secret could very well be out.

Vin remained on that rooftop for a few moments, but knew she'd find nothing. A man clever enough to escape her at the exact moment when her tin was down would also be clever enough to remain hidden until she was gone. In fact, it made her wonder why he had let her see him in the first . . .

Vin stood bolt upright, then downed a metal vial and Pushed herself off the rooftop, jumping with a furious anxiety back toward the camp.

She found the soldiers cleaning up the wreckage and bodies at the camp's perimeter. Elend was moving among them calling out orders, congratulating the men, and generally letting himself be seen. Indeed, sight of his white-clothed form immediately brought Vin a sense of relief.

She landed beside him. "Elend, were you attacked?"

He glanced at her. "What? Me? No, I'm fine."

Then the Allomancer wasn't sent to distract me from an attack on Elend, she thought, frowning. It had seemed so obvious. It—

Elend pulled her aside, looking worried. "*I'm* fine, Vin, but there's something else—something's happened."

"What?" Vin asked.

Elend shook his head. "I think this all was just a distraction—the entire attack on the camp."

"But, if they weren't after you," Vin said, "and they

weren't after our supplies, then what was there to distract us from?"

Elend met her eyes. "The koloss."

"How did we miss *this*?" Vin asked, sounding frustrated.

Elend stood with a troop of soldiers on a plateau, waiting as Vin and Ham inspected the burned siege equipment. Down below, he could see Fadrex City, and his own army camped outside it. The mists had retreated a short time ago. It was disturbing that from this distance he couldn't even make out the canal—the falling ash had darkened its waters and covered the landscape to the point that everything just looked black.

At the base of the plateau's cliffs lay the remnants of their koloss army. Twenty thousand had become ten thousand in a few brief moments as a well-laid trap had rained down destruction on the beasts while Elend's troops were distracted. The daymists had kept his men from seeing what was going on until it was too late. Elend himself had felt the deaths, but had misinterpreted them as koloss sensing the battle.

"Caves in the back of those cliffs," Ham said, poking at a bit of charred wood. "Yomen probably had the trebuchets stored in the caves in anticipation of our arrival, though I'd guess they were originally being built for an assault on Luthadel. Either way, this plateau was a perfect staging area for a barrage. I'd say Yomen set them up here intending to attack our army, but when we camped the koloss just beneath the plateau . . ."

Elend could still hear the screams in his head—the koloss, full of bloodlust and frothing to fight, yet unable to attack their enemies, which were high atop the plateau. The falling rocks had done a lot of damage. And then the creatures had slipped away from him. Their frustration had been too powerful, and for a time, he hadn't been able to keep them from turning on each other. Most of the deaths had come as the koloss attacked each other. Roughly one of every two had died as they had paired off and killed each other.

I lost control of them, he thought. It had only been for a short while, and it had only happened because they hadn't been able to get at their enemies. However, it set a dangerous precedent.

Vin, frustrated, kicked a large chunk of burned wood, sending it tumbling down the side of the plateau.

"This was a *very* well-planned attack, El," Ham said, speaking in a soft voice. "Yomen must have seen us sending out extra patrols in the mornings, and correctly guessed that we were expecting an attack during those hours. So, he gave us one—then hit us where we should have been the strongest."

"It cost him a lot, though," Elend said. "He had to burn his own siege equipment to keep it away from us, and he has to have lost hundreds of soldiers—plus their mounts—in the attack on our camp."

"True," Ham said. "But would you trade a couple dozen siege weapons and five hundred men for ten thousand koloss? Plus, Yomen has to be worried about keeping that cavalry mobile—the Survivor only knows where he got enough grain to feed those horses as long as he did. Better for him to strike now and lose them in battle than to have them starve."

Elend nodded slowly. *This makes things more difficult. With ten thousand fewer koloss . . .* Suddenly, the forces were much more evenly matched. Elend could maintain his siege, but storming the city would be far more risky.

He sighed. "We shouldn't have left the koloss so far outside of the main camp. We'll have to move them in."

Ham didn't seem to like that.

"They're not dangerous," Elend said. "Vin and I can control them." *Mostly.*

Ham shrugged. He moved back through the smoking wreckage, preparing to send messengers. Elend walked forward, approaching Vin, who stood at the very edge of the cliff. Being up so high still made him a bit uncomfortable. Yet, she barely even noticed the sheer drop in front of her.

"I should have been able to help you regain control of them," she said quietly, staring out into the distance. "Yomen distracted me."

"He distracted us all," Elend said. "I felt the koloss in my head, but even so, I couldn't figure out what was going on. I'd regained control of them by the time you got back, but by then, a lot of them were dead."

"Yomen has a Mistborn," Vin said.

"You're sure?"

Vin nodded.

One more thing, he thought. He contained his frustration, however. His men needed to see him confident. "I'm giving a thousand of the koloss to you," he said. "We should have split them up earlier."

"You're stronger," Vin said.

"Not strong enough, apparently."

Vin sighed, then nodded. "Let me go down below." They'd found that proximity helped with taking control of koloss.

"I'll pull off a section of a thousand or so, then let go. Be ready to grab them as soon as I do."

Vin nodded, then stepped off the side of the plateau.

I should have realized that I was getting caught up in the excitement of the fighting, Vin thought as she fell through the air. It seemed so obvious to her now. And, unfortunately, the results of the attack left her feeling even more pent-up and anxious than she had before.

She tossed a coin and landed. Even a drop of several hundred feet didn't bother her anymore. It was odd to think about. She remembered timidly standing atop the Luthadel city wall, afraid to use her Allomancy to jump off, despite Kelsier's coaxing. Now she could step off a cliff and muse thoughtfully to herself on the way down.

She walked across the powdery ground. The ash came up to the top of her calves and would have been difficult to walk in without pewter to give her strength. The ashfalls were growing increasingly dense.

Human approached her almost immediately. She couldn't tell if the koloss was simply reacting to their bond, or if he was actually aware and interested enough to pick her out. He had a new wound on his arm, a result of the fighting. He fell into step beside her as she moved up to the other koloss, his massive form obviously having no trouble with the deep ash.

As usual, there was very little emotion to the koloss camp. Just a short time before, they had been screaming in bloodlust, attacking each other as stones crashed down from above. Now they simply sat in the ash, gathered in small groups, ignoring their wounds. They would have had fires going if there had been wood available. Some few dug, finding handfuls of dirt to chew on.

"Don't your people care, Human?" Vin asked.

The massive koloss looked down at her, ripped face bleeding slightly. "Care?"

"That so many of you died," Vin said. She could see corpses lying about, forgotten in the ash save for the ritual flaying that was the koloss form of burial. Several koloss still worked, moving between bodies, ripping off the skin.

"We take care of them," Human said.

"Yes," Vin said. "You pull their skin off. Why do you do that, anyway?"

"They are dead," Human said, as if that were enough of an explanation.

To the side, a large group of koloss stood up, commanded by Elend's silent orders. They separated themselves from the main camp, trudging out into the ash. A moment later, they began to look around, no longer moving as one.

Vin reacted quickly. She turned off her metals, burned duralumin, then flared zinc in a massive Pull, Rioting the koloss emotions. As expected, they snapped under her control, just as Human was.

Controlling this many was more difficult, but still well within her abilities. Vin ordered them to be calm, and to not kill, then let them return to the camp. From now on, they would remain in the back of her mind, no longer requiring Allomancy to manipulate. They were easy to ignore unless their passions grew strong.

Human watched them. "We are . . . fewer," he finally said.

Vin started. "Yes," she said. "You can tell that?"

"I . . ." Human trailed off, beady little eyes watching his camp. "We fought. We died. We need more. We have too many swords." He pointed in the distance, to a large pile of metal. Wedge-shaped koloss swords that no longer had owners.

You can control a koloss population through the swords, Elend had once told her. *They fight to get bigger swords as they grow. Extra swords go to the younger, smaller koloss.*

But nobody knows where those come from.

"You need koloss to use those swords, Human," Vin said.

Human nodded.

"Well," she said. "You'll need to have more children, then."

"Children?"

"More," Vin said. "More koloss."

"You need to give us more," Human said, looking at her.

"Me?"

"You fought," he said, pointing at her shirt. There was blood there, not her own.

"Yes, I did," Vin said.

"Give us more."

"I don't understand," Vin said. "Please, just show me."

"I can't," Human said, shaking his head as he spoke in his slow tone. "It's not right."

"Wait," Vin said. "Not right?" It was the first real statement of values she'd gotten from a koloss.

Human looked at her, and she could see consternation on his face. So, Vin gave him an Allomantic nudge. She didn't know exactly what to ask him to do, and that made her control of him weaker. Yet, she Pushed him to do as he was thinking, trusting—for some reason—that his mind was fighting with his instincts.

He screamed.

Vin backed away, shocked, but Human didn't attack her. He ran into the koloss camp, a massive blue monster on two legs, kicking up ash. Others backed away from him—not out of fear, for they wore their characteristic impassive faces. They simply appeared to have enough sense to stay out of the way of an enraged koloss of Human's size.

Vin followed carefully as Human approached one of the dead bodies of a koloss who still wore his skin. Human didn't rip the skin off, however, but flung the corpse over his shoulder and took off running toward Elend's camp.

Uh, oh, Vin thought, dropping a coin and taking to the air. She bounded after Human, careful not to outpace him. She considered ordering him back, but did not. He was acting unusually, true, but that was a good thing. Koloss generally didn't do *anything* unusual. They were predictable to a fault.

She landed at the camp's guard post and waved the soldiers back. Human continued on, barreling into the camp, startling soldiers. Vin stayed with him, keeping the soldiers away.

Human paused in the middle of camp, a bit of his passion wearing off. Vin nudged him again. After looking about, Human took off toward the broken section of camp, where Yomen's soldiers had attacked.

Vin followed, growing more and more curious. Human hadn't taken out his sword. Indeed, he didn't seem angry at all, just . . . intense. He arrived at a section where tents had fallen and men had died. The battle was still only a few hours old, and soldiers moved about, cleaning up. Triage tents had been set up just beside the battlefield. Human headed for those.

Vin rushed ahead, cutting him off just as he reached the tent with the wounded. "Human," she said warily. "What are you doing?"

He ignored her, slamming the dead koloss down on the ground. Now, finally, Human ripped the skin off the corpse. It came off easily—this was one of the smaller koloss, whose skin hung in folds, far too large for its body.

Human pulled the skin free, causing several of the watching guards to groan in disgust. Vin watched closely despite the stomach-wrenching sight. She felt like she was on the verge of understanding something very important.

Human reached down, and pulled something out of the koloss corpse.

"Wait," Vin said, stepping forward. "What was that?"

Human ignored her. He pulled out something else, and this time Vin caught a flash of bloodied metal. She followed his fingers as he moved, and this time saw the item before he pulled it free and hid it in his palm.

A spike. A small metal spike driven into the side of the dead koloss. There was a rip of blue skin beside the spike-head, as if . . .

As if the spikes were holding the skin in place, Vin thought. *Like nails holding cloth to a wall.*

Spikes. Spikes like . . .

Human retrieved a fourth spike, then stepped forward into the tent. Surgeons and soldiers moved back in fear, crying out for Vin to do something as Human approached the bed of a wounded soldier. Human looked from one unconscious man to another, then reached for one of them.

Stop! Vin commanded in her mind.

Human froze in place. Only then did the complete horror of what was happening occur to her. "Lord Ruler," she whispered. "You were going to turn them into koloss, weren't you? That's where you come from. That's why there are no koloss children."

"I am *human,*" the large beast said quietly.

Hemalurgy can be used to steal Allomantic or Feruchemical powers and give them to another person. However, a Hemalurgic spike can also be created by killing a normal person, one who is neither an Allomancer nor a Feruchemist. In that case, the spike instead steals the very power of Preservation existing within the soul of the person. (The power that, in fact, gives all people sentience.)

A Hemalurgic spike can extract this power, then transfer it to another, granting them residual abilities similar to those of Allomancy. After all, Preservation's body—a tiny trace of which is carried by every human being—is the very same essence that fuels Allomancy.

And so, a kandra granted the Blessing of Potency is actually acquiring a bit of innate strength similar to that of burning pewter. The Blessing of Presence grants mental capacity in a similar way, while the Blessing of Awareness is the ability to sense with greater acuity and the rarely used Blessing of Stability grants emotional fortitude.

38

SOMETIMES, SPOOK FORGOT THE MIST was even there. It had become such a pale, translucent thing to him. Nearly invisible. Stars in the sky blazed like a million limelights shining down on him. It was a beauty only he could see.

He turned, looking across the burned remains of the building. Skaa workers carefully sifted through the mess. It was hard for Spook to remember that they couldn't see well in the night's darkness. He had to keep them packed closely together, working as much by touch as by sight.

The scent was, of course, terrible. Yet, burning pewter seemed to help mitigate that. Perhaps the strength it gave him extended to his ability to avoid unintentional reactions, such as retching or coughing. During his youth, he had wondered about the pairing of tin and pewter. Other Allomantic pairs were opposites—steel Pushed on metals, iron Pulled on them. Copper hid Allomancers, bronze revealed Allomancers. Zinc enflamed emotions, brass depressed them. Yet, tin and pewter didn't seem opposites—one enhanced the body, the other the senses.

And yet, these *were* opposites. Tin made his sense of touch so sharp that each step had once been uncomfortable. Pewter enhanced his body, making it resistant to pain—and so as he picked his way across the blackened ruin, his feet didn't hurt as much. In a similar way, where light had once blinded him, pewter let him endure far more before needing his blindfold.

The two were opposites, yet complements—just like the other pairs of Allomantic metals. He felt *right* having the one to go with the other. How had he survived without pewter? He had been a man with only one half of an ability. Now he was complete.

And yet, he did wonder what it would be like to have the other powers too. Kelsier had given him pewter. Could he, perhaps, bless Spook with iron and steel as well?

A man directed the line of working figures. His name was Franson; he was the one who had asked Spook to rescue his sister. The execution was only a day away. Soon, the child would be thrown into a burning building of her own, but Spook was working on ways to stop that. There wasn't much he could do at the moment. So, in the meantime, Franson and his men dug.

It had been some time since Spook had gone to spy on the Citizen and his councillors. He'd shared the information he'd gleaned with Sazed and Breeze, and they'd seemed appreciative. However, with the increased security around the Citizen's home, they'd suggested that it was foolhardy to risk more spying until they'd figured out their plans for the city. Spook had accepted their guidance, though he felt himself growing anxious. He missed going to see Beldre, the quiet girl with the lonely eyes.

He didn't know her. He couldn't fool himself that he did. Yet, when they'd met and spoken that once, she hadn't screamed or betrayed him. She'd seemed intrigued by him. That was a good sign, right?

Fool, he thought. *She's the Citizen's own sister! Talking to her nearly got you killed. Focus on the task at hand.*

Spook watched the work for a time longer. Finally, Franson—dirty and exhausted in the starlight—approached him. "My lord," Franson said, "we've gone over this section four times now. The men in the basement pit have moved all the debris and ash to the sides, and have sifted through it twice. Whatever we were going to find, we've found it."

Spook nodded. Franson was probably right. Spook removed a small pouch from his pocket, handing it to Franson. It clinked, and the large skaa man raised an eyebrow.

"Payment," Spook said, "for the other men. They've worked here for three nights."

"They're friends, my lord," he said. "They just want to see my sister rescued."

"Pay them anyway," Spook said. "And tell them to spend the coins on food and supplies as soon as they can—before Quellion abolishes coinage in the city."

"Yes, my lord," Franson said. Then, he glanced to the side, where a mostly burned banister still stood upright. This is where the workers had placed the objects they had located in the wreckage: nine human skulls. They cast eerie shadows in the starlight. Leering, burned, and blackened.

"My lord," Franson said. "May I ask the point of this?"

"I watched this building burn down," Spook said. "I was there when these poor people were herded into the mansion, then locked inside. I couldn't do anything."

"I'm . . . sorry, my lord," Franson said.

Spook shook his head. "It's past now. However, there is something their deaths can teach us."

"My lord?"

Spook regarded the skulls. The day Spook had watched this building burn—the first time he had witnessed one of the Citizen's executions—Durn had told him something. Spook had wanted information about the Citizen's weaknesses, something to help him beat the man. Durn had only said one thing in response to this.

Count the skulls.

Spook had never had the chance to investigate that tip. He knew Durn would probably explain himself if pushed, but they both seemed to understand something important. Spook needed to see it for himself. He needed to know what the Citizen was doing.

And now he did. "Ten people were sent into this building to die, Franson," Spook said. "Ten people. Nine skulls."

The man frowned. "What does that tell us?"

"It tells us there's a way to get your sister out."

"I'm not certain what to make of this, Lord Breeze," Sazed said. They sat at a table in one of Urteau's skaa bars. The alcohol flowed freely, and skaa workers packed the place, despite the darkness and the mists.

"What do you mean?" Breeze asked. They sat alone, though Goradel and three of his toughs sat wearing street clothing at the next table over.

"This is very strange to me," Sazed said. "Skaa having their own bars is odd enough. But, skaa going out at night?"

Breeze shrugged. "Perhaps their fear of the night was more a product of the Lord Ruler's influence than the mists. With his troops on the streets watching for thieves, there were reasons other than mist to stay inside at night."

Sazed shook his head. "I have studied these things, Lord Breeze. The skaa fear of the mists was an ingrained superstitious mind-set—it was a part of their lives. And, Quellion has broken it down in little over a year."

"Oh, I think the wine and beer probably did the breaking," Breeze noted. "You'd be surprised at what men will go through in order to get themselves properly intoxicated."

Sazed eyed Breeze's own cup—the man had taken quite a liking to the skaa bars, despite the fact that he was forced to wear very mundane clothing. Of course, the clothing probably wasn't necessary anymore. If the city had even a halfway decent rumor mill, people would have already connected Breeze to the visitors who had met with Quellion a few days before. And, now that Sazed had come to the bar, any suspicions would have been confirmed. There was no way to hide Sazed's identity. His nationality was obvious. He was too tall, too bald, and he had the typical Terris long face with drooping features and earlobes stretched out by the application of numerous earrings.

The time for anonymity had passed, though Breeze had

used it well. During the few days when people hadn't known who he was, he'd managed to build both goodwill and contacts in the local underground. Now, he and Sazed could sit and enjoy a quiet drink without really drawing much attention. Breeze would, of course, be Soothing the people to ensure that—but, even so, Sazed was impressed. For one as fond of high society as Breeze, the man did a remarkable job of relating to ordinary skaa workers.

A group of men laughed at the next table, and Breeze smiled, then stood and made his way over to join them. Sazed remained where he was, a mug of untouched wine on the table before him. In his opinion, there was an obvious reason why the skaa were no longer afraid to go out in the mists. Their superstitions had been overcome by something stronger: Kelsier. The one they were now calling the Lord of the Mists.

The Church of the Survivor had spread much further than Sazed had expected. It wasn't organized the same way in Urteau as in Luthadel, and the focus seemed to be different, but the fact remained that men were worshipping Kelsier. In fact, the differences were part of what made the whole phenomenon fascinating.

What am I missing? Sazed thought. *What is the connection here?*

The mists killed. Yet, these people went out in the mists. Why weren't the people terrified of them?

This is not my problem, Sazed told himself. *I need to remain focused. I've let my studies of the religions in my portfolio lapse.* He was getting close to being finished, and that worried him. So far, every single religion had proven full of inconsistencies, contradictions, and logical flaws. He was growing more and more worried that, even among the hundreds of religions in his metalminds, he would never be able to find the truth.

A wave from Breeze distracted him. So, Sazed stood—forcing himself not to show the despair he felt—and moved over to the table. The men there made room.

"Thank you," Sazed said, sitting.

"You forgot your cup, friend Terrisman," one of the men pointed out.

"I apologize," Sazed said. "I have never been one fond of intoxicants. Please, do not take offense. Your thoughtful gift was nevertheless appreciated."

"Does he always talk like that?" one of the men asked, looking at Breeze.

"You've never known a Terrisman, have you?" asked another.

Sazed flushed, to which Breeze chuckled, laying a hand on Sazed's shoulder. "All right, gentlemen. I've brought you the Terrisman, as requested. Go ahead, ask your questions."

There were six local men at the table—all mine workers, from what Sazed could tell. One of the men leaned forward, hands clasped in front of him, knuckles scarred by rock. "Breeze here says a lot of things," the man said in a low voice. "But people like him always make promises. Quellion said a lot of the same things a year ago, when he was taking control after Straff Venture left."

"Yes," Sazed. "I can understand your skepticism."

"But," the man said, raising a hand. "Terrismen don't lie. They're good people. Everyone knows that—lords, skaa, thieves, and obligators."

"So, we wanted to talk to you," another of the men said. "Maybe you're different; maybe you'll lie to us. But, better to hear it from a Terrisman than a Soother."

Breeze blinked, revealing just a faint hint of surprise. Apparently, he hadn't realized they'd been aware of his abilities.

"Ask your questions," Sazed said.

"Why did you come to this city?" one of the men asked.

"To take control of it," Sazed said.

"Why do you care?" another asked. "Why does Venture's son even want Urteau?"

"Two reasons," Sazed said. "First, because of the resources it offers. I cannot go into details, but suffice it to say that your city is very desirable for economic reasons. The second reason, however, is equally important. Lord Elend Venture is one of the best men I have ever known. He believes he can do better for this people than the current government."

"That wouldn't be hard," one of the men grumbled.

Another man shook his head. "What? You want to give the city back to the Ventures? One year, and you've forgotten the things that Straff used to do in this city?"

"Elend Venture is not his father," Sazed said. "He is a man worthy of being followed."

"And the Terris people?" one of the skaa asked. "Do they follow him?"

"In a way," Sazed said. "Once, my people tried to rule themselves, as your people now do. However, they realized the advantages of an alliance. My people have moved to the Central Dominance, and they accept the protection of Elend Venture." *Of course,* Sazed thought, *they'd rather follow me. If I would be their king.*

The table fell silent.

"I don't know," one of the men said. "What business do we have even talking about this? I mean, Quellion is in charge, and these strangers don't have an army to take his throne away from him. What's the point?"

"The Lord Ruler fell to us when we had no army," Breeze pointed out, "and Quellion himself seized the government from noble rule. Change can occur."

"We're not trying to form an army or rebellion," Sazed quickly added. "We just want you to start . . . thinking. Talking with your friends. You are obviously influential men. Perhaps if Quellion hears of discontent among his people, he will begin to change his ways."

"Maybe," one of the men said.

"We don't need these outsiders," the other man repeated. "The Survivor of the Flames has come to deal with Quellion."

Sazed blinked. *Survivor of the Flames?* He caught a sly smile on Breeze's lips—the Soother had apparently heard the term before, and now he appeared to be watching Sazed for a reaction.

"The Survivor doesn't enter into this," one of the men said. "I can't believe we're even *thinking* of rebellion. Most of the world is in chaos, if you hear the reports! Shouldn't we just be happy with what we've got?"

The Survivor? Sazed thought. *Kelsier? But, they seem to have given him a new title. Survivor of the Flames?*

"You're starting to twitch, Sazed," Breeze whispered. "You might as well just ask. No harm in asking, right?"

No harm in asking.

"The . . . Survivor of the Flames?" Sazed asked. "Why do you call Kelsier that?"

"Not Kelsier," one of the men said. "The other Survivor. The new one."

"The Survivor of Hathsin came to overthrow the Lord Ruler," one of the men said. "So, can't we assume the Survivor of the Flames has come to overthrow Quellion? Maybe we *should* listen to these men."

"If the Survivor is here to overthrow Quellion," another man said, "then he won't need the help of these types. They just want the city for themselves."

"Excuse me," Sazed said. "But . . . might we meet this new Survivor?"

The group of men shared looks.

"Please," Sazed said. "I was a friend to the Survivor of Hathsin. I should very much like to meet a man whom you have deemed worthy of Kelsier's stature."

"Tomorrow," one of the men said. "Quellion tries to keep the dates quiet, but they get out. There will be executions near Marketpit. Be there."

Even now, I can barely grasp the scope of all this. The events surrounding the end of the world seem even larger than the Final Empire and the people within it. I sense shards of something from long ago, a fractured presence, something spanning the void.

I have delved and searched, and have only been able to come up with a single name: Adonasium. Who, or what, it was, I do not yet know.

39

TENSOON SAT ON HIS HAUNCHES. Horrified.

Ash rained down like shards of a broken sky, floating, making the very air look pocked and sickly. Even where he sat, atop a windswept hill, there was a layer of ash smothering the plant life. Some trees had branches broken by the weight of repeated ash pileups.

How could they not see? he thought. *How can they hide in their hole of a Homeland, content to let the land above die?*

Yet, TenSoon had lived for hundreds of years, and a part of him understood the tired complacency of the First and Second Generations. At times he'd felt the same thing himself. A desire to simply wait. To spend years idly, content in the Homeland. He'd seen the outside world—seen more of it than any human or koloss would ever know. What need had he of experiencing more?

The Seconds had seen him as more orthodox and obedient than his brethren, all because he had continually wanted to leave the Homeland and serve Contracts. The Second Generation had always misunderstood him. TenSoon hadn't served out of a desire to be obedient. He'd done it out of fear: fear that he'd become content and apathetic like the Seconds and begin to think that the outside world didn't matter to the kandra people.

He shook his head, then rose to all fours and loped off down the side of the hill, scattering ash into the air with each bound. As frightening as things had gotten, he was happy for one thing. The wolfhound's body felt good on him. There was such a power in it—a capacity for movement—that no human form could match. It was almost as if this were the form he *always* should have worn. What better body for a kandra with an incurable wanderlust? A kandra who had left his Homeland behind more often than any other, serving under the hated hands of human masters, all because of his fear of complacency?

He made his way through the thin forest cover, over hills, hoping that the blanket of ash wouldn't make it too difficult for him to navigate. The falling ash did affect the kandra people—it affected them greatly. They had legends about this exact event. What good was the First Contract, what good was the waiting, the protection of the Trust? To most of the kandra, apparently, these things had become a point unto themselves.

Yet, these things *meant* something. They had an origin. TenSoon hadn't been alive back then. However, he had known the First Generation and been raised by the Second. He grew up during days when the First Contract—the Trust, the Resolution—had been more than just words. The First Contract was a set of instructions. Actions to take when the world began to fail. Not just ceremony, and not just metaphor. He knew that its contents frightened some of the kandra. For them, it was better that the First Contract be a philosophical, abstract thing—for if it were still concrete, still relevant, it would require great sacrifices of them.

TenSoon stopped running; he was up to his wolfhound knees in deep black ash. The location looked vaguely familiar. He turned south, moving through a small rocky hollow—the stones now just dark lumps—looking for a place he had been over a year before. A place he'd visited after he had turned against Zane, his master, and left Luthadel to return to the Homeland.

He scrambled up a few rocks, then rounded the side of a stone outcrop, knocking lumps of ash off with his passing. They broke apart as they fell, throwing more flakes into the air.

And there it was. The hollow in rock, the place where he had stopped a year before. He remembered it, despite how the ash had transformed the landscape. The Blessing of Presence, serving him again. How would he get along without it?

I would not be sentient without it, he thought, smiling

grimly. It was the bestowing of a Blessing on a mistwraith that brought the creature to wakefulness and true life. Each kandra got one of the four: Presence, Potency, Stability, or Awareness. It didn't matter which one a kandra gained; any of the four would give him or her sentience, changing the mistwraith into a fully conscious kandra.

In addition to sentience, each Blessing gave something else. A power. But there were stories of kandra who had gained more than one by taking them from others.

TenSoon stuck a paw into the depression, digging out the ash, working to uncover the things he had hidden a year before. He found them quickly, rolling one—then the other—out onto the rock shelf in front of him. Two small, polished iron spikes. It took two spikes to form a single Blessing. TenSoon didn't know why this was. It was simply the way of things.

TenSoon lay down, commanding the skin of his shoulder to part, and absorbed the spikes into his body. He moved them through muscles and ligaments—dissolving several organs, then re-forming them with the spikes piercing them.

Immediately, he felt power wash through him. His body became stronger. It was more than the simple adding of muscles—he could do that by re-forming his body. No, this gave each muscle an extra innate strength, making them work much better, much more powerfully, than they would have otherwise.

The Blessing of Potency. He'd stolen the two spikes from OreSeur's body. Without this Blessing, TenSoon would never have been able to follow Vin as he had during their year together. It more than doubled the power and endurance of each muscle. He couldn't regulate or change the level of that added strength—this was not Feruchemy or Allomancy, but something different. Hemalurgy.

A person had died to create each spike. TenSoon tried not to think about that too much; just as he tried not to think about how he only had this Blessing because he had killed one of his own generation. The Lord Ruler had provided the spikes each century, giving the number requested, so that the kandra could craft a new generation.

He now had four spikes, two Blessings, and was one of the most powerful kandra alive. His muscles strengthened, TenSoon jumped confidently from the top of the rock formation, falling some twenty feet to land safely on the ash-covered ground below. He took off, running far more quickly now. The Blessing of Potency resembled the power of an Allomancer burning pewter, but it was not the same. It would not keep TenSoon moving indefinitely, nor could he flare it for an extra burst of power. On the other hand, it required no metals to fuel it.

He made his path eastward. The First Contract was very explicit. When Ruin returned, the kandra were to seek out the Father to serve him. Unfortunately, the Father was dead. The First Contract didn't take that possibility into consideration. So—unable to go to the Father—TenSoon did the next best thing. He went looking for Vin.

Originally, we assumed that a koloss was a combination of two people into one. That was wrong. Koloss are not the melding of two people, but five, as evidenced by the four spikes needed to make them. Not five bodies, of course, but five souls.

Each pair of spikes grants what the kandra would call the Blessing of Potency. However, each spike also distorts the koloss body a little more, making it increasingly inhuman. Such is the cost of Hemalurgy.

40

"NOBODY KNOWS PRECISELY HOW INQUISITORS are made," Elend said from the front of the tent, addressing a small group, which included Ham, Cett, the scribe Noorden, and the mostly recovered Demoux. Vin sat at the back, still trying to sort through what she had discovered. Human . . . all koloss . . . they had once been people.

"There are lots of theories about it, however," Elend said. "Once the Lord Ruler fell, Sazed and I did some research, and discovered some interesting facts from the obligators we interviewed. For instance, Inquisitors are made from ordinary men—men who remember who they were, but gain new Allomantic abilities."

"Our experience with Marsh proves that as well," Ham said. "He remembered who he was, even after he had all of those spikes driven through his body. And he gained the powers of a Mistborn when he became an Inquisitor."

"Excuse me," Cett said, "but will someone please explain what the hell this has to do with our siege of the city? There aren't any Inquisitors here."

Elend folded his arms. "This is important, Cett, because we're at war with more than just Yomen. Something we don't understand, something far greater than those soldiers inside of Fadrex."

Cett snorted. "You still believe in this talk of doom and gods and the like?"

"Noorden," Elend said, looking at the scribe. "Please tell Lord Cett what you told me earlier today."

The former obligator nodded. "Well, my lord, it's like this. Those numbers relating to the percentage of people who fall ill to the mists, they're just *too* regular to be natural. Nature works in organized chaos—randomness on the small scale, with trends on the large scale. I cannot believe that anything natural could have produced such precise results."

"What do you mean?" Cett asked.

"Well, my lord," Noorden said. "Imagine that you hear a tapping sound somewhere outside your tent. If it repeats occasionally, with no exact set pattern, then it might be the wind blowing a loose flap against a pole. However, if it repeats with exact regularity, you know that it must be a person, beating against a pole. You'd be able to make the distinction immediately, because you've learned that nature can be repetitive in a case like that, but not *exact*. These numbers are the same, my lord. They're just too organized, too repetitive, to be natural. They had to have been crafted by somebody."

"You're saying that a person made those soldiers sick?" Cett asked.

"A person? . . . No, not a person, I'd guess," Noorden said. "But *something* intelligent must have done it. That's the only conclusion I can draw. Something with an agenda, something that cares to be precise."

The room fell silent.

"And, this relates to Inquisitors somehow, my lord?" Demoux asked carefully.

"It does," Elend said. "At least, it does if you think as I do—which, I'll admit, not many people do."

"For better or for worse . . ." Ham said, smiling.

"Noorden, what do you know of how Inquisitors are made?" Elend asked.

The scribe grew uncomfortable. "I was in the Canton of Orthodoxy, as you may know, not the Canton of Inquisition."

"Surely there were rumors," Elend asked.

"Well, of course," Noorden said. "More than rumors, actually. The higher obligators were *always* trying to discover how the Inquisitors got their power. There was a rivalry between the Cantons, you see, and . . . well, I supposed you don't care about that. Regardless, we *did* have rumors."

"And?" Elend asked.

"They said . . ." Noorden began. "They said that an Inquisitor was a fusion of many different people. In order to make an Inquisitor, the Canton of Inquisition had to get a whole group of Allomancers, then combine their powers into one."

Again, silence in the room. Vin pulled her legs up, wrapping her arms around her knees. She didn't like talking about Inquisitors.

"Lord Ruler!" Ham swore quietly. "That's it! *That's* why the Inquisitors were so keen on hunting down skaa Mistings! Don't you see! It wasn't just because the Lord Ruler ordered half-breeds to be killed—it was so that the Inquisitors could perpetuate themselves! They needed Allomancers to kill so that they could make new Inquisitors!"

Elend nodded from his place at the front of the room. "Somehow, those spikes in the Inquisitors' bodies transfer Allomantic ability. You kill eight Mistings, and you give all their powers to one other man, such as Marsh. Sazed once told me that Marsh was always hesitant to speak of the day he was made an Inquisitor, but he did say that it was . . . 'messy.' "

Ham nodded. "And when Kelsier and Vin found his room the day he was taken and made an Inquisitor, they found a corpse in there. One they initially assumed was Marsh!"

"Later, Marsh said that more than one person had been killed there," Vin said quietly. "There just hadn't been enough . . . left of them to tell."

"Again," Cett said, "does this all have a point?"

"Well, it seems to be doing a good job of annoying you," Ham said lightly. "Do we *need* any other point?"

Elend gave them both hard looks. "The point is, Cett, that Vin discovered something earlier this week."

The group turned toward her.

"Koloss," Vin said. "They're made from humans."

"What?" Cett asked, frowning. "That's absurd."

"No," Vin said, shaking her head. "I'm sure of it. I've checked living koloss. Hidden in those folds and rips of skin on their bodies, they are pierced by spikes. Smaller than the Inquisitor spikes, and made from different metals, but all of the koloss have them."

"Nobody has been able to figure out where new koloss come from," Elend said. "The Lord Ruler guarded the secret, and it's become one of the great mysteries of our time. Koloss seem to kill each other with regularity when someone isn't actively controlling them. Yet, there always seem to be more of the creatures. How?"

"Because they are constantly replenishing their numbers," Ham said, nodding slowly. "From the villages they pillage."

"Did you ever wonder," Elend said, "back during the siege

of Luthadel, why Jastes's koloss army attacked a random village before coming for us? The creatures needed to replenish their numbers."

"They always walk about," Vin said, "wearing clothing, talking about being human. Yet, they can't quite remember what it was like. Their minds have been broken."

Elend nodded. "The other day, Vin finally got one of them to show her how to make new koloss. From what he did, and from what he's said since, we believe that he was going to try to *combine* two men into one. That would make a creature with the strength of two men, but the mind of neither."

"A third art," Ham said, looking up. "A third way to use the metals. There is Allomancy, which draws power from the metals themselves. There is Feruchemy, which uses metals to draw power from your own body, and there is . . ."

"Marsh called it Hemalurgy," Vin said quietly.

"Hemalurgy . . ." Ham said. "Which uses the metals to draw power from *someone else's* body."

"Great," Cett said. "Point?"

"The Lord Ruler created servants to help him," Elend said. "Using this art . . . this Hemalurgy . . . he made soldiers, which we call koloss. He made spies, which we call kandra. And he made priests, which we call Inquisitors. He built them all with weaknesses, so that he could control them."

"I first learned how to take control of the koloss because of TenSoon," Vin said. "He inadvertently showed me the secret. He mentioned that the kandra and koloss were cousins, and I realized I could control one just as I had the other."

"I . . . still don't see where you're heading with this," Demoux said, glancing from Vin to Elend.

"The Inquisitors must have the same weakness, Demoux," Elend said. "This Hemalurgy leaves the mind . . . wounded. It allows an Allomancer to creep in and take control. The nobility always wondered what made the Inquisitors so fanatically devoted to the Lord Ruler. They weren't like regular obligators—they were far more obedient. Zealous to a fault."

"It happened to Marsh," Vin whispered. "The first time I

met him after he'd been made an Inquisitor, he seemed different. But, he only grew even odder during the year following the Collapse. Finally, he turned on Sazed, tried to kill him."

"What we're trying to suggest," Elend said, "is that something is controlling the Inquisitors and the koloss. Something is exploiting the weakness the Lord Ruler built into the creatures and is using them as its pawns. The troubles we've been suffering, the chaos following the Collapse—it's *not* simply chaos. No more than the patterns of people who fall sick to the mists are chaotic. I know it seems obvious, but the important thing here is that we now know the method. We understand why they can be controlled and how they're being controlled."

Elend continued to pace, his feet marking the dirty tent floor. "The more I think about Vin's discovery, the more I come to believe that this is all connected. The koloss, the kandra, and the Inquisitors are not three separate oddities, but part of a single cohesive phenomenon. Now, on the surface, knowledge of this third art . . . this Hemalurgy . . . doesn't seem like much. We don't intend to use it to make more koloss, so what good is the knowledge?"

Cett nodded, as if Elend had spoken the man's own thoughts. Elend, however, had drifted off a bit, staring out the open tent flaps, losing himself in thought. It was something he'd once done frequently, back when he spent more time on scholarship. He wasn't addressing Cett's questions. He was speaking his own concerns, following his own logical path.

"This war we're fighting," Elend continued, "it isn't just about soldiers. It isn't just about koloss, or about taking Fadrex City. It's about the sequence of events we inadvertently started the moment we struck down the Lord Ruler. Hemalurgy—the origins of the koloss—is part of a pattern. The percentages that fall sick from the mists are also part of the pattern. The less we see chaos, and the more we see the *pattern,* the better we're going to be at understanding just what we fight—and just how to defeat it."

Elend turned toward the group. "Noorden, I want you to change the focus of your research. Up until now, we've assumed that the movements of the koloss were random. I'm no longer convinced that is true. Research our old scout reports. Draw up lists and plot movements. Pay particular attention to bodies of koloss that we specifically know *weren't* under the control of an Inquisitor. I want to see if we can discover why they went where they did."

"Yes, my lord," Noorden said.

"The rest of you stay vigilant," Elend said. "I don't want another mistake like last week's. We can't afford to lose any more troops, even koloss."

They nodded, and Elend's posture indicated the end of the meeting. Cett was carried away to his tent, Noorden bustled off to begin this new research, and Ham went in search of something to eat. Demoux, however, stayed. Vin stood and trailed forward, stepping up to Elend's side and taking his arm as he turned to address Demoux.

"My lord . . ." Demoux said, looking a bit embarrassed. "I assume General Hammond has spoken to you?"

What's this? Vin thought, perking up.

"Yes, Demoux," Elend said with a sigh. "But I really don't think it's something to worry about."

"What?" Vin asked.

"There is a certain level of . . . ostracism happening in the camp, my lady," Demoux said. "Those of us who fell sick for two weeks, rather than a few days, are being regarded with a measure of suspicion."

"Suspicion that you no longer agree with, right, Demoux?" Elend punctuated this remark with a very kingly stern look.

Demoux nodded. "I trust your interpretation, my lord. It's just that . . . well, it is difficult to lead men who distrust you. And, it's much harder for the others like me. They've taken to eating together, staying away from the others during their free time. It's reinforcing the division."

"What do you think?" Elend asked. "Should we try to force reintegration?"

"That depends, my lord," Demoux said.

"On?"

"On several factors," Demoux said. "If you're planning to attack soon, then reintegrating would be a bad idea—I don't want men fighting alongside those they don't trust. However, if we're going to continue the siege for some time, then forcing them back together might make sense. The larger segment of the army would have time to learn to trust the mistfallen again."

Mistfallen, Vin thought. *Interesting name.*

Elend looked down at her, and she knew what he was thinking. The ball at the Canton of Resource was only a few days away. If Elend's plan went well, then perhaps they wouldn't have to attack Fadrex.

Vin didn't have great hopes for that option. Plus, without resupply from Luthadel, they couldn't count on much anymore. They could continue the siege as planned for months, or they might end up having to attack within a few weeks.

"Organize a new company," Elend said, turning to Demoux. "Fill it with these mistfallen. We'll worry about dealing with superstition after we hold Fadrex."

"Yes, my lord," Demoux said. "I think that . . ."

They continued talking, but Vin stopped paying attention as she heard voices approaching the command tent. It was probably nothing. Even so, she moved around so that she was between the approaching people and Elend, then checked her metal reserves. Within moments, she could determine who was talking. One was Ham. She relaxed as the tent flap opened, revealing Ham in his standard vest and trousers, leading a wearied red-haired soldier. The exhausted man had ash-stained clothing and wore the leathers of a scout.

"Conrad?" Demoux asked with surprise.

"You know this man?" Elend asked.

"Yes, my lord," Demoux said. "He's one of the lieutenants I left back in Luthadel with King Penrod."

Conrad saluted, though he looked rather the worse for

wear. "My lord," the man said. "I bring news from the capital."

"Finally!" Elend said. "What word from Penrod? Where are those supply barges I sent for?"

"Supply barges, my lord?" Conrad asked. "My lord, King Penrod sent me to ask *you* for resupply. There are riots in the city, and some of the food stores have been pillaged. King Penrod sent me to ask you for a contingent of troops to help him restore order."

"Troops?" Elend asked. "What of the garrison I left with him? He should have plenty of men!"

"They're not enough, my lord," Conrad said. "I don't know why. I can only relay the message I was sent to deliver."

Elend cursed, slamming his fist against the command tent's table. "Can Penrod not do the *one* thing I asked of him? All he needed to do was hold lands we already have secure!"

The soldier jumped at the outburst, and Vin watched with concern. Elend, however, managed to keep his temper under control. He took a deep breath, waving to the soldier. "Rest yourself, Lieutenant Conrad, and get some food. I will want to speak with you further about this later."

Vin found Elend later that night, standing on the perimeter of the camp, looking up at the Fadrex watch fires on the cliffs above. She laid a hand on his shoulder, and the fact that he didn't jump indicated that he'd heard her coming. It was still a little strange to her that Elend, who had always seemed slightly oblivious of the world around him, was now a capable Mistborn, with tin to enhance his ears that let him hear even the softest footsteps approaching.

"You talked to the messenger?" she asked as he put his arm around her, still looking up at the night sky. Ash fell around them. A couple of Elend's soldier Tineyes passed on patrol, carrying no lights, silently walking the perimeter of the camp. Vin herself had just gotten back from a similar patrol, though hers had been around the perimeter of Fadrex

She did a couple of rounds every night, watching the city for unusual activity.

"Yes," Elend said. "Once he'd had some rest, I spoke to him in depth."

"Bad news?"

"Much of what he said before. Penrod apparently never got my orders to send food and troops. Conrad was one of four messengers Penrod sent to us. We don't know what happened to the other three. Conrad himself was chased by a group of koloss, and he only got away by baiting them with his horse, sending it one direction and hiding as they chased it down and butchered it. He slipped away while they were feasting."

"Brave man," Vin said.

"Lucky as well," Elend said. "Either way, it seems unlikely that Penrod will be able to send us support. There are food stores in Luthadel, but if the news of riots is true, Penrod won't be able to spare the soldiers it would take to guard supplies on their way to us."

"So . . . where does that leave us?" Vin asked.

Elend looked at her, and she was surprised to see determination in his eyes, not frustration. "With knowledge."

"What?"

"Our enemy has exposed himself, Vin. Attacking our messengers directly with hidden pockets of koloss? Trying to undermine our supply base in Luthadel?" Elend shook his head. "Our enemy *wants* this to look random, but I see the pattern. It's too focused, too intelligent, to be happenstance. He's trying to make us pull away from Fadrex."

Vin felt a chill. Elend made to say more, but she reached up and laid a hand on his lips, quieting him. He seemed confused, but then apparently understood, for he nodded. *Whatever we say, Ruin can hear,* Vin thought. *We can't give away what we know.*

Still, something passed between them. A knowledge that they had to stay at Fadrex, that they *had* to find out what was in that storage cavern. For their enemy was working hard to keep them from doing so. Was Ruin, indeed, behind the chaos in Luthadel? A ploy to draw Elend and his forces back to restore order, thereby abandoning Fadrex?

It was only speculation, but it was all they had. Vin nodded to Elend, indicating that she agreed with his determination to stay. Still, she worried. Luthadel was to have been their rock in all of this—their secure position. If it was falling apart, what did they have?

More and more, she was beginning to understand that there would be no falling back. No retreat to develop alternative plans. The world was collapsing around them, and Elend had committed himself to Fadrex.

If they failed here, there would be nowhere else to go.

Eventually, Elend squeezed her shoulder, then walked off into the mists to check on some of the guard posts. Vin remained alone, staring up at those watch fires, feeling a worrisome sense of foreboding. Her thoughts from before, in the fourth storage cavern, returned to her. Fighting wars, besieging cities, playing at politics—it wasn't enough. These things wouldn't save them if the very land itself died.

But, what else could they do? The only option they had was to take Fadrex and hope the Lord Ruler had left them some clue to help. She still felt an inexplicable desire to find the atium. Why was she so certain it would help?

She closed her eyes, not wanting to face the mists, which—as always—pulled away from her, leaving a half-inch or so of empty air around her. She'd drawn upon them once, back when she'd fought the Lord Ruler. Why had she been able to fuel her Allomancy with their power that one time?

She reached out to them, trying again, as she had so many times. She called to them, pleaded with them in her mind, tried to access their power. And, she felt as if she *should* be able to. There was a strength to the mists. Trapped within them. But it wouldn't yield to her. It was as if something kept them back, some blockage perhaps? Or, maybe, a simple whim on their part.

"Why?" she whispered, eyes still closed. "Why help me that once, but never again? Am I mad, or did you really give me power when I demanded it?"

The night gave her no answers. Finally, she sighed and turned away, seeking refuge inside of the tent.

Hemalurgic spikes change people physically, depending on which powers are granted, where the spike is placed, and how many spikes someone has. Inquisitors, for instance, are changed drastically from the humans they used to be. Their hearts are in different places from those of humans, and their brains rearrange to accommodate the lengths of metal jabbed through their eyes. Koloss are changed in even more drastic ways.

One might think that kandra are changed most of all. However, one must remember that new kandra are made from mistwraiths, and not humans. The spikes worn by the kandra cause only a small transformation in their hosts—leaving their bodies mostly like that of a mistwraith, but allowing their minds to begin working. Ironically, while the spikes dehumanize the koloss, they give a measure of humanity to the kandra.

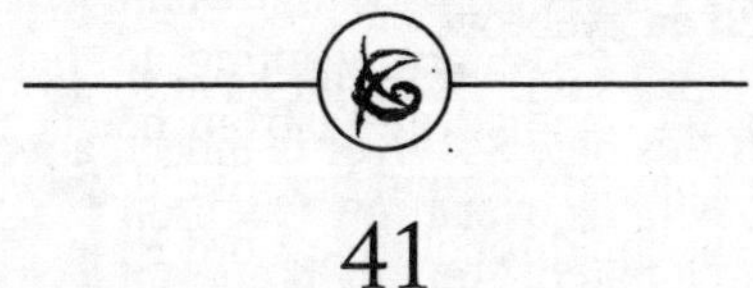

41

"DON'T YOU SEE, BREEZE?" SAZED said eagerly. "This is an example of what we call ostention—a legend being emulated in real life. The people believed in the Survivor of Hathsin, and so they have made for themselves *another* survivor to help them in their time of need."

Breeze raised an eyebrow. They stood near the back of a crowd gathering in the market district, waiting for the Citizen to arrive.

"It is fascinating," Sazed said. "This is an evolution of the Survivor legend that I never anticipated. I knew that they might deify him—in fact, that was almost inevitable. However, since Kelsier was once an 'ordinary' person, those who worship him can imagine *other* people achieving the same status."

Breeze nodded distractedly. Allrianne stood beside him, looking quite petulant that she'd been required to wear drab skaa clothing.

Sazed ignored their lack of excitement. "I wonder what the future of this will be. Perhaps there will be a *succession* of Survivors for this people. This could be the foundation of a religion with true lasting potential, since it could reinvent itself to suit the needs of the populace. Of course, new Survivors mean new leaders—each one with different opinions. Rather than a line of priests who promote orthodoxy, each new Survivor would seek to establish himself as distinct from those he succeeded. It could make for numerous factions and divisions in the body of worshippers."

"Sazed," Breeze said. "What ever happened to not collecting religions?"

Sazed paused. "I'm not really collecting this religion. I'm just theorizing about its potential."

Breeze raised an eyebrow.

"Besides," Sazed said. "It might have to do with our current mission. If this new Survivor is indeed a real person, he may be able to help us overthrow Quellion."

"Or," Allrianne noted, "he might present a challenge to us for leadership of the city once Quellion does fall."

"True," Sazed admitted. "Either way, I do not see why you are complaining, Breeze. Did you not *want* me to become interested in religions again?"

"That was before I realized you'd spend the entire evening, then the next morning, chattering about it," Breeze said. "Where is Quellion, anyway? If I miss lunch because of his executions, I'll be rather annoyed."

Executions. In his excitement, Sazed had nearly forgotten just what it was they had come to see. His eagerness deflated, and he remembered why Breeze was acting so solemnly. The man spoke lightly, but the concern in his eyes indicated that he was disturbed by the thought of the Citizen burning innocent people to death.

"There," Allrianne said, pointing toward the other side of the market. Something was making a stir: the Citizen, wearing a bright blue costume. It was a new "approved" color—one only he was allowed to wear. His councillors surrounded him in red.

"Finally," Breeze said, following the crowd as they bunched up around the Citizen.

Sazed followed, his steps growing reluctant. Now that he thought about it, he was tempted to use his troops to try to stop what was about to occur. Of course, he knew that would be foolish. Playing his hand now to save a few would ruin their chances of saving the entire city. With a sigh, he followed Breeze and Allrianne, moving with the crowd. He also suspected that watching the murders would remind him of the pressing nature of his duties in Urteau. Theological studies would wait for another time.

"You're going to have to kill them," Kelsier said.

Spook crouched quietly atop a building in the wealthier section of Urteau. Below, the Citizen's procession was approaching; Spook watched it through cloth-wrapped eyes. It had taken many coins—nearly the last of what he'd brought with him from Luthadel—to bribe out the location of the executions sufficiently in advance so that he could get into position.

He could see the sorry individuals that Quellion had decided to murder. Many of them were like Franson's sister—people who had been discovered to have noble parentage. Several others, however, were only spouses of those with noble blood. Spook also knew of one man in this group who had spoken out too loudly against Quellion. The man's connection to the nobility was tenuous. He had once been a craftsman catering specifically to a noble clientele.

"I know you don't want to do it," Kelsier said. "But you can't lose your nerve now."

Spook felt powerful—pewter lent him an air of invincibility that he'd never before imagined. He had slept barely a few hours in the last six days, but he didn't feel tired. He had a sense of balance that any cat would have envied, and he had strength his muscles shouldn't have been able to produce.

And yet, power wasn't everything. His palms were sweating beneath his cloak, and he felt beads of perspiration creeping down his brow. He was no Mistborn. He wasn't Kelsier or Vin. He was just Spook. What was he thinking?

"I can't do it," he whispered.

"You can," Kelsier said. "You've practiced with the cane—I've watched. Plus, you stood against those soldiers in the market. They nearly killed you, but you were fighting two Thugs. You did very well, considering."

"I . . ."

"You need to save those people, Spook. Ask yourself: What would *I* do if I were there?"

"I'm not you."

"Not yet," Kelsier whispered.

Not yet.

Below, Quellion preached against the people about to be executed. Spook could see Beldre, the Citizen's sister, at his side. Spook leaned forward. Was that really a look of sympathy, even pain, in her eyes as she watched the unfortunate prisoners herded toward the building? Or, was that just what Spook wanted to see in her? He followed her gaze, watching the prisoners. One of them was a child, holding fearfully to a woman as the group was prodded into the building that would become their pyre.

Kelsier's right, Spook thought. *I can't let this happen. I may not succeed, but at least I have to try.* His hands continued to shake as he moved through the hatch atop his building and dashed down the steps, cloak whipping behind him. He rounded a corner, heading for the wine cellar.

Noblemen were strange creatures. During the days of

the Lord Ruler, they had often feared for their lives as much as skaa thieves did, for court intrigue often led to imprisonment or assassination. Spook should have realized what he was missing from the beginning. No thieving crew would build a lair without a bolt-hole for emergency escapes.

Why would the nobility be any different?

He leaped, cloak flapping as he dropped the last few steps. He hit the dusty floor, and his enhanced ears heard Quellion begin to rant up above. The skaa crowds were murmuring. The flames had started. There, in the darkened basement of the building, Spook found a section of the wall already open, a secret passageway leading from the building next door. A group of soldiers stood in the passageway.

"Quickly," Spook heard one of them say, "before the fire gets here."

"Please!" another voice cried, her words echoing through the passageway. "At least take the child!"

People grunted. The soldiers moved on the opposite side of the passage from Spook, keeping the people in the other basement from escaping. They had been sent by Quellion to save one of the prisoners. On the outside, the Citizen made a show of denouncing anyone with noble blood. Allomancers, however, were too valuable to kill. And so, he chose his buildings carefully—only burning those with hidden exits through which he could carefully extract the Allomancers.

It was the perfect way to show orthodoxy, yet maintain a grip on the city's most powerful resource. But it wasn't this hypocrisy that made Spook's hands stop shaking as he charged the soldiers.

It was the crying child.

"*Kill them!*" Kelsier screamed.

Spook whipped out his dueling cane. One of the soldiers finally noticed him, spinning in shock.

He fell first.

Spook hadn't realized how hard he could swing. The soldier's helmet flew through the hidden passageway, its metal crumpled. The other soldiers cried out as Spook leaped over their fallen companion in the close confines. They carried swords, but had trouble drawing them.

Spook, however, had brought daggers.

He pulled one free, wielding it with a swing powered by both pewter and fury, enhanced senses guiding his steps. He cut through two soldiers, elbowing their dying bodies aside, pressing his advantage. At the end of the passageway, four soldiers stood with a short skaa man.

Fear shone in their eyes.

Spook threw himself forward, and the shocked soldiers finally overcame their surprise. They pushed backward, throwing open the secret door and stumbling over themselves as they entered the building basement on the other side.

The structure was already well on its way to burning down. Spook could smell the smoke. The rest of the condemned people were in the room—they had probably been trying to get through the doorway to follow their friend who had escaped. Now they were forced backward as the soldiers shoved their way into the room, finally drawing their swords.

Spook gutted the slowest of the four soldiers, then left his dagger in the body, pulling out a second dueling cane. The firm length of wood felt good in his hand as he spun between shocked civilians, attacking the soldiers.

"The soldiers can't be allowed to escape," Kelsier whispered. "Otherwise, Quellion will know that the people were rescued. You have to leave him confused."

Light flickered in a hallway beyond the well-furnished basement room. Firelight. Spook could feel the heat already. Grimly, the three backlit soldiers raised their swords. Smoke began to creep in along the ceiling, spreading like a dark black mist. Prisoners cringed, confused.

Spook dashed forward, spinning as he swung both of his canes at one of the soldiers. The man took the bait, sidestepping Spook's attack, then lunging forward. In an ordinary fight, Spook would have been skewered.

Pewter and tin saved him. Spook moved on feet made light, feeling the wind of the oncoming sword, knowing where it would pass. His heart thudded inside his chest as the sword sliced through the fabric at his side, but missed the flesh. He brought a cane down, cracking the man's sword arm, then smacked another into his skull.

The soldier fell, surprise visible in his dying eyes as Spook pushed past him.

The next soldier was already swinging. Spook brought up both of his canes, crossing them to block. The sword bit through one, spinning half of the cane into the air, but got caught in the second. Spook snapped his weapon to the side, pushing the blade away, then spun inside the man's reach and took him down with an elbow to the stomach.

Spook punched the man's head as he fell. The sound of bone on bone cracked in the burning room. The soldier slumped at Spook's feet.

I can actually do this! Spook thought. *I am like them. Vin and Kelsier. No more hiding in basements or fleeing from danger. I can fight!*

He spun, smiling.

And found the final soldier standing with Spook's own knife held to the neck of a young girl. The soldier stood with his back to the burning hallway, eyeing escape through the hidden passage. Behind the man, flames were curling around the wooden doorframe, licking the room.

"The rest of you, get out!" Spook said, not turning from the soldier. "Go out the back door of the building you find at the end of this tunnel. You'll find men there. They'll hide you in the underground, then get you out of the city. Go!"

Some had already fled, and those who remained moved at his command. The soldier stood, watching, obviously trying to decide his course. He must have known he was facing an Allomancer—no ordinary man could have taken down so many soldiers so quickly. Fortunately, it appeared that Quellion hadn't sent his own Allomancers into the building. He likely kept them above, protecting him.

Spook stood still. He dropped the broken dueling cane, but held the other tightly to keep his hand from shaking. The girl whimpered quietly.

What would Kelsier have done?

Behind him, the last of the prisoners was fleeing into the passage. "You!" Spook said without turning. "Bar that door from the outside. Quickly!"

"But—"

"Do it!" Spook yelled.

"No!" the soldier said, pressing the knife against the girl's neck. "I'll kill her!"

"Do and you die," Spook said. "You know that. Look at me. You're not getting past me. You're—"

The door thunked closed.

The soldier cried out, dropping the girl, rushing toward the door, obviously trying to get to it before the bar fell on the other side. "That's the only way out! You'll get us—"

Spook broke the man's knees with a single crack of the dueling cane. The soldier screamed, falling to the ground. Flames burned on three of the walls, now. The heat was already intense.

The bar clicked into place on the other side of the door. Spook looked down at the soldier. Still alive.

"Leave him," Kelsier said. "Let him burn in the building."

Spook hesitated.

"He would have let all of those people die," Kelsier said. "Let him feel what he would have done to these—what he has already done several times, at Quellion's command."

Spook left the groaning man on the ground, moving over to the secret door. He threw his weight against it.

It held.

Spook cursed quietly, raising a boot and kicking the door. It, however, remained solid.

"That door was built by noblemen who feared they would be pursued by assassins," Kelsier said. "They were familiar with Allomancy, and would make certain the door was strong enough to resist a Thug's kick."

The fire was growing hotter. The girl huddled on the floor, whimpering. Spook whirled, staring down the flames, feeling their heat. He stepped forward, but his amplified senses were so keen that the heat seemed amazingly powerful to him.

He gritted his teeth, picking up the girl.

I have pewter now, he thought. *It can balance the power of my senses.*

That will have to be enough.

Smoke billowed out the windows of the condemned building. Sazed waited with Breeze and Allrianne, standing at the back of a solemn crowd. The people were oddly silent as they watched the flames claim their prize. Perhaps they sensed the truth.

That they could be taken and killed as easily as the poor wretches who died inside.

"How quickly we come around," Sazed whispered. "It wasn't long ago that men were forced to watch the Lord Ruler cut the heads from innocent people. Now we do it to ourselves."

Silence. What sounded like yells came from inside the building. The screams of dying men.

"Kelsier was wrong," Breeze said.

Sazed frowned, turning.

"He blamed the noblemen," Breeze said. "He thought that if we got rid of them, things like this wouldn't happen."

Sazed nodded. Then, oddly, the crowd began to grow restless, shuffling about, murmuring. And, Sazed felt himself agreeing with them. Something needed to be done about this atrocity. Why did nobody fight? Quellion stood there, surrounded by his proud men in red. Sazed gritted his teeth, growing angry.

"Allrianne, dear," Breeze said, "this isn't the time."

Sazed started. He turned, glancing at the young woman. She was crying.

By the Forgotten Gods, Sazed thought, finally recognizing her touch on his emotions, Rioting them to make him angry at Quellion. *She's as good as Breeze is.*

"Why not?" she said. "He deserves it. I could make this crowd rip him apart."

"And his second-in-command would take control," Breeze said, "then execute these people. We haven't prepared enough."

"It seems that you're never done preparing, Breeze," she snapped.

"These things require—"

"Wait," Sazed said, raising a hand. He frowned, watching the building. One of the building's boarded windows—one high in a peaked attic section on top of the roof itself—seemed to be shaking.

"Look!" Sazed said. "There!"

Breeze raised an eyebrow. "Perhaps our Flame God is about to make his appearance, eh?" He smiled at what he obviously found a ridiculous concept. "I wonder what we were supposed to learn during this revolting little experience. Personally, I think the men who sent us here didn't know what they—"

One of the planks suddenly flew off of the window, spinning in the air, swirling smoke behind it. Then the window burst outward.

A figure in dark clothing leaped through the shattering mess of boards and smoke, landing on the rooftop. His long cloak actually appeared to be on fire in places, and he carried a small bundle in his arms. A child. The figure rushed along the top of the burning rooftop, then leaped off the front of the building, trailing smoke as he fell to the ground.

He landed with the grace of a man burning pewter, not stumbling despite the two-story fall, his burning cloak billowing out around him. People backed away, surprised, and Quellion spun in shock.

The man's hood fell back as he stood upright. Only then did Sazed recognize him.

Spook stood tall, seeming in the sunlight to be older than he really was. Or, perhaps, Sazed had never looked at him as anything but a child until that moment. Either way, the young man regarded Quellion proudly, eyes wrapped with a blindfold, his body smoking as he held the coughing child in his arms. He didn't seem the least bit intimidated by the troop of twenty soldiers that surrounded the building.

Breeze cursed quietly. "Allrianne, we're going to need that Riot after all!"

Sazed suddenly felt a weight pressing against him. Breeze Soothed away his distracting emotions—his confusion, his concern—and left Sazed, along with the crowd, completely open to Allrianne's focused burst of enraged anger.

The crowd exploded with motion, people crying out in the name of the Survivor, rushing the guards. For a moment, Sazed feared that Spook wouldn't take the opportunity to run. Despite the strange bandage on Spook's eyes, Sazed could tell that the boy was staring straight at Quellion—as if in challenge.

Fortunately, however, Spook finally turned away. The crowd distracted the advancing soldiers, and Spook ran on feet that seemed to move far too quickly. He ducked down an alleyway, carrying the girl he had rescued, his cloak trailing smoke. As soon as Spook had a safe head start, Breeze smothered the crowd's will to rebel, keeping them from getting themselves cut down by the soldiers. The people backed away, dispersing. The Citizen's soldiers, however, stayed close around their leader. Sazed could hear frustration in the Citizen's voice as he called for the inevitable retreat. He couldn't spare more than a few men to chase down Spook, not with the potential of a riot. He had to get himself to safety.

As soldiers marched away, Breeze turned an eye toward Sazed. "Well," he noted, "*that* was somewhat unexpected."

I think that the koloss were more intelligent than we wanted to give them credit for being. For instance, originally, they used only spikes the Lord Ruler gave them to make new members. He would provide the metal and the unfortunate skaa captives, and the koloss would create new "recruits."

At the Lord Ruler's death, then, the koloss should quickly have died out. This was how he had designed them. If they got free from his control, he expected them to kill themselves off and end their own rampage. However, they somehow made the deduction that spikes in the bodies of fallen koloss could be harvested, then reused.

They then no longer required a fresh supply of spikes. I often wonder what effect the constant reuse of spikes had on their population. A spike can only hold so much of a Hemalurgic charge, so they could not create spikes that granted infinite strength, no matter how many people those spikes killed and drew power from. However, did the repeated reuse of spikes perhaps bring more humanity to the koloss they made?

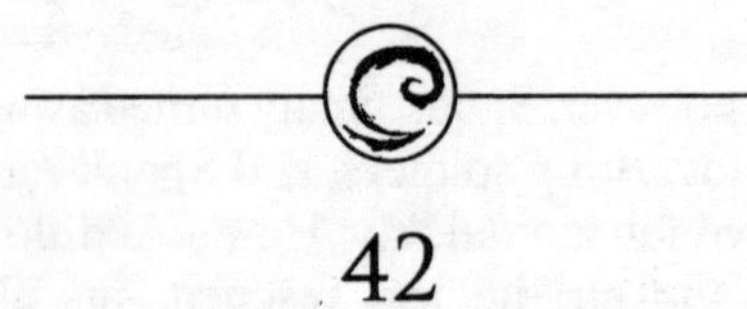

42

WHEN MARSH ENTERED LUTHADEL, HE was far more careful than he had been when he'd entered the nameless town at the western border of the dominance. An Inquisitor moving through the capital of Elend's empire would not go unreported, and might draw undue attention. The emperor was gone, and he had left his playground open to be used by others. No need to spoil that.

So, Marsh moved at night, hooded cloak up, burning steel and jumping about on coins. Even so, seeing the magnificent city—sprawling, dirty, yet still *home*—was hard for the watching, waiting part of Marsh. Once, Marsh himself had run the skaa rebellion in this city. He felt responsible for its occupants, and the thought of Ruin doing to them what he'd done to the people of the other town, the one where the ashmount had blown . . .

There was no ashmount that close to Luthadel. Unfortunately, there were things Ruin could do to a city that didn't involve natural forces. On his way to Luthadel, Marsh had stopped at no fewer than four villages, where he had secretly killed the men guarding their food stores, then set fire to the buildings that contained them. He knew that the other Inquisitors went about the world, committing similar atrocities as they searched for the thing Ruin desired above all others. The thing Preservation had taken from him.

He had yet to find it.

Marsh leaped over a street, landing atop a peaked rooftop, running along its edge and making his way toward the northeastern side of the city. Luthadel had changed during the year since he'd last seen it. The Lord Ruler's forced labor projects had brutalized the skaa, but had kept things clean of ash and given even the oversized city a sense of order. There was none of that now. Growing food was obviously a priority—and keeping the city clean could wait for later, if there was a later.

There were far more trash heaps now, and mounds of ash—which would have once been scraped into the river at the center of the city—slumped in alleys and against buildings. Marsh felt himself begin to smile at the beauty of the disrepair, and his little, rebellious part withdrew and hid.

He couldn't fight. Now was not the time.

He soon arrived at Keep Venture, seat of Elend's government. It had been invaded by koloss during the siege of Luthadel, its lower stained-glass windows shattered by the beasts. The windows had been replaced only by boards. Marsh smiled, then Steelpush-leaped up to a balcony on the second floor. He was familiar with this building. Before he'd been taken by Ruin, he had spent several months living here, helping Emperor Venture keep control in his city.

Marsh found Penrod's rooms easily. They were the only ones occupied, and the only ones guarded. Marsh crouched a few corridors down, watching with his inhuman eyes as he considered his next course of action.

Impaling an unwilling subject with a Hemalurgic spike was a very tricky prospect. The spike's size was, in this case, immaterial. Just as a pinch of metal dust could fuel Allomancy for a time, or a small ring could hold a small Feruchemical charge, a rather small bit of metal could work for Hemalurgy. Inquisitor spikes were made large to be intimidating, but a small pin could, in many instances, be just as effective as a massive spike. It depended on how long one wanted to leave the spike outside of a person's body after using it to kill someone.

For Marsh's purposes this day, a small spike was preferable; he didn't want to give Penrod powers, just pierce him with metal. Marsh pulled out the spike he had made from the Allomancer in the doomed town a few days back. It was about five inches long—actually bigger than it needed to be, strictly speaking. However, Marsh would need to drive this spike forcefully into a man's body, which meant it needed to be at least large enough to hold its shape. There were some two or three hundred bind points across a human's body. Marsh didn't know them all; Ruin would guide his hand when the time came to strike, making sure the spike was delivered to the right place. His master's direct attention was focused elsewhere at the moment, and he was giving Marsh general commands to get into position and prepare for the attack.

Hemalurgic spikes. The hidden part of himself shivered, remembering the day when he had unexpectedly been made into an Inquisitor. He'd thought that he had been discovered. He'd been working as a spy for Kelsier in the Steel Priesthood. Little did he know that he hadn't been singled out as suspicious—he'd been singled out as extraordinary.

The Inquisitors had come for him at night, while he'd waited nervously to meet with Kelsier and pass on what he assumed would be his final message to the rebellion. They'd burst through the door, moving more quickly than Marsh could react. They gave him no option. They'd simply slammed him down against the ground, then thrown a screaming woman on top of him.

Then, the Inquisitors had pounded a spike right through her heart and into Marsh's eye.

The pain was too great for him to remember. That moment

was a hole in his memory, filled with vague images of the Inquisitors repeating this process, killing other unfortunate Allomancers and pounding their powers—their very souls, it seemed—into Marsh's body. When it was finished, he lay groaning on the floor, a new flood of sensory information making it difficult for him even to think. Around him, the other Inquisitors had danced about, cutting apart the other bodies with their axes, rejoicing in the addition of another member to their ranks.

That was, in a way, the day of his birth. What a wonderful day. Penrod, however, would not have such joy. He wasn't to be made into an Inquisitor—he would get only a single, small spike. One that had been made days ago, and been allowed to sit outside a body—leaking power—all that time.

Marsh waited for Ruin to come to him in force. Not only would the spike have to be planted precisely, but Penrod would have to leave it in long enough for Ruin to begin influencing his thoughts and emotions. The spike had to touch the blood—at first, at least. After the spike was pounded in, the skin could heal around the metal, and the spike would still work. However, to begin with, there would be blood.

How did one make a person forget about five inches of metal sprouting from their body? How did one make others ignore it? Ruin had tried to get a spike into Elend Venture on several occasions now, and had always failed. In fact, most attempts failed. The few people claimed with the process, however, were worth the effort.

Ruin came upon him, and he lost control of his body. He moved without knowing what he was going to do, following direct orders. *Down the corridor. Don't attack the guards. In through the door.*

Marsh shoved aside the two watching soldiers, kicking the door down and bursting into the antechamber.

Right. To the bedchamber.

Marsh was through the room in a heartbeat, the two soldiers

belatedly screaming for help outside. Penrod was an aging man with a dignified air. He had the presence of mind to leap from his bed at the sounds, grabbing a hardwood dueling cane from its place atop his nightstand.

Marsh smiled. A dueling cane? Against an Inquisitor? He pulled his obsidian hand axe from the sheath at his side.

Fight him, Ruin said, *but do not kill him. Make it a difficult battle, but allow him to feel that he's holding you off.*

It was an odd request, but Marsh's mind was so directly controlled that he couldn't even pause to think about it. He could simply leap forward to attack.

It was harder than it seemed. He had to make sure to strike with the axe in ways that Penrod could block. Several times, he had to tap speed from one of his spikes—which doubled as a Feruchemical metalmind—to suddenly inch his axe in the right direction, lest he accidentally behead the king of Luthadel.

Yet, Marsh did it. He cut Penrod a few times, fighting all the while with the small spike held hidden in his left palm, letting the king think he was doing well. Within moments, the guards had joined the fight, which allowed Marsh to keep up appearances even better. Three normal men against an Inquisitor was still no contest, but from their perspectives, maybe it would seem like one.

It wasn't long before a troop of some dozen guards burst into the chamber outside the bedroom, coming to aid their king.

Now, Ruin said. *Act frightened, get ready to put the spike in, and prepare to flee out the window.*

Marsh tapped speed and moved. Ruin guided his hand precisely as he slammed his left hand into Penrod's chest, driving the spike directly into the man's heart. Marsh heard Penrod scream, smiled at the sound, and leaped out the window.

A short time later, Marsh hung outside that same window, unseen and unnoticed, even by the numerous guard patrols.

He was far too skilled, far too careful, to be spotted listening with tin-enhanced ears, hanging underneath an outcropping of stone near the window. Inside, surgeons conferred.

"When we try to pull the spike out, the bleeding increases dramatically, my lord," one voice explained.

"The shard of metal got dangerously close to your heart," said another.

Dangerously close? Marsh thought with a smile from his upside-down perch. *The spike pierced his heart.* But, of course, the surgeons couldn't know that. Since Penrod was conscious, they would assume that the spike had come close, but somehow just barely missed.

"We fear pulling it out," the first surgeon said. "How . . . do you feel?"

"Remarkably good, actually," said Penrod. "There is an ache, and some discomfort. But I feel strong."

"Then let us leave the shard, for now," the first surgeon said, sounding concerned. But, what else could he do? If he *did* pull the spike out, it *would* kill Penrod. A clever move by Ruin.

They would wait for Penrod to regain his strength, then try again to remove the spike. Again, it would threaten Penrod's life. They'd have to leave it. And, with Ruin now able to touch his mind—not control him, just nudge things in certain directions—Penrod would soon forget about the spike. The discomfort would fade, and with the spike under his clothing, no one would find it irregular.

And then he would be Ruin's as surely as any Inquisitor. Marsh smiled, let go of the outcropping, and dropped to the dark streets below.

For all that it disgusts me, I cannot help but be impressed by Hemalurgy as an art.

In Allomancy and Feruchemy, skill and subtlety come through the application of one's powers. The best Allomancer might not be the most powerful, but instead the one who can best manipulate the Pushes and Pulls of metals. The best Feruchemist is the one who is most capable of sorting the information in his copperminds, or best able to manipulate his weight with iron.

The art that is unique to Hemalurgy, however, is the knowledge of where to place the spikes.

43

VIN LANDED WITH A HUSHED rustle of cloth. She crouched in the night, holding up her dress to keep it from brushing the ashen rooftop, then peered into the mists.

Elend dropped beside her, then fell into a crouch, asking no questions. She smiled, noting that his instincts were getting better. He watched the mists too, though he obviously didn't know what he was looking for.

"He's following us," Vin whispered.

"Yomen's Mistborn?" Elend asked.

Vin nodded.

"Where?" he asked.

"Three houses back," Vin said.

Elend squinted, and she felt one of his Allomantic pulses suddenly increase in speed. He was flaring tin.

"That lump on the right side?" Elend asked.

"Close enough," Vin said.

"So . . ."

"So, he knows I've spotted him," Vin said. "Otherwise, I wouldn't have stopped. Right now, we're studying one another."

Elend reached to his belt, slipping out an obsidian knife.

"He won't attack," Vin said.

"How do you know?"

"Because," Vin said. "When he intends to kill us, he'll try

to do it when you and I aren't together—or when we're sleeping."

That seemed to make Elend even more nervous. "Is that why you've been staying up all night lately?"

Vin nodded. Forcing Elend to sleep alone was a small price to pay for keeping him safe. *Is it you back there following us, Yomen?* she wondered. *On the night of your own party? That would be quite the feat.* It didn't seem likely; but still, Vin was suspicious. She had a habit of suspecting *everyone* of being Mistborn. She still thought it was healthy, even if she had been wrong more often than not.

"Come on," she said, rising. "Once we get into the party, we shouldn't have to worry about him."

Elend nodded, and the two continued along their path to the Canton of Resource.

The plan is simple, Elend had said just hours before. *I'll confront Yomen, and the nobility won't be able to help gathering around to gawk. At that point, you sneak away and see if you can find your way to the storage chamber.*

It really was a simple plan—the best ones usually were. If Elend confronted Yomen, it would keep the attention of the guards on him, hopefully letting Vin slip out. She'd have to move quickly and quietly, and would probably have to eliminate some guards—all without raising an alarm. Yet, this appeared to be the only way in. Not only was Yomen's fortress-like building well lit and extremely well guarded, but his Mistborn was good. The man had detected her every other time she'd tried to sneak in—always remaining at a distance, his mere presence warning her that he could raise the alarm in a heartbeat.

Their best chance was the ball. Yomen's defenses, and his Mistborn, would be focused on their master, keeping him safe.

They landed in the courtyard, causing carriages to stop and guards to turn in shock. Vin glanced to Elend in the misty darkness. "Elend," she said quietly, "I need you to promise me something."

He frowned. "What?"

"Eventually, I'm going to get spotted," Vin said. "I'll sneak as best I can, but I doubt we'll get through this without creating a disturbance. When it hits, I want you to get out."

"Vin, I can't do that. I have to—"

"No," Vin said sharply. "Elend, you don't have to help me. You *can't* help me. I love you, but you're just not as good at this as I am. I can take care of myself, but I need to know that I won't have to take care of you, too. If anything goes wrong—or, if things go right, but the building goes on alert—I want you to get out. I'll meet you at the camp."

"And if you get into trouble?" Elend said.

Vin smiled. "Trust me."

He paused, then nodded. Trusting her was one thing he could obviously do—something he'd always done.

The two strode forward. It felt very strange to be attending a ball at a Ministry building. Vin was accustomed to stained glass and ornamentation, but Canton offices were generally austere—and this one was no exception. It was only a single story tall, and it had sharp, flat walls with very small windows. No limelights illuminated the outside, and while a couple of large tapestry banners fluttered against the stonework, the only indication that this night was special was the cluster of carriages and nobility in the courtyard. The soldiers in the area had noted Vin and Elend, but made no move to engage—or even slow—them.

Those watching—both nobility and soldiers—were interested, but few of them looked surprised. Vin and Elend were expected. Vin's hunch about that was confirmed when she moved up the steps, and nobody moved to intercept them. The guards at the door watched suspiciously, but let her and Elend pass.

Inside, she found a long entry hall, lit by lamps. The flow of people turned left, so Vin and Elend followed, twisting through a few labyrinthine corridors until they approached a larger meeting hall.

"Not exactly the most impressive place for a ball, eh?" Elend said as they waited their turn to be announced.

Vin nodded. Most noble keeps had exterior entrances directly into their ballroom. The room ahead—from what she could see of it—had been adapted from a standard Ministry meeting room. Rivets covered the floor where benches had once been, and there was a stage on the far side of the room, where obligators had probably once stood to give instruction to their subordinates. This was where Yomen's table had been set up.

It was too small to be a truly practical ballroom. The people inside weren't cramped, exactly, but neither did they have the space the nobility preferred for forming separate little groups where they could gossip.

"Looks like there are other party rooms," Elend said, nodding to several corridors leading from the main "ballroom." People were trailing in and out of them.

"Places for people to go if they feel too crowded," Vin said. "This is going to be a tough place to escape, Elend. Don't let yourself get cornered. Looks like an exit over there to the left."

Elend followed her gaze as they walked into the main room. Flickering torchlight and trails of mist indicated a courtyard or atrium. "I'll stay close to it," he said. "And avoid going to any of the smaller side rooms."

"Good," Vin said. She also noted something else—twice during the trip through the corridors to the ballroom, she'd seen stairwells leading down. That implied a fairly large basement, something uncommon back in Luthadel. *The Canton building goes down, rather than up,* she decided. It made sense, assuming that there really was a storage cache below.

The door herald announced them without needing a card to read from, and the two entered the room. The party was nowhere near as lavish as the one at Keep Orielle had been. There were snacks, but no dinner—likely because there wasn't room for dining tables. There was music and dancing, but the room was not draped in finery. Yomen had elected to leave the simple, stark Ministry walls uncovered.

"I wonder why he even bothers to hold balls," Vin whispered.

"He probably had to start them," Elend said. "To prompt the other nobility. Now he's part of the rotation. It's smart of him, though. It gives a man some measure of power to be able to draw the nobility into his home and be their host."

Vin nodded, then eyed the dance floor. "One dance before we split up?"

Elend wavered. "To tell you the truth, I feel a bit too nervous."

Vin smiled, then kissed him lightly, completely breaking noble protocol. "Give me about an hour before the distraction. I want to get a feel for the party before I sneak away."

He nodded, and they split, Elend heading directly for a group of men that Vin didn't recognize. Vin herself kept moving. She didn't want to get bogged down by conversation, so she avoided the women she recognized from Keep Orielle. She knew that she should probably have worked to reinforce her contacts, but the truth was that she felt a little bit of what Elend did. Not truly nervousness, but rather a desire to avoid typical ball activities. She wasn't here to mingle. She had more important tasks to be concerned with.

So, she meandered through the ballroom, sipping a cup of wine and studying the guards. There were a lot of them, which was probably good. The more guards there were in the ballroom, the fewer there would be in the rest of the building. Theoretically.

Vin kept moving, nodding to people, but withdrawing anytime one of them tried to make conversation with her. If she had been Yomen, she would have ordered a few particular soldiers to keep watch on her, just to make certain that she didn't stray anywhere sensitive. Yet, none of the men seemed to be all that focused on her. As the hour passed, she grew more and more frustrated. Was Yomen really so incompetent that he wouldn't keep watch on a known Mistborn who entered his home base?

Annoyed, Vin burned bronze. Perhaps there were Allomancers nearby. She nearly jumped in shock when she felt the Allomantic pulsings coming from just beside her.

There were two of them. Courtly puffs—women whose

names she didn't know, but who looked distinctly dismissible. That was probably the idea. They stood chatting with a couple of other women a short distance from Vin. One was burning copper, the other was burning tin—Vin would never have picked them out if she hadn't had the ability to pierce copperclouds.

As Vin drifted through the room, the two followed, moving with an impressive level of skill as they slid in and out of conversations. They always stuck close enough to Vin to be within tin-enhanced hearing range, yet stayed far enough away in the relatively crowded room that Vin would never have picked them out without Allomantic help.

Interesting, she thought, moving toward the perimeter of the room. At least Yomen wasn't underestimating her. But now, how to give the women the slip? They wouldn't be distracted by Elend's disturbance, and they certainly wouldn't let Vin sneak away without raising an alarm.

As she wandered, working on the problem, she noted a familiar figure sitting at the edge of the ballroom. Slowswift sat in his usual suit, smoking his pipe as he relaxed in one of the chairs set out for the elderly or the overdanced. She trailed over toward him.

"I thought you didn't come to these things," she noted, smiling. Behind, her two shadows expertly worked their way into a conversation a short distance away.

"I only come when my king holds them," Slowswift said.

"Ah," Vin said, then she drifted away. Out of the corner of her eye, she noted Slowswift frowning. He'd obviously expected her to speak to him further, but she couldn't risk his saying anything incriminating. At least, not yet. Her tails extricated themselves from their conversation, the speed of Vin's departure forcing them to do so awkwardly. After walking for a bit, Vin paused, giving the women the chance to get themselves into yet another conversation.

Then, Vin spun and walked quickly back to Slowswift, trying to look as if she'd just remembered something. Her tails, intent on looking natural, had trouble following. They hesitated, and Vin gained just a few short breaths of freedom.

She leaned down to Slowswift as she passed. "I need two men," she said. "Ones you trust against Yomen. Have them meet me in a part of the party that is more secluded, a place where people can sit and chat."

"The patio," Slowswift said. "Down the left corridor, then outside."

"Good," Vin said. "Tell your men to go there, but then wait until I approach them. Also, please send a messenger to Elend. Tell him I need another half hour."

Slowswift nodded to the cryptic comment, and Vin smiled as her shadows trailed closer. "I hope you feel better soon," she said, putting on a fond smile.

"Thank you, my dear," Slowswift said, coughing slightly.

Vin trailed away again. She slowly made her way in the direction Slowswift had indicated, the exit she'd picked out earlier. Sure enough, a few moments later she passed into mist. *The mist vanishes inside buildings, eventually,* Vin thought. *Everyone always assumes it has something to do with heat, or perhaps the lack of airflow. . . .*

In a few seconds, she found herself standing on a lantern-lit garden patio. Though tables had been set up for people to relax, the patio was sparsely populated. Servants wouldn't go out in the mists, and most nobility—though they didn't like to admit it—found the mists disconcerting. Vin wandered over to an ornate metal railing, then leaned against it, looking up at the sky, feeling the mists around her and idly fingering her earring.

Soon, her two shadows appeared, chatting quietly, and Vin's tin let her hear that they were talking about how stuffy the other room had been. Vin smiled, maintaining her posture as the two women took chairs a distance away, continuing to chat. After that, two young men wandered in and sat down at another table. They weren't as natural about the process as the women, but Vin hoped they weren't suspicious enough to draw attention.

Then, she waited.

Life as a thief—a life spent preparing for jobs, watching in spy holes, and carefully choosing just the right opportunity to pick a pocket—had taught her patience. It was one urchin attribute she had never lost. She stood, staring at the sky, giving no indication at all that she intended to leave. Now, she simply had to wait for the distraction.

You shouldn't have relied on him for the distraction, Reen whispered in her mind. *He'll fail. Never let your life depend on the competence of someone whose life isn't also on the line.*

It had been one of Reen's favorite sayings. She didn't think of him very often, anymore—or, really, anyone from her old life. That life had been one of pain and sorrow. A brother who beat her to keep her safe, a crazy mother who had inexplicably slaughtered Vin's baby sister.

However, that life was only a faint echo, now. She smiled to herself, amused at how far she had come. Reen might have called her a fool, but she trusted Elend—trusted him to succeed, trusted him with her life. That was something she could never have done during her early years.

After about ten minutes, someone came out from the party and wandered over to the pair of women. He spoke with them just briefly, then returned to the party. Another man came twenty minutes after that, doing the same thing. Hopefully, the women were passing on the information Vin wished: that Vin had apparently decided to spend an indeterminate amount of time outside, staring at the mists. Those inside wouldn't expect her to return anytime soon.

A few moments after the second messenger returned to the party, a man rushed out and approached one of the tables. "You have to come hear this!" he whispered to the people at the table—the only ones currently on the patio who had nothing to do with Vin. That group left. Vin smiled. Elend's distraction had come.

Vin jumped into the air, then Pushed against the railing beside her, launching herself across the patio.

The women had obviously grown bored, chatting idly to themselves. It took them a few moments to notice Vin's movement. In those moments, Vin shot across the now-empty patio, dress flapping as she flew. One of the women opened her mouth to yell.

Vin extinguished her metals, then burned duralumin and brass, *Pushing* on the emotions of both women.

She'd done this only once before, to Straff Venture. A duralumin-fueled Brasspush was a terrible thing; it flattened a person's emotions, making them feel empty, completely void of all feeling. Both women gasped, and the one who had been standing stumbled to the ground instead, falling silent.

Vin landed hard, her pewter still off lest she mix it with duralumin. She put her pewter back on immediately, however, rolling up to her feet. She took one of the women with an elbow to the stomach, then grabbed her face and slammed it down into the table, knocking her out. The other woman sat dazedly on the ground. Vin grimaced, then grabbed the woman by the throat, choking her.

It felt brutal, but Vin didn't let up until the woman fell unconscious—proven by the fact that she let her Allomantic coppercloud fall. Vin sighed, releasing the woman. The unconscious spy slumped to the floor.

Vin turned. Slowswift's young men stood by anxiously. Vin waved them over.

"Stash these two in the bushes," Vin said quickly, "then sit at the table. If anyone asks after them, say that you saw them follow me back into the party. Hopefully, that will keep everyone confused."

The men flushed. "We—"

"Do as I say or flee," Vin snapped. "Don't argue with me. I left them both alive, and I can't afford to let them report that I've escaped their watch. If they stir, you'll have to knock them out again."

The men nodded reluctantly.

Vin reached up and unbuttoned her dress, letting the garment fall to the ground and revealing the sleek, dark clothing she wore underneath. She gave the dress to the men to hide as well, then moved into the building, away from the party. Inside the misty corridor, she found a stairwell, and slipped down it. Elend's distraction would be in full progress by now. Hopefully, it would last long enough.

"That's right," Elend said, arms folded, staring down Yomen. "A duel. Why make the armies fight for the city? You and I could settle this ourselves."

Yomen didn't laugh at the ridiculous idea. He simply sat at his table, his thoughtful eyes set in a bald, tattooed head, the single bead of atium tied to his forehead sparkling in the lantern-light. The rest of the crowd was reacting just as Elend had expected. Conversations had died, and people had rushed in, packing into the main ballroom to watch the confrontation between emperor and king.

"Why do you think that I would consent to such a thing?" Yomen finally asked.

"All accounts say that you are a man of honor."

"But you are not," Yomen said, pointing at Elend. "This very offer proves that. You are an Allomancer—there would be no contest between us. What honor would there be in that?"

Elend didn't really care. He just wanted Yomen occupied as long as possible. "Then choose a champion," he said. "I'll fight him instead."

"Only a Mistborn would be a match for you," Yomen said.

"Then send one against me."

"Alas, I have none. I won my kingdom through fairness, legality, and the Lord Ruler's grace—not through threat of assassination, like yourself."

No Mistborn, you say? Elend thought, smiling. *So, your "fairness, legality, and grace" don't preclude lying?* "You would really let your people die?" Elend said loudly, sweeping his hand across the room. More and more people were gathering to watch. "All because of your pride?"

"Pride?" Yomen said, leaning forward. "You call it pride to defend your own rule? I call it pride to march your armies into another man's kingdom, seeking to intimidate him with barbaric monsters."

"Monsters your own Lord Ruler created and used to intimidate and conquer as well," Elend said.

Yomen paused. "Yes, the Lord Ruler created the koloss," he said. "It was his prerogative to determine how they were used. Besides, he kept them far away from civilized cities—yet you march them right up to our doorstep."

"Yes," Elend said, "and they haven't attacked. That's because I can control them as the Lord Ruler did. Wouldn't that suggest that I have inherited his right to rule?"

Yomen frowned, perhaps noticing that Elend's arguments kept changing—that he was saying whatever came to mind in order to keep the discussion going.

"You may be unwilling to save this city," Elend said, "but there are others in it who are wiser. You don't think I came here without allies, do you?"

Yomen paused again.

"Yes," Elend said, scanning the crowd. "You're not just fighting me, Yomen. You're fighting your own people. Which ones will betray you, when the time comes? How well can you trust them, exactly?"

Yomen snorted. "Idle threats, Venture. What is this really about?" However, Elend could tell that his words bothered Yomen. The man *didn't* trust the local nobility. He would have been a fool to do so.

Elend smiled, preparing his next argument. He could keep this discussion going for quite some time. For, if there was one thing in particular that he had learned by growing up in his father's house it was this: how to annoy people.

You have your distraction, Vin, Elend thought. *Let's hope you can end the fight for this city before it really begins.*

Each spike, positioned very carefully, can determine how the recipient's body is changed by Hemalurgy. A spike in one place creates a monstrous, near-mindless beast. In another place, a spike will create a crafty—yet homicidal—Inquisitor.

Without the instinctive knowledge granted by taking the power at the Well of Ascension, Rashek would never have been able to use Hemalurgy. With his mind expanded, and with a little practice, he was able to intuit where to place spikes that would create the servants he wanted.

It is a little-known fact that the Inquisitors' torture chambers were actually Hemalurgic laboratories. The Lord Ruler was constantly trying to develop new breeds of servant. It is a testament to Hemalurgy's complexity that, despite a thousand years of trying, he never managed to create anything with it beyond the three kinds of creatures he developed during those few brief moments holding the power.

44

VIN CREPT DOWN THE STONE stairwell, small sounds echoing eerily from below. She had no torch or lantern, and the stairwell was not lit, but enough light reflected up from below to let her tin-enhanced eyes see.

The more she thought about it, the more the large basement made sense. This was the Canton of Resource—the arm of the Ministry that had been in charge of feeding the people, maintaining the canals, and supplying the other Cantons. Vin supposed that this basement had once been well stocked with supplies. If the cache really was here, it would be the first that she had discovered hidden beneath a Canton of Resource building. Vin expected great things from it. What better place to hide your atium and your most important resources than with an organization that was in charge of transportation and storage across the entire empire?

The stairwell was simple, utilitarian, and steep. Vin wrinkled her nose at the musty air, which seemed all the more stuffy to her tin-enhanced sense of smell. Still, she was grateful for tin's enhanced vision, not to mention the enhanced hearing, which let her hear clinking armor below—an indication that she needed to move quite carefully.

And so she did. She reached the bottom of the stairwell and peeked around the corner. Three narrow stone corridors split off from the stairwell landing, each heading in a different direction at ninety-degree angles. The sounds were coming from the right, and as Vin leaned out a bit more, she nearly jumped as she saw a pair of guards standing lazily against the wall a short distance away.

Guards standing in the corridors, Vin thought, ducking back into the stairwell. *Yomen definitely wants to protect something down here.*

Vin crouched down on the rough, cool stone. Pewter, steel, and iron were of relatively little use at the moment. She could take down both guards, but it would be risky, since she couldn't afford to make any noise. She didn't know where the cache was—and therefore couldn't afford to make a disturbance, not yet.

Vin closed her eyes, burning brass and zinc. She carefully—and slowly—Soothed the emotions of the two soldiers. She heard them settle back, leaning against the side of the corridor. Then, she Rioted their sense of boredom, tugging on that single emotion. She peeked around the corner again, keeping the pressure on, waiting.

One of the men yawned. A few seconds later, the other one did. Then they both yawned at once. And Vin scuttled straight across the landing and into the shadowed hallway beyond. She pressed herself up against the wall, heart beating quickly, and waited. No cry came, though one of the guards did mumble something about being tired.

Vin smiled in excitement. It had been a long time since she'd had to truly sneak. She had spied and scouted, but had trusted on the mists, the darkness, and her ability to move quickly to protect her. This was different. It reminded her of the days when she and Reen had burgled houses.

What would my brother say now? she wondered, padding down the corridor on unnaturally light, quiet feet. *He'd think*

I've gone crazy, sneaking into a building not for wealth, but for information. To Reen, life had been about survival—the simple, harsh facts of survival. Trust nobody. Make yourself invaluable to your team, but don't be too threatening. Be ruthless. Stay alive.

She hadn't abandoned his lessons. They'd always be part of her—they were what had kept her alive and careful, even during her years with Kelsier's crew. She just no longer listened to them exclusively. She tempered them with trust and hope.

Your trust will get you killed someday, Reen seemed to whisper in the back of her mind. But, of course, even Reen himself hadn't stuck to his code perfectly. He'd died protecting Vin, refusing to give her up to the Inquisitors, even though doing so might have saved his life.

Vin continued forward. It soon became evident that the basement was an extensive grid of narrow corridors surrounding larger rooms. She peeked into one, creaking the door open, and found some supplies. They were basic kinds of things, flour and the like—not the carefully canned, organized, and catalogued long-term supplies of a storage cache.

There must be a loading dock down one of these corridors, Vin guessed. *It probably slopes up, leading to that subcanal that runs into the city.*

Vin moved on, but she knew she wouldn't have time to search each of the basement's many rooms. She approached another intersection of corridors, and crouched down, frowning. Elend's diversion wouldn't last forever, and someone would eventually discover the women she'd knocked unconscious. She needed to get to the cache quickly.

She glanced around. The corridors were sparsely lit by the occasional lamp. Yet, there seemed to be more light coming from the left. She moved down this corridor, and the lamps became more frequent. Soon, she caught the sound of voices, and she moved more carefully, approaching another intersection. She peeked down it. To the left, she noted a pair of soldiers standing in the distance. To her right, there were four.

Right it is, then, she thought. However, this was going to be a little more difficult.

She closed her eyes, listening carefully. She could hear both groups of soldiers, but there seemed to be something else. Other groups in the distance. Vin picked one of these and begin to Pull with a powerful Riot of emotions. Soothing and Rioting weren't blocked by stone or steel—during the days of the Final Empire, the Lord Ruler had set up Soothers in various sections of the skaa slums, letting them Soothe away the emotions of everyone nearby, affecting hundreds, even thousands, of people at once.

She waited. Nothing happened. She was trying to Riot the men's sense of anger and irritability. However, she didn't even know if she was Pulling in the right direction. In addition, Rioting and Soothing weren't as precise as Pushing steel. Breeze always explained that the emotional makeup of a person was a complex jumble of thoughts, instincts, and feelings. An Allomancer couldn't control minds or actions. He could only nudge.

Unless . . .

Taking a deep breath, Vin extinguished all of her metals. Then, she burned duralumin and zinc, and *Pulled* in the direction of the distant guards, hitting them with a powerfully enhanced burst of emotional Allomancy.

Immediately, a curse echoed through the hallway. Vin cringed. Fortunately, the noise wasn't directed at her. The guards in the corridor perked up, and the argument in the distance grew louder, more fervent. Vin didn't need to burn tin to hear when the scuffle broke out, men yelling at each other.

The guards to the left rushed away, moving to find out what the source of the disturbance was. The ones to her right left two men behind, however, and so Vin drank a vial of metal, then Rioted their emotions, enhancing their senses of curiosity to the point of breaking.

The two men left, rushing after their companions, and Vin

scurried down the corridor. She soon saw that her instincts had proven right—the four men had been guarding a door into one of the storage rooms. Vin took a deep breath, then opened the door and ducked inside. The trapdoor inside was closed, but she knew what to look for. She pulled it open, then jumped into the darkness beneath her.

She Pushed down a coin as she fell, using the sound of its hitting to let her know how far down the floor was. She landed on rough stonework, standing in complete darkness—pitch black beyond even what tin would let her see in. She felt around, however, and found a lantern on the wall. She pulled out her flint, and soon had light.

And there it was, the door in the wall leading into the storage cavern. The rock mountings had been torn apart, the door forced. The wall was still there, and the door itself was intact, but getting it open had obviously taken some great amount of work. The door was open slightly, barely wide enough for a person to get through. It had obviously taken Yomen a lot of effort to even get it that far.

He must have known it was here, Vin thought, standing up straight. *But . . . why break it open like this? He has a Mistborn who could have opened the door with a Steelpull.*

Heart fluttering in anticipation, Vin slipped through the opening and into the silent storage cache. She immediately jumped down to the cache floor and began searching for the plate that would contain the Lord Ruler's information. She just had to—

Stone scraped against stone behind her.

Vin spun, feeling an instant of sharp and dreadful realization.

The stone door shut behind her.

". . . and *that*," Elend said, "is why the Lord Ruler's system of government *had* to fall."

He was losing them. He could tell—more and more people were trailing away from the argument. The problem was, Yomen actually *was* interested.

"You make a mistake, young Venture," the obligator said, tapping the table idly with his fork. "The sixth-century stewardship program was not even devised by the Lord Ruler. The newly formed Canton of Inquisition proposed it as a means of population control for the Terris, and the Lord Ruler agreed to it provisionally."

"That provision turned into a means of subjugating an entire race of people," Elend said.

"That subjugation started far earlier," Yomen said. "Everyone knows the history of this, Venture. The Terris were a people who absolutely refused to submit to imperial rule, and they had to be strictly reined in. However, can you honestly say that Terris stewards were treated poorly? They're the most honored servants in all of the empire!"

"I'd hardly call being made into a favored slave a fair return for losing one's manhood," Elend said, raising an eyebrow and folding his arms.

"There are at least a dozen sources I could quote you on that," Yomen said with a wave of his hand. "What about Trendalan? He claimed that being made a eunuch had left him free to pursue more potent thoughts of logic and of harmony, since he wasn't distracted by worldly lusts."

"He didn't have a choice in the matter," Elend said.

"Few of us have choice in our stations," Yomen replied.

"I prefer people to have that choice," Elend said. "You'll notice that I have given the skaa freedom in my lands, and given the nobility a parliamentary council by which they have a hand in ruling the city in which they live."

"High ideals," Yomen said, "and I recognize Trendalan's own words in what you claim to have done. However, even he said that it would be unlikely for such a system to continue in stability for very long."

Elend smiled. It had been a long time since he'd had such a good argument. Ham never delved deeply into topics—he liked philosophical questions, but not scholarly debates—and Sazed just didn't like to argue.

I wish I could have met Yomen when I was younger, Elend

thought. *Back when I had time to simply worry about philosophy. Oh, the discussions we could have had. . . .*

Of course, those discussions probably would have ended up with Elend in the hands of the Steel Inquisitors for being a revolutionary. Still, he had to admit that Yomen was no fool. He knew his history and his politics—he just happened to have completely erroneous beliefs. Another day, Elend would have been happy to persuade him of that fact.

Unfortunately, this particular argument was growing increasingly tense for Elend. He couldn't maintain both Yomen's attention and that of the crowd. Each time he tried to do something to get the crowd back, Yomen seemed to get suspicious—and each time Elend actually tried to engage the king, the crowd itself grew bored with the philosophical debate.

So it was that Elend was actually relieved when the yells of surprise finally came. Seconds later, a pair of soldiers rushed into the room, carrying a dazed and bloodied young woman in a ball gown.

Lord Ruler, Vin! Elend thought. *Was that really necessary?*

Elend glanced back at Yomen, and the two shared a look. Then Yomen stood. "Where is the empress Venture!" he demanded.

Time to go, Elend thought, remembering his promise to Vin. However, something occurred to him. *I'll probably never have another chance to get this close to Yomen,* Elend thought. *And there's one sure way to prove whether or not he's an Allomancer.*

Try to kill him.

It was bold, perhaps foolish, but he was growing certain he'd never convince Yomen to surrender his city. He'd claimed that he wasn't Mistborn; it was very important to see if he was lying or not. So, trusting his instincts in this matter, Elend dropped a coin and Pushed himself up onto the stage. Ballgoers began to cry out, their idyllic world shattering as Elend whipped out a pair of glass daggers. Yomen paled and backed away. Two guards who had been pretending to be Yomen's dinner partners stood up from their seats, pulling staves from beneath the table.

"You liar," Yomen spat as Elend landed on the dining table. "Thief, butcher, *tyrant*!"

Elend shrugged, then shot coins at the two guards, easily dropping them both. He jumped for Yomen, grabbing the man around the neck, yanking him backward. Gasps and screams came from the crowd.

Elend squeezed, choking Yomen. No strength flooded the man's limbs. No Allomantic Pull or Push tried to shake him from Elend's grasp. The obligator barely even struggled.

Either he's no Allomancer, Elend thought, *or he's one hell of an actor.*

He let Yomen go, pushing the king back toward his dining table. Elend shook his head—that was one mystery that was—

Yomen jumped forward, pulling out a glass knife, slashing. Elend started, ducking backward, but the knife hit, slicing a gash in his forearm. The cut blazed with pain, enhanced by Elend's tin, and Elend cursed, stumbling away.

Yomen struck again, and Elend *should* have been able to dodge. He had pewter, and Yomen was still moving with the clumsiness of an unenhanced man. Yet, the attack moved with Elend, somehow managing to take him in the side. Elend grunted, blood hot on his skin, and he looked into Yomen's eyes. The king pulled the knife free, easily dodging Elend's counterstrike. It was almost like . . .

Elend burned electrum, giving himself a bubble of false atium images. Yomen hesitated immediately, looking confused.

He's burning atium, Elend thought with shock. *That means he* is *Mistborn!*

Part of Elend wanted to stay and fight, but the cut in his side was bad—bad enough that he knew he needed to get it taken care of soon. Cursing his own stupidity, he Pushed himself into the air, dropping blood on the terrified nobility clustered below. He should have listened to Vin—he was going to get a serious lecture when he got back to camp.

He landed, and noted that Yomen had chosen not to follow. The obligator king stood behind his table, holding a knife red with Elend's blood, watching with anger.

Elend turned, throwing up a handful of coins and Pushing them into the air above the heads of the ballgoers—careful not to hit any of them. They cowered in fear, throwing themselves to the ground. Once the coins landed, Elend Pushed off of them to send himself in a short, low jump through the room and toward the exit Vin had indicated. Soon, he entered an outdoor patio cloaked with mist.

He glanced back at the building, feeling frustrated, though he didn't know why. He had done his part—he'd kept Yomen and his guests distracted for a good half hour. True, he'd gotten himself wounded, but he *had* discovered that Yomen was an Allomancer. That was worth knowing.

He dropped a coin and shot himself into the air.

Three hours later, Elend sat in the command tent with Ham, waiting quietly.

He got his side and arm patched. Vin didn't arrive.

He told the others about what had happened. Vin didn't arrive.

Ham forced him to get something to eat. Elend paced for an hour after that, and still Vin did not return.

"I'm going back," Elend said, standing.

Ham looked up. "El, you lost *a lot* of blood. I'd guess that only pewter is keeping you on your feet."

It was true. Elend could feel the edges of fatigue beneath his veil of pewter. "I can handle it."

"You'll kill yourself that way," Ham said.

"I don't care. I—" Elend cut off as his tin-enhanced ears heard someone approaching the tent. He pulled back the flaps before the man even arrived, startling him.

"My lord!" the man said. "Message from the city."

Elend snatched the letter, ripping it open.

Pretender Venture, the note said, *I have her, as you have probably guessed. There's one thing I've always noted about Mistborn. To a man, they are overconfident. Thank you for the stimulating conversation. I'm glad I was able to keep you distracted for so long.*

King Yomen.

Vin sat quietly in the dark cavern. Her back rested against the stone block that was the door to her prison. Beside her, on the rock floor, sat the dwindling lantern she'd brought into the massive room.

She'd Pushed and she'd Pulled, trying to force her way out. However, she'd soon realized that the broken stones she'd seen on the outside—the work project she'd assumed had been used to open the door—had actually had a different purpose. Yomen had apparently removed the metal plates inside the door, the ones that an Allomancer could Push or Pull on to open it. That left the door as simply a stone block. With duralumin-enhanced pewter, she should have been able to push even that open. Unfortunately, she found it difficult to get leverage on the floor, which sloped down away from the block. In addition, they must have done something to the hinges—or perhaps even piled up more rock against the other side—for she couldn't get the door to budge.

She ground her teeth in frustration, sitting with her back to the stone door. Yomen had set an intentional trap for her. Had she and Elend been that predictable? Regardless, it was a brilliant move. Yomen knew he couldn't fight them. So, instead, he'd simply captured Vin. It had the same effect, but without any of the risks. And she'd fallen right into the trap.

She'd searched the entire room, trying to find a way out, but had come up with nothing. Even worse, she'd located no hidden stock of atium. It was hard to tell with all the cans of food and other sources of metal, but her initial search hadn't been promising.

"Of course it won't be in here," she muttered to herself. "Yomen wouldn't have had time to pull out all of these cans, but if he were planning to trap me, he certainly would have removed the atium. I'm such an *idiot*!"

She leaned back, annoyed, frustrated, exhausted.

I hope Elend did what I said, Vin thought. If he had gotten captured too . . .

Vin knocked her head back against the obstinate stones, frustrated.

Something sounded in the darkness.

Vin froze, then quickly scrambled up into a crouch. She checked her metal reserves—she had plenty, for the moment.

I'm probably just—

It came again. A soft footfall. Vin shivered, realizing that she had only cursorily checked the chamber, and then she'd been searching for atium and other ways out. Could someone have been hiding inside the entire time?

She burned bronze, and felt him. An Allomancer. Mistborn. The one she had felt before; the man she had chased.

So that's it! she thought. *Yomen* did *want his Mistborn to fight us—but he knew he had to separate us first!* She smiled, standing. It wasn't a perfect situation, but it was better than thinking about the immobile door. A Mistborn she could beat, then hold hostage until they released her.

She waited until the man was close—she could tell by the beating of the Allomantic pulses that she hoped he didn't know she could feel—then spun, kicking her lantern toward him. She jumped forward, guiding herself toward her enemy, who stood outlined by the lantern's last flickers. He looked up at her as she soared through the air, her daggers out.

And she recognized his face.

Reen.

PART FOUR

BEAUTIFUL DESTROYER

A man with a given power—such as an Allomantic ability—who then gained a Hemalurgic spike granting that same power would be nearly twice as strong as a natural unenhanced Allomancer.

An Inquisitor who was a Seeker before his transformation would therefore have an enhanced ability to use bronze. This simple fact explains how many Inquisitors were able to pierce copperclouds.

45

VIN LANDED, ABORTING HER ATTACK, but still tense, eyes narrow with suspicion. Reen was backlit by the fitful lantern-light, looking much as she remembered. The four years had changed him, of course—he was taller, broader of build—but he had the same hard face, unrelieved by humor. His posture was familiar to her; during her childhood, he had often stood as he did now, arms folded in disapproval.

It all returned to her. Things she thought she'd banished into the dark, quarantined parts of her mind: blows from Reen's hand, harsh criticism from his tongue, furtive moves from city to city.

And yet, tempering these memories was an insight. She was no longer the young girl who had borne her beatings in confused silence. Looking back, she could see the fear Reen had shown in the things he had done. He'd been terrified that his half-breed Allomancer of a sister would be discovered and slaughtered by the Steel Inquisitors. He'd beaten her when she made herself stand out. He'd yelled at her when she was too competent. He'd moved her when he'd feared that the Canton of Inquisition had caught their trail.

Reen had died protecting her. He had taught her paranoia and distrust out of a twisted sense of duty, for he'd believed that was the only way she would survive on the streets of the Final Empire. And, she'd stayed with him, enduring the treatment. Inside—not even buried all that deeply—she'd known something very important. Reen had loved her.

She looked up and met the eyes of the man standing in the cavern. Then, she slowly shook her head. *No,* she thought. *It looks like him, but those eyes are* not *his.*

"Who are you?" she demanded.

"I'm your brother," the creature said, frowning. "It's only been a few years, Vin. You've grown brash—I thought I'd taught you better than that."

He certainly has the mannerisms down, Vin thought, walking forward warily. *How did he learn them? Nobody thought that Reen was of any importance during his life. They wouldn't have known to study him.*

"Where did you get his bones?" Vin asked, circling the creature. The cavern floor was rough and lined with burgeoning shelves. Darkness extended in all directions. "And how did you get the face so perfect? I thought kandra had to digest a body to make a good copy."

He had to be a kandra, after all. How else would someone manage such a perfect imitation? The creature turned, regarding her with a confused expression. "What is this nonsense? Vin, I realize that we're not exactly the type to reunite with a fond embrace, but I *did* at least expect you to recognize me."

Vin ignored the complaints. Reen, then Breeze, had taught her too well. She'd know Reen if she saw him. "I need information," she said. "About one of your kind. He is called TenSoon, and he returned to your Homeland a year ago. He said he was going to be put on trial. Do you know what happened to him? I would like to contact him, if possible."

"Vin," the false Reen said firmly, "I am *not* a kandra."

We'll see about that, Vin thought, reaching out with zinc and hitting the impostor with a duralumin-fueled blast of emotional Allomancy.

He didn't even stumble. Such an attack would have put a kandra under Vin's control, just as it did with koloss. Vin wavered. It was growing difficult to see the impostor in the waning lantern-light, even with tin enhancing her eyes.

The failed emotional Allomancy meant that he wasn't a kandra. But he wasn't Reen either. There seemed only one logical course to follow.

She attacked.

Whoever the impostor was, he knew her well enough to anticipate this move. Though he exclaimed in mock surprise, he immediately jumped back, getting out of her reach. He moved on light feet—light enough that Vin was reasonably certain he was burning pewter. In fact, she could still feel the Allomantic pulses coming from him, though for some reason it was hard for her to pin down exactly which metals he was burning.

Either way, the Allomancy was an additional confirmation of her suspicions. Reen had not been an Allomancer. True, he could have Snapped during their time apart, but she didn't think he had any noble blood to impart him an Allomantic heritage. Vin had gotten her powers from her father, the parent she and Reen had not shared.

She attacked experimentally, testing this impostor's skill. He stayed out of her reach, watching carefully as she alternately prowled and attacked. She tried to corner him against the shelves, but he was too careful to be caught.

"This is pointless," the impostor said, jumping away from her again.

No coins, Vin thought. *He doesn't use coins to jump.*

"You'd have to expose yourself too much to actually hit me, Vin," the impostor said, "and I'm obviously good enough to stay out of your reach. Can't we stop this and get on to more important matters? Aren't you even a bit curious as to what I've been doing these last four years?"

Vin backed into a crouch, like a cat preparing to pounce, and smiled.

"What?" the impostor asked.

At that moment, her stalling paid off. Behind them, the overturned lantern finally flickered out, plunging the cavern into darkness. But Vin, with her ability to pierce copper-clouds, could still sense her enemy. She'd dropped her coin pouch back when she'd first sensed someone in the room—she bore no metal to give him warning of her approach.

She launched herself forward, intending to grab her enemy around the neck and pull him into a pin. The Allomantic pulses didn't let her see him, but they did tell her exactly where he was. That would be enough of an edge.

She was wrong. He dodged her just as easily as he had before.

Vin fell still. *Tin,* she thought. *He can hear me coming.*

So, she kicked over a storage shelf, then attacked again as the crash of the falling shelf echoed loudly in the chamber, spilling cans across the floor.

The impostor evaded her again. Vin froze. Something was very wrong. Somehow, he always sensed her. The cavern fell silent. Neither sound nor light bounced off its walls. Vin crouched, the fingers of one hand resting lightly on the cool stone before her. She could feel the thumping, his Allomantic power washing across her in waves. She focused on it, trying to differentiate the metals that had produced it. Yet, the pulses felt opaque. Muddled.

There's something familiar about them, she realized. *When I first sensed this impostor, I thought . . . I thought he was the mist spirit.*

There was a reason the pulses felt familiar. Without the light to distract her, making her connect the figure with Reen, she could see what she'd been missing.

Her heart began to beat quickly, and for the first time this evening—imprisonment included—she began to feel afraid. The pulses felt just like the ones she'd felt a year ago. The pulses that had led her to the Well of Ascension.

"Why have you come here?" she whispered to the blackness.

Laughter. It rang in the empty cavern, loud, free. The thumpings approached, though no footsteps marked the thing's movement. The pulses suddenly grew enormous and overpowering. They washed across Vin, unbounded by the cavern's echoes, an unreal sound that passed through things both living and dead. She stepped backward in the darkness, and nearly tripped over the shelves she'd knocked down.

I should have known you wouldn't be fooled, a kindly voice said in her head. The thing's voice. She'd heard it only once before, a year ago, when she'd released it from its imprisonment in the Well of Ascension.

"What do you want?" she whispered.

You know what I want. You've always known.

And she did. She had sensed it in the moment when she had touched the thing. Ruin, she called it. It had very simple desires. To see the world come to its end.

"I will stop you," she said. Yet, it was hard to not feel foolish speaking the words to a force she did not understand, a thing that existed beyond men and beyond worlds.

It laughed again, though this time the sound was only inside her head. She could still feel Ruin pulsing—though not from any one specific place. It surrounded her. She forced herself to stand up straight.

Ah, Vin, Ruin said, its voice almost fatherly in tone. *You act as if I were your enemy.*

"You are my enemy. You seek to end the things I love."

And is an ending always bad? it asked. *Must not all things, even worlds, someday end?*

"There is no need to hasten that end," Vin said. "No reason to force it."

All things are subject to their own nature, Vin, Ruin said, seeming to flow around her. She could feel its touch upon her—wet and delicate, like mist. *You cannot blame me for being what I am. Without me, nothing would end. Nothing* could *end. And therefore, nothing could grow. I am life. Would you fight life itself?*

Vin fell silent.

Do not mourn because the day of this world's end has arrived, Ruin said. *That end was ordained the very day of the world's conception. There is a beauty in death—the beauty of finality, the beauty of completion.*

For nothing is truly complete until the day it is finally destroyed.

"Enough," Vin snapped, feeling alone and smothered in the chill darkness. "Stop taunting me. Why have you come here?"

Come here? it asked. *Why do you ask that?*

"What is your purpose in appearing now?" Vin said. "Have you simply come to gloat over my imprisonment?"

I have not "just appeared," Vin, Ruin said. *Why, I have never left. I've always been with you. A part of you.*

"Nonsense," Vin said. "You only just revealed yourself."

I revealed myself to your eyes, yes, Ruin said. *But, I see that you do not understand. I've always been with you, even when you could not see me.*

It paused, and there was silence, both outside and inside of her head.

When you're alone, no one can betray you, a voice whispered in the back of her mind. Reen's voice. The voice she heard sometimes, almost real, like a conscience. She'd taken it for granted that the voice was just part of her psyche—a leftover from Reen's teachings. An instinct.

Anyone will betray you, Vin, the voice said, repeating a bit of advice it commonly gave. As it spoke, it slowly slid from Reen's voice into that of Ruin. *Anyone.*

I've always been with you. You've heard me in your mind since your first years of life.

Ruin's escape deserves some explanation. This is a thing that even I had a problem understanding.

Ruin could not have used the power at the Well of Ascension. It was of Preservation, Ruin's fundamental opposite. Indeed, a direct confrontation of these two forces would have caused the destruction of both.

Ruin's prison, however, was fabricated of that power. Therefore, it was attuned to the power of Preservation—the very power of the Well. When that power was released and dispersed, rather than utilized, it acted as a key. The subsequent "unlocking" is what finally freed Ruin.

46

"ALL RIGHT," BREEZE SAID, "SO does somebody want to speculate on how our team's spy ended up becoming a pseudo-religious vigilante freedom fighter?"

Sazed shook his head. They sat in their cavern lair beneath the Canton of Inquisition. Breeze, declaring that he was tired of travel rations, had ordered several of the soldiers to break open some of the cavern's supplies to prepare a more suitable meal. Sazed might have complained, but the truth was that the cavern was so well stocked that even a determinedly eating Breeze wouldn't be able to make a dent in it.

They had waited all day for Spook to return to the lair. Tensions in the city were high, and most of their contacts had gone to ground, weathering the Citizen's paranoia regarding a rebellion. Soldiers walked the streets, and a sizable contingent had set up camp just outside the Ministry building. Sazed was worried that the Citizen had associated Breeze and Sazed with Spook's appearance at the executions. It appeared that their days of moving about freely in the city were at an end.

"Why hasn't he come back?" Allrianne asked. She and Breeze sat at a fine table, pilfered from an empty nobleman's mansion. They had, of course, changed back to their fine clothing—a suit on Breeze, a peach dress on Allrianne. They always changed as soon as possible, as if eager to reaffirm to themselves who they really were.

Sazed did not dine with them; he didn't have much of an appetite. Captain Goradel leaned against a bookcase a short distance away, determined to keep a close eye on his charges. Though the good-natured man wore his usual smile, Sazed could tell from the orders he'd given to his soldiers that he was worried about the possibility of an assault. He made very certain that Breeze, Allrianne, and Sazed stayed within the protective confines of the cavern. Better to be trapped than dead.

"I'm sure the boy is fine, my dear," Breeze said, finally answering Allrianne's question. "It's likely he hasn't come back because he fears implicating us in what he did today."

"Either that," Sazed said, "or he can't get past the soldiers watching outside."

"He snuck into a burning building while we were watching, my dear man," Breeze said, "I doubt he'd have trouble with a bunch of toughs, especially now that it's dark out."

Allrianne shook her head. "It would have been better if he'd managed to sneak *out* of that building as well, rather than jumping off the roof in front of everyone."

"Perhaps," Breeze said. "But, part of being a vigilante rebel is letting your enemies know what you are about. The psychological effect produced by leaping from a burning building carrying a child is quite sound. And, to do that right in front of the tyrant who tried to execute said child? I wasn't aware that dear little Spook had such a flair for drama!"

"He's not so little anymore, I think," Sazed said quietly. "We have a habit of ignoring Spook too much."

"Habits come from reinforcement, my dear man," Breeze said, wagging a fork at Sazed. "We paid little attention to the lad because he rarely had an important role to play. It isn't his fault—he was simply young."

"Vin was young as well," Sazed noted.

"Vin, you must admit, is something of a special case."

Sazed couldn't argue with that.

"Either way," Breeze said, "when we look at the facts, what happened isn't really all that surprising. Spook has had months to become known to Urteau's underground population, and he is of the Survivor's own crew. It is logical that they would begin to look to him to save them, much as Kelsier saved Luthadel."

"We're forgetting one thing, Lord Breeze," Sazed said. "He jumped from a rooftop ledge two stories up and landed on a cobbled street. Men do not survive falls like that without broken bones."

Breeze paused. "Staged, you think? Perhaps he worked out some kind of landing platform to soften the fall?"

Sazed shook his head. "I believe it a stretch to assume that Spook could plan, and execute, a staged rescue like that. He would have needed the aid of the underground, which would have ruined the effect. If they knew that his survival was a trick, then we wouldn't have heard the rumors we did about him."

"What, then?" Breeze asked, shooting a glance at Allrianne. "You're not truly suggesting that Spook has been *Mistborn* all this time, are you?"

"I do not know," Sazed said softly.

Breeze shook his head, chuckling. "I doubt he could have hidden that from us, my dear man. Why, he would have had to go through that entire mess of overthrowing the Lord Ruler, then the fall of Luthadel, without ever revealing that he was anything more than a Tineye! I refuse to accept that."

Or, Sazed thought, *you refuse to accept that you wouldn't have detected the truth.* Still, Breeze had a point. Sazed had known Spook as a youth. The boy had been awkward and shy, but he hadn't been deceitful. It was truly a stretch to imagine him to have been a Mistborn from the beginning.

Yet, Sazed had seen that fall. He had seen the grace of the jump, the distinctive poise and natural dexterity of one burning pewter. Sazed found himself wishing for his copperminds so that he could search for references about people spontaneously manifesting Allomantic powers. Could a man be a Misting early in life, then transform to a full Mistborn later?

It was a simple thing, related to his duties as an ambassador. Perhaps he could spend just a little time looking through his stored memories, seeking examples. . . .

He paused. *Don't be silly,* he thought. *You're just looking for excuses. You* know *that it's impossible for an Allomancer to gain new powers. You won't find any examples because there aren't any.*

He didn't need to look through his metalminds. He had set those aside for a very good reason—he could not be a Keeper, could not share the knowledge he'd collected, until he could sort the truth from the lies.

I've let myself get distracted lately, he thought with determination, rising from his place and leaving the others behind. He walked over to his "room" in the cache, with the sheets hung there cutting off his view of the others. Sitting on the table was his portfolio. In the corner, next to a shelf full of cans, sat his sack full of metalminds.

No, Sazed thought. *I made a promise to myself. I will keep it. I will not allow myself to become a hypocrite simply because some new religion appears and waves at me. I will be strong.*

He sat down at the table, opening his portfolio, taking out the next sheet in the line. It listed the tenets of the Nelazan people, who had worshipped the god Trell. Sazed had always been partial to this religion because of its focus on learning and study of mathematics and the heavens. He'd saved it for near the end, but had done so more out of worry than anything else. He'd wanted to put off what he'd known would happen.

Sure enough, as he read about the religion, he saw the holes in its doctrines. True, the Nelazan had known a great deal about astronomy, but their teachings on the afterlife were sketchy—almost whimsical. Their doctrine was purposefully vague, they'd taught, allowing all men to discover truth for themselves. Reading this, however, left Sazed frustrated. What good was a religion without answers? Why believe in something if the response to half of his questions was "Ask Trell, and he will answer"?

He didn't dismiss the religion immediately. He forced himself to put it aside, acknowledging to himself that he wasn't in the right mood for studying. He didn't feel like he was in the mood for much, actually.

What if Spook really has become Mistborn? he wondered, mind getting drawn back to the previous conversation. It seemed impossible. Yet, a lot of things they thought they'd known about Allomancy—such as the existence of only ten metals—had turned out to be falsehoods taught by the Lord Ruler to hide some powerful secrets.

Perhaps it *was* possible for an Allomancer to spontaneously manifest new powers. Or, perhaps there was a more mundane reason Spook had managed such a long fall. It could be related to the thing that made Spook's eyes so sensitive. Drugs, perhaps?

Either way, Sazed's worry about what was happening kept him from being able to focus on studying the Nelazan religion as he should. He kept getting the feeling that something very important was occurring. And Spook was at the center of it.

Where was that boy?

"I know why you're so sad," Spook said.

Beldre turned, shock showing on her face. She didn't see him at first. He must have been too deep in the misty shadows. It was growing hard for him to tell.

He stepped forward, moving across the plot of land that had once been a garden outside the Citizen's home. "I figured it out," Spook said. "At first, I thought that sadness had to do with this garden. It must have been beautiful, once. You would have seen it in its fullness, before your brother ordered all gardens plowed under. You were related to nobility, and probably lived in their society."

She looked surprised at this.

"Yes, I know," Spook said. "Your brother is an Allomancer. He's a Coinshot; I felt his Pushes. That day at Marketpit."

She remained silent—more beautiful herself than the garden could ever have been—though she did take a step backward as her eyes finally found him in the mists.

"Eventually," Spook continued, "I decided that I must be wrong. Nobody mourns so much for a simple garden, no matter how lovely. After that, I thought the sadness in your eyes must come from being forbidden to take part in your brother's councils. He always sends you out, into the garden, when he meets with his most important officials. I know what it's like to feel useless and excluded among important people."

He took another step forward. The rough earth lay torn beneath his feet, covered by an inch of ash, the dreary remnants of what had once been fertile ground. To his right stood the lone shrub that Beldre often came to gaze at. He didn't look toward it; he kept his eyes on her.

"I was wrong," he said. "Being forbidden your brother's conferences would lead to frustration, but not such pain. Not such regret. I know that sorrow now. I killed for the first time this afternoon. I helped overthrow empires, then helped build them anew. And I'd never killed a man. Not until today."

He stopped, then looked into her eyes. "Yes, I know that sorrow. What I'm trying figure out is why *you* feel it."

She turned away. "You shouldn't be here," she said. "There are guards watching—"

"No," Spook said. "Not anymore. Quellion sent too many men into the city—he's afraid that he'll suffer a revolution, like happened in Luthadel. Like he himself inspired here when he seized power. He's right to be afraid, but he was wrong to leave his own palace so poorly guarded."

"Kill him," Kelsier whispered. "Quellion is inside; this is the perfect chance. He deserves it, you know he does."

No, Spook thought. *Not today. Not in front of her.*

Beldre glanced back at him, her eyes growing hard. "Why have you come? To taunt me?"

"To tell you that I understand," Spook said.

"How can you say that?" she said. "You don't understand me—you don't know me."

"I think I do," Spook said. "I saw your eyes today, when you watched those people being marched to their deaths. You feel guilty. Guilty for your brother's murders. You sorrow because you feel you should be able to stop him." He took a step forward. "You can't, Beldre. He's been corrupted by his power. He might once have been a good man, but no longer. Do you realize what he's doing? Your brother is murdering people simply to get Allomancers. He captures them, then threatens to kill their families unless they do as he asks. Are those the actions of a good man?"

"You are a simplistic fool," Beldre whispered, though she wouldn't meet his eyes.

"I know," Spook said. "What are a few deaths when it comes to securing the stability of a kingdom?" He paused, then shook his head. "He's killing children, Beldre. And he's doing it simply to cover up the fact that he's gathering Allomancers."

Beldre was silent for a moment. "Go," she finally said.

"I want you to come with me."

She looked up.

"I'm going to overthrow your brother," Spook said. "I am a member of the Survivor's own crew. We took down the Lord Ruler—Quellion will hardly provide us with a challenge. You don't have to be here when he falls."

Beldre snorted quietly in derision.

"It's not just about your safety," Spook said. "If you join with us, it will be a strong blow to your brother. Perhaps it will convince him that he is wrong. There could be a more peaceful way of making this happen."

"I'm going to start screaming in three heartbeats," Beldre said.

"I don't fear your guards," Spook said.

"I don't doubt that," Beldre said. "But if they come, you'll have to kill again."

Spook wavered. He stayed where he was, however, calling her bluff.

And so she started screaming.

"Go kill him!" Kelsier said over her screams. "Now, before it's too late! Those guards you killed—they were just following orders. *Quellion,* he's the true monster."

Spook ground his teeth in frustration, then finally ran, fleeing from Beldre and her screams, leaving Quellion alive.

For the moment.

The group of rings, clasps, ear loops, bracelets, and other bits of metal gleamed on the table like a treasure hoard of legend. Of course, most of the metals were rather mundane. Iron, steel, tin, copper. No gold or atium.

Yet, to a Feruchemist, the metals were worth far more than their economic value. They were batteries, stores that could be filled, then drawn upon. One made of pewter, for instance, could be filled with strength. Filling it would drain the Feruchemist of strength for a time—making him weak enough that simple tasks grew difficult—but the price was worthwhile. For, when necessary, he could draw that strength forth.

Many of these metalminds, spread out on the table in front of Sazed, were empty at the moment. Sazed had last used them during the horrific battle that had ended with the fall—then rescue—of Luthadel over a year before. That battle had left him drained in more ways than one. Ten rings, lined up on the side of the table, had been used to nearly kill him. Marsh had shot them at Sazed like coins, piercing his skin. That, however, had allowed Sazed to draw forth their power and heal himself.

At the very center of the collection were the most important metalminds of all. Four bracers—meant to clasp on to the upper or lower arms—sat gleaming and polished, made of the purest copper. They were the largest of his metalminds, for they held the most. Copper carried memories. A Feruchemist could take images, thoughts, or sounds that were fresh in his mind, then store them away. While inside, they wouldn't decay or change, as memories could while held in the mind.

When Sazed had been a young man, an older Feruchemist had read out the entire contents of his copperminds. Sazed had stored the knowledge in his own copperminds; they contained the sum total of Keeper knowledge. The Lord Ruler had worked hard to smother people's memories of the past. But the Keepers had gathered them—stories of how the world had been before the ash came and the sun had turned red. The Keepers had memorized the names of places and of kingdoms, had gathered the wisdom of those who were lost.

And they had memorized the religions that had been forbidden by the Lord Ruler. These he had worked the most diligently to destroy, and so the Keepers had worked with equal diligence to rescue them—to secure them away inside of metalminds, so someday they could be taught again. Above all, the Keepers had searched for one thing: knowledge of their own religion, the beliefs of the Terris people. Those had been forgotten during the destructive chaos following the Lord Ruler's ascension. However, despite centuries of work, the Keepers had never recovered this most precious knowledge of all.

I wonder what would have happened if we had *found it,* Sazed thought, picking up a steelmind and quietly polishing it. *Probably nothing.* He'd given up on his work with the religions in his portfolio for the moment, feeling too discouraged to study.

There were fifty religions left in his portfolio. Why was he deluding himself, hoping to find any more truth in them than he had in the previous two hundred and fifty? None of the religions had managed to survive the years. Shouldn't he just let them be? Looking through them seemed to be part of the great fallacy in the work of the Keepers. They'd struggled to remember the beliefs of men, but those beliefs had already proven they lacked the resilience to survive. Why bring them back to life? That seemed as pointless as reviving a sickly animal so it could fall to predators again.

He continued to polish. Out of the corner of his eye, he saw Breeze watching him. The Soother had come to Sazed's "room," complaining that he couldn't sleep, not with Spook still outside somewhere. Sazed had nodded, but continued polishing. He didn't wish to get into a conversation; he just wanted to be alone.

Breeze, unfortunately, stood and came over. "Sometimes, I don't understand you, Sazed," Breeze said.

"I do not endeavor to be mysterious, Lord Breeze," Sazed said, moving on to polish a small bronze ring.

"Why take such good care of them?" Breeze asked. "You never wear them anymore. In fact, you seem to spurn them."

"I do not spurn the metalminds, Lord Breeze. They are, in a way, the only sacred thing I have left in my life."

"But you don't wear them, either."

Sazed continued polishing. "No. I do not."

"But why?" Breeze asked. "You think that she would have wanted this? She was a Keeper too—do you honestly think she'd want you to give up your metalminds?"

"This particular habit of mine is *not* about Tindwyl."

"Oh?" Breeze asked, sighing as he seated himself at the table. "What do you mean? Because honestly, Sazed, you're confusing me. I understand people. It bothers me that I can't understand you."

"After the Lord Ruler's death," Sazed said, putting down the ring, "do you know what I spent my time doing?"

"Teaching," Breeze said. "You left to go and restore the lost knowledge to the people of the Final Empire."

"And did I ever tell you how that teaching went?"

Breeze shook his head.

"Poorly," Sazed said, picking up another ring. "The people didn't really care. They weren't interested in the religions of the past. And why should they have been? Why worship something that people *used* to believe in?"

"People are always interested in the past, Sazed."

"Interested, perhaps," Sazed said, "but interest is not faith. These metalminds, they are a thing of museums and old libraries. They are of little use to modern people. During the years of the Lord Ruler's reign, we Keepers pretended that we were doing vital work. We *believed* that we were doing vital work. And yet, in the end, nothing we did had any real value. Vin didn't need this knowledge to kill the Lord Ruler.

"I am probably the last of the Keepers. The thoughts in these metalminds will die with me. And, at times, I can't make myself regret that fact. This is not an era for scholars and philosophers. Scholars and philosophers do not help feed starving children."

"And so you don't wear them anymore?" Breeze said. "Because you think they're useless?"

"More than that," Sazed said. "To wear these metalminds would be to pretend. I would be pretending that I find the things in them to be of use, and I have not yet decided if I do or not. To wear them now would seem like a betrayal. I set them aside, for I can do them no justice. I'm just not ready to believe, as we did before, that gathering knowledge and religions is more important than taking action. Perhaps if the Keepers had fought, rather than just memorized, the Lord Ruler would have fallen centuries ago."

"But *you* resisted, Sazed," Breeze said. "You fought."

"I don't represent myself any longer, Lord Breeze," Sazed said softly. "I represent all Keepers, since I am apparently the last. And I, as the last, do not believe in the things I once taught. I cannot with good conscience imply that I am the Keeper I once was."

Breeze sighed, shaking his head. "You don't make sense."

"It makes sense to me."

"No, I think you're just confused. This may not seem to you like a world for scholars, my dear friend, but I think you'll be proven wrong. It seems to me that now—suffering in the darkness that might just be the end of everything—is when we need knowledge the most."

"Why?" Sazed said. "So I can teach a dying man a religion that I don't believe? To speak of a god, when I know there is no such being?"

Breeze leaned forward. "Do you really believe that? That nothing is watching over us?"

Sazed sat quietly, slowing in his polishing. "I have yet to decide for certain," he finally said. "At times, I have hoped to find some truth. However, today, that hope seems very distant to me. There is a darkness upon this land, Breeze, and I am not sure that we can fight it. I am not sure that I want to fight it."

Breeze looked troubled at that. He opened his mouth, but before he could respond, a rumble rolled through the cavern. The rings and bracers on the table quivered and clinked together as the entire room shook, and there was a clatter as some foodstuffs fell—though not too many, for Captain Goradel's men had done good work in moving most of the stockpile off of shelves and to the ground, in order to deal with the quakes.

Eventually, the shaking subsided. Breeze sat with a white face, looking up at the ceiling of the cavern. "I tell you, Sazed," he said. "Every time one of those quakes comes, I wonder at the wisdom of hiding in a cave. Not the safest place during an earthquake, I should think."

"We really have no other option at the moment," Sazed said.

"True, I suppose. Do . . . does it seem to you like those quakes are coming more frequently?"

"Yes," Sazed said, picking up a few fallen bracelets from the floor. "Yes, they are."

"Maybe . . . this region is just more prone to them," Breeze said, not sounding convinced. He turned, looking to the side as Captain Goradel rounded a shelf and approached them in a rush.

"Ah, come to check on us, I see," Breeze said. "We survived the quake quite handily. No need for urgency, my dear captain."

"It's not that," Goradel said, puffing slightly. "It's Lord Spook. He's back."

Sazed and Breeze shared a look, then rose from their chairs, following Goradel to the front of the cavern. They found Spook walking down the steps. His eyes were uncovered, and Sazed saw a new hardness in the young man's expression.

We really haven't *been paying enough attention to the lad.*

The soldiers backed away. There was blood on Spook's clothing, though he didn't appear wounded. His cloak was burned in places, and the bottom ended in a charred rip.

"Good," Spook said, noticing Breeze and Sazed, "you're here. Did that quake cause any damage?"

"Spook?" Breeze asked. "No, we're all fine here. No damage. But—"

"We have little time for chatter, Breeze," Spook said, walking past them. "Emperor Venture wants Urteau, and we're going to deliver it to him. I need you to start spreading rumors in the city. It should be easy—some of the more important elements in the underworld already know the truth."

"What truth?" Breeze asked, joining Sazed as they followed Spook through the cavern.

"That Quellion is using Allomancers," Spook said, his voice echoing in the cavern. "I've now confirmed what I suspected before—Quellion recruits Mistings from the people he arrests. He rescues them from his own fires, then holds their families hostage. He relies on the very thing he's preaching against. The entire foundation for his rule, therefore, is a lie. Exposing that lie should cause the entire system to collapse."

"That's capital, we can certainly do that . . ." Breeze said, glancing at Sazed again. Spook kept walking, and Sazed followed, trailing Spook as he moved through the cavern. Breeze moved away, probably to fetch Allrianne.

Spook stopped beside the water's edge. He stood there for a moment, then turned toward Sazed. "You said that you have been studying the construction that brought the water down here, diverting it from the canals."

"Yes," Sazed said.

"Is there a way to reverse the process?" Spook asked. "Make the water flood the streets again?"

"Perhaps," Sazed said. "I am not certain that I have the engineering expertise to accomplish the feat, however."

"Is there knowledge in your metalminds that would help you?" Spook asked.

"Well . . . yes."

"Then use them," Spook said.

Sazed paused, looking uncomfortable.

"Sazed," Spook said. "We don't have much time—we have to take this city before Quellion decides to attack and destroy us. Breeze is going to spread the rumors, then I am going to find a way to expose Quellion as a liar before his people. He's an Allomancer himself."

"Will that be enough?"

"It will if we give them someone else to follow," Spook said, turning back to look across the waters. "Someone who can survive fires; someone who can restore water to the city streets. We'll give them miracles and a hero, then expose their leader as a hypocrite and a tyrant. Confronted with that, what would *you* do?"

Sazed didn't respond immediately. Spook made good points, even about Sazed's metalminds still being useful. Yet Sazed wasn't certain what he thought of the changes in the young man. Spook seemed to have grown far more competent, but . . .

"Spook," Sazed said, stepping in closer, speaking quietly enough that the soldiers standing behind couldn't hear. "What is it you aren't sharing with us? How did you survive the leap from that building? Why do you cover your eyes with cloth?"

"I . . ." Spook faltered, showing a hint of the insecure boy he had once been. For some reason, seeing that made Sazed more comfortable. "I don't know if I can explain, Saze," Spook said, some of his pretension evaporating. "I'm still trying to figure it out myself. I'll explain eventually. For now, can you just trust me?"

The lad had always been a sincere one. Sazed searched those eyes, so eager.

And found something important. Spook cared. He cared about this city, about overthrowing the Citizen. He'd saved those people earlier, when Sazed and Breeze had just stood outside, watching.

Spook cared, and Sazed did not. Sazed tried—he grew frustrated with himself because of his depression, which had been worse this evening than it usually was.

His emotions had been so traitorous lately. He had trouble studying, had trouble leading, had trouble being of any use whatsoever. But, looking into Spook's eager eyes, he was almost able to forget his troubles for a moment.

If the lad wanted to take the lead, then who was Sazed to argue?

He glanced toward his room, where the metalminds lay. He had gone so long without them. They tempted him with their knowledge.

As long as I don't preach the religions they contain, he thought, *I'm not a hypocrite. Using this specific knowledge Spook requests will, at least, bring some small meaning to the suffering of those who worked to gather knowledge of engineering.*

It seemed a weak excuse. But, in the face of Spook taking the lead and offering a good reason to use the metalminds, it was enough.

"Very well," Sazed said. "I shall do as you request."

Ruin's prison was not like those that hold men. He wasn't bound by bars. In fact, he could move about freely.

His prison, rather, was one of impotence. In the terms of forces and gods, this meant balance. If Ruin were to push, the prison would push back, essentially rendering Ruin powerless. And because much of his power was stripped away and hidden, he was unable to affect the world in any but the most subtle of ways.

I should stop here and clarify something. We speak of Ruin being "freed" from his prison. But that is misleading. Releasing the power at the Well tipped the aforementioned balance back toward Ruin, but he was still too weak to destroy the world in the blink of an eye as he yearned to do. This weakness was caused by part of Ruin's power—his very body—having been taken and hidden from him.

Which was why Ruin became so obsessed with finding the hidden part of his self.

47

ELEND STOOD IN THE MISTS.

Once, he had found them disconcerting. They had been the unknown—something mysterious and uninviting, something that belonged to Allomancers and not to ordinary men.

Yet, now he was an Allomancer himself. He stared up at the shifting, swirling, spinning banks of vapor. Rivers in the sky. He almost felt as if he should get pulled along in some phantom current. When he'd first displayed Allomantic powers, Vin had explained Kelsier's now-infamous motto. *The mists are our friend. They hide us. Protect us. Give us power.*

Elend continued to stare upward. It had been three days since Vin's capture.

I shouldn't have let her go, he thought again, heart twisting within him. *I shouldn't have agreed to such a risky plan.*

Vin had always been the one to protect him. What did they do now, when she was in danger? Elend felt so inadequate. Had their situations been reversed, Vin would have found a way to get into the city and rescue him. She'd have assassinated Yomen, would have done *something.*

And yet, Elend didn't have her flair of brash determination. He was too much of a planner and was too well acquainted with politics. He *couldn't* risk himself to save her. He'd already put himself into danger once, and in so doing, had risked the fate of his entire army. He couldn't leave them behind again and put himself in danger, particularly not by going into Fadrex, where Yomen had already proven himself a skilled manipulator.

No further word had come from Yomen. Elend expected ransom demands, and was terrified of what he might have to do if they came. Could he trade the fate of the world for Vin's life? No. Vin had faced a similar decision at the Well of Ascension, and had chosen the right option. Elend had to follow her example, had to be strong.

Yet the thought of her captured came close to paralyzing him with dread. Only the spinning mists seemed to somehow comfort him.

She'll be all right, he told himself, not for the first time. *She's Vin. She'll figure a way out of it. She'll be all right. . . .*

It felt odd, to Elend, that after a lifetime of finding the mists unsettling he would now find them so comforting. Vin didn't see them that way, not anymore. Elend could sense it in the way she acted, in the words she spoke. She distrusted the mists. Hated them, even. And Elend couldn't really blame her. They had, after all, changed somehow—bringing destruction and death.

Yet, Elend found it hard to distrust the mists. They just *felt* right. How could they be his enemy? They spun, swirling around him just slightly as he burned metals, like leaves spinning in a playful wind. As he stood there, they seemed to soothe away his concerns about Vin's captivity, giving him confidence that she would find a way out.

He sighed, shaking his head. Who was he to trust his own instincts about the mists over Vin's? She had the instincts born of a lifetime of struggling to survive. What did Elend have? Instincts born of a lifetime of partygoing and dancing?

Sound came from behind him. People walking. Elend turned, eyeing a pair of servants carrying Cett in his chair.

"That damn Thug isn't around here, is he?" Cett asked as the servants set him down.

Elend shook his head as Cett waved the servants away. "No," Elend said. "He's investigating some kind of disturbance in the ranks."

"What happened this time?" Cett asked.

"Fistfight," Elend said, turning away, looking back toward Fadrex City's watch fires.

"The men are restless," Cett said. "They're a little like koloss, you know. Leave them too long, and they'll get themselves into trouble."

Koloss are like them, actually, Elend thought. *We should have seen it earlier. They are men—just men reduced to their most base emotions.*

Cett sat quietly in the mists for a time, and Elend continued his contemplations.

Eventually, Cett spoke, his voice uncharacteristically soft. "She's as good as dead, son. You know that."

"No, I don't," Elend said.

"She's not invincible," Cett said. "She's a damn good Allomancer, true. But, take her metals away . . ."

She'll surprise you, Cett.

"You don't even look worried," Cett said.

"Of course I'm worried," Elend said, growing more certain. "I just . . . well, I trust her. If anyone can get out, Vin will."

"You're in denial," Cett said.

"Perhaps," Elend admitted.

"Are we going to attack?" Cett asked. "Try and get her back?"

"This is a siege, Cett," Elend said. "The point is to *not* attack."

"And our supplies?" Cett asked. "Demoux had to put the soldiers on half rations today. We'll be lucky not to starve ourselves before we can get Yomen to surrender."

"We have time yet," Elend said.

"Not much. Not with Luthadel in revolt." Cett was silent for a moment, then continued. "Another of my raiding parties returned today. They had the same things to report."

The same news as all the others. Elend had authorized Cett to send soldiers into nearby villages, to scare the people, perhaps pillage some supplies. Yet, each of the raiding groups had come back empty-handed, bearing the same story.

The people in Yomen's kingdom were starving. Villages barely survived. The soldiers hadn't the heart to hurt them any further, and there wasn't anything to take, anyway.

Elend turned toward Cett. "You think me a bad leader, don't you?"

Cett looked up, then scratched at his beard. "Yes," he admitted. "But, well . . . Elend, you've got one thing going for you as a king that I never did."

"And that is?"

Cett shrugged. "The people like you. Your soldiers trust you, and they know you have too good a heart for your own good. You have a strange effect on them. Lads like those, they should have been eager to rob villages, even poor ones. Especially considering how on-edge our men are and how many fights there have been in camp. And yet, they didn't. Hell, one of the groups felt so sorry for the villagers that they stayed for a few days and helped water the fields and do repairs to some of the homes!"

Cett sighed, shaking his head. "A few years ago, I would have laughed at anyone who chose loyalty as a basis for rule. But, well . . . with the world falling apart as it is, I think even *I* would rather have someone to trust, as opposed to someone to fear. I guess that's why the soldiers act as they do."

Elend nodded.

"I thought a siege was a good idea," Cett said. "But, I don't think it will work anymore, son. The ash is falling too hard now, and we don't have supplies. This whole thing is becoming a damn mess. We need to strike and take what we can from Fadrex, then retreat to Luthadel and try to hold it through the summer while our people grow crops."

Elend fell silent, then turned, looking to the side as he heard something else in the mists. Shouting and cursing. It was faint—Cett probably couldn't hear it. Elend left, hurrying toward the sound, leaving Cett behind.

Another fight, Elend realized as he approached one of the cooking fires. He heard yells, blustering, and the sounds of men brawling. *Cett's right. Goodhearted or not, our men are getting too restless. I need—*

"Stop this immediately!" a new voice called. Just ahead, through the dark mists, Elend could see figures moving about the firelight. He recognized the voice; General Demoux had arrived on the scene.

Elend slowed. Better to let the general deal with the disturbance. There was a big difference between being disciplined by one's military commander and one's emperor. The men would be better off if Demoux were the one to punish them.

The fighting, however, did not stop.

"Stop this!" Demoux yelled again, moving into the conflict. A few of the brawlers listened to him, pulling back. The rest, however, just continued to fight. Demoux pushed himself into the melee, reaching to pull apart two of the combatants.

And one of them punched him. Square in the face, throwing Demoux to the ground.

Elend cursed, dropping a coin and Pushing himself forward. He fell directly into the middle of the firelight, Pushing out with a Soothing to dampen the emotions of those fighting.

"Stop!" he bellowed.

They did, freezing, one of the soldiers standing over the fallen General Demoux.

"What is going on here?" Elend demanded, furious. The soldiers looked down. "Well?" Elend said, turning toward the man who had punched Demoux.

"I'm sorry, my lord," the man grumbled. "We just . . ."

"Speak, soldier," Elend said, pointing, Soothing the man's emotions, leaving him compliant and docile.

"Well, my lord," the man said. "They're cursed, you know. They're the reason Lady Vin got taken. They were speaking of the Survivor and his blessings, and that just smacked me as hypocrisy, you know? Then, *of course* their leader would show, demanding that we stop. I just . . . well, I'm tired of listening to them, is all."

Elend frowned in anger. As he did so, a group of the army's Mistings—Ham at their head—shoved through the crowd. Ham met Elend's eyes, and Elend nodded toward the men who had been fighting. Ham made quick work of them, gathering them up for reprimand. Elend walked over, pulling Demoux to his feet. The grizzled general looked more shocked than anything.

"I'm sorry, my lord," Demoux said quietly. "I should have seen that coming . . . I should have been ready for it."

Elend just shook his head. The two of them watched quietly until Ham joined them, his police pushing the troublemakers away. The rest of the crowd dispersed, returning to their duties. The solitary bonfire burned alone in the night, as if shunned as a new symbol of bad luck.

"I recognized a number of those men," Ham said, joining Elend and Demoux as the troublemakers were led away. "Mistfallen."

Mistfallen. The men who, like Demoux, had lain sick from the mists for weeks, instead of a single day. "This is *ridiculous,*" Elend said. "So they remained sick awhile longer. That doesn't make them cursed!"

"You don't understand superstition, my lord," Demoux said, shaking his head and rubbing his chin. "The men *look* for someone to blame for their ill luck. And . . . well, it's easy to see why they'd be feeling their luck was bad lately. They've been hard on *anyone* who was sickened by the mists; they're just most hard on we who were out the longest."

"I refuse to accept such idiocy in my army," Elend said. "Ham, did you see one of those men strike Demoux?"

"They *hit* him?" Ham asked with surprise. "Their general?"

Elend nodded. "The big man I was talking to. Brill is his name, I think. You know what will have to be done."

Ham cursed, looking away.

Demoux looked uncomfortable. "Maybe we could just . . . throw him in solitary or something."

"No," Elend said through his teeth. "No, we hold to the law. If he'd struck his captain, maybe we could let him off. But deliberately striking one of my generals? The man will have to be executed. Discipline is falling apart as it is."

Ham wouldn't look at him. "The other fight I had to break up was also between a group of regular soldiers and a group of mistfallen."

Elend ground his teeth in frustration. Demoux, however,

met his eyes. *You know what needs to be done,* he seemed to say.

Being a king isn't always about doing what you want, Tindwyl had often said. *It's about doing what needs to be done.*

"Demoux," Elend said. "I think the problems in Luthadel are even more serious than our difficulties with discipline. Penrod looked toward us for support. I want you to gather a group of men and take them back along the canal with the messenger, Conrad. Lend aid to Penrod and bring the city back under control."

"Yes, my lord," Demoux said. "How many soldiers should I take?"

Elend met his eyes. "About three hundred should suffice." It was the number who were mistfallen. Demoux nodded, then withdrew into the night.

"It's the right thing to do, El," Ham said softly.

"No, it's not," Elend said. "Just like it's not right to have to execute a soldier because of a single lapse in judgment. But, we need to keep this army together."

"I guess," Ham said.

Elend turned, glancing up through the mists. Toward Fadrex City. "Cett's right," he finally said. "We can't just continue to sit out here, not while the world is dying."

"So, what do we do about it?" Ham asked.

Elend wavered. What to do about it indeed? Retreat and leave Vin—and probably the entire empire—to its doom? Attack, causing the deaths of thousands, becoming the conqueror he feared? Was there no other way to take the city?

Elend turned and struck out into the night. He found his way to Noorden's tent, Ham following curiously. The former obligator was awake, of course. Noorden kept odd hours. He stood hurriedly as Elend entered his tent, bowing in respect.

There, on the table, Elend found what he wanted. The thing he had ordered Noorden to work on. Maps. Troop movements. The locations of koloss bands.

Yomen refuses to be intimidated by my forces, Elend thought. *Well, let's see if I can turn the odds back against him.*

Once "freed," Ruin was able to affect the world more directly. The most obvious way he did this was by making the ashmounts emit more ash and the earth begin to break apart. As a matter of fact, I believe that much of Ruin's energy during those last days was dedicated to these tasks.

He was also able to affect and control far more people than before. Where he had once influenced only a few select individuals, he could now direct entire koloss armies.

48

AS DAYS PASSED IN THE cavern, Vin regretted knocking over the lantern. She tried to salvage it, searching with blind fingers. However, the oil had spilled. She was locked in darkness.

With a thing that wanted to destroy the world.

Sometimes she could sense it, pulsing near her, watching silently—like some fascinated patron at a carnival show. Other times, it vanished. Obviously, walls meant nothing to it. The first time it disappeared, she felt a sense of relief. However, just moments after it vanished, she heard Reen's voice in her mind. *I haven't left you,* it said. *I'm always here.*

The words chilled her, and she thought—just briefly—that it had read her mind. However, she decided that her thoughts would have been easy to guess. Looking back through her life, she realized that Ruin couldn't have spoken each and every time she heard Reen's voice in her head. A lot of the time she heard Reen, it was in response to things she'd been thinking, rather than things she'd been doing. Since Ruin couldn't read minds, those comments couldn't have come from it.

Ruin had been speaking to her for so long, it was difficult

to separate her own memories from its influence. Yet, she had to trust in the Lord Ruler's promise that Ruin couldn't read her mind. The alternative was to abandon hope. And she wouldn't do that. Each time Ruin spoke to her, it gave her clues about its nature. Those clues might give her the means to defeat it.

Defeat it? Vin thought, leaning back against a rough stone wall of the cavern. *It's a force of nature, not a man. How could I even think to defeat something like that?*

Time was very difficult to gauge in the perpetual blackness, but she figured from her sleep patterns that it had been around three or four days since her imprisonment.

Everyone called the Lord Ruler a god, Vin reminded herself. *I killed him.*

Ruin had been imprisoned once. That meant that it *could* be defeated, or at least bottled up. But, what did it mean to imprison an abstraction—a force—like Ruin? It had been able to speak to her while imprisoned. But its words had felt less forceful then. Less . . . directed. Ruin had acted more as an influence, giving the child Vin impressions that manifested through memories of Reen. Almost like . . . it had influenced her emotions. Did that mean it used Allomancy? It did indeed pulse with Allomantic power.

Zane heard voices, Vin realized. *Right before he died, he seemed to be talking to something.* She felt a chill as she rested her head back against the wall.

Zane had been mad. Perhaps there was no connection between the voices he heard and Ruin. Yet, it seemed like too much of a coincidence. Zane had tried to get her to go with him, to seek out the source of the pulsings—the pulsings that had eventually led her to free Ruin.

So, Vin thought, *Ruin can influence me regardless of distance or containment. However, now that it has been freed, it can manifest directly. That brings up another question. Why hasn't it already destroyed us all? Why play games with armies?*

The answer to that one, at least, seemed obvious. She sensed Ruin's boundless will to destroy. She felt as if she knew its mind. One drive. One impulse. Ruin. So, if it hadn't accomplished its goal yet, that meant it couldn't. That it was hindered. Limited to indirect, gradual means of destruction—like falling ash and the light-stealing mists.

Still, those methods *would* eventually be effective. Unless Ruin was stopped. But how?

It was imprisoned before . . . but what did the imprisoning? She'd once assumed that the Lord Ruler had been the one behind Ruin's imprisonment. But that was wrong. Ruin had *already* been imprisoned when the Lord Ruler had traveled to the Well of Ascension. The Lord Ruler, then known as Rashek, had gone on the quest with Alendi, in order to slay the presumed Hero of Ages. Rashek's purpose had been to *stop* Alendi from doing what Vin had eventually done: accidentally releasing Ruin.

Ironically, it had been *better* that a selfish man like Rashek had taken the power. For, a selfish man kept the power for himself, rather than giving it up and freeing Ruin.

Regardless, Ruin had already been imprisoned before the quest began. That meant that the Deepness—the mists—weren't related to Ruin. Or, at least, the connection wasn't as simple as she'd assumed. Letting Ruin go hadn't been what had prompted the mists to start coming during the day and killing people. In fact, the daymists had started to appear as much as a year *before* she'd released Ruin, and the mists had started killing people some hours before Vin had found her way to the Well.

So . . . what do I know? That Ruin was imprisoned long ago. Imprisoned by something that, perhaps, I can find and use again?

She stood up. Too much sitting and thinking had made her restless, and she began to walk, feeling her way along the wall.

During her first day of imprisonment she'd begun, by touch, to scout the cavern. It was huge, like the other caches, and the process had taken her several days. However, she'd had nothing else to do. Unlike the cache in Urteau, this one had no pool or source of water. And, as Vin investigated it, she discovered that Yomen had removed all of the water barrels from what she assumed was their place on the far right corner. He'd left the canned food and other supplies—the cavern was so enormous that he would have had trouble finding time to remove everything, let alone finding a place to store it somewhere else—however, he'd taken all of the water.

That left Vin with a problem. She felt her way along the wall, locating a shelf where she'd left an open can of stew. Even with pewter and a rock, it had taken her a frightfully long time to get into the can. Yomen had been clever enough to remove the tools she could have used for opening the food stores, and Vin only had one vial's worth of pewter remaining. She'd opened some ten cans of food on her first day, burning away what pewter she'd had inside of her. That food was already dwindling, however, and she was feeling the need for water—the stew did little to quench her thirst.

She picked up the can of stew, carefully eating only a mouthful. It was almost gone. The taste reminded her of the hunger that was a growing complement to her thirst. She pushed the feeling away. She'd dealt with hunger for her entire childhood. It was nothing new, even if it had been years since she'd last felt it.

She moved on, trailing fingers on the side of the wall to keep her bearings. It seemed like such a clever way to kill a Mistborn. Yomen couldn't defeat her, and he trapped her instead. Now, he could simply wait for her to die of dehydration. Simple, effective.

Perhaps Ruin is speaking to Yomen, too, she thought. *My imprisonment could all be part of Ruin's plan.*

Whatever that is.

Why had Ruin chosen her? Why not lead someone else to the Well of Ascension? Someone easier to control? She could understand why Ruin had chosen Alendi, all those years before. During Alendi's time, the Well had been sequestered high in the mountains. It would have been a very difficult trek, and Ruin would have needed just the right person to plan, then survive, the expedition.

However, during Vin's day, the Well had somehow been

moved to Luthadel. Or, perhaps Luthadel had been built on top of the Well. Either way, it was there, right beneath the Lord Ruler's palace. Why had Ruin waited so long to free himself? And, of all the people he could have chosen as his pawn, why Vin?

She shook her head as she arrived at her destination—the only other thing of interest in the vast cavern. A metal plate on the wall. She reached up, brushing her fingers across the slick steel. She'd never been an excellent reader, and the last year—spent in war and travel—hadn't afforded her much time to improve her abilities. And so, it had taken her some time, feeling her way across each groove carved into the metal, to figure out what was written on the plate.

There was no map. Or, at least, not like the ones in the previous storage caverns. Instead, there was a simple circle, with a dot at the center. Vin wasn't certain what it was supposed to mean. The text was equally frustrating. Vin ran her fingers across the grooves, though she had long since memorized what the words said.

I have failed you.

I have planned these caverns, knowing a calamity is coming, hoping that I might find some secret that might be of use should I fall to the thing's scheming. Yet, I have nothing. I do not know how to defeat it. The only thing I can think of is to keep it at bay by taking the power at the Well for myself when it returns.

However, if you are reading this, I have failed. That means I am dead. As I write this, I find that prospect to be less tragic than I might previously have assumed. I would rather not deal with the thing. It has been my constant companion, the voice that whispers to me always, telling me to destroy, begging me to give it freedom.

I fear that it has corrupted my thoughts. It cannot sense what I think, but it can speak inside of my head. Eight hundred years of this has made it difficult to trust my own mind. Sometimes, I hear the voices, and simply assume that I am mad.

That would certainly be preferable.

I do know that these words must be written in steel to be

preserved. I have written them in a steel sheet, then ordered them scribed into a plate, knowing that in doing so, I reveal my weakness to my own priests. The thing has whispered to me that I am a fool to expose myself by writing this and letting others see it.

That is primarily why I decided to go through with the creation of this plate. Doing so seemed to make the thing angry. That is reason enough, I think. It is good that some few of my loyal priests know of my weakness, if only for the good of the empire, should I somehow fall.

I have tried to be a good ruler. At first, I was too young, too angry. I made mistakes. Yet, I have tried so hard. I nearly destroyed the world with my arrogance, and yet I fear I have nearly destroyed it again through my rule. I can do better. I will do better. I will create a land of order.

The thoughts in my mind, however, make me wonder just how much of what I do has been twisted from my original intentions. At times, my empire seems a place of peace and justice. Yet, if that is so, why can I not stop the rebellions? They cannot defeat me, and I must order them slaughtered each time they rise up. Can they not see the perfection of my system?

Regardless, this is not the place for justification. I need no justification, for I am—after a form—God. Yet, I know there is something greater than I. If I can be destroyed, It will be the cause of that destruction.

I have no advice to give. It is more powerful than I am. It is more powerful than this world. It claims to have created this world, in fact. It will destroy us all eventually.

Perhaps these stores will let mankind survive a little longer. Perhaps not. I am dead. I doubt that I should care.

Still, I do. For you are my people. I am the Hero of Ages. That is what it must mean: Hero of Ages, a hero that lives through the ages, as I do.

Know that the thing's power is not complete. Fortunately, I have hidden his body well.

And that was the end. Vin tapped the plate with frustration. Everything about the words on it seemed contrived to frustrate her. The Lord Ruler had led them on this grand chase, then at the end, he offered no hope? Elend was betting so much on what this plaque would contain, and yet, it was virtually worthless. At least the other ones had contained some relevant information about a new metal or the like.

I have failed you. It was infuriating—almost crushingly so—to come all this way, then find that the Lord Ruler had been as stumped as they were. And, if he'd known more—as his words implied that he did—why hadn't he *shared* it on the plate? And yet, she could sense his instability even through these words—his washing back and forth from contrition to arrogance. Perhaps that was Ruin's influence on him. Or, perhaps it was simply the way he had always been. Either way, Vin suspected that the Lord Ruler couldn't have told her much more that would have been of use. He'd done what he could, holding Ruin at bay for a thousand years. It had corrupted him, perhaps even driven him mad.

That didn't stop her from feeling a sharp sense of disappointment at what the plate contained. The Lord Ruler had been given a thousand years to worry about what would happen to the land if he were killed before the power returned to the Well, and even he hadn't been able to come up with a way out of the problem.

She looked up toward the plate, though in the darkness, she could not see it.

There has to be a way! she thought, refusing to accept the Lord Ruler's implication that they were doomed. *What was it you wrote at the bottom? "I have hidden his body well."*

That part seemed important. However, she hadn't been—

A sound rung through the darkness.

Vin turned immediately, growing tense, feeling for her last metal vial. Proximity to Ruin had made her jumpy, and she found her heart beating with anxiety as she listened to the echoing sounds—sounds of stone grinding against stone.

The door to the cavern was opening.

One might ask why Ruin couldn't have used Inquisitors to release him from his prison. The answer to this is simple enough, if one understands the workings of power.

Before the Lord Ruler's death, he maintained too tight a grip on them to let Ruin control them directly. Even after the Lord Ruler's death, however, such a servant of Ruin could never have rescued him. The power in the Well was of Preservation, and an Inquisitor could only have taken it by first removing his Hemalurgic spikes. That, of course, would have killed him.

Thus, Ruin needed a much more indirect way to achieve his purpose. He needed someone he hadn't tainted too much, but someone he could lead by the nose, carefully manipulating.

49

SAZED MADE A SMALL NOTATION on his diagram, comparing measurements of the waterway. From what he could tell, the Lord Ruler hadn't really needed to do much to create the underground lake. Water had already been flowing into the cavern. The Lord Ruler's engineers had simply widened the passageways, bringing in a steadier, surer flow that outpaced the natural drainage.

The result was an aquifer of good size. Some machinery in a side cave proved to be a mechanism for plugging the outlets at the bottom—presumably so that one could keep the water reserve from escaping, should something happen to the incoming supply. Unfortunately, there was no existing way to block off the inlets.

Before the Lord Ruler's creation of the reservoir, only a small amount of the water had passed into the cavern. The rest flowed instead into what were now the streets, filling the canals. So, Sazed assumed, if he could stop the water from entering the cavern, it would refill the canals.

I'll need to know more about water pressure, Sazed thought, *so I can provide enough weight to plug those inlets.* He thought he'd seen a book on the subject inside his metalmind.

He leaned back in his chair, tapping his metalmind. Memory blossomed inside his head as he withdrew a section of text: an index he'd made listing the titles of books he had in his storage. As soon as he pulled the text out, the words became as clear to him as if he'd just read and memorized them. He scanned through the list quickly, seeking the title he needed. When he found it, he scribbled it on a piece of paper. Then, he placed the list back inside his coppermind.

The experience was odd. After replacing the list, he could recollect having drawn the material out—but, he had no memory whatsoever of what the index had contained. There was a blank in his mind. Only thc words scribbled on the paper explained things that he'd known just seconds before. With that title, he could draw the appropriate book into his mind in its entirety. He selected the chapters he wanted, then stuck the rest back into the coppermind, lest they decay.

And, with those chapters, his knowledge of engineering was as fresh as if he'd just read and studied the book. He easily figured out the proper weights and balances he'd need to craft barriers that would, he hoped, return water to the streets above.

He worked alone, sitting at a fine stolen desk, a lantern lighting the cavern around him. Even with the knowledge provided by his copperminds, it was difficult work, with many calculations—not exactly the kind of research he was accustomed to. Fortunately, a Keeper's copperminds were not limited to his own interests. Each Keeper kept all of the knowledge. Sazed could vaguely remember the years he'd spent listening and memorizing. He'd only needed to know the information well enough to remember it for a short time, then he could dump it into a coppermind. In that way, he was both one of the smartest and most ignorant men who had ever lived—he had memorized so much, but had intentionally forgotten it all.

Regardless, he had access to texts on engineering as well as religion. Knowing such things did not make him a brilliant mathematician or architect—however, it did give him enough competence to make him a good deal better than a layman.

And, as he worked, he was finding it more and more difficult to deny that scholarship was something at which he excelled. He was not a leader. He was not an ambassador. Even while he served as Elend's chief ambassador, he'd spent much of his time looking through his religions. Now, when he should be heading the team in Urteau, more and more he found himself letting Spook take the lead.

Sazed was a man of research and of letters. He found contentment in his studies. Even though engineering wasn't an area he particularly enjoyed, the truth was, he'd much rather study—no matter what the topic—than do anything else. *Is it such a shameful thing,* he thought, *to be the man who likes to provide information for others, rather than be the one who has to use that information?*

The tapping of a cane on the ground announced Breeze's arrival. The Soother didn't need a cane to walk; he just preferred to carry one to look more gentlemanly. Of all the skaa thieves Sazed had known, Breeze did by far the best job of imitating a nobleman.

Sazed quickly jotted down a few more notations, then returned the chapters on water pressure to his coppermind. No need to let them decay while speaking to Breeze. For, of course, Breeze would want to talk. Sure enough, as soon as Breeze sat at Sazed's table, he scanned the diagrams, then raised an eyebrow. "That's coming along nicely, my dear man. You may have missed your calling."

Sazed smiled. "You are kind, Lord Breeze, though I fear an engineer would find this plan unsightly. Still, I think it will be sufficient."

"You really think you can do it?" Breeze asked. "Make

the waters flow as the lad asked? Is it even possible?"

"Oh, it is quite possible," Sazed said. "My expertise—not the plausibility of the task—is the item in question. The waters once filled those canals, and they can do so again. In fact, I believe that their return will be far more spectacular than the original flow. Before, much of the water was already diverted into these caverns. I should be able to block most of that and return the waters above in force. Of course, if Lord Spook wishes to keep the canals flowing, then we will have to let some of the water escape down here again. Canal works generally don't have much of a current, especially in an area where there are many locks."

Breeze raised an eyebrow.

"Actually," Sazed continued, "canals are far more fascinating than you might expect. Take, for instance, the methods of transforming a natural river into a canal—making it what is called a navigation—or perhaps look at the methods of dredging used to remove silt and ash from the depths. I have one particular book by the infamous Lord Fedre, who—despite his reputation—was an absolute genius when it came to canal architecture. Why, I've had to . . ." Sazed trailed off, then smiled wanly. "I apologize. You're not interested in this, are you?"

"No," Breeze said, "but it's enough that *you* are, Sazed. It's good to see you excited about your studies again. I don't know what it was you were working on before, but it always bothered me that you wouldn't share it with anyone. Seemed like you were almost ashamed of what you were doing. Now, however—this is like the Sazed I remember!"

Sazed looked down at his scribbled notes and diagrams. It was true. The last time that he had been so excited about a line of study was . . .

When he'd been with her. Working on their collection of myths and references regarding the Hero of Ages.

"In truth, Lord Breeze," Sazed said, "I do feel somewhat guilty."

Breeze rolled his eyes. "Sazed. Do you *always* have to be feeling guilty about something? Back in the original crew, you felt you weren't doing enough to help us overthrow the Lord Ruler. Then, once we killed him, you were distraught because you weren't doing what the other Keepers told you to. Do you want to tell me exactly how you go about feeling guilty for *studying,* of all things?"

"I enjoy it."

"That's wonderful, my dear man," Breeze said. "Why be ashamed of that enjoyment? It's not like you enjoy killing puppies or something like that. True, I think you're a bit crazy, but if you want to enjoy something so particularly esoteric, then you should feel free. It leaves more room for those of us who prefer more common delights—such as getting drunk on Straff Venture's finest wines."

Sazed smiled. He knew that Breeze was Pushing on his emotions, making him feel better, but he did not rebel against the emotions. The truth was, he *did* feel good. Better than he had in some time.

Though, still . . .

"It is not so simple, Lord Breeze," Sazed said, setting down his pen. "I feel happy being able to simply sit and read, without having to be in charge. That is why I feel guilty."

"Not everybody is meant to be a leader, Sazed."

"No," Sazed said, "but Lord Elend did put me in charge of securing this city. I should be planning our overthrow of the Citizen, not letting Lord Spook do it."

"My dear man!" Breeze said, leaning down. "Have I taught you nothing? Being in charge isn't about *doing* anything—it's about making certain that other people do what they're supposed to! Delegation, my friend. Without it, we would have to bake our own bread and dig our own latrines!" Then, Breeze leaned in. "And, trust me. You don't want to taste anything I've had a hand in baking. Ever. Particularly after I've cleaned a latrine."

Sazed shook his head. "This isn't what Tindwyl would have wanted of me. She respected leaders and politicians."

"Correct me if you must," Breeze said, "but didn't she fall in love with *you,* not some king or prince?"

"Well, love is perhaps—"

"Come now, Sazed," Breeze said. "You were mooning about as surely as any teenage boy with a new fancy. And, while she was a bit more reserved, she did love you. One didn't have to be a Soother to see that much."

Sazed sighed, looking down.

"Is this what she'd want of you, Sazed?" Breeze said. "To deny who you are? To become yet another stuffy politician?"

"I do not know, Lord Breeze," Sazed said softly. "I . . . I don't have her anymore. And so, perhaps, I can remember her by being involved in what she loved."

"Sazed," Breeze said frankly, "how is it you can be so wise in so many areas, yet be so completely *stupid* about this?"

"I . . ."

"A man *is* what he has passion about," Breeze said. "I've found that if you give up what you want most for what you *think* you should want more, you'll just end up miserable."

"And if what I want isn't what society needs?" Sazed said. "Sometimes, we just have to do what we don't enjoy. That is a simple fact of life, I think."

Breeze shrugged. "I don't worry about that. I just do what I'm good at. In my case, that's making other people do things that I don't want to. It all fits together, in the end."

Sazed shook his head. It wasn't that simple, and his depression lately hadn't *only* been tied to Tindwyl and her death. He had put off his study of the religions, but he knew that he would be driven to return to them. The work with the canals was a welcome distraction, but even so, Sazed could feel his earlier conclusions and work looming.

He didn't *want* to discover that the last religions in the group held no answers. That was part of why it was so relaxing for him to study something else, for engineering didn't threaten his worldview. However, he could not distract himself forever. He would find the answers, or the lack of answers, eventually. His portfolio sat beneath the desk, resting against the sack of metalminds.

For now, however, he allowed himself a reprieve. But even

with his concern over the religions abated for the moment, there were concerns that needed addressing. He nodded his head in the direction of the lake. Spook, just barely visible, stood at the edge, speaking with Goradel and some of the soldiers.

"And what of him, Lord Breeze?" Sazed asked in a whisper, low enough that even Spook wouldn't be able to hear. "As I said, Emperor Venture placed me in charge of this matter. What if I let Spook take control, and then he fails? I worry that the young man is not . . . seasoned enough for this task."

Breeze shrugged. "He seems to be doing well so far. Remember how young Vin was when she killed the Lord Ruler."

"Yes," Sazed whispered, "but this situation is different. Spook seems . . . odd, lately. He is certainly hiding things from us. Why is he so determined to take this city?"

"I think it's good for the boy to show a little determination," Breeze said, sitting back in his chair. "That lad has been far too passive for most of his life."

"Do you not worry about his plan? This could easily collapse around us."

"Sazed," Breeze said. "Do you remember our meeting a few weeks back? Spook asked me why we couldn't just topple Quellion like we did the Lord Ruler."

"I remember," Sazed said. "You told him the reason we couldn't was because we didn't have Kelsier anymore."

Breeze nodded. "Well," he said softly, pointing his cane toward Spook, "my opinion has been revised. We don't have Kelsier, but it's looking more and more like we have something similar."

Sazed frowned.

"I'm not saying the lad has Kelsier's force of personality. His . . . presence. However, you've heard the reputation the boy is gaining among the people. Kelsier succeeded not because of who he was, but because of who people *thought* he was. That's something I didn't believe we could replicate. I'm starting to think I was wrong."

Sazed wasn't as easily convinced. Yet, he kept his reservations to himself as he turned back to his research. Spook must have noticed them looking over at him, for a few minutes later he made his way to Sazed's table. The boy blinked against the lantern-light, soft though it was, and pulled up a chair. The fine furniture looked odd to Sazed, contrasted against the rows of dusty, utilitarian shelves.

Spook looked fatigued. *How long has it been since he slept?* Sazed thought. *He's still up whenever I bed down, and awake before I rise.*

"Something doesn't feel right here," Spook said.

"Oh?" Breeze asked. "Other than the fact that we're chatting beside an underground lake in a storehouse built by the Lord Ruler underneath an Inquisitor fortress?"

Spook gave the Soother a flat look, then glanced at Sazed. "I feel like we should have been attacked by now."

"What makes you say that?" Sazed asked.

"I know Quellion, Saze. The man's a bully after the classical style. He came to power through force, and he keeps control by giving the people plenty of alcohol and tiny freedoms, like letting them go to bars at night. At the same time, however, he keeps everyone on the edge of fear."

"How *did* he take charge, anyway?" Breeze asked. "How did he get control before some nobleman with a good set of house guards could do it?"

"Mists," Spook said. "He went out in them, and declared that anyone faithful to the Survivor would be safe in them. Then, the mists started killing, and gave a handy confirmation of what he'd said. He made a big deal about the mists killing those who had evil in their hearts. The people were so worried about what was happening that they listened to him. He managed to make a law that required everyone to go out in the mists, so that they could see who died and who didn't. The ones who survived were—he declared—pure. He told them they could set up a nice little utopia. After that, they started killing nobility."

"Ah," Breeze said. "Clever."

"Yeah," Spook said. "He completely glossed over the fact that the nobility never got taken by the mists."

"Wait," Sazed said. "*What?*"

Spook shrugged. "Hard to confirm now, but that's what the stories say. The nobility seemed immune to the mistsickness. Not skaa who had noble blood, but actually nobility."

"How odd," Breeze noted.

More than odd, Sazed thought. *Downright strange. Does Elend know about this connection?* As Sazed considered it, it seemed unlikely that Elend did. Their army and allies were all made up of skaa. The only nobility they knew were those back in Luthadel, and they had all chosen to stay inside at night, rather than risk going into the mists.

"Either way," Spook said, "Quellion's a bully. And bullies don't like anyone in their turf who can challenge them. We should have had some kind of attempt on our lives by now."

"The lad has a point," Breeze said. "Quellion's type doesn't kill just in fancy executions. I'd bet that for every person he throws into one of those buildings, there are three dead in an alley somewhere, slowly being buried in ash."

"I've told Goradel and his men to be particularly careful," Spook said, "and I've prowled our perimeter. However, I haven't caught any assassins so much as spying on us. Quellion's troops just sit out there, watching us, but not doing anything."

Breeze rubbed his chin. "Perhaps Quellion is more afraid of us than you assume."

"Perhaps," Spook said, sighing. He rubbed his forehead.

"Lord Spook," Sazed said carefully, "you should sleep."

"I'm fine," Spook said.

If I didn't know better, I'd say he was burning pewter to stay awake, Sazed thought. *Or, am I just looking for signs to confirm what I worried about before?*

We never questioned when Vin or Kelsier manifested powers beyond what even normal Allomancers were capable of. Why should I be so suspicious of Spook? Is it simply be-

cause I know him too well? Do I focus on my memories of the boy when he has obviously become a man?

"Anyway," Spook said, "how goes the research?"

"Rather well, actually," Sazed said, turning around several of his diagrams so that Spook could see them. "I am about ready to begin work on the actual construction."

"How long will it take, do you think?"

"A few weeks, perhaps," Sazed said. "A rather short time, all things considered. Fortunately, the people who drained the canals left behind a large amount of rubble, which I can use. In addition, the Lord Ruler stocked this storehouse quite well. There is timber, as well as some basic carpentry supplies, and even some pulley networks."

"What was that creature preparing for?" Breeze said. "Food and water, I can understand. But, blankets? Timber? *Pulleys*?"

"Disaster, Lord Breeze," Sazed said. "He included everything that a people would need in the event that the city itself was destroyed. He even included bedrolls for sleeping and infirmary supplies. Perhaps he feared koloss rampages."

"No," Spook said. "He prepared for exactly what is happening. Now, you'll be building something to plug the water? I kind of thought you'd just collapse the tunnels."

"Oh, goodness no," Sazed said. "We don't have the manpower or equipment to cause a cave-in. Also, I wouldn't want to do anything that would risk bringing the cavern down upon us. My plans are to build a wooden blocking mechanism that can be lowered into the current. Enough weight, along with the proper framework, should provide reinforcement to stop the flow. It's actually not unlike the mechanisms used in the locks of canals."

"Which," Breeze added, "he'll be happy to tell you about. At length."

Sazed smiled. "I do think that—"

He was cut off, however, as Captain Goradel arrived, looking a fair bit more solemn than usual.

"Lord Spook," Goradel said. "Someone is waiting for you above."

"Who?" Spook asked, pulling his spectacles and bandage from a pocket. "Durn?"

"No, my lord. She says she's the Citizen's sister."

"I'm not here to join with you," the woman—Beldre—said.

They sat in an austere audience chamber in the Inquisition building above their cavern. The room's chairs lacked any sort of cushioning, and steel plates hung on the wooden walls as decoration—to Sazed, they were uncomfortable reminders of what he had seen when he had visited the Conventical of Seran.

Beldre was a young woman with auburn hair. She wore a simple, Citizen-approved dress, dyed red. She sat with hands in lap, and while she met the eyes of those in the room, there was a nervous apprehension to her that weakened her position considerably.

"Why *are* you here then, my dear?" Breeze asked carefully. He sat in a chair across from Beldre. Allrianne sat at his side, watching the girl with an air of disapproval. Spook paced in the background, occasionally turning toward the window.

He thinks this is a feint, Sazed realized. *That the girl is a distraction to throw us off before we get attacked.* The boy wore his dueling canes, strapped to his waist like swords. How well did Spook even know how to fight?

"I'm here . . ." Beldre said, looking down. "I'm here because you're going to kill my brother."

"Now, where did you get an idea like that!" Breeze said. "We're in the city to forge a treaty with your brother, not assassinate him! Do we look like the types who would be very good at that sort of thing?"

Beldre shot a glance at Spook.

"Him excluded," Breeze said. "Spook is harmless. Really, you shouldn't—"

"Breeze," Spook interrupted, glancing over with his strange, bandaged eyes, spectacles hidden underneath and bulging out from the face just slightly under the cloth. "That's enough. You're making us both seem like idiots. Beldre knows why we're here—everyone in the city knows why we're here."

The room fell silent.

He . . . looks a little bit like an Inquisitor, wearing those spectacles beneath the bandages, Sazed thought, shivering.

"Beldre," Spook said. "You honestly expect us to think that you came here simply to plead for your brother's life?"

She glanced at Spook, defiantly meeting his eyes—or, rather, his lack thereof. "You can try to sound harsh, but I know you won't hurt me. You're of the Survivor's crew."

Spook folded his arms.

"Please," Beldre said. "Quellion is a good man, like you. You have to give him more time. Don't kill him."

"What makes you think we'd kill him, child?" Sazed asked. "You just said that you thought we would never harm you. Why is your brother different?"

Beldre glanced down. "You're the ones who killed the Lord Ruler. You overthrew the entire empire. My brother doesn't believe it—he thinks that you rode the Survivor's popularity, claiming to be his friends after he'd sacrificed himself."

Spook snorted. "I wonder where your brother got an idea like that. Perhaps he knows someone else who's claimed to have the Survivor's blessing, *killing* people in his name . . ."

Beldre blushed.

"Your brother doesn't trust us," Sazed said. "Why do you?"

Beldre shrugged. "I don't know," she said quietly. "I guess . . . men who lie don't save children from burning buildings."

Sazed glanced at Spook, but couldn't read anything in the young man's hard expression. Finally, Spook spoke. "Breeze, Sazed, Allrianne, outside with me. Goradel, watch the woman."

Spook pushed his way out into the hallway, and Sazed followed with the others. Once the door was closed, Spook turned to regard the rest of them. "Well?"

"I don't like her," Allrianne said, folding her arms.

"Of course you don't, dear," Breeze said. "You never like competition."

"Competition?" Allrianne huffed. "From a timid little thing like that? Honestly."

"What do you think, Breeze?" Spook asked.

"About the girl, or about you insulting me in there?"

"The first," Spook said. "Your pride isn't important right now."

"My dear fellow," Breeze said, "my pride is *always* important. As for the girl, I'll tell you this—she's terrified. Despite what she says, she's very, very frightened—which means that she hasn't done this sort of thing very often. My guess is that she's noble."

Allrianne nodded. "Definitely. Just look at her hands—when they're not shaking from fright, you can see that they're clean and soft. She grew up being pampered."

"She's obviously a bit naive," Sazed said. "Otherwise she wouldn't have come here, expecting that we'd just listen to her, then let her go."

Spook nodded. He cocked his head, as if listening to something. Then he walked forward, pushing open the door to the room.

"Well?" Beldre asked, maintaining her false air of forcefulness. "Have you decided to listen to me?"

"In a way," Spook said. "I'm going to give you more time to explain your point. Plenty of time, actually."

"I . . . don't have long," Beldre said. "I need to get back to my brother. I didn't tell him I was leaving, and . . ." She trailed off, apparently seeing something in Spook's expression. "You're going to take me captive, aren't you?"

"Breeze," Spook said, turning. "How do you think the people would respond if I started spreading the rumor that the Citizen's own sister has turned against him, fleeing to our embassy for protection?"

Breeze smiled. "Well now. That's clever! Almost makes up for how you treated me. Have I mentioned yet how rude that was?"

"You can't!" Beldre said, standing, facing Spook. "Nobody will believe that I've deserted!"

"Oh?" Spook asked. "Did you speak to the soldiers outside before you came in here?"

"Of course not," Beldre said. "They'd have tried to stop me. I ran up the steps before they could."

"So, they can confirm that you entered the building of your own will," Spook said. "Sneaking around a guard post."

"Doesn't look good," Breeze agreed.

Beldre wilted slightly, sitting down in her chair. *By the Forgotten Gods,* Sazed thought. *She really* is *naive. The Citizen must have expended a great deal of effort in sheltering her so.*

Of course, from what Sazed had heard, Quellion rarely let the girl out of his sight. She was always with him, being watched over. *How will he react?* Sazed thought with a chill. *What will he do when he learns we have her? Attack?*

Perhaps that was the plan. If Spook could force an outright attack on the Citizen's part, it would look bad. Especially bad when Quellion was turned back by a few soldiers—he couldn't know how well fortified their position was.

When did Spook get so clever?

Beldre looked up from her seat, a few tears of frustration gleaming in her eyes. "You can't do this. This is deceitful! What would the Survivor say if he knew what you were planning?"

"The Survivor?" Spook asked, chuckling. "I have a feeling he'd approve. If he were here, actually, I think he'd suggest that we do this very thing . . ."

One can see Ruin's craftiness in the meticulousness of his planning. He managed to orchestrate the downfall of the Lord Ruler only a short time before Preservation's power returned to the Well of Ascension. And then, within a few years of that event, he had freed himself.

On the time scale of gods and their power, this very tricky timing was as precise as an expert cut performed by the most talented of surgeons.

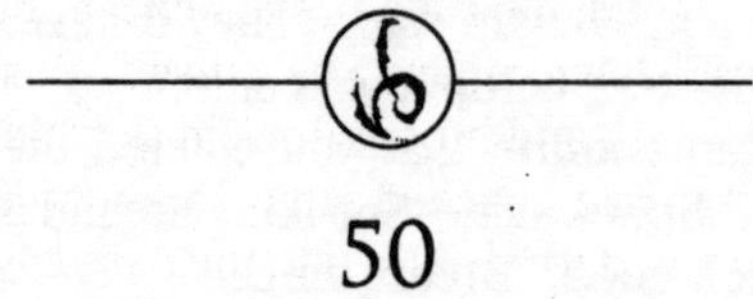

50

THE DOOR TO THE CAVERN opened.

Vin immediately downed her last vial of metals.

She jumped, tossing a coin behind herself, leaping up onto the top of one of the freestanding shelves. The cavern echoed with the sound of stone on stone as its door opened. Vin threw herself forward—Pushing off the coin—to shoot toward the front of the room. A crack of light outlined the door, and even this small amount of illumination hurt her eyes.

She gritted her teeth against the light, blinking as she landed. She threw herself up against the wall just to the side of the door, clutching her knives, flaring pewter to help herself deal with the sudden pain of light. Tears crept down her cheeks.

The door stopped moving. A solitary man stepped into the cavern, bearing a raised lantern. He wore a fine black suit and gentleman's hat.

Vin ignored him.

She slipped around the man and ducked through the door, entering the small chamber beyond. A group of startled workers shied back, dropping ropes which were connected to the door's opening mechanisms. Vin ignored these men as well, other than to shove her way through them. Dropping a coin, she Pushed herself upward. The wooden ladder's rungs became a blur beside her as she soared up and slammed into the trapdoor in the ceiling.

And bounced off it with a grunt of pain.

She desperately caught rungs of the ladder as she began to

fall, ignoring the sudden sting in her shoulder from hitting so hard. She flared pewter and pushed down on a rung with her legs, then slammed her back up against the trapdoor, trying to force it up and open.

She strained. Then, the rung broke beneath her feet, sending her toppling down again. She cursed, Pushing off her coin to slow her fall, and hit the floor in a crouch.

The workers had backed into a huddle—uncertain whether they wanted to venture into the dark cavern, but also uncertain whether they wanted to remain in the small room with a Mistborn. The suited nobleman had turned. He held his lantern high, illuminating Vin. A bit of broken ladder rung fell free and cracked to the stone floor beside her.

"The trapdoor is well secured with a very large rock on top of it, Lady Venture," the nobleman said. Vin vaguely recognized him. He was a bit overweight, but was kempt, with very short hair and a thoughtful face.

"Tell the men up above to remove the stone," Vin said quietly, raising a dagger.

"That is not going to happen, I'm afraid."

"I can make it happen," Vin said, stepping forward. The workers pulled back even further.

The nobleman smiled. "Lady Venture, let me assure you of several things. The first is that you are the only Allomancer among us, and so I have no doubt that you could slaughter us with the barest of efforts. The second is that the stone above is not moving anytime soon, so we might as well sit down and have a pleasant chat, as opposed to brandishing weapons and threatening each other."

There was something . . . disarming about the man. Vin checked with bronze, but he wasn't burning any metals. Just to be certain, she Pulled a bit on his emotions, making him more trusting and friendly, then tried to Soothe away any sense of guile he might have felt.

"I see that you're at least considering my offer," the nobleman said, waving to one of the workers. The worker hastily opened his pack, pulling out two folding chairs, then arranging them on the ground before the open stone door. The nobleman placed the lantern to the side, then sat down.

Vin crept a little closer. "Why do I recognize you?"

"I'm a friend of your husband," the nobleman said.

"Telden," Vin said, placing him. "Telden Hasting."

Telden nodded. She had seen him at the ball a few weeks back, the first one they had attended. But, she'd known him from someplace earlier than that. He'd been one of Elend's friends in Luthadel, before the Collapse.

Warily, Vin took the offered seat, trying to figure out Yomen's game. Did he think she wouldn't kill Telden, just because he'd been Elend's friend?

Telden lounged in his chair, somewhat less proper than the average nobleman. He waved a worker forward, and the man presented two bottles. "Wine," Telden said. "One is pure, the other contains an extremely powerful sedative."

Vin raised an eyebrow. "This is to be some sort of guessing game?"

"Hardly," Telden said, opening one of the bottles. "I'm far too thirsty—and from what I hear, you're not the type who possesses an excessive amount of patience for games."

Vin cocked her head as Telden accepted two cups from a servant, then poured some of the ruby wine into each. As she watched, she realized why he was so disarming. He reminded her of Elend—the old, carefree Elend. From what she could tell, this Telden was genuinely still like that.

I have to grant Yomen that much, she thought. *His city may not be perfect, but he has created a place where men like Telden can retain some of their innocence.*

Telden took a drink of his wine, proffering the other cup to Vin. She slid one of her knives into her sheath, then took the cup. She didn't drink—and had no intention of doing so.

"This is the wine without the sedative," Telden said. "Good vintage, too. Yomen is a true gentleman—if he's going to send one of his friends down into a pit to die, he'll at least provide them with expensive wine to soften the blow."

"I'm supposed to believe that you're here to be imprisoned too?" Vin asked flatly.

"Of course not," Telden said. "Though many consider my mission to be hopeless."

"And that mission is?"

"To get you to drink some of the drugged wine, so that you can be safely transported up above."

Vin snorted.

"I see that you agree with my detractors," Telden said.

"You just gave yourself away," Vin said. "You just said that I'm supposed to drink the wine and fall unconscious. That means you have a way to signal to those above that I've been dealt with, so they can remove the stone and let you out. You have the power to free us. And I have the power to make you do as I wish."

"Emotional Allomancy cannot control me to that extent," Telden said. "I'm no Allomancer, but I do know something of it. I suspect that you're manipulating my emotions right now, actually—which really isn't necessary, since I'm being completely frank with you."

"I don't need Allomancy to make you talk," Vin said, glancing down at the knife she still had in her other hand.

Telden laughed. "You think that King Yomen—yes, he's up above—won't be able to tell if I'm speaking under duress? I have no doubt that you'd be able to break me, but I'm not going to betray my word simply on threats, so you'd have to cut off a few fingers or something before I'd do as you ask. I'm pretty certain that Yomen and the others would hear me screaming."

"I could kill the servants," Vin said. "One at a time, until you agree to tell Yomen that I'm unconscious and have him open the door."

Telden smiled. "You think that I'd care if you kill them?"

"You're one of Elend's friends," Vin said. "You were one of those who talked philosophy with him."

"Philosophy," Telden said, "and politics. Elend, however, was the only one of us interested in the skaa. I assure you, the rest of us really didn't understand where he got such a fascination with them." He shrugged. "However, I'm not a heartless man. If you kill enough of them, perhaps I *would* break down and do as you ask. Might as well get started, then."

Vin glanced at the servants. They seemed terrified of her, and Telden's words didn't help. After a few moments of silence, Telden chuckled.

"You are Elend's wife," he noted. "Yomen is aware of this, you see. He was mostly convinced that you wouldn't kill any of us, despite your rather fearsome reputation. From what we hear, you have a habit of killing kings and gods, perhaps the occasional soldier. Skaa servants, however . . ."

Vin looked away from the servants, but didn't meet Telden's eyes, fearing that he'd see confirmation in them. He was wrong about her—she would kill those servants if she thought it would get her out. However, she was uncertain. If Yomen heard screams, he wouldn't be likely to open the trapdoor, and Vin would have slaughtered innocents for no reason.

"So," Telden said, finishing off his wine. "We are at a stalemate. We assume that you're running low on food down here, unless you've found a way to open those cans. Even if you have, there's nothing you can do down here to help up above. My guess is that unless you take the wine, we'll all end up starving to death in this cavern."

Vin sat back in her chair. *There has to be a way out—a chance to exploit this.*

However, it was incredibly unlikely that she'd be able to break through that door above. She could *maybe* use duralumin and steel to Push her way through. However, her steel and pewter would be gone, and she was out of metal vials.

Telden's words, unfortunately, held a great deal of truth. Even if Vin could survive in the cavern, she'd be stagnant and useless. The siege would continue up above—she didn't even know how that was going—and the world would continue to die by Ruin's machinations.

She needed to get out of the cavern. Even if that meant being put into Yomen's hands. She eyed the bottle of drugged wine.

Damn, she thought. *That obligator is far cleverer than we expected.* The wine would certainly have been prepared with enough strength to knock out an Allomancer.

However . . .

Pewter made the body resistant to all kinds of drugs. If she flared pewter with duralumin after drinking the wine, would it perhaps burn away the poison and leave her awake? She could pretend to be unconscious, then escape above.

It seemed like a stretch. And yet, what was she to do? Her food was almost gone, and her chances for escaping were slim. She didn't know what Yomen wanted of her—and Telden would be very unlikely to tell her—but he must not want her dead. If that had been the case, he'd simply have left her to starve.

She had a choice. Either wait longer in the cavern, or gamble on a better chance to escape up above. She thought for just a moment, then made up her mind. She reached for the bottle. Even if her trick with pewter didn't work, she'd rather gamble on getting into a better situation up above.

Telden chuckled. "They did say that you were a decisive one. That's rather refreshing—I've spent far too long with stuffy noblemen who take years to come to any firm decisions."

Vin ignored him. She easily popped the cork off of the bottle, then raised it and took a swig. The drugs began to take effect almost immediately. She settled back in her chair, letting her eyes droop, trying to give the impression that she was falling asleep. Indeed, it was very difficult to remain awake. Her mind was clouding despite flared pewter.

She slumped, feeling herself drift away. *Here goes,* she thought, then burned duralumin. Her body flared with hyper-enhanced pewter. Immediately, the feeling of tiredness went away. She almost bolted upright from the sudden burst of energy. Telden was chuckling. "I'll be," he said to one of the servants. "She actually went for it."

"You'd be dead if she hadn't, my lord," the servant said. "We'd all be dead."

And then the duralumin ran out. Her pewter disappeared with a puff, and with it went her immunity to the drug, which hadn't burned away. It had been a long shot anyway.

She barely heard her weapon click as it slipped from her fingers and hit the floor. Then, she fell unconscious.

Once Ruin was free from his prison, he was able to influence people more strongly—but impaling someone with a Hemalurgic spike was difficult no matter what the circumstances.

To achieve such things, he apparently began with people who already had a tenuous grip on reality. Their insanity made them more open to his touch, and he could use them to spike more stable people. Either way, it's impressive how many important people Ruin managed to spike. King Penrod, ruling Luthadel at the time, is a very good example of this.

51

ELEND FLEW THROUGH THE MISTS. He'd never quite been able to manage Vin's horseshoe trick. Somehow, she could keep herself in the air, bounding from Push to Push, then Pulling each horseshoe back up behind her after she used it. To Elend, the process looked like a cyclone of potentially lethal chunks of metal with Vin at the center.

He dropped a coin, then Pushed himself in a powerful leap. He'd given up on the horseshoe method after four or five failed attempts. Vin had seemed puzzled that he couldn't get it down—she'd apparently figured it out on her own, needing only about a half hour's practice to perfect it.

But, well, that was Vin.

Elend made do with coins, of which he carried a rather large bag. Copper clips, the smallest of the old imperial coins, worked perfectly for his purposes—particularly since he was apparently much more powerful than other Mistborn. Each of his Pushes carried him farther than they should have, and he really didn't use that many coins, even when traveling a long distance.

It felt good to be away. He felt free as he plunged down from his leap, dropping through the shifting darkness, then flared pewter and landed with a muffled thump. The ground in this particular valley was relatively free of ash—it had drifted, leaving a small corridor where it only came up to his mid-calf. So, he ran for a few minutes, for the change.

A mistcloak fluttered behind him. He wore dark clothing, rather than one of his white uniforms. It seemed appropriate; besides, he'd never really had a chance to be a true Mistborn. Since discovering his powers, he'd spent his life at war. There wasn't all that much need for him to go scuttling about in the darkness, particularly not with Vin around to do it better.

I can see why Vin would find this intoxicating, he thought, dropping another coin and bounding between two hilltops. Even with the stress of Vin's capture and the threat to the empire, there was an exhilarating freedom about cruising through the mists. It almost allowed him to forget about the wars, the destruction, and the responsibility.

Then, he landed, ash coming up to nearly his waist. He stood for a few moments, looking down at the soft black powder. He couldn't escape it. Vin was in danger, the empire was collapsing, and his people were starving. It was his job to fix these things—that was the burden he'd taken upon himself when he'd become emperor.

He Pushed himself into the air, leaving a trail of ash fluttering in the mists behind him.

I certainly hope Sazed and Breeze are having better luck in Urteau, he thought. He was worried about his chances with Fadrex, and the Central Dominance was going to need the grain in the Urteau cache if they were going to plant enough food for the coming winter.

He couldn't worry about that now. He simply had to count

on his friends to be effective. Elend's job was to do something to help Vin. He couldn't just sit and wait in the camp, letting Yomen pull the strings. And yet, he didn't dare try to assassinate Yomen—not after the man had tricked both of them so cleverly.

And so, Elend ran, heading northeast, toward the last known location of a koloss army. The time for subtlety and diplomacy was over. Elend needed a threat—something he could hold over Yomen's head and, if necessary, use to batter him. And nothing was better at battering a city than koloss. Perhaps he was a fool for seeking out the brutes on his own. Perhaps it was wrong to give up on diplomacy. Yet, he had made his decision. It seemed he had failed in so many things lately—protecting Vin, keeping Luthadel safe, defending his people—that he simply *needed* to act.

Ahead, he saw a light in the mists. He landed, running through a field of knee-deep ash. Only flared pewter gave him the strength to manage it. When he got closer, he saw a village. He heard screams. He saw shadows scrambling about in fright.

He leaped, dropping a coin, flaring his metals. He passed through curling mist, looming over the village and its frightened occupants, his mistcloak flaring. Several of the homes were burning. And, by that light, he could see the hulking dark forms of koloss moving through the streets. Elend picked a beast who was raising its weapon to strike, then Pulled. Below, he heard the koloss grunt, but it managed to hang onto its weapon. However, the koloss itself wasn't that much heavier than Elend—and so it was Pulled up into the air by one arm as Elend was yanked downward. Elend Pulled himself against a door hinge as he fell, edging himself just to the side of the confused flying koloss. He sprayed the beast with coins as he passed.

Beast and weapon spun in the air. Elend landed in the street before a huddled group of skaa. The flying koloss's weapon hit the ashen earth point-first beside him. The koloss itself dropped dead on the other side of the street.

A large group of koloss turned, bloodred eyes shining in

the firelight, frenzy making them excited about the prospect of a challenge. He would have to frighten them first, before he'd be able to take control of them. He was looking forward to that this time.

How could they possibly have once been people? Elend wondered, dashing forward and yanking the fallen koloss sword from the ground as he passed it, throwing out a spray of black soil. The Lord Ruler had created the creatures. Was this what had happened to those who had opposed him? Had they become koloss to make his army? The creatures had great strength and fortitude, and could subsist on the barest of sustenance. Yet, to make men—even your enemies—into monsters such as this?

Elend ducked forward, dropping one beast by shearing its legs at the knees. Then he jumped, lopping off the arm of another. He spun, slamming his crude sword through the chest of a third. He felt no remorse at killing what had once been innocents. Those people were dead. The creatures that remained would propagate themselves by using other humans unless they were stopped.

Or unless they were controlled.

Elend cried out, spinning through the group of koloss, wielding a sword that should have been too heavy for him. More and more creatures took notice, turning to tromp down streets lit by the light of burning buildings. This was a very large group, by scout reports—some thirty thousand in number. That many would quickly overrun such a small village, annihilating it like a small pile of ash before storm winds.

Elend would not let that happen. He fought, killing beast after beast. He'd come to gain himself a new army, but as the time passed, he found himself fighting for another reason. How many villages such as this one had been destroyed without anyone in Luthadel pausing to give so much as a passing thought? How many subjects—claimed by Elend, even if they didn't know it—had he lost to the koloss? How many had he failed to protect already?

Elend sheared a koloss head free, then spun, Pushing two smaller beasts away by their swords. A massive twelve-footer was stomping forward, weapon raised. Elend gritted his teeth, then raised his own sword, flaring pewter.

Weapon met weapon in the blazing village, metal ringing like a forge under the hammer. And Elend stood his ground, matching strength with a monster twice his height.

The koloss stood, dumbfounded.

Stronger than I should be, Elend thought, twisting and cutting the surprised creature's arm free. *Why can't that strength protect the people I rule?*

He cried out, slicing the koloss clean through at the waist—if only to show that he could. The beast fell into two gory pieces.

Why? Elend thought with rage. *What strength must I possess, what must I do, to protect them?*

Vin's words, spoken months ago back in the city of Vetitan, returned to him. She'd called everything he did short-term. But, what more could he do? He was no slayer of gods, no divine hero of prophecy. He was just a man.

And, it seemed that these days, ordinary men—even Allomancers—weren't worth very much. He screamed as he killed, ripping through another pack of koloss. And yet, like his efforts back at Fadrex, it just didn't seem like enough.

Around him, the village still burned. As he fought, he could hear women crying, children screaming, men dying. Even the efforts of a Mistborn were negligible. He could kill and kill, but that would not save the people of the village. He screamed, Pushing out with a Soothing, yet the koloss resisted him. He didn't bring even a single one under his control. Did that mean that an Inquisitor controlled them? Or were they simply not frightened enough?

He fought on. And, as he did, the prevalence of death around him seemed a metaphor for all he had done over the last three years. He should have been able to protect the people—he'd tried *so hard* to protect the people. He'd stopped armies, overthrown tyrants, reworked laws, and scavenged supplies. And yet, all of that was a tiny drop of salvation in a vast ocean of death, chaos, and pain. He couldn't save the empire by protecting a corner of it, just as he couldn't save the village by killing a small fraction of the koloss.

What good was killing another monster if it was just replaced by two more? What good was food to feed his people if the ash just smothered everything anyway? What good was he, an emperor who couldn't even defend the people of a single village?

Elend had never lusted for power. He'd been a theorist and a scholar—ruling an empire had mostly been an academic exercise for him. Yet, as he fought on that dark night in the burning mists and falling ash, he began to understand. As people died around him despite his most frenzied efforts, he could see what would drive men for more and more power.

Power to protect. At that moment, he would have accepted the powers of godhood, if it would mean having the strength to save the people around him.

He dropped another koloss, then spun as he heard a scream. A young woman was being pulled from a nearby house, despite an older man holding onto her arm, both yelling for help. Elend reached to his sash, pulling free his bag of coins. He tossed it into the air, then simultaneously Pushed on some of the coins inside and Pulled on others. The sack exploded with twinkling bits of metal, and Elend shot some forward into the body of the koloss yanking on the woman.

It grunted, but did not stop. Coins rarely worked against koloss—you had to hit them just right to kill them. Vin could do it.

Elend wasn't in a mood for such subtlety, even had he possessed it. He yelled in defiance, snapping more coins at the beast. He flipped them up off the ground toward himself, then flung them forward, shooting missile after glittering missile into the creature's blue body. Its back became a glistening mass of too-red blood, and finally it slumped over.

Elend spun, turning from the relieved father and daughter to face down another koloss. It raised its weapon to strike, but Elend just screamed at it in anger.

I should be able to protect them! he thought. He needed to take control of the entire group, not waste time fighting them one at a time. But, they resisted his Allomancy, even as he Pushed on their emotions again. Where was the Inquisitor guardian?

As the koloss swung its weapon, Elend flared pewter and flung himself to the side, then sheared the creature's hand free at the wrist. As the beast screamed in pain, Elend threw himself back into the fight. The villagers began to rally around him. They obviously had no training for war—they were likely under Yomen's protection and didn't need to worry about bandits or roving armies. Yet, despite their lack of skill, they obviously knew to stay close to the Mistborn. Their desperate, pleading eyes prodded Elend on, drove him to cut down koloss after koloss.

For the moment, he didn't have to worry about the right or wrong of the situation. He could simply *fight*. The desire for battle burned within him like metal—the desire, even, to kill. And so he fought on—fought for the surprise in the eyes of the townspeople, for the hope each of his blows seemed to inspire. They had given their lives up for lost, and then a man had dropped from the sky to defend them.

Two years before, during the siege of Luthadel, Vin had attacked Cett's fortification and slaughtered three hundred of his soldiers. Elend had trusted that she had good reasons for the attack, but he'd never understood how she could do such a thing. At least, not until this night, fighting in an unnamed village, too much ash in the dark sky, the mists on fire, koloss dying in ranks before him.

The Inquisitor didn't appear. Frustrated, Elend spun away from a group of koloss, leaving one dying in his wake, then extinguished his metals. The creatures surrounded him, and he burned duralumin, then burned zinc, and *Pulled*.

The village fell silent.

Elend paused, stumbling slightly as he finished his spin. He looked through the falling ash, turning toward the remaining koloss—thousands and thousands of them—who now suddenly stood motionless and patient around him, under his control at last.

There's no way I took them all at once, he thought warily. What had happened to the Inquisitor? There was usually one with a mob of koloss this big. Had it fled? That would explain why suddenly Elend had been able to control the koloss.

Worried, yet uncertain what else to do, he turned to scan the village. Some people had gathered to stare at him. They seemed to be in shock—instead of doing something about the burning buildings, they simply stood in the mists, watching him.

He should have felt triumphant. And yet, his victory was spoiled by the Inquisitor's absence. In addition, the village was in flames—by this point, very few structures remained that weren't burning. Elend hadn't saved the village. He'd found his koloss army, as he'd planned, but he felt as if he'd failed in some greater way. He sighed, dropping his sword from tired, bloody fingers, then walked toward the villagers. As he moved, he was disturbed by the number of koloss bodies he passed. Had he really slain so many?

Another part of him—quiescent now, but still aflame—was sorry that the time for killing had ended. He stopped before a silent group of villagers.

"You're him, aren't you?" an elderly man asked.

"Who?" Elend asked.

"The Lord Ruler," the man whispered.

Elend looked down at his black uniform, encased in a mistcloak, both of which were slick with blood.

"Close enough," he said, turning to the east—toward where his human army camped many miles away, waiting for him to return with a new koloss force to aid them. There was only one reason for him to do that. Finally, he acknowledged what he'd decided, unconsciously, the moment he'd set out to find more of the creatures.

The time for killing hasn't ended at all, he thought. *It has just begun.*

Near the end, the ash began to pile up in frightening amounts. I've spoken of the special microbes that the Lord Ruler devised to help the world deal with the ashfalls. They did not "feed" on ash, really. Rather, they broke it down as an aspect of their metabolic functions. Volcanic ash itself is, actually, good for soil, depending on what one wishes to grow.

Too much of anything, however, is deadly. Water is necessary for survival, yet too much will drown. During the history of the Final Empire, the land balanced on the very knife-edge of disaster via the ash. The microbes broke it down about as rapidly as it fell, but when there was so much of it that it oversaturated the soil, it became more difficult for plants to survive.

In the end, the entire system fell apart. Ash fell so steadily that it smothered and killed, and the world's plant life died off. The microbes had no chance of keeping up, for they needed time and nutrients to reproduce.

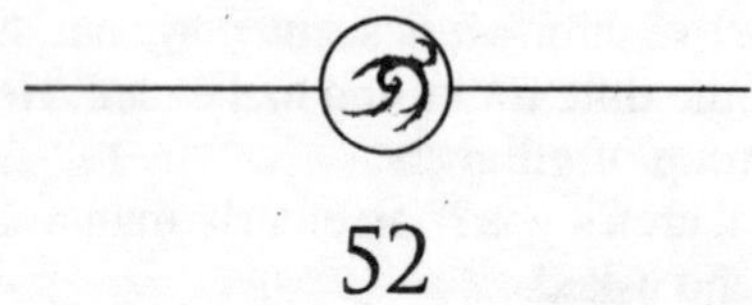

52

DURING THE DAYS OF THE Lord ruler, Luthadel had been the most crowded city in the world. Filled with three- and four-story tenements, it had been packed with the skaa who'd worked its numerous furnaces and forges, with the noble merchants who'd sold its goods, and with the high nobility who'd simply wanted to be near the imperial court. TenSoon had assumed that now, with the Lord Ruler dead and the imperial government shattered, Luthadel would become far less densely populated.

He had, apparently, been wrong.

Still wearing the wolfhound's body, he trotted along in amazement as he explored the streets. It seemed that every nook—every alleyway, every street corner, each and every tenement—had become home to a skaa family. The city smelled terrible, and refuse clogged the streets, buried in ash.

What is going on? he wondered. The skaa lived in filth, many of them looking sick, coughing piteously in their ash-filled gutters. TenSoon made his way toward Keep Venture. If there were answers to be found, he hoped to locate them there. Occasionally, he had to growl menacingly at skaa who looked at him hungrily, and twice he had to run from gangs that ignored his growls.

Surely Vin and Elend would not have let this city fall so far, he thought as he hid in an alley. It was a foreboding sign. He'd left Luthadel without knowing whether or not his friends would even survive the city's siege. Elend's banner—the spear and the scroll—flew at the front of the city, but could someone else have taken Elend's sign as their own? And what of the koloss army that had threatened to destroy Luthadel a year ago?

I should never have left her, TenSoon thought, feeling a stab of anxiety. *My foolish kandra sense of duty. I should have stayed here, and told her what I know, little though it is.*

The world could end because of my foolish honor.

He poked his head out of the alleyway, looking at Keep Venture. TenSoon's heart sank to see that its beautiful stained-glass windows had been shattered. Crude boards blocked the broken holes. There were guards at the front gates, however, which seemed a better sign.

TenSoon crept forward, trying to look like a mangy stray. He kept to the shadows, edging his way up to the gate. Then, he lay down in some refuse to watch the soldiers. He expanded his eardrums, craning to hear what the men were saying.

It turned out to be nothing. The two guards stood quietly, looking bored and not a little disconsolate as they leaned against their obsidian-tipped spears. TenSoon waited, wishing that Vin were there to Pull on the emotions of the guards, making them more talkative.

Of course, if Vin were here, I wouldn't have to be poking

about for information, TenSoon thought with frustration. And so, he waited. Waited as the ash fell, waited even until the sky darkened and the mists came out. Their appearance finally sparked some life into the guards. "I hate night duty," one of them muttered.

"Nothing wrong with night," the other one said. "Not for us. Mists didn't kill us. We're safe from them."

What? TenSoon thought, frowning to himself.

"Are we safe from the king?" the first guard said quietly.

His companion shot him a glance. "Don't say such things."

The first guard shrugged. "I just hope the emperor gets back soon."

"King Penrod has all of the emperor's authority," the second guard said sternly.

Ah, TenSoon thought. *So Penrod managed to keep the throne. But . . . what's this about an emperor?* TenSoon feared that the emperor was Straff Venture. That terrible man had been the one poised to take Luthadel when TenSoon had left.

But what of Vin? Somehow, TenSoon just couldn't bring himself to believe that she had been defeated. He had watched her kill Zane Venture, a man who had been burning atium when Vin had none. She'd done the impossible three times, to TenSoon's count. She'd slain the Lord Ruler. She'd defeated Zane.

And she'd befriended a kandra who had been determined to hate her.

The guards fell silent again. *This is foolish,* TenSoon thought. *I don't have time to hide in corners and eavesdrop. The world is ending!* He rose, shaking the ash from his body—an action that caused the guards to start, raising their spears anxiously as they searched the darkening night for the source of the sound.

TenSoon hesitated, their nervousness giving him an idea. He turned and loped off into the night. He'd grown to know the city quite well during his year serving with Vin—she had liked to patrol the city, particularly the areas around Keep

Venture. Even with his knowledge, however, it took TenSoon some time to find his way to where he was going. He had never visited the location, but he had heard it described.

Described by a person whom TenSoon had been killing at the time.

The memory still brought him chills. Kandra served Contracts—and in Contracts, they usually were required to imitate specific individuals. A master would provide the proper body—kandra were forbidden to kill humans themselves—and the kandra would emulate it. However, before any of that happened, the kandra would usually study its quarry, learning as much about them as possible.

TenSoon had killed OreSeur, his generation brother. OreSeur, who had helped overthrow the Father. At Kelsier's command, OreSeur had pretended to be a nobleman named Lord Renoux so that Kelsier would have an apparent nobleman as a front to use in his plan to overthrow the empire. But, there had been a more important part for OreSeur to play in Kelsier's plot. A secret part that not even the other members of the crew had known until after Kelsier's death.

TenSoon arrived at the old warehouse. It stood where OreSeur had said it would. TenSoon shuddered, remembering OreSeur's screams. The kandra had died beneath TenSoon's torture, torture which had been necessary, for TenSoon had needed to learn all that he could. Every secret. All that he would need in order to convincingly imitate his brother.

That day, TenSoon's hatred of humans—and at himself for serving them—had burned more deeply than ever before. How Vin had overcome that, he still didn't know.

The warehouse before TenSoon was now a holy place, ornamented and maintained by the Church of the Survivor. A plaque hung out front, displaying the sign of the spear—the weapon by which both Kelsier and the Lord Ruler had died—and giving a written explanation of why the warehouse was important.

TenSoon knew the story already. This was the place where the crew had found a stockpile of weapons, left by the Survivor to arm the skaa people for their revolution. It had been discovered the same day that Kelsier had died, and rumors whispered that the spirit of the Survivor had appeared in this place, giving guidance to his followers. Those rumors were true, after a fashion. TenSoon rounded the building, following instructions OreSeur had given as he died. The Blessing of Presence let TenSoon recall the precise words, and despite the ash, he found the spot—a place where the cobbles were disturbed. Then, he began to dig.

Kelsier, the Survivor of Hathsin, had indeed appeared to his followers that night years ago. Or, at least, his bones had. OreSeur had been commanded to take the Survivor's own body and digest it, then appear to the faithful skaa and give them encouragement. The legends of the Survivor, the whole religion that had sprung up around him, had been started by a kandra.

And TenSoon had eventually killed that kandra. But not before learning his secrets. Secrets such as where OreSeur had buried the bones of the Survivor, and how the man had looked.

TenSoon smiled as he unearthed the first bone. They were years old now, and he hated using old bones. Plus, there would be no hair, so the one he created would be bald. Still, the opportunity was too valuable to pass up. He'd only seen the Survivor once, but with his expertise in imitation . . .

Well, it was worth a try.

Wellen leaned against his spear, watching those mists again. Rittle—his companion guard—said they weren't dangerous. But, Rittle hadn't seen what they could do. What they could reveal. Wellen figured that he had survived because he respected them. That, and because he didn't think too hard about the things he had seen.

"You think Skiff and Jaston will be late to relieve us again?" Wellen asked, trying again to start a conversation.

Rittle just grunted. "Dunno, Wells." Rittle never did care for small talk.

"I think maybe one of us should go see," Wellen said, eyeing the mist. "You know, ask if they've come in yet. . . ." He trailed off.

Something was out there.

Lord Ruler! he thought, cringing back. *Not again!*

But, no attack came from the mists. Instead, a dark figure strode forward. Rittle perked up, lowering his spear. "Halt!"

A man walked from the mists, wearing a deep black cloak, arms at his sides, hood up. His face, however, was visible. Wellen frowned. Something about this man looked familiar. . . .

Rittle gasped, then fell to his knees, clutching something at his neck—the pendant of a silver spear that he always wore. Wellen frowned. Then he noticed the scars on this newcomer's arms.

Lord Ruler! Wellen thought in shock, realizing where he'd seen this man's face. It had been in a painting, one of many available in the city, that depicted the Survivor of Hathsin.

"Rise," the stranger said, speaking in a benevolent voice.

Rittle stood on shaking feet. Wellen backed away, uncertain whether to be awed or terrified, and feeling a little of both.

"I have come to commend your faith," the Survivor said.

"My lord . . ." Rittle said, his head still bowed.

"Also," Kelsier said, raising a finger. "I have come to tell you I do not approve of how this city is being run. My people are sick, they starve, and they die."

"My lord," Rittle said, "there is not enough food, and there have been riots seizing that which was stockpiled. My lord, and the mists kill! Please, why have you sent them to kill us!"

"I did no such thing," Kelsier said. "I know that food is scarce, but you must share what you have and have hope. Tell me of the man who rules this city."

"King Penrod?" Rittle asked. "He rules for Emperor Elend Venture, who is away at war."

"Lord *Elend* Venture? And he approves of how this city is being treated?" Kelsier looked angry. Wellen cringed.

"No, my lord!" Rittle said, shaking. "I . . ."

"Lord Penrod is mad," Wellen found himself saying.

The Survivor turned toward him.

"Wells, you shouldn't . . ." Rittle said, but then trailed off, the Survivor shooting him a stern look.

"Speak," the Survivor said to Wellen.

"He speaks to the air, my lord," Wellen said, averting his eyes. "Talks to himself—claims that he can see the Lord Ruler standing beside him. Penrod . . . he's given lots of strange orders, lately. Forcing the skaa to fight each other for food, claiming that only the strong should survive. He kills those who disagree with him. That kind of thing."

"I see," the Survivor said.

Surely he knows this already, Wellen thought. *Why bother asking?*

"Where is my Heir?" the Survivor asked. "The Hero of Ages, Vin."

"The Lady Empress?" Wellen asked. "She's with the emperor."

"Where?"

"Nobody knows for certain, my lord," Rittle said, still shaking. "She hasn't returned in a long time. My sergeant says that she and the emperor are fighting in the South, fighting koloss. But I've heard other men say the army went to the west."

"That's not very helpful," Kelsier said.

Wellen perked up, remembering something.

"What?" the Survivor asked, apparently noticing Wellen's change in posture.

"An army troop stopped by the city a few months ago," Wellen said, feeling proud. "They kept it quiet, but I was in the group that helped them resupply. Lord Breeze was with them, and he spoke of meeting up with others of your crew."

"Where?" Kelsier asked. "Where were they going?"

"North," Wellen said. "To Urteau. That must be where the emperor is, my lord. The Northern Dominance is in rebellion. He must have taken his armies to quell it."

The Survivor nodded. "Very well," he said. He turned as if

to go, then paused, looking back. "Pass what news you can," he said. "There isn't much time left. Tell the people that when the mists leave, they should immediately find shelter. A place underground, if possible."

Wellen paused, then nodded. "The caverns," he said. "Where you trained your army?"

"That will do," Kelsier said. "Farewell."

The Survivor disappeared into the mists.

TenSoon left the gates of Keep Venture behind, running off into the mists. He could, perhaps, have gotten himself into the building. However, he wasn't certain how well his imitation of the Survivor would hold up under closer scrutiny.

He didn't know how reliable the two guards' information was. However, he had no better leads. Other people he had talked to in the night hadn't been able to provide any information about the army's movements. Evidently, Vin and Elend had been gone from Luthadel for quite some time.

He rushed back to the patch of earth behind the warehouse where he'd found Kelsier's body. He knelt in the darkness, uncovering the sack he'd stuffed with bones. He needed to get the dog's body back and head north. Hopefully he would—

"You there!" a voice said.

TenSoon looked up reflexively. A man stood in the doorway of the warehouse, looking through the mists at TenSoon. A lantern flared to life behind him, revealing a group of people who had apparently taken up residence inside of the holy place.

Uh, oh . . . TenSoon thought as those at the front adopted shocked expressions.

"My lord!" the man in front said, quickly kneeling in his sleeping robe. "You've returned!"

TenSoon stood, stepping carefully to hide the sack of bones behind him. "I have," he said.

"We knew that you would," the man said as others began to whisper and cry out behind him. Many fell to their knees.

"We stayed in this place, praying for you to come give us counsel. The king is mad, my lord! What do we do?"

TenSoon was tempted to expose himself as a kandra, but looking into their hopeful eyes, he found that he could not. Besides, perhaps he could do some good. "Penrod has been corrupted by Ruin," he said. "The thing that seeks to destroy the world. You must gather the faithful and escape this city before Penrod kills you all."

"My lord, where should we go?"

TenSoon hesitated. Where? "There are a pair of guards at the front of Keep Venture. They know of a place. Listen to them. You *must* get to a place underground. Do you understand?"

"Yes, lord," the man said. Behind, more and more people were edging forward, straining to catch a glimpse of TenSoon. He bore their scrutiny with some nervousness. Finally, he bid them be careful, then fled into the night.

He found an empty building and quickly changed back to the dog's bones before anyone else could see him. When he was done, he eyed the Survivor's bones, feeling a strange . . . reverence.

Don't be silly, he told himself. *They're just bones, like hundreds of other sets you've used.* Still, it seemed foolish to leave such a potentially powerful tool behind. He carefully packed them into the sack he'd pilfered, then—using paws he'd created to have more dexterity than those of a real wolfhound—he tied the sack on his back.

After that, TenSoon left the city by the northern gate, running at full wolfhound speed. He would go to Urteau and hope that he was on the right path.

The pact between Preservation and Ruin is a thing of gods, and difficult to explain in human terms. Indeed, initially, there was a stalemate between them. On one hand, each knew that only by working together could they create. On the other hand, both knew that they would never have complete satisfaction in what

they created. Preservation would not be able to keep things perfect and unchanging, and Ruin would not be able to destroy completely.

Ruin, of course, eventually acquired the ability to end the world and gain the satisfaction he wanted. But, then, that wasn't originally part of the bargain.

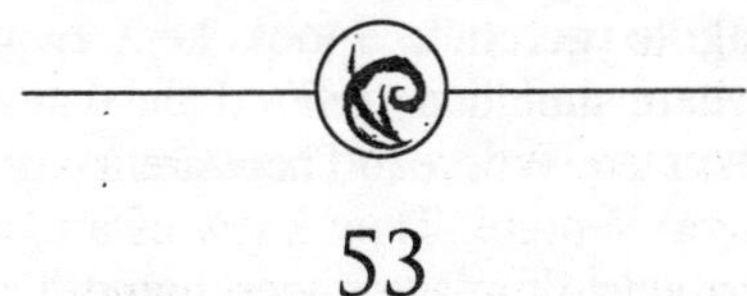

53

SPOOK FOUND HER SITTING ON the rocky lakeshore, looking out across the deep black waters, so still in the cavern's windless air. In the near distance, Spook could hear Sazed—with a large contingent of Goradel's men—working on their project to stanch the flow of water into the cavern.

Spook approached Beldre quietly, carrying a mug of warmed tea. It almost seemed to burn his flesh, which meant that it would be just right for normal people. He let his own food and drinks sit out until they cooled to room temperature.

He didn't wear his eye bandage. With pewter, he'd found that he could withstand a little lantern-light. She didn't turn as he approached, so he cleared his throat. She jumped slightly. It was no wonder that Quellion worked so hard to shelter the girl—one could not fake Beldre's level of innocence. She wouldn't survive three heartbeats in the underground. Even Allrianne, who did her best to look like a puff, had an edge to her that bespoke an ability to be as hard as necessary in order to survive. Beldre, though . . .

She's normal, Spook thought. *This is how people would be, if they didn't have to deal with Inquisitors, armies, and assassins.* For that, he actually envied her. It was a strange feeling, after so many years spent wishing that he were someone more important.

She turned back toward the waters, and he approached

and sat beside her. "Here," he said, handing her the mug. "I know it gets a bit chilly down here, with the lake and the water."

She paused, then took the mug. "Thank you," she whispered. Spook let her roam free in the cavern—there was very little she could sabotage, though he had warned Goradel's men to keep an eye on her. Either way, there was no way she was going to get out. Spook kept two dozen men guarding the exit, and had ordered the ladder up to the trapdoor above removed, to be replaced only with proper authorization.

"Hard to believe this place was beneath your city all along, isn't it?" Spook said, trying to work into a conversation. Oddly, it had seemed easier to speak to her when he was confronting her in her gardens, surrounded by danger.

Beldre nodded. "My brother would have loved to find this place. He worries about food supplies. Fewer and fewer fish are being caught in the northern lakes. And crops . . . well, they're not doing so well, I hear."

"The mists," Spook said. "They don't let enough sunlight through for most plants."

Beldre nodded, looking down at her mug. She hadn't taken a sip yet.

"Beldre," Spook said, "I'm sorry. I actually considered kidnapping you from those gardens, but decided against it. However, with you showing up here, alone . . ."

"It was just too good an opportunity," she said bitterly. "I understand. It's my own fault. My brother always says I'm too trusting."

"There are times that would be an advantage."

Beldre sniffed quietly. "I've never known such times as that. It seems my entire life, I've just trusted and been hurt. This is no different."

Spook sat, feeling frustrated with himself. *Kelsier, tell me what to say!* he thought. Yet, God remained silent. The Survivor didn't seem to have much advice about things that didn't relate to securing the city.

It had all seemed so simple when Spook had given the

order to capture her. Why, now, was he sitting here with this empty pit in his stomach?

"I believed in him, you know," Beldre said.

"Your brother?"

"No," she said with a slight shake of her head. "The Lord Ruler. I was a good little noblewoman. I always gave my payments to the obligators—paying extra, even, and calling them in to witness the smallest things. I also paid them to come tutor me in the history of the empire. I thought everything was perfect. So neat; so peaceful. And then, they tried to kill me. Turns out I'm half skaa. My father wanted a child so desperately, and my mother was barren. He had two children with one of the maidservants—my mother even approved."

She shook her head. "Why would someone do that?" she continued. "I mean, why not pick a noblewoman? No. My father chose the servant woman. I guess he fancied her or something. . . ." She looked down.

"For me, it was my grandfather," Spook said. "I never knew him. Grew up on the streets."

"Sometimes I wish *I* had," Beldre said. "Then maybe this would all make sense. What do you do when the priests you've been paying to tutor you since you were a child—men you trusted more than your own parents—come to take you away for execution? I would have died, too. I just went with them. Then . . ."

"Then what?" Spook asked.

"You saved me," she whispered. "The Survivor's crew. You overthrew the Lord Ruler, and in the chaos, everybody forgot about people like me. The obligators were too busy trying to please Straff."

"And then, your brother took over."

She nodded quietly. "I thought he'd be a good ruler. He really is a good man! He just wants everything to be stable and secure. Peace for everyone. Yet, sometimes, the things he *does* to people . . . the things he *asks* of people . . ."

"I'm sorry," Spook said.

She shook her head. "And then you came. You rescued

that child, right in front of Quellion and me. You came to my gardens, and you didn't even threaten me. I thought . . . maybe he really is as the stories say. Maybe he'll help. And, like the idiot I always am, I just came."

"I wish things were simple, Beldre," Spook said. "I wish I could let you go. But, this is for the greater good."

"That's just what Quellion always says, you know," she said.

Spook paused.

"You're a lot alike, you two," she said. "Forceful. Commanding."

Spook chuckled. "You really don't know me very well, do you?"

She flushed. "You're the Survivor of the Flames. Don't think I haven't heard the rumors—my brother can't keep me out of *all* of his conferences."

"Rumors," Spook said, "are rarely reliable."

"You're a member of the Survivor's crew."

Spook shrugged. "That's true. Though, I became a member by accident."

She frowned, glancing at him.

"Kelsier handpicked the others," Spook said. "Ham, Breeze, Sazed—even Vin. He chose my uncle too. And, by doing so, he got me as a bonus. I . . . I was never really part of it all, Beldre. I was kind of like an observer. They posted me on watch and things like that. I sat in on the planning sessions, and everyone just treated me like an errand boy. I must have refilled Breeze's cup a hundred times during that first year!"

A hint of amusement showed on her face. "You make it sound like you were a servant."

"Pretty much," Spook said, smiling. "I couldn't talk very well—I'd grown used to speaking in an Eastern street slang, and everything I said came out garbled. I've still got an accent, they tell me. So, I just stayed quiet most of the time, embarrassed. The crew was nice to me, but I knew I was pretty much just ignored."

"And now you're in charge of them all."

Spook laughed. "No. Sazed's the one really in charge of us here. Breeze ranks me too, but he lets me give orders because he's too lazy to do so. He likes to make people do things without them knowing it. Half the time, I'm certain that the things I'm saying are just ideas he somehow got into my head."

Beldre shook her head. "The Terrisman is in charge? But, he looks to you!"

"He just lets me do what he doesn't want to," Spook said. "Sazed's a great man—one of the best I've known. But, well, he's a scholar. He's better off studying a project and writing notes than he is giving commands. So, that only leaves me. I'm just doing the job that everyone else is too busy to do."

Beldre sat quietly for a moment, then finally took a sip of her tea. "Ah," she said. "It's good!"

"The Lord Ruler's own brew, for all we know," Spook said. "We found it down here, with the rest of this stuff."

"This is why you came, isn't it?" Beldre asked, nodding to the cavern. "I wondered why your emperor cared about Urteau. We haven't really been an important force in the world since the Venture line moved its center of power to Luthadel."

Spook nodded. "This is part of it, though Elend is also worried about the rebellion up here. It's dangerous, having a foe who is slaughtering noblemen controlling one of the major cities just a short distance north of Luthadel. That's all I can really tell you, though. Most of the time, I feel like I'm *still* just a bystander in all of this. Vin and Elend, they're the ones who really know what's going on. To them, I'm the guy they could spare to spend months spying in Urteau while they did important work in the South."

"They are wrong to treat you so," Beldre said.

"No, it's all right," Spook said. "I've kind of enjoyed being up here. I feel like I've been able to do something, finally."

She nodded. After a short time, she set down her cup, wrapping her arms around her knees. "What are they like?" she asked. "I've heard so many stories. They say that Emperor

Venture always wears white, and that the ash refuses to stick to him! He can quell an army just by looking at them. And his wife, the Survivor's heir. Mistborn . . ."

Spook smiled. "Elend is a forgetful scholar—twice as bad as Sazed ever was. He gets lost in his books and forgets about meetings he himself called. He only dresses with any sense of fashion because a Terriswoman bought him a new wardrobe. War has changed him some, but on the inside, I think he's still just a dreamer caught in a world with too much violence.

"And Vin . . . well, she really *is* different. I've never been sure what to make of her. Sometimes, she seems as frail as a child. And then she kills an Inquisitor. She can be fascinating and frightening at the same time. I tried to court her once."

"Really?" Beldre said, perking up.

Spook smiled. "I gave her a handkerchief. I heard that's how you do it in noble society."

"Only if you're a romantic," Beldre said, smiling wistfully.

"Well, I gave her one," Spook said. "But I don't think she knew what I meant by it. And, of course, once she *did* figure it out, she turned me down. I'm not sure what I was thinking, trying to court her. I mean, I'm just Spook. Quiet, incomprehensible, forgettable Spook."

He closed his eyes. *What am I saying?* Women didn't want to hear men talk about how insignificant they were. He'd heard that much. *I shouldn't have come to talk to her. I should have just gone about, giving orders. Looking like I was in charge.*

The damage had been done, however. She knew the truth about him. He sighed, opening his eyes.

"I don't think you're forgettable," Beldre said. "Of course, I'd be *more* likely to think fondly of you if you were to let me go."

Spook smiled. "Eventually. I promise."

"Are you going to use me against him?" Beldre asked. "Threaten to kill me if he doesn't give in?"

"Threats like that are hollow if you know you'll never do

what you say," Spook said. "Honestly, Beldre, I'm not going to hurt you. In fact, I've got a feeling you'll be safer here than back in your brother's palace."

"Please don't kill him, Spook," Beldre said. "Maybe . . . maybe you can help him somehow, help him see that he's being too extreme."

Spook nodded. "I'll . . . try."

"Do you promise?" she said.

"All right," Spook said. "I promise to at least try to save your brother. If I can."

"And the city too."

"And the city," Spook said. "Trust me. We've done this before—the transition will go smoothly."

Beldre nodded, and she actually seemed to believe him. *What kind of woman is still able to trust people after everything she's been through?* If she'd been Vin, she would have stabbed him in the back at the first opportunity, and that would have probably been the right thing to do. Yet, this girl just continued to trust. It was like finding a beautiful plant growing alone in a field of burnt ash.

"Once we're done, maybe you could introduce me to the emperor and empress," Beldre said. "They sound like interesting people."

"I'll never argue with that statement," Spook said. "Elend and Vin . . . well, they're certainly *interesting*. Interesting people with heavy burdens. Sometimes, I wish I were powerful enough to do important works like them."

Beldre laid a hand on his arm, and he glanced down, a bit surprised. *What?*

"Power can be a terrible thing, Spook," she said quietly. "I'm . . . not pleased with what it's done to my brother. Don't wish so hard for it."

Spook met her eyes, then nodded and rose. "If you need anything, ask Sazed. He'll see to your comforts."

She looked up. "Where are you going?"

"To be seen."

* * *

"I want primary trade contracts on all the canals," Durn said. "And a title from the emperor."

"You?" Spook said. "A title? You think a 'lord' in front of your name is going to make that face any less ugly?"

Durn raised an eyebrow.

Spook just chuckled. "Both are yours. I cleared it with Sazed and Breeze—they'll even draft you a contract, if you want."

Durn nodded appreciatively. "I do. Lords pay attention to things like that." They sat in one of his many backroom chambers—not in his private home, but in a place attached to a particular inn. An old set of drums hung on the wall.

Spook had had little trouble sneaking out past Quellion's soldiers standing watch at the front of the Ministry building. Even before he'd gained enhanced abilities with tin, and long before he'd been able to burn pewter, he'd learned to sneak about in the night and spy. A group of soldiers had barely posed an obstacle for him. He couldn't remain cooped up in the cavern like the others. He had too much work to do.

"I want the Harrows dammed off," Spook said. "We'll flood the canals during the evening, when the markets are empty. Nobody lives in the streetslots except for those of you here in the slums. If you want to keep this place from flooding, you'll need a good *watertight* blockade in place."

"Already taken care of," Durn said. "When the Harrows were new, we pulled off the lock system from its mouth, but I know where it is. It'll fit back in place well enough to keep the water out, assuming we can install it correctly."

"You'd better," Spook said. "I don't want the deaths of half the city's beggar population on my conscience. I'll warn you the day we intend to pull this off. See if you can get some of the goods out of the market, as well as keep people out of the streetslots. That, plus what you're doing for my reputation, will guarantee you the title you want."

Durn nodded, rising. "Well, let's go work on that reputation, then." He led the way out of the back room, bringing Spook out into the commons of the bar. As always, Spook wore his burned cloak—it had become something of a symbol for him. He'd never worn a mistcloak, but somehow, this felt even better.

The people rose when he entered. He smiled, motioning for Durn's men to bring out wineskins—stolen from the storage cavern and carried by Spook as he snuck out several nights in a row. "Tonight," he said, "you don't have to pay for Quellion's stolen liquor. That's his way of keeping you happy and content."

And that was the only speech he gave. He wasn't Kelsier, able to impress people with his words. Instead—at Breeze's suggestion—he stayed mostly quiet. He visited tables, trying to not be aloof, but also speaking little. He looked thoughtful, and asked the people about their problems. He listened to stories of loss and hardship, and drank with them to the memory of those Quellion had murdered. And, with his pewter, he never got drunk. He already had a reputation for that—the people regarded it mystically, as they did his ability to survive fire.

After that bar, they visited another, and another after that, Durn careful to keep him to the safest—and yet most populated—of the locations. Some were in the Harrows, others were above. Through it all, Spook felt an amazing thing: his confidence growing. He really *was* a little like Kelsier. Vin might have been the one trained by the Survivor, but Spook was the one who was doing just what he'd done—encouraging the people, leading them to rise up for their own sakes.

As the evening passed, the various bars became a blur. Spook breathed curses against Quellion, speaking of the murders and of the Allomancers the Citizen retained. Spook didn't spread the rumors that Quellion was himself an Allomancer—he let Breeze do that more carefully. That way, it wouldn't look like Spook was too eager to set the man up.

* * *

"To the Survivor!"

Spook looked up, holding his mug of wine, smiling as the bar patrons cheered.

"To the Survivor!" another said, pointing at Spook. "Survivor of the Flames!"

"To the death of the Citizen!" Durn said, raising his own mug—though he rarely drank from it. "Down with the man who said he'd let us rule, then took it all for himself!"

Spook smiled, taking a drink. He hadn't realized how exhausting it could be to simply sit around and speak to people. His flared pewter kept his body's weariness at bay, but it couldn't prevent the mental fatigue.

I wonder what Beldre would think if she saw this, he thought. *The men cheering me. She'd be impressed, wouldn't she? She'd forget about how I droned on about how useless I was.*

Perhaps the visits to the bars had been fatiguing simply because he had something else he wished he could be doing. It was silly—she was his captive. He'd betrayed her trust. She was obviously just warming up to him in an effort to get him to let her go. Yet, he couldn't help thinking back to their conversation, going over it again and again in his mind. Despite the stupid things he'd said, she'd laid her hand on his arm. That meant something, didn't it?

"You all right?" Durn asked, leaning in. "That's your tenth mug tonight."

"I'm fine," Spook said.

"You were looking a little distant there."

"I have a lot on my mind," Spook said.

Durn leaned back, frowning, but didn't say anything more.

Some things about his conversation with Beldre bothered Spook, even more than his own stupid comments. She seemed to really be worried by the things that her brother had done. When Spook himself was in power, would she see him as she did Quellion? Would that be a bad thing, or a good thing? She already said they were similar.

Power can be a terrible thing. . . .

He looked up, glancing at the people of the bar as they cheered him again, just as the men had in the other bars. Kelsier had been able to handle adulation like this. If Spook wanted to be like Kelsier, then he'd have to deal with it as well, right?

Wasn't it a good thing to be liked? To have people willing to follow him? He could finally break away from the old Spook. He could stop being that boy, the one so insignificant and easily forgotten. He could leave that child behind, and become a man who was respected. And why shouldn't he be respected? He *wasn't* that boy anymore. He wore his bandages across his eyes, heightening his mystical reputation as a man who did not need light to see. Some even said that anywhere that fire burned, Spook could see.

"They love you," Kelsier whispered. "You deserve it."

Spook smiled. That was all the confirmation he needed. He stood, raising his arms before the crowd. They cheered in response.

It had been a long time coming. And it felt all the sweeter for the wait.

Preservation's desire to create sentient life was what eventually broke the stalemate. In order to give mankind awareness and independent thought, Preservation knew that he would have to give up part of himself—his own soul—to dwell within mankind. This would leave him just a tiny bit weaker than his opposite, Ruin.

That tiny bit seemed inconsequential, compared with their total vast sums of power. However, over aeons, this tiny flaw would allow Ruin to overcome Preservation, thereby bringing an end to the world.

This, then, was their bargain. Preservation got mankind, the only creations that had more Preservation than Ruin in them, rather than a balance. Independent life that could think and feel. In exchange, Ruin was given a promise—and proof—that he could bring an end to all they had created together. It was the pact.

And Preservation eventually broke it.

54

WHEN VIN AWOKE, SHE WAS not surprised to find herself bound. She *was* surprised to feel that she was wearing metal manacles.

The first thing she did—even before she opened her eyes—was reach inside for her metals. With steel and iron, perhaps she could use the manacles as weapons. With pewter . . .

Her metals were gone.

She kept her eyes closed, trying not to display the panic she felt, thinking through what had happened. She'd been in the cavern, trapped with Ruin. Elend's friend had come in, given her the wine, and she'd taken it. Gambled.

How long had it been since she'd fallen unconscious?

"Your breathing has changed," a voice reported. "You are obviously awake."

Vin cursed herself quietly. There was a very easy way to take away an Allomancer's powers—easier, even, than making them burn aluminum. You just had to keep them drugged long enough for them to pass the metals through their body. As she thought about it, her mind shrugging off the effects of extended sleep, she realized this was what must have happened to her.

The silence continued. Finally, Vin opened her eyes. She expected to see cell bars. Instead, she saw a sparsely furnished, utilitarian room. She lay on a bench, head cushioned by a hard pillow. Her manacles were connected to a chain several feet long, which was in turn locked to the base of the bench. She tugged on the chain carefully, and determined that it was very well affixed.

The motion drew the attention of a pair of guards who stood beside the bench. They jumped slightly, raising staffs and eyeing her warily. Vin smiled to herself; part of her was proud that she could evoke such a response even when chained and metalless.

"You, Lady Venture, present something of a problem." The voice came from the side. Vin raised herself up on one arm, looking over the bench's armrest. On the other side of the room—perhaps fifteen feet away—a bald figure in robes stood with his back to her. He stared out a large window, facing west, and the setting sun was a violent crimson blaze around his silhouette.

"What do I do?" Yomen asked, still not turning toward her. "A single flake of steel, and you could slaughter my guards with their own buttons. A taste of pewter, and you could lift that bench and smash your way out of the room. The logical thing to do would be to gag you, keep you drugged at all times, or kill you."

Vin opened her mouth to reply, but all that came out was a cough. She immediately tried to burn pewter to strengthen her body. The lack of metal was like missing a limb. As she sat up, coughing further and growing dizzy, she found herself craving the metal more than she'd imagined that she ever would. Allomancy wasn't supposed to be addictive, not like certain herbs or poisons. However, at that moment, she could have sworn that all the scientists and philosophers were flat-out wrong.

Yomen made a sharp gesture with one arm, still not turning from the sunset. A servant approached, bearing a cup for Vin. She eyed it uncertainly.

"If I wanted to poison you, Lady Venture," Yomen said without turning, "I could do it without guile."

Good point, Vin thought wryly, accepting the cup and drinking the water it contained.

"Water," Yomen said. "Collected from rain, then strained

and purified. You will find no trace metals in it to burn. I specifically ordered it kept in wooden containers only."

Clever, Vin thought. Years before she'd become consciously aware of her Allomantic powers, she'd been burning the tiny bits of metal she haphazardly got from groundwater or dining utensils.

The water quenched her thirst and stilled her cough. "So," she finally said, "if you're so worried about me eating metals, why leave me ungagged?"

Yomen stood quietly for a moment. Finally, he turned, and she could see the tattoos across his eyes and face, his skin reflecting the deep colors of the falling sun outside. On his forehead, he wore his single, silvery bead of atium.

"Various reasons," said the obligator king.

Vin studied him, then raised the cup to take another drink. The motion jangled her manacles, which she eyed in annoyance as they again restricted her movement.

"They're made of silver," Yomen said. "A particularly frustrating metal for Mistborn, or so I am told."

Silver. Useless, unburnable silver. Like lead, it was one of the metals that provided no Allomantic powers at all.

"An unpopular metal indeed . . ." Yomen said, nodding to the side. A servant approached Vin, bearing something on a small platter. Her mother's earring. It was a dull thing, Allomantically, made of bronze with some silver plating. Much of the gilding had worn off years ago, and the brownish bronze showed through, making the earring look to be the cheap bauble it was.

"Which is why," Yomen continued, "I am so curious as to why you would bother with an ornament such as this. I have had it tested. Silver on the outside, bronze on the inside. Why those metals? One useless to Allomancers, the other granting what is considered the weakest of Allomantic powers. Would not an earring of steel or of pewter make more sense?"

Vin eyed the earring. Her fingers itched to grab it, if only to feel metal between her fingers. If she'd had steel, she could have Pushed on the earring, using it as a weapon.

Kelsier had once told her to keep wearing it for that simple reason. Yet, it had been given to her by her mother. A woman Vin had never known. A woman who had tried to kill her.

Vin snatched the earring. Yomen watched curiously as she stuck it in her ear. He seemed . . . wary. As if waiting for something.

If I really did have some trick planned, she thought, *he'd be dead in an instant. How can he stand there so calmly? Why give me my earring? Even if it isn't made of useful metals, I might find a way to use it against him.*

Her instincts told her he was trying an old street ploy—kind of like throwing your enemy a dagger to make him attack. Yomen wanted to spring any traps she was planning. It seemed a silly move. How could he possibly hope to best a Mistborn?

Unless he himself is a Mistborn, Vin thought. *He feels he can beat me.*

He has atium, and is ready to burn it when I try something.

Vin did nothing; made no attack. She wasn't certain if her instincts about Yomen were right, but that didn't really matter. She couldn't attack, for the earring had no hidden secret. The truth was, she simply wanted it back because it felt comfortable in her ear. She was accustomed to wearing it.

"Interesting," Yomen said. "Regardless, you are about to discover one of the reasons I have left you without a gag . . ." With that, he raised a hand toward the door. He clasped his hands behind his back as a servant opened the door, showing in an unarmed soldier in the white and brown of Elend's livery.

You should kill him, Ruin whispered in her mind. *All of them.*

"Lady Venture," Yomen said without looking at her. "I must ask you not to speak to this man except when I indicate, and answer only as I request. Otherwise, he will have to be executed, and a fresh messenger sent for from your army."

The soldier paled. Vin just frowned, eyeing the obligator king. Yomen was obviously a calm man, and he wanted to appear harsh. How much of it was an act?

"You can see that she is alive, as promised," Yomen said to the soldier.

"How do we know this is not a kandra in disguise?" the soldier asked.

"You can ask your question," Yomen said.

"Lady Venture," the soldier said, "what did you have for dinner the night before you went to the party inside the city?"

It was a good question to ask. A kandra would have interrogated her about important moments—such as her first meeting with Elend. Something like a meal, however, was so random that no kandra would have thought to ask about it. Now, if Vin could remember. . . .

She looked at Yomen. He nodded—she could answer. "Eggs," she said. "Fresh eggs that I bought in the city, during one of my spying trips."

The man nodded.

"You have your answer, soldier," Yomen said. "Report to your king that his wife is still alive."

The soldier withdrew and the servants closed the door. Vin sat back on the bench, waiting for a gag.

Yomen remained where he was, looking at her.

Vin looked back. Finally, she spoke. "How long do you think that you can keep Elend placated? If you know anything of him at all, then you will realize that he is a king first, and a man second. He will do what he needs to do, even if it means my death."

"Eventually, perhaps," Yomen said. "However, for now, the stall is effective. They say that you are a blunt woman, and appreciate brevity. Therefore, I will be straightforward with you. My purpose in capturing you was not to use you as leverage against your husband."

"Is that so," she said flatly. "Why *did* you capture me, then?"

"It is simple, Lady Venture," Yomen said. "I captured you so that I could execute you."

If he expected surprise from her, she didn't give it. She just shrugged. "Sounds like an unnecessarily formal term. Why not just cut my throat while I was drugged?"

"This city is a place of law," Yomen said. "We do not kill indiscriminately."

"This is war," Vin said. "If you wait for 'discrimination' before you kill, you'll have a lot of unhappy soldiers."

"Your crime is not one of war, Lady Venture."

"Oh? And am I to know this crime, then?"

"It is the most simple of all crimes. Murder."

Vin raised an eyebrow. Had she killed someone close to this man? Perhaps one of the noble soldiers in Cett's retinue, back a year ago when she'd assaulted Keep Hasting?

Yomen met her eyes, and she saw something in them. A loathing that he kept hidden behind the calm front. No, she hadn't killed one of his friends or relatives. She'd killed someone far more important to him.

"The Lord Ruler," she said.

Yomen turned away again.

"You can't honestly intend to try me for *that,*" Vin said. "It's ridiculous."

"There will be no trial," Yomen said. "I am the authority in this city, and need no ceremony to give me direction or permission."

Vin snorted. "I thought you said this was a place of law."

"And I am that law," Yomen said calmly. "I believe in letting a person speak for themselves before I make my decision. I will give you time to prepare your thoughts—however, the men who will be guarding you have orders to kill you if it ever looks like you are putting something unapproved into your mouth."

Yomen glanced back at her. "I'd be very careful while I eat or drink, if I were you. Your guards have been told to err on the side of safety, and they know that I will not punish them if they accidentally kill you."

Vin paused, cup of water still held lightly in her fingers.

Kill him, Ruin's voice whispered. *You could do it. Take a weapon from one of those soldiers, then use it on Yomen.*

Vin frowned. Ruin still used Reen's voice—it was familiar, something that had always seemed a part of her. Discovering that it belonged to that *thing* . . . it was like finding out that her reflection really belonged to someone else, and that she'd never actually seen herself.

She ignored the voice. She wasn't sure why Ruin would want her to try killing Yomen. After all, Yomen had captured her—the obligator king was working on Ruin's side. Plus, Vin doubted her ability to cause the man any harm. Chained, lacking offensive metals . . . she'd be a fool to attack.

She also didn't trust Yomen's comments about keeping her alive so that she could "speak" in her defense. He was up to something. Yet, she couldn't fathom what it might be. Why leave her alive? He was too clever a man to lack a reason.

Giving no hint of his motivations, Yomen turned away from her again, looking back out his window. "Take her away."

By sacrificing most of his consciousness, Preservation created Ruin's prison, breaking their deal and trying to keep Ruin from destroying what they had created. This event left their powers again nearly balanced—Ruin imprisoned, only a trace of himself capable of leaking out. Preservation reduced to a mere wisp of what he once was, barely capable of thought and action.

These two minds were, of course, independent of the raw force of their powers. Actually, I am uncertain of how thoughts and personalities came to be attached to the powers in the first place—but I believe they were not there originally. For both powers could be detached from the minds that ruled them.

55

IT TOOK ELEND MUCH LONGER to get back from the village than it had taken to get there. For one thing, he had left a lot of his coins with the villagers. He wasn't certain how much good money would do them in the coming weeks, but he'd felt that he had to do something. They were going to have a rough time of it the next few months. Their food stores nearly depleted, their homes burned by koloss, their water sources contaminated by ash, their capital—and king—besieged by Elend himself . . .

I have to stay focused, he told himself, walking through the falling ash. *I can't help every village. I have to worry about the larger picture.*

A picture that included using a force of koloss to destroy another man's city. Elend gritted his teeth, continuing to walk. The sun was creeping toward the horizon, and the mists had already started to appear, lit by the blazing fire of red sunlight. Behind him tromped some thirty thousand koloss. His new army.

That was another reason it took him a bit longer to get back. He wanted to walk with the koloss army, rather than jumping ahead of them, in case their Inquisitor appeared to steal them back. He still couldn't believe that such a large group hadn't been under any kind of direction.

I attacked a koloss army on my own, he thought as he slogged through a patch of thigh-deep ash. *I did it without Vin's help, intent on defeating their Inquisitor by myself.*

How had he thought to fight an Inquisitor on his own? Kelsier himself had only barely been able to defeat one of the things.

Vin has killed three now, he thought. *We took them on together, but she was the one who killed each one.*

He didn't begrudge her the abilities she had, but he did feel occasional glimmers of envy. That amused him. It had never bothered him when he'd been an ordinary man, but now that he was Mistborn too, he found himself coveting her skill.

And even with her skill, she had been captured. Elend tromped along, feeling a weight he couldn't shake. Everything just seemed *wrong* to him. Vin imprisoned, while he was free. Mist and ash suffocating the land. Elend, despite all his powers, was unable to do anything to protect the people—and the woman—he loved.

And that was the third reason that he walked ploddingly

with his koloss, rather than returning immediately to his camp. He needed some time to think. Some time alone. Perhaps that was what had driven him to leave in the first place.

He'd known that their work was dangerous, but he'd never *really* thought that he might lose her. She was Vin. She always got out. She survived.

But what if, this time, she didn't?

He'd always been the vulnerable one—the common person in a world of Mistborn and koloss. The scholar who couldn't fight, who had to depend on Vin for protection. Even during the last year of fighting, she'd stayed close to him. If she'd been in danger, he'd been in danger, and there hadn't really been time to think about what would happen if he survived and she didn't.

He shook his head, pushing through the ash. He could have used koloss to force a trail for him. For the moment, however, he wanted to be apart even from them. So, he walked ahead, a lone figure in black on a field of solid ash backlit by a setting red sun.

The ashfalls were getting far worse. Before he'd left the village, he'd spent a day having his koloss clear the streets and rebuild some of the homes. Yet, with the rate at which the ash was falling, the mist and even the possibility of other wandering koloss were becoming secondary problems. The ash. *It* alone would kill them. Already, it buried trees and hills. It was up to his waist in places.

Perhaps if I'd stayed in Luthadel, he thought, *working with my scholars, we could have discovered a way to stop this. . . .*

No, that was foolish. What would they do? Plug the ashmounts? Find a way to wash all of the ash out into the sea? In the distance ahead of him through the evening mists, he could see a red glow in the sky, even though the sun set on the opposite horizon. He could only assume that the light to the east came from fire and lava rising out of the ashmounts.

What did he do about a dying sky, ash so thick he could barely move through it, and erupting volcanoes? So far, his way of dealing with these things had been to ignore them.

Or, rather, to let Vin worry about them.

That's really what has me worried, he thought. *Losing the woman I love is bad enough. But, losing the one I trusted to fix all this . . . that's truly frightening.*

It was an odd realization. The deep truth was, he really *did* trust Vin as more than a person. She was more like a force. Almost a god, even? It seemed silly, thinking about that directly. She was his wife. Even if he was a member of the Church of the Survivor, it felt wrong to worship her, to think her divine.

And he didn't, not really. But he did trust her. Vin was a person of instinct, while Elend was one of logic and thought. Sometimes, it seemed she could do the impossible simply because she didn't stop to *think* about how impossible it really was. If Elend came to a cliff, he stopped, gauging the distance to the other side. Vin just jumped.

What would happen on the day she didn't reach the other side? What if the events they were tied up in were bigger than two people could hope to solve, even if one of those people was Vin? As he considered it, even the possibility of discovering helpful information in the cache at Fadrex had been a slim hope.

We need help, Elend thought with frustration. He stopped in the ash, the darkness closing around him as night proper finally fell. The mists swirled.

Help. So, what did that mean? Help from some mysterious god like the ones that Sazed had once preached about? Elend had never known a god other than the Lord Ruler. And he'd never really had faith in that creature—though, meeting Yomen had changed his perspective on how some people worshipped the Lord Ruler.

Elend stood, looking up at the sky, watching the flakes of ash fall. Continuing their silent, yet ceaseless, barrage against the land. Like the raven feathers of a soft pillow used to suffocate a sleeping victim.

We are doomed, he thought. Behind him, the koloss stopped their march, waiting upon his silent order. *That's it. It's all going to end.*

The realization wasn't crushing. It was gentle, like a final tendril of smoke from a dying candle. He suddenly knew that they couldn't fight—that everything they'd done over the last year had been pointless.

Elend slumped to his knees. The ash came up to his chest. Perhaps this was one final reason why he'd wanted to walk home alone. When others were around, he felt as if he had to be optimistic. But, alone, he could face the truth.

And there, in the ash, he finally just gave up.

Someone knelt down beside him.

Elend jumped backward, scrambling to his feet and scattering ash. He flared pewter belatedly, giving himself the tense strength of a Mistborn about to attack. But, there was nobody beside him. He froze, wondering if he'd been imagining things. And then, burning tin and squinting in the darkness of the ashen night, he finally saw it. A creature of mist.

It wasn't really *composed* of mist. Rather, it was outlined in mist. The random shiftings suggested its figure, which was roughly that of a man. Elend had seen this creature twice before. The first time, it had appeared to him in the wilderness of the Northern Dominance.

The second time, it had stabbed him in the gut, leaving him to bleed to death.

Yet, that had been an attempt to get Vin to take the power at the Well of Ascension and use it to heal Elend. The thing's intentions had been good, even if it had nearly killed Elend. Plus, Vin said that this creature had led her to the bit of metal that had somehow turned Elend into an Allomancer.

The mist spirit watched him, its figure barely distinguishable in the patterns of flowing mists.

"What?" Elend asked. "What do you want of me?"

The mist spirit raised its arm and pointed to the northeast.

That's what it did the first time it met me. It just pointed, as if trying to get me to go somewhere. I didn't understand what it meant then *either.*

"Look," Elend said, suddenly feeling exhausted. "If you want to say something, why not just say it?"

The mist spirit stood quietly in the mists.

"At least write it," Elend said. "The pointing just isn't working." He knew that the creature—whatever it was—had some corporeality. After all, it had managed to stab Elend handily enough.

He expected the creature to just continue standing there. However, to Elend's surprise, it followed the command, kneeling down in the ash. It reached out with a misty hand, and began to scratch in the ash. Elend took a step forward, cocking his head to see what the thing was writing.

I will kill you, the words said. *Death, death, death.*

"Well . . . that's pleasant," Elend said, feeling an eerie chill.

The mist spirit seemed to slump. It knelt in the ash, making no impression in the ground.

Such odd words to write, Elend thought, *when it seemed to be trying to get me to trust it . . .* "It can change your words, can't it?" Elend asked. "The other force. It can rewrite pieces of text on paper, so why not things scratched in ash?"

The mist spirit looked up.

"That's why you ripped the corners off of Sazed's papers," Elend said. "You couldn't write him a note, because the words would just get changed. So, you had to do other things. More blunt things—like pointing."

The creature stood.

"So, write more slowly," Elend said. "Use exaggerated motions. I'll watch the movements of your arm, and form the letters in my mind."

The mist spirit began immediately, waving its arms about. Elend cocked his head, watching its motions. He couldn't make any sense of them, let alone form letters out of them.

"Wait," he said, holding up a hand. "That isn't working. Either it's changing things, or you just don't know your letters."

Silence.

Wait, Elend thought, glancing at the text on the ground. *If the text changed . . .*

"It's here, isn't it," he said, feeling a sudden and icy chill. "It's here with us now."

The mist spirit remained still.

"Bounce around for a yes," Elend said.

The mist spirit began to wave its arms as it had before.

"Close enough," Elend said, shivering. He glanced around,

but could see nothing else in the mists. If the thing Vin had released was there, then it made no impression. Yet, Elend thought he *could* feel something different. A slight increase in wind, a touch of ice in the air, the mists moving about more agitatedly. Perhaps he was just imagining things.

He focused his attention back on the mist spirit. "You're . . . not as solid as you were before."

The creature remained still.

"Is that a no?" Elend said, frustrated. The creature remained still.

Elend closed his eyes. Forcing himself to focus, thinking back to the logic puzzles of his youth. *I need to approach this more directly. Use questions that can be answered with a simple yes or no.* Why would the mist spirit be harder to see now than before? Elend opened his eyes.

"Are you weaker than you were before?" he asked.

The thing waved its arms.

Yes, Elend thought.

"Is it because the world is ending?" Elend asked.

More waving.

"Are you weaker than the other thing? The thing Vin set free?"

Waving.

"*A lot* weaker?" Elend asked.

It waved, though it seemed a bit disconsolate this time.

Great, Elend thought. Of course, he could have guessed that. Whatever the mist spirit was, it wasn't a magical answer to their problems. If it were, it would have saved them by now.

What we lack most is information, Elend thought. *I need to learn what I can from this thing.*

"Are you related to the ash?" he asked.

No motion.

"Are you causing the ashfalls?" he asked.

No motion.

"Is the other thing causing the ashfalls?"

This time, it waved.

Okay. "Is it causing the mists to come in the day too?"

No motion.

"Are *you* causing the mists to come in the day?"

It seemed to pause in thought at this one, then it waved about less vigorously than before.

Is that a "maybe"? Elend wondered. *Or a "partially"?*

The creature fell still. It was getting harder and harder to see it in the mists. Elend flared his tin, but that didn't make the creature any more distinct. It seemed to be . . . fading.

"Where was it you wanted me to go?" Elend asked, more for himself than expecting an answer. "You pointed . . . east? Did you want me to go back to Luthadel?"

It waved with half-enthusiasm again.

"Do you want me to attack Fadrex City?"

It stood still.

"Do you *not* want me to attack Fadrex City?"

It waved vigorously.

Interesting, he thought.

"The mists," Elend said. "They're connected to all this, aren't they?"

Waving.

"They're killing my men," Elend said.

It stepped forward, then stood still, somehow looking urgent.

Elend frowned. "You reacted to that. You mean to say they *aren't* killing my men?"

It waved.

"That's ridiculous. I've *seen* the men fall dead."

It stepped forward, pointing at Elend. He glanced down at his sash. "The coins?" he asked, looking up.

It pointed again. Elend reached into his sash. All that was there were his metal vials. He pulled one out. "Metals?"

It waved vigorously. It just continued to wave and wave. Elend looked down at the vial. "I don't understand."

The creature fell still. It was getting more and more vague, as if it were evaporating.

"Wait!" Elend said, stepping forward. "I have another question. One more before you go!"

It stared him in the eyes.

"Can we beat it?" Elend asked softly. "Can we survive?"

Stillness. Then, the creature waved just briefly. Not a vigorous wave—more of a hesitant one. An uncertain one. It evaporated, maintaining that same wave, the mists becoming indistinct and leaving no sign that the creature had been there.

Elend stood in the darkness. He turned and glanced at his koloss army, who waited like the trunks of dark trees in the distance. Then he turned back, scanning for any further signs of the mist spirit. Finally, he just turned and began to tromp his way back to Fadrex. The koloss followed.

He felt . . . stronger. It was silly—the mist spirit hadn't really given him any useful information. It had been almost like a child. The things it had told him were mostly just confirmations of what he'd already suspected.

Yet, as he walked, he moved with more determination. If only because he knew there were things in the world he didn't understand—and that meant, perhaps, there were possibilities he didn't see. Possibilities for survival.

Possibilities to land safely on the other side of the chasm, even when logic told him not to jump.

I don't know why Preservation decided to use his last bit of life appearing to Elend during his trek back to Fadrex. From what I understand, Elend didn't really learn that much from the meeting. By then, of course, Preservation was but a shadow of himself—and that shadow was under immense destructive pressure from Ruin.

Perhaps Preservation—or, the remnants of what he had been—wanted to get Elend alone. Or, perhaps he saw Elend kneeling in that field, and knew that the emperor of men was very close to just lying down in the ash, never to rise again. Either way, Preservation did appear, and in doing so exposed himself to Ruin's attacks. Gone were the days when Preservation could turn away an Inquisitor with a bare gesture, gone—even—were the days when he could strike a man down to bleed and die.

By the time Elend saw the "mist spirit," Preservation must have been barely coherent. I wonder what Elend would have done, had he known that he was in the presence of a dying god—that on that night, he had been the last witness of Preservation's passing. If Elend had waited just a few more minutes on that ashen field, he would have seen a body—short of stature, black hair, prominent nose—fall from the mists and slump dead into the ash.

As it was, the corpse was left alone to be buried in ash. The world was dying. Its gods had to die with it.

56

SPOOK STOOD IN THE DARK cavern, looking at his board and paper. He had it propped up, like an artist's canvas, though he wasn't sketching images, but ideas. Kelsier had always outlined his plans for the crew on a charcoal board. It seemed like a good idea, even though Spook wasn't explaining plans to a crew, but rather trying to work them out for himself.

The trick was going to be getting Quellion to expose himself as an Allomancer before the people. Durn had told them what to look for, and the crowds would be ready, waiting for confirmation of what they had been told. However, for Spook's plan to work, he'd have to catch the Citizen in a public place, then get the man to use his powers in a way that was obvious to those watching.

I can't let him just Push on a distant metal, then, he thought, scratching a note to himself on the charcoal board. *I'll need him to shoot into the air, or perhaps blast some coins. Something visible, something we can tell everyone to watch for.*

That would be tough, but Spook was confident. He had several ideas scratched up on the board, ranging from attacking

Quellion at a rally to tricking him into using his powers when he thought nobody was looking. Slowly, the thoughts were jelling into a cohesive plan.

I really can *do this,* Spook thought, smiling. *I always felt such awe for Kelsier's leadership abilities. But, it's not as hard as I thought.*

Or, at least, that was what he told himself. He tried not to think about the consequences of a failure. Tried not to think about the fact that he still held Beldre hostage. Tried not to worry about the fact that when he awoke some mornings—his tin having burned away during the night—his body felt completely numb, unable to feel anything until he got more metal as fuel. Tried not to focus on the riots and incidents his appearances, speeches, and work among the people were causing.

Kelsier kept telling him not to worry. That should be enough for him. Shouldn't it?

After a few minutes, he heard someone approaching, footsteps quiet—but not too quiet for him—on the stone. The rustle of a dress, yet without perfume, let him know exactly who it was.

"Spook?"

He lowered the charcoal and turned. Beldre stood at the far side of his "room." He'd made himself an alcove between several of the storage shelves, partitioned off with sheets—his own personal office. The Citizen's sister wore a beautiful noble gown of green and white.

Spook smiled. "You like the dresses?"

She looked down, flushing slightly. "I . . . haven't worn anything like this in years."

"Nobody in this city has," Spook said, setting down the charcoal and wiping his fingers on a rag. "But, then, that makes it pretty easy to get them, if you know which buildings to loot. It looks like I matched your size pretty well, eh?"

"Yes," she said quietly, drifting forward. The gown really did look good on her, and Spook found it a little difficult to focus as she drew closer. She eyed his charcoal board, then frowned. "Is . . . that supposed to make any sense?"

Spook shook himself free of his trance. The charcoal board was a mess of scratches and notations. That, in itself, would have made it difficult enough to read. There was, however, something else that made it even more incomprehensible.

"It's mostly written in Eastern street slang," Spook said.

"The language you grew up speaking?" she said, fingering the board's edge, careful not to touch the writing itself, lest she smudge it.

Spook nodded.

"Even the words are different," she said. "Wasing?"

"It kind of means 'was doing,'" Spook explained. "You start sentences with it. 'Wasing the run of there' would mean 'I was running to that place.'"

"Wasing the where of how of the finds," Beldre said, smiling slightly to herself as she read from the board. "It sounds like gibberish!"

"Wasing the how of wanting the doing," Spook said, smiling, falling into a full accent. Then he flushed, turning away.

"What?" she asked.

Why do I always act so foolish around her? he thought. *The others always made fun of my slang—even Kelsier thought it was silly. Now I start speaking it before her?*

He'd been feeling confident and sure as he studied his plans before she arrived. Why was it that the girl could always make him fall out of his leadership role and go back to being the old Spook? The Spook who had never been important.

"You shouldn't be ashamed of the accent," Beldre said. "I think it's kind of charming."

"You just said it was gibberish," Spook said, turning back to her.

"But that's the best part!" Beldre said. "It's gibberish on *purpose,* right?"

Spook remembered with fondness how his parents had responded to his adoption of the slang. It had been a kind of power, being able to say things that only his friends could understand. Of course, he'd started speaking in it so much that it had been hard to switch back.

"So," Beldre said, eyeing the board. "What does it say?"

Spook hesitated. "Just random thoughts," he said. She was his enemy—he had to remember that.

"Oh," she said. Something unreadable crossed her face, then she turned away from the board.

Her brother always banished her from his conferences, Spook thought. *Never told her anything important. Left her feeling like she was useless. . . .*

"I need to get your brother to use his Allomancy in front of the people," Spook found himself saying. "To let them see that he's a hypocrite."

Beldre looked back.

"The board is filled with my ideas," Spook said. "Most of them aren't very good. I'm kind of leaning toward just attacking him, making him defend himself."

"That won't work," Beldre said.

"Why not?"

"He won't use Allomancy against you. He wouldn't expose himself like that."

"If I threaten him strongly enough he will."

Beldre shook her head. "You promised not to hurt him. Remember?"

"No," Spook said, raising a finger. "I promised to *try* to find another way. And, I don't intend to kill him. I just need to make him *think* that I'd kill him."

Beldre fell silent again. His heart lurched.

"I won't do it, Beldre," Spook said. "I won't kill him."

"You promise that?"

Spook nodded.

She looked up at him, then smiled. "I want to write him a letter. Perhaps I can talk him into listening to you; we could avoid the need for this in the first place."

"All right . . ." Spook said. "But, you realize I'll have to read the letter to make certain you're not revealing anything that could hurt my position."

Beldre nodded.

Of course, he'd do more than read it. He'd rewrite it on another sheet of paper, changing the line order, and then add a few unimportant words. He'd worked on too many thieving crews to be unaware of ciphers. But, assuming that Beldre was being honest with him, a letter from her to Quellion was a good idea. It couldn't help but strengthen Spook's position.

He opened his mouth to ask whether or not her sleeping accommodations were acceptable, but cut himself off as he heard someone approaching. Harder footsteps this time. Captain Goradel, he guessed.

Sure enough, the soldier appeared around the corner to Spook's "room" a short time later.

"My lord," the soldier said. "You should see this."

The soldiers were gone.

Sazed looked through the window with the others, inspecting the empty plot of ground where Quellion's troops had been camped for the last few weeks, watching the Ministry building.

"When did they leave?" Breeze asked, rubbing his chin thoughtfully.

"Just now," Goradel explained.

The move felt ominous to Sazed for some reason. He stood beside Spook, Breeze, and Goradel—though the others seemed to take the soldiers' retreat as a good sign.

"Well, it will make sneaking out easier," Goradel noted.

"More than that," Spook said. "It means I can incorporate our own soldiers in the plan against Quellion. We'd never have gotten them out of the building secretly with half an army on our doorstep, but now . . ."

"Yes," Goradel said. "But where did they go? Do you think Quellion is suspicious of us?"

Breeze snorted. "That, my dear man, sounds like a question for your scouts. Why not have them search out where that army went?"

Goradel nodded. But then, to Sazed's slight surprise, the soldier looked toward Spook for a confirmation. Spook nodded, and the captain moved off to give the orders.

He looks to the boy over Breeze and I, Sazed thought. He shouldn't have been surprised. Sazed himself had agreed to let Spook take the lead, and to Goradel, all three of them—Sazed, Breeze, Spook—were probably equal. All were in Elend's inner circle, and of the three, Spook was the best warrior. It made sense for Goradel to look to him as a source of authority.

It just felt strange to see Spook giving orders to the soldiers. Spook had always been so quiet during the days of the original crew. And yet, Sazed was beginning to respect the boy too. Spook knew how to give orders in a way that Sazed could not, and he had shown remarkable foresight in his preparations in Urteau, as well as his plans to overthrow Quellion. He had a flair for the dramatic that Breeze kept saying was remarkable.

And yet, there was that bandage on the boy's eyes, and the other things he hadn't explained. Sazed knew that he should have pushed harder for answers, but the truth was that he trusted Spook. Sazed had known Spook from the lad's young teenage years, when he'd barely been capable of communicating with others.

As Goradel moved off, Spook looked to Sazed and Breeze. "Well?"

"Quellion is planning something," Breeze said. "Seems too early to jump to conclusions, though."

"I agree," Spook said. "For now, we go forward with the plan."

With that, they split up. Sazed turned, making his way back down and over to the far side of the cavern—to where a large group of soldiers worked in an area well lit with lanterns. On his arms, he wore the familiar weight of his copperminds—two on his forearms, two on his upper arms. In them sat the knowledge of engineering he needed to complete the task Spook had assigned him.

Lately, Sazed didn't know what to think. Each time he climbed the ladder and looked out over the city, he saw worse signs. The ashfalls were heavier. The earthquakes were growing more and more frequent, and more and more violent. The mists were lingering later and later in the day. The sky grew dark, the red sun more like a vast bleeding scar than a source of light and life. The ashmounts made the horizon red even during the night.

It seemed to him that the end of the world should be a time when men *found* faith, not a time when they lost it. Yet, the little time that he'd devoted to studying the religions in his portfolio had not been encouraging. Twenty more religions eliminated, leaving just thirty potential candidates.

He shook his head to himself, moving among the toiling soldiers. Several groups worked on wooden contraptions filled with rocks—weight systems that would fall to block off the water running into the cavern. Others worked on the system of pulleys that would lower the mechanism. After about a half hour or so, Sazed determined that they were all doing their tasks well, and returned to his calculations. However, as he walked to his table, he saw Spook approaching him.

"Riots," Spook said, falling into step beside Sazed.

"Excuse me, Lord Spook?"

"That's where the soldiers went. Some people started a fire, and the soldiers guarding us were needed to put it out before the whole city went up. There's a lot more wood here than there is in Central Dominance cities."

Sazed frowned. "Our actions here are becoming dangerous, I fear."

Spook shrugged. "Seems like a good thing to me. This city is on the edge of snapping, Saze. Just like Luthadel was when we took control."

"Only the presence of Elend Venture kept that city from destroying itself," Sazed said quietly. "Kelsier's revolution could easily have turned into a disaster."

"It will be all right," Spook said.

Sazed eyed the young man as the two of them walked through the cavern. Spook seemed to be trying very hard to project an air of confidence. Perhaps Sazed was just growing cynical, but he found it difficult to be as optimistic as Spook.

"You don't believe me," Spook said.

"I'm sorry, Lord Spook," Sazed said. "It's not that . . . it's just that I seem to have trouble having faith in anything lately."

"Oh."

They walked silently for a while, eventually finding themselves at the edge of the glassy underground lake. Sazed paused beside the waters, his worries chewing at his insides. He stood for a long moment, feeling frustrated, but not really having an outlet.

"Don't you even worry, Spook?" Sazed finally asked. "Worry that we'll fail?"

"I don't know," Spook said, shuffling.

"And, it's so much more than *this,*" Sazed said, waving back at the work crews. "The very sky seems to be our enemy. The land is dying. Don't you wonder what good any of this is? Why we even struggle? We're all doomed anyway!"

Spook flushed. Then, finally, he looked down. "I don't know," he repeated. "I . . . I understand what you're doing, Sazed. You're trying to find out if I doubt myself. I guess you can see through me."

Sazed frowned, but Spook wasn't looking.

"You're right," the young man said then, wiping his brow, "I *do* wonder if I'll fail. I guess Tindwyl would be annoyed at me, wouldn't she? She didn't think that leaders should doubt themselves."

That gave Sazed pause. *What am I doing?* he thought, horrified at his outburst. *Is this what I've really become? During most of my life, I resisted the Synod, rebelling against my own people. Yet, I was at peace, confident that I was doing the right thing.*

Now I come here, where people need me most, and I just sit around and snap at my friends, telling them that we're just going to die?

"But," Spook said, looking up, "though I doubt myself, I still think we'll be all right."

Sazed was surprised at the hope he saw in the boy's eyes. *That's what I've lost.*

"How can you say that?" Sazed asked.

"I don't know, really," Spook said. "I just . . . Well, do you remember that question you asked me when you first got here? We were standing by the lake, just over there. You asked me about faith. You asked what good it was, if it just led people to hurt each other, like Quellion's faith in the Survivor has done."

Sazed looked out over the lake. "Yes," he said softly. "I remember."

"I've been thinking about that ever since," Spook said. "And . . . I think I might have an answer."

"Please."

"Faith," Spook said, "means that it doesn't matter what happens. You can trust that somebody is watching. Trust that somebody will make it all right."

Sazed frowned.

"It means that there will always be a way," Spook whispered, staring forward, eyes glazed, as if seeing things that Sazed could not.

Yes, Sazed thought. *That is what I have lost. And it's what I need to get back.*

I have come to see that each power has three aspects: a physical one, which can be seen in the creations made by Ruin and Preservation; a spiritual one in the unseen energy that permeates all of the world; and a cognitive one in the minds which controlled that energy.

There is more to this. Much more that even I do not yet comprehend.

57

YOU SHOULD KILL THEM.

Vin looked up as she heard a pair of guards pass the door to her cell. There was one good thing about Ruin's voice—it tended to warn her when people were nearby, even if it did always tell her to kill them.

A part of her did wonder if, in fact, she was mad. After all, she saw and heard things that nobody else could. However, if she were mad, there would really be no way for her to realize it. So, she simply decided to accept what she heard, and move on.

In truth, she was glad for Ruin's voice on occasion. Other than Ruin, she was alone in the cell. All was still. Even the soldiers did not speak—likely at Yomen's orders. Plus, each time Ruin spoke, she felt as if she learned something. For instance, she had learned that Ruin could either manifest in person or affect her from a distance. When its actual presence was not with her in the cell, Ruin's words were far more simple and vague.

Take, for instance, Ruin's order that she kill the guards. She couldn't follow that suggestion, not from within the cell. It wasn't so much a specific order as it was an attempt to change her inclinations. Again, that reminded her of Allomancy, which could exert a general influence over a person's emotions.

General influence . . .

Something suddenly occurred to her. She quested out, and—sure enough—she could still feel the thousand koloss that Elend had given her. They were under her control still, distant, obeying the general orders she'd given them before.

Could she use them somehow? Deliver a message to Elend, perhaps? Get them to attack the city and free her? As she considered them, both plans seemed flawed. Sending them to Fadrex would just get them killed, as well as risk upsetting whatever plans Elend had for a potential attack. She could send them to find Elend, but that would probably just get them killed by the camp guards, who would be afraid they were bloodlusting. Plus, what would she have them do if they did get to him? She could order them to take actions, like attack or pick someone up, but she'd never tried something as delicate as ordering one to speak certain words.

She tried forming those words in her head and getting

them to the koloss, but all she sensed back was confusion. She'd have to work on that some more. And, as she considered, she wondered if getting a message to Elend would really be the best way to use them. It would let Ruin know about a potential tool she had that, maybe, he hadn't noticed.

"I see that he finally found a cell for you," a voice said.

Vin looked up, and there he was. Still wearing Reen's form, Ruin stood in the small cell with her. He maintained a straight-backed posture, standing almost benevolently over her. Vin sat up on her cot. She'd never thought that of all her metals, she would miss bronze so much. When Ruin returned to visit in "person," burning bronze had let her feel him via bronzepulses and gave her warning that he had arrived, even if he didn't appear to her.

"I'll admit that I'm disappointed in you, Vin," Ruin said. He used Reen's voice, but he imbued it with a sense of . . . age. Of quiet wisdom. The fatherly nature of that voice, mixed with Reen's face and her own knowledge of the thing's desire to destroy, was disturbing.

"The last time you were captured and locked away without metals," Ruin continued, "not a night passed before you'd killed the Lord Ruler and overthrown the empire. Now you've been soundly imprisoned for what . . . a week now?"

Vin didn't respond. *Why come taunt me? Does it expect to learn something?*

Ruin shook its head. "I would have thought at the very least that you'd have killed Yomen."

"Why are you so concerned with his death?" Vin asked. "It seems to me that he's on your side."

Ruin shook its head, standing with hands clasped behind its back. "You still don't understand, I see. You're *all* on my side, Vin. I created you. You're my tools—each and every one of you. Zane, Yomen, you, your dear Emperor Venture . . ."

"No. Zane was yours, and Yomen is obviously misguided. But Elend . . . he'll fight against you."

"But he can't," Ruin said. "That's what you refuse to understand, child. You *cannot* fight me, for by the mere act of fighting you advance my goals."

"Evil men, perhaps, help you," Vin said. "But not Elend. He's a good person, and not even you can deny that."

"Vin, Vin. *Why* can't you see? This isn't about good or evil. Morality doesn't even enter into it. Good men will kill as quickly for what they want as evil men—only the things they want are different."

Vin fell silent.

Ruin shook its head. "I keep trying to explain. This process we are engaged in, the end of all things—it's not a *fight,* but a simple culmination of inevitability. Can any man make a pocket watch that won't eventually wind down? Can you imagine a lantern that won't eventually burn out? All things end. Think of me as a caretaker—the one who watches the shop and makes certain that the lights are turned out, that everything is cleaned up, once closing time arrives."

For a moment, he made her question. There was some truth in his words, and seeing the changes in the land these last few years—changes that started before Ruin was even released—did make her wonder.

Yet, something about the conversation bothered her. If what Ruin said was completely true, then why did he care about her? Why return and speak to her?

"I guess that you've won, then," she said quietly.

"Won?" Ruin asked. "Don't you understand? There was nothing for me to win, child. Things happen as they must."

"I see," Vin said.

"Yes, perhaps you do," Ruin said. "I think that *you* just might be able to." It turned and began to walk quietly from one side of the cell toward the other. "You are a piece of me, you know. Beautiful destroyer. Blunt and effective. Of all those I've claimed over this brief thousand years, you are the only one I think just might be able to understand me."

Why, Vin thought, *it's gloating! That's why Ruin is here—because it wants to make certain that someone understands what it has accomplished!* There was a feeling of pride and victory in Ruin's eyes. They were human emotions, emotions that Vin could understand.

At that moment, Ruin stopped being an *it* in her mind, and instead became a *he*.

Vin began to think—for the first time—that she could find a way to beat Ruin. He was powerful, perhaps even incomprehensible. But she had seen humanity in him, and that humanity could be deceived, manipulated, and broken. Perhaps it was this same conclusion that Kelsier had drawn, after looking into the Lord Ruler's eyes that fateful night when he had been captured. She finally felt as if she understood him, and what it must have felt like to undertake something so bold as the defeat of the Lord Ruler.

But Kelsier had years to plan, Vin thought. *I . . . I don't even know how long I have. Not long, I would guess.* Even as she thought, another earthquake began. The walls trembled, and Vin heard guards cursing in the hallway as something fell and broke. And Ruin . . . he seemed to be in a state of bliss, his eyes closed, mouth open slightly and looking pleasured as the building and city rumbled.

Eventually, all fell still. Ruin opened his eyes, staring her down. "This work I do, it's about *passion,* Vin. It's about dynamic events; it's about change! That is why you and your Elend are so important to me. People with passion are people who will destroy—for a man's passion is not *true* until he proves how much he's willing to sacrifice for it. Will he kill? Will he go to war? Will he break and discard that which he has, all in the name of what he *needs*?"

It's not just that Ruin feels that he's accomplished something, Vin thought, *he feels that he's overcome. Despite what he claims, he feels that he's won—that he's defeated something . . . but who or what? Us? We would be no adversary for a force like Ruin.*

A voice from the past seemed to whisper to her from long ago. *What's the first rule of Allomancy, Vin?*

Consequence. Action and reaction. If Ruin had power to destroy, then there was something that opposed him. It had to be. Ruin had an opposite, an opponent. Or, he once had.

"What did you do to him?" Vin asked.

Ruin hesitated, frowning as he turned toward her.

"Your opposite," Vin said. "The one who once stopped you from destroying the world."

Ruin was silent for a long moment. Then he smiled, and Vin saw something chilling in that smile. A knowledge that he was right. Vin *was* part of him. She understood him.

"Preservation is dead," Ruin said.

"You killed him?"

Ruin shrugged. "Yes, but no. He gave of himself to craft a cage. Though his throes of agony have lasted several thousand years, now, finally, he is gone. And the bargain has come to its fruition."

Preservation, Vin thought, a piece of a gigantic whole clicking into place. *The opposite of Ruin. A force like that couldn't have* destroyed *his enemy, because he would represent the opposite of destruction. But imprisonment, that would be within his powers.*

Imprisonment that ended when I gave up the power at the Well.

"And so you see the inevitability," Ruin said softly.

"You couldn't create it yourself, could you?" Vin asked. "The world, life. You can't create, you can only destroy."

"He couldn't create either," Ruin said. "He could only preserve. Preservation is not creation."

"And so you worked together," Vin said.

"Both with a promise," Ruin said. "My promise was to work with him to create you—life that thinks, life that loves."

"And his promise?" Vin asked, fearing that she knew the answer.

"That I could destroy you eventually," Ruin said softly. "And I have come to claim what was promised me. The only point in creating something is to watch it die. Like a story that must come to a climax, what I have done will not be fulfilled until the end has arrived."

It can't be true, Vin thought. *Preservation. If he really represents a power in the universe, then he couldn't really have been destroyed, could he?*

"I know what you are thinking," Ruin said. "You cannot

enlist Preservation's power. He is dead. He couldn't kill me, you see. He could only imprison me."

Yes. I figured that last part out already. You really can't read my mind, can you?

Ruin continued. "It was a villainous act, I must say. Preservation tried to escape our bargain. Would you not call that an evil deed? It is as I said before—good and evil have little to do with ruin or preservation. An evil man will protect that which he desires as surely as a good man."

But something is keeping Ruin from destroying the world now, she thought. *For all his words about stories and endings, he is not a force that would wait for an "appropriate" moment. There is more to this, more that I'm not understanding. What is holding him back?*

"I've come to you," Ruin said, "because I want you, at least, to watch and see. To know. For it has come."

Vin perked up. "What? The end?"

Ruin nodded.

"How long?" Vin asked.

"Days," Ruin said. "But not weeks."

Vin felt a chill, realizing something. He had come to her, finally revealing himself, because she was captured. He thought that there was no further chance for mankind. He assumed that he had won.

Which means that there is a way to beat him, she thought with determination. *And it involves me. But I can't do it here, or he wouldn't have come to gloat.*

And that meant she had to get free. Quickly.

Once you begin to understand these things, you can see how Ruin was trapped even though Preservation's mind was gone, expended to create the prison. Though Preservation's consciousness was mostly destroyed, his spirit and body were still in force. And, as an opposite force of Ruin, these could still prevent Ruin from destroying.

Or, at least, keep him from destroying things too quickly. Once his mind was "freed" from its prison the destruction accelerated quickly.

58

"THROW YOUR WEIGHT HERE," SAZED said, pointing at a wooden lever. "The counterweights will fall, swinging down all four floodgates and stemming the flow into the cavern. I warn you, however—the explosion of water above will be rather spectacular. We should be able to fill the city's canals in a matter of hours, and I suspect that a portion of the northern city will be flooded."

"To dangerous levels?" Spook asked.

"I do not think so," Sazed said. "The water will burst out through the conduits in the interchange building beside us. I've inspected the equipment there, and it appears sound. The water *should* flow directly into the canals, and from there exit the city. Either way, I would not want to be in those street-slots when this water comes. The current will be quite swift."

"I've taken care of that," Spook said. "Durn is going to make certain the people know to be clear of the waterways."

Sazed nodded. Spook couldn't help but be impressed. The complicated construct of wood, gears, and wire looked like it should have taken months to build, not weeks. Large nets of rocks weighed down the four gates, which hung, ready to block off the river.

"This is amazing, Saze," Spook said. "With a sign as spectacular as the reappearance of the canal waters, the people will be *certain* to listen to us instead of the Citizen." Breeze and Durn's men had been working hard over the last few weeks, whispering to the people to watch for a miracle from the Survivor of the Flames. Something extraordinary, something to prove—once and for all—who was the rightful master of the city.

"It is the best I could do," Sazed said with a modest bow of the head. "The seals won't be perfectly tight, of course. However, that should matter little."

"Men?" Spook said, turning to four of Goradel's soldiers. "You understand what you are to do?"

"Yes, sir," the lead soldier said. "We wait for a messenger, then throw the lever there."

"If no messenger comes," Spook said, "throw the switch at nightfall."

"And," Sazed said, raising a finger, "don't forget to twist the sealing mechanism in the other room, plugging the water flow *out* of this chamber. Otherwise, the lake will eventually empty. Better that we keep this reservoir full, just in case."

"Yes, sir," the soldier said with a nod.

Spook turned, looking back over the cavern. Soldiers bustled about, preparing. He was going to need most of them for the night's activities. They looked eager—they'd spent too long holed up in the cavern and the building above. To the side, Beldre regarded Sazed's contraption with interest. Spook broke away from the soldiers, approaching her with a quick step.

"You're really going to do it?" she said. "Return the water to the canals?"

Spook nodded.

"I sometimes imagined what it would be like to have the waters back," she said. "The city wouldn't feel as barren—it would become important, like it was during the early days of the Final Empire. All those beautiful waterways. No more ugly gashes in the ground."

"It will be a wonderful sight," Spook said, smiling.

Beldre just shook her head. "It . . . amazes me that you can be such different people at the same time. How can the man who would do such a beautiful thing for my city also plan such destruction?"

"Beldre, I'm not planning to destroy your city."

"Just its government."

"I do what needs to be done."

"Men say that so easily," Beldre said. "Yet, everybody seems to have a different opinion of what 'needs' to be done."

"Your brother had his chance," Spook said.

Beldre looked down. She still carried with her the letter they'd received earlier in the day—a response from Quellion. Beldre's plea had been heartfelt, but the Citizen had responded with insults, implying that she had been forced to write the words because she was being held prisoner.

I do not fear a usurper, the letter read. *I am protected by the Survivor himself. You will not have this city, tyrant.*

Beldre looked up. "Don't do it," she whispered. "Give him more time. Please."

Spook hesitated.

"There is no more time," Kelsier whispered. "Do what must be done."

"I'm sorry," Spook said, turning from her. "Stay with the soldiers—I'm leaving four men to guard you. Not to keep you from fleeing, though they will do that. I want you inside this cavern. I can't promise that the streets will be safe."

He heard her sniffle quietly behind him. He left her standing there, then walked toward the gathering group of soldiers. One man brought Spook his dueling canes and singed cloak. Goradel stood at the front of his soldiers, looking proud. "We're ready, my lord."

Breeze walked up beside him, shaking his head, dueling cane tapping the ground. He sighed. "Well, here we go again. . . ."

The evening's occasion was a speech Quellion had been publicizing for some time. He had stopped executions recently, as if finally realizing that the deaths were contributing to the instability of his rule. He apparently intended to swing back toward benevolence, holding rallies, emphasizing the wonderful things he was doing for the city.

Spook walked alone, a little ahead of Breeze, Allrianne,

and Sazed, who chatted behind. Some of Goradel's soldiers followed as well, wearing common Urteau garb. Spook had split their force, sending it by different paths. It wasn't dark yet—to Spook the falling sun was bright, forcing him to wear his blindfold and spectacles. Quellion liked to hold his speeches in the evening, so that the mists arrived during them. He liked the implied connection to the Survivor.

A figure hobbled out of a side streetslot next to Spook. Durn walked with a stooped posture, a cloak obscuring his figure. Spook respected the twisted man's insistence on leaving the security of the Harrows, going out to run jobs himself. Perhaps that was why he'd ended up as leader of the city's underground.

"People are gathering, as expected," Durn said, coughing quietly. "Some of your soldiers are already there."

Spook nodded.

"Things are . . . unsettled in the city," Durn said. "It worries me. Segments I can't control have already started looting some of the prohibited noble mansions. My men are all busy trying to get people out of the streetslots."

"It will be all right," Spook said. "Most of the populace will be at the speech."

Durn was silent for a moment. "Word is that Quellion is going to use his speech to denounce you, then finally order an attack on the Ministry building where you're staying."

"It's a good thing we won't be there, then," Spook said. "He shouldn't have withdrawn his soldiers, even if he *did* need them to keep order in the city."

Durn nodded.

"What?" Spook said.

"I just hope you can handle this, lad. Once this night is through, the city will be yours. Treat it better than Quellion did."

"I will," Spook said.

"My men will create a disturbance for you at the meeting. Farewell." Durn took the next left, disappearing down another streetslot alleyway.

Ahead, the crowds were already gathering. Spook put up

the hood of his cloak, keeping his eyes obscured as he wove his way through the crowd. He quickly left Sazed and the others behind, pushing his way up a ramp to the old city square—the place Quellion had chosen for his speech. His men had erected a wooden stage, from which the Citizen could face the crowd. The speech was already in progress. Spook stopped just a short distance away from a guard patrol. Many of Quellion's soldiers surrounded the stage, eyeing the crowd.

Minutes passed, and Spook spent them listening to Quellion's voice ring, yet paying no attention to the words. Ash fell around him, dusting the crowd. Mists began to twist in the air.

He listened, listened with ears no other man had. He used Allomancy's strange ability to filter and ignore—hearing through the chatter and whispers and shuffles and coughs, just as he could somehow see through the obscuring mists. He heard the city. Yells in the distance.

It was beginning.

"Too fast!" a voice whispered, a beggar moving up to Spook's side. "Durn sends word. Riots in the streets, ones he didn't start! Durn cannot control them. My lord, the city is beginning to burn!"

"It was a night not unlike this one," another voice whispered. Kelsier's voice. "A glorious night. When I took the city of Luthadel, and made it mine."

A disturbance began at the back of the crowd; Durn's men were causing their distraction. Some of Quellion's guards pulled away to quell this nearby riot. The Citizen continued to shout his accusations. Spook heard his own name in Quellion's words, but the context was simply noise.

Spook tilted his head back, looking up at the sky. Ash fell toward him, as if he were sailing through it into the air. Like a Mistborn.

His hood fell back. Men around him whispered in surprise.

A clock rang in the distance. Goradel's soldiers rushed the stage. Around him, Spook could feel a glow rising. The fires of rebellion, burning in the city. Just like the night he had overthrown the Lord Ruler. The torches of revolution. Then the people had put Elend on the throne.

This time, it would be Spook they elevated.

Weak no more, he thought. *Never weak again!*

The last of Quellion's soldiers rushed away from the stage, moving into combat with Goradel's men. The crowd shied away from the battle, but nobody ran. They had been prepared well for the night's events. Many would be waiting, watching for the signs Spook and Durn had promised—signs revealed just a few hours before, to minimize the risk of Quellion's spies learning Spook's plan. A miracle in the canals, and proof that Quellion was an Allomancer.

If the Citizen—or even any of his guards on the stage—shot coins or used Allomancy to leap into the air, the people would see. They would know that they had been deceived. And that would be the end. The crowd surged away from the cursing soldiers, and their withdrawal left Spook standing alone. Quellion's voice finally trailed off. Some of his soldiers were rushing up to get him off the stage.

Quellion's eyes found Spook. Only then did they show fear.

Spook leaped. He couldn't Steelpush himself, but his legs were fueled by the power of flared pewter. He soared up, easily cresting the lip of the stage, landing in a crouch. He pulled free a dueling cane, then rushed the Citizen.

Behind him, people began to cry out. Spook heard his name, Survivor of the Flames. Survivor. He wouldn't just kill Quellion, but destroy him. Undermining his rule, just as Breeze had suggested. At that moment, the Soother and Allrianne would be manipulating the crowd, keeping them from running away in a panic. Holding them there.

So they could watch the show Spook was about to give.

The guards at Quellion's side saw Spook too late. He dropped the first one easily, crushing the man's skull inside his helmet. Quellion screamed for more help.

Spook swung at another man, but his target moved out of the way, supernaturally quick. Spook pulled to the side just in time to dodge a blow, the weapon grazing the side of his cheek. The man was an Allomancer—a pewter burner. The large brute who carried no sword, but instead an obsidian-edged cudgel.

Pewter isn't spectacular enough, Spook thought. *The people won't know how to tell if a man is swinging too quickly or enduring too much. I have to make Quellion shoot coins.*

The Thug backed away, obviously noting Spook's own increased speed. He kept his weapon raised warily, but did not attack. He just had to stall, letting his companion pull Quellion away. The Thug would be no easy fight—he would be more skilled than Spook, and even stronger.

"Your family is free," Spook lied quietly. "We saved them earlier. Help us capture Quellion—he no longer has a hold on you."

The Thug paused, lowering his weapon.

"Kill him!" Kelsier snapped.

That hadn't been Spook's plan, but he responded to the prompting. He dodged inside the Thug's reach. The man turned in shock, and as he did, Spook delivered a backhanded blow to the skull. Spook's dueling cane shattered. The Thug stumbled to the ground, and Spook snatched up the man's fallen weapon, the obsidian-lined cudgel.

Quellion was at the edge of the stage. Spook jumped, sailing across the wooden platform. It was all right for him to use Allomancy; he hadn't preached against it. Only Quellion the hypocrite needed to fear using his powers.

Spook cut down the remaining guard as he landed—the jagged shards of obsidian ripping through flesh. The soldier fell, and Quellion spun.

"I don't fear you!" Quellion said, voice shaking. "I'm protected!"

"Kill him," Kelsier ordered, appearing visibly on the stage a short distance away. Usually, the Survivor only spoke in his mind; he hadn't actually appeared since that day in the burning building. It meant important things were happening.

Spook grabbed the Citizen by the front of his shirt, yanking him forward. Spook raised the length of wood, blood dripping from the obsidian shards onto the side of his hand.

"*No!*"

Spook froze at that voice, then glanced to the side. *She* was there, shoving her way through the crowd, approaching the open space before the stage.

"*Beldre?*" Spook asked. "How did you get out of the cavern?"

But, of course, she couldn't hear him. Only Spook's supernatural hearing had allowed him to pick her voice out of the sounds of fear and battle. He met her eyes across the distance, and saw her whispered words more than he heard them.

Please. You promised.

"Kill him!"

Quellion chose that moment to try and pull away. Spook turned, yanking back again—harder this time, nearly ripping Quellion's shirt free as he threw the man down to the wooden platform. Quellion cried out in pain, and Spook raised his brutal weapon with both hands.

Something sparked in the firelight. Spook barely felt the impact, though it shook him. He stumbled, looking down, seeing blood on his side. Something had pierced the flesh of his left arm and shoulder. Not an arrow, though it had moved like one. His arm drooped, and though he couldn't feel the pain, it seemed that his muscles weren't working properly.

Something hit me. A . . . coin.

He turned. Beldre stood at the front of the crowd, crying, her hand raised toward him.

She was there that day I was captured, Spook thought numbly, *at her brother's side. He always keeps her near. To protect her, we thought.*

Or the other way around?

Spook stood up straighter, Quellion whimpering in front of him. Spook's arm dripped a trail of blood from where Beldre's coin had hit, but he ignored it, staring at her.

"You were always the Allomancer," he whispered. "Not your brother."

And then, the crowd began to scream—likely prompted by Breeze. "The Citizen's sister is an Allomancer!"

"Hypocrite!"

"Liar!"

"He killed my uncle, yet left his own sister alive!"

Beldre cried out as the people, carefully prepared and planted, saw the proof that Spook had promised them. It didn't have the target he had intended, but the machine he had set in motion could not be halted now. The people gathered around Beldre, yelling in anger, shoving her among themselves.

Spook stepped toward her, raising his wounded arm. Then a shadow fell on him.

"She was always planning to betray you, Spook," Kelsier said.

Spook turned, looking at the Survivor. He stood tall and proud, like the day when he'd faced the Lord Ruler.

"You kept waiting for an assassin," Kelsier said. "You didn't realize that Quellion had already sent one. His sister. Didn't it strike you as strange that he'd let her get away from him and enter the enemy's own base? She was sent there to kill you. You, Sazed, and Breeze. The problem is, she was raised a pampered rich girl. She's not used to killing. She never was. You were never really in danger from her."

The crowd surged, and Spook spun, worried about Beldre. However, he calmed a bit as he realized that the people were simply pulling her toward the stage. "Survivor!" people were chanting. "Survivor of the Flames!"

"King!"

They cast Beldre before him, pushing her up onto the platform. Her scarlet clothing was ripped, her figure battered, her auburn hair a mess. To the side, Quellion groaned. Spook appeared to have broken his arm without realizing it.

Spook moved to help Beldre. She was bleeding from several small cuts, but she was alive. And she was crying.

"She was his bodyguard," Kelsier said, stepping over to Beldre. "That's why she was always with him. Quellion isn't an Allomancer. He never was."

Spook knelt beside the girl, cringing at her bruised form.

"Now, you must kill her," Kelsier said.

Spook looked up, blood seeping from the cut on the side of his face, where the Thug had grazed him. Blood dripped from his chin. "*What?*"

"You want power, Spook?" Kelsier said, stepping forward. "You want to be a better Allomancer? Well, power must come from somewhere. It is never free. This woman is a Coinshot. Kill her, and you can have her ability. I will give it to you."

Spook looked down at the weeping woman. He felt surreal, as if he were not quite there. His breathing was labored, each breath coming as a gasp, his body shaking despite his pewter. People chanted his name. Quellion was mumbling something. Beldre continued to cry.

Spook reached up with his bloodied hand, ripping off his blindfold, spectacles tumbling free. He stumbled to his feet, looking out over the city.

And saw it burning.

The sounds of rioting echoed through the streets. Flames burned in a dozen different spots, lighting the mists, casting a hellish haze over the city. Not the fires of rebellion at all. The fires of destruction.

"This is wrong . . ." Spook whispered.

"You will take the city, Spook," Kelsier said. "You will have what you always wanted! You'll be like Elend, and like Vin. Better than either! You'll have Elend's titles and Vin's power! You'll be like a god!"

Spook turned away from the burning city as something caught his attention. Quellion was reaching out with his good arm, reaching toward . . .

Toward Kelsier.

"Please," Quellion whispered. It seemed as if he could *see* the Survivor, though nobody else around them could. "My lord Kelsier, why have you forsaken me?"

"I gave you pewter, Spook," Kelsier said angrily, not looking at Quellion. "Will you deny me now? You must pull free one of the steel spikes that support this stage. Then, you must take the girl, and press her to your chest. Kill her with the spike, and drive it into your own body. That is the only way!"

Kill her with the spike . . . Spook thought, feeling numb. *This all began that day when I nearly died. I was fighting a Thug in the market; I used him as a shield. But . . . the other soldier struck anyway, stabbing through his friend and into me.*

Spook stumbled away from Beldre, kneeling beside Quellion. The man cried out as Spook forced him down against the wooden planks.

"That's right," Kelsier said. "Kill him first."

But Spook wasn't listening. He ripped Quellion's shirt, looking at the shoulder and chest. There was nothing odd about either. The Citizen's upper arm, however, had a length of metal piercing it. It appeared to be bronze. Hand shaking, Spook pulled the metal free. Quellion screamed.

But so did Kelsier.

Spook turned, bloodied bronze spike in his hand. Kelsier was enraged, hands like claws, stepping forward.

"What *are* you?" Spook asked.

The thing screamed, but Spook ignored it, looking down at his own chest. He ripped open his shirt, exposing the mostly healed wound in his shoulder. A glimmer of metal still shone there, the tip of the sword. The sword that had passed through an Allomancer—killing the man—and then entered Spook's own body. Kelsier had told him to leave the broken shard there. As a symbol of what Spook had gone through.

The point of the shard protruded from Spook's skin. How had he forgotten about it? How had he ignored such a relatively large piece of metal inside of his body? Spook reached for it.

"No!" Kelsier said. "Spook, do you want to go back to being normal? Do you want to be useless again? You'll lose your pewter, and go back to being weak, like you were when you let your uncle die!"

Spook wavered.

No, Spook thought. *Something is wrong. I was supposed*

to expose Quellion, get him to use his Allomancy, but I just attacked instead. I wanted to kill. I forgot about plans and preparation. I brought destruction to this city.

This is not right!

He pulled the glass dagger from his boot. Kelsier screamed terribly in his ears, but Spook reached up anyway, slicing the flesh of his chest. He reached in with pewter-enhanced fingers and grabbed the steel shard that was embedded inside.

Then, he ripped the bit of metal free, casting it across the stage, crying out at the shock of pain. Kelsier vanished immediately. And so did Spook's ability to burn pewter.

It hit him all at once—the fatigue of pushing himself so hard during his time in Urteau. The wounds he'd been ignoring. The sudden explosion of light, sound, smell, and sensation that pewter had let him resist. It overcame him like a physical force, crushing him down. He collapsed to the platform.

He groaned, unable to think anymore. He could simply let the blackness take him. . . .

Her city is burning.

Blackness . . .

Thousands will die in the flames.

The mists tickled his cheeks. In the cacophony, Spook had let his tin dim, relieving him of sensation, leaving him feeling blissfully numb. It was better that way.

You want to be like Kelsier? Really like Kelsier? Then fight when you are beaten!

"Lord Spook!" The voice was faint.

Survive!

With a scream of pain, Spook flared tin. As the metal always did, it brought a wave of sensations—thousands of them, shocking him at once. Pain. Feeling. Hearing. Sounds, smells, lights.

And lucidity.

Spook forced himself to his knees, coughing. Blood still streamed down his arm. He looked up. Sazed was running toward the platform.

"Lord Spook!" Sazed said, puffing as he arrived. "Lord Breeze is trying to damp down riots, but we pushed this city too far, I think! The people will destroy it in their rage."

"The flames," Spook croaked. "We have to put out the fires. The city is too dry; it has too much wood. It will burn, with everyone in it."

Sazed looked grave. "There is no way. We must get out! This riot will destroy us."

Spook glanced to the side. Beldre was kneeling beside her brother. She'd bound his wound, and then made a makeshift sling for his arm. Quellion glanced at Spook, looking dazed. As if he'd just awoken from a dream.

Spook stumbled to his feet. "We won't abandon the city, Sazed."

"But—"

"*No!*" Spook said. "I ran from Luthadel and left Clubs to die. I will not run again! We can stop the flames. We just need water."

Sazed paused.

"Water," Beldre said, standing.

"The canals will fill soon," Spook said. "We can organize fire brigades—use the flood to stop the flames."

Beldre glanced down. "There will be no flood, Spook. The guards you left . . . I attacked them with coins."

Spook felt a chill. "Dead?"

She shook her head, hair disheveled, her face scratched. "I don't know," she said quietly. "I didn't look."

"The waters have not come yet," Sazed said. "They . . . should have been released by now."

"Then we will bring them!" Spook snapped. He spun at Quellion, then stumbled, feeling dizzy. "You!" he said, pointing at the Citizen. "You would be king of this city? Well, lead this people, then. Get control of them and prepare them to put out the fires."

"I can't," Quellion said. "They'll kill me for what I've done."

Spook wobbled, light-headed. He steadied himself against a beam, holding his head. Beldre took a step toward him.

Spook looked up, meeting Quellion's eyes. The fires of the city were so bright that his flared tin made it difficult to see. Yet, he dared not release the metal—only the power of noise, heat, and pain was keeping him conscious.

"You *will* go to them," Spook said. "I don't give a damn if they rip you apart, Quellion. You're going to try to save this city. If you don't, I'll kill you myself. *Do you understand?*"

The Citizen froze, then nodded.

"Sazed," Spook said, "take him to Breeze and Allrianne. I'm going to the cache. I'll bring the floodwaters to the canals, one way or another. Have Breeze and the others form fire brigades to douse the flames as soon as there is water."

Sazed nodded. "It is a good plan. But Goradel will lead the Citizen. I am coming with you."

Spook nodded wearily. Then, as Sazed moved off to get the guard captain—who had apparently established a defensive perimeter around the square—Spook climbed from the stage and forced himself to begin moving toward the cache.

Soon, he noticed someone catch up to him. Then, after a few moments, that person passed him and ran on. Part of his mind knew it was a good thing that Sazed had decided to move on—the Terrisman had created the mechanism that would flood the city. He would throw the lever. Spook wasn't needed.

Keep moving.

He did, walking on, as if each step were in atonement for what he had done to the city. After a short time, he realized that someone was at his side, tying a bandage on his arm.

He blinked. "Beldre?"

"I betrayed you," she said, looking down. "But, I didn't have a choice. I couldn't let you kill him. I . . ."

"You did the right thing," Spook said. "Something . . . something was interfering, Beldre. It had your brother. It almost had me. I don't know. We have to keep walking, though. The lair is close. Just up the ramp."

She supported him as they walked. Spook smelled the smoke before he got there. He saw the light, and felt the heat. He and Beldre climbed up to the top of the ramp, practically crawling, for she was nearly as battered as he was. However, Spook knew what he would find.

The Ministry building, like so much of the town, was burning. Sazed stood before it, hand raised before his eyes. To Spook's overenhanced senses, the brilliance of the flames was so great that he had to look away. The heat made him feel as if he were standing just inches from the sun.

Sazed tried to get closer to the building, but was forced back. He turned toward Spook, shielding his face. "It's too hot!" he said. "We need to find some water, or perhaps some sand. Put out the fire before we can get below."

"Too late . . ." Spook whispered. "It will take too long."

Beldre turned, looking over her city. To Spook's eyes, smoke seemed to twist and rise everywhere in the bright sky, reaching up, as if to meet the falling ash.

He set his jaw, then stumbled forward, toward the fire.

"Spook!" she cried out. But, she needn't have worried. The flames were too hot. The pain was so strong that he had to pull back before he'd crossed even half the distance. He stumbled away, joining Beldre and Sazed, gasping quietly, blinking tears. His heightened senses made it even more difficult for him to approach the flames.

"There is nothing we can do here," Sazed said. "We must gather crews and come back."

"I've failed," Spook whispered.

"No more than any of us," Sazed said. "This is my fault. The emperor put me in command."

"We were supposed to bring security to the city," Spook said. "Not destruction. I should be able to stop those fires. But, it hurts too much."

Sazed shook his head. "Ah, Lord Spook. You are no god, to command fire at your whim. You are a man, like the rest of us. We're all just . . . men."

Spook allowed them to pull him away. Sazed was right, of course. He was just a man. Just Spook. Kelsier had chosen his crew with care. He'd left a note for them, when he died. It had listed the others—Vin, Breeze, Dockson, Clubs, and Ham. He'd spoken of them, of why he'd picked them.

But not Spook. The only one who didn't fit in.

I named you, Spook. You were my friend.

Isn't that enough?

Spook froze, forcing the others to stop. Sazed and Beldre looked at him. Spook stared into the night. A night that was far too bright. The fires burned. The smoke was pungent.

"No," Spook whispered, feeling fully lucid for the first time since the evening's violence had started. He pulled himself free of Sazed's grip and ran back toward the burning building.

"Spook!" Two voices yelled in the night.

Spook approached the flames. His breathing grew forced, and his skin grew hot. The fire was bright—consuming. He dashed right for it. Then, at the moment when the pain became too great, he extinguished his tin.

And became numb.

It happened just as it had before, when he had been trapped in the building without any metals. Flaring tin for so long had expanded his senses, but now that he wasn't burning it at all, those same senses became dull. His entire body grew deadened, lacking feeling or sensation.

He burst through the doorway into the building, flames raining around him.

His body burned. But, he couldn't feel the flames, and the pain could not drive him back. The fire was bright enough that even his weakened eyes could still see. He dashed forward, ignoring fire, heat, and smoke.

Survivor of the Flames.

He knew the fires were killing him. Yet, he forced himself onward, continuing to move long after the pain should have rendered him unconscious. He reached the room at the back, skidding and sliding down the broken ladder.

The cavern was dark. He stumbled through it, pushing his way past shelves and furniture, making his way along the wall, moving with a desperation that warned him that his time was short. His body wasn't working right anymore—he had pushed it too far, and he no longer had pewter.

He was glad for the darkness. As he finally stumbled

against Sazed's machine, he knew that he would have been horrified to see what the flames had done to his arms.

Groaning quietly, he felt for and found the lever—or, through numb hands, what he hoped was the lever. His fingers no longer worked. So, he simply threw his weight against it, moving the gears as required.

Then he slid down to the ground, feeling only cold and dark.

PART FIVE

TRUST

I do not know what went on in the minds of the koloss—what memories they retained, what human emotions they truly still knew. I do know that our discovery of the one creature, who named himself Human, was tremendously fortunate. Without his struggle to become human again, we might never have understood the link between the koloss, Hemalurgy, and the Inquisitors.

Of course, there was another part for him to play. Granted, not large, but still important, all things considered.

59

URTEAU HAD SEEN BETTER DAYS.

Vin certainly did her work here well, TenSoon thought as he padded through the city, shocked at the destruction. About two years ago—before he'd been sent to spy on Vin—he had been Straff Venture's kandra, and had often visited Urteau. While it had never matched Luthadel's noble majesty or sprawling poverty, it had been a fine city, worthy of being the seat of a Great House.

Now, a good third of the city was a burned ruin. Those buildings that hadn't burned down were either abandoned or overcrowded—an odd mixture, in TenSoon's opinion. Apparently, noble homes were avoided, while skaa buildings were overpacked.

More remarkable, however, were the canals. They had been

refilled somehow. TenSoon sat on his haunches, watching the occasional makeshift boat push its way through a canal, displacing the patina of ash that covered the water. Here and there, debris and refuse clogged the waterways, but they were passable in most places.

He rose, shaking his canine head, continuing on his way. He'd stowed the bag with Kelsier's bones outside, not wanting to look odd carrying a pack on his back.

What had been the purpose of burning the city, then restoring its canals? He would likely have to wait to find the answer. He'd seen no army camped outside; if Vin had been here, she'd already moved on to another location. His goal now was to find what passed for leadership in the remains of the city, then continue on his way, hunting down the Hero of Ages.

As he walked, he heard the people talking—speaking of how they'd managed to survive the fires that had claimed much of the city. They actually seemed cheerful. There was despair, too, but there seemed an inordinate amount of happiness. This was not a city whose people had been conquered.

They feel they defeated the fire, TenSoon thought, making his way along a more crowded street. *They don't see losing a third of the city as a disaster—they see saving two-thirds of it as a miracle.*

He followed the flow of traffic toward the center of town, where he finally found the soldiers he'd expected. They were definitely Elend's, bearing the spear and the scroll on the arms of their uniforms. However, they defended an unlikely location: a Ministry building.

TenSoon sat back on his haunches, cocking his head. The building was obviously a center of operations. People bustled about under the eyes of the watchful soldiers, moving in and out. If he wanted answers, he'd need to get inside. He briefly considered going to fetch Kelsier's bones from outside the city. However, he discarded that thought. He wasn't certain if he wanted to deal with the ramifications of making the Survivor appear again. There was another way to get in—equally shocking, perhaps, but far less theologically disturbing.

He padded over to the front of the building and walked up the steps, drawing a few startled looks. As he approached the front doors, one of the guards shouted at him, waving the butt of a spear in his direction.

"Here now!" the man said. "This is no place for dogs. Whose hound is this?"

TenSoon sat back on his haunches. "I belong to no man," he said.

The guard jumped back in shock, and TenSoon got a twisted sense of pleasure. He immediately chided himself. The world was ending, and he went about startling random soldiers. Still, it *was* an advantage of wearing a dog's body that he'd never considered. . . .

"Wha . . ." the soldier said, looking around to see if he were the victim of some joke.

"I said," TenSoon repeated, "that I belong to no man. I am my own master."

It was a strange concept—the weight of which, undoubtedly, the guard could never grasp. TenSoon, a kandra, was outside of the Homeland without a Contract. As far as he knew, he was the first of his people to do such a thing in seven hundred years. It felt oddly . . . satisfying.

Several people were staring at him now. Other guards had approached, looking to their comrade for an explanation.

TenSoon gambled. "I've come from Emperor Venture," he said. "I bear a message for your leaders here."

To TenSoon's satisfaction, several of the other guards jumped. The first one, however—now an old hand when it came to talking dogs—raised a hesitant finger, pointing into the building. "In there."

"Thank you," TenSoon said, rising and walking through a now-quiet crowd as he made his way into the Ministry offices. He heard comments about "trick" and "well-trained" behind him, and noticed several guards running past him, faces urgent. He wound his way through groups and lines of people, all ignorant of the odd occurrence at the entrance to the building. At the end of the lines, TenSoon found . . .

Breeze. The Soother sat in a throne-like chair, holding a cup of wine, looking very pleased with himself as he made proclamations and settled disputes. He looked much as he had when TenSoon had served as Vin's servant. One of the guards stood whispering to Breeze. Both eyed TenSoon as he padded up to the front of the line. The guard paled slightly, but Breeze just leaned forward, smiling.

"So," he said, tapping his cane lightly against the marble floor. "Were you always a kandra, or did you eat the bones of Vin's hound recently?"

TenSoon sat. "I was always a kandra."

Breeze nodded. "I knew there was something odd about you—far too well behaved for a wolfhound." He smiled, sipping his wine. "Lord Renoux, I presume? It's been a while."

"I'm not him, actually," TenSoon said. "I'm a different kandra. It's . . . complicated."

That gave Breeze pause. He eyed TenSoon, and TenSoon felt just a moment of panic. Breeze was a Soother—and, like all Soothers, he held the power to take control of TenSoon's body. The Secret.

No, TenSoon told himself forcefully. *Allomancers are weaker now than they once were. Only with duralumin could they take control of a kandra, and Breeze is only a Misting—he can't burn duralumin.*

"Drinking on the job, Breeze?" TenSoon asked, raising a canine eyebrow.

"Of course," Breeze said, raising the cup. "What good is being in charge if you can't set your own working conditions?"

TenSoon snorted. He hadn't ever really liked Breeze—though perhaps that came from his bias against Soothers. Or, perhaps, his bias against all humans. Regardless, he wasn't inclined toward small talk. "Where is Vin?" he asked.

Breeze frowned. "I thought you brought a message from her?"

"I lied to the guards," TenSoon said. "I've actually come searching for her. I bring news she needs to hear—news regarding the mists and ash."

"Well, then, my dear man . . . um . . . I suppose I mean my dear *doggie.* Anyway, let us retire; you can talk to Sazed. He's far more useful than I am regarding these sorts of things."

". . . and, with Spook barely having survived the ordeal," said the Terrisman, "I thought it best to let Lord Breeze take command. We set up shop in a different Ministry building—it seemed equipped to be a bureaucratic center—and had Breeze start listening to petitions. He is better at dealing with people than I am, I think, and seems to enjoy taking care of the day-to-day concerns of the citizenry."

The Terrisman sat in his chair, a portfolio open on the desk before him, a pile of notes beside it. Sazed looked different to TenSoon for some reason that he couldn't pin down. The Keeper wore the same robes, and had the same Feruchemical bracers on his arms. There was something missing, however.

That, however, was the least of TenSoon's problems.

"*Fadrex City?*" TenSoon asked, sitting on his own chair. They were in one of the smaller rooms at the Ministry building—one that had once been an obligator's sleeping quarters. Now, it simply held a desk and chairs, the walls and floor as austere as one might expect for Ministry furnishings.

Sazed nodded. "She and the emperor hoped to find another of these storage caverns there."

TenSoon slumped. Fadrex was halfway across the empire. Even with the Blessing of Potency, it would take weeks for him to get there. He had a very, very long run ahead of him.

"Might I ask what business you have with Lady Vin, kandra?" Sazed asked.

TenSoon paused. It felt very odd, in a way, to speak so openly with Breeze, and now Sazed. These were men that

TenSoon had watched for months while he acted like a dog. They'd never known him, yet he felt as if he knew them.

He knew, for instance, that Sazed was dangerous. The Terrisman was a Keeper—a group that TenSoon and his brethren had been trained to avoid. Keepers were always prying for rumors, legends, and tales. The kandra had many secrets; if the Keepers were ever to discover the riches of kandra culture, it could be disastrous. They'd want to study, ask questions, and record what they found.

TenSoon opened his mouth to say "Nothing." However, he stopped. Didn't he *want* someone to help with kandra culture? Someone who focused on religions, and who—perhaps—knew much of theology? Someone who knew about the legends of the Hero of Ages? Of all the members of the crew other than Vin, TenSoon had held Sazed in the highest regard.

"It has to do with the Hero of Ages," TenSoon said carefully. "And the advent of the world's end."

"Ah," Sazed said, rising. "Very well then. I shall give you whatever provisions you need. Will you be starting out immediately? Or, will you be staying here to rest for a time?"

What? TenSoon thought. Sazed hadn't even twitched at the mention of religious matters. It didn't seem like him at all.

Yet, Sazed continued speaking, as if TenSoon hadn't just hinted at one of the greatest religious secrets of their age.

I'll never understand humans, he thought, shaking his head.

The prison Preservation created for Ruin was not created out of Preservation's power, though it was of *Preservation. Rather, Preservation sacrificed his consciousness—one could say his mind—to fabricate that prison. He left a shadow of himself, but Ruin, once escaped, began to suffocate and isolate this small remnant vestige of his rival. I wonder if Ruin ever thought it strange that Preservation had cut himself off from his own power, relinquishing it and leaving it in the world, to be gathered and used by men.*

In Preservation's gambit, I see nobility, cleverness, and desperation. He knew that he could not defeat Ruin. He had given too much of himself and, beyond that, he was the embodiment of stasis and stability. He could not destroy, not even to protect. It was against his nature. Hence the prison.

Mankind, however, had been created by both Ruin and Preservation—with a hint of Preservation's own soul to give them sentience and honor. In order for the world to survive, Preservation knew he had to depend upon his creations. To give them his trust.

I wonder what he thought when those creations repeatedly failed him.

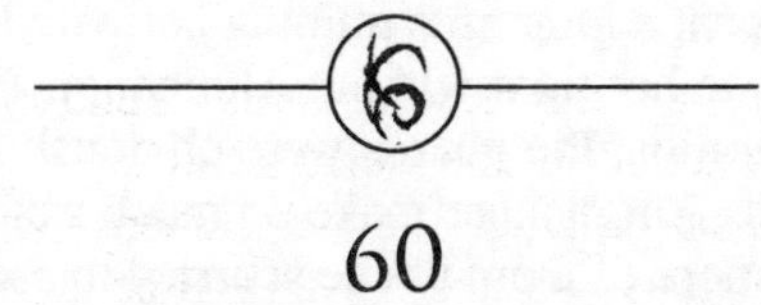

60

THE BEST WAY TO FOOL someone, in Vin's estimation, was to give them what they wanted. Or, at the very least, what they expected. As long as they assumed that they were one step ahead, they wouldn't look back to see if there were any steps that they'd completely missed.

Yomen had designed her prison well. Any metal used in the construction of her cot or facilities was Allomantically useless. Silver, while expensive, seemed the metal of choice—and there was very little even of that. Just a few screws in the cot that Vin managed to work free with her fingernails.

Her meals—a greasy, flavorless gruel—were served in wooden bowls, with wooden spoons. The guards were hazekillers: men who carried staves and wore no metal on their bodies, and who had been trained to fight Allomancers. Her room was a simple stone construction with a solid wooden door, its hinges and bolts made of silver.

She knew from her guards' behavior that they expected something from her. Yomen had prepared them well, and so when they slid her food through the slit, she could see the tension in their bodies and the speed of their retreat. It was like they were feeding a viper.

So, the next time they came to take her to Yomen, she attacked.

She moved as soon as the door opened, wielding a wooden leg she'd pulled off her cot. She dropped the first guard with a club to the arm, then a second hit on the back of his head. Her blows felt weak without pewter, but it was the best she could manage. She scrambled past the second guard in line, then slammed her shoulder into the stomach of the third. She didn't weigh much, but it was enough to get him to drop his staff—which she immediately grabbed.

Ham had spent a long time training her with the staff, and he'd often made her fight without Allomancy. Even with all of their preparation, the guards were obviously surprised to see a metalless Allomancer make so much trouble, and she dropped two more of them as she scurried to escape.

Unfortunately, Yomen was not a fool. He had sent so many guards to bring her that even dropping four of them made little difference. There had to be at least twenty men in the hallway outside her cell, clogging her exit, if nothing else.

Her goal was to give them what they expected, not get herself killed. So, as soon as she confirmed that her "escape attempt" really was doomed, she let one of the soldiers hit her on the shoulder and she dropped her staff with a grunt. Disarmed, she raised her hands and backed away. The soldiers, of course, swept her feet out from beneath her and piled on top of her, holding her down while one manacled her arms.

Vin suffered the treatment, shoulder pulsing with pain. How long would she have to go without metal before she'd stop instinctively trying to burn pewter? She hoped she'd never actually find out.

Eventually, the soldiers pulled her to her feet and pushed

her down the hallway. The three she'd knocked down—not to mention the one that she'd disarmed—grumbled a bit, rubbing their wounds. All twenty men regarded her even more warily, if that was possible.

She didn't give them any trouble until they got her into Yomen's audience chamber. When they moved to chain her manacles to the bench, she squirmed a bit, earning herself a knee in the stomach. She gasped, then slumped to the floor beside the bench. There, groaning, she rubbed her hands and wrists with the gruel grease that she'd soaked into her undershirt. It was smelly and grimy, but it was very slick—and the guards, distracted by her escape attempt, had completely forgotten to search her.

"Surely you didn't think to escape without any metals to burn," Yomen asked.

Vin lifted her head. He stood with his back to her again, though this time he was looking out a dark window. Vin found it very odd to see the mists curling up against the window glass. Most skaa couldn't afford glass, and most noblemen chose the colored kind. The darkness outside of Yomen's window seemed a waiting beast, the mists its fur brushing against the glass as it shifted.

"I would think that you'd be flattered," Yomen continued. "I didn't know if you were really as dangerous as reported, but I decided to assume that you were. You see, I—"

Vin didn't give him any more time. There were only two ways she could escape from the city: the first would be to find some metals, the second would be to take Yomen captive. She planned to try both.

She yanked her greased hands free from the manacles, which had been fastened to her arms when they were squirming and flexed. She ignored the pain and the blood as the manacles scraped her hands, then she leaped to her feet, reaching into a fold in her shirt and pulling out the silver screws that she'd taken from her cot. These, she threw at the soldiers.

The men, of course, yelled in surprise and threw themselves to the ground, ducking her presumed Steelpush. Their own preparation and worry worked against them—for Vin had no steel. The screws bounced against the wall ineffectively, and the guards lay confused by her feint. She was halfway to Yomen before the first one thought to scramble back to his feet.

Yomen turned. As always, he wore the little drop of atium at his forehead. Vin lunged for it.

Yomen stepped casually out of the way. Vin lunged again, this time feinting, then trying to elbow him in the stomach. Her attack didn't land, however, as Yomen—hands still clasped behind his back—sidestepped her again.

She knew that look on his face—that look of complete control, of power. Yomen obviously had very little battle training, but he dodged her anyway.

He was burning atium.

Vin stumbled to a halt. *No wonder he wears that bit on his forehead,* she thought. *It's for emergencies.* She could see in his smile that he really *had* anticipated her. He'd known that she would try something, and he'd baited her, letting her get close. But, he'd never really been in danger.

The guards finally caught up with her, but Yomen raised a hand, waving them back. Then he gestured toward the bench. Quietly, Vin returned and sat down. She had to think, and she certainly wasn't going to get anywhere with Yomen burning atium.

As she sat, Ruin appeared next to her—materializing as if from dark smoke, wearing Reen's body. None of the others reacted; they obviously couldn't see him.

"Too bad," Ruin said. "In a way, you almost had him. But . . . then, in a way, you were never really close, either."

She ignored Ruin, looking up at Yomen. "You're Mistborn."

"No," he said, shaking his head. He didn't turn back toward his window, however. He stood facing her, wary. He'd probably turned off his atium—it was far too valuable to leave burning—but he'd have it in reserve, careful to watch her for signs of another attack.

"No?" Vin said, raising a skeptical eyebrow. "You were burning atium, Yomen. I saw that much."

"Believe as you wish," Yomen said. "But know this, woman: I do not lie. I've never needed lies, and I find that is particularly true now, when the entire world is in chaos. People need truth from those they follow."

Vin frowned.

"Regardless, it is time," Yomen said.

"Time?" Vin asked.

Yomen nodded. "Yes. I apologize for leaving you for so long in your cell. I have been . . . distracted."

Elend, Vin thought. *What has he been doing? I feel so blind!*

She glanced at Ruin, who stood on the other side of the bench, shaking his head as if he understood far more than he was telling her. She turned back to Yomen. "I still don't understand," she said. "Time for what?"

Yomen met her eyes. "Time for me to make a decision about your execution, Lady Venture."

Oh, she thought. *Right.* Between her dealings with Ruin and her plans to escape, she'd nearly forgotten Yomen's declaration that he intended to let her "defend" herself before he executed her.

Ruin walked across the room, circling Yomen in a leisurely stroll. The obligator king stood, still meeting Vin's eyes. If he could see Ruin, he didn't show it. Instead, he waved to a guard, who opened a side door, leading in several obligators in gray robes. They seated themselves on a bench across the room from Vin.

"Tell me, Lady Venture," Yomen said, turning back to her, "why did you come to Fadrex City?"

Vin cocked her head. "I thought this wasn't to be a trial. You said that you didn't need that sort of thing."

"I would think," Yomen replied, "that you would be pleased with any delay in the process."

A delay meant more time to think—more time to possibly escape. "Why did we come?" Vin asked. "We knew you had one of the Lord Ruler's supply caches beneath your city."

Yomen raised an eyebrow. "How did you know about it?"

"We found another one," Vin said. "It had directions to Fadrex."

Yomen nodded to himself. She could tell that he believed her, but there was something . . . else. He seemed to be making connections that she didn't understand, and probably didn't have the information to understand. "And the danger my kingdom posed to yours?" Yomen asked. "That didn't have anything at all to do with your invasion of my lands?"

"I wouldn't say that," Vin said. "Cett had been pushing Elend to move into this dominance for some time."

The obligators conferred quietly at this comment, though Yomen stood aloof, arms folded as he regarded her. Vin found the experience unnerving. It had been years—from her days in Camon's crew—since she had felt so much in another's power. Even when she'd faced the Lord Ruler, she'd felt differently. Yomen seemed to see her as a tool.

But a tool to do what? And, how could she manipulate his needs so that he kept her alive long enough for her to escape?

Make yourself indispensable, Reen had always taught. *Then a crewleader can't get rid of you without losing power himself.* Even now, the voice of her brother still seemed to whisper the words in her mind. Were they memories, interpretations of his wisdom, or effects of Ruin's influence? Regardless, it seemed like good advice at the moment.

"So, you came with the express purpose of invasion?" Yomen asked.

"Elend intended to try diplomacy first," Vin said carefully. "However, we both knew that it's a bit hard to play the diplomat when you camp an army outside of someone's city."

"You admit to being conquerors, then," Yomen said. "You *are* more honest than your husband."

"Elend is more sincere than either of us, Yomen," Vin snapped. "Just because he interprets things differently from you or me does not mean he's being dishonest when he expresses his view."

Yomen raised an eyebrow, perhaps at the quickness of her response. "A valid point."

Vin sat back on the bench, wrapping her cut hands with a bit of clean cloth from her shirt. Yomen stood beside the windows of the large, stark room. It felt very odd to be speaking to him. On one hand, she and he seemed very different. He was a bureaucrat obligator whose lack of muscle or warrior's grace proved that he'd spent his life concerned with forms and records. She was a child of the streets and an adult practiced in war and assassination.

Yet, his mannerisms, his way of speaking, seemed to resemble her own. *Is this what I might have been more like*, she wondered, *had I not been born a skaa? A blunt bureaucrat rather than a terse warrior?*

As Yomen contemplated her, Ruin walked in a slow circle around the obligator king. "This one is a disappointment," Ruin said quietly.

Vin glanced at Ruin just briefly. He shook his head. "Such destruction this one could have caused, had he struck out, rather than staying huddled in his little city, praying to his dead god. Men would have followed him. I could never get through to him on the long term, unfortunately. Not every ploy can be successful, particularly when the will of fools like him must be accounted for."

"So," Yomen said, drawing her attention back to him, "you came to take my city because you heard of my stockpile, and because you feared a return of the Lord Ruler's power."

"I didn't say that," Vin said, frowning.

"You said that you feared me."

"As a foreign power," Vin said, "with a proven ability to undermine a government and take it over."

"I didn't take over," Yomen said. "I returned this city, and the dominance, to its rightful rule. But that is beside the point. I want you to tell me of this religion your people preach."

"The Church of the Survivor?"

"Yes," Yomen said. "You are one of its heads, correct?"

"No," Vin said. "They revere me. But I've never felt that I properly fit as part of the religion. Mostly, it's focused around Kelsier."

"The Survivor of Hathsin," Yomen said. "He died. How is it that people worship him?"

Vin shrugged. "It used to be common to worship gods that one couldn't see."

"Perhaps," Yomen said. "I have . . . read of such things, though I find them difficult to understand. Faith in an unseen god—what sense does that make? Why reject the god that they lived with for so long—the one that they could see, and feel—in favor of one that died? One that the Lord Ruler himself struck down?"

"You do it," Vin said. "You're still worshipping the Lord Ruler."

"He's not gone," Yomen said.

Vin paused.

"No," Yomen said, apparently noting her confusion. "I haven't seen or heard of him since his disappearance. However, neither do I put any credence in reports of his death."

"He was rather dead," Vin said. "Trust me."

"I don't trust you, I'm afraid," Yomen said. "Tell me of that evening. Tell me precisely what happened."

So Vin did. She told him of her imprisonment, and of her escape with Sazed. She told him of her decision to fight the Lord Ruler, and of her reliance on the Eleventh Metal. She left out her strange ability to draw upon the power of the mists, but she explained pretty much everything else—including Sazed's theory that the Lord Ruler had been immortal through the clever manipulation of his Feruchemy and Allomancy in combination.

And Yomen actually listened. Her respect for the man increased as she spoke, and as he didn't interrupt her. He wanted to hear her story, even if he didn't believe it. He was a man who accepted information for what it was—another tool to be used, yet to be trusted no more than any other tool.

"And so," Vin finished, "he is dead. I stabbed him through the heart myself. Your faith in him is admirable, but it can't change what happened."

Yomen stood silently. The older obligators—who still sat on their benches—had grown white in the face. She knew that her testimony might have damned her, but for some reason she felt that honesty—plain, blunt honesty—would serve her better than guile. That's how she usually felt.

An odd conviction for one who grew up in thieving crews, she thought. Ruin had apparently grown bored during her account, and had walked over to look out the window.

"What I need to find out," Yomen finally said, "is why the Lord Ruler thought it necessary for you to *think* that you had killed him."

"Didn't you listen to what I just said?" Vin demanded.

"I did," Yomen said calmly. "And do not forget that you are a prisoner here—one who is very close to death."

Vin forced herself to be quiet.

"You find my words ridiculous?" Yomen said. "More ridiculous than your own? Think of how I see you, claiming to have slain a man I *know* to be God. Is it not plausible that he wanted this to happen? That he's out there, still, watching us, waiting . . ."

That's what this is all about, she realized. *Why he captured me, why he's so eager to speak with me. He's convinced that the Lord Ruler is still alive. He just wants to figure out where I fit into all of this. He wants me to give him the proof that he's so desperately wishing for.*

"Why don't you think you should be part of the skaa religion, Vin?" Ruin whispered.

She turned, trying not to look directly at him, lest Yomen see her staring into empty space.

"Why?" Ruin asked. "Why don't you want them worshipping you? All of those happy skaa? Looking toward you for hope?"

"The Lord Ruler *must* be behind all of this," Yomen mused out loud. "That means that he wanted the world to see you as his killer. He wanted the skaa to worship you."

"Why?" Ruin repeated. "Why be so uncomfortable? Is it because you know you *can't* offer them hope? What is it they call him, the one you are supposed to have replaced? The Survivor? A word of Preservation, I think. . . ."

"Perhaps he intends to return dramatically," Yomen said. "To depose you and topple you, to prove that faith in him is the only true faith."

Why don't you fit? Ruin whispered in her head.

"Why else would he want them to worship you?" Yomen asked.

"*They're wrong!*" Vin snapped, raising hands to her head, trying to stop the thoughts. Trying to stop the guilt.

Yomen paused.

"They're wrong about me," Vin said. "They don't worship me, they worship what they think I should be. But I'm not the Heir of the Survivor. I didn't do what Kelsier did. He freed them."

You conquered them, Ruin whispered.

"Yes," Vin said, looking up. "You're looking in the wrong direction, Yomen. The Lord Ruler won't return."

"I told you that—"

"No," Vin said, standing. "No, he's not coming back. He doesn't need to. *I* took his place."

Elend had worried that he was becoming another Lord Ruler, but his concern had always seemed flawed to Vin. He hadn't been the one to conquer and reforge an empire, she had. She'd been the one who made the other kings submit.

She'd done exactly as the Lord Ruler had. A Hero had risen up, and the Lord Ruler had killed him, then taken the power of the Well of Ascension. Vin had killed the Lord Ruler, then taken that same power. She'd given up the power, true, but she'd filled the same role.

It all came to a head. The reason why the skaa worshipping her, calling her their savior, felt so wrong. Suddenly, her real role in it all seemed to snap into place.

"I'm not the Survivor's Heir, Yomen," she said sickly. "I'm the Lord Ruler's."

He shook his head dismissively.

"When you first captured me," she said, "I wondered why you kept me alive. An enemy Mistborn? Why not just kill me and be done with it? You claimed that you wanted to give me a trial, but I saw through that. I knew you had another motive. And now I know what it is." She looked him in the eyes. "You said earlier that you planned to execute me for the Lord Ruler's murder, but you just admitted that you think he's still alive. You say that he'll return to topple me from my place, so you can't kill me, lest you interfere with your god's plans."

Yomen turned away from her.

"You *can't* kill me," she said. "Not until you're certain of my place in your theology. That's why you kept me alive, and that's why you risk bringing me in here to talk. You need information only I can give—you have to get testimony from me in a trial of sorts because you want to know what happened that night. So you can try to convince yourself that your god still lives."

Yomen didn't respond.

"Admit it. I'm in no danger here." She stepped forward.

And Yomen moved. His steps suddenly became more fluid—he didn't have the grace of pewter or the knowledge of a warrior, but he moved just *right.* She dodged instinctively, but his atium let him anticipate her, and before she could so much as think, he'd thrown her to the floor, holding her pinned with a knee against her back.

"I may not kill you yet," he said calmly, "but that hardly means that you're in 'no danger,' Lady Venture."

Vin grunted.

"I want something from you," he said. "Something more than what we've discussed. I want you to tell your husband to send his army away."

"Why would I do that?" Vin said, face pressed against the cold stone of the floor.

"Because," Yomen said, "you claim to want my storage cache, yet you claim to be good people. You now know that I will use the food in it wisely, to feed my people. If your Elend really is as altruistic as you claim, he certainly won't be so selfish as to throw away lives to war, just so you can steal away our food and use it to feed your own."

"We can grow crops," Vin said. "We get enough light in the Central Dominance, while you don't. The seed stock you have will be useless to you!"

"Then trade me for it."

"You won't *talk* to us!"

Yomen stepped back, releasing the pressure on her back. She rubbed her neck, sitting up, feeling frustrated. "It's about more than the food in that cache, Yomen," she said. "We control the other four of them. The Lord Ruler, he left clues in them. There is something to the whole group that can save us."

Yomen snorted. "You were down there all that time, and you didn't read the plaque that the Lord Ruler left?"

"Of course I did."

"Then you know that there *is* nothing more in those caches," Yomen said. "They're all part of his plan, true. And for some reason that plan requires that men think he is dead. Regardless, you know now what he said. So, why take the city from me?"

Why take the city from me? The real reason itched inside of Vin. Elend had always found it an unimportant one, but to her, it held powerful appeal. "You know full well why we have to take the city," Vin said. "As long as you have *it,* we have reason to conquer you."

"It?" Yomen asked.

Ruin stepped forward, curious.

"You know what I mean. The atium. The Lord Ruler's supply."

"That?" Yomen asked, laughing. "This is all about the atium? Atium is worthless!"

Vin frowned. "Worthless? It's the single most valuable commodity in the Final Empire!"

"Oh?" Yomen asked. "And how many people are there around to burn it? How many noble houses remain to play petty politics and vie for power by showing how much atium they can leach from the Lord Ruler? The value of atium was based in the economy of an empire, Lady Venture. Without the trappings of a reserve system and an upper class giving the metal implied worth, atium has no real value." Yomen shook his head. "To a starving man, what is more important—a loaf of bread, or an entire jar of atium he can't use, eat, or sell?"

He waved for the guards to take her. They pulled her to her feet, and she struggled, holding Yomen's eyes.

Yomen turned away from her again. "Those lumps of metal do me no good, save—perhaps—to keep you in check. No, the food was the real resource. The Lord Ruler left me the riches I required to establish his power again. I just need to figure out what he wants me to do next."

The soldiers finally succeeded in pulling her away.

I don't wonder that we focused far too much on the mists during those days. But from what I now know of sunlight and plant development, I realize that our crops weren't in as much danger from misty days as we feared. We might very well have been able to find plants to eat that did not need as much light to survive.

True, the mists did also cause some deaths in those who went out in them, but the number killed was not a large enough percentage of the population to be a threat to our survival as a species. The ash, that was our real problem. The smoke filling the atmosphere, the black flakes covering up everything beneath, the eruptions of the volcanic ashmounts . . . Those were what would kill the world.

61

"ELEND!" HAM CALLED, RUSHING UP to him. "You're back!"

"Surprised?" Elend asked, reading his friend's expression.

"Of course not," Ham said, a little too quickly. "The scouts reported your approach."

My arrival may not surprise you, Elend thought tiredly, *but the fact that I'm still alive does. Did you think I'd run off to get myself killed, or did you simply think that I'd wander away and abandon you?*

It wasn't a line of reasoning he wanted to pursue. So, he simply smiled, resting a hand on Ham's shoulder and looking toward the camp. It looked strange, bunkered down as it was, ash piled up outside of it. It looked a little like it was dug into the ground several feet. There was so much ash. . . .

I can't worry about everything at once, Elend thought with determination. *I just have to trust. Trust in myself and keep going.*

He had pondered the mist spirit the rest of his trip. Had it really told him not to attack Fadrex, or was Elend simply misinterpreting its gestures? What had it wanted him to learn by pointing at his vial of metals?

Beside him, Ham was regarding the mass of new koloss. To the side of the army, his other koloss sat—still under his control. Though he had grown increasingly adept at keeping a hold on the creatures, it was still nice to be back close to them. It made him feel more comfortable.

Ham whistled quietly. "Twenty-eight thousand?" he asked. "Or, at least, that's what the scouts say."

Elend nodded.

"I hadn't realized how large the group was," Ham said. "With that many . . ."

Thirty-seven thousand total, Elend thought. *More than enough to storm Fadrex.*

He began to walk down the incline, toward the camp. Though he hadn't needed much pewter to help him through the hike, he was still tired. "Any news of Vin?" he said hopefully, though he knew that if she'd managed to escape, she would have already found him.

"We sent a messenger into the city while you were gone," Ham said as they began to walk. "Yomen said a soldier could come and confirm that Vin was still alive, and so we complied in your name, thinking it best if Yomen thought you were here."

"You did well," Elend said.

"It's been a while since then," Ham said. "We haven't heard anything of her since."

"She's still alive," Elend said.

Ham nodded. "I believe so too."

Elend smiled. "It's not just faith, Ham," he said, nodding toward the koloss that had remained behind. "Before she was captured, I gave some of those to her. If she'd died, then they would have gone out of control. As long as she lives—whether or not she has metals—she will remain bonded to them."

Ham paused. "That . . . would have been something good to tell us earlier, El."

"I know," Elend said. "It's too easy to forget how many I'm controlling—I didn't even think that not all of those are mine. Post scouts, keep an eye on them. I'll take them back if they go wild."

Ham nodded. "Could you contact her through them?"

Elend shook his head. How did he explain? Controlling the koloss wasn't a subtle thing—their minds were too dull for much beyond simple commands. He could order them to attack, or to freeze, or to follow and carry things. But he couldn't direct them precisely, couldn't instruct them to speak a message or even *how* to accomplish a goal. He could only say "Do this" and watch them go.

"We've had scout reports from the Central Dominance, El," Ham said, voice troubled.

Elend looked at him.

"Most of our scouts didn't return. Nobody knows what happened to Demoux and the men you sent—we hope they reached Luthadel, but the capital is in bad shape. The scouts who have returned bear some pretty frustrating news. We've lost many of the cities you conquered during this last year. The people are starving, and a lot of villages are empty save for the dead. Those who can flee to Luthadel, leaving trails of corpses on the road, buried in ash."

Elend closed his eyes. But Ham wasn't done.

"There are tales of cities swallowed by the rumbling

earth," Ham said, voice almost a whisper. "King Lekal and his city fell to lava from one of the ashmounts. We haven't heard from Janarle in weeks; his entire retinue seems to have vanished, and the Northern Dominance is in chaos. The entire Southern Dominance is said to be burning. . . . Elend, what do we do?"

Elend continued to stride forward, walking onto an ash-free pathway and then into the camp proper. Soldiers were gathering about, whispering, looking at him. He didn't know how to answer Ham's question. What did he do? What *could* he do?

"We'll help them, Ham," he said. "We won't give up."

Ham nodded, looking slightly bolstered. "Though, before you do anything else, what you should probably do is go change your clothing. . . ."

Elend glanced down, remembering that he was still wearing the black uniform, bloodied from killing koloss, then stained by ash. His appearance caused quite a stir in the men. *They've only seen me in the white, pristine outfit. Many of them have never even seen me fight—never seen me bloodied, never seen me dirtied by ash.*

He wasn't certain what bothered him about that.

Ahead, Elend could see a bearded figure sitting in a chair beside the pathway, as if he were simply out there for an afternoon repast. Cett eyed him as he passed. "More koloss?"

Elend nodded.

"We're going to attack, then?" Cett asked.

Elend stopped.

The mist spirit apparently didn't want him to attack. But, he couldn't be certain what it had wanted him to know or think—he didn't even know if he should trust it. Could he base the future of his empire on vague impressions he got from a ghost in the mists?

He had to get into that storage, and he couldn't afford to wait in siege—not any longer. Plus, attacking seemed the best way to get Vin back safely. Yomen would never return her—Elend either had to sit around and wait, or he had to attack, hoping that in the chaos of battle, Yomen would leave her in a dungeon somewhere. True, attacking risked an execution, but letting Yomen use her as a bargaining chip seemed just as dangerous for her.

I have to be the man who makes the hard decisions, he told himself. *It's what Vin was trying to teach me at the ball—that I can be both Elend the man, and Elend the king. I took these koloss for a purpose. Now I need to use them.*

"Inform the soldiers," Elend said. "But don't have them form ranks. We attack in the morning, but do so in surprise—koloss first, breaking through their defenses. The men can form up after that, then go in and seize control."

We'll rescue Vin, get into that cavern, then get back to Luthadel with the food supplies.

And survive as long as we can.

I suspect that Alendi, the man Rashek killed, was himself a Misting—a Seeker. Allomancy, however, was a different thing in those days, and much more rare. The Allomancers alive in our day are the descendants of the men who ate those few beads of Preservation's power. They formed the foundation of the nobility, and were the first to name him emperor.

The power in those few beads was so concentrated that it could last through ten centuries of breeding and inheritance.

62

SAZED STOOD OUTSIDE THE ROOM, looking in. Spook lay in his bed, still swaddled in bandages. The boy had not awakened since his ordeal, and Sazed wasn't certain if he ever would. Even if he did live, he'd be horribly scarred for the rest of his life.

Though, Sazed thought, *this proves one thing. The boy*

doesn't have pewter. If Spook *had* been able to burn pewter, then he would have healed far more quickly. Sazed had administered a vial of pewter just in case, and it had made no difference. The boy hadn't mystically become a Thug.

It was comforting, in a way. It meant that Sazed's world still made sense.

Inside the room, the girl—Beldre—sat at Spook's side. She came every day to spend time with the lad. More time, even, than she spent with her brother, Quellion. The Citizen had a broken arm and some other wounds, but nothing lethal. Though Breeze ruled in Urteau, Quellion was still an authority, and he seemed to have grown far more . . . civil. He now seemed willing to consider an alliance with Elend.

It seemed strange to Sazed that Quellion would become so accommodating. They had entered his city, sown chaos, and nearly killed him. Now he listened to their offers of peace? Sazed was suspicious, to be sure. Time would tell.

Inside, Beldre turned slightly, finally noticing Sazed at the doorway. She smiled, standing.

"Please, Lady Beldre," he said, entering. "Don't stand."

She seated herself again as Sazed walked forward. He surveyed his bandage work on Spook, checking the young man's condition, comparing notes from inside the medical texts of his copperminds. Beldre watched quietly.

Once he was finished, he turned to leave.

"Thank you," Beldre said from behind.

Sazed stopped.

She glanced at Spook. "Do you think . . . I mean, has his condition changed?"

"I am afraid that it has not, Lady Beldre. I cannot promise anything in regard to his recovery."

She smiled faintly, turning back toward the wounded lad. "He'll make it," she said.

Sazed frowned.

"He's not just a man," Beldre said. "He's something special. I don't know what he did to bring my brother back, but Quellion is just like his old self—the way he was before all of this insanity began. And the city. The people have hope again. That's what Spook wanted."

Hope . . . Sazed thought, studying the girl's eyes. *She really does love him.*

It seemed, in a way, silly to Sazed. How long had she known the boy? A few weeks? During that short time, Spook had not only earned Beldre's love, but had become a hero to the people of an entire city.

She sits and hopes, having faith that he will recover, Sazed thought. *Yet, upon seeing him, the first thing I thought of was how relieved I was that he wasn't a Pewterarm.* Had Sazed really become that callous? Just two years before, he had been willing to fall hopelessly in love with a woman who had spent most of her life chastising him. A woman with whom he had only had a few precious days.

He turned and left the room.

Sazed walked to his quarters in the nobleman's mansion they had taken, their new home now that their former residence was a burned-out ruin. It was nice to have ordinary walls and steps again, rather than endless shelves bounded by cavern walls.

On his desk sat the open portfolio, its cloth-wrapped coverboard stained with ash. One stack of pages sat to its left, and one stack sat to its right. There were only ten pages left in the right stack.

Taking a deep breath, Sazed approached and sat down. It was time to finish.

It was late morning the next day before he set the final sheet onto the top of the left stack. He'd moved quickly through these last ten, but he'd been able to give them his undivided attention, not being distracted by riding as he worked or other concerns. He felt that he'd given each one due consideration.

He sat for a time, feeling fatigued, and not just from lack of sleep. He felt . . . numb. His task was done. After a year's work, he'd sifted through each and every religion in his stack. And he'd eliminated every one.

It was odd, how many common features they all had. Most claimed ultimate authority, denouncing other faiths. Most taught of an afterlife, but could offer no proof. Most taught about a god or gods, yet—again—had little justification for their teachings. And every single one of them was riddled with inconsistencies and logical fallacies.

How did men believe in something that preached love on one hand, yet taught destruction of unbelievers on the other? How did one rationalize belief with no proof? How could they honestly expect him to have faith in something that taught of miracles and wonders in the far past, but carefully gave excuses for why such things didn't occur in the present day?

And then, of course, there was the final flake of ash on the pile—the thing that each and every faith had, in his opinion, failed to prove. All taught that believers would be blessed. And all had absolutely no answer as to why their gods had allowed the faithful to be captured, imprisoned, enslaved, and slaughtered by a heretic known as Rashek, the Lord Ruler.

The stack of pages sat face down on the desk before him. They meant that there was no truth. No faith that would bring Tindwyl back to him. Nothing watching over men, contrary to what Spook had affirmed so strongly. Sazed ran his fingers across the final page, and finally, the depression he'd been fighting—barely holding at bay for so long—was too strong for him to overcome. The portfolio had been his final line of defense.

It was pain. That's what the loss felt like. Pain and numbness at the same time; a barb-covered wire twisting around his chest combined with an absolute inability to do anything about it. He felt like huddling in a corner, crying, and just letting himself die.

No! he thought. *There must be something. . . .*

He reached under his desk, trembling fingers seeking his sack of metalminds. However, he didn't pull one of these out, but instead removed a large, thick tome. He put it on the table beside his portfolio, then opened it to a random page. Words written in two different hands confronted him. One was careful and flowing. His own. The other was terse and determined. Tindwyl's.

He rested his fingers on the page. He and Tindwyl had compiled this book together, deciphering the history, prophecies, and meanings surrounding the Hero of Ages. Back before Sazed had stopped caring.

That's a lie, he thought, forming a fist. *Why do I lie to myself? I still care. I never stopped caring. If I'd stopped caring, then I wouldn't still be searching. If I didn't care so much, then being betrayed wouldn't feel so painful.*

Kelsier had spoken of this. Then Vin had done the same. Sazed had never expected to have similar feelings. Who was there that could hurt him so deeply that he felt betrayed? He was not like other men. He acknowledged that not out of arrogance, but out of simple self-knowledge. He forgave people, perhaps to a fault. He simply wasn't the type to feel bitter.

He'd assumed, therefore, that he would never have to deal with these emotions. That's why he'd been so unprepared to be betrayed by the only thing he couldn't accept as being flawed.

He couldn't believe. If he believed, it meant that God—or the universe, or whatever it was that watched over man—had failed. Better to believe that there was nothing at all. Then, all of the world's inadequacies were simply mere chance. Not caused by a god who had failed them.

Sazed glanced at his open tome, noticing a little slip of paper sticking out between its pages. He pulled it free, surprised to find the picture of a flower that Vin had given him, the one that Kelsier's wife had carried. The one she'd used to give herself hope. To remind her of a world that had existed before the coming of the Lord Ruler.

He glanced upward. The ceiling was of wood, but red sunlight—refracted by the window—sprayed across it. "Why?" he whispered. "Why leave me like this? I studied everything about you. I learned the religions of *five hundred* different peoples and sects. I taught about you when other men had given up a thousand years before.

"Why leave *me* without hope, when others can have faith? Why leave *me* to wonder? Shouldn't I be more certain than any other? Shouldn't my knowledge have protected me?"

And yet, his faith had made him even more susceptible. *That's what trust is,* Sazed thought. *It's about giving someone else power over you. Power to hurt you.* That's why he'd given up his metalminds. That's why he had decided to sort through the religions one at a time, trying to find one that had no faults. Nothing to fail him.

It just made sense. Better to not believe, rather than be proven wrong. Sazed looked back down. Why did he think to talk to the heavens? There was nothing there.

There never had been.

Outside, in the hallway, he could hear voices. "My dear doggie," Breeze said, "surely you'll stay for another day."

"No," said TenSoon the kandra, speaking in his growling voice. "I must find Vin as soon as possible."

Even the kandra, Sazed thought. *Even an inhuman creature has more faith than I.*

And yet, how could they understand? Sazed closed his eyes tight, feeling a pair of tears squeeze from the corners. How could anyone understand the pain of a faith betrayed? He had *believed.* And yet, when he had needed hope the most, he had found only emptiness.

He picked up the book, then snapped closed his portfolio, locking the inadequate summaries inside. He turned toward the hearth. Better to simply burn it all.

Belief . . . He remembered a voice from the past. His own voice, speaking to Vin on that terrible day after Kelsier's death. *Belief isn't simply a thing for fair times and bright days, I think. What is belief—what is faith—if you don't continue in it after failure. . . .*

How innocent he had been.

Better to trust and be betrayed, Kelsier seemed to whisper. It had been one of the Survivor's mottos. *Better to love and be hurt.*

Sazed gripped the tome. It was such a meaningless thing. Its text could be changed by Ruin at any time. *And do I believe in that*? Sazed thought with frustration. *Do I have faith in this Ruin, but not in something better?*

He stood quietly in the room, holding the book, listening to Breeze and TenSoon outside. The book was a symbol to him. It represented what he had once been. It represented failure. He glanced upward again. *Please,* he thought. *I want to believe. I really do. I just . . . I just need something. Something more than shadows and memories. Something real.*

Something true. Please?

"Farewell, Soother," TenSoon said. "Give my regards to the Announcer." Then, Sazed heard Breeze thump away. TenSoon padded down the hallway on his quieter dog's feet.

Announcer. . . .

Sazed froze.

That word. . . .

Sazed stood, stunned for a moment. Then, he threw his door open and burst into the hallway. The door slammed back against the wall, making Breeze jump. TenSoon stopped at the end of the hallway, near the stairs. He turned back, looking at Sazed.

"What did you call me?" Sazed demanded.

"The Announcer," TenSoon said. "You are, are you not, the one who pointed out Lady Vin as the Hero of Ages? That, then, is your title."

Sazed fell to his knees, slapping his tome—the one he had written with Tindwyl—on the floor before him. He flipped through the pages, locating one in particular, penned in his own hand. *I thought myself the Holy Witness,* it said, *the prophet foretold to discover the Hero of Ages.* They were the words of Kwaan, the man who had originally named Alendi the Hero. From these writings, which were their only clues about the original Terris religion, Sazed and the others had gleaned what little they knew of the prophecies about the Hero of Ages.

"What is this?" Breeze asked, leaning down, scanning the words. "Hum. Looks like you've got the wrong term, my dear doggie. Not 'Announcer' at all, but 'Holy Witness.' "

Sazed looked up. "This is one of the passages that Ruin changed, Breeze," he said quietly. "When I wrote it, it read differently—but Ruin altered it, trying to trick me and Vin into fulfilling his prophecies. The skaa had started to call me the Holy Witness, their own term. So Ruin retroactively changed Kwaan's writings so that they seemed prophetic and reference me."

"Is that so?" Breeze asked, rubbing his chin. "What did it say before?"

Sazed ignored the question, instead meeting TenSoon's canine eyes. "How did you know?" he demanded. "How do you know the words of the ancient Terris prophecies?"

TenSoon fell back on his haunches. "It strikes me as odd, Terrisman. There's one great inconsistency in this all, a problem *no one* has ever thought to point out. What happened to the packmen who traveled with Rashek and Alendi up to the Well of Ascension?"

Rashek. The man who had become the Lord Ruler.

Breeze stood up straight. "That's easy, kandra," he said, waving his cane. "Everyone knows that when the Lord Ruler took the throne of Khlennium, he made his trusted friends into noblemen. That's why the nobility of the Final Empire were so pampered—they were the descendants of Rashek's good friends."

TenSoon sat quietly.

No, Sazed thought with wonder. *No . . . that couldn't be!* "He *couldn't* have made those packmen into nobles."

"Why ever not?" Breeze asked.

"Because the nobility gained Allomancy," Sazed said, standing. "Rashek's friends were *Feruchemists.* If he'd made them into noblemen, then . . ."

"Then they could have challenged him," TenSoon said. "They could have become both Allomancers and Feruchemists as he was, and had his same powers."

"Yes," Sazed said. "He spent ten centuries trying to breed Feruchemy *out* of the Terris population—all in fear that someday someone would be born with both Feruchemy and Allomancy! His friends who went to the Well with him would have been dangerous, since they were obviously powerful Feruchemists, and they knew what Rashek had done to Alendi. Rashek would have had to do something else with them. Something to sequester them, perhaps even kill them. . . ."

"No," TenSoon said. "He didn't kill them. You call the Father a monster, but he was not an evil man. He didn't kill his friends, though he did recognize the threat their powers posed to him. So, he offered them a bargain, speaking directly to their minds while he was holding the power of creation."

"What bargain?" Breeze asked, obviously confused.

"Immortality," TenSoon said quietly. "In exchange for their Feruchemy. They gave it up, along with something else."

Sazed stared at the creature in the hallway, a creature who thought like a man but had the form of a beast. "They gave up their humanity," Sazed whispered.

TenSoon nodded.

"They live on?" Sazed asked, stepping forward. "The Lord Ruler's companions? The very Terrismen who climbed to the Well with him?"

"We call them the First Generation," TenSoon said. "The founders of the kandra people. The Father transformed every living Feruchemist into a mistwraith, beginning that race. His good friends, however, he returned to sentience with a few Hemalurgic spikes. You've done your work poorly, Keeper. I expected that you'd drag this out of me *long* before I had to leave."

I've been a fool, Sazed thought, blinking away tears. *Such a fool.*

"What?" Breeze asked, frowning. "What's going on? Sazed? My dear man, why are you so flustered? What do this creature's words mean?"

"They mean hope," Sazed said, pushing into his room, hurriedly throwing some of his clothing into a travel pack.

"Hope?" Breeze asked, peeking in.

Sazed looked back, toward where Breeze stood. The kandra had walked up, and stood behind him in the hallway. "The Terris religion, Breeze," Sazed said. "The thing my sect was founded for, the thing my people have spent lifetimes searching to discover. It lives on. Not in written words that can be corrupted or changed. But in the minds of men who actually practiced it. *The Terris faith is not dead!*"

There was one more religion to add to his list. His quest was not yet over.

"Quickly, Keeper," TenSoon said. "I was prepared to go without you, since everyone agreed that you had stopped caring about these things. However, if you will come, I will show you the way to my Homeland—it is along the path I must travel to find Vin. Hopefully, you will be able to convince the First Generation of the things I have not."

"And that is?" Sazed asked, still packing.

"That the end has arrived."

Ruin tried many times to get spikes into other members of the crew. Though some of what happened makes it seem like it was easy for him to gain control of people, it really was not.

Sticking the metal in just the right place—at the right time—was incredibly difficult, even for a subtle creature like Ruin. For instance, he tried very hard to spike both Elend and Yomen. Elend managed to avoid it each time, as he did on the field outside of the small village that contained the next-to-last storage cache.

Ruin did actually manage to get a spike into Yomen, once. Yomen, however, removed the spike before Ruin got a firm grip on him. It was much easier for Ruin to get a hold on people who were passionate and impulsive than it was for him to hold on to people who were logical and prone to working through their actions in their minds.

63

"WHAT I DON'T UNDERSTAND," VIN said, "is why you chose me. You had a thousand years and hundreds of thousands of people to choose from. Why lead *me* to the Well of Ascension to free you?"

She was in her cell, sitting on her cot—which now lay legless on the floor, having collapsed when she removed the screws. She'd asked for a new one. She'd been ignored.

Ruin turned toward her. He came often, wearing Reen's body, still indulging himself in what Vin could only assume was a kind of gloating. As he often did, however, he ignored her question. Instead, he turned to the east, eyes seeming as if they could see directly through the cell wall.

"I wish you could see it," he said. "The ashfalls have grown beautiful and deep, as if the sky itself has shattered, raining down shards of its corpse in flakes of black. You feel the ground tremble?"

Vin didn't respond.

"Those quakes are the earth's final sighs," Ruin said. "Like an old man, moaning as he dies, calling for his children so that he can pass on his last bits of wisdom. The very ground is pulling itself apart. The Lord Ruler did much of this himself. You can blame him, if you wish."

Vin perked up. She didn't draw attention to herself by asking more questions, but instead just let Ruin ramble on. Again, she noted just how *human* some of his mannerisms seemed.

"He thought he could solve the problems himself," Ruin continued. "He rejected me, you know."

And that happened exactly a thousand years ago, Vin thought. *A thousand years has passed since Alendi failed in his quest; a thousand years since Rashek took the power for himself and became the Lord Ruler. That's part of the answer to my question. The glowing liquid at the Well of Ascension—it was gone by the time I finished freeing Ruin. It must have disappeared after Rashek used it too.*

A thousand years. Time for the Well to regenerate its power? But what was that power? Where did it come from?

"The Lord Ruler didn't really save the world," Ruin continued. "He just postponed its destruction—and, in doing so, he helped me. That's the way it must always be, as I told you. When men think they are helping the world, they actually do more harm than good. Just like you. You tried to help, but you just ended up freeing me."

Ruin glanced at her, then smiled in a fatherly way. She didn't react.

"The ashmounts," Ruin continued, "the dying landscape, the broken people—those were all Rashek's. The twisting of men to become koloss, kandra, and Inquisitor, all his . . ."

"But, you hated him," Vin said. "He didn't free you—so you had to wait another thousand years."

"True," Ruin said. "But a thousand years is not much time. Not much time at all. Besides, I couldn't refuse to help Rashek. I help everyone, for my power is a tool—the only tool by which things can change."

It's all ending, Vin thought. *It really is. I don't have time to sit and wait. I need to do something.* Vin stood, causing Ruin to glance toward her as she walked to the front of the cell. "Guards!" she called. Her voice echoed in her own chamber. "Guards!" she repeated.

Eventually, she heard a thump outside. "What?" a rough voice demanded.

"Tell Yomen that I want to deal."

There was a pause.

"Deal?" the guard finally asked.

"Yes," Vin said. "Tell him I have information that I want to give him."

She wasn't certain how to read the guard's response, since it was simply more silence. She thought she heard him walking away, but without tin, she couldn't tell.

Eventually, however, the guard returned. Ruin watched her, curious, as the door unlocked and then opened. The customary troop of soldiers stood outside.

"Come with us."

As Vin entered Yomen's audience chamber, she was immediately struck by the differences in the man. He looked much more haggard than he had the last time they'd met, as if he'd gone far too long without sleep.

But . . . he's Mistborn, Vin thought with confusion. *That means he could burn pewter to keep that fatigue out of his eyes.*

Why doesn't he? Unless . . . he can't burn it. Unless there's only one metal available to him.

She'd always been taught that there was no such thing as an atium Misting. But, more and more, she was realizing that the Lord Ruler perpetuated a lot of misinformation to keep himself in control and in power. She had to learn to stop depending on what she'd been *told* was true, and focus on the facts as she found them.

Yomen watched her as she entered, guards surrounding her. She could read the expectation of a trick in his eyes—yet, as always, he waited for her to act first. Hovering very close to the edge of danger seemed his way. The guards took stations at the doors, leaving her standing in the middle of the room.

"No manacles?" she asked.

"No," Yomen said. "I don't expect you to be here long. The guards tell me that you've offered information."

"I have."

"Well," Yomen said, arms clasped behind his back, "I told them to bring you to me if they even so much as suspected a trick. Apparently, they didn't believe your pleas that you want to deal. I wonder why." He raised an eyebrow toward her.

"Ask me a question," Vin said. To the side, Ruin trailed through the wall, stepping with an idle, unconcerned gait.

"Very well," Yomen said. "How does Elend control the koloss?"

"Allomancy," Vin said. "Emotional Allomancy, when used on a koloss, will bring them under the Allomancer's control."

"I find that hard to believe," Yomen said flatly. "If it were that simple, someone other than yourself would have discovered it."

"Most Allomancers are too weak to manage it," Vin said. "You need to use a metal that enhances your power."

"There is no such metal."

"You know of aluminum?"

Yomen paused, but Vin could see in his eyes that he did.

"Duralumin is the Allomantic alloy of aluminum," Vin said. "Where aluminum dampens the power of other metals, duralumin enhances them. Mix duralumin and zinc or brass, then Pull on the emotions of a koloss, and he will be yours."

Yomen didn't dismiss her comments as lies. Ruin, however, strolled forward, walking around Vin in a circle.

"Vin, Vin. What is your game now?" Ruin asked, amused. "Lead him on with little tidbits, then betray him?"

Yomen apparently came to the same conclusion. "Your facts are interesting, Empress, but completely unprovable in my present situation. Therefore, they are—"

"There were five of these storage caverns," Vin said, stepping forward. "We found the others. They led us here."

Yomen shook his head. "And? Why should I care?"

"Your Lord Ruler planned something for those caverns—you can tell that much from the plate he left here in this one. He says that he came up with no way to fight what is happening to us in the world, but do you believe that? I feel there has to be more, some clue hidden in the text of all five plaques."

"You expect me to believe that *you* care what the Lord Ruler wrote?" Yomen asked. "You, his purported murderer?"

"I couldn't care less about him," Vin admitted. "But Yomen, you *have* to believe that I care what happens to the people of the empire! If you've gathered any intelligence about Elend or myself, you know that is true."

"Your Elend is a man who thinks far too highly of himself," Yomen said. "He has read many books, and assumes that his learning makes him capable of being a king. You . . . I still don't know what to think about you." His eyes showed a bit of the hatred she had seen in him during their last meeting. "You claim to have killed the Lord Ruler. Yet . . . he couldn't really have died. You're part of all this, somehow."

That's it, Vin thought. *That's my in.* "He wanted us to meet," Vin said. She didn't believe it, but Yomen would.

Yomen raised an eyebrow.

"Can't you see?" Vin said. "Elend and I discovered the other storage caverns, the first one under Luthadel itself.

Then, we came here. This was the *last* of the five. The end of the trail. For some reason, the Lord Ruler wanted to lead us here. To you."

Yomen stood for a few moments. To the side, Ruin mimed applause.

"Send for Lellin," Yomen said, turning toward one of his soldiers. "Tell him to bring his maps."

The soldier saluted and left. Yomen turned to Vin, still frowning. "This is not to be an exchange. You will give me the information I request, then I will decide what to do with it."

"Fine," Vin said. "But, you yourself just said that I was connected to all of this. It's *all* connected, Yomen. The mists, the koloss, me, you, the storage caverns, the ash . . ."

He flinched slightly as Vin mentioned that last one.

"The ash is getting worse, isn't it?" she asked. "Falling more thickly?"

Yomen nodded.

"We were always worried about the mists," Vin said. "But the ash, it's going to be what kills us. It will block the sunlight, bury our cities, cover our streets, choke our fields. . . ."

"The Lord Ruler won't let that happen," Yomen said.

"And if he really is dead?"

Yomen met her eyes. "Then you have doomed us all."

Doomed. . . . The Lord Ruler had said something similar right before Vin had killed him. She shivered, waiting in awkward silence, suffering Ruin's smiling stare until a scribe scuttled into the room, bearing several rolled maps.

Yomen took one of the maps, waving the man away. He spread it out on a table, waving Vin forward. "Show me," he said, stepping back to keep out of her reach as she approached.

She picked up a piece of charcoal, then began to mark the locations of the storage caverns. Luthadel. Satren. Vetitan. Urteau. All five that she had found—all near the Central Dominance, one in the center, the other four forming a box around it. She put a final "X" beside Fadrex City.

Then, with charcoal gripped in her fingers, she noticed

something. *Sure are a lot of mines shown on this map around Fadrex*, she thought. *A lot of metal in the area.*

"Step back," Yomen said.

Vin moved away. He approached, scanning the map. Vin stood in silence, thinking. *Elend's scribes could never find a pattern to the cache locations. Two were in small cities, two in large ones. Some near canals, others not. The scribes claimed that they just didn't have a large enough set from which to determine patterns.*

"This seems completely random," Yomen said, echoing her own thoughts.

"I didn't make up those locations, Yomen," she said, folding her arms. "Your spies can confirm where Elend has taken his armies and sent his emissaries."

"Not all of us have the resources for extensive spy networks, Empress," Yomen said flatly, looking back at the map. "There should be some pattern. . . ."

Vetitan, Vin thought. *The place where we found the cavern just before this one. It was a mining town as well. And Urteau too.*

"Yomen?" she said, looking up. "Does one of those maps list mineral deposits?"

"Of course," he said distractedly. "We *are* the Canton of Resource, after all."

"Get it out."

Yomen raised an eyebrow, indicating what he thought of her giving him orders. However, he waved for his scribe to do as she had requested. A second map overlaid the first, and Vin walked forward. Yomen immediately shied backward, keeping out of reach.

He has good instincts, for a bureaucrat, she thought, slipping the charcoal out from underneath the map. She quickly made her five marks again. With each one, her hand grew more tense. Each cavern was in a rocky area, near metal mines. Even Luthadel bore rich mineral deposits. Lore said that the Lord Ruler had constructed his capital in that location *because* of the mineral content in the area, particularly the groundwater. That much the better for Allomancers.

"What are you trying to imply?" Yomen asked. He'd edged close enough to see what she'd marked.

"This is the connection," Vin said. "He built his storages near sources of metal."

"Or, it was simple chance."

"No," Vin said, looking up, glancing at Ruin. "No, metal equals Allomancy, Yomen. There's a pattern here."

Yomen waved her away again, approaching the map. He snorted. "You've included marks near each of the most productive mines in the inner empire. You expect me to believe that you're not just playing me, offering some phantom 'evidence' that these really are the locations of the storage caverns?"

Vin ignored him. *Metal. The words of Kwaan were written in metal, because he said they were safe. Safe. Safe from being changed, we assumed.*

Or, did he mean safe from being read?

The Lord Ruler had drawn his maps on metal plates.

So, what if Ruin couldn't find the storages on his own because of the metal shielding them? He would have needed someone to lead him. Someone to visit each one, read the map it contained, then lead him on. . . .

Lord Ruler! We've made the same mistake again! We did exactly what he wanted. No wonder he's let us live!

However, instead of feeling ashamed, this time Vin felt herself growing angry. She glanced over at Ruin, who stood there with his air of cosmic wisdom. His knowing eyes, his fatherly tone, and his deific arrogance.

Not again, Vin thought, gritting her teeth. *This time, I'm on to him. That means I can trick him. But . . . I need to know why. Why was he so interested in the storages? What is it he needs before he wins this battle? What is the reason he's waited so long?*

Suddenly, the answer seemed obvious to her. As she examined her feelings, she realized that one of her main reasons for searching out the caches had repeatedly been discredited by Elend. Yet, Vin had continued to pursue the caches, searching for this one thing. She'd *felt,* for reasons she couldn't explain, that it was important.

The thing that had driven the imperial economy for a thousand years. The most powerful of Allomantic metals.

Atium.

Why had she been so infatuated with it? Elend and Yomen were both right—atium was of little importance in the current world. But, her feelings denied that. Why? Was it because *Ruin* wanted it, and Vin had some unexplained connection to him?

The Lord Ruler had said Ruin couldn't read her mind. But she knew that he could affect her emotions. Change how she regarded things, push her forward. Drive her to search out the thing he wanted.

Looking at the emotions that had affected her, she could see Ruin's plan, the way he had manipulated her, the way he thought. Ruin wanted the atium! And, with a chill of terror, Vin realized that she had led him right to it. *No wonder he was so smug before!* Vin thought. *No wonder he assumed that he'd won!*

Why would a god-like force be so interested in a simple thing like an Allomantic metal? The question made her doubt her conclusions slightly. But at that moment, the doors to the chamber burst open.

And an Inquisitor stood beyond them.

Immediately, Yomen and the soldiers all fell to one knee. Vin took an involuntary step backward. The creature stood tall, like most of its kind, and still wore the gray robes of its pre-Collapse office. The bald head was wrinkled with intricate tattoos, mostly black, one stark red. And, of course, there were the spikes driven point-first through its eyes. One of the spikes had been pounded in farther than the other, crushing the socket around the spikehead. The creature's face, twisted by an inhuman sneer, had once been familiar to Vin.

"Marsh?" Vin whispered in horror.

"My lord," Yomen said, spreading his hands out. "You

have finally come! I sent messengers, searching for—"

"Silence," Marsh said in a grating voice, striding forward. "On your feet, obligator."

Yomen hastily stood. Marsh glanced at Vin, smiled slightly, but then pointedly ignored her. He did, however, look directly at Ruin and bow his head in subservience.

Vin shivered. Marsh's features, even twisted as they were, reminded her of his brother. Kelsier.

"You are about to be attacked, obligator," Marsh said, sweeping forward, throwing open the large window at the other side of the room. Through it, Vin could see over the rocky shelves to where Elend's army camped beside the canal.

Except, there was no canal. There were no rocky shelves. Everything was just a uniform black. Ash filled the sky, as thick as a snowstorm.

Lord Ruler! Vin thought. *It's gotten so bad!*

Yomen hurried over to the window. "Attacked, my lord? But, they haven't even broken camp!"

"The koloss will attack in surprise," the Inquisitor said. "They don't need to form up ranks—they will simply charge."

Yomen froze for a second, then turned to his soldiers. "Hasten to the defenses. Gather the men on the forward rises!"

Soldiers scuttled from the room. Vin stood quietly. *The man I know as Marsh is dead,* she thought. *He tried to kill Sazed, now he's fully one of them. Ruin has . . .*

Has taken control of him. . . .

An idea began to spark in her mind.

"Quickly, obligator," Marsh said. "I did not come to protect your foolish little city. I've come for the thing you discovered in that cache."

"My lord?" Yomen said, surprised.

"Your atium, Yomen," the Inquisitor said. "Give it to me. It *cannot* be in this city when that attack comes, just in case you fall. I shall take it someplace safe."

Vin closed her eyes.

"My . . . lord?" Yomen finally said. "You are, of course, welcome to anything I possess. But, there was no atium in the storage cache. Just the seven beads I had gathered myself, held as a reserve for the Canton of Resource."

Vin opened her eyes. "*What?*"

"Impossible!" Marsh roared. "But, you told the girl earlier that you had it!"

Yomen paled. "Misdirection, my lord. She seemed convinced that I had some wealth of atium, so I let her think that she was right."

"*NO!*"

Vin jumped at the sudden yell. However, Yomen didn't even flinch—and a second later, she realized why. Ruin was the one who had screamed. He had become indistinct, losing Reen's form, his figure blossoming outward in a kind of tempest of whirling darkness. Almost like mist, only far, far blacker.

She'd seen that blackness before. She'd walked through it, in the cavern beneath Luthadel, on her way to the Well of Ascension.

A second later, Ruin was back. He looked like Reen again. He folded his arms behind his back, and didn't look at her, as if trying to pretend that he had not lost control. In his eyes, however, she could see frustration. Anger. She edged away from him—edging *closer* to Marsh.

"You fool!" Marsh said, walking away from her, speaking to Yomen. "You idiot!"

Damn, Vin thought in annoyance.

"I . . ." Yomen said, confused. "My lord, why do you care for atium? It is worthless without Allomancers and house politicians to pay for it."

"You know nothing," Marsh snapped. Then, he smiled. "But you are doomed. Yes . . . doomed indeed. . . ."

Outside, she could see that Elend's army was breaking camp. Yomen turned back to the window, and Vin edged closer, ostensibly to give herself a better look. Elend's forces were gathering—men and koloss. Most likely, they had noticed the buildup of city defenses, and had realized that they'd lost any opportunity for surprise.

"He's going to ravage this city," Ruin said, stepping up beside Vin. "Your Elend is a good servant, child. One of my finest. You should be proud of him."

"So many koloss . . ." she heard Yomen whisper. "My lord, there is no way we can fight so many. We need your help."

"Why should I help you?" Marsh asked. "You who fail to deliver to me what I need?"

"But I've remained faithful," Yomen said. "When all others abandoned the Lord Ruler, I have continued to serve him."

"The Lord Ruler is dead," Marsh said with a snort. "He was an unprofitable servant as well."

Yomen paled.

"Let this city burn before the wrath of forty thousand koloss," Marsh said.

Forty thousand koloss, Vin thought. He'd found more, somewhere. Attacking seemed the logical thing to do—he could finally capture the city, perhaps giving Vin a chance to escape in the chaos. Very logical, very smart. And yet, suddenly, Vin became sure of one thing.

"Elend won't attack," she announced.

Six eyes—two steel, two flesh, and two incorporeal—turned toward her.

"Elend won't loose that many koloss upon the city," she said. "He's trying to intimidate you, Yomen. And you should listen. Would you still obey this creature, this Inquisitor? He disdains you. He wants you to die. Join with us instead."

Yomen frowned.

"You could fight him with me," Vin said. "You're an Allomancer. These monsters *can* be defeated."

Marsh smiled. "Idealism from you, Vin?"

"Idealism?" she asked, facing the creature. "You think it's idealistic to believe I can kill an Inquisitor? You know I've done it before."

Marsh waved a dismissive hand. "I'm not talking about your foolish threats. I'm talking about *him.*" He nodded toward the army outside. "Your Elend belongs to Ruin, just as

I do—just as you do. We all resist, but we all bow before him eventually. Only then do we understand the beauty there is in destruction."

"Your god does not control Elend," Vin said. "He keeps trying to claim that he does, but that only makes him a liar. Or, perhaps, something of an idealist himself."

Yomen watched, confused.

"And if he *does* attack?" Marsh asked with a quiet, eager voice. "What would that mean, Vin? What if he does send his koloss against this city in a blood frenzy, sends them to slaughter and kill, all so that he can get what he *thinks* he needs so badly? Atium and food couldn't get him to come in . . . but you? How would that make you feel? You killed for him. What makes you think that Elend won't do the same for you?"

Vin closed her eyes. Memories of her assault upon Cett's tower returned to her. Memories of wanton killing, Zane at her side. Memories of fire, and death, and an Allomancer loosed.

She'd never killed like that again.

She opened her eyes. Why wouldn't Elend attack? Attacking made so much sense. He knew he could take the city easily. However, he also knew he had trouble controlling the koloss when they reached too great a frenzy. . . .

"Elend won't attack," she said quietly. "Because he's a better person than I am."

One might notice that Ruin did not send his Inquisitors to Fadrex until after Yomen had—apparently—confirmed that the atium was there in the city. Why not send them as soon as the final cache was located? Where were his minions in all of this?

One must realize that, in Ruin's mind, all men were his minions, particularly those whom he could manipulate directly. He didn't send an Inquisitor because they were busy doing other tasks. Instead, he sent someone who—in his mind—was exactly the same thing as an Inquisitor.

He tried to spike Yomen, failed, and by that time, Elend's army had arrived. So, he used a different pawn to investigate the cache for him and discover if the atium really was there or not. He didn't commit too many resources to the city at first, fearing a deception on the Lord Ruler's part. Like him, I still wonder if the caches were, in part, intended for just that purpose—to distract Ruin and keep him occupied.

64

". . . AND THAT'S WHY YOU ABSOLUTELY *must* get that message sent, Spook. The pieces of this thing are all spinning about, cast to the wind. You have a clue that nobody else does. Send it flying for me."

Spook nodded, feeling fuzzy. Where was he? What was going on? And why, suddenly, did everything hurt so much?

"Good lad. You did well, Spook. I'm proud."

He tried to nod again, but everything was fuzz and blackness. He coughed, prompting some gasps from a place far off. He groaned. Parts of him hurt quite sharply, though others just tingled. Still others . . . well, those he couldn't feel at all, though he thought he *should* have been able to.

I was dreaming, he realized as he slowly came to consciousness. *Why have I been asleep? Was I on watch? Should I go on watch? The shop . . .*

His thoughts trailed off as he opened his eyes. There was someone standing above him. A face. One . . . quite a bit uglier than the face he'd hoped to see.

"Breeze?" he tried to say, though it came out as a croak.

"Ha!" Breeze said with uncharacteristic tears in his eyes. "He *is* waking!"

Another face hovered over him, and Spook smiled. *That's* the one he'd been waiting for. Beldre. "What's going on?" Spook whispered.

Hands brought something to his lips—a water skin. They poured carefully, giving him a drink. He coughed, but got it down. "Why . . . why can't I move?" Spook asked. The only thing he seemed able to twitch was his left hand.

"Your body is being held in casts and bandages, Spook," Beldre said. "Sazed's orders."

"The burns," Breeze said. "Well, they aren't *that* bad, but . . ."

"To hell with the burns," Spook croaked. "I'm alive. I wasn't expecting that."

Breeze looked up at Beldre, smiling.

Send it flying. . . .

"Where is Sazed?" Spook asked.

"You should really try to rest," Beldre said, rubbing his cheek softly. "You've been through a lot."

"And slept through more, I expect," Spook said. "Sazed?"

"Gone, my dear boy," Breeze said. "He went off south with Vin's kandra."

Vin.

Feet clomped across the floor, and a second later, Captain Goradel's face appeared beside the other two. The square-jawed soldier smiled broadly. "Survivor of the Flames indeed!"

You have a clue that nobody else does. . . .

"How is the city?" Spook asked.

"Mostly safe," Beldre said. "The canals flooded, and my brother organized fire brigades. Most of the buildings that burned weren't inhabited anyway."

"You saved it, my lord," Goradel said.

I'm proud. . . .

"The ash is falling even more thickly, isn't it?" Spook asked.

The three above shared looks. Their troubled expressions were enough of a confirmation.

"We're getting a lot of refugees into the city," Beldre said. "From surrounding cities and villages, some as far as Luthadel. . . ."

"I need to send a message," Spook said. "To Vin."

"All right," Breeze said soothingly. "We'll do that as soon as you are better."

"Listen to me, Breeze," Spook said, staring up at the ceiling, unable to do much more than twitch. "Something was controlling me and the Citizen. I *saw* it—the thing that Vin released at the Well of Ascension. The thing that is bringing ash down to destroy us. It wanted this city, but we fought it off. Now, I need to warn Vin."

That's what he'd been sent to do in Urteau. Find information, then report it back to Vin and Elend. He was only just beginning to understand how important a duty that could be.

"Travel is difficult right now, my boy," Breeze said. "It isn't exactly perfect conditions for sending messages."

"Rest some more," Beldre said. "We'll worry about it when you're healed."

Spook gritted his teeth in frustration.

You must *get that message sent, Spook. . . .*

"I'll take it," Goradel said quietly.

Spook looked to the side. Sometimes, it was easy to ignore the soldier, with his simple, straightforward manner and his pleasant demeanor. However, the determination in his voice made Spook smile.

"Lady Vin saved my life," Goradel said. "The night of the Survivor's rebellion, she could have left me to die at the hands of the mob. She could have killed me herself. But she took the time to tell me that she understood what I'd been through, and convinced me to switch sides. If she needs this information, Survivor, then I *will* get it to her, or I will die trying."

Spook tried to nod, but his head was held tight by the bandages and wrappings. He flexed his hand. It seemed to work . . . or, at least, work well enough.

He met Goradel's eyes. "Go to the armory and have a sheet of metal pounded thin," Spook said. "Then, return here with something I can use to scratch the metal. These words must be written in steel, and I cannot speak them aloud."

In those moments when the Lord Ruler both held the power at the Well and was feeling it drain away from him, he understood a great many things. He saw the power of Feruchemy, and rightly feared it. Many of the Terris people, he knew, would reject him as the Hero, for he didn't fulfill their prophecies well. They'd see him as a usurper who killed the Hero they sent. Which, in truth, he was.

I think, over the years, Ruin would subtly twist him and make him do terrible things to his own people. But at the beginning, I suspect his decision against them was motivated more by logic than emotion. He was about to unveil a grand power in the Mistborn.

He could have, I suppose, kept Allomancy secret and used Feruchemists as his primary warriors and assassins. However, I think he was wise to choose as he did. Feruchemists, by the nature of their powers, have a tendency toward scholarship. With their incredible memories, they would have been very difficult to control over the centuries. Indeed, they were *difficult to control, even when he suppressed them. Allomancy not only provided a spectacular new ability without that drawback, it offered a mystical power he could use to bribe kings to his side.*

65

ELEND STOOD UPON A SMALL rock outcropping to look over his troops. Below, the koloss stalked forward, stomping a pathway in the ash for his humans to use after the initial koloss assault.

Elend waited, Ham standing just a few steps below.

I wear white, Elend thought. *The color of purity. I try to represent what is good and right. For my men.*

"The koloss should have no trouble with those fortifications," Ham said quietly. "They can leap to the top of city walls; they'll be able to climb those broken stone ridges."

Elend nodded. There probably wouldn't be any need for the human soldiers to attack. With his koloss alone, Elend had the numerical advantage, and it was unlikely Yomen's soldiers had ever fought the creatures before.

The koloss sensed a fight. He could feel them getting excited. They strained against him, wishing to attack.

"Ham," he said, glancing down. "Is this right?"

Ham shrugged. "This move does make sense, El," he said, rubbing his chin. "Attacking is our only real chance of saving Vin. And, we can't hold the siege—not any longer." Ham paused, then shook his head, his tone of voice taking on that uncertain quality it always did when he considered one of his logic problems. "Yet, loosing a group of koloss on a city does seem immoral. I wonder if you'll be able to control them, once they begin to rampage. Is saving Vin worth the possibility of killing even one innocent child? I don't know. Then again, maybe we'll save more children by bringing them into our empire. . . ."

I shouldn't have bothered to ask Ham, Elend thought. *He never has been able to give a straight answer.* He looked out over the field, blue koloss against a plain of black. With tin, he could see men cowering on the tops of the Fadrex City ridges.

"No," Ham said.

Elend glanced down at the Thug.

"No," Ham repeated. "We shouldn't attack."

"Ham?" Elend said, feeling a surreal amusement. "Did you actually come to a *conclusion*?"

Ham nodded. "Yes." He didn't offer explanation or rationalization.

Elend looked up. *What would Vin do?* His first instinct was to think that she'd attack. But then, he remembered when he had discovered her years before, after she'd assaulted Cett's tower. She'd been huddled up in a corner, crying.

No, he thought. *No, she wouldn't do this thing. Not to protect me. She's learned better.*

"Ham," he said, surprising himself. "Tell the men to pull

back and disassemble camp. We're returning to Luthadel."

Ham looked back, surprised—as if he hadn't expected Elend to come to the same conclusion he had. "And Vin?"

"I'm not going to attack this city, Ham," Elend said. "I won't conquer these people, even if it is for their own good. We'll find another way to get Vin free."

Ham smiled. "Cett's going to be furious."

Elend shrugged. "He's a paraplegic. What's he going to do? Bite us? Come on, let's get down off this rock and go deal with Luthadel."

"They're pulling back, my lord," the soldier said.

Vin sighed in relief. Ruin stood, expression unreadable, hands folded behind his back. Marsh stood with one hand claw-like on Yomen's shoulder, both watching out the window.

Ruin brought in an Inquisitor, she thought. *He must have grown tired of my efforts to get the truth out of Yomen, and instead brought in someone he knew the obligator would obey.*

"This is very odd," Ruin finally said.

Vin took a breath, then gambled. "Don't you see?" she asked quietly.

Ruin turned toward her.

She smiled. "You really don't understand, do you?"

This time, Marsh turned as well.

"You think I didn't realize?" Vin asked. "You think I didn't know you were after the atium all along? That you were following us from cavern to cavern, Pushing on my emotions, forcing me to search it out for you? You were so obvious. Your koloss always drew close to a city only *after* we discovered that it was the next in line. You moved in to threaten us, make us move more quickly, but you never got your koloss there *too* fast. The thing is, we knew all along."

"Impossible," Ruin whispered.

"No," Vin said. "Quite possible. Atium is metal, Ruin. You

can't see it. Your vision gets fuzzy when too much of it is around, doesn't it? Metal is your power; you use it to make Inquisitors, but it's like light to you—blinding. You never saw when we actually discovered the atium. You just followed along with our ruse."

Marsh let go of Yomen, then rushed across the room, grabbing Vin by the arms.

"*WHERE IS IT!*" the Inquisitor demanded, lifting her, shaking her.

She laughed, distracting Marsh as she carefully reached for his sash. Marsh shook her too much, however, and her fingers couldn't find their mark.

"You will tell me where the atium is, child," Ruin said calmly. "Haven't I explained this? There is no fighting against me. You think yourself clever, perhaps, but you really don't understand. You don't even know what that atium is."

Vin shook her head. "You think I'd actually lead you to it?"

Marsh shook her again, rattling her, making her grit her teeth. When he stopped, her vision swam. To the side, she could barely make out Yomen watching with a frown. "Yomen," she said. "Your people are safe now—can you not finally trust that Elend is a good man?"

Marsh tossed her aside. She hit hard, rolling.

"Ah, child," Ruin said, kneeling down beside her. "Must I *prove* that you cannot fight me?"

"Yomen!" Marsh said, turning. "Prepare your men. I want you to order an assault!"

"What?" Yomen said. "My lord, an assault?"

"Yes," Marsh said. "I want you to take all of your soldiers and have them attack Elend Venture's position."

Yomen paled. "Leave behind our fortifications? Charge an army of *koloss*?"

"That is my order," Marsh said.

Yomen stood quietly for a moment.

"Yomen . . ." Vin said, crawling to her knees. "Don't you see that he's manipulating you?"

Yomen didn't respond. He looked troubled. *What would make him even consider an order like that?*

"You see," Ruin whispered. "You see my power? You see how I manipulate even their faith?"

"Give the order," Yomen said, turning from Vin, facing his soldier captains. "Have the men attack. Tell them that the Lord Ruler will protect them."

"Well," Ham said, standing beside Elend in the camp. "I didn't expect that."

Elend nodded slowly, watching the flood of men pour through the Fadrex gateway. Some stumbled in the deep ash; others pushed their way forward, their charge hampered to a slow crawl.

"Some stayed back," Elend said, pointing up at the wall top. Not having tin, Ham wouldn't be able to see the men who lined the wall, but he'd trust Elend's words. Around them, Elend's human soldiers were breaking camp. The koloss still waited silently in their positions, surrounding the camp.

"What is Yomen thinking?" Ham asked. "He's throwing an inferior force against an army of koloss?"

Like we did, attacking the koloss camp back in Vetitan. Something about it made Elend very uncomfortable.

"Retreat," Elend said.

"Huh?" Ham asked.

"I said sound the retreat!" Elend said. "Abandon position. Pull the soldiers back!"

At his silent command, the koloss began to charge away from the city. Yomen's soldiers were still pushing their way through the ash. Elend's koloss, however, would clear the way for his men. They should be able to stay ahead.

"Strangest retreat *I've* ever seen," Ham noted, but moved back to give the orders.

That's it, Elend thought in annoyance. *It's time to figure out what the hell is going on in that city.*

* * *

Yomen was crying. They were small, quiet tears. He stood straight-backed, not facing the window.

He fears that he's ordered his men to their deaths, Vin thought. She moved up to him, limping slightly from where she'd hit the ground. Marsh stood watching out the window. Ruin eyed her curiously.

"Yomen," she said.

Yomen turned toward her. "It's a test," he said. "The Inquisitors are the Lord Ruler's most holy priests. I'll do as commanded, and the Lord Ruler will protect my men and this city. Then you will see."

Vin gritted her teeth. Then, she turned and forced herself to walk up beside Marsh. She glanced out the window—and was surprised to see that Elend's army was retreating away from Yomen's soldiers. Yomen's force wasn't running with very much conviction. Obviously, they were content to let their superior enemy run away before them. The sun was finally setting.

Marsh did not seem to find Elend's retreat amusing. That was enough to make Vin smile—which made Marsh grab her again.

"You think you have won?" Marsh asked, leaning down, his uneven spikeheads hanging just before Vin's face.

Vin reached for his sash. *Just a little farther. . . .*

"You claim to have been playing with me, child," Ruin said, stepping up next to her. "But you are the one who has been played. The koloss who serve you, they get their strength from *my* power. You think that I would let you control them if it weren't for my eventual gain?"

Vin felt a moment of chill.

Oh, no. . . .

Elend felt a terrible *ripping* sensation. It was like a part of his innards had been suddenly, and forcibly, pulled away from him. He gasped, releasing his Steelpush. He fell through the ash-filled sky, and landed unevenly on a rock shelf outside of Fadrex City.

He gasped, breathing in and out, trembling.

What in the hell was that? he thought, standing up, holding his thumping head.

And then he realized it. He couldn't feel the koloss anymore. In the distance, the massive blue creatures stopped running away. And then, to Elend's horror, he watched them turn around.

They began to charge his men.

Marsh held her. "Hemalurgy is *his* power, Vin!" he said. "The Lord Ruler used it unwittingly! The fool! Each time he built an Inquisitor or a koloss, he made another servant for his enemy! Ruin waited patiently, knowing that when he finally broke free, he'd have an entire army waiting for him!"

Yomen was at another window. He gasped quietly, watching. "You did deliver my men!" the obligator said. "The koloss have turned to attack their own army!"

"They'll come after your men next, Yomen," Vin said, dizzily. "Then they'll destroy your city."

"It is ending," Ruin whispered. "Everything needs to fit into place. Where is the atium? It's the last piece."

Marsh shook her. She finally managed to reach his sash—and slipped her fingers into it. Fingers trained by her brother, and by a lifetime on the street.

The fingers of a thief.

"You can't fool me, Vin," Ruin said. "I am God."

Marsh raised one hand—releasing her arm—then raised a fist as if to hit her. He moved with power, pewter obviously burning inside of him. He was an Allomancer, like all Inquisitors. Which meant he tended to keep metals on his person. Vin flipped her hand up and downed the vial of metals she'd stolen from his sash.

Marsh froze, and Ruin fell silent.

Vin smiled.

Pewter flared in her stomach, restoring her to life. Marsh moved to complete his slap, but she pulled out of the way, then yanked him off balance by pulling her other arm—

which he still held—to the side. He hung on, barely, but when he turned to face Vin, he found her holding her earring in one hand.

And she duralumin-Pushed it directly into his forehead. It was a tiny bit of metal, but it threw up a drop of blood as it hit, ripping through his head and passing out the other side.

Marsh dropped, and Vin was thrown backward by her own Push. She crashed into the wall, causing soldiers to scatter and yell, raising weapons. Yomen turned toward her, surprised.

"Yomen!" she said. "Bring your men back! Fortify the city!" Ruin had disappeared in the chaos of her escape. Perhaps he was out overseeing the control of the koloss.

Yomen seemed indecisive. "I . . . No. I will not lose faith. I must be strong."

Vin gritted her teeth, climbing to her feet. *Nearly as frustrating as Elend is at times,* she thought, scrambling over to Marsh's body. She reached into his sash, pulling out the second—and final—vial he had stored there. She downed this, restoring the metals she'd lost to duralumin.

Then, she hopped up on the windowsill. Mist puffed around her—the sun was still up, but the mists were arriving earlier and earlier. Outside, she could see Elend's forces beleaguered by rampaging koloss on one side, Yomen's soldiers not attacking—yet blocking retreat—on the other. She moved to jump out and join the fight, and then she noticed something.

A small group of koloss. A thousand in number, small enough to apparently have been ignored by both Elend's forces and Yomen's. Even Ruin appeared to have paid them no heed, for they simply stood in the ash, partially buried, like a collection of quiet stones.

Vin's koloss. The ones that Elend had given her, Human at their lead. With a devious smile, she ordered them forward.

To attack Yomen's men.

"I'm telling you, Yomen," she said, hopping off of the windowsill and back into the room. "Those koloss don't care which side the humans are on—they'll kill anyone. The Inquisitors have gone mad, now that the Lord Ruler is dead. Didn't you pay any attention to what this one said?"

Yomen looked thoughtful.

"He even admitted that the Lord Ruler was dead, Yomen," Vin said with exasperation. "Your faith is commendable. But sometimes, you just have to know when to *give up and move on*!"

One of the soldier captains yelled something, and Yomen spun back toward the window. He cursed.

Immediately, Vin felt something. Something *Pulling* on her koloss. She cried out as they were yanked away from her, but the damage had been done. Yomen looked troubled. He'd seen the koloss attack his soldiers. He looked into Vin's eyes, silent for a moment. "Retreat into the city!" he finally yelled, turning to his messengers. "And order the men to allow Venture's soldiers refuge inside as well!"

Vin sighed in relief. And then, something grabbed her leg. She looked down with shock as Marsh climbed to his knees. She had sliced through his brain itself, but the amazing Inquisitor healing powers seemed to be able to deal even with that.

"Fool," Marsh said, standing. "Even if Yomen turns against me, I can kill him, and his soldiers will follow me. He's given them a belief in the Lord Ruler, and I hold that belief by right of inheritance."

Vin took a deep breath, then hit Marsh with a duralumin-Soothing. If it worked on koloss and kandra, why not Inquisitors?

Marsh stumbled. Vin's Push lasted a brief moment, but during it she *felt* something. A wall, like she'd felt the first time she'd tried to control TenSoon or the first time she'd taken control of a group of koloss.

She *Pushed,* Pushed with everything she had. In a burst of power, she came close to seizing control of Marsh's body, but not close enough. The wall within his mind was too strong, and she only had one vial's worth of metal to use. The wall shoved her back. She cried out in frustration.

Marsh reached out, growling, and grabbed her by the neck. She gasped, eyes widening as Marsh began to grow in size. Getting stronger, like . . .

A Feruchemist, she realized. *I'm in serious trouble.*

People in the room were yelling, but she couldn't hear them. Marsh's hand—now large and beefy—gripped her throat, strangling her. Only flared pewter was keeping her alive. She flashed back to the day, many years ago, when she'd been held by another Inquisitor. Standing in the Lord Ruler's throne room.

On that day, Marsh himself had saved her life. It seemed a twisted irony that she would struggle now, being strangled by him.

Not. Yet.

The mists began to swirl around her.

Marsh started, though he continued to hold her.

Vin drew upon the mists.

It happened again. She didn't know how, or why, but it just *happened.* She breathed the mists into her body, as she had on that day so long ago when she'd killed the Lord Ruler. She somehow pulled them into her and used them to fuel her body with an incredible Allomantic surge of power.

And, with that power, she *Pushed* on Marsh's emotions.

The wall inside of him cracked, then burst. For a moment, Vin felt a sense of vertigo. She saw things through Marsh's eyes—indeed, she felt like she *understood* him. His love of destruction, and his hatred of himself. And through him, she caught a brief glimpse of something. A hateful, destructive thing that hid behind a mask of civility.

Ruin was *not* the same thing as the mists.

Marsh cried out, dropping her. Her strange burst of power dissipated, but it didn't matter, for Marsh fled out the window and Pushed himself away through the mists. Vin picked herself up, coughing.

I did it. I drew upon the mists again. But why now? Why, after all the trying, did it happen now?

There was no time to consider it at the moment—not with the koloss attacking. She turned to the baffled Yomen. "Continue to retreat into the city!" she said. "I'm going out to help."

* * *

Elend fought desperately, cutting down koloss after koloss. It was difficult, dangerous work, even for him. These koloss couldn't be controlled—no matter how he Pushed or Pulled on their emotions, he couldn't bring even one of them under his power.

That only left fighting. And, his men weren't prepared for battle—he'd forced them to abandon camp too quickly.

A koloss swung, its sword whooshing dangerously close to Elend's head. He cursed, dropping a coin and Pushing himself backward through the air, over his fighting men and back into camp. They'd managed to retreat back to the positioning of their original fortification, which meant that they had a small hill for defense and didn't have to fight in ash. A group of his Coinshots—he only had ten—stood firing wave after wave of coins into the main bulk of the koloss, and archers threw similar volleys. The main line of soldiers was supported by Lurchers from behind, who would Pull on koloss weapons and throw them off balance, giving the regular men extra openings. Thugs ran around the perimeter in groups of two or three, shoring up weak spots and acting as reserves.

Even with all of that, they were in serious trouble. Elend's army couldn't stand against so many koloss any more easily than Fadrex could have. Elend landed in the middle of the half-disassembled camp, breathing heavily, covered in koloss blood. Men yelled as they fought a short distance away, holding the camp perimeter with the help of Elend's Allomancers. The bulk of the koloss army was still bunched around the northern section of camp, but Elend couldn't pull his men back any farther toward Fadrex without exposing them to Yomen's archers.

Elend tried to catch his breath as a servant rushed up with a cup of water for him. Cett sat a short distance away, directing the battle tactics. Elend tossed aside the empty cup and moved over to the general, who sat at a small table. It held a map of the area, but hadn't been marked on. The koloss were so close, the battle happening just yards away, that it wasn't really necessary to keep an abstract battle map.

"Never did like having those things in the army," Cett said

as he downed a cup of water himself. A servant moved over, leading a surgeon, who pulled out a bandage to begin working on Elend's arm—which, up until that moment, he hadn't noticed was bleeding.

"Well," Cett noted, "at least we'll die in battle, rather than of starvation!"

Elend snorted, picking up his sword again. The sky was nearly dark. They didn't have much time before—

A figure landed on the table in front of Cett. "Elend!" Vin said. "Retreat to the city. Yomen will let you in."

Elend started. "Vin!" Then, he smiled. "What took you so long?"

"I got delayed by an Inquisitor and a dark god," she said. "Now, hustle. I'll go see if I can distract some of those koloss."

Inquisitors had little chance of resisting Ruin. They had more spikes than any of his other Hemalurgic creations, and that put them completely under his domination.

Yes, it would have taken a man of supreme will to resist Ruin even slightly while bearing the spikes of an Inquisitor.

66

SAZED TRIED NOT TO THINK about how dark the ash was in the sky, or how terrible the land looked.

I've been such a fool, he thought, riding in the saddle. *Of all the times that the world needed something to believe in, this is it. And I wasn't there to give it to them.*

He hurt from so much riding, yet he clung to the saddle, still somewhat amazed at the creature who ran beneath him. When Sazed had first decided to go with TenSoon south, he had despaired at making the trip. Ash fell like the snows of a blizzard, and it had piled terribly high in most places. Sazed had known travel would be difficult, and he'd feared slowing TenSoon, who could obviously travel far more quickly as a wolfhound.

TenSoon considered this concern, then had ordered a horse and a large hog to be brought to him. TenSoon first ingested the hog to give himself extra mass, then molded his gel-like flesh around the horse to digest it as well. Within an hour, he'd formed his body into a replica of the horse—but one with enhanced muscles and weight, creating the enormous, extra-strong marvel which Sazed now rode.

They'd been running nonstop since then. Fortunately, Sazed had some wakefulness he'd stored in a metalmind a year ago, after the siege of Luthadel. He used this to keep himself from falling asleep. It still amazed him that TenSoon could enhance a horse's body so well. It moved with ease through the thick ash, where a real horse—and certainly a human—would have balked at the difficulty. *Another thing I've been a fool about. These last few days, I could have been interrogating TenSoon about his powers. How much more is there that I don't know?*

Despite his shame, however, Sazed felt something of peace within himself. If he'd continued to teach about religions after he'd stopped believing in them, then he would have been a true hypocrite. Tindwyl had believed in giving people hope, even if one had to tell them lies to do so. That's the credit she had given to religion: lies that made people feel better.

Sazed couldn't have acted the same way—at least, he couldn't have done so and remained the person he wanted to be. However, he now had hope. The Terris religion was the one that had taught about the Hero of Ages in the first place. If any contained the truth, it would be this one. Sazed needed to interrogate the First Generation of kandra and discover what they knew.

Though, if I do find the truth, what will I do with it?

The trees they passed were stripped of leaves. The landscape was covered in a good four feet of ash. "How can you keep going like this?" Sazed asked as the kandra galloped over a hilltop, shoving aside ash and ignoring obstructions.

"My people are created from mistwraiths," TenSoon explained, not even sounding winded. "The Lord Ruler turned the Feruchemists into mistwraiths, and they began to breed true as a species. You add a Blessing to a mistwraith, and they become awakened, turning into a kandra. One such as I, created centuries after the Ascension, was born as a mistwraith but became awakened when I received my Blessing."

". . . Blessing?" Sazed asked.

"Two small metal spikes, Keeper," TenSoon said. "We are created like Inquisitors, or like koloss. However, we are more subtle creations than either of those. We were made third and last, as the Lord Ruler's power waned."

Sazed frowned, leaning low as the horse ran beneath some skeletal tree branches.

"What is different about you?"

"We have more independence of will than the other two," TenSoon said. "We only have two spikes in us, while the others have more. An Allomancer can still take control of us, but free we remain more independent of mind than koloss or Inquisitors, who are both affected by Ruin's impulses even when he isn't directly controlling them. Did you never wonder why both of them are driven so powerfully to kill?"

"That doesn't explain how you can carry me, all our baggage, and still run through this ash."

"The metal spikes we carry grant us things," TenSoon said. "Much as Feruchemy gives you strength, or Allomancy gives Vin strength, my Blessing gives me strength. It will never run out, but it isn't as spectacular as the bursts your people can create. Still, my Blessing—mixed with my ability to craft my body as I wish—allows me a high level of endurance."

Sazed fell silent. They continued to gallop.

"There isn't much time left," TenSoon noted.

"I can see that," Sazed said. "It makes me wonder what we can do."

"This is the only time in which we could succeed," TenSoon said. "We must be poised, ready to strike. Ready to aid the Hero of Ages when she comes."

"Comes?"

"She will lead an army of Allomancers to the Homeland," TenSoon said, "and there will save all of us—kandra, human, koloss, and Inquisitor."

An army of Allomancers? "Then . . . what am I to do?"

"You must convince the kandra how dire the situation is," TenSoon explained, slowing to a stop in the ash. "For there is . . . something they must be prepared to do. Something very difficult, yet necessary. My people will resist it, but perhaps you can show them the way."

Sazed nodded, then climbed off of the kandra to stretch his legs.

"Do you recognize this location?" TenSoon asked, turning to look at him with a horse's head.

"I do not," Sazed said. "With the ash . . . well, I haven't really been able to follow our path for days."

"Over that ridge, you will find the place where the Terris people have set up their refugee camp."

Sazed turned with surprise. "The Pits of Hathsin?"

TenSoon nodded. "We call it the Homeland."

"The *Pits*?" Sazed asked with shock. "But . . ."

"Well, not the Pits themselves," TenSoon said. "You know that this entire area has cave complexes beneath it?"

Sazed nodded. The place where Kelsier had trained his original army of skaa soldiers was just a short trip to the north.

"Well, one of those cave complexes is the kandra Homeland. It abuts the Pits of Hathsin—in fact, several of the kandra passages run into the Pits, and had to be kept closed off, lest workers in the Pits find their way into the Homeland."

"Does your Homeland grow atium?" Sazed asked.

"Grow it? No, it does not. That is, I suppose, what separates the Homeland from the Pits of Hathsin. Either way, the entrance to my people's caverns is right there."

Sazed turned with a start. "Where?"

"That depression in the ash," TenSoon said, nodding his large head toward it. "Good luck, Keeper. I have my own duties to attend to."

Sazed nodded, feeling shocked that they had traveled so far so quickly, and untied his pack from the kandra's back. He left the bag containing bones—those of the wolfhound, and another set that looked human. Probably a body TenSoon carried to use should he need it.

The enormous horse turned to go.

"Wait!" Sazed said, raising a hand.

TenSoon looked back.

"Good luck," Sazed said. "May . . . our god preserve you."

TenSoon smiled with a strange equine expression, then took off, galloping through the ash.

Sazed turned to the depression in the ground. Then, he hefted his pack—filled with metalminds and a solitary tome—and walked forward. Even moving that short distance in the ash was difficult. He reached the depression and—taking a breath—began to dig his way into the ash.

He didn't get far before he slid down into a tunnel. It didn't open straight down, fortunately, and he didn't fall far. The cavern around him came up at an incline, opening to the outside world in a hole that was half pit, half cave. Sazed stood up in the cavern, then reached into his pack and pulled out a tinmind. With this, he tapped eyesight, improving his vision as he walked into the darkness.

A tinmind didn't work as well as an Allomancer's tin—or, rather, it didn't work in the same way. It could allow one to see very great distances, but it was of far less help in poor illumination. Soon, even with his tinmind, Sazed was walking in darkness, feeling his way along the tunnel.

And then, he saw light.

"Halt!" a voice called. "Who returns from Contract?"

Sazed continued forward. A part of him was frightened, but another part was just curious. He knew a very important fact.

Kandra could not kill humans.

Sazed stepped up to the light, which turned out to be a melon-sized rock atop a pole, its porous material coated with some kind of glowing fungus. A pair of kandra blocked his path. They were easily identifiable as such since they wore no clothing and their skins were translucent. They appeared to have bones carved from rock.

Fascinating! Sazed thought. *They make their own bones. I really do have a new culture to explore. A whole new society—art, religion, mores, gender interactions. . . .*

The prospect was so exciting that, for a moment, even the end of the world seemed trivial by comparison. He had to remind himself to focus. He needed to investigate their religion first. Other things were secondary.

"Kandra, who are you? Which bones do you wear?"

"You are going to be surprised, I think," Sazed said as gently as he could. "For, I am no kandra. My name is Sazed, Keeper of Terris, and I have been sent to speak with the First Generation."

Both kandra guards started.

"You don't have to let me pass," Sazed said. "Of course, if you don't take me into your Homeland, then I'll have to leave and tell everyone on the outside where it is. . . ."

The guards turned to each other. "Come with us," one of them finally said.

Koloss also had little chance of breaking free.. Four spikes, and their diminished mental capacity, left them fairly easy to dominate. Only in the throes of a blood frenzy did they have any form of autonomy.

Four spikes also made them easier for Allomancers to con-

trol. In our time, it required a duralumin Push to take control of a kandra. Koloss, however, could be taken by a determined regular Push, particularly when they were frenzied.

67

ELEND AND VIN STOOD ATOP the Fadrex City fortifications. The rock ledge had once held the bonfires they'd watched in the night sky—she could see the blackened scar from one of them just to her left.

It felt good to be held by Elend again. His warmth was a comfort, particularly when looking out of the city, over the field that Elend's army had once occupied. The koloss army was growing. It stood silently in the blizzard-like ash, thousands strong. More and more of the creatures were arriving each day, amassing to an overwhelming force.

"Why don't they just attack?" Yomen asked with annoyance. He was the only other one who stood on the overlook; Ham and Cett were down below, seeing to the army's preparation. They'd need to be ready to defend the moment that the koloss assaulted the city.

"He wants us to know just how soundly he's going to beat us," Vin said. *Plus,* she added in her mind, *he's waiting. Waiting on that last bit of information.*

Where is the atium?

She'd fooled Ruin. She'd proven to herself that it could be done. Yet, she was still frustrated. She felt like she'd spent the last few years of her life reacting to every wiggle of Ruin's fingers. Each time she thought herself clever, wise, or self-sacrificing, she discovered that she'd simply been doing his will the entire time. It made her angry.

But what could she do?

I have to make Ruin play his hand, she thought. *Make* him *act, expose himself.*

For a brief moment, back in Yomen's throne room, she had felt something amazing. With the strange power she'd gained from the mists, she'd touched Ruin's own mind—via Marsh—and seen something therein.

Fear. She remembered it, distinct and pure. At that moment, Ruin had been afraid of her. That's why Marsh had fled.

Somehow, she'd taken the power of the mists into her, then used them to perform Allomancy of surpassing might. She'd done it before, when fighting the Lord Ruler in his palace. Why could she only draw on that power at random, unpredictable times? She'd wanted to use it against Zane, but had failed. She'd tried a dozen times during the last few days, just as she'd tried during the days following the Lord Ruler's death. She'd never been able to access even a hint of that power.

It struck like a thunderclap.

A massive, overpowering quake rolled across the land. The rock ledges around Fadrex broke, some of them tumbling to the ground. Vin remained on her feet, but only with the help of pewter, and she barely snatched Yomen by the front of his obligator robes as he careened and almost fell from their ledge. Elend grabbed her arm, reinforcing her as the sudden quake shook the land. Inside the city, several buildings fell.

Then, all went still. Vin breathed heavily, forehead slicked with sweat, Yomen's robes clutched in her grip. She glanced at Elend.

"That one was far worse than the previous ones," he said, cursing quietly to himself.

"We're doomed," Yomen said softly, forcing himself to his feet. "If the things you say are true, then not only is the Lord Ruler dead, but the thing he spent his life fighting has now come to destroy the world."

"We've survived this long," Elend said firmly. "We'll make it yet. Earthquakes may hurt us, but they hurt the koloss too—look, and you'll see that some of them were crushed by toppling rocks. If things get rough up here, we can retreat inside the cavern."

"And will it survive quakes like that one?" Yomen asked.

"Better than the buildings up here will. None of this was built for earthquakes—but if I know the Lord Ruler, he anticipated the quakes, and picked caverns that were solid and capable of withstanding them."

Yomen seemed to take little comfort in the words, but Vin smiled. Not because of what Elend said, but because of how he said it. Something about him had changed. He seemed confident in a way he'd never been before. He had some of the same idealistic air he'd expressed when he'd been a youth at court—yet he also had the hardness of the man who'd led his people in war.

He'd finally found the balance. And, oddly enough, it had come from deciding to retreat.

"He does have a point, however, Vin," Elend said in a softer tone. "We need to figure out our next step. Ruin obviously intended to defeat us here, but he has been pushed back for a time, at least. What now?"

We have to trick him, she thought. *Perhaps . . . use the same strategy Yomen used on me?*

She paused, considering the idea. She reached up, fingering her earring. It had been mangled after its trip through Marsh's head, of course, but it had been a simple matter to have a smith bend it back into shape.

The first time she'd met with Yomen, he'd given her back the earring. It had seemed like a strange move, giving metal to an Allomancer. Yet, in a controlled environment, it had been very clever. He'd been able to test and see if she had any hidden metals—all the while reserving the fact that he could burn atium and protect himself.

Later, he'd been able to get her to reveal her hand, to attack and show him what she was planning, so that he could defuse it in a situation where he was in power. Could she do the same to Ruin?

That thought mixed with another one. Both times when

the mists had helped her, they had come in a moment of pure desperation. It was as if they reacted to her need. So, was there a way to put herself in a situation where her need was even greater than before? It was a thin hope, but—mixed with her desire to force Ruin's hand—it formed a plan in her head.

Put herself in danger. Make Ruin bring his Inquisitors, putting Vin in a situation where the mists *had* to help her. If that didn't work, maybe she could get Ruin to play his hand or spring any hidden traps he had waiting for her.

It was incredibly risky, but she could feel that she didn't have much time. Ruin would win soon—very soon—unless she did *something*. And, this was all she could think of to do. But, how could she make it happen without explaining it to Elend? She couldn't speak of the plan, lest she reveal to Ruin what she was doing.

She looked up at Elend, a man she seemed to know better than herself. He hadn't needed to tell her that he'd reconciled the two halves of himself, she'd simply been able to tell it from looking at him. With a person like that, did she even really need to speak her plans? Perhaps . . . "Elend," she said, "I think there's only one way to save this city."

"And that is?" he said slowly.

"I have to go get *it*."

Elend frowned, then opened his mouth. She looked into his eyes, hoping. He paused.

"The . . . atium?" he guessed.

Vin smiled. "Yes. Ruin knows that we have it. He'll find it even if we don't use it. But, if we bring it here, at least we can fight."

"It would be safer here anyway," Elend said slowly, eyes confused, but trusting her. "I'd rather have an army between those riches and our enemies. Perhaps we could use it to bribe some local warlords to help us."

It seemed a flimsy ruse to her. And yet, she knew that was because she could see Elend's confusion, could read his lies in his eyes. She understood him, as he understood her. It was an understanding that required love.

And she suspected that was something that Ruin would never be able to comprehend.

"I need to leave, then," she said, embracing him tightly, closing her eyes.

"I know."

She held him close for a few moments longer, feeling the ash fall around her, blow against her skin and cheek. Feeling Elend's heart beat beneath her ear. She leaned up and kissed him. Finally, she pulled back, then checked her metals. She met his eyes, and he nodded, so she jumped down into the city to gather some horseshoes.

A few moments later, she was shooting through the ashy air toward Luthadel, a maelstrom of metal around her. Elend stood silently behind, on the rock ledge, watching her go.

Now, she thought to Ruin, who she knew was watching her carefully, even though he hadn't revealed himself since she'd drawn upon the mists. *Let's have a chase, you and I.*

When the Lord Ruler offered his plan to his Feruchemist friends—the plan to change them into mistwraiths—he was making them speak on behalf of all the land's Feruchemists. Though he changed his friends into kandra to restore their minds and memories, the rest he left as nonsentient mistwraiths. These bred more of their kind, living and dying, becoming a race unto themselves. From these children of the original mistwraiths, he made the next generations of kandra.

However, even gods can make mistakes, I have learned. Rashek, the Lord Ruler, thought to transform all of the living Feruchemists into mistwraiths. However, he did not think of the genetic heritage left in the other Terris people, whom he left alive. So it was that Feruchemists continued being born, if only rarely.

This oversight cost him much, but gained the world so much more.

68

SAZED WALKED IN WONDER, LED by his guards. He saw kandra after kandra, each one with a more interesting body than the one before. Some were tall and willowy, with bones made of white wood. Others were stocky, with bones thicker than any human's. All stuck generally to human body shapes, however.

They used to be *human,* he reminded himself. *Or, at least, their ancestors were.*

The caverns around him felt old. The pathways were worn smooth, and while there were no real "buildings," he passed many smaller caverns, varied drapery hanging in front of their openings. There was a sense of exquisite craftsmanship to it all, from the carved poles that held the fungus lights, to the very bones of the people around him. It wasn't the detailed ornamentation of a nobleman's keep, for there were no patterns, leaves, or knots carved into the stonework or bones. Instead, things were polished smooth, carved with rounded sides, or woven in broad lines and shapes.

The kandra seemed afraid of him. It was a strange experience for Sazed. He had been many things in his life: rebel, servant, friend, scholar. However, never before had he found himself an object of fear. Kandra ducked around corners, peeking at him. Others stood in shock, watching him pass. Obviously, news of his arrival had spread quickly, otherwise they would have just assumed him to be a kandra wearing human bones.

His guards led him to a steel door set into a large cavern

wall. One of them moved inside, while the other guarded Sazed. Sazed noticed shards of metal twinkling in the kandra's shoulders. They appeared to be spikes, one in each shoulder.

Smaller than Inquisitor spikes, Sazed thought. *But still very effective. Interesting.*

"What would you do if I were to run?" Sazed asked.

The kandra started. "Um . . ."

"Can I assume from your hesitance that you are still forbidden to harm, or at least kill, a human?" Sazed asked.

"We follow the First Contract."

"Ah," Sazed said. "Very interesting. And, with whom did you make the First Contract?"

"The Father."

"The Lord Ruler?" Sazed asked.

The kandra nodded.

"He is, unfortunately and truly, dead. So, is your Contract no longer valid?"

"I don't know," the kandra said, looking away.

So, Sazed thought, *not all of them are as forceful of personality as TenSoon. Even when he was playing the part of a simple wolfhound, I found him to be intense.*

The other soldier returned. "Come with me," he said.

They led Sazed through the open metal doors. The room beyond had a large metal pedestal a few feet high. The guards did not step on it, but led Sazed around it toward a place before a group of stone lecterns. Many of the lecterns were empty, though kandra with twinkling bones stood behind two of them. These creatures were tall—or, at least, they used tall bones—and very fine-featured.

Aristocrats, Sazed thought. He had found that class of people very easy to identify, no matter what the culture or—apparently—species.

Sazed's guards gestured for him to stand before the lecterns. Sazed ignored the gestures, walking in a circle around the room. As he had expected, his guards didn't know what to do—they followed, but refrained from putting their hands on him.

"There is metal plating surrounding the entire chamber," Sazed noted. "Is it ornamental, or does it serve a function?"

"We will be asking the questions here, Terrisman!" said one of the aristocratic kandra.

Sazed paused, turning. "No," he said. "No, you will not. I am Sazed, Keeper of Terris. However, among your people, I have another name. Holy Announcer."

The other kandra leader snorted. "What does an outsider know of such things?"

"An outsider?" Sazed asked. "You should better learn your own doctrine, I think." He began to walk forward. "I am Terris, as are you. Yes, I know your origins. I know how you were created—and I know the heritage you bring with you."

He stopped before their lecterns. "I announce to you that I have discovered the Hero. I have lived with her, worked with her, and watched her. I handed her the very spear she used to slay the Lord Ruler. I have seen her take command of kings, watched her overcome armies of both men and koloss. I have come to announce this to you, so that you may prepare yourselves."

He paused, eyeing them. "For the end is here," he added.

The two kandra stood quietly for a few moments. "Go get the others," one finally said, his voice shaking.

Sazed smiled. As one of the guards ran off, Sazed turned to face down the second soldier. "I shall require a table and chair, please. Also, something with which to write."

A few minutes later, all was ready. His kandra attendants had swelled from four to over twenty—twelve of them being the aristocratic ones with the twinkling bones. Some attendants had set up a small table for Sazed, and he seated himself as the kandra nobles spoke together in anxious whispers.

Carefully, Sazed placed his pack on the table and began to remove his metalminds. Small rings, smaller earrings and studs, and large bracers soon lined the table. He pushed up his sleeves, then clasped on his copperminds—two large bracers on the upper arms, then two bracers on the forearms. Finally, he removed his tome from the pack and set it on the table. Some kandra approached with thin plates of metal. Sazed watched curiously as they arranged them for him, along with what appeared to be a steel pen, capable of making indentations in the soft writing metal. The kandra servants bowed and withdrew.

Excellent, Sazed thought, picking up the metal pen and clearing his throat. The kandra leaders turned toward him.

"I assume," Sazed said, "that you are the First Generation?"

"We are the Second Generation, Terrisman," one of the kandra said.

"Well, I apologize for taking your time, then. Where can I find your superiors?"

The lead kandra snorted. "Do not think you have us quelled just because you were able to draw us together. I see no reason for you to speak with the First Generation, even if you can blaspheme quite accurately."

Sazed raised an eyebrow. "Blaspheme?"

"You are not the Announcer," the kandra said. "This is not the end."

"Have you seen the ash up above?" Sazed said. "Or, has it stopped up the entrances to this cavern complex so soundly that nobody can escape to see that the world is falling apart?"

"We have lived a very long time, Terrisman," one of the other kandra said. "We have seen periods where the ash fell more copiously than others."

"Oh?" Sazed asked. "And you have, perhaps, seen the Lord Ruler die before as well?"

Some of the kandra looked uncomfortable at this, though the one at the lead shook his head. "Did TenSoon send you?"

"He did," Sazed admitted.

"You can make no arguments other than those he has already made," the kandra said. "Why would he think that you—an outsider—could persuade us, when he could not?"

"Perhaps because he understood something about me," Sazed said, tapping his book with his pen. "Are you aware of the ways of Keepers, kandra?"

"My name is KanPaar," the kandra said. "And yes, I understand what Keepers do—or, at least, what they did, before the Father was killed."

"Then," Sazed said, "perhaps you know that every Keeper has an area of specialty. The intention was that when the Lord Ruler finally did fall, we would already be divided into specialists who could teach our knowledge to the people."

"Yes," KanPaar said.

"Well," Sazed said, rubbing fingers over his book. "My specialty was religion. Do you know how many religions there were before the Lord Ruler's Ascension?"

"I don't know. Hundreds."

"We have record of five hundred and sixty-three," Sazed said. "Though that includes sects of the same religions. In a more strict count, there were around three hundred."

"And?" KanPaar asked.

"Do you know how many of these survived until this day?" Sazed asked.

"None?"

"One," Sazed said, holding up a finger. "Yours. The Terris religion. Do you think it a coincidence that the religion you follow not only still exists, but also foretells this exact day?"

KanPaar snorted. "You are saying nothing new. So my religion is real, while others were lies. What does that explain?"

"That you should listen, perhaps, to members of your faith who bring you tidings." Sazed began to flip through his book. "At the very least, I would think that you'd be interested in this book, as it contains the collected information about the Hero of Ages that I was able to discover. Since I knew little of the true Terris religion, I had to get my information from secondhand accounts—from tales and stories, and from texts written during the intermediate time.

"Unfortunately," Sazed continued, "much of this text was changed by Ruin when he was trying to persuade the Hero to visit the Well of Ascension and set him free. Therefore, it is quite well corrupted and tainted by his touch."

"And why would I be interested?" KanPaar asked. "You just told me that your information is corrupt and useless."

"Useless?" Sazed asked. "No, not useless at all. Corrupt, yes. Changed by Ruin. My friend, I have a tome here filled with Ruin's lies. You have a mind filled with the original truths. Apart, we know very little. However, if we were to *compare*—discovering precisely which items Ruin changed—would it not tell us exactly what his plan is? At the very least, it would tell us what he didn't want us to focus on, I think."

The room fell silent.

"Well," KanPaar finally said, "I—"

"That will be enough, KanPaar," a voice said.

Sazed paused, cocking his head. The voice hadn't come from any of those beside the pedestals. Sazed glanced around the room, trying to discover who had spoken.

"You may leave, Seconds," another voice said.

One of the Seconds gasped. "Leave? Leave you with this one, an outsider?"

"A descendant," one of the voices said. "A Worldbringer. We will hear him."

"Leave us," said another voice.

Sazed raised an eyebrow, sitting as the Second Generationers—looking rattled—left their lecterns and quietly made their way from the room. A pair of guards pushed the doors shut, blocking the view of those kandra who had been watching outside. Sazed was left alone in the room with the phantoms who had spoken.

Sazed heard a scraping sound. It echoed through the steel-lined chamber, and then a door opened at the back of the room. From this came what he assumed was the First Generation. They looked . . . old. Their kandra flesh literally hung from their bodies, drooping, like translucent tree moss dripping from bone branches. They were stooped, seeming older than the other kandra he had seen, and they didn't walk so much as shuffle.

They wore simple robes, with no sleeves, but the garments still looked odd on the creatures. In addition, beneath their translucent skin, he could see that they had white, normal skeletons. "Human bones?" Sazed asked as the elderly creatures made their way forward, walking with canes.

"Our own bones," one of them said, speaking with a tired near-whisper of a voice. "We hadn't the skill or knowledge to form True Bodies when this all began, and so took our original bones again when the Lord Ruler gave them to us."

The First Generation appeared to have only ten members. They arranged themselves on the benches. And, out of respect, Sazed moved his table so that he was seated before them, like a presenter before an audience.

"Now," he said, raising his metal scratching pen. "Let us begin—we have much work to do."

The question remains, where did the original prophecies about the Hero of Ages come from? I now know that Ruin changed them, but did not fabricate them. Who first taught that a Hero would come, one who would be an emperor of all mankind, yet would be rejected by his own people? Who first stated he would carry the future of the world on his arms, or that he would repair that which had been sundered?

And who decided to use the neutral pronoun, so that we wouldn't know if the Hero was a woman or a man?

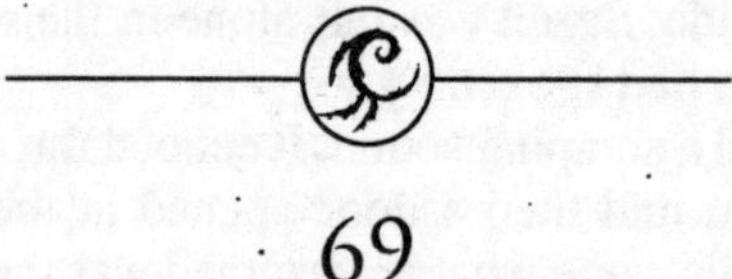

69

MARSH KNELT IN A PILE of ash, hating himself and the world. The ash fell without cease, drifting onto his back, covering him, and yet he did not move.

He had been cast aside, told to sit and wait. Like a tool forgotten in the yard, slowly being covered in snow.

I was there, he thought. *With Vin. Yet . . . I couldn't speak to her. Couldn't tell her anything.*

Worse . . . he hadn't wanted to. During his entire conversation with her, his body and mind had belonged to Ruin completely. Marsh had been helpless to resist, hadn't been able to do anything that might have let Vin kill him.

Except for a moment. A moment near the end, when she'd almost taken control of him. A moment when he'd seen something inside of his master—his god, his *self*—that gave him hope.

For in that moment, Ruin had feared her.

And then, Ruin had forced Marsh to run, leaving behind his army of koloss—the army that Marsh had been ordered to let Elend Venture steal, then bring to Fadrex. The army that Ruin had eventually stolen back.

And now Marsh waited in the ash.

What is the point? he thought. His master wanted something . . . needed something . . . and he feared Vin. Those two things gave Marsh hope, but what could he do? Even in Ruin's moment of weakness, Marsh had been unable to take control.

Marsh's plan—to wait, keeping the rebellious sliver of himself secret until the right moment, then pull out the spike in his back and kill himself—seemed increasingly foolish. How could he hope to break free, even for that long?

Stand.

The command came wordlessly, but Marsh reacted instantly. And Ruin was back, controlling his body. With effort, Marsh retained some small control of his mind, though only because Ruin seemed distracted. Marsh started dropping coins, Pushing off them, using and reusing them in the same way Vin used horseshoes. Horseshoes—which had far more metal—would have been better, for they would have let him Push farther with each one. But, he made coins work.

He propelled himself through the late-afternoon sky. The red air was unpleasantly abrasive, so crowded with ash. Marsh watched it, trying to keep himself from seeing beauty in the destruction without alerting Ruin that he wasn't completely dominated.

It was difficult.

After some time—after night had long since fallen—Ruin commanded Marsh to the ground. He descended quickly, robes flapping, and landed atop a short hill. The ash came up to his waist, and he was probably standing on a few feet of packed ash underneath.

In the distance, down the slope, a solitary figure pushed resolutely through the ash. The man wore a pack and led an exhausted horse.

Who is this? Marsh thought, looking closer. The man had the build of a soldier, with a square face and balding head, his jaw bearing several days' worth of beard. Whoever he was, he had an impressive determination. Few people would brave the mists—yet this man not only walked through them, but forged his way through ash that was as high as his chest. The man's uniform was stained black, as was his skin. Dark . . . ashen . . .

Beautiful.

Marsh launched himself from the hilltop, hurling through the mist and ash on a Push of steel. The man below must have heard him coming, for he spun, reaching anxiously for the sword at his side.

Marsh landed atop the horse's back. The creature cried out, rearing, and Marsh jumped, placing one foot on the beast's face as he flipped over it and landed in the ash. The soldier had worn a path straight ahead, and Marsh felt as if he were looking down a tight, black corridor.

The man whipped his sword free. The horse whinnied nervously, stamping in the ash.

Marsh smiled, and pulled an obsidian axe from the sheath by his side. The soldier backed away, trying to clear room in the ash for a fight. Marsh saw the worry in the man's eyes, the dreadful anticipation.

The horse whinnied again. Marsh spun and sheared off its front legs, causing it to scream in pain. Behind, the soldier moved. And—surprisingly—instead of running, he attacked.

The man rammed his sword through Marsh's back. It hit a spike, veering to the side, but still impaled him. Marsh turned, smiling, and tapped healing to keep himself standing.

The man kept moving, reaching up for Marsh's back, obviously intending to try and pull free the back spike. Marsh burned pewter, however, and spun out of the way, ripping away the soldier's weapon.

Should have let him grab it . . . the free sliver said, struggling, yet useless.

Marsh swung for the man's head, intending to take it off with a single sweep of the axe, but the soldier rolled in the ash, whipping a dagger from his boot and swiping in an attempt to hamstring Marsh. A clever move, which would have left Marsh on the ground, healing power or not.

However, Marsh tapped speed. He suddenly moved several times faster than a normal person, and he easily dodged the slice, instead planting a kick in the soldier's chest.

The man grunted as his ribs cracked. He fell in the ash, rolling and coughing, blood on his lips. He came to a stop, covered in ash. Weakly, he reached for his pocket.

Another dagger? Marsh thought. However, the man pulled out a folded sheet. Metal?

Marsh had a sudden and overpowering desire to grab that sheet of metal. The soldier struggled to crumple the thin sheet, to destroy its contents, but Marsh screamed and brought his axe down on the man's arm, shearing it off. Marsh raised the axe again, and this time took off the man's head.

He didn't stop, however, the blood fury driving him to slam his axe into the corpse over and over again. In the back of his head, he could feel Ruin exulting in the death—yet, he could also sense frustration. Ruin tried to pull him away from the killing, to make him grab that slip of metal, but in the grip of the bloodlust, Marsh couldn't be controlled. Just like koloss.

Couldn't be controlled. . . . That's—

He froze, Ruin taking control once again. Marsh shook his head, the man's blood rolling down his face, dripping from his chin. He turned and glanced at the dying horse, which screamed in the quiet night. Marsh stumbled to his feet, then reached for the disembodied arm, pulling free the sheet of metal the soldier had tried to destroy with his dying strength.

Read it!

The words were distinct in Marsh's mind. Rarely did Ruin bother to address him—it just used him like a puppet.

Read it aloud!

Marsh frowned, slowly unfolding the letter, trying to give himself time to think. Why would Ruin need him to read it? Unless . . . Ruin couldn't read? But, that didn't make sense. The creature had been able to change the words in books.

It had to be able to read. Then, was it the metal that stopped Ruin?

He had the flap of metal unfolded. There were indeed words scratched into its inside surface. Marsh tried to resist reading the words. In fact, he longed to grab his axe from where it had fallen dripping blood in the ash, then use it to kill himself. But, he couldn't manage. He didn't even have enough freedom to drop the letter. Ruin pushed and pulled, manipulating Marsh's emotions, eventually getting him so that . . .

Yes. Why should he bother disagreeing? Why argue with his god, his lord, his self? Marsh held the sheet up, flaring his tin to get a better look at its contents in the darkness.

" 'Vin,' " he read. " 'My mind is clouded. A part of me wonders what is real anymore. Yet, one thing seems to press on me again and again. I must tell you something. I don't know if it will matter, but I must say it nonetheless.

" 'The thing we fight is real. I have seen it. It tried to destroy me, and it tried to destroy the people of Urteau. It got control of me through a method I wasn't expecting. Metal. A little sliver of metal piercing my body. With that, it was able to twist my thoughts. It couldn't take complete control of me, like you control the koloss, but it did something similar, I think. Perhaps the piece of metal wasn't big enough. I don't know.

" 'Either way, it appeared to me, taking the form of Kelsier. It did the same thing to the king here in Urteau. It is clever. It is subtle.

" 'Be careful, Vin. Don't trust anyone pierced by metal! Even the smallest bit can taint a man.

" 'Spook.' "

Marsh, again completely controlled by Ruin, crumpled the metal up until its scratchings were unreadable. Then, he tossed it into the ash and used it as an anchor to Push himself into the air. Toward Luthadel.

He left the corpses of horse, man, and message to lie dead in the ash, slowly being buried.

Like forgotten tools.

Quellion actually placed his spike himself, as I understand it. The man was never entirely stable. His fervor for following Kelsier and killing the nobility was enhanced by Ruin, but Quellion had already had the impulses. His passionate paranoia bordered on insanity at times, and Ruin was able to prod him into placing that crucial spike.

Quellion's spike was bronze, and he made it from one of the first Allomancers he captured. That spike made him a Seeker, which was one of the ways he was able to find and blackmail so many Allomancers during his time as king of Urteau.

The point, however, is that people with unstable personalities were more susceptible to Ruin's influence, even if they didn't have a spike in them. That, indeed, is likely how Zane got his spike.

70

"I STILL DON'T SEE WHAT good this does," Yomen said, walking beside Elend as they passed Fadrex's gate.

Elend ignored the comment, waving a greeting to a group of soldiers. He stopped beside another group—not his, but

Yomen's—and inspected their weapons. He gave them a few words of encouragement, then moved on. Yomen watched quietly, walking at Elend's side as an equal, not a captured king.

The two had an uneasy truce, but the field of koloss outside was more than enough of a motivation to keep them working together. Elend had the larger army of the two, but not by much—and they were growing increasingly outnumbered as more and more koloss arrived.

"We should be working on the sanitation problem," Yomen continued once they were out of the men's earshot. "An army exists on two principles: health and food. Provide those two things, and you will be victorious."

Elend smiled, recognizing the reference. Trentison's *Supplying in Scale.* A few years earlier, he would have agreed with Yomen, and the two would probably have spent the afternoon discussing the philosophy of leadership in Yomen's palace. However, Elend had learned things in the last few years that he simply hadn't been able to get from his studies.

Unfortunately, that meant he really couldn't explain them to Yomen—particularly not in the time they had. So, instead, he nodded down the street. "We can move on to the infirmary now, if you wish, Lord Yomen."

Yomen nodded, and the two turned toward another section of the city. The obligator had a no-nonsense approach to just about everything. Problems should be dealt with quickly and directly. He had a good mind, despite his fondness for making snap judgments.

As they walked, Elend was careful to keep an eye out for soldiers—on duty or off—in the streets. He nodded to their salutes, met their eyes. Many were working to repair the damages caused by the increasingly powerful earthquakes. Perhaps it was just in Elend's mind, but it seemed that the soldiers walked a little taller after he passed.

Yomen frowned slightly as he watched Elend do this. The obligator still wore the robes of his station, despite the little bead of atium at his brow that he used to mark his kingship. The tattoos on the man's forehead almost seemed to curl toward the bead, as if they had been designed with it in mind.

"You don't know much about leading soldiers, do you, Yomen?" Elend asked.

The obligator raised an eyebrow. "I know more than you ever will about tactics, supply lines, and the running of armies between distinct points."

"Oh?" Elend said lightly. "So, you've read Bennitson's *Armies in Motion,* have you?" The "distinct points" line was a dead giveaway.

Yomen's frown deepened.

"One thing that we scholars tend to forget about, Yomen, is the impact *emotion* can have on a battle. It isn't just about food, shoes, and clean water, necessary as those are. It's about hope, courage, and the will to live. Soldiers need to know that their leader will be in the fight—if not killing enemies, then directing things personally from behind the lines. They can't think of him as an abstract force up on a tower somewhere, watching out a window and pondering the depths of the universe."

Yomen fell silent as they walked through streets that, despite being cleaned of ash, had a forlorn cast to them. Most of the people had retreated to the back portions of the city, where the koloss would go last, if they broke through. They were camping outside, since buildings were unsafe in the quakes.

"You are an . . . interesting man, Elend Venture," Yomen finally said.

"I'm a bastard," Elend said.

Yomen raised an eyebrow.

"In composition, not in temperament or by birth," Elend said with a smile. "I'm an amalgamation of what I've needed to be. Part scholar, part rebel, part nobleman, part Mistborn, and part soldier. Sometimes, I don't even know myself. I had a devil of a time getting all those pieces to work together. And, just when I'm starting to get it figured out, the world up and ends on me. Ah, here we are."

Yomen's infirmary was a converted Ministry building—which, in Elend's opinion, showed that Yomen was willing to be flexible. His religious buildings weren't so sacred to him that he couldn't acknowledge that they were the best facilities for taking care of the sick and wounded. Inside, they found physicians tending those who had survived the initial clash with the koloss. Yomen bustled off to speak with the infirmary bureaucrats—apparently, he was worried about the number of infections that the men had suffered. Elend walked over to the section with the most serious cases, and began visiting them, offering encouragement.

It was tough work, looking at the soldiers who had suffered because of his foolishness. How could he have missed seeing that Ruin could take the koloss back? It made so much sense. And yet, Ruin had played its hand well—it had misled Elend, making him think that the Inquisitors were controlling the koloss. Making him feel the koloss could be counted on.

What would have happened, he thought, *if I'd attacked this city with them as originally planned?* Ruin would have ransacked Fadrex, slaughtering everyone inside, and *then* turned the koloss on Elend's soldiers. Now the fortifications defended by Elend and Yomen's men had given Ruin enough pause to make it build up its forces before attacking.

I have doomed this city, Elend thought, sitting beside the bed of a man who had lost his arm to a koloss blade.

It frustrated him. He knew he'd made the right decision. And, in truth, he'd rather be inside the city—almost certainly doomed—than be outside besieging it, and winning. For he knew that the winning side wasn't always the right side.

Still, it came back to his continuing frustration at his inability to protect his people. And, despite Yomen's rule of Fadrex, Elend considered its people to be his people. He'd taken the Lord Ruler's throne, named himself emperor. The entirety of the Final Empire was his to care for. What good was a ruler who couldn't even protect one city, let alone an empire full of them?

A disturbance at the front of the infirmary room caught

his attention. He cast aside his dark thoughts, then bid farewell to the soldier. He rushed to the front of the hospital, where Yomen had already appeared to see what the ruckus was about. A woman stood holding a young boy, who was shaking uncontrollably with the fits.

One of the physicians rushed forward, taking the boy. "Mistsickness?" he asked.

The woman, weeping, nodded. "I kept him inside until today. I knew! I knew that it wanted him! Oh, please . . ."

Yomen shook his head as the physician took the boy to a bed. "You should have listened to me, woman," he said firmly. "Everyone in the city was to have been exposed to the mists. Now your son will take a bed that we may need for wounded soldiers."

The woman slumped down, still crying. Yomen sighed, though Elend could see the concern in the man's eyes. Yomen was not a heartless man, just a pragmatic one. In addition, his words made sense. It was no use hiding someone inside all of their lives, just because of the possibility that they might fall to the mists.

Fall to the mists . . . Elend thought idly, glancing at the boy in bed. He had stopped convulsing, though his face was twisted in an expression of pain. It looked like he hurt so much. Elend had only hurt that much once in his life.

We never did figure out what this mistsickness was all about, he thought. The mist spirit had never returned to him. But, perhaps Yomen knew something.

"Yomen," he said, walking up to the man, distracting him from his discussion with the surgeons. "Did any of your people ever figure out the reason for the mistsickness?"

"Reason?" Yomen asked. "Does there need to be a reason for a sickness?"

"There does for one this strange," Elend said. "Did you realize that it strikes down exactly sixteen percent of the population? Sixteen percent—to the man."

Instead of being surprised, Yomen just shrugged. "Makes sense."

"Sense?" Elend asked.

"Sixteen is a powerful number, Venture," Yomen said, looking over some reports. "It was the number of days it took the Lord Ruler to reach the Well of Ascension, for instance. It figures prominently in Church doctrine."

Of course, Elend thought. *Yomen wouldn't be surprised to find order in nature—he believes in a god who ordered that nature.*

"Sixteen . . ." Elend said, glancing at the sick boy.

"The number of original Inquisitors," Yomen said. "The number of Precepts in each Canton charter. The number of Allomantic metals. The—"

"Wait," Elend said, looking up. "What?"

"Allomantic metals," Yomen said.

"There are only fourteen of those."

Yomen shook his head. "Fourteen we know of, assuming your lady was right about the metal paired to aluminum. However, fourteen is not a number of power. Allomantic metals come in sets of two, with groupings of four. It seems likely that there are two more we haven't discovered, bringing the number to sixteen. Two by two by two by two. Four physical metals, four mental metals, four enhancement metals, and four temporal metals."

Sixteen metals . . .

Elend glanced at the boy again. Pain. Elend had known such pain once—the day his father had ordered him beaten. Beaten to give him such pain that he thought he might die. Beaten to bring his body to a point near death, so that he would Snap.

Beaten to discover if he was an Allomancer.

Lord Ruler! Elend thought with shock. He dashed away from Yomen, pushing back into the soldiers' section of the infirmary.

"Who here was taken by the mists?" Elend demanded.

The wounded regarded him with quizzical looks.

"Did any of you get sick?" Elend asked. "When I made you stand out in the mists? Please, I must know!"

Slowly, the man with one arm raised his remaining hand.

"I was taken, my lord. I'm sorry. This wound is probably punishment for—"

Elend cut the man off, rushing forward, pulling out his spare metal vial. "Drink this," he commanded.

The man paused, then did as asked. Elend knelt beside the bed eagerly, waiting. His heart pounded in his chest. "Well?" he finally asked.

"Well . . . what, my lord?" the soldier asked.

"Do you feel anything?" Elend asked.

The soldier shrugged. "Tired, my lord?"

Elend closed his eyes, sighing. *It was a silly—*

"Well, that's odd," the soldier suddenly said.

Elend snapped his eyes open.

"Yes," the soldier said, looking a bit distracted. "I . . . I don't know what to make of *that*."

"Burn it," Elend said, turning on his bronze. "Your body knows how, if you let it."

The soldier's frown deepened, and he cocked his head. Then, he began to thump with Allomantic power.

Elend closed his eyes again, exhaling softly.

Yomen was walking up behind Elend. "What is this?"

"The mists were never our enemy, Yomen," Elend said, eyes still closed. "They were just trying to help."

"Help? Help how? What are you talking about?"

Elend opened his eyes, turning. "They weren't killing us, Yomen. They weren't making us sick. They were *Snapping* us. Bringing us power. Making us able to fight."

"My lord!" a voice suddenly called. Elend turned as a frazzled soldier stumbled into the room. "My lords! The koloss are attacking! They're charging the city!"

Elend felt a start. *Ruin. It knows what I just discovered—it knows it needs to attack now, rather than wait for more troops.*

Because I know the secret!

"Yomen, gather every bit of powdered metal you can find in this city!" Elend yelled. "Pewter, tin, steel, and iron! Get it to anyone who has been stricken by the mists! Make them drink it down!"

"Why?" Yomen said, still confused.

Elend turned, smiling. "Because they are now Allomancers. This city isn't going to fall as easily as everyone assumed. If you need me, I'll be on the front lines!"

There is something special about the number sixteen. For one thing, it was Preservation's sign to mankind.

Preservation knew, even before he imprisoned Ruin, that he wouldn't be able to communicate with humankind once he diminished himself. And so, he left clues—clues that couldn't be altered by Ruin. Clues that related back to the fundamental laws of the universe. The number was meant to be proof that something unnatural was happening, and that there was help to be found.

It may have taken us long to figure this out, but when we eventually did understand the clue—late though it was—it provided a much-needed boost.

As for the other aspects of the number . . . well, even I am still investigating that. Suffice it to say that it has great ramifications regarding how the world, and the universe itself, works.

71

SAZED TAPPED HIS PEN AGAINST the metal paper, frowning slightly. "Very little of this last chunk is different from what I knew before," he said. "Ruin changed small things—perhaps to keep me from noticing the alterations. It's obvious that he wanted to make me realize that Vin was the Hero of Ages."

"He wanted her to release him," said Haddek, leader of the First Generation. His companions nodded.

"Perhaps she was never the Hero," one of the others offered.

Sazed shook his head. "I believe that she is. These prophecies still refer to her—even the unaltered ones that you have told me. They talk of one who is separate from the Terris people, a king of men, a rebel caught between two worlds. Ruin just *emphasized* that Vin was the one, since he wanted her to come and free him."

"We always assumed that the Hero would be a man," Haddek said in his wheezing voice.

"So did everyone else," Sazed said. "But, you said yourself that all the prophecies use gender-neutral pronouns. That had to be intentional—one does not use such language in old Terris by accident. The neutral case was chosen so that we wouldn't know whether the Hero was male or female."

Several of the ancient Terrismen nodded. They worked by the quiet blue light of the glowing stones, still sitting in the chamber with the metal walls—which, from what Sazed had been able to gather, was something of a holy place for the kandra.

He tapped his pen, frowning. What was bothering him? *They say I will hold the future of the entire world on my arms. . . .* Alendi's words, from his logbook written so long ago. The words of the First Generation confirmed that was true.

There was still something for Vin to do. Yet, the power at the Well of Ascension was gone. Used up. How could she fight without it? Sazed looked up at his audience of ancient kandra. "What *was* the power at the Well of Ascension, anyway?"

"Even we are not certain of that, young one," Haddek said. "By the time we lived as men, our gods had already passed from this world, leaving the Terris with only the hope of the Hero."

"Tell me of this thing," Sazed said, leaning forward. "How did your gods pass from this world?"

"Ruin and Preservation," said one of the others. "They created our world, and our people."

"Neither could create alone," Haddek said. "No, they

could not. For, to preserve something is not to create it—and neither can you create through destruction only."

It was a common theme in mythology—Sazed had read it in dozens of the religions he'd studied. The world being created out of a clash between two forces, sometimes rendered as chaos and order, sometimes named destruction and protection. That bothered him a little bit. He was hoping to discover something *new* in the things men were telling him.

And yet . . . just because something was common, did that make it false? Or, could all of those mythologies have a shared, and true, root?

"They created the world," Sazed said. "Then left?"

"Not immediately," Haddek said. "But, here is the trick, young one. They had a deal, those two. Preservation wanted to create men—to create life capable of emotion. He obtained a promise from Ruin to help make men."

"But at a cost," one of the others whispered.

"What cost?" Sazed asked.

"That Ruin could one day be allowed to destroy the world," Haddek replied.

The circular chamber fell silent.

"Hence the betrayal," Haddek said. "Preservation gave his life to imprison Ruin, to keep him from destroying the world."

Another common mythological theme—the martyr god. It was one that Sazed himself had witnessed in the birth of the Church of the Survivor.

Yet . . . this time it's my own religion, he thought. He frowned, leaning back, trying to decide how he felt. For some reason, he had assumed that the truth would be *different.* The scholarly side of him argued with his desire for belief. How could he believe in something so filled with mythological clichés?

He'd come all this way, believing that he'd been given one last chance to find the truth. Yet, now that he studied it, he was finding that it was shockingly similar to religions he had rejected as false.

"You seem disturbed, child," Haddek said. "Are you that worried about the things we say?"

"I apologize," Sazed said. "This is a personal problem, not related to the fate of the Hero of Ages."

"Please, speak," one of the others said.

"It is complicated," Sazed said. "For some time now, I have been searching through the religions of mankind, trying to ascertain which of their teachings were true. I had begun to despair that I would *ever* find a religion that offered the answers I sought. Then, I learned that my own religion still existed, protected by the kandra. I came here, hoping to find the truth."

"This is the truth," one of the kandra said.

"That's what *every* religion teaches," Sazed said, frustration mounting. "Yet, in each of them I find inconsistencies, logical leaps, and demands of faith I find impossible to accept.

"It sounds to me, young one," Haddek said, "that you're searching for something that cannot be found."

"The truth?" Sazed said.

"No," Haddek replied. "A religion that requires no faith of its believers."

Another of the kandra elders nodded. "We follow the Father and the First Contract, but our faith is not in him. It's in . . . something higher. We trust that Preservation planned for this day, and that his desire to protect will prove more powerful than Ruin's desire to destroy."

"But you don't know," Sazed said. "You are offered proof only once you believe, but if you believe, you can find proof in anything. It is a logical conundrum."

"Faith isn't about logic, son," Haddek said. "Perhaps that's your problem. You cannot 'disprove' the things you study, any more than we can prove to you that the Hero will save us. We simply must believe it, and accept the things Preservation has taught us."

It wasn't enough for Sazed. However, for the moment, he decided to move on. He didn't have all the facts about the Terris religion yet. Perhaps once he had them, he would be able to sort this all out.

"You spoke of the prison of Ruin," Sazed said. "Tell me how this relates to the power that Lady Vin used."

"Gods don't have bodies like those of men," Haddek said. "They are . . . forces. Powers. Preservation's mind passed, but he left his power behind."

"In the form of a pool of liquid?" Sazed said.

The members of the First Generation nodded.

"And the dark black smoke outside?" Sazed asked.

"Ruin," Haddek said. "Waiting, watching, during his imprisonment."

Sazed frowned. "The cavern of smoke was very much larger than the Well of Ascension. Why the disparity? Was Ruin *that* much more powerful?"

Haddek snorted quietly. "They were equally powerful, young one. They were *forces,* not men. Two aspects of a single power. Is one side of a coin more 'powerful' than the other? They pushed equally upon the world around them."

"Though," one of the others added, "there is a story that Preservation gave too much of himself to make mankind, to create something that had *more* of Preservation in them than they had of Ruin. Yet, it would be only a small amount in each individual. Tiny . . . easy to miss, except over a long, long time . . ."

"So, why the difference in size?" Sazed asked.

"You aren't seeing, young one," Haddek said. "The power in that pool, that wasn't Preservation."

"But, you just said—"

"It was *part* of Preservation, to be sure," Haddek continued. "But, he was a force—his influence is everywhere. Some of it, perhaps, concentrated into that pool. The rest is . . . elsewhere and everywhere."

"But Ruin, his mind was focused there," another kandra said. "And so, his power tended to coalesce there. Much more of it, at least, than that of Preservation."

"But not all of it," another one said, laughing.

Sazed cocked his head. "Not all of it? It, too, was spread out across the world, I assume?"

"In a way," Haddek said.

"We now speak of things in the First Contract," one of the other kandra warned.

Haddek paused, then turned, studying Sazed's eyes. "If what this man says is true, then Ruin has escaped. That means he will be coming for his body. His . . . power."

Sazed felt a chill. "It's here?" he asked quietly.

Haddek nodded. "We were to gather it. The First Contract, the Lord Ruler named it—our charge in this world."

"The other Children had a purpose," another kandra added. "The koloss, they were created to fight. The Inquisitors, they were created to be priests. Our task was different."

"Gather the power," Haddek said. "And protect it. Hide it. Keep it. For the Father knew Ruin would escape one day. And on that day, he would begin searching for his body."

The group of aged kandra looked past Sazed. He frowned, turning to follow their eyes. They were looking toward the metal dais.

Slowly, Sazed stood, walking across the stone floor. The dais was large—perhaps twenty feet across—but not very high. He stepped onto it, causing one of the kandra behind him to gasp. Yet, none of them called out to stop him.

There was a seam down the middle of the circular platform, and a hole—perhaps the size of a large coin—at the center. Sazed peered through the hole, but it was too dark to see anything.

He stepped back.

I should have a little left, he thought, glancing toward his table, with its metalminds. *I refilled that ring for a few months before I gave up on my metalminds.*

He walked over quickly, selecting a small pewter ring off of the table. He slipped it on, then looked up at the members of the First Generation. They turned from his querying look.

"Do what you must, child," Haddek said, his aged voice echoing in the room. "We could not stop you if we wished."

Sazed walked back to the dais, then tapped his pewtermind for the strength he had stored in it over a year ago. His body immediately grew several times stronger than normal, and his robes suddenly felt tight. With hands now thick with muscles, he reached down and—bracing himself against the rough floor—shoved against one side of the disk on the floor.

It ground against stone as it moved, uncovering a large pit. Something glittered beneath.

Sazed froze, his strength—and body—deflating as he released his pewtermind. His robes became loose again. The room was silent. Sazed stared at the half-covered pit, and at the enormous pile of nuggets hidden in the floor.

"The Trust, we call it," Haddek said with a soft voice. "Given for our safekeeping by the Father."

Atium. Thousands upon thousands of beads of it. Sazed gasped. "The Lord Ruler's atium stockpile . . . It was here all along."

"Most of that atium never left the Pits of Hathsin," Haddek said. "There were obligators on staff at all times—but never Inquisitors, for the Father knew that they could be corrupted. The obligators broke the geodes in secret, inside of a metal room constructed for the purpose, then took out the atium. The noble family then transported the empty geodes to Luthadel, never knowing that they didn't have any atium in their possession at all. What atium the Lord Ruler did get, and distribute, to the nobility was brought in by the obligators. They disguised the atium as Ministry funds and hid the beads in piles of coins so that Ruin wouldn't see them as they were transported in convoys full of new acolytes to Luthadel."

Sazed stood, dumbstruck. *Here . . . all along. Just a short distance from the very caves where Kelsier raised his army. A short journey from Luthadel, completely unprotected all these years.*

Yet hidden so well.

"You worked for atium," Sazed said, looking up. "The kandra Contracts, they were paid in atium."

Haddek nodded. "We were to gather all of it we could. What didn't end up in our hands, the Mistborn burned away. Some of the houses kept small stockpiles, but the Father's taxes and fees kept most of the atium flowing back to him as payments. And, eventually, almost all of it ended up here."

Sazed looked down. *Such a fortune,* he thought. *Such . . . power.* Atium never *had* fit in with the other metals. Every one of them, even aluminum and duralumin, could be mined or created through natural processes. Atium, however—it had only ever come from a single place, its appearance mysterious and strange. Its power had allowed one to do something unlike anything else in Allomancy or Feruchemy.

It let one see the future. Not a thing of men at all, more . . . a thing of gods.

It was more than just a metal. It was condensed concentrated power.

Power that Ruin would want. Very badly.

TenSoon pushed toward the crest of the hill, moving through ash that was so high that he was glad he had switched to the horse's body, for a wolfhound could never have moved through piles so deep.

The ash fell strongly where he was, limiting his visibility. *I will never make it to Fadrex at this rate,* he thought with anger. Even pushing hard, moving in the massive horse's body, he was moving too slowly to get far from the Homeland.

He finally crested the hill, his breath coming in puffing snorts out the horse's snout.

At the top of the hill he froze, shocked. The landscape before him was burning.

Tyrian, closest of the ashmounts to Luthadel, stood in the near distance, half of its top blown free from some violent eruption. The air itself seemed to burn with tongues of flame, and the broad plain in front of TenSoon was clogged with flowing lava. It was a deep, powerful red. Even from a distance, he could feel the heat pushing against him.

He stood for a long moment, deep in ash, gazing upon a landscape that had once contained villages, forests, and roads. All was now gone, burnt away. The earth had cracked in the distance, and more lava seemed to be spilling out of it.

By the First Contract, he thought with despair. He could detour to the south, continue on to Fadrex as if he'd come in a straight line from Luthadel, but for some reason, he found it hard to get up the motivation.

It was too late.

Yes, there are sixteen metals. I find it highly unlikely that the Lord Ruler did not know of them all. Indeed, the fact that he spoke of several on the plates in the storage caches meant that he knew at least of those.

I must assume that he did not tell mankind of them earlier for a reason. Perhaps he held them back to give him a secret edge, much as he kept back the single nugget of Preservation's body that made men into Mistborn.

Or, perhaps he simply decided that mankind had enough power in the ten metals they already understood. Some things we shall never know. Part of me still finds what he did regrettable. During the thousand-year reign of the Lord Ruler, how many people were born, Snapped, lived, and died never knowing that they were Mistings, simply because their metals were unknown?

Of course, this did give us a slight advantage, at the end. Ruin had a lot of trouble giving duralumin to his Inquisitors, since they'd need an Allomancer who could burn it to kill before they could use it. And, since none of the duralumin Mistings in the world knew about their power, they didn't burn it and reveal themselves to Ruin. That left most Inquisitors without the power of duralumin, save in a few important cases—such as Marsh—where they got it from a Mistborn. This was usually considered a waste, for if one killed a Mistborn with Hemalurgy, one could draw out only one of their sixteen powers and lost the rest. Ruin considered it much better to try to subvert them and gain access to all of their power.

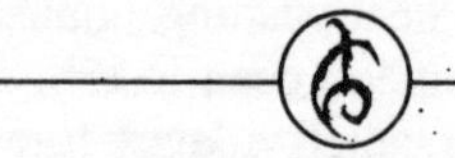

72

IT BEGAN RAINING JUST BEFORE Vin reached Luthadel. A quiet, cold drizzle that wetted the night, but did not banish the mists.

She flared her bronze. In the distance, she could sense

Allomancers. Mistborn. Chasing her. There were at least a dozen of them, homing in on her position.

She landed on the city wall, bare feet slipping just slightly on the stones. Beyond her stretched Luthadel, even now proud in its sprawl. Founded a thousand years before by the Lord Ruler, it was built atop the Well of Ascension itself. During the ten centuries of his reign, Luthadel had burgeoned, becoming the most important—and most crowded—place in all of the empire.

And it was dying.

Vin stood up straight, looking out over the vast city. Pockets of flame flared where buildings had caught fire. The flames defied the rain, illuminating the various slums and other neighborhoods like watch fires in the night. In their light, she could see that the city was a wreck. Entire swathes of the town had been torn apart, the buildings broken or burned. The streets were eerily vacant—nobody fought the fires, nobody huddled in the gutters.

The capital, once home to hundreds of thousands, seemed empty. Wind blew through Vin's rain-wetted hair and she felt a shiver. The mists, as usual, stayed away from her—pushed aside by her Allomancy. She was alone in the largest city in the world.

No. Not alone. She could feel them approaching—Ruin's minions. She had led them here, made them assume that she was bringing them to the atium. There would be far more of them than she could fight. She was doomed.

That was the idea.

She launched off the wall, shooting through the mist, ash, and rain. She wore her mistcloak, more out of nostalgia than utility. It was the same one she'd always had—the one that Kelsier had given her on her very first night of training.

She landed with a splash atop a building, then leaped again, bounding over the city. She wasn't certain if it was poetic or ominous that it was raining this night. There had been another night when she had visited Kredik Shaw in the rain. A part of her still thought she should have died that night.

She landed on the street, then stood upright, her tasseled

mistcloak falling around her, hiding her arms and chest. She stood quietly, looking up at Kredik Shaw, the Hill of a Thousand Spires. The Lord Ruler's palace, location of the Well of Ascension.

The building was an assemblage of several low wings topped by dozens of rising towers, spires, and spines. The awful near-symmetry of the amalgamation was only made more unsettling by the presence of the mists and ash. The building had been abandoned since the Lord Ruler's death. The doors were broken, and she could see shattered windows in the walls. Kredik Shaw was as dead as the city it once had dominated.

A figure stepped up beside her. "Here?" Ruin said. "This is where you lead me? We have searched this place."

Vin remained quiet, looking up at the spires. Black fingers of metal reaching up into a blacker sky.

"My Inquisitors are coming," Ruin whispered.

"You shouldn't have revealed yourself," Vin said, not looking toward him. "You should have waited until I retrieved the atium. I'll never do it now."

"Ah, but I no longer believe that you *have* it," Ruin said in his fatherly voice. "Child . . . child. I believed you at first—indeed, I gathered my powers, ready to face you. When you came here, however, I knew that you had misled me."

"You don't know that for certain," Vin said softly, voice complemented by the quiet rain.

Silence. "No," Ruin finally said.

"Then you'll have to try to make me talk," she whispered.

"*Try*? You realize the forces I can bring to bear against you, child? You realize the power I have, the destruction I represent? I am mountains that crush. I am waves that crash. I am storms that shatter. I am *the end*."

Vin continued to stare up into the falling rain. She didn't question her plan—it wasn't really her way. She'd decided what to do. It was time to spring Ruin's trap.

She was tired of being manipulated.

"You will never have it," Vin said. "Not while I live."

Ruin screamed, a sound of primal anger, of something

that *had* to destroy. Then, he vanished. Lightning flared, its light a wave of power moving through the mist. It illuminated robed figures in the blackened rain, walking toward her. Surrounding her.

Vin turned toward a ruined building a short distance away, watching as a figure climbed up over the rubble. Now lit only faintly by starlight, the figure had a bare chest, a stark rib cage, and taut muscles. Rain ran down his skin, dripping from the spikes that sprouted from his chest. One between each set of ribs. His face bore spikes in the eyes—one of which had been pounded back into his skull, crushing the socket.

Normal Inquisitors had nine spikes. The one she'd killed with Elend had ten. Marsh appeared to have upward of twenty. He growled softly.

And the fight began.

Vin flung back her cloak, spraying water from the tassels, and Pushed herself forward. Thirteen Inquisitors hurtled through the night sky toward her. Vin ducked a flight of axe swings, then slammed a Push toward a pair of Inquisitors, burning duralumin. The creatures were thrown backward by their spikes, and Vin accelerated in a sudden lurch to the side.

She hit another Inquisitor, feet against his chest. Water sprayed, flecked with ash, as Vin reached down and grabbed one of the spikes in the Inquisitor's eyes. Then she Pulled herself backward and flared pewter.

She lurched, and the spike came free. The Inquisitor screamed, but did not fall dead. It looked at her, one side of the head a gaping hole, and hissed. Removing one eye-spike, apparently, wasn't enough to kill.

Ruin laughed in her head.

The spikeless Inquisitor reached for her, and Vin Pulled herself into the sky, yanking on one of the metal spires of Kredik Shaw. She downed the contents of a metal vial as she flew, restoring her steel.

A dozen figures in black robes sprang up through the falling rain to follow. Marsh remained below, watching.

Vin gritted her teeth, then whipped out a pair of daggers and Pushed herself back down—directly toward the Inquisitors. She passed among them, surprising several, who had probably expected her to jump away. She slammed directly into the creature she'd pulled the spike from, spinning him in the air, ramming her daggers into his chest. He gritted his teeth, laughing, then slapped her arms apart and kicked her back toward the ground.

She fell with the rain.

Vin hit hard, but managed to land on her feet. The Inquisitor hit the cobblestones back-first, her daggers still in his chest. But he stood up easily, tossing the daggers aside, shattering them on the cobblestones.

Then he moved suddenly. *Too* quickly. Vin didn't have time to think as he splashed through the misty rain, grabbing her by the throat.

I've seen that speed before, she thought as she struggled. *Not just from Inquisitors. From Sazed. That's a Feruchemical power. Just like the strength Marsh used earlier.*

That was the reason for the new spikes. These other Inquisitors didn't have as many as Marsh, but they obviously had some new powers. Strength. Speed. Each of these creatures was, essentially, another Lord Ruler.

You see? Ruin asked.

Vin cried out, duralumin-Pushing against the Inquisitor, tearing herself out of his grasp. The move left her throat bleeding from his fingernails, and she had to down another vial of metals—her last—to restore her steel as she hydroplaned across the wet ground.

Feruchemical storages run out, she told herself. *Even Allomancers make mistakes. I can win.*

Yet, she wavered, breathing heavily as she came to a rest, one hand to the ground, up to the wrist in cold rainwater. Kelsier had struggled fighting one Inquisitor. What was she doing fighting thirteen?

Sodden-robed figures landed around her. Vin kicked, slamming a foot into an Inquisitor chest, then Pulled herself off to spin away from another one. She rolled across the slick cobblestones, an obsidian axe nearly taking off her head as she came up and kicked two pewter-enhanced feet at the knees of an opponent.

Bones crunched. The Inquisitor screamed and fell. Vin pushed herself to her feet with one hand, then Pulled on the spires up above, throwing herself up about ten feet to dodge the multitude of swings that came after her.

She landed back on the ground, grabbing the handle of the fallen Inquisitor's axe. She swung it up, spraying water, her skin stained with wet ash as she blocked a blow.

You cannot fight, Vin, Ruin said. *Each blow only helps me. I am Ruin.*

She screamed, throwing herself forward in a reckless attack, shouldering aside one Inquisitor, then slamming her axe into the side of another. They growled and swung, but she stayed a step ahead, barely dodging their attacks. The one she had knocked down stood back up, his knees healed. He was smiling.

A blow she didn't see took her in the shoulder, throwing her forward. She felt warm blood running down her back, but pewter deadened the pain. She threw herself to the side, regaining her feet, clutching her axe.

The Inquisitors stalked forward. Marsh watched quietly, rain dripping down his face, spikes protruding from his body like the spires of Kredik Shaw. He did not join the fight.

Vin growled, then Pulled herself into the sky again. She shot ahead of her foes, and bounded from spire to spire, using their metal as anchors. The twelve Inquisitors followed like a flock of ravens, leaping between spires, robes flapping, taking different paths than she. She lurched through the mists, which continued to spin around her in defiance of the rain.

An Inquisitor landed against the spike she was aiming for. She yelled, swinging her axe in an overhand blow as she landed, but he Pushed off—dodging her swing—then Pulled himself right back. She kicked at his feet, sending both herself and her opponent sprawling into the air. Then, she grabbed his robe as they fell.

He looked up, teeth clenched in a smile, knocking her axe out of her hand with an inhumanly strong hand. His body began to swell, gaining the unnatural bulk of a Feruchemist tapping strength. He laughed at Vin, grabbing her neck. He didn't even notice as Vin Pulled them both slightly to the side as they fell through the air.

They hit one of the lower spikes, the metal piercing the surprised Inquisitor's chest. Vin wrenched herself to the side, out of the way, but hung on to his head, her weight pulling him down the spire. She didn't look as the spike ripped through his body, but when she hit the ground below, she was holding only a head. A disembodied spike splashed into an ashen puddle beside her, and she dropped the dead creature's head beside it.

Marsh screamed in anger. Four more Inquisitors landed around her. Vin kicked at one, but it moved with Feruchemical speed, catching her foot. Another grabbed her by the arm and wrenched her to the side. She cried out, kicking her way free, but a third one grabbed her, his grip enhanced by both Allomantic and Feruchemical strength. The other three followed, holding her with claw-like fingers.

Taking a deep breath, Vin extinguished her tin, then burned duralumin, steel, and pewter. She Pushed outward with a sudden wave of power; Inquisitors were thrown back by their spikes. They sprawled, falling to the ground, cursing.

Vin hit the cobblestones. Suddenly, the pain in her back and her throat seemed impossibly strong. She flared tin to clear her mind, but still stumbled, woozily, as she climbed to her feet. She'd used up all of her pewter in that one burst.

She moved to run, and found a figure standing in front of her. Marsh was silent, though another wave of lightning lit the mists.

Her pewter was gone. She was bleeding from a wound that probably would have killed anyone else. She was desperate.

Okay. Now! she thought as Marsh slapped her. The blow threw her to the ground.

Nothing happened.

Come on! Vin thought, trying to draw upon the mists. Terror twisted within her as Marsh loomed, a black figure in the night. *Please!*

Each time the mists had helped her, they had done so when she was most desperate. This was her plan, weak though it seemed: to put herself in more trouble than she'd ever been in before, then count on the mists to help her. As they had twice before.

Marsh knelt over her. Images flashed like bursts of lightning through her tired mind.

Camon, raising a meaty hand to beat her. Rain falling on her as she huddled in a dark corner, her side aching from a deep gash. Zane turning toward her as they stood at the top of Keep Hasting, one of his hands dripping a slow stream of blood.

Vin tried to scramble away across the slick, cold cobblestones, but her body wasn't working right. She could barely crawl. Marsh slammed a fist down on her leg, shattering the bone, and she cried out in shocked, icy pain. No pewter tempered the blow. She tried to pull herself up to grab one of Marsh's spikes, but he snatched her leg—the broken one—and her own effort just made her scream in agony.

Now, Ruin said in his kindly voice, *we will begin. Where is the atium, Vin? What do you know of it?*

"Please . . ." Vin whispered, reaching toward the mists. "Please, please, please . . ."

Yet, they remained aloof. Once, they had swirled playfully around her body, but now they pulled back instead. Just as they'd done for the entire last year. She was crying, reaching for them, but they puffed away. Shunning her like a victim of the plague.

It was the same way the mists treated the Inquisitors.

The creatures rose, surrounding her, silhouettes in the dark night. Marsh yanked her back to him, then reached for her arm. She heard her bone snap before she felt the pain. It came, however, and she screamed.

It had been a long time since she'd known torture. The streets had not been kind, but during the last few years, she'd been able to repress most of those experiences. She'd become a Mistborn. Powerful. Protected.

Not this time, she realized through the haze of agony. *Sazed won't come for me this time. Kelsier won't save me. Even the mists have abandoned me. I'm alone.*

Her teeth began to chatter, and Marsh raised her other arm. He looked down at her with spiked eyes, expression unreadable. Then snapped the bone.

Vin screamed, more from the terror than the pain.

Marsh watched her scream, listening to its sweetness. He smiled, then reached down for her unbroken leg. If only Ruin weren't holding him back. Then he could kill her. He strained against his bonds, lusting to do her more harm.

No . . . a tiny piece of him thought.

The rain fell, marking a beautiful night. The city of Luthadel lay bedecked in its funereal best, smoldering, some parts still burning despite the wet night. How he wished he'd arrived in time to see the riots and the death. He smiled, the passionate love of a fresh kill rising in him.

No, he thought.

He knew, somehow, that the end was very near. The ground trembled beneath his feet, and he had to steady himself with one hand before continuing his work, snapping Vin's other leg. The final day had arrived. The world would not survive this night. He laughed gleefully, fully in the throes of a blood frenzy, barely controlled as he broke Vin's body.

NO!

Marsh awakened. Though his hands still moved as ordered, his mind rebelled. He took in the ash, and the rain, the blood and the soot, and it disgusted him. Vin lay nearly dead.

Kelsier treated her like a daughter, he thought as he broke her fingers, one at a time. She was screaming. *The daughter he never had with Mare.*

I've given up. Just like I did with the rebellion.

It was the great shame of his life. Years ago, before the Collapse, he had led the skaa rebellion. But, he'd given in. He'd withdrawn, giving up leadership of the group. And he'd done it only one year before the rebellion—with Kelsier's help—finally overthrew the Final Empire. Marsh had been its leader, but had given up. Just before the victory.

No, he thought as he broke the fingers on her other hand. *Not again. No more giving up!*

His hand moved up to her collarbone. And then he saw it. A single bit of metal, glittering in Vin's ear. Her earring. She'd explained it to him once.

I don't remember it, Vin's voice whispered to him from the past. A memory of when Marsh himself had sat with her on a quiet veranda at Mansion Renoux, watching Kelsier organize a caravan below, just before Marsh left to infiltrate the ranks of the Steel Priesthood.

Vin had spoken of her insane mother. *Reen said that he came home one day and found my mother covered in blood,* Vin had said. *She'd killed my baby sister. Me, however, she hadn't touched—except to give me an earring . . .*

Don't trust anyone pierced by metal. Spook's letter. *Even the smallest bit can taint a man.*

The smallest bit.

As he looked closer, the earring—though twisted and chipped—looked almost like a tiny spike.

He didn't think. He didn't give Ruin time to react. Amid the thrill of killing the Hero of Ages, Ruin's control was weaker than it had ever been. Summoning all the will he had remaining, Marsh reached out.

And ripped the earring from Vin's ear.

Vin's eyes snapped open.

Ash and water fell on her. Her body burned with pain, and the echoing screams of Ruin's demands still reverberated in her head.

But the voice spoke no further. It had been stifled midsentence.

What?

The mists returned to her with a snap. They flowed around her, sensing the Allomancy of her tin, which she still burned faintly. They spun around her as they once had, playful, friendly.

She was dying. She knew it. Marsh was done with her bones, and was obviously growing impatient. He screamed, holding his head. Then, he reached down, grabbing his axe from the puddle beside him. Vin couldn't have run if she'd wanted to.

Fortunately, the pain was fading. Everything was fading. It was black.

Please, she thought, reaching out to the mists with one final plea. They felt so familiar all of a sudden. Where had she felt that feeling before? Where did she know them?

From the Well of Ascension, of course, a voice whispered in her head. *It's the same power, after all. Solid in the metal you fed to Elend. Liquid in the pool you burned. And vapor in the air, confined to night. Hiding you. Protecting you.*

Giving you power!

Vin gasped, drawing in breath—a breath that sucked in the mists. She felt suddenly warm, the mists surging within her, lending her their strength. Her entire body burned like metal, and the pain disappeared in a flash.

Marsh swung his axe for her head, spraying water.

And she caught his arm.

I have spoken of Inquisitors, and their ability to pierce copperclouds. As I said, this power is easily understood when one realizes that many Inquisitors were Seekers before their transformation, and that meant their bronze became twice as strong.

There is at least one other case of a person who could pierce copperclouds. In her case, however, the situation was slightly different. She was a Mistborn from birth, and her sister was the Seeker. The death of that sister—and subsequent inheritance of power via the Hemalurgic spike used to kill that sister—left her twice as good at burning bronze as a typical Mistborn. And that let her see through the copperclouds of lesser Allomancers.

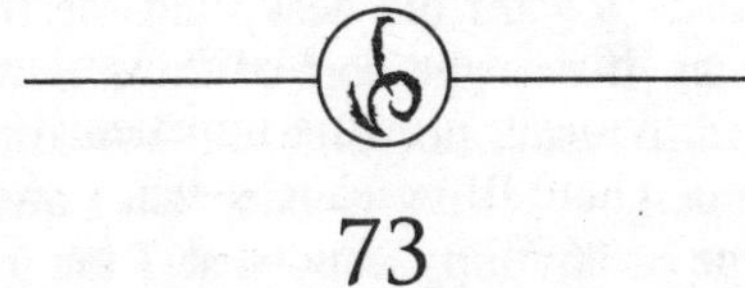

73

THE MISTS CHANGED.

TenSoon looked up through the ash. He lay, exhausted and numb, atop the hill before the field of lava that barred his path eastward. His muscles felt lethargic—signs that he had been pushing too hard. Even the Blessing of Potency could only do so much.

He stood, forcing his horse's body to rise, looking at his nighttime surroundings. Endless fields of ash extended behind him; even the track he had worn up to the top of the hill was close to being filled in. The lava burned ahead of him. However, something seemed different. What?

The mists flowed, moving about, swirling. Generally, the mists had a very chaotic pattern. Some parts would flow one way, while others would spin about in other directions. There were often rivers of motion, but they never conformed to one another. Most often, they followed the wind; this night the wind was still.

And yet, the mist seemed to be flowing in one direction. As soon as he noticed it, TenSoon found it one of the most singularly strange sights he had ever beheld. Instead of swirling or spinning, the mists moved together in a seemingly purposeful flow. They coursed around him, and he felt like a stone in a huge, incorporeal river.

The mists flowed toward Luthadel. *Perhaps I'm not too late!* he thought, regaining some of his hope. He shook himself from his stupor, and took off in a gallop back the way he had come.

* * *

"Breezy, come look at this."

Breeze rubbed his eyes, looking across the room to where Allrianne sat in her nightgown, looking out the window. It was late—too late. He should have been asleep.

He looked back toward his desk, and the treaty he had been working on. It was the sort of thing Sazed or Elend should have had to write, not Breeze. "You know," he said, "I distinctly remember telling Kelsier that I did *not* want to end up in charge of anything important. Running kingdoms and cities is work for fools, not thieves! Government is far too inefficient to provide a suitable income."

"Breezy!" Allrianne said insistently, Pulling on his emotions quite blatantly.

He sighed, rising. "Very well," he grumbled. *Honestly,* he thought. *How is it, of all the qualified people in Kelsier's little crew, that* I *end up the one leading a city?*

He joined Allrianne at the window, peeking out. "What is it exactly I'm supposed to see, dear? I don't . . ."

He trailed off, frowning. Beside him, Allrianne touched his arm, seeming concerned as she looked out the window.

"Now, that *is* strange," he said. The mists flowed by outside, moving like a river—and they seemed to be accelerating.

The door to his room slammed open. Breeze jumped, and Allrianne squeaked. They spun to find Spook standing in the doorway, still half covered in bandages.

"Gather the people," the boy croaked, holding the doorframe to keep from collapsing. "We need to move."

"My dear boy," Breeze said, unsettled. Allrianne took Breeze's arm, holding on quietly, yet tightly. "My dear boy, what is this? You should be in bed!"

"Gather them, Breeze!" Spook said, suddenly sounding very authoritative. "Take them to the storage cavern. Pack them in! Quickly! We don't have much time!"

"What do you make of it?" Ham asked, wiping his brow. Blood immediately oozed from the cut again, running down the side of his face.

Elend shook his head, breathing deeply—almost in gasps—as he leaned back against the side of a jagged rock outcropping. He closed his eyes, fatigue making his body shake despite his pewter. "I don't really care about mists right now, Ham," he whispered. "I can barely think straight."

Ham grunted in agreement. Around them, men screamed and died, fighting the endless waves of koloss. They had some of the creatures bottled up in the natural stone corridor leading into Fadrex, but the real fights were happening on the rugged rock formations that enclosed the city. Too many koloss, tired of waiting outside, had begun crawling up to attack from the sides.

It was a precarious battlefield, one that often demanded Elend's attention. They had a large number of Allomancers, but most of them were inexperienced—they hadn't even known about their powers until this very day. Elend was a one-man reserve force, bounding across the defensive lines, plugging holes while Cett directed tactics below.

More screams. More death. More metal hitting metal, rock, and flesh. *Why?* Elend thought with frustration. *Why can't I protect them?* He flared pewter, taking a deep breath and standing up in the night.

The mists flowed overhead, as if pulled by some invisible force. For a moment, even exhausted as he was, he froze.

"Lord Venture!" someone shouted. Elend spun, looking toward the sound. A youthful messenger scrambled up the side of the rock outcropping, wide-eyed.

Oh, no . . . Elend thought, tensing.

"My lord, they're retreating!" the lad said, stumbling to a halt before Elend.

"What?" Ham asked, standing.

"It's true, my lord. They pulled back from the city gates! They're leaving."

Elend immediately dropped a coin, shooting himself into the sky. Mist flowed around him, its tendrils a million tiny strings being yanked eastward. Below, he saw the hulking, dark forms of the koloss running away in the night.

So many of them, he thought, landing on a rock formation. *We'd never have beaten them. Even with Allomancers.*

But, they were leaving. Running away at an inhuman speed. Moving . . .

Toward Luthadel.

Vin fought like a tempest, spraying rainwater through the dark night as she threw back Inquisitor after Inquisitor.

She shouldn't have been alive. She'd run out of pewter, yet she felt it flaring inside, burning brighter than it ever had before. She felt as if the bleeding sun itself blazed within her, running molten through her veins.

Her every Steelpush or Ironpull slammed against her as if it were made with the power of duralumin. Yet, the metal reserves within her did not vanish. Instead, they grew stronger. Vaster. She wasn't certain what was happening to her. However, she *did* know one thing.

Suddenly, fighting twelve Inquisitors at once did not seem like an impossible task.

She cried out, slapping an Inquisitor to the side, then ducking a pair of axes. She crouched, then jumped, leaping in an arc through the rain, coming down beside Marsh, who still lay stunned from where she had thrown him after her rebirth.

He looked up, finally seeming to focus on her, then cursed and rolled away as Vin punched downward. Her fist shattered a cobblestone, throwing back a ripple of dark rainwater, splashing her arms and face, leaving specks of black ash behind.

She looked up toward Marsh. He stood erect, barechested, his spikes glistening in the darkness.

Vin smiled, then spun on the Inquisitors rushing her from behind. She yelled, dodging a swinging axe. Had these creatures ever seemed quick to her? Within the embrace of limitless pewter, she seemed to move as the mist itself did. Light. Quick.

Unchained.

The sky spun in a tempest of its own as she attacked, moving in a swirling frenzy. The mists whirled around her arm in a vortex as she punched one Inquisitor in the face, throwing him backward. The mists danced before her as she caught the fallen Inquisitor's axe, then sheared the arm off another of the creatures. She took his head next, leaving the others stunned with the speed of her motion.

That's two dead.

They attacked again. She bounded backward, Pulling herself toward the spires above. The trail of ravens launched after her, their robes snapping in the wet darkness. She hit a spire feet-first, then launched upward and Pulled on an Inquisitor's spikes, something that was easy to do with her new power. Her chosen quarry lurched upward ahead of his companions.

Vin shot downward, meeting the Inquisitor in the air. She grabbed him by the eye-spikes and pulled, ripping them out with her newfound strength. Then she kicked off the creature and Pushed against the spikes in his chest.

She shot upward in the air, leaving a corpse flipping end over end in the rain beneath her, massive gaps in its head where the spikes had been. They could lose some spikes and live, she knew, but the removal of others was deadly. Losing both eye-spikes appeared to be enough to kill them.

Three.

Inquisitors hit the spire she had Pushed off of, and they leaped up to follow her. Vin smiled, then threw the spikes she still carried, catching one of the Inquisitors in the chest with them. Then, she Pushed. The unfortunate Inquisitor was thrown downward, and he hit a flat rooftop so violently that it pushed several of his spikes up out of his body. They sparkled and spun in the air, then fell beside his immobile corpse.

Four.

Vin's mistcloak fluttered as she shot upward in the sky. Eight Inquisitors still chased her, reaching for her. Crying out, Vin raised her hands toward the creatures as she began to fall. Then, she *Pushed.*

She hadn't realized how strong her new powers were. They were obviously akin to duralumin, since she could affect the spikes inside of an Inquisitor's body. Her overpowering Push forced the whole flock of them downward, as if they'd been swatted. In fact, her Push also hit the metal spire directly beneath her.

The stone architecture holding the spire in place exploded, spraying chips and dust outward as the spire itself crushed the building beneath it. And Vin was thrown upward.

Very quickly.

She blasted through the sky, mists streaking past her, the force of her Push straining even her mist-enhanced body with the stress of sudden acceleration.

And then she was out. She emerged into the open air, like a fish leaping from the water. Beneath her, the mists covered the nighttime land like an enormous white blanket. Around her, there was only open air. Unsettling, strange. Above her, a million stars—normally visible only to Allomancers—watched her like the eyes of those long dead.

Her momentum ran out, and she spun quietly, whiteness below, light above. She notice that she'd trailed a line of mist up out of the main cloud. This hung like a tether ready to pull her back down. In fact, all the mists were spinning slightly in what looked like an enormous weather pattern. A whirlpool of white.

The heart of the whirlpool was directly beneath her.

She fell, plummeting back down toward the earth below. She entered the mists, drawing them behind her, breathing them in. Even as she fell, she could feel them surging about her in a massive, empire-wide spiral. She welcomed them into herself, and the vortex of mist around her grew more and more violent.

Instants later, Luthadel appeared, a massive black welt upon the land. She fell down, streaking toward Kredik Shaw and its spires, which seemed to be pointing toward her. The Inquisitors were still there—she could see them standing on a flat rooftop amid the spires, looking up. Waiting. There were only eight, not counting Marsh. One lay impaled on a nearby spike from her last push; the blow had apparently torn the center spike out of his back.

Five, Vin thought, landing a short distance from the Inquisitors.

If a single Push could throw her up so far she passed out of the mists, then what would happen if she Pushed outward?

She waited quietly as the Inquisitors charged. She could see desperation in their movements. Whatever was happening to Vin, Ruin was apparently willing to risk every one of the creatures in the hopes that they would kill her before she was complete. Mists pulled toward her, moving more and more quickly, drawn into her like water being sucked down a drain.

When the Inquisitors had almost reached her, she *Pushed* outward again, throwing metal away from her with all the force as she could muster, while at the same time strengthening her body with a massive flare of pewter. Stone cracked. Inquisitors cried out.

And Kredik Shaw exploded.

Towers toppled from their foundations. Doors ripped free from their frames. Windows shattered. Blocks burst, the entire structure torn to pieces as its metals lurched away. She screamed as she Pushed, the ground trembling beneath her. Everything—even the rock and stone, which obviously contained residual traces of metal ore—was thrown violently back.

She gasped, stopping her Push. She drew in breath, feeling the rain splatter against her. The building that had been the Lord Ruler's palace was gone, flattened to rubble which spread out and away from her like an impact crater.

An Inquisitor burst from the rubble, face bleeding from where one of his spikes had ripped free. Vin raised a hand, Pulling and steadying herself from behind. The Inquisitor's head lurched, his other eye-spike pulling free. He toppled forward, and Vin caught the spike, Pushing it toward another

Inquisitor who was rushing her. He raised a hand to Push it back at her.

And she drove it forward anyway, ignoring his Push with a quick Push backward to stabilize herself. He was thrown away and slammed into the remnants of a wall. The spike continued forward, Pushed like a fish darting through water, ignoring the current. The spike slammed into the Inquisitor's face, crushing it, pinning his head back against the granite.

Six and seven.

Vin stalked across the rubble, mists storming. Overhead, they swirled furiously, forming a funnel cloud with her at its focus. It was like a tornado, but with no air currents. Just impalpable mists, as if painted on the air. Spinning, swirling, coming to her silent command.

She stepped over an Inquisitor corpse that had been crushed by the rubble; she kicked his head free to make certain he was dead.

Eight.

Three rushed her at once. She screamed, turning, Pulling on a fallen spire. The massive piece of metal—nearly as big as a building itself—lurched into the air, spinning at her command. She slammed it into the Inquisitors like a club, crushing them. She turned, leaving the enormous iron pillar resting atop their corpses.

Nine. Ten. Eleven.

The storm broke, though the mists continued to swirl. The rain let up as Vin walked across the shattered building, eyes searching for Allomantic blue lines that were moving. She found one trembling before her, and she picked up and tossed aside an enormous marble disk. An Inquisitor groaned beneath; she reached for him, and realized that her hand was leaking mist. It didn't just swirl around her, it came from her, smoking forth from the pores in her skin. She breathed out, and mist puffed before her, then immediately entered the vortex and was pulled in again.

She grabbed the Inquisitor, pulling him up. His skin began to heal as he used his Feruchemical powers, and he struggled, growing stronger. Yet, even the awesome strength of Feruchemy made little difference against Vin. She pulled his eye-spikes free, tossed them aside, then left the corpse slumping in the rubble.

Twelve.

She found the last Inquisitor huddled in a pool of rainwater. It was Marsh. His body was broken, and he was missing one of the spikes from his side. The spike hole was bleeding, but that one apparently wasn't enough to kill him. He turned his pair of spikeheads to look up at her, expression stiff.

Vin paused, breathing deeply, feeling rainwater trail down her arms and drip off her fingers. She still burned within, and she looked up, staring into the vortex of mists. It was spinning so powerfully, twisting down. She was having trouble thinking for all the energy that coursed through her.

She looked down again.

This isn't Marsh, she thought. *Kelsier's brother is long dead. This is something else. Ruin.*

The mist swirled in a final tempest, the circular motion growing faster—yet tighter—as the final wisps of mist spun down and were pulled into Vin's body.

Then the mists were gone. Starlight shone above, and flecks of ash fell in the air. The night landscape was eerie in its stillness, blackness, and clarity. Even with tin—which let her see at night far better than a normal person could—the mists had always been there. To see the night landscape without them was . . . wrong.

Vin began to tremble. She gasped, feeling the fire within her blaze hotter and hotter. It was Allomancy as she'd never known it. It felt as if she had never understood it. The power was far greater than metals, mere Pushes and Pulls. It was something awesomely more vast. A power that men had used, yet never comprehended.

She forced her eyes open. There was one Inquisitor left. She had drawn them to Luthadel, forced them to expose themselves, laying a trap for someone far more powerful than herself. And the mists had responded.

It was time to finish what she had come to do.

Marsh watched limply as Vin fell to her knees. Shaking, she reached for one of his eye-spikes.

There was nothing he could do. He'd used up most of the healing in his metalmind, and the rest would do him no good. Stored healing worked by way of speed. He could either heal himself a small amount very quickly, or wait and heal himself slowly, yet completely. Either way, he was dead as soon as Vin pulled those spikes free.

Finally, he thought with relief as she grabbed the first spike. *Whatever I did . . . it worked. Somehow.*

He felt Ruin's rage, felt his master realizing his mistake. In the end, Marsh had mattered. In the end, Marsh hadn't given up. He'd done Mare proud.

Vin pulled the spike free. It hurt, of course—hurt far more than Marsh would have thought possible. He screamed—both in pain and in joy—as Vin reached for the other eye-spike.

And then, she hesitated. Marsh waited expectantly. She shook, then coughed, cringing. She gritted her teeth, reaching toward him. Her fingers touched the spike.

And then, Vin vanished.

She left behind the misty outline of a young woman. That dissipated and was soon gone, too, leaving Marsh alone in the wreckage of a palace, head blazing with pain, body covered in sickly, sodden ash.

She once asked Ruin why he had chosen her. The primary answer is simple. It had little to do with her personality, attitudes, or even skill with Allomancy.

She was simply the only child Ruin could find who was in a position to gain the right Hemalurgic spike—one that would grant her heightened power with bronze, which would then let her sense the location of the Well of Ascension. She had an insane mother, a sister who was a Seeker, and was—herself—Mistborn. That was precisely the combination Ruin needed.

There were other reasons, of course. But even Ruin didn't know them.

74

DAY BROKE WITH NO MISTS.

Elend stood atop the rocky heights in front of Fadrex City, looking out. He felt far better with a night's rest behind him, though his body ached from fighting, his arm throbbed where he'd been wounded, and his chest hurt where he'd carelessly allowed a koloss to punch him. The massive bruise would have crippled another man.

Koloss corpses littered the ground before the city, piled particularly high in the corridor leading into Fadrex itself. The whole area smelled of death and dried blood. Far more often than Elend would have liked, the field of blue corpses was broken by the lighter skin of a human. Still, Fadrex had survived—if only because of the last-minute addition of several thousand Allomancers and the eventual retreat of the koloss.

Why did they leave? Elend wondered, thankful yet frustrated. *And, perhaps more importantly, where are they going?*

Elend turned at the sound of footsteps on rock and saw Yomen climbing the rough-hewn steps to join him, puffing slightly, still pristine in his obligator's robes. Nobody had expected him to fight. He was, after all, a scholar, and not a warrior.

Like me, Elend thought, smiling wryly.

"The mists are gone," Yomen said.

Elend nodded. "Both day and night."

"The skaa fled inside when the mists vanished. Some still refuse to leave their homes. For centuries, they feared being out at night because of the mists. Now the mists disappear, and they find it so unnatural that they hide again."

Elend turned away, looking back out. The mists were gone, but the ash still fell. And it fell hard. The corpses that had fallen during the night hours were nearly buried.

"Has the sun always been this hot?" Yomen asked, wiping his brow.

Elend frowned, noticing for the first time that it *did* seem hot. It was still early morning, yet it already felt like noon.

Something is still wrong, he thought. *Very wrong. Worse, even.* The ash choked the air, blowing in the breeze, coating everything. And the heat . . . shouldn't it have been getting *colder* as more ash flew into the air, blocking the sunlight? "Form crews, Yomen," Elend said. "Have them pick through the bodies and search for wounded among that mess down there. Then, gather the people and begin moving them into the storage cavern. Tell the soldiers to be ready for . . . for something. I don't know what."

Yomen frowned. "You sound as if you're not going to be here to help me."

Elend turned eastward. "I won't be."

Vin was still out there somewhere. He didn't understand why she had said what she had about the atium, but he trusted her. Perhaps she had intended to distract Ruin with lies. Elend suspected that somehow, the people of Fadrex owed her their lives. She'd drawn the koloss away—she'd figured something out, something that he couldn't even guess at.

She always complains that she's not a scholar, he thought, smiling to himself. *But that's just because she lacks education. She's twice as quick-witted as half the "geniuses" I knew during my days at court.*

He couldn't leave her alone. He needed to find her. Then . . . well, he didn't know what they'd do next. Find Sazed, perhaps? Either way, Elend could do no more in Fadrex. He moved to walk down the steps, intending to find Ham and Cett. However, Yomen caught his shoulder.

Elend turned.

"I was wrong about you, Venture," Yomen said. "The things I said were undeserved."

"You let me into your city when my men were surrounded by their own koloss," Elend said. "I don't care *what* you said about me. You're a good man in my estimation."

"You're wrong about the Lord Ruler, though," Yomen said. "He's guiding this all."

Elend just smiled.

"It doesn't bother me that you don't believe," Yomen said, reaching up to his forehead. "I've learned something. The Lord Ruler uses unbelievers as well as believers. We're all part of his plan. Here."

Yomen pulled the bead of atium free from its place at his brow. "My last bead. In case you need it."

Elend accepted the bit of metal, rolling it over in his fingers. He'd never burned atium. For years, his family had overseen its mining—but, by the time Elend himself had become Mistborn, he'd already either spent what he'd been able to obtain, or had given it to Vin to be burned.

"How did you do it, Yomen?" he asked. "How did you make it seem you were an Allomancer?"

"I *am* an Allomancer, Venture."

"Not a Mistborn," Elend said.

"No," Yomen said. "A Seer—an atium Misting."

Elend nodded. He'd assumed that was impossible, but it was hard to rely on assumptions about *anything* anymore. "The Lord Ruler knew about your power?"

Yomen smiled. "Some secrets, he worked very hard to guard."

Atium Mistings, Elend thought. *That means there are others too . . . gold Mistings, electrum Mistings . . .* Though, as he thought about it, some—like aluminum Mistings or duralumin Mistings—would be impossible to find because they couldn't use their metals without being able to burn other metals.

"Atium was too valuable to use in testing people for Allomantic powers anyway," Yomen said, turning away. "I never really found the power all that useful. How often does one have both atium and the desire to use it up in a few heartbeats? Take that bit and go find your wife."

Elend stood for a moment, then tucked the bead of atium away and went down to give Ham some instructions. A few minutes later, he was streaking across the landscape, doing his best to fly with the horseshoes as Vin had taught him.

Each Hemalurgic spike driven through a person's body gave Ruin some small ability to influence them. This was mitigated, however, by the mental fortitude of the one being controlled.

In most cases—depending on the size of the spike and the length of time it had been worn—a single spike gave Ruin only minimal powers over a person. He could appear to them, and could warp their thoughts slightly, making them overlook certain oddities—for instance, their compulsion for keeping and wearing a simple earring.

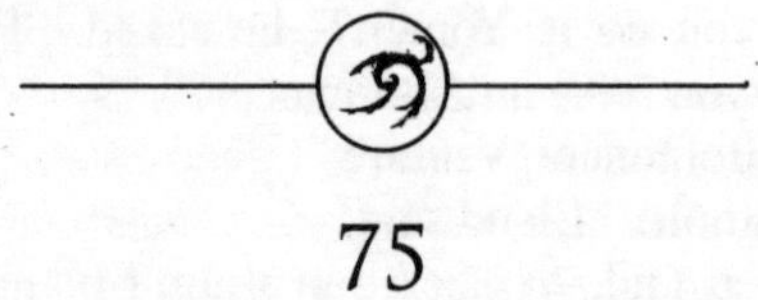

75

SAZED GATHERED HIS NOTES, CAREFULLY stacking the thin sheets of metal. Though the metal served an important function in keeping Ruin from modifying—or perhaps even reading—their contents, Sazed found them a bit frustrating. The plates were easily scratched, and they couldn't be folded or bound.

The kandra elders had given him a place to stay, and it was surprisingly lush for a cave. Kandra apparently enjoyed human comforts—blankets, cushions, mattresses. Some even preferred to wear clothing, though those who didn't declined to create genitals for their True Bodies. That left him wondering about scholarly sorts of questions. They reproduced by transforming mistwraiths into kandra, so genitals would be redundant. Yet, the kandra identified themselves by gender—each was definitely a "he" or a "she." So, how did they know? Did they choose arbitrarily, or did they actually know what they would have been, had they been born human rather than as a mistwraith?

He wished he had more time to study their society. So far, everything he'd done in the Homeland had been focused on learning more of the Hero of Ages and the Terris religion. He'd made a sheet of notes about what he'd discovered, and it sat at the top of his metallic stack. It looked surprisingly, even depressingly, similar to any number of sheets in his portfolio.

The Terris religion, as one might have expected, focused heavily on knowledge and scholarship. The Worldbringers—their word for Keepers—were holy men and women who imparted knowledge, but also wrote of their god, Terr. It was the ancient Terris word for "to preserve." A central focus of the religion had been the histories of how Preservation—or Terr—and Ruin had interacted, and these included various prophecies about the Hero of Ages, who was seen as a successor to Preservation.

Aside from the prophecies, however, the Worldbringers had taught temperance, faith, and understanding to their people. They had taught that it was better to build than to destroy, a principle at the core of their teachings. Of course there had been rituals, rites, initiations, and traditions. There were also lesser religious leaders, required offerings, and codes of conduct. It all seemed good, but hardly original. Even the focus on scholarship was something shared by several dozen other religions Sazed had studied.

That, for some reason, depressed him. It was just another religion.

What had he expected? Some astounding doctrine that would prove to him once and for all that there was a god? He felt like a fool. Yet, he also felt betrayed. This was what he'd ridden across the empire, feeling elated and anticipatory, to discover? This was what he'd expected to save them? These were just more words. Pleasant ones, like most in his portfolio, but hardly compelling. Was he supposed to believe just because it was the religion his people had followed?

There were no promises here that Tindwyl still lived. Why was it that people had followed this, or any, of the religions? Frustrated, Sazed dipped into his metalminds, dumping a group of accounts into his mind. Writings the Keepers had discovered—journals, letters, other sources from which scholars had pieced together what had once been believed. He looked through them, thought of them, read them.

What had made these people so willing to accept their religions? Were they simply products of their society, believing because it was tradition? He read of their lives, and tried to persuade himself that the people were simpletons, that they hadn't ever truly questioned their beliefs. Surely they would have seen the flaws and inconsistencies if they'd just taken the time to be rational and discerning.

Sazed sat with closed eyes, a wealth of information from journals and letters in his mind, searching for what he expected to find. However, as the time passed, he did not discover what he sought. The people did not seem like fools to him. As he sat, something began to occur to him. Something about the words, the feelings, of the people who had believed.

Before, Sazed had looked at the doctrines themselves. This time, he found himself studying the people who had believed, or what he could find of them. As he read their words over again in his mind, he began to see something. The faiths he had looked at, they couldn't be divorced from the people who had adhered to them. In the abstract, those religions were stale. However, as he read the words of the people—really *read* them—he began to see patterns.

Why did they believe? Because they saw miracles. Things one man took as chance, a man of faith took as a sign. A loved one recovering from disease, a fortunate business deal, a chance meeting with a long lost friend. It wasn't the grand doctrines or the sweeping ideals that seemed to make believers out of men. It was the simple magic in the world around them.

What was it Spook said? Sazed thought, sitting in the shadowy kandra cavern. *That faith was about trust. Trusting that somebody was watching. That somebody would make it all right in the end, even though things looked terrible at the moment.*

To believe, it seemed, one had to *want* to believe. It was a conundrum, one Sazed had wrestled with. He wanted someone, something, to force him to have faith. He wanted to have to believe because of the proof shown to him.

Yet, the believers whose words now filled his mind would have said he already had proof. Had he not, in his moment of despair, received an answer? As he had been about to give up, TenSoon had spoken. Sazed had begged for a sign, and received it.

Was it chance? Was it providence?

In the end, apparently, it was up to him to decide. He slowly returned the letters and journals to his metalminds, leaving his specific memory of them empty—yet retaining the feelings they had prompted in him. Which would he be? Believer or skeptic? At that moment, neither seemed a patently foolish path.

I do *want to believe,* he thought. *That's why I've spent so much time searching. I can't have it both ways. I simply have to decide.*

Which would it be? He sat for a few moments, thinking, feeling, and—most important—remembering.

I sought help, Sazed thought. *And something answered.*

Sazed smiled, and everything seemed a little bit brighter. *Breeze was right,* he thought, standing and organizing his things as he prepared to go. *I was not meant to be an atheist.*

The thought seemed a little too flippant for what had just happened to him. As he picked up his metal sheets and prepared to go meet with the First Generation, he realized that kandra passed outside his humble little cavern, completely oblivious to the important decision he'd just made.

But, that was how things often went, it seemed. Some important decisions were made on a battlefield or in a conference room. But others happened quietly, unseen by others. That didn't make the decision any less important to Sazed. He would believe. Not because something had been proven to him beyond his ability to deny. But because he chose to.

As, he realized, Vin had once chosen to believe and trust in the crew. Because of what Kelsier had taught her. *You taught me too, Survivor,* Sazed thought, moving out into the stone tunnel to meet with the kandra leaders. *Thank you.*

Sazed made his way through the cavern corridors, suddenly eager at the prospect of another day interviewing the members of the First Generation. Now that he had covered most of their religion, he planned to find out more about the First Contract.

As far as he knew, he was the only human other than the Lord Ruler to have ever read its words. The members of the First Generation treated the metal bearing the contract with noticeably less reverence than the other kandra. That had surprised him.

Of course, Sazed thought, turning a corner, *it does make some kind of sense. To the members of the First Generation, the Lord Ruler was a friend. They remember climbing that mountain with him—their leader, yes, but not a god. Kind of like the members of the crew, who had trouble seeing Kelsier in a religious light.*

Still lost in thought, Sazed wandered into the Trustwarren, whose broad metallic doors were open. He paused, however, just inside. The First Generation waited in their alcoves, as was common. They didn't come down until Sazed closed the doors. Oddly, however, the members of the Second Generation stood at their lecterns, addressing the crowds of kandra—who, despite being far more reserved than a similar group of humans would have been, still displayed an air of anxiety.

". . . does it mean, KanPaar?" one lesser kandra was asking. "Please, we are confused. Ask the First Generation."

"We have spoken of this thing already," said KanPaar,

leader of the Seconds. "There is no need for alarm. Look at you, crowding together, murmuring and rumormongering as if you were humans!"

Sazed moved up to one of the younger kandra, who stood gathered outside the doorway to the Trustwarren. "Please," he whispered. "What is the source of this concern?"

"The mists, Holy Worldbringer," the kandra—a female, he thought—whispered back.

"What of them?" Sazed asked. "The fact that they are staying later and later in the day?"

"No," the kandra girl replied. "The fact that they're *gone*."

Sazed started. "*What?*"

The kandra nodded. "Nobody noticed it until early this morning. It was still dark out, and a guard walked by to check one of the exits. He says there was no mist at all outside, despite it being night! Others went out too. They all agree."

"This is a simple matter," KanPaar said to the chamber. "We know that it was raining last night, and sometimes rain disperses the mists for a short time. They will return tomorrow."

"But, it's not raining now," one of the kandra said. "And, it wasn't raining when TarKavv went out on patrol. There have been mists in the morning for months now. Where are they?"

"Bah," KanPaar said, waving his hand. "You worried when the mists started staying in the mornings, now you complain that they are gone? We are *kandra.* We are eternal—we outwait everything and anything. We don't gather in rowdy mobs. Go back to what you were doing. This means nothing."

"No," a voice whispered into the cavern. Heads turned up, and the entire group hushed.

"No," Haddek—leader of the First Generation—whispered from his hidden alcove. "This is important. We have been wrong, KanPaar. Very . . . very wrong. Clear the Trustwarren. Leave only the Keeper behind. And spread the word. The day of the Resolution may have come."

This comment only served to agitate the kandra further.

Sazed stood frozen with wonder; he had never seen such a reaction in the normally calm creatures. They did as they were told—kandra appeared to be very good at that—and left the room, but there were whispers and debates. The Seconds slunk out last, looking humiliated. Sazed watched them go, thinking about KanPaar's words.

We are eternal—we outwait everything and anything. Suddenly, the kandra began to make more sense to Sazed. How easy it would be to ignore the outside world if one were immortal. They had outlasted so many problems and predicaments, upheavals and riots, that anything occurring on the outside must have seemed trivial.

So trivial, in fact, that it was even possible to ignore the prophecies of one's own religion as they started to come true. Eventually, the room was empty, and a pair of beefy members of the Fifth Generation pushed the doors closed from outside, leaving Sazed alone on the floor of the room. He waited patiently, arranging his notes on his desk as the members of the First Generation hobbled out of their hidden stairwells and joined him on the floor of the Trustwarren.

"Tell me, Keeper," Haddek said as his brothers seated themselves, "what do you make of this event?"

"The departure of the mists?" Sazed asked. "It does seem portentous—though, admittedly, I cannot give a specific reason why."

"That is because there are things we have not yet explained to you," Haddek said, looking toward the others. They seemed very troubled. "Things relating to the First Contract, and the promises of the kandra."

Sazed readied a sheet of metal paper. "Please, continue."

"I must ask that you not record these words," Haddek said.

Sazed paused, then set down his pen. "Very well—though I warn you. The memory of a Keeper, even without his metalminds, is very long."

"That cannot be helped," said one of the others. "We need your counsel, Keeper. As an outsider."

"As a son," another whispered.

"When the Father made us," Haddek said. "He . . . gave us a charge. Something different from the First Contract."

"To him, it was almost an afterthought," one of the others added. "Though once he mentioned it, he implied it was very important."

"He made us promise," Haddek said. "Each of us. He told us that someday, we might be required to remove our Blessings."

"Pull them from our bodies," one of the others added.

"Kill ourselves," Haddek said.

The room fell silent.

"You are certain this would kill you?" Sazed asked.

"It would change us back to mistwraiths," Haddek said. "That is the same thing, essentially."

"The Father said we would have to do it," another said. "There wasn't a 'might' about it. He said that we would have to make certain the other kandra knew of this charge."

"We call it the Resolution," Haddek said. "Each kandra is told of it when he or she is first birthed. They are given the charge—sworn and ingrained—to pull their Blessing free, should the First Generation command it. We have never invoked this charge."

"But you're considering it now?" Sazed asked, frowning. "I do not understand. Simply because of the way that the mists are acting?"

"The mists are the body of Preservation, Keeper," Haddek said. "This is a *very* portentous event."

"We have been listening to our children discuss it all morning," another said. "And it troubles us. They do not know all the mists represent, but they are aware of their importance."

"Rashek said that we'd know," another said. "He told us. 'The day will come when you have to remove your Blessings. You'll know when it arrives.' "

Haddek nodded. "He said that we'd know. And . . . we are very worried."

"How can we order the deaths of all of our people?" another asked. "The Resolution has always bothered me."

"Rashek saw the future," Haddek said, turning. "He held the power of Preservation and wielded it. He is the only man ever to have done so! Even this girl of whom the Keeper speaks did not *use* the power. Only Rashek! The Father."

"Where, then, are the mists?" another asked.

The room fell silent again. Sazed sat, pen held in his hand, yet not writing anything. He leaned forward. "The mists are the body of Preservation?"

The others nodded.

"And . . . it has disappeared?"

Again, a nod.

"Does this not mean, then, that Preservation has returned?"

"That is impossible," Haddek said. "Preservation's power remains, for power cannot be destroyed. His mind, however, was all but destroyed—for this was the sacrifice he made to imprison Ruin."

"The sliver remains," another reminded. "The shadow of self."

"Yes," Haddek said. "But that is not Preservation, just an image—a remnant. Now that Ruin has escaped, I think we can assume that even it has been destroyed."

"I think it is more," another began. "We could—"

Sazed held up his hands, getting their attention. "If Preservation has not returned, then has, perhaps, someone else taken up his power to use in this fight? Is that not what your teachings say will happen? That which has been sundered must again begin to find its whole."

Silence.

"Perhaps," Haddek said.

Vin, Sazed thought, growing excited. *This is what it means to be the Hero of Ages! I am right to believe. She* can *save us!*

Sazed took a piece of metal paper, beginning to scribble down his thoughts. At that moment, however, the doors to the Trustwarren burst open.

Sazed paused, turning with a frown. A group of rock-boned Fifth Generationers clomped into the room, followed by the willowy members of the Second Generation. Outside, the cavern hallway was empty of its earlier crowd.

"Take them," KanPaar said furtively, pointing.

"What is this!" Haddek exclaimed.

Sazed sat where he was, pen held in his fingers. He recognized the urgent, tense posture in the figures of the Second Generationers. Some looked frightened, others determined. The Fifth Generationers moved forward quickly, their movements enhanced by the Blessing of Potency.

"KanPaar!" Haddek said. "What is this?"

Sazed slowly stood up. Four Fifth Generationers came over to surround him, bearing hammers as weapons.

"It's a coup," Sazed said.

"You can no longer lead," KanPaar said to the First Generation. "You would destroy what we have here, polluting our land with outsiders, letting the talk of revolutionaries cloud kandra wisdom."

"This is not the time, KanPaar," Haddek said, the members of the First Generation crying out as they were prodded and grappled.

"Not the time?" KanPaar asked angrily. "You spoke of the Resolution! Have you no idea the panic this has caused? You would destroy *everything* we have."

Sazed turned calmly, looking at KanPaar. Despite his angry tone, the kandra was smiling slightly through translucent lips.

He had to strike now, Sazed thought, *before the First Generation said more to the common people—making the Seconds redundant. KanPaar can stuff them all away somewhere, and then prop up dummies in the alcoves.*

Sazed reached for his pewtermind. One of the Fifths snapped it away with a too-quick grab of the hand, and two others took Sazed by the arms. He struggled, but his kandra captors were inhumanly strong.

"KanPaar!" Haddek yelled. The First's voice was surprisingly strong. "You are of the Second Generation—you owe obedience to me. We created you!"

KanPaar ignored him, directing his kandra to bind the

members of the First Generation. The other Seconds stood in a cluster behind him, looking increasingly apprehensive and shocked at what they were doing.

"The time for the Resolution may indeed be here!" Haddek said. "We must—" He cut off as one of the Fifths gagged him.

"That is exactly why I must take leadership," KanPaar said, shaking his head. "You are too unstable, old one. I will not trust the future of our people to a creature who could, at a whim, order them to kill themselves."

"You fear change," Sazed said, meeting the kandra's eyes.

"I fear instability," KanPaar said. "I will make certain the kandra people have a firm and immutable leadership."

"You make the same argument as many revolutionaries," Sazed said. "And I can see your concern. However, you *must* not do this thing. Your own prophecies are coming to a head. I understand now! Without the part the kandra are to play, you could inadvertently cause the end of all things. Let me continue my research—lock us in this room if you must—but do not—"

"Gag him," KanPaar said, turning.

Sazed struggled, with no success, as his mouth was bound and he was pulled from the Trustwarren, leaving the atium—the body of a god—behind, and in the hands of traitors.

I've always wondered about the strange ability Allomancers have to pierce the mists. When one burned tin, he or she could see farther at night, looking through the mists. To the layman, this might seem like a logical connection—tin, after all, enhances the senses.

The logical mind, however, may find a puzzle in this ability. How, exactly, would tin let one see through the mists? As an obstruction, they are unconnected with the quality of one's eyesight. Both the nearsighted scholar and the long-sighted scout would have the same trouble seeing into the distance if there were a wall in the way.

This, then, should have been our first clue. Allomancers could see through the mists because the mists were, indeed, composed of the very same power as Allomancy. Once attuned by burning tin, the Allomancer was almost part of the mists. And therefore, they became more translucent to him.

76

VIN . . . FLOATED. SHE WASN'T ASLEEP, but she didn't quite feel awake either. She was disoriented, uncertain. Was she still lying in the broken courtyard of Kredik Shaw? Was she sleeping in her cabin aboard the narrowboat with Elend? Was she in her palace quarters, back in Luthadel, the city under siege? Was she in Clubs's shop, worried and confused by the kindness of this strange new crew?

Was she huddled in an alleyway, crying, back hurting from another of Reen's beatings?

She felt about her, trying to make sense of her surroundings. Her arms and legs didn't seem to work. In fact, she couldn't even really focus on them. The longer she floated, however, the clearer her vision became. She was . . . in Luthadel. After killing the Inquisitors.

Why couldn't she feel anything? She tried to reach down, to push herself to her knees, but the ground seemed strangely far away. And, she saw no arms in front of her. She just continued to float.

I'm dead, she thought.

Even as that occurred to her, she woke up a bit more. She could see, though it was as if she looked through a very blurry, distorting pane of glass. She felt . . . a power buzzing within her. A strength unlike that of limbs—but somehow more versatile.

She managed to turn, getting a sweeping view of the city. And, halfway through her turn, she came face-to-face with something dark.

She couldn't tell how far away it was. It seemed close and distant at the same time. She could view it with detail—far more detail than she could see in the actual world—but she couldn't touch it. She knew, instinctively, what it was.

Ruin no longer looked like Reen. Instead, he manifested as a large patch of shifting black smoke. A thing without a body, but with a consciousness greater than that of a simple human.

That . . . is what I've become, Vin realized, thoughts becoming clearer.

Vin, Ruin spoke. His voice was not that of Reen, but instead something more . . . guttural. It was a vibration that washed across her, like an Allomantic pulse.

Welcome, Ruin said, *to godhood.*

Vin remained silent, though she quested out with her power, trying to get a sense of what she could do. Understanding seemed to open to her. It was like before, when she'd taken the power at the Well of Ascension. She immediately *knew* things. Only this time, the power was so vast—the understanding so great—that it seemed to have shocked her mind. Fortunately, that mind was expanding, and she was growing.

Awakening.

She rose above the city, knowing that the power spinning through her—the core of her existence—was simply a hub. A focus for power that stretched across the entire world. She could be anywhere she wished. Indeed, a part of her was in all places at once. She could see the world as a whole.

And it was dying. She felt its tremors, saw its life ebbing. Already, most of the plant life on the planet was dead. Animals would go quickly—the ones who survived were those who could find a way to chew on dead foliage now covered by ash. Humans would not be far behind, though Vin found it interesting to note that a surprising percentage of them had found their way down into one or another of the storage caverns.

Not storage caverns . . . Vin thought, finally understanding the Lord Ruler's purpose. *Shelters. That's why they're so vast. They're like fortresses for people to hide in. To wait, to survive a little longer.*

Well, she would fix that. She felt electrified with power. She reached out and plugged the ashmounts. She soothed them, deadened them, smothered their ability to spray ash and lava. Then, she reached into the sky and wiped the smoke and darkness from the atmosphere—like a maid wiping soot from a dirty window. She did all of this in a matter of instants; not more than five minutes would have passed on the world below.

Immediately, the land began to burn.

The sun was amazingly powerful—she hadn't realized how much the ash and smoke had done to shield the land. She cried out, spinning the world quickly so that the sun moved to its other side. Darkness fell. And, as soon as she did that, tempests began to swoop across the landscape. Weather patterns were disrupted by the motion, and in the sea a sudden wave appeared, enormously large. It rolled toward the coast, threatening to wipe away several cities.

Vin cried out again, reaching to stop the wave. And something blocked her.

She heard laughter. She turned in the air, looking to where Ruin sat like a shifting, undulating thundercloud.

Vin, Vin . . . he said. *Do you realize how like the Lord Ruler you are? When he first took the power, he tried to solve everything. All of man's ills.*

She saw it. She wasn't omniscient—she couldn't see the entirety of the past. However, she *could* see the history of the power she held. She could see when Rashek had taken it, and she could see him, frustrated, trying to pull the planet into a proper orbit. Yet, he pulled it too far, leaving the world cold and freezing. He pushed it back again, but his power was too vast—too terrible—for him to control properly at that time. So, he again left the world too hot. All life would have perished.

He opened the ashmounts, clogging the atmosphere, turning the sun red. And, in doing so, he saved the planet—but doomed it as well.

You are so impetuous, Ruin thought. *I have held this power for a period of time longer than you can imagine. It takes care and precision to use it correctly.*

Unless, of course, you just want to destroy.

He reached out with a power Vin could feel. Immediately, without knowing how or why, she blocked him. She threw her power up against his, and he halted, unable to act.

Below, the tsunami crashed into the coast. There were still people down there. People who had hidden from the koloss, who had survived on fish from the sea when their crops failed. Vin felt their pain, their terror, and she cried out as she reached to protect them.

And, again, was stopped.

Now you know the frustration, Ruin said as the tsunami destroyed villages. *What was it your Elend said? For every Push, there is a Pull. Throw something up, and it will come back down. Opposition.*

For Ruin, there is Preservation. Time immemorial! Eternity! And each time I push, YOU push back. Even when dead, you stopped me, for we are forces. I can do nothing! And you can do nothing! Balance! The curse of our existence.

Vin suffered as the people below were crushed, washed away, and drowned. *Please,* she said. *Please just let me save them.*

Why? Ruin asked. *What is it I told you before? Everything you do serves me. It is out of kindness that I stop you. For, even if you were to reach your hand out for them, you would destroy more than you preserve.*

That is always the way it is.

Vin hung, listening to the screams. And yet, a part of her mind—now so vast, now capable of many thoughts at once—dissected Ruin's words.

They were untrue. He said that all things destroyed, yet he complained about balance. He warned that she would only destroy more, but she could not believe that he would stop her out of kindness. He wanted her to destroy.

It couldn't be both ways. She knew herself as his opposite. She *could* have saved those people, if he hadn't stopped her. True, she probably didn't have the accuracy to do it yet. That wasn't the power's fault, however, but hers. He had to stop her so that she wouldn't learn, as the Lord Ruler had, and become more capable with the power.

She spun away from him, moving back toward Luthadel. Her awareness was still expanding, but she was confused by something she saw. Bright points of light, dotting the landscape, shining like flares. She drew closer, trying to figure out what they were. Yet, just as it was difficult to look directly at a bright lantern and see what was emitting the light, it was difficult to discern the source of this power.

She figured it out as she reached Luthadel. A large glow was coming from the broken palace. Most of the light was shaped vaguely like . . .

Spires. Metal. *That's* what caused the glowing power. *I was right. Metal is power, and it's why Ruin couldn't read things written in steel.* Vin turned away from a brightly shining spire. Ruin was there, as always, watching her.

I was surprised when Preservation said he wanted to create you, Ruin said, a bit of curiosity in his voice. *Other life is ordered by way of nature. Balanced. But Preservation . . . he wanted to create something intentionally unbalanced. Something that could choose to preserve at times, but to ruin at others. Something in the form of that which we'd seen before. It was intriguing.*

I find it odd that he expended so much of himself to create you. Why would he weaken himself, eventually giving me the strength to destroy the world, simply to place human beings on his world? I know that others call his death to imprison me a sacrifice, but that *wasn't the sacrifice. His sacrifice came much earlier.*

Yes, he still tried to betray me—to imprison me. But, he could not stop me. He could only slow me. Forestall. Delay. Since the day we created you, there has been an imbalance. I was stronger. And he knew it.

Vin frowned—or, at least, she felt as if she were frowning, though she no longer had a body. His words . . .

He says he's stronger, Vin thought. *Yet, we are equally matched. Is he lying again?*

No . . . he didn't lie. Looking back with her ever-expanding mind, she saw that everything Ruin said, he *believed.* He truly thought that whatever she did helped him. He saw the world through the lenses of destruction.

He wasn't lying about being more powerful than she. Yet, they were obviously matched at the moment. Which meant . . .

There's another piece of Ruin out there, Vin thought. *Preservation* is *weaker because he gave up a piece of himself to create mankind. Not his consciousness—that he used to fuel Ruin's prison—but an actual bit of his power.*

What she had suspected before, she now knew with certainty. Ruin's power was concentrated, hidden somewhere by Preservation. *The atium.* Ruin *was* stronger. Or, he would be, once he recovered the last part of his self. Then, he would be able to destroy completely—they would no longer be balanced.

She swung about in frustration, a glowing white aura of mist with wispy tendrils expanding across the entire world. *There's so much I still don't know,* Vin thought.

It was an odd thing to acknowledge, with her mind broadening to include so much. Yet, her ignorance was no longer that of a person. Her ignorance was related to experience. Ruin had such a huge head start on her. He had created for himself servants who could act without his direction, and so she could not block them.

She saw his planning manifest in the world. She saw him subtly influencing the Lord Ruler a thousand years ago. Even while Rashek held the power of Preservation, Ruin had whispered in his ear, directing him toward an understanding of Hemalurgy. And, Rashek had obeyed without realizing it, creating minions—armies—for Ruin to take when the time was right.

Vin could see them—the koloss—converging toward Luthadel.

I will give you credit, Vin, Ruin said, hovering nearby. *You destroyed my Inquisitors. All but one, at least. They were very difficult to make. I . . .*

She stopped focusing on him, at least with most of her mind. Something else drew her attention. Something moving into Luthadel, flying on spears of light.

Elend.

Looking back, we should have been able to see the connection between the mists, Allomancy, and the power at the Well of Ascension. Not only could Allomancers' vision pierce the mists, but there was the fact that the mists swirled slightly around the body of a person using any kind of Allomancy.

More telling, perhaps, was the fact that when a Hemalurgist used his abilities, it drove the mists away. The closer one came to Ruin, the more under his influence, and the longer one bore his spikes, the more the mists were repelled.

77

ELEND STOOD IN THE RUBBLE of Kredik Shaw, mind numb as he contemplated the destruction.

It seemed . . . impossible. What force could have leveled such an enormous, majestic building? What could have caused such destruction, breaking apart buildings and flinging rubble several streets away? And, all of the destruction was focused here, at what had once been the center of the Lord Ruler's power.

Elend skidded down some rubble, approaching the center of what looked like an impact crater. He turned around in the dark night, looking at the fallen blocks and spires.

"Lord Ruler . . ." he swore quietly, unable to help himself. Had something happened at the Well of Ascension? Had it exploded?

Elend turned, looking across his city. It appeared to be empty. Luthadel, largest metropolis in the Final Empire, seat of his government. Empty. Much of it in ruins, a good third of it burned, and Kredik Shaw itself flattened as if it had been pounded by the fist of a god.

Elend dropped a coin and shot away, heading along his

original path toward the northeastern section of the city. He'd come to Luthadel hoping to find Vin, but had been forced to take a slight detour to the south in order to get around a particularly large swath of lava burning the plains around Mount Tyrian. That sight, along with the sight of Luthadel in ruin, left him very disturbed.

Where was Vin?

He jumped from building to building. He kicked up ash with each leap. Things were happening. The ash was slowly trickling away—in fact, it had mostly stopped falling. That was good, but he remembered well a short time ago when the sun had suddenly blazed with an amazing intensity. Those few moments had burned him so that his face still hurt.

Then, the sun had . . . dropped. It had fallen below the horizon in less than a second, the ground lurching beneath Elend's feet. Part of him assumed that he was going mad. Yet, he could not deny that it was now nighttime, even if his body—and one of the city clocks he had visited—indicated that it should have been afternoon.

He landed on a building, then jumped off, Pushing against a broken door handle. He shivered as he moved in the open air of darkness. It was night—the stars blazing uncomfortably above—and there was no mist. Vin had told him that the mists would protect him. What would protect him now that they were gone?

He made his way to Keep Venture, his palace. He found the building to be a burned-out husk. He landed in the courtyard, staring up at his home—the place he had been raised—trying to make sense of the destruction. Several guards in the brown colors of his livery lay decomposing on the cobblestones. All was still.

What in the hell happened here? he thought with frustration. He poked through the building, but found no clues. All had been burned. He left via a broken window on the top floor, then paused at something he saw in the rear courtyard.

He dropped to the ground. And there, beneath a patio canopy that had kept off much of the ash, he found a corpse in a fine gentlemen's suit lying on the cobbles. Elend rolled it over, noting the sword thrust through its stomach and the posture of a suicide. The corpse's fingers still held the weapon. *Penrod,* he thought, recognizing the face. Dead, presumably, by his own hand.

Something lay scrawled in charcoal on the patio floor. Elend wiped away the drifted ash, smudging the letters in the process. Fortunately, he could still read them. *I'm sorry,* it read. *Something has taken control of me . . . of this city. I am lucid only part of the time. Better to kill myself than to cause more destruction. Look toward the Terris Dominance for your people.*

Elend turned toward the north. Terris? That seemed like a very odd place in which to seek refuge. If the people of the city had fled, then why would they have left the Central Dominance, the place where the mists were the weakest?

He eyed the scribbles.

Ruin . . . a voice seemed to whisper. *Lies . . .*

Ruin could change text. Words like Penrod's couldn't be trusted. Elend bid a silent farewell to the corpse, wishing he had the time to bury the old statesman, then dropped a coin to Push himself into the air.

The people of Luthadel had gone *somewhere.* If Ruin had found a way to kill them, then Elend would have found more corpses. He suspected that if he took the time to search, he could probably find people still hiding in the city. Likely, the disappearance of the mists—then the sudden change from day to night—had driven them into hiding. Perhaps they had made it to the storage cavern beneath Kredik Shaw. Elend hoped that not many had gone there, considering the damage that had been done to the palace. If there were people there, they would be sealed in.

West . . . the wind seemed to whisper. *Pits . . .*

Ruin usually changes text so that it's very similar to what it said before, Elend thought. *So . . . Penrod probably did write most of those words, trying to tell me where to go to find my people. Ruin made it sound like they went to the Terris Dominance, but what if Penrod originally wrote that they went to the Terris people?*

It made good sense. If he'd fled Luthadel, he would have

gone there—it was a place where there was already an established group of refugees, a group with herds, crops, and food.

Elend turned west, leaving the city, cloak flapping with each Allomantic bound.

Suddenly, Ruin's frustration made even more sense to Vin. She felt she held the power of all creation. Yet, it took everything she had to get even a few words to Elend.

She wasn't even certain if he'd heard her or not. She knew him so well, however, that she felt a . . . connection. Despite Ruin's efforts to block her, she felt as if some part of her had been able to get through to some part of Elend. Perhaps in the same way Ruin was able to communicate with his Inquisitors and followers?

Still, her near-impotence was infuriating.

Balance, Ruin spat. *Balance imprisoned me. Preservation's sacrifice—that was to siphon off the part of me that was stronger, to lock it away, to leave me equal with him again. For a time.*

Only for a time. And what is time to us, Vin?

Nothing.

It may seem odd to those reading this that atium was part of the body of a god. However, it is necessary to understand that when we said "body" we generally meant "power." As my mind has expanded, I've come to realize that objects and energy are actually composed of the very same things, and can change state from one to another. It makes perfect sense to me that the power of godhood would be manifest within the world in physical form. Ruin and Preservation were not nebulous abstractions. They were integral parts of existence. In a way, every object that existed in the world was composed of their power.

Atium, then, was an object that was one-sided. Instead of being composed of half Ruin and half Preservation—as, say, a rock would be—atium was completely of Ruin. The Pits of Hathsin were crafted by Preservation as a place to hide the chunk of Ruin's body that he had stolen away during the betrayal and imprisonment. Kelsier didn't truly destroy this place by shattering those crystals, for they would have regrown eventually—in a few hundred years—and continued to deposit atium, as the place was a natural outlet for Ruin's trapped power.

When people burned atium, then, they were drawing upon the power of Ruin—which is, perhaps, why atium turned people into such efficient killing machines. They didn't use up this power, however, but simply made use of it. Once a nugget of atium was expended, the power would return to the Pits and begin to coalesce again—just as the power at the Well of Ascension would return there again after it had been used.

78

THIS IS, SAZED THOUGHT, *WITHOUT a doubt, the oddest dungeon I have ever been in.*

Granted, it was only the second time he had been imprisoned. Still, he had observed several prisons in his lifetime, and had read of others. Most were like cages. This one, however, consisted only of a hole in the ground with an iron grate covering the top. Sazed scrunched down inside of it, stripped of his metalminds, his legs cramped.

It was probably built for a kandra, he thought. *One without bones, perhaps?* What would a kandra without bones be like? A pile of goo? Or, perhaps, a pile of muscles?

Either way, this prison had not been meant to hold a man—particularly not one as tall as Sazed. He could barely move. He reached up, pushing against the grate, but it was secure. A large lock held it in place.

He wasn't certain how long he had been in the pit. Hours? Perhaps even days. They still hadn't given him anything to eat, though a member of the Third Generation had poured some water on him. Sazed was still wet with it, and he had taken to sucking on the cloth of his robes to assuage his thirst.

This is silly, he thought, not for the first time. *The world is ending, and I'm in prison?* He was the final Keeper, the Announcer. He should be up above, recording events.

Because, truth be told, he was beginning to believe that the world would not end. He had accepted that something, perhaps Preservation itself, was watching over and protecting mankind. He was more and more determined to follow the Terris religion—not because it was perfect, but because he would rather believe and have hope.

The Hero *was* real. Sazed believed that. And he had faith in her.

He had lived with Kelsier and had helped the man. He had chronicled the rise of the Church of the Survivor during the first years of its development. He had even researched the Hero of Ages with Tindwyl and taken it upon himself to announce Vin as the one who fulfilled the prophecies. But it was only recently that he'd started to have faith in her. Perhaps it was his decision to be someone who saw miracles. Perhaps it was the daunting fear of the ending that seemed to loom just ahead. Perhaps it was the tension and anxiety. Regardless, somehow, from the chaos, he drew peace.

She would come. She would preserve the world. However, Sazed needed to be ready to help. And that meant escaping.

He eyed the metal grate. The lock was of fine steel, the grate itself of iron. He reached up tentatively, touching the bars, draining a bit of his weight and putting it into the iron. Immediately, his body grew lighter. In Feruchemy, iron stored physical weight, and the grate was pure enough to hold a Feruchemical charge. It went against his instincts to use the grate as a metalmind—it wasn't portable, and if he had to flee, he'd leave behind all of the power he'd saved. Yet, what good would it be to simply sit in the pit and wait?

He reached up with the other hand, touching the steel lock with one finger. Then, he began to fill it as well, draining his body of speed. He instantly began to feel lethargic, as if his every motion—even his breathing—was more difficult. It was like he had to push through some thick substance each time he moved.

He stayed that way. He had learned to enter a kind of meditative trance when he filled metalminds. Often, he would fill many at once, leaving himself sickly, weak, slow, and dull-minded. When he could, it was better to simply . . .

Drift.

He wasn't certain how long the meditation lasted. Occasionally, the guard came to pour water on him. When the sounds came, Sazed would let go and huddle down, pretending to sleep. But, as soon as the guard withdrew, he would reach back up and continue to fill the metalminds.

More time passed. Then, he heard sounds. Sazed huddled down again, then waited expectantly for the shower of water.

"When I sent you back to save my people," a voice growled, "this wasn't exactly what I had in mind."

Sazed popped his eyes open, glancing upward, and was surprised to see a canine face looking through the grate. "TenSoon?" Sazed asked.

The kandra grunted and stepped back. Sazed perked up as another kandra appeared. She wore a delicate True Body made of wood, willowy and almost inhuman. And, she held some keys.

"Quickly, MeLaan," TenSoon growled with his dog's voice. He had apparently switched back to the wolfhound, which made sense. Moving as a horse through the sometimes steep and narrow tunnels of the Homeland would have been difficult.

The female kandra unlocked the grate, then pulled it back. Sazed eagerly climbed free. In the room, he found several other kandra wearing deviant True Bodies. In the corner, the prison guard lay bound and gagged.

"I was seen entering the Homeland, Terrisman," TenSoon said. "So we have little time. What has happened here? MeLaan told me of your imprisonment—KanPaar announced that the First Generation had ordered you taken. What did you do to antagonize them?"

"Not them," Sazed said, stretching his cramped legs. "It was the Second Generation. They have taken the Firsts captive, and plan to rule in their stead."

The girl—MeLaan—gasped. "They would never!"

"They did," Sazed said, standing. "I fear for the safety of the Firsts. KanPaar may have been afraid to kill me because I am human. However, the Firsts . . ."

"But," MeLaan said, "the Seconds are kandra. They wouldn't do something like that! We're not that kind of people."

TenSoon and Sazed shared a look. *All societies have people who break the rules, child,* Sazed thought. *Particularly when power is concerned.*

"We have to find the Firsts," TenSoon said. "And recover the Trustwarren."

"We will fight with you, TenSoon," one of the other kandra said.

"We're finally throwing them off!" another said. "The Seconds, and their insistence that we serve the humans!"

Sazed frowned at this. What did humans have to do with this conflict? Then, however, he noticed how the others regarded TenSoon. *The dog's body,* he realized. *To them, TenSoon is a revolutionary of the highest order—all because of something Vin ordered him to do.*

TenSoon met Sazed's eyes again, opening his mouth to speak. Then, however, he paused. "They're coming," he said with a curse, his dog's ears flattening.

Sazed spun with concern, noticing shadows on the rock wall of the corridor leading into the prison chamber. The chamber was small, with six or so pit cells in the floor. There were no other entrances.

Despite their brave words, TenSoon's companions immediately shied back, huddling against the wall. They were obviously not accustomed to conflict, particularly with their own kind. TenSoon shared none of their timidity. He charged forward as soon as the group of Fifths entered the room, ramming his shoulder into one's chest, howling and clawing at another.

There is a kandra who fits in with his people as poorly as I do with my own, Sazed thought, smiling. He stepped backward, moving up onto the top of the prison grate, touching its metals with his bare feet.

The Fifths had trouble fighting TenSoon—he had trained with Vin, and was apparently quite confident in his dog's body. He kept moving, knocking them over. However, there were five of them, and only one TenSoon. He was forced to retreat.

The wounds in his body close as he orders them, Sazed noticed. *That must be why the guards usually carry hammers.*

Which made it fairly obvious how one had to fight kandra. TenSoon backed up beside Sazed. "I apologize," the dog growled. "This isn't much of a rescue."

"Oh, I don't know," Sazed said with a smile, the Fifths surrounding them. "You needn't give up so quickly, I think."

The Fifths charged, and Sazed tapped iron from the grate beneath his bare feet. Immediately, his body grew several times heavier than normal, and he grabbed a kandra guard by the arms.

Then fell on him.

Sazed always said he wasn't a warrior. However, the number of times he'd said that, then been forced to fight anyway, made him think he was losing that excuse. The truth was, he'd been in far more battles over the last few years than he felt he had any right to have survived.

Either way, he knew some rudimentary moves—and, with both Feruchemy and surprise to aid him, that was about all he needed. Tapping weight increased the density of his body and of his bones, keeping him from damaging himself as he collapsed on top of the soldier. Sazed felt a satisfying crack as they hit the grate, Sazed's greatly increased weight crushing the kandra guard's bones. They used stone True Bodies, but even that wasn't enough.

Sazed released the metalmind, then began to fill it instead, making his body incredibly light. He touched his foot to the steel lock, and tapped speed. Suddenly, he was faster than any man had a right to be. He stood up even as the other four guards turned toward him in surprise.

He stopped filling his ironmind, regaining normal weight, then reached with a blurring speed to pick up the hammer of the fallen soldier. He didn't have enhanced strength, but he had speed. He slammed the hammer down on a kandra shoulder, growing heavier to add to the momentum of his blow.

The kandra's bones shattered. Sazed snapped his foot on the lock and tapped all of the remaining speed. He crouched, pivoting, and slammed his hammer into the knees of two kandra who were trying to attack him with their own hammers.

They cried out, falling, as Sazed's speed ran out.

He stood up straight. TenSoon was sitting atop the final guard, pinning him to the ground. "I thought you were a scholar," the dog noted, his captive squirming.

Sazed tossed aside the hammer. "I am," he said. "Vin would have fought her way free from this prison days ago. Now, I believe we should deal with these . . ." He waved toward the fallen Fifths, who seemed to have quite a bit of trouble moving with their bones broken.

TenSoon nodded. He motioned for some of his friends to help him with the one he was sitting on. They held the captive tentatively, but there were enough of them to keep the prisoner still.

"What have you done here, FhorKood?" TenSoon demanded of the captive. Sazed kept an eye on the other Fifths, and was forced to slam a mallet against one of them, breaking more bones as he tried to sneak away.

FhorKood spat. "Dirty Third," he muttered.

"*You* are the traitor this time," TenSoon said, smiling slightly. "KanPaar brands me a Contract-breaker, then he overthrows the First Generation? If the world weren't ending, I'd find that far more amusing. Now, speak!"

Sazed paused as he noticed something. The other cells in the floor were occupied. He leaned down, recognizing something about the muscles he saw inside. They were . . . discolored, and a bit deformed. Like . . . hanging moss.

"TenSoon!" he said, looking up. "Perhaps the First Generation *is* still alive. Come here."

TenSoon moved over, then looked down at the pit, frowning with canine lips. "MeLaan! The keys!"

She rushed over, unlocking the grate. With some consternation, Sazed was able to determine that there were multiple sets of squirming muscles in the pit, each of a slightly different color.

"We need bones," TenSoon said, standing.

MeLaan nodded, rushing from the room. Sazed shared a look with TenSoon.

"They must have killed the other kandra in these cells," TenSoon said softly. "Traitors to our kind, imprisoned endlessly. It was to have been my fate. Either way, it is clever—everyone thinks that these cells hold dire criminals. It wouldn't be odd for the Fifths to continue feeding them, and nobody would suspect that the occupants had been replaced with the First Generation, assuming they didn't look too closely at the color of the muscles."

"We need to keep moving," Sazed said. "Get to KanPaar."

TenSoon shook his head. "We won't get far without the Firsts to tell our story, Terrisman. Go and store more of your Feruchemy. We may need it."

With that, TenSoon moved, crouching over their captive. "You have two options, FhorKood," he said. "Either relinquish those bones, or I'll digest your body and kill you, as I did OreSeur."

Sazed frowned, watching. The captured kandra seemed terrified of TenSoon. The Fifth's body liquefied, and he moved slug-like away from the granite bones. TenSoon smiled.

"What is that for?" Sazed asked.

"Something Zane taught me," TenSoon said, his dog's body beginning to melt, the hair falling out. "Nobody expects a *kandra* to be an impostor. In a few moments, FhorKood here will return to the Second Generation and tell them that the traitor TenSoon has been captured. I should be able to stall long enough for the Firsts to regenerate—they will take far longer than I do to make bodies."

Sazed nodded. MeLaan returned a short time later with a large sack full of bones, and TenSoon—having re-created FhorKood's body with incredible speed—moved out of the chamber on his mission.

Then, Sazed sat down, removing the lock and holding it to use as a metalmind, using an iron hammer in the other hand to store weight. It felt odd to just sit there, but apparently the Firsts would need a few hours to regenerate their bodies.

There really isn't a rush, is there? Sazed thought. *I have the First Generation here—they're the ones I needed. I can continue to question them, learn what I want. TenSoon will have KanPaar distracted. It doesn't matter that the Seconds will be in charge for a few more hours.*

What harm could they possibly do?

I believe that the mists were searching for someone to become a new host for them. The power needed a consciousness to direct it. In this matter, I am still rather confused. Why would power used to create and destroy need a mind to oversee it? And yet, it seems to have only a vague will of its own, tied in to the mandate of its abilities. Without a consciousness to direct it, nothing could actually be created or destroyed. It's as if the power of Preservation understands that its tendency to reinforce stability is not enough. If nothing changed, nothing would ever come to exist.

That makes me wonder who or what the minds of Preservation and Ruin were.

Regardless, the mists—the power of Preservation—chose someone to become their host long before all of this happened. That someone, however, was immediately seized by Ruin and used as a pawn. He must have known that by giving her a disguised Hemalurgic spike, he would keep the mists from investing themselves in her as they wished.

The three times she drew upon their power, then, were the three times when her earring had been removed from her body. When she had fought the Lord Ruler, his Allomancy had ripped it free. When fighting Marsh in Fadrex, she had used the earring as a weapon.

And, at the end, Marsh ripped it out, freeing her and allowing the mists—which were now desperate for a host, since Preservation's last wisp was gone—to finally pour themselves into her.

79

SOMETHING CHANGED.

Vin arose from her contemplation of the world. Something important was happening. She didn't have enough experience to tell what it was immediately, but she did see Ruin's nexus suddenly shoot away.

She followed. Speed wasn't an issue. In fact, she didn't even really feel like she was moving. She "followed" because that was how her mind interpreted the experience of instantly moving her consciousness to the place where Ruin had focused his.

She recognized the area. The Pits of Hathsin, or a place nearby. As a portion of her mind had noticed earlier, the Pits themselves had become a massive refugee camp, the people there quickly consuming the resources that the Terris people had carefully stored. A part of her smiled. The Terris gave of their goods freely, helping those who had fled Luthadel. The Lord Ruler had worked to breed the Terris so they were docile. However, had he expected that in making his perfect servants, he would also create a thoughtful, kindly people who would give of their last flocks to help those who were starving?

The thing that she'd noticed earlier didn't have to do with the Terris or their guests. She saw it as she drew closer. A shining blaze of . . . something. Powerful, more mighty than the sun itself to her eyes. She focused on it, but could see little. What could shine so magnificently?

"Take this," a voice said. "Find humans, and trade for weapons and supplies."

"Yes, Lord KanPaar," a second voice said. They were

coming from the center of the shining area. It was to the side of the Pits, only a few minutes' travel from the refugees.

Oh, no . . . Vin thought, feeling a sudden dread.

"The foolish Firsts have sat on this treasure for far too long," KanPaar said. "With these riches, we could be *ruling,* not serving, mankind."

"I . . . thought we didn't want to change things?" the second voice said.

"Oh, we won't. Not quickly, at least. For now, just this small amount needs to be sold . . ."

Hidden beneath the ground, Vin thought, heightened mind making the connections. *In a place that already shines because of the large number of metal deposits. Ruin would never have been able to know where the atium was.*

The depth of the Lord Ruler's strategies amazed her. He had held on for a thousand years, maintaining such an amazing secret, keeping atium safe. She imagined obligators communicating only on metal plates, giving instructions for the operations at the Pits. She imagined caravans traveling from the Pits, carrying atium mixed with gold and coins to hide where it was moving and what exactly was going on.

You don't know what I do for mankind, the Lord Ruler had said.

And I didn't, Vin thought. *Thank you.*

She felt Ruin surge with power, and she blocked him. But just as she had been able to get a tendril of power past Ruin to Elend, Ruin was able to get the tiniest thread through. It was enough, for the one who had spoken was tainted with Hemalurgy. A spike in each shoulder drew Ruin's power and allowed him to speak to their bearer.

A kandra? Vin thought, her senses finally managing to peer through the atium glare to see a creature with a translucent body standing in a cavern, just beneath the ground. Another kandra was crawling out of a hole nearby, carrying a small pouch of atium.

Ruin seized control of the kandra KanPaar. The creature stiffened, his metal spikes betraying him.

Speak of this, Ruin said to KanPaar, Vin feeling his words as they pulsed into the kandra. *How much atium is there?*

"Wha . . . who are you?" KanPaar said. "Why are you in my head?"

I am God, the voice said. *And you are mine.*

All of you are mine.

Elend landed outside the Pits of Hathsin, throwing up a puff of ash. Oddly, some of his own soldiers were there, guarding the perimeter. They rushed forward, spears held anxiously, then froze when they recognized him.

"Lord *Venture*?" one of the men asked with shock.

"I know you," Elend said, frowning. "From my army at Fadrex."

"You sent us back, my lord," the other soldier said. "With General Demoux. To help Lord Penrod in Luthadel."

Elend glanced up at the night sky, speckled with stars. Some time had passed during his travel to the Pits from Luthadel. If time were now passing normally, the night was halfway through. What would happen when the sun rose again?

"Quickly," Elend said. "I need to speak with the leaders of this camp."

The return of the First Generation was accomplished with as much flair as Sazed had hoped. The old kandra, now wearing larger bodies, still bore the distinctive colorings and aged skin of their generation. He had feared that the ordinary kandra would not recognize them. However, he hadn't counted on the long life spans of the kandra people. Even if the Firsts only emerged once every century, most of the kandra would have seen them several times.

Sazed smiled as the group of Firsts moved into the main kandra chamber, continuing to cause shock and surprise in the others. They proclaimed KanPaar had betrayed them and imprisoned them, then called the kandra people to assemble. Sazed stayed back behind MeLaan and the others, watching for snags in their plan.

To the side, he saw a familiar kandra approaching.

"Keeper," TenSoon said, still wearing the body of a Fifth. "We need to be careful. There are strange things afoot."

"Such as?" Sazed asked.

Then, TenSoon attacked him.

Sazed started, and his moment of confusion cost him dearly. TenSoon—or whoever it was—got his hands around Sazed's throat and began to choke him. They fell backward, drawing the attention of the surrounding kandra. Sazed's assailant—bearing bones of rock—weighed far more than Sazed, and was easily able to roll to the top, his hands still on Sazed's neck.

"TenSoon?" MeLaan asked, sounding terrified.

It's not him, Sazed thought. *It can't be. . . .*

"Keeper," his assailant said between clenched teeth. "Something is very wrong."

You're telling me! Sazed tried to gasp for breath, reaching toward the pocket of his robe, struggling to grab the metalmind lock inside.

"I can barely keep myself from crushing your throat right now," the kandra continued. "Something has control of me. It wants me to kill you."

You're doing a pretty good job! Sazed thought.

"I'm sorry," TenSoon said.

The Firsts had gathered around them. Sazed was barely able to focus, panic controlling him as he fought a much stronger, much heavier foe. He grabbed hold of his impromptu steelmind, but only then realized that speed would do him little good when he was being held so tightly.

"It has come, then," whispered Haddek, leader of the Firsts. Sazed barely noticed as one of the other Firsts began to shake. People were crying out but the blood thumping in Sazed's ears kept him from hearing what they were saying.

Haddek turned away from the gasping Sazed. And then, in a loud voice, yelled something. "The Resolution has come!"

Above him, TenSoon jerked. Something within the kandra seemed to be fighting—tradition and a lifetime of training warred against the control of an outside force. TenSoon released Sazed with one hand, but kept choking him with the other. Then, with his free hand, the kandra reached toward his own shoulder.

Sazed blacked out.

The kandra people always said they were of Preservation, while the koloss and Inquisitors were of Ruin. Yet, the kandra bore Hemalurgic spikes, just like the others. Was their claim, then, simple delusion?

No, I think not. They were created by the Lord Ruler to be spies. When they said such things, most of us interpreted that as meaning he planned to use them as spies in his new government, because of their ability to imitate other people. Indeed, they were used for this purpose.

But I see something much more grand in their existence. They were the Lord Ruler's double agents, planted with Hemalurgic spikes, yet trusted—taught, bound—to pull them free when Ruin tried to seize them. In Ruin's moment of triumph, when he'd always assumed the kandra would be his on a whim, the vast majority of them immediately switched sides and left him unable to seize his prize.

They were *of Preservation all along.*

80

"THE TERRISMEN DID A GOOD job with this place, my lord," Demoux said.

Elend nodded, walking through the quiet nighttime camp with hands clasped behind his back. He was glad he'd stopped to change into a fresh white uniform before leaving Fadrex. As it was supposed to, the clothing attracted attention. The people seemed to take hope simply from seeing him. Their lives had been cast into chaos—they needed to know that their leader was aware of their situation.

"The camp is enormous, as you can see," Demoux continued. "Several hundred thousand people now live here. Without the Terrismen, I doubt that the refugees would have survived. As it is, they managed to keep sickness to a minimum, to organize crews to filter and bring fresh water to the camp, and to distribute food and blankets."

Demoux hesitated, glancing at Elend. "Food is running out, however," the general said quietly. Apparently, when he'd discovered that Penrod was dead and that most of Luthadel's population was at the Pits, he decided to keep his men there to help.

They passed another campfire, and the people there rose. They watched Elend and his general with hope. At this campfire, Demoux stopped as a young Terriswoman approached and handed him and Elend some warm tea to drink. Her eyes lingered fondly on Demoux, and he thanked her by name. The Terris people were affectionate toward Demoux—they were thankful to him for bringing soldiers to help organize and police the mass of refugees.

The people needed leadership and order in these times. "I shouldn't have left Luthadel," Elend said quietly.

Demoux didn't respond immediately. The two of them finished their tea, then continued on, walking with an honor guard of about ten soldiers, all from Demoux's group. The general had sent several messengers back to Elend. They had never arrived. Perhaps they hadn't been able to get around the lava field. Or perhaps they had run afoul of the very same army of koloss Elend had passed on his way to Luthadel.

Those koloss . . . Elend thought. *The ones we drove away from Fadrex, plus more, are coming directly in this direction. There are even more people here than there were in Fadrex. And they don't have a city wall, or many soldiers at all, to protect them.*

"Have you been able to figure out what happened in Luthadel, Demoux?" Elend asked quietly, pausing in a darkened area between campfires. It still felt so strange to be out with no mists to obscure the night. He could see so much further—yet, oddly, the night didn't seem as bright.

"Penrod, my lord," Demoux said softly. "They say he went mad. He began finding traitors in the nobility, even within his own army. He divided the city, and it turned into another house war. Almost all of the soldiers killed one another, and the city half burned down. The majority of the people escaped, but they have very little by way of protection. A determined group of bandits could probably wreak havoc on this whole group."

Elend fell silent. *House war,* he thought with frustration. *Ruin, using our own tricks against us. That's the same method Kelsier used to seize the city.*

"My lord . . ." Demoux said tentatively.

"Speak," Elend said.

"You were right to send me and my men back," Demoux said. "The Survivor is behind this, my lord. He wanted us here for some reason."

Elend frowned. "What makes you say that?"

"These people," Demoux said, "they fled Luthadel because of Kelsier. He appeared to a pair of soldiers, then a group of people, in the city. They say he'd told them to be ready for disaster, and to lead the people out of the city. It's because of them that so many escaped. Those two soldiers and their friends had supplies prepared, and they had the presence of mind to come here."

Elend's frown deepened. Yet, he had seen too much to reject even such a strange story. "Send for these men," he said.

Demoux nodded, waving for a soldier.

"Also," Elend said, remembering that Demoux and his men had been sick from the mists, "see if anyone here has any Allomantic metals. Pass them out to your soldiers and have them ingest them."

"My lord?" Demoux said, confused, as he turned.

"It's a long story, Demoux," Elend said. "Suffice it to say that your god—or somebody—has made you and your men into Allomancers. Divide your men by the metal it turns out they can burn. We're going to need all of the Coinshots, Thugs, and Lurchers we can get."

Sazed's eyes fluttered open, and he shook his head, groaning. How long had he been out? Probably not long, he realized, as his vision cleared. He'd passed out from lack of air. That kind of thing usually only left one unconscious for a short time.

Assuming one woke up at all.

Which I did, he thought, coughing and rubbing his throat, sitting up. The kandra cavern glowed with the quiet light of its blue phosphorescent lanterns. By that light, he could see that he was surrounded by something strange.

Mistwraiths. The cousins of the kandra, the scavengers that hunted at night and fed on corpses. They moved about Sazed, masses of muscle, flesh, and bone—but with those bones combined in strange, unnatural ways. Feet hanging off at angles, heads connected to arms. Ribs used like legs.

Except, these bones were not actually bone at all, but stone, metal, or wood. Sazed stood up solemnly as he looked over the remnants of the kandra people. Littered across the floor, among the jumbled mass of mistwraiths—who oozed about like giant, translucent slugs—were discarded spikes. Kandra Blessings. The things that had brought them sentience.

They had done it. They had held to their oath, and had removed their spikes rather than be taken over by Ruin. Sazed looked over them with pity, amazement, and respect.

The atium, he thought. *They did this to stop Ruin from getting the atium. I have to protect it!*

He stumbled away from the main chamber, regaining his strength as he made his way to the Trustwarren. He paused, however, as he approached, noticing sounds. He peeked around a corner, and looked down the corridor through the open Trustwarren doorway. Inside, he found a group of kandra—perhaps twenty in number—working to push back the plate on the floor that covered the atium.

Of course they didn't all become mistwraiths, he thought. Some would have been outside of the hearing of the Firsts, or wouldn't have had the courage to pull their spikes free. In fact, as he thought about it, he was even more impressed that so many *had* obeyed the command from the First Generation.

Sazed easily recognized KanPaar directing the work inside. The kandra would take the atium and would deliver it to Ruin. Sazed had to stop them. But it was twenty against one—with Sazed having only one small metalmind. It didn't seem like good odds for him.

However, then Sazed noticed something sitting outside the doors of the Trustwarren. A simple cloth sack, of little note save for the fact that Sazed recognized it. He'd carried his metalminds in it for years. They must have tossed it there after taking Sazed captive. It lay about twenty feet down the corridor from him, right beside the doorway into the Trustwarren.

In the other room, KanPaar looked up, staring directly toward Sazed's position. Ruin had noticed him.

Sazed didn't pause to think further. He reached into his pocket, grabbed the steel lock, and tapped it. He rushed through the corridor on inhumanly quick feet, snatching his sack from the ground as kandra began to cry out.

Sazed snapped open the sack, and found a collection of bracelets, rings, and bracers inside. He dumped them out, spilling the precious metalminds to the floor and grabbed two particular ones. Then, still moving at blurring speed, he dashed to the side.

His steelmind ran out. One of the rings he'd grabbed was pewter. He tapped it for strength, growing in size and bulk. Then, he slammed the doors to the Trustwarren closed, causing those now trapped inside to cry out in shock. Finally, he tapped the other ring—this one iron. He grew several times heavier, making himself into a doorstop, holding the massive metal doors to the Trustwarren closed.

It was a delaying tactic. He stood, holding the doors shut, his metalminds depleting at an alarming rate. They were the same rings he'd worn at the siege of Luthadel, the ones that had been embedded within him. He'd replenished them following the siege, before he'd given up Feruchemy. They would not last long. What would he do when the kandra burst through the door? He searched desperately for a way to bar or block the portal, but could see nothing. And, if he let go for even a moment, the kandra inside would burst free.

"Please," he whispered, hoping that—like before—the thing that listened would give him a miracle. "I'm going to need help. . . ."

"I swear it was him, my lord," said the soldier, a man named Rittle. "I've believed in the Church of the Survivor since the day of Kelsier's own death, my lord. He preached to me, converted me to the rebellion. I was there when he visited the caves and had Lord Demoux fight for his honor. I'd know Kelsier like I'd know my father. It *was* the Survivor."

Elend turned to the other soldier, who nodded in agreement. "I didn't know him, my lord," said this man. "However, he matched the descriptions. I think it was really him, I do."

Elend turned to Demoux, who nodded. "They described Lord Kelsier very accurately, my lord. He *is* watching over us."

Elend. . . .

A messenger arrived and whispered something to Demoux. The night was dark, and in the torchlight, Elend turned to study the two soldiers who had seen Kelsier. They didn't look like highly reliable witnesses—Elend hadn't exactly left his best soldiers behind when he'd gone campaigning. Still, others had apparently seen the Survivor too. Elend would want to speak with them.

He shook his head. And, where in the world was Vin?

Elend. . . .

"My lord," Demoux said, touching his arm, looking concerned. Elend dismissed the two soldier witnesses. Accurate or not, he owed them a great debt—they had saved many lives with their preparation.

"Scout's report, my lord," Demoux said, face illuminated by a pole-top torch flickering in the night breeze. "Those koloss you saw, they *are* heading this way. Moving quickly.

Scouts saw them approaching in the distance from a hilltop. They . . . could be here before the night is over."

Elend cursed quietly.

Elend. . . .

He frowned. Why did he keep hearing his name on the wind? He turned, looking into the darkness. Something was pulling him, guiding him, whispering to him. He tried to ignore it, turning back to Demoux. And yet, it was there, in his heart.

Come. . . .

It seemed like Vin's voice.

"Gather an honor guard," Elend said, grabbing the torch by its shaft, then throwing on an ashcloak and buttoning it down to his knees. Then, he turned toward the darkness.

"My lord?" Demoux said.

"Just do it!" Elend said, striding off into the darkness.

Demoux called for some soldiers, following in a hurry.

What am I doing? Elend thought, pushing his way through the waist-deep ash, using the cloak to keep his uniform somewhat clean. *Chasing at dreams? Maybe I'm going mad.*

He could see something in his mind. A hillside with a hole in it. A memory, perhaps? Had he come this way before? Demoux and his soldiers followed quietly, looking apprehensive.

Elend pushed onward. He was almost—

He stopped. There it was, the hillside. It would have been indistinguishable from the others around it, except there were tracks leading up to it. Elend frowned, pushing forward through the deep ash, moving to the point where the tracks ended. There, he found a hole in the ground, leading down.

A cave, he thought. *Perhaps . . . a place for my people to hide?*

It wouldn't be big enough for that, likely. Still, the caves Kelsier had used for his rebellion had been large enough to hold some ten thousand men. Curious, Elend poked down into the cave, walking down its steep incline, throwing off the cloak. Demoux and his men followed with curiosity.

The tunnel went down for a bit, and Elend was surprised to find that there was light coming from ahead. Immediately, he flared pewter, growing tense. He tossed aside his torch, then burned tin, enhancing his vision. He could see several poles that glowed blue at the top. They appeared to be made of rock.

What in the world . . . ?

He moved forward quickly, motioning for Demoux and his men to follow. The tunnel led to a vast cavern. Elend stopped. It was as large as one of the storage caverns. Larger, perhaps. Down below, something moved.

Mistwraiths? he realized with surprise. *Is this where they hide? In holes in the ground?*

He dropped a coin, shooting himself through the poorly lit cavern to land on the stone floor a distance away from Demoux and the others. The mistwraiths weren't as large as others he had seen. And . . . why were they using rocks and wood in place of bones?

He heard a sound. Only tin-enhanced ears let him catch it, but it sounded distinctly unlike a sound a mistwraith would make. Stone against metal. He waved sharply to Demoux, then moved carefully down a side corridor.

At its end, he stopped in surprise. A familiar figure stood against a pair of large metal doors, grunting, apparently trying to hold them closed.

"*Sazed?*" Elend asked, standing up straighter.

Sazed looked up, saw Elend, and was apparently so surprised that he lost control of the doors. They burst open, throwing the Terrisman aside, revealing a group of angry, translucent-skinned kandra.

"Your Majesty!" Sazed said. "Do not let them escape!"

Demoux and his soldiers clanked up behind Elend. *That's either Sazed, or a kandra who ate his bones,* Elend thought. He made a snap decision. He'd trusted the voice in his ear. He'd trust that this was Sazed.

The group of kandra tried to get past Demoux's soldiers. However, the kandra weren't particularly good warriors, and their weapons were made of metal. It took Elend and Demoux all of about two minutes to subdue the group, breaking their bones to keep them from healing and escaping.

Afterward, Elend walked over to Sazed, who had stood up and dusted himself off. "How did you find me, Your Majesty?"

"I honestly don't know," Elend said. "Sazed, what is this place?"

"The Homeland of the kandra people, Your Majesty," Sazed said. "And the hiding place of the Lord Ruler's atium hoard."

Elend raised an eyebrow, following Sazed's pointed finger. There was a room beyond the doors, and a pit in the floor.

Great, Elend thought. *Now we find it.*

"You don't look too excited, Your Majesty," Sazed noted. "Kings, armies, Mistborn—even Kelsier himself—have been searching for this cache for years."

"It's worthless," Elend said. "My people are starving, and they can't eat metal. This cavern, however . . . it might prove useful. What do you think, Demoux?"

"If there are any other chambers like that first one, my lord, it could hold a substantial percentage of our people."

"There are four large caverns," Sazed said. "And four entrances that I know of."

Elend turned to Demoux. He was already giving orders to his soldiers. *We have to get the people down here before the sun rises,* Elend thought, remembering the heat. *At the very least, before those koloss arrive.*

After that . . . well, they would have to see. For now, Elend had only one goal.

Survival.

Snapping has always been the dark side of Allomancy. A person's genetic endowment may make them a potential Allomancer, but in order for the power to manifest, the body must be put through extraordinary trauma. Though Elend spoke of how terrible his beating was, during our day, unlocking Allomancy in a person was easier than it had once been, for we had the infusion of

Preservation's power into the human bloodlines via the nuggets granted to nobility by the Lord Ruler.

When Preservation set up the mists, he was afraid of Ruin escaping his prison. In those early days, before the Ascension, the mists began to Snap people as they did during our time—but this action of the mists was one of the only ways to awaken Allomancy in a person, for the genetic attributes were buried too deeply to be brought out by a simple beating. The mists of that day created Mistings only, of course—there were no Mistborn until the Lord Ruler made use of the nuggets.

The people misinterpreted the mists' intent, as the process of Snapping Allomancers caused some—particularly the young and the old—to die. This hadn't been Preservation's desire, but he'd given up most of his consciousness to form Ruin's prison, and the mists had to be left to work as best they could without specific direction.

Ruin, subtle as ever, knew that he couldn't stop the mists from doing their work. However, he could do the unexpected and encourage *them. And so, he helped make them stronger. That brought death to the plants of the world, and created the threat that became known as the Deepness.*

81

VIN TURNED TOWARD RUIN, PROJECTING a smile. The cloud of twisting black mist seemed agitated.

So, you can influence a single minion, Ruin snapped, turning upon itself, rising in the air. Vin followed, streaking up to loom over the entire Central Dominance. Below, she could see Demoux's soldiers rushing to the camp, waking the people, organizing them to flight. Already, some of them were making their way along the tracks in the ash toward the safety of the caverns.

She could feel the sun, and knew that the planet was far

too near it to be safe. Yet, she could do nothing more. Not only would Ruin have stopped her, but she didn't understand her power yet. She felt as the Lord Ruler must have—almighty, yet clumsy. If she tried to move the world, she would only make things worse.

But, she had accomplished something. Ruin had his koloss pounding toward them at breakneck speed, but they still wouldn't arrive at the Pits for several hours. Plenty of time to get the people to the caverns.

Ruin must have noticed what she was studying, or perhaps he sensed her smugness. *You think you've won?* he asked, sounding amused. *Why, because you managed to stop a few kandra? They were always the weakest of the minions the Lord Ruler created for me. I have made a habit of ignoring them. Either way, Vin, you cannot really think that you have beaten me.*

Vin waited, watching as the people fled to the relative safety of the caverns. Even as the bulk of them arrived—soldiers separating them into groups, sending them to the different entrances—her good humor began to fade. She had managed to get through to Elend, and while it had seemed like a great victory at the moment, she could now see that it was little more than another stalling tactic.

Have you counted the koloss in my army, Vin? Ruin asked. *I've made them from your people, you know. I've gathered hundreds of thousands.*

Vin focused, enumerating instantly. He was telling the truth.

This is the force I could have thrown at you at any time, Ruin said. *Most of them kept to the Outer Dominances, but I've been bringing them in, marching them toward Luthadel. How many times must I tell you, Vin? You can't win. You could never win. I've just been playing with you.*

Vin pulled back, ignoring his lies. He hadn't been playing with them—he'd been trying to discover the secrets that Preservation had left, the secret that the Lord Ruler had kept. Still, the numbers Ruin had finally managed to marshal were awe-inspiring. There were far more koloss than there were people climbing into the caverns. With a force like that, Ruin could assault even a well-fortified position. And, by Vin's count, Elend had fewer than a thousand men with any battle training.

On top of that, there was the sun and its destructive heat, the death of the world's crops, the tainting of water and land with several feet of ash . . . Even the lava flows, which she had stopped, were beginning again, her plugging of the ash-mounts having provided only a temporary solution. A bad one, even. Now that the mountains couldn't erupt, great cracks were appearing in the land, and the magma, the earth's burning blood, was boiling out that way.

We're just so far behind! Vin thought. *Ruin had centuries to plan this. Even when we thought we were being clever, we fell for his plots. What good is it to sequester my people beneath the ground if they're just going to starve?*

She turned toward Ruin, who sat billowing and shifting upon himself, watching his koloss army. She felt a hatred that seemed incompatible with the power she held. The hatred made her sick, but she didn't let go of it.

This thing before her . . . it would destroy everything she knew, everything she loved. It couldn't understand love. It built only so that it could destroy. At that moment, she reversed her earlier decision. She'd never again call Ruin a "him." Humanizing the creature gave it too much respect.

Seething, watching, she didn't know what else to do. So, she attacked.

She wasn't even certain how she did it. She threw herself at Ruin, forcing her power up against its power. There was friction between them, a clash of energy, and it tormented her divine body. Ruin cried out, and—mixing with Ruin—she knew its mind.

Ruin was surprised. It didn't expect Preservation to be able to attack. Vin's move smacked too much of destruction. Ruin didn't know how to respond, but it threw its power back against her in a protective reflex. Their selves crashed, threatening to dissolve. Finally, Vin pulled back, lacerated, rebuffed.

Their power was too well matched. Opposite, yet similar. Like Allomancy.

Opposition, Ruin whispered. *Balance. You'll learn to hate it, I suspect, though Preservation never could.*

"So, *this* is the body of a god?" Elend asked, rolling the bead of atium around in his palm. He held it up next to the one that Yomen had given him.

"Indeed, Your Majesty," Sazed said. The Terrisman looked eager. Didn't he understand how dangerous their situation was? Demoux's scouts—the ones that had returned—reported that the koloss were only minutes away. Elend had ordered his troops posted at the doorways to the Homeland, but his hope—that the koloss wouldn't know where to find his people—was a slim one, considering what Sazed had told him about Ruin.

"Ruin can't help but come for it," Sazed explained. They stood in the metal-lined cavern called the Trustwarren, the place where the kandra had spent the last thousand years gathering and guarding the atium. "This atium is *part* of him. It's what he's been searching for all this time."

"Which means we'll have a couple hundred thousand koloss trying to climb down our throats, Sazed," Elend said, handing back the bead of atium. "I say we give it to him."

Sazed paled. "Give it to him? Your Majesty, my apologies, but that would mean the end of the world. Instantly. I am certain of it."

Great, Elend thought.

"It will be all right, Elend," Sazed said.

Elend frowned up at the Terrisman, who stood peacefully in his robes.

"Vin will come," Sazed explained. "She is the Hero of Ages—she will arrive to save this people. Don't you see how perfect this all is? It's arranged, planned. That you would come here, find me, at this exact moment . . . That you'd be able to lead the people to safety in these caverns . . . Well, it all fits together. She'll come."

Interesting time for him to get his faith back, Elend thought. He rolled Yomen's bead between his fingers, thinking. Outside the room, he could hear whispers. People—Terris stewards, skaa leaders, even a few soldiers—stood listening. Elend could hear the anxiety in their voices. They had heard of the approaching army. As Elend watched, Demoux carefully pushed his way through them and entered the room.

"Soldiers posted, my lord," the general said.

"How many do we have?" Elend asked.

Demoux looked grim. "The two hundred and eighty I brought with me," he said. "Plus about five hundred from the city. Another hundred ordinary citizens that we armed with those kandra hammers, or spare weapons from our soldiers. And, we have four different entrances to this cavern complex we need to guard."

Elend closed his eyes.

"She'll come," Sazed said.

"My lord," Demoux said, pulling Elend aside. "This is bad."

"I know," Elend said, exhaling softly. "Did you give the men metals?"

"What we could find," Demoux said quietly. "The people didn't think to bring powdered metal with them when they fled Luthadel. We've found a couple of noblemen who were Allomancers, but they were only Copperclouds or Seekers."

Elend nodded. He'd bribed or pressed the useful nobleman Allomancers into his army already.

"We gave those metals to my soldiers," Demoux said. "But none of them could burn them. Even if we had Allomancers, we cannot hold this location, my lord! Not with so few soldiers, not against that many koloss. We'll delay them at first, because of the narrow entrances. But . . . well . . ."

"I realize that, Demoux," Elend said with frustration. "But do you have any other options?"

Demoux was silent. "I was hoping you'd have some, my lord."

"None here," Elend said.

Demoux grew grim. "Then we die."

"What about faith, Demoux?" Elend asked.

"I believe in the Survivor, my lord. But . . . well, this looks pretty bad. I've felt like a man waiting his turn before the headsman ever since we spotted those koloss. Maybe the Survivor doesn't want us to succeed here. Sometimes, people just have to die."

Elend turned away, frustrated, clenching and unclenching his fist around the bead of atium. It was the same problem, the same trouble he always had. He'd failed back during the siege of Luthadel—it had taken Vin to protect the city. He'd failed in Fadrex City—only the koloss getting distracted had rescued him there.

A ruler's most basic duty was to protect his people. In this one area, Elend continually felt impotent. Useless.

Why can't I do it? Elend thought with frustration. *I spend a year searching out storage caverns to provide food, only to end up trapped with my people starving. I search all that time looking for the atium—hoping to use it to buy safety for my people—and then I find it too late to spend it on anything.*

Too late. . . .

He paused, glancing back toward the metal plate in the floor.

Years searching for . . . atium.

None of the metals Demoux had given his soldiers had worked. Elend had been working under the assumption that Demoux's group would be like the other mistfallen back in Urteau—that they'd be composed of all kinds of Mistings. Yet, there had been something *different* about Demoux's group. They had fallen sick for far longer than the others.

Elend pushed forward, rushing past Sazed, grabbing a handful of beads. A vast wealth, unlike anything any man had ever possessed. Valuable for its rarity. Valuable for its economic power. Valuable for its *Allomancy.*

"Demoux," he snapped, rising and tossing the bead to him. "Eat this."

Demoux frowned. "My lord?"

"Eat it," Elend said.

Demoux did as asked. He stood for a moment.

Two hundred and eighty men, Elend thought. *Sent away from my army because of all the ones who fell sick, they were the* most *sick. Sixteen days.*

Two hundred and eighty men. One-sixteenth of those who fell sick. One out of sixteen Allomantic metals.

Yomen had proven that there was such a thing as an atium Misting. If Elend hadn't been so distracted, he would have made the connection earlier. If one out of sixteen who fell sick remained that way the longest, would that not imply that they'd gained the most powerful of the sixteen abilities?

Demoux looked up, eyes widening.

And Elend smiled.

Vin hovered outside the cavern, watching with dread as the koloss approached. They were already in a blood frenzy—Ruin had that much control over them. There were thousands upon thousands of them. The slaughter was about to begin.

Vin cried out as they drew closer, throwing herself against Ruin again, trying to drive her power to destroy the thing. As before, she was rebuffed. She felt herself screaming, trembling as she thought about the impending deaths below. It would be like the tsunami deaths on the coast, only worse.

For these were people she knew. People she loved.

She turned back toward the entrance. She didn't want to watch, but she wouldn't be able to do anything else. Her self was everywhere. Even if she pulled her nexus away, she knew that she'd still feel the deaths—that they would make her tremble and weep.

From within the cavern, echoing, she sensed a familiar voice. "Today, men, I ask of you your lives." Vin hovered down, listening, though she couldn't see into the cavern because of the metals in the rock. She could hear, however. If she'd had eyes, she would have been crying, she knew.

"I ask of you your lives," Elend said, voice echoing, "and your courage. I ask of you your faith, and your honor—your strength, and your compassion. For today, I lead you to die. I will not ask you to welcome this event. I will not insult you by calling it well, or just, or even glorious. But I will say this.

"Each moment you fight is a gift to those in this cavern. Each second we fight is a second longer that thousands of people can draw breath. Each stroke of the sword, each koloss felled, each breath earned is a victory! It is a person protected for a moment longer, a life extended, an enemy frustrated!"

There was a brief pause.

"In the end, they will kill us," Elend said, voice loud, ringing in the cavern. "But first, they shall *fear* us!"

The men yelled at this, and Vin's enhanced mind could pick out around two hundred and fifty distinct voices. She heard them split, rushing toward the different cavern entrances. A moment later, someone appeared from the front entrance near her.

A figure in white slowly stepped out into the ash, brilliant white cape fluttering. He held a sword in one hand.

Elend! she tried to cry at him. *No! Go back! Charging them is madness! You'll be killed!*

Elend stood tall, watching the waves of koloss as they approached, trampling down the black ash, an endless sea of death with blue skin and red eyes. Many carried swords, the others just bore rocks and lengths of wood. Elend was a tiny white speck before them, a single dot on an endless canvas of blue.

He raised his sword high and charged.

ELEND!

Suddenly, Elend burst with a brilliant energy, so bright that Vin gasped. He met the first koloss head-on, ducking beneath the swinging sword and decapitating the creature in one stroke. Then, instead of jumping away, he spun to the side, swinging. Another koloss fell. Three swords flashed around him, but all missed by just a breath. Elend ducked to the side, taking a koloss in the stomach, then whipped his sword around—his head barely passing beneath another swing—and took off a koloss arm.

He still didn't Push himself away. Vin froze, watching as

he took down one koloss, then beheaded another in a single, fluid stroke. Elend moved with a grace she had never seen from him—she had always been the better warrior, yet at this moment, he put her to shame. He wove between koloss blades as if he were taking part in a prerehearsed stage fight, body after body falling before his gliding blade.

A group of soldiers in Elend's colors burst from the cavern entrance, charging. Like a wave of light, their forms exploded with power. They, too, moved into the koloss ranks, striking with incredible precision. Not a single one of them fell as Vin watched. They fought with miraculous skill and fortune, each koloss blade falling just a little too late. Blue corpses began to pile up around the glowing force of men.

Somehow, Elend had found an entire army who could burn atium.

Elend was a god.

He'd never burned atium before, and his first experience with the metal filled him with wonder. The koloss around him all emitted atium shadows—images that moved before they did, showing Elend exactly what they would do. He could see into the future, if only a few seconds. In a battle, that was just what one needed.

He could feel the atium enhancing his mind, making him capable of reading and using all of the new information. He didn't even have to pause and think. His arms moved of their own volition, swinging his sword with awesome precision.

He spun amid a cloud of phantom images, striking at flesh, feeling almost as if he were in the mists again. No koloss could stand against him. He felt energized—he felt amazing. For a time, he was invincible. He'd swallowed so many atium beads he felt as if he'd throw up. For its entire history, atium had been a thing that men had needed to save and hoard. Burning it had seemed such a shame that it had been used only sparingly, only in instances of great need.

Elend didn't need to worry about any of that. He just burned as much as he wanted. And it made him into a disaster for the koloss—a whirlwind of exact strikes and impossible dodges, always a few steps ahead of his opponents. Foe after foe fell before him. And, when he began to get low on atium, he Pushed himself off a fallen sword back to the entrance. There, with plenty of water to wash it down, Sazed waited with another bag of atium.

Elend downed the beads quickly, then returned to the battle.

Ruin raged and spun, trying to stop the slaughter. Yet, this time, Vin was the force of balance. She blocked Ruin's every attempt to destroy Elend and the others, keeping it contained.

I can't decide if you're a fool, Vin thought toward it, *or if you simply exist in a way that makes you incapable of considering some things.*

Ruin screamed, buffeting against her, trying to destroy her as she had tried to destroy it. However, once again, their powers were too evenly matched. Ruin was forced to pull back.

Life, Vin said. *You said that the only reason to create something was so that you could destroy it.*

She hovered beside Elend, watching him fight. The deaths of the koloss should have pained her. Yet, she did not think of the death. Perhaps it was the influence of Preservation's power, but she saw only a man, struggling, fighting, even when hope seemed impossible. She didn't see death, she saw life. She saw faith.

We create things to watch them grow, Ruin, she said. *To take pleasure in seeing that which we love become more than it was before. You said that you were invincible—that all things break apart. All things are Ruined. But there are things that fight against you—and the ironic part is, you can't even understand those things. Love. Life. Growth.*

The life of a person is more than the chaos of its passing. Emotion, Ruin. This is your defeat.

* * *

Sazed watched anxiously from the mouth of the cavern. A small group of men huddled around him. Garv, leader of the Church of the Survivor in Luthadel. Harathdal, foremost of the Terris stewards. Lord Dedri Vasting, one of the surviving Assembly members from the city government. Aslydin, the young woman whom Demoux had apparently come to love during his few short weeks at the Pits of Hathsin. A smattering of others, important—or faithful—enough to get near the front of the crowd and watch.

"Where is she, Master Terrisman?" Garv asked.

"She'll come," Sazed promised, hand resting on the rock wall. The men fell quiet. Soldiers—those without the blessing of atium—waited nervously with them, knowing they were next in line, should Elend's assault fail.

She has to come, Sazed thought. *Everything points toward her arrival.*

"The Hero *will* come," he repeated.

Elend sheared through two heads at once, dropping the koloss. He spun his blade, taking off an arm, then stabbed another koloss through the neck. He hadn't seen that one approaching, but his mind had seen and interpreted the atium shadow before the real attack came.

Already he stood atop of carpet of blue corpses. He did not stumble. With atium, his every step was exact, his blade guided, his mind crisp. He took down a particularly large koloss, then stepped back, pausing briefly.

The sun crested the horizon in the east. It started to grow hotter.

They had been fighting for hours, yet the army of koloss still seemed endless. Elend slew another koloss, but his motions were beginning to feel sluggish. Atium enhanced the mind, but it did not boost the body, and he'd started to rely on his pewter to keep him going. Who would have known that one could get tired—exhausted, even—while burning atium? Nobody had ever used as much of the metal as Elend had.

But he had to keep going. His atium was running low. He turned back toward the mouth of the cavern, just in time to see one of his atium soldiers go down in a spray of blood.

Elend cursed, spinning as an atium shadow passed through him. He ducked the swing that followed, then took off the creature's arm. He beheaded the one that followed, then cut another's legs out from beneath it. For most of the battle, he hadn't used fancy Allomantic jumps or attacks, just straightforward swordplay. His arms were growing tired, however, and he was forced to begin Pushing koloss away from him to manage the battlefield. The reserve of atium—of *life*—within him was dwindling. Atium burned so quickly.

Another man screamed. Another soldier dead.

Elend began to back toward the cavern. There were just *so many* koloss. His band of two hundred and eighty had slain thousands, yet the koloss didn't care. They kept attacking, a brutal wave of endless determination, resisted only by the pockets of atium Mistings protecting each of the entrances to the Homeland.

Another man died. They were running out of atium.

Elend screamed, swinging his sword about him, taking down three koloss in a maneuver that never should have worked. He flared steel and Pushed the rest away from him.

The body of a god, burning within me, he thought. He gritted his teeth, attacking as more of his men fell. He scrambled up a pile of koloss, slicing off arms, legs, heads. Stabbing chests, necks, guts. He fought on, alone, his clothing long since stained from white to red.

Something moved behind him, and he spun, raising his blade, letting the atium lead him. Yet, he froze, uncertain. The creature behind him was no koloss. It stood in a black robe, one eye socket empty and bleeding, the other bearing a spike that had been crushed back into its skull. Elend could see straight into the empty eye socket, through the creature's head, and out the back.

Marsh. He had a cloud of atium shadows around him—he was burning the metal too, and would be immune to Elend's own atium.

* * *

Human led his koloss soldiers through the tunnels. They killed any person in their path.

Some had stood at the entrance. They had fought long. They had been strong. They were dead now.

Something drove Human on. Something stronger than anything that had controlled him before. Stronger than the little woman with the black hair, though she had been very strong. This thing was stronger. It was Ruin. Human knew this.

He could not resist. He could only kill. He cut down another human.

Human burst into a large open chamber filled with other little people. Controlling him, Ruin made him turn away and not kill them. Not that Ruin didn't want him to kill them. It just wanted something else *more.*

Human rushed forward. He crawled over tumbled rocks and stones. He shoved aside crying humans. Other koloss followed him. For the moment, all of his own desires were forgotten. There was only his overpowering desire to get to . . .

A small room. There. In front of him. Human threw open the doors. Ruin yelled in pleasure as he entered this room. It contained the thing Ruin wanted.

"Guess what I found," Marsh growled, stepping up, Pushing against Elend's sword. The weapon was ripped from his fingers, flying away. "Atium. A kandra was carrying it, looking to sell it. Foolish creature."

Elend cursed, ducking out of the way of a koloss swing, pulling his obsidian dagger from the sheath at his leg.

Marsh stalked forward. Men screamed—cursing, falling—as their atium died out. Elend's soldiers were being overrun. The screams tapered off as the last of his men guarding this entrance died. He doubted the others would last much longer.

Elend's atium warned him of attacking koloss, letting him dodge—barely—but he couldn't kill them very effectively with the dagger. And, as the koloss took his attention, Marsh struck with an obsidian axe. The blade fell, and Elend leaped away, but the dodge left him off balance.

Elend tried to recover, but his metals were running low—not just his atium, but his basic metals. Iron, steel, pewter. He hadn't been paying much attention to them, since he had atium, but he'd been fighting for so long now. If Marsh had atium, then they were equal—and without basic metals, Elend would die.

An attack from the Inquisitor forced Elend to flare pewter to get away. He cut down three koloss with ease, his atium still helping him, but Marsh's immunity was a serious challenge. The Inquisitor crawled over the fallen bodies of koloss, scrambling toward Elend, his single spikehead reflecting the too-bright light of the sun overhead.

Elend's pewter ran out.

"You cannot beat me, Elend Venture," Marsh said in a voice like gravel. "We've killed your wife. I will kill you."

Vin. Elend didn't believe it. *Vin will come,* he thought. *She'll save us.*

Faith. It was a strange thing to feel at that moment. Marsh swung.

Pewter and iron suddenly flared to life within Elend. He didn't have time to think about the oddity; he simply reacted, Pulling on his sword, which lay stuck into the ground a distance away. It flipped through the air and he caught it, swinging with a too-quick motion, blocking Marsh's axe. Elend's body seemed to pulse, powerful and vast. He struck forward instinctively, forcing Marsh backward across the ashen field. Koloss backed away for the moment, shying from Elend, as if frightened. Or awed.

Marsh raised a hand to Push on Elend's sword, but nothing happened. It was . . . as if something deflected the blow. Elend screamed, charging, beating back Marsh with the strikes of his silvery weapon. The Inquisitor looked shocked as it blocked with the obsidian axe, its motions too quick for even Allomancy to explain. Yet Elend still forced him to retreat, across fallen corpses of blue, ash stirring beneath a red sky.

A powerful peace swelled in Elend. His Allomancy flared

bright, though he knew the metals inside of him should have burned away. Only atium remained, and its strange power did not—could not—give him the other metals. But it didn't matter. For a moment, he was embraced by something greater. He looked up, toward the sun.

And he saw—just briefly—an enormous figure in the air just above him. A shifting, brilliant personage of pure white. Her hands held to his shoulders with her head thrown back, white hair streaming, mist flaring behind her like wings that stretched across the sky.

Vin, he thought with a smile.

Elend looked back down as Marsh screamed and leaped forward, attacking with his axe in one hand, seeming to trail something vast and black like a cloak behind him. Marsh raised his other hand across his face, as if to shield his dead eyes from the image in the air above Elend.

Elend burned the last of his atium, flaring it to life in his stomach. He raised his sword in two hands and waited for Marsh to draw close. The Inquisitor was stronger and was a better warrior. Marsh had the powers of both Allomancy and Feruchemy, making him another Lord Ruler. This was not a battle Elend could win. Not with a sword.

Marsh arrived, and Elend thought he understood what it had been like for Kelsier to face the Lord Ruler on that square in Luthadel, all those years ago. Marsh struck with his axe; Elend raised his sword in return and prepared to strike.

Then, Elend burned duralumin with his atium.

Sight, Sound, Strength, Power, Glory, Speed!

Blue lines sprayed from his chest like rays of light. But those were all overshadowed by one thing. Atium plus duralumin. In a flash of knowledge, Elend felt a mind-numbing wealth of information. All became white around him as knowledge saturated his mind.

"I see now," he whispered as the vision faded, and along with it his remaining metals. The battlefield returned. He stood upon it, his sword piercing Marsh's neck. It had gotten caught on the spikehead jutting out of Marsh's back, between the shoulder blades.

Marsh's axe was buried in Elend's chest.

The phantom metals Vin had given him burned to life within Elend again. They took the pain away. However, there was only so much that pewter could do, no matter how high it was flared. Marsh ripped his axe free, and Elend stumbled backward, bleeding, letting go of his sword. Marsh pulled the blade free from his neck, and the wound vanished, healed by the powers of Feruchemy.

Elend fell, slumping into a pile of koloss bodies. He would have been dead already, save for the pewter. Marsh stepped up to him, smiling. His empty eye socket was wreathed in tattoos, the mark that Marsh had taken upon himself. The price he had paid to overthrow the Final Empire.

Marsh grabbed Elend by the throat, pulling him back up. "Your soldiers are dead, Elend Venture," the creature whispered. "Our koloss rampage inside the kandra caverns. Your metals are gone. You have lost."

Elend felt his life dripping away; the last trickle from an empty glass. He'd been here before, back in the cavern at the Well of Ascension. He should have died then and he'd been terrified. This time, oddly, he was not. There was no regret. Just satisfaction.

Elend looked up at the Inquisitor. Vin, like a glowing phantom, still hovered above them both. "Lost?" Elend whispered. "We've won, Marsh."

"Oh, and how is that?" Marsh asked, dismissive.

Human stood at the side of the pit in the center of the cavern room. The pit where Ruin's body had been. The place of victory.

Human stood, dumbfounded, a group of other koloss stepping up to him, looking equally confused.

The pit was empty.

"Atium," Elend whispered, tasting blood. "Where is the atium, Marsh? Where do you think we got the power to fight?

You came for that atium? Well it's *gone.* Tell your master that! You think my men and I expected to kill all of these koloss? There are tens of thousands of them! That wasn't the point at all."

Elend's smile widened. "Ruin's body is gone, Marsh. We burned it all away, the others and I. You might be able to kill me, but you'll *never* get what you came for. And that is why we win."

Marsh screamed in anger, demanding the truth, but Elend had spoken it. The deaths of the others meant that they had run out of atium. His men had fought until it was gone, as Elend had commanded, burning away every last bit.

The body of a god. The power of a god. Elend had held it for a moment. More important, he'd destroyed it. Hopefully, that would keep his people safe.

It's up to you now, Vin, he thought, still feeling the peace of her touch upon his soul. *I've done what I can.*

He smiled at Marsh again, defiantly, as the Inquisitor raised his axe.

The axe took off Elend's head.

Ruin raged and thrashed about, enraged and destructive. Vin only sat quietly, watching Elend's headless body slump back into the pile of blue corpses.

How do you like that! Ruin screamed. *I killed him! I Ruined everything you love! I took it from you!*

Vin floated above Elend's body, looking down. She reached out with incorporeal fingers, touching his head, remembering how it had felt to use her power to fuel his Allomancy. She didn't know what she had done. Something akin to what Ruin did when it controlled the koloss, perhaps. Only opposite. Liberating. Serene.

Elend was dead. She knew that, and knew that there was nothing she could do. That brought pain, true, but not the pain she had expected. *I let him go long ago,* she thought, stroking his face. *At the Well of Ascension. Allomancy brought him back to me for a time.*

She didn't feel the pain or terror that she had known before, when she'd thought him dead. This time, she felt only peace. These last few years had been a blessing—an extension. She'd given Elend up to be his own man, to risk himself as he wished, and perhaps to die. She would always love him. But she would not cease to function because he was gone.

The opposite, perhaps. Ruin floated directly above her, throwing down insults, telling her how it would kill the others. Sazed. Breeze. Ham. Spook.

So few left of the original crew, she thought. *Kelsier dead so long ago. Dockson and Clubs slaughtered at the Battle of Luthadel. Yeden dead with his soldiers. OreSeur taken at Zane's command. Marsh, fallen to become an Inquisitor. And the others who joined us, now gone as well. Tindwyl, TenSoon, Elend . . .*

Did Ruin think she would let their sacrifices be for nothing? She rose, gathering her power. She forced it against the power of Ruin, as she had the other times. Yet, this time was different. When Ruin pushed back, she didn't retreat. She didn't preserve herself. She drove onward.

The confrontation made her divine body tremble in pain. It was the pain of a cold and hot meeting, the pain of two rocks being smashed together and ground to dust. Their forms undulated and rippled in a tempest of power.

And Vin drove on.

Preservation could never destroy you! she thought, almost screaming it against the agony. *He could only protect. That's why he needed to create humankind. All along, Ruin, this was part of his plan!*

He didn't give up part of himself, making himself weaker, simply so that he could create intelligent life! He knew he needed something of both Preservation and of Ruin. Something that could both protect and destroy. Something that could destroy to protect.

He gave up his power at the Well, and into the mists, giving it to us so that we could take it. He always intended this to happen. You think this was your plan? It was his. His all along.

Ruin cried out. Still, she drove on.

You created the thing that can kill you, Ruin, Vin said. *And you just made one huge final mistake. You shouldn't have killed Elend.*

You see, he was the only reason I had left to live.

She didn't shy back, though the conflict of opposites ripped her apart. Ruin screamed in terror as the force of her power completely melded with Ruin's.

Her consciousness—now formed and saturated with Preservation—moved to touch that of Ruin. Neither would yield. And, with a surge of power, Vin bid farewell to the world, then pulled Ruin into the abyss with her.

Their two minds puffed away, like mist under a hot sun.

Once Vin died, the end came quickly. We were not prepared for it—but even all of the Lord Ruler's planning could not have prepared us for this. How did one prepare for the end of the world itself?

82

SAZED WATCHED QUIETLY FROM THE mouth of the cavern. Outside, the koloss raged and stomped about, looking confused. Most of the men who had been watching with Sazed had fled. Even most of the soldiers had retreated into the caverns, calling him a fool for waiting. Only General Demoux, who had managed to crawl back to the cavern after his atium ran out, remained, just a few steps into the tunnel. The man was bloody, his arm ending in a tourniquet, his leg crushed. He coughed quietly, waiting for Aslydin to return with more bandages.

Outside, the sun rose into the sky. The heat was incredible, like an oven. Cries of pain echoed from deep within the cavern behind Sazed. Koloss were inside.

"She'll come," Sazed whispered.

He could see Elend's body. It had fallen back down the pile of koloss corpses. It was stark, bright white and red against the black and blue of the koloss and ash.

"Vin will come," Sazed said insistently.

Demoux looked dazed. Too much blood lost. He slumped back, closing his eyes. Koloss began to move toward the cavern mouth, though they didn't have the direction or frenzy they'd displayed before.

"The Hero *will* come!" Sazed said.

Outside, something appeared, as if from mists, then slumped down in the bodies beside Elend's corpse. It was followed immediately by something else, a second figure, which also fell motionless.

There! Sazed thought, scrambling out of the cavern. He dashed past several koloss. They tried to swing for him, but Sazed wore his metalminds. He felt he should have his copperminds to use in case he needed to record something important. He wore his ten rings, the ones he'd used to fight during the siege of Luthadel, for he knew that he might need them.

He tapped a bit of steel and dodged the koloss attacks. He moved quickly through the mass of confused-looking koloss, climbing over bodies, moving up to the scrap of white cloak that marked Elend's resting place. His corpse was there, headless.

A small body lay beside his. Sazed fell to his knees, grabbing Vin by the shoulders. Beside her, atop the pile of dead koloss, lay another body. It was that of a man with red hair, one whom Sazed did not recognize, but he ignored it.

For Vin was not moving.

No! he thought, checking for a pulse. There was none. Her eyes were closed. She looked peaceful, but very, very dead.

"This can *not* be!" he yelled, shaking her body again. Several koloss lumbered toward him.

He glanced upward. The sun was rising. It was getting hard to breathe for the heat. He felt his skin burning. By the time the sun reached its zenith, it would likely be so hot the land would burn.

"Is this how it ends?" he screamed toward the sky. "Your Hero is dead! Ruin's power may be broken, the koloss may be lost to him as an army, but *the world will still die*!"

The ash had killed the plants. The sun would burn away anything that remained. There was no food. Sazed blinked out tears, but they dried on his face.

"This is how you leave us?" he whispered.

And then, he felt something. He looked down. Vin's body was smoking slightly. Not from the heat. It seemed to be leaking something . . . or, no. It was connected to something. The twists of mist he saw, they led to a vast white light. He could just barely see it.

He reached out and touched the mist, and felt an awesome power. A power of stability. To the side, the other corpse—the one he didn't recognize—was also leaking something. A deep black smoke. Sazed reached out with his other hand, touching the smoke, and felt a different power—more violent. The power of change.

He knelt, stunned, between the bodies. And, only then, did it start to make sense.

The prophecies always used the gender-neutral, he thought. *So that they could refer to either a man or a woman, we assumed. Or . . . perhaps because they referred to a Hero who wasn't really either one?*

He stood up. The sun's power overhead felt insignificant compared to the twin—yet opposite—powers that surrounded him.

The Hero would be rejected of his people, Sazed thought. *Yet, he would save them. Not a warrior, though he would fight. Not born a king, but would become one anyway.*

He looked upward again.

Is this what you planned all along?

He tasted of the power, but drew back, daunted. How could he use such a thing? He was just a man. In the brief glimpse of forces that he touched, he knew that he'd have no hope of using it. He didn't have the training.

"I can't do this," he said through cracked lips, reaching to the sky. "I don't know how. I cannot make the world as it was—I never saw it. If I take this power, I will do as the Lord Ruler did, and will only make things worse for my trying. I am simply a man."

Koloss cried out in pain from the burning. The heat was terrible, and around Sazed, trees began to pop and burst into flames. His touch on the twin powers kept him alive, he knew, but he did not embrace them.

"I am no Hero," he whispered, still reaching to the sky.

His arms twinkled, golden. His copperminds, worn on his forearms, reflected the light of the sun. They had been with him for so long, his companions. His knowledge.

Knowledge. . . .

The words of the prophecy were very precise, he thought suddenly. *They say . . . they say that the Hero will bear the future of the world on his arms.*

Not on his shoulders. Not in his hands. On his arms.

By the Forgotten Gods!

He slammed his arms into the twin mists and seized the powers offered to him. He drew them in, feeling them infuse his body, making him burn. His flesh and bones evaporated, but as they did, he tapped his copperminds, dumping their entire contents into his expanding consciousness.

The copperminds, now empty, dropped with his rings to the pile of blue corpses beside the bodies of Vin, Elend, and Ruin's nameless body. Sazed opened eyes as large as the world itself, drawing in power that latticed all of creation.

The Hero will have the power to save the world. But he will also have the power to destroy it.

We never understood. He wouldn't simply bear the power of Preservation. He needed the power of Ruin as well.

The powers were opposites. As he drew them in, they threatened to annihilate each other. And yet, because he was of one mind on how to use them, he could keep them separate. They could touch *without* destroying each other, if he willed it. For these two powers had been used to create all things. If they fought, they destroyed. If they were used together, they created.

Understanding swelled within him. Over a thousand

years, the Keepers had collected the knowledge of mankind and stored it in their copperminds. They had passed it down from Keeper to Keeper, each man or woman carrying the entire bulk of knowledge, so that he or she could pass it on when necessary. Sazed had it all.

And, in a moment of transcendence, he understood it all. He saw the patterns, the clues, the secrets. Men had believed and worshipped for as long as they had existed, and within those beliefs, Sazed found the answers he needed. Gems, hidden from Ruin in all the religions of mankind.

There had been a people called the Bennett. They had considered mapmaking to be a solemn duty; Sazed had once preached their religion to Kelsier himself. From their detailed maps and charts, Sazed discovered how the world had once looked. He used his powers to restore the continents and oceans, the islands and coastlines, the mountains and rivers.

There had been a people known as the Nelazan. They had worshipped the stars, had called them the Thousand Eyes of their god, Trell, watching them. Sazed remembered well offering the religion to the young Vin while she had sat, captive, undergoing her first haircut with the crew. From the Nelazan, the Keepers had recovered star charts, and had dutifully recorded them—even though scholars had called them useless, since they hadn't been accurate since the days before the Ascension. Yet, from these star charts, and from the patterns and movements of the other planets in the solar system they outlined, Sazed could determine exactly where the world was supposed to sit in orbit. He put the planet back into its old place—not pushing too hard, as the Lord Ruler once had, for he had a frame of reference by which to measure.

There had been a people known as the Canzi who had worshipped death; they had provided detailed notes about the human body. Sazed had offered one of their prayers over the bodies they had found in Vin's old crew hideout, back when Kelsier had still lived. From the Canzi teachings about the body, Sazed determined that the physiology of mankind had changed—either by the Lord Ruler's intention or by simple evolution—to adapt to breathing ash and eating brown plants. In a wave of power, Sazed restored the bodies of men to the way they had been before, leaving each person the same, yet fixing the problems that living for a thousand years on a dying world had caused. He didn't destroy men, warping and twisting them as the Lord Ruler had when he'd created the kandra, for Sazed had a guide by which to work.

He learned other things too. Dozens of secrets. One religion worshipped animals, and from it Sazed drew forth pictures, explanations, and references regarding the life that *should* have lived on the earth. He restored it. From another—Dadradah, the religion he had preached to Clubs before the man died—Sazed learned about colors and hues. It was the last religion Sazed had ever taught, and with its poems about color and nature, he could restore the plants, sky, and landscape to the way they had once been. Every religion had clues in it, for the faiths of men contained the hopes, loves, wishes, and lives of the people who had believed them.

Finally, Sazed took the religion of the Larsta, the religion that Kelsier's wife—Mare—had believed in. Its priests had composed poetry during their times of meditation. From these poems—and from a scrap of paper that Mare had given to Kelsier, who had given it to Vin, who had given it to Sazed—he learned of the beautiful things that the world had once held.

And he restored flowers to the plants that had once borne them.

The religions in my portfolio weren't useless after all, he thought, the power flowing from him and remaking the world. *None of them were. They weren't all true.*

But they all had truth.

Sazed hovered over the world, changing things as he felt he must. He cradled the hiding places of mankind, keeping the caverns safe—even if he did move them about—as he reworked the world's tectonics. Finally, he exhaled softly, his work finished. And yet, the power did not evaporate from him, as he had expected it to.

Rashek and Vin only touched small pieces of it at the Well of Ascension, he realized. *I have something more. Something endless.*

Ruin and Preservation were dead, and their powers had been joined together. In fact, they belonged together. How had they been split? Someday, perhaps, he would discover the answer to that question.

Somebody would need to watch over the world, care for it, now that its gods were gone. It wasn't until that moment that Sazed understood the term Hero of Ages. Not a Hero that came once in the ages.

But a Hero who would span the ages. A Hero who would preserve mankind throughout all its lives and times. Neither Preservation nor Ruin, but both.

God.

Vin was special.

Preservation chose her from a very young age, as I have mentioned. I believe that he was grooming her to take his power. Yet, the mind of Preservation was very weak at that point, reduced only to the fragment that we knew as the mist spirit.

What made him choose this girl? Was it because she was a Mistborn? Was it because she had Snapped so early in life, coming to her powers even as she went through the pains of the unusually difficult labor her mother went through to bear her?

Vin was unusually talented and strong with Allomancy, even from the beginning. I believe that she must have drawn some of the mist into her when she was still a child, in those brief times when she wasn't wearing the earring. Preservation had mostly gotten her to stop wearing it by the time Kelsier recruited her, though she put it back in for a moment before joining the crew. Then, she'd left it there at his suggestion.

Nobody else could draw upon the mists. I have determined this. Why were they open to Vin and not others? I suspect that she couldn't have taken them all in until after she'd touched the power at the Well of Ascension. It was always meant, I believe, to be something of an attuning force. Something that, once touched, would adjust a person's body to be able to accept the mists.

Yet, she did make use of a small crumb of Preservation's power when she defeated the Lord Ruler, a year before she even began hearing the thumping of the power's return to the Well.

There is much more to this mystery. Perhaps I will tease it out eventually, as my mind grows more and more accustomed to its expanded nature. Perhaps I will determine why I was able to take the powers myself. For now, I only wish to make a simple acknowledgment of the woman who held the power just before me.

Of all of us who touched it, I feel she was the most worthy.

EPILOGUE

SPOOK AWOKE FROM THE NIGHTMARE, then sat up. The cavern around him was dark, lit only by candles and lamps.

He stood, stretching. Around him, people gasped. He walked past them, seeking out his friends. The cavern was packed—holding everyone from Urteau who had been willing to come and hide. As such, it was difficult for Spook to pick his way through the shuffling, coughing, chatting bodies. As he walked, the whispers grew louder, and people stood, following.

Beldre came running up to him, wearing a white dress. "Spook?" she asked with wonder. "What . . . what happened?"

He just smiled, putting his arm around her. They made their way to the front of the cavern. Breeze sat at a table—of course, *he* would have furniture, while pretty much everyone else sat on the rock floor. Spook smiled at him, and the Soother raised an eyebrow.

"You're looking well, my boy," Breeze said, taking a drink of his wine.

"You could say that," Spook said.

"That's all you're going to say?" Beldre said to Breeze. "Look at him! He's been healed!"

Breeze shrugged, putting down his wine and standing. "My dear, with all the oddities that have been happening lately, young Spook's appearance doesn't measure up. A simple healing? Why, that's rather mundane, if you ask me."

Breeze smiled, catching Spook's eye.

"Shall we then?" Spook asked.

Breeze shrugged. "Why not? What do you think that we'll find?"

"I'm not sure," Spook admitted, stepping into the antechamber beyond the cavern. He started to climb the ladder.

"Spook," Beldre said warily. "You know what the scouts said. The entire city was burning from the heat of the sun. . . ."

Spook looked up, noting the light shining between the cracks of the trapdoor. He smiled, then pushed it open.

There was no city outside. Just a field of grass. Green grass. Spook blinked at the strange sight, then crawled out onto the soft earth, making room for Breeze. The Soother's head popped out, then cocked to the side. "Now, *there's* a sight," he said, crawling out beside Spook.

Spook stood up in the grass. It came up to his thighs. Green. Such a strange color for plants.

"And . . . the sky," Breeze said, shading his eyes. "Blue. Not a hint of ash or smoke. Very odd. Very odd indeed. I'll bet Vin had something to do with this mess. That girl never *could* do things the proper way."

Spook heard a gasp from behind, and turned to see Beldre climbing out of the cavern. He helped her step up onto the ground, then they walked in silent wonder through the tall grass. The sun was so bright overhead, yet it wasn't uncomfortably hot.

"What happened to the city?" Beldre whispered, holding Spook's arm.

He shook his head. Then, however, he heard something. He turned, thinking he saw motion on the horizon. He walked forward, Beldre at his side, Breeze calling down for Allrianne to come up and see what had happened.

"Are those . . . people?" Beldre asked, finally seeing what Spook had. The people in the distance saw them, too, and as soon as they drew close, Spook smiled and waved at one.

"Spook?" Ham called. "Kid, is that you?"

Spook and Beldre hurried forward. Ham stood with others, and behind them Spook could see another trapdoor in the middle of the grassy meadow floor. People he didn't recognize—some wearing uniforms from Elend's army—were climbing out. Ham rushed over, wearing his usual vest and trousers, and grabbed Spook in an embrace.

"What are you doing here?" Ham asked, letting go.

"I don't know," Spook said. "Last I knew, I was in Urteau."

Ham looked up at the sky. "I was in Fadrex! What happened?"

Spook shook his head. "I don't know if the places we used to know have meaning anymore, Ham. . . ."

Ham nodded, turning as one of the soldiers pointed. Another batch of people was emerging from a hole a short distance away. Spook and Ham walked forward—at least, until Ham saw someone in the other batch of people. Spook vaguely recognized her as Ham's wife, who had been back in Luthadel. The Thug let out a cry of excitement, then rushed forward to greet his family.

Spook made his way from hole to hole. There appeared to be six of them, some well populated, others not so much. One stood out. It wasn't a trapdoor, like the others, but a slanted cave entrance. Here, he found General Demoux speaking with a small group of people, a pretty Terriswoman holding his arm.

"I was in and out of consciousness for it," Demoux was saying, "but I saw him. The Survivor. It *had* to be him—hanging in the sky, glowing. Waves of color moved through the air, and the ground trembled, the land spinning and moving. He came. Just like Sazed said he would."

"Sazed?" Spook spoke up, Demoux noticing him for the first time. "Where is he?"

Demoux shook his head. "I don't know, Lord Spook." Then he paused. "Where did you come from, anyway?"

Spook ignored the question. The openings and holes formed a pattern. Spook walked through the thick grass, leading Beldre, making his way to the very center of the pattern. The wind blew softly, bending the stalks of grass in wave-like undulations. Ham and Breeze rushed to catch up to him, already arguing about something trivial, Ham with a child on one arm, his other around his wife's shoulders.

Spook froze as he caught sight of a bit of color in the

grass. He held up a hand, warning the others, and they stepped forward more quietly. There, in the center of the grass, was a field of . . . somethings. Colorful somethings, growing from the ground, with tops like bright-colored leaves. They were shaped like upside-down bells, with long straight stalks, the petals at the top open toward the sun. As if reaching for its light and gaping to drink it in.

"Beautiful . . ." Beldre whispered.

Spook stepped forward, moving among the plants. *Flowers,* he thought, recognizing them from the picture Vin had carried. *Kelsier's dream finally came true.*

At the center of the flowers, he found two people. Vin lay wearing her customary mistcloak, shirt, and trousers. Elend was in a brilliant white uniform, complete with cape. They were holding hands as they lay amid the flowers.

And they were both dead.

Spook knelt beside them, listening to Ham and Breeze cry out. They examined the bodies, checking for vital signs, but Spook focused on something else, almost hidden in the grass. He picked it up—a large leather tome.

He opened it, reading the first page.

I am, unfortunately, the Hero of Ages, read the delicate, careful letters. Spook thought he recognized the handwriting. As he flipped through the book, a slip of paper fell free. Spook picked it up—one side had a faded drawing of a flower, the very picture he'd been thinking about moments before. On the other side was a note scrawled in the same handwriting as the book.

Spook, it read. *I tried to bring them back, but apparently fixing the bodies doesn't return the souls. I will get better at this with time, I expect. However, be assured that I have spoken with our friends, and they are quite happy where they are. They deserve a rest, I think.*

The book contains a short record of the events that led up to the world dying and being reborn, along with some musings I have made about the history, philosophy, and science of recent occurrences. If you look to your right, you will find a much larger group of books in the grass. These contain all of the knowledge—repeated verbatim—that was contained in my metalminds. Let the knowledge of the past not be forgotten.

Rebuilding will be difficult, I think—but likely far easier than living beneath the Lord Ruler or surviving Ruin's attempt to destroy the world. I think you'll be surprised at the number of people who fled to the storage caverns. Rashek planned very well for this day. He suffered much beneath Ruin's hand, but he was a good man, who ultimately had honorable intentions.

You did well. Know that the message you sent via Captain Goradel saved us all, in the end. The people will need leadership in the years to come. Likely, they will look to you. I'm sorry that I cannot be there in person to help you, but know that I am . . . about.

I have made you Mistborn, and healed the damage you did to your body by flaring tin so much. I hope you don't mind. It was Kelsier's request, actually. Consider it a parting gift from him.

Watch over them for me.

P.S. There are still two metals that nobody knows about. You might want to poke about and see if you can figure out what they are. I think they'll interest you.

Spook looked up, staring at the strangely empty, blue sky. Beldre came over and knelt beside him, looking over his paper, then giving him a quizzical look.

"You look troubled," she said.

Spook shook his head. "No," he said, folding up the little slip of paper and putting it in his pocket. "No, I'm not troubled. In fact, I actually think everything is going to be all right. Finally."

ARS ARCANUM

1. Metals Quick Reference Chart

2. Names and Terms

3. Summaries of Previous Books

You can also find extensive annotations of every chapter in the book, along with deleted scenes, a very active blog, and expanded world information, at www.brandonsanderson.com.

METALS QUICK REFERENCE CHART

METAL	ALLOMANTIC POWER	FERUCHEMICAL POWER	HEMALURGIC POWER
Iron	Pulls on Nearby Sources of Metal	Stores Physical Weight	Steals Human Strength
Steel	Pushes on Nearby Sources of Metal	Stores Physical Speed	Steals Allomantic Physical Powers
Tin	Increases Senses	Stores Senses	Steals Human Senses
Pewter	Increases Physical Abilities	Stores Physical Strength	Steals Feruchemical Physical Powers
Brass	Soothes (dampens) Emotions	Stores Warmth	Steals Feruchemical Mental Attributes

METAL	ALLOMANTIC POWER	FERUCHEMICAL POWER	HEMALURGIC POWER
Zinc	Riots (enflames) Emotions	Stores Mental Speed	Steals Human Emotional Fortitude
Copper	Hides Allomantic Pulses	Stores Memories	Steals Human Mental Fortitude
Bronze	Allows One to Hear Allomantic Pulses	Stores Wakefulness	Steals Allomantic Mental Powers
Aluminum	Destroys All of the Allomancer's Reserves	Unknown	Steals Allomantic Enhancement Powers
Duralumin	Enhances the Next Metal Burned	Unknown	Unknown
Atium	See into Other People's Futures	Stores Age	Steals Allomantic Temporal Powers
Malatium	See into Other People's Pasts	Unknown	Unknown
Gold	See into Your Own Past	Stores Health	Unknown
Electrum	See into Your Own Future	Unknown	Unknown

NAMES AND TERMS

ALENDI: A man who conquered the world a thousand years ago, before the Lord Ruler's Ascension. Vin found his journal in the Lord Ruler's palace, and thought—at first—that he had become the Lord Ruler. It was later discovered that his servant, Rashek, killed Alendi and took his place. Alendi was a friend and protégé of Kwaan, a Terris scholar who thought that Alendi might be the Hero of Ages.

ALLOMANCY: A mystical hereditary power allowing the burning of metals inside the body to gain special abilities.

ALLOMANTIC METALS: There are eight basic Allomantic metals. These come in pairs, comprising a base metal and its alloy. They can also be divided into two groups of four as internal metals (tin, pewter, copper, bronze) and external metals (iron, steel, zinc, brass). It was long assumed that there were only ten Allomantic metals: the eight basic metals, along with gold and atium. However, the discovery of active alloys for gold and atium expanded the number of metals to twelve. The discovery of aluminum and duralumin brought this number to fourteen.

ALLOMANTIC PULSE: The signal given off by an Allomancer who is burning metals. Only someone who is burning bronze can "hear" an Allomantic pulse.

ALLRIANNE: Lord Ashweather Cett's only daughter. She is romantically involved with Breeze.

ALUMINUM: Once known only to the Steel Inquisitors, this metal—when burned—depletes all of an Allomancer's other metal reserves.

ANCHOR (ALLOMANTIC): A term used to refer to a piece of metal that an Allomancer Pushes on or Pulls on when burning steel or iron.

ASCENSION (OF THE LORD RULER): The Ascension is the term used to describe what happened to Rashek when he took the power at the Well of Ascension and became the Lord Ruler. It is also sometimes used in connection with Vin, as she did something similar in taking the power, though she released it instead of using it.

ASCENSION, WELL OF: Historically the location of a great power, the Well of Ascension was the place to which it was prophecied the Hero of Ages would travel in order to gain the power he needed to defeat the Deepness. Vin located it beneath Kredik Shaw in Luthadel (though it had always been thought to be in the Terris Mountains). It was deep within a large cavern filled with supplies and foodstuffs. (*See also* Storage Cavern.)

ASHFALLS: A term that refers to the rain of ash, which falls frequently from the sky in the Final Empire because of the ashmounts.

ASHMOUNTS: Seven large ash volcanoes which appeared in the Final Empire during the Ascension. They eject mainly ash, rather than magma.

ASHWEATHER: Lord Cett's first name.

ATIUM: A strange metal formerly produced in the Pits of Hathsin. It condensed inside of small geodes that formed in crystalline pockets within caves there.

BELDRE: Quellion's sister.

BLESSING, KANDRA: Each kandra was granted one of four powers by the Lord Ruler. These are the Blessing of Potency, the Blessing of Presence, the Blessing of Awareness, and the Blessing of Stability.

BOXING: The slang name for an imperial gold coin. The name comes from the picture on its back of Kredik Shaw, the Lord Ruler's palace—or, the "box" in which he lived.

BREEZE: A Soother on Kelsier's crew, now one of Elend's foremost counselors and diplomats. He is thought by the rest of the crew to be half-skaa, like all of them, but he's actually a full-blooded nobleman who was forced during his youth to hide in the underground. He is romantically involved with Allrianne Cett.

BRONZEPULSE: Another term for an Allomantic pulse.

BURN (ALLOMANCY): Allomancers utilizing or expending the metals in their stomachs are said to be "burning" them. They must swallow a metal, usually in an alcohol suspension, then Allomantically metabolize it to access its power.

BURNLANDS: The deserts at the edges of the Final Empire.

CAMON: Vin's old crewleader. A harsh man who often beat her, Camon was cast out by Kelsier. The Inquisitors eventually killed him.

CANTON: A department of the Steel Ministry.

CETT: Lord Ashweather Cett marched on the Central Dominance during the siege of Luthadel. He feared that Straff Venture would capture the city, and its atium, and was himself suffering rebellions in his homeland. He escaped Fadrex with an army and made a desperate play for the capital. He eventually joined with Elend's forces at the end of the siege, helping Vin fight Straff Venture, and earning himself a place of trust as one of Elend's advisors. Although known as "King" Cett, he rules no lands, for they are still in rebellion. (*See also* Yomen.)

CHANNEREL, RIVER: The river that runs through the middle of Luthadel.

CITIZEN, THE: Quellion's title. (*See also* Quellion.)

CLADENT: Clubs's real name.

CLIP: The nickname for an imperial copper coin in the Final Empire. Commonly used by Mistborn and Coinshots for jumping and attacking.

CLUBS: A Smoker on Kelsier's crew, Spook's uncle, once general of Elend's armies. Clubs was killed by koloss during the siege of Luthadel.

COINSHOT: A Misting who can burn steel.

COLLAPSE, THE: A term used to refer to the death of the Lord Ruler and the fall of the Final Empire.

CONVENTICAL OF SERAN: A stronghold of the Inquisitors where Sazed and Marsh discovered Kwaan's last words.

COPPERCLOUD: The invisible, obscuring field set up by someone burning copper. If an Allomancer burns metals while within a coppercloud, their Allomantic pulses are hidden from those burning bronze. The term *Coppercloud* can also refer to a Smoker (a Misting who can burn copper).

DEEPNESS, THE: The mysterious monster or force that threatened the world just before the rise of the Lord Ruler and the Final Empire. The Lord Ruler claimed to have defeated it when he Ascended, but it was later revealed that the Deepness was the mists, and that the Lord Ruler didn't defeat them so much as hold them back. The Deepness is attacking again, the mists increasingly covering the land during the day now, causing crops to fail.

DEMOUX, GENERAL: An officer in Elend's army, known for his faith in the Survivor.

DOCKSON: Kelsier's old right-hand man, a member of the original crew. He was killed during the siege of Luthadel.

DOMINANCE (FINAL EMPIRE): A province of the Final Empire. Luthadel is in the Central Dominance. The four surrounding dominances are called the Inner Dominances, and include most of the population and culture of the Final Empire. After the Collapse, the Final Empire shattered, and different kings took power, trying to claim leadership of the various dominances, effectively turning each one into a separate kingdom. Elend now rules the Central Dominance along with most of the Northern Dominance and portions of the Eastern and Southern Dominances.

DOX: Dockson's nickname.

DURALUMIN: The Allomantic alloy of aluminum, duralumin is a mixture of aluminum, copper, manganese, and magnesium. If an Allomancer burns duralumin, the next metal (or metals) he or she burns will be given explosive power, at the cost of burning away all at once every bit of that metal inside the Allomancer.

ELEND VENTURE: Emperor of the New Empire, husband of Vin Venture, a Mistborn and scholar.

EXTINGUISH (ALLOMANTIC): To cease burning an Allomantic metal.

FADREX: A modestly sized, well-fortified city in the Western Dominance. Once home and capital city of Ashweather Cett, it was an important warehousing and distribution center for the Canton of Resource. As Cett left, it was seized by the obligator known as Lord Yomen.

FATREN: Also known as Fats. The skaa man who rules the city of Vetitan.

FEDRE, LORD: An infamous scoundrel of a nobleman who

lived in the eighth century of the Lord Ruler's reign. Known for his fondness for cats and canals.

FELT: Once one of Straff's spies, the man was (like most of Straff's employees) left behind at the fall of Luthadel. He gave his allegiance to Elend instead, and now serves as an officer in Elend's army.

FINAL EMPIRE: The empire established by the Lord Ruler. The name came from his certainty that since he was immortal, it would be the last empire the world would ever know.

FLARE (ALLOMANTIC): To draw a little extra power from an Allomantic metal at the expense of making it burn faster.

GENERATIONS, KANDRA: The kandra people are divided into generations, based on when they were created. The First Generation is made up of the original kandra and still survives. Each century after them, the Lord Ruler allowed another group of kandra to be created, and they were named the Second Generation, the Third Generation, and so forth.

GNEORNDIN: Ashweather Cett's only son.

GORADEL, CAPTAIN: Once a soldier in the Luthadel Garrison, Goradel was guarding the palace when Vin decided to infiltrate and kill the Lord Ruler. Vin convinced him to switch sides, and he later led Elend through the palace to try and rescue her. He is now an officer in Elend's army.

HADDEK: Leader of the First Generation of kandra.

HAM: A Thug on Kelsier's crew, now a general in Elend's army. Known for his enjoyment of philosophical puzzles, and for wearing only a vest no matter what the temperature.

HAMMOND: Ham's real name.

HATHSIN: *See* Pits of Hathsin.

HAZEKILLER: A soldier with no Allomantic or Feruchemical powers who is trained to fight and kill Allomancers.

HERO OF AGES, THE: The prophecied savior of the Terris people. It was foretold that he would come, take the power at the Well of Ascension, then be selfless enough to give it up in order to save the world from the Deepness. Alendi was thought to be the Hero of Ages, but was killed before he could complete his quest. Vin followed in his footsteps, and got further, taking the power, then giving it up. The prophecies, however, proved to be falsified—a ruse intended to allow a force named Ruin to escape imprisonment. (*See also* Ruin.)

HOID: A mystery yet to be solved.

HOMELAND, KANDRA: The cavern complex that the kandra use as their secret home. It is known to no human other than the Lord Ruler (who is now dead). Kandra who serve well in Contracts are allowed periods of rest in the Homeland.

INQUISITOR, STEEL: A group of strange priests who served the Lord Ruler. They have spikes driven completely through their heads—point-first through the eyes—yet continue to live. They were fanatically devoted to him, and were used primarily to hunt out and kill skaa with Allomantic powers. They have the abilities of a Mistborn granted to them via Hemalurgy, and some other powers gained by that art as well.

IRONEYES: Marsh's nickname when he was a member of the crew, before he became an Inquisitor.

IRONPULL: Pulling on a metal when Allomantically burning iron. This Pull exerts a force on the metal item, yanking it directly toward the Allomancer. If the metallic item, known as an "anchor," is heavier than the Allomancer, he or she will instead be Pulled toward it.

JANARLE, KING: Once Straff Venture's second-in-command, Janarle was forced to swear allegiance to Elend Venture. He now rules the Northern Dominance on Elend's behalf.

JASTES LEKAL: Heir to the Lekal house title and one of Elend's former friends. He and Elend often discussed politics and philosophy along with Telden. Jastes gathered an army of koloss and marched on Luthadel during the siege begun by Straff and Cett, then lost control of them. Elend executed Jastes for the death and destruction he caused.

KANDRA: A race of creatures who can ingest a person's dead body, then reproduce that body with their own flesh. As relatives of mistwraiths, kandra have no bones, so they keep and use the bones of the person they imitate. Natural spies, they serve Contracts with mankind—which must be paid for with atium. Kandra are immortal. (*See also* Homeland *and* Generations.)

KANPAAR: Foremost of the Second Generation of kandra.

KEEPER (TERRIS): Often used loosely as another term for a Feruchemist. The Keepers were actually an organization of Feruchemists dedicated to discovering, then memorizing, all of the knowledge and religions that existed before the Ascension. The Lord Ruler hunted them to near-extinction, forcing them to remain hidden. After the Collapse, they began teaching and revealing their knowledge. However, they were attacked by the Inquisitors about the time of the siege of Luthadel, and are all presumed dead, save Sazed.

KELL: Kelsier's nickname.

KELSIER: The most famous thieving crewleader in the Final Empire, Kelsier raised a rebellion of skaa and overthrew the Lord Ruler, but was killed in the process. He was Mistborn, and was Vin's teacher. His death spawned a religion known as the Church of the Survivor.

KHLENNIUM: An ancient kingdom that existed before the rise of the Final Empire. It was Alendi's homeland.

KOLOSS: A race of bestial warriors created by the Lord Ruler during his Ascension, then used by him to conquer the world.

KREDIK SHAW: The Lord Ruler's palace in Luthadel. It means "the Hill of a Thousand Spires" in the old Terris language.

KWAAN: A Terris scholar before the Collapse. He was a Worldbringer, and was the first to mistake Alendi for the Hero of Ages. He later changed his mind, betraying his former friend by recruiting Rashek to stop him.

LADRIAN: Breeze's real name.

LEKAL, KING: A distant relative of Jastes Lekal, King Audil Lekal took power over Jastes's kingdom after the siege of Luthadel. He has slowly lost most of that kingdom to banditry and koloss incursions.

LESTIBOURNES: Spook's real name.

LLAMAS, MISTBORN: Brandon's former writing group, who helped and advised on all three Mistborn books. Mistborn

Llamas chew various kinds of plants to gain super-llaman powers. T-shirts can be found on the Web site, if you know where to look.

LORD RULER: The emperor who ruled the Final Empire for a thousand years. He was once named Rashek, and was a Terris servant who was hired by Alendi. He killed Alendi, however, and went to the Well of Ascension in his place, and there took the power and Ascended. He was finally killed by Vin, but not before warning her that she was making a terrible mistake.

LURCHER: A Misting who can burn iron.

LUTHADEL: Capital of the Final Empire, and largest city in the land. Luthadel is known for its textiles, its forges, and its majestic noble keeps. It was nearly destroyed during the siege of Luthadel by rampaging koloss and is now ruled by King Penrod, one of the subject kings under Elend.

MALATIUM: The metal discovered by Kelsier, often dubbed the Eleventh Metal. Nobody knows where he found it, or why he thought it could kill the Lord Ruler, but it is an alloy of atium and gold. Malatium eventually provided the clue Vin needed to defeat the Lord Ruler, as it allows an Allomancer to see a shadow from another person's past.

MARE: Kelsier's wife, a friend of Sazed's who was very active in the skaa rebellion before her death in the Pits of Hathsin.

MELAAN: A kandra of the Seventh Generation. She was trained and "raised" by TenSoon.

METALMIND: A piece of metal that a Feruchemist uses as a kind of battery, filling it with certain attributes that he or she can later withdraw. Specific metalminds are named after the different metals they are made of: tinmind, steelmind, etc.

MIST: The strange, omnipresent fog that falls on the Final Empire every night. Thicker than a common fog, it swirls and churns about, almost as if it were alive. Just before Vin took the power at the Well of Ascension, the mists changed and began randomly killing people who went out in them.

MISTBORN: An Allomancer who can burn all of the Allomantic metals.

MISTCLOAK: A garment worn by many Mistborn as a mark

of their station. Mistcloaks are constructed from dozens of thick ribbons of cloth that are sewn together at the top, but allowed to spread free from the chest down.

MISTING: An Allomancer who can burn only one metal. They are much more common than Mistborn. (Note: An Allomancer either has one power or all of them. There are no in-betweens with two or three.) The Lord Ruler and his priests always taught that there were only eight kinds of Mistings, based on the first eight Allomantic metals.

MISTSICKNESS: The name used for the strange malady that strikes people who go out into the mists. Though most who do so are unharmed, a sizable minority fall to the shakes and grow sick. This sickness can last just a few days or over two weeks, and is sometimes fatal. One need only go out in the mists once, however, to become inoculated—and immune—to mistsickness. Nobody knows why it began, though the first reports of it came just before Vin took the power at the Well of Ascension.

MISTWRAITH: A nonsentient relative of the kandra people. Mistwraiths are globs of boneless flesh that scavenge the land at night, eating any carcass they find, then using the skeletons for their own bodies. Kandra are actually made from mistwraiths, which they call the "unbirthed."

NEW EMPIRE: The name Elend gave his realm after he took power from Cett and Straff at the end of the siege of Luthadel. It currently includes the Central Dominance and the Northern Dominance, with parts of the Eastern and Southern Dominances as well.

NOORDEN: One of the only obligators who chose to stay in Luthadel and serve Elend.

OBLIGATOR: A member of the Lord Ruler's priesthood. Obligators were more than just religious figures, however—they were civil bureaucrats, and even a spy network. A business deal or promise that wasn't witnessed by an obligator was not considered legally or morally binding.

ORESEUR: A kandra employed by Kelsier. OreSeur once played the part of Lord Renoux, Vin's uncle. He was killed by TenSoon, who impersonated him to get close to Vin.

PATRESEN, LADY: A noblewoman in Fadrex known for her proofreading abilities.

PENROD, FERSON: One of the most prominent noblemen who remained in Luthadel after the Collapse, Penrod made a play for the throne, eventually succeeding in taking it away from Elend via a democratic process. He later accepted Elend as his emperor, and now rules Luthadel.

PEWTERARM: Another term for a Thug, a Misting who can burn pewter.

PITS OF HATHSIN, THE: A network of caverns and crevasses that were the only place in the Final Empire that produced atium. The Lord Ruler used prisoners to work them. Kelsier destroyed their ability to produce atium shortly before he died. Now home to the Terris refugees.

PRESERVATION: An ancient Terris god, Preservation was Ruin's opposite—the force for stability, stasis, and continuity. He gave up most of his mental force to imprison Ruin at the Well of Ascension.

PULL (ALLOMANTIC): Using Allomancy to Pull on something—either on people's emotions with zinc, or on metals with iron.

PUSH (ALLOMANTIC): Using Allomancy to Push on something—either on people's emotions with brass, or on metals with steel.

QUELLION: Ruler of Urteau, Quellion considers himself a pure follower of the Survivor, and tries to uphold Kelsier's injunction to overthrow and execute the nobility. Beldre is his sister.

RASHEK: A Terris packman before the Ascension, Rashek was hired by Alendi to help him make the trek to the Well of Ascension. Rashek deeply resented Alendi, and eventually killed him. He took the power at the Well himself, and became the Lord Ruler.

REEN: Vin's half-brother, who protected her and trained her as a thief. Reen was brutal and unforgiving, but he did save Vin from their insane mother, then protect her during her childhood. He was killed by the Inquisitors when he refused to give them Vin's location. Sometimes, Vin hears the words of his lessons in her memory, and he has come to represent the more brutal side of life in Vin's mind.

RELEASE (FERUCHEMICAL): When a Feruchemist stops tapping a metalmind, no longer drawing forth its power.

RENOUX, LORD: A nobleman whom Kelsier killed, then hired the kandra OreSeur to impersonate. Before the Collapse, Vin played the part of his niece, Valette Renoux.

RIOT (ALLOMANTIC): When an Allomancer burns zinc and Pulls on a person's emotions, enflaming them.

RIOTER (ALLOMANTIC): A Misting who can burn zinc.

RUIN: An ancient Terris god, Ruin is the force of destruction, entropy, and decay in the world. Once imprisoned near the Well of Ascension, Ruin was accidentally released by Vin. Ruin's power is not yet complete, and he mostly affects the world subtly, by whispering in the ears of his servants and by changing the text of documents. He cannot change things written in metal.

SATREN: A city in the East that has a storage cavern.

SAZE: Sazed's nickname on the crew.

SAZED: A Terris Keeper who joined Kelsier's crew against the wishes of his people, then helped overthrow the Final Empire. He was romantically involved with Tindwyl, and her death has pushed him into a long bout of depression. He now serves as chief ambassador in Elend's empire, and has been named by Elend third in line for the throne, should Elend and Vin both die.

SEEKER (ALLOMANTIC): A Misting who can burn bronze.

SHAN ELARIEL: Elend's former fiancée, a Mistborn whom Vin killed.

SIEGE OF LUTHADEL: The term used to refer to the month-long attack upon the Central Dominance by Ashweather Cett, Straff Venture, and Jastes Lekal. It ended with Jastes losing control of his koloss army, which attacked Luthadel. Vin managed to stop this army, then turn it against Straff. At the last minute, Cett joined her.

SKAA: The peasantry of the Final Empire. They were once of

different races and nationalities. Over the thousand-year span of the empire the Lord Ruler worked hard to stamp out any sense of identity in the people, eventually succeeding in creating a single, homogeneous race of slave workers. Elend freed them when he took over Luthadel. Many of them have now joined the Church of the Survivor.

SLOWSWIFT: The nickname of a certain nobleman in Fadrex. He bears a striking resemblance to a well-known storyteller.

SMOKER (ALLOMANTIC): Misting who can burn copper. Also known as a Coppercloud.

SOOTHE (ALLOMANTIC): When an Allomancer burns brass and Pushes on a person's emotions, dampening them.

SOOTHER: A Misting who can burn brass.

SPOOK: A Tineye from Kelsier's crew. The youngest member of the crew, Spook was only fifteen when the Lord Ruler was overthrown. He is Clubs's nephew, and was once known for his use of garbled street slang. At the command of the other members of the crew, he fled Luthadel before its fall, but felt terribly guilty for doing so. He now serves as a scout and spy for Elend, and has been stationed in Urteau, where he is gathering information about the rebels there.

STEEL MINISTRY: The Lord Ruler's priesthood, consisting of a small number of Steel Inquisitors and a larger body of priests called obligators. The Steel Ministry was more than just a religious organization; it was the civic framework of the Final Empire.

STORAGE CAVERN: The Lord Ruler left behind five caches of supplies hidden in caverns beneath certain cities. Each one contains a metal plate giving the location of the next cavern, and providing some advice from the Lord Ruler. The first cavern was discovered beneath Luthadel itself.

STRAFF VENTURE: Elend's father, once king of the Northern Dominance. He was killed by Vin at the climax of the siege of Luthadel.

STREETSLOT: The name for the sunken streets of Urteau. They are really just drained canals. Rather than fill them in, the people of the city walk along their bottoms.

SURVIVOR OF HATHSIN: A cognomen of Kelsier, referring to the fact that he is the only known prisoner to ever escape the prison camps at the Pits of Hathsin.

SYNOD (TERRIS): Once the elite leaders of the Terris Keepers, the entire Synod was attacked and carried off by the Inquisitors. They are presumed dead.

TAP (FERUCHEMICAL): Drawing power from within a Feruchemist's metalminds. It is parallel to the term "burn" used by Allomancers.

TATHINGDWEN: Once capital of the Terris Dominance, Tathingdwen was burned by the Inquisitors during their assault on the Keepers.

TELDEN: One of Elend's old friends, with whom he talked politics and philosophy. Known for being something of a playboy and dandy.

TENSOON: Once Straff Venture's kandra, TenSoon was loaned to Zane for use in spying on Vin. TenSoon killed OreSeur and took his place, acting as Vin's companion. He came to like her, despite his natural inclination to hate all humans, and eventually betrayed Zane—breaking his Contract—to help her. In consequence of this action, he returned to the Homeland to accept punishment from his people. He has the Blessing of Presence, as well as the Blessing of Potency, which he stole from OreSeur.

TERRIS: The dominance in the far north of the Final Empire. During the days of the Lord Ruler, it was the only dominance to retain the name of the kingdom it used to be, perhaps a sign of the Lord Ruler's fondness for his homeland. (Though it was later discovered that the current Dominance of Terris is not actually where the old kingdom stood.) The Terris people abandoned their homeland after the Inquisitor assault a year ago, fleeing to the Central Dominance, where Elend took them in. They now make their home in the valleys surrounding the Pits of Hathsin.

THUG (ALLOMANTIC): A Misting who can burn pewter.

TINDWYL: A Terris Keeper and a member of the Synod. Once romantically involved with Sazed, Tindwyl was killed during the siege of Luthadel. She was one of Elend's primary teachers in the art of leadership.

TINEYE: A Misting who can burn tin.

TRUSTWARREN: The holiest place in the kandra Homeland.

TYRIAN, MOUNT: The closest of the ashmounts to Luthadel.

UNBIRTHED: *See* Mistwraith.

URTEAU: Capital of the Northern Dominance, and once the seat of House Venture. Now in rebellion, it is ruled by a man known as Quellion the Citizen. Site of a storage cavern.

VALETTE RENOUX: The alias that Vin used when infiltrating noble society during the days before the Collapse.

VEDLEW: A senior elder of the Terris people.

WELL OF ASCENSION: *See* Ascension, Well of.

WELLEN: Also known as Wells. One of Cett's soldiers whom he brought with him into Luthadel during the siege. Wells was the sole survivor of a large group of men who were on watch the night when Vin and Zane assaulted Cett's position.

WORLDBRINGERS: A sect of scholarly Terris Feruchemists before the Collapse, of which Kwaan was a member. The later order of Keepers was based on the Worldbringers.

YEDEN: A member of Kelsier's crew and the skaa rebellion. He was killed during the fight against the Lord Ruler.

YOMEN, LORD ARADAN: An obligator in Urteau who was politically opposed to Cett. A member of the Canton of Resource, Yomen took control of Fadrex—and Cett's kingdom—when Cett left to besiege Luthadel.

SUMMARIES OF PREVIOUS BOOKS

BOOK ONE

Mistborn: The Final Empire introduces the Final Empire, a land ruled over by a powerful immortal known as the Lord Ruler. A thousand years ago, the Lord Ruler took the power at the Well of Ascension and supposedly defeated a powerful force or creature known only as the Deepness.

The Lord Ruler conquered the known world and founded the Final Empire. He ruled for a thousand years, stamping out all remnants of the individual kingdoms, cultures, religions, and languages that used to exist in his land. In their place he set up his own system. Certain peoples were dubbed "skaa," a word that meant something akin to slave or peasant. Other peoples were dubbed nobility, and most of these were descendants of those who had supported the Lord Ruler during his years of conquest. The Lord Ruler had supposedly given them the power of Allomancy in order to gain powerful assassins and warriors with intelligence, as opposed to the brutish koloss, and had used them well in conquering and maintaining his empire.

Skaa and nobility were forbidden to interbreed. During the thousand years of the Lord Ruler's reign, many rebellions occurred among the skaa, but none were successful.

Finally, a half-breed Mistborn known as Kelsier decided to challenge the Lord Ruler. Once the most famous gentleman thief in the Final Empire, Kelsier was known for his daring schemes. Those eventually ended with his capture, however, and he was sent to the Lord Ruler's death camp at the Pits of Hathsin, the secret source of atium.

It was said that nobody ever escaped the Pits of Hathsin alive—but Kelsier did just that. He gained the powers of a Mistborn during that time, and managed to free himself, earning the title "the Survivor of Hathsin." At this point, he turned from his selfish ways and decided to try his most daring plan yet: the overthrow of the Final Empire.

He recruited a team of thieves, mostly half-breed Mistings, to help him achieve his goal. During this time, he also discovered a young half-breed Mistborn girl named Vin. Vin was as yet unaware of her powers, and Kelsier brought her into the crew to train her, theoretically to have someone to whom he could pass his legacy.

Kelsier's crew slowly gathered an underground army of skaa rebels. Despite their progress, the crew began to wonder if Kelsier was setting himself up to be another Lord Ruler. He sought to make himself a legend among the skaa, becoming almost a religious figure to them. At the same time, Vin—who had been raised on the streets by a cruel brother—grew to trust people for the first time in her life. As this happened, Vin began to believe in Kelsier and his purpose.

Even before mastering her Allomantic talents, Vin was used as a spy among the nobility, and was trained to infiltrate their balls and parties playing the part of "Valette Renoux," a young noblewoman from the countryside. During the first of these balls, she met Elend Venture, a young, idealistic nobleman and heir of his house. He eventually convinced her that not all noblemen were deserving of their poor reputation, and the two fell in love, despite Kelsier's best efforts.

The crew also discovered a journal, apparently written by the Lord Ruler himself during the days before the Ascension. This book painted a different picture of the tyrant—it depicted a melancholy, tired man who was trying his best to protect the people against the Deepness, despite the fact that he didn't really understand it.

In the end, it was revealed that Kelsier's plan had been much broader than simply using a skaa army to overthrow the empire. In part the effort to raise troops provided an opportunity to spread rumors about himself. He also used it to train his crew in the arts of leadership and persuasion. The true extent of his plan was revealed when he sacrificed his life in a very visible way, making himself a martyr to the skaa and finally convincing them to rise up and overthrow the Lord Ruler.

One of Kelsier's crewmembers—a man who had been playing the part of "Lord Renoux," Valette's uncle—turned out to be a kandra named OreSeur. OreSeur took on Kelsier's form, then went about creating rumors that Kelsier had returned from the grave, further inspiring the skaa. After this, OreSeur's Contract passed to Vin.

It was Vin who actually killed the Lord Ruler. She discovered that he wasn't actually a god, or even immortal—he had simply found a way to extend his life and his power by using

Allomancy and Feruchemy at the same time. He wasn't the hero from the logbook—but, instead, was that man's servant, a Feruchemist of some great power. Still, he was much stronger in Allomancy than Vin. While she was fighting him, she drew upon the mists somehow, burning them in place of metals. She still doesn't know why or how this happened. With that power—and with the knowledge of his true nature—she was able to defeat and kill the Lord Ruler.

The Final Empire was thrown into chaos. Elend Venture took control of Luthadel, the capital, and put Kelsier's crew in prime governmental positions.

BOOK TWO

The Well of Ascension describes how the fledgling kingdom managed to survive for a year under Elend's leadership. Elend set up a type of parliament, named the Assembly, and gave them a great deal of power. While Elend showed expertise in the theories of leadership, he lacked practical experience. His rule became unstable as various members of the Assembly began to jockey for power.

Rumors of the Lord Ruler's atium cache—combined with the prize that was Luthadel, the largest city in the empire—eventually drew several predators to the Central Dominance. The worst of these was Straff Venture, Elend's own father. Straff marched a sizable army to Luthadel, secretly bringing with him a Mistborn son, named Zane. Fortunately for Luthadel, Breeze managed to convince a second army—led by Ashweather Cett—to march on the city as well. Surprised by the presence of the other, each tyrant realized that he couldn't afford to attack the city, for afterward he would be vulnerable to the other army. So, they settled down into a siege, more worried about each other than they were about Elend.

About this time, a Keeper named Tindwyl arrived in Luthadel. Sazed invited her to come and help Elend learn to be a better king. She worked with him, trying to teach him to temper his idealism with a measure of realism. Elend convinced the crew to help him play Straff and Cett against each other, with the ultimate goal of getting them to fight. Elend hoped that if the two invaders weakened their armies against one another, his own force—by far the smallest of the three—could defeat the remnants. He began to meet with Straff and Cett, trying to manipulate them. During his maneuvering, however, a faction in the Assembly managed to depose him via a law he himself had written.

Elend refused to use his army to seize back the city, a decision that Tindwyl and the crew thought was foolishly idealistic. Instead, he decided to play the political game and try to convince the Assembly to reinstate him.

During all of this, Vin had troubles of her own. She had discovered a mysterious "mist spirit" that came out at nights, watching her. She noticed that the logbook author—Alendi—had seen a similar manifestation before he arrived at the Well of Ascension. In addition, Vin began to hear strange thumpings when she burned bronze.

Vin's emotions regarding Elend and her own worth to him went through a great deal of turmoil. She loved him, but didn't think that the two of them were right for each other. She worried that she was too brutal, and not enough of a politician, to make him a good wife. Complicating this was Zane, Straff's Mistborn son and Elend's half-brother, who spent many evenings sparring with Vin, tempting her and driving a wedge between her and Elend. Vin began to rely upon the kandra OreSeur, who was—by Elend's order—to remain by her side at all times and watch over her. The two became friends despite their initial dislike for one another.

About this time, Sazed returned to Luthadel, having discovered some very alarming facts during his wanderings. First, it appeared that the mists were beginning to come during the day. Second, the mists were somehow causing people to fall sick and die. Third, there was a large army of koloss marching on Luthadel, led by Jastes Lekal. Sazed began to work on researching these things, along with translating a strange inscription he had discovered in the South while traveling with Marsh. This inscription turned out to record the last words of

Kwaan, a scholar who—some thousand years earlier—had been deeply involved with Alendi, Rashek, and the Terris prophecies. Sazed also began to interact with Tindwyl, who disapproved of his rebellious nature, yet harbored some deep feelings for him.

Elend's campaign in the Assembly failed, and they elected Ferson Penrod as their king instead of Elend. Oddly, however, being deposed finally made Elend begin to understand what it meant to be a king and leader. He began to intertwine his philosophies about justice with the things Tindwyl was teaching him, and actually started to become an inspiring and effective leader—even if he no longer held the throne. The city's problems, however, grew even worsc as Jastes Lekal's koloss arrived. It quickly became clear that he had only marginal control over the murderous beasts.

Eventually, Zane prompted Vin to assault Cett's base inside of Luthadel. (Cett had entered to make a play for the throne himself.) She and Zane slaughtered their way to the top floor of the keep, where Vin had a breakdown prompted by what she'd just done. She fled, leaving Cett alive. Soon after, Zane attacked her, driven to madness by strange voices in his head. Vin and Zane fought, and OreSeur revealed himself as a spy, another kandra named TenSoon, who had killed and impersonated the real OreSeur. Vin managed to kill Zane, even though he had atium, then she ran to Elend. Her emotional problems in remission, she convinced Sazed to marry Elend and her.

Following his near-assassination, Cett retreated from Luthadel and withdrew his armies from the siege. Elend's attempts to get Jastes to withdraw were unsuccessful. Outside, Straff realized that if he simply pulled back, the koloss would probably attack and destroy the city—leaving Straff himself to return and take control once the beasts had exhausted themselves in combat.

Many of the crewmembers realized that this was what would happen. Sazed convinced them that they should lie to Vin and Elend, telling them that the city would be safe and sending them north to search for the Well of Ascension. This ploy succeeded. Vin and Elend left, taking Spook with them, and in their absence the koloss finally attacked. The city's army fought well, Sazed himself holding one of the city gates against terrible odds. During the fighting, Clubs, Dockson, and Tindwyl were killed. As the koloss were about to destroy everything, Vin returned to the city, having learned from Spook that she had been deceived.

Vin exploited an Allomantic weakness in the koloss revealed to her by TenSoon/OreSeur the kandra, taking control of the koloss in the same way the Lord Ruler once had. She used those koloss to attack Straff's army when it returned, and she was joined by Cett at the last moment. With Straff dead, Vin forced Penrod, Cett, and Straff's second-in-command to swear allegiance to Elend, naming him emperor.

The city was saved. However, Vin continued to hear the strange thumpings in her mind. She'd become convinced that she—not the ancient man Alendi—was the Hero of Ages. She soon realized that the Well of Ascension wasn't actually in the northern mountains, but instead beneath Luthadel. She and Elend investigated this, discovering that beneath Kredik Shaw, there was a large secret cavern stockpiled with food. Beyond that cavern was another, filled with dark smoke. Beyond that, a pool of glowing power. The Well of Ascension.

Sazed, up above, was still reeling from Tindwyl's death. He had thrown himself into his studies, and discovered—to his alarm—that something was very wrong with the prophecies. He rushed after Vin and Elend, intent on stopping them from taking the power at the Well, but was blocked by Marsh. As the two fought, Vin took the power and did what she thought was the right thing. Though the mist spirit stabbed Elend, Vin didn't use the Well's power to heal him. Instead, she released it as the prophecies said she had to do in order to stop the mists from destroying the world.

She made the wrong choice. A dark force imprisoned near the Well of Ascension had altered the prophecies and led Vin to do what was necessary to release it. The thing burst free, leaving Vin with the horror of what she had done. The mist spirit, however, provided a way for her to save Elend by making him into a Mistborn.

The book ends with Vin and Elend on the walls of Luthadel, having saved the city but also having released a terrible force upon the world. Sazed, crushed by Tindwyl's death, had come to believe that his faith was worthless. Spook was riddled with guilt for abandoning Clubs to die in the city, and both Breeze and Ham bore emotional scars from their seemingly hopeless fight against the koloss. On top of all this, as Sazed had reported, the mists had changed somehow, and they now killed people who went into them.

Elend, however, was determined to consolidate their new empire and find a way to fight the thing that Vin had released. When she asked him what they were going to do now, he had only one answer for her: They were going to survive. No matter what.

One year has passed.

Brandon Sanderson was born in Nebraska in 1975. Since then he has written the Mistborn series, amongst others, become a *New York Times* bestselling author and been hailed as the natural successor to Robert Jordan. He lives in Utah.

www.brandonsanderson.com

Praise for Brandon Sanderson and

THE WELL OF ASCENSION:

'This entertaining read will especially please those who always wanted to know what happened after the good guys won' *Publishers Weekly*

'All the explosive action any adventure fan could want' *Locus*

'A great epic fantasy . . . Fans of Terry Goodkind and Terry Brooks will find *The Well of Ascension* fulfilling, satisfying, and incredibly exciting' *SFRevu.com*

'Brandon Sanderson is the real thing – an exciting storyteller with a unique and powerful vision' *David Farland*

'Sanderson is astonishingly wise' *Orson Scott Card*

Also by Brandon Sanderson from Gollancz:

The Final Empire

THE WELL OF ASCENSION

Mistborn Book Two

BRANDON SANDERSON

First published in Great Britain in 2009 by
Gollancz
An imprint of the Orion Publishing Group
Carmelite House, 50 Victoria Embankment,
London EC4Y 0DZ
An Hachette UK Company

34

A CIP catalogue record for this book is available from the British Library

ISBN 978 0 575 08993 8

Printed in Great Britain by Clays Ltd, Elcograf S.p.A.

www.brandonsanderson.com

www.orionbooks.co.uk

The Orion Publishing Group's policy is to use papers that are natural, renewable and recyclable products and made from wood grown in sustainable forests. The logging and manufacturing processes are expected to conform to the environmental regulations of the country of origin.

FOR PHYLLIS CALL,

Who may never understand my fantasy books,
yet who taught me more about life
—and therefore writing—
than she can probably ever know

(Thanks, Grandma!)

CONTENTS

[illegible]

ACKNOWLEDGMENTS

First off, as always, my excellent agent, Joshua Bilmes, and editor, Moshe Feder, deserve high praise for their efforts. This book in particular required some thoughtful drafting, and they were up to the task. They have my thanks, as do their assistants, Steve Mancino (an excellent agent in his own right) and Denis Wong.

There are some other fine folks at Tor who deserve my thanks. Larry Yoder (the best sales rep in the nation) did a wonderful job selling the book. Seth Lerner, Tor's mass-market art director, is a genius at matching books to artists. And, speaking of artists, I think the amazing Christian McGrath did a brilliant job with this cover. More can be seen at christianmcgrath.com. Isaac Stewart, a good friend of mine and a fellow writer, did all of the map work and the symbols for the chapter headings. Find him at nethermore.com. Shawn Boyles is the official Mistborn Llama artist, and a great guy to boot. Check my Web site for more information. Finally, I'd like to thank the Tor publicity department—specifically Dot Lin—which has been wonderful in promoting my books and taking care of me. Thank you so much, all of you!

Another round of thanks needs to go out to my alpha readers. These tireless folks provide feedback on my novels in the early stages, dealing with all of the problems, typos, and inconsistencies before I get them worked out. In no particular order, these people are:

Ben Olson, Krista Olsen, Nathan Goodrich, Ethan Skarstedt, Eric J. Ehlers, Jillena O'Brien, C. Lee Player, Kimball Larsen, Bryce Cundick, Janci Patterson, Heather Kirby, Sally Taylor, The Almighty Pronoun, Bradley Reneer, Holly Venable, Jimmy, Alan Layton, Janette Layton, Kaylynn ZoBell, Rick Stranger, Nate Hatfield, Daniel A. Wells, Stacy Whitman, Sarah Bylund, and Benjamin R. Olsen.

A special thanks goes to the people at the Provo Waldenbooks for their support. Sterling, Robin, Ashley, and the terrible duo of Steve "Bookstore Guy" Diamond and Ryan McBride (who were also alpha readers). Also, I must acknowledge my brother, Jordan, for his work on my Web site (along with Jeff Creer). Jordo also is the official "keep Brandon's head on straight" guy, with his solemn duty being to make fun of me and my books.

My mother, father, and sisters are always a wonderful help as well. If I forgot any alpha readers, I'm sorry! I'll put you in twice next time. Note, Peter Ahlstrom, I didn't forget you—I just decided to stick you in late to make you sweat a bit.

Finally, my thanks go out to my wonderful wife, whom I married during the editing process of this book. Emily, I love you!

Terris Dominance
Farmost Dominance
Western Dominance
Northern Dominance
Central Dominance
Crescent Dominance
Southern Dominance
Eastern Dominance
Southern Islands
Remote Dominance
16. Lake Tyrian
17. Lake Luthadel
18. The Black Lake
19. River Searan
20. North Seran
21. South Seran
22. The River Channerel
The Final Empire
1. Luthadel
2. Pits of Hathsin
3. Urteau 4. Fadrex City
5. Tremredare 6. Tathingdwen
7. Conventical of Seran
8. Mount Derytatith, historic location of The Well of Ascension
The Ashmounts: 9. Tyrian
10. Zerinah 11. Faleast 12. Doriel
13. Morag 14. Kalling 15. Torinost
2006

LUTH

Steel Gate

Ashwarrens

Aspen Row

The Twists

Hotel District

Iron Gate

Old Gate

Commercial District

Bronze Gate

1. Square of the Survivor
2. Kredik Shaw
3. Bilmes' Books
4. Assembly Building
5. Luthadel Garrison
6. Keep Venture
7. Keep Hasting
8. Keep Lekal
9. Keep Erikeller
10. Clubs' Shop
11. Camon's Safehouse
12. Old Wall Street
13. Kenton Street
14. Ahlstrom Square
15. Feder Canal
16. Canal Street
17. Skaa Market

ADEL
TIN GATE
SOOTWARRENS
PEWTER GATE
BLOCKSTREET
ZINC GATE
INDUSTRIAL DISTRICT
SOUTHBRIDGE
BRASSGATE
BRASS GATE
COPPER GATE
CHANNEREL
2006

PART ONE

HEIR OF THE SURVIVOR

I write these words in steel, for anything not set in metal cannot be trusted.

1

THE ARMY CREPT LIKE A dark stain across the horizon.

King Elend Venture stood motionless upon the Luthadel city wall, looking out at the enemy troops. Around him, ash fell from the sky in fat, lazy flakes. It wasn't the burnt white ash that one saw in dead coals; this was a deeper, harsher black ash. The Ashmounts had been particularly active lately.

Elend felt the ash dust his face and clothing, but he ignored it. In the distance, the bloody red sun was close to setting. It backlit the army that had come to take Elend's kingdom from him.

"How many?" Elend asked quietly.

"Fifty thousand, we think," Ham said, leaning against the parapet, beefy arms folded on the stone. Like everything in the city, the wall had been stained black by countless years of ashfalls.

"Fifty thousand soldiers . . ." Elend said, trailing off. Despite heavy recruitment, Elend barely had twenty thousand men under his command—and they were peasants with less than a year of training. Maintaining even that small number was straining his resources. If they'd been able to find the Lord Ruler's atium, perhaps things would be different. As it was, Elend's rule was in serious danger of economic disaster.

"What do you think?" Elend asked.

"I don't know, El," Ham said quietly. "Kelsier was always the one with the vision."

"But you helped him plan," Elend said. "You and the others, you were his crew. You were the ones who came up with a strategy for overthrowing the empire, then made it happen."

Ham fell silent, and Elend felt as if he knew what the man was thinking. *Kelsier was central to it all. He was the one who organized, the one who took all of the wild brainstorming and turned it into a viable operation. He was the leader. The genius.*

And he'd died a year before, on the very same day that the people—as part of his secret plan—had risen up in fury to overthrow their god emperor. Elend had taken the throne in the ensuing chaos. Now it was looking more and more like he would lose everything that Kelsier and his crew had worked so hard to accomplish. Lose it to a tyrant who might be even worse than the Lord Ruler. A petty, devious bully in "noble" form. The man who had marched his army on Luthadel.

Elend's own father, Straff Venture.

"Any chance you can . . . talk him out of attacking?" Ham asked.

"Maybe," Elend said hesitantly. "Assuming the Assembly doesn't just surrender the city."

"They close?"

"I don't know, honestly. I worry that they are. That army has frightened them, Ham." *And with good reason,* he thought. "Anyway, I have a proposal for the meeting in two days. I'll try to talk them out of doing anything rash. Dockson got back today, right?"

Ham nodded. "Just before the army's advance."

"I think we should call a meeting of the crew," Elend said. "See if we can come up with a way out of this."

"We'll still be pretty shorthanded," Ham said, rubbing his chin. "Spook isn't supposed to be back for another week, and the Lord Ruler only knows where Breeze went. We haven't had a message from him in months."

Elend sighed, shaking his head. "I can't think of anything else, Ham." He turned, staring out over the ashen landscape again. The army was lighting campfires as the sun set. Soon, the mists would appear.

I need to get back to the palace and work on that proposal, Elend thought.

"Where'd Vin run off to?" Ham asked, turning back to Elend.

Elend paused. "You know," he said, "I'm not sure."

Vin landed softly on the damp cobblestones, watching as the mists began to form around her. They puffed into existence as darkness fell, growing like tangles of translucent vines, twisting and wrapping around one another.

The great city of Luthadel was still. Even now, a year after the Lord Ruler's death and the rise of Elend's new free government, the common people stayed in their homes at night. They feared the mists, a tradition that went far deeper than the Lord Ruler's laws.

Vin slipped forward quietly, senses alert. Inside herself, as always, she burned tin and pewter. Tin enhanced her senses, making it easier for her to see in the night. Pewter made her body stronger, made her lighter on her feet. These, along with copper—which had the power to hide her use of Allomancy from others who were burning bronze—were metals that she left on almost all the time.

Some called her paranoid. She thought herself prepared. Either way, the habit had saved her life on numerous occasions.

She approached a quiet street corner and paused, peeking out. She'd never really understood *how* she burned metals; she could remember doing it for as long as she'd been alive, using Allomancy instinctively even before she was formally trained by Kelsier. It didn't really matter to her. She wasn't like Elend; she didn't need a logical explanation for everything. For Vin, it was enough that when she swallowed bits of metal, she was able to draw upon their power.

Power she appreciated, for she well knew what it was like to lack it. Even now, she was not what one would likely envision as a warrior. Slight of frame and barely five feet tall, with dark hair and pale skin, she knew she had an almost frail look about her. She no longer displayed the underfed look she had during her childhood on the streets, but she certainly wasn't someone any man would find intimidating.

She liked that. It gave her an edge—and she needed every edge she could get.

She also liked the night. During the day, Luthadel was cramped and confining despite its size. But at night the mists fell like a deep cloud. They dampened, softened, shaded. Massive keeps became shadowed mountains, and crowded tenements melted together like a chandler's rejected wares.

Vin crouched beside her building, still watching the intersection. Carefully, she reached within herself and burned steel—one of the other metals she'd swallowed earlier. Immediately, a group of translucent blue lines sprang up around her. Visible only to her eyes, the lines pointed from her chest to nearby sources of metal—all metals, no matter what type. The thickness of the lines was proportionate to the size of the metal pieces they met. Some pointed to bronze door latches, others to crude iron nails holding boards together.

She waited silently. None of the lines moved. Burning steel was an easy way to tell if someone was moving nearby. If they were wearing bits of metal, they would trail telltale moving lines of blue. Of course, that wasn't the main purpose of steel. Vin reached her hand carefully into her belt pouch and pulled out one of the many coins that sat within, muffled by cloth batting. Like all other bits of metal, this coin had a blue line extending from its center to Vin's chest.

She flipped the coin into the air, then mentally grabbed its line and—burning steel—Pushed on the coin. The bit of metal shot into the air, arcing through the mists, forced away by the Push. It plinked to the ground in the middle of the street.

The mists continued to spin. They were thick and mysterious, even to Vin. More dense than a simple fog and more constant than any normal weather pattern, they churned and flowed, making rivulets around her. Her eyes could pierce them; tin made her sight more keen. The night seemed lighter to her, the mists less thick. Yet, they were still there.

A shadow moved in the city square, responding to her coin—which she had Pushed out into the square as a signal. Vin crept forward, and recognized OreSeur the kandra. He wore a different body than he had a year ago, during the days when he had acted the part of Lord Renoux. Yet, this balding, nondescript body had now become just as familiar to Vin.

OreSeur met up with her. "Did you find what you were looking for, Mistress?" he asked, tone respectful—yet somehow still a little hostile. As always.

Vin shook her head, glancing around in the darkness. "Maybe I was wrong," she said. "Maybe I *wasn't* being followed." The acknowledgment made her a bit sad. She'd been looking forward to sparring with the Watcher again tonight. She still didn't even know who he was; the first night, she'd mistaken him for an assassin. And maybe he was. Yet, he seemed to display very little interest in Elend—and a whole lot of interest in Vin.

"We should go back to the wall," Vin decided, standing up. "Elend will be wondering where I went."

OreSeur nodded. At that moment, a burst of coins shot through the mists, spraying toward Vin.

I have begun to wonder if I am the only sane man left. Can the others not see? They have been waiting so long for their hero to come—the one spoken of in Terris prophecies—that they quickly jump between conclusions, presuming that each story and legend applies to this one man.

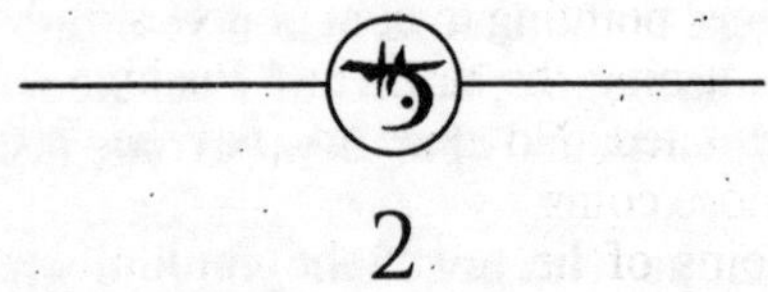

2

VIN REACTED IMMEDIATELY, SPRINGING AWAY. She moved with incredible speed, tasseled cloak swirling as she skidded across the wet cobblestones. The coins hit the ground behind her, throwing up chips of stone, then leaving trails in the mist as they ricocheted away.

"OreSeur, go!" she snapped, though he was already fleeing toward a nearby alleyway.

Vin spun into a low crouch, hands and feet on the cool stones, Allomantic metals flaring in her stomach. She burned steel, watching the translucent blue lines appear around her. She waited, tense, watching for . . .

Another group of coins shot from the dark mists, each one trailing a blue line. Vin immediately flared steel and Pushed against the coins, deflecting them out into the darkness.

The night fell still again.

The street around her was wide—for Luthadel—though tenements rose high on either side. Mist spun lazily, making the ends of the street disappear into a haze.

A group of eight men appeared from the mists and approached. Vin smiled. She *had* been right: Someone was following her. These men weren't, however, the Watcher. They didn't have his solid grace, his sense of power. These men were something far more blunt. Assassins.

It made sense. If *she* had just arrived with an army to

conquer Luthadel, the first thing she'd have done was send in a group of Allomancers to kill Elend.

She felt a sudden pressure at her side, and she cursed as she was thrown off balance, her coin pouch jerking away from her waist. She ripped its string free, letting the enemy Allomancer Push the coins away from her. The assassins had at least one Coinshot—a Misting who had the power to burn steel and Push on metals. In fact, two of the assassins trailed blue lines pointing to coin pouches of their own. Vin considered returning the favor and Pushing their pouches away, but hesitated. No need to play her hand yet. She might need those coins.

Without coins of her own, she couldn't attack from a distance. However, if this was a good team, then attacking from a distance would be pointless—their Coinshots and Lurchers would be ready to deal with shot coins. Fleeing wasn't an option either. These men hadn't come for her alone; if she fled, they'd continue on to their real goal.

Nobody sent assassins to kill bodyguards. Assassins killed important men. Men like Elend Venture, king of the Central Dominance. The man she loved.

Vin flared pewter—body growing tense, alert, dangerous. *Four Thugs at the front,* she thought, eyeing the advancing men. The pewter burners would be inhumanly strong, capable of surviving a great deal of physical punishment. Very dangerous up close. *And the one carrying the wooden shield is a Lurcher.*

She feinted forward, causing the approaching Thugs to jump backward. Eight Mistings against one Mistborn was decent odds for them—but only if they were careful. The two Coinshots moved up the sides of the street, so that they'd be able to Push at her from both directions. The last man, standing quietly beside the Lurcher, had to be a Smoker—relatively unimportant in a fight, his purpose was to hide his team from enemy Allomancers.

Eight Mistings. Kelsier could have done it; he'd killed an Inquisitor. She wasn't Kelsier, however. She had yet to decide if that was a bad or a good thing.

Vin took a deep breath, wishing she had a bit of atium to

spare, and burned iron. This let her Pull on a nearby coin—one of those that had been shot at her—much as steel would have let her Push on it. She caught it, dropped it, then jumped, making as if to Push on the coin and shoot herself into the air.

One of the Coinshots, however, Pushed against the coin, shooting it away. Since Allomancy would only let a person Push directly away from—or Pull directly toward—their body, Vin was left without a decent anchor. Pushing against the coin would only shoot her sideways.

She dropped back to the ground.

Let them think they have me trapped, she thought, crouching in the center of the street. The Thugs approached a little more confidently. *Yes,* Vin thought. *I know what you're thinking. This is the Mistborn who killed the Lord Ruler? This scrawny thing? Can it be possible?*

I wonder the same thing myself.

The first Thug ducked in to attack, and Vin burst into motion. Obsidian daggers flashed in the night as she ripped them free from their sheaths, and blood sprayed black in the darkness as she ducked beneath the Thug's staff and slashed her weapons across his thighs.

The man cried out. The night was no longer silent.

Men cursed as Vin moved through them. The Thug's partner attacked her—blurringly fast, his muscles fueled by pewter. His staff whipped a tassel from Vin's mistcloak as she threw herself to the ground, then pushed herself back up out of a third Thug's reach.

A spray of coins flew toward her. Vin reached out and Pushed on them. The Coinshot, however, continued to Push—and Vin's Push smashed against his.

Pushing and Pulling metals was all about weight. And—with the coins between them—that meant Vin's weight was slammed against the assassin's weight. Both were tossed backward. Vin shot out of a Thug's reach; the Coinshot fell to the ground.

A flurry of coins came at her from the other direction. Still tumbling in the air, Vin flared steel, giving herself an extra burst of power. Blue lines were a jumbled mess, but she didn't need to isolate the coins to Push them all away.

This Coinshot let go of his missiles as soon as he felt Vin's touch. The bits of metal scattered out into the mists.

Vin hit the cobblestones shoulder-first. She rolled—flaring pewter to enhance her balance—and flipped to her feet. At the same time, she burned iron and Pulled hard on the disappearing coins.

They shot back toward her. As soon as they got close, Vin jumped to the side and Pushed them toward the approaching Thugs. The coins, however, immediately veered away, twisting through the mists toward the Lurcher. He was unable to Push the coins away—like all Mistings, he only had one Allomantic power, and his was to Pull with iron.

He did this effectively, protecting the Thugs. He raised his shield and grunted from the impact as the coins hit it and bounced away.

Vin was already moving again. She ran directly for the now exposed Coinshot to her left, the one who had fallen to the ground. The man yelped in surprise, and the other Coinshot tried to distract Vin, but he was too slow.

The Coinshot died with a dagger in his chest. He was no Thug; he couldn't burn pewter to enhance his body. Vin pulled out her dagger, then yanked his pouch free. He gurgled quietly and collapsed back to the stones.

One, Vin thought, spinning, sweat flying from her brow. She now faced seven men down the corridor-like street. They probably expected her to flee. Instead, she charged.

As she got close to the Thugs, she jumped—then threw down the pouch she'd taken from the dying man. The remaining Coinshot cried out, immediately Pushing it away. Vin, however, got some lift from the coins, throwing herself in a leap directly over the heads of the Thugs.

One of them—the wounded one—had unfortunately been smart enough to remain behind to protect the Coinshot. The Thug raised his cudgel as Vin landed. She ducked his first attack, raised her dagger, and—

A blue line danced into her vision. Quick. Vin reacted immediately, twisting and Pushing against a door latch to throw herself out of the way. She hit the ground on her side, then flung herself up with one hand. She landed skidding on mist-wetted feet.

A coin hit the ground behind her, bouncing against the cobbles. It hadn't come close to hitting her. In fact, it had seemed aimed at the remaining assassin Coinshot. He'd probably been forced to Push it away.

But who had fired it?

OreSeur? Vin wondered. But, that was foolish. The kandra was no Allomancer—and besides, he wouldn't have taken the initiative. OreSeur did only what he was expressly told.

The assassin Coinshot looked equally confused. Vin glanced up, flaring tin, and was rewarded with the sight of a man standing atop a nearby building. A dark silhouette. He didn't even bother to hide.

It's him, she thought. *The Watcher.*

The Watcher remained atop his perch, offering no further interference as the Thugs rushed Vin. She cursed as she found three staves coming at her at once. She ducked one, spun around the other, then planted a dagger in the chest of the man holding the third. He stumbled backward, but didn't drop. Pewter kept him on his feet.

Why did the Watcher interfere? Vin thought as she jumped away. *Why would he shoot that coin at a Coinshot who could obviously Push it away?*

Her preoccupation with the Watcher nearly cost her her life as an unnoticed Thug charged her from the side. It was the man whose legs she'd slashed. Vin reacted just in time to dodge his blow. This, however, put her into range of the other three.

All attacked at once.

She actually managed to twist out of the way of two of the strikes. One, however, crashed into her side. The powerful blow tossed her across the street, and she collided with a shop's wooden door. She heard a crack—from the door, fortunately, and not her bones—and she slumped to the ground, daggers lost. A normal person would be dead. Her pewter-strengthened body, however, was tougher than that.

She gasped for breath, forcing herself up to her feet, and flared tin. The metal enhanced her senses—including her sense of pain—and the sudden shock cleared her mind.

Her side ached where she'd been struck. But she couldn't stop. Not with a Thug charging her, swinging his staff in an overhead blow.

Crouching before the doorway, Vin flared pewter and caught the staff in both hands. She growled, pulling back her left hand, then cracking her fist against the weapon, shattering the fine hardwood in a single blow. The Thug stumbled, and Vin smashed her half of the staff across his eyes.

Though dazed, he stayed on his feet. *Can't fight the Thugs,* she thought. *I have to keep moving.*

She dashed to the side, ignoring her pain. The Thugs tried to follow, but she was lighter, thinner, and—much more important—faster. She circled them, coming back toward the Coinshot, Smoker, and Lurcher. A wounded Thug had again retreated to protect these men.

As Vin approached, the Coinshot threw a double handful of coins at her. Vin Pushed the coins away, then reached out and Pulled on the ones in the bag at the man's waist.

The Coinshot grunted as the bag whipped toward Vin. It was tied by a short tether to his waist, and the pull of her weight jerked him forward. The Thug grabbed and steadied him.

And since her anchor couldn't move, Vin was instead Pulled toward it. She flared her iron, flying through the air, raising a fist. The Coinshot cried out and he pulled a tie to free the bag.

Too late. Vin's momentum carried her forward, and she drove her fist into the Coinshot's cheek as she passed. His head spun around, neck snapping. As Vin landed, she brought her elbow up into the surprised Thug's chin, tossing him backward. Her foot followed, crashing against the Thug's neck.

Neither rose. That was three down. The discarded coin pouch fell to the ground, breaking and throwing a hundred sparkling bits of copper across the cobblestones around Vin. She ignored the throbbing in her elbow and faced down the Lurcher. He stood with his shield, looking strangely unworried.

A *crack* sounded behind her. Vin cried out, her tin-enhanced ears overreacting to the sudden sound. Pain shot through her head, and she raised hands to her ears. She'd forgotten the Smoker, who stood holding two lengths of wood, crafted to make sharp noises when pounded together.

Movements and reactions, actions and consequences—these were the essence of Allomancy. Tin made her eyes pierce the mists—giving her an edge over the assassins. However, the tin also made her ears extremely acute. The Smoker raised his sticks again. Vin growled and yanked a handful of coins off the cobblestones, then shot them at the Smoker. The Lurcher, of course, Pulled them toward him instead. They hit the shield and bounced free. And as they sprayed into the air, Vin carefully Pushed one so it fell behind him.

The man lowered his shield, unaware of the coin Vin had manipulated. Vin Pulled, whipping the single coin directly toward her—and into the back of the Lurcher's chest. He fell without a sound.

Four.

All fell still. The Thugs running toward her drew to a stop, and the Smoker lowered his sticks. They had no Coinshots and no Lurchers—nobody that could Push or Pull metal—and Vin stood amid a field of coins. If she used them, even the Thugs would fall quickly. All she had to do was—

Another coin shot through the air, fired from the Watcher's rooftop. Vin cursed, ducking. The coin, however, didn't strike her. It took the stick-holding Smoker directly in the forehead. The man toppled backward, dead.

What? Vin thought, staring at the dead man.

The Thugs charged, but Vin retreated, frowning. *Why kill the Smoker? He wasn't a threat anymore.*

Unless . . .

Vin extinguished her copper, then burned bronze, the metal that let her sense when other Allomancers were using powers nearby. She couldn't feel the Thugs burning pewter. They were still being Smoked, their Allomancy hidden.

Someone else was burning copper.

Suddenly, it all made sense. It made sense that the group

would risk attacking a full Mistborn. It made sense that the Watcher had fired at the Coinshot. It made sense that he had killed the Smoker.

Vin was in grave danger.

She only had a moment to make her decision. She did so on a hunch, but she'd grown up on the streets, a thief and a scam artist. Hunches felt more natural to her than logic ever would.

"OreSeur!" she yelled. "Go for the palace!"

It was a code, of course. Vin jumped back, momentarily ignoring the Thugs as her servant ducked out of an alleyway. He pulled something off his belt and whipped it toward Vin: a small glass vial, the kind that Allomancers used to store metal shavings. Vin quickly Pulled the vial to her hand. A short distance away, the second Coinshot—who had lain there, as if dead—now cursed and scrambled to his feet.

Vin spun, drinking the vial with a quick gulp. It contained only a single bead of metal. Atium. She couldn't risk carrying it on her own body—couldn't risk having it Pulled away from her during a fight. She'd ordered OreSeur to remain close this night, ready to give her the vial in an emergency.

The "Coinshot" pulled a hidden glass dagger from his waist, charging at Vin ahead of the Thugs, who were getting close. Vin paused for just a moment—regretting her decision, but seeing its inevitability.

The men had hidden a Mistborn among their numbers. A Mistborn like Vin, a person who could burn all ten metals. A Mistborn who had been waiting for the right moment to strike at her, to catch her unprepared.

He would have atium, and there was only one way to fight someone who had atium. It was the ultimate Allomantic metal, usable only by full Mistborn, and it could easily decide the fate of a battle. Each bead was worth a fortune—but what good was a fortune if she died?

Vin burned her atium.

The world around her seemed to change. Every moving object—swinging shutters, blowing ash, attacking Thugs, even trails of mist—shot out a translucent replica of itself.

The replicas moved just in front of their real counterparts, showing Vin exactly what would happen a few moments in the future.

Only the Mistborn was immune. Rather than shooting out a single atium shadow, he released dozens—the sign that he was burning atium. He paused just briefly. Vin's own body would have just exploded with dozens of confusing atium shadows. Now that she could see the future, she could see what he was going to do. That, in turn, changed what she was going to do. That changed what he was going to do. And so, like the reflections in two mirrors facing each other, the possibilities continued into infinity. Neither had an advantage.

Though their Mistborn paused, the four unfortunate Thugs continued to charge, having no way to know that Vin burned atium. Vin turned, standing beside the body of the fallen Smoker. With one foot, she kicked the soundsticks into the air.

A Thug arrived, swinging. His diaphanous atium shadow of a staff blow passed through her body. Vin twisted, ducking to the side, and could feel the real staff pass over her ear. The maneuver seemed easy within the aura of atium.

She snatched one of the soundsticks from the air, then slammed it up into the Thug's neck. She spun, catching the other soundstick, then twisted back and cracked it against the man's skull. He fell forward, groaning, and Vin spun again, easily dodging between two more staves.

She smashed the noise sticks against the sides of a second Thug's head. They shattered—ringing with a hollow sound like that of a musician's beat—as the Thug's skull cracked.

He fell, and did not move again. Vin kicked his staff into the air, then dropped the broken soundsticks and caught it. She spun, twisting the staff and tripping both remaining Thugs at once. In a fluid motion, she delivered two swift—yet powerful—blows to their faces.

She fell to a crouch as the men died, holding the staff in one hand, her other hand resting against the mist-wetted cobbles. The Mistborn held back, and she could see uncertainty in his eyes. Power didn't necessarily mean competence, and his two best advantages—surprise and atium—had been negated.

He turned, Pulling a group of coins up off the ground, then shot them. Not toward Vin—but toward OreSeur, who still stood in the mouth of an alleyway. The Mistborn obviously hoped that Vin's concern for her servant would draw her attention away, perhaps letting him escape.

He was wrong.

Vin ignored the coins, dashing forward. Even as OreSeur cried out in pain—a dozen coins piercing his skin—Vin threw her staff at the Mistborn's head. Once it left her fingers, however, its atium shadow became firm and singular.

The Mistborn assassin ducked, dodging perfectly. The move distracted him long enough for her to close the distance, however. She needed to attack quickly; the atium bead she'd swallowed had been small. It would burn out quickly. And, once it was gone, she'd be exposed. Her opponent would have total power over her. He—

Her terrified opponent raised his dagger. At that moment, his atium ran out.

Vin's predatory instincts reacted instantly, and she swung a fist. He raised an arm to block her blow, but she saw it coming, and she changed the direction of her attack. The blow took him square in the face. Then, with deft fingers, she snatched his glass dagger before it could fall and shatter. She stood and swung it through her opponent's neck.

He fell quietly.

Vin stood, breathing heavily, the group of assassins dead around her. For just a moment, she felt overwhelming power. With atium, she was invincible. She could dodge any blow, kill any enemy.

Her atium ran out.

Suddenly, everything seemed to grow dull. The pain in her side returned to her mind, and she coughed, groaning. She'd have bruises—large ones. Perhaps some cracked ribs.

But she'd won again. Barely. What would happen when she failed? When she didn't watch carefully enough, or fight skillfully enough?

Elend would die.

Vin sighed, and looked up. *He* was still there, watching her from atop a roof. Despite a half-dozen chases spread across several months, she'd never managed to catch him. Someday she would corner him in the night.

But not today. She didn't have the energy. In fact, a part of her worried that he'd strike her down. *But* . . . she thought. *He saved me. I would have died if I'd gotten too close to that hidden Mistborn. An instant of him burning atium with me unaware, and I'd have found his daggers in my chest.*

The Watcher stood for a few more moments—wreathed, as always, in the curling mists. Then he turned, jumping away into the night. Vin let him go; she had to deal with OreSeur.

She stumbled over to him, then paused. His nondescript body—in a servant's trousers and shirt—had been pelted with coins, and blood seeped from the several wounds.

He looked up at her. "What?" he asked.

"I didn't expect there to be blood."

OreSeur snorted. "You probably didn't expect me to feel pain either."

Vin opened her mouth, then paused. Actually, she hadn't ever thought about it. Then she hardened herself. *What right does this* thing *have to chastise me?*

Still, OreSeur had proven useful. "Thank you for throwing me the vial," she said.

"It was my duty, Mistress," OreSeur said, grunting as he pulled his broken body up against the side of the alleyway. "I was charged with your protection by Master Kelsier. As always, I serve the Contract."

Ah, yes. The almighty Contract. "Can you walk?"

"Only with effort, Mistress. The coins shattered several of these bones. I will need a new body. One of the assassins, perhaps?"

Vin frowned. She glanced back toward the dead men, and her stomach twisted slightly at the gruesome sight of their fallen bodies. She'd killed them, eight men, with the cruel efficiency that Kelsier had trained in her.

This is what I am, she thought. *A killer, like those men.* That was how it had to be. Someone had to protect Elend.

However, the thought of OreSeur eating one of them—digesting the corpse, letting his strange kandra senses memorize the positioning of muscles, skin, and organs, so that he could reproduce them—sickened her.

She glanced to the side, and saw the veiled scorn in OreSeur's eyes. They both knew what she thought of him eating human bodies. They both knew what he thought of her prejudice.

"No," Vin said. "We won't use one of these men."

"You'll have to find me another body, then," OreSeur said. "The Contract states that I cannot be forced to kill men."

Vin's stomach twisted again. *I'll think of something,* she thought. His current body was that of a murderer, taken after an execution. Vin was still worried that someone in the city would recognize the face.

"Can you get back to the palace?" Vin asked.

"With time," OreSeur said.

Vin nodded, dismissing him, then turned back toward the bodies. Somehow she suspected that this night would mark a distinct turning point in the fate of the Central Dominance.

Straff's assassins had done more damage than they would ever know. That bead of atium had been her last. The next time a Mistborn attacked her, she would be exposed.

And would likely die as easily as the Mistborn she'd slain this night.

My brethren ignore the other facts. They cannot connect the other strange things that are happening. They are deaf to my objections and blind to my discoveries.

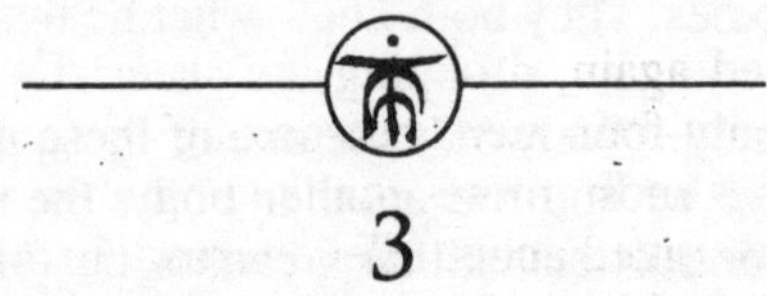

3

ELEND DROPPED HIS PEN TO his desk with a sigh, then leaned back in his chair and rubbed his forehead.

Elend figured that he knew as much about political theory as any living man. He'd certainly read more about economics, studied more about governments, and held more political debates than anyone he knew. He understood all the theories about how to make a nation stable and fair, and had tried to implement those in his new kingdom.

He just hadn't realized how incredibly frustrating a parliamentary council would be.

He stood up and walked over to get himself some chilled wine. He paused, however, as he glanced out his balcony doors. In the distance, a glowing haze shone through the mists. The campfires of his father's army.

He put down the wine. He was already exhausted, and the alcohol probably wouldn't help. *I can't afford to fall asleep until I get this done!* he thought, forcing himself to return to his seat. The Assembly would meet soon, and he needed to have the proposal finished tonight.

Elend picked up the sheet, scanning its contents. His handwriting looked cramped even to him, and the page was scattered with crossed-out lines and notations—reflections of his frustration. They'd known about the army's approach for weeks now, and the Assembly still quibbled about what to do.

Some of its members wanted to offer a peace treaty; others thought they should simply surrender the city. Still others felt they should attack without delay. Elend feared that the surrender faction was gaining strength; hence his proposal. The motion, if passed, would buy him more time. As king, he already had prime right of parlay with a foreign dictator. The proposal would forbid the Assembly from doing anything rash until he'd at least met with his father.

Elend sighed again, dropping the sheet. The Assembly was only twenty-four men, but getting them to agree on anything was almost more challenging than any of the problems they argued about. Elend turned, looking past the solitary lamp on his desk, out through the open balcony doors and toward the fires. Overhead, he heard feet scuttling on the rooftop—Vin, going about her nightly rounds.

Elend smiled fondly, but not even thinking of Vin could restore his good temper. *That group of assassins she fought tonight. Can I use that somehow?* Perhaps if he made the attack public, the Assembly would be reminded of the disdain Straff had for human life, and then be less likely to surrender the city to him. But . . . perhaps they'd also get frightened that he'd send assassins after *them,* and be more likely to surrender.

Sometimes Elend wondered if the Lord Ruler had been right. Not in oppressing the people, of course—but in retaining all of the power for himself. The Final Empire had been nothing if not stable. It had lasted a thousand years, weathering rebellions, maintaining a strong hold on the world.

The Lord Ruler was immortal, though, Elend thought. *That's an advantage I'll certainly never have.*

The Assembly was a better way. By giving the people a parliament with real legal authority, Elend would craft a stable government. The people would have a king—a man to provide continuity, a symbol of unity. A man who wouldn't be tainted by the need to get reappointed. However, they would also have an Assembly—a council made up of their peers that could voice their concerns.

It all sounded wonderful in theory. Assuming they survived the next few months.

Elend rubbed his eyes, then dipped his pen and began to scratch new sentences at the bottom of the document.

The Lord Ruler was dead.

Even a year later, Vin sometimes found that concept difficult to grasp. The Lord Ruler had been . . . everything. King and god, lawmaker and ultimate authority. He had been eternal and absolute, and now he was dead.

Vin had killed him.

Of course, the truth wasn't as impressive as the stories. It hadn't been heroic strength or mystical power that had let Vin defeat the emperor. She'd just figured out the trick that he'd been using to make himself immortal, and she'd fortunately—almost accidentally—exploited his weakness. She wasn't brave or clever. Just lucky.

Vin sighed. Her bruises still throbbed, but she had suffered far worse. She sat atop the palace—once Keep Venture—just above Elend's balcony. Her reputation might have been unearned, but it had helped keep Elend alive. Though dozens of warlords squabbled in the land that had once been the Final Empire, none of them had marched on Luthadel.

Until now.

Fires burned outside the city. Straff would soon know that his assassins had failed. What then? Assault the city? Ham and Clubs warned that Luthadel couldn't hold against a determined attack. Straff had to know that.

Still, for the moment, Elend was safe. Vin had gotten pretty good at finding and killing assassins; barely a month passed that she didn't catch someone trying to sneak into the palace. Many were just spies, and very few were Allomancers. However, a normal man's steel knife would kill Elend just as easily as an Allomancer's glass one.

She wouldn't let that occur. Whatever else happened—whatever sacrifices it required—Elend *had* to stay alive.

Suddenly apprehensive, she slipped over to the skylight to check on him. Elend sat safely at his desk below, scribbling away on some new proposal or edict. Kingship had changed the man remarkably little. About four years her senior—placing him in his early twenties—Elend was a man who put great stock in learning, but little in appearance. He only bothered to comb his hair when he attended an important function, and he somehow managed to wear even well-tailored outfits with an air of dishevelment.

He was probably the best man she had ever known. Earnest, determined, clever, and caring. And, for some reason, he loved her. At times, that fact was even more amazing to her than her part in the Lord Ruler's death.

Vin looked up, glancing back at the army lights. Then she looked to the sides. The Watcher had not returned. Often on nights like this he would tempt her, coming dangerously close to Elend's room before disappearing into the city.

Of course, if he'd wanted to kill Elend, he could just have done it while I was fighting the others. . . .

It was a disquieting thought. Vin couldn't watch Elend every moment. He was exposed a frightening amount of the time.

True, Elend had other bodyguards, and some were even Allomancers. They, however, were stretched as thin as she was. This night's assassins had been the most skilled, and most dangerous, that she had ever faced. She shivered, thinking about the Mistborn who had hid among them. He hadn't been very good, but he wouldn't have needed much skill to burn atium, then strike Vin directly in the right place.

The shifting mists continued to spin. The army's presence whispered a disturbing truth: The surrounding warlords were beginning to consolidate their domains, and were thinking about expansion. Even if Luthadel stood against Straff somehow, others would come.

Quietly, Vin closed her eyes and burned bronze, still worried that the Watcher—or some other Allomancer—might be nearby, planning to attack Elend in the supposedly safe aftermath of the assassination attempt. Most Mistborn considered bronze to be a relatively useless metal, as it was easily negated. With copper, a Mistborn could mask their Allomancy—not to mention protect themselves from emotional manipulation by zinc or brass. Most Mistborn considered it foolish not to have their copper on at all times.

And yet . . . Vin had the ability to pierce copperclouds.

A coppercloud wasn't a visible thing. It was far more vague. A pocket of deadened air where Allomancers could burn their metals and not worry that bronze burners would be able to sense them. But Vin could sense Allomancers who used metals inside of a coppercloud. She still wasn't certain why. Even Kelsier, the most powerful Allomancer she had known, hadn't been able to pierce a coppercloud.

Tonight, however, she sensed nothing.

With a sigh, she opened her eyes. Her strange power was confusing, but it wasn't unique to her. Marsh had confirmed that Steel Inquisitors could pierce copperclouds, and she was certain that the Lord Ruler had been able to do so. But . . . why her? Why could Vin—a girl who barely had two years' training as a Mistborn—do it?

There was more. She still remembered vividly the morning when she'd fought the Lord Ruler. There was something about that event that she hadn't told anyone—partially because it made her fear, just a bit, that the rumors and legends about her were true. Somehow, she'd drawn upon the mists, using *them* to fuel her Allomancy instead of metals.

It was only with that power, the power of the mists, that she had been able to beat the Lord Ruler in the end. She liked to tell herself that she had simply been lucky in figuring out the Lord Ruler's tricks. But . . . there *had* been something strange that night, something that she'd done. Something that she shouldn't have been able to do, and had never been able to repeat.

Vin shook her head. There was so much they didn't know, and not just about Allomancy. She and the other leaders of Elend's fledgling kingdom tried their best, but without Kelsier to guide them, Vin felt blind. Plans, successes, and even goals were like shadowy figures in the mist, formless and indistinct.

You shouldn't have left us, Kell, she thought. *You saved the world—but you should have been able to do it without dying.* Kelsier, the Survivor of Hathsin, the man who had conceived and implemented the collapse of the Final Empire. Vin had known him, worked with him, been trained by him. He was a legend and a hero. Yet, he had also been a man. Fallible. Imperfect. It was easy for the skaa to revere him, then blame Elend and the others for the dire situation that Kelsier had created.

The thought left her feeling bitter. Thinking about Kelsier often did that. Perhaps it was the sense of abandonment, or perhaps it was just the uncomfortable knowledge that Kelsier—like Vin herself—didn't fully live up to his reputation.

Vin sighed, closing her eyes, still burning bronze. The evening's fight had taken a lot out of her, and she was beginning to dread the hours she still intended to spend watching. It would be difficult to remain alert when—

She sensed something.

Vin snapped her eyes open, flaring her tin. She spun and stooped against the rooftop to obscure her profile. There was someone out there, burning metal. Bronze pulses thumped weakly, faint, almost unnoticeable—like someone playing drums very quietly. They were muffled by a coppercloud. The person—whoever it was—thought that their copper would hide them.

So far, Vin hadn't left anyone alive, save Elend and Marsh, who knew of her strange power.

Vin crept forward, fingers and toes chilled by the roof's copper sheeting. She tried to determine the direction of the pulses. Something was . . . odd about them. She had trouble distinguishing the metals her enemy was burning. Was that the quick, beating thump of pewter? Or was it the rhythm of iron? The pulses seemed indistinct, like ripples in a thick mud.

They were coming from somewhere very close. . . . On the rooftop . . .

Just in front of her.

Vin froze, crouching, the night breezes blowing a wall of mist across her. Where was he? Her senses argued with each other; her bronze said there was something right in front of her, but her eyes refused to agree.

She studied the dark mists, glanced upward just to be certain, then stood. *This is the first time my bronze has been wrong,* she thought with a frown.

Then she saw it.

Not something *in* the mists, but something *of* the mists. The figure stood a few feet away, easy to miss, for its shape was only faintly outlined by the mist. Vin gasped, stepping backward.

The figure continued to stand where it was. She couldn't tell much about it; its features were cloudy and vague, outlined by the chaotic churnings of windblown mist. If not for the form's persistence, she could have dismissed it—like the shape of an animal seen briefly in the clouds.

But it stayed. Each new curl of the mist added definition to thin its body and long head. Haphazard, yet persistent. It suggested a human, but it lacked the Watcher's solidity. It felt . . . looked . . . wrong.

The figure took a step forward.

Vin reacted instantly, throwing up a handful of coins and Pushing them through the air. The bits of metal zipped through the mist, trailing streaks, and passed right through the shadowy figure.

It stood for a moment. Then, it simply puffed away, dissipating into the mists' random curls.

Elend wrote the final line with a flair, though he knew he'd simply have a scribe rewrite the proposal. Still, he was proud. He thought that he'd been able to work out an argument that would finally convince the Assembly that they could not simply surrender to Straff.

He glanced unconsciously toward a stack of papers on his desk. On their top sat an innocent-seeming yellow letter, still folded, bloodlike smudge of wax broken at the seal. The letter had been short. Elend remembered its words easily.

Son,

I trust you've enjoyed seeing after Venture interests in Luthadel. I have secured the Northern Dominance,

and will shortly be returning to our keep in Luthadel. You may turn over control of the city to me at that time.
King Straff Venture

Of all the warlords and despots that had afflicted the Final Empire since the Lord Ruler's death, Straff was the most dangerous. Elend knew this firsthand. His father was a true imperial nobleman: He saw life as a competition between lords to see who could earn the greatest reputation. He had played the game well, making House Venture the most powerful of the pre-Collapse noble families.

Elend's father would not see the Lord Ruler's death as a tragedy or a victory—just as an opportunity. The fact that Straff's supposedly weak-willed fool of a son now claimed to be king of the Central Dominance probably gave him no end of mirth.

Elend shook his head, turning back to the proposal. *A few more rereads, a few tweaks, and I'll finally be able to get some sleep. I just—*

A cloaked form dropped from the skylight in the roof and landed with a quiet thump behind him.

Elend raised an eyebrow, turning toward the crouching figure. "You know, I leave the balcony open for a reason, Vin. You could come in that way, if you wanted."

"I know," Vin said. Then she darted across the room, moving with an Allomancer's unnatural litheness. She checked beneath his bed, then moved over to his closet and threw open the doors. She jumped back with the tension of an alert animal, but apparently found nothing inside that met with her disapproval, for she moved over to peek through the door leading into the rest of Elend's chambers.

Elend watched her with fondness. It had taken him some time to get used to Vin's particular . . . idiosyncrasies. He teased her about being paranoid; she just claimed she was careful. Regardless, half the time she visited his chambers she checked underneath his bed and in his closet. The other times, she held herself back—but Elend often caught her glancing distrustfully toward potential hiding places.

She was far less jumpy when she didn't have a particular reason to worry about him. However, Elend was only just beginning to understand that there was a very complex person hiding behind the face he had once known as Valette Renoux's. He had fallen in love with her courtly side without ever knowing the nervous, furtive Mistborn side. It was still a little difficult to see them as the same person.

Vin closed the door, then paused briefly, watching him with her round, dark eyes. Elend found himself smiling. Despite her oddities—or, more likely *because* of them—he loved this thin woman with the determined eyes and blunt temperament. She was like no one he had ever known—a woman of simple, yet honest, beauty and wit.

She did, however, sometimes worry him.

"Vin?" he asked, standing.

"Have you seen anything strange tonight?"

Elend paused. "Besides you?"

She frowned, striding across the room. Elend watched her small form, clothed in black trousers and a man's buttoning shirt, mistcloak tassels trailing behind her. She wore the cloak's hood down, as usual, and she stepped with a supple grace—the unconscious elegance of a person burning pewter.

Focus! he told himself. *You really* are *getting tired.* "Vin? What's wrong?"

Vin glanced toward the balcony. "That Mistborn, the Watcher, is in the city again."

"You're sure?"

Vin nodded. "But . . . I don't think he's going to come for you tonight."

Elend frowned. The balcony doors were still open, and trails of mist puffed through them, creeping along the floor until they finally evaporated. Beyond those doors was . . . darkness. Chaos.

It's just mist, he told himself. *Water vapor. Nothing to fear.* "What makes you think the Mistborn won't come for me?"

Vin shrugged. "I just feel he won't."

She often answered that way. Vin had grown up a creature of the streets, and she trusted her instincts. Oddly, so did Elend. He eyed her, reading the uncertainty in her posture. Something else had unsettled her this night. He looked into her eyes, holding them for a moment, until she glanced away.

"What?" he asked.

"I saw . . . something else," she said. "Or, I thought I did. Something in the mist, like a person formed from smoke. I could feel it, too, with Allomancy. It disappeared, though."

Elend frowned more deeply. He walked forward, putting his arms around her. "Vin, you're pushing yourself too hard. You can't keep prowling the city at night and then staying up all day. Even Allomancers need rest."

She nodded quietly. In his arms, she didn't seem to him like the powerful warrior who had slain the Lord Ruler. She felt like a woman past the edge of fatigue, a woman overwhelmed by events—a woman who probably felt a lot like Elend did.

She let him hold her. At first, there was a slight stiffness to her posture. It was as if a piece of her still expected to be hurt—a primal sliver that couldn't understand that it was possible to be touched out of love rather than anger. Then, however, she relaxed. Elend was one of the few she could do that around. When she held him—really held him—she clung with a desperation that bordered on terror. Somehow, despite her powerful skill as an Allomancer and her stubborn determination, Vin was frighteningly vulnerable. She seemed to need Elend. For that, he felt lucky.

Frustrated, at times. But lucky. Vin and he hadn't discussed his marriage proposal and her refusal, though Elend often thought of the encounter.

Women are difficult enough to understand, he thought, *and I had to go and pick the oddest one of the lot.* Still, he couldn't really complain. She loved him. He could deal with her idiosyncrasies.

Vin sighed, then looked up at him, finally relaxing as he leaned down to kiss her. He held it for a long moment, and she sighed. After the kiss, she rested her head on his shoulder. "We do have another problem," she said quietly. "I used the last of the atium tonight."

"Fighting the assassins?"

Vin nodded.

"Well, we knew it would happen eventually. Our stockpile couldn't last forever."

"Stockpile?" Vin asked. "Kelsier only left us six beads."

Elend sighed, then pulled her tight. His new government was supposed to have inherited the Lord Ruler's atium reserves—a supposed cache of the metal comprising an amazing treasure. Kelsier had counted on his new kingdom holding those riches; he had died expecting it. There was only one problem. Nobody had ever found the reserve. They had found some small bit—the atium that had made up the bracers that the Lord Ruler had used as a Feruchemical battery to store up age. However, they had spent those on supplies for the city, and they had actually contained only a very small bit of atium. Nothing like the cache was said to have. There should still be, somewhere in the city, a wealth of atium thousands of times larger than those bracers.

"We'll just have to deal with it," Elend said.

"If a Mistborn attacks you, I won't be able to kill him."

"Only if he has atium," Elend said. "It's becoming more and more rare. I doubt the other kings have much of it."

Kelsier had destroyed the Pits of Hathsin, the only place where atium could be mined. Still, if Vin *did* have to fight someone with atium . . .

Don't think about that, he told himself. *Just keep searching. Perhaps we can buy some. Or maybe we'll find the Lord Ruler's cache. If it even exists. . . .*

Vin looked up at him, reading the concern in his eyes, and he knew she had arrived at the same conclusions as he. There was little that could be accomplished at the moment; Vin had done well to conserve their atium as long as she had. Still, as Vin stepped back and let Elend return to his table, he couldn't help thinking about how they could have spent that atium. His people would need food for the winter.

But, by selling the metal, he thought, sitting, *we would have put more of the world's most dangerous Allomantic weapon into the hands of our enemies.* Better that Vin used it up.

As he began to work again, Vin poked her head over his shoulder, obscuring his lamplight. "What is it?" she asked.

"The proposal blocking the Assembly until I've had my right of parlay."

"Again?" she asked, cocking her head and squinting as she tried to make out his handwriting.

"The Assembly rejected the last version."

Vin frowned. "Why don't you just tell them that they *have* to accept it? You're the king."

"Now, see," Elend said, "that's what I'm trying to prove by all this. I'm just one man, Vin—maybe my opinion isn't better than theirs. If we all work on the proposal together, it will come out better than if one man had done it himself."

Vin shook her head. "It will be too weak. No teeth. You should trust yourself more."

"It's not about trust. It's about what's right. We spent a thousand years fighting off the Lord Ruler—if I do things the same way he did, then what will be the difference?"

Vin turned and looked him in the eyes. "The Lord Ruler was an evil man. You're a good one. *That's* the difference."

Elend smiled. "It's that easy for you, isn't it?"

Vin nodded.

Elend leaned up and kissed her again. "Well, some of us have to make things a little more complicated, so you'll have to humor us. Now, kindly remove yourself from my light so I can get back to work."

She snorted, but stood up and rounded the desk, leaving behind a faint scent of perfume. Elend frowned. *When'd she put that on?* Many of her motions were so quick that he missed them.

Perfume—just another of the apparent contradictions that made up the woman who called herself Vin. She wouldn't have been wearing it out in the mists; she usually put it on just for him. Vin liked to be unobtrusive, but she loved wearing scents—and got annoyed at him if he didn't notice when she was trying out a new one. She seemed suspicious and paranoid, yet she trusted her friends with a dogmatic loyalty. She went out at night in black and gray, trying so hard to hide—but Elend had seen her at the balls a year ago, and she had looked natural in gowns and dresses.

For some reason she had stopped wearing those. She hadn't ever explained why.

Elend shook his head, turning back to his proposal. Next to Vin, politics seemed simplistic. She rested her arms on the desktop, watching him work, yawning.

"You should get some rest," he said, dipping his pen again.

Vin paused, then nodded. She removed her mistcloak, wrapped it around herself, then curled up on the rug beside his desk.

Elend paused. "I didn't mean *here,* Vin," he said with amusement.

"There's still a Mistborn out there somewhere," she said with a tired, muffled voice. "I'm not leaving you." She twisted in the cloak, and Elend caught a brief grimace of pain on her face. She was favoring her left side.

She didn't often tell him the details of her fights. She didn't want to worry him. It didn't help.

Elend pushed down his concern and forced himself to start reading again. He was almost finished—just a bit more and—

A knock came at his door.

Elend turned with frustration, wondering at this new interruption. Ham poked his head in the doorway a second later.

"Ham?" Elend said. "You're still awake?"

"Unfortunately," Ham said, stepping into the room.

"Mardra is going to kill you for working late again," Elend said, setting down his pen. Complain though he might about some of Vin's quirks, at least she shared Elend's nocturnal habits.

Ham just rolled his eyes at the comment. He still wore his standard vest and trousers. He'd agreed to be the captain of Elend's guard on a single condition: that he would never have to wear a uniform. Vin cracked an eye as Ham wandered into the room, then relaxed again.

"Regardless," Elend said. "To what do I owe the visit?"

"I thought you might want to know that we identified those assassins who tried to kill Vin."

Elend nodded. "Probably men I know." Most Allomancers were noblemen, and he was familiar with all of those in Straff's retinue.

"Actually, I doubt it," Ham said. "They were Westerners."

Elend paused, frowning, and Vin perked up. "You're sure?"

Ham nodded. "Makes it a bit unlikely that your father sent them—unless he's done some heavy recruiting in Fadrex City. They were of Houses Gardre and Conrad, mostly."

Elend sat back. His father was based in Urteau, hereditary home of the Venture family. Fadrex was halfway across the empire from Urteau, several months' worth of travel. The chances were slim that his father would have access to a group of Western Allomancers.

"Have you heard of Ashweather Cett?" Ham asked.

Elend nodded. "One of the men who's set himself up as king in the Western Dominance. I don't know much about him."

Vin frowned, sitting. "You think he sent these?"

Ham nodded. "They must have been waiting for a chance to slip into the city, and the traffic at the gates these last few days would have provided the opportunity. That makes the arrival of Straff's army and the attack on Vin's life something of a coincidence."

Elend glanced at Vin. She met his eyes, and he could tell that she wasn't completely convinced that Straff hadn't sent the assassins. Elend, however, wasn't so skeptical. Pretty much every tyrant in the area had tried to take him out at one point or another. Why not Cett?

It's that atium, Elend thought with frustration. He'd never found the Lord Ruler's cache—but that didn't stop the despots in the empire from assuming he was hiding it somewhere.

"Well, at least your father didn't send the assassins," Ham said, ever the optimist.

Elend shook his head. "Our relationship wouldn't stop him, Ham. Trust me."

"He's your father," Ham said, looking troubled.

"Things like that don't matter to Straff. He probably hasn't sent assassins because he doesn't think I'm worth the trouble. If we last long enough, though, he will."

Ham shook his head. "I've heard of sons killing their fathers to take their place . . . but fathers killing their sons . . . I wonder what that says about old Straff's mind, that he'd be willing to kill you. You think that—"

"Ham?" Elend interrupted.

"Hum?"

"You know I'm usually good for a discussion, but I don't really have time for philosophy right now."

"Oh, right." Ham smiled wanly, standing and moving to go. "I should get back to Mardra anyway."

Elend nodded, rubbing his forehead and picking up his pen yet again. "Make sure you gather the crew for a meeting. We need to organize our allies, Ham. If we don't come up with something incredibly clever, this kingdom may be doomed."

Ham turned back, still smiling. "You make it sound so desperate, El."

Elend looked over at him. "The Assembly is a mess, a half-dozen warlords with superior armies are breathing down my neck, barely a month passes without someone sending assassins to kill me, and the woman I love is slowly driving me insane."

Vin snorted at this last part.

"Oh, is that all?" Ham said. "See? It's not so bad after all. I mean, we *could* be facing an immortal god and his all-powerful priests instead."

Elend paused, then chuckled despite himself. "Good night, Ham," he said, turning back to his proposal.

"Good night, Your Majesty."

Perhaps they are right. Perhaps I am mad, or jealous, or simply daft. My name is Kwaan. Philosopher, scholar, traitor. I am the one who discovered Alendi, and I am the one who first proclaimed him to be the Hero of Ages. I am the one who started this all.

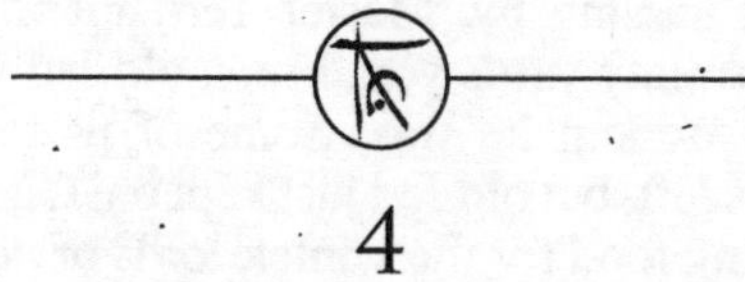

4

THE BODY SHOWED NO OVERT wounds. It still lay where it had fallen—the other villagers had been afraid to move it. Its arms and legs were twisted in awkward positions, the dirt around it scuffed from predeath thrashings.

Sazed reached out, running his fingers along one of the marks. Though the soil here in the Eastern Dominance held far more clay than soil did in the north, it was still more black than it was brown. Ashfalls came even this far south. Ashless soil, washed clean and fertilized, was a luxury used only for the ornamental plants of noble gardens. The rest of the world had to do what it could with untreated soil.

"You say that he was alone when he died?" Sazed asked, turning to the small cluster of villagers standing behind him.

A leather-skinned man nodded. "Like I said, Master Terrisman. He was just standing there, no one else about. He paused, then he fell and wiggled on the ground for a bit. After that, he just . . . stopped moving."

Sazed turned back to the corpse, studying the twisted muscles, the face locked in a mask of pain. Sazed had brought his medical coppermind—the metal armband wrapped around his upper right arm—and he reached into it with his mind, pulling out some of the memorized books he had stored therein. Yes, there were some diseases that killed with shakes and spasms. They rarely took a man so suddenly, but it sometimes happened. If it hadn't been for other circumstances, Sazed would have paid the death little heed.

"Please, repeat to me again what you saw," Sazed asked.

The leather-skinned man at the front of the group, Teur, paled slightly. He was in an odd position—his natural desire for notoriety would make him want to gossip about his experience. However, doing so could earn the distrust of his superstitious fellows.

"I was just passing by, Master Terrisman," Teur said. "On the path twenty yards yon. I seen old Jed working his field—a hard worker, he was. Some of us took a break when the lords left, but old Jed just kept on. Guess he knew we'd be needing food for the winter, lords or no lords."

Teur paused, then glanced to the side. "I know what people say, Master Terrisman, but I seen what I seen. It was day when I passed, but there was *mist* in the valley here. It stopped me, because I've never been out in the mist—my wife'll vouch me that. I was going to turn back, and then I seen old Jed. He was just working away, as if he hadn't seen the mist.

"I was going to call out to him, but before I could, he just . . . well, like I told you. I seen him standing there, then he froze. The mist swirled about him a bit, then he began to jerk and twist, like something really strong was holding him and shaking him. He fell. Didn't get up after that."

Still kneeling, Sazed looked back at the corpse. Teur apparently had a reputation for tall tales. Yet, the body was a chilling corroboration—not to mention Sazed's own experience several weeks before.

Mist during the day.

Sazed stood, turning toward the villagers. "Please fetch for me a shovel."

Nobody helped him dig the grave. It was slow, muggy work in the southern heat, which was strong despite the advent of autumn. The clay earth was difficult to move—but, fortunately, Sazed had a bit of extra stored-up strength inside a pewtermind, and he tapped it for help.

He needed it, for he wasn't what one would call an athletic man. Tall and long-limbed, he had the build of a scholar, and still wore the colorful robes of a Terris steward. He also still kept his head shaved, after the manner of the station he had served in for the first forty-some years of his life. He didn't wear much of his jewelry now—he didn't want to tempt highway bandits—but his earlobes were stretched out and pierced with numerous holes for earrings.

Tapping strength from his pewtermind enlarged his muscles slightly, giving him the build of a stronger man. Even with the extra strength, however, his steward's robes were stained with sweat and dirt by the time he finished digging. He rolled the body into the grave, and stood quietly for a moment. The man had been a dedicated farmer.

Sazed searched through his religions coppermind for an appropriate theology. He started with an index—one of the many that he had created. When he had located an appropriate religion, he pulled free detailed memories about its practices. The writings entered his mind as fresh as when he had just finished memorizing them. They would fade, with time, like all memories—however, he intended to place them back in the coppermind long before that happened. It was the way of the Keeper, the method by which his people retained enormous wealths of information.

This day, the memories he selected were of HaDah, a southern religion with an agricultural deity. Like most religions—which had been oppressed during the time of the Lord Ruler—the HaDah faith was a thousand years extinct.

Following the dictates of the HaDah funeral ceremony, Sazed walked over to a nearby tree—or, at least, one of the shrublike plants that passed for trees in this area. He broke off a long branch—the peasants watching him curiously—and carried it back to the grave. He stooped down and drove it into the dirt at the bottom of the hole, just beside the corpse's head. Then he stood and began to shovel dirt back into the grave.

The peasants watched him with dull eyes. *So depressed,*

Sazed thought. The Eastern Dominance was the most chaotic and unsettled of the five Inner Dominances. The only men in this crowd were well past their prime. The press gangs had done their work efficiently; the husbands and fathers of this village were likely dead on some battlefield that no longer mattered.

It was hard to believe that anything could actually be worse than the Lord Ruler's oppression. Sazed told himself that these people's pain would pass, that they would someday know prosperity because of what he and the others had done. Yet, he had seen farmers forced to slaughter each other, had seen children starve because some despot had "requisitioned" a village's entire food supply. He had seen thieves kill freely because the Lord Ruler's troops no longer patrolled the canals. He had seen chaos, death, hatred, and disorder. And he couldn't help but acknowledge that he was partially to blame.

He continued to refill the hole. He had been trained as a scholar and a domestic attendant; he was a Terrisman steward, the most useful, most expensive, and most prestigious of servants in the Final Empire. That meant almost nothing now. He'd never dug a grave, but he did his best, trying to be reverent as he piled dirt on the corpse. Surprisingly, about halfway through the process, the peasants began to help him, pushing dirt from the pile into the hole.

Perhaps there is hope for these yet, Sazed thought, thankfully letting one of the others take his shovel and finish the work. When they were done, the very tip of the HaDah branch breached the dirt at the head of the grave.

"Why'd you do that?" Teur asked, nodding to the branch.

Sazed smiled. "It is a religious ceremony, Goodman Teur. If you please, there is a prayer that should accompany it."

"A prayer? Something from the Steel Ministry?"

Sazed shook his head. "No, my friend. It is a prayer from a previous time, a time before the Lord Ruler."

The peasants eyed each other, frowning. Teur just rubbed his wrinkled chin. They all remained quiet, however, as Sazed said a short HaDah prayer. When he finished, he turned toward the peasants. "It was known as the religion of HaDah. Some of your ancestors might have followed it, I think. If any of you wish, I can teach you of its precepts."

The assembled crowd stood quietly. There weren't many of them—two dozen or so, mostly middle-aged women and a few older men. There was a single young man with a club leg; Sazed was surprised that he'd lived so long on a plantation. Most lords killed invalids to keep them from draining resources.

"When is the Lord Ruler coming back?" asked a woman.

"I do not believe that he will," Sazed said.

"Why did he abandon us?"

"It is a time of change," Sazed said. "Perhaps it is also time to learn of other truths, other ways."

The group of people shuffled quietly. Sazed sighed quietly; these people associated faith with the Steel Ministry and its obligators. Religion wasn't something that skaa worried about—save, perhaps, to avoid it when possible.

The Keepers spent a thousand years gathering and memorizing the dying religions of the world, Sazed thought. *Who would have thought that now—with the Lord Ruler gone—people wouldn't care enough to want what they'd lost?*

Yet, he found it hard to think ill of these people. They were struggling to survive, their already harsh world suddenly made unpredictable. They were tired. Was it any wonder that talk of beliefs long forgotten failed to interest them?

"Come," Sazed said, turning toward the village. "There are other things—more practical things—that I can teach you."

And I am the one who betrayed Alendi, for I now know that he must never be allowed to complete his quest.

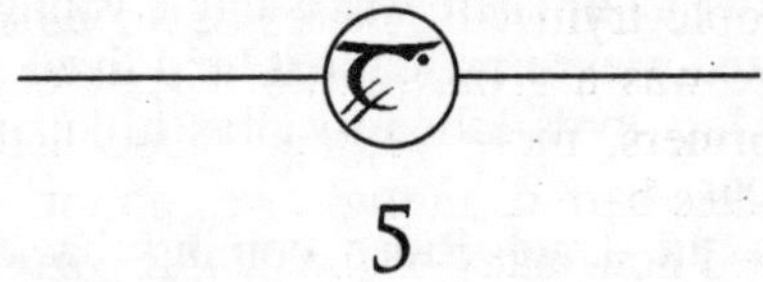

5

VIN COULD SEE SIGNS OF anxiety reflected in the city. Workers milled anxiously and markets bustled with an edge of concern—showing that same apprehension that one might see in a cornered rodent. Frightened, but not sure what to do. Doomed with nowhere to run.

Many had left the city during the last year—noblemen fleeing, merchants seeking some other place of business. Yet, at the same time, the city had swelled with an influx of skaa. They had somehow heard of Elend's proclamation of freedom, and had come with optimism—or, at least, as much optimism as an overworked, underfed, repeatedly beaten populace could manage.

And so, despite predictions that Luthadel would soon fall, despite whispers that its army was small and weak, the people had stayed. Worked. Lived. Just as they always had. The life of a skaa had never been very certain.

It was still strange for Vin to see the market so busy. She walked down Kenton Street, wearing her customary trousers and buttoned shirt, thinking about the time when she'd visited the street during the days before the Collapse. It had been the quiet home of some exclusive tailoring shops.

When Elend had abolished the restrictions on skaa merchants, Kenton Street had changed. The thoroughfare had blossomed into a wild bazaar of shops, pushcarts, and tents. In order to target the newly empowered—and newly waged—skaa workers, the shop owners had altered their selling methods. Where once they had coaxed with rich window displays, they now called and demanded, using criers, salesmen, and even jugglers to try to attract trade.

The street was so busy that Vin usually avoided it, and this day was even worse than most. The arrival of the army had sparked a last-minute flurry of buying and selling, the people trying to get ready for whatever was to come. There was a grim tone to the atmosphere. Fewer street performers, more yelling. Elend had ordered all eight city gates barred, so flight was no longer an option. Vin wondered how many of the people regretted their decision to stay.

She walked down the street with a businesslike step, hands clasped to keep the nervousness out of her posture. Even as a child—an urchin on the streets of a dozen different cities—she hadn't liked crowds. It was hard to keep track of so many people, hard to focus with so much going on. As a child, she'd stayed near the edges of crowds, hiding, venturing out to snatch the occasional fallen coin or ignored bit of food.

She was different now. She forced herself to walk with a straight back, and kept her eyes from glancing down or looking for places to hide. She was getting so much better but seeing the crowds reminded her of what she had once been. What she would always—at least in part—still be.

As if in response to her thoughts, a pair of street urchins scampered through the throng, a large man in a baker's apron screaming at them. There were still urchins in Elend's new world. In fact, as she considered it, paying the skaa population probably made for a far better street life for urchins. There were more pockets to pick, more people to distract the shop owners, more scraps to go around, and more hands to feed beggars.

It was difficult to reconcile her childhood with such a life. To her, a child on the street was someone who learned to be quiet and hide, someone who went out at night to search through garbage. Only the most brave of urchins had dared cut purses; skaa lives had been worthless to many noblemen. During her childhood, Vin had known several urchins who been killed or maimed by passing noblemen who found them offensive.

Elend's laws might not have eliminated the poor, something he so much wanted to do, but he had improved the lives of even the street urchins. For that—among other things—she loved him.

There were still some noblemen in the crowd, men who had been persuaded by Elend or circumstances that their fortunes would be safer in the city than without. They were desperate, weak, or adventuresome. Vin watched one man pass, surrounded by a group of guards. He didn't give her a second glance; to him, her simple clothing was reason enough to ignore her. No noblewoman would dress as she did.

Is that what I am? she wondered, pausing beside a shop window, looking over the books inside—the sale of which had always been a small, but profitable, market for the idle imperial nobility. She also used the glass reflection to make certain no one snuck up behind her. *Am I a noblewoman?*

It could be argued that she was noble simply by association. The king himself loved her—had asked her to marry him—and she had been trained by the Survivor of Hathsin. Indeed, her father had been noble, even if her mother had been skaa. Vin reached up, fingering the simple bronze earring that was the only thing she had as a memento of Mother.

It wasn't much. But, then, Vin wasn't sure she wanted to think about her mother all that much. The woman had, after all, tried to kill Vin. In fact, she *had* killed Vin's full sister. Only the actions of Reen, Vin's half brother, had saved her. He had pulled Vin, bloody, from the arms of a woman who had shoved the earring into Vin's ear just moments before.

And still Vin kept it. As a reminder, of sorts. The truth was, she didn't feel like a noblewoman. At times, she thought she had more in common with her insane mother than she did with the aristocracy of Elend's world. The balls and parties she had attended before the Collapse—they had been a charade. A dreamlike memory. They had no place in this world of collapsing governments and nightly assassinations.

Plus, Vin's part in the balls—pretending to be the girl Valette Renoux—had always been a sham.

She pretended still. Pretended not to be the girl who had grown up starving on the streets, a girl who had been beaten far more often than she had been befriended. Vin sighed, turning from the window. The next shop, however, drew her attention despite herself.

It contained ball gowns.

The shop was empty of patrons; few thought of gowns on the eve of an invasion. Vin paused before the open doorway, held almost as if she were metal being Pulled. Inside, dressing dummies stood posed in majestic gowns. Vin looked up at the garments, with their tight waists and tapering, bell-like skirts. She could almost imagine she was at a ball, soft music in the background, tables draped in perfect white, Elend standing up on his balcony, leafing through a book. . . .

She almost went in. But why bother? The city was about to be attacked. Besides, the garments were expensive. It had been different when she'd spent Kelsier's money. Now she spent Elend's money—and Elend's money was the kingdom's money.

She turned from the gowns and walked back out onto the street. *Those aren't me anymore. Valette is useless to Elend—he needs a Mistborn, not an uncomfortable girl in a gown that she doesn't quite fill.* Her wounds from the night before, now firm bruises, were a reminder of her place. They were healing well—she'd been burning pewter heavily all day—but she'd be stiff for a while yet.

Vin quickened her pace, heading for the livestock pens. As she walked, however, she caught sight of someone tailing her.

Well, perhaps "tailing" was too generous a word—the man certainly wasn't doing a very good job of going unnoticed. He was balding on top, but wore the sides of his hair long. He wore a simple skaa's smock: a single-piece tan garment that was stained dark with ash.

Great, Vin thought. There was another reason she avoided the market—or any place where crowds of skaa gathered.

She sped up again, but the man hurried as well. Soon, his awkward movements gained attention—but, instead of cursing him, most people paused reverently. Soon others joined him, and Vin had a small crowd trailing her.

A part of her wanted to just slap down a coin and shoot away. *Yes,* Vin thought to herself wryly, *use Allomancy in the daylight. That'll make you inconspicuous.*

So, sighing, she turned to confront the group. None of them looked particularly threatening. The men wore trousers and dull shirts; the women wore one-piece, utilitarian dresses. Several more men wore single-piece, ash-covered smocks.

Priests of the Survivor.

"Lady Heir," one of them said, approaching and falling to his knees.

"Don't call me that," Vin said quietly.

The priest looked up at her. "Please. We need direction. We have cast off the Lord Ruler. What do we do now?"

Vin took a step backward. Had Kelsier understood what he was doing? He had built up the skaa's faith in him, then had died a martyr to turn them in rage against the Final Empire. What had he thought would happen after that? Could he have foreseen the Church of the Survivor—had he known that they would replace the Lord Ruler with Kelsier himself as God?

The problem was, Kelsier had left his followers with no doctrine. His only goal had been to defeat the Lord Ruler; partially to get his revenge, partially to seal his legacy, and partially—Vin hoped—because he had wanted to free the skaa.

But now what? These people must feel as she did. Set adrift, with no light to guide them.

Vin could not be that light. "I'm not Kelsier," she said quietly, taking another step backward.

"We know," one of the men said. "You're his heir—he passed on, and this time *you* Survived."

"Please," a woman said, stepping forward, holding a young child in her arms. "Lady Heir. If the hand that struck down the Lord Ruler could touch my child . . ."

Vin tried to back away farther, but realized she was up against another crowd of people. The woman stepped closer, and Vin finally raised an uncertain hand to the baby's forehead.

"Thank you," the woman said.

"You'll protect us, won't you, Lady Heir?" asked a young man—no older than Elend—with a dirty face but honest eyes. "The priests say that you'll stop that army out there, that its soldiers won't be able to enter the city while you're here."

That was too much for her. Vin mumbled a halfhearted response, but turned and pushed her way through the crowd. The group of believers didn't follow her, fortunately.

She was breathing deeply, though not from exertion, by the time she slowed. She moved into an alley between two shops, standing in the shade, wrapping her arms around herself. She had spent her life learning to remain unnoticed, to be quiet and unimportant. Now she could be none of those things.

What did the people expect of her? Did they really think that she could stop an army by herself? That was one lesson she'd learned very early into her training: Mistborn weren't invincible. One man, she could kill. Ten men could give her trouble. An army . . .

Vin held herself and took a few calming breaths. Eventually, she moved back out onto the busy street. She was near her destination now—a small, open-sided tent surrounded by four pens. The merchant lounged by it, a scruffy man who had hair on only half of his head—the right half. Vin stood for a moment, trying to decide if the odd hairstyle was due to disease, injury, or preference.

The man perked up when he saw her standing at the edge of his pens. He brushed himself off, throwing up a small amount of dust. Then he sauntered up to her, smiling with what teeth he still had, acting as if he hadn't heard—or didn't care—that there was an army just outside.

"Ah, young lady," he said. "Lookin' for a pup? I've got some wee scamps that any girl is sure to love. Here, let me grab one. You'll agree it's the cutest thing you ever seen."

Vin folded her arms as the man reached down to grab a puppy from one of the pens. "Actually," she said, "I was looking for a wolfhound."

The merchant looked up. "Wolfhound, miss? 'Tis no pet for a girl like yourself. Mean brutes, those. Let me find you a nice bobbie. Nice dogs, those—smart, too."

"No," Vin said, drawing him up short. "You will bring me a wolfhound."

The man paused again, looking at her, scratching himself in several undignified places. "Well, I guess I can see . . ."

He wandered toward the pen farthest from the street. Vin waited quietly, nose downturned at the smell as the merchant yelled at a few of his animals, selecting an appropriate one. Eventually, he pulled a leashed dog up to Vin. It was a wolfhound, if a small one—but it had sweet, docile eyes, and an obviously pleasant temperament.

"The runt of the litter," the merchant said. "A good animal for a young girl, I'd say. Will probably make an excellent hunter, too. These wolfhounds, they can smell better than any beast you seen."

Vin reached for her coin purse, but paused, looking down at the dog's panting face. It almost seemed to be smiling at her.

"Oh, for the Lord Ruler's sake," she snapped, pushing past the dog and master, stalking toward the back pens.

"Young lady?" the merchant asked, following uncertainly.

Vin scanned the wolfhounds. Near the back, she spotted a massive black and gray beast. It was chained to a post, and it regarded her defiantly, a low growl rising in its throat.

Vin pointed. "How much for that one in the back?"

"*That?*" the merchant asked. "Good lady, that's a watchbeast. It's meant to be set loose on a lord's grounds to attack anyone who enters! It's the one of the meanest things you'll ever see!"

"Perfect," Vin said, pulling out some coins.

"Good lady, I couldn't possibly sell you that beast. Not possibly at all. Why, I'll bet it weighs half again as much as you do."

Vin nodded, then pulled open the pen gate and strode in. The merchant cried out, but Vin walked right up to the wolfhound. He began to bark wildly at her, frothing.

Sorry about this, Vin thought. Then, burning pewter, she ducked in and slammed her fist into the animal's head.

The animal froze, wobbled, then fell unconscious in the dirt. The merchant stopped up short beside her, mouth open.

"Leash," Vin ordered.

He gave her one. She used it to tie the wolfhound's feet together, and then—with a flare of pewter—she threw the animal over her shoulders. She cringed only slightly at the pain in her side.

This thing better not get drool on my shirt, she thought, handing the merchant some coins and walking back toward the palace.

Vin slammed the unconscious wolfhound to the floor. The guards had given her some strange looks as she entered the palace, but she was getting used to those. She brushed off her hands.

"What is that?" OreSeur asked. He'd made it back to her rooms at the palace, but his current body was obviously unusable. He'd needed to form muscles in places that men didn't normally have them to even keep the skeleton together, and while he'd healed his wounds, his body looked unnatural. He still wore the bloodstained clothing from the night before.

"This," Vin said, pointing at the wolfhound, "is your new body."

OreSeur paused. "*That?* Mistress, that is a dog."

"Yes," Vin said.

"I am a man."

"You're a kandra," Vin said. "You can imitate flesh and muscle. What about fur?"

The kandra did not look pleased. "I cannot imitate it," he said, "but I can use the beast's own fur, like I use its bones. However, surely there is—"

"I'm not going to kill for you, kandra," Vin said. "And

even if I did kill someone, I wouldn't let you . . . eat them. Plus, this will be more inconspicuous. People will begin to talk if I keep replacing my stewards with unknown men. I've been telling people for months that I was thinking of dismissing you. Well, I'll tell them that I finally did—nobody will think to realize that my new pet hound is actually my kandra."

She turned, nodding toward the carcass. "This will be very useful. People pay less attention to hounds than they do to humans, and so you'll be able to listen in on conversations."

OreSeur's frown deepened. "I will not do this thing easily. You will need to compel me, by virtue of the Contract."

"Fine," Vin said. "You're commanded. How long will it take?"

"A regular body only takes a few hours," OreSeur said. "This could take longer. Getting that much fur to look right will be challenging."

"Get started, then," Vin said, turning toward the door. On her way, however, she noticed a small package sitting on her desk. She frowned, walking over and taking off the lid. A small note sat inside.

Lady Vin,

Here is the next alloy you requested. Aluminum is very difficult to acquire, but when a noble family recently left the city, I was able to buy some of their diningware.

I do not know if this one will work, but I believe it worth a try. I have mixed the aluminum with four percent copper, and found the outcome quite promising. I have read of this composition; it is called duralumin.

Your servant, Terion

Vin smiled, setting aside the note and removing the rest of the box's contents: a small pouch of metal dust and a thin silvery bar, both presumably of this "duralumin" metal. Terion was a master Allomantic metallurgist. Though not an Allomancer himself, he had been mixing alloys and creating dusts for Mistborn and Mistings for most of his life.

Vin pocketed both pouch and bar, then turned toward OreSeur. The kandra regarded her with a flat expression.

"This came for me today?" Vin asked, nodding to the box.

"Yes, Mistress," OreSeur said. "A few hours ago."

"And you didn't tell me?"

"I'm sorry, Mistress," OreSeur said in his toneless way, "but you did not *command* me to tell you if packages arrived."

Vin ground her teeth. He knew how anxiously she'd been waiting for another alloy from Terion. All of the previous aluminum alloys they'd tried had turned out to be duds. It bothered her to know that there was another Allomantic metal out there somewhere, waiting to be discovered. She wouldn't be satisfied until she found it.

OreSeur just sat where he was, bland expression on his face, unconscious wolfhound on the floor in front of him.

"Just get to work on that body," Vin said, spinning and leaving the room to search for Elend.

Vin finally found Elend in his study, going over some ledgers with a familiar figure.

"Dox!" Vin said. He'd retired to his rooms soon after his arrival the day before, and she hadn't seen much of him.

Dockson looked up and smiled. Stocky without being fat, he had short dark hair and still wore his customary half beard. "Hello, Vin."

"How was Terris?" she asked.

"Cold," Dockson replied. "I'm glad to be back. Though I wish I hadn't arrived to find that army here."

"Either way, we're glad you've returned, Dockson," Elend said. "The kingdom practically fell apart without you."

"That hardly seems the case," Dockson said, closing his ledger and setting it on the stack. "All things—and armies—considered, it looks like the royal bureaucracy held together fairly well in my absence. You hardly need me anymore!"

"Nonsense!" Elend said.

Vin leaned against the door, eyeing the two men as they continued their discussion. They maintained their air of forced joviality. Both were dedicated to making the new kingdom work, even if it meant pretending that they liked each other. Dockson pointed at places in the ledgers, talking about finances and what he'd discovered in the outlying villages under Elend's control.

Vin sighed, glancing across the room. Sunlight streamed through the room's stained-glass rose window, throwing colors across the ledgers and table. Even now, Vin still wasn't accustomed to the casual richness of a noble keep. The window—red and lavender—was a thing of intricate beauty. Yet, noblemen apparently found its like so commonplace that they had put this one in the keep's back rooms, in the small chamber that Elend now used as his study.

As one might expect, the room was piled with stacks of books. Shelves lined the walls from floor to ceiling, but they were no match for the sheer volume of Elend's growing collection. She'd never cared much for Elend's taste in books. They were mostly political or historical works, things with topics as musty as their aged pages. Many of them had once been forbidden by the Steel Ministry, but somehow the old philosophers could make even salacious topics seem boring.

"Anyway," Dockson said, finally closing his ledgers. "I have some things to do before your speech tomorrow, Your Majesty. Did Ham say there's a city defense meeting that evening as well?"

Elend nodded. "Assuming I can get the Assembly to agree not to hand the city over to my father, we'll need to come up with a strategy to deal with this army. I'll send someone for you tomorrow night."

"Good," Dockson said. With that, he nodded to Elend, winked at Vin, then made his way from the cluttered room.

As Dockson shut the door, Elend sighed, then relaxed back in his oversized plush chair.

Vin walked forward. "He really is a good man, Elend."

"Oh, I realize he is. Being a good man doesn't always make one likable, however."

"He's nice, too," Vin said. "Sturdy, calm, stable. The crew relied on him." Even though Dockson wasn't an Allomancer, he had been Kelsier's right-hand man.

"He doesn't like me, Vin," Elend said. "It's . . . very hard to get along with someone who looks at me like that."

"You're not giving him a fair chance," Vin complained, stopping beside Elend's chair.

He looked up at her, smiling wanly, his vest unbuttoned, his hair an absolute mess. "Hum . . ." he said idly, taking her hand. "I really like that shirt. Red looks good on you."

Vin rolled her eyes, letting him gently pull her into the chair and kiss her. There was a passion to the kiss—a need, perhaps, for something stable. Vin responded, feeling herself relax as she pulled up against him. A few minutes later, she sighed, feeling much better snuggled into the chair beside him. He pulled her close, leaning the chair back into the window's sunlight.

He smiled and glanced at her. "That's a . . . new perfume you're wearing."

Vin snorted, putting her head against his chest. "It's not perfume, Elend. It's dog."

"Ah, good," Elend said. "I was worried that you'd departed from your senses. Now, is there any particular reason *why* you smell like dog?"

"I went to the market and bought one, then carried it back and fed it to OreSeur, so it can be his new body."

Elend paused. "Why, Vin. That's brilliant! Nobody will suspect a dog to be a spy. I wonder if anyone's ever thought of that before. . . ."

"Someone must have," Vin said. "I mean, it makes such sense. I suspect those who thought of it, however, didn't share the knowledge."

"Good point," Elend said, relaxing back. Yet, from as close as they were, she could still feel a tension in him.

Tomorrow's speech, Vin thought. *He's worried about it.*

"I must say, however," Elend said idly, "that I find it a bit disappointing that you're *not* wearing dog-scented perfume. With your social station, I could see some of the local noblewomen trying to imitate you. That could be amusing indeed."

She leaned up, looking at his smirking face. "You know, Elend—sometimes it's bloody difficult to tell when you're teasing, and when you're just being dense."

"That makes me more mysterious, right?"

"Something like that," she said, snuggling up against him again.

"Now, see, you don't understand how clever that is of me," he said. "If people can't tell when I'm being an idiot and when I'm being a genius, perhaps they'll assume my blunders are brilliant political maneuverings."

"As long as they don't mistake your actual brilliant moves for blunders."

"That shouldn't be difficult," Elend said. "I fear I have few enough of *those* for people to mistake."

Vin looked up with concern at the edge in his voice. He, however, smiled, shifting the topic. "So, OreSeur the dog. Will he still be able to go out with you at nights?"

Vin shrugged. "I guess. I wasn't really planning on bringing him for a while."

"I'd like it if you did take him," Elend said. "I worry about you out there, every night, pushing yourself so hard."

"I can handle it," Vin said. "Someone needs to watch over you."

"Yes," Elend said, "but who watches over you?"

Kelsier. Even now, that was still her immediate reaction. She'd known him for less than a year, but that year had been the first in her life that she had felt protected.

Kelsier was dead. She, like the rest of the world, had to live without him.

"I know you were hurt when you fought those Allomancers the other night," Elend said. "It would be really nice for my psyche if I knew someone was with you."

"A kandra's no bodyguard," Vin said.

"I know," Elend said. "But they're incredibly loyal—I've never heard of one breaking Contract. He'll watch out for you. I worry about you, Vin. You wonder why I stay up so late, scribbling at my proposals? I can't sleep, knowing that you might be out there fighting—or, worse, lying somewhere in a street, dying because nobody was there to help you."

"I take OreSeur with me sometimes."

"Yes," Elend said, "but I know you find excuses to leave him behind. Kelsier bought you the services of an incredibly valuable servant. I can't understand why you work so hard to avoid him."

Vin closed her eyes. "Elend. He *ate* Kelsier."

"So?" Elend asked. "Kelsier was already dead. Besides, he himself gave that order."

Vin sighed, opening her eyes. "I just . . . don't trust that thing, Elend. The creature is unnatural."

"I know," Elend said. "My father always kept a kandra. But, OreSeur is something, at least. Please. Promise me you'll take him with you."

"All right. But I don't think he's going to like the arrangement much either. He and I didn't get along very well even when he was playing Renoux, and I his niece."

Elend shrugged. "He'll hold to his Contract. That's what is important."

"He holds to the Contract," Vin said, "but only grudgingly. I swear that he enjoys frustrating me."

Elend looked down at her. "Vin, kandra are excellent servants. They don't do things like that."

"No, Elend," Vin said. "*Sazed* was an excellent servant. He enjoyed being with people, helping them. I never felt that he resented me. OreSeur may do everything I command, but he doesn't like me; he never has. I can tell."

Elend sighed, rubbing her shoulder. "Don't you think you might be a little irrational? There's no real reason to hate him so."

"Oh?" Vin asked. "Just like there's no reason you shouldn't get along with Dockson?"

Elend paused. Then he sighed. "I guess you have a point," he said. He continued to rub Vin's shoulder as he stared upward, toward the ceiling, contemplative.

"What?" Vin asked.

"I'm not doing a very good job of this, am I?"

"Don't be foolish," Vin said. "You're a wonderful king."

"I might be a passable king, Vin, but I'm not *him*."

"Who?"

"Kelsier," Elend said quietly.

"Elend, nobody expects you to be Kelsier."

"Oh?" he said. "That's why Dockson doesn't like me. He hates noblemen; it's obvious in the way that he talks, the way he acts. I don't know if I really blame him, considering the life he's known. Regardless, he doesn't think I should be king. He thinks that a skaa should be in my place—or, even better, Kelsier. They all think that."

"That's nonsense, Elend."

"Really? And if Kelsier still lived, would I be king?"

Vin paused.

"You see? They accept me—the people, the merchants, even the noblemen. But in the back of their minds, they wish they had Kelsier instead."

"I don't wish that."

"Don't you?"

Vin frowned. Then she sat up, turning so that she was kneeling over Elend in the reclined chair, their faces just inches apart. "Don't you *ever* wonder that, Elend. Kelsier was my teacher, but I didn't love him. Not like I love you."

Elend stared into her eyes, then nodded. Vin kissed him deeply, then snuggled down beside him again.

"Why not?" Elend eventually asked.

"Well, he was old, for one thing."

Elend chuckled. "I seem to recall you making fun of *my* age as well."

"That's different," Vin said. "You're only a few years older than me—Kelsier was ancient."

"Vin, thirty-eight is not ancient."

"Close enough."

Elend chuckled again, but she could tell that he wasn't satisfied. Why *had* she chosen Elend, rather than Kelsier? Kelsier had been the visionary, the hero, the Mistborn.

"Kelsier was a great man," Vin said quietly as Elend began to stroke her hair. "But . . . there were things about him, Elend. Frightening things. He was intense, reckless, even a little bit cruel. Unforgiving. He'd slaughter people without guilt or concern, just because they upheld the Final Empire or worked for the Lord Ruler.

"I could love him as a teacher and a friend. But I don't think I could ever love—not *really* love—a man like that. I don't blame him; he was of the streets, like me. When you struggle so hard for life, you grow strong—but you can grow harsh, too. His fault or not, Kelsier reminded me too much of men I . . . knew when I was younger. Kell was a far better person than they—he really could be kind, and he did sacrifice his life for the skaa. However, he was just so hard."

She closed her eyes, feeling Elend's warmth. "You, Elend Venture, are a good man. A *truly* good man."

"Good men don't become legends," he said quietly.

"Good men don't need to become legends." She opened her eyes, looking up at him. "They just do what's right anyway."

Elend smiled. Then he kissed the top of her head and leaned back. They lay there for a time, in a room warm with sunlight, relaxing.

"He saved my life, once," Elend finally said.

"Who?" Vin asked with surprise. "Kelsier?"

Elend nodded. "That day after Spook and OreSeur were captured, the day Kelsier died. There was a battle in the square when Ham and some soldiers tried to free the captives."

"I was there," Vin said. "Hiding with Breeze and Dox in one of the alleyways."

"Really?" Elend said, sounding a bit amused. "Because I came looking for you. I thought that they'd arrested you, along with OreSeur—he was pretending to be your uncle, then. I tried to get to the cages to rescue you."

"You did *what*? Elend, it was a battlefield in that square! There was an Inquisitor there, for the Lord Ruler's sake!"

"I know," Elend said, smiling faintly. "See, that Inquisitor is the one who tried to kill me. It had its axe raised and everything. And then . . . Kelsier was there. He smashed into the Inquisitor, throwing it to the ground."

"Probably just a coincidence," Vin said.

"No," Elend said softly. "He meant it, Vin. He looked at me while he struggled with the Inquisitor, and I saw it in his eyes. I've always wondered about that moment; everyone tells me that Kelsier hated the nobility even more than Dox does."

Vin paused. "He . . . started to change a little at the end, I think."

"Change enough that he'd risk himself to protect a random nobleman?"

"He knew that I loved you," Vin said, smiling faintly. "I guess, in the end, that proved stronger than his hatred."

"I didn't realize . . ." He trailed off as Vin turned, hearing something. Footsteps approaching. She sat up, and a second later, Ham poked his head into the room. He paused when he saw Vin sitting in Elend's lap, however.

"Oh," Ham said. "Sorry."

"No, wait," Vin said. Ham poked his head back in, and Vin turned to Elend. "I almost forgot why I came looking for you in the first place. I got a new package from Terion today."

"*Another* one?" Elend asked. "Vin, when are you going to give this up?"

"I can't afford to," she said.

"It can't be all that important, can it?" he asked. "I mean, if everybody's forgotten what that last metal does, then it must not be very powerful."

"Either that," Vin said, "or it was so amazingly powerful that the Ministry worked very hard to keep it a secret." She slid off of the chair to stand up, then took the pouch and thin bar out of her pocket. She handed the bar to Elend, who sat up in his plush chair.

Silvery and reflective, the metal—like the aluminum from which it was made—felt too light to be real. Any Allomancer who accidentally burned aluminum had their other metal reserves stripped away from them, leaving them powerless. Aluminum had been kept secret by the Steel Ministry; Vin had only found out about it on the night when she'd been captured by the Inquisitors, the same night she'd killed the Lord Ruler.

They had never been able to figure out the proper Allomantic alloy of aluminum. Allomantic metals always came in pairs—iron and steel, tin and pewter, copper and bronze, zinc and brass. Aluminum and . . . something. Something powerful, hopefully. Her atium was gone. She needed an edge.

Elend sighed, handing back the bar. "The last time you tried to burn one of those it left you sick for two days, Vin. I was terrified."

"It can't kill me," Vin said. "Kelsier promised that burning a bad alloy would only make me sick."

Elend shook his head. "Even Kelsier was wrong on occasion, Vin. Didn't you say that he misunderstood how bronze worked?"

Vin paused. Elend's concern was so genuine that she felt herself being persuaded. However . . .

When that army attacks, Elend is going to die. The city's skaa might survive—no ruler would be foolish enough to slaughter the people of such a productive city. The king, however, would be killed. She couldn't fight off an entire army, and she could do little to help with preparations.

She did know Allomancy, however. The better she got at it, the better she'd be able to protect the man she loved.

"I have to try it, Elend," she said quietly. "Clubs says that Straff won't attack for a few days—he'll need that long to rest his men from the march and scout the city for attack. That means I can't wait. If this metal does make me sick, I'll be better in time to help fight—but only if I try it now."

Elend's face grew grim, but he did not forbid her. He had learned better than that. Instead, he stood. "Ham, you think this is a good idea?"

Ham nodded. He was a warrior; to him, her gamble would make sense. She'd asked him to stay because she'd need someone to carry her back to her bed, should this go wrong.

"All right," Elend said, turning back to Vin, looking resigned.

Vin climbed into the chair, sat back, then took a pinch of the duralumin dust and swallowed it. She closed her eyes, and felt at her Allomantic reserves. The common eight were all there, well stocked. She didn't have any atium or gold, nor did she have either of their alloys. Even if she'd had atium, it was too precious to use except in an emergency—and the other three had only marginal usefulness.

A new reserve appeared. Just as one had the four times before. Each time she'd burned an aluminum alloy, she'd immediately felt a blinding headache. *You'd think I'd have learned* . . . she thought. Gritting her teeth, she reached inside and burned the new alloy.

Nothing happened.

"Have you tried it yet?" Elend asked apprehensively.

Vin nodded slowly. "No headache. But . . . I'm not sure if the alloy is doing anything or not."

"But it's burning?" Ham asked.

Vin nodded. She felt the familiar warmth from within, the tiny fire that told her that a metal was burning. She tried moving about a bit, but couldn't distinguish any change to her physical self. Finally she just looked up and shrugged.

Ham frowned. "If it didn't make you sick, then you've found the right alloy. Each metal only has one valid alloy."

"Or," Vin said, "that's what we've always been told."

Ham nodded. "What alloy was this?"

"Aluminum and copper," Vin said.

"Interesting," Ham said. "You don't feel anything at all?"

Vin shook her head.

"You'll have to practice some more."

"Looks like I'm lucky," Vin said, extinguishing the duralumin. "Terion came up with forty different alloys he thought we could try, once we had enough aluminum. This was only the fifth."

"Forty?" Elend asked incredulously. "I wasn't aware that there were so many metals you could make an alloy from!"

"You don't have to have two metals to make an alloy," Vin said absently. "Just one metal and something else. Look at steel—it's iron and carbon."

"Forty . . ." Elend repeated. "And you would have tried them all?"

Vin shrugged. "Seemed like a good place to start."

Elend looked concerned at that thought, but didn't say anything further. Instead, he turned to Ham. "Anyway, Ham, was there something you wanted to see us about?"

"Nothing important," Ham said. "I just wanted to see if Vin was up for some sparring. That army has me feeling antsy, and I figure Vin could still use some practice with the staff."

Vin shrugged. "Sure. Why not?"

"You want to come, El?" Ham asked. "Get in some practice?"

Elend laughed. "And face one of you two? I've got my royal dignity to think of!"

Vin frowned slightly, looking up at him. "You really should practice more, Elend. You barely know how to hold a sword, and you're *terrible* with a dueling cane."

"Now, see, why would I worry about that when I have you to protect me?"

Vin's concern deepened. "We can't always be around you, Elend. I'd worry a lot less if you were better at defending yourself."

He just smiled and pulled her to her feet. "I'll get to it eventually, I promise. But, not today—I've got too much to think about right now. How about if I just come watch you two? Perhaps I'll pick up something by observation—which is, by the way, the preferable method of weapons training, since it doesn't involve me getting beaten up by a girl."

Vin sighed, but didn't press the point further.

I write this record now, pounding it into a metal slab, because I am afraid. Afraid for myself, yes—I admit to being human. If Alendi does return from the Well of Ascension, I am certain that my death will be one of his first objectives. He is not an evil man, but he is a ruthless one. That is, I think, a product of what he has been through.

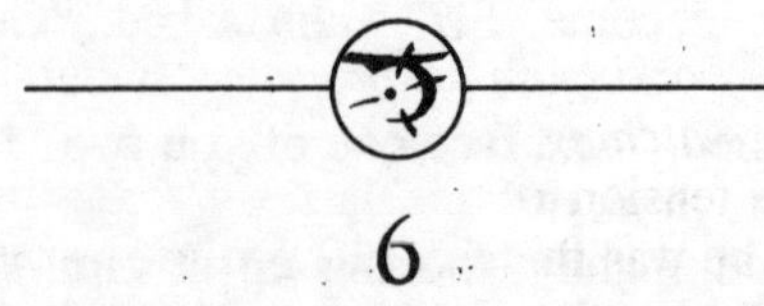

6

ELEND LEANED DOWN AGAINST THE railing, looking in at the sparring yard. Part of him did wish to go out and practice with Vin and Ham. However, the larger part of him just didn't see the point.

Any assassin likely to come after me will be an Allomancer, he thought. *I could train ten years and be no match for one of them.*

In the yard itself, Ham took a few swings with his staff, then nodded. Vin stepped up, holding her own staff, which was a good foot taller than she was. Watching the two of them, Elend couldn't help remarking on the disparity. Ham had the firm muscles and powerful build of a warrior. Vin looked even thinner than usual, wearing only a tight buttoned shirt and a pair of trousers, with no cloak to mask her size.

The inequality was enhanced by Ham's next words. "We're practicing with the staff, not practicing Pushing and Pulling. Don't use anything but pewter, all right?"

Vin nodded.

It was the way they often sparred. Ham claimed that there was no substitute for training and practice, no matter how powerful an Allomancer one was. He let Vin use pewter, however, because he said the enhanced strength and dexterity was disorienting unless one was accustomed to it.

The sparring field was like a courtyard. Situated in the palace barracks, it had an open-sided hallway built around it. Elend stood in this, roof overhead keeping the red sun out of his eyes. That was nice, for a light ashfall had begun, and occasional flakes of ash floated down from the sky. Elend crossed his arms on the railing. Soldiers passed occasionally in the hallway behind, bustling with activity. Some, however, paused to watch; Vin and Ham's sparring sessions were something of a welcome diversion to the palace guards.

I should be working on my proposal, Elend thought. *Not standing here watching Vin fight.*

But . . . the tension of the last few days had been so pressing that he was finding it difficult to get up the motivation to do yet *another* read-through of the speech. What he really needed was to just spend a few moments thinking.

So, he simply watched. Vin approached Ham warily, staff held in a firm, two-handed stance. Once, Elend probably would have found trousers and shirt on a lady to be inappropriate, but he'd been around Vin too long to still be bothered by that. Ball gowns and dresses were beautiful—but there was something *right* about Vin in simple garb. She wore it more comfortably.

Besides, he kind of liked how the tight clothing looked on her.

Vin usually let others strike first, and this day was no exception. Staves rapped as Ham engaged her, and despite her size, Vin held her own. After a quick exchange, they both backed away, circling warily.

"My money's on the girl."

Elend turned as he noticed a form limping down the hallway toward him. Clubs stepped up beside Elend, setting a ten-boxing coin down on the railing with a snap. Elend smiled to the general, and Clubs scowled back—which was generally accepted as Clubs's version of a smile. Dockson excluded, Elend had taken quickly to the other members of Vin's crew. Clubs, however, had taken a little getting used to. The stocky man had a face like a gnarled toadstool, and he always seemed to be squinting in displeasure—an expression usually matched by his tone of voice.

However, he was a gifted craftsman, not to mention an Allomancer—a Smoker, actually, though he didn't get to use his power much anymore. For the better part of a year, Clubs had acted as general of Elend's military forces. Elend didn't know where Clubs had learned to lead soldiers, but the man had a remarkable knack for it. He'd probably gotten the skill in the same place that he'd acquired the scar on his leg—a scar that produced the hobble from which Clubs drew his nickname.

"They're just sparring, Clubs," Elend said. "There won't be a 'winner.'"

"They'll end with a serious exchange," Clubs said. "They always do."

Elend paused. "You're asking me to bet against Vin, you know," he noted. "That could be unhealthy."

"So?"

Elend smiled, pulling out a coin. Clubs still kind of intimidated him, and he didn't want to risk offending the man.

"Where's that worthless nephew of mine?" Clubs asked as he watched the sparring.

"Spook?" Elend asked. "He's back? How'd he get into the city?"

Clubs shrugged. "He left something on my doorstep this morning."

"A gift?"

Clubs snorted. "It was a woodcarving from a master carpenter up in Yelva City. The note said, 'I just wanted to show you what *real* carpenters are up to, old man.'"

Elend chuckled, but trailed off as Clubs eyed him with a discomforting stare. "Whelp was never this insolent before," Clubs muttered. "I swear, you lot have corrupted the lad."

Clubs almost seemed to be smiling. Or, was he serious? Elend couldn't ever decide if the man was as crusty as he seemed, or if Elend was the butt of some elaborate joke.

"How is the army doing?" Elend finally asked.

"Terribly," Clubs said. "You want an army? Give me more than one year to train it. Right now, I'd barely trust those boys against a mob of old women with sticks."

Great, Elend thought.

"Can't do much right now, though," Clubs grumbled. "Straff is digging in some cursory fortifications, but mostly he's just resting his men. The attack will come by the end of the week."

In the courtyard, Vin and Ham continued to fight. It was slow, for the moment, Ham taking time to pause and explain principles or stances. Elend and Clubs watched for a short time as the sparring gradually became more intense, the rounds taking longer, the two participants beginning to sweat as their feet kicked up puffs of ash in the packed, sooty earth.

Vin gave Ham a good contest despite the ridiculous differences in strength, reach, and training, and Elend found himself smiling slightly despite himself. She was something special—Elend had realized that when he'd first seen her in the Venture ballroom, nearly two years before. He was only now coming to realize how much of an understatement "special" was.

A coin snapped against the wooden railing. "My money's on Vin, too."

Elend turned with surprise. The man who had spoken was a soldier who had been standing with the others watching behind. Elend frowned. "Who—"

Then, Elend cut himself off. The beard was wrong, the posture too straight, but the man standing behind him was familiar. "Spook?" Elend asked incredulously.

The teenage boy smiled behind an apparently fake beard. "Wasing the where of calling out."

Elend's head immediately began to hurt. "Lord Ruler, don't tell me you've gone back to the dialect?"

"Oh, just for the occasional nostalgic quip," Spook said with a laugh. His words bore traces of his Easterner accent; during the first few months Elend had known the boy, Spook had been utterly unintelligible. Fortunately, the boy had grown out of using his street cant, just as he'd managed to grow out of most of his clothing. Well over six feet tall, the sixteen-year-old young man hardly resembled the gangly boy Elend had met a year before.

Spook leaned against the railing beside Elend, adopting a teenage boy's lounging posture and completely destroying his image as a soldier—which, indeed, he wasn't.

"Why the costume, Spook?" Elend asked with a frown.

Spook shrugged. "I'm no Mistborn. We more mundane spies have to find ways to get information without flying up to windows and listening outside."

"How long you been standing there?" Clubs asked, glaring at his nephew.

"Since before you got here, Uncle Grumbles," Spook said. "And, in answer to your question, I got back a couple days ago. Before Dockson, actually. I just thought I'd take a bit of a break before I went back to duty."

"I don't know if you've noticed, Spook," Elend said, "but we're at war. There isn't a lot of time to take breaks."

Spook shrugged. "I just didn't want you to send me away again. If there's going to be war here, I want to be around. You know, for the excitement."

Clubs snorted. "And where did you get that uniform?"

"Uh . . . Well . . ." Spook glanced to the side, displaying just a hint of the uncertain boy Elend had known.

Clubs grumbled something about insolent boys, but Elend just laughed and clapped Spook on the shoulder. The boy looked up, smiling; though he'd been easy to ignore at first, he was proving as valuable as any of the other members of Vin's former crew. As a Tineye—a Misting who could burn tin to enhance his senses—Spook could listen to conversations from far away, not to mention notice distant details.

"Anyway, welcome back," Elend said. "What's the word from the west?"

Spook shook his head. "I hate to sound too much like Uncle Crusty over there, but the news isn't good. You know those rumors about the Lord Ruler's atium being in Luthadel? Well, they're back. Stronger this time."

"I thought we were past that!" Elend said. Breeze and

his team had spent the better part of six months spreading rumors and manipulating the warlords into believing that the atium must have been hidden in another city, since Elend hadn't found it in Luthadel.

"Guess not," Spook said. "And . . . I think someone's spreading these rumors intentionally. I've been on the street long enough to sense a planted story, and this rumor smells wrong. Someone really wants the warlords to focus on you."

Great, Elend thought. "You don't know where Breeze is, do you?"

Spook shrugged, but he no longer seemed to be paying attention to Elend. He was watching the sparring. Elend glanced back toward Vin and Ham.

As Clubs had predicted, the two had fallen into a more serious contest. There was no more instruction; there were no more quick, repetitive exchanges. They sparred in earnest, fighting in a swirling melee of staffs and dust. Ash flew around them, blown up by the wind of their attacks, and even more soldiers paused in the surrounding hallways to watch.

Elend leaned forward. There was something *intense* about a duel between two Allomancers. Vin tried an attack. Ham, however, swung simultaneously, his staff blurringly quick. Somehow, Vin got her own weapon up in time, but the power of Ham's blow threw her back in a tumble. She hit the ground on one shoulder. She gave barely a grunt of pain, however, and somehow got a hand beneath her, throwing herself up to land on her feet. She skidded for a moment, retaining her balance, holding her staff up.

Pewter, Elend thought. It made even a clumsy man dexterous. And, for a person normally graceful like Vin . . .

Vin's eyes narrowed, her innate stubbornness showing in the set of her jaw, the displeasure in her face. She didn't like being beaten—even when her opponent was obviously stronger than she was.

Elend stood up straight, intending to suggest an end to the sparring. At that moment, Vin dashed forward.

Ham brought his staff up expectantly, swinging as Vin

came within reach. She ducked to the side, passing within inches of the attack, then brought her weapon around and slammed it into the back of Ham's staff, throwing him off balance. Then she ducked in for the attack.

Ham, however, recovered quickly. He let the force of Vin's blow spin him around, and he used the momentum to bring his staff around in a powerful blow aimed directly at Vin's chest.

Elend cried out.

Vin jumped.

She didn't have metal to Push against, but that didn't seem to matter. She sprang a good seven feet in the air, easily cresting Ham's staff. She flipped as the swing passed beneath her, her fingers brushing the air just above the weapon, her own staff spinning in a one-handed grip.

Vin landed, her staff already howling in a low swing, its tip throwing up a line of ash as it ran along the ground. It slammed into the back of Ham's legs. The blow swept Ham's feet out from beneath him, and he cried out as he fell.

Vin jumped into the air again.

Ham slammed to the earth on his back, and Vin landed on his chest. Then, she calmly rapped him on the forehead with the end of her staff. "I win."

Ham lay, looking dazed, Vin crouching on his chest. Dust and ash settled quietly in the courtyard.

"Damn . . ." Spook whispered, voicing a sentiment that seemed to be shared by the dozen or so watching soldiers.

Finally, Ham chuckled. "Fine. You beat me—now, if you would, kindly get me something to drink while I try to massage some feeling back into my legs."

Vin smiled, hopping off his chest and scampering away to do as requested. Ham shook his head, climbing to his feet. Despite his words, he walked with barely a limp; he'd probably have a bruise, but it wouldn't bother him for long. Pewter not only enhanced one's strength, balance, and speed, it also made one's body innately stronger. Ham could shrug off a blow that would have shattered Elend's legs.

Ham joined them, nodding to Clubs and punching Spook lightly on the arm. Then he leaned against the railing and rubbed his left calf, cringing slightly. "I swear, Elend—sometimes sparring with that girl is like trying to fight with a gust of wind. She's never where I think she'll be."

"How did she do that, Ham?" Elend asked. "The jump, I mean. That leap seemed inhuman, even for an Allomancer."

"Used steel, didn't she?" Spook said.

Ham shook his head. "No, I doubt it."

"Then how?" Elend asked.

"Allomancers draw strength from their metals," Ham said, sighing and putting his foot down. "Some can squeeze out more than others—but the real power comes from the metal itself, not the person's body."

Elend paused. "So?"

"So," Ham said, "an Allomancer doesn't have to be physically strong to be incredibly powerful. If Vin were a Feruchemist, it would be different—if you ever see Sazed increase *his* strength, his muscles will grow larger. But with Allomancy, all the strength comes directly from the metal.

"Now, most Thugs—myself included—figure that making their bodies strong will only add to their power. After all, a muscular man burning pewter will be that much stronger than a regular man of the same Allomantic power."

Ham rubbed his chin, eyeing the passage Vin had left through. "But . . . well, I'm beginning to think that there might be another way. Vin's a thin little thing, but when she burns pewter, she grows several times stronger than any normal warrior. She packs all that strength into a small body, and doesn't have to bother with the weight of massive muscles. She's like . . . an insect. Far stronger than her mass or her body would indicate. So, when she jumps, she can *jump*."

"But you're still stronger than she is," Spook said.

Ham nodded. "And I can make use of that—assuming I can ever hit her. That's getting harder and harder to do."

Vin finally returned, carrying a jug of chilled juice—apparently she'd decided to go all the way to the keep, rather than grabbing some of the warm ale kept on hand in the courtyard. She handed a flagon to Ham, and had thought to bring cups for Elend and Clubs.

"Hey!" Spook said as she poured. "What about me?"

"That beard looks silly on you," Vin said as she poured.

"So I don't get anything to drink?"

"No."

Spook paused. "Vin, you're a strange girl."

Vin rolled her eyes; then she glanced toward the water barrel in the corner of the courtyard. One of the tin cups lying beside it lurched into the air, shooting across the courtyard. Vin stuck her hand out, catching it with a slapping sound, then set it on the railing before Spook. "Happy?"

"I will be once you pour me something to drink," Spook said as Clubs grunted, taking a slurp from his own cup. The old general then reached over, sliding two of the coins off the railing and pocketing them.

"Hey, that's right!" Spook said. "You owe me, El. Pay up."

Elend lowered his cup. "I never agreed to the bet."

"You paid Uncle Irritable. Why not me?"

Elend paused, then sighed, pulling out a ten-boxing coin and setting it beside Spook's. The boy smiled, plucking both up in a smooth street-thief gesture. "Thanks for winning the bout, Vin," he said with a wink.

Vin frowned at Elend. "You bet against me?"

Elend laughed, leaning across the railing to kiss her. "I didn't mean it. Clubs bullied me."

Clubs snorted at that comment, downed the rest of his juice, then held out his cup for a refill. When Vin didn't respond, he turned to Spook and gave the boy a telling scowl. Finally, Spook sighed, picking up the jug to refill the cup.

Vin was still regarding Elend with dissatisfaction.

"I'd be careful, Elend," Ham said with a chuckle. "She can hit pretty hard. . . ."

Elend nodded. "I should know better than to antagonize her when there are weapons lying around, eh?"

"Tell me about it," Ham said.

Vin sniffed at that comment, rounding the railing so that she could stand next to Elend. Elend put his arm around her, and as he did, he caught a bare flash of envy in Spook's eyes. Elend suspected that the boy'd had a crush on Vin for some time—but, well, Elend couldn't really blame him for that.

Spook shook his head. "I've got to find myself a woman."

"Well, that beard isn't going to help," Vin said.

"It's just a disguise, Vin," Spook said. "El, I don't suppose you could give me a title or something?"

Elend smiled. "I don't think that will matter, Spook."

"It worked for you."

"Oh, I don't know," Elend said. "Somehow, I think Vin fell in love with me *despite* my title, rather than because of it."

"But you had others before her," Spook said. "Noble girls."

"A couple," Elend admitted.

"Though Vin has a habit of killing off her competition," Ham quipped.

Elend laughed. "Now, see, she only did that once. And I think Shan deserved it—she was, after all, trying to assassinate me at the time." He looked down fondly, eyeing Vin. "Though, I do have to admit, Vin *is* a bit hard on other women. With her around, everybody else looks bland by comparison."

Spook rolled his eyes. "It's more interesting when she kills them off."

Ham chuckled, letting Spook pour him some more juice. "Lord Ruler only knows what she'd do to you if you ever tried to leave her, Elend."

Vin stiffened immediately, pulling him a little tighter. She'd been abandoned far too many times. Even after what they'd been through, even after his proposal of marriage, Elend had to keep promising Vin that he wasn't going to leave her.

Time to change the topic, Elend thought, the joviality of the moment fading. "Well," he said, "I think I'm going to go visit the kitchens and get something to eat. You coming, Vin?"

Vin glanced at the sky—likely checking to see how soon it would grow dark. Finally, she nodded.

"I'll come," Spook said.

"No you won't," Clubs said, grabbing the boy by the back of the neck. "You're going to stay right here and explain exactly where you got one of my soldiers' uniforms."

Elend chuckled, leading Vin away. Truth be told, even with the slightly sour end of conversation, he felt better for having come to watch the sparring. It was strange how the members of Kelsier's crew could laugh and make light, even during the most terrible of situations. They had a way of making him forget about his problems. Perhaps that was a holdover from the Survivor. Kelsier had, apparently, insisted on laughing, no matter how bad the situation. It had been a form of rebellion to him.

None of that made the problems go away. They still faced an army several times larger than their own, in a city that they could barely defend. Yet, if anyone could survive such a situation, it would be Kelsier's crew.

Later that night, having filled her stomach at Elend's insistence, Vin made her way with Elend to her rooms.

There, sitting on the floor, was a perfect replica of the wolfhound she had bought earlier. It eyed her, then bowed its head. "Welcome back, Mistress," the kandra said in a growling, muffled voice.

Elend whistled appreciatively, and Vin walked in a circle around the creature. Each hair appeared to have been placed perfectly. If it hadn't spoken, one would never have been able to tell it wasn't the original dog.

"How do you manage the voice?" Elend asked curiously.

"A voice box is a construction of flesh, not bone, Your Majesty," OreSeur said. "Older kandra learn to manipulate their bodies, not just replicate them. I still need to digest a person's corpse to memorize and re-create their exact features. However, I can improvise some things."

Vin nodded. "Is that why making this body took you so much longer than you'd said?"

"No, Mistress," OreSeur said. "The hair. I'm sorry I didn't warn you—placing fur like this takes a great deal of precision and effort."

"Actually, you did mention it," Vin said, waving her hand.

"What do you think of the body, OreSeur?" Elend asked.

"Honestly, Your Majesty?"

"Of course."

"It is offensive and degrading," OreSeur said.

Vin raised an eyebrow. *That's forward of you, Renoux,* she thought. *Feeling a little belligerent today, are we?*

He glanced at her, and she tried—unsuccessfully—to read his canine expression.

"But," Elend said, "you'll wear the body anyway, right?"

"Of course, Your Majesty," OreSeur said. "I would die before breaking the Contract. It is life."

Elend nodded to Vin, as if he'd just made a major point.

Anyone can claim loyalty, Vin thought. *If someone has a "Contract" to ensure their honor, then all the better. That makes the surprise more poignant when they do turn on you.*

Elend was obviously waiting for something. Vin sighed. "OreSeur, we'll be spending more time together in the future."

"If that is what you wish, Mistress."

"I'm not sure if it is or not," Vin said. "But it's going to happen anyway. How well can you move about in that body?"

"Well enough, Mistress."

"Come on," she said, "let's see if you can keep up."

I am also afraid, however, that all I have known—that my story—will be forgotten. I am afraid for the world that is to come. Afraid that my plans will fail.

Afraid of a doom worse, even, than the Deepness.

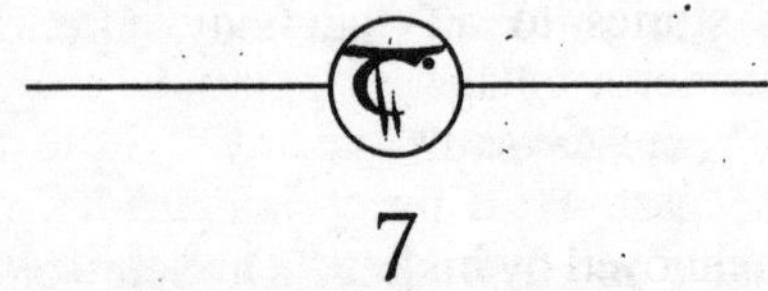

7

SAZED NEVER THOUGHT HE'D HAVE reason to appreciate dirt floors. However, they proved remarkably useful in writing instruction. He drew several words in the dirt with a long stick, giving his half-dozen students a model. They proceeded to scribble their own copies, rewriting the words several times.

Even after living among various groups of rural skaa for a year, Sazed was still surprised by their meager resources. There wasn't a single piece of chalk in the entire village, let alone ink or paper. Half the children ran around naked, and the only shelters were the hovels—long, one-room structures with patchy roofs. The skaa had farming tools, fortunately, but no manner of bows or slings for hunting.

Sazed had led a scavenging mission up to the plantation's abandoned manor. The leavings had been meager. He'd suggested that the village elders relocate their people to the manor itself for the winter, but he doubted they would do so. They had visited the manor with apprehension, and many hadn't been willing to leave Sazed's side. The place reminded them of lords—and lords reminded them of pain.

His students continued to scribble. He had spent quite a bit of effort explaining to the elders why writing was so important. Finally, they had chosen him some students—partially, Sazed was sure, just to appease him. He shook his head slowly as he watched them write. There was no passion in their learning. They came because they were ordered, and because "Master Terrisman" willed it, not because of any real desire for education.

During the days before the Collapse, Sazed had often imagined what the world would be like once the Lord Ruler was gone. He had pictured the Keepers emerging, bringing forgotten knowledge and truths to an excited, thankful populace. He'd imagined teaching before a warm hearth at night, telling stories to an eager audience. He'd never paused to consider a village, stripped of its working men, whose people were too exhausted at night to bother with tales from the past. He'd never imagined a people who seemed more annoyed by his presence than thankful.

You must be patient with them, Sazed told himself sternly. His dreams now seemed like hubris. The Keepers who had come before him, the hundreds who had died keeping their knowledge safe and quiet, had never expected praise or accolades. They had performed their great task with solemn anonymity.

Sazed stood up and inspected his students' writings. They were getting better—they could recognize all of the letters. It wasn't much, but it was a start. He nodded to the group, dismissing them to help prepare the evening meal.

They bowed, then scattered. Sazed followed them out, then realized how dim the sky was; he had probably kept his students too late. He shook his head as he strolled between the hill-like hovels. He again wore his steward's robes, with their colorful V-shaped patterns, and he had put in several of his earrings. He kept to the old ways because they were familiar, even though they were also a symbol of oppression. How would future Terris generations dress? Would a lifestyle forced upon them by the Lord Ruler become an innate part of their culture?

He paused at the edge of the village, glancing down the corridor of the southern valley. It was filled with blackened soil occasionally split by brown vines or shrubs. No mist, of course; mist came only during the night. The stories had to be mistakes. The thing he'd seen had to have been a fluke.

And what did it matter if it wasn't? It wasn't his duty to investigate such things. Now that the Collapse had come, he had to disperse his knowledge, not waste his time chasing after foolish stories. Keepers were no longer investigators, but instructors. He carried with him thousands of books—information about farming, about sanitation, about government, and about medicine. He needed to give these things to the skaa. That was what the Synod had decided.

And yet, a part of Sazed resisted. That made him feel deeply guilty; the villagers needed his teachings, and he wished dearly to help them. However . . . he felt that he was *missing* something. The Lord Ruler was dead, but the story did not seem finished. Was there something he had overlooked?

Something larger, even, than the Lord Ruler? Something so large, so big, that it was effectively invisible?

Or, do I just want *there to be something else?* he wondered. *I've spent most of my adult life resisting and fighting, taking risks that the other Keepers called mad. I wasn't content with feigned subservience—I had to get involved in the rebellion.*

Despite that rebellion's success, Sazed's brethren still hadn't forgiven him for his involvement. He knew that Vin and the others saw him as docile, but compared with other Keepers he was a wild man. A reckless, untrustworthy fool who threatened the entire order with his impatience. They had believed their duty was to wait, watching for the day when the Lord Ruler was gone. Feruchemists were too rare to risk in open rebellion.

Sazed had disobeyed. Now he was having trouble living the peaceful life of a teacher. Was that because some subconscious part of him knew that the people were still in danger, or was it because he simply couldn't accept being marginalized?

"Master Terrisman!"

Sazed spun. The voice was terrified. *Another death in the mists?* he thought immediately.

It was eerie how the other skaa remained inside their hovels despite the horrified voice. A few doors creaked, but nobody rushed out in alarm—or even curiosity—as the screamer dashed up to Sazed. She was one of the field-workers, a stout, middle-aged woman. Sazed checked his reserves as she approached; he had on his pewtermind for strength, of course, and a very small steel ring for speed. Suddenly, he wished he'd chosen to wear just a few more bracelets this day.

"Master Terrisman!" the woman said, out of breath. "Oh, he's come back! He's come for us!"

"Who?" Sazed asked. "The man who died in the mists?"

"No, Master Terrisman. The *Lord Ruler.*"

Sazed found him standing just outside the village. It was already growing dark, and the woman who'd fetched Sazed had returned to her hovel in fear. Sazed could only imagine how the poor people felt—trapped by the onset of the night and its mist, yet huddled and worried at the danger that lurked outside.

And an ominous danger it was. The stranger waited quietly on the worn road, wearing a black robe, standing almost as tall as Sazed himself. The man was bald, and he wore no jewelry—unless, of course, you counted the massive iron spikes that had been driven point-first through his eyes.

Not the Lord Ruler. A Steel Inquisitor.

Sazed still didn't understand how the creatures continued to live. The spikes were wide enough to fill the Inquisitor's entire eye sockets; the nails had destroyed the eyes, and pointed tips jutted out the back of the skull. No blood dripped from the wounds—for some reason, that made them seem more strange.

Fortunately, Sazed knew this particular Inquisitor. "Marsh," Sazed said quietly as the mists began to form.

"You are a very difficult person to track, Terrisman," Marsh said—and the sound of his voice shocked Sazed. It had changed, somehow, becoming more grating, more gristly. It now had a grinding quality, like that of a man with a cough. Just like the other Inquisitors Sazed had heard.

"Track?" Sazed asked. "I wasn't planning on others needing to find me."

"Regardless," Marsh said, turning south. "I did. You need to come with me."

Sazed frowned. "What? Marsh, I have a work to do here."

"Unimportant," Marsh said, turning back, focusing his eyeless gaze on Sazed.

Is it me, or has he become stranger since we last met? Sazed shivered. "What is this about, Marsh?"

"The Conventical of Seran is empty."

Sazed paused. The Conventical was a Ministry stronghold to the south—a place where the Inquisitors and high obligators of the Lord Ruler's religion had retreated after the Collapse.

"Empty?" Sazed asked. "That isn't likely, I think."

"True nonetheless," Marsh said. He didn't use body language as he spoke—no gesturing, no movements of the face.

"I . . ." Sazed trailed off. *What kinds of information, wonders, secrets, the Conventical's libraries must hold.*

"You must come with me," Marsh said. "I may need help, should my brethren discover us."

My brethren. Since when are the Inquisitors Marsh's "brethren"? Marsh had infiltrated their numbers as part of Kelsier's plan to overthrow the Final Empire. He was a traitor to their numbers, not their brother.

Sazed hesitated. Marsh's profile looked . . . unnatural, even unnerving, in the dim light. Dangerous.

Don't be foolish, Sazed chastised himself. Marsh was Kelsier's brother—the Survivor's only living relative. As an Inquisitor, Marsh had authority over the Steel Ministry, and many of the obligators had listened to him despite his involvement with the rebellion. He had been an invaluable resource for Elend Venture's fledgling government.

"Go get your things," Marsh said.

My place is here, Sazed thought. *Teaching the people, not gallivanting across the countryside, chasing my own ego.*

And yet . . .

"The mists are coming during the day," Marsh said quietly.

Sazed looked up. Marsh was staring at him, the heads of his spikes shining like round disks in the last slivers of sunlight. Superstitious skaa thought that Inquisitors could read minds, though Sazed knew that was foolish. Inquisitors had the powers of Mistborn, and could therefore influence other people's emotions—but they could *not* read minds.

"Why did you say that?" Sazed asked.

"Because it is true," Marsh said. "This is not over, Sazed. It has not yet begun. The Lord Ruler . . . he was just a delay. A cog. Now that he is gone, we have little time remaining. Come with me to the Conventical—we must search it while we have the opportunity."

Sazed paused, then nodded. "Let me go explain to the villagers. We can leave tonight, I think."

Marsh nodded, but he didn't move as Sazed retreated to the village. He just remained, standing in the darkness, letting the mist gather around him.

It all comes back to poor Alendi. I feel bad for him, and for all the things he has been forced to endure. For what he has been forced to become.

8

VIN THREW HERSELF INTO THE mists. She soared in the night air, passing over darkened homes and streets. An occasional, furtive bob of light glowed in the mists—a guard patrol, or perhaps an unfortunate late-night traveler.

Vin began to descend, and she immediately flipped a coin out before herself. She Pushed against it, her weight plunging it down into the quiet depths. As soon as it hit the street below, her Push forced her upward, and she sprang back into the air. Soft Pushes were very difficult—so each coin she Pushed against, each jump she made, threw her into the air at a terrible speed. The jumping of a Mistborn wasn't like a bird's flight. It was more like the path of a ricocheting arrow.

And yet, there was a grace to it. Vin breathed deeply as she arced above the city, tasting the cool, humid air. Luthadel by day smelled of burning forges, sun-heated refuse, and fallen ash. At night, however, the mists gave the air a beautiful chill crispness—almost a cleanliness.

Vin crested her jump, and she hung for just a brief moment as her momentum changed. Then she began to plummet back toward the city. Her mistcloak tassels fluttered around her, mingling with her hair. She fell with her eyes closed, remembering her first few weeks in the mist, training beneath Kelsier's relaxed—yet watchful—tutelage. He had given her this. Freedom. Despite two years as a Mistborn, she had never lost the sense of intoxicating wonder she felt when soaring through the mists.

She burned steel with her eyes closed; the lines appeared anyway, visible as a spray of threadlike blue lines set against the blackness of her eyelids. She picked two, pointing downward behind her, and Pushed, throwing herself into another arc.

What did I ever do without this? Vin thought, opening her eyes, whipping her mistcloak behind her with a throw of the arm.

Eventually, she began to fall again, and this time she didn't toss a coin. She burned pewter to strengthen her limbs, and landed with a thump on the wall surrounding Keep Venture's grounds. Her bronze showed no signs of Allomantic activity nearby, and her steel revealed no unusual patterns of metal moving toward the keep.

Vin crouched on the dark wall for a few moments, right at the edge, toes curling over the lip of the stone. The rock was cool beneath her feet, and her tin made her skin far more sensitive than normal. She could tell that the wall needed to be cleaned; lichens were beginning to grow along its side, encouraged by the night's humidity, protected from the day's sun by a nearby tower.

Vin remained quiet, watching a slight breeze push and churn the mists. She heard the movement on the street below before she saw it. She tensed, checking her reserves, before she was able to discern a wolfhound's shape in the shadows.

She dropped a coin over the side of the wall, then leapt off. OreSeur waited as she landed quietly before him, using a quick Push on the coin to slow her descent.

"You move quickly," Vin noted appreciatively.

"All I had to do was round the palace grounds, Mistress."

"Still, you stuck closer to me this time than you ever did before. That wolfhound's body *is* faster than a human one."

OreSeur paused. "I suppose," he admitted.

"Think you can follow me through the city?"

"Probably," OreSeur said. "If you lose me, I will return to this point so you can retrieve me."

Vin turned and dashed down a side street. OreSeur then took off quietly behind her, following.

Let's see how well he does in a more demanding chase, she thought, burning pewter and increasing her speed. She sprinted along the cool cobbles, barefoot as always. A normal man could never have maintained such a speed. Even a trained runner couldn't have kept pace with her, for he would have quickly tired.

With pewter, however, Vin could run for hours at breakneck speeds. It gave her strength, lent her an unreal sense of balance, as she shot down the dark, mist-ruled street, a flurry of cloak tassels and bare feet.

OreSeur kept pace. He loped beside her in the night, breathing heavily, focused on his running.

Impressive, Vin thought, then turned down an alleyway. She easily jumped the six-foot-tall fence at the back, passing into the garden of some lesser nobleman's mansion. She spun, skidding on the wet grass, and watched.

OreSeur crested the top of the wooden fence, his dark, canine form dropping through the mists to land in the loam before Vin. He came to a stop, resting on his haunches, waiting quietly, panting. There was a look of defiance in his eyes.

All right, Vin thought, pulling out a handful of coins. *Follow this.*

She dropped a coin and threw herself backward up into the air. She spun in the mists, twisting, then Pushed herself sideways off a well spigot. She landed on a rooftop and jumped off, using another coin to Push herself over the street below.

She kept going, leaping from rooftop to rooftop, using coins when necessary. She occasionally shot a glance behind, and saw a dark form struggling to keep up. He'd rarely followed her as a human; usually, she had checked in with him at specific points. Moving out in the night, jumping through the mists . . . this was the true domain of the Mistborn. Did Elend understand what he asked when he told her to bring OreSeur with her? If she stayed down on the streets, she'd expose herself.

She landed on a rooftop, jarring to a sudden halt as she grabbed hold of the building's stone lip, leaning out over a street three stories below. She maintained her balance, mist swirling below her. All was silent.

Well, that didn't take long, she thought. *I'll just have to explain to Elend that—*

OreSeur's canine form thumped to the rooftop a short distance away. He padded over to her, then sat down on his haunches, waiting expectantly.

Vin frowned. She'd traveled for a good ten minutes, running over rooftops with the speed of a Mistborn. "How . . . how did you get up here?" she demanded.

"I jumped atop a shorter building, then used it to reach these tenements, Mistress," OreSeur said. "Then I followed you along the rooftops. They are placed so closely together that it was not difficult to jump from one to another."

Vin's confusion must have shown, for OreSeur continued. "I may have been . . . hasty in my judgment of these bones, Mistress. They certainly do have an impressive sense of smell—in fact, all of their senses are quite keen. It was surprisingly easy to track you, even in the darkness."

"I . . . see," Vin said. "Well, that's good."

"Might I ask, Mistress, the purpose of that chase?"

Vin shrugged. "I do this sort of thing every night."

"It seemed like you were particularly intent on losing me. It will be very difficult to protect you if you don't let me stay near you."

"Protect me?" Vin asked. "You can't even fight."

"The Contract forbids me from killing a human," OreSeur said. "I could, however, go for help should you need it."

Or throw me a bit of atium in a moment of danger, Vin admitted. *He's right—he could be useful. Why am I so determined to leave him behind?*

She glanced over at OreSeur, who sat patiently, his chest puffing from exertion. She hadn't realized that kandra even needed to breathe.

He ate Kelsier.

"Come on," Vin said. She jumped from the building, Pushing herself off a coin. She didn't pause to see if OreSeur followed.

As she fell, she reached for another coin, but decided not to use it. She Pushed against a passing window bracket instead. Like most Mistborn, she often used clips—the smallest denomination of coin—to jump. It was very convenient that the economy supplied a prepackaged bit of metal of an ideal size and weight for jumping and shooting. To most Mistborn, the cost of a thrown clip—or even a bag of them—was negligible.

But Vin was not most Mistborn. In her younger years, a handful of clips would have seemed an amazing treasure. That much money could have meant food for weeks, if she scrimped. It also could have meant pain—even death—if the other thieves had discovered that she'd obtained such a fortune.

It had been a long time since she'd gone hungry. Though she still kept a pack of dried foods in her quarters, she did so more out of habit than anxiety. She honestly wasn't sure what she thought of the changes within her. It was nice not to have to worry about basic necessities—and yet, those worries had been replaced by ones far more daunting. Worries involving the future of an entire nation.

The future of . . . a people. She landed on the city wall—a structure much higher, and much better fortified, than the small wall around Keep Venture. She hopped up on the battlements, fingers seeking a hold on one of the merlons as she leaned over the edge of the wall, looking out over the army's fires.

She had never met Straff Venture, but she had heard enough from Elend to be worried.

She sighed, pushing back off the battlement and hopping onto the wall walk. Then she leaned back against one of the merlons. To the side, OreSeur trotted up the wall steps and approached. Once again, he went down onto his haunches, watching patiently.

For better or for worse, Vin's simple life of starvation and beatings was gone. Elend's fledgling kingdom was in serious danger, and she'd burned away the last of his atium trying to keep herself alive. She'd left him exposed—not just to armies, but to any Mistborn assassin who tried to kill him.

An assassin like the Watcher, perhaps? The mysterious figure who had interfered in her fight against Cett's Mistborn. What did he want? Why did he watch her, rather than Elend?

Vin sighed, reaching into her coin pouch and pulling out her bar of duralumin. She still had the reserve of it within her, the bit she'd swallowed earlier.

For centuries, it had been assumed that there were only ten Allomantic metals: the four base metals and their alloys, plus atium and gold. Yet, Allomantic metals always came in pairs—a base metal and an alloy. It had always bothered Vin that atium and gold were considered a pair, when neither was an alloy of the other. In the end, it had turned out that they weren't actually paired; they each had an alloy. One of these—malatium, the so-called Eleventh Metal—had eventually given Vin the clue she'd needed to defeat the Lord Ruler.

Somehow Kelsier had found out about malatium. Sazed still hadn't been able to trace the "legends" that Kelsier had supposedly uncovered teaching of the Eleventh Metal and its power to defeat the Lord Ruler.

Vin rubbed her finger on the slick surface of the duralumin bar. When Vin had last seen Sazed, he'd seemed frustrated—or, at least, as frustrated as Sazed ever grew—that he couldn't find even hints regarding Kelsier's supposed legends. Though Sazed claimed he'd left Luthadel to teach the people of the Final Empire—as was his duty as a Keeper—Vin hadn't missed the fact that Sazed had gone south. The direction in which Kelsier claimed to have discovered the Eleventh Metal.

Are there rumors about this metal, too? Vin wondered, rubbing the duralumin. *Ones that might tell me what it does?*

Each of the other metals produced an immediate, visible effect; only copper, with its ability to create a cloud that masked an Allomancer's powers from others, didn't have an obvious sensory clue to its purpose. Perhaps duralumin was similar. Could its effect be noticed only by another Allomancer, one trying to use his or her powers on Vin? It was the opposite of aluminum, which made metals disappear. Did that mean duralumin would make other metals last longer?

Movement.

Vin just barely caught the hint of shadowed motion. At first, a primal bit of terror rose in her: Was it the misty form, the ghost in the darkness she had seen the night before?

You were just seeing things, she told herself forcefully. *You were too tired.* And, in truth, the glimmer of motion proved too dark—too *real*—to be the same ghostly image.

It was him.

He stood atop one of the watchtowers—not crouching, not even bothering to hide. Was he arrogant or foolish, this unknown Mistborn? Vin smiled, her apprehension turning to excitement. She prepared her metals, checking her reserves. Everything was ready.

Tonight I catch you, my friend.

Vin spun, throwing out a spray of coins. Either the Mistborn knew he'd been spotted, or he was ready for an attack, for he easily dodged. OreSeur hopped to his feet, spinning, and Vin whipped her belt free, dropping her metals.

"Follow if you can," she whispered to the kandra, then sprang into the darkness after her prey.

The Watcher shot away, bounding through the night. Vin had little experience chasing another Mistborn; her only real chance to practice had come during Kelsier's training sessions. She soon found herself struggling to keep up with the Watcher, and she felt a stab of guilt for what she had done to OreSeur earlier. She was learning firsthand how difficult it was to follow a determined Mistborn through the mists. And she didn't have the advantage of a dog's sense of smell.

She did, however, have tin. It made the night clearer and enhanced her hearing. With it, she managed to follow the Watcher as he moved toward the center of the city. Eventually, he let himself drop down toward one of the central fountain squares. Vin fell as well, hitting the slick cobblestones with a flare of pewter, then dodging to the side as he threw out a handful of coins.

Metal rang against stone in the quiet night, coins plinging against statues and cobblestones. Vin smiled as she landed on all fours; then she bounded forward, jumping with pewter-enhanced muscles and Pulling one of the coins up into her hand.

Her opponent leaped backward, landing on the edge of a nearby fountain. Vin landed, then dropped her coin, using it to throw herself upward over the Watcher's head. He stooped, watching warily as she passed over him.

Vin caught of one of the bronze statues at the center of the fountain itself and pulled herself to a stop atop it. She crouched on the uneven footing, looking down at her opponent. He stood balanced on one foot at the edge of the fountain, quiet and black in the churning mists. There was a . . . challenge in his posture.

Can you catch me? he seemed to ask.

Vin whipped her daggers out and jumped free of the statue. She Pushed herself directly toward the Watcher, using the cool bronze as an anchor.

The Watcher used the statue as well, Pulling himself forward. He shot just beneath Vin, throwing up a wave of water, his incredible speed letting him skid like a stone across the fountain's still surface. As he jumped clear of the water, he Pushed himself away, shooting across the square.

Vin landed on the fountain lip, chill water spraying across her. She growled, jumping after the Watcher.

As he landed, he spun and whipped out his own daggers. She rolled beneath his first attack, then brought her daggers up in a two-handed double jab. The Watcher jumped quickly out of the way, his daggers sparkling and dropping beads of fountain water. He had a lithe power about him as he came to rest in a crouch. His body looked tense and sure. Capable.

Vin smiled again, breathing quickly. She hadn't felt like this since . . . since those nights so long ago, when she'd sparred with Kelsier. She remained in a crouch, waiting, watching the mist curl between her and her opponent. He was of medium height, had a wiry build, and he wore no mistcloak.

Why no cloak? Mistcloaks were the ubiquitous mark of her kind, a symbol of pride and security.

She was too far away to distinguish his face. She thought she saw a hint of a smile, however, as he jumped backward and Pushed against another statue. The chase began again.

Vin followed him through the city, flaring steel, landing on roofs and streets, Pushing herself in great arcing leaps. The two bounded through Luthadel like children on a playground—Vin trying to cut off her opponent, he cleverly managing to stay just a little bit ahead of her.

He was good. Far better than any Mistborn she had known or faced, save perhaps for Kelsier. However, she'd grown greatly in skill since she'd sparred with the Survivor. Could this newcomer be even better? The thought thrilled her. She'd always considered Kelsier a paradigm of Allomantic ability, and it was easy to forget that he'd had his powers for only a couple of years before the Collapse.

That's the same amount of time that I've been training, Vin realized as she landed in a small, cramped street. She frowned, crouching, remaining still. She'd seen the Watcher fall toward this street.

Narrow and poorly maintained, the street was practically an alleyway, lined on both sides by three- and four-story buildings. There was no motion—either the Watcher had slipped away or he was hiding nearby. She burned iron, but the iron-lines revealed no motion.

However, there was another way. . . .

Vin pretended to still be looking around, but she turned on her bronze, flaring it, trying to pierce the coppercloud that she thought might be close.

And there he was. Hiding in a room behind the mostly closed shutters of a derelict building. Now that she knew where to look, she saw the bit of metal he'd probably used to jump up to the second story, the latch he must have Pulled on to quickly close the shutters behind him. He'd probably scouted this street beforehand, always intending to lose her here.

Clever, Vin thought.

He couldn't have anticipated her ability to pierce copperclouds. But, attacking him now might give away that ability. Vin stood quietly, thinking of him crouching above, tensely waiting for her to move off.

She smiled. Reaching inside, she examined the duralumin reserve. There was a possible way to discover if burning it created some change in the way she looked to another Mistborn. The Watcher was likely burning most of his metals, trying to determine what her next move would be.

So, thinking herself incredibly clever, Vin burned the fourteenth metal.

A massive explosion sounded in her ears. Vin gasped, dropping to her knees in shock. Everything grew bright around her, as if some crack of energy had illuminated the entire street. And she felt cold; frigidly, stunningly cold.

She moaned, trying to make sense of the sound. It . . . it wasn't an explosion, but many explosions. A rhythmic thudding, like a drum pounding just beside her. Her heartbeat. And the breeze, loud as a howling wind. The scratchings of a dog searching for food. Someone snoring in their sleep. It was as if her hearing had been magnified a hundred times.

And then . . . nothing. Vin fell backward against the cobblestones, the sudden rush of light, coldness, and sound evaporating. A form moved in the shadows nearby, but she couldn't make it out—she couldn't see in the darkness anymore. Her tin was . . .

Gone, she realized, coming to. *My entire store of tin has been burned away. I was . . . burning it, when I turned on the duralumin.*

I burned them both at once. That's the secret. The duralumin had burned away all her tin in a single, massive burst. It had made her senses amazingly acute for a very short time, but had stolen away her entire reserve. And, looking, she could see that her bronze and her pewter—the other metals she'd been burning at the time—were gone as well. The onrush of sensory information had been so vast that she hadn't noticed the effects of the other two.

Think about it later, Vin told herself, shaking her head. She felt like she should be deafened and blinded, but she wasn't. She was just a bit stunned.

The dark form moved up beside her in the mists. She didn't have time to recover; she pushed herself to her feet, stumbling. The form, it was too short to be the Watcher. It was . . .

"Mistress, do you require assistance?"

Vin paused as OreSeur padded up to her, then sat on his haunches.

"You . . . managed to follow," Vin said.

"It was not easy, Mistress," OreSeur said flatly. "Do you require assistance?"

"What? No, no assistance." Vin shook her head, clearing her mind. "I guess that's one thing I didn't think of by making you a dog. You can't carry metals for me now."

The kandra cocked his head, then padded over into an alleyway. He returned a moment later with something in his mouth. Her belt.

He dropped it by her feet, then returned to his waiting position. Vin picked up the belt, pulling off one of her extra metal vials. "Thank you," she said slowly. "That is very . . . thoughtful of you."

"I fulfill my Contract, Mistress," the kandra said. "Nothing more."

Well, this is more than you've ever done before, she thought, downing a vial and feeling her reserves return. She burned tin, restoring her night vision, releasing a veil of tension from her mind; since she'd discovered her powers, she'd never had to go out at night in complete darkness.

The shutters of the Watcher's room were open; he had apparently fled during her fit. Vin sighed.

"Mistress!" OreSeur snapped.

Vin spun. A man landed quietly behind her. He looked . . . familiar, for some reason. He had a lean face—topped with dark hair—and his head was cocked slightly in confusion. She could see the question in his eyes. Why had she fallen down?

Vin smiled. "Maybe I just did it to lure you closer," she whispered—softly, yet loud enough that she knew tin-enhanced ears would hear her.

The Mistborn smiled, then tipped his head to her as if in respect.

"Who are you?" Vin asked, stepping forward.

"An enemy," he replied, holding up a hand to ward her back.

Vin paused. Mist swirled between them on the quiet street. "Why, then, did you help me fight those assassins?"

"Because," he said. "I'm also insane."

Vin frowned, eyeing the man. She had seen insanity before in the eyes of beggars. This man was not insane. He stood proudly, eyes controlled as he regarded her in the darkness.

What kind of game is he playing? she wondered.

Her instincts—a lifetime's worth of instincts—warned her to be wary. She had only just learned to trust her friends, and she wasn't about to offer the same privilege to a man she had met in the night.

And yet, it had been over a year since she'd spoken with another Mistborn. There were conflicts within her that she couldn't explain to the others. Even Mistings, like Ham and Breeze, couldn't understand the strange dual life of a Mistborn. Part assassin, part bodyguard, part noblewoman . . . part confused, quiet girl. Did this man have similar troubles with his identity?

Perhaps she could make an ally out of him, bringing a second Mistborn to the defense of the Central Dominance. Even if she couldn't, she certainly couldn't afford to fight him. A spar in the night was one thing, but if their contest grew dangerous, atium might come into play.

If that happened, she'd lose.

The Watcher studied her with a careful eye. "Answer something for me," he said in the mists.

Vin nodded.

"Did you really kill Him?"

"Yes," Vin whispered. There was only one person he could mean.

He nodded slowly. "Why do you play their games?"

"Whose games?"

The Watcher gestured into the mists, toward Keep Venture.

"Those aren't games," Vin said. "It's no game when the people I love are in danger."

The Watcher stood quietly, then shook his head, as if . . . disappointed. Then, he pulled something from his sash.

Vin jumped back immediately. The Watcher, however, simply flipped a coin to the ground between them. It bounced a couple of times, coming to a rest on the cobbles. Then, the Watcher Pushed himself backward into the air.

Vin didn't follow. She reached up, rubbing her head; she still felt like she should have a headache.

"You're letting him go?" OreSeur asked.

Vin nodded. "We're done for tonight. He fought well."

"You sound almost respectful," the kandra said.

Vin turned, frowning at the hint of disgust in the kandra's voice. OreSeur sat patiently, displaying no further emotion.

She sighed, tying her belt around her waist. "We're going to need to come up with a harness or something for you," she said. "I want you to carry extra metal vials for me, like you did as a human."

"A harness won't be necessary, Mistress," OreSeur said.

"Oh?"

OreSeur rose, padding forward. "Please get out one of your vials."

Vin did as requested, pulling out a small glass vial. OreSeur stopped, then turned one shoulder toward her. As she watched, the fur parted and the flesh itself split, showing forth veins and layers of skin. Vin pulled back a bit.

"There is no need to be worried, Mistress," OreSeur said. "My flesh is not like your own. I have more . . . control over it, you might say. Place the metal vial inside my shoulder."

Vin did as asked. The flesh sealed around the vial, obscuring it from view. Experimentally, Vin burned iron. No blue lines appeared pointing toward the hidden vial. Metal inside of a person's stomach couldn't be affected by another Allomancer; indeed, metal piercing a body, like Inquisitor spikes or Vin's own earring, couldn't be Pushed or Pulled by someone else. Apparently, the same rule applied to metals hidden within a kandra.

"I will deliver this to you in an emergency," OreSeur said.

"Thank you," Vin said.

"The Contract, Mistress. Do not give me thanks. I do only what I am required."

Vin nodded slowly. "Let's go back to the palace, then," she said. "I want to check on Elend."

But, let me begin at the beginning. I met Alendi first in Khlennium; he was a young lad then, and had not yet been warped by a decade spent leading armies.

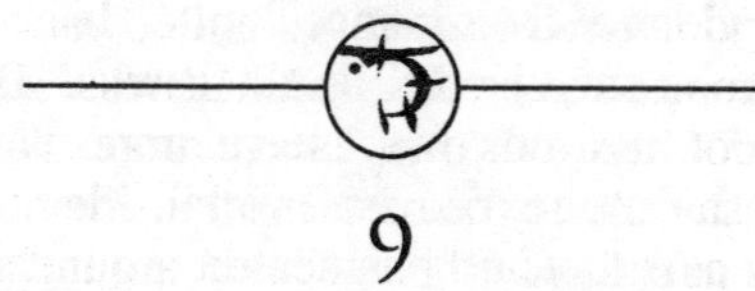

9

MARSH HAD CHANGED. THERE WAS something . . . harder about the former Seeker. Something in the way he always seemed to be staring at things Sazed couldn't see, something in his blunt responses and terse language.

Of course, Marsh had always been a straightforward man. Sazed eyed his friend as the two strode down the dusty highway. They had no horses; even if Sazed had possessed one, most beasts wouldn't go near an Inquisitor.

What did Spook say that Marsh's nickname was? Sazed thought to himself as they walked. *Before his transformation, they used to call him . . . Ironeyes.* The name that had turned out to be chillingly prophetic. Most of the others found Marsh's transformed state discomforting, and had left him isolated. Though Marsh hadn't seemed to mind the treatment, Sazed had made a special effort to befriend the man.

He still didn't know if Marsh appreciated the gesture or not. They did seem to get along well; both shared an interest in scholarship and history, and both were interested in the religious climate of the Final Empire.

And, he did come looking for me, Sazed thought. *Of course, he did claim that he wanted help in case the Inquisitors weren't all gone from the Conventical of Seran.* It was a weak excuse. Despite his powers as a Feruchemist, Sazed was no warrior.

"You should be in Luthadel," Marsh said.

Sazed looked up. Marsh had spoken bluntly, as usual, without preamble. "Why do you say that?" Sazed asked.

"They need you there."

"The rest of the Final Empire has need of me too, Marsh. I am a Keeper—one group of people should not be able to monopolize all of my time."

Marsh shook his head. "These peasants, they will forget your passing. No one will forget the things that will soon happen in the Central Dominance."

"You would be surprised, I think, at what men can forget. Wars and kingdoms may seem important now, but even the Final Empire proved mortal. Now that it has fallen, the Keepers have no business being involved in politics." *Most would say we never had any business being involved in politics at all.*

Marsh turned toward him. Those eyes, sockets filled entirely with steel. Sazed did not shiver, but he felt distinctly uncomfortable.

"And your friends?" Marsh asked.

This touched on something more personal. Sazed looked away, thinking of Vin, and of his vow to Kelsier that he would protect her. *She needs little protection now,* he thought. *She's grown more adept at Allomancy than even Kelsier was.* And yet, Sazed knew that there were modes of protection that didn't relate to fighting. These things—support, counsel, kindness—were vital to every person, and most especially to Vin. So much rested on that poor girl's shoulders.

"I have . . . sent help," Sazed said. "What help I can."

"Not good enough," Marsh said. "The things happening in Luthadel are too important to ignore."

"I am not ignoring them, Marsh," Sazed said. "I am simply performing my duty as best I can."

Marsh finally turned away. "The wrong duty. You will return to Luthadel once we are finished here."

Sazed opened his mouth to argue, but said nothing. What was there to say? Marsh was right. Though he had no proof, Sazed knew that there *were* important things happening in Luthadel—things that would require his aid to fight. Things that likely affected the future of the entire land once known as the Final Empire.

So, he closed his mouth and trudged after Marsh. He

would return to Luthadel, proving himself a rebel once again. Perhaps, in the end, he would realize that there was no ghostly threat facing the world—that he had simply returned because of his own selfish desire to be with his friends.

In fact, he hoped that proved to be the truth. The alternative made him very uncomfortable.

Alendi's height struck me the first time I saw him. Here was a man who towered over others, a man who—despite his youth and his humble clothing—demanded respect.

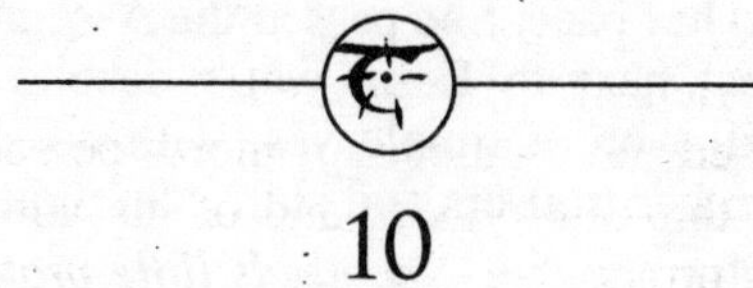

10

THE ASSEMBLY HALL WAS in the former Steel Ministry Canton of Finance headquarters. It was a low-ceilinged space, more of a large lecture room than an assembly hall. There were rows of benches fanning out in front of a raised stage. On the right side of the stage, Elend had constructed a tier of seats for the Assembly members. On the left of the stage, he had constructed a single lectern for speakers.

The lectern faced the Assemblymen, not the crowd. The common people were, however, encouraged to attend. Elend thought that everyone should be interested in the workings of their government; it pained him that the Assembly's weekly meetings usually had a small audience.

Vin's seat was on the stage, but at the back, directly opposite the audience. From her vantage with the other bodyguards, she would look past the lectern toward the crowd. Another row of Ham's guards—in regular clothing—sat in the first row of the audience, providing a first line of protection. Elend had balked at Vin's demands to having guards both in front of the stage and behind it—he thought that bodyguards sitting right behind the speakers would be distracting. Ham and Vin, however, had insisted. If Elend was going to stand up in front of a crowd every week, Vin wanted to be certain she could keep a close eye on him—and on those watching him.

Getting to her chair, therefore, required Vin to walk across the stage. Stares followed her. Some of the watching crowd were interested in the scandal; they assumed that she was Elend's mistress, and a king sleeping with his personal assassin made for good gossip. Others were interested in the politics; they wondered how much influence Vin had over Elend, and whether they could use her to get the king's ear. Still others were curious about the growing legends; they wondered if a girl like Vin could really have slain the Lord Ruler.

Vin hurried her pace. She passed the Assemblymen and found her seat next to Ham, who—despite the formal occasion—still wore a simple vest with no shirt. Sitting next to him in her trousers and shirt, Vin didn't feel quite so out of place.

Ham smiled, clapping her affectionately on the shoulder. She had to force herself not to jump at the touch. It wasn't that she disliked Ham—quite the opposite, actually. She loved him as she did all of the former members of Kelsier's band. It was just that . . . well, she had trouble explaining it, even to herself. Ham's innocent gesture made her want to squirm. It seemed to her that people shouldn't be so casual with the way that they touched others.

She pushed those thoughts away. She had to learn to be like other people. Elend deserved a woman who was normal.

He was already there. He nodded to Vin as he noticed her arrival, and she smiled. Then he turned back to speaking quietly with Lord Penrod, one of the noblemen in the Assembly.

"Elend will be happy," Vin whispered. "Place is packed."

"They're worried," Ham said quietly. "And worried people pay more attention to things like this. Can't say I'm happy—all these people make our job harder."

Vin nodded, scanning the audience. The crowd was a strangely mixed one—a collection of different groups who would never have met together during the days of the Final Empire. A major part were noblemen, of course. Vin frowned, thinking of how often various members of the nobility tried to manipulate Elend, and of the promises he made to them. . . .

"What's that look for?" Ham asked, nudging her.

Vin eyed the Thug. Expectant eyes twinkled in his firm, rectangular face. Ham had an almost supernatural sense when it came to arguments.

Vin sighed. "I don't know about this, Ham."

"This?"

"This," Vin said quietly, waving her hand at the Assembly. "Elend tries so hard to make everyone happy. He gives so much away—his power, his money. . . ."

"He just wants to see that everyone is treated fairly."

"It's more than that, Ham," Vin said. "It's like he's determined to make everyone a nobleman."

"Would that be such a bad thing?"

"If everyone is a nobleman, then there is no such thing as a nobleman. Everyone *can't* be rich, and everyone can't be in charge. That's just not the way things work."

"Perhaps," Ham said thoughtfully. "But, doesn't Elend have a civic duty to try and make sure justice is served?"

Civic duty? Vin thought. *I should have known better than to talk to Ham about something like this. . . .*

Vin looked down. "I just think he could see that everyone was treated well without having an Assembly. All they do is argue and try to take his power away. And he lets them."

Ham let the discussion die, and Vin turned back to her study of the audience. It appeared that a large group of mill workers had arrived first and managed to get the best seats. Early in the Assembly's history—perhaps ten months before—the nobility had sent servants to reserve seats for them, or had bribed people to give up their places. As soon as Elend had discovered this, however, he had forbidden both practices.

Other than the noblemen and the mill workers, there was a large number of the "new" class. Skaa merchants and craftsmasters, now allowed to set their own prices for their services. They were the true winners in Elend's economy. Beneath the Lord Ruler's oppressive hand, only the few most extraordinarily skilled skaa had been able to rise to positions of even moderate comfort. Without those restrictions, these same people had quickly proven to have abilities and acumen far above their noble counterparts'. They represented a faction in the Assembly at least as powerful as that of the nobility.

Other skaa peppered the crowd. They looked much the same as they had before Elend's rise to power. While noblemen generally wore suits—complete with dayhats and coats—these skaa wore simple trousers. Some of them were still dirty from their day's labor, their clothing old, worn, and stained with ash.

And yet . . . there *was* something different about them. It wasn't in their clothing, but their postures. They sat a little straighter, their heads held a little higher. And they had enough free time to attend an Assembly meeting.

Elend finally stood to begin the meeting. He had let his attendants dress him this morning, and the result was attire that was almost completely free of dishevelment. His suit fit well, all the buttons were done up, and his vest was of an appropriate dark blue. His hair was even neatly styled, the short, brown curls lying flat.

Normally, Elend would begin the meeting by calling on other speakers, Assemblymen who would drone on for hours about various topics like taxation rates or city sanitation. However, this day, there were more pressing matters.

"Gentlemen," Elend said. "I beg your leave to depart from our usual agenda this afternoon, in the light of our current . . . state of city affairs."

The group of twenty-four Assemblymen nodded, a few muttering things under their breath. Elend ignored them. He was comfortable before crowds, far more comfortable than Vin would ever be. As he unrolled his speech, Vin kept one eye on the crowd, watching for reactions or problems.

"The dire nature of our situation should be quite obvious," Elend said, beginning the speech he had prepared earlier. "We face a danger that this city has never known. Invasion and siege from an outside tyrant.

"We are a new nation, a kingdom founded on principles unknown during the days of the Lord Ruler. Yet, we are already a kingdom of tradition. Freedom for the skaa. Rule by our own choice and of our own design. Noblemen who don't have to cower before the Lord Ruler's obligators and Inquisitors.

"Gentlemen, one year is not enough. We have tasted freedom, and we need time to savor it. During the last month, we have frequently discussed and argued regarding what to do should this day arrive. Obviously, we are of many minds on the issue. Therefore, I ask for a vote of solidarity. Let us promise ourselves, and these people, that we will not give this city over to a foreign power without due consideration. Let us resolve to gather more information, to seek for other avenues, and even to fight should it be deemed necessary."

The speech went on, but Vin had heard it a dozen times as Elend practiced it. As he spoke, she found herself eying the crowd. She was most worried about the obligators she saw sitting in the back. They showed little reaction to the negative light in which Elend's remarks cast them.

She'd never understood why Elend allowed the Steel Ministry to continue teaching. It was the last real remnant of the Lord Ruler's power. Most obligators obstinately refused to lend their knowledge of bureaucracy and administration to Elend's government, and they still regarded skaa with contempt.

And yet, Elend let them remain. He maintained a strict rule that they were not allowed to incite rebellion or violence. However, he also didn't eject them from the city, as Vin had suggested. Actually, if the choice had been solely hers, she probably would have executed them.

Eventually, Elend's speech drew to a close, and Vin turned her attention back to him. "Gentlemen," he said, "I make this proposal out of faith, and I make it in the names of those we represent. I ask for time. I propose that we forgo all votes regarding the future of the city until a proper royal delegation has been allowed to meet with the army outside and determine what, if any, opportunity there is for negotiations."

He lowered his sheet, looking up, waiting for comments.

"So," said Philen, one of the merchants on the Assembly. "You're asking us to give *you* the power to decide the city's fate." Philen wore his rich suit so well that an observer would never have known that he'd first put one on about a year ago.

"What?" Elend asked. "I said nothing of the sort—I'm simply asking for more time. To meet with Straff."

"He's rejected all of our earlier messages," said another Assemblyman. "What makes you think he'll listen now?"

"We're approaching this wrong!" said one of the noble representatives. "We should be resolving to *beg* Straff Venture not to attack, not resolving to meet with him and chat. We need to establish quickly that we're willing to work with him. You've all seen that army. He's planning to destroy us!"

"Please," Elend said, raising a hand. "Let us stay on topic!"

One of the other Assemblymen—one of the skaa—spoke up, as if he hadn't heard Elend. "You say that because you're noble," he said, pointing at the noble Elend had interrupted. "It's easy for you to talk about working with Straff, since you've got very little to lose!"

"Very little to lose?" the nobleman said. "I and all of my house could be executed for supporting Elend against his father!"

"Bah," said one of the merchants. "This is all pointless. We should have hired mercenaries months ago, as I'd suggested."

"And where would we have gotten the funds for that?" asked Lord Penrod, senior of the noble Assemblymen.

"Taxes," the merchant said with a wave of his hand.

"Gentlemen!" Elend said; then, louder, "Gentlemen!"

This garnered him some small measure of attention.

"We *have* to make a decision," Elend said. "Stay focused, if you please. What of my proposal?"

"It's pointless," said Philen the merchant. "Why should we wait? Let's just invite Straff into the city and be done. He's going to take it anyway."

Vin sat back as the men began to argue again. The problem was, the merchant Philen—as little as she liked him—

had a point. Fighting was looking like a very unattractive option. Straff had such a large army. Would stalling really do that much good?

"Look, see," Elend said, trying to get their attention again—and only partially succeeding. "Straff is my father. Maybe I could talk to him. Get him to listen? Luthadel was his home for years. Perhaps I can convince him not to attack it."

"Wait," said one of the skaa representatives. "What of the food issue? Have you seen what the merchants are charging for grain? Before we worry about that army, we should talk about bringing prices down."

"Always blaming us for your problems," one of the merchant Assemblymen said, pointing. And the squabbling began again. Elend slumped just slightly behind the lectern. Vin shook her head, feeling sorry for Elend as the discussion degenerated. This was what often happened at Assembly meetings; it seemed to her that they simply didn't give Elend the respect he deserved. Perhaps that was his own fault, for elevating them to his near equals.

Finally, the discussion wound down, and Elend got out a piece of paper, obviously planning to record the vote on his proposal. He did not look optimistic.

"All right," Elend said. "Let's vote. Please remember—giving me time will *not* play our hand. It will simply give me a chance to try and make my father reconsider his desire to take our city away from us."

"Elend, lad," said Lord Penrod. "We all lived here during the Lord Ruler's reign. We all know what kind of man your father is. If he wants this city, he *is* going to take it. All we can decide, then, is how to best give up. Perhaps we can find a way for the people to retain some freedom under his rule."

The group sat quietly, and for the first time nobody brought up a new squabble. A few of them turned toward Penrod, who sat with a calm, in-control expression. Vin knew little of the man. He was one of the more powerful noblemen who had remained in the city after the Collapse, and he was politically conservative. However, she had never heard him speak derogatively of the skaa, which was probably why he was so popular with the people.

"I speak bluntly," Penrod said, "for it is the truth. We are not in a position to bargain."

"I agree with Penrod," Philen said, jumping in. "If Elend wants to meet with Straff Venture, then I guess that's his right. As I understand it, kingship grants him authority to negotiate with foreign monarchs. However, we don't have to promise not to give Straff the city."

"Master Philen," Lord Penrod said. "I think you misjudged my intent. I said that giving up the city was inevitable—but that we should try to gain as much from it as possible. *That* means at least meeting with Straff to assess his disposition. Voting to give him the city now would be to play our hand too soon."

Elend looked up, looking hopeful for the first time since the discussion had first degenerated. "So, you support my proposal?" he asked.

"It is an awkward way to achieve the pause I think necessary," Penrod said. "But . . . seeing as how the army is already here, then I doubt we have time for anything else. So, yes, Your Majesty. I support your proposal."

Several other members of the Assembly nodded as Penrod spoke, as if giving the proposal consideration for the first time. *That Penrod has too much power,* Vin thought, eyes narrowing as she regarded the elderly statesman. *They listen to him more than they do Elend.*

"Should we vote, then?" one of the other Assemblymen asked.

And they did. Elend recorded votes as they moved down the line of Assemblymen. The eight noblemen—seven plus Elend—voted for the proposal, giving Penrod's opinion a great deal of weight. The eight skaa were mostly for it, and the merchants mostly against it. In the end, however, Elend got the two-thirds vote he needed.

"Proposal accepted," Elend said, making the final tally, looking a bit surprised. "The Assembly divests itself of the right to surrender the city until after the king has met with Straff Venture in official parlay."

Vin sat back in her seat, trying to decide what she thought of the vote. It was good that Elend had gotten his way, but the manner in which he'd achieved it bothered her.

Elend finally relinquished the lectern, sitting and letting a disgruntled Philen take the lead. The merchant read a proposal calling for a vote to turn control of city food stockpiles over to the merchants. However, this time Elend himself led the dissent, and the arguing began again. Vin watched with interest. Did Elend even realize how much like the others he acted while he was arguing against their proposals?

Elend and a few of the skaa Assemblymen managed to filibuster long enough that the lunch break arrived with no vote cast. The people in the audience stood, stretching, and Ham turned toward her. "Good meeting, eh?"

Vin just shrugged.

Ham chuckled. "We really have to do something about your ambivalence toward civic duty, kid."

"I already overthrew one government," Vin said. "I figure that takes care of my 'civic duty' for a while."

Ham smiled, though he kept a wary eye on the crowd—as did Vin. Now, with everyone moving about, would be the perfect time for an attempt on Elend's life. One person in particular caught her attention, and she frowned.

"Be back in a few seconds," she said to Ham, rising.

"You did the right thing, Lord Penrod," Elend said, standing beside the older nobleman, whispering quietly as break proceeded. "We need more time. You know what my father will do to this city if he takes it."

Lord Penrod shook his head. "I didn't do this for you, son. I did it because I wanted to make certain that fool Philen didn't hand the city over before the nobility extracted promises from your father about our rights to title."

"Now, see," Elend said, holding up a finger. "There has to be another way! The Survivor would never have given this city away without a fight."

Penrod frowned, and Elend paused, quietly cursing himself. The old lord was a traditionalist—quoting the Survivor at him would have little positive effect. Many of the noblemen felt threatened by Kelsier's influence with the skaa.

"Just think about it," Elend said, glancing to the side as Vin approached. She waved him away from the Assemblymen seats, and he excused himself. He crossed the stage, joining her. "What is it?" he asked quietly.

"Woman at the back," Vin said quietly, eyes suspicious. "Tall one, in the blue."

The woman in question wasn't hard to find; she wore a bright blue blouse and colorful red skirt. She was middle-aged, of lean build, and had her waist-length hair pulled back in a braid. She waited patiently as people moved about the room.

"What about her?" Elend asked.

"Terris," Vin said.

Elend paused. "You're sure?"

Vin nodded. "Those colors . . . that much jewelry. She's a Terriswoman for sure."

"So?"

"So, I've never met her," Vin said. "And she was watching you, just now."

"People watch me, Vin," Elend noted. "I *am* the king, after all. Besides, why should you have met her?"

"All of the other Terris people have come to meet me right after they enter the city," Vin said. "I killed the Lord Ruler; they see me as the one that freed their homeland. But, I don't recognize her. She hasn't ever come thank me."

Elend rolled his eyes, grabbing Vin by the shoulders and turning her away from the woman. "Vin, I feel it's my gentlemanly duty to tell you something."

Vin frowned. "What?"

"You're gorgeous."

Vin paused. "What does that have to do with anything?"

"Absolutely nothing," Elend said with a smile. "I'm just trying to distract you."

Slowly, Vin relaxed, smiling slightly.

"I don't know if anyone's ever told you this, Vin," Elend noted, "but you can be a bit paranoid at times."

She raised an eyebrow. "Oh?"

"I know it's hard to believe, but it's true. Now, I happen to find it rather charming, but do you honestly think that a *Terriswoman* would try to kill me?"

"Probably not," Vin admitted. "But, old habits . . ."

Elend smiled. Then, he glanced back at the Assemblymen, most of whom were speaking quietly in groups. They didn't mix. Noblemen spoke with noblemen, merchants with merchants, skaa workers with other skaa workers. They seemed so fragmented, so obstinate. The simplest proposals sometimes met with arguments that could take hours.

They need to give me more time! he thought. Yet, even as he thought, he realized the problem. More time for what? Penrod and Philen had accurately attacked his proposal.

The truth was, the entire city was in over its head. Nobody really knew what to do about a superior invading force, least of all Elend. He just knew that they couldn't give up. Not yet. There *had* to be a way to fight.

Vin was still looking to the side, out over the audience. Elend followed her gaze. "Still watching that Terriswoman?"

Vin shook her head. "Something else . . . something odd. Is that one of Clubs's messengers?"

Elend paused, turning. Indeed, several soldiers were working their way through the crowd, approaching the stage. At the back of the room, people had begun whispering and shuffling, and some were already moving quickly out of the chamber.

Elend felt Vin stiffen in anxiety, and fear stabbed him. *We're too late. The army has attacked.*

One of the soldiers finally reached the stage, and Elend rushed over. "What?" he asked. "Has Straff attacked?"

The soldier frowned, looking concerned. "No, my lord."

Elend sighed slightly. "What, then?"

"My lord, it's a second army. It just arrived outside the city."

Oddly, it was Alendi's simple ingenuousness that first led me to befriend him. I employed him as an assistant during his first months in the grand city.

11

FOR THE SECOND TIME IN two days, Elend stood atop the Luthadel city wall, studying an army that had come to invade his kingdom. Elend squinted against the red afternoon sunlight, but he was no Tineye; he couldn't make out details about the new arrival.

"Any chance they're here to help us?" Elend asked hopefully, looking toward Clubs, who stood beside him.

Clubs just scowled. "They fly Cett's banner. Remember him? Guy who sent eight Allomancer assassins to kill you two days back?"

Elend shivered in the chill autumn weather, glancing back out over the second army. It was making camp a good distance from Straff's army, close to the Luth-Davn Canal, which ran out the west side of the River Channerel. Vin stood at Elend's side, though Ham was off organizing things among the city guard. OreSeur, wearing the wolfhound's body, sat patiently on the wall walk beneath Vin.

"How did we miss their approach?" Elend asked.

"Straff," Clubs said. "This Cett came in from the same direction, and our scouts were focused on him. Straff probably knew about this other army a few days ago, but we had virtually no chance of seeing them."

Elend nodded.

"Straff is setting up a perimeter of soldiers, watching the enemy army," Vin said. "I doubt they're friendly to each other." She stood atop one of the sawtooth parapet crenels, feet positioned dangerously close to the wall's edge.

"Maybe they'll attack each other," Elend said hopefully.

Clubs snorted. "I doubt it. They're too evenly matched, though Straff might be a little stronger. I doubt Cett would take the chance by attacking him."

"Why come, then?" Elend asked.

Clubs shrugged. "Maybe he hoped he'd beat Venture to Luthadel, and get to take it first."

He spoke of the event—the capture of Luthadel—as if it were a given. Elend's stomach twisted as he leaned against the battlement, looking out through a merlon. Vin and the others were thieves and skaa Allomancers—outcasts who had been hunted for most of their lives. Perhaps they were accustomed to dealing with this pressure—this fear—but Elend was not.

How did they live with the lack of control, the sense of inevitability? Elend felt powerless. What could he do? Flee, and leave the city to fend for itself? That, of course, was not an option. But, confronted with not one, but two armies preparing to destroy his city and take his throne, Elend found it hard to keep his hands steady as he gripped the rough stone of the battlement.

Kelsier would have found a way out of this, he thought.

"There!" Vin's voice interrupted Elend's thoughts. "What's that?"

Elend turned. Vin was squinting, looking toward Cett's army, using tin to see things that were invisible to Elend's mundane eyes.

"Someone's leaving the army," Vin said. "Riding on horseback."

"Messenger?" Clubs asked.

"Maybe," Vin said. "He's riding pretty fast. . . ." She began to run from one stone tooth to the next, moving along the wall. Her kandra immediately followed, padding quietly across the wall beneath her.

Elend glanced at Clubs, who shrugged, and they began to follow. They caught up with Vin standing on the wall near one of the towers, watching the oncoming rider. Or, at least, Elend assumed that was what she watched—he still couldn't see what she had.

Allomancy, Elend thought, shaking his head. Why couldn't he have at least ended up with one power—even one of the weaker ones, like copper or iron?

Vin cursed suddenly, standing up straight. "Elend, that's *Breeze*!"

"What!" Elend said. "Are you sure?"

"Yes! He's being chased. Archers on horseback."

Clubs cursed, waving to a messenger. "Send riders! Cut off his pursuit!"

The messenger dashed away. Vin, however, shook her head. "They won't make it in time," she said, almost to herself. "The archers will catch him, or at least shoot him. Even I couldn't get there fast enough, not running. But, maybe . . ."

Elend frowned, looking up at her. "Vin, that's way too far to jump—even for you."

Vin glanced at him, smiled, then leaped off the wall.

Vin readied the fourteenth metal, duralumin. She had a reserve, but she didn't burn it—not yet. *I hope this works,* she thought, seeking an appropriate anchor. The tower beside her had a reinforced iron bulwark on the top—that would work.

She Pulled on the bulwark, yanking herself up to the top of the tower. She immediately jumped again, Pushing herself up and out, angling into the air away from the wall. She extinguished all of her metals except for steel and pewter.

Then, still Pushing against the bulwark, she burned duralumin.

A sudden force smashed against her. It was so powerful, she was certain that only an equally powerful flash of pewter held her body together. She blasted away from the keep, hurtling through the sky as if tossed by some giant, invisible god. The air rushed by so quickly that it roared, and the pressure of sudden acceleration made it difficult to think.

She floundered, trying to regain control. She had, fortunately, picked her trajectory well: she was shooting right toward Breeze and his pursuers. Whatever Breeze had done, it had been enough to make someone extremely angry—for there were a full two dozen men charging after him, arrows nocked.

Vin fell, her steel and pewter completely burned away in that single duralumin-fueled flash of power. She grabbed a metal vial off her belt, downing its contents. However, as she tossed the vial away, she suddenly felt an odd sense of vertigo. She wasn't accustomed to jumping during the day. It was strange to see the ground coming at her, strange not to have a mistcloak flapping behind her, strange not to have the mist. . . .

The lead rider lowered his bow, taking sight at Breeze. Neither appeared to have noticed Vin, swooping down like a bird of prey above.

Well, not exactly swooping. Plummeting.

Suddenly snapped back to the moment, Vin burned pewter and threw a coin toward the quickly approaching ground. She Pushed against the coin, using it to slow her momentum and to nudge her to the side. She hit right between Breeze and the archers, landing with a jarring crash, throwing up dust and dirt.

The archer released his arrow.

Even as Vin rebounded, dirt spraying around her, she reached out and Pushed herself back into the air straight at the arrow. Then she Pushed against it. The arrowhead ripped backward—throwing out shards of wood as it split its own shaft in midair—then smacked directly into the forehead of the archer who had released it.

The man toppled from his mount. Vin landed from her rebound. She reached out, Pushing against the horseshoes of the two beasts behind the leader, causing the animals to stumble. The Push threw Vin backward into the air, and cries of equine pain sounded amid the crash of bodies hitting the ground.

Vin continued to Push, flying along the road just a few feet above the ground, quickly catching up with Breeze. The portly man turned in shock, obviously stunned to find Vin hanging in the air beside his galloping horse, her clothing flapping in the wind of her passage. She winked at him, then reached out and Pulled against the armor of another rider.

She immediately lurched in the air. Her body protested the sudden shift in momentum, but she ignored the twist of pain. The man she Pulled against managed to stay in his saddle—until Vin smashed into him feet-first, throwing him backward.

She landed on the black earth, the rider tumbling to the ground beside her. A short distance away, the remaining riders finally reined in their mounts, coming to an abrupt stop a few feet away.

Kelsier probably would have attacked. There were a lot of them, true, but they were wearing armor and their horses were shod. Vin, however, was not Kelsier. She had delayed the riders long enough for Breeze to get away. That was enough.

Vin reached out and Pushed against one of the soldiers, throwing herself backward, leaving the riders to gather their wounded. The soldiers, however, promptly pulled out stone-tipped arrows and nocked their bows.

Vin hissed in frustration as the group took sight. *Well, friends,* she thought, *I suggest that you hang on tightly.*

She Pushed slightly against them all, then burned duralumin. The sudden crash of force was expected—the wrench in her chest, the massive flare in her stomach, the howling wind. What she didn't expect was the effect she'd have on her anchors. The blast of power scattered men and horses, throwing them into the air like leaves in the wind.

I'm going to have to be very careful with this, Vin thought, gritting her teeth and spinning herself in the air. Her steel and pewter were gone again, and she was forced to down her last metal vial. She'd have to start carrying more of those.

She hit the ground running, pewter keeping her from tripping despite her terrific speed. She slowed just slightly, letting the mounted Breeze catch up to her, then increased her pace to keep up with him. She dashed like a sprinter, letting pewter's strength and balance keep her upright as she paced the tiring horse. The beast eyed her as they ran, seeming to display a hint of animal frustration to see a human matching it.

They reached the city a few moments later. Breeze reined

in as the doors to Iron Gate began to open, but, rather than wait, Vin simply threw down a coin and Pushed, letting her forward momentum carry her toward the walls. As the gates swung open, she Pushed against their studs, and this second Push sent her sailing straight up. She just barely crested the battlements—passing between a pair of startled soldiers—before dropping over the other side. She landed in the courtyard, steadying herself with one hand against the cool stones, as Breeze entered through the gate.

Vin stood. Breeze patted his forehead with a handkerchief as he trotted his animal up beside her. He'd let his hair grow longer since she'd last seen him, and he kept it slicked back, its lower edges tickling his collar. It wasn't graying yet, though he was in his mid-forties. He wore no hat—it had probably blown free—but he had on one of his rich suits and silken vests. They were powdered with black ash from his hurried ride.

"Ah, Vin, my dear," Breeze said, breathing almost as deeply as his horse. "I must say, that was a timely arrival on your part. Impressively flamboyant as well. I do hate to force a rescue—but, well, if one is necessary, then it might as well happen with style."

Vin smiled as he climbed down from the horse—proving he was hardly the most adroit man in the square—and stablehands arrived to care for the beast. Breeze wiped his brow again as Elend, Clubs, and OreSeur scrambled down the steps to the courtyard. One of the aides must have finally found Ham, for he ran up through the courtyard.

"Breeze!" Elend said, approaching and clasping arms with the shorter man.

"Your Majesty," Breeze said. "You are in good health and good humor, I assume?"

"Health, yes," Elend said. "Humor . . . well, there *is* an army crouching just outside my city."

"Two armies, actually," Clubs grumbled as he hobbled up.

Breeze folded up his handkerchief. "Ah, and dear Master Cladent. Optimistic as always, I see."

Clubs snorted. To the side, OreSeur padded up to sit next to Vin.

"And Hammond," Breeze said, eyeing Ham, who was

smiling broadly. "I'd almost managed to delude myself into forgetting that *you* would be here when I returned."

"Admit it," Ham said. "You're glad to see me."

"See you, perhaps. *Hear* you, never. I had grown quite fond of my time spent away from your perpetual, pseudo-philosophical pratterings."

Ham just smiled a little broader.

"I'm glad to see you, Breeze," Elend said. "But your timing could have been a little better. I was hoping that you would be able to stop some of these armies from marching on us."

"*Stop* them?" Breeze asked. "Now, why would I want to do that, my dear man? I did, after all, just spend three months working to get Cett to march his army down here."

Elend paused, and Vin frowned to herself, standing just outside the group. Breeze looked rather pleased with himself—though that was, admittedly, rather common for him.

"So . . . Lord Cett's on our side?" Elend asked hopefully.

"Of course not," Breeze said. "He's here to ravage the city and steal your presumed atium supply."

"You," Vin said. "You're the one who has been spreading the rumors about the Lord Ruler's atium stash, aren't you?"

"Of course," Breeze said, eyeing Spook as the boy finally arrived at the gates.

Elend frowned. "But . . . why?"

"Look outside your walls, my dear man," Breeze said. "I knew that your father was going to march on Luthadel eventually—even *my* powers of persuasion wouldn't have been enough to dissuade him. So, I began spreading rumors in the Western Dominance, then made myself one of Lord Cett's advisors."

Clubs grunted. "Good plan. Crazy, but good."

"Crazy?" Breeze said. "*My* mental stability is no issue here, Clubs. The move was not crazy, but brilliant."

Elend looked confused. "Not to insult your brilliance, Breeze. But . . . how exactly is bringing a hostile army to our city a good idea?"

"It's basic negotiating strategy, my good man," Breeze

explained as a packman handed him his dueling cane, taken off the horse. Breeze used it to gesture westward, toward Lord Cett's army. "When there are only two participants in a negotiation, one is generally stronger than the other. That makes things very difficult for the weaker party—which, in this case, would have been us."

"Yes," Elend said, "but with three armies, we're still the weakest."

"Ah," Breeze said, holding up the cane, "but those other two parties are fairly even in strength. Straff is likely stronger, but Cett has a very large force. If either of those warlords risks attacking Luthadel, his army will suffer losses—enough losses that he won't be able to defend himself from the third army. To attack us is to expose oneself."

"And that makes this a standoff," Clubs said.

"Exactly," Breeze said. "Trust me, Elend my boy. In this case, two large, enemy armies are far better than a single large, enemy army. In a three-way negotiation, the weakest party actually has the most power—because his allegiance added to either of the other two will choose the eventual winner."

Elend frowned. "Breeze, we don't want to give our allegiance to *either* of these men."

"I realize that," Breeze said. "However, our opponents do not. By bringing a second army in, I've given us time to think. Both warlords thought they could get here first. Now that they've arrived at the same time, they'll have to reevaluate. I'm guessing we'll end up in an extended siege. A couple of months at least."

"That doesn't explain how we're going to get rid of them," Elend said.

Breeze shrugged. "I got them here—you get to decide what to do with them. And I'll tell you, it was no easy task to make Cett arrive on time. He was due to come in a full five days before Venture. Fortunately, a certain . . . malady spread through camp a few days ago. Apparently, someone poisoned the main water supply and gave the entire camp diarrhea."

Spook, standing behind Clubs, snickered.

"Yes," Breeze said, eyeing the boy. "I thought you might appreciate that. You still an unintelligible nuisance, boy?"

"Wassing the where of not," Spook said, smiling and slipping back into his Eastern street slang.

Breeze snorted. "You still make more sense than Hammond, half the time," he mumbled, turning to Elend. "So, isn't anyone going to send for a carriage to drive me back to the palace? I've been Soothing you ungrateful lot for the better part of five minutes—looking as tired and pathetic as I can—and not one of you has had the good graces to pity me!"

"You must be losing your touch," Vin said with a smile. Breeze was a Soother—an Allomancer who could burn brass to calm another person's emotions. A very skilled Soother—and Vin knew of none more skilled than Breeze—could dampen all of a person's emotions but a single one, effectively making them feel exactly as he wanted.

"Actually," Elend said, turning and looking back up at the wall, "I was hoping we could go back up on the wall and study the armies some more. If you spent time with Lord Cett's force, then you could probably tell us a lot about it."

"I can; I will; I am *not* going to climb those steps. Can't you see how tired I am, man?"

Ham snorted, clapping Breeze on the shoulder—and throwing up a puff of dust. "How can you be tired? Your poor horse did all the running."

"It was emotionally exhausting, Hammond," Breeze said, rapping the larger man's hand with his cane. "My departure was somewhat disagreeable."

"What happened, anyway?" Vin asked. "Did Cett find out you were a spy?"

Breeze looked embarrassed. "Let's just say that Lord Cett and I had a . . . falling-out."

"Caught you in bed with his daughter, eh?" Ham said, earning a chuckle from the group. Breeze was anything but a ladies' man. Despite his ability to play with emotions, he had expressed no interest in romance for as long as Vin had known him. Dockson had once noted that Breeze was just too focused on himself to consider such things.

Breeze simply rolled his eyes at Ham's comment. "Honestly, Hammond. I think your jokes are getting worse as you age. One too many hits on the head while sparring, I suspect."

Ham smiled, and Elend sent for a couple of carriages. While they waited, Breeze launched into a narrative of his travels. Vin glanced down at OreSeur. She still hadn't found a good opportunity to tell the rest of the crew about the body change. Perhaps now that Breeze was back, Elend would hold a conference with his inner circle. That would be a good time. She had to be quiet about it, since she wanted the palace staff to think that she'd sent OreSeur away.

Breeze continued his story, and Vin looked back at him, smiling. Not only was Breeze a natural orator, but he had a very subtle touch with Allomancy. She could barely feel his fingers on her emotions. Once, she had found his intrusions offensive, but she was growing to understand that touching people's emotions was simply part of who Breeze was. Just as a beautiful woman demanded attention by virtue of her face and figure, Breeze drew it by near unconscious use of his powers.

Of course, that didn't make him any less a scoundrel. Getting others to do as he wished was one of Breeze's main occupations. Vin just no longer resented him for using Allomancy to do it.

The carriage finally approached, and Breeze sighed in relief. As the vehicle pulled up, he eyed Vin, then nodded toward OreSeur. "What's that?"

"A dog," Vin said.

"Ah, blunt as ever, I see," Breeze said. "And, why is it that you now have a dog?"

"I gave it to her," Elend said. "She wanted one, so I bought it for her."

"And you chose a *wolfhound*?" Ham asked, amused.

"You've fought with her before, Ham," Elend said, laughing. "What would you have given her? A poodle?"

Ham chuckled. "No, I guess not. It fits, actually."

"Though it's almost as big as she is," Clubs added, regarding her with a squinty-eyed look.

Vin reached down, resting her hand on OreSeur's head.

Clubs did have a point; she'd chosen a big animal, even for a wolfhound. He stood over three feet tall at the shoulder—and Vin knew from experience how heavy that body was.

"Remarkably well-behaved for a wolfhound," Ham said, nodding. "You chose well, El."

"Regardless," Breeze said. "Can we please return to the palace? Armies and wolfhounds are all well and good, but I believe supper is more pressing at this point."

"So, why didn't we tell them about OreSeur?" Elend asked, as their carriage bumped its way back toward Keep Venture. The three of them had taken a carriage of their own, leaving the other four to follow in the other vehicle.

Vin shrugged. OreSeur sat on the seat across from her and Elend, quietly watching the conversation. "I'll tell them eventually," Vin said. "A busy city square didn't seem the right place for the revelation."

Elend smiled. "Keeping secrets is a hard habit to break, eh?"

Vin flushed. "I'm not keeping him secret, I'm just . . ." She trailed off, looking down.

"Don't feel bad, Vin," Elend said. "You lived a long time on your own, without anyone to trust. Nobody expects you to change overnight."

"It hasn't been one night, Elend," she said. "It's been two years."

Elend laid a hand on her knee. "You're getting better. The others talk about how much you've changed."

Vin nodded. *Another man would be afraid that I'm keeping secrets from him, too. Elend just tries to make me feel less guilty.* He was a better man than she deserved.

"Kandra," Elend said, "Vin says you do well at keeping up with her."

"Yes, Your Majesty," OreSeur said. "These bones, though distasteful, are well equipped for tracking and quick movement."

"And if she gets hurt?" Elend said. "Will you be able to pull her to safety?"

"Not with any speed, Your Majesty. I will, however, be

able to go for aid. These bones have many limitations, but I will do my best to fulfill the Contract."

Elend must have caught Vin's raised eyebrow, for he chuckled. "He'll do as he says, Vin."

"The Contract is everything, Mistress," OreSeur said. "It demands more than simple service. It requires diligence and devotion. It *is* the kandra. By serving it, we serve our people."

Vin shrugged. The group fell silent, Elend pulling a book from his pocket, Vin leaning against him. OreSeur lay down, filling the entire seat opposite the humans. Eventually, the carriage rolled into the Venture courtyard, and Vin found herself looking forward to a warm bath. As they were climbing from the carriage, however, a guard rushed up to Elend. Tin allowed Vin to hear what the man said, even though he spoke before she could close the distance.

"Your Majesty," the guard whispered, "our messenger reached you, then?"

"No," Elend said with a frown as Vin walked over. The soldier gave her a look, but continued speaking; the soldiers all knew that Vin was Elend's primary bodyguard and confidant. Still, the man looked oddly concerned when he saw her.

"We . . . ah, don't want to be intrusive," the soldier said. "That's why we've kept this quiet. We were just wondering if . . . everything is all right." He looked at Vin as he spoke.

"What is this about?" Elend asked.

The guard turned back toward the king. "The corpse in Lady Vin's room."

The "corpse" was actually a skeleton. One completely picked clean, without a hint of blood—or even tissue—marring its shiny white surfaces. A good number of the bones were broken, however.

"I'm sorry, Mistress," OreSeur said, speaking low enough that only she could hear. "I assumed that you were going to dispose of these."

Vin nodded. The skeleton was, of course, the one OreSeur had been using before she gave him the animal body.

Finding the door unlocked—Vin's usual sign that she wanted a room cleaned—the maids had entered. Vin had stashed the bones in a basket, intending to deal with them later. Apparently, the maids had decided to check and see what was in the basket, and been somewhat surprised.

"It's all right, Captain," Elend said to the young guard—Captain Demoux, second-in-command of the palace guard. Despite the fact that Ham shunned uniforms, this man seemed to take great pride in keeping his own uniform very neat and smart.

"You did well by keeping this quiet," Elend said. "We knew about these bones already. They aren't a reason for concern."

Demoux nodded. "We figured it was something intentional." He didn't look at Vin as he spoke.

Intentional, Vin thought. *Great. I wonder what this man thinks I did.* Few skaa knew what kandra were, and Demoux wouldn't know what to make of remains like these.

"Could you dispose of these quietly for me, Captain?" Elend asked, nodding to the bones.

"Of course, Your Majesty," the guard said.

He probably assumes I ate the person or something, Vin thought with a sigh. *Sucked the flesh right off his bones.*

Which, actually, wasn't that far from the truth.

"Your Majesty," Demoux said. "Would you like us to dispose of the other body as well?"

Vin froze.

"Other one?" Elend asked slowly.

The guard nodded. "When we found this skeleton, we brought in some dogs to sniff about. The dogs didn't turn up any killers, but they did find another body. Just like this one—a set of bones, completely cleaned of flesh."

Vin and Elend shared a look. "Show us," Elend said.

Demoux nodded, and led them out of the room, giving a few whispered orders to one of his men. The four of them—three humans and one kandra—traveled a short distance down the palace hallway, toward a less used section of visitors' chambers. Demoux dismissed a soldier standing at a particular door, then led them inside.

"This body wasn't in a basket, Your Majesty," Demoux

said. "It was stuffed in a back closet. We'd probably never have found it without the dogs—they picked up the scent pretty easily, though I can't see how. These corpses are completely clean of flesh."

And there it was. Another skeleton, like the first, sitting piled beside a bureau. Elend glanced at Vin, then turned to Demoux. "Would you excuse us, Captain?"

The young guard nodded, walking from the room and closing the door.

"Well?" Elend said, turning to OreSeur.

"I do not know where this came from," the kandra said.

"But it is another kandra-eaten corpse," Vin said.

"Undoubtedly, Mistress," OreSeur said. "The dogs found it because of the particular scent our digestive juices leave on recently excreted bones."

Elend and Vin shared a look.

"However," OreSeur said, "it is probably not what you think. This man was probably killed far from here."

"What do you mean?"

"They are discarded bones, Your Majesty," OreSeur said. "The bones a kandra leaves behind . . ."

"After he finds a new body," Vin finished.

"Yes, Mistress," OreSeur said.

Vin looked at Elend, who frowned. "How long ago?" he asked. "Maybe the bones were left a year before, by my father's kandra."

"Perhaps, Your Majesty," OreSeur said. But he sounded hesitant. He padded over, sniffing at the bones. Vin picked one up herself, holding it to her nose. With tin, she easily picked out a sharp scent that reminded her of bile.

"It's very strong," she said, glancing at OreSeur.

He nodded. "These bones haven't been here long, Your Majesty. A few hours at most. Perhaps even less."

"Which means we have another kandra somewhere in the palace," Elend said, looking a bit sick. "One of my staff has been . . . eaten and replaced."

"Yes, Your Majesty," OreSeur said. "There is no way to tell from these bones whom it could be, since these are the discards. The kandra would have taken the new bones, eating their flesh and wearing their clothing."

Elend nodded, standing. He met Vin's eyes, and she knew he was thinking the same thing she was. It was possible that a member of the palace staff had been replaced, which would mean a slight breach in security. There was a far more dangerous possibility, however.

Kandra were incomparable actors; OreSeur had imitated Lord Renoux so perfectly that even people who'd known him had been fooled. Such talent could have been used for the imitation of a maid or a servant. However, if an enemy had wanted to get a spy into Elend's closed meetings, he would need to replace a person far more important.

It would be someone that we haven't seen during the last few hours, Vin thought, dropping the bone. She, Elend, and OreSeur had been on the wall for most of the afternoon and evening—ever since the end of the Assembly meeting—but the city and palace had been in chaos since the second army had arrived. The messengers had had trouble finding Ham, and she still wasn't certain where Dockson was. In fact, she hadn't seen Clubs until he'd joined her and Elend on the wall just a bit before. And Spook had been the last to arrive.

Vin looked down at the pile of bones, feeling a sickening sense of unease. There was a very good chance that someone in their core team—a member of Kelsier's former band—was now an impostor.

THE END OF PART ONE

PART TWO

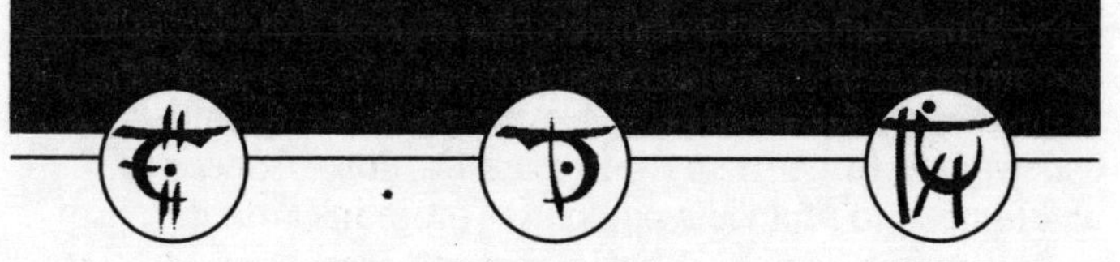

GHOSTS IN THE MIST

It wasn't until years later that I became convinced that Alendi was the Hero of Ages. Hero of Ages: the one called Rabzeen in Khlennium, the Anamnesor.

Savior.

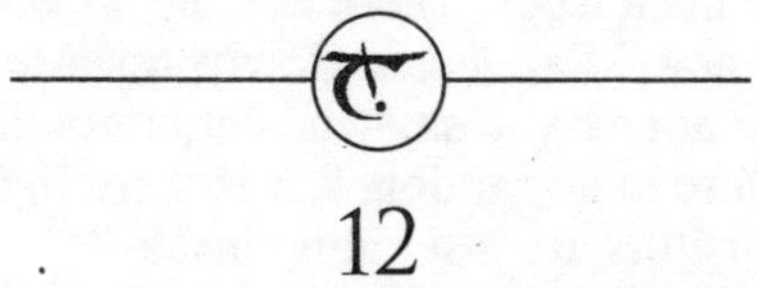

12

A FORTRESS SAT IN THE misty murk of evening.

It rested at the bottom of a large depression in the land. The steep-sided, craterlike valley was so wide that even in daylight Sazed would barely have been able to see the other side. In the oncoming darkness, obscured by mist, the far edge of the massive hole was only a deep shadow.

Sazed knew very little about tactics and strategy; though his metalminds held dozens of books on the subjects, he had forgotten their contents in order to create the stored records. The little he did know told him that this fortress—the Conventical of Seran—was not very defensible. It relinquished the high ground, and the crater sides would provide an excellent location for siege engines to pelt rocks down at the walls.

This fortress, however, had not been built to defend against enemy soldiers. It had been built to provide solitude. The crater made it difficult to find, for a slight rise in the land around the crater's lip made it practically invisible until one drew near. No roads or paths marked the way, and travelers would have great trouble getting down the sheer sides.

The Inquisitors did not want visitors.

"Well?" Marsh asked.

He and Sazed stood on the crater's northern lip, before a drop of several hundred feet. Sazed tapped his vision tinmind, drawing forth some of the eyesight he had stored within it. The edges of his vision fuzzed, but things directly in front of him seemed to grow much closer. He tapped a little more sight, ignoring the nausea that came from compounding so much vision.

The increased eyesight let him study the Conventical as if he stood before it. He could see each notch in the dark stone walls—flat, broad, imposing. He could discern each bit of rust on the large steel plates that hung bolted into outside stones of the wall. He could see each lichen-encrusted corner and ash-stained ledge. There were no windows.

"I do not know," Sazed said slowly, releasing his vision tinmind. "It is not easy to say whether or not the fortress is inhabited. There is no motion, nor is there light. But, perhaps the Inquisitors are just hiding inside."

"No," Marsh said, his stiff voice uncomfortably loud in the evening air. "They are gone."

"Why would they leave? This is a place of great strength, I think. Poor defense against an army, but a great defense against the chaos of the times."

Marsh shook his head. "They are gone."

"How are you so certain?"

"I do not know."

"Where did they go, then?"

Marsh looked at him, then turned and glanced over his shoulder. "North."

"Toward Luthadel?" Sazed asked, frowning.

"Among other things," Marsh said. "Come. I do not know if they will return, but we should exploit this opportunity."

Sazed nodded. This was why they had come, after all. Still, a part of him hesitated. He was a man of books and genteel service. Traveling the countryside to visit villages was enough removed from his experience to be discomforting. Infiltrating the Inquisitor stronghold . . .

Marsh obviously didn't care about his companion's inner struggles. The Inquisitor turned and began to walk along the rim of the crater. Sazed threw his pack over his shoulder, then followed. They eventually arrived at a cage-like contraption, obviously meant to be lowered down to the bottom by ropes and pulleys. The cage sat locked in place at the top ledge, and Marsh stopped at its side, but did not enter.

"What?" Sazed asked.

"The pulley system," Marsh said. "The cage is meant to be lowered by men holding it from below."

Sazed nodded, realizing this was true. Marsh stepped forward and threw a lever. The cage fell. Ropes began to smoke, and pulleys squealed as the massive cage plummeted toward the chasm floor. A muted crash echoed against the rocks.

If there is anyone down there, Sazed thought, *they now know we're here.*

Marsh turned toward him, the heads of his eye-spikes glistening slightly in the failing sunlight. "Follow however you wish," he said. Then, he tied off the counterrope and began to climb down the ropes.

Sazed stepped up to the platform's edge, watching Marsh shimmy down the dangling rope into the shadowed, misty abyss. Then, Sazed knelt and opened his pack. He unhooked the large metal bracers around his upper and lower arms—his core copperminds. They contained the memories of a Keeper, the stored knowledge of centuries past. He reverently placed them to the side, then pulled a pair of much smaller bracelets—one iron, one pewter—from the pack. Metalminds for a warrior.

Did Marsh understand how unskilled Sazed was in this area? Amazing strength did not a warrior make. Regardless, Sazed snapped the two bracelets around his ankles. Next, he pulled out two rings—tin and copper. These he slipped on his fingers.

He closed the pack and threw it over his shoulder, then picked up his core copperminds. He carefully located a good hiding place—a secluded hollow between two boulders—and slid them inside. Whatever happened below, he didn't want to risk them being taken and destroyed by the Inquisitors.

In order to fill a coppermind with memories, Sazed had

listened to another Keeper recite his entire collection of histories, facts, and stories. Sazed had memorized each sentence, then shoved those memories into the copper-mind for later retrieval. Sazed remembered very little of the actual experience—but he could draw forth any of the books or essays he wished, placing them back into his mind, gaining the ability to recollect them as crisply as when he'd first memorized them. He just had to have the bracers on.

Being without his copperminds made him anxious. He shook his head, walking back over to the platform. Marsh was moving very quickly down toward the chasm floor; like all Inquisitors, he had the powers of a Mistborn. Though how he had gotten those powers—and how he managed to live despite the spikes that had been driven directly through his brain—was a mystery. Marsh had never answered Sazed's questions on the subject.

Sazed called down, drawing Marsh's attention, then held up his pack and dropped it. Marsh reached out, and the pack lurched, Pulled by its metals into Marsh's hand. The Inquisitor threw it over his shoulder before continuing his descent.

Sazed nodded thankfully, then stepped off the platform. As he began to fall, he mentally reached into his ironmind, searching for the power he had stored therein. Filling a metalmind always had a cost: in order to store up sight, Sazed had been forced to spend weeks with poor eyesight. During that time, he had worn a tin bracelet, stowing away the excess sight for later use.

Iron was a bit different from the others. It didn't store up sight, strength, endurance—or even memories. It stored something completely different: weight.

This day, Sazed didn't tap the power stored inside the ironmind; that would have made him more heavy. Instead, he began to fill the ironmind, letting it suck away his weight. He felt a familiar sense of lightness—a sense that his own body wasn't pressing upon itself as forcefully.

His fall slowed. The Terris philosophers had much to say on using an ironmind. They explained that the power didn't actually change a person's bulk or size—it just somehow changed the way that the ground pulled against them. Sazed's fall didn't slow because of his decrease in weight—it slowed because he suddenly had a relatively large amount of surface exposed to the wind of his fall, and a lighter body to go along with it.

Regardless of the scientific reasons, Sazed didn't fall as quickly. The thin metal bracelets on his legs were the heaviest things on his body, and they kept him pointed feet-downward. He held out his arms and bent his body slightly, letting the wind push against him. His descent was not terribly slow—not like that of a leaf or a feather. However, he didn't plummet either. Instead, he fell in a controlled—almost leisurely—manner. Clothing flapping, arms outspread, he passed Marsh, who watched with a curious expression.

As he approached the ground, Sazed tapped his pewtermind, drawing forth a tiny bit of strength to prepare. He hit the ground—but, because his body was so light, there was very little shock. He barely even needed to bend his knees to absorb the force of impact.

He stopped filling the ironmind, released his pewter, and waited quietly for Marsh. Beside him, the carrying cage lay in shambles. Sazed noticed several broken iron shackles with discomfort. Apparently, some of those who had visited the Conventical had not come by choice.

By the time Marsh neared the bottom, the mists were thick in the air. Sazed had lived with them all of his life, and had never before felt uncomfortable in them. Yet, now he half expected the mists to begin choking him. To kill him, as they seemed to have done to old Jed, the unfortunate farmer whose death Sazed had investigated.

Marsh dropped the last ten feet or so, landing with an Allomancer's increased agility. Even after spending so much time with Mistborn, Sazed was impressed with Allomancy's gifts. Of course, he'd never been jealous of them—not really. True, Allomancy was better in a fight; but it could not expand the mind, giving one access to the dreams, hopes, and beliefs of a thousand years of culture. It could not give the knowledge to treat a wound, or help teach a poor village to use modern fertilization techniques.

The metalminds of Feruchemy weren't flamboyant, but they had a far more lasting value to society.

Besides, Sazed knew a few tricks with Feruchemy that were bound to surprise even the most prepared warrior.

Marsh handed him the pack. "Come."

Sazed nodded, shouldering the pack and following the Inquisitor across the rocky ground. Walking next to Marsh was odd, for Sazed wasn't accustomed to being around people who were as tall as he was. Terrismen were tall by nature, and Sazed even more so: his arms and legs were a bit too long for his body, a medical condition brought on by his having been castrated as a very young boy. Though the Lord Ruler was dead, Terris culture would long feel the effects of his stewardship and breeding programs—the methods by which he had tried to breed Feruchemical powers out of the Terris people.

The Conventical of Seran loomed in the darkness, looking even more ominous now that Sazed stood within the crater. Marsh strode right up to the front doors, and Sazed followed behind. He wasn't afraid, not really. Fear had never been a strong motivator in Sazed's life. However, he did worry. There were so few Keepers left; if he died, that was one fewer person who could travel, restoring lost truths and teaching the people.

Not that I'm doing such at the moment anyway. . . .

Marsh regarded the massive steel doors. Then he threw his weight against one, obviously burning pewter to enhance his strength. Sazed joined him, pushing hard. The door did not budge.

Regretting the expenditure of power, Sazed reached into his pewtermind and tapped strength. He used far more than he had when landing, and his muscles immediately increased in size. Unlike Allomancy, Feruchemy often had direct effects on a person's body. Beneath his robes, Sazed gained the bulk and build of a lifetime warrior, easily becoming twice as strong as he had been a moment earlier. With their combined effort, the two of them managed to push the door open.

It did not creak. It slid slowly, but evenly, inward, exposing a long, dark hallway.

Sazed released his pewtermind, reverting to his normal self. Marsh strode into the Conventical, his feet kicking up the mist that had begun to pour through the open doorway.

"Marsh?" Sazed asked.

The Inquisitor turned.

"I won't be able to see inside there."

"Your Feruchemy . . ."

Sazed shook his head. "It can let me see better in darkness, but only if there's some light to begin with. In addition, tapping that much sight would drain my tinmind in a matter of minutes. I'll need a lantern."

Marsh paused, then nodded. He turned into the darkness, quickly disappearing from Sazed's view.

So, Sazed thought, *Inquisitors don't need light to see.* It was to be expected: the spikes filled Marsh's entire sockets, completely destroying the eyeballs. Whatever strange power allowed Inquisitors to see, it apparently worked just as well in pure darkness as it did in daylight.

Marsh returned a few moments later, carrying a lamp. From the chains Sazed had seen on the descent cage, Sazed suspected that the Inquisitors had kept a sizable group of slaves and servants to attend their needs. If that was the case, where had the people gone? Had they fled?

Sazed lit the lamp with a flint from his pack. The lamp's ghostly light illuminated a stark, daunting hallway. He stepped into the Conventical, holding the lamp high, and began to fill the small copper ring on his finger, the process transforming it into a coppermind.

"Large rooms," he whispered, "without adornment." He didn't really need to say the words, but he'd found that speaking helped him form distinct memories. He could then place them into the coppermind.

"The Inquisitors, obviously, had a fondness for steel," he continued. "This is not surprising, considering that their religion was often referred to as the Steel Ministry. The walls are hung with massive steel plates, which bear no rust, unlike the ones outside. Many of those here are not completely smooth, but instead crafted with some interesting patterns etched . . . almost *buffed* . . . into their surfaces."

Marsh frowned, turning toward him. "What are you doing?"

Sazed held up his right hand, showing the copper ring. "I must make an account of this visit. I will need to repeat this experience back to other Keepers when the opportunity presents itself. There is much to be learned from this place, I think."

Marsh turned away. "You should not care about the Inquisitors. They are not worthy of your record."

"It isn't a matter of worthiness, Marsh," Sazed said, holding up his lamp to study a square pillar. "Knowledge of all religions is valuable. I must make certain these things persist."

Sazed regarded the pillar for a moment, then closed his eyes and formed an image of it inside his head, which he then added to the coppermind. Visual memories, however, were less useful than spoken words. Visualizations faded very quickly once taken out of a coppermind, suffering from the mind's distortion. Plus, they could not be passed to other Keepers.

Marsh didn't respond to Sazed's comment about religion; he just turned and walked deeper into the building. Sazed followed at a slower pace, speaking to himself, recording the words in his coppermind. It was an interesting experience. As soon as he spoke, he felt the thoughts sucked from his mind, leaving behind a blank hollowness. He had difficulty remembering the specifics of what he had just been saying. However, once he was done filling his coppermind, he would be able to tap those memories later and know them with crisp clarity.

"The room is tall," he said. "There are a few pillars, and they are also wrapped in steel. They are blocky and square, rather than round. I get a sense that this place was created by a people who cared little for subtlety. They ignored small details in favor of broad lines and full geometries.

"As we move beyond the main entryway, this architectural theme continues. There are no paintings on the walls, nor are there wooden adornments or tile floors. Instead, there are only the long, broad hallways with their harsh lines and reflective surfaces. The floor is constructed of steel squares, each a few feet across. They are . . . cold to the touch.

"It is strange not to see the tapestries, stained-glass windows, and sculpted stones that are so common in Luthadel's architecture. There are no spires or vaultings here. Just squares and rectangles. Lines . . . so many lines. Nothing here is soft. No carpet, no rugs, no windows. It is a place for people who see the world differently from ordinary men.

"Marsh walked straight down this massive hallway, as if oblivious to its decor. I will follow him, then come back to record more later. He seems to be following something . . . something I cannot sense. Perhaps it is . . ."

Sazed trailed off as he stepped around a bend and saw Marsh standing in the doorway of a large chamber. The lamplight flickered unevenly as Sazed's arm quivered.

Marsh had found the servants.

They had been dead long enough that Sazed hadn't noticed the scent until he had come close. Perhaps that was what Marsh had been following; the senses of a man burning tin could be quite acute.

The Inquisitors had done their work thoroughly. These were the remnants of a slaughter. The room was large, but had only one exit, and the bodies were piled high near the back, killed by what looked like harsh sword or axe strokes. The servants had huddled up against the back wall as they died.

Sazed turned away.

Marsh, however, remained in the doorway. "There is a bad air about this place," he finally said.

"You have only just noticed that?" Sazed asked.

Marsh turned, glancing at him, demanding his gaze. "We should not spend much time here. There are stairs at the end of the hallway behind us. I will go up—that is where the Inquisitors' quarters will be. If the information I seek is here, I will find it there. You may stay, or you may descend. However, do not follow me."

Sazed frowned. "Why?"

"I must be alone here. I cannot explain it. I do not care if you witness Inquisitor atrocities. I just . . . do not wish to be with you when you do."

Sazed lowered his lamp, turning its light away from the horrific scene. "Very well."

Marsh turned, brushing past Sazed and disappearing into the dark hallway. And Sazed was alone.

He tried not to think about that very much. He returned to the main hallway, describing the slaughter to his coppermind before giving a more detailed explanation of the architecture and the art—if, indeed, that was what the different patterns on the wall plates could be called.

As he worked—his voice echoing quietly against the rigid architecture, his lamp a weak drop of light reflected in steel—his eyes were drawn toward the back of the hallway. There was a pool of darkness there. A stairwell, leading down.

Even as he turned back to his description of one of the wall mounts, he knew that he would eventually find himself walking toward that darkness. It was the same as ever—the curiosity, the *need* to understand the unknown. This sense had driven him as a Keeper, had led him to Kelsier's company. His search for truths could never be completed, but neither could it be ignored. So, he eventually turned and approached the stairwell, his own whispering voice his only companion.

"The stairs are akin to what I saw in the hallway. They are broad and expansive, like the steps leading up to a temple or palace. Except, these go down, into darkness. They are large, likely cut from stone and then lined with steel. They are tall, meant for a determined stride.

"As I walk, I wonder what secrets the Inquisitors deemed worthy of hiding below the earth, in the basement of their stronghold. This entire building is a secret. What did they do here, in these massive hallways and open, empty rooms?

"The stairwell ends in another large, square room. I've noticed something—there are no doors in the doorways here. Each room is open, visible to those outside. As I walk, peeking into the rooms beneath the earth, I find cavernous chambers with few furnishings. No libraries, no lounges. Several contain large metal blocks that could be altars.

"There is . . . something different here in this last room, at the back of the main landing. I'm not certain what to make of it. A torture chamber, perhaps? There are tables—metal tables—set into the floor. They are bloody, though there are no corpses. Blood flakes and powders at my feet—a lot of men have died in this room, I think. There don't appear to be torture implements beyond . . .

"Spikes. Like the ones in Inquisitor eyes. Massive, heavy things—like the spikes one might pound into the ground with a very large mallet. Some are tipped with blood, though I don't think I'll handle those. These other ones . . . yes, they look indistinguishable from the ones in Marsh's eyes. Yet, some are of different metals."

Sazed set the spike down on a table, metal clinking against metal. He shivered, scanning the room again. A place to make new Inquisitors, perhaps? He had a sudden horrific vision of the creatures—once only several dozen in number—having swelled their ranks during their months sequestered in the Conventical.

But that didn't seem right. They were a secretive, exclusive bunch. Where would they have found enough men worthy of joining their ranks? Why not make Inquisitors from the servants above, rather than just killing them?

Sazed had always suspected that a man had to be an Allomancer to be changed into an Inquisitor. Marsh's own experience substantiated that premise: Marsh had been a Seeker, a man who could burn bronze, before his transformation. Sazed looked again at the blood, the spikes, and the tables, and decided he wasn't certain that he wanted to know how one made a new Inquisitor.

Sazed was about to leave the room when his lamp revealed something at the back. Another doorway.

He moved forward, trying to ignore the dried blood at his feet, and entered a chamber that didn't seem to match the rest of the Conventical's daunting architecture. It was cut directly into the stone, and it twisted down into a very small stairwell. Curious, Sazed walked down the set of worn stone steps. For the first time since entering the building, he felt cramped, and he had to stoop as he reached the bottom of the stairwell and entered a small chamber. He stood up straight, and held up his lamp to reveal . . .

A wall. The room ended abruptly, and his light sparkled off the wall. It held a steel plate, like those above. This one was a good five feet across, and nearly as tall. And it bore writing. Suddenly interested, Sazed set down his pack and stepped forward, raising his lamp to read the top words on the wall.

The text was in Terris.

It was an old dialect, certainly, but one that Sazed could make out even without his language coppermind. His hand trembled as he read the words.

I write these words in steel, for anything not set in metal cannot be trusted.

I have begun to wonder if I am the only sane man remaining. Can the others not see? They have been waiting so long for their hero to come—the one spoken of in Terris prophecies—that they quickly jump between conclusions, presuming that each story and legend applies to this one man.

My brethren ignore the other facts. They cannot connect the other strange things that are happening. They are deaf to my objections and blind to my discoveries.

Perhaps they are right. Perhaps I am mad, or jealous, or simply daft. My name is Kwaan. Philosopher, scholar, traitor. I am the one who discovered Alendi, and I am the one who first proclaimed him to be the Hero of Ages. I am the one who started this all.

And I am the one who betrayed him, for I now know that he must never be allowed to complete his quest.

"Sazed."

Sazed jumped, nearly dropping the lamp. Marsh stood in the doorway behind him. Imperious, discomforting, and so dark. He fit this place, with its lines and hardness.

"The upstairs quarters are empty," Marsh said. "This trip

has been a waste—my brethren took anything of use with them."

"Not a waste, Marsh," Sazed said, turning back to the plate of text. He hadn't read all of it; he hadn't even gotten close. The script was written in a tight, cramped hand, its etchings coating the wall. The steel had preserved the words despite their obvious age. Sazed's heart beat a little faster.

This was a fragment of text from before the Lord Ruler's reign. A fragment written by a Terris philosopher—a holy man. Despite ten centuries of searching, the Keepers had never fulfilled the original goal of their creation: they had never discovered their own Terris religion.

The Lord Ruler had squelched Terris religious teachings soon after his rise to power. His persecution of the Terris people—his own people—had been the most complete of his long reign, and the Keepers had never found more than vague fragments regarding what their own people had once believed.

"I have to copy this down, Marsh," Sazed said, reaching for his pack. Taking a visual memory wouldn't work—no man could stare at a wall of so much text, then remember the words. He could, perhaps, read them into his coppermind. However, he wanted a physical record, one that perfectly preserved the structure of lines and punctuation.

Marsh shook his head. "We will not stay here. I do not think we should even have come."

Sazed paused, looking up. Then he pulled several large sheets of paper from his pack. "Very well, then," he said. "I'll take a rubbing. That will be better anyway, I think. It will let me see the text exactly as it was written."

Marsh nodded, and Sazed got out his charcoal.

This discovery . . . he thought with excitement. *This will be like Rashek's logbook. We are getting close!*

However, even as he began the rubbing—his hands moving carefully and precisely—another thought occurred to him. With a text like this in his possession, his sense of duty would no longer let him wander the villages. He had to return to the north to share what he had found, lest he die and this text be lost. He had to go to Terris.

Or . . . to Luthadel. From there he could send messages north. He had a valid excuse to get back to the center of action, to see the other crewmembers again.

Why did that make him feel even more guilty?

When I finally had the realization—finally connected all of the signs of the Anticipation to Alendi—I was so excited. Yet, when I announced my discovery to the other Worldbringers, I was met with scorn.

Oh, how I wish that I had listened to them.

13

MIST SWIRLED AND SPUN, LIKE monochrome paints running together on a canvas. Light died in the west, and night came of age.

Vin frowned. "Does it seem like the mists are coming earlier?"

"Earlier?" OreSeur asked in his muffled voice. The kandra wolfhound sat next to her on the rooftop.

Vin nodded. "Before, the mists didn't start to appear until after it grew dark, right?"

"It is dark, Mistress."

"But they're already here—they started to gather when the sun was barely beginning to set."

"I don't see that it matters, Mistress. Perhaps the mists are simply like other weather patterns—they vary, sometimes."

"Doesn't it even seem a little strange to you?"

"I will think it strange if you wish me to, Mistress," OreSeur said.

"That isn't what I meant."

"I apologize, Mistress," OreSeur said. "Tell me what you *do* mean, and I will be certain to believe as commanded."

Vin sighed, rubbing her brow. *I wish Sazed were back . . .* she thought. It was an idle wish, however. Even if Sazed were in Luthadel, he wouldn't be her steward. The Terrismen no longer called any man master. She'd have to make do with OreSeur. The kandra, at least, could provide information that Sazed could not—assuming she could get it out of him.

"We need to find the impostor," Vin said. "The one who . . . replaced someone."

"Yes, Mistress," OreSeur said.

Vin sat back in the mists, reclining on a slanted rooftop, resting her arms back on the tiles. "Then, I need to know more about you."

"Me, Mistress?"

"Kandra in general. If I'm going to find this impostor, I need to know how he thinks, need to understand his motivations."

"His motivations will be simple, Mistress," OreSeur said. "He will be following his Contract."

"What if he's acting without a Contract?"

OreSeur shook his canine head. "Kandra always have a Contract. Without one, they are not allowed to enter human society."

"Never?" Vin asked.

"Never."

"And what if this is some kind of rogue kandra?" Vin said.

"Such a thing does not exist," OreSeur said firmly.

Oh? Vin thought skeptically. However, she let the matter drop. There was little reason for a kandra to infiltrate the palace on his own; it was far more likely that one of Elend's enemies had sent the creature. One of the warlords, perhaps, or maybe the obligators. Even the other nobility in the city would have had good reason to spy on Elend.

"Okay," Vin said. "The kandra is a spy, sent to gather information for another human."

"Yes."

"But," Vin said, "if he did take the body of someone in the palace, he didn't kill them himself. Kandra can't kill humans, right?"

OreSeur nodded. "We are all bound by that rule."

"So, somebody snuck into the palace, murdered a member of the staff, then had their kandra take the body." She paused, trying to work through the problem. "The most dangerous possibilities—the crewmembers—should be considered first. Fortunately, since the killing happened yesterday, we can eliminate Breeze, who was outside the city at the time."

OreSeur nodded.

"We can eliminate Elend as well," Vin said. "He was with us on the wall yesterday."

"That still leaves the majority of the crew, Mistress."

Vin frowned, sitting back. She'd tried to establish solid alibis for Ham, Dockson, Clubs, and Spook. However, all of them had had at least a few hours unaccounted for. Long enough for a kandra to digest them and take their place.

"All right," she said. "So, how do I find the impostor? How can I tell him from other people?"

OreSeur sat quietly in the mists.

"There has to be a way," Vin said. "His imitation can't be perfect. Would cutting him work?"

OreSeur shook his head. "Kandra replicate a body perfectly, Mistress—blood, flesh, skin, and muscle. You have seen that when I split my skin."

Vin sighed, standing and stepping up on the tip of the peaked rooftop. The mists were already full, and the night was quickly becoming black. She began to walk idly back and forth on the ridge, an Allomancer's balance keeping her from falling.

"Perhaps I can just see who isn't acting oddly," she said. "Are most kandra as good at imitation as you are?"

"Among kandra, my own skill is average. Some are worse, others are better."

"But no actor is perfect," Vin said.

"Kandra don't often make mistakes, Mistress," OreSeur said. "But, this is probably your best method. Be warned, however—he could be anyone. My kind are very skilled."

Vin paused. *It's not Elend,* she told herself forcibly. *He was with me all day yesterday.* Except in the morning.

Too long, she decided. *We were on the wall for hours, and those bones were freshly expelled. Besides, I'd know if it were him . . . wouldn't I?*

She shook her head. "There has to be another way. Can I spot a kandra with Allomancy somehow?"

OreSeur didn't answer immediately. She turned toward him in the darkness, studying his canine face. "What?" she asked.

"These are not things we speak of with outsiders."

Vin sighed. "Tell me anyway."

"Do you command me to speak?"

"I don't really care to command you in anything."

"Then I may leave?" OreSeur asked. "You do not wish to command me, so our Contract is dissolved?"

"That isn't what I meant," Vin said.

OreSeur frowned—a strange expression to see on a dog's face. "It would be easier for me if you would try to say what you mean, Mistress."

Vin gritted her teeth. "Why is it you're so hostile?"

"I'm not hostile, Mistress. I am your servant, and will do as you command. That is part of the Contract."

"Sure. Are you like this with all of your masters?"

"With most, I am fulfilling a specific role," OreSeur said. "I have bones to imitate—a person to become, a personality to adopt. You have given me no direction; just the bones of this . . . animal."

So that's it, Vin thought. *Still annoyed by the dog's body.* "Look, those bones don't really change anything. You are still the same person."

"You do not understand. It is not who a kandra *is* that's important. It's who a kandra *becomes.* The bones he takes, the role he fulfills. None of my previous masters have asked me to do something like this."

"Well, I'm not like other masters," Vin said. "Anyway, I asked you a question. Is there a way I can spot a kandra with Allomancy? And yes, I command you to speak."

A flash of triumph shone in OreSeur's eyes, as if he enjoyed forcing her into her role. "Kandra cannot be affected by mental Allomancy, Mistress."

Vin frowned. "Not at all?"

"No, Mistress," OreSeur said. "You can try to Riot or Soothe our emotions, if you wish, but it will have no effect. We won't even know that you are trying to manipulate us."

Like someone who is burning copper. "That's not exactly the most useful bit of information," she said, strolling past the kandra on the roof. Allomancers couldn't read minds or emotions; when they Soothed or Rioted another person, they simply had to hope that the person reacted as intended.

She could "test" for a kandra by Soothing someone's emotions, perhaps. If they didn't react, that might mean they were a kandra—but it could also just mean that they were good at containing their emotions.

OreSeur watched her pacing. "If it were easy to detect kandra, Mistress, then we wouldn't be worth much as impostors, would we?"

"I suppose not," Vin acknowledged. However, thinking about what he'd said made her consider something else. "Can a kandra *use* Allomancy? If they eat an Allomancer, I mean?"

OreSeur shook his head.

That's another method, then, Vin thought. *If I catch a member of the crew burning metals, then I know he's not the kandra.* Wouldn't help with Dockson or the palace servants, but it would let her eliminate Ham and Spook.

"There's something else," Vin said. "Before, when we were doing the job with Kelsier, he said that we had to keep you away from the Lord Ruler and his Inquisitors. Why was that?"

OreSeur looked away. "This is not a thing we speak of."

"Then I command you to speak of it."

"Then I must refuse to answer," OreSeur said.

"Refuse to answer?" Vin asked. "You can do that?"

OreSeur nodded. "We are not required to reveal secrets about kandra nature, Mistress. It is—"

"In the Contract," Vin finished, frowning. *I really need to read that thing again.*

"Yes, Mistress. I have, perhaps, said too much already."

Vin turned away from OreSeur, looking out over the city. The mists continued to spin. Vin closed her eyes, questing out with bronze, trying to feel the telltale pulse of an Allomancer burning metals nearby.

OreSeur rose and padded over beside her, then settled down on his haunches again, sitting on the inclined roof. "Shouldn't you be at the meeting the king is having, Mistress?"

"Perhaps later," Vin said, opening her eyes. Out beyond the city, watchfires from the armies lit the horizon. Keep Venture blazed in the night to her right, and inside of it, Elend was holding council with the others. Many of the most important men in the government, sitting together in one room. Elend would call her paranoid for insisting that she be the one who watched for spies and assassins. That was fine; he could call her whatever he wanted, as long as he stayed alive.

She settled back down. She was glad Elend had decided to pick Keep Venture as his palace, rather than moving into Kredik Shaw, the Lord Ruler's home. Not only was Kredik Shaw too big to be properly defended, but it also reminded her of him. The Lord Ruler.

She thought of the Lord Ruler often, lately—or, rather, she thought of Rashek, the man who had become the Lord Ruler. A Terrisman by birth, Rashek had killed the man who should have taken the power at the Well of Ascension and . . .

And done what? They still didn't know. The Hero had been on a quest to protect the people from a danger simply known as the Deepness. So much had been lost; so much had been intentionally destroyed. Their best source of information about those days came in the form of an aged journal, written by the Hero of Ages during the days before Rashek had killed him. However, it gave precious few clues about his quest.

Why do I even worry about these things? Vin thought. *The Deepness is a thing a thousand years forgotten. Elend and the others are right to be concerned about more pressing events.*

And still, Vin found herself strangely detached from them. Perhaps that was why she found herself scouting outside. It wasn't that she didn't worry about the armies.

She just felt . . . removed from the problem. Even now, as she considered the threat to Luthadel, her mind was drawn back to the Lord Ruler.

You don't know what I do for mankind, he had said. *I was your god, even if you couldn't see it. By killing me, you have doomed yourselves.* Those were the Lord Ruler's last words, spoken as he lay dying on the floor of his own throne room. They worried her. Chilled her, even still.

She needed to distract herself. "What kinds of things do you like, kandra?" she asked, turning to the creature, who still sat on the rooftop beside her. "What are your loves, your hatreds?"

"I do not want to answer that."

Vin frowned. "Do not want to, or do not *have* to?"

OreSeur paused. "Do not want to, Mistress." The implication was obvious. *You're going to have to command me.*

She almost did. However, something gave her pause, something in those eyes—inhuman though they were. Something familiar.

She'd known resentment like that. She'd felt it often during her youth, when she'd served crewleaders who had lorded over their followers. In the crews, one did what one was commanded—especially if one was a small waif of a girl, without rank or means of intimidation.

"If you don't wish to speak of it," Vin said, turning away from the kandra, "then I won't force you."

OreSeur was silent.

Vin breathed in the mist, its cool wetness tickling her throat and lungs. "Do you know what *I* love, kandra?"

"No, Mistress."

"The mists," she said, holding out her arms. "The power, the freedom."

OreSeur nodded slowly. Nearby, Vin felt a faint pulsing with her bronze. Quiet, strange, unnerving. It was the same odd pulsing that she had felt atop Keep Venture a few nights before. She had never been brave enough to investigate it again.

It's time to do something about that, she decided. "Do you know what I hate, kandra?" she whispered, falling to a crouch, checking her knives and metals.

"No, Mistress."

She turned, meeting OreSeur's eyes. "I hate being afraid."

She knew that others thought her jumpy. Paranoid. She had lived with fear for so long that she had once seen it as something natural, like the ash, the sun, or the ground itself.

Kelsier had taken that fear away. She was careful, still, but she didn't feel a constant sense of terror. The Survivor had given her a life where the ones she loved didn't beat her, had shown her something better than fear. Trust. Now that she knew of these things, she would not quickly surrender them. Not to armies, not to assassins . . .

Not even to spirits.

"Follow if you can," she whispered, then dropped off the rooftop to the street below.

She dashed along the mist-slicked street, building momentum before she had time to lose her nerve. The source of the bronze pulses was close; it came from only one street over, in a building. Not the top, she decided. One of the darkened windows on the third floor, the shutters open.

Vin dropped a coin and jumped into the air. She shot upward, angling herself by Pushing against a latch across the street. She landed in the window's pitlike opening, arms grabbing the sides of the frame. She flared tin, letting her eyes adjust to the deep darkness within the abandoned room.

And it was there. Formed entirely of mists, it shifted and spun, its outline vague in the dark chamber. It had a vantage to see the rooftop where Vin and OreSeur had been talking.

Ghosts don't spy on people . . . do they? Skaa didn't speak of things like spirits or the dead. It smacked too much of religion, and religion was for the nobility. To worship was death for skaa. That hadn't stopped some, of course—but thieves like Vin had been too pragmatic for such things.

There was only one thing in skaa lore that this creature matched. Mistwraiths. Creatures said to steal the souls of men foolish enough to go outside at night. But, Vin now knew what mistwraiths were. They were cousins to the kandra—strange, semi-intelligent beasts who used the bones of those they ingested. They were odd, true—but hardly phantoms, and not really even that dangerous. There were no dark wraiths in the night, no haunting spirits or ghouls.

Or so Kelsier had said. The thing standing in the dark room—its insubstantial form writhing in the mists—seemed a powerful counterexample. She gripped the sides of the window, fear—her old friend—returning.

Run. Flee. Hide.

"Why have you been watching me?" she demanded.

The thing did not move. Its form seemed to draw the mists forward, and they spun slightly, as if in an air current.

I can sense it with bronze. That means it's using Allomancy—and Allomancy attracts the mist.

The thing stepped forward. Vin tensed.

And then the spirit was gone.

Vin paused, frowning. That was it? She had—

Something grabbed her arm. Something cold, something terrible, but something very real. A pain shot through her head, moving as if from her ear and into her mind. She yelled, but cut off as her voice failed. With a quiet groan—her arm quivering and shaking—she fell backward out of the window.

Her arm was still cold. She could feel it whipping in the air beside her, seeming to exude chill air. Mist passed like trailing clouds.

Vin flared tin. Pain, cold, wetness, and lucidity burst into her mind, and she threw herself into a twist and flared pewter just as she hit the ground.

"Mistress?" OreSeur said, darting from the shadows.

Vin shook her head, pushing herself up to her knees, her palms cool against the slick cobblestones. She could still feel the trailing chill in her left arm.

"Shall I go for aid?" the wolfhound asked.

Vin shook her head, forcing herself into a wobbling stand. She looked upward, through swirling mists, toward the black window above.

She shivered. Her shoulder was sore from where she

had hit the ground, and her still bruised side throbbed, but she could feel her strength returning. She stepped away from the building, still looking up. Above her, the deep mists seemed . . . ominous. Obscuring.

No, she thought forcefully. *The mists are my freedom; the night is my home! This is where I belong. I haven't needed to be afraid in the night since Kelsier taught me otherwise.*

She couldn't lose that. She wouldn't go back to the fear. Still, she couldn't help the quick urgency in her step as she waved to OreSeur and scampered away from the building. She gave no explanation for her strange actions.

He didn't ask for one.

Elend set a third pile of books onto the table, and it slumped against the other two, threatening to topple the entire lot to the floor. He steadied them, then glanced up.

Breeze, in a prim suit, regarded the table with amusement as he sipped his wine. Ham and Spook were playing a game of stones as they waited for the meeting to begin; Spook was winning. Dockson sat in the corner of the room, scribbling on a ledger, and Clubs sat in a deep plush chair, eyeing Elend with one of his stares.

Any of these men could be an impostor, Elend thought. The thought still seemed insane to him. What was he to do? Exclude them all from his confidence? No, he needed them too much.

The only option was to act normally and watch them. Vin had told him to try and spot inconsistencies in their personalities. He intended to do his best, but the reality was he wasn't sure how much he would be able to see. This was more Vin's area of expertise. He needed to worry about the armies.

Thinking of her, he glanced at the stained-glass window at the back of the study, and was surprised to see it was dark.

That late already? Elend thought.

"My dear man," Breeze noted. "When you told us you

needed to 'go and gather a few important references,' you might have warned us that you were planning to be gone for two full hours."

"Yes, well," Elend said, "I kind of lost track of time. . . ."

"For two hours?"

Elend nodded sheepishly. "There were books involved."

Breeze shook his head. "If the fate of the Central Dominance weren't at stake—and if it weren't so fantastically enjoyable to watch Hammond lose an entire month's earnings to the boy there—I'd have left an hour ago."

"Yes, well, we can get started now," Elend said.

Ham chuckled, standing up. "Actually, it's kind of like the old days. Kell always arrived late, too—and he liked to hold his meetings at night. Mistborn hours."

Spook smiled, his coin pouch bulging.

We still use boxings—Lord Ruler imperials—as our coinage, Elend thought. *We'll have to do something about that.*

"I miss the charcoal board, though," Spook said.

"I certainly don't," Breeze replied. "Kell had atrocious handwriting."

"Absolutely atrocious," Ham said with a smile, sitting. "You have to admit, though—it was distinctive."

Breeze raised an eyebrow. "It *was* that, I suppose."

Kelsier, the Survivor of Hathsin, Elend thought. *Even his handwriting is legendary.* "Regardless," he said, "I think perhaps we should get to work. We've still got two armies waiting out there. We're not leaving tonight until we have a plan to deal with them!"

The crewmembers shared looks.

"Actually, Your Majesty," Dockson said, "we've already worked on that problem for a bit."

"Oh?" Elend asked, surprised. *Well, I guess I did leave them alone for a couple of hours.* "Let me hear it, then."

Dockson stood, pulling his chair a bit closer to join the rest of the group, and Ham began to speak.

"Here's the thing, El," Ham said. "With two armies here, we don't have to worry about an immediate attack. But, we're still in serious danger. This will probably turn into an extended siege as each army tries to outlast the other."

"They'll try to starve us out," Clubs said. "Weaken us, and their enemies, before attacking."

"And," Ham continued, "that puts us in a bind—because we can't last very long. The city is already on the edge of starvation—and the enemy kings are probably aware of that fact."

"What are you saying?" Elend asked slowly.

"We have to make an alliance with one of those armies, Your Majesty," Dockson said. "They both know it. Alone, they can't reliably defeat one another. With our help, however, the balance will be tipped."

"They'll hem us in," Ham said. "Keep us blockaded until we get desperate enough to side with one of them. Eventually, we'll have to do so—either that, or let our people starve."

"The decision comes down to this," Breeze said. "We can't outlast the others, so we have to choose *which* of those men we want to take over the city. And, I would suggest making our decision quickly as opposed to waiting while our supplies run out."

Elend stood quietly. "By making a deal with one of those armies, we'll essentially be giving away our kingdom."

"True," Breeze said, tapping the side of his cup. "However, what I gained us by bringing a second army is bargaining power. You see, at least we are in a position to demand something in exchange for our kingdom."

"What good is that?" Elend asked. "We still lose."

"It's better than nothing," Breeze said. "I think that we might be able to persuade Cett to leave you as a provisional leader in Luthadel. He doesn't like the Central Dominance; he finds it barren and flat."

"Provisional leader of the city," Elend said with a frown. "That is somewhat different from king of the Central Dominance."

"True," Dockson said. "But, every emperor needs good men to administrate the cities under their rule. You wouldn't be king, but you—and our armies—would live through the next few months, and Luthadel wouldn't be pillaged."

Ham, Breeze, and Dockson all sat resolutely, looking him in the eye. Elend glanced down at his pile of books, thinking of his research and study. Worthless. How long had the crew known that there was only one course of action?

The crew seemed to take Elend's silence as assent.

"Cett really is the best choice, then?" Dockson asked. "Perhaps Straff would be more likely to make an agreement with Elend—they are, after all, family."

Oh, he'd make an agreement, Elend thought. *And he'd break it the moment it was convenient. But . . . the alternative? Give the city over to this Cett? What would happen to this land, this people, if he were in charge?*

"Cett is best, I think," Breeze said. "He is very willing to let others rule, as long as he gets his glory and his coins. The problem is going to be that atium. Cett thinks it is here, and if he doesn't find it . . ."

"We just let him search the city," Ham said.

Breeze nodded. "You'd have to persuade him that I misled him about the atium—and that shouldn't be too hard, considering what he thinks of me. Which is another small matter—you'll have to convince him that I've been dealt with. Perhaps he'd believe that I was executed as soon as Elend found out I had raised an army against him."

The others nodded.

"Breeze?" Elend asked. "How does Lord Cett treat the skaa in his lands?"

Breeze paused, then glanced away. "Not well, I'm afraid."

"Now, see," Elend said. "I think we need to consider how to best protect our people. I mean, if we give everything over to Cett, then we'd save my skin—but at the cost of the entire skaa population of the dominance!"

Dockson shook his head. "Elend, it's not a betrayal. Not if this is the only way."

"That's easy to say," Elend said. "But I'm the one who'd have to bear the guilty conscience for doing such a thing. I'm not saying that we should throw out your suggestion, but I do have a few ideas that we might talk about. . ."

The others shared looks. As usual, Clubs and Spook remained quiet during proceedings; Clubs only spoke when he felt it absolutely necessary, and Spook tended to stay on the periphery of the conversations. Finally, Breeze, Ham, and Dockson looked back at Elend.

"This is your country, Your Majesty," Dockson said carefully. "We're simply here to give advice." *Very good advice,* his tone implied.

"Yes, well," Elend said, quickly selecting a book. In his haste, he knocked over one of the stacks, sending a clatter of books across the table and landing a volume in Breeze's lap.

"Sorry," Elend said, as Breeze rolled his eyes and sat the book back up on the table. Elend pulled open his own book. "Now, this volume had some very interesting things to say about the movement and arrangement of troop bodies—"

"Uh, El?" Ham asked, frowning. "That looks like a book on shipping grain."

"I know," Elend said. "There weren't a lot of books about warfare in the library. I guess that's what we get for a thousand years without any wars. However, this book does mention how much grain it took to keep the various garrisons in the Final Empire stocked. Do you have any idea how much food an army needs?"

"You have a point," Clubs said, nodding. "Usually, it's a blasted pain to keep soldiers fed; we often had supply problems fighting on the frontier, and we were only small bands, sent to quell the occasional rebellion."

Elend nodded. Clubs didn't often speak of his past fighting in the Lord Ruler's army—and the crew didn't often ask him about it.

"Anyway," Elend said, "I'll bet both Cett and my father are unaccustomed to moving large bodies of men. There will be supply problems, especially for Cett, since he marched so hastily."

"Maybe not," Clubs said. "Both armies have secured canal routes into Luthadel. That will make it easy for them to send for more supplies."

"Plus," Breeze added, "though much of Cett's land is

in revolt right now, he *does* still hold the city of Haverfrex, which held one of the Lord Ruler's main canneries. Cett has a remarkable amount of food a short canal trip away."

"Then, we disrupt the canals," Elend said. "We find a way to stop those supplies from coming. Canals make resupply quick, but also vulnerable, since we know exactly which route it will take. And, if we can take away their food, perhaps they'll be forced to turn around and march home."

"Either that," Breeze said, "or they'll just decide to risk attacking Luthadel."

Elend paused. "That's a possibility," he said. "But, well, I've been researching how to hold the city as well." He reached across the table, picking up a book. "Now, this is Jendellah's *City Management in the Modern Era.* He mentions how difficult Luthadel is to police because of its extreme size and large number of skaa slums. He suggests using roving bands of city watchmen. I think we could adapt his methods to use in a battle—our wall is too long to defend in detail, but if we had mobile bands of troops that could respond to—"

"Your Majesty," Dockson interrupted.

"Hum? Yes?"

"We've got a troop of boys and men who have barely a year's training, and we're facing not one overwhelming force, but *two*. We can't win this battle by force."

"Oh, yes," Elend said. "Of course. I was just saying that if we *did* have to fight, I have some strategies. . . ."

"If we fight, we lose," Clubs said. "We'll probably lose anyway."

Elend paused for a moment. "Yes, well, I just . . ."

"Attacking the canal routes is a good idea, though," Dockson said. "We can do that covertly, perhaps hire some of the bandits in the area to attack supply barges. It probably won't be enough to send Cett or Straff home, but we could make them more desperate to make alliances with us."

Breeze nodded. "Cett's already worried about instability back in his home dominance. We should send him a preliminary messenger, let him know we're interested in an alliance. That way, as soon as his supply problems begin, he'll think of us."

"We could even send him a letter explaining Breeze's execution," Dockson said, "as a sign of good faith. That—"

Elend cleared his throat. The others paused.

"I, uh, wasn't finished yet," Elend said.

"I apologize, Your Majesty," Dockson said.

Elend took a deep breath. "You're right—we can't afford to fight those armies. But, I think we need to find a way to get them to fight each other."

"A pleasant sentiment, my dear man," Breeze said. "But getting those two to attack one another isn't as simple as persuading Spook over there to refill my wine." He turned, holding out his empty cup. Spook paused, then sighed, rising to fetch the wine bottle.

"Well, yes," Elend said. "But, while there aren't a lot of books on warfare, there *are* a lot about politics. Breeze, you said the other day that being the weakest party in a three-way stalemate gives us power."

"Exactly," Breeze said. "We can tip the battle for either of the two larger sides."

"Yes," Elend said, opening a book. "Now that there are three parties involved, it's not warfare—it's politics. This is just like a contest between houses. And in house politicking, even the most powerful houses can't stand without allies. The small houses are weak individually, but they are strong when considered as a group.

"We're like one of those small houses. If we want to make any gains, we're going to have to get our enemies to forget about us—or, at least, make them think us inconsequential. If they both assume that they have the better of us—that they can use us to defeat the other army, then turn on us at their leisure—then they'll leave us alone and concentrate on each other."

Ham rubbed his chin. "You're talking about playing both sides, Elend. It's a dangerous position to put ourselves in."

Breeze nodded. "We'd have to switch our allegiance to whichever side seems weaker at the moment, keep them snapping at each other. And there's no guarantee that the winner between the two would be weakened enough for us to defeat."

"Not to mention our food problems," Dockson said. "What you propose would take time, Your Majesty. Time during which we'd be under siege, our supplies dwindling. It's autumn right now. Winter will soon be upon us."

"It will be tough," Elend agreed. "And risky. But, I think we can do it. We make them *both* think we're allied with them, but we hold back our support. We encourage them against one another, and we wear away at their supplies and morale, pushing them into a conflict. When the dust settles, the surviving army might just be weak enough for us to beat."

Breeze looked thoughtful. "It has style," he admitted. "And, it does kind of sound fun."

Dockson smiled. "You only say that because it involves making someone else do our work for us."

Breeze shrugged. "Manipulation works so well on a personal level, I don't see why it wouldn't be an equally viable national policy."

"That's actually how most rulership works," Ham mused. "What is a government but an institutionalized method of making sure somebody *else* does all the work?"

"Uh, the plan?" Elend asked.

"I don't know, El," Ham said, getting back on topic. "It sounds like one of Kell's plans—foolhardy, brave, and a little insane." He sounded as if he were surprised to hear Elend propose such a measure.

I can be as foolhardy as any man, Elend thought indignantly, then paused. Did he really want to follow that line of thought?

"We could get ourselves into some serious trouble," Dockson said. "If either side decides it's tired of our games . . ."

"They'll destroy us," Elend said. "But . . . well, gentlemen, you're gamblers. You can't tell me that this plan doesn't appeal to you more than simply bowing before Lord Cett."

Ham shared a look with Breeze, and they seemed to be considering the idea. Dockson rolled his eyes, but seemed like he was objecting simply out of habit.

No, they didn't want to take the safe way out. These were the men who had challenged the Lord Ruler, men who had made their livelihood scamming noblemen. In some ways, they were very careful; they could be precise in their attention to detail, cautious in covering their tracks and protecting their interests. But when it came time to gamble for the big prize, they were often willing.

No, not willing. Eager.

Great, Elend thought. *I've filled my inner council with a bunch of thrill-seeking masochists. Even worse, I've decided to join them.* But, what else could he do?

"We could at least consider it," Breeze said. "It does sound exciting."

"Now, see, I didn't suggest this because it was exciting, Breeze," Elend said. "I spent my youth trying to plan how I would make a better city of Luthadel once I became leader of my house. I'm not going to throw away those dreams at the first sign of opposition."

"What about the Assembly?" Ham said.

"That's the best part," Elend said. "They voted in my proposal at the meeting two days back. They can't open the city gates to any invader until I meet with my father in parlay."

The crew sat quietly for a few moments. Finally, Ham turned to Elend, shaking his head. "I really don't know, El. It sounds appealing. We actually discussed a few more daring plans like this while we were waiting for you. But . . ."

"But what?" Elend asked.

"A plan like this depends a lot on you, my dear man," Breeze said, sipping his wine. "You'd have to be the one to meet with the kings—the one to persuade them both that we're on their side. No offense, but you're new to scamming. It's difficult to agree to a daring plan that puts a newcomer in as the linchpin member of the team."

"I can do this," Elend said. "Really."

Ham glanced at Breeze, then both glanced at Clubs. The

gnarled general shrugged. "If the kid wants to try it, then let him."

Ham sighed, then looked back. "I guess I agree. As long as you're up to this, El."

"I think I am," Elend said, covering his nervousness. "I just know we can't give up, not easily. Maybe this won't work—maybe, after a couple months of being besieged, we'll just end up giving away the city anyway. However, that gives us a couple of months during which *something* could happen. It's worth the risk to wait, rather than fold. Wait, and plan."

"All right, then," Dockson said. "Give us some time to come up with some ideas and options, Your Majesty. We'll meet again in a few days to talk about specifics."

"All right," Elend said. "Sounds good. Now, if we can move on to other matters, I'd like to mention—"

A knock came at the door. At Elend's call, Captain Demoux pushed open the door, looking a little embarrassed. "Your Majesty?" he said. "I apologize, but . . . I think we caught someone listening in on your meeting."

"What?" Elend said. "Who?"

Demoux turned to the side, waving in a pair of his guards. The woman they led into the room was vaguely familiar to Elend. Tall, like most Terris, she wore a bright-colored, but utilitarian, dress. Her ears were stretched downward, the lobes elongated to accommodate numerous earrings.

"I recognize you," Elend said. "From the Assembly hall a few days ago. You were watching me."

The woman didn't answer. She looked over the room's occupants, standing stiffly—even haughtily—despite her bound wrists. Elend had never actually met a Terriswoman before; he'd only met stewards, eunuchs trained from birth to work as manservants. For some reason, Elend had expected a Terriswoman to seem a bit more servile.

"She was hiding in the next room over," Demoux said. "I'm sorry, Your Majesty. I don't know how she got past us. We found her listening against the wall, though I doubt she heard anything. I mean, those walls are made of stone."

Elend met the woman's eyes. Older—perhaps fifty—she wasn't beautiful, but neither was she homely. She was sturdy, with a straightforward, rectangular face. Her stare was calm and firm, and it made Elend uncomfortable to hold it for long.

"So, what did you expect to overhear, woman?" Elend asked.

The Terriswoman ignored the comment. She turned to the others, and spoke in a lightly accented voice. "I would speak with the king alone. The rest of you are excused."

Ham smiled. "Well, at least she's got nerve."

Dockson addressed the Terriswoman. "What makes you think that we would leave our king alone with you?"

"His Majesty and I have things to discuss," the woman said in a businesslike manner, as if oblivious of—or unconcerned about—her status as a prisoner. "You needn't be worried about his safety; I'm certain that the young Mistborn hiding outside the window will be more than enough to deal with me."

Elend glanced to the side, toward the small ventilation window beside the more massive stained-glass one. How would the Terriswoman have known that Vin was watching? Her ears would have to be extraordinarily keen. Keen enough, perhaps, to listen in on the meeting through a stone wall?

Elend turned back to the newcomer. "You're a Keeper."

She nodded.

"Did Sazed send you?"

"It is because of him that I am here," she said. "But I was not 'sent.'"

"Ham, it's all right," Elend said slowly. "You can go."

"Are you sure?" Ham asked, frowning.

"Leave me bound, if you wish," the woman said.

If she really is a Feruchemist, that won't be much of a hindrance, Elend thought. *Of course, if she really is a Feruchemist—a Keeper, like Sazed—I shouldn't have anything to fear from her. Theoretically.*

The others shuffled from the room, their postures indicating what they thought of Elend's decision. Though they were no longer thieves by profession, Elend suspected that they—like Vin—would always bear the effects of their upbringing.

"We'll be just outside, El," Ham—the last one out—said, then pulled the door shut.

And yet, any who know me will realize that there was no chance I would give up so easily. Once I find something to investigate, I become dogged in my pursuit.

14

THE TERRISWOMAN SNAPPED HER BONDS, and the ropes dropped to the floor.

"Uh, Vin?" Elend said, beginning to wonder about the logic of meeting with this woman. "Perhaps it's time you came in."

"She's not actually there," the Terriswoman said offhandedly, walking forward. "She left a few minutes ago to do her rounds. That is why I let myself be caught."

"Um, I see," Elend said. "I'll be calling for the guards now."

"Don't be a fool," the Terriswoman said. "If I wanted to kill you, I could do it before the others got back in. Now be quiet for a moment."

Elend stood uncomfortably as the tall woman walked around the table in a slow circle, studying him as a merchant might inspect a piece of furniture up for auction. Finally she stopped, placing her hands on her hips.

"Stand up straight," she commanded.

"Excuse me?"

"You're slouching," the woman said. "A king must maintain an air of dignity at all times, even when with his friends."

Elend frowned. "Now, while I appreciate advice, I don't—"

"No," the woman said. "Don't hedge. Command."

"Excuse me?" Elend said again.

The woman stepped forward, placing a hand on his shoulder and pressing his back firmly to improve his posture. She stepped back, then nodded slightly to herself.

"Now, see," Elend said. "I don't—"

"No," the woman interrupted. "You must be stronger in the way that you speak. Presentation—words, actions, postures—will determine how people judge you and react to you. If you start every sentence with softness and uncertainty, you will seem soft and uncertain. Be forceful!"

"What is going on here?" Elend demanded, exasperated.

"There," the woman said. "Finally."

"You said that you know Sazed?" Elend asked, resisting the urge to slouch back into his earlier posture.

"He is an acquaintance," the woman said. "My name is Tindwyl; I am, as you have guessed, a Keeper of Terris." She tapped her foot for a moment, then shook her head. "Sazed warned me about your slovenly appearance, but I honestly assumed that no king could have such a poor sense of self-presentation."

"Slovenly?" Elend asked. "Excuse me?"

"Stop saying that," Tindwyl snapped. "Don't ask questions; say what you mean. If you object, object—don't leave your words up to my interpretation."

"Yes, well, while this is fascinating," Elend said, walking toward the door, "I'd rather avoid further insults this evening. If you'll excuse me . . ."

"Your people think you are a fool, Elend Venture," Tindwyl said quietly.

Elend paused.

"The Assembly—a body you yourself organized—ignores your authority. The skaa are convinced that you won't be able to protect them. Even your own council of friends makes their plans in your absence, assuming your input to be no great loss."

Elend closed his eyes, taking a slow, deep breath.

"You have good ideas, Elend Venture," Tindwyl said.

"Regal ideas. However, you are not a king. A man can only lead when others accept him as their leader, and he has only as much authority as his subjects give to him. All of the brilliant ideas in the world cannot save your kingdom if no one will listen to them."

Elend turned. "This last year I've read every pertinent book on leadership and governance in the four libraries."

Tindwyl raised an eyebrow. "Then, I suspect that you spent a great deal of time in your room that you *should* have been out, being seen by your people and learning to be a ruler."

"Books have great value," Elend said.

"Actions have greater value."

"And where am I to learn the proper actions?"

"From me."

Elend paused.

"You may know that every Keeper has an area of special interest," Tindwyl said. "While we all memorize the same store of information, one person can only study and understand a limited amount of that store. Our mutual friend Sazed spends his time on religions."

"And your specialty?"

"Biographies," she said. "I have studied the lives of generals, kings, and emperors whose names you have never heard. Understanding theories of politics and leadership, Elend Venture, is not the same as understanding the lives of men who lived such principles."

"And . . . you can teach me to emulate those men?"

"Perhaps," Tindwyl said. "I haven't yet decided whether or not you're a hopeless case. But, I am here, so I will do what I can. A few months ago, I received a letter from Sazed, explaining your predicament. He did not ask me to come to train you—but, then, Sazed is perhaps another man who could learn to be more forceful."

Elend nodded slowly, meeting the Terriswoman's eyes.

"Will you accept my instruction, then?" she asked.

Elend thought for a moment. *If she's anywhere near as useful as Sazed, then . . . well, I could certainly use some help at this.* "I will," he said.

Tindwyl nodded. "Sazed also mentioned your humility. It could be an asset—assuming you don't let it get in the way. Now, I believe that your Mistborn has returned."

Elend turned toward the side window. The shutter swung open, allowing mist to begin streaming into the room and revealing a crouching, cloaked form.

"How did you know I was here?" Vin asked quietly.

Tindwyl smiled—the first such expression Elend had seen on her face. "Sazed mentioned you as well, child. You and I should speak soon in private, I think."

Vin slipped into the room, drawing mist in behind her, then closed the shutter. She didn't bother to hide her hostility or mistrust as she put herself between Elend and Tindwyl.

"Why are you here?" Vin demanded.

Tindwyl smiled again. "It took your king there several minutes to get to that question, and here you ask it after a few bare moments. You are an interesting couple, I think."

Vin's eyes narrowed.

"Regardless, I should withdraw," Tindwyl said. "We shall speak again, I assume, Your Majesty?"

"Yes, of course," Elend said. "Um . . . is there anything I should begin practicing?"

"Yes," Tindwyl said, walking to the door. "Stop saying 'um.' "

"Right."

Ham poked his head in the door as soon as Tindwyl opened it. He immediately noticed her discarded bonds. He didn't say anything, however; he likely assumed that Elend had freed her.

"I think we're done for the night, everyone," Elend said. "Ham, would you see that Mistress Tindwyl is given quarters in the palace? She's a friend of Sazed's."

Ham shrugged. "All right, then." He nodded to Vin, then withdrew. Tindwyl did not bid them good night as she left.

Vin frowned, then glanced at Elend. He seemed . . . distracted. "I don't like her," she said.

Elend smiled, stacking up the books on his table. "You don't like anyone when you first meet them, Vin."

"I liked you."

"Thereby demonstrating that you are a terrible judge of character."

Vin paused, then smiled. She walked over and began picking through the books. They weren't typical Elend fare—far more practical than the kinds of things he usually read. "How did it go tonight?" she asked. "I didn't have much time to listen."

Elend sighed. He turned, sitting down on the table, looking up at the massive rose window at the back of the room. It was dark, its colors only hinted as reflections in the black glass. "It went well, I suppose."

"I told you they'd like your plan. It's the sort of thing they'll find challenging."

"I suppose," Elend said.

Vin frowned. "All right," she said, hopping up to stand on the table. She sat down beside him. "What is it? Is it something that woman said? What did she want, anyway?"

"Just to pass on some knowledge," he said. "You know how Keepers are, always wanting an ear to listen to their lessons."

"I suppose," Vin said slowly. She hadn't ever seen Elend depressed, but he did get discouraged. He had so many ideas, so many plans and hopes, that she sometimes wondered how he kept them all straight. She would have said that he lacked focus; Reen had always said that focus kept a thief alive. Elend's dreams, however, were so much a part of who he was. She doubted he could discard them. She didn't think she would want him to, for they were part of what she loved about him.

"They agreed to the plan, Vin," Elend said, still looking up at the window. "They even seemed excited, like you said they'd be. It's just . . . I can't help thinking that their suggestion was far more rational than mine. They wanted to side with one of the armies, giving it our support in exchange for leaving me as a subjugated ruler in Luthadel."

"That would be giving up," Vin said.

"Sometimes, giving up is better than failing. I just committed my city to an extended siege. That will mean hunger, perhaps starvation, before this is over with."

Vin put a hand on his shoulder, watching him uncertainly. Usually, he was the one who reassured her. "It's still a better way," she said. "The others probably just suggested a weaker plan because they thought you wouldn't go along with something more daring."

"No," Elend said. "They weren't pandering to me, Vin. They really thought that making a strategic alliance was a good, safe plan." He paused, then looked at her. "Since when did *that* group represent the reasonable side of my government?"

"They've had to grow," Vin said. "They can't be the men they once were, not with this much responsibility."

Elend turned back toward the window. "I'll tell you what worries me, Vin. I'm worried that their plan *wasn't* reasonable—perhaps it itself was a bit foolhardy. Perhaps making an alliance would have been a difficult enough task. If that's the case, then what *I'm* proposing is just downright ludicrous."

Vin squeezed his shoulder. "We fought the Lord Ruler."

"You had Kelsier then."

"Not *that* again."

"I'm sorry," Elend said. "But, really, Vin. Maybe my plan to try and hold on to the government is just arrogance. What was it you told me about your childhood? When you were in the thieving crews, and everyone was bigger, stronger, and meaner than you, what did you do? Did you stand up to the leaders?"

Memories flashed in her mind. Memories of hiding, of keeping her eyes down, of weakness.

"That was then," she said. "You can't let others beat on you forever. That's what Kelsier taught me—that's why we fought the Lord Ruler. That's why the skaa rebellion fought the Final Empire all those years, even when there was no chance of winning. Reen taught me that the rebels were fools. But Reen is dead now—and so is the Final Empire. And . . ."

She leaned down, catching Elend's eyes. "You can't give up the city, Elend," she said quietly. "I don't think I'd like what that would do to you."

Elend paused, then smiled slowly. "You can be very wise sometimes, Vin."

"You think that?"

He nodded.

"Well," she said, "then obviously you're as poor a judge of character as I am."

Elend laughed, putting his arm around her, hugging her against his side. "So, I assume the patrol tonight was uneventful?"

The mist spirit. Her fall. The chill she could still feel—if only faintly remembered—in her forearm. "It was," she said. The last time she'd told him of the mist spirit, he'd immediately thought she'd been seeing things.

"See," Elend said, "you should have come to the meeting; I would have liked to have had you here."

She said nothing.

They sat for a few minutes, looking up at the dark window. There was an odd beauty to it; the colors weren't visible because of the lack of back light, and she could instead focus on the patterns of glass. Chips, slivers, slices, and plates woven together within a framework of metal.

"Elend?" she finally said. "I'm worried."

"I'd be concerned if you weren't," he said. "Those armies have *me* so worried that I can barely think straight."

"No," Vin said. "Not about that. I'm worried about other things."

"Like what?"

"Well . . . I've been thinking about what the Lord Ruler said, right before I killed him. Do you remember?"

Elend nodded. He hadn't been there, but she'd told him.

"He talked about what he'd done for mankind," Vin said. "He saved us, the stories say. From the Deepness."

Elend nodded.

"But," Vin said, "what *was* the Deepness? You were a nobleman—religion wasn't forbidden to you. What did the Ministry teach about the Deepness and the Lord Ruler?"

Elend shrugged. "Not much, really. Religion wasn't forbidden, but it wasn't encouraged either. There was something proprietary about the Ministry, an air that implied they would take care of religious things—that we didn't need to worry ourselves."

"But they did teach you about some things, right?"

Elend nodded. "Mostly, they talked about why the nobility were privileged and the skaa cursed. I guess they wanted us to understand how fortunate we were—though honestly, I always found the teachings a little disturbing. See, they claimed that we were noble because our ancestors supported the Lord Ruler before the Ascension. But, that means that we were privileged because of what other people had done. Not really fair, eh?"

Vin shrugged. "Fair as anything else, I guess."

"But, didn't you get angry?" Elend said. "Didn't it frustrate you that the nobility had so much while you had so little?"

"I didn't think about it," Vin said. "The nobility had a lot, so we could take it from them. Why should I care how they got it? Sometimes, when I had food, other thieves beat me and took it. What did it matter how I got my food? It was still taken from me."

Elend paused. "You know, sometimes I wonder what the political theorists I've read would say if they met you. I have a feeling they'd throw up their hands in frustration."

She poked him in the side. "Enough politics. Tell me about the Deepness."

"Well, I think it was a creature of some sort—a dark and evil thing that nearly destroyed the world. The Lord Ruler traveled to the Well of Ascension, where he was given the power to defeat the Deepness and unite mankind. There are several statues in the city depicting the event."

Vin frowned. "Yes, but they never really show what the Deepness looked like. It's depicted as a twisted lump at the Lord Ruler's feet."

"Well, the last person who actually saw the Deepness died a year ago, so I guess we'll have to make do with the statues."

"Unless it comes back," Vin said quietly.

Elend frowned, looking at her again. "Is that what this is about, Vin?" His face softened slightly. "Two armies aren't enough? You have to worry about the fate of the world as well?"

Vin glanced down sheepishly, and Elend laughed, pulling her close. "Ah, Vin. I know you're a bit paranoid—honestly, considering our situation, I'm starting to feel the same—but I think this is one problem you don't have to worry about. I haven't heard any reports of monstrous incarnations of evil rampaging across the land."

Vin nodded, and Elend leaned back a bit, obviously assuming that he'd answered her question.

The Hero of Ages traveled to the Well of Ascension to defeat the Deepness, she thought. *But the prophecies all said that the Hero shouldn't take the Well's power for himself. He was supposed to give it, trust in the power itself to destroy the Deepness.*

Rashek didn't do that—he took the power for himself. Wouldn't that mean that the Deepness was never defeated? Why, then, wasn't the world destroyed?

"The red sun and brown plants," Vin said. "Did the Deepness do that?"

"Still thinking about that?" Elend frowned. "Red sun and brown plants? What other colors would they be?"

"Kelsier said that the sun was once yellow, and plants were green."

"That's an odd image."

"Sazed agrees with Kelsier," Vin said. "The legends all say that during the early days of the Lord Ruler, the sun changed colors, and ash began to fall from the skies."

"Well," Elend said, "I guess the Deepness *could* have had something to do with it. I don't know, honestly." He sat musingly for a few moments. "Green plants? Why not purple or blue? So odd. . . ."

The Hero of Ages traveled north, to the Well of Ascension, Vin thought again. She turned slightly, her eyes drawn toward the Terris mountains so far away. Was it still up there? The Well of Ascension?

"Did you have any luck getting information out of OreSeur?" Elend asked. "Anything to help us find the spy?"

Vin shrugged. "He told me that kandra can't use Allomancy."

"So, you can find our impostor that way?" Elend said, perking up.

"Maybe," Vin said. "I can test Spook and Ham, at least. Regular people will be more difficult—though kandra can't be Soothed, so maybe that will let me find the spy."

"That sounds promising," Elend said.

Vin nodded. The thief in her, the paranoid girl that Elend always teased, itched to use Allomancy on him—to test him, to see if he reacted to her Pushes and Pulls. She stopped herself. This one man she would trust. The others she would test, but she would not question Elend. In a way, she'd rather trust him and be wrong than deal with the worry of mistrust.

I finally understand, she thought with a start. *Kelsier. I understand what it was like for you with Mare. I won't make your same mistake.*

Elend was looking at her.

"What?" she asked.

"You're smiling," he said. "Do I get to hear the joke?"

She hugged him. "No," she said simply.

Elend smiled. "All right then. You can test Spook and Ham, but I'm pretty sure the impostor isn't one of the crew—I talked to them all today, and they were all themselves. We need to search the palace staff."

He doesn't know how good kandra can be. The enemy kandra had probably studied his victim for months and months, learning and memorizing their every mannerism.

"I've spoken to Ham and Demoux," Elend said. "As members of the palace guard, they know about the bones—and Ham was able to guess what they were. Hopefully, they can sort through the staff with minimal disturbance and locate the impostor."

Vin's senses itched at how trusting Elend was. *No,* she thought. *Let him assume the best. He has enough to worry about. Besides, perhaps the kandra* is *imitating someone outside our core team. Elend can search that avenue.*

And, if the impostor is a member of the crew . . . Well,

that's the sort of situation where my paranoia comes in handy.

"Anyway," Elend said, standing. "I have a few things to check on before it gets too late."

Vin nodded. He gave her a long kiss, then left. She sat on the table for a few moments longer, not looking at the massive rose window, but at the smaller window to the side, which she'd left slightly open. It stood, a doorway into the night. Mist churned in the blackness, tentatively sending tendrils into the room, evaporating quietly in the warmth.

"I will not fear you," Vin whispered. "And I will find your secret." She climbed off the table and slipped out the window, back out to meet with OreSeur and do another check of the palace grounds.

I had determined that Alendi was the Hero of Ages, and I intended to prove it. I should have bowed before the will of the others; I shouldn't have insisted on traveling with Alendi to witness his journeys.

It was inevitable that Alendi himself would find out what I believed him to be.

15

ON THE EIGHTH DAY OUT of the Conventical, Sazed awoke to find himself alone.

He stood, pushing off his blanket and the light film of ash that had fallen during the night. Marsh's place beneath the tree's canopy was empty, though a patch of bare earth indicated where the Inquisitor had slept.

Sazed stood, following Marsh's footsteps out into the harsh red sunlight. The ash was deeper here, without the cover of trees, and there was also more wind blowing it into drifts. Sazed regarded the windswept landscape. There was no further sign of Marsh.

Sazed returned to camp. The trees here—in the middle of the Eastern Dominance—rose twisted and knotted, but they had shelflike, overlapping branches, thick with brown needles. These provided decent shelter, though the ash seemed capable of infiltrating any sanctuary.

Sazed made a simple soup for breakfast. Marsh did not return. Sazed washed his brown travel robes in a nearby stream. Marsh did not return. Sazed sewed a rent in his sleeve, oiled his walking boots, and shaved his head. Marsh did not return. Sazed got out the rubbing he'd made in the Conventical, transcribed a few words, then forced himself to put the sheet away—he worried about blurring the words by opening it too often or by getting ash on it. Better to wait until he could have a proper desk and clean room.

Marsh did not return.

Finally, Sazed left. He couldn't define the sense of urgency that he felt—part excitement to share what he had learned, part desire to see how Vin and the young king Elend Venture were handling events in Luthadel.

Marsh knew the way. He would catch up.

Sazed raised his hand, shading his eyes against the red sunlight, looking down from his hilltop vantage. There was a slight darkness on the horizon, to the east of the main road. He tapped his geography coppermind, seeking out descriptions of the Eastern Dominance.

The knowledge swelled his mind, blessing him with recollection. The darkness was a village named Urbene. He searched through one of his indexes, looking for the right gazetteer. The index was growing fuzzy, its information difficult to remember—which meant that he'd switched it from coppermind to memory and back too many times. Knowledge inside a coppermind would remain pristine, but anything inside his head—even for only a few moments—would decay. He'd have to re-memorize the index later.

He found what he was looking for, and dumped the right

memories into his head. The gazetteer listed Urbene as "picturesque," which probably meant that some important nobleman had decided to make his manor there. The listing said that the skaa of Urbene were herdsmen.

Sazed scribbled a note to himself, then redeposited the gazetteer's memories. Reading the note told him what he had just forgotten. Like the index, the gazetteer memories had inevitably decayed slightly during their stay in his head. Fortunately, he had a second set of copperminds hidden back up in Terris, and would use those to pass his knowledge on to another Keeper. His current copperminds were for everyday use. Unapplied knowledge benefited no one.

He shouldered his pack. A visit to the village would do him some good, even if it slowed him down. His stomach agreed with the decision. It was unlikely the peasants would have much in the way of food, but perhaps they would be able to provide something other than broth. Besides, they might have news of events at Luthadel.

He hiked down the short hill, taking the smaller, eastern fork in the road. Once, there had been little travel in the Final Empire. The Lord Ruler had forbidden skaa to leave their indentured lands, and only thieves and rebels had dared disobey. Still, most of the nobility had made their livings by trading, so a village such as this one might be accustomed to visitors.

Sazed began to notice the oddities immediately. Goats roamed the countryside along the road, unwatched. Sazed paused, then dug a coppermind from his pack. He searched through it as he walked. One book on husbandry claimed that herdsmen sometimes left their flocks alone to graze. Yet, the unwatched animals made him nervous. He quickened his pace.

Just to the south, the skaa starve, he thought. *Yet here, livestock is so plentiful that nobody can be spared to keep it safe from bandits or predators?*

The small village appeared in the distance. Sazed could almost convince himself that the lack of activity—the lack of movement in the streets, the derelict doors and shutters swinging in the breeze—was due to his approach. Perhaps the people were so scared that they were hiding. Or, perhaps they simply were all out. Tending flocks. . . .

Sazed stopped. A shift in the wind brought a telltale scent from the village. The skaa weren't hiding, and they hadn't fled. It was the scent of rotting bodies.

Suddenly urgent, Sazed pulled out a small ring—a scent tinmind—and slipped it on his thumb. The smell on the wind, it didn't seem like that of a slaughter. It was a mustier, dirtier smell. A smell not only of death, but of corruption, unwashed bodies, and waste. He reversed the use of the tinmind, filling it instead of tapping it, and his ability to smell grew very weak—keeping him from gagging.

He continued on, carefully entering the village proper. Like most skaa villages, Urbene was organized simply. It had a group of ten large hovels built in a loose circle with a well at the center. The buildings were wood, and for thatching they used the same needle-bearing branches from the trees he'd seen. Overseers' huts, along with a fine nobleman's manor, stood a little farther up the valley.

If it hadn't been for the smell—and the sense of haunted emptiness—Sazed might have agreed with his gazetteer's description of Urbene. For skaa residences, the hovels looked well maintained, and the village lay in a quiet hollow amid the rising landscape.

It wasn't until he got a little closer that he found the first bodies. They lay scattered around the doorway to the nearest hovel, about a half-dozen of them. Sazed approached carefully, but could quickly see that the corpses were at least several days old. He knelt beside the first one, that of a woman, and could see no visible cause of death. The others were the same.

Nervous, Sazed forced himself to reach up and pull open the door to the hovel. The stench from inside was so strong that he could smell it through his tinmind.

The hovel, like most, was only a single chamber. It was filled with bodies. Most lay wrapped in thin blankets; some sat with backs pressed up against the walls, rotting heads hanging limply from their necks. They had gaunt, nearly fleshless bodies with withered limbs and protruding ribs. Haunted, unseeing eyes sat in desiccated faces.

These people had died of starvation and dehydration.

Sazed stumbled from the hovel, head bowed. He didn't expect to find anything different in the other buildings, but he checked anyway. He saw the same scene repeated again and again. Woundless corpses on the ground outside; many more bodies huddled inside. Flies buzzing about in swarms, covering faces. In several of the buildings he found gnawed human bones at the center of the room.

He stumbled out of the final hovel, breathing deeply through his mouth. Dozens of people, over a hundred total, dead for no obvious reason. What possibly could have caused so many of them to simply sit, hidden in their houses, while they ran out of food and water? How could they have starved when there were beasts running free? And what had killed those that he'd found outside, lying in the ash? They didn't seem as emaciated as the ones inside, though from the level of decomposition, it was difficult to tell.

I must be mistaken about the starvation, Sazed told himself. *It must have been a plague of some sort, a disease. That is a much more logical explanation.* He searched through his medical coppermind. Surely there were diseases that could strike quickly, leaving their victims weakened. And the survivors must have fled. Leaving behind their loved ones. Not taking any of the animals from their pastures. . . .

Sazed frowned. At that moment, he thought he heard something.

He spun, drawing auditory power from his hearing tinmind. The sounds were there—the sound of breathing, the sound of movement, coming from one of the hovels he'd visited. He dashed forward, throwing open the door, looking again on the sorry dead. The corpses lay where they had been before. Sazed studied them very carefully, this time watching until he found the one whose chest was moving.

By the forgotten gods . . . Sazed thought. The man didn't need to work hard to feign death. His hair had fallen out, and his eyes were sunken into his face. Though he didn't look particularly starved, Sazed must have missed seeing him because of his dirty, almost corpselike body.

Sazed stepped toward the man. "I am a friend," he said quietly. The man remained motionless. Sazed frowned as he walked forward and laid a hand on the man's shoulder.

The man's eyes snapped open, and he cried out, jumping to his feet. Dazed and frenzied, he scrambled over corpses, moving to the back of the room. He huddled down, staring at Sazed.

"Please," Sazed said, setting down his pack. "You mustn't be afraid." The only food he had besides broth spices was a few handfuls of meal, but he pulled some out. "I have food."

The man shook his head. "There is no food," he whispered. "We ate it all. Except . . . the food." His eyes darted toward the center of the room. Toward the bones Sazed had noticed earlier. Uncooked, gnawed on, placed in a pile beneath a ragged cloth, as if to hide them.

"I didn't eat the food," the man whispered.

"I know," Sazed said, taking a step forward. "But, there is other food. Outside."

"Can't go outside."

"Why not?"

The man paused, then looked down. "Mist."

Sazed glanced toward the doorway. The sun was nearing the horizon, but wouldn't set for another hour or so. There was no mist. Not now, anyway.

Sazed felt a chill. He slowly turned back toward the man. "Mist . . . during the day?"

The man nodded.

"And it stayed?" Sazed asked. "It didn't go away after a few hours?"

The man shook his head. "Days. Weeks. All mist."

Lord Ruler! Sazed thought, then caught himself. It had been a long time since he'd sworn by that creature's name, even in his thoughts.

But for the mist to come during the day, then to stay—if this man were to be believed—for weeks . . . Sazed could imagine the skaa, frightened in their hovels, a thousand years of terror, tradition, and superstition keeping them from venturing outside.

But to remain inside until they starved? Even their fear of the mist, deep-seated though it was, wouldn't have been enough to make them starve themselves to death, would it?

"Why didn't you leave?" Sazed asked quietly.

"Some did," the man said, nodding as if to himself. "Jell. You know what happened to him."

Sazed frowned. "Dead?"

"Taken by the mist. Oh, how he shook. Was a bull-headed one, you know. Old Jell. Oh, how he shook. How he writhed when it took him."

Sazed closed his eyes. *The corpses I found outside the doors.*

"Some got away," the man said.

Sazed snapped his eyes open. "What?"

The crazed villager nodded again. "Some got away, you know. They called to us, after leaving the village. Said it was all right. It didn't take them. Don't know why. It killed others, though. Some, it shook to the ground, but they got up later. Some it killed."

"The mist let some survive, but it killed others?"

The man didn't answer. He'd sat down, and now he lay back, staring unfocused at the ceiling.

"Please," Sazed said. "You must answer me. Who did it kill and who did it let pass? What is the connection?"

The man turned toward him. "Time for food," he said, then rose. He wandered over to a corpse, then pulled on an arm, ripping the rotted meat free. It was easy to see why he hadn't starved to death like the others.

Sazed pushed aside nausea, striding across the room and grabbing the man's arm as he raised the near fleshless bone to his lips. The man froze, then looked up at Sazed. "It's not mine!" he yelped, dropping the bone and running to the back of the room.

Sazed stood for a moment. *I must hurry. I must get to Luthadel. There is more wrong with this world than bandits and armies.*

The wild man watched with a feral sort of terror as Sazed picked up his pack, then paused and set it down again. He pulled out his largest pewtermind. He fastened the wide metal bracer to his forearm, then turned and walked toward the villager.

"No!" the man screamed, trying to dash to the side. Sazed tapped the pewtermind, pulling out a burst of strength. He felt his muscles enlarge, his robes growing tight. He snatched the villager as the man ran passed, then held him out, far enough away that the man couldn't do either of them much harm.

Then he carried the man outside of the building.

The man stopped struggling as soon as they emerged into the sunlight. He looked up, as if seeing the sun for the first time. Sazed set him down, then released his pewtermind.

The man knelt, looking up at the sun, then turned to Sazed. "The Lord Ruler . . . why did he abandon us? Why did he go?"

"The Lord Ruler was a tyrant."

The man shook his head. "He loved us. He ruled us. Now that he's gone, the mists can kill us. They hate us."

Then, surprisingly adroit, the man leaped to his feet and scrambled down the pathway out of the village. Sazed took a step forward, but paused. What would he do? Pull the man all the way to Luthadel? There was water in the well and there were animals to eat. Sazed could only hope that the poor wretch would be able to manage.

Sighing, Sazed returned to the hovel and retrieved his pack. On his way out, he paused, then pulled out one of his steelminds. Steel held one of the very most difficult attributes to store up: physical speed. He had spent months filling this particular steelmind in preparation for the possibility that someday he might need to run somewhere very, very quickly.

He put it on now.

Yes, he was the one who fueled the rumors after that. I could never have done what he himself did, convincing and persuading the world that he was indeed the Hero. I don't know if he himself believed it, but he made others think that he must be the one.

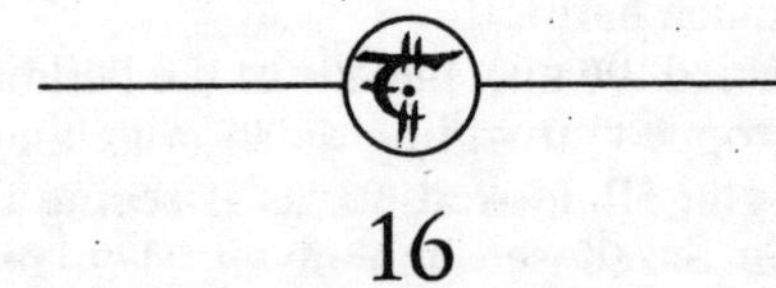

16

VIN RARELY USED HER QUARTERS. Elend had assigned her spacious rooms—which was, perhaps, part of the problem. She'd spent her childhood sleeping in nooks, lairs, or alleys. Having three separate chambers was a bit daunting.

It didn't really matter, however. During her time awake she was with either Elend or the mists. Her rooms existed for her to sleep in. Or, in this case, for her to make a mess in.

She sat on the floor in the center of her main chamber. Elend's steward, concerned that Vin didn't have any furniture, had insisted on decorating her rooms. This morning, Vin had pushed some of this aside, bunching up rugs and chairs on one side so that she could sit on the cool stones with her book.

It was the first real book she had ever owned, though it was just a collection of pages bound loosely at one side. That suited her just fine; the simple binding had made the book that much easier to pull apart.

She sat amid stacks of paper. It was amazing how many pages there were in the book, once she had separated them. Vin sat next to one pile, looking over its contents. She shook her head, then crawled over to another pile. She leafed through the pages, eventually selecting one.

Sometimes I wonder if I'm going mad, the words read.

Perhaps it is due to the pressure of knowing that I must somehow bear the burden of an entire world. Perhaps it is caused by the death I have seen, the friends I have lost. The friends I have been forced to kill.

Either way, I sometimes see shadows following me. Dark creatures that I don't understand, nor do I wish to understand. They are, perhaps, some figment of my overtaxed mind?

Vin sat for a moment, rereading the paragraphs. Then she moved the sheet over to another pile. OreSeur lay on the side of the room, head on paws, eyeing her. "Mistress," he said as she set down the page, "I have been watching you work for the last two hours, and will admit that I am thoroughly confused. What is the point of all this?"

Vin crawled over to another stack of pages. "I thought you didn't care how I spent my time."

"I don't," OreSeur said. "But I do get bored."

"And annoyed, apparently."

"I like to understand what is going on around me."

Vin shrugged, gesturing toward the stacks of paper. "This is the Lord Ruler's logbook. Well, actually, it's not the logbook of the Lord Ruler we knew, but the logbook of the man who *should* have been the Lord Ruler."

"Should have been?" OreSeur asked. "You mean he should have conquered the world, but didn't?"

"No," Vin said. "I mean he should have been the one who took the power at the Well of Ascension. This man, the man who wrote this book—we don't actually know his name—was some kind of prophesied hero. Or . . . everyone thought he was. Anyway, the man who became the Lord Ruler—Rashek—was this hero's packman. Don't you remember us talking about this, back when you were imitating Renoux?"

OreSeur nodded. "I recall you briefly mentioning it."

"Well, this is the book Kelsier and I found when we infiltrated the Lord Ruler's palace. We thought it was written by the Lord Ruler, but it turns out it was written by the man the Lord Ruler killed, the man whose place he took."

"Yes, Mistress," OreSeur said. "Now, why exactly are you tearing it to pieces?"

"I'm not," Vin said. "I just took off the binding so I could move the pages around. It helps me think."

"I . . . see," OreSeur said. "And, what exactly are you looking for? The Lord Ruler is dead, Mistress. Last I checked, you killed him."

What am I looking for? Vin thought, picking up another page. *Ghosts in the mist.*

She read the words on this page slowly.

It isn't a shadow.

This dark thing that follows me, the thing that only I can see—it isn't really a shadow. It is blackish and translucent, but it doesn't have a shadowlike solid outline. It's insubstantial—wispy and formless. Like it's made out of black fog.

Or mist, perhaps.

Vin lowered the page. *It watched him, too,* she thought. She remembered reading the words over a year before, thinking that the Hero must have started to go mad. With all the pressures on him, who would have been surprised?

Now, however, she thought she understood the nameless logbook author better. She knew he was not the Lord Ruler, and could see him for what he might have been. Uncertain of his place in the world, but forced into important events. Determined to do the best he could. Idealistic, in a way.

And the mist spirit had chased him. What did it mean? What did seeing it imply for her?

She crawled over to another pile of pages. She'd spent the morning scanning through the logbook for clues about the mist creature. However, she was having trouble digging out much beyond these two, familiar passages.

She made piles of pages that mentioned anything strange or supernatural. She made a small pile with pages that referenced the mist spirit. She also had a special pile for references to the Deepness. This last one, ironically, was both the largest and least informative of the group.

The logbook author had a habit of mentioning the Deepness, but not saying much about it.

The Deepness was dangerous, that much was clear. It had ravaged the land, slaying thousands. The monster had sown chaos wherever it stepped, bringing destruction and fear, but the armies of mankind had been unable to defeat it. Only the Terris prophecies and the Hero of Ages had offered any hope.

If only he had been more specific! Vin thought with frustration, riffling papers. However, the tone of the logbook really was more melancholy than it was informative. It was something that the Hero had written for himself, to stay sane, to let him put his fears and hopes down on paper. Elend said he wrote for similar reasons, sometimes. To Vin, it seemed a silly method of dealing with problems.

With a sigh, she turned to the last stack of papers—the one with pages she had yet to study. She lay down on the stone floor and began to read, searching for useful information.

It took time. Not only was she a slow reader, but her mind kept wandering. She'd read the logbook before—and, oddly, hints and phrases from it reminded her of where she'd been at the time. Two years and a world away in Fellise, still recovering from her near death at the hands of a Steel Inquisitor, she'd been forced to spend her days pretending to be Valette Renoux, a young, inexperienced country noblewoman.

Back then, she still hadn't believed in Kelsier's plan to overthrow the Final Empire. She'd stayed with the crew because she valued the strange things they offered her—friendship, trust, and lessons in Allomancy—not because she accepted their goals. She would never have guessed where that would lead her. To balls and parties, to actually growing—just a bit—to become the noblewoman she had pretended to be.

But that had been a farce, a few months of make-believe. She forced her thoughts away from the frilly clothing and the dances. She needed to focus on practical matters.

And . . . is this practical? she thought idly, setting a page in one of the stacks. *Studying things I barely comprehend, fearing a threat nobody else even cares to notice?*

She sighed, folding her arms under her chin as she lay on her stomach. What was she really worried about? That the Deepness would return? All she had were a few phantom visions in the mist—things that could, as Elend implied, have easily been fabricated by her overworked mind. More important was another question. Assuming that the Deepness was real, what did she expect to do about it? She was no hero, general, or leader.

Oh, Kelsier, she thought, picking up another page. *We could use you now.* Kelsier had been a man beyond convention . . . a man who had somehow been able to defy reality. He'd thought that by giving his life to overthrow the Lord Ruler, he would secure freedom for the skaa. But, what if his sacrifice had opened the way for a greater danger, something so destructive that the Lord Ruler's oppression was a preferable alternative?

She finally finished the page, then placed it in the stack of those that contained no useful information. Then she paused. She couldn't even remember what she'd just read. She sighed, picking the page back up, looking at it again. How did Elend do it? He could study the same books over and over again. But, for Vin, it was hard to—

She paused. *I must assume that I am not mad,* the words said. *I cannot, with any rational sense of confidence, continue my quest if I do not believe this. The thing following me must, therefore, be real.*

She sat up. She only vaguely remembered this section of the logbook. The book was organized like a diary, with sequential—but dateless—entries. It had a tendency to ramble, and the Hero had been fond of droning on about his insecurities. This section had been particularly dry.

But there, in the middle of his complaining, was a tidbit of information.

I believe that it would kill me, if it could, the text continued.

There is an evil feel to the thing of shadow and fog, and my skin recoils at its touch. Yet, it seems limited in what it can do, especially to me.

It can affect this world, however. The knife it placed in

Fedik's chest proves that much. I'm still not certain which was more traumatic for him—the wound itself, or seeing the thing that did it to him.

Rashek whispers that I stabbed Fedik myself, for only Fedik and I can give witness to that night's events. However, I must make a decision. I must determine that I am not mad. The alternative is to admit that it was I who held that knife.

Somehow, knowing Rashek's opinion on the matter makes it much easier for me to believe the opposite.

The next page continued on about Rashek, and the next several entries contained no mention of the mist spirit. However, Vin found even these few paragraphs exciting.

He made a decision, she thought. *I have to make the same one.* She'd never worried that she was mad, but she had sensed some logic in Elend's words. Now she rejected them. The mist spirit was not some delusion brought on by a mixture of stress and memories of the logbook. It was real.

That didn't mean the Deepness was returning, nor did it mean that Luthadel was in any sort of supernatural danger. Both, however, were possibilities.

She set this page with the two others that contained concrete information about the mist spirit, then turned back to her studies, determined to pay closer attention to her reading.

The armies were digging in.

Elend watched from atop the wall as his plan, vague though it was, began to take form. Straff was making a defensive perimeter to the north, holding the canal route back a relatively short distance to Urteau, his home city and capital. Cett was digging in to the west of the city, holding the Luth-Davn Canal, which ran back to his cannery in Haverfrex.

A cannery. That was something Elend wished he had in the city. The technology was newer—perhaps fifty years old—but he'd read of it. The scholars had considered its main use that of providing easily carried supplies for soldiers fighting at the fringes of the empire. They hadn't considered stockpiles for sieges—particularly in Luthadel. But, then, who would have?

Even as Elend watched, patrols began to move out from the separate armies. Some moved to watch the boundaries between the two forces, but others moved to secure other canal routes, bridges across the River Channerel, and roads leading away from Luthadel. In a remarkably short time, the city felt completely surrounded. Cut off from the world, and the rest of Elend's small kingdom. No more moving in or out. The armies were counting on disease, starvation, and other weakening factors to bring Elend to his knees.

The siege of Luthadel had begun.

That's a good thing, he told himself. *For this plan to work, they have to think me desperate. They have to be so sure that I'm willing to side with them, that they don't consider that I might be working with their enemies, too.*

As Elend watched, he noticed someone climbing up the steps to the wall. Clubs. The general hobbled over to Elend, who had been standing alone. "Congratulations," Clubs said. "Looks like you now have a full-blown siege on your hands."

"Good."

"It'll give us a little breathing room, I guess," Clubs said. Then he eyed Elend with one of his gnarled looks. "You'd better be up to this, kid."

"I know," Elend whispered.

"You've made yourself the focal point," Clubs said. "The Assembly can't break this siege until you meet officially with Straff, and the kings aren't likely to meet with anyone on the crew other than yourself. This is all about you. Useful place for a king to be, I suppose. If he's a good one."

Clubs fell silent. Elend stood, looking out over the separate armies. The words spoken to him by Tindwyl the Terriswoman still bothered him. *You are a fool, Elend Venture. . . .*

So far, neither of the kings had responded to Elend's requests for a meeting—though the crew was sure that they soon would. His enemies would wait, to make Elend sweat a bit. The Assembly had just called another meeting, probably to try and bully him into releasing them from their earlier proposal. Elend had found a convenient reason to skip the meeting.

He looked at Clubs. "And am I a good king, Clubs? In your opinion."

The general glanced at him, and Elend saw a harsh wisdom in his eyes. "I've known worse leaders," he said. "But I've also known a *hell* of a lot better."

Elend nodded slowly. "I want to be good at this, Clubs. Nobody else is going to look after the skaa like they deserve. Cett, Straff. They'd just make slaves of the people again. I . . . I want to be more than my ideas, though. I want to—*need to*—be a man that others can look to."

Clubs shrugged. "My experience has been that the man is usually made by the situation. Kelsier was a selfish dandy until the Pits nearly broke him." He glanced at Elend. "Will this siege be *your* Pits of Hathsin, Elend Venture?"

"I don't know," he said honestly.

"Then we'll have to wait and see, I guess. For now, someone wants to speak with you." He turned, nodding down toward the street some forty feet below, where a tall, feminine figure stood in colorful Terris robes.

"She told me to send you down," Clubs said. He paused, then glanced at Elend. "It isn't often you meet someone who feels like they can order me around. And a Terriswoman at that. I thought those Terris were all docile and kindly."

Elend smiled. "I guess Sazed spoiled us."

Clubs snorted. "So much for a thousand years of breeding, eh?"

Elend nodded.

"You sure she's safe?" Clubs asked.

"Yes," Elend said. "Her story checks out—Vin brought in several of the Terris people from the city, and they knew and recognized Tindwyl. She's apparently a fairly important person back in her homeland."

Plus, she had performed Feruchemy for him, growing

stronger to free her hands. That meant she wasn't a kandra. All of it together meant that she was trustworthy enough; even Vin admitted that, even if she continued to dislike the Terriswoman.

Clubs nodded to him, and Elend took a deep breath. Then he walked down the stairs to meet Tindwyl for another round of lessons.

"Today, we will do something about your clothing," Tindwyl said, closing the door to Elend's study. A plump seamstress with bowl-cut white hair waited inside, standing respectfully with a group of youthful assistants.

Elend glanced down at his clothing. It actually wasn't bad. The suit coat and vest fit fairly well. The trousers weren't as stiff as those favored by imperial nobility, but he was the king now; shouldn't he be able to set the trends?

"I don't see what's wrong with it," he said. He held up a hand as Tindwyl began to speak. "I know it's not quite as formal as what other men like to wear, but it suits me."

"It's disgraceful," Tindwyl said.

"Now, I hardly see—"

"Don't argue with me."

"But, see, the other day you said that—"

"Kings don't argue, Elend Venture," Tindwyl said firmly. "They *command.* And, part of your ability to command comes from your bearing. Slovenly clothing invites other slovenly habits—such as your posture, which I've already mentioned, I believe."

Elend sighed, rolling his eyes as Tindwyl snapped her fingers. The seamstress and her assistants started unpacking a pair of large trunks.

"This isn't necessary," Elend said. "I already have some suits that fit more snugly; I wear them on formal occasions."

"You're not going to wear suits anymore," Tindwyl said.

"Excuse me?"

Tindwyl eyed him with a commanding stare, and Elend sighed.

"Explain yourself!" he said, trying to sound commanding.

Tindwyl nodded. "You have maintained the dress code preferred by the nobility sanctioned by the Final Emperor. In some respects, this was a good idea—it gave you a connection to the former government, and made you seem less of a deviant. Now, however, you are in a different position. Your people are in danger, and the time for simple diplomacy is over. You are at war. Your dress should reflect that."

The seamstress selected a particular costume, then brought it over to Elend while the assistants set up a changing screen.

Elend hesitantly accepted the costume. It was stiff and white, and the front of the jacket appeared to button all the way up to a rigid collar. All and all, it looked like . . .

"A uniform," he said, frowning.

"Indeed," Tindwyl said. "You want your people to believe that you can protect them? Well, a king isn't simply a lawmaker—he's a general. It is time you began to act like you deserve your title, Elend Venture."

"I'm no warrior," Elend said. "This uniform is a lie."

"The first point we will soon change," Tindwyl said. "The second is not true. You command the armies of the Central Dominance. That makes you a military man whether or not you know how to swing a sword. Now, go change."

Elend acceded with a shrug. He walked around the changing screen, pushed aside a stack of books to make room, then began to change. The white trousers fit snugly and fell straight around the calves. While there was a shirt, it was completely obscured by the large, stiff jacket—which had military shoulder fittings. It had an array of buttons—all of which, he noticed, were wood instead of metal—as well as a strange shieldlike design over the right breast. It seemed to have some sort of arrow, or perhaps spear, emblazoned in it.

Stiffness, cut, and design considered, Elend was surprised how well the uniform fit. "It's sized quite well," he noted, putting on the belt, then pulling down the bottom of the jacket, which came all the way to his hips.

"We got your measurements from your tailor," Tindwyl said.

Elend stepped around the changing screen, and several assistants approached. One politely motioned for him to step into a pair of shiny black boots, and the other attached a white cape to fastenings at his shoulders. The final assistant handed him a polished hardwood dueling cane and sheath. Elend hooked it onto the belt, then pulled it through a slit in the jacket so it hung outside; that much, at least, he had done before.

"Good," Tindwyl said, looking him up and down. "Once you learn to stand up straight, that will be a decent improvement. Now, sit."

Elend opened his mouth to object, but thought better of it. He sat down, and an assistant approached to attach a sheet around his shoulders. She then pulled out a pair of shears.

"Now, wait," Elend said. "I see where this is going."

"Then voice an objection," Tindwyl said. "Don't be vague!"

"All right, then," Elend said. "I like my hair."

"Short hair is easier to care for than long hair," Tindwyl said. "And you have proven that you cannot be trusted in the area of personal grooming."

"You aren't cutting my hair," Elend said firmly.

Tindwyl paused, then nodded. The apprentice backed away, and Elend stood, pulling off the sheet. The seamstress produced a large mirror, and Elend walked forward to inspect himself.

And froze.

The difference was surprising. All his life, he'd seen himself as a scholar and socialite, but also as just a bit of a fool. He was Elend—the friendly, comfortable man with the funny ideas. Easy to dismiss, perhaps, but difficult to hate.

The man he saw now was no dandy of the court. He was a serious man—a formal man. A man to be taken seriously. The uniform made him want to stand up straighter, to rest one hand on the dueling cane. His hair—slightly curled, long on the top and sides, and blown loose by the wind atop the city wall—didn't fit.

Elend turned. "All right," he said. "Cut it."

Tindwyl smiled, then nodded for him to sit. He did so, waiting quietly while the assistant worked. When he stood again, his head matched the suit. It wasn't extremely short, not like Ham's hair, but it was neat and precise. One of the assistants approached and handed him a loop of silver-painted wood. He turned to Tindwyl, frowning.

"A crown?" he asked.

"Nothing ostentatious," Tindwyl said. "This is a more subtle era than some of those gone by. The crown isn't a symbol of your wealth, but of your authority. You will wear it from now on, whether you are in private or in public."

"The Lord Ruler didn't wear a crown."

"The Lord Ruler didn't need to remind people that he was in charge," Tindwyl said.

Elend paused, then slipped on the crown. It bore no gemstones or ornamentation; it was just a simple coronet. As he might have expected, it fit perfectly.

He turned back toward Tindwyl, who waved for the seamstress to pack up and leave. "You have six uniforms like this one waiting for you in your rooms," Tindwyl said. "Until this siege is over, you will wear nothing else. If you want variety, change the color of the cape."

Elend nodded. Behind him, the seamstress and her assistants slipped out the door. "Thank you," he told Tindwyl. "I was hesitant at first, but you are right. This makes a difference."

"Enough of one to deceive people for now, at least," Tindwyl said.

"Deceive people?"

"Of course. You didn't think that this was it, did you?"

"Well . . ."

Tindwyl raised an eyebrow. "A few lessons, and you think you're through? We've barely begun. You are still a fool, Elend Venture—you just don't look like one anymore. Hopefully, our charade will begin reversing some of the damage you've done to your reputation. However, it is going to take a lot more training before I'll actually trust you to interact with people and not embarrass yourself."

Elend flushed. "What do you—" He paused. "Tell me what you plan to teach me, then."

"Well, you need to learn how to walk, for one thing."

"Something's wrong with the way I walk?"

"By the forgotten gods, yes!" Tindwyl said, sounding amused, though no smile marred her lips. "And your speech patterns still need work. Beyond that, of course, there is your inability to handle weapons."

"I've had some training," Elend said. "Ask Vin—I rescued her from the Lord Ruler's palace the night of the Collapse!"

"I know," Tindwyl said. "And, from what I've heard, it was a miracle you survived. Fortunately, the girl was there to do the actual fighting. You apparently rely on her quite a bit for that sort of thing."

"She's Mistborn."

"That is no excuse for your slovenly lack of skill," Tindwyl said. "You cannot always rely on your woman to protect you. Not only is it embarrassing, but your people—your soldiers—will expect you to be able to fight with them. I doubt you will ever be the type of leader who can lead a charge against the enemy, but you should at least be able to handle yourself if your position gets attacked."

"So, you want me to begin sparring with Vin and Ham during their training sessions?"

"Goodness, no! Can't you imagine how terrible it would be for morale if the men saw you being beaten up in public?" Tindwyl shook her head. "No, we'll have you trained discreetly by a dueling master. Given a few months, we should have you competent with the cane and the sword. Hopefully, this little siege of yours will last that long before the fighting starts."

Elend flushed again. "You keep talking down to me. It's like I'm not even king in your eyes—like you see me as some kind of placeholder."

Tindwyl didn't answer, but her eyes glinted with satisfaction. *You said it, not I,* her expression seemed to say.

Elend flushed more deeply.

"You can, perhaps, learn to be a king, Elend Venture,"

Tindwyl said. "Until then, you'll just have to learn to fake it."

Elend's angry response was cut off by a knock at the door. Elend gritted his teeth, turning. "Come in."

The door swung open. "There's news," Captain Demoux said, his youthful face excited as he entered. "I—" He froze.

Elend cocked his head. "Yes?"

"I . . . uh . . ." Demoux paused, looked Elend over again before continuing. "Ham sent me, Your Majesty. He says that a messenger from one of the kings has arrived."

"Really?" Elend said. "From Lord Cett?"

"No, Your Majesty. The messenger is from your father."

Elend frowned. "Well, tell Ham I'll be there in a moment."

"Yes, Your Majesty," Demoux said, retreating. "Uh, I like the new uniform, Your Majesty."

"Thank you, Demoux," Elend said. "Do you, by chance, know where Lady Vin is? I haven't seen her all day."

"I think she's in her quarters, Your Majesty."

Her quarters? She never stays there. Is she sick?

"Do you want me to summon her?" Demoux asked.

"No, thank you," Elend said. "I'll get her. Tell Ham to make the messenger comfortable."

Demoux nodded, then withdrew.

Elend turned to Tindwyl, who was smiling to herself with a look of satisfaction. Elend brushed by her, walking over to grab his notebook. "I'm going to learn to do more than just 'fake' being king, Tindwyl."

"We'll see."

Elend shot a glance at the middle-aged Terriswoman in her robes and jewelry.

"Practice expressions like that one," Tindwyl noted, "and you just might do it."

"Is that all it is, then?" Elend asked. "Expressions and costumes? Is that what makes a king?"

"Of course not."

Elend stopped by the door, turning back. "Then, what does? What do *you* think makes a man a good king, Tindwyl of Terris?"

"Trust," Tindwyl said, looking him in the eyes. "A good king is one who is trusted by his people—and one who deserves that trust."

Elend paused, then nodded. *Good answer,* he acknowledged, then pulled open the door and rushed out to find Vin.

If only the Terris religion, and belief in the Anticipation, hadn't spread beyond our people.

17

THE PILES OF PAPER SEEMED to multiply as Vin found more and more ideas in the logbook that she wanted to isolate and remember. What were the prophecies about the Hero of Ages? How did the logbook author know where to go, and what did he think he'd have to do when he got there?

Eventually, lying amid the mess—overlapping piles turned in odd directions to keep them separate—Vin acknowledged a distasteful fact. She was going to have to take notes.

With a sigh, she rose and crossed the room, stepping carefully over several stacks and approaching the room's desk. She'd never used it before; in fact, she'd complained about it to Elend. What need did she have of a writing desk?

So she'd thought. She selected a pen, then pulled out a little jar of ink, remembering the days when Reen had taught her to write. He'd quickly grown frustrated with her scratchings, complaining about the cost of ink and paper. He'd taught her to read so that she could decipher contracts and imitate a noblewoman, but he'd thought that writing was less useful. In general, Vin shared this opinion.

Apparently, however, writing had uses even if one wasn't a scribe. Elend was always scribbling notes and memos to himself; she'd often been impressed by how quickly he could write. How did he make the letters come so easily?

She grabbed a couple of blank sheets of paper and walked back over to her sorted piles. She sat down with crossed legs and unscrewed the top of the ink bottle.

"Mistress," OreSeur noted, still lying with his paws before him, "you do realize that you just left the writing desk behind to sit on the floor."

Vin looked up. "And?"

"The purpose of a writing desk is, well, writing."

"But my papers are all over here."

"Papers can be moved, I believe. If they prove too heavy, you could always burn pewter to give yourself more strength."

Vin eyed his amused face as she inked the nib of her pen. *Well, at least he's displaying something other than his dislike of me.* "The floor is more comfortable."

"If you say so, Mistress, I will believe it to be true."

She paused, trying to determine if he was still mocking her or not. *Blasted dog's face,* she thought. *Too hard to read.*

With a sigh, she leaned down and began to write out the first word. She had to make each line precisely so that the ink didn't smudge, and she had to pause often to sound out words and find the right letters. She'd barely written a couple of sentences before a knock came at her door. She looked up with a frown. Who was bothering her?

"Come in," she called.

She heard a door open in the other room, and Elend's voice called out. "Vin?"

"In here," she said, turning back to her writing. "Why did you knock?"

"Well, you might have been changing," he said, entering.

"So?" Vin asked.

Elend chuckled. "Two years, and privacy is still a strange concept to you."

Vin looked up. "Well, I did—"

For just the briefest flash of a moment, she thought he was someone else. Her instincts kicked in before her brain, and she reflexively dropped the pen, jumping up and flaring pewter.

Then she stopped.

"That much of a change, eh?" Elend asked, holding out his arms so she could get a better look at his costume.

Vin put a hand to her chest, so shocked that she stepped right on one of her stacks. It was Elend, but it wasn't. The brilliant white costume, with its sharp lines and firm figure, looked so different from his normal loose jacket and trousers. He seemed more commanding. More regal.

"You cut your hair," she said, walking around him slowly, studying the costume.

"Tindwyl's idea," he said. "What do you think?"

"Less for people to grab on to in a fight," Vin said.

Elend smiled. "Is that all you think about?"

"No," Vin said absently, reaching up to tug his cape. It came free easily, and she nodded approvingly. Mistcloaks were the same; Elend wouldn't have to worry about someone grabbing his cape in a fight.

She stepped back, arms folded. "Does this mean I can cut my hair, too?"

Elend paused just briefly. "You're always free to do what you want, Vin. But, I kind of think it's pretty longer."

It stays, then.

"Anyway," Elend said. "You approve?"

"Definitely," Vin said. "You look like a king." Though, she suspected a part of her would miss the tangle-haired, disheveled Elend. There had been something . . . endearing about that mixture of earnest competence and distracted inattention.

"Good," Elend said. "Because I think we're going to need the advantage. A messenger just . . ." He trailed off, looking over her stacks of paper. "Vin? Were you doing *research*?"

Vin flushed. "I was just looking through the logbook, trying to find references to the Deepness."

"You were!" Elend stepped forward excitedly. To her chagrin, he quickly located the paper with her fledgling notes on it. He held the paper up, then looked over at her. "Did you write this?"

"Yes," she said.

"Your penmanship is beautiful," he said, sounding a bit surprised. "Why didn't you tell me you could write like this?"

"Didn't you say something about a messenger?"

Elend put the sheet back down, looking oddly like a proud parent. "Right. A messenger from my father's army has arrived. I'm making him wait for a bit—it didn't seem wise to appear too eager. But, we should probably go meet with him."

Vin nodded, waving to OreSeur. The kandra rose and padded to her side, and the three of them left her quarters.

That was one nice thing about books and notes. They could always wait for another time.

They found the messenger waiting in the third-floor Venture atrium. Vin and Elend walked in, and she stopped immediately.

It was *him*. The Watcher.

Elend stepped forward to meet the man, and Vin grabbed his arm. "Wait," she hissed quietly.

Elend turned, confused.

If that man has atium, Vin thought with a stab of panic, *Elend is dead. We're all dead.*

The Watcher stood quietly. He didn't look much like a messenger or courier. He wore all black, even a pair of black gloves. He wore trousers and a silken shirt, with no cloak or cape. She remembered that face. It was him.

But . . . she thought, *if he'd wanted to kill Elend, he could have done so already.* The thought frightened her, yet she had to admit it was true.

"What?" Elend asked, standing in the doorway with her.

"Be careful," she whispered. "This is no simple messenger. That man is Mistborn."

Elend paused, frowning. He turned back toward the

Watcher, who stood quietly, clasping his hands behind his back, looking confident. Yes, he was Mistborn; only a man such as he could walk into an enemy palace, completely surrounded by guards, and not be the slightest bit unsettled.

"All right," Elend said, finally stepping into the room. "Straff's man. You bring a message for me?"

"Not just a message, Your Majesty," the Watcher said. "My name is Zane, and I am something of an . . . ambassador. Your father was very pleased to receive your invitation for an alliance. He's glad that you are finally seeing reason."

Vin studied the Watcher, this "Zane." What was his game? Why come himself? Why reveal who he was?

Elend nodded, keeping a distance from Zane. "Two armies," Elend said, "camped outside my door . . . well, that's not the kind of thing I can ignore. I'd like to meet with my father and discuss possibilities for the future."

"I think he would enjoy that," Zane said. "It has been some time since he saw you, and he has long regretted your falling-out. You are, after all, his only son."

"It's been hard on both of us," Elend said. "Perhaps we could set up a tent in which to meet outside the city?"

"I'm afraid that won't be possible," Zane said. "His Majesty rightly fears assassins. If you wish to speak with him, he'd be happy to host you at his tent in the Venture camp."

Elend frowned. "Now, I don't think that makes much sense. If he fears assassins, shouldn't I?"

"I'm certain he could protect you in his own camp, Your Majesty," Zane said. "You have nothing to fear from Cett's assassins there."

"I . . . see," Elend said.

"I'm afraid that His Majesty was quite firm on this point," Zane said. "You are the one who is eager for an alliance—if you wish a meeting, you will have to come to him."

Elend glanced at Vin. She continued to watch Zane. The man met her eyes, and spoke. "I have heard reports of the beautiful Mistborn who accompanies the Venture heir. She who slew the Lord Ruler, and was trained by the Survivor himself."

There was silence in the room for a moment.

Elend finally spoke. "Tell my father that I will consider his offer."

Zane finally turned away from Vin. "His Majesty was hoping for us to set a date and time, Your Majesty."

"I will send another message when I have made my decision," Elend said.

"Very well," Zane said, bowing slightly, though he used the move to catch Vin's eyes once again. Then he nodded once to Elend, and let the guards escort him away.

In the cold mist of early evening, Vin waited on the short wall of Keep Venture, OreSeur sitting at her side.

The mists were quiet. Her thoughts were far less serene.

Who else would he work for? she thought. *Of course he's one of Straff's men.*

That explained many things. It had been quite a while since their last encounter; Vin had begun to think that she wouldn't see the Watcher again.

Would they spar again, then? Vin tried to suppress her eagerness, tried to tell herself that she simply wanted to find this Watcher because of the threat he posed. But, the thrill of another fight in the mists—another chance to test her abilities against a Mistborn—made her tense with anticipation.

She didn't know him, and she certainly didn't trust him. That only made the prospect of a fight all the more exciting.

"Why are we waiting here, Mistress?" OreSeur asked.

"We're just on patrol," Vin said. "Watching for assassins or spies. Just like every night."

"Do you command me to believe you, Mistress?"

Vin shot him a flat stare. "Believe as you wish, kandra."

"Very well," OreSeur said. "Why did you not tell the king that you've been sparring with this Zane?"

Vin turned back toward the dark mists. "Assassins and

Allomancers are my concern, not Elend's. No need to worry him yet—he has enough troubles at the moment."

OreSeur sat back on his haunches. "I see."

"You don't believe I'm right?"

"I believe as I wish," OreSeur said. "Isn't that what you just commanded me, Mistress?"

"Whatever," Vin said. Her bronze was on, and she had to try very hard not to think about the mist spirit. She could feel it waiting in the darkness to her right. She didn't look toward it.

The logbook never did mention what became of that spirit. It nearly killed one of the Hero's companions. After that, there was barely a mention of it.

Problems for another night, she thought as another source of Allomancy appeared to her bronze senses. A stronger, more familiar source.

Zane.

Vin hopped up onto the battlements, nodded farewell to OreSeur, then jumped out into the night.

Mist twisted in the sky, different breezes forming silent streams of white, like rivers in the air. Vin skimmed them, burst through them, and rode them like a bouncing stone cast upon the waters. She quickly reached the place where she and Zane had last parted, the lonely abandoned street.

He waited in the center, still wearing black. Vin dropped to the cobbles before him in a flurry of mistcloak tassels. She stood up straight.

He never wears a cloak. Why is that?

The two stood opposite one another for a few silent moments. Zane had to know of her questions, but he offered no introduction, greeting, or explanation. Eventually, he reached into a pocket and pulled out a coin. He tossed it to the street between them, and it bounced—metal ringing against stone—and came to a stop.

He jumped into the air. Vin did likewise, both Pushing against the coin. Their separate weights nearly canceled each other out, and they shot up and back, like the two arms of a "V."

Zane spun, throwing a coin behind him. It slammed

against the side of a building and he Pushed, throwing himself toward Vin. Suddenly, she felt a force slam against her coin pouch, threatening to toss her back down to the ground.

What is the game tonight, Zane? she thought even as she yanked the tie on her pouch, dropping it free from her belt. She Pushed against it, and it shot downward, forced by her weight. When it hit the ground, Vin had the better upward force: she was Pushing against the pouch from directly above, while Zane was only pushing from the side. Vin lurched upward, streaking past Zane in the cool night air, then threw her weight against the coins in his own pocket.

Zane began to drop. However, he grabbed the coins—keeping them from ripping free—and Pushed down on her pouch. He froze in the air—Vin Pushing him from above, his own Push forcing him upward. And, because he stopped, Vin's Push suddenly threw her backward.

Vin let go of Zane and allowed herself to drop. Zane, however, didn't let himself fall. He Pushed himself back up into the air, then began to bound away, never letting his feet touch rooftops or cobblestones.

He tried to force me to the ground, Vin thought. *First one to fall loses, is that it?* Still tumbling, Vin spun herself in the air. She retrieved her coin pouch with a careful Pull, then threw it down toward the ground and Pushed herself upward.

She Pulled the pouch back into her hand even as she flew, then jumped after Zane, Pushing recklessly through the night, trying to catch up. In the darkness, Luthadel seemed cleaner than it did during the day. She couldn't see the ash-stained buildings, the dark refineries, the haze of smoke from the forges. Around her, the empty keeps of the old high nobility watched like silent monoliths. Some of the majestic buildings had been given to lesser nobles, and others had become government buildings. The rest—after being plundered at Elend's command—lay unused, their stained-glass windows dark, their vaultings, statues, and murals ignored.

Vin wasn't certain if Zane purposely headed to Keep

Hasting, or if she simply caught up to him there. Either way, the enormous structure loomed as Zane noticed her proximity and turned, throwing a handful of coins at her.

Vin Pushed against them tentatively. Sure enough, as soon as she touched them, Zane flared steel and Pushed harder. If she'd been Pushing hard, the force of his attack would have thrown her backward. As it was, she was able to deflect the coins to her sides.

Zane immediately Pushed against her coin pouch again, throwing himself upward along one of Keep Hasting's walls. Vin was ready for this move as well. Flaring pewter, she grabbed the pouch in a two-handed grip and ripped it in half.

Coins sprayed beneath her, shooting toward the ground under the force of Zane's Push. She selected one and Pushed herself, gaining lift as soon as it hit the ground. She spun, facing upward, her tin-enhanced ears hearing a shower of metal hit the stones far below. She'd still have access to the coins, but she didn't have to carry them on her body.

She shot up toward Zane, one of the keep's outer towers looming in the mists to her left. Keep Hasting was one of the finest in the city. It had a large tower at the center—tall, imposing, wide—with a ballroom at the very top. It also had six smaller towers rising equidistant around the central structure, each one connected to it by a thick wall. It was an elegant, majestic building. Somehow, she suspected that Zane had sought it out for that reason.

Vin watched him now, his Push losing power as he got too far from the coin anchor below. He spun directly above her, a dark figure against a shifting sky of mist, still well below the top of the wall. Vin yanked sharply on several coins below, Pulling them into the air in case she needed them.

Zane plummeted toward her. Vin reflexively Pushed against the coins in his pocket, then realized that was probably what he'd wanted: it gave him lift while forcing her down. She let go as she fell, and she soon passed the group of coins she'd Pulled into the air. She Pulled on one, bringing it into her hand, then Pushed on another, sending it sideways into the wall.

Vin shot to the side. Zane whooshed by her in the air, his passing churning the mists. He soon bobbed back up—probably using a coin from below—and flung a double handful of coins straight at her.

Vin spun, again deflecting the coins. They shot around her, and she heard several *pling* against something in the mists behind her. Another wall. She and Zane were sparring between a pair of the keep's outer towers; there was an angled wall to either side of them, with the central tower just a short distance in front of them. They were fighting near the tip of an open-bottomed triangle of stone walls.

Zane shot toward her. Vin reached out to throw her weight against him, but realized with a start that he was no longer carrying any coins. He was Pushing on something behind him, though—the same coin Vin had slammed against the wall with her weight. She Pushed herself upward, trying to get out of the way, but he angled upward as well.

Zane crashed into her, and they began to fall. As they spun together, Zane grabbed her by the upper arms, holding his face close to hers. He didn't seem angry, or even very forceful.

He just seemed calm.

"This is what we are, Vin," he said quietly. Wind and mist whipped around them as they fell, the tassels of Vin's mistcloak writhing in the air around Zane. "Why do you play their games? Why do you let them control you?"

Vin placed her hand lightly against Zane's chest, then Pushed on the coin that had been in her palm. The force of the Push lurched her free of his grip, flipping him up and backward. She caught herself just a few feet from the ground, Pushing against fallen coins, throwing herself upward again.

She passed Zane in the night, and saw a smile on his face as he fell. Vin reached downward, locking on to the blue lines extending toward the ground far below, then flared iron and Pulled against all of them at once. Blue lines zipped around her, the coins rising and rising shooting past the surprised Zane.

She Pulled a few choice coins into her hands. *Let's see if you can stay in the air now,* Vin thought with a smile, Pushing outward, spraying the other coins away into the night. Zane continued to fall.

Vin began to fall as well. She threw a coin to each side, then Pushed. The coins shot into the mists, flying toward the stone walls to either side. Coins slapped against stone, and Vin lurched to a halt in the air.

She Pushed hard, holding herself in place, anticipating a Pull from below. *If he pulls, I Pull, too,* she thought. *We both fall, and I keep the coins between us in the air. He'll hit the ground first.*

A coin shot past her in the air.

What! Where did he get that! She'd been sure that she'd Pushed away every coin below.

The coin arced upward, through the mists, trailing a blue line visible to her Allomancer's eyes. It crested the top of the wall to her right. Vin glanced down just in time to see Zane slow, then lurch upward—Pulling on the coin that was now held in place atop the wall by the stone railing.

He passed her with a self-satisfied look on his face.

Show-off.

Vin let go of the coin to her left while still Pushing to her right. She lurched to the left, nearly colliding with the wall before she threw another coin at it. She Pushed on this one, throwing herself upward and to the right. Another coin sent her back upward to the left, and she continued to bounce between the walls, back and forth, until she crested the top.

She smiled as she twisted in the air. Zane—hovering in the air above the wall's top—nodded appreciatively as she passed. She noticed that he'd grabbed a few of her discarded coins.

Time for a little attack myself, Vin thought.

She slammed a Push against the coins in Zane's hand, and they shot her upward. However, Zane was still Pushing against the coin on the wall top below, and so he didn't fall. Instead he hung in the air between the two forces—his own Push forcing him upward, Vin's Push forcing him downward.

Vin heard him grunt in exertion, and she Pushed harder. She was so focused, however, that she barely saw him open his other hand and Push a coin up toward her. She reached out to Push against it, but fortunately his aim was off, and the coin missed her by a few inches.

Or perhaps it didn't. Immediately, the coin zipped back downward and hit her in the back. Zane Pulled on it forcefully, and the bit of metal dug into Vin's skin. She gasped, flaring pewter to keep the coin from cutting through her.

Zane didn't relent. Vin gritted her teeth, but he weighed much more than she did. She inched down toward him in the night, her Push straining to keep the two of them apart, the coin digging painfully into her back.

Never get into a raw Pushing match, Vin, Kelsier had warned her. *You don't weigh enough—you'll lose every time.*

She stopped Pushing on the coin in Zane's hand. Immediately, she fell, Pulled by the coin on her back. She Pushed on it slightly, giving herself a little leverage, then threw her final coin to the side. It hit at the last moment, and Vin's Push scooted her out from between Zane and his coin.

Zane's coin snapped him in the chest, and he grunted: he had obviously been trying to get Vin to collide with him again. Vin smiled, then Pulled against the coin in Zane's hand.

Give him what he wants, I guess.

He turned just in time to see her slam feet-first into him. Vin spun, feeling him crumple beneath her. She exulted in the victory, spinning in the air above the wall walk. Then she noticed something: several faint lines of blue disappearing into the distance. Zane had pushed all of their coins away.

Desperately, Vin grabbed one of the coins and Pulled it back. Too late, however. She searched frantically for a closer source of metal, but all was stone or wood. Disoriented, she hit the stone wall walk, tumbling amid her mistcloak until she came to a halt beside the wall's stone railing.

She shook her head and flared tin, clearing her vision with a flash of pain and other senses. Surely Zane hadn't fared better. He must have fallen as—

Zane hung a few feet away. He'd found a coin—Vin

couldn't fathom how—and was Pushing against it below him. However, he didn't shoot away. He hovered above the wall top, just a few feet in the air, still in a half tumble from Vin's kick.

As Vin watched, Zane rotated slowly in the air, hand outstretched beneath him, twisting like a skilled acrobat on a pole. There was a look of intense concentration on his face, and his muscles—all of them, arms, face, chest—were taut. He turned in the air until he was facing her.

Vin watched with awe. It was possible to Push just slightly against a coin, regulating the amount of force with which one was thrown backward. It was incredibly difficult, however—so difficult that even Kelsier had struggled with it. Most of the time, Mistborn simply used short bursts. When Vin fell, for instance, she slowed herself by throwing a coin and Pushing against it briefly—but powerfully—to counteract her momentum.

She'd never seen an Allomancer with as much control as Zane. His ability to push slightly against that coin would be of little use in a fight; it obviously took too much concentration. Yet, there was a grace to it, a beauty to his movements that implied something Vin herself had felt.

Allomancy wasn't just about fighting and killing. It was about skill and grace. It was something beautiful.

Zane rotated until he was upright, standing in a gentleman's posture. Then he dropped to the wall walk, his feet slapping quietly against the stones. He regarded Vin—who still lay on the stones—with a look that lacked contempt.

"You are very skilled," he said. "And quite powerful."

He was tall, impressive. *Like . . . Kelsier*. "Why did you come to the palace today?" she asked, climbing to her feet.

"To see how they treated you. Tell me, Vin. What is it about Mistborn that makes us—despite our powers—so willing to act as slaves to others?"

"Slaves?" Vin said. "I'm no slave."

Zane shook his head. "They use you, Vin."

"Sometimes it's good to be useful."

"Those words are spoken of insecurity."

Vin paused; then she eyed him. "Where did you get that coin, at the end? There were none nearby."

Zane smiled, then opened his mouth and pulled out a coin. He dropped it to the stones with a *pling*. Vin opened her eyes wide. *Metal inside a person's body can't be affected by another Allomancer. . . . That's such an easy trick! Why didn't I think of it?*

Why didn't Kelsier think of it?

Zane shook his head. "We don't belong with them, Vin. We don't belong in *their* world. We belong here, in the mists."

"I belong with those who love me," Vin said.

"Love you?" Zane asked quietly. "Tell me. Do they understand you, Vin? *Can* they understand you? And, can a man love something he doesn't understand?"

He watched her for a moment. When she didn't respond, he nodded to her slightly, then Pushed against the coin he had dropped moments before, throwing himself back into the mists.

Vin let him go. His words held more weight than he probably understood. *We don't belong in their world. . . .* He couldn't know that she'd been pondering her place, wondering whether she was noblewoman, assassin, or something else.

Zane's words, then, meant something important. He felt himself to be an outsider. A little like herself. It was a weakness in him, certainly. Perhaps she could turn him against Straff—his willingness to spar with her, his willingness to reveal himself, hinted at that much.

She breathed in deeply of the cool, mist air, her heart still beating quickly from the exchange. She felt tired, yet alive, from fighting someone who might actually be better than she was. Standing in the mists atop the wall of an abandoned keep, she decided something.

She had to keep sparring with Zane.

If only the Deepness hadn't come when it did, providing a threat that drove men to desperation both in action and belief.

18

"KILL HIM," GOD WHISPERED.

Zane hung quietly in the mists, looking through Elend Venture's open balcony doors. The mists swirled around him, obscuring him from the king's view.

"You should kill him," God said again.

In a way, Zane hated Elend, though he had never met the man before today. Elend was everything that Zane should have been. Favored. Privileged. Pampered. He was Zane's enemy, a block in the road to domination, the thing that was keeping Straff—and therefore Zane—from ruling the Central Dominance.

But he was also Zane's brother.

Zane let himself drop through the mists, falling silently to the ground outside Keep Venture. He Pulled his anchors up into his hand—three small bars he had been pushing on to hold himself in place. Vin would be returning soon, and he didn't want to be near the keep when she did. She had a strange ability to know where he was; her senses were far more keen than any Allomancer he had ever known or fought. Of course, she had been trained by the Survivor himself.

I would have liked to have known him, Zane thought as he moved quietly across the courtyard. *He was a man who understood the power of being Mistborn. A man who didn't let others control him.*

A man who did what had to be done, no matter how ruthless it seemed. Or so the rumors said.

Zane paused beside the outer keep wall, below a buttress. He stooped, removing a cobblestone, and found the message left there by his spy inside Elend's palace. Zane retrieved it, replaced the cobblestone, then dropped a coin and launched himself out into the night.

Zane did not slink. Nor did he creep, skulk, or cower. In fact, he didn't even like to hide.

So, he approached the Venture army camp with a determined stride. It seemed to him that Mistborn spent too much of their existence hiding. True, anonymity offered some limited freedom. However, his experience had been that it bound them more than it freed them. It let them be controlled, and it let society pretend that they didn't exist.

Zane strode toward a guard post, where two soldiers sat beside a large fire. He shook his head; they were virtually useless, blinded by the firelight. Normal men feared the mists, and that made them less valuable. That wasn't arrogance; it was a simple fact. Allomancers were more useful, and therefore more valuable, than normal men. That was why Zane had Tineyes watching in the darkness as well. These regular soldiers were more a formality than anything else.

"Kill them," God commanded as Zane walked up to the guard post. Zane ignored the voice, though it was growing more and more difficult to do so.

"Halt!" one of the guards said, lowering a spear. "Who is that?"

Zane Pushed the spear offhandedly, flipping up the tip. "Who else would it be?" he snapped, walking into the firelight.

"Lord Zane!" the other soldier said.

"Summon the king," Zane said, passing the guard post. "Tell him to meet me in the command tent."

"But, my lord," the guard said. "The hour is late. His Majesty is probably . . ."

Zane turned, giving the guard a flat stare. The mists swirled between them. Zane didn't even have to use emotional Allomancy on the soldier; the man simply saluted, then rushed off into the night to do as commanded.

Zane strode through the camp. He wore no uniform or

mistcloak, but soldiers stopped and saluted as he passed. *This* was the way it should be. They knew him, knew what he was, knew to respect him.

And yet, a part of him acknowledged that if Straff hadn't kept his bastard son hidden, Zane might not be the powerful weapon that he was today. That secrecy had forced Zane to live a life of near squalor while his half brother, Elend, had been privileged. But it also meant that Straff had been able to keep Zane hidden for most of his life. Even still, while rumors were growing about the existence of Straff's Mistborn, few realized that Zane was Straff's son.

Plus, living a harsh life had taught Zane to survive on his own. He had become hard, and powerful. Things he suspected Elend would never understand. Unfortunately, one side effect of his childhood was that it had apparently driven him mad.

"Kill him," God whispered as Zane passed another guard. The voice spoke every time he saw a person—it was Zane's quiet, constant companion. He understood that he was insane. It hadn't really been all that hard to determine, all things considered. Normal people did not hear voices. Zane did.

He found insanity no excuse, however, for irrational behavior. Some men were blind, others had poor tempers. Still others heard voices. It was all the same, in the end. A man was defined not by his flaws, but by how he overcame them.

And so, Zane ignored the voice. He killed when he wanted to, not when it commanded. In his estimation, he was actually quite lucky. Other madmen saw visions, or couldn't distinguish their delusions from reality. Zane, at least, could control himself.

For the most part.

He Pushed on the metal clasps on the flaps of the command tent. The flaps flipped backward, opening for him as the soldiers to either side saluted. Zane ducked inside.

"My lord!" said the nightwatch officer of command.

"Kill him," God said. "He's really not that important."

"Paper," Zane ordered, walking to the room's large

table. The officer scrambled to comply, grabbing a stack of sheets. Zane Pulled on the nib of a pen, flipping it across the room to his waiting hand. The officer brought the ink.

"These are troop concentrations and night patrols," Zane said, scribbling down some numbers and diagrams on the paper. "I observed them tonight, while I was in Luthadel."

"Very good, my lord," the soldier said. "We appreciate your help."

Zane paused. Then he slowly continued to write. "Soldier, you are not my superior. You aren't even my equal. I am not 'helping' you. I am seeing to the needs of my army. Do you understand?"

"Of course, my lord."

"Good," Zane said, finishing his notes and handing the paper to the soldier. "Now, leave—or I'll do as a friend has suggested and ram this pen through your throat."

The soldier accepted the paper, then quickly withdrew. Zane waited impatiently. Straff did not arrive. Finally, Zane cursed quietly and Pushed open the tent flaps and strode out. Straff's tent was a blazing red beacon in the night, well lit by numerous lanterns. Zane passed the guards, who knew better than to bother him, and entered the king's tent.

Straff was having a late dinner. He was a tall man, brown of hair like both his sons—the two important ones, at least. He had fine nobleman's hands, which he used to eat with finesse. He didn't react as Zane entered.

"You're late," Straff said.

"Kill him," God said.

Zane clinched his fists. This command from the voice was the hardest to ignore. "Yes," he said. "I'm late."

"What happened tonight?" Straff asked.

Zane glanced at the servants. "We should do this in the command tent."

Straff continued to sip his soup, staying where he was, implying that Zane had no power to order him about. It was frustrating, but not unexpected. Zane had used virtually the same tactic on the nightwatch officer just moments before. He had learned from the best.

Finally, Zane sighed, taking a seat. He rested his arms on

the table, idly spinning a dinner knife as he watched his father eat. A servant approached to ask Zane if he wanted a meal, but he waved the man away.

"Kill Straff," God commanded. "You should be in his place. You are stronger than he is. You are more competent."

But I'm not as sane, Zane thought.

"Well?" Straff asked. "Do they have the Lord Ruler's atium or not?"

"I'm not sure," Zane said.

"Does the girl trust you?" Straff asked.

"She's beginning to," Zane said. "I did see her use atium, that once, fighting Cett's assassins."

Straff nodded thoughtfully. He really was competent; because of him, the Northern Dominance had avoided the chaos that prevailed in the rest of the Final Empire. Straff's skaa remained under control, his noblemen quelled. True, he had been forced to execute a number of people to prove that he was in charge. But, he did what needed to be done. That was one attribute in a man that Zane respected above all others.

Especially since he had trouble displaying it himself.

"Kill him!" God yelled. "You hate him! He kept you in squalor, forcing you to fight for your survival as a child."

He made me strong, Zane thought.

"Then use that strength to kill him!"

Zane grabbed the carving knife off the table. Straff looked up from his meal, then flinched just slightly as Zane sliced the flesh of his own arm. He cut a long gash into the top of his forearm, drawing blood. The pain helped him resist the voice.

Straff watched for a moment, then waved for a servant to bring Zane a towel so he wouldn't get blood on the rug.

"You need to get her to use atium again," Straff said. "Elend may have been able to gather one or two beads. We'll only know the truth if she runs out." He paused, turning back to his meal. "Actually, what you need to do is get her to tell you where the stash is hidden, if they even have it."

Zane sat, watching the blood seep from the gash on his forearm. "She's more capable than you think, Father."

Straff raised an eyebrow. "Don't tell me you believe those stories, Zane? The lies about her and the Lord Ruler?"

"How do you know they are lies?"

"Because of Elend," Straff said. "That boy is a fool; he only controls Luthadel because every nobleman with half a wit in his head fled the city. If that girl were powerful enough to defeat the Lord Ruler, I sincerely doubt that your brother could ever have gained her loyalty."

Zane cut another slice in his arm. He didn't cut deeply enough to do any real damage, and the pain worked as it usually did. Straff finally turned from his meal, masking a look of discomfort. A small, twisted piece of Zane took pleasure from seeing that look in his father's eyes. Perhaps it was a side effect of his insanity.

"Anyway," Straff said, "did you meet with Elend?"

Zane nodded. He turned to a serving girl. "Tea," he said, waving his uncut arm. "Elend was surprised. He wanted to meet with you, but he obviously didn't like the idea of coming into your camp. I doubt he'll come."

"Perhaps," Straff said. "But, don't underestimate the boy's foolishness. Either way, perhaps now he understands how our relationship will proceed."

So much posturing, Zane thought. By sending this message, Straff took a stand: he wouldn't be ordered about, or even inconvenienced, on Elend's behalf.

Being forced into a siege inconvenienced you, though, Zane thought with a smile. What Straff would have liked to do was attack directly, taking the city without parlay or negotiations. The arrival of the second army made that impossible. Attack now, and Straff would be defeated by Cett.

That meant waiting, waiting in a siege, until Elend saw reason and joined with his father willingly. But, waiting was something Straff disliked. Zane didn't mind as much. It would give him more time to spar with the girl. He smiled.

As the tea arrived, Zane closed his eyes, then burned tin to enhance his senses. His wounds burst to life, minor pains becoming great, shocking him to wakefulness.

There was a part of all this he wasn't telling Straff. *She is coming to trust me,* he thought. *And there's something else about her. She's like me. Perhaps . . . she could understand me.*

Perhaps she could save me.

He sighed, opening his eyes and using the towel to clean his arm. His insanity frightened him sometimes. But, it seemed weaker around Vin. That was all he had to go on for the moment. He accepted his tea from the serving girl—long braid, firm chest, homely features—and took a sip of the hot cinnamon.

Straff raised his own cup, then hesitated, sniffing delicately. He eyed Zane. "Poisoned tea, Zane?"

Zane said nothing.

"Birchbane, too," Straff noted. "That's a depressingly unoriginal move for you."

Zane said nothing.

Straff made a cutting motion. The girl looked up with terror as one of Straff's guards stepped toward her. She glanced at Zane, expecting some sort of aid, but he just looked away. She yelled pathetically as the guard pulled her off to be executed.

She wanted the chance to kill him, he thought. *I told her it probably wouldn't work.*

Straff just shook his head. Though not a full Mistborn, the king was a Tineye. Still, even for one with such an ability, sniffing birchbane amid the cinnamon was an impressive feat.

"Zane, Zane . . ." Straff said. "What would you do if you actually managed to kill me?"

If I actually wanted to kill you, Zane thought, *I'd use that knife, not poison.* But, he let Straff think what he wished. The king expected assassination attempts. So Zane provided them.

Straff held something up—a small bead of atium. "I was going to give you this, Zane. But I see that we'll have to wait. You need to get over these foolish attempts on my life. If you were ever to succeed, where would you get your atium?"

Straff didn't understand, of course. He thought that atium was like a drug, and assumed that Mistborn relished using it.

Therefore, he thought he could control Zane with it. Zane let the man continue in his misapprehension, never explaining that he had his own personal stockpile of the metal.

That, however, brought him to face the real question that dominated his life. God's whispers were returning, now that the pain was fading. And, of all the people the voice whispered about, Straff Venture was the one who most deserved to die.

"Why?" God asked. "Why won't you kill him?"

Zane looked down at his feet. *Because he's my father,* he thought, finally admitting his weakness. Other men did what they had to. They were stronger than Zane.

"You're insane, Zane," Straff said.

Zane looked up.

"Do you really think you could conquer the empire yourself, if you were to kill me? Considering your . . . particular malady, do you think you could run even a city?"

Zane looked away. "No."

Straff nodded. "I'm glad we both understand that."

"You should just attack," Zane said. "We can find the atium once we control Luthadel."

Straff smiled, then sipped the tea. The *poisoned* tea.

Despite himself, Zane started, sitting up straight.

"Don't presume to think you know what I'm planning, Zane," Straff said. "You don't understand *half* as much as you assume."

Zane sat quietly, watching his father drink the last of the tea.

"What of your spy?" Straff asked.

Zane lay the note on the table. "He's worried that they might suspect him. He has found no information about the atium."

Straff nodded, setting down the empty cup. "You'll return to the city and continue to befriend the girl."

Zane nodded slowly, then turned and left the tent.

Straff thought he could feel the birchbane already, seeping through his veins, making him tremble. He forced himself to remain in control. Waiting for a few moments.

Once he was sure Zane was distant, he called for a guard. "Bring me Amaranta!" Straff ordered. "Quickly!"

The soldier rushed to do his master's bidding. Straff sat quietly, tent rustling in the evening breeze, a puff of mist floating to the floor from the once open flap. He burned tin, enhancing his senses. Yes . . . he could feel the poison within him. Deadening his nerves. He had time, however. As long as an hour, perhaps, and so he relaxed.

For a man who claimed he didn't want to kill Straff, Zane certainly spent a lot of effort trying. Fortunately, Straff had a tool even Zane didn't know about—one that came in the form of a woman. Straff smiled as his tin-enhanced ears heard soft footsteps approaching in the night.

The soldiers sent Amaranta right in. Straff hadn't brought all of his mistresses with him on the trip—just his ten or fifteen favorites. Mixed in with the ones he was currently bedding, however, were some women that he kept for their effectiveness rather than their beauty. Amaranta was a good example. She had been quite attractive a decade before, but now she was creeping up into her late twenties. Her breasts had begun to sag from childbirth, and every time Straff looked at her, he noticed the wrinkles that were appearing on her forehead and around her eyes. He got rid of most women long before they reached her age.

This one, however, had skills that were useful. If Zane heard that Straff had sent for the woman this night, he'd assume that Straff had simply wanted to bed her. He'd be wrong.

"My lord," Amaranta said, getting down on her knees. She began to disrobe.

Well, at least she's optimistic, Straff thought. He would have thought that after four years without being called to his bed, she would understand. Didn't women realize when they were too old to be attractive?

"Keep your clothing on, woman," he snapped.

Amaranta's face fell, and she laid her hands in her lap, leaving her dress half undone, one breast exposed—as if she were trying to tempt him with her aging nudity.

"I need your antidote," he said. "Quickly."

"Which one, my lord?" she asked. She wasn't the only herbalist Straff kept; he learned scents and tastes from four different people. Amaranta, however, was the best of them.

"Birchbane," Straff said. "And . . . maybe something else. I'm not sure."

"Another general potion, then, my lord?" Amaranta asked.

Straff nodded curtly. Amaranta rose, walking to his poison cabinet. She lit the burner at the side, boiling a small pot of water as she quickly mixed powders, herbs, and liquids. The concoction was her particular specialty—a mixture of all of the basic poison antidotes, remedies, and reagents in her repertoire. Straff suspected that Zane had used the birchbane to cover something else. Whatever it was, however, Amaranta's concoction would deal with—or at least identify—it.

Straff waited uncomfortably as Amaranta worked, still half naked. The concoction needed to be prepared freshly each time, but it was worth the wait. She eventually brought him a steaming mug. Straff gulped it, forcing down the harsh liquid despite its bitterness. Immediately, he began to feel better.

He sighed—another trap avoided—as he drank the rest of the cup to be certain. Amaranta knelt expectantly again.

"Go," Straff ordered.

Amaranta nodded quietly. She put her arm back through the dress's sleeve, then retreated from the tent.

Straff sat stewing, empty cup cooling in his hand. He knew he held the edge. As long as he appeared strong before Zane, the Mistborn would continue to do as commanded.

Probably.

If only I had passed over Alendi when looking for an assistant, all those years ago.

19

SAZED UNCLASPED HIS FINAL STEELMIND. He held it up, the braceletlike band of metal glistening in the red sunlight. To another man, it might seem valuable. To Sazed, it was now just another empty husk—a simple steel bracelet. He could refill it if he wished, but for the moment he didn't consider the weight worth carrying.

With a sigh, he dropped the bracelet. It fell with a clank, tossing up a puff of ash from the ground. *Five months of storing, of spending every fifth day drained of speed, my body moving as if impeded by a thick molasses. And now it's all gone.*

The loss had purchased something valuable, however. In just six days of travel, using steelminds on occasion, he had traveled the equivalent of six weeks' worth of walking. According to his cartography coppermind, Luthadel was now a little over a week away. Sazed felt good about the expenditure. Perhaps he'd overreacted to the deaths he'd found in the little southern village. Perhaps there was no need for him to hurry. But, he'd created the steelmind to be used.

He hefted his pack, which was much lighter than it had been. Though many of his metalminds were small, they were heavy in aggregate. He'd decided to discard some of the less valuable or less full ones as he ran. Just like the steel bracelet, which he left sitting in the ash behind him as he went on.

He was definitely in the Central Dominance now. He'd passed Faleast and Tyrian, two of the northern Ashmounts. Tyrian was still just barely visible to the south—a tall, solitary peak with a cut-off, blackened top. The landscape had grown flat, the trees changing from patchy brown pines to the willowy white aspens common around Luthadel. The aspens rose like bones growing from the black soil, clumping, their ashen white bark scarred and twisted. They—

Sazed paused. He stood near the central canal, one of the main routes to Luthadel. The canal was empty of boats at the moment; travelers were rare these days, even more rare than they had been during the Final Empire, for bandits were far more common. Sazed had outrun several groups of them during his hurried flight to Luthadel.

No, solitary travelers were rare. Armies were far more common—and, judging from the several dozen trails of smoke he saw rising ahead of him, he had run afoul of one. It stood directly between him and Luthadel.

He thought quietly for a moment, flakes of ash beginning to fall lightly around him. It was midday; if that army had scouts, Sazed would have a very difficult time getting around it. In addition, his steelminds were empty. He wouldn't be able to run from pursuit.

And yet, an army within a week of Luthadel. . . . Whose was it, and what threat did it pose? His curiosity, the curiosity of a scholar, prodded him to seek a vantage from which to study the troops. Vin and the others could use any information he gathered.

Decision made, Sazed located a hill with a particularly large stand of aspens. He dropped his pack at the base of a tree, then pulled out an ironmind and began to fill it. He felt the familiar sensation of decreased weight, and he easily climbed to the top of the thin tree—his body was now light enough that it didn't take much strength to pull himself upward.

Hanging from the very tip of the tree, Sazed tapped his tinmind. The edges of his vision fuzzed, as always, but with the increased vision he could make out details about the large group settled into a hollow before him.

He was right about it being an army. He was wrong about it being made up of men.

"By the forgotten gods . . ." Sazed whispered, so shocked

that he nearly lost his grip. The army was organized in only the most simplistic and primitive way. There were no tents, no vehicles, no horses. Just hundreds of large cooking fires, each ringed with figures.

And those figures were of a deep blue. They varied greatly in size; some were just five feet tall, others were lumbering hulks of ten feet or more. They were both the same species, Sazed knew. Koloss. The creatures—though similar to men in base form—never stopped growing. They simply continued to get bigger as they aged, growing until their hearts could no longer support them. Then they died, killed by their body's own growth imperative.

Before they died, however, they got very large. And very dangerous.

Sazed dropped from the tree, making his body light enough that he hit the ground softly. He hurriedly searched through his copperminds. When he found the one he wanted, he strapped it to his upper left arm, then climbed back up the tree.

He searched an index quickly. Somewhere, he'd taken notes on a book about the koloss—he'd studied it trying to decide if the creatures had a religion. He'd had someone repeat the notes back to him, so he could store them in the coppermind. He had the book memorized, too, of course, but placing so much information directly in his mind would ruin the—

There, he thought, recovering the notes. He tapped them from the coppermind, filling his mind with knowledge.

Most koloss bodies gave out before they reached twenty years of age. The more "ancient" creatures were often a massive twelve feet in height, with stocky, powerful bodies. However, few koloss lived that long—and not just because of heart failure. Their society—if it could be called that—was extremely violent.

Excitement suddenly overcoming apprehension, Sazed tapped tin for vision again, searching through the thousands of blue humanoids, trying to get visual proof of what he'd read. It wasn't hard to find fights. Scuffles around the fires seemed common, and, interestingly, they were always between koloss of nearly the same size.

Sazed magnified his view even further—gripping the tree tightly to overcome the nausea—and got his first good look at a koloss.

It was a creature of smaller size—perhaps six feet tall. It was man-shaped, with two arms and legs, though its neck was hard to distinguish. It was completely bald. The oddest feature, however, was its blue skin, which hung loose and folded. The creature looked like a fat man might, had all his fat been drained away, leaving the stretched skin behind.

And . . . the skin didn't seem to be *connected* very well. Around the creature's red, blood-drop eyes, the skin sagged, revealing the facial muscles. The same was true around the mouth: the skin sagged a few inches below the chin, the lower teeth and jaw completely exposed.

It was a stomach-turning sight, especially for a man who was already nauseated. The creature's ears hung low, flopping down beside its jawline. Its nose was formless and loose, with no cartilage supporting it. Skin hung baggily from the creature's arms and legs, and its only clothing was a crude loincloth.

Sazed turned, selecting a larger creature—one perhaps eight feet tall—to study. The skin on this beast wasn't as loose, but it still didn't seem to fit quite right. Its nose twisted at a crooked angle, pulled flat against the face by an enlarged head that sat on a stumpy neck. The creature turned to leer at a companion, and again, the skin around its mouth didn't quite fit: the lips didn't close completely, and the holes around the eyes were too big, so they exposed the muscles beneath.

Like . . . a person wearing a mask made of skin, Sazed thought, trying to push away his disgust. *So . . . their body continues to grow, but their skin doesn't?*

His thought was confirmed as a massive, ten-foot-tall beast of a koloss wandered into the group. Smaller creatures scattered before this newcomer, who thumped up to the fire, where several horses were roasting.

This largest creature's skin was pulled so tight it was beginning to tear. The hairless blue flesh had ripped around the eyes, at the edges of the mouth, and around the massive chest muscles. Sazed could see little trails of red blood dripping from the rips. Even where the skin wasn't torn, it was pulled taut—the nose and ears were so flat they were almost indistinguishable from the flesh around them.

Suddenly, Sazed's study didn't seem so academic. Koloss had come to the Central Dominance. Creatures so violent and uncontrollable that the Lord Ruler had been forced to keep them away from civilization. Sazed extinguished his tinmind, welcoming the return to normal vision. He had to get to Luthadel and warn the others. If they—

Sazed froze. One problem with enhancing his vision was that he temporarily lost the ability to see close up—so it wasn't odd that he hadn't noticed the koloss patrol surrounding his aspens.

By the forgotten gods! He held firm to the tip of the tree, thinking quickly. Several koloss were already pushing their way into the stand. If he dropped to the ground, he'd be too slow to escape. As always, he wore a pewtermind; he could easily become as strong as ten men, and maintain it for a good amount of time. He could fight, perhaps. . . .

Yet, the koloss carried crude-looking, but massive, swords. Sazed's notes, his memory, and his lore all agreed: Koloss were very dangerous warriors. Strong as ten men or not, Sazed wouldn't have the skill to defeat them.

"Come down," called a deep, slurred voice from below. "Come down now."

Sazed looked down. A large koloss, skin just beginning to stretch, stood at the tree's base. It gave the aspen a shake.

"Come down now," the creature repeated.

The lips don't work very well, Sazed thought. *He sounds like a man trying to talk without moving his lips.* He wasn't surprised that the creature could talk; his notes mentioned that. He was, however, surprised at how calm it sounded.

I could run, he thought. He could keep to the tops of trees, perhaps cross the distance between patches of aspens by dropping his metalminds and trying to ride gusts of wind. But it would be very difficult—and very unpredictable.

And he would have to leave his copperminds—a thousand years of history—behind.

So, pewtermind ready in case he needed strength, Sazed let go of the tree. The koloss leader—Sazed could only assume that was what he was—watched Sazed fall to the ground with a red-eyed stare. The creature did not blink. Sazed wondered if it even *could* blink, its skin stretched as it was.

Sazed plunked to the ground beside the tree, then reached for his pack.

"No," the koloss snapped, grabbing the pack with an inhumanly quick swipe of the arm. It tossed the pack to another koloss.

"I need that," Sazed said. "I will be much more cooperative if—"

"Quiet!" the koloss yelled with a rage so sudden that Sazed took a step backward. Terrismen were tall—especially Terrismen eunuchs—and it was very disconcerting to be dwarfed by this beastly creature, well over nine feet in height, its skin a blackish blue, its eyes the color of the sun at dusk. It loomed over Sazed, and he cringed in spite of himself.

Apparently, that was the proper reaction, for the lead koloss nodded and turned away. "Come," it slurred, lumbering through the small aspen forest. The other koloss—about seven of them—followed.

Sazed didn't want to find out what would happen if he disobeyed. He chose a god—Duis, a god once said to watch over wearied travelers—and said a quick, silent prayer. Then he hurried forward, staying with the pack of koloss as they walked toward the camp.

At least they didn't kill me out of hand, Sazed thought. He'd half expected that, considering what he'd read. Of course, even the books didn't know much. The koloss had been kept separate from mankind for centuries; the Lord Ruler only called upon them in times of great martial need, to quell revolts, or to conquer new societies discovered on the inner islands. At those times, the koloss had caused absolute destruction and slaughter—or so the histories claimed.

Could all that have been propaganda? Sazed wondered. *Maybe the koloss aren't as violent as we assumed.*

One of the koloss beside Sazed howled in sudden anger. Sazed spun as the koloss jumped at one of its companions. The creature ignored the sword on its back, instead punching his enemy's head with a blocky fist. The others paused, turning to watch the fight, but none of them seemed alarmed.

Sazed watched with growing horror as the aggressor proceeded to repeatedly pummel his enemy. The defender tried to protect himself, getting out a dagger and managing to score a cut on the aggressor's arm. The blue skin tore, seeping bright red blood, as the aggressor got his hands around his opponent's thick head and twisted.

There was a snap. The defender stopped moving. The aggressor removed the sword from his victim's back and strapped it on beside his own weapon, then removed a small pouch that was tied beside the sword. After that, he stood, ignoring the wound on his arm, and the group began to walk again.

"Why?" Sazed asked, shocked. "What was that for?"

The wounded koloss turned around. "I hated him," he said.

"Move!" the lead koloss snapped at Sazed.

Sazed forced himself to start walking. They left the corpse lying in the road. *The pouches,* he thought, trying to find something to focus on besides the brutality. *They all carry those pouches.* The koloss kept them tied to their swords. They didn't carry the weapons in sheaths; they were simply bound on their backs with leather straps. And tied to those straps were pouches. Sometimes there was just one, though the two largest creatures in the group each had several.

They look like coin pouches, Sazed thought. *But, the koloss don't have an economy. Perhaps they keep personal possessions in them? But what would beasts like these value?*

They entered the camp. There didn't appear to be sentries at the borders—but, then, why would guards be necessary? It would be very difficult for a human to sneak into this camp.

A group of smaller koloss—the five-foot-tall ones—rushed forward as soon as the group arrived. The murderer threw his extra sword to one of them, then pointed into the distance. He kept the pouch for himself, and the small ones rushed off, following the road in the direction of the body.

Burial detail? Sazed wondered.

He walked uncomfortably behind his captors as they penetrated into the camp. Beasts of all sorts were being roasted over the firepits, though Sazed didn't think any of them had once been human. In addition, the ground around the camp had been completely stripped of plant life, as if it had been grazed by a group of particularly aggressive goats.

And, according to his coppermind, that wasn't far off the truth. Koloss could, apparently, subsist on practically anything. They preferred meat, but would eat any kind of plant—even grass, going so far as to pull it up by the roots to eat. Some reports even spoke of them eating dirt and ash, though Sazed found that a little difficult to believe.

He continued to walk. The camp smelled of smoke, grime, and a strange musk that he assumed was koloss body odor. Some of the creatures turned as he passed, watching him with steady red eyes.

It's like they only have two emotions, he thought, jumping as a fireside koloss suddenly screamed and attacked a companion. *They're either indifferent or they're enraged.*

What would it take to set them all off at once? And . . . what kind of a disaster would they cause if that happened? He nervously revised his earlier thoughts. No, the koloss had not been maligned. The stories he had heard—stories of koloss running wild in the Farmost Dominance, causing widespread destruction and death—were obviously true.

But something kept this group marginally reined in. The Lord Ruler had been able to control the koloss, though no book explained how. Most writers simply accepted this ability as part of what had made the Lord Ruler God. The man had been immortal—compared with that, other powers seemed mundane.

His immortality, however, was a trick, Sazed thought. *Simply a clever combination of Feruchemical and Allomantic powers.* The Lord Ruler had been just a normal man—albeit one with an unusual combination of abilities and opportunities.

That being the case, how had he controlled the koloss? *There* was *something different about the Lord Ruler. Something more than his powers. He did something at the Well of Ascension, something that forever changed the world. Perhaps his ability to control the koloss came from that.*

Sazed's captors ignored the occasional fights around firepits. There didn't appear to be any female koloss in the camp—or, if there were, they were indistinguishable from the males. Sazed did, however, notice a koloss corpse lying forgotten near one of the fires. It had been flayed, the blue skin ripped free.

How could any society exist like this? he thought with horror. His books said the koloss bred and aged quickly—a fortunate situation for them, considering the number of deaths he had already seen. Even so, it seemed to him that this species killed too many of its members to continue.

Yet they did continue. Unfortunately. The Keeper in him believed strongly that nothing should be lost, that every society was worth remembering. However, the brutality of the koloss camp—the wounded creatures who sat, ignoring the gashes in their skin, the flayed corpses along the path, the sudden bellows of anger and subsequent murders—tested this belief.

His captors led him around a small hillock in the land, and Sazed paused as he saw something very unexpected.

A tent.

"Go," the lead koloss said, pointing.

Sazed frowned. There were several dozen humans outside the tent, carrying spears and dressed like imperial guards. The tent was large, and behind it stood a line of boxy carts.

"Go!" the koloss yelled.

Sazed did as he was told. Behind him, one of the koloss indifferently tossed Sazed's pack toward the human guards.

The metalminds inside clinked together as they hit the ashy ground, causing Sazed to cringe. The soldiers watched the koloss retreat with a wary eye; then one picked up the pack. Another leveled his spear at Sazed.

Sazed held up his hands. "I am Sazed, a Keeper of Terris, once steward, now teacher. I am not your enemy."

"Yes, well," the guard said, still watching the retreating koloss. "You're still going to have to come with me."

"May I have my possessions back?" Sazed asked. This hollow appeared free of koloss; apparently, the human soldiers wanted to keep their distance.

The first guard turned to his companion, who was perusing Sazed's pack. The second guard looked up and shrugged. "No weapons. Some bracelets and rings, maybe worth something."

"None of them are of precious metals," Sazed said. "They are the tools of a Keeper, and are of little value to anyone but myself."

The second guard shrugged, handing the bag to the first man. Both were of standard Central Dominance coloring—dark hair, light skin, the build and height of those who'd had proper nutrition as children. The first guard was the older of the two, and was obviously in charge. He took the bag from his companion. "We'll see what His Majesty says."

Ah, Sazed thought. "Let us speak with him then."

The guard turned, pushing aside the tent door and motioning for Sazed to enter. Sazed stepped from red sunlight into a functional—if sparsely furnished—tent room. This main chamber was large, and contained several more guards. Sazed had seen perhaps two dozen so far.

The lead guard walked forward and poked his head into a room at the back. A few moments later, he waved Sazed forward and pulled back the tent door.

Sazed entered the second chamber. The man inside wore the pants and suit jacket of a Luthadel nobleman. He was balding—his hair reduced to a few struggling wisps—despite his youth. He stood, tapping the side of his leg with a nervous hand, and jumped slightly when Sazed entered.

Sazed recognized the man. "Jastes Lekal."

"*King* Lekal," Jastes snapped. "Do I know you, Terrisman?"

"We have not met, Your Majesty," Sazed said, "but I have had some dealings with a friend of yours, I think. King Elend Venture of Luthadel?"

Jastes nodded absently. "My men say the koloss brought you. They found you poking around the camp?"

"Yes, Your Majesty," Sazed said carefully, watching as Jastes began to pace. *This man isn't much more stable than the army he apparently leads,* he thought with dissatisfaction. "How is it that you have persuaded the creatures to serve you?"

"You are a prisoner, Terrisman," Jastes snapped. "No questions. Did Elend send you to spy on me?"

"I was sent by no man," Sazed said. "You happened to be in my path, Your Majesty. I meant no harm by my observations."

Jastes paused, eyeing Sazed, before beginning to pace again. "Well, never mind. I've been without a proper steward for some time now. You will serve me now."

"I apologize, Your Majesty," Sazed said, bowing slightly. "But that will not be possible."

Jastes frowned. "You're a steward—I can tell that from the robes. Is Elend so great a master that you would deny me?"

"Elend Venture is not my master, Your Majesty," Sazed said, meeting the young king's eyes. "Now that we are free, the Terrismen no longer call any man master. I cannot be your servant, for I can be no man's servant. Keep me as prisoner, if you must. But I will not serve you. I apologize."

Jastes paused again. Instead of being angry, however, he simply seemed . . . embarrassed. "I see."

"Your Majesty," Sazed said calmly, "I realize that you commanded me to ask no questions, so I will instead make observations. You appear to have placed yourself in a very poor position. I know not how you control these koloss, but I cannot help but think that your grip is tenuous. You are in danger, and you appear intent on sharing that danger with others."

Jastes flushed. "Your 'observations' are flawed, Terrisman.

I *am* in control of this army. They obey me completely. How many other noblemen have you seen gather koloss armies? None—only I have been successful."

"They do not seem very much under control, Your Majesty."

"Oh?" Jastes asked. "And did they tear you apart when they found you? Pummel you to death for sport? Ram a stick through you and roast you over one of their fires? No. They don't do these things because *I* commanded them otherwise. It may not seem like much, Terrisman, but trust me—this is a sign of great restraint and obedience for koloss."

"Civilization is no great achievement, Your Majesty."

"Do not try me, Terrisman!" Jastes snapped, running a hand through the remnants of his hair. "These are koloss we speak of—we can't expect much from them."

"And you bring them to Luthadel?" Sazed asked. "Even the Lord Ruler feared these creatures, Your Majesty. He kept them away from cities. You bring them to the most populated area in all of the Final Empire!"

"You don't understand," Jastes said. "I tried overtures of peace, but nobody listens unless you have money or an army. Well, I have one, and I'll soon have the other. I know Elend's sitting on that stash of atium—and I'm just come to . . . to make an alliance with him."

"An alliance where you take over control of the city?"

"Bah!" Jastes said with a wave of his hand. "Elend doesn't control Luthadel—he's just a placeholder waiting for someone more powerful to come along. He's a good man, but he's an innocent idealist. He's going to lose his throne to one army or another, and I'll give him a better deal than Cett or Straff will, that's certain."

Cett? Straff? What kind of trouble has young Venture gotten himself into? Sazed shook his head. "Somehow I doubt that a 'better' deal' involves the use of koloss, Your Majesty."

Jastes frowned. "You certainly are smart-mouthed, Terrisman. You're a sign—your entire people are a sign—of what has gone wrong with the world. I used to respect the Terris people. There's no shame in being a good servant."

"There's often little pride in it either," Sazed said. "But, I apologize for my attitude, Your Majesty. It is not a manifestation of Terris independence. I have always been too free with my comments, I think. I never made the best of stewards." *Or the best of Keepers,* he added to himself.

"Bah," Jastes said again, resuming his pacing.

"Your Majesty," Sazed said. "I must continue to Luthadel. There are . . . events I need to deal with. Think what you will of my people, but you must know that we are honest. The work I do is beyond politics and wars, thrones and armies. It is important for all men."

"Scholars always say things like that," Jastes said. He paused. "Elend always said things like that."

"Regardless," Sazed continued, "I must be allowed to leave. In exchange for my freedom, I will deliver a message from you to His Majesty King Elend, if you wish."

"I could send a messenger of my own at any time!"

"And leave yourself with one less man to protect you from the koloss?" Sazed said.

Jastes paused just briefly.

Ah, so he does fear them. Good. At least he's not insane.

"I *will* be leaving, Your Majesty," Sazed said. "I do not mean to be arrogant, but I can see that you don't have the resources to keep prisoners. You can let me go, or you can give me to the koloss. I would be wary, however, of letting them get into a habit of killing humans."

Jastes eyed him. "Fine," he said. "Deliver this message, then. Tell Elend that I don't care if he knows I'm coming—I don't even care if you give our numbers. Be sure you're accurate, though! I have over twenty thousand koloss in this army. He can't fight me. He can't fight the others, either. But, if I had those city walls . . . well, I could hold off both other armies for him. Tell him to be logical. If he gives over the atium, I'll even let him keep Luthadel. We can be neighbors. Allies."

One bankrupt of coin, the other bankrupt of common sense, Sazed thought. "Very well, Your Majesty. I will speak with Elend. I will need the return of my possessions, however."

The king waved a hand in annoyance, and Sazed withdrew, waiting quietly as the lead guard entered the king's chambers again and received his orders. As he waited for the soldiers to prepare—his pack thankfully returned to him—Sazed thought about what Jastes had said. *Cett or Straff*. Just how many forces were working on Elend to take his city?

If Sazed had wanted a quiet place to study, he'd apparently chosen the wrong direction to run.

It wasn't until a few years later that I began to notice the signs. I knew the prophecies—I am a Terris Worldbringer, after all. And yet, not all of us are religious men; some, such as myself, are more interested in other topics. However, during my time with Alendi, I could not help but become more interested in the Anticipation. He seemed to fit the signs so well.

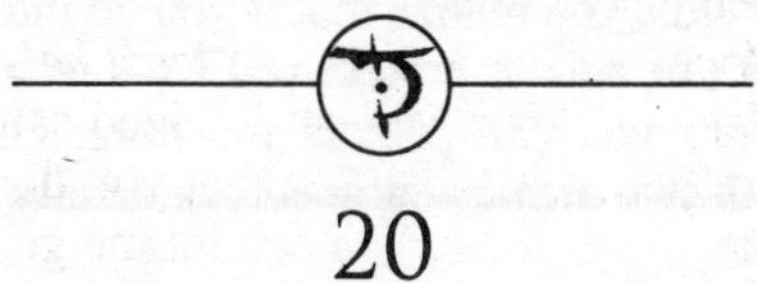

20

"THIS IS GOING TO BE dangerous, Your Majesty," Dockson said.

"It's our only option," Elend said. He stood behind his table; it was, as usual, stacked with books. He was backlit by the study's window, and its colors fell upon the back of his white uniform, dyeing it a brilliant maroon.

He certainly does look more commanding in that outfit, Vin thought, sitting in Elend's plush reading chair, OreSeur resting patiently on the floor beside her. She still wasn't sure what to think of the changes in Elend. She knew the alterations were mostly visual—new clothing, new haircut—but other things about him seemed to be changing as well. He stood up straighter when he spoke, and was more authoritative. He was even training in the sword and the cane.

Vin glanced at Tindwyl. The matronly Terriswoman sat in a stiff chair at the back of the room, watching the proceedings. She had perfect posture, and was ladylike in her colorful skirt and blouse. She didn't sit with her legs folded beneath her, as Vin currently did, and she'd never wear trousers.

What is it about her? Vin thought. *I've spent a year trying to get Elend to practice his swordsmanship. Tindwyl's been here less than a month, and she already has him sparring.*

Why did Vin feel bitter? Elend wouldn't change that much, would he? She tried to quiet the little piece of her that worried about this new confident, well-dressed warrior of a king—worried that he would turn out to be different from the man she loved.

What if he stopped needing her?

She pulled down into the chair just a little bit farther as Elend continued to speak with Ham, Dox, Clubs, and Breeze.

"El," Ham said, "you realize that if you go into the enemy camp, we won't be able to protect you."

"I'm not sure you can protect me here, Ham," Elend said. "Not with two armies camped practically against the walls."

"True," Dockson said, "but I'm worried that if you enter that camp, you'll never come out."

"Only if I fail," Elend said. "If I follow the plan—convince my father that we're his allies—he'll let me return. I didn't spend a lot of time politicking in the court when I was younger. However, one thing I *did* learn to do was manipulate my father. I know Straff Venture—and I know that I can beat him. Besides, he doesn't want me dead."

"Can we be sure of that?" Ham asked, rubbing his chin.

"Yes," Elend said. "After all, Straff hasn't sent assassins after me, while Cett has. It makes sense. What better person for Straff to leave in control of Luthadel than his own son? He thinks he can control me—he'll assume that he can make me give him Luthadel. If I play into that, I should be able to get him to attack Cett."

"He does have a point . . ." Ham said.

"Yes," Dockson said, "but what is to keep Straff from just taking you hostage and forcing his way into Luthadel?"

"He'll still have Cett at his back," Elend said. "If he fights us, he'll lose men—a lot of men—and expose himself to attack from behind."

"But he'll have you, my dear man," Breeze said. "He wouldn't have to attack Luthadel—he could force us to give in."

"You'll have orders to let me die first," Elend said. "That's why I set up the Assembly. It has the power to choose a new king."

"But why?" Ham asked. "Why take this risk, El? Let's wait a bit longer and see if we can get Straff to meet with you in a more neutral location."

Elend sighed. "You *have* to listen to me, Ham. Siege or no siege, we can't just sit here. If we do, either we'll get starved out, or one of those armies will decide to break the siege and attack us, hoping to take our walls, then turn and immediately defend against its enemies. They won't do that easily, but it could happen. It *will* happen, if we don't begin to play the kings against one another."

The room fell silent. The others slowly turned toward Clubs, who nodded. He agreed.

Good job, Elend, Vin thought.

"Someone has to meet with my father," Elend said. "And, I need to be that person. Straff thinks I am a fool, so I can convince him that I'm no threat. Then, I'll go and persuade Cett that I'm on his side. When they finally attack each other—each one thinking we're on their side—we'll withdraw instead and force them to fight it out. The winner won't have enough strength left to take the city from us!"

Ham and Breeze nodded their heads. Dockson, however, shook his. "The plan is good in theory, but going into the enemy camp unguarded? That seems foolish."

"Now, see," Elend said. "I think this is to our advantage. My father believes strongly in control and domination. If I walk into his camp, I'll essentially be telling him that I agree he has authority over me. I'll seem weak, and he'll assume that he can take me whenever he wants. It's a risk, but if I don't do this, *we die.*"

The men eyed each other.

Elend stood up a little straighter and pulled his hands into fists at his sides. He always did that when he was nervous.

"I'm afraid that this isn't a discussion," Elend said. "I've made my decision."

They're not going to accept a declaration like that, Vin thought. The crew were an independent lot.

Yet, surprisingly, none of them objected.

Dockson finally nodded his head. "All right, Your Majesty," he said. "You're going to need to walk a dangerous line—make Straff believe that he can count on our support, but also convince him that he can betray us at his leisure. You have to make him want our strength of arms while at the same time dismissing our strength of will."

"And," Breeze added, "you need to do so without him figuring out that you're playing both sides."

"Can you do it?" Ham asked. "Honestly, Elend?"

Elend nodded. "I can do it, Ham. I've gotten much better at politics this last year." He said the words with confidence, though Vin noticed that he still had his fists clenched. *He'll have to learn not to do that.*

"You may, perhaps, understand politics," Breeze said, "but *this* is scamming. Face it, my friend, you're dreadfully honest—always talking about how to defend the rights of skaa and the like."

"Now, see, you're being unfair," Elend said. "Honesty and good intentions are completely different. Why, I can be just as dishonest as—" He paused. "Why am I arguing this point? We admit what has to be done, and we know that I'm the one who has to do it. Dox, would you draft a letter to my father? Suggest that I would be happy to visit him. In fact . . ."

Elend paused, glancing at Vin. Then, he continued. "In fact, tell him that I want to discuss the future of Luthadel, and because I want to introduce him to someone special."

Ham chuckled. "Ah, nothing like bringing a girl home to meet the father."

"Especially when that girl happens to be the most dangerous Allomancer in the Central Dominance," Breeze added.

"You think he'll agree to letting her come?" Dockson said.

"If he doesn't, there's no deal," Elend said. "Make sure he knows that. Either way, I do think he'll agree. Straff has a habit of underestimating me—probably with good reason. However, I'll bet that sentiment extends to Vin as well. He'll assume she isn't as good as everyone says."

"Straff has his own Mistborn," Vin added. "To protect him. It will only be fair for Elend to be able to bring me. And, if I'm there, I can get him out should something go wrong."

Ham chuckled again. "That probably wouldn't make for a very dignified retreat—getting slung over Vin's shoulder and carried to safety."

"Better than dying," Elend said, obviously trying to act good-natured, but flushing slightly at the same time.

He loves me, but he's still a man, Vin thought. *How many times have I hurt his pride by being Mistborn while he is simply a normal person? A lesser man would never have fallen in love with me.*

But, doesn't he deserve a woman that he feels he can protect? A woman who's more like . . . a woman?

Vin pulled down in her chair again, seeking warmth within its plushness. However, it was Elend's study chair, where he read. Didn't he also deserve a woman who shared his interests, one who didn't find reading a chore? A woman with whom he could talk about his brilliant political theories?

Why am I thinking about our relationship so much lately? Vin thought.

We don't belong in their world, Zane had said. *We belong here, in the mists.*

You don't belong with them. . . .

"There is something else I wanted to mention, Your

Majesty," Dockson said. "You should meet with the Assembly. They've been growing impatient to get your ear—something about counterfeit coins being passed in Luthadel."

"I don't really have time for city business right now," Elend said. "The prime reason I set up the Assembly was so that they could deal with these kinds of issues. Go ahead and send them a message, telling them that I trust their judgment. Apologize for me, and explain that I'm seeing to the city's defense. I'll try and make the Assembly meeting next week."

Dockson nodded, scribbling a note to himself. "Though," he noted, "that is something else to consider. By meeting with Straff, you'll give up your hold on the Assembly."

"This isn't an official parlay," Elend said. "Just an informal meeting. My resolution from before will still stand."

"In all honesty, Your Majesty," Dockson said, "I highly doubt that *they* will see it that way. You know how angry they are to be left without recourse until you decide to hold the parlay."

"I know," Elend said. "But the risk is worthwhile. We *need* to meet with Straff. Once that is done, I can return with—hopefully—good news for the Assembly. At that point, I can argue that the resolution hasn't been fulfilled. For now, the meeting goes forward."

More decisive indeed, Vin thought. *He's changing. . . .*

She had to stop thinking about things like that. Instead, she focused on something else. The conversation turned to specific ways that Elend could manipulate Straff, each of the crewmembers giving him tips on how to scam effectively. Vin, however, found herself watching them, looking for discrepancies in their personalities, trying to decide if any of them might be the kandra spy.

Was Clubs being even quieter than normal? Was Spook's shift in language patterns due to growing maturity, or because the kandra had difficulty mimicking his slang? Was Ham, perhaps, too jovial? He also seemed to focus less on his little philosophical puzzles than he once had. Was that because he was more serious now, or because the kandra didn't know how to imitate him properly?

It was no good. If she thought too much, she could spot seeming discrepancies in anyone. Yet, at the same time, they all seemed like themselves. People were just too complex to reduce to simple personality traits. Plus, the kandra would be good—very good. He would have a lifetime of training in the art of imitating others, and he had probably been planning his insertion for a long time.

It came down to Allomancy, then. With all of the activities surrounding the siege and her studies about the Deepness, however, she hadn't had a chance to test her friends. As she thought about it, she admitted that the lack of time excuse was a weak one. The truth was that she was probably distracting herself because the thought of one of the crew—one of her first group of friends—being a traitor was just too upsetting.

She had to get over that. If there really were a spy in the group, that would be the end of them. If the enemy kings found out about the tricks Elend was planning . . .

This in mind, she tentatively burned bronze. Immediately, she sensed an Allomantic pulse from Breeze—dear, incorrigible Breeze. He was so good at Allomancy that even Vin couldn't detect his touch most of the time, but he was also compulsive about using his power.

He wasn't currently using it on her, however. She closed her eyes, focusing. Once, long ago, Marsh had tried to train her in the fine art of using bronze to read Allomantic pulses. She hadn't realized at the time just how large a task he'd begun.

When an Allomancer burned a metal, they gave off an invisible, drumlike beat that only another Allomancer burning bronze could sense. The rhythm of these pulses—how quickly the beats came, the way they "sounded"—told exactly what metal was being burned.

It took practice, and was difficult, but Vin was getting better at reading the pulses. She focused. Breeze was burning brass—the internal, mental Pushing metal. And . . .

Vin focused harder. She could feel a pattern washing over her, a double *dum-dum* beat with each pulse. They felt oriented to her right. The pulses were washing against something else, something that was sucking them in.

Elend. Breeze was focused on Elend. Not surprising, considering the current discussion. Breeze was always Pushing on the people he interacted with.

Satisfied, Vin sat back. But then she paused. *Marsh implied there was much more to bronze than many people thought. I wonder. . . .*

She squeezed her eyes shut—ignoring the fact that any of the others who saw her would think her actions strange—and focused again on the Allomantic pulses. She flared the bronze, concentrating so hard she felt she'd give herself a headache. There was a . . . vibration to the pulses. But what that could mean, she wasn't certain.

Focus! she told herself. However, the pulses stubbornly refused to yield any further information.

Fine, she thought. *I'll cheat.* She turned off her tin—she almost always had it on a little bit—then reached inside and burned the fourteenth metal. Duralumin.

The Allomantic pulses became so loud . . . so powerful . . . she swore she could feel their vibrations shaking her apart. They pounded like beats from a massive drum set right beside her. But she got something from them.

Anxiety, nervousness, worry, insecurity, anxiety, nervousness, worry—

It was gone, her bronze expended in one massive flare of power. Vin opened her eyes; no one in the room was looking at her except OreSeur.

She felt drained. The headache she'd predicted before now came in full force, thudding inside her head like the tiny brother of the drum she'd now banished. However, she held to the information she'd gleaned. It hadn't come in words, but feelings—and her first fear was that Breeze was making these emotions appear. Anxiety, nervousness, worry. However, she immediately realized that Breeze was a Soother. If he focused on emotions, it would be the ones he was *dampening*. The ones he was using his powers to Soothe away.

She looked from him to Elend. *Why . . . he's making Elend more confident!* If Elend stood a little taller, it was because Breeze was quietly helping, Soothing away anxiety and worry. And Breeze did this even as he argued and made his usual mocking comments.

Vin studied the plump man, ignoring her headache, feeling a newfound sense of admiration. She'd always wondered just a little at Breeze's placement in the crew. The other men were all, to an extent, idealists. Even Clubs, beneath his crotchety exterior, had always struck her as a solidly good man.

Breeze was different. Manipulative, a little selfish—he seemed like he'd joined the crew for the challenge, not because he really wanted to help the skaa. But, Kelsier had always claimed that he'd chosen his crew carefully, picking the men for their integrity, not just their skill.

Perhaps Breeze wasn't an exception after all. Vin watched him pointing his cane at Ham as he said something flippant. And yet, on the inside, he was completely different.

You're a good man, Breeze, she thought, smiling to herself. *You just try your best to hide it.*

And he also wasn't the impostor. She'd known that before, of course; Breeze hadn't been in the city when the kandra had made the switch. However, having a second confirmation lifted a tiny bit of her burden.

Now if she could just eliminate some of the others.

Elend bid the crew farewell after the meeting. Dockson went to pen the requested letters, Ham to go over security, Clubs back to training the soldiers, and Breeze to try and placate the Assembly regarding Elend's lack of attention.

Vin trailed out of the study, shooting him a glance, then eyeing Tindwyl. *Suspicious of her still, eh?* Elend thought with amusement. He nodded reassuringly, and Vin frowned, looking just a little annoyed. He would have let her stay, but . . . well, facing Tindwyl was embarrassing enough alone.

Vin left the room, wolfhound kandra at her side. *Looks like she's growing more attached to the creature,* Elend thought with satisfaction. It was good to know that someone watched over her.

Vin shut the door behind her, and Elend sighed, rubbing his shoulder. Several weeks of training with the sword and cane were taking a lot out of him, and his body was bruised. He tried to keep the pain from showing—or, rather, from letting Tindwyl see him show the pain. *At least I proved that I'm learning,* he thought. *She had to see how well I did today.*

"Well?" he asked.

"You are an embarrassment," Tindwyl said, standing before her chair.

"So you like to say," Elend said, walking forward to begin piling up a stack of books. Tindwyl said that he needed to let servants keep his study clean, something he'd always resisted. The clutter of books and papers felt right to him, and he certainly didn't want someone else moving them around.

With her standing there looking at him, however, it was difficult not to feel self-conscious about the mess. He stacked another book on the pile.

"Surely you noticed how well I did," Elend said. "I got them to let me go into Straff's camp."

"You are king, Elend Venture," Tindwyl said, arms folded. "Nobody 'lets' you do anything. The first change in attitude has to be your own—you have to stop thinking that you need permission or agreement from those who follow you."

"A king should lead by consent of his citizens," Elend said. "I will not be another Lord Ruler."

"A king should be strong," Tindwyl said firmly. "He accepts counsel, but only when he asks for it. He makes it clear that the final decision is his, not his counselors'. You need better control over your advisors. If they don't respect you, then your enemies won't either—and the masses never will."

"Ham and the others respect me."

Tindwyl raised an eyebrow.

"They do!"

"What do they call you?"

Elend shrugged. "They're my friends. They use my name."

"Or a close approximation of it. Right, 'El'?"

Elend flushed, setting one final book on the stack. "You'd have me force my friends to address me by my title?"

"Yes," Tindwyl said. "Especially in public. You should be addressed as 'Your Majesty,' or at least as 'my lord.' "

"I doubt Ham would deal well with that," Elend said. "He has some issues with authority."

"He will get over them," Tindwyl said, wiping her finger along a bookcase. She didn't need to hold it up for Elend to know there would be dust on its tip.

"What about you?" Elend challenged.

"Me?"

"You call me 'Elend Venture,' not 'Your Majesty.' "

"I am different," Tindwyl said.

"Well, I don't see why you should be. You can call me 'Your Majesty' from now on."

Tindwyl smiled slyly. "Very well, Your Majesty. You can unclench your fists now. You're going to have to work on that—a statesman should not give visual clues of his nervousness."

Elend glanced down, relaxing his hands. "All right."

"In addition," Tindwyl continued, "you still hedge too much in your language. It makes you seem timid and hesitant."

"I'm working on that."

"Don't apologize unless you really mean it," Tindwyl said. "And don't make excuses. You don't need them. A leader is often judged by how well he bears responsibility. As king, everything that happens in your kingdom—regardless of who commits the act—is your fault. You are even responsible for unavoidable events such as earthquakes or storms."

"Or armies," Elend said.

Tindwyl nodded. "Or armies. It is your responsibility to deal with these things, and if something goes wrong, it is your fault. You simply have to accept this."

Elend nodded, picking up a book.

"Now, let's talk about guilt," Tindwyl said, seating herself. "Stop cleaning. That isn't a job for a king."

Elend sighed, setting down the book.

"Guilt," Tindwyl said, "does not become a king. You have to stop feeling sorry for yourself."

"You just told me everything that happens in the kingdom is my fault!"

"It is."

"How can I *not* feel guilty, then?"

"You have to feel confident that your actions are the best," Tindwyl explained. "You have to know that no matter how bad things get, they would be worse without you. When disaster occurs, you take responsibility, but you don't wallow or mope. You aren't allowed that luxury; guilt is for lesser men. You simply need to do what is expected."

"And that is?"

"To make everything better."

"Great," Elend said flatly. "And if I fail?"

"Then you accept responsibility, and make everything better on the second try."

Elend rolled his eyes. "And what if I can't ever make things better? What if I'm really not the best man to be king?"

"Then you remove yourself from the position," Tindwyl said. "Suicide is the preferred method—assuming, of course, that you have an heir. A good king knows not to foul up the succession."

"Of course," Elend said. "So, you're saying I should just kill myself."

"No. I'm telling you to have pride in yourself, Your Majesty."

"That's not what it sounds like. Every day you tell me how poor a king I am, and how my people will suffer because of it! Tindwyl, I'm *not* the best man for this position. He got himself killed by the Lord Ruler."

"That is enough!" Tindwyl snapped. "Believe it or not, Your Majesty, you *are* the best person for this position."

Elend snorted.

"You are best," Tindwyl said, "because you hold the throne now. If there is anything worse than a mediocre king, it is chaos—which is what this kingdom would have if *you* hadn't taken the throne. The people on both sides, noblemen and skaa, accept you. They may not believe in you, but they accept you. Step down now—or even die accidentally—and there would be confusion, collapse, and destruction. Poorly trained or not, weak of character or not, mocked or not, you are all this country has. You are *king*, Elend Venture."

Elend paused. "I'm . . . not sure if you're making me feel any better about myself, Tindwyl."

"It's—"

Elend raised a hand. "Yes, I know. It's not about how I feel."

"You have no place for guilt. Accept that you're king, accept that you can do nothing constructive to change that, and accept responsibility. Whatever you do, be confident—for if you weren't here, there would be chaos."

Elend nodded.

"Arrogance, Your Majesty," Tindwyl said. "Successful leaders all share one common trait—they believe that they can do a better job than the alternatives. Humility is fine when considering your responsibility and duty, but when it comes time to make a decision, you must not question yourself."

"I'll try."

"Good," Tindwyl said. "Now, perhaps, we can move on to another matter. Tell me, why haven't you married that young girl?"

Elend frowned. *Wasn't expecting that. . . .* "That's a very personal question, Tindwyl."

"Good."

Elend deepened his frown, but she sat expectantly, watching him with one of her unrelenting stares.

"I don't know," Elend finally said, sitting back in his chair, sighing. "Vin isn't . . . like other women."

Tindwyl raised an eyebrow, her voice softening slightly. "I think that the more women you come to know, Your Majesty, the more you'll find that statement applies to all of them."

Elend nodded ruefully.

"Either way," Tindwyl said, "things are not well as they stand. I will not pry further into your relationship, but—as we've discussed—appearances are very important to a king. It isn't appropriate for you to be seen as having a mistress. I realize that sort of thing was common for imperial nobility. The skaa, however, want to see something better in you. Perhaps because many noblemen were so frivolous with their sexual lives, the skaa have always prized monogamy. They wish desperately for you to respect their values."

"They'll just have to be patient with us," Elend said. "I actually want to marry Vin, but she won't have it."

"Do you know why?"

Elend shook his head. "She . . . doesn't seem to make sense a lot of the time."

"Perhaps she isn't right for a man in your position."

Elend looked up sharply. "What does that mean?"

"Perhaps you need someone a little more refined," Tindwyl said. "I'm certain she's a fine bodyguard, but as a lady, she—"

"Stop," Elend snapped. "Vin is fine as she is."

Tindwyl smiled.

"What?" Elend demanded.

"I've insulted you all afternoon, Your Majesty, and you barely grew sullen. I mentioned your Mistborn in a mildly disparaging way, and now you're ready to throw me out."

"So?"

"So, you do love her?"

"Of course," Elend said. "I don't understand her, but yes. I love her."

Tindwyl nodded. "I apologize, then, Your Majesty. I had to be certain."

Elend frowned, relaxing in his chair slightly. "So, this was some kind of test, then? You wanted to see how I would react to your words about Vin?"

"You will always be tested by those you meet, Your Majesty. You might as well grow accustomed to it."

"But, why do you care about my relationship with Vin?"

"Love is not easy for kings, Your Majesty," Tindwyl said in an uncharacteristically kind voice. "You will find that your affection for the girl can cause far more trouble than any of the other things we've discussed."

"And that's a reason to give her up?" Elend asked stiffly.

"No," Tindwyl said. "No, I don't think so."

Elend paused, studying the stately Terriswoman with her square features and her stiff posture. "That . . . seems odd, coming from you. What about kingly duty and appearances?"

"We must make allowances for the occasional exception," Tindwyl said.

Interesting, Elend thought. He wouldn't have considered her the type to agree to any sort of "exceptions." *Perhaps she's a little deeper than I've assumed.*

"Now," Tindwyl said. "How are your training sessions going?"

Elend rubbed his sore arm. "All right, I suppose. But—"

He was interrupted by a knock at the door. Captain Demoux entered a moment later. "Your Majesty, a visitor has arrived from Lord Cett's army."

"A messenger?" Elend said, standing.

Demoux paused, looking a little embarrassed. "Well . . . sort of. She says she's Lord Cett's daughter, and she's come looking for Breeze."

He was born of a humble family, yet married the daughter of a king.

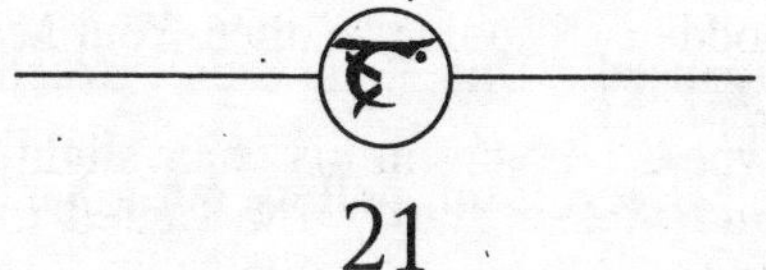

21

THE YOUNG WOMAN'S EXPENSIVE DRESS—light red silk with a shawl and lace sleeves—might have lent her an air of dignity, had she not scampered forward as soon as Breeze entered the room. Her light Western hair bouncing, she made a squeal of happiness as she threw her arms around Breeze's neck.

She was, perhaps, eighteen years old.

Elend glanced at Ham, who stood dumbfounded.

"Well, looks like you were right about Breeze and Cett's daughter," Elend whispered.

Ham shook his head. "I didn't think . . . I mean I joked, because it was Breeze, but I didn't expect to be *right*!"

Breeze, for his part, at least had the decency to look terribly uncomfortable in the young woman's arms. They stood inside the palace atrium, the same place where Elend had met with his father's messenger. Floor-to-ceiling windows let in the afternoon light, and a group of servants stood at one side of the room to wait on Elend's orders.

Breeze met Elend's eyes, blushing deeply. *I don't think I've ever seen him do that before,* Elend thought.

"My dear," Breeze said, clearing his throat, "perhaps you should introduce yourself to the king?"

The girl finally let go of Breeze. She stepped back, curtsying to Elend with a noblewoman's grace. She was a bit plump, her hair long after pre-Collapse fashion, and her cheeks were red with excitement. She was a cute thing, obviously well trained for the court—exactly the sort of girl that Elend had spent his youth trying to avoid.

"Elend," Breeze said, "might I introduce Allrianne Cett, daughter to Lord Ashweather Cett, king of the Western Dominance?"

"Your Majesty," Allrianne said.

Elend nodded. "Lady Cett." He paused, then—with a hopeful voice—continued. "Your father sent you as an ambassador?"

Allrianne paused. "Um . . . he didn't exactly send me, Your Majesty."

"Oh, dear," Breeze said, pulling out a handkerchief to dab his brow.

Elend glanced at Ham, then back at the girl. "Perhaps you should explain," he said, gesturing toward the atrium's seats. Allrianne nodded eagerly, but stayed close to Breeze as they sat. Elend waved for some servants to bring chilled wine.

He had a feeling he was going to want something to drink.

"I seek asylum, Your Majesty," Allrianne said, speaking with a quick voice. "I had to go. I mean, Breezy must have told you how my father is!"

Breeze sat uncomfortably, and Allrianne put an affectionate hand on his knee.

"How your father is?" Elend asked.

"He is so manipulative," Allrianne said. "So *demanding*. He drove Breezy away, and I absolutely had to follow. I wouldn't spend another moment in that camp. A war camp! He brought me, a young lady, along with him to war! Why, do you know what it is like to be leered at by every passing soldier? Do you understand what it is like to live in a tent?"

"I—"

"We rarely had fresh water," Allrianne continued. "And I couldn't take a decent bath without fear of peeping soldiers! During our travels, there was dreadful nothing to do all day but sit in the carriage and bounce, bounce, bounce. Why, until Breezy came, I hadn't had a refined conversation in weeks. And then, Father drove him away. . . ."

"Because?" Ham asked eagerly.

Breeze coughed.

"I had to get away, Your Majesty," Allrianne said. "You have to give me asylum! I know things that could help you. Like, I saw my father's camp. I'll bet you don't know that he is getting supplies from the cannery in Haverfrex! What do you think of that?"

"Um . . . impressive," Elend said hesitantly.

Allrianne nodded curtly.

"And, you came to find Breeze?" Elend asked.

Allrianne flushed slightly, glancing to the side. However, when she spoke, she displayed little tact. "I had to see him again, Your Majesty. So charming, so . . . wonderful. I wouldn't have expected Father to understand a man such as he."

"I see," Elend said.

"Please, Your Majesty," Allrianne said. "You have to take me in. Now that I've left Father, I have nowhere else to go!"

"You may stay—for a time, at least," Elend said, nodding greetings to Dockson, who had entered through the atrium doors. "But, you've obviously had a difficult trip. Perhaps you would like an opportunity to refresh yourself . . . ?"

"Oh, I would much appreciate that, Your Majesty!"

Elend eyed Cadon, one of the palace stewards, who stood at the back of the room with other servants. He nodded; rooms were prepared. "Then," Elend said, standing, "Cadon will lead you to some rooms. We will take dinner this evening at seven, and can speak again then."

"Thank you, Your Majesty!" Allrianne said, jumping up from her chair. She gave Breeze another hug, then stepped forward, as if to do the same for Elend. Fortunately, she thought better of it, instead allowing the servants to lead her away.

Elend sat. Breeze sighed deeply, leaning back in a wearied posture as Dockson walked forward, taking the girl's seat.

"That was . . . unexpected," Breeze noted.

There was an awkward pause, the atrium trees shifting slightly in the breeze from the balcony. Then—with a sharp bark—Ham began to laugh. The noise sparked Elend, and—despite the danger, despite the gravity of the problem—he found himself laughing as well.

"Oh, honestly," Breeze huffed, which only prompted them further. Perhaps it was the sheer incongruity of the situation, perhaps it was because he needed to release tension, but Elend found himself laughing so hard he almost fell from the chair. Ham wasn't doing much better, and even Dockson cracked a smile.

"I fail to see the levity in this situation," Breeze said. "The daughter of Lord Cett—a man who is currently besieging our home—just demanded asylum in the city. If Cett wasn't determined to kill us before, he certainly will be now!"

"I know," Elend said, taking deep breaths. "I know. It's just . . ."

"It's the image of you," Ham said, "being hugged by that courtly fluffcake. I can't think of anything more awkward than you being confronted by an irrational young woman!"

"This throws another wrinkle into things," Dockson noted. "Although, I'm not accustomed to *you* being the one to bring us a problem of this nature, Breeze. Honestly, I thought we would be able to avoid unplanned female attachments now that Kell is gone."

"This isn't my fault," Breeze said pointedly. "The girl's affection is completely misplaced."

"That's for sure," Ham mumbled.

"All right," a new voice said. "What was that pink thing I just passed in the hallway?"

Elend turned to find Vin standing, arms folded, in the atrium doorway. *So quiet. Why does she walk stealthily even in the palace?* She never wore shoes that clicked, never wore skirts that could rustle, and never had metal on her clothing that could clink or be Pushed by Allomancers.

"That wasn't pink, my dear," Breeze said. "That was red."

"Close enough," Vin said, walking forward. "She was bubbling to the servants about how hot her bath needed to be, and making certain they wrote down her favorite foods."

Breeze sighed. "That's Allrianne. We'll probably have to get a new pastry chef—either that, or have desserts ordered in. She's rather particular about her pastries."

"Allrianne Cett is the daughter of Lord Cett," Elend explained as Vin—ignoring the chairs—sat on the edge of a planter beside his chair, laying a hand on his arm. "Apparently, she and Breeze are something of an item."

"Excuse me?" Breeze huffed.

Vin, however, wrinkled her nose. "That's disgusting, Breeze. You're old. She's young."

"There was no relationship," Breeze snapped. "Besides, I'm not *that* old—nor is she *that* young."

"She sounded like she was about twelve," Vin said.

Breeze rolled his eyes. "Allrianne was a child of the country court—a little innocent, a little spoiled—but she hardly deserves to be spoken of in that manner. She's actually quite witty, in the right circumstances."

"So, was there anything between you?" Vin pressed.

"Of course not," Breeze said. "Well, not really. Nothing

real, though it could have been taken the wrong way. *Was* taken the wrong way, actually, once her father discovered . . . Anyway, who are you to talk, Vin? I seem to remember a certain *young* girl pining for an *old* Kelsier a few years back."

Elend perked up at this.

Vin flushed. "I never pined over Kelsier."

"Not even at the beginning?" Breeze asked. "Come now, a dashing man like him? He saved you from being beaten by your old crewleader, took you in . . ."

"You're a sick man," Vin declared, folding her arms. "Kelsier was like a father to me."

"Eventually, perhaps," Breeze said, "but—"

Elend held up a hand. "Enough," he said. "This line of discussion is useless."

Breeze snorted, but fell silent. *Tindwyl is right,* Elend thought. *They will listen to me if I act like I expect them to.*

"We have to decide what to do," Elend said.

"The daughter of the man threatening us could be a very powerful bargaining chip," Dockson said.

"You mean take her hostage?" Vin said, eyes narrowing.

Dockson shrugged. "Someone has to state the obvious, Vin."

"Not really a hostage," Ham said. "She came to us, after all. Simply letting her stay could have the same effect as taking her hostage."

"That would risk antagonizing Cett," Elend said. "Our original plan was to make him think we're his ally."

"We could give her back, then," Dockson said. "That could get us a long way in the negotiations."

"And her request?" Breeze asked. "The girl wasn't happy in her father's camp. Shouldn't we at least consider her wishes?"

All eyes turned toward Elend. He paused. Just a few weeks ago, they would have kept on arguing. It seemed strange that they should so quickly begin to look to him for decisions.

Who was he? A man who had haphazardly ended up on the throne? A poor replacement for their brilliant leader? An idealist who hadn't considered the dangers his philosophies would bring? A fool? A child? An impostor?

The best they had.

"She stays," Elend said. "For now. Perhaps we'll be forced to return her eventually, but this will make a useful distraction for Cett's army. Let them sweat for a bit. It will only buy us more time."

The crewmembers nodded, and Breeze looked relieved.

I'll do what I can, make the decisions as I see they must be made, Elend thought.

Then accept the consequences.

He could trade words with the finest of philosophers, and had an impressive memory. Nearly as good, even, as my own. Yet, he was not argumentative.

22

CHAOS AND STABILITY, THE MIST was both. Upon the land there was an empire, within that empire were a dozen shattered kingdoms, within those kingdoms were cities, towns, villages, plantations. And above them all, within them all, around them all, was the mist. It was more constant than the sun, for it could not be hidden by clouds. It was more powerful than the storms, for it would outlast any weather's fury. It was always there. Changing, but eternal.

Day was an impatient sigh, awaiting the night. When the darkness did come, however, Vin found that the mists did not calm her as they once had.

Nothing seemed certain anymore. Once the night had been her refuge; now she found herself glancing behind, watching for ghostly outlines. Once Elend had been her peace, but he was changing. Once she had been able to protect the things she loved—but she was growing more and more afraid that the forces moving against Luthadel were beyond her capacity to stop.

Nothing frightened her more than her own impotence. During her childhood she had taken it for granted that she couldn't change things, but Kelsier had given her pride in herself.

If she couldn't protect Elend, what good was she?

There are still some things I can do, she thought forcefully. She crouched quietly on a ledge, mistcloak tassels hanging down, waving slightly in the wind. Just below her, torches burned fitfully at the front of Keep Venture, illuminating a pair of Ham's guards. They stood alert in the swirling mists, showing impressive diligence.

The guards wouldn't be able to see her sitting just above them; they'd barely be able to see twenty feet in the thick mists. They weren't Allomancers. Besides the core crew, Elend had access to barely half a dozen Mistings—which made him Allomantically weak compared with most of the other new kings in the Final Empire. Vin was supposed to make up the difference.

The torches flickered as the doors opened, and a figure left the palace. Ham's voice echoed quietly in the mist as he greeted his guards. One reason—perhaps the main reason—that the guards were so diligent was because of Ham. He might have been a bit of an anarchist at heart, but he could be a very good leader if he was given a small team. Though his guards weren't the most disciplined, polished soldiers Vin had seen, they were fiercely loyal.

Ham talked with the men for a time, then he waved farewell and walked out into the mists. The small courtyard between the keep and its wall contained a couple of guard posts and patrols, and Ham would visit each one in turn. He walked boldly in the night, trusting to diffused starlight to see, rather than blinding himself with a torch. A thief's habit.

Vin smiled, leaping quietly to the ground, then scampering after Ham. He walked on, ignorant of her presence.

What would it be like to have only one Allomantic power? Vin thought. *To be able to make yourself stronger, but to have ears as weak as those of any normal man?* It had been only two years, but already she had come to rely so heavily on her abilities.

Ham continued forward, Vin following discreetly, until they reached the ambush. Vin tensed, flaring her bronze.

OreSeur howled suddenly, jumping from a pile of boxes. The kandra was a dark silhouette in the night, his inhuman baying disturbing even to Vin. Ham spun, cursing quietly.

And he instinctively flared pewter. Focused on her bronze, Vin confirmed that the pulses were definitely coming from him. Ham spun around, searching in the night as OreSeur landed. Vin, however, simply smiled. Ham's Allomancy meant he wasn't the impostor. She could cross another name off her list.

"It's okay, Ham," Vin said, walking forward.

Ham paused, lowering his dueling cane. "Vin?" he asked, squinting in the mist.

"It's me," she said. "I'm sorry, you startled my hound. He can get jumpy at night."

Ham relaxed. "We all can, I guess. Anything happening tonight?"

"Not that I can tell," she said. "I'd let you know."

Ham nodded. "I'd appreciate it—though I doubt you'd need me. I'm captain of the guard, but you're the one who does all the work."

"You're more valuable than you think, Ham," Vin said. "Elend confides in you. Since Jastes and the others left him, he's needed a friend."

Ham nodded. Vin turned, glancing into the mists, where OreSeur sat waiting on his haunches. He seemed to be getting more and more comfortable with his hound's body.

Now that she knew Ham was not an impostor, there was something she needed to discuss with him. "Ham," she said, "your protection of Elend is more valuable than you know."

"You're talking about the impostor," Ham said quietly. "El has me searching through the palace staff to see who might have gone missing for a few hours on that day. It's a tough task, though."

She nodded. "There's something else, Ham. I'm out of atium."

He stood quietly in the mists for a moment, and then she heard him mutter a curse.

"I'll die the next time I fight a Mistborn," she said.

"Not unless he has atium," Ham said.

"What are the chances that someone would send a Mistborn without atium to fight me?"

He hesitated.

"Ham," she said, "I need to find a way to fight against someone who is burning atium. Tell me that you know a way."

Ham shrugged in the darkness. "There are lots of theories, Vin. I once had a long conversation with Breeze about this—though he spent most of it grumbling that I was annoying him."

"Well?" Vin asked. "What can I do?"

He rubbed his chin. "Most people agree that the best way to kill a Mistborn with atium is to surprise them."

"That doesn't help if they attack me first," Vin said.

"Well," Ham said. "Barring surprise, there isn't much. Some people think that you *might* be able to kill an atium-using Mistborn if you catch them in an unavoidable situation. It's like a game of fets—sometimes, the only way to take a piece is to corner it so that no matter which way it moves, it dies.

"Doing that to a Mistborn is pretty tough, though. The thing is, atium lets the Mistborn see the future—so he knows when a move will trap him, and so he can avoid the situation. The metal is supposed to enhance his mind somehow, too."

"It does. When I'm burning atium, I often dodge before I even register the attacks that are coming."

Ham nodded.

"So," Vin said, "what else?"

"That's it, Vin," Ham said. "Thugs talk about this topic a lot—we're all afraid of going up against a Mistborn. Those are your two options: Surprise him or overwhelm him. I'm sorry."

Vin frowned. Neither option would do her much good if she got ambushed. "Anyway, I need to keep moving. I promise to tell you about any corpses I produce."

Ham laughed. "How about you just try and avoid getting into situations where you have to produce them, eh? The Lord only knows what this kingdom would do if we lost you. . . ."

Vin nodded, though she wasn't certain how much Ham could see of her in the darkness. She waved to OreSeur, heading out toward the keep wall, leaving Ham on the cobbled path.

"Mistress," OreSeur said as they reached the top of the wall, "might I know the purpose of surprising Master Hammond like that? Are you that fond of startling your friends?"

"It was a test," Vin said, pausing beside a merlon gap, looking out over the city proper.

"A test, Mistress?"

"To see if he would use Allomancy. That way, I could know that he wasn't the impostor."

"Ah," the kandra said. "Clever, Mistress."

Vin smiled. "Thank you," she said. A guard patrol was moving toward them. Not wanting to have to deal with them, Vin nodded to the wall-top stone guardhouse. She jumped, pushing off a coin, and landed on top of it. OreSeur bounded up beside her, using his strange kandra musculature to leap the ten feet.

Vin sat down cross-legged to think, and OreSeur padded over to the roof's side and lay down, paws hanging over the edge. As they sat, Vin considered something. *OreSeur told me that a kandra didn't gain Allomantic powers if he ate an Allomancer . . . but, can a kandra be an Allomancer on his own? I never did finish that conversation.*

"This will tell me if a person isn't a kandra, won't it?" Vin asked, turning to OreSeur. "Your people don't have Allomantic powers, right?"

OreSeur didn't answer.

"OreSeur?" Vin said.

"I'm not required to answer that question, Mistress."

Yes, Vin thought with a sigh. *The Contract. How am I supposed to catch this other kandra if OreSeur won't answer any of my questions?* She leaned back in frustration, staring up into the endless mists, using her mistcloak to cushion her head.

"Your plan will work, Mistress," OreSeur said quietly.

Vin paused, rolling her head to look at him. He lay with head on forepaws, staring over the city. "If you sense Allomancy from someone, then they aren't a kandra."

Vin sensed a hesitant reluctance to his words, and he didn't look at her. It was as if he spoke grudgingly, giving up information that he'd rather have kept to himself.

So secretive, Vin thought. "Thank you," she said.

OreSeur shrugged a pair of canine shoulders.

"I know you'd rather not have to deal with me," she said. "We'd both rather keep our distance from each other. But, we'll just have to make things work this way."

OreSeur nodded again, then turned his head slightly and looked at her. "Why is it that you hate me?"

"I don't hate you," Vin said.

OreSeur raised a canine eyebrow. There was a wisdom in those eyes, an understanding that Vin was surprised to see. She'd never seen such things in him before.

"I . . ." Vin trailed off, looking away. "I just haven't ever gotten over the fact that you ate Kelsier's body."

"That isn't it," OreSeur said, turning back to look at the city. "You're too smart to be bothered by that."

Vin frowned indignantly, but the kandra wasn't looking at her. She turned, staring back up at the mists. *Why did he bring this up?* she thought. *We were just starting to get along.* She'd been willing to forget.

You really want to know? she thought. *Fine.*

"It's because you knew," she whispered.

"Excuse me, Mistress?"

"You knew," Vin said, still looking into the mists. "You were the only one on the crew who knew Kelsier was going to die. He told you that he was going to let himself be killed, and that you were to take his bones."

"Ah," OreSeur said quietly.

Vin turned accusing eyes at the creature. "Why didn't you say something? You knew how we felt about Kelsier. Did you even *consider* telling us that the idiot planned to kill himself? Did it even cross your mind that we might be able to stop him, that we might be able to find another way?"

"You are being quite harsh, Mistress."

"Well, you wanted to know," Vin said. "It was worst right after he died. When you came to be my servant, by his order. You never even spoke of what you'd done."

"The Contract, Mistress," OreSeur said. "You do not wish to hear this, perhaps, but I was bound. Kelsier did not wish you to know of his plans, so I could not tell you. Hate me if you must, but I do not regret my actions."

"I don't hate you." *I got over that.* "But, honestly, you wouldn't even break the Contract for his own good? You served Kelsier for two years. Didn't it even hurt you to know he was going to die?"

"Why should I care if one master or another dies?" OreSeur said. "There is always another to take their place."

"Kelsier wasn't that kind of master," Vin said.

"Wasn't he?"

"No."

"I apologize, Mistress," OreSeur said. "I will believe as commanded, then."

Vin opened her mouth to reply, then snapped it closed. If he was determined to keep thinking like a fool, then it was his right to do so. He could continue to resent masters, just as . . .

Just as she resented him. For keeping his word, for holding to his Contract.

Ever since I've known him, I've done nothing but treat him poorly, Vin thought. *First, when he was Renoux, I reacted against his haughty bearing—but that bearing wasn't his, it was part of the act he had to play. Then, as OreSeur, I avoided him. Hated him, even, for letting Kelsier die. Now I've forced him into an animal's body.*

And, in two years of knowing him, the only times I've asked about his past, I did it so that I could glean more information about his people so that I could find the impostor.

Vin watched the mists. Of all the people in the crew, only OreSeur had been an outsider. He hadn't been invited to their conferences. He hadn't inherited a position in the government. He'd helped as much as any of them, playing a vital role—that of the "spirit" Kelsier, who had returned from the grave to incite the skaa to their final rebellion. Yet, while the rest of them had titles, friendships, and duties, the only thing OreSeur had gained from overthrowing the Final Empire was another master.

One who hated him.

No wonder he reacts like he does, Vin thought. Kelsier's last words to her returned to her mind: *You have a lot to learn about friendship, Vin. . . .* Kell and the others had invited her in, treated her with dignity and friendliness, even when she hadn't deserved it.

"OreSeur," she said, "what was your life like before you were recruited by Kelsier?"

"I don't see what that has to do with finding the impostor, Mistress," OreSeur said.

"It doesn't have anything to do with that," Vin said. "I just thought maybe I should get to know you better."

"My apologies, Mistress, but I don't want you to know me."

Vin sighed. *So much for that.*

But . . . well, Kelsier and the others hadn't turned away when she'd been blunt with them. There was a familiar tone to OreSeur's words. Something in them that she recognized.

"Anonymity," Vin said quietly.

"Mistress?"

"Anonymity. Hiding, even when you're with others. Being quiet, unobtrusive. Forcing yourself to stay apart—emotionally, at least. It's a way of life. A protection."

OreSeur didn't answer.

"You serve beneath masters," Vin said. "Harsh men who fear your competence. The only way to keep them from hating you is to make certain they don't pay attention to you. So, you make yourself look small and weak. Not a threat. But sometimes you say the wrong thing, or you let your rebelliousness show."

She turned toward him. He was watching her. "Yes," he finally said, turning to look back over the city.

"They hate you," Vin said quietly. "They hate you because of your powers, because they can't make you break your word, or because they worry that you are too strong to control."

"They become afraid of you," OreSeur said. "They grow paranoid—terrified, even as they use you, that you will take their place. Despite the Contract, despite knowing that no kandra would break his sacred vow, they fear you. And men hate what they fear."

"And so," Vin said, "they find excuses to beat you. Sometimes, even your efforts to remain harmless seem to provoke them. They hate your skill, they hate the fact that they don't have more reasons to beat you, so they beat you."

OreSeur turned back to her. "How do you know these things?" he demanded.

Vin shrugged. "That's not only how they treat kandra, OreSeur. That's the same way crewleaders treat a young girl—an anomaly in a thieving underground filled with men. A child who had a strange ability to make things happen—to influence people, to hear what she shouldn't, to move more quietly and quickly than others. A tool, yet a threat at the same time."

"I . . . didn't realize, Mistress. . . ."

Vin frowned. *How could he not have known about my past? He knew I was a street urchin.* Except . . . had he? For the first time, Vin realized how OreSeur must have seen her two years before, when she'd first met him. He had arrived in the area after her recruitment; he probably assumed that she'd been part of Kelsier's team for years, like the others.

"Kelsier recruited me for the first time just a few days before I met you," Vin said. "Well, actually, he didn't so much *recruit* me as *rescue* me. I spent my childhood serving in one thieving crew after another, always working for the least reputable and most dangerous men, for those were the only ones who would take in a couple of transients like my brother and me. The smart crewleaders learned that I was a good tool. I'm not sure if they figured out that I was an Allomancer—some probably did, others just thought I was 'lucky.' Either way, they needed me. And that made them hate me."

"So they beat you?"

Vin nodded. "The last one especially. That was when I was really beginning to figure out how to use Allomancy, even though I didn't know what it was. Camon knew, though. And he hated me even as he used me. I think he was afraid that I would figure out how to use my powers fully. And on that day, he worried that I would kill him . . ." Vin turned her head, looking at OreSeur. "Kill him and take his place as crewleader."

OreSeur sat quietly, up on his haunches now, regarding her.

"Kandra aren't the only ones that humans treat poorly," Vin said quietly. "We're pretty good at abusing each other, too."

OreSeur snorted. "With you, at least, they had to hold back for fear they'd kill you. Have you ever been beaten by a master who knows that no matter how hard he hits, you won't die? All he has to do is get you a new set of bones, and you'll be ready to serve again the next day. We are the ultimate servant—you can beat us to death in the morning, then have us serve you dinner that night. All the sadism, none of the cost."

Vin closed her eyes. "I understand. I wasn't a kandra, but I did have pewter. I think Camon knew he could beat me far harder than he should have been able to."

"Why didn't you run?" OreSeur asked. "You didn't have a Contract bonding you to him."

"I . . . don't know," Vin said. "People are strange, OreSeur, and loyalty is so often twisted. I stayed with Camon because he was familiar, and I feared leaving more than I did staying. That crew was all I had. My brother was gone, and I was terrified of being alone. It seems kind of strange now, thinking back."

"Sometimes a bad situation is still better than the alternative. You did what you needed to do to survive."

"Perhaps," Vin said. "But there's a better way, OreSeur. I didn't know it until Kelsier found me, but life doesn't have to be like that. You don't have to spend your years mistrusting, staying in the shadows and keeping yourself apart."

"Perhaps if you are human. I am kandra."

"You can still trust," Vin said. "You don't *have* to hate your masters."

"I don't hate them all, Mistress."

"But you don't trust them."

"It is nothing personal, Mistress."

"Yes it is," Vin said. "You don't trust us because you're afraid we'll hurt you. I understand that—I spent months with Kelsier wondering when I was going to get hurt again."

She paused. "But OreSeur, nobody betrayed us. Kelsier was *right*. It seems incredible to me even now, but the men in this crew—Ham, Dockson, Breeze—they're good people. And, even if one of them were to betray me, I'd still rather have trusted them. I can sleep at night, OreSeur. I can feel peace, I can laugh. Life is different. Better."

"You are human," OreSeur said stubbornly. "You can have friends because they don't worry that you'll eat them, or some other foolishness."

"I don't think that about you."

"Don't you? Mistress, you just admitted that you resent me because I ate Kelsier. Beyond that, you hate the fact that I followed my Contract. You, at least, have been honest.

"Human beings find us disturbing. They hate that we eat their kind, even though we only take bodies that are already dead. Your people find it unsettling that we can take their forms. Don't tell me that you haven't heard the legends of my people. Mistwraiths, they call us—creatures that steal the shapes of men who go into the mists. You think a monster like that, a legend used to frighten children, will ever find acceptance in your society?"

Vin frowned.

"This is the reason for the Contract, Mistress," OreSeur said, his muffled voice harsh as he spoke through dog's lips.

"You wonder why we don't just run away from you? Meld into your society, and become unseen? We tried that. Long ago, when the Final Empire was new. Your people found us, and they started to destroy us. They used Mistborn to hunt us down, for there were many more Allomancers in those days. Your people hated us because they feared we would replace them. We were almost completely destroyed—and then we came up with the Contract."

"But, what difference does that make?" Vin asked. "You're still doing the same things, aren't you?"

"Yes, but now we do them at *your* command," OreSeur said. "Men like power, and they love controlling something powerful. Our people offered to serve, and we devised a binding contract—one that every kandra vowed to uphold. We will not kill men. We will take bones only when we are commanded. We will serve our masters with absolute obedience. We began to do these things, and men stopped killing us. They still hated and feared us—but they also knew they could command us.

"We became your tools. As long as we remain subservient, Mistress, we survive. And that is why I obey. To break the Contract would be to betray my people. We cannot fight you, not while you have Mistborn, and so we must serve you."

Mistborn. Why are Mistborn so important? He implied that they could find kandra. . . .

She kept this tidbit to herself; she sensed that if she pointed it out, he'd close up again. So, instead, she sat up and met his eyes in the darkness. "If you wish, I will free you from your Contract."

"And what would that change?" OreSeur asked. "I'd just get another Contract. By our laws I must wait another decade before I have time for freedom—and then only two years, during which time I won't be able to leave the kandra Homeland. To do otherwise would risk exposure."

"Then, at least accept my apology," she asked. "I was foolish to resent you for following your Contract."

OreSeur paused. "That still doesn't fix things, Mistress. I still have to wear this cursed dog's body—I have no personality or bones to imitate!"

"I'd think that you would appreciate the opportunity simply to be yourself."

"I feel naked," OreSeur said. He sat quietly for a moment; then he bowed his head. "But . . . I have to admit that there are advantages to these bones. I didn't realize how unobtrusive they would make me."

Vin nodded. "There were times in my life when I would have given anything to be able to take the form of a dog and just live my life being ignored."

"But not anymore?"

Vin shook her head. "No. Not most of the time, anyway. I used to think that everyone was like you say—hateful, hurtful. But there are good people in the world, OreSeur. I wish I could prove that to you."

"You speak of this king of yours," OreSeur said, glancing toward the keep.

"Yes," Vin said. "And others."

"You?"

Vin shook her head. "No, not me. I'm not a good person or a bad person. I'm just here to kill things."

OreSeur watched her for a moment, then settled back down. "Regardless," he said, "you are not my worst master. That is, perhaps, a compliment among our people."

Vin smiled, but her own words left her a bit haunted. *Just here to kill things. . . .*

She glanced toward the light of the armies outside the city. A part—the part that had been trained by Reen, the part that still occasionally used his voice in the back of her mind—whispered that there was another way to fight these armies. Rather than rely on politics and parlays, the crew could use Vin. Send her on a quiet visit into the night that left the kings and generals of the armies dead.

But, she knew that Elend wouldn't approve of something like that. He'd argue against using fear to motivate, even on one's enemies. He'd point out that if she killed Straff or Cett, they'd just be replaced by other men, men even more hostile toward the city.

Even so, it seemed like such a brutal, logical answer. A piece of Vin itched to do it, if only to be doing something other than waiting and talking. She was not a person meant to be besieged.

No, she thought. *That's not my way. I don't have to be like Kelsier was. Hard. Unyielding. I can be something better. Something that trusts in Elend's way.*

She shoved aside that part of her that wanted to just go assassinate both Straff and Cett, then turned her attention to other things. She focused on her bronze, watching for signs of Allomancy. Though she liked to jump around and "patrol" the area, the truth was that she was just as effective staying in one place. Assassins would be likely to scout the front gates, for that was where patrols began and the largest concentration of soldiers waited.

Still, she felt her mind wandering. There were forces moving in the world, and Vin wasn't certain if she wanted to be part of them.

What is my place? she thought. She never felt that she'd discovered it—not back when she'd been playing as Valette Renoux, and not now, when she acted as the bodyguard to the man she loved. Nothing quite fit.

She closed her eyes, burning tin and bronze, feeling the touch of wind-borne mist on her skin. And, oddly, she felt something else, something very faint. In the distance she could sense Allomantic pulsings. They were so dull she almost missed them.

They were kind of like the pulses given off by the mist spirit. She could hear it, too, much closer. Atop a building out in the city. She was getting used to its presence, not that she had much choice. Still, as long as it only watched. . . .

It tried to kill one of the Hero's companions, she thought. *It knifed him, somehow.* Or so the logbook claimed.

But . . . what was that pulsing in the far distance? It was soft . . . yet powerful. Like a faraway drum. She squeezed her eyes shut, focusing.

"Mistress?" OreSeur said, suddenly perking up.

Vin snapped her eyes open. "What?"

"Didn't you hear that?"

Vin sat up. "Wha—" Then she picked it out. Footsteps outside the wall a short distance away. She leaned closer, noticing a dark figure walking down the street toward the keep. She'd been so focused on her bronze that she'd completely tuned out real sounds.

"Good job," she said, approaching the edge of the guard station's roof. Only then did she realize something important. OreSeur had taken the initiative: he'd alerted her of the danger without specifically being ordered to listen.

It was a small thing, but it seemed important.

"What do you think?" she asked quietly, watching the figure approach. He carried no torch, and he seemed very comfortable in the mists.

"Allomancer?" OreSeur asked, crouching beside her.

Vin shook her head. "There's no Allomantic pulse."

"So if he is one, he's Mistborn," OreSeur said. He still didn't know she could pierce copperclouds. "He's too tall to be your friend Zane. Be careful, Mistress."

Vin nodded, dropped a coin, then threw herself into the mists. Behind her, OreSeur jumped down from the guardhouse, then leapt off the wall and dropped some twenty feet to the ground.

He certainly does like to push the limits of those bones, she thought. Of course, if a fall couldn't kill him, then she could perhaps understand his courage.

She guided herself by Pulling on the nails in a wooden roof, landing just a short distance from the dark figure. She pulled out her knives and prepared her metals, making certain she had duralumin. Then she moved quietly across the street.

Surprise, she thought. Ham's suggestion still left her nervous. She couldn't always depend on surprise. She followed the man, studying him. He was tall—very tall. And in robes. In fact, those robes . . .

Vin stopped short. "Sazed?" she asked with shock.

The Terrisman turned, face now visible to her tin-enhanced eyes. He smiled. "Ah, Lady Vin," he said with his familiar, wise voice. "I was beginning to wonder how long it would take you to find me. You are—"

He was cut off as Vin grabbed him in an excited embrace. "I didn't think you were going to come back so soon!"

"I was not planning to return, Lady Vin," Sazed said. "But events are such that I could not avoid this place, I think. Come, we must speak with His Majesty. I have news of a rather disconcerting nature."

Vin let go, looking up at his kindly face, noting the tiredness in his eyes. Exhaustion. His robes were dirty and smelled of ash and sweat. Sazed was usually very meticulous, even when he traveled. "What is it?" she asked.

"Problems, Lady Vin," he said quietly. "Problems and troubles."

The Terris rejected him, but he came to lead them.

23

"KING LEKAL CLAIMED THAT HE had twenty thousand of the creatures in his army," Sazed said quietly.

Twenty thousand! Elend thought in shock. That was easily as dangerous as Straff's fifty thousand men. Probably more so.

The table fell silent, and Elend glanced at the others. They sat in the palace kitchen, where a couple of cooks hurriedly prepared a late-night dinner for Sazed. The white room had an alcove at the side with a modest table for servant meals. Not surprisingly, Elend had never dined in the room, but Sazed had insisted that they not wake the servants it would require to prepare the main dining hall, though he apparently hadn't eaten all day.

So, they sat on the low wooden benches, waiting while the cooks worked—far enough away that they couldn't hear the hushed conversation in the alcove. Vin sat beside Elend, arm around his waist, her wolfhound kandra on the floor beside her. Breeze sat on the other side of him, looking disheveled; he'd been rather annoyed when they'd woken him. Ham had already been up, as had Elend himself. Another proposal had needed work—a letter he would send to the Assembly explaining that he was meeting with Straff informally, rather than in official parlay.

Dockson pulled over a stool, choosing a place away from Elend, as usual. Clubs sat slumped on his side of the bench, though Elend couldn't tell if the posture was from weariness or from general Clubs grumpiness. That left only Spook, who sat on one of the serving tables a distance away, legs swinging over the side as he occasionally pilfered a tidbit of food from the annoyed cooks. He was, Elend noticed with amusement, flirting quite unsuccessfully with a drowsy kitchen girl.

And then there was Sazed. The Terrisman sat directly across from Elend with the calm sense of collectedness that only Sazed could manage. His robes were dusty, and he looked odd without his earrings—removed to not tempt thieves, Elend would guess—but his face and hands were clean. Even dirtied from travel, Sazed still gave off a sense of tidiness.

"I do apologize, Your Majesty," Sazed said. "But I do not think that Lord Lekal is trustworthy. I realize that you were friends with him before the Collapse, but his current state seems somewhat . . . unstable."

Elend nodded. "How is he controlling them, you think?"

Sazed shook his head. "I cannot guess, Your Majesty."

Ham shook his head. "I have men in the guard who came up from the South after the Collapse. They were soldiers, serving in a garrison near a koloss camp. The Lord Ruler hadn't been dead a day before the creatures went crazy. They attacked everything in the area—villages, garrisons, cities."

"The same happened in the Northwest," Breeze said. "Lord Cett's lands were being flooded with refugees running from rogue koloss. Cett tried to recruit the koloss garrison near his own lands, and they followed him for a time. But then, something set them off, and they just attacked his army. He had to slaughter the whole lot—and lost nearly two thousand soldiers killing a small garrison of five hundred koloss."

The group grew quiet again, the clacking and talking of the cooking staff sounding a short distance away. *Five hundred koloss killed two thousand men,* Elend thought. *And the Jastes force contains twenty thousand of the beasts. Lord Ruler . . .*

"How long?" said Clubs. "How far away?"

"It took me a little over a week to get here," Sazed said. "Though it looked as if King Lekal had been camped there for a time. He is obviously coming this direction, but I don't know how quickly he intends to march."

"Probably wasn't expecting to find that two other armies beat him to the city," Ham noted.

Elend nodded. "What do we do, then?"

"I don't see that we *can* do anything, Your Majesty," Dockson said, shaking his head. "Sazed's report doesn't give me much hope that we'll be able to reason with Jastes. And, with the siege we're already under, there is little we can do."

"He might just turn around and go," Ham said. "With two armies already here . . ."

Sazed looked hesitant. "He knew about the armies, Lord Hammond. He seemed to trust in his koloss over the human armies."

"With twenty thousand," Clubs said, "he could probably take *either* of those other armies."

"But he'd have trouble with both of them," Ham said. "*That* would give me pause, if I were him. By showing up with a pile of volatile koloss, he could easily worry Cett and Straff enough that they would join forces against him."

"Which would suit us just fine," Clubs said. "The more that *other* people fight, the better off we are."

Elend sat back. He felt a looming anxiety, and it was good to have Vin next to him, arm around him, even if she didn't say much. Sometimes, he felt stronger simply because of her presence. *Twenty thousand koloss.* This single threat scared him more than either of the other armies.

"This could be a good thing," Ham said. "If Jastes *were* to lose control of those beasts near Luthadel, there's a good chance they'd attack one of those other armies."

"Agreed," Breeze said tiredly. "I think we need to keep stalling, draw out this siege until the koloss army arrives. One more army in the mix means only more advantage for us."

"I don't like the idea of koloss in the area," Elend said, shivering slightly. "No matter what advantage they offer us. If they attack the city . . ."

"I say we worry about that when, and if, they arrive," Dockson said. "For now, we have to continue our plan as we intended. His Majesty meets with Straff, trying to manipulate him into a covert alliance with us. With luck, the imminent koloss presence will make him more willing to deal."

Elend nodded. Straff had agreed to meet, and they'd set a date for a few days away. The Assembly was angry that he hadn't consulted with them about the time and place, but there was little they could do about the matter.

"Anyway," Elend finally said, sighing. "You said you had other news, Saze? Better, hopefully?"

Sazed paused. A cook finally walked over, setting a plate of food before him: steamed barley with strips of steak and some spiced lagets. The scents were enough to make Elend a little hungry. He nodded thankfully to the palace chef, who had insisted on preparing the meal himself despite the late hour, and who waved to his staff and began to withdraw.

Sazed sat quietly, waiting to speak until the staff were again out of earshot. "I hesitate to mention this, Your Majesty, for your burdens already seem great."

"You might as well just tell me," Elend said.

Sazed nodded. "I fear that we may have exposed the world to something when we killed the Lord Ruler, Your Majesty. Something unanticipated."

Breeze raised a tired eyebrow. "Unanticipated? You mean other than ravaging koloss, power-hungry despots, and bandits?"

Sazed paused. "Um, yes. I speak of items a little more nebulous, I fear. There is something wrong with the mists."

Vin perked up slightly beside Elend. "What do you mean?"

"I have been following a trail of events," Sazed explained. He looked down as he spoke, as if embarrassed. "I have been performing an investigation, you might say. You see, I have heard numerous reports of the mists coming during the daytime."

Ham shrugged. "That happens sometimes. There are foggy days, especially in the fall."

"That is not what I mean, Lord Hammond," Sazed said. "There is a difference between the mist and ordinary fog. It is difficult to spot, perhaps, but it is noticeable to a careful eye. The mist is thicker, and . . . well . . ."

"It moves in larger patterns," Vin said quietly. "Like rivers in the sky. It never just hangs in one place; it floats in the breeze, almost like it makes the breeze."

"And it can't enter buildings," Clubs said. "Or tents. It evaporates soon after it does."

"Yes," Sazed said. "When I first heard these reports of day mist, I assumed that the people were just letting their superstitions get out of control. I have known many skaa who refused to go out on a foggy morning. However, I was curious about the reports, so I traced them to a village in the South. I taught there for some time, and never received confirmation of the stories. So, I made my way from that place."

He paused, frowning slightly. "Your Majesty, please do not think me mad. During those travels I passed a secluded valley, and saw what I swear was mist, not fog. It was moving across the landscape, creeping toward me. During the full light of day."

Elend glanced at Ham. He shrugged. "Don't look at me."

Breeze snorted. "He was asking your opinion, my dear man."

"Well, I don't have one."

"Some philosopher you are."

"I'm not a philosopher," Ham said. "I just like to think about things."

"Well, think about *this,* then," Breeze said.

Elend glanced at Sazed. "Have those two always been this way?"

"Honestly, I am not certain, Your Majesty," Sazed said, smiling slightly. "I have known them for only slightly longer than yourself."

"Yes, they've always been like this," Dockson said, sighing quietly. "If anything, they've gotten worse over the years."

"Aren't you hungry?" Elend asked, nodding to Sazed's plate.

"I can eat once our discussion is finished," Sazed said.

"Sazed, you're not a servant anymore," Vin said. "You don't have to worry about things like that."

"It is not a matter of serving or not, Lady Vin," Sazed said. "It is a matter of being polite."

"Sazed," Elend said.

"Yes, Your Majesty?"

He pointed at the plate. "Eat. You can be polite another time. Right now, you look famished—and you're among friends."

Sazed paused, giving Elend an odd look. "Yes, Your Majesty," he said, picking up a knife and spoon.

"Now," Elend began, "why does it matter if you saw mist during the day? We know that the things the skaa say aren't true—there's no reason to fear the mist."

"The skaa may be more wise than we credit them, Your Majesty," Sazed said, taking small, careful bites of food. "It appears that the mist has been killing people."

"What?" Vin asked, leaning forward.

"I have never seen it myself, Lady Vin," Sazed said. "But I have seen its effects, and have collected several separate reports. They all agree that the mist has been killing people."

"That's preposterous," Breeze said. "Mist is harmless."

"That is what I thought, Lord Ladrian," Sazed said. "However, several of the reports are quite detailed. The incidents always occurred during the day, and each one tells of the mist curling around some unfortunate individual, who then died—usually in a seizure. I gathered interviews with witnesses myself."

Elend frowned. From another man, he'd dismiss the news. But Sazed . . . he was not a man that one dismissed. Vin, sitting beside Elend, watched the conversation with interest, chewing slightly on her bottom lip. Oddly, she didn't object to Sazed's words—though the others seemed to be reacting as Breeze had.

"It doesn't make sense, Saze," Ham said. "Thieves, nobles, and Allomancers have gone out in the mists for centuries."

"Indeed they have, Lord Hammond," Sazed said with a nod. "The only explanation I can think of involves the Lord Ruler. I heard no substantive reports of mist deaths before the Collapse, but I have had little trouble finding them since. The reports are concentrated in the Outer Dominances, but the incidents appear to be moving inward. I found one . . . very disturbing incident several weeks to the south, where an entire village seems to have been trapped in their hovels by the mists."

"But, why would the Lord Ruler's death have anything to do with the mists?" Breeze asked.

"I am not certain, Lord Ladrian," Sazed said. "But it is the only connection I have been able to hypothesize."

Breeze frowned. "I wish you wouldn't call me that."

"I apologize, Lord Breeze," Sazed said. "I am still accustomed to calling people by their full names."

"Your name is Ladrian?" Vin asked.

"Unfortunately," Breeze said. "I've never been fond of it, and with dear Sazed putting 'Lord' before it . . . well, the alliteration makes it even more atrocious."

"Is it me," Elend said, "or are we going off on even more tangents than usual tonight?"

"We get that way when we're tired," Breeze said with a yawn. "Either way, our good Terrisman must have his facts wrong. Mist doesn't kill."

"I can only report what I have discovered," Sazed said. "I will need to do some more research."

"So, you'll be staying?" Vin asked, obviously hopeful.

Sazed nodded.

"What about teaching?" Breeze asked, waving his hand. "When you left, I recall that you said something about spending the rest of your life traveling, or some nonsense like that."

Sazed blushed slightly, glancing down again. "That duty will have to wait, I fear."

"You're welcome to stay as long as you want, Sazed," Elend said, shooting a glare at Breeze. "If what you say is true, then you'll be doing a greater service through your studies than you would by traveling."

"Perhaps," Sazed said.

"Though," Ham noted with a chuckle, "you probably could have picked a safer place to set up shop—one that isn't being pushed around by two armies and twenty thousand koloss."

Sazed smiled, and Elend gave an obligatory chuckle. *He said that the incidents involving the mist were moving inward, toward the center of the empire. Toward us.*

Something else to worry about.

"What's going on?" a voice suddenly asked. Elend turned toward the kitchen doorway, where a disheveled-looking Allrianne stood. "I heard voices. Is there a party?"

"We were just discussing matters of state interest, my dear," Breeze said quickly.

"The other girl is here," Allrianne said, pointing at Vin. "Why didn't you invite me?"

Elend frowned. *She heard voices? The guest quarters aren't anywhere near the kitchens.* And Allrianne was dressed, wearing a simple noblewoman's gown. She'd taken the time to get out of her sleeping clothing, but she'd left her hair disheveled. Perhaps to make herself look more innocent?

I'm starting to think like Vin, Elend told himself with a sigh. As if to corroborate his thoughts, he noticed Vin narrowing her eyes at the new girl.

"Go back to your rooms, dear," Breeze said soothingly. "Don't trouble His Majesty."

Allrianne sighed dramatically, but turned and did as he

asked, trailing off into the hallway. Elend turned back to Sazed, who was watching the girl with a curious expression. Elend gave him an "ask later" look, and the Terrisman turned back to his meal. A few moments later, the group began to break up. Vin hung back with Elend as the others left.

"I don't trust that girl," Vin said as a couple of servants took Sazed's pack and guided him away.

Elend smiled, turning to look down at Vin. "Do I have to say it?"

She rolled her eyes. "I know. 'You don't trust anyone, Vin.' This time I'm right. She was dressed, but her hair was disheveled. She must have done that intentionally."

"I noticed."

"You did?" She sounded impressed.

Elend nodded. "She must have heard the servants waking up Breeze and Clubs, so she got up. That means she spent a good half an hour eavesdropping. She kept her hair mussed so that we'd assume that she'd just come down."

Vin opened her mouth slightly, then frowned, studying him. "You're getting better," she eventually said.

"Either that, or Miss Allrianne just isn't very good."

Vin smiled.

"I'm still trying to figure out why you didn't hear her," Elend noted.

"The cooks," Vin said. "Too much noise. Besides, I was a little distracted by what Sazed was saying."

"And what do you think of it?"

Vin paused. "I'll tell you later."

"All right," Elend said. To Vin's side, the kandra rose and stretched its wolfhound body. *Why did she insist on bringing OreSeur to the meeting?* he wondered. *Wasn't it just a few weeks ago that she couldn't stand the thing?*

The wolfhound turned, glancing at the kitchen windows. Vin followed its gaze.

"Going back out?" Elend asked.

Vin nodded. "I don't trust this night. I'll stay near your balcony, in case there's trouble."

She kissed him; then she moved away. He watched her

go, wondering why she had been so interested in Sazed's stories, wondering what it was she wasn't telling him.

Stop it, he told himself. Perhaps he was learning her lessons a little too well—of all the people in the palace, Vin was the last one he needed to be paranoid about. However, every time he felt like he was beginning to figure Vin out, he realized just how little he understood her.

And that made everything else seem a little more depressing. With a sigh, he turned to seek out his rooms, where his half-finished letter to the Assembly waited to be completed.

Perhaps I should not have spoken of the mists, Sazed thought, following a servant up the stairs. *Now I've troubled the king about something that might just be my delusion.*

They reached the top of the stairs, and the servant asked if he wished a bath drawn. Sazed shook his head. In most other circumstances he would have welcomed the opportunity to get clean. However, running all the way to the Central Dominance, being captured by the koloss, then marching the rest of the way up to Luthadel had left him wearied to the farthest fringe of exhaustion. He'd barely had the strength to eat. Now he just wanted to sleep.

The servant nodded and led Sazed down a side corridor.

What if he was imagining connections that didn't exist? Every scholar knew that one of the greatest dangers in research was the desire to find a specific answer. He had not imagined the testimonies he had taken, but had he exaggerated their importance? What did he really have? The words of a frightened man who had seen his friend die of a seizure? The testimony of a lunatic, crazed to the point of cannibalism? The fact remained that Sazed himself had never seen the mists kill.

The servant led him to a guest chamber, and Sazed thankfully bid the man good night. He watched the man walk away, holding only a candle, his lamp left for Sazed to use. During most of Sazed's life, he had belonged to a class of servants prized for their refined sense of duty and decorum. He'd been in charge of households and manors, supervising servants just like the one who had led him to his rooms.

Another life, he thought. He had always been a little frustrated that his duties as a steward had left him little time for study. How ironic it was that he should help overthrow the Final Empire, then find himself with even less time.

He reached to push open the door, and froze almost immediately. There was already a light inside the room.

Did they leave a lamp on for me? he wondered. He slowly pushed the door open. Someone was waiting for him.

"Tindwyl," Sazed said quietly. She sat beside the room's writing desk, collected and neatly dressed, as always.

"Sazed," she replied as he stepped in, shutting the door. Suddenly, he was even more acutely aware of his dirty robes.

"You responded to my request," he said.

"And you ignored mine."

Sazed didn't meet her eyes. He walked over, setting his lamp on top of the room's bureau. "I noticed the king's new clothing, and he appears to have gained a bearing to match them. You have done well, I think."

"We are only just started," she said dismissively. "You were right about him."

"King Venture is a very good man," Sazed said, walking to the washbasin to wipe down his face. He welcomed the cold water; dealing with Tindwyl was bound to tire him even further.

"Good men can make terrible kings," Tindwyl noted.

"But bad men cannot make good kings," Sazed said. "It is better to start with a good man and work on the rest, I think."

"Perhaps," Tindwyl said. She watched him with her normal hard expression. Others thought her cold—harsh, even. But Sazed had never seen that in her. Considering what she had been through, he found it remarkable—amazing, even—that she was so confident. Where did she get it?

"Sazed, Sazed . . ." she said. "Why did you return to the Central Dominance? You know the directions the Synod gave you. You are supposed to be in the Eastern Dominance, teaching the people on the borders of the burnlands."

"That is where I was," Sazed said. "And now I am here. The South will get along for a time without me, I think."

"Oh?" Tindwyl asked. "And who will teach them irrigation techniques, so they can produce enough food to survive the cold months? Who will explain to them basic lawmaking principles so that they may govern themselves? Who will show them how to reclaim their lost faiths and beliefs? You were always so passionate about that."

Sazed set down the washcloth. "I will return to teach them when I am certain there is not a greater work I need to do."

"What greater work could there be?" Tindwyl demanded. "This is our life's duty, Sazed. This is the work of our entire *people*. I know that Luthadel is important to you, but there is nothing for you here. I will care for your king. You must go."

"I appreciate your work with King Venture," Sazed said. "My course has little to do with him, however. I have other research to do."

Tindwyl frowned, eyeing him with a cool stare. "You're still looking for this phantom connection of yours. This foolishness with the mists."

"There *is* something wrong, Tindwyl," he said.

"No," Tindwyl said, sighing. "Can't you see, Sazed? You spent ten years working to overthrow the Final Empire. Now, you can't content yourself with regular work, so you have invented some grand threat to the land. You're afraid of being irrelevant."

Sazed looked down. "Perhaps. If you are correct, then I will seek the forgiveness of the Synod. I should probably seek it anyway, I think."

"Oh, Sazed," Tindwyl said, shaking her head slightly. "I can't understand you. It makes sense when young fireheads like Vedzan and Rindel buck the Synod's advice. But you? You are the soul of what it means to be Terris—so calm, so humble, so careful and respectful. So wise. Why are you the one who consistently defies our leaders? It doesn't make sense."

"I am not so wise as you think, Tindwyl," Sazed said quietly. "I am simply a man who must do as he believes. Right now, I believe there to be a danger in the mists, and I must investigate my impressions. Perhaps it is simply arrogance and foolishness. But I would rather be known as arrogant and foolish than risk danger to the people of this land."

"You will find nothing."

"Then I will be proven wrong," Sazed said. He turned, looking into her eyes. "But kindly remember that the last time I disobeyed the Synod, the result was the collapse of the Final Empire and the freedom of our people."

Tindwyl made a tight-lipped frown. She didn't like being reminded of that fact—none of the Keepers did. They held that Sazed had been wrong to disobey, but they couldn't very well punish him for his success.

"I don't understand you," she repeated quietly. "You should be a leader among our people, Sazed. Not our greatest rebel and dissident. Everyone wants to look up to you—but they can't. Must you defy every order you are given?"

He smiled wanly, but did not answer.

Tindwyl sighed, rising. She walked toward the door, but paused, taking his hand as she passed. She looked into his eyes for a moment; then he removed the hand.

She shook her head and left.

He commanded kings, and though he sought no empire, he became greater than all who had come before.

24

SOMETHING IS GOING ON, VIN thought, sitting in the mists atop Keep Venture.

Sazed was not prone to exaggeration. He was meticulous—that much showed in his mannerisms, his cleanliness, and even the way he spoke. And, he was even more meticulous when it came to his studies. Vin was inclined to believe his discoveries.

And she'd certainly seen things in the mists. Dangerous things. Could the mist spirit explain the deaths Sazed had encountered? *But, if that's the case, why didn't Sazed speak of figures in the mist?*

She sighed, closing her eyes and burning bronze. She could hear the spirit, watching nearby. And, she could hear *it* again as well, the strange thumping in the distance. She opened her eyes, leaving her bronze on, and quietly unfolded something from her pocket: a sheet from the logbook. By the light from Elend's balcony below, and with tin, she could easily read the words.

> *I sleep but a few hours each night. We must press forward, traveling as much as we can each day—but when I finally lie down, I find sleep elusive. The same thoughts that trouble me during the day are only compounded by the stillness of night.*
>
> *And, above it all, I hear the thumping sounds from above, the pulsings from the mountains. Drawing me closer with each beat.*

She shivered. She had asked one of Elend's seekers to

burn bronze, and he had claimed to hear nothing from the north. Either he was the kandra, lying to her about his ability to burn bronze, or Vin could hear a rhythm that nobody else could. Nobody except a man a thousand years dead.

A man everyone had assumed was the Hero of Ages.

You're being silly, she told herself, refolding the paper. *Jumping to conclusions.* To her side, OreSeur rustled, lying quietly and staring out over the city.

And yet, she kept thinking of Sazed's words. Something was happening with the mists. Something was wrong.

Zane didn't find her atop Keep Hasting.

He stopped in the mists, standing quietly. He'd expected to find her waiting, for this was the place of their last fight. Even thinking of the event made him tense with anticipation.

During the months of sparring, they had always met again at the place where he'd eventually lost her. Yet, he'd returned to this location on several nights, and had never found her. He frowned, thinking of Straff's orders, and of necessity.

Eventually, he would likely be ordered to kill this girl. He wasn't certain what bothered him more—his growing reluctance to consider such an act, or his growing worry that he might not actually be able to beat her.

She could be it, he thought. *The thing that finally lets me resist. The thing that convinces me to just . . . leave.*

He couldn't explain why he needed a reason. Part of him simply ascribed it to his insanity, though the rational part of him felt that was a weak excuse. Deep down, he admitted that Straff was all he had ever known. Zane wouldn't be able to leave until he knew he had someone else to rely on.

He turned away from Keep Hasting. He'd had enough of waiting; it was time to seek her out. Zane threw a coin, bounding across the city for a time. And, sure enough, there she was: sitting atop Keep Venture, watching over his foolish brother.

Zane rounded the keep, keeping far enough away that even tin-enhanced eyes wouldn't see him. He landed on the back of the keep's roof, then walked forward quietly. He approached, watching her sit on the edge of the roof. The air was silent.

Finally, she turned around, jumping slightly. He swore that she could sense him when she shouldn't be able to.

Either way, he was discovered.

"Zane," Vin said flatly, easily identifying the silhouette. He wore his customary black on black, with no mistcloak.

"I've been waiting," he said quietly. "Atop Keep Hasting. Hoping you'd come."

She sighed, careful to keep an eye on him, but relaxing slightly. "I'm not really in the mood for sparring right now."

He watched her. "Pity," he finally said. He walked over, prompting Vin to rise cautiously to her feet. He paused beside the lip of the rooftop, looking down at Elend's lit balcony.

Vin glanced at OreSeur. He was tense, alternately watching her and Zane.

"You're so worried about him," Zane said quietly.

"Elend?" Vin asked.

Zane nodded. "Even though he uses you."

"We've had this discussion, Zane. He isn't using me."

Zane looked up at her, meeting her eyes, standing straight-backed and confident in the night.

He's so strong, she thought. *So sure of himself. So different from . . .*

She stopped herself.

Zane turned away. "Tell me, Vin," he said, "when you were younger, did you ever wish for power?"

Vin cocked her head, frowning at the strange question. "What do you mean?"

"You grew up on the streets," Zane said. "When you were younger, did you wish for power? Did you dream of having the ability to free yourself, to kill those who brutalized you?"

"Of course I did," Vin said.

"And now you have that power," Zane said. "What

would the child Vin say if she could see you? A Mistborn who is bent and bowed by the weight of another's will? Powerful, yet somehow still subservient?"

"I'm a different person now, Zane," Vin said. "I'd like to think that I've learned things since I was a child."

"I've found that a child's instincts are often the most honest," Zane said. "The most natural."

Vin didn't respond.

Zane turned quietly, looking out over the city, seemingly unconcerned that he was exposing his back to her. Vin eyed him, then dropped a coin. It plinked against the metal rooftop, and he immediately glanced back toward her.

No, she thought, *he doesn't trust me.*

He turned away again, and Vin watched him. She did understand what he meant, for she had once thought as he did. Idly, she wondered what kind of person she might have become if she'd gained full access to her powers without—at the same time—learning of friendship and trust from Kelsier's crew.

"What would you do, Vin?" Zane asked, turning back toward her. "Assuming you didn't have any constraints—assuming there were no repercussions for your actions?"

Go north. The thought was immediate. *Find out what is causing that thumping.* She didn't say it, however. "I don't know," she said instead.

He turned, eyeing her. "You aren't taking me seriously, I see. I apologize for wasting your time."

He turned to go, walking directly between her and OreSeur. Vin watched him, and felt a sudden stab of concern. He'd come to her, willing to talk rather than just fight—and she'd wasted the opportunity. She was never going to turn him to her side if she didn't talk to him.

"You want to know what I'd do?" she asked, her voice ringing in the silent mists.

Zane paused.

"If I could just use my power as I wanted?" Vin asked. "No repercussions? I'd protect him."

"Your king?" Zane asked, turning.

Vin nodded sharply. "These men who brought armies against him—your master, this man named Cett. I'd kill them. I'd use my power to make certain that nobody could threaten Elend."

Zane nodded quietly, and she saw respect in his eyes. "And why don't you?"

"Because . . ."

"I see the confusion in your eyes," Zane said. "You know that your instincts to kill those men are right—yet you hold back. Because of him."

"There *would* be repercussions, Zane," Vin said. "If I killed those men, their armies might just attack. Right now, diplomacy could still work."

"Perhaps," Zane said. "Until he *asks* you to go kill someone for him."

Vin snorted. "Elend doesn't work that way. He doesn't give me orders, and the only people I kill are the ones who try to kill him first."

"Oh?" Zane said. "You may not act at his order, Vin, but you certainly refrain from action at it. You are his toy. I don't say this to insult you—you see, I'm as much a toy as you are. Neither of us can break free. Not alone."

Suddenly, the coin Vin had dropped snapped into the air, flying toward Zane. She tensed, but it simply streaked into Zanc's waiting hand.

"It's interesting," he said, turning the coin in his fingers. "Many Mistborn stop seeing the value in coins. To us, they simply become something to be used for jumping. It's easy to forget the value of something when you use it so often. When it becomes commonplace and convenient to you. When it becomes . . . just a tool."

He flipped the coin up, then shot it out into the night. "I must go," he said, turning.

Vin raised a hand. Seeing him use Allomancy made her realize that there was another reason she wanted to speak with him. It had been so long since she'd talked with another Mistborn, one who understood her powers. Someone like her.

But, it seemed to her that she was too desperate for him to stay. So she let him go, and returned to her vigil.

He fathered no children, yet all of the land became his progeny.

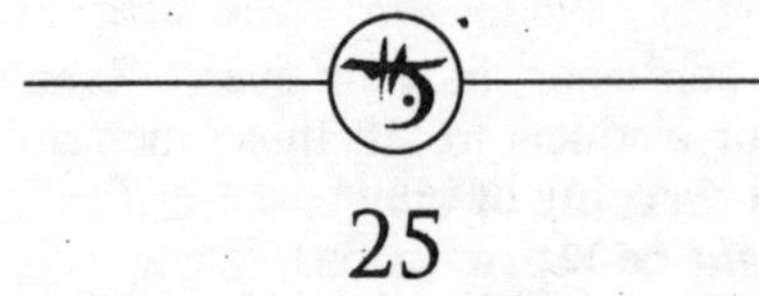

25

VIN WAS A VERY LIGHT sleeper—a heritage from her youth. Thieving crews worked together out of necessity, and any man who couldn't guard his own possessions was considered to be unworthy of them. Vin, of course, had been at the very bottom of the hierarchy—and while she hadn't had many possessions to protect, being a young girl in a primarily male environment gave her other reasons to be a light sleeper.

So it was that when she awoke to a quiet bark of warning, she reacted without thinking. She tossed off her covers, reaching immediately for the vial on her bedstand. She didn't sleep with metals inside of her; many of the Allomantic metals were, to some small extent, poisonous. It was unavoidable that she'd have to deal with some of that danger, but she had been warned to burn away excess metals at the end of each day.

She downed this vial even as she reached for the obsidian daggers hidden beneath her pillow. The door to her sleeping chamber swung open, and Tindwyl walked in. The Terriswoman froze in midstep as she saw Vin crouching on the bed's footboard a few feet away, twin daggers glistening, body tense.

Tindwyl raised an eyebrow. "So you are awake."

"Now."

The Terriswoman smiled.

"What are you doing in my rooms?" Vin demanded.

"I came to wake you. I thought we might go shopping."

"Shopping?"

"Yes, dear," Tindwyl said, walking over to pull open the curtains. It was far earlier in the day than Vin usually rose.

"From what I hear, you're going to meet with His Majesty's father on the morrow. You'll want a suitable dress for the occasion, I assume?"

"I don't wear dresses anymore." *What is your game?*

Tindwyl turned, eyeing Vin. "You sleep in your clothing?"

Vin nodded.

"You don't keep any ladies-in-waiting?"

Vin shook her head.

"Very well, then," Tindwyl said, turning to walk from the room. "Bathe and change. We'll leave when you're ready."

"I don't take commands from you."

Tindwyl paused by the door, turning. Then her face softened. "I know you don't, child. You may come with me if you wish—the choice is yours. However, do you really want to meet with Straff Venture in trousers and a shirt?"

Vin hesitated.

"At least come browse," Tindwyl said. "It will help take your mind off things."

Finally, Vin nodded. Tindwyl smiled again, then left.

Vin glanced at OreSeur, who sat beside her bed. "Thanks for the warning."

The kandra shrugged.

Once, Vin wouldn't have been able to imagine living in a place like Keep Venture. The young Vin had been accustomed to hidden lairs, skaa hovels, and the occasional alley. Now she lived in a building bespeckled with stained glass, bounded by mighty walls and grand archways.

Of course, Vin thought as she left the stairwell, *many things have happened that I didn't expect. Why think about them now?*

Her youth in the thieving crews had been much on her mind of late, and Zane's comments—ridiculous though they were—itched in her mind. Did Vin belong in a place like this keep? She had a great many skills, but few of them were beautiful hallway kinds of skills. They were more . . . ash-stained alleyway kinds of skills.

She sighed, OreSeur at her side as she made her way to the southern entryway, where Tindwyl said she'd be waiting. The hallway here grew wide and grand, and opened directly into the courtyard. Usually, coaches came right up into the entryway to pick up their occupants—that way the noblemen wouldn't be exposed to the elements.

As she approached, her tin let her hear voices. One was Tindwyl, the other . . .

"I didn't bring much," Allrianne said. "A couple hundred boxings. But I *do* so need something to wear. I can't survive on borrowed gowns forever!"

Vin paused as she turned into the last part of the hallway.

"The king's gift will surely be enough to pay for a dress, dear," Tindwyl said, noticing Vin. "Ah, here she is."

A sullen-looking Spook stood with the two women. He had on his palace guard's uniform, though he wore the jacket undone and the trousers loose. Vin walked forward slowly. "I wasn't expecting company," she said.

"Young Allrianne was trained as a courtly noblewoman," Tindwyl said. "She will know the current fashions, and will be able to advise on your purchases."

"And Spook?"

Tindwyl turned, eyeing the boy. "Packman."

Well, that explains his mood, Vin thought.

"Come," Tindwyl said, walking toward the courtyard. Allrianne followed quickly, walking with a light, graceful step. Vin glanced at Spook, who shrugged, and they followed as well.

"How did you get pulled into this?" Vin whispered to Spook.

"Was up too early, sneaking food," Spook grumbled. "Miss Imposing there noticed me, smiled like a wolfhound, and said, 'We'll be needing your services this afternoon, young man.' "

Vin nodded. "Stay alert and keep your tin burning. Remember, we're at war."

Spook obediently did what she said. Standing close to him as she was, Vin easily picked up and identified his tin's Allomantic pulses—meaning he wasn't the spy.

Another one off the list, Vin thought. *At least this trip won't be a total waste.*

A coach waited for them by the front keep gates. Spook climbed up beside the coachman, and the women piled into the back. Vin sat down inside, and OreSeur climbed in and took the seat next to her. Allrianne and Tindwyl sat across from her, and Allrianne eyed OreSeur with a frown, wrinkling her nose. "Does the animal have to sit on the seats with us?"

"Yes," Vin said as the carriage started moving.

Allrianne obviously expected more of an explanation, but Vin didn't give one. Finally, Allrianne turned to look out the window. "Are you sure we'll be safe, traveling with only one manservant, Tindwyl?"

Tindwyl eyed Vin. "Oh, I think that we'll be all right."

"Oh, that's right," Allrianne said, looking back at Vin. "You're an Allomancer! Are the things they say true?"

"What things?" Vin asked quietly.

"Well, they say you killed the Lord Ruler, for one. And that you're kind of . . . um . . . well." Allrianne bit her lip. "Well, just a little bit rickety."

"Rickety?"

"And dangerous," Allrianne said. "But, well, that can't be true. I mean, you're going shopping with us, right?"

Is she trying to provoke me on purpose?

"Do you always wear clothing like that?" Allrianne asked.

Vin was in her standard gray trousers and tan shirt. "It's easy to fight in."

"Yes, but . . . well." Allrianne smiled. "I guess that's why we're here today, right, Tindwyl?"

"Yes, dear," Tindwyl said. She'd been studying Vin through the entire conversation.

Like what you see? Vin thought. *What is it you want?*

"You have to be the strangest noblewoman I've ever met," Allrianne declared. "Did you grow up far from court? I did, but my mother was quite certain to train me well. Of course, she was just trying to make me into a good catch so Father could auction me off to make an alliance."

Allrianne smiled. It had been a while since Vin had been

forced to deal with women like her. She remembered hours spent at court, smiling, pretending to be Valette Renoux. Often when she thought of those days, she remembered the bad things. The spite she'd faced from court members, her own lack of comfort in the role.

But, there had also been good things. Elend was one. She would never have met him if she hadn't been pretending to be a noblewoman. And the balls—with their colors, their music, and their gowns—had held a certain transfixing charm. The graceful dancing, the careful interactions, the perfectly decorated rooms . . .

Those things are gone now, she told herself. *We don't have time for silly balls and gatherings, not when the dominance is on the verge of collapse.*

Tindwyl was still watching her.

"Well?" Allrianne asked.

"What?" Vin asked.

"Did you grow up far from court?"

"I'm not noble, Allrianne. I'm skaa."

Allrianne paled, then flushed, then raised her fingers to her lips. "Oh! You poor thing!" Vin's augmented ears heard something beside her—a light chuckling from OreSeur, soft enough that only an Allomancer could have heard him.

She resisted the urge to shoot the kandra a flat look. "It wasn't so bad," she said.

"But, well, no wonder you don't know how to dress!" Allrianne said.

"I know how to dress," Vin said. "I even own a few gowns." *Not that I've put one on in months. . . .*

Allrianne nodded, though she obviously didn't believe Vin's comment. "Breezy is skaa, too," she said quietly. "Or, half skaa. He told me. Good thing he didn't tell Father—Father never has been very nice to skaa."

Vin didn't reply.

Eventually, they reached Kenton Street, and the crowds made the carriage a liability. Vin climbed out first, OreSeur hopping down to the cobblestones beside her. The market street was busy, though not as packed as it had been the last time she'd visited. Vin glanced over the prices at some nearby shops as the others exited the coach.

Five boxings for a bin of aging apples, Vin thought with dissatisfaction. *Food is already going at a premium.* Elend had stores, fortunately. But how long would they last before the siege? Not through the approaching winter, certainly—not with so much of the dominance's grain still unharvested in the outer plantations.

Time may be our friend now, Vin thought, *but it will turn on us eventually.* They had to get those armies to fight each other. Otherwise, the city's people might die of starvation before the soldiers even tried to take the walls.

Spook hopped down from the carriage, joining them as Tindwyl surveyed the street. Vin eyed the bustling crowds. The people were obviously trying to go about their daily activities, despite the threat from outside. What else could they do? The siege had already lasted for weeks. Life had to go on.

"There," Tindwyl said, pointing to a dressmaker's shop.

Allrianne scampered forward. Tindwyl followed behind, walking with modest decorum. "Eager young thing, isn't she?" the Terriswoman asked.

Vin shrugged. The blond noblewoman had already gotten Spook's attention; he was following her with a lively step. Of course, it wasn't hard to get Spook's attention. You just had to have breasts and smell nice—and the second was sometimes optional.

Tindwyl smiled. "She probably hasn't had an opportunity to go shopping since she left with her father's army weeks ago."

"You sound like you think she went through some awful ordeal," Vin said. "Just because she couldn't go shopping."

"She obviously enjoys it," Tindwyl said. "Surely you can understand being taken from that which you love."

Vin shrugged as they reached the shop. "I have trouble feeling sympathy for a courtly puff who is tragically taken from her dresses."

Tindwyl frowned slightly as they entered the shop, Ore-Seur settling down to wait outside. "Do not be so hard on the child. She is a product of her upbringing, just as you are. If you judge her worth based on frivolities, then you are doing the same as those who judge you based on your simple clothing."

"I like it when people judge me based on my simple clothing," Vin said. "Then they don't expect too much."

"I see," Tindwyl said. "Then, you haven't missed this at all?" She nodded toward the shop's inner room.

Vin paused. The room burst with colors and fabric, lace and velvet, bodices and skirts. Everything was powdered with a light perfume. Standing before the dressing dummies in their brilliant hues, Vin was—for just a moment—again taken back to the balls. Back to when she was Valette. Back to when she had an *excuse* to be Valette.

"They say you enjoyed noble society," Tindwyl said lightly, walking forward. Allrianne was already standing near the front of the room, running her fingers across a bolt of fabric, talking to the dressmaker in a firm voice.

"Who told you that?" Vin asked.

Tindwyl turned back. "Why, your friends, dear. It's quite curious—they say you stopped wearing dresses a few months after the Collapse. They all wonder why. They say you seemed to like dressing like a woman, but I guess they were wrong."

"No," Vin said quietly. "They were right."

Tindwyl raised an eyebrow, pausing beside a dressmaker's dummy in a bright green dress, edged with lace, the bottom flaring wide with several underskirts.

Vin approached, looking up at the gorgeous costume. "I was beginning to like dressing like this. That was the problem."

"I don't see a problem in that, dear."

Vin turned away from the gown. "This isn't me. It never was—it was just an act. When wearing a dress like that, it's too easy to forget who you really are."

"And these dresses can't be part of who you really are?"

Vin shook her head. "Dresses and gowns are part of who *she* is." She nodded toward Allrianne. "I need to be something else. Something harder." *I shouldn't have come here.*

Tindwyl laid a hand on Vin's shoulder. "Why haven't you married him, child?"

Vin looked up sharply. "What kind of question is that?"

"An honest one," Tindwyl said. She seemed far less harsh than she had been the other times Vin had met her. Of course, during those times, she had mostly been addressing Elend.

"That topic is not your concern," Vin said.

"The king has asked me to help him improve his image," Tindwyl said. "And I have taken it upon myself to do more than that—I want to make a real king of him, if I can. There is some great potential in him, I think. However, he's not going to be able to realize it until he's more sure about certain things in his life. You in particular."

"I . . ." Vin closed her eyes, remembering his marriage proposal. That night, on the balcony, ash lightly falling in the night. She remembered her terror. She'd known, of course, where the relationship was going. Why had she been so frightened?

That was the day she'd stopped wearing dresses.

"He shouldn't have asked me," Vin said quictly, opening her eyes. "He can't marry me."

"He loves you, child," Tindwyl said. "In a way, that is unfortunate—this would all be much easier if he could feel otherwise. However, as things stand . . ."

Vin shook her head. "I'm wrong for him."

"Ah," Tindwyl said. "I see."

"He needs something else," Vin said. "Something better. A woman who can be a queen, not just a bodyguard. Someone . . ." Vin's stomach twisted. "Someone more like her."

Tindwyl glanced toward Allrianne, who laughed at a comment made by the elderly dressmaker as he took her measurements.

"You are the one he fell in love with, child," Tindwyl said.

"When I was pretending to be like her."

Tindwyl smiled. "Somehow, I doubt that you could be like Allrianne, no matter how hard you practiced."

"Perhaps," Vin said. "Either way, it was my courtly performance that he loved. He didn't know what I really was."

"And has he abandoned you now that he does know of it?"

"Well, no. But—"

"All people are more complex than they first appear," Tindwyl said. "Allrianne, for instance, is eager and young—perhaps a bit too outspoken. But she knows more of the court than many would expect, and she seems to know how to recognize what is good in a person. That is a talent many lack.

"Your king is a humble scholar and thinker, but he has the will of a warrior. He is a man who has the nerve to fight, and I think—perhaps—you have yet to see the best of him. The Soother Breeze is a cynical, mocking man—until he looks at young Allrianne. Then he softens, and one wonders how much of his harsh unconcern is an act."

Tindwyl paused, looking at Vin. "And you. You are so much more than you are willing to accept, child. Why look at only one side of yourself, when your Elend sees so much more?"

"Is that what this is all about?" Vin said. "You trying to turn me into a queen for Elend?"

"No, child," Tindwyl said. "I wish to help you turn into whoever you are. Now, go let the man take your measurements so you can try on some stock dresses."

Whoever I am? Vin thought, frowning. However, she let the tall Terriswoman push her forward, and the elderly dressmaker took his tape and began to measure.

A few moments and a changing room later, Vin stepped back into the room wearing a memory. Silky blue with white lace, the gown was tight at the waist and through the bust, but had a large, flowing bottom. The numerous skirts made it flare out, tapering down in a triangular shape, her feet completely covered, the bottom of the skirt flush with the floor.

It was terribly impractical. It rustled when she moved, and she had to be careful where she stepped to keep it from catching or brushing a dirty surface. But it was beautiful, and it made her feel beautiful. She almost expected a band to start playing, Sazed to stand over her shoulder like a protective sentry, and Elend to appear in the distance, lounging and watching couples dance as he flipped through a book.

Vin walked forward, letting the dressmaker watch where the garment pinched and where it bunched, and Allrianne let out an "Ooo" as she saw Vin. The old dressmaker leaned on his cane, dictating notes to a young assistant. "Move around a bit more, my lady," he requested. "Let me see how it fits when you do more than just walk in a straight line."

Vin spun slightly, turning on one foot, trying to remember the dancing moves Sazed had taught her.

I never did get to dance with Elend, she realized, stepping to the side, as if to music she could only faintly remember. *He always found an excuse to wiggle out of it.*

She twirled, getting a feel for the dress. She would have thought that her instincts would have decayed. Now that she had one on again, however, she was surprised at how easy it was to fall back into those habits—stepping lightly, turning so that the bottom of the dress flared just a bit. . . .

She paused. The dressmaker was no longer dictating. He watched her quietly, smiling.

"What?" Vin asked, flushing.

"I'm sorry, my lady," he said, turning to tap on his assistant's notebook, sending the boy away with a point of his finger. "But I don't rightly think I've ever seen someone move so gracefully. Like a . . . passing breath."

"You flatter me," Vin said.

"No, child," Tindwyl said, standing to the side. "He's right. You move with a grace that most women can only envy."

The dressmaker smiled again, turning as his assistant approached with a group of square cloth color samples. The old man began to sort through them with a wizened hand, and Vin stepped over to Tindwyl, holding her hands at the sides, trying not to let the traitorous dress take control of her again.

"Why are you being so nice to me?" Vin demanded quietly.

"Why shouldn't I be?" Tindwyl asked.

"Because you're mean to Elend," Vin said. "Don't deny it—I've listened in on your lessons. You spend the time insulting and disparaging him. But now you're pretending to be nice."

Tindwyl smiled. "I am not pretending, child."

"Then why are you so mean to Elend?"

"The lad grew up as a pampered son of a great lord," Tindwyl said. "Now that he's king, he needs a little harsh truth, I think." She paused, glancing down at Vin. "I sense that you've had quite enough of that in your life."

The dressmaker approached with his swatches, spreading them out on a low table. "Now, my lady," he said, tapping one group with a bent finger. "I think your coloring would look particularly good with dark cloth. A nice maroon, perhaps?"

"What about a black?" Vin asked.

"Heavens, no," Tindwyl said. "Absolutely no more black or gray for you, child."

"What about this one, then?" Vin asked, pulling out a royal blue swatch. It was nearly the shade she'd worn the first night she'd met Elend, so long ago.

"Ah, yes," the dressmaker said. "That would look wonderful against that light skin and dark hair. Hum, yes. Now, we'll have to pick a style. You need this by tomorrow evening, the Terriswoman said?"

Vin nodded.

"Ah, then. We'll have to modify one of the stock dresses, but I think I have one in this color. We'll have to take it in quite a bit, but we can work through the night for a beauty like yourself, can't we, lad? Now, as for the style . . ."

"This is fine, I guess," Vin said, looking down. The gown was the standard cut of those she'd worn at previous balls.

"Well, we're not looking for 'fine,' now, are we?" the dressmaker said with a smile.

"What if we removed some of the pettiskirts?" Tindwyl said, pulling at the sides of Vin's dress. "And perhaps raised the hem just a bit, so that she could move more freely?"

Vin paused. "You could do that?"

"Of course," the dressmaker said. "The lad says thinner skirts are more popular to the south, though they tend to lag in fashion a bit behind Luthadel." He paused. "Though, I don't know that Luthadel even really *has* a fashion anymore. . . ."

"Make cuffs of the sleeves wide," Tindwyl said. "And sew a couple of pockets into them for certain personal items."

The old man nodded as his quiet assistant scribbled down the suggestion.

"The chest and waist can be tight," Tindwyl continued, "but not restrictive. Lady Vin needs to be able to move freely."

The old man paused. "Lady Vin?" he asked. He looked a little closer at Vin, squinting, then turned to his assistant. The boy nodded quietly.

"I see . . ." the man said, paling, hand shaking just a little bit more. He placed it on the top of his cane, as if to give himself a little more stability. "I'm . . . I'm sorry if I offended you, my lady. I didn't know."

Vin flushed again. *Another reason why I shouldn't go shopping.* "No," she said, reassuring the man. "It's all right. You haven't offended me."

He relaxed slightly, and Vin noticed Spook strolling over.

"Looks like we've been found," Spook said, nodding to the front windows.

Vin glanced past dressing dummies and bales of cloth to see a crowd gathering outside. Tindwyl watched Vin with curiosity.

Spook shook his head. "Why do you get to be so popular?"

"I killed their god," Vin said quietly, ducking around a dressing dummy, hiding from the dozens of peeking eyes.

"I helped too," Spook said. "I even got my nickname from Kelsier himself! But nobody cares about poor little Spook."

Vin scanned the room for windows. *There's got to be a back door. Of course, there might be people in the alley.*

"What are you doing?" Tindwyl asked.

"I have to go," Vin said. "Get away from them."

"Why don't you go out and talk to them?" Tindwyl asked. "They're obviously very interested in seeing you."

Allrianne emerged from a dressing room—wearing a gown of yellow and blue—and twirled dramatically. She was obviously put out when she didn't even get Spook's attention.

"I'm not going out there," Vin said. "Why would I want to do something like that?"

"They need hope," Tindwyl said. "Hope you can give them."

"A false hope," Vin said. "I'd only encourage them to think of me as some object of worship."

"That's not true," Allrianne said suddenly, walking forward, looking out the windows without the least bit of embarrassment. "Hiding in corners, wearing strange clothing, and being mysterious—*that's* what has gotten you this amazing reputation. If people knew how ordinary you were, they wouldn't be so crazy to get a look at you." She paused, then looked back. "I . . . uh, didn't mean that like I think it sounded."

Vin flushed. "I'm not Kelsier, Tindwyl. I don't want people to worship me. I just want to be left alone."

"Some people don't have that choice, child," Tindwyl said. "You struck down the Lord Ruler. You were trained by the Survivor, and you are the king's consort."

"I'm not his consort," Vin said, flushing. "We're just . . ." *Lord, even* I *don't understand our relationship. How am I supposed to explain it?*

Tindwyl raised an eyebrow.

"All right," Vin said, sighing and walking forward.

"I'll go with you," Allrianne said, grabbing Vin's arm as if they had been friends since childhood. Vin resisted, but couldn't figure a way to pry her off without making a scene.

They stepped out of the shop. The crowd was already large, and the periphery was filling as more and more people came to investigate. Most were skaa in brown, ash-stained work coats or simple gray dresses. The ones in the front backed away as Vin stepped out, giving her a little ring of empty space, and a murmur of awed excitement moved through the crowd.

"Wow," Allrianne said quietly. "There sure are a lot of them. . . ."

Vin nodded. OreSeur sat where he had before, near the door, and he watched her with a curious canine expression.

Allrianne smiled at the crowd, waving with a sudden hesitance. "You can, you know, fight them off or something if this turns messy, right?"

"That won't be necessary," Vin said, finally slipping her arm free of Allrianne's grasp and giving the crowd a bit of a Soothing to calm them. After that, she stepped forward, trying to push down her sense of itching nervousness. She'd grown to no longer feel she needed to hide when she went out in public, but standing before a crowd like this . . . well, she almost turned and slinked back into the dressmaker's shop.

A voice, however, stopped her. The speaker was a middle-aged man with an ash-stained beard and a dirty black cap held nervously in his hands. He was a strong man, probably a mill worker. His quiet voice seemed a contrast to his powerful build. "Lady Heir. What will become of us?"

The terror—the uncertainty—in the large man's voice was so piteous that Vin hesitated. He regarded her with hopeful eyes, as did most of the others.

So many, Vin thought. *I thought the Church of the Survivor was small.* She looked at the man, who stood wringing his cap. She opened her mouth, but then . . . couldn't do it. She couldn't tell him that she didn't know what would happen; she couldn't explain to those eyes that she wasn't the savior that he needed.

"Everything will be all right," Vin heard herself say, increasing her Soothing, trying to take away some of their fear.

"But the armies, Lady Heir!" one of the women said.

"They're trying to intimidate us," Vin said. "But the king won't let them. Our walls are strong, as are our soldiers. We can outlast this siege."

The crowd was silent.

"One of those armies is led by Elend's father, Straff Venture," Vin said. "Elend and I are going to go meet with Straff tomorrow. We will persuade him to be our ally."

"The king is going to surrender!" a voice said. "I heard it. He's going to trade the city for his life."

"No," Vin said. "He would never do that!!"

"He won't fight for us!" a voice called. "He's not a soldier. He's a politician!"

Other voices called out in agreement. Reverence disappeared as people began to yell out concerns, while others began to demand help. The dissidents continued to rail against Elend, yelling that there was no way he could protect them.

Vin raised her hands to her ears. Trying to ward off the crowd, the chaos. *"Stop!"* she yelled, Pushing out with steel and brass. Several people stumbled back away from her, and she could see a wave in the crowd as buttons, coins, and buckles suddenly pressed backward.

The people grew suddenly quiet.

"I will suffer no ill words spoken of our king!" Vin said, flaring her brass and increasing her Soothing. "He is a good man, and a good leader. He has sacrificed much for you—your freedom comes because of his long hours spent drafting laws, and your livelihoods come because of his work securing trade routes and agreements with merchants."

Many members of the crowd looked down. The bearded man at the front continued to twist his cap, however, looking at Vin. "They're just right frightened, Lady Heir. Right frightened."

"We'll protect you," Vin said. *What am I saying?* "Elend and I, we'll find a way. We stopped the Lord Ruler. We can stop these armies . . ." She trailed off, feeling foolish.

Yet, the crowd responded. Some were obviously still unsatisfied, but many seemed calmed. The crowd began to break up, though some of its members came forward, leading or carrying small children. Vin paused nervously. Kelsier had often met with and held the children of the skaa, as if giving them his blessing. She bid the group a hasty farewell and ducked back into the shop, pulling Allrianne after her.

Tindwyl waited inside, nodding with satisfaction.

"I lied," Vin said, pushing the door closed.

"No you didn't," Tindwyl said. "You were optimistic. The truth or fiction of what you said has yet to be proven."

"It won't happen," Vin said. "Elend can't defeat three armies, not even with my help."

Tindwyl raised an eyebrow. "Then you should leave. Run away, leave the people to deal with the armies themselves."

"I didn't mean that," Vin said.

"Well, make a decision then," Tindwyl said. "Either give up on the city or believe in it. Honestly, the pair of you. . . ." She shook her head.

"I thought you weren't going to be harsh with me," Vin noted.

"I have trouble with that sometimes," Tindwyl said. "Come, Allrianne. Let's finish your fitting."

They moved to do so. However, at that moment—as if to belie Vin's assurances of safety—several warning drums began to beat atop the city wall.

Vin froze, glancing through the window, out over the anxious crowd.

One of the armies was attacking. Cursing the delay, she rushed into the back of the shop to change out of the bulky dress.

Elend scrambled up the steps to the city wall, nearly tripping on his dueling cane in his haste. He stumbled out of the stairwell, moving onto the wall top, rearranging the cane at his side with a curse.

The wall top was in chaos. Men scrambled about, calling to each other. Some had forgotten their armor, others their bows. So many tried to get up after Elend that the stairwell got clogged, and he watched hopelessly as men crowded around the openings below, creating an even larger jam of bodies in the courtyard.

Elend spun, watching a large group of Straff's men—thousands of them—rush toward the wall. Elend stood near Tin Gate, at the north of the city, nearest Straff's army. He could see a separate group of soldiers rushing toward Pewter Gate, a little to the east.

"Archers!" Elend yelled. "Men, where are your bows?"

His voice, however, was lost in the shouting. Captains moved about, trying to organize the men, but apparently too many footmen had come to the wall, leaving a lot of the archers trapped in the courtyard below.

Why? Elend thought desperately, turning back toward the charging army. *Why is he attacking? We had an a agreement to meet!*

Had he, perhaps, gotten wind of Elend's plan to play both sides of the conflict? Perhaps there really *was* a spy in the inner crew.

Either way, Elend could only watch hopelessly as the army approached his wall. One captain managed to get off a pathetic volley of arrows, but it didn't do much good. As the army approached, arrows began to zip up toward the wall, mixed with flying coins. Straff had Allomancers in the group.

Elend cursed, ducking down below a merlon as coins bounced against the stonework. A few soldiers fell. Elend's soldiers. Killed because he'd been too proud to surrender the city.

He peeked carefully over the wall. A group of men carrying a battering ram were approaching, their bodies carefully protected by men with shields. The care probably meant that the rammers were Thugs, a suspicion confirmed by the sound the ram made when it smashed into the gate. That was not the blow of ordinary men.

Hooks followed next. Shot up toward the wall by Coinshots below, falling far more accurately than if they'd been thrown. Soldiers moved to pull them off, but coins shot up, taking the men almost as quickly as they made the attempt. The gate continued to thump beneath him, and he doubted it would last for long.

And so we fall, Elend thought. *With barely a hint of resistance.*

And there was nothing he could do. He felt impotent, forced to keep ducking down lest his white uniform make him a target. All of his politicking, all of his preparations, all of his dreams and his plans. Gone.

And then Vin was there. She landed atop the wall, breathing hard, amid a group of wounded men. Coins and arrows that came near to her deflected back out into the air. Men rallied around her, moving to remove hooks and pull the wounded to safety. Her knives cut ropes, dropping them back down below. She met Elend's eyes, looking determined, then moved as if to leap over the side of the wall and confront the Thugs with their battering ram.

Elend raised a hand, but someone else spoke.

"Vin, wait!" Clubs bellowed, bursting out of the stairwell.

She paused. Elend had never heard such a forceful command from the gnarled general.

Arrows stopped flying. The booming calmed. Elend stood hesitantly, watching with a frown as the army retreated back across the ash-strewn fields toward their camp. They left a couple of corpses behind; Elend's men had actually managed to hit a few with their arrows. His own army had taken far heavier casualties: some two dozen men appeared to be wounded.

"What . . . ?" Elend asked, turning to Clubs.

"They weren't putting up scaling ladders," Clubs said, eyeing the retreating force. "This wasn't an actual attack."

"What was it then?" Vin asked, frowning.

"A test," Clubs said. "It's common in warfare—a quick skirmish to see how your enemy responds, to feel out their tactics and preparations."

Elend turned, watching the disorganized soldiers make way for healers to care for the wounded. "A test," he said, glancing at Clubs. "My guess is that we didn't do very well."

Clubs shrugged. "Far worse than we should have. Maybe this will scare the lads into paying better attention during drills." He paused, and Elend could see something he wasn't expressing. Worry.

Elend glanced out over the wall, watching the retreating

army. Suddenly, it made sense. It was exactly the kind of move that his father liked to make.

The meeting with Straff would take place as planned. However, before it happened, Straff wanted Elend to know something.

I can take this city any time, the attack seemed to say. *It's mine, no matter what you do. Remember that.*

He was forced into war by a misunderstanding—and always claimed he was no warrior—yet he came to fight as well as any man.

26

"THIS IS NOT A GOOD idea, Mistress." OreSeur sat on his haunches, watching Vin unpack a large, flat box.

"Elend thinks it's the only way," she said, pulling off the top of the box. The luxurious blue dress lay wrapped within. She pulled it out, noting its comparatively light weight. She walked over to the changing screen and began to disrobe.

"And the assault on the walls yesterday?" OreSeur asked.

"That was a warning," she said, continuing to unbutton her shirt. "Not a serious attack." Though, apparently, it had really unsettled the Assembly. Perhaps that had been the point. Clubs could say all he wished about strategy and testing the walls, but from Vin's standpoint, the thing Straff had gained most was even more fear and chaos inside Luthadel.

Only a few weeks of being besieged, and the city was already strained near to breaking. Food was terribly expensive, and Elend had been forced to open the city stockpiles. The people were on edge. Some few thought the attack had been a victory for Luthadel, taking it as a good sign that the army had been "repelled." Most, however, were simply even more scared than they had been before.

But, again, Vin was left with a conundrum. How to react, facing such an overpowering force? Cower, or try to continue with life? Straff had tested the walls, true—but he had maintained the larger part of his army back and in position, should Cett have tried to make an opportunistic attack at that time. He'd wanted information, and he'd wanted to intimidate the city.

"I still don't know if this meeting is a good idea," OreSeur said. "The attack aside, Straff is not a man to be trusted. Kelsier had me study all of the major noblemen in the city when I was preparing to become Lord Renoux. Straff is deceitful and harsh, even for a human."

Vin sighed, removing her trousers, then pulled on the dress's slip. It wasn't as tight as some, and gave her a lot of room to move through the thigh and legs. *Good so far.*

OreSeur's objection was logical. One of the first things she had learned on the street was to avoid situations where it was difficult to flee. Her every instinct rebelled at the idea of walking into Straff's camp.

Elend had made his decision, however. And, Vin understood that she needed to support him. In fact, she was even coming to agree with the move. Straff wanted to intimidate the entire city—but he really wasn't as threatening as he thought. Not as long as he had to worry about Cett.

Vin had had enough of intimidation in her life. In a way, Straff's attack on the walls left her feeling even more determined to manipulate him to their own ends. Going into his camp seemed a bit crazy on first impression, but the more she thought about it, the more she realized that it was the only way they were going to get to Straff. He had to see them as weak, had to feel that his bullying tactics had worked. That was the only way they would win.

That meant doing something she didn't like. It meant being surrounded, entering the enemy's den. However, if

Elend did manage to get out of the camp safely, it would provide a large morale boost for the city. Beyond that, it would make Ham and the rest of the crew more confident in Elend. Nobody would even have questioned the idea of Kelsier entering an enemy camp to negotiate; in fact, they probably would have expected him to come back from the negotiations somehow having convinced Straff to surrender.

I just need to make sure he comes back out safely, Vin thought, pulling on the dress. *Straff can display all the muscle he wants—none of it will matter if we're the ones directing his attacks.*

She nodded to herself, smoothing her dress. Then she walked out from behind the changing screen, studying herself in her mirror. Though the dressmaker had obviously sewn it to retain a traditional form, it didn't have a completely triangular bell shape, but instead fell a bit straighter down along her thighs. It was cut open near the shoulders—though it had tight sleeves and open cuffs—and the waist bent with her and gave her a good range of motion.

Vin stretched a bit, jumping, twisting. She was surprised at how light the dress felt, and how well she moved in it. Of course, any skirt would hardly be ideal for fighting—but this one would be an enormous improvement over the bulky creations she had worn to the parties a year before.

"Well?" she asked, spinning.

OreSeur raised a canine eyebrow. "What?"

"What do you think?"

OreSeur cocked his head. "Why ask me?"

"Because I care what you think," Vin said.

"The dress is very nice, Mistress. Though, to be honest, I have always found the garments to be a little ridiculous. All of that cloth and color, it doesn't seem very practical."

"Yes, I know," Vin said, using a pair of sapphire barrettes to pin the sides of her hair back a bit from her face. "But . . . well, I'd forgotten how much fun these things could be to wear."

"I fail to see why that would be, Mistress."

"That's because you're a man."

"Actually, I'm a kandra."

"But you're a boy kandra."

"How do you know that?" OreSeur asked. "Gender is not easy to tell in my people, since our forms are fluid."

Vin looked at him, raising an eyebrow. "I can tell." Then she turned back to her jewelry cabinet. She didn't have much; though the crew had outfitted her with a good sampling of jewelry during her days as Valette, she had given most of it to Elend to help fund various projects. She had, however, kept a few of her favorites—as if she'd known that she'd someday find her way back into a dress.

I'm just wearing it this once, she thought. *This still isn't me.*

She snapped on a sapphire bracelet. Like her barrettes, it contained no metal; the gemstones were set into a thick hardwood that closed with a wooden twist-clasp. The only metal on her body, then, would be her coins, her metal vial, and the single earring. Kept, by Kelsier's suggestion, as a bit of metal she could Push on in an emergency.

"Mistress," OreSeur said, pulling something out from under her bed with his paw. A sheet of paper. "This fell from the box as you were opening it." He grabbed it between two of his surprisingly dexterous paw fingers and held it up for her.

Vin accepted the paper. *Lady Heir,* it read.

I made the chest and bodice extra tight to give support—and cut the skirts so they would resist flaring—in case you need to jump. There are slits for metal vials in each of the cuffs, as well as a ripple in the cloth cut to obscure a dagger strapped around each forearm. I hope you find the alterations suitable.

Feldeu, Dressmaker.

She glanced down, noting the cuffs. They were thick and wide, and the way they pointed at the sides made perfect hiding places. Though the sleeves were tight around the upper arms, the forearms were looser, and she could see where the daggers could be strapped.

"It seems that he has made dresses for Mistborn before," OreSeur noted.

"Probably," Vin said. She moved over to her dressing mirror to apply a little makeup, and found that several of her makeup pads had dried out. *Guess I haven't done this for a while either. . . .*

"What time are we leaving, Mistress?" OreSeur asked.

Vin paused. "Actually, OreSeur, I wasn't planning to bring you. I still intend to keep your cover with the other people in the palace, and I think it would look very suspicious of me to bring my pet dog on this particular trip."

OreSeur was silent for a moment. "Oh," he said. "Of course. Good luck, then, Mistress."

Vin felt only a tiny stab of disappointment; she'd expected him to object more. She pushed the emotion aside. Why should she fault him? He'd been the one to rightly point out the dangers of going into the camp.

OreSeur simply lay down, resting head on paws as he watched her continue applying her makeup.

"But, El," Ham said, "you should at least let us send you in our own carriage."

Elend shook his head, straightening his jacket as he looked in the mirror. "That would require sending in a coachman, Ham."

"Right," Ham said. "Who would be me."

"One man won't make a difference in getting us out of that camp. And, the fewer people I take with me, the fewer people Vin and I have to worry about."

Ham shook his head. "El, I . . ."

Elend laid a hand on Ham's shoulder. "I appreciate the concern, Ham. But, I can do this. If there's one man in this world I can manipulate, it's my father. I'll come out of this with him feeling assured that he has the city in his pocket."

Ham sighed. "All right."

"Oh, one other thing," Elend said hesitantly.

"Yes?"

"Would you mind calling me 'Elend' instead of just 'El'?"

Ham chuckled. "I suppose that one's easy enough to do."

Elend smiled thankfully. *It's not what Tindwyl wanted, but it's a start. We'll worry about the "Your Majesty"s later.*

The door opened, and Dockson walked in. "Elend," he said. "This just arrived for you." He held up a sheet of paper.

"From the Assembly?" Elend asked.

Dockson nodded. "They're not happy about you missing the meeting this evening."

"Well, I can't change the appointment with Straff just because they want to meet a day early," Elend said. "Tell them I'll try and visit when I get back."

Dockson nodded, then turned as a rustling sounded from behind him. He stepped to the side, a strange look on his face, as Vin walked up to the doorway.

And she was wearing a dress—a beautiful blue gown that was sleeker than the common courtly fare. Her black hair sparkled with a pair of sapphire barrettes, and she seemed . . . different. More feminine—or, rather, more confident in her femininity.

How much she's changed since I first met her, Elend thought, smiling. Almost two years had passed. Then she had been a youth, albeit one with the life experiences of someone far older. Now she was a woman—a very dangerous woman, but one who still looked up at him with eyes that were just a bit uncertain, just a bit insecure.

"Beautiful," Elend whispered. She smiled.

"Vin!" Ham said, turning. "You're wearing a dress!"

Vin flushed. "What did you expect, Ham? That I would meet with the king of the Northern Dominance in trousers?"

"Well . . ." Ham said. "Actually, yes."

Elend chuckled. "Just because *you* insist on going about everywhere in casual clothing, Ham, doesn't mean that everyone does. Honestly, don't you get tired of those vests?"

Ham shrugged. "They're easy. And simple."

"And cold," Vin said, rubbing her arms. "I'm glad I asked for something with sleeves."

"Be thankful for the weather," Ham said. "Every chill you suffer will seem far worse to the men out in those armies."

Elend nodded. Winter had, technically, started. The weather probably wouldn't get bad enough to be more than a mild discomfort—they rarely got snow in the Central Dominance—but the chill nights certainly wouldn't improve morale.

"Well, let's go," Vin said. "The sooner we get this over with, the better."

Elend stepped forward, smiling, taking Vin's hands. "I appreciate this, Vin," he said quietly. "And you really do look gorgeous. If we weren't marching off to near certain doom, I'd be tempted to command a ball be held tonight just for the opportunity to show you off."

Vin smiled. "Near certain doom is that compelling?"

"Guess I've been spending too much time with the crew." He leaned down to kiss her, but she yelped and jumped back.

"It took me the better part of an hour to get this makeup on right," she snapped. "No kissing!"

Elend chuckled as Captain Demoux poked his head in the door. "Your Majesty, the carriage has arrived."

Elend looked at Vin. She nodded.

"Let's go," he said.

Sitting inside the carriage Straff had sent for them, Elend could see a solemn group standing on the wall, watching them roll away. The sun was near to setting.

He commands us to come in the evening; we'll have to leave when the mists are out, Elend thought. *A crafty way of pointing out how much power he has over us.*

It was his father's way—a move, in a way, that was similar to the attack on the walls a day before. To Straff, everything was about posturing. Elend had watched his father at court, and had seen him manipulate even obligators. By holding the contract to oversee the Lord Ruler's atium mine, Straff Venture had played a game even more dangerous than his fellow noblemen. And he had played that game very well. He hadn't factored in Kelsier throwing chaos into the mix, but who had?

Since the Collapse, Straff had secured the most stable,

and most powerful, kingdom in the Final Empire. He was a crafty, careful man who knew how to plan for years to get what he wanted. And this was the man Elend had to manipulate.

"You look worried," Vin said. She was across from him in the carriage, sitting in a prim, ladylike posture. It was as if donning a dress somehow granted her new habits and mannerisms. Or just a return to old ones—she'd once been able to act like a noblewoman well enough to fool Elend.

"We'll be all right," she said. "Straff won't hurt you—even if things go bad, he won't dare make a martyr of you."

"Oh, I'm not worried about my safety," Elend said.

Vin raised an eyebrow. "Because?"

"Because I have you," Elend said with a smile. "You're worth an army, Vin."

This, however, didn't seem to console her.

"Come here," he said, scooting over and waving her to the seat beside him.

She rose and moved across the carriage—but paused, eyeing him. "Makeup."

"I'll be careful," Elend promised.

She nodded, sitting and letting him put an arm around her. "Be careful of the hair, too," she said. "And your suit coat—don't get anything on it."

"When did you get so fashion-conscious?" he asked.

"It's the dress," Vin said with a sigh. "As soon as I put it on, all of Sazed's lessons started coming back to me."

"I really do like the dress on you," Elend said.

Vin shook her head.

"What?" Elend asked as the carriage bumped, pushing her a bit closer to him. *Another new perfume,* he thought. *At least that's one habit she never got out of.*

"This isn't me, Elend," she said quietly. "This dress, these mannerisms. They're a lie."

Elend sat quietly for a moment.

"No objections?" Vin said. "Everyone else thinks I'm speaking nonsense."

"I don't know," Elend said honestly. "Changing into my new clothes made *me* feel different, so what you say makes sense. If wearing dresses feels wrong to you, then you don't have to wear them. I want you to be happy, Vin."

Vin smiled, looking up at him. Then she leaned up and kissed him.

"I thought you said none of that," he said.

"From you," she said. "I'm Mistborn—we're more precise."

Elend smiled, though he couldn't quite feel jovial. Conversation, however, did keep him from fretting. "I feel uncomfortable in these clothes, sometimes. Everyone expects so much more from me when I wear them. They expect a king."

"When I wear a dress," Vin said, "they expect a lady. Then they're disappointed when they find me instead."

"Anyone who would feel disappointed to find *you* is too dense to be of any relevance," Elend said. "I don't want you to be like them, Vin. They're not honest. They don't care. I like you as you are."

"Tindwyl thinks that I can be both," Vin said. "A woman and a Mistborn."

"Tindwyl is wise," Elend said. "A bit brutal, but wise. You should listen to her."

"You just told me you liked me how I am."

"I do," Elend said. "But I'd like you *however* you were, Vin. I love you. The question is, how do you like yourself?"

That gave her pause.

"Clothing doesn't really change a man," Elend said. "But it changes how others react to him. Tindwyl's words. I think . . . I think the trick is convincing yourself that you *deserve* the reactions you get. You can wear the court's dresses, Vin, but make them your own. Don't worry that you aren't giving people what they want. Give them who you are, and let that be enough." He paused, smiling. "It was for me."

She smiled back, then carefully leaned against him. "All right," she said. "Enough insecurity for the moment. Let's review. Tell me more about your father's disposition."

"He's a perfect imperial nobleman. Ruthless, clever, and infatuated with power. You remember my . . . experience when I was thirteen?"

Vin nodded.

"Well, Father was very fond of skaa brothels. I think that he liked how strong he felt by taking a girl while knowing that she would be killed for his passion. He keeps several dozen mistresses, and if they don't please him, they get removed."

Vin muttered something quietly in response to this.

"He's the same way with political allies. One didn't ally with House Venture—one agreed to be dominated by House Venture. If you weren't willing to be our slave, then you didn't get to contract with us."

Vin nodded. "I've known crewleaders like that."

"And how did you survive when they turned an eye toward you?"

"By acting unimportant," Vin said. "By crawling on the ground when they passed and by never giving them reason to challenge me. Exactly what you're planning to do tonight."

Elend nodded.

"Be careful," Vin said. "Don't let Straff think that you're mocking him."

"All right."

"And don't promise too much," Vin said. "Act like you're trying to seem tough. Let him think he's bullying you into doing what he wants—he'll enjoy that."

"You've had experience with this before, I see."

"Too much of it," Vin said. "But, you've heard this before."

Elend nodded. They'd planned and replanned this meeting. Now he simply had to do what the crew had taught him. *Make Straff think we're weak, imply we'll give him the city—but only if he helps us against Cett first.*

Outside the window, Elend could see that they were approaching Straff's army. *So big!* he thought. *Where did Father learn to administrate a force like this?*

Elend had hoped, perhaps, that his father's lack of military experience would translate to a poorly run army. Yet, the tents were arranged in a careful pattern, and the soldiers wore neat uniforms. Vin moved over to her window, looking out with avid eyes, showing far more interest than an imperial noblewoman would have dared. "Look," she said, pointing.

"What?" Elend asked, leaning over.

"Obligator," Vin said.

Elend looked over her shoulder, spotting the former imperial priest—the skin around his eyes tattooed in a wide pattern—directing a line of soldiers outside a tent. "So that's it. He's using obligators to administrate."

Vin shrugged. "It makes sense. They'd know how to manage large groups of people."

"And how to supply them," Elend said. "Yes, it's a good idea—but it's still surprising. It implies that he still needs obligators—and that he's still subject to the Lord Ruler's authority. Most of the other kings threw off the obligators as soon as they could."

Vin frowned. "I thought you said your father likes being in power."

"He does," Elend said. "But also likes powerful tools. He always keeps a kandra, and he has a history of associating with dangerous Allomancers. He believes that he can control them—and he probably believes the same thing about the obligators."

The carriage slowed, then stopped beside a large tent. Straff Venture emerged a moment later.

Elend's father had always been a large man, firm of figure with a commanding posture. The new beard only heightened the effect. He wore a sharp, well-cut suit, just like the suits he had tried to get Elend to wear as a boy. That was when Elend had begun wearing his clothing disheveled—the buttons undone, the jackets too large. Anything to separate him from his father.

Elend's defiance had never been meaningful, however. He had annoyed Straff, pulling small stunts and acting foolish when he knew he could get away with it. None of it had mattered.

Not until that final night. Luthadel in flames, the skaa rebellion running out of control, threatening to bring down the entire city. A night of chaos and destruction, with Vin trapped somewhere within it.

Then Elend had stood up to Straff Venture.

I'm not the same boy you pushed around, Father. Vin squeezed his arm, and Elend climbed out of the carriage as the coachman opened the door. Straff waited quietly, a strange look on his face as Elend raised a hand to help Vin down.

"You came," Straff said.

"You seem surprised, Father."

Straff shook his head. "I see that you're just as big an idiot as ever, boy. You're in my power now—I could have you killed with a bare wave of my hand." He raised his arm, as if to do just that.

Now's the moment, Elend thought, heart thumping. "I've *always* been in your power, Father," he said. "You could have had me killed months ago, could have taken my city away at a bare whim. I don't see how my coming here changes anything."

Straff hesitated.

"We came for dinner," Elend said. "I had hoped to give you a chance to meet Vin, and had hoped that we might discuss certain . . . issues of particular import to you."

Straff frowned.

That's right, Elend thought. *Wonder if I have some offer yet to make. You know that the first man to play his hand usually loses.*

Straff wouldn't pass up an opportunity for gain—even a slim opportunity, like the one Elend represented. He probably figured there was nothing Elend could say that was of real importance. But could he be sure? What did he have to lose?

"Go and confirm with my chef that there will be three for dinner," Straff said to a servant.

Elend let out a lightly held breath.

"That girl's your Mistborn, then?" Straff asked.

Elend nodded.

"Cute little thing," Straff said. "Tell her to stop Soothing my emotions."

Vin flushed.

Straff nodded toward the tent. Elend led Vin forward, though she glanced over her shoulder, obviously not liking the idea of exposing her back to Straff.

Little bit late for that . . . Elend thought.

The tent chamber was what Elend would have expected of his father: stuffed with pillows and rich furniture, very little of which Straff would actually use. Straff furnished to suggest his power. Like the massive keeps of Luthadel, a nobleman's surroundings were an expression of how important he was.

Vin waited quietly, tensely, at Elend's side in the center of the room. "He's good," she whispered. "I was as subtle as I can manage, and he still noticed my touch."

Elend nodded. "He's also a Tineye," he said in a normal voice. "So he's probably listening to us right now."

Elend looked toward the door. Straff walked in a few moments later, giving no indication as to whether he had heard Vin or not. A group of servants entered a few moments later, carrying a large dining table.

Vin inhaled sharply. The servants were skaa—imperial skaa, after the old tradition. They were ragged, their clothing made of torn smocks, and showed bruises from a recent beating. They carried their loads with lowered eyes.

"Why the reaction, girl?" Straff asked. "Oh, that's right. You're skaa, aren't you—pretty dress notwithstanding? Elend is very kind; I wouldn't let you wear something like that." *Or much at all,* his tone implied.

Vin shot Straff a look, but pulled a little closer to Elend, grabbing his arm. Again, Straff's words were only about posturing; Straff was cruel, but only insofar as it served him. He wanted to make Vin uncomfortable.

Which he seemed to be doing. Elend frowned, glancing down, and caught just a hint of a sly smile on her lips.

Breeze has told me that Vin is more subtle with her Allomancy than most Soothers, he recalled. *Father's good, but for him to pick out her touch . . .*

She let him, of course.

Elend looked back at Straff, who hit one of the skaa servants on their way out. "I hope none of them are relatives of yours," Straff said to Vin. "They haven't been very diligent lately. I might have to execute a few."

"I'm not skaa anymore," Vin said quietly. "I'm a noblewoman."

Straff just laughed. He had already dismissed Vin as a threat. He knew she was Mistborn, he must have heard that she was dangerous, and yet he now assumed that she was weak and inconsequential.

She is *good at this,* Elend thought with wonder. Servants began to bring in a feast that was impressive considering the circumstances. As they waited, Straff turned to an aide. "Send in Hoselle," he ordered. "And tell her to be quick."

He seems less reserved than I remember, Elend thought. In the Lord Emperor's day, a good nobleman had been stiff and inhibited when in public, though many had turned to extravagant indulgence when in private. They would dance and have quiet dinner conversation at the ball, for instance, but enjoy whores and drunkenness in the small hours of night.

"Why the beard, Father?" Elend asked. "Last I knew, those weren't in fashion."

"I set the fashion now, boy," Straff said. "Sit." Vin waited respectfully, Elend noticed, until Elend was seated before taking her place. She managed to maintain an air of half jumpiness: she'd look Straff in the eyes, but always gave a reflexive twitch, as if part of her wanted to glance away.

"Now," Straff said, "tell me why you're here."

"I thought it was obvious, Father," Elend said. "I'm here to discuss our alliance."

Straff raised an eyebrow. "Alliance? We both just agreed that your life is mine. I don't see a need to ally with you."

"Perhaps," Elend said. "But, there are other factors at play here. I assume that you weren't expecting Cett's arrival?"

"Cett is of little concern," Straff said, turning his attention to the meal: big slabs of barely cooked beef. Vin wrinkled her nose, though Elend couldn't tell if that was part of her act or not.

Elend cut his steak. "A man with an army nearly as large as your own is hardly of 'little' concern, Father."

Straff shrugged. "He'll be of no trouble to me once I have the city walls. You'll turn those over to me as part of our alliance, I assume?"

"And invite Cett to attack the city?" Elend said. "Yes, together you and I could hold against him, but why go on the defensive? Why let him weaken our fortifications, and possibly just continue this siege until both of our armies are starving? We need to *attack* him, Father."

Straff snorted. "You think I need your help to do so?"

"You do if you want to beat him with any measure of assured success," Elend said. "We can take him easily together—but never alone. We need each other. Let's attack, you leading your armies, me leading mine."

"Why are you so eager?" Straff asked, narrowing his eyes.

"Because I want to prove something," Elend said. "Look, we both know you're going to take Luthadel from me. But, if we ride together against Cett first, it will look like I *wanted* to ally with you all along. I'll be able to give you the city without looking like a complete buffoon. I can spin it that I brought in my father to help us against the army I knew was coming. I turn the city over to you, and then become your heir again. We both get what we want. But *only* once Cett is dead."

Straff paused, and Elend could see that his words were having an effect. *Yes,* he thought. *Think that I'm just the same boy you left behind—eccentric, eager to resist you for silly reasons. And, saving face is a very Venture thing to do.*

"No," Straff said.

Elend started.

"No," Straff said again, turning to his meal. "That's not how we're going to do this, boy. I'll decide when—or even *if*—I attack Cett."

That should have worked! Elend thought. He studied Straff, trying to judge what was wrong. There was a faint hesitance about his father.

I need more information, he thought. He glanced to his side, to where Vin sat, spinning something lightly in her hand. Her fork. She met his eyes, then tapped it lightly.

Metal, Elend thought. *Good idea.* He looked over at Straff. "You came for the atium," he said. "You don't have to conquer my city to get it."

Straff leaned forward. "Why haven't you spent it?"

"Nothing brings sharks faster than fresh blood, Father," Elend said. "Spending large amounts of atium would only have indicated for certain that I had it—a bad idea, considering the trouble we took to squelch those rumors."

There was a sudden motion at the front of the tent, and soon a flustered young girl entered. She wore a ball gown—red—and had her black hair pulled back into a long, flowing tail. She was, perhaps, fifteen.

"Hoselle," Straff said, pointing to the chair next to him.

The girl nodded obediently, scurrying forward to sit beside Straff. She was done up in makeup, and the dress was low-cut. Elend had little doubt as to her relationship with Straff.

Straff smiled and chewed his food, calm and gentlemanly. The girl looked a little bit like Vin—same almond face, similar dark hair, same fine features and thin build. It was a statement. *I can get one just like yours—only younger and prettier.* More posturing.

It was that moment—that smirk in Straff's eyes—which reminded Elend more than ever why he hated his father.

"Perhaps we *can* make a deal, boy," Straff said. "Deliver the atium to me, and I'll deal with Cett."

"Getting it to you will take time," Elend said.

"Why?" Straff asked. "Atium is light."

"There's a lot of it."

"Not so much you couldn't pack it on a cart and send it out," Straff said.

"It's more complicated than that," Elend said.

"I don't think it is," Straff said, smiling. "You just don't want to give it to me."

Elend frowned.

"We don't have it," Vin whispered.

Straff turned.

"We never found it," she said. "Kelsier overthrew the Lord Ruler just so he could get that atium. But we never could find out where the metal was. It probably wasn't ever in the city."

Wasn't expecting that . . . Elend thought. Of course, Vin tended to do things by instinct, much as Kelsier was said to have done. All the planning in the world could go out the window with Vin around—but what she did instead was usually better.

Straff sat for a moment. He seemed to believe Vin. "So you really have nothing at all to offer me."

I need to act weak, Elend remembered. *Need him to think he can take the city any time, but also think it isn't worth taking right now.* He began to tap the table quietly with his index finger, trying to look nervous. *If Straff thinks we don't have the atium . . . then he'll be a lot less likely to risk attacking the city. Less gain. That's why Vin said what she did.*

"Vin doesn't know what she's talking about," Elend said. "I've kept the atium hidden, even from her. I'm sure we can arrange something, Father."

"No," Straff said, now sounding amused. "You really *don't* have it. Zane said . . . but, well, I didn't believe . . ."

Straff shook his head, turning back toward his meal. The girl at his side didn't eat; she sat quietly, like the ornament she was expected to be. Straff took a long drink of his wine, then let out a satisfied sigh. He looked at his child mistress. "Leave us," he said.

She immediately did as commanded.

"You, too," Straff said to Vin.

Vin stiffened slightly. She looked toward Elend.

"It's all right," he said slowly.

She paused, then nodded. Straff himself was little danger to Elend, and she was a Mistborn. If something went wrong, she could get to Elend quickly. And, if she left, it would do what they wanted—make Elend look less powerful. In a better position to deal with Straff.

Hopefully.

"I'll wait just outside," Vin said quietly, withdrawing.

He was no simple soldier. He was a force of leadership—a man that fate itself seemed to support.

27

"ALL RIGHT," STRAFF SAID, setting down his fork. "Let's be honest, boy. I'm this close to simply having you killed."

"You'd execute your only son?" Elend asked.

Straff shrugged.

"You need me," Elend said. "To help you fight Cett. You can kill me, but you'd gain nothing. You'd still have to take Luthadel by force, and Cett would still be able to attack—and defeat you—in your weakened state."

Straff smiled, folding his arms, leaning forward so he loomed over the table. "You are wrong on both counts, boy. First, I think that if I killed you, the next leader of Luthadel would be more accommodating. I have certain interests in the city who indicate that is true. Second, I don't need your help to fight Cett. He and I already have a treaty."

Elend paused. "What?"

"What do you think I've been doing these last few weeks? Sitting and waiting on your whims? Cett and I have exchanged pleasantries. He's not interested in the city—he just wants the atium. We agreed to split what we discover in Luthadel, then work together to take the rest of the Final Empire. He conquers to the west and north, I head east and south. Very accommodating man, Cett."

He's bluffing, Elend thought with reasonable certainty. That wasn't Straff's way; he wouldn't make an alliance with someone so near to him in strength. Straff feared betrayal too much.

"You think I would believe that?" Elend said.

"Believe what you wish," Straff said.

"And the koloss army marching this way?" Elend asked, playing one of their trump cards.

This made Straff pause.

"If you want to take Luthadel before those koloss get here, Father," Elend said, "then I think you might want to be a little more accommodating toward the man who's come, offering you everything you want. I only ask one thing—let me have a victory. Let me fight Cett, secure my legacy. *Then* you can have the city."

Straff thought about it, thought about it long enough that Elend dared to hope he might just have won. Then, however, Straff shook his head. "No, I think not. I'll take my chances with Cett. I don't know why he is willing to let me have Luthadel, but he doesn't seem to care much about it."

"And you do?" Elend said. "You know we don't have the atium. What does the city matter to you now?"

Straff leaned forward a bit farther. Elend could smell his breath, odorous from the dinner spices. "That's where you are wrong about me, boy. That's why—even if you'd been able to promise me that atium—you would never have left this camp tonight. I made a mistake a year ago. If I'd stayed in Luthadel, I would have been the one on that throne. Instead, it was you. I can't imagine why—I guess a weak Venture was still better than the other alternatives."

Straff was everything Elend had hated about the old empire. Presumptuous. Cruel. Arrogant.

Weakness, Elend thought, calming himself. *I can't be threatening.* He shrugged. "It's only a city, Father. From my position, it doesn't matter half as much as your army."

"It's more than a city," Straff said. "It's the Lord Ruler's city—and it has my home in it. My keep. I understand that you're using it as your palace."

"I didn't really have any other place to go."

Straff turned back to his meal. "All right," he said in between cutting chunks of steak, "at first, I thought you were an idiot for coming tonight, but now I'm not so certain. You must have seen the inevitable."

"You're stronger," Elend said. "I can't stand up to you."

Straff nodded. "You've impressed me, boy. Wearing

proper clothing, getting yourself a Mistborn mistress, maintaining control of the city. I'm going to let you live."

"Thank you," Elend said.

"And, in exchange, you're going to give me Luthadel."

"As soon as Cett is dealt with."

Straff laughed. "No, that's not the way these things work, boy. We're not negotiating. You're listening to my orders. Tomorrow, we'll ride to the city together, and you'll order the gates opened. I'll march my army in and take command, and Luthadel will become the new capital of my kingdom. If you stay in line and do as I say, I'll name you heir again."

"We can't do that," Elend said. "I left orders that the gates weren't to be opened to you, no matter what."

Straff paused.

"My advisors thought you might try and use Vin as a hostage, forcing me to relinquish the city," Elend said. "If we go together, they'll assume you're threatening me."

Straff's mood darkened. "You'd better hope that they don't."

"They will," Elend said. "I know these men, Father. They'd be eager for an excuse to take the city away from me."

"Then, why come here?"

"To do as I said," Elend said. "To negotiate an alliance against Cett. I can deliver Luthadel to you—but I still need time. Let's take down Cett first."

Straff grabbed his dinner knife by the hilt and slammed it down into the table. "I said this wasn't a negotiation! You don't make demands, boy. I could have you killed!"

"I'm just stating facts, Father," Elend said quickly. "I don't want to—"

"You've gotten smooth," Straff said, eyes narrowing. "What did you hope to accomplish with this game? Coming to my camp? Bringing nothing to offer . . ." He paused, then continued. "Nothing to offer except for that girl. Pretty little thing, she is."

Elend flushed. "That won't get you into the city. Remember, my advisors thought you might try threatening her."

"Fine," Straff snapped. "You die; I take the city by force."

"And Cett attacks you from behind," Elend said. "Pinning you against our wall and forcing you to fight surrounded."

"He'd take heavy losses," Straff said. "He wouldn't be able to take and hold the city after that."

"Even with diminished forces, he'd have a better chance of taking it from us than he would if he waited and then tried to take it from you."

Straff stood. "I'll have to take that chance. I left you behind before. I'm not going to let you loose again, boy. Those cursed skaa were supposed to kill you and leave me free of you."

Elend stood as well. However, he could see the resolve in Straff's eyes.

It isn't working, Elend thought, panic beginning to set in. This plan had been a gamble, but he hadn't ever really thought that he'd fail. Indeed, he'd played his cards well. But, something was wrong—something he hadn't anticipated, and still didn't understand. Why was Straff resisting so much?

I'm too new to this, Elend thought. Ironically, if he had let his father train him better as a child, he might have known what he'd done wrong. As it was, he suddenly realized the gravity of his situation. Surrounded by a hostile army. Separated from Vin.

He was going to die.

"Wait!" Elend said desperately.

"Ah," Straff said smiling. "Finally realized what you've gotten yourself into?" There was pleasure in Straff's smile. Eagerness. There had always been something inside Straff that had enjoyed hurting others, though Elend had rarely seen it applied to him. Propriety had always been there to stop Straff.

Propriety enforced by the Lord Ruler. At that moment, Elend saw murder in his father's eyes.

"You never intended to let me live," Elend said. "Even if I'd given you the atium, even if I'd gone with you to the city."

"You were dead the moment I decided to march here," Straff said. "Idiot boy. I do thank you for bringing me that girl, though. I'll take her tonight. We'll see if she cries my name or yours while I'm—"

Elend laughed.

It was a desperate laugh, a laugh at the ridiculous situation he'd gotten himself into, a laugh at his sudden worry and fear—but most of all, it was a laugh at the idea of Straff trying to force himself upon Vin. "You have no idea how foolish you sound," Elend said.

Straff flushed. "For that, boy, I'll be extra rough with her."

"You are a pig, Father," Elend said. "A sick, disgusting man. You thought you were a brilliant leader, but you were barely competent. You nearly got our house destroyed—only the Lord Ruler's own death saved you!"

Straff called for his guards.

"You may take Luthadel," Elend said, "but you'll lose it! I may have been a bad king, but you'll be a terrible one. The Lord Ruler was a tyrant, but he was also a genius. You're neither. You're just a selfish man who'll use up his resources, then end up dead from a knife in the back."

Straff pointed at Elend as soldiers rushed in. Elend didn't cringe. He'd grown up with this man, been raised by him, been tortured by him. And, despite it all, Elend had never spoken his mind. He'd rebelled with the petty timidity of a teenage boy, but he'd never spoken the truth.

It felt good. It felt right.

Perhaps playing the weak hand was a mistake against Straff. He always was fond of crushing things.

And suddenly Elend knew what he had to do. He smiled, looking Straff in the eyes.

"Kill me, Father," he said, "and you'll die, too."

"Kill me, Father," Elend said, "and you'll die, too."

Vin paused. She stood outside the tent, in the darkness of early night. She'd been standing with Straff's soldiers, but they'd rushed in at his command. She'd moved into the darkness, and now stood on the north side of the tent, watching the shadowed forms move within.

She'd been about to burst in. Elend hadn't been doing very well—not that he was a bad negotiator. He was just too honest by nature. It wasn't difficult to tell when he was bluffing, especially if you knew him well.

But, this new proclamation was different. It wasn't a sign of Elend attempting to be clever, nor was it an angry outburst like the one he'd made moments before. Suddenly, he seemed calm and forceful.

Vin waited quietly, her daggers out, tense in the mists before the glowing tent. Something told her she had to give Elend just a few more moments.

Straff laughed at Elend's threat.

"You are a fool, Father," Elend said. "You think I came here to negotiate? You think I would willingly deal with one such as you? No. You know me better than that. You know that I'd never submit to you."

"Then why?" Straff asked.

She could almost hear Elend's smile. "I came to get near you, Father . . . and to bring my Mistborn to the very heart of your camp."

Silence.

Finally, Straff laughed. "You threaten me with that wisp of a girl? If that's the great Mistborn of Luthadel I've been hearing of, then I'm sorely disappointed."

"That's because she wants you to feel that way," Elend said. "Think, Father. You were suspicious, and the girl confirmed those suspicions. But, if she's as good as the rumors say—and I know you've heard the rumors—then how would you have spotted her touch on your emotions?

"You caught her Soothing you, and you called her on it. Then, you didn't feel the touch anymore, so you assumed that she was cowed. But, after that, you began to feel confident. Comfortable. You dismissed Vin as a threat—but would any rational man dismiss a Mistborn, no matter how small or quiet? In fact, you'd think that the small, quiet ones would be the assassins you'd want to pay the *most* attention to."

Vin smiled. *Clever,* she thought. She reached out, Rioting Straff's emotions, flaring her metal and stoking his sense of anger. He gasped in sudden shock. *Take the clue, Elend.*

"Fear," Elend said.

She Soothed away Straff's anger and exchanged it for fear.

"Passion."

She complied.

"Calmness."

She soothed everything away. Inside the tent, she saw Straff's shadow standing stiffly. An Allomancer couldn't force a person to do anything—and usually, strong Pushes or Pulls on an emotion were less effective, since they alerted the target that something was wrong. In this case, however, Vin wanted Straff to know for certain she was watching.

She smiled, extinguishing her tin. Then she burned duralumin and Soothed Straff's emotions with explosive pressure, wiping away all capacity for feeling within him. His shadow stumbled beneath the attack.

Her brass was gone a moment later, and she turned on her tin again, watching the black patterns on the canvas.

"She's powerful, Father," Elend said. "She's more powerful than any Allomancer you've known. She killed the Lord Ruler. She was trained by the Survivor of Hathsin. And if you kill me, *she'll kill you.*"

Straff righted himself, and the tent fell silent again.

A footstep sounded. Vin spun, ducking, raising her dagger.

A familiar figure stood in the night mists. "Why is it I can never sneak up on you?" Zane asked quietly.

Vin shrugged and turned back to the tent—but moved herself so she could keep an eye on Zane, too. He walked over and crouched beside her, watching the shadows.

"That's hardly a useful threat," Straff finally said from within. "You'll be dead, even if your Mistborn does get to me."

"Ah, Father," Elend said. "I was wrong about your interest in Luthadel. However, you're also wrong about me—you've *always* been wrong about me. I don't care if I die, not if it brings safety to my people."

"Cett will take the city if I'm gone," Straff said.

"I think my people might be able to hold against him," Elend said. "After all, he has the smaller army."

"This is idiocy!" Straff snapped. He didn't, however, order his soldiers forward any farther.

"Kill me, and you die, too," Elend said. "And not just you. Your generals. Your captains. Even your obligators. She has orders to slaughter you all."

Zane took a step closer to Vin, his feet crunching slightly on the packed-down weeds that made up the floor of the camp. "Ah," he whispered, "clever. No matter how strong your opponent is, he can't attack if you've got a knife at his throat."

Zane leaned even closer, and Vin looked up at him, their faces just inches from each other. He shook his head in the soft mists. "But tell me—why is it that people like you and me always have to be the knives?"

Inside the tent, Straff was growing concerned. "No one is that powerful, boy," he said, "not even a Mistborn. She might be able to kill some of my generals, but she'd never get to me. I have my own Mistborn."

"Oh?" Elend said. "And why hasn't he killed her? Because he's afraid to attack? If you kill me, Father—if you even make so much as a *move* toward my city—then she'll begin the slaughter. Men will die like prisoners before the fountains on a day of execution."

"I thought you said he was above this kind of thing," Zane whispered. "You claimed you weren't his tool. You said he wouldn't use you as an assassin. . . ."

Vin shuffled uncomfortably. "He's bluffing, Zane," she said. "He'd never actually do anything like that."

"She is an Allomancer like you've never seen, Father," Elend said, voice muffled by the tent. "I've seen her fight other Allomancers—none of them can even touch her."

"Is that true?" Zane asked.

Vin paused. Elend hadn't actually ever seen her attack other Allomancers. "He saw me attack some soldiers once, and I've told him about my fights with other Allomancers."

"Ah," Zane said softly. "So it's only a small lie, then. Those are fine when one is king. Many things are. Exploiting one person to save an entire kingdom? What leader wouldn't pay such a cheap price? Your freedom in exchange for his victory."

"He's not using me," Vin said.

Zane stood. Vin turned slightly, watching carefully as he walked into the mists, away from tents, torches, and soldiers. He paused, standing a short distance away, looking up. Even with the light of tent and fires, this camp was claimed by the mists. It spun all around them. From within it, the torchlight and campfires seemed insignificant. Like dying coals.

"What is this to *him*," Zane said quietly, sweeping a hand around him. "Can he ever understand the mists? Can he ever understand you?"

"He loves me," Vin said, glancing back at the shadowed forms. They had fallen quiet for a moment, Straff obviously considering Elend's threats.

"He loves *you*?" Zane asked. "Or he loves *having you*?"

"Elend isn't like that," Vin said. "He's a good man."

"Good or not, you aren't like him," Zane said, voice echoing in the night to her tin-enhanced ears. "Can he understand what it is like to be one of us? Can he know the things we know, care about the things we love? Has he ever seen those?" Zane gestured upward, toward the sky. Far beyond the mists, lights shone in the sky, like tiny freckles. Stars, invisible to the normal eye. Only a person burning tin could penetrate the mists and see them shining.

She remembered the first time Kelsier had shown them to her. She remembered how stunned she had been that the stars had been there all along, invisible beyond the mists. . . .

Zane continued to point upward. "Lord Ruler!" Vin whispered, taking a small step away from the tent. Through the swirling mists, in the reflected light of the tent, she could see something on Zane's arm.

The skin was covered with thin white streaks. Scars.

Zane immediately lowered his arm, hiding the scarred flesh with his sleeve.

"You were in the Pits of Hathsin," Vin said quietly. "Like Kelsier."

Zane looked away.

"I'm sorry," Vin said.

Zane turned back, smiling in the night. It was a firm,

confident smile. He stepped forward. "I understand you, Vin."

Then he bowed slightly to her and jumped away, disappearing into the mists. Inside the room, Straff spoke to Elend.

"Go. Leave here."

The carriage rolled away. Straff stood outside his tent, heedless of the mists, still feeling a bit stunned.

I let him go. Why did I let him go?

Yet—even now—he could feel her touch slamming against him. One emotion after another, like a treasonous maelstrom within him, and then . . . nothing. Like a massive hand, grabbing his soul and squeezing it into painful submission. It had felt the way he thought death might.

No Allomancer could be that powerful.

Zane respects her, Straff thought. *And everyone says she killed the Lord Ruler. That little thing. It couldn't be.*

It seemed impossible. And apparently, that was just the way she wanted it to seem.

Everything had been going so well. The information provided by Zane's kandra spy had been accurate: Elend *did* try to make an alliance. The frightening thing about it was that Straff might have gone along with it, assuming Elend to be of no consequence, if the spy hadn't sent warning.

Even so, Elend had bested him. Straff had even been *prepared* for their feint of weakness, and he had still fallen.

She's so powerful. . . .

A figure in black stepped out of the mists and walked up to Straff. "You look like you've seen a ghost, Father," Zane said with a smile. "Your own, perhaps?"

"Was there anyone else out there, Zane?" Straff asked, too shaken for repartee at the moment. "Another couple of Mistborn, perhaps, helping her?"

Zane shook his head. "No. She really is that strong." He turned to walk back out into the mists.

"Zane!" Straff snapped, making the man pause. "We're going to change plans. I want you to kill her."

Zane turned. "But—"

"She's too dangerous. Plus, we now have the information we wanted to get from her. They don't have the atium."

"You believe them?" Zane asked.

Straff paused. After how thoroughly he'd been manipulated this evening, he wasn't going to trust anything he thought he'd learned. "No," he decided. "But we'll find it another way. I want that girl *dead*, Zane."

"Are we attacking the city for real, then?"

Straff almost gave the order right then, commanding his armies to prepare for a morning assault. The preliminary attack had gone well, showing that the defenses were hardly impressive. Straff could take that wall, then use it against Cett.

However, Elend's final words before departing this evening made him stop. *Send your armies against my city, Father,* the boy had said, *and die. You've felt her power—you know what she can do. You can try and hide, you can even conquer my city.*

But she will find you. And she will kill you.

Your only option is to wait. I'll contact you when my armies are prepared to attack Cett. We'll strike together, as I said earlier.

Straff couldn't depend on that. The boy had changed—had become strong, somehow. If Straff and Elend attacked together, Straff had no illusions as to how quickly he'd be betrayed. But Straff couldn't attack Luthadel while that girl was alive. Not knowing her strength, having felt her touch on his emotions.

"No," he finally said to Zane's question. "We won't attack. Not until you kill her."

"That might be harder than you make it sound, Father," Zane said. "I'll need some help."

"What kind of help?"

"A strike team. Allomancers that can't be traced."

Zane was speaking of a particular group. Most Allomancers were easy to identify because of their noble lineages. Straff, however, had access to some special resources. There was a reason that he had so many mistresses—dozens and dozens of them. Some thought it was just because he was lustful.

That wasn't it at all. More mistresses meant more children. And more children, born from a high noble line like his, meant more Allomancers. He'd only spawned one Mistborn, but there were many Mistings.

"It will be done," Straff said.

"They might not survive the encounter, Father," Zane warned, still standing in the mists.

That awful sensation returned. The sense of nothingness, the horrible knowledge that someone else had complete and total control over his emotions. Nobody should have that much power over him. Especially not Elend.

He should be dead. He came right to me. And I let him go.

"Get rid of her," Straff said. "Do anything you need to, Zane. Anything."

Zane nodded, then walked away with a self-satisfied stroll.

Straff returned to his tent and sent for Hoselle again. She looked enough like Elend's girl. It would do him good to remind himself that most of the time, he really was in control.

Elend sat back in the carriage, a little stunned. *I'm still alive!* he thought with growing excitement. *I did it! I convinced Straff to leave the city alone.*

For a time, at least. Luthadel's safety depended on Straff remaining frightened of Vin. But . . . well, any victory was an enormous one for Elend. He hadn't failed his people. He was their king, and his plan—crazy though it might have seemed—had worked. The small crown on his head suddenly didn't seem as heavy as it had before.

Vin sat across from him. She didn't look nearly as pleased as she could have.

"We did it, Vin!" Elend said. "It wasn't what we planned, but it worked. Straff won't dare attack the city now."

She nodded quietly.

Elend frowned. "Um, it's because of you that the city

will be safe. You know that, right? If you hadn't been there . . . well, of course, if it hadn't been for you, the entire Final Empire would still be enslaved."

"Because I killed the Lord Ruler," she said quietly.

Elend nodded.

"But it was *Kelsier's* plan—the crew's skills, the people's strength of will—that freed the empire. I just held the knife."

"You make it sound like a trivial thing, Vin," he said. "It's not! You're a fantastic Allomancer. Ham says he can't beat you even in an *unfair* fight anymore, and you've kept the palace free of assassins. There's nobody like you in all of the Final Empire!"

Strangely, his words made her huddle into the corner just a little farther. She turned, watching out the window, eyes staring into the mists. "Thank you," she said softly.

Elend wrinkled his brow. *Every time I begin to think I've figured out what's going on in her head . . .* He moved over, putting an arm around her. "Vin, what's wrong?"

She was silent, then finally shook her head, forcing a smile. "It's nothing, Elend. You're right to be excited. You were brilliant in there—I doubt even Kelsier could have manipulated Straff so neatly."

Elend smiled, and pulled her close, impatient as the carriage rolled up to the dark city. The doors of Tin Gate opened hesitantly, and Elend saw a group of men standing just inside of the courtyard. Ham held aloft a lantern in the mists.

Elend didn't wait for the carriage to stop on its own. He opened the door and hopped down as it was rolling to a halt. His friends began to smile eagerly. The gates thumped closed.

"It worked?" Ham asked hesitantly as Elend approached. "You did it?"

"Kind of," Elend said with a smile, clasping hands with Ham, Breeze, Dockson, and finally Spook. Even the kandra, OreSeur, was there. He padded over to the carriage, waiting for Vin. "The initial feint didn't go so well—my father didn't bite on an alliance. But then I told him I'd kill him!"

"Wait. How was that a good idea?" Ham asked.

"We overlooked one of our greatest resources, my friends," Elend said as Vin climbed down from the carriage. Elend turned, waving his hand toward her. "We have a weapon like nothing they can match! Straff expected me to come begging, and he was ready to control that situation. However, when I mentioned what would happen to him and his army if Vin's anger was roused . . ."

"My dear man," Breeze said. "You went into the camp of the strongest king in the Final Empire, and you *threatened* him?"

"Yes I did!"

"Brilliant!"

"I know!" Elend said. "I told my Father that he *was* going to let me leave his camp and that he *was* going to leave Luthadel alone, otherwise I'd have Vin kill him and every general in his army." He put his arm around Vin. She smiled at the group, but he could tell that something was still troubling her.

She doesn't think I did a good job, Elend realized. *She saw a better way to manipulate Straff, but she doesn't want to spoil my enthusiasm.*

"Well, guess we won't need a new king," Spook said with a smile. "I was kind of looking forward to taking the job. . . ."

Elend laughed. "I don't intend to vacate the position for quite some time yet. We'll let the people know that Straff has been cowed, if temporarily. That should boost morale a bit. Then, we deal with the Assembly. Hopefully, they'll pass a resolution to wait for me to meet with Cett like I just did with Straff."

"Shall we have a celebration back at the palace?" Breeze asked. "As fond as I am of the mists, I doubt the courtyard is an appropriate place to be discussing these issues."

Elend patted him on the back and nodded. Ham and Dockson joined him and Vin, while the others took the carriage they'd come in. Elend glanced oddly at Dockson as he climbed into the carriage. Ordinarily, the man would have chosen the other vehicle—the one Elend wasn't in.

"Honestly, Elend," Ham said as he settled into his seat.

"I'm impressed. I half thought we were going to have to raid that camp to get you back."

Elend smiled, eyeing Dockson, who sat down as the carriage began moving. He pulled open his satchel and took out a sealed envelope. He looked up and met Elend's eyes. "This came from the Assembly members for you a short time ago, Your Majesty."

Elend paused. Then he took it and broke the seal. "What is it?"

"I'm not sure," Dockson said. "But . . . I've already started hearing rumors."

Vin leaned in, reading over Elend's arm as he scanned the sheet inside. *Your Majesty,* it read.

This note is to inform you that by majority vote, the Assembly has decided to invoke the charter's no-confidence clause. We appreciate your efforts on behalf of the city, but the current situation calls for a different kind of leadership than Your Majesty can provide. We take this step with no hostility, but only resignation. We see no other alternative, and must act for the good of Luthadel.

We regret to have to inform you of this by letter.

It was signed by all twenty-three members of the Assembly.

Elend lowered the paper, shocked.

"What?" Ham asked.

"I've just been deposed," Elend said quietly.

THE END OF PART TWO

PART THREE

KING

He left ruin in his wake, but it was forgotten. He created kingdoms, and then destroyed them as he made the world anew.

28

"LET ME SEE IF I understand this correctly," Tindwyl said, calm and polite, yet somehow still stern and disapproving. "There is a clause in the kingdom's legal code that lets the Assembly overthrow their king?"

Elend wilted slightly. "Yes."

"And you wrote the law yourself?" Tindwyl demanded.

"Most of it," Elend admitted.

"You wrote into your own law a way that you could be deposed?" Tindwyl repeated. Their group—expanded from those who had met in the carriages to include Clubs, Tindwyl, and Captain Demoux—sat in Elend's study. The group's size was such that they'd run out of chairs, and Vin sat quietly at the side, on a stack of Elend's books, having quickly changed to trousers and shirt. Tindwyl and Elend were standing, but the rest were seated—Breeze prim, Ham relaxed, and Spook trying to balance his chair as he leaned back on two legs.

"I put in that clause intentionally," Elend said. He stood at the front of the room, leaning with one arm against the glass of his massive stained-glass window, looking up at its dark shards. "This land wilted beneath the hand of an oppressive ruler for a thousand years. During that time, philosophers and thinkers dreamed of a government where a bad ruler could be ousted without bloodshed. I took this throne through an unpredictable and unique series of events, and I didn't think it right to unilaterally impose my will—or the will of my descendants—upon the people. I wanted to start a government whose monarchs would be responsible to their subjects."

Sometimes, he talks like those books he reads, Vin thought. *Not like a normal man at all . . . but like words on a page.*

Zane's words came back to her, seeming to whisper in her mind. *You aren't like him.* She pushed the thought out.

"With respect, Your Majesty," Tindwyl said, "this has to be one of the most foolish things I've ever seen a leader do."

"It was for the good of the kingdom," Elend said.

"It was sheer idiocy," Tindwyl snapped. "A king doesn't subject himself to the whims of another ruling body. He is valuable to his people because he is an absolute authority!"

Vin had rarely seen Elend so sorrowful, and she cringed a bit at the sadness in his eyes. However, a different piece of her was rebelliously happy. He wasn't king anymore. Now maybe people wouldn't work so hard to kill him. Maybe he could just be Elend again, and they could leave. Go somewhere. A place where things weren't so complicated.

"Regardless," Dockson said to the quiet room, "something must be done. Discussing the prudence of decisions already past has little current relevance."

"Agreed," Ham said. "So, the Assembly tried to kick you out. What are we going to do about it?"

"We obviously can't let them have their way," Breeze said. "Why, the people overthrew a government just last year! This is a bad habit to be getting into, I should think."

"We need to prepare a response, Your Majesty," Dockson said. "Something decrying this deceitful maneuver, performed while you were negotiating for the very safety of the city. Now that I look back, it's obvious that they arranged this meeting so that you *couldn't* be present and defend yourself."

Elend nodded, still staring up at the dark glass. "There's probably no need to call me Your Majesty anymore, Dox."

"Nonsense," Tindwyl said, arms folded as she stood beside a bookcase. "You are still king."

"I've lost the mandate of the people," Elend said.

"Yes," Clubs said, "but you've still got the mandate of my armies. That makes you king no matter what the Assembly says."

"Exactly," Tindwyl said. "Foolish laws aside, you're still in a position of power. We need to tighten martial law, restrict movement within the city. Seize control of key points, and sequester the members of the Assembly so that your enemies can't raise a resistance against you."

"I'll have my men on the streets before light," Clubs said.

"No," Elend said quietly.

There was a pause.

"Your Majesty?" Dockson asked. "It really is the best move. We can't let this faction against you gain momentum."

"It's not a faction, Dox," Elend said. "It's the elected representatives of the Assembly."

"An Assembly you formed, my dear man," Breeze said. "They have power because *you* gave it to them."

"The law gives them their power, Breeze," Elend said. "And we are all subject to it."

"Nonsense," Tindwyl said. "As king, you are the law. Once we secure the city, you can call in the Assembly and explain to its members that you need their support. Those who disagree can be held until the crisis is over."

"No," Elend said, a little more firm. "We will do none of that."

"That's it, then?" Ham asked. "You're giving up?"

"I'm not giving up, Ham," Elend said, finally turning to regard the group. "But I'm not going to use the city's armies to pressure the Assembly."

"You'll lose your throne," Breeze said.

"See reason, Elend," Ham said with a nod.

"I will *not* be an exception to my own laws!" Elend said.

"Don't be a fool," Tindwyl said. "You should—"

"Tindwyl," Elend said, "respond to my ideas as you wish, but do not call me a fool again. I will not be belittled because I express my opinion!"

Tindwyl paused, mouth partially open. Then she pressed her lips together and took her seat. Vin felt a quiet surge of satisfaction. *You trained him, Tindwyl,* she thought with a smile. *Can you really complain if he stands up to you?*

Elend walked forward, placing his hands on the table as he regarded the group. "Yes, we will respond. Dox, you write a letter informing the Assembly of our disappointment and feelings of betrayal—inform them of our success with Straff, and lay on the guilt as thickly as possible.

"The rest of us will begin planning. We'll get the throne back. As has been stated, I know the law. I wrote it. There are ways to deal with this. Those ways do *not,* however, include sending our armies to secure the city. I will not be like the tyrants who would take Luthadel from us! I will not force the people to do my will, even if I know it is best for them."

"Your Majesty," Tindwyl said carefully, "there is nothing immoral about securing your power during a time of chaos. People react irrationally during such times. That is one of the reasons why they need strong leadership. They need you."

"Only if they want me, Tindwyl," Elend said.

"Forgive me, Your Majesty," Tindwyl said, "but that statement seems somewhat naive to me."

Elend smiled. "Perhaps it is. You can change my clothing and my bearing, but you can't change the soul of who I am. I'll do what I think is right—and that includes letting the Assembly depose me, if that is their choice."

Tindwyl frowned. "And if you can't get your throne back through lawful means?"

"Then I accept that fact," Elend said. "And do my best to help the kingdom anyway."

So much for running away, Vin thought. However, she couldn't help smiling. Part of what she loved about Elend was his sincerity. His simple love for the people of Luthadel—his determination to do what was right for them—was what separated him from Kelsier. Even in martyrdom, Kelsier had displayed a hint of arrogance. He'd made certain that he would be remembered like few men who had ever lived.

But Elend—to him, ruling the Central Dominance wasn't about fame or glory. For the first time, completely and honestly, she decided something. Elend was a far better king than Kelsier would ever have been.

"I'm . . . not certain what I think of this experience, Mistress," a voice whispered beside her. Vin paused, looking down as she realized that she had begun idly scratching OreSeur's ears.

She pulled her hand back with a start. "Sorry," she said.

OreSeur shrugged, resting his head back on his paws.

"So, you said there's a legal way to get the throne back," Ham said. "How do we go about it?"

"The Assembly has one month to choose a new king," Elend said. "Nothing in the law says that the new king can't be the same as the old one. And, if they can't come up with a majority decision by that deadline, the throne reverts to me for a minimum of one year."

"Complicated," Ham said, rubbing his chin.

"What did you expect?" Breeze said. "It's the law."

"I didn't mean the law itself," Ham said. "I meant getting the Assembly to either choose Elend or not choose anyone. They wouldn't have deposed him in the first place unless they had another person in mind for the throne."

"Not necessarily," Dockson said. "Perhaps they simply meant this as a warning."

"Perhaps," Elend said. "Gentlemen, I think this is a sign. I've been ignoring the Assembly—we thought that they were taken care of, since I got them to sign that proposal giving me right of parlay. However, we never realized that an easy way for them to get around that proposal was to choose a new king, then have *him* do as they wished."

He sighed, shaking his head. "I have to admit, I've never been very good at handling the Assembly. They don't see me as a king, but as a colleague—and because of that, they can easily see themselves taking my place. I'll bet one of the Assemblymen has convinced the others to put him on the throne instead."

"So, we just make him disappear," Ham said. "I'm sure Vin could . . ."

Elend frowned.

"I'm joking, El," Ham said.

"You know, Ham," Breeze noted. "The only funny thing about your jokes is how often they lack any humor whatsoever."

"You're only saying that because they usually involve you in the punch line."

Breeze rolled his eyes.

"You know," OreSeur muttered quietly, obviously counting on her tin to let Vin hear him, "it seems that these meetings would be more productive if someone forgot to invite those two."

Vin smiled. "They're not *that* bad," she whispered.

OreSeur raised an eyebrow.

"Okay," Vin said. "They do distract us a little bit."

"I could always eat one of them, if you wish," OreSeur said. "That might speed things up."

Vin paused.

OreSeur, however, had a strange little smile on his lips. "Kandra humor, Mistress. I apologize. We can be a bit grim."

Vin smiled. "They probably wouldn't taste very good anyway. Ham's far too stringy, and you don't want to know the kinds of things that Breeze spends his time eating. . . ."

"I'm not sure," OreSeur said. "One is, after all, named 'Ham.' As for the other . . ." He nodded to the cup of wine in Breeze's hand. "He does seem quite fond of marinating himself."

Elend was picking through his stacks of books, pulling out several relevant volumes on law—including the book of Luthadel law that he himself had written.

"Your Majesty," Tindwyl said, emphasizing the term. "You have two armies on your doorstep, and a group of koloss making their way into the Central Dominance. Do you honestly think that you have time for a protracted legal battle now?"

Elend set down the books and pulled his chair to the table. "Tindwyl," he said. "I have two armies on my doorstep, koloss coming to pressure them, and I myself am the main obstacle keeping the leaders of this city from handing the kingdom over to one of the invaders. Do you honestly think that it's a coincidence that I get deposed *now*?"

Several members of the crew perked up at this, and Vin cocked her head.

"You think one of the invaders might be behind this?" Ham asked, rubbing his chin.

"What would you do, if you were them?" Elend said, opening a book. "You can't attack the city, because it will cost you too many troops. The siege has already lasted weeks, your troops are getting cold, and the men Dockson hired have been attacking your canal supply barges, threatening your food supply. Add on top of that, you know that a large force of koloss are marching this way . . . and, well, it makes sense. If Straff and Cett's spies are any good, they'll know that the Assembly just about capitulated and gave the city away when that army first arrived. Assassins have failed to kill me, but if there were another way to remove me . . ."

"Yes," Breeze said. "This does sound like something Cett would do. Turn the Assembly against you, put a sympathizer on the throne, then get him to open the gates."

Elend nodded. "And my father seemed hesitant to side with me this evening, as if he felt he had some other way to get the city. I can't be certain if either monarch is behind this move, Tindwyl, but we certainly can't ignore the possibility. This isn't a distraction—this is very much part of the same siege tactics we've been fighting since those armies arrived. If I can put myself back on the throne, then Straff and Cett will know that I'm the only one they can work with—and that will, hopefully, make them more likely to side with me in desperation, particularly as those koloss draw near."

With that, Elend began riffling through a stack of books. His depression seemed to be abating in face of this new academic problem. "There might be a few other clauses of relevance in the law," he half mumbled. "I need to do some studying. Spook, did you invite Sazed to this meeting?"

Spook shrugged. "I couldn't get him to wake up."

"He's recovering from his trip here," Tindwyl said, turning away from her study of Elend and his books. "It's an issue of the Keepers."

"Needs to refill one of his metalminds?" Ham asked.

Tindwyl paused, her expression darkening. "He explained that to you, then?"

Ham and Breeze nodded.

"I see," Tindwyl said. "Regardless, he could not help with this problem, Your Majesty. I give you some small aid in the area of government because it is my duty to train leaders in knowledge of the past. However, traveling Keepers such as Sazed do not take sides in political matters."

"Political matters?" Breeze asked lightly. "You mean, perhaps, like overthrowing the Final Empire?"

Tindwyl closed her mouth, lips growing thin. "You should not encourage him to break his vows," she finally said. "If you were his friends, you would see that to be true, I think."

"Oh?" Breeze asked, pointing at her with his cup of wine. "Personally, I think you're just embarrassed that he disobeyed you all, but then actually ended up freeing your people."

Tindwyl gave Breeze a flat stare, her eyes narrow, her posture stiff. They sat that way for a long moment. "Push on my emotions all you wish, Soother," Tindwyl said. "My feelings are my own. You will have no success here."

Breeze finally turned back to his drink, muttering something about "damn Terrismen."

Elend, however, wasn't paying attention to the argument. He already had four books open on the table before him, and was flipping through a fifth. Vin smiled, remembering the days—not so long ago—when his courtship of her had often involved him plopping himself down in a nearby chair and opening a book.

He is the same man, she thought. *And that soul, that man, is the one who loved me before he knew I was Mistborn. He loved me even after he discovered I was a thief, and thought I was trying to rob him. I need to remember that.*

"Come on," she whispered to OreSeur, standing as Breeze

and Ham got into another argument. She needed time to think, and the mists were still fresh.

This would be a lot easier if I weren't so skilled, Elend thought with amusement, poking through his books. *I set up the law too well.*

He followed a particular passage with his finger, rereading it as the crew slowly trailed away. He couldn't remember if he'd dismissed them or not. Tindwyl would probably chastise him for that.

Here, he thought, tapping the page. *I might have grounds to argue for a revote if any of the members of the Assembly arrived late to the meeting, or made their votes in absentia.* The vote to depose had to be unanimous—save, of course, for the king being deposed.

He paused, noticing movement. Tindwyl was the only one still in the room with him. He looked up from his books with resignation. *I probably have this coming. . . .*

"I apologize for treating you with disrespect, Your Majesty," she said.

Elend frowned. *Wasn't expecting that.*

"I have a habit of treating people like children," Tindwyl said. "It is not something that I should be proud of, I think."

"It's—" Elend paused. Tindwyl had taught him never to excuse people's failings. He could accept people with failings—even forgive them—but if he glossed over the problems, then they would never change. "I accept your apology," he said.

"You've learned quickly, Your Majesty."

"I haven't had much choice," Elend said with a smile. "Of course, I didn't change fast enough for the Assembly."

"How did you let this happen?" she asked quietly. "Even considering our disagreement over how a government should be run, I should think that these Assemblymen would be supporters of yours. You gave them their power."

"I ignored them, Tindwyl. Powerful men, friends or not, never like being ignored."

She nodded. "Though, perhaps we should pause to take

note of your successes, rather than simply focusing on your failings. Vin tells me that your meeting with your father went well."

Elend smiled. "We scared him into submission. It felt very good to do something like that to Straff. But, I think I might have offended Vin somehow."

Tindwyl raised an eyebrow.

Elend set down his book, leaning forward with his arms on the desk. "She was in an odd mood on the way back. I could barely get her to talk to me. I'm not sure what it was."

"Perhaps she was just tired."

"I'm not convinced that Vin *gets* tired," Elend said. "She's always moving, always doing something. Sometimes, I worry that she thinks I'm lazy. Maybe that's why . . ." He trailed off, then shook his head.

"She doesn't think that you are lazy, Your Majesty," Tindwyl said. "She refused to marry you because she doesn't think that she is worthy of you."

"Nonsense," Elend said. "Vin's Mistborn, Tindwyl. She knows she's worth ten men like me."

Tindwyl raised an eyebrow. "You understand very little about women, Elend Venture—especially young women. To them, their competence has a surprisingly small amount to do with how they feel about themselves. Vin is insecure. She doesn't believe that she deserves to be with you—it is less that she doesn't think she deserves you personally, and more that she isn't convinced that she deserves to be happy at all. She has led a very confusing, difficult life."

"How sure are you about this?"

"I've raised a number of daughters, Your Majesty," Tindwyl said. "I understand the things of which I speak."

"Daughters?" Elend asked. "You have children?"

"Of course."

"I just . . ." The Terrismen he'd known were eunuchs, like Sazed. The same couldn't be true for a woman like Tindwyl, of course, but he'd assumed that the Lord Ruler's breeding programs would have affected her somehow.

"Regardless," Tindwyl said curtly, "you must make some decisions, Your Majesty. Your relationship with Vin is going to be difficult. She has certain issues that will provide more problems than you would find in a more conventional woman."

"We've already discussed this," Elend said. "I'm not looking for a more 'conventional' woman. I love Vin."

"I'm not implying that you shouldn't," Tindwyl said calmly. "I am simply giving you instruction, as I have been asked to do. You need to decide how much you're going to let the girl, and your relationship with her, distract you."

"What makes you think I'm distracted?"

Tindwyl raised an eyebrow. "I asked you about your success with Lord Venture this evening, and all you wanted to talk about was how Vin felt during the ride home."

Elend hesitated.

"Which is more important to you, Your Majesty?" Tindwyl asked. "This girl's love, or the good of your people?"

"I'm not going to answer a question like that," Elend said.

"Eventually, you may not have a choice," Tindwyl said. "It is a question most kings face eventually, I fear."

"No," Elend said. "There's no reason that I can't both love Vin and protect my people. I've studied too many hypothetical dilemmas to be caught in a trap like that."

Tindwyl shrugged, standing. "Believe as you wish, Your Majesty. However, I already see a dilemma, and I find it not at all hypothetical." She bowed her head slightly in deference, then withdrew from the room, leaving him with his books.

There were other proofs to connect Alendi to the Hero of Ages. Smaller things, things that only one trained in the lore of the Anticipation would have noticed. The birthmark on his arm. The way his hair turned gray when he was barely twenty and five years of age. The way he spoke, the way he treated people, the way he ruled.

He simply seemed to fit.

29

"TELL ME, MISTRESS," ORESEUR SAID, lying lazily, head on paws. "I have been around humans for a goodly number of years. I was under the impression that they needed regular sleep. I guess I was mistaken."

Vin sat on a wall-top stone ledge, one leg up against her chest, the other dangling over the side of the wall. Keep Hasting's towers were dark shadows in the mists to her right and to her left. "I sleep," she said.

"Occasionally." OreSeur yawned a deep, tongue-stretching yawn. Was he adopting more canine mannerisms?

Vin turned away from the kandra, looking east, over the slumbering city of Luthadel. There was a fire in the distance, a growing light that was too large to be of man's touch. Dawn had arrived. Another night had passed, making it nearly a week since she and Elend had visited Straff's army. Zane had yet to appear.

"You're burning pewter, aren't you?" OreSeur asked. "To stay awake?"

Vin nodded. Beneath a light burn of pewter, her fatigue was only a mild annoyance. She could feel it deep within her, if she looked hard, but it had no power over her. Her senses were keen, her body strong. Even the night's cold wasn't as bothersome. The moment she extinguished her pewter, however, she'd feel the exhaustion in force.

"That cannot be healthy, Mistress," OreSeur said. "You sleep barely three or four hours a day. Nobody—Mistborn, man, or kandra—can survive on a schedule like that for long."

Vin looked down. How could she explain her strange insomnia? She should be over that; she no longer had to be frightened of the other crewmembers around her. And yet, no matter how exhausted she grew, she was finding sleep more and more difficult to claim. How could she sleep, with that quiet thumping in the distance?

It seemed to be getting closer, for some reason. Or simply stronger? *I hear the thumping sounds from above, the pulsings from the mountains. . . .* Words from the logbook.

How could she sleep, knowing that the spirit watched her from the mist, ominous and hateful? How could she sleep when armies threatened to slaughter her friends, when Elend's kingdom had been taken from him, when everything she thought she'd known and loved was getting muddled and obscure?

. . . when I finally lie down, I find sleep elusive. The same thoughts that trouble me during the day are only compounded by the stillness of night. . . .

OreSeur yawned again. "He's not coming, Mistress."

Vin turned, frowning. "What do you mean?"

"This is the last place you sparred with Zane," OreSeur said. "You're waiting for him to come."

Vin paused. "I could use a spar," she finally said.

Light continued to grow in the east, slowly brightening the mists. The mists persisted, however, reticent to give way before the sun.

"You shouldn't let that man influence you so, Mistress," OreSeur said. "I do not think he is the person you believe him to be."

Vin frowned. "He's my enemy. What else would I believe?"

"You do not treat him like an enemy, Mistress."

"Well, he hasn't attacked Elend," Vin said. "Maybe Zane isn't fully under Straff's control."

OreSeur sat quietly, head on paws. Then he turned away.

"What?" Vin asked.

"Nothing, Mistress. I will believe as I'm told."

"Oh, no," Vin said, turning on the ledge to look at him. "You're not going back to that excuse. What were you thinking?"

OreSeur sighed. "I was thinking, Mistress, that your fixation with Zane is disconcerting."

"Fixation?" Vin said. "I'm just keeping an eye on him. I don't like having another Mistborn—enemy or not—running around in my city. Who knows what he could be up to?"

OreSeur frowned, but said nothing.

"OreSeur," Vin said, "if you have things to say, speak!"

"I apologize, Mistress," OreSeur said. "I'm not accustomed to chatting with my masters—especially not candidly."

"It's all right. Just speak your mind."

"Well, Mistress," OreSeur said, raising his head off his paws, "I do not like this Zane."

"What do you know of him?"

"Nothing more than you," OreSeur admitted. "However, most kandra are very good judges of character. When you practice imitation for as long as I have, you learn to see to the hearts of men. I do not like what I have seen of Zane. He seems too pleased with himself. He seems too deliberate in the way he has befriended you. He makes me uncomfortable."

Vin sat on the ledge, legs parted, hands before her with palms down, resting on the cool stone. *He might be right.*

But, OreSeur hadn't flown with Zane, hadn't sparred in the mists. Through no fault of his own, OreSeur was like Elend. Not an Allomancer. Neither of them could understand what it was to soar on a Push of steel, to flare tin and experience the sudden shock of five heightened senses. They couldn't know. They couldn't understand.

Vin leaned back. Then, she regarded the wolfhound in the growing light. There was something she'd been meaning to mention, and now seemed as good a time as any. "OreSeur, you can switch bodies, if you want."

The wolfhound raised an eyebrow.

"We have those bones that we found in the palace," Vin said. "You can use those, if you're tired of being a dog."

"I couldn't use them," OreSeur said. "I haven't digested their body—I wouldn't know the proper arrangement of muscles and organs to make the person look correct."

"Well, then," Vin said. "We could get you a criminal."

"I thought you liked these bones on me," OreSeur said.

"I do," Vin said. "But, I don't want you to stay in a body that makes you unhappy."

OreSeur snorted. "My happiness is not an issue."

"It is to me," Vin said. "We could—"

"Mistress," OreSeur interrupted.

"Yes?"

"I shall keep these bones. I've grown accustomed to them. It is very frustrating to change forms often."

Vin hesitated. "All right," she finally said.

OreSeur nodded. "Though," he continued, "speaking of bodies, Mistress, are we ever planning to return to the palace? Not all of us have the constitution of a Mistborn—some people need sleep and food on occasion."

He certainly complains a lot more now, Vin thought. However, she found the attitude to be a good sign; it meant OreSeur was growing more comfortable with her. Comfortable enough to tell her when he thought she was being stupid.

Why do I even bother with Zane? she thought, rising and turning eyes northward. The mist was still moderately strong, and she could barely make out Straff's army, still holding the northern canal, maintaining the siege. It sat like a spider, waiting for the right time to spring.

Elend, she thought. *I should be more focused on Elend.* His motions to dismiss the Assembly's decision, or to force a revote, had all failed. And, stubbornly lawful as always, Elend continued to accept his failures. He still thought he had a chance to persuade the Assembly to choose him as king—or at least not vote anybody else to the position.

So he worked on speeches and planned with Breeze and Dockson. This left him little time for Vin, and rightly so. The last thing he needed was her distracting him. This was something she couldn't help him with—something she couldn't fight or scare away.

His world is of papers, books, laws, and philosophies, she thought. *He rides the words of his theories like I ride the mists. I always worry that he can't understand me . . . but can I really even understand him?*

OreSeur stood, stretched, and placed his forepaws on the wall's railing to raise himself and look north, like Vin.

Vin shook her head. "Sometimes, I wish Elend weren't so . . . well, noble. The city doesn't need this confusion right now."

"He did the right thing, Mistress."

"You think so?"

"Of course," OreSeur said. "He made a contract. It is his duty to keep that contract, no matter what. He must serve his master—in his case, that would be the city—even if that master makes him do something very distasteful."

"That's a very kandralike way of seeing things," Vin said.

OreSeur looked up at her, raising a canine eyebrow, as if to ask *Well, what did you expect?* She smiled; she had to suppress a chuckle every time she saw that expression on his dog face.

"Come on," Vin said. "Let's get back to the palace."

"Excellent," OreSeur said, dropping down to all fours. "That meat I set out should be perfect by now."

"Unless the maids found it again," Vin said with a smile.

OreSeur's expression darkened. "I thought you were going to warn them."

"What would I say?" Vin asked with amusement. "Please don't throw away this rancid meat—my dog likes to eat it?"

"Why not?" OreSeur asked. "When I imitate a human, I almost never get to have a good meal, but dogs eat aged meat sometimes, don't they?"

"I honestly don't know," Vin said.

"Aged meat is delicious."

"You mean 'rotten' meat."

"Aged," OreSeur said insistently as she picked him up, preparing to carry him down from the wall. The top of Keep Hasting was a good hundred feet tall—far too high up for OreSeur to jump, and the only path down would be through the inside of the abandoned keep. Better to carry him.

"Aged meat is like aged wine or aged cheese," OreSeur continued. "It tastes better when it's a few weeks old."

I suppose that's one of the side effects of being related to scavengers, Vin thought. She hopped up on the lip of the wall, dropping a few coins. However, as she prepared to jump—OreSeur a large bulk in her arms—she hesitated. She turned one last time, looking out at Straff's army. It was fully visible now; the sun had risen completely above the horizon. Yet, a few insistent swirls of mist wavered in the air, as if trying to defy the sun, to continue to cloak the city, to stave off the light of day. . . .

Lord Ruler! Vin thought, struck by a sudden insight. She'd been working on this problem so long, it had begun to frustrate her. And now, when she'd been ignoring it, the answer had come to her. As if her subconscious had still been picking it apart.

"Mistress?" OreSeur asked. "Is everything all right?"

Vin opened her mouth slightly, cocking her head. "I think I just realized what the Deepness was."

But, I must continue with the sparsest of detail. Space is limited. The other Worldbringers must have thought themselves humble when they came to me, admitting that they had been wrong. Even then, I was beginning to doubt my original declaration.

But, I was prideful.

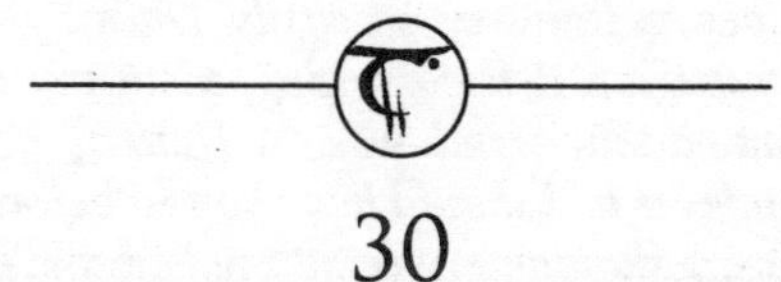

30

I write this record now, Sazed read, *pounding it into a metal slab, because I am afraid. Afraid for myself, yes—I admit to being human. If Alendi does return from the Well of Ascension, I am certain that my death will be one of his first objectives. He is not an evil man, but he is a ruthless one. That is, I think, a product of what he has been through.*

I am also afraid, however, that all I have known—that my story—will be forgotten. I am afraid for the world that is to come. Afraid that Alendi will fail. Afraid of a doom brought by the Deepness.

It all comes back to poor Alendi. I feel bad for him, and for all the things he has been forced to endure. For what he has been forced to become.

But, let me begin at the beginning. I met Alendi first in Khlennium; he was a young lad then, and had not yet been warped by a decade spent leading armies.

Alendi's height struck me the first time I saw him. Here was a man who was small of stature, but who seemed to tower over others, a man who demanded respect.

Oddly, it was Alendi's simple ingenuousness that first led me to befriend him. I employed him as an assistant during his first months in the grand city.

It wasn't until years later that I became convinced that Alendi was the Hero of Ages. Hero of Ages: the one called Rabzeen in Khlennium, the Anamnesor.

Savior.

When I finally had the realization—finally connected all of the signs of the Anticipation to him—I was so excited. Yet, when I announced my discovery to the other Worldbringers, I was met with scorn. Oh, how I wish that I had listened to them.

And yet, any who know me will realize that there was no chance I would give up so easily. Once I find something to investigate, I become dogged in my pursuit. I had determined that Alendi was the Hero of Ages, and I intended to prove it. I should have bowed before the will of the others; I shouldn't have insisted on traveling with Alendi to witness his journeys. It was inevitable that Alendi himself would find out what I believed him to be.

Yes, he was the one who fueled the rumors after that. I could never have done what he himself did, convincing and persuading the world that he was indeed the Hero. I don't know if he himself believed it, but he made others think that he must be the one.

If only the Terris religion, and belief in the Anticipation, hadn't spread beyond our people. If only the Deepness hadn't come, providing a threat that drove men to desperation both in action and belief. If only I had passed over Alendi when looking for an assistant, all those years ago.

Sazed sat back from his work of transcribing the rubbing. There was still a great deal to do—it was amazing how much writing this Kwaan had managed to cram onto the relatively small sheet of steel.

Sazed looked over his work. He'd spent his entire trip north anticipating the time when he could finally begin work on the rubbing. A part of him had been worried. Would the dead man's words seem as important sitting in a well-lit room as they had when in the dungeons of the Conventical of Seran?

He scanned to another part of the document, reading a few choice paragraphs. Ones of particular importance to him.

As the one who found Alendi, however, I became someone important. Foremost amongst the Worldbringers.

There was a place for me, in the lore of the Anticipation—I thought myself the Announcer, the prophet foretold to discover the Hero of Ages. Renouncing Alendi then would have been to renounce my new position, my acceptance, by the others.

And so I did not.

But I do so now. Let it be known that I, Kwaan, Worldbringer of Terris, am a fraud.

Sazed closed his eyes. *Worldbringer.* The term was known to him; the order of the Keepers had been founded upon memories and hopes from Terris legends. The Worldbringers had been teachers, Feruchemists who had traveled the lands bearing knowledge. They had been a prime inspiration for the secret order of Keepers.

And now he had a document made by a Worldbringer's own hand.

Tindwyl is going to be very annoyed with me, Sazed thought, opening his eyes. He'd read the entire rubbing, but he would need to spend time studying it. Memorizing it. Cross-referencing it with other documents. This one bit of writing—perhaps twenty pages total—could easily keep him busy for months, even years.

His window shutters rattled. Sazed looked up. He was in his quarters at the palace—a tasteful collection of well-decorated rooms that were far too lavish for one who had spent his life as a servant. He rose, walked over to the window, undid the latch, and pulled open the shutters. He smiled as he found Vin crouching on the ledge outside.

"Um . . . hi," Vin said. She wore her mistcloak over gray shirt and black trousers. Despite the onset of morning, she obviously hadn't yet gone to bed after her nightly prowling. "You should leave your window unlatched. I can't get in if it's locked. Elend got mad at me for breaking too many latches."

"I shall try to remember that, Lady Vin," Sazed said, and gesturing for her to enter.

Vin hopped spryly through the window, mistcloak rustling. "*Try* to remember?" she asked. "You never forget anything. Not even the things you don't have stuck in a metalmind."

She's grown so much more bold, he thought as she walked over to his writing desk, peering over his work. *Even in the months I've been away.*

"What's this?" Vin asked, still looking at the desk.

"I found it at the Conventical of Seran, Lady Vin," Sazed said, walking forward. It felt so good to be wearing clean robes again, to have a quiet and comfortable place in which to study. Was he a bad man for preferring this to travel?

One month, he thought. *I will give myself one month of study. Then I will turn the project over to someone else.*

"What is it?" Vin asked, holding up the rubbing.

"If you please, Lady Vin," Sazed said apprehensively. "That is quite fragile. The rubbing could be smudged. . . ."

Vin nodded, putting it down and scanning his transcription. There had been a time when she would have avoided anything that smelled of stuffy writing, but now she looked intrigued. "This mentions the Deepness!" she said with excitement.

"Among other things," Sazed said, joining her at the desk. He sat down, and Vin walked over to one of the room's low-backed, plush chairs. However, she didn't sit on it as an ordinary person would; instead, she hopped up and sat down on the top of the chair's back, her feet resting on the seat cushion.

"What?" she asked, apparently noticing Sazed's smile.

"Just amused at a proclivity of Mistborn, Lady Vin," he said. "Your kind has trouble simply sitting—it seems you always want to perch instead. That is what comes from having such an incredible sense of balance, I think."

Vin frowned, but passed over the comment. "Sazed," she said, "what was the Deepness?"

He laced his fingers before himself, regarding the young woman as he mused. "The Deepness, Lady Vin? That is a subject of much debate, I think. It was supposedly something great and powerful, though some scholars have dismissed the entire legend as a fabrication concocted by the Lord Ruler. There is some reason to believe this theory, I think, for the only real records of those times are the ones sanctioned by the Steel Ministry."

"But, the logbook mentions the Deepness," Vin said. "And so does that thing you're translating now."

"Indeed, Lady Vin," Sazed said. "But, even among those who assume the Deepness was real, there is a great deal of debate. Some hold to the Lord Ruler's official story, that the Deepness was a horrible, supernatural beast—a dark god, if you will. Others disagree with this extreme interpretation. They think the Deepness was more mundane—an army of some sort, perhaps invaders from another land. The Farmost Dominance, during pre-Ascension times, was apparently populated with several breeds of men who were quite primitive and warlike."

Vin was smiling. He looked at her questioningly, and

she just shrugged. "I asked Elend this same question," she explained, "and I got barely a sentence-long response."

"His Majesty has different areas of scholarship; pre-Ascension history may be too stuffy a topic even for him. Besides, anyone who asks a Keeper about the past should be prepared for an extended conversation, I think."

"I'm not complaining," Vin said. "Continue."

"There isn't much more to say—or, rather, there is a great deal more to say, but I doubt much of it has relevance. Was the Deepness an army? Was it, perhaps, the first attack from koloss, as some theorize? That would explain much—most stories agree that the Lord Ruler gained some power to defeat the Deepness at the Well of Ascension. Perhaps he gained the support of the koloss, and then used them as his armies."

"Sazed," Vin said. "I don't think the Deepness was the koloss."

"Oh?"

"I think it was the mist."

"That theory has been proposed," Sazed said with a nod.

"It has?" Vin asked, sounding a bit disappointed.

"Of course, Lady Vin. During the thousand-year reign of the Final Empire, there are few possibilities that *haven't* been discussed, I think. The mist theory has been advanced before, but there are several large problems with it."

"Such as?"

"Well," Sazed said, "for one thing, the Lord Ruler is said to have defeated the Deepness. However, the mist is obviously still here. Also, if the Deepness was simply mist, why call it by such an obscure name? Of course, others point out that much of what we know or have heard of the Deepness comes from oral lore, and something very common can take on mystical properties when transferred verbally through generations. The 'Deepness' therefore could mean not just the mist, but the event of its coming or alteration.

"The larger problem with the mist theory, however, is one of malignance. If we trust the accounts—and we have little else to go on—the Deepness was terrible and destructive. The mist seems to display none of this danger."

"But it kills people now."

Sazed paused. "Yes, Lady Vin. It apparently does."

"And what if it did so before, but the Lord Ruler stopped it somehow? You yourself said that you think we did something—something that changed the mist—when we killed the Lord Ruler."

Sazed nodded. "The problems I have been investigating are quite terrible, to be certain. However, I do not see that they could be a threat on the same level as the Deepness. Certain people have been killed by the mists, but many are elderly or otherwise lacking in constitution. It leaves many people alone."

He paused, tapping his thumbs together. "But, I would be remiss if I didn't admit some merit to the suggestion, Lady Vin. Perhaps even a few deaths would be enough to cause a panic. The danger could have been exaggerated by retelling—and, perhaps the killings were more widespread before. I haven't been able to collect enough information to be certain of anything yet."

Vin didn't respond. *Oh, dear,* Sazed thought, sighing to himself. *I've bored her. I really do need to be more careful, watching my vocabulary and my language. One would think that after all my travels among the skaa, I would have learned—*

"Sazed?" Vin said, sounding thoughtful. "What if we're looking at it wrong? What if these random deaths in the mists aren't the problem at all?"

"What do you mean, Lady Vin?"

She sat quietly for a moment, one foot tapping back idly against the chair's back cushion. She finally looked up, meeting his eyes. "What would happen if the mists came during the day permanently?"

Sazed mused on that for a moment.

"There would be no light," Vin continued. "Plants would die, people would starve. There would be death . . . chaos."

"I suppose," Sazed said. "Perhaps that theory has merit."

"It's not a theory," Vin said, hopping down from her chair. "It's what happened."

"You're so certain, already?" Sazed asked with amusement.

Vin nodded curtly, joining him at the desk. "I'm right," she said with her characteristic bluntness. "I know it." She pulled something out of a trouser pocket, then drew over a stool to sit beside him. She unfolded the wrinkled sheet and flattened it on the desk.

"These are quotes from the logbook," Vin said. She pointed at a paragraph. "Here the Lord Ruler talks about how armies were useless against the Deepness. At first, I thought this meant that the armies hadn't been able to defeat it—but look at the wording. He says 'The swords of my armies are useless.' What's more useless than trying to swing a sword at mist?"

She pointed at another paragraph. "It left destruction in its wake, right? Countless thousands died because of it. But, he never says that the Deepness actually attacked them. He says that they 'died because of it.' Maybe we've just been looking at this the wrong way all along. Those people weren't crushed or eaten. They starved to death because their land was slowly being swallowed by the mists."

Sazed studied her paper. She seemed so certain. Did she know nothing of proper research techniques? Of questioning, of studying, of postulating and devising answers?

Of course she doesn't, Sazed chastised himself. *She grew up on the streets—she doesn't use research techniques.*

She just uses instinct. And she's usually right.

He smoothed the paper again, reading its passages. "Lady Vin? Did you write this yourself?"

She flushed. "Why is everybody so surprised about that?"

"It just doesn't seem in your nature, Lady Vin."

"You people have corrupted me," she said. "Look, there isn't a single comment on this sheet that contradicts the idea that the Deepness was mist."

"Not contradicting a point and proving it are different things, Lady Vin."

She waved indifferently. "I'm right, Sazed. I *know* I am."

"What about this point, then?" Sazed asked, pointing to

a line. "The Hero implies that he can sense a sentience to the Deepness. The mist isn't alive."

"Well, it does swirl around someone using Allomancy."

"That isn't the same thing, I think," Sazed said. "He says that the Deepness was mad . . . destructively insane. Evil."

Vin paused. "There is something, Sazed," she admitted.

He frowned.

She pointed at another section of notes. "Do you recognize these paragraphs?" *It isn't a shadow,* the words read.

This dark thing that follows me, the thing that only I can see—it isn't really a shadow. It is blackish and translucent, but it doesn't have a shadowlike solid outline. It's insubstantial—wispy and formless. Like it's made out of a dark fog.

Or mist, perhaps.

"Yes, Lady Vin," Sazed said. "The Hero saw a creature following him. It attacked one of his companions, I think."

Vin looked in his eyes. "I've seen it, Sazed."

He felt a chill.

"It's out there," she said. "Every night, in the mists. Watching me. I can *feel* it, with Allomancy. And, if I get close enough, I can see it. As if formed from the mist itself. Insubstantial, yet somehow still there."

Sazed sat quietly for a moment, not certain what to think.

"You think me mad," Vin accused.

"No, Lady Vin," he said quietly. "I don't think any of us are in a position to call such things madness, not considering what is happening. Just . . . are you certain?"

She nodded firmly.

"But," Sazed said. "Even if this is true, it does not answer my question. The logbook author saw that same creature, and he didn't refer to it as the Deepness. It was not the Deepness, then. The Deepness was something else—something dangerous, something he could feel as evil."

"That's the secret, then," Vin said. "We have to figure out why he spoke of the mists that way. Then we'll know . . ."

"Know what, Lady Vin?" Sazed asked.

Vin paused, then looked away. She didn't answer, instead turning to a different topic. "Sazed, the Hero never did what he was supposed to. Rashek killed him. And, when Rashek took the power at the Well, he didn't give it up like he was supposed to—he kept it for himself."

"True," Sazed said.

Vin paused again. "And the mists have started killing people. They've started coming during the day. It's . . . like things are repeating again. So . . . maybe that means that the Hero of Ages will have to come again."

She glanced back at him, looking a bit . . . embarrassed? *Ah* . . . Sazed thought, sensing her implication. She saw things in the mists. The previous Hero had seen the same things. "I am not certain that is a valid statement, Lady Vin."

She snorted. "Why can't you just come out and say 'you're wrong,' like regular people?"

"I apologize, Lady Vin. I have had much training as a servant, and we are taught to be nonconfrontational. Nevertheless, I do not think that you are wrong. However, I also think that, perhaps, you haven't fully considered your position."

Vin shrugged.

"What makes you think that the Hero of Ages will return?"

"I don't know. Things that happen; things I feel. The mists are coming again, and someone needs to stop them."

Sazed ran his fingers across his translated section of the rubbing, looking over its words.

"You don't believe me," Vin said.

"It isn't that, Lady Vin," Sazed said. "It's just that I am not prone to rushing to decisions."

"But, you've thought about the Hero of Ages, haven't you?" Vin said. "He was part of your religion—the lost religion of Terris, the thing you Keepers were founded to try and discover."

"That is true," Sazed admitted. "However, we do not know much about the prophecies that our ancestors used to find their Hero. Besides, the reading I've been doing lately suggests that there was something wrong with their interpretations. If the greatest theologians of pre-Ascension Terris were unable to properly identify their Hero, how are we supposed to do so?"

Vin sat quietly. "I shouldn't have brought it up," she finally said.

"No, Lady Vin, please don't think that. I apologize—your theories have great merit. I simply have a scholar's mind, and must question and consider information when I am given it. I am far too fond of arguing, I think."

Vin looked up, smiling slightly. "Another reason you never made a good Terris steward?"

"Undoubtedly," he said with a sigh. "My attitude also tends to cause conflicts with the others of my order."

"Like Tindwyl?" Vin asked. "She didn't sound happy when she heard that you'd told us about Feruchemy."

Sazed nodded. "For a group dedicated to knowledge, the Keepers can be rather stingy with information about their powers. When the Lord Ruler still lived—when Keepers were hunted—the caution was warranted, I think. But, now that we are free from that, my brethren and sisters seem to have found the habit of secrecy a difficult one to break."

Vin nodded. "Tindwyl doesn't seem to like you very much. She says that she came because of your suggestion, but every time someone mentions you, she seems to get . . . cold."

Sazed sighed. Did Tindwyl dislike him? He thought, perhaps, that her inability to do so was a large part of the problem. "She is simply disappointed in me, Lady Vin. I'm not sure how much you know of my history, but I had been working against the Lord Ruler for some ten years before Kelsier recruited me. The other Keepers thought that I endangered my copperminds, and the very order itself. They believed that the Keepers should remain quiet—waiting for the day when the Lord Ruler fell, but not seeking to make it happen."

"Seems a bit cowardly to me," Vin said.

"Ah, but it was a very prudent course. You see, Lady Vin, had I been captured, there are many things I could have revealed. The names of other Keepers, the location of our safe houses, the means by which we managed to hide ourselves in Terris culture. My brethren worked for many decades to make the Lord Ruler think that Feruchemy had finally been exterminated. By revealing myself, I could have undone all of that."

"That would only have been bad had we failed," Vin said. "We didn't."

"We could have."

"We didn't."

Sazed paused, then smiled. Sometimes, in a world of debate, questions, and self-doubt, Vin's simple bluntness was refreshing. "Regardless," he continued, "Tindwyl is a member of the Synod—a group of Keeper elders who guide our sect. I have been in rebellion against the Synod a number of times during my past. And, by returning to Luthadel, I am defying them once again. She has good reason to be displeased with me."

"Well, *I* think you're doing the right thing," Vin said. "We need you."

"Thank you, Lady Vin."

"I don't think you have to listen to Tindwyl," she said. "She's the type who acts like she knows more than she does."

"She is very wise."

"She's hard on Elend."

"Then she probably does so because it is best for him," Sazed said. "Do not judge her too harshly, child. If she seems off-putting, it is only because she has lived a very hard life."

"Hard life?" Vin asked, tucking her notes back into her pocket.

"Yes, Lady Vin," Sazed said. "You see, Tindwyl spent most of her life as a Terris mother."

Vin hesitated, hand in pocket, looking surprised. "You mean . . . she was a Breeder?"

Sazed nodded. The Lord Ruler's breeding program included selecting a few, special individuals to use for birthing new children—with the goal being to breed Feruchemy out of the population.

"Tindwyl had, at last count, birthed over twenty children," he said. "Each with a different father. Tindwyl had her first child when she was fourteen, and spent her entire life being taken repeatedly by strange men until she became pregnant. And, because of the fertility drugs the Breeding masters forced upon her, she often bore twins or triplets."

"I . . . see," Vin said softly.

"You are not the only one who knew a terrible childhood, Lady Vin. Tindwyl is perhaps the strongest woman I know."

"How did she bear it?" Vin asked quietly. "I think . . . I think I would probably have just killed myself."

"She is a Keeper," Sazed said. "She suffered the indignity because she knew that she did a great service for her people. You see, Feruchemy is hereditary. Tindwyl's position as a mother ensured future generations of Feruchemists among our people. Ironically, she is exactly the sort of person that the Breeding masters were supposed to avoid letting reproduce."

"But, how did such a thing happen?"

"The breeders assumed they'd already cut Feruchemy out of the population," Sazed said. "They started looking to create other traits in the Terris—docility, temperance. They bred us like fine horses, and it was a great stroke when the Synod managed to get Tindwyl chosen for their program.

"Of course, Tindwyl has very little training in Feruchemy. She did, fortunately, receive some of the copperminds that we Keepers carry. So, during her many years locked away, she was able to study and read biographies. It was only during the last decade—her childbearing years through—that she was able to join and gain fellowship with the other Keepers."

Sazed paused, then shook his head. "By comparison, the rest of us have known a life of freedom, I think."

"Great," Vin mumbled, standing and yawning. "Another reason for you to feel guilty."

"You should sleep, Lady Vin," Sazed noted.

"For a few hours," Vin said, walking toward the door, leaving him alone again with his studies.

In the end, my pride may have doomed us all.

31

PHILEN FRANDEU WAS NOT SKAA. He had *never* been skaa. Skaa made things or grew things. Philen sold things. There was an enormous difference between the two.

Oh, some people had called him skaa. Even now, he could see that word in the eyes of some of the other Assemblymen. They regarded Philen and his fellow merchants with the same disdain that they gave the eight skaa workers on the Assembly. Couldn't they see that the two groups were completely different?

Philen shifted a bit on the bench. Shouldn't the Assembly hall at least have comfortable seating? They were waiting on just a few members; the tall clock in the corner said that fifteen minutes still remained until the meeting began. Oddly, one of those who had yet to arrive was Venture himself. King Elend was usually early.

Not king anymore, Philen thought with a smile. *Just plain old Elend Venture.* It was a poor name—not as good as Philen's own. Of course, he had been just "Lin" until a year and a half ago. Philen Frandeu was what he had dubbed himself after the Collapse. It delighted him to no end that the others had taken to calling him the name without pause. But, why shouldn't he have a grand name? A lord's name? Was Philen not as good as any of the "noblemen" sitting aloofly in their places?

Oh, he was just as good. Better, even. Yes, they had called him skaa—but during those years, they had come to him out of need, and so their arrogant sneers had lacked power. He'd seen their insecurity. They'd needed him. A man they called skaa. But he'd also been a merchant. A merchant who wasn't noble. Something that wasn't supposed to have existed in the Lord Ruler's perfect little empire.

But, noblemen merchants had to work with the obligators. And, where there had been obligators, nothing illegal could occur. Hence Philen. He'd been . . . an intermediary, of sorts. A man capable of arranging deals between interested parties who, for various reasons, wanted to avoid the watchful eyes of the Lord Ruler's obligators. Philen hadn't been part of a thieving crew—no, that was far too dangerous. And far too mundane.

He had been born with an eye for finances and trades. Give him two rocks, and he'd have a quarry by the end of the week. Give him a spoke, and he'd change it to a fine horse-drawn carriage. Two bits of corn, and he'd eventually have a massive shipment of grain sailing to the Farmost Dominance markets. Actual noblemen had done the trades, of course, but Philen had been behind it all. A vast empire of his own.

And still, they couldn't see. He wore a suit as fine as theirs; now that he could trade openly, he had become one of the wealthiest men in Luthadel. Yet, the noblemen ignored him, just because he lacked a valid pedigree.

Well, they would see. After today's meeting . . . yes, they would see. Philen looked out into the crowd, looking anxiously for the person he had hidden there. Reassured, he looked toward the noblemen of the Assembly, who sat chatting a short distance away. One of their last members—Lord Ferson Penrod—had just arrived. The older man walked up onto the Assembly's dais, passing by the members, greeting each in turn.

"Philen," Penrod said, noticing him. "A new suit, I see. The red vest suits you."

"Lord Penrod! Why, you're looking well. You got over the other night's ailment, then?"

"Yes, it passed quickly," the lord said, nodding a head topped with silver hair. "Just a touch of stomach ills."

Pity, Philen thought, smiling. "Well, we'd best be seated. I see that young Venture isn't here, though. . . ."

"Yes," Penrod said, frowning. He'd been most difficult to convince to vote against Venture; he had something of a fondness for the boy. He had come around in the end. They all had.

Penrod moved on, joining the other noblemen. The old fool probably thought he was going to end up as king. Well, Philen had other plans for that throne. It wasn't Philen's own posterior that would sit in it, of course; he had no interest in running a country. Seemed like a terrible way to make money. Selling things. That was a much better way. More stable, less likely to lose one his head.

Oh, but Philen had plans. He'd always had those. He had to keep himself from glancing at the audience again.

Philen turned, instead, to study the Assembly. They had all arrived except Venture. Seven noblemen, eight merchants, and eight skaa workers: twenty-four men, with Venture. The three-way division was supposed to give the commoners the most power, since they ostensibly outnumbered the noblemen. Even Venture hadn't understood that merchants weren't skaa.

Philen wrinkled his nose. Even though the skaa Assemblymen usually cleaned up before coming to the meetings, he could smell the stink of forges, mills, and shops on them. Men who made things. Philen would have to be certain they were put back in their place, once this was over. An Assembly was an interesting idea, but it should be filled only with those who deserved the station. Men like Philen.

Lord Philen, he thought. *Not long now.*

Hopefully, Elend would be late. Then, maybe they could avoid his speech. Philen could imagine how it would go anyway.

Um . . . now, see, this wasn't fair. I should be king. Here, let me read you a book about why. Now, um, can you all please give some more money to the skaa?

Philen smiled.

The man next to him, Getrue, nudged him. "You think he's going to show up?" he whispered.

"Probably not. He must know that we don't want him. We kicked him out, didn't we?"

Getrue shrugged. He'd gained weight since the Collapse—a lot of it. "I don't know, Lin. I mean . . . we didn't mean. He was just . . . the armies . . . We have to have a strong king, right? Someone who will keep the city from falling?"

"Of course," Philen said. "And my name isn't Lin."

Getrue flushed. "Sorry."

"We did the right thing," Philen continued. "Venture is a weak man. A fool."

"I wouldn't say that," Getrue said. "He has good ideas. . . ." Getrue glanced downward uncomfortably.

Philen snorted, glancing at the clock. It was time, though he couldn't hear the chimes over the crowd. The Assembly meetings had become busy since Venture's fall. Benches fanned out before the stage, benches crowded with people, mostly skaa. Philen wasn't sure why they were allowed to attend. They couldn't vote or anything.

More Venture foolishness, he thought, shaking his head. At the very back of the room—behind the crowd, opposite the stage—sat two large, broad doors letting in the red sunlight. Philen nodded toward some men, and they pushed the doors shut. The crowds hushed.

Philen stood to address the Assembly. "Well, since—"

The Assembly hall doors burst back open. A man in white stood with a small crowd of people, backlit by red sunlight. Elend Venture. Philen cocked his head, frowning.

The former king strode forward, white cape fluttering behind him. His Mistborn was at his side, as usual, but she was wearing a dress. From the few times Philen had spoken with her, he would have expected her to look awkward in a noblewoman's gown. And yet, she seemed to wear it well, walking gracefully. She actually looked rather fetching.

At least, until Philen met her eyes. She did not have a warm look for the Assembly members, and Philen glanced away. Venture had brought all of his Allomancers with him—the former thugs of the Survivor's crew. Elend apparently wanted to remind everyone who his friends were. Powerful men. Frightening men.

Men who killed gods.

And Elend had not one, but two Terrismen with him. One was only a woman—Philen had never seen a Terriswoman before—but still, it was impressive. Everyone had heard how the stewards had left their masters after the Collapse; they refused to work as servants anymore. Where had Venture found not one, but two of the colorful-robed stewards to serve him?

The crowd sat quietly, watching Venture. Some seemed uncomfortable. How were they to treat this man? Others seemed . . . awed? Was that right? Who would be awed by Elend Venture—even if the Elend Venture in question was clean-shaven, had styled hair, wore new clothing and . . . ? Philen frowned. Was that a dueling cane the king was wearing? And a wolfhound at his side?

He's not king anymore! Philen reminded himself again.

Venture strode up onto the Assembly stage. He turned, waving for his people—all eight of them—to sit with the guards. Venture then turned and glanced at Philen. "Philen, did you want to say something?"

Philen realized he was still standing. "I . . . was just—"

"Are you Assembly chancellor?" Elend asked.

Philen paused. "Chancellor?"

"The king presides at Assembly meetings," Elend said. "We now have no king—and so, by law, the Assembly should have elected a chancellor to call speakers, adjudicate time allotments, and break tie votes." He paused, eyeing Philen. "Someone needs to lead. Otherwise there is chaos."

Despite himself, Philen grew nervous. Did Venture know that Philen had organized the vote against him? No, no he didn't, he couldn't. He was looking at each of the Assembly members in turn, meeting their eyes. There was none of the jovial, dismissible boy that had attended these meetings before. Standing in the militaristic suit, firm instead of hesitant . . . he almost seemed like a different person.

You found a coach, it appears, Philen thought. *A little too late. Just wait. . . .*

Philen sat down. "Actually, we didn't get a chance to choose a chancellor," he said. "We were just getting to that."

Elend nodded, a dozen different instructions rattling in his head. Keep eye contact. Use subtle, but firm, expressions. Never appear hurried, but don't seem hesitant. Sit down without wiggling, don't shuffle, use a straight posture, don't form your hands into fists when you're nervous. . . .

He shot a quick glance at Tindwyl. She gave him a nod. *Get back to it, El,* he told himself. *Let them sense the differences in you.*

He walked over to take his seat, nodding to the other seven noblemen on the Assembly. "Very well," he said, taking the lead. "Then, might I nominate a chancellor?"

"Yourself?" asked Dridel, one of the noblemen; his sneer seemed permanent, as far as Elend could tell. It was a passably appropriate expression for one with such a sharp face and dark hair.

"No," Elend said. "I'm hardly an unbiased party in today's proceedings. Therefore, I nominate Lord Penrod. He's as honorable a man as we're likely to find, and I believe he can be trusted to mediate our discussions."

The group was quiet for a moment.

"That seems logical," Hettel, a forge worker, finally said.

"All in favor?" Elend said, raising his hand. He got a good eighteen hands—all of the skaa, most of the nobility, only one of the merchants. It was a majority, however.

Elend turned to Lord Penrod. "I believe that means that you are in charge, Ferson."

The stately man nodded appreciatively, then rose to formally open the meeting, something Elend had once done. Penrod's mannerisms were polished, his posture strong as he stood in his well-cut suit. Elend couldn't help but feel a little jealous, watching Penrod act so naturally in the things that Elend was struggling to learn.

Maybe he would make a better king than I, Elend thought. *Perhaps . . .*

No, he thought firmly. *I have to be confident. Penrod is a decent man and an impeccable noble, but those things do not make a leader. He hasn't read what I've read, and doesn't understand legislative theory as I do. He's a good man, but he's still a product of his society—he doesn't consider skaa animals, but he'll never be able to think of them as equals.*

Penrod finished the introductions, then turned to Elend. "Lord Venture, you called this meeting. I believe that the law grants you first opportunity to address the Assembly."

Elend nodded thankfully, rising.

"Will twenty minutes be enough time?" Penrod asked.

"It should be," Elend said, passing Penrod as they traded places. Elend stood up at the lectern. To his right, the floor of the hall was packed with shuffling, coughing, whispering people. There was a tension to the room—this was the first time Elend had confronted the group that had betrayed him.

"As many of you know," Elend said to the twenty-three Assembly members, "I recently returned from a meeting with Straff Venture—the warlord who is, unfortunately, my father. I would like to give a report of this encounter. Realize that because this is an open meeting, I will adjust my report to avoid mentioning sensitive matters of national security."

He paused just slightly, and saw the looks of confusion he had expected. Finally, Philen the merchant cleared his throat.

"Yes, Philen?" Elend asked.

"This is all well and good, Elend," Philen said. "But aren't you going to address the matter that brought us here?"

"The reason we meet together, Philen," Elend said, "is so that we can discuss how to keep Luthadel safe and prosperous. I think the people are most worried about the armies—and we should, primarily, seek to address their concerns. Matters of leadership in the Assembly can wait."

"I . . . see," Philen said, obviously confused.

"The time is yours, Lord Venture," Penrod said. "Proceed as you wish."

"Thank you, Chancellor," Elend said. "I wish to make it very clear that my father is *not* going to attack this city. I can understand why people would be concerned, particularly because of last week's preliminary assault on our walls. That, however, was simply a test—Straff fears attacking too much to commit all of his resources.

"During our meeting, Straff told me that he had made an alliance with Cett. However, I believe this to have been a bluff—if, unfortunately, a bluff with teeth. I suspect that he was, indeed, planning to risk attacking us, despite Cett's presence. That attack has been halted."

"Why?" asked one of the worker representatives. "Because you're his son?"

"No, actually," Elend said. "Straff is not one to let familial relationships hamper his determination." Elend paused, glancing at Vin. He was beginning to realize that she didn't like being the one who held the knife at Straff's throat, but she had given him permission to speak of her in his speech.

Still . . .

She said it was all right, he told himself. *I'm not choosing duty over her!*

"Come now, Elend," Philen said. "Stop with the theatrics. What did you promise Straff to keep his armies out of the city?"

"I threatened him," Elend said. "My fellow Assemblymen, when facing down my father in parlay, I realized that we—as a group—have generally ignored one of our greatest resources. We think of ourselves as an honorable body, created by the mandate of the people. However, we are not here because of anything we ourselves did. There is only one reason we have the positions we do—and that reason is the Survivor of Hathsin."

Elend looked the members of the Assembly in the eyes as he continued. "I have, at times, felt as I suspect that many of you do. The Survivor is a legend already, one we cannot hope to emulate. He has power over this people—a power stronger than our own, even though he is dead. We're jealous. Insecure, even. These are natural, human feelings. Leaders feel them just as acutely as other people—perhaps even more so.

"Gentlemen, we cannot afford to continue thinking like this. The Survivor's legacy doesn't belong to one group, or even to this city alone. He is our progenitor—the father of everyone who is free in this land. Whether or not you accept his religious authority, you must admit that without his bravery and sacrifice, we would not now enjoy our current freedom."

"What does this have to do with Straff?" Philen snapped.

"Everything," Elend said. "For, though the Survivor is gone, his legacy remains. Specifically, in the form of his apprentice." Elend nodded toward Vin. "She is the most powerful Mistborn alive—something Straff now knows for himself. Gentlemen, I know my father's temperament. He will not attack this city while he fears retribution from a source he cannot stop. He now realizes that if he attacks, he will incur the wrath of the Survivor's heir—a wrath not even the Lord Ruler himself could withstand."

Elend fell silent, listening to the whispered conversations move through the crowd. News of what he'd just said would reach the populace, and bring them strength. Perhaps, even, news would reach Straff's army through the spies Elend knew must be in the audience. He'd noticed his father's Allomancer sitting in the crowd, the one named Zane.

And when news reached Straff's army, the men there might think twice about obeying any orders to attack. Who would want to face the very force that had destroyed the Lord Ruler? It was a weak hope—the men of Straff's army probably didn't believe all of the stories out of Luthadel—but every little bit of weakened morale would help.

It also wouldn't hurt for Elend to associate himself a little more strongly with the Survivor. He was just going to have to get over his insecurity; Kelsier had been a great man, but he was gone. Elend would just have to do his best to see that the Survivor's legacy lived on.

For that was what would be best for his people.

Vin sat with a twisted stomach, listening to Elend's speech.

"You okay with this?" Ham whispered, leaning over to her as Elend gave a more detailed account of his visit with Straff.

Vin shrugged. "Whatever helps the kingdom."

"You were never comfortable with the way that Kell set himself up with the skaa—none of us were."

"It's what Elend needs," Vin said.

Tindwyl, who sat just before them, turned and gave her a flat look. Vin expected some recrimination for whispering during the Assembly proceedings, but apparently the Terriswoman had a different kind of castigation in mind.

"The king—" She still referred to Elend that way. "—needs this link with the Survivor. Elend has very little of his own authority to rely upon, and Kelsier is currently the most well loved, most celebrated man in the Central Dominance. By implying that the government was founded by the Survivor, the king will make the people think twice about meddling with it."

Ham nodded thoughtfully. Vin glanced downward, however. *What's the problem? Just earlier, I was beginning to wonder if I were the Hero of Ages, and now I'm worried about the notoriety Elend is giving me?*

She sat uncomfortably, burning bronze, feeling the pulsing from far away. It was growing even louder. . . .

Stop it! she told herself. *Sazed doesn't think the Hero would return, and he knows the histories better than anyone. It was foolish, anyway. I need to focus on what's happening here.*

After all, Zane was in the audience.

Vin sought out his face near the back of the room, a light burn of tin—not enough to blind her—letting her study his features. He wasn't looking at her, but watching the Assembly. Was he working at Straff's command, or was this visit his own? Straff and Cett both undoubtedly had spies in the audience—and, of course, Ham had guards mixed with the people as well. Zane unnerved her, however. Why didn't he turn toward her? Wasn't't—

Zane met her eyes. He smiled slightly, then turned back to his study of Elend.

Vin felt a shiver despite herself. So, did this mean he wasn't avoiding her? *Focus!* She told herself. *You need to pay attention to what Elend is saying.*

He was almost done, however. He wrapped up his speech with a few comments on how he thought they could keep Straff off-balance. Again, he couldn't be too detailed—not without giving away secrets. He glanced at the large clock in the corner; done three minutes early, he moved to leave the lectern.

Lord Penrod cleared his throat. "Elend, aren't you forgetting something?"

Elend hesitated, then looked back at the Assembly. "What is it that you all want me to say?"

"Don't you have a reaction?" one of the skaa workers said. "About . . . what happened at the last meeting?"

"You received my missive," Elend said. "You know how I feel about the matter. However, this public forum is not a place for accusations or denunciations. The Assembly is too noble a body for that kind of thing. I wish that a time of danger were not when the Assembly had chosen to voice its concerns, but we cannot alter what has happened."

He moved to sit again.

"That's it?" asked one of the skaa. "You're not even going to argue for yourself, try and persuade us to reinstate you?"

Elend paused again. "No," he said. "No, I don't think that I will. You have made your opinions known to me, and I am disappointed. However, you are the representatives chosen by the people. I believe in the power that you have been given.

"If you have questions, or challenges, I will be happy to defend myself. However, I am not going to stand and preach my virtues. You all know me. You know what I can do, and what I intend to do, for this city and the surrounding populace. Let that stand as my argument."

He returned to his seat. Vin could see hints of a frown on Tindwyl's face. Elend hadn't given the speech that she and he had prepared, a speech giving the very arguments the Assembly was obviously expecting.

Why the change? Vin wondered. Tindwyl obviously didn't think it was a good idea. And yet, oddly, Vin found herself trusting Elend's instincts more than she did Tindwyl's.

"Well," Lord Penrod said, approaching the lectern again. "Thank you for that report, Lord Venture. I'm not certain if we have other items of business. . . ."

"Lord Penrod?" Elend asked.

"Yes?"

"Perhaps you should hold the nominations?"

Lord Penrod frowned.

"The nominations for king, Penrod," Philen snapped.

Vin paused, eyeing the merchant. *He certainly seems up on things,* she noted.

"Yes," Elend said, eyeing Philen as well. "In order for the Assembly to choose a new king, nominations must be held at least three days before the actual voting. I suggest we hold the nominations now, so that we can hold the vote as soon as possible. The city suffers each day it is without a leader."

Elend paused, then smiled. "Unless, of course, you intend to let the month lapse without choosing a new king. . . ."

Good to confirm that he still wants the crown, Vin thought.

"Thank you, Lord Venture," Penrod said. "We'll do that now, then. . . . And, how exactly do we proceed?"

"Each member of the Assembly may make one nomination, if he wishes," Elend said. "So that we don't become overburdened with options, I would recommend that we all exercise restraint—only choose someone that you honestly and sincerely think would make the finest king. If you have a nomination to make, you may stand and announce it to the rest of the group."

Penrod nodded, returning to his seat. Almost as soon as he sat, however, one of the skaa stood. "I nominate Lord Penrod."

Elend had to expect that, Vin thought. *After nominating Penrod to be chancellor. Why give such authority to the man that he knew would be his greatest contender for the throne?*

The answer was simple. Because Elend knew that Lord Penrod was the best choice for chancellor. *Sometimes, he's a little* too *honorable,* Vin thought, not for the first time. She turned to study the skaa Assemblyman who had nominated Penrod. Why were the skaa so quick to unify behind a nobleman?

She suspected that it was still too soon. The skaa were accustomed to being led by noblemen, and even with their freedom, they were traditional beings—more traditional, even, than the noblemen. A lord like Penrod—calm, commanding—seemed inherently better suited to the title of king than a skaa.

They'll have to get over that, eventually, Vin thought. *At least, they will if they're ever going to be the people that Elend wants them to be.*

The room remained quiet, no other nominations being made. A few people coughed in the audience, even the whispers now dead. Finally, Lord Penrod himself stood.

"I nominate Elend Venture," he said.

"Ah . . ." someone whispered behind her.

Vin turned, glancing at Breeze. "What?" she whispered.

"Brilliant," Breeze said. "Don't you see? Penrod is an honorable man. Or, at least, as honorable as noblemen get—which means that he insists on being *seen* as honorable. Elend nominated Penrod for chancellor. . . ."

Hoping, in turn, that Penrod would feel obligated to nominate Elend for king, Vin realized. She glanced at Elend, noting a slight smile on his lips. Had he really crafted the exchange? It seemed a move subtle enough for Breeze himself.

Breeze shook his head appreciatively. "Not only did Elend not have to nominate himself—which would have made him look desperate—but now everyone on the Assembly thinks that the man they respect, the man they would probably choose as king, would rather have Elend hold the title. Brilliant."

Penrod sat, and the room remained quiet. Vin suspected that he also had made the nomination so that he wouldn't go uncontested to the throne. The entire Assembly probably thought that Elend deserved a chance to reclaim his place; Penrod was just the one who was honorable enough to voice the feeling.

But, what about the merchants? Vin thought. *They've got to have their own plan.* Elend thought that it was probably Philen who had organized the vote against him. They'd want to put one of their own on the throne, one who could open the city gates to whichever of the kings was manipulating them—or whichever one paid the best.

She studied the group of eight men, in their suits that seemed—somehow—even more fine than those of the noblemen. They all seemed to be waiting on the whims of a single man. What was Philen planning?

One of the merchants moved as if to stand, but Philen shot him a harsh glance. The merchant did not rise. Philen sat quietly, a nobleman's dueling cane across his lap. Finally, when most of the room had noticed the merchant's focus on him, he slowly rose to his feet.

"I have a nomination of my own," he said.

There was a snort from the skaa section. "Now who's being melodramatic, Philen?" one of the Assemblymen there said. "Just go ahead and do it—nominate yourself."

Philen raised an eyebrow. "Actually, I'm *not* going to nominate myself."

Vin frowned, and she saw confusion in Elend's eyes.

"Though I appreciate the sentiment," Philen continued, "I am but a simple merchant. No, I think that the title of king should go to someone whose skills are a little more specialized. Tell me, Lord Venture, must our nominations be for people on the Assembly?"

"No," Elend said. "The king doesn't have to be an Assemblyman—I accepted this position after the fact. The king's primary duty is that of creating, then enforcing, the law. The Assembly is only an advisory council with some measure of counterbalancing power. The king himself can be anyone—actually, the title was intended to be hereditary. I didn't expect . . . certain clauses to be invoked quite so quickly."

"Ah, yes," Philen said. "Well, then. I think the title should go to someone who has a little practice with it. Someone who has shown skill with leadership. Therefore, I nominate Lord Ashweather Cett to be our king!"

What? Vin thought with shock as Philen turned, gesturing toward the audience. A man sitting there removed his skaa cloak, pulling down the hood, revealing a suit and a face with a bristling beard.

"Oh dear . . ." Breeze said.

"It's actually him?" Vin asked incredulously as the whispers began in the audience.

Breeze nodded. "Oh, that's him. Lord Cett himself." He paused, then eyed her. "I think we might be in trouble."

I had never received much attention from my brethren; they thought that my work and my interests were unsuitable to a Worldbringer. The couldn't see how my work, studying nature instead of religion, benefited the people of the fourteen lands.

32

VIN SAT QUIETLY, TENSELY, SCANNING the crowd. *Cett wouldn't have come alone,* she thought.

And then she saw them, now that she knew what she was looking for. Soldiers in the crowd, dressed like skaa, forming a small protective buffer around Cett's seat. The king did not rise, though a young man at his side did.

Maybe thirty guards, Vin thought. *He may not be foolish enough to come alone . . . but entering the very city you're besieging?* It was a bold move—one that bordered on stupidity. Of course, many had said the same about Elend's visit to Straff's army.

But Cett wasn't in the same position as Elend. He wasn't desperate, wasn't in danger of losing everything. Except . . . he had a smaller army than Straff, and the koloss were coming. And if Straff did secure the supposed atium supply, Cett's days as leader in the West would certainly be numbered. Coming into Luthadel might not have been an act of desperation, but it also wasn't the act of a man who held the upper hand. Cett was gambling.

And he seemed to be enjoying it.

Cett smiled as the room waited in silence, Assemblymen and audience alike too shocked to speak. Finally, Cett waved to a few of his disguised soldiers, and the men picked up Cett's chair and carried it to the stage. Assemblymen whispered and commented, turning to aides or companions, seeking confirmation of Cett's identity. Most of the noblemen sat quietly—which should have been enough of a confirmation, in Vin's mind.

"He's not what I expected," Vin whispered to Breeze as the soldiers climbed up on the dais.

"Nobody told you he was crippled?" Breeze asked.

"Not just that," Vin said. "He's not wearing a suit." He had on a pair of trousers and a shirt, but instead of a nobleman's suit coat, he was wearing a worn black jacket. "Plus, that beard. He couldn't have grown a beast like that in one year—he must have had it before the Collapse."

"You only knew noblemen in Luthadel, Vin," Ham said. "The Final Empire was a big place, with a lot of different societies. Not everybody dresses like they do here."

Breeze nodded. "Cett was the most powerful nobleman in his area, so he needn't worry about tradition and propriety. He did what he wished, and the local nobility pandered. There were a hundred different courts with a hundred different little 'Lord Rulers' in the empire, each region having its own political dynamic."

Vin turned back to the stage front. Cett sat in his chair, having yet to speak. Finally, Lord Penrod stood. "This is most unexpected, Lord Cett."

"Good!" Cett said. "That was, after all, the point!"

"Do you wish to address the Assembly?"

"I thought I already was."

Penrod cleared his throat, and Vin's tin-enhanced ears heard a disparaging mutter from the noblemen's section regarding "Western noblemen."

"You have ten minutes; Lord Cett," Penrod said, sitting.

"Good," Cett said. "Because—unlike the boy over there—I intend to tell you exactly *why* you should make me king."

"And that is?" one of the merchant Assemblymen asked.

"Because I've got an army on your damn doorstep!" Cett said with a laugh.

The Assembly looked taken aback.

"A threat, Cett?" Elend asked calmly.

"No, Venture," Cett replied. "Just honesty—something you Central noblemen seem to avoid at all cost. A threat is only a promise turned around. What was it you told these people? That your mistress had her knife at Straff's throat? So, were you implying that if you *weren't* elected, you'd have your Mistborn withdraw, and let the city be destroyed?"

Elend flushed. "Of course not."

"Of course not," Cett repeated. He had a loud voice—unapologetic, forceful. "Well, I don't pretend, and I don't hide. My army is here, and my intention is to take this city. However, I'd much rather that you just give it to me."

"You, sir, are a tyrant," Penrod said flatly.

"So?" Cett asked. "I'm a tyrant with forty thousand soldiers. That's *twice* what you've got guarding these walls."

"What's to stop us from simply taking you hostage?" asked one of the other noblemen. "You seem to have delivered yourself to us quite neatly."

Cett bellowed a laugh. "If I don't return to my camp this evening, my army has orders to attack and raze the city immediately—no matter what! They'll probably get destroyed by Venture afterward—but it won't matter to me, or to you, at that point! We'll all be dead."

The room fell silent.

"See, Venture?" Cett asked. "Threats work wonderfully."

"You honestly expect us to make you our king?" Elend asked.

"Actually, I do," Cett said. "Look, with your twenty thousand added to my forty, we could easily hold these walls against Straff—we could even stop that army of koloss."

Whispers began immediately, and Cett raised a bushy eyebrow, turning to Elend. "You didn't tell them about the koloss, did you?"

Elend didn't respond.

"Well, they'll know soon enough," Cett said. "Regardless, I don't see that you have any other option but to elect me."

"You're not an honorable man," Elend said simply. "The people expect more from their leaders."

"I'm not an honorable man?" Cett asked with amusement. "And you *are*? Let me ask you a direct question, Venture. During the proceedings of this meeting, have any of your Allomancers over there been Soothing members of the Assembly?"

Elend paused. His eyes glanced to the side, finding Breeze. Vin closed her eyes. *No, Elend, don't—*

"Yes, they have," Elend admitted.

Vin heard Tindwyl groan quietly.

"And," Cett continued, "can you honestly say that you've never doubted yourself? Never wondered if you were a good king?"

"I think every leader wonders these things," Elend said.

"Well, I haven't," Cett said. "I've always known I was meant to be in charge—and I've always done the best job of making certain that I stayed in power. I know how to make myself strong, and that means I know how to make those who associate with me strong as well.

"Here's the deal. You give me the crown, and I'll take charge here. You all get to keep your titles—and those of the Assembly who don't have titles will *get* them. In addition, you'll get to keep your heads—which is a far better deal than Straff would offer, I assure you.

"The people get to keep working, and I'll make certain

that they're fed this winter. Everything goes back to normal, the way it was before this insanity began a year back. The skaa work, the nobility administrates."

"You think they'd go back to that?" Elend asked. "After all we fought for, you think I will simply let you force the people back into slavery?"

Cett smiled beneath his large beard. "I wasn't under the impression that the decision was yours, Elend Venture."

Elend fell silent.

"I want to meet with each of you," Cett said to the Assemblymen. "If you'll allow, I wish to move into Luthadel with some of my men. Say, a force of five thousand—enough to make me feel safe, but not to be of any real danger to you. I'll take up residence in one of the abandoned keeps, and wait until your decision next week. During that time, I'll meet with each of you in turn and explain the . . . benefits that would come from choosing me as your king."

"Bribes," Elend spat.

"Of course," Cett said. "Bribes for all of the people of this city—the foremost bribe being that of peace! You're so fond of name-calling, Venture. 'Slaves,' 'threats,' 'honorable.' 'Bribe' is just a word. Looked at another way, a bribe is just a promise, turned on *its* head." Cett smiled.

The group of Assemblymen was silent. "Shall we vote, then, on whether to let him enter the city?" Penrod asked.

"Five thousand is way too many," one of the skaa Assemblymen said.

"Agreed," Elend said. "There's no way we can let that many foreign troops into Luthadel."

"I don't like it at all," another said.

"What?" said Philen. "A monarch inside our city will be less dangerous than one outside, wouldn't you say? And besides, Cett has promised us all titles."

This gave the group something to think about.

"Why not just give me the crown now?" Cett said. "Open your gates to my army."

"You can't," Elend said immediately. "Not until there is a king—or unless you can get a unanimous vote right now."

Vin smiled. Unanimous wouldn't happen in that case as long as Elend was on the Assembly.

"Bah," Cett said, but he obviously was smooth enough not to insult the legislative body further. "Let me take up residence in the city, then."

Penrod nodded. "All in favor of allowing Lord Cett to take up residence inside with . . . say . . . a thousand troops?"

A full nineteen of the Assemblymen raised their hands. Elend was not one of them.

"It is done, then," Penrod said. "We adjourn for two weeks."

This can't be happening, Elend thought. *I thought maybe Penrod would provide a challenge, Philen a lesser one. But . . . one of the very tyrants who is threatening the city? How could they? How could they even consider his suggestion?*

Elend stood, catching Penrod's arm as he turned to walk off the dais. "Ferson," Elend said quietly, "this is insanity."

"We have to consider the option, Elend."

"Consider selling out the people of this city to a tyrant?"

Penrod's face grew cold, and he shook Elend's arm free. "Listen, lad," he said quietly. "You are a good man, but you've always been an idealist. You've spent time in books and philosophy—I've spent my life fighting politics with the members of the court. You know theories; I know people."

He turned, nodding to the audience. "Look at them, lad. They're *terrified.* What good do your dreams do them when they're starving? You talk of freedom and justice when two armies are preparing to slaughter their families."

Penrod turned back to Elend, staring him in the eyes. "The Lord Ruler's system wasn't perfect, but it kept these people safe. We don't even have that anymore. Your ideals can't face down armies. Cett might be a tyrant, but given the choice between him and Straff, I'd have to choose Cett. We'd probably have given him the city weeks ago, if you hadn't stopped us."

Penrod nodded to Elend, then turned and joined a few

of the noblemen who were leaving. Elend stood quietly for a moment.

We have seen a curious phenomenon associated with rebel groups that break off of the Final Empire and attempt to seek autonomy, he thought, recalling a passage from Ytves's book *Studies in Revolution. In almost all cases, the Lord Ruler didn't need to send his armies to reconquer the rebels. By the time his agents arrived, the groups had overthrown themselves.*

It seems that the rebels found the chaos of transition more difficult to accept than the tyranny they had known before. They joyfully welcomed back authority—even oppressive authority—for it was less painful for them than uncertainty.

Vin and the others joined him on the stage, and he put his arm around her shoulders, standing quietly as he watched people trail from the building. Cett sat surrounded by a small group of Assemblymen, arranging meetings with them.

"Well," Vin said quietly. "We know *he's* Mistborn."

Elend turned toward her. "You sensed Allomancy from him?"

Vin shook her head. "No."

"Then, how do you know?" Elend asked.

"Well, look at him," Vin said with a wave of her hand. "He acts like he can't walk—that *has* to be covering up something. What would be more innocent than a cripple? Can you think of a better way to hide the fact that you're a Mistborn?"

"Vin, my dear," Breeze said, "Cett has been crippled since childhood, when a disease rendered his legs useless. He's not Mistborn."

Vin raised an eyebrow. "That has to be one of the best cover stories I've ever heard."

Breeze rolled his eyes, but Elend just smiled.

"What now, Elend?" Ham asked. "We obviously can't deal with things the same way now that Cett has entered the city."

Elend nodded. "We have to plan. Let's . . ." He trailed off as a young man left Cett's group, walking toward Elend. It was the same man who had been sitting next to Cett.

"Cett's son," Breeze whispered. "Gneorndin."

"Lord Venture," Gneorndin said, bowing slightly. He was, perhaps, about Spook's age. "My father wishes to know when you would like to meet with him."

Elend raised an eyebrow. "I have no intention of joining the line of Assemblymen waiting upon Cett's bribes, lad. Tell your father that he and I have nothing to discuss."

"You don't?" Gneorndin asked. "And what about my sister? The one you kidnapped?"

Elend frowned. "You know that isn't true."

"My father would still like to discuss the event," Gneorndin said, shooting a hostile glance at Breeze. "Besides, he thinks that a conversation between you two might be in the city's best interests. You met with Straff in his camp—don't tell me that you aren't willing to do the same for Cett inside your own city?"

Elend paused. *Forget your biases,* he told himself. *You need to talk to this man, if only for the information the meeting might provide.*

"All right," Elend said. "I'll meet with him."

"Dinner, in one week?" Gneorndin asked.

Elend nodded curtly.

As the one who found Alendi, however, I became someone important. Foremost among the Worldbringers.

33

VIN LAY ON HER STOMACH, arms folded, head resting on them as she studied a sheet of paper on the floor in front of her. Considering the last few days of chaos, it was surprising to her that she found returning to her studies to be a relief.

A small one, however, for her studies held their own problems. *The Deepness* has *returned,* she thought. *Even if the mists only kill infrequently, they've begun to turn hostile again. That means the Hero of Ages needs to come again too, doesn't it?*

Did she honestly think that might be her? It sounded ridiculous, when she considered it. Yet, she heard the thumping in her head, saw the spirit in the mists. . . .

And what of that night, over a year gone, when she'd confronted the Lord Ruler? That night when somehow, she'd drawn the mists into herself, burning them as if they were metal?

That's not enough, she told herself. *One freak event—one I've never been able to replicate—doesn't mean I'm some mythological savior.* She didn't even really know most of the prophecies about the Hero. The logbook mentioned that he was supposed to come from humble origins—but that pretty much described every skaa in the Final Empire. He was supposed to have hidden royal bloodlines, but that made every half-breed in the city a candidate. In fact, she'd be willing to bet that most skaa had one or another hidden nobleman progenitor.

She sighed, shaking her head.

"Mistress?" OreSeur asked, turning. He stood on a chair, his forepaws up against the window as he looked out at the city.

"Prophecies, legends, foretellings," Vin said, slapping her hand down on her sheet of notes. "What's the point? Why did the Terris even believe in these things? Shouldn't a religion teach something practical?"

OreSeur settled down on his haunches upon the chair. "What would be more practical than gaining knowledge of the future?"

"If these actually said something useful, I'd agree. But even the logbook acknowledges that the Terris prophecies could be understood many different ways. What good are promises that could be interpreted so liberally?"

"Do not dismiss someone's beliefs because you do not understand them, Mistress."

Vin snorted. "You sound like Sazed. A part of me is

tempted to think that all these prophecies and legends were devised by priests who wanted to make a living."

"Only a part of you?" OreSeur asked, sounding amused.

Vin paused, then nodded. "The part that grew up on the streets, the part that always expects a scam." That part didn't want to acknowledge the other things she felt.

The thumpings were getting stronger and stronger.

"Prophecies do not have to be a scam, Mistress," OreSeur said. "Or even, really, a promise for the future. They can simply be an expression of hope."

"What do you know of such things?" Vin said dismissively, setting aside her sheet.

There was a moment of silence. "Nothing, of course, Mistress," OreSeur eventually said.

Vin turned toward the dog. "I'm sorry, OreSeur. I didn't mean . . . Well, I've just been feeling distracted lately."

Thump. Thump. Thump. . . .

"You need not apologize to me, Mistress," OreSeur said. "I am only kandra."

"Still a person," Vin said. "If one with dog breath."

OreSeur smiled. "You chose these bones for me, Mistress. You must deal with the consequences."

"The bones might have something to do with it," Vin said, rising. "But I don't think that carrion you eat is helping. Honestly, we have to get you some mint leaves to chew."

OreSeur raised a canine eyebrow. "And you don't think a dog with sweet breath would attract attention?"

"Only from anyone you happen to kiss in the near future," Vin said, returning her stacks of paper to her desk.

OreSeur chuckled softly in his canine way, turning back to study the city.

"Is the procession finished yet?" Vin asked.

"Yes, Mistress," OreSeur said. "It is difficult to see, even from a height. But, it does look like Lord Cett has finished moving in. He certainly did bring a lot of carts."

"He's Allrianne's father," Vin said. "Despite how much that girl complains about accommodations in the army, I'd bet that Cett likes to travel in comfort."

OreSeur nodded. Vin turned, leaning against the desk,

watching him and thinking of what he'd said earlier. *Expression of hope. . . .*

"The kandra have a religion, don't they?" Vin guessed.

OreSeur turned sharply. That was enough of a confirmation.

"Do the Keepers know of it?" Vin asked.

OreSeur stood on his hind legs, paws against the windowsill. "I should not have spoken."

"You needn't be afraid," Vin said. "I won't give away your secret. But, I don't see why it has to be secret anymore."

"It is a kandra thing, Mistress," OreSeur said. "It wouldn't be of any interest to anyone else."

"Of course it would," Vin said. "Don't you see, OreSeur? The Keepers believe that the last independent religion was destroyed by the Lord Ruler centuries ago. If the kandra managed to keep one, that suggests that the Lord Ruler's theological control of the Final Empire *wasn't* absolute. That has to mean something."

OreSeur paused, cocking his head, as if he hadn't considered such things.

His theological control wasn't absolute? Vin thought, a bit surprised at the words. *Lord Ruler—I'm starting to sound like Sazed and Elend. I've been studying too much lately.*

"Regardless, Mistress," OreSeur said. "I'd rather you didn't mention this to your Keeper friends. They would probably begin asking discomforting questions."

"They're like that," Vin said with a nod. "What is it your people have prophecies about, anyway?"

"I don't think you want to know, Mistress."

Vin smiled. "They talk about overthrowing us, don't they?"

OreSeur sat down, and she could almost see a flush on his canine face. "My . . . people have dealt with the Contract for a great long time, Mistress. I know it is difficult for you to understand why we would live under this burden, but we find it necessary. Yet, we do dream of a day when it may not be."

"When all the humans are subject to you?" Vin asked.

OreSeur looked away. "When they're all dead, actually."

"Wow."

"The prophecies are not literal, Mistress," OreSeur said. "They're metaphors—expressions of hope. Or, at least, that is how I have always seen them. Perhaps your Terris prophecies are the same? Expressions of a belief that if the people were in danger, their gods would send a Hero to protect them? In this case, the vagueness would be intentional—and rational. The prophecies were never meant to mean someone specific, but more to speak of a general feeling. A general hope."

If the prophecies weren't specific, why could only she sense the drumming beats?

Stop it, she told herself. *You're jumping to conclusions.* "All the humans dead," she said. "How do we die off? The kandra kill us?"

"Of course not," OreSeur said. "We honor our Contract, even in religion. The stories say that you'll kill yourselves off. You're of Ruin, after all, while the kandra are of Preservation. You're . . . actually supposed to destroy the world, I believe. Using the koloss as your pawns."

"You actually sound sorry for them," Vin noted with amusement.

"The kandra actually tend to think well of the koloss, Mistress," OreSeur said. "There is a bond between us; we both understand what it is to be slaves, we both are outsiders to the culture of the Final Empire, we both—"

He paused.

"What?" Vin asked.

"Might I speak no further?" OreSeur asked. "I have said too much already. You put me off balance, Mistress."

Vin shrugged. "We all need secrets." She glanced toward the door. "Though there's one I still need to figure out."

OreSeur hopped down from his chair, joining her as she strode out the door.

There was still a spy somewhere in the palace. She'd been forced to ignore that fact for far too long.

Elend looked deeply into the well. The dark pit—wide-mouthed to accommodate the comings and goings of numerous skaa—seemed a large mouth opening up, stone lips spread and preparing to swallow him down. Elend glanced to the side, where Ham stood speaking with a group of healers.

"We first noticed when so many people came to us complaining of diarrhea and abdominal pains," the healer said. "The symptoms were unusually strong, my lord. We've . . . already lost several to the malady."

Ham glanced at Elend, frowning.

"Everyone who grew sick lived in this area," the healer continued. "And drew their water from this well or another in the next square."

"Have you brought this to the attention of Lord Penrod and the Assembly?" Elend asked.

"Um, no, my lord. We figured that you . . ."

I'm not king anymore, Elend thought. However, he couldn't say the words. Not to this man, looking for help.

"I'll take care of it," Elend said, sighing. "You may return to your patients."

"They are filling our clinic, my lord," he said.

"Then appropriate one of the empty noble mansions," Elend said. "There are plenty of those. Ham, send him with some of my guard to help move the sick and prepare the building."

Ham nodded, waving over a soldier, telling him to gather twenty on-duty men from the palace to meet with the healer. The healer smiled, looking relieved, and bowed to Elend as he left.

Ham walked up, joining Elend beside the well. "Coincidence?"

"Hardly," Elend said, gripping the edge if the well with frustrated fingers. "The question is, which one poisoned it?"

"Cett just came into the city," Ham said, rubbing his chin. "Would have been easy to send out some soldiers to covertly drop in the poison."

"Seems more like something my father would do," Elend said. "Something to increase our tension, to get back at us for playing him for a fool in his camp. Plus, he's got that Mistborn who could have easily placed the poison."

Of course, Cett had had this same thing happen to him—Breeze poisoning his water supply back before he reached the city. Elend ground his teeth. There was really no way to know which one was behind the attack.

Either way, the poisoned wells meant trouble. There were others in the city, of course, but they were just as vulnerable. The people might have to start relying on the river for their water, and it was far less healthy, its waters muddy and polluted by waste from both the army camps and the city itself.

"Set guards around these wells," Elend said, waving a hand. "Board them up, post warnings, and then tell the healers to watch with particular care for other outbreaks."

We just keep getting wound tighter and tighter, he thought as Ham nodded. *At this rate, we'll snap long before winter ends.*

After a detour for a late dinner—where some talk about servants getting sick left her concerned—Vin went in and checked on Elend, who had just returned from walking the city with Ham. After that, Vin and OreSeur continued their original quest: that of finding Dockson.

They located him in the palace library. The room had once been Straff's personal study; Elend seemed to find the room's new purpose amusing for some reason.

Personally, Vin didn't find the library's location nearly as amusing as its contents. Or, rather, lack thereof. Though the room was lined with shelves, nearly all of them showed signs of having been pillaged by Elend. The rows of books lay pocked by forlorn empty spots, their companions taken away one by one, as if Elend were a predator, slowly whittling down a herd.

Vin smiled. It probably wouldn't be too long before Elend had stolen every book in the small library, carrying the tomes up to his study, then forgetfully placing them in one of his piles—ostensibly for return. Still, there were a large number of volumes left—ledgers, books of figures, and notebooks on finances; things that Elend usually found of little interest.

Dockson sat at the library's desk now, writing in a ledger. He noticed her arrival, and glanced over with a smile, but then turned back to his notations—apparently not wanting to lose his place. Vin waited for him to finish, OreSeur at her side.

Of all the members of the crew, Dockson seemed to have changed the most during the last year. She remembered her first impressions of him, back in Camon's lair. Dockson had been Kelsier's right-hand man, and the more "realistic" of the pair. And yet, there had always been an edge of humor to Dockson—a sense that he enjoyed his role as the straight man. He hadn't foiled Kelsier so much as complemented him.

Kelsier was dead. Where did that leave Dockson? He wore a nobleman's suit, as he always had—and of all the crewmembers, the suits seemed to fit him the best. If he shaved off the half beard, he could pass for a nobleman—not a rich high courtier, but a lord in early middle age who had lived his entire life trading goods beneath a great house master.

He wrote in his ledgers, but he had always done that. He still played the role of the responsible one in the crew. So, what was different? He was the same person, did the same things. He just *felt* different. The laughter was gone; the quiet enjoyment of the eccentricity in those around him. Without Kelsier, Dockson had somehow changed from temperate to . . . boring.

And that was what made her suspicious.

This has to be done, she thought, smiling at Dockson as he set down his pen and waved her to take a seat.

Vin sat down, OreSeur padding over to stand beside her chair. Dockson eyed the dog, shaking his head slightly. "That's such a remarkably well-trained beast, Vin," he said. "I don't think I've ever seen one quite like it. . . ."

Does he know? Vin wondered with alarm. *Would one kandra be able to recognize another in a dog's body?* No, that couldn't be. Otherwise OreSeur could find the impostor for her. So, she simply smiled again, patting OreSeur's head. "There is a trainer in the market. He teaches wolfhounds to be protective—to stay with young children and keep them out of danger."

Dockson nodded. "So, any purpose to this visit?"

Vin shrugged. "We never chat anymore, Dox."

Dockson sat back in his chair. "This might not be the best time for chatting. I have to prepare the royal finances to be taken over by someone else, should the vote go against Elend."

Would a kandra be able to do the ledgers? Vin wondered. *Yes. They'd have known—they'd have been prepared.*

"I'm sorry," Vin said. "I don't mean to bother you, but Elend has been so busy lately, and Sazed has his project. . . ."

"It's all right," Dockson said. "I can spare a few minutes. What's on your mind?"

"Well, do you remember that conversation we had, back before the Collapse?"

Dockson frowned. "Which one?"

"You know. . . . The one about your childhood."

"Oh," Dockson said, nodding. "Yes, what about it?"

"Well, do you still think the same way?"

Dockson paused thoughtfully, fingers slowly tapping on the desktop. Vin waited, trying not to show her tension. The conversation in question had been between the two of them, and during it, Dockson had first spoken to her of how much he'd hated the nobility.

"I suppose I don't," Dockson said. "Not anymore. Kell always said that you gave the nobility too much credit, Vin. But you started to change even him there at the end. No, I don't think that noble society needs to be completely destroyed. They aren't all monsters as once presumed."

Vin relaxed. He not only knew the conversation, he knew the details of the tangents they'd discussed. She had been the only one there with him. That had to mean that he wasn't the kandra, right?

"This is about Elend, isn't it?" Dockson asked.

Vin shrugged. "I suppose."

"I know that you wish he and I could get along better,

Vin. But, all things considered, I think we're doing pretty well. He is a decent man; I can acknowledge that. He has some faults as a leader: he lacks boldness, lacks presence."

Not like Kelsier.

"But," Dockson continued, "I don't want to see him lose his throne. He has treated the skaa fairly, for a nobleman."

"He's a good person, Dox," Vin said quietly.

Dockson looked away. "I know that. But . . . well, every time I talk to him, I see Kelsier standing over his shoulder, shaking his head at me. Do you know how long Kell and I dreamed of toppling the Lord Ruler? The other crewmembers, they thought Kelsier's plan was a newfound passion—something that came to him in the Pits. But it was older than that, Vin. Far older.

"We always hated the nobility, Kell and I. When we were youths, planning our first jobs, we wanted to be rich—but we also wanted to hurt them. Hurt them for taking from us things they had no right to. My love . . . Kelsier's mother. . . . Every coin we stole, every nobleman we left dead in an alleyway—this was our way of waging war. Our way of punishing them."

Vin sat quietly. It was these kinds of stories, these memories of a haunted past, that had always made her just a little uncomfortable with Kelsier—and with the person he had been training her to become. It was this sentiment that gave her pause, even when her instincts whispered that she should go and exact retribution on Straff and Cett with knives in the night.

Dockson held some of that same hardness. Kell and Dox weren't evil men, but there was an edge of vengefulness to them. Oppression had changed them in ways that no amount of peace, reformation, or recompense could redeem.

Dockson shook his head. "And we put one of them on the throne. I can't help but think that Kell would be angry with me for letting Elend rule, no matter how good a man he is."

"Kelsier changed at the end," Vin said quietly. "You said it yourself, Dox. Did you know that he saved Elend's life?"

Dockson turned, frowning. "When?"

"On that last day," Vin said. "During the fight with the Inquisitor. Kell protected Elend, who came looking for me."

"Must have thought he was one of the prisoners."

Vin shook her head. "He knew who Elend was, and knew that I loved him. In the end, Kelsier was willing to admit that a good man was worth protecting, no matter who his parents were."

"I find that hard to accept, Vin."

"Why?"

Dockson met her eyes. "Because if I accept that Elend bears no guilt for what his people did to mine, then I must admit to being a monster for the things that I did to them."

Vin shivered. In those eyes, she saw the truth behind Dockson's transformation. She saw the death of his laughter. She saw the guilt. The murders.

This man is no impostor.

"I can find little joy in this government, Vin," Dockson said quietly. "Because I know what we did to create it. The thing is, I'd do it all again. I tell myself it's because I believe in skaa freedom. I still lie awake at nights, however, quietly satisfied for what we've done to our former rulers. Their society undermined, their god dead. Now they know."

Vin nodded. Dockson looked down, as if ashamed, an emotion she'd rarely seen in him. There didn't seem to be anything else to say. Dockson sat quietly as she withdrew, his pen and ledger forgotten on the desktop.

"It's not him," Vin said, walking down an empty palace hallway, trying to shake the haunting sound of Dockson's voice from her mind.

"You are certain, Mistress?" OreSeur asked.

Vin nodded. "He knew about a private conversation that Dockson and I had before the Collapse."

OreSeur was silent for a moment. "Mistress," he finally said, "my brethren can be *very* thorough."

"Yes, but how could he have known about such an event?"

"We often interview people before we take their bones, Mistress," OreSeur explained. "We'll meet them several times, in different settings, and find ways to talk about their lives. We'll also talk to their friends and acquaintances. Did you ever tell anyone about this conversation you had with Dockson?"

Vin stopped to lean against the side of the stone hallway. "Maybe Elend," she admitted. "I think I mentioned it to Sazed too, just after it happened. That was almost two years ago."

"That could have been enough, Mistress," OreSeur said. "We cannot learn everything about a person, but we try our best to discover items like this—private conversations, secrets, confidential information—so that we can mention them at appropriate times and reinforce our illusion."

Vin frowned.

"There are . . . other things as well, Mistress," OreSeur said. "I hesitate because I do not wish you to imagine your friends in pain. However, it is common for our master—the one who actually does the killing—to torture their victim for information."

Vin closed her eyes. Dockson felt so real . . . his guilt, his reactions . . . that couldn't be faked, could it?

"Damn," she whispered quietly, opening her eyes. She turned, sighing as she pushed open the shutters of a hallway window. It was dark out, and the mists curled before her as she leaned against the stone windowsill and looked out at the courtyard two stories below.

"Dox isn't an Allomancer," she said. "How can I find out for certain if he's the impostor or not?"

"I do not know, Mistress," OreSeur said. "This is never an easy task."

Vin stood quietly. Absently, she pulled out her bronze earring—her mother's earring—and worked it between her fingers, watching it reflect light. It had once been gilded with silver, but that had worn off in most places.

"I hate this," she finally whispered.

"What, Mistress?"

"This . . . distrust," she said. "I hate being suspicious of my friends. I thought I was through mistrusting those around me. I feel like a knife is twisting inside of me, and it cuts deeper every time I confront one of the crew."

OreSeur sat on his haunches beside her, and he cocked his head. "But, Mistress. You've managed to eliminate several of them as impostors."

"Yes," Vin said. "But that only narrows the field—brings me one step closer to knowing which one of them is dead."

"And that knowledge isn't a good thing?"

Vin shook her head. "I don't want it to be any of them, OreSeur. I don't want to distrust them, don't want to find out that we're right. . . ."

OreSeur didn't respond at first, leaving her to stare out the window, mists slowly streaming to the floor around her.

"You are sincere," OreSeur finally said.

She turned. "Of course I am."

"I'm sorry, Mistress," OreSeur said. "I did not wish to be insulting. I just . . . Well, I have been kandra to many masters. So many of them are suspicious and hateful of everyone around them, I had begun to think that your kind lacked the capacity for trust."

"That's silly," Vin said, turning back to the window.

"I know it is," OreSeur said. "But people often believe silly things, if given enough proof. Either way, I apologize. I do not know which of your friends is dead, but I am sorry that one of my kind brought you this pain."

"Whoever he is, he's just following his Contract."

"Yes, Mistress," OreSeur said. "The Contract."

Vin frowned. "Is there a way that you could find out which kandra has a Contract in Luthadel?"

"I'm sorry, Mistress," OreSeur said. "That is not possible."

"I figured as much," she said. "Are you likely to know him, whoever he is?"

"The kandra are a close-knit group, Mistress," OreSeur said. "And our numbers are small. There is a good chance that I know him quite well."

Vin tapped her finger against the windowsill, frowning as she tried to decide if the information was useful.

"I still don't think it's Dockson," she finally said, replacing the earring. "We'll ignore him for now. If I can't get any other leads, we'll come back . . ." She trailed off as something caught her attention. A figure walking in the courtyard, bearing no light.

Ham, she thought. But the walk wasn't right.

She Pushed on the shield of the lamp hanging on the wall a short distance away. It snapped closed, the lamp shaking as the hallway fell into darkness.

"Mistress?" OreSeur asked as Vin climbed up into the window, flaring her tin as she squinted into the night.

Definitely not Ham, she thought.

Her first thought was of Elend—a sudden terror that assassins had come while she was talking to Dockson. But, it was early in the night, and Elend would still be speaking with his counselors. It was an unlikely time for an assassination.

And only one man? Not Zane, not judging from the height.

Probably just a guard, Vin thought. *Why do I have to be so paranoid all the time?*

And yet . . . she watched the figure walking into the courtyard, and her instincts kicked in. He seemed to be moving suspiciously, as if he were uncomfortable—as if he didn't want to be seen.

"In my arms," she said to OreSeur, tossing a padded coin out the window.

He hopped up obligingly, and she leaped out the window, fell twenty-five feet, and landed with the coin. She released OreSeur and nodded into the mists. He followed closely as she moved into the darkness, stooping and hiding, trying to get a good look at the lone figure. The man walked briskly, moving toward the side of the palace, where the servants' entrances were. As he passed, she finally saw his face.

Captain Demoux? she thought.

She sat back, crouching with OreSeur beside a small stack of wooden supply boxes. What did she really know of Demoux? He was one of the skaa rebels recruited by Kelsier almost two years before. He'd taken to command,

and had been promoted quickly. He was one of the loyal men who had stayed behind when the rest of the army had followed Yeden to their doom.

After the Collapse, he'd stayed in with the crew, eventually becoming Ham's second. He had received no small amount of training from Ham—which might explain why he'd go out at night without a torch or lantern. But, even so. . . .

If I were going to replace someone on the crew, Vin thought, *I wouldn't pick an Allomancer—that would make the impostor too easy to spot. I'd pick someone ordinary, someone who wouldn't have to make decisions or attract notice.*

Someone close to the crew, but not necessarily on it. Someone who is always near important meetings, but someone that others don't really know that well. . . .

She felt a small thrill. If the impostor were Demoux, it would mean that one of her good friends *hadn't* been killed. And it would mean that the kandra's master was even smarter than she'd given him credit for being.

He rounded the keep, and she followed quietly. However, whatever he'd been doing this night, it was already completed—for he moved in through one of the entrances on the side of the building, greeting the guards posted there to watch.

Vin sat back in the shadows. He'd spoken to the guards, so he hadn't snuck out of the palace. And yet . . . she recognized the stooped posture, the nervous movements. He'd been nervous about something.

That's him, she thought. *The spy.*

But now, what should she do about it?

There was a place for me, in the lore of the Anticipation—I thought myself the Announcer, the prophet foretold to discover the Hero of Ages. Renouncing Alendi then would have been to renounce my new position, my acceptance, by the others.

And so I did not.

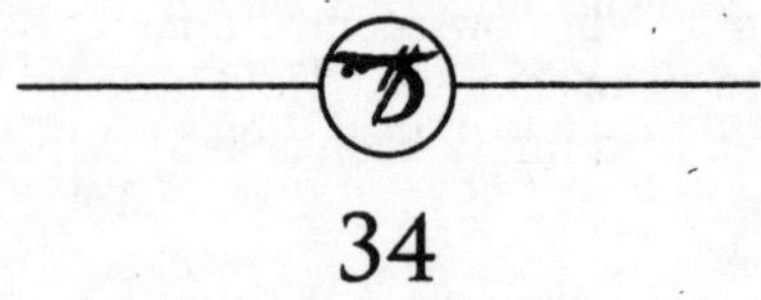

34

"THAT WON'T WORK," ELEND SAID, shaking his head. "We need a unanimous decision—minus the person being ousted, of course—in order to depose a member of the Assembly. We'd never manage to vote out all eight merchants."

Ham looked a bit deflated. Elend knew that Ham liked to consider himself a philosopher; indeed, Ham had a good mind for abstract thinking. However, he wasn't a scholar. He liked to think up questions and answers, but he didn't have experience studying a text in detail, searching out its meaning and implications.

Elend glanced at Sazed, who sat with a book open on the table before him. The Keeper had at least a dozen volumes stacked around him—though, amusingly, his stacks were neatly arranged, spines pointing the same direction, covers flush. Elend's own stacks were characteristically haphazard, pages of notes sticking out at odd angles.

It was amazing how many books one could fit into a room, assuming one didn't want to move around very much. Ham sat on the floor, a small pile of books beside him, though he spent most of his time voicing one random idea or another. Tindwyl had a chair, and did not study. The Terriswoman found it perfectly acceptable to train Elend as a king; however, she refused to research and give suggestions about keeping his throne. This seemed, in her eyes, to cross some unseen line between being an educator and a political force.

Good thing Sazed isn't like that, Elend thought. *If he were, the Lord Ruler might still be in charge. In fact, Vin and I would probably both be dead—Sazed was the one who actually rescued her when she was imprisoned by the Inquisitors. It wasn't me.*

He didn't like to think about that event. His bungled attempt at rescuing Vin now seemed a metaphor for all he had done wrong in his life. He'd always been well-intentioned, but he'd rarely been able to deliver. That was going to change.

"What about this, Your Majesty?" The one who spoke was the only other person in the room, a scholar named Noorden. Elend tried to ignore the intricate tattoos around the man's eyes, indications of Noorden's former life as an obligator. He wore large spectacles to try to hide the tattoos, but he had once been relatively well placed in the Steel Ministry. He could renounce his beliefs, but the tattoos would always remain.

"What have you found?" Elend asked.

"Some information on Lord Cett, Your Majesty," Noorden said. "I found it in one of the ledgers you took from the Lord Ruler's palace. It seems Cett isn't as indifferent to Luthadel politics as he'd like us to think." Noorden chuckled to himself at the thought.

Elend had never met a cheerful obligator before. Perhaps that was why Noorden hadn't left the city like most of his kind; he certainly didn't seem to fit into their ranks. He was only one of several men that Elend had been able to find to act as scribes and bureaucrats in his new kingdom.

Elend scanned Noorden's page. Though the page was filled with numbers rather than words, his scholar's mind easily parsed the information. Cett had done a lot of trading with Luthadel. Most of his work had been done using lesser houses as fronts. That might have fooled noblemen, but not the obligators, who had to be informed of the terms of any deal.

Noorden passed the ledger over to Sazed, who scanned the numbers.

"So," Noorden said, "Lord Cett wanted to appear unconnected to Luthadel—the beard and the attitude only serving to reinforce that impression. Yet, he always had a very quiet hand in things here."

Elend nodded. "Maybe he realized that you can't avoid politics by pretending you're not part of them. There's no way he would have been able to grab as much power as he did without some solid political connections."

"So, what does this tell us?" Sazed asked.

"That Cett is far more accomplished at the game than he wants people to believe," Elend said, standing, then stepping over a pile of books as he made his way back to his chair. "But, I think that much was obvious by the way he manipulated me and the Assembly yesterday."

Noorden chuckled. "You should have seen the way you all looked, Your Majesty. When Cett revealed himself, a few of the noble Assemblymen actually jumped in their seats! I think the rest of you were too shocked to—"

"Noorden?" Elend said.

"Yes, Your Majesty?"

"Please focus on the task at hand."

"Um, yes, Your Majesty."

"Sazed?" Elend asked. "What do you think?"

Sazed looked up from his book—a codified and annotated version of the city's charter, as written by Elend himself. The Terrisman shook his head. "You did a very good job with this, I think. I can see very few methods of preventing Lord Cett's appointment, should the Assembly choose him."

"Too competent for your own good?" Noorden said.

"A problem which, unfortunately, I've rarely had," Elend said, sitting and rubbing his eyes.

Is this how Vin feels all the time? he wondered. She got less sleep than he, and she was always moving about, running, fighting, spying. Yet, she always seemed fresh. Elend was beginning to droop after just a couple of days of hard study.

Focus, he told himself. *You have to know your enemies so that you can fight them. There has to be a way out of this.*

Dockson was still composing letters to the other Assemblymen. Elend wanted to meet with those who were willing. Unfortunately, he had a feeling that number would be small. They had voted him out, and now they had been presented with an option that seemed an easy way out of their problems.

"Your Majesty . . ." Noorden said slowly. "Do you think, maybe, that we should just let Cett take the throne? I mean, how bad could he be?"

Elend stopped. One of the reasons he employed the former obligator was because of Noorden's different viewpoint. He wasn't a skaa, nor was he a high nobleman. He wasn't a thief. He was just a scholarly little man who had joined the Ministry because it had offered an option other than becoming a merchant.

To him, the Lord Ruler's death had been a catastrophe that had destroyed his entire way of life. He wasn't a bad man, but he had no real understanding of the plight of the skaa.

"What do you think of the laws I've made, Noorden?" Elend asked.

"They're brilliant, Your Majesty," Noorden said. "Keen representations of the ideals spoken of by old philosophers, along with a strong element of modern realism."

"Will Cett respect these laws?" Elend asked.

"I don't know. I haven't ever really met the man."

"What do your instincts tell you?"

Noorden hesitated. "No," he finally said. "He isn't the type of man who rules by law. He just does what he wants."

"He would bring only chaos," Elend said. "Look at the information we have from his homeland and the places he's conquered. They are in turmoil. He's left a patchwork of half alliances and promises—threats of invasion acting as the thread that—barely—holds it all together. Giving him rule of Luthadel would just set us up for another collapse."

Noorden scratched his cheek, then nodded thoughtfully and turned back to his reading.

I can convince him, Elend thought. *If only I could do the same for the Assemblymen.*

But Noorden was a scholar; he thought the way Elend did. Logical facts were enough for him, and a promise of stability was more powerful than one of wealth. The Assembly was a different beast entirely. The noblemen wanted a return to what they'd known before; the merchants saw an opportunity to grab the titles they'd always envied; and the skaa were simply worried about a brutal slaughter.

And yet, even those were generalizations. Lord Penrod saw himself as the city's patriarch—the ranking nobleman, the one who needed to bring a measure of conservative temperance to their problems. Kinaler, one of the steelworkers, was worried that the Central Dominance needed a kinship with the kingdoms around it, and saw an alliance with Cett as the best way to protect Luthadel in the long run.

Each of the twenty-three Assemblymen had their own thoughts, goals, and problems. That was what Elend had intended; ideas proliferated in such an environment. He just hadn't expected so many of their ideas to contradict his own.

"You were right, Ham," Elend said, turning.

Ham looked up, raising an eyebrow.

"At the beginning of this all, you and the others wanted to make an alliance with one of the armies—give them the city in exchange for keeping it safe from the other armies."

"I remember," Ham said.

"Well, that's what the people want," Elend said. "With or without my consent, it appears they're going to give the city to Cett. We should have just gone with your plan."

"Your Majesty?" Sazed asked quietly.

"Yes?"

"My apologies, but it is not your duty to do what the people want."

Elend blinked. "You sound like Tindwyl."

"I have known few people as wise as she, Your Majesty," Sazed said, glancing at her.

"Well, I disagree with both of you," Elend said. "A ruler should only lead by the consent of the people he rules."

"I do not disagree with that, Your Majesty," Sazed said. "Or, at least, I do believe in the theory of it. Regardless, I still do not believe that your duty is to do as the people wish. Your duty is to lead as best you can, following the dictates of your conscience. You must be true, Your Majesty, to the man you wish to become. If that man is not whom the people wish to have lead them, then they will choose someone else."

Elend paused. *Well, of course. If I shouldn't be an exception to my own laws, I shouldn't be an exception to my own ethics, either.* Sazed's words were really just a rephrasing of things Tindwyl had said about trusting oneself, but Sazed's explanation seemed a better one. A more honest one.

"Trying to guess what people wish of you will only lead to chaos, I think," Sazed said. "You cannot please them all, Elend Venture."

The study's small ventilation window bumped open, and Vin squeezed through, pulling in a puff of mist behind her. She closed the window, then surveyed the room.

"More?" she asked incredulously. "You found more books?"

"Of course," Elend said.

"How many of those things have people written?" she asked with exasperation.

Elend opened his mouth, then paused as he saw the twinkle in her eye. Finally, he just sighed. "You're hopeless," he said, turning back to his letters.

He heard rustling from behind, and a moment later Vin landed on one of his stacks of books, somehow managing to balance atop it. Her mistcloak tassels hung down around her, smudging the ink on his letter.

Elend sighed.

"Oops," Vin said, pulling back the mistcloak. "Sorry."

"Is it really necessary to leap around like that all the time, Vin?" Elend asked.

Vin jumped down. "Sorry," she repeated, biting her lip. "Sazed says it's because Mistborn like to be up high, so we can see everything that's going on."

Elend nodded, continuing the letter. He preferred them to be in his own hand, but he'd need to have a scribe rewrite this one. He shook his head. *So much to do. . . .*

Vin watched Elend scribble. Sazed sat reading, as did one of Elend's scribes—the obligator. She eyed the man, and he shrank down a little in his seat. He knew that she'd never trusted him. Priests shouldn't be cheerful.

She was excited to tell Elend what she'd discovered about Demoux, but she hesitated. There were too many people around, and she didn't really have any evidence—just her instincts. So, she held herself back, looking over the stacks of books.

There was a dull quiet in the room. Tindwyl sat with her eyes slightly glazed; she was probably studying some ancient biography in her mind. Even Ham was reading, though he flipped from book to book, hopping topics. Vin felt as if she should be studying something, too. She thought of the notes she'd been making about the Deepness and the Hero of Ages, but couldn't bring herself to get them out.

She couldn't tell him about Demoux, yet, but there *was* something else she'd discovered.

"Elend," she said quietly. "I have something to tell you."

"Humm?"

"I heard the servants talking when OreSeur and I got dinner earlier," Vin said. "Some people they know have been sick lately—a lot of them. I think that someone might be fiddling with our supplies."

"Yes," Elend said, still writing. "I know. Several wells in the city have been poisoned."

"They have?"

He nodded. "Didn't I tell you when you checked on me earlier? That's where Ham and I were."

"You didn't tell me."

"I thought I did," Elend said, frowning.

Vin shook her head.

"I apologize," he said, leaned up and kissed her, then turned back to his scribbling.

And a kiss is supposed to make it all right? she thought sullenly, sitting back on a stack of books.

It was a silly thing; there was really no reason that Elend *should* have told her so quickly. And yet, the exchange left her feeling odd. Before, he would have asked her to do something about the problem. Now, he'd apparently handled it all on his own.

Sazed sighed, closing his tome. "Your Majesty, I can find no holes. I have read your laws over six times now."

Elend nodded. "I feared as much. The only advantage we could gain from the law is to misinterpret it intentionally—which I will not do."

"You are a good man, Your Majesty," Sazed said. "If you had seen a hole in the law, you would have fixed it. Even if you hadn't caught the flaws, one of us would have, when you asked for our opinions."

He lets them call him "Your Majesty," Vin thought. *He tried to get them to stop that. Why let them use it now?*

Odd, that Elend would finally start to think of himself as king after the throne had been taken from him.

"Wait," Tindwyl said, eyes unglazing. "You read over this law before it was ratified, Sazed?"

Sazed flushed.

"He did," Elend said. "In fact, Sazed's suggestions and ideas were instrumental in helping me craft the current code."

"I see," Tindwyl said through tight lips.

Elend frowned. "Tindwyl, you were not invited to this meeting. You are suffered at it. Your advice has been well appreciated, but I will not allow you to insult a friend and guest of my household, even if those insults are indirect."

"I apologize, Your Majesty."

"You will not apologize to me," Elend said. "You will apologize to Sazed, or you will leave this conference."

Tindwyl sat for a moment; then she stood and left the room. Elend didn't appear offended. He simply turned back to writing his letters.

"You didn't need to do that, Your Majesty," Sazed said. "Tindwyl's opinions of me are well founded, I think."

"I will do as I see fit, Sazed," Elend said, still writing.

"No offense, my friend, but you have a history of letting people treat you poorly. I won't stand for it in my house—by insulting your help with my laws, she insulted me as well."

Sazed nodded, then reached over to pick up a new volume.

Vin sat quietly. *He's changing so quickly. How long has it been since Tindwyl arrived? Two months?* None of the things Elend said were that different from what he would have said before—but the way he said them was completely different. He was firm, demanding in a way that implied he expected respect.

It's the collapse of his throne, the danger of the armies, Vin thought. *The pressures are forcing him to change, to either step up and lead or get crushed.* He'd known about the wells. What other things had he discovered, and not told her?

"Elend?" Vin asked. "I've thought more about the Deepness."

"That's wonderful, Vin," Elend said, smiling at her. "But, I really don't have time right now. . . ."

Vin nodded, and smiled at him. However, her thoughts were more troubled. *He's not uncertain, like he once was. He doesn't have to rely on people as much for support.*

He doesn't need me anymore.

It was a foolish thought. Elend loved her; she knew that. His aptitude wouldn't make her less valuable to him. And yet, she couldn't stamp out her worries. He'd left her once before, when he'd been trying to juggle the needs of his house with his love for her, and the action had nearly crushed her.

What would happen if he abandoned her now?

He won't, she told herself. *He's a better man than that.*

But, good men had failed relationships, didn't they? People grew apart—particularly people who were so different to begin with. Despite herself—despite her self-assurances—she heard a small voice pop up in the back of her mind.

It was a voice she'd thought banished, a voice she hadn't ever expected to hear again.

Leave him first, Reen, her brother, seemed to whisper in her head. *It will hurt less.*

Vin heard a rustling outside. She perked up slightly, but it had been too soft for the others to hear. She stood, walking over to the ventilation window.

"Going back on patrol?" Elend asked.

She turned, then nodded.

"You might want to scout out Cett's defenses at Keep Hasting," Elend said.

Vin nodded again. Elend smiled at her, then turned back to his letters. Vin pulled open the window and stepped out into the night. Zane stood in the mists, feet barely resting against the stone lip running beneath the window. He stood at a skewed angle, feet against the wall, body jutting out into the night.

Vin glanced to the side, noting the bit of metal that Zane was Pulling against to hold himself stationary. Another feat of prowess. He smiled at her in the night.

"Zane?" she whispered.

Zane glanced upward, and Vin nodded. A second later, they both landed atop Keep Venture's metal roof.

Vin turned to Zane. "Where have you been?"

He attacked.

Vin jumped back in surprise as Zane spun forward, a swirling form in black, knives twinkling. She came down with her feet half off the rooftop, tense. *A spar, then?* she thought.

Zane struck, his knife coming dangerously close to her neck as she dodged to the side. There was something different about his attacks this time. Something more dangerous.

Vin cursed and pulled out her own daggers, jumping back from another attack. As she moved, Zane sliced through the air, cutting the tip off one of her mistcloak tassels.

She turned to face him. He walked forward, but held no combat posture. He seemed confident, yet unconcerned, as if he were strolling up to an old friend, not entering a fight.

All right then, she thought, jumping forward, swiping with her daggers.

Zane stepped forward casually, turning just slightly to the side, easily dodging one knife. He reached out, grabbing her other hand with an effortless motion, stopping its blow.

Vin froze. Nobody was that good. Zane looked down at her, eyes dark. Unconcerned. Unworried.

He was burning atium.

Vin pulled free of his grip, jumping backward. He let her go, watching as she fell into a crouch, sweat beading on her brow. She felt a sudden, sharp stab of terror—a guttural, primal feeling. She had feared this day from the moment she'd learned of atium. It was the terror of knowing she was powerless, despite all of her skills and abilities.

It was the terror of knowing she was going to die.

She turned to jump away, but Zane leaped forward before she even began to move. He knew what she would do before she did herself. He grabbed her shoulder from behind, pulling her backward, throwing her down to the rooftop.

Vin slammed against the metal roofing, gasping in pain. Zane stood above her, looking down, as if waiting.

I won't be beaten this way! Vin thought with desperation. *I won't be killed like a trapped rat!*

She reached and swung a knife at his leg, but it was useless. He pulled the leg back slightly—just enough—so that her swing didn't even nick the cloth of his trousers. She was like a child, being held at a distance by a much larger, more powerful foe. This was what it must be like, being a normal person, trying to fight her.

Zane stood in the darkness.

"What?" she finally demanded.

"You really don't have it," he said quietly. "The Lord Ruler's atium stash."

"No," she said.

"You don't have any at all," he said flatly.

"I used the last bead the day I fought Cett's assassins."

He stood for a moment; then he turned, stepping away from her. Vin sat up, heart thumping, hands shaking just a bit. She forced herself to her feet, then stooped and retrieved her fallen daggers. One had cracked against the roof's copper top.

Zane turned back toward her, quiet in the mists.

Zane watched her in the darkness, saw her fear—yet also her determination.

"My father wants me to kill you," Zane said.

She stood, watching him, eyes still afraid. She was strong, and she repressed the fear well. The news from their spy, the words Vin had spoken while visiting Straff's tent, were all true. There was no atium to be had in this city.

"Is that why you stayed away?" she asked.

He nodded, turning away from her.

"So?" she asked. "Why let me live?"

"I'm not sure," he admitted. "I may still kill you. But . . . I don't have to. Not to fulfill his order. I could just take you away—that would have the same effect."

He turned back toward her. She was frowning, a small, quiet figure in the mists.

"Come with me," he said. "Both of us could leave—Straff would lose his Mistborn, and Elend would lose his. We could deny them *both* their tools. And we could be free."

She didn't respond immediately. Finally, she shook her head. "This . . . thing between us, Zane. It isn't what you think."

"What do you mean?" he said, stepping forward.

She looked up at him. "I love Elend, Zane. I really do."

And you think that means you can't feel anything for me? Zane thought. *What of that look I've seen in your eyes, that longing? No, it isn't as easy as you imply, is it?*

It never is.

And yet, what else had he expected? He turned away. "It makes sense. That's the way it has always been."

"What is that supposed to mean?" she demanded.

Elend. . . .

"Kill him," God whispered.

Zane squeezed his eyes shut. She would not be fooled; not a woman who had grown up on the streets, a woman who was friends with thieves and scammers. This was the difficult part. She would need to see things that terrified Zane.

She would need truth.

"Zane?" Vin asked. She still seemed a bit shaken by his attack, but she was the type who recovered quickly.

"Can't you see the resemblance?" Zane asked, turning. "The same nose, the same slant of the face? I cut my hair shorter than he, but it has the same curl. Is it so hard to see?"

Her breath caught in her throat.

"Who else would Straff Venture trust as his Mistborn?" Zane asked. "Why else would he let me get so close, why else would he feel so comfortable letting me in on his plans?"

"You're his son," Vin whispered. "Elend's brother."

Zane nodded.

"Elend . . ."

"Doesn't know of me," Zane said. "Ask him about our father's sexual habits sometime."

"He's told me," Vin said. "Straff likes mistresses."

"For more than one reason," Zane said. "More women means more children. More children means more Allomancers. More Allomancers means more chances at having a Mistborn son to be your assassin."

Breeze-blown mist washed over them. In the distance, a soldier's armor clinked as he patrolled.

"While the Lord Ruler lived, I could never inherit," Zane said. "You know how strict the obligators were. I grew up in the shadows, ignored. You lived on the streets—I assume that was terrible. But, think of what it would be like to be a scavenger in your own home, unacknowledged by your father, treated like a beggar. Think of watching your brother, a boy your same age, growing up privileged. Think of watching his disdain for the things you longed to have. Comfort, idleness, love . . ."

"You must hate him," Vin whispered.

"Hate?" Zane asked. "No. Why hate a man for what he is? Elend has done nothing to me, not directly. Besides, Straff found a reason to need me, eventually—after I

Snapped, and he finally got what he'd been gambling to get for the last twenty years No, I don't hate Elend. Sometimes, however, I do envy him. He has everything. And still . . . it seems to me like he doesn't appreciate it."

Vin stood quietly. "I'm sorry."

Zane shook his head sharply. "Don't pity me, woman. If I were Elend, I wouldn't be Mistborn. I wouldn't understand the mists, nor would I know what it was like to grow up alone and hated." He turned, looking into her eyes. "Don't you think a man better appreciates love when he has been forced for so long to go without?"

"I . . ."

Zane turned away. "Anyway," he said, "I didn't come here tonight to lament my childhood. I came with a warning."

Vin grew tense.

"A short time ago," Zane said, "my father let several hundred refugees through his barricade to approach the city. You know of the koloss army?"

Vin nodded.

"It attacked and pillaged the city of Suisna earlier."

Vin felt a start of fright. Suisna was only a day away from Luthadel. The koloss were close.

"The refugees came to my father for help," Zane said. "He sent them on to you."

"To make the people of the city more afraid," Vin said. "And to provide a further drain on our resources."

Zane nodded. "I wanted to give you warning. Both of the refugees, and of my orders. Think about my offer, Vin. Think about this man who claims to love you. You know he doesn't understand you. If you leave, it will be better for both of you."

Vin frowned. Zane bowed his head slightly to her, then jumped into the night, Pushing against the metal rooftop. She still didn't believe him about Elend. He could see that in her eyes.

Well, proof was coming. She'd soon see. She'd soon understand what Elend Venture truly thought of her.

But I do so now. Let it be known that I, Kwaan, Worldbringer of Terris, am a fraud.

35

IT FELT LIKE SHE WAS going to a ball again.

The beautiful maroon gown would have fit in perfectly at one of the parties she had attended during the months before the Collapse. The dress was untraditional, but not unfashionable. The changes simply made the dress seem distinctive.

The alterations left her freer to move; let her walk more gracefully, turn more naturally. That, in turn, made her feel even more beautiful. Standing before her mirror, Vin thought of what it might have been like to wear the dress to a real ball. To be herself—not Valette, the uncomfortable country noblewoman. Not even Vin, the skaa thief. To be herself.

Or, at least, as she could imagine herself. Confident because she accepted her place as a Mistborn. Confident because she accepted her place as the one who had struck down the Lord Ruler. Confident because she knew that the king loved her.

Maybe I could *be both,* Vin thought, running her hands down the sides of the dress, feeling the soft satin.

"You look beautiful, child," Tindwyl said.

Vin turned, smiling hesitantly. "I don't have any jewelry. I gave the last of it to Elend to help feed the refugees. It was the wrong color to go with this dress anyway."

"Many women use jewelry to try and hide their own plainness," Tindwyl said. "You don't have that need."

The Terriswoman stood with her usual posture, hands clasped before her, rings and earrings sparkling. None of her jewelry, however, had gemstones; in fact, most of it was made from simple materials. Iron, copper, pewter. Feruchemical metals.

"You haven't been in to see Elend lately," Vin said, turning back to the mirror and using a few wooden barrettes to hold her hair back.

"The king is quickly approaching the point where he no longer needs my instruction."

"He's that close then?" Vin asked. "To being like the men from your biographies?"

Tindwyl laughed. "Goodness, no, child. He's quite far from that."

"But—"

"I said he would no longer need my instruction," Tindwyl said. "He is learning that he can rely only so much upon the words of others, and has reached the point where he will have to learn more for himself. You would be surprised, child, how much about being a good leader simply comes from experience."

"He seems very different to me," Vin said quietly.

"He is," Tindwyl said, walking forward to lay a hand on Vin's shoulder. "He is becoming the man that he always knew he would have to be—he just didn't know the path. Though I am hard on him, I think he would have found his way, even if I hadn't come. A man can only stumble for so long before he either falls or stands up straight."

Vin looked at her mirror self, pretty in its maroon dressings. "This is what *I* have to become. For him."

"For him," Tindwyl agreed. "And for yourself. This is where *you* were heading, before you got distracted."

Vin turned. "Are you going to come with us tonight?"

Tindwyl shook her head. "That is not my place. Now, go meet your king."

This time, Elend did not intend to enter his enemy's lair without a proper escort. Two hundred soldiers stood in the courtyard, waiting to accompany him to Cett's dinner, and Ham—fully armed—was playing personal bodyguard. Spook would act as Elend's coachman. That only left

Breeze, who—understandably—was a bit nervous about the idea of going to the dinner.

"You don't have to come," Elend told the portly man as they assembled in the Venture courtyard.

"I don't?" Breeze said. "Well then, I shall remain here. Enjoy the dinner!"

Elend paused, frowning.

Ham clapped Elend on the shoulder. "You should know better than to give that one any wiggle room, Elend!"

"Well, I meant my words," Elend said. "We could really use a Soother, but he doesn't have to come if he doesn't want to."

Breeze looked relieved.

"You don't even feel a bit guilty, do you?" Ham asked.

"Guilty?" Breeze asked, hand resting on his cane. "My dear Hammond, have you *ever* known me to express such a dreary and uninspired emotion? Besides, I have a feeling Cett will be more amiable without me around."

He's probably right, Elend thought as his coach pulled up.

"Elend," Ham said. "Don't you think bringing two hundred soldiers with us is . . . well, a little obvious?"

"Cett is the one who said we should be honest with our threats," Elend said. "Well, I'd say two hundred men is on the conservative side of how well I trust the man. He'll still have us outnumbered five to one."

"But you'll have a Mistborn sitting a few seats from him," a soft voice said from behind.

Elend turned, smiling at Vin. "How can you possibly move so quietly in a dress like that?"

"I've been practicing," she said, taking his arm.

Thing is, she probably has, he thought, inhaling her perfume, imagining Vin creeping through the palace hallways in a massive ball gown.

"Well, we should get moving," Ham said. He gestured for Vin and Elend to enter the carriage, and they left Breeze behind on the palace steps.

After a year of passing Keep Hasting in the night, its windows darkened, it felt right to see them glowing again.

"You know," Elend said from beside her, "we never did get to attend a ball together."

Vin turned from her contemplation of the approaching keep. Around her, the carriage bounced along to the sound of several hundred tromping feet, the evening just beginning to grow dark.

"We met up several times at the balls," Elend continued, "but we never officially attended one together. I never got the chance to pick you up in my carriage."

"Is that really so important?" Vin asked.

Elend shrugged. "It's all part of the experience. Or, it was. There was a comfortable formality to it all; the gentleman arriving to accompany the lady, then everyone watching you enter and evaluating how you look together. I did it dozens of times with dozens of women, but never with the one that would have made the experience special."

Vin smiled. "Do you think we'll ever have balls again?"

"I don't know, Vin. Even if we survive all of this . . . well, could you dance while so many people starved?" He was probably thinking about the hundreds of refugees, wearied from their travels, stripped of all food and equipment by Straff's soldiers, huddled together in the warehouse Elend had found for them.

You danced before, she thought. *People starved then, too.* But that was a different time; Elend hadn't been king then. In fact, as she thought about it, he had never actually danced at those balls. He had studied and met with his friends, planning how he could make a better place out of the Final Empire.

"There has to be a way to have both," Vin said. "Maybe we could throw balls, and ask the nobility who came to donate money to help feed the people."

Elend smiled. "We'd probably spend twice as much on the party as we got in donations."

"And the money we spent would go to skaa merchants."

Elend paused thoughtfully, and Vin smirked to herself. *Odd that I would end up with the only frugal nobleman in the city.* What a pair they were—a Mistborn who felt guilty wasting coins to jump and a nobleman who thought balls were too expensive. It was a wonder that Dockson could pry enough money out of them to keep the city running.

"We'll worry about that later," Elend said as the Hasting gates opened, revealing a field of soldiers at attention.

You can bring your soldiers if you want, the display seemed to say. *I've got more.* In reality, they were entering a strange allegory of Luthadel itself. Elend's two hundred were now surrounded by Cett's thousand—which, in turn, were surrounded by Luthadel's twenty thousand. The city, of course, was then surrounded by nearly a hundred thousand troops on the outside. Layer upon layer of soldiers, all tensely waiting for a fight. Thoughts of balls and parties fled her mind.

Cett did not greet them at the door. That duty was performed by a soldier in a simple uniform.

"Your soldiers can remain here," the man said as they entered the main entryway. Once, the large, pillared room had been draped in fine rugs and wall hangings, but Elend had taken those to fund his government. Cett, obviously, hadn't brought replacements, and that left the inside of the keep feeling austere. Like a battlefront fortress, rather than a mansion.

Elend turned, waving to Demoux, and the captain ordered his men to wait indoors. Vin stood for a moment, consciously keeping herself from shooting a glare at Demoux. If he *was* the kandra, as her instincts warned, then it was dangerous to have him too close. Part of her itched to simply throw him in a dungeon.

And yet, a kandra couldn't hurt humans, so he wasn't a direct threat. He was simply there to relay information. Plus, he'd already know their most sensitive secrets; there was little point in striking now, playing her hand so quickly. If she waited, saw where he went when he slipped out of the city, then maybe she could find out which army—or sect in the city—he was reporting to. Learn what information he had betrayed.

And so, she stayed her hand, waiting. The time to strike would come.

Ham and Demoux arranged their men, and then a smaller honor guard—including Ham, Spook, and Demoux—gathered to stay with Vin and Elend. Elend nodded to Cett's man, and the soldier led them down a side passageway.

We're not heading toward the lifts, Vin thought. The Hasting ballroom was at the very top of the keep's central tower; the times she had attended balls in the structure, she had been taken to the top on one of four human-drawn lifts. Either Hasting didn't want to waste the manpower, or . . .

He picked the tallest keep in the city, Vin thought. *The one with the fewest windows as well.* If Cett pulled all the lifts to the top, it would be very difficult for an invading force to claim the keep.

Fortunately, it didn't appear that they would have to go all the way to the top this evening. After they climbed two flights in a twisting stone stairwell—Vin having to pull her dress in at the sides to keep from brushing against the stones—their guide led them out into a large, circular room with stained-glass windows running around the entire perimeter, broken only by columns to support the ceiling. The single room was nearly as wide around as the tower itself.

A secondary ballroom, perhaps? Vin wondered, taking in the beauty. The glass wasn't lit, though she suspected that there were clefts for limelights on the outside. Cett didn't appear to care about such things. He had set up a large table in the very center of the room, and sat at its head. He was already eating.

"You're late," he called out to Elend, "so I started without you."

Elend frowned. To this, Cett laughed a full bellow, holding up a drumstick. "You seem more aghast at my breach of etiquette than you do about the fact that I brought an army to conquer you, boy! But, I suppose that's Luthadel. Sit down before I eat this all myself."

Elend held out an arm for Vin, leading her to the table. Spook took up position near the stairwell, his Tineye's ears listening for danger. Ham led their ten men to a position from which they could watch the only entrances to the room—the entry from the stairs and the door the serving staff used.

Cett ignored the soldiers. He had a group of his own bodyguards standing near the wall on the other side of the room, but he seemed unconcerned that Ham's troop had them slightly outnumbered. His son—the young man who had attended him at the Assembly meeting—stood at his side, waiting quietly.

One of the two has to be Mistborn, Vin thought. *And I still think it is Cett.*

Elend seated her, then took a chair next to her, both of them sitting directly across from Cett. He barely paused in his eating as the servers brought Vin's and Elend's dishes.

Drumsticks, Vin thought, *and vegetables in gravy. He wants this to be a messy meal—he wants to make Elend uncomfortable.*

Elend didn't start on his food immediately. He sat, watching Cett, his expression thoughtful.

"Damn," Cett said. "This is good food. You have no idea how hard it is to get proper meals when traveling!"

"Why did you want to speak with me?" Elend asked. "You know I won't be convinced to vote for you."

Cett shrugged. "I thought it might be interesting."

"Is this about your daughter?" Elend asked.

"Lord Ruler, no!" Cett said with a laugh. "Keep the silly thing, if you want. The day she ran off was one of the few joys I've had this last month."

"And if I threaten to harm her?" Elend asked.

"You won't," Cett said.

"You're certain?"

Cett smiled through his thick beard, leaning toward Elend. "I know you, Venture. I'd been watching you, studying you, for months. And then, you were kind enough to send one of your friends to spy on me. I learned a lot about you from him!"

Elend looked troubled.

Cett laughed. "Honestly, you didn't think I'd recognize one of the Survivor's own crewmembers? You Luthadel noblemen must assume that everyone outside the city is a damn fool!"

"And yet, you listened to Breeze," Elend said. "You let him join you, listened to his advice. And then, you only chased him away when you found him being intimate with your daughter—the one you claim to have no affection for."

"Is *that* why he told you he left the camp?" Cett asked, laughing. "Because I caught him with Allrianne? Goodness, what do I care if the girl seduced him?"

"You think *she* seduced *him*?" Vin asked.

"Of course," Cett said. "Honestly, I only spent a few weeks with him, and even *I* know how useless he is with women."

Elend was taking all this in stride. He watched Cett with narrow, discerning eyes. "So why *did* you chase him away?"

Cett leaned back. "I tried to turn him. He refused. I figured killing him would be preferable to letting him return to you. But, he's remarkably agile for a man his size."

If Cett really is Mistborn, there's no way Breeze got away without Cett letting him, Vin thought.

"So you see, Venture," Cett said. "I know you. I know you better, perhaps, than you know yourself—for I know what your friends think of you. It takes a pretty extraordinary man to earn the loyalty of a weasel like Breeze."

"So you think I won't harm your daughter," Elend said.

"I *know* you won't," Cett said. "You're honest—I happen to like that about you. Unfortunately, honesty is very easy to exploit—I knew, for instance, that you'd admit Breeze was Soothing that crowd." Cett shook his head. "Honest men weren't meant to be kings, lad. It's a damn shame, but it's true. That's why I have to take the throne from you."

Elend was silent for a moment. Finally, he looked to Vin. She took his plate, sniffing it with an Allomancer's senses.

Cett laughed. "Think I'd poison you?"

"No, actually," Elend said as Vin set the plate down. She wasn't as good as some, but she'd leaned the obvious scents.

"You wouldn't use poison," Elend said. "That isn't your way. You seem to be a rather honest man yourself."

"I'm just blunt," Cett said. "There's a difference."

"I haven't heard you tell a lie yet."

"That's because you don't know me well enough to discern the lies," Cett said. He held up several grease-stained fingers. "I've already told you three lies tonight, lad. Good luck guessing which ones they were."

Elend paused, studying Cett. "You're playing with me."

"Of course I am!" Cett said. "Don't you see, boy? This is why you shouldn't be king. Leave the job to men who understand their own corruption; don't let it destroy you."

"Why do you care?" Elend asked.

"Because I'd rather not kill you," Cett said.

"Then don't."

Cett shook his head. "That isn't how all this works, lad. If there is an opportunity to stabilize your power, or to get more power, you'd damn well better take it. And I will."

The table fell silent again. Cett eyed Vin. "No comments from the Mistborn?"

"You swear a lot," Vin said. "You're not supposed to do that in front of ladies."

Cett laughed. "That's the funny thing about Luthadel, lass. They're all so concerned about doing what is 'proper' when people can see them—but, at the same time, they find nothing wrong with going and raping a couple skaa women when the party is through. At least *I* swear to your face."

Elend still hadn't touched his food. "What will happen if you win the vote for the throne?"

Cett shrugged. "Honest answer?"

"Always."

"First thing, I'd have you assassinated," Cett said. "Can't have old kings sticking around."

"And if I step down?" Elend said. "Withdraw from the vote?"

"Step down," Cett said, "vote for me, and then leave town, and I'll let you live."

"And the Assembly?" Elend asked.

"Dissolved," Cett said. "They're a liability. Any time you give a committee power, you just end up with confusion."

"The Assembly gives the people power," Elend said. "That's what a government should provide."

Surprisingly, Cett didn't laugh at that comment. Instead,

he leaned in again, setting one arm on the table, discarding a half-eaten drumstick. "That's the thing, boy. Letting the people rule themselves is fine when everything is bright and happy, but what about when you have two armies facing you? What about when there's a band of insane koloss destroying villages on your frontier? Those aren't the times when you can afford to have an Assembly around to depose you." Cett shook his head. "The price is too high. When you can't have both freedom and safety, boy, which do you choose?"

Elend was silent. "I make my own choice," he finally said. "And I leave the others to make their own as well."

Cett smiled, as if he'd expected such a reply. He started in on another drumstick.

"Let's say I leave," Elend said. "And let's say you do get the throne, protect the city, and dissolve the Assembly. What then? What of the people?"

"Why do you care?"

"You need ask?" Elend said. "I thought you 'understood' me."

Cett smiled. "I put the skaa back to work, in the way the Lord Ruler did. No pay, no emancipated peasant class."

"I can't accept that," Elend said.

"Why not?" Cett said. "It's what they want. You gave them a choice—and they chose to throw you out. Now they're going to choose to put me on the throne. They know that the Lord Ruler's way was the best. One group must rule, and another must serve. Someone has to grow the food and work the forges, boy."

"Perhaps," Elend said. "But you're wrong about one thing."

"And what is that?"

"They're not going to vote for you," Elend said, standing. "They're going to choose me. Faced with the choice between freedom and slavery, they will choose freedom. The men of the Assembly are the finest of this city, and they will make the best choice for its people."

Cett paused, then he laughed. "The best thing about you, lad, is that you can say that and sound serious!"

"I'm leaving, Cett," Elend said, nodding to Vin.

"Oh, sit down, Venture," Cett said, waving toward Elend's chair. "Don't act indignant because I'm being honest with you. We still have things to discuss."

"Such as?" Elend asked.

"Atium," Cett said.

Elend stood for a moment, apparently forcing down his annoyance. When Cett didn't speak immediately, Elend finally sat and began to eat. Vin just picked quietly at her food. As she did, however, she studied the faces of Cett's soldiers and servants. There were bound to be Allomancers mixed among them—finding out how many could give Elend an advantage.

"Your people are starving," Cett said. "And, if my spies are worth their coin, you just got another influx of mouths. You can't last much longer under this siege."

"And?" Elend asked.

"I have food," Cett said. "A lot of it—more than my army needs. Canned goods, packed with the new method the Lord Ruler developed. Long-lasting, no spoilage. Really a marvel of technology. I'd be willing to trade you some of them. . . ."

Elend paused, fork halfway to his lips. Then he lowered it and laughed. "You still think I have the Lord Ruler's atium?"

"Of course you have it," Cett said, frowning. "Where else would it be?"

Elend shook his head, taking a bite of gravy-drenched potato. "Not here, for certain."

"But . . . the rumors . . ." Cett said.

"Breeze spread those rumors," Elend said. "I thought you'd figured out why he joined your group. He wanted you to come to Luthadel so that you'd stop Straff from taking the city."

"But, Breeze did everything he could to *keep* me from coming here," Cett said. "He downplayed the rumors, he tried to distract me, he . . ." Cett trailed off, then he bellowed a laugh. "I thought he was just there to spy! It seems we both underestimated each other."

"My people could still use that food," Elend said.

"And they'll have it—assuming I become king."

"They're starving now," Elend said.

"And their suffering will be your burden," Cett said, his face growing hard. "I can see that you have judged me, Elend Venture. You think me a good man. You're wrong. Honesty does not make a man less of a tyrant. I slaughtered thousands to secure my rule. I put burdens on the skaa that make even the Lord Ruler's hand seem pleasant. I made certain that I stayed in power. I will do the same here."

The men fell silent. Elend ate, but Vin only mixed her food around. If she had missed a poison, she wanted one of them to remain alert. She still wanted to find those Allomancers, and there was only one way to be certain. She turned off her copper, then burned bronze.

There was no Coppercloud burning; Cett apparently didn't care if someone recognized his men as Allomancers. Two of his men were burning pewter. Neither, however, were soldiers; both were pretending to be members of the serving staff who were bringing meals. There was also a Tineye pulsing in the other room, listening.

Why hide Thugs as servants, then use no copper to hide their pulses? In addition, there were no Soothers or Rioters. Nobody was trying to influence Elend's emotions. Neither Cett nor his youthful attendant were burning any metals. Either they weren't actually Allomancers, or they feared exposing themselves. Just to be certain, Vin flared her bronze, seeking to pierce any hidden copperclouds that might be nearby. She could see Cett putting out some obvious Allomancers as a distraction, then hiding the others inside a cloud.

She found nothing. Finally satisfied, she returned to picking at her meal. *How many times has this ability of mine—the ability to pierce copperclouds—proven useful?* She'd forgotten what it was like to be blocked from sensing Allomantic pulses. This one little ability—simple though it seemed—provided an enormous advantage. And the Lord Ruler and his Inquisitors had probably been able to do it from the beginning. What other tricks was she missing, what other secrets had died with the Lord Ruler?

He knew the truth about the Deepness, Vin thought. *He must have. He tried to warn us, at the end. . . .*

Elend and Cett were talking again. Why couldn't she focus on the problems of the city?

"So you don't have any atium at all?" Cett said.

"None that we're willing to sell," Elend said.

"You've searched the city?" Cett asked.

"A dozen times."

"The statues," Cett said. "Perhaps the Lord Ruler hid the metal by melting it down, then building things out of it."

Elend shook his head. "We thought of that. The statues aren't atium, and they aren't hollow either—that would have been a good place to hide metal from Allomancer eyes. We thought maybe that it would be hidden in the palace somewhere, but even the spires are simple iron."

"Caves, tunnels. . . ."

"None that we can find," Elend said. "We've had Allomancers patrol, searching for large sources of metals. We've done everything we can think of, Cett, short of tearing holes in the ground. Trust me. We've been working on this problem for a while."

Cett nodded, sighing. "So, I suppose holding you for ransom would be pointless?"

Elend smiled. "I'm not even king, Cett. The only thing you'd do is make the Assembly less likely to vote for you."

Cett laughed. "Suppose I'll have to let you go, then."

Alendi was never the Hero of Ages. At best, I have amplified his virtues, creating a Hero where there was none. At worst, I fear that all we believe may have been corrupted.

36

ONCE THIS WAREHOUSE HAD HELD swords and armor, scattered across its floor in heaps, like some mythical treasure. Sazed remembered walking through it, marveling at the preparations Kelsier had made without alerting any of his crewmembers. Those weapons had armed the rebellion on the eve of the Survivor's own death, letting it take the city.

Those weapons were now stored in lockers and armories. In their place, a desperate, beaten people huddled in what blankets they could find. There were very few men, none of fighting quality; Straff had pressed those into his army. These others—the weak, the sickly, the wounded—he had allowed to Luthadel, knowing that Elend wouldn't turn them away.

Sazed moved among them, offering what comfort he could. They had no furniture, and even changes of clothing were becoming scarce in the city. The merchants, realizing that warmth would be a premium for the upcoming winter, had begun raising prices on all their wares, not just foodstuffs.

Sazed knelt beside a crying woman. "Peace, Genedere," he said, his coppermind reminding him of her name.

She shook her head. She had lost three children in the koloss attack, two more in the flight to Luthadel. Now the final one—the babe she had carried the entire way—was sick. Sazed took the child from her arms, carefully studying his symptoms. Little had changed from the day before.

"Is there hope, Master Terrisman?" Genedere asked.

Sazed glanced down at the thin, glassy-eyed baby. The chances were not good. How could he tell her such a thing?

"As long as he breathes, there is hope, dear woman," Sazed said. "I will ask the king to increase your portion of food—you need strength to give suck. You *must* keep him warm. Stay near the fires, and use a damp cloth to drip water in his mouth even when he is not eating. He has great need of liquids."

Genedere nodded dully, taking back the baby. How Sazed wished he could give her more. A dozen different religions passed through his mind. He had spent his entire life trying to encourage people to believe in something other than the Lord Ruler. Yet, for some reason, at this moment he found it difficult to preach one of them to Genedere.

It had been different before the Collapse. Each time he'd spoken of a religion, Sazed had felt a subtle sense of rebellion. Even if people hadn't accepted the things he taught—and they rarely had—his words had reminded them that there had once been beliefs other than the doctrines of the Steel Ministry.

Now there was nothing to rebel against. In the face of the terrible grief he saw in Genedere's eyes, he found it difficult to speak of religions long dead, gods long forgotten. Esoterica would not ease this woman's pain.

Sazed stood, moving on to the next group of people.

"Sazed?"

Sazed turned. He hadn't noticed Tindwyl entering the warehouse. The doors of the large structure were closed against approaching night, and the firepits gave an inconsistent light. Holes had been knocked in the roof to let out the smoke; if one looked up, trails of mist could be seen creeping into the room, though they evaporated before they reached halfway to the floor.

The refugees didn't often look up.

"You've been here nearly all day," Tindwyl said. The room was remarkably quiet, considering its occupancy. Fires crackled, and people lay silent in their pain or numbness.

"There are many wounded here," Sazed said. "I am the

best one to look after them, I think. I am not alone—the king has sent others and Lord Breeze is here, Soothing the people's despair."

Sazed nodded to the side, where Breeze sat in a chair, ostensibly reading a book. He looked terribly out of place in the room, wearing his fine three-piece suit. Yet, his mere presence said something remarkable, in Sazed's estimation.

These poor people, Sazed thought. *Their lives were terrible under the Lord Ruler. Now even what little they had has been taken from them.* And they were only a tiny number—four hundred compared with the hundreds of thousands who still lived in Luthadel.

What would happen when the final stores of food ran out? Rumors were already abroad regarding the poisoned wells, and Sazed had just heard that some of their stored food had been sabotaged as well. What would happen to these people? How long could the siege continue?

In fact, what would happen when the siege ended? What would happen when the armies finally began to attack and pillage? What destruction, what grief, would the soldiers cause in searching for hidden atium?

"You do care for them," Tindwyl said quietly, stepping up.

Sazed turned toward her. Then he looked down. "Not as much as I should, perhaps."

"No," Tindwyl said. "I can see it. You confuse me, Sazed."

"I seem to have a talent in that area."

"You look tired. Where is your bronzemind?"

Suddenly, Sazed felt the fatigue. He'd been ignoring it, but her words seemed to bring it in like a wave, rolling over him.

He sighed. "I used most of my wakefulness in my run to Luthadel. I was so eager to get here. . . ." His studies had languished recently. With the problems in the city, and the arrival of the refugees, he hadn't had much time. Besides, he had already transcribed the rubbing. Further work would require detailed cross-referencing to other works, searching for clues. He probably wouldn't even have time to . . .

He frowned, noting the odd look in Tindwyl's eyes.

"All right," she said, sighing. "Show me."

"Show you?"

"Whatever it was you found," she said. "The discovery that prompted you to run across two dominances. Show it to me."

Suddenly, everything seemed to lighten. His fatigue, his worry, even his sorrow. "I would love to," he said quietly.

Another job well done, Breeze thought, congratulating himself as he watched the two Terrismen leave the warehouse.

Most people, even noblemen, misunderstood Soothing. They thought of it as some kind of mind control, and even those who knew more presumed that Soothing was an invasive, terrible thing.

Breeze had never seen it that way. Soothing wasn't invasive. If it was, then ordinary interaction with another person was comparably invasive. Soothing, when done right, was no more a violation of another person than it was for a woman to wear a low-cut gown or speak in a commanding voice. All three produced common, understandable, and—most important—natural reactions in people.

Take Sazed, for example. Was it "invasive" to make the man less fatigued, so he could better go about his ministrations? Was it wrong to Soothe away his pain—just a bit—thereby making him better able to cope with the suffering?

Tindwyl was an even better example. Perhaps some would call Breeze a meddler for Soothing her sense of responsibility, and her disappointment, when she saw Sazed. But, Breeze had not created the emotions that the disappointment had been overshadowing. Emotions like curiosity. Respect. Love.

No, if Soothing were simple "mind control," Tindwyl would have turned away from Sazed as soon as the two left Breeze's area of influence. But Breeze knew that she wouldn't. A crucial decision had been made, and Breeze had not made that decision for her. The moment had been building for weeks; it would have occurred with or without Breeze.

He had just helped it happen sooner.

Smiling to himself, Breeze checked his pocket watch. He still had a few more minutes, and he settled back in his chair, sending out a general Soothing wave, lessening people's grief and pain. Focusing on so many at once, he couldn't be very specific; some would find themselves made a little emotionally numb as he Pushed too strongly against them. But, it would be good for the group as a whole.

He didn't read his book; in truth, he couldn't understand how Elend and the rest spent so much time with them. Dreadfully boring things. Breeze could only see himself reading if there were no people around. Instead, he went back to what he'd been doing before Sazed had drawn his attention. He studied the refugees, trying to decide what each one was feeling.

This was the other great misunderstanding about Soothing. Allomancy wasn't nearly as important as observational talent. True, having a subtle touch certainly helped. However, Soothing didn't give an Allomancer the ability to know someone's feelings. Those, Breeze had to guess on his own.

It all came back to what was natural. Even the most inexperienced skaa would realize they were being Soothed if unexpected emotions began bouncing around inside of them. True subtlety in Soothing was about encouraging natural emotions, all done by carefully making the right other emotions less powerful. People were a patchwork of feelings; usually, what they thought they were "feeling" at the moment only related to which emotions were currently most dominant within them.

The careful Soother saw what was beneath the surface. He understood what a man was feeling, even when that man himself didn't understand—or acknowledge—those emotions. Such was the case with Sazed and Tindwyl.

Odd pair, that one, Breeze thought to himself, idly Soothing one of the skaa to make him more relaxed as he tried to sleep. *The rest of the crew is convinced that those two are enemies. But, hatred rarely creates that measure of bitterness and frustration. No, those two emotions come from an entirely different set of problems.*

Of course, isn't Sazed supposed to be a eunuch? I wonder how this all came about. . . .

His speculations trailed off as the warehouse doors opened. Elend walked in—Ham, unfortunately, accompanying him. Elend was wearing one of his white uniforms, complete with white gloves and a sword. The white was an important symbol; with all of the ash and soot in the city, a man in white was quite striking. Elend's uniforms had to been crafted of special fabrics designed to be resistant to ash, and they still had to be scrubbed every day. The effect was worth the effort.

Breeze immediately picked at Elend's emotions, making the man less tired, less uncertain—though the second was becoming almost unnecessary. That was partially the Terriswoman's doing; Breeze had been impressed with her ability to change how people felt, considering her lack of Allomancy.

Breeze left Elend's emotions of disgust and pity; both were appropriate considering the environment. He did, however, give Ham a nudge to make him less argumentative; Breeze wasn't in a mood to deal with the man's prattlings at the moment.

He stood as the two men approached. People perked up as they saw Elend, his presence somehow bringing them a hope that Breeze couldn't emulate with Allomancy. They whispered, calling Elend King.

"Breeze," Elend said, nodding. "Is Sazed here?"

"He just left, I'm afraid," Breeze said.

Elend seemed distracted. "Ah, well," he said. "I'll find him later." Elend looked around the room, lips downturned. "Ham, tomorrow, I want you to round up the clothing merchants on Kenton Street and bring them here to see this."

"They might not like that, Elend," Ham said.

"I hope they don't," Elend said. "But we'll see how they feel about their prices once they visit this room. I can understand food's expense, considering its scarcity. However, there is no reason but greed to deny the people clothing."

Ham nodded, but Breeze could see the reticence in his posture. Did the others realize how strangely nonconfrontational Ham was? He liked to argue with friends, but he rarely actually came to any conclusions in his philosophizing. Plus, he absolutely hated fighting with strangers; Breeze had always found that an odd attribute in one who was hired, essentially, to hit people. He gave Ham a bit of a Soothing to make him less worried about confronting the merchants.

"You aren't going to stay here all night, are you, Breeze?" Elend asked.

"Lord Ruler, no!" Breeze said. "My dear man, you're lucky you managed to get me to come at all. Honestly, this is no place for a gentleman. The dirt, the depressing atmosphere—and that's not even making mention of the smell!"

Ham frowned. "Breeze, someday you're going to have to learn to think about other people."

"As long as I can think about them from a distance, Hammond, I shall be happy to engage in the activity."

Ham shook his head. "You're hopeless."

"Are you heading back to the palace then?" Elend asked.

"Yes, actually," Breeze said, checking his pocket watch.

"Do you need a ride?"

"I brought my own carriage," Breeze said.

Elend nodded, then turned to Ham, and the two retreated the way they had come, talking about Elend's next meeting with one of the other Assemblymen.

Breeze wandered into the palace a short time later. He nodded to the door guards, Soothing away their mental fatigue. They perked up in response, watching the mists with renewed vigilance. It wouldn't last long, but little touches like that were second nature to Breeze.

It was getting late, and few people were in the hallways. He made his way through the kitchens, Nudging the scullery maids to make them more chatty. It would make their cleaning pass more quickly. Beyond the kitchens he found a small stone room, lit by a couple of plain lamps, set with a small table. It was one of the palace's boothlike, solitary dining rooms.

Clubs sat in one corner of the booth, gimped leg stretched out on the bench. He eyed Breeze with a scowl. "You're late."

"You're early," Breeze said, sliding into the bench across from Clubs.

"Same thing," Clubs grumbled.

There was a second cup on the table, along with a bottle of wine. Breeze unbuttoned his vest, sighed quietly, and poured himself a cup as he leaned back with his legs up on his bench.

Clubs sipped his wine.

"You have your cloud up?" Breeze asked.

"Around you?" Clubs said. "Always."

Breeze smiled, taking a sip, and relaxed. Though he rarely had opportunities to use his powers anymore, Clubs was a Smoker. When he was burning copper, every Allomancer's abilities were invisible to those burning bronze. But more important—at least to Breeze—burning copper made Clubs immune to any form of emotional Allomancy.

"Don't see why that makes you so happy," Clubs said. "I thought you liked playing with emotions."

"I do," Breeze said.

"Then why come drink with me every night?" Clubs asked.

"You mind the company?"

Clubs didn't answer. That was pretty much his way of saying he didn't mind. Breeze eyed the grumpy general. Most of the other crewmembers stayed away from Clubs; Kelsier had brought him in at the last moment, since the Coppercloud they usually used had died.

"Do you know what it's like, Clubs?" Breeze asked. "Being a Soother?"

"No."

"It gives you remarkable control. It's a wonderful feeling, being able to influence those around you, always feeling like you have a handle on how people will react."

"Sounds delightful," Clubs said flatly.

"And yet, it does things to you. I spend most of my time watching people—tweaking, Nudging, and Soothing. That's changed me. I don't . . . look at people the same way. It's hard to just be friends with someone when you see them as something to be influenced and changed."

Clubs grunted. "So that's why we never used to see you with women."

Breeze nodded. "I can't help it anymore. I always touch the emotions of everyone around me. And so, when a woman comes to love me . . ." He liked to think he wasn't invasive. Yet, how could he trust anyone who said they loved him? Was it he, or his Allomancy, that they responded to?

Clubs filled his cup. "You're a lot sillier than you act."

Breeze smiled. Clubs was one of the few people who was completely immune to his touch. Emotional Allomancy wouldn't work on him, and he was always completely forthcoming with his emotions: everything made him grumpy. Manipulating him through non-Allomantic means had proven to be a fruitless waste of time.

Breeze regarded his wine. "The amusing thing is, you almost didn't join the crew because of me."

"Damn Soothers," Clubs muttered.

"But you're immune to us."

"To your Allomancy, maybe," Clubs said. "But that isn't the only way you people do things. A man always has to watch himself around Soothers."

"Then why let me join you every evening for wine?"

Clubs was silent for a moment, and Breeze almost thought he wasn't going to respond. Finally, Clubs muttered, "You're not as bad as most."

Breeze took a gulp of wine. "That is as honest a compliment as I think I've ever received."

"Don't let it ruin you," Clubs said.

"Oh, I think I'm too late for ruining," Breeze said, topping off his cup. "This crew . . . Kell's plan . . . has already done a thorough job of that."

Clubs nodded in agreement.

"What happened to us, Clubs?" Breeze asked. "I joined Kell for the challenge. I never did know why you joined."

"Money."

Breeze nodded. "His plan fell apart, his army got destroyed, and we stayed. Then he died, and we *still* stayed. This blasted kingdom of Elend's is doomed, you know."

"We won't last another month," Clubs said. It wasn't idle pessimism; Breeze knew people well enough to tell when they were serious.

"And yet, here we are," Breeze said. "I spent all day making skaa feel better about the fact that their families had been slaughtered. You spent all day training soldiers that—with or without your help—will barely last a few heartbeats against a determined foe. We follow a boy of a king who doesn't seem to have a shade of a clue just how bad his predicament is. Why?"

Clubs shook his head. "Kelsier. Gave us a city, made us think we were responsible for protecting it."

"But we aren't that kind of people," Breeze said. "We're thieves and scammers. We shouldn't care. I mean . . . I've gotten so bad that I Soothe scullery maids so that they'll have a happier time at work! I might as well start dressing in pink and carrying around flowers. I could probably make quite a bundle at weddings."

Clubs snorted. Then he raised his cup. "To the Survivor," he said. "May he be damned for knowing us better than we knew ourselves."

Breeze raised his own cup. "Damn him," he agreed quietly.

The two fell silent. Talking to Clubs tended to turn into . . . well, not talking. However, Breeze felt a simple contentment. Soothing was wonderful; it made him who he was. But it was also work. Even birds couldn't fly all the time.

"*There* you are."

Breeze snapped his eyes open. Allrianne stood at the entrance to the room, just at the edge of the table. She wore light blue; where had she gotten so many dresses? Her makeup was, of course, immaculate—and there was a bow in her hair. That long blond hair—common in the West but almost unheard of in the Central Dominance—and that perky, inviting figure.

Desire immediately blossomed inside of him. *No!* Breeze thought. *She's half your age. You're a dirty old man. Dirty!* "Allrianne," he said uncomfortably, "shouldn't you be in bed or something?"

She rolled her eyes, shooing his legs out of the way so she could sit on the bench beside him. "It's only nine o'clock, Breeze. I'm eighteen, not ten."

You might as well be, he thought, looking away from her, trying to focus on something else. He knew that he should be stronger, shouldn't let the girl get near him, but he did nothing as she slid up to him and took a drink from his cup.

He sighed, putting his arm around her shoulders. Clubs just shook his head, the hint of a smile on his lips.

"Well," Vin said quietly, "that answers one question."

"Mistress?" OreSeur said, sitting across the table from her in the dark room. With her Allomancer's ears, she could hear exactly what was going on in the next boothlike room over.

"Allrianne is an Allomancer," Vin said.

"Really?"

Vin nodded. "She's been Rioting Breeze's emotions ever since she arrived, making him more attracted to her."

"One would think that he'd notice," OreSeur said.

"You'd think," Vin said. She probably shouldn't feel as amused as she did. The girl could be a Mistborn—though the idea of that puff flying through the mists seemed ridiculous.

Which is probably exactly how she wants me to think, Vin thought. *I have to remember Kliss and Shan—neither one of them turned out to be the person I thought they were.*

"Breeze probably just doesn't think his emotions are unnatural," Vin said. "He must be attracted to her already."

OreSeur closed his mouth and cocked his head—his dog's version of a frown.

"I know," Vin agreed. "But, at least we know he isn't the one using Allomancy to seduce *her*. Either way, that's irrelevant. Clubs isn't the kandra."

"How could you possibly know that, Mistress?"

Vin paused. Clubs always turned his copper on around Breeze; it was one of the few times he used it. However, it was difficult to tell if someone was burning copper. After all, if they turned on their metal, they hid themselves by default.

But Vin could pierce copperclouds. She could sense Allrianne's Rioting; she could even sense a faint thumping coming from Clubs himself, copper's own Allomantic pulse, something that Vin suspected few people beyond herself and the Lord Ruler had ever heard.

"I just know," Vin said.

"If you say so, Mistress," OreSeur said. "But . . . didn't you already decide the spy was Demoux?"

"I wanted to check Clubs anyway," she said. "Before I did anything drastic."

"Drastic?"

Vin sat quietly for a moment. She didn't have much proof, but she did have her instincts—and those instincts told her Demoux was the spy. That sneaking way he'd gone out the other night . . . the obvious logic of choosing him . . . it all fit.

She stood. Things were getting too dangerous, too sensitive. She couldn't ignore it any longer. "Come on," she said, leaving the booth behind. "It's time to put Demoux in prison."

"What do you mean you *lost* him?" Vin asked, standing outside the door to Demoux's room.

The servant flushed. "My lady, I'm sorry. I watched him, like you told me—but he went out on patrol. Should I have followed? I mean, don't you think that would have looked suspicious?"

Vin cursed quietly to herself. She knew that she didn't have much right to be angry, however. *I should have told Ham straight off,* she thought with frustration.

"My lady, he only left a few minutes ago," the servant said.

Vin glanced at OreSeur, then took off down the corridor. As soon as they reached a window, Vin leaped out into the dark night, OreSeur following behind her, dropping the short distance to the courtyard.

Last time, I saw him come back in through the gates to

the palace grounds, she thought, running through the mist. She found a couple of soldiers there, guarding.

"Did Captain Demoux come this way?" she demanded, bursting into their ring of torchlight.

They perked up, at first shocked, then confused.

"Lady Heir?" one of them said. "Yes, he just went out, on patrol just a minute or two ago."

"By himself?" Vin asked.

They nodded.

"Isn't that a little odd?"

They shrugged. "He goes by himself sometimes," one said. "We don't question. He's our superior, after all."

"Which way?" Vin demanded.

One pointed, and Vin took off, OreSeur at her side. *I should have watched better. I should have hired real spies to keep an eye on him. I should have—*

She froze. Up ahead, walking down a quite street in the mists, was a figure, walking into the city. Demoux.

Vin dropped a coin and threw herself into the air, passing far over his head, landing on top of a building. He continued, oblivious. Demoux or kandra, neither would have Allomantic powers.

Vin paused, daggers out, ready to spring. But . . . she still didn't have any real proof. The part of her that Kelsier had transformed, the part that had come to trust, thought of the Demoux she knew.

Do I really believe he's the kandra? she thought. *Or do I just* want *him to be the kandra, so that I don't have to suspect my real friends?*

He continued to walk below, her tin-enhanced ears easily picking out his footfalls. Behind, OreSeur scrambled up onto the top of the roof, then padded over and sat down beside her.

I can't just attack, she thought. *I need to at least watch, see where he's going. Get proof.* Perhaps learn something in the process.

She waved to OreSeur, and they quietly followed along the rooftops, trailing Demoux. Soon, Vin noticed something odd—a flicker of firelight illuminating the mists a few streets over, making haunted shadows of buildings.

Vin glanced at Demoux, trailing him with her eyes as he wandered down an alleyway, moving toward the illumination.

What . . . ?

Vin threw herself off the roof. It took only three bounds for her to reach the source of the light. A modest bonfire crackled in the center of a small square. Skaa huddled around it for warmth, looking a little frightened in the mists. Vin was surprised to see them. She hadn't seen skaa go out in the mists since the night of the Collapse.

Demoux approached down a side street, greeting several of the others. In the firelight she could confirm for certain that it was him—or, at least, a kandra with his face.

There were, perhaps, two hundred people in the square. Demoux moved as if to sit on the cobblestones, but someone quickly approached with a chair. A young woman brought him a mug of something steaming, which he received gratefully.

Vin leaped to a rooftop, staying low to keep from being exposed by the firelight. More skaa arrived, mostly in groups, but some brave individuals came alone.

A sound came from behind her, and Vin turned as OreSeur—apparently having barely made the jump—scrambled the last few feet over the edge onto the roof. He glanced down at the street below, shook his head, then padded over to join her. She raised a finger to her lips, nodding down at the growing group of people. OreSeur cocked his head at the sight, but said nothing.

Finally, Demoux stood, holding the still steaming cup in his hands. People gathered around, sitting on the cold cobblestones, huddled beneath blankets or cloaks.

"We shouldn't fear the mists, my friends," Demoux said. His wasn't the voice of a strong leader or forceful battle commander—it was the voice of hardened youth, a little hesitant, but compelling nonetheless.

"The Survivor taught us of this," he continued. "I know it's very hard to think of the mists without remembering stories of mistwraiths or other horrors. But, the Survivor gave the mists to us. We should try and remember him, through them."

Lord Ruler . . . Vin thought with shock. *He's one of them—a member of the Church of the Survivor!* She wavered, uncertain what to think. Was he the kandra or wasn't he? Why would the kandra meet with a group of people like this? But . . . why would Demoux himself do it?

"I know it's hard," Demoux said below, "without the Survivor. I know you're afraid of the armies. Trust me, I know. I see them too. I know you suffer beneath this siege. I . . . don't know if I can even tell you not to worry. The Survivor himself knew great hardship—the death of his wife, his imprisonment in the Pits of Hathsin. But he survived. That's the point, isn't it? We have to live on, no matter how hard this all gets. We'll win, in the end. Just like he did."

He stood with his mug in his hands, looking nothing like the skaa preachers Vin had seen. Kelsier had chosen a passionate man to found his religion—or, more precisely, to found the revolution the religion had come from. Kelsier had needed leaders who could enflame supporters, whip them up into a destructive upheaval.

Demoux was something different. He didn't shout, but spoke calmly. Yet, people paid attention. They sat on the stones around him, looking up with hopeful—even worshipful—eyes.

"The Lady Heir," one of them whispered. "What of her?"

"Lady Vin bears a great responsibility," Demoux said. "You can see the weight bowing her down, and how frustrated she is with the problems in the city. She is a straightforward woman, and I don't think she likes the Assembly's politicking."

"But, she'll protect us, right?" one asked.

"Yes," Demoux said. "Yes, I believe she will. Sometimes, I think that she's even more powerful than the Survivor was. You know that he only had two years to practice as a Mistborn? She's barely had that much time herself."

Vin turned away. *It comes back to that,* she thought. *They sound rational until they talk about me, and then . . .*

"She'll bring us peace, someday," Demoux said. "The heir will bring back the sun, stop the ash from falling. But we have to survive until then. And we have to fight. The Survivor's entire work was to see the Lord Ruler dead and make us free. What gratitude do we show if we run now that armies have come?

"Go and tell your Assemblymen that you don't want Lord Cett, or even Lord Penrod, to be your king. The vote happens in one day, and we *need* to make certain the right man is made king. The Survivor chose Elend Venture, and that is whom we must follow."

That's new, Vin thought.

"Lord Elend is weak," one of the people said. "He won't defend us."

"Lady Vin loves him," Demoux said. "She wouldn't love a weak man. Penrod and Cett treat you like the skaa *used* to be treated, and that's why you think they're strong. But that's not strength—it's oppression. We have to be better than that! We have to trust the Survivor's judgment!"

Vin relaxed against the lip of the roof, tension melting a bit. If Demoux really was the spy, then he wasn't going to give her any evidence this night. So, she put her knives away, then rested with her arms folded on the rooftop's edge. The fire crackled in the cool winter evening, sending billows of smoke to mix with the mists, and Demoux continued to speak in his quiet, reassuring voice, teaching the people about Kelsier.

It's not even really a religion, Vin thought as she listened. *The theology is so simple—not at all like the complex beliefs that Sazed speaks about.*

Demoux taught basic concepts. He held up Kelsier as a model, talking about survival, and about enduring hardships. Vin could see why the direct words would appeal to the skaa. The people really only had two choices: to struggle on, or to give up. Demoux's teachings gave them an excuse to keep living.

The skaa didn't need rituals, prayers, or codes. Not yet. They were too inexperienced with religion in general, too frightened of it, to want such things. But, the more she listened, the more Vin understood the Church of the Survivor. It was what they needed; it took what the skaa already knew—a life filled with hardship—and elevated it to a higher, more optimistic plane.

And the teachings were still evolving. The deification of Kelsier she had expected; even the reverence for her was understandable. But, where did Demoux get the promises that Vin would stop the ash and bring back the sun? How did he know to preach of green grasses and blue skies, describing the world as it was known only in some of the world's most obscure texts?

He described a strange world of colors and beauty—a place foreign and difficult to conceive, but somehow wonderful all the same. Flowers and green plants were strange, alien things to these people; even Vin had trouble visualizing them, and she had heard Sazed's descriptions.

Demoux was giving the skaa a paradise. It had to be something completely removed from normal experience, for the mundane world was not a place of hope. Not with a foodless winter approaching, not with armies threatening and the government in turmoil.

Vin pulled back as Demoux finally ended the meeting. She lay for a moment, trying to decide how she felt. She'd been near certain about Demoux, but now her suspicions seemed unfounded. He'd gone out at night, true, but she saw now what he was doing. Plus, he'd acted so suspiciously when sneaking out. It seemed to her, as she reflected, that a kandra would know how to go about things in a much more natural way.

It's not him, she thought. *Or, if it is, he's not going to be as easy to unmask as I thought.* She frowned in frustration. Finally, she just sighed, rising, and walked to the other side of the roof. OreSeur followed, and Vin glanced at him. "When Kelsier told you to take his body," she said, "what did he want you to preach to these people?"

"Mistress?" OreSeur asked.

"He had you appear, as if you were him returned from the grave."

"Yes."

"Well, what did he have you say?"

OreSeur shrugged. "Very simple things, Mistress. I told them that the time for rebellion had arrived. I told them that I—Kelsier—had returned to give them hope for victory."

I represent that thing you've never been able to kill, no matter how hard you try. They had been Kelsier's final words, spoken face-to-face with the Lord Ruler. *I am hope.*

I am hope.

Was it any wonder that this concept would become central to the church that sprang up around him? "Did he have you teach things like we just heard Demoux say?" Vin asked. "About the ash no longer falling, and the sun turning yellow?"

"No, Mistress."

"That's what I thought," Vin said as she heard rustling on the stones below. She glanced over the side of the building, and saw Demoux returning to the palace.

Vin dropped to the alleyway floor behind him. To the man's credit, he heard her, and he spun, hand on dueling cane.

"Peace, Captain," she said, rising.

"Lady Vin?" he asked with surprise.

She nodded, approaching closer so that he'd be able to see her better in the night. Fading torchlight still lit the air from behind, swirls of mist playing with shadows.

"I didn't know you were a member of the Church of the Survivor," she said softly.

He looked down. Though he was easily two hands taller than she, he seemed to shrink a bit before her. "I . . . I know it makes you uncomfortable. I'm sorry."

"It's all right," she said. "You do a good thing for the people. Elend will appreciate hearing of your loyalty."

Demoux looked up. "Do you have to tell him?"

"He needs to know what the people believe, Captain. Why would you want me to keep it quiet?"

Demoux sighed. "I just . . . I don't want the crew to think I'm out here pandering to the people. Ham thinks preaching about the Survivor is silly, and Lord Breeze says the only reason to encourage the church is to make people more pliant."

Vin regarded him in the darkness. "You really believe, don't you?"

"Yes, my lady."

"But you knew Kelsier," she said. "You were with us from near the beginning. You know he's no god."

Demoux looked up, a bit of a challenge in his eyes. "He died to overthrow the Lord Ruler."

"That doesn't make him divine."

"He taught us how to survive, to have hope."

"You survived before," Vin said. "People had hope before Kelsier got thrown in those pits."

"Not like we do now," Demoux said. "Besides . . . he had power, my lady. I felt it."

Vin paused. She knew the story; Kelsier had used Demoux as an example to the rest of the army in a fight with a skeptic, directing his blows with Allomancy, making Demoux seem as if he had supernatural powers.

"Oh, I know about Allomancy now," Demoux said. "But . . . I felt him Pushing on my sword that day. I felt him use me, making me more than I was. I think I can still feel him, sometimes. Strengthening my arm, guiding my blade. . . ."

Vin frowned. "Do you remember the first time we met?"

Demoux nodded. "Yes. You came to the caverns where we were hiding on the day when the army was destroyed. I was on guard duty. You know, my lady—even then, I knew that Kelsier would come for us. I knew that he'd come and get those of us who had been faithful and guide us back to Luthadel."

He went to those caves because I forced him to. He wanted to get himself killed fighting an army on his own.

"The destruction of the army was a test," Demoux said, looking up into the mists. "These armies . . . the siege . . . they're just tests. To see if we will survive or not."

"And the ash?" Vin asked. "Where did you hear that it would stop falling?"

Demoux turned back to her. "The Survivor taught that, didn't he?"

Vin shook her head.

"A lot of the people are saying it," Demoux said. "It must be true. It fits with everything else—the yellow sun, the blue sky, the plants. . . ."

"Yes, but where did you first hear those things?"

"I'm not sure, my lady."

Where did you hear that I would be the one to bring them about? she thought, but she somehow couldn't bring herself to voice the question. Regardless, she knew the answer: Demoux wouldn't know. Rumors were propagating. It would be difficult indeed to trace them back to their source now.

"Go back to the palace," Vin said. "I have to tell Elend what I saw, but I'll ask him not to tell the rest of the crew."

"Thank you, my lady," Demoux said, bowing. He turned and hurried away. A second later, Vin heard a thump from behind: OreSeur, jumping down to the street.

She turned. "I was sure it was him."

"Mistress?"

"The kandra," Vin said, turning back toward the disappearing Demoux. "I thought I'd discovered him."

"And?"

She shook her head. "It's like Dockson—I think Demoux knows too much to be faking. He feels . . . real to me."

"My brethren—"

"Are quite skilled," Vin said with a sigh. "Yes, I know. But we're not going to arrest him. Not tonight, at least. We'll keep an eye on him, but I just don't think it's him anymore."

OreSeur nodded.

"Come on," she said. "I want to check on Elend."

And so, I come to the focus of my argument. I apologize. Even forcing my words into steel, sitting and scratching in this frozen cave, I am prone to ramble.

37

SAZED GLANCED AT THE WINDOW SHUTTERS, noting the hesitant beams of light that were beginning to shine through the cracks. *Morning already?* he thought. *We studied all night?* It hardly seemed possible. He had tapped no wakefulness, yet he felt more alert—more alive—than he had in days.

Tindwyl sat in the chair beside him. Sazed's desk was filled with loose papers, two sets of ink and pen waiting to be used. There were no books; Keepers had no need of such.

"Ah!" Tindwyl said, grabbing a pen and beginning to write. She didn't look tired either, but she had likely dipped into her bronzemind, tapping the wakefulness stored within.

Sazed watched her write. She almost looked young again; he hadn't seen such overt excitement in her since she had been abandoned by the Breeders some ten years before. On that day, her grand work finished, she had finally joined her fellow Keepers. Sazed had been the one to present her with the collected knowledge that had been discovered during her thirty years of cloistered childbirth.

It hadn't taken her long to achieve a place in the Synod. By then, however, Sazed had been ousted from their ranks.

Tindwyl finished writing. "The passage is from a biography of King Wednegon," she said. "He was one of the last leaders who resisted the Lord Ruler in any sort of meaningful combat."

"I know who he was," Sazed said, smiling.

She paused. "Of course." She obviously wasn't accustomed to studying with someone who had access to as much information as she did. She pushed the written passage over to Sazed; even with his mental indexes and self-notes, it would be faster for her to write out the passage than it would be for him to try and find it within his own copperminds.

I spent a great deal of time with the king during his final weeks, the text read.

> *He seemed frustrated, as one might imagine. His soldiers could not stand against the Conqueror's koloss, and his men had been beaten back repeatedly ever since FellSpire. However, the king didn't blame his soldiers. He thought that his problems came from another source: food.*
>
> *He mentioned this idea several times during those last days. He thought that if he'd had more food, he could have held out. In this, Wednegon blamed the Deepness. For, though the Deepness had been defeated—or at least weakened—its touch had depleted Darrelnai's food stores.*
>
> *His people could not both raise food and resist the Conqueror's demon armies. In the end, that was why they fell.*

Sazed nodded slowly. "How much of this text do we have?"

"Not much," Tindwyl said. "Six or seven pages. This is the only section that mentions the Deepness."

Sazed sat quietly for a moment, rereading the passage. Finally, he looked up at Tindwyl. "You think Lady Vin is right, don't you? You think the Deepness was mist."

Tindwyl nodded.

"I agree," Sazed said. "At the very least, what we now call 'the Deepness' was some sort of change in the mist."

"And your arguments from before?"

"Proven wrong," Sazed said, setting down the paper. "By your words and my own studies. I did not wish this to be true, Tindwyl."

Tindwyl raised an eyebrow. "You defied the Synod again to seek after something you didn't even want to believe?"

He looked into her eyes. "There is a difference between fearing something and desiring it. The return of the Deepness could destroy us. I did not want this information—but neither could I pass by the opportunity to discover it."

Tindwyl looked away. "I do not believe that this will destroy us, Sazed. You have made a grand discovery, that I will admit. The writings of the man Kwaan tell us much. Indeed, if the Deepness was the mists, then our understanding of the Lord Ruler's Ascension has been enhanced greatly."

"And if the mists are growing stronger?" Sazed asked. "If, by killing the Lord Ruler, we also destroyed whatever force was keeping the mists chained?"

"We have no proof that the mists are coming by day," Tindwyl said. "And on the possibility of them killing people, we have only your hesitant theories."

Sazed glanced away. On the table, his fingers had smudged Tindwyl's hurriedly written words. "That is true," he said.

Tindwyl sighed softly in the dim room. "Why do you never defend yourself, Sazed?"

"What defense is there?"

"There must be some. You apologize and ask forgiveness, but your apparent guilt never seems to change your behavior! Do you never think that, perhaps, if you had been more outspoken, you might be leading the Synod? They cast you out because you refused to offer arguments on your own behalf. You're the most contrite rebel I've ever known."

Sazed didn't respond. He glanced to the side, seeing her concerned eyes. Beautiful eyes. *Foolish thoughts,* he told himself, looking away. *You've always known that. Some things were meant for others, but never for you.*

"You were right about the Lord Ruler, Sazed," Tindwyl said. "Perhaps the others would have followed you if you had been just a little more . . . insistent."

Sazed shook his head. "I am not a man from one of your biographies, Tindwyl. I am not even, really, a man."

"You are a better man than they, Sazed," Tindwyl said quietly. "The frustrating part is, I've never been able to figure out why."

They fell silent. Sazed rose and walked to the window, opening the shutters, letting in the light. Then he extinguished the room's lamp.

"I will leave today," Tindwyl said.

"Leave?" Sazed asked. "The armies might not let you pass."

"I wasn't going to pass them, Sazed. I plan to visit them. I have given knowledge to young Lord Venture; I need to offer the same aid to his opponents."

"Ah," Sazed said. "I see. I should have realized this."

"I doubt they will listen as he has," Tindwyl said, a hint of fondness slipping into her voice. "Venture is a fine man."

"A fine king," Sazed said.

Tindwyl didn't respond. She looked at the table, with its scattered notations, each drawn from one or another of their copperminds, scribbled in haste, then shown and reread.

What was this night, then? This night of study, this night sharing thoughts and discoveries?

She was still beautiful. Auburn hair graying, but kept long and straight. Face marked by a lifetime of hardship that had not broken her. And eyes . . . keen eyes, with the knowledge and love of learning that only a Keeper could claim.

I should not consider these things, Sazed thought again. *There is no purpose to them. There never was.* "You must go, then," he said, turning.

"Again, you refuse to argue," she said.

"What would be the point of argument? You are a wise and determined person. You must be guided by your own conscience."

"Sometimes, people only seem determined upon one course because they have been offered no other options."

Sazed turned toward her. The room was quiet, the only sounds coming from the courtyard below. Tindwyl sat half in sunlight, her bright robes slowly growing more illuminated as the shadows fell away. She seemed to be implying something, something he had not expected to ever hear from her.

"I am confused," he said, sitting back down in a slow motion. "What of your duty as a Keeper?"

"It is important," she admitted. "But . . . certain, occasional exceptions must be allowed. This rubbing you found . . . well, perhaps it merits further study before I depart."

Sazed watched her, trying to read her eyes. *What is it I feel?* he wondered. Confused? Dumbfounded?

Afraid?

"I cannot be what you wish, Tindwyl," he said. "I am not a man."

She waved her hand indifferently. "I have had more than enough of 'men' and childbearing over the years, Sazed. I have done my duty to the Terris people. I should like to stay away from them for a time, I think. A part of me resents them, for what was done to me."

He opened his mouth to speak, but she held up a hand. "I know, Sazed. I took that duty upon myself, and am glad for my service. But . . . during the years spent alone, meeting with the Keepers only on occasion, I found it frustrating that all their planning seemed to be directed at maintaining their status as a conquered people.

"I only ever saw one man pushing the Synod toward active measures. While they planned how to keep themselves hidden, one man wanted to attack. While they decided the best ways to foil the Breeders, one man wanted to plot the downfall of the Final Empire. When I rejoined my people, I found that man still fighting. Alone. Condemned for fraternizing with thieves and rebels, he quietly accepted his punishment."

She smiled. "That man went on to free us all."

She took his hand. Sazed sat, astonished.

"The men I read about, Sazed," Tindwyl said quietly, "these were not men who sat and planned the best ways to hide. They fought; they sought victory. Sometimes, they were reckless—and other men called them fools. Yet, when the dice were cast and the bodies counted, they were men who *changed* things."

Sunlight entered the room in full, and she sat, cupping his hand in hers. She seemed . . . anxious. Had he ever seen that emotion in her? She was strong, the strongest woman he knew. That couldn't possibly be apprehension he saw in her eyes.

"Give me an excuse, Sazed," she whispered.

"I should . . . very much like it if you stayed," Sazed said, one hand in hers, the other resting on the tabletop, fingers trembling slightly.

Tindwyl raised an eyebrow.

"Stay," Sazed said. "Please."

Tindwyl smiled. "Very well—you have persuaded me. Let us return to our studies, then."

Elend walked the top of the city wall in the morning light, sword at his hip clicking against the side of the stonework with each step.

"You almost look like a king," a voice noted.

Elend turned as Ham climbed the last few steps up to the wall walk. The air was brisk, frost still crystalline in shadows on the stone. Winter was approaching. Perhaps it had arrived. Yet, Ham wore no cloak—only his usual vest, trousers, and sandals.

I wonder if he even knows what it is like to be cold, Elend thought. *Pewter. Such an amazing talent.*

"You say I nearly look like a king," Elend said, turning to continue walking along the wall as Ham joined him. "I guess Tindwyl's clothing has done wonders for my image."

"I didn't mean the clothing," Ham said. "I was talking about that look on your face. How long have you been up here?"

"Hours," Elend said. "How did you find me?"

"The soldiers," Ham said. "They're starting to see you as a commander, Elend. They watch where you are; they stand a little straighter when you're around, polish their weapons if they know you'll be stopping by."

"I thought you didn't spend much time with them," Elend said.

"Oh, I never said that," Ham said. "I spend lots of time with the soldiers—I just can't be intimidating enough to be their commander. Kelsier always wanted me to be a general—I think, deep down, he thought that befriending people was inferior to leading them. Perhaps he was right; men need leaders. I just don't want to be one of them."

"I do," Elend said, surprised to hear himself say so.

Ham shrugged. "That's probably a good thing. You are, after all, king."

"Kind of," Elend said.

"You're still wearing the crown."

Elend nodded. "It felt wrong to go without it. It sounds silly, I know—I only wore it for a short time. But, people need to know that someone is still in charge. For a few more days at least."

They continued to walk. In the distance, Elend could see a shadow upon the land: the third army had finally arrived in the wake of the refugees it had sent. Their scouts weren't certain why the koloss force had taken so long to get to Luthadel. The villagers' sad tale, however, gave some clue.

The koloss had not attacked Straff or Cett. They lay waiting. Apparently, Jastes had enough control over them to keep them in check. And so they joined the siege, another beast waiting for the opportunity to spring on Luthadel.

When you can't have both freedom and safety, which do you choose . . . ?

"You seem surprised to realize that you want to be in charge," Ham said.

"I just haven't ever voiced the desire before," Elend said. "It sounds so arrogant, when I actually say it. I want to be king. I don't want another man to take my place. Not Penrod, not Cett . . . not anyone. The position is mine. This city is mine."

"I don't know if 'arrogant' is the right word, El," Ham said. "Why do you want to be king?"

"To protect this people," Elend said. "To guard their safety—and their rights. But, also to make certain that the noblemen don't end up on the wrong end of another rebellion."

"That's not arrogance."

"It is, Ham," Elend said. "But it's an understandable arrogance. I don't think a man could lead without it. Actually, I think it's what I've been missing through most of my reign. Arrogance."

"Self-confidence."

"A nicer word for the same concept," Elend said. "I can do a better job for this people than another man could. I just have to find a way to prove that fact to them."

"You will."

"You're an optimist, Ham," Elend said.

"So are you," Ham noted.

Elend smiled. "True. But this job is changing me."

"Well, if you want to keep the job, we should probably get back to studying. We only have one day left."

Elend shook his head. "I've read all I can, Ham. I will not take advantage of the law, so there's no reason to search for loopholes, and studying other books looking for inspiration just isn't working. I need time to think. Time to walk. . . ."

They continued to do so. As they did, Elend noticed something out in the distance. A group of enemy soldiers doing something he couldn't distinguish. He waved over one of his men.

"What is that?" he asked.

The soldier shaded his eyes, looking. "Looks like another skirmish between Cett's men and Straff's, Your Majesty."

Elend raised an eyebrow. "That happens often?"

The soldier shrugged. "More and more often, lately. Usually the scouting patrols run afoul of each other and get into a conflict. Leave a few bodies behind when they retreat. Nothing big, Your Majesty."

Elend nodded, dismissing the man. *Big enough,* he thought to himself. *Those armies must be as tense as we are. The soldiers can't enjoy remaining so long in a siege, particularly with the winter weather.*

They were close. The arrival of the koloss would only cause more chaos. If he shoved right, Straff and Cett would be pushed into a head-on battle. *I just need a little more time!* he thought, continuing to walk, Ham at his side.

Yet, first he needed to get his throne back. Without that authority, he was nothing—and could do nothing.

The problem gnawed at his mind. As the walk continued, however, something distracted him—this time, something inside the walls rather than outside of them. Ham was right—the soldiers *did* stand a little taller when Elend approached their posts. They saluted him, and he nodded to them, walking with hand on pommel, as Tindwyl had instructed.

If I do keep my throne, I owe it to that woman, he thought. Of course, she'd chastise him for that thought. She would tell him that he kept his throne because he deserved to—because he was king. In changing himself, he had simply used the resources at hand to overcome his challenges.

He wasn't certain if he'd ever be able to see things that way. But, her final lesson to him the day before—he somehow knew that it was her last—had taught him only one new concept: that there was no one mold for kingship. He would not be like the kings of the past, any more than he would be like Kelsier.

He would be Elend Venture. His roots were in philosophy, so he would be remembered as a scholar. He'd best use that to his advantage, or he wouldn't be remembered at all. No kings could admit their weaknesses, but they were certainly wise to admit their strengths.

And what are my strengths? he thought. *Why should I be the one who rules this city, and those around it?*

Yes, he was a scholar—and an optimist, as Ham had noted. He was no master duelist, though he was improving. He wasn't an excellent diplomat, though his meetings with Straff and Cett proved that he could hold his own.

What was he?

A nobleman who loved the skaa. They'd always fascinated him, even before the Collapse—before he'd met Vin and the others. It had been one of his pet philosophical puzzles to try and prove them no different from men of noble birth. It sounded idealistic, even a little prim, when he thought about it—and, if he was truthful, much of his interest in the skaa before the Collapse had been academic. They had been unknown, and so they had seemed exotic and interesting.

He smiled. *I wonder what the plantation workers would have thought, had anyone told them they were "exotic."*

But then the Collapse had come—the rebellion predicted in his books and theories coming to life. His beliefs hadn't been able to continue as mere academic abstractions. And he'd come to know the skaa—not just Vin and the crew, but the workers and the servants. He'd seen the hope beginning to grow within them. He'd seen the awakening of self-respect, and of self-worth, in the people of the city, and it excited him.

He would not abandon them.

That's what I am, Elend thought, pausing as he walked the wall. *An idealist. A melodramatic idealist who, despite his books and learning, never did make a very good nobleman.*

"What?" Ham asked, stopping next to him.

Elend turned toward him. "I've got an idea," he said.

This is the problem. Though I believed in Alendi at first, I later became suspicious. It seemed that he fit the signs, true. But, well, how can I explain this?

Could it be that he fit them too well?

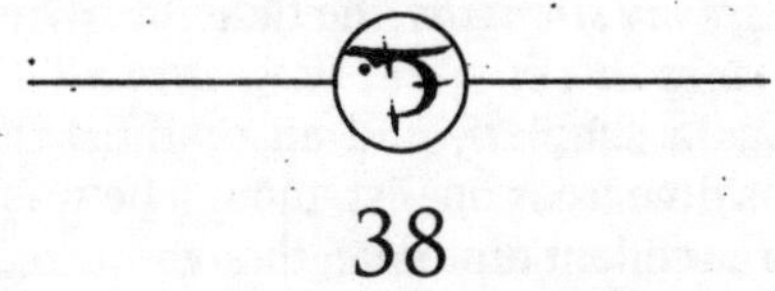

38

HOW CAN HE POSSIBLY LOOK so *confident when I feel so nervous?* Vin thought, standing beside Elend as the Assembly Hall began to fill. They had arrived early; this time, Elend said he wanted to appear in control by being the one who greeted each Assemblyman as he arrived.

Today, the vote for king would occur.

Vin and Elend stood on the stage, nodding to the Assemblymen as they entered through the room's side door. On the floor of the room, the benches were already growing crowded. The first few rows, as always, were seeded with guards.

"You look beautiful today," Elend said, looking at Vin.

Vin shrugged. She had worn her white gown, a flowing garment with a few diaphanous layers on the top. Like the others, it was designed for mobility, and it matched Elend's new outfits—especially with the dark embroidery on the sleeves. Her jewelry was gone, but she did have a few white wooden barrettes for her hair.

"It's odd," she said, "how quickly wearing these gowns became natural for me again."

"I'm glad you made the switch," Elend said. "The trousers and shirt are you . . . but this is you, too. The part of you I remember from the balls, when we barely knew each other."

Vin smiled wistfully, looking up at him, the gathering crowd growing a bit more distant. "You never did dance with me."

"I'm sorry," he said, holding her arm with a light touch. "We haven't had much time for each other lately, have we?"

Vin shook her head.

"I'll fix that," Elend said. "Once this confusion is all through, once the throne is secure, we can get back to us."

Vin nodded, then turned sharply as she noticed movement behind her. An Assemblyman walking across the stage.

"You're jumpy," Elend said, frowning slightly. "Even more than usual. What am I missing?"

Vin shook her head. "I don't know."

Elend greeted the Assemblyman—one of the skaa representatives—with a firm handshake. Vin stood at his side, her earlier wistfulness evaporating like mist as her mind returned to the moment. *What* is *bothering me?*

The room was packed—everyone wanted to witness the events of the day. Elend had been forced to post guards at the doors to maintain order. But, it wasn't just the number of people that made her edgy. It was a sense of . . . wrongness to the event. People were gathering like carrion feeders to a rotting carcass.

"This isn't right," Vin said, holding Elend's arm as the Assemblyman moved off. "Governments shouldn't change hands based on arguments made from a lectern."

"Just because it hasn't happened that way in the past doesn't mean it *shouldn't* happen," Elend said.

Vin shook her head. "Something is going to go wrong, Elend. Cett will surprise you, and maybe Penrod will, too. Men like them won't sit still and let a vote decide their future."

"I know," Elend said. "But they aren't the only ones who can offer up surprises."

Vin looked at him quizzically. "You're planning something?"

He paused, then glanced at her. "I . . . well, Ham and I came up with something last night. A ploy. I've been trying to find a way to talk to you about it, but there just hasn't been time. We had to move quickly."

Vin frowned, sensing his apprehension. She started to say something, but then stopped, studying his eyes. He seemed a little embarrassed. "What?" she asked.

"Well . . . it kind of involves you, and your reputation. I was going to ask permission, but . . ."

Vin felt a slight chill. Behind them, the last Assemblyman took his seat, and Penrod stood up to conduct the meeting. He glanced toward Elend, clearing his throat.

Elend cursed quietly. "Look, I don't have time to explain," he said. "But, it's really not a big deal—it might not even get me that many votes. But, well, I had to try. And it doesn't change anything. Between us, I mean."

"What?"

"Lord Venture?" Penrod said. "Are you ready for this meeting to begin?"

The hall grew quiet. Vin and Elend still stood in the center of the stage, between the lectern and the seats of the Assembly members. She looked at him, torn between a sense of dread, a sense of confusion, and a slight sense of betrayal.

Why didn't you tell me? she thought. *How can I be ready if you don't tell me what you're planning? And . . . why are you looking at me like that?*

"I'm sorry," Elend said, moving over to take his seat.

Vin remained standing alone before the audience. Once, so much attention would have terrified her. It still made her uncomfortable. She ducked her head slightly, walking toward the back benches and her empty spot.

Ham wasn't there. Vin frowned, turning as Penrod opened the proceedings. *There,* she thought, finding Ham in the audience, sitting calmly with a group of skaa. The group was obviously conversing quietly, but even with tin, Vin would never be able to pick out their voices in the large crowd. Breeze stood with some of Ham's soldiers at the back of the room. It didn't matter if they knew about Elend's plan—they were too far away for her to interrogate them.

Annoyed, she arranged her skirts, then sat. She hadn't felt so blind since . . .

Since that night a year ago, she thought, *that moment just before we figured out Kelsier's true plan, that moment when I thought everything was collapsing around me.*

Perhaps that was a good sign. Had Elend cooked up some last-minute flash of political brilliance? It didn't really matter that he hadn't shared it with her; she probably wouldn't understand the legal basis for it anyway.

But . . . he always shared his plans with me before.

Penrod continued to drone on, likely maximizing his time in front of the Assembly. Cett was on the front bench of the audience, surrounded by a good twenty soldiers, sitting with a look of self-satisfaction. As well he should. From the accounts she'd heard, Cett stood to take the vote with ease.

But what was Elend planning?

Penrod will vote for himself, Vin thought. *So will Elend. That leaves twenty-two votes. The merchants are behind Cett, and so are the skaa. They're too afraid of that army to vote for anyone else.*

That only leaves the nobility. Some of them will vote for Penrod—he's the strongest nobleman in the city; many of the members of the Assembly are longtime political allies of his. But, even if he takes half of the nobility—which he probably won't—Cett will win. Cett only needs a two-thirds majority to get the throne.

Eight merchants, eight skaa. Sixteen men on Cett's side. He was going to win. What could Elend possibly do?

Penrod finally finished his opening announcements. "But, before we vote," he said, "I would like to offer time to the candidates to make any final addresses they wish. Lord Cett, would you care to go first?"

In the audience, Cett shook his head. "I've made my offers and my threats, Penrod. You all know you have to vote for me."

Vin frowned. He seemed certain of himself, and yet . . . She scanned the crowd, eyes falling on Ham. He was talking to Captain Demoux. And seated next to them was one of the men who had followed her in the market. A priest of the Survivor.

Vin turned, studying the Assembly. The skaa representatives looked uncomfortable. She glanced at Elend, who stood up to take his turn at the front of the lectern. His earlier confidence had returned, and he looked regal in his sharp white uniform. He still wore his crown.

It doesn't change things, he'd said. *Between us. . . .*

I'm sorry.

Something that would use her reputation to gain him votes. Her reputation was Kelsier's reputation, and only the skaa really cared about that. And there was one easy way to gain influence with them. . . .

"You joined the Church of the Survivor, didn't you?" she whispered.

The reactions of the skaa Assemblymen, the logic of the moment, Elend's words to her before, all of them suddenly made sense. If Elend joined the Church, the skaa Assemblymen might be afraid to vote against him. And, Elend didn't need sixteen votes to gain the throne; if the Assembly deadlocked, he won. With the eight skaa and his own vote, the others would never be able to oust him.

"Very clever," she whispered.

The ploy might not work. It would depend on how much hold the Church of the Survivor had on the skaa Assemblymen. Yet, even if some skaa voted against Elend, there were still the noblemen who would probably vote for Penrod. If enough did, Elend would still deadlock the Assembly and keep his throne.

All it would cost was his integrity.

That's unfair, Vin told herself. If Elend had joined with the Church of the Survivor, he would hold to whatever promises he had made. And, if the Church of the Survivor gained official backing, it could become as powerful in Luthadel as the Steel Ministry had once been. And . . . how would that change the way Elend saw her?

This doesn't change anything, he had promised.

She dully heard him begin to speak, and his references to Kelsier now seemed obvious to her. Yet, the only thing she could feel was a slight sense of anxiety. It was as Zane had said. She was the knife—a different kind of knife, but still a tool. The means by which Elend would protect the city.

She should be furious, or at least sick. Why did her eyes keep darting toward the crowd? Why couldn't she focus on what Elend was saying, on how he was elevating her? Why was she suddenly so on edge?

Why were those men subtly moving their way around the edges of the room?

"So," Elend said, "by the blessing of the Survivor himself, I ask you to vote for me."

He waited quietly. It was a drastic move; joining the Church of the Survivor put Elend under the spiritual authority of an external group. But, Ham and Demoux both had thought it a good idea. Elend had spent the better part of the previous day getting the word out to the skaa citizens about his decision.

It felt like a good move. The only thing he worried about was Vin. He glanced at her. She didn't like her place in the Church of the Survivor, and having Elend join it meant that he—technically—accepted her part in the mythology. He tried to catch her eye and smile, but she wasn't watching him. She was looking out into the audience.

Elend frowned. Vin stood up.

A man from the audience suddenly shoved aside two soldiers in the front row, then leaped supernaturally far to land up on the dais. The man pulled out a dueling cane.

What? Elend thought in shock. Fortunately, months spent sparring at Tindwyl's command had given him instincts he didn't know he had. As the Thug charged, Elend tucked and rolled. He hit the ground, scrambling, and turned to see the beefy man bearing down on him, dueling cane raised.

A flurry of white lace and skirts fluttered through the air over Elend. Vin slammed feet-first into the Thug, throwing him backward as she spun, skirts flaring.

The man grunted. Vin landed with a thump directly in front of Elend. The Assembly Hall echoed with sudden screaming and shouts.

Vin kicked the lectern out of the way. "Stay behind me," she whispered, an obsidian dagger glittering in her right hand.

Elend nodded hesitantly, unbuckling the sword at his waist as he climbed to his feet. The Thug wasn't alone; three small groups of armed men were moving through the room. One attacked the front row, distracting the guards there. Another group was climbing onto the dais. The third group seemed occupied by something in the crowd. Cett's soldiers.

The Thug had regained his feet. He didn't look like he had suffered much from Vin's kick.

Assassins, Elend thought. *But who sent them?*

The man smiled as he was joined by a group of five friends. Chaos filled the room, Assemblymen scattering, their bodyguards rushing to surround them. Yet, the fighting in front of the stage kept anyone from escaping in that direction. The Assemblymen clogged around the stage's side exit. The attackers, however, didn't seem concerned with them.

Only with Elend.

Vin remained in her crouch, waiting for the men to attack first, her posture threatening despite the frilly dress. Elend thought he actually heard her growl quietly.

The men attacked.

Vin snapped forward, swiping at the lead Thug with a dagger. His reach was too great, however, and he easily fended her off with a swipe of his staff. There were six men in total; three who were obviously Thugs, leaving the other three to likely be Coinshots or Lurchers. A strong component of metal-controllers. Someone didn't want her ending this fight quickly with coins.

They didn't understand that she would never use coins in this situation. Not with Elend standing so close and with so many people in the room. Coins couldn't be deflected safely. If she shot a handful at her enemies, random people would die.

She had to kill these men fast. They were already fanning out, surrounding her and Elend. They moved in pairs—one Thug and one Coinshot in each team. They would attack from the sides, trying to get past her to Elend.

Vin reached behind herself with iron, Pulling Elend's sword from its sheath with a ringing squeal. She caught it by the hilt, throwing it at one of the teams. The Coinshot Pushed it back at her, and she in turn Pushed it to the side, spinning it toward a second pair of Allomancers.

One of them Pushed it back at her again. Vin Pulled from behind, whipping Elend's metal-tipped sheath out of his hands and shooting it through the air by its clasp. Sheath passed sword in the air. This time, the enemy Coinshots Pushed both items out of the way, deflecting them toward the fleeing audience.

Men shouted in desperation as they trampled and tried to force their way out of the room. Vin gritted her teeth. She needed a better weapon.

She flung a stone dagger at one assassin pair, then jumped toward another, spinning beneath the attacking Thug's weapon. The Coinshot didn't have any metal on him that she could sense; he was just there to keep her from killing the Thug with coins. They probably assumed that Vin would be easy to defeat, as she was deprived of the ability to shoot coins.

The Thug brought his staff back around, trying to catch her with the end. She caught the weapon, yanking it forward and jumping up as she Pushed against the Assembly bleachers behind her. Her feet hit the Thug in the chest, and she kicked hard with flared pewter. As he grunted, Vin Pulled herself back toward the nails in the bleachers as hard as she could.

The Thug managed to stay on his feet. He seemed completely surprised, however, to find Vin streaking away from him, holding his staff in her hands.

She landed and spun toward Elend. He'd found himself a weapon—a dueling cane—and had the good sense to back himself against a wall. To her right, some of the Assemblymen stood in a huddle, surrounded by their guards. The room was too full, the exits too small and cramped, for them all to escape.

The Assemblymen made no moves to help Elend.

One of the assassins cried out, pointing as Vin Pushed against the bleachers and shot toward them, moving herself in front of Elend. Two Thugs raised their weapons as Vin turned in the air, lightly Pulling against a door's hinges to spin herself. Her gown fluttered as she landed.

I really have to thank that dressmaker, she thought as she raised the staff. She briefly considered ripping the dress free anyway, but the Thugs were upon her too quickly. She blocked both blows at once, then threw herself between the men, flaring pewter, moving faster than even they.

One of them cursed, trying to bring his staff around. Vin broke his leg before he could. He dropped with a howl, and Vin leaped onto his back, forcing him to the ground as she swung an overhand blow at the second Thug. He blocked, then shoved his weapon against hers to throw her back off his companion.

Elend attacked. The king's actions, however, seemed sluggish compared with the movements of men burning pewter. The Thug turned almost nonchalantly, smashing Elend's weapon with an easy blow.

Vin cursed as she fell. She hurled her staff at the Thug, forcing him to turn away from Elend. He barely ducked out of the way as Vin hit the ground, bounced to her feet, and whipped out a second dagger. She dashed forward before the Thug could turn back to Elend.

A spray of coins flew toward her. She couldn't Push them back, not toward the crowd. She cried out—throwing herself between the coins and Elend—then Pushed to the sides, dividing them as best she could so they sprayed against the wall. Even so, she felt a flash of pain from her shoulder.

Where did he get the coins? she thought with frustration. However, as she glanced to the side, she saw the Coinshot standing beside a cowering Assemblyman, who had been forced to give up his coin pouch.

Vin gritted her teeth. Her arm still worked. That was all that mattered. She yelled and threw herself at the closest Thug. However, the third Thug had regained his weapon—the one Vin had thrown—and was now circling with his Coinshot to try and get behind Vin.

One at a time, Vin thought.

The Thug nearest her swung his weapon. She needed to surprise him. So, she didn't dodge or block. She simply took his blow in the side, burning duralumin and pewter to resist. Something cracked within her as she was hit, but with duralumin, she was strong enough to stay up. Wood shattered, and she continued forward, slamming her dagger into the Thug's neck.

He dropped, revealing a surprised Coinshot behind him. Vin's pewter evaporated with the duralumin, and pain blossomed like a sunrise in her side. Even so, she yanked her dagger free as the Thug fell, still moving quickly enough to drop the Coinshot with a dagger in the chest.

Then she stumbled, gasping quietly, holding her side as two men died at her feet.

One Thug left, she thought desperately. *And two Coinshots.*

Elend needs me. To the side, she saw one of the Coinshots fire a spray of stolen coins at Elend. She cried out, Pushing them away, and she heard the Coinshot cursing.

She turned—counting on the blue lines from her steel to warn her if the Coinshots tried shooting anything else at Elend—and ripped her backup vial of metal from her sleeve, where it had been tied tightly to keep it from being Pulled away. However, even as she yanked the stopper open, the vial lurched from her now undexterous hand. The second Coinshot grinned as he Pushed the vial away, tipping it and spraying its contents across the floor.

Vin growled, but her mind was growing fuzzy. She needed pewter. Without it, the large coin wound in her shoulder—its blood turning her lacy sleeve red—and the crushing pain in her side were too much. She almost couldn't think.

A staff swung toward her head. She jerked to the side, rolling. However, she no longer had the grace or speed of pewter. A normal man's blow she could have dodged, but the attack of an Allomancer was another thing.

I shouldn't have burned duralumin! she thought. It had been a gamble, letting her kill two assassins, but it had left her too exposed. The staff descended toward her.

Something large slammed into the Thug, bearing him to the ground in a growling flurry of claws. Vin came out of her dodge as the Thug punched OreSeur in the head, cracking his skull. Yet, the Thug was bleeding and cursing, and his staff had rolled free. Vin snatched it up, scrambling to her feet and gritting her teeth as she drove the butt of the staff down into the man's face. He took the blow with a curse, swiping her feet out from under her with a kick.

She fell beside OreSeur. The wolfhound, oddly, was smiling. There was a wound in his shoulder.

No, not a wound. An opening in the flesh—and a vial of metal hidden inside. Vin snatched it, rolling, keeping it hidden as the Thug regained his feet. She downed the liquid, and the flakes of metal it contained. On the floor before her, she could see the shadow of the Thug raising his weapon in a mighty overhand blow.

Pewter flared to life inside of her, and her wounds became

mere annoying buzzes. She jerked to the side as the blow fell, hitting the floor, throwing up bits of wood. Vin flipped to her feet, slamming her fist into the arm of her surprised opponent.

It wasn't enough to break the bones, but it obviously hurt. The Thug—now missing two teeth—grunted in pain. To the side, Vin saw OreSeur on his feet, his dog's jaw hanging unnaturally. He nodded to her; the Thug would think him dead from the cracked skull.

More coins flew at Elend. She Pushed them away without even looking. In front of her, OreSeur struck the Thug from behind, making him spin in surprise just as Vin attacked. The Thug's staff passed within a finger's width of her head as it smashed into OreSeur's back, but her own hand took the man in the face. She didn't punch, however; that wouldn't do much against a Thug.

She had one finger out, and she had incredible aim. The Thug's eye popped as she rammed her finger into the socket.

She hopped back as he cried out, raising a hand to his face. She smashed her fists into his chest, throwing him to the ground, then jumped over OreSeur's crumpled form and grabbed her dagger off the ground.

Thc Thug died, clutching his face in agony, her dagger in his chest.

Vin spun, searching desperately for Elend. He'd taken one of the fallen Thugs' weapons and was fending off the two remaining Coinshots, who had apparently grown frustrated by her Pushing away all of their coin attacks. Instead, they had pulled out dueling canes to attack him directly. Elend's training had apparently been enough to keep him alive—but only because his opponents had to keep an eye on Vin to make certain she didn't try using coins herself.

Vin kicked up the staff of the man she'd just killed, catching it. A Coinshot cried out as she growled and dashed toward them, spinning her weapon. One had the presence of mind to Push off the bleachers and launch himself away. Vin's weapon still caught him in midair, throwing him to the side. The next swing took down his companion, who had tried to dash away.

Elend stood breathing heavily, his costume disheveled.

He did better than I thought he would, Vin admitted, flexing, trying to judge the damage to her side. She needed to get a bandage on that shoulder. The coin hadn't hit bone, but the bleeding would—

"Vin!" Elend cried out.

Something very strong suddenly grabbed her from behind. Vin choked as she was jerked backward and thrown to the ground.

The first Thug. She'd broken his leg, then forgotten—

He got his hands around her neck, squeezing as he knelt above her, his legs pressing against her chest, his face wild with rage. His eyes bulged, adrenaline mixing with pewter.

Vin gasped for breath. She was taken back to years before, to beatings performed by men looming above her. Camon, and Reen, and a dozen others.

No! she thought, flaring her pewter, struggling. He had her pinned, however, and he was much larger then she was. Much stronger. Elend slammed his staff against the man's back, but the Thug barely even flinched.

Vin couldn't breathe. She felt her throat being crushed. She tried to pry the Thug's hands apart, but it was as Ham had always said. Her small size was a great advantage to her in most situations—but when it came down to brute strength, she was no match for a man of bulk and muscle. She tried Pulling herself to the side, but the man's grip was too strong, her weight too small compared with his.

She struggled in vain. She had duralumin still—burning it only made other metals vanish, not the duralumin itself—but last time that had nearly gotten her killed. If she didn't take the Thug down quickly, she'd be left without pewter once again.

Elend pounded, yelling for help, but his voice sounded distant. The Thug pressed his face almost up against Vin's, and she could see his fury. At that moment, incredibly, a thought occurred to her.

Where have I seen this man before?

Her vision darkened. However, as the Thug constricted his grip, he leaned closer, closer, closer. . . .

She didn't have a choice. Vin burned duralumin and

flared her pewter. She flung her opponent's hands aside and smashed her head upward into his face.

The man's head exploded as easily as the eyeball had earlier.

Vin gasped for breath and pushed the headless corpse off her. Elend stumbled back, his suit and face sprayed red. Vin stumbled to her feet. Her vision swam as her pewter dissipated—but even through that, she could see an emotion on Elend's face, stark as the blood on his brilliant white uniform.

Horror.

No, she thought, her mind fading. *Please, Elend, not that. . . .*

She fell forward, unable to maintain consciousness.

Elend sat in his ruined suit, hands against forehead, the wreckage of the Assembly Hall hauntingly empty around him.

"She'll live," Ham said. "She actually isn't hurt that badly. Or . . . well, not that badly for Vin. She just needs plenty of pewter and some of Sazed's care. He says the ribs aren't even broken, just cracked."

Elend nodded absently. Some soldiers were clearing away the corpses, among them the six men that Vin had killed, including the one at the end. . . .

Elend squeezed his eyes shut.

"What?" Ham asked.

Elend opened his eyes, forming his hand into a fist to keep it from shaking. "I know you've seen a lot of battles, Ham," he said. "But, I'm not used to them. I'm not used to . . ." He turned away as the soldiers dragged away the headless body.

Ham watched the corpse go.

"I've only actually seen her fight once before, you know," Elend said quietly. "In the palace, a year ago. She only threw a few men against the walls. It was nothing like this."

Ham took a seat beside Elend on the benches. "She's Mistborn, El. What did you expect? A single Thug can easily take down ten men—dozens, if he has a Coinshot to support him. A Mistborn . . . well, they're like an army in one person."

Elend nodded. "I know, Ham. I know she killed the Lord Ruler—she's even told me how she faced several Steel Inquisitors. But . . . I've just never seen . . ."

He closed his eyes again. The image of Vin stumbling toward him at the end, her beautiful white ball gown covered in the gore of a man she'd just killed with her forehead . . .

She did it to protect me, he thought. *But that doesn't make it any less disturbing.*

Maybe that even makes it a little more disturbing.

He forced his eyes open. He couldn't afford to be distracted; he had to be strong. He was king.

"You think Straff sent them?" Elend asked.

Ham nodded. "Who else? They targeted you and Cett. I guess your threat to kill Straff wasn't as binding as we assumed."

"How is Cett?"

"He barely escaped alive. As it is, they slaughtered half of his soldiers. In the fray, Demoux and I couldn't even see what was happening up on the stage with you and Vin."

Elend nodded. By the time Ham had arrived, Vin had already dealt with the assassins. It had taken her only a few minutes to wipe out all six of them.

Ham was silent for a moment. Finally, he turned to Elend. "I'll admit, El," he said quietly. "I'm impressed. I didn't see the fight, but I saw the aftermath. It's one thing to fight six Allomancers, but it's another to do that while trying to protect a regular person, and to keep any bystanders from harm. And that last man . . ."

"Do you remember when she saved Breeze?" Elend asked. "It was so far away, but I swear I saw her throw horses into the air with her Allomancy. Have you ever heard of anything like that?"

Ham shook his head.

Elend sat quietly for a moment. "I think we need to do some planning. What with today's events, we can't . . ."

Ham looked up as Elend trailed off. "What?"

"Messenger," Elend said, nodding toward the doorway.

Sure enough, the man presented himself to the soldiers, then was escorted up to the stage. Elend stood, walking over to meet the short man, who wore Penrod's heraldry on his coat.

"My lord," the man said, bowing. "I've been sent to inform you that the voting will proceed at Lord Penrod's mansion."

"The voting?" Ham asked. "What nonsense is this? His Majesty was nearly killed today!"

"I'm sorry, my lord," the aide said. "I was simply told to deliver the message."

Elend sighed. He'd hoped that, in the confusion, Penrod wouldn't remember the deadline. "If they don't choose a new leader today, Ham, then I get to retain the crown. They've already wasted their grace period."

Ham sighed. "And if there are more assassins?" he asked quietly. "Vin will be laid up for a few days, at least."

"I can't rely on her to protect me all the time," Elend said. "Let's go."

"I vote for myself," Lord Penrod said.

Not unexpected, Elend thought. He sat in Penrod's comfortable lounge, accompanied by a group of shaken Assemblymen—none of whom, thankfully, had been hurt in the attack. Several held drinks, and there was a veritable army of guards waiting around the perimeter, eyeing each other warily. The crowded room also held Noorden and three other scribes, who were there to witness the voting, according to the law.

"I vote for Lord Penrod as well," said Lord Dukaler.

Also not unexpected, Elend thought. *I wonder how much that cost Penrod.*

Mansion Penrod was not a keep, but it was lavishly decorated. The plushness of Elend's chair was welcome as a relief from the tensions of the day. Yet, Elend feared that it was too soothing. It would be very easy to drift off. . . .

"I vote for Cett," said Lord Habren.

Elend perked up. It was the second for Cett, which put him behind Penrod by three.

Everyone turned to Elend. "I vote for myself," he said, trying to project a firmness that was hard to maintain after everything that had happened. The merchants were next. Elend settled back, prepared for the expected run of votes for Cett.

"I vote for Penrod," Philen said.

Elend sat upright, alert. *What!*

The next merchant voted for Penrod as well. As did the next, and the next. Elend sat stunned, listening. *What did I miss?* he thought. He glanced at Ham, who shrugged in confusion.

Philen glanced at Elend, smiling pleasantly. Elend couldn't tell if there was bitterness or satisfaction in that look, however. *They switched allegiances? That quickly?* Philen had been the one to sneak Cett into the city in the first place.

Elend looked down the row of merchants, trying with little success to gauge their reactions. Cett himself wasn't in the meeting; he had retreated to Keep Hasting to nurse his wound.

"I vote for Lord Venture," said Haws, foremost of the skaa faction. This also managed to get a stir out of the room. Haws met Elend's eye, and nodded. He was a firm believer in the Church of the Survivor, and while the different preachers of the religion were beginning to disagree on how to organize their followers, they all agreed that a believer on the throne would be better for them than handing the city over to Cett.

There will be a price to pay for this allegiance, Elend thought as the skaa voted. They knew Elend's reputation for honesty, and he would not betray their trust.

He had told them he would become an open member of their sect. He hadn't promised them belief, but he had promised them devotion. He still wasn't certain what he had given away, but both of them knew they would need each other.

"I vote for Penrod," said Jasten, a canal worker.

"As do I," said Thurts, his brother.

Elend gritted his teeth. He'd known they would be trouble; they never had liked the Church of the Survivor. But, four of the skaa had already given him their votes. With only two remaining, he had a very good shot at a deadlock.

"I vote for Venture," said the next man.

"I do, too," said the final skaa. Elend gave the man, Vet, a smile of appreciation.

That left fifteen votes for Penrod, two for Cett, and seven for Elend. Deadlock. Elend reclined slightly, head resting against the chair's pillowed back, sighing softly.

You did your job, Vin, he thought. *I did mine. Now we just need to keep this country in one piece.*

"Um," a voice asked, "am I allowed to change my vote?"

Elend opened his eyes. It was Lord Habren, one of the votes for Cett.

"I mean, it's obvious now that Cett isn't going to win," Habren said, flushing slightly. The young man was a distant cousin of the Elariel family, which was probably how he'd gotten his seat. Names still meant power in Luthadel.

"I'm not sure if you can change or not," Lord Penrod said.

"Well, I'd rather my vote meant something," Habren said. "There are only two votes for Cett, after all."

The room fell silent. One by one, the members of the Assembly turned to Elend. Noorden the scribe met Elend's eyes. There was a clause allowing for men to change their votes, assuming that the chancellor hadn't officially closed the voting—which, indeed, he hadn't.

The clause was a rather oblique; Noorden was probably the only other one in the room who knew the law well enough to interpret it. He nodded slightly, still meeting Elend's eyes. He would hold his tongue.

Elend sat still in a room full of men who trusted him, even as they rejected him. He could do as Noorden did. He could say nothing, or could say that he didn't know.

"Yes," Elend said softly. "The law allows for you to change your vote, Lord Habren. You may only do so once, and must do so before the winner is declared. Everyone else has the same opportunity."

"Then I vote for Lord Penrod," Habren said.

"As do I," said Lord Hue, the other who had voted for Cett.

Elend closed his eyes.

"Are there any other alterations?" Lord Penrod asked.

No one spoke.

"Then," Penrod said, "I see seventeen votes for myself, seven votes for Lord Venture. I officially close the voting and humbly accept your appointment as king. I shall serve as best I can in this capacity."

Elend stood, then slowly removed his crown. "Here," he said, setting it on the mantle. "You'll need this."

He nodded to Ham, then left without looking back at the men who had discarded him.

THE END OF PART THREE

PART FOUR

KNIVES

I know your argument. We speak of the Anticipation, of things foretold, of promises made by our greatest prophets of old. Of course the Hero of Ages will fit the prophecies. He will fit them perfectly. That's the idea.

39

STRAFF VENTURE RODE QUIETLY IN the misty twilight air. Though he would have preferred a carriage, he felt it important to travel by horseback and present a compelling image for the troops. Zane, not surprisingly, chose to walk. He sauntered along beside Straff's horse, the two of them leading a group of fifty soldiers.

Even with the troops, Straff felt exposed. It wasn't just the mists, and it wasn't just the darkness. He could still remember her touch on his emotions.

"You've failed me, Zane," Straff said.

The Mistborn looked up, and—burning tin—Straff could see a frown on his face. "Failed?"

"Venture and Cett still live. Beyond that, you sent a batch of my best Allomancers to their deaths."

"I warned you that they might die," Zane said.

"For a purpose, Zane," Straff said sternly. "Why did you need a group of secret Allomancers if you were just going to send them on a suicide mission in the middle of a public gathering? You may assume our resources to be unlimited, but let me assure you—those six men can*not* be replaced."

It had taken Straff decades of work with his mistresses to gather so many hidden Allomancers. It had been pleasurable work, but work all the same. In one reckless gambit, Zane had destroyed a good third of Straff's Allomancer children.

My children dead, our hand exposed, and that . . . creature of Elend's still lives!

"I'm sorry, Father," Zane said. "I thought that the chaos and crowded quarters would keep the girl isolated, and force her not to use coins. I really thought this would work."

Straff frowned. He well knew that Zane thought himself more competent than his father; what Mistborn wouldn't think such a thing? Only a delicate mixture of bribery, threats, and manipulation kept Zane under control.

Yet, no matter what Zane thought, Straff was no fool. He knew, at that moment, that Zane was hiding something. *Why send those men to die?* Straff thought. *He must have intended them to fail—otherwise he would have helped them fight the girl.*

"No," Zane said softly, talking to himself as he sometimes did. "He's my father . . ." He trailed off, then shook his head sharply. "No. Not them either."

Lord Ruler, Straff thought, looking down at the muttering madman beside him. *What have I gotten myself into?* Zane was growing more unpredictable. Had he sent those men to die out of jealousy, out of lust for violence, or had he simply been bored? Straff didn't *think* that Zane had turned on him, but it was difficult to tell. Either way, Straff didn't like having to rely on Zane for his plans to work. He didn't really like having to rely on Zane for *anything.*

Zane looked up at Straff, and stopped talking. He did a good job of hiding his insanity, most of the time. A good enough job that Straff sometimes forgot about it. Yet, it still lurked there, beneath the surface. Zane was as dangerous a tool as Straff had ever used. The protection provided by a Mistborn outweighed the danger of Zane's insanity.

Barely.

"You needn't worry, Father," Zane said. "The city will still be yours."

"It will never be mine as long as that woman lives," Straff said. He shivered. *Perhaps that's what this was all about. Zane's attack was so obvious that everyone in the city knows I was behind it, and when that Mistborn demon wakes, she will come after me in retribution.*

But, if that were Zane's goal, then why not just kill me himself? Zane didn't make sense. He didn't have to. That was, perhaps, one of the advantages of being insane.

Zane shook his head. "I think you will be surprised, Father. One way or another, you will soon have nothing to fear from Vin."

"She thinks I tried to have her beloved king assassinated."

Zane smiled. "No, I don't think that she does. She's far too clever for that."

Too clever to see the truth? Straff thought. However, his tin-enhanced ears heard shuffling in the mists. He held up a hand, halting his procession. In the distance, he could just barely pick out the flickering blobs of wall-top torches. They were close to the city—uncomfortably close.

Straff's procession waited quietly. Then, from the mists before them, a man on horseback appeared, accompanied by fifty soldiers of his own. Ferson Penrod.

"Straff," Penrod said, nodding.

"Ferson."

"Your men did well," Penrod said. "I'm glad your son didn't have to die. He's a good lad. A bad king, but an earnest man."

A lot of my sons died today, Ferson, Straff thought. *The fact that Elend still lives isn't fortunate—it's irony.*

"You are ready to deliver the city?" Straff asked.

Penrod nodded. "Philen and his merchants want assurances that they will have titles to match those Cett promised them."

Straff waved a dismissive hand. "You know me, Ferson." *You used to practically grovel before me at parties every week.* "I always honor business agreements. I'd be an idiot not to appease those merchants—they're the ones who will bring me tax revenue from this dominance."

Penrod nodded. "I'm glad we could come to an understanding, Straff. I don't trust Cett."

"I doubt you trust me," Straff said.

Penrod smiled. "But I do know you, Straff. You're one of us—a Luthadel nobleman. Besides, you have produced the most stable kingdom in the dominances. That's all we're looking for right now. A little stability for this people."

"You almost sound like that fool son of mine."

Penrod paused, then shook his head. "Your boy isn't a fool, Straff. He's just an idealist. In truth, I'm sad to see his little utopia fall."

"If you are sad for him, Ferson, then you are an idiot, too."

Penrod stiffened. Straff caught the man's proud eyes, holding them with his stare, until Penrod looked down. The exchange was a simple one, mostly meaningless—but it did serve as a very important reminder.

Straff chuckled. "You're going to have to get used to being a small fish again, Ferson."

"I know."

"Be cheerful," Straff said. "Assuming this turnover of power happens as you promised, no one will have to end up dead. Who knows, maybe I'll let you keep that crown of yours."

Penrod looked up.

"For a long time, this land didn't have kings," Straff said quietly. "It had something greater. Well, I'm not the Lord Ruler—but I can be an emperor. You want to keep your crown and rule as a subject king under me?"

"That depends on the cost, Straff," Penrod said carefully.

Not completely quelled, then. Penrod had always been clever; he'd been the most important nobleman to stay behind in Luthadel, and his gamble had certainly worked.

"The cost is exorbitant," Straff said. "Ridiculously so."

"The atium," Penrod guessed.

Straff nodded. "Elend hasn't found it, but it's here, somewhere. I was the one who mined those geodes—my men spent decades harvesting them and bringing them to Luthadel. I know how much of it we harvested, and I know that nowhere near the same amount came back out in disbursements to the nobility. The rest is in that city, somewhere."

Penrod nodded. "I'll see what I can find, Straff."

Straff raised an eyebrow. "You need to get back into practice, Ferson."

Penrod paused, then bowed his head. "I'll see what I can find, *my lord.*"

"Good. Now, what news did you bring of Elend's mistress?"

"She collapsed after the fight," Penrod said. "I employ a spy on the cooking staff, and she said she delivered a bowl of broth to Lady Vin's room. It returned cold."

Straff frowned. "Could this woman of yours slip the Mistborn something?"

Penrod paled slightly. "I . . . don't think that would be wise, my lord. Besides, you know Mistborn constitutions."

Perhaps she really is incapacitated, Straff thought. *If we moved in . . .* The chill of her touch on his emotions returned. Numbness. Nothingness.

"You needn't fear her so, my lord," Penrod said.

Straff raised an eyebrow. "I'm not afraid, I'm wary. I will not move into that city until my safety is assured—and until I move in, your city is in danger from Cett. Or, worse. What would happen if those koloss decide to attack the city, Ferson? I'm in negotiations with their leader, and he seems to be able to control them. For now. Have you ever seen the aftermath of a koloss slaughter?"

He probably hadn't; Straff hadn't until just recently. Penrod just shook his head. "Vin won't attack you. Not if the Assembly votes to put you in command of the city. The transfer will be perfectly legal."

"I doubt she cares about legality."

"Perhaps," Penrod said. "But Elend *does.* And, where he commands, the girl follows."

Unless he has as little control over her as I have over Zane, Straff thought, shivering. No matter what Penrod said, Straff wasn't going to take the city until that horrible creature was dealt with. In this, he could rely only on Zane.

And that thought frightened him almost as much as Vin did.

Without further discussion, Straff waved to Penrod, dismissing him. Penrod turned and retreated into the mists with his entourage. Even with his tin, Straff barely heard Zane land on the ground beside him. Straff turned, looking at the Mistborn.

"You really think he'd turn the atium over to you if he found it?" Zane asked quietly.

"Perhaps," Straff said. "He has to know that he'd never be able to hold on to it—he doesn't have the military might to protect a treasure like that. And, if he doesn't give it to me . . . well, it would probably be easier to take the atium from him than it would be to find it on my own."

Zane seemed to find the answer satisfactory. He waited for a few moments, staring into the mists. Then he looked at Straff, a curious expression on his face. "What time is it?"

Straff checked his pocket watch, something no Mistborn would carry. Too much metal. "Eleven seventeen," he said.

Zane nodded, turning back to look at the city. "It should have taken effect by now."

Straff frowned. Then he began to sweat. He flared tin, clamping his eyes shut. *There!* he thought, noticing a weakness inside of him. "More poison?" he asked, keeping the fear from his voice, forcing himself to be calm.

"How do you do it, Father?" Zane asked. "I thought for certain you'd missed this one. Yet, here you are, just fine."

Straff was beginning to feel weak. "One doesn't need to be Mistborn to be capable, Zane," he snapped.

Zane shrugged, smiling in the haunting way only he could—keenly intelligent, yet eerily unstable. Then he just shook his head. "You win again," he said, then shot upward into the sky, churning mists with his passing.

Straff immediately turned his horse, trying to maintain his decorum as he urged it back toward the camp. He could feel the poison. Feel it stealing his life. Feel it threatening him, overcoming him. . . .

He went, perhaps, too quickly. It was difficult to maintain an air of strength when you were dying. Finally, he broke into a gallop. He left his startled guards behind, and they called in surprise, breaking into a jog to try and keep up.

Straff ignored their complaints. He kicked the horse faster. Could he feel the poison slowing his reactions? Which one had Zane used? Gurwraith? No, it required injection. Tompher, perhaps? Or . . . perhaps he had found one that Straff didn't even know about.

He could only hope that wasn't the case. For, if Straff didn't know of the poison, then Amaranta probably wouldn't know of it either, and wouldn't be able to put the antidote into her catch-all healing potion.

The lights of camp illuminated the mists. Soldiers cried out as Straff approached, and he was nearly run through as one of his own men leveled a spear at the charging horse. Fortunately, the man recognized him in time. Straff rode the man down even as he turned aside his spear.

Straff charged right up to his tent. By now, his men were scattering, preparing as if for an invasion, or some other attack. There was no way he could hide this from Zane.

I wouldn't be able to hide my death either.

"My lord!" a captain said, dashing up to him.

"Send for Amaranta," Straff said, stumbling off his horse.

The soldier paused. "Your mistress, lord?" the man said, frowning. "Why—"

"Now!" Straff commanded, throwing back his tent flap, walking inside. He paused, legs trembling as the tent flap closed. He wiped his brow with a hesitant hand. Too much sweat.

Damn him! he thought with frustration. *I have to kill him, contain him . . . I have to do something. I can't rule like this!*

But what? He'd sat up nights, he'd wasted days, trying to decide what to do about Zane. The atium he used to bribe the man no longer seemed a good motivator. Zane's actions this day—slaughtering Straff's children in an obviously hopeless attempt to kill Elend's mistress—proved that he could no longer be trusted, even in a small way.

Amaranta arrived with surprising speed, and she immediately began mixing her antidote. Eventually, as Straff slurped down the horrid-tasting concoction—feeling its healing effects immediately—he came to an uneasy conclusion.

Zane had to die.

And yet . . . something about all this seemed so convenient. It felt almost as if we constructed a hero to fit our prophecies, rather than allowing one to arise naturally. This was the worry I had, the thing that should have given me pause when my brethren came to me, finally willing to believe.

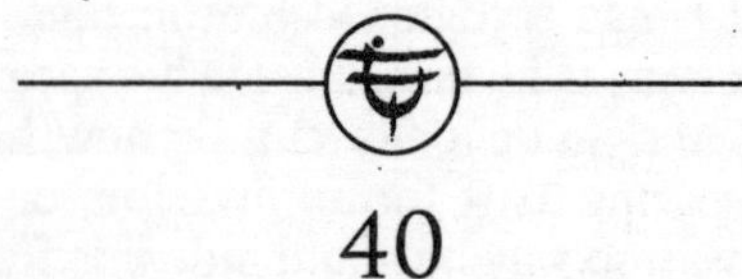

40

ELEND SAT BESIDE HER BED.

That comforted her. Though she slept fitfully, a piece of her knew that he was there, watching over her. It felt odd to be beneath his protective care, for she was the one who usually did the guarding.

So, when she finally woke, she wasn't surprised to find him in the chair beside her bed, reading quietly by soft candlelight. As she came fully awake, she didn't jump up, or search the room with apprehension. Instead, she sat up slowly, pulling the blanket up under her arms, then took a sip of the water that had been left for her beside the bed.

Elend closed the book and turned toward her, smiling. Vin searched those soft eyes, delving for hints of the horror she had seen before. The disgust, the terror, the shock.

He knew her for a monster. How could he smile so kindly?

"Why?" she asked quietly.

"Why what?" he asked.

"Why wait here?" she said. "I'm not dying—I remember that much."

Elend shrugged. "I just wanted to be near you."

She said nothing. A coal stove burned in the corner, though it needed more fuel. Winter was close, and it was looking to be a cold one. She wore only a nightgown; she'd asked the maids not to put one on her, but by then Sazed's draught—to help her sleep—had already begun taking effect, and she hadn't had the energy to argue.

She pulled the blanket closer. Only then did she realize something she should have noticed earlier. "Elend! You're not wearing your uniform."

He looked down at his clothing—a nobleman's suit from his old wardrobe, with an unbuttoned maroon vest. The jacket was too big for him. He shrugged. "No need to continue the charade anymore, Vin."

"Cett is king?" she asked with a sinking feeling.

Elend shook his head. "Penrod."

"That doesn't make sense."

"I know," he said. "We aren't sure why the merchants betrayed Cett—but it doesn't really matter anymore. Penrod is a far better choice anyway. Than either Cett, or me."

"You know that's not true."

Elend sat back contemplatively. "I don't know, Vin. I thought I was the better man. Yet, while I thought up all kinds of schemes to keep the throne from Cett, I never really considered the one plan that would have been certain to defeat him—that of giving my support to Penrod, combining our votes. What if my arrogance had landed us with Cett? I wasn't thinking of the people."

"Elend . . ." she said, laying a hand on his arm.

And he flinched.

It was slight, almost unnoticeable, and he covered it quickly. But the damage was done. Damage she had caused, damage within him. He had finally seen—really seen—what she was. He'd fallen in love with a lie.

"What?" he said, looking into her face.

"Nothing," Vin said. She withdrew her hand. Inside, something cracked. *I love him so much. Why? Why did I let him see? If only I'd had a choice!*

He's betraying you, Reen's voice whispered in the back of her mind. *Everyone will leave you eventually, Vin.*

Elend sighed, glancing toward the shutters to her room. They were closed, keeping the mists out, though Vin could see the darkness beyond.

"The thing is, Vin," he said quietly, "I never really thought it would end this way. I trusted them, right to the end. The people—the Assemblymen they chose—I trusted that they would do the right thing. When they didn't choose me, I was actually surprised. I shouldn't have been. We *knew* that I was the long shot. I mean, they had already voted me out once. But, I'd convinced myself that was just a warning. Inside, in my heart, I thought that they would reinstate me."

He shook his head. "Now, I either have to admit that my faith in them was wrong, or I have to trust in their decision."

That was what she loved: his goodness, his simple honesty. Things as odd and exotic to a skaa urchin as her own Mistborn nature must be to most people. Even among all the good men of Kelsier's crew, even amid the best of the nobility, she had never found another man like Elend Venture. A man who would rather believe that the people who had dethroned him were just trying to do the right thing.

At times, she had felt a fool for falling in love with the first nobleman whom she grew to know. But now she realized that her love of Elend had not come about because of simple convenience or proximity. It had come because of who Elend was. The fact that she had found him first was an event of incredible fortune.

And now . . . it was over. At least, in the form it had once had. But, she'd known all along that it would turn out this way. That was why she'd refused his marriage proposal, now over a year old. She couldn't marry him. Or, rather, she couldn't let him marry her.

"I know that sorrow in your eyes, Vin," Elend said softly.

She looked at him with shock.

"We can get past this," he said. "The throne wasn't everything. We might be better off this way, actually. We did our best. Now it's someone else's turn to try."

She smiled wanly. *He doesn't know. He must* never *know how much this hurts. He's a good man—he'd try to force himself to keep loving me.*

"But," he said, "you should get some more rest."

"I feel fine," Vin said, stretching slightly. Her side hurt, and her neck ached, but pewter burned within her, and none of her wounds were debilitating. "I need to—"

She cut herself off as a realization hit her. She sat upright, the sudden motion making her rigid with pain. The day before was a blur, but . . .

"OreSeur!" she said, pushing aside the blanket.

"He's fine, Vin," Elend said. "He's a kandra. Broken bones mean nothing to him."

She paused, half out of bed, suddenly feeling foolish. "Where is he?"

"Digesting a new body," Elend said, smiling.

"Why the smile?" she asked.

"I've just never heard someone express that much concern for a kandra before."

"Well, I don't see why not," Vin said, climbing back in bed. "OreSeur risked his life for me."

"He's a kandra, Vin," Elend repeated. "I don't think those men could have killed him; I doubt even a Mistborn could."

Vin paused. *Not even a Mistborn could.* . . . What bothered her about that statement? "Regardless," she said. "He feels pain. He took two serious blows on my behalf."

"Just fulfilling his Contract."

His Contract. . . . OreSeur had attacked a human. He had *broken* his Contract. For her.

"What?" Elend asked.

"Nothing," Vin said quickly. "Tell me about the armies."

Elend eyed her, but allowed the conversation to change directions. "Cett is still holed up in Keep Hasting. We're not sure what his reaction will be. The Assembly didn't choose him, which can't be good. And yet, he hasn't protested—he has to realize that he's trapped in here now."

"He must have really believed that we'd choose him," Vin said, frowning. "Why else would he come into the city?"

Elend shook his head. "It was an odd move in the first place. Anyway, I have advised the Assembly to try and make a deal with him. I think he believes that the atium isn't in the city, so there's really no reason for him to want Luthadel."

"Except for the prestige."

"Which wouldn't be worth losing his army," Elend's said. "Or his life."

Vin nodded. "And your father?"

"Silent," Elend said. "It's strange, Vin. This isn't like him—those assassins were so blatant. I'm not sure what to make of them."

"The assassins," Vin said, sitting back in the bed. "You've identified them?"

Elend shook his head. "Nobody recognizes them."

Vin frowned.

"Maybe we aren't as familiar with the noblemen out in the Northern Dominance as we thought we were."

No, Vin thought. *No, if they were from a city as close as Urteau—Straff's home—some of them would be known, wouldn't they?* "I thought I recognized one of them," Vin finally said.

"Which one?"

"The . . . last one."

Elend paused. "Ah. Well, I guess we won't be able to identify him now."

"Elend, I'm sorry you had to see that."

"What?" Elend asked. "Vin, I've seen death before. I was forced to attend the Lord Ruler's executions, remember?" He paused. "Not that what you did was like that, of course."

Of course.

"You were amazing," Elend said. "I'd be dead right now if you hadn't stopped those Allomancers—and it's likely that Penrod and the other Assemblymen would have fared the same. You saved the Central Dominance."

We always have to be the knives. . . .

Elend smiled, standing. "Here," he said, walking to the side of the room. "This is cold, but Sazed said you should eat it when you awoke." He returned with a bowl of broth.

"Sazed sent it?" Vin asked skeptically. "Drugged, then?"

Elend smiled. "He warned me not to taste it myself—he

said it was filled with enough sedatives to knock me out for a month. It takes a lot to affect you pewter burners."

He set the bowl on the bedstand. Vin eyed it through narrowed eyes. Sazed was probably worried that, despite her wounds, she'd go out and prowl the city if she were left on her own. He was probably right. With a sigh, Vin accepted the bowl and began to sip at it.

Elend smiled. "I'll send someone to bring you more coal for the stove," he said. "There are some things I need to do."

Vin nodded, and he left, pulling the door shut behind him.

When Vin next awoke, she saw that Elend was still there. He stood in the shadows, watching her. It was still dark outside. The shutters to her window were open, and mist coated the floor of the room.

The shutters were *open.*

Vin sat upright and turned toward the figure in the corner. It wasn't Elend. "Zane," she said flatly.

He stepped forward. It was so easy to see the similarities between him and Elend, now that she knew what to look for. They had the same jaw, the same wavy dark hair. They even had similar builds, now that Elend had been exercising.

"You sleep too soundly," Zane said.

"Even a Mistborn's body needs sleep to heal."

"You shouldn't have been hurt in the first place," Zane said. "You should have been able to kill those men with ease, but you were distracted by my brother, and by trying to keep the people of the room from harm. *This* is what he's done to you—he's changed you, so that you no longer see what needs to be done, you just see what he wants you to do."

Vin raised an eyebrow, quietly feeling beneath her pillow. Her dagger was there, fortunately. *He didn't kill me in my sleep,* she thought. *That has to be a good sign.*

He took another step forward. She tensed. "What is your game, Zane?" she said. "First, you tell me that you've decided not to kill me—then you send a group of assassins. What now? Have you come to finish the job?"

"We didn't send those assassins, Vin," Zane said quietly.

Vin snorted.

"Believe as you wish," Zane said, taking another step forward so that he stood right beside her bed, a tall figure of blackness and solemnity. "But, my father is still terrified of you. Why would he risk retribution by trying to kill Elend?"

"It was a gamble," Vin said. "He hoped those assassins would kill me."

"Why use them?" Zane asked. "He has me—why use a bunch of Mistings to attack you in the middle of a crowded room, when he could just have me use atium in the night and kill you?"

Vin hesitated.

"Vin," he said, "I watched the corpses being carried away from the Assembly Hall, and I recognized some of them from Cett's entourage."

That's it! Vin thought. *That's where I saw that Thug whose face I smashed! He was at Keep Hasting, peeking out from the kitchen while we ate with Cett, pretending to be a servant.*

"But, the assassins attacked Cett too . . ." Vin trailed off. It was basic thieving strategy: if you had a front that you wanted to escape suspicion as you burgled the shops around it, you made certain to "steal" from yourself as well.

"The assassins who attacked Cett were all normal men," Vin said. "No Allomancers. I wonder what he told them—that they'd be allowed to 'surrender' once the battle turned? But why fake an attack in the first place? He was favored for the throne."

Zane shook his head. "Penrod made a deal with my father, Vin. Straff offered the Assembly wealth beyond anything Cett could provide. That's why the merchants changed their votes. Cett must have gotten wind of their betrayal. He has spies enough in the city."

Vin sat, dumbfounded. *Of course!* "And the only way that Cett could see to win . . ."

"Was to send the assassins," Zane said with a nod.

"They were to attack all three candidates, killing Penrod and Elend, but leaving Cett alive. The Assembly would assume that they'd been betrayed by Straff, and Cett would become king."

Vin gripped her knife with a shaking hand. She was growing tired of games. Elend had almost died. She had almost failed.

Part of her, a burning part, wanted to do what she'd first been inclined to. To go out and kill Cett and Straff, to remove the danger the most efficient way possible.

No, she told herself forcefully. *No, that was Kelsier's way. It's not my way. It's not . . . Elend's way.*

Zane turned away, facing toward her window, staring at the small waterfall-like flow of mist spilling through. "I should have arrived sooner to the fight. I was outside, with the crowds that came too late to get a seat. I didn't even know what was happening until the people started piling out."

Vin raised an eyebrow. "You almost sound sincere, Zane."

"I have no wish to see you dead," he said, turning. "And I certainly don't want to see harm befall Elend."

"Oh?" Vin asked. "Even though he's the one who had all the privileges, while you were despised and kept locked away?"

Zane shook his head. "It isn't like that. Elend is . . . pure. Sometimes—when I hear him speak—I wonder if I would have become like him, if my childhood had been different."

He met her eyes in the dark room. "I'm . . . broken, Vin. Maddened. I can never be like Elend. But, killing him wouldn't change me. It's probably best that he and I were raised apart—it's far better that he doesn't know about me. Better that he remain as he is. Untainted."

"I . . ." Vin floundered. What could she say? She could see actual sincerity in Zane's eyes.

"I'm not Elend," Zane said. "I never will be—I'm not a part of his world. But, I don't think that I *should* be. Neither should you. After the fighting was done, I finally got into the Assembly Hall. I saw Elend standing over you, at the end. I saw the look in his eyes."

She turned away.

"It's not his fault that he is what he is," Zane said. "As I said, he's pure. But, that makes him different from us. I've tried to explain it to you. I wish you could have seen that look in his eyes. . . ."

I saw it, Vin thought. She didn't want to remember it, but she *had* seen it. That awful look of horror, a reaction to something terrible and alien, something beyond understanding.

"I can't be Elend," Zane said quietly, "but you don't want me to be." He reached over and dropped something on her bedstand. "Next time, be prepared."

Vin snatched the object as Zane began to walk toward the window. The ball of metal rolled in her palm. The shape was bumpy, but the texture was smooth—like a nugget of gold. She knew it without having to swallow it. *"Atium?"*

"Cett may send other assassins," Zane said, hopping up onto the windowsill.

"You're *giving* it to me?" she asked. "There's enough here for a good two minutes of burning!" It was a small fortune, easily worth twenty thousand boxings before the Collapse. Now, with the scarcity of atium . . .

Zane turned back toward her. "Just keep yourself safe," he said, then launched himself out into the mists.

Vin did not like being injured. Logically, she knew that other people probably felt the same way; after all, who would enjoy pain and debilitation? Yet, when the others got sick, she sensed frustration from them. Not terror.

When sick, Elend would spend the day in bed, reading books. Clubs had taken a bad blow during practice several months before, and he had grumbled about the pain, but had stayed off his leg for a few days without much prodding.

Vin was growing to be more like them. She could lie in bed as she did now, knowing that nobody would try to slit her throat while she was too weak to call for help. Still, she itched to rise, to show that she wasn't very badly wounded. Lest someone think otherwise, and try to take advantage.

It isn't like that anymore! she told herself. It was light outside, and though Elend had been back to visit several times, he was currently away. Sazed had come to check on her wounds, and had begged her to stay in bed for "at least one more day." Then he'd gone back to his studies. With Tindwyl.

What ever happened to those two hating each other? she thought with annoyance. *I barely get to see him.*

Her door opened. Vin was pleased that her instincts were still keen enough that she immediately grew tense, reaching for her daggers. Her pained side protested the sudden motion.

Nobody entered.

Vin frowned, still tense, until a canine head popped up over the top of her footboard. "Mistress?" said a familiar, half growl of a voice.

"OreSeur?" Vin said. "You're wearing another dog's body!"

"Of course, Mistress," OreSeur said, hopping up onto the bed. "What else would I have?"

"I don't know," Vin said, putting away her daggers. "When Elend said you'd had him get you a body, I just assumed that you'd asked for a human. I mean, everyone saw my 'dog' die."

"Yes," OreSeur said, "but it will be simple to explain that you got a new animal. You are expected to have a dog with you now, and so *not* having one would provoke notice."

Vin sat quietly. She'd changed back to trousers and shirt, despite Sazed's protests. Her dresses hung in the other room, one noticeably absent. At times, when she looked at them, she thought she saw the gorgeous white gown hanging there, sprayed with blood. Tindwyl had been wrong: Vin couldn't be both Mistborn and lady. The horror she had seen in the eyes of the Assemblymen was enough proof for her.

"You didn't need to take a dog's body, OreSeur," Vin said quietly. "I'd rather that you were happy."

"It is all right, Mistress," OreSeur said. "I have grown . . . fond of these kinds of bones. I should like to explore their advantages a little more before I return to human ones."

Vin smiled. He'd chosen another wolfhound—a big brute of a beast. The colorings were different: more black than gray, without any patches of white. She approved.

"OreSeur . . ." Vin said, looking away. "Thank you for what you did for me."

"I fulfill my Contract."

"I've been in other fights," Vin said. "You never intervened in those."

OreSeur didn't answer immediately. "No, I didn't."

"Why this time?"

"I did what felt right, Mistress," OreSeur said.

"Even if it contradicted the Contract?"

OreSeur sat up proudly on his haunches. "I did *not* break my Contract," he said firmly.

"But you attacked a human."

"I didn't kill him," OreSeur said. "We are cautioned to stay out of combat, lest we accidentally cause a human death. Indeed, most of my brethren think that helping someone kill is the same as killing, and feel it is a breach of the Contract. The words are distinct, however. I did nothing wrong."

"And if that man you tackled had broken his neck?"

"Then I would have returned to my kind for execution," OreSeur said.

Vin smiled. "Then you *did* risk your life for me."

"In a small way, I suppose," OreSeur said. "The chances of my actions directly causing that man's death were slim."

"Thank you anyway."

OreSeur bowed his head in acceptance.

"Executed," Vin said. "So you can be killed?"

"Of course, Mistress," OreSeur said. "We aren't immortal."

Vin eyed him.

"I will say nothing specific, Mistress," OreSeur said. "As you might imagine, I would rather not reveal the weaknesses of my kind. Please suffice it to say that they exist."

Vin nodded, but frowned in thought, bringing her knees up to her chest. Something was still bothering her, something about what Elend had said earlier, something about Ore-Seur's actions. . . .

"But," she said slowly, "you couldn't have been killed by swords or staves, right?"

"Correct," OreSeur said. "Though our flesh looks like yours, and though we feel pain, beating us has no permanent effect."

"Then why are you afraid?" Vin said, finally lighting upon what was bothering her.

"Mistress?"

"Why did your people make the Contract?" Vin asked. "Why subjugate yourselves to mankind? If our soldiers couldn't hurt you, then why even worry about us?"

"You have Allomancy," OreSeur said.

"So, Allomancy can kill you?"

"No," OreSeur said, shaking his canine head. "It cannot. But, perhaps we should change the topic. I'm sorry, Mistress. This is very dangerous ground for me."

"I understand," Vin said, sighing. "It's just so frustrating. There's so much I don't know—about the Deepness, about the legal politics . . . even about my own friends!" She sat back, looking up at the ceiling. *And there's still a spy in the palace.. Demoux or Dockson, likely. Maybe I should just order them both taken and held for a time? Would Elend even do such a thing?*

OreSeur was watching her, apparently noting her frustration. Finally, he sighed. "Perhaps there are some things I can speak of, Mistress, if I am careful. What do you know of the origin of the kandra?"

Vin perked up. "Nothing."

"We did not exist before the Ascension," he said.

"You mean to say that the Lord Ruler created you?"

"That is what our lore teaches," OreSeur said. "We are not certain of our purpose. Perhaps we were to be Father's spies."

"Father?" Vin said. "It seems strange to hear him spoken of that way."

"The Lord Ruler created us, Mistress," OreSeur said. "We are his children."

"And I killed him," Vin said. "I . . . feel like I should apologize."

"Just because he is our Father does not mean we accepted everything he did, Mistress," OreSeur said. "Cannot a human man love his father, yet not believe he is a good person?"

"I suppose."

"Kandra theology about Father is complex," OreSeur said. "Even for us, it is difficult to sort through it sometimes."

Vin frowned. "OreSeur? How old are you?"

"Old," he said simply.

"Older than Kelsier?"

"Much," OreSeur. "But not as old as you are thinking. I do not remember the Ascension."

Vin nodded. "Why tell me all of this?"

"Because of your original question, Mistress. Why do we serve the Contract? Well, tell me—if you were the Lord Ruler, and had his power, would you have created servants without building into them a way that you could control them?"

Vin nodded slowly in understanding.

"Father took little thought of the kandra from about the second century after his Ascension," OreSeur said. "We tried to be independent for a time, but it was as I explained, humankind resented us. Feared us. And, some of them knew of our weaknesses. When my ancestors considered their options, they eventually chose voluntary servitude as opposed to forced slavery."

He created them, Vin thought. She had always shared a bit of Kelsier's view regarding the Lord Ruler—that he was more man than deity. But, if he'd truly created a completely new species, then there had to have been some divinity in him.

The power of the Well of Ascension, she thought. *He took it for himself—but it didn't last. It must have run out, and quickly. Otherwise, why would he have needed armies to conquer?*

An initial burst of power, the ability to create, to change—perhaps to save. He'd pushed back the mists, and in the process he'd somehow made the ash begin to fall and the sky turn red. He'd created the kandra to serve him—and probably the koloss, too. He might even have created Allomancers themselves.

And after that, he had returned to being a normal man. Mostly. The Lord Ruler had still held an inordinate amount of power for an Allomancer, and had managed to keep control of his creations—and he had somehow kept the mists from killing.

Until Vin had slain him. Then the koloss had begun to rampage, and the mists had returned. The kandra hadn't been beneath his control at that time, so they remained as they were. But, he built into them a method of control, should he need it. A way to make the kandra serve him. . . .

Vin closed her eyes, and quested out lightly with her Allomantic senses. OreSeur had said that kandra couldn't be affected by Allomancy—but she knew something else about the Lord Ruler, something that had distinguished him from other Allomancers. His inordinate power had allowed him to do things he shouldn't have been able to.

Things like pierce copperclouds, and affect metals inside of a person's body. Maybe *that* was how he controlled the kandra, the thing that OreSeur was speaking of. The reason they feared Mistborn.

Not because Mistborn could kill them, but because Mistborn could do something else. Enslave them, somehow. Tentatively, testing what he'd said earlier, Vin reached out with a Soothing and touched OreSeur's emotions. Nothing happened.

I can do some of the same things as the Lord Ruler, she thought. *I can pierce copperclouds. Perhaps, if I just Push harder . . .*

She focused, and *Pushed* on his emotions with a powerful Soothing. Again, nothing happened. Just as he'd told her. She sat for a moment. And then, impulsively, she burned duralumin and tried one final, massive Push.

OreSeur immediately let out a howl so bestial and unexpected that Vin jumped to her feet in shock, flaring pewter.

OreSeur fell to the bed, shaking.

"OreSeur!" she said, dropping to her knees, grabbing his head. "I'm sorry!"

"Said too much . . ." he muttered, still shaking. "I knew I'd said too much."

"I didn't mean to hurt you," Vin said.

The shaking subsided, and OreSeur fell still for a moment, breathing quietly. Finally, he pulled his head out of her arms. "What you meant is immaterial, Mistress," he said flatly. "The mistake was mine. Please, never do that again."

"I promise," she said. "I'm sorry."

He shook his head, crawling off the bed. "You shouldn't even have been able to do it. There are strange things about you, Mistress—you are like the Allomancers of old, before the passage of generations dulled their powers."

"I'm sorry," Vin said again, feeling helpless. *He saved my life, nearly broke his Contract, and I do this to him. . . .*

OreSeur shrugged. "It is done. I need to rest. I suggest that you do the same."

After that, I began to see other problems.

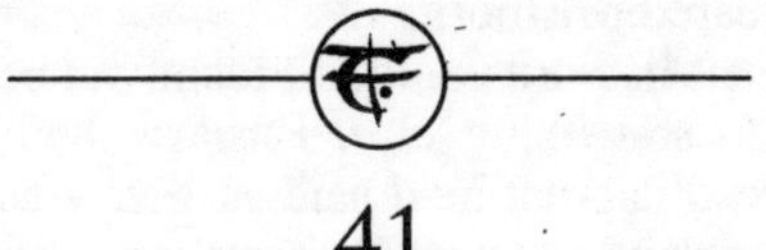

41

"'I WRITE THIS RECORD NOW,'" Sazed read out loud, "'pounding it into a metal slab, because I am afraid. Afraid for myself, yes—I admit to being human. If Alendi does return from the Well of Ascension, I am certain that my death will be one of his first objectives. He is not an evil man, but he is a ruthless one. That is, I think, a product of what he has been through.'"

"That fits what we know of Alendi from the logbook," Tindwyl said. "Assuming that Alendi is that book's author."

Sazed glanced at his pile of notes, running over the basics in his mind. Kwaan had been an ancient Terris scholar. He had discovered Alendi, a man he began to think—through his studies—might be the Hero of Ages, a figure from Terris prophecy. Alendi had listened to him, and had become a political leader. He had conquered much of the world, then traveled north to the Well of Ascension. By then, however, Kwaan had apparently changed his mind about Alendi—and had tried to stop him from getting to the Well.

It fit together. Even though the logbook author never mentioned his own name, it was obvious that he was Alendi. "It is a very safe assumption, I think," Sazed said. "The logbook even speaks of Kwaan, and the falling-out they had."

They sat beside each other in Sazed's rooms. He had requested, and received, a larger desk to hold their multitudinous notes and scribbled theories. Beside the door sat the remnants of their afternoon meal, a soup they had hurriedly gulped down. Sazed itched to take the dishes down to the kitchens, but he hadn't been able to pull himself away yet.

"Continue," Tindwyl requested, sitting back in her chair, looking more relaxed than Sazed had ever seen her. The rings running down the sides of her ears alternated in color—a gold or copper followed by a tin or iron. It was such a simple thing, but there was a beauty to it.

"Sazed?"

Sazed started. "I apologize," he said, then turned back to his reading. " 'I am also afraid, however, that all I have known—that my story—will be forgotten. I am afraid for the world that may come. Afraid because my plans failed. Afraid of a doom brought by the Deepness.' "

"Wait," Tindwyl said. "Why did he fear that?"

"Why would he not?" Sazed asked. "The Deepness—which we assume is the mist—was killing his people. Without sunlight, their crops would not grow, and their animals could not graze."

"But, if Kwaan feared the Deepness, then he should not have opposed Alendi," Tindwyl said. "He was climbing to the Well of Ascension to *defeat* the Deepness."

"Yes," Sazed said. "But by then, Kwaan was convinced that Alendi wasn't the Hero of Ages."

"But why would that matter?" Tindwyl said. "It didn't take a specific person to stop the mists—Rashek's success proves that. Here, skip to the end. Read that passage about Rashek."

" 'I have a young nephew, one Rashek,' " Sazed read. " 'He hates all of Khlennium with the passion of envious youth. He hates Alendi even more acutely—though the two have never met—for Rashek feels betrayed that one of our oppressors should have been chosen as the Hero of Ages.

" 'Alendi will need guides through the Terris mountains. I have charged Rashek with making certain that he and his trusted friends are chosen as those guides. Rashek is to try and lead Alendi in the wrong direction, to discourage him or otherwise foil his quest. Alendi won't know that he has been deceived.

" 'If Rashek fails to lead Alendi astray, then I have instructed the lad to kill my former friend. It is a distant hope. Alendi has survived assassins, wars, and catastrophes. And yet, I hope that in the frozen mountains of Terris, he may finally be exposed. I hope for a miracle.

" 'Alendi must not reach the Well of Ascension. He must not take the power for himself.' "

Tindwyl sat back, frowning.

"What?"

"Something is wrong there, I think," she said. "But I cannot tell you precisely what."

Sazed scanned the text again. "Let us break it down to simple statements, then. Rashek—the man who became the Lord Ruler—was Kwaan's nephew."

"Yes," Tindwyl said.

"Kwaan sent Rashek to mislead, or even kill, his once-friend Alendi the Conqueror—a man climbing the mountains of Terris to seek the Well of Ascension."

Tindwyl nodded.

"Kwaan did this because he feared what would happen if Alendi took the Well's power for himself."

Tindwyl raised a finger. "Why did he fear that?"

"It seems a rational fear, I think," Sazed said.

"Too rational," Tindwyl replied. "Or, rather, perfectly rational. But, tell me, Sazed. When you read Alendi's logbook, did you get the impression that he was the type who would take that power for himself?"

Sazed shook his head. "Actually, the opposite. That is part of what made the logbook so confusing—we couldn't figure out why the man represented within would have done as we assumed he must have. I think that is part of what eventually led Vin to guess that the Lord Ruler wasn't Alendi at all, but Rashek, his packman."

"And Kwaan says that he knew Alendi well," Tindwyl said. "In fact, in this very rubbing, he compliments the man on several occasions. Calls him a good person, I believe."

"Yes," Sazed said, finding the passage. " 'He is a good man—despite it all, he is a good man. A sacrificing man. In truth, all of his actions—all of the deaths, destructions, and pains that he has caused—have hurt him deeply.' "

"So, Kwaan knew Alendi well," Tindwyl said. "And thought highly of him. He also, presumably, knew his nephew Rashek well. Do you see my problem?"

Sazed nodded slowly. "Why send a man of wild temperament, one whose motivations are based on envy and hatred, to kill a man you thought to be good and of worthy temperament? It does seem an odd choice."

"Exactly," Tindwyl said, resting her arms on the table.

"But," Sazed said, "Kwaan says right here that he 'doubts that if Alendi reaches the Well of Ascension, he will take the power and then—in the name of the greater good—give it up.' "

Tindwyl shook her head. "It doesn't make sense, Sazed. Kwaan wrote several times about how he feared the Deepness, but then he tried to foil the hope of stopping it by sending a hateful youth to kill a respected, and presumably wise, leader. Kwaan practically *set up* Rashek to take the power—if letting Alendi take the power was such a concern, wouldn't he have feared that Rashek might do the same?"

"Perhaps we simply see things with the clarity of those regarding events that have already occurred," Sazed said.

Tindwyl shook her head. "We're missing something, Sazed. Kwaan is a very rational, even deliberate, man—one can tell that from his narrative. He was the one who discovered Alendi, and was the first to tout him as the Hero of Ages. Why would he turn against him as he did?"

Sazed nodded, flipping through his translation of the rubbing. Kwaan had gained much notoriety by discovering the Hero. He found the place he was looking for.

There was a place for me in the lore of the Anticipation, the text read. *I thought myself the Announcer, the prophet foretold to discover the Hero of Ages. Renouncing Alendi then would have been to renounce my new position, my acceptance, by the others.*

"Something dramatic must have happened," Tindwyl said. "Something that would make him turn against his friend, the source of his own fame. Something that pricked his conscience so sharply that he was willing to risk opposing the most powerful monarch in the land. Something so frightening that he took a ridiculous chance by sending this Rashek on an assassination mission."

Sazed leafed through his notes. "He fears both the Deepness and what would happen if Alendi took the power. Yet, he cannot seem to decide which one is the greater threat, and neither seems more present in the narrative than the other. Yes, I can see the problem here. Do you think, perhaps, Kwaan was trying to imply something by the inconsistency in his own arguments?"

"Perhaps," Tindwyl said. "The information is just so slim. I cannot judge a man without knowing the context of his life!"

Sazed looked up, eyeing her. "Perhaps we have been studying too hard," he said. "Shall we take a break?"

Tindwyl shook her head. "We don't have the time, Sazed."

He met her eyes. She was right on that point.

"You sense it too, don't you?" she asked.

He nodded. "This city will soon fall. The forces pressing upon it . . . the armies, the koloss, the civil confusion . . ."

"I fear it will be more violent than your friends hope, Sazed," Tindwyl said quietly. "They seem to believe that they can just continue to juggle their problems."

"They are an optimistic group," he said with a smile. "Unaccustomed to being defeated."

"This will be worse than the revolution," Tindwyl said. "I have studied these things, Sazed. I know what happens when a conqueror takes a city. People will die. Many people."

Sazed felt a chill at her words. There was a tension to Luthadel; war was coming to the city. Perhaps one army or another would enter by the blessing of the Assembly, but the other would still strike. The walls of Luthadel would run red when the siege finally ended.

And he feared that end was coming very, very soon.

"You are right," he said, turning back to the notes on his desktop. "We must continue to study. We should collect more of what we can find about the land before the Ascension, so that you may have the context you seek."

She nodded, showing a fatalistic resolve. This was not a task they could complete in the time they had. Deciphering the meaning of the rubbing, comparing it to the logbook, and relating it to the context of the period was a scholarly undertaking that would require the determined work of years.

Keepers had much knowledge—but in this case, it was almost too much. They had been gathering and transmitting records, stories, myths, and legends for so long that it took years for one Keeper to recite the collected works to a new initiate.

Fortunately, included with the mass of information were indexes and summaries created by the Keepers. On top of this came the notes and personal indexes each individual Keeper made. And yet, these only helped the Keeper understand just how much information he had. Sazed himself had spent his life reading, memorizing, and indexing religions. Each night, before he slept, he read some portion of a note or story. He was probably the world's foremost scholar on pre-Ascension religions, and yet he felt as if he knew so little.

Compounding all of that was the inherent unreliability of their information. A great deal of it came from the mouths of simple people, doing their best to remember what their lives had once been like—or, more often, what the lives of their grandparents had once been like. The Keepers hadn't been founded until late in the second century of the Lord Ruler's reign. By then, many religions had already been wiped out in their pure forms.

Sazed closed his eyes, dumped another index from a coppermind into his head, then began to search it. There wasn't much time, true, but Tindwyl and he were Keepers. They were accustomed to beginning tasks that others would have to finish.

Elend Venture, once king of the Central Dominance, stood on the balcony of his keep, overlooking the vast city of Luthadel. Though the first snows had yet to fall, the weather had grown cold. He wore an overcloak, tied at the front, but it didn't protect his face. A chill tingled his cheeks as a wind blew across him, whipping at his cloak. Smoke rose from chimneys, gathering like an ominous shadow above the city before rising up to meld with the ashen red sky.

For every house that produced smoke, there were two that did not. Many of those were probably deserted; the city held nowhere near the population it once had. However, he knew that many of those smokeless houses were still inhabited. Inhabited, and freezing.

I should have been able to do more for them, Elend thought, eyes open to the piercing cold wind. *I should have found a way to get more coal; I should have managed to provide for them all.*

It was humbling, even depressing, to admit that the Lord Ruler had done better than Elend himself. Despite being a heartless tyrant, the Lord Ruler had at least kept a significant portion of the population from starving or freezing. He had kept armies in check, and had kept crime at a manageable level.

To the northeast, the koloss army waited. It had sent no

emissaries to the city, but it was more frightening than either Cett's or Straff's armies. The cold wouldn't scare away its occupants; despite their bare skin, they apparently took little notice of weather changes. This final army was the most disturbing of the three—more dangerous, more unpredictable, and impossible to deal with. Koloss did not bargain.

We haven't been paying enough attention to that threat, he thought as he stood on the balcony. *There's just been so much to do, so much to worry about, that we couldn't focus on an army that might be as dangerous to our enemies as it is to us.*

It was looking less and less likely that the koloss would attack Cett or Straff. Apparently, Jastes was enough in control to keep them waiting to take a shot at Luthadel itself.

"My lord," said a voice from behind. "Please, come back in. That's a fell wind. No use killing yourself from a chill."

Elend turned back. Captain Demoux stood dutifully in the room, along with another bodyguard. In the aftermath of the assassination attempt, Ham had insisted that Elend go about guarded. Elend hadn't complained, though he knew there was little reason for caution anymore. Straff wouldn't want to kill him now that he wasn't king.

So earnest, Elend thought, studying Demoux's face. *Why do I find him youthful? We're nearly the same age.*

"Very well," Elend said, turning and striding into the room. As Demoux closed the balcony doors, Elend removed his cloak. The suit below felt wrong on him. Sloppy, even though he had ordered it cleaned and pressed. The vest was too tight—his practice with the sword was slowly modifying his body—while the coat hung loosely.

"Demoux," Elend said. "When is your next Survivor rally?"

"Tonight, my lord."

Elend nodded. He'd feared that; it would be a cold night.

"My lord," Demoux said, "do you still intend to come?"

"Of course," Elend said. "I gave my word that I would join with your cause."

"That was before you lost the vote, my lord."

"That is immaterial," Elend said. "I am joining your movement because it is important to the skaa, Demoux, and I want to understand the will of my . . . of the people. I promised you dedication—and you shall have it."

Demoux seemed a bit confused, but spoke no further. Elend eyed his desk, considering some studying, but found it hard to motivate himself in the chill room. Instead, he pushed open the door and strode out into the hallway. His guards followed.

He stopped himself from turning toward Vin's rooms. She needed her rest, and it didn't do her much good to have him peeking in every half hour to check on her. So instead he turned to wander down a different passageway.

The back hallways of Keep Venture were tight, dark, stone constructions of labyrinthine complexity. Perhaps it was because he'd grown up in these passages, but he felt at home in their dark, secluded confines. They had been the perfect place for a young man who didn't really care to be found. Now he used them for another reason; the corridors provided a perfect place for extended walking. He didn't point himself in any particular direction, he just moved, working out his frustration to the beating of his own footsteps.

I can't fix the city's problems, he told himself. *I have to let Penrod handle that—he's the one the people want.*

That should have made things easier for Elend. It let him focus on his own survival, not to mention let him spend time revitalizing his relationship with Vin. She, however, seemed different lately. Elend tried to tell himself it was just her injury, but he sensed something deeper. Something in the way she looked at him, something in the way she reacted to his affection. And, despite himself, he could think of only one thing that had changed.

He was no longer king.

Vin was not shallow. She had shown him nothing but devotion and love during their two years together. And yet, how could she not react—even if unconsciously—to his colossal failure? During the assassination attempt, he had watched her fight. *Really* watched her fight, for the first time. Until that day, he hadn't realized just how amazing she was. She wasn't just a warrior, and she wasn't just an Allomancer. She was a force, like thunder or wind. The way she had killed that last man, smashing his head with her own . . .

How could she love a man like me? he thought. *I couldn't even hold my throne. I wrote the very laws that deposed me.*

He sighed, continuing to walk. He felt like he should be scrambling, trying to figure out a way to convince Vin that he was worthy of her. But that would just make him seem more incompetent. There was no correcting past mistakes, especially since he could see no real "mistakes" he had made. He had done the best he could, and that had proven insufficient.

He paused at an intersection. Once, a relaxing dip into a book would have been enough to calm him. Now he felt nervous. Tense. A little . . . like he assumed Vin usually felt.

Maybe I could learn from her, he thought. *What would Vin do in my situation?* She certainly wouldn't just wander around, brooding and feeling sorry for herself. Elend frowned, looking down a hallway lighted by flickering oil lamps, only half of them lit. Then he took off, waking with a determined stride toward a particular set of rooms.

He knocked quietly, and got no response. Finally, he poked his head in. Sazed and Tindwyl sat quietly before a desk piled high with scraps of paper and ledgers. They both sat staring, as if at nothing, their eyes bearing the glazed-over look of someone who had been stunned. Sazed's hand rested on the table. Tindwyl's rested on top of it.

Sazed shook himself alert suddenly, turning to regard Elend. "Lord Venture! I am sorry. I did not hear you enter."

"It's all right, Saze," Elend said, walking into the room. As he did, Tindwyl shook awake as well, and she removed her hand from Sazed's. Elend nodded to Demoux and his companion—who were still following—indicating that they should remain outside, then closed the door.

"Elend," Tindwyl said, her voice laced with its typical

undercurrent of displeasure. "What is your purpose in bothering us? You have already proven your incompetence quite soundly—I see no need for further discussion."

"This is still my home, Tindwyl," Elend replied. "Insult me again, and you will find yourself ejected from the premises."

Tindwyl raised an eyebrow.

Sazed paled. "Lord Venture," he said quickly, "I don't think that Tindwyl meant to—"

"It's all right, Sazed," Elend said, raising a hand. "She was just testing to see if I had reverted back to my previous state of insultability."

Tindwyl shrugged. "I have heard reports of your moping through thc palacc hallways like a lost child."

"Those reports are true," Elend said. "But that doesn't mean that my pride is completely gone."

"Good," Tindwyl said, nodding to a chair. "Seat yourself, if you wish."

Elend nodded, pulling the chair over before the two and sitting. "I need advice."

"I've given you what I can already," Tindwyl said. "In fact, I've perhaps given you too much. My continued presence here makes it seem that I'm taking sides."

"I'm not king anymore," Elend said. "Therefore, I have no side. I'm just a man seeking truth."

Tindwyl smiled. "Ask your questions, then."

Sazed watched the exchange with obvious interest.

I know, Elend thought, *I'm not sure I understand our relationship either.* "Here is my problem," he said. "I lost the throne, essentially, because I wasn't willing to lie."

"Explain," Tindwyl said.

"I had a chance to obscure a piece of the law," Elend said. "At the last moment, I could have made the Assembly take me as king. Instead, I gave them a bit of information that was true, but which ended up costing me the throne."

"I'm not surprised," Tindwyl said.

"I doubted that you would be," Elend said. "Now, do you think I was foolish to do as I did?"

"Yes."

Elend nodded.

"But," Tindwyl said, "that moment isn't what cost you the throne, Elend Venture. That moment was a small thing, far too simple to credit with your large-scale failure. You lost the throne because you wouldn't command your armies to secure the city, because you insisted on giving the Assembly too much freedom, and because you don't employ assassins or other forms of pressure. In short, Elend Venture, you lost the throne because you are a good man."

Elend shook his head. "Can you not be both a man who follows his conscience *and* a good king, then?"

Tindwyl frowned in thought.

"You ask an age-old question, Elend," Sazed said quietly. "A question that monarchs, priests, and humble men of destiny have always asked. I do not know that there is an answer."

"Should I have told the lie, Sazed?" Elend asked.

"No," Sazed said, smiling. "Perhaps another man should have, in your same position. But, a man must be cohesive with himself. You have made your decisions in life, and changing yourself at the last moment—telling this lie—would have been against who you are. It is better for you to have done as you did and lost the throne, I think."

Tindwyl frowned. "His ideals are nice, Sazed. But what of the people? What if they die because Elend wasn't capable of controlling his own conscience?"

"I do not wish to argue with you, Tindwyl," Sazed said. "It is simply my opinion that he chose well. It is his right to follow his conscience, then trust in providence to fill in the holes caused by the conflict between morality and logic."

Providence. "You mean God," Elend said.

"I do."

Elend shook his head. "What is God, Sazed, but a device used by obligators?"

"Why do you make the choices that you do, Elend Venture?"

"Because they're right," Elend said.

"And why are these things right?"

"I don't know," Elend said with a sigh, leaning back. He caught a disapproving glance from Tindwyl at his posture, but he ignored her. He wasn't king; he could slouch if he wanted to. "You talk of God, Sazed, but don't you preach of a hundred different religions?"

"Three hundred, actually," Sazed said.

"Well, which one do *you* believe?" Elend asked.

"I believe them all."

Elend shook his head. "That doesn't make sense. You've only pitched a half-dozen to me, but I can already see that they're incompatible."

"It is not my position to judge truth, Lord Venture," Sazed said, smiling. "I simply carry it."

Elend sighed. *Priests . . .* he thought. *Sometimes, talking to Sazed is like talking to an obligator.*

"Elend," Tindwyl said, her tone softening. "I think you handled this situation in the wrong way. However, Sazed does have a point. You were true to your own convictions, and that is a regal attribute, I think."

"And what should I do now?" he asked.

"Whatever you wish," Tindwyl said. "It was never my place to tell you what to do. I simply gave you knowledge of what men in your place did in the past."

"And what would they have done?" Elend asked. "These great leaders of yours, how would they have reacted to my situation?"

"It is a meaningless question," she said. "They would not have found themselves in this situation, for they would not have lost their titles in the first place."

"Is that what it's about, then?" Elend asked. "The title?"

"Isn't that what we were discussing?" Tindwyl asked.

Elend didn't answer. *What do you think makes a man a good king?* he had once asked of Tindwyl. *Trust,* she had replied. *A good king is one who is trusted by his people—and one who deserves that trust.*

Elend stood up. "Thank you, Tindwyl," he said.

Tindwyl frowned in confusion, then turned to Sazed. He looked up and met Elend's eyes, cocking his head slightly. Then he smiled. "Come, Tindwyl," he said. "We should return to our studies. His Majesty has work to do, I think."

Tindwyl continued to frown as Elend left the room. His

guards followed behind as he quickly strode down the hallway.

I won't go back to the way I was, Elend thought. *I won't continue to fret and worry. Tindwyl taught me better than that, even if she never really understood me.*

Elend arrived at his rooms a few moments later. He stalked directly in, then opened his closet. The clothing Tindwyl had chosen for him—the clothing of a king—waited inside.

Some of you may know of my fabled memory. It is true; I need not a Feruchemist's metalmind to memorize a sheet of words in an instant.

42

"GOOD," ELEND SAID, USING A charcoal stick to circle another section on the city map before him. "What about here?"

Demoux scratched his chin. "Grainfield? That's a nobleman's neighborhood, my lord."

"It used to be," Elend said. "Grainfield was filled with cousin houses to the Ventures. When my father pulled out of the city, so did most of them."

"Then we'll probably find the homes filled with skaa transients, I'd guess."

Elend nodded. "Move them out."

"Excuse me, my lord?" Demoux said. The two stood in Keep Venture's large carriage landing. Soldiers moved in a bustle through the spacious room. Many of them didn't wear uniforms; they weren't on official city business. Elend was no longer king, but they had still come at his request.

That said something, at least.

"We need to move the skaa out of those homes," Elend continued. "Noblemen's houses are mostly stone mansions with a lot of small rooms. They're extremely hard to heat, requiring a separate hearth or a stove for every room. The skaa tenements are depressing, but they have massive hearths and open rooms."

Demoux nodded slowly.

"The Lord Ruler couldn't have his workers freezing," Elend said. "Those tenements are the best way to efficiently look after a large population of people with limited resources."

"I understand, my lord," Demoux said.

"Don't force them, Demoux," Elend said. "My personal guard—even augmented with army volunteers—has no official authority in the city. If a family wants to stay in their pilfered aristocratic house, let them. Just make certain that they know there's an alternative to freezing."

Demoux nodded, then moved over to pass on the commands. Elend turned as a messenger arrived. The man had to weave his way through an organized jumble of soldiers receiving orders and making plans.

Elend nodded to the newcomer. "You're on the demolitions scout group, correct?"

The man nodded as he bowed. He wasn't in uniform; he was a soldier, not one of Elend's guards. He was a younger man, with a square jaw, balding head, and honest smile.

"Don't I know you?" Elend said.

"I helped you a year ago, my lord," the man said. "I led you into the Lord Ruler's palace to help rescue Lady Vin. . . ."

"Goradel," Elend said, remembering. "You used to be in the Lord Ruler's personal guard."

The man nodded. "I joined up in your army after that day. Seemed like the thing to do."

Elend smiled. "Not my army anymore, Goradel, but I do appreciate you coming to help us today. What's your report?"

"You were right, my lord," Goradel said, "the skaa have already robbed the empty homes for furniture. But, not many thought of the walls. A good half of the abandoned mansions have wooden walls on the inside, and a lot of the tenements were made of wood. Most all of them have wooden roofs."

"Good," Elend said. He surveyed the gathering mass of men. He hadn't told them his plans; he'd simply asked for volunteers to help him with some manual labor. He hadn't expected the response to number in the hundreds.

"It looks like we're gathering quite a group, my lord," Demoux said, rejoining Elend.

Elend nodded, giving leave for Goradel to withdraw. "We'll be able to try an even more ambitious project than I'd planned."

"My lord," Demoux said. "Are you certain you want to start tearing the city down around ourselves?"

"We either lose buildings or we lose people, Demoux," Elend said. "The buildings go."

"And if the king tries to stop us?"

"Then we obey," Elend said. "But I don't think Lord Penrod will object. He's too busy trying to get a bill through the Assembly that hands the city over to my father. Besides, it's probably better for him to have these men here, working, than it is to have them sitting and worrying in the barracks."

Demoux fell silent. Elend did as well; both knew how precarious their position was. Only a short time had passed since the assassination attempt and the transfer of power, and the city was in shock. Cett was still holed up inside of Keep Hasting, and his armies had moved into position to attack the city. Luthadel was like a man with a knife pressed very closely to his throat. Each breath cut the skin.

I can't do much about that now, Elend thought. *I have to make certain the people don't freeze these next few nights.* He could feel the bitter cold, despite the daylight, his cloak, and the shelter. There were a lot of people in Luthadel, but if he could get enough men tearing down enough buildings, he just might be able to do some good.

"My lord!"

Elend turned as a short man with a drooping mustache approached. "Ah, Felt," he said. "You have news?" The man was working on the poisoned-food problem—specifically how the city was being breached.

The scout nodded. "I do indeed, my lord. We interrogated the refugees with a Rioter, and we came up dry. Then, however, I started thinking. The refugees seemed too obvious to me. Strangers in the city? Of course they'd be the first ones we'd suspect. I figured, with how much has been going wrong with the wells and the food and the like, someone *has* to be sneaking in and out of the city."

Elend nodded. They'd been watching Cett's soldiers inside Keep Hasting very carefully, and none of them was responsible. Straff's Mistborn was still a possibility, but Vin had never believed that he was behind the poisoning. Elend hoped that the trail—if it could be found—would lead back to someone in his own palace, hopefully revealing who on his serving staff had been replaced by a kandra.

"Well?" Elend asked.

"I interrogated the people who run passwalls," Felt continued. "I don't think they're to blame."

"Passwalls?"

Felt nodded. "Covert passages out of the city. Tunnels or the like."

"Such things exist?" Elend asked with surprise.

"Of course, my lord," Felt said. "Moving between cities was very difficult for skaa thieves during the Lord Ruler's reign. Everyone who entered Luthadel was subject to interview and interrogation. So, ways to get into the city covertly were very prevalent. Most of those have shut down—the ones who used to lower people up and down by ropes over the walls. A few are still running, but I don't think they are letting the spies in. Once that first well was poisoned, the passwalls all got paranoid that you'd come after them. Since then, they've only been letting people *out* of the city—ones who want to run from the besieged city and the like."

Elend frowned. He wasn't certain what he thought of the fact that people were disobeying his order that the gates be shut, with no passage out.

"Next," Felt said, "I tried the river."

"We thought of that," Elend said. "The grates covering the water are all secure."

Felt smiled. "That they are. I sent some men down under the water to search about, and we found several locks down below, keeping the river grates in place."

"What?"

"Someone pried the grates free, my lord," Felt said, "then locked them back into place so it wouldn't look suspicious. That way, they could swim in and out at their leisure."

Elend raised an eyebrow.

"You want us to replace the grates?" Felt asked.

"No," Elend said. "No, just replace those locks with new ones, then post men to watch. Next time those prisoners try and get into the city, I want them to find themselves trapped."

Felt nodded, retreating with a happy smile on his face. His talents as a spy hadn't been put to much good use lately, and he seemed to be enjoying the tasks Elend was giving him. Elend made a mental note to think about putting Felt to work on locating the kandra spy—assuming, of course, that Felt himself wasn't the spy.

"My lord," Demoux said, approaching. "I think I might be able to offer a second opinion on how the poisonings are occurring."

Elend turned. "Oh?"

Demoux nodded, waving for a man to approach from the side of the room. He was younger, perhaps eighteen, and had the dirty face and clothing of a skaa worker.

"This is Larn," Demoux said. "A member of my congregation."

The young man bowed to Elend, posture nervous.

"You may speak, Larn," Demoux said. "Tell Lord Venture what you saw."

"Well, my lord," the young man said. "I tried to go tell this to the king. The new king, I mean." He flushed, embarrassed.

"It's all right," Elend said. "Continue."

"Well, the men there turned me away. Said the king didn't

have time for me. So, I came to Lord Demoux. I figured he might believe me."

"About what?" Elend asked.

"Inquisitor, my lord," the man said quietly. "I saw one in the city."

Elend felt a chill. "You're sure?"

The young man nodded. "I've lived in Luthadel all my life, my lord. Watched executions a number of times. I'd recognize one of those monsters, sure I would. I saw him. Spikes through the eyes, tall and robed, slinking about at night. Near the center squares of the city. I promise you."

Elend shared a look with Demoux.

"He's not the only one, my lord," Demoux said quietly. "Some other members of my congregation claimed to have seen an Inquisitor hanging around Kredik Shaw. I dismissed the first few, but Larn, he's trustworthy. If he said he saw something, he did. Eyes nearly as good as a Tineye, that one."

Elend nodded slowly, and ordered a patrol from his personal guard to keep watch in the area indicated. After that, he turned his attention back to the wood-gathering effort. He gave the orders, organizing the men into teams, sending some to begin working, others to gather recruits. Without fuel, many of the city's forges had shut down, and the workers were idle. They could use something to occupy their time.

Elend saw energy in the men's eyes as they began to split up. Elend knew that determination, that firmness of eye and arm. It came from the satisfaction of doing something, of not just sitting around and waiting for fate—or kings—to act.

Elend turned back to the map, making a few notations. From the corner of his eye, he saw Ham saunter in. "So this is where they all went!" Ham said. "The sparring grounds are empty."

Elend looked up, smiling.

"You're back to the uniform, then?" Ham asked.

Elend glanced down at his white outfit. Designed to stand out, to set him apart from a city stained by ash. "Yes."

"Too bad," Ham said with a sigh. "Nobody should have to wear a uniform."

Elend raised an eyebrow. In the face of undeniable winter, Ham had finally taken to wearing a shirt beneath his vest. He wore no cloak or coat, however.

Elend turned back to the map. "The clothing suits me," he said. "It just feels right. Anyway, that vest of yours is as much a uniform as this is."

"No it's not."

"Oh?" Elend asked. "Nothing screams Thug like a man who goes about in the winter without a coat, Ham. You've used your clothing to change how people react to you, to let them know who you are and what you represent—which is essentially what a uniform does."

Ham paused. "That's an interesting way of looking at it."

"What?" Elend said. "You never argued about something like this with Breeze?"

Ham shook his head as he turned to look over the groups of men, listening to the men Elend had appointed to give orders.

He's changed, Elend thought. *Running this city, dealing with all of this, it's even changed him.* The Thug was more solemn, now—more focused. Of course, he had even more stake in the city's safety than the rest of the crew. It was sometimes hard to remember that the free-spirited Thug was a family man. Ham tended to not talk much about Mardra or his two children. Elend suspected it was habit; Ham had spent much of his marriage living apart from his family in order to keep them safe.

This whole city is my family, Elend thought, watching the soldiers leave to do their work. Some might have thought something as simple as gathering firewood to be a mundane task, of little relevance in a city threatened by three armies. However, Elend knew that the freezing skaa people would receive the fuel with as much appreciation as they would salvation from the armies.

The truth was that Elend felt a little like his soldiers did. He felt a satisfaction—a thrill even—from doing something, *anything,* to help.

"What if Cett's attack comes?" Ham said, still looking over the soldiers. "A good portion of the army will be out scattered through the city."

"Even if we have a thousand men in my teams, that's not much of a dent in our forces. Besides, Clubs thinks there will be plenty of time to gather them. We've got messengers set up."

Elend looked back at his map. "Anyway, I don't think Cett's going to attack just yet. He's pretty safe in that keep, there. We'll never take him—we'd have to pull too many men away from the city defenses, leaving ourselves exposed. The only thing he really has to worry about is my father . . ."

Elend trailed off.

"What?" Ham said.

"That's why Cett is here," Elend said, blinking in surprise. "Don't you see? He intentionally left himself without options. If Straff attacks, Cett's armies will end up fighting alongside our own. He's locked in his fate with ours."

Ham frowned. "Seems like a pretty desperate move."

Elend nodded, thinking back to his meeting with Cett. " 'Desperate,' " he said. "That's a good word. Cett is desperate for some reason—one I haven't been able to figure out. Anyway, by putting himself in here, he sides with us against Straff—whether we want the alliance or not."

"But, what if the Assembly gives the city to Straff? If our men join with him and attack Cett?"

"That's the gamble he took," Elend said. *Cett never intended to be able to walk away from the confrontation here in Luthadel. He intends to take the city or be destroyed.*

He is waiting, hoping Straff will attack, worrying that we'll just give into him. But neither can happen as long as Straff is afraid of Vin. A three-way standoff. With the koloss as a fourth element that nobody can predict.

Someone needed to do something to tip the scales. "Demoux," Elend said. "Are you ready to take over here?"

Captain Demoux looked over, nodding.

Elend turned to Ham. "I have a question for you, Ham."

Ham raised an eyebrow.

"How insane are you feeling at the moment?

Elend led his horse out of the tunnel into the scraggly landscape outside of Luthadel. He turned, craning to look up at the wall. Hopefully, the soldiers there had gotten his message, and wouldn't mistake him for a spy or a scout of one of the enemy armies. He'd rather not end up in Tindwyl's histories as the ex-king who'd died by an arrow from one of his own men.

Ham led a small, grizzled woman from the tunnel. As Elend had guessed, Ham had easily found a suitable passwall to get them out of the city.

"Well, there you go," said the elderly woman, resting on her cane.

"Thank you, good woman," Elend said. "You have served your dominance well this day."

The woman snorted, raising an eyebrow—though, from what Elend could tell, she was quite nearly blind. Elend smiled, pulling out a pouch and handing it to her. She reached into it with gnarled, but surprisingly dexterous, fingers and counted out the contents. "Three extra?"

"To pay you to leave a scout here," Elend said. "To watch for our return."

"Return?" the woman asked. "You aren't running?"

"No," Elend said. "I just have some business with one of the armies."

The woman raised the eyebrow again. "Well, none of Granny's business," she muttered, turning back down the hole with a tapping cane. "For three clips, I can find a grandson to sit out here for a few hours. Lord Ruler knows, I have enough of them."

Ham watched her go, a spark of fondness in his eyes.

"How long have you known about this place?" Elend asked, watching as a couple of burly men pulled closed the hidden section of stone. Half burrowed, half cut from the wall's stones themselves, the tunnel was a remarkable feat. Even after hearing about the existence of such things from

Felt earlier, it was still a shock to travel through one hidden not a few minutes' ride from Keep Venture itself.

Ham turned back to him as the false wall snapped shut. "Oh, I've known of this for years and years," he said. "Granny Hilde used to give me sweets when I was a kid. Of course, that was really just a cheap way of getting some quiet—yet well-targeted—publicity for her passwall. When I was grown, I used to use this to sneak Mardra and the kids in and out of the city when they came to visit."

"Wait," Elend said. "You grew up in Luthadel?"

"Of course."

"On the streets, like Vin?"

Ham shook his head. "Not really like Vin," he said in a subdued voice, scanning the wall. "I don't really think anyone grew up like Vin. I had skaa parents—my grandfather was the nobleman. I was involved with the underground, but I had my parents for a good portion of my childhood. Besides, I was a boy—and a large one." He turned toward Elend. "I suspect that makes a big difference."

Elend nodded.

"You're not going to shut this place down, are you?" Ham asked.

Elend turned with shock. "Why would I?"

Ham shrugged. "It doesn't exactly seem like the kind of honest enterprise that you would approve of. There are probably people fleeing from the city nightly through this hole. Granny Hilde is known to take coin and not ask questions—even if she does grumble at you a bit."

Ham did have a point. *Probably why he didn't tell me about the place until I specifically asked.* His friends walked a fine line, close to their old ties with the underground, yet working hard to build up the government they'd sacrificed so much to create.

"I'm not king," Elend said, leading his horse away from the city. "What Granny Hilde does isn't any of my business."

Ham moved up beside him, looking relieved. Elend could see that relief dissipate, however, as the reality of what they were doing settled in. "I don't like this, El."

They stopped walking as Elend mounted. "Neither do I."

Ham took a deep breath, then nodded.

My old nobleman friends would have tried to talk me out of this, Elend thought with amusement. *Why did I surround myself with people who had been loyal to the Survivor? They* expect *their leaders to take irrational risks.*

"I'll go with you," Ham said.

"No," Elend said. "It won't make a difference. Stay here, wait to see if I get back. If I don't, tell Vin what happened."

"Sure, I'll tell her," Ham said wryly. "Then I'll proceed to remove her daggers from my chest. Just make sure you come back, all right?"

Elend nodded, barely paying attention. His eyes were focused on the army in the distance. An army without tents, carriages, food carts, or servants. An army who had eaten the foliage to the ground in a wide swath around them. Koloss.

Sweat made the reins slick in Elend's hands. This was different from before, when he'd gone into Straff's army and Cett's keep. This time he was alone. Vin couldn't get him out if things went bad; she was still recovering from her wounds, and nobody knew what Elend was doing but Ham.

What do I owe the people of this city? Elend thought. *They rejected me. Why do I still insist on trying to protect them?*

"I recognize that look, El," Ham said. "Let's go back."

Elend closed his eyes, letting out a quiet sigh. Then he snapped his eyes open and kicked his horse into a gallop.

It had been years since he'd seen koloss, and that experience had come only at his father's insistence. Straff hadn't trusted the creatures, and had never liked having garrisons of them in the Northern Dominance, one just a few days' march from his home city of Urteau. Those koloss had been a reminder, a warning, from the Lord Ruler.

Elend rode his horse hard, as if using its momentum to bolster his own will. Aside from one brief visit to the Urteau koloss garrison, everything he knew of the creatures came from books—but Tindwyl's instruction had weakened his once absolute, and slightly naive, trust in his learning.

It will have to be enough, Elend thought as he approached the camp. He gritted his teeth, slowing his animal as he approached a wandering squad of Koloss.

It was as he remembered. One large creature—its skin revoltingly split and cracked by stretch marks—led a few medium-sized beasts, whose bleeding rips were only beginning to appear at the corners of their mouths and the edges of their eyes. A smattering of smaller creatures—their baggy skin loose and sagging beneath their eyes and arms—accompanied their betters.

Elend reined in his horse, trotting it over to the largest beast. "Take me to Jastes."

"Get off your horse," the koloss said.

Elend looked the creature directly in the eyes. Atop his horse, he was nearly the same height. "Take me to Jastes."

The koloss regarded him with a set of beady, unreadable eyes. It bore a rip from one eye to the other, above the nose, a secondary rip curving down to one of the nostrils. The nose itself was pulled so tight it was twisted and flattened, held to the bone a few inches off-center.

This was the moment. The books said the creature would either do as commanded or simply attack him. Elend sat tensely.

"Come," the koloss snapped, turning to walk back toward the camp. The rest of the creatures surrounded Elend's horse, and the beast shuffled nervously. Elend kept a tight hold on his reins and nudged the animal forward. It responded skittishly.

He should have felt good at his small victory, but his tension only increased. They moved forward into the koloss camp. It was like being swallowed. Like letting a rockslide collapse around you. Koloss looked up as he passed, watching him with their red, emotionless eyes. Many others just stood silently around their cooking fires, unresponsive, like men who had been born dull-minded and witless.

Others fought. They killed each other, wrestling on the ground before their uncaring companions. No philosopher, scientist, or scholar had been able to determine exactly what set off a koloss. Greed seemed a good motivation. Yet, they would sometimes attack when there was plenty of food, killing a companion for *his* hunk of beef. Pain was another good motivator, apparently, as was a challenge to authority. Carnal, visceral reasons. And yet, there seemed to be times when they attacked without any cause or reason.

And after fighting, they would explain themselves in calm tones, as if their actions were perfectly rational. Elend shivered as he heard yells, telling himself that he would probably be all right until he reached Jastes. Koloss usually just attacked each other.

Unless they got into a blood frenzy.

He pushed that thought away, instead focusing on the things that Sazed had mentioned about his trip into the koloss camp. The creatures wore the wide, brutish iron swords that Sazed had described. The bigger the koloss, the bigger the weapon. When a koloss reached a size where he thought he needed a larger sword, he had only two choices: find one that had been discarded, or kill someone and take theirs. A koloss population could often be crudely controlled by increasing or decreasing the number of swords available to the group.

None of the scholars knew how the creatures bred.

As Sazed had explained, these koloss also had strange little pouches tied to their sword straps. *What are they?* Elend thought. *Sazed said he saw the largest koloss carrying three or four. But that one leading my group has almost twenty.* Even the small koloss in Elend's group had three pouches.

That's the difference, he thought. *Whatever is in those pouches, could it be the way Jastes controls the creatures?*

There was no way to know, save begging one of the pouches off a koloss—and he doubted they would let them go.

As he walked, he noticed another oddity: some of the koloss were wearing clothing. Before, he'd seen them only in loincloths, as Sazed had reported. Yet, many of these koloss had pants, shirts, or skirts pulled onto their bodies. They wore the clothing without regard for size, and most pieces were so tight they had torn. Others were so loose they had to be tied on. Elend saw a few of the larger koloss wearing garments like bandanas tied around their arms or heads.

"We are not koloss," the lead koloss suddenly said, turning to Elend as they walked.

Elend frowned. "Explain."

"You think we are koloss," it said through lips that were stretched too tightly to work properly. "We are humans. We will live in your city. We will kill you, and we will take it."

Elend shivered, realizing the source of the mismatched garments. They had come from the village that the koloss had attacked, the one whose refugees had trickled into Luthadel. This appeared to be a new development in koloss thinking. Or, had it always been there, repressed by the Lord Ruler? The scholar in Elend was fascinated. The rest of him was simply horrified.

His koloss guide paused before a small group of tents, the only such structures in the camp. Then the lead koloss turned and yelled, startling Elend's horse. Elend fought to keep his mount from throwing him as the koloss jumped and attacked one of its companions, proceeding to pummel it with a massive fist.

Elend won his struggle. The lead koloss, however, did not.

Elend climbed off his horse, patting the beast on the neck as the victimized koloss pulled his sword from the chest of his former leader. The survivor—who now bore several cuts in his skin that hadn't come from stretching—bent down to harvest the pouches tied to the corpse's back. Elend watched with a muted fascination as the koloss stood and spoke.

"He was never a good leader," it said in a slurred voice.

I can't let these monsters attack my city, Elend thought. *I have to do something.* He pulled his horse forward, turning his back on the koloss as he entered the secluded section of camp, watched over by a group of nervous young men in uniforms. Elend handed his reins to one of them.

"Take care of this for me," Elend said, striding forward.

"Wait!" one of the soldiers said. "Halt!"

Elend turned sharply, facing the shorter man, who was trying to both level his spear at Elend and keep an eye on the koloss. Elend didn't try to be harsh; he just wanted to keep his own anxiety under control and keep moving. Either way, the resulting glare probably would have impressed even Tindwyl.

The soldier jerked to a halt.

"I am Elend Venture," Elend said. "You know that name?"

The man nodded.

"You may announce me to Lord Lekal," Elend said. "Just get to the tent before I do."

The young man took off at a dash. Elend followed, striding up to the tent, where other soldiers stood hesitantly.

What must it have done to them, Elend wondered, *living surrounded by koloss, so terribly outnumbered?* Feeling a stab of pity, he didn't try to bully his way in. He stood with faux patience until a voice called from inside. "Let him in."

Elend brushed past the guards and threw open the tent flap.

The months had not been kind to Jastes Lekal. Somehow, the few wisps of hair on his head looked far more pathetic than complete baldness would have. His suit was sloppy and stained, his eyes underlined by a pair of deep bags. He was pacing, and jumped slightly when Elend entered.

Then he froze for a moment, eyes wide. Finally, he raised a quivering hand to push back hair he didn't have. "Elend?" he asked. "What in the Lord Ruler's name happened to you?"

"Responsibility, Jastes," Elend said quietly. "It appears that neither of us were ready for it."

"Out," Jastes said, waving to his guards. They shuffled past Elend, closing the tent flap behind them.

"It's been a while, Elend," Jastes said, chuckling weakly.

Elend nodded.

"I remember those days," Jastes said, "sitting in your den

or mine, sharing a drink with Telden. We were so innocent, weren't we?"

"Innocent," Elend said, "but hopeful."

"Want something to drink?" Jastes said, turning toward the room's desk. Elend eyed the bottles and flasks lying in the corner of the room. They were all empty. Jastes removed a full bottle from the desk and poured Elend a small cup, the size and clear color an indication that this was no simple dinner wine.

Elend accepted the small cup, but did not drink. "What happened, Jastes? How did the clever, thoughtful philosopher I knew turn into a tyrant?"

"Tyrant?" Jastes snapped, downing his cup in a single shot. "I'm no tyrant. Your father's the tyrant. I'm just a realist."

"Sitting at the center of a koloss army doesn't seem to be a very realistic position to me."

"I can control them."

"And Suisna?" Elend asked. "The village they slaughtered?"

Jastes wavered. "That was an unfortunate accident."

Elend looked down at the drink in his hand, then threw it aside, the liquor splashing on the dusty tent floor. "This isn't my father's den, and we are not friends any longer. I will call no man friend who leads something like *this* against my city. What happened to your honor, Jastes Lekal?"

Jastes snorted, glancing at the spilled liquor. "That's always been the problem with you, Elend. So certain, so optimistic, so self-righteous."

"It was *our* optimism," Elend said, stepping forward. "We wanted to change things, Jastes, not destroy them!"

"Is that so?" Jastes countered, showing a temper Elend had never seen in his friend. "You want to know why I'm here, Elend? Did you even *pay attention* to what was happening in the Southern Dominance while you played in Luthadel?"

"I'm sorry about what happened to your family, Jastes."

"Sorry?" Jastes said, snatching the bottle off his desk. "You're *sorry*? I implemented your plans, Elend. I did everything we talked about—freedom, political honesty. I trusted my allies rather than crushing them into submission. And you know what happened?"

Elend closed his eyes.

"They killed everyone, Elend," Jastes said. "That's what you do when you take over. You kill your rivals and their families—even the young girls, even the babies. And you leave their bodies, as a warning. That's good politics. That's how you stay in power!"

"It's easy to believe in something when you win all the time, Jastes," Elend said, opening his eyes. "The losses are what define a man's faith."

"Losses?" Jastes demanded. "My sister was a *loss*?"

"No, I mean—"

"Enough!" Jastes snapped, slamming the bottle down on his desk. "Guards!"

Two men threw back the tent flap and moved into the room.

"Take His Majesty captive," Jastes said, with an unsteady wave of his hand. "Send a messenger to the city, tell them that we want to negotiate."

"I'm not king anymore, Jastes," Elend said.

Jastes stopped.

"Do you think I'd come here and let myself get captured if I were king?" Elend asked. "They deposed me. The Assembly invoked a no-confidence clause and chose a new king."

"You bloody idiot," Jastes said.

"Losses, Jastes," Elend said. "It hasn't been as hard for me as it was for you, but I do think I understand."

"So," Jastes said, running a hand through his "hair," "that fancy suit and haircut didn't save you, eh?"

"Take your koloss and go, Jastes."

"That sounded like a threat, Elend," Jastes said. "You aren't king, you don't have an army, and I don't see your Mistborn around. What grounds do you have for threats?"

"They're *koloss,*" Elend said. "Do you really want them getting into the city? It's your home, Jastes—or, it was once. There are thousands of people inside!"

"I can . . . control my army," Jastes said.

"No, I doubt you can," Elend said. "What happened, Jastes? Did they decide they needed a king? They decided that's the way that 'humans' did it, so they should do it, too? What is it that they carry in those pouches?"

Jastes didn't answer.

Elend sighed. "What happens when one of them just snaps and attacks you?"

Jastes shook his head. "I'm sorry, Elend," he said quietly. "I can't let Straff get that atium."

"And my people?"

Jastes paused only briefly, then lowered his eyes and motioned to the guards. One laid a hand on Elend's shoulder.

Elend's reaction surprised even himself. He slammed his elbow up into the man's face, shattering his nose, then took the other man down with a kick to the leg. Before Jastes could do more than cry out, Elend jumped forward.

Elend ripped an obsidian knife—given to him by Vin—from his boot and caught Jastes by the shoulder. Elend slammed the whimpering man around, pushing him backward onto the desk and—barely thinking to consider his actions—rammed the knife into his old friend's shoulder.

Jastes emitted a loud, pathetic scream.

"If killing you would do anything useful, Jastes," Elend growled, "I'd do it right now. But I don't know how you control these things, and I don't want to set them loose."

Soldiers piled into the room. Elend didn't look up. He slapped Jastes, stopping his cries of pain.

"You listen," Elend said. "I don't care if you've been hurt, I don't care if you don't believe in the philosophies anymore, and I don't really care if you get yourself killed playing politics with Straff and Cett.

"But I *do* care if you threaten my people. I want you to march your army out of my dominance—go attack Straff's homeland, or maybe Cett's. They're both undefended. I promise I won't let your enemies get the atium.

"And, as a friend, I'll give you a bit of counsel. Think about that wound in your arm for a little while, Jastes. I was your best friend, and I nearly killed you. What the *hell* are you doing sitting in the middle of an entire army of deranged koloss?"

Soldiers surrounded him. Elend stood, ripping the knife from Jastes's body and spinning the man around, pressing the weapon against his throat.

The guards froze.

"I'm leaving," Elend said, pushing the confused Jastes ahead of him, moving out of the tent. He noticed with some concern that there were barely a dozen human guards. Sazed had counted more. Where had Jastes lost them?

There was no sign of Elend's horse. So he kept a wary eye on the soldiers, pulling Jastes toward the invisible line between the human camp and the koloss one. Elend turned as he reached the perimeter, then pushed Jastes back toward his men. They caught him, one pulling out a bandage for the arm. Others made moves as if to chase Elend, but they paused, hesitant.

Elend had crossed the line into the koloss camp. He stood quietly, watching the pathetic group of young soldiers, Jastes at their center. Even as they ministered to him, Elend could see the look in Jastes's eyes. Hatred. He wouldn't retreat. The man Elend had known was dead, replaced by this product of a new world that didn't kindly regard philosophers and idealists.

Elend turned away, walking among the koloss. A group of them quickly approached. The same one as before? He couldn't tell for certain.

"Take me out," Elend commanded, meeting the eyes of the largest koloss in the team. Either Elend seemed more commanding now, or this koloss was more easily cowed, for there was no argument. The creature simply nodded and began to shuffle out of the camp, his team surrounding Elend.

This trip was a waste, Elend thought with frustration. *All I did was antagonize Jastes. I risked my life for nothing.*

If only I could find out what was in those pouches!

He eyed the group of koloss around him. It was a typical group, ranging in size from five feet to one ten-foot monstrosity. They walked along with slumped, unengaged postures. . . .

Elend still had his knife out.

This is stupid, he thought. For some reason, that didn't stop him from choosing the smallest koloss in the group, taking a deep breath, and attacking.

The rest of the koloss paused to watch. The creature Elend had chosen spun—but in the wrong direction. It turned to face its companion koloss, the one nearest to it in size, as Elend tackled it, ramming the knife into its back.

Even at five feet with a small build, the koloss was incredibly strong. It tossed Elend off, bellowing in pain. Elend, however, managed to keep hold of his dagger.

Can't let it get out that sword, he thought, scrambling to his feet and ramming his knife into the creature's thigh. The koloss dropped again, punching at Elend with one arm, fingers reaching for its sword with the other. Elend took the punch to the chest, and fell back to the sooty ground.

He groaned, gasping. The koloss pulled out its sword, but had trouble standing. Both knife wounds bled stark red blood; the liquid seemed brighter, more reflective, than that of a human, but that might have just been a contrast with the deep blue skin.

The koloss finally managed to gain its feet, and Elend realized his mistake. He'd let the adrenaline of his confrontation with Jastes—his frustration at his inability to stop the armies—drive him. He'd sparred a lot lately, but he was in no position to take a koloss.

But it was far too late to worry about that now.

Elend rolled out of the way as a thick, clublike sword smashed to the ground beside him. Instincts overrode terror, and he mostly managed to avoid the backswing. It took him a bit in the side, spraying a patch of blood across his once white uniform, but he barely even felt the cut.

Only one way to win a knife fight against a guy with a sword . . . Elend thought, gripping his knife. The thought, oddly, hadn't come from one of his trainers, or even from Vin. He wasn't sure where it came from, but he trusted it.

Close in tight as fast as possible, and kill quickly.

And Elend attacked. The koloss swung as well. Elend

could see the attack, but couldn't do anything about it. He could only throw himself forward, knife raised, teeth clenched.

He rammed his knife into the koloss's eye, barely managing to get inside the creature's reach. Even so, the hilt of the sword hit him in the stomach.

Both dropped.

Elend groaned quietly, slowly becoming aware of the hard, ash-packed earth and weeds eaten down to their roots. A fallen twig was scratching his cheek. Odd that he would notice that, considering the pain in his chest. He stumbled to his feet. The koloss he'd attacked did not rise. Its companions stood, looking unconcerned, though their eyes were focused on him. They seemed to want something.

"He ate my horse," Elend said, saying the first thing that came to his clouded mind.

The group of koloss nodded. Elend stumbled forward, wiping the ash from his cheek with a dazed hand as he knelt beside the dead creature. He ripped his knife out, then slid it back in his boot. Next he unfastened the pouches; this koloss had two.

Finally, not certain why, he grabbed the creature's large sword and rested it up on his shoulder. It was so weighty that he could barely carry it, and certainly wouldn't be able to swing it. *How does a creature so small use something like this?*

The koloss watched him work without comment; then they led him out of the camp. Once they had retreated, Elend pulled open one of the pouches and looked inside.

He shouldn't have been surprised by what he found inside. Jastes had decided to control his army the old-fashioned way.

He was paying them.

The others call me mad. As I have said, that may be true.

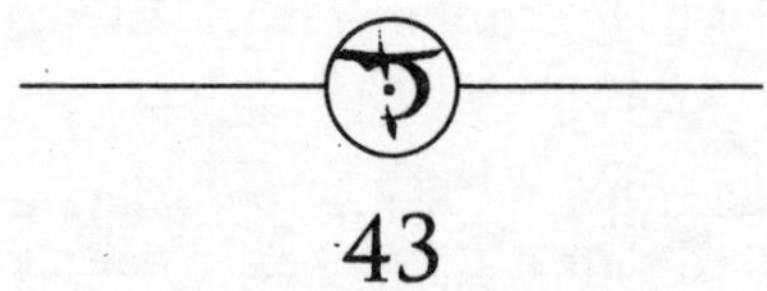

43

MIST POURED INTO THE DARK room, collapsing around Vin like a waterfall as she stood in the open balcony doorway. Elend was a motionless lump sleeping in his bed a short distance away.

Apparently, Mistress, OreSeur had explained, *he went into the koloss camp alone. You were asleep, and none of us knew what he was doing. I don't think he managed to persuade the creatures not to attack, but he did come back with some very useful information.*

OreSeur sat on his haunches beside her. He had not asked why Vin had come to Elend's rooms, nor why she stood, quietly watching the former king in the night.

She couldn't protect him. She tried so hard, but the impossibility of keeping even *one person* safe suddenly seemed so real—so tangible—to her that she felt sick.

Elend had been right to go out. He was his own man, competent, kingly. What he had done would only put him in more danger, however. Fear had been a companion of hers for such a long time that she had grown accustomed to it, and it rarely caused a physical reaction in her. Yet, watching him sleep quietly, she found her hands traitorously unsteady.

I saved him from the assassins. I protected him. I'm a powerful Allomancer. Why, then, do I feel so helpless?

So alone.

She walked forward, bare feet silent as she stepped up to Elend's bed. He did not wake. She stood for a long moment, just looking at him peaceful in his slumber.

OreSeur growled quietly.

Vin spun. A figure stood on the balcony, straight-backed and black, a near silhouette even to her tin-enhanced eyes. Mist fell before him, pooling on the floor, spreading out like an ethereal moss.

"Zane," she whispered.

"He is not safe, Vin," he said, stepping slowly into the room, pushing a wave of mist before him.

She looked back at Elend. "He never will be."

"I came to tell you that there is a traitor in your midst."

Vin looked up. "Who?" she asked.

"The man, Demoux," Zane said. "He contacted my father a short time before the assassination attempt, offering to open the gates and give up the city."

Vin frowned. *That makes no sense.*

Zane stepped forward. "Cett's work, Vin. He is a snake, even among high lords. I don't know how he bribed away one of your own men, but I do know that Demoux tried to provoke my father to attack the city during the voting."

Vin paused. If Straff had attacked at that moment, it would have reinforced the impression that he had sent the assassins in the first place.

"Elend and Penrod were supposed to die," Zane said. "With the Assembly in chaos, Cett could have taken charge. He could have led his forces—along with your own—against Straff's attacking army. He would have become the savior who protected Luthadel against the tyranny of an invader. . . ."

Vin stood quietly. Just because Zane said it didn't mean it was true. Yet, her investigations whispered that Demoux was the traitor.

She'd recognized the assassin at the assembly, and he *had* been from Cett's retinue, so she knew that Zane was telling the truth about at least one thing. Plus, Cett had precedent for sending Allomancer assassins: he had sent the ones months ago, when Vin had used the last of her atium. Zane had saved her life during that fight.

She clenched her fists, frustration biting at her chest. *If he's right, then Demoux is dead, and an enemy kandra has been in the palace, spending his days just steps away from*

Elend. Even if Zane lies, we still have a tyrant inside the city, another without. A force of koloss salivating over the people. And Elend doesn't need me.

Because there's nothing I can do.

"I see your frustration," Zane whispered, stepping up beside Elend's bed, looking down at his sleeping brother. "You keep listening to him. You want to protect him, but he won't let you." Zane looked up, meeting her eyes. She saw an implication in them.

There *was* something she could do—the thing a part of her had wanted to do from the beginning. The thing she'd been trained to do.

"Cett almost killed the man you love," Zane said. "Your Elend does as he wishes. Well, let us do as *you* wish." He looked into her eyes. "We have been someone else's knives for too long. Let's show Cett why he should fear us."

Her fury, her frustration at the siege, yearned to do as Zane suggested. Yet, she wavered, her thoughts in chaos. She had killed—killed well—just a short time before, and it had terrified her. Yet . . . Elend could take risks—insane risks, traveling into an army of koloss on his own. It almost felt like a betrayal. She had worked so hard to protect him, straining herself, exposing herself. Then, just a few days later, he wandered alone into a camp full of monsters.

She gritted her teeth. Part of her whispered that if Elend wouldn't be reasonable and stay out of danger, she'd just have to go and make *sure* the threats against him were removed.

"Let's go," she whispered.

Zane nodded. "Realize this," he said. "We can't just assassinate him. Another warlord will take his place, and take his armies. We have to attack *hard*. We have to hit that army so soundly that whoever takes over for Cett is so frightened that he withdraws."

Vin paused, looking away from him, nails biting into her own palms.

"Tell me," he said, stepping closer to her. "What would your Kelsier tell you to do?"

The answer was simple. Kelsier would never have gotten into this situation. He had been a hard man, a man with little tolerance for any who threatened those he loved. Cett and Straff wouldn't have lasted a single night at Luthadel without feeling Kelsier's knife.

There was a part of her that had always been awed by his powerful, utilitarian brutality.

There are two ways to stay safe, Reen's voice whispered to her. *Either be so quiet and harmless that people ignore you, or be so dangerous that they're terrified of you.*

She met Zane's eyes and nodded. He smiled, then moved over and jumped out the window.

"OreSeur," she whispered once he was gone. "My atium."

The dog paused, then padded up to her, his shoulder splitting. "Mistress . . ." he said slowly. "Do not do this."

She glanced at Elend. She couldn't protect him from everything. But she could do something.

She took the atium from OreSeur. Her hands no longer shook. She felt cold.

"Cett has threatened all that I love," she whispered. "He will soon know that there is something in this world more deadly than his assassins. Something more powerful than his army. Something more terrifying than the Lord Ruler himself.

"And I am coming for him."

Mist duty, they called it.

Every soldier had to take his turn, standing in the dark with a sputtering torch. Someone had to watch. Had to stare into those shifting, deceitful mists and wonder if anything was out there. Watching.

Wellen knew there was.

He knew it, but he never spoke. Soldiers laughed at such superstitions. They had to go out in the mists. They were used to it. They knew better than to fear it.

Supposedly.

"Hey," Jarloux said, stepping up to the edge of the wall. "Wells, do you see something out there?"

Of course he didn't. They stood with several dozen others on the perimeter of Keep Hasting, watching from the outer keep wall—a low fortification, perhaps fifteen feet tall, that surrounded the grounds. Their job was to look for anything suspicious in the mists.

"Suspicious." That was the word they used. It was *all* suspicious. It was mist. That shifting darkness, that void made of chaos and hatred. Wellen had never trusted it. They were out there. He knew.

Something moved in the darkness. Wellen stepped back, staring into the void, his heart beginning to flutter, hands beginning to sweat as he raised his spear.

"Yeah," Jarloux said, squinting. "I swear, I see . . ."

It came, as Wellen had always known it would. Like a thousand gnats on a hot day, like a hail of arrows shot by an entire army. Coins sprayed across the battlements. A wall of shimmering death, hundreds of trails zipping through the mists. Metal rang against stone, and men cried out in pain.

Wellen stepped back, raising his spear, as Jarloux yelled the alarm. Jarloux died halfway through the call, a coin snapping through his mouth, throwing out a chip of tooth as it proceeded out the back of his head. Jarloux collapsed, and Wellen stumbled away from the corpse, knowing that it was too late to run.

The coins stopped. Silence in the air. Men lay dying or groaning at his feet.

Then they came. Two dark shadows of death in the night. Ravens in the mist. They flew over Wellen with a rustle of black cloth.

And they left him behind, alone amid the corpses of what had once been a squad of forty men.

Vin landed in a crouch, bare feet on the cool stone cobbles of the Hasting courtyard. Zane landed upright, standing—as always—with his towering air of self-confidence.

Pewter blazed within her, giving her muscles the taut energy of a thousand excited moments. She easily ignored the pain of her wounded side. Her sole bead of atium rested in her stomach, but she didn't use it. Not yet. Not unless she was right, and Cett proved to be Mistborn.

"We'll go from the bottom up," Zane said.

Vin nodded. The central tower of Keep Hasting was many stories high, and they couldn't know which one Cett was on. If they started low, he wouldn't be able to escape.

Besides. Going up would be more difficult. The energy in Vin's limbs cried for release. She'd waited, remained coiled, for far too long. She was tired of weakness, tired of being restrained. She had spent months as a knife, held immobile at someone's throat.

It was time to cut.

The two dashed forward. Torches began to light around them as Cett's men—those who camped in the courtyard—awakened to the alarm. Tents unfurled and collapsed, men yelling in surprise, looking for the army that assailed them. They could only wish that they were so lucky.

Vin jumped straight up into the air, and Zane spun, throwing a bag of coins around him. Hundreds of bits of copper sparkled in the air beneath her—a peasant's fortune. Vin landed with a rustle, and they both Pushed, their power throwing the coins outward. The torch-sparkled missiles ripped through the camp, dropping surprised, drowsy men.

Vin and Zane continued toward the central tower. A squad of soldiers had formed up at the tower's front. They still seemed disoriented, confused, and sleepy, but they were armed. Armed with metal armor and steel weapons—a choice that, had they actually been facing an enemy army, would have been wise.

Zane and Vin slid into the midst of the soldiers. Zane tossed a single coin into the air between them. Vin reached out and Pushed against it, feeling Zane's weight as he also Pushed against it.

Braced against each other, they both Pushed in opposite directions, throwing their weight against the breastplates of the soldiers to either side. With flared pewter—holding each other steady—their Pushes scattered the soldiers as if they had been slapped by enormous hands. Spears and swords twisted in the night, clattering to the cobbles. Breastplates towed bodies away.

Vin extinguished her steel as she felt Zane's weight come off the coin. The sparkling bit of metal bounced to the ground between them, and Zane turned, throwing up his hand toward the single soldier who remained standing directly between Zane and the keep doors.

A squad of soldiers raced up behind Zane, but they suddenly halted as he Pushed against them—then sent the transfer of weight directly into the lone soldier. The unfortunate man crashed backward into the keep doors.

Bones crunched. The doors flung open as the soldier burst into the room beyond. Zane ducked through the open doorway, and Vin moved smoothly behind him, her bare feet leaving rough cobbles and falling on smooth marble instead.

Soldiers waited inside. These didn't wear armor, and they carried large wooden shields to block coins. They were armed with staves or obsidian swords. Hazekillers—men trained specifically to fight Allomancers. There were, perhaps, fifty of them.

Now it begins in earnest, Vin thought, leaping into the air and Pushing off the door's hinges.

Zane led by Pushing on the same man he'd used to break open the doors, throwing the corpse toward a group of hazekillers. As the soldier crashed into them, Vin landed amid a second group. She spun on the floor, whipping out her legs and flaring pewter, tripping a good four men. As the others tried to strike, she Pushed downward against a coin in her pouch, ripping it free and throwing herself upward. She spun in the air, catching a falling staff discarded by a tripped soldier.

Obsidian cracked against the white marble where she had been. Vin came down with her own weapon and struck, attacking faster than anyone should be able to, hitting ears, chins, and throats. Skulls cracked. Bones broke. She was barely breathing hard when she found all ten of her opponents down.

Ten men . . . didn't Kelsier once tell me he had trouble with half a dozen hazekillers?

No time to think. A large group of soldiers charged her. She yelled and jumped toward them, throwing her staff into the face of the first man she met. The others raised their shields, surprised, but Vin whipped out a pair of obsidian daggers as she landed. She rammed them into the thighs of two men before her, then spun past them, attacking flesh where she saw it.

An attack flickered from the corner of her eye, and she snapped up an arm, blocking the wooden staff as it came for her head. The wood cracked, and she took the man down with a wide sweep of the dagger, nearly beheading him. She jumped backward as the others moved in, braced herself, then yanked on the armored corpse Zane had used before, Pulling it toward her.

Shields did little good against a missile so large. Vin smashed the corpse into her opponents, sweeping them before her. To the side, she could see the remnants of the hazekillers who had attacked Zane. Zane stood among them, a black pillar before the fallen, arms outstretched. He met her eyes, then nodded toward the rear of the chamber.

Vin ignored the few remaining hazekillers. She Pushed against the corpse and sent herself sliding across the floor. Zane jumped up, Pushing back, shattering his way through a window and into the mists. Vin quickly did a check of the back rooms: no Cett. She turned and took down a straggling hazekiller as she ducked into the lift shaft.

She needed no elevator. She shot straight up on a Pushed coin, bursting out onto the third floor. Zane would take the second.

Vin landed quietly on the marble floor, hearing footsteps come down a stairwell beside her. She recognized this large, open room: it was the chamber where she and Elend had met Cett for dinner. It was now empty, even the table removed, but she recognized the circular perimeter of stained-glass windows.

Hazekillers burst from the kitchen room. Dozens. *There must be another stairwell back there,* Vin thought as she darted toward the stairwell beside her. Dozens more were coming out there, however, and the two groups moved to surround her.

Fifty-to-one must have seemed like good odds for the

men, and they charged confidently. She glanced at the open kitchen doors, and saw no Cett beyond. This floor was clear.

Cett certainly brought a lot of hazekillers, she thought, backing quietly to the center of the room. Save for the stairwell, kitchens, and pillars, the room was mostly surrounded in arched stained-glass windows.

He planned for my attack. Or, he tried to.

Vin ducked down as the waves of men surrounded her. She turned her head up, eyes closed, and burned duralumin.

Then she Pulled.

Stained-glass windows—set in metal frames inside their arches—exploded around the room. She felt the metal frames burst inward, twisting on themselves before her awesome power. She imagined twinkling slivers of multicolored glass in the air. She heard men scream as glass and metal hit them, embedding in their flesh.

Only the outer layer of men would die from the blast. Vin opened her eyes and jumped as a dozen dueling canes fell around her. She passed through a hail of attacks. Some hit. It didn't matter. She couldn't feel pain at the moment.

She Pushed against a broken metal frame, throwing herself over the heads of soldiers, landing outside the large circle of attackers. The outer line of men was down, impaled by glass shards and twisted metal frames. Vin raised a hand and bowed her head.

Duralumin and steel. She Pushed. The world lurched.

Vin shot out into the mists through a broken window as she Pushed against the line of corpses impaled by metal frames. The bodies were thrown away from her, smashing into the men who were still alive in the center.

Dead, dying, and unharmed were swept from the room, Pushed out the window opposite Vin. Bodies twisted in the mists, fifty men thrown into the night, leaving the room empty save for trails of blood and discarded bits of glass.

Vin downed a vial of metals as the mists rushed around her; then she Pulled herself back toward the keep, using a window on the fourth floor. As she approached, a corpse crashed through the window, falling out into the night. She caught a glimpse of Zane disappearing out another window on the opposite side. This level was clear.

Lights burned on the fifth floor. They probably could have come here first, but that wasn't the plan. Zane was right. They didn't just need to kill Cett. They needed to terrify his entire army.

Vin Pushed against the same corpse that Zane had thrown out the window, using its metal armor as an anchor. It shot down at an angle, passing just inside a broken window, and Vin soared upward in an angle away from the building. A quick Pull directed her back to the building once she reached the elevation she needed. She landed at a window on the fifth floor.

Vin grasped the stone sill, heart thumping, breaths coming in deep gasps. Sweat made her face cold in the winter breeze, despite the heat burning within her. She gulped, eyes wide, and flared her pewter.

Mistborn.

She shattered the window with a slap. The soldiers that waited beyond jumped backward, spinning. One wore a metal belt buckle. He died first. The other twenty barely knew how to react as the buckle buzzed through their ranks, twisting between Vin's Pushes and Pulls. They had been trained, instructed, and perhaps even tested against Allomancers.

But they had never fought Vin.

Men screamed and fell, Vin ripping through their ranks with only the buckle as a weapon. Before the force of her pewter, tin, steel, and iron, the possible use of atium seemed an incredible waste. Even without it, she was a terrible weapon—one that, until this moment, even she hadn't understood.

Mistborn.

The last man fell. Vin stood among them, feeling a numbing sense of satisfaction. She let the belt buckle slip from her fingers. It hit carpet. She stood in a room that wasn't unadorned as the rest of the building had been; there was furniture here, and there were some minor decorations. Perhaps Elend's clearing crews hadn't gotten this far before Cett's arrival, or perhaps he'd simply brought some of his own comforts.

Behind her was the stairwell. In front of her was a fine wooden wall set with a door—the inner apartments. Vin stepped forward quietly, mistcloak rustling as she Pulled four lamps off the brackets behind her. They whipped forward, and she sidestepped, letting them crash into the wall. Fire blossomed across splattered oil, billowing across the wall, the force of the lamps breaking the door on its hinges. She raised a hand, Pushing it fully open.

Fire dripped around her as she stepped into the room beyond. The richly decorated chamber was quiet, and eerily empty save for two figures. Cett sat in a simple wooden chair, bearded, sloppily dressed, and looking very, very tired. Cett's young son stepped in between Cett and Vin. The boy held a dueling cane.

So, which one is Mistborn?

The boy swung. Vin caught the weapon, then shoved the boy to the side. He crashed into the wooden wall, then slumped to the ground. Vin eyed him.

"Leave Gneorndin alone, woman," Cett said. "Do what you came to do."

Vin turned toward the nobleman. She remembered her frustration, her rage, her cool, icy anger. She stepped forward and grabbed Cett by the front of his suit. "Fight me," she said, and tossed him backward.

He slammed against the back wall, then slumped to the ground. Vin prepared her atium, but he did not rise. He simply rolled to the side, coughing.

Vin walked over, pulling him up by one arm. He balled a fist, trying to strike her, but he was pathetically weak. She let the blows bounce off her side.

"Fight me," she commanded, tossing him to the side. He tumbled across the floor—head hitting hard—and came to rest against the burning wall, a trickle of blood running from his brow. He didn't rise.

Vin gritted her teeth, striding forward.

"Leave him alone!" The boy, Gneorndin, stumbled in front of Cett, raising his dueling cane in a wavering hand.

Vin paused, cocking her head. The boy's brow was

streaked with sweat, and he was unsteady on his feet. She looked into his eyes, and saw absolute terror therein. This boy was no Mistborn. Yet, he held his ground. Pathetically, hopelessly, he stood before the body of the fallen Cett.

"Step aside, son," Cett said in a tired voice. "There is nothing you can do here."

The boy started to shake, then began to weep.

Tears, Vin thought, feeling an oddly surreal feeling cloud her mind. She reached up, surprised to find wet streaks on her own cheeks.

"You have no Mistborn," she whispered.

Cett had struggled to a half-reclining position, and he looked into her eyes.

"No Allomancers faced us this night," she said. "You used them all on the assassination attempt in the Assembly Hall?"

"The only Allomancers I had, I sent against you months ago," Cett said with a sigh. "They were all I ever had, my only hope of killing you. Even they weren't from my family. My whole line has been corrupted by skaa blood—Allrianne is the only Allomancer to be born to us for centuries."

"You came to Luthadel . . ."

"Because Straff would have come for me eventually," Cett said. "My best chance, lass, was to kill *you* early on. That's why I sent them all against you. Failing that, I knew I had to try and take this damn city and its atium so I could buy myself some Allomancers. Didn't work."

"You could have just offered us an alliance."

Cett chuckled, pulling himself up to a sitting position. "It doesn't work that way in real politics. You take, or you get taken. Besides, I've always been a gambling man." He looked up at her, meeting her eyes. "Do what you came to," he repeated.

Vin shivered. She couldn't feel her tears. She could barely feel anything.

Why? Why can't I make sense of anything anymore?

The room began to shake. Vin spun, looking toward the back wall. The wood there quivered and spasmed like a dying animal. Nails began to pop, ripping backward through the paneling; then the entire wall burst away from Vin. Burning boards, splinters, nails, and shingles sprayed in the air, flying around a man in black. Zane stood sideways in the room beyond, death strewn at his feet, hands at his sides.

Red streamed from the tips of his fingers, running in a steady drip. He looked up through the burning remnants of the wall, smiling. Then he stepped toward Cett's room.

"No!" Vin said, dashing at him.

Zane paused, surprised. He stepped to the side, easily dodging Vin, walking toward Cett and the boy.

"Zane, leave them!" Vin said, turning toward him, Pushing herself in a skid across the room. She reached for his arm. The black fabric glistened wet with blood that was only his own.

Zane dodged. He turned toward her, curious. She reached for him, but he moved out of the way with supernatural ease, outstepping her like a master swordsman facing a young boy.

Atium, Vin thought. *He probably burned it this entire time. But, he didn't need it to fight those men . . . they didn't have a chance against us anyway.*

"Please," she asked. "Leave them."

Zane turned toward Cett, who sat expectant. The boy was at his side, trying to pull his father away.

Zane looked back at her, head cocked.

"Please," Vin repeated.

Zane frowned. "He still controls you, then," he said, sounding disappointed. "I thought, maybe, if you could fight and see just how powerful you were, you'd shake yourself free of Elend's grip. I guess I was wrong."

Then he turned his back on Cett and walked out through the hole he had made. Vin followed quietly, feet crunching splinters of wood as she slowly withdrew, leaving a broken keep, shattered army, and humiliated lord behind.

But must not even a madman rely on his own mind, his own experience, rather than that of others?

44

IN THE COLD CALM OF morning, Breeze watched a very disheartening sight: Cett's army withdrawing.

Breeze shivered, breath puffing as he turned toward Clubs. Most people wouldn't have been able to read beyond the sneer on the squat general's face. But Breeze saw more: he saw the tension in the taut skin around Clubs's eyes, he noticed the way that Clubs tapped his finger against the frosty stone wall. Clubs was not a nervous man. The motions meant something.

"This is it, then?" Breeze asked quietly.

Clubs nodded.

Breeze couldn't see it. There were still two armies out there; it was still a standoff. Yet, he trusted Clubs's assessment. Or, rather, he trusted his own knowledge of people enough to trust his assessment of Clubs.

The general knew something he didn't.

"Kindly explain," Breeze said.

"This'll end when Straff figures it out," Clubs said.

"Figures what out?"

"That those koloss will do his job for him, if he lets them."

Breeze paused. *Straff doesn't really care about the people in the city—he just wants to take it for the atium. And for the symbolic victory.*

"If Straff pulls back . . ." Breeze said.

"Those koloss will attack," Clubs said with a nod. "They'll slaughter everyone they find and generally make rubble out of the city. Then Straff can come back and find his atium once the koloss are done."

"Assuming they leave, my dear man."

Clubs shrugged. "Either way, he's better off. Straff will face one weakened enemy instead of two strong ones."

Breeze felt a chill, and pulled his cloak closer. "You say that all so . . . straightforwardly."

"We were dead the moment that first army got here, Breeze," Clubs said. "We're just good at stalling."

Why in the name of the Lord Ruler do I spend my time with this man? Breeze thought. *He's nothing more than a pessimistic doomsayer.* And yet, Breeze knew people. This time, Clubs wasn't exaggerating.

"Bloody hell," Breeze muttered.

Clubs just nodded, leaning against the wall and looking out at the disappearing army.

"Three hundred men," Ham said, standing in Elend's study. "Or, at least, that's what our scouts say."

"That's not as bad as I'd feared," Elend said. They stood in Elend's study, the only other occupant being Spook, who sat lounging beside the table.

"El," Ham said, "Cett only had a thousand men with him here in Luthadel. That means that during Vin's attack, Cett took thirty percent casualties in *less than ten minutes.* Even on a battlefield, most armies will break if they take thirty or forty percent casualties in the course of an *entire day's* fighting."

"Oh," Elend said, frowning.

Ham shook his head, sitting down, pouring himself something to drink. "I don't get it, El. Why'd she attack him?"

"She's loony," Spook said.

Elend opened his mouth to counter that comment, but found it difficult to explain his feelings. "I'm not sure why she did it," he finally admitted. "She did mention that she didn't believe those assassins at the Assembly came from my father."

Ham shrugged. He looked . . . haggard. This wasn't his element, dealing with armies and worrying about the fate of kingdoms. He preferred to concern himself with smaller spheres.

Of course, Elend thought, *I'd just prefer to be in my chair, reading quietly. We do what we must.*

"Any news of her yet?" Elend asked.

Spook shook his head. "Uncle Grumpy has the scouts searching the city, but so far nothing."

"If Vin doesn't want to be found . . ." Ham said.

Elend began to pace. He couldn't keep still; he was beginning to think he must look like Jastes, wandering in circles, running his hand through his hair.

Be firm, he told himself. *You can afford to seem worried, but you mustn't ever seem uncertain.*

He continued to pace, though he slowed his step, and he didn't voice his concerns to Ham or Spook. What if Vin was wounded? What if Cett had killed her? Their scouts had seen very little of the attack the night before. Vin had definitely been involved, and there were conflicting reports that said she'd been fighting another Mistborn. She had left the keep with one of the top floors in flames—and, for some reason, she had left Cett alive.

Since then, nobody had seen her.

Elend closed his eyes, pausing as he leaned a hand against the stone wall. *I've been ignoring her lately. I've helped the city . . . but what good will it do to save Luthadel if I lose her? It's almost like I don't know her anymore.*

Or did I ever know her in the first place?

It felt wrong to not have her with him. He had come to rely on her simple bluntness. He needed her genuine realism—her sheer sense of concreteness—to keep him grounded. He needed to hold her, so that he could know that there was something more important than theories and concepts.

He loved her.

"I don't know, El," Ham finally said. "I never thought that Vin would be a liability, but she had a hard youth. I remember once she exploded at the crew for little reason, yelling and screaming about her childhood. I . . . don't know that she's completely stable."

Elend opened his eyes. "She's stable, Ham," he said firmly. "And she's more capable than any of us."

Ham frowned. "But—"

"She had a good reason for attacking Cett," Elend said. "I trust her."

Ham and Spook exchanged glances, and Spook just shrugged.

"It's more than last night, El," Ham said. "Something's not right with that girl—not just mentally, either. . . ."

"What do you mean?" Elend asked.

"Remember the attack on the Assembly?" Ham said. "You told me you saw her get hit square-on by a Thug's staff."

"And?" Elend asked. "It laid her out for three full days."

Ham shook his head. "Her complete collection of wounds—getting hit in the side, the shoulder wound, nearly being choked to death—those all together laid her out for a couple of days. But, if she'd really gotten hit that hard by a Thug, she shouldn't have been out for days, Elend. She should have been out for weeks. Maybe longer. She certainly shouldn't have escaped without broken ribs."

"She was burning pewter," Elend said.

"Presumably, so was the Thug."

Elend paused.

"You see?" Ham said. "If both were flaring pewter, then they should have balanced each other out. That leaves Vin—a girl who can't weigh more than a hundred pounds—getting clobbered full-on by a trained soldier with three times her weight. She shrugged it off with barely a few days' rest."

"Vin's special," Elend finally said.

"I won't argue with that," Ham said. "But she's also hiding things from us. Who was that other Mistborn? Some of the reports make it sound like they were working together."

She said there was another Mistborn in the city, Elend thought. *Zane—Straff's messenger. She hasn't mentioned him in a very long while.*

Ham rubbed his forehead. "This is all falling apart around us, El."

"Kelsier could have kept it together," Spook mumbled.

"When he was here, even our failures were part of his plan."

"The Survivor is dead," Elend said. "I never knew him, but I've listened to enough about him to learn one thing. He didn't give in to despair."

Ham smiled. "That much is true. He was laughing and joking the day after we lost our entire army to a miscalculation. Arrogant bastard."

"Callous," Spook said.

"No," Ham said, reaching for his cup. "I used to think that. Now . . . I just think he was determined. Kell always looked toward tomorrow, no matter what the consequences."

"Well, we have to do the same," Elend said. "Cett is gone—Penrod let him leave. We can't change that fact. But, we do have information on the koloss army."

"Oh, about that," Spook said, reaching into his pouch. He tossed something to the table. "You're right—they're the same."

The coin rolled to a stop, and Elend picked it up. He could see where Spook had scraped it with a knife, peeling off the gold paint to reveal the dense hardwood beneath. It was a poor representation of a boxing; it was little wonder that the fakes had been so easy to pick out. Only a fool would try to pass them off as real. A fool, or a koloss.

Nobody was certain how some of Jastes's fake boxings had worked their way up to Luthadel; perhaps he had tried giving them to peasants or beggars in his home dominance. Either way, it was fairly apparent what he was doing. He'd needed an army, and had needed cash. He'd fabricated the one to get the other. Only koloss would have fallen for such a ploy.

"I don't get it," Ham said as Elend passed him the coin. "How come the koloss have suddenly decided to take money? The Lord Ruler never paid them."

Elend paused, thinking back to his experience with the camp. *We are humans. We will live in your city. . . .*

"The koloss are changing, Ham," Elend said. "Or maybe we never really understood them in the first place. Either way, we need to be strong. This isn't over yet."

"It would be easier to be strong if I knew our Mistborn wasn't insane. She didn't even discuss this with us!"

"I know," Elend said.

Ham rose, shaking his head. "There's a reason the Great Houses were always so reluctant to use their Mistborn against each other. Things just got a whole lot more dangerous. If Cett does have a Mistborn, and he decides to retaliate . . ."

"I know," Elend said again, bidding the two farewell.

Ham waved to Spook, and the two of them left, off to check with Breeze and Clubs.

They all act so glum, Elend thought, leaving his rooms to find something to eat. *It's like they think we're doomed because of one setback. But, Cett's withdrawal is a good thing. One of our enemies is leaving—and there are still two armies out there. Jastes won't attack if doing so exposes him to Straff, and Straff himself is too scared of Vin to do anything. In fact, her attack on Cett will only make my father more frightened. Maybe that's why she did it.*

"Your Majesty?" a voice whispered.

Elend spun, searching the hallway.

"Your Majesty," said a short figure in the shadows. OreSeur. "I think I've found her."

Elend didn't bring anyone with him save for a few guards. He didn't want to explain to Ham and the others how he'd gotten his information; Vin still insisted on keeping OreSeur secret.

Ham's right about one thing, Elend thought as his carriage pulled to a stop. *She is hiding things. She does it all the time.*

But that didn't stop him from trusting her. He nodded to OreSeur, and they left the carriage. Elend waved his guards back as he approached a dilapidated building. It had probably once been a poor merchant's shop—a place run by extremely low nobility, selling meager necessities to skaa workers in exchange for food tokens, which could in turn be exchanged for money from the Lord Ruler.

The building was in a sector that Elend's fuel-collection crews hadn't reached yet. It was obvious, however, that it hadn't seen a lot of use lately. It had been ransacked long ago, and the ash coating the floor was a good four inches deep. A small trail of footprints led toward a back stairwell.

"What is this place?" Elend asked with a frown.

OreSeur shrugged a pair of dog's shoulders.

"Then how did you know she was here?"

"I followed her last night, Your Majesty," OreSeur said. "I saw the general direction she went. After that, it was simply a process of careful searching."

Elend frowned. "That still must have taken some pretty mean tracking abilities, kandra."

"These bones have unusually keen senses."

Elend nodded. The stairwell led up into a long hallway with several rooms at the ends. Elend began to walk down the hallway, then paused. To one side, a panel on the wall had been slid back, revealing a small cubby. He could hear movement within.

"Vin?" he asked, poking his head into the cubby.

There was a small room hidden behind the wall, and Vin sat on the far side. The room—more of a nook—was only a few feet across, and even Vin wouldn't have been able to stand up in it. She didn't respond to him. She simply sat, leaning against the far wall, head turned away from him.

Elend crawled inside the small chamber, getting ash on his knees. It was barely large enough for him to enter without bumping into her. "Vin? Are you all right?"

She sat, twisting something between her fingers. And she was looking at the wall—looking through a narrow hole. Elend could see sunlight shining through.

It's a peephole, he realized. *To watch the street below. This isn't a shop—it's a thieving hideout. Or, it was.*

"I used to think Camon was a terrible man," Vin said quietly.

Elend paused, on hands and knees. Finally, he settled back into a cramped seated position. At least Vin didn't look hurt. "Camon?" he asked. "Your old crewleader, before Kelsier?"

Vin nodded. She turned away from the slit, sitting with her arms around her knees. "He beat people, he killed those who disagreed with him. Even among street thugs, he was brutal."

Elend frowned.

"But," Vin said quietly, "I doubt he killed as many people during his entire life as I killed last night."

Elend closed his eyes. Then he opened them and shuffled a little closer, laying a hand on Vin's shoulder. "Those were enemy soldiers, Vin."

"I was like a child in a room full of bugs," Vin whispered. He could finally see what was in her fingers. It was her earring, the simple bronze stud that she always wore. She looked down at it, twisting it between her fingers.

"Did I ever tell you how I got this?" she asked. He shook his head. "My mother gave it to me," she said. "I don't remember it happening—Reen told me about it. My mother . . . she heard voices sometimes. She killed my baby sister, slaughtered her. And that same day she gave me this, one of her own earrings. As if . . . as if choosing me over my sister. A punishment for one, a twisted present for another."

Vin shook her head. "My entire life has been death, Elend. Death of my sister, the death of Reen. Crewmembers dead around me, Kelsier falling to the Lord Ruler, then my own spear in the Lord Ruler's chest. I try to protect, and tell myself that I'm escaping it all. And then . . . I do something like I did last night."

Not certain what else to do, Elend pulled her close. She was stiff, however. "You had a good reason for what you did," he said.

"No I didn't," Vin said. "I just wanted to hurt them. I wanted to scare them and make them leave you alone. It sounds childish, but that's how I felt."

"It's not childish, Vin," Elend said. "It was good strategy. You gave our enemies a show of force. You frightened away one of our major opponents, and now my father will be even more afraid to attack. You've bought us more time!"

"Bought it with the lives of hundreds of men."

"Enemy soldiers who marched into our city," Elend said. "Men who were protecting a tyrant who oppresses his people."

"That's the same rationale Kelsier used," Vin said quietly, "when he killed noblemen and their guards. He said they were upholding the Final Empire, so they deserved to die. He frightened me."

Elend didn't know what to say to that.

"It was like he thought himself a god," Vin whispered. "Taking life, giving life, where he saw fit. I don't want to be like him, Elend. But, everything seems to be pushing me in that direction."

"I . . ." *You're not like him,* he wanted to say. It was true, but the words wouldn't come out. They rang hollow to him.

Instead, he pulled Vin close, her shoulder up against his chest, head beneath his chin. "I wish I knew the right things to say, Vin," he whispered. "Seeing you like this makes every protective instinct inside of me twist. I want to make it better—I want to fix everything—but I don't know how. Tell me what to do. Just tell me how I can help!"

She resisted his embrace a little at first, but then sighed quietly and slid her arms around him, holding him tightly. "You can't help with this," she said softly. "I have to do it alone. There are . . . decisions I have to make."

He nodded. "You'll make the right ones, Vin."

"You don't even know what I'm deciding."

"It doesn't matter," he said. "I know I can't help—I couldn't even hold on to my own throne. You're ten times as capable as I am."

She squeezed his arm. "Don't say things like that. Please?"

He frowned at the tension in her voice, then nodded. "All right. But, either way, I trust you, Vin. Make your decisions—I'll support you."

She nodded, relaxing a bit beneath his arms. "I think . . ." she said. "I think I have to leave Luthadel."

"Leave? And go where?"

"North," she said. "To Terris."

Elend sat back, resting against the wooden wall. *Leave?*

he thought with a twisting feeling. *Is this what I've earned by being so distracted lately?*

Have I lost her?

And yet, he'd just told her that he'd support her decisions. "If you feel you have to go, Vin," he found himself saying, "then you should do so."

"If I were to leave, would you go with me?"

"Now?"

Vin nodded, head rubbing his chest.

"No," he finally said. "I couldn't leave Luthadel, not with those armies still out there."

"But the city rejected you."

"I know," he said, sighing. "But . . . I can't leave them, Vin. They rejected me, but I won't abandon them."

Vin nodded again, and something told him this was the answer she had expected.

Elend smiled. "We're a mess, aren't we?"

"Hopeless," she said softly, sighing as she finally pulled away from him. She seemed so tired. Outside the room, Elend could hear footsteps. OreSeur appeared a moment later, poking his head into the hidden chamber.

"Your guards are growing restless, Your Majesty," he said to Elend. "They will soon come looking for you."

Elend nodded, shuffling over to the exit. Once in the hallway, he offered a hand to help Vin out. She took the hand, crawling out, then stood and dusted off her clothing—her typical shirt and trousers.

Will she ever go back to dresses now? he wondered.

"Elend," she said, fishing in a pocket. "Here, you can spend this, if you want."

She opened up her hand, dropping a bead into his hand.

"Atium?" he asked incredulously. "Where did you get it?"

"From a friend," she said.

"And you didn't burn it last night?" Elend asked. "When you were fighting all those soldiers?"

"No," Vin said. "I swallowed it, but I didn't end up needing it, so I forced it back up."

Lord Ruler! Elend thought. *I didn't even consider that she didn't have atium. What could she have done if she'd burned that bit?* He looked up at her. "Some reports say that there's another Mistborn in the city."

"There is. Zane."

Elend dropped the bead back into her hand. "Then keep this. You might need it to fight him."

"I doubt that," Vin said quietly.

"Keep it anyway," Elend said. "This is worth a small fortune—but we'd need a very *large* fortune to make any difference now. Besides, who would buy it? If I used it to bribe Straff or Cett, they'd only become more certain I'm holding atium against them."

Vin nodded, then glanced at OreSeur. "Keep this," she said, handing the bead toward him. "It's big enough that another Allomancer could pull it off me if he wanted."

"I will guard it with my life, Mistress," OreSeur said, his shoulder splitting open to make room for the bit of metal.

Vin turned to join Elend as they walked down the steps, moving to meet with the guards below.

I know what I have memorized. I know what is now repeated by the other Worldbringers.

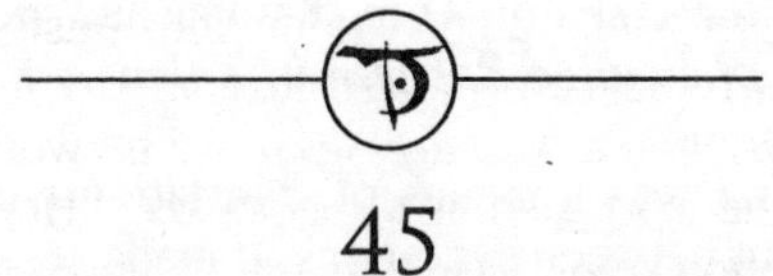

45

"THE HERO OF AGES WON'T be Terris," Tindwyl said, scribbling a note at the bottom of their list.

"We knew that already," Sazed said. "From the logbook."

"Yes," Tindwyl said, "but Alendi's account was only a reference—a thirdhand mention of the effects of a prophecy. I found someone quoting the prophecy itself."

"Truly?" Sazed asked, excited. "Where?"

"The biography of Helenntion," Tindwyl said. "One of the last survivors of the Council of Khlennium."

"Write it for me," Sazed said, scooting his chair a bit closer to hers. He had to blink a few times as she wrote, his head clouding for a moment from fatigue.

Stay alert! he told himself. *There isn't much time left. Not much at all. . . .*

Tindwyl was doing a little better than he, but her wakefulness was obviously beginning to run out, for she was starting to droop. He'd taken a quick nap during the night, rolled up on her floor, but she had carried on. As far as he could tell, she'd been awake for over a week straight.

There was much talk of the Rabzeen, during those days, Tindwyl wrote. *Some said he would come to fight the Conqueror. Others said he was the Conqueror. Helenntion didn't make his thoughts on the matter known to me. The Rabzeen is said to be "He who is not of his people, yet fulfills all of their wishes." If this is the case, then perhaps the Conqueror is the one. He is said to have been of Khlennium.*

She stopped there. Sazed frowned, reading the words again. Kwaan's last testimony—the rubbing Sazed had taken at the Conventical of Seran—had proven useful in more than one way. It had provided a key.

It wasn't until years later that I became convinced that he was the Hero of Ages, Kwaan had written. *Hero of Ages: the one called Rabzeen in Khlennium, the Anamnesor. . . .*

The rubbing was a means of translation—not between languages, but between synonyms. It made sense that there would be other names for the Hero of Ages; a figure so important, so surrounded by lore, would have many titles. Yet, so much had been lost from those days. The Rabzeen and the Anamnesor were both mythological figures vaguely familiar to Sazed—but they were only two among hosts. Until the discovery of the rubbing, there had been no way to connect their names to the Hero of Ages.

Now Tindwyl and he could search their metalminds with open eyes. Perhaps, in the past, Sazed had read this very passage from Helenntion's biography; he had at least skimmed many of the older records, searching for religious references. Yet, he would never have been able to realize that the passage was referring to the Hero of Ages, a figure from Terris lore that the Khlenni people had renamed into their own tongue.

"Yes . . ." he said slowly. "This is good, Tindwyl. Very good." He reached over, laying his hand on hers.

"Perhaps," she said, "though it tells us nothing new."

"Ah, but the wording might be important, I think," Sazed said. "Religions are often very careful with their writings."

"Especially prophecies," Tindwyl said, frowning just a bit. She was not fond of anything that smacked of superstition or soothsaying.

"I would have thought," Sazed noted, "that you would no longer have this prejudice, considering our current enterprise."

"I gather information, Sazed," she said. "Because of what it says of people, and because of what the past can teach us. However, there is a reason I took to studying history as opposed to theology. I don't approve of perpetuating lies."

"Is that what you think I do when I teach of religions?" he asked in amusement.

Tindwyl looked toward him. "A bit," she admitted. "How can you teach the people to look toward the gods of the dead, Sazed? Those religions did their people little good, and their prophecies are now dust."

"Religions are an expression of hope," Sazed said. "That hope gives people strength."

"Then you don't believe?" Tindwyl asked. "You just give the people something to trust, something to delude themselves?"

"I would not call it so."

"Then you think the gods you teach of *do* exist?"

"I . . . think that they deserved to be remembered."

"And their prophecies?" Tindwyl said. "I see scholarly value in what we do—the bringing to light of facts from the past could give us information about our current problems. Yet, this soothsaying for the future is, at its core, foolishness."

"I would not say that," Sazed said. "Religions are promises—promises that there is something watching over us, guiding us. Prophecies, therefore, are natural extensions of the hopes and desires of the people. Not foolishness at all."

"So, your interest is purely academic?" Tindwyl said.

"I wouldn't say that."

Tindwyl studied him, watching his eyes. She frowned slowly. "You believe it, don't you?" she asked. "You believe that this girl is the Hero of Ages."

"I have not yet decided," Sazed said.

"How can you even consider such a thing, Sazed?" Tindwyl asked. "Don't you see? Hope is a good thing—a wonderful thing—but you must have hope in something appropriate. If you perpetuate the dreams of the past, then you stifle your own dreams of the future."

"What if the past dreams are worthy of being remembered?"

Tindwyl shook her head. "Look at the odds, Sazed. What are the chances we would end up where we are, studying this rubbing, in the very same household as the Hero of Ages?"

"Odds are irrelevant when a foretelling is involved."

Tindwyl closed her eyes. "Sazed . . . I think religion is a good thing, and belief is a good thing, but it is foolishness to look for guidance in a few vague phrases. Look at what happened last time someone assumed they had found this Hero. The Lord Ruler, the Final Empire, was the result."

"Still, I will hope. If you did not believe the prophecies, then why work so hard to discover information about the Deepness and the Hero?"

"It's simple," Tindwyl said. "We are obviously facing a danger that has come before—a recurring problem, like a plague that plays itself out, only to return again centuries later. The ancient people knew of this danger, and had information about it. That information, naturally, broke down and became legends, prophecies, and even religions. There will be, then, clues to our situation hidden in the past. This is not a matter of soothsaying, but of research."

Sazed lay his hand on hers. "I think, perhaps, that this is something we cannot agree upon. Come, let us return to our studies. We must use the time we have left."

"We should be all right," Tindwyl said, sighing and reaching to tuck a bit of hair back into her bun. "Apparently, your Hero scared off Lord Cett last night. The maid who brought breakfast was speaking of it."

"I know of the event," Sazed said.

"Then things are growing better for Luthadel."

"Yes," Sazed said. "Perhaps."

She frowned. "You seem hesitant."

"I do not know," he said, glancing down. "I do not feel that Cett's departure is a good thing, Tindwyl. Something is very wrong. We need to be finished with these studies."

Tindwyl cocked her head. "How soon?"

"We should try to be done tonight, I think," Sazed said, glancing toward the pile of unbound sheets they had stacked on the table. That stack contained all the notes, ideas, and connections that they'd made during their furious bout of study. It was a book, of sorts—a guidebook that told of the Hero of Ages and the Deepness. It was a good document—incredible, even, considering the time they'd been given. It was not comprehensive. It was, however, probably the most important thing he'd ever written.

Even if he wasn't certain why.

"Sazed?" Tindwyl asked, frowning. "What is this?" She reached to the stack of papers, pulling out a sheet that was slightly askew. As she held it up, Sazed was shocked to see that a chunk from the bottom right corner had been torn off.

"Did you do this?" she asked.

"No," Sazed said. He accepted the paper. It was one of the transcriptions of the rubbing; the tear had removed the last sentence or so. There was no sign of the missing piece.

Sazed looked up, meeting Tindwyl's confused gaze. She turned, shuffling through a stack of papers to the side. She pulled out another copy of the transcription and held it up.

Sazed felt a chill. The corner was missing.

"I referenced this yesterday," Tindwyl said quietly. "I

haven't left the room save for a few minutes since then, and you were always here."

"Did you leave last night?" Sazed asked. "To visit the privy while I slept?"

"Perhaps. I don't remember."

Sazed sat for a moment, staring at the page. The tear was eerily similar in shape to the one from their main stack. Tindwyl, apparently thinking the same thing, laid it over its companion. It matched perfectly; even the smallest ridges in the tears were identical. Even if they'd been torn lying right on top of one another, the duplication wouldn't have been so perfect.

Both of them sat, staring. Then they burst into motion, riffling through their stacks of pages. Sazed had four copies of the transcription. All were missing the same exact chunk.

"Sazed . . ." Tindwyl said, her voice shaking just a bit. She held up a sheet of paper—one that had only half of the transcription on it, ending near the middle of the page. A hole had been torn directly in the middle of the page, removing the exact same sentence.

"The rubbing!" Tindwyl said, but Sazed was already moving. He left his chair, rushing to the trunk where he stored his metalminds. He fumbled with the key at his neck, pulling it off and unlocking the trunk. He threw it open, removed the rubbing, then unfolded it delicately on the ground. He withdrew his fingers suddenly, feeling almost as if he'd been bitten, as he saw the tear at the bottom. The same sentence, removed.

"How is this possible?" Tindwyl whispered. "How could someone know so much of our work—so much of us?"

"And yet," Sazed said, "how could they know so little of our abilities? I have the entire transcription stored in my metalmind. I can remember it right now."

"What does the missing sentence say?"

" 'Alendi must not reach the Well of Ascension; he must not be allowed to take the power for himself.' "

"Why remove this sentence?" Tindwyl asked.

Sazed stared at the rubbing. *This seems impossible. . . .*

A noise sounded at the window. Sazed spun, reaching

reflexively into his pewtermind and increasing his strength. His muscles swelled, his robe growing tight.

The shutters swung open. Vin crouched on the sill. She paused as she saw Sazed and Tindwyl—who had also apparently tapped strength, growing to have almost masculine bulk.

"Did I do something wrong?" Vin asked.

Sazed smiled, releasing his pewtermind. "No, child," he said. "You simply startled us." He met Tindwyl's eye, and she began to gather up the ripped pieces of paper. Sazed folded up the rubbing; they would discuss it further later.

"Have you seen anyone spending too much time around my room, Lady Vin?" Sazed asked as he replaced the rubbing. "Any strangers—or even any particular guards?"

"No," Vin said, climbing into the room. She walked barefoot, as usual, and she didn't wear her mistcloak; she rarely did in the daytime. If she had fought the night before, she had changed clothing, for there were no stains of blood—or even sweat—on this outfit. "Do you want me to watch for anyone suspicious?" she asked.

"Yes, please," Sazed said, locking the chest. "We fear that someone has been riffling through our work, though why they would wish to do so is confusing."

Vin nodded, remaining where she was as Sazed returned to his seat. She regarded him and Tindwyl for a moment.

"I need to talk to you, Sazed," Vin said.

"I can spare a few moments, I think," Sazed said. "But, I must warn you that my studies are very pressing."

Vin nodded, then glanced at Tindwyl. Finally, she sighed, rising. "I guess I will go and see about lunch, then."

Vin relaxed slightly as the door closed; then she moved over to the table, sitting down in Tindwyl's chair, pulling her legs up before her on the wooden seat.

"Sazed," she asked, "how do you know if you're in love?"

Sazed blinked. "I . . . I do not think *I* am one to speak on this topic, Lady Vin. I know very little about it."

"You always say things like that," Vin said. "But really, you're an expert on just about everything."

Sazed chuckled. "In this case, I assure you that my insecurity is heartfelt, Lady Vin."

"Still, you've got to know something."

"A bit, perhaps," Sazed said. "Tell me, how do you feel when you are with young Lord Venture?"

"I want him to hold me," Vin said quietly, turning to the side, looking out the window. "I want him to talk to me, even if I don't understand what he's saying. Anything to keep him there, with me. I want to be better because of him."

"That seems like a very good sign, Lady Vin."

"But . . ." Vin glanced down. "I'm not good for him, Sazed. He's scared of me."

"Scared?"

"Well, he's at least uncomfortable with me. I saw the look in his eyes when he saw me fighting on the day of the Assembly attack. He stumbled away from me, Sazed, horrified."

"He'd just seen a man slain," Sazed said. "Lord Venture is somewhat innocent in these matters, Lady Vin. It wasn't you, I think—it was simply a natural reaction to the horror of death."

"Either way," Vin said, glancing back out the window. "I don't want him to see me that way. I want to be the girl he needs—the girl who can support his political plans. The girl who can be pretty when he needs her on his arm, and who can comfort him when he's frustrated. Except, that's not me. You're the one who trained me to act like a courtly woman, Saze, but we both know that I wasn't all that good at it."

"And Lord Venture fell in love with you," Sazed said, "because you *didn't* act like the other women. Despite Lord Kelsier's interference, despite your knowledge that all noblemen were our enemies, Elend fell in love with you."

"I shouldn't have let him," Vin said quietly. "I need to stay away from him, Saze—for his own good. That way, he can fall in love with someone else. Someone who is a better match for him. Someone who doesn't go kill a hundred people when she gets frustrated. Someone who deserves his love."

Sazed rose, robes swishing as he stepped to Vin's chair. He stooped down, placing his head even with hers, laying a hand on her shoulder. "Oh, child. When will you stop worrying and simply let yourself be loved?"

Vin shook her head. "It's not that easy."

"Few things are. Yet, I tell you this, Lady Vin. Love must be allowed to flow both ways—if it is not, then it is not truly love, I think. It is something else. Infatuation, perhaps? Either way, there are some of us who are far too quick to make martyrs of ourselves. We stand at the side, watching, thinking that we do the right thing by inaction. We fear pain—our own, or that of another."

He squeezed her shoulder. "But . . . is that love? Is it love to assume for Elend that he has no place with you? Or, is it love to let him make his own decision in the matter?"

"And if I'm wrong for him?" Vin asked.

"You must love him enough to trust his wishes, even if you disagree with them. You must respect him—no matter how wrong you think he may be, no matter how poor you think his decisions, you must respect his desire to make them. Even if one of them includes loving you."

Vin smiled slightly, but she still seemed troubled. "And . . ." she said very slowly, "if there is someone else? For me?"

Ah. . . .

She tensed immediately. "You mustn't tell Elend I said that."

"I won't," Sazed promised. "Who is this other man?"

Vin shrugged. "Just . . . someone more like myself. The kind of man I *should* be with."

"Do you love him?"

"He's strong," Vin said. "He makes me think of Kelsier."

So there is *another Mistborn,* Sazed thought. In this matter, he knew he should remain unbiased. He didn't know enough about this second man to make a judgment—and Keepers were supposed to give information, but avoid specific advice.

Sazed, however, had never been very good at following that rule. He didn't know this other Mistborn, true, but he *did* know Elend Venture. "Child," he said, "Elend is the best of men, and you have been so much happier since you've been with him."

"But, he's really the first man I loved," Vin said quietly. "How do I know it's right? Shouldn't I pay more attention to the man who is a better match for me?"

"I don't know, Lady Vin. I honestly don't know. I warned you of my ignorance in this area. But, can you really hope to find a better person than Lord Elend?"

She sighed. "It's all so frustrating. I should be worrying about the city and the Deepness, not which man to spend my evenings with!"

"It is hard to defend others when our own lives are in turmoil," Sazed said.

"I just have to decide," Vin said, standing, walking over toward the window. "Thank you, Sazed. Thank you for listening . . . thank you for coming back to the city."

Sazed nodded, smiling. Vin shot backward out the open window, shoving herself against some bit of metal. Sazed sighed, rubbing his eyes as he walked over to the room's door and pulled it open.

Tindwyl stood outside, arms crossed. "I think I would feel more comfortable in this city," she said, "if I didn't know that our Mistborn had the volatile emotions of a teenage girl."

"Lady Vin is more stable than you think," Sazed said.

"Sazed, I've raised some fifteen daughters," Tindwyl said, entering the room. "*No* teenage girl is stable. Some are just better at hiding it than others."

"Then, be glad she didn't hear you eavesdropping," Sazed said. "She is usually rather paranoid about such things."

"Vin has a weak spot regarding Terris people," Tindwyl said with a wave of her hand. "We can likely thank you for that. She seems to give great value to your advice."

"Such as it is."

"I thought what you said was very wise, Sazed," Tindwyl said, sitting. "You would have made an excellent father."

Sazed bowed his head in embarrassment, then moved over to sit down. "We should—"

A knock came at the door.

"Now what?" Tindwyl asked.

"Did you not order us lunch?"

Tindwyl shook her head. "I never even left the hallway."

A second later, Elend poked his head into the room. "Sazed? Could I talk to you for a bit?"

"Of course, Lord Elend," Sazed said, rising.

"Great," Elend said, striding into the room. "Tindwyl, you are excused."

She rolled her eyes, shooting an exasperated glance at Sazed, but stood and walked from the room.

"Thank you," Elend said as she shut the door. "Please, sit," he said, waving to Sazed.

Sazed did so, and Elend took a deep breath, standing with hands clasped behind his back. He had gone back to his white uniforms, and stood with a commanding posture despite his obvious frustration.

Someone stole my friend the scholar away, Sazed thought, *and left a king in his place.* "I assume this is about Lady Vin, Lord Elend?"

"Yes," Elend said, beginning to pace, gesturing with one hand as he spoke. "She doesn't make any sense, Sazed. I expect that—hell, I count on it. She's not just female, she's *Vin*. But, I'm left unsure how to react. One minute she seems warm to me—like we were before this mess hit the city—and the next minute she's distant and stiff."

"Perhaps she's just confused herself."

"Perhaps," Elend agreed. "But shouldn't at least *one* of us know what is going on in our relationship? Honestly, Saze, sometimes I just think we're too different to be together."

Sazed smiled. "Oh, I don't know about that, Lord Elend. You may be surprised at how similarly the two of you think."

"I doubt that," Elend said, continuing to pace. "She's Mistborn; I'm just a regular man. She grew up on the streets; I grew up in a mansion. She is wily and clever; I'm book-learned."

"She is extremely competent, and so are you," Sazed said. "She was oppressed by her brother, you by your father. Both of you hated the Final Empire, and fought it. And both of you think far too much about what *should* be, rather than what is."

Elend paused, looking at Sazed. "What does that mean?"

"It means that I think you two are right for each other," Sazed said. "I am not supposed to make such judgments, and truly, this is just the opinion of a man who hasn't seen much of you two in the last few months. But, I believe it to be true."

"And our differences?" Elend asked.

"At first glance, the key and the lock it fits may seem very different," Sazed said. "Different in shape, different in function, different in design. The man who looks at them without knowledge of their true nature might think them opposites, for one is meant to open, and the other to keep closed. Yet, upon closer examination, he might see that without one, the other becomes useless. The wise man then sees that both lock and key were created for the same purpose."

Elend smiled. "You need to write a book sometime, Sazed. That's as profound as anything I've read."

Sazed flushed, but glanced at the stack of papers on the desktop. Would they be his legacy? He wasn't certain if they were profound, but they did represent the most cohesive attempt that he'd ever made at writing something original. True, most of the sheets contained quotes or references, but a great deal of the text also included his thoughts and annotations.

"So," Elend said, "what should I do?"

"About Lady Vin?" Sazed asked. "I would suggest simply giving her—and yourself—a little more time."

"Time is at a premium these days, Saze."

"When is it not?"

"When your city isn't besieged by two armies," Elend said, "one of them led by a megalomaniac tyrant, the other by a reckless fool."

"Yes," Sazed said slowly. "Yes, I think you may be right. I should return to my studies."

Elend frowned. "What are you working on, anyway?"

"Something that has little relevance to your current problem, I fear," Sazed said. "Tindwyl and I are collecting and compiling references about the Deepness and the Hero of Ages."

"The Deepness . . . Vin mentioned it, too. You really think it might return?"

"I think it has returned, Lord Elend," Sazed said. "It never left, really. I believe the Deepness was—*is*—the mists."

"But, why . . ." Elend said, then held up a hand. "I'll read your conclusions when you have finished. I can't afford to get sidetracked right now. Thank you, Sazed, for your advice."

Yes, a king indeed, Sazed thought.

"Tindwyl," Elend said, "you may come back in now. Sazed, good day." Elend turned toward the door, and it cracked open slowly. Tindwyl strode in, hiding her embarrassment.

"How did you know I was out there?" she asked.

"I guessed," Elend said. "You're as bad as Vin. Anyway, good day, both of you."

Tindwyl frowned as he left; then she glanced at Sazed.

"You really did do a fine job with him," Sazed said.

"Too fine a job," Tindwyl said, sitting. "I actually think that if the people had let him remain in command, he might have found a way to save the city. Come, we must return to work—this time, I actually did send someone for lunch, so we should get as much done as possible before it arrives."

Sazed nodded, seating himself and picking up his pen. Yet, he found it difficult to focus on his work. His mind kept returning to Vin and Elend. He wasn't certain why it was so important to him that they make their relationship work. Perhaps it was simply because they were both friends of his, and he wished to see them happy.

Or perhaps there was something else. Those two were the best Luthadel had to offer. The most powerful Mistborn of the skaa underground, and the most noble leader of the aristocratic culture. They needed each other, and the Final Empire needed them both.

Plus, there was the work he was doing. The specific pronoun used in much of the Terris prophetic language was gender neutral. The actual word meant "it," though it was commonly translated into modern tongues as "he." Yet each "he" in his book could also have been written as "she." If Vin really was the Hero of Ages. . . .

I need to find a way to get them out of the city, Sazed thought, a sudden realization washing over him. *Those two must not be here when Luthadel falls.*

He put aside his notes and immediately began writing a quick series of letters.

The two are not the same.

46

BREEZE COULD SMELL INTRIGUE FROM two streets away. Unlike many of his fellow thieves, he hadn't grown up impoverished, nor had he been forced to live in the underground. He'd grown up in a place far more cutthroat: an aristocratic court. Fortunately, the other crewmembers didn't treat him differently because of his full-blooded noble origin.

That was, of course, because they didn't know about it.

His upbringing afforded him certain understandings. Things that he doubted any skaa thief, no matter how competent, knew. Skaa intrigue made a brutal kind of sense; it was a matter of naked life and death. You betrayed your allies for money, for power, or to protect yourself.

In the noble courts, intrigue was more abstract. Betrayals wouldn't often end with either party dead, but the ramifications could span generations. It was a game—so much of one, in fact, that the young Breeze had found the open brutality of the skaa underground to be refreshing.

He sipped his warm mug of mulled wine, eyeing the note in his fingers. He'd come to believe that he wouldn't have to worry about intracrew conspiracies anymore: Kelsier's crew was an almost sickeningly tight group, and Breeze did everything within his Allomantic powers to keep it that way. He'd seen what infighting could do to a family.

That was why he was so surprised to receive this letter. Despite its mock innocence, he could easily pick out the signs. The hurried pace of the writing, smudged in places but not rewritten. Phrases like "No need to tell others of this" and "do not wish to cause alarm." The extra drops of sealing wax, spread gratuitously on the lip of the letter, as if to give extra protection against prying eyes.

There was no mistaking the tone of the missive. Breeze had been invited to a conspiratorial conference. But, why in the Lord Ruler's name would *Sazed,* of all people, want to meet in secret?

Breeze sighed, pulling out his dueling cane and using it to steady himself. He grew light-headed sometimes when he stood; it was a minor malady he'd always had, though it seemed to have grown worse during the last few years. He glanced over his shoulder as his vision cleared, toward where Allrianne slept in his bed.

I should probably feel more guilty about her, he thought, smiling despite himself and reaching to put his vest and jacket on over his trousers and shirt. *But . . . well, we're all going to be dead in a few days anyway.* An afternoon spent speaking with Clubs could certainly put one's life in perspective.

Breeze wandered out into the hallway, making his way though the gloomy, inadequately lit Venture passageways. *Honestly,* he thought, *I understand the value in saving lamp oil, but things are depressing enough right now without the dark corridors.*

The meeting place was only a few short twists away. Breeze located it easily because of the two soldiers standing watch outside the door. Demoux's men—soldiers who reported to the captain religiously, as well as vocationally.

Interesting, Breeze thought, remaining hidden in the side hallway. He quested out with his Allomantic powers and Soothed the men, taking away their relaxation and certainty, leaving behind anxiety and nervousness. The guards began to grow restless, shuffling. Finally, one turned and opened the door, checking on the room inside. The motion gave Breeze a full view of the room's contents. Only one man sat within. Sazed.

Breeze stood quietly, trying to decide his next course of action. There was nothing incriminating in the letter; this couldn't all simply be a trap on Elend's part, could it? An obscure attempt at finding out which crewmembers would betray him and which wouldn't? Seemed like too distrustful a move for the good-natured boy. Besides, if that were the case, Sazed would have to try and get Breeze to do more than simply meet in a clandestine location.

The door swung closed, the soldier returning to his place. *I can trust Sazed, can't I?* Breeze thought. But, if that was the case, why the quiet meeting? Was Breeze overreacting?

No, the guards proved that Sazed worried about this meeting being discovered. It was suspicious. If it were anyone else, Breeze would have gone straight to Elend. But Sazed . . .

Breeze sighed, then wandered into the hallway, dueling cane clicking against the floor. *Might as well see what he has to say. Besides, if he* is *planning something devious, it'd almost be worth the danger to see it.* Despite the letter, despite the strange circumstances, Breeze had trouble imagining a Terrisman being involved in something that wasn't completely honest.

Perhaps the Lord Ruler had had the same problem.

Breeze nodded to the soldiers, Soothing away their anxiety and restoring them to a more temperate humor. There was another reason why he was willing to chance the meeting. Breeze was only just beginning to realize how dangerous his predicament was. Luthadel would soon fall. Every instinct he'd nurtured during thirty years in the underground was telling him to run.

That feeling made him more likely to take risks. The Breeze of a few years earlier would already have abandoned the city. *Damn you, Kelsier,* he thought as he pushed open the door.

Sazed looked up with surprise from his table. The room was sparse, with several chairs and only two lamps. "You're early, Lord Breeze," Sazed said, standing quickly.

"Of course I am," Breeze snapped. "I had to make certain this wasn't a trap of some sort." He paused. "This isn't a trap of some sort, right?"

"Trap?" Sazed asked. "What are you talking about?"

"Oh, don't sound so shocked," Breeze said. "This is no simple meeting."

Sazed wilted slightly. "It's . . . that obvious, is it?"

Breeze sat, laying his cane across his lap, and eyed Sazed tellingly, Soothing the man to make him feel a little more self-conscious. "You may have helped us overthrow the Lord Ruler, my dear man—but you have a lot to learn about being sneaky."

"I apologize," Sazed said, sitting. "I simply wanted to meet quickly, to discuss certain . . . sensitive issues."

"Well, I'd recommend getting rid of those guards," Breeze said. "They make the room stand out. Then, light a few more lamps and get us something to eat or drink. If Elend walks in—I assume it's Elend we're hiding from?"

"Yes."

"Well, if he comes and sees us sitting here in the dark, eyeing each other insidiously, he'll know something is up. The less natural the occasion, the more natural you want to appear."

"Ah, I see," Sazed said. "Thank you."

The door opened and Clubs hobbled in. He eyed Breeze, then Sazed, then wandered over toward a chair. Breeze glanced at Sazed—no surprise there. Clubs was obviously invited as well.

"Lose those guards," Clubs snapped.

"Immediately, Lord Cladent," Sazed said, standing and shuffling over to the door. He spoke briefly with the guards, then returned. As Sazed was sitting, Ham poked his head into the room, looking suspicious.

"Wait a minute," Breeze said. "How many people are coming to this secret meeting?"

Sazed gestured for Ham to sit. "All of the more . . . experienced members of the crew."

"You mean everyone but Elend and Vin," Breeze said.

"I did not invite Lord Lestibournes either," Sazed said.

Yes, but Spook isn't the one we're hiding from.

Ham sat down hesitantly, shooting a questioning glance at Breeze. "So . . . why exactly are we meeting behind the backs of our Mistborn and our king?"

"King no longer," a voice noted from the door. Dockson walked in and sat. "In fact, it could be argued that Elend isn't leader of this crew anymore. He fell into that position by happenstance—just like he fell into the throne."

Ham flushed. "I know you don't like him, Dox, but I'm not here to talk treason."

"There's no treason if there's no throne to betray," Dockson said, sitting. "What are we going to do—stay here and be servants in his house? Elend doesn't need us. Perhaps it's time to transfer our services to Lord Penrod."

"Penrod is a nobleman, too," Ham said. "You can't tell me you like him any better than you do Elend."

Dockson thumped the table quietly with his fist. "It's not about who I *like,* Ham. It's about seeing that this damn kingdom Kelsier threw at us remains standing! We've spent a year and a half cleaning up his mess. Do you want to see that work wasted?"

"Please, gentlemen," Sazed said, trying—without success—to break into the conversation.

"Work, Dox?" Ham said, flushed. "What work have you done? I haven't seen you do much of anything besides sit and complain every time someone offers a plan."

"Complain?" Dockson snapped. "Do you have any idea how much administrative work it has taken to keep this city from falling upon itself? What have you done, Ham? You refused to take command of the army. All you do is drink and spar with your friends!"

That's enough of that, Breeze thought, Soothing the men. *At this rate, we'll strangle each other before Straff can have us executed.*

Dockson settled back in his chair, waving a dismissive hand at Ham, who still sat red-faced. Sazed waited, obviously chagrined by the outbreak. Breeze Soothed away his insecurity. *You're in charge here, Sazed. Tell us what is going on.*

"Please," Sazed said. "I did not bring us together so that we could argue. I understand that you are all tense—that is understandable, considering the circumstances."

"Penrod is going to give our city to Straff," Ham said.

"That's better than letting him slaughter us," Dockson countered.

"Actually," Breeze said, "I don't think we have to worry about Straff slaughtering us."

"No?" Dockson asked, frowning. "Do you have some information you haven't been sharing with us, Breeze?"

"Oh, get over yourself, Dox," Ham snapped. "You've never been happy that you didn't end up in charge when Kell died. That's the real reason you never liked Elend, isn't it?"

Dockson flushed, and Breeze sighed, slapping both of them with a powerful blanket Soothing. They both jumped slightly, as if they'd been stung—though the sensation would be quite the opposite. Their emotions, once volatile, would suddenly have become numb and unresponsive.

Both looked at Breeze.

"Yes," he said, "of course I'm Soothing you. Honestly, I know Hammond is a bit immature—but you, Dockson?"

Dockson sat back, rubbing his forehead. "You can let go, Breeze," he said after a moment. "I'll keep my tongue."

Ham just grumbled, settling one hand on the table. Sazed watched the exchange with a little bit of shock.

This is what cornered men are like, my dear Terrisman, Breeze thought. *This is what happens when they lose hope. They might be able to keep up appearances in front of the soldiers, but put them alone with their friends . . .*

Sazed was a Terrisman; his entire life had been one of oppression and loss. But these men, Breeze himself included, were accustomed to success. Even against overwhelming odds, they were confident. They were the type of men who could go up against a god, and expect to win. They wouldn't deal well with losing. Of course, when losing meant death, who would?

"Straff's armies are getting ready to break camp," Clubs finally said. "He's doing it subtly, but the signs are there."

"So, he's coming for the city," Dockson said. "My men in Penrod's palace say the Assembly has been sending missive after missive to Straff, all but begging him to come take up occupation of Luthadel."

"He's not going to take the city," Clubs said. "At least, not if he's smart."

"Vin is still a threat," Breeze said. "And it doesn't look like Straff has a Mistborn to protect him. If he came into Luthadel, I doubt there is a single thing he could do to keep her from slitting his throat. So, he'll do something else."

Dockson frowned, and glanced at Ham, who shrugged.

"It's really quite simple," Breeze said, tapping the table with his dueling cane. "Why, even I figured it out." Clubs snorted at this. "If Straff makes it look like he's withdrawing, the koloss will probably attack Luthadel for him. They're too literal to understand the threat of a hidden army."

"If Straff withdraws," Clubs said, "Jastes won't be able to keep them from the city."

Dockson blinked. "But they'd . . ."

"Slaughter?" Clubs asked. "Yes. They'd pillage the richest sectors of the town—probably end up killing most of the noblemen in the city."

"Eliminating the men that Straff has been forced—against his will, knowing that man's pride—to work with," Breeze added. "In fact, there's a good chance the creatures will kill Vin. Can you imagine her not joining the fight if koloss broke in?"

The room fell silent.

"But, that doesn't really help Straff get the city," Dockson said. "He'll still have to fight the koloss."

"Yes," Clubs said, scowling. "But, they'll probably take down some of the city gates, not to mention level a lot of the homes. That will leave Straff with a clear field to attack a weakened foe. Plus, koloss don't strategize—for them, city walls won't be much help. Straff couldn't ask for a better setup."

"He'd be seen as a liberator," Breeze said quietly. "If he returns at the right time—after the koloss have broken into the city and fought the soldiers, but before they've done serious damage to the skaa quarter—he could free the people and establish himself as their protector, not their conqueror. Knowing how the people feel, I think they'd welcome him. Right now, a strong leader would mean more to them than coins in their pockets and rights in the Assembly."

As the group thought on this, Breeze eyed Sazed, who still sat quietly. He'd said so little; what was his game? Why gather the crew? Was he subtle enough to know that they'd simply needed to have an honest discussion like this, without Elend's morals to clutter things up?

"We could just let Straff have it," Dockson finally said. "The city, I mean. We could promise to call Vin off. If that is where this is heading anyway . . ."

"Dox," Ham said quietly, "what would Kell think, to hear you talk like that?"

"We could give the city to Jastes Lekal," Breeze said. "Perhaps he can be persuaded to treat the skaa with dignity."

"And let twenty thousand koloss into the city?" Ham asked. "Breeze, have you ever *seen* what those things can do?"

Dockson pounded the table. "I'm just giving options, Ham. What else are we going to do?"

"Fight," Clubs said. "And die."

The room fell silent again.

"You sure know how to kill a conversation, my friend," Breeze finally said.

"It needed to be said," Clubs muttered. "No use fooling yourselves anymore. We can't win a fight, and a fight is where this was always going. The city is going to get attacked. We're going to defend it. And we'll lose.

"You wonder if we should just give up. Well, we're not going to do that. Kell wouldn't let us, and so we won't let ourselves. We'll fight, and we'll die with dignity. Then, the city will burn—but we'll have said something. The Lord Ruler pushed us around for a thousand years, but now we skaa have pride. We fight. We resist. And we die."

"What was this all worth, then?" Ham said with frustration. "Why overthrow the Final Empire? Why kill the Lord Ruler? Why do anything, if it was just going to end like this? Tyrants ruling every dominance, Luthadel smashed to rubble, our crew dead?"

"Because," Sazed said softly, "someone had to begin it. While the Lord Ruler ruled, society could not progress. He kept a stabilizing hand on the empire, but it was an oppressive hand as well. Fashion stayed remarkably unchanged for a thousand years, the noblemen always trying to fit the Lord Ruler's ideals. Architecture and science did not progress, for the Lord Ruler frowned on change and invention.

"And the skaa could not be free, for he would not let them. However, killing him did not free our peoples, my friends. Only time will do that. It will take centuries, perhaps—centuries of fighting, learning, and growth. At the beginning, unfortunately and unavoidably, things will be very difficult. Worse even than they were beneath the Lord Ruler."

"And we die for nothing," Ham said with a scowl.

"No," Sazed said. "Not nothing, Lord Hammond. We will die to show that there are skaa who will not be bullied, who will not back down. This is a very important precedent, I think. In the histories and legends, this is the kind of event that inspires. If the skaa are ever to take rule of themselves, there will need to be sacrifices they can look to for motivation. Sacrifices like that of the Survivor himself."

The men sat in silence.

"Breeze," Ham said, "I could use a little more confidence right now."

"Of course," Breeze said, carefully Soothing away the man's anxiety and fear. His face lost some of its pale pallor, and he sat up a little straighter. Just for good measure, Breeze gave the rest of the crew a little of the same treatment.

"How long have you known?" Dockson asked Sazed.

"For some time now, Lord Dockson," Sazed said.

"But, you couldn't have known that Straff would pull back and give us to the koloss. Only Clubs figured that out."

"My knowledge was general, Lord Breeze," Sazed said in his even voice. "It did not relate to the koloss specifically. I have thought for some time that this city would fall. In all honesty, I am deeply impressed with your efforts. This people should long since have been defeated, I think. You have done something grand—something that will be remembered for centuries."

"Assuming anyone survives to tell the story," Clubs noted.

Sazed nodded. "That, actually, is why I called this gathering. There is little chance of those of us who remain in the city surviving—we will be needed to help with defenses, and if we do survive the koloss attack, Straff will try to execute us. However, it is not necessary for us *all* to remain in Luthadel for its fall—someone, perhaps, should be sent out to organize further resistance against the warlords."

"I won't leave my men," Clubs grumbled.

"Nor I," Ham said. "Though I *did* send my family to ground yesterday." The simple phrase meant that he'd had them leave, perhaps to hide in the city's underground, perhaps to escape through one of the passwalls. Ham wouldn't know—and that way he couldn't betray their location. Old habits died hard.

"If this city falls," Dockson said, "I'll be here with it. That's what Kell would expect. I'm not leaving."

"I'll go," Breeze said, looking at Sazed. "Is it too early to volunteer?"

"Um, actually, Lord Breeze," Sazed said, "I wasn't—"

Breeze held up a hand. "It's all right, Sazed. I believe it's obvious whom you think should be sent away. You didn't invite them to the meeting."

Dockson frowned. "We're going to defend Luthadel to the death, and you want to send away our only Mistborn?"

Sazed nodded his head. "My lords," he said softly, "the

men of this city will need our leadership. We gave them this city and put them in this predicament. We cannot abandon them now. But . . . there are great things at work in this world. Greater things than us, I think. I am convinced that Mistress Vin is part of them.

"Even if these matters are delusions on my part, then Lady Vin still *must* not be allowed to die in this city. She is the people's most personal and powerful link to the Survivor. She has become a symbol to them, and her skills as a Mistborn give her the best chance of being able to get away, then survive the attacks Straff will undoubtedly send. She will be a great value in the fight to come—she can move quickly and stealthily, and can fight alone, doing much damage, as she proved last night."

Sazed bowed his head. "My lords, I called you here today so that we could decide how to convince her to run, when the rest of us stay to fight. It will not be an easy task, I think."

"She won't leave Elend," Ham said. "He'll have to go, too."

"My thoughts as well, Lord Hammond," Sazed said.

Clubs chewed his lip in thought. "That boy won't be easily convinced to flee. He still thinks we can win this fight."

"And we may yet," Sazed said. "My lords, my purpose is not to leave you without any hope at all. But, the dire circumstances, the likelihood of success . . ."

"We know, Sazed," Breeze said. "We understand."

"There have to be others of the crew who can go," Ham said, looking down. "More than just the two."

"I would send Tindwyl with them," Sazed said. "She will carry to my people many discoveries of great importance. I also plan to send Lord Lestibournes. He would do little good in the battle, and his abilities as a spy could be of help to Lady Vin and Lord Elend as they try to rally resistance among the skaa.

"However, those four will not be the only ones who survive. Most of the skaa should be safe—Jastes Lekal seems to be able to control his koloss somehow. Even if he cannot, then Straff should arrive in time to protect the city's people."

"Assuming Straff is planning what Clubs thinks he is," Ham said. "He could actually be withdrawing, cutting his losses and leaving Luthadel behind."

"Either way," Clubs said. "Not many can get out. Neither Straff nor Jastes are likely to allow large groups of people to flee the city. Right now, confusion and fear in the streets will serve their purposes far better than depopulation. We might be able to get a few riders on horseback out—especially if one of those riders is Vin. The rest of the people will have to take their chances with the koloss."

Breeze felt his stomach turn. Clubs spoke so bluntly . . . so callously. But that was Clubs. He wasn't even really a pessimist; he just said the things that he didn't think others wanted to acknowledge.

Some of the skaa will survive to become slaves for Straff Venture, Breeze thought. *But those who fight—and those who have led the city this last year—are doomed. That includes me.*

It's true. This time there really is no way out.

"Well?" Sazed asked, hands spread before him. "Are we in agreement that these four should go?"

The members of the group nodded.

"Let us discuss, then," Sazed said, "and devise a plan for sending them away."

"We could just make Elend think that the danger isn't that great," Dockson said. "If he believes that the city is in for a long siege, he might be willing to go with Vin on a mission somewhere. They wouldn't realize what was happening back here until it was too late."

"A good suggestion, Lord Dockson," Sazed said. "I think, also, that we could work with Vin's concept of the Well of Ascension."

The discussion continued, and Breeze sat back, satisfied. *Vin, Elend, and Spook will survive,* he thought. *I'll have to convince Sazed to let Allrianne go with them.* He glanced around the room, noticing a release of tension in the postures of the others. Dockson and Ham seemed at peace, and even Clubs was nodding quietly to himself, looking satisfied as they talked through suggestions.

The disaster was still coming. But, somehow, the possibility that some would escape—the youngest crewmembers, the ones still inexperienced enough to hope—made everything else a little easier to accept.

Vin stood quietly in the mists, looking up at the dark spires, columns, and towers of Kredik Shaw. In her head, two sounds thumped. The mist spirit and the larger, vaster sound.

It was growing more and more demanding.

She continued forward, ignoring the thumps as she approached Kredik Shaw. The Hill of a Thousand Spires, once home of the Lord Ruler. It had been abandoned for well over a year, but no vagrants had made their home here. It was too ominous. Too terrible. Too much a reminder of *him*.

The Lord Ruler had been a monster. Vin remembered well the night, over a year before, when she had come to this palace intending to kill him. To do the job that Kelsier had unwittingly trained her to do. She had walked through this very courtyard, had passed guards at the doors before her.

And she had let them live. Kelsier would have just fought his way in. But Vin had talked them into leaving, into joining the rebellion. That act had saved her life when one of those very men, Goradel, had led Elend to the palace dungeons to help rescue Vin.

In a way, the Final Empire had been overthrown because she *hadn't* acted like Kelsier.

And yet, could she base future decisions upon a coincidence like that? Looking back, it seemed too perfectly allegorical. Like a neat little tale told to children, intended to teach a lesson.

Vin had never heard those tales as a child. And, she had survived when so many others had died. For every lesson like the one with Goradel, it seemed that there were a dozen that ended in tragedy.

And then there was Kelsier. He'd been right, in the end. His lesson was very different from the ones taught by the children's tales. Kelsier had been bold, even excited, when he executed those who stood in his path. Ruthless. He had looked toward the greater good; he'd always had his eyes focused on the fall of the empire, and the eventual rise of a kingdom like Elend's.

He had succeeded. Why couldn't she kill as he had, knowing she was doing her duty, never feeling guilt? She'd always been frightened by the edge of danger Kelsier had displayed. Yet, wasn't that very edge the thing that had let him succeed?

She passed into the tunnel-like corridors of the palace, feet and mistcloak tassels trailing marks in the dust. The mists, as always, remained behind. They didn't enter buildings—or, if they did, they usually didn't remain for long. With them, she left behind the mist spirit.

She had to make a decision. She didn't like the decision, but she was accustomed to doing things she didn't like. That was life. She hadn't wanted to fight the Lord Ruler, but she had.

It soon became too dark even for Mistborn eyes, and she had to light a lantern. When she did, she was surprised to see that her footsteps weren't the only ones in the dust. Apparently, someone else had been haunting the corridors. However, whoever it was, she didn't encounter them as she walked through the hallways.

She entered the chamber a few moments later. She wasn't sure what had drawn her to Kredik Shaw, let alone the hidden chamber at its center. It seemed, however, that she had been feeling a kinship with the Lord Ruler lately. Her walkings had brought her here, to a place she hadn't visited since that night when she'd slain the only God she'd ever known.

He had spent a lot of time in this hidden chamber, a place he had apparently built to remind him of his homeland. The chamber had a domed roof that arced overhead. The walls were filled with silvery murals and the floor was filled with metallic inlays. She ignored these, walking forward toward the room's central feature—a small stone building that had been built within the larger chamber.

It was here that Kelsier and his wife had been captured many years before, during Kelsier's first attempt to rob the

Lord Ruler. Mare had been murdered at the Pits. But Kelsier had survived.

It was here, in this same chamber, that Vin had first faced an Inquisitor, and had nearly been killed herself. It was also here that she had come months later in her first attempt to kill the Lord Ruler. She had been defeated that time, too.

She stepped into the small building-within-a-building. It had only one room. The floor had been torn up by Elend's crews, searching for the atium. The walls were still hung, however, with the trappings the Lord Ruler had left behind. She raised her lantern, looking at them.

Rugs. Furs. A small wooden flute. The things of his people, the Terris people, from a thousand years before. Why had he built his new city of Luthadel here, to the south, when his homeland—and the Well of Ascension itself—had been to the north? Vin had never really understood that.

Perhaps it came down to decision. Rashek, the Lord Ruler, had been forced to make a decision, too. He could have continued as he was, the pastoral villager. He would probably have had a happy life with his people.

But he had decided to become something more. In doing so, he had committed terrible atrocities. Yet, could she blame him for the decision itself? He had become what he'd thought he needed to be.

Her decision seemed more mundane, but she knew that other things—the Well of Ascension, the protection of Luthadel—could not be considered until she was certain what she wanted and who she was. And yet, standing in that room where Rashek had spent much of his time, thinking about the Well, the demanding thumps in her head sounded louder than they ever had before.

She had to decide. Elend was the one she wanted to be with. He represented peace. Happiness. Zane, however, represented what she felt she had to become. For the good of everyone involved.

The Lord Ruler's palace held no clues or answers for her. A few moments later, frustrated and baffled at why she had even come, she left it behind, walking back out into the mists.

Zane awoke to the sound of a tent spike being pounded in a specific rhythm. His reaction was immediate.

He burned steel and pewter. He always swallowed a new bit of each before sleeping. He knew the habit would probably kill him someday; metals were poisonous if allowed to linger.

Dying someday was better, in Zane's opinion, than dying today.

He flipped out of his cot, tossing his blanket toward the opening tent flap. He could barely see in the darkness of night. Even as he jumped, he heard something ripping. The tent walls being slit.

"Kill them!" God screamed.

Zane thumped to the ground and grabbed a handful of coins from the bowl beside his bed. He heard cries of surprise as he spun, throwing coins in a spinning spray around him.

He Pushed. Tiny plunks of sound thumped around him as coins met canvas, then continued on.

And men began to scream.

Zane fell to a crouch, waiting silently as the tent collapsed around him. Someone was thrashing the cloth to his right. He shot a few coins, and heard a satisfying grunt of pain. In the stillness, canvas resting atop him like a blanket, he heard footsteps running away.

He sighed, relaxing, and used a dagger to slice away the top of his tent. He emerged to a misty night. He'd gone to sleep later today than he usually did; it was probably near midnight. Time to be up anyway.

He strode across the fallen top of his tent—moving over to the now cloaked form of his cot—and cut a hole so he could reach through and pluck out the vial of metal he'd stored in a pocket beneath it. He downed the metals, and tin brought near light to his surroundings. Four men lay dying or dead around his tent. They were soldiers, of course—Straff's soldiers. The attack had come later than Zane had expected.

Straff trusts me more than I assumed. Zane stepped over the dead form of an assassin and cut his way into a storage chest, then pulled out his clothing. He changed quietly, then removed a small bag of coins from the chest. *It must have been the attack on Cett's keep,* he thought. *It finally convinced Straff that I was too dangerous to let live.*

Zane found his man working quietly beside a tent a short distance away, ostensibly testing the strength of a tent cord. He watched every night, paid to pound on a tent spike should anyone approach Zane's tent. Zane tossed the man a bag of coins, then moved off into the darkness, passing the canal waters with their supply barges on his way to Straff's tent.

His father had some few limitations. Straff was fine at large-scale planning, but the details—the subtleties—often got away from him. He could organize an army and crush his enemies. He, however, liked to play with dangerous tools. Like the atium mines at the Pits of Hathsin. Like Zane.

Those tools often ended up burning him.

Zane walked up to the side of Straff's tent, then ripped a hole in the canvas and strode in. Straff waited for him. Zane gave the man credit: Straff watched his death coming with defiance in his eyes. Zane stopped in the middle of the room, in front of Straff, who sat in his hard wooden chair.

"Kill him," God commanded.

Lamps burned in the corners, illuminating the canvas. The cushions and blankets in the corner were rumpled; Straff had taken one last romp with his favorite mistresses before sending his assassins. The king displayed his characteristic air of strong defiance, but Zane saw more. He saw a face too slick with sweat, and he saw hands trembling, as if from a disease.

"I have atium for you," Straff said. "Buried in a place only I know."

Zane stood quietly, staring at his father.

"I will proclaim you openly," Straff said. "Name you my heir. Tomorrow, if you wish."

Zane didn't respond. Straff continued to sweat.

"The city is yours," Zane finally said, turning away.

He was rewarded with a startled gasp from behind.

Zane glanced back. He'd never seen such a look of shock on his father's face. That alone was almost worth everything.

"Pull your men back, as you are planning," Zane said, "but don't return to the Northern Dominance. Wait for those koloss to invade the city, let them take down the defenses and kill the defenders. Then, you can sweep in and rescue Luthadel."

"But, Elend's Mistborn . . ."

"Will be gone," Zane said. "She's leaving with me, tonight. Farewell, Father." He turned and left through the slit he'd made.

"Zane?" Straff called from inside the tent.

Zane paused again.

"Why?" Straff asked, looking out through the slit. "I sent assassins to kill you. Why are you letting me live?"

"Because you're my father," Zane said. He turned away, looking into the mists. "A man shouldn't kill his father."

With that, Zane bid a final farewell to the man who had created him. A man whom Zane—despite his insanity, despite the abuse he'd known over the years—loved.

In the dark mists he threw down a coin and shot out over the camp. Outside its confines, he landed and easily located the bend in the canal he used as a marker. From the hollow of a small tree there, he pulled a bundle of cloth. A mistcloak, the first gift Straff had given him, years before when Zane had first Snapped. To him, it was too precious to wear around, to soil and use.

He knew himself a fool. However, he could not help how he felt. One could not use emotional Allomancy on one's self.

He unwrapped the mistcloak and withdrew the things it protected—several vials of metal and a pouch filled with beads. Atium.

He knelt there for a long moment. Then, he reached up

to his chest, feeling the space just above his rib cages. Where his heart thumped.

There was a large bump there. There always had been. He didn't think about it often; his mind seemed to get distracted when he did. It, however, was the real reason he never wore cloaks.

He didn't like the way that cloaks rubbed against the small point of the spike that stuck out of his back just between the shoulder blades. The head was against his sternum, and couldn't be seen beneath clothing.

"It is time to go," God said.

Zane stood, leaving the mistcloak behind. He turned from his father's camp, leaving behind that which he had known, instead seeking the woman who would save him.

Alendi believes as they do.

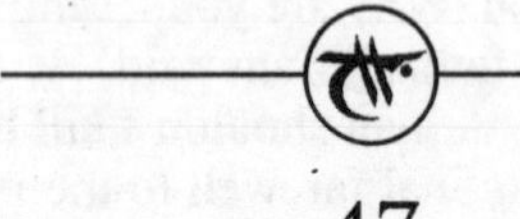

47

A PART OF VIN WASN'T EVEN bothered by how many people she had killed. That very indifference, however, terrified her.

She sat on her balcony a short time after her visit to the palace, the city of Luthadel lost in darkness before her. She sat in the mists—but knew better, now, than to think she'd find solace in their swirling patterns. Nothing was that simple anymore.

The mist spirit watched her, as always. It was too distant to see, but she could feel it. And, even stronger than the mist spirit, she could feel something else. That powerful thumping, growing louder and louder. It had once seemed distant, but no longer.

The Well of Ascension.

That was what it had to be. She could *feel* its power returning, flowing back into the world, demanding to be taken up and used. She kept finding herself glancing north, toward Terris, expecting to see something on the horizon. A burst of light, a blazing fire, a tempest of winds. Something. But there was just mist.

It seemed that she couldn't succeed at anything, lately. Love, protection, duty. *I've let myself get stretched too thin,* she thought.

There were so many things that demanded her attention, and she'd tried to give heed to them all. As a result, she had accomplished nothing. Her research about the Deepness and the Hero of Ages lay untouched for days, still arranged in piles scattered across her floor. She knew next to nothing about the mist spirit—only that it watched her, and that the logbook author had thought it dangerous. She hadn't dealt with the spy in her crew; she didn't know if Zane's claims regarding Demoux were true.

And Cett still lived. She couldn't even perform a proper massacre without stumbling halfway through. It was Kelsier's fault. He had trained her to take his place, but could anyone ever really do that?

Why do we always have to be someone else's knives? Zane's voice whispered in her head.

His words had seemed to make sense sometimes, but they had a flaw. Elend. Vin wasn't his knife—not really. He didn't want her to assassinate or kill. But, his ideals had left him without a throne, and had left his city surrounded by enemies. If she really loved Elend—if she really loved the people of Luthadel—wouldn't she have done more?

The pulsings thumped against her, like the beats of a drum the size of the sun. She burned bronze almost constantly now, listening to the rhythm, letting it pull her away. . . .

"Mistress?" OreSeur asked from behind. "What are you thinking about?"

"The end," Vin said quietly, staring outward.

Silence.

"The end of what, Mistress?"

"I don't know."

OreSeur padded over to the balcony, walking into the mists and sitting down beside her. She was getting to know him well enough that she could see concern in his canine eyes.

She sighed, shaking her head. "I just have decisions to make. And, no matter which choice I make, it will mean an end."

OreSeur sat for a moment, head cocked. "Mistress," he finally said, "that seems excessively dramatic to me."

Vin shrugged. "No advice for me, then?"

"Just make the decision," OreSeur said.

Vin sat for a moment, then smiled. "Sazed would have said something wise and comforting."

OreSeur frowned. "I fail to see why he should be part of this conversation, Mistress."

"He was my steward," Vin said. "Before he left, and before Kelsier switched your Contract to me."

"Ah," OreSeur said. "Well, I never did much like Terrismen, Mistress. Their self-important sense of subservience is very difficult to imitate—not to mention the fact that their muscles are far too stringy to taste good."

Vin raised an eyebrow. "You've imitated Terrismen? I didn't think there would be much cause for that—they weren't a very influential people during the days of the Lord Ruler."

"Ah," OreSeur said. "But they were always *around* influential people."

Vin nodded, standing. She walked back into her empty room and lit a lamp, extinguishing her tin. Mist carpeted the room, flowing over her stacks of paper, her feet throwing up puffs as she walked toward the bedroom.

She paused, That was a bit strange. Mist rarely remained long when it came indoors. Elend said it had to do with heat and enclosed spaces. Vin had always ascribed to it something more mystical. She frowned, watching it.

Even without tin, she heard the creak.

Vin spun. Zane stood on the balcony, his figure a black silhouette in the mists. He stepped forward, the mist following around him, as it did around anyone burning metals. And yet . . . it also seemed to be pushing *away* from him slightly.

OreSeur growled quietly.

"It's time," Zane said.

"Time for what?" Vin asked, setting the lamp down.

"To go," Zane said. "To leave these men and their armies. To leave the squabbling. To be free."

Free.

"I . . . don't know, Zane," Vin said, looking away.

She heard him step forward. "What do you owe him, Vin? He doesn't know you. He fears you. The truth is, he was never worthy of you."

"No," Vin said, shaking her head. "That's not it at all, Zane. You don't understand. I was never worthy of him. Elend deserves someone better. He deserves . . . someone who shares his ideals. Someone who thinks he was right to give up his throne. Someone who sees more honor—and less foolishness—in that."

"Either way," Zane said, stopping a short distance from her. "He cannot understand you. Us."

Vin didn't reply.

"Where would you go, Vin?" Zane asked. "If you weren't bound to this place, bound to him? If you were free, and could do whatever you wished, where would you go?"

The thumpings seemed louder. She glanced toward OreSeur, who sat quietly by the side wall, mostly in the dark. Why feel guilty? What did she have to prove to him?

She turned back to Zane. "North," she said. "To Terris."

"We can go there. Wherever you want. Location is irrelevant to me, as long as it is not this place."

"I can't abandon them," Vin said.

"Even if by doing so, you steal away Straff's only Mistborn?" Zane asked. "The trade is a good one. My father will know that I have disappeared, but he will not realize that you aren't still in Luthadel. He'll be even more afraid to attack. By giving yourself freedom, you'll also be leaving your allies with a precious gift."

Zane took her hand, forcing her to look at him. He did

look like Elend—like a hard version of Elend. Zane had been broken by life, just as she had been, but both had put themselves back together. Had the re-forming made them stronger, or more fragile?

"Come," Zane whispered. "You can save me, Vin."

A war is coming to the city, Vin thought with a chill. *If I stay, I will have to kill again.*

And slowly, she let him draw her away from her desk, toward the mists and the comforting darkness beyond. She reached up, pulling out a metal vial for the journey, and the motion caused Zane to spin suspiciously.

He has good instincts, Vin thought. *Instincts like my own. Instincts that won't let him trust, but that keep him alive.*

He relaxed as he saw what she was doing, and smiled and turned away again. Vin followed him, walking again, but she felt a sudden stab of fear. *This is it,* she thought. *After this, everything changes. The time for decisions has passed.*

And I made the wrong choice.

Elend wouldn't have jumped like that when I took out the vial.

She froze. Zane tugged on her wrist, but she didn't move. He turned toward her in the mists, frowning as he stood at the edge of her balcony.

"I'm sorry," Vin whispered, slipping her hand free. "I can't go with you."

"What?" Zane asked. "Why not?"

Vin shook her head, turning and walking back into the room.

"Tell me what it is!" Zane said, tone rising. "What is it about him that draws you? He isn't a great leader. He's not a warrior. He's no Allomancer or general. *What is it about him?*"

The answer came to her simply and easily. *Make your decisions—I'll support you in them.* "He trusts me," she whispered.

"What?" Zane asked incredulously.

"When I attacked Cett," Vin said, "the others thought I was acting irrationally—and they were right. But Elend told them I had a good reason, even if he didn't know what it was."

"So he's a fool," Zane said.

"When we spoke later," Vin continued, not looking at Zane, "I was cold to him. I think he knew that I was trying to decide whether to stay with him or not. And . . . he told me that he trusted my judgment. He'd support me if I chose to leave him."

"So he's also unappreciative," Zane said.

Vin shook her head. "No. He just loves me."

"I love you."

Vin paused, looking at Zane. He looked angry. Desperate, even. "I believe you. I still can't go with you."

"But *why*?"

"Because it would require leaving Elend," she said. "Even if I can't share his ideals, I can respect them. Even if I don't deserve him, I can be near him. I'm staying, Zane."

Zane stood quietly for a moment, mist falling around his shoulders. "I've failed, then."

Vin turned away from him. "No. It isn't that you've failed. You aren't flawed simply because I—"

He slammed into her, throwing her toward the mist-covered floor. Vin turned her head, shocked, as she crashed into the wooden floor, the breath going out of her.

Zane loomed above her, his face dark. "You were supposed to save me," he hissed.

Vin flared every metal she had in a sudden jolt. She shoved Zane backward and Pulled herself against the door hinges. She flew backward and hit the door hard, the wood cracking slightly, but she was too tense—too shocked—to feel anything but the thud.

Zane rose quietly, standing tall, dark. Vin rolled forward into a crouch. Zane was attacking her. Attacking her for real.

But . . . he . . .

"OreSeur!" Vin said, ignoring her mind's objections, whipping out her daggers. "Run away!"

The code given, she charged, trying to distract Zane's attention from the wolfhound. Zane sidestepped her attacks with a casual grace. Vin whipped a dagger toward his neck. It barely missed as Zane tipped his head backward. She struck at his side, at his arm, at his chest. Each strike missed.

She'd known he'd burn atium. She'd expected that. She skidded to a stop, looking at him. He hadn't even bothered to pull out his own weapons. He stood before her, face dark, mist a growing lake at his feet. "Why didn't you listen to me, Vin?" he asked. "Why force me to keep being Straff's tool? We both know where that must lead."

Vin ignored him. Gritting her teeth, she launched into an attack. Zane backhanded her indifferently, and she Pushed slightly against the deskmounts behind him—tossing herself backward, as if thrown by the force of his blow. She slammed into the wall, then slumped to the ground.

Directly beside the startled OreSeur.

He hadn't opened his shoulder to give her the atium. Hadn't he understood the code? "The atium I gave you," Vin hissed. "I need it. *Now.*"

"Kandra," Zane said. "Come to me."

OreSeur met her eyes, and she saw something within them. Shame. He glanced away, then padded across the floor, mist up to his knees, as he joined Zane in the center of the room.

"No . . ." Vin whispered. "OreSeur—"

"You will no longer obey her commands, TenSoon," Zane said.

OreSeur bowed his head.

"The Contract, OreSeur!" Vin said, climbing to her knees. "You *must* obey my orders!"

"My servant, Vin," Zane said. "My Contract. *My* orders."

My servant. . . .

And suddenly, it clicked. She'd suspected everyone—Dockson, Breeze, even Elend—but she'd never connected the spy to the one person that made the most sense. There *had* been a kandra in the palace all along. And he had been at her side.

"I'm sorry, Mistress," OreSeur whispered.

"How long?" Vin asked, bowing her head.

"Since you gave my predecessor—the real OreSeur—the dog's body," the kandra said. "I killed him that day and took his place, wearing the body of a dog. You never saw him as a wolfhound."

What easier way to mask the transformation? Vin thought. "But, the bones we discovered in the palace," she said. "You were with me on the wall when they appeared. They—"

She'd taken his word on how fresh those bones had been; she'd taken his word on when they had been produced. She'd assumed all along that the switch must have happened that day, when she was with Elend on the city wall—but she'd done so primarily because of what OreSeur had said.

Idiot! she thought. OreSeur—or, TenSoon, as Zane had called him—had led her to suspect everyone but himself. What was wrong with her? She was usually so good at sniffing out traitors, at noticing insincerity. How had she missed spotting her own kandra?

Zane walked forward. Vin waited, on her knees. *Weak,* she told herself. *Look weak. Make him leave you alone. Try to—*

"Soothing me will do no good," Zane said quietly, grabbing her by the front of her shirt, picking her up, then throwing her back down. Mist sprayed beneath her, puffing up in a splash as she slammed to the floor. Vin stifled her cry of pain.

I have to stay quiet. If guards come, he'll kill them. If Elend comes . . .

She had to stay quiet, quiet even as Zane kicked her in her wounded side. She grunted, eyes watering.

"You could have saved me," Zane said, peering down at her. "I was willing to go with you. Now, what is left? Nothing. Nothing, but Straff's orders." He punctuated that sentence with a kick.

Stay small, she told herself through the pain. *He'll leave you alone eventually. . . .*

But it had been years since she'd had to bow before anyone. Her days of cringing before Camon and Reen were almost misty shadows, forgotten before the light offered by

Elend and Kelsier. As Zane kicked again, Vin found herself growing angry.

He brought his foot back, angling it toward her face, and Vin moved. As his foot arced down, she threw herself backward, Pushing against the window latches to scoot herself through the mists. She flared pewter, throwing herself up to her feet, trailing mist from the floor. It was up past her knees now.

She glared at Zane, who looked back with a dark expression. Vin ducked forward, but Zane moved faster—moved *first*—stepping between her and the balcony. Not that getting to it would do her any good; with atium, he could chase her down easily.

It was like before, when he'd attacked her with atium. Only this time it was worse. Before, she'd been able to believe—if just a little—that they were still sparring. Still not enemies, even if they weren't friends. She hadn't really believed that he wanted to kill her.

She had no such illusions this time. Zane's eyes were dark, his expression flat—just like that night a few days before, when slaughtering Cett's men.

Vin was going to die.

She hadn't felt such fear in a long time. But now she saw it, felt it, smelled it on herself as she shied away from the approaching Zane. She felt what it was like to face a Mistborn—what it must have been like for those soldiers she'd killed. There was no fighting. There was no chance.

No, she told herself forcefully, holding her side. *Elend didn't back down against Straff. He doesn't have Allomancy, but he marched into the center of the koloss camp.*

I can beat this.

With a cry, Vin dashed toward TenSoon. The dog backed away in shock, but he needn't have worried. Zane was there again. He slammed a shoulder into Vin, then whipped his dagger around and slashed a wound across her cheek as she fell backward. The cut was precise. Perfect. Matching the wound on her other cheek, one given to her during her first fight with a Mistborn, nearly two years before.

Vin gritted her teeth, burning iron as she fell. She Pulled on a pouch on her desk, whipping the coins into her hand.

She hit the ground on her side, other hand down, and threw herself back to her feet. She dumped a shower of coins from the pouch into her hand, then raised them at Zane.

Blood dripped from her chin. She threw the coins out. Zane moved to Push them away.

Vin smiled, then burned duralumin as she Pushed. The coins snapped forward, and the wind of their sudden passing parted the mist on the ground, revealing the floor beneath.

The room shook.

And in an eyeblink, Vin found herself slammed back against the wall. She gasped in surprise, breath knocked from her lungs, her vision swimming. She looked up, disoriented, surprised to find herself on the ground again.

"Duralumin," Zane said, still standing with a hand up before him. "TenSoon told me about it. We deduced you must have a new metal from the way you can sense me when my copper is on. After that, a little searching, and he found that note from your metallurgist, which handily had the instructions for making duralumin."

Her addled mind struggled to connect ideas. Zane had duralumin. He'd used the metal, and had Pushed against one of the coins she'd shot at him. He must have Pushed behind himself as well, to keep from being forced backward as his weight met hers.

And her own duralumin-enhanced Push had slammed her against the wall. She had trouble thinking. Zane walked forward. She looked up, dazed, then scrambled away on hands and knees, crawling in the mists. It was at face level, and her nostrils tickled as she inhaled the cool, quiet chaos.

Atium. She needed atium. But, the bead was in TenSoon's shoulder; she couldn't Pull it to herself. The reason he carried it there was that the flesh protected it from being affected by Allomancers. Just like the spikes piercing an Inquisitor's body, just like her own earring. Metal inside—or even piercing—a person's body could not be Pulled or Pushed except with the most extreme of Allomantic forces.

But she'd done it once. When fighting the Lord Ruler. It hadn't been her own power, or even duralumin, that had let her accomplish it. It had been something else. The mists.

She'd drawn upon them.

Something hit her on her back, pushing her down. She rolled over, kicking upward, but her foot missed Zane's face by a few atium-aided inches. Zane slapped her foot aside, then reached down, slamming her against the floor by her shoulders.

Mists churned around him as he looked down at her. Through her terror, she reached out for the mists, as she had over a year before when fighting the Lord Ruler. That day, they had fueled her Allomancy, giving her a strength that she shouldn't have had. She reached out for them, begging for their help.

And nothing happened.

Please. . . .

Zane slammed her down again. The mists continued to ignore her pleas.

She twisted, Pulling against the window frame to get leverage, and pushed Zane to the side. They rolled, Vin coming around on top.

Suddenly, both of them lurched off the floor, bursting out of the mists and flying toward the ceiling, thrown upward as Zane Pushed against coins on the floor. They slammed against the ceiling, Zane's body pushing against hers, pinning her to the wooden planks. He was on top again—or, rather, he was on the bottom, but that was now the point of leverage.

Vin gasped. He was so strong. Stronger than she. His fingers bit into the flesh of her arms despite her pewter, and her side ached from her earlier wounds. She was in no condition to fight—not against another Mistborn.

Especially not one with atium.

Zane continued to Push them against the ceiling. Vin's hair fell toward him, and mists churned the floor below, like a whirlpool vortex that was slowly rising.

Zane released his Push, and they fell. Yet, he was still in control. He spun her, throwing her down below him as they entered the mists again. They hit the ground, the blow knocking the wind from Vin's lungs yet again. Zane loomed above her, speaking through gritted teeth.

"All that effort, wasted," he hissed. "Hiding an Allomancer in Cett's hirelings so that you would suspect him of attacking you at the Assembly. Forcing you to fight in front of Elend so that he'd be intimidated by you. Pushing you to explore your powers and kill so that you'd realize just how powerful you truly are. All wasted!"

He leaned down. "You. Were. Supposed. To. *Save me!*" he said, his face just inches from hers, breathing heavily. He pinned one of her struggling arms to the floor with his knee, and then, in a strangely surreal moment, he kissed her.

And at the same time, he rammed his dagger into the side of one of her breasts. Vin tried to cry out, but his mouth held hers as the dagger cut her flesh.

"Be careful, Master!" OreSeur—TenSoon—suddenly yelled. "She knows much about kandra!"

Zane looked up, his hand stilled. The voice, the pain, brought lucidity to Vin. She flared tin, using the pain to shock herself awake, clearing her mind.

"What?" Zane asked, looking down toward the kandra.

"She knows, Master," TenSoon said. "She knows our secret. The reason why we served the Lord Ruler. The reason why we serve the Contract. She knows *why we fear Allomancers so much.*"

"Be silent," Zane commanded. "And speak no more."

TenSoon fell silent.

Our secret . . . Vin thought, glancing over at the wolfhound, sensing the anxiety in his canine expression. *He's trying to tell me something. Trying to help me.*

Secret. The secret of the kandra. The last time she'd tried Soothing him, he'd howled with pain. Yet, she saw permission in his expression. It was enough.

She slammed TenSoon with a Soothing. He cried out, howling, but she Pushed harder. Nothing happened. Gritting her teeth, she burned duralumin.

Something broke. She was in two places at once. She could feel TenSoon standing by the wall, and she could feel her own body in Zane's grip. TenSoon was hers, totally and completely. Somehow, not quite knowing how, she ordered him forward, controlling his body.

The massive wolfhound's body slammed into Zane, throwing him off Vin. The dagger flipped to the ground, and Vin stumbled to her knees, grabbing her chest, feeling warm blood there. Zane rolled, obviously shocked, but he came to his feet and kicked TenSoon.

Bones broke. The wolfhound tumbled across the floor—right toward Vin. She snatched the dagger off the ground as he rolled to her feet, then plunged it into his shoulder, cutting the shoulder, her fingers feeling in the muscle and sinew. She came up with bloodied hands and a single bead of atium. She swallowed it with a gulp, spinning toward Zane.

"Now let's see how you fare," she hissed, burning atium. Dozens of atium shadows burst from Zane, showing her possible actions he could take—all of them ambiguous. She would be giving off the same confusing mess to his eyes. They were even.

Zane turned, looking into her eyes, and his atium shadows disappeared.

Impossible! she thought. TenSoon groaned at her feet as she realized that her atium reserve was gone. Burned away. But the bead had been so large. . . .

"Did you think I'd give you the very weapon you needed to fight me?" Zane asked quietly. "Did you think I'd really give up atium?"

"But—"

"A lump of lead," Zane said, walking forward. "Plated with a thin layer of atium around it. Oh, Vin. You really need to be more careful whom you trust."

Vin stumbled backward, feeling her confidence wilt. *Make him talk!* she thought. *Try to get his atium to run out.*

"My brother said that I shouldn't trust anyone . . ." she mumbled. "He said . . . anyone would betray me."

"He was a wise man," Zane said quietly, standing chest-deep in mists.

"He was a paranoid fool," Vin said. "He kept me alive, but he left me broken."

"Then he did you a favor."

Vin glanced toward TenSoon's mangled, bleeding form. He was in pain; she could see it in his eyes. In the distance she could hear . . . thumping. She'd turned her bronze back on. She looked up slowly. Zane was walking toward her. Confident.

"You've been playing with me," she said. "You drove a

wedge between me and Elend. You made me think he feared me, made me think he was using me."

"He was," Zane said.

"Yes," Vin said. "But it doesn't matter—not the way you made it seem. Elend uses me. Kelsier used me. We use each other, for love, for support, for trust."

"Trust will kill you," he said.

"Then it is better to die."

"I trusted you," he said, stopping before her. "And you betrayed me."

"No," Vin said, raising her dagger. "I'm going to save you. Just like you want." She snapped forward and struck, but her hope—that he'd run out of atium—was in vain. He sidestepped indifferently; he let her dagger come within an inch of striking, but he was never really in danger.

Vin spun to attack, but her blade cut only air, skimming along the top of the rising mists.

Zane moved before her next attack came, dodging even before she knew what she was going to do. Her dagger stabbed the place where he had been standing.

He's too fast, she thought, side burning, mind thumping. Or was that the Well of Ascension thumping. . . .

Zane stopped just in front of her.

I can't hit him, she thought with frustration. *Not when he knows where I'll strike before I do!*

Vin paused.

Before I do. . . .

Zane stepped away to a place near the center of the room, then kicked her fallen dagger into the air and caught it. He turned back toward her, mist trailing from the weapon in his hand, jaw set and eyes dark.

He knows where I'll strike before I do.

Vin raised her dagger, blood trickling down face and side, thunderous drumbeats booming in her mind. The mist was nearly up to her chin.

She cleared her mind. She didn't plan an attack. She didn't react to Zane as he ran toward her, dagger raised. She loosened her muscles and closed her eyes, listening to his footsteps. She felt the mist rise around her, churned by Zane's advent.

She snapped her eyes open. He had the dagger raised; it glittered as it swung. Vin prepared to attack, but didn't think about the strike; she simply let her body react.

And she watched Zane very, very carefully.

He flinched just slightly to the left, open hand moving upward, as if to grab something.

There! Vin thought, immediately wrenching herself to the side, forcing her instinctive attack out of its natural trajectory. She twisted her arm—and dagger—midswing. She had been about to attack left, as Zane's atium had anticipated.

But, by reacting, Zane had shown her what she was going to do. Let her see the future. And if she could see it, she could change it.

They met. Zane's weapon took her in the shoulder. But Vin's knife took him in the neck. His left hand closed on empty air, snatching at a shadow that should have told him where her arm would be.

Zane tried to gasp, but her knife had pierced his windpipe. Air sucked through blood around the blade, and Zane stumbled back, eyes wide with shock. He met her eyes, then collapsed into the mists, his body thumping against the wooden floor.

Zane looked up through the mists, looked up at her. *I'm dying,* he thought.

Her atium shadow had *split* at the last moment. Two shadows, two possibilities. He'd counteracted the wrong one. She'd tricked him, defeated him somehow. And now he was dying.

Finally.

"You know why I thought you'd save me?" he tried to whisper to her, though he somehow knew that his lips weren't properly forming the words. "The voice. You were the first person I ever met that it didn't tell me to kill. The only person."

"Of course I didn't tell you to kill *her,*" God said.

Zane felt his life seeping away.

"You know the really funny thing, Zane?" God asked. "The most amusing part of this all? You're not insane.

"You never were."

Vin watched quietly as Zane sputtered, blood coming from his lips. She watched cautiously; a knife to the throat should have been enough to kill even a Mistborn, but sometimes pewter could let one do awesome things.

Zane died. She checked his pulse, then retrieved her dagger. After that, she stood for a moment, feeling . . . numb, in both mind and body. She raised a hand to her wounded shoulder—and in doing so, she brushed her wounded breast. She was bleeding too much, and her mind was growing fuzzy again.

I killed him.

She flared pewter, forcing herself to keep moving. She stumbled over to TenSoon, kneeling beside him.

"Mistress," he said. "I'm sorry. . . ."

"I know," she said, staring at the terrible wound she'd made. His legs no longer worked, and his body lay in an unnatural twist. "How can I help?"

"Help?" TenSoon said. "Mistress, I nearly got you killed!"

"I know," she said again. "How can I make the pain go away? Do you need another body?"

TenSoon was quiet for a moment. "Yes."

"Take Zane's," Vin said. "For the moment, at least."

"He is dead?" TenSoon asked with surprise.

He couldn't see, she realized. *His neck is broken.*

"Yes," she whispered.

"How, Mistress?" TenSoon asked. "He ran out of atium?"

"No," Vin said.

"Then, how?"

"Atium has a weakness," she said. "It lets you see the future."

"That . . . doesn't sound like a weakness, Mistress."

Vin sighed, wobbling slightly. *Focus!* she thought. "When you burn atium, you see a few moments into the future—and you can change what will happen in that future. You can grab an arrow that should have kept flying. You can dodge a blow that should have killed you. And you can move to block an attack before it even happens."

TenSoon was quiet, obviously confused.

"He showed me what *I* was going to do," Vin said. "I couldn't change the future, but Zane could. By reacting to my attack before I even knew what I was going to do, he inadvertently showed me the future. I reacted against him, and he tried to block a blow that never came. That let me kill him."

"Mistress . . ." TenSoon whispered. "That is brilliant."

"I'm sure I'm not the first to think of it," Vin said wearily. "But it isn't the sort of secret that you share. Anyway, take his body."

"I . . . would rather not wear the bones of that creature," TenSoon said. "You don't know how broken he was, Mistress."

Vin nodded tiredly. "I could just find you another dog body, if you want."

"That won't be necessary, Mistress," TenSoon said quietly. "I still have the bones of the other wolfhound you gave me, and most of them are still good. If I replace a few of them with the good bones from this body, I should be able to form a complete skeleton to use."

"Do it, then. We're going to need to plan what to do next."

TenSoon was quiet for a moment. Finally, he spoke. "Mistress, my Contract is void, now that my master is dead. I . . . need to return to my people for reassignment."

"Ah," Vin said, feeling a wrench of sadness. "Of course."

"I do not want to go," TenSoon said. "But, I must at least report to my people. Please, forgive me."

"There is nothing to forgive," Vin said. "And thank you for that timely hint at the end."

TenSoon lay quietly. She could see guilt in his canine eyes. *He shouldn't have helped me against his current master.*

"Mistress," TenSoon said. "You know our secret now. Mistborn can control a kandra's body with Allomancy. I don't know what you will do with it—but realize that I have entrusted you with a secret that my people have kept sacred for a thousand years. The way that Allomancers could take control of our bodies and make slaves of us."

"I . . . don't even understand what happened."

"Perhaps it is better that way," TenSoon said. "Please, leave me. I have the other dog's bones in the closet. When you return, I will be gone."

Vin rose, nodding. She left, then, pushing through the mists and seeking the hallway outside. Her wounds needed tending. She knew that she should go to Sazed, but somehow she couldn't force herself in that direction. She walked faster, feet taking her down the hallway, until she was running.

Everything was collapsing around her. She couldn't manage it all, couldn't keep things straight. But she did know what she wanted.

And so she ran to him.

He is a good man—despite it all, he is a good man. A sacrificing man. In truth, all of his actions—all of the deaths, destructions, and pains that he has caused—have hurt him deeply. All of these things were, in truth, a kind of sacrifice for him.

48

ELEND YAWNED, LOOKING OVER THE letter he'd penned to Jastes. Perhaps he could persuade his former friend to see reason.

If he couldn't . . . well, a duplicate of the wooden coin Jastes had been using to "pay" the koloss sat on Elend's desk. It was a perfect copy, whittled by Clubs himself.

Elend was pretty certain that he had access to more wood than Jastes did. If he could help Penrod stall for a few more weeks, they might be able to make enough "money" to bribe the koloss away.

He set down his pen, rubbing his eyes. It was late. Time to—

His door slammed open. Elend spun, and caught sight of a flustered Vin dashing across the room and into his arms. She was crying.

And she was bloody.

"Vin!" he said. "What happened?"

"I killed him," she said, head buried in Elend's chest.

"Who?"

"Your brother," she said. "Zane. Straff's Mistborn. I killed him."

"Wait. What? My *brother*?"

Vin nodded. "I'm sorry."

"Forget about that, Vin!" Elend said, gently prying her back and pushing her into his chair. She had a gash on her cheek, and her shirt was slick with blood. "Lord Ruler! I'm going to get Sazed right now."

"Don't leave me," she said, holding his arm.

Elend paused. Something had changed. She seemed to need him again. "Come with me, then. We'll both go see him."

Vin nodded, standing. She teetered just a bit, and Elend felt a spike of fear, but the determined look in her eyes wasn't something he wanted to challenge. He put his arm around her, letting her lean on him as they walked to Sazed's quarters. Elend paused to knock, but Vin simply pushed her way into the dark room, then wobbled and sat down on the floor just inside.

"I'll . . . sit here," she said.

Elend paused worriedly by her side, then raised his lamp and called toward the bedchamber. "Sazed!"

The Terrisman appeared a moment later, looking exhausted and wearing a white sleeping robe. He noticed Vin, blinked a few times, then disappeared into his chambers. He returned a moment later with a metalmind bracer strapped to his forearm and a bag of medical equipment.

"Now, Lady Vin," Sazed said, setting the bag down.

"What would Master Kelsier think, seeing you in this condition? You ruin more clothing in this manner, I think. . . ."

"This isn't a time for levity, Sazed," Elend said.

"I apologize, Your Majesty," Sazed said, carefully cutting the clothing away from Vin's shoulder. "However, if she is still conscious, then she isn't in serious danger." He peered closer at the wound, absently lifting clean cloths from his bag.

"You see?" Sazed asked. "This gash is deep, but the blade was deflected by the bone, and missed hitting any major vessels. Hold this here." He pressed a cloth to the wound, and Elend put his hand on it. Vin sat with her eyes closed, resting back against the wall, blood dripping slowly from her chin. She seemed more exhausted than in pain.

Sazed took his knife and cut away the front of Vin's shirt, exposing her wounded chest.

Elend paused. "Perhaps I should . . ."

"Stay," Vin said. It wasn't a plea, but a command. She raised her head, opening her eyes as Sazed tisked quietly at the wound, then got out a numbing agent and some needle and thread.

"Elend," she said, "I need to tell you something."

He paused. "All right."

"I've realized something about Kelsier," she said quietly. "I always focus on the wrong things, when it comes to him. It's hard to forget the hours he spent training me to be an Allomancer. Yet, it wasn't his ability to fight that made him great—it wasn't his harshness or his brutality, or even his strength or his instincts."

Elend frowned.

"Do you know what it was?" she asked.

He shook his head, still pressing the cloth against her shoulder.

"It was his ability to trust," she said. "It was the way that he made good people into *better* people, the way that he inspired them. His crew worked because he had confidence in them—because he respected them. And, in return, they respected each other. Men like Breeze and Clubs became heroes because Kelsier had faith in them."

She looked up at him, blinking tired eyes. "And you are far better at that than Kelsier ever was, Elend. He had to work at it. You do it instinctively, treating even weasels like Philen as if they were good and honorable men. It's not naiveté, as some think. It's what Kelsier had, only greater. He could have learned from you."

"You give me too much credit," he said.

She shook a tired head. Then she turned to Sazed.

"Sazed?" she asked.

"Yes, child?"

"Do you know any wedding ceremonies?"

Elend nearly dropped the cloth in shock.

"I know several," Sazed said as he tended the wound. "Some two hundred, actually."

"Which one is the shortest?" Vin asked.

Sazed pulled a stitch tight. "The people of Larsta only required a profession of love before a local priest. Simplicity was a tenet of their belief structure—a reaction, perhaps, to the traditions of the land they were banished from, which was known for its complex system of bureaucratic rules. It is a good religion, one that focused on simple beauty found in nature."

Vin looked at Elend. Her face was bloody, her hair a mess.

"Now, see," he said. "Vin, don't you think that maybe this should wait until, you know—"

"Elend?" she interrupted. "I love you."

He froze.

"Do you love me?" she asked.

This is insane. "Yes," he said quietly.

Vin turned to Sazed, who was still working. "Well?"

Sazed looked up, fingers bloodied. "This is a very strange time for such an event, I think."

Elend nodded in agreement.

"It's just a little bit of blood," Vin said tiredly. "I'm really all right, now that I've sat down."

"Yes," Sazed said, "but you seem somewhat distraught, Lady Vin. This isn't a decision to be made lightly, under the influence of strong emotions."

Vin smiled. "The decision to get married shouldn't be made because of strong emotions?"

Sazed floundered. "That isn't exactly what I meant. I'm simply not certain that you are fully in control of your faculties, Lady Vin."

Vin shook her head. "I'm more in control than I have been for months. It's time for me to stop hesitating, Sazed—time to stop worrying, time to accept my place in this crew. I know what I want, now. I love Elend. I don't know what kind of time we'll have together, but I want some, at least."

Sazed sat for a moment, then returned to his sewing. "And you, Lord Elend? What are your thoughts?"

What *were* his thoughts? He remembered just the day before, when Vin had spoken of leaving, and the wrenching he had felt. He thought of how much he depended on her wisdom, and her bluntness, and her simple—but not simplistic—devotion to him. Yes, he did love her.

The world had gone chaotic recently. He had made mistakes. Yet, despite everything that had happened, and despite his frustrations, he still felt strongly that he wanted to be with Vin. It wasn't the idyllic infatuation he'd felt a year and a half ago, at the parties. But it felt more solid.

"Yes, Sazed," he said. "I do want to marry her. I have wanted it for some time. I . . . I don't know what's going to happen to the city, or my kingdom, but I want to be with Vin when it comes."

Sazed continued to work. "Very well, then," he finally said. "If it is my witness you require, then you have it."

Elend knelt, still pressing the cloth on Vin's shoulder, feeling a little bit stunned. "That's it then?"

Sazed nodded. "It is as valid as any witness the obligators could give you, I think. Be warned, the Larsta love oath is binding. They knew no form of divorce in their culture. Do you accept my witness of this event?"

Vin nodded. Elend felt himself doing the same.

"Then you are married," Sazed said, tying off his thread, then draping a cloth across Vin's chest. "Hold this for a bit, Lady Vin, and stanch the rest of the bleeding." Then he moved on to her cheek.

"I feel like there should be a ceremony or something," Elend said.

"I could give one, if you wish," Sazed said, "but I do not think you need one. I have known you both for some time, and am willing to give my blessing to this union. I simply offer counsel. Those who take lightly promises they make to those they love are people who find little lasting satisfaction in life. This is not an easy time in which to live. That does not mean that it has to be a difficult time to love, but it does mean that you will find unusual stresses upon your lives and your relationship.

"Do not forget the love oath you made to each other this evening. It will give you much strength in the days to come, I think." With that, he pulled the last stitch tight on Vin's face, then finally moved to the shoulder. The bleeding there had mostly stopped, and Sazed studied the wound for a moment before beginning work on it.

Vin looked up at Elend, smiling, looking a bit drowsy. He stood and walked over to the room's washbasin, and returned with a damp cloth to wipe off her face and cheek.

"I'm sorry," she said quietly as Sazed moved around and took the place Elend had been kneeling in.

"Sorry?" Elend said. "About my father's Mistborn?"

Vin shook her head. "No. For taking so long."

Elend smiled. "You're worth the wait. Besides, I think I had to figure a few things out as well."

"Like how to be a king?"

"And how to stop being one."

Vin shook her head. "You never stopped being one, Elend. They can take your crown, but they can't take your honor."

Elend smiled. "Thank you. However, I don't know how much good I've done the city. By even being here, I divided the people, and now Straff will end up in control."

"I'll kill Straff if he puts one foot in this city."

Elend gritted his teeth. *Back to the same problems again.* They could only hold Vin's knife against his neck for so long. He'd figure out a way to wiggle around, and there was always Jastes and those koloss. . . .

"Your Majesty," Sazed said as he worked, "perhaps I can offer a solution."

Elend glanced down at the Terrisman, raising an eyebrow.

"The Well of Ascension," Sazed said.

Vin opened her eyes immediately.

"Tindwyl and I have been researching the Hero of Ages," Sazed continued. "We are convinced that Rashek never did what the Hero was supposed to. In fact, we aren't even convinced that this Alendi of a thousand years ago *was* the Hero. There are too many discrepancies, too many problems and contradictions. In addition, the mists—the Deepness—are still here. And now they are killing people."

Elend frowned. "What are you saying?"

Sazed pulled a stitch tight. "Something still needs to be done, Your Majesty. Something important. Looking at it from a smaller perspective, it might seem that the events at Luthadel and the rise of the Well of Ascension are unrelated. However, from a larger view, they may be solutions to one another."

Elend smiled. "Like the lock and the key."

"Yes, Your Majesty," Sazed said, smiling. "Precisely like that."

"It thumps," Vin whispered, eyes closing. "In my head. I can *feel* it."

Sazed paused, then wrapped a bandage around Vin's arm. "Can you feel where it is?"

Vin shook her head. "I . . . There doesn't seem to be a direction to the pulses. I thought they were distant, but they're getting louder."

"That must be the Well returning to power," Sazed said. "It is fortunate that I know where to find it."

Elend turned, and Vin opened her eyes again.

"My research has revealed the location, Lady Vin," Sazed said. "I can draw you a map, from my metalminds."

"Where?" Vin whispered.

"North," Sazed said. "In the mountains of Terris. Atop one of the lower peaks, known as Derytatith. Travel there will be difficult this time of year. . . ."

"I can do it," Vin said firmly as Sazed turned to working

on her chest wound. Elend flushed again, then paused as he turned away.

I'm . . . married. "You're going to leave?" Elend asked, looking to Vin. "Now?"

"I have to," Vin whispered. "I *have* to go to it, Elend."

"You should go with her, Your Majesty," Sazed said.

"What?"

Sazed sighed, looking up. "We have to face facts, Your Majesty. As you said earlier, Straff will soon take this city. If you are here, you will be executed. However, Lady Vin will undoubtedly need help securing the Well."

"It's supposed to hold great power," Elend said, rubbing his chin. "Could we, you think, destroy those armies?"

Vin shook her head. "We couldn't use it," she whispered. "The power is a temptation. That's what went wrong last time. Rashek took the power instead of giving it up."

"Giving it up?" Elend asked. "What does that mean?"

"Letting it go, Your Majesty," Sazed said. "Letting *it* defeat the Deepness on its own."

"Trust," Vin whispered. "It's about trust."

"However," Sazed said, "I think that releasing this power could do great things for the land. Change things, and undo much of the damage the Lord Ruler did. I have a strong suspicion that it would destroy the koloss, since they were created by the Lord Ruler's misuse of the power."

"But Straff would hold the city," Elend said.

"Yes," Sazed said, "but if you leave, the transition will be peaceful. The Assembly has all but decided to accept him as their emperor, and it appears that he'll let Penrod rule as a subject king. There will be no bloodshed, and you will be able to organize resistance from outside. Besides, who knows what releasing the power will do? Lady Vin could be left changed, much as the Lord Ruler was. With the crew in hiding within the city, it should not be so difficult to oust your father—particularly when he grows complacent in a year or so."

Elend gritted his teeth. *Another revolution.* Yet, what Sazed said made sense. *For so long, we've been worrying about the small-scale.* He glanced at Vin, feeling a surge of warmth and love. *Maybe it's time I started listening to the things she's been trying to tell me.*

"Sazed," Elend said, a sudden thought occurring to him, "do you think that I could convince the Terris people to help us?"

"Perhaps, Your Majesty," Sazed said. "My prohibition against interfering—the one I have been ignoring—comes because I was given a different assignment by the Synod, not because we believe in avoiding all action. If you could convince the Synod that the future of the Terris people will be benefited by having a strong ally in Luthadel, you may just be able to get yourself military aid from Terris."

Elend nodded, thoughtful.

"Remember the lock and the key, Your Majesty," Sazed said, finishing off Vin's second wound. "In this case, leaving seems like the opposite of what you should do. However, if you look at the larger picture, you will see that it's precisely what you *need* to do."

Vin opened her eyes, looking up at him, smiling. "We can do this, Elend. Come with me."

Elend stood for a moment. *Lock and key.* . . . "All right," he said. "We'll leave as soon as Vin is able."

"She should be able to ride tomorrow," Sazed said. "You know what pewter can do for a body."

Elend nodded. "All right. I should have listened to you earlier, Vin. Besides, I've always wanted to see your homeland, Sazed. You can show it to us."

"I will need to stay here, I fear," Sazed said. "I should soon leave for the South to continue my work there. Tindwyl, however, can go with you—she has important information that needs to be passed on to my brethren the Keepers."

"It will need to be a small group," Vin said. "We'll have to outrun—or perhaps sneak past—Straff's men."

"Just you three, I think," Sazed said. "Or, perhaps one other person to help with watches while you sleep, someone skilled in hunting and scouting. Lord Lestibournes, perhaps?"

"Spook would be perfect," Elend said, nodding. "You're sure the other crewmembers will be safe in the city?"

"Of course they won't," Vin said, smiling. "But they're experts. They hid from the Lord Ruler—they'll be able to hide from Straff. Particularly if they don't have to worry about keeping you safe."

"Then it is decided," Sazed said, standing. "You two should try to rest well tonight, despite the recent change in your relationship. Can you walk, Lady Vin?"

"No need," Elend said, leaning down and picking her up. She wrapped her arms around him, though her grip was not tight, and he could see that her eyes were already drooping again.

He smiled. Suddenly, the world seemed a much simpler place. He would take some time and spend it on what was really important; then, once he and Vin had sought help from the North, they could return. He actually looked forward to coming back and tackling their problems with renewed vigor.

He held Vin tight, nodding good night to Sazed, then walking out toward his rooms. It seemed that everything had worked out fine in the end.

Sazed stood slowly, watching the two leave. He wondered what they would think of him, when they heard of Luthadel's fall. At least they would have each other for support.

His wedding blessing was the last gift he could give them—that, and their lives. *How will history judge me for my lies?* he wondered. *What will it think of the Terrisman who took such a hand in politics, the Terrisman who would fabricate mythology to save the lives of his friends?* The things he'd said about the Well were, of course, falsehoods. If there was such a power, he had no idea where it was, nor what it would do.

How history judged him would probably depend on what Elend and Vin did with their lives. Sazed could only hope that he had done the right thing. Watching them go, knowing that their youthful love would be spared, he couldn't help but smile at his decision.

With a sigh, he stooped down and gathered up his medical items; then he retreated to his rooms to fabricate the map he had promised Vin and Elend.

THE END OF PART FOUR

PART FIVE

SNOW AND ASH

He is accustomed to giving up his own will before the greater good, as he sees it.

49

"YOU ARE A FOOL, ELEND Venture," Tindwyl snapped, arms folded, eyes wide with displeasure.

Elend pulled a strap tight on his saddle. Part of the wardrobe Tindwyl had made for him included a black and silver riding uniform, and he wore this now, fingers snug within the leather gloves, and a dark cloak to keep off the ash.

"Are you listening to me?" Tindwyl demanded. "You can't leave. Not now! Not when your people are in such danger!"

"I'll protect them in another way," he said, checking on the packhorses.

They were in the keep's covered way, used for arrivals and departures. Vin sat on her own horse, enveloped almost completely in her cloak, hands holding her reins tensely. She had very little experience riding, but Elend refused to let her run. Pewter or no pewter, the wounds from her fight at the Assembly still hadn't healed completely, not to mention the damage she'd taken the night before.

"Another way?" Tindwyl asked. "You should be with them. You're their king!"

"No, I'm *not*," Elend snapped, turning toward the Terriswoman. "They rejected me, Tindwyl. Now I have to worry about more important events on a larger stage. They wanted a traditional king? Well, let them have my father. When I return from Terris, perhaps they will have realized what they lost."

Tindwyl shook her head and stepped forward, speaking in a quiet voice. "Terris, Elend? You go north. For her. You know why she wants to go there, don't you?"

He paused.

"Ah, so you do know," Tindwyl said. "What do you think of it, Elend? Don't tell me you believe these delusions. She thinks she's the Hero of Ages. She supposes that she'll find something in the mountains up there—some power, or perhaps some revelation, that will transform her into a divinity."

Elend glanced at Vin. She looked down at the ground, hood down, still sitting quietly on her horse.

"She's trying to follow her master, Elend," Tindwyl whispered. "The Survivor became a god to these people, so she thinks she has to do the same."

Elend turned to Tindwyl. "If that is what she truly believes, then I support her."

"You support her madness?" Tindwyl demanded.

"Do not speak of my wife in that manner," Elend said, his commanding tone causing Tindwyl to flinch. He swung up into his saddle. "I trust her, Tindwyl. Part of trust is belief."

Tindwyl snorted. "You can't possibly believe that she is some prophesied messiah, Elend. I know you—you're a scholar. You may have professed allegiance to the Church of the Survivor, but you don't believe in the supernatural any more than I do."

"I believe," he said firmly, "that Vin is my wife, and that I love her. Anything important to her is important to me—and anything she believes has at least that much weight of truth to me. We are going north. We will return once we've released the power there."

"Fine," Tindwyl said. "Then you will be remembered as a coward who abandoned his people."

"Leave us!" Elend ordered, raising his finger and pointing toward the keep.

Tindwyl spun, stalking toward the doorway. As she

passed it, she pointed at the supply table, where she had previously placed a book-sized package, wrapped in brown paper, tied with a thick string. "Sazed wishes you to deliver this to the Keeper Synod. You'll find them in the city of Tathingdwen. Enjoy your exile, Elend Venture." Then, she left.

Elend sighed, moving his horse over beside Vin's.

"Thank you," she said quietly.

"For what?"

"For what you said."

"I meant it, Vin," Elend said, reaching over to lay a hand on her shoulder.

"Tindwyl might be right, you know," she said. "Despite what Sazed said, I could be mad. Do you remember when I told you that I'd seen a spirit in the mists?"

Elend nodded slowly.

"Well, I've seen it again," Vin said. "It's like a ghost, formed from the patterns in mist. I see it all the time, watching me, following me. And I hear those rhythms in my head—majestic, powerful thumpings, like Allomantic pulses. Only, I don't need bronze anymore to hear them."

Elend squeezed her shoulder. "I believe you, Vin."

She looked up, reserved. "Do you, Elend? Do you really?"

"I'm not sure," he admitted. "But I'm trying very hard to. Either way, I think going north is the right thing to do."

She nodded slowly. "That's enough, I think."

He smiled, turning back to the doorway. "Where is Spook?"

Vin shrugged beneath her cloak. "I assume Tindwyl won't be coming with us, then."

"Probably not," Elend said, smiling.

"How will we find our way to Terris?"

"It won't be hard," Elend said. "We'll just follow the imperial canal to Tathingdwen." He paused, thinking of the map Sazed had given them. It led straight into the Terris Mountains. They'd have to get supplies in Tathingdwen, and the snows would be high, but . . . well, that was a problem for another time.

Vin smiled, and Elend walked over to pick up the package

Tindwyl had left. It appeared to be a book of some sort. A few moments later, Spook arrived. He wore his soldier's uniform, and had saddlebags slung over his shoulder. He nodded to Elend, handed Vin a large bag, then moved to his own horse.

He looks nervous, Elend thought as the boy slung his bags over his horse. "What's in the bag?" he asked, turning to Vin.

"Pewter dust," she said. "I think we might need it."

"Are we ready?" Spook asked, looking over at them.

Elend glanced at Vin, who nodded. "I guess we—"

"Not quite yet," a new voice said. "I'm not ready at *all.*"

Elend turned as Allrianne swept into the passage. She wore a rich brown and red riding skirt, and had her hair tied up beneath a scarf. *Where'd she get that outfit?* Elend wondered. Two servants followed her, bearing bundles.

Allrianne paused, tapping her lip with a thoughtful expression. "I think I'm going to need a packhorse."

"What are you doing?" Vin demanded.

"Going with you," Allrianne said. "Breezy says I have to leave the city. He's a very silly man, sometimes, but he can be quite stubborn. He spent the entire conversation Soothing me—as if I couldn't recognize his touch by now!"

Allrianne waved to one of the servants, who ran to get a stablehand.

"We're going to be riding very hard," Elend said. "I'm not sure if you'll be able to keep up."

Allrianne rolled her eyes. "I rode all the way out here from the Western Dominance! I think I can manage. Besides, Vin is hurt, so you probably won't be going *that* fast."

"We don't want you along," Vin said. "We don't trust you—and we don't like you."

Elend closed his eyes. *Dear, blunt Vin.*

Allrianne just twittered a laugh as the servant returned with two horses, then began to load one. "Silly Vin," she said. "How can you say that after all we've shared?"

"Shared?" Vin asked. "Allrianne, we went shopping together *one time.*"

"And I felt we bonded quite well," Allrianne said. "Why, we're practically sisters!"

Vin gave the girl a flat stare.

"Yes," Allrianne said, "and you're *definitely* the older, boring sister." She smiled sweetly, then swung easily up into her saddle, suggesting considerable horsemanship. One of the servants led her packhorse over, then tied the reins into place behind Allrianne's saddle.

"All right, Elend dear," she said. "I'm ready. Let's go."

Elend glanced at Vin, who shook her head with a dark look.

"You can leave me behind if you wish," Allrianne said, "but I'll just follow and get into trouble, and then you'll have to come save me. And don't even try and pretend that you wouldn't!"

Elend sighed. "Very well," he said. "Let's go."

They made their way slowly through the city, Elend and Vin at the lead, Spook bringing their packhorses, Allrianne riding to the side. Elend kept his head up, but that only let him see the faces that poked out of windows and doorways as he passed. Soon, a small crowd was trailing them—and while he couldn't hear their whispers, he could imagine what they were saying.

The king. The king is abandoning us. . . .

He knew that many of them still couldn't understand that Lord Penrod held the throne. Elend glanced away from an alleyway, where he saw many eyes watching him. There was a haunted fear in those eyes. He had expected to see accusations, but somehow their despondent acceptance was even more disheartening. They expected him to flee. They expected to be abandoned. He was one of the few rich enough, and powerful enough, to get away. Of course he'd run.

He squeezed his own eyes shut, trying to force down his guilt. He wished that they could have left at night, sneaking out the passwall as Ham's family had. However, it was important that Straff saw Elend and Vin leaving, so that he understood he could take the city without attacking.

I'll be back, Elend promised the people. *I'll save you. For now, it's better if I leave.*

The broad doors of Tin Gate appeared ahead of them. Elend kicked his horse forward, speeding ahead of his silent wave of followers. The guards at the gate already had their orders. Elend gave them a nod, reining in his horse, and the men swung the doors open. Vin and the others joined him before the opening portal.

"Lady Heir," one of the guards asked quietly. "Are you leaving, too?"

Vin looked to the side. "Peace," she said. "We're not abandoning you. We're going for help."

The soldier smiled.

How can he trust her so easily? Elend thought. *Or, is hope all he has left?*

Vin turned her horse around, facing the crowd of people, and she lowered her hood. "We will return," she promised. She didn't seem as nervous as she had before when dealing with people who revered her.

Ever since last night, something has changed in her, Elend thought.

As a group, the soldiers saluted them. Elend saluted back; then he nodded to Vin. He led the way as they galloped out the gates, angling toward the northern highway—a path that would allow them to skirt just west of Straff's army.

They hadn't gone far before a group of horsemen moved to intercept them. Elend rode low on his horse, sparing a glance for Spook and the packhorses. What caught Elend's attention, however, was Allrianne: she rode with amazing proficiency, a look of determination on her face. She didn't seem the least bit nervous.

To the side, Vin whipped her cloak back, bringing out a handful of coins. She flung them into the air, and they shot forward with a speed Elend had never seen, even from other Allomancers. *Lord Ruler!* he thought with shock as the coins zipped away, disappearing faster than he could track.

Soldiers fell, and Elend barely heard the *pling*ing of metal against metal over the sound of wind and hoofbeats. He rode directly through the center of the chaotic group of men, many of them down and dying.

Arrows began to fall, but Vin scattered these without

even waving a hand. She had opened the bag of pewter, he noticed, and was releasing the dust in a shower behind her as she rode, Pushing some of it to the sides.

The next arrows won't have metal heads, Elend thought nervously. Soldiers were forming up behind, shouting.

"I'll catch up," Vin said, then jumped off her horse.

"Vin!" Elend yelled, turning his beast. Allrianne and Spook shot past him, riding hard. Vin landed and, amazingly, didn't even stumble as she began to run. She downed a vial of metal, then looked toward the archers.

Arrows flew. Elend cursed, but kicked his horse into motion. There was little he could do now. He rode low, galloping as the arrows fell around him. One passed within inches of his head, falling to stick into the road.

And then they stopped falling. He glanced backward, teeth gritted. Vin stood before a rising cloud of dust. *The pewter dust,* he thought. *She's Pushing on it—Pushing the flakes along the ground, stirring up the dust and ash.*

A massive wave of dust, metal, and ash slammed into the archers, washing over them. It blew around the soldiers, making them curse and shield their eyes, and some fell to the ground, holding their faces.

Vin swung back onto her horse, then galloped away from the billowing mass of wind-borne particles. Elend slowed his horse, letting her catch up. The army was in chaos behind them, men giving orders, people scattering.

"Speed up!" Vin said as she approached. "We're almost out of bowshot!"

Soon they joined Allrianne and Spook. *We aren't out of danger—my father could still decide to send pursuit.*

But, the soldiers couldn't have mistaken Vin. If Elend's instincts were right, Straff would let them run. His prime target was Luthadel. He could go after Elend later; for now, he would simply be happy to see Vin leaving.

"Thank you kindly for the help getting out," Allrianne suddenly said, watching the army. "I'll be going now."

With that, she veered her two horses away, angling toward a group of low hills to the west.

"What?" Elend asked with surprise, pulling up next to Spook.

"Leave her," Vin said. "We don't have time."

Well, that solves one problem, Elend thought, turning his horse to the northern highway. *Farewell, Luthadel. I'll be back for you later.*

"Well, that solves one problem," Breeze noted, standing atop the city wall and watching Elend's group disappear around a hillside. To the east, a large—and still unexplained—pillar of smoke rose from the koloss camp. To the west, Straff's army was buzzing about, stirred by the escape.

At first, Breeze had worried about Allrianne's safety—but then he'd realized that, enemy army notwithstanding, there was no safer place for her than beside Vin. As long as Allrianne didn't get too far away from the others, she would be safe.

It was a quiet group that stood atop the wall with him, and for once, Breeze barely touched their emotions. Their solemnity seemed appropriate. The young Captain Demoux stood beside the aging Clubs, and the peaceful Sazed stood with Ham the warrior. Together, they watched the seed of hope they'd cast to the winds.

"Wait," Breeze said, frowning as he noticed something. "Wasn't Tindwyl supposed to be with them?"

Sazed shook his head. "She decided to stay."

"Why would she do that?" Breeze asked. "Didn't I hear her babbling something about not interfering in local disputes?"

Sazed shook his head. "I do not know, Lord Breeze. She is a difficult woman to read."

"They all are," Clubs muttered.

Sazed smiled. "Either way, it appears our friends have escaped."

"May the Survivor protect them," Demoux said quietly.

"Yes," Sazed said. "May he indeed."

Clubs snorted. Resting one arm on the battlements, he turned to eye Sazed with a gnarled face. "Don't encourage him."

Demoux flushed, then turned and walked away.

"What was that about?" Breeze asked curiously.

"The boy has been preaching to my soldiers," Clubs said. "Told him I didn't want his nonsense cluttering their minds."

"It is not nonsense, Lord Cladent," Sazed said, "it's faith."

"Do you honestly think," Clubs said, "that *Kelsier* is going to protect these people?"

Sazed wavered. "They believe it, and that is—"

"No," Clubs interrupted, scowling. "That *isn't* enough, Terrisman. These people fool themselves by believing in the Survivor."

"You believed in him," Sazed said. Breeze was tempted to Soothe him, make the argument less tense, but Sazed already seemed completely calm. "You followed him. You believed in the Survivor enough to overthrow the Final Empire."

Clubs scowled. "I don't like your ethics, Terrisman—I never have. Our crew—Kelsier's crew—fought to free this people because it was *right*."

"Because you believed it to be right," Sazed said.

"And what do you believe to be right, Terrisman?"

"That depends," Sazed said. "There are many different systems with many different worthy values."

Clubs nodded, then turned, as if the argument were over.

"Wait, Clubs," Ham said. "Aren't you going to respond to that?"

"He said enough," Clubs said. "His belief is situational. To him, even the Lord Ruler was a deity because people worshipped him—or were forced to worship him. Aren't I right, Terrisman?"

"In a way, Lord Cladent," Sazed said. "Though, the Lord Ruler might have been something of an exception."

"But you still keep records and memories of the Steel Ministry's practices, don't you?" Ham asked.

"Yes," Sazed admitted.

"Situational," Clubs spat. "At least that fool Demoux had the sense to choose *one* thing to believe in."

"Do not deride someone's faith simply because you do not share it, Lord Cladent," Sazed said quietly.

Clubs snorted again. "It's all very easy for you, isn't it?" he asked. "Believing everything, never having to choose?"

"I would say," Sazed replied, "that it is more difficult to believe as I do, for one must learn to be inclusionary and accepting."

Clubs waved a dismissive hand, turning to hobble toward the stairs. "Suit yourself. I have to go prepare my boys to die."

Sazed watched him go, frowning. Breeze gave him a Soothing—taking away his self-consciousness—for good measure.

"Don't mind him, Saze," Ham said. "We're all a little on edge, lately."

Sazed nodded. "Still, he makes good points—ones I have never before had to face. Until this year, my duty was to collect, study, and remember. It is still very hard for me to consider setting one belief beneath another, even if that belief is based on a man that I know to have been quite mortal."

Ham shrugged. "Who knows? Maybe Kell *is* out there somewhere, watching over us."

No, Breeze thought. *If he were, we wouldn't have ended up here—waiting to die, locked in a city we were supposed to save.*

"Anyway," Ham said, "I still want to know where that smoke is coming from."

Breeze glanced at the koloss camp. The dark pillar was too centralized to be coming from cooking fires. "The tents?"

Ham shook his head. "El said there were only a couple of tents—far too few to make that much smoke. That fire has been burning for some time."

Breeze shook his head. *Doesn't really matter now, I guess.*

Straff Venture coughed again, curling over in his chair. His arms were slick with sweat, his hands trembling.

He wasn't getting better.

At first, he'd assumed that the chills were a side effect of his nervousness. He'd had a hard evening, sending assassins after Zane, then somehow escaping death at the insane Mistborn's hands. Yet, during the night, Straff's shakes hadn't gotten better. They'd grown worse. They weren't just from nervousness; he must have a disease of some sort.

"Your Majesty!" a voice called from outside.

Straff straightened himself, trying to look as presentable as possible. Even so, the messenger paused as he entered the tent, apparently noting Straff's wan skin and tired eyes.

"My . . . lord," the messenger said.

"Speak, man," Straff said curtly, trying to project a regality he didn't feel. "Out with it."

"Riders, my lord," the man said. "They left the city!"

"What!" Straff said, throwing off his blanket and standing. He managed to stand upright despite a bout of dizziness. "Why wasn't I informed?"

"They passed quickly, my lord," the messenger said. "We barely had time to send the interception crew."

"You caught them, I assume," Straff said, steadying himself on his chair.

"Actually, they escaped, my lord," the messenger said slowly.

"What?" Straff said, spinning in rage. The motion was too much. The dizziness returned, blackness creeping across his field of vision. He stumbled, catching himself on the chair, managing to collapse into it rather than onto the floor.

"Send for the healer!" he heard the messenger shout. "The king is sick!"

No, Straff thought groggily. *No, this came too quickly. It can't be a disease.*

Zane's last words. What had they been? *A man shouldn't kill his father. . . .*

Liar.

"Amaranta," Straff croaked.

"My lord?" a voice asked. Good. Someone was with him.

"Amaranta," he said again. "Send for her."

"Your mistress, my lord?"

Straff forced himself to remain conscious. As he sat, his vision and balance returned somewhat. One of his door guards was at his side. What was the man's name? Grent.

"Grent," Straff said, trying to sound commanding. "You must bring Amaranta to me. Now!"

The soldier hesitated, then rushed from the room. Straff focused on his breathing. In and out. In and out. Zane was a snake. In and out. In and out. Zane hadn't wanted to use the knife—no, that was expected. In and out. But when had the poison come? Straff had been feeling ill the entire day before.

"My lord?"

Amaranta stood at the doorway. She had been beautiful once, before age had gotten to her—as it got to all of them. Childbirth destroyed a woman. So succulent she had been, with her firm breasts and smooth, unblemished skin. . . .

Your mind is wandering, Straff told himself. Focus.

"I need . . . antidote," Straff forced out, focusing on the Amaranta of the now: the woman in her late twenties, the old—yet still useful—thing that kept him alive in the face of Zane's poisons.

"Of course, my lord," Amaranta said, walking over to his poison cabinet, getting out the necessary ingredients.

Straff settled back, focusing on his breathing. Amaranta must have sensed his urgency, for she hadn't even tried to get him to bed her. He watched her work, getting out her burner and ingredients. He needed . . . to find . . . Zane. . . .

She wasn't doing it the right way.

Straff burned tin. The sudden flash of sensitivity nearly blinded him, even in the shade of his tent, and his aches and shivers became sharp and excruciating. But his mind cleared, as if he'd suddenly bathed in frigid water.

Amaranta was preparing the wrong ingredients. Straff didn't know a great deal about the making of antidotes. He'd been forced to delegate this duty, instead focusing his efforts on learning to recognize the details—the scents, the tastes, the discolorations—of poisons. Yet, he had watched Amaranta prepare her catch-all antidote on numerous occasions. And she was doing it differently this time.

He forced himself out of his chair, keeping tin flared, though it caused his eyes to water. "What are you doing?" he said, walking on unsteady feet toward her.

Amaranta looked up, shocked. The guilt that flashed in her eyes was enough confirmation.

"What are you doing!" Straff bellowed, fear giving him strength as he grabbed her by the shoulders, shaking her. He was weakened, but he was still much stronger than she.

The woman looked down. "Your antidote, my lord . . ."

"You're making it the wrong way!" Straff said.

"I thought, you looked fatigued, so I might add something to help you stay awake."

Straff paused. The words seemed logical, though he was having trouble thinking. Then, looking down at the chagrined woman, he noticed something. His eyes enhanced beyond natural detail, he caught a slight glimpse of a bit of uncovered flesh beneath her bodice.

He reached down and ripped off the side of her dress, exposing her skin. Her left breast—disgusting to him, for it sagged a slight bit—was scarred and cut, as if by a knife. None of the scars were fresh, but even in his addled state, Straff recognized Zane's handiwork.

"You're his lover?" Straff said.

"It's your fault," Amaranta hissed. "You abandoned me, once I aged and bore you a few children. Everyone told me you would, but yet, I hoped . . ."

Straff felt himself growing weak. Dizzy, he rested a hand on the wooden poisons cabinet.

"Yet," Amaranta said, tears on her cheeks. "Why did you have to take Zane from me, too? What did you do, to draw him off? To make him stop coming to me?"

"You let him poison me," Straff said, falling to one knee.

"Fool," Amaranta spat. "He never poisoned you—not a single time. Though, at my request, he often made you think that he had. And then, each time, you ran to me. You suspected everything Zane did—and yet, you never once paused to think what was in the 'antidote' I gave you."

"It made me better," Straff mumbled.

"That's what happens when you're addicted to a drug,

Straff," Amaranta whispered. "When you get it, you feel better. When you don't get it . . . you die."

Straff closed his eyes.

"You're mine now, Straff," she said. "I can make you—"

Straff bellowed, gathering what strength he had and throwing himself at the woman. She cried in surprise as he tackled her, pushing her to the ground.

Then she said nothing, for Straff's hands choked her windpipe. She struggled for a bit, but Straff weighed far more than she did. He'd intended to demand the antidote, to force her to save him, but he wasn't thinking clearly. His vision began to fuzz, his mind dim.

By the time he regained his wits, Amaranta was blue and dead on the ground before him. He wasn't certain how long he'd been strangling her corpse. He rolled off her, toward the open cabinet. On his knees, he reached up for the burner, but his shaking hands toppled it to the side, spilling hot liquid across the floor.

Cursing to himself, he grabbed a flagon of unheated water and began to throw handfuls of herbs into it. He stayed away from the drawers that held the poisons, sticking to those that held antidotes. Yet, there were many crossovers. Some things were poisonous in large doses, but could cure in smaller amounts. Most were addictive. He didn't have time to worry about that; he could feel the weakness in his limbs, and he could barely grab the handfuls of herbs. Bits of brown and red shook from his fingers as he dumped handful after handful into the mixture.

One of these was the herb that she'd gotten him addicted to. Any one of the others might kill him. He wasn't even sure what the odds were.

He drank the concoction anyway, gulping it down between choking gasps for air, then let himself slip into unconsciousness.

I have no doubt that if Alendi reaches the Well of Ascension, he will take the power and then—in the name of the presumed greater good—give it up.

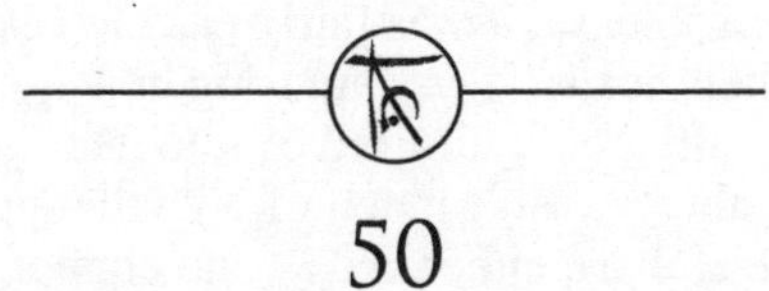

50

"ARE THOSE THE FELLOWS YOU want, Lady Cett?"

Allrianne scanned the valley—and the army it contained—then looked down at the bandit, Hobart. He smiled eagerly—or, well, he *kind* of smiled. Hobart had fewer teeth than he had fingers, and he was missing a couple of those.

Allrianne smiled back from atop her horse. She sat sidesaddle, reins held lightly in her fingers. "Yes, I do believe that it is, Master Hobart."

Hobart looked back at his band of thugs, grinning. Allrianne Rioted them all a bit, reminding them how much they wanted her promised reward. Her father's army spread out before them in the distance. She had wandered for an entire day, traveling west, looking for it. But, she'd been heading in the wrong direction. If she hadn't run afoul of Hobart's helpful little gang, she would have been forced to sleep outside.

And that would have been rather unpleasant.

"Come, Master Hobart," she said, moving her horse forward. "Let's go and meet with my father."

The group followed happily, one of them leading her packhorse. There was a certain charm to simple men, like Hobart's crew. They really only wanted three things: money, food, and sex. And they could usually use the first to get the other two. When she'd first run across this group, she'd blessed her fortune—despite the fact that they had been running down a hillside in ambush, intent on robbing and raping her. Another charm about men like these was that they were rather inexperienced with Allomancy.

She kept a firm hold on their emotions as they rode down toward the camp. She didn't want them reaching any disappointing conclusions—such as "Ransoms are usually bigger than rewards." She couldn't control them completely, of course—she could only influence them. However, with men so base, it was fairly easy to read what was going on in their heads. It was amusing how quickly a little promise of wealth could turn brutes into near gentlemen.

Of course, there wasn't much of a challenge in dealing with men like Hobart, either. No . . . no challenge, as there had been with Breezy. Now, *that* had been fun. And rewarding, too. She doubted she'd ever find a man as aware of his emotions, and as aware of the emotions of others, as Breezy. Getting a man like him—a man so expert in Allomancy, so determined that his age made him inappropriate for her—to love her . . . well, that had been a true accomplishment.

Ah, Breezy, she thought as they passed out of the forest and onto the hillside before the army. *Do any of your friends even understand what a noble man you are?*

They really didn't treat him well enough. Of course, that was to be expected. That was what Breezy wanted. People who underestimated you were easier to manipulate. Yes, Allrianne understood this concept quite well—for there were few things more quickly dismissed than a young, silly girl.

"Halt!" a soldier said, riding up with an honor guard. They had swords drawn. "Step away from her, you!"

Oh, honestly, Allrianne thought, rolling her eyes. She Rioted the group of soldiers, enhancing their sense of calmness. She didn't want any accidents.

"Please, Captain," she said as Hobart and his crew drew weapons, huddling around her uncertainly. "These men have rescued me from the savage wilderness and brought me safely home, at much personal cost and danger."

Hobart nodded firmly, an action undermined just a bit as he wiped his nose on his sleeve. The soldier captain looked over the ash-stained, motley-clothed group of bandits, then frowned.

"See that these men have a good meal, Captain," she said airily, kicking her horse forward. "And give them space for the night. Hobart, I'll send your reward once I meet with my father."

Bandits and soldiers moved in behind her, and Allrianne made sure to Riot them both, enhancing their senses of trust. It was a tough sell for the soldiers, especially as the wind shifted, blowing the full stench of the bandit crew across them. Still, they all reached the camp without incident.

The groups parted, Allrianne giving her horses to an aide and calling for a page to warn her father that she'd returned. She dusted off her riding dress, then strode through camp, smiling pleasantly and looking forward to a bath and the other comforts—such as they were—that the army could provide. However, first there were things she needed to attend to.

Her father liked to spend evenings in his open-sided planning pavilion, and he sat there now, arguing with a messenger. He looked over as Allrianne swished into the pavilion, smiling sweetly at Lords Galivan and Detor, her father's generals.

Cett sat on a high-legged chair so he could get a good view of his table and its maps. "Well, damn it," he said. "You *are* back."

Allrianne smiled, wandering around his planning table, looking at the map. It detailed the supply lines back to the Western Dominance. What she saw was not good.

"Rebellions back home, Father?" she asked.

"And ruffians attacking my supply carts," Cett said. "That boy Venture bribed them, I'm sure of it."

"Yes, he did," Allrianne said. "But, that's all pointless now. Did you miss me?" She made sure to Tug strongly on his sense of devotion.

Cett snorted, pulling at his beard. "Fool of a girl," he said. "I should have left you home."

"So I could have fallen to your enemies when they raised a rebellion?" she asked. "We both know that Lord

Yomen was going to move the moment you pulled your armies out of the dominance."

"And I should have let that damn obligator have you!"

Allrianne gasped. "Father! Yomen would have held me for ransom. You know how terribly I wilt when I'm locked up."

Cett glanced at her, and then—apparently despite himself—he started to chuckle. "You'd've had him feeding you gourmet foods before the day was through. Maybe I *should* have left you behind. Then, at least, I'd have known where you were—rather than worrying where you'd run off to next. You didn't bring that idiot Breeze back with you, did you?"

"Father!" Allrianne said. "Breezy is a good man."

"Good men die quickly in this world, Allrianne," Cett said. "I know—I've killed enough of them."

"Oh, yes," Allrianne said, "you're very wise. And taking an aggressive stance against Luthadel had *such* a positive outcome, didn't it? Chased away with your tail between your legs? You'd be dead now, if dear Vin had as little conscience as you."

"That 'conscience' didn't stop her from killing some three hundred of my men," Cett said.

"She's a very confused young lady," Allrianne said. "Either way, I do feel obliged to remind you that I was right. You should have made an alliance with the Venture boy, instead of threatening him. That means you owe me five new dresses!"

Cett rubbed his forehead. "This isn't a damn game, girl."

"Fashion, Father, is no *game*," Allrianne said firmly. "I can't very well enchant bandit troops into leading me safely home if I look like a street rat, now can I?"

"More bandits, Allrianne?" Cett asked with a sigh. "You know how long it took us to get rid of the last group?"

"Hobart's a wonderful man," Allrianne said testily. "Not to mention well-connected with the local thieving community. Give him some gold and some prostitutes, and you might just be able to talk him into helping you with those brigands that are attacking your supply lines."

Cett paused, glancing at the map. Then he began to pull at

his beard thoughtfully. "Well, you're back," he finally said. "Guess we'll have to take care of you. I suppose you want someone to carry a litter for you as we head home. . . ."

"Actually," Allrianne said, "we're not going back to the dominance. We're returning to Luthadel."

Cett didn't immediately dismiss the comment; he could usually tell when she was being serious. Instead, he simply shook his head. "Luthadel holds nothing for us, Allrianne."

"We can't go back to the dominance, either," Allrianne said. "Our enemies are too strong, and some of them have Allomancers. That's why we had to come here in the first place. We can't leave the area until we have either money or allies."

"There's no money in Luthadel," Cett said. "I believe Venture when he says the atium isn't there."

"I agree," Allrianne said. "I searched that palace well, never found a bit of the stuff. That means we need to leave here with friends, instead of money. Go back, wait for a battle to start, then help whichever side looks like it's going to win. They'll feel indebted to us—they might even decide to let us live."

Cett stood quietly for a moment. "That's not going to help save your friend Breeze, Allrianne. His faction is by far the weakest—even teaming with the Venture boy, I doubt we could beat Straff or those koloss. Not without access to the city walls and plenty of time to prepare. If we go back, it will be to help your Breeze's enemies."

Allrianne shrugged. *You can't help him if you're not there, Father,* she thought. *They're going to lose anyway—if you* are *in the area, then there's a chance you'll end up helping Luthadel.*

A very small chance, Breeze. That's the best I can give you. I'm sorry.

Elend Venture awoke on their third day out of Luthadel, surprised at how rested he could feel after a night spent in a tent out in the wilderness. Of course, part of that might have been the company.

Vin lay curled up beside him in their bedroll, her head resting against his chest. He would have expected her to be a light sleeper, considering how jumpy she was, but she seemed to feel comfortable sleeping beside him. She even seemed to become just a little less anxious when he put his arms around her.

He looked down at her fondly, admiring the form of her face, the slight curl of her black hair. The cut on her cheek was almost invisible now, and she'd already pulled out the stitches. A constant, low burn of pewter gave the body remarkable strength for recovery. She didn't even favor her right arm anymore—despite the cut shoulder—and her weakness from the fight seemed completely gone.

She still hadn't given him much of an explanation regarding that night. She had fought Zane—who had apparently been Elend's half brother—and TenSoon the kandra had left. Yet, neither of those things seemed like they could have caused the distress in her he'd sensed when she'd come to him in his rooms.

He didn't know if he'd ever get the answers he wanted. Yet, he was coming to realize that he could love her even if he didn't completely understand her. He bent down and kissed the top of her head.

She immediately tensed, eyes opening. She sat up, exposing a bare torso, then glanced around their small tent. It was dimly lit with the light of dawn. Finally, she shook her head, looking over at him. "You're a bad influence on me."

"Oh?" he asked, smiling as he rested on one arm.

Vin nodded, running a hand through her hair. "You're making me get used to sleeping at night," she said. "Plus, I don't sleep in my clothing anymore."

"If you did, it would make things a little awkward."

"Yes," she said, "but what if we get attacked during the night? I'd have to fight them naked."

"I wouldn't mind watching that."

She gave him a flat stare, then reached for a shirt.

"You're having a bad influence on me, too, you know," he said as he watched her dress.

She raised an eyebrow.

"You're making me relax," he said. "And letting me stop

worrying. I've been so tied up with things in the city lately that I'd forgotten what it was like to be an impolite recluse. Unfortunately, during our trip, I've had time to read not only one, but all *three* volumes of Troubeld's *Arts of Scholarship.*"

Vin snorted, kneeling in the low tent as she pulled her belt tight; then she crawled over to him. "I don't know how you read while riding," she said.

"Oh, it's quite easy—if you aren't afraid of horses."

"I'm not afraid of them," Vin said. "They just don't like me. They know I can outrun them, and that makes them surly."

"Oh, is that it?" Elend asked, smiling, pulling her over to straddle him.

She nodded, then leaned down to kiss him. She ended it after a moment, however, moving to stand. She swatted his hand away as he tried to pull her back down.

"After all the trouble I took to get dressed?" she asked. "Besides, I'm hungry."

He sighed, reclining back as she scampered out of the tent, into the red morning sunlight. He lay for a moment, quietly remarking to himself on his fortune. He still wasn't sure how their relationship had worked out, or even why it made him so happy, but he was more than willing to enjoy the experience.

Eventually, he looked over at his clothing. He had brought only one of his nice uniforms—along with the riding uniform—and he didn't want to wear either too often. He didn't have servants anymore to wash the ash out of his clothing; in fact, despite the tent's double flap, some ash had managed to work its way inside during the night. Now that they were out of the city, there were no workers to sweep the ash away, and it was getting everywhere.

So, he dressed in an outfit far more simple: a pair of riding trousers, not unlike the pants that Vin often wore, with a buttoning gray shirt and a dark jacket. He'd never been forced to ride long distances before—carriages were generally preferred—but Vin and he were taking the trip relatively slowly. They had no real urgency. Straff's scouts hadn't followed them for long, and nobody was expecting them at their destination. They had time to ride leisurely, taking breaks, occasionally walking so that they wouldn't get too sore from riding.

Outside, he found Vin stirring up the morning fire and Spook caring for the horses. The young man had done some extensive traveling, and he knew how to tend horses—something that Elend was embarrassed to have never learned.

Elend joined Vin at the firepit. They sat for a few moments, Vin poking at the coals. She looked pensive.

"What?" Elend asked.

She glanced southward. "I . . ." Then she shook her head. "It's nothing. We're going to need more wood." She glanced to the side, toward where their axe lay beside the tent. The weapon flipped up into the air, shooting toward her blade-first. She stepped to the side, snatching the handle as it passed between her and Elend. Then she stalked over to a fallen tree. She took two swings at it, then easily kicked it down and broke it in two.

"She has a way of making the rest of us feel a little redundant, doesn't she?" Spook asked, stepping up beside Elend.

"At times," Elend said with a smile.

Spook shook his head. "Whatever I see or hear, she can sense better—and she can fight whatever it is that she finds. Every time I come back to Luthadel, I just feel . . . useless."

"Imagine being a regular person," Elend said. "At least you're an Allomancer."

"Maybe," Spook said, the sound of Vin chopping coming from the side. "But people respect you, El. They just dismiss me."

"I don't dismiss you, Spook."

"Oh?" the young man asked. "When's the last time I did anything important for the crew?"

"Three days ago," Elend said. "When you agreed to come with Vin and me. You're not just here to tend horses, Spook—you're here because of your skills as a scout and a Tineye. Do you still think we're being followed?"

Spook paused, then shrugged. "I can't be sure. I think

Straff's scouts turned back, but I keep catching sight of someone back there. I never get a good glimpse of them, though."

"It's the mist spirit," Vin said, walking by and dumping an armload of wood beside the firepit. "It's chasing us."

Spook and Elend shared a look. Then Elend nodded, refusing to act on Spook's uncomfortable stare. "Well, as long as it stays out of our way, it's not a problem, right?"

Vin shrugged. "I hope not. If you see it, though, call for me. The records say it can be dangerous."

"All right," Elend said. "We'll do that. Now, let's decide what to have for breakfast."

Straff woke up. That was his first surprise.

He lay in bed, inside his tent, feeling like someone had picked him up and slammed him against the wall a few times. He groaned, sitting up. His body was free from bruises, but he ached, and his head was pounding. One of the army healers, a young man with a full beard and bulging eyes, sat beside his bed. The man studied Straff for a moment.

"You, my lord, should be dead," the young man said.

"I'm not," Straff said, sitting up. "Give me some tin."

A soldier approached with a metal vial. Straff downed it, then scowled at how dry and sore his throat was. He burned the tin only lightly; it made his wounds feel worse, but he had come to depend on the slight edge the enhanced senses gave him.

"How long?" he asked.

"Better part of three days, my lord," the healer said. "We . . . weren't sure what you'd eaten, or why. We thought about trying to get you to vomit, but it appeared that you'd taken the draught of your own choice, so . . ."

"You did well," Straff said, holding his arm up in front of him. It still shook a bit, and he couldn't make it stop. "Who is in charge of the army?"

"General Janarle," the healer said.

Straff nodded. "Why hasn't he had me killed?"

The healer blinked in surprise, glancing at the soldiers.

"My lord," said Grent the soldier, "who would dare betray you? Any man who tried would end up dead in his tent. General Janarle was *most* worried about your safety."

Of course, Straff realized with shock. *They don't know that Zane is gone. Why . . . if I did die, then everyone assumes that Zane would either take control himself, or get revenge on those he thought responsible.* Straff laughed out loud, shocking those watching over him. Zane had tried to kill him, but had accidentally saved his life by sheer force of reputation.

I beat you, Straff realized. *You're gone, and I'm alive.* That didn't, of course, mean that Zane wouldn't return—but, then again, he might not. Perhaps . . . just maybe . . . Straff was rid of him forever.

"Elend's Mistborn," Straff said suddenly.

"We followed her for a while, my lord," Grent said. "But, they got too far from the army, and Lord Janarle ordered the scouts back. It appears she's making for Terris."

He frowned. "Who else was with her?"

"We think your son Elend escaped as well," the soldier said. "But it could have been a decoy."

Zane did it, Straff thought with shock. *He actually got rid of her.*

Unless it's a trick of some sort. But, then . . .

"The koloss army?" Straff asked.

"There's been a lot of fighting in its ranks lately, sir," Grent said. "The beasts seem more restless."

"Order our army to break camp," Straff said. "Immediately. We're retreating back toward the Northern Dominance."

"My lord?" Grent said with shock. "I think Lord Janarle is planning an assault, waiting only for your word. The city is weak, and their Mistborn is gone."

"We're pulling back," Straff said, smiling. "For a while, at least." *Let's see if this plan of yours works, Zane.*

Sazed sat in a small kitchen alcove, hands on the table before him, a metallic ring glittering on each finger. They were small, for metalminds, but storing up Feruchemical attributes took time. It would take weeks to fill even a ring's worth of metal—and he barely had days. In fact, Sazed was surprised the koloss had waited so long.

Three days. Not much time at all, but he suspected he would need every available edge in the approaching conflict. So far he'd been able to store up a small amount of each attribute. Enough for a boost in an emergency, once his other metalminds ran out.

Clubs hobbled into the kitchen. He seemed a blur to Sazed. Even wearing his spectacles—to help compensate for the vision he was storing in a tinmind—it was difficult for him to see.

"That's it," Clubs said, his voice muffled—another tinmind was taking Sazed's hearing. "They're finally gone."

Sazed paused for a moment, trying to decipher the comment. His thoughts moved as if through a thick, turgid soup, and it took him a moment to understand what Clubs had said.

They're gone. Straff's troops. They've withdrawn. He coughed quietly before replying. "Did he ever respond to any of Lord Penrod's messages?"

"No," Clubs said. "But he did execute the last messenger."

Well, that isn't a very good sign, Sazed thought slowly. Of course, there hadn't been very many good signs over the last few days. The city was on the edge of starvation, and their brief respite of warmth was over. It would snow this evening, if Sazed guessed right. That made him feel even more guilty to be sitting in the kitchen nook, beside a warm hearth, sipping broth as his metalminds sapped his strength, health, senses, and power of thought. He had rarely tried to fill so many at once.

"You don't look so good," Clubs noted, sitting.

Sazed blinked, thinking through the comment. "My . . . goldmind," he said slowly. "It draws my health, storing it up." He glanced at his bowl of broth. "I must eat to maintain my strength," he said, mentally preparing himself to take a sip.

It was an odd process. His thoughts moved so slowly that it took him a moment to decide to eat. Then his body reacted slowly, the arm taking a few seconds to move. Even then, the muscles quivered, their strength sapped away and stored in his pewtermind. Finally, he was able to get a spoonful to his lips and take a quiet sip. It tasted bland; he was filling scent as well, and without it, his sense of taste was severely hampered.

He should probably be lying down—but if he did that, he was liable to sleep. And, while sleeping, he couldn't fill metalminds—or, at least, he could fill only one. A bronzemind, the metal that stored wakefulness, would force him to sleep longer in exchange for letting him go longer without sleep on another occasion.

Sazed sighed, carefully setting down his spoon, then coughing. He'd done his best to help avert the conflict. His best plan had been to send a letter to Lord Penrod, urging him to inform Straff Venture that Vin was gone from the city. He had hoped that Straff would then be willing to make a deal. Apparently, that tactic had been unsuccessful. Nobody had heard from Straff in days.

Their doom approached like the inevitable sunrise. Penrod had allowed three separate groups of townspeople—one of them composed of nobility—to try to flee Luthadel. Straff's soldiers, more wary after Elend's escape, had caught and slaughtered each group. Penrod had even sent a messenger to Lord Jastes Lekal, hoping to strike some deal with the Southern leader, but the messenger had not returned from the koloss camp.

"Well," Clubs said, "at least we kept them off for a few days."

Sazed thought for a moment. "It was simply a delay of the inevitable, I fear."

"Of course it was," Clubs said. "But it was an important delay. Elend and Vin will be almost four days away by now. If the fighting had started too soon, you can bet that little Miss Mistborn would have come back and gotten herself killed trying to save us."

"Ah," Sazed said slowly, forcing himself to reach for another spoonful of broth. The spoon was a dull weight in his numb fingers; his sense of touch, of course, was being siphoned into a tinmind. "How are the city defenses coming?" he asked as he struggled with the spoon.

"Terribly," Clubs said. "Twenty thousand troops may sound like a lot—but try stringing them out through a city this big."

"But the koloss won't have any siege equipment," Sazed said, focused on his spoon. "Or archers."

"Yes," Clubs said. "But we have eight city gates to protect—and any of five are within quick reach of the koloss. None of those gates was built to withstand an attack. And, as it stands, I can barely post a couple thousand guards at each gate, since I really don't know which way the koloss will come first."

"Oh," Sazed said quietly.

"What did you expect, Terrisman?" Clubs asked. "Good news? The koloss are bigger, stronger, and far crazier than we are. And they have an advantage in numbers."

Sazed closed his eyes, quivering spoon held halfway to his lips. He suddenly felt a weakness unrelated to his metalminds. *Why didn't she go with them? Why didn't she escape?*

As Sazed opened his eyes, he saw Clubs waving for a servant to bring him something to eat. The young girl returned with a bowl of soup. Clubs eyed it with dissatisfaction for a moment, but then lifted a knotted hand and began to slurp. He shot a glance at Sazed. "You expecting an apology out of me, Terrisman?" he asked between spoonfuls.

Sazed sat shocked for a moment. "Not at all, Lord Cladent," he finally said.

"Good," Clubs said. "You're a decent enough person. You're just confused."

Sazed sipped his soup, smiling. "That is comforting to hear. I think." He thought for a moment. "Lord Cladent. I have a religion for you."

Clubs frowned. "You don't give up, do you?"

Sazed looked down. It took him a moment to gather together what he'd been thinking about before. "What you said earlier, Lord Cladent. About situational morality. It made me think of a faith, known as Dadradah. Its practitioners spanned many countries and peoples; they believed that there was only one God, and that there was only one right way to worship."

Clubs snorted. "I'm really not interested in one of your dead religions, Terrisman. I think that—"

"They were artists," Sazed said quietly.

Clubs hesitated.

"They thought art drew one closer to God," Sazed said. "They were most interested in color and hue, and they were fond of writing poetry describing the colors they saw in the world around them."

Clubs was silent. "Why preach this religion to me?" he demanded. "Why not pick one that is blunt, like I am? Or one that worshipped warfare and soldiers?"

"Because, Lord Cladent," Sazed said. He blinked, recalling memories with effort through his muddled mind. "That is not you. It is what you must do, but it is not you. The others forget, I think, that you were a woodworker. An artist. When we lived in your shop, I often saw you, putting the finishing touches on pieces your apprentices had carved. I saw the care you used. That shop was no simple front for you. You miss it, I know."

Clubs didn't respond.

"You must live as a soldier," Sazed said, pulling something from his sash with a weak hand. "But you can still dream like an artist. Here. I had this made for you. It is a symbol of the Dadradah faith. To its people, being an artist was a higher calling, even, than being a priest."

He set the wooden disk on the table. Then, with effort, he smiled at Clubs. It had been a long time since he had preached a religion, and he wasn't certain what had made him decide to offer this one to Clubs. Perhaps it was to prove to himself that there was value in them. Perhaps it was stubbornness, reacting against the things Clubs had said earlier. Either way, he found satisfaction in the way that Clubs stared at the simple wooden disk with the carved picture of a brush on it.

The last time I preached a religion, he thought, *I was in that village to the south, the one where Marsh found me.*

Whatever happened to him, anyway? Why didn't he return to the city?

"Your woman has been looking for you," Clubs finally said, looking up, leaving the disk on the table.

"*My* woman?" Sazed said. "Why, we are not . . ." He trailed off as Clubs eyed him. The surly general was quite proficient at meaningful looks.

"Very well," Sazed said, sighing. He glanced down at his fingers and the ten glittering rings they bore. Four were tin: sight, hearing, scent, and touch. He continued to fill these; they wouldn't handicap him much. He released his pewtermind, however, as well as his steelmind and his zincmind.

Immediately, strength refilled his body. His muscles stopped sagging, reverting from emaciated to healthy. The fuzz lifted from his mind, allowing him to think clearly, and the thick, swollen slowness evaporated. He stood, invigorated.

"That's fascinating," Clubs mumbled.

Sazed looked down.

"I could see the change," Clubs said. "Your body grew stronger, and your eyes focused. Your arms stopped shaking. I guess you don't want to face that woman without all of your faculties, eh? I don't blame you." Clubs grunted to himself, then continued to eat.

Sazed bid farewell to the man, then strode out of the kitchen. His feet and hands still seemed like nearly unfeeling lumps. Yet, he felt an energy. There was nothing like simple contrast to awaken a man's sense of indomitability.

And there was nothing that could sap that sensation more quickly than the prospect of meeting with the woman he loved. Why had Tindwyl stayed? And, if she was determined not to go back to Terris, why had she avoided him these last few days? Was she mad that he had sent Elend away? Was she disappointed that he insisted on staying to help?

He found her inside Keep Venture's grand ballroom. He paused for a moment, impressed—as always—by the room's unquestionable majesty. He released his sight tinmind for just a moment, removing his spectacles as he looked around the awesome space.

Enormous, rectangular stained-glass windows reached to the ceiling along both walls of the huge room. Standing at the side, Sazed was dwarfed by massive pillars that supported a small gallery that ran beneath the windows on either side of the chamber. Every bit of stone in the room seemed carved—every tile a part of one mosaic or another, every bit of glass colored to sparkle in the early-evening sunlight.

It's been so long . . . he thought. The first time he'd seen this chamber, he had been escorting Vin to her first ball. It was then, while playing the part of Valette Renoux, she had met Elend. Sazed had chastised her for carelessly attracting the attention of so powerful a man.

And now he himself had performed their marriage. He smiled, replacing his spectacles and filling his eyesight tinmind again. *May the Forgotten Gods watch over you, children. Make something of our sacrifice, if you can.*

Tindwyl stood speaking with Dockson and a small group of functionaries at the center of the room. They were crowded around a large table, and as Sazed approached, he could see what was spread atop it.

Marsh's map, he thought. It was an extensive and detailed representation of Luthadel, complete with notations about Ministry activity. Sazed had a visual image of the map, as well as a detailed description of it, in one of his copperminds—and he had sent a physical copy to the Synod.

Tindwyl and the others had covered the large map with their own notations. Sazed approached slowly, and as soon as Tindwyl saw him, she waved for him to approach.

"Ah, Sazed," Dockson said in a businesslike tone, voice muddled to Sazed's weak ears. "Good. Please, come here."

Sazed stepped up onto the low dance floor, joining them at the table. "Troop placements?" he asked.

"Penrod has taken command of our armies," Dockson said. "And he's put noblemen in charge of all twenty battalions. We're not certain we like that situation."

Sazed looked over the men at the table. They were a group of scribes that Dockson himself had trained—all skaa. *Gods!* Sazed thought. *He can't be planning a rebellion* now *of all times, can he?*

"Don't look so frightened, Sazed," Dockson said. "We're not going to do anything too drastic—Penrod is still letting Clubs organize the city defenses, and he seems to be taking advice from his military commanders. Besides, it's far too late to try something too ambitious."

Dockson almost seemed disappointed.

"However," Dockson said, pointing at the map, "I don't trust these commanders he's put in charge. They don't know anything about warfare—or even about survival. They've spent their lives ordering drinks and throwing parties."

Why do you hate them so? Sazed thought. Ironically, Dockson was the one in the crew who *looked* most like a nobleman. He was more natural in a suit than Breeze, more articulate than Clubs or Spook. Only his insistence on wearing a very unaristocratic half beard made him stand out.

"The nobility may not know warfare," Sazed said, "but they are experienced with command, I think."

"True," Dockson said. "But so are we. That's why I want one of our people near each gate, just in case things go poorly and someone really competent needs to take command."

Dockson pointed at the table, toward one of the gates—Steel Gate. It bore a notation of a thousand men in a defensive formation. "This is your battalion, Sazed. Steel Gate is the farthest the koloss are likely to reach, and so you might not even see any fighting. However, when the battle begins, I want you there with a group of messengers to bring word back to Keep Venture in case your gate gets attacked. We'll set up a command post here in the main ballroom—it's easily accessible with those broad doors, and can accommodate a lot of motion."

And it was a not-so-subtle smack in the face of Elend Venture, and nobility in general, to use such a beautiful chamber as a setting from which to run a war. *No wonder he supported me in sending Elend and Vin away. With them gone, he's gained undisputed control of Kelsier's crew.*

It wasn't a bad thing. Dockson was an organizational genius and a master of quick planning. He did have certain prejudices, however.

"I know you don't like to fight, Saze," Dockson said, leaning down on the table with both hands. "But we need you."

"I think he is preparing for battle, Lord Dockson," Tindwyl said, eyeing Sazed. "Those rings on his fingers give good indication of his intentions."

Sazed glanced across the table at her. "And what is your place in this, Tindwyl?"

"Lord Dockson came to me for advice," Tindwyl said. "He has little experience with warfare himself, and wished to know the things I have studied about the generals of the past."

"Ah," Sazed said. He turned to Dockson, frowning in thought. Eventually, he nodded. "Very well. I will take part in your project—but, I must warn you against divisiveness. Please, tell your men not to break the chain of command unless they absolutely must."

Dockson nodded.

"Now, Lady Tindwyl," Sazed said. "Might we speak for a moment in private?"

She nodded, and they excused themselves, walking under the nearest overhanging gallery. In the shadows, behind one of the pillars, Sazed turned toward Tindwyl. She looked so pristine—so poised, so calm—despite the dire situation. How did she do that?

"You're storing quite a large number of attributes, Sazed," Tindwyl noted, glancing at his fingers again. "Surely you have other metalminds prepared from before?"

"I used all of my wakefulness and speed making my way to Luthadel," Sazed said. "And I have no health stored at all—I used up the last of it overcoming a sickness when I was teaching in the South. I always intended to fill another one, but we've been too busy. I do have some large amount of strength and weight stored, as well as a good selection of tinminds. Still, one can never be *too* well prepared, I think."

"Perhaps," Tindwyl said. She glanced back at the group

around the table. "If it gives us something to do other than think about the inevitable, then preparation has not been wasted, I think."

Sazed felt a chill. "Tindwyl," he said quietly. "Why did you stay? There is no place for you here."

"There is no place for you either, Sazed."

"These are my friends," he said. "I will not leave them."

"Then why did you convince their leaders to leave?"

"To flee and live," Sazed said.

"Survival is not a luxury often afforded to leaders," Tindwyl said. "When they accept the devotion of others, they must accept the responsibility that comes with it. This people will die—but they need not die feeling betrayed."

"They were not—"

"They expect to be saved, Sazed," Tindwyl hissed quietly. "Even those men over there—even *Dockson,* the most practical one in this bunch—think that they'll survive. And do you know why? Because, deep down, they believe that something will save them. Something that saved them before, the only piece of the Survivor they have left. She represents hope to them now. And you sent her away."

"To live, Tindwyl," Sazed repeated. "It would have been a waste to lose Vin and Elend here."

"Hope is never wasted," Tindwyl said, eyes flashing. "I thought you of all people would understand that. You think it was stubbornness that kept me alive all those years in the hands of the Breeders?"

"And is it stubbornness or hope that kept you here, in the city?" he asked.

She looked up at him. "Neither."

Sazed looked at her for a long moment in the shadowed alcove. Planners talked in the ballroom, their voices echoing. Shards of light from the windows reflected off the marble floors, throwing slivers of illumination across the walls. Slowly, awkwardly, Sazed put his arms around Tindwyl. She sighed, letting him hold her.

He released his tinminds and let his senses return in a flood.

Softness from her skin and warmth from her body washed across him as she moved farther into the embrace, resting her head against his chest. The scent of her hair—unperfumed, but clean and crisp—filled his nose, the first thing he'd smelled in three days. With a clumsy hand, Sazed pulled free his spectacles so he could see her clearly. As sounds returned fully to his ears, he could hear Tindwyl breathing beside him.

"Do you know why I love you, Sazed?" she asked quietly.

"I cannot fathom," he answered honestly.

"Because you never give in," she said. "Other men are strong like bricks—firm, unyielding, but if you pound on them long enough, they crack. You . . . you're strong like the wind. Always there, so willing to bend, but never apologetic for the times when you must be firm. I don't think any of your friends understand what a power they had in you."

Had, he thought. *She already thinks of all this in the past tense. And . . . it feels right for her to do so.* "I fear that whatever I have won't be enough to save them," Sazed whispered.

"It was enough to save three of them, though," Tindwyl said. "You were wrong to send them away . . . but maybe you were right, too."

Sazed just closed his eyes and held her, cursing her for staying, yet loving her for it all the same.

At that moment, the wall-top warning drums began to beat.

And so, I have made one final gamble.

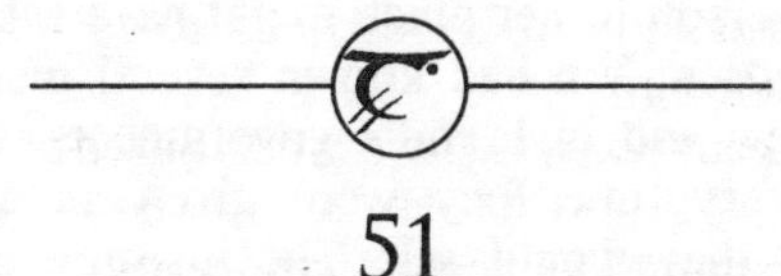

51

THE MISTY RED LIGHT OF morning was a thing that should not have existed. Mist died before daylight. Heat made it evaporate; even locking it inside of a closed room made it condense and disappear. It shouldn't have been able to withstand the light of the rising sun.

Yet it did. The farther they'd gotten from Luthadel, the longer the mists lingered in the mornings. The change was slight—they were still only a few days' ride from Luthadel—but Vin knew. She saw the difference. This morning, the mists seemed even stronger than she'd anticipated—they didn't even weaken as the sun came up. They obscured its light.

Mist, she thought. *Deepness.* She was increasingly sure that she was right about it, though she couldn't know for certain. Still, it felt right to her for some reason. The Deepness hadn't been some monster or tyrant, but a force more natural—and therefore more frightening. A creature could be killed. The mists . . . they were far more daunting. The Deepness wouldn't oppress with priests, but use the people's own superstitious terror. It wouldn't slaughter with armies, but with starvation.

How did one fight something larger than a continent? A thing that couldn't feel anger, pain, hope, or mercy?

Yet, it was Vin's task to do just that. She sat quietly on a large boulder beside the night's firepit, her legs up, knees to her chest. Elend still slept; Spook was out scouting.

She didn't question her place any longer. She was either mad or she was the Hero of Ages. It was her task to defeat the mists. *Yet . . .* she thought, frowning. *Shouldn't the thumpings be getting louder, not softer?* The longer they traveled, the weaker the thumpings seemed. Was she too late? Was something happening at the Well to dampen its power? Had someone else already taken it?

We have to keep moving.

Another person in her place might have asked why he had been chosen. Vin had known several men—both in Camon's crew and in Elend's government—who would complain every time they were given an assignment. "Why me?" they would ask. The insecure ones didn't think they were up to the task. The lazy ones wanted out of the work.

Vin didn't consider herself to be either self-assured or self-motivated. Still, she saw no point in asking why. Life had taught her that sometimes things simply happened. Often, there hadn't been any specific reason for Reen to beat her. And, reasons were weak comforts, anyway. The reasons that Kelsier had needed to die were clear to her, but that didn't make her miss him any less.

She had a job to do. The fact that she didn't understand it didn't stop her from acknowledging that she had to try to accomplish it. She simply hoped that she'd know what to do when the time came. Though the thumpings were weaker, they were still there. They drew her forward. To the Well of Ascension.

Behind her, she could feel the lesser vibration of the mist spirit. It never disappeared until the mists themselves did. It had been there all morning, standing just behind her.

"Do you know the secret to this all?" she asked quietly, turning toward the spirit in the reddish mists. "Do you have—"

The Allomantic pulse of the mist spirit was coming from directly inside the tent she shared with Elend.

Vin jumped off the rock, landing on the frosted ground and scrambling to the tent. She threw open the flaps. Elend slept inside, head just barely visible as it poked out of the blankets. Mist filled the small tent, swirling, twisting—and that was odd enough. Mist didn't usually enter tents.

And there, in the middle of the mists, was the spirit. Standing directly above Elend.

It wasn't even really there. It was just an outline in the

mists, a repeating pattern caused by chaotic movements. And yet it was real. She could feel it, and she could see it—see it as it looked up, meeting her gaze with invisible eyes.

Hateful eyes.

It raised an insubstantial arm, and Vin saw something flash. She reacted immediately, whipping out a dagger, bursting into the tent and swinging. Her blow met something tangible in the mist spirit's hand. A metallic sound rang in the calm air, and Vin felt a powerful, numbing chill in her arm. The hairs across her entire body prickled.

And then it disappeared. Fading away, like the ringing of its somehow substantial blade. Vin blinked, then turned to look through the blowing tent flap. The mists outside were gone; day had finally won.

It didn't seem to have many victories remaining.

"Vin?" Elend asked, yawning and stirring.

Vin calmed her breathing. The spirit had gone. The daylight meant safety, for now. *Once, it was the nights that I found safe,* she thought. *Kelsier gave them to me.*

"What's wrong?" Elend asked. How could someone, even a nobleman, be so slow to rise, so unconcerned about thc vulnerability he displayed while sleeping?

She sheathed her dagger. *What can I tell him? How can I protect him from something I can barely see?* She needed to think. "It was nothing," she said quietly. "Just me . . . being jumpy again."

Elend rolled over, sighing contentedly. "Is Spook doing his morning scout?"

"Yes."

"Wake me when he gets back."

Vin nodded, but he probably couldn't see her. She knelt, looking at him as the sun rose behind her. She'd given herself to him—not just her body, and not just her heart. She'd abandoned her rationalizations, given away her reservations, all for him. She could no longer afford to think that she wasn't worthy of him, no longer give herself the false comfort of believing they couldn't ever be together.

She'd never trusted anyone this much. Not Kelsier, not

Sazed, not Reen. Elend had everything. That knowledge made her tremble inside. If she lost him, she would lose herself.

I mustn't think about that! she told herself, rising. She left the tent, quietly closing the flaps behind her. In the distance, shadows moved. Spook appeared a moment later.

"Someone's definitely back there," he said quietly. "Not spirits, Vin. Five men, with a camp."

Vin frowned. "Following us?"

"They must be."

Straff's scouts, she thought. "We'll let Elend decide what to do about them."

Spook shrugged, walking over to sit on her rock. "You going to wake him?"

Vin turned back. "Let him sleep a little longer."

Spook shrugged again. He watched as she walked over to the firepit and unwrapped the wood they'd covered the night before, then began to build a fire.

"You've changed, Vin," Spook said.

She continued to work. "Everyone changes," she said. "I'm not a thief anymore, and I have friends to support me."

"I don't mean that," Spook said. "I mean recently. This last week. You're different than you were."

"Different how?"

"I don't know. You don't seem as frightened all the time."

Vin paused. "I've made some decisions. About who I am, and who I will be. About what I want."

She worked quietly for a moment, and finally got a spark to catch. "I'm tired of putting up with foolishness," she finally said. "Other people's foolishness, and my own. I've decided to act, rather than second-guess. Perhaps it's a more immature way of looking at things. But it feels right, for now."

"It's not immature," Spook said.

Vin smiled, looking up at him. Sixteen and hardly grown into his body, he was the same age that she'd been when Kelsier had recruited her. He was squinting against the light, even though the sun was low.

"Lower your tin," Vin said. "No need to keep it on so strong."

Spook shrugged. She could see the uncertainty in him. He wanted so badly to be useful. She knew that feeling.

"What about you, Spook?" she said, turning to gather the breakfast supplies. Broth and mealcakes again. "How have you been lately?"

He shrugged yet again.

I'd almost forgotten what it was like to try and have a conversation with a teenage boy, she thought, smiling.

"Spook . . ." she said, just testing out the name. "What do you think of that nickname, anyway? I remember when everyone called you by your real name." Lestibournes—Vin had tried to spell it once. She'd gotten about five letters in.

"Kelsier gave me my name," Spook said, as if that were reason enough to keep it. And perhaps it was. Vin saw the look in Spook's eyes when he mentioned Kelsier; Clubs might be Spook's uncle, but Kelsier had been the one he looked up to.

Of course, they all had looked up to Kelsier.

"I wish I were powerful, Vin," Spook said quietly, arms folded on his knees as he sat on the rock. "Like you."

"You have your own skills."

"Tin?" Spook asked. "Almost worthless. If I were Mistborn, I could do great things. Be someone important."

"Being important isn't all that wonderful, Spook," Vin said, listening to the thumpings in her head. "Most of the time, it's just annoying."

Spook shook his head. "If I were Mistborn, I could save people—help people, who need it. I could stop people from dying. But . . . I'm just Spook. Weak. A coward."

Vin looked at him, frowning, but his head was bowed, and he wouldn't meet her eyes.

What was that about? she wondered.

Sazed used a bit of strength to help him take the steps three at a time. He burst out of the stairwell just behind Tindwyl, the two of them joining the remaining members of the crew on the wall top. The drums still sounded; each had a different rhythm as it sounded over the city. The mixing beats echoed chaotically from buildings and alleyways.

The northern horizon seemed bare without Straff's army. If only that same emptiness had extended to the northeast, where the koloss camp seemed in turmoil.

"Can anyone make out what's going on?" Breeze asked.

Ham shook his head. "Too far."

"One of my scouts is a Tineye," Clubs said, hobbling over. "He raised the alarm. Said the koloss were fighting."

"My good man," Breeze said, "aren't the foul creatures *always* fighting?"

"More than usual," Clubs said. "Massive brawl."

Sazed felt a swift glimmer of hope. "They're fighting?" he said. "Perhaps they will kill each other!"

Clubs eyed him with one of those looks. "Read one of your books, Terrisman. What do they say about koloss emotions?"

"They only have two," Sazed said. "Boredom and rage. But—"

"This is how they always begin a battle," Tindwyl said quietly. "They start to fight among themselves, enraging more and more of their members, and then . . ."

She trailed off, and Sazed saw it. The dark smudge to the east growing lighter. Dispersing. Resolving into individual members.

Charging the city.

"Bloody hell," Clubs swore, then quickly began to hobble down the steps. "Messengers away!" he bellowed. "Archers to the wall! Secure the river grates! Battalions, form positions! Get ready to fight! Do you want those things breaking in here and getting at your children!"

Chaos followed. Men began to dash in all directions. Soldiers scrambled up the stairwells, clogging the way down, keeping the crew from moving.

It's happening, Sazed thought numbly.

"Once the stairwells are open," Dockson said quietly, "I want each of you to go to your battalion. Tindwyl, you have Tin Gate, in the north by Keep Venture. I might need your advice, but for now, stay with those boys. They'll listen to you—they respect Terrismen. Breeze, you have one of your Soothers in each of battalions four through twelve?"

Breeze nodded. "They aren't much, though. . . ."

"Just have them keep those boys fighting!" Dockson said. "Don't let our men break!"

"A thousand men are far too many for one Soother to handle, my friend," Breeze said.

"Have them do the best they can," Dockson said. "You and Ham take Pewter Gate and Zinc Gate—looks like the koloss are going to hit here first. Clubs should bring in reinforcements."

The two men nodded; then Dockson looked at Sazed. "You know where to go?"

"Yes . . . yes, I think so," Sazed said, gripping the wall. In the air, flakes of ash began to fall from the sky.

"Go, then!" Dockson said as one final squad of archers made its way out of the stairwell.

"My lord Venture!"

Straff turned. With some stimulants, he was able to remain strong enough to stay atop his saddle—though he wouldn't have dared to fight. Of course, he wouldn't have fought anyway. That wasn't his way. One brought armies to do such things.

He turned his animal as the messenger approached. The man puffed, putting hands on knees as he stopped beside Straff's mount, bits of ash swirling on the ground at his feet.

"My lord," the man said. "The koloss army has attacked Luthadel!"

Just as you said, Zane, Straff thought in wonder.

"The koloss, attacking?" Lord Janarle asked, moving his horse up beside Straff's. The handsome lord frowned, then eyed Straff. "You expected this, my lord?"

"Of course," Straff said, smiling.

Janarle looked impressed.

"Pass an order to the men, Janarle," Straff said. "I want this column turned back toward Luthadel."

"We can be there in an hour, my lord!" Janarle said.

"No," Straff said. "Let's take our time. We wouldn't want to overwork our troops, would we?"

Janarle smiled. "Of course not, my lord."

Arrows seemed to have little effect on the koloss.

Sazed stood, transfixed and appalled, atop his gate's watchtower. He wasn't officially in charge of the men, so he didn't have any orders to give. He simply stood with the scouts and messengers, waiting to see if he was needed or not.

That left him plenty of time to watch the horror unfolding. The koloss weren't charging his section of the wall yet, thankfully, and his men stood watching tensely as the creatures barreled toward Tin Gate and Pewter Gate in the distance.

Even far away—the tower letting him see over a section of the city to where Tin Gate lay—Sazed could see the koloss running straight through hailstorms of arrows. Some of the smaller ones appeared to fall dead or wounded, but most just continued to charge. Men murmured on the tower near him.

We aren't ready for this, Sazed thought. *Even with months to plan and anticipate, we aren't ready.*

This is what we get, being ruled over by a god for a thousand years. A thousand years of peace—tyrannical peace, but peace nonetheless. We don't have generals, we have men who know how to order a bath drawn. We don't have tacticians, we have bureaucrats. We don't have warriors, we have boys with sticks.

Even as he watched the oncoming doom, his scholar's mind was analytical. Tapping sight, he could see that many of the distant creatures—especially the larger ones—carried small uprooted trees. They were ready, in their own way, to break into the city. The trees wouldn't be as effective as real battering rams—but then, the city gates weren't built to withstand a real battering in the first place.

Those koloss are smarter than we give them credit for,

he thought. *They can recognize the abstract value of coins, even if they don't have an economy. They can see that they'll need tools to break down our doors, even if they don't know how to make those tools.*

The first koloss wave reached the wall. Men began to toss down rocks and other items. Sazed's own section had similar piles, one just next to the gate arch, beside which he stood. But arrows had almost no effect; what good would a few rocks do? Koloss clumped around the base of the wall, like the water of a dammed-up river. Distant thumps sounded as the creatures began to beat against the gates.

"Battalion sixteen!" a messenger called from below, riding up to Sazed's gate. "Lord Culee!"

"Here!" a man called from the wall top beside Sazed's tower.

"Pewter Gate needs reinforcements immediately! Lord Penrod commands you to bring six companies and follow me!"

Lord Culee began to give the orders. *Six companies . . .* Sazed thought. *Six hundred of our thousand.* Clubs's words from earlier returned to him: Twenty thousand men might seem like a lot, until one saw how thinly they had to be stretched.

The six companies marched away, leaving the courtyard before Sazed's gate disturbingly empty. The four hundred remaining men—three hundred in the courtyard, one hundred on the wall—shuffled quietly.

Sazed closed his eyes and tapped his hearing tinmind. He could hear . . . wood beating on wood. Screams. Human screams. He released the tinmind quickly, then tapped eyesight again, leaning out and looking toward the section of the wall where the battle was being fought. The koloss were throwing back the fallen rocks—and they were far more accurate than the defenders. Sazed jumped as he saw a young soldier's face crushed, his body thrown back off the wall top by the rock's force. Sazed released his tinmind, breathing quickly.

"Be firm, men!" called one of the soldiers on the wall.

He was barely a youth—a nobleman, but he couldn't be more than sixteen. Of course, a lot of the men in the army were that age.

"Stand firm . . ." the young commander repeated. His voice sounded uncertain, and it trailed off as he noticed something in the distance. Sazed turned, following the man's gaze.

The koloss had gotten tired of standing around, piling up at a single gate. They were moving to surround the city, large groups of them breaking up, fording the River Channerel toward other gates.

Gates like Sazed's.

Vin landed directly in the middle of the camp. She tossed a handful of pewter dust into the firepit, then Pushed, blowing coals, soot, and smoke across a pair of surprised guards, who had been fixing breakfast. She reached out and Pulled out the stakes of the three small tents.

All three collapsed. One was unoccupied, but cries came from the other two. The canvas outlined struggling, confused figures—one inside the larger tent, two inside the smaller one.

The guards scrambled back, raising their arms to protect their eyes from the soot and sparks, their hands reaching for swords. Vin raised a fist toward them—and, as they blinked their eyes clear, she let a single coin drop to the ground.

The guards froze, then took their hands off their swords. Vin eyed the tents. The person in charge would be inside the larger one—and he was the man she would need to deal with. Probably one of Straff's captains, though the guards didn't wear Venture heraldry. Perhaps—

Jastes Lekal poked his head out of his tent, cursing as he extricated himself from the canvas. He'd changed much in the two years since Vin had last seen him. However, there had been hints of what the man would become. His thin figure had become spindly; his balding head had fulfilled its promise. Yet, how had his face come to look so haggard . . . so old? He was Elend's age.

"Jastes," Elend said, stepping out of his hiding place in the forest. He walked into the clearing, Spook at his side. "Why are you here?"

Jastes managed to stand as his other two soldiers cut their way out of their tent. He waved them down. "El," he said. "I . . . didn't know where else to go. My scouts said that you were fleeing, and it seemed like a good idea. Wherever you're going, I want to go with you. We can hide there, maybe. We can—"

"Jastes!" Elend snapped, striding forward to stand beside Vin. "Where are your koloss? Did you send them away?"

"I tried," Jastes said, looking down. "They wouldn't go—not once they'd seen Luthadel. And then . . ."

"What?" Elend demanded.

"A fire," Jastes said. "In our . . . supply carts."

Vin frowned.

"Your supply carts?" Elend said. "The carts where you carried your wooden coins?"

"Yes."

"Lord Ruler, man!" Elend said stepping forward. "And you just *left* them there, without leadership, outside our home?"

"They would have killed me, El!" Jastes said. "They were beginning to fight so much, to demand more coins, to demand we attack the city. If I'd stayed, they'd have slaughtered me! They're beasts—beasts that only barely have the shape of man."

"And you left," Elend said. "You abandoned Luthadel to them."

"You abandoned it, too," Jastes said. He walked forward, hands pleading as he approached Elend. "Look, El. I know I was wrong. I thought I could control them. I didn't mean for this to happen!"

Elend fell silent, and Vin could see a hardness growing in his eyes. Not a dangerous hardness, like Kelsier. More of a . . . regal bearing. The sense that he was more than he wanted to be. He stood straight, looking down at the man pleading before him.

"You raised an army of violent monsters and led them in

a tyrannical assault, Jastes," Elend said. "You caused the slaughter of innocent villages. Then, you abandoned that army without leadership or control outside the most populated city in the whole of the Final Empire."

"Forgive me," Jastes said.

Elend looked the man in the eyes. "I forgive you," he said quietly. Then, in one fluid stroke, he drew his sword and sheared Jastes's head from his shoulders. "But my kingdom cannot."

Vin stared, dumbfounded, as the corpse fell to the ground. Jastes's soldiers cried out, drawing their weapons. Elend turned, his face solemn, and raised the point of his bloodied sword toward them. "You think this execution was performed in error?"

The guards paused. "No, my lord," one of them finally said, looking down.

Elend knelt and cleaned his sword on Jastes's cloak. "Considering what he did, this was a better death than he deserved." Elend snapped his sword back into its sheath. "But he was my friend. Bury him. Once you are through, you are welcome to travel with me to Terris, or you may go back to your homes. Choose as you wish." With that, he walked back into the woods.

Vin paused, watching the guards. Solemnly, they moved forward to collect the body. She nodded to Spook, then dashed out into the forest after Elend. She didn't have to go far. She found him sitting on a rock a short distance away, staring at the ground. An ashfall had begun, but most of the flakes got caught in the trees, coating their leaves like black moss.

"Elend?" she asked.

He looked out, staring into the forest. "I'm not sure why I did it, Vin," he said quietly. "Why should I be the one to bring justice? I'm not even king. And yet, it had to be done. I felt it. I feel it still."

She laid a hand on his shoulder.

"He's the first man I've ever killed," Elend said. "He and I had such dreams, once: We'd ally two of the most powerful imperial houses, uniting Luthadel as never before. Ours wasn't to have been a treaty of greed, but a true political alliance intended to help make the city a better place."

He looked up at her. "I think I understand now, Vin, what it is like for you. In a way, we're both knives—both tools. Not for each other, but for this kingdom. This people."

She wrapped her arms around him, holding him, pulling his head to her chest. "I'm sorry," she whispered.

"It had to be done," he said. "The saddest part is, he's right. I abandoned them, too. I should take my own life with this sword."

"You left for a good reason, Elend," Vin said. "You left to protect Luthadel, to make it so Straff wouldn't attack."

"And if the koloss attack before Straff can?"

"Maybe they won't," Vin said. "They don't have a leader—maybe they'll attack Straff's army instead."

"No," Spook's voice said. Vin turned, seeing him approach through the forest, eyes squinting against the light. *That boy burns way too much tin,* she thought.

"What do you mean?" Elend asked, turning.

Spook looked down. "They won't attack Straff's army, El. It won't be there anymore."

"What?" Vin asked.

"I . . ." Spook looked away, shame showing in his face.

I'm a coward. His words from earlier returned to her. "You knew," Vin said. "You knew the koloss were going to attack!"

Spook nodded.

"That's ridiculous," Elend said. "You couldn't have known that Jastes would follow us."

"I didn't," Spook said, a lump of ash falling from a tree behind him, bursting before the wind, and fluttering in a hundred different flakes to the ground. "But my uncle figured that Straff would withdraw his army and let the koloss attack the city. That's why Sazed decided to send us away."

Vin felt a sudden chill.

I've found the location of the Well of Ascension, Sazed had said. *To the north. In the Terris Mountains. . . .*

"Clubs told you this?" Elend was saying.

Spook nodded.

"And you didn't tell me?" Elend demanded, standing.

Oh, no. . . .

Spook paused, then shook his head. "You would have wanted to go back! I didn't want to die, El! I'm sorry. I'm a coward." He cringed, glancing at Elend's sword, shying away.

Elend paused, as if realizing he'd been stepping toward the boy. "I'm not going to hurt you, Spook," he said. "I'm just ashamed of you." Spook lowered his eyes, then sank down to the ground, sitting with his back to an aspen.

The thumpings, getting softer. . . .

"Elend," Vin whispered.

He turned.

"Sazed lied. The Well isn't to the north."

"What?"

"It's at Luthadel."

"Vin, that's ridiculous. We'd have found it."

"We didn't," she said firmly, standing, looking south. Focusing, she could feel the thumpings, washing across her. Pulling her.

South.

"The Well can't be to the south," Elend said. "The legends *all* place it north, in the Terris Mountains."

Vin shook her head, confused. "It's there," she said. "I know it is. I don't know how, but it *is* there."

Elend looked at her, then nodded, trusting her instincts.

Oh, Sazed, she thought. *You probably had good intentions, but you may have doomed us all.* If the city fell to the koloss . . .

"How fast can we get back?" Elend asked.

"That depends," she said.

"Go back?" Spook asked, looking up. "El, they're all *dead.* They told me to tell you the truth once you got to Tathingdwen, so you wouldn't kill yourselves climbing the mountains in the winter for nothing. But, when Clubs talked to me, it was also to say goodbye. I could see it in his eyes. He knew he'd never see me again."

Elend paused, and Vin could see a moment of uncertainty

in his eyes. A flash of pain, of terror. She knew those emotions, because they hit her at the same time.

Sazed, Breeze, Ham. . . .

Elend grabbed her arm. "You have to go, Vin," he said. "There might be survivors . . . refugees. They'll need your help."

She nodded, the firmness of his grip—the determination in his voice—giving her strength.

"Spook and I will follow," he said. "It should only take us a couple of days' hard riding. But an Allomancer with pewter can go faster than any horse over long distances."

"I don't want to leave you," she whispered.

"I know."

It was still hard. How could she run off and leave him, when she'd only just rediscovered him? Yet, she could feel the Well of Ascension even more urgently now that she was sure of its location. And if some of her friends *did* survive the attack . . .

Vin gritted her teeth, then opened up her pouch and pulled out the last of her pewter dust. She drank it down with a mouthful of water from her flask. It scratched her throat going down. *It's not much,* she thought. *It won't let me pewter-drag for long.*

"They're all dead . . ." Spook mumbled again.

Vin turned. The pulses thumped demandingly. From the south.

I'm coming.

"Elend," she said. "Please do something for me. Don't sleep during the night, when the mists are out. Travel during the night, if you can, and keep your wits about you. Watch for the mist spirit—I think it may mean you harm."

He frowned, but nodded.

Vin flared pewter, then took off at a run toward the highway.

My pleas, my teachings, my objections, and even my treasons were all ineffectual. Alendi has other counselors now, ones who tell him what he wants to hear.

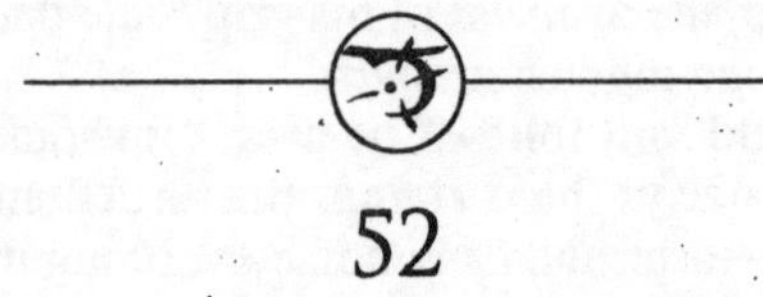

52

BREEZE DID HIS BEST TO pretend he was *not* in the middle of a war. It didn't work very well.

He sat on his horse at the edge of Zinc Gate's courtyard. Soldiers shuffled and clanked, standing in ranks before the gates, waiting and watching their companions atop the wall.

The gates thumped. Breeze cringed, but continued his Soothing. "Be strong," he whispered. "Fear, uncertainty—I take these away. Death may come through those doors, but you can fight it. You can win. Be strong. . . ."

Brass flared like a bonfire within his stomach. He had long since used up his vials, and had taken to choking down handfuls of brass dust and mouthfuls of water, which he had in a steady supply thanks to Dockson's mounted messengers.

How long can this possibly last? he thought, wiping his brow, continuing to Soothe. Allomancy was, fortunately, very easy on the body; Allomantic power came from within the metals themselves, not from the one who burned them. Yet, Soothing was much more complex than other Allomantic skills, and it demanded constant attention.

"Fear, terror, anxiety . . ." he whispered. "The desire to run or give up. I take these from you. . . ." The speaking wasn't necessary, of course, but it had always been his way—it helped keep him focused.

After a few more minutes of Soothing, he checked his pocket watch, then turned his horse and trotted over to the other side of the courtyard. The gates continued to boom, and Breeze wiped his brow again. He noted, with dissatisfaction, that his handkerchief was nearly too damp to do him any good. It was also beginning to snow. The wetness would make the ash stick to his clothing, and his suit would be absolutely ruined.

The suit will be ruined by your blood, Breeze, he told himself. *The time for silliness is over. This is serious. Far too serious. How did you even end up here?*

He redoubled his efforts, Soothing a new group of soldiers. He was one of the most powerful Allomancers in the Final Empire—especially when it came to emotional Allomancy. He could Soothe hundreds of men at once, assuming they were packed close enough together, and assuming that he was focusing on simple emotions. Even Kelsier hadn't been able to manage those numbers.

Yet, the entire crowd of soldiers was beyond even his ability, and he had to do them in sections. As he began work on the new group, he saw the ones he had left begin to wilt, their anxiety taking over.

When those doors burst, these men are going to scatter.

The gates boomed. Men clustered on the walls, throwing down rocks, shooting arrows, fighting with a frantic lack of discipline. Occasionally, an officer would push his way past them, yelling orders, trying to coordinate their efforts, but Breeze was too far away to tell what they were saying. He could just see the chaos of men moving, screaming, and shooting.

And, of course, he could see the return fire. Rocks zipped into the air from below, some cracking against the ramparts. Breeze tried not to think about what was on the other side of the wall, the thousands of enraged koloss beasts. Occasionally, a soldier would drop. Blood dripped down into the courtyard from several sections of the ramparts.

"Fear, anxiety, terror . . ." Breeze whispered.

Allrianne had escaped. Vin, Elend, and Spook were safe. He had to keep focusing on those successes. *Thank you, Sazed, for making us send them away,* he thought.

Hoofbeats clopped behind him. Breeze continued his Soothing, but turned to see Clubs riding up. The general rode his horse with a hunched-over slouch, eyeing the soldiers with one eye open, the other perpetually squeezed closed in a squint. "They're doing well," he said.

"My dear man," Breeze said. "They're *terrified*. Even the ones beneath my Soothing watch those gates like they were some terrible void waiting to suck them in."

Clubs eyed Breeze. "Feeling poetic today, are we?"

"Impending doom has that effect on me," Breeze said as the gates shook. "Either way, I doubt the men are doing 'well.' "

Clubs grunted. "Men are always nervous before a fight. But, these are good lads. They'll hold."

The gates shook and quivered, splinters appearing at the edges. *Those hinges are straining* . . . Breeze thought.

"Don't suppose you can Soothe those koloss?" Clubs asked. "Make them less ferocious?"

Breeze shook his head. "Soothing those beasts has no effect. I've tried it."

They fell silent again, listening to the booming gates. Eventually, Breeze glanced over at Clubs, who sat, unperturbed, on his horse. "You've been in combat before," Breeze said. "How often?"

"Off and on for the better part of twenty years, when I was younger," Clubs said. "Fighting rebellions in the distant dominances, warring against the nomads out in the barrens. The Lord Ruler was pretty good about keeping those conflicts quiet."

"And . . . how did you do?" Breeze asked. "Were you often victorious?"

"Always," Clubs said.

Breeze smiled slightly.

"Of course," Clubs said, glancing at Breeze, "we were the ones with koloss on our side. Damn hard to kill, those beasts."

Great, Breeze thought.

Vin ran.

She'd only been on one "pewter drag" before—with Kelsier, two years ago. While burning pewter at a steady flare, one could run with incredible speed—like a sprinter in their quickest dash—without ever growing tired.

Yet, the process did something to a body. Pewter kept her moving, but it also bottled up her natural fatigue. The juxtaposition made her mind fuzz, bringing on a trancelike state of exhausted energy. Her soul wanted so badly to rest, yet her body just kept running, and running, and running, following the canal towpath toward the south. Toward Luthadel.

Vin was prepared for the effects of pewter dragging this time, and so she handled them far better. She fought off the trance, keeping her mind focused on her goal, not the repetitive motions of her body. However, that focus led her to discomforting thoughts.

Why am I doing this? she wondered. *Why push myself so hard? Spook said it—Luthadel has to have already fallen. There is no need for urgency.*

And yet, she ran.

She saw images of death in her mind. Ham, Breeze, Dockson, Clubs, and dear, dear Sazed. The first real friends she had ever known. She loved Elend, and part of her blessed the others for sending him away from danger. However, the other piece of her was furious at them for sending her away. That fury guided her.

They let me abandon them. They forced *me to abandon them!*

Kelsier had spent months teaching her how to trust. His last words to her in life had been ones of accusation, and they were words she had never been able to escape. *You still have a lot to learn about friendship, Vin.*

He had gone on to risk his life to get Spook and OreSeur out of danger, fighting off—and eventually killing—a Steel Inquisitor. He had done this despite Vin's protests that the risk was pointless.

She had been wrong.

How dare they! she thought, feeling the tears on her cheeks as she dashed down the canal's highwaylike towpath. Pewter gave her inhuman balance, and the speed—which would have been perilous for anyone else—felt natural to her. She didn't trip, she didn't stumble, but an outside observer would think her pace reckless.

Trees whipped by. She leapt washouts and dips in the land. She ran as she had done only once before, and pushed herself even harder than she had on that day. Before, she had been running simply to keep up with Kelsier. Now she ran for those she loved.

How dare they! she thought again. *How dare they not give me the same chance that Kelsier had! How dare they refuse my protection, refuse to let me help them!*

How dare they die. . . .

Her pewter was running low, and she was only a few hours into her run. True, she had probably covered an entire day's worth of walking in those few hours. Yet, somehow, she knew it wouldn't be enough. They were already dead. She was going to be too late, just as when she'd run years before. Too late to save their army. Too late to save her friends.

Vin continued to run. And she continued to cry.

"How did we get here, Clubs?" Breeze asked quietly, still on the floor of the courtyard, before the booming gate. He sat on his horse, amid a muddy mixture of falling snow and ash. The simple, quiet flutterings of white and black seemed to belie the screaming men, the breaking gate, and the falling rocks.

Clubs looked over at him, frowning. Breeze continued stare up, at the ash and snow. Black and white. Lazy.

"We aren't men of principle," Breeze said quietly. "We're thieves. Cynics. You, a man tired of doing the Lord Ruler's bidding, a man determined to see himself get ahead for once. Me, a man of wavering morals who loves to toy with others, to make their emotions my game. How did we end up here? Standing at the head of an army, fighting an idealist's cause? Men like us shouldn't be leaders."

Clubs watched the men in the courtyard. "Guess we're just idiots," he finally said.

Breeze paused, then noticed that glimmer in Clubs's eyes. That spark of humor, the spark that was hard to recognize unless one knew Clubs very well. It was that spark that told the truth—that showed Clubs to be a man of rare understanding.

Breeze smiled. "I guess we are. Like we said before. It's Kelsier's fault. He turned us into idiots who would stand at the front of a doomed army."

"That bastard," Clubs said.

"Indeed," Breeze said.

Ash and snow continued to fall. Men yelled in alarm.

And the gates burst open.

"The eastern gate has been breached, Master Terrisman!" Dockson's messenger said, puffing slightly as he crouched beside Sazed. They both sat beneath the wall-top battlements, listening to the koloss pound on their own gate. The one that had fallen would be Zinc Gate, the one on the easternmost side of Luthadel.

"Zinc Gate is the most well defended," Sazed said quietly. "They will be able to hold it, I think."

The messenger nodded. Ash blew along the wall top, piling in the cracks and alcoves in the stone, the black flakes adulterated by the occasional bit of bone-white snow.

"Is there anything you wish me to report to Lord Dockson?" the messenger asked.

Sazed paused, glancing along his wall's defenses. He'd climbed down from the watchtower, joining the regular ranks of men. The soldiers had run out of stones, though the archers were still working. He peeked over the side of the wall and saw the koloss corpses piling up. However, he also saw the splintered front of the gate. *It's amazing they can maintain such rage for so long,* he thought, ducking back. The creatures continued to howl and scream, like feral dogs.

He sat back against the wet stone, shivering in the chill wind, his toes growing numb. He tapped his brassmind, drawing out the heat he'd stored therein, and his body suddenly flooded with a pleasant sensation of warmth.

"Tell Lord Dockson that I fear for this gate's defenses,"

Sazed said quietly. "The best men were stolen away to help with the eastern gates, and I have little confidence in our leader. If Lord Dockson could send someone else to be in charge, that would be for the best, I think."

The messenger paused.

"What?" Sazed asked.

"Isn't that why he sent you, Master Terrisman?"

Sazed frowned. "Please tell him I have even less confidence in my own ability to lead . . . or to fight . . . than I do in that of our commander."

The messenger nodded and took off, scrambling down the steps toward his horse. Sazed cringed as a rock hit the wall just above him. Chips flipped over the merlon, scattering to the battlement in front of him. *By the Forgotten Gods* . . . Sazed thought, wringing his hands. *What am I doing here?*

He saw motion on the wall beside him, and turned as the youthful soldier captain—Captain Bedes—moved up to him, careful to keep his head down. Tall, with thick hair that grew down around his eyes, he was spindly even beneath his armor. The young man looked like he should have been dancing at balls, not leading soldiers in battle.

"What did the messenger say?" Bedes asked nervously.

"Zinc Gate has fallen, my lord," Sazed replied.

The young captain paled. "What . . . what should we do?"

"Why ask me, my lord?" Sazed asked. "You are in command."

"Please," the man said, grabbing Sazed's arm. "I don't . . . I . . ."

"My lord," Sazed said sternly, forcing down his own nervousness. "You are a nobleman, are you not?"

"Yes . . ."

"Then you are accustomed to giving orders," Sazed said. "Give them now."

"Which orders?"

"It doesn't matter," Sazed said. "Let the men see that you are in charge."

The young man wavered, then yelped and ducked as a

rock took one of the nearby archers in the shoulder, throwing him back into the courtyard. The men below scrambled out of the way of the corpse, and Sazed noticed something odd. A group of people had gathered at the back of the courtyard. Civilians—skaa—in ash-stained clothing.

"What are they doing here?" Sazed asked. "They should be hiding, not standing here to tempt the koloss once the creatures break through!"

"*Once* they break through?" Captain Bedes asked.

Sazed ignored the man. Civilians he could deal with. He was accustomed to being in charge of a nobleman's servants.

"I will go speak to them," Sazed said.

"Yes . . ." Bedes said. "That sounds like a good idea."

Sazed made his way down the steps, which were growing slick and wet with ashen slush, then approached the group of people. There were even more of them than he had assumed; they extended back into the street a short distance. The hundred or so people stood huddled together, watching the gates through the falling snow, looking cold, and Sazed felt a little guilty for his brassmind's warmth.

Several of the people bowed their heads as Sazed approached.

"Why are you here?" Sazed asked. "Please, you must seek shelter. If your homes are near the courtyard, then go hide near the middle of the city. The koloss are likely to begin pillaging as soon as they finish with the army, so the edges of the city are more dangerous."

None of the people moved.

"Please!" Sazed said. "You *must* go. If you stay, you will die!"

"We are not here to die, Holy First Witness," said an elderly man at the front. "We are here to watch the koloss fall."

"Fall?" Sazed asked.

"The Lady Heir will protect us," said another woman.

"The Lady Heir has left the city!" Sazed said.

"Then we will watch you, Holy First Witness," the man said, leaning with one hand on a young boy's shoulder.

"Holy First Witness?" Sazed said. "Why call me this name?"

"You are the one who brought news of the Lord Ruler's death," the man said. "You gave the Lady Heir the spear she used to slay our lord. You were the witness to her actions."

Sazed shook his head. "That may be true, but I am not worthy of reverence. I'm not a holy man, I'm just a . . ."

"A witness," the old man said. "If the Heir is to join this fight, she will appear near you."

"I . . . am sorry . . ." Sazed said, flushing. *I sent her away. I sent your god to safety.*

The people watched him, their eyes reverent. It was wrong; they should not worship him. He was simply an observer.

Except, he wasn't. He had made himself part of this all. It was as Tindwyl had indirectly warned him. Now that Sazed had participated in events, he had become an object of worship himself.

"You should not look at me like that," Sazed said.

"The Lady Heir says the same thing," the old man said, smiling, breath puffing in the cold air.

"That is different," Sazed said. "She is . . ." He cut off, turning as he heard cries from behind. The archers on the wall were waving in alarm, and young Captain Bedes was rushing over to them. *What is—*

A bestial blue creature suddenly pulled itself up onto the wall, its skin streaked and dripping with scarlet blood. It shoved aside a surprised archer, then grabbed Captain Bedes by the neck and tossed him backward. The boy disappeared, falling to the koloss below. Sazed heard the screams even from a distance. A second koloss pulled itself up onto the wall, then a third. Archers stumbled away in shock, dropping their weapons, some shoving others off the ramparts in their haste.

The koloss are jumping up, Sazed realized. *Enough corpses must have piled below. And yet, to jump so high . . .*

More and more creatures were pulling themselves onto the top of the wall. They were the largest of the monsters, the ones over ten feet in height, but that only made it easier for them to sweep the archers out of their way. Men fell to the courtyard, and the pounding on the gates redoubled.

"Go!" Sazed said, waving at the people behind him. Some of them backed away. Many stood firm.

Sazed turned desperately back toward the gates. The wooden structures began to crack, splinters spraying through the snowy, ash-laden air. The soldiers backed away, postures frightened. Finally, with a snap, the bar broke and the right gate burst open. A howling, bleeding, wild mass of koloss began to scramble across the wet stones.

Soldiers dropped their weapons and fled. Others remained, frozen with terror. Sazed stood at their back, between the horrified soldiers and the mass of skaa.

I am not a warrior, he thought, hands shaking as he stared at the monsters. It had been difficult enough to stay calm inside their camp. Watching them scream—their massive swords out, their skin ripped and bloodied as they fell upon the human soldiers—Sazed felt his courage begin to fail.

But if I don't do something, nobody will.

He tapped pewter.

His muscles grew. He drew deeply upon his steelmind as he dashed forward, taking more strength than he ever had before. He had spent years storing up strength, rarely finding occasion to use it, and now he tapped that reserve.

His body changed, weak scholar's arms transforming into massive, bulky limbs. His chest widened, bulging, and his muscles grew taut with power. Days spent fragile and frail focused on this single moment. He shoved his way through the ranks of soldiers, pulling his robe over his head as it grew too restrictive, leaving himself wearing only a vestigial loincloth.

The lead koloss turned to find himself facing a creature nearly his own size. Despite its rage, despite its inhumanness, the beast froze, surprise showing in its beady red eyes.

Sazed punched the monster. He hadn't practiced for war, and knew next to nothing about combat. Yet, at that moment, his lack of skill didn't matter. The creature's face folded around his fist, its skull cracking.

Sazed turned on thick legs, looking back at the startled soldiers. *Say something brave!* he told himself.

"Fight!" Sazed bellowed, surprised at the sudden deepness and strength of his voice.

And, startlingly, they did.

Vin fell to her knees, exhausted on the muddy, ash-soaked highway. Her fingers and knees hit the slushy cold, but she didn't care. She simply knelt, wheezing. She couldn't run any farther. Her pewter was gone. Her lungs burned and her legs ached. She wanted to collapse and curl up, coughing.

It's just the pewter drag, she thought forcibly. She'd pushed her body hard, but hadn't had to pay for it until now.

She coughed a moment longer, groaning, then reached a dripping hand into her pocket and pulled out her last two vials. They had a mixture of all eight base metals, plus duralumin. Their pewter would keep her going for a little bit longer. . . .

But not long enough. She was still hours away from Luthadel. Even with pewter, she wouldn't arrive until long after dark. She sighed, replacing her vials, forcing herself to her feet.

What would I do if I arrived? Vin thought. *Why work so hard? Am I that eager to fight again? To slaughter?*

She knew that she wouldn't arrive in time for the battle. In fact, the koloss had probably attacked days ago. Still, this worried her. Her attack on Cett's keep still flashed horrific images in her head. Things she had done. Death she had caused.

And yet, something felt different to her now. She had accepted her place as a knife. But what was a knife, but another tool? It could be used for evil or for good; it could kill, or it could protect.

That point was moot, considering how weak she felt. It was hard to keep her legs from trembling as she flared tin, clearing her head. She stood on the imperial highway, a sodden, pockmarked roadway that looked—in the softly falling snow—to twist onward for eternity. It ran directly beside the imperial canal, which was a snakelike cut in the land, wide but empty, extending beside the highway.

Before, with Elend, this road had seemed bright and new. Now it looked dark and depressing. The Well thumped, its pulsings growing more powerful with each step she took back toward Luthadel. Yet, it wasn't happening fast enough. Not fast enough for her to stop the koloss from taking the city.

Not fast enough for her friends.

I'm sorry . . . she thought, teeth chattering as she pulled her cloak tight, pewter no longer aiding her against the cold. *I'm so sorry that I failed you.*

She saw a line of smoke in the distance. She looked east, then west, but didn't see much. The flat landscape was clouded in ashen snows.

A village, thought her still-numb mind. *One of many in the area.* Luthadel was by far the dominant city of the small dominance, but there were others. Elend hadn't been able to keep the others completely free of banditry, but they had fared far better than towns in other areas of the Final Empire.

Vin stumbled forward, pressing on through the slushy black puddles toward the village. After about fifteen minutes of walking, she turned off the main highway and made her way up a side road to the village. It was small, even by skaa standards. Just a few hovels, along with a couple of nicer structures.

Not a plantation, Vin thought. *This was once a way village—a place for traveling noblemen to stop for the evening.* The small manor—which would have once been run by a minor noble landlord—was dark. Two of the skaa hovels, however, had light shining through the cracks. The gloomy weather must have convinced the people to retire from their labors early.

Vin shivered, walking up to one of the buildings, her tin-enhanced ears picking out sounds of talking inside. She paused, listening. Children laughed, and men spoke with gusto. She smelled what must have been the beginnings of the evening meal—a simple vegetable stew.

Skaa . . . laughing, she thought. A hovel like this one would have been a place of fear and gloom during the days of the Lord Ruler. Happy skaa had been considered underworked skaa.

We've meant something. It's all meant something.

But was it worth the deaths of her friends? The fall of Luthadel? Without Elend's protection, even this little village would soon be taken by one tyrant or another.

She drank in the sounds of laughter. Kelsier hadn't given up. He had faced the Lord Ruler himself, and his last words had been defiant. Even when his plans had seemed hopeless, his own corpse lying in the street, he had secretly been victorious.

I refuse to give up, she thought, straightening. *I refuse to accept their deaths until I hold their corpses in my arms.*

She raised a hand and pounded on the door. Immediately, the sounds inside stopped. Vin extinguished her tin as the door creaked open. Skaa, especially country skaa, were skittish things. She'd probably have to—

"Oh, you poor thing!" the woman exclaimed, pulling the door open the rest of the way. "Come in out of that snow. What are you doing out there!"

Vin hesitated. The woman was dressed simply, but the clothing was well made to stave off the winter. The firepit in the center of the room glowed with a welcome warmth.

"Child?" the woman asked. Behind, a stocky, bearded man rose to place a hand on the woman's shoulder and study Vin.

"Pewter," Vin said quietly. "I need pewter."

The couple looked at each other, frowning. They probably thought her mind addled. After all, how must she look, hair drenched by the snow, clothing wet and stuck with ash? She only wore simple riding clothing—trousers and a nondescript cloak.

"Why don't you come inside, child?" the man suggested. "Have something to eat. Then we can talk about where you came from. Where are your parents?"

Lord Ruler! Vin thought with annoyance. *I don't look* that *young, do I?*

She threw a Soothing on the couple, suppressing their

concern and suspicion. Then, she Rioted their willingness to help. She wasn't as good as Breeze, but she wasn't unpracticed, either. The couple immediately relaxed.

"I don't have much time," Vin said. "Pewter."

"The lord had some fine diningware in his home," the man said slowly. "But we traded most of that for clothing and farming equipment. I think there are a couple of goblets left. Master Cled—our elder—has them in the other hovel. . . ."

"That might work," Vin said. *Though the metal probably won't be mixed with Allomantic percentages in mind.* It would probably have too much silver or not enough tin, making the pewter work more weakly than it would otherwise.

The couple frowned, then looked at the others in the hovel.

Vin felt despair crawl back into her chest. What was she thinking? Even if the pewter were of the right alloy, it would take time to shave it and produce enough for her to use in running. Pewter burned relatively quickly. She'd need a lot of it. Preparing it could take almost as much time as simply walking to Luthadel.

She turned, looking south, through the dark, snowy sky. Even with pewter, it would take hours more running. What she really needed was a spikeway—a path marked by spikes driven in the ground that an Allomancer could push against, throwing themselves through the air again and again. On such an organized pathway, she'd once traveled from Luthadel to Fellise—an hour's carriage ride—in under ten minutes.

But there was no spikeway from this village to Luthadel; there weren't even ones along the main canal routes. They were too hard to set up, too specific in their usefulness, to be worth the bother of running them long distances. . . .

Vin turned, causing the skaa couple to jump. Perhaps they'd noticed the daggers in her belt, or perhaps it was the look in her eyes, but they no longer looked quite as friendly as they had before.

"Is that a stable?" Vin said, nodding toward one of the dark buildings.

"Yes," the man said hesitantly. "But we have no horses. Only a couple of goats and cows. Surely you don't want to—"

"Horseshoes," Vin said.

The man frowned.

"I need horseshoes," Vin said. "A lot of them."

"Follow me," the man said, responding to her Soothing. He led her out into the cold afternoon. Others followed behind them, and Vin noticed a couple of men casually carrying cudgels. Perhaps it wasn't just Elend's protection that had allowed these people to remain unmolested.

The stocky man threw his weight against the stable door, pushing it to the side. He pointed to a barrel inside. "They were getting rusty anyway," he said.

Vin walked up to the barrel and took out a horseshoe, testing its weight. Then she tossed it up in front of her and Pushed it with a solid flare of steel. It shot away, arcing far through the air until it splashed into a pool some hundred paces away.

Perfect, she thought.

The skaa men were staring. Vin reached into her pocket and pulled out one of her metal vials, downing its contents and restoring her pewter. She didn't have much of it left by pewter-dragging standards, but she had plenty of steel and iron. Both burned slowly. She could Push and Pull on metals for hours yet.

"Prepare your village," she said, burning pewter, then counting out ten horseshoes. "Luthadel is besieged—it might have fallen already. If you get word that it has, I suggest you take your people and move to Terris. Follow the imperial canal directly to the north."

"Who are you?" the man asked.

"Nobody of consequence."

He paused. "You're *her,* aren't you?"

She didn't need to ask what he meant. She simply dropped a horseshoe to the ground behind her.

"Yes," she said quietly, then Pushed off of the shoe.

Immediately, she shot into the air at an angle. As she began to fall, she dropped another horseshoe. However, she waited until she was near the ground to Push against this one; she needed to keep herself going more forward than up.

She'd done all this before. It wasn't that different from using coins to jump around. The trick was going to be to keep herself moving. As she Pushed against the second horseshoe—propelling herself into the snowy air again—she reached behind herself and Pulled hard on the first horseshoe.

The horseshoe wasn't connected to anything, so it leaped into the air after her, crossing the distance through the sky as Vin dropped a third shoe to the ground. She let go of the first shoe, its momentum carrying it through the air above her head. It fell to the ground as she Pushed against the third shoe and Pulled on the second one, now far behind her.

This is going to be tough, Vin thought, frowning with concentration as she passed over the first shoe and Pushed on it. However, she didn't get the angle right, and she fell too far before Pushing. The horseshoe shot out behind her, and didn't give her enough upward momentum to keep her in the air. She hit the ground hard, but immediately Pulled the shoe to herself and tried again.

The first few tries were slow. The biggest problem was getting the angle down. She had to hit the shoe just right, giving it enough downward force to keep it in place on the ground, but enough forward motion to keep her moving in the right direction. She had to land often that first hour, going back to fetch horseshoes. However, she didn't have time for much experimentation, and her determination insisted that she get the process right.

Eventually, she had three shoes working pretty well; it helped that the ground was wet, and that her weight pressed the horseshoes down in the mud, giving her a stronger anchor to use when Pushing herself forward. Soon she was able to add a fourth shoe. The more frequently she Pushed—the more horseshoes she had to Push against—the faster she would go.

By the time she was an hour out of the village, she added a fifth shoe. The result was a continuous flow of flipping metal chunks. Vin Pulled, then Pushed, then Pulled, then

Pushed, moving with continual single-mindedness, juggling herself through the air.

The ground raced beneath her and horseshoes shot through the air above her. The wind became a roar as she Pushed herself faster and faster, steering her pathway to the south. She was a flurry of metal and motion—as Kelsier had been, near the end, when he had killed the Inquisitor.

Except, her metal wasn't meant to kill, but save. *I might not arrive in time,* she thought, air rushing around her. *But I'm not going to give up halfway.*

I have a young nephew, one Rashek. He hates all of Khlennium with the passion of envious youth. He hates Alendi even more acutely—though the two have never met—for Rashek feels betrayed that one of our oppressors should have been chosen as the Hero of Ages.

53

STRAFF WAS ACTUALLY STARTING TO feel quite well as his army crested the last hill to overlook Luthadel. He'd discreetly tried a few drugs from his cabinet, and he was pretty certain he knew which one Amaranta had given him: Black Frayn. A nasty drug indeed. He'd have to wean himself from it slowly—but, for now, a few swallowed leaves made him stronger and more alert than he'd ever been before. In fact, he felt wonderful.

He was sure the same couldn't be said for those in Luthadel. The koloss pooled around the outer wall, still beating on several of the gates on the north and east sides. Smoke rose from inside the city.

"Our scouts say the creatures have broken through four of

the city gates, my lord," said Lord Janarle. "They breached the eastern gate first, and there met with heavy resistance. The northeastern gate fell next, then the northwestern gate, but the troops at both are holding as well. The main breach happened in the north. The koloss are apparently ravaging from that direction, burning and looting."

Straff nodded. *The northern gate,* he thought. *The one closest to Keep Venture.*

"Do we attack, my lord?" Janarle asked.

"How long ago did the northern gate fall?"

"Perhaps an hour ago, my lord."

Straff shook his head leisurely. "Then, let us wait. The creatures worked quite hard to break into the city—we should at least let them have a little fun before we slaughter them."

"Are you sure, my lord?"

Straff smiled. "Once they lose their bloodlust in a few hours, they'll be tired from all the fighting and calm down. *That* will be the best time to strike. They'll be dispersed through the city and weakened from the resistance. We can take them easily, that way."

Sazed gripped his koloss opponent by the throat, forcing back its snarling, distorted face. The beast's skin was stretched so tightly that it had split down the center of the face, revealing bloody muscles above the teeth, around the nose holes. It breathed with husky rage, spraying droplets of spittle and blood across Sazed with each exhalation.

Strength! Sazed thought, tapping his pewtermind for more power. His body became so massive that he feared splitting his own skin. Fortunately, his metalminds had been built to expand, braces and rings that didn't connect on one side so that they could bend. Still, his bulk was daunting. He probably wouldn't have been able to walk or maneuver with such size—but it didn't matter, for the koloss had already knocked him to the ground. All he needed was some extra power in his grip. The creature clawed him in the arm with one hand, reaching behind with the other, grasping its sword. . . .

Sazed's fingers finally crushed the beast's thick neck.

The creature tried to snarl, but no breath came, and it instead thrashed about in frustration. Sazed forced himself to his feet, then hurled the creature toward its companions. With such unnatural strength, even a body eleven feet tall felt light in his fingers. It smashed into a pile of attacking koloss, forcing them backward.

Sazed stood, gasping. *I'm using my strength up so quickly,* he thought, releasing his pewtermind, his body deflating like a wineskin. He couldn't continue tapping his reserves so much. He'd already used up a good half of his strength—strength that had taken decades to store. He still hadn't used his rings, but he had only a few minutes of each attribute in those. They would wait for an emergency.

And that might be what I'm facing now, he thought with dread. They still held Steel Gate Square. Though koloss had broken through the gate, only a few could pass through at once—and only the most massive seemed able to jump up to the wall.

Sazed's little troop of soldiers was sorely pressed, however. Bodies lay scattered in the courtyard. The skaa faithful at the back had begun pulling the wounded to safety. Sazed could hear them groaning behind him.

Koloss corpses littered the square as well, and despite the carnage, Sazed couldn't help but feel a sense of pride at how much it was costing the creatures to force their way inside this portal. Luthadel was not falling easily. Not at all.

The koloss seemed rebuffed for the moment, and though several skirmishes still continued in the courtyard, a new group of monsters was gathering outside the gate.

Outside the gate, Sazed thought, glancing to the side. The creatures had cared to break open only one of the massive door gates, the right one. There were corpses in the square—dozens, perhaps hundreds—but the koloss themselves had cleared many out of the way of the gate itself so that they could get into the courtyard.

Perhaps . . .

Sazed didn't have time to think. He dashed forward, tapping his pewtermind again, giving himself the strength of five men. He picked up the body of a smaller koloss and threw it out the gate. The creatures outside snarled, scattering. There were still hundreds waiting for the chance to get in, but they tripped over the dead in their haste to get out of the way of his projectile.

Sazed slipped on blood as he grabbed a second body, throwing it to the side. "To me!" he screamed, hoping that there were men who could hear, and who could respond.

The koloss realized what he was doing too late. He kicked another body out of the way, then slammed his body against the open door and tapped his ironmind, drawing forth the weight he had stored within it. Immediately, he became far heavier, and that weight crashed against the gate, slamming it closed.

Koloss rushed at the doorway from the other side. Sazed scrambled up against the gate, pushing corpses out of the way, forcing the massive portal closed all the way. He tapped his ironmind further, draining its precious reserve at an alarming rate. He became so heavy he felt his own weight crushing him to the ground, and only his increased strength managed to keep him on his feet. Frustrated koloss pounded on the gate, but he held. Held them back, hands and chest pressed against the rough wood, toes wedged back against uneven cobbles. With his brassmind, he didn't even feel the cold, though ash, snow, and blood mixed at his feet.

Men cried out. Some died. Others slammed their own weight against the gate, and Sazed spared a glance behind. The rest of his soldiers set up a perimeter, protecting the gate from the koloss inside the city. The men fought bravely, backs to the gate, only Sazed's power keeping the portal from flying open.

And yet, they fought. Sazed cried out in defiance, feet slipping, holding the gate as his soldiers killed the remaining koloss in the courtyard. Then, a group of them rushed in from the side, bearing with them a large length of wood. Sazed didn't know where they'd gotten it, nor did he care, as they slid it into place where the gate bar had been.

His weight ran out, the ironmind empty. *I should have stored more of that, over the years,* he thought with a sigh of exhaustion, sinking down before the closed gate. It had seemed like a lot, until he'd been forced to use it so often, using it to shove away koloss or the like.

I usually just stored up weight as a side effect of making myself lighter. That always seemed the more useful way to use iron.

He released pewter, and felt his body deflating. Fortunately, stretching his body in such a manner didn't leave his skin loose. He went back to his usual self, only bearing a dreadful sense of exhaustion and a faint soreness. The koloss continued to beat on the gate. Sazed opened tired eyes, lying bare-chested in the falling snow and ash. His soldiers stood solemnly before him.

So few, he thought. Barely fifty remained of his original four hundred. The square itself was red—as if painted—with bright koloss blood, and it mixed with the darker human kind. Sickly blue lumps of bodies lay alone or in heaps, interspersed with the twisted and torn pieces that were often all that remained of human bodies once they were hit by the brutal koloss swords.

The thumping continued, like low drums, on the other side of the gate. The beating picked up to a frenzied pace, the gate shaking, as the koloss grew more frustrated. They could probably smell the blood, feel the flesh that had so nearly been theirs.

"That board won't hold for long," one of the soldiers said quietly, a bit of ash floating down in front of his face. "And the hinges are splintering. They're going to get through again."

Sazed stumbled to his feet. "And we will fight again."

"My lord!" a voice said. Sazed turned to see one of Dockson's messengers ride around a pile of corpses. "Lord Dockson says that . . ." He trailed off, noticing for the first time that Sazed's gate was closed. "How . . ." the man began.

"Deliver your message, young man," Sazed said tiredly.

"Lord Dockson says you won't get any reinforcements," the man said, reining in his horse. "Tin Gate has fallen, and—"

"Tin Gate?" Sazed asked. *Tindwyl!* "When?"

"Over an hour ago, my lord."

An hour? he thought with shock. *How long have we been fighting?*

"You have to hold here, my lord!" the young man said, turning and galloping back the way he had come.

Sazed took a step to the east. *Tindwyl. . . .*

The thumping on his gate grew louder, and the board began to crack. The men ran for something else to use to secure the gate, but Sazed could see that the mountings that kept the board in place were beginning to pull apart. Once they went, there would be no way to hold the gate closed.

Sazed closed his eyes, feeling the weight of fatigue, reaching into his pewtermind. It was nearly drained. After it was gone, he'd only have the tiny bit of strength in one of the rings.

Yet, what else could he do?

He heard the board snap, and men yelled.

"Back!" Clubs yelled. "Fall into the city!"

The remnants of their army broke apart, pulling back from Zinc Gate. Breeze watched with horror as more and more koloss spilled into the square, overrunning the few men too weak or too wounded to retreat. The creatures swept forward like a great blue tide, a tide with swords of steel and eyes of red.

In the sky, the sun—only faintly visible behind storm clouds—was a bleeding scar that crept toward the horizon.

"Breeze," Clubs snapped, pulling him back. "Time to go."

Their horses had long since bolted. Breeze stumbled after the general, trying not to listen to the snarling from behind.

"Fall back to the harrying positions!" Clubs called to those men who could hear him. "First squad, shore up inside Keep Lekal! Lord Hammond should be there by now, preparing the defenses! Squad two, with me to Keep Hasting!"

Breeze continued on, his mind as numb as his feet. He'd been virtually useless in the battle. He'd tried to take away the men's fear, but his efforts had seemed so inadequate. Like . . . holding a piece of paper up to the sun to make shade.

Clubs held up a hand, and the squad of two hundred men stopped. Breeze looked around. The street was quiet in the falling ash and snow. Everything seemed . . . dull. The sky was dim, the city's features softened by the blanket of black-speckled snow. It seemed so strange to have fled the horrific scene of scarlet and blue to find the city looking so lazy.

"Damn!" Clubs snapped, pushing Breeze out of the way as a raging group of koloss burst from a side street. Clubs's soldiers fell into a line, but another group of koloss—the creatures that had just burst through the gate—came up behind them.

Breeze stumbled, falling in the snow. *That other group . . . it came from the north! The creatures have infiltrated the city this far already?*

"Clubs!" Breeze said, turning. "We—"

Breeze looked just in time to see a massive koloss sword sheer through Clubs's upraised arm, then continue on to hit the general in the ribs. Clubs grunted, thrown to the side, his sword arm—weapon and all—flying free. He stumbled on his bad leg, and the koloss brought his sword down in a two-handed blow.

The dirty snow finally got some color. A splash of red.

Breeze stared, dumbfounded, at the remains of his friend's corpse. Then the koloss turned toward Breeze, snarling.

The likelihood of his own impending death hit, stirring him as even the cold snow couldn't. Breeze scrambled back, sliding in the snow, instinctively reaching out to try and Soothe the creature. Of course, nothing happened. Breeze tried to get to his feet, and the koloss—along with several others—began to bear down on him. At that moment, however, another troop of soldiers fleeing the gate appeared from a cross street, distracting the koloss.

Breeze did the only thing that seemed natural. He crawled inside a building and hid.

"This is all Kelsier's fault," Dockson muttered, making another notation on his map. According to messengers, Ham had reached Keep Lekal. It wouldn't last long.

The Venture grand hall was a flurry of motion and chaos as panicked scribes ran this way and that, finally realizing that koloss didn't care if a man were skaa, scholar, nobleman, or merchant. The creatures just liked to kill.

"He should have seen this coming," Dockson continued. "He left us with this mess, and then he just assumed that we'd find a way to fix it. Well, I can't hide a city from its enemies—not like I hid a crew. Just because we were excellent thieves doesn't mean we'd be any good at running a kingdom!"

Nobody was listening to him. His messengers had all fled, and his guards fought at the keep gates. Each of the keeps had its own defenses, but Clubs—rightly—had decided to use them only as a fallback option. They weren't designed to repel a large-scale attack, and they were too secluded from each other. Retreating to them only fractured and isolated the human army.

"Our real problem is follow-through," Dockson said, making a final notation at Tin Gate, explaining what had happened there. He looked over the map. He'd never expected Sazed's gate to be the last one to hold.

"Follow-through," he continued. "We assumed we could do a better job than the noblemen, but once we had the power, we put them back in charge. If we'd killed the whole lot, perhaps then we could have started fresh. Of course, that would have meant invading the other dominances—which would have meant sending Vin to take care of the most important, most problematic, noblemen. There would have been a slaughter like the Final Empire had never seen. And, if we'd done that . . ."

He trailed off, looking up as one of the massive, majestic stained-glass windows shattered. The others began to explode as well, broken by thrown rocks. A few large koloss jumped through the holes, landing on the shard-strewn marble floor. Even broken, the windows were beautiful, the spiked glass edges twinkling in the evening light. Through one of them, Dockson could see that the storm was breaking, letting sunlight through.

"If we'd done that," Dockson said quietly, "we'd have been no better than beasts."

Scribes screamed, trying to flee as the koloss began the slaughter. Dockson stood quietly, hearing noise behind—grunts, harsh breathing—as koloss approached through the back hallways. He reached for the sword on his table as men began to die.

He closed his eyes. *You know, Kell,* he thought. *I almost started to believe that they were right, that you were watching over us. That you were some sort of god.*

He opened his eyes and turned, pulling the sword from its sheath. Then he froze, staring at the massive beast approaching from behind. *So big!*

Dockson gritted his teeth, sending a final curse Kelsier's way, then charged, swinging.

The creature caught his weapon in an indifferent hand, ignoring the cut it caused. Then, it brought its own weapon down, and blackness followed.

"My lord," Janarle said. "The city has fallen. Look, you can see it burning. The koloss have penetrated all but one of the four gates under attack, and they run wild in the city. They aren't stopping to pillage—they're just killing. Slaughtering. There aren't many soldiers left to oppose them."

Straff sat quietly, watching Luthadel burn. It seemed . . . a symbol to him. A symbol of justice. He'd fled this city once, leaving it to the skaa vermin inside, and when he'd come back to demand it be returned to him, the people had resisted.

They had been defiant. They had earned this.

"My lord," Janarle said. "The koloss army is weakened enough already. Their numbers are hard to count, but the corpses they left behind indicate that as much as a third of their force has fallen. We can take them!"

"No," Straff said, shaking his head. "Not yet."

"My lord?" Janarle said.

"Let the koloss have the damn city," Straff said quietly. "Let them clear it out and burn the whole thing to the ground. Fires can't hurt our atium—in fact, they'll probably make the metal easier to find."

"I . . ." Janarle seemed shocked. He didn't object further, but his eyes were rebellious.

I'll have to take care of him later, Straff thought. *He'll rise against me if he finds that Zane is gone.*

That didn't matter at the moment. The city had rejected him, and so it would die. He'd build a better one in its place.

One dedicated to Straff, not the Lord Ruler.

"Father!" Allrianne said urgently.

Cett shook his head. He sat on his horse, beside his daughter's horse, on a hill to the west of Luthadel. He could see Straff's army, gathered to the north, watching—as he watched—the death throes of a doomed city.

"We have to help!" Allrianne insisted.

"No," Cett said quietly, shrugging off the effects of her Raging his emotions. He'd grown used to her manipulations long ago. "Our help wouldn't matter now."

"We have to do something!" Allrianne said, pulling his arm.

"No," Cett said more forcefully.

"But you came back!" she said. "Why did we return, if not to help?"

"We will help," Cett said quietly. "We'll help Straff take the city when he wishes, then we'll submit to him and hope he doesn't kill us."

Allrianne paled. "That's it?" she hissed. "That's why we returned, so that you can give our kingdom to that monster?"

"What else did you expect?" Cett demanded. "You know me, Allrianne. You know that this is the choice I have to make."

"I thought I knew you," she snapped. "I thought you were a good man, down deep."

Cett shook his head. "The good men are all dead, Allrianne. They died inside that city."

Sazed fought on. He was no warrior; he didn't have honed instincts or training. He calculated that he should have died hours before. And yet, somehow, he managed to stay alive.

Perhaps it was because the koloss didn't fight with skill, either. They were blunt—like their giant, wedgelike swords—and they simply threw themselves at their opponents with little thought of tactics.

That should have been enough. Yet, Sazed held—and where he held, his few men held with him. The koloss had rage on their side, but Sazed's men could see the weak and elderly standing, waiting, just at the edge of the square. The soldiers knew why they fought. This reminder seemed enough to keep them going, even when they began to be surrounded, the koloss working their way into the edges of the square.

Sazed knew, by now, that no relief was going to come. He'd hoped, perhaps, that Straff would decide to take the city, as Clubs had suggested. But it was too late for that; night was approaching, the sun inching toward the horizon.

The end is finally here, Sazed thought as the man next to him was struck down. Sazed slipped on blood, and the move saved him as the koloss swung over his head.

Perhaps Tindwyl had found a way to safety. Hopefully, Elend would deliver the things he and she had studied. *They were important,* Sazed thought, even if he didn't know why.

Sazed attacked, swinging the sword he'd taken from a koloss. He enhanced his muscles in a final burst as he swung, giving them strength right as the sword met koloss flesh.

He hit. The resistance, the wet sound of impact, the shock up his arm—these were familiar to him now. Bright koloss blood sprayed across him, and another of the monsters fell.

And Sazed's strength was gone.

Pewter tapped clean, the koloss sword was now heavy in his hands. He tried to swing it at the next koloss in line, but the weapon slipped from his weak, numb, tired fingers.

This koloss was a big one. Nearing twelve feet tall, it was the largest of the monsters Sazed had seen. Sazed tried to step away, but he stumbled over the body of a recently killed soldier. As he fell, his men finally broke, the last dozen scattering. They'd held well. Too well. Perhaps if he'd let them retreat . . .

No, Sazed thought, looking up at his death. *I did well, I think. Better than any mere scholar should have been able to.*

He thought about the rings on his fingers. They could, perhaps, give him a little bit of an edge, let him run. Flee. Yet, he couldn't summon the motivation. Why resist? Why had he resisted in the first place? He'd known that they were doomed.

You're wrong about me, Tindwyl, he thought. *I do give up, sometimes. I gave up on this city long ago.*

The koloss loomed over Sazed, who still lay half sprawled in the bloody slush, and raised its sword. Over the creature's shoulder, Sazed could see the red sun hanging just above the top of the wall. He focused on that, rather than on the falling sword. He could see rays of sunlight, like . . . shards of glass in the sky.

The sunlight seemed to sparkle, twinkling, coming for him. As if the sun itself were welcoming him. Reaching down to accept his spirit.

And so, I die. . . .

A twinkling droplet of light sparkled in the beam of sunlight, then hit the koloss directly in the back of the skull. The creature grunted, stiffening, dropping its sword. It collapsed to the side, and Sazed lay, stupefied, on the ground for a moment. Then he looked up at the top of the wall.

A small figure stood silhouetted by the sun. Black before the red light, a cloak flapped gently on her back. Sazed blinked. The bit of sparkling light he'd seen . . . it had been a coin. The koloss before him was dead.

Vin had returned.

She jumped, leaping as only an Allomancer could, to soar in a graceful arc above the square. She landed directly in the midst of the koloss and spun. Coins shot out like angry insects, cutting through blue flesh. The creatures didn't drop as easily as humans would have, but the attack got their attention. The koloss turned away from the fleeing soldiers and defenseless townspeople.

The skaa at the back of the square began to chant. It was a bizarre sound to hear in the middle of a battle. Sazed sat up, ignoring his pains and exhaustion as Vin jumped. The city gate suddenly lurched, its hinges twisting. The koloss had already beaten on it so hard. . . .

The massive wooden portal burst free from the wall, Pulled by Vin. *Such power,* Sazed thought numbly. *She must be Pulling on something behind herself—but, that would mean that poor Vin is being yanked between two weights as heavy as that gate.*

And yet, she did it, lifting the gate door with a heave, Pulling it toward herself. The huge hardwood gate crashed through the koloss ranks, scattering bodies. Vin twisted expertly in the air, Pulling herself to the side, swinging the gate to the side as if it were tethered to her by a chain.

Koloss flew in the air, bones cracking, sprayed like splinters before the enormous weapon. In a single sweep, Vin cleared the entire courtyard.

The gate dropped. Vin landed amid a group of crushed bodies, silently kicking a soldier's war staff up into her hands. The remaining koloss outside the gate paused only briefly, then charged. Vin began to attack swiftly, but precisely. Skulls cracked, koloss falling dead in the slush as they tried to pass her. She spun, sweeping a few of them to the ground, spraying ashen red slush across those running up behind.

I . . . I have to do something, Sazed thought, shaking off his stupefaction. He was still bare-chested, the cold ignored because of his brassmind—which was nearly empty. Vin continued to fight, felling koloss after koloss. *Even her strength won't last forever. She can't save the city.*

Sazed forced himself to his feet, then moved toward the back of the square. He grabbed the old man at the front of the crowd of skaa, shaking the man out of his chanting. "You were right," Sazed said. "She returned."

"Yes, Holy First Witness."

"She will be able to give us some time, I think," Sazed said. "The koloss have broken into the city. We need to gather what people we can and escape."

The old man paused, and for a moment Sazed thought he would object—that he would claim Vin would protect them, would defeat the entire army. Then, thankfully, he nodded.

"We'll run out the northern gate," Sazed said urgently. "That is where the koloss first entered the city, and so it is likely that they have moved on from that area."

I hope, Sazed thought, rushing off to raise the warning. The fallback defensive positions were supposed to be the high noble keeps. Perhaps they would find survivors there.

So, Breeze thought, *it turns out that I'm a coward.*

It was not a surprising revelation. He had always said that it was important for a man to understand himself, and he had always been aware of his selfishness. So, he was not at all shocked to find himself huddling against the flaking bricks of an old skaa home, shutting his ears to the screams just outside.

Where was the proud man now? The careful diplomat, the Soother with his immaculate suits? He was gone, leaving behind this quivering, useless mass. He tried several times to burn brass, to Soothe the men fighting outside. However, he couldn't accomplish this most simple of actions. He couldn't even move.

Unless one counted trembling as movement.

Fascinating, Breeze thought, as if looking at himself from the outside, seeing the pitiful creature in the ripped, bloodied suit. *So this is what happens to me, when the stress gets too strong? It's ironic, in a way. I've spent a lifetime controlling the emotions of others. Now I'm so afraid, I can't even function.*

The fighting continued outside. It was going on an awful long time. Shouldn't those soldiers be dead?

"Breeze?"

He couldn't move to see who it was. *Sounds like Ham. That's funny. He should be dead, too.*

"Lord Ruler!" Ham said, coming into Breeze's view. He wore a bloodied sling on one arm. He fell urgently to Breeze's side. "Breeze, can you hear me?"

"We saw him duck in here, my lord," another voice said.

A soldier? "Took shelter from the fight. We could feel him Soothing us, though. Kept us fighting, even when we should have given up. After Lord Cladent died . . ."

I'm a coward.

Another figure appeared. Sazed, looking concerned. "Breeze," Ham said, kneeling. "My keep fell, and Sazed's gate is down. We haven't heard anything from Dockson in over an hour, and we found Clubs's body. Please. The koloss are destroying the city. We need to know what to do."

Well, don't ask me, Breeze said—or tried to say. He thought it came out as a mumble.

"I can't carry you, Breeze," Ham said. "My arm is nearly useless."

Well, that's all right, Breeze mumbled. *You see, my dear man, I don't think I'm of much use anymore. You should move on. It's quite all right if you just leave me here.*

Ham looked up at Sazed, helpless.

"Hurry, Lord Hammond," Sazed said. "We can have the soldiers carry the wounded. We will make our way to Keep Hasting. Perhaps we can find sanctuary there. Or . . . perhaps the koloss will be distracted enough to let us slip out of the city."

Distracted? Breeze mumbled. *Distracted by the killing of other people, you mean. Well, it is somewhat comforting to know that we're* all *cowards. Now, if I could just lie here for a little longer, I might be able to fall asleep . . .*

And forget all of this.

Alendi will need guides through the Terris Mountains. I have charged Rashek with making certain that he and his trusted friends are chosen as those guides.

54

VIN'S STAFF BROKE AS SHE slammed it across a koloss face.

Not again, she thought with frustration, spinning and ramming the broken shard into another creature's chest. She turned and came face-to-face with one of the big ones, a good five feet taller than she.

It thrust its sword toward her. Vin jumped, and the sword collided with broken cobblestones beneath her. She shot upward, not needing any coins to carry herself up to eye level with the creature's twisted face.

They always looked surprised. Even after watching her fight dozens of their companions, they seemed shocked to see her dodge their blows. Their minds seemed to equate size with power; a larger koloss always beat a smaller one. A five-foot-tall human should have been no problem for a monster this big.

Vin flared pewter as she smashed her fist into the beast's head. The skull cracked beneath her knuckles, and the beast fell backward as she dropped back to the ground. Yet, as always, there was another to take its place.

She was getting tired. No, she'd *started* the battle tired. She'd pewter-dragged, then used a convoluted personal spikeway to carry herself across an entire dominance. She was exhausted. Only the pewter in her last metal vial was keeping her upright.

I should have asked Sazed for one of his empty pewterminds! she thought. Feruchemical and Allomantic metals were the same. She could have burned that—though it would probably have been a bracer or a bracelet. To large to swallow.

She ducked to the side as another koloss attacked. Coins didn't stop these things, and they all weighed too much for her to Push them away without an anchor. Besides, her steel and iron reserves were extremely low.

She killed koloss after koloss, buying time for Sazed and the people to get a good head start. Something was different this time—different from when she'd killed at Cett's palace. She felt good. It wasn't just because she killed monsters.

It was because she understood her purpose. And she agreed with it. She *could* fight, *could* kill, if it meant defending those who could not defend themselves. Kelsier might have been able to kill for shock or retribution, but that wasn't good enough for Vin.

And she would never let it be again.

That determination fueled her attacks against the koloss. She used a stolen sword to cut off the legs of one, then threw the weapon at another, Pushing on it to impale the koloss in the chest. Then she Pulled on the sword of a fallen soldier, yanking it into her hand. She ducked backward, but nearly stumbled as she stepped on another body.

So tired, she thought.

There were dozens—perhaps even hundreds—of corpses in the courtyard. In fact, a pile was forming beneath her. She climbed it, retreating slightly as the creatures surrounded her again. They crawled over the corpses of their fallen brethren, rage frothing in their blood-drop eyes. Human soldiers would have given up, going to seek easier fights. The koloss, however, seemed to multiply as she fought them, others hearing the sounds of battle and coming to join in.

She swiped, pewter aiding her strength as she cut off an arm from one koloss, then a leg from another, before finally going for the head of a third. She ducked and dodged, jumping, staying out of their reach, killing as many as she could.

But as desperate as her determination—as strong as her newfound resolve to defend—she knew that she couldn't keep fighting, not like this. She was only one person. She couldn't save Luthadel, not alone.

"Lord Penrod!" Sazed yelled, standing at the gates to Keep Hasting. "You *must* listen to me."

There was no response. The soldiers at the top of the short keep wall were quiet, though Sazed could sense their discomfort. They didn't like ignoring him. In the distance, the battle still raged. Koloss screamed in the night. Soon they would find their way to Sazed and Ham's growing band of several thousand, who now huddled quietly outside Keep Hasting's gate.

A haggard messenger approached Sazed. He was the same one that Dockson had been sending to Steel Gate. He'd lost his horse somewhere, and they'd found him with a group of refugees in the Square of the Survivor.

"Lord Terrisman," the messenger said quietly. "I . . . just got back from the command post. Keep Venture has fallen. . . ."

"Lord Dockson?"

The man shook his head. "We found a few wounded scribes hiding outside the keep. They saw him die. The koloss are still in the building, breaking windows, rooting about. . . ."

Sazed turned back, looking over the city. So much smoke billowed in the sky that it seemed the mists had come already. He'd begun filling his scent tinmind to keep the stench away.

The battle for the city might be over, but now the true tragedy would begin. The koloss in the city had finished killing soldiers. Now they would slaughter the people. There were hundreds of thousands of them, and Sazed knew the creatures would gleefully extend the devastation. No looting. Not when there was killing to be done.

More screams sounded in the night. They'd lost. Failed. And now, the city would *truly* fall.

The mists can't be far away, he thought, trying to give himself some hope. *Perhaps that will give us some cover.*

Still, one image stood out to him. Clubs, dead in the

snow. The wooden disk Sazed had given him earlier that same day tied to a loop around his neck.

It hadn't helped.

Sazed turned back to Keep Hasting. "Lord Penrod," he said loudly. "We are going to try and slip out of the city. I would welcome your troops and your leadership. If you stay here, the koloss will attack this keep and kill you."

Silence.

Sazed turned, sighing as Ham—arm still in a sling—joined him. "We have to go, Saze," Ham said quietly.

"You're bloody, Terrisman."

Sazed turned. Ferson Penrod stood on the top of his wall, looking down. He still looked immaculate in his nobleman's suit. He even wore a hat against the snow and ash. Sazed looked down at himself. He still wore only his loincloth. He hadn't had time to worry about clothing, particularly with his brassmind to keep him warm.

"I've never seen a Terrisman fight," Penrod said.

"It is not a common occurrence, my lord," Sazed replied.

Penrod looked up, staring out over the city. "It's falling, Terrisman."

"That is why we must go, my lord," Sazed said.

Penrod shook his head. He still wore Elend's thin crown. "This is my city, Terrisman. I will not abandon it."

"A noble gesture, my lord," Sazed said. "But these with me are your people. Will you abandon them in their flight northward?"

Penrod paused. Then he just shook his head again. "There will be no flight northward, Terrisman. Keep Hasting is among the tallest structures in the city—from it, we can see what the koloss are doing. They will not let you escape."

"They may turn to pillaging," Sazed said. "Perhaps we can get by them and escape."

"No," Penrod said, his voice echoing hauntingly across the snowy streets. "My Tineye claims the creatures have already attacked the people you sent to escape through the northern gate. Now the koloss have turned this way. They're coming for us."

As cries began to echo through the distant streets, coming

closer, Sazed knew that Penrod's words must be true. "Open your gates, Penrod!" Sazed yelled. "Let the refugees in!" *Save their lives for a few more pitiful moments.*

"There is no room," Penrod said. "And there is no time. We are doomed."

"You must let us in!" Sazed screamed.

"It is odd," Penrod said, voice growing softer. "By taking this throne from the Venture boy, I saved his life—and I ended my own. I could not save the city, Terrisman. My only consolation is that I doubt Elend could have done so either."

He turned to go, walking down somewhere beyond the wall.

"Penrod!" Sazed yelled.

He did not reappear. The sun was setting, the mists were appearing, and the koloss were coming.

Vin cut down another koloss, then jumped back, Pushing herself off of a fallen sword. She shot away from the pack, breathing heavily, bleeding from a couple of minor cuts. Her arm was growing numb; one of the creatures had punched her there. She could kill—kill better than anyone she knew. However, she couldn't fight forever.

She landed on a rooftop, then stumbled, falling to kneel in a pile of snow. The koloss called and howled behind her, and she knew they would come, chasing her, hounding her. She'd killed hundreds of them, but what was a few hundred when compared with an army of over twenty thousand?

What did you expect? she thought to herself. *Why keep fighting once you knew Sazed was free? Did you think to stop them all? Kill every koloss in the army?*

Once, she'd stopped Kelsier from rushing an army by himself. He had been a great man, but still just one person. He couldn't have stopped an entire army—no more than she could.

I have to find the Well, she thought with determination, burning bronze, the thumpings—which she'd been ignoring during the battle—becoming loud to her ears.

And yet, that left her with the same problem as before.

She knew it was in the city now; she could feel the thumpings all around her. Yet, they were so powerful, so omnipresent, that she couldn't sense a direction from them.

Besides, what proof did she have that finding the Well would even help? If Sazed had lied about the location—had gone so far as to draw up a fake map—then what else had he lied about? The power might stop the mists, but what good would that do for Luthadel, burning and dying?

She knelt in frustration, pounding the top of the roof with her fists. She had proven too weak. What good was it to return—what good was it to decide to protect—if she couldn't do anything to help?

She knelt for a few moments, breathing in gasps. Finally, she forced herself to her feet and jumped into the air, throwing down a coin. Her metals were nearly gone. She barely had enough steel to carry her through a few jumps. She ended up slowing near Kredik Shaw, the Hill of a Thousand Spires. She caught one of the spikes at the top of the palace, spinning in the night, looking out over the darkening city.

It was burning.

Kredik Shaw itself was silent, quiet, left alone by looters of both races. Yet, all around her, Vin saw light in the darkness. The mists glowed with a haunting light.

It's like . . . like that day two years ago, she thought. *The night of the skaa rebellion.* Except, on that day, the firelight had come from the torches of the rebels as they marched on the palace. This night, a revolution of a different type was occurring. She could hear it. She had her tin burning, and she forced herself to flare it, opening her ears. She heard the screams. The death. The koloss hadn't finished their killing work by destroying the army. Not by far.

They had only just begun.

The koloss are killing them all, she thought, shivering as the fires burned before her. *Elend's people, the ones he left behind because of me. They're dying.*

I am his knife. Their knife. Kelsier trusted me with them. I should be able to do something. . . .

She dropped toward the ground, skidding off an angled rooftop, landing in the palace courtyard. Mists gathered around her. The air was thick. And not just with ash and snow; she could smell death in its breezes, hear screams in its whispers.

Her pewter ran out.

She slumped to the ground, a wave of exhaustion hitting her so hard that everything else seemed inconsequential. She suddenly knew she shouldn't have relied on the pewter so much. Shouldn't have pushed herself so hard. But, it had seemed like the only way.

She felt herself begin to slip into unconsciousness.

But people were screaming. She could hear them—had heard them before. Elend's city . . . Elend's people . . . dying. Her friends were out there somewhere. Friends that Kelsier had trusted her to protect.

She gritted her teeth, shoving aside the exhaustion for a moment longer, struggling up to her feet. She looked through the mists, toward the phantom sounds of terrified people. She began to dash toward them.

She couldn't jump; she was out of steel. She couldn't even run very fast, but as she forced her body to move, it responded better and better, fighting off the dull numbness that she'd earned from relying on pewter so long.

She burst out of an alleyway, skidding in the snow, and found a small group of people running before a koloss raiding party. There were six of the beasts, small ones, but still dangerous. Even as Vin watched, one of the creatures cut down an elderly man, slicing him nearly in two. Another picked up a small girl, slamming her against the side of a building.

Vin dashed forward, past the fleeing skaa, whipping out her daggers. She still felt exhausted, but adrenaline helped her somewhat. She had to keep moving. Keep going. To stop was to die.

Several of the beasts turned toward her, eager to fight. One swung for her, and Vin let herself slide in the slush—slipping closer to him—before cutting the back of his leg. He howled in pain as her knife got caught in his baggy skin. She managed to yank it free as a second creature swung.

I feel so slow! she thought with frustration, barely sliding to her feet before backing away from the creature's reach. His sword sprayed chill water across her, and she jumped forward, planting a dagger in the creature's eye.

Suddenly thankful for the times Ham had made her practice without Allomancy, she caught the side of a building to steady herself in the slush. Then she threw herself forward, shouldering the koloss with the wounded eye—he was clawing at the dagger and yelling—into his companions. The koloss with the young girl turned, shocked, as Vin rammed her other dagger into his back. He didn't drop, but he did let go of the child.

Lord Ruler, these things are tough! she thought, cloak whipping as she grabbed the child and dashed away. *Especially when you're not tough yourself. I need some more metals.*

The girl in Vin's arms cringed as a koloss howl sounded, and Vin spun, flaring her tin to keep herself from falling unconscious from her fatigue. The creatures weren't following, however—they were arguing over a bit of clothing the dead man had been wearing. The howl sounded again, and this time, Vin realized, it had come from another direction.

People began to scream again. Vin looked up, only to find those she'd just rescued facing down an even larger group of koloss.

"No!" Vin said, raising a hand. But, they'd run far while she'd been fighting. She wouldn't even have been able to see them, save for her tin. As it was, she was able to see painfully well as the creatures began to lay into the small group with their thick-bladed swords.

"No!" Vin screamed again, the deaths startling her, shocking her, standing as a reminder of all the deaths she'd been unable to prevent.

"No. No! *No!*"

Pewter, gone. Steel, gone. Iron, gone. She had nothing.

Or . . . she had one thing. Not even pausing to think on what prompted her to use it, she threw a duralumin-enhanced Soothing at the beasts.

It was as if her mind slammed into Something. And then, that Something shattered. Vin skidded to a halt, shocked, child still in her arms as the koloss stopped, frozen in their horrific act of slaughter.

What did I just do? she thought, tracing through her muddled mind, trying to connect why she had reacted as she had. Was it because she had been frustrated?

No. She knew that the Lord Ruler had built the Inquisitors with a weakness: Remove a particular spike from their back, and they'd die. He had also built the kandra with a weakness. The koloss had to have a weakness, too.

TenSoon called the koloss . . . his cousins, she thought.

She stood upright, the dark street suddenly quiet save for the whimpering skaa. The koloss waited, and she could feel herself in their minds. As if they were an extension of her own body, the same thing she had felt when she'd taken control of TenSoon's body.

Cousins indeed. The Lord Ruler had built the koloss with a weakness—the same weakness as the kandra. He *had* given himself a way to keep them in check.

And suddenly she understood how he'd controlled them all those long years.

Sazed stood at the head of his large band of refugees, snow and ash—the two now indistinguishable in the misty darkness—falling around him. Ham sat to one side, looking drowsy. He'd lost too much blood; a man without pewter would have died by now. Someone had given Sazed a cloak, but he had used it to wrap the comatose Breeze. Even though be barely tapped his brassmind for warmth, Sazed himself wasn't cold.

Maybe he was just getting too numb to care.

He held two hands up before him, forming fists, ten rings sparkling against the light of the group's single lantern. Koloss approached from the dark alleyways, their forms huddled shadows in the night.

Sazed's soldiers backed away. There was little hope left in them. Sazed alone stood in the quiet snow, a spindly, bald scholar, nearly naked. He, the one who preached the religions of the fallen. He, who had given up hope at the end. He, who should have had the most faith of all.

Ten rings. A few minutes of power. A few minutes of life.

He waited as the koloss gathered. The beasts grew strangely silent in the night. They stopped approaching. They stood still, a line of dark, moundlike silhouettes in the night.

Why don't they attack! Sazed thought, frustrated.

A child whimpered. Then, the koloss began to move again. Sazed tensed, but the creatures didn't walk forward. They split, and a quiet figure walked through the center of them.

"Lady Vin?" Sazed asked. He still hadn't had a chance to speak with her since she'd saved him at the gate. She looked exhausted.

"Sazed," she said tiredly. "You lied to me about the Well of Ascension."

"Yes, Lady Vin," he said.

"That isn't important now," she said. "Why are you standing naked *outside* of the keep's walls?"

"I . . ." He looked up at the koloss. "Lady Vin, I—"

"Penrod!" Vin shouted suddenly. "Is that you up there?"

The king appeared. He looked as confused as Sazed felt.

"Open your gates!" Vin yelled.

"Are you mad?" Penrod yelled back.

"I'm not sure," Vin said. She turned, and a group of koloss moved forward, walking quietly as if commanded. The largest one picked Vin up, holding her up high, until she was nearly level with the top of the keep's low wall. Several guards atop the wall shied away from her.

"I'm tired, Penrod," Vin said. Sazed had to tap his hearing tinmind to listen in on her words.

"We're all tired, child," Penrod said.

"I'm particularly tired," Vin said. "I'm tired of the games. I'm tired of people dying because of arguments between their leaders. I'm tired of good men being taken advantage of."

Penrod nodded quietly.

"I want you to gather our remaining soldiers," Vin said, turning to look over the city. "How many do you have in there?"

"About two hundred," he said.

Vin nodded. "The city is not lost—the koloss have fought against the soldiers, but haven't had much time to turn on the population yet. I want you to send out your soldiers to find any groups of koloss that are pillaging or killing. Protect the people, but don't attack the koloss if you can help it. Send a messenger for me instead."

Remembering Penrod's bullheadedness earlier, Sazed thought the man might object. He didn't. He just nodded.

"What do we do then?" Penrod asked.

"I'll take care of the koloss," Vin said. "We'll go reclaim Keep Venture first—I'm going to need more metals, and there are plenty stored there. Once the city is secure, I want you and your soldiers to put out those fires. It shouldn't be too hard; there aren't a lot of buildings left that can burn."

"Very well," Penrod said, turning to call out his orders.

Sazed watched in silence as the massive koloss lowered Vin to the ground. It stood quietly, as if it were a monster hewn of stone, and not a breathing, bleeding, living creature.

"Sazed," Vin said softly. He could sense the fatigue in her voice.

"Lady Vin," Sazed said. To the side, Ham finally shook himself out of his stupor, looking up in shock as he noticed Vin and the koloss.

Vin continued to look at Sazed, studying him. Sazed had trouble meeting her eyes. But, she was right. They could talk about his betrayal later. There were other, more important tasks that had to be accomplished. "I realize you probably have work for me to do," Sazed said, breaking the silence. "But, might I instead be excused? There is . . . a task I wish to perform."

"Of course, Sazed," Vin said. "But first, tell me. Do you know if any of the others survived?"

"Clubs and Dockson are dead, my lady," Sazed said. "I have not seen their bodies, but the reports were from reliable sources. You can see that Lord Hammond is here, with us, though he has suffered a very bad wound."

"Breeze?" she asked.

Sazed nodded to the lump that lay huddled beside the wall. "He lives, thankfully. His mind, however, appears to be reacting poorly to the horrors he saw. It could simply be a form of shock. Or . . . it could be something more lasting."

Vin nodded, turning to Ham. "Ham. I need pewter."

He nodded dully, pulling out a vial with his good hand. He tossed it to her. Vin downed it, and immediately her fatigue seemed to lessen. She stood up straighter, her eyes becoming more alert.

That can't be healthy, Sazed thought with worry. *How much of that has she been burning?*

Step more energetic, she turned to walk toward her koloss.

"Lady Vin?" Sazed asked, causing her to turn around. "There is still an army out there."

"Oh, I know," Vin said, turning to take one of the large, wedgelike koloss swords from its owner. It was actually a few inches taller than she was.

"I am well aware of Straff's intentions," she said, hefting the sword up onto her shoulder. Then she turned in to the snow and mist, walking toward Keep Venture, her strange koloss guards tromping after her.

It took Sazed well into the night to complete his self-appointed task. He found corpse after corpse in the frigid night, many of them iced over. The snow had stopped falling, and the wind had picked up, hardening the slush to slick ice. He had to break some of the corpses free to turn them over and inspect their faces.

Without his brassmind to provide heat, he could never have performed his grisly job. Even so, he had found himself some warmer clothing—a simple brown robe and a set of boots. He continued working through the night, the wind swirling flakes of snow and ice around him. He started at the gate, of course. That was where the most corpses were. However, he eventually had to move into alleyways and thoroughfares.

He found her body sometime near morning.

The city had stopped burning. The only light he had was his lantern, but it was enough to reveal the strip of fluttering cloth in a snowbank. At first, Sazed thought it was just another bloodied bandage that had failed in its purpose. Then he saw a glimmer of orange and yellow, and he moved over—he no longer had the strength to rush—and reached into the snow.

Tindwyl's body cracked slightly as he rolled it out. The blood on her side was frozen, of course, and her eyes were iced open. Judging from the direction of her flight, she had been leading her soldiers to Keep Venture.

Oh, Tindwyl, he thought, reaching down to touch her face. It was still soft, but dreadfully cold. After years of being abused by the Breeders, after surviving so much, she had found this. Death in a city where she hadn't belonged, with a man—no, a *half* man—who did not deserve her.

He released his brassmind, and let the night's cold wash over him. He didn't want to feel warm at the moment. His lantern flickered uncertainly, illuminating the street, shadowing the icy corpse. There, in that frozen alley of Luthadel, looking down at the corpse of the woman he loved, Sazed realized something.

He didn't know what to do.

He tried to think of something proper to say—something proper to think—but suddenly, all of his religious knowledge seemed hollow. What was the use in giving her a burial? What was the value in speaking the prayers of a long-dead god? What good was he? The religion of Dadradah hadn't helped Clubs; the Survivor hadn't come to rescue the thousands of soldiers who had died. What was the point?

None of Sazed's knowledge gave him comfort. He accepted the religions he knew—believed in their value—but that didn't give him what he needed. They didn't assure him that Tindwyl's spirit still lived. Instead, they made him question. If so many people believed so many different things, how could any one of them—or, even, anything at all—actually be true?

The skaa called Sazed holy, but at that moment he

realized that he was the most profane of men. He was a creature who knew three hundred religions, yet had faith in none of them.

So, when his tears fell—and nearly began to freeze to his face—they gave him as little comfort as his religions. He moaned, leaning over the frozen corpse.

My life, he thought, *has been a sham.*

Rashek is to try and lead Alendi in the wrong direction, to discourage him, or otherwise foil his quest. Alendi doesn't know that he has been deceived, that we've all been deceived, and he will not listen to me now.

55

STRAFF WOKE IN THE COLD morning and immediately reached for a leaf of Black Frayn. He was beginning to see the benefits of his addiction. It woke him quickly and easily, making his body feel warm despite the early hour. When he might have once taken an hour to get ready, he was up in minutes, dressed, prepared for the day.

And glorious that day would be.

Janarle met him outside his tent, and the two walked through the bustling camp. Straff's boots cracked on half ice, half snow as he made his way to his horse.

"The fires are out, my lord," Janarle explained. "Probably due to the snows. The koloss probably finished their rampaging and took shelter from the cold. Our scouts are afraid to get too close, but they say the city is like a graveyard. Quiet and empty, save for the bodies."

"Maybe they actually killed each other off," Straff said cheerfully, climbing into his saddle, breath puffing in the crisp morning air. Around him, the army was forming up.

Fifty thousand soldiers, eager at the prospect of taking the city. Not only was there plundering to be done, but moving into Luthadel would mean roofs and walls for all of them.

"Perhaps," Janarle said, mounting.

Wouldn't that be convenient, Straff thought with a smile. *All of my enemies dead, the city and its riches mine, and no skaa to worry about.*

"My lord!" someone cried.

Straff looked up. The field between his camp and Luthadel was colored gray and white, the snow stained by ash. And gathering on the other side of that field were koloss.

"Looks like they are alive after all, my lord," Janarle said.

"Indeed," Straff said, frowning. There were still a lot of the creatures. They piled out of the western gate, not attacking immediately, instead gathering in a large body.

"Scout counts say there are fewer of them than there were," Janarle said after a short time. "Perhaps two-thirds their original number, maybe a bit fewer. But, they *are* koloss. . . ."

"But they're abandoning their fortifications," Straff said, smiling, Black Frayn warming his blood, making him feel like he was burning metals. "And they're coming to us. Let them charge. This should be over quickly."

"Yes, my lord," Janarle said, sounding a little less certain. He frowned, then, pointing toward the southern section of the city. "My . . . lord?"

"What now?"

"Soldiers, my lord," Janarle said. "Human ones. Looks to be several thousand of them."

Straff frowned. "They should all be dead!"

The koloss charged. Straff's horse shuffled slightly as the blue monsters ran across the gray field, the human troops falling into more organized ranks behind.

"Archers!" Janarle shouted. "Prepare first volley!"

Perhaps I shouldn't be at the front, Straff thought suddenly. He turned his horse, then noticed something. An arrow suddenly shot from the midst of the charging koloss.

But, koloss didn't use bows. Besides, the monsters were

still far away, and that object was far too big to be an arrow anyway. A rock, perhaps? It seemed larger than . . .

It began to fall down toward Straff's army. Straff stared into the sky, riveted by the strange object. It grew more distinct as it fell. It wasn't an arrow, nor was it a rock.

It was a person—a person with a flapping mistcloak.

"No!" Straff yelled. *She's supposed to be gone!*

Vin screamed down from her duralumin-fueled Steeljump, massive koloss sword light in her hands. She hit Straff directly in the head with the sword, then continued on downward, slamming into the ground, throwing up snow and frozen dirt with the power of her impact.

The horse fell into two pieces, front and back. What remained of the former king slid to the ground with the equine corpse. She looked at the remnants, smiled grimly, and bid Straff farewell.

Elend had, after all, warned him what would happen if he attacked the city.

Straff's generals and attendants stood around her in a stunned circle. Behind her, the koloss army barreled forward, confusion in Straff's ranks making the archer volleys ragged and less effective.

Vin kept a tight hold on her sword, then Pushed outward with a duralumin-enhanced Steelpush. Riders were thrown, their beasts tripped by their shoes, and soldiers sprayed backward from her in a circle of several dozen yards. Men screamed.

She downed another vial, restoring both steel and pewter. Then she jumped up, seeking out generals and other officers to attack. As she moved, her koloss troops hit the front ranks of Straff's army, and the real carnage began.

"What are they doing?" Cett asked, hurriedly throwing on his cloak as he was placed and tied into his saddle.

"Attacking, apparently," said Bahmen, one of his aides. "Look! They're working *with* the koloss."

Cett frowned, doing up his cloak clasp. "A treaty?"

"With koloss?" Bahmen asked.

Cett shrugged. "Who's going to win?"

"No way to tell, my lord," the man said. "Koloss are—"

"What is this!" Allrianne demanded, riding up the snowy incline, accompanied by a couple of abashed guards. Cett had, of course, ordered them to keep her in the camp—but he had also, of course, expected that she'd get past them eventually.

At least I can count on her to be slowed down by getting ready in the morning, he thought with amusement. She wore one of her dresses, immaculately arranged, her hair done. If a building were burning down, Allrianne would still pause to do her makeup before escaping.

"Looks like the battle has begun," Cett said, nodding toward the fighting.

"*Outside* the city?" Allrianne asked, riding up next to him. Then she brightened. "They're attacking Straff's position!"

"Yes," Cett said. "And that leaves the city—"

"We have to help them, Father!"

Cett rolled his eyes. "You know we're going to do nothing of the sort. We'll see who wins. If they're weak enough—which I hope they will be—we'll attack them. I didn't bring all of my forces back with me, but maybe . . ."

He trailed off as he noticed the look in Allrianne's eyes. He opened his mouth to speak, but before he could do so, she kicked her horse into motion.

Her guards cursed, dashing forward—too late—to try and grab her reins. Cett sat, stunned. This was a little insane, even for her. She wouldn't dare . . .

She galloped down the hill toward the battle. Then she paused, as he had expected. She turned, looking back at him.

"If you want to protect me, Father," she yelled, "you'd better charge!"

With that, she turned and started galloping again, her horse throwing up puffs of snow.

Cett didn't move.

"My lord," Bahmen said. "Those forces look almost evenly matched. Fifty thousand men against a force of some twelve thousand koloss and about five thousand men. If we were to add our strength to either side . . ."

Damn fool girl! he thought, watching Allrianne gallop away.

"My lord?" Bahmen asked.

Why did I come to Luthadel in the first place? Was it because I really thought I could take the city? Without Allomancers, with my homeland in revolt? Or, was it because I was looking for something? A confirmation of the stories. A power like I saw on that night, when the Heir almost killed me.

How exactly did they get the koloss to fight with them, anyway?

"Gather our forces!" Cett commanded. "We're marching to the defense of Luthadel. And somebody send riders after that fool daughter of mine!"

Sazed rode quietly, his horse moving slowly in the snow. Ahead of him, the battle raged, but he was far enough behind it to be out of danger. He'd left the city behind, where Luthadel's surviving women and elderly watched from the walls. Vin had saved them from the koloss. The real miracle would be to see if she could save them from the other two armies.

Sazed didn't ride into the fight. His metalminds were mostly empty, and his body was nearly as tired as his mind. He simply brought his horse to a halt, its breath puffing in the cold as he sat alone on the snowy plain.

He didn't know how to deal with Tindwyl's death. He felt . . . hollow. He wished that he could just stop feeling. He wished that he could go back and defend her gate, instead of his own. Why hadn't he gone in search of her when he'd heard of the northern gate's fall? She'd still been alive then. He might have been able to protect her. . . .

Why did he even care anymore? Why bother?

But, the ones who had faith were right, he thought. *Vin came back to defend the city. I lost hope, but they never did.*

He started his horse forward again. The sounds of battle

came in the distance. He tried to focus on anything but Tindwyl, but his thoughts kept returning to things he had studied with her. The facts and stories became more precious, for they were a link to her. A painful link, but one he couldn't bear to discard.

The Hero of Ages was not simply to be a warrior, he thought, still riding slowly toward the battlefield. *He was a person who united others, who brought them together. A leader.*

He knew that Vin thought she was the Hero. But Tindwyl was right: it was too much of a coincidence. And, he wasn't even certain what he believed anymore. If anything.

The Hero of Ages was removed from the Terris people, he thought, watching the koloss attack. *He was not royalty himself, but came to it eventually.*

Sazed pulled his horse up, pausing in the center of the open, empty field. Arrows stuck from the snow around him, and the ground was thoroughly trampled. In the distance, he heard a drum. He turned, watching as an army of men marched over a rise to the west. They flew Cett's banner.

He commanded the forces of the world. Kings rode to his aid.

Cett's forces joined the battle against Straff. There was a crash of metal against metal, bodies grunting, as a new front came under attack. Sazed sat on the field between the city and the armies. Vin's forces were still outnumbered, but as Sazed watched, Straff's army began to pull back. It broke into pieces, its members fighting without direction. Their movements bespoke terror.

She's killing their generals, he thought.

Cett was a clever man. He himself rode to battle, but he stayed near the back of his ranks—his infirmities requiring him to remain tied into his saddle and making it difficult for him to fight. Still, by joining the battle, he ensured that Vin would not turn her koloss on him.

For there was really no doubt in Sazed's mind who would win this conflict. Indeed, before even an hour had passed, Straff's troops began to surrender in large groups.

The sounds of battle died down, and Sazed kicked his horse forward.

Holy First Witness, he thought. *I don't know that I believe that. But, either way, I should be there for what happens next.*

The koloss stopped fighting, standing silently. They parted for Sazed as he rode up through their ranks. Eventually, he found Vin standing, bloodied, her massive koloss sword held on one shoulder. Some koloss pulled a man forward—a lord in rich clothing and a silvery breastplate. They dropped him before Vin.

From behind, Penrod approached with an honor guard, led by a koloss. Nobody spoke. Eventually, the koloss parted again, and this time a suspicious Cett rode forward, surrounded by a large group of soldiers and led by a single koloss.

Cett eyed Vin, then scratched his chin. "Not much of a battle," he said.

"Straff's soldiers were afraid," Vin said. "They're cold, and they have no desire to fight koloss."

"And their leaders?" Cett asked.

"I killed them," Vin said. "Except this one. Your name?"

"Lord Janarle," said Straff's man. His leg appeared broken, and koloss held him by either arm, supporting him.

"Straff is dead," Vin said. "You control this army now."

The nobleman bowed his head. "No, I don't. You do."

Vin nodded. "On your knees," she said.

The koloss dropped Janarle. He grunted in pain, but then bowed forward. "I swear my army to you," he whispered.

"No," Vin said sharply. "Not to me—to the rightful heir of House Venture. He is your lord now."

Janarle paused. "Very well," he said. "Whatever you wish. I swear loyalty to Straff's son, Elend Venture."

The separate groups stood in the cold. Sazed turned as Vin did, looking at Penrod. Vin pointed at the ground. Penrod quietly dismounted, then bowed himself to the ground.

"I swear as well," he said. "I give my loyalty to Elend Venture."

Vin turned to Lord Cett.

"You expect this of me?" the bearded man said, amused.

"Yes," Vin said quietly.

"And if I refuse?" Cett asked.

"Then I'll kill you," Vin said quietly. "You brought armies to attack my city. You threatened my people. I won't slaughter your soldiers, make them pay for what you did, but I *will* kill you, Cett."

Silence. Sazed turned, looking back at the lines of immobile koloss, standing in the bloodied snow.

"That is a threat, you know," Cett said. "Your own Elend would never stand for such a thing."

"He's not here," Vin said.

"And what do you think he'd say?" Cett asked. "He'd tell me not to give in to such a demand—the honorable Elend Venture would never give in simply because someone threatened his life."

"You're not the man that Elend is," Vin said. "And you know it."

Cett paused, then smiled. "No. No, I'm not." He turned to his aides. "Help me down."

Vin watched quietly as the guards undid Cett's legs, then lifted him down to the snowy ground. He bowed. "Very well, then. I swear myself to Elend Venture. He's welcome to my kingdom . . . assuming he can take it back from that damn obligator who now controls it."

Vin nodded, turning to Sazed. "I need your help, Sazed."

"Whatever you command, Mistress," Sazed said quietly.

Vin paused. "Please don't call me that."

"As you wish," Sazed said.

"You're the only one here I trust, Sazed," Vin said, ignoring the three kneeling men. "With Ham wounded and Breeze . . ."

"I will do my best," Sazed said, bowing his head. "What is it you want me to do?"

"Secure Luthadel," Vin said. "Make certain the people are sheltered, and send for supplies from Straff's storehouses. Get these armies situated so that they won't kill each other, then send a squad to fetch Elend. He'll be coming south on the canal highway."

Sazed nodded, and Vin turned to the three kneeling kings. "Sazed is my second. You will obey him as you would Elend or myself."

They each nodded in turn.

"But, where will you be?" Penrod asked, looking up.

Vin sighed, suddenly looking terribly weak. "Sleeping," she said, and dropped her sword. Then she Pushed against it, shooting backward into the sky, toward Luthadel.

He left ruin in his wake, but it was forgotten, Sazed thought, turning to watch her fly. *He created kingdoms, and then destroyed them as he made the world anew.*

We had the wrong gender all along.

THE END OF PART FIVE

PART SIX

WORDS IN STEEL

If Rashek fails to lead Alendi astray, then I have instructed the lad to kill Alendi.

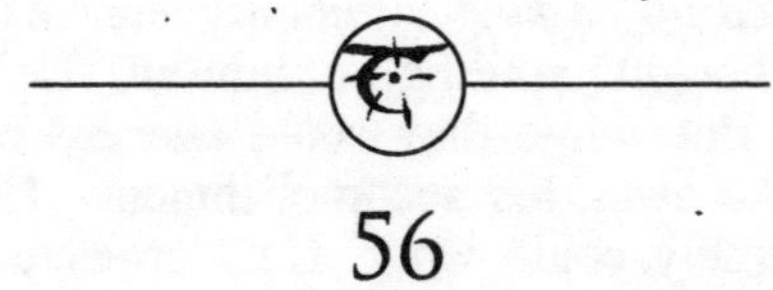

56

HOW CAN VIN STAND THIS? Elend wondered. He could barely see twenty feet in the mists. Trees appeared as apparitions around him as he walked, their branches curling around the road. The mist almost seemed to live: it moved, swirled, and blew in the cold night air. It snatched up his puffs of breath, as if drawing a piece of him into it.

He shivered and kept walking. The snow had melted patchily over the last few days, leaving heaps in shadowed areas. The canal road, thankfully, was mostly clear.

He walked with a pack over his shoulder, carrying only the necessities. At Spook's suggestion, they'd traded their horses at a village several days back. They'd rode the creatures hard the last few days, and it was Spook's estimation that trying to keep them fed—and alive—for the last leg of their trip to Luthadel wouldn't be worth the effort.

Besides, whatever was going to happen at the city had likely already occurred. So Elend walked, alone, in the darkness. Despite the eeriness, he kept his word and traveled only at night. Not only was it Vin's will, but Spook claimed that night was safer. Few travelers braved the mists. Therefore, most bandits didn't bother watching roadways at night.

Spook prowled ahead, his keen senses allowing him to detect danger before Elend blundered into it. *How does that work, anyway?* Elend wondered as he walked. *Tin is supposed to make you see better. But what does it matter how far you can see, if the mists just obscure everything?*

Writers claimed that Allomancy could help a person pierce the mists, somehow. Elend had always wondered what that was like. Of course, he had also wondered what it felt like to feel the strength of pewter, or to fight with atium. Allomancers were uncommon, even among Great Houses. Yet, because of the way Straff had treated him, Elend had always felt guilty that he hadn't been one.

But, I ended up as king eventually, even without Allomancy, he thought, smiling to himself. He'd lost the throne, true. But, while they could take his crown, they could not take away his accomplishments. He'd proved that an Assembly could work. He'd protected the skaa, given them rights, and a taste of freedom they'd never forget. He'd done more than anyone would have expected of him.

Something rustled in the mists.

Elend froze, staring out into the darkness. *Sounds like leaves,* he thought nervously. *Something moving across them? Or . . . just the wind blowing them?*

He decided at that moment that there was nothing more unnerving than staring into the misty darkness, seeing ever-shifting silhouettes. A part of him would rather face down a koloss army than stand alone, at night, in an unknown forest.

"Elend," someone whispered.

Elend spun. He put a hand to his chest as he saw Spook approaching. He thought about chastising the boy for sneaking up on him—but, well, there wasn't really any other way to approach in the mists.

"Did you see something?" Spook asked quietly.

Elend shook his head. "But I think I heard something."

Spook nodded, then darted off into the mists again. Elend stood, uncertain whether he should continue on, or just wait. He didn't have to debate for very long. Spook returned a few moments later.

"Nothing to worry about," Spook said. "Just a mistwraith."

"What?" Elend asked.

"Mistwraith," Spook said. "You know. Big goopy things? Related to kandra? Don't tell me you haven't read about them?"

"I have," Elend said, nervously scanning the darkness. "But, I never thought I'd be out in the mists with one."

Spook shrugged. "It's probably just following our scent, hoping that we'll leave some trash for it to eat. The things are harmless, mostly."

"Mostly?" Elend asked.

"You probably know more about them than I do. Look, I didn't come back here to chat about scavengers. There's light up ahead."

"A village?" Elend asked, thinking back to when they'd come this way before.

Spook shook his head. "Looks like watchfires."

"An army?"

"Maybe. I'm just thinking you should wait behind for a bit. It could be awkward if you wander into a scout post."

"Agreed," Elend said.

Spook nodded, then took off into the mists.

And Elend was alone in the darkness again. He shivered, pulling his cloak close, and eyed the mists in the direction from which he'd heard the mistwraith. Yes, he'd read about them. He knew they were supposed to be harmless. But the thought of something crawling out there—its skeleton made from random sets of bones—watching him . . .

Don't focus on that, Elend told himself.

He turned his attention, instead, to the mists. Vin was right about one thing, at least. They were lingering longer and longer despite the sunrise. Some mornings, they remained a full hour after the sun came up. He could easily imagine the disaster that would befall the land should the mists persist all day. Crops would fail, animals would starve, and civilization would collapse.

Could the Deepness really be something so simple? Elend's own impressions of the Deepness were seated in scholarly tradition. Some writers dismissed the entire thing as a legend—a rumor used by the obligators to enhance their god's aura of divinity. The majority accepted the historical definition of the Deepness—a dark monster that had been slain by the Lord Ruler.

And yet, thinking of it as the mist made some sense. How could a single beast, no matter how dangerous, threaten an entire land? The mists, though . . . they could be destructive. Kill plants. Perhaps even . . . kill people, as Sazed had suggested?

He eyed it shifting around him, playful, deceptive. Yes, he could see it as the Deepness. Its reputation—more frightening than a monster, more dangerous than an army—was one it would deserve. In fact, watching it as he was, he could see it trying to play tricks on his mind. For instance, the mist bank directly in front of him seemed to be forming shapes. Elend smiled as his mind picked out images in the mists. One almost looked like a person standing there, in front of him.

The person stepped forward.

Elend jumped, taking a slight step backward, his foot crunching on a bit of ice-crusted snow. *Don't be silly,* he told himself. *Your mind is playing tricks on you. There's nothing—*

The shape in the mists took another step forward. It was indistinct, almost formless, and yet it seemed real. Random movements in the mists outlined its face, its body, its legs.

"Lord Ruler!" Elend yelped, jumping back. The thing continued to regard him.

I'm going mad, he thought, hands beginning to shake. The mist figure stopped a few feet in front of him and then raised its right arm and pointed.

North. Away from Luthadel.

Elend frowned, glancing in the direction the figure pointed. There was nothing but more empty mists. He turned back toward it, but it stood quietly, arm upraised.

Vin spoke of this thing, he remembered, forcing down his fear. *She tried to tell me about it. And I thought she was making things up!* She was right—just as she'd been right about the mists staying longer in the day, and the possibility of the mists being the Deepness. He was beginning to wonder which of them was the scholar.

The mist figure continued to point.

"What?" Elend asked, his own voice sounding haunting in the silent air.

It stepped forward, arm still raised. Elend put a useless hand to his sword, but held his ground.

"Tell me what you wish of me!" he said forcefully.

The thing pointed again. Elend cocked his head. It certainly didn't seem threatening. In fact, he felt an unnatural feeling of peace coming from it.

Allomancy? he thought. *It's Pulling on my emotions!*

"Elend?" Spook's voice drifted out of the mists.

The figure suddenly dissolved, its form melting into the mists. Spook approached, his face dark and shadowed in the night. "Elend? What were you saying?"

Elend took his hand off his sword, standing upright. He eyed the mists, still not completely convinced that he wasn't seeing things. "Nothing," he said.

Spook glanced back the way he had come. "You should come look at this."

"The army?" Elend asked, frowning.

Spook shook his head. "No. The refugees."

"The Keepers are dead, my lord," the old man said, sitting across from Elend. He didn't have a tent, only a blanket stretched between several poles. "Either dead, or captured."

Another man brought Elend a cup of warm tea, his demeanor servile. Both wore the robes of stewards, and while their eyes bespoke exhaustion, their robes and hands were clean.

Old habits, Elend thought, nodding thankfully and taking a sip of the tea. *Terris's people might have declared themselves independent, but a thousand years of servitude cannot be so easily thrown off.*

The camp was an odd place. Spook said he counted nearly a thousand people in it—a nightmare of a number to care for, feed, and organize in the cold winter. Many were elderly, and the men were mostly stewards: eunuchs bred for genteel service, with no experience in hunting.

"Tell me what happened," Elend said.

The elderly steward nodded, his head shaking. He didn't seem particularly frail—actually, he had that same air of controlled dignity that most stewards exhibited—but his body had a slow, chronic tremble.

"The Synod came out into the open, my lord, once the empire fell." He accepted a cup of his own, but Elend noticed that it was only half full—a precaution that proved wise as the elderly steward's shaking nearly spilled its contents. "They became our rulers. Perhaps it was not wise to reveal themselves so soon."

Not all Terrismen were Feruchemists; in fact, very few were. The Keepers—people like Sazed and Tindwyl—had been forced into hiding long ago by the Lord Ruler. His paranoia that Feruchemical and Allomantic lines might mix—thereby potentially producing a person with his same powers—had led him to try and destroy all Feruchemists.

"I've known Keepers, friend," Elend said softly. "I find it hard to believe that they could have been easily defeated. Who did this?"

"Steel Inquisitors, my lord," the old man said.

Elend shivered. *So that's where they've been.*

"There were dozens of them, my lord," the old man said. "They attacked Tathingdwen with an army of koloss brutes. But, that was just a distraction, I think. Their real goal was the Synod and the Keepers themselves. While our army, such as it was, fought the beasts, the Inquisitors themselves struck at the Keepers."

Lord Ruler . . . Elend thought, stomach twisting. *So, what do we do with the book Sazed told us to deliver to the Synod? Do we pass it on to these men, or keep it?*

"They took the bodies with them, my lord," the old man said. "Terris is in ruins, and that is why we are going south. You said you know King Venture?"

"I . . . have met him," Elend said. "He ruled Luthadel, where I am from."

"Will he take us in, do you think?" the old man asked. "We have little hope anymore. Tathingdwen was the Terris capital, but even it wasn't large. We are few, these days—the Lord Ruler saw to that."

"I . . . do not know if Luthadel can help you, friend."

"We can serve well," the old man promised. "We were prideful to declare ourselves free, I think. We struggled to survive even before the Inquisitors attacked. Perhaps they did us a favor by casting us out."

Elend shook his head. "Koloss attacked Luthadel just over a week ago," he said quietly. "I am a refugee myself, Master Steward. For all I know, the city itself has fallen."

The old man fell silent. "Ah, I see," he finally said.

"I'm sorry," Elend said. "I was traveling back to see what happened. Tell me—I traveled this way not long ago. How is it that I missed you in my journey north?"

"We didn't come by the canal route, my lord," the old man said. "We cut across country, straight down, so that we could gather supplies at Suringshath. You . . . have no further word of events at Luthadel, then? There was a senior Keeper in residence there. We were hoping, perhaps, to seek her counsel."

"Lady Tindwyl?" Elend asked.

The old man perked up. "Yes. You know her?"

"She was an attendant at the king's court," Elend said.

"Keeper Tindwyl could be considered our leader now, I think," the old man said. "We aren't certain how many traveling Keepers there are, but she is the only known member of the Synod who was out of the city when we were attacked."

"She was still in Luthadel when I left," Elend said.

"Then she might live still," the old man said. "We can hope, I think. I thank you, traveler, for your information. Please, make yourself comfortable in our camp."

Elend nodded, rising. Spook stood a short distance away, in the mists near a pair of trees. Elend joined him.

The people kept large fires burning in the night, as if to defy the mists. The light did some good in dispelling the mists' power—and yet the light seemed to accentuate them as well, creating three-dimensional shadows that bewildered the eye. Spook leaned against the scraggly tree trunk, looking around at things Elend couldn't see. Elend could hear, however, some of what Spook must be inspecting. Crying children. Coughing men. Shuffling livestock.

"It doesn't look good, does it?" Elend said quietly.

Spook shook his head. "I wish they'd take down all these fires," he muttered. "The light hurts my eyes."

Elend glanced to the side. "They aren't *that* bright."

Spook shrugged. "They're just wasting wood."

"Forgive them their comfort, for now. They'll have little enough of it in the weeks to come." Elend paused, looking over at a passing squad of Terris "soldiers"—a group of men who were obviously stewards. Their posture was excellent, and they walked with a smooth grace, but Elend doubted they knew how to use any weapons beyond a cooking knife.

No, there is no army in Terris to help my people.

"You sent Vin back to gather our allies," Spook said quietly. "To bring them up to meet with us, perhaps to seek refuge in Terris."

"I know," Elend said.

"We can't gather in Terris, though," Spook said. "Not with the Inquisitors up there."

"I know," Elend said again.

Spook was silent for a moment. "The whole world is falling apart, El," he finally said. "Terris, Luthadel . . ."

"Luthadel has *not* been destroyed," Elend said, looking sharply at Spook.

"The koloss—"

"Vin will have found a way to stop them," Elend said. "For all we know, she already found the power at the Well of Ascension. We need to keep going. We can, and will, rebuild whatever was lost. Then we'll worry about helping Terris."

Spook paused, then nodded and smiled. Elend was surprised to see how much his confident words seemed to soothe the boy's concerns. Spook leaned back, eyeing Elend's still steaming cup of tea, and Elend handed it over with a mumble that he didn't like heartroot tea. Spook drank happily.

Elend, however, found matters more troubling than he'd admitted. *The Deepness returning, ghosts in the mist, and Inquisitors making a play for the Terris Dominance. What else have I been ignoring?*

It is a distant hope. Alendi has survived assassins, wars, and catastrophes. And yet, I hope that in the frozen mountains of Terris, he may finally be exposed. I hope for a miracle.

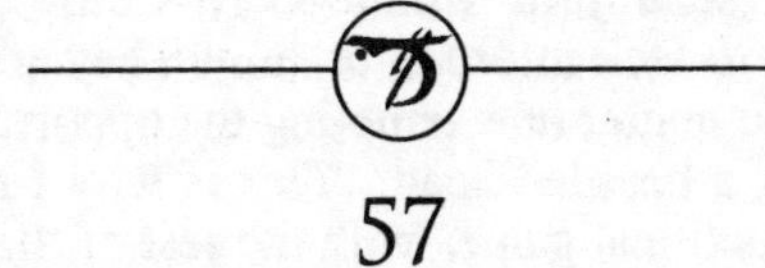

57

"LOOK, WE ALL KNOW WHAT we need to do," Cett said, pounding the table. "We've got our armies here, ready and willing to fight. Now, let's go get my damn country back!"

"The empress gave us no command to do such a thing," Janarle said, sipping his tea, completely unfazed by Cett's lack of decorum. "I, personally, think that we should wait at least until the emperor returns."

Penrod, the oldest of the men in the room, had enough tact to look sympathetic. "I understand that you are concerned for your people, Lord Cett. But we haven't even had a week to rebuild Luthadel. It is far too early to be worrying about expanding our influence. We cannot possibly authorize these preparations."

"Oh, leave off, Penrod," Cett snapped. "You're not in charge of us."

All three men turned to Sazed. He felt very awkward, sitting at the head of the table in Keep Venture's conference chamber. Aides and attendants, including some of Dockson's bureaucrats, stood at the perimeter of the sparse room, but only the three rulers—now kings beneath Elend's imperial rule—sat with Sazed at the table.

"I think that we should not be hasty, Lord Cett," Sazed said.

"This isn't haste," Cett said, pounding the table again. "I just want to order scout and spy reports, so that we can have information we need when we invade!"

"If we *do* invade," Janarle said. "If the emperor decides to recover Fadrex City, it won't happen until this summer, at the very earliest. We have far more pressing concerns. My armies have been away from the Northern Dominance for too long. It is basic political theory that we should stabilize what we have *before* we move into new territory."

"Bah!" Cett said, waving an indifferent hand.

"You may send your scouts, Lord Cett," Sazed said. "But they are to seek information only. They are to engage in no raids, no matter how tempting the opportunity."

Cett shook a bearded head. "*This* is why I never bothered to play political games with the rest of the Final Empire. Nothing gets done because everyone is too busy scheming!"

"There is much to be said for subtlety, Lord Cett," Penrod said. "Patience brings the greater prize."

"Greater prize?" Cett asked. "What did the Central Dominance earn itself by waiting? You waited right up until the moment that your city fell! If you hadn't been the ones with the best Mistborn . . ."

"Best Mistborn, my lord?" Sazed asked quietly. "Did you not see her take command of the koloss? Did you not see her leap across the sky like an arrow in flight? Lady Vin isn't simply the 'best Mistborn.' "

The group fell silent. *I have to keep them focused on her,* Sazed thought. *Without Vin's leadership—without the threat of her power—this coalition would dissolve in three heartbeats.*

He felt so inadequate. He couldn't keep the men ontopic, and he couldn't do much to help them with their various problems. He could just keep reminding them of Vin's power.

The trouble was, he didn't really want to. He was feeling something very odd in himself, feelings he usually didn't have. Disconcern. Apathy. Why did anything that these men talked about matter? Why did anything matter, now that Tindwyl was dead?

He gritted his teeth, trying to force himself to focus.

"Very well," Cett said, waving a hand. "I'll send the scouts. Has that food arrived from Urteau yet, Janarle?"

The younger nobleman grew uncomfortable. "We . . . may have trouble with that, my lord. It seems that an unwholesome element has been rabble-rousing in the city."

"No wonder you want to send troops back to the Northern Dominance!" Cett accused. "You're planning to conquer your kingdom back and leave mine to rot!"

"Urteau is *much* closer than your capital, Cett," Janarle said, turning back to his tea. "It only makes sense to set me up there before we turn our attention westward."

"We will let the empress make that decision," Penrod said. He liked to act the mediator—and by doing so, he made himself seem above the issues. In essence, he put himself in control by putting himself in between the other two.

Not all that different from what Elend tried to do, Sazed thought, *with our armies.* The boy had more of a sense of political strategy than Tindwyl had ever credited him with.

I shouldn't think about her, he told himself, closing his eyes. Yet, it was hard not to. Everything Sazed did, everything he thought, seemed wrong because she was gone. Lights seemed dimmer. Motivations were more difficult to reach. He found that he had trouble even *wanting* to pay attention to the kings, let alone give them direction.

It was foolish, he knew. How long had Tindwyl been back in his life? Only a few months. Long ago, he had resigned himself to the fact that he would never be loved—in general—and that he certainly would never have *her* love. Not only did he lack manhood, but he was a rebel and a dissident—a man well outside of the Terris orthodoxy.

Surely her love for him had been a miracle. Yet, whom did he thank for that blessing, and whom did he curse for stealing her away? He knew of hundreds of gods. He would hate them all, if he thought it would do any good.

For the sake of his own sanity, he forced himself to get distracted by the kings again.

"Listen," Penrod was saying, leaning forward, arms on the tabletop. "I think we're looking at this the wrong way, gentlemen. We shouldn't be squabbling, we should be happy. We are in a very unique position. In the time since the Lord Ruler's empire fell, dozens—perhaps hundreds—of men have tried to set themselves up as kings in various ways. The one thing they shared, however, was that they all lacked stability.

"Well, it appears that *we* are going to be forced to work together. I am starting to see this in a favorable light. I will give my allegiance to the Venture couple—I'll even live with Elend Venture's eccentric views of government—if it means that I'll still be in power ten years from now."

Cett scratched at his beard for a moment, then nodded. "You make a good point, Penrod. Maybe the first good one I've ever heard out of you."

"But we can't continue trying to assume that we know what we are to do," Janarle said. "We need direction. Surviving the next ten years, I suspect, is going to depend heavily on my not ending up dead on the end of that Mistborn girl's knife."

"Indeed," Penrod said, nodding curtly. "Master Terrisman. When can we expect the empress to take command again?"

Once again, all three pairs of eyes turned to Sazed.

I don't really care, Sazed thought, then immediately felt guilty. Vin was his friend. He did care. Even if it was hard to care about anything for him. He looked down in shame. "Lady Vin is suffering greatly from the effects of an extended pewter drag," he said. "She pushed herself very hard this last year, and then ended it by running all the way back to Luthadel. She is in great need of rest. I think we should let her be for a time longer."

The others nodded, and returned to their discussion. Sazed's mind, however, turned to Vin. He'd understated her malady, and he was beginning to worry. A pewter drag drained the body, and he suspected that she'd been forcing herself to stay awake with the metal for months now.

When a Keeper stored up wakefulness, he slept as if in a coma for a time. He could only hope that the effects of such a terrible pewter drag were the same, for Vin hadn't awoken a single time since her return a week before. Perhaps she'd awake soon, like a Keeper who came out of sleep.

Perhaps it would last longer. Her koloss army waited outside the city, controlled—apparently—even though she was unconscious. But for how long? Pewter dragging could kill, if the person had pushed themselves too hard.

What would happen to the city if she never woke up?

Ash was falling. *A lot of ashfalls lately,* Elend thought as he and Spook emerged from the trees and looked out over the Luthadel plain.

"See," Spook said quietly, pointing. "The city gates are broken."

Elend frowned. "But the koloss are camped *outside* the city." Indeed, Straff's army camp was also still there, right where it had been.

"Work crews," Spook said, shading his face against the sunlight to protect his overly sensitive Allomancer's eyes. "Looks like they're burying corpses outside the city."

Elend's frown deepened. *Vin. What happened to her? Is she all right?*

He and Spook had cut across country, taking a cue from the Terrismen, to make certain that they didn't get discovered by patrols from the city. Indeed, this day they'd broken their pattern, traveling a little bit during the day so that they could arrive at Luthadel just before nightfall. The mists would soon be coming, and Elend was fatigued—both from rising early and from walking so long.

More than that, he was tired of not knowing what had happened to Luthadel. "Can you see whose flag is set over the gates?" he asked.

Spook paused, apparently flaring his metals. "Yours," he finally said, surprised.

Elend smiled. *Well, either they managed to save the city somehow, or this is a very elaborate trap to capture me.* "Come on," he said, pointing to a line of refugees who were being allowed back into the city—likely those who had fled before, returning for food now that the danger was past. "We'll mix with those and make our way in."

Sazed sighed quietly, shutting the door to his room. The kings were finished with the day's arguments. Actually, they were starting to get along quite well, considering the fact that they'd all tried to conquer each other just a few weeks before.

Sazed knew he could take no credit for their newfound amiability, however. He had other preoccupations.

I've seen many die, in my days, he thought, walking into the room. *Kelsier. Jadendwyl. Crenda. People I respected. I never wondered what had happened to their spirits.*

He set his candle on the table, the fragile light illuminating a few scattered pages, a pile of strange metal nails taken from koloss bodies, and one manuscript. Sazed sat down at the table, fingers brushing the pages, remembering the days spent with Tindwyl, studying.

Maybe this is why Vin put me in charge, he thought. *She knew I'd need something to take my mind off Tindwyl.*

And yet, he was finding more and more that he didn't *want* to take his mind off her. Which was more potent? The pain of memory, or the pain of forgetting? He was a Keeper—it was his life's work to remember. Forgetting, even in the name of personal peace, was not something that appealed to him.

He flipped through the manuscript, smiling fondly in the dark chamber. He'd sent a cleaned-up, rewritten version with Vin and Elend to the north. This, however, was the original. The frantically—almost desperately—scribbled manuscript made by two frightened scholars.

As he fingered the pages, the flickering candlelight revealed Tindwyl's firm, yet beautiful, script. It mixed easily with paragraphs written in Sazed's own, more reserved hand. At times, a page would alternate between their different hands a dozen different times.

He didn't realize that he was crying until he blinked, sending loose a tear, which hit the page. He looked down, stunned as the bit of water caused a swirl in the ink.

"What now, Tindwyl?" he whispered. "Why did we do this? You never believed in the Hero of Ages, and I never believed in anything, it appears. What was the point of all this?"

He reached up and dabbed the tear with his sleeve, preserving the page as best he could. Despite his tiredness, he began to read, selecting a random paragraph. He read to remember. To think of days when he hadn't worried about why they were studying. He had simply been content to do what he enjoyed best, with the person he had come to love most.

We gathered everything we could find on the Hero of Ages and the Deepness, he thought, reading. *But so much of it seems contradictory.*

He flipped through to a particular section, one that Tindwyl had insisted that they include. It contained the several most blatant self-contradictions, as declared by Tindwyl. He read them over, giving them fair consideration for the first time. This was Tindwyl the scholar—a cautious skeptic. He fingered through the passages, reading her script.

The Hero of Ages will be tall of stature, one read. *A man who cannot be ignored by others.*

The power must not be taken, read another. *Of this, we are certain. It must be held, but not used. It must be released.* Tindwyl had found that condition foolish, since other sections talked about the Hero using the power to defeat the Deepness.

All men are selfish, read another. *The Hero is a man who can see the needs of all beyond his own desires.* "If all men are selfish," Tindwyl had asked, "then how can the Hero be selfless, as is said in other passages? And, indeed, how can a humble man be expected to conquer the world?"

Sazed shook his head, smiling. At times, her objections had been very well conceived—but at other times, she had just been struggling to offer another opinion, no matter how much of a stretch it required. He ran his fingers across the page again, but paused on the first paragraph.

Tall of stature, it said. That wouldn't refer to Vin. It hadn't come from the rubbing, but another book. Tindwyl had included it because the rubbing, the more trustworthy source, said he'd be short. Sazed flipped through the book to the complete transcription of Kwaan's iron-plate testimony, searching for the passage.

Alendi's height struck me the first time I saw him, it read. *Here was a man who was small of stature, but who seemed to tower over others, a man who demanded respect.*

Sazed frowned. Before, he'd argued that there was no contradiction, for one passage could be interpreted as referring to the Hero's presence or character, rather than just his physical height. Now, however, Sazed paused, really seeing Tindwyl's objections for the first time.

And something felt wrong to him. He looked back at his book, scanning the contents of the page.

There was a place for me in the lore of the Anticipation, he read. *I thought myself the Holy First Witness, the prophet foretold to discover the Hero of Ages. Renouncing Alendi then would have been to renounce my new position, my acceptance, by the others.*

Sazed's frown deepened. He traced the paragraph. Outside, it was growing dark, and a few trails of mist curled around the shutters, creeping into the room before vanishing.

Holy First Witness, he read again. *How did I miss that? It's the same name the people called me, back at the gates. I didn't recognize it.*

"Sazed."

Sazed jumped, nearly toppling his book to the floor as he turned. Vin stood behind him, a dark shadow in the poorly lit room.

"Lady Vin! You're up!"

"You shouldn't have let me sleep so long," she said.

"We tried to wake you," he said softly. "You were in a coma."

She paused.

"Perhaps it is for the best, Lady Vin," Sazed said. "The fighting is done, and you pushed yourself hard these last few months. It is good for you to get some rest, now that this is over."

She stepped forward, shaking her head, and Sazed could

see that she looked haggard, despite her days of rest. "No, Sazed," she said. "This is not 'over.' Not by far."

"What do you mean?" Sazed asked, growing concerned.

"I can still hear it in my head," Vin said, raising a hand to her forehead. "It's here. In the city."

"The Well of Ascension?" Sazed asked. "But, Lady Vin, I lied about that. Truly and apologetically, I don't even know if there *is* such a thing."

"Do you believe me to be the Hero of Ages?"

Sazed looked away. "A few days ago, on the field outside the city, I felt certain. But . . . lately . . . I don't seem to know what I believe anymore. The prophecies and stories are a jumble of contradictions."

"This isn't about prophecies," Vin said, walking over to his table and looking at his book. "This is about what needs to be done. I can feel it . . . pulling me."

She glanced at the closed window, with the mists curling at the edges. Then, she walked over and threw the shutters open, letting in the cold winter air. Vin stood, closing her eyes and letting the mists wash over her. She wore only a simple shirt and trousers.

"I drew upon it once, Sazed," she said. "Do you know that? Did I tell you? When I fought the Lord Ruler. I drew power from the mists. That's how I defeated him."

Sazed shivered, not just from the cold. From the tone in her voice, and the air of her words. "Lady Vin . . ." he said, but wasn't sure how to continue. Drew upon the mists? What did she mean?

"The Well is here," she repeated, looking out the window, mist curling into the room.

"It can't be, Lady Vin," Sazed said. "All of the reports agree. The Well of Ascension was found in the Terris Mountains."

Vin shook her head. "He changed the world, Sazed."

He paused, frowning. "What?"

"The Lord Ruler," she whispered. "He created the Ashmounts. The records say he made the vast deserts around the empire, that he broke the land in order to preserve it. Why should we assume that things look like they did when he first climbed to the Well? He created mountains. Why couldn't he have flattened them?"

Sazed felt a chill.

"It's what I would do," Vin said. "If I knew the power would return, if I wanted to preserve it. I'd hide the Well. I'd let the legends remain, talking about mountains to the north. Then, I would build my city around the Well so that I could keep an eye on it."

She turned, looking at him. "It's here. The power waits."

Sazed opened his mouth to object, but could find nothing. He had no faith. Who was he to argue with such things? As he paused, he heard voices below, from outside.

Voices? he thought. *At night? In the mists?* Curious, he strained to hear what was being said, but they were too far away. He reached into the bag beside his table. Most of his metalminds were empty; he wore only his copperminds, with their stores of ancient knowledge. Inside the sack, he found a small pouch. It contained the ten rings he had prepared for the siege, but had never used. He pulled it open, took out one of the ten, then tucked the bag into his sash.

With this ring—a tinmind—he could tap hearing. The words below became distinct to him.

"The king! The king has returned!"

Vin leaped out the window.

"I don't fully understand how she does it either, El," Ham said, walking with his arm in a sling.

Elend walked through the city streets, people trailing behind him, speaking in excited tones. The crowd was growing larger and larger as people heard that Elend had returned. Spook eyed them uncertainly, but seemed to be enjoying the attention.

"I was out cold for the last part of the battle," Ham was saying. "Only pewter kept me alive—koloss slaughtered my team, breached the walls of the keep I was defending. I got out, and found Sazed, but my mind was growing muddled by then. I remember falling unconscious outside Keep

Hasting. When I woke up, Vin had already taken the city back. I . . ."

They paused. Vin stood in front of them in the city street. Quiet, dark. In the mists, she almost looked like the spirit Elend had seen earlier.

"Vin?" he asked in the eerie air.

"Elend," she said, rushing forward, into his arms, and the air of mystery was gone. She shivered as she held him. "I'm sorry. I think I did something bad."

"Oh?" he asked. "What is that?"

"I made you emperor."

Elend smiled. "I noticed, and I accept."

"After all you did to make certain the people had a choice?"

Elend shook his head. "I'm beginning to think my opinions were simplistic. Honorable, but . . . incomplete. We'll deal with this. I'm just glad to find that my city is still standing."

Vin smiled. She looked tired.

"Vin?" he asked. "Are you still pewter-dragging?"

"No," she said. "This is something else." She glanced to the side, face thoughtful, as if deciding something.

"Come," she said.

Sazed watched out the window, a second tinmind enhancing his sight. It was indeed Elend below. Sazed smiled, one of the weights on his soul removed. He turned, intending to go and meet the king.

And then he saw something blowing on the floor in front of him. A scrap of paper. He knelt down, picking it up, noticing his own handwriting on it. Its edges were jagged from having been ripped. He frowned, walking over to his table, opening the book to the page with Kwaan's narrative. A piece was missing. The same piece as before, the one that had been ripped free that time with Tindwyl. He'd almost forgotten the strange occurrence with the pages all missing the same sentence.

He'd rewritten this page, from his metalmind, after they'd found the torn sheets. Now the same bit had been torn free, the last sentence. Just to make certain, he put it up next to his book. It fit perfectly. *Alendi must not reach the Well of Ascension,* it read, *for he must not be allowed to take the power for himself.* It was the exact wording Sazed had in his memory, the exact wording of the rubbing.

Why would *Kwaan have worried about this?* he thought, sitting down. *He says he knew Alendi better than anyone else. In fact, he called Alendi an honorable man on several occasions.*

Why would Kwaan be so worried about Alendi taking the power for himself?

Vin walked through the mists. Elend, Ham, and Spook trailed behind her, the crowd dispersed by Elend's order—though some soldiers did stay close to protect Elend.

Vin continued on, feeling the pulsings, the thumpings, the power that shook her very soul. Why couldn't the others feel it?

"Vin?" Elend asked. "Where are we going?"

"Kredik Shaw," she said softly.

"But . . . why?"

She just shook her head. She knew the truth, now. The Well was in the city. With how strong the pulsings were growing, she might have assumed that their direction would be harder to discern. But that wasn't the way it was at all. Now that they were loud and full, she found it easier.

Elend glanced back at the others, and she could sense his concern. Up ahead, Kredik Shaw loomed in the night. Spires, like massive spikes, jutted from the ground in an off-balance pattern, reaching accusingly toward the stars above.

"Vin," Elend said. "The mists are acting . . . strangely."

"I know," she said. "They're guiding me."

"No, actually," Elend said. "They kind of look like they're pulling *away* from you."

Vin shook her head. This felt *right.* How could she explain? Together, they entered the remnants of the Lord Ruler's palace.

The Well was here all along, Vin thought, amused. She

could feel the pulses vibrating through the building. Why hadn't she noticed it before?

The pulses were still too weak, then, she realized. *The Well wasn't full yet. Now it is.* And it called to her.

She followed the same path as before. The path she'd followed with Kelsier, breaking into Kredik Shaw on a doomful night when she had nearly died. The path she'd followed on her own, the night she had come to kill the Lord Ruler. The tight stone corridors opened into the room shaped like an upside-down bowl. Elend's lantern glistened against the fine stonework and murals, mostly in black and gray. The stone shack stood in the center of the room, abandoned, enclosed.

"I think we're finally going to find your atium, Elend," Vin said, smiling.

"What?" Elend said, his voice echoing in the chamber. "Vin, we searched here. We tried everything."

"Not enough, apparently," Vin said, eyeing the small building-within-a-building, but not moving toward it.

This is where I'd put it, she thought. *It makes sense. The Lord Ruler would have wanted to keep the Well close so that when the power returned, he'd be able to take it.*

But I killed him before that could happen.

The booming came from below. They'd torn up sections of the floor, but had stopped when they'd hit solid rock. There had to be a way down. She walked over, searching through the building-within-a-building, but found nothing. She left, passing her confused friends, frustrated.

Then she tried burning her metals. As always, the blue lines shot up around her, pointing to sources of metal. Elend was wearing several, as was Spook, though Ham was clean. Some of the stonework bore metal inlays, and lines pointed to those.

Everything was as expected. There was nothing . . .

Vin frowned, stepping to the side. One of the inlays bore a particularly thick line. Too thick, in fact. She frowned, inspecting the line as it—like the others—pointed from her chest directly at the stone wall. This one seemed to be pointing *beyond* the wall.

What?

She Pulled on it. Nothing happened. So, she Pulled harder, grunting as she was yanked toward the wall. She released the line, glancing about. There were inlays on the floor. Deep ones. Curious, she anchored herself by Pulling on these, then Pulled on the wall again. She thought she felt something budge.

She burned duralumin and Pulled as hard as she could. The explosion of power nearly ripped her apart, but her anchor held, and duralumin-fueled pewter kept her alive. And a section of the wall slid open, stone grinding against stone in the quiet room. Vin gasped, letting go as her metals ran out.

"Lord Ruler!" Spook said. Ham was quicker, however, moving with the speed of pewter and peeking into the opening. Elend stayed at her side, grabbing her arm as she nearly fell.

"I'm fine," Vin said, downing a vial and restoring her metals. The power of the Well thumped around her. It almost seemed to shake the room.

"There are stairs in here," Ham said, poking his head back out.

Vin steadied herself and nodded to Elend, and the two of them followed Ham and Spook through the false section of the wall.

•

But, I must continue with the sparsest of detail, Kwaan's account read.

> *Space is limited. The other Worldbringers must have thought themselves humble when they came to me, admitting that they had been wrong about Alendi. Even then, I was beginning to doubt my original declaration. But, I was prideful.*
>
> *In the end, my pride may have doomed us all. I had never received much attention from my brethren; they thought that my work and my interests were unsuitable to a Worldbringer. The couldn't see how my studies, which focused on nature instead of religion, benefited the people of the fourteen lands.*

As the one who found Alendi, however, I became someone important. Foremost among the Worldbringers. There was a place for me in the lore of the Anticipation—I thought myself the Holy First Witness, the prophet foretold to discover the Hero of Ages. Renouncing Alendi then would have been to renounce my new position, my acceptance, by the others.

And so I did not. But I do so now.

Let it be known that I, Kwaan, Worldbringer of Terris, am a fraud. Alendi was never the Hero of Ages. At best, I have amplified his virtues, creating a hero where there was none. At worst, I fear that I have corrupted all we believe.

Sazed sat at his table, reading from his book.

Something is not right here, he thought. He traced back a few lines, looking at the words "Holy First Witness" again. Why did that line keep bothering him?

He sat back, sighing. Even if the prophecies did speak about the future, they wouldn't be things to follow or use as guideposts. Tindwyl was right on that count. His own study had proven them to be unreliable and shadowed.

So what was the problem?

It just doesn't make sense.

But, then again, sometimes religion didn't make literal sense. Was that the reason, or was that his own bias? His growing frustration with the teachings he had memorized and taught, but which had betrayed him in the end?

It came down to the scrap of paper on his desk. The torn one. *Alendi must not be allowed to reach the Well of Ascension. . . .*

Someone was standing next to his desk.

Sazed gasped, stumbling back, nearly tripping over his chair. It wasn't actually a person. It was a shadow—formed, it seemed, from streams of mist. They were very faint, still trailing through the window that Vin had opened, but they made a person. Its head seemed turned toward the table, toward the book. Or . . . perhaps the scrap of paper.

Sazed felt like running, like scrambling away in fear, but

his scholar's mind dredged something up to fight his terror. *Alendi,* he thought. *The one everyone thought was the Hero of Ages. He said he saw a thing made of mist following him.*

Vin claimed to have seen it as well.

"What . . . do you want?" he asked, trying to remain calm.

The spirit didn't move.

Could it be . . . her? he wondered with shock. Many religions claimed that the dead continued to walk the world, just beyond the view of mortals. But this thing was too short to be Tindwyl. Sazed was sure that he would have recognized her, even in such an amorphous form.

Sazed tried to gauge where it was looking. He reached out a hesitant hand, picking up the scrap of paper.

The spirit raised an arm, pointing toward the center of the city. Sazed frowned.

"I don't understand," he said.

The spirit pointed more insistently.

"Write down for me what you want me to do."

It just pointed.

Sazed stood for a long moment in the room with only one candle, then glanced at the open book. The wind flipped its pages, showing his handwriting, then Tindwyl's, then his again.

Alendi must not be allowed to reach the Well of Ascension. He must not be allowed to take the power for himself.

Perhaps . . . perhaps Kwaan knew something that nobody else had. Could the power corrupt even the best of people? Could that be why he turned against Alendi, trying to stop him?

The mist spirit pointed again.

If the spirit tore free that sentence, perhaps it was trying to tell me something. But . . . Vin wouldn't take the power for herself. She wouldn't destroy, as the Lord Ruler did, would she?

And if she didn't have a choice?

Outside, someone screamed. The yell was of pure terror, and it was soon joined by others. A horrible, echoing set of sounds in a dark night.

There wasn't time to think. Sazed grabbed the candle, spilling wax on the table in his haste, and left the room.

The winding set of stone stairs led downward for quite some time. Vin walked down them, Elend at her side, the thumping sounding loudly in her ears. At the bottom, the stairwell opened into . . .

A vast chamber. Elend held his lantern high, looking down into a huge stone cavern. Spook was already halfway down the stone steps leading to the floor. Ham was following.

"Lord Ruler . . ." Elend whispered, standing at Vin's side. "We'd have never found this without tearing down the entire building!"

"That was probably the idea," Vin said. "Kredik Shaw isn't simply a palace, but a capstone. Built to hide something. *This.* Above, those inlays on the walls hid the cracks of the doorway, and the metal in them obscured the opening mechanism from Allomantic eyes. If I hadn't had a hint . . ."

"Hint?" Elend asked, turning to her.

Vin shook her head, nodding to the steps. The two began down them. Below, she heard Spook's voice ring.

"There's food down here!" hc yelled. "Cans and cans of it!"

Indeed, they found rank upon rank of shelves sitting on the cavern floor, meticulously packed as if set aside in preparation for something important. Vin and Elend reached the cavern floor as Ham chased after Spook, calling for him to slow down. Elend made as if to follow, but Vin grabbed his arm. She was burning iron.

"Strong source of metal that way," she said, growing eager.

Elend nodded, and they rushed through the cavern, passing shelf after shelf. *The Lord Ruler must have prepared these,* she thought. *But for what purpose?*

She didn't care at the moment. She didn't really care about the atium either, but Elend's eagerness to find it was too much to ignore. They rushed up to the end of the cavern, where they found the source of the metal line.

A large metal plaque hung on the wall, like the one Sazed had described finding in the Conventical of Seran. Elend was clearly disappointed when they saw it. Vin, however, stepped forward, looking through tin-enhanced eyes to see what it contained.

"A map?" Elend asked. "That's the Final Empire."

Indeed, a map of the empire was carved into the metal. Luthadel was marked at the center. A small circle marked another city nearby.

"Why is Statlin City circled?" Elend asked, frowning.

Vin shook her head. "This isn't what we came for," she said. "There." A tunnel split off from the main cavern. "Come on."

Sazed ran through the streets, not even certain what he was doing. He followed the mist spirit, which was difficult to trace in the night, as his candle had long since puffed out.

People screamed. Their panicked sounds gave him chills, and he itched to go and see what the problem was. Yet the mist spirit was demanding; it paused to catch his attention if it lost him. It could simply be leading him to his death. And yet . . . he felt a trust for it that he could not explain.

Allomancy? he thought. *Pulling on my emotions?*

Before he could consider that further, he stumbled across the first body. It was a skaa man in simple clothing, skin stained with ash. His face was twisted in a grimace of pain, and the ash on the ground was smeared from his thrashings.

Sazed gasped as he pulled to a halt. He knelt, studying the body by the dim light of an open window nearby. This man had not died easily.

It's . . . like the killings I was studying, he thought. *Months ago, in the village to the south. The man there said that the mists had killed his friend. Caused him to fall to the ground and thrash about.*

The spirit appeared in front of Sazed, its posture insistent. Sazed looked up, frowning. "You did this?" he whispered.

The thing shook its head violently, pointing. Kredik Shaw was just ahead. It was the direction Vin and Elend had gone earlier.

Sazed stood. *Vin said she thought the Well was still in the city,* he thought. *The Deepness has come upon us, as its tendrils have been doing in the far reaches of the empire for some time. Killing.*

Something greater than we comprehend is going on.

He still couldn't believe that Vin going to the Well would be dangerous. She had read; she knew Rashek's story. She wouldn't take the power for herself. He was confident. But not completely certain. In fact, he was no longer certain *what* they should do with the Well.

I have to get to her. Stop her, talk to her, prepare her. We can't rush into something like this. If, indeed, they were going to take the power at the Well, they needed to think about it first and decide what the best course was.

The mist spirit continued to point. Sazed stood and ran forward, ignoring the horror of the screams in the night. He approached the doors of the massive palace structure with its spires and spikes, then dashed inside.

The mist spirit remained behind, in the mists that had birthed it. Sazed lit his candle again with a flint, and waited. The mist spirit did not move forward. Still feeling an urgency, Sazed left it behind, continuing into the depths of the Lord Ruler's former home. The stone walls were cold and dark, his candle a wan light.

The Well couldn't be here, he thought. *It's supposed to be in the mountains.*

Yet, so much about that time was vague. He was beginning to doubt that he'd ever understood the things he'd studied.

He quickened his step, shading his candle with his hand, knowing where he needed to go. He'd visited the building-within-a-building, the place where the Lord Ruler had once spent his time. Sazed had studied the place after the empire's fall, chronicling and cataloguing. He stepped into the outer room, and was halfway across it before he noticed the unfamiliar opening in the wall.

A figure stood in doorway, head bowed. Sazed's candlelight reflected the polished marble walls, the silvery inlayed murals, and the spikes in the man's eyes.

"Marsh?" Sazed asked, shocked. "Where have you been?"

"What are you doing, Sazed?" Marsh whispered.

"I'm going to Vin," he said, confused. "She has found the Well, Marsh. We have to get to her, stop her from doing anything with it until we're sure what it does."

Marsh remained silent for a short time. "You should not have come here, Terrisman," he finally said, head still bowed.

"Marsh? What is going on?" Sazed took a step forward, feeling urgent.

"I wish I knew. I wish . . . I wish I understood."

"Understood what?" Sazed asked, voice echoing in the domed room.

Marsh stood silently for a moment. Then he looked up, focusing his sightless spikeheads on Sazed.

"I wish I understood why I have to kill you," he said, then lifted a hand. An Allomantic Push slammed into the metal bracers on Sazed's arms, throwing him backward, crashing him into the hard stone wall.

"I'm sorry," Marsh whispered.

Alendi must not reach the Well of Ascension. . . .

58

"LORD RULER!" ELEND WHISPERED, pausing at the edge of the second cavern.

Vin joined him. They had walked in the passage for some time, leaving the storage cavern far behind, walking through a natural stone tunnel. It had ended here, at a second, slightly smaller cavern that was clogged with a thick, dark smoke. It didn't seep out of the cavern, as it should have, but billowed and churned upon itself.

Vin stepped forward. The smoke didn't choke her, as she expected. There was something oddly welcoming about it. "Come on," she said, walking through it across the cavern floor. "I see light up ahead."

Elend joined her nervously.

Thump. Thump. Thump.

Sazed slammed into the wall. He was no Allomancer; he had no pewter to strengthen his body. As he collapsed to the ground, he felt a sharp pain in his side, and knew he had cracked a rib. Or worse.

Marsh strode forward, faintly illuminated by Sazed's candle, which burned fitfully where Sazed had dropped it.

"Why did you come?" Marsh whispered as Sazed struggled to his knees. "Everything was going so well." He watched with iron eyes as Sazed slowly crawled away. Then Marsh Pushed again, throwing Sazed to the side.

Sazed skidded across the beautiful white floor, crashing into another wall. His arm snapped, cracking, and his vision shuddered.

Through his pain, he saw Marsh stoop down and pick something up. A small pouch. It had fallen from Sazed's sash. It was filled with bits of metal; Marsh obviously thought it was a coin pouch.

"I'm sorry," Marsh said again, then raised a hand and Pushed the bag at Sazed.

The pouch shot across the room and hit Sazed, ripping, the bits of metal inside tearing into Sazed's flesh. He didn't have to look down to know how badly he was injured. Oddly, he could no longer feel his pain—but he could feel the blood, warm, on his stomach and legs.

I'm . . . sorry, too, Sazed thought as the room grew dark, and he fell to his knees. *I've failed . . . though I know not at what. I can't even answer Marsh's question. I don't know why I came here.*

He felt himself dying. It was an odd experience. His mind

was resigned, yet confused, yet frustrated, yet slowly . . . having . . . trouble . . .

Those weren't coins, a voice seemed to whisper.

The thought rattled in his dying mind.

The bag Marsh shot at you. Those weren't coins. They were rings, Sazed. Eight of them. You took out two—eyesight and hearing. You left the other ones where they were.

In the pouch, tucked into your sash.

Sazed collapsed, death coming upon him like a cold shadow. And yet, the thought rang true. Ten rings, embedded into his flesh. Touching him. Weight. Speed of body. Sight. Hearing. Touch. Scent. Strength. Speed of mind. Wakefulness.

And health.

He tapped gold. He didn't have to be wearing the metalmind to use it—he only had to be touching it. His chest stopped burning, and his vision snapped back into focus. His arm straightened, the bones reknitting as he drew upon several days' worth of health in a brief flash of power. He gasped, his mind recovering from its near death, but the goldmind restored a crisp clarity to his thoughts.

The flesh healed around the metal. Sazed stood, pulling the empty bag from where it stuck from his skin, leaving the rings inside of him. He dropped it to the ground, the wound sealing, draining the last of the power from the goldmind. Marsh stopped at the mouth of the doorway, turning in surprise. Sazed's arm still throbbed, probably cracked, and his ribs were bruised. Such a short burst of health could only do so much.

But he was alive.

"You have betrayed us, Marsh," Sazed said. "I did not realize those spikes stole a man's soul, as well as his eyes."

"You cannot fight me," Marsh replied quietly, his voice echoing in the dark room. "You are no warrior."

Sazed smiled, feeling the small metalminds within him give him power. "Neither, I think, are you."

I am involved in something that is far over my head, Elend thought as they passed through the strange, smoke-filled cavern. The floor was rough and uneven, and his lantern seemed dim—as if the swirling black smoke were sucking in the light.

Vin walked confidently. No, determinedly. There was a difference. Whatever was at the end of this cavern, she obviously wanted to discover it.

And . . . what will it be? Elend thought. *The Well of Ascension?*

The Well was a thing of mythology—something spoken of by obligators when they taught about the Lord Ruler. And yet . . . he had followed Vin northward, expecting to find it, hadn't he? Why be so tentative now?

Perhaps because he was finally beginning to accept what was happening. And it worried him. Not because he feared for his life, but because suddenly he didn't understand the world. Armies he could understand, even if he didn't know how to defeat them. But a thing like the Well? A thing of gods, a thing beyond the logic of scholars and philosophers?

That was terrifying.

They finally approached the other side of the smoky cavern. Here, there appeared to be a final chamber, one much smaller than the first two. As they stepped into it, Elend noticed something immediately: this room was man-made. Or, at least, it had the *feel* of something man-made. Stalactites formed pillars through the low-ceilinged room, and they were spaced far too evenly to be random. Yet, at the same time, they looked as if they had grown naturally, and showed no signs of being worked.

The air seemed warmer inside—and, thankfully, they passed out of the smoke as they entered. A low light came from something on the far side of the chamber, though Elend couldn't distinguish the source. It didn't look like torchlight. It was the wrong color, and it shimmered rather than flickered.

Vin wrapped an arm around him, staring toward the back of the chamber, suddenly seeming apprehensive.

"Where is that light coming from?" Elend asked, frowning.

"A pool," Vin said quietly, her eyes far keener than his. "A glowing white pool."

Elend frowned. But, the two of them didn't move. Vin seemed hesitant. "What?" he asked.

She pulled against him. "That's the Well of Ascension. I can *feel* it inside of my head. Beating."

Elend forced a smile, feeling a surreal sense of displacement. "That's what we came for, then."

"What if I don't know what to do?" Vin asked quietly. "What if I take the power, but I don't know how to use it? What if I . . . become like the Lord Ruler?"

Elend looked down at her, arms wrapped around him, and his fear lessened a bit. He loved her. The situation they faced, it couldn't easily fit into his logical world. But Vin had never really needed logic. And he didn't need it either, if he trusted her.

He took her head in his hands, rotating it up to look at him. "Your eyes are beautiful."

She frowned. "What—"

"And," Elend continued, "part of the beauty in them comes from your sincerity. You won't become the Lord Ruler, Vin. You'll know what to do with that power. I trust you."

She smiled hesitantly, then nodded. However, she didn't move forward into the cavern. Instead, she pointed at something over Elend's shoulder. "What's that?"

Elend turned, noticing a ledge on the back wall of the small room. It grew straight out of the rock just beside the doorway they had entered. Vin approached the ledge, and Elend followed behind her, noticing the shards that lay upon it.

"It looks like broken pottery," Elend said. There were several patches of it, and more of it was scattered on the floor beneath the ledge.

Vin picked up a piece, but there didn't seem to be anything distinctive about it. She looked at Elend, who was fishing through the pottery pieces. "Look at this," he said, holding up one that hadn't been broken like the others. It was a disklike piece of fired clay with a single bead of some metal at the center.

"Atium?" she asked.

"It looks like the wrong color," he said, frowning.

"What is it, then?"

"Maybe we'll find the answers over there," Elend said, turning and looking down the rows of pillars toward the light. Vin nodded, and they walked forward.

Marsh immediately tried to Push Sazed away by the metal bracers on his arms. Sazed was ready, however, and he tapped his ring ironmind—drawing forth the weight he had stored within it. His body grew denser, and he felt its weight pulling him down, his fists feeling like balls of iron on the ends of lead arms.

Marsh immediately lurched away, thrown violently backward by his own Push. He slammed into the back wall, a cry of surprise escaping his lips. It echoed in the small, domed room.

Shadows danced in the room as the candle grew weaker. Sazed tapped sight, enhancing his vision, and released iron as he dashed toward the addled Inquisitor. Marsh, however, recovered quickly. He reached out, Pulling an unlit lamp off the wall. It zipped through the air, flying toward Marsh.

Sazed tapped zinc. He felt something like a twisted hybrid of an Allomancer and a Feruchemist, his sources of metal embedded within him. The gold had healed his insides, made him whole, but the rings still remained within his flesh. This was what the Lord Ruler had done, keeping his metalminds inside of him, piercing his flesh so that they would be harder to steal.

That had always seemed morbid to Sazed. Now, he saw how useful it could be. His thoughts sped up, and he quickly saw the trajectory of the lamp. Marsh would be able to use it as a weapon against him. So Sazed tapped steel. Allomancy and Feruchemy had one fundamental difference: Allomancy drew its powers from the metals themselves, and so the amount of power was limited; in Feruchemy, one could compound an attribute many times, drawing out months' worth of power in a few minutes.

Steel stored physical speed. Sazed zipped across the room, air rushing in his ears as he shot past the open doorway. He snatched the lamp out of the air, then tapped iron hard—increasing his weight manyfold—and tapped pewter to give himself massive strength.

Marsh didn't have time to react. He was now Pulling on a lamp held in Sazed's inhumanly strong, inhumanly heavy, hand. Again, Marsh was yanked by his own Allomancy. The Pull threw him across the room, directly toward Sazed.

Sazed turned, slamming the lamp into Marsh's face. The metal bent in his hand, and the force threw Marsh backward. The Inquisitor hit the marble wall, a spray of blood misting in the air. As Marsh slumped to the ground, Sazed could see that he'd driven one of the eye-spikes back into the front of the skull, crushing the bone around the socket.

Sazed returned his weight to normal, then jumped forward, raising his impromptu weapon again. Marsh, however, threw an arm up and Pushed. Sazed skidded back a few feet before he was able to tap the ironmind again, increasing his weight.

Marsh grunted, his Push forcing him back against the wall. It also, however, kept Sazed at bay. Sazed struggled to step forward, but the pressure of Marsh's Push—along with his own bulky, weighed-down body—made walking difficult. The two strained for a moment, Pushing against each other in the darkening light. The room's inlays sparkled, quiet murals watching them, open doorway leading down to the Well just to the side.

"Why, Marsh?" Sazed whispered.

"I don't know," Marsh said, his voice coming out in a growl.

With a flash of power, Sazed released his ironmind and instead tapped steel, increasing his speed again. He dropped the lamp, ducking to the side, moving more quickly than Marsh could track. The lamp was forced backward, but then fell to the ground as Marsh let go of his Push, jumping forward, obviously trying to keep from being trapped against the wall.

But Sazed was faster. He spun, raising a hand to try to pull out Marsh's linchpin spike—the one in between his shoulder blades, pounded down lengthwise into the back. Pulling this one spike would kill an Inquisitor; it was the weakness the Lord Ruler had built into them.

Sazed skidded around Marsh to attack from behind. The spike in Marsh's right eye protruded several extra inches out the back of his skull, and it dribbled blood.

Sazed's steelmind ran out.

The rings had never been intended to last long, and his two extreme bursts had drained this one in seconds. He slowed with a dreadful lurch, but his arm was still raised, and he still had the strength of ten men. He could see the bulge of the linchpin spike underneath Marsh's robe. If he could just—

Marsh spun, then dexterously knocked aside Sazed's hand. He rammed an elbow into Sazed's stomach, then brought a backhand up and crashed it into his face.

Sazed fell backward, and his pewtermind ran out, his strength disappearing. He hit the hard steel ground with a grunt of pain, and rolled.

Marsh loomed in the dark room. The candle flickered.

"You were wrong, Sazed," Marsh said quietly. "Once, I was not a warrior, but that has changed. You spent the last two years teaching, but I spent them killing. Killing so many people. . . ."

Marsh stepped forward, and Sazed coughed, trying to get his bruised body to move. He worried that he'd rebroken his arm. He tapped zinc again, speeding up his thoughts, but that didn't help his body move. He could only watch—more fully aware of his predicament and unable to do a thing to stop it—as Marsh picked up the fallen lamp.

The candle went out.

Yet, Sazed could still see Marsh's face. Blood dripped from the crushed socket, making the man's expression even harder to read. The Inquisitor seemed . . . sorrowful as he raised the lamp in a clawlike grip, intending to smash it down into Sazed's face.

Wait, Sazed thought. *Where is that light coming from?*

A dueling cane smashed against the back of Marsh's head, shattering and throwing up splinters.

•

Vin and Elend walked up to the pool. Elend knelt quietly beside it, but Vin just stood. Staring at the glittering waters.

They were gathered in a small depression in the rock, and they looked thick—like metal. A silvery white, glowing liquid metal. The Well was only a few feet across, but its power loomed in her mind.

Vin was so enraptured by the beautiful pool, in fact, that she didn't notice the mist spirit until Elend's grip tightened on her arm. She looked up, noticing the spirit standing before them. It seemed to have its head bowed, but as she turned, its shadowy form stood up straighter.

She'd never seen the creature outside of the mist. It still wasn't completely . . . whole. Mist puffed from its body, flowing downward, creating its amorphous form. A persistent pattern.

Vin hissed quietly, pulling out a dagger.

"Wait!" Elend said, standing.

She frowned, shooting him a glance.

"I don't think it's dangerous, Vin," he said, stepping away from her, toward the spirit.

"Elend, no!" she said, but he gently shook her free.

"It visited me while you were gone, Vin," he explained. "It didn't hurt me. It just . . . seemed like it wanted me to know something." He smiled, still wearing his nondescript cloak and traveling clothing, and walked slowly up to the mist spirit. "What is it you want?"

The mist spirit stood immobile for a moment, then it raised its arm. Something flashed, reflecting the pool's light.

"No!" Vin screamed, dashing forward as the spirit slashed across Elend's gut. Elend grunted in pain, then stumbled back.

"Elend!" Vin said, scrambling to Elend's side as he slipped and fell to the ground. The spirit backed away, dripping blood from somewhere within its deceptively incorporeal form. Elend's blood.

Elend lay, shocked, eyes wide. Vin flared pewter and ripped open the front of his jacket, exposing the wound. The spirit had cut deeply into his stomach, slashing the gut open.

"No . . . no . . . no . . ." Vin said, mind growing numb, Elend's blood on her hands.

The wound was very bad. Deadly.

Ham dropped the broken cane, one arm still in a sling. The beefy Thug looked incredibly pleased with himself as he stepped over Marsh's body and reached his good hand toward Sazed.

"Didn't expect to find you here, Saze," the Thug said.

Dazed, Sazed took the hand and climbed to his feet. He stumbled over Marsh's body, somehow distractedly knowing that a simple club to the head wouldn't be enough to kill the creature. Yet Sazed was too addled to care. He picked up his candle, lit it from Ham's lantern, then made his way toward the stairs, forcing himself onward.

He had to keep going. He had to get to Vin.

Vin cradled Elend in her arms, her cloak forming a hasty—and dreadfully inadequate—bandage around his torso.

"I love you," she whispered, tears warm on her cold cheeks. "Elend, I love you. I love you. . . ."

Love wouldn't be enough. He was trembling, eyes staring upward, barely able to focus. He gasped, and blood bubbled in his spittle.

She turned to the side, numbly realizing where she knelt. The pool glowed beside her, just inches from where Elend had fallen. Some of his blood had dribbled into the pool, though it didn't mix with the liquid metal.

I can save him, she realized. *The power of creation rests just inches from my fingers.* This was the place where Rashek had ascended to godhood. The Well of Ascension.

She looked back at Elend, at his dying eyes. He tried to focus on her, but he seemed to be having trouble controlling his muscles. It seemed like . . . he was trying to smile.

Vin rolled up her coat and put it beneath his head. Then, wearing just her trousers and shirt, she walked up to the pool. She could hear it thumping. As if . . . calling to her. Calling for her to join with it.

She stepped onto the pool. It resisted her touch, but her foot began to sink, slowly. She stepped forward, moving into the center of the pool, waiting as she sank. Within seconds, the pool was up to her chest, the glowing liquid all around her.

She took a breath, then leaned her head back, looking up as the pool absorbed her, covering her face.

Sazed stumbled down the stairs, candle held in quivering fingers. Ham was calling after him. He passed a confused Spook on the landing below, and ignored the boy's questions.

However, as he began to make his way down to the cavern floor, he slowed. A small tremor ran through the rock.

Somehow, he knew that he was too late.

The power came upon her suddenly.

She felt the liquid pressing against her, creeping into her body, crawling, forcing its way through the pores and openings in her skin. She opened her mouth to scream, and it rushed in that way too, choking her, gagging her.

With a sudden flare, her earlobe began to hurt. She cried out, pulling her earring free, dropping it into the depths. She pulled off her sash, letting it—and her Allomantic vials—go as well, removing the only metals on her person.

Then she started to burn. She recognized the sensation: it was exactly like the feeling of burning metals in her stomach, except it came from her entire body. Her skin flared, her muscles flamed, and her very bones seemed on fire. She gasped, and realized the metal was gone from her throat.

She was glowing. She felt the power within, as if it were trying to burst back out. It was like the strength she gained by burning pewter, but amazingly more potent. It was a force of incredible capacity. It would have been beyond her ability to understand, but it expanded her mind, forcing her to grow and comprehend what she now possessed.

She could remake the world. She could push back the mists. She could feed millions with the wave of her hand, punish the evil, protect the weak. She was in awe of herself. The cavern was as if translucent around her, and she saw the entire world spreading, a magnificent sphere upon which life could exist only in a small little area at the poles. She could fix that. She could make things better. She could . . .

She could save Elend.

She glanced down and saw him dying. She immediately understood what was wrong with him. She could fix his damaged skin and sliced organs.

You mustn't do it, child.

Vin looked up with shock.

You know what you must do, the Voice said, whispering to her. It sounded aged. Kindly.

"I have to save him!" she cried.

You know what you must do.

And she did know. She saw it happen—she saw, as if in a vision, Rashek when he'd taken the power for himself. She saw the disasters he created.

It was all or nothing—like Allomancy, in a way. If she took the power, she would have to burn it away in a few moments. Remaking things as she pleased, but only for a brief time.

Or . . . she could give it up.

I must defeat the Deepness, the Voice said.

She saw that, too. Outside the palace, in the city, across the land. People in the mists, shaking, falling. Many stayed indoors, thankfully. The traditions of the skaa were still strong within them.

Some were out, however. Those who trusted in Kelsier's words that the mists could not hurt them. But now the mists could. They had changed, bringing death.

This was the Deepness. Mists that killed. Mists that were slowly covering the entire land. The deaths were sporadic; Vin saw many falling dead, but saw others simply falling sick, and still others going about in the mists as if nothing were wrong.

It will get worse, the Voice said quietly. *It will kill and destroy. And, if you try to stop it yourself, you will ruin the world, as Rashek did before you.*

"Elend . . ." she whispered. She turned toward him, bleeding on the floor.

At that moment, she remembered something. Something Sazed had said. *You must love him enough to trust his wishes,* he had told her. *It isn't love unless you learn to respect him—not what you* assume *is best, but what he actually wants. . . .*

She saw Elend weeping. She saw him focusing on her, and she knew what he wanted. He wanted his people to live. He wanted the world to know peace, and the skaa to be free.

He wanted the Deepness to be defeated. The safety of his people meant more to him than his own life. Far more.

You'll know what to do, he'd told her just moments before. *I trust you. . . .*

Vin closed her eyes, and tears rolled down her cheeks. Apparently, gods could cry.

"I love you," she whispered.

She let the power go. She held the capacity to become a deity in her hands, and she gave it away, releasing it to the waiting void. She gave up Elend.

Because she knew that was what he wanted.

The cavern immediately began to shake. Vin cried out as the flaring power within her was ripped away, soaked up greedily by the void. She screamed, her glow fading, then fell into the now empty pool, head knocking against the rocks.

The cavern continued to shake, dust and chips falling from the ceiling. And then, in a moment of surreal clarity, Vin heard a single, distinct sentence ringing in her mind.

I am FREE!

. . . for he must not be allowed to release the thing that is imprisoned there.

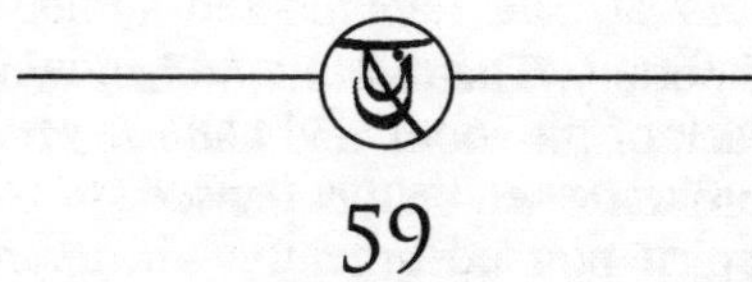

59

VIN LAY, QUIETLY, WEEPING.

The cavern was still, the tempest over. The thing was gone, and the thumping in her mind was finally quiet. She sniffled, arms around Elend, holding him as he gasped his final few breaths. She'd screamed for help, calling for Ham and Spook, but had gotten no response. They were too far away.

She felt cold. Empty. After holding that much power, then having it ripped from her, she felt like she was nothing. And, once Elend died, she would be.

What would be the point? she thought. *Life doesn't mean anything. I've betrayed Elend. I've betrayed the world.*

She wasn't certain what had happened, but somehow she'd made a horrible, horrible mistake. The worst part was, she had tried so hard to do what was right, even if it hurt.

Something loomed above her. She looked up at the mist spirit, but couldn't even really feel rage. She was having trouble feeling anything at the moment.

The spirit raised an arm, pointing.

"It's over," she whispered.

It pointed more demandingly.

"I won't get to them in time," she said. "Besides, I *saw* how bad the cut was. Saw it with the power. There's nothing any of them could do, not even Sazed. So, you should be pleased. You got what you wanted . . ." She trailed off. Why had the spirit stabbed Elend?

To make me heal him, she thought. *To keep me . . . from releasing the power.*

She blinked her eyes. The spirit waved its arm.

Slowly, numbly, she got to her feet. She watched the spirit in a trance as it floated a few steps over and pointed at something on the ground. The room was dark, now that the pool was empty, and was illuminated only by Elend's lantern. She had to flare tin to see what the spirit was pointing at.

A piece of pottery. The disk Elend had taken from the shelf in the back of the room, and had been holding in his hand. It had broken when he'd collapsed.

The mist spirit pointed urgently. Vin approached and bent over, fingers finding the small nugget of metal that had been at the disk's center.

"What is it?" she whispered.

The mist spirit turned and drifted back to Elend. Vin walked up quietly.

He was still alive. He seemed to be getting weaker, and was trembling less. Eerily, as he grew closer to death, he actually seemed a bit more in control. He looked at her as she knelt, and she could see his lips moving.

"Vin . . ." he whispered.

She knelt beside him, looked at the bead of metal, then looked up at the spirit. It stood motionless. She rolled the bead between her fingers, then moved to eat it.

The spirit moved urgently, shaking its hands. Vin paused, and the spirit pointed at Elend.

What? she thought. However, she wasn't really in a state to think. She held the nugget up to Elend. "Elend," she whispered, leaning close. "You must swallow this."

She wasn't certain if he understood her or not, though he did appear to nod. She placed the bit of metal in his mouth. His lips moved, but he started to choke.

I have to get him something to wash it down, she thought. The only thing she had was one of her metal vials. She reached into the empty well, retrieving her earring and her sash. She pulled free a vial, then poured the liquid into his mouth.

Elend continued to cough weakly, but the liquid did its work well, washing down the bead of metal. Vin knelt, feeling so powerless, a depressing contrast to how she had been just moments before. Elend closed his eyes.

Then, oddly, the color seemed to return to his cheeks. Vin knelt, confused, watching him. The look on his face, the way he lay, the color of his skin . . .

She burned bronze, and with shock, felt pulses coming from Elend.

He was burning pewter.

EPILOGUE

TWO WEEKS LATER, A SOLITARY figure arrived at the Conventical of Seran.

Sazed had left Luthadel quietly, troubled by his thoughts and by the loss of Tindwyl. He'd left a note. He couldn't stay in Luthadel. Not at the moment.

The mists still killed. They struck random people who went out at night, with no discernible pattern. Many of the people did not die, but only became sick. Others, the mists murdered. Sazed didn't know what to make of the deaths. He wasn't even certain if he cared. Vin spoke of something terrible she had released at the Well of Ascension. She had expected Sazed to want to study and record her experience.

Instead, he had left.

He made his way through the solemn, steel-plated rooms. He half expected to be confronted by one Inquisitor or another. Perhaps Marsh would try to kill him again. By the time he and Ham had returned from the storage cavern beneath Luthadel, Marsh had vanished again. His work had, apparently, been done. He'd stalled Sazed long enough to keep him from stopping Vin.

Sazed made his way down the steps, through the torture chamber, and finally into the small rock room he'd visited on his first trip to the Conventical, so many weeks before. He dropped his pack to the ground, working it open with tired fingers, then looked up at the large steel plate.

Kwaan's final words stared back at him. Sazed knelt, pulling a carefully tied portfolio from his pack. He undid the string, and then removed his original rubbing, made in this very room months before. He recognized his fingerprints on the thin paper, knew the strokes of the charcoal to be his own. He recognized the smudges he had made.

With growing nervousness, he held the rubbing up and slapped it against the steel plate on the wall.

And the two did not match.

Sazed stepped back, uncertain what to think now that his suspicions had been confirmed. The rubbing slipped limply from his fingers, and his eyes found the sentence at the end of the plate. The last sentence, the one that the mist spirit had ripped free time and time again. The original one on the steel plate was different from the one Sazed had written and studied.

Alendi must not reach the Well of Ascension, Kwaan's ancient words read, *for he must not be allowed to release the thing that is imprisoned there.*

Sazed sat down quietly. *It was all a lie,* he thought numbly. *The religion of the Terris people . . . the thing the Keepers spent millennia searching for, trying to understand, was a lie. The so-called prophecies, the Hero of Ages . . . a fabrication.*

A trick.

What better way for such a creature to gain freedom? Men would die in the name of prophecies. They wanted to believe, to hope. If someone—something—could harness that energy, twist it, what amazing things could be accomplished. . . .

Sazed looked up, reading the words on the wall, reading the second half once again. It contained paragraphs that were different from his rubbing.

Or, rather, his rubbing had been changed somehow. Changed to reflect what the thing had wished Sazed to read. *I write these words in steel,* Kwaan's first words said, *for anything not set in metal cannot be trusted.*

Sazed shook his head. They should have paid attention to that sentence. Everything he had studied after that had, apparently, been a lie. He looked up at the plate, scanning its contents, coming to the final section.

And so, they read, *I come to the focus of my argument. I apologize. Even forcing my words into steel, sitting and scratching in this frozen cave, I am prone to ramble.*

This is the problem. Though I believed in Alendi at first, I later became suspicious. It seemed that he fit the signs, true. But, well, how can I explain this?

Could it be that he fit them too well?

I know your argument. We speak of the Anticipation, of things foretold, of promises made by our greatest prophets of old. Of course the Hero of Ages will fit the prophecies. He will fit them perfectly. That's the idea.

And yet . . . something about all this seems so convenient. It feels almost as if we constructed a hero to fit our prophecies, rather than allowing one to arise naturally. This was the worry I had, the thing that should have given me pause when my brethren came to me, finally willing to believe.

After that, I began to see other problems. Some of you may know of my fabled memory. It is true; I need not a Feruchemist's metalmind to memorize a sheet of words in an instant. And I tell you, call me daft, but the words of the prophecies are changing.

The alterations are slight. Clever, even. A word here, a slight twist there. But the words on the pages are different from the ones in my memory. The other Worldbringers scoff at me, for they have their metalminds to prove to them that the books and prophecies have not changed.

And so, this is the great declaration I must make. There is something—some force—that wants us to believe that the Hero of Ages has come, and that he must travel to the Well of Ascension. Something is making the prophecies change so that they refer to Alendi more perfectly.

And whatever this power is, it can change words within a Feruchemist's metalmind.

The others call me mad. As I have said, that may be true. But must not even a madman rely on his own mind, his own experience, rather than that of others? I know what I have memorized. I know what is now repeated by the other Worldbringers. The two are not the same.

I sense a craftiness behind these changes, a manipulation subtle and brilliant. I have spent the last two years in exile, trying to decipher what the alterations could mean. I have come to only one conclusion. Something has taken control of our religion, something nefarious, something that cannot be trusted. It misleads, and it shadows. It uses Alendi to destroy, leading him along a path of death and sorrow. It is pulling him toward the Well of Ascension, where the millennial power has gathered. I can only guess that it sent the Deepness as a method of making mankind more desperate, of pushing us to do as it wills.

The prophecies have changed. They now tell Alendi that he must give up the power once he takes it. This is not what was once implied by the texts—they were more vague. And yet, the new version seems to make it a moral imperative. The texts now outline a terrible consequence if the Hero of Ages takes the power for himself.

Alendi believes as they do. He is a good man—despite it all, he is a good man. A sacrificing man. In truth, all of his actions—all of the deaths, destructions, and pains that he has caused—have hurt him deeply. All of these things were, in truth, a kind of sacrifice for him. He is accustomed to giving up his own will for the common good, as he sees it.

I have no doubt that if Alendi reaches the Well of Ascension, he will take the power and then—in the name of the presumed greater good—will give it up. Give it away to this same force that has changed the texts. Give it up to this force of destruction that has brought him to war, that has tempted him to kill, that has craftily led him to the north.

This thing wants the power held in the Well, and it has raped our religion's holiest tenets in order to get it.

And so, I have made one final gamble. My pleas, my teachings, my objections, and even my treasons were all ineffectual. Alendi has other counselors now, ones who tell him what he wants to hear.

I have a young nephew, one Rashek. He hates all of Khlennium with the passion of envious youth. He hates Alendi even more acutely—though the two have never met—for Rashek feels betrayed that one of our oppressors should have been chosen as the Hero of Ages.

Alendi will need guides through the Terris Mountains. I have charged Rashek with making certain that he and his trusted friends are chosen as those guides. Rashek is to try and lead Alendi in the wrong direction, to dissuade him, discourage him, or otherwise foil his quest. Alendi doesn't know that he has been deceived, that we've all been deceived, and he will not listen to me now.

If Rashek fails to lead the trek astray, then I have instructed the lad to kill Alendi. It is a distant hope. Alendi has survived assassins, wars, and catastrophes. And yet, I hope that in the frozen mountains of Terris, he may finally be exposed. I hope for a miracle.

Alendi must not reach the Well of Ascension, for he must not be allowed to release the thing that is imprisoned there.

Sazed sat back. It was the final blow, the last strike that killed whatever was left of his faith.

He knew at that moment that he would never believe again.

Vin found Elend standing on the city wall, looking over the city of Luthadel. He wore a white uniform, one of the ones that Tindwyl had made for him. He looked . . . harder than he had just a few weeks before.

"You're awake," she said, moving up beside him.

He nodded. He didn't look at her, but continued to watch the city, with its bustling people. He'd spent quite a bit of time delirious and in bed, despite the healing power of his newfound Allomancy. Even with pewter, the surgeons had been uncertain if he'd survive.

He had. And, like a true Allomancer, he was up and about the first day he was lucid.

"What happened?" he asked.

She shook her head, leaning against the stones of the battlement. She could still hear that terrible, booming voice. *I am FREE. . . .*

"I'm an Allomancer," Elend said.

She nodded.

"Mistborn, apparently," he continued.

"I think . . . we know where they came from, now," Vin said. "The first Allomancers."

"What happened to the power? Ham didn't have a straight answer for me, and all anyone else knows are rumors."

"I set something free," she whispered. "Something that shouldn't have been released; something that led me to the Well. I should never have gone looking for it, Elend."

Elend stood in silence, still regarding the city.

She turned, burying her head in his chest. "It was terrible," she said. "I could feel that. And I set it free."

Finally, Elend wrapped his arms around her. "You did the best you could, Vin," he said. "In fact, you did the right thing. How could you have known that everything you'd been told, trained, and prepared to do was wrong?"

Vin shook her head. "I am worse than the Lord Ruler. In the end, maybe he realized he was being tricked, and knew he had to take the power rather than release it."

"If he'd been a good man, Vin," Elend said, "he wouldn't have done the things he did to this land."

"I may have done far worse," Vin said. "This thing I released . . . the mists killing people, and coming during the day . . . Elend, what are we going to do?"

He looked at her for a moment, then turned back toward the city and its people. "We're going to do what Kelsier taught us, Vin. We're going to survive."

THE END OF BOOK TWO

ARS ARCANUM

1. Metals Quick-Reference Chart

2. Names and Terms

3. Summary of Book One

You can also find extensive annotations of every chapter in the book, along with deleted scenes, a very active blog, and expanded world information at www.brandonsanderson.com.

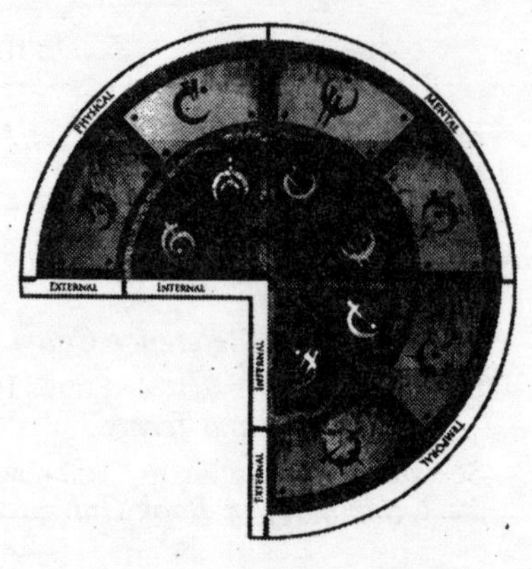

METALS QUICK-REFERENCE CHART

METAL	ALLOMANTIC POWER	FERUCHEMICAL POWER
Iron	Pushes on Nearby Sources of Metals	Stores Physical Weight
Steel	Pulls on Nearby Sources of Metal	Stores Physical Speed
Tin	Increases Senses	Stores Senses
Pewter	Increases Physical Abilities	Stores Physical Strength
Brass	Soothes (Dampens) Emotions	Stores Warmth
Zinc	Riots (Enflames) Emotions	Stores Mental Speed
Copper	Hides Allomantic Pulses	Stores Memories
Bronze	Allows One to Hear Allomantic Pulses	Stores Wakefulness

METAL	ALLOMANTIC POWER	FERUCHEMICAL POWER
Atium	See into Other People's Futures	Stores Age
Malatium	See into Other People's Pasts	Unknown
Gold	See into Your Own Past	Stores Health
Electrum	See into Your Own Future	Unknown

NAMES AND TERMS

ALENDI: A man who conquered the world a thousand years ago, before the Lord Ruler's Ascension. Vin found his journal in the Lord Ruler's palace, and thought—at first—that he had become the Lord Ruler. It was later discovered that his servant, Rashek, killed him and took his place. Alendi was a friend and protégé of Kwaan, a Terris scholar who thought that Alendi might be the Hero of Ages.

ALLOMANCY: A mystical hereditary power involving the burning of metals inside the body to gain special abilities.

ALLOMANTIC METALS: There are eight basic Allomantic metals. These come in pairs, comprising a base metal and its alloy. They can also be divided into two groups of four as internal metals (tin, pewter, copper, bronze) and external metals (iron, steel, zinc, brass). It was long assumed that there were only two other Allomantic metals: gold and atium. However, the discovery of alloys for gold and atium has expanded the number of metals to twelve. There have been rumors of other metals, one of which has been discovered. (See also: Aluminum.)

ALLOMANTIC PULSE: The signal given off by an Allomancer who is burning metals. Only someone who is burning bronze can "hear" an Allomantic pulse.

ALLRIANNE: Lord Ashweather Cett's only daughter.

ALUMINUM: A metal Vin was forced to burn in the Lord Ruler's palace. Once known only to the Steel Inquisitors, this metal, when burned, depletes all of an Allomancer's other metal reserves. Its alloy, if it has one, is unknown.

AMARANTA: One of Straff Venture's mistresses. An herbalist.

ANCHOR (ALLOMANTIC): A term used to refer to a piece of metal that an Allomancer Pushes on or Pulls on when burning iron or steel.

ASCENSION (OF THE LORD RULER): The Ascension is the term used to describe what happened to Rashek when he took the power at the Well of Ascension and became the Lord Ruler.

ASHFALLS: Ash falls frequently from the sky in the Final Empire because of the Ashmounts.

ASHMOUNTS: Seven large ash volcanoes that appeared in the Final Empire during the Ascension.

ASHWEATHER: Lord Cett's first name.

ATIUM: A strange metal formerly produced in the Pits of Hathsin. It collected inside of small geodes that formed in crystalline pockets in caves beneath the ground.

BIRCHBANE: A common poison.

BOXING: The slang name for an imperial gold coin. The name comes from the picture on its back of Kredik Shaw, the Lord Ruler's palace—or, the "box" in which he lives.

BREEZE: A Soother on Kelsier's crew, now one of Elend's foremost counselors.

BRONZEPULSE: Another term for an Allomantic pulse.

BURN (ALLOMANCY): An Allomancer utilizing or expending the metals in their stomachs. First, they must swallow a metal, then Allomantically metabolize it inside of them to access its power.

BURNLANDS: The deserts at the edges of the Final Empire.

CAMON: Vin's old crewleader. A harsh man who often beat her, Camon was cast out by Kelsier. The Inquisitors eventually killed him.

CANTON: A suboffice within the Steel Ministry.

CETT: Lord Ashweather Cett is the most prominent king who has managed to gain power in the Western Dominance. His home city is Fadrex.

CHANNEREL: The river that runs through Luthadel.

CLADENT: Clubs's real name.

CLIP (COINAGE): The nickname for an imperial copper coin in the Final Empire. Commonly used by Mistborn and Coinshots for jumping and attacking.

CLUBS: A Smoker on Kelsier's crew, now general of Elend's armies. He once was a skaa carpenter.

COINSHOT: A Misting who can burn steel.

COLLAPSE, THE: The death of the Lord Ruler and the fall of the Final Empire.

COPPERCLOUD: The invisible, obscuring field set up by someone burning copper. If an Allomancer burns metals while within a coppercloud, their Allomantic pulses are hidden from those burning bronze. The term "Coppercloud" is also, sometimes, used to refer to a Smoker (a Misting who can burn copper).

DEEPNESS, THE: The mythological monster or force that threatened the land just before the rise of the Lord Ruler and the Final Empire. The term comes from Terris lore, and the Hero of Ages was the one prophesied to come and eventually defeat the Deepness. The Lord Ruler claims to have defeated it when he Ascended.

DEMOUX, CAPTAIN: Ham's second-in-command, a soldier in Elend's palace guard.

DOCKSON: Kelsier's old right-hand man, informal leader of his crew now that Kelsier is dead. He has no Allomantic powers.

DOMINANCE (FINAL EMPIRE): A province of the Final Empire. Luthadel is in the Central Dominance. The four surrounding dominances are called the Inner Dominances, and include most of the population and culture of the Final Empire. After the Collapse, the Final Empire shattered, and different kings took power, trying to claim leadership of the various dominances, effectively turning each one into a kingdom of its own.

DOX: Dockson's nickname.

ELEND VENTURE: King of the Central Dominance, son of Straff Venture.

EXTINGUISH (ALLOMANTIC): To cease burning an Allomantic metal.

FADREX: A modestly sized, well-fortified city in the Western Dominance. Capital city and home to Ashweather Cett. A main place of stockpile for the Canton of Resource.

FELT: Once one of Straff's spies, the man was (like most of Straff's employees) left behind at the fall of Luthadel. He gave his allegiance to Elend instead.

FINAL EMPIRE: The empire established by the Lord Ruler. The name came from the fact that, being immortal, he felt that it would be the last empire the world ever knew, since it would never fall or end.

FLARE (ALLOMANTIC): To draw a little extra power from an Allomantic metal at the expense of making it burn faster.

GNEORNDIN: Ashweather Cett's only son.

GORADEL: Once a soldier in the Luthadel Garrison, Goradel was guarding the palace when Vin decided to infiltrate and kill the Lord Ruler. Vin convinced him to switch sides, and he later led Elend through the palace to try and rescue her. Now a member of Elend's guard.

HAM: A Thug on Kelsier's crew, now captain of Elend's palace guard.

HAMMOND: Ham's real name.

HATHSIN: See Pits of Hathsin.

HERO OF AGES, THE: The mythological prophesied savior of the Terris people. It was foretold that he would come, take the power at the Well of Ascension, then be selfless enough to give it up in order to save the world from the Deepness. Alendi was thought to be the Hero of Ages, but was killed before he could complete his quest.

INQUISITORS, STEEL: A group of strange creatures, priests who served the Lord Ruler. They have spikes driven completely through their heads—point-first through the eyes—yet continue to live. They were fanatically devoted to him, and were used primarily to hunt out and kill skaa with

Allomantic powers. They have the abilities of a Mistborn, and some others.

IRONEYES: Marsh's nickname in the crew.

IRONPULL: Pulling on a metal when Allomantically burning iron. This Pull exerts a force on the metal item, yanking it directly toward the Allomancer. If the metallic item, known as an anchor, is heavier than the Allomancer, he or she will instead be Pulled toward the metal source.

JANARLE: Straff Venture's second-in-command.

JASTES LEKAL: Heir to the Lekal house title, one of Elend's former friends. He and Elend often talked politics and philosophy together with Telden.

KANDRA: A race of strange creatures who can ingest the dead body of a person, then reproduce that body with their own flesh. They keep the bones of the person they imitate, using them, as kandra themselves have no bones. They serve Contracts with mankind—which must be bought with atium—and are relatives of mistwraiths.

KEEPER (TERRIS): "Keeper" is often used as simply another term for a Feruchemist. The Keepers are actually an organization of Feruchemists dedicated to discovering, then memorizing, all of the knowledge and religions that existed before the Ascension. The Lord Ruler hunted them to near extinction, forcing them to remain hidden.

KELL: Kelsier's nickname.

KELSIER: The most famous thieving crewleader in the Final Empire, Kelsier raised a rebellion of skaa and overthrew the Lord Ruler, but was killed in the process. He was Mistborn, and was Vin's teacher.

KHLENNIUM: An ancient kingdom that existed before the rise of the Final Empire. It was Alendi's homeland.

KLISS: A woman whom Vin knew in the court at Luthadel. She eventually turned out to be an informant for hire.

KOLOSS: A race of bestial warriors created by the Lord Ruler during his Ascension, then used by him to conquer the world.

KREDIK SHAW: The Lord Ruler's palace in Luthadel. It means "the Hill of a Thousand Spires" in the old Terris language.

KWAAN: A Terris scholar before the Collapse. He was a Worldbringer, and was the first to mistakenly think that Alendi was the Hero of Ages. He later changed his mind, betraying his former friend.

LADRIAN: Breeze's real name.

LESTIBOURNES: Spook's real name.

LLAMAS, MISTBORN: Brandon's writing group. Mistborn Llamas burn various kinds of plants to gain super-llaman powers. T-shirts can be found on the Web site.

LORD RULER: The emperor who ruled the Final Empire for a thousand years. He was once named Rashek, and was a Terris servant who was hired by Alendi. He killed Alendi, however, and went to the Well of Ascension in his place, and there took the power and Ascended. He was finally killed by Vin.

LURCHER: A Misting who can burn steel.

LUTHADEL: Capital of the Final Empire, and largest city in the land. Luthadel is known for its textiles, its forges, and its majestic noble keeps.

MALATIUM: The metal discovered by Kelsier, often dubbed the Eleventh Metal. Nobody knows where he found it, or why he thought it could kill the Lord Ruler. It did, however, eventually lead Vin to the clue she needed to defeat the emperor.

MARDRA: Ham's wife. She doesn't like to be involved in his thieving practices, or exposing their children to the danger of his lifestyle, and generally keeps her distance from the members of the crew.

METALMIND: A piece of metal that a Feruchemist uses as a kind of battery, filling it with certain attributes that he or she can later withdraw. Specific metalminds are named after the different metals: tinmind, steelmind, etc.

MIST: The strange, omnipresent fog that falls on the Final Empire every night. Thicker than a regular fog, it swirls and churns about, almost as if it were alive.

MISTBORN: An Allomancer who can burn all of the Allomantic metals.

MISTCLOAK: A garment worn by many Mistborn as a mark of their station. It is constructed from dozens of thick ribbons of cloth that are sewn together at the top, but allowed to spread free from the shoulders down.

MISTING: An Allomancer who can burn only one metal. They are much more common than Mistborn. (Note: In Allomancy, an Allomancer has either one power or all of them. There are no in-betweens with two or three.)

MISTWRAITH: A nonsentient relative of the kandra people. Mistwraiths are globs of boneless flesh that scavenge the land at night, eating bodies they find, then using the skeletons for their own bodies.

MOORDEN: One of the only obligators who chose to stay in Luthadel and serve Elend.

OBLIGATOR: A member of the Lord Ruler's priesthood. Obligators were more than just religious figures, however; they were civil bureaucrats, and even a spy network. A business deal or promise that wasn't witnessed by an obligator was not considered legally or morally binding.

ORESEUR: A kandra employed by Kelsier. He once played the part of Lord Renoux, Vin's uncle. Vin now holds his Contract.

PENROD, FERSON: One of the most prominent noblemen left in Luthadel. A member of Elend's Assembly.

PEWTERARM: Another term for a Thug, a Misting who can burn pewter.

PHILEN: A prominent merchant in Luthadel and a member of Elend's Assembly.

PITS OF HATHSIN, THE: A network of caverns that were once the only place in the Final Empire that produced atium. The Lord Ruler used prisoners to work them. Kelsier destroyed their ability to produce atium shortly before he died.

PULL (ALLOMANTIC): Using Allomancy to Pull on something—either people's emotions with zinc, or metals with iron.

PUSH (ALLOMANTIC): Using Allomancy to Push on something—either people's emotions with brass, or metals with steel.

RASHEK: A Terris packman before the Ascension, Rashek was hired by Alendi to help him make the trek to the Well of Ascension. Rashek never got along well with Alendi, and eventually killed him. He took the power himself, and became the Lord Ruler.

REEN: Vin's brother, the one who protected her and trained her as a thief. Reen was brutal and unforgiving, but he did save Vin from their insane mother, then protected her during her childhood.

RELEASE (FERUCHEMICAL): When a Feruchemist stops tapping a metalmind, no longer drawing forth its power.

RENOUX, LORD: A nobleman that Kelsier killed, then hired the kandra OreSeur to imitate. Vin played the part of his niece, Valette Renoux.

RIOT (ALLOMANTIC): When an Allomancer burns zinc and Pulls on a person's emotions, enflaming them.

RIOTER (ALLOMANTIC): A Misting who can burn zinc.

SAZE: Sazed's nickname on the crew.

SAZED: A Terris Keeper who joined Kelsier's crew against the wishes of his people, then helped overthrow the Final Empire.

SEEKER (ALLOMANTIC): A Misting who can burn bronze.

SHAN ELARIEL: Elend's former fiancée, a Mistborn whom Vin killed.

SKAA: The peasantry of the Final Empire. They were once of different races and nationalities, but over the thousand-year span of the empire the Lord Ruler worked hard to stamp out any sense of identity in the people, eventually succeeding in creating a single, homogeneous race of slave workers.

SMOKER (ALLOMANTIC): An Allomancer who can burn copper. Also known as a Coppercloud.

SOOTHE (ALLOMANTIC): When an Allomancer burns brass and Pushes on a person's emotions, dampening them.

SOOTHER: A Misting who can burn brass.

SPOOK: A Tineye on Kelsier's crew. The youngest member of the crew, Spook was only fifteen when the Lord Ruler was overthrown. He is Clubs's nephew, and was once known for his use of garbled street slang.

STEEL MINISTRY: The Lord Ruler's priesthood, consisting of a small number of Steel Inquisitors and a larger body of priests called obligators. The Steel Ministry was more than just a religious organization; it was the civic framework of the Final Empire as well.

STRAFF VENTURE: Elend's father, king of the Northern Dominance. He makes his home in Urteau.

SURVIVOR OF SATHSIN: A cognomen of Kelsier, referring to the fact that he is the only known prisoner to ever escape the prison camps at the Pits of Hathsin.

SYNOD (TERRIS): The elite leaders of the Terris Keeper organization.

TAP (FERUCHEMICAL): Drawing power from within a Feruchemist's metalminds. It is parallel to the term "burn" used by Allomancers.

TATHINGDWEN: Capital of the Terris Dominance.

TELDEN: One of Elend's old friends, with whom he would talk politics and philosophy.

TENSOON: Straff Venture's kandra.

TERRIS: The dominance in the far north of the Final Empire. It is the only dominance to retain the name of the kingdom it used to be, perhaps a sign of the Lord Ruler's fondness for his homeland.

THUG (ALLOMANTIC): A Misting who can burn pewter.

TINDWYL: A Terris Keeper and a member of the Synod.

TINEYE: A Misting who can burn tin.

URTEAU: Capital of the Northern Dominance, and seat of House Venture.

VALETTE RENOUX: The alias that Vin used when infiltrating noble society during the days before the Collapse.

WELL OF ASCENSION: A mythological center of power from Terris lore. The Well of Ascension was said to hold a magical reserve of power that could be drawn upon by one who made the trek to visit it at the right time.

WORLDBRINGER: A sect of scholarly Terris Feruchemists before the Collapse. The subsequent Order of Keepers was based on the Worldbringers.

YEDEN: A member of Kelsier's crew and the skaa rebellion. He was killed during the fight against the Lord Ruler.

YOMEN, LORD: An obligator in Urteau who was politically opposed to Cett.

SUMMARY OF BOOK ONE

Mistborn: The Final Empire introduced the land of the Final Empire, ruled over by a powerful immortal known as the Lord Ruler. A thousand years before, the Lord Ruler took the power at the Well of Ascension and supposedly defeated a powerful force or creature known only as the Deepness.

The Lord Ruler conquered the known world and founded the Final Empire. He ruled for a thousand years, stamping out all remnants of the individual kingdoms, cultures, religions, and languages that used to exist in his land. In their place he set up his own system. Certain peoples were dubbed "skaa," a word that meant something akin to "slave" or "peasant." Other peoples were dubbed nobility, and most of these were descendants of those people who had supported the Lord Ruler during his years of conquest. The Lord Ruler had supposedly given them the power of Allomancy in order to gain powerful assassins and warriors who had minds that could think, as opposed to the brutish koloss, and had used them well in conquering and maintaining his empire.

Skaa and nobility were forbidden to interbreed, and the nobility were somehow given the power of Allomancy. During the thousand years of the Lord Ruler's reign, many rebellions occurred among the skaa, but none were successful.

Finally, a half-breed Mistborn known as Kelsier decided to challenge the Lord Ruler. Once the most famous of gentleman thieves in the Final Empire, Kelsier had been known for his daring schemes. Those eventually ended with his capture, however, and he had been sent to the Lord Ruler's death camp at the Pits of Hathsin, the secret source of atium.

It was said that nobody ever escaped the Pits of Hathsin alive—but Kelsier did just that. He gained his powers as a Mistborn during that time, and managed to free himself, earning thc title the Survivor of Hathsin. At this point, he turned from his selfish ways and decided to try his most daring plan yet: the overthrow of the Final Empire.

He recruited a team of thieves, mostly half-breed Mistings, to help him achieve his goal. During this time, he also recruited a young half-breed Mistborn girl named Vin. Vin was unaware of her powers, and Kelsier brought her into the crew to train her, theoretically to have someone to whom he could pass his legacy.

Kelsier's crew slowly gathered an underground army of skaa rebels. The crew began to fear that Kelsier was setting himself up to be another Lord Ruler. He sought to make himself a legend among the skaa, becoming almost a religious figure to them. Meanwhile, Vin—who had been raised on the streets by a cruel brother—was growing to trust people for the first time in her life. As this happened, Vin began to believe in Kelsier and his purpose.

During the process of working on their plan, Vin was

used as a spy among the nobility, and was trained to infiltrate their balls and parties playing the part of "Valette Renoux," a young noblewoman from the countryside. During the first of these balls, she met Elend Venture, a young, idealistic nobleman. He eventually showed her that not all noblemen were deserving of their poor reputation, and the two became enamored of each other, despite Kelsier's best efforts.

The crew also discovered a journal, apparently written by the Lord Ruler himself during the days before the Ascension. This book painted a different picture of the tyrant; it depicted a melancholy, tired man who was trying his best to protect the people against the Deepness, despite the fact that he didn't really understand it.

In the end, it was revealed that Kelsier's plan had been much more broad than simple use of the army to overthrow the empire. He'd partially spent so much effort on raising troops so that he would have an excuse to spread rumors about himself. He also used it to train his crew in the arts of leadership and persuasion. The true extent of his plan was revealed when he sacrificed his life in a very visible way, making himself a martyr to the skaa and finally convincing them to rise up and overthrow the Lord Ruler.

One of Kelsier's crewmembers—a man who had been playing the part of "Lord Renoux," Valette's uncle—turned out to be a kandra named OreSeur. OreSeur took on Kelsier's form, then went about spreading rumors that Kelsier had returned from the grave, inspiring the skaa. After this, he became Contractually bound to Vin, and was charged with watching over her after Kelsier's death.

Vin was the one who in fact killed the Lord Ruler. She discovered that he wasn't actually a god, or even immortal—he had simply found a way to extend his life and his power by making use of both Allomancy and Feruchemy at the same time. He wasn't the hero from the logbook—but, instead, was that man's servant, a Feruchemist of some great power. Still, he was much stronger in Allomancy than Vin. While she was fighting him, she drew upon the mists somehow, burning them in place of metals. She still doesn't know why or how this happened. With that power—and with the knowledge of his true nature—she was able to defeat and kill him.

The Final Empire was thrown into chaos. Elend Venture took control of Luthadel, the capital, and put Kelsier's crew in prime governmental positions.

One year has passed.

Please turn the page for a sneak preview of . . .

. . . the final book in the MISTBORN series

Coming soon from Gollancz.

PROLOGUE

MARSH STRUGGLED TO KILL HIMSELF.

His hand trembled as he tried to summon the strength to make himself reach up and pull the spike free from his back and end his monstrous life. He had given up on trying to break free. Three years. Three years as an Inquisitor, three years imprisoned in his own thoughts. Those years had proven that there was no escape. Even now, his mind clouded.

And then *It* took control. The world seemed to vibrate around him; then suddenly he could see clearly. Why had he struggled? Why had he worried? All was as it should be.

He stepped forward. Though he could no longer see as normal men did – after all, he had large steel spikes driven point-first through his eyes – he could sense the room around him. The spikes protruded from the back of his skull; if he reached up to touch the back of his head, he could feel the sharp points. There was no blood.

The spikes gave him power. Everything was outlined in faint blue Allomantic lines, highlighting the world. The room was of modest size, and several companions – also outlined in blue, the Allomantic lines pointing at the metals contained in their very blood – stood with Marsh. Each one had spikes through his eyes.

Each one that is, except for the man tied to the table in front of him. Marsh smiled, taking a spike off of the table beside him, then hefting it. His prisoner wore no gag. That would have stopped the screams.

'Please,' the prisoner whispered, trembling. Even a Terrisman steward would break down when confronted by his own violent death. The man struggled weakly. He was in a very awkward position, as he had been tied to the table on top of another person. The table had been designed that way, with depressions to allow for the body underneath.

'What is it that you want?' the Terrisman asked. 'I can tell you no more about the Synod!'

Marsh fingered the brass spike, feeling its tip. There was work to do, but he hesitated, relishing the pain and terror of the man's voice. Hesitated so that he could . . .

Marsh grabbed control of his own mind. The room's scents lost their sweetness, and instead reeked with the stench of blood and death. His joy turned to horror. His prisoner was a Keeper of Terris – a man who had worked his entire life for the good of others. Killing him would not only be a crime, but a tragedy. Marsh tried to take command, tried to force his arm up and around to grab the linchpin spoke from its back – its removal would kill him.

Yet, *It* was too strong. The force. Somehow,

it had control over Marsh – and it needed him and the other Inquisitors to be its hands. It was free – Marsh could still feel it exulting in that – but something kept it from affecting the world too much by itself. An opposition. A force that lay over the land like a shield.

It was not yet complete. It needed more. Something else . . . something hidden. And Marsh would find that something, bring it to its master. The master that Vin had freed. The entity that had been imprisoned within the Well of Ascension.

It called itself Ruin.

Marsh smiled as his prisoner began to cry; then he stepped forward, raising the spike in his hand. He placed it against the whimpering man's chest. The spike would need to pierce the man's body, passing through the heart, then be driven into the body of the Inquisitor tied below. Hemalurgy was a messy art.

That was why it was so much fun. Marsh picked up a mallet and began to pound.

Brandon Sanderson was born in Nebraska in 1975. Since then he has written the Mistborn series, amongst others, become a *New York Times* bestselling author and been hailed as the natural successor to Robert Jordan. He lives in Utah.

http://www.brandonsanderson.com/

Praise for Brandon Sanderson and THE FINAL EMPIRE:

'[Sanderson] has created a fascinating world here, one that deserves a sequel'

The Washington Post

'Intrigue, politics, and conspiracies mesh complexly in a world Sanderson realises in satisfying depth and peoples with impressive characters'

Booklist

'An enjoyable, adventurous read'
Locus

'Brandon Sanderson is the real thing – an exciting storyteller with a unique and powerful vision'

David Farland

'Sanderson is astonishingly wise'

Orson Scott Card

BRANDON SANDERSON

First published in Great Britain in 2009 by
Gollancz
An imprint of the Orion Publishing Group
Carmelite House, 50 Victoria Embankment,
London EC4Y 0DZ
An Hachette UK Company

40

A CIP catalogue record for this book is available
from the British Library

ISBN 978 0 575 08991 4

Printed in Great Britain by Clays Ltd, Elcograf S.p.A.

www.brandonsanderson.com

www.orionbooks.co.uk

The Orion Publishing Group's policy is to use papers that are natural, renewable and recyclable products and made from wood grown in sustainable forests. The logging and manufacturing processes are expected to conform to the environmental regulations of the country of origin.

FOR BETH SANDERSON,

Who's been reading fantasy
For longer than I've been alive,
And fully deserves
To have a grandson as loony as she is.

ACKNOWLEDGMENTS

Once again, I find myself in need of thanking my wonderful agent, Joshua Bilmes, and equally amazing editor, Moshe Feder. They did a wonderful job with this book, and I'm proud to have the opportunity to work with them.

As always, my tireless writing groups have consistently provided feedback and encouragement: Alan Layton, Janette Layton, Kaylynne ZoBell, Nate Hatfield, Bryce Cundick, Kimball Larsen, and Emily Scorup. Alpha readers, who saw a version of this book in a much rougher form and helped me shape it into what you see now, included Krista Olson, Benjamin R. Olson, Micah Demoux, Eric Ehlers, Izzy Whiting, Stacy Whitman, Kristina Kugler, Megan Kauffman, Sarah Bylund, C. Lee Player, Ethan Skarstedt, Jillena O'Brien, Ryan Jurado, and the incalculable Peter Ahlstrom.

There are also a few people in particular whom I would like to thank. Isaac Stewart, who did the map work for this novel, was an invaluable resource both in the idea department and with visual cues. Heather Kirby had excellent advice to help me with the mysterious inner workings of a young woman's mind. The proofreading done by Chersti Stapely and Kayleena Richins was much appreciated.

In addition, I'd like to acknowledge some of the very important people who work behind the scenes on the books that you buy. Irene Gallo, the art director at Tor, does a brilliant job—it's because of her that both this book and *Elantris* have the wonderful covers that they do. Also, David Moench, in the Tor publicity department, went far beyond the call of duty in helping make *Elantris* a success. Both have my thanks.

Finally, as always, I am thankful to my family for their continued support and enthusiasm.

In particular, I'd like to thank my brother, Jordan, for his enthusiasm, support, and loyalty. Check out his handiwork at my Web site: www.brandonsanderson.com.

Terris Dominance
Farmost Dominance
Western Dominance
Northern Dominance
Central Dominance
Crescent Dominance
Southern Dominance
Southern Islands
Eastern Dominance
Remote Dominance
9. Lake Tyrian
10. Lake Luthadel
11. The Black Lake
12. River Searan
13. North Searan
14. South Searan
15. The River Channerel
The Final Empire
1. Luthadel
The Ashmounts
2. Tyrian 3. Zerinah
4. Faleast 5. Doriel
6. Morag 7. Kalling 8. Torinost
2005

LUTH

Steel Gate

Aspen Row

The Twists

Hotel District

Iron Gate

Old Gate

Commercial District

Bronze Gate

1. Fountain Square
2. Kredik Shaw
3. Canton of Orthodoxy Headquarters
4. Canton of Finance Headquarters
5. Luthadel Garrison
6. Keep Venture
7. Keep Hasting
8. Keep Lekal
9. Keep Erikeller
10. Clubs' Shop
11. Camon's Safehouse
12. Old Wall Street
13. Kenton Street
14. Ahlstrom Square
15. 15th Crossroads
16. Canal Street
17. Skaa Market
18. Canton of Resource Headquarters
19. Canton of Inquisition Headquarters

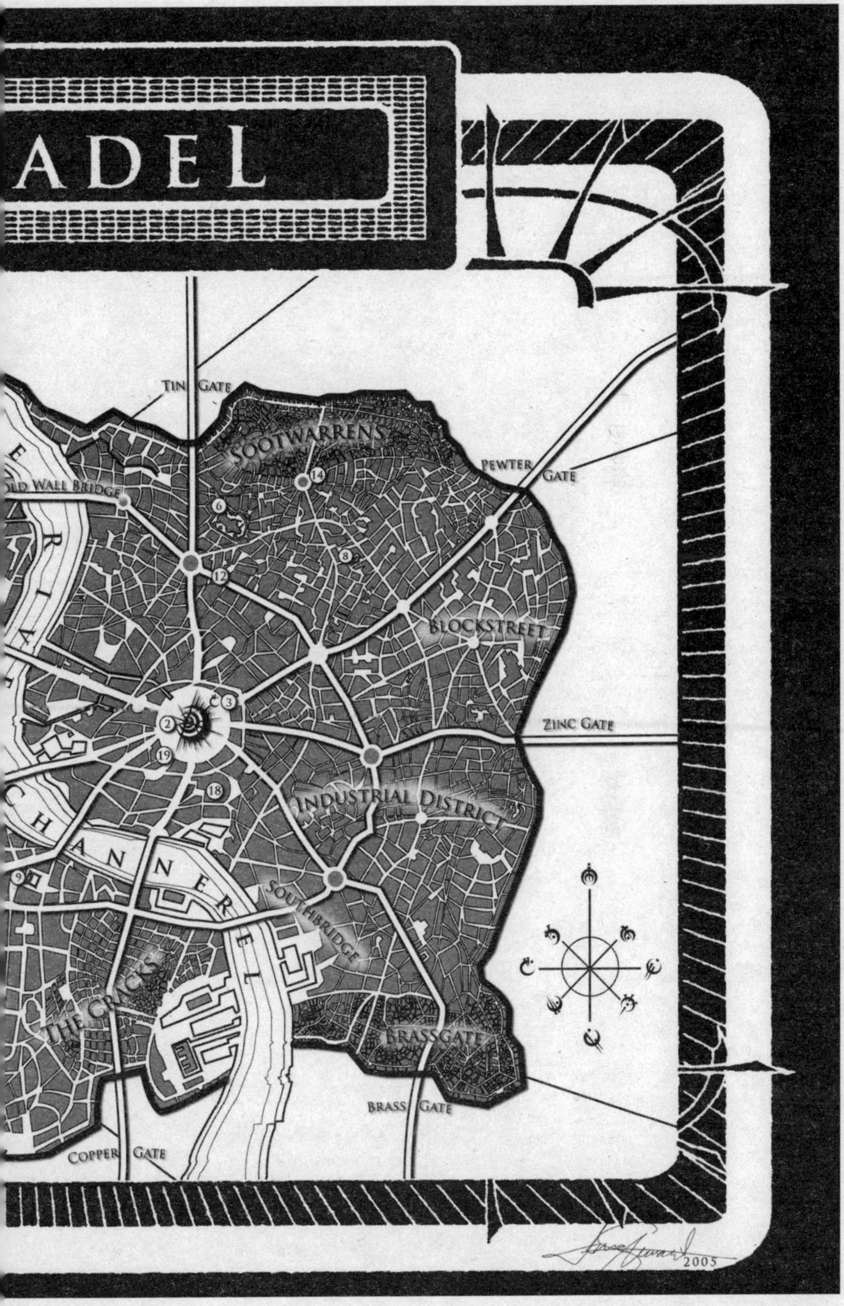

ADEL

TIN GATE
SOOTWARRENS
OLD WALL BRIDGE
PEWTER GATE
BLOCKSTREET
ZINC GATE
INDUSTRIAL DISTRICT
CHANNEREL
SOUTHBRIDGE
BRASSGATE
BRASS GATE
COPPER GATE

14
6
8
12
3
2
19
18
9

2005

Sometimes, I worry that I'm not the hero everyone thinks I am.

The philosophers assure me that this is the time, that the signs have been met. But I still wonder if they have the wrong man. So many people depend on me. They say I will hold the future of the entire world on my arms.

What would they think if they knew that their champion—the Hero of Ages, their savior—doubted himself? Perhaps they wouldn't be shocked at all. In a way, this is what worries me most. Maybe, in their hearts, they wonder—just as I do.

When they see me, do they see a liar?

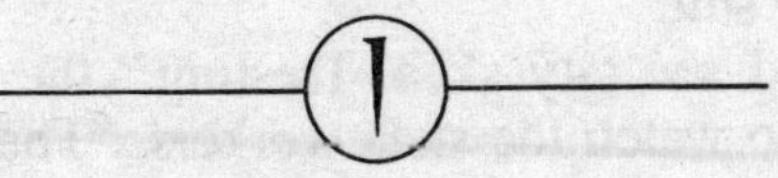

PROLOGUE

ASH FELL FROM THE SKY.

Lord Tresting frowned, glancing up at the ruddy midday sky as his servants scuttled forward, opening a parasol over Tresting and his distinguished guest. Ashfalls weren't that uncommon in the Final Empire, but Tresting had hoped to avoid getting soot stains on his fine new suit coat and red vest, which had just arrived via canal boat from Luthadel itself. Fortunately, there wasn't much wind; the parasol would likely be effective.

Tresting stood with his guest on a small hilltop patio that overlooked the fields. Hundreds of people in brown smocks worked in the falling ash, caring for the crops. There was a sluggishness to their efforts—but, of course, that was the way of the skaa. The peasants were an indolent, unproductive lot.

They didn't complain, of course; they knew better than that. Instead, they simply worked with bowed heads, moving about their work with quiet apathy. The passing whip of a taskmaster would force them into dedicated motion for a few moments, but as soon as the taskmaster passed, they would return to their languor.

Tresting turned to the man standing beside him on the hill. "One would think," Tresting noted, "that a thousand years of working in fields would have bred them to be a little more effective at it."

The obligator turned, raising an eyebrow—the motion done as if to highlight his most distinctive feature, the intricate tattoos that laced the skin around his eyes. The tattoos were enormous, reaching all the way across his brow and up the sides of his nose. This was a full prelan—a very important obligator indeed. Tresting had his own, personal obligators back at the manor, but they were only minor functionaries, with barely a few marks around their eyes. This man had arrived from Luthadel with the same canal boat that had brought Tresting's new suit.

"You should see city skaa, Tresting," the obligator said, turning back to watch the skaa workers. "These are actually quite diligent compared to those inside Luthadel. You have more . . . direct control over your skaa here. How many would you say you lose a month?"

"Oh, a half dozen or so," Tresting said. "Some to beatings, some to exhaustion."

"Runaways?"

"Never!" Tresting said. "When I first inherited this land from my father, I had a few runaways—but I executed their families. The rest quickly lost heart. I've never understood men who have trouble with their skaa—I find the creatures easy to control, if you show a properly firm hand."

The obligator nodded, standing quietly in his gray robes. He seemed pleased—which was a good thing. The skaa weren't actually Tresting's property. Like all skaa, they belonged to the Lord Ruler; Tresting only leased the workers from his God, much in the same way he paid for the services of His obligators.

The obligator looked down, checking his pocket watch, then glanced up at the sun. Despite the ashfall, the sun was bright this day, shining a brilliant crimson red behind the smoky blackness of the upper sky. Tresting removed a handkerchief and wiped his brow, thankful for the parasol's shade against the midday heat.

"Very well, Tresting," the obligator said. "I will carry your proposal to Lord Venture, as requested. He will have a favorable report from me on your operations here."

Tresting held in a sigh of relief. An obligator was required to witness any contract or business deal between noblemen. True, even a lowly obligator like the ones Tresting employed could serve as such a witness—but it meant so much more to impress Straff Venture's own obligator.

The obligator turned toward him. "I will leave back down the canal this afternoon."

"So soon?" Tresting asked. "Wouldn't you care to stay for supper?"

"No," the obligator replied. "Though there is another matter I wish to discuss with you. I came not only at the behest of Lord Venture, but to . . . look in on some matters for the Canton of Inquisition. Rumors say that you like to dally with your skaa women."

Tresting felt a chill.

The obligator smiled; he likely meant it to be disarming, but Tresting only found it eerie. "Don't worry yourself, Tresting," the obligator said. "If there had been any *real* worries about your actions, a Steel Inquisitor would have been sent here in my place."

Tresting nodded slowly. Inquisitor. He'd never seen one of the inhuman creatures, but he had heard . . . stories.

"I have been satisfied regarding your actions with the skaa women," the obligator said, looking back over the fields. "What I've seen and heard here indicate that you always clean up your messes. A man such as yourself—efficient, productive—could go far in Luthadel. A few more years of work, some inspired mercantile deals, and who knows?"

The obligator turned away, and Tresting found himself smiling. It wasn't a promise, or even an endorsement—for the most part, obligators were more bureaucrats and witnesses than they were priests—but to hear such praise from one of the Lord Ruler's own servants . . . Tresting knew that some nobility considered the obligators to be unsettling—some men even considered them a bother—but at that moment, Testing could have kissed his distinguished guest.

Tresting turned back toward the skaa, who worked quietly beneath the bloody sun and the lazy flakes of ash. Tresting had always been a country nobleman, living on his plantation, dreaming of perhaps moving into Luthadel itself. He had heard of the balls and the parties, the glamour and the intrigue, and it excited him to no end.

I'll have to celebrate tonight, he thought. There was that young girl in the fourteenth hovel that he'd been watching for some time. . . .

He smiled again. A few more years of work, the obligator had said. But could Tresting perhaps speed that up, if he worked a little harder? His skaa population had been growing lately. Perhaps if he pushed them a bit more, he could bring in an extra harvest this summer and fulfill his contract with Lord Venture in extra measure.

Tresting nodded as he watched the crowd of lazy skaa, some working with their hoes, others on hands and knees, pushing the ash away from the fledgling crops. They didn't complain. They didn't hope. They barely dared think. That was the way it should be, for they were skaa. They were—

Tresting froze as one of the skaa looked up. The man met Tresting's eyes, a spark—no, a fire—of defiance showing in his expression. Tresting had never seen anything like it, not in the face of a skaa. Tresting stepped backward reflexively, a chill running through him as the strange, straight-backed skaa held his eyes.

And smiled.

Tresting looked away. "Kurdon!" he snapped.

The burly taskmaster rushed up the incline. "Yes, my lord?"

Tresting turned, pointing at . . .

He frowned. Where had that skaa been standing? Working with their heads bowed, bodies stained by soot and sweat, they were so hard to tell apart. Tresting paused, searching. He thought he knew the place . . . an empty spot, where nobody now stood.

But, no. That couldn't be it. The man couldn't have disappeared from the group so quickly. Where would he have gone? He must be in there, somewhere, working with his head now properly bowed. Still, his moment of apparent defiance was inexcusable.

"My lord?" Kurdon asked again.

The obligator stood at the side, watching curiously. It would not be wise to let the man know that one of the skaa had acted so brazenly.

"Work the skaa in that southern section a little harder," Tresting ordered, pointing. "I see them being sluggish, even for skaa. Beat a few of them."

Kurdon shrugged, but nodded. It wasn't much of a reason for a beating—but, then, he didn't need much of a reason to give the workers a beating.

They were, after all, only skaa.

Kelsier had heard stories.

He had heard whispers of times when once, long ago, the sun had not been red. Times when the sky hadn't been clogged by smoke and ash, when plants hadn't struggled to grow, and when skaa hadn't been slaves. Times before the Lord Ruler. Those days, however, were nearly forgotten. Even the legends were growing vague.

Kelsier watched the sun, his eyes following the giant red disk as it crept toward the western horizon. He stood quietly for a long moment, alone in the empty fields. The day's work was done; the skaa had been herded back to their hovels. Soon the mists would come.

Eventually, Kelsier sighed, then turned to pick his way across the furrows and pathways, weaving between large heaps of ash. He avoided stepping on the plants—though he wasn't sure why he bothered. The crops hardly seemed worth the effort. Wan, with wilted brown leaves, the plants seemed as depressed as the people who tended them.

The skaa hovels loomed in the waning light. Already, Kelsier could see the mists beginning to form, clouding the air, and giving the moundlike buildings a surreal, intangible look. The hovels stood unguarded; there was no need for watchers, for no skaa would venture outside once night arrived. Their fear of the mists was far too strong.

I'll have to cure them of that someday, Kelsier thought as he approached one of the larger buildings. *But, all things in their own time.* He pulled open the door and slipped inside.

Conversation stopped immediately. Kelsier closed the door, then turned with a smile to confront the room of about thirty skaa. A firepit burned weakly at the center, and the large cauldron beside it was filled with vegetable-dappled water—the beginnings of an evening meal. The soup would be bland, of course. Still, the smell was enticing.

"Good evening, everyone," Kelsier said with a smile, resting his pack beside his feet and leaning against the door. "How was your day?"

His words broke the silence, and the women returned to their dinner preparations. A group of men sitting at a crude table, however, continued to regard Kelsier with dissatisfied expressions.

"Our day was filled with work, traveler," said Tepper, one of the skaa elders. "Something you managed to avoid."

"Fieldwork hasn't ever really suited me," Kelsier said. "It's far too hard on my delicate skin." He smiled, holding up hands and arms that were lined with layers and layers of thin scars. They covered his skin, running lengthwise, as if some beast had repeatedly raked its claws up and down his arms.

Tepper snorted. He was young to be an elder, probably barely into his forties—at most, he might be five years Kelsier's senior. However, the scrawny man held himself with the air of one who liked to be in charge.

"This is no time for levity," Tepper said sternly. "When we harbor a traveler, we expect him to behave himself and avoid suspicion. When you ducked away from the fields this morning, you could have earned a whipping for the men around you."

"True," Kelsier said. "But those men could also have been

whipped for standing in the wrong place, for pausing too long, or for coughing when a taskmaster walked by. I once saw a man beaten because his master claimed that he had 'blinked inappropriately.' "

Tepper sat with narrow eyes and a stiff posture, his arm resting on the table. His expression was unyielding.

Kelsier sighed, rolling his eyes. "Fine. If you want me to go, I'll be off then." He slung his pack up on his shoulder and nonchalantly pulled open the door.

Thick mist immediately began to pour through the portal, drifting lazily across Kelsier's body, pooling on the floor and creeping across the dirt like a hesitant animal. Several people gasped in horror, though most of them were too stunned to make a sound. Kelsier stood for a moment, staring out into the dark mists, their shifting currents lit feebly by the cooking pit's coals.

"Close the door." Tepper's words were a plea, not a command.

Kelsier did as requested, pushing the door closed and stemming the flood of white mist. "The mist is not what you think. You fear it far too much."

"Men who venture into the mist lose their souls," a woman whispered. Her words raised a question. Had Kelsier walked in the mists? What, then, had happened to his soul?

If you only knew, Kelsier thought. "Well, I guess this means I'm staying." He waved for a boy to bring him a stool. "It's a good thing, too—it would have been a shame for me to leave before I shared my news."

More than one person perked up at the comment. This was the real reason they tolerated him—the reason even the timid peasants would harbor a man such as Kelsier, a skaa who defied the Lord Ruler's will by traveling from plantation to plantation. A renegade he might be—a danger to the entire community—but he brought news from the outside world.

"I come from the north," Kelsier said. "From lands where the Lord Ruler's touch is less noticeable." He spoke in a clear voice, and people leaned unconsciously toward him as they worked. On the next day, Kelsier's words would be repeated to the several hundred people who lived in other hovels. The skaa might be subservient, but they were incurable gossips.

"Local lords rule in the West," Kelsier said, "and they are far from the iron grip of the Lord Ruler and his obligators. Some of these distant noblemen are finding that happy skaa make better workers than mistreated skaa. One man, Lord Renoux, has even ordered his taskmasters to stop unauthorized beatings. There are whispers that he's considering paying wages to his plantation skaa, like city craftsmen might earn."

"Nonsense," Tepper said.

"My apologies," Kelsier said. "I didn't realize that Goodman Tepper had been to Lord Renoux's estates recently. When you dined with him last, did he tell you something that he did not tell me?"

Tepper blushed: Skaa did not travel, and they certainly didn't dine with lords. "You think me a fool, traveler," Tepper said, "but I know what you're doing. You're the one they call the Survivor; those scars on your arms give you away. You're a troublemaker—you travel the plantations, stirring up discontent. You eat our food, telling your grand stories and your lies, then you disappear and leave people like me to deal with the false hopes you give our children."

Kelsier raised an eyebrow. "Now, now, Goodman Tepper," he said. "Your worries are completely unfounded. Why, I have no intention of eating your food. I brought my own." With that, Kelsier reached over and tossed his pack onto the earth before Tepper's table. The loose bag slumped to the side, dumping an array of foods to the ground. Fine breads, fruits, and even a few thick, cured sausages bounced free.

A summerfruit rolled across the packed earthen floor and bumped lightly against Tepper's foot. The middle-aged skaa regarded the fruit with stunned eyes. "That's nobleman's food!"

Kelsier snorted. "Barely. You know, for a man of renowned prestige and rank, your Lord Tresting has remarkably poor taste. His pantry is an embarrassment to his noble station."

Tepper paled even further. "That's where you went this afternoon," he whispered. "You went to the manor. You . . . *stole from the master!*"

"Indeed," Kelsier said. "And, might I add that while your lord's taste in food is deplorable, his eye for soldiers is far more impressive. Sneaking into his manor during the day was quite a challenge."

Tepper was still staring at the bag of food. "If the taskmasters find this here . . ."

"Well, I suggest you make it disappear then," Kelsier said. "I'd be willing to bet that it tastes a fair bit better than watered-down farlet soup."

Two dozen sets of hungry eyes studied the food. If Tepper intended further arguments, he didn't make them quickly enough, for his silent pause was taken as agreement. Within a few minutes, the bag's contents had been inspected and distributed, and the pot of soup sat bubbling and ignored as the skaa feasted on a meal far more exotic.

Kelsier settled back, leaning against the hovel's wooden wall and watching the people devour their food. He had spoken correctly: The pantry's offerings had been depressingly mundane. However, this was a people who had been fed on nothing but soup and gruel since they were children. To them, breads and fruits were rare delicacies—usually eaten only as aging discards brought down by the house servants.

"Your storytelling was cut short, young man," an elderly skaa noted, hobbling over to sit on a stool beside Kelsier.

"Oh, I suspect there will be time for more later," Kelsier said. "Once all evidence of my thievery has been properly devoured. Don't you want any of it?"

"No need," the old man said. "The last time I tried lords' food, I had stomach pains for three days. New tastes are like new ideas, young man—the older you get, the more difficult they are for you to stomach."

Kelsier paused. The old man was hardly an imposing sight. His leathered skin and bald scalp made him look more frail than they did wise. Yet, he had to be stronger than he looked; few plantation skaa lived to such ages. Many lords didn't allow the elderly to remain home from daily work, and the frequent beatings that made up a skaa's life took a terrible toll on the elderly.

"What was your name again?" Kelsier asked.

"Mennis."

Kelsier glanced back at Tepper. "So, Goodman Mennis, tell me something. Why do you let him lead?"

Mennis shrugged. "When you get to be my age, you have to be very careful where you waste your energy. Some battles just aren't worth fighting." There was an implication in Mennis's eyes; he was referring to things greater than his own struggle with Tepper.

"You're satisfied with this, then?" Kelsier asked, nodding toward the hovel and its half-starved, overworked occupants. "You're content with a life full of beatings and endless drudgery?"

"At least it's a life," Mennis said. "I know what wages, malcontent, and rebellion bring. The eye of the Lord Ruler, and the ire of the Steel Ministry, can be far more terrible than a few whippings. Men like you preach change, but I wonder. Is this a battle we can really fight?"

"You're fighting it already, Goodman Mennis. You're just losing horribly." Kelsier shrugged. "But, what do I know? I'm just a traveling miscreant, here to eat your food and impress your youths."

Mennis shook his head. "You jest, but Tepper might have been right. I fear your visit will bring us grief."

Kelsier smiled. "That's why I didn't contradict him—at least, not on the troublemaker point." He paused, then smiled more deeply. "In fact, I'd say calling me a troublemaker is probably the only accurate thing Tepper has said since I got here."

"How do you do that?" Mennis asked, frowning.

"What?"

"Smile so much."

"Oh, I'm just a happy person."

Mennis glanced down at Kelsier's hands. "You know, I've only seen scars like those on one other person—and he was dead. His body was returned to Lord Tresting as proof that his punishment had been carried out." Mennis looked up at Kelsier. "He'd been caught speaking of rebellion. Tresting sent him to the Pits of Hathsin, where he had worked until he died. The lad lasted less than a month."

Kelsier glanced down at his hands and forearms. They still burned sometimes, though he was certain the pain was only in his mind. He looked up at Mennis and smiled. "You ask why I smile, Goodman Mennis? Well, the Lord Ruler thinks he has claimed laughter and joy for himself. I'm disinclined to let him do so. This is one battle that doesn't take very much effort to fight."

Mennis stared at Kelsier, and for a moment Kelsier thought the old man might smile in return. However, Mennis eventually just shook his head. "I don't know. I just don't—"

The scream cut him off. It came from outside, perhaps to the north, though the mists distorted sounds. The people in the hovel fell silent, listening to the faint, high-pitched yells. Despite the distance and the mist, Kelsier could hear the pain contained in those screams.

Kelsier burned tin.

It was simple for him now, after years of practice. The tin sat with other Allomantic metals within his stomach, swallowed earlier, waiting for him to draw upon them. He reached inside with his mind and touched the tin, tapping powers he still barely understood. The tin flared to life within him, burning his stomach like the sensation of a hot drink swallowed too quickly.

Allomantic power surged through his body, enhancing his senses. The room around him became crisp, the dull firepit flaring to near blinding brightness. He could feel the grain in the wood of the stool beneath him. He could still taste the remnants of the loaf of bread he'd snacked on earlier. Most importantly, he could hear the screams with supernatural ears. Two separate people were yelling. One was an older woman, the other a younger woman—perhaps a child. The younger screams were getting farther and farther away.

"Poor Jess," a nearby woman said, her voice booming in Kelsier's enhanced ears. "That child of hers was a curse. It's better for skaa not to have pretty daughters."

Tepper nodded. "Lord Tresting was sure to send for the girl sooner or later. We all knew it. Jess knew it."

"Still a shame, though," another man said.

The screams continued in the distance. Burning tin, Kelsier was able to judge the direction accurately. Her voice was moving toward the lord's manor. The sounds set something off within him, and he felt his face flush with anger.

Kelsier turned. "Does Lord Tresting ever return the girls after he's finished with them?"

Old Mennis shook his head. "Lord Tresting is a law-abiding nobleman—he has the girls killed after a few weeks. He doesn't want to catch the eye of the Inquisitors."

That was the Lord Ruler's command. He couldn't afford to have half-breed children running around—children who might possess powers that skaa weren't even supposed to know existed. . . .

The screams waned, but Kelsier's anger only built. The yells reminded him of other screams. A woman's screams from the past. He stood abruptly, stool toppling to the ground behind him.

"Careful, lad," Mennis said apprehensively. "Remember what I said about wasting energy. You'll never raise that rebellion of yours if you get yourself killed tonight."

Kelsier glanced toward the old man. Then, through the screams and the pain, he forced himself to smile. "I'm not here to lead a rebellion among you, Goodman Mennis. I just want to stir up a little trouble."

"What good could that do?"

Kelsier's smile deepened. "New days are coming. Survive a little longer, and you just might see great happenings in the Final Empire. I bid you all thanks for your hospitality."

With that, he pulled open the door and strode out into the mist.

Mennis lay awake in the early hours of morning. It seemed that the older he became, the more difficult it was for him to sleep. This was particularly true when he was troubled about something, such as the traveler's failure to return to the hovel.

Mennis hoped that Kelsier had come to his senses and decided to move on. However, that prospect seemed unlikely; Mennis had seen the fire in Kelsier's eyes. It seemed such a shame that a man who had survived the Pits would instead find death here, on a random plantation, trying to protect a girl everyone else had given up for dead.

How would Lord Tresting react? He was said to be particularly harsh with anyone who interrupted his nighttime enjoyments. If Kelsier had managed to disturb the master's pleasures, Tresting might easily decide to punish the rest of his skaa by association.

Eventually, the other skaa began to awake. Mennis lay on the hard earth—bones aching, back complaining, muscles exhausted—trying to decide if it was worth rising. Each day, he nearly gave up. Each day, it was a little harder. One day, he would just stay in the hovel, waiting until the taskmasters came to kill those who were too sick or too elderly to work.

But not today. He could see too much fear in the eyes of the skaa—they knew that Kelsier's nighttime activities would bring trouble. They needed Mennis; they looked to him. He needed to get up.

And so he did. Once he started moving, the pains of age decreased slightly, and he was able to shuffle out of the hovel toward the fields, leaning on a younger man for support.

It was then that he caught a scent in the air. "What's that?" he asked. "Do you smell smoke?"

Shum—the lad upon whom Mennis leaned—paused. The last remnants of the night's mist had burned away, and the red sun was rising behind the sky's usual haze of blackish clouds.

"I always smell smoke, lately," Shum said. "The Ashmounts are violent this year."

"No," Mennis said, feeling increasingly apprehensive. "This is different." He turned to the north, toward where a group of skaa were gathering. He let go of Shum, shuffling toward the group, feet kicking up dust and ash as he moved.

At the center of the group of people, he found Jess. Her daughter, the one they all assumed had been taken by Lord Tresting, stood beside her. The young girl's eyes were red from lack of sleep, but she appeared unharmed.

"She came back not long after they took her," the woman was explaining. "She came and pounded on the door, crying in the mist. Flen was sure it was just a mistwraith impersonating her, but I had to let her in! I don't care what he says, I'm not giving her up. I brought her out in the sunlight, and she didn't disappear. That proves she's not a mistwraith!"

Mennis stumbled back from the growing crowd. Did none of them see it? No taskmasters came to break up the group. No soldiers came to make the morning population counts. Something was very wrong. Mennis continued to the north, moving frantically toward the manor house.

By the time he arrived, others had noticed the twisting line of smoke that was just barely visible in the morning light. Mennis wasn't the first to arrive at the edge of the short hilltop plateau, but the group made way for him when he did.

The manor house was gone. Only a blackened, smoldering scar remained.

"By the Lord Ruler!" Mennis whispered. "What happened here?"

"He killed them all."

Mennis turned. The speaker was Jess's girl. She stood looking down at the fallen house, a satisfied expression on her youthful face.

"They were dead when he brought me out," she said. "All of them—the soldiers, the taskmasters, the lords . . . dead. Even Lord Tresting and his obligators. The master had left me, going to investigate when the noises began. On the way out, I saw him lying in his own blood, stab wounds in his chest. The man who saved me threw a torch in the building as we left."

"This man," Mennis said. "He had scars on his hands and arms, reaching past the elbows?"

The girl nodded silently.

"What kind of demon was that man?" one of the skaa muttered uncomfortably.

"Mistwraith," another whispered, apparently forgetting that Kelsier had gone out during the day.

But he did go out into the mist, Mennis thought. *And, how did he accomplish a feat like this . . . ? Lord Tresting kept over two dozen soldiers! Did Kelsier have a hidden band of rebels, perhaps?*

Kelsier's words from the night before sounded in his ears. *New days are coming. . . .*

"But, what of us?" Tepper asked, terrified. "What will happen when the Lord Ruler hears this? He'll think that we did it! He'll send us to the Pits, or maybe just send his koloss to slaughter us outright! Why would that troublemaker do something like this? Doesn't he understand the damage he's done?"

"He understands," Mennis said. "He warned us, Tepper. He came to stir up trouble."

"But, why?"

"Because he knew we'd never rebel on our own, so he gave us no choice."

Tepper paled.

Lord Ruler, Mennis thought. *I can't do this. I can barely get up in the mornings—I can't save this people.*

But what other choice was there?

Mennis turned. "Gather the people, Tepper. We must flee before word of this disaster reaches the Lord Ruler."

"Where will we go?"

"The caves to the east," Mennis said. "Travelers say there are rebel skaa hiding in them. Perhaps they'll take us in."

Tepper paled further. "But . . . we'd have to travel for days. Spend nights *in the mist.*"

"We can do that," Mennis said, "or we can stay here and die."

Tepper stood frozen for a moment, and Mennis thought the shock of it all might have overwhelmed him. Eventually, however, the younger man scurried off to gather the others, as commanded.

Mennis sighed, looking up toward the trailing line of smoke, cursing the man Kelsier quietly in his mind.

New days indeed.

PART ONE

THE SURVIVOR OF HATHSIN

I consider myself to be a man of principle. But, what man does not? Even the cutthroat, I have noticed, considers his actions "moral" after a fashion.

Perhaps another person, reading of my life, would name me a religious tyrant. He could call me arrogant. What is to make that man's opinion any less valid than my own?

I guess it all comes down to one fact: In the end, I'm the one with the armies.

1

ASH FELL FROM THE SKY.

Vin watched the downy flakes drift through the air. Leisurely. Careless. Free. The puffs of soot fell like black snowflakes, descending upon the dark city of Luthadel. They drifted in corners, blowing in the breeze and curling in tiny whirlwinds over the cobblestones. They seemed so uncaring. What would that be like?

Vin sat quietly in one of the crew's watch-holes—a hidden alcove built into the bricks on the side of the safe house. From within it, a crewmember could watch the street for signs of danger. Vin wasn't on duty; the watch-hole was simply one of the few places where she could find solitude.

And Vin liked solitude. *When you're alone, no one can betray you.* Reen's words. Her brother had taught her so many things, then had reinforced them by doing what he'd always promised he would—by betraying her himself. *It's the only way you'll learn. Anyone will betray you, Vin. Anyone.*

The ash continued to fall. Sometimes, Vin imagined she was like the ash, or the wind, or the mist itself. A thing without thought, capable of simply *being*, not thinking, caring, or hurting. Then she could be . . . free.

She heard shuffling a short distance away, then the trapdoor at the back of the small chamber snapped open.

"Vin!" Ulef said, sticking his head into the room. "There you are! Camon's been searching for you for a half hour."

That's kind of why I hid in the first place.

"You should get going," Ulef said. "The job's almost ready to begin."

Ulef was a gangly boy. Nice, after his own fashion—naive, if one who had grown up in the underworld could ever really be called "naive." Of course, that didn't mean he wouldn't betray her. Betrayal had nothing to do with friendship; it was a simple fact of survival. Life was harsh on the streets, and if a skaa thief wanted to keep from being caught and executed, he had to be practical.

And ruthlessness was the very most practical of emotions. Another of Reen's sayings.

"Well?" Ulef asked. "You should go. Camon's mad."

When is he not? However, Vin nodded, scrambling out of the cramped—yet comforting—confines of the watch-hole. She brushed past Ulef and hopped out of the trapdoor, moving into a hallway, then a run-down pantry. The room was one of many at the back of the store that served as a front for the safe house. The crew's lair itself was hidden in a tunneled stone cavern beneath the building.

She left the building through a back door, Ulef trailing behind her. The job would happen a few blocks away, in a richer section of town. It was an intricate job—one of the most complex Vin had ever seen. Assuming Camon wasn't caught, the payoff would be great indeed. If he was caught . . . Well, scamming noblemen and obligators was a very dangerous profession—but it certainly beat working in the forges or the textile mills.

Vin exited the alleyway, moving out onto a dark, tenement-lined street in one of the city's many skaa slums. Skaa too sick to work lay huddled in corners and gutters, ash drifting around them. Vin kept her head down and pulled up her cloak's hood against the still falling flakes.

Free. No, I'll never be free. Reen made certain of that when he left.

"There you are!" Camon lifted a squat, fat finger and jabbed it toward her face. "Where were you?"

Vin didn't let hatred or rebellion show in her eyes. She simply looked down, giving Camon what he expected to see. There were other ways to be strong. That lesson she had learned on her own.

Camon growled slightly, then raised his hand and backhanded her across the face. The force of the blow threw Vin back against the wall, and her cheek blazed with pain. She slumped against the wood, but bore the punishment silently. Just another bruise. She was strong enough to deal with it. She'd done so before.

"Listen," Camon hissed. "This is an important job. It's worth thousands of boxings—worth more than you a hundred times over. I won't have you fouling it up. Understand?"

Vin nodded.

Camon studied her for a moment, his pudgy face red with anger. Finally, he looked away, muttering to himself.

He was annoyed about something—something more than just Vin. Perhaps he had heard about the skaa rebellion several days to the north. One of the provincial lords, Themos Tresting, had apparently been murdered, his manor burned to the ground. Such disturbances were bad for business; they made the aristocracy more alert, and less gullible. That, in turn, could cut seriously into Camon's profits.

He's looking for someone to punish, Vin thought. *He always gets nervous before a job.* She looked up at Camon, tasting blood on her lip. She must have let some of her confidence show, because he glanced at her out of the corner of his eye, and his expression darkened. He raised his hand, as if to strike her again.

Vin used up a bit of her Luck.

She expended just a smidgen; she'd need the rest for the job. She directed the Luck at Camon, calming his nervousness. The crewleader paused—oblivious of Vin's touch, yet feeling its effects nonetheless. He stood for a moment; then he sighed, turning away and lowering his hand.

Vin wiped her lip as Camon waddled away. The thiefmaster looked very convincing in his nobleman's suit. It was as rich a costume as Vin had ever seen—it had a white shirt overlaid by a deep green vest with engraved gold buttons. The black suit coat was long, after the current fashion, and he wore a matching black hat. His fingers sparkled with rings, and he even carried a fine dueling cane. Indeed, Camon did an excellent job of imitating a nobleman; when it came to playing a role, there were few thieves more competent than Camon. Assuming he could keep his temper under control.

The room itself was less impressive. Vin pulled herself to her feet as Camon began to snap at some of the other crewmembers. They had rented one of the suites at the top of a local hotel. Not too lavish—but that was the idea. Camon was going to be playing the part of "Lord Jedue," a country nobleman who had hit upon hard financial times and come to Luthadel to get some final, desperate contracts.

The main room had been transformed into a sort of audience chamber, set with a large desk for Camon to sit behind, the walls decorated with cheap pieces of art. Two men stood beside the desk, dressed in formal stewards' clothing; they would play the part of Camon's manservants.

"What is this ruckus?" a man asked, entering the room. He was tall, dressed in a simple gray shirt and a pair of slacks, with a thin sword tied at his waist. Theron was the other crewleader—this particular scam was actually his. He'd brought in Camon as a partner; he'd needed someone to play Lord Jedue, and everyone knew that Camon was one of the best.

Camon looked up. "Hum? Ruckus? Oh, that was just a minor discipline problem. Don't bother yourself, Theron." Camon punctuated his remark with a dismissive wave of the hand—there was a reason he played such a good aristocrat.

He was arrogant enough that he could have been from one of the Great Houses.

Theron's eyes narrowed. Vin knew what the man was probably thinking: He was deciding how risky it would be to put a knife in Camon's fat back once the scam was over. Eventually, the taller crewleader looked away from Camon, glancing at Vin. "Who's this?" he asked.

"Just a member of my crew," Camon said.

"I thought we didn't need anyone else."

"Well, we need her," Camon said. "Ignore her. My end of the operation is none of your concern."

Theron eyed Vin, obviously noting her bloodied lip. She glanced away. Theron's eyes lingered on her, however, running down the length of her body. She wore a simple white buttoned shirt and a pair of overalls. Indeed, she was hardly enticing; scrawny with a youthful face, she supposedly didn't even look her sixteen years. Some men preferred such women, however.

She considered using a bit of Luck on him, but eventually he turned away. "The obligator is nearly here," Theron said. "Are you ready?"

Camon rolled his eyes, scttling his bulk down into the chair behind the desk. "Everything is perfect. Leave me be, Theron! Go back to your room and wait."

Theron frowned, then spun and walked from the room, muttering to himself.

Vin scanned the room, studying the decor, the servants, the atmosphere. Finally, she made her way to Camon's desk. The crewleader sat riffling through a stack of papers, apparently trying to decide which ones to put out on the desktop.

"Camon," Vin said quietly, "the servants are too fine."

Camon frowned, looking up. "What is that you're babbling?"

"The servants," Vin repeated, still speaking in a soft whisper. "Lord Jedue is supposed to be desperate. He'd have rich clothing left over from before, but he wouldn't be able to afford such rich servants. He'd use skaa."

Camon glared at her, but he paused. Physically, there was little difference between noblemen and skaa. The servants Camon had appointed, however, were dressed as minor noblemen—they were allowed to wear colorful vests, and they stood a little more confidently.

"The obligator has to think that you're nearly impoverished," Vin said. "Pack the room with a lot of skaa servants instead."

"What do you know?" Camon said, scowling at her.

"Enough." She immediately regretted the word; it sounded too rebellious. Camon raised a bejeweled hand, and Vin braced herself for another slap. She couldn't afford to use up any more Luck. She had precious little remaining anyway.

However, Camon didn't hit her. Instead, he sighed and rested a pudgy hand on her shoulder. "Why do you insist on provoking me, Vin? You know the debts your brother left when he ran away. Do you realize that a less merciful man than myself would have sold you to the whoremasters long ago? How would you like that, serving in some nobleman's bed until he grew tired of you and had you executed?"

Vin looked down at her feet.

Camon's grip grew tight, his fingers pinching her skin where neck met shoulder, and she gasped in pain despite herself. He grinned at the reaction.

"Honestly, I don't know why I keep you, Vin," he said, increasing the pressure of his grip. "I should have gotten rid of you months ago, when your brother betrayed me. I suppose I just have too kindly a heart."

He finally released her, then pointed for her to stand over by the side of the room, next to a tall indoor plant. She did as ordered, orienting herself so she had a good view of the entire room. As soon as Camon looked away, she rubbed her shoulder. *Just another pain. I can deal with pain.*

Camon sat for a few moments. Then, as expected, he waved to the two "servants" at his side.

"You two!" he said. "You're dressed too richly. Go put on something that makes you look like skaa servants instead—and bring back six more men with you when you come."

Soon, the room was filled as Vin had suggested. The obligator arrived a short time later.

Vin watched Prelan Laird step haughtily into the room. Shaved bald like all obligators, he wore a set of dark gray robes. The Ministry tattoos around his eyes identified him as a prelan, a senior bureaucrat in the Ministry's Canton of Finance. A set of lesser obligators trailed behind him, their eye tattoos far less intricate.

Camon rose as the prelan entered, a sign of respect—something even the highest of Great House noblemen would show to an obligator of Laird's rank. Laird gave no bow or acknowledgment of his own, instead striding forward and taking the seat in front of Camon's desk. One of the crewmen impersonating a servant rushed forward, bringing chilled wine and fruit for the obligator.

Laird picked at the fruit, letting the servant stand obediently, holding the platter of food as if he were a piece of furniture. "Lord Jedue," Laird finally said. "I am glad we finally have the opportunity to meet."

"As am I, Your Grace," Camon said.

"Why is it, again, that you were unable to come to the Canton building, instead requiring that I visit you here?"

"My knees, Your Grace," Camon said. "My physicians recommend that I travel as little as possible."

And you were rightly apprehensive about being drawn into a Ministry stronghold, Vin thought.

"I see," Laird said. "Bad knees. An unfortunate attribute in a man who deals in transportation."

"I don't have to go on the trips, Your Grace," Camon said, bowing his head. "Just organize them."

Good, Vin thought. *Make sure you remain subservient, Camon. You need to seem desperate.*

Vin needed this scam to succeed. Camon threatened her and he beat her—but he considered her a good-luck charm. She wasn't sure if he knew why his plans went better when she was in the room, but he had apparently made the connection. That made her valuable—and Reen had always said that the surest way to stay alive in the underworld was to make yourself indispensable.

"I see," Laird said again. "Well, I fear that our meeting has come too late for your purposes. The Canton of Finance has already voted on your proposal."

"So soon?" Camon asked with genuine surprise.

"Yes," Laird replied, taking a sip of his wine, still not dismissing the servant. "We have decided not to accept your contract."

Camon sat for a moment, stunned. "I'm sorry to hear that, Your Grace."

Laird came to meet you, Vin thought. *That means he's still in a position to negotiate.*

"Indeed," Camon continued, seeing what Vin had. "That is especially unfortunate, as I was ready to make the Ministry an even better offer."

Laird raised a tattooed eyebrow. "I doubt it will matter. There is an element of the Council who feels that the Canton would receive better service if we found a more stable house to transport our people."

"That would be a grave mistake," Camon said smoothly. "Let us be frank, Your Grace. We both know that this contract is House Jedue's last chance. Now that we've lost the Farwan deal, we cannot afford to run our canal boats to Luthadel anymore. Without the Ministry's patronage, my house is financially doomed."

"This is doing very little to persuade me, Your Lordship," the obligator said.

"Isn't it?" Camon asked. "Ask yourself this, Your Grace—who will serve you better? Will it be the house that has dozens of contracts to divide its attention, or the house that views your contract as its last hope? The Canton of Finance will not find a more accommodating partner than a desperate one. Let my boats be the ones that bring your acolytes down from the north—let my soldiers escort them—and you will not be disappointed."

Good, Vin thought.

"I . . . see," the obligator said, now troubled.

"I would be willing to give you an extended contract, locked in at the price of fifty boxings a head per trip, Your Grace. Your acolytes would be able to travel our boats at their leisure, and would always have the escorts they need."

The obligator raised an eyebrow. "That's half the former fee."

"I told you," Camon said. "We're desperate. My house *needs* to keep its boats running. Fifty boxings will not make us a profit, but that doesn't matter. Once we have the Ministry contract to bring us stability, we can find other contracts to fill our coffers."

Laird looked thoughtful. It was a fabulous deal—one that might ordinarily have been suspicious. However, Camon's presentation created the image of a house on the brink of financial collapse. The other crewleader, Theron, had spent five years building, scamming, and finagling to create this moment. The Ministry would be remiss not to consider the opportunity.

Laird was realizing just that. The Steel Ministry was not just the force of bureaucracy and legal authority in the Final Empire—it was like a noble house unto itself. The more wealth it had, the better its own mercantile contracts, the more leverage the various Ministry Cantons had with each other—and with the noble houses.

Laird was still obviously hesitant, however. Vin could see the look in his eyes, the suspicion she knew well. He was not going to take the contract.

Now, Vin thought, *It's my turn.*

Vin used her Luck on Laird. She reached out tentatively—not even really sure what she was doing, or why she could even do it. Yet her touch was instinctive, trained through years of subtle practice. She'd been ten years old before she'd realized that other people couldn't do what she could.

She pressed against Laird's emotions, dampening them. He became less suspicious, less afraid. Docile. His worries melted away, and Vin could see a calm sense of control begin to assert itself in his eyes.

Yet, Laird still seemed slightly uncertain. Vin pushed harder. He cocked his head, looking thoughtful. He opened his mouth to speak, but she pushed against him again, desperately using up her last pinch of Luck.

He paused again. "Very well," he finally said. "I will take this new proposal to the Council. Perhaps an agreement can still be reached."

If men read these words, let them know that power is a heavy burden. Seek not to be bound by its chains. The Terris prophecies say that I will have the power to save the world.

They hint, however, that I will have the power to destroy it as well.

2

IN KELSIER'S OPINION, THE CITY of Luthadel—seat of the Lord Ruler—was a gloomy sight. Most of the buildings had been built from stone blocks, with tile roofs for the wealthy, and simple, peaked wooden roofs for the rest. The structures were packed closely together, making them seem squat despite the fact that they were generally three stories high.

The tenements and shops were uniform in appearance; this was not a place to draw attention to oneself. Unless, of course, you were a member of the high nobility.

Interspersed throughout the city were a dozen or so monolithic keeps. Intricate, with rows of spearlike spires or deep archways, these were the homes of the high nobility. In fact, they were the *mark* of a high noble family: Any family who could afford to build a keep and maintain a high-profile presence in Luthadel was considered to be a Great House.

Most of the open ground in the city was around these keeps. The patches of space amid the tenements were like clearings in a forest, the keeps themselves like solitary mounts rising above the rest of the landscape. Black mountains. Like the rest of the city, the keeps were stained by countless years of ashfalls.

Every structure in Luthadel—virtually every structure Kelsier had ever seen—had been blackened to some degree. Even the city wall, upon which Kelsier now stood, was blackened by a patina of soot. Structures were generally darkest at the top, where the ash gathered, but rainwaters and evening condensations had carried the stains over ledges and down walls. Like paint running down a canvas, the darkness seemed to creep down the sides of buildings in an uneven gradient.

The streets, of course, were completely black. Kelsier stood waiting, scanning the city as a group of skaa workers worked in the street below, clearing away the latest mounds of ash. They'd take it to the River Channerel, which ran through the center of the city, sending the piles of ash to be washed away, lest it pile up and eventually bury the city. Sometimes, Kelsier wondered why the entire empire wasn't just one big mound of ash. He supposed the ash must break down into soil eventually. Yet, it took a ridiculous amount of effort to keep cities and fields clear enough to be used.

Fortunately, there were always enough skaa to do the work. The workers below him wore simple coats and trousers, ash-stained and worn. Like the plantation workers he had left behind several weeks before, they worked with beaten-down, despondent motions. Other groups of skaa passed the workers, responding to the bells in the distance, chiming the hour and calling them to their morning's work at the forges or mills. Luthadel's main export was metal; the city was home to hundreds of forges and refineries. However, the surgings of the river provided excellent locations for mills, both to grind grains and make textiles.

The skaa continued to work. Kelsier turned away from them, looking up into the distance, toward the city center, where the Lord Ruler's palace loomed like some kind of massive, multi-spined insect. Kredik Shaw, the Hill of a Thousand Spires. The palace was several times the size of any nobleman's keep, and was by far the largest building in the city.

Another ashfall began as Kelsier stood contemplating the city, the flakes falling lightly down upon the streets and buildings. *A lot of ashfalls, lately,* he thought, glad for the excuse to pull up the hood on his cloak. *The Ashmounts must be active.*

It was unlikely that anyone in Luthadel would recognize him—it had been three years since his capture. Still, the hood was reassuring. If all went well, there would come a time when Kelsier would want to be seen and recognized. For now, anonymity was probably better.

Eventually, a figure approached along the wall. The man, Dockson, was shorter than Kelsier, and he had a squarish face that seemed well suited to his moderately stocky build. A nondescript brown hooded cloak covered his black hair, and he wore the same short half beard that he'd sported since his face had first put forth whiskers some twenty years before.

He, like Kelsier, wore a nobleman's suit: colored vest, dark coat and trousers, and a thin cloak to keep off the ash. The clothing wasn't rich, but it was aristocratic—indicative of the Luthadel middle class. Most men of noble birth weren't wealthy enough to be considered part of a Great House—yet, in the Final Empire, nobility wasn't just about money. It was about lineage and history; the Lord Ruler was immortal, and he apparently still remembered the men who had supported him during the early years of his reign. The descendants of those men, no matter how poor they became, would always be favored.

The clothing would keep passing guard patrols from asking too many questions. In the cases of Kelsier and Dockson, of course, that clothing was a lie. Neither was actually noble—though, technically, Kelsier was a half-blood. In many ways, however, that was worse than being just a normal skaa.

Dockson strolled up next to Kelsier, then leaned against the battlement, resting a pair of stout arms on the stone. "You're a few days late, Kell."

"I decided to make a few extra stops in the plantations to the north."

"Ah," Dockson said. "So you *did* have something to do with Lord Tresting's death."

Kelsier smiled. "You could say that."

"His murder caused quite a stir among the local nobility."

"That was kind of the intention," Kelsier said. "Though, to be honest, I wasn't planning anything quite so dramatic. It was almost more of an accident than anything else."

Dockson raised an eyebrow. "How do you 'accidentally' kill a nobleman in his own mansion?"

"With a knife in the chest," Kelsier said lightly. "Or, rather, a pair of knives in the chest—it always pays to be careful."

Dockson rolled his eyes.

"His death isn't exactly a loss, Dox," Kelsier said. "Even among the nobility, Tresting had a reputation for cruelty."

"I don't care about Tresting," Dockson said. "I'm just considering the state of insanity that led me to plan another job with you. Attacking a provincial lord in his manor house, surrounded by guards . . . Honestly, Kell, I'd nearly forgotten how foolhardy you can be."

"Foolhardy?" Kelsier asked with a laugh. "That wasn't foolhardy—that was just a small diversion. You should see some of the things I'm *planning* to do!"

Dockson stood for a moment, then he laughed too. "By the Lord Ruler, it's good to have you back, Kell! I'm afraid I've grown rather boring during the last few years."

"We'll fix that," Kelsier promised. He took a deep breath, ash falling lightly around him. Skaa cleaning crews were already back at work on the streets below, brushing up the dark ash. Behind, a guard patrol passed, nodding to Kelsier and Dockson. They waited in silence for the men to pass.

"It's good to be back," Kelsier finally said. "There's something homey about Luthadel—even if it is a depressing, stark pit of a city. You have the meeting organized?"

Dockson nodded. "We can't start until this evening, though. How'd you get in, anyway? I had men watching the gates."

"Hmm? Oh, I snuck in last night."

"But how—" Dockson paused. "Oh, right. That's going to take some getting used to."

Kelsier shrugged. "I don't see why. You always work with Mistings."

"Yes, but this is different," Dockson said. He held up a hand to forestall further argument. "No need, Kell. I'm not hedging—I just said it would take some getting used to."

"Fine. Who's coming tonight?"

"Well, Breeze and Ham will be there, of course. They're very curious about this mystery job of ours—not to mention rather annoyed that I won't tell him what you've been up to these last few years."

"Good," Kelsier said with a smile. "Let them wonder. How about Trap?"

Dockson shook his head. "Trap's dead. The Ministry finally caught up with him a couple months ago. Didn't even bother sending him to the Pits—they beheaded him on the spot."

Kelsier closed his eyes, exhaling softly. It seemed that the Steel Ministry caught up with everyone eventually. Sometimes, Kelsier felt that a skaa Misting's life wasn't so much about surviving as it was about picking the right time to die.

"This leaves us without a Smoker," Kelsier finally said, opening his eyes. "You have any suggestions?"

"Ruddy," Dockson said.

Kelsier shook his head. "No. He's a good Smoker, but he's not a good enough man."

Dockson smiled. "Not a good enough man to be on a thieving crew . . . Kell, I *have* missed working with you. All right, who then?"

Kelsier thought for a moment. "Is Clubs still running that shop of his?"

"As far as I know," Dockson said slowly.

"He's supposed to be one of the best Smokers in the city."

"I suppose," Dockson said. "But . . . isn't he supposed to be kind of hard to work with?"

"He's not so bad," Kelsier said. "Not once you get used to him. Besides, I think he might be . . . amenable to this particular job."

"All right," Dockson said, shrugging. "I'll invite him. I think one of his relatives is a Tineye. Do you want me to invite him too?"

"Sounds good," Kelsier said.

"All right," Dockson said. "Well, beyond that, there's just Yeden. Assuming he's still interested . . ."

"He'll be there," Kelsier said.

"He'd better be," Dockson said. "He'll be the one paying us, after all."

Kelsier nodded, then frowned. "You didn't mention Marsh."

Dockson shrugged. "I warned you. Your brother never did approve of our methods, and now . . . well, you know Marsh. He won't even have anything to do with Yeden and the rebellion anymore, let alone with a bunch of criminals like us. I think we'll have to find someone else to infiltrate the obligators."

"No," Kelsier said. "He'll do it. I'll just have to stop by to persuade him."

"If you say so." Dockson fell silent then, and the two stood for a moment, leaning against the railing and looking out over the ash-stained city.

Dockson finally shook his head. "This is insane, eh?"

Kelsier smiled. "Feels good, doesn't it?"

Dockson nodded. "Fantastic."

"It will be a job like no other," Kelsier said, looking north—across the city and toward the twisted building at its center.

Dockson stepped away from the wall. "We have a few hours before the meeting. There's something I want to show you. I think there's still time—if we hurry."

Kelsier turned with curious eyes. "Well, I *was* going to go and chastise my prude of a brother. But . . ."

"This will be worth your time," Dockson promised.

Vin sat in the corner of the safe house's main lair. She kept to the shadows, as usual; the more she stayed out of sight, the more the others would ignore her. She couldn't afford to expend Luck keeping the men's hands off of her. She'd barely had time to regenerate what she'd used a few days before, during the meeting with the obligator.

The usual rabble lounged at tables in the room, playing at dice or discussing minor jobs. Smoke from a dozen different pipes pooled at the top of the chamber, and the walls were stained dark from countless years of similar treatment. The floor was darkened with patches of ash. Like most thieving crews, Camon's group wasn't known for its tidiness.

There was a door at the back of the room, and beyond it lay a twisting stone stairway that led up to a false rain grate in an alleyway. This room, like so many others hidden in the imperial capital of Luthadel, wasn't supposed to exist.

Rough laughter came from the front of the chamber, where Camon sat with a half-dozen cronies enjoying a typical afternoon of ale and crass jokes. Camon's table sat beside the bar, where the overpriced drinks were simply another way Camon exploited those who worked for him. The Luthadel criminal element had learned quite well from the lessons taught by the nobility.

Vin tried her best to remain invisible. Six months before, she wouldn't have believed that her life could actually get worse without Reen. Yet, despite her brother's abusive anger, he had kept the other crewmembers from having their way with Vin. There were relatively few women on thieving crews; generally, those women who got involved with the underworld ended up as whores. Reen had always told her that a girl needed to be tough—tougher, even, than a man—if she wanted to survive.

You think some crewleader is going to want a liability like you on his team? he had said. *I don't even want to have to work with you, and I'm your brother.*

Her back still throbbed; Camon had whipped her the day before. The blood would ruin her shirt, and she wouldn't be able to afford another one. Camon was already retaining her wages to pay the debts Reen had left behind.

But, I am strong, she thought.

That was the irony. The beatings almost didn't hurt anymore, for Reen's frequent abuses had left Vin resilient, while at the same time teaching her how to look pathetic and broken. In a way, the beatings were self-defeating. Bruises and welts mended, but each new lashing left Vin more hardened. Stronger.

Camon stood up. He reached into his vest pocket and pulled out his golden pocket watch. He nodded to one of his companions, then he scanned the room, searching for . . . her. His eyes locked on Vin. "It's time."

Vin frowned. *Time for what?*

The Ministry's Canton of Finance was an imposing structure—but, then, *everything* about the Steel Ministry tended to be imposing.

Tall and blocky, the building had a massive rose window in the front, though the glass was dark from the outside. Two large banners hung down beside the window, the soot-stained red cloth proclaiming praises to the Lord Ruler.

Camon studied the building with a critical eye. Vin could sense his apprehension. The Canton of Finance was hardly the most threatening of Ministry offices—the Canton of Inquisition, or even the Canton of Orthodoxy, had a far more ominous reputation. However, voluntarily entering any Ministry office . . . putting yourself in the power of the obligators . . . well, it was a thing to do only after serious consideration.

Camon took a deep breath, then strode forward, his dueling cane tapping against the stones as he walked. He wore his rich nobleman's suit, and he was accompanied by a half-dozen crewmembers—including Vin—to act as his "servants."

Vin followed Camon up the steps, then waited as one of the crewmembers jumped forward to pull the door open for his "master." Of the six attendants, only Vin seemed to have been told nothing of Camon's plan. Suspiciously, Theron—Camon's supposed partner in the Ministry scam—was nowhere to be seen.

Vin entered the Canton building. Vibrant red light, sparkled with lines of blue, fell from the rose window. A single obligator, with midlevel tattoos around his eyes, sat behind a desk at the end of the extended entryway.

Camon approached, his cane thumping against the carpet as he walked. "I am Lord Jedue," he said.

What are you doing, Camon? Vin thought. *You insisted to Theron that you wouldn't meet with Prelan Laird in his Canton office. Yet, now you're here.*

The obligator nodded, making a notation in his ledger. He waved to the side. "You may take one attendant with you into the waiting chamber. The rest must remain here."

Camon's huff of disdain indicated what he thought of that prohibition. The obligator, however, didn't look up from his ledger. Camon stood for a moment, and Vin couldn't tell if he was genuinely angry or just playing the part of an arrogant nobleman. Finally, he jabbed a finger at Vin.

"Come," he said, turning and waddling toward the indicated door.

The room beyond was lavish and plush, and several noblemen lounged in various postures of waiting. Camon chose a chair and settled into it, then pointed toward a table set with wine and red-frosted cakes. Vin obediently fetched him a glass of wine and a plate of food, ignoring her own hunger.

Camon began to pick hungrily at the cakes, smacking quietly as he ate.

He's nervous. More nervous, even, than before.

"Once we get in, you will say nothing," Camon grumbled between bites.

"You're betraying Theron," Vin whispered.

Camon nodded.

"But, how? Why?" Theron's plan was complex in execution, but simple in concept. Every year, the Ministry transferred its new acolyte obligators from a northern training facility south to Luthadel for final instruction. Theron had discovered, however, that those acolytes and their overseers brought down with them large amounts of Ministry funds—disguised as baggage—to be strongholded in Luthadel.

Banditry was very difficult in the Final Empire, what with the constant patrols along canal routes. However, if one were running the very canal boats that the acolytes were sailing upon, a robbery could become possible. Arranged at just the right time . . . the guards turning on their passengers . . . a man could make quite a profit, then blame it all on banditry.

"Theron's crew is weak," Camon said quietly. "He expended too many resources on this job."

"But, the return he'll make—" Vin said.

"Will never happen if I take what I can now, then run," Camon said, smiling. "I'll talk the obligators into a down payment to get my caravan boats afloat, then disappear and leave Theron to deal with the disaster when the Ministry realizes that it's been scammed."

Vin stood back, slightly shocked. Setting up a scam like this would have cost Theron thousands upon thousands of boxings—if the deal fell through now, he would be ruined. And, with the Ministry hunting him, he wouldn't even have time to seek revenge. Camon would make a quick profit, as well as rid himself of one of his more powerful rivals.

Theron was a fool to bring Camon into this, she thought.

But, then, the amount Theron had promised to pay Camon was great; he probably assumed that Camon's greed would keep him honest until Theron himself could pull a double cross. Camon had simply worked faster than anyone, even Vin, had expected. How could Theron have known that Camon would undermine the job itself, rather than wait and try and steal the entire haul from the caravan boats?

Vin's stomach twisted. *It's just another betrayal,* she thought sickly. *Why does it still bother me so? Everyone betrays everyone else. That's the way life is. . . .*

She wanted to find a corner—someplace cramped and secluded—and hide. Alone.

Anyone will betray you. Anyone.

But there was no place to go. Eventually, a minor obligator entered and called for Lord Jedue. Vin followed Camon as they were ushered into an audience chamber.

The man who waited inside, sitting behind the audience desk, was not Prelan Laird.

Camon paused in the doorway. The room was austere, bearing only the desk and simple gray carpeting. The stone walls were unadorned, the only window barely a handspan wide. The obligator who waited for them had some of the most intricate tattoos around his eyes that Vin had ever seen. She wasn't even certain what rank they implied, but they extended all the way back to the obligator's ears and up over his forehead.

"Lord Jedue," the strange obligator said. Like Laird, he wore gray robes, but he was very different from the stern, bureaucratic men Camon had dealt with before. This man was lean in a muscular way, and his clean-shaven, triangular head gave him an almost predatory look.

"I was under the impression that I would be meeting with Prelan Laird," Camon said, still not moving into the room.

"Prelan Laird has been called away on other business. I am High Prelan Arriev—head of the board that was reviewing your proposal. You have a rare opportunity to address me directly. I normally don't hear cases in person, but Laird's absence has made it necessary for me to share in some of his work."

Vin's instincts made her tense. *We should go. Now.*

Camon stood for a long moment, and Vin could see him considering. Run now? Or, take a risk for the greater prize? Vin didn't care about prizes; she just wanted to live. Camon, however, had not become crewleader without the occasional gamble. He slowly moved into the room, eyes cautious as he took the seat opposite the obligator.

"Well, High Prelan Arriev," Camon said with a careful voice. "I assume that since I have been called back for another appointment, the board is considering my offer?"

"Indeed we are," the obligator said. "Though I must admit, there are some Council members who are apprehensive about dealing with a family that is so near to economic disaster. The Ministry generally prefers to be conservative in its financial operations."

"I see."

"But," Arriev said, "there are others on the board who are quite eager to take advantage of the savings you offered us."

"And with which group do you identify, Your Grace?"

"I, as of yet, have not made my decision." The obligator leaned forward. "Which is why I noted that you have a rare opportunity. Convince me, Lord Jedue, and you will have your contract."

"Surely Prelan Laird outlined the details of our offer," Camon said.

"Yes, but I would like to hear the arguments from you personally. Humor me."

Vin frowned. She remained near the back of the room, standing near the door, still half convinced she should run.

"Well?" Arriev asked.

"We need this contract, Your Grace," Camon said. "Without it we won't be able to continue our canal shipping operations. Your contract would give us a much needed period of stability—a chance to maintain our caravan boats for a time while we search for other contracts."

Arriev studied Camon for a moment. "Surely you can do better than that, Lord Jedue. Laird said that you were very persuasive—let me hear you *prove* that you deserve our patronage."

Vin prepared her Luck. She could make Arriev more inclined to believe . . . but something restrained her. The situation felt wrong.

"We are your best choice, Your Grace," Camon said. "You fear that my house will suffer economic failure? Well, if it does, what have you lost? At worst, my narrowboats would stop running, and you would have to find other merchants to deal with. Yet, if your patronage is enough to maintain my house, then you have found yourself an enviable long-term contract."

"I see," Arriev said lightly. "And why the Ministry? Why not make your deal with someone else? Surely there are other options for your boats—other groups who would jump at such rates."

Camon frowned. "This isn't about money, Your Grace, it is about the victory—the showing of confidence—that we would gain by having a Ministry contract. If you trust us, others will too. I *need* your support." Camon was sweating now. He was probably beginning to regret this gamble. Had he been betrayed? Was Theron behind the odd meeting?

The obligator waited quietly. He could destroy them, Vin knew. If he even suspected that they were scamming him, he could give them over to the Canton of Inquisition. More than one nobleman had entered a Canton building and never returned.

Gritting her teeth, Vin reached out and used her Luck on the obligator, making him less suspicious.

Arriev smiled. "Well, you have convinced me," he suddenly declared.

Camon sighed in relief.

Arriev continued, "Your most recent letter suggested that you need three thousand boxings as an advance to refurbish your equipment and resume shipping operations. See the scribe in the main hallway to finish the paperwork so that you may requisition the necessary funds."

The obligator pulled a sheet of thick bureaucratic paper from a stack, then stamped a seal at the bottom. He proffered it to Camon. "Your contract."

Camon smiled deeply. "I knew coming to the Ministry was the wise choice," he said, accepting the contract. He stood, nodding respectfully to the obligator, then motioned for Vin to open the door for him.

She did so. *Something is wrong. Something is* very *wrong.* She paused as Camon left, looking back at the obligator. He was still smiling.

A happy obligator was always a bad sign.

Yet, no one stopped them as they passed through the waiting room with its noble occupants. Camon sealed and delivered the contract to the appropriate scribe, and no soldiers appeared to arrest them. The scribe pulled out a small chest filled with coins, and then handed it to Camon with an indifferent hand.

Then, they simply left the Canton building, Camon gathering his other attendants with obvious relief. No cries of alarm. No tromping of soldiers. They were free. Camon had successfully scammed both the Ministry and another crewleader.

Apparently.

•

Kelsier stuffed another one of the little red-frosted cakes into his mouth, chewing with satisfaction. The fat thief and his scrawny attendant passed through the waiting room, entering the entryway beyond. The obligator who had interviewed the two thieves remained in his office, apparently awaiting his next appointment

"Well?" Dockson asked. "What do you think?"

Kelsier glanced at the cakes. "They're quite good," he said, taking another one. "The Ministry has always had excellent taste—it makes sense that they would provide superior snacks."

Dockson rolled his eyes. "About the girl, Kell."

Kelsier smiled as he piled four of the cakes in his hand, then nodded toward the doorway. The Canton waiting room was growing too busy for the discussion of delicate matters. On the way out, he paused and told the obligator secretary in the corner that they needed to reschedule.

Then the two crossed through the entry chamber—passing the overweight crewleader, who stood speaking with a scribe.

Kelsier stepped out onto the street, pulled his hood up against the still falling ash, then led the way across the street. He paused beside an alleyway, standing where he and Dockson could watch the Canton building's doors.

Kelsier munched contentedly on his cakes. "How'd you find out about her?" he asked between bites.

"Your brother," Dockson replied. "Camon tried to swindle Marsh a few months ago, and he brought the girl with him then, too. Actually, Camon's little good-luck charm is becoming moderately famous in the right circles. I'm still not sure if he knows what she is or not. You know how superstitious thieves can get."

Kelsier nodded, dusting off his hands. "How'd you know she'd be here today?"

Dockson shrugged. "A few bribes in the right place. I've been keeping an eye on the girl ever since Marsh pointed her out to me. I wanted to give you an opportunity to see her work for yourself."

Across the street, the Canton building's door finally opened, and Camon made his way down the steps surrounded by a group of "servants." The small, short-haired girl was with him. The sight of her made Kelsier frown. She had a nervous anxiety to her step, and she jumped slightly whenever someone made a quick move. The right side of her face was still slightly discolored from a partially healed bruise.

Kelsier eyed the self-important Camon. *I'll have to come up with something particularly suitable to do to that man.*

"Poor thing," Dockson muttered.

Kelsier nodded. "She'll be free of him soon enough. It's a wonder no one discovered her before this."

"Your brother was right then?"

Kelsier nodded. "She's at least a Misting, and if Marsh says she's more, I'm inclined to believe him. I'm a bit surprised to see her using Allomancy on a member of the Ministry, especially inside a Canton building. I'd guess that she doesn't know that she's even using her abilities."

"Is that possible?" Dockson asked.

Kelsier nodded. "Trace minerals in the water can be burned, if just for a tiny bit of power. That's one of the reasons the Lord Ruler built his city here—lots of metals in the ground. I'd say that . . ."

Kelsier trailed off, frowning slightly. Something was wrong. He glanced toward Camon and his crew. They were still visible in the near distance, crossing the street and heading south.

A figure appeared in the Canton building's doorway. Lean with a confident air, he bore the tattoos of a high prelan of the Canton of Finance around his eyes. Probably the very man Camon had met with shortly before. The obligator stepped out of the building, and a second man exited behind him.

Beside Kelsier, Dockson suddenly grew stiff.

The second man was tall with a strong build. As he turned, Kelsier was able to see that a thick metal spike had been pounded tip-first through each of the man's eyes. With shafts as wide as an eye socket, the nail-like spikes were long enough that their sharp points jutted out about an inch from the back of the man's clean-shaven skull. The flat spike ends shone like two silvery disks, sticking out of the sockets in the front, where the eyes should have been.

A Steel Inquisitor.

"What's *that* doing here?" Dockson asked.

"Stay calm," Kelsier said, trying to force himself to do the same. The Inquisitor looked toward them, spiked eyes regarding Kelsier, before turning in the direction that Camon and the girl had gone. Like all Inquisitors, he wore intricate eye tattoos—mostly black, with one stark red line—that marked him as a high-ranking member of the Canton of Inquisition.

"He's not here for us," Kelsier said. "I'm not burning anything—he'll think that we're just ordinary noblemen."

"The girl," Dockson said.

Kelsier nodded. "You say Camon's been running this scam on the Ministry for a while. Well, the girl must have been detected by one of the obligators. They're trained to recognize when an Allomancer tampers with their emotions."

Dockson frowned thoughtfully. Across the street, the Inquisitor conferred with the other obligator, then the two of them turned to walk in the direction that Camon had gone. There was no urgency to their pace.

"They must have sent a tail to follow them," Dockson said.

"This is the Ministry," Kelsier said. "There'll be two tails, at least."

Dockson nodded. "Camon will lead them directly back to his safe house. Dozens of men will die. They're not all the most admirable people, but . . ."

"They fight the Final Empire, in their own way," Kelsier said. "Besides, I'm not about to let a possible Mistborn slip away from us—I want to talk to that girl. Can you deal with those tails?"

"I said I'd become boring, Kell," Dockson said. "Not sloppy. I can handle a couple of Ministry flunkies."

"Good," Kelsier said, reaching into his cloak pocket and pulling out a small vial. A collection of metal flakes floated in an alcohol solution within. Iron, steel, tin, pewter, copper, bronze, zinc, and brass—the eight basic Allomantic metals. Kelsier pulled off the stopper and downed the contents in a single swift gulp.

He pocketed the now empty vial, wiping his mouth. "I'll handle that Inquisitor."

Dockson looked apprehensive. "You're going to try and take him?"

Kelsier shook his head. "Too dangerous. I'll just divert him. Now, get going—we don't want those tails finding the safe house."

Dockson nodded. "Meet back at the fifteenth crossroad," he said before taking off down the alley and disappearing around a corner.

Kelsier gave his friend a count of ten before reaching within himself and burning his metals. His body came awash with strength, clarity, and power.

Kelsier smiled; then—burning zinc—he reached out and yanked firmly on the Inquisitor's emotions. The creature froze in place, then spun, looking back toward the Canton building.

Let's have a chase now, you and I, Kelsier thought.

We arrived in Terris earlier this week, and, I have to say, I find the countryside beautiful. The great mountains to the north—with their bald snowcaps and forested mantles—stand like watchful gods over this land of green fertility. My own lands to the south are mostly flat; I think that they might look less dreary if there were a few mountains to vary the terrain.

The people here are mostly herdsmen—though timber harvesters and farmers are not uncommon. It is a pastoral land, certainly. It seems odd that a place so remarkably agrarian could have produced the prophecies and theologies upon which the entire world now relies.

3

CAMON COUNTED HIS COINS, DROPPING the golden boxings one by one into the small chest on his table. He still looked a bit stunned, as well he should have. Three thousand boxings was a fabulous amount of money—far more than Camon would earn in even a very good year. His closest cronies sat at the table with him, ale—and laughter—flowing freely.

Vin sat in her corner, trying to understand her feelings of dread. Three thousand boxings. The Ministry should never have let such a sum go so quickly. Prelan Arriev had seemed too cunning to be fooled with ease.

Camon dropped another coin into the chest. Vin couldn't decide if he was being foolish or clever by making such a display of wealth. Underworld crews worked under a strict agreement: Everyone received a cut of earnings in proportion to their status in the group. While it was sometimes tempting to kill the crewleader and take his money for yourself, a successful leader created more wealth for everyone. Kill him prematurely, and you would cut off future earnings—not to mention earn the wrath of the other crewmembers.

Still, three thousand boxings . . . that would be enough to tempt even the most logical thief. It was all wrong.

I have to get out of here, Vin decided. *Get away from Camon, and the lair, in case something happens.*

And yet . . . leave? By herself? She'd never been alone before; she'd always had Reen. He'd been the one to lead her from city to city, joining different thieving crews. She loved solitude. But the thought of being by herself, out in the city, horrified her. That was why she'd never run away from Reen; that was why she'd stayed with Camon.

She couldn't go. But she had to. She looked up from her corner, scanning the room. There weren't many people in the crew for whom she felt any sort of attachment. Yet, there were a couple that she would be sorry to see hurt, should the obligators actually move against the crew. A few men who hadn't tried to abuse her, or—in very rare cases—who had actually shown her some measure of kindness.

Ulef was at the top of that list. He wasn't a friend, but he was the closest thing she had now that Reen was gone. If he would go with her, then at least she wouldn't be alone. Cautiously, Vin stood and moved along the side of the room to where Ulef sat drinking with some of the other younger crewmembers.

She tugged on Ulef's sleeve. He turned toward her, only slightly drunk. "Vin?"

"Ulef," she whispered. "We need to go."

He frowned. "Go? Go where?"

"Away," Vin whispered. "Out of here."

"Now?"

Vin nodded urgently.

Ulef glanced back at his friends, who were chuckling among themselves, shooting suggestive looks at Vin and Ulef.

Ulef flushed. "You want to go somewhere, just you and I?"

"Not like that," Vin said. "Just . . . I need to leave the lair. And I don't want to be alone."

Ulef frowned. He leaned closer, a slight stink of ale on his breath. "What is this about, Vin?" he asked quietly.

Vin paused. "I . . . think something might happen, Ulef," she whispered. "Something with the obligators. I just don't want to be in the lair right now."

Ulef sat quietly for a moment. "All right," he finally said. "How long will this take?"

"I don't know," Vin said. "Until evening, at least. But we have to go. *Now.*"

He nodded slowly.

"Wait here for a moment," Vin whispered, turning. She shot a glance at Camon, who was laughing at one of his own jokes. Then she quietly moved through the ash-stained, smoky chamber into the lair's back room.

The crew's general sleeping quarters consisted of a simple, elongated corridor lined with bedrolls. It was crowded and uncomfortable, but it was far better than the cold alleyways she'd slept in during her years traveling with Reen.

Alleyways that I might have to get used to again, she thought. She had survived them before. She could do so again.

She moved to her pallet, the muffled sounds of men laughing and drinking sounding from the other room. Vin knelt down, regarding her few possessions. If something did happen to the crew, she wouldn't be able to come back to the lair. Ever. But, she couldn't take the bedroll with her now—it was far too obvious. That left only the small box that contained her personal effects: a pebble from each city she'd visited, the earring Reen said Vin's mother had given her, and a bit of obsidian the size of a large coin. It was chipped into an irregular pattern—Reen had carried it as some kind of good luck charm. It was the only thing he'd left behind when he'd snuck away from the crew half a year before. Abandoning her.

Just like he always said he would, Vin told herself sternly. *I never thought he'd actually go—and that's exactly why he had to leave.*

She gripped the bit of obsidian in her hand and pocketed the pebbles. The earring she put in her ear—it was a very simple thing. Little more than a stud, not even worth stealing, which was why she didn't fear leaving it in the back room. Still, Vin had rarely worn it, for fear that the ornamentation would make her look more feminine.

She had no money, but Reen had taught her how to scavenge and beg. Both were difficult in the Final Empire, especially in Luthadel, but she would find a way, if she had to.

Vin left her box and bedroll, slipping back out into the common room. Maybe she was overreacting; perhaps nothing would happen to the crew. But, if it did . . . well, if there was one thing Reen had taught her, it was how to protect her neck. Bringing Ulef was a good idea. He had contacts in Luthadel. If something happened to Camon's crew, Ulef could probably get her and him jobs on—

Vin froze just inside the main room. Ulef wasn't at the table where she had left him. Instead, he stood furtively near the front of the room. Near the bar. Near . . . Camon.

"What is this!" Camon stood, his face red as sunlight. He pushed his stool out of the way, then lurched toward her, half drunk. "Running away? Off to betray me to the Ministry, are you!"

Vin dashed toward the stairwell door, desperately scrambling around tables and past crewmembers.

Camon's hurled wooden stool hit her square in the back, throwing her to the ground. Pain flared between her shoulders; several crewmembers cried out as the stool bounced off of her and thumped against the floorboards nearby.

Vin lay in a daze. Then . . . something within her—something she knew of but didn't understand—gave her strength. Her head stopped swimming, her pain becoming a focus. She climbed awkwardly to her feet.

Camon was there. He backhanded her even as she stood. Her head snapped to the side from the blow, twisting her neck so painfully that she barely felt herself hit the floor again.

Camon bent over, grabbing her by the front of her shirt and pulling her up, raising his fist. Vin didn't pause to think or to speak; there was only one thing to do. She used up all of her Luck in a single furious effort, pushing against Camon, calming his fury.

Camon teetered. For a moment, his eyes softened. He lowered her slightly.

Then the anger returned to his eyes. Hard. Terrifying.

"Damn wench," Camon muttered, grabbing her by the

shoulders and shaking her. "That backstabbing brother of yours never respected me, and you're the same. I was too easy on you both. Should have . . ."

Vin tried to twist free, but Camon's grip was firm. She searched desperately for aid from the other crewmembers—however, she knew what she would find. Indifference. They turned away, their faces embarrassed but not concerned. Ulef still stood near Camon's table, looking down guiltily.

In her mind, she thought she heard a voice whispering to her. Reen's voice. *Fool! Ruthlessness—it's the most logical of emotions. You don't have any friends in the underworld. You'll never have any friends in the underworld!*

She renewed her struggles, but Camon hit her again, knocking her to the ground. The blow stunned her, and she gasped, breath knocked from her lungs.

Just endure, she thought, mind muddled. *He won't kill me. He needs me.*

Yet, as she turned weakly, she saw Camon looming above her in the caliginous room, drunken fury showing in his face. She knew this time would be different; it would be no simple beating. He thought that she intended to betray him to the Ministry. He wasn't in control.

There was murder in his eyes.

Please! Vin thought with desperation, reaching for her Luck, trying to make it work. There was no response. Luck, such as it was, had failed her.

Camon bent down, muttering to himself as he grabbed her by the shoulder. He raised an arm—his meaty hand forming another fist, his muscles tensing, an angry bead of sweat slipping off his chin and hitting her on the cheek.

A few feet away, the stairwell door shook, then burst open. Camon paused, arm upraised as he glared toward the door and whatever unfortunate crewmember had chosen such an inopportune moment to return to the lair.

Vin seized the distraction. Ignoring the newcomer, she tried to shake herself free from Camon's grip, but she was too weak. Her face blazed from where he'd hit her, and she tasted blood on her lip. Her shoulder had been twisted awkwardly, and her side ached from where she'd fallen. She clawed at

Camon's hand, but she suddenly felt weak, her inner strength failing her just as her Luck had. Her pains suddenly seemed greater, more daunting, more . . . demanding.

She turned toward the door desperately. She was close—painfully close. She had nearly escaped. Just a little farther . . .

Then she saw the man standing quietly in the stairwell doorway. He was unfamiliar to her. Tall and hawk-faced, he had light blond hair and wore a relaxed nobleman's suit, his cloak hanging free. He was, perhaps, in his mid-thirties. He wore no hat, nor did he carry a dueling cane.

And he looked very, very angry.

"What is this?" Camon demanded. "Who are you?"

How did he get by the scouts . . . ? Vin thought, struggling to get her wits back. Pain. She could deal with pain. *The obligators . . . did they send him?*

The newcomer looked down at Vin, and his expression softened slightly. Then he looked up at Camon and his eyes grew dark.

Camon's angry demands were cut off as he was thrown backward as if had been punched by a powerful force. His arm was ripped free from Vin's shoulder, and he toppled to the ground, causing the floorboards to shake.

The room fell quiet.

Have to get away, Vin thought, forcing herself up to her knees. Camon groaned in pain from a few feet away, and Vin crawled away from him, slipping beneath an unoccupied table. The lair had a hidden exit, a trapdoor beside the far back wall. If she could crawl to it—

Suddenly, Vin felt an overwhelming peace. The emotion slammed into her like a sudden weight, her emotions squished silent, as if crushed by a forceful hand. Her fear puffed out like an extinguished candle, and even her pain seemed unimportant.

She slowed, wondering why she had been so worried. She stood up, pausing as she faced the trapdoor. She breathed heavily, still a little dazed.

Camon just tried to kill me! the logical part of her mind warned. *And someone else is attacking the lair. I have to get away!* However, her emotions didn't match the logic. She felt . . . serene. Unworried. And more than a little bit curious.

Someone had just used Luck on her.

She recognized it somehow, even though she'd never felt it upon her before. She paused beside the table, one hand on the wood, then slowly turned around. The newcomer still stood in the stairwell doorway. He studied her with a critical eye, then smiled in a disarming sort of way.

What is going on?

The newcomer finally stepped into the room. The rest of Camon's crew remained sitting at their tables. They looked surprised, but oddly unworried.

He's using Luck on them all. But . . . how can he do it to so many at once? Vin had never been able to store up enough Luck to do more than give the occasional, brief push.

As the newcomer entered the room, Vin could finally see that a second person stood in the stairwell behind him. This second man was less imposing. He was shorter, with a dark half beard and close-cropped straight hair. He also wore a nobleman's suit, though his was less sharply tailored.

On the other side of the room, Camon groaned and sat up, holding his head. He glanced at the newcomers. "Master Dockson! Why, uh, well, this is a surprise!"

"Indeed," said the shorter man—Dockson. Vin frowned, realizing she sensed a slight familiarity to these men. She recognized them from somewhere.

The Canton of Finance. They were sitting in the waiting room when Camon and I left.

Camon climbed to his feet, studying the blond newcomer. Camon looked down at the man's hands, both of which were lined with strange, overlapping scars. "By the Lord Ruler . . ." Camon whispered. "The Survivor of Hathsin!"

Vin frowned. The title was unfamiliar to her. Should she know this man? Her wounds still throbbed despite the peace she felt, and her head was dizzy. She leaned on the table for support, but did not sit.

Whoever this newcomer was, Camon obviously thought him important. "Why, Master Kelsier!" Camon sputtered. "This is a rare honor!"

The newcomer—Kelsier—shook his head. "You know, I'm not really interested in listening to you."

Camon let out an "urk" of pain as he was thrown backward again. Kelsier made no obvious gesture to perform the feat. Yet, Camon collapsed to the ground, as if shoved by some unseen force.

Camon fell quiet, and Kelsier scanned the room. "The rest of you know who I am?"

Many of the crewmembers nodded.

"Good. I've come to your lair because you, my friends, owe me a great debt."

The room was silent save for Camon's groans. Finally, one of the crewmen spoke. "We . . . do, Master Kelsier?"

"Indeed you do. You see, Master Dockson and I just saved your lives. Your rather incompetent crewleader left the Ministry's Canton of Finance about an hour ago, returning directly to this safe house. He was followed by two Ministry scouts, one high-ranking prelan . . . and a single Steel Inquisitor."

No one spoke.

Oh, Lord . . . Vin thought. She'd been right—she just hadn't been fast enough. If there was an Inquisitor—

"I dealt with the Inquisitor," Kelsier said. He paused, letting the implication hang in the air. What kind of person could so lightly claim to have "dealt" with an Inquisitor? Rumors said the creatures were immortal, that they could see a man's soul, and that they were unmatched warriors.

"I require payment for services rendered," Kelsier said.

Camon didn't get up this time; he had fallen hard, and he was obviously disoriented. The room remained still. Finally, Milev—the dark-skinned man who was Camon's second—scooped up the coffer of Ministry boxings and dashed forward with it. He proffered it to Kelsier.

"The money Camon got from the Ministry," Milev explained. "Three thousand boxings."

Milev is so eager to please him, Vin thought. *This is more than just Luck—either that, or it's some sort of Luck I've never been able to use.*

Kelsier paused, then accepted the coin chest. "And you are?"

"Milev, Master Kelsier."

"Well, Crewleader Milev, I will consider this payment satisfactory—assuming you do one other thing for me."

Milev paused. "What would that be?"

Kelsier nodded toward the near-unconscious Camon. "Deal with him."

"Of course," Milev said.

"I want him to live, Milev," Kelsier said, holding up a finger. "But I don't want him to enjoy it."

Milev nodded. "We'll make him a beggar. The Lord Ruler disapproves of the profession—Camon won't have an easy time of it here in Luthadel."

And Milev will dispose of him anyway as soon as he thinks this Kelsier isn't paying attention.

"Good," Kelsier said. Then he opened the coin chest and began counting out some golden boxings. "You're a resourceful man, Milev. Quick on your feet, and not as easily intimidated as the others."

"I've had dealings with Mistings before, Master Kelsier," Milev said.

Kelsier nodded. "Dox," he said, addressing his companion, "where were we going to have our meeting tonight?"

"I was thinking that we should use Clubs's shop," said the second man.

"Hardly a neutral location," Kelsier said. "Especially if he decides not to join us."

"True."

Kelsier looked to Milev. "I'm planning a job in this area. It would be useful to have the support of some locals." He held out a pile of what looked like a hundred boxings. "We'll require use of your safe house for the evening. This can be arranged?"

"Of course," Milev said, taking the coins eagerly.

"Good," Kelsier said. "Now, get out."

"Out?" Milev asked hesitantly.

"Yes," Kelsier said. "Take your men—including your former leader—and leave. I want to have a private conversation with Mistress Vin."

The room grew silent again, and Vin knew she wasn't the only one wondering how Kelsier knew her name.

"Well, you heard him!" Milev snapped. He waved for a group of thugs to go grab Camon, then he shooed the rest of the crewmembers up the stairs. Vin watched them go, growing apprehensive. This Kelsier was a powerful man, and instinct told her that powerful men were dangerous. Did he know of her Luck? Obviously; what other reason would he have for singling her out?

How is this Kelsier going to try and use me? she thought, rubbing her arm where she'd hit the floor.

"By the way, Milev," Kelsier said idly. "When I say 'private,' I mean that I don't want to be spied on by the four men watching us through peek-holes behind the far wall. Kindly take them up into the alley with you."

Milev paled. "Of course, Master Kelsier."

"Good. And, in the alleyway you'll find the two dead Ministry spies. Kindly dispose of the corpses for us."

Milev nodded, turning.

"And Milev," Kelsier added.

Milev turned back again.

"See that none of your men betray us," Kelsier said quietly. And Vin felt it again—a renewed pressure on her emotions. "This crew already has the eye of the Steel Ministry—do not make an enemy of me as well."

Milev nodded sharply, then disappeared into the stairwell, pulling the door closed behind him. A few moments later, Vin heard footsteps from the peek room; then all was still. She was alone with a man who was—for some reason—so singularly impressive that he could intimidate an entire room full of cutthroats and thieves.

She eyed the bolt door. Kelsier was watching her. What would he do if she ran?

He claims to have killed an Inquisitor, Vin thought. *And . . . he used Luck. I have to stay, if just long enough to find out what he knows.*

Kelsier's smile deepened, then finally he laughed. "That was *far* too much fun, Dox."

The other man, the one Camon had called Dockson, snorted and walked toward the front of the room. Vin tensed, but he didn't move toward her, instead strolled to the bar.

"You were insufferable enough before, Kell," Dockson said. "I don't know how I'm going to handle this new reputation of yours. At least, I'm not sure how I'm going to handle it and maintain a straight face."

"You're jealous."

"Yes, that's it," Dockson said. "I'm terribly jealous of your ability to intimidate petty criminals. If it's of any note to you, I think you were too harsh on Camon."

Kelsier walked over and took a seat at one of the room's tables. His mirth darkened slightly as he spoke. "You saw what he was doing to the girl."

"Actually, I didn't," Dockson said dryly, rummaging through the bar's stores. "Someone was blocking the doorway."

Kelsier shrugged. "Look at her, Dox. The poor thing's been beaten nearly senseless. I don't feel any sympathy for the man."

Vin remained where she was, keeping watch on both men. As the tension of the moment grew weaker, her wounds began to throb again. The blow between her shoulder blades—that would be a large bruise—and the slap to her face burned as well. She was still a little dizzy.

Kelsier was watching her. Vin clinched her teeth. Pain. She could deal with pain.

"You need anything, child?" Dockson asked. "A wet handkerchief for that face, perhaps?"

She didn't respond, instead remaining focused on Kelsier. *Come on. Tell me what you want with me. Make your play.*

Dockson finally shrugged, then ducked beneath the bar for a moment. He eventually came up with a couple of bottles.

"Anything good?" Kelsier asked, turning.

"What do you think?" Dockson asked. "Even among thieves, Camon isn't exactly known for his refinement. I have socks worth more than this wine."

Kelsier sighed. "Give me a cup anyway." Then he glanced back at Vin. "You want anything?"

Vin didn't respond.

Kelsier smiled. "Don't worry—we're far less frightening than your friends think."

"I don't think they were her friends, Kell," Dockson said from behind the bar.

"Good point," Kelsier said. "Regardless, child, you don't have anything to fear from us. Other than Dox's breath."

Dockson rolled his eyes. "Or Kell's jokes."

Vin stood quietly. She could act weak, the way she had with Camon, but instincts told her that these men wouldn't respond well to that tactic. So, she remained where she was, assessing the situation.

The calmness fell upon her again. It encouraged her to be at ease, to be trusting, to simply do as the men were suggesting. . . .

No! She stayed where she was.

Kelsier raised an eyebrow. "That's unexpected."

"What?" Dockson asked as he poured a cup of wine.

"Nothing," Kelsier said, studying Vin.

"You want a drink or not, lass?" Dockson asked.

Vin said nothing. All her life, as long as she could remember, she'd had her Luck. It made her strong, and it gave her an edge over other thieves. It was probably why she was still alive. Yet, all that time, she'd never really known what it was or why she could use it. Logic and instinct now told her the same thing—that she needed to find out what this man knew.

However he intended to use her, whatever his plans were, she needed to endure them. She had to find out how he'd grown so powerful.

"Ale," she finally said.

"Ale?" Kelsier asked. "That's it?"

Vin nodded, watching him carefully. "I like it."

Kelsier rubbed his chin. "We'll have to work on that," he said. "Anyway, have a seat."

Hesitant, Vin walked over and sat down opposite Kelsier at the small table. Her wounds throbbed, but she couldn't afford to show weakness. Weakness killed. She had to pretend to ignore the pain. At least, sitting as she was, her head cleared.

Dockson joined them a moment later, giving Kelsier a glass of wine and Vin her mug of ale. She didn't take a drink.

"Who are you?" she asked in a quiet voice.

Kelsier raised an eyebrow. "You're a blunt one, eh?"

Vin didn't reply.

Kelsier sighed. "So much for my intriguing air of mystery."

Dockson snorted quietly.

Kelsier smiled. "My name is Kelsier. I'm what you might

call a crewleader—but I run a crew that isn't like any you've probably known. Men like Camon, along with his crew, like to think of themselves as predators, feeding off of the nobility and the various organizations of the Ministry."

Vin shook her head. "Not predators. Scavengers." One would have thought, perhaps, that so close to the Lord Ruler, such things as thieving crews would not be able to exist. Yet, Reen had shown her that the opposite was true: Powerful, rich nobility congregated around the Lord Ruler. And, where power and riches existed, so did corruption—especially since the Lord Ruler tended to police his nobility far less than he did the skaa. It had to do, apparently, with his fondness for their ancestors.

Either way, thieving crews like Camon's were the rats who fed on the city's corruption. And, like rats, they were impossible to entirely exterminate—especially in a city with the population of Luthadel.

"Scavengers," Kelsier said, smiling; apparently he did that a lot. "That's an appropriate description, Vin. Well, Dox and I, we're scavengers too . . . we're just a higher quality of scavenger. We're more well-bred, you might say—or perhaps just more ambitious."

She frowned. "You're noblemen?"

"Lord, no," Dockson said.

"Or, at least," Kelsier said, "not full-blooded ones."

"Half-breeds aren't supposed to exist," Vin said carefully. "The Ministry hunts them."

Kelsier raised an eyebrow. "Half-breeds like you?"

Vin felt a shock. *How . . . ?*

"Even the Steel Ministry isn't infallible, Vin," Kelsier said. "If they can miss you, then they can miss others."

Vin paused thoughtfully. "Milev. He called you Mistings. Those are some kind of Allomancer, right?"

Dockson glanced at Kelsier. "She's observant," the shorter man said with an appreciative nod.

"Indeed," Kelsier agreed. "The man did call us Mistings, Vin—though the appellation was a bit hasty, since neither Dox nor I are technically Mistings. We do, however, associate with them quite a bit."

Vin sat quietly for a moment, sitting beneath the scrutiny

of the two men. Allomancy. The mystical power held by the nobility, granted to them by the Lord Ruler some thousand years before as a reward for their loyalty. It was basic Ministry doctrine; even a skaa like Vin knew that much. The nobility had Allomancy and privilege because of their ancestors; the skaa were punished for the same reason.

The truth was, however, that she didn't really know what Allomancy was. It had something to do with fighting, she'd always assumed. One "Misting," as they were called, was said to be dangerous enough to kill an entire thieving team. Yet, the skaa she knew spoke of the power in whispered, uncertain tones. Before this moment, she'd never even paused to consider the possibility that it might simply be the same thing as her Luck.

"Tell me, Vin," Kelsier said, leaning forward with interest. "Do you realize what you did to that obligator in the Canton of Finance?"

"I used my Luck," Vin said quietly. "I use it to make people less angry."

"Or less suspicious," Kelsier said. "Easier to scam."

Vin nodded.

Kelsier held up a finger. "There are a lot of things you're going to have to learn. Techniques, rules, and exercises. One lesson, however, cannot wait. *Never* use emotional Allomancy on an obligator. They're all trained to recognize when their passions are being manipulated. Even the high nobility are forbidden from Pulling or Pushing the emotions of an obligator. You are what caused that obligator to send for an Inquisitor."

"Pray the creature never catches your trail again, lass," Dockson said quietly, sipping his wine.

Vin paled. "You didn't kill the Inquisitor?"

Kelsier shook his head. "I just distracted him for a bit—which was quite dangerous enough, I might add. Don't worry, many of the rumors about them aren't true. Now that he's lost your trail, he won't be able to find you again."

"Most likely," Dockson said.

Vin glanced at the shorter man apprehensively.

"Most likely," Kelsier agreed. "There are a lot of things we don't know about the Inquisitors—they don't seem to follow the normal rules. Those spikes through their eyes, for instance, should kill them. Nothing I've learned about Allomancy has ever provided an explanation for how those creatures keep living. If it were only a regular Misting Seeker on your trail, we wouldn't need to worry. An Inquistor . . . well, you'll want to keep your eyes open. Of course, you already seem pretty good at that."

Vin sat uncomfortably for a moment. Eventually, Kelsier nodded to her mug of ale. "You aren't drinking."

"You might have slipped something in it," Vin said.

"Oh, there was no need for me to sneak something into your drink," Kelsier said with a smile, pulling an object out of his suit coat pocket. "After all, you're going to drink this vial of mysterious liquid quite willingly."

He set a small glass vial on the tabletop. Vin frowned, regarding the liquid within. There was a dark residue at its bottom. "What is it?" she asked.

"If I told you, it wouldn't be mysterious," Kelsier said with a smile.

Dockson rolled his eyes. "The vial is filled with an alcohol solution and some flakes of metal, Vin."

"Metal?" she asked with a frown.

"Two of the eight basic Allomantic metals," Kelsier said. "We need to do some tests."

Vin eyed the vial.

Kelsier shrugged. "You'll have to drink it if you want to know any more about this Luck of yours."

"You drink half first," Vin said.

Kelsier raised an eyebrow. "A bit on the paranoid side, I see."

Vin didn't respond.

Finally, he sighed, picking up the vial and pulling off the plug.

"Shake it up first," Vin said. "So you get some of the sediment."

Kelsier rolled his eyes, but did as requested, shaking the vial, then downing half of its contents. He set it back on the table with a click.

Vin frowned. Then she eyed Kelsier, who smiled. He knew

that he had her. He had shown off his power, had tempted her with it. *The only reason to be subservient to those with power is so that you can learn to someday take what they have.* Reen's words.

Vin reached out and took the vial, then she downed its contents. She sat, waiting for some magical transformation or surge of power—or even signs of poison. She felt nothing.

How . . . anticlimactic. She frowned, leaning back in her chair. Out of curiosity, she felt at her Luck.

And felt her eyes widen in shock.

It was there, like a massive golden hoard. A storage of power so incredible that it stretched her understanding. Always before, she had needed to be a scrimp with her Luck, holding it in reserve, using up morsels sparingly. Now she felt like a starving woman invited to a high nobleman's feast. She sat, stunned, regarding the enormous wealth within her.

"So," Kelsier said with a prodding voice. "Try it. Soothe me."

Vin reached out, tentatively touching her newfound mass of Luck. She took a bit, and directed it at Kelsier.

"Good." Kelsier leaned forward eagerly. "But we already knew you could do that. Now the real test, Vin. Can you go the other way? You can dampen my emotions, but can you enflame them too?"

Vin frowned. She'd never used her Luck in such a way; she hadn't even realized that she could. Why was he so eager?

Suspicious, Vin reached for her source of Luck. As she did so, she noticed something interesting. What she had first interpreted as one massive source of power was actually two different sources of power. There were different types of Luck.

Eight. He'd said there were eight of them. But . . . what do the others do?

Kelsier was still waiting. Vin reached to the second, unfamiliar source of Luck, doing as she'd done before and directing it at him.

Kelsier's smile deepened, and he sat back, glancing at Dockson. "That's it then. She did it."

Dockson shook his head. "To be honest, Kell, I'm not sure what to think. Having one of you around was unsettling enough. Two, though . . ."

Vin regarded them with narrowed, dubious eyes. "Two what?"

"Even among the nobility, Vin, Allomancy is modestly rare," Kelsier said. "True, it's a hereditary skill, with most of its powerful lines among the high nobility. However, breeding alone doesn't guarantee Allomantic strength.

"Many high noblemen only have access to a single Allomantic skill. People like that—those who can only perform Allomancy in one of its eight basic aspects—are called Mistings. Sometimes these abilities appear in skaa—but only if that skaa has noble blood in his or her near ancestry. You can usually find one Misting in . . . oh, about ten thousand mixed-breed skaa. The better, and closer, the noble ancestry, the more likely the skaa is to be a Misting."

"Who were your parents, Vin?" Dockson asked. "Do you remember them?"

"I was raised by my half brother, Reen," Vin said quietly, uncomfortable. These were not things she discussed with others.

"Did he speak of your mother and father?" Dockson asked.

"Occasionally," she admitted. "Reen said that our mother was a whore. Not out of choice, but the underworld . . ." She trailed off. Her mother had tried to kill her, once, when she was very young. She vaguely remembered the event. Reen had saved her.

"What about your father, Vin?" Dockson asked.

Vin looked up. "He is a high prelan in the Steel Ministry."

Kelsier whistled softly. "Now, *that's* a slightly ironic breach of duty."

Vin looked down at the table. Finally, she reached over and took a healthy pull on her mug of ale.

Kelsier smiled. "Most ranking obligators in the Ministry are high noblemen. Your father gave you a rare gift in that blood of yours."

"So . . . I'm one of these Mistings you mentioned?"

Kelsier shook his head. "Actually, no. You see, this is what made you so interesting to us, Vin. Mistings only have access to one Allomantic skill. You just proved you have two. And, if you have access to at least two of the eight, then you have access to the rest as well. That's the way it works—if you're an

Allomancer, you either get one skill or you get them all."

Kelsier leaned forward. "You, Vin, are what is generally called a Mistborn. Even amongst the nobility, they're incredibly rare. Amongst skaa . . . well, let's just say I've only met one other skaa Mistborn in my entire life."

Somehow, the room seemed to grow more quiet. More still. Vin stared at her mug with distracted, uncomfortable eyes. *Mistborn.* She'd heard the stories, of course. The legends.

Kelsier and Dockson sat quietly, letting her think. Eventually, she spoke. "So . . . what does this all mean?"

Kelsier smiled. "It means that you, Vin, are a very special person. You have a power that most high noblemen envy. It is a power that, had you been born an aristocrat, would have made you one of the most deadly and influential people in all of the Final Empire."

Kelsier leaned forward again. "But, you weren't born an aristocrat. You're not noble, Vin. You don't have to play by their rules—and that makes you even *more* powerful."

Apparently, the next stage of my quest will take us up into the highlands of Terris. This is said to be a cold, unforgiving place—a land where the mountains themselves are made of ice.

Our normal attendants will not do for such a trip. We should probably hire some Terris packmen to carry our gear.

4

"YOU HEARD WHAT HE SAID! He's planning a job." Ulef's eyes shone with excitement. "I wonder which of the Great Houses he's going to strike."

"It'll be one of the most powerful ones," said Disten, one

of Camon's head pointmen. He was missing a hand, but his eyes and ears were among the keenest in the crew. "Kelsier never bothers himself with small-time jobs."

Vin sat quietly, her mug of ale—the same one Kelsier had given her—still sitting mostly full on the tabletop. Her table was crowded with people; Kelsier had let the thieves return to their home for a bit before his meeting began. Vin, however, would have preferred to remain by herself. Life with Reen had accustomed her to loneliness—if you let someone get too close, it would just give them better opportunities to betray you.

Even after Reen's disappearance, Vin had kept to herself. She hadn't been willing to leave; however, she also hadn't felt the need to become familiar with the other crewmembers. They had, in turn, been perfectly willing to let her alone. Vin's position had been precarious, and associating with her could have tainted them by association. Only Ulef had made any moves to befriend her.

If you let someone get close to you, it will only hurt more when they betray you, Reen seemed to whisper in her mind.

Had Ulef even really been her friend? He'd certainly sold her out quickly enough. In addition, the crewmembers had taken Vin's beating and sudden rescue in stride, never mentioning their betrayal or refusal to help her. They'd only done what was expected.

"The Survivor hasn't bothered himself with *any* jobs lately," said Harmon, an older, scraggly-bearded burglar. "He's barely been seen in Luthadel a handful of times during the last few years. In fact, he hasn't pulled any jobs since . . ."

"This is the first one?" Ulef asked eagerly. "The first since he escaped the Pits? Then it's bound to be something spectacular!"

"Did he say anything about it, Vin?" Disten asked. "Vin?" He waved a stumpy arm in her direction, catching her attention.

"What?" she asked, looking up. She had cleaned herself slightly since her beating at Camon's hand, finally accepting a handkerchief from Dockson to wipe the blood from her face. There was little she could do about the bruises, however. Those still throbbed. Hopefully, nothing was broken.

"Kelsier," Disten repeated. "Did he say anything about the job he's planning?"

Vin shook her head. She glanced down at the bloodied handkerchief. Kelsier and Dockson had left a short time ago, promising to return after she'd had some time to think about the things they had told her. There was an implication in their words, however—an offer. Whatever job they were planning, she was invited to participate.

"Why'd he pick you to be his twixt, anyway, Vin?" Ulef asked. "Did he say anything about that?"

That's what the crew assumed—that Kelsier had chosen her to be his contact with Camon's . . . Milev's . . . crew.

There were two sides to the Luthadel underground. There were the regular crews, like Camon's. Then there were . . . the *special* ones. Groups composed of the extremely skillful, the extremely foolhardy, or the extremely talented. Allomancers.

The two sides of the underworld didn't mix; regular thieves left their betters alone. However, occasionally one of these Misting crews hired a regular team to do some of its more mundane work, and they would choose a twixt—a go-between—to work with both crews. Hence Ulef's assumption about Vin.

Milev's crewmembers noticed her unresponsiveness, and turned to another topic: Mistings. They spoke of Allomancy with uncertain, whispered tones, and she listened, uncomfortable. How could she be associated with something they held in such awe? Her Luck . . . her Allomancy . . . was something small, something she used to survive, but something really quite unimportant.

But, such power . . . she thought, looking in at her Luck reserve.

"What's Kelsier been doing these last few years, I wonder?" Ulef asked. He had seemed a bit uncomfortable around her at the beginning of the conversation, but that had passed quickly. He'd betrayed her, but this was the underworld. No friends.

It didn't seem that way between Kelsier and Dockson. They appeared to trust each other. A front? Or were they simply one of those rare teams that actually didn't worry about each other's betrayal?

The most unsettling thing about Kelsier and Dockson had

been their openness with her. They seemed willing to trust, even accept, Vin after a relatively short time. It couldn't be genuine—no one could survive in the underworld following such tactics. Still, their friendliness was disconcerting.

"Two years . . ." said Hrud, a flat-faced, quiet thug. "He must have spent the entire time planning for this job."

"It must be some job indeed. . . ." Ulef said.

"Tell me about him," Vin said quietly.

"Kelsier?" Disten asked.

Vin nodded.

"They didn't talk about Kelsier down south?"

Vin shook her head.

"He was the best crewleader in Luthadel," Ulef explained. "A legend, even among the Mistings. He robbed some of the wealthiest Great Houses in the city."

"And?" Vin asked.

"Someone betrayed him," Harmon said in a quiet voice.

Of course, Vin thought.

"The Lord Ruler himself caught Kelsier," Ulef said. "Sent Kelsier and his wife to the Pits of Hathsin. But *he escaped.* He escaped from the Pits, Vin! He's the only one who ever has."

"And the wife?" Vin asked.

Ulef glanced at Harmon, who shook his head. "She didn't make it."

So, he's lost someone too. How can he laugh so much? So honestly?

"That's where he got those scars, you know," Disten said. "The ones on his arms. He got them at the Pits, from the rocks on a sheer wall he had to climb to escape."

Harmon snorted. "That's not how he got them. He killed an Inquisitor while escaping—that's where he got the scars."

"I heard he got them fighting one of the monsters that guard the Pits," Ulef said. "He reached into its mouth and strangled it *from the inside.* The teeth scraped his arms."

Disten frowned. "How do you strangle someone from the inside?"

Ulef shrugged. "That's just what I heard."

"The man isn't natural," Hrud muttered. "Something happened to him in the Pits, something bad. He wasn't an Allomancer before then, you know. He entered the Pits a regular skaa, and now . . . Well, he's a Misting for sure—if he's even human anymore. Been out in the mists a lot, that one has. Some say that the real Kelsier is dead, that the thing wearing his face is . . . something else."

Harmon shook his head. "Now, that's just plantation-skaa foolishness. We've all gone out in the mists."

"Not in the mists outside the city," Hrud insisted. "The mistwraiths are out there. They'll grab a man and take his face, sure as the Lord Ruler."

Harmon rolled his eyes.

"Hrud's right about one thing," Disten said. "That man isn't human. He might not be a mistwraith, but he's not skaa either. I've heard of him doing things, things like only *they* can do. The ones that come out at night. You saw what he did to Camon."

"Mistborn," Harmon muttered.

Mistborn. Vin had heard the term before Kelsier had mentioned it to her, of course. Who hadn't? Yet, the rumors about Mistborn made stories of Inquisitors and Mistings seem rational. It was said that Mistborn were heralds of the mists themselves, endowed with great powers by the Lord Ruler. Only high noblemen could be Mistborn; they were said to be a secret sect of assassins who served him, only going out at night. Reen had always taught her that they were a myth, and Vin had assumed he was right.

And Kelsier says I—like he himself—am one of them. How could she be what he said? Child of a prostitute, she was nobody. She was nothing.

Never trust a man who tells you good news, Reen had always said. *It's the oldest, but easiest, way to con someone.*

Yet, she did have her Luck. Her Allomancy. She could still sense the reserves Kelsier's vial had given her, and had tested her powers on the crewmembers. No longer limited to just a bit of Luck a day, she found she could produce far more striking effects.

Vin was coming to realize that her old goal in life—simply

staying alive—was uninspired. There was so much more she could be doing. She had been a slave to Reen; she had been a slave to Camon. She would be a slave to this Kelsier too, if it would lead her to eventual freedom.

At his table, Milev looked at his pocket watch, then stood. "All right, everyone out."

The room began to clear in preparation for Kelsier's meeting. Vin remained where she was; Kelsier had made it quite clear to the others that she was invited. She sat quietly for a bit, the room feeling far more comfortable to her now that it was empty. Kelsier's friends began to arrive a short time later.

The first man down the steps had the build of a soldier. He wore a loose, sleeveless shirt that exposed a pair of well-sculpted arms. He was impressively muscular, but not massive, and had close-cropped hair that stuck up slightly on his head.

The soldier's companion was a sharply dressed man in a nobleman's suit—plum vest, gold buttons, black overcoat—complete with short-brimmed hat and dueling cane. He was older than the soldier, and was a bit portly. He removed his hat upon entering the room, revealing a head of well-styled black hair. The two men were chatting amiably as they walked, but they paused when they saw the empty room.

"Ah, this must be our twixt," said the man in the suit. "Has Kelsier arrived yet, my dear?" He spoke with a simple familiarity, as if they were longtime friends. Suddenly, despite herself, Vin found herself liking this well-dressed, articulate man.

"No," she said quietly. Though overalls and a work shirt had always suited her, she suddenly wished that she owned something nicer. This man's very bearing seemed to demand a more formal atmosphere.

"Should have known that Kell would be late to his own meeting," the soldier said, sitting down at one of the tables near the center of the room.

"Indeed," said the suited man. "I suppose his tardiness leaves us with a chance for some refreshment. I could so use something to drink. . . ."

"Let me get you something," Vin said quickly, jumping to her feet.

"How gracious of you," the suited man said, choosing a

chair next to the soldier. He sat with one leg crossed over the other, his dueling cane held to the side, tip against the floor, one hand resting on the top.

Vin walked to the bar and began rummaging for drinks.

"Breeze . . ." the soldier said with a warning tone as Vin selected a bottle of Camon's most expensive wine and began pouring a cup.

"Hum . . . ?" the suited man said, raising an eyebrow.

The soldier nodded toward Vin.

"Oh, very well," the suited man said with a sigh.

Vin paused, wine half poured, and frowned slightly. *What am I doing?*

"I swear, Ham," the suited man said, "you are dreadfully stiff sometimes."

"Just because you can Push someone around doesn't mean you should, Breeze."

Vin stood, dumbfounded. *He . . . used Luck on me.* When Kelsier had tried to manipulate her, she'd felt his touch and had been able to resist. This time, however, she hadn't even realized what she was doing.

She looked up at the man, thinning her eyes. "Mistborn."

The suited man, Breeze, chuckled. "Hardly. Kelsier's the only skaa Mistborn you're likely to ever meet, my dear—and pray you never are in a situation where you meet a noble one. No, I am just an ordinary, humble Misting."

"Humble?" Ham asked.

Breeze shrugged.

Vin looked down at the half-full cup of wine. "You Pulled on my emotions. With . . . Allomancy, I mean."

"I Pushed on them, actually," Breeze said. "Pulling makes a person less trusting and more determined. Pushing on emotions—Soothing them—makes a person more trusting."

"Regardless, you controlled me," Vin said. "You made me fetch you a drink."

"Oh, I wouldn't say that I *made* you do it," Breeze said. "I just altered your emotions slightly, putting you in a frame of mind where you'd be more likely to do as I wished."

Ham rubbed his chin. "I don't know, Breeze. It's an interesting question. By influencing her emotions, did you take away her ability to choose? If, for instance, she were to kill or steal while under your control, would the crime be hers or yours?"

Breeze rolled his eyes. "There's really no question to it at all. You shouldn't think about such things, Hammond—you'll hurt your brain. I offered her encouragement, I simply did it through an irregular means."

"But—"

"I'm not going to argue it with you, Ham."

The beefy man sighed, looking a little bit forlorn.

"Are you going to bring me the drink . . . ?" Breeze asked hopefully, looking at Vin. "I mean, you're already up, and you're going to have to come back this direction to reach your seat anyway. . . ."

Vin examined her emotions. Did she feel irregularly drawn to do as the man asked? Was he manipulating her again? Finally, she simply walked away from the bar, leaving the drink where it was.

Breeze sighed. He didn't stand to go get the drink himself, however.

Vin walked tentatively toward the two men's table. She was accustomed to shadows and corners—close enough to eavesdrop, but far enough away to escape. Yet, she couldn't hide from these men—not while the room was so empty. So, she chose a chair at the table beside the one that the two men were using, then sat cautiously. She needed information—as long as she was ignorant, she was going to be at a severe disadvantage in this new world of Misting crews.

Breeze chuckled. "Nervous little thing, aren't you?"

Vin ignored the comment. "You," Vin said, nodding to Ham. "You're a . . . a Misting too?"

Ham nodded. "I'm a Thug."

Vin frowned in confusion.

"I burn pewter," Ham said.

Again, Vin looked at him questioningly.

"He can make himself stronger, my dear," Breeze said. "He hits things—particularly other people—who try to interfere with what the rest of us are doing."

"There's much more to it than that," Ham said. "I run general security for jobs, providing my crewleader with manpower and warriors, assuming such are necessary."

"And he'll try and bore you with random philosophy when it isn't," Breeze added.

Ham sighed. "Breeze, honestly, sometimes I don't know why I . . ." Ham trailed off as the door opened again, admitting another man.

The newcomer wore a dull tan overcoat, a pair of brown trousers, and a simple white shirt. However, his face was far more distinctive than his clothing. It was knotted and gnarled, like a twisted piece of wood, and his eyes shone with the level of disapproving dissatisfaction only the elderly can display. Vin couldn't quite place his age—he was young enough that he wasn't stooped over, yet he was old enough that he made even the middle-aged Breeze look youthful.

The newcomer looked over Vin and the others, huffed disdainfully, then walked to a table on the other side of the room and sat down. His steps were marked by a distinct limp.

Breeze sighed. "I'm going to miss Trap."

"We all will," Ham said quietly. "Clubs is very good, though. I've worked with him before."

Breeze studied the newcomer. "I wonder if I could get *him* to bring my drink over. . . ."

Ham chuckled. "I'd pay money to see you try it."

"I'm sure you would," Breeze said.

Vin eyed the newcomer, who seemed perfectly content to ignore her and the other two men. "What's he?"

"Clubs?" Breeze asked. "He, my dear, is a Smoker. He is what will keep the rest of us from being discovered by an Inquisitor."

Vin chewed on her lip, digesting the new information as she studied Clubs. The man shot her a glare, and she looked away. As she turned, she noticed that Ham was looking at her.

"I like you, kid," he said. "The other twixts I've worked with have either been too intimidated to talk to us, or they've been jealous of us for moving into their territory."

"Indeed," Breeze said. "You're not like most crumbs. Of

course, I'd like you a great deal more if you'd go fetch me that glass of wine. . . ."

Vin ignored him, glancing at Ham. "Crumb?"

"That's what some of the more self-important members of our society call lesser thieves," Ham said. "They call you crumbs, since you tend to be involved with . . . less inspired projects."

"No offense intended, of course," Breeze said.

"Oh, I wouldn't ever take offense at—" Vin paused, feeling an irregular desire to please the well-dressed man. She glared at Breeze. "Stop that!"

"See, there," Breeze said, glancing at Ham. "She still retains her ability to choose."

"You're hopeless."

They assume I'm a twixt, Vin thought. *So Kelsier hasn't told them what I am. Why?* Time constraints? Or, was the secret too valuable to share? How trustworthy were these men? And, if they thought her a simple "crumb," why were they being so nice to her?

"Who else are we waiting upon?" Breeze asked, glancing at the doorway. "Besides Kell and Dox, I mean."

"Yeden," Ham said.

Breeze frowned with a sour expression. "Ah, yes."

"I agree," Ham said. "But, I'd be willing to bet that he feels the same way about us."

"I don't even see why he was invited," Breeze said.

Ham shrugged. "Something to do with Kell's plan, obviously."

"Ah, the infamous 'plan,'" Breeze said musingly. "What job could it be, what indeed . . . ?"

Ham shook his head. "Kell and his cursed sense of drama."

"Indeed."

The door opened a few moments later, and the one they had spoken of, Yeden, entered. He turned out to be an unassuming man, and Vin had trouble understanding why the other two were so displeased about his attendance. Short with curly brown hair, Yeden was dressed in simple gray skaa clothing and a patched, soot-stained brown worker's coat. He regarded the surroundings with a look of disapproval, but he was nowhere near as openly hostile as Clubs, who still sat on the other side of the room scowling at anyone who looked in his direction.

Not a very big crew, Vin thought. *With Kelsier and Dockson, that makes six of them.* Of course, Ham had said that he led a group of "Thugs." Were the men at this meeting simply representatives? The leaders of smaller, more specialized groups? Some crews worked that way.

Breeze checked his pocket watch three more times before Kelsier finally arrived. The Mistborn crewleader burst through the door with his cheery enthusiasm, Dockson sauntering along behind. Ham stood immediately, smiling broadly and clasping hands with Kelsier. Breeze stood as well, and while his greeting was a bit more reserved, Vin had to admit that she had never seen any crewleader welcomed so happily by his men.

"Ah," Kelsier said, looking toward the other side of the room. "Clubs and Yeden too. So, everyone's here. Good—I absolutely loathe being made to wait."

Breeze raised an eyebrow as he and Ham settled back into their chairs, Dockson taking a seat at the same table. "Are we to receive any explanation for your tardiness?"

"Dockson and I were visiting my brother," Kelsier explained, walking toward the front of the lair. He turned and leaned back against the bar, scanning the room. When Kelsier's eyes fell on Vin, he winked.

"Your brother?" Ham said. "Is Marsh coming to the meeting?"

Kelsier and Dockson shared a look. "Not tonight," Kelsier said. "But he'll join the crew eventually."

Vin studied the others. They were skeptical. *Tension between Kelsier and his brother, perhaps?*

Breeze raised his dueling cane, pointing the tip at Kelsier. "All right, Kelsier, you've kept this 'job' secret from us for eight months now. We know it's big, we know you're excited, and we're all properly annoyed at you for being so secretive. So, why don't you just go ahead and tell us what it is?"

Kelsier smiled. Then he stood up straight, waving a hand toward the dirty, plain-looking Yeden. "Gentlemen, meet your new employer."

This was, apparently, quite a shocking statement.

"*Him?*" Ham asked.

"Him," Kelsier said with a nod.

"What?" Yeden asked, speaking for the first time. "You have trouble working with someone who actually has morals?"

"It's not that, my dear man," Breeze said, setting his dueling cane across his lap. "It's just that, well, I was under the strange impression that you didn't *like* our types very much."

"I don't," Yeden said flatly. "You're selfish, undisciplined, and you've turned your backs on the rest of the skaa. You dress nicely, but on the inside you're dirty as ash."

Ham snorted. "I can already see that this job is going to be *great* for crew morale."

Vin watched quietly, chewing on her lip. Yeden was obviously a skaa worker, probably a member of a forge or textile mill. What connection did he have with the underground? And . . . how would he be able to afford the services of a thieving crew, especially one as apparently specialized as Kelsier's team?

Perhaps Kelsier noticed her confusion, for she found him looking at her as the others continued to speak.

"I'm still a little confused," Ham said. "Yeden, we're all aware of how you regard thieves. So . . . why hire us?"

Yeden squirmed a bit. "Because," he finally said, "everyone knows how effective you are."

Breeze chuckled. "Disapproving of our morals doesn't make you unwilling to make use of our skills, I see. So, what is the job, then? What does the skaa rebellion wish of us?"

Skaa rebellion? Vin thought, a piece of the conversation falling into place. There were two sides to the underworld. The far larger portion was made up of the thieves, crews, whores, and beggars who tried to survive outside of mainstream skaa culture.

And then there were the rebels. The people who worked against the Final Empire. Reen had always called them fools—a sentiment shared by most of the people, both underworlders and regular skaa, that Vin had met.

All eyes slowly turned to Kelsier, who leaned back against the bar again. "The skaa rebellion, courtesy of its leader, Yeden, has hired us for something very specific."

"What?" Ham asked. "Robbery? Assassination?"

"A little of both," Kelsier said, "and, at the same time, neither one. Gentlemen, this isn't going to be a regular job. It's going to be different from anything any crew has ever tried to pull. We're going to help Yeden overthrow the Final Empire."

Silence.

"Excuse me?" Ham asked.

"You heard me right, Ham," Kelsier said. "That's the job I've been planning—the destruction of the Final Empire. Or, at least, its center of government. Yeden has hired us to supply him with an army, then provide him with a favorable opportunity to seize control of this city."

Ham sat back, then shared a glance with Breeze. Both men turned toward Dockson, who nodded solemnly. The room remained quiet for a moment longer; then the silence was broken as Yeden began to laugh ruefully to himself.

"I should never have agreed to this," Yeden said, shaking his head. "Now that you say it, I realize how ridiculous it all sounds."

"Trust me, Yeden," Kelsier said. "These men have made a habit of pulling off plans that seem ridiculous at first glance."

"That may be true, Kell," Breeze said. "But, in this case, I find myself agreeing with our disapproving friend. Overthrow the Final Empire . . . that is something that skaa rebels have been working toward for a thousand years! What makes you think that we can achieve anything where those men have failed?"

Kelsier smiled. "We'll succeed because we have vision, Breeze. That's something the rebellion has always lacked."

"Excuse me?" Yeden said indignantly.

"It's true, unfortunately," Kelsier said. "The rebellion condemns people like us because of our greed, but for all their high morals—which, by the way, I respect—they never get anything done. Yeden, your men hide in woods and in hills, plotting how they'll someday rise up and lead a glorious war against the Final Empire. But your kind has no idea how to develop and execute a proper plan."

Yeden's expression grew dark. "And *you* have no idea what you are talking about."

"Oh?" Kelsier said lightly. "Tell me, what has your rebellion accomplished during its thousand-year struggle? Where are your successes and your victories? The Massacre of Tougier three centuries ago, where seven thousand skaa rebels were slaughtered? The occasional raid of a traveling canal boat or the kidnapping of a minor noble official?"

Yeden flushed. "That's the best we can manage with the people we have! Don't blame my men for their failures—blame the rest of the skaa. We can't ever get them to help. They've been beaten down for a millennium; they haven't got any spirit left. It's difficult enough to get one in a thousand to listen to us, let alone rebel!"

"Peace, Yeden," Kelsier said, holding up a hand. "I'm not trying to insult your courage. We're on the same side, remember? You came to me specifically because you were having trouble recruiting people for your army."

"I'm regretting that decision more and more, thief," Yeden said.

"Well, you've already paid us," Kelsier said. "So it's a little late to back out now. But, we'll get you that army, Yeden. The men in this room are the most capable, most clever, and most skilled Allomancers in the city. You'll see."

The room grew quiet again. Vin sat at her table, watching the interaction with a frown. *What is your game, Kelsier?* His words about overthrowing the Final Empire were obviously a front. It seemed most likely to her that he intended to scam the skaa rebellion. But . . . if he'd already been paid, then why continue the charade?

Kelsier turned from Yeden to Breeze and Ham. "All right, gentlemen. What do you think?"

The two men shared a look. Finally Breeze spoke. "Lord Ruler knows, I've never been one to turn down a challenge. But, Kell, I do question your reasoning. Are you sure we can do this?"

"I'm positive," Kelsier said. "Previous attempts to overthrow the Lord Ruler have failed because they lacked proper organization and planning. We're thieves, gentlemen—and we're extraordinarily good ones. We can rob the unrobbable and fool the unfoolable. We know how to take an incredibly large task and break it down to manageable pieces, then deal with each of those pieces. We know how to get what we want. These things make us perfect for this particular task."

Breeze frowned. "And . . . how much are we getting paid for achieving the impossible?"

"Thirty thousand boxings," Yeden said. "Half now, half when you deliver the army."

"Thirty thousand?" Ham said. "For an operation this big? That will barely cover expenses. We'll need a spy among the nobility to watch for rumors, we'll need a couple of safe houses, not to mention someplace big enough to hide and train an entire army. . . ."

"No use haggling now, thief," Yeden snapped. "Thirty thousand may not sound like much to *your* type, but it's the result of decades of saving on our part. We can't pay you more because we don't have anything more."

"It's good work, gentlemen," Dockson noted, joining the conversation for the first time.

"Yes, well, that's all great," Breeze said. "I consider myself a nice enough fellow. But . . . this just seems a bit too altruistic. Not to mention stupid."

"Well . . ." Kelsier said, "there might be a little bit more in it for us. . . ."

Vin perked up, and Breeze smiled.

"The Lord Ruler's treasury," Kelsier said. "The plan, as it stands now, is to provide Yeden with an army and an opportunity to seize the city. Once he takes the palace, he'll capture the treasury and use its funds to secure power. And, central to that treasury . . ."

"Is the Lord Ruler's atium," Breeze said.

Kelsier nodded. "Our agreement with Yeden promises us half of the atium reserves we find in the palace, no matter how vast they may be."

Atium. Vin had heard of the metal, but she had never actually seen any. It was incredibly rare, supposedly used only by noblemen.

Ham was smiling. "Well, now," he said slowly, "that's almost a big enough prize to be tempting."

"That atium stockpile is supposed to be enormous," Kelsier said. "The Lord Ruler sells the metal only in small bits, charging outrageous sums to the nobility. He *has* to keep a huge reserve of it to make certain he controls the market, and to make certain he has enough wealth for emergencies."

"True . . ." Breeze said. "But, are you sure you want to try something like this so soon after . . . what happened the last time we tried getting into the palace?"

"We're going to do things differently this time," Kelsier said. "Gentlemen, I'll be frank with you. This isn't going to be an easy job, but it *can* work. The plan is simple. We're going to find a way to neutralize the Luthadel Garrison—leaving the area without a policing force. Then, we're going to throw the city into chaos."

"We've got a couple of options on how to do that," Dockson said. "But we can talk about that later."

Kelsier nodded. "Then, in that chaos, Yeden will march his army into Luthadel and seize the palace, taking the Lord Ruler prisoner. While Yeden secures the city, we'll pilfer the atium. We'll give half to him, then disappear with the other half. After that, it's his job to hang on to what he's grabbed."

"Sounds a little dangerous for you, Yeden," Ham noted, glancing at the rebel leader.

He shrugged. "Perhaps. But, if we do, by some miracle, end up in control of the palace, then we'll have at least done something no skaa rebellion has ever achieved before. For my men, this isn't just about riches—it isn't even about surviving. It's about doing something grand, something wonderful, to give the skaa hope. But, I don't expect you people to understand things like that."

Kelsier shot a quieting glance at Yeden, and the man sniffed and sat back. *Did he use Allomancy?* Vin wondered. She'd seen employer-crew relationships before, and it seemed that Yeden was much more in Kelsier's pocket than the other way around.

Kelsier turned back to Ham and Breeze. "There's more to all this than simply a show of daring. If we do manage to steal that atium, it will be a sound blow to the Lord Ruler's financial foundation. He depends on the money that atium provides—without it, he could very well be left without the means to pay his armies.

"Even if he escapes our trap—or, if we decide to take the city when he's gone to minimize having to deal with him—he'll be financially ruined. He won't be able to march soldiers in to take the city away from Yeden. If this works right, we'll have the city in chaos anyway, and the nobility will be too weak to react against the rebel forces. The Lord Ruler will be left confused, and unable to mount a sizable army."

"And the koloss?" Ham asked quietly.

Kelsier paused. "If he marches those creatures on his own capital city, the destruction it would cause could be even more dangerous than financial instability. In the chaos, the provincial noblemen will rebel and set themselves up as kings, and the Lord Ruler won't have the troops to bring them into line. Yeden's rebels will be able to hold Luthadel, and we, my friends, will be very, very rich. Everyone gets what they want."

"You're forgetting the Steel Ministry," Clubs snapped, sitting almost forgotten at the side of the room. "Those Inquisitors won't just let us throw their pretty theocracy into chaos."

Kelsier paused, turning toward the gnarled man. "We will have to find a way to deal with the Ministry—I've got a few plans for that. Either way, problems like that are the things that we—as a crew—will have to work out. We have to get rid of the Luthadel Garrison—there's no way we'll be able to get anything done with them policing the streets. We'll have to come up with an appropriate way to throw the city into chaos, and we'll have to find a way to keep the obligators off our trail.

"But, if we play this right, we might be able to force the Lord Ruler to send the palace guard—maybe even the Inquisitors—into the city to restore order. That will leave the palace itself exposed, giving Yeden a perfect opportunity to strike. After that, it won't matter what happens with the

Ministry or the Garrison—the Lord Ruler won't have the money to maintain control of his empire."

"I don't know, Kell," Breeze said, shaking his head. His flippancy was subdued; he seemed to be honestly considering the plan. "The Lord Ruler got that atium somewhere. What if he just goes and mines some more?"

Ham nodded. "No one even knows where the atium mine is."

"I wouldn't say *no one*," Kelsier said with a smile.

Breeze and Ham shared a look.

"You know?" Ham asked.

"Of course," Kelsier said. "I spent a year of my life working there."

"The Pits?" Ham asked with surprise.

Kelsier nodded. "That's why the Lord Ruler makes certain nobody survives working there—he can't afford to let his secret out. It's not just a penal colony, not just a hellhole where skaa are sent to die. It's a mine."

"Of course . . ." Breeze said.

Kelsier stood up straight, stepping away from the bar and walking toward Ham and Breeze's table. "We have a chance here, gentlemen. A chance to do something great—something no other thieving crew has ever done. We'll rob from the Lord Ruler himself!

"But, there's more. The Pits nearly killed me, and I've seen things . . . differently since I escaped. I see the skaa, working without hope. I see the thieving crews, trying to survive on aristocratic leavings, often getting themselves—and other skaa—killed in the process. I see the skaa rebellion trying so hard to resist the Lord Ruler, and never making any progress.

"The rebellion fails because it's too unwieldy and spread out. Anytime one of its many pieces gains momentum, the Steel Ministry crushes it. That's not the way to defeat the Final Empire, gentlemen. But, a small team—specialized and highly skilled—has a hope. We can work without great risk of exposure. We know how to avoid the Steel Ministry's tendrils. We understand how the high nobility thinks, and how to exploit its members. We can do this!"

He paused beside Breeze and Ham's table.

"I don't know, Kell," Ham said. "It's not that I'm disagreeing with your motives. It's just that . . . well, this seems a bit foolhardy."

Kelsier smiled. "I know it does. But you're going to go along with it anyway, aren't you?"

Ham paused, then nodded. "You know I'll join your crew no matter what the job. This sounds crazy, but so do most of your plans. Just . . . just tell me. Are you serious about overthrowing the Lord Ruler?"

Kelsier nodded. For some reason, Vin was almost tempted to believe him.

Ham nodded firmly. "All right, then. I'm in."

"Breeze?" Kelsier asked.

The well-dressed man shook his head. "I'm not sure, Kell. This is a bit extreme, even for you."

"We need you, Breeze," Kell said. "No one can Soothe a crowd like you can. If we're going to raise an army, we'll need your Allomancers—and your powers."

"Well, that much is true," Breeze said. "But, even still . . ."

Kelsier smiled, then he set something on the table—the cup of wine Vin had poured for Breeze. She hadn't even noticed that Kelsier had grabbed it off of the bar.

"Think of the challenge, Breeze," Kelsier said.

Breeze glanced at the cup, then looked up at Kelsier. Finally, he laughed, reaching for the wine. "Fine. I'm in."

"It's impossible," a gruff voice said from the back of the room. Clubs sat with folded arms, regarding Kelsier with a scowl. "What are you really planning, Kelsier?"

"I'm being honest," Kelsier replied. "I plan to take the Lord Ruler's atium and overthrow his empire."

"You can't," the man said. "It's idiocy. The Inquisitors will hang us all by hooks through our throats."

"Perhaps," Kelsier said. "But think of the reward if we succeed. Wealth, power, and a land where the skaa can live like men, rather than slaves."

Clubs snorted loudly. Then he stood, his chair toppling backward onto the floor behind him. "No reward would be enough. The Lord Ruler tried to have you killed once—I see that you won't be satisfied until he gets it right." With that, the older man turned and stalked in a limping gait from the room, slamming the door behind him.

The lair grew quiet.

"Well, guess we'll need a different Smoker," Dockson said.

"You're just going to let him go?" Yeden demanded. "He knows everything!"

Breeze chuckled. "Aren't you supposed to be the moral one in this little group?"

"Morals doesn't have anything to do with it," Yeden said. "Letting someone go like that is foolish! He could bring the obligators down on us in minutes."

Vin nodded in agreement, but Kelsier just shook his head. "I don't work that way, Yeden. I invited Clubs to a meeting where I outlined a dangerous plan—one some people might even call stupid. I'm not going to have him assassinated because he decided it was too dangerous. If you do things like that, pretty soon nobody will come listen to your plans in the first place."

"Besides," Dockson said. "We wouldn't invite someone to one of these meetings unless we trusted him not to betray us."

Impossible, Vin thought, frowning. He had to be bluffing to keep up crew morale; nobody was that trusting. After all, hadn't the others said that Kelsier's failure a few years before—the event that had sent him to the Pits of Hathsin—had come because of a betrayal? He probably had assassins following Clubs at that very moment, watching to make certain he didn't go to the authorities.

"All right, Yeden," Kelsier said, getting back to business. "They accepted. The plan is on. Are you still in?"

"Will you give the rebellion's money back if I say no?" Yeden asked.

The only response to that was a quiet chuckle from Ham. Yeden's expression darkened, but he just shook his head. "If I had any other option . . ."

"Oh, stop complaining," Kelsier said. "You're officially part of a thieving crew now, so you might as well come over here and sit with us."

Yeden paused for a moment, then sighed and walked over to sit at Breeze, Ham, and Dockson's table, beside which Kelsier was still standing. Vin still sat at the next table over.

Kelsier turned, looking over toward Vin. "What about you, Vin?"

She paused. *Why is he asking me? He already knows he has a hold over me. The job doesn't matter, as long as I learn what he knows.*

Kelsier waited expectantly.

"I'm in," Vin said, assuming that was what he wanted to hear.

She must have guessed correctly, for Kelsier smiled, then nodded to the last chair at the table.

Vin sighed, but did as he indicated, standing and walking over to take the last seat.

"Who is the child?" Yeden asked.

"Twixt," Breeze said.

Kelsier cocked an eyebrow. "Actually, Vin is something of a new recruit. My brother caught her Soothing his emotions a few months back."

"Soother, eh?" Ham asked. "Guess we can always use another of those."

"Actually," Kelsier noted, "it seems she can Riot people's emotions as well."

Breeze started.

"Really?" Ham asked.

Kelsier nodded. "Dox and I tested her just a few hours ago."

Breeze chuckled. "And here I was telling her that she'd probably never meet another Mistborn besides yourself."

"A second Mistborn on the team . . ." Ham said appreciatively. "Well, that increases our chances somewhat."

"What are you saying?" Yeden sputtered. "Skaa can't be Mistborn. I'm not even sure if Mistborn exist! *I've* certainly never met one."

Breeze raised an eyebrow, then laid a hand on Yeden's shoulder. "You should try not to talk so much, friend," he suggested. "You'll sound far less stupid that way."

Yeden shook off Breeze's hand, and Ham laughed. Vin, however, sat quietly, considering the implications of what Kelsier had said. The part about stealing the atium reserves was tempting, but seizing the city to do it? Were these men really that reckless?

Kelsier pulled a chair over to the table for himself and sat down on it the wrong way, resting his arms on the seatback. "All right," he said. "We have a crew. We'll plan specifics at the next meeting, but I want you all to be thinking about the job. I have some plans, but I want fresh minds to consider our task. We'll need to discuss ways to get the Luthadel Garrison out of the city, and ways that we can throw this place into so much chaos that the Great Houses can't mobilize their forces to stop Yeden's army when it attacks."

The members of the group, save Yeden, nodded.

"Before we end for the evening, however," Kelsier continued, "there is one more part of the plan I want to warn you about."

"More?" Breeze asked with a chuckle. "Stealing the Lord Ruler's fortune and overthrowing his empire aren't enough?"

"No," Kelsier said. "If I can, I'm going to kill him too."

Silence.

"Kelsier," Ham said slowly. "The Lord Ruler is the Sliver of Infinity. He's a piece of God Himself. You can't kill him. Even *capturing* him will probably prove impossible."

Kelsier didn't reply. His eyes, however, were determined.

That's it, Vin thought. *He has to be insane.*

"The Lord Ruler and I," Kelsier said quietly, "we have an unsettled debt. He took Mare from me, and he nearly took my own sanity as well. I'll admit to you all that part of my reason for this plan is to get revenge on him. We're going to take his government, his home, and his fortune from him.

"However, for that to work, we'll have to get rid of him. Perhaps imprison him in his own dungeons—at the very least, we'll have to get him out of the city. However, I can think of something far better than either option. Down those pits where he sent me, I Snapped and came to an awakening of my Allomantic powers. Now I intend to use them to kill him."

Kelsier reached into his suit pocket and pulled something out. He set it on the table.

"In the north, they have a legend," Kelsier said. "It teaches that the Lord Ruler isn't immortal—not completely. They say he can be killed with the right metal. The Eleventh Metal. That metal."

Eyes turned toward the object on the table. It was a thin bar of metal, perhaps as long and wide as Vin's small finger, with straight sides. It was silvery white in color.

"The Eleventh Metal?" Breeze asked uncertainly. "I've heard of no such legend."

"The Lord Ruler has suppressed it," Kelsier said. "But it can still be found, if you know where to look. Allomantic theory teaches of ten metals: the eight basic metals, and the two high metals. There is another one, however, unknown to most. One far more powerful, even, than the other ten."

Breeze frowned skeptically.

Yeden, however, appeared intrigued. "And, this metal can somehow kill the Lord Ruler?"

Kelsier nodded. "It's his weakness. The Steel Ministry wants you to believe that he's immortal, but even he can be killed—by an Allomancer burning this."

Ham reached out, picking up the thin bar of metal. "Where did you get it?"

"In the north," Kelsier said. "In a land near the Far Peninsula, a land where people still remember what their old kingdom was called in the days before the Ascension."

"How does it work?" Breeze asked.

"I'm not sure," Kelsier said frankly. "But I intend to find out."

Ham regarded the porcelain-colored metal, turning it over his fingers.

Kill the Lord Ruler? Vin thought. The Lord Ruler was a force, like the winds or the mists. One did not kill such things. They didn't live, really. They simply *were.*

"Regardless," Kelsier said, accepting the metal back from Ham, "you don't need to worry about this. Killing the Lord Ruler is my task. If it proves impossible, we'll settle for tricking him outside of the city, then robbing him silly. I just thought that you should know what I'm planning."

I've bound myself to a madman, Vin thought with resignation. But that didn't really matter—not as long as he taught her Allomancy.

I don't even understand what I'm supposed to do. The Terris philosophers claim that I'll know my duty when the time comes, but that's a small comfort.

The Deepness must be destroyed, and apparently I'm the only one who can do so. It ravages the world even now. If I don't stop it soon, there will be nothing left of this land but bones and dust.

5

"AHA!" KELSIER'S TRIUMPHANT FIGURE POPPED up from behind Camon's bar, a look of satisfaction on his face. He brought his arm up and thunked a dusty wine bottle down on the countertop.

Dockson looked over with amusement. "Where'd you find it?"

"One of the secret drawers," Kelsier said, dusting off the bottle.

"I thought I'd found all of those," Dockson said.

"You did. One of them had a false back."

Dockson chuckled. "Clever."

Kelsier nodded, unstoppering the bottle and pouring out three cups. "The trick is to never stop looking. There's *always* another secret." He gathered up the three cups and walked over to join Vin and Dockson at the table.

Vin accepted her cup with a tentative hand. The meeting had ended a short time earlier, Breeze, Ham, and Yeden leaving to ponder the things Kelsier had told them. Vin felt that she should have left as well, but she had nowhere to go. Dockson and Kelsier seemed to take it for granted that she would remain with them.

Kelsier took a long sip of the rubicund wine, then smiled. "Ah, that's *much* better."

Dockson nodded in agreement, but Vin didn't taste her own drink.

"We're going to need another Smoker," Dockson noted.

Kelsier nodded. "The others seemed to take it well, though."

"Breeze is still uncertain," Dockson said.

"He won't back out. Breeze likes a challenge, and he'll never find a challenge greater than this one." Kelsier smiled. "Besides, it'd drive him insane to know that we were pulling a job that he wasn't in on."

"Still, he's right to be apprehensive," Dockson said. "I'm a little worried myself."

Kelsier nodded his agreement, and Vin frowned. *So, are they serious about the plan? Or is this still a show for my sake?* The two men seemed so competent. Yet, overthrowing the Final Empire? They'd sooner stop the mists from flowing or the sun from rising.

"When do your other friends get here?" Dockson asked.

"A couple days," Kelsier said. "We'll need to have another Smoker by then. I'm also going to need some more atium."

Dockson frowned. "Already?"

Kelsier nodded. "I spent most of it buying OreSeur's Contract, then used my last bit at Tresting's plantation."

Tresting. The nobleman who had been killed in his manor the week before. *How was Kelsier involved? And, what was it Kelsier said before about atium?* He'd claimed that the Lord Ruler kept control of the high nobility by maintaining a monopoly on the metal.

Dockson rubbed his bearded chin. "Atium's not easy to come by, Kell. It took nearly eight months of planning to steal you that last bit."

"That's because you had to be delicate," Kelsier said with a devious smile.

Dockson eyed Kelsier with a look of slight apprehension. Kelsier just smiled more broadly, and finally Dockson rolled his eyes, sighing. Then he glanced at Vin. "You haven't touched your drink."

Vin shook her head.

Dockson waited for an explanation, and eventually Vin was

forced to respond. "I don't like to drink anything I didn't prepare myself."

Kelsier chuckled. "She reminds me of Vent."

"Vent?" Dockson said with a snort. "The lass is a bit paranoid, but she's not *that* bad. I swear, that man was so jumpy that his own heartbeat could startle him."

The two men shared a laugh. Vin, however, was only made more uncomfortable by the friendly air. *What do they expect from me? Am I to be an apprentice of some sort?*

"Well, then," Dockson said, "are you going to tell me how you plan on getting yourself some atium?"

Kelsier opened his mouth to respond, but the stairs clattered with the sound of someone coming down. Kelsier and Dockson turned; Vin, of course, had seated herself so she could see both entrances to the room without having to move.

Vin expected the newcomer to be one of Camon's crewmembers, sent to see if Kelsier was done with the lair yet. Therefore, she was completely surprised when the door swung open to reveal the surly, gnarled face of the man called Clubs.

Kelsier smiled, eyes twinkling.

He's not surprised. Pleased, perhaps, but not surprised.

"Clubs," Kelsier said.

Clubs stood in the doorway, giving the three of them an impressively disapproving stare. Finally, he hobbled into the room. A thin, awkward-looking teenage boy followed him.

The boy fetched Clubs a chair and put it by Kelsier's table. Clubs settled down, grumbling slightly to himself. Finally, he eyed Kelsier with a squinting, wrinkle-nosed expression. "The Soother is gone?"

"Breeze?" Kelsier asked. "Yes, he left."

Clubs grunted. Then he eyed the bottle of wine.

"Help yourself," Kelsier said.

Clubs waved for the boy to go fetch him a cup from the bar, then turned back to Kelsier. "I had to be sure," he said. "Never can trust yourself when a Soother is around—especially one like him."

"You're a Smoker, Clubs," Kelsier said. "He couldn't do much to you, not if you didn't want him to."

Clubs shrugged. "I don't like Soothers. It's not just Allomancy—men like that . . . well, you can't trust that you aren't being manipulated when they are around. Copper or no copper."

"I wouldn't rely on something like that to get your loyalty," Kelsier said.

"So I've heard," Clubs said as the boy poured him a cup of wine. "Had to be sure, though. Had to think about things without that Breeze around." He scowled, though Vin had trouble determining why, then took the cup and downed half of it in one gulp.

"Good wine," he said with a grunt. Then he looked over at Kelsier. "So, the Pits really did drive you insane, eh?"

"Completely," Kelsier said with a straight face.

Clubs smiled, though on his face the expression had a decidedly twisted look. "You mean to go through with this, then? This so-called job of yours?"

Kelsier nodded solemnly.

Clubs downed the rest of his wine. "You've got yourself a Smoker then. Not for the money, though. If you're really serious about toppling this government, then I'm in."

Kelsier smiled.

"And don't smile at me," Clubs snapped. "I hate that."

"I wouldn't dare."

"Well," Dockson said, pouring himself another drink, "that solves the Smoker problem."

"Won't matter much," Clubs said. "You're going to fail. I've spent my life trying to hide Mistings from the Lord Ruler and his obligators. He gets them all eventually anyway."

"Why bother helping us, then?" Dockson asked.

"Because," Clubs said, standing. "The Lord's going to get me sooner or later. At least this way, I'll be able to spit in his face as I go. Overthrowing the Final Empire . . ." He smiled. "It's got style. Let's go, kid. We've got to get the shop ready for visitors."

Vin watched them go, Clubs limping out the door, the boy pulling it closed behind them. Then she glanced at Kelsier. "You knew he'd come back."

He shrugged, standing and stretching. "I hoped. People are

attracted to vision. The job I'm proposing . . . well, it just isn't the sort of thing you walk away from—at least, not if you're a bored old man who's generally annoyed at life. Now, Vin, I assume that your crew owns this entire building?"

Vin nodded. "The shop upstairs is a front."

"Good," Kelsier said, checking his pocket watch, then handing it to Dockson. "Tell your friends that they can have their lair back—the mists are probably already coming out."

"And us?" Dockson asked.

Kelsier smiled. "We're going to the roof. Like I told you, I have to fetch some atium."

By day, Luthadel was a blackened city, scorched by soot and red sunlight. It was hard, distinct, and oppressive.

At night, however, the mists came to blur and obscure. High noble keeps became ghostly, looming silhouettes. Streets seemed to grow more narrow in the fog, every thoroughfare becoming a lonely, dangerous alleyway. Even noblemen and thieves were apprehensive about going out at night—it took a strong heart to brave the foreboding, misty silence. The dark city at night was a place for the desperate and the foolhardy; it was a land of swirling mystery and strange creatures.

Strange creatures like me, Kelsier thought. He stood upon the ledge that ran around the lip of the flat-roofed lair. Shadowed buildings loomed in the night around him, and the mists made everything seem to shift and move in the darkness. Weak lights peeked from the occasional window, but the tiny beads of illumination were huddled, frightened things.

A cool breeze slipped across the rooftop, shifting the haze, brushing against Kelsier's mist-wetted cheek like an exhaled breath. In days past—back before everything had gone wrong—he had always sought out a rooftop on the evening before a job, wishing to overlook the city. He didn't realize he was observing his old custom this night until he glanced to the side, expecting Mare to be there next to him, as she always had been.

Instead, he found only the empty air. Lonely. Silent. The mists had replaced her. Poorly.

He sighed and turned. Vin and Dockson stood behind him on the rooftop. Both looked apprehensive to be out in the mists, but they dealt with their fear. One did not get far in the underworld without learning to stomach the mists.

Kelsier had learned to do far more than "stomach" them. He had gone among them so often during the last few years that he was beginning to feel more comfortable at night, within the mists' obscuring embrace, than he did at day.

"Kell," Dockson said, "do you *have* to stand on the ledge like that? Our plans may be a bit crazy, but I'd rather not have them end with you splattered across the cobblestones down there."

Kelsier smiled. *He still doesn't think of me as a Mistborn,* he thought. *It will take some getting used to for all of them.*

Years before, he had become the most infamous crewleader in Luthadel, and he had done it without even being an Allomancer. Mare had been a Tineye, but he and Dockson . . . they had just been regular men. One a half-breed with no powers, the other a runaway plantation skaa. Together, they had brought Great Houses to their knees, stealing brashly from the most powerful men in the Final Empire.

Now Kelsier was more, so much more. Once he had dreamed of Allomancy, wishing for a power like Mare's. She had been dead before he'd Snapped, coming to his powers. She would never see what he would do with them.

Before, the high nobility had feared him. It had taken a trap set by the Lord Ruler himself to capture Kelsier. Now . . . the Final Empire itself would shake before he was finished with it.

He scanned the city once more, breathing in the mists, then hopped down off the ledge and strolled over to join Dockson and Vin. They carried no lights; ambient starlight diffused by the mists was enough to see by in most cases.

Kelsier took off his jacket and vest, handing them to Dockson, then he untucked his shirt, letting the long garment hang loose. The fabric was dark enough that it wouldn't give him away in the night.

"All right," Kelsier said. "Who should I try?"

Dockson frowned. "You're sure you want to do this?"

Kelsier smiled.

Dockson sighed. "Houses Urbain and Teniert have been hit recently, though not for their atium."

"Which house is the strongest right now?" Kelsier asked, squatting down and undoing the ties on his pack, which rested by Dockson's feet. "Who would no one consider hitting?"

Dockson paused. "Venture," he finally said. "They've been on top for the last few years. They keep a standing force of several hundred men, and the local house nobility includes a good two dozen Mistings."

Kelsier nodded. "Well, that's where I'll go, then. They're certain to have some atium." He pulled open the pack, then whipped out a dark gray cloak. Large and enveloping, the cloak wasn't constructed from a single piece of cloth—rather, it was made up of hundreds of long, ribbonlike strips. They were sewn together at the shoulders and across the chest, but mostly they hung separate from one another, like overlapping streamers.

Kelsier threw on the garment, its strips of cloth twisting and curling, almost like the mists themselves.

Dockson exhaled softly. "I've never been so close to someone wearing one of those."

"What is it?" Vin asked, her quiet voice almost haunting in the night mists.

"A Mistborn cloak," Dockson said. "They all wear the things—it's kind of like a . . . sign of membership in their club."

"It's colored and constructed to hide you in the mist," Kelsier said. "And it warns city guards and other Mistborn not to bother you." He spun, letting the cloak flare dramatically. "I think it suits me."

Dockson rolled his eyes.

"All right," Kelsier said, bending down and pulling a cloth belt from his pack. "House Venture. Is there anything I need to know?"

"Lord Venture supposedly has a safe in his study," Dockson said. "That's where he'd probably keep his atium stash. You'll find the study on the third floor, three rooms in from the upper southern balcony. Be careful, House Venture keeps about a dozen hazekillers in addition to its regular troops and Mistings."

Kelsier nodded, tying on the belt—it had no buckle, but it did contain two small sheaths. He pulled a pair of glass daggers from the bag, checked them for nicks, and slid them into the sheaths. He kicked off his shoes and stripped off his stockings, leaving himself barefoot on the chill stones. With the shoes also went the last bit of metal on his person save for his coin pouch and the three vials of metals in his belt. He selected the largest one, downed its contents, then handed the empty vial to Dockson.

"That it?" Kelsier asked.

Dockson nodded. "Good luck."

Beside him, the girl Vin was watching Kelsier's preparations with intense curiosity. She was a quiet, small thing, but she hid an intensity that he found impressive. She was paranoid, true, but not timid.

You'll get your chance, kid, he thought. *Just not tonight.*

"Well," he said, pulling a coin from his pouch and tossing it off the side of the building. "Guess I'll be going. I'll meet you back at Clubs's shop in a bit."

Dockson nodded.

Kelsier turned and walked back up onto the roof's ledge. Then he jumped off the building.

Mist curled in the air around him. He burned steel, second of the basic Allomantic metals. Translucent blue lines sprang into existence around him, visible only to his eyes. Each one led from the center of his chest out to a nearby source of metal. The lines were all relatively faint—a sign that they pointed to metal sources that were small: door hinges, nails, and other bits. The type of source metal didn't matter. Burning iron or steel would point blue lines at all kinds of metal, assuming they were close enough and large enough to be noticeable.

Kelsier chose the line that pointed directly beneath him, toward his coin. Burning steel, he Pushed against the coin.

His descent immediately stopped, and he was thrown back up into the air in the opposite direction along the blue line. He reached out to the side, selected a passing window clasp, and Pushed against it, angling himself to the side. The careful nudge sent him up and over the lip of the building directly across the street from Vin's lair.

Kelsier landed with a lithe step, falling into a crouch and running across the building's peaked roof. He paused in the darkness at the other side, peering through the swirling air. He burned tin, and felt it flare to life in his chest, enhancing his senses. Suddenly the mists seemed less deep. It wasn't that the night around him grew any lighter; his ability to perceive simply increased. In the distance to the north, he could just barely make out a large structure. Keep Venture.

Kelsier left his tin on—it burned slowly, and he probably didn't need to worry about running out. As he stood, the mists curled slightly around his body. They twisted and spun, running in a slight, barely noticeable current beside him. The mists knew him; they claimed him. They could sense Allomancy.

He jumped, Pushing against a metal chimney behind him, sending himself in a wide horizontal leap. He tossed a coin even as he jumped, the tiny bit of metal flickering through the darkness and fog. He Pushed against the coin before it hit the ground, the force of his weight driving it downward in a sharp motion. As soon as it hit the cobblestones, Kelsier's Pushing forced him upward, turning the second half of his leap into a graceful arc.

Kelsier landed on another peaked wooden rooftop. Steelpushing and Ironpulling were the first things that Gemmel had taught him. *When you Push on something, it's like you're throwing your weight against it,* the old lunatic had said. *And you can't change how much you weigh—you're an Allomancer, not some northern mystic. Don't Pull on something that weighs less than you unless you want it to come flying at you, and don't Push on something heavier than you unless you want to get tossed in the other direction.*

Kelsier scratched his scars, then pulled his mistcloak tight as he crouched on the roof, the wooden grain biting his unshod toes. He often wished that burning tin didn't enhance all of the senses—or, at least, not all of them at once. He needed the improved eyesight to see in the darkness, and he made good use of the improved hearing as well. However, burning tin made the night seem even more chilly to his overly sensitive skin, and his feet registered every pebble and wooden ripple they touched.

Keep Venture rose before him. Compared with the murky city, the keep seemed to blaze with light. High nobles kept different schedules from regular people; the ability to afford, even squander, lamp oil and candles meant that the wealthy didn't have to bow before the whims of season or sun.

The keep was majestic—that much was visible simply from the architecture. While it maintained a defensive wall around the grounds, the keep itself was more an artistic construction than a fortification. Sturdy buttressings arched out from the sides, allowing for intricate windows and delicate spires. Brilliant stained-glass windows stretched high along the sides of the rectangular building, and they shone with light from within, giving the surrounding mists a variegated glow.

Kelsier burned iron, flaring it strong and searching the night for large sources of metal. He was too far away from the keep to use small items like coins or hinges. He'd need a larger anchor to cover this distance.

Most of the blue lines were faint. Kelsier marked a couple of them moving in a slow pattern up ahead—probably a pair of guards standing on the rooftop. Kelsier would be sensing their breastplates and weapons. Despite Allomantic considerations, most noblemen still armed their soldiers with metal. Mistings who could Push or Pull metals were uncommon, and full Mistborn were even more so. Many lords thought it impractical to leave one's soldiers and guards relatively defenseless in order to counter such a small segment of the population.

No, most high noblemen relied on other means to deal with Allomancers. Kelsier smiled. Dockson had said that Lord Venture kept a squad of hazekillers; if that was true, Kelsier would probably meet them before the night was through. He ignored the soldiers for the moment, instead focusing on a solid line of blue pointing toward the keep's lofty top. It likely had bronze or copper sheeting on the roof. Kelsier flared his iron, took a deep breath, and Pulled on the line.

With a sudden jerk, he was yanked into the air.

Kelsier continued to burn iron, pulling himself toward the keep at a tremendous speed. Some rumors claimed that Mistborn could fly, but that was a wistful exaggeration. Pulling and Pushing against metals usually felt less like flying than it did like falling—only in the wrong direction. An Allomancer had to Pull hard in order to get the proper momentum, and this sent him hurtling toward his anchor at daunting speeds.

Kelsier shot toward the keep, mists curling around him. He easily cleared the protective wall surrounding the keep's grounds, but his body dropped slightly toward the ground as he moved. It was his pesky weight again; it tugged him down. Even the swiftest of arrows angled slightly toward the ground as it flew.

The drag of his weight meant that instead of shooting right up to the roof, he swung in an arc. He approached the keep wall several dozen feet below the rooftop, still traveling at a terrible speed.

Taking a deep breath, Kelsier burned pewter, using it to enhance his physical strength much in the same way that tin enhanced his senses. He turned himself in the air, hitting the stone wall feet-first. Even his strengthened muscles protested at the treatment, but he stopped without breaking any bones. He immediately released his hold on the roof, dropping a coin and Pushing against it even as he began to fall. He reached out, selecting a source of metal above him—one of the wire housings of a stained-glass window—and Pulled on it.

The coin hit the ground below and was suddenly able to support his weight. Kelsier launched himself upward, Pushing on the coin and Pulling on the window at the same time. Then, extinguishing both metals, he let momentum carry him the last few feet up through the dark mists. Cloak flapping quietly, he crested the lip of the keep's upper service walkway, flipped himself up over the stone railing, and landed quietly on the ledge.

A startled guard stood not three paces away. Kelsier was upon the man in a second, jumping into the air, Pulling slightly on the guard's steel breastplate and throwing the man off balance. Kelsier whipped out one of his glass daggers, allowing the strength of his Ironpull to bring him toward the guard. He landed with both feet against the man's chest, then crouched and sliced with a pewter-enhanced swing.

The guard collapsed with a slit throat. Kelsier landed lithely beside him, ears straining in the night, listening for sounds of alarm. There were none.

Kelsier left the guard to his gurgling demise. The man was likely a lesser nobleman. The enemy. If he were, instead, a skaa soldier—enticed into betraying his people in exchange for a few coins . . . Well, then, Kelsier was even happier to send such men into their eternity.

He Pushed off the dying man's breastplate, hopping up off the stone service walkway and onto the rooftop itself. The bronze roof was chill and slick beneath his feet. He scurried along it, heading toward the southern side of the building, looking for the balcony Dockson had mentioned. He wasn't too worried about being spotted; one purpose of this evening was to steal some atium, the tenth and most powerful of the generally known Allomantic metals. His other purpose, however, was to cause a commotion.

He found the balcony with ease. Wide and broad, it was probably a sitting balcony, used to entertain small groups. It was quiet at the moment, however—empty save for two guards. Kelsier crouched silently in the night mists above the balcony, furled gray cloak obscuring him, toes curling out over the side of the roof's metallic lip. The two guards chatted unwittingly below.

Time to make a bit of noise.

Kelsier dropped to the ledge directly between the guards. Burning pewter to strengthen his body, he reached out and fiercely Steelpushed against both men at the same time. Braced as he was at the center, his Push threw the guards away in opposite directions. The men cried out in surprise as the sudden force threw them backward, hurling them over the balcony railing into the darkness beyond.

The guards screamed as they fell. Kelsier threw open the balcony doors, letting a wall of mist fall inward around him, its tendrils creeping forward to claim the darkened room beyond.

Third room in, Kelsier thought, moving forward in a crouching run. The second room was a quiet, greenhouse-like conservatory. Low beds containing cultivated bushes and small trees ran through the room, and one wall was made up of enormous floor-to-ceiling windows to provide sunlight for the plants. Though it was dark, Kelsier knew that the plants would all be of slightly different colors than the typical brown—some would be white, others ruddy, and perhaps even a few light yellow. Plants that weren't brown were a rarity cultivated and kept by the nobility.

Kelsier moved quickly through the conservatory. He paused at the next doorway, noting its lighted outline. He extinguished his tin lest his enhanced eyes be blinded when he entered the lit room, and threw open the door.

He ducked inside, blinking against the light, a glass dagger in each hand. The room, however, was empty. It was obviously a study; a lantern burned on each wall beside bookcases, and it had a desk in the corner.

Kelsier replaced his knives, burning steel and searching for sources of metal. There was a large safe in the corner of the room, but it was too obvious. Sure enough, another strong source of metal shone from inside the eastern wall. Kelsier approached, running his fingers along the plaster. Like many walls in noble keeps, this one was painted with a soft mural. Foreign creatures lounged beneath a red sun. The false section of wall was under two feet square, and it had been placed so that its cracks were obscured by the mural.

There's always another secret, Kelsier thought. He didn't bother trying to figure out how to open the contraption. He simply burned steel, reaching in and tugging against the weak source of metal that he assumed was the trapdoor's locking mechanism. It resisted at first, pulling him against the wall, but he burned pewter and yanked harder. The lock snapped, and the panel swung open, revealing a small safe embedded in the wall.

Kelsier smiled. It looked small enough for a pewter-enhanced man to carry, assuming he could get it out of the wall.

He jumped up, Ironpulling against the safe, and landed with his feet against the wall, one foot on either side of the open panel. He continued to Pull, holding himself in place, and flared his pewter. Strength flooded his legs, and he flared his steel as well, Pulling against the safe.

He strained, grunting slightly at the exertion. It was a test to see which would give out first—the safe, or his legs.

The safe shifted in its mountings. Kelsier Pulled harder, muscles protesting. For an extended moment, nothing happened. Then the safe shook and ripped free of the wall. Kelsier fell backward, burning steel and Pushing against the safe to get out of the way. He landed maladroitly, sweat dripping from his brow as the safe crashed to the wooden floor, throwing up splinters.

A pair of startled guards burst into the room.

"About time," Kelsier noted, raising a hand and Pulling on one of the soldier's swords. It whipped out of the sheath, spinning in the air and streaking toward Kelsier point-first. He extinguished his iron, stepping to the side and catching the sword by its hilt as momentum carried it past.

"Mistborn!" the guard screamed.

Kelsier smiled and jumped forward.

The guard pulled out a dagger. Kelsier Pushed it, tearing the weapon out of the man's hand, then swung, shearing the guard's head from his body. The second guard cursed, tugging free the release tie on his breastplate.

Kelsier Pushed on his own sword even as he completed his swing. The sword ripped from his fingers and hissed directly toward the second guard. The man's armor dropped free—preventing Kelsier from Pushing against it—just as the first guard's corpse fell to the ground. A moment later, Kelsier's sword planted itself in the second guard's now unarmored chest. The man stumbled quietly, then collapsed.

Kelsier turned from the bodies, cloak rustling. His anger was quiet, not as fierce as it had been the night he'd killed Lord Tresting. But he felt it still, felt it in the itching of his scars and in the remembered screams of the woman he loved. As far as Kelsier was concerned, any man who upheld the Final Empire also forfeited his right to live.

He flared his pewter, strengthening his body, then squatted down and lifted the safe. He teetered for a second beneath its weight, then got his balance and began to shuffle back toward the balcony. Perhaps the safe held atium; perhaps it didn't. However, he didn't have time to search out other options.

He was halfway through the conservatory when he heard footsteps from behind. He turned to see the study flooding with figures. There were eight of them, each one wearing a loose gray robe and carrying a dueling cane and a shield instead of a sword. Hazekillers.

Kelsier let the safe drop to the ground. Hazekillers weren't Allomancers, but they were trained to fight Mistings and Mistborn. There wouldn't be a single bit of metal on their bodies, and they would be ready for his tricks.

Kelsier stepped back, stretching and smiling. The eight men fanned into the study, moving with quiet precision.

This should be interesting.

The hazekillers attacked, dashing by twos into the conservatory. Kelsier pulled out his daggers, ducking beneath the first attack and slicing at a man's chest. The hazekiller jumped back, however, and forced Kelsier away with a swing of his cane.

Kelsier flared his pewter, letting strengthened legs carry him back in a powerful jump. With one hand, he whipped out a handful of coins and Pushed them against his opponents. The metal disks shot forward, zipping through the air, but his enemies were ready for this: They raised their shields, and the coins bounced off the wood, throwing up splinters but leaving the men unharmed.

Kelsier eyed the other hazekillers as they filled the room, advancing on him. They couldn't hope to fight him in an extended battle—their tactic would be to rush him at once, hoping for a quick end to the fight, or to at least stall him until Allomancers could be awakened and brought to fight. He glanced at the safe as he landed.

He couldn't leave without it. He needed to end the fight quickly as well. Flaring pewter, he jumped forward, trying an experimental dagger swipe, but he couldn't get inside his opponent's defenses. Kelsier barely ducked away in time to avoid getting cracked on the head by the end of a cane.

Three of the hazekillers dashed behind him, cutting off his retreat into the balcony room. *Great*, Kelsier thought, trying to keep an eye on all eight men at once. They advanced on him with careful precision, working as a team.

Gritting his teeth, Kelsier flared his pewter again; it was running low, he noticed. Pewter was the fastest-burning of the basic eight metals.

No time to worry about that now. The men behind him attacked, and Kelsier jumped out of the way—Pulling on the safe to tug himself toward the center of the room. He Pushed as soon as he hit the ground near the safe, launching himself into the air at an angle. He tucked, flipping over the heads of two attackers, and landed on the ground beside a well-cultivated tree bed. He spun, flaring his pewter and raising his arm in defense against the swing he knew would come.

The dueling cane connected with his arm. A burst of pain ran down his forearm, but his pewter-enhanced bone held. Kelsier kept moving, driving his other hand forward and slamming a dagger into his opponent's chest.

The man stumbled back in surprise, the motion ripping away Kelsier's dagger. A second hazekiller attacked, but Kelsier ducked, then reached down with his free hand, ripping his coin pouch off of his belt. The hazekiller prepared to block Kelsier's remaining dagger, but Kelsier raised his other hand instead, slamming the coin pouch into the man's shield.

Then he Pushed on the coins inside.

The hazekiller cried out, the force of the intense Steelpush throwing him backward. Kelsier flared his steel, Pushing so hard that he tossed himself backward as well—away from the pair of men who tried to attack him. Kelsier and his enemy flew away from each other, hurled in opposite directions. Kelsier collided with the far wall, but kept Pushing, smashing his opponent—pouch, shield, and all—against one of the massive conservatory windows.

Glass shattered, sparkles of lanternlight from the study playing across its shards. The hazekiller's desperate face disappeared into the darkness beyond, and mist—quiet, yet ominous—began to creep in through the shattered window.

The other six men advanced relentlessly, and Kelsier was forced to ignore the pain in his arm as he ducked two swings. He spun out of the way, brushing past a small tree, but a third hazekiller attacked, smashing his cane into Kelsier's side.

The attack threw Kelsier into the tree bed. He tripped, then collapsed near the entrance to the lit study, dropping his dagger. He gasped in pain, rolling to his knees and holding his side. The blow would have broken another man's ribs. Even Kelsier would have a massive bruise.

The six men moved forward, spreading to surround him again. Kelsier stumbled to his feet, vision growing dizzy from pain and exertion. He gritted his teeth, reaching down and pulling out one of his remaining vials of metal. He downed its contents in a single gulp, replenishing his pewter, then burned tin. The light nearly blinded him, and the pain in his arm and side suddenly seemed more acute, but the burst of enhanced senses cleared his head.

The six hazekillers advanced in a sudden, coordinated attack.

Kelsier whipped his hand to the side, burning iron and searching for metal. The closest source was a thick silvery paperweight on a desk just inside the study. Kelsier flipped it into his hand, then turned, arm held toward the advancing men, falling into an offensive stance.

"All right," he growled.

Kelsier burned steel with a flash of strength. The rectangular ingot ripped from his hand, streaking through the air. The foremost hazekiller raised his shield, but he moved too slowly. The ingot hit the man's shoulder with a crunch, and he dropped, crying out.

Kelsier spun to the side, ducking a staff swing and putting a hazekiller between himself and the fallen man. He burned iron, Pulling the ingot back toward him. It whipped through the air, cracking the second hazekiller in the side of the head. The man collapsed as the ingot flipped into the air.

One of the remaining men cursed, rushing forward to attack. Kelsier Pushed the still airborne ingot, flipping it away from him—and away from the attacking hazekiller, who had his shield raised. Kelsier heard the ingot hit the ground behind him, and he reached up—burning pewter—and caught the hazekiller's cane mid-swing.

The hazekiller grunted, struggling against Kelsier's enhanced strength. Kelsier didn't bother trying to pull the weapon free; instead he Pulled sharply on the ingot behind him, bringing it toward his own back at a deadly speed. He twisted at the last moment, using his momentum to spin the hazekiller around—right into the ingot's path.

The man dropped.

Kelsier flared pewter, steadying himself against attacks. Sure enough, a cane smashed against his shoulders. He stumbled to his knees as the wood cracked, but flared tin kept him conscious. Pain and lucidity flashed through his mind. He Pulled on the ingot—ripping it out of the dying man's back—and stepped to the side, letting the impromptu weapon shoot past him.

The two hazekillers nearest him crouched warily. The ingot snapped into one of the men's shields, but Kelsier didn't continue Pushing, lest he throw himself off balance. Instead, he burned iron, wrenching the ingot back toward himself. He ducked, extinguishing iron and feeling the ingot whoosh through the air above him. There was a crack as it collided with the man who had been sneaking up on him.

Kelsier spun, burning iron then steel to send the ingot soaring toward the final two men. They stepped out of the way, but Kelsier tugged on the ingot, dropping it to the ground directly in front of them. The men regarded it warily, distracted as Kelsier ran and jumped, Steelpushing himself against the ingot and flipping over the men's heads. The hazekillers cursed, spinning. As Kelsier landed, he Pulled the ingot again, bringing it up to smash into a man's skull from behind.

The hazekiller fell silently. The ingot flipped a few times in the darkness, and Kelsier snatched it from the air, its cool surface slick with blood. Mist from the shattered window flowed by his feet, curling up around his legs. He brought his hand down, pointing it directly at the last remaining hazekiller.

Somewhere in the room, a fallen man groaned.

The remaining hazekiller stepped back, then dropped his weapon and dashed away. Kelsier smiled, lowering his hand.

Suddenly, the ingot was Pushed from his fingers. It shot across the room, smashing through another window. Kelsier cursed, spinning to see another, larger group of men pouring into the study. They wore the clothing of noblemen. Allomancers.

Several of them raised hands, and a flurry of coins shot toward Kelsier. He flared steel, Pushing the coins out of the way. Windows shattered and wood splintered as the room was sprayed with coins. Kelsier felt a tug on his belt as his final vial of metal was ripped away, Pulled toward the other room. Several burly men ran forward in a crouch, staying beneath the shooting coins. Thugs—Mistings who, like Ham, could burn pewter.

Time to go, Kelsier thought, deflecting another wave of coins, gritting his teeth against the pain in his side and arm. He glanced behind him; he had a few moments, but he was never going to make it back to the balcony. As more Mistings advanced, Kelsier took a deep breath and dashed toward one of the broken, floor-to-ceiling windows. He leapt out into the mists, turning in the air as he fell, and reached out to Pull firmly on the fallen safe.

He jerked in midair, swinging down toward the side of the building as if tied to the safe by a tether. He felt the safe slide forward, grinding against the floor of the conservatory as Kelsier's weight pulled against it. He slammed against the side of the building, but continued to Pull, catching himself on the upper side of a windowsill. He strained, standing upside down in the window well, Pulling on the safe.

The safe appeared over the lip of the floor above. It teetered, then fell out the window and began to plummet directly toward Kelsier. He smiled, extinguishing his iron and pushing away from the building with his legs, throwing himself out into the mists like some insane diver. He fell backward through the darkness, barely catching sight of an angry face poking out of the broken window above.

Kelsier Pulled carefully against the safe, moving himself in the air. Mists curled around him, obscuring his vision, making him feel as if he weren't falling at all—but hanging in the middle of nothingness.

He reached the safe, then twisted in the air and Pushed against it, throwing himself upward.

The safe crashed into the cobblestones just below. Kelsier Pushed against the safe slightly, slowing himself until he eventually jerked to a halt in the air just a few feet above the ground. He hung in the mists for a moment, ribbons from his cloak curling and flapping in the wind, then let himself drop to the ground beside the safe.

The strongbox had been shattered by the fall. Kelsier pried open its mangled front, tin-enhanced ears listening to calls of alarm from the building above. Inside the safe, he found a small pouch of gemstones and a couple of ten-thousand boxing letters of credit, all of which he pocketed. He felt around inside, suddenly worried that the night's work had been for naught. Then his fingers found it—a small pouch at the very back.

He pulled it open, revealing a grouping of dark, beadlike bits of metal. Atium. His scars flared, memories of his time in the Pits returning to him.

He pulled the pouch tight and stood. With amusement, he noticed a twisted form lying on the cobblestones a short distance away—the mangled remains of the hazekiller he'd thrown out the window. Kelsier walked over, and retrieved his coin pouch with a tug of Ironpulling.

No, this night was not a waste. Even if he hadn't found the atium, any night that ended with a group of dead noblemen was a successful one, in Kelsier's opinion.

He gripped his pouch in one hand and the bag of atium in the other. He kept his pewter burning—without the strength it lent his body, he'd probably collapse from the pain of his wounds—and dashed off into the night, heading toward Clubs's shop.

I never wanted this, true. But somebody has to stop the Deepness. And, apparently, Terris is the only place this can be done.

On this fact, however, I don't have to take the word of the philosophers. I can feel our goal now, can sense it, though the others cannot. It . . . pulses, in my mind, far off in the mountains.

6

VIN AWOKE TO A QUIET room, red morning sunlight peeking through cracks in the shutters. She lay in bed for a moment, unsettled. Something felt wrong. It wasn't that she was waking up in an unfamiliar place—traveling with Reen had accustomed her to a nomadic lifestyle. It took her a moment to realize the source of her discomfort.

The room was empty.

Not only was it empty, it was open. Uncrowded. And it was . . . comfortable. She lay on an actual mattress, raised on posts, with sheets and a plush quilt. The room was decorated with a sturdy wooden armoire, and even had a circular rug. Perhaps another might have found the room cramped and spartan, but to Vin it seemed lavish.

She sat up, frowning. It felt wrong to have a room all to herself. She had always been crammed into tight bunkrooms filled with crewmembers. Even while traveling, she had slept in beggars' alleys or rebel caves, and Reen had been there with her. She had always been forced to fight to find privacy. Being given it so easily seemed to devalue the years she had spent relishing her brief moments of solitude.

She slipped out of bed, not bothering to open the shutters. The sunlight was faint, which meant it was still early morning, but she could already hear people moving in the hallway. She crept to the door, creaking it open and peeking out.

After leaving Kelsier the night before, Dockson had led

Vin to Clubs's shop. Because of the late hour, Clubs had immediately led them to their separate rooms. Vin, however, had not gone to bed immediately. She had waited until everyone was asleep, then had snuck out to inspect her surroundings.

The residence was almost more of an inn than it was a shop. Though it had a showroom below and a large workshop in the back, the building's second floor was dominated by several long hallways lined with guestrooms. There was a third floor, and the doors were more widely spaced there, implying larger rooms. She hadn't tapped for trapdoors or false walls—the noise might have awakened someone—but experience told her that it wouldn't be a proper lair if it didn't have at least a secret basement and some bolt-holes.

Overall, she was impressed. The carpentry equipment and half-finished projects below indicated a reputable, working front. The lair was secure, well stocked, and well maintained. Watching through the crack in her door, Vin made out a group of about six groggy young men coming out of the hallway opposite her own. They wore simple clothing, and made their way down the stairs toward the workroom.

Apprentice carpenters, Vin thought. *That's Clubs's front—he's a skaa craftsman.* Most skaa lived lives of drudgery on the plantations; even those who lived in a city were generally forced to do menial labor. However, some talented few were allowed a trade. They were still skaa; they were paid poorly and were always subject to the whims of the nobility. However, they had a measure of freedom that most skaa would envy.

Clubs was probably a master carpenter. What would entice such a man—one who had, by skaa standards, an amazing life—to risk joining the underground?

He is a Misting, Vin thought. *Kelsier and Dockson called him a "Smoker."* She would probably have to figure out what that meant on her own; experience told her that a powerful man like Kelsier would withhold knowledge from her as long as he could, stringing her along with occasional tidbits. His knowledge was what bound her to him—it would be unwise to give away too much too quickly.

Footsteps sounded outside, and Vin continued to peek through the crack.

"You'll want to get ready, Vin," Dockson said as he passed her door. He wore a nobleman's dress shirt and slacks, and he already looked awake and trim. He paused, continuing. "There's a fresh bath for you in the room at the end of the hallway, and I had Clubs scrounge you up a few changes of clothing. They should fit well enough until we can get you something more appropriate. Take your time in the bath—Kell's planned a meeting for this afternoon, but we can't start until Breeze and Ham arrive."

Dockson smiled, eyeing her through the cracked door, then continued on down the hallway. Vin flushed at being caught. *These are observant men. I'm going to have to remember that.*

The hallway grew quiet. She slipped out her door and crept down to the indicated room, and was half surprised to find that there was indeed a warm bath waiting for her. She frowned, studying the tiled chamber and metal tub. The water smelled scented, after the fashion of noble ladies.

These men are more like noblemen than skaa, Vin thought. She wasn't certain what she thought of that. However, they obviously expected her to do as they did, so she closed and bolted the door, then disrobed and crawled into the tub.

She smelled funny.

Even though the scent was faint, Vin still caught whiffs of herself occasionally. It was the smell of a passing noblewoman, the scent of a perfumed drawer opened by her brother's burgling fingers. The smell grew less noticeable as the morning progressed, but it still worried her. It would distinguish her from other skaa. If this crew expected her to take those baths regularly, she would have to request that the perfumes be removed.

The morning meal was more up to her expectations. Several skaa women of various ages worked the shop's kitchen, preparing baywraps—rolls of thin, flat bread stuffed with boiled barley and vegetables. Vin stood by the kitchen doorway, watching the women work. None of them smelled like she did, though they were far more cleanly and well groomed than average skaa.

In fact, there was an odd sense of cleanliness to the entire building. She hadn't noticed it the night before, because of the darkness, but the floor was scrubbed clean. All of the workers—kitchen women or apprentices—had clean faces and hands. It felt odd to Vin. She was accustomed to her own fingers being black with ashstains; with Reen, if she'd ever washed her face, she had quickly rubbed it with ash again. A clean face stood out on the streets.

No ash in the corners, she thought, eyeing the floor. *The room is kept swept.* She'd never lived in such a place before. It was almost like living in some nobleman's house.

She glanced back at the kitchen women. They wore simple dresses of white and gray, with scarves around the tops of their heads and long tails of hair hanging out the back. Vin fingered her own hair. She kept it short, like a boy's—her current, ragged cut had been given by one of the other crewmembers. She wasn't like these women—she never had been. By Reen's command, Vin had lived so that other crewmembers would think of her as a thief first and a girl second.

But, what am I now? Perfumed by her bath, yet wearing the tan trousers and buttoning shirt of an apprentice craftsman, she felt distinctly out of place. And that was bad—if she felt awkward, then she undoubtedly looked awkward too. Something else to make her stand out.

Vin turned, eyeing the workroom. The apprentices were already about their morning labors, working on various bits of furniture. They stayed in the back while Clubs worked in the main showroom, putting detailed finishing touches on the pieces.

The back kitchen door suddenly slammed open. Vin slipped reflexively to the side, putting her back to a wall and peeking around into the kitchen.

Ham stood in the kitchen doorway, framed by red sunlight. He wore a loose shirt and vest, both sleeveless, and carried several large packs. He wasn't dirtied by soot—none of the crew had ever been, the few times Vin had seen them.

Ham walked through the kitchen and into the workroom. "So," he said, dropping his packs, "anyone know which room is mine?"

"I'll ask Master Cladent," one of the apprentices said, moving into the front room.

Ham smiled, stretching, then turned toward Vin. "Morning, Vin. You know, you don't have to hide from me. We're on the same team."

Vin relaxed but remained where she was, standing beside a line of mostly finished chairs. "You're going to live here too?"

"It always pays to stay near the Smoker," Ham said, turning and disappearing back into the kitchen. He returned a moment later with a stack of four large baywraps. "Anyone know where Kell is?"

"Sleeping," Vin said. "He came in late last night, and hasn't gotten up yet."

Ham grunted, taking a bite of a baywrap. "Dox?"

"In his room on the third floor," Vin said. "He got up early, came down to get something to eat, and went back upstairs." She didn't add that she knew, from peeking through the keyhole, that he was sitting at his desk scribbling on some papers.

Ham raised an eyebrow. "You always keep track of where everyone is like that?"

"Yes."

Ham paused, then chuckled. "You're an odd kid, Vin." He gathered up his packs as the apprentice returned, and the two moved up the stairs. Vin stood, listening to their footsteps. They stopped about halfway down the first hallway, perhaps a few doors from her room.

The scent of steamed barley enticed her. Vin eyed the kitchen. Ham had gone in and taken food. Was she allowed to do the same?

Trying to look confident, Vin strode into the kitchen. A pile of baywraps sat on a platter, probably to be delivered to the apprentices as they worked. Vin picked up two of them. None of the women objected; in fact, a few of them even nodded respectfully toward her.

I'm an important person now, she thought with a measure of discomfort. Did they know that she was . . . Mistborn? Or was she simply treated with respect because she was a guest?

Eventually, Vin took a third baywrap and fled to her room. It was more food than she could possibly eat; however, she intended to scrape out the barley and save the flatbread, which would keep well should she need it later.

A knock came at her door. Vin answered it, pulling the door open with a careful motion. A young man stood outside—the boy who had been with Clubs back at Camon's lair the night before.

Thin, tall, and awkward-looking, he was dressed in gray clothing. He was perhaps fourteen, though his height might have made him look older than he was. He seemed nervous for some reason.

"Yes?" Vin asked.

"Um . . ."

Vin frowned. "What?"

"You're wanted," he said in a thick Eastern accent. "Ups in the where above with the doing. With Master Jumps to the third floor. Uh, I've gotta go." The boy blushed, then turned and hurried away, scrambling up the stairs.

Vin stood in the doorway of her room, dumbfounded. *Was that supposed to make any sense?* she wondered.

She peeked into the hallway. The boy had seemed like he expected her to follow him. Finally, she decided to do so, carefully making her way up the steps.

Voices were coming from an open door at the end of the hallway. Vin approached and peeked around the corner to find a well-decorated room, set with a fine rug and comfortable-looking chairs. A hearth burned at the side of the room, and the chairs were arranged to point toward a large charcoal writing board set atop an easel.

Kelsier stood, leaning one elbow resting against the brick hearth, a cup of wine in his hand. Angling herself slightly, Vin could see that he was talking to Breeze. The Soother had arrived well into midday, and had appropriated half of Clubs's apprentices to unload his possessions. Vin had watched from her window as the apprentices had carried the luggage—disguised as boxes of lumber scraps—up to Breeze's room. Breeze himself hadn't bothered to help.

Ham was there, as was Dockson, and Clubs was settling himself into the large, overstuffed chair farthest from Breeze. The boy who had fetched Vin sat on a stool beside Clubs, and he was obviously making a point of trying not to look at her. The final occupied chair held the man Yeden, dressed—as before—in common skaa worker's clothing. He sat in his chair without resting against its back, as if he disapproved of its plushness. His face was darkened with soot, as Vin expected of a skaa worker.

There were two empty chairs. Kelsier noticed Vin standing by the doorway, and gave her one of his inviting smiles. "Well, there she is. Come in."

Vin scanned the room. There was a window, though its shutters were closed against approaching gloom. The only chairs were the ones in Kelsier's half circle. Resigned, she moved forward and took the empty chair beside Dockson. It was too big for her, and she settled into it with her knees folded beneath her.

"That's all of us," Kelsier said.

"Who's the last chair for?" Ham asked.

Kelsier smiled, winked, but ignored the question. "All right, let's talk. We've got something of a task ahead of ourselves, and the sooner we begin outlining a plan, the better."

"I thought you had a plan," Yeden said uncomfortably.

"I have a framework," Kelsier said. "I know what needs to happen, and I have a few ideas on how to do it. But, you don't gather a group like this and just tell them what to do. We need to work this out together, beginning with a list of problems we need to deal with if we want the plan to work."

"Well," Ham said, "let me get the framework straight first. The plan is to gather Yeden an army, cause chaos in Luthadel, secure the palace, steal the Lord Ruler's atium, then leave the government to collapse?"

"Essentially," Kelsier said.

"Then," Ham said, "our main problem is the Garrison. If we want chaos in Luthadel, then we can't have twenty thousand troops here to keep the peace. Not to mention the fact that Yeden's troops will never take the city while there is any sort of armed resistance on the walls."

Kelsier nodded. Picking up a piece of chalk, he wrote *Luthadel Garrison* up on the board. "What else?"

"We'll need a way to make said chaos in Luthadel," Breeze

said, gesturing with a cup of wine. "Your instincts are right, my dear man. This city is where the Ministry makes its headquarters and the Great Houses run their mercantile empires. We'll need to bring Luthadel down if we want to break the Lord Ruler's ability to govern."

"Mentioning the nobility brings up another point," Dockson added. "The Great Houses all have guard forces in the city, not to mention their Allomancers. If we're going to deliver the city to Yeden, we'll have to deal with those noblemen."

Kelsier nodded, writing *Chaos* and *Great Houses* beside *Luthadel Garrison* on his board.

"The Ministry," Clubs said, leaning back in his plush chair so much that Vin almost couldn't see his grumpy face. "There'll be no change in government as long as the Steel Inquisitors have anything to say about it."

Kelsier added *Ministry* to the board. "What else?"

"Atium," Ham said. "You might as well write it up there—we'll need to secure the palace quickly, once general mayhem starts, and make certain nobody else takes the opportunity to slip into the treasury."

Kelsier nodded, writing *Atium: Secure Treasury* on the board.

"We will need to find a way to gather Yeden's troops," Breeze added. "We'll have to be quiet, but quick, and train them somewhere that the Lord Ruler won't find them."

"We also might want to make certain that the skaa rebellion is ready to take control of Luthadel," Dockson added. "Seizing the palace and digging in will make for a spectacular story, but it would be nice if Yeden and his people were actually ready to govern, once this is all over."

Troops and *Skaa Rebellion* were added to the board. "And," Kelsier said, "I'm going to add 'Lord Ruler.' We'll at least want a plan to get him out of the city, should other options fail." After writing *Lord Ruler* on the list, he turned back toward the group. "Did I forget anything?"

"Well," Yeden said dryly, "if you're listing problems we'll have to overcome, you should write up there that we're all bloody insane—though I doubt we can fix that fact."

The group chuckled, and Kelsier wrote *Yeden's Bad Atti-*

tude on the board. Then he stepped back, looking over the list. "When you break it down like that, it doesn't sound so bad, does it?"

Vin frowned, trying to decide if Kelsier was attempting a joke or not. The list wasn't just daunting—it was disturbing. Twenty thousand imperial soldiers? The collected forces and power of the high nobility? The Ministry? One Steel Inquisitor was said to be more powerful than a thousand troops.

More discomforting, however, was how matter-of-factly they regarded the issues. How could they even think of resisting the Lord Ruler? He was . . . well, he was the *Lord*. He ruled all of the world. He was the creator, protector, and punisher of mankind. He had saved them from the Deepness, then had brought the ash and the mists as a punishment for the people's lack of faith. Vin wasn't particularly religious—intelligent thieves knew to avoid the Steel Ministry—but even she knew the legends.

And yet, the group regarded their list of "problems" with determination. There was a grim mirth about them—as if they understood that they had a better chance of making the sun rise at night than they did of overthrowing the Final Empire. Yet, they were still going to try.

"By the Lord Ruler," Vin whispered. "You're *serious*. You really mean to do this."

"Don't use his name as an oath, Vin," Kelsier said. "Even blasphemy honors him—when you curse by that creature's name, you acknowledge him as your god."

Vin fell silent, sitting back in her chair, a bit numb.

"Anyway," Kelsier said, smiling lightly. "Anyone have any ideas on how to overcome these problems? Besides Yeden's attitude, of course—we all know he's hopeless."

The room was quiet and thoughtful.

"Thoughts?" Kelsier asked. "Angles? Impressions?"

Breeze shook his head. "Now that it's all up there, I can't help wondering if the child has a point. This is a daunting task."

"But it *can* be done," Kelsier said. "Let's start by talking about how to break the city. What can we do that would be so threatening that it would throw the nobility into chaos, maybe even get the palace guard out into the city, exposing them to our troops? Something that would distract the Ministry, and the Lord Ruler himself, while we move our troops in to attack?"

"Well, a general revolution among the populace comes to mind," Ham said.

"Won't work," Yeden said firmly.

"Why not?" Ham asked. "You know how the people are treated. They live in slums, work in mills and smithies the entire day, and half of them *still* starve."

Yeden shook his head. "Don't you understand? The rebellion has been trying for a *thousand years* to get the skaa in this city to rise up. It never works. They're too beaten down—they don't have the will or the hope to resist. That's why I had to come to you to get an army."

The room fell still. Vin, however, slowly nodded her head. She'd seen it—she'd *felt* it. One didn't fight the Lord Ruler. Even living as a thief, crouching at the edge of society, she knew that. There would be no rebellion.

"He's right, I'm afraid," Kelsier said. "The skaa won't rise up, not in their current state. If we're going to overthrow this government, we'll need to do it without the help of the masses. We can probably recruit our soldiers from among them, but we can't count on the general populace."

"Could we cause a disaster of some sort?" Ham asked. "A fire maybe?"

Kelsier shook his head. "It might disrupt trade for a while, but I doubt it would have the effect we want. Besides, the cost in skaa lives would be too high. The slums would burn, not stone nobleman keeps."

Breeze sighed. "What, then, would you have us do?"

Kelsier smiled, eyes twinkling. "What if we turned the Great Houses against each other?"

Breeze paused. "A house war . . ." he said, taking a speculative sip of his wine. "It's been a while since the city had one of those."

"Which means that tensions have had plenty of time to brew," Kelsier said. "The high nobility are growing increasingly powerful—the Lord Ruler barely has control over them anymore, which is why we have a chance of shattering his grip. Luthadel's Great Houses are the key—they control imperial trade, not to mention enslave the greatest majority of the skaa."

Kelsier pointed at the board, moving his finger between the line that said *Chaos* and the line that said *Great Houses*.

"If we can turn the houses inside Luthadel against each other, we can bring down the city. Mistborn will start assassinating house leaders. Fortunes will collapse. It won't take long before there is open warfare in the streets. Part of our contract with Yeden states that we'll give him an opening to seize the city for himself. Can you think of a better one than that?"

Breeze nodded with a smile. "It has flair—and I do like the idea of having the noblemen kill each other."

"You *always* like it better when someone else does the work, Breeze," Ham noted.

"My dear friend," Breeze replied, "the entire point of life is to find ways to get others to do your work for you. Don't you know anything about basic economics?"

Ham raised an eyebrow. "Actually, I—"

"It was a rhetorical question, Ham," Breeze interrupted, rolling his eyes.

"Those are the best kind!" Ham replied.

"Philosophy later, Ham," Kelsier said. "Stay on task. What do you think of my suggestion?"

"It could work," Ham said, settling back. "But I can't see the Lord Ruler letting things go that far."

"It's our job to see that he doesn't have a choice," Kelsier said. "He's known to let his nobility squabble, probably to keep them off-balance. We fan those tensions, then we somehow force the Garrison to pull out. When the houses start fighting in earnest, the Lord Ruler won't be able to do anything to stop them—except, perhaps, send his palace guard into the streets, which is exactly what we want him to do."

"He could also send for a koloss army," Ham noted.

"True," Kelsier said. "But they're stationed a moderate distance away. That's a flaw we need to exploit. Koloss troops make wonderful grunts, but they have to be kept away from civilized cities. The very center of the Final Empire is exposed, yet the Lord Ruler is confident in his strength—and why shouldn't he be? He hasn't faced a serious threat in centuries. Most cities only need small policing forces."

"Twenty thousand men is hardly a 'small' number," Breeze said.

"It is on a national scale," Kelsier said, holding up a finger. "The Lord Ruler keeps most of his troops on the edges of his empire, where the threat of rebellion is strongest. That's why we're going to strike him here, in Luthadel itself—and that's why we're going to succeed."

"Assuming we can deal with that Garrison," Dockson noted.

Kelsier nodded, turning to write *House War* underneath *Great Houses* and *Chaos*. "All right, then. Let's talk about the Garrison. What are we going to do about it?"

"Well," Ham said speculatively, "historically, the best way to deal with a large force of soldiers is to have your own large force of soldiers. We're going to raise Yeden an army—why not let them attack the Garrison? Isn't that kind of the point of raising the army in the first place?"

"That won't work, Hammond," Breeze said. He regarded his empty cup of wine, then held it up toward the boy sitting beside Clubs, who immediately scurried over to refill it.

"If we wanted to defeat the Garrison," Breeze continued, "we'd need our own force of *at least* its same size. We'd probably want one much larger, since our men will be newly trained. We might be able to raise Yeden an army—we might even be able to get him one large enough to hold the city for a while. But, getting him one large enough to take on the Garrison inside its fortifications? We might as well give up now, if that's our plan."

The group fell silent. Vin squirmed in her chair, looking over each man in turn. Breeze's words had a profound effect. Ham opened his mouth to speak, then closed it again, sitting back to reconsider.

"All right," Kelsier finally said. "We'll get back to the Garrison in a moment. Let's look at our own army. How can we raise one of substantial size and hide it from the Lord Ruler?"

"Again, that will be difficult," Breeze said. "There is a very good reason why the Lord Ruler feels safe in the Central Dominance. There are constant patrols on the roadways and canals, and you can hardly spend a day traveling without running into a village or plantation. This isn't the sort of place where you can raise an army without attracting notice."

"The rebellion has those caves up to the north," Dockson said. "We might be able to hide some men there."

Yeden paled. "You *know* about the Arguois caverns?"

Kelsier rolled his eyes. "Even the Lord Ruler knows about them, Yeden. The rebels there just aren't dangerous enough to bother him yet."

"How many people do you have, Yeden?" Ham asked. "In Luthadel and around it, caves included? What do we have to start with?"

Yeden shrugged. "Maybe three hundred—including women and children."

"And how many do you think those caves could hide?" Ham asked.

Yeden shrugged again.

"The caves could support a larger group, for certain," Kelsier said. "Perhaps ten thousand. I've been there—the rebellion has been hiding people in them for years, and the Lord Ruler has never bothered to destroy them."

"I can imagine why," Ham said. "Cave fighting is nasty business, especially for the aggressor. The Lord Ruler likes to keep defeats to a minimum—he's nothing if not vain. Anyway, ten thousand. That's a decent number. It could hold the palace with ease—might even be able to hold the city, if it had the walls."

Dockson turned to Yeden. "When you asked for an army, what size were you thinking?"

"Ten thousand sounds like a good number, I suppose," Yeden said. "Actually . . . it's a bit larger than I was thinking."

Breeze tipped his cup slightly, swirling the wine. "I hate to sound contrary again—that's usually Hammond's job—but I do have to return to our earlier problem. Ten thousand men. That won't even *frighten* the Garrison. We're talking about twenty thousand well-armed, well-trained troops."

"He has a point, Kell," Dockson said. He had found a small book somewhere, and had begun taking notes on the meeting.

Kelsier frowned.

Ham nodded. "Any way you look at it, Kell, that Garrison is going to be a tough stone to break. Perhaps we should just focus on the nobility. Maybe we can cause enough chaos that even the Garrison won't be able to suppress it."

Kelsier shook his head. "Doubtful. The Garrison's primary duty is to maintain order in the city. If we can't deal with those troops, we'll never pull this off." He paused, then eyed Vin. "What do you think, Vin? Any suggestions?"

She froze. Camon had never asked her opinion. What did Kelsier want from her? She pulled back into her chair slightly as she realized that the other members of the crew had turned, looking at her.

"I . . ." Vin said slowly.

"Oh, don't intimidate the poor thing, Kelsier," Breeze said with a wave of his hand.

Vin nodded, but Kelsier didn't turn away from her. "No, really. Tell me what you're thinking, Vin. You've got a much larger enemy threatening you. What do you do?"

"Well," she said slowly. "You don't fight him, that's for certain. Even if you won somehow, you'd be so hurt and broken that you couldn't fight off anyone else."

"Makes sense," Dockson said. "But we might not have a choice. We have to get rid of that army somehow."

"And if it just left the city?" she asked. "That would work too? If I had to deal with someone big, I'd try and distract him first, get him to leave me alone."

Ham chuckled. "Good luck getting the Garrison to leave Luthadel. The Lord Ruler sends squads out on patrol sometimes, but the only time I know of the entire Garrison leaving was when that skaa rebellion broke out down in Courteline a half century ago."

Dockson shook his head. "Vin's idea is too good to dismiss that easily, I think. Really, we can't fight the Garrison—at least, not while they're entrenched. So, we need to get them to leave the city somehow."

"Yes," Breeze said, "but it would take a particular crisis to require involving the Garrison. If the problem weren't threatening enough, the Lord Ruler wouldn't send the entire Garrison. If it were too dangerous, he'd hunker down and send for his koloss."

"A rebellion in one of the nearby cities?" Ham suggested.

"That leaves us with the same problem as before," Kelsier said, shaking his head. "If we can't get the skaa here to rebel, we'll never get ones outside the city to do so."

"What about a feint of some sort, then?" Ham asked. "We're assuming that we'll be able to raise a sizable group of soldiers. If they pretend to attack someplace nearby, perhaps the Lord Ruler would send the Garrison out to help."

"I doubt he'd send them away to protect another city," Breeze said. "Not if it left him exposed in Luthadel."

The group fell silent, thinking again. Vin glanced around, then found Kelsier's eyes on her.

"What?" he asked.

She squirmed a bit, glancing down. "How far away are the Pits of Hathsin?" she finally asked.

The crew paused.

Finally, Breeze laughed. "Oh, now *that's* devious. The nobility don't know that the Pits produce atium, so the Lord Ruler couldn't make much of a fuss—not without revealing that there's something very special about those Pits. That means no koloss."

"They wouldn't arrive in time anyway," Ham said. "The Pits are only a couple of days away. If they were threatened, the Lord Ruler would have to respond quickly. The Garrison would be the only force in striking distance."

Kelsier smiled, eyes alight. "And it wouldn't take much of an army to threaten the Pits, either. A thousand men could do it. We send them to attack, then when the Garrison leaves, we march our second, larger force in and seize Luthadel itself. By the time the Garrison realized that they'd been duped, they wouldn't be able to get back in time to stop us from taking the city walls."

"Could we keep them, though?" Yeden asked apprehensively.

Ham nodded eagerly. "With ten thousand skaa, I could hold this city against the Garrison. The Lord Ruler would have to send for his koloss."

"By then, we'd have the atium," Kelsier said. "And the Great Houses won't be in any position to stop us—they'll be weakened and frail because of their internal fighting."

Dockson was scribbling furiously on his pad. "We'll need to use Yeden's caves, then. They're within striking distance of both our targets, and they're closer to Luthadel than the Pits are. If our army left from there, it could get here before the Garrison could return from the Pits."

Kelsier nodded.

Dockson continued to scribble. "I'll have to start stockpiling supplies in those caves, maybe make a trip out to check conditions there."

"And, how are we going to get the soldiers there?" Yeden asked. "That's a week outside the city—and skaa aren't allowed to travel on their own."

"I've already got someone who can help us there," Kelsier said, writing *Attack Pits of Hathsin* beneath *Luthadel Garrison* on his board. "I have a friend that can give us a front to run canal boats to the north."

"Assuming," Yeden said, "you can even make good on your first and primary promise. I paid you to gather me an army. Ten thousand men is a great number, but I've still to see an adequate explanation of how you're going to raise them. I've already told you the kinds of problems we've had trying to recruit in Luthadel."

"We won't need the general population to support us," Kelsier said. "Just a small percentage of them—there are nearly a million workers in and around Luthadel. This should actually be the easiest part of the plan, since we happen to be in the presence of one of the world's greatest Soothers. Breeze, I'm counting on you and your Allomancers to force us up a nice selection of recruits."

Breeze sipped his wine. "Kelsier, my good man. I wish you wouldn't use words like 'force' in reference to my talents. I simply encourage people."

"Well, can you encourage us up an army?" Dockson asked.

"How much time do I have?" Breeze asked.

"A year," Kelsier said. "We'll plan this to go off next fall. Assuming the Lord Ruler does gather his forces to attack Yeden once we take the city, we might as well make him do it in the winter."

"Ten thousand men," Breeze said with a smile, "gathered from a resistant population in less than a year. It would certainly be a challenge."

Kelsier chuckled. "From you, that's as good as a yes. Start in Luthadel, then move to the surrounding cities. We need people who are close enough to gather at the caves."

Breeze nodded.

"We'll also need weapons and supplies," Ham said. "And we'll need to train the men."

"I've already got a plan to get weapons," Kelsier said. "Can you find some men to do the training?"

Ham paused thoughtfully. "Probably. I know some skaa soldiers who fought in one of the Lord Ruler's Suppression Campaigns."

Yeden paled. "Traitors!"

Ham shrugged. "Most of them aren't proud of what they did," he said. "But most of them also like to eat. It's a hard world, Yeden."

"My people will never work with such men," Yeden said.

"They'll have to," Kelsier said sternly. "A large number of skaa rebellions fail because their men are poorly trained. We're going to give you an army of well-equipped, well-fed men—and I'll be damned if I'm going to let you get them slaughtered because they were never taught which end of the sword to hold."

Kelsier paused, then eyed Ham. "However, I do suggest that you find men who are bitter against the Final Empire for what it forced them to do. I don't trust men whose loyalty only goes as far as the boxings in their pockets."

Ham nodded, and Yeden quieted. Kelsier turned, writing *Ham: Training* and *Breeze: Recruitment* beneath *Troops* on the board.

"I'm interested in your plan to get weapons," Breeze said. "How, exactly, do you intend to arm ten thousand men without making the Lord Ruler suspicious? He keeps a *very* careful eye on the armament flows."

"We could make the weapons," Clubs said. "I have enough extra wood that we could churn out a war staff or two every day. Could probably get you some arrows too."

"I appreciate the offer, Clubs," Kelsier said. "And I think that's a good idea. However, we're going to need more than staves. We'll need swords, shields, and armor—and we need them quickly enough to begin training."

"How, then, are you going to do it?" Breeze asked.

"The Great Houses can get weapons," Kelsier said. "They don't have any problems arming their personal retinues."

"You want us to steal from them?"

Kelsier shook his head. "No, for once we're going to do things somewhat legally—we're going to buy our weapons. Or, rather, we're going to have a sympathetic nobleman buy them for us."

Clubs laughed bluntly. "A nobleman sympathetic to the skaa? It will never happen."

"Well, 'never' happened a short time ago, then," Kelsier said lightly. "Because I've already found someone to help us."

The room fell silent save for the crackling of the fireplace. Vin squirmed slightly in her chair, glancing at the others. They seemed shocked.

"Who?" Ham asked.

"His name is Lord Renoux," Kelsier said. "He arrived in the area a few days back. He's staying in Fellise—he doesn't quite have enough influence to establish himself in Luthadel. Besides, I think it's prudent to keep Renoux's activities a bit removed from the Lord Ruler."

Vin cocked her head. Fellise was a small, suburb-style city an hour outside of Luthadel; she and Reen had worked there before moving into the capital city. How had Kelsier recruited this Lord Renoux? Had he bribed the man, or was it some sort of scam?

"I know of Renoux," Breeze said slowly. "He's a Western lord; he has a great deal of power in the Farmost Dominance."

Kelsier nodded. "Lord Renoux recently decided to try and elevate his family to high noble status. His official story is that he came south in order to expand his mercantile efforts. He hopes that by shipping fine Southern weaponry to the North, he can earn enough money—and make enough connections—to build himself a keep in Luthadel by the end of the decade."

The room was quiet.

"But," Ham said slowly, "those weapons will be coming to us instead."

Kelsier nodded. "We'll have to fake the shipping records, just in case."

"That's . . . quite an ambitious front, Kell," Ham said. "A lord's family working on our side."

"But," Breeze said, looking confused. "Kelsier, you *hate* noblemen."

"This one's different," Kelsier said with a sly smile.

The crew studied Kelsier. They didn't like working with a nobleman; Vin could tell that much easily. It probably didn't help that Renoux was so powerful.

Suddenly, Breeze laughed. He leaned back in his chair, downing the last of his wine. "You blessed madman! You killed him, didn't you? Renoux—you killed him and replaced him with an impostor."

Kelsier's smile broadened.

Yeden cursed, but Ham simply smiled. "Ah. Now *that* makes sense. Or, at least, it makes sense if you're Kelsier the Foolhardy."

"Renoux is going to take up permanent residence in Fellise," Kelsier said. "He'll be our front if we need to do anything official. I'll use him to purchase armaments and supplies, for instance."

Breeze nodded thoughtfully. "Efficient."

"Efficient?" Yeden asked. "You've killed a nobleman! A very important one."

"You're planning to overthrow the entire empire, Yeden," Kelsier noted. "Renoux isn't going to be the last aristocratic casualty in this little endeavor."

"Yes, but impersonating him?" Yeden asked. "That sounds a little risky to me."

"You hired us because you wanted extraordinary results, my dear man," Breeze said, sipping his wine. "In our line of work, extraordinary results usually require extraordinary risks."

"We minimize them as best we can, Yeden," Kelsier said. "My actor is *very* good. However, these are the sorts of things we're going to be doing in this job."

"And if I order you to stop a few of them?" Yeden asked.

"You can shut down the job at any time," Dockson said, not looking up from his ledgers. "But as long as it is in motion,

Kelsier has final say on plans, objectives, and procedures. That is how we work; you knew that when you hired us."

Yeden shook his head ruefully.

"Well?" Kelsier asked. "Do we continue or not? The call is yours, Yeden."

"Feel free to call an end to it, friend," Breeze said with a helpful voice. "Don't be afraid of offending us. I, for one, look favorably upon free money."

Vin saw Yeden pale slightly. In Vin's estimation, he was fortunate that Kelsier hadn't simply taken his money and stabbed him in the chest. But, she was becoming increasingly convinced that wasn't the way things worked around here.

"This is insane," Yeden said.

"Trying to overthrow the Lord Ruler?" Breeze asked. "Why, yes, as a matter of fact, it is."

"All right," Yeden said, sighing. "We continue."

"Good," Kelsier said, writing *Kelsier: Equipment* under *Troops*. "The Renoux front will also give us an 'in' with Luthadel high society. This will be a very important advantage—we'll need to keep careful track of Great House politics if we're going to start a war."

"This house war might not be as easy to pull off as you think, Kelsier," Breeze warned. "The current lot of high noblemen is a careful, discriminating group."

Kelsier smiled. "Then it's good that you're here to help, Breeze. You're an expert at making people do what you want—together, you and I will plan how to make the high nobility turn on each other. Major house wars seem to happen every couple of centuries or so. The current group's competence will only make them more dangerous, so getting them riled up shouldn't be *that* hard. In fact, I've already started the process. . . ."

Breeze raised an eyebrow, then glanced at Ham. The Thug grumbled a bit, pulling out a golden ten-boxing coin and flipping it across the room to the self-satisfied Breeze.

"What was that about?" Dockson asked.

"We had a bet," Breeze said, "regarding whether or not Kelsier was involved in last night's disturbance."

"Disturbance?" Yeden asked. "What disturbance?"

"Someone attacked House Venture," Ham said. "The rumors claim that three full Mistborn were sent to assassinate Straff Venture himself."

Kelsier snorted. "Three? Straff certainly has an elevated opinion of himself. I didn't go anywhere near His Lordship. I was there for the atium—and to make certain that I was seen."

"Venture isn't sure who to blame," Breeze said. "But because Mistborn were involved, everyone assumes that it was one of the Great Houses."

"That was the idea," Kelsier said happily. "The high nobility take Mistborn attacks very seriously—they have an unspoken agreement that they won't use Mistborn to assassinate each other. A few more strikes like this, and I'll have them snapping at each other like frightened animals."

He turned, adding *Breeze: Planning* and *Kelsier: General Mayhem* beneath *Great Houses* on the board.

"Anyway," Kelsier continued, "we'll need to keep an eye on local politics to find out which Houses are making alliances. That means sending a spy to some of their functions."

"Is that really necessary?" Yeden asked uncomfortably.

Ham nodded. "It's standard procedure for *any* Luthadel job, actually. If there is information to be had, it will pass through the lips of the court's powerful. It always pays to keep an open set of ears moving through their circles."

"Well, that should be easy," Breeze said. "We just bring up your impostor and send him into the parties."

Kelsier shook his head. "Unfortunately, Lord Renoux himself won't be able to come to Luthadel."

Yeden frowned. "Why not? Won't your impostor hold up to close scrutiny?"

"Oh, he looks just like Lord Renoux," Kelsier said. "*Exactly* like Lord Renoux, actually. We just can't let him get near an Inquisitor. . . ."

"Ah," Breeze said, exchanging a glance with Ham. "One of *those*. Well, then."

"What?" Yeden asked. "What does he mean?"

"You don't want to know," Breeze said.

"I don't?"

Breeze shook his head. "You know how unsettled you just were when Kelsier said he'd replaced Lord Renoux with an impostor? Well, this is about a dozen times worse. Trust me—the less you know, the more comfortable you'll be."

Yeden looked toward Kelsier, who was smiling broadly. Yeden paled, then leaned back in his chair. "I think you're probably right."

Vin frowned, eying the others in the room. They seemed to know what Kelsier was talking about. She'd have to study this Lord Renoux sometime.

"Anyway," Kelsier said, "we have to send someone to the social functions. Dox, therefore, will be playing Renoux's nephew and heir, a scion of the family who has recently gained favor with Lord Renoux."

"Wait a moment, Kell," Dockson said. "You didn't tell me about this."

Kelsier shrugged. "We're going to need someone to be our dupe with the nobility. I assumed that you'd fit the role."

"Can't be me," Dockson said. "I got marked during the Eiser job just a couple months back."

Kelsier frowned.

"What?" Yeden asked. "Do I want to know what they're talking about this time?"

"He means that thc Ministry is watching for him," Breeze said. "He pretended to be a nobleman, and they found out."

Dockson nodded. "The Lord Ruler himself saw me on one occasion, and he's got a flawless memory. Even if I managed to avoid him, someone's bound to recognize me eventually."

"So . . ." Yeden said.

"So," Kelsier said, "we'll need someone else to play Lord Renoux's heir."

"Don't look at me," Yeden said apprehensively.

"Trust me," Kelsier said flatly, "nobody was. Clubs is out too—he's far too prominent a local skaa craftsman."

"I'm out as well," Breeze said. "I already have several aliases among the nobility. I suppose I could use one of them, but I couldn't go to any major balls or parties—it would be rather embarrassing if I met someone who knew me by a different alias."

Kelsier frowned thoughtfully.

"I could do it," Ham said. "But you know I'm no good at acting."

"What about my nephew?" Clubs said, nodding to the young man at his side.

Kelsier studied the boy. "What's your name, son?"

"Lestibournes."

Kelsier raised an eyebrow. "That's a mouthful. You don't have a nickname?"

"Not of the yetting yet."

"We'll have to work on that," Kelsier said. "Do you always speak in that Eastern street slang?"

The boy shrugged, obviously nervous at being such a center of attention. "Wasing the place when I was young."

Kelsier glanced at Dockson, who shook his head. "I don't think it's a good idea, Kell."

"Agreed." Kelsier turned to Vin, then smiled. "I guess that leaves you. How good are you at imitating a noblewoman?"

Vin paled slightly. "My brother gave me a few lessons. But, I've never actually tried to. . . ."

"You'll do fine," Kelsier said, writing *Vin: Infiltration* underneath *Great Houses*. "All right. Yeden, you should probably begin planning how you're to keep control of the empire once this is all through."

Yeden nodded. Vin felt a little sorry for the man, seeing how much the planning—the sheer outrageousness of it all—seemed to be overwhelming him. Still, it was hard to feel sympathy for him, considering what Kelsier had just said regarding *her* part in all this.

Playing a noblewoman? she thought. *Surely there's someone else who could do a better job. . . .*

Breeze's attention was still on Yeden and his obvious discomfort. "Don't look so solemn, my dear fellow," Breeze said. "Why, you'll probably never actually have to *rule* the city. Chances are, we'll all get caught and executed long before that happens."

Yeden smiled wanly. "And if we don't? What's to keep you all from just knifing me and taking the empire for yourselves?"

Breeze rolled his eyes. "We're thieves, my dear man, not politicians. A nation is far too unwieldy a commodity to be worth our time. Once we have our atium, we'll be happy."

"Not to mention rich," Ham added.

"The two words are synonyms, Hammond," Breeze said.

"Besides," Kelsier said to Yeden. "We won't be giving you the entire empire—hopefully, it will shatter once Luthadel destabilizes. You'll have this city, and probably a good piece of the Central Dominance—assuming you can bribe the local armies into supporting you."

"And . . . the Lord Ruler?" Yeden asked.

Kelsier smiled. "I'm still planning to deal with him personally—I just have to figure out how to make the Eleventh Metal work."

"And if you don't?"

"Well," Kelsier said, writing *Yeden: Preparation and Rule* beneath *Skaa Rebellion* on the board, "we'll try and find a way to trick him out of the city. Perhaps we can get him to go with his army to the Pits and secure things there."

"Then what?" Yeden asked.

"You find some way to deal with him," Kelsier said. "You didn't hire us to kill the Lord Ruler, Yeden—that's just a possible perk I intend to throw in if I can."

"I wouldn't worry *too* much, Yeden," Ham added. "He won't be able to do much without funds or armies. He's a powerful Allomancer, but by no means omnipotent."

Breeze smiled. "Though, if you think about it, hostile, dethroned pseudodeities probably make disagreeable neighbors. You'll have to figure out something to do with him."

Yeden didn't appear to like that idea much, but he didn't continue the argument.

Kelsier turned. "That should be it, then."

"Uh," Ham said, "what about the Ministry? Shouldn't we at least find a way to keep an eye on those Inquisitors?"

Kelsier smiled. "We'll let my brother deal with them."

"Like hell you will," a new voice said from the back of the room.

Vin jumped to her feet, spinning and glancing toward the room's shadowed doorway. A man stood there. Tall and broad-shouldered, he had a statuesque rigidity. He wore modest clothing—a simple shirt and trousers with a loose skaa jacket. His arms were folded in dissatisfaction, and he had a hard, square face that looked a bit familiar.

Vin glanced back at Kelsier. The similarity was obvious.

"Marsh?" Yeden said, standing. "Marsh, it *is* you! He promised you'd be joining the job, but I . . . well . . . welcome back!"

Marsh's face remained impassive. "I'm not certain if I'm 'back' or not, Yeden. If you all don't mind, I'd like to speak privately with my little brother."

Kelsier didn't seem intimidated by Marsh's harsh tone. He nodded to the group. "We're done for the evening, folks."

The others rose slowly, giving Marsh a wide berth as they left. Vin followed them, pulling the door shut and walking down the stairs to give the appearance of retiring to her room.

Less than three minutes later she was back at the door, listening carefully to the conversation going on inside.

Rashek is a tall man—of course, most of these Terrismen are tall. He is young to receive so much respect from the other packmen. He has charisma, and the women of court would probably describe him as handsome, in a rugged sort of way.

Yet, it amazes me that anyone would give heed to a man who speaks such hatred. He has never seen Khlennium, yet he curses the city. He does not know me, yet I can already see the anger and hostility in his eyes.

7

THREE YEARS HADN'T CHANGED MARSH'S appearance much. He was still the stern, commanding person Kelsier had known since childhood. There was still that glint of disappointment in his eyes, and he spoke with the same air of disapproval.

Yet, if Dockson were to be believed, Marsh's attitudes had

changed much since that day three years before. Kelsier still found it hard to believe that his brother had given up leadership of the skaa rebellion. He had always been so passionate about his work.

Apparently, that passion had dimmed. Marsh walked forward, regarding the charcoal writing board with a critical eye. His clothing was stained slightly by dark ash, though his face was relatively clean, for a skaa. He stood for a moment, looking over Kelsier's notes. Finally, Marsh turned and tossed a sheet of paper onto the chair beside Kelsier.

"What is this?" Kelsier asked, picking it up.

"The names of the eleven men you slaughtered last night," Marsh said. "I thought you might at least want to know."

Kelsier tossed the paper into the crackling hearth. "They served the Final Empire."

"They were *men*, Kelsier," Marsh snapped. "They had lives, families. Several of them were skaa."

"Traitors."

"People," Marsh said. "People who were just trying to do the best with what life gave them."

"Well, I'm just doing the same thing," Kelsier said. "And, fortunately, life gave *me* the ability to push men like them off the tops of buildings. If they want to stand against me like noblemen, then they can die like noblemen."

Marsh's expression darkened. "How can you be so flippant about something like this?"

"Because, Marsh," Kelsier said, "humor is the only thing I've got left. Humor and determination."

Marsh snorted quietly.

"You should be happy," Kelsier said. "After decades of listening to your lectures, I've finally decided to do something worthwhile with my talents. Now that you're here to help, I'm sure—"

"I'm not here to help," Marsh interrupted.

"Then why did you come?"

"To ask you a question." Marsh stepped forward, stopping right in front of Kelsier. They were about the same height, but Marsh's stern personality always made him seem to loom taller.

"How dare you do this?" Marsh asked quietly. "I dedicated my life to overthrowing the Final Empire. While you and your thieving friends partied, I hid runaways. While you planned petty burglaries, I organized raids. While you lived in luxury, I watched brave people die of starvation."

Marsh reached up, stabbing a finger at Kelsier's chest. "*How dare you?* How dare you try and hijack the rebellion for one of your little 'jobs'? How dare you use this dream as a way of enriching yourself?"

Kelsier pushed Marsh's finger away. "That's not what this is about."

"Oh?" Marsh asked, tapping the word *atium* on the board. "Why the games, Kelsier? Why lead Yeden along, pretending to accept him as your 'employer'? Why act like you care about the skaa? We both know what you're really after."

Kelsier clenched his jaw, a bit of his humor melting away. *He always could do that to me.* "You don't know me anymore, Marsh," Kelsier said quietly. "This isn't about money—I once had more wealth than any man could spend. This job is about something different."

Marsh stood close, studying Kelsier's eyes, as if searching for truth in them. "You always were a good liar," he finally said.

Kelsier rolled his eyes. "Fine, think what you want. But don't preach to me. Overthrowing the empire might have been your dream once—but now you've become a good little skaa, staying in your shop and fawning over noblemen when they visit."

"I've faced reality," Marsh said. "Something you've never been good at. Even if you're serious about this plan, you'll fail. Everything the rebellion has done—the raids, the thefts, the deaths—has accomplished nothing. Our best efforts were never even a mild annoyance for the Lord Ruler."

"Ah," Kelsier said, "but being an annoyance is something that *I* am very good at. In fact, I'm far more than just a 'mild' annoyance—people tell me I can be downright frustrating. Might as well use this talent for the cause of good, eh?"

Marsh sighed, turning away. "This isn't about a 'cause,' Kelsier. It's about revenge. It's about you, just like everything always is. I'll believe that you aren't after the money—I'll even believe that you intend to deliver Yeden this army he's apparently paying you for. But I won't believe that you care."

"That's where you are wrong, Marsh," Kelsier said quietly. "That's where you've always been wrong about me."

Marsh frowned. "Perhaps. How did this start, anyway? Did Yeden come to you, or did you go to him?"

"Does it matter?" Kelsier asked. "Look, Marsh. I need someone to infiltrate the Ministry. This plan won't go anywhere if we don't discover a way to keep an eye on those Inquisitors."

Marsh turned. "You actually expect me to help you?"

Kelsier nodded. "That's why you came here, no matter what you say. You once told me that you thought I could do great things if I ever applied myself to a worthy goal. Well, that's what I'm doing now—and you're going to help."

"It's not that easy anymore, Kell," Marsh said with a shake of his head. "Some people are different now. Others are . . . gone."

Kelsier let the room grow quiet. Even the hearth's fire was starting to die out. "I miss her too."

"I'm sure that you do—but I have to be honest with you, Kell. Despite what she did . . . sometimes I wish that you hadn't been the one to survive the Pits."

"I wish the same thing every day."

Marsh turned, studying Kelsier with his cold, discerning eyes. The eyes of a Seeker. Whatever he saw reflected inside of Kelsier must have finally met with his approval.

"I'm leaving," Marsh said. "But, for some reason you actually seem sincere this time. I'll come back and listen to whatever insane plan you've concocted. Then . . . well, we'll see."

Kelsier smiled. Beneath it all, Marsh was a good man—a better one than Kelsier had ever been. As Marsh turned toward the door, Kelsier caught a flicker of shadowed movement from beneath the doorway. He immediately burned iron, and the translucent blue lines shot out from his body, connecting him to nearby sources of metal. Marsh, of course, had none on his person—not even any coins. Traveling through skaa sectors of town could be very dangerous for a man who looked even marginally prosperous.

Someone else, however, hadn't yet learned not to carry

metal on her person. The blue lines were thin and weak—they didn't do well penetrating wood—but they were just strong enough to let Kelsier locate the belt latch of a person out in the hallway, moving quickly away from the door on silent feet.

Kelsier smiled to himself. The girl was remarkably skilled. Her time on the streets, however, had also left her with remarkable scars. Hopefully, he would be able to encourage the skills while helping heal the scars.

"I'll return tomorrow," Marsh said as he reached the door.

"Just don't come by too early," Kelsier said with a wink. "I've got some things to do tonight."

Vin waited quietly in her darkened room, listening to footsteps clomp down the stairs to the ground floor. She crouched beside her door, trying to determine if both sets had continued down the steps or not. The hallway fell silent, and eventually she breathed a quiet sigh of relief.

A knock sounded on the door just inches from her head.

Her start of surprise nearly knocked her to the ground. *He's good!* she thought.

She quickly ruffled her hair and rubbed her eyes, trying to make it appear as if she had been sleeping. She untucked her shirt, and waited until the knock came again before pulling open the door.

Kelsier lounged against the doorframe, backlit by the hallway's single lantern. The tall man raised an eyebrow at her disheveled state.

"Yes?" Vin asked, trying to sound drowsy.

"So, what do you think of Marsh?"

"I don't know," Vin said, "I didn't see much of him before he kicked us out."

Kelsier smiled. "You're not going to admit that I caught you, are you?"

Vin almost smiled back. Reen's training came to her rescue. *The man who wants you to trust him is the one you must fear the most.* Her brother's voice almost seemed to whisper in her head. It had grown stronger since she'd met Kelsier, as if her instincts were on edge.

Kelsier studied her for a moment, then stepped back from the doorframe. "Tuck in that shirt and follow me."

Vin frowned. "Where are we going?"

"To begin your training."

"Now?" Vin asked, glancing at the dark shutters to her room.

"Of course," Kelsier said. "It's a perfect night for a stroll."

Vin straightened her clothing, joining him in the hallway. If he actually planned to begin teaching her, then she wasn't going to complain, no matter what the hour. They walked down the steps to the first floor. The workroom was dark, furniture projects lying half finished in the shadows. The kitchen, however, was bright with light.

"Just a minute," Kelsier said, walking toward the kitchen.

Vin paused just inside the shadows of the workroom, letting Kelsier enter the kitchen without her. She could just barely see inside. Dockson, Breeze, and Ham sat with Clubs and his apprentices around a wide table. Wine and ale were present, though in small amounts, and the men were munching on a simple evening snack of puffed barley cakes and battered vegetables.

Laughter trickled out into the workroom. Not raucous laughter, such as had often sounded from Camon's table. This was something softer—something indicative of genuine mirth, of good-natured enjoyment.

Vin wasn't certain what kept her out of the room. She hesitated—as if the light and the humor were a barrier—and she instead remained in the quiet, solemn workroom. She watched from the darkness, however, and wasn't completely able to suppress her longing.

Kelsier returned a moment later, carrying his pack and a small cloth bundle. Vin regarded the bundle with curiosity, and he handed it to her with a smile. "A present."

The cloth was slick and soft in Vin's fingers, and she quickly realized what it was. She let the gray material unroll in her fingers, revealing a Mistborn cloak. Like the garment Kelsier had worn the night before, it was tailored completely from separate, ribbonlike strips of cloth.

"You look surprised," Kelsier noted.

"I . . . assumed that I'd have to earn this somehow."

"What's there to earn?" Kelsier said, pulling out his own cloak. "This is who you are, Vin."

She paused, then threw the cloak over her shoulders and tied it on. It felt . . . different. Thick and heavy on her shoulders, but light and unconstraining around her arms and legs. The ribbons were sewn together at the top, allowing her to pull it tight by the mantle if she wished. She felt . . . enveloped. Protected.

"How does it feel?" Kelsier asked.

"Good," Vin said simply.

Kelsier nodded, pulling out several glass vials. He handed two to her. "Drink one; keep the other in case you need it. I'll show you how to mix new vials later."

Vin nodded, downing the first vial and tucking the second into her belt.

"I'm having some new clothing tailored for you," Kelsier said. "You'll want to get into the habit of wearing things that don't have any metal on them: belts with no buckles, shoes that slip on and off, trousers without clasps. Perhaps later, if you're feeling daring, we'll get you some women's clothing."

Vin flushed slightly.

Kelsier laughed. "I'm just teasing you. However, you're entering a new world now—you may find that there are situations where it will be to your advantage to look less like a crew thief and more like a young lady."

Vin nodded, following Kelsier as he walked to the shop's front door. He pushed the portal open, revealing a wall of darkly shifting mists. He stepped out into them. Taking a deep breath, Vin followed.

Kelsier shut the door behind them. The cobbled street felt muffled to Vin, the shifting mists making everything just a bit damp. She couldn't see far in either direction, and the street ends seemed to fade into nothingness, paths into eternity. Above, there was no sky, just swirling currents of gray upon gray.

"All right, let's begin," Kelsier said. His voice felt loud in the quiet, empty street. There was a confidence to his tone, something that—confronted with the mists all around—Vin certainly didn't feel.

"Your first lesson," Kelsier said, strolling down the street,

Vin trailing along beside him, "isn't about Allomancy, but attitude." He swept his hand forward. "This, Vin. This is *ours*. The night, the mists—they belong to us. Skaa avoid the mists as if they were death. Thieves and soldiers go out at night, but they fear it nonetheless. Noblemen feign nonchalance, but the mist makes them uncomfortable."

He turned, regarding her. "The mists are your friend, Vin. They hide you, they protect you . . . and they give you power. Ministry doctrine—something rarely shared with skaa—claims that the Mistborn are descendants of the only men who remained true to the Lord Ruler during the days before his Ascension. Other legends whisper that we are something beyond even the Lord Ruler's power, something that was born on that day when the mists first came upon the land."

Vin nodded slightly. It seemed odd to hear Kelsier speak so openly. Buildings filled with sleeping skaa loomed on either side of the street. And yet, the dark shutters and quiet air made Vin feel as if she and Kelsier were alone. Alone in the most densely populated, overcrowded city in all of the Final Empire.

Kelsier continued to walk, the spring in his step incongruent with the dark gloom.

"Shouldn't we be worried about soldiers?" Vin asked quietly. Her crews always had to be careful of nighttime Garrison patrols.

Kelsier shook his head. "Even if we were careless enough to be spotted, no imperial patrol would dare bother Mistborn. They'd see our cloaks and pretend not to see us. Remember, nearly all Mistborn are members of the Great Houses—and the rest are from lesser Luthadel houses. Either way, they're very important individuals."

Vin frowned. "So, the guards just ignore the Mistborn?"

Kelsier shrugged. "It's bad etiquette to acknowledge that the skulking rooftop figure you see is actually a very distinguished and proper high lord—or even high lady. Mistborn are so rare that houses can't afford to apply gender prejudices to them.

"Anyway, most Mistborn live two lives—the life of the courtgoing aristocrat, and the life of the sneaking, spying Allomancer. Mistborn identities are closely guarded house secrets—rumors regarding who is Mistborn are always a focus of high noble gossip."

Kelsier turned down another street, Vin following, still a bit nervous. She wasn't certain where he was taking her; it was easy to get lost in the night. Perhaps he didn't even have a destination, and was just accustoming her to the mists.

"All right," Kelsier said, "let's get you used to the basic metals. Can you feel your metal reserves?"

Vin paused. If she focused, she could distinguish eight sources of power within her—each one far larger, even, than her two had been on the day when Kelsier had tested her. She had been reticent to use her Luck much since then. She was coming to realize that she had been using a weapon she'd never really understood—a weapon that had accidentally drawn the attention of a Steel Inquisitor.

"Begin burning them, one at a time," Kelsier said.

"Burning?"

"That's what we call it when you activate an Allomantic ability," Kelsier said. "You 'burn' the metal associated with that power. You'll see what I mean. Start with the metals you don't know about yet—we'll work on Soothing and Raging emotions some other time."

Vin nodded, pausing in the middle of the street. Tentatively, she reached out to one of the new sources of power. One of them was slightly familiar to her. Had she used it before without realizing it? What would it do?

Only one way to find out... Uncertain what, exactly, she was supposed to do, Vin gripped the source of power and tried to use it.

Immediately, she felt a flare of heat from within her chest. It wasn't discomforting, but it was obvious and distinct. Along with the warmth came something else—a feeling of rejuvenation, and of power. She felt . . . more *solid*, somehow.

"What happened?" Kelsier asked.

"I feel different," Vin said. She held up her hand, and it seemed as if the limb reacted just a bit too quickly. The muscles were eager. "My body is strange. I don't feel tired anymore, and I feel alert."

"Ah," Kelsier said. "That's pewter. It enhances your physical abilities, making you stronger, more able to resist fatigue and pain. You'll react more quickly when you're burning it, and your body will be tougher."

Vin flexed experimentally. Her muscles didn't seem any bigger, yet she could feel their strength. It wasn't just in her muscles, however—it was everything about her. Her bones, her flesh, her skin. She reached out to her reserve, and could feel it shrinking.

"I'm running out," she said.

Kelsier nodded. "Pewter burns relatively quickly. The vial I gave you was measured to contain about ten minutes' worth of continuous burning—though it will go faster if you flare often and slower if you are careful about when you use it."

"Flare?"

"You can burn your metals a little more powerfully if you try," Kelsier said. "It makes them run out much faster, and it's difficult to maintain, but it can give you an extra boost."

Vin frowned, trying to do as he said. With a push of effort, she was able to stoke the flames within her chest, flaring the pewter.

It was like the inhaled breath before a daring leap. A sudden rush of strength and power. Her body grew tense with anticipation, and for just a moment she felt invincible. Then it passed, her body relaxing slowly.

Interesting, she thought, noting how quickly her pewter had burned during that brief moment.

"Now, there's something you need to know about Allomantic metals," Kelsier said as they strolled forward in the mists. "The more pure they are, the more effective they are. The vials we prepare contain absolutely pure metals, prepared and sold specifically for Allomancers.

"Alloys—like pewter—are even trickier, since the metal percentages have to be mixed just right, if you want maximum power. In fact, if you aren't careful when you buy your metals, you could end up with the wrong alloy entirely."

Vin frowned. "You mean, someone might scam me?"

"Not intentionally," Kelsier said. "The thing is, most of the terms that people use—words like 'brass,' 'pewter,' and 'bronze'—are really quite vague, when you get down to it. Pewter, for instance, is generally accepted as an alloy of tin mixed with lead, with perhaps some copper or silver, depending on the use and the circumstances. *Allomancer's pewter*, however, is an alloy of ninety-one percent tin, nine percent lead. If you want maximum strength from your metal, you have to use those percentages."

"And . . . if you burn the wrong percentage?" Vin asked.

"If the mixture is only off by a bit, you'll still get some power out of it," Kelsier said. "However, if it's too far off, burning it will make you sick."

Vin nodded slowly. "I . . . think I've burned this metal before. Once in a while, in very small amounts."

"Trace metals," Kelsier said. "From drinking water contaminated by metals, or by eating with pewter utensils."

Vin nodded. Some of the mugs in Camon's lair had been pewter.

"All right," Kelsier said. "Extinguish the pewter and let's move on to another metal."

Vin did as asked. The withdrawal of power left her feeling weak, tired, and exposed.

"Now," Kelsier said, "you should be able to notice a kind of pairing between your reserves of metal."

"Like the two emotion metals," Vin said.

"Exactly. Find the metal linked to pewter."

"I see it," Vin said.

"There are two metals for every power," Kelsier said. "One Pushes, one Pulls—the second is usually an alloy of the first. For emotions—the external mental powers—you Pull with zinc and Push with brass. You just used pewter to Push your body. That's one of the internal physical powers."

"Like Ham," Vin said. "He burns pewter."

Kelsier nodded. "Mistings who can burn pewter are called Thugs. A crude term, I suppose—but they tend to be rather crude people. Our dear Hammond is something of an exception to that rule."

"So, what does the other internal physical metal do?"

"Try it and see."

Vin did so eagerly, and the world suddenly became

brighter around her. Or . . . well, that wasn't quite right. She could see better, and she could see farther, but the mists were still there. They were just . . . more translucent. The ambient light around her seemed brighter, somehow.

There were other changes. She could feel her clothing. She realized that she had always been able to feel it, but she usually ignored it. Now, however, it felt closer. She could sense the textures, and was acutely aware of the places where the cloth was tight on her.

She was hungry. That, too, she had been ignoring—yet now her hunger seemed far more pressing. Her skin felt wetter, and she could smell the crisp air mixed with scents of dirt, soot, and refuse.

"Tin enhances your senses," Kelsier said, his voice suddenly seeming quite loud. "And it's one of the slowest-burning metals—the tin in that vial is enough to keep you going for hours. Most Mistborn leave their tin on whenever they're out in the mists—I've had mine on since we left the shop."

Vin nodded. The wealth of sensations was nearly overwhelming. She could hear creaks and scuffles in the darkness, and they made her want to jump in alarm, certain that someone was sneaking up behind her.

This is going to take some getting used to.

"Leave it burning," Kelsier said, waving for her to walk beside him as he continued down the street. "You'll want to accustom yourself to the enhanced senses. Just don't flare it all the time. Not only would you run out of it very quickly, but perpetually flaring metals does . . . strange things to people."

"Strange?" Vin asked.

"Metals—especially tin and pewter—stretch your body. Flaring the metals only pushes this stretching further. Stretch it too far for too long, and things start to break."

Vin nodded uncomfortably. Kelsier fell quiet, and they continued to walk, letting Vin explore her new sensations and the detailed world that tin revealed. Before, her vision had been restricted to a tiny pocket within the night. Now, however, she saw an entire city enveloped by a blanket of shifting, swirling mist. She could make out keeps like small, dark mountains in the distance, and could see specks of light from windows, like pin-pricked holes in the night. And above . . . she saw lights in the sky.

She stopped, gazing up with wonder. They were faint, blurred to even her tin-enhanced eyes, but she could just barely make them out. Hundreds of them. Thousands of them. So small, like the dying embers of candles recently extinguished.

"Stars," Kelsier said, strolling up beside her. "You can't see them very often, even with tin. It must be a particularly clear night. People used to be able to look up and see them every night—that was before the mists came, before the Ashmounts erupted ash and smoke into the sky."

Vin glanced at him. "How do you know?"

Kelsier smiled. "The Lord Ruler has tried very hard to crush memories of those days, but still some remain." He turned, not really having answered her question, and continued to walk. Vin joined him. Suddenly, with tin, the mists around her didn't seem so ominous. She was beginning to see how Kelsier could walk about at night with such confidence.

"All right," Kelsier eventually said. "Let's try another metal."

Vin nodded, leaving her tin on but picking another metal to burn as well. When she did so, a very strange thing happened—a multitude of faint blue lines sprung from her chest, streaking out into the spinning mists. She froze, gasping slightly and looking down at her chest. Most of the lines were thin, like translucent pieces of twine, though a couple were as thick as yarn.

Kelsier chuckled. "Leave that metal and its partner alone for the moment. They're a bit more complicated than the others."

"What . . . ?" Vin asked, tracing the lines of blue light with her eyes. They pointed at random objects. Doors, windows—a couple even pointed at Kelsier.

"We'll get to it," he promised. "Extinguish that one and try one of the last two."

Vin extinguished the strange metal and ignored its companion, picking one of the last metals. Immediately, she felt a strange vibration. Vin paused. The pulses didn't make a sound that she could hear, yet she could feel them washing across her. They seemed to be coming from Kelsier. She looked at him, frowning.

"That's probably bronze," Kelsier said. "The internal mental Pulling metal. It lets you sense when someone is using Allomancy nearby. Seekers, like my brother, use it. Generally it's not that useful—unless you happen to be a Steel Inquisitor searching for skaa Mistings."

Vin paled. "Inquisitors can use Allomancy?"

Kelsier nodded. "They're all Seekers—I'm not sure if that's because Seekers are chosen to become Inquisitors, or if the process of becoming an Inquisitor grants the power. Either way, since their main duties are to find half-breed children and noblemen who use Allomancy improperly, it's a useful skill for them to have. Unfortunately, 'useful' for them means 'rather annoying' for us."

Vin began to nod, then froze. The pulsing had stopped.

"What happened?" she asked.

"I started burning copper," Kelsier said, "the companion to bronze. When you burn copper, it hides your use of powers from other Allomancers. You can try burning it now, if you want, though you won't sense much."

Vin did so. The only change was a feeling of slight vibration within her.

"Copper is a vital metal to learn," Kelsier said. "It will hide you from Inquisitors. We probably don't have anything to worry about tonight—the Inquisitors would assume us to be regular noble Mistborn, out for training. However, if you're ever in a skaa guise and need to burn metals, make sure you turn on your copper first."

Vin nodded appreciatively.

"In fact," Kelsier said, "many Mistborn keep their copper on all the time. It burns slowly, and it makes you invisible to other Allomancers. It hides you from bronze, and it also prevents others from manipulating your emotions."

Vin perked up.

"I thought that might interest you," Kelsier said. "Anyone burning copper is immune to emotional Allomancy. In addition, copper's influence occurs in a bubble around you. This cloud—called a coppercloud—hides anyone inside of it from the senses of a Seeker, though it won't make them immune to emotional Allomancy, like it will you."

"Clubs," Vin said. "That's what a Smoker does."

Kelsier nodded. "If one of our people is noticed by a Seeker, they can run back to the lair and disappear. They can also practice their abilities without fear of being discovered. Allomantic pulses coming from a shop in a skaa sector of town would be a quick giveaway to a passing Inquisitor."

"But, you can burn copper," Vin said. "Why were you so worried about finding a Smoker for the crew?"

"I can burn copper, true," Kelsier said. "And so can you. We can use all of the powers, but we can't be everywhere. A successful crewleader needs to know how to divide labor, especially on a job as big as this one. Standard practice has a coppercloud going at all times in the lair. Clubs doesn't do it all himself—several of those apprentices are Smokers too. When you hire a man like Clubs, it's understood that he'll provide you with a base of operations and a team of Smokers competent enough to keep you hidden at all times."

Vin nodded. However, she was more interested in copper's ability to protect her emotions. She would need to locate enough of it to keep it burning all the time.

They started walking again, and Kelsier gave her more time to get used to burning tin. Vin's mind, however, began to wander. Something didn't feel . . . right to her. Why was Kelsier telling her all of these things? It seemed like he was giving away his secrets too easily.

Except one, she thought suspiciously. *The metal with the blue lines. He hasn't gone back to it yet.* Perhaps that was the thing he was going to keep from her, the power he would hold in reserve to maintain control over her.

It must be strong. The most powerful of the eight.

As they walked through the quiet streets, Vin reached tentatively inside. She eyed Kelsier, then carefully burned that unknown metal. Again, the lines sprang up around her, pointing in seemingly random directions.

The lines moved with her. One end of each thread stayed stuck to her chest, while the other end remained attached to a given place along the street. New lines appeared as she walked, and old ones faded, disappearing behind. The lines came in various widths, and some of them were brighter than others.

Curious, Vin tested the lines with her mind, trying to discover their secret. She focused on a particularly small and innocent-looking one, and found that she could feel it individually if she concentrated. She almost felt like she could touch it. She reached out with her mind and gave it a slight tug.

The line shook, and something immediately flew out of the darkness toward her. Vin yelped, trying to jump away, but the object—a rusty nail—shot directly toward her.

Suddenly, something grabbed the nail, ripping it away and throwing it back out into the darkness.

Vin came up from her roll in a tense crouch, mistcloak fluttering around her. She scanned the darkness, then glanced at Kelsier, who was chuckling softly.

"I should have known you'd try that," he said.

Vin flushed in embarrassment.

"Come on," he said, waving her over. "No harm done."

"The nail attacked me!" Did that metal bring objects to life? That would be an incredible power indeed.

"Actually, you kind of attacked yourself," Kelsier said.

Vin stood carefully, then joined him as he began to walk down the street again.

"I'll explain what you did in a moment," he promised. "First, there's something you have to understand about Allomancy."

"Another rule?"

"More a philosophy," Kelsier said. "It has to do with consequences."

Vin frowned. "What do you mean?"

"Every action we take has consequences, Vin," Kelsier said. "I've found that in both Allomancy and life, the person who can best judge the consequences of their actions will be the most successful. Take burning pewter, for instance. What are its consequences?"

Vin shrugged. "You get stronger."

"What happens if you're carrying something heavy when your pewter runs out?"

Vin paused. "I suppose you'd drop it."

"And, if it's too heavy, you could hurt yourself seriously. Many a Misting Thug has shrugged off a dire wound while fighting, only to die from that same wound once their pewter ran out."

"I see," Vin said quietly.

"*Ha!*"

Vin jumped in shock, throwing her hands up over her enhanced ears. "Ow!" she complained, glaring at Kelsier.

He smiled. "Burning tin has consequences too. If someone produces a sudden light or sound, you can be blinded or stunned."

"But, what does that have to do with those last two metals?"

"Iron and steel give you the ability to manipulate other metals around you," Kelsier explained. "With iron, you can Pull a metal source toward yourself. With steel, you can Push one away. Ah, here we are."

Kelsier stopped, looking up ahead.

Through the mist, Vin could see the massive city wall looming above them. "What are we doing here?"

"We're going to practice Ironpulling and Steelpushing," Kelsier said. "But first, some basics." He pulled something out of his belt—a clip, the smallest denomination of coin. He held it up before her, standing to the side. "Burn steel, the opposite of the metal you burned a few moments ago."

Vin nodded. Again, the blue lines sprang up around her. One of them pointed directly at the coin in Kelsier's hand.

"All right," Kelsier said. "Push on it."

Vin reached toward the proper thread and Pushed slightly. The coin flipped out of Kelsier's fingers, traveling directly away from Vin. She continued to focus on it, Pushing the coin through the air until it snapped against the wall of a nearby house.

Vin was thrown violently backward in a sudden, jerking motion. Kelsier caught her and kept her from falling to the ground.

Vin stumbled and righted herself. Across the street, the coin—now released from her control—plinked to the ground.

"What happened?" Kelsier asked her.

She shook her head. "I don't know. I Pushed on the coin, and it flew away. But when it hit the wall, I was pushed away."

"Why?"

Vin frowned thoughtfully. "I guess . . . I guess the coin

couldn't go anywhere, so I had to be the one that moved."

Kelsier nodded approvingly. "Consequences, Vin. You use your own weight when you Steelpush. If you're a lot heavier than your anchor, it will fly away from you like that coin did. However, if the object is heavier than you are—or if it runs into something that is—you'll be Pushed away. Ironpulling is similar—either you'll be Pulled toward the object or it will be Pulled toward you. If your weights are similar, then you'll both move.

"This is the great art of Allomancy, Vin. Knowing how much, or how little, you will move when you burn steel or iron will give you a major advantage over your opponents. You'll find that these two are the most versatile and useful of your abilities."

Vin nodded.

"Now, remember," he continued. "In both cases, the force of your Push or Pull is *directly* away from or toward you. You can't flip things around with your mind, controlling them to go wherever you want. That's not the way that Allomancy works, because that's not the way the physical world works. When you push against something—whether with Allomancy or with your hands—it goes directly in the opposite direction. Force, reactions, consequences. Understand?"

Vin nodded again.

"Good," Kelsier said happily. "Now, let's go jump over that wall."

"*What?*"

He left her standing dumbfounded in the street. She watched him approach the base of the wall, then scurried over to him.

"You're insane!" she said quietly.

Kelsier smiled. "I think that's the second time today you've said that to me. You need to pay better attention—if you'd been listening to everyone else, you'd know that my sanity departed long ago."

"Kelsier," she said, looking up at the wall. "I can't. . . . I mean, I've never really even used Allomancy before this evening!"

"Yes, but you're such a quick learner," Kelsier said, pulling something out from beneath his cloak. It appeared to be a belt. "Here, put this on. It's got metal weights strapped to it. If something goes wrong, I'll probably be able to catch you."

"Probably?" Vin asked nervously, strapping on the belt.

Kelsier smiled, then dropped a large metal ingot at his feet. "Put the ingot directly below you, and remember to Steelpush, not Ironpull. Don't stop Pushing until you reach the top of the wall."

Then he bent down and jumped.

Kelsier shot into the air, his dark form vanishing into the curling mists. Vin waited for a moment, but he didn't plummet back down to his doom.

All was still, even to her enhanced ears. The mists whirled playfully around her. Taunting her. Daring her.

She glanced down at the ingot, burning steel. The blue line glowed with a faint, ghostly light. She stepped over to the ingot, standing with one foot on either side of it. She glanced up at the mists, then down one last time.

Finally, she took a deep breath and Pushed against the ingot with all of her strength.

"He shall defend their ways, yet shall violate them. He will be their savior, yet they shall call him heretic. His name shall be Discord, yet they shall love him for it."

8

VIN SHOT INTO THE AIR. She suppressed a scream, remembering to continue Pushing despite her fear. The stone wall was a blur of motion just a few feet away from her. The ground disappeared below, and the line of blue pointing toward the ingot grew fainter and fainter.

What happens if it disappears?

She began to slow. The fainter the line grew, the more her speed decreased. After just a few moments of flight, she crept to a halt—and was left hanging in the air above a nearly invisible blue line.

"I've always liked the view from up here."

Vin glanced to the side. Kelsier stood a short distance away; she had been so focused that she hadn't noticed that she was hovering just a few feet from the top of the wall.

"Help!" she said, continuing to Push desperately, lest she fall. The mists below her shifted and spun, like some dark ocean of damned souls.

"You don't have to worry too much," Kelsier said. "It's easier to balance in the air if you have a tripod of anchors, but you can do fine with a single anchor. Your body is used to balancing itself. Part of what you've been doing since you learned to walk transfers to Allomancy. As long as you stay still, hanging at the very edge of your Pushing ability, you'll be pretty stable—your mind and body will correct any slight deviations from the base center of your anchor below, keeping you from falling to the sides.

"If you were to Push on something else, or move too much to one side, though . . . well, you'd lose your anchor below, and wouldn't be pushing directly up anymore. Then you'd have problems—you'd tip over like a lead weight on the top of a very tall pole."

"Kelsier . . ." Vin said.

"I hope you aren't afraid of heights, Vin," Kelsier said. "That's quite a disadvantage for a Mistborn."

"I'm . . . not . . . afraid . . . of . . . heights," Vin said through gritted teeth. *"But I'm also not accustomed to hanging in the air a hundred feet above the bloody street!"*

Kelsier chuckled, but Vin felt a force tug against her belt, pulling her through the air toward him. He grabbed her and pulled her up over the stone railing, then set her down beside him. He reached an arm over the side of the wall. A second later, the ingot shot up through the air, scraping along the side of the wall, until it flipped into his waiting hand.

"Good job," he said. "Now we go back down." He tossed

the ingot over his shoulder, casting it into the dark mists on the other side of the wall.

"We're really going outside?" Vin asked. "Outside the city walls? *At night?*"

Kelsier smiled in that infuriating way of his. He walked over and climbed onto the battlements. "Varying the strength with which you Push or Pull is difficult, but possible. It's better to just fall a bit, then Push to slow yourself. Let go and fall some more, then Push again. If you get the rhythm right, you'll reach the ground just fine."

"Kelsier," Vin said, approaching the wall. "I don't . . ."

"You're at the top of the city wall now, Vin," he said, stepping out into the air. He hung, hovering, balanced as he'd explained to her before. "There are only two ways down. Either you jump off, or you try and explain to that guard patrol why a Mistborn needs to use their stairwell."

Vin turned with concern, noting an approaching bob of lanternlight in the dark mists.

She turned back to Kelsier, but he was gone. She cursed, bending over the side of the wall and looking down into the mists. She could hear the guards behind her, speaking softly to one another as they walked along the wall.

Kelsier was right: She didn't have many options. Angry, she climbed up onto the battlement. She wasn't afraid of heights in particular, but who wouldn't be apprehensive, standing atop the wall, looking down at her doom? Vin's heart fluttered, her stomach twisting.

I hope Kelsier's out of the way, she thought, checking the blue line to make certain she was above the ingot. Then, she stepped off.

She immediately began to plummet toward the ground. She Pushed reflexively with her steel, but her trajectory was off; she had fallen to the side of the ingot, not directly toward it. Consequently, her Push nudged her to the side even farther, and she began to tumble through the air.

Alarmed, she Pushed again—harder this time, flaring her steel. The sudden effort launched her back upward. She arced sideways through the air, popping up into the air alongside the walltop. The passing guards spun with surprise, but their faces soon became indistinct as Vin fell back down toward the ground.

Mind muddled by terror, she reflexively reached out and Pulled against the ingot, trying to yank herself toward it. And, of course, it obediently shot up toward her.

I'm dead.

Then her body lurched, pulled upward by the belt. Her descent slowed until she was drifting quietly through the air. Kelsier appeared in the mists, standing on the ground beneath her; he was—of course—smiling.

He let her drop the last few feet, catching her, then setting her upright on the soft earth. She stood quivering for a moment, breathing in terse, anxious breaths.

"Well, that was fun," Kelsier said lightly.

Vin didn't respond.

Kelsier sat down on a nearby rock, obviously giving her time to gather her wits. Eventually, she burned pewter, using the sensation of solidness it provided to steady her nerves.

"You did well," Kelsier said.

"I nearly died."

"Everybody does, their first time," Kelsier said. "Ironpulling and Steelpushing are dangerous skills. You can impale yourself with a bit of metal that you Pull into your own body, you can jump and leave your anchor too far behind, or you can make a dozen other mistakes.

"My experience—limited though it is—has been that it's better to get into those extreme circumstances early, when someone can watch over you. Anyway, I assume you can understand why it's important for an Allomancer to carry as little metal on their body as possible."

Vin nodded, then paused, reaching up to her ear. "My earring," she said. "I'll have to stop wearing it."

"Does it have a clip on the back?" Kelsier asked.

Vin shook her head. "It's just a small stud, and the pin on the back bends down."

"Then you'll be all right," Kelsier said. "Metal in your body—even if only a bit of it is in your body—can't be Pushed or Pulled. Otherwise another Allomancer could rip the metals out of your stomach while you were burning them."

Good to know, Vin thought.

"It's also why those Inquisitors can walk around so confidently with a pair of steel spikes sticking out of their heads. The metal pierces their bodies, so it can't be affected by another Allomancer. Keep the earring—it's small, so you won't be able to do much with it, but you could use it as a weapon in an emergency."

"All right."

"Now, you ready to go?"

She looked up at the wall, preparing to jump again, then nodded.

"We're not going back up," Kelsier said. "Come on."

Vin frowned as Kelsier began to walk out into the mists. *So, does he have a destination after all—or has he just decided to wander some more?* Oddly, his affable nonchalance made him very difficult to read.

Vin hurried to keep up, not wanting to be left alone in the mists. The landscape around Luthadel was barren save for scrub and weeds. Prickles and dried leaves—both dusted with ash from an earlier ashfall—rubbed against her legs as they walked. The underbrush crunched as they walked, quiet and a bit sodden with mist dew.

Occasionally, they passed heaps of ash that had been carted out of the city. Most of the time, however, ash was thrown into the River Channerel, which passed through the city. Water broke it down eventually—or, at least, that was what Vin assumed. Otherwise the entire continent would have been buried long ago.

Vin stayed close to Kelsier as they walked. Though she had traveled outside cities before, she had always moved as part of a group of boatmen—the skaa workers who ran narrowboats and barges up and down the many canal routes in the Final Empire. It had been hard work—most noblemen used skaa instead of horses to pull the boats along the towpath—but there had been a certain freedom to knowing that she was traveling at all, for most skaa, even skaa thieves, never left their plantation or town.

The constant movement from city to city had been Reen's choice; he had been obsessive about never getting locked down. He usually got them places on canal boats run by underground crews, never staying in one place for more than a year. He had kept moving, always going. As if running from something.

They continued to walk. At night, even the barren hills and scrub-covered plains took on a forbidding air. Vin didn't speak, though she tried to make as little noise as possible. She had heard tales of what went abroad in the land at night, and the cover of the mists—even pierced by tin as it now was—made her feel as if she were being watched.

The sensation grew more unnerving as they traveled. Soon, she began to hear noises in the darkness. They were muffled and faint—crackles of weeds, shuffles in the echoing mist.

You're just being paranoid! she told herself as she jumped at some half-imagined sound. Eventually, however, she could stand it no more.

"Kelsier!" she said with an urgent whisper—one that sounded betrayingly loud to her enhanced ears. "I think there's something out there."

"Hum?" Kelsier asked. He looked lost in his thoughts.

"I think something is following us!"

"Oh," Kelsier said. "Yes, you're right. It's a mistwraith."

Vin stopped dead in her tracks. Kelsier, however, kept going.

"Kelsier!" she said, causing him to pause. "You mean *they're real?*"

"Of course they are," Kelsier said. "Where do you think all the stories came from?"

Vin stood in dumbfounded shock.

"You want to go look at it?" Kelsier asked.

"Look at the mistwraith?" Vin asked. "Are you—" She stopped.

Kelsier chuckled, strolling back to her. "Mistwraiths might be a bit disturbing to look at, but they're relatively harmless. They're scavengers, mostly. Come on."

He began to retrace their footsteps, waving her to follow. Reluctant—but morbidly curious—Vin followed. Kelsier walked at a brisk pace, leading her to the top of a relatively scrub-free hill. He crouched down, motioning for Vin to do likewise.

"Their hearing isn't very good," he said as she knelt in the rough, ashen dirt beside him. "But their sense of smell—or, rather, taste—is quite acute. It's probably following our trail, hoping that we'll discard something edible."

Vin squinted in the darkness. "I can't see it," she said, searching the mists for a shadowed figure.

"There," Kelsier said, pointing toward a squat hill.

Vin frowned, imagining a creature crouching atop the hill, watching her as she looked for it.

Then the hill moved.

Vin jumped slightly. The dark mound—perhaps ten feet tall and twice as long—lurched forward in a strange, shuffling gait, and Vin leaned forward, trying to get a better look.

"Flare your tin," Kelsier suggested.

Vin nodded, calling upon a burst of extra Allomantic power. Everything immediately became lighter, the mists becoming even less of an obstruction.

What she saw caused her to shiver—fascinated, revolted, and more than a little disturbed. The creature had smoky, translucent skin, and Vin could see its bones. It had dozens upon dozens of limbs, and each one looked as if it had come from a different animal. There were human hands, bovine hooves, canine haunches, and others she couldn't identify.

The mismatched limbs let the creature walk—though it was more of a shamble. It crawled along slowly, moving like an awkward centipede. Many of the limbs, in fact, didn't even look functional—they jutted from the creature's flesh in a twisted, unnatural fashion.

Its body was bulbous and elongated. It wasn't just a blob, though . . . there was a strange logic to its form. It had a distinct skeletal structure, and—squinting through tin-enhanced eyes—she thought she could make out translucent muscles and sinew wrapping the bones. The creature flexed odd jumbles of muscles as it moved, and appeared to have a dozen different rib cages. Along the main body, arms and legs hung at unnerving angles.

And heads—she counted six. Despite the translucent skin, she could make out a horse head sitting beside that of a deer. Another head turned toward her, and she could see its human skull. The head sat atop a long spinal cord attached to some kind of animal torso, which was in turn attached to a jumble of strange bones.

Vin nearly retched. "What . . . ? How . . . ?"

"Mistwraiths have malleable bodies," Kelsier said. "They can shape their skin around any skeletal structure, and can even re-create muscles and organs if they have a model to mimic."

"You mean . . . ?"

Kelsier nodded. "When they find a corpse, they envelop it and slowly digest the muscles and organs. Then, they use what they've eaten as a pattern, creating an exact duplicate of the dead creature. They rearrange the parts a little bit—excreting the bones they don't want, while adding the ones they do want to their body—forming a jumble like what you see out there."

Vin watched the creature shamble across the field, following her tracks. A flap of slimy skin drooped from its underbelly, trailing along the ground. *Tasting for scents*, Vin thought. *Following the smell of our passing.* She let her tin return to normal, and the mistwraith once again became a shadowed mound. The silhouette, however, only seemed to heighten its abnormality.

"Are they intelligent, then?" Vin asked. "If they can split up a . . . body and put the pieces where they want?"

"Intelligent?" Kelsier asked. "No, not one this young. More instinctual than intelligent."

Vin shivered again. "Do people know about these things? I mean, other than the legends?"

"What do you mean by 'people'?" Kelsier asked. "A lot of Allomancers know about them, and I'm sure the Ministry does. Regular people . . . well, they just don't go out at night. Most skaa fear and curse mistwraiths, but go their entire lives without actually seeing one."

"Lucky for them," Vin muttered. "Why doesn't someone do something about these things?"

Kelsier shrugged. "They're not that dangerous."

"That one has a human head!"

"It probably found a corpse," Kelsier said. "I've never heard of a mistwraith attacking a full-grown, healthy adult. That's probably why everyone leaves them alone. And, of course, the high nobility have devised their own uses for the creatures."

Vin looked at him questioningly, but he said no more, rising and walking down the hillside. She shot one more glance at the unnatural creature, then took off, following Kelsier.

"Is that what you brought me out here to see?" Vin asked.

Kelsier chuckled. "Mistwraiths might look eerie, but they're hardly worth such a long trip. No, we're heading over there."

She followed his gesture, and was able to make out a change in the landscape ahead. "The imperial highroad? We've circled around to the front of the city."

Kelsier nodded. After a short walk—during which Vin glanced backward no less than three times to make certain the mistwraith hadn't gained on them—they left the scrub and stepped onto the flat, packed earth of the imperial highroad. Kelsier paused, scanning the road in either direction. Vin frowned, wondering what he was doing.

Then she saw the carriage. It was parked by the side of the highroad, and Vin could see that there was a man waiting beside it.

"Ho, Sazed," Kelsier said, walking forward.

The man bowed. "Master Kelsier," he said, his smooth voice carrying well in the night air. It had a higher pitch to it, and he spoke with an almost melodic accent. "I almost thought that you had decided not to come."

"You know me, Saze," Kelsier said, jovially slapping the man on the shoulder. "I'm the soul of punctuality." He turned and waved a hand toward Vin. "This apprehensive little creature is Vin."

"Ah, yes," Sazed said, speaking in a slow, well-enunciated way. There was something strange about his accent. Vin approached cautiously, studying the man. Sazed had a long, flat face and a willowy body. He was even taller than Kelsier—tall enough to be a bit abnormal—and his arms were unusually long.

"You're a Terrisman," Vin said. His earlobes had been stretched out, and the ears themselves contained studs that ran around their perimeter. He wore the lavish, colorful robes of a Terris steward—the garments were made of embroidered, overlapping V shapes, alternating among the three colors of his master's house.

"Yes, child," Sazed said, bowing. "Have you known many of my people?"

"None," Vin said. "But I know that the high nobility prefer Terrismen stewards and attendants."

"Indeed they do, child," Sazed said. He turned to Kelsier. "We should go, Master Kelsier. It is late, and we are still an hour away from Fellise."

Fellise, Vin thought. *So, we're going to see the impostor Lord Renoux.*

Sazed opened the carriage door for them, then closed it after they climbed in. Vin settled on one of the plush seats as she heard Sazed climb atop the vehicle and set the horses in motion.

Kelsier sat quietly in the carriage. The window shades were closed against the mist, and a small lantern, half shielded, hung in the corner. Vin rode on the seat directly across from him—her legs tucked up underneath her, her enveloping mistcloak pulled close, hiding her arms and legs.

She always does that, Kelsier thought. *Wherever she is, she tries to be as small and unnoticeable as possible. So tense.* Vin didn't sit, she crouched. She didn't walk, she prowled. Even when she was sitting in the open, she seemed to be trying to hide.

She's a brave one, though. During his own training, Kelsier hadn't been quite so willing to throw himself off of a city wall—old Gemmel had been forced to push him.

Vin watched him with those quiet, dark eyes of hers. When she noticed his attention, she glanced away, huddling down a little more within her cloak. Unexpectedly, however, she spoke.

"Your brother," she said in her soft near-whisper of a voice. "You two don't get along very well."

Kelsier raised an eyebrow. "No. We never have, really. It's a shame. We should, but we just . . . don't."

"He's older than you?"

Kelsier nodded.

"Did he beat you often?" Vin asked.

Kelsier frowned. "Beat me? No, he didn't beat me at all."

"You stopped him, then?" Vin said. "Maybe that's why he doesn't like you. How did you escape? Did you run, or were you just stronger than him?"

"Vin, Marsh never *tried* to beat me. We argued, true—but we never really wanted to hurt one another."

Vin didn't contradict him, but he could see in her eyes that she didn't believe him.

What a life . . . Kelsier thought, falling silent. There were so many children like Vin in the underground. Of course, most died before reaching her age. Kelsier had been one of the lucky ones: His mother had been a resourceful mistress of a high nobleman, a clever woman who had managed to hide the fact that she was skaa from her lord. Kelsier and Marsh had grown up privileged—considered illegitimate, but still noble—until their father had finally discovered the truth.

"Why did you teach me those things?" Vin asked, interrupting his thoughts. "About Allomancy, I mean."

Kelsier frowned. "I promised you that I would."

"Now that I know your secrets, what is to keep me from running away from you?"

"Nothing," Kelsier said.

Once again, her distrusting glare told him that she didn't believe his answer. "There are metals you didn't tell me about. Back in our meeting on the first day, you said there were ten."

Kelsier nodded, leaning forward. "There are. But I didn't leave the last two out because I wanted to keep things from you. They're just . . . difficult to get used to. It will be easier if you practice with the basic metals first. However, if you want to know about the last two, I can teach you once we arrive in Fellise."

Vin's eyes narrowed.

Kelsier rolled his eyes. "I'm not trying to trick you, Vin. People serve on my crews because they want to, and I'm effective because they can rely on one another. No distrust, no betrayals."

"Except one," Vin whispered. "The betrayal that sent you to the Pits."

Kelsier froze. "Where did you hear that?"

Vin shrugged.

Kelsier sighed, rubbing his forehead with one hand. That wasn't what he wanted to do—he wanted to scratch his scars, the ones that ran all along his fingers and hands, twisting up his arms toward his shoulders. He resisted.

"That isn't something worth talking about," he said.

"But there was a traitor," Vin said.

"We don't know for certain." That sounded weak, even to him. "Regardless, my crews rely on trust. That means no coercions. If you want out, we can go back to Luthadel right now. I'll show you the last two metals, then you can be on your way."

"I don't have enough money to survive on my own," Vin said.

Kelsier reached inside of his cloak and pulled out a bag of coins, then tossed it onto the seat beside her. "Three thousand boxings. The money I took from Camon."

Vin glanced at the bag distrustfully.

"Take it," Kelsier said. "You're the one who earned it—from what I've been able to gather, your Allomancy was behind most of Camon's recent successes, and you were the one who risked Pushing the emotions of an obligator."

Vin didn't move.

Fine, Kelsier thought, reaching up and knocking on the underside of the coachman's chair. The carriage stopped, and Sazed soon appeared at his window.

"Turn the carriage around please, Saze," Kelsier said. "Take us back to Luthadel."

"Yes, Master Kelsier."

Within moments, the carriage was rolling back in the direction it had come. Vin watched in silence, but she seemed a little less certain of herself. She eyed the bag of coins.

"I'm serious, Vin," Kelsier said. "I can't have someone on my team who doesn't want to work with me. Turning you away isn't a punishment; it's just the way things must be."

Vin didn't respond. Letting her go would be a gamble—but forcing her to stay would be a bigger one. Kelsier sat, trying to read her, trying to understand her. Would she betray them to the Final Empire if she left? He thought not. She wasn't a bad person.

She just thought that everybody else was.

"I think your plan is crazy," she said quietly.

"So do half the people on the crew."

"You can't defeat the Final Empire."

"We don't have to," Kelsier said. "We just have to get Yeden an army, then seize the palace."

"The Lord Ruler will stop you," Vin said. "You can't beat him—he's immortal."

"We have the Eleventh Metal," Kelsier said. "We'll find a way to kill him."

"The Ministry is too powerful. They'll find your army and destroy it."

Kelsier leaned forward, looking Vin in the eye. "You trusted me enough to jump off the top of the wall, and I caught you. You're going to have to trust me this time too."

She obviously didn't like the word "trust" very much. She studied him in the weak lanternlight, remaining quiet long enough that the silence grew uncomfortable.

Finally, she snatched the bag of coins, quickly hiding it beneath her cloak. "I'll stay," she said. "But not because I trust you."

Kelsier raised an eyebrow. "Why, then?"

Vin shrugged, and she sounded perfectly honest when she spoke. "Because I want to see what happens."

Having a keep in Luthadel qualified a house for high noble status. However, having a keep didn't mean that one had to live in it, especially not all of the time. Many families also maintained a residence in one of Luthadel's outskirt cities.

Less crowded, cleaner, and less strict in its observance of imperial laws, Fellise was a rich town. Rather than containing imposing, buttressed keeps, it was filled with lavish manors and villas. Trees even lined some of the streets; most of them were aspens, whose bone-white bark was somehow resistant to the discoloring of the ash.

Vin watched the mist-cloaked city through her window, the carriage lantern extinguished at her request. Burning tin, she was able to study the neatly organized and well-groomed streets. This was a section of Fellise she had rarely seen; despite the town's opulence, its slums were remarkably similar to the ones in every other city.

Kelsier watched the city through his own window, frowning.

"You disapprove of the waste," Vin guessed, her voice a whisper. The sound would carry to Kelsier's enhanced ears. "You see the riches of this city and think of the skaa who worked to create it."

"That's part of it," Kelsier said, his own voice barely a whisper. "There's more, though. Considering the amount of money spent on it, this city should be beautiful."

Vin cocked her head. "It is."

Kelsier shook his head. "The homes are still stained black. The soil is still arid and lifeless. The trees still grow leaves of brown."

"Of course they're brown. What else would they be?"

"Green," Kelsier said. "Everything should be green."

Green? Vin thought. *What a strange thought.* She tried to imagine trees with green leaves, but the image seemed silly. Kelsier certainly had his quirks—though, anyone who had spent so long at the Pits of Hathsin was bound to be left a bit strange.

He turned back toward her. "Before I forget, there are a couple more things you should know about Allomancy."

Vin nodded.

"First," Kelsier said, "remember to burn away any unused metals you have inside of you at the end of the night. Some of the metals we use can be poisonous if digested; it's best not to sleep with them in your stomach."

"All right," Vin said.

"Also," Kelsier said, "never try to burn a metal that isn't one of the ten. I warned you that impure metals and alloys can make you sick. Well, if you try to burn a metal that isn't Allomantically sound at all, it could be deadly."

Vin nodded solemnly. *Good to know,* she thought.

"Ah," Kelsier said, turning back toward the window. "Here

we are: the newly purchased Manor Renoux. You should probably take off your cloak—the people here are loyal to us, but it always pays to be careful."

Vin agreed completely. She pulled off the cloak, letting Kelsier tuck it in his pack. Then she peeked out the carriage window, peering through the mists at the approaching manor. The grounds had a low stone wall and an iron gate; a pair of guards opened the way as Sazed identified himself.

The roadway inside was lined with aspens, and atop the hill ahead Vin could see a large manor house, phantom light spilling from its windows.

Sazed pulled the carriage up before the manor, then handed the reins to a servant and climbed down. "Welcome to Manor Renoux, Mistress Vin," he said, opening the door and gesturing to help her down.

Vin eyed his hand, but didn't take it, instead scrambling down on her own. The Terrisman didn't seem offended by her refusal.

The steps to the manor house were lit by a double line of lantern poles. As Kelsier hopped from the carriage, Vin could see a group of men gathering at the top of the white marble stairs. Kelsier climbed the steps with a springy stride; Vin followed behind, noticing how clean the steps were. They would have to be scrubbed regularly to keep the ash from staining them. Did the skaa who maintained the building know that their master was an imposter? How was Kelsier's "benevolent" plan to overthrow the Final Empire helping the common people who cleaned these steps?

Thin and aging, "Lord Renoux" wore a rich suit and a pair of aristocratic spectacles. A sparse, gray mustache colored his lip, and—despite his age—he didn't carry a cane for support. He nodded respectfully to Kelsier, but maintained a dignified air. Immediately, Vin was struck by one obvious fact: *This man knows what he is doing.*

Camon had been skilled at impersonating noblemen, but his self-importance had always struck Vin as a bit juvenile. While there were noblemen like Camon, the more impressive ones were like this Lord Renoux: calm, and self-confident. Men whose nobility was in their bearing rather than their ability to speak scornfully to those around them. Vin had to resist cringing when the impostor's eyes fell on her—he seemed far too much a nobleman, and she had been trained to reflexively avoid their attention.

"The manor is looking much better," Kelsier said, shaking hands with Renoux.

"Yes, I'm impressed with its progress," Renoux said. "My cleaning crews are quite proficient—give us a bit more time, and the manor will be so grand that I wouldn't hesitate to host the Lord Ruler himself."

Kelsier chuckled. "Wouldn't *that* be an odd dinner party." He stepped back, gesturing toward Vin. "This is the young lady I spoke of."

Renoux studied her, and Vin glanced away. She didn't like it when people looked at her that way—it made her wonder how they were going to try and use her.

"We will need to speak further of this, Kelsier," Renoux said, nodding toward the mansion's entrance. "The hour is late, but . . ."

Kelsier stepped into the building. "Late? Why, it's barely midnight. Have your people prepare some food—Lady Vin and I missed dinner."

A missed meal was nothing new to Vin. However, Renoux immediately waved to some servants, and they leapt into motion. Renoux walked into the building, and Vin followed. She paused in the entryway, however, Sazed waiting patiently behind her.

Kelsier paused, turning when he noticed that she wasn't following. "Vin?"

"It's so . . . clean," Vin said, unable to think of any other description. On jobs, she'd occasionally seen the homes of noblemen. However, those times had happened at night, in dark gloom. She was unprepared for the well-lit sight before her.

The white marble floors of Manor Renoux seemed to glow, reflecting the light of a dozen lanterns. Everything was . . . pristine. The walls were white except where they had been wash-painted with traditional animal murals. A brilliant chandelier sparkled above a double staircase, and the room's other decorations—crystal sculptures, vases set with bundles of aspen branches—glistened, unmarred by soot, smudge, or fingerprint.

Kelsier chuckled. "Well, her reaction speaks highly of your efforts," he said to Lord Renoux.

Vin allowed herself to be led into the building. The group turned right, entering a room whose whites were muted slightly by the addition of maroon furnishings and drapes.

Renoux paused. "Perhaps the lady could enjoy some refreshment here for a moment," he said to Kelsier. "There are some matters of a . . . delicate nature that I would discuss with you."

Kelsier shrugged. "Fine with me," he said, following Renoux toward another doorway. "Saze, why don't you keep Vin company while Lord Renoux and I talk?"

"Of course, Master Kelsier."

Kelsier smiled, eyeing Vin, and somehow she knew that he was leaving Sazed behind to keep her from eavesdropping.

She shot the departing men an annoyed look. *What was that you said about "trust," Kelsier?* However, she was even more annoyed at herself for getting unsettled. Why should she care if Kelsier excluded her? She had spent her entire life being ignored and dismissed. It had never bothered her before when other crewleaders left her out of their planning sessions.

Vin took a seat in one of the stiffly upholstered maroon chairs, tucking her feet up beneath her. She knew what the problem was. Kelsier had been showing her too much respect, making her feel too important. She was beginning to think that she *deserved* to be part of his secret confidences. Reen's laughter in the back of her mind discredited those thoughts, and she sat, annoyed at both herself and Kelsier, feeling ashamed, but not exactly certain why.

Renoux's servants brought her a platter of fruits and breads. They set up a small stand beside her chair, and even gave her a crystalline cup filled with a glistening red liquid. She couldn't tell if it was wine or juice, and she didn't intend to find out. She did, however, pick at the food—her instincts wouldn't let her pass up a free meal, even if it was prepared by unfamiliar hands.

Sazed walked over and took a position standing just behind her chair to the right. He waited with a stiff posture, hands clasped in front of him, eyes forward. The stance was obviously intended to be respectful, but his looming posture didn't help her mood any.

Vin tried to focus on her surroundings, but this only reminded her of how rich the furnishings were. She was uncomfortable amid such finery; she felt as if she stood out like a black spot on a clean rug. She didn't eat the breads for fear that she would drop crumbs on the floor, and she worried at her feet and legs—which had been stained with ash while walking through the countryside—marring the furnishings.

All of this cleanliness came at some skaa's expense, Vin thought. *Why should I worry about disturbing it?* However, she had trouble feeling outraged, for she knew this was only a front. "Lord Renoux" had to maintain a certain level of finery. It would be suspicious to do otherwise.

In addition, something else kept her from resenting the waste. The servants were happy. They went about their duties with a businesslike professionalism, no sense of drudgery about their efforts. She heard laughter in the outer hallway. These were not mistreated skaa; whether they had been included in Kelsier's plans or not was irrelevant.

So, Vin sat and forced herself to eat fruit, yawning occasionally. It was turning out to be a long night indeed. The servants eventually left her alone, though Sazed continued to loom just behind her.

I can't eat like this, she finally thought with frustration. "Could you not stand over my shoulder like that?"

Sazed nodded. He took two steps forward so that he stood next to her chair, rather than behind it. He adopted the same stiff posture, looming above her just as he had before.

Vin frowned in annoyance, then noticed the smile on Sazed's lips. He glanced down at her, eyes twinkling at his joke, then walked over and seated himself in the chair beside hers.

"I've never known a Terrisman with a sense of humor before," Vin said dryly.

Sazed raised an eyebrow. "I was under the impression that

you hadn't known any Terrismen at all, Mistress Vin."

Vin paused. "Well, I've never *heard* of one with a sense of humor. You're supposed to be completely rigid and formal."

"We're just subtle, Mistress," Sazed said. Though he sat with a stiff posture, there was still something . . . relaxed about him. It was as if he were as comfortable when sitting properly as other people were when lounging.

That's how they're supposed to be. The perfect serving men, completely loyal to the Final Empire.

"Is something troubling you, Mistress Vin?" Sazed asked as she studied him.

How much does he know? Perhaps he doesn't even realize that Renoux is an imposter. "I was just wondering how you . . . came here," she finally said.

"You mean, how did a Terrisman steward end up as part of a rebellion intending to overthrow the Final Empire?" Sazed asked in his soft voice.

Vin flushed. Apparently he was well versed indeed.

"That is an intriguing question, Mistress," Sazed said. "Certainly, my situation is not common. I would say that I arrived at it because of belief."

"Belief?"

"Yes," Sazed said. "Tell me, Mistress. What is it that you believe?"

Vin frowned. "What kind of question is that?"

"The most important kind, I think."

Vin sat for a moment, but he obviously expected a reply, so she finally shrugged. "I don't know."

"People often say that," Sazed said, "but I find that it is rarely true. Do you believe in the Final Empire?"

"I believe that it is strong," Vin said.

"Immortal?"

Vin shrugged. "It has been so far."

"And the Lord Ruler? Is he the Ascended Avatar of God? Do you believe that he, as the Ministry teaches, is a Sliver of Infinity?"

"I . . . I've never thought about it before."

"Perhaps you should," Sazed said. "If, upon examination,

you find that the Ministry's teachings do not suit you, then I would be pleased to offer you an alternative."

"What alternative?"

Sazed smiled. "That depends. The right belief is like a good cloak, I think. If it fits you well, it keeps you warm and safe. The wrong fit, however, can suffocate."

Vin paused, frowning slightly, but Sazed just smiled. Eventually, she turned her attention back to her meal. After a short wait, the side door opened, and Kelsier and Renoux returned.

"Now," Renoux said as he and Kelsier seated themselves, a group of servants bringing another plate of food for Kelsier, "let us discuss this child. The man you were going to have play my heir will not do, you say?"

"Unfortunately," Kelsier said, making quick work of his food.

"That complicates things greatly," Renoux said.

Kelsier shrugged. "We'll just have Vin be your heir."

Renoux shook his head. "A girl her age *could* inherit, but it would be suspicious for me to pick her. There are any number of legitimate male cousins in the Renoux line who would be far more suitable choices. It was going to bc difficult enough to get a middle-aged man past courtly scrutiny. A young girl . . . no, too many people would investigate her background. Our forged family lines will survive passing scrutiny, but if someone were to actually send messengers to search out her holdings . . ."

Kelsier frowned.

"Besides," Renoux added. "There is another issue. If I were to name a young, unmarried girl as my heir, hers would instantly become one of the most sought-after hands in Luthadel. It would be very difficult for her to spy if she were to receive that much attention."

Vin flushed at the thought. Surprisingly, she found her heart sinking as the old imposter spoke. *This was the only part Kelsier gave me in the plan. If I can't do it, what good am I to the crew?*

"So, what do you suggest?" Kelsier asked.

"Well, she doesn't *have* to be my heir," Renoux said. "What if, instead, she were simply a young scion I brought with me to Luthadel? Perhaps I promised her parents—distant but favored cousins—that I would introduce their daughter to the court? Everyone would assume that my ulterior motive is to marry her off to a high noble family, thereby gaining myself another connection to those in power. However, she wouldn't draw much attention—she would be of low status, not to mention somewhat rural."

"Which would explain why she's a bit less refined than other court members," Kelsier said. "No offense, Vin."

Vin looked up from hiding a piece of napkin-wrapped bread in her shirt pocket. "Why would I be offended?"

Kelsier smiled. "Never mind."

Renoux nodded to himself. "Yes, this will work much better. Everyone assumes that House Renoux will eventually join the high nobility, so they'll accept Vin into their ranks out of courtesy. However, she herself will be unimportant enough that most people will ignore her. That is the ideal situation for what we will want her to do."

"I like it," Kelsier said. "Few people expect a man of your age and mercantile concerns to bother himself with balls and parties, but having a young socialite to send instead of a rejection note will serve as an advantage to your reputation."

"Indeed," Renoux said. "She'll need some refinement, however—and not just in appearance."

Vin squirmed a bit beneath their scrutiny. It looked as if her part in the plan would go forward, and she suddenly realized what that meant. Being around Renoux made her uncomfortable—and he was a *fake* nobleman. How would she react to an entire room full of real ones?

"I'm afraid I'll have to borrow Sazed from you for a while," Kelsier said.

"Quite all right," Renoux said. "He's really not my steward, but yours."

"Actually," Kelsier said, "I don't think he's *anybody's* steward anymore, eh Saze?"

Sazed cocked his head. "A Terrisman without a master is like a soldier with no weapon, Master Kelsier. I have enjoyed my time attending to Lord Renoux, as I am certain that I shall enjoy returning to your service."

"Oh, you won't be returning to my service," Kelsier said.

Sazed raised an eyebrow.

Kelsier nodded toward Vin. "Renoux is right, Saze. Vin needs some coaching, and I know plenty of high noblemen who are less refined than yourself. Do you think you could help the girl prepare?"

"I am certain that I could offer the young lady some aid," Sazed said.

"Good," Kelsier said, popping one last cake in his mouth, then rising. "I'm glad that's settled, because I'm starting to feel tired—and poor Vin looks like she's about to nod off in the middle of her fruit plate."

"I'm fine," Vin said immediately, the assertion weakened slightly by a stifled yawn.

"Sazed," Renoux said, "would you show them to the appropriate guest chambers?"

"Of course, Master Renoux," Sazed said, rising from his seat in a smooth motion.

Vin and Kelsier trailed the tall Terrisman from the room as a group of servants took away the remnants of the meal. *I left food behind,* Vin noticed, feeling a bit drowsy. She wasn't certain what to think of the occurrence.

As they crested the stairs and turned into a side hallway, Kelsier fell into place beside Vin. "I'm sorry for excluding you back there, Vin."

She shrugged. "There's no reason for me to know all of your plans."

"Nonsense," Kelsier said. "Your decision tonight makes you as much a part of this team as anyone else. Renoux's words in private, however, were of a personal nature. He is a marvelous actor, but he feels very uncomfortable with people knowing the specifics of how he took Lord Renoux's place. I promise you, nothing we discussed has any bearing on your part in the plan."

Vin continued walking. "I . . . believe you."

"Good," Kelsier said with a smile, clapping her on the shoulder. "Saze, I know my way to the men's guest quarters—I was, after all, the one who bought this place. I can make my way from here."

"Very well, Master Kelsier," Sazed said with a respectful nod. Kelsier shot Vin a smile, then turned down a hallway, walking with his characteristically lively step.

Vin watched him go, then followed Sazed down a different side passage, pondering the Allomancy training, her discussion with Kelsier in the carriage, and finally Kelsier's promise just a few moments before. The three thousand boxings—a fortune in coins—was a strange weight tied to her belt.

Eventually, Sazed opened a particular door for her, walking in to light the lanterns. "The linens are fresh, and I will send maids to prepare you a bath in the morning." He turned, handing her his candle. "Will you require anything else?"

Vin shook her head. Sazed smiled, bid her good evening, then walked back out in the hallway. Vin stood quietly for a short moment, studying the room. Then she turned, glancing once again in the direction Kelsier had gone.

"Sazed?" she said, peeking back out into the hallway.

The steward paused, turning back. "Yes, Mistress Vin?"

"Kelsier," Vin said quietly. "He's a good man, isn't he?"

Sazed smiled. "A very good man, Mistress. One of the best I've known."

Vin nodded slightly. "A good man . . ." she said softly. "I don't think I've ever known one of those before."

Sazed smiled, then bowed his head respectfully and turned to leave.

Vin let the door swing shut.

THE END OF PART ONE

PART TWO

REBELS BENEATH A SKY OF ASH

In the end, I worry that my arrogance shall destroy us all.

9

VIN PUSHED AGAINST THE COIN and threw herself up into the mist. She flew away from earth and stone, soaring through the dark currents of the sky, wind fluttering her cloak.

This is freedom, she thought, breathing deeply of the cool, damp air. She closed her eyes, feeling the passing wind. *This was what I was always missing, yet never knew it.*

She opened her eyes as she began to descend. She waited until the last moment, then flicked a coin. It hit the cobblestones, and she Pushed against it lightly, slowing her descent. She burned pewter with a flash and hit the ground running, dashing along Fellise's quiet streets. The late-autumn air was cool, but winters were generally mild in the Central Dominance. Some years passed without even a flake of snow.

She tossed a coin backward, then used it to Push herself slightly up and to the right. She landed on a low stone wall, barely breaking stride as she ran spryly along the wall's top. Burning pewter enhanced more than muscles—it increased all the body's physical abilities. Keeping pewter at a low burn gave her a sense of balance that any night burglar would have envied.

The wall turned north, and Vin paused at the corner. She fell into a crouch, bare feet and sensitive fingers gripping the chill stone. Her copper on to hide her Allomancy, she flared tin to strain her senses.

Stillness. Aspens made insubstantial ranks in the mist, like emaciated skaa standing in their work lines. Estates rolled in the distance—each one walled, manicured, and well guarded. There were far fewer dots of light in the city than there were in Luthadel. Many of the homes were only part-time residences, their masters away visiting some other sliver of the Final Empire.

Blue lines suddenly appeared before her—one end of each pointing at her chest, the other disappearing into the mists. Vin immediately jumped to the side, dodging as a pair of coins shot past in the night air, leaving trails in the mist. She flared pewter, landing on the cobbled street beside the wall. Her tin-enhanced ears picked out a scraping sound; then a dark form shot into the sky, a few blue lines pointing to his coin pouch.

Vin dropped a coin and threw herself into the air after her opponent. They soared for a moment, flying over the grounds of some unsuspecting nobleman. Vin's opponent suddenly changed course in the air, jerking toward the mansion itself. Vin followed, letting go of the coin below her, instead burning iron and Pulling on one of the mansion's window latches.

Her opponent hit first, and she heard a thud as he ran into the side of the building. He was off a second later.

A light brightened, and a confused head poked out of a window as Vin spun in the air, landing feet-first against the mansion. She immediately kicked off of the vertical surface, angling herself slightly and Pushing against the same window latch. Glass cracked, and she shot away into the night before gravity could reclaim her.

Vin flew through the mists, eyes straining to keep track of her quarry. He shot a couple of coins back at her, but she Pushed them away with a dismissive thought. A hazy blue line fell downward—a dropped coin—and her opponent moved to the side again.

Vin dropped her own coin and Pushed. However, her coin suddenly jerked backward along the ground—the result of a Push from her opponent. The sudden move changed the trajectory of Vin's jump, throwing her sideways. She cursed, flicking another coin to the side, using it to Push herself back on track. By then, she'd lost her quarry.

All right . . . she thought, hitting the soft ground just inside the wall. She emptied a few coins into her hand, then tossed the mostly full pouch into the air, giving it a strong Push in the direction she had seen her quarry disappear. The pouch disappeared into the mists, trailing a faint blue Allomantic line.

A scattering of coins suddenly shot from the bushes ahead, streaking toward her bag. Vin smiled. Her opponent had assumed that the flying pouch was Vin herself. He was too far away to see the coins in her hand, just as he had been too far away for her to see the coins he carried.

A dark figure jumped out of the bushes, hopping up onto the stone wall. Vin waited quietly as the figure ran along the wall and slipped down onto the other side.

Vin launched herself straight up into the air, then threw her handful of coins at the figure passing below. He immediately Pushed, sending the coins streaking away—but they were only a distraction. Vin landed on the ground before him, twin glass knives whipping from her sheathes. She lunged, slashing, but her opponent jumped backward.

Something's wrong. Vin ducked and threw herself to the side as a handful of glittering coins—her coins, the ones her opponent had Pushed away—shot back down from the sky into her opponent's hand. He turned and sprayed them in her direction.

Vin dropped her daggers with a quiet yelp, thrusting her hands forward and Pushing on the coins. Immediately, she was thrown backward as her Push was matched by her opponent.

One of the coins lurched in the air, hanging directly between the two of them. The rest of the coins disappeared into the mists, pushed sideways by conflicting forces.

Vin flared her steel as she flew, and heard her opponent grunt as he was Pushed backward as well. Her opponent hit the wall. Vin slammed into a tree, but she flared pewter and ignored the pain. She used the wood to brace herself, continuing to Push.

The coin quivered in the air, trapped between the amplified strength of two Allomancers. The pressure increased. Vin gritted her teeth, feeling the small aspen bend behind her.

Her opponent's Pushing was relentless.

Will . . . not . . . be beaten! Vin thought, flaring both steel and pewter, grunting slightly as she threw the entire force of her strength at the coin.

There was a moment of silence. Then Vin lurched backward, the tree cracking with a loud snap in the night air.

Vin hit the ground in a tumble, splinters of wood scattering around her. Even tin and pewter weren't enough to keep her mind clear as she rolled across the cobblestones, eventually coming to a dizzy rest. A dark figure approached, mistcloak ribbons billowing around him. Vin lurched to her feet, grasping for knives she'd forgotten that she'd dropped.

Kelsier put down his hood and held her knives toward her. One was broken. "I know it's instinctual, Vin, but you don't have to put your hands forward when you Push—nor do you have to drop what you're holding."

Vin grimaced in the darkness, rubbing her shoulder and nodding as she accepted the daggers.

"Nice job with the pouch," Kelsier said. "You had me for a moment."

"For all the good it did," Vin grumbled.

"You've only been doing this for a few months, Vin," he said lightly. "All things considered, your progress is fantastic. I would, however, recommend that you avoid Push-matches with people who weigh more than you." He paused, eyeing Vin's short figure and thin frame. "Which probably means avoiding them with pretty much everybody."

Vin sighed, stretching slightly. She'd have more bruises. *At least they won't be visible.* Now that the bruises Camon had given her face were finally gone, Sazed had warned her to be careful. Makeup could only cover so much, and she would have to look like a "proper" young noblewoman if she were going to infiltrate the court.

"Here," Kelsier said, handing her something. "A souvenir."

Vin held up the object—the coin they had Pushed between them. It was bent and flattened from the pressure.

"I'll see you back at the mansion," Kelsier said.

Vin nodded, and Kelsier disappeared into the night. *He's right,* she thought. *I'm smaller, I weigh less, and I have a shorter reach than anyone I'm likely to fight. If I attack someone head on, I'll lose.*

The alternative had always been her method anyway—to struggle quietly, to stay unseen. She had to learn to use Allomancy the same way. Kelsier kept saying that she was developing amazingly fast as an Allomancer. He seemed to think it was his teaching, but Vin felt it was something else. The mists . . . the night prowling . . . it all felt *right* to her. She was not worried about mastering Allomancy in time to help Kelsier against other Mistborn.

It was her other part in the plan that worried her.

Sighing, Vin hopped over the wall to search for her coin pouch. Up at the mansion—not Renoux's home, but one owned by some other nobleman—lights were on and people milled about. None of them ventured deeply into the night. The skaa would fear mistwraiths; the nobility would have guessed that Mistborn had caused the disturbance. Neither one was something a sane person would want to confront.

Vin eventually traced her pouch by steel-line to the upper branches of a tree. She Pulled it slightly, tugging it down into her hand, then made her way back out to the street. Kelsier probably would have left the pouch behind—the two dozen or so clips it contained wouldn't have been worth his time. However, for most of her life Vin had scrounged and starved. She just couldn't force herself to be wasteful. Even tossing coins to jump with made her uncomfortable.

So, she used her coins sparingly as she traveled back toward Renoux's mansion, instead Pushing and Pulling off of buildings and discarded bits of metal. The half-jumping, half-running gait of a Mistborn came naturally to her now, and she didn't have to think much about her movements.

How would she fare, trying to pretend to be a noblewoman? She couldn't hide her apprehensions, not from herself. Camon had been good at imitating noblemen because of his self-confidence, and that was one attribute Vin knew she didn't have. Her success with Allomancy only proved that her place was in corners and shadows, not striding around in pretty dresses at courtly balls.

Kelsier, however, refused to let her back out. Vin landed in a crouch just outside Mansion Renoux, puffing slightly from exertion. She regarded the lights with a slight feeling of apprehension.

You've got to learn to do this, Vin, Kelsier kept telling her. *You're a talented Allomancer, but you'll need more than Steelpushes to succeed against the nobility. Until you can move in their society as easily as you do in the mists, you'll be at a disadvantage.*

Letting out a quiet sigh, Vin rose from her crouch, then took off her mistcloak and stuffed it away for later retrieval. Then she walked up the steps and into the building. When she asked after Sazed, the mansion servants directed her to the kitchens, so she made her way into the closed-off, hidden section of the mansion that was the servants' quarters.

Even these parts of the building were kept immaculately clean. Vin was beginning to understand why Renoux made such a convincing impostor: He didn't allow for imperfection. If he maintained his impersonation half as well as he maintained order in his mansion, then Vin doubted anyone would ever discover the ruse.

But, she thought, *he must have some flaw. Back in the meeting two months ago, Kelsier said that Renoux wouldn't be able to withstand scrutiny by an Inquisitor. Perhaps they'd be able to sense something about his emotions, something that gives him away?*

It was a small item, but Vin had not forgotten it. Despite Kelsier's words about honesty and trust, he still had his secrets. Everyone did.

Sazed was, indeed, to be found in the kitchens. He stood with a middle-aged servant. She was tall for a skaa woman—though standing next to Sazed made her look diminutive. Vin recognized her as a member of the mansion staff; Cosahn was her name. Vin had made an effort to memorize all of the names of the local staff, if only to keep tabs on them.

Sazed looked over as Vin entered. "Ah, Mistress Vin. Your

return is quite timely." He gestured to his companion. "This is Cosahn."

Cosahn studied Vin with a businesslike air. Vin longed to return to the mists, where people couldn't look at her like that.

"It is long enough now, I think," Sazed said.

"Probably," Cosahn said. "But I cannot perform miracles, Master Vaht."

Sazed nodded. "Vaht" was, apparently, the proper title for a Terrisman steward. Not quite skaa, but definitely not noblemen, the Terrismen held a very strange place in imperial society.

Vin studied the two of them suspiciously.

"Your hair, Mistress," Sazed said with a calm tone. "Cosahn is going to cut it for you."

"Oh," Vin said, reaching up. Her hair was getting a bit long for her taste—though somehow she doubted that Sazed was going to let her have it cropped boyishly short.

Cosahn waved to a chair, and Vin reluctantly seated herself. She found it unnerving to sit docilely while someone worked with shears so close to her head, but there was no getting around it.

After a few moments of running her hands through Vin's hair, "tisk"ing quietly, Cosahn began to snip. "Such beautiful hair," she said, almost as if to herself, "thick, with a nice deep black color. It's a shame to see it cared for so poorly, Master Vaht. Many courtly women would die for hair like this—it has just enough body to lie full, but is straight enough to work with easily."

Sazed smiled. "We'll have to see that it receives better care in the future," he said.

Cosahn continued her work, nodding to herself. Eventually, Sazed walked over and took a seat just a few feet in front of Vin.

"Kelsier hasn't returned yet, I assume?" Vin asked.

Sazed shook his head, and Vin sighed. Kelsier didn't think she was practiced enough go with him on his nightly raids, many of which he went on directly following his training sessions with Vin. During the last two months, Kelsier had put in appearances on the properties of a dozen different noble houses, both in Luthadel and in Fellise. He varied his disguises and apparent motives, trying to create an air of confusion among the Great Houses.

"What?" Vin asked, eyeing Sazed, who was regarding her with a curious look.

The Terrisman nodded his head slightly with respect. "I was wondering if you might be willing to listen to another proposal."

Vin sighed, rolling her eyes. "Fine." *It isn't like I can do anything else but sit here.*

"I think I have the perfect religion for you," Sazed said, his normally stoic face revealing a glimmer of eagerness. "It is called 'Trelagism,' after the god Trell. Trell was worshipped by a group known as the Nelazan, a people who lived far to the north. In their land, the day and night cycle was very odd. During some months of the year, it was dark for most of the day. During the summer, however, it only grew dark for a few hours at a time.

"The Nelazan believed that there was beauty in darkness, and that the daylight was more profane. They saw the stars as the Thousand Eyes of Trell watching them. The sun was the single, jealous eye of Trell's brother, Nalt. Since Nalt only had one eye, he made it blaze brightly to outshine his brother. The Nelazan, however, were not impressed, and preferred to worship the quiet Trell, who watched over them even when Nalt obscured the sky."

Sazed fell silent. Vin wasn't sure how to respond, so she didn't say anything.

"It really is a good religion, Mistress Vin," Sazed said. "Very gentle, yet very powerful. The Nelazan were not an advanced people, but they were quite determined. They mapped the entire night sky, counting and placing every major star. Their ways suit you—especially their preference of the night. I can tell you more, if you wish."

Vin shook her head. "That's all right, Sazed."

"Not a good fit, then?" Sazed said, frowning slightly. "Ah, well. I shall have to consider it some more. Thank you, Mistress—you are very patient with me, I think."

"Consider it some more?" Vin asked. "That's the fifth religion you've tried to convert me to, Saze. How many more can there be?"

"Five hundred and sixty two," Sazed said. "Or, at least, that is the number of belief systems I know. There are, likely and unfortunately, others that have passed from this world without leaving traces for my people to collect."

Vin paused. "And you have all of these religions *memorized?*"

"As much as is possible," Sazed said. "Their prayers, their beliefs, their mythologies. Many are very similar—breakoffs or sects of one another."

"Even still, how can you remember all of that?"

"I have . . . methods," Sazed said.

"But, what's the point?"

Sazed frowned. "The answer should be obvious, I think. People are valuable, Mistress Vin, and so—therefore—are their beliefs. Since the Ascension a thousand years ago, so many beliefs have disappeared. The Steel Ministry forbids the worship of anyone but the Lord Ruler, and the Inquisitors have quite diligently destroyed hundreds of religions. If *someone* doesn't remember them, then they will simply disappear."

"You mean," Vin said incredulously, "you're trying to get me to believe in religions that have been dead for a thousand years?"

Sazed nodded.

Is everyone involved with Kelsier insane?

"The Final Empire cannot last forever," Sazed said quietly. "I do not know if Master Kelsier will be the one who finally brings its end, but that end *will* come. And when it does—when the Steel Ministry no longer holds sway—men will wish to return to the beliefs of their fathers. On that day they will look to the Keepers, and on that day we shall return to mankind his forgotten truths."

"Keepers?" Vin asked as Cosahn moved around to begin snipping at her bangs. "There are more like you?"

"Not many," Sazed said. "But some. Enough to pass the truths on to the next generation."

Vin sat thoughtfully, resisting the urge to squirm beneath Cosahn's ministrations. The woman certainly was taking her time—when Reen had cut Vin's hair, he had been finished after just a few quick hacks.

"Shall we go over your lessons while we wait, Mistress Vin?" Sazed asked.

Vin eyed the Terrisman, and he smiled just slightly. He knew that he had her captive; she couldn't hide, or even sit at the window, staring out into the mists. All she could do was sit and listen. "Fine."

"Can you name all ten Great Houses of Luthadel in order of power?"

"Venture, Hasting, Elariel, Tekiel, Lekal, Erikeller, Erikell, Haught, Urbain, and Buvidas."

"Good," Sazed said. "And you are?"

"I am the Lady Valette Renoux, fourth cousin to Lord Teven Renoux, who owns this mansion. My parents—Lord Hadren and Lady Fellette Renoux—live in Chakath, a city in the Western Dominance. Major export, wool. My family works in trading dyes, specifically blushdip red, from the snails that are common there, and callowfield yellow, made from tree bark. As part of a trade agreement with their distant cousin, my parents sent me down here to Luthadel, so I can spend some time at court."

Sazed nodded. "And how do you feel about this opportunity?"

"I am amazed and a little overwhelmed," Vin said. "People will pay attention to me because they wish to curry favor with Lord Renoux. Since I'm not familiar with the ways of court, I will be flattered by their attention. I will ingratiate myself to the court community, but I will stay quiet and out of trouble."

"Your memorization skills are admirable, Mistress," Sazed said. "This humble attendant wonders how much more successful might you be if you dedicated yourself to learning, rather than dedicating yourself to avoiding our lessons."

Vin eyed him. "Do all Terrisman 'humble attendants' give their masters as much lip as you do?"

"Only the successful ones."

Vin eyed him for a moment, then sighed. "I'm sorry, Saze. I don't mean to avoid your lessons. I just . . . the mists . . . I get distracted sometimes."

"Well, fortunately and honestly, you are very quick to learn. However, the people of the court have had their entire lives to study etiquette. Even as a rural noblewoman, there are certain things you would know."

"I know," Vin said. "I don't want to stand out."

"Oh, you can't avoid that, Mistress. A newcomer, from a distant part of the empire? Yes, they will notice you. We just don't want to make them suspicious. You must be considered, then dismissed. If you act too much like a fool, that will be suspect in and of itself."

Great.

Sazed paused, cocking his head slightly. A few seconds later, Vin heard footsteps in the hallway outside. Kelsier sauntered into the room, bearing a self-satisfied smile. He pulled off his mistcloak, then paused as he saw Vin.

"What?" she asked, sinking a little further into the chair.

"The haircut looks good," Kelsier said. "Nice job, Cosahn."

"It was nothing, Master Kelsier." Vin could hear the blush in her voice. "I just work with what I have."

"Mirror," Vin said, holding out her hand.

Cosahn handed her one. Vin held it up, and what she saw gave her pause. She looked . . . like a girl.

Cosahn had done a remarkable job of evening out the hair, and she had managed to get rid of the snags. Vin had always found that if her hair got too long, it had a tendency to stand up. Cosahn had done something about this too. Vin's hair still wasn't very long—it barely hung down over her ears—but at least it lay flat.

You don't want them to think of you as a girl, Reen's voice warned. Yet, for once, she found herself wanting to ignore that voice.

"We might actually turn you into a lady, Vin!" Kelsier said with a laugh, earning him a glare from Vin.

"First we'll have to persuade her not to scowl so often, Master Kelsier," Sazed noted.

"That's going to be hard," Kelsier said. "She's quite fond of making faces. Anyway, well done, Cosahn."

"I've still got a little bit of trimming to do, Master Kelsier," the woman said.

"By all means, continue," Kelsier said. "But I'm going to filch Sazed for a moment."

Kelsier winked at Vin, smiled at Cosahn, then he and Sazed retreated from the room—once again leaving Vin where she couldn't eavesdrop.

Kelsier peeked into the kitchen, watching Vin sit sullenly in her chair. The haircut really was good. However, his compliments had an ulterior motive—he suspected that Vin had spent far too much of her life being told that she was worthless. Perhaps if she had a bit more self-confidence, she wouldn't try to hide so much.

He let the door slide shut, turning to Sazed. The Terrisman waited, as always, with restful patience.

"How is the training going?" Kelsier asked.

"Very well, Master Kelsier," Sazed said. "She already knew some things from training she received at her brother's hands. Above that, however, she is an extremely intelligent girl—perceptive and quick to memorize. I didn't expect such skill from one who grew up in her circumstances."

"A lot of the street children are clever," Kelsier said. "The ones who aren't dead."

Sazed nodded solemnly. "She is extremely reserved, and I sense that she doesn't see the full value in my lessons. She is very obedient, but is quick to exploit mistakes or misunderstandings. If I don't tell her exactly when and where to meet, I often have to search the entire mansion for her."

Kelsier nodded. "I think it's her way of maintaining a bit of control in her life. Anyway, what I really wanted to know is whether she's ready or not."

"I'm not sure, Master Kelsier," Sazed replied. "Pure knowledge is not the equivalent of skill. I'm not certain if she has the . . . poise to imitate a noblewoman, even a young and inexperienced one. We've done practice dinners, gone over conversational etiquette, and memorized gossip. She seems skilled at it all, in a controlled situation. She's even done well sitting in on tea meetings when Renoux entertains noble guests. However, we won't really be able to tell if she can do this until we put her alone in a party full of aristocrats."

"I wish she could practice some more," Kelsier said with a shake of his head. "But every week we spend preparing increases the chances that the Ministry will discover our budding army in the caves."

"It is a test of balance, then," Sazed said. "We must wait long enough to gather the men we need, yet move soon enough to avoid discovery."

Kelsier nodded. "We can't pause for one crewmember—we'll have to find someone else to be our mole if Vin does badly. Poor girl—I wish I had time to train her better in Allomancy. We've barely covered the first four metals. I just don't have enough *time*!"

"If I might make a suggestion . . ."

"Of course, Saze."

"Send the child with some of the Misting crewmembers," Sazed said. "I hear that the man Breeze is a very accomplished Soother, and surely the others are equally skilled. Let them show Mistress Vin how to use her abilities."

Kelsier paused thoughtfully. "That's a good idea, Saze."

"But?"

Kelsier glanced back toward the door, beyond which Vin was still petulantly getting her haircut. "I'm not sure. Today, when we were training, we got into a Steelpush shoving match. The kid has to weigh less than half what I do, but she gave me a decent pummeling anyway."

"Different people have different strengths in Allomancy," Sazed said.

"Yes, but the variance isn't usually this great," Kelsier said. "Plus, it took me months and months to learn how to manipulate my Pushes and Pulls. It's not as easy as it sounds—even something as simple as Pushing yourself up onto a rooftop requires an understanding of weight, balance, and trajectory.

"But Vin . . . she seems to know all these things instinctively. True, she can only use the first four metals with any skill, but the progress she's made is amazing."

"She is a special girl."

Kelsier nodded. "She deserves more time to learn about her powers. I feel a little guilty about pulling her into our plans. She'll probably end up at a Ministry execution ceremony with the rest of us."

"But that guilt won't stop you from using her to spy on the aristocracy."

Kelsier shook his head. "No," he said quietly. "It won't. We'll need every advantage we can get. Just . . . watch over her, Saze. From now on, you'll act as Vin's steward and guardian at the functions she attends—it won't be odd for her to bring a Terrisman servant with her."

"Not at all," Sazed agreed. "In fact, it would be strange to send a girl her age to courtly functions without an escort."

Kelsier nodded. "Protect her, Saze. She might be a powerful Allomancer, but she's inexperienced. I'll feel a lot less guilty about sending her into those aristocratic dens if I know you're with her."

"I will protect her with my life, Master Kelsier. I promise you this."

Kelsier smiled, resting a thankful hand on Sazed's shoulder. "I feel pity for the man who gets in your way."

Sazed bowed his head humbly. He looked innocuous, but Kelsier knew the strength that Sazed hid. Few men, Allomancers or not, would fare well in a fight with a Keeper whose anger had been roused. That was probably why the Ministry had hunted the sect virtually to extinction.

"All right," Kelsier said. "Get back to your teaching. Lord Venture is throwing a ball at the end of the week, and—ready or not—Vin is going to be there."

It amazes me how many nations have united behind our purpose. There are still dissenters, of course—and some kingdoms, regrettably, have fallen to wars that I could not stop.

Still, this general unity is glorious, even humbling, to contemplate. I wish that the nations of mankind hadn't required such a dire threat to make them see the value of peace and cooperation.

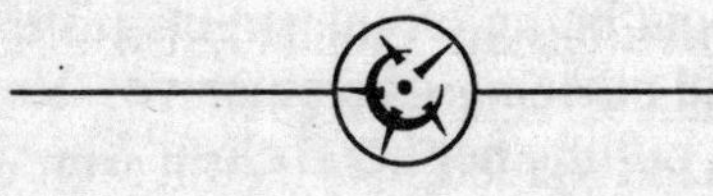

10

VIN WALKED ALONG A STREET in the Cracks—one of Luthadel's many skaa slums—with her hood up. For some reason, she found the muffled heat of a hood preferable to the oppressive red sunlight.

She walked with a slouch, eyes down, sticking near to the side of the street. The skaa she passed had similar airs of dejection. No onc looked up; no one walked with a straight back or an optimistic smile. In the slums, those things would make one look suspicious.

She'd almost forgotten how oppressive Luthadel could be. Her weeks in Fellise had accustomed her to trees and washed stone. Here, there was nothing white—no creeping aspens, no whitewashed granite. All was black.

Buildings were stained by countless, repetitive ashfalls. Air curled with smoke from the infamous Luthadel smithies and a thousand separate noble kitchens. Cobblestones, doorways, and corners were clogged with soot—the slums were rarely swept clean.

It's like . . . things are actually brighter at night than they are during the day, Vin thought, pulling her patched skaa cloak close, turning a corner. She passed beggars, huddled on corners, hands outstretched and hoping for an offering, their pleadings falling vainly on the ears of people who were themselves starving. She passed workers, walking with heads and shoulders bowed, caps or hoods pulled down to keep ash out of their eyes. Occasionally, she passed squads of Garrison town guards, walking with full armor—breastplate, cap, and black cloak—trying to look as intimidating as possible.

This last group moved through the slums, acting as the Lord Ruler's hands in an area most obligators found too distasteful to visit. The Garrisoners kicked at beggars to make certain they were truly invalids, stopped wandering workers to harass them about being on the streets instead of working, and made a general nuisance of themselves. Vin ducked down as a group passed, pulling her hood close. She was old enough that she should have been either bearing children or working in a mill, but her size often made her look younger in profile.

Either the ruse worked, or this particular squad wasn't interested in looking for ditchers, for they let her pass with barely a glance. She ducked around a corner, walking down an ash-drifted alley, and approached the soup kitchen at the end of the small street.

Like most of its kind, the kitchen was dingy and poorly maintained. In an economy where workers were rarely, if ever, given direct pay, kitchens had to be supported by the nobility. Some local lords—probably the owners of the mills and forges in the area—paid the kitchen owner to provide food for the local skaa. The workers would be given meal tokens for their time, and would be allowed a short break at midday to go eat. The central kitchen would allow the smaller businesses to avoid the costs of providing on-site meals.

Of course, since the kitchen owner was paid directly, he could pocket whatever he could save on ingredients. In Vin's experience, kitchen food was about as tasty as ashwater.

Fortunately, she hadn't come to eat. She joined the line at the door, waiting quietly as workers presented their meal chips. When her turn came, she pulled out a small wooden disk and passed it to the skaa man at the door. He accepted the chip with a smooth motion, nodding almost imperceptibly to his right.

Vin walked in the indicated direction, passing through a filthy dining room, floor scattered with tracked-in ash. As she approached the far wall, she could see a splintery wooden door set in the room's corner. A man seated by the door caught her eyes, nodded slightly, and pushed the door open. Vin passed quickly into the small room beyond.

"Vin, my dear!" Breeze said, lounging at a table near the center of the room. "Welcome! How was Fellise?"

Vin shrugged, taking a seat at the table.

"Ah," Breeze said. "I'd almost forgotten what a fascinating conversationalist you are. Wine?"

Vin shook her head.

"Well, I would certainly like some." Breeze wore one of his extravagant suits, dueling cane resting across his lap. The chamber was only lit by a single lantern, but it was far cleaner than the room outside. Of the four other men in the room, Vin recognized only one—an apprentice from Clubs's shop. The two by the door were obviously guards. The last man appeared to be a regular skaa worker—complete with blackened jacket and ashen face. His self-confident air, however, proved that he was a member of the underground. Probably one of Yeden's rebels.

Breeze held up his cup, tapping its side with his fingernail. The rebel regarded it darkly.

"Right now," Breeze said, "you're wondering if I'm using Allomancy on you. Perhaps I am, perhaps I am not. Does it matter? I'm here by your leader's invitation, and he ordered you to see that I was made comfortable. And, I assure you, a cup of wine in my hand is *absolutely* necessary for my comfort."

The skaa man waited for a moment, then snatched the cup and stalked away, grumbling under his breath about foolish costs and wasted resources.

Breeze raised an eyebrow, turning to Vin. He seemed quite pleased with himself.

"So, did you Push him?" she asked.

Breeze shook his head. "Waste of brass. Did Kelsier tell you why he asked you to come here today?"

"He told me to watch you," Vin said, a bit annoyed at being handed off to Breeze. "He said he didn't have time to train me in all the metals."

"Well," Breeze said, "let us begin, then. First, you must understand that Soothing is about more than just Allomancy. It's about the delicate and noble art of manipulation."

"Noble indeed," Vin said.

"Ah, you sound like one of *them*," Breeze said.

"Them who?"

"Them everyone else," Breeze said. "You saw how that skaa gentleman treated me? People don't like us, my dear. The idea of someone who can play with their emotions, who can 'mystically' get them to do certain things, makes them uncomfortable. What they do not realize—and what you *must* realize—is that manipulating others is something that all people do. In fact, manipulation is at the core of our social interaction."

He settled back, raising his dueling cane and gesturing with it slightly as he spoke. "Think about it. What is a man doing when he seeks the affection of a young lady? Why, he is trying to manipulate her to regard him favorably. What happens when old two friends sit down for a drink? They tell stories, trying to impress each other. Life as a human being is about posturing and influence. This isn't a bad thing—in fact, we depend upon it. These interactions teach us how to respond to others."

He paused, pointing at Vin with the cane. "The difference between Soothers and regular people is that we are aware of what we're doing. We also have a slight . . . advantage. But, is it really that much more 'powerful' than having a charismatic personality or a fine set of teeth? I think not."

Vin paused.

"Besides," Breeze added, "as I mentioned, a good Soother must be skilled far beyond his ability to use Allomancy. Allomancy can't let you read minds or even emotions—in a way, you're as blind as anyone else. You fire off pulses of emotions, targeted at a single person or in an area, and your subjects will have their emotions altered—hopefully producing the effect that you wished. However, great Soothers are those who can successfully use their eyes and instincts to know how a person is feeling *before* they get Soothed."

"What does it matter how they're feeling?" Vin said, trying to cover her annoyance. "You're just going to Soothe them anyway, right? So, when you're done, they'll feel how you want them to."

Breeze sighed, shaking his head. "What would you say if you knew I'd Soothed you on three separate occasions during our conversation?"

Vin paused. "When?" she demanded.

"Does it matter?" Breeze asked. "This is the lesson you must learn, my dear. If you can't read how someone is feeling, then you'll never have a subtle touch with emotional Allomancy. Push someone too hard, and even the most blind of skaa will realize that they're being manipulated somehow. Touch too softly, and you won't produce a noticeable effect—other, more powerful emotions will still rule your subject."

Breeze shook his head. "It's all about understanding people," he continued. "You have to read how someone is feeling, change that feeling by nudging it in the proper direction, then channel their newfound emotional state to your advantage. That, my dear, is the challenge in what we do! It is difficult, but for those who can do it well . . ."

The door opened, and the sullen skaa man returned, bearing an entire bottle of wine. He put it and a cup on the table before Breeze, then went over to stand on the other side of the room, beside peepholes looking into the dining room.

"There are vast rewards," Breeze said with a quiet smile. He winked at her, then poured some wine.

Vin wasn't certain what to think. Breeze's opinion seemed cruel. Yet, Reen had trained her well. If she didn't have power over this thing, others would gain power over her through it. She started burning copper—as Kelsier had taught her—to shield herself from further manipulations on Breeze's part.

The door opened again, and a familiar vest-wearing form tromped in. "Hey, Vin," Ham said with a friendly wave. He walked over to the table, eyeing the wine. "Breeze, you know that the rebellion doesn't have the money for that kind of thing."

"Kelsier will reimburse them," Breeze said with a dismissive wave. "I simply cannot work with a dry throat. How is the area?"

"Secure," Ham said. "But I've got Tineyes on the corners just in case. Your bolt-exit is behind that hatch in the corner."

Breeze nodded, and Ham turned, looking at Clubs's apprentice. "You Smoking back there, Cobble?"

The boy nodded.

"Good lad," Ham said. "That's everything, then. Now we just have to wait for Kell's speech."

Breeze checked his pocket watch. "He's not scheduled for another few minutes. Shall I have someone fetch you a cup?"

"I'll pass," Ham said.

Breeze shrugged, sipping his wine.

There was a moment of silence. Finally, Ham spoke. "So . . ."

"No," Breeze interrupted.

"But—"

"Whatever it is, we don't want to hear about it."

Ham gave the Soother a flat stare. "You can't Push me into complacence, Breeze."

Breeze rolled his eyes, taking a drink.

"What?" Vin asked. "What were you going to say?"

"Don't encourage him, my dear," Breeze said.

Vin frowned. She glanced at Ham, who smiled.

Breeze sighed. "Just leave me out of it. I'm not in the mood for one of Ham's inane debates."

"Ignore him," Ham said eagerly, pulling his chair a little bit closer to Vin. "So, I've been wondering. By overthrowing the Final Empire are we doing something good, or are we doing something bad?"

Vin paused. "Does it matter?"

Ham looked taken aback, but Breeze chuckled. "Well answered," the Soother said.

Ham glared at Breeze, then turned back to Vin. "Of course it matters."

"Well," Vin said, "I guess we're doing something good. The Final Empire has oppressed the skaa for centuries."

"Right," Ham said. "But, there's a problem. The Lord Ruler is God, right?"

Vin shrugged. "Does it matter?"

Ham glared at her.

She rolled her eyes. "All right. The Ministry claims that he is God."

"Actually," Breeze noted, "the Lord Ruler is only a *piece* of God. He is the Sliver of Infinity—not omniscient or omnipresent, but an independent section of a consciousness that *is*."

Ham sighed. "I thought you didn't want to be involved."

"Just making certain everyone has their facts correct," Breeze said lightly.

"Anyway," Ham said. "God is the creator of all things, right? He is the force that dictates the laws of the universe, and is therefore the ultimate source of ethics. He is absolute morality."

Vin blinked.

"You see the dilemma?" Ham asked.

"I see an idiot," Breeze mumbled.

"I'm confused," Vin said. "What's the problem?"

"We claim to be doing good," Ham said. "But, the Lord Ruler—as God—*defines* what is good. So, by opposing him we're actually evil. But, since he's doing the wrong thing, does evil actually count as good in this case?"

Vin frowned.

"Well?" Ham asked.

"I think you gave me a headache," Vin said.

"I warned you," Breeze noted.

Ham sighed. "But, don't you think it's worth thinking about?"

"I'm not sure."

"I am," Breeze said.

Ham shook his head. "No one around here likes to have decent, intelligent discussions."

The skaa rebel in the corner suddenly perked up. "Kelsier's here!"

Ham raised an eyebrow, then stood. "I should go watch the perimeter. Think about that question, Vin."

"All right . . ." Vin said as Ham left.

"Over here, Vin," Breeze said, rising. "There are peepholes on the wall for us. Be a dear and bring my chair over, would you?"

Breeze didn't look back to see if she did as requested. She paused, uncertain. With her copper on, he couldn't Soothe her, but . . . Eventually, she sighed and carried both chairs over to the side of the room. Breeze slid back a long, thin slat in the wall, revealing a view of the dining room.

A group of dirtied skaa men sat around tables, wearing brown work coats or ragged cloaks. They were a dark group, with ash-stained skin and slumped postures. However, their presence at the meeting meant that they were willing to listen. Yeden sat at a table near the front of the room, wearing his usual patched worker's coat, his curly hair cut short during Vin's absence.

Vin had expected some kind of grand entrance from Kelsier. Instead, however, he simply walked quietly out of the kitchen. He paused by Yeden's table, smiling and speaking quietly with the man for a moment, then he stepped up before the seated workers.

Vin had never seen him in such mundane clothing before. He wore a brown skaa coat and tan trousers, like many of the audience. Kelsier's outfit, however, was clean. No soot stained the cloth, and while it was of the same rough material that skaa commonly used, it bore no patches or tears. The difference was stark enough, Vin decided—if he'd come in a suit, it would have been too much.

He put his arms behind his back, and slowly the crowd of workers quieted. Vin frowned, watching through the peep slit, wondering at Kelsier's ability to quiet a room of hungry men by simply standing before them. Was he using Allomancy, perhaps? Yet, even with her copper on, she felt a . . . presence from him.

Once the room fell quiet, Kelsier began to speak. "You've probably all heard of me, by now," he said. "And, you wouldn't be here if you weren't at least a little bit sympathetic to my cause."

Beside Vin, Breeze sipped his drink. "Soothing and Rioting aren't like other kinds of Allomancy," he said quietly. "With most metals, Pushing and Pulling have opposite effects. With emotions, however, you can often produce the same result regardless of whether you Soothe or Riot.

"This doesn't hold for extreme emotional states—complete emotionlessness or utter passion. However, in most cases, it doesn't matter which power you use. People are not like solid bricks of metal—at any given time, they will have a dozen different emotions churning within them. An experienced Soother can dampen everything but the emotion he wants to remain dominant."

Breeze turned slightly. "Rudd, send in the blue server, please."

One of the guards nodded, cracking the door and whispering something to the man outside. A moment later, Vin saw a serving girl wearing a faded blue dress move through the crowd, filling drinks.

"My Soothers are mixed with the crowd," Breeze said, his voice growing distracted. "The serving girls are a sign, telling my men which emotions to Soothe away. They will work, just as I do. . . ." He trailed off, concentrating as he looked into the crowd.

"Fatigue . . ." he whispered. "That's not a necessary emotion right now. Hunger . . . distracting. Suspicion . . . definitely not helpful. Yes, and as the Soothers work, the Rioters enflame the emotions we want the crowd to be feeling. Curiosity . . . that's what they need now. Yes, listen to Kelsier. You've heard legends and stories. See the man for yourself, and be impressed."

"I know why you came today," Kelsier said quietly. He spoke without much of the flamboyance Vin associated with the man, his tone quiet, but direct. "Twelve-hour days in a mill, mine, or forge. Beatings, lack of pay, poor food. And, for what? So that you can return to your tenements at the day's end to find another tragedy? A friend, slain by an uncaring taskmaster. A daughter, taken to be some nobleman's plaything. A brother, dead at the hand of a passing lord who was having an unpleasant day."

"Yes," Breeze whispered. "Good. Red, Rudd. Send in the girl in light red."

Another serving girl entered the room.

"Passion and anger," Breeze said, his voice almost a mumble. "But just a bit. Just a nudge—a reminder."

Curious, Vin extinguished her copper for a moment, burning bronze instead, trying to sense Breeze's use of Allomancy. No pulses came from him.

Of course, she thought. *I forgot about Clubs's apprentice—he'd keep me from sensing any Allomantic pulses.* She turned her copper back on.

Kelsier continued to speak. "My friends, you're not alone in your tragedy. There are millions, just like you. And they need you. I've not come to beg—we've had enough of that in our lives. I simply ask you to think. Where would you rather your energy be spent? On forging the Lord Ruler's weapons? Or, on something more valuable?"

He's not mentioning our troops, Vin thought. *Or even what those who join with him are going to do. He doesn't want the workers to know details. Probably a good idea—those he recruits can be sent to the army, and the rest won't be able to give away specific information.*

"You know why I am here," Kelsier said. "You know my friend, Yeden, and what he represents. Every skaa in the city knows about the rebellion. Perhaps you've considered joining it. Most of you will not—most of you will go back to your soot-stained mills, to your burning forges, to your dying homes. You'll go because this terrible life is familiar. But some of you . . . some of you will come with me. And those are the men who will be remembered in the years to come. Remembered for having done something grand."

Many of the workers shared glances, though some just stared at their half-empty soup bowls. Finally, someone near the back of the room spoke. "You're a fool," the man said. "The Lord Ruler will kill you. You don't rebel against God in his *own city.*"

The room fell silent. Tense. Vin sat up as Breeze whispered to himself.

In the room, Kelsier stood quietly for a moment. Finally, he reached up and pulled back the sleeves on his jacket, revealing the crisscrossed scars on his arms. "The Lord Ruler is not our god," he said quietly. "And he cannot kill me. He tried, but he failed. For I am the thing that he can never kill."

With that, Kelsier turned, walking from the room the way he had come.

"Hum," Breeze said, "well, that was a little dramatic. Rudd, bring back the red and send out the brown."

A serving woman in brown walked into the crowd.

"Amazement," Breeze said. "And, yes, pride. Soothe the anger, for now. . . ."

The crowd sat quietly for a moment, the dining room eerily motionless. Finally, Yeden stood up to speak and give some further encouragement, as well as an explanation of what the men should do, should they wish to hear more. As he talked, the men returned to their meals.

"Green, Rudd," Breeze said. "Hum, yes. Let's make you all thoughtful, and give you a nudge of loyalty. We wouldn't want anyone to run to the obligators, would we? Kell's covered his tracks quite well, but the less the authorities hear, the better, eh? Oh, and what about you, Yeden? You're a bit too nervous. Let's Soothe that, take away your worries. Leave only that passion of yours—hopefully, it will be enough to cover up that stupid tone in your voice."

Vin continued to watch. Now that Kelsier had gone, she found it easier to focus on the crowd's reactions, and on Breeze's work. As Yeden spoke, the workers outside seemed to react exactly according to Breeze's mumbled instructions. Yeden, too, showed effects of the Soothing: He grew more comfortable, his voice more confident, as he spoke.

Curious, Vin let her copper drop again. She concentrated, seeing if she could sense Breeze's touch on her emotions; she would be included in his general Allomantic projections. He didn't have time to pick and choose individuals, except maybe Yeden. It was very, very difficult to sense. Yet, as Breeze sat mumbling to himself, she began to feel the exact emotions he described.

Vin couldn't help but be impressed. The few times that Kelsier had used Allomancy on her emotions, his touch has been like a sudden, blunt punch to the face. He had strength, but very little subtlety.

Breeze's touch was incredibly delicate. He Soothed certain emotions, dampening them while leaving others unaffected. Vin thought she could sense his men Rioting on her emotions, too, but these touches weren't nearly as subtle as Breeze's. She left her copper off, watching for touches on her emotions as Yeden continued his speech. He explained that the men who joined with them would have to leave family and friends for a time—as long as a year—but would be fed well during that time.

Vin felt her respect for Breeze continue to rise. Suddenly, she didn't feel so annoyed with Kelsier for handing her off. Breeze could only do one thing, but he obviously had a great deal of practice at it. Kelsier, as a Mistborn, had to learn all of the Allomantic skills; it made sense that he wouldn't be as focused in any one power.

I need to make certain he sends me to learn from the others, Vin thought. *They'll be masters at their own powers.*

Vin turned her attention back to the dining room as Yeden wrapped up. "You heard Kelsier, the Survivor of Hathsin," he said. "The rumors about him are true—he's given up his thieving ways, and turned his considerable attention toward working for the skaa rebellion! Men, we are preparing for something grand. Something that may, indeed, end up being our last struggle against the Final Empire. Join with us. Join with your brothers. Join with the Survivor himself!"

The dining room fell silent.

"Bright red," Breeze said. "I want those men to leave feeling passionate about what they've heard."

"The emotions will fade, won't they?" Vin said as a red-clothed serving girl entered the crowd.

"Yes," Breeze said, sitting back and sliding the panel closed. "But memories stay. If people associate strong emotion with an event, they'll remember it better."

A few moments later, Ham entered through the back door. "That went well. The men are leaving invigorated, and a number of them are staying behind. We'll have a good set of volunteers to send off to the caves."

Breeze shook his head. "It's not enough. Dox takes a few days to organize each of these meetings, and we only get about twenty men from each one. At this rate, we'll never hit ten thousand in time."

"You think we need more meetings?" Ham asked. "That's going to be tough—we have to be very careful with these things, so only those who can be reasonably trusted are invited."

Breeze sat for a moment. Finally, he downed the rest of his

wine. "I don't know—but we'll have to think of something. For now, let's return to the shop. I believe Kelsier wishes to hold a progress meeting this evening."

Kelsier looked to the west. The afternoon sun was a poisonous red, shining angrily through a sky of smoke. Just below it, Kelsier could see the silhouetted tip of a dark peak. Tyrian, closest of the Ashmounts.

He stood atop Clubs's flat-roofed shop, listening to workers returning home on the streets below. A flat roof meant having to shovel off ash occasionally, which was why most skaa buildings were peaked, but in Kelsier's opinion the view was often worth a bit of trouble.

Below him, the skaa workers trudged in despondent ranks, their passing kicking up a small cloud of ash. Kelsier turned away from them, looking toward the northern horizon . . . toward the Pits of Hathsin.

Where does it go? he thought. *The atium reaches the city, but then disappears. It isn't the Ministry—we've watched them—and no skaa hands touch the metal. We assume it goes into the treasury. We hope it does, at least.*

While burning atium, a Mistborn was virtually unstoppable, which was part of why it was so valuable. But, his plan was about more than just wealth. He knew how much atium was harvested at the pits, and Dockson had researched the amounts that the Lord Ruler doled out—at exorbitant prices—to the nobility. Barely a tenth of what was mined eventually found its way into noble hands.

Ninety percent of the atium produced in the world had been stockpiled, year after year, for a thousand years. With that much of the metal, Kelsier's team could intimidate even the most powerful of the noble houses. Yeden's plan to hold the palace probably seemed futile to many—indeed, on its own, it was doomed to fail. However, Kelsier's other plans . . .

Kelsier glanced down at the small, whitish bar in his hand. The Eleventh Metal. He knew the rumors about it—he'd started them. Now, he just had to make good on them.

He sighed, turning eyes east, toward Kredik Shaw, the Lord Ruler's palace. The name was Terris; it meant "The Hill of a Thousand Spires." Appropriate, since the imperial palace resembled a patch of enormous black spears thrust into the ground. Some of the spires twisted, others were straight. Some were thick towers, others were thin and needlelike. They varied in height, but each one was tall. And each one ended in a point.

Kredik Shaw. That's where it had ended three years before. And he needed to go back.

The trapdoor opened, and a figure climbed onto the roof. Kelsier turned with a raised eyebrow as Sazed brushed off his robe, then approached in his characteristically respectful posture. Even a rebellious Terrisman maintained the form of his training.

"Master Kelsier," Sazed said with a bow.

Kelsier nodded, and Sazed stepped up beside him, looking toward the imperial palace. "Ah," he said to himself, as if understanding Kelsier's thoughts.

Kelsier smiled. Sazed had been a valuable find indeed. Keepers were necessarily secretive, for the Lord Ruler had hunted them practically since the Day of Ascension itself. Some legends claimed that the Ruler's complete subjugation of the Terris people—including the breeding and stewardship programs—was simply an outgrowth of his hatred for Keepers.

"I wonder what he would think if he knew a Keeper was in Luthadel," Kelsier said, "barely a short walk from the palace itself."

"Let us hope we never find out, Master Kelsier," Sazed said.

"I appreciate your willingness to come here to the city, Saze. I know it's a risk."

"This is a good work," Sazed said. "And this plan is dangerous for all involved. Indeed, simply living is dangerous for me, I think. It is not healthy to belong to a sect that the Lord Ruler himself fears."

"Fears?" Kelsier asked, turning to look up at Sazed. Despite Kelsier's above-average height, the Terrisman was still a good head taller. "I'm not sure if he fears anything, Saze."

"He fears the Keepers," Sazed said. "Definitely and inexplicably. Perhaps it is because of our powers. We are not Allomancers, but . . . something else. Something unknown to him."

Kelsier nodded, turning back toward the city. He had so many plans, so much work to do—and at the core of it all were the skaa. The poor, humble, defeated skaa.

"Tell me about another one, Saze," Kelsier said. "One with power."

"Power?" Sazed asked. "That is a relative term when applied to religion, I think. Perhaps you would like to hear of Jaism. Its followers were quite faithful and devout."

"Tell me about them."

"Jaism was founded by a single man," Sazed said. "His true name is lost, though his followers simply called him 'the Ja.' He was murdered by a local king for preaching discord—something he was apparently very good at—but that only made his following larger.

"The Jaists thought that they earned happiness proportional to their overt devotion, and were known for frequent and fervent professions of faith. Apparently, speaking with a Jaist could be frustrating, since they tended to end nearly every sentence with 'Praise the Ja.' "

"That's nice, Saze," Kelsier said. "But power is more than just words."

"Oh, quite indeed," Sazed agreed. "The Jaists were strong in their faith. Legends say that the Ministry had to wipe them out completely, since not one Jaist would accept the Lord Ruler as God. They didn't last long past the Ascension, but only because they were so blatant that they were easy to hunt down and kill."

Kelsier nodded, then he smiled, eyeing Sazed. "You didn't ask me if I wanted to convert."

"My apologies, Master Kelsier," Sazed said, "but the religion does not suit you, I think. It has a level of brashness that you might find appealing, but you would find the theology simplistic."

"You're getting to know me too well," Kelsier said, still regarding the city. "In the end, after kingdoms and armies had fallen, the religions were still fighting, weren't they?"

"Indeed," Sazed said. "Some of the more resilient religions lasted all the way until the fifth century."

"What made them so strong?" Kelsier said. "How did they do it, Saze? What gave these theologies such power over people?"

"It wasn't any one thing, I think," Sazed said. "Some were strong through honest faith, others because of the hope they promised. Others were coercive."

"But they all had passion," Kelsier said.

"Yes, Master Kelsier," Sazed said with a nod. "That is a quite true statement."

"That's what we've lost," Kelsier said, looking over the city with its hundreds of thousands, barely a handful of whom would dare fight. "They don't have faith in the Lord Ruler, they simply fear him. They don't have anything left to believe in."

"What do *you* believe in, if I may ask, Master Kelsier?"

Kelsier raised an eyebrow. "I'm not exactly sure yet," he admitted. "But overthrowing the Final Empire seems like a good start. Are there any religions on your list that include the slaughter of noblemen as a holy duty?"

Sazed frowned disapprovingly. "I do not believe so, Master Kelsier."

"Maybe I should found one," Kelsier said with an idle smile. "Anyway, have Breeze and Vin returned yet?"

"They arrived just before I came up here."

"Good," Kelsier said with a nod. "Tell them I'll be down in a moment."

Vin sat in her overstuffed chair in the conference room, legs tucked beneath her, trying to study Marsh out of the corner of her eye.

He looked so much like Kelsier. He was just . . . stern. He wasn't angry, nor was he grumpy like Clubs. He just wasn't happy. He sat in his chair, a neutral expression on his face.

The others had all arrived except for Kelsier, and they were chatting quietly amongst themselves. Vin caught Lestibournes's eye and waved him over. The teenage boy approached and crouched beside her chair.

"Marsh," Vin whispered beneath the general hum of the room. "Is that a nickname?"

"Notting without the call of his parents."

Vin paused, trying to decipher the boy's eastern dialect. "Not a nickname, then?"

Lestibournes shook his head. "He wasing one though."

"What was it?"

"Ironeyes. Others stopped using it. Too calling close to an iron in the real eyes, eh? Inquisitor."

Vin glanced at Marsh again. His expression was hard, his eyes unwavering, almost like they *were* made of iron. She could see why people would stop using the nickname; even referring to a Steel Inquisitor made her shiver.

"Thanks."

Lestibournes smiled. He was an earnest boy. Strange, intense, and jumpy—but earnest. He retreated to his stool as Kelsier finally arrived.

"All right, crew," he said. "What've we got?"

"Besides the bad news?" Breeze asked.

"Let's hear it."

"It's been twelve weeks, and we've gathered under two thousand men," Ham said. "Even with the numbers the rebellion already has, we're going to fall short."

"Dox?" Kelsier asked. "Can we get more meetings?"

"Probably," Dockson said from his seat beside a table stacked with ledgers.

"Are you sure you want to take that risk, Kelsier?" Yeden asked. His attitude had improved during the last few weeks—especially once Kelsier's recruits had begun to file in. As Reen had always said, results made quick friends.

"We're already in danger," Yeden continued. "Rumors are all over the underground. If we make any more of a stir, the Ministry is going to realize that something major is happening."

"He's probably right, Kell," Dockson said. "Besides, there are only so many skaa willing to listen. Luthadel is big, true, but our movement here is limited."

"All right," Kelsier said. "So, we'll start working the other towns in the area. Breeze, can you split your crew into two effective groups?"

"I suppose," Breeze said hesitantly.

"We can have one team work in Luthadel and the other work in surrounding towns. I can probably make it to all of the meetings, assuming we organize them so they don't happen at the same time."

"That many meetings will expose us even more," Yeden said.

"And that, by the way, brings up another problem," Ham said. "Weren't we supposed to be working on infiltrating the Ministry's ranks?"

"Well?" Kelsier asked, turning to Marsh.

Marsh shook his head. "The Ministry is tight—I need more time."

"It's not going to happen," Clubs grumbled. "Rebellion's already tried it."

Yeden nodded. "We've tried to get spies into the Inner Ministries a dozen times. It's impossible."

The room fell silent.

"I have an idea," Vin said quietly.

Kelsier raised an eyebrow.

"Camon," she said. "He was working on a job before you recruited me. Actually, it was the job that got us spotted by the obligators. The core of that plan was organized by another thief, a crewleader named Theron. He was setting up a fake canal convoy to carry Ministry funds to Luthadel."

"And?" Breeze asked.

"Those same canal boats would have brought new Ministry acolytes to Luthadel for the final part of their training. Theron has a contact along the route, a lesser obligator who was open to bribes. Maybe we could get him to add an 'acolyte' to the group from his local chapter."

Kelsier nodded thoughtfully. "It's worth looking into."

Dockson scribbled something on a sheet with his fountain pen. "I'll contact Theron and see if his informant is still viable."

"How are our resources coming?" Kelsier asked.

Dockson shrugged. "Ham found us two ex-soldier instructors. The weapons, however . . . well, Renoux and I are making contacts and initiating deals, but we can't move very quickly. Fortunately, when the weapons come, they should come in bulk."

Kelsier nodded. "That's everything, right?"

Breeze cleared his throat. "I've . . . been hearing a lot of rumors on the streets, Kelsier," he said. "The people are talking about this Eleventh Metal of yours."

"Good," Kelsier said.

"Aren't you worried that the Lord Ruler will hear? If he has forewarning of what you're going to do, it will be much more difficult to . . . resist him."

He didn't say "kill," Vin thought. *They don't think that Kelsier can do it.*

Kelsier just smiled. "Don't worry about the Lord Ruler—I've got things under control. In fact, I intend to pay the Lord Ruler a personal visit sometime during the next few days."

"*Visit?*" Yeden asked uncomfortably. "You're going to visit the Lord Ruler? Are you insa . . ." Yeden trailed off, then glanced at the rest of the room. "Right. I forgot."

"He's catching on," Dockson noted.

Heavy footsteps sounded in the hallway, and one of Ham's guards entered a moment later. He made his way to Ham's chair and whispered a brief message.

Ham frowned.

"What?" Kelsier asked.

"An incident," Ham said.

"Incident?" Dockson asked. "What kind of incident?"

"You know that lair we met in a few weeks back?" Ham said. "The one where Kell first introduced his plan?"

Camon's lair, Vin thought, growing apprehensive.

"Well," Ham said, "apparently the Ministry found it."

It seems Rashek represents a growing faction in Terris culture. A large number of the youths think that their unusual powers should be used for more than just fieldwork, husbandry, and stonecarving. They are rowdy, even violent—far different from the quiet, discerning Terris philosophers and holy men that I have known.

They will have to be watched carefully, these Terrismen. They could be very dangerous, if given the opportunity and the motivation.

11

KELSIER PAUSED IN THE DOORWAY, blocking Vin's view. She stooped down, trying to peek past him into the lair, but too many people were in the way. She could only tell that the door hung at an angle, splintered, the upper hinge torn free.

Kelsier stood for a long moment. Finally, he turned, looking past Dockson toward her. "Ham is right, Vin. You may not want to see this."

Vin stood where she was, looking at him resolutely. Finally, Kelsier sighed, stepping into the room. Dockson followed, and Vin could finally see what they had been blocking.

The floor was scattered with corpses, their twisted limbs shadowed and haunting in the light of Dockson's solitary lantern. They weren't rotting yet—the attack had happened only that morning—but there was still a smell of death about the room. The scent of blood drying slowly, the scent of misery and of terror.

Vin remained in the doorway. She'd seen death before—seen it often, on the streets. Knifings in alleys. Beatings in lairs. Children dead of starvation. She had once seen an old woman's neck snapped by the backhand of an annoyed lord.

The body had lain in the street for three days before a skaa corpse crew had finally come for it.

Yet, none of those incidents had the same air of intentional butchery that she saw in Camon's lair. These men hadn't simply been killed, they had been torn apart. Limbs lay separated from torsos. Broken chairs and tables impaled chests. There were only a few patches of floor that were not covered in sticky, dark blood.

Kelsier glanced at her, obviously expecting some sort of reaction. She stood, looking over the death, feeling . . . numb. What should her reaction be? These were the men who had mistreated her, stolen from her, beaten her. And yet, these were the men who had sheltered her, included her, and fed her when others might have simply given her to the whoremasters.

Reen probably would have berated her for the traitorous sadness she felt at the sight. Of course, he had always been angry when—as a child—she'd cried as they left one town for another, not wanting to leave the people she'd grown to know, no matter how cruel or indifferent they were. Apparently, she hadn't quite gotten over that weakness. She stepped into the room, not shedding any tears for these men, yet at the same time wishing that they had not come to such an end.

In addition, the gore itself was disturbing. She tried to force herself to maintain a stiff face in front of the others, but she found herself cringing occasionally, glancing away from mangled corpses. The ones who had performed the attack had been quite . . . thorough.

This seems extreme, even for the Ministry, she thought. *What kind of person would do something like this?*

"Inquisitor," Dockson said quietly, kneeling by a corpse.

Kelsier nodded. Behind Vin, Sazed stepped into the room, careful to keep his robes clear of the blood. Vin turned toward the Terrisman, letting his actions distract her from a particularly grisly corpse. Kelsier was a Mistborn, and Dockson was supposedly a capable warrior. Ham and his men were securing the area. However, others—Breeze, Yeden, and Clubs—had stayed behind. The area was too dangerous. Kelsier had even resisted Vin's desire to come.

Yet, he had brought Sazed without apparent hesitation. The

move, subtle though it was, made Vin regard the steward with a new curiosity. Why would it be too dangerous for Mistings, yet safe enough for a Terrisman steward? Was Sazed a warrior? How would he have learned to fight? Terrismen were supposedly raised from birth by very careful trainers.

Sazed's smooth step and calm face gave her few clues. He didn't appear shocked by the carnage, however.

Interesting, Vin thought, picking her way through shattered furniture, stepping clear of blood pools, making her way to Kelsier's side. He crouched beside a pair of corpses. One, Vin noticed in a moment of shock, had been Ulef. The boy's face was contorted and pained, the front of his chest a mass of broken bones and ripped flesh—as if someone had forcibly torn the rib cage apart with his hands. Vin shivered, looking away.

"This isn't good," Kelsier said quietly. "Steel Inquisitors don't generally bother with simple thieving crews. Usually, the obligators would just come down with their troops and take everyone captive, then use them to make a good show on an execution day. An Inquisitor would only get involved if it had a special interest in the crew."

"You think . . ." Vin said. "You think it might be the same one as before?"

Kelsier nodded. "There are only about twenty Steel Inquisitors in the whole of the Final Empire, and half of them are out of Luthadel at any given time. I find it too much of a coincidence that you would catch one's interest, escape, and then have your old lair get hit."

Vin stood quietly, forcing herself to look down at Ulef's body and confront her sorrow. He had betrayed her in the end, but for a time he had almost been a friend.

"So," she said quietly, "the Inquisitor still has my scent?"

Kelsier nodded, standing.

"Then this is my fault," Vin said. "Ulef and the others . . ."

"It was Camon's fault," Kelsier said firmly. "He's the one who tried to scam an obligator." He paused, then looked over at her. "You going to be all right?"

Vin looked up from Ulef's mangled corpse, trying to remain strong. She shrugged. "None of them were my friends."

"That's kind of coldhearted, Vin."

"I know," she said with a quiet nod.

Kelsier regarded her for a moment, then crossed the room to speak with Dockson.

Vin looked back at Ulef's wounds. They looked like the work of some crazed animal, not a single man.

The Inquisitor must have had help, Vin told herself. *There is no way one person, even an Inquisitor, could have done all this.* There was a pileup of bodies near the bolt exit, but a quick count told her that most—if not all—of the crew was accounted for. One man couldn't have gotten to all of them quickly enough . . . could he have?

There are a lot of things we don't know about the Inquisitors, Kelsier had told her. *They don't quite follow the normal rules.*

Vin shivered again.

Footsteps sounded on the stairs, and Vin grew tense, crouching and preparing to run.

Ham's familiar figure appeared in the stairwell. "Area's secure," he said, holding up a second lantern. "No sign of obligators or Garrisoners."

"That's their style," Kelsier said. "They want the massacre to be discovered—they left the dead as a sign."

The room fell silent save for a low mumbling from Sazed, who stood at the far left side of the room. Vin picked her way over to him, listening to the rhythmic cadence of his voice. Eventually, he stopped speaking, then bowed his head and closed his eyes.

"What was that?" Vin asked as he looked up again.

"A prayer," Sazed said. "A death chant of the Cazzi. It is meant to awaken the spirits of the dead and entice them free from their flesh so that they may return to the mountain of souls." He glanced at her. "I can teach you of the religion, if you wish, Mistress. The Cazzi were an interesting people—very familiar with death."

Vin shook her head. "Not right now. You said their prayer—is this the religion you believe in, then?"

"I believe in them all."

Vin frowned. "None of them contradict each other?"

Sazed smiled. "Oh, often and frequently they do. But, I respect the truths behind them all—and I believe in the need for each one to be remembered."

"Then, how did you decide which religion's prayer to use?" Vin asked.

"It just seemed . . . appropriate," Sazed said quietly, regarding the scene of shadowed death.

"Kell," Dockson called from the back of the room. "Come look at this."

Kelsier moved to join him, as did Vin. Dockson stood by the long corridor-like chamber that had been her crew's sleeping quarters. Vin poked her head inside, expecting to find a scene similar to the one in the common room. Instead, there was only a single corpse tied to a chair. In the weak light she could barely make out that his eyes had been gouged out.

Kelsier stood quietly for a moment. "That's the man I put in charge."

"Milev," Vin said with a nod. "What about him?"

"He was killed slowly," Kelsier said. "Look at the amount of blood on the floor, the way his limbs are twisted. He had time to scream and struggle."

"Torture," Dockson said, nodding.

Vin felt a chill. She glanced up at Kelsier.

"Shall we move our base?" Ham asked.

Kelsier slowly shook his head. "When Clubs came to this lair, he would have worn a disguise to and from the meeting, hiding his limp. It's his job as a Smoker to make certain that you can't find him just by asking around on the street. None of the people in this crew could have betrayed us—we should still be safe."

No one spoke the obvious. *The Inquisitor shouldn't have been able to find this lair either.*

Kelsier stepped back into the main room, pulling Dockson aside and speaking to him in a quiet voice. Vin edged closer, trying to hear what they were saying, but Sazed placed a restraining hand on her shoulder.

"Mistress Vin," he said disapprovingly, "if Master Kelsier wanted us to hear what he was saying, would he not speak in a louder voice?"

Vin shot the Terrisman an angry glance. Then she reached inside and burned tin.

The sudden stench of blood almost staggered her. She could hear Sazed's breathing. The room was no longer dark—in fact, the brilliant light of two lanterns made her eyes water. She became aware of the stuffy, unventilated air.

And she could hear, quite distinctly, Dockson's voice.

". . . went to check on him a couple times, like you asked. You'll find him three streets west of the Fourwell Crossroads."

Kelsier nodded. "Ham," he said in a loud voice, causing Vin to jump.

Sazed looked down at her with disapproving eyes.

He knows something of Allomancy, Vin thought, reading the man's expression. *He guessed what I was doing.*

"Yes, Kell?" Ham said, peeking out of the back room.

"Take the others back to the shop," Kelsier said. "And be careful."

"Of course," Ham promised.

Vin eyed Kelsier, then resentfully allowed herself to be ushered from the lair with Sazed and Dockson.

I should have taken the carriage, Kelsier thought, frustrated by his slow pace. *The others could have walked back from Camon's lair.*

He itched to burn steel and begin jumping toward his destination. Unfortunately, it was very difficult to remain inconspicuous when flying through the city during the full light of day.

Kelsier adjusted his hat and continued walking. A nobleman pedestrian was not an irregular sight, especially in the commercial district, where more fortunate skaa and less fortunate noblemen mixed on the streets—though each group did its best to ignore the other.

Patience. Speed doesn't matter. If they know about him, he's already dead.

Kelsier entered a large crossroad square. Four wells sat in its corners, and a massive copper fountain—its green skin caked and blackened by soot—dominated the square's center.

The statue depicted the Lord Ruler, standing dramatically in cloak and armor, a formless representation of the Deepness dead in the water at his feet.

Kelsier passed the fountain, its waters flaked from a recent ashfall. Skaa beggars called out from the streetsides, their pitiful voices walking a fine line between audibility and annoyance. The Lord Ruler barely suffered them; only skaa with severe disfigurements were allowed to beg. Their pitiful life, however, was not something even plantation skaa would envy.

Kelsier tossed them a few clips, not caring that doing so made him stand out, and continued to walk. Three streets over, he found a much smaller crossroads. It was also rimmed by beggars, but no fine fountain splashed the center of this intersection, nor did the corners contain wells to draw traffic.

The beggars here were even more pathetic—these were the sorry individuals who were too wretched to fight themselves a spot in a major square. Malnourished children and age-withered adults called out with apprehensive voices; men missing two or more limbs huddled in corners, their soot-stained forms almost invisible in the shadows.

Kelsier reached reflexively for his coin purse. *Stay on track,* he told himself. *You can't save them all, not with coins. There will be time for these once the Final Empire is gone.*

Ignoring the piteous cries—which became louder once the beggars realized he was watching them—Kelsier studied each face in turn. He had only seen Camon briefly, but he thought that he'd recognize the man. However, none of the faces looked right, and none of the beggars had Camon's girth, which should have still been noticeable despite weeks of starvation.

He's not here, Kelsier thought with dissatisfaction. Kelsier's order—given to Milev, the new crewleader—that Camon be made a beggar had been carried out. Dockson had checked on Camon to make certain.

Camon's absence in the square could simply mean that he'd gained a better spot. It could also mean that the Ministry had found him. Kelsier stood quietly for a moment, listening to the beggars' haunted moanings. A few flakes of ash began to float down from the sky.

Something was wrong. There weren't any beggars near the

north corner of the intersection. Kelsier burned tin, and smelled blood on the air.

He kicked off his shoes, then pulled his belt free. His cloak clasp went next, the fine garment dropping to the cobblestones. That done, the only metal remaining on his body was in his coin pouch. He dumped a few coins into his hand, then carefully made his way forward, leaving his discarded garments for the beggars.

The smell of death grew stronger, but he didn't hear anything except scrambling beggars behind him. He edged onto the northern street, immediately noticing a thin alleyway to his left. Taking a breath, he flared pewter and ducked inside.

The thin, dark alley was clogged with refuse and ash. No one waited for him—at least, no one living.

Camon, crewleader turned beggar, hung quietly from a rope tied far above. His corpse spun leisurely in the breeze, ash falling lightly around it. He hadn't been hanged in the conventional fashion—the rope had been tied to a hook, then rammed down his throat. The bloodied end of the hook jutted from his skin below the chin, and he swung with head tipped back, rope running out of his mouth. His hands were tied, his still plump body showing signs of torture.

This isn't good.

A foot scraped the cobblestones behind, and Kelsier spun, flaring steel and spraying forth a handful of coins.

With a girlish yelp, a small figure ducked to the ground, coins deflected as she burned steel.

"Vin?" Kelsier said. He cursed, reaching out and yanking her into the alleyway. He glanced around the corner, watching the beggars perk up as they heard coins hit the cobblestones.

"What are you doing here?" he demanded, turning back. Vin wore the same brown overalls and gray shirt she had before, though she at least had the sense to wear a nondescript cloak with the hood up.

"I wanted to see what you were doing," she said, cringing slightly before his anger.

"This could have been dangerous!" Kelsier said. "What were you thinking?"

Vin cowered further.

Kelsier calmed himself. *You can't blame her for being curious,* he thought as a few brave beggars scuttled in the street after the coins. *She's just—*

Kelsier froze. It was so subtle he almost missed it. Vin was Soothing his emotions.

He glanced down. The girl was obviously trying to make herself invisible against the corner of the wall. She seemed so timid, yet he caught a hidden glimmer of determination in her eyes. This child had made an art of making herself seem harmless.

So subtle! Kelsier thought. *How did she get so good so quickly?*

"You don't have to use Allomancy, Vin," Kelsier said softly. "I'm not going to hurt you. You know that."

She flushed. "I didn't mean it . . . it's just habit. Even still."

"It's all right," Kelsier said, laying a hand on her shoulder. "Just remember—no matter what Breeze says, it's bad manners to touch the emotions of your friends. Plus, the noblemen consider it an insult to use Allomancy in formal settings. Those reflexes will get you into trouble if you don't learn to control them."

She nodded, rising to study Camon. Kelsier expected her to turn away in disgust, but she just stood quietly, a look of grim satisfaction on her face.

No, this one isn't weak, Kelsier thought. *No matter what she'd have you believe.*

"They tortured him here?" she asked. "Out in the open?"

Kelsier nodded, imagining the screams reverberating out to the uncomfortable beggars. The Ministry liked to be very visible with its punishments.

"Why the hook?" Vin asked.

"It's a ritual killing reserved for the most reprehensible of sinners: people who misuse Allomancy."

Vin frowned. "Camon was an Allomancer?"

Kelsier shook his head. "He must have admitted to something heinous during his torture." Kelsier glanced at Vin. "He must have known what you were, Vin. He used you intentionally."

She paled slightly. "Then . . . the Ministry knows that I'm a Mistborn?"

"Perhaps. It depends on whether Camon knew or not. He could have assumed you were just a Misting."

She stood quietly for a moment. "What does this mean for my part in the job, then?"

"We'll continue as planned," Kelsier said. "Only a couple of obligators saw you at the Canton building, and it takes a very rare man to connect the skaa servant and the well-dressed noblewoman as the same person."

"And the Inquisitor?" Vin asked softly.

Kelsier didn't have an answer to that one. "Come on," he finally said. "We've already attracted too much attention."

What would it be like if every nation—from the isles in the South to the Terris hills in the North—were united under a single government? What wonders could be achieved, what progress could be made, if mankind were to permanently set aside its squabblings and join together?

It is too much, I suppose, to even hope for. A single, unified empire of man? It could never happen.

12

VIN RESISTED THE URGE TO pick at her noblewoman's dress. Even after a half week of being forced to wear one—Sazed's suggestion—she found the bulky garment uncomfortable. It pulled tightly at her waist and chest, then fell to the floor with several layers of ruffled fabric, making it difficult to walk. She kept feeling as if she were going to trip—

and, despite the gown's bulk, she felt as if she were somehow exposed by how tight it was through the chest, not to mention the neckline's low curve. Though she had exposed nearly as much skin when wearing normal, buttoning shirts, this seemed different somehow.

Still, she had to admit that the gown made quite a difference. The girl who stood in the mirror before her was a strange, foreign creature. The light blue dress, with its white ruffles and lace, matched the sapphire barrettes in her hair. Sazed claimed he wouldn't be happy until her hair was at least shoulder-length, but he had still suggested that she purchase the broochlike barrettes and put them just above each ear.

"Often, aristocrats don't hide their deficiencies," he had explained. "Instead, they highlight them. Draw attention to your short hair, and instead of thinking you're unfashionable, they might be impressed by the statement you are making."

She also wore a sapphire necklace—modest by noble standards, but still worth more than two hundred boxings. It was complemented by a single ruby bracelet for accentuation. Apparently, the current fashion dictated a single splash of a different color to provide contrast.

And it was all hers, paid for by crew funds. If she ran, taking the jewelry and her three thousand boxings, she could live for decades. It was more tempting than she wanted to admit. Images of Camon's men, their corpses twisted and dead in the quiet lair, kept returning to her. That was probably what waited for her if she remained.

Why, then, didn't she go?

She turned from the mirror, putting on a light blue silken shawl, the female aristocrat's version of a cloak. Why didn't she leave? Perhaps it was her promise to Kelsier. He had given her the gift of Allomancy, and he depended on her. Perhaps it was her duty to the others. In order to survive, crews needed each person to do their separate job.

Reen's training told her that these men were fools, but she was tempted, enticed, by the possibility that Kelsier and the others offered. In the end, it wasn't the wealth or the job's thrill that made her stay. It was the shadowed prospect—unlikely and unreasonable, but still seductive—of a group whose members actually trusted one another. She had to stay. She *had* to know if it lasted, or if it was—as Reen's growing whispers promised—all a lie.

She turned and left her room, walking toward the front of Mansion Renoux, where Sazed waited with a carriage. She had decided to stay, and that meant she had to do her part.

It was time to make her first appearance as a noblewoman.

The carriage shook suddenly, and Vin jumped in surprise. The vehicle continued normally, however, and Sazed didn't move from his place in the driver's seat.

A sound came from above. Vin flared her metals, tensing, as a figure dropped down off the top of the carriage and landed on the footman's rest just outside her door. Kelsier smiled as he peeked his head in the window.

Vin let out a relieved breath, settling back into her seat. "You could have just asked us to pick you up."

"No need," Kelsier said, pulling open the carriage door and swinging inside. It was already dark outside, and he wore his mistcloak. "I warned Sazed I'd be dropping by sometime during the trip."

"And you didn't tell me?"

Kelsier winked, pulling the door shut. "I figured I still owed you for surprising me in that alleyway last week."

"How very adult of you," Vin said flatly.

"I've always been very confident in my immaturity. So, are you ready for this evening?"

Vin shrugged, trying to hide her nervousness. She glanced down. "How . . . uh, do I look?"

"Splendid," Kelsier said. "Just like a noble young lady. Don't be nervous, Vin—the disguise is perfect."

For some reason, that didn't feel like the answer she'd wanted to hear. "Kelsier?"

"Yes?"

"I've been meaning to ask this for a while," she said, glancing out the window, though all she could see is mist. "I understand that you think this is important—having a spy among the nobility. But . . . well, do we really have to do it this way?

Couldn't we get street informants to tell us what we need to know about house politics?"

"Perhaps," Kelsier said. "But those men are called 'informants' for a reason, Vin. Every question you ask them gives a clue about your true motives—even meeting with them reveals a bit of information that they could sell to someone else. It's better to rely on them as little as possible."

Vin sighed.

"I don't send you into danger heedlessly, Vin," Kelsier said, leaning forward. "We do need a spy among the nobility. Informants generally get their information from servants, but most aristocrats are not fools. Important meetings go on where no servant can overhear them."

"And you expect me to be able to get into such meetings?"

"Perhaps," Kelsier said. "Perhaps not. Either way, I've learned that it's always useful to have someone infiltrate the nobility. You and Sazed will overhear vital items that street informants wouldn't think important. In fact, just by being at these parties—even if you don't overhear anything—you will get us information."

"How so?" Vin asked, frowning.

"Make note of the people who seem interested in you," Kelsier said. "Those will be of the houses we want to watch. If they pay attention to you, they're probably paying attention to Lord Renoux—and there's one good reason why they would be doing that."

"Weapons," Vin said.

Kelsier nodded. "Renoux's position as a weapons merchant will make him valuable to those who are planning military action. These are the houses on which I'll need to focus my attention. There should already be a sense of tension among the nobility—hopefully, they're starting to wonder which houses are turning against the others. There hasn't been an all-out war among the Great Houses for over a century, but the last one was devastating. We need to replicate it."

"That could mean the deaths of a lot of noblemen," Vin said.

Kelsier smiled. "I can live with that. How about you?"

Vin smiled despite her tension.

"There's another reason for you to do this," Kelsier said.

"Sometime during this fiasco of a plan of mine, we might need to face the Lord Ruler. I have a feeling that the fewer people we need to sneak into his presence, the better. Having a skaa Mistborn hiding among the nobility . . . well, it could be a powerful advantage."

Vin felt a slight chill. "The Lord Ruler . . . will he be there tonight?"

"No. There will be obligators in attendance, but probably no Inquisitors—and certainly not the Lord Ruler himself. A party like this is far beneath his attention."

Vin nodded. She'd never seen the Lord Ruler before—she'd never wanted to.

"Don't worry so much," Kelsier said. "Even if you were to meet him, you'd be safe. He can't read minds."

"Are you sure?"

Kelsier paused. "Well, no. But, if he *can* read minds, he doesn't do it to everyone he meets. I've known several skaa who pretended to be noblemen in his presence—I did it several times myself, before . . ." He trailed off, glancing down toward his scar-covered hands.

"He caught you eventually," Vin said quietly.

"And he'll probably do so again," Kelsier said with a wink. "But, don't worry about him for now—our goal this evening is to establish Lady Valette Renoux. You won't need to do anything dangerous or unusual. Just make an appearance, then leave when Sazed tells you. We'll worry about building confidences later."

Vin nodded.

"Good girl," Kelsier said, reaching out and pushing open the door. "I'll be hiding near the keep, watching and listening."

Vin nodded gratefully, and Kelsier jumped out of the carriage door, disappearing into the dark mists.

Vin was unprepared for how bright Keep Venture would be in the darkness. The massive building was enveloped in an aura of misty light. As the carriage approached, Vin could see that eight enormous lights blazed along the outside of the rectangular building. They were as bright as bonfires, yet far more steady, and they had mirrors arranged behind them to make them shine directly on the keep. Vin had trouble determining their purpose. The ball would happen indoors—why light the outside of the building?

"Head inside, please, Mistress Vin," Sazed said from his position above. "Proper young ladies do not gawk."

Vin shot him a glare he couldn't see, but ducked her head back inside, waiting with impatient nervousness as the carriage pulled up to the massive keep. It eventually rolled to a stop, and a Venture footman immediately opened her door. A second footman approached and held out a hand to help her down.

Vin accepted his hand, trying with as much grace as possible to pull the frilled, bulky bottom of her dress out of the carriage. As she carefully descended—trying not to trip—she was grateful for the footman's steadying hand, and she finally realized why men were expected to help a lady out of her carriage. It wasn't a silly custom after all—the clothing was the silly part.

Sazed surrendered the carriage and took his place a few steps behind her. He wore robes even more fine than his standard fare; though they still maintained the same V-like pattern, they had a belted waist and wide, enveloping sleeves.

"Forward, Mistress," Sazed coached quietly from behind. "Up the carpet, so that your dress doesn't rub on the cobbles, and in through the main doors."

Vin nodded, trying to swallow her discomfort. She walked forward, passing noblemen and ladies in various suits and gowns. Though they weren't looking at her, she felt exposed. Her steps were nowhere near as graceful as those of the other ladies, who looked beautiful and comfortable in their gowns. Her hands began to sweat inside her silky, blue-white gloves.

She forced herself to continue. Sazed introduced her at the door, presenting her invitation to the attendants. The two men, dressed in black and red servant's suits, bowed and waved her in. A crowd of aristocrats was pooling slightly in the foyer, waiting to enter the main hall.

What am I doing? she thought frantically. She could challenge mist and Allomancy, thieves and burglaries, mistwraiths and beatings. Yet, facing these noblemen and their ladies . . . going amongst them in the light, visible, unable to hide . . . this terrified her.

"Forward, Mistress," Sazed said in a soothing voice. "Remember your lessons."

Hide! Find a corner! Shadows, mists, anything!

Vin kept her hands clasped rigidly before her, walking forward. Sazed walked beside her. Out of the corner of her eyes, she could see concern on his normally calm face.

And well he should worry! Everything he had taught her seemed fleeting—vaporous, like the mists themselves. She couldn't remember names, customs, anything.

She stopped just inside the foyer, and an imperious-looking nobleman in a black suit turned to regard her. Vin froze.

The man looked her over with a dismissive glance, then turned away. She distinctly heard the word "Renoux" whispered, and she glanced apprehensively to the side. Several women were looking at her.

And yet, it didn't feel like they were seeing her at all. They were studying the gown, the hair, and the jewelry. Vin glanced to the other side, where a group of younger men were watching her. They saw the neckline, the pretty dress and the makeup, but they didn't see *her*.

None of them could see Vin, they could only see the face she had put on—the face she wanted them to see. They saw Lady Valette. It was as if Vin weren't there.

As if . . . she were hiding, hiding right in front of their eyes.

And suddenly, her tension began to retreat. She let out a long, calming breath, anxiety flowing away. Sazed's training returned, and she adopted the look of a girl amazed by her first formal ball. She stepped to the side, handing her shawl to an attendant, and Sazed relaxed beside her. Vin shot him a smile, then swept forward into the main hall.

She could *do* this. She was still nervous, but the moment of panic was over. She didn't need shadows or corners—she just needed a mask of sapphires, makeup, and blue fabric.

The Venture main hall was a grand and imposing sight. Four or five daunting stories high, the hall was several times as long as it was wide. Enormous, rectangular stained-glass windows ran in rows along the hall, and the strange, powerful lights outside shone on them directly, throwing a cascade of colors across the room. Massive, ornate stone pillars were set into the walls, running between the windows. Just before the pillars met the floor, the wall fell away, indenting and creating a single-story gallery beneath the windows themselves. Dozens of white-clothed tables sat in this area, shadowed behind the pillars and beneath the overhang. In the distance, at the far end of the hallway, Vin could make out a low balcony set into the wall, and this held a smaller group of tables.

"The dining table of Lord Straff Venture," Sazed whispered, gesturing toward the far balcony.

Vin nodded. "And those lights outside?"

"Limelights, Mistress," Sazed explained. "I'm not certain the process used—somehow, the quicklime stones can be heated to brilliance without melting them."

A string orchestra played on a platform to her left, providing music for the couples who danced in the very center of the hall. To her right, serving tables held platter upon platter of foods being attended by scurrying serving men in white.

Sazed approached an attendant and presented Vin's invitation. The man nodded, then whispered something in a younger servant's ear. The young man bowed to Vin, then led the way into the room.

"I asked for a small, solitary table," Sazed said. "You won't need to mingle during this visit, I think. Just be seen."

Vin nodded gratefully.

"The solitary table will mark you as single," Sazed warned. "Eat slowly—once your meal is through, men will come to ask you to dance."

"You didn't teach me to dance!" Vin said in an urgent whisper.

"There wasn't time, Mistress," Sazed said. "Worry not—respectfully and rightly, you can refuse these men. They will assume that you are simply flustered by your first ball, and no harm will be done."

Vin nodded, and the serving man led them to a small table near the center of the hallway. Vin seated herself in the only chair while Sazed ordered her meal. He then stepped up to stand behind her chair.

Vin sat primly, waiting. Most of the tables lay just beneath the overhang of the gallery—up close to the dancing—and that left a corridorlike walkway behind them, near the wall. Couples and groups passed along this, speaking quietly. Occasionally someone gestured or nodded toward Vin.

Well, that part of Kelsier's plan is working. She was getting noticed. She had to force herself not to cringe or sink down in her chair, however, as a high prelan strolled along the pathway behind her. He wasn't the one she had met, fortunately, though he had the same gray robes and dark tattoos around his eyes.

Actually, there were a fair number of obligators at the party. They strolled about, mingling with the partygoers. And yet, there was an . . . aloofness to them. A division. They hovered about, almost like chaperones.

The Garrison watches the skaa, Vin thought. *Apparently, the obligators perform a similar function for the nobility.* It was an odd sight—she'd always thought of the noblemen as being free. And, truthfully, they were far more confident than the skaa. Many seemed to be enjoying themselves, and the obligators didn't seem to be acting really as police, or even specifically as spies. And yet, they were there. Hovering about, joining in conversations. A constant reminder of the Lord Ruler and his empire.

Vin turned her attention away from the obligators—their presence still made her a bit uncomfortable—and instead focused on something else: the beautiful windows. Sitting where she was, she could see some of the ones directly across and up from where she sat.

They were religious, like many scenes preferred by the aristocracy. Perhaps it was to show devotion, or perhaps it was required. Vin didn't know enough—but, likely, that was something Valette wouldn't know either, so it was all right.

She did, fortunately, recognize some of the scenes—mostly because of Sazed's teachings. He seemed to know as much about the Lord Ruler's mythology as he did about other religions, though it seemed odd to her that he would study the very religion he found so oppressive.

Central to many of the windows was the Deepness. Dark black—or, in window terms, violet—it was formless, with vengeful, tentaclelike masses creeping across several windows. Vin looked up at it, along with the brilliantly colored depictions of the Lord Ruler, and found herself a little bit transfixed by the backlit scenes.

What was it? she wondered. *The Deepness? Why depict it so formlessly—why not show what it really was?*

She'd never really wondered about the Deepness before, but Sazed's lessons left her wondering. Her instincts whispered scam. The Lord Ruler had invented some terrible menace that he'd been able to destroy in the past, therefore "earning" his place as emperor. And yet, staring up at the horrible, twisting thing, Vin could almost believe.

What if something like that *had* existed? And, if it had, how had the Lord Ruler managed to defeat it?

She sighed, shaking her head at the thoughts. Already, she was beginning to think too much like a noblewoman. She was admiring the beauty of the decorations—thinking about what they meant—without giving more than a passing thought to the wealth that had created them. It was just that everything here was so wondrous and ornate.

The pillars in the hall weren't just normal columns, they were carved masterpieces. Wide banners hung from the ceiling just above the windows, and the arching, lofty ceiling was crisscrossed by structural buttressings and dotted with capstones. Somehow she knew each of those capstones was intricately carved, despite the fact that they were too far away to be seen from below.

And the dancers matched, perhaps even outshone, the exquisite setting. Couples moved gracefully, stepping to the soft music with seemingly effortless motions. Many were even chatting with one another while they danced. The ladies moved freely in their dresses—many of which, Vin noticed, made her own frilly garment look plain by comparison. Sazed was right: Long hair was certainly the fashion, though an equal number kept their hair up as left it down.

Surrounded by the majestic hall, the sharp-suited noblemen looked different, somehow. Distinguished. Were these the same creatures that beat her friends and enslaved the skaa? They seemed too . . . perfect, too well-mannered, for such horrible acts.

I wonder if they even notice the outside world, she thought, crossing her arms on the table as she watched the dancing. *Perhaps they can't see beyond their keeps and their balls—just like they can't see past my dress and makeup.*

Sazed tapped her shoulder, and Vin sighed, adopting a more ladylike posture. The meal arrived a few moments later—a feast of such strange flavors that she would have been daunted, had she not eaten similar fare often during the last few months. Sazed's lessons might have omitted dancing, but they had been quite extensive regarding dining etiquette, for which Vin was grateful. As Kelsier had said, her main purpose of the evening was to make an appearance—and so it was important that she make a proper one.

She ate delicately, as instructed, and that allowed her to be slow and meticulous. She didn't relish the idea of being asked to dance; she was half afraid she'd panic again if anyone actually spoke to her. However, a meal could only be extended so long—especially one with a lady's small portions. She soon finished, and set her fork across the plate, indicating that she was done.

The first suitor approached not two minutes later. "Lady Valette Renoux?" the young man asked, bowing just slightly. He wore a green vest beneath his long, dark suit coat. "I am Lord Rian Strobe. Would you care to dance?"

"My lord," Vin said, glancing down demurely. "You are kind, but this is my first ball, and everything here is so grand! I fear that I'll stumble from nervousness on the dance floor. Perhaps, next time . . . ?"

"Of course, my lady," he said with a courteous nod, then withdrew.

"Very well done, Mistress," Sazed said quietly. "Your accent was masterful. You will, of course, have to dance with him at the next ball. We shall surely have you trained by then, I think."

Vin flushed slightly. "Maybe he won't attend."

"Perhaps," Sazed said. "But not likely. The young nobility are quite fond of their nightly diversions."

"They do this every night?"

"Nearly," Sazed said. "The balls are, after all, a prime reason people come to Luthadel. If one is in town and there is a ball—and there almost always is—one generally attends, especially if one is young and unmarried. You won't be expected to attend quite so frequently, but we should probably get you up to attending two or three a week."

"Two or three . . ." Vin said. "I'm going to need more gowns!"

Sazed smiled. "Ah, thinking like a noblewoman already. Now, Mistress, if you will excuse me . . ."

"Excuse you?" Vin asked, turning.

"To the steward's dinner," Sazed said. "A servant of my rank is generally dismissed once my master's meal is finished. I hesitate to go and leave you, but that room will be filled with the self-important servants of the high nobility. There will be conversations there that Master Kelsier wishes me to overhear."

"You're leaving me by myself?"

"You've done well so far, Mistress," Sazed said. "No major mistakes—or, at least, none that wouldn't be expected of a lady new to court."

"Like what?" Vin asked apprehensively.

"We shall discuss them later. Just remain at your table, sipping your wine—try not to get it refilled too often—and wait for my return. If other young men approach, turn them away as delicately as you did the first."

Vin nodded hesitantly.

"I shall return in about an hour," Sazed promised. He remained, however, as if waiting for something.

"Um, you are dismissed," Vin said.

"Thank you, Mistress," he said, bowing and withdrawing. Leaving her alone.

Not alone, she thought. *Kelsier's out there somewhere, watching in the night.* The thought comforted her, though she wished she didn't feel the empty space beside her chair quite so keenly.

Three more young men approached her for dances, but each one accepted her polite rejection. No others came after them; word had probably gotten around that she wasn't interested in dancing. She memorized the names of the four men who had approached her—Kelsier would want to know them—and began to wait.

Oddly, she soon found herself growing bored. The room was well ventilated, but she still felt hot beneath the layers of fabric. Her legs were especially bad, since they had to deal with her ankle-long undergarments. The long sleeves didn't help either, though the silky material was soft against her skin. The dancing continued, and she watched with interest for a time. However, her attention soon turned to the obligators.

Interestingly, they did seem to serve some sort of function at the party. Though they often stood apart from the groups of chatting nobility, occasionally they would join in. And, every so often, a group would pause and seek out an obligator, waving one over with a respectful gesture.

Vin frowned, trying to decide what she was missing. Eventually, a group at a nearby table waved to a passing obligator. The table was too far away to hear unaided, but with tin . . .

She reached inside to burn the metal, but then paused. *Copper first,* she thought, turning the metal on. She would have to grow accustomed to leaving it on almost all the time, so that she wouldn't expose herself.

Her Allomancy hidden, she burned tin. Immediately, the light in the room became blinding, and she had to close her eyes. The band's music became louder, and a dozen conversations around her turned from buzzes to audible voices. She had to try hard to focus on the one she was interested in, but the table was the one closest to her, so she eventually singled out the appropriate voices.

". . . swear that I'll share news of my engagement with him before anyone else," one of the people said. Vin opened her eyes a slit—it was one of the noblemen at the table.

"Very well," said the obligator. "I witness and record this."

The nobleman reached out a hand, and coins clinked. Vin extinguished her tin, opening her eyes all the way in time to see the obligator wandering away from the table, slipping something—likely the coins—into a pocket of his robes.

Interesting, Vin thought.

Unfortunately, the people at that table soon rose and went their separate ways, leaving Vin without anyone close enough to eavesdrop upon. Her boredom returned as she watched the obligator stroll across the room toward one of his companions. She began to tap on the table, idly watching the two obligators until she realized something.

She recognized one of them. Not the one who had taken the money earlier, but his companion, an older man. Short and firm-featured, he stood with an imperious air. Even the other obligator seemed deferential to him.

At first, Vin thought her familiarity came from her visit to the Canton of Finance with Camon, and she felt a stab of panic. Then, however, she realized that this wasn't the same man. She'd seen him before, but not there. He was . . .

My father, she realized with stupefaction.

Reen had pointed him out once, when they had first come to Luthadel, a year ago; he had been inspecting the workers at a local forge. Reen had taken Vin, sneaking her in, insisting that she at least see her father once—though she still didn't understand why. She had memorized the face anyway.

She resisted the urge to shrink down in her chair. There was no way the man would be able to recognize her—he didn't even know she existed. She forcibly turned her attention away from him, looking up at the windows instead. She couldn't get that good a look at them, however, because the pillars and overhang restricted her view.

As she sat, she noticed something she hadn't seen before—a lofty, inset balcony that ran just above the entire far wall. It was like a counterpart to the alcove beneath the windows, except it ran at the top of the wall, between the stained-glass windows and the ceiling. She could see movement upon it, couples and singles strolling along, looking down upon the party below.

Her instincts drew her toward the balcony, from where she could watch the party without being seen herself. It would also give her a wonderful view of the banners and the windows directly above her table, not to mention let her study the stonework without seeming to gawk.

Sazed had told her to stay, but the more she sat, the more she found her eyes drawn toward the hidden balcony. She itched to stand up and move, to stretch her legs and perhaps air them out a bit. The presence of her father—oblivious of her or not—served only as another motivation for her to leave the main floor.

It isn't like anyone else is asking me to dance, she thought. *And I've done what Kelsier wanted, I've been seen by the nobility.*

She paused, then waved for a serving boy.

He approached with alacrity. "Yes, Lady Renoux?"

"How do I get up there?" Vin asked, pointing toward the balcony.

"There are stairs just to the side of the orchestra, my lady," the boy said. "Climb them to the top landing."

Vin nodded her thanks. Then, determined, she stood and made her way to the front of the room. No one gave her passing more than a glance, and she walked with more confidence as she crossed the hallway to the stairwell.

The stone corridor twisted upward, curling upon itself, its steps short but steep. Little stained glass windows, no wider than her hand, ran up the outside wall—though they were dark in color, lacking backlight. Vin climbed eagerly, working away her restless energy, but she soon began to puff from the weight of the dress and the difficulty of holding it up so that she didn't trip. A spark of burned pewter, however, made the climb effortless enough that she didn't sweat and ruin her makeup.

The climb proved to be worth the effort. The upper balcony was dark—lit only by several small blue-glassed lanterns on the walls—and it gave an amazing view of the stained-glass windows. The area was quiet, and Vin felt practically alone as she approached the iron railing between two pillars, looking down. The stone tiles of the floor below formed a pattern she hadn't noticed, a kind of freeform curving of gray upon white.

Mists? she wondered idly, leaning against the railing. It, like the lantern bracket behind her, was intricate and detailed—both had been wrought in the form of thick, curving vines. To her sides, the tops of the pillars were carved into stone animals that appeared frozen in the motion of jumping off of the balcony.

"Now, see, here's the problem with going to refill your cup of wine."

The sudden voice made Vin jump, and she spun. A young man stood behind her. His suit wasn't the finest she had seen, nor was his vest as bright as most. Both coat and shirt seemed to fit too loosely, and his hair was just a bit disheveled. He carried a cup of wine, and the outer pocket of his suit coat bulged with the shape of a book that was just a bit too big for its confines.

"The problem is," the young man said, "you return to find that your favorite spot has been stolen by a pretty girl. Now, a gentleman would move on to another place, leaving the lady to her contemplations. However, this *is* the best spot on the balcony—it's the only place close enough to a lantern to have good reading light."

Vin flushed. "I'm sorry, my lord."

"Ah, see, now I feel guilty. All for a cup of wine. Look, there's plenty of room for two people here—just scoot over a bit."

Vin paused. Could she politely refuse? He obviously wanted her to stay near him—did he know who she was? Should she try to find out his name, so she could tell Kelsier?

She stepped a bit to the side, and the man took a place next to her. He leaned back against the side pillar, and, surprisingly, took out his book and began to read. He was right: The lantern shined directly on the pages. Vin stood for a moment, watching him, but he seemed completely absorbed. He didn't even pause to look up at her.

Isn't he going to pay me any attention at all? Vin thought, puzzled at her own annoyance. *Maybe I should have worn a fancier dress.*

The man sipped at his wine, focused on the book.

"Do you always read at balls?" she asked.

The young man looked up. "Whenever I can get away with it."

"Doesn't that kind of defeat the purpose of coming?" Vin asked. "Why attend if you're just going to avoid socializing?"

"You're up here too," he pointed out.

Vin flushed. "I just wanted to get a brief view of the hall."

"Oh? And why did you refuse all three men who asked you to dance?"

Vin paused. The man smiled, then turned back to his book.

"There were four," Vin said with a huff. "And I refused them because I don't know how to dance very well."

The man lowered his book slightly, eyeing her. "You know, you're a lot less timid than you look."

"Timid?" Vin asked. "I'm not the one staring at his book when there's a young lady standing by him, never having properly introduced himself."

The man raised a speculative eyebrow. "Now, see, you sound like my father. Far better looking, but just as grumpy."

Vin glared at him. Finally, he rolled his eyes. "Very well, let me be a gentleman, then." He bowed to her with a refined, formal step. "I am Lord Elend. Lady Valette Renoux, might I have the pleasure of sharing this balcony with you whilst I read?"

Vin folded her arms. *Elend? Family name or given name? Should I even care? He just wanted his spot back. But . . . how did he know that I'd refused dancing partners?* Somehow, she had a suspicion that Kelsier would want to hear about this particular conversation.

Oddly, she didn't feel a desire to shrug this man away as she had the others. Instead, she felt another stab of annoyance as he again raised his book.

"You still haven't told me why you would rather read than participate," she said.

The man sighed, lowering the book again. "Well, see, I'm not exactly the best dancer either."

"Ah," Vin said.

"But," he said, raising a finger, "that's only part of it. You may not realize this yet, but it's not that hard to get overpartied. Once you attend five or six hundred of these balls, they start to feel a bit repetitive."

Vin shrugged. "You'd probably learn to dance better if you practiced."

Elend raised an eyebrow. "You're not going to let me get back to my book, are you?"

"I wasn't intending to."

He sighed, tucking the book back into his jacket pocket—which was beginning to show signs of book-shaped wear. "Well, then. Do you want to go dance instead?"

Vin froze. Elend smiled nonchalantly.

Lord! He's either incredibly smooth or socially incompetent. It was disturbing that she couldn't determine which.

"That's a no, I assume?" Elend said. "Good—I thought I should offer, since we've established that I'm a gentleman. However, I doubt the couples below would appreciate us trampling their toes."

"Agreed. What were you reading?"

"Dilisteni," Elend said. "*Trials of Monument.* Heard of it?"

Vin shook her head.

"Ah, well. Not many have." He leaned over the railing, looking below. "So, what do you think of your first experience at court?"

"It's very . . . overwhelming."

Elend chuckled. "Say what you will about House Venture—they know how to throw a party."

Vin nodded. "You don't like House Venture, then?" she said. Perhaps this was one of the rivalries Kelsier was watching for.

"Not particularly, no," Elend said. "They're an ostentatious lot, even for high nobility. They can't just have a party, they have to throw the *best* party. Never mind that they run their servants ragged setting it up, then beat the poor things in retribution when the hall isn't perfectly clean the very next morning."

Vin cocked her head. *Not words I'd expect to hear from a nobleman.*

Elend paused, looking a little embarrassed. "But, well, never mind that. I think your Terrisman is looking for you."

Vin started, glancing over the side of the balcony. Sure enough, Sazed's tall form stood by her now-empty table, speaking to a serving boy.

Vin yelped quietly. "I've got to go," she said, turning toward the stairwell.

"Ah, well then," Elend said, "back to reading it is." He gave her a half wave of farewell, but he had his book open before she passed the first step.

Vin reached the bottom out of breath. Sazed saw her immediately.

"I'm sorry," she said, chagrined as she approached.

"Do not apologize to me, Mistress," Sazed said quietly. "It is both unseemly and unnecessary. Moving about a bit was a good idea, I think. I would have suggested it, had you not seemed so nervous."

Vin nodded. "Is it time for us to go, then?"

"It is a proper time to withdraw, if you wish," he said, glancing up at the balcony. "May I ask what you were doing up there, Mistress?"

"I wanted to get a better look at the windows," Vin said. "But I ended up talking to someone. He seemed interested in me at first, but now I don't think he ever intended to pay me much attention. It doesn't matter—he didn't seem important enough to bother Kelsier with his name."

Sazed paused. "Who was it you were speaking to?"

"The man in the corner there, on the balcony," Vin said.

"One of Lord Venture's friends?"

Vin froze. "Is one of them named Elend?"

Sazed paled visibly. "You were chatting with Lord *Elend Venture?*"

"Um . . . yes?"

"Did he ask you to dance?"

Vin nodded. "But I don't think he meant it."

"Oh, dear," Sazed said. "So much for controlled anonymity."

"Venture?" Vin asked, frowning. "Like, Keep Venture?"

"Heir to the house title," Sazed said.

"Hum," Vin said, realizing that she should probably be a bit more intimidated than she felt. "He was a bit annoying—in a pleasant sort of way."

"We shouldn't be discussing this here," Sazed said. "You're far, far below his station. Come, let us retire. I shouldn't have gone away to the dinner. . . ."

He trailed off, mumbling to himself as he led Vin to the entryway. She got one more glimpse into the main chamber as she retrieved her shawl, and she burned tin, squinting against the light and seeking the balcony above.

He held the book, closed, in one hand—and she could have sworn that he was looking down in her direction. She smiled, and let Sazed usher her to their carriage.

I know that I shouldn't let a simple packman perturb me. However, he is from Terris, where the prophecies originated. If anyone could spot a fraud, would it not be he?

Nevertheless, I continue my trek, going where the scribbled auguries proclaim that I will meet my destiny—walking, feeling Rashek's eyes on my back. Jealous. Mocking. Hating.

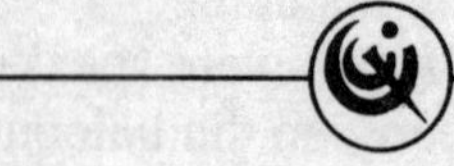

13

VIN SAT WITH HER LEGS crossed beneath her on one of Lord Renoux's fine easy chairs. It felt good to be rid of the bulky dress, instead getting back to a more familiar shirt and trousers.

However, Sazed's calm displeasure made her want to squirm. He stood on the other side of the room, and Vin got the distinct impression that she was in trouble. Sazed had questioned her in depth, seeking out every detail of her conversation with Lord Elend. Sazed's inquiries had been respectful, of course, but they had also been forceful.

The Terrisman seemed, in Vin's opinion, unduly worried about her exchange with the young nobleman. They hadn't really talked about anything important, and Elend himself was decidedly unspectacular for a Great House lord.

But, there *had* been something odd about him—something Vin hadn't admitted to Sazed. She'd felt . . . comfortable with

Elend. Looking back on the experience, she realized that for those few moments, she hadn't really been Lady Valette. Nor had she been Vin, for that part of her—the timid crewmember—was almost as fake as Valette was.

No, she'd simply been . . . whoever she was. It was a strange experience. She had occasionally felt the same way during her time with Kelsier and the others, but in a more limited manner. How had Elend been able to evoke her true self so quickly and so thoroughly?

Maybe he used Allomancy on me! she thought with a start. Elend was a high nobleman; perhaps he was a Soother. Maybe there was more to the conversation than she had thought.

Vin sat back in her chair, frowning to herself. She'd had copper on, and that meant he *couldn't* have used emotional Allomancy on her. Somehow, he had simply gotten her to let her guard down. Vin thought back to the experience, thinking about how oddly comfortable she'd felt. In retrospect, it was clear that she hadn't been careful enough.

I'll be more cautious next time. She assumed that they would meet again. They'd better.

A servant entered and whispered quietly to Sazed. A quick burn of tin let Vin hear the conversation—Kelsier had finally returned.

"Please send word to Lord Renoux," Sazed said. The white-clothed servant nodded, leaving the room with a quick step.

"The rest of you may leave," Sazed said calmly, and the room's attendants scampered away. Sazed's quiet vigil had forced them to stand, waiting in the tense room, not speaking or moving.

Kelsier and Lord Renoux arrived together, chatting quietly. As always, Renoux wore a rich suit cut in the unfamiliar Western style. The aging man kept his gray mustache trimmed thin and neat, and he walked with a confident air. Even after spending an entire evening among the nobility, Vin was again struck by his aristocratic bearing.

Kelsier still wore his mistcloak. "Saze?" he said as he entered. "You have news?"

"I am afraid so, Master Kelsier," Sazed said. "It appears

that Mistress Vin caught the attention of Lord Elend Venture at the ball tonight."

"Elend?" Kelsier asked, folding his arms. "Isn't he the heir?"

"He is indeed," Renoux said. "I met the lad perhaps four years ago, when his father visited the West. He struck me as a bit undignified for one of his station."

Four years? Vin thought. *There's no way he's been imitating Lord Renoux for that long. Kelsier only escaped the Pits two years ago!* She eyed the impostor, but—as always—was unable to detect a flaw in his bearing.

"How attentive was the boy?" Kelsier asked.

"He asked her to dance," Sazed said. "But Mistress Vin was wise enough to decline. Apparently, their meeting was a matter of idle happenstance—but I fear she may have caught his eye."

Kelsier chuckled. "You taught her too well, Saze. In the future, Vin, perhaps you should try to be a little less charming."

"Why?" Vin asked, trying to mask her annoyance. "I thought we *wanted* me to be well liked."

"Not by a man as important as Elend Venture, child," Lord Renoux said. "We sent you to court so you could make alliances—not scandals."

Kelsier nodded. "Venture is young, eligible, and heir to a powerful house. Your having a relationship with him could make serious problems for us. The women of the court would be jealous of you, and the older men would disapprove of the rank difference. You'd alienate yourself from large sections of the court. To get the information we need, we need the aristocracy to see you as uncertain, unimportant, and—most importantly—unthreatening."

"Besides, child," Lord Renoux said. "It is unlikely that Elend Venture has any real interest in you. He is known to be a court eccentric—he is probably just trying to heighten his reputation by doing the unexpected."

Vin felt her face flush. *He's probably right,* she told herself sternly. Still, she couldn't help feeling annoyed at the three of them—especially Kelsier, with his flippant, unconcerned attitude.

"Yes," Kelsier said, "it's probably best that you avoid Venture completely. Try to offend him or something. Give him a couple of those glares you do."

Vin regarded Kelsier with a flat look.

"That's the one!" Kelsier said with a laugh.

Vin clinched her teeth, then forced herself to relax. "I saw my father at the ball tonight," she said, hoping to distract Kelsier and the others away from Lord Venture.

"Really?" Kelsier asked with interest.

Vin nodded. "I recognized him from a time my brother pointed him out to me."

"What is this?" Renoux asked.

"Vin's father is an obligator," Kelsier said. "And, apparently an important one if he has enough pull to go to a ball like this. Do you know what his name is?"

Vin shook her head.

"Description?" Kelsier asked.

"Uh . . . bald, eye tattoos . . ."

Kelsier chuckled. "Just point him out to me sometime, all right?"

Vin nodded, and Kelsier turned to Sazed. "Now, did you bring me the names of which noblemen asked Vin to dance?"

Sazed nodded. "She gave me a list, Master Kelsier. I also have several interesting tidbits to share from the stewards' meal."

"Good," Kelsier said, glancing at the grandfather clock in the corner. "You'll have to save them for tomorrow morning, though. I've got to be going."

"Going?" Vin asked, perking up. "But you just got in!"

"That's the funny thing about arriving somewhere, Vin," he said with a wink. "Once you're there, the only thing you can really do is leave again. Get some sleep—you're looking a bit ragged."

Kelsier waved a farewell to the group, then ducked out of the room, whistling amiably to himself.

Too nonchalant, Vin thought. *And too secretive. He usually tells us which families he plans to hit.*

"I think I *will* retire," Vin said, yawning.

Sazed eyed her suspiciously, but let her go as Renoux began speaking quietly to him. Vin scrambled up the stairs to her room, threw on her mistcloak, and pushed open her balcony doors.

Mist poured into the room. She flared iron, and was rewarded with the sight of a fading blue metal line, pointing into the distance.

Let's see where you're going, Master Kelsier.

Vin burned steel, Pushing herself into the cold, humid autumn night. Tin enhanced her eyes, making the wet air tickle her throat as she breathed. She Pushed hard behind her, then Pulled slightly on the gates below. The maneuver swung her in a soaring arc over the steel gates, which she then Pushed against to throw herself farther into the air.

She kept an eye on the trail of blue that pointed toward Kelsier, following him at enough of a distance to remain unseen. She wasn't carrying any metal—not even coins—and she kept her copper burning to hide her use of Allomancy. Theoretically, only sound could alert Kelsier of her presence, and so she moved as quietly as possible.

Surprisingly, Kelsier didn't head into town. After passing the mansion's gates, he turned north out of the city. Vin followed, landing and running quietly on the rough ground.

Where is he going? she thought with confusion. *Is he circling Fellise? Heading for one of the peripheral mansions?*

Kelsier continued northward for a short time, then his metal line suddenly began to grow dim. Vin paused, stopping beside a group of stumpy trees. The line faded at a rapid rate: Kelsier had suddenly sped up. She cursed to herself, breaking into a dash.

Ahead, Kelsier's line vanished into the night. Vin sighed, slowing. She flared her iron, but it was barely enough to catch a glimpse of him disappearing again in the distance. She'd never keep up.

Her flared iron, however, showed her something else. She frowned, continuing forward until she reached a stationary source of metal—two small bronze bars stuck into the ground a couple feet from each other. She flipped one up into her hand, then looked into the swirling mists to the north.

He's jumping, she thought. *But why?* Jumping *was* faster than walking, but there didn't seem much point to it in the empty wilderness.

Unless . . .

She walked forward, and she soon found two more bronze bars embedded in the earth. Vin glanced backward. It was hard to tell in the night, but it seemed that the four bars made a line that pointed directly toward Luthadel.

So that's how he does it, she thought. Kelsier had an uncanny ability to move between Luthadel and Fellise with remarkable speed. She'd assumed that he was using horses, but it appeared that there was a better way. He—or perhaps someone before him—had laid down an Allomantic road between the two cities.

She gripped the first bar in her palm—she'd need it to soften her landing if she was wrong—then stepped up in front of the second pair of bars and launched herself into the air.

She Pushed hard, flaring her steel, throwing herself as far up into the sky as she could. As she flew, she flared her iron, searching for other sources of metal. They soon appeared—two directly north, and two more in the distance to either side of her.

The ones on the sides are for course corrections, she realized. She'd have to keep moving directly north if she wanted to stay on the bronze highway. She nudged herself slightly to the left—moving so that she passed directly between the two adjacent bars of the main path—then hurled herself forward again in an arcing leap.

She got the hang of it quickly, hopping from point to point, never dropping even close to the ground. In just a few minutes, she had the rhythm down so well that she barely had to do any corrections from the sides.

Her progress across the scraggly landscape was incredibly swift. The mists blew by, her mistcloak whipping and flapping behind her. Still, she forced herself to speed up. She'd spent too long studying the bronze bars. She had to catch up to Kelsier; otherwise she'd arrive in Luthadel, but not know where to go from there.

She began to throw herself from point to point at an almost reckless speed, watching desperately for some sign of Allomantic motion. After about ten minutes of leaping, a line of blue finally appeared ahead of her—one pointing up, rather than down toward bars in the ground. She breathed in relief.

Then a second line appeared, and a third.

Vin frowned, letting herself drop to the ground with a muted thump. She flared tin, and a massive shadow appeared in the night before her, its top sparkling with balls of light.

The city wall, she thought with amazement. *So soon? I made the trip twice as fast as a man on horseback!*

However, that meant she'd lost Kelsier. Frowning to herself, she used the bar she'd been carrying to throw herself up onto the battlements. Once she landed on the damp stone, she reached behind and Pulled the bar up into her hand. Then she approached the other side of the wall, hopping up and crouching on the stone railing as she scanned the city.

What now? she thought with annoyance. *Head back to Fellise? Stop by Clubs's shop and see if he went there?*

She sat uncertainly for a moment, then threw herself off the wall and began making her way across the rooftops. She wandered randomly, pushing off of window clasps and bits of metal, using the bronze bar—then pulling it back into her hand—when long jumps were necessary. It wasn't until she arrived that she realized she'd unconsciously gone to a specific destination.

Keep Venture rose before her in the night. The limelights had been extinguished, and only a few phantom torches burned near guard posts.

Vin crouched on the lip on a rooftop, trying to decide what had led her back to the massive keep. The cool wind ruffled her hair and cloak, and she thought she felt a few tiny raindrops on her cheek. She sat for a long moment, her toes growing cold.

Then she noticed motion to her right. She crouched immediately, flaring her tin.

Kelsier sat on a rooftop not three houses away, just barely lit by ambient light. He didn't seem to have noticed her. He was watching the keep, his face too distant for her to read his expression.

Vin watched him with suspicious eyes. He'd dismissed her

meeting with Elend, but perhaps it worried him more than he'd admitted. A sudden spike of fear made her tense.

Could he be here to kill Elend? The assassination of a high noble heir would certainly create tension amongst the nobility.

Vin waited apprehensively. Eventually, however, Kelsier stood and walked away, Pushing himself off the rooftop and into the air.

Vin dropped her bronze bar—it would give her away—and dashed after him. Her iron showed blue lines moving in the distance, and she hurriedly jumped out over the street and Pushed herself off a sewer grate below, determined not to lose him again.

He moved toward the center of the city. Vin frowned, trying to guess his destination. Keep Erikeller was in that direction, and it was a major supplier of armaments. Perhaps Kelsier planned to do something to interrupt its supplies, making House Renoux more vital to the local nobility.

Vin landed on a rooftop and paused, watching Kelsier shoot off into the night. *He's moving fast again. I—*

A hand fell on her shoulder.

Vin yelped, jumping back, flaring pewter.

Kelsier regarded her with a cocked eyebrow. "You're supposed to be in bed, young lady."

Vin glanced to the side, toward the line of metal. "But—"

"My coin pouch," Kelsier said, smiling. "A good thief can steal clever tricks as easily as he steals boxings. I've started being more careful since you tailed me last week—at first, I assumed you were a Venture Mistborn."

"They have some?"

"I'm sure they do," Kelsier said. "Most of the Great Houses do—but your friend Elend isn't one of them. He's not even a Misting."

"How do you know? He could be hiding it."

Kelsier shook his head. "He nearly died in a raid a couple of years ago—if there were ever a time to show your powers, it would have been then."

Vin nodded, still looking down, not meeting Kelsier's eyes.

He sighed, sitting down on the slanted rooftop, one leg hanging over the side. "Have a seat."

Vin settled herself on the tile roof across from him. Above, the cool mists continued to churn, and it had begun to drizzle slightly—but that wasn't much different from the regular nightly humidity.

"I can't have you tailing me like this, Vin," Kelsier said. "Do you remember our discussion about trust?"

"If you trusted me, you'd tell me where you were going."

"Not necessarily," Kelsier said. "Maybe I just don't want you and the others to worry about me."

"Everything you do is dangerous," Vin said. "Why would we worry any more if you told us specifics?"

"Some tasks are even more dangerous than others," Kelsier said quietly.

Vin paused, then glanced to the side, in the direction Kelsier had been going. Toward the center of the city.

Toward Kredik Shaw, the Hill of a Thousand Spires. The Lord Ruler's palace.

"You're going to confront the Lord Ruler!" Vin said quietly. "You said last week that you were going to pay him a visit."

" 'Visit' is, perhaps, too strong a word," Kelsier said. "I *am* going to the palace, but I sincerely hope I don't run into the Lord Ruler himself. I'm not ready for him yet. Regardless, *you* are going straight to Clubs's shop."

Vin nodded.

Kelsier frowned. "You're just going to try and follow me again, aren't you?"

Vin paused, then she nodded again.

"Why?"

"Because I want to help," Vin said quietly. "So far, my part in this all has essentially boiled down to going to a party. But, I'm Mistborn—you've trained me yourself. I'm not going to sit back and let everyone else do dangerous work while I sit, eat dinner, and watch people dance."

"What you're doing at those balls is important," Kelsier said.

Vin nodded, glancing down. She'd just let him go, then she'd follow him. Part of her reasoning was what she'd said before: She was beginning to feel a camaraderie for this crew, and it was like nothing she had ever known. She wanted to be part of what it was doing; she wanted to help.

However, another part of her whispered that Kelsier wasn't telling her everything. He might trust her; he might not. However, he certainly had secrets. The Eleventh Metal, and therefore the Lord Ruler, were involved in those secrets.

Kelsier caught her eyes, and he must have seen her intention to follow in them. He sighed, leaning back. "I'm serious, Vin! You can't go with me."

"Why not?" she asked, abandoning pretense. "If what you're doing is so dangerous, wouldn't it be safer if you had another Mistborn watching your back?"

"You still don't know all of the metals," Kelsier said.

"Only because you haven't taught me."

"You need more practice."

"The best practice is doing," Vin said. "My brother trained me to steal by taking me on burglaries."

Kelsier shook his head. "It's too dangerous."

"Kelsier," she said in a serious tone. "We're planning to *overthrow the Final Empire.* I don't really expect to live until the end of the year anyway.

"You keep telling the others what an advantage it is to have two Mistborn on the team. Well, it's not going to be much of an advantage unless you actually let me *be* a Mistborn. How long are you going to wait? Until I'm 'ready'? I don't think that will ever happen."

Kelsier eyed her for a moment, then he smiled. "When we first met, half the time I couldn't get you to say a word. Now you're lecturing me."

Vin blushed. Finally, Kelsier sighed, reaching beneath his cloak to pull something out. "I can't believe I'm considering this," he muttered, handing her the bit of metal.

Vin studied the tiny, silvery ball of metal. It was so reflective and bright that it almost seemed to be a drop of liquid, yet it was solid to the touch.

"Atium," Kelsier said. "Tenth, and most powerful, of the known Allomantic metals. That bead is worth more than the entire bag of boxings I gave you before."

"This little bit?" she asked with surprise.

Kelsier nodded. "Atium only comes from one place—the Pits of Hathsin—where the Lord Ruler controls its production and distribution. The Great Houses get to buy a monthly stipend of atium, which is one of the main ways the Lord Ruler controls them. Go ahead and swallow it."

Vin eyed the bit of metal, uncertain she wanted to waste something so valuable.

"You can't sell it," Kelsier said. "Thieving crews try, but they get tracked down and executed. The Lord Ruler is very protective of his atium supply."

Vin nodded, then swallowed the metal. Immediately, she felt a new well of power appear within her, waiting to be burned.

"All right," Kelsier said, standing. "Burn it as soon as I start walking."

Vin nodded. As he began to walk forward, she drew upon her new well of strength and burned atium.

Kelsier seemed to fuzz slightly to her eyes; then a translucent, wraithlike image shot out into the mists in front of him. The image looked just like Kelsier, and it walked just a few steps in front of him. A very faint, trailing after-image extended from the duplicate back to Kelsier himself.

It was like . . . a reverse shadow. The duplicate did everything Kelsier did—except, the image moved *first*. It turned, and then Kelsier followed its same path.

The image's mouth began moving. A second later, Kelsier spoke. "Atium lets you see just a bit into the future. Or, at least, it lets you see what people are going to do a little bit in the future. In addition, it enhances your mind, allowing you to deal with the new information, allowing you to react more quickly and collectedly."

The shadow stopped, then Kelsier walked up to it, stopping as well. Suddenly, the shadow reached out and slapped her, and Vin moved reflexively, putting her hand up just as Kelsier's real hand began to move. She caught his arm midswing.

"While you're burning atium," he said, "nothing can surprise you. You can swing a dagger, knowing confidently that your enemies will run right into it. You can dodge attacks with ease because you'll be able to see where every blow will fall. Atium makes you quite nearly invincible. It enhances your mind, making you able to make use of all the new information."

Suddenly, dozens of other images shot from Kelsier's body. Each one sprang in a different direction, some striding across the roof, others jumping into the air. Vin released his arm, rising and backing away in confusion.

"I just burned atium too," Kelsier said. "I can see what you're going to do, and that changes what I'm going to do—which in turn changes what you're going to do. The images reflect each of the possible actions we might take."

"It's confusing," Vin said, watching the insane jumble of images, old ones constantly fading, new ones constantly appearing.

Kelsier nodded. "The only way to defeat someone who is burning atium is to burn it yourself—that way, neither of you has an advantage."

The images vanished.

"What did you do?" Vin asked with a start.

"Nothing," Kelsier said. "Your atium probably ran out."

Vin realized with surprise that he was right—the atium was gone. "It burns so quickly!"

Kelsier nodded, sitting down again. "That's probably the fastest fortune you've ever blown, eh?"

Vin nodded, stunned. "It seems likc such a waste."

Kelsier shrugged. "Atium is only valuable because of Allomancy. So, if we didn't burn it, it wouldn't be worth the fortune that it is. Of course, if we do burn it, we make it even more rare. It's kind of an interesting relationship—ask Ham about it sometimes. He loves talking about atium economics.

"Anyway, any Mistborn you face will probably have atium. However, they'll be reluctant to use it. In addition, they won't have swallowed it yet—atium is fragile, and your digestive juices will ruin it in a matter of hours. So, you have to walk a line between conservation and effectiveness. If it looks like your opponent is using atium, then you'd better use yours too—however, make sure he doesn't lure you into using up your reserve before he does."

Vin nodded. "Does this mean you're taking me tonight?"

"I'll probably regret it," Kelsier said, sighing. "But I don't see any way to make you stay behind—short of tying you up, perhaps. But, I warn you Vin. This could be dangerous. *Very* dangerous. I don't intend to meet the Lord Ruler, but I do intend to sneak into his stronghold. I think I know where we might find a clue on how to defeat him."

Vin smiled, stepping forward as Kelsier waved her toward him. He reached into his pouch and pulled out a vial, which he handed to her. It was like regular Allomantic vials, except the liquid inside held only a single drop of metal. The atium bead was several times larger than the one he had given her to practice on.

"Don't use it unless you have to," Kelsier warned. "You need any other metals?"

Vin nodded. "I burned up most of my steel getting here."

Kelsier handed her another vial. "First, let's go retrieve my coin pouch."

Sometimes I wonder if I'm going mad.

Perhaps it is due to the pressure of knowing that I must somehow bear the burden of an entire world. Perhaps it is caused by the death I have seen, the friends I have lost. The friends I have been forced to kill.

Either way, I sometimes see shadows following me. Dark creatures that I don't understand, nor wish to understand. Are they, perhaps, some figment of my overtaxed mind?

14

IT STARTED RAINING JUST AFTER they located the coin pouch. It wasn't a hard rain, but it seemed to clear the mist slightly. Vin shivered, pulling up her hood, crouching beside Kelsier on a rooftop. He didn't pay the weather much heed, so neither did she. A little dampness wouldn't hurt—in fact, it would probably help, as the rainfall would cover the sounds of their approach.

Kredik Shaw lay before them. The peaked spires and sheer towers rose like dark talons in the night. They varied greatly in thickness—some were wide enough to house stairwells and large rooms, but others were simply thin rods of steel jutting up into the sky. The variety gave the mass a twisted, off-center symmetry—an almost-balance.

The spikes and towers had a foreboding cast in the damp, misty night—like the ash-blackened bones of a long-weathered carcass. Looking at them, Vin thought she felt something . . . a *depression*, as if simply being close to the building was enough to suck away her hope.

"Our target is a tunnel complex at the base of one of the far right spires," Kelsier said, his voice barely carrying over the quiet hush of the falling rain. "We're heading for a room at the very center of that complex."

"What's inside?"

"I don't know," Kelsier said. "That's what we're going to find out. Once every three days—and today isn't one of them—the Lord Ruler visits this chamber. He stays for three hours, then leaves. I tried to get in once before. Three years ago."

"The job," Vin whispered. "The one that . . ."

"Got me captured," Kelsier said with a nod. "Yes. At the time, we thought that the Lord Ruler stored riches in the room. I don't think that's true, now, but I'm still curious. The way he visits is so regular, so . . . odd. Something's in that room, Vin. Something important. Maybe it holds the secret to his power and immortality."

"Why do we need to worry about that?" Vin asked. "You have the Eleventh Metal to defeat him, right?"

Kelsier frowned slightly. Vin waited for an answer, but he didn't ever give one. "I failed to get in last time, Vin," he said instead. "We got close, but we got there too easily. When we arrived, there were Inquisitors outside the room. Waiting for us."

"Someone told them you were coming?"

Kelsier nodded. "We planned that job for months. We were overconfident, but we had reason to be. Mare and I were the best—the job should have gone flawlessly." Kelsier paused, then he turned to Vin. "Tonight, I didn't plan at all. We're just going in—we'll quiet anyone who tries to stop us, then break into that room."

Vin sat quietly, feeling the chill rainwater on her wet hands and damp arms. Then she nodded.

Kelsier smiled slightly. "No objections?"

Vin shook her head. "I made you take me with you. It's not my place to object now."

Kelsier chuckled. "Guess I've been hanging out with Breeze too long. I just don't feel right unless someone tells me I'm crazy."

Vin shrugged. However, as she moved on the rooftop, she felt it again—the sense of depression coming from Kredik Shaw.

"There is something, Kelsier," she said. "The palace feels . . . wrong, somehow."

"That's the Lord Ruler," Kelsier said. "He radiates like an incredibly powerful Soother, smothering the emotions of everyone who gets close to him. Turn on your copper; that will make you immune."

Vin nodded, burning copper. Immediately, the sensation went away.

"Good?" Kelsier asked.

She nodded again.

"All right, then," he said, giving her a handful of coins. "Stay close to me, and keep your atium handy—just in case."

With that, he threw himself off the roof. Vin followed, her cloak tassels spraying rainwater. She burned pewter as she fell, and hit the ground with Allomantically strengthened legs.

Kelsier took off at a dash, and she followed. Her speed on the wet cobblestones would have been reckless, but her pewter-fueled muscles reacted with precision, strength, and balance. She ran in the wet, misty night, burning tin and copper—one to let her see, the other to let her hide.

Kelsier rounded the palace complex. Oddly, the grounds had no outer wall. *Of course they don't. Who would dare attack the Lord Ruler?*

Flat space, covered in cobblestones, was all that surrounded the Hill of a Thousand Spires. No tree, foliage, or structure stood to distract one's eye from the disturbing, asymmetric collection of wings, towers, and spires that was Kredik Shaw.

"Here we go," Kelsier whispered, his voice carrying to her tin-enhanced ears. He turned, dashing directly toward a squat, bunkerlike section of the palace. As they approached, Vin saw a pair of guards standing by an ornate, gatelike door.

Kelsier was on the men in a flash, cutting one down with slashing knives. The second man tried to cry out, but Kelsier jumped, slamming both feet into the man's chest. Thrown to the side by the inhumanly strong kick, the guard crashed into the wall, then slumped to the ground. Kelsier was on his feet a second later, slamming his weight against the door and pushing it open.

Weak lanternlight spilled out of a stone corridor within. Kelsier ducked through the door. Vin dimmed her tin, then followed in a crouching dash, her heart pounding. Never, in all her time as a thief, had she done something like this. Hers had been a life of sneaky burgling and scamming, not raids or muggings. As she followed Kelsier down the corridor—their feet and cloaks leaving a wet trail on the smooth stonework—she nervously pulled out a glass dagger, gripping the leather-wrapped handle in a sweaty palm.

A man stepped into the hallway just ahead, exiting what appeared to be some sort of guard chamber. Kelsier jumped forward and elbowed the soldier in the stomach, then slammed him against the wall. Even as the guard collapsed, Kelsier ducked into the room.

Vin followed, stepping into chaos. Kelsier Pulled a metal candelabrum from the corner up into his hands, then began to spin with it, striking down soldier after soldier. Guards cried out, scrambling and grabbing staves from the side of the room. A table covered in half-eaten meals was thrown to the side as men tried to make room.

A soldier turned toward Vin, and she reacted without thinking. She burned steel and threw out a handful of coins. She Pushed, and the missiles shot forward, tearing through the guard's flesh and dropping him.

She burned iron, Pulling the coins back to her hand. She turned with a bloodied fist, spraying the room with metal, dropping three soldiers. Kelsier felled the last with his impromptu staff.

I just killed four men, Vin thought, stunned. Before, Reen had always done the killing.

There was rustling behind. Vin spun to see another squadron of soldiers enter through a door opposite her. To the side, Kelsier dropped his candelabrum and stepped forward. The room's four lanterns suddenly ripped from their mountings, slamming directly toward him. He ducked to the side, letting the lanterns crash together.

The room fell dark. Vin burned tin, her eyes adapting to light from the corridor outside. The guards, however, stumbled to a halt.

Kelsier was amidst them a second later. Daggers flashing in the darkness. Men screaming. Then all was silent.

Vin stood surrounded by death, bloodied coins dribbling from her stunned fingers. She kept a tight grip on her dagger, however—if only to steady her quivering arm.

Kelsier lay a hand on her shoulder, and she jumped.

"These were evil men, Vin," he said. "Every skaa knows in his heart that it is the greatest of crimes to take up arms in defense of the Final Empire."

Vin nodded numbly. She felt . . . wrong. Maybe it was the death, but now that she was actually within the building, she swore that she could still feel the Lord Ruler's power. Something seemed to Push her emotions, making her more depressed despite her copper.

"Come. Time is short." Kelsier took off again, hopping lithely over corpses, and Vin felt herself following.

I made him bring me, she thought. *I wanted to fight, like him. I'm going to have to get used to this.*

They dashed into a second corridor, and Kelsier jumped into the air. He lurched, then shot forward. Vin did the same, leaping and seeking an anchor far down the corridor, then using it to Pull herself through the air.

Side corridors whipped past, the air a rushing howl in her tin-enhanced ears. Ahead, two soldiers stepped into the corridor. Kelsier slammed feet-first into one, then flipped up and rammed a dagger into the other's neck. Both men fell.

No metal, Vin thought, dropping to the ground. *None of the guards in this place wear metal.* Hazekillers, they were called. Men trained to fight Allomancers.

Kelsier ducked down a side corridor, and Vin had to sprint to keep up with him. She flared pewter, willing her legs to move faster. Ahead, Kelsier paused, and Vin lurched to a stop beside him. To their right was an open, arching doorway, and it shone with a light far brighter than that of the small corridor lanterns. Vin extinguished her tin, following Kelsier through the archway and into the room.

Six braziers burned with open flames at the corners of the large, dome-roofed chamber. In contrast to the simple corridors, this room was covered with silver-inlayed murals. Each obviously represented the Lord Ruler; they were like the windows she had seen earlier, except less abstract. She saw a mountain. A large cavern. A pool of light.

And something very dark.

Kelsier strode forward, and Vin turned. The center of the room was dominated by a small structure—a building within the building. Ornate, with carved stone and flowing patterns, the single-story building stood reverently before them. All in all, the quiet, empty chamber gave Vin a strange feeling of solemnity.

Kelsier walked forward, bare feet falling on smooth black marble. Vin followed in a nervous crouch; the room seemed empty, but there had to be other guards. Kelsier walked up to a large oaken door set into the inner building, its surface carved with letterings Vin didn't recognize. He reached out and pulled open the door.

A Steel Inquisitor stood inside. The creature smiled, lips curling in an eerie expression beneath the two massive spikes that had been pounded point-first through its eyes.

Kelsier paused for just a moment. Then he yelled, "*Vin, run!*" as the Inquisitor's hand snapped forward, grabbing him by the throat.

Vin froze. To the sides, she saw two other black-robed Inquisitors stride through open archways. Tall, lean, and bald, they were also marked by their spikes and intricate Ministry eye tattoos.

The closest Inquisitor lifted Kelsier up into the air by his neck. "Kelsier, the Survivor of Hathsin," the creature said in a grinding voice. Then he turned toward Vin. "And . . . you. I've been looking for you. I'll let this one die quickly if you'll tell me which nobleman spawned you, half-breed."

Kelsier coughed, struggling for breath as he pried at the creature's grip. The Inquisitor turned, regarding Kelsier with spike-end eyes. Kelsier coughed again, as if trying to say something, and the Inquisitor curiously pulled Kelsier a bit closer.

Kelsier's hand whipped out, ramming a dagger into the creature's neck. As the Inquisitor stumbled, Kelsier slammed his fist into the creature's forearm, shattering the bone with a snap. The Inquisitor dropped him, and Kelsier fell to the reflective marble floor, coughing.

Gasping for breath, Kelsier looked up at Vin with intense eyes. "I said *run!*" he croaked, tossing something to her.

Vin paused, reaching out to catch the coin pouch. However, it lurched suddenly in the air, shooting forward. Abruptly, she realized Kelsier wasn't throwing it to her, but *at* her.

The bag hit her in the chest. Pushed by Kelsier's Allomancy, it hurled her across the room—past the two surprised Inquisitors—until she finally dropped awkwardly to the floor, skidding on the marble.

Vin looked up, slightly dazed. In the distance, Kelsier regained his feet. The main Inquisitor, however, didn't seem very concerned about the dagger in his neck. The other two Inquisitors stood between her and Kelsier. One turned toward her, and Vin felt chilled by its horrifying, unnatural gaze.

"*RUN!*" The word echoed in the domed chamber. And this time, finally, it struck home.

Vin scrambled to her feet—fear shocking her, screaming at her, making her move. She dashed toward the nearest archway, uncertain if it was the one she had come in through. She clutched Kelsier's coin pouch and burned iron, frantically seeking an anchor down the corridor.

Must get away!

She grabbed the first bit of metal she saw and yanked, tearing herself off the ground. She shot down the corridor at an uncontrolled speed, terror flaring her iron.

She lurched suddenly, and everything spun. She hit the

ground at an awkward angle—her head slamming against the rough stone—then lay dizzily, wondering what had happened. The coin pouch . . . someone had Pulled on it, using its metal to yank her backward.

Vin rolled over and saw a dark form shooting down the corridor. The Inquisitor's robes fluttered as he dropped lightly to his feet a short distance from Vin. He strode forward, his face impassive.

Vin flared tin and pewter, clearing her mind and pushing away the pain. She whipped out a few coins, Pushing them at the Inquisitor.

He raised a hand, and both coins froze in the air. Vin's own Push suddenly threw her backward, and she tumbled across the stones, skidding and sliding.

She heard the coins pling against the floor as she came to a rest. She shook her head, a dozen new bruises flaring angrily across her body. The Inquisitor stepped over the discarded coins, walking toward her with a smooth gait.

I have to get away! Even Kelsier had been afraid to face an Inquisitor. If he couldn't fight one, what chance did she have?

None. She dropped the pouch and jumped to her feet, then she ran, ducking through the first doorway she saw. The room beyond was empty of people, but a golden altar stood at its center. Between the altar, the four candelabra at the corners, and the cluttering of other religious paraphernalia, the space was cramped.

Vin turned, Pulling a candelabrum into her hands, remembering Kelsier's trick from before. The Inquisitor stepped into the room, then raised an almost amused hand, ripping the candelabra from her hands in an easy Allomantic Pull.

He's so strong! Vin thought with horror. He was probably steadying himself by Pulling against the lantern brackets behind. However, the force of his Ironpulls was far more powerful than Kelsier's had ever been.

Vin jumped, Pulling herself slightly up and over the altar. At the doorway, the Inquisitor reached over to a bowl that sat atop a short pillar, pulling out what appeared to be a handful of small metal triangles. They were sharp on all sides, and they cut the creature's hand in a dozen different places. He ignored the wounds, raising a bloody hand toward her.

Vin yelped, ducking behind the altar as pieces of metal sprayed against the back wall.

"You are trapped," the Inquisitor said in a scratchy voice. "Come with me."

Vin glanced to the side. There weren't any other doors in the room. She peeked up, glancing at the Inquisitor, and a piece of metal shot at her face. She Pushed against it, but the Inquisitor was too strong. She had to duck and let the metal go, lest his power pin her back against the wall.

I'll need something to block with. Something that isn't made of metal.

As she heard the Inquisitor step into the room, she found what she needed—a large, leather-bound book sitting beside the altar. She grabbed it, then paused. There was no use in being rich if she died. She pulled out Kelsier's vial and downed the atium, then burned it.

The Inquisitor's shadow stepped around the side of the altar, then the actual Inquisitor followed a second later. The atium-shadow opened its hand, and a spray of tiny, translucent daggers shot at her.

Vin raised her book as the real daggers followed. She swung the book through the shadow trails just as the real daggers shot toward her. She caught every one, their sharp, jagged edges digging deeply into the book's leather cover.

The Inquisitor paused, and she was rewarded by what seemed to be a look of confusion on its twisted face. Then a hundred shadow images shot from his body.

Lord Ruler! Vin thought. He had atium too.

Not pausing to worry about what that meant, Vin hopped over the altar, carrying the book with her as protection against further missiles. The Inquisitor spun, spike-eyes following her as she ducked back into the hallway.

A squad of soldiers stood waiting for her. However, each one bore a future-shadow. Vin ducked between them, barely watching where their weapons would fall, somehow avoiding the attacks of twelve different men. And, for a moment, she almost forgot the pain and fear—and they were replaced by an incredible sense of power. She dodged effortlessly, staves swinging above and beside her, each one missing by just inches. She was invincible.

She spun through the ranks of the men, not bothering to kill or hurt them—she only wanted to escape. As she passed the last one, she turned around a corner.

And a second Inquisitor, his body springing with shadow images, stepped up and slammed something sharp into her lower side.

Vin gasped in pain. There was a sickening sound as the creature pulled his weapon free of her body; it was a length of wood affixed with sharp obsidian blades. Vin grasped her side, stumbling backward, feeling a terrifying amount of warm blood seeping from the wound.

The Inquisitor looked familiar. *The first one, from the other room,* she thought through the pain. *Does . . . that mean that Kelsier is dead?*

"Who is your father?" the Inquisitor asked.

Vin kept her hand at her side, trying to stop the blood. It was a large wound. A bad wound. She had seen such wounds before. They always killed.

Yet, she still stood. *Pewter,* her confused mind thought. *Flare pewter!*

She did so, the metal giving her body strength, letting her stay on her feet. The soldiers stepped back to let the second Inquisitor approach her from the side. Vin looked in horror from one Inquisitor to the other, both descending upon her, blood pouring between her fingers and down her side. The lead Inquisitor still carried the axelike weapon, its edge coated with blood. Her blood.

I'm going to die, she thought with terror.

And then she heard it. Rain. It was faint, but her tin-ears picked it out behind her. She spun, lurching through a door, and was rewarded by the sight of a large archway on the other side of the room. Mist pooled at the room's floor, and rain slapped the stones outside.

Must have been where the guards came from, she thought. She kept her pewter flared, amazed at how well her body still worked, and stumbled out into the rain, reflexively clutching the leather book to her chest.

"You think to escape?" the lead Inquisitor asked from behind, his voice amused.

Numbly, Vin reached into the sky and Pulled against one of the palace's many spires. She heard the Inquisitor curse as she pitched into the air, hurling up into the dark night.

The thousand spires rose around her. She Pulled against one, then switched to another. The rain was strong now, and it made the night black. There was no mist to reflect ambient light, and the stars were hidden by clouds above. Vin couldn't see where she was going; she had to use Allomancy to sense the metallic tips of the spires, and hope there was nothing in between.

She hit a spire, catching hold of it in the night and pulling to a stop. *Have to bandage the wound . . .* she thought weakly. She was beginning to grow numb, her head cloudy despite her pewter and tin.

Something slammed against the spire above her, and she heard a low growl. Vin Pushed off even as she felt the Inquisitor slash the air beside her.

She had one chance. Midjump, she Pulled herself sideways, toward a different spire. At the same time, she Pushed against the book in her hands—it still had bits of metal embedded into its cover. The book continued in the direction she had been going, metal lines glowing weakly in the night. It was the only metal she had on her.

Vin caught the next spire lightly, trying to make as little sound as possible. She strained in the night, burning tin, the rainfall becoming a thunder in her ears. Over it, she thought she heard the distinct sound of something hitting a spire in the direction she had Pushed the book.

The Inquisitor had fallen for her ruse. Vin sighed, hanging from the spire, rain splattering her body. She made sure her copper was still burning, Pulled lightly against the spire to hold herself in place, and ripped off a piece of her shirt to bandage the wound. Despite her numb mind, she couldn't help noticing how big the gash was.

Oh, Lord, she thought. Without pewter, she would have fallen unconscious long ago. She should be dead.

Something sounded in the darkness. Vin felt a chill, looking up. All was black around her.

It can't be. He can't—

Something slammed into her spire. Vin cried out, jumping away. She Pulled herself toward another spire, caught it weakly, then immediately Pushed off again. The Inquisitor followed, thuds sounding as he jumped from spire to spire behind her.

He found me. He couldn't see me, hear me, or sense me. But he found me.

Vin hit a spire, holding it by one hand, limply hanging in the night. Her strength was nearly gone. *I . . . have to get away . . . hide. . . .*

Her hands were numb, and her mind felt nearly the same. Her fingers slipped from the cold, wet metal of the spire, and she felt herself drop free into the darkness.

She fell with the rain.

However, she went only a short distance before thudding against something hard—the roof of a particularly tall bit of the palace. Dazed, she climbed to her knees, crawling away from the spire, seeking a corner.

Hide . . . hide . . . hide . . .

She crawled weakly to the nook formed by another tower. She huddled against the dark corner, lying in a deep puddle of ashy rainwater, arms wrapped around herself. Her body was wet with rain and blood.

She thought, for just a moment, that she might have escaped.

A dark form thumped to the rooftop. The rain was letting up, and her tin revealed a head set with two spikes, a body cloaked in a dark robe.

She was too weak to move, too weak to do more than shiver in the puddle of water, clothing plastered to her skin. The Inquisitor turned toward her.

"Such a small, troubling thing you are," he said. He stepped forward, but Vin could barely hear his words.

It was growing dark again . . . no, it was just her mind. Her vision grew dark, her eyes closing. Her wound didn't hurt anymore. She couldn't . . . even . . . think. . . .

A sound, like shattering branches.

Then arms gripped her. Warm arms, not the arms of death. She forced her eyes open.

"Kelsier?" she whispered.

But it wasn't Kelsier's face that looked back at her, streaked with concern. It was a different, kinder face. She sighed in relief, drifting away as the strong arms pulled her close, making her feel oddly safe in the terrible storms of night.

I don't know why Kwaan betrayed me. Even still, this event haunts my thoughts. He was the one who discovered me; he was the Terris philosopher who first called me the Hero of Ages. It seems ironically surreal that now—after his long struggle to convince his colleagues—he is the only major Terris holy man to preach against my reign.

15

"YOU TOOK HER WITH YOU?" Dockson demanded, bursting into the room. "You took Vin into Kredik Shaw? Are you *bloody insane*?"

"Yes," Kelsier snapped. "You've been right all along. I'm a madman. A lunatic. Perhaps I should have just died in the Pits and never come back to bother any of you!"

Dockson paused, taken aback by the force in Kelsier's words. Kelsier pounded the table in frustration, and the wood splintered from the force of the blow. He still burned pewter, the metal helping him resist his several wounds. His mistcloak lay in tatters, his body sliced by a half-dozen different small cuts. His entire right side burned with pain. He'd have a massive bruise there, and he'd be lucky if none of his ribs were cracked.

Kelsier flared the pewter. The fire within felt good—it gave him a focus for his anger and self-loathing. One of the apprentices worked quickly, tying a bandage around Kelsier's largest gash. Clubs sat with Ham at the side of the kitchen; Breeze was away visiting a suburb.

"By the Lord Ruler, Kelsier," Dockson said quietly.

Even Dockson, Kelsier thought. *Even my oldest friend swears by the Lord Ruler's name. What are we doing? How can we face this?*

"There were three Inquisitors waiting for us, Dox," Kelsier said.

Dockson paled. "And you *left* her there?"

"She got out before I did. I tried to distract the Inquisitors as long as I could, but . . ."

"But?"

"One of the three followed her. I couldn't get to it—maybe the other two Inquisitors were simply trying to keep me busy so that their companion could find her."

"Three Inquisitors," Dockson said, accepting a small cup of brandy from one of the apprentices. He downed it.

"We must have made too much noise going in," Kelsier said. "Either that, or they were already there for some reason. And we *still* don't know what's in that room!"

The kitchen fell silent. The rain outside picked up again, assaulting the building with a reproachful fury.

"So . . ." Ham said, "what of Vin?"

Kelsier glanced at Dockson, and saw pessimism in his eyes. Kelsier had barely escaped, and he had years of training. If Vin was still in Kredik Shaw . . .

Kelsier felt a sharp, twisting pain in his chest. *You let her die too. First Mare, then Vin. How many more will you lead to slaughter before this is through?*

"She might be hiding somewhere in the city," Kelsier said. "Afraid to come to the shop because the Inquisitors are looking for her. Or . . . perhaps for some reason she went back to Fellise."

Maybe she's out there somewhere, dying alone in the rain.

"Ham," Kelsier said, "you and I are heading back to the palace. Dox, take Lestibournes and visit other thieving crews. Maybe one of their scouts saw something. Clubs, send an apprentice to Renoux's mansion to see if she went there."

The solemn group started to move, but Kelsier didn't need

to state the obvious. He and Ham wouldn't be able to get close to Kredik Shaw without running afoul of guard patrols. Even if Vin was hiding in the city somewhere, the Inquisitors would probably find her first. They would have—

Kelsier froze, his sudden jerk causing the others to pause. He'd heard something.

Hurried footsteps sounded as Lestibournes rushed down the stairs and into the room, his lanky form wet with rain. "Someone's coming! Out the night with the calling!"

"Vin?" Ham asked hopefully.

Lestibournes shook his head. "Big man. Robe."

This is it, then. I've brought death to the crew—I've led the Inquisitors right to them.

Ham stood, picking up a wooden stave. Dockson pulled out a pair of daggers, and Clubs's six apprentices moved to the back of the room, eyes wide with fright.

Kelsier flared his metals.

The back door to the kitchen slammed open. A tall, dark form in wet robes stood in the rain. And he carried a cloth-wrapped figure in his arms.

"Sazed!" Kelsier said.

"She is badly wounded," Sazed said, stepping quickly into the room, his fine robes streaming with rainwater. "Master Hammond, I require some pewter. Her supply is exhausted, I think."

Ham rushed forward as Sazed set Vin on the kitchen table. Her skin was clammy and pale, her thin frame soaked and wet.

She's so small, Kelsier thought. *Barely more than a child. How could I have thought to take her with me?*

She bore a massive, bloody wound in her side. Sazed set something aside—a large book he'd been carrying in his arms beneath Vin—and accepted a vial from Hammond, then bent down and poured the liquid down the unconscious girl's throat. The room fell silent, the sound of pounding rain coming through the still open door.

Vin's face flushed slightly with color, and her breathing seemed to steady. To Kelsier's Allomantic bronze senses, she began to pulse softly with a rhythm not unlike a second heartbeat.

"Ah, good," Sazed said, undoing Vin's makeshift bandage. "I feared that her body was too unfamiliar with Allomancy to burn metals unconsciously. There is hope for her, I think. Master Cladent, I shall require a pot of boiled water, some bandages, and the medical bag from my rooms. Quickly, now!"

Clubs nodded, waving for his apprentices to do as instructed. Kelsier cringed as he watched Sazed's work. The wound was bad—worse than any he himself had survived. The cut went deeply into her gut; it was the type of wound that killed slowly, but consistently.

Vin, however, was no ordinary person—pewter would keep an Allomancer alive long after their body should have given out. In addition, Sazed was no ordinary healer. Religious rites were not the only things that Keepers stored in their uncanny memories; their metalminds contained vast wealths of information on culture, philosophy, and science.

Clubs ushered his apprentices from the room as the surgery began. The procedure took an alarming amount of time, Ham applying pressure to the wound as Sazed slowly stitched Vin's insides back together. Finally, Sazed closed the outer wound and applied a clean bandage, then asked Ham to carefully carry the girl up to her bed.

Kelsier stood, watching Ham carry Vin's weak, limp form out of the kitchen. Then, he turned to Sazed questioningly. Dockson sat in the corner, the only other one still in the room.

Sazed shook his head gravely. "I do not know, Master Kelsier. She could survive. We will need to keep her supplied with pewter—it will help her body make new blood. Even still, I have seen many strong men die from wounds smaller than this one."

Kelsier nodded.

"I arrived too late, I think," Sazed said. "When I found her gone from Renoux's mansion, I came to Luthadel as quickly as I could. I used up an entire metalmind to make the trip with haste. I was still too late. . . ."

"No, my friend," Kelsier said. "You've done well this night. Far better than I."

Sazed sighed, then reached over and fingered the large book he'd set aside before beginning the surgery. The tome was wet with rainwater and blood. Kelsier regarded it, frowning. "What is that, anyway?"

"I don't know," Sazed said. "I found it at the palace, while I was searching for the child. It is written in Khlenni."

Khlenni, the language of Khlennium—the ancient, pre-Ascension homeland of the Lord Ruler. Kelsier perked up a bit. "Can you translate it?"

"Perhaps," Sazed said, suddenly sounding very tired. "But . . . not for a time, I think. After this evening, I shall need to rest."

Kelsier nodded, calling for one of the apprentices to prepare Sazed a room. The Terrisman nodded thankfully, then walked wearily up the stairs.

"He saved more than Vin's life tonight," Dockson said, approaching quietly from behind. "What you did was stupid, even for you."

"I had to know, Dox," he said. "I had to go back. What if the atium really is in there?"

"You said that it isn't."

"I said that," Kelsier said with a nod, "and I'm mostly sure. But what if I'm wrong?"

"That's no excuse," Dockson said angrily. "Now Vin is dying and the Lord Ruler is alerted to us. Wasn't it enough that you got Mare killed trying to get into that room?"

Kelsier paused, but he was too drained to feel any anger. He sighed, sitting down. "There's more, Dox."

Dockson frowned.

"I've avoided talking about the Lord Ruler to the others," Kelsier said, "but . . . I'm worried. The plan is good, but I have this terrible, haunting feeling that we'll never succeed as long as he's alive. We can take his money, we can take his armies, we can trick him out of the city . . . but I still worry that we won't be able to stop him."

Dockson frowned. "You're serious about this Eleventh Metal business, then?"

Kelsier nodded. "I searched for two years to find a way to kill him. Men have tried everything—he ignores normal wounds, and decapitation only annoys him. A group of soldiers burned down his inn during one of the early wars. The

Lord Ruler walked out as barely more than a skeleton, then healed in a matter of seconds.

"Only the stories of the Eleventh Metal offered any hope. But I can't make it work! That's why I had to go back to the palace. The Lord Ruler's hiding *something* in that room—I can feel it. I can't help thinking that if we knew what it was, we'd be able to stop him."

"You didn't have to take Vin with you."

"She followed me," Kelsier said. "I worried that she'd try to get in on her own if I left her. The girl has a headstrong streak, Dox—she hides it well, but she's blasted stubborn when she wants to be."

Dockson sighed, then nodded quietly. "And we *still* don't know what's in that room."

Kelsier eyed the book Sazed had set on the table. The rainwater had marked it, but the tome was obviously designed to endure. It was strapped tightly to prevent water from seeping in, and the cover was of well-cured leather.

"No," Kelsier finally said. "We don't." *But we do have that, whatever it is.*

"Was it worth it, Kell?" Dockson asked. "Was this insane stunt really worth nearly getting yourself—and the child—killed?"

"I don't know," Kelsier said honestly. He turned to Dockson, meeting his friend's eyes. "Ask me once we know whether or not Vin will live."

THE END OF PART TWO

PART THREE

CHILDREN OF A BLEEDING SUN

Many think that my journey started in Khlennium, that great city of wonder. They forget that I was no king when my quest began. Far from it.

I think it would do men well to remember that this task was not begun by emperors, priests, prophets, or generals. It didn't start in Khlennium or Kordel, nor did it come from the great nations to the east or the fiery empire of the West.

It began in a small, unimportant town whose name would mean nothing to you. It began with a youth, the son of a blacksmith, who was unremarkable in every way—except, perhaps, in his ability to get into trouble.

It began with me.

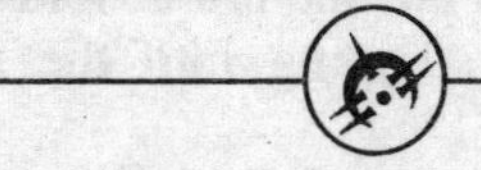

16

WHEN VIN AWOKE, THE PAIN told her that Reen had beaten her again. What had she done? Had she been too friendly to one of the other crewmembers? Had she made a foolish comment, drawing the crewleader's ire? She was to remain quiet, always quiet, staying away from the others, never calling attention to herself. Otherwise he would beat her. She had to learn, he said. She had to learn. . . .

But, her pain seemed too strong for that. It had been a long time since she could remember hurting this much.

She coughed slightly, opening her eyes. She lay in a bed that was far too comfortable, and a lanky teenage boy sat in a chair beside her bed.

Lestibournes, she thought. *That's his name. I'm in Clubs's shop.*

Lestibournes jumped to his feet. "You're awaking!"

She tried to speak, but just coughed again, and the boy hurriedly gave her a cup of water. Vin sipped it thankfully, grimacing at the pain in her side. In fact, her entire body felt like it had been pummeled soundly.

"Lestibournes," she finally croaked.

"Notting as the now," he said. "Kelsier wasing the hit with my name; changed it to Spook."

"Spook?" Vin asked. "It fits. How long have I been asleep?"

"Two weeks," the boy said. "Wait here." He scrambled away, and she could hear him calling out in the distance.

Two weeks? She sipped at the cup, trying to organize her muddled memories. Reddish afternoon sunlight shone through the window, lighting the room. She set the cup aside, checking her side, where she found a large white bandage.

That's where the Inquisitor hit me, she thought. *I should be dead.*

Her side was bruised and discolored from where she'd hit the roof after falling, and her body bore a dozen other nicks, bruises, and scrapes. All in all, she felt absolutely terrible.

"Vin!" Dockson said, stepping into the room. "You're awake!"

"Barely," Vin said with a groan, lying back against her pillow.

Dockson chuckled, walking over and sitting on Lestibournes's stool. "How much do you remember?"

"Most everything, I think," she said. "We fought our way into the palace, but there were Inquisitors. They chased us, and Kelsier fought—" She stopped, looking at Dockson. "Kelsier? Is he—"

"Kell's fine," Breeze said. "He came out of the incident in far better shape than you did. He knows the palace fairly well, from the plans we made three years ago, and he . . ."

Vin frowned as Dockson trailed off. "What?"

"He said the Inquisitors didn't seem very focused on killing him. They left one to chase him, and sent two after you."

Why? Vin thought. *Did they simply want to concentrate*

their energy on the weakest enemy first? Or, is there another reason? She sat back thoughtfully, working through the events of that night.

"Sazed," Vin she finally said. "He saved me. The Inquisitor was about to kill me, but . . . Dox, what *is* he?"

"Sazed?" Dockson asked. "That's probably a question I should let him answer."

"Is he here?"

Dockson shook his head. "He had to return to Fellise. Breeze and Kell are out recruiting, and Ham left last week to inspect our army. He won't be back for another month at least."

Vin nodded, feeling drowsy.

"Drink the rest of your water," Dockson suggested. "There's something in it to help with the pain."

Vin downed the rest of the drink, then rolled over and let sleep take her again.

Kelsier was there when she awoke. He sat on the stool by her bed, hands clasped with his elbows on his knees, watching her by the faint light of a lantern. He smiled when she opened her eyes. "Welcome back."

She immediately reached for the cup of water on the bedstand. "How's the job going?"

He shrugged. "The army is growing, and Renoux has begun to purchase weapons and supplies. Your suggestion regarding the Ministry turned out to be a good one—we found Theron's contact, and we've nearly negotiated a deal that will let us place someone as a Ministry acolyte."

"Marsh?" Vin asked. "Will he do it himself?"

Kelsier nodded. "He's always had a . . . certain fascination with the Ministry. If any skaa can pull off imitating an obligator, it will be Marsh."

Vin nodded, sipping her drink. There was something different about Kelsier. It was subtle—a slight alteration in his air and attitude. Things had changed during her sickness.

"Vin," Kelsier said hesitantly. "I owe you an apology. I nearly got you killed."

Vin snorted quietly. "It's not your fault. I made you take me."

"You shouldn't have been able to make me," Kelsier said. "My original decision to send you away was the right one. Please accept the apology."

Vin nodded quietly. "What do you need me to do now? The job has to go forward, right?"

Kelsier smiled. "Indeed it does. As soon as you're up to it, I'd like you to move back to Fellise. We created a cover story saying that Lady Valette has taken sick, but rumors are starting to appear. The sooner you can be seen in the flesh by visitors, the better."

"I can go tomorrow," Vin said.

Kelsier chuckled. "I doubt it, but you can go soon. For now, just rest." He stood, moving to leave.

"Kelsier?" Vin asked, causing him to pause. He turned, looking at her.

Vin struggled to formulate what she wanted to say. "The palace . . . the Inquisitors . . . We're not invincible, are we?" She flushed; it sounded stupid when she said it that way.

Kelsier, however, just smiled. He seemed to understand what she meant. "No, Vin," he said quietly. "We're far from it."

Vin watched the landscape pass outside her carriage window. The vehicle, sent from Mansion Renoux, had supposedly taken Lady Valette for a ride through Luthadel. In reality, it hadn't picked up Vin until it had stopped briefly by Clubs's street. Now, however, her window shades were open, showing her again to the world—assuming anyone cared.

The carriage made its way back toward Fellise. Kelsier had been right: She'd had to rest three more days in Clubs's shop before feeling strong enough to make the trip. In part, she'd waited simply because she had dreaded struggling into a noblewoman's dresses with her bruised arms and wounded side.

Still, it felt good to be up again. There had been something . . . wrong about simply recovering in bed. Such a lengthy period of rest wouldn't have been given to a regular thief; thieves either got back to work quickly or were abandoned for dead. Those who couldn't bring in money for food couldn't be allowed to take up space in the lair.

But, that isn't the only way people live, Vin thought. She was still uncomfortable with that knowledge. It hadn't mattered to Kelsier and the others that she drained their resources—they hadn't exploited her weakened state, but had cared for her, each one spending time at her bedside. Most notable among the vigilists had been the young Lestibournes. Vin didn't even feel that she knew him very well, yet Kelsier said that the boy had spent hours watching over her during her coma.

What did one make of a world where a crewleader agonized over his people? In the underground, each person bore responsibility for what happened to them—the weaker segment of a crew had to be allowed to die, lest they keep everyone else from earning enough to survive. If a person got captured by the Ministry, you left them to their fate and hoped that they didn't betray too much. You didn't worry about your own guilt at putting them in danger.

They're fools, Reen's voice whispered. *This entire plan will end in disaster—and your death will be your own fault for not leaving when you could.*

Reen had left when he could. Perhaps he'd known that the Inquisitors would eventually hunt her down for the powers she unwittingly possessed. He always had known when to leave—it was no accident, she thought, that he hadn't ended up slaughtered with the rest of Camon's crew.

And yet, she ignored Reen's promptings in her head, instead letting the carriage pull her toward Fellise. It wasn't that she felt completely secure in her place with Kelsier's crew—indeed, in a way, her place with these people was making her even more apprehensive. What if they stopped needing her? What if she became useless to them?

She had to prove to them that she could do what they needed her to. There were functions to attend, a society to infiltrate. She had so much work to do; she couldn't afford to spend any more of it sleeping.

In addition, she needed to return to her Allomantic practice sessions. It had only taken a few short months for her to grow dependent upon her powers, and she longed for the freedom of leaping through the mists, of Pulling and Pushing her way through the skies. Kredik Shaw had taught her that she wasn't invincible—but Kelsier's survival with barely a scratch proved that it was possible to be much better than she was. Vin needed to practice, to grow in strength, until she too could escape Inquisitors like Kelsier had.

The carriage turned a bend and rolled into Fellise. The familiar, pastoral suburb made Vin smile to herself, and she leaned against the open carriage window, feeling the breeze. With luck, some streetgoers would gossip that Lady Valette had been seen riding through the city. She arrived at Mansion Renoux a few short turns later. A footman opened the door, and Vin was surprised to see Lord Renoux himself waiting outside the carriage to help her down.

"My lord?" she said, giving him her hand. "Surely you have more important things to attend to."

"Nonsense," he said. "A lord must be allowed time to dote upon his favored niece. How was your ride?"

Does he ever break character? He didn't ask after the others in Luthadel, or give any indication that he knew of her wound.

"It was refreshing, Uncle," she said as they walked up the steps to the mansion doors. Vin was thankful for the pewter burning lightly in her stomach to give strength to her still weak legs. Kelsier had warned against using it too much, lest she grow dependent upon its power, but she saw little alternative until she was healed.

"That is wonderful," Renoux said. "Perhaps, once you are feeling better, we should take lunch together on the garden balcony. It has been warm lately, despite the coming winter."

"That would be very pleasant," Vin said. Before, she'd found the impostor's noble bearing intimidating. Yet, as she slipped into the persona of Lady Valette, she experienced the same calmness as before. Vin the thief was nothing to a man such as Renoux, but Valette the socialite was another matter.

"Very good," Renoux said, pausing inside the entryway. "However, let us attend to that on another day—for now, you would likely prefer to rest from your journey."

"Actually, my lord, I'd like to visit Sazed. I have some matters I must discuss with the steward."

"Ah," Renoux said. "You will find him in the library, working on one of my projects."

"Thank you," Vin said.

Renoux nodded, then walked away, his dueling cane clicking against the white marble floor. Vin frowned, trying to decide if he was completely sane. Could someone really adopt a persona that wholly?

You do it, Vin reminded herself. *When you become Lady Valette, you show a completely different side of yourself.*

She turned, flaring pewter to help her climb the northern set of stairs. She let her flare lapse as she reached the top, returning to a normal burn. As Kelsier said, it was dangerous to flare metals for too extended a period; an Allomancer could quickly make their body dependent.

She took a few breaths—climbing the stairs had been difficult, even with pewter—then walked down the corridor to the library. Sazed sat at a desk beside a small coal stove on the far side of the small room, writing on a pad of paper. He wore his standard steward's robes, and a pair of thin spectacles sat at the end of his nose.

Vin paused in the doorway, regarding the man who had saved her life. *Why is he wearing spectacles? I've seen him read before without them.* He seemed completely absorbed by his work, periodically studying a large tome on the desk, then turning to scribble notes on his pad.

"You're an Allomancer," Vin said quietly.

Sazed paused, then set down his pen and turned. "What makes you say that, Mistress Vin?"

"You got to Luthadel too quickly."

"Lord Renoux keeps several swift messenger horses in his stables. I could have taken one of those."

"You found me at the palace," Vin said.

"Kelsier told me of his plans, and I correctly assumed that you had followed him. Locating you was a stroke of luck, one that nearly took me too long to achieve."

Vin frowned. "You killed the Inquisitor."

"Killed?" Sazed asked. "No, Mistress. It takes far more power than I possess to kill one of those monstrosities. I simply . . . distracted him."

Vin stood in the doorway for a moment longer, trying to figure out why Sazed was being so ambiguous. "So, are you an Allomancer or not?"

He smiled, then he pulled a stool out from beside the desk. "Please, sit down."

Vin did as requested, crossing the room and sitting on the stool, her back to a massive bookshelf.

"What would you think if I told you that I wasn't an Allomancer?" Sazed asked.

"I'd think that you were lying," Vin said.

"Have you known me to lie before?"

"The best liars are those who tell the truth most of the time."

Sazed smiled, regarding her through bespectacled eyes. "That is true, I think. Still, what proof have you that I am an Allomancer?"

"You did things that couldn't have been done without Allomancy."

"Oh? A Mistborn for two months, and already you know all that is possible in the world?"

Vin paused. Up until just recently, she hadn't even known much about Allomancy. Perhaps there was more to the world than she had assumed.

There's always another secret. Kelsier's words.

"So," she said slowly, "what exactly *is* a 'Keeper'?"

Sazed smiled. "Now, *that* is a far more clever question, Mistress. Keepers are . . . storehouses. We remember things, so that they can be used in the future."

"Like religions," Vin said.

Sazed nodded. "Religious truths are my particular specialty."

"But, you remember other things too?"

Sazed nodded.

"Like what?"

"Well," Sazed said, closing the tome he had been studying. "Languages, for instance."

Vin immediately recognized the glyph-covered cover. "The book I found in the palace! How did you get it?"

"I happened across it while searching for you," the Terrisman said. "It is written in a very old language, one that hasn't been spoken regularly in nearly a millennium."

"But you speak it?" Vin asked.

Sazed nodded. "Enough to translate this, I think."

"And . . . how many languages do you know?"

"A hundred and seventy-two," Sazed said. "Most of them, such as Khlenni, are no longer spoken. The Lord Ruler's unity movement of the fifth century made certain of that. The language people now speak is actually a distant dialect of Terris, the language of my homeland."

A hundred and seventy-two, Vin thought with amazement. "That . . . sounds impossible. One man couldn't remember that much."

"Not one man," Sazed said. "One Keeper. What I do is similar to Allomancy, but not the same. You draw power from metals. I . . . use them to create memories."

"How?" Vin asked.

Sazed shook his head. "Perhaps another time, Mistress. My kind . . . we prefer to maintain our secrets. The Lord Ruler hunts us with a remarkable, confusing passion. We are far less threatening than Mistborn—yet, he ignores Allomancers and seeks to destroy us, hating the Terris people because of us."

"Hating?" Vin asked. "You're treated better than regular skaa. You're given positions of respect."

"That is true, Mistress," Sazed said. "But, in a way, the skaa are more free. Most Terrismen are raised from birth to be stewards. There are very few of us left, and the Lord Ruler's breeders control our reproduction. No Terrisman steward is allowed to have a family, or even to bear children."

Vin snorted. "That seems like it would be hard to enforce."

Sazed paused, hand laying on the cover of the large book. "Why, not at all," he said with a frown. "All Terrisman stewards are eunuchs, child. I assumed you knew that."

Vin froze, then she blushed furiously. "I . . . I'm . . . sorry. . . ."

"Truly and surely, no apology is required. I was castrated soon after my birth, as is standard for those who will be stewards. Often, I think I would have easily traded my life for that of a common skaa. My people are less than slaves . . . they're fabricated automatons, created by breeding programs, trained from birth to fulfill the Lord Ruler's wishes."

Vin continued to blush, cursing her lack of tact. Why hadn't anyone told her? Sazed, however, didn't seem offended—he never seemed to get angry about anything.

Probably a function of his . . . condition, Vin thought. *That's what the breeders must want. Docile, even-tempered stewards.*

"But," Vin said, frowning, "you're a rebel, Sazed. You're fighting the Lord Ruler."

"I am something of a deviant," Sazed said. "And, my people are not as completely subjugated as the Lord Ruler would believe, I think. We hide Keepers beneath his very eyes, and some of us even gather the courage to break our training."

He paused, then shook his head. "It is not an easy thing, however. We are a weak people, Mistress. We are eager to do as we are told, quick to seek subjugation. Even I, whom you dub a rebel, immediately sought out a position of stewardship and subservience. We are not so brave as we would wish, I think."

"You were brave enough to save me," Vin said.

Sazed smiled. "Ah, but there was an element of obedience in that too. I promised Master Kelsier that I would see to your safety."

Ah, she thought. She had wondered if he'd had a reason for his actions. After all, who would risk their life simply to save Vin? She sat for a moment in thought, and Sazed turned back to his book. Finally, she spoke again, drawing the Terrisman's attention. "Sazed?"

"Yes, Mistress?"

"Who betrayed Kelsier three years ago?"

Sazed paused, then set down his fountain pen. "The facts

are unclear, Mistress. Most of the crew assumes it was Mare, I think."

"Mare?" Vin asked. "Kelsier's wife?"

Sazed nodded. "Apparently, she was one of the only people who could have done it. In addition, the Lord Ruler himself implicated her."

"But, wasn't she sent to the Pits too?"

"She died there," Sazed said. "Master Kelsier is reticent about the Pits, but I sense that the scars he bears from that horrid place go much deeper than the ones you see on his arms. I don't think he ever knew if she was the traitor or not."

"My brother said that anyone would betray you, if they had the right chance and a good enough motive."

Sazed frowned. "Even if such a thing were true, I would not want to live believing it."

It seems better than what happened to Kelsier: being turned over to the Lord Ruler by one you thought you loved.

"Kelsier is different lately," Vin said. "He seems more reserved. Is that because he feels guilty for what happened to me?"

"I suspect that is part of it," Sazed said. "However, he is also coming to realize that there is a large difference between heading a small crew of thieves and organizing a large rebellion. He can't take the risks he once did. The process is changing him for the better, I think."

Vin wasn't so certain. However, she remained silent, realizing with frustration how tired she was. Even sitting on a stool seemed strenuous to her now.

"Go and sleep, Mistress," Sazed said, picking up his pen and relocating his place in the tome with his finger. "You survived something that probably should have killed you. Give your body the thanks it deserves; let it rest."

Vin nodded tiredly, then climbed to her feet and left him scribbling quietly in the afternoon light.

Sometimes I wonder what would have happened if I'd remained there, in that lazy village of my birth. I'd have become a smith, like my father. Perhaps I'd have a family, sons of my own.

Perhaps someone else would have come to carry this terrible burden. Someone who could bear it far better than I. Someone who deserved to be a hero.

17

BEFORE COMING TO MANSION RENOUX, Vin had never seen a cultivated garden. On burglaries or scouting missions, she had occasionally seen ornamental plants, but she'd never given them much heed—they, like many noble interests, had seemed frivolous to her.

She hadn't realized how beautiful the plants could be when arranged carefully. Mansion Renoux's garden balcony was a thin, oval structure that overlooked the grounds below. The gardens weren't large—they required too much water and attention to form more than a thin perimeter around the back of the building.

Still, they were marvelous. Instead of mundane browns and whites, the cultivated plants were of deeper, more vibrant colors—shades of red, orange, and yellow, with the colors concentrated in their leaves. The groundskeepers had planted them to make intricate, beautiful patterns. Closer to the balcony, exotic trees with colorful yellow leaves gave shade and protected from ashfalls. It was a very mild winter, and most of the trees still held their leaves. The air felt cool, and the rustling of branches in the wind was soothing.

Almost soothing enough, in fact, to make Vin forget how annoyed she was.

"Would you like more tea, child?" Lord Renoux asked. He

didn't wait for an answer; he simply waved for a servant to rush forward and refill her cup.

Vin sat on a plush cushion, her wicker chair designed for comfort. During the last four weeks, her every whim and desire had been met. Servants cleaned up after her, primped her, fed her, and even helped bathe her. Renoux saw that anything she asked for was given her, and she certainly wasn't expected to do anything strenuous, dangerous, or even slightly inconvenient.

In other words, her life was maddeningly boring. Before, her time at Mansion Renoux had been monopolized by Sazed's lessons and Kelsier's training. She'd slept during the days, having only minimal contact with the mansion staff.

Now, however, Allomancy—at least, the nighttime jumping kind—was forbidden her. Her wound was only partially healed, and too much motion reopened it. Sazed still gave her occasional lessons, but his time was dominated by translating the book. He spent long hours in the library, poring over its pages with an uncharacteristically excited air.

He's found a new bit of lore, Vin thought. *To a Keeper, that's probably as intoxicating as streetspice.*

She sipped at her tea with repressed petulance, eyeing the nearby servants. They seemed like scavenger birds, roosting and waiting for any opportunity to make Vin as comfortable—and as frustrated—as possible.

Renoux wasn't much help either. His idea of "taking lunch" with Vin was to sit and attend to his own duties—making notes on ledgers or dictating letters—while eating. Her attendance seemed important to him, but he rarely paid much attention to her other than to ask how her day had been.

Yet, she forced herself to act the part of a prim noblewoman. Lord Renoux had hired some new servants that didn't know about the job—not house staff, but gardeners and workmen. Kelsier and Renoux had worried that the other houses would grow suspicious if they couldn't get at least a few servant-spies onto the Renoux grounds. Kelsier didn't see it as a danger to the job, but it did mean that Vin had to maintain her persona whenever possible.

I can't believe that people live like this, Vin thought as some servants began clearing away the meal. *How can noblewomen fill their days with so much nothing? No wonder everyone's eager to attend those balls!*

"Is your respite pleasant, dear?" Renoux asked, pouring over another ledger.

"Yes, Uncle," Vin said through tight lips. "Quite."

"You should be up to a shopping trip soon," Renoux said, looking up at her. "Perhaps you would like to visit Kenton Street? Get some new earrings to replace that pedestrian stud you wear?"

Vin reached a hand to her ear, where her mother's earring still sat. "No," she said. "I'll keep this."

Renoux frowned, but said no more, for a servant approached and drew his attention. "My lord," the servant said to Renoux. "A carriage just arrived from Luthadel."

Vin perked up. That was the servants' way of saying that a member of the crew had arrived.

"Ah, very good," Renoux said. "Show them up, Tawnson."

"Yes, my lord."

A few minutes later, Kelsier, Breeze, Yeden, and Dockson walked out onto the balcony. Renoux discreetly waved to the servants, who closed the glass balcony doors and left the crew in privacy. Several men took up position just inside, watching to make certain that the wrong people didn't have an opportunity to eavesdrop.

"Are we interrupting your meal?" Dockson asked.

"No!" Vin said quickly, cutting off Lord Renoux's reply. "Sit, please."

Kelsier strolled over to the balcony's ledge, looking out over the garden and grounds. "Nice view you have here."

"Kelsier, is that wise?" Renoux asked. "Some of the gardeners are men for whom I cannot vouch."

Kelsier chuckled. "If they can recognize me from this distance, they deserve more than the Great Houses are paying them." However, he did leave the balcony edge, walking over to the table and spinning a chair, then sitting down on it the wrong way. Over the last few weeks, he had mostly returned to his old, familiar self. Yet, there were still changes. He held meetings more often, discussed more of his plans with the crew. He also still seemed different, more . . . thoughtful.

Sazed was right, Vin thought. *Our attack on the palace might have been near-deadly for me, but it has changed Kelsier for the better.*

"We thought we'd have our meeting here this week," Dockson said, "since you two rarely get to participate."

"That was most thoughtful of you, Master Dockson," Lord Renoux said. "But your concern is unnecessary. We are doing just fine—"

"No," Vin interrupted. "No, *we* aren't. Some of us need information. What's happening with the crew? How is the recruitment going?"

Renoux eyed her with dissatisfaction. Vin, however, ignored him. *He's not really a lord,* she told herself. *He's just another crewmember. My opinion counts as much as his! Now that the servants are gone, I can speak how I want.*

Kelsier chuckled. "Well, captivity's made her a bit more outspoken, if nothing else."

"I don't have anything to *do,*" Vin said. "It's driving me insane."

Breeze set his cup of wine on the table. "Some would find your state quite enviable, Vin."

"Then they must *already* be insane."

"Oh, they're mostly noblemen," Kelsier said. "So, yes, they're quite mad."

"The job," Vin reminded. "What's happening?"

"Recruitment is still too slow," Dockson said. "But we're improving."

"We may have to sacrifice further security for numbers, Kelsier," Yeden said.

That's a change too, she thought, impressed as she noted Yeden's civility. He had taken to wearing nicer clothing—not quite a full gentlemen's suit like Dockson or Breeze, but at least a well-cut jacket and trousers, with a buttoning shirt beneath, all kept clean of soot.

"That can't be helped, Yeden," Kelsier said. "Fortunately, Ham's doing well with the troops. I had a message from him just a few days ago. He's impressed with their progress."

Breeze snorted. "Be warned—Hammond does tend to be a bit optimistic about these kinds of things. If the army were made up of one-legged mutes, he would praise their balance and their listening skills."

"I should like to see the army," Yeden said eagerly.

"Soon," Kelsier promised.

"We should be able to get Marsh into the Ministry within the month," Dockson said, nodding to Sazed as the Terrisman passed their sentries and entered the balcony. "Hopefully, Marsh will be able to give some insight as to how to deal with the Steel Inquisitors."

Vin shivered.

"They are a concern," Breeze agreed. "Considering what a couple of them did to you two, I don't envy capturing the palace with them in there. They are as dangerous as Mistborn."

"More," Vin said quietly.

"Can the army really fight them?" Yeden asked uncomfortably. "I mean, they're supposed to be immortal, aren't they?"

"Marsh will find the answer," Kelsier promised.

Yeden paused, then nodded, accepting Kelsier's word.

Yes, changed indeed, Vin thought. It appeared that not even Yeden could resist Kelsier's charisma for an extended period of time.

"In the meantime," Kelsier said, "I'm hoping to hear what Sazed has learned about the Lord Ruler."

Sazed sat, laying his tome on the tabletop. "I will tell you what I can, though this is not the book that I first assumed it to be. I thought that Mistress Vin had recovered some ancient religious text—but it is of a far more mundane nature."

"Mundane?" Dockson asked. "How?"

"It is a journal, Master Dockson," Sazed said. "A record that appears to have been penned by the Lord Ruler himself—or, rather, the man who became the Lord Ruler. Even Ministry teachings agree that before the Ascension, he was a mortal man.

"This book tells of his life just prior to his final battle at the Well of Ascension a thousand years ago. Mostly, it is a record of his travels—a narration of the people he met, the places he visited, and the trials he faced during his quest."

"Interesting," Breeze said, "but how does it help us?"

"I am not certain, Master Ladrian," Sazed said. "However, understanding the real history behind the Ascension will be of use, I think. At the very least, it will give us some insight to the Lord Ruler's mind."

Kelsier shrugged. "The Ministry thinks it's important—Vin said she found it in some kind of shrine in the central palace complex."

"Which, of course," Breeze noted, "doesn't at *all* raise any questions regarding its authenticity."

"I do not believe it to be a fabrication, Master Ladrian," Sazed said. "It contains a remarkable level of detail, especially regarding unimportant issues—like packmen and supplies. In addition, the Lord Ruler it depicts is very conflicted. If the Ministry were going to devise a book for worship, they would present their god with more . . . divinity, I think."

"I'll want to read it when you are done, Saze," Dockson said.

"And I," Breeze said.

"Some of Clubs's apprentices occasionally work as scribes," Kelsier said. "We'll have them make a copy for each of you."

"Handy lot, those," Dockson noted.

Kelsier nodded. "So, where does that leave us?"

The group paused, then Dockson nodded to Vin. "With the nobility."

Kelsier frowned slightly.

"I can go back to work," Vin said quickly. "I'm mostly healed, now."

Kelsier shot a look at Sazed, who raised an eyebrow. He checked on her wound periodically. Apparently, he didn't like what he saw.

"Kell," Vin said. "I'm going *insane*. I grew up as a thief, scrambling for food and space—I can't just sit around and let these servants pamper me." *Besides, I have to prove that I can still be useful to this crew.*

"Well," Kelsier said. "You're one of the reasons we came here today. There's a ball this weekend that—"

"I'll go," Vin said.

Kelsier held up a finger. "Hear me out, Vin. You've been through a lot lately, and this infiltration could get dangerous."

"Kelsier," Vin said flatly. "My whole *life* has been dangerous. I'm going."

Kelsier didn't look convinced.

"She has to do it, Kell," Dockson said. "For one thing, the nobility is going to get suspicious if she doesn't start going to parties again. For another, we need to know what she sees. Having servant spies on the staff isn't the same as having a spy listening to local plots. You know that."

"All right, then," Kelsier finally said. "But you have to promise not to use physical Allomancy until Sazed says otherwise."

Later that evening, Vin still couldn't believe how eager she was to go the ball. She stood in her room, looking over the different gown ensembles that Dockson had found for her. Since she had been forced to wear noblewoman's attire for a good month straight, she was beginning to find dresses just a shade more comfortable than she once had.

Not that they aren't frivolous, of course, she thought, inspecting the four gowns. *All of that lace, the layers of material . . . a simple shirt and trousers are so much more practical.*

Yet, there *was* something special about the gowns—something in their beauty, like the gardens outside. When regarded as static items, like a solitary plant, the dresses were only mildly impressive. However, when she considered attending the ball, the gowns took on a new meaning. They were beautiful, and they would make her beautiful. They were the face she would show to the court, and she wanted to choose the right one.

I wonder if Elend Venture will be there. . . . Didn't Sazed say that most of the younger aristocrats attended every ball?

She lay a hand on one dress, black with silver embroiderings. It would match her hair, but was it too dark? Most of the other women wore colorful dresses; muted colors seemed reserved for men's suits. She eyed a yellow gown, but it just seemed a little too . . . perky. And the white one was too ornate.

That left the red. The neckline was lower—not that she had a lot to show—but it was beautiful. A bit gossamer, with full sleeves that were made of translucent mesh in places, it enticed her. But it seemed so . . . blatant. She picked it up, feeling the soft material in her fingers, imagining herself wearing it.

How did I get to this? Vin thought. *This thing would be impossible to hide in! These frilly creations, these aren't me.*

And yet . . . part of her longed to be back at the ball again. The daily life of a noblewoman frustrated her, but her memories of that one night were alluring. The beautiful couples dancing, the perfect atmosphere and music, the marvelous crystalline windows . . .

I don't even realize when I'm wearing perfume anymore, she realized with shock. She found it preferable to bathe in scented water each day, and the servants even perfumed her clothing. It was all subtle, of course, but it would be enough to give her away while sneaking.

Her hair had grown longer, and had been carefully cut by Renoux's stylist so that it fell around her ears, curling just slightly. She no longer looked quite so scrawny in the mirror, despite her lengthy sickness; regular meals had filled her out.

I'm becoming . . . Vin paused. She didn't know what she was becoming. Certainly not a noblewoman. Noblewomen didn't get annoyed when they couldn't to go out stalking at night. Yet, she wasn't really Vin the urchin anymore. She was . . .

Mistborn.

Vin carefully laid the beautiful red dress back on her bed, then crossed the room to look out the window. The sun was close to setting; soon, the mists would come—though, as usual, Sazed would have guards posted to make certain that she didn't go on any unauthorized Allomantic romps. She hadn't complained at the precautions. He was right: Unwatched, she probably would have broken her promise long ago.

She caught a glimpse of motion to her right, and could just barely make out a figure standing out on the garden balcony. Kelsier. Vin stood for a moment, then left her rooms.

Kelsier turned as she walked onto the balcony. She paused,

not wanting to interrupt, but he gave her one of his characteristic smiles. She walked forward, joining him at the carved stone balcony railing.

He turned and looked westward—not at the grounds, but beyond them. Toward the wilderness, lit by a setting sun, outside of town. "Does it ever look wrong to you, Vin?"

"Wrong?" she asked.

Kelsier nodded. "The dry plants, the angry sun, the smoky-black sky."

Vin shrugged. "How can those things be right or wrong? That's just the way things are."

"I suppose," Kelsier said. "But, I think your mind-set is part of the wrongness. The world shouldn't look like this."

Vin frowned. "How do you know that?"

Kelsier reached into his vest pocket and pulled out a piece of paper. He unfolded it with a gentle touch, then handed it to Vin.

She accepted the sheet, holding it carefully; it was so old and worn that it seemed close to breaking at the creases. It didn't contain any words, just an old, faded picture. It depicted a strange shape—something like a plant, though not one Vin had ever seen. It was too . . . flimsy. It didn't have a thick stalk, and its leaves were far too delicate. At its top, it had a strange collection of leaves that were a different color from the rest.

"It's called a flower," Kelsier said. "They used to grow on plants, before the Ascension. Descriptions of them appear in the old poems and stories—things that only Keepers and rebel sages know about anymore. Apparently, these plants were beautiful, and they had a pleasant smell."

"Plants that smell?" Vin asked. "Like fruit?"

"Something like that, I think. Some of the reports even claim that these flowers *grew into* fruit, in the days before the Ascension."

Vin stood quietly, frowning, trying to imagine such a thing.

"That picture belonged to my wife, Mare," Kelsier said quietly. "Dockson found it in her things after we were taken. He kept it, hoping that we would return. He gave it to me after I escaped."

Vin looked down at the picture again.

"Mare was fascinated by pre-Ascension times," Kelsier said, still staring out over the gardens. In the distance, the sun touched the horizon, and grew an even deeper red. "She collected things like that paper: pictures and descriptions of the old times. I think that fascination—along with the fact that she was a Tineye—is part of what led her to the underground, and to me. She's the one who first introduced me to Sazed, though I didn't use him in my crew at the time. He wasn't interested in thieving."

Vin folded up the paper. "And you keep this picture still? After . . . what she did to you?"

Kelsier fell silent for a moment. Then he eyed her. "Been listening at doors again, have we? Oh, don't worry. I suppose it's common enough knowledge." In the distance, the setting sun became a blaze, its ruddy light illuminating clouds and smoke alike.

"Yes, I keep the flower," Kelsier said. "I'm not really sure why. But . . . do you stop loving someone just because they betray you? I don't think so. That's what makes the betrayal hurt so much—pain, frustration, anger . . . and I still loved her. I still do."

"How?" Vin asked. "How can you? And, how can you possibly trust people? Didn't you learn from what she did to you?"

Kelsier shrugged. "I think . . . I think given the choice between loving Mare—betrayal included—and never knowing her, I'd choose love. I risked, and I lost, but the risk was still worth it. It's the same with my friends. Suspicion is healthy in our profession—but only to an extent. I'd rather trust my men than worry about what will happen if they turn on me."

"That sounds foolish," Vin said.

"Is happiness foolish?" Kelsier asked, turning toward her. "Where have you been happier, Vin? On my crew, or back with Camon?"

Vin paused.

"I don't know for sure if Mare betrayed me," Kelsier said, looking back at the sunset. "She always claimed that she didn't."

"And she was sent to the Pits, right?" Vin said. "That doesn't make sense, if she sided with the Lord Ruler."

Kelsier shook his head, still staring into the distance. "She showed up at the Pits a few weeks after I was sent there—we were separated, after we were caught. I don't know what happened during that time, or why she was eventually sent to Hathsin. The fact that she *was* sent to die hints that maybe she really didn't betray me, but . . ."

He turned toward Vin. "You didn't hear him when he caught us, Vin. The Lord Ruler . . . he thanked her. Thanked her for betraying me. His words—spoken with such an eerie sense of honesty—mixed with the way that the plan was set up . . . well, it was hard to believe Mare. That didn't change my love, though—not deep down. I nearly died when she did a year later, beaten before the slavemasters at the Pits. That night, after her corpse was taken away, I Snapped."

"You went mad?" Vin asked.

"No," Kelsier said. "Snapping is an Allomantic term. Our powers are latent at first—they only come out after some traumatic event. Something intense—something almost deadly. The philosophers say that a man can't command the metals until he has seen death and rejected it."

"So . . . when did it happen to me?" Vin asked.

Kelsier shrugged. "It's hard to tell. Growing up as you did, there were probably ample opportunities for you to Snap."

He nodded as if to himself. "For me," he said, "it was that night. Alone in the Pits, my arms bleeding from the day's work. Mare was dead, and I feared that I was responsible—that my lack of faith took away her strength and will. She died knowing that I questioned her loyalty. Maybe, if I'd really loved her, I wouldn't have ever questioned. I don't know."

"But, you didn't die," Vin said.

Kelsier shook his head. "I decided that I'd see her dream fulfilled. I'd make a world where flowers returned, a world with green plants, a world where no soot fell from the sky. . . ." He trailed off, then sighed. "I know. I'm insane."

"Actually," Vin said quietly, "it kind of makes sense. Finally."

Kelsier smiled. The sun sank beneath the horizon, and while its light was still a flare in the west, the mists began to appear. They didn't come from one specific place, they just sort of . . . grew. They extended like translucent, twisting vines in the sky—curling back and forth, lengthening, dancing, melding.

"Mare wanted children," Kelsier said suddenly. "Back when we were first married, a decade and a half ago. I . . . didn't agree with her. I wanted to become the most famous skaa thief of all time, and didn't have time for things that would slow me down.

"It's probably a good thing that we didn't have children. The Lord Ruler might have found and killed them. But, he might not have—Dox and the others survived. Now, sometimes, I wish that I had a piece of her with me. A child. A daughter, perhaps, with Mare's same dark hair and resilient stubbornness."

He paused, then looked down at Vin. "I don't want to be responsible for something happening to you, Vin. Not again."

Vin frowned. "I'm not spending any more time locked in this mansion."

"No, I don't suppose you will. If we try and keep you in much longer, you'll probably just show up at Clubs's shop one night having done something very foolish. We're a bit too much alike that way, you and I. Just . . . be careful."

Vin nodded. "I will."

They stood for a few more minutes, watching the mists gather. Finally, Kelsier stood up straight, stretching. "Well, for what it's worth, I'm glad you decided to join us, Vin."

Vin shrugged. "To tell you the truth, I'd kind of like to see one of those flowers for myself."

You could say that circumstances forced me to leave my home behind—certainly, if I had stayed, I would now be dead. During those days—running without knowing why, carrying a burden I didn't understand—I assumed that I would lose myself in Khlennium and seek a life of indistinction.

I am slowly coming to understand that anonymity, like so many other things, has already been lost to me forever.

18

SHE DECIDED TO WEAR THE red dress. It was definitely the boldest choice, but that felt right. After all, she hid her true self behind an aristocratic appearance; the more visible that appearance was, the easier it should be for her to hide.

A footman opened the carriage door. Vin took a deep breath—chest a little confined by the special corset she was wearing to hide her bandages—then accepted the footman's hand and climbed down. She straightened her dress, nodded to Sazed, then joined the other aristocrats making their way up the steps to Keep Elariel. It was a bit smaller than the keep of House Venture. However, Keep Elariel apparently had a separate party ballroom, while House Venture had its gatherings in the enormous main hall.

Vin eyed the other noblewomen, and felt a bit of her confidence vanish. Her dress was beautiful, but the other women had so much more than just gowns. Their long, flowing hair and self-assured airs matched their bejeweled figures. They filled out the upper portions of their dresses with voluptuous curves, and moved elegantly in the frilled splendor of the lower folds. Vin occasionally caught glimpses of the women's feet, and they didn't wear simple slippers like her own, but rather high-heeled shoes.

"Why don't I have shoes like that?" she asked quietly as they climbed the carpet-covered stairs.

"Heels take practice to walk in, Mistress," Sazed replied. "Since you've only just learned to dance, it might be best if you wore regular shoes for a time."

Vin frowned, but accepted the explanation. Sazed's mention of dancing, however, increased her discomfort. She remembered the flowing poise of the dancers at her last ball. She certainly wouldn't be able to imitate that—she barely even knew the basic steps.

That won't matter, she thought. *They won't see me—they'll see Lady Valette. She's supposed to be new and uncertain, and everyone thinks she's been ill lately. It will make sense for her to be a poor dancer.*

That thought in mind, Vin reached the top of the stairs feeling a bit more secure.

"I must say, Mistress," Sazed said. "You seem far less nervous this time—in fact, you even seem excited. This is the proper attitude for Valette to display, I think."

"Thank you," she said, smiling. He was right: She *was* excited. Excited to be part of the job again—excited, even, to be back among the nobility, with their splendor and grace.

They stepped up to the squat ballroom building—one of several low wings extending from the main keep—and a servant took her shawl. Vin paused a moment just inside the doorway, waiting as Sazed arranged her table and meal.

The Elariel ballroom was very different from the majestic Venture grand hall. The dim room was only a single story high, and while it had a lot of stained-glass windows, they were all in the ceiling. Circular rose-window skylights shone from above, lit by small limelights on the roof. Each table was set with candles, and despite the light from above, there was a reserved darkness about the room. It seemed . . . private, despite the numerous people in attendance.

This room had obviously been designed to accommodate parties. A sunken dancing floor lay at its center, and this was better lit than the rest of the room. There were two tiers of tables circling the dancing floor: The first tier was only a few feet above, the other was farther back and about twice as high.

A servant led her to a table at the rim of the room. She sat, Sazed taking his customary place beside her, and began to wait for her meal to arrive.

"How exactly am I supposed to get the information Kelsier wants?" she asked quietly, scanning the dark room. The deep, crystalline colors from above projected patterns across tables and people, creating an impressive atmosphere, yet making it difficult to distinguish faces. Was Elend here somewhere amidst the ball-goers?

"Tonight, some men should ask you to dance," Sazed said. "Accept their invitations—this will give you an excuse to seek them out later and mingle in their groups. You don't need to participate in conversations—you just have to listen. At future balls, perhaps some of the young men will begin to ask you to accompany them. Then you'll be able to sit at their table and listen to all of their discussions."

"You mean, sit with one man the entire time?"

Sazed nodded. "It's not uncommon. You would dance only with him that night as well."

Vin frowned. However, she let the matter drop, turning to inspect the room again. *He's probably not even here—he said he avoided balls when possible. Even if he were here, he'd be off on his own. You won't even—*

A muted thump sounded as someone dropped a stack of books onto her table. Vin jumped in startlement, turning as Elend Venture pulled over a chair, then sat down with a relaxed posture. He leaned back in the chair, angling toward a candelabrum beside her table, and opened a book to begin reading.

Sazed frowned. Vin hid a smile, eyeing Elend. He still didn't look as if he had bothered to brush his hair, and again wore his suit without the buttons done up. The garment wasn't shabby, but nor was it as rich as others at the party. It seemed to have been tailored to be loose and relaxed, defying the traditional sharp, well-cut fashion.

Elend flipped through his book. Vin waited patiently for him to acknowledge her, but he just continued to read. Finally, Vin raised an eyebrow. "I don't remember giving you permission to sit at my table, Lord Venture," she said.

"Don't mind me," Elend said, not looking up. "You've got a big table—there's plenty of room for both of us."

"Both of us, perhaps," Vin said. "But I'm not sure about those books. Where are the servers going to put my meal?"

"There's a bit of space to your left," Elend said offhandedly.

Sazed's frown deepened. He stepped forward, gathering up the books and setting them on the floor beside Elend's chair.

Elend continued to read. He did, however, raise a hand to gesture. "See, now, that's why I don't ever use Terrismen servants. They're an insufferably efficient lot, I must say."

"Sazed is hardly insufferable," Vin said coolly. "He is a good friend, and is probably a better man than you will ever be, Lord Venture."

Elend finally looked up. "I'm . . . sorry," he said in a frank tone. "I apologize."

Vin nodded. Elend, however, opened his book and began reading again.

Why sit with me if he's just going to read? "What did you do at these parties before you had me to pester?" she asked in an annoyed tone.

"See, now, how can I be pestering you?" he asked. "I mean, really, Valette. I'm just sitting here, reading quietly to myself."

"At *my* table. I'm certain you could get your own—you're the Venture heir. Not that you were forthcoming about that fact during our last meeting."

"True," Elend said. "I *do*, however, recall telling you that the Ventures were an annoying lot. I'm just trying to live up to the description."

"You're the one that made up the description!"

"Convenient, that," Elend said, smiling slightly as he read.

Vin sighed in frustration, scowling.

Elend peeked up over his book. "That's a stunning dress. It's almost as beautiful as you are."

Vin froze, jaw hanging open slightly. Elend smiled mischievously, then turned back to his book, eyes sparkling as if to indicate that he'd made the comment simply because he knew the reaction he'd get.

Sazed loomed over the table, not bothering to mask his disapproval. Yet, he said nothing. Elend was obviously too important to be chastised by a simple steward.

Vin finally found her tongue. "How is it, Lord Venture, that an eligible man like yourself comes to these balls alone?"

"Oh, I don't," Elend said. "My family usually has one girl or another lined up to accompany me. Tonight's fare is the Lady Stase Blanches—she's the one in the green dress sitting on the lower tier across from us."

Vin glanced across the room. Lady Blanches was a gorgeous blond woman. She kept glancing up at Vin's table, covering a scowl.

Vin flushed, turning away. "Um, shouldn't you be down there with her?"

"Probably," Elend said. "But, see, I'll tell you a secret. The truth is, I'm not really much of a gentleman. Besides, *I* didn't invite her—it wasn't until I got into the carriage that I was informed regarding my accompaniment."

"I see," Vin said with a frown.

"My behavior is, nonetheless, deplorable. Unfortunately, I'm quite prone to such bouts of deplorability—take, for instance, my fondness for reading books at the dinner table. Excuse me for a moment; I'm going to go get something to drink."

He stood, tucking the book into his pocket, and walked toward one of the room's bar tables. Vin watched him go, both annoyed and bemused.

"This is not good, Mistress," Sazed said in a low tone.

"He's not *that* bad."

"He's using you, Mistress," Sazed said. "Lord Venture is infamous for his unconventional, disobedient attitude. Many people dislike him—precisely because he does things like this."

"Like this?"

"He is sitting with you because he knows that it will annoy his family," Sazed said. "Oh, child—I do not wish to bring you pain, but you must understand the ways of the court. This young man is not romantically interested in you. He is a young, arrogant lord who chafes at his father's restrictions—so he rebels, acting rude and offensive. He knows that his father will relent if he acts spoiled enough for long enough."

Vin felt her stomach twist. *Sazed's probably right, of course. Why else would Elend seek me out? I'm exactly what he needs—someone lowborn enough to annoy his father, but inexperienced enough not to see the truth.*

Her meal arrived, but Vin didn't have much of an appetite anymore. She began to pick at the food as Elend returned, settling down with a large goblet filled with some mixed drink. He sipped as he read.

Let's see how he reacts if I don't interrupt his reading, Vin thought in annoyance, remembering her lessons, and eating her food with a lady's grace. It wasn't a large meal—mostly some rich, buttered vegetables—and the sooner she finished, the sooner she could get to dancing. At least then she wouldn't have to sit with Elend Venture.

The young lord paused several times as she ate, peeking at her over the top of his book. He obviously expected her to say something, but she never did. As she ate, however, her anger faded. She glanced at Elend, studying his slightly disheveled appearance, watching the earnestness with which he read his book. Could this man really hide the twisted sense of manipulation Sazed implied? Was he really just using her?

Anyone will betray you, Reen whispered. *Everyone will betray you.*

Elend just seemed so . . . genuine. He felt like a real person, not a front or a face. And it did seem like he wanted her to talk to him. It felt like a personal victory to Vin when he finally sat the book down and looked at her.

"Why are you here, Valette?" he asked.

"Here at the party?"

"No, here in Luthadel."

"Because it's the center of everything," Vin said.

Elend frowned. "I suppose it is. But, the empire is a big place to have such a small center. I don't think we really understand how large it is. How long did it take you to get here?"

Vin felt a moment of panic, but Sazed's lessons snapped quickly into her mind. "Almost two months by canal, with some stops."

"Such a long time," Elend said. "They say it can take half a year to travel from one end of the empire to the other, yet most of us ignore everything but this little bit at the center."

"I . . ." Vin trailed off. With Reen, she'd been all across the Central Dominance. It was the smallest of the dominances, however, and she'd never visited the more exotic places in the empire. This central area was good for thieves; oddly, the place closest to the Lord Ruler was also the one with the most corruption, not to mention the most riches.

"What do you think of the city, then?" Elend asked.

Vin paused. "It's . . . dirty," she said honestly. In the dim light, a servant arrived to remove her empty plate. "It's dirty, and it's full. The skaa are treated terribly, but I guess that's true everywhere."

Elend cocked his head, giving her a strange look.

I shouldn't have mentioned the skaa. That wasn't very noble-like.

He leaned forward. "You think the skaa here are treated worse than the ones on your plantation? I always thought they would be better off in the city."

"Um . . . I'm not sure. I didn't go to the fields very often."

"So, you didn't interact with them very much?"

Vin shrugged. "Why does it matter? They're just skaa."

"See, now, that's what we always say," Elend said. "But I don't know. Maybe I'm too curious, but they interest me. Did you ever hear them talk to one another? Did they sound like regular people?"

"What?" Vin asked. "Of course they did. What else would they sound like?"

"Well, you know what the Ministry teaches."

She didn't. However, if it was regarding the skaa, it probably wasn't flattering. "I make it a rule to never completely believe anything the Ministry says."

Elend paused again, cocking his head. "You're . . . not what I expected, Lady Valette."

"People rarely are."

"So, tell me about the plantation skaa. What are they like?"

Vin shrugged. "Like skaa everywhere else."

"Are they intelligent?"

"Some are."

"But, not like you and me, right?" Elend asked.

Vin paused. *How would a noblewoman respond?* "No, of course not. They're just skaa. Why are you so interested in them?"

Elend seemed . . . disappointed. "No reason," he said, sitting back in his chair and opening his book. "I think some of those men over there want to ask you to dance."

Vin turned, noticing that there was indeed a group of young men standing a short distance from her table. They looked away as soon as she turned. After a few moments, one of the men pointed at another table; then he walked over and asked a young lady to dance.

"Several people have noticed you, my lady," Sazed said. "However, they never approach. Lord Venture's presence intimidates them, I think."

Elend snorted. "They should know that I am anything but intimidating."

Vin frowned, but Elend just continued to read. *Fine!* she thought, turning back toward the young men. She caught one man's eye, smiling slightly.

A few moments later, the young man approached. He spoke to her in a stiff, formal tone. "Lady Renoux, I am Lord Melend Liese. Would you care to dance?"

Vin shot a glance at Elend, but he didn't look up from his book.

"I would love to, Lord Liese," Vin said, taking the young man's hand and rising.

He led her down to the dance floor, and as they approached, Vin's nervousness returned. Suddenly, one week of practice didn't seem like enough. The music stopped, allowing for couples to leave or enter the floor, and Lord Liese led her forward.

Vin fought down her paranoia, reminding herself that everyone saw the dress and the rank, not Vin herself. She looked up into Lord Liese's eyes and saw, surprisingly, apprehension.

The music began, as did the dancing. Lord Liese's face took on a look of consternation. She could feel his palm sweating in her hands. *Why, he's just as nervous as I am! Perhaps even more.*

Liese was younger than Elend, closer to her own age. He probably wasn't very experienced with balls—he certainly didn't look like he'd danced much. He focused so much on the steps that his motions felt rigid.

It makes sense, Vin realized, relaxing and letting her body move in the motions Sazed had taught. *The experienced ones wouldn't ask me to dance, not when I'm so new. I'm beneath their notice.*

But, why is Elend paying attention to me? Is it simply what Sazed said—a ploy to annoy his father? Why, then, does he seem interested in what I have to say?

"Lord Liese," Vin said. "Do you know much of Elend Venture?"

Liese looked up. "Um, I . . ."

"Don't focus so much on the dancing," Vin said. "My instructor says that it will flow more naturally if you don't try too hard."

He blushed.

Lord Ruler! Vin thought. *How fresh* is *this boy?*

"Um, Lord Venture . . ." Liese said. "I don't know. He's a very important person. Far more important than I am."

"Don't let his lineage intimidate you," Vin said. "From what I've seen, he's pretty harmless."

"I don't know, my lady," Liese said. "Venture is a very influential house."

"Yes, well, Elend doesn't live up to that reputation. He seems very fond of ignoring those in his company—does he do that to everyone?"

Liese shrugged, dancing more naturally now that they were talking. "I don't know. You . . . seem to know him better than I, my lady."

"I . . ." Vin trailed off. She *felt* as if she knew him well—far better than she should know a man after two brief encounters. She couldn't very well explain that to Liese, however.

But, maybe . . . Didn't Renoux say that he'd met Elend once?

"Oh, Elend is a friend of the family," Vin said as they spun beneath a crystalline skylight.

"He is?"

"Yes," Vin said. "It was very kind of my uncle to ask Elend

to watch over me at these parties, and so far he's been quite a dear. I do wish that he'd pay less attention to those books of his and more attention to introducing me, though."

Liese perked up, and he seemed to grow a little less insecure. "Oh. Why, that makes sense."

"Yes," Vin said, "Elend has been like an older brother to me during my time here in Luthadel."

Liese smiled.

"I ask you about him because he doesn't speak much of himself," Vin said.

"The Ventures have all been quiet lately," Liese said. "Ever since the attack on their keep several months back."

Vin nodded. "You know much about that?"

Liese shook his head. "No one tells me anything." He glanced down, watching their feet. "You're very good at dancing, Lady Renoux. You must have attended many balls back in your home city."

"You flatter me, my lord," Vin said.

"No, really. You're so . . . graceful."

Vin smiled, feeling a slight surge of confidence.

"Yes," Liese said, almost to himself. "You're not at all like Lady Shan said—" He stopped, jerking slightly, as if realizing what he was saying.

"What?" Vin said.

"Nothing," Liese said, his blush rising. "I'm sorry. It was nothing."

Lady Shan, Vin thought. *Remember that name.*

She prodded Liese further as the dance progressed, but he was obviously too inexperienced to know much. He did feel that there was a tension rising between the houses; though the balls continued, there were more and more absences as people didn't attend parties thrown by their political rivals.

When the dance ended, Vin felt good about her efforts. She probably hadn't discovered much of value to Kelsier—however, Liese was only the beginning. She'd work up to more important people.

Which means, Vin thought as Liese led her back to her table, *I'm going to have to attend a lot more of these balls.* It wasn't that the balls themselves were unpleasant—especially now that she was more confident in her dancing. However, more balls meant fewer chances to be out in the mists.

Not that Sazed would let me go anyway, she thought with an inward sigh, smiling politely as Liese bowed and retreated.

Elend had spread his books across the table, and her alcove was lit by several more candelabra—apparently filched from other tables.

Well, Vin thought, *we've at least got thieving in common.*

Elend hunched over the table, making notations in a small, pocket-sized book. He didn't look up as she sat. Sazed, she noticed, was nowhere to be seen.

"I sent the Terrisman to dinner," Elend said distractedly as he scribbled. "No need for him to go hungry while you twirled down below."

Vin raised an eyebrow, regarding the books that dominated her tabletop. Even as she watched, Elend pushed one tome aside—leaving it open to a specific page—and pulled over another. "So, how was the aforementioned twirling, anyway?" he said.

"It was actually kind of fun."

"I thought you weren't very good at it."

"I wasn't," Vin said. "I practiced. You may find this information surprising, but sitting in the back of a room reading books in the dark doesn't exactly help one become a better dancer."

"Is that a proposition?" Elend asked, pushing aside his book and selecting another. "It's unladylike to ask a man to dance, you know."

"Oh, I wouldn't want to take you away from your reading," Vin said, turning a book toward her. She grimaced—the text was written in a small, cramped hand. "Besides, dancing with you would undermine all of the work I just did."

Elend paused. Then he finally looked up. "Work?"

"Yes," Vin said. "Sazed was right—Lord Liese finds you intimidating, and he found me intimidating by association. It could be quite disastrous to a young lady's social life if all of the young men assumed her unavailable simply because an annoying lord decided to study at her table."

"So . . ." Elend said.

"So I told him that you were simply showing me the ways of court. Kind of like an . . . older brother."

"Older brother?" Elend asked, frowning.

"*Much* older," Vin said, smiling. "I mean, you've got to be at least twice my age."

"Twice your . . . Valette, I'm *twenty-one*. Unless you're a *very* mature ten-year-old, I'm nowhere near 'twice your age.' "

"I've never been good with math," Vin said offhandedly.

Elend sighed, rolling his eyes. Nearby, Lord Liese was speaking quietly with his group of friends, gesturing toward Vin and Elend. Hopefully, one would come ask her to dance soon.

"Do you know a Lady Shan?" Vin asked idly as she waited.

Surprisingly, Elend looked up. "Shan Elariel?"

"I assume so," Vin said. "Who is she?"

Elend turned back to his book. "Nobody important."

Vin raised an eyebrow. "Elend, I've only been doing this for a few months, but even *I* know not to trust a comment like that."

"Well . . ." Elend said. "I might be engaged to her."

"You have a fiancée?" Vin asked with exasperation.

"I'm not exactly sure. We haven't really done anything about the situation for a year or so. Everyone's likely forgotten the matter by now."

Great, Vin thought.

A moment later, one of Liese's friends approached. Glad to be rid of the frustrating Venture heir, Vin stood, accepting the young lord's hand. As she walked to the dance floor, she glanced at Elend, and caught him peeking over the book at her. He immediately turned back to his research with an overtly indifferent air.

Vin sat down at her table, feeling a remarkable level of exhaustion. She resisted the urge to pull off her shoes and massage her feet; she suspected that wouldn't be very ladylike. She quietly turned on her copper, then burned pewter, strengthening her body and washing away a bit of her fatigue.

She let her pewter, then her copper, lapse. Kelsier had assured her that with copper on, she couldn't be spotted as an Allomancer. Vin wasn't so certain. With pewter burning, her reactions were too fast, her body too strong. It seemed to her that an observant person would be able to notice such inconsistencies, whether or not they themselves were an Allomancer.

With the pewter off, her fatigue returned. She'd been trying to wean herself off constant pewter lately. Her wound was to the point that it only hurt badly if she twisted the wrong way, and she wanted to recover her strength on her own, if she could.

In a way, her fatigue this evening was a good thing—it was a result of an extended period of dancing. Now that the young men regarded Elend as a guardian, rather than a romantic interest, they had no qualms about asking Vin to dance. And, worried that she would make an unintended political statement by refusing, Vin had agreed to each request. A few months ago, she would have laughed at the idea of exhaustion from dancing. However, her sore feet, aching side, and tired legs were only part of it. The effort of memorizing names and houses—not to mention putting up with her dancing partners' fluffy conversation—left her mentally drained.

It's a good thing Sazed had me wear slippers instead of heels, Vin thought with a sigh, sipping her chilled juice. The Terrisman hadn't returned from his dinner yet. Notably, Elend wasn't at the table either—though his books still lay scattered across its top.

Vin eyed the tomes. Perhaps if she appeared to be reading, the young men would leave her alone for a bit. She reached over, riffling through the books for a likely candidate. The one she was most interested in—Elend's small, leather-bound notebook—was missing.

Instead, she picked a large, blue tome and hefted it over to her side of the table. She had picked it for its large lettering—was paper really so expensive that scribes needed to cram as many lines to a page as possible? Vin sighed, leafing through the volume.

I can't believe people read books this big, she thought. Despite the large lettering, each page was filled with words. It would take days and days to read the entire thing. Reen had taught her reading so that she would be able to decipher contracts, write notes, and perhaps play a noblewoman. However, her training hadn't extended to texts this massive.

Historical Practices in Imperial Political Rule, the first page read. The chapters had titles like "The Fifth Century Governorship Program" and "The Rise of Skaa Plantations." She flipped through to the end of the book, figuring it would probably be the most interesting. The final chapter was titled "Current Political Structure."

So far, she read, *the plantation system has produced a far more stable government than previous methodologies. The structure of Dominances with each provincial lord taking command of—and responsibility for—his skaa has fostered a competitive environment where discipline is harshly enforced.*

The Lord Ruler apparently finds this system troubling because of the freedom it allows the aristocracy. However, the relative lack of organized rebellion is undoubtedly enticing; during the two hundred years that the system has been in place, there hasn't been a major uprising in the Five Inner Dominances.

Of course, this political system is only an extension of the greater theocratic rulership. The aristocracy's independence has been tempered by a renewed vigor in obligator enforcement. No lord, no matter how lofty, would be advised to think himself above their law. The call from an Inquisitor can come to anyone.

Vin frowned. While the text itself was dry, she was surprised that the Lord Ruler allowed such analytical discussions of his empire. She settled back in her chair, holding up the book, but she didn't read any more. She was too exhausted from the hours she had spent covertly trying to wiggle information out of her dancing partners.

Unfortunately, politics didn't pay heed to Vin's state of exhaustion. Though she did her best to appear absorbed in Elend's book, a figure soon approached her table.

Vin sighed, preparing herself for another dance. She soon realized, however, that the newcomer wasn't a nobleman, but a Terrisman steward. Like Sazed, he wore robes with overlapping V designs, and was very fond of jewelry.

"Lady Valette Renoux?" the tall man asked in a faintly accented voice.

"Yes," Vin said hesitantly.

"My mistress, Lady Shan Elariel, requires your presence at her table."

Requires? Vin thought. She already didn't like that tone, and she had little desire to meet with Elend's former betrothed. Unfortunately, House Elariel was one of the more powerful Great Houses—probably not someone to dismiss offhandedly.

The Terrisman waited expectantly.

"Very well," Vin said, rising with as much grace as she could muster.

The Terrisman led Vin toward a table a short distance from her own. The table was well attended, with five women seated around it, and Vin picked out Shan immediately. Lady Elariel was obviously the statuesque woman with long dark hair. She wasn't participating in the conversation, but seemed to dominate it nonetheless. Her arms sparkled with lavender bracelets that matched her dress, and she turned dismissive eyes toward Vin as she approached.

Those dark eyes, however, were keen. Vin felt exposed before them—stripped of her fine dress, reduced to a dirty urchin once again.

"Excuse us, ladies," Shan said. The women immediately did as ordered, departing the table in a stately flurry.

Shan picked up a fork and began to meticulously dissect and devour a small piece of dessert cake. Vin stood uncertainly, the Terrisman steward taking up a position behind Shan's chair.

"You may sit," Shan said.

I feel like a skaa again, Vin thought, sitting. *Noblemen treat each other this way too?*

"You are in an enviable position, child," Shan said.

"How is that?" Vin asked.

"Address me as 'Lady Shan,'" Shan said, her tone unchanged. "Or, perhaps, 'Your Ladyship.'"

Shan waited expectantly, taking petite bites of the cake. Finally, Vin said, "Why is that, Your Ladyship?"

"Because young Lord Venture has decided to use you in his games. That means you have the opportunity to be used by me as well."

Vin frowned. *Remember to stay in character. You're the easily intimidated Valette.*

"Wouldn't it be better to not be used at all, Your Ladyship?" Vin said carefully.

"Nonsense," Shan replied. "Even an uncultured simpleton like yourself must see the importance of being useful to your betters." Shan said the words, even the insult, without vehemence; she simply seemed to take it for granted that Vin would agree.

Vin sat, dumbfounded. None of the other nobility had treated her in such a manner. Of course, the only member of a Great House she'd met so far was Elend.

"I trust from your vapid look that you accept your place," Shan said. "Do well, child, and perhaps I will let you join my retinue. You could learn much from the ladies here in Luthadel."

"Such as?" Vin asked, trying to keep the snappishness out of her voice.

"Look at yourself sometime, child. Hair like you've undergone some terrible disease, so scrawny that your dress hangs like a bag. Being a noblewoman in Luthadel requires . . . perfection. Not *that*." She said the last word while waving her hand dismissively toward Vin.

Vin flushed. There was a strange power to this woman's demeaning attitude. With a start, Vin realized that Shan reminded her of some crewleaders she had known, Camon the latest of them—men who would hit a person, fully expecting no resistance. Everyone knew that resisting such men only made the beating worse.

"What do you want from me?" Vin asked.

Shan raised an eyebrow as she set aside her fork, the cake only half-eaten. The Terrisman took the plate and walked off with it. "You really are a dull-minded thing, aren't you?" Shan asked.

Vin paused. "What does *Her Ladyship* want from me?"

"I'll tell you eventually—assuming Lord Venture decides to keep playing with you." Vin caught just the barest flash of hatred in her eyes when she said Elend's name.

"For now," Shan continued, "tell me of your conversation with him this evening."

Vin opened her mouth to respond. But . . . something felt wrong. She only caught the barest flicker of it—she wouldn't have even noticed that much without Breeze's training.

A Soother? Interesting.

Shan was trying to make Vin complacent. So that she would talk, perhaps? Vin began to relate her conversation with Elend, staying away from anything interesting. However, something still felt odd to her—something about the way that Shan was playing with her emotions. From the corner of her eye, Vin saw Shan's Terrisman return from the kitchens. However, he didn't walk back toward Shan's table—he headed in the other direction.

Toward Vin's own table. He paused beside it, and began to poke through Elend's books.

Whatever he wants, I can't let him find it.

Vin stood suddenly, finally provoking an overt reaction in Shan as the woman looked up with surprise.

"I just remembered that I told my Terrisman to find me at my table!" Vin said. "He'll be worried if I'm not sitting there!"

"Oh, for the Lord Ruler's sake," Shan muttered under her breath. "Child, there is no need—"

"I'm sorry, Your Ladyship," Vin said. "I've got to go."

It was a bit obvious, but it was the best she could manage. Vin curtsied and withdrew from Shan's table, leaving the displeased woman behind. The Terrisman was good—by the time Vin was a few steps away from Shan's table, he had noticed Vin and continued on his way, his motions impressively smooth.

Vin arrived back at her table, wondering if she'd made a blunder by leaving Shan so rudely. However, she was growing too tired to care. As she noticed another group of young men eyeing her, she hurriedly sat, plopping open one of Elend's books.

Fortunately, the ploy worked better this time. The young men eventually trailed away, leaving Vin in peace, and she sat back, relaxing slightly with the book open before her. The evening was growing late, and the ballroom was slowly beginning to empty.

The books, she thought with a frown, picking up her cup of juice to take a sip. *What did the Terrisman want with them?*

She scanned the table, trying to notice if anything had been disturbed, but Elend had left the books in such a state of disarray that it was hard to tell. However, a small book sitting beneath another tome caught her eye. Most of the other texts lay open to a specific page, and she had seen Elend perusing them. This particular book, however, was closed—and she couldn't remember him ever opening it. It had been there before—she recognized it because it was so much thinner than the others—so the Terrisman hadn't left it behind.

Curious, Vin reached over and slid the book out from underneath the larger book. It had had a black leather cover, and the spine read *Weather Patterns of the Northern Dominance.* Vin frowned, turning the book over in her hands. There was no title page, nor was an author listed. It launched directly into text.

When regarding the Final Empire in its entirety, one certain fact is unmistakable. For a nation ruled by a self-proclaimed divinity, the empire has experienced a frightening number of colossal leadership errors. Most of these have been successfully covered up, and can only be found in the metalminds of Feruchemists or on the pages of banned texts. However, one only need look to the near past to note such blunders as the Massacre at Devanex, the revision of the Deepness Doctrine, and the relocation of the Renates peoples.

The Lord Ruler does not age. That much, at least, is undeniable. This text, however, purports to prove that he is by no means infallible. During the days before the Ascension, mankind suffered chaos and uncertainty caused by an endless cycle of kings, emperors, and other monarchs. One would think that now, with a single, immortal governor, society would finally have an opportunity to find stability and enlightenment. It is the remarkable lack of either attribute in the Final Empire that is the Lord Ruler's most grievous oversight.

Vin stared at the page. Some of the words were beyond her skill, but she was able to grasp the author's meaning. He was saying . . .

She snapped the book closed and hurriedly put it back in its place. What would happen if the obligators discovered that

Elend owned such a text? She glanced to the sides. They were there, of course, mingling with the crowds like at the other ball, marked by their gray robes and tattooed faces. Many sat at tables with noblemen. Friends? Or spies for the Lord Ruler? Nobody seemed quite as comfortable when an obligator was nearby.

What is Elend doing with a book like that? A powerful nobleman like himself? Why would he read texts that malign the Lord Ruler?

A hand fell on her shoulder, and Vin spun reflexively, pewter and copper flaring in her stomach.

"Whoa," Elend said, stepping back and raising his hand. "Has anyone ever told you how jumpy you are, Valette?"

Vin relaxed, sitting back in her chair and extinguishing her metals. Elend sauntered over to his place and sat down. "Enjoying Heberen?"

Vin frowned, and Elend nodded to the larger, thick book that still sat before her.

"No," Vin said. "It's boring. I was just pretending to read so that the men would leave me alone for a bit."

Elend chuckled. "Now, see, your cleverness is coming back to snap at you."

Vin raised an eyebrow as Elend began to gather up his books, stacking them on the table. He didn't appear to notice that she'd moved the "weather" book, but he did carefully slide it into the middle of the stack.

Vin turned her eyes from the book. *I probably shouldn't tell him about Shan—not until I talk to Sazed.* "I think my cleverness did its job well," she said instead. "After all, *I* came to the ball to dance."

"I find dancing overrated."

"You can't remain aloof from the court forever, Lord Venture—you're the heir of a very important house."

He sighed, stretching and leaning back in his chair. "I suppose you're right," he said with surprising frankness. "But the longer I hold out, the more annoyed my father will become. That, in itself, is a worthy goal."

"He's not the only one you hurt," Vin said. "What of the

girls that never get asked to dance because you're too busy rummaging through your books?"

"As I recall," Elend said, setting the last book on the top of his pile, "someone was just pretending to read in order to *avoid* dancing. I don't think the ladies have any trouble finding more amicable partners than myself."

Vin raised an eyebrow. "I didn't have trouble because I'm new and I'm low-ranked. I suspect that the ladies closer to your station have trouble finding partners, amicable or not. As I understand it, noblemen are uncomfortable dancing with women above their station."

Elend paused, obviously searching for a comeback.

Vin leaned forward. "What is it, Elend Venture? Why are you so intent on avoiding your duty?"

"Duty?" Elend asked, leaning toward her, his posture earnest. "Valette, this isn't duty. This ball . . . this is fluff and distraction. A waste of time."

"And women?" Vin asked. "Are they a waste too?"

"Women?" Elend asked. "Women are like . . . thunderstorms. They're beautiful to look at, and sometimes they're nice to listen to—but most of the time they're just plain inconvenient."

Vin felt her jaw drop slightly. Then she noticed the twinkle in his eye, the smile at the edges of his lips, and she found herself smiling as well. "You say these things just to provoke me!"

His smile deepened. "I'm charming that way." He stood, looking at her fondly. "Ah, Valette. Don't let them trick you into taking yourself too seriously. It's not worth the effort. But, I must bid you a good evening. Try not to let months pass between balls you attend in the future."

Vin smiled. "I'll think about it."

"Please do," Elend said, bending down and scooting the tall stack of books off the table and into his arms. He teetered for a moment, then steadied himself and peeked to the side. "Who knows—maybe one of these days you'll actually get me to dance."

Vin smiled, nodding as the nobleman turned and walked

off, circling the perimeter of the ballroom's second tier. He was soon met by two other young men. Vin watched curiously as one of the men clapped Elend on the shoulder in a friendly way, then took half of the books. The three began to walk together, chatting.

Vin didn't recognize the newcomers. She sat thoughtfully as Sazed finally appeared out of a side hallway, and Vin eagerly waved him forward. He approached with a hurried step.

"Who are those men with Lord Venture?" Vin asked, pointing toward Elend.

Sazed squinted behind his spectacles. "Why . . . one of them is Lord Jastes Lekal. The other is a Hasting, though I don't know his given name."

"You sound surprised."

"Houses Lekal and Hasting are both political rivals of House Venture, Mistress. Noblemen often visit with each other in smaller, after-ball parties, making alliances. . . ." The Terrisman paused, turning back to her. "Master Kelsier will wish to hear of this, I think. It is time we retire."

"I agree," Vin said, rising. "And so do my feet. Let's go."

Sazed nodded, and the two of them made their way to the front doors. "What took you so long?" Vin asked as they waited for an attendant to fetch her shawl.

"I came back several times, Mistress," Sazed said. "But you were always dancing. I decided I would be of far more use speaking with the servants than I would be standing beside your table."

Vin nodded, accepting her shawl, then walked out the front steps and down the carpeted stairs, Sazed just behind her. Her step was quick—she wanted to get back and tell Kelsier the names she'd memorized before she forgot the whole list. She paused at the landing, waiting for a servant to fetch her carriage. As she did, she noticed something odd. A small disturbance was going on a short distance away in the mists. She stepped forward, but Sazed put a hand on her shoulder, holding her back. A lady wouldn't wander off into the mists.

She reached to burn copper and tin, but waited—the disturbance was getting closer. It resolved as a guard appeared from the mists, pulling a small, struggling form: a skaa boy in dirty clothing, face soot-stained. The soldier gave Vin a wide berth, nodding apologetically to her as he approached one of the guard captains. Vin burned tin to hear what was said.

"Kitchen boy," the soldier said quietly. "Tried to beg from one of the noblemen inside a carriage when they stopped for the gates to open."

The captain simply nodded. The soldier pulled his captive back out into the mists, walking toward the far courtyard. The boy struggled, and the soldier grunted with annoyance, keeping a tight grip. Vin watched him go, Sazed's hand on her shoulder, as if to hold her back. Of course she couldn't help the boy. He shouldn't have—

In the mists, beyond the eyesight of regular people, the soldier drew out a dagger and slit the boy's throat. Vin jumped, shocked, as the sounds of the boy's struggling tapered off. The guard dropped the body, then grabbed it by a leg and began to drag it away.

Vin stood, stunned, as her carriage pulled up.

"Mistress," Sazed prompted, but she simply stood there.

They killed him, she thought. *Right here, just a few paces away from where noblemen wait for their carriages. As if . . . the death were nothing out of the ordinary. Just another skaa, slaughtered. Like an animal.*

Or less than an animal. Nobody would slaughter pigs in a keep courtyard. The guard's posture as he'd performed the murder indicated that he'd simply been too annoyed with the struggling boy to wait for a more appropriate location. If any of the other nobility around Vin had noticed the event, they paid it no heed, continuing their chatting as they waited. Actually, they seemed a little more chatty, now that the screams had stopped.

"Mistress," Sazed said again, pushing her forward.

She allowed herself to be led into the carriage, her mind still distracted. It seemed such an impossible contrast to her. The pleasant nobility, dancing, just inside a room sparkling with light and dresses. Death in the courtyard. Didn't they care? Didn't they know?

This is the Final Empire, Vin, she told herself as the carriage rolled away. *Don't forget the ash because you see a little silk. If those people in there knew you were skaa, they'd have you slaughtered just as easily as they did that poor boy.*

It was a sobering thought—one that absorbed her during the entire trip back to Fellise.

Kwaan and I met by happenstance—though, I suppose, he would use the word "providence."

I have met many other Terris philosophers since that day. They are, every one, men of great wisdom and ponderous sagaciousness. Men with an almost palpable importance.

Not so Kwaan. In a way, he is as unlikely a prophet as I am a hero. He never had an air of ceremonious wisdom—nor was he even a religious scholar. When we first met, he was studying one of his ridiculous interests in the great Khlenni library—I believe he was trying to determine whether or not trees could think.

That he should be the one who finally discovered the great Hero of Terris prophecy is a matter that would cause me to laugh, had events turned out just a little differently.

19

KELSIER COULD FEEL ANOTHER ALLOMANCER pulsing in the mists. The vibrations washed over him like rhythmic waves brushing up against a tranquil shore. They were faint, but unmistakable.

He crouched atop a low garden wall, listening to the vibrations. The curling white mist continued its normal, placid wafting—indifferent, save for the bit closest to his body, which curled in the normal Allomantic current around his limbs.

Kelsier squinted in the night, flaring tin and seeking out the other Allomancer. He thought he saw a figure crouching atop a wall in the distance, but he couldn't be certain. He recognized the Allomantic vibrations, however. Each metal, when burned, gave off a distinct signal, recognizable to one who was well practiced with bronze. The man in the distance burned tin, as did the four others Kelsier had sensed hiding around Keep Tekiel. The five Tineyes formed a perimeter, watching the night, searching for intruders.

Kelsier smiled. The Great Houses were growing nervous. Keeping five Tineyes on watch wouldn't be that hard for a house like Tekiel, but the noblemen Allomancers would resent being forced into simple guard duty. And if there were five Tineyes on watch, chances were good that a number of Thugs, Coinshots, and Lurchers were on call as well. Luthadel was quietly in a state of alert.

The Great Houses were growing so wary, in fact, that Kelsier had trouble finding cracks in their defenses. He was only one man, and even Mistborn had limits. His success so far had been achieved through surprise. However, with five Tineyes on watch, Kelsier wouldn't be able to get very close to the keep without serious risk of being spotted.

Fortunately, Kelsier didn't need to test Tekiel's defenses this night. Instead, he crept along the wall toward the outer grounds. He paused near the garden well, and—burning bronze to make certain no Allomancers were near—reached into a stand of bushes to retrieve a large sack. It was heavy enough that he had to burn pewter to pull it free and throw it over his shoulder. He paused in the night for a moment, straining for sounds in the mist, then hauled the sack back toward the keep.

He stopped near a large, whitewashed garden veranda that sat beside a small reflecting pool. Then, he heaved the sack off his shoulder and dumped its contents—a freshly killed corpse—onto the ground.

The body—which had belonged to one Lord Charrs Entrone—rolled to a stop with its face in the dirt, twin dagger wounds glistening in its back. Kelsier had ambushed the half-drunken man on a street just outside of a skaa slum, ridding the world of another nobleman. Lord Entrone, in particular, would not be missed—he was infamous for his twisted sense of pleasure. Skaa bloodfights, for instance, were a particular enjoyment of his. That was where he had spent this evening.

Entrone had, not coincidentally, been a major political ally of House Tekiel. Kelsier left the corpse sitting in its own blood. The gardeners would locate it first—and once the servants knew about the death, no amount of noble obstinacy would keep it quiet. The murder would cause an outcry, and immediate blame would probably be placed upon House Izenry, House Tekiel's rival. However, Entrone's suspiciously unexpected death might make House Tekiel wary. If they began poking around, they would find that Entrone's gambling opponent at the night's bloodfight had been Crews Geffenry—a man whose house had been petitioning the Tekiels for a stronger alliance. Crews was a known Mistborn, and a very competent knife-fighter.

And so, the intrigue would begin. Had House Izenry done the murder? Or, perhaps, had the death been an attempt by House Geffenry to push Tekiel into a higher state of alarm—thereby encouraging them to seek allies among the lesser nobility? Or, was there a third answer—a house that wanted to strengthen the rivalry between Tekiel and Izenry?

Kelsier hopped off the garden wall, scratching at the fake beard he wore. It didn't really matter whom House Tekiel decided to blame; Kelsier's real purpose was to make them question and worry, to make them mistrust and misunderstand. Chaos was his strongest ally in fostering a house war. When that war finally came, each noblemen killed would be one less person that the skaa would have to face in their rebellion.

As soon as Kelsier got a short distance from Keep Tekiel, he flipped a coin and went to the rooftops. Occasionally, he wondered what the people in the houses beneath him thought, hearing footsteps from above. Did they know that Mistborn found their homes a convenient highway, a place where they could move without being bothered by guards or thieves? Or, did the people attribute the knockings to the ever-blamable mistwraiths?

They probably don't even notice. Sane people are asleep when the mists come out. He landed on a peaked roof, retrieved his pocket watch from a nook to check the time, then stowed it—and the dangerous metal from which it was made—away again. Many nobility blatantly wore metal, a foolish form of bravado. The habit had been inherited directly from the Lord Ruler. Kelsier, however, didn't like carrying any metal—watch, ring, or bracelet—on him that he didn't have to.

He launched himself into the air again, making his way toward the Sootwarrens, a skaa slum on the far northern side of town. Luthadel was an enormous, sprawling city; every few decades or so, new sections were added, the city wall expanded through the sweat and effort of skaa labor. With the advent of the modern canal era, stone was growing relatively cheap and easy to move.

I wonder why he even bothers with the wall, Kelsier thought, moving along rooftops parallel to the massive structure. *Who would attack? The Lord Ruler controls everything. Not even the western isles resist anymore.*

There hadn't been a true war in the Final Empire for centuries. The occasional "rebellion" consisted of nothing more than a few thousand men hiding in hills or caves, coming out for periodic raids. Even Yeden's rebellion wouldn't rely much on forcc—thcy wcrc counting on thc chaos of a housc war, mixed with the strategic misdirection of the Luthadel Garrison, to give them an opening. If it came down to an extended campaign, Kelsier would lose. The Lord Ruler and the Steel Ministry could marshal literally millions of troops if the need arose.

Of course, there was his other plan. Kelsier didn't speak of it, he barely even dared consider it. He probably wouldn't even have an opportunity to implement it. But, if the opportunity did arrive . . .

He dropped to the ground just outside of the Sootwarrens, then pulled his mistcloak tight and walked along the street with a confident step. His contact sat in the doorway of a closed shop, puffing quietly on a pipe. Kelsier raised an eyebrow; tobacco was an expensive luxury. Hoid was either very wasteful, or he was just as successful as Dockson implied.

Hoid calmly put away the pipe, then climbed to his feet—though that didn't make him much taller. The scrawny bald man bowed deeply in the misty night. "Greetings, my lord."

Kelsier paused in front of the man, arms tucked carefully inside his mistcloak. It wouldn't do for a street informant to realize that the unidentified "nobleman" he was meeting with had the scars of Hathsin on his arms.

"You come highly recommended," Kelsier said, mimicking the haughty accent of a nobleman.

"I am one of the best, my lord."

Anyone who can survive as long as you have must be good, Kelsier thought. Lords didn't like the idea of other men knowing their secrets. Informants generally didn't live very long.

"I need to know something, informant," Kelsier said. "But first you must vow never to speak of this meeting to anyone."

"Of course, my lord," Hoid said. He'd likely break the promise before the night was out—another reason informants didn't tend to live very long. "There is, however, the matter of payment. . . ."

"You'll have your money, skaa," Kelsier snapped.

"Of course, my lord," Hoid said with a quick bob of the head. "You requested information regarding House Renoux, I believe. . . ."

"Yes. What is known about it? Which houses is it aligned with? I must know these things."

"There isn't really much to know, my lord," Hoid said. "Lord Renoux is very new to the area, and he is a careful man. He's making neither allies nor enemies at the moment—he's buying a large number of weapons and armor, but is probably just purchasing from a wide variety of houses and merchants, thereby ingratiating himself to them all. A wise tactic. He will, perhaps, have an excess of merchandise, but he will also have an excess of friends, yes?"

Kelsier snorted. "I don't see why I should pay you for that."

"He'll have too much merchandise, my lord," Hoid said quickly. "You could make a clever profit, knowing that Renoux is shipping at a loss."

"I'm no merchant, skaa," Kelsier said. "I don't care about profits and shipping!" *Let him chew on that. Now he thinks I'm of a Great House—of course, if he hadn't suspected that because of the mistcloak, then he doesn't deserve his reputation.*

"Of course, my lord," Hoid said quickly. "There is more, of course. . . ."

Ah, and here we see it. Does the street know that House Renoux is connected to the rumblings of rebellion? If anyone had discovered that secret, then Kelsier's crew was in serious jeopardy.

Hoid coughed quietly, holding out his hand.

"Insufferable man!" Kelsier snapped, tossing a pouch at Hoid's feet.

"Yes, my lord," Hoid said, falling to his knees and searching about with his hand. "I apologize, my lord. My eyesight is weak, you know. I can barely see my own fingers held in front of my face."

Clever, Kelsier thought as Hoid found the pouch and tucked it away. The comment about eyesight was, of course, a lie—no man would get far in the underground with such an impediment. However, a nobleman who thought his informant to be half blind would be far less paranoid about being identified. Not that Kelsier himself was worried—he wore one of Dockson's best disguises. Beside the beard, he had a fake, but realistic, nose, along with platforms in the shoes and makeup to lighten his skin.

"You said there was more?" Kelsier said. "I swear, skaa, if it isn't good . . ."

"It is," Hoid said quickly. "Lord Renoux is considering a union between his niece, the Lady Valette, and Lord Elend Venture."

Kelsier paused. *Wasn't expecting that . . .* "That's silly. Venture is *far* above Renoux."

"The two youths were seen speaking—at length—at the Venture ball a month ago."

Kelsier laughed derisively. "Everyone knows about that. It meant nothing."

"Did it?" Hoid asked. "Does everyone know that Lord Elend Venture spoke very highly of the girl to his friends, the group of nobleling philosophers that lounge at the Broken Quill?"

"Young men speak of girls," Kelsier said. "It means nothing. You will be returning those coins."

"Wait!" Hoid said, sounding apprehensive for the first

time. "There is more. Lord Renoux and Lord Venture have had secret dealings."

What?

"It is true," Hoid continued. "This is fresh news—I heard it barely an hour ago myself. There is a connection between Renoux and Venture. And, for some reason, Lord Renoux was able to demand that Elend Venture be assigned to watch over Lady Valette at balls." He lowered his voice. "It is even whispered that Lord Renoux has some kind of . . . leverage over House Venture."

What happened at that ball tonight? Kelsier thought. Out loud, however, he said, "This all sounds very weak, skaa. You have nothing more than idle speculations?"

"Not about House Renoux, my lord," Hoid said. "I tried, but your worry over this house is meaningless! You should pick a house more central to politics. Like, say, House Elariel . . ."

Kelsier frowned. By mentioning Elariel, Hoid was implying that he had some important tidbit that would be worth Kelsier's payment. It seemed that House Renoux's secrets were safe. It was time to move the discussion along to other houses, so that Hoid wouldn't get suspicious of Kelsier's interest in Renoux.

"Very well," Kelsier said. "But if this isn't worth my time . . ."

"It is, my lord. Lady Shan Elariel is a Soother."

"Proof?"

"I felt her touch on my emotions, my lord," Hoid said. "During a fire at Keep Elariel a week ago, she was there calming the emotions of the servants."

Kelsier had started that fire. Unfortunately, it hadn't spread beyond the guardhouses. "What else?"

"House Elariel has recently given her leave to use her powers more at court functions," Hoid said. "They fear a house war, and wish her to make whatever allegiances possible. She always carries a thin envelope of shaved brass in her right glove. Get a Seeker close to her at a ball, and you shall see. My lord, I do not lie! My life as an informant depends solely upon my reputation. Shan Elariel *is* a Soother."

Kelsier paused, as if musing. The information was useless to him, but his true purpose—finding out about House

Renoux—had already been fulfilled. Hoid had earned his coins, whether he realized it or not.

Kelsier smiled. *Now to sow a little more chaos.*

"What of Shan's covert relationship with Salmen Tekiel?" Kelsier said, picking the name of a likely young nobleman. "Do you think that she used her powers to gain his favor?"

"Oh, most certainly, my lord," Hoid said quickly. Kelsier could see the glimmer of excitement in his eyes; he assumed that Kelsier had given him a luscious bit of political gossip free of charge.

"Perhaps she was the one who secured Elariel the deal with House Hasting last week," Kelsier said musingly. There had been no such deal.

"Most likely, my lord."

"Very well, skaa," Kelsier said. "You have earned your coins. Perhaps I shall call upon you another time."

"Thank you, my lord," Hoid said, bowing very low.

Kelsier dropped a coin and launched himself into the air. As he landed on a rooftop, he caught a glimpse of Hoid scuttling over to pluck the coin off the ground. Hoid didn't have any trouble locating it, despite his "weak eyesight." Kelsier smiled, then kept moving. Hoid hadn't mentioned Kelsier's tardiness, but Kelsier's next appointment would not be so forgiving.

He made his way eastward, toward Ahlstrom Square. He pulled off his mistcloak as he moved, then ripped off his vest, revealing the tattered shirt hidden beneath. He dropped to an alleyway, discarding cloak and vest, then grabbed a double handful of ash from the corner. He rubbed the crusty, dark flakes on his arms, masking his scars, then ground them onto his face and false beard.

The man who stumbled out of the alleyway seconds later was very different from the nobleman who had met with Hoid. The beard, once neat, now jutted out in an unkempt frazzle. A few, select bits had been removed, making it look patchy and sickly. Kelsier stumbled, pretending to have a lame leg, and called out to a shadowed figure standing near the square's quiet fountain.

"My lord?" Kelsier asked in a raspy voice. "My lord, is that you?"

Lord Straff Venture, leader of House Venture, was a domineering man, even for a nobleman. Kelsier could make out a pair of guards standing at his side; the lord himself didn't seem the least bit bothered by the mists—it was openly known that he was a Tineye. Venture stepped forward firmly, dueling cane tapping the ground beside him.

"You are late, skaa!" he snapped.

"My lord, I . . . I . . . I was waiting in the alley, my lord, like we agreed!"

"We agreed to no such thing!"

"I'm sorry, my lord," Kelsier said again, bowing—then stumbling because of his "lame" leg. "I'm sorry, I'm sorry. I was just in the alley. I didn't mean to make you wait."

"Couldn't you see us, man?"

"I'm sorry, my lord," Kelsier said. "My eyesight . . . it isn't very good, you know. I can barely see my own hands in front of my face." *Thanks for the tip, Hoid.*

Venture snorted, handing his dueling cane to a guard, then slapped Kelsier smartly across the face.

Kelsier stumbled to the ground, holding his cheek. "I'm sorry, my lord," he mumbled again.

"Next time you make me wait, it will be the cane," Venture said curtly.

Well, I know where to go next time I need a corpse to dump on someone's lawn, Kelsier thought, stumbling to his feet.

"Now," Venture said. "Let us get down to business. What is this important news you promised to deliver?"

"It's about House Erikell, my lord," Kelsier said. "I know Your Lordship has had dealings with them in the past."

"And?"

"Well, my lord, they are cheating you dearly. They have been selling their swords and canes to House Tekiel for half the price you've been paying!"

"Proof?"

"You need only look to Tekiel's new armaments, my lord," Kelsier said. "My word is true. I have nothing but my reputation! If I have not that, I have not my life."

And he wasn't lying. Or, at least, not completely. It would be useless of Kelsier to spread information that Venture could corroborate or dismiss with ease. Some of what he said was true—Tekiel was giving a slight advantage to Erikell. Kelsier was overstating it, of course. If he played the game well, he could start a rift between Erikell and Venture, while at the same time making Venture jealous of Tekiel. And, if Venture came to Renoux for weapons instead of Erikell . . . well, that would just be a side benefit.

Straff Venture snorted. His house was powerful—incredibly powerful—and relied on no specific industry or enterprise to fuel its wealth. That was a very difficult position to achieve in the Final Empire, considering the Lord Ruler's taxes and atium costs. It also made Venture a powerful tool to Kelsier. If he could give this man the right mixture of truth and fiction . . .

"This is of little use to me," Venture said suddenly. "Let's see how much you *really* know, informant. Tell me about the Survivor of Hathsin."

Kelsier froze. "Excuse me, my lord?"

"You want to get paid?" Venture asked. "Well, tell me about the Survivor. Rumors say he's returned to Luthadel."

"Rumors only, my lord," Kelsier said quickly. "I have never met this Survivor, but I doubt he is in Luthadel—if, indeed, he even lives."

"I've heard that he's gathering a skaa rebellion."

"There are always fools whispering rebellion to the skaa, my lord," Kelsier said. "And there are always those who try to use the name of the Survivor, but I do not believe that any man could have lived through the Pits. I could seek more information on this, if you wish, but I worry you will be disappointed in what I find. The Survivor is dead—the Lord Ruler . . . he does not allow such oversights."

"True," Venture said contemplatively. "But the skaa seem convinced about this rumor of an 'Eleventh Metal.' Have you heard of it, informant?"

"Ah, yes," Kelsier said, covering his shock. "A legend, my lord."

"One I've never heard of," Venture said. "And I pay *very* close attention to such things. This is no 'legend.' Someone very clever is manipulating the skaa."

"An . . . interesting conclusion, my lord," Kelsier said.

"Indeed," Venture said. "And, assuming the Survivor *did* die in the Pits, and if someone had gotten ahold of his corpse . . . his bones . . . there are ways to imitate a man's appearance. You know of what I speak?"

"Yes, my lord," Kelsier said.

"Watch for this," Venture said. "I don't care about your gossip—bring me something about this man, or whatever he is, that leads the skaa. *Then* you'll get some coin of me."

Venture spun in the darkness, waving to his men and leaving a thoughtful Kelsier behind.

Kelsier arrived at Mansion Renoux a short time later; the spikeway between Fellise and Luthadel made for quick travel between the cities. He hadn't placed the spikes himself; he didn't know who had. He often wondered what he would do if, while traveling the spikeway, he met another Mistborn traveling in the opposite direction.

We'd probably just ignore each other, Kelsier thought as he landed in Mansion Renoux's courtyard. *We're pretty good at doing that.*

He peered through the mists at the lantern-lit mansion, his recovered mistcloak flapping slightly in the calm wind. The empty carriage indicated that Vin and Sazed had returned from House Elariel. Kelsier found them inside, waiting in the sitting room and speaking quietly with Lord Renoux.

"That's a new look for you," Vin noted as Kelsier walked into the room. She still wore her dress—a beautiful red gown—though she sat in an unladylike position, legs tucked beneath her.

Kelsier smiled to himself. *A few weeks ago she would have changed out of that gown as soon as she got back. We'll turn her into a lady yet.* He found a seat, picking at the fake, soot-stained beard. "You mean this? I hear beards are going to make a return soon. I'm just trying to stay on the edge of fashionability."

Vin snorted. "The edge of beggar fashion, maybe."

"How did the evening go, Kelsier?" Lord Renoux asked.

Kelsier shrugged. "Like most others. Fortunately, it appears that House Renoux remains free of suspicion—though I myself am something of a concern to some of the nobility."

"You?" Renoux asked.

Kelsier nodded as a servant brought him a warm, damp cloth to clean his face and arms—though Kelsier wasn't certain if the servants were worried about his comfort or the ash he might get on the furniture. He wiped off his arms, exposing the pale white scratch scars, then began to pick off the beard.

"It seems that the general skaa have gotten wind of the Eleventh Metal," he continued. "Some of the nobility have heard the building rumors, and the more intelligent ones are growing worried."

"How does this affect us?" Renoux asked.

Kelsier shrugged. "We'll spread opposite rumors to make the nobility focus more on each other and less on me. Though, amusingly, Lord Venture encouraged me to search out information about myself. A man could get very confused from this kind of playacting—I don't know how you do it, Renoux."

"It is who I am," the kandra said simply.

Kelsier shrugged again, turning to Vin and Sazed. "So, how did your evening go?"

"Frustratingly," Vin said with a surly tone.

"Mistress Vin is a tad annoyed," Sazed said. "On the way back from Luthadel, she told me the secrets she'd gathered while dancing."

Kelsier chuckled. "Not much of interest?"

"Sazed already knew it all!" Vin snapped. "I spent hours twirling and twittering for those men, and it was all worthless!"

"Hardly worthless, Vin," Kelsier said, pulling off the last bit of false beard. "You made some contacts, you were seen, and you practiced your twittering. As for information—well, nobody's going to tell you anything important yet. Give it some time."

"How much time?"

"Now that you're feeling better, we can have you start attending the balls regularly. After a few months, you should have gathered enough contacts to begin finding the kind of information we need."

Vin nodded, sighing. She didn't seem quite as opposed to the idea of regularly attending balls as she once had, however.

Sazed cleared his throat. "Master Kelsier, I feel that I must mention something. Our table was attended by Lord Elend Venture for most of the evening, though Mistress Vin did find a way to make his attentions less threatening to the court."

"Yes," Kelsier said, "so I understand. What did you tell those people, Vin? That Renoux and Venture are friends?"

Vin paled slightly. "How do you know?"

"I'm mysteriously powerful," Kelsier said with a wave of his hand. "Anyway, everyone thinks that House Renoux and House Venture have had secret business dealings. They probably assume that Venture has been stockpiling weapons."

Vin frowned. "I didn't mean it to go that far. . . ."

Kelsier nodded, rubbing the glue from his chin. "That's the way court is, Vin. Things can get out of hand quickly. However, this isn't much of a problem—though it does mean that you're going to have to be very careful when dealing with House Venture, Lord Renoux. We'll want to see what kind of reaction they have to Vin's comments."

Lord Renoux nodded. "Agreed."

Kelsier yawned. "Now, if there isn't anything else, playing both nobleman and beggar in one evening has made me dreadfully tired. . . ."

"There is one other thing, Master Kelsier," Sazed said. "At the end of the evening, Mistress Vin saw Lord Elend Venture leaving the ball with young lords of Houses Lekal and Hasting."

Kelsier paused, frowning. "That's an odd combination."

"So I thought," Sazed said.

"He's probably just trying to annoy his father," Kelsier said musingly. "Fraternizing with the enemy in public . . ."

"Perhaps," Sazed said. "But the three did seem to be good friends."

Kelsier nodded, standing. "Investigate this further, Saze. There's a chance that Lord Venture and his son are playing us all for fools."

"Yes, Master Kelsier," Sazed said.

Kelsier left the room, stretching and handing his mistcloak to a servant. As he walked up the eastern stairway, he heard quick footsteps. He turned to find Vin scooting up behind him, shimmering red dress held up as she climbed the steps.

"Kelsier," she said quietly. "There was something else. Something I'd like to talk about."

Kelsier raised an eyebrow. *Something she doesn't even want Sazed to hear?* "My room," he said, and she followed him up the stairs and into the chamber.

"What is this about?" he asked as she shut the door behind her.

"Lord Elend," Vin said, looking down, seeming a bit embarrassed. "Sazed already doesn't like him, so I didn't want to mention this in front of the others. But, I found something strange tonight."

"What?" Kelsier asked curiously, leaning back against his bureau.

"Elend had a stack of books with him," Vin said.

First name, Kelsier thought with disapproval. *She* is *falling for the boy.*

"He's known to read a lot," Vin continued, "but some of these books . . . well, when he was gone, I picked through them."

Good girl. The streets gave you at least a few good instincts.

"One of them drew my attention," she said. "The title said something about the weather, but the words inside spoke about the Final Empire and its flaws."

Kelsier raised an eyebrow. "What exactly did it say?"

Vin shrugged. "Something about how since the Lord Ruler is immortal, his empire should be more advanced and peaceful."

Kelsier smiled. "*Book of the False Dawn*—any Keeper can quote the entire thing to you. I didn't think there were any physical copies left. Its author—Deluse Couvre—went on to write some books that were even more damning. Though he didn't blaspheme against Allomancy, the obligators made an exception in his case and strung him up on a hook anyway."

"Well," Vin said, "Elend has a copy. I think one of the other noblewomen was trying to find the book. I saw one of her servants rifling through them."

"Which noblewoman?"

"Shan Elariel."

Kelsier nodded. "Former fiancée. She's probably searching for something to blackmail the Venture boy with."

"I think she's an Allomancer, Kelsier."

Kelsier nodded distractedly, thinking about the information. "She's a Soother. She probably had the right idea with those books—if the Venture heir is reading a book like *False Dawn*, not to mention foolish enough to carry it around with him . . ."

"Is it that dangerous?" Vin asked.

Kelsier shrugged. "Moderately. It's an older book, and it didn't actually encourage rebellion, so it might slide."

Vin frowned. "The book sounded pretty critical of the Lord Ruler. He allows the nobility to read things like that?"

"He doesn't really 'allow' them to do such things," Kelsier said. "More, he sometimes ignores it when they do. Banning books is tricky business, Vin—the more stink the Ministry makes about a text, the more attention it will draw, and the more people will be tempted to read it. *False Dawn* is a stuffy volume, and by *not* forbidding it, the Ministry doomed it to obscurity."

Vin nodded slowly.

"Besides," Kelsier said, "the Lord Ruler is far more lenient with the nobility than he is with skaa. He sees them as the children of his long-dead friends and allies, the men who supposedly helped him defeat the Deepness. He occasionally lets them get away with things like reading edgy texts or assassinating family members."

"So . . . the book is nothing to worry about?" Vin asked.

Kelsier shrugged. "I wouldn't say that either. If young Elend has *False Dawn*, he might also have other books that *are* explicitly forbidden. If obligators had proof of that, they'd hand young Elend over to the Inquisitors—nobleman or not. The question is, how do we make certain that happens? If the Venture heir were to be executed, it would certainly add to Luthadel's political turmoil."

Vin paled visibly.

Yes, Kelsier thought with an internal sigh. *She's definitely falling for him. I should have foreseen this. Sending a young, pretty girl into noble society? One vulture or another was bound to latch on to her.*

"I didn't tell you this so we could get him killed, Kelsier!" she said. "I thought, maybe . . . well, he's reading forbidden books, and he seems like a good man. Maybe we can use him as an ally or something."

Oh, child, Kelsier thought. *I hope he doesn't hurt you too much when he discards you. You should know better than this.*

"Don't count on it," he said out loud. "Lord Elend might be reading a forbidden book, but that doesn't make him our friend. There have always been noblemen like him—young philosophers and dreamers who think that their ideas are new. They like to drink with their friends and grumble about the Lord Ruler; but, in their hearts, they're still noblemen. They'll never overthrow the establishment."

"But—"

"No, Vin," Kelsier said. "You have to trust me. Elend Venture doesn't care about us or the skaa. He's a gentleman anarchist because it's fashionable and exciting."

"He talked to me about the skaa," Vin said. "He wanted to know if they were intelligent, and if they acted like real people."

"And was his interest compassionate or intellectual?"

She paused.

"See," Kelsier said. "Vin, that man is *not* our ally—in fact, I distinctly recall telling you to stay away from him. When you spend time with Elend Venture, you put the operation—and your fellow crewmembers—in jeopardy. Understand?"

Vin looked down, nodding.

Kelsier sighed. *Why do I suspect that staying away from him is the last thing she intends to do? Bloody hell—I don't have time to deal with this right now.*

"Go get some sleep," Kelsier said. "We can talk more about this later."

It isn't a shadow.

This dark thing that follows me, the thing that only I can see— It isn't really a shadow. It's blackish and translucent, but it doesn't have a shadowlike solid outline. It's insubstantial—wispy and formless. Like it's made out of a dark fog.

Or mist, perhaps.

20

VIN WAS GROWING VERY TIRED of the scenery between Luthadel and Fellise. She'd made the same trip at least a dozen times during the last few weeks—watching the same brown hills, scraggly trees, and rug of weedy underbrush. She was beginning to feel as if she could individually identify each and every bump in the road.

She attended numerous balls—but they were only the beginning. Luncheons, sitting parties, and other forms of daily entertainment were just as popular. Often, Vin traveled between the cities two or even three times a day. Apparently, young noblewomen didn't have anything better to do than sit in carriages for six hours a day.

Vin sighed. In the near distance, a group of skaa trudged along the towpath beside a canal, pulling a barge toward Luthadel. Her life could be much worse.

Still, she felt frustration. It was still midday, but there weren't any important events happening until the evening, so she had nowhere to go but back to Fellise. She kept thinking about how much faster she could make the trip if she used the spikeway. She longed to leap through the mists again, but Kelsier had been reluctant to continue her training. He allowed her out for a short time each night to maintain her skills, but she wasn't allowed any extreme, exciting leaps.

Just some basic moves—mostly Pushing and Pulling small objects while standing on the ground.

She was beginning to grow frustrated with her continued weakness. It had been over three months since her encounter with the Inquisitor; the worst of winter had passed without even a flake of snow. How long was it going to take her to recover?

At least I can still go to balls, she thought. Despite her annoyance at the constant traveling, Vin was coming to enjoy her duties. Pretending to be a noblewoman was actually far less tense than regular thieving work. True, her life would be forfeit if her secret were ever discovered, but for now the nobility seemed willing to accept her—to dance with her, dine with her, and chat with her. It was a good life—a bit unexciting, but her eventual return to Allomancy would fix that.

That left her with two frustrations. The first was her inability to gather useful information; she was getting increasingly annoyed at having her questions avoided. She was growing experienced enough to tell that there was a great deal of intrigue going on, yet she was still too new to be allowed a part in it.

Still, while her outsider status was annoying, Kelsier was confident that it would eventually change. Vin's second major annoyance wasn't so easily dealt with. Lord Elend Venture had been notably absent from several balls during the last few weeks, and he had yet to repeat his act of spending the entire evening with her. While she rarely had to sit alone anymore, she was quickly coming to realize that none of the other noblemen had the same . . . depth as Elend. None of them had his droll wit, or his honest, earnest eyes. The others didn't feel *real*. Not like he did.

He didn't seem to be avoiding her. However, he also didn't seem to be making much of an effort to spend time with her.

Did I misread him? she wondered as the carriage reached Fellise. Elend was so hard to understand sometimes. Unfortunately, his apparent indecision hadn't changed his former fiancée's temperament. Vin was beginning to realize why Kelsier had warned her to avoid catching the attention of anyone too important. She didn't run into Shan Elariel often, thankfully—but when they did meet, Shan took every occasion to deride, insult, and demean Vin. She did it with a calm, aristocratic manner, even her bearing reminding Vin just how inferior she was.

Perhaps I'm just becoming too attached to my Valette persona, Vin thought. Valette was just a front; she was supposed to be all the things Shan said. However, the insults still stung.

Vin shook her head, putting both Shan and Elend out of her mind. Ash had fallen during her trip to the city, and though it was done now, its aftermath was visible in small drifts and flurries of black blowing across the town's streets. Skaa workers moved about, sweeping the soot into bins and carrying it out of the city. They occasionally had to hurry to get out of the way of a passing noble carriage, none of which bothered to slow for the workers.

Poor things, Vin thought, passing a group of ragged children who were shaking aspen trees to get the ash out so that it could be swept up—it wouldn't do for a passing nobleman to get an unexpected dump of tree-borne ash on his head. The children shook, two to a tree, bringing furious black showers down on their heads. Careful, cane-wielding taskmasters walked up and down the street, making certain the work continued.

Elend and the others, she thought. *They must not understand how bad life is for the skaa. They live in their pretty keeps, dancing, never really understanding the extent of the Lord Ruler's oppression.*

She could see beauty in the nobility—she wasn't like Kelsier, hating them outright. Some of them seemed quite kind, in their own way, and she was beginning to think some of the stories skaa told about their cruelty must be exaggerated. And yet, when she saw events like that poor boy's execution or the skaa children, she had to wonder. How could the nobility not see? How could they not understand?

She sighed, looking away from the skaa as the carriage finally rolled up to Mansion Renoux. She immediately noticed a large gathering in the inner courtyard, and she grabbed a fresh vial of metals, worrying that the Lord Ruler had sent soldiers to arrest Lord Renoux. However, she quickly realized that the crowd wasn't made up of soldiers, but of skaa in simple worker's clothing.

The carriage rolled through the gates, and Vin's confusion deepened. Boxes and sacks lay in heaps among the skaa—many of them dusted with soot from the recent ashfall. The workers themselves bustled with activity, loading a series of carts. Vin's carriage pulled to a stop in front of the mansion, and she didn't wait for Sazed to open the door. She hopped out on her own, holding up her dress and stalking over to Kelsier and Renoux, who stood surveying the operation.

"You're running goods to the caves out of *here*?" Vin asked under her breath as she reached the two men.

"Curtsey to me, child," Lord Renoux said. "Maintain appearances while we can be seen."

Vin did as ordered, containing her annoyance.

"Of course we are, Vin," Kelsier said. "Renoux has to do *something* with all of the weapons and supplies he's been gathering. People would start getting suspicious if they didn't see him sending them away."

Renoux nodded. "Ostensibly, we're sending this all via canal barges to my plantation in the west. However, the barges will stop to drop off supplies—and many of the canalmen—at the rebellion caverns. The barges and a few men will continue on to keep up appearances."

"Our soldiers don't even know that Renoux is in on the plan," Kelsier said, smiling. "They think he's a nobleman that I'm scamming. Besides, this will be a great opportunity for us to go and inspect the army. After a week or so at the caves, we can return to Luthadel on one of Renoux's barges coming east."

Vin paused. " 'We'?" she asked, suddenly imagining weeks spent on the barge, watching the same, dull scenery day, after day, after day as they traveled. That would be even worse than traveling back and forth between Luthadel and Fellise.

Kelsier raised an eyebrow. "You sound worried. Apparently, someone's coming to enjoy her balls and parties."

Vin flushed. "I just thought that I should be here. I mean, after all the time I missed by being sick, I—"

Kelsier held up his hand, chuckling. "You're staying; Yeden

and I are the ones going. I need to inspect the troops, and Yeden is going to take a turn watching over the army so that Ham can come back to Luthadel. We'll also take my brother with us, then drop him at his insertion point with the Ministry acolytes up in Vennias. It's a good thing you're back—I want you to spend a little time with him before we leave."

Vin frowned. "With Marsh?"

Kelsier nodded. "He's a Misting Seeker. Bronze is one of the less useful metals, especially for a full Mistborn, but Marsh claims he can show you a few tricks. This will probably be your last chance to train with him."

Vin glanced toward the gathering caravan. "Where is he?"

Kelsier frowned. "He's late."

Runs in the family, I guess.

"He should be here soon, child," Lord Renoux said. "Perhaps you'd like to go take some refreshment inside?"

I've had plenty of refreshment lately, she thought, controlling her annoyance. Instead of going into the mansion, she wandered across the courtyard, studying the goods and workers, who were packing the supplies onto carts for transport to the local canal docks. The grounds were kept well maintained, and though the ash hadn't been cleaned up yet, the low-cut grass meant that she didn't have to hold her dress up much to keep it from dragging.

Beyond that, ash was surprisingly easy to get out of clothing. With proper washing, and some expensive soaps, even a white garment could be rendered clean of ash. That was why the nobility could always have new-looking clothing. It was such an easy, simple thing to divide the skaa and the aristocracy.

Kelsier's right, Vin thought. *I am coming to enjoy being a noblewoman.* And she was concerned about the changes her new lifestyle was encouraging inside of her. Once, her problems had been things like starvation and beatings—now they were things like extended carriage rides and companions who arrived late for appointments. What did a transformation like that do to a person?

She sighed to herself, walking amidst the supplies. Some of the boxes would be filled with weapons—swords, war staves, bows—but the bulk of the material was sacked foodstuffs. Kelsier said that forming an army required far more grain than it did steel.

She trailed her fingers along one stack of boxes, careful not to brush the ash that was on top of them. She'd known that they'd be sending out a barge this day, but she hadn't expected Kelsier to go with it. Of course, he probably hadn't made the decision to go until a short time before—even the new, more responsible Kelsier was an impulsive man. Perhaps that was a good attribute in a leader. He wasn't afraid to incorporate new ideas, no matter when they occurred to him.

Maybe I should ask to go with him, Vin thought idly. *I've been playing the noblewoman far too much lately.* The other day, she'd caught herself sitting straight-backed in her carriage with a prim posture, despite the fact that she was alone. She feared that she was losing her instincts—being Valette was almost more natural to her now than being Vin was.

But of course she couldn't leave. She had a lunch appointment with Lady Flavine to attend, not to mention the Hasting ball—it was going to be the social event of the month. If Valette was absent, it would take weeks to repair the damage. Besides, there was always Elend. He'd probably forget about her if she disappeared again.

He's already forgotten you, she told herself. *He's barely spoken to you during the last three parties. Keep your head on, Vin. This is all just another scam—a game, like the ones you pulled before. You're building your reputation to gain information, not so that you can flirt and play.*

She nodded to herself, resolute. To her side, a few skaa men loaded one of the carts. Vin paused, standing beside a large stack of boxes and watching the men work. According to Dockson, the army's recruitment was picking up.

We're gaining momentum, Vin thought. *I guess word is spreading.* That was good—assuming it didn't spread *too* far.

She watched the packmen for a moment, sensing something . . . odd. They seemed unfocused. After a few moments, she was able to determine the source of their distraction. They kept shooting looks at Kelsier, whispering as they worked. Vin inched closer—keeping to the side of the boxes—and burned tin.

". . . no, that's him for certain," one of the men whispered. "I saw the scars."

"He's tall," another said.

"Of course he is. What did you expect?"

"He spoke at the meeting where I was recruited," another said. "The Survivor of Hathsin." There was awe in his tone.

The men moved on, walking over to gather more boxes. Vin cocked her head, then began to move among the workers, listening. Not all of them were discussing Kelsier, but a surprising number were. She also heard a number of references to the "Eleventh Metal."

So that's why, Vin thought. *The rebellion's momentum isn't gathering—Kelsier's is.* The men spoke of him in quiet, almost reverent, tones. For some reason, that made Vin uncomfortable. She would never have been able to stand hearing similar things said about her. Yet, Kelsier took them in stride; his charismatic ego probably just fueled the rumors even more.

I wonder if he'll be able to let it go when this is all through. The other crewmembers obviously had no interest in leadership, but Kelsier seemed to thrive on it. Would he really let the skaa rebellion take over? Would any man be able to relinquish that kind of power?

Vin frowned. Kelsier was a good man; he'd probably make a good ruler. However, if he did try to take control, it would smell of betrayal—a reneging on the promises that he had made to Yeden. She didn't want to see that from Kelsier.

"Valette," Kelsier called.

Vin jumped slightly, feeling a bit guilty. Kelsier pointed toward a carriage that was pulling onto the mansion grounds. Marsh had arrived. She walked back as the carriage pulled up, and she reached Kelsier about the same time that Marsh did.

Kelsier smiled, nodding toward Vin. "We won't be ready to leave for a while yet," he said to Marsh. "If you have time, could you show the kid a few things?"

Marsh turned toward her. He shared Kelsier's lanky build and blond hair, but he wasn't as handsome. Maybe it was the lack of a smile.

He pointed up, toward the mansion's fore-balcony. "Wait for me up there."

Vin opened her mouth to reply, but something about Marsh's expression made her shut it again. He reminded her of the old times, several months ago, when she had not questioned her superiors. She turned, leaving the three, and made her way into the mansion.

It was a short trip up the stairs to the fore-balcony. When she arrived, she pulled over a chair and seated herself beside the whitewashed wooden railing. The balcony had, of course, already been scrubbed clean of ash. Below, Marsh was still speaking with Kelsier and Renoux. Beyond them, beyond even the sprawling caravan, Vin could see the barren hills outside of the city, lit by red sunlight.

Only a few months playing noblewoman, and I already find anything that isn't cultivated to be inferior. She'd never thought of the landscape as "barren" during the years she'd traveled with Reen. *And Kelsier says the entire land used to be even more fertile than a nobleman's garden.*

Did he think to reclaim such things? Keepers could, perhaps, memorize languages and religions, but they couldn't create seeds for plants that had long been extinct. They couldn't make the ash stop falling or the mists go away. Would the world really change that much if the Final Empire were gone?

Besides, didn't the Lord Ruler have *some* right to his place? He'd defeated the Deepness, or so he claimed. He'd saved the world, which—in a twisted sort of way—made it his. What right did they have to try and take it from him?

She wondered about such things often, though she didn't express her worries to the others. They all seemed committed to Kelsier's plan; some even seemed to share his vision. But Vin was more hesitant. She had learned, as Reen had taught, to be skeptical of optimism.

And if there were ever a plan to be hesitant about, this was the one.

However, she was getting past the point where she questioned herself. She knew the reason she stayed in the crew. It wasn't the plan; it was the people. She liked Kelsier. She liked Dockson, Breeze, and Ham. She even liked the strange little Spook and his crotchety uncle. This was a crew unlike any other she'd worked with.

Is that a good enough reason to let them get you killed? Reen's voice asked.

Vin paused. She had been hearing his whispers in her mind less frequently lately, but they were still there. Reen's teachings, drilled into her over sixteen years of life, could not be idly discarded.

Marsh arrived on the balcony a few moments later. He glanced at her with those hard eyes of his, then spoke. "Kelsier apparently expects me to spend the evening training you in Allomancy. Let us get started."

Vin nodded.

Marsh eyed her, obviously expecting more of a response. Vin sat quietly. *You're not the only one who can be terse, friend.*

"Very well," Marsh said, sitting beside her, resting one arm on the balcony railing. His voice sounded a little less annoyed when he continued. "Kelsier says that you have spent very little time training with the internal mental abilities. Correct?"

Vin nodded again.

"I suspect that many full Mistborn neglect these powers," Marsh said. "And that is a mistake. Bronze and copper may not be as flashy as other metals, but they can be very powerful in the hands of someone properly trained. The Inquisitors work through their manipulation of bronze, and the Misting underground survives because of its reliance upon copper.

"Of the two powers, bronze is by far the more subtle. I can teach you how to use it properly—if you practice what I show you, then you will have an advantage that many Mistborn dismiss."

"But, don't other Mistborn know to burn copper?" Vin asked. "What is the use of learning bronze if everyone you fight is immune to its powers?"

"I see that you already think like one of them," Marsh said. "Not everyone is Mistborn, girl—in fact, very, very few people are. And, despite what your kind likes to think, normal Mistings can kill people too. Knowing that the man attacking you is a Thug rather than a Coinshot could very easily save your life."

"All right," Vin said.

"Bronze will also help you identify Mistborn," Marsh said. "If you see someone using Allomancy when there is no Smoker nearby, and yet don't sense them giving off Allomantic pulses, then you know that they are Mistborn—either that, or they're an Inquisitor. In either case, you should run."

Vin nodded silently, the wound in her side throbbing slightly.

"There are great advantages to burning bronze, rather than just running around with your copper on. True, you Smoke yourself by using copper—but in a way you also blind yourself. Copper makes you immune to having your emotions Pushed or Pulled."

"But that's a good thing."

Marsh cocked his head slightly. "Oh? And what would be the greater advantage? Being immune to—but ignorant of—some Soother's attentions? Or instead knowing—from your bronze—exactly which emotions he is trying to suppress?"

Vin paused. "You can see something that specific?"

Marsh nodded. "With care and practice, you can recognize very minute changes in your opponents' Allomantic burnings. You can identify precisely which parts of a person's emotions a Soother or Rioter intends to influence. You'll also be able to tell when someone is flaring their metal. If you grow very skilled, you might even be able to tell when they're running low on metals."

Vin paused in thought.

"You begin to see the advantage," Marsh said. "Good. Now burn bronze."

Vin did so. Immediately, she felt two rhythmic thumpings in the air. The soundless pulses washed over her, like the beating of drums or the washings of ocean waves. They were mixed and muddled.

"What do you sense?" Marsh asked.

"I . . . think there are two different metals being burned. One's coming from Kelsier down below; the other is coming from you."

"Good," Marsh said appreciatively. "You've practiced."

"Not much," Vin admitted.

He cocked an eyebrow. "Not much? You can already determine pulse origins. That takes practice."

Vin shrugged. "It seems natural to me."

Marsh was still for a moment. "Very well," he eventually said. "Are the two pulses different?"

Vin concentrated, frowning.

"Close your eyes," Marsh said. "Remove other distractions. Focus only on the Allomantic pulses."

Vin did so. It wasn't like hearing—not really. She had to concentrate to distinguish anything specific about the pulses. One felt . . . like it was beating against her. The other, in a strange sensation, felt like it was actually pulling her toward it with each beat.

"One's a Pulling metal, isn't it?" Vin asked, opening her eyes. "That one's Kelsier. You're Pushing."

"Very good," Marsh said. "He is burning iron, as I asked him to so that you could practice. I—of course—am burning bronze."

"Do they all do that?" Vin asked. "Feel distinct, I mean?"

Marsh nodded. "You can tell a Pulling metal from a Pushing metal by the Allomantic signature. Actually, that's how some of the metals were originally divided into their categories. It isn't intuitive, for instance, that tin Pulls while pewter Pushes. I didn't tell you to open your eyes."

Vin shut them.

"Focus on the pulses," Marsh said. "Try and distinguish their lengths. Can you tell the difference between them?"

Vin frowned. She focused as hard as she could, but her sense of the metals seemed . . . muddled. Fuzzy. After a few minutes, the lengths of the separate pulses still seemed the same to her.

"I can't sense anything," she said, dejected.

"Good," Marsh said flatly. "It took me six months of practice to distinguish pulse lengths—if you'd done it on the first try, I'd have felt incompetent."

Vin opened her eyes. "Why ask me to do it, then?"

"Because you need to practice. If you can tell Pulling metals from Pushing metals already . . . well, you apparently have talent. Perhaps as much talent as Kelsier has been bragging about."

"What was I supposed to see, then?" Vin asked.

"Eventually, you'll be able to sense two different pulse lengths. Internal metals, like bronze and copper, give off longer pulses than external metals, like iron and steel. Practice will also let you sense the three patterns within the pulses: one for the physical metals, one for the mental metals, and one for the two greater metals.

"Pulse length, metal group, and Push-Pull variance—once you know these three things, you will be able to tell exactly which metals your opponent is burning. A long pulse that beats against you and has a quick pattern will be pewter—the internal Pushing physical metal."

"Why the names?" Vin asked. "External and internal?"

"Metals come in groups of four—or, at least, the lower eight do. Two external metals, two internal metals—one each that Pushes, one each that Pulls. With iron, you Pull on something outside of yourself, with steel you Push on something outside of yourself. With tin you Pull on something inside of yourself, with pewter you Push on something inside of yourself."

"But, bronze and copper," Vin said. "Kelsier called them internal metals, but it seems like they affect external things. Copper keeps people from sensing when you use Allomancy."

Marsh shook his head. "Copper doesn't change your opponents, it changes something within yourself that has an effect on your opponents. That's why it is an internal metal. Brass, however, alters another person's emotions directly—and is an external metal."

Vin nodded thoughtfully. Then she turned, glancing toward Kelsier. "You know a lot about all the metals, but you're just a Misting, right?"

Marsh nodded. He didn't look like he intended to respond, though.

Let's try something, then, Vin thought, extinguishing her bronze. She lightly began burning copper to mask her Allomancy. Marsh didn't react, instead continuing to look down at Kelsier and the caravan.

I should be invisible to his senses, she thought, carefully burning both zinc and brass. She reached, just as Breeze had been training her to do, and subtly touched Marsh's emotions. She suppressed his suspicions and inhibitions, while at the same time bringing out his sense of wistfulness. Theoretically, that would make him more likely to talk.

"You must have learned somewhere?" Vin asked carefully. *He'll see what I did for sure. He's going to get angry and—*

"I Snapped when I was very young," Marsh said. "I've had a long time to practice."

"So have a lot of people," Vin said.

"I . . . had reasons. They're hard to explain."

"They always are," Vin said, slightly increasing her Allomantic pressure.

"You know how Kelsier feels about the nobility?" Marsh asked, turning toward her, his eyes like ice.

Ironeyes, she thought. *Like they said.* She nodded to his question.

"Well, I feel the same way about the obligators," he said, turning away. "I'll do anything to hurt them. They took our mother—that's when I Snapped, and that's when I vowed to destroy them. So, I joined the rebellion and started learning all I could about Allomancy. Inquisitors use it, so I had to understand it—understand everything I could, be as *good* as I could, and are you Soothing me?"

Vin started, abruptly extinguishing her metals. Marsh turned back toward her again, his expression cold.

Run! Vin thought. She almost did. It was nice to know that the old instincts were still there, if buried just a bit.

"Yes," she said meekly.

"You *are* good," Marsh said. "I'd have never known if I hadn't started rambling. Stop it."

"I already have."

"Good," Marsh said. "That's the second time you've altered my emotions. Never do it again."

Vin nodded. "Second time?"

"The first was in my shop, eight months ago."

That's right. Why don't I remember him? "I'm sorry."

Marsh shook his head, finally turning away. "You're Mistborn—that's what you do. He does the same thing." He was looking down at Kelsier.

They sat quietly for a few moments.

"Marsh?" Vin asked. "How did you know I was Mistborn? I only knew how to Soothe back then."

Marsh shook his head. "You knew the other metals instinctively. You were burning pewter and tin that day—just a tiny bit, barely noticeable. You probably got the metals from water and dining utensils. Did you ever wonder why you survived when so many others died?"

Vin paused. *I did live through a lot of beatings. A lot of days with no food, nights spent in alleys during rain or ashfalls . . .*

Marsh nodded. "Very few people, even Mistborn, are so attuned to Allomancy that they burn metals instinctively. That's what interested me in you—that's why I kept track of you and told Dockson where to find you. And, are you Pushing my emotions again?"

Vin shook her head. "I promise."

Marsh frowned, studying her with one of his stony gazes.

"So stern," Vin said quietly. "Like my brother."

"Were you close?"

"I hated him," Vin whispered.

Marsh paused, then turned away. "I see."

"Do you hate Kelsier?"

Marsh shook his head. "No, I don't hate him. He's frivolous and self-important, but he's my brother."

"And that's enough?" Vin asked.

Marsh nodded.

"I . . . have trouble understanding that," Vin said honestly, looking out over the field of skaa, boxes, and sacks.

"Your brother didn't treat you well, I presume?"

Vin shook her head.

"What about your parents?" Marsh said. "One was a nobleman. The other?"

"Mad," Vin said. "She heard voices. It got so bad that my brother was afraid to leave us alone with her. But, of course, he didn't have a choice. . . ."

Marsh sat quietly, not speaking. *How did this get turned back to me?* Vin thought. *He's no Soother, yet he's getting as much out of me as I'm getting out of him.*

Still, it was good to speak it finally. She reached up, idly fingering her earring. "I don't remember it," she said, "but

Reen said that he came home one day and found my mother covered in blood. She'd killed my baby sister. Messily. Me, however, she hadn't touched—except to give me an earring. Reen said . . . He said she was holding me on her lap, babbling and proclaiming me a queen, my sister's corpse at our feet. He took me from my mother, and she fled. He saved my life, probably. That's part of why I stayed with him, I guess. Even when it was bad."

She shook her head, glancing at Marsh. "Still, you don't know how lucky you are, having Kelsier as a brother."

"I suppose," Marsh said. "I just . . . wish he wouldn't treat people like playthings. I've been known to kill obligators, but murdering men just because they're noble . . ." Marsh shook his head. "It's not just that, either. He likes people to fawn over him."

He had a point. However, Vin also detected something in his voice. Jealousy? *You're the older brother, Marsh. You were the responsible one—you joined the rebellion instead of working with thieves. It must have hurt that Kelsier was the one everybody liked.*

"Still," Marsh said, "he's getting better. The Pits changed him. Her . . . death changed him."

What's this? Vin thought, perking up slightly. There was definitely something here, too. Hurt. Deep hurt, more than a man should feel for a sister-in-law.

So that's it. It wasn't just "everyone" who liked Kelsier more, it was one person in particular. Someone you loved.

"Anyway," Marsh said, his voice growing more firm. "The arrogance of the past is behind him. This plan of his is insane, and I'm sure he's partially doing it just so he can enrich himself, but . . . well, he didn't have to go to the rebellion. He's trying to do something good—though it will probably get him killed."

"Why go along if you're so sure he'll fail?"

"Because he's going to get me into the Ministry," Marsh said. "The information I gather there will help the rebellion for centuries after Kelsier and I are dead."

Vin nodded, glancing down at the courtyard. She spoke hesitantly. "Marsh, I don't think it's *all* behind him. The way he's setting himself up with the skaa . . . the way they're starting to look at him . . ."

"I know," Marsh said. "It started with that 'Eleventh Metal' scheme of his. I don't know that we have to worry—this is just Kell playing his usual games."

"It makes me wonder why he's leaving on this trip," Vin said. "He'll be away from the action for a good month."

Marsh shook his head. "He'll have an entire army full of men to perform for. Besides, he needs to get out of the city. His reputation is growing too unwieldy, and the nobility is becoming too interested in the Survivor. If rumors got out that a man with scars on his arms is staying with Lord Renoux . . ."

Vin nodded, understanding.

"Right now," Marsh said, "he's playing the part of one of Renoux's distant relatives. That man has to leave before someone connects him to the Survivor. When Kell gets back, he'll have to keep a low profile—sneaking into the mansion instead of walking up the steps, keeping his hood up when he's in Luthadel."

Marsh trailed off, then stood. "Anyway, I've given you the basics. Now you just need to practice. Whenever you're with Mistings, have them burn for you and focus on their Allomantic pulses. If we meet again, I'll show you more, but there's nothing else I can do until you've practiced."

Vin nodded, and Marsh walked out the door without any other farewell. A few moments later, she saw him approach Kelsier and Renoux again.

They really don't hate each other, Vin thought, resting with both arms crossed atop the railing. *What would that be like?* After some thought, she decided that the concept of loving siblings was a little like the Allomantic pulse lengths she was supposed to be looking for—they were just too unfamiliar for her to understand at the moment.

"The Hero of Ages shall be not a man, but a force. No nation may claim him, no woman shall keep him, and no king may slay him. He shall belong to none, not even himself."

21

KELSIER SAT QUIETLY, READING AS his boat moved slowly along the canal to the north. *Sometimes, I worry that I'm not the hero everyone thinks I am,* the text said.

> What proof do we have? The words of men long dead, only now deemed divinatory? Even if we accept the prophecies, only tenuous interpretation links them to me. Is my defense of the Summer Hill really the "Burden by which the Hero shall be dubbed"? My several marriages could give me a "Bloodless bond to the world's kings," if you look at it the right way. There are dozens of similar phrases that could refer to events in my life. But, then again, they could all just be coincidences.
>
> The philosophers assure me that this is the time, that the signs have been met. But I still wonder if they have the wrong man. So many people depend on me. They say I will hold the future of the entire world on my arms. What would they think if they knew that their champion—the Hero of Ages, their savior—doubted himself?
>
> Perhaps they wouldn't be shocked at all. In a way, this is what worries me most. Maybe, in their hearts, they wonder—just like I do. When they see me, do they see a liar?
>
> Rashek seems to think so. I know that I shouldn't let a simple packman perturb me. However, he is from Terris, where the prophecies originated. If anyone could spot a fraud, would it not be he?

Nevertheless, I continue my trek, going where the scribbled auguries proclaim that I will meet my destiny—walking, feeling Rashek's eyes on my back. Jealous. Mocking. Hating.

In the end, I worry that my arrogance shall destroy us all.

Kelsier lowered the booklet, his cabin shaking slightly from the efforts of the pullers outside. He was glad that Sazed had provided him with a copy of the translated portions of the Lord Ruler's logbook before the caravan boats' departure. There was blessed little else to do during the trip.

Fortunately, the logbook was fascinating. Fascinating, and eerie. It was disturbing to read words that had originally been written by the Lord Ruler himself. To Kelsier the Lord Ruler was less a man, and more a . . . creature. An evil force that needed to be destroyed.

Yet, the person presented in the logbook seemed all too mortal. He questioned and pondered—he seemed a man of depth, and even of character.

Though, it would be best not to trust his narrative too closely, Kelsier thought, running his fingers across the page. *Men rarely see their own actions as unjustified.*

Still, the Lord Ruler's story reminded Kelsier of the legends he had heard—stories whispered by skaa, discussed by noblemen, and memorized by Keepers. They claimed that once, before the Ascension, the Lord Ruler had been the greatest of men. A beloved leader, a man entrusted with the fate of all mankind.

Unfortunately, Kelsier knew how the story ended. The Final Empire itself was the logbook's legacy. The Lord Ruler hadn't saved mankind; he had enslaved it instead. Reading a firsthand account, seeing the Lord Ruler's self-doubt and internal struggles, only made the story that much more tragic.

Kelsier raised the booklet to continue; however, his boat began to slow. He glanced out the window of his cabin, looking up the canal. Dozens of men trudged along the towpath—a small road alongside the canal—pulling the four barges and two narrowboats that made up their convoy. It was an efficient, if labor-intensive, way to travel; men pulling a barge across a canal could move hundreds more pounds of weight than they could if forced to carry packs.

The men had pulled to a stop, however. Ahead, Kelsier could make out a lock mechanism, beyond which the canal split into two sections. A kind of crossroads of waterways. *Finally,* Kelsier thought. His weeks of travel were over.

Kelsier didn't wait for a messenger. He simply stepped out onto the deck of his narrowboat and slipped a few coins from his pouch into his hand. *Time to be a bit ostentatious,* he thought, dropping a coin to the wood. He burned steel and Pushed himself into the air.

He lurched upward at an angle, quickly gaining a height where he could see the entire line of men—half pulling the boats, half walking and waiting for their shifts. Kelsier flew in an arc, dropping another coin as he passed over one of the supply-laden barges, then Pushing against it when he began to descend. Would-be soldiers looked up, pointing in awe as Kelsier soared above the canal.

Kelsier burned pewter, strengthening his body as he thumped to the deck of the narrowboat leading the caravan.

Yeden stepped out of his cabin, surprised. "Lord Kelsier! We've, uh, arrived at the crossroads."

"I can see that," Kelsier said, glancing back along the line of boats. The men on the towpath spoke excitedly, pointing. It felt strange to use Allomancy so obviously in the daylight, and before so many people.

There's no help for it, he thought. *This visit is the last chance the men will have to see me for months. I need to make an impression, give them something they can hold on to, if this is all going to work. . . .*

"Shall we go see if the group from the caves has arrived to meet us?" Kelsier asked, turning back to Yeden.

"Of course," Yeden said, waving for a servant to pull his narrowboat up to the side of the canal and throw out the plank. Yeden looked excited; he really was an earnest man, and that much Kelsier could respect, even if he was a bit lacking in presence.

Most of my life, I've had the opposite problem, Kelsier

thought with amusement, walking with Yeden off of the boat. *Too much presence, not enough earnestness.*

The two of them walked up the line of canal workers. Near the front of the men, one of Ham's Thugs—playing the part of Kelsier's guard captain—saluted. "We've reached the crossroads, Lord Kelsier."

"I can see that," Kelsier repeated. A dense stand of birch trees grew ahead, running up a slope into the hills. The canals ran away from the woods—there were better sources of wood in other parts of the Final Empire. The forest stood alone and ignored by most.

Kelsier burned tin, wincing slightly at the suddenly blinding sunlight. His eyes adjusted, however, and he was able to pick out detail—and a slight bit of motion—in the forest.

"There," he said, flipping a coin into the air, then Pushing it. The coin zipped forward and thocked against a tree. The prearranged sign given, a small group of camouflaged men left the tree line, crossing the ash-stained earth toward the canal.

"Lord Kelsier," the foremost man said, saluting. "My name is Captain Demoux. Please, gather the recruits and come with me General Hammond is eager to meet with you."

"Captain" Demoux was a young man to be so disciplined. Barely into his twenties, he led his small squad of men with a level of solemnity that might have seemed self-important had he been any less competent.

Younger men than he have led soldiers into battle, Kelsier thought. *Just because I was a fop when I was that age doesn't mean that everyone is. Look at poor Vin—only sixteen, already a match for Marsh in seriousness.*

They took a roundabout passage through the forest—by Ham's order, each troop took a different path to avoid wearing a trail. Kelsier glanced back at the two hundred or so men behind, frowning slightly. Their trail would probably still be visible, but there was little he could do about that—the movements of so many men would be nearly impossible to mask.

Demoux slowed, waving, and several members of his

squad scrambled forward; they didn't have half their leader's sense of military decorum. Still, Kelsier was impressed. The last time he'd visited, the men had been typically ragtag and uncoordinated, like most skaa outcasts. Ham and his officers had done their work well.

The soldiers pulled away some false underbrush, revealing a crack in the ground. It was dark within, the sides jutting with crystalline granite. It wasn't a regular hillside cavern, but instead a simple rend in the ground leading directly down.

Kelsier stood quietly, looking down at the black, stone-laced rift. He shivered slightly.

"Kelsier?" Yeden asked, frowning. "What is it?"

"It reminds me of the Pits. They looked like this—cracks in the ground."

Yeden paled slightly. "Oh. I, uh . . ."

Kelsier waved dismissively. "I knew this was coming. I climbed down inside those caves every day for a year, and I always came back out. I beat them. They have no power over me."

To prove his words, he stepped forward and climbed down into the thin crack. It was just wide enough for a large man to slip through. As Kelsier descended, he saw the soldiers—both Demoux's squad and the new recruits—watching quietly. He had intentionally spoken loud enough for them to hear.

Let them see my weakness, and let them see me overcome it.

They were brave thoughts. However, once he passed beneath the surface, it was as if he were back again. Smashed between two walls of stone, questing downward with shaking fingers. Cold, damp, dark. Slaves had to be the ones who recovered the atium. Allomancers might have been more effective, but using Allomancy near atium crystals shattered them. So, the Lord Ruler used condemned men. Forcing them into the pits. Forcing them to crawl downward, ever downward . . .

Kelsier forced himself onward. This wasn't Hathsin. The crack wouldn't go down for hours, and there would be no crystal-lined holes to reach through with torn, bleeding arms—stretching, seeking the atium geode hidden within. One geode; that bought one more week of life. Life beneath the taskmasters' lashes. Life beneath the rule of a sadistic god. Life beneath the sun gone red.

I will change things for the others, Kelsier thought. *I will make it better!*

The climb was difficult for him, more difficult than he ever would have admitted. Fortunately, the crack soon opened up to a larger cavern beneath, and Kelsier caught a glimpse of light from below. He let himself drop the rest of the way, landing on the uneven stone floor, and smiled at the man who stood waiting.

"Hell of an entryway you've got there, Ham," Kelsier said, dusting off his hands.

Ham smiled. "You should see the bathroom."

Kelsier laughed, moving to make way for the others. Several natural tunnels led off of the chamber, and a small rope ladder hung from the bottom of the rift to facilitate going back up. Yeden and Demoux soon climbed down the ladder into the cavern, their clothing scraped and dirtied from the descent. It wasn't an easy entrance to get through. That, however, was the idea.

"It's good to see you, Kell," Ham said. It was odd to see him in clothing that wasn't missing the sleeves. In fact, his militaristic outfit looked rather formal, with square-cut lines and buttons down the front. "How many have you brought me?"

"Just over two hundred and forty."

Ham raised his eyebrows. "Recruitment has picked up, then?"

"Finally," Kelsier said with a nod. Soldiers began to drop into the cavern, and several of Ham's aides moved forward, helping the newcomers and directing them down a side tunnel.

Yeden moved over to join Kelsier and Ham. "This cavern is amazing, Lord Kelsier! I've never actually been to the caves myself. No wonder the Lord Ruler hasn't found the men down here!"

"The complex is completely secure," Ham said proudly. "There are only three entrances, all of them cracks like this one. With proper supplies, we could hold this place indefinitely against an invading force."

"Plus," Kelsier said, "this isn't the only cave complex beneath these hills. Even if the Lord Ruler were determined to destroy us, his army could spend weeks searching and still not find us."

"Amazing," Yeden said. He turned, eyeing Kelsier. "I was wrong about you, Lord Kelsier. This operation . . . this army . . . well, you've done something impressive here."

Kelsier smiled. "Actually, you were right about me. You believed in me when this started—we're only here because of you."

"I . . . guess I did, didn't I?" Yeden said, smiling.

"Either way," Kelsier said, "I appreciate the vote of confidence. It's probably going to take some time to get all these men down the crack—would you mind directing things here? I'd like to talk to Hammond for a bit."

"Of course, Lord Kelsier." There was respect—even a growing bit of adulation—in his voice.

Kelsier nodded to the side. Ham frowned slightly, picking up a lantern, then followed Kelsier from the first chamber. They entered a side tunnel, and once they were out of earshot, Ham paused, glancing backward.

Kelsier stopped, raising an eyebrow.

Ham nodded back toward the entry chamber. "Yeden certainly has changed."

"I have that effect on people."

"Must be your awe-inspiring humility," Ham said. "I'm serious, Kell. How do you do it? That man practically hated you; now he looks at you like a kid idolizing his big brother."

Kelsier shrugged. "Yeden's never been part of an effective team before—I think he's started to realize that we might actually have a chance. In little over half a year, we've gathered a rebellion larger than he's ever seen. Those kind of results can convert even the stubborn."

Ham didn't look convinced. Finally, he just shrugged, beginning to walk again. "What was it you wanted to talk about?"

"Actually, I'd like to visit the other two entrances, if we could," Kelsier said.

Ham nodded, pointing to a side tunnel and leading the way. The tunnel, like most of the others, hadn't been hollowed by human hands; it was a natural growth of the cave complex. There were hundreds of similar cave systems in the Central Dominance, though most weren't as extensive. And only one—the Pits of Hathsin—grew atium geodes.

"Anyway, Yeden's right," Ham said, twisting his way through a narrow place in the tunnel. "You picked a great place to hide these people."

Kelsier nodded. "Various rebel groups have been using the cavern complexes in these hills for centuries. They're frighteningly close to Luthadel, but the Lord Ruler has never led a successful raid against anyone here. He just ignores the place now—one too many failures, probably."

"I don't doubt it," Ham said. "With all the nooks and bottlenecks down here, this would be a nasty place to have a battle." He stepped out of the passageway, entering another small cavern. This one also had a rift in the ceiling, and faint sunlight trickled down. A squad of ten soldiers stood guard in the room, and they snapped to attention as soon as Ham entered.

Kelsier nodded approvingly. "Ten men at all times?"

"At each of the three entrances," Ham said.

"Good," Kelsier said. He walked forward, inspecting the soldiers. He wore his sleeves up, his scars showing, and he could see the men eyeing them. He didn't really know what to inspect, but he tried to look discriminating. He examined their weapons—staves for eight of the men, swords for two—and dusted off a few shoulders, though none of the men wore uniforms.

Finally, he turned to a soldier who bore an insignia on his shoulder. "Who do you let out of the caverns, soldier?"

"Only men bearing a letter sealed by General Hammond himself, sir!"

"No exceptions?" Kelsier asked.

"No, sir!"

"And if I wanted to leave right now?"

The man paused. "Uh . . ."

"You'd stop me!" Kelsier said. "No one is exempt, soldier. Not me, not your bunkmate, not an officer—no one. If they don't have that seal, they don't leave!"

"Yes, sir!" the soldier said.

"Good man," Kelsier said. "If all of your soldiers are this fine, General, then the Lord Ruler has good reason to be afraid."

The soldiers puffed up slightly at the words.

"Carry on, men," Kelsier said, waving for Ham to follow as he left the room.

"That was kind of you," Ham said softly. "They've been anticipating your visit for weeks."

Kelsier shrugged. "I just wanted to see that they were guarding the crack properly. Now that you have more men, I want you to post guards at any tunnels leading to these exit caverns."

Ham nodded. "Seems a bit extreme, though."

"Humor me," Kelsier said. "A single runaway or malcontent could betray us all to the Lord Ruler. It's nice that you feel that you could defend this place, but if there's an army camped outside trapping you in, this army will effectively become useless to us."

"All right," Ham said. "You want to see the third entrance?"

"Please," Kelsier said.

Ham nodded, leading him down another tunnel.

"Oh, one other thing," Kelsier said after a bit of walking. "Get together groups of a hundred men—all ones you trust—to go tromp around up in the forest. If someone comes looking for us, we won't be able to hide the fact that lots of people have passed through the area. However, we might be able to muddle the tracks so much that the trails all lead nowhere."

"Good idea."

"I'm full of 'em," Kelsier said as they stepped into another cave chamber, this one far larger than the previous two. It wasn't an entrance rift, but instead a practice room. Groups of men stood with swords or staves, sparring beneath the eye of uniformed instructors. Uniforms for the officers had been Dockson's idea. They couldn't afford to outfit all the men—it would be too expensive, and obtaining that many uniforms would look suspicious. However, maybe seeing their leaders in uniform would help give the men a sense of cohesion.

Ham paused at the edge of the room rather than continuing onward. He eyed the soldiers, speaking softly. "We need to talk about this sometime, Kell. The men are starting to feel like soldiers, but . . . Well, they're skaa. They've spent their lives working in mills or fields. I don't know how well they'll do when we actually get them onto a battlefield."

"If we do everything right, they won't have to do much fighting," Kelsier said. "The Pits are only guarded by a couple hundred soldiers—the Lord Ruler can't have too many men there, lest he hint at the location's importance. Our thousand men can take the Pits with ease, then retreat as soon as the Garrison arrives. The other nine thousand might have to face a few Great House guard squads and the palace soldiers, but our men should have the upper hand in numbers."

Ham nodded, though his eyes still seemed uncertain.

"What?" Kelsier asked, leaning against the smooth, crystalline mouth of the cavern juncture.

"And when we're done with them, Kell?" Ham asked. "Once we have our atium, we give the city—and the army—over to Yeden. Then what?"

"That's up to Yeden," Kelsier said.

"They'll be slaughtered," Ham said very softly. "Ten thousand men can't hold Luthadel against the entire Final Empire."

"I intend to give them a better chance than you think, Ham," Kelsier said. "If we can turn the nobility against each other and destabilize the government . . ."

"Maybe," Ham said, still not convinced.

"You agreed to the plan, Ham," Kelsier said. "This was what we were intending all along. Raise an army, deliver it to Yeden."

"I know," Ham said, sighing and leaning back against the cavern wall. "I guess . . . Well, it's different, now that I've been leading them. Maybe I'm just not meant to be in charge like this. I'm a bodyguard, not a general."

I know how you feel, my friend, Kelsier thought. *I'm a thief, not a prophet. Sometimes, we just have to be what the job requires.*

Kelsier laid a hand on Ham's shoulder. "You did a fine job here."

Ham paused. " 'Did' fine?"

"I brought Yeden to replace you. Dox and I decided it would be better to rotate him in as the army's commander—that way, the troops get used to him as their leader. Besides, we need you back in Luthadel. Someone has to visit the Garrison and gather intelligence, and you're the only one with any military contacts."

"So, I'm going back with you?" Ham asked.

Kelsier nodded.

Ham looked crestfallen for just a moment, then he relaxed, smiling. "I'll finally be able get out of this uniform! But, do you think Yeden can handle it?"

"You said yourself, he's changed a lot during the last few months. And, he really is an excellent administrator—he's done a fine job with the rebellion since my brother left."

"I suppose. . . ."

Kelsier shook his head ruefully. "We're spread thin, Ham. You and Breeze are two of the only men I know I can trust, and I need you back in Luthadel. Yeden's not perfect for the job here, but the army is going to be his, eventually. Might as well let him lead it for a time. Besides, it will give him something to do; he's growing a bit touchy about his place in the crew." Kelsier paused, then smiled in amusement. "I think he's jealous of the attention I pay the others."

Ham smiled. "That *is* a change."

They began to walk again, leaving the practice chamber behind. They entered another twisting stone tunnel, this one leading slightly downward, Ham's lantern providing their only light.

"You know," Ham said after a few minutes of walking, "there's something else nice about this place. You've probably noticed this before, but it certainly is beautiful down here sometimes."

Kelsier hadn't noticed. He glanced to the side as they walked. One edge of the chamber had been formed of dripping minerals from the ceiling, thin stalactites and stalagmites—like dirty icicles—melding together to form a kind of banister. Minerals twinkled in Ham's light, and the path in front of them seemed to be frozen in the form of a tumbling molten river.

No, Kelsier thought. *No, I don't see its beauty, Ham.* Other men might see art in the layers of color and melted rock. Kelsier only saw the Pits. Endless caves, most of them going straight down. He'd been forced to wiggle through cracks, plunging downward in the darkness, not even given a light to brighten his way.

Often, he'd considered not climbing back up. But, then he would find a corpse in the caves—the body of another prisoner, a man who had gotten lost, or who had perhaps just given up. Kelsier would feel their bones and promise himself more. Each week, he'd found an atium geode. Each week he'd avoided execution by brutal beating.

Except that last time. He didn't deserve to be alive—he should have been killed. But, Mare had given him an atium geode, promising him that she'd found two that week. It wasn't until after he'd turned it in that he'd discovered her lie. She'd been beaten to death the next day. Beaten to death right in front of him.

That night, Kelsier had Snapped, coming into his powers as a Mistborn. The next night, men had died.

Many men.

Survivor of Hathsin. A man who shouldn't live. Even after watching her die, I couldn't decide if she'd betrayed me or not. Did she give me that geode out of love? Or did she do it out of guilt?

No, he couldn't see beauty in the caverns. Other men had been driven mad by the Pits, becoming terrified of small, enclosed spaces. That hadn't happened to Kelsier. However, he knew that no matter what wonders the labyrinths held—no matter how amazing the views or delicate the beauties—he would never acknowledge them. Not with Mare dead.

I can't think about this anymore, Kelsier decided, the cavern seeming to grow darker around him. He glanced to the side. "All right, Ham. Go ahead. Tell me what you're thinking about."

"Really?" Ham said eagerly.

"Yes," Kelsier said with a sense of resignation.

"All right," Ham said. "So, here's what I've been worried about lately: Are skaa different from noblemen?"

"Of course they are," Kelsier said. "The aristocracy has the money and the land; the skaa don't have anything."

"I don't mean economics—I'm talking about physical differences. You know what the obligators say, right?"

Kelsier nodded.

"Well, is it true? I mean, skaa really do have a lot of children, and I've heard that aristocrats have trouble reproducing."

The Balance, it was called. It was supposedly the way that the Lord Ruler ensured that there weren't too many noblemen for the skaa to support, and the way he made certain that—despite beatings and random killings—there were always enough skaa to grow food and work in mills.

"I've always just assumed it to be Ministry rhetoric," Kelsier said honestly.

"I've known skaa women to have as many as a dozen children," Ham said. "But I can't name a single major noble family with more than three."

"It's just cultural."

"And the height difference? They say you used to be able to tell skaa and noblemen apart by sight alone. That's changed, probably through interbreeding, but most skaa are still kind of short."

"That's nutritional. Skaa don't get enough to eat."

"What about Allomancy?"

Kelsier frowned.

"You have to admit that there's a physical difference there," Ham said. "Skaa never become Mistings unless they have aristocratic blood somewhere in their last five generations."

That much, at least, was true.

"Skaa think differently from noblemen, Kell," Ham said. "Even these soldiers are kind of timid, and they're the brave ones! Yeden's right about the general skaa population—it will never rebel. What if . . . what if there really is something physically different about us? What if the noblemen are *right* to rule over us?"

Kelsier froze in the hallway. "You don't really mean that."

Ham stopped as well. "I guess . . . no, I don't. But I do wonder sometimes. The noblemen have Allomancy, right? Maybe they're meant to be in charge."

"Meant by who? The Lord Ruler?"

Ham shrugged.

"No, Ham," Kelsier said. "It isn't right. *This* isn't right. I know it's hard to see—things have been this way for so long—but something very serious is wrong with the way skaa live. You *have* to believe that."

Ham paused, then nodded.

"Let's go," Kelsier said. "I want to visit that other entrance."

The week passed slowly. Kelsier inspected the troops, the training, the food, the weapons, the supplies, the scouts, the guards, and just about everything else he could think of. More important, he visited the men. He complimented and encouraged them—and he made certain to use Allomancy frequently in front of them.

While many skaa had heard of "Allomancy," very few knew specifically what it could do. Nobleman Mistings rarely used their powers in front of other people, and half-breeds had to be even more careful. Ordinary skaa, even city skaa, didn't know of things like Steelpushing or Pewter-burning. When they saw Kelsier flying through the air or sparring with supernatural strength, they would just attribute it to formless "Allomancy Magics." Kelsier didn't mind the misunderstanding at all.

Despite all of the week's activities, however, he never forgot his conversation with Ham.

How could he even wonder if skaa are inferior? Kelsier thought, poking at his meal as he sat at the high table in the central meeting cavern. The massive "room" was large enough to hold the entire army of seven thousand men, though many sat in side chambers or halfway out into tunnels. The high table sat on a raised rock formation at the far end of the chamber.

I'm probably worrying too much. Ham was prone to think about things that no sane man would consider; this was just another of his philosophical dilemmas. In fact, he already seemed to have forgotten his earlier concerns. He laughed with Yeden, enjoying his meal.

As for Yeden, the gangly rebel leader looked quite satisfied with his general's uniform, and had spent the week taking very serious notes from Ham regarding the army's operation. He seemed to be falling quite naturally into his duties.

In fact, Kelsier seemed to be the only one who wasn't enjoying the feast. The evening's foods—brought on the barges especially for the occasion—were humble by aristocratic standards, but were much finer than what the soldiers were used to. The men relished the meal with a joyful boisterousness, drinking their small allotment of ale and celebrating the moment.

And still, Kelsier worried. What did these men think they were fighting for? They seemed enthusiastic about their training, but that might have just been due to the regular meals. Did they actually believe that they deserved to overthrow the Final Empire? Did they think that skaa were inferior to noblemen?

Kelsier could sense their reservations. Many of the men realized the impending danger, and only the strict exit rules kept them from fleeing. While they were eager to speak of their training, they avoided talking about their final task—that of seizing the palace and city walls, then holding off the Luthadel Garrison.

They don't think they can succeed, Kelsier guessed. *They need confidence. The rumors about me are a start, but . . .*

He nudged Ham, getting the man's attention.

"Are there any men who have given you discipline problems?" Kelsier asked quietly.

Ham frowned at the odd question. "There are a couple, of course. I'd think there are always dissidents in a group this large."

"Anyone in particular?" Kelsier asked. "Men who have wanted to leave? I need someone outspoken in their opposition to what we're doing."

"There are a couple in the brig right now," Ham said.

"Anyone here?" Kelsier asked. "Preferably someone sitting at a table we can see?"

Ham thought for a moment, scanning the crowd. "The man sitting at the second table with the red cloak. He was caught trying to escape a couple weeks ago."

The man in question was scrawny and twitchy; he sat at his table with a hunched, solitary posture.

Kelsier shook his head. "I need someone a bit more charismatic."

Ham rubbed his chin in thought. Then he paused, and nodded toward another table. "Bilg. The big guy sitting at the fourth table over on the right."

"I see him," Kelsier said. Bilg was a brawny man wearing a vest and a full beard.

"He's too clever to be insubordinate," Ham said, "but he's been making trouble quietly. He doesn't think we have a chance against the Final Empire. I'd lock him up, but I can't really punish a man for expressing fear—or, at least, if I did, I'd have to do the same for half the army. Besides, he's too good a warrior to discard idly."

"He's perfect," Kelsier said. He burned zinc, then looked toward Bilg. While zinc wouldn't let him read the man's emotions, it was possible—when burning the metal—to isolate just a single individual for Soothing or Rioting, much as one was able to isolate a single bit of metal from hundreds to Pull on.

Even still, it was difficult to single Bilg out from such a large crowd, so Kelsier just focused on the entire tableful of men, keeping their emotions "in hand" for later use. Then he stood. Slowly, the cavern quieted.

"Men, before I leave, I wish to express one last time how much I was impressed by this visit." His words rang through the room, amplified by the cavern's natural acoustics.

"You are becoming a fine army," Kelsier said. "I apologize for stealing General Hammond, but I leave a very competent man in his place. Many of you know General Yeden—you know of his many years serving as rebellion leader. I have confidence in his ability to train you even further in the ways of soldiers."

He began to Riot Bilg and his companions, enflaming their emotions, counting on the fact that they'd be feeling disagreeable.

"It is a great task I ask of you," Kelsier said, not looking at Bilg. "Those skaa outside of Luthadel—indeed, most skaa everywhere—have no idea what you are about to do for them. They aren't aware of the training you endure or the battles you prepare to fight. However, they will reap the rewards. Someday, they will call you heroes."

He Rioted Bilg's emotions even harder.

"The Garrison of Luthadel is strong," Kelsier said, "but we can defeat it—especially if we take the city walls quickly. Do not forget why you came here. This isn't simply about learning to swing a sword or wear a helm. This is about a revolution such as the world has never seen—it is about taking the government for ourselves, about ousting the Lord Ruler. Do not lose sight of your goal."

Kelsier paused. From the corner of his eye, he could see dark expressions from the men at Bilg's table. Finally, in the silence, Kelsier heard a muttered comment from the table—carried by cavern acoustics to many ears.

Kelsier frowned, turning toward Bilg. The entire cavern seemed to grow even more still. "Did you say something?" Kelsier asked. *Now, the moment of decision. Will he resist, or will he be cowed?*

Bilg looked back. Kelsier hit the man with a flared Riot. His reward came as Bilg stood from his table, face red.

"Yes, *sir*," the brawny man snapped. "I did say something. I said that some of us haven't lost sight of our 'goal.' We think about it every day."

"And why is that?" Kelsier asked. Rumbling whispers began to sound at the back of the cavern as soldiers passed the news to those too far away to hear.

Bilg took a deep breath. "Because, *sir*, we think that this is suicide you're sending us to. The Final Empire's armies are bigger than just one garrison. It won't matter if we take the walls—we'll get slaughtered eventually anyway. You don't overthrow an empire with a couple thousand soldiers."

Perfect, Kelsier thought. *I'm sorry, Bilg. But someone needed to say it, and it certainly couldn't be me.*

"I see we have a disagreement," Kelsier said loudly. "*I* believe in these men, and in their purpose."

"I believe that you are a deluded fool," Bilg bellowed. "And I was a bigger fool for coming to these bloody caves. If you're so certain about our chances, then why can't anyone leave? We're trapped here until you send us to die!"

"You insult me," Kelsier snapped. "You know very well why men aren't allowed to leave. Why do you want to go, soldier? Are you that eager to sell out your companions to the Lord Ruler? A few quick boxings in exchange for four thousand lives?"

Bilg's face grew redder. "I would never do such a thing, but

I'm certainly not going to let you send me to my death, either! This army is a waste."

"You speak treason," Kelsier said. He turned, scanning the crowd. "It is not fitting for a general to fight a man beneath his command. Is there a soldier here who is willing to defend the honor of this rebellion?"

Immediately, a couple dozen men stood up. Kelsier noticed one in particular. He was smaller than the rest, but he had the simple earnestness that Kelsier had noticed earlier. "Captain Demoux."

Immediately, the young captain jumped forward.

Kelsier reached over, grabbing his own sword and tossing it down to the man. "You can use a sword, lad?"

"Yes, sir!"

"Someone fetch a weapon for Bilg and a pair of studded vests." Kelsier turned toward Bilg. "Noblemen have a tradition. When two men have a dispute, they settle it with a duel. Defeat my champion, and you are free to leave."

"And if he defeats me?" Bilg asked.

"Then you'll be dead," Kelsier said.

"I'm dead if I stay," Bilg said, accepting a sword from a nearby soldier. "I accept the terms."

Kelsier nodded, waving for some men to pull aside tables and make an open space before the high table. Men began to stand, crowding around to watch the contest.

"Kell, what are you doing!" Ham hissed at his side.

"Something that needs to be done."

"Needs to be . . . Kelsier, that boy is no match for Bilg! I trust Demoux—that's why I promoted him—but he's not that great a warrior. Bilg's one of the finest swordsmen in the army!"

"The men know this?" Kelsier asked.

"Of course," Ham said. "Call this off. Demoux is nearly half Bilg's size—he's at a disadvantage in reach, strength, and skill. He'll get slaughtered!"

Kelsier ignored the request. He sat quietly as Bilg and Demoux hefted their weapons, a pair of soldiers tying on their leather cuirasses. When they were done, Kelsier waved a hand, motioning for the battle to begin.

Ham groaned.

It would be a short fight. Both men had longswords and little armor. Bilg stepped forward with confidence, making a few testing swings toward Demoux. The boy was at least competent—he blocked the blows, but he revealed a great deal about his abilities as he did so.

Taking a deep breath, Kelsier burned steel and iron.

Bilg swung, and Kelsier nudged the blade to the side, giving Demoux room to escape. The boy tried a thrust, but Bilg easily knocked it away. The larger warrior then attacked with a barrage, sending Demoux stumbling backward. Demoux tried to jump out of the way of the last swing, but he was too slow. The blade fell with awful inevitability.

Kelsier flared iron—stabilizing himself by Pulling against a lantern bracket behind—then grabbed the iron studs on Demoux's vest. Kelsier Pulled as Demoux jumped, yanking the boy backward in a small arc away from Bilg.

Demoux landed with a maladroit stumble as Bilg's sword smashed into the stone ground. Bilg looked up with surprise, and a low rumble of amazement moved through the crowd.

Bilg growled, running forward with weapon held high. Demoux blocked the powerful swing, but Bilg knocked the boy's weapon aside with a careless sweep. Bilg struck again, and Demoux raised a hand in reflexive defense.

Kelsier Pushed, freezing Bilg's sword in midswing. Demoux stood, hand forward, as if he had stopped the attacking weapon with a thought. The two stood like that for a moment, Bilg trying to force the sword forward, Demoux staring in awe at his hand. Standing up a bit straighter, Demoux tentatively forced his hand forward.

Kelsier Pushed, throwing Bilg backward. The large warrior tumbled to the ground with a cry of surprise. When he rose a moment later, Kelsier didn't have to Riot his emotions to make him angry. He bellowed in rage, grabbing his sword in two hands and rushing toward Demoux.

Some men don't know when to quit, Kelsier thought as Bilg swung.

Demoux began to dodge. Kelsier shoved the boy to the side, getting him out of the way. Then Demoux turned, gripping his own weapon in two hands and swinging at Bilg. Kelsier grabbed Demoux's weapon in mid-arc and Pulled against it forcefully, ripping the steel forward with a mighty flare of iron.

The swords smashed together, and Demoux's Kelsier-enhanced blow knocked Bilg's weapon out of his hands. There was a loud snap, and the large miscreant fell to the floor—thrown completely off balance by the force of Demoux's blow. Bilg's weapon bounced to the stone floor a distance away.

Demoux stepped forward, raising his weapon over the stunned Bilg. And then, he stopped. Kelsier burned iron, reaching out to grab the weapon and Pull it down, to force the killing blow, but Demoux resisted.

Kelsier paused. *This man should die,* he thought angrily. On the ground, Bilg groaned quietly. Kelsier could just barely see his twisted arm, its bone shattered by the powerful strike. It was bleeding.

No, Kelsier thought. *This is enough.*

He released Demoux's weapon. Demoux lowered his sword, staring down at Bilg. Then, Demoux raised his hands, regarding them with wonder, his arms quivering slightly.

Kelsier stood, and the crowd fell to a hush once again.

"Do you think I would send you against the Lord Ruler unprepared?" Kelsier demanded in a loud voice. "Do you think I would just send you off to die? You fight for what is just, men! You fight for *me*. I will not leave you unaided when you go against the soldiers of the Final Empire."

Kelsier thrust his hand into the air, holding aloft a tiny bar of metal. "You've heard of this, haven't you? You know the rumors of the Eleventh Metal? Well, I have it—and I will use it. The Lord Ruler will die!"

The men began to cheer.

"This is not our only tool!" Kelsier bellowed. "You soldiers have power untold inside of you! You have heard of the arcane magics that the Lord Ruler uses? Well, we have some of our own! Feast, my soldiers, and don't fear the battle to come. Look forward to it!"

The room erupted in a riot of cheers, and Kelsier waved for

more ale to be delivered. A couple of servants rushed forward to help Bilg from the room.

When Kelsier sat, Ham was frowning deeply. "I don't like this, Kell," he said.

"I know," Kelsier said quietly.

Ham was about to speak further, but Yeden leaned across him. "That was amazing! I . . . Kelsier, I didn't know! You should have told me you could pass your powers to others. Why, with these abilities, how can we possibly lose?"

Ham laid a hand on Yeden's shoulder, pushing the man back into his seat. "Eat," he ordered. Then, he turned to Kelsier, pulling his chair closer and speaking in a low voice. "You just lied to my entire army, Kell."

"No, Ham," Kelsier said quietly. "I lied to *my* army."

Ham paused. Then his face darkened.

Kelsier sighed. "It was only a partial lie. They don't need to be warriors, they just have to look threatening long enough for us to grab the atium. With it, we can bribe the Garrison, and our men won't even have to fight. That's virtually the same thing as what I promised them."

Ham didn't respond.

"Before we leave," Kelsier said, "I want you to select a few dozen of our most trustworthy and devoted soldiers. We'll send them back to Luthadel—with vows that they can't reveal where the army is—so that word of this evening can spread amongst the skaa."

"So this is about your ego?" Ham snapped.

Kelsier shook his head. "Sometimes we need to do things that we find distasteful, Ham. My ego may be considerable, but this is about something else entirely."

Ham sat for a moment, then turned back to his meal. He didn't eat, however—he just sat staring at the blood on the ground before the high table.

Ah, Ham, Kelsier thought. *I wish I could explain everything to you.*

Plots behind plots, plans beyond plans.

There was always another secret.

At first, there were those who didn't think the Deepness was a serious danger, at least not to them. However, it brought with it a blight that I have seen infect nearly every part of the land. Armies are useless before it. Great cities are laid low by its power. Crops fail, and the land dies.

This is the thing I fight. This is the monster I must defeat. I fear that I have taken too long. Already, so much destruction has occurred that I fear for mankind's survival.

Is this truly the end of the world, as many of the philosophers predict?

22

We arrived in Terris earlier this week, *Vin read*, and, I have to say, I find the countryside beautiful. The great mountains to the north—with their bald snowcaps and forested mantles—stand like watchful gods over this land of green fertility. My own lands to the south are mostly flat; I think that they might look less dreary if there were a few mountains to vary the terrain.

The people here are mostly herdsmen—though timber harvesters and farmers are not uncommon. It is a pastoral land, certainly. It seems odd that a place so remarkably agrarian could have produced the prophecies and theologies upon which the entire world now relies.

We picked up a group of Terris packmen to guide us through the difficult mountain passages. Yet, these are no ordinary men. The stories are apparently true—some Terrismen have a remarkable ability that is most intriguing.

Somehow, they can store up their strength for use on the next day. Before they sleep at night, they spend an hour lying in their bedrolls, during which time they suddenly grow very frail in appearance—almost as if they had aged by half a century. Yet, when they wake the next morning, they become quite muscular. Apparently, their powers have something to do with the metal bracelets and earrings that they always wear.

The leader of the packmen is named Rashek, and he is rather taciturn. Nevertheless, Braches—inquisitive, as always—has promised to interrogate him in the hopes of discovering exactly how this wondrous strength-storing is achieved.

Tomorrow, we begin the final stage of our pilgrimage—the Far Mountains of Terris. There, hopefully, I will find peace—both for myself, and for our poor land.

AS SHE READ HER COPY of the logbook, Vin was quickly coming to several decisions. First was the firm belief that she did *not* like reading. Sazed didn't listen to her complaints; he just claimed that she hadn't practiced enough. Couldn't he see that reading was hardly as practical a skill as being able to handle a dagger or use Allomancy?

Still, she continued to read as per his orders—if only to stubbornly prove that she could. Many of the logbook's words were difficult to her, and she had to read in a secluded part of Renoux's mansion where she could sound out the words to herself, trying to decipher the Lord Ruler's odd style of writing.

The continued reading led to her second conclusion: The Lord Ruler was far more whiny than any god had a right to be. When pages of the logbook weren't filled with boring notes about the Lord Ruler's travels, they were instead packed with internal contemplations and lengthy moralistic ramblings. Vin was beginning to wish that she'd never found the book in the first place.

She sighed, settling back into her wicker chair. A cool early-spring breeze blew through the lower gardens, passing over the petite fountain brook to her left. The air was comfortably moist, and the trees overhead shaded her from the afternoon sun. Being nobility—even fake nobility—certainly did have its perks.

A quiet footfall sounded behind her. It was distant, but Vin had grown into the habit of burning a little bit of tin at all times. She turned, shooting a covert glance over her shoulder.

"Spook?" she said with surprise as young Lestibournes walked down the garden path. "What are you doing here?"

Spook froze, blushing. "Wasing with the Dox to come and be without the stay."

"Dockson?" Vin said. "He's here too?" *Maybe he has news of Kelsier!*

Spook nodded, approaching. "Weapons for the getting, giving for the time to be."

Vin paused. "You lost me on that one."

"We needed the drop off some more weapons," Spook said, struggling to speak without his dialect. "Storing them here for a while."

"Ah," Vin said, rising and brushing off her dress. "I should go see him."

Spook looked suddenly apprehensive, flushing again, and Vin cocked her head. "Was there something else?"

With a sudden movement, Spook reached into his vest and pulled something out. Vin flared pewter in response, but the item was simply a pink-and-white handkerchief. Spook thrust it toward her.

Vin took it hesitantly. "What's this for?"

Spook flushed again, then turned and dashed away.

Vin watched him go, dumbfounded. She looked down at the handkerchief. It was made of soft lace, but there didn't seem to be anything unusual about it.

That is one strange boy, she thought, tucking the handkerchief inside her sleeve. She picked up her copy of the logbook, then began to work her way up the garden path. She was growing so accustomed to wearing a dress that she barely had to pay attention to keep the gown's lower layers from brushing against underbrush or stones.

I guess that in itself is a valuable skill, Vin thought as she reached the mansion's garden entrance without having snagged her dress on a single branch. She pushed open the many-paned glass door and stopped the first servant she saw.

"Master Delton has arrived?" she asked, using Dockson's fake name. He played the part of one of Renoux's merchant contacts inside Luthadel.

"Yes, my lady," the servant said. "He's in conference with Lord Renoux."

Vin let the servant go. She could probably force her way into the conference, but it would look bad. Lady Valette had no reason to attend a mercantile meeting between Renoux and Delton.

Vin chewed her lower lip in thought. Sazed was always telling her she had to keep up appearances. *Fine,* she thought. *I'll wait. Maybe Sazed can tell me what that crazy boy expects me to do with this handkerchief.*

She sought out the upper library, maintaining a pleasant ladylike smile, inwardly trying to guess what Renoux and Dockson were talking about. Dropping off the weapons was an excuse; Dockson wouldn't have come personally to do something so mundane. Perhaps Kelsier had been delayed. Or, maybe Dockson had finally gotten a communication from Marsh—Kelsier's brother, along with the other new obligator initiates, should be arriving back in Luthadel soon.

Dockson and Renoux could have sent for me, she thought with annoyance. Valette often entertained guests with her uncle.

She shook her head. Even though Kelsier had named her a full member of the crew, the others obviously still regarded her as something of a child. They were friendly and accepting, but they didn't think to include her. It was probably unintentional, but that didn't make it any less frustrating.

Light shone from the library ahead. Sure enough, Sazed sat inside, translating the last group of pages from the logbook. He looked up as Vin entered, smiling and nodding respectfully.

No spectacles this time either, Vin noted. *Why did he wear them for that short time before?*

"Mistress Vin," he said, rising and fetching her a chair. "How are your studies of the logbook going?"

Vin looked down at the loosely bound pages in her hand. "All right, I suppose. I don't see why I have to bother reading them—you gave copies to Kell and Breeze too, didn't you?"

"Of course," Sazed said, setting the chair down beside his desk. "However, Master Kelsier asked every member of the crew to read the pages. He is correct to do so, I think. The more eyes that read those words, the more likely we will be to discover the secrets hidden within them."

Vin sighed slightly, smoothing her dress and seating herself. The white and blue dress was beautiful—though intended for daily use, it was only slightly less luxurious than one of her ball gowns.

"You must admit, Mistress," Sazed said as he sat, "the text is amazing. This work is a Keeper's dream. Why, I'm discovering things about my culture that even I did not know!"

Vin nodded. "I just got to the part where they reach Terris." *Hopefully, the next part will contain fewer supply lists. Honestly, for an evil god of darkness, he certainly can be dull.*

"Yes, yes," Sazed said, speaking with uncharacteristic enthusiasm. "Did you see what he said, how he described Terris as a place of 'green fertility'? Keeper legends speak of this. Terris is now a tundra of frozen dirt—why, almost no plants can survive there. But, once it was green and beautiful, like the text says."

Green and beautiful, Vin thought. *Why would green be beautiful? That would be like having blue or purple plants—it would just be weird.*

However, there was something about the logbook that made her curious—something that both Sazed and Kelsier had been strangely closemouthed about. "I just read the part where the Lord Ruler gets some Terris packmen," Vin said carefully. "He talked about how they grow stronger during the day because they let themselves be weak at night."

Sazed suddenly grew more subdued. "Yes, indeed."

"You know something about this? Does it have to do with being a Keeper?"

"It does," Sazed said. "But, this should remain a secret, I think. Not that you aren't worthy of trust, Mistress Vin. However, if fewer people know about Keepers, then fewer rumors will be told of us. It would be best if the Lord Ruler began to believe that he had destroyed us completely, as has been his goal for the last thousand years."

Vin shrugged. "Fine. Hopefully, none of the secrets Kelsier wants us to discover in this text are related to the Terrisman powers—if they are, I'll miss them completely."

Sazed paused.

"Ah, well," Vin said nonchalantly, flipping through the pages she hadn't read. "Looks like he spends a lot of time talking about the Terrismen. Guess I won't be able to give much input when Kelsier gets back."

"You make a good point," Sazed said slowly. "Even if you make it a bit melodramatically."

Vin smiled pertly.

"Very well," Sazed said with a sigh. "We should not have let you spend so much time with Master Breeze, I think."

"The men in the logbook," Vin said. "They're Keepers?"

Sazed nodded. "What we now call Keepers were far more common back then—perhaps even more common than Mistings are among modern nobility. Our art is called 'Feruchemy,' and it grants the ability to store certain physical attributes inside bits of metal."

Vin frowned. "You burn metals too?"

"No, Mistress," Sazed said with a shake of his head. "Feruchemists aren't like Allomancers—we don't 'burn' away our metals. We use them as storage. Each piece of metal, dependent upon size and alloy, can store a certain physical quality. The Feruchemist saves up an attribute, then draws upon that reserve at a later time."

"Attribute?" Vin asked. "Like strength?"

Sazed nodded. "In the text, the Terris packmen make themselves weaker during the evening, storing up strength in their bracelets for use on the next day."

Vin studied Sazed's face. "That's why you wear so many earrings!"

"Yes, Mistress," he said, reaching over to pull up his sleeves. Underneath his robe, he wore thick iron bracers around his upper arms. "I keep some of my reserves hidden—but wearing many rings, earrings, and other items of jewelry has always been a part of Terris culture. The Lord Ruler once tried to enforce a ban upon Terrismen touching or owning any metal—in fact, he tried to make wearing metal a noble privilege, rather than a skaa one."

Vin frowned. "That's odd," she said. "One would think that the nobility *wouldn't* want to wear metal, because that would make them vulnerable to Allomancy."

"Indeed," Sazed said. "However, it has long been imperial fashion to accent one's wardrobe with metal. It began, I suspect, with the Lord Ruler's desire to deny the Terrismen the right to touch metal. He himself began wearing metal rings and bracelets, and the nobility always follows him in fashion. Nowadays, the most wealthy often wear metal as a symbol of power and pride."

"Sounds foolish," Vin said.

"Fashion often is, Mistress," Sazed said. "Regardless, the ploy failed—many of the nobility only wear wood painted to look like metal, and the Terris managed to weather the Lord Ruler's discontent in this area. It was simply too impractical to never let stewards handle metal. That hasn't stopped the Lord Ruler from trying to exterminate the Keepers, however."

"He fears you."

"And hates us. Not just Feruchemists, but all Terrismen." Sazed laid a hand on the still untranslated portion of the text. "I hope to find that secret in here as well. No one remembers why the Lord Ruler persecutes the Terris people, but I suspect that it has something to do with those packmen—their leader, Rashek, appears to be a very contrary man. The Lord Ruler often speaks of him in the narrative."

"He mentioned religion," Vin said. "The Terris religion. Something about prophecies?"

Sazed shook his head. "I cannot answer that question, Mistress, for I don't know any more of the Terris religion than you do."

"But, you collect religions," Vin said. "You don't know about your own?"

"I do not," Sazed said solemnly. "You see, Mistress, this was why the Keepers were formed. Centuries ago, my people hid away the last few Terris Feruchemists. The Lord Ruler's purges of the Terris people were growing quite violent—this was before he began the breeding program. Back then, we weren't stewards or servants—we weren't even skaa. We were something to be destroyed.

"Yet, something kept the Lord Ruler from wiping us out completely. I don't know why—perhaps he thought genocide too kind a punishment. Anyway, he successfully destroyed our religion during the first two centuries of his rule. The organization of Keepers was formed during the next century, its members intent upon discovering that which had been lost, then remembering for the future."

"With Feruchemy?"

Sazed nodded, rubbing his fingers across the bracer on his right arm. "This one is made of copper; it allows for the storage of memories and thoughts. Each Keeper carries several bracers like this, filled with knowledge—songs, stories, prayers, histories, and languages. Many Keepers have a particular area of interest—mine is religion—but we all remember the entire collection. If just one of us survives until the death of the Lord Ruler, then the world's people will be able to recover all that they have lost."

He paused, then pulled down his sleeve. "Well, not *all* that was lost. There are still things we are missing."

"Your own religion," Vin said quietly. "You never found it, did you?"

Sazed shook his head. "The Lord Ruler implies in this logbook that it was our prophets that led him to the Well of Ascension, but even this is new information for us. What did we believe? What, or whom, did we worship? Where did these Terris prophets come from, and how did they predict the future?"

"I'm . . . sorry."

"We continue to look, Mistress. We will find our answers eventually, I think. Even if we do not, we will still have provided an invaluable service for mankind. Other people call us docile and servile, but we have fought him, in our own way."

Vin nodded. "So, what other things can you store? Strength and memories. Anything else?"

Sazed eyed her. "I have said too much already, I think. You understand the mechanics of what we do—if the Lord Ruler mentions these things in his text, you will not be confused."

"Sight," Vin said, perking up. "That's why you wore glasses for a few weeks after you rescued me. You needed to be able to see better that night when you saved me, so you used up your storage. Then you spent a few weeks with weak vision so that you could refill it."

Sazed didn't respond to the comment. He picked up his pen, obviously intending to turn back to his translation. "Was there anything else, Mistress?"

"Yes, as a matter of fact," Vin said, pulling the handkerchief from her sleeve. "Do you have any idea what this is?"

"It appears to be a handkerchief, Mistress."

Vin raised a droll eyebrow. "Very funny. You've spent far too long around Kelsier, Sazed."

"I know," he said with a quiet sigh. "He has corrupted me, I think. Regardless, I do not understand your question. What is distinctive about that particular handkerchief?"

"That's what *I* want to know," Vin said. "Spook gave it to me just a little bit ago."

"Ah. That makes sense, then."

"What?" Vin demanded.

"In noble society, Mistress, a handkerchief is the traditional gift a young man gives a lady that he wishes to seriously court."

Vin paused, regarding the handkerchief with shock. "*What?* Is that boy crazy?"

"Most young men his age are somewhat crazy, I think," Sazed said with a smile. "However, this is hardly unexpected. Haven't you noticed how he stares at you when you enter the room?"

"I just thought he was creepy. What is he thinking? He's so much younger than me."

"The boy is fifteen, Mistress. That only makes him one year your junior."

"Two," Vin said. "I turned seventeen last week."

"Still, he isn't really that much younger than you."

Vin rolled her eyes. "I don't have time for his attentions."

"One would think, Mistress, that you would appreciate the opportunities you have. Not everyone is so fortunate."

Vin paused. *He's a eunuch, you fool.* "Sazed, I'm sorry. I . . ."

Sazed waved a hand. "It is something I have never known enough of to miss, Mistress. Perhaps I am fortunate—a life in the underground does not make it easy to raise a family. Why, poor Master Hammond has been away from his wife for months."

"Ham's *married?*"

"Of course," Sazed said. "So is Master Yeden, I believe. They protect their families by separating them from underground activities, but this necessitates spending large periods of time apart."

"Who else?" Vin asked. "Breeze? Dockson?"

"Master Breeze is a bit too . . . self-motivated for a family, I think. Master Dockson hasn't spoken of his romantic life, but I suspect that there is something painful in his past. That is not uncommon for plantation skaa, as you might expect."

"Dockson is from a plantation?" Vin asked with surprise.

"Of course. Don't you ever spend time talking with your friends, Mistress?"

Friends. I have friends. It was an odd realization.

"Anyway," Sazed said, "I should continue my work. I am sorry to be so dismissive, but I am nearly finished with the translation. . . ."

"Of course," Vin said, standing and smoothing her dress. "Thank you."

She found Dockson sitting in the guest study, writing quietly on a piece of paper, a pile of documents organized neatly on the desktop. He wore a standard nobleman's suit, and always looked more comfortable in the clothing than the others did. Kelsier was dashing, Breeze immaculate and lavish, but Dockson . . . he simply looked natural in the outfit.

He looked up as she entered. "Vin? I'm sorry—I should have sent for you. For some reason I assumed you were out."

"I often am, these days," she said, closing the door behind her. "I stayed home today; listening to noblewomen prattle over their lunches can get a bit annoying."

"I can imagine," Dockson said, smiling. "Have a seat."

Vin nodded, strolling into the room. It was a quiet place, decorated in warm colors and deep woods. It was still somewhat light outside, but Dockson already had the evening drapes drawn and was working by candlelight.

"Any news from Kelsier?" Vin asked as she sat.

"No," Dockson said, setting aside his document. "But that's not unexpected. He wasn't going to stay at the caves for long, so sending a messenger back would have been a bit silly—as an Allomancer, he might even be able to get back before a man on horseback. Either way, I suspect he'll be a few days late. This is Kell we're talking about, after all."

Vin nodded, then sat quietly for a moment. She hadn't spent as much time with Dockson as she had with Kelsier and Sazed—or even Ham and Breeze. He seemed like a kind man, however. Very stable, and very clever. While most of the others contributed some kind of Allomantic power to the crew, Dockson was valuable because of his simple ability to organize.

When something needed to be purchased—such as Vin's dresses—Dockson saw that it got done. When a building needed to be rented, supplies procured, or a permit secured, Dockson made it happen. He wasn't out front, scamming noblemen, fighting in the mists, or recruiting soldiers. Without him, however, Vin suspected that the entire crew would fall apart.

He's a nice man, she told herself. *He won't mind if I ask him.* "Dox, what was it like living on a plantation?"

"Hmm? The plantation?"

Vin nodded. "You grew up on one, right? You're a plantation skaa?"

"Yes," Dockson said. "Or, at least, I was. What was it like? I'm not sure how to answer, Vin. It was a hard life, but most skaa live hard lives. I wasn't allowed to leave the plantation—or even go outside of the hovel community—without permission. We ate more regularly than a lot of the street skaa, but we were worked as hard as any millworker. Perhaps more.

"The plantations are different from the cities. Out there, every lord is his own master. Technically, the Lord Ruler owns the skaa, but the noblemen rent them, and are allowed to kill as many as they want. Each lord just has to make certain that his crops come in."

"You seem so . . . unemotional about it," Vin said.

Dockson shrugged. "It's been a while since I lived there, Vin. I don't know that the plantation was overly traumatic. It was just life—we didn't know anything better. In fact, I now know that amongst plantation lords, mine was actually rather lenient."

"Why did you leave, then?"

Dockson paused. "An event," he said his voice growing almost wistful. "You know that the law says that a lord can bed any skaa woman that he wishes?"

Vin nodded. "He just has to kill her when he's done."

"Or soon thereafter," Dockson said. "Quickly enough that she can't birth any half-breed children."

"The lord took a woman you loved, then?"

Dockson nodded. "I don't talk about it much. Not because I can't, but because I think it would be pointless. I'm not the only skaa to lose a loved one to a lord's passion, or even to a lord's indifference. In fact, I'll bet you'd have trouble finding a skaa who *hasn't* had someone they love murdered by the aristocracy. That's just . . . the way it is."

"Who was she?" Vin asked.

"A girl from the plantation. Like I said, my story isn't that original. I remember . . . sneaking between the hovels at night to spend time with her. The entire community played along, hiding us from the taskmasters—I wasn't supposed to be out after dark, you see. I braved the mists for the first time for her, and while many thought me foolish to go out at night, others got over their superstition and encouraged me. I think the romance inspired them; Kareien and I reminded everyone that there was something to live for.

"When Kareien was taken by Lord Devinshae—her corpse returned the next morning for burial—something just . . . died in the skaa hovels. I left that next evening. I didn't know there was a better life, but I just couldn't stay, not with Kareien's family there, not with Lord Devinshae watching us work. . . ."

Dockson sighed, shaking his head. Vin could finally see some emotion in his face. "You know," he said, "it amazes me sometimes that we even try. With everything they've done to us—the deaths, the tortures, the agonies—you'd think that we would just give up on things like hope and love. But we don't. Skaa still fall in love. They still try to have families, and they still struggle. I mean, here we are . . . fighting Kell's insane little war, resisting a god we know is just going to slaughter us all."

Vin sat quietly, trying to comprehend the horror of what he described. "I . . . thought you said that your lord was a kind one."

"Oh, he was," Dockson said. "Lord Devinshae rarely beat his skaa to death, and he only purged the elderly when the population got completely out of control. He has an impeccable reputation among the nobility. You've probably seen him at some of the balls—he's been in Luthadel lately, over the winter, between planting seasons."

Vin felt cold. "Dockson, that's horrible! How could they let a monster like that among them?"

Dockson frowned, then he leaned forward slightly, resting his arms on the desktop. "Vin, they're *all* like that."

"I know that's what some of the skaa say, Dox," Vin said. "But, the people at the balls, they aren't like that. I've met them, danced with them. Dox, a lot of them are good people. I don't think they realize how terrible things are for the skaa."

Dockson looked at her with a strange expression. "Am I really hearing this from you, Vin? Why do you think we're fighting against them? Don't you realize the things those people—all of those people—are capable of?"

"Cruelty, perhaps," Vin said. "And indifference. But they aren't monsters, not all of them—not like your former plantation lord."

Dockson shook his head. "You just aren't seeing well enough, Vin. A nobleman can rape and murder a skaa woman one night, then be praised for his morality and virtue the next day. Skaa just aren't people to them. Noblewomen don't even consider it cheating when their lord sleeps with a skaa woman."

"I . . ." Vin trailed off, growing uncertain. This was the one area of noble culture she hadn't wanted to confront. Beatings, she could perhaps forgive, but this . . .

Dockson shook his head. "You're letting them dupe you, Vin. Things like this are less visible in the cities because of whorehouses, but the murders still happen. Some brothels use women of very poor—but noble—birth. Most, however, just kill off their skaa whores periodically to keep the Inquisitors placated."

Vin felt a little weak. "I . . . know about the brothels, Dox. My brother always threatened to sell me to one. But, just because brothels exist doesn't mean that all the men go to them. There are lots of workers who don't visit the skaa whorehouses."

"Noblemen are different, Vin," Dockson said sternly.

"They're horrible creatures. Why do you think I don't complain when Kelsier kills them? Why do you think I'm working with him to overthrow their government? You should ask some of those pretty boys you dance with how often they've slept with a skaa woman they knew would be killed a short time later. They've all done it, at one point or another."

Vin looked down.

"They can't be redeemed, Vin," Dockson said. He didn't seem as passionate about the topic as Kelsier, he just seemed . . . resigned. "I don't think that Kell will be happy until they're all dead. I doubt we have to go that far—or even that we can—but I, for one, would be more than happy to see their society collapse."

Vin sat quietly. *They can't* all *be like that,* she thought. *They're so beautiful, so distinguished. Elend has never taken and murdered a skaa woman . . . has he?*

I sleep but a few hours each night. We must press forward, traveling as much as we can each day—but when I finally lie down, I find sleep elusive. The same thoughts that trouble me during the day are only compounded by the stillness of night.

And, above it all, I hear the thumping sounds from above, the pulsings from the mountains. Drawing me closer with each beat.

23

"THEY SAY THAT THE DEATHS of the Geffenry brothers were a retaliation for the murder of Lord Entrone," Lady Kliss said quietly. Behind Vin's group, the musicians played upon their stage, but the evening was growing late, and few people danced.

Lady Kliss's circle of partygoers frowned at the news. There were about six of them, including Vin and her companion—one Milen Davenpleu, a young heir to a minor house title.

"Kliss, really," Milen said. "Houses Geffenry and Tekiel are allies. Why would Tekiel assassinate two Geffenry noblemen?"

"Why indeed?" Kliss said, leaning forward conspiratorially, her massive blond bun wobbling slightly. Kliss had never displayed much fashion sense. She was an excellent source of gossip, however.

"You remember when Lord Entrone was found dead in the Tekiel gardens?" Kliss asked. "Well, it *seemed* obvious that one of House Tekiel's enemies had killed him. But, House Geffenry has been petitioning Tekiel for an alliance—apparently, a faction within the house thought that if something happened to enflame the Tekiels, they would be more willing to seek allies."

"You're saying that Geffenry *purposely* killed a Tekiel ally?" asked Rene, Kliss's date. He scrunched up his ample brow in thought.

Kliss patted Rene's arm. "Don't worry about it too much, dear," she advised, then turned eagerly back to the conversation. "Don't you see? By secretly killing Lord Entrone, Geffenry hoped to get the allegiance it needs. *That* would give it access to those Tekiel canal routes through the eastern plains."

"But it backfired," Milen said thoughtfully. "Tekiel discovered the ruse, and killed Ardous and Callins."

"I danced with Ardous a couple of times at the last ball," Vin said. *Now he's dead, his corpse left on the streets outside a skaa slum.*

"Oh?" Milen asked. "Was he any good?"

Vin shrugged. "Not very." *That's all you can ask, Milen? A man is dead, and you just want to know if I liked him more than you?*

"Well, now he's dancing with the worms," said Tyden, the final man in the group.

Milen gave the quip a pity laugh, which was more than it deserved. Tyden's attempts at humor generally left something to be desired. He seemed like the type who would have been more at home with the ruffians of Camon's crew than the noblemen of the dance hall.

Of course, Dox says they're all like that, underneath.

Vin's conversation with Dockson still dominated her thoughts. When she'd started coming to the noblemen's balls back on that first night—the night she'd nearly been killed—she'd thought about how fake everything seemed. How had she forgotten that original impression? How had she let herself get taken in, to begin admiring their poise and their splendor?

Now, every nobleman's arm around her waist made her cringe—as if she could feel the rot within their hearts. How many skaa had Milen killed? What about Tyden? He seemed like the type who would enjoy a night with the whores.

But, still she played along. She had finally worn her black gown this evening, somehow feeling the need to set herself apart from the other women with their bright colors and often brighter smiles. However, she couldn't avoid the others' company; Vin had finally begun to gain the confidences her crew needed. Kelsier would be delighted to know that his plan for House Tekiel was working, and that wasn't the only thing she had been able to discover. She had dozens of little tidbits that would be of vital use to the crew's efforts.

One such tidbit was about House Venture. The family was bunkering up for what it expected to be an extended house war; one evidence of this was the fact that Elend attended far fewer balls than he once had. Not that Vin minded. When he did come, he generally avoided her, and she didn't really want to talk to him anyway. Memories of what Dockson had said made her think that she might have trouble remaining civil toward Elend.

"Milen?" Lord Rene asked. "Are you still planning on joining us for a game of shelldry tomorrow?"

"Of course, Rene," Milen said.

"Didn't you promise that last time?" Tyden asked.

"I'll be there," Milen said. "Something came up last time."

"And it won't come up again?" Tyden asked. "You know we can't play unless we have a fourth man. If you're not going to be there, we could ask someone else. . . ."

Milen sighed, then held up a hand, sharply gesturing to the side. The motion caught Vin's attention—she had only been half listening to the conversation. She looked to the side, and nearly jumped in shock as she saw an obligator approaching the group.

So far she'd managed to avoid obligators at the balls. After her first run-in with a high prelan, some months ago—and the subsequent alerting of an Inquisitor—she'd been apprehensive to even go near one.

The obligator approached, smiling in a creepy sort of way. Perhaps it was the arms clasped before him, hands hidden inside the gray sleeves. Perhaps it was the tattoos around the eyes, wrinkled with the aging skin. Perhaps it was the way his eyes regarded her; it seemed like they could see through her guise. This wasn't just a nobleman, this was an *obligator*—eyes of the Lord Ruler, enforcer of His law.

The obligator stopped at the group. His tattoos marked him as a member of the Canton of Orthodoxy, the primary bureaucratic arm of the Ministry. He eyed the group, speaking in a smooth voice. "Yes?"

Milen pulled out a few coins. "I promise to meet these two for shelldry tomorrow," he said, handing the coins to the aging obligator.

It seemed like such a silly reason to call over an obligator—or, at least, so Vin thought. The obligator, however, didn't laugh or point out the frivolity of the demand. He simply smiled, palming the coins as deftly as any thief. "I witness this, Lord Milen," he said.

"Satisfied?" Milen asked of the other two.

They nodded.

The obligator turned, not giving Vin a second glance, and strolled away. She released a quiet breath, watching his shuffling form.

They must know everything that happens in court, she realized. *If nobility call them over to witness things this simple . . .* The more she knew about the Ministry, the more she realized how clever the Lord Ruler had been in organizing them. They witnessed every mercantile contract; Dockson and Renoux had to deal with obligators nearly every day. Only they could authorize weddings, divorces, land purchases, or ratify inheritance of titles. If an obligator hadn't witnessed an event, it hadn't happened, and if one hadn't sealed a document, then it might as well not have been written.

Vin shook her head as the conversation turned to other topics. It had been a long night, and her mind was full of information to scribble down on her way back to Fellise.

"Excuse me, Lord Milen," she said, laying a hand on his arm—though touching him made her shiver slightly. "I think perhaps it is time for me to retire."

"I'll walk you to your carriage," he said.

"That won't be necessary," she said sweetly. "I want to refresh myself, and then I have to wait for my Terrisman anyway. I'll just go sit down at our table."

"Very well," he said, nodding respectfully.

"Go if you must, Valette," Kliss said. "But you'll never know the news I have about the Ministry. . . ."

Vin paused. "What news?"

Kliss's eyes twinkled, and she glanced at the disappearing obligator. "The Inquisitors are buzzing like insects. They've hit *twice* as many skaa thieving bands these last few months as usual. They don't even take prisoners for executions—they just leave them all dead."

"How do you know this?" Milen asked skeptically. He seemed so straight-backed and noble. You would never know what he really was.

"I have my sources," Kliss said with a smile. "Why, the Inquisitors found another band just this afternoon. One headquartered not far from here."

Vin felt a chill. They weren't *that* far from Clubs's shop. . . . *No, it couldn't be them. Dockson and the rest are too clever. Even without Kelsier in town, they'll be safe.*

"Cursed thieves," Tyden spat. "Damn skaa don't know their place. Isn't the food and clothing we give enough of a theft from our pockets?"

"It's amazing the creatures can even survive as thieves," said Carlee, Tyden's young wife, in her normal purring voice. "I can't imagine what kind of incompetent would let himself get robbed by skaa."

Tyden flushed, and Vin eyed him with curiosity. Carlee

rarely spoke except to make some jab against her husband. *He must have been robbed himself. A scam, perhaps?*

Filing away the information for later investigation, Vin turned to go—a motion that put her face-to-face with a newcomer to the group: Shan Elariel.

Elend's former betrothed was immaculate, as always. Her long auburn hair had an almost luminous sheen, and her beautiful figure only reminded Vin how scrawny she herself was. Self-important in a way that could make even a confident person uncertain, Shan was—as Vin was beginning to realize—exactly what most of the aristocracy thought was the perfect woman.

The men in Vin's group nodded their heads in respect, and the women curtsied, honored to have their conversation joined by one so important. Vin glanced to the side, trying to escape, but Shan was standing right before her.

Shan smiled. "Ah, Lord Milen," she said to Vin's companion, "it's a pity that your original date this evening took sick. It appears you were left with few other options."

Milen flushed, Shan's comment expertly placing him in a difficult position. Did he defend Vin, possibly earning the ire of a very powerful woman? Or, did he instead agree with Shan, thereby insulting his date?

He took the coward's way out: He ignored the comment. "Lady Shan, it is a pleasure to have you join us."

"Indeed," Shan said smoothly, eyes glittering with pleasure as she regarded Vin's discomfort.

Cursed woman! Vin thought. It seemed that whenever Shan grew bored, she would seek out Vin and embarrass her for sport.

"However," Shan said, "I am afraid I didn't come to chat. Unpleasant though it may be, I have business with the Renoux child. Will you excuse us?"

"Of course, my lady," Milen said, backing away. "Lady Valette, thank you for your company this evening."

Vin nodded to him and the others, feeling a little like a wounded animal being abandoned by the herd. She *really* didn't want to deal with Shan this evening.

"Lady Shan," Vin said once they were alone. "I think your

interest in me is unfounded. I haven't really been spending much time with Elend lately."

"I know," Shan said. "It appears I overestimated your competence, child. One would think that once you'd gained favor with a man so much more important than yourself, you wouldn't have let him slip away so easily."

Shouldn't she be jealous? Vin thought, suppressing a cringe as she felt the inevitable touch of Shan's Allomancy on her emotions. *Shouldn't she hate me for taking her place?*

But, that wasn't the noble way. Vin was nothing—a momentary diversion. Shan wasn't interested in recapturing Elend's affection; she just wanted a way to strike back at the man who had slighted her.

"A wise girl would put herself in a position where she could make use of the only advantage she has," Shan said. "If you think any other important nobleman will ever pay any attention to you, then you are mistaken. Elend likes to shock the court—and so, naturally, he chose to do so with the most homely and lumpish woman he could find. Take this opportunity; you shall not soon find another."

Vin gritted her teeth against the insults and the Allomancy; Shan had obviously made an art out of forcing people to take whatever abuse she sought fit to deliver.

"Now," Shan said, "I require information regarding certain texts Elend has in his possession. You *can* read, can't you?"

Vin nodded curtly.

"Good," Shan said. "All you need to do is memorize the titles of his books—don't look on the outside covers, they can be misleading. Read the first few pages, then report back to me."

"And if I should instead tell Elend what you're planning?"

Shan laughed. "My dear, you don't *know* what I'm planning. Besides, you seem to be making some headway in court. Surely you realize that betraying *me* is not something you want to even contemplate."

With that, Shan walked off, immediately gathering a collection of hangers-on from the surrounding nobility. Shan's Soothing weakened, and Vin felt her frustration and anger rise. There had been a time when she would have simply scampered away, ego already too beaten down to be bothered by Shan's insults. This night, however, she found herself wishing for a way to strike back.

Calm yourself. This is a good thing. You've become a pawn in Great House plans—most lesser nobility probably dream of such an opportunity.

She sighed, retreating toward the now empty table she had shared with Milen. The ball this evening was being held at the marvelous Keep Hasting. Its tall, round central keep was attended by six auxiliary towers, each set off from the main building a short distance and connected to it by walltop walkways. All seven towers were set with winding, curving patterns of stained glass.

The ballroom was at the top of the wide central tower. Fortunately, a system of skaa-powered pulley platforms kept noble guests from having to walk all the way to the top. The ballroom itself wasn't as spectacular as some Vin had visited—just a squarish chamber with vaulted ceilings and colored glass running around the perimeter.

Funny, how easily one can become jaded, Vin thought. *Perhaps that's how the noblemen can do such terrible things. They've been killing for so long that it doesn't unsettle them anymore.*

She asked a servant to go fetch Sazed, then sat down to rest her feet. *I wish Kelsier would hurry up and get back,* she thought. The crew, Vin included, seemed less motivated without him around. It wasn't that she didn't want to work; Kelsier's snappy wit and optimism just helped keep her moving.

Vin looked up idly, and her eyes caught sight of Elend Venture standing just a short distance away, chatting with a small group of young noblemen. She froze. Part of her—the Vin part—wanted to scurry away and hide. She'd fit beneath a table, dress and all.

Oddly, however, she found her Valette side stronger. *I have to talk to him,* she thought. *Not because of Shan, but because I have to find out the truth. Dockson was exaggerating. He* had *to be.*

When had she grown so confrontational? Even as she stood, Vin was amazed at her firm resolve. She crossed the ballroom—checking her black dress briefly as she walked. One of Elend's companions tapped him on the shoulder, nodding toward Vin. Elend turned, and the other two men withdrew.

"Why, Valette," he said as she paused in front of him. "I arrived late. I didn't even know you were here."

Liar. Of course you knew. Valette wouldn't miss the Hasting Ball. How to broach it? How to ask? "You've been avoiding me," she said.

"Now, I wouldn't say that. I've just been busy. House issues, you know. Besides, I warned you that I was rude, and . . ." he trailed off. "Valette? Is everything all right?"

Vin realized she was sniffling slightly, and she felt a tear on her cheek. *Idiot!* she thought, dabbing her eyes with Lestibournes's handkerchief. *You'll ruin your makeup!*

"Valette, you're shaking!" Elend said with concern. "Here, let's go to the balcony and get you some fresh air."

She let him lead her away from the sounds of music and chattering people, and they stepped into the quiet, dark air. The balcony—one of many jutting from the top of the central Hasting tower—was empty. A single stone lantern stood as part of the railing, and some tastefully placed plants lined the corners.

Mist floated in the air, prevalent as ever, though the balcony was close enough to the keep's warmth that the mist was weak. Elend didn't pay any attention to it. He, like most noblemen, considered fear of the mist to be a foolish skaa superstition—which, Vin supposed, was right.

"Now, what is this about?" Elend asked. "I'll admit, I have been ignoring you. I'm sorry. You didn't deserve it, I just . . . well, it seemed like you were fitting in so well that you didn't need a troublemaker like me being—"

"Have you ever slept with a skaa woman?" Vin asked.

Elend paused, taken aback. "Is *that* what this is all about? Who told you this?"

"Have you?" Vin demanded.

Elend paused.

Lord Ruler. It's true.

"Sit down," Elend said, fetching her a chair.

"It's true, isn't it?" Vin said, sitting. "You've done it. He was right, you're *all* monsters."

"I . . ." He laid a hand on Vin's arm, but she pulled it away, only to feel a teardrop drip down her face and stain her dress. She reached up, wiping her eyes, the handkerchief coming back colored with makeup.

"It happened when I was thirteen," Elend said quietly. "My father thought it was time that I became 'a man.' I didn't even know they were going to kill the girl afterward, Valette. Honestly, I didn't."

"And after that?" she demanded, growing angry. "How many girls have you murdered, Elend Venture?"

"None! Never again, Valette. Not after I found out what had happened that first time."

"You expect me to believe you?"

"I don't know," Elend said. "Look, I know that it's fashionable for the women of court to label all men brutes, but you have to believe me. We're not all like that."

"I was told that you are," Vin said.

"By whom? Country nobility? Valette, they don't know us. They're jealous because we control most of the canal systems—and they might just have a right to be. Their envy doesn't make us terrible people, however."

"What percentage?" Vin asked. "How many noblemen do these things?"

"Maybe a third," Elend said. "I'm not sure. They aren't the types I spend my time with."

She wanted to believe him, and that desire should have made her more skeptical. But, looking into those eyes—eyes she had always found so honest—she found herself swayed. For the first time she could remember, she completely pushed aside Reen's whispers, and simply believed.

"A third," she whispered. *So many. But, that's better than all of them.* She reached up to dab her eyes, and Elend eyed her handkerchief.

"Who gave you that?" he asked curiously.

"A suitor," Vin said.

"Is he the one who's been telling you these things about me?"

"No, that was another," Vin said. "He . . . said that all noblemen—or, rather, all Luthadel noblemen—were terrible people. He said that court women don't even consider it cheating when their men sleep with skaa whores."

Elend snorted. "Your informant doesn't know women very well, then. I dare you to find me one lady who isn't bothered when her husband dallies with another—skaa or noble."

Vin nodded, taking a deep breath, calming herself. She felt ridiculous . . . but she also felt at peace. Elend knelt beside her chair, still obviously concerned.

"So," she said, "your father is one of the third?"

Elend flushed in the wan light, looking down. "He likes all kinds of mistresses—skaa, noble, it doesn't matter to him. I still think about that night, Valette. I wish . . . I don't know."

"It wasn't your fault, Elend," she said. "You were just a thirteen-year-old boy who was doing what his father told him."

Elend looked away, but she had already seen the anger and guilt in his eyes. "Someone needs to stop these kinds of things from happening," he said quietly, and Vin was struck by the intensity in his voice.

This is a man who cares, she thought. *A man like Kelsier, or like Dockson. A good man. Why can't they see that?*

Finally, Elend sighed, standing and pulling over a chair for himself. He sat down, elbow resting against the railing, running his hand through his messy hair. "Well," he noted, "you probably aren't the first lady I've made cry at a ball, but you *are* the first one I've made cry that I sincerely care about. My gentlemanly prowess has reached new depths."

Vin smiled. "It's not you," she said, leaning back. "It's just been . . . a very draining few months. When I found out about these things, I just couldn't handle it all."

"The corruption in Luthadel needs to be dealt with," Elend said. "The Lord Ruler doesn't even see it—he doesn't want to."

Vin nodded, then she eyed Elend. "Why exactly *have* you been avoiding me lately, anyway?"

Elend flushed again. "I just figured you had enough new friends to keep you occupied."

"What is that supposed to mean?"

"I don't like a lot of the people you've been spending your time with, Valette," Elend said. "You've managed to fit very well into Luthadel society, and I generally find that playing politics changes people."

"That's easy to say," Vin snapped. "Especially when you're at the very *top* of the political structure. You can afford to ignore politics—some of us aren't so fortunate."

"I suppose."

"Besides," Vin said, "you play politics just as well as the rest. Or, are you going to try and tell me that your initial interest in me wasn't sparked by a desire to spite your father?"

Elend held up his hands. "All right, consider me suitably chastised. I was a fool and a twit. It runs in the family."

Vin sighed, sitting back and feeling the cool whisper of the mists on her tear-wetted cheeks. Elend wasn't a monster; she believed him on that count. Perhaps she was a fool, but Kelsier was having an effect on her. She was beginning to trust those around her, and there was no one she wanted to let herself trust more than Elend Venture.

And, when it wasn't connected directly to Elend, she found the horrors of the noble-skaa relationship easier to deal with. Even if a third of the noblemen were murdering skaa women, something was probably salvageable of the society. The nobility wouldn't have to be purged—that was *their* tactic. Vin would have to make certain that sort of thing didn't happen, no matter what bloodline one had.

Lord Ruler, Vin thought. *I'm starting to think like the others—it's almost like I think that we can change things.*

She glanced across at Elend, who sat with his back to the curling mists beyond. He looked morose.

I brought out bad memories, Vin thought guiltily. *No wonder he hates his father so much.* She longed to do something to make him feel better.

"Elend," she said, drawing his attention. "They're just like us."

He paused. "What?"

"The plantation skaa," Vin said. "You asked me about them once. I was afraid, so I acted like a proper noblewoman—but you seemed disappointed when I didn't have more to say."

He leaned forward. "So, you *did* spend time with the skaa?"

Vin nodded. "A lot of time. Too much, if you ask my family. That might be why they sent me out here. I knew some of the skaa very well—one older man, in particular. He lost someone, a woman he loved, to a nobleman who wanted a pretty thing for the evening's entertainment."

"At your plantation?"

Vin shook her head quickly. "He ran away and came to my father's lands."

"And you hid him?" Elend asked with surprise. "Runaway skaa are supposed to be executed!"

"I kept his secret," Vin said. "I didn't know him for very long, but . . . well, I can promise you this, Elend: His love was as strong as that of any nobleman. Stronger than most of them here in Luthadel, certainly."

"And intelligence?" Elend asked eagerly. "Did they seem . . . slow?"

"Of course not," Vin snapped. "I should think, Elend Venture, that I knew several skaa more clever than yourself. They may not have education, but they're still intelligent. And they're angry."

"Angry?" he asked.

"Some of them," Vin said. "About the way they're treated."

"They know, then? About the disparities between us and them?"

"How could they not?" Vin said, reaching up to wipe her nose with the handkerchief. She paused, however, noting just how much makeup she had rubbed across it.

"Here," Elend said, handing her his own handkerchief. "Tell me more. How do you know these things?"

"They told me," Vin said. "They trusted me. I know that they're angry because they would complain about their lives. I know they're intelligent because of the things they keep hidden from the nobility."

"Like what?"

"Like, the underground movement network," Vin said. "Skaa help runaways travel the canals from plantation to plantation. The noblemen don't notice because they never pay attention to skaa faces."

"Interesting."

"Plus," Vin said, "there are the thieving crews. I figure that those skaa must be fairly clever if they're able to hide from the obligators and the nobility, stealing from the Great Houses right beneath the Lord Ruler's nose."

"Yes, I know," Elend said. "I wish I could meet one of them, to ask them how they hide so well. They must be fascinating people."

Vin almost spoke further, but she held her tongue. *I've probably said too much already.*

Elend looked over at her. "You're fascinating too, Valette. I should have known better than to assume you'd been corrupted by the rest of them. Perhaps you'll be able to corrupt them instead."

Vin smiled.

"But," Elend said, rising. "I need to be leaving. I actually came to the party tonight for a specific purpose—some friends of mine are meeting together."

That's right! Vin thought. *One of the men Elend met with before—the ones that Kelsier and Sazed thought it was strange that he would associate with—was a Hasting.*

Vin stood as well, handing Elend back his handkerchief.

He didn't take it. "You might want to keep that. It wasn't intended to be simply functional."

Vin looked down at the handkerchief. *When a nobleman wants to court a lady seriously, he gives her a handkerchief.*

"Oh!" she said, pulling the handkerchief back. "Thank you."

Elend smiled, stepping close to her. "That other man, whoever he is, might have a lead on me because of my foolishness. However, I am not so foolish that I would pass up the chance to give him a little competition." He winked, bowed slightly, and walked back toward the central ballroom.

Vin waited a moment, then walked forward and slipped through the balcony doorway. Elend met up with the same two as before—a Lekal and a Hasting, political enemies of the Venture. They paused for a moment, then all three walked toward a stairwell at the side of the room.

Those stairwells only lead to one place, Vin thought, slipping back into the room. *The auxiliary towers.*

"Mistress Valette?"

Vin jumped, turning to find Sazed approaching. "Are we ready to go?" he asked.

Vin moved over to him quickly. "Lord Elend Venture just disappeared down that stairwell with his Hasting and Lekal friends."

"Interesting," Sazed said. "And why would . . . Mistress, what happened to your makeup!"

"Never mind," Vin said. "I think I should follow them."

"Is that *another* handkerchief, Mistress?" Sazed asked. "You have been busy."

"Sazed, are you listening to me?"

"Yes, Mistress. I suppose you could follow them if you wish, but you would be fairly obvious. I don't know that it would be the best method of gaining information."

"I wouldn't follow them overtly," Vin said quietly. "I'd use Allomancy. But, I need your permission for that."

Sazed paused. "I see. How is your side?"

"It's been healed for ages," Vin said. "I don't even notice it anymore."

Sazed sighed. "Very well. Master Kelsier intended to begin your training in earnest again when he returned, anyway. Just . . . be careful. This is a ridiculous thing to say to a Mistborn, I think, but I ask anyway."

"I will," Vin said. "I'll meet you on that balcony over there in an hour."

"Good luck, Mistress," Sazed said.

Vin was already rushing back toward the balcony. She stepped around the corner, then stood before the stone railing and the mists beyond. The beautiful, swirling void. *It's been far too long,* she thought, reaching into her sleeve and pulling out a vial of metals. She downed it eagerly and got out a small handful of coins.

Then, blissfully, she hopped up onto the railing and threw herself out into the dark mists.

Tin gave her sight as the wind flapped at her dress. Pewter gave her strength as she turned her eyes toward the buttresslike wall running between the tower and the main keep.

Steel gave her power as she threw a coin downward, sending it into the darkness.

She lurched in the air. The air resistance fluttered her dress, and she felt like she was trying to pull a bale of cloth behind her, but her Allomancy was strong enough to deal with that. Elend's tower was the next one over; she needed to get onto the walltop walkway that ran between it and the central tower. Vin flared steel, Pushing herself up a bit higher, then flung another coin into the mists behind her. When it hit the wall, she used it to shoot herself forward.

She slammed into her target wall just a bit too low—folds of cloth cushioning the blow—but she managed to grab the lip of the walkway above. An unenhanced Vin would have had trouble pulling herself up onto the wall, but Vin the Allomancer easily scrambled over the side.

She crouched in her black dress, moving quietly across the walltop pathway. There were no guards, but the tower ahead of her had a lit sentrypost at its base.

Can't go that way, she thought, glancing upward instead. The tower appeared to have several rooms, and a couple of them were lit. Vin dropped a coin and catapulted herself upward, then Pulled against a window mounting and yanked herself over to land lightly on the stone window ledge. The shutters were closed against the night, and she had to lean close, flaring tin, to hear what was going on inside.

". . . balls always last well into the night. We'll probably have to pull double duty."

Guards, Vin thought, jumping and Pushing against the top of the window. It rattled as she shot up the side of the tower. She caught the base of the next window ledge and pulled herself up.

". . . don't regret my tardiness," a familiar voice said from inside. Elend. "She happens to be far more attractive than you are, Telden."

A masculine voice laughed. "The mighty Elend Venture, finally captured by a pretty face."

"She's more than that, Jastes," Elend said. "She's kindhearted—she helped skaa runaways on her plantation. I think we should bring her in to talk with us."

"Not a chance," said a deep-voiced man. "Look, Elend, I don't mind if you want to talk philosophy. Hell, I'll even share a few drinks with you when you do. But I'm not going to let random people come join us."

"I agree with Telden," Jastes said. "Five people is enough."

"See, now," Elend's voice said. "I don't think you're being fair."

"Elend . . ." another voice said sufferingly.

"All right," Elend said. "Telden, did you read the book I gave you?"

"I tried," Telden said. "It's a bit thick."

"But it's good, right?" Elend said.

"Good enough," Telden said. "I can see why the Lord Ruler hates it so much."

"Redalevin's works are better," Jastes said. "More concise."

"I don't mean to be contrary," said a fifth voice. "But, is this all we're going to do? Read?"

"What's wrong with reading?" Elend asked.

"It's a bit boring," the fifth voice said.

Good man, Vin thought.

"Boring?" Elend asked. "Gentlemen, these ideas—these words—they're *everything*. These men knew that they'd be executed for their words. Can you not sense their passion?"

"Passion, yes," the fifth voice said. "Usefulness, no."

"We can change the world," Jastes said. "Two of us are house heirs, the other three are second heirs."

"Someday, we'll be the ones in charge," Elend said. "If we put these ideas into effect—fairness, diplomacy, moderation—we can exert pressure even on the Lord Ruler!"

The fifth voice snorted. "You might be heir to a powerful house, Elend, but the rest of us aren't as important. Telden and Jastes will probably never inherit, and Kevoux—no offense—is hardly that influential. We can't change the world."

"We can change the way our houses work," Elend said. "If the houses would stop squabbling, we might be able to gain some real power in the government—rather than just bow to the whims of the Lord Ruler."

"Every year, the nobility grows weaker," Jastes said in agreement. "Our skaa belong to the Lord Ruler, as does our land. His obligators determine who we can marry and what we can believe. Our canals, even, are officially 'his' property. Ministry assassins kill men who speak out too openly, or who are too successful. This is no way to live."

"I agree with you there," Telden said. "Elend's prattling about class imbalance seems like silliness to me, but I can see the importance of presenting a unified front before the Lord Ruler."

"Exactly," Elend said. "This is what we have to—"

"Vin!" a voice whispered.

Vin jumped, nearly falling off the window ledge in shock. She glanced around in alarm.

"Above you," the voice whispered.

She glanced up. Kelsier hung from another window ledge just above. He smiled, winked, then nodded down toward the wall-walkway below.

Vin glanced back at Elend's room as Kelsier dropped through the mists beside her. Finally, she pushed herself off and followed Kelsier down, using her same coin to slow her descent.

"You're back!" she said eagerly as she landed.

"Got back this afternoon."

"What are you doing here?"

"Checking up on our friend in there," Kelsier said. "Doesn't seem like much has changed since the last time."

"Last time?"

Kelsier nodded. "I've spied on that little group a couple of times since you told me about them. I shouldn't have bothered—they're not a threat. Just a bunch of noblelings getting together to drink and debate."

"But, they want to overthrow the Lord Ruler!"

"Hardly," Kelsier said with a snort. "They're just doing what noblemen do—planning alliances. It's not that unusual for the next generation to start organizing their house coalitions before they come to power."

"This is different," Vin said.

"Oh?" Kelsier asked with amusement. "You've been a noble so long that you can tell that already?"

She flushed, and he laughed, putting a friendly arm around

her shoulders. "Oh, don't get like that. They seem like nice enough lads, for noblemen. I promise not to kill any of them, all right?"

Vin nodded.

"Perhaps we can find a way to use them—they do seem more open-minded than most. I just don't want you to be disappointed, Vin. They're still noblemen. Perhaps they can't help what they are, but that doesn't change their nature."

Just like Dockson, Vin thought. *Kelsier assumes the worst about Elend.* But, did she really have any reason to expect otherwise? To fight a battle like Kelsier and Dockson were, it was probably more effective—and better for the psyche—to assume that all of their enemies were evil.

"What happened to your makeup, by the way?" Kelsier asked.

"I don't want to talk about it," Vin said, thinking back to her conversation with Elend. *Why did I have to cry? I'm such an idiot! And, the way I blurted out that question about him sleeping with skaa.*

Kelsier shrugged. "Okay, then. We should get going—I doubt young Venture and his comrades will discuss anything relevant."

Vin paused.

"I've listened to them on three separate occasions, Vin," Kelsier said. "I'll summarize for you, if you want."

"All right," she said with a sigh. "But I told Sazed I'd meet him back up at the party."

"Off you go, then," Kelsier said. "I promise not to tell him you were sneaking around and using Allomancy."

"He told me I could," Vin said defensively.

"He did?"

Vin nodded.

"My mistake," Kelsier said. "You should probably have Saze fetch you a cloak before you leave the party—you've got ash all over the front of your dress. I'll meet you back at Clubs's shop—have the carriage drop you and Sazed off there, then continue on out of the city. That'll keep up appearances."

Vin nodded again, and Kelsier winked and jumped off the wall into the mists.

In the end, I must trust in myself. I have seen men who have beaten from themselves the ability to recognize truth and goodness, and I do not think I am one of them. I can still see the tears in a young child's eyes and feel pain at his suffering.

If I ever lose this, then I will know that I've passed beyond hope of redemption.

24

KELSIER WAS ALREADY AT THE shop when Vin and Sazed arrived. He sat with Ham, Clubs, and Spook in the kitchen, enjoying a late-night drink.

"Ham!" Vin said eagerly as she came in the back door. "You're back!"

"Yup," he said happily, raising his cup.

"It seems like you've been gone forever!"

"You're telling me," Ham said, his voice earnest.

Kelsier chuckled, rising to refill his drink. "Ham's a bit tired of playing general."

"I had to wear a uniform," Ham complained, stretching. He now wore his customary vest and trousers. "Even plantation skaa don't have to deal with that kind of torture."

"Try wearing a formal gown sometime," Vin said, seating herself. She'd brushed off the front of her dress, and it didn't look half as bad as she'd feared. The blackish gray ash still showed up a bit against the dark fabric, and the fibers were rough where she'd rubbed against stone, but both were barely noticeable.

Ham laughed. "It seems that you've turned into a proper young lady while I was gone."

"Hardly," Vin said as Kelsier handed her a cup of wine. She paused briefly, then took a sip.

"Mistress Vin is being modest, Master Hammond," Sazed

said, taking a seat. "She's growing quite proficient at courtly arts—better than many actual nobles that I have known."

Vin flushed, and Ham laughed again. "Humility, Vin? Where'd you ever learn a bad habit like that?"

"Not from me, certainly," Kelsier said, offering Sazed a cup of wine. The Terrisman raised his hand in a respectful refusal.

"Of course she didn't get it from *you*, Kell," Ham said. "Maybe Spook taught her. He seems to be the only one in this crew who knows how to keep his mouth shut, eh, kid?"

Spook flushed, obviously trying to avoid looking at Vin.

I'll have to deal with him sometime, she thought. *But . . . not tonight. Kelsier's back and Elend's not a murderer—this is a night to relax.*

Footsteps sounded on the stairs, and a moment later Dockson strolled into the room. "A party? And no one sent for me?"

"You seemed busy," Kelsier said.

"Besides," Ham added, "we know you're too responsible to sit around and get drunk with a bunch of miscreants like us."

"*Someone* has to keep this crew running," Dockson said lightheartedly, pouring himself a drink. He paused, frowning at Ham. "That vest looks familiar. . . ."

Ham smiled. "I ripped the arms off of my uniform coat."

"You didn't!" Vin said with a smile.

Ham nodded, looking self-satisfied.

Dockson sighed, continuing to fill his cup. "Ham, those things cost money."

"Everything costs money," Ham said. "But, what *is* money? A physical representation of the abstract concept of effort. Well, wearing that uniform for so long was a pretty mean effort. I'd say that this vest and I are even now."

Dockson just rolled his eyes. In the main room, the shop's front door opened and closed, and Vin heard Breeze bid hello to the apprentice on watch.

"By the way, Dox," Kelsier said, leaning with his back against a cupboard. "I'm going to need a few 'physical representations of the concept of effort' myself. I'd like to rent a small warehouse to conduct some of my informant meetings."

"That can probably be arranged," Dockson said. "Assuming we keep Vin's wardrobe budget under control, I—" He broke off, glancing at Vin. "What did you do to that gown, young lady!"

Vin flushed, scrunching down in her chair. *Perhaps it's a bit more noticeable than I thought. . . .*

Kelsier chuckled. "You may have to get used to dirtied clothing, Dox. Vin's back on Mistborn duty as of this evening."

"Interesting," Breeze said, entering the kitchen. "Might I suggest that she avoid fighting three Steel Inquisitors at once this time?"

"I'll do my best," Vin said.

Breeze strolled over to the table and chose a seat with his characteristic decorum. The portly man raised his dueling cane, pointing it at Ham. "I see that my period of intellectual respite has come to an end."

Ham smiled. "I thought up a couple beastly questions while I was gone, and I've been saving them just for you, Breeze."

"I'm dying of anticipation," Breeze said. He turned his cane toward Lestibournes. "Spook, drink."

Spook rushed over and fetched Breeze a cup of wine.

"He's such a fine lad," Breeze noted, accepting the drink. "I barely even have to nudge him Allomantically. If only the rest of you ruffians were so accommodating."

Spook frowned. "Niceing the not on the playing without."

"I have no idea what you just said, child," Breeze said. "So I'm simply going to pretend it was coherent, then move on."

Kelsier rolled his eyes. "Losing the stress on the nip," he said. "Notting without the needing of care."

"Riding the rile of the rids to the right," Spook said with a nod.

"What are you two babbling about?" Breeze said testily.

"Wasing the was of brightness," Spook said. "Nip the having of wishing of this."

"Ever wasing the doing of this," Kelsier agreed.

"Ever wasing the wish of having the have," Ham added with a smile. "Brighting the wish of wasing the not."

Breeze turned to Dockson with exasperation. "I believe our companions have finally lost their minds, dear friend."

Dockson shrugged. Then, with a perfectly straight face, he said, "Wasing not of wasing is."

Breeze sat, dumbfounded, and the room burst into laughter. Breeze rolled his eyes indignantly, shaking his head and muttering about the crew's gross childishness.

Vin nearly choked on her wine as she laughed. "What did you even say?" she asked of Dockson as he sat down beside her.

"I'm not sure," he confessed. "It just sounded right."

"I don't think you said anything, Dox," Kelsier said.

"Oh, he said something," Spook said. "It just didn't *mean* anything."

Kelsier laughed. "That's true pretty much all the time. I've found you can ignore half of what Dox tells you and not miss much—except for maybe the occasional complaint that you're spending too much."

"Hey!" Dockson said. "Once again, must I point out that *someone* has to be responsible? Honestly, the way you people go through boxings . . ."

Vin smiled. Even Dockson's complaints seemed good-natured. Clubs sat quietly by the side wall, looking as curmudgeonly as ever, but Vin caught sight of a slight smile on his lips. Kelsier rose and opened another bottle of wine, refilling cups as he told the crew about the skaa army's preparations.

Vin felt . . . contented. As she sipped at her wine, she caught sight of the open doorway leading into the darkened workshop. She imagined, just for a moment, that she could see a figure out in the shadows—a frightened wisp of a girl, untrusting, suspicious. The girl's hair was ragged and short, and she wore a simple, untucked dirty shirt and a pair of brown trousers.

Vin remembered that second night in Clubs's shop, when she had stood out in the dark workroom, watching the others share late-night conversation. Had she really been that girl—one who would hide in the cold darkness, watching the laughter and friendship with a hidden envy, but never daring to join it?

Kelsier made some particularly witty comment, drawing laughter from the entire room.

You're right, Kelsier, Vin thought with a smile. *This* is *better.*

She wasn't like them yet—not completely. Six months couldn't silence Reen's whispers, and she couldn't see herself ever being as trusting as Kelsier was. But . . . she could finally understand, at least a little bit, why he worked the way he did.

"All right," Kelsier said, pulling over a chair and sitting on it the wrong way. "It looks like the army will be ready on schedule, and Marsh is in place. We need to get this plan moving. Vin, news from the ball?"

"House Tekiel is vulnerable," she said. "Its allies are scattering, and the vultures are moving in. Some whisper that debts and lost business will force the Tekiel to sell off their keep by the end of the month. There's no way they can afford to continue paying the Lord Ruler's keep tax."

"Which effectively eliminates one entire Great House from the city," Dockson said. "Most of the Tekiel nobility—including Mistings and Mistborn—will have to move to outer plantations to try and recoup losses."

"Nice," Ham noted. Any noble houses they could frighten out of the city would make seizing it that much easier.

"That still leaves nine Great Houses in the city," Breeze noted.

"But they've started killing each other at night," Kelsier said. "That's only one step away from open war. I suspect we'll see an exodus start here pretty soon—anyone who isn't willing to risk assassination to maintain dominance in Luthadel will leave town for a couple of years."

"The strong houses don't seem very afraid, though," Vin said. "They're still throwing balls, anyway."

"Oh, they'll keep doing that right up until the end," Kelsier said. "Balls make great excuses to meet with allies and keep an eye on enemies. House wars are primarily political, and so they demand political battlefields."

Vin nodded.

"Ham," Kelsier said, "we need to keep an eye on the Luthadel Garrison. You're still planning to visit your soldier contacts tomorrow?"

Ham nodded. "I can't promise anything, but I should be able to reestablish some connections. Give me a bit of time, and I'll find out what the military is up to."

"Good," Kelsier said.

"I'd like to go with him," Vin said.

Kelsier paused. "With Ham?"

Vin nodded. "I haven't trained with a Thug yet. Ham could probably show me a few things."

"You already know how to burn pewter," Kelsier said. "We've practiced that."

"I know," Vin said. How could she explain? Ham had practiced with pewter exclusively—he was bound to be better at it than Kelsier.

"Oh, stop pestering the child," Breeze said. "She's probably just tired of balls and parties. Let her go be a normal street urchin again for a bit."

"Fine," Kelsier said, rolling his eyes. He poured himself another drink. "Breeze, how well could your Soothers manage if you were gone for a little while?"

Breeze shrugged. "I am, of course, the most effective member of the team. But, I *did* train the others—they'll recruit effectively without me, especially now that stories about the Survivor are getting so popular."

"We need to talk about that by the way, Kell," Dockson said, frowning. "I'm not sure if I like all this mysticism about you and the Eleventh Metal."

"We can discuss it later," Kelsier said.

"Why ask about my men?" Breeze said. "Have you finally grown so jealous of my impeccable fashion sense that you've decided to have me disposed of?"

"You might say that," Kelsier said. "I was thinking of sending you to replace Yeden in a few months."

"Replace Yeden?" Breeze asked with surprise. "You mean for *me* to lead the army?"

"Why not?" Kelsier asked. "You're great at giving orders."

"From the background, my dear man," Breeze said. "I don't stand out in front. Why, I'd be a *general*. Do you have any idea how ludicrous that sounds?"

"Just consider it," Kelsier said. "Our recruitment should be mostly done by then, so you might be most effective if you were to go to the caves and let Yeden come back to prepare his contacts here."

Breeze frowned. "I suppose."

"Regardless," Kelsier said, rising. "I don't think I've had

nearly enough wine. Spook, be a good lad and run down to the cellar for another bottle, eh?"

The boy nodded, and the conversation turned back to lighter topics. Vin settled back in her chair, feeling the warmth of the coal stove at the side of the room, content for the moment to simply enjoy the peace of not having to worry, fight, or plan.

If only Reen could have known something like this, she thought, idly fingering her earring. *Perhaps then, things would have been different for him. For us.*

Ham and Vin left the next day to visit the Luthadel Garrison.

After so many months of playing a noblewoman, Vin had thought that it would feel strange to wear street clothing again. Yet, it really didn't. True, it was a bit *different*—she didn't have to worry about sitting properly or walking so that her dress didn't brush against dirty walls or floors. Yet, the mundane clothing still felt natural to her.

She wore a simple pair of brown trousers and a loose white shirt, tucked in at the waist, then overlaid by a leather vest. Her still lengthening hair was pulled up under a cap. Casual passersby might think her a boy, though Ham didn't seem to think it mattered.

And it really didn't. Vin had grown accustomed to having people study and evaluate her, but no one on the street even bothered to give her a glance. Shuffling skaa workers, unconcerned low noblemen, even high-placed skaa like Clubs—they all ignored her.

I'd almost forgotten what it was like to be invisible, Vin thought. Fortunately, the old attitudes—looking down when she walked, stepping out of people's way, slouching to make herself inconspicuous—returned to her easily. Becoming Vin the street skaa felt as simple as remembering an old, familiar melody she used to hum.

This really is just another disguise, Vin thought as she walked beside Ham. *My makeup is a light coat of ash, carefully rubbed on my cheeks. My gown is a pair of trousers, rubbed to make them seem old and well used.*

Who, then, was she really? Vin the urchin? Valette the

lady? Neither? Did any of her friends really know her? Did she even really know herself?

"Ah, I've missed this place," Ham said, walking happily beside her. Ham always seemed happy; she couldn't imagine him dissatisfied, despite what he'd said about his time leading the army.

"It's kind of strange," he said, turning to Vin. He didn't walk with the same careful air of despondence that Vin had cultivated; he didn't even seem to care that he stood out from other skaa. "I probably shouldn't miss this place—I mean, Luthadel is the dirtiest, most crowded city in the Final Empire. But, there's also something about it. . . ."

"Is this where your family lives?" Vin asked.

Ham shook his head. "They live in a smaller city outside of town. My wife is a seamstress there; she tells people I'm in the Luthadel Garrison."

"Don't you miss them?"

"Of course I do," Ham said. "It's hard—I only get to spend a few months at a time with them—but it's better this way. If I were to get killed on a job, the Inquisitors would have a tough time tracking my family. I haven't even told Kell which city they live in."

"You think the Ministry would go to that much trouble?" Vin asked. "I mean, you'd already be dead."

"I'm a Misting, Vin—that means that all of my descendants will have some noble blood. My children might turn out to be Allomancers, as might their children. No, when the Inquisitors kill a Misting, they make certain to wipe out his children too. The only way to keep my family safe is to stay away from them."

"You could just not use your Allomancy," Vin said.

Ham shook his head. "I don't know if I could do that."

"Because of the power?"

"No, because of the money," Ham said frankly. "Thugs—or, Pewterarms, as the nobility prefer to call them—are the most sought-after Mistings. A competent Thug can stand against a half-dozen regular men, and he can lift more, endure more, and move faster than any other hired muscle. Those things mean a lot when you have to keep your crews small. Mix a couple of

Coinshots with five or so Thugs, and you've got yourself a small, mobile army. Men will pay a lot for protection like that."

Vin nodded. "I can see how the money would be tempting."

"It's more than tempting, Vin. My family doesn't have to live in packed skaa tenements, nor do they have to worry about starving. My wife only works to keep up appearances—they have a good life, for skaa. Once I have enough, we'll move away from the Central Dominance. There are places in the Final Empire that a lot of people don't know about—places where a man with enough money can live the life of a nobleman. Places where you can stop worrying and just live."

"That sounds . . . appealing."

Ham nodded, turning and leading them down a larger thoroughfare toward the main city gates. "I got the dream from Kell, actually. That's what he always said he wanted to do. I just hope I have more luck than he did. . . ."

Vin frowned. "Everyone says he was rich. Why didn't he leave?"

"I don't know," Ham said. "There was always another job—each one bigger than the last. I guess when you're a crewleader like him, the game can get addicting. Soon, money didn't even seem to matter to him. Eventually, he heard that the Lord Ruler was storing some incalculable secret in that hidden sanctum of his. If he and Mare had walked away before that job . . . But, well, they didn't. I don't know—maybe they wouldn't have been happy living lives where they *didn't* have to worry."

The concept seemed to intrigue him, and Vin could see another of his "questions" working within his mind.

I guess when you're a crewleader like him, the game can get addicting. . . .

Her earlier apprehensions returned. What would happen if Kelsier seized the imperial throne for himself? He couldn't possibly be as bad as the Lord Ruler, but . . . she was reading more and more of the logbook. The Lord Ruler hadn't always been a tyrant. He'd been a good man, once. A good man whose life had gone wrong.

Kelsier's different, Vin told herself forcefully. *He'll do the right thing.*

Still, she wondered. Ham might not understand, but Vin could see the enticement. Despite noble depravity, there was something intoxicating about high society. Vin was captivated by the beauty, the music, and the dancing. Her fascination wasn't the same as Kelsier's—she wasn't as interested in political games or even scams—but she could understand why he would have been reluctant to leave Luthadel behind.

That reluctance had destroyed the old Kelsier. But, it had produced something better—a more determined, less self-serving Kelsier. Hopefully.

Of course, his plans before also cost him the woman he loved. Is that why he hates the nobility so much?

"Ham?" she asked. "Has Kelsier always hated the nobility?"

Ham nodded. "It's worse now, though."

"He frightens me sometimes. It seems like he wants to kill *all* of them, no matter who they are."

"I'm concerned about him too," Ham said. "This Eleventh Metal business . . . it's almost like he's making himself out to be some kind of holy man." He paused, then he looked toward her. "Don't worry too much. Breeze, Dox, and I have already talked about this. We're going to confront Kell, see if we can rein him in a bit. He means well, but he has a tendency to go a little overboard sometimes."

Vin nodded. Ahead, the customary crowded lines of people waited for permission to pass through the city gates. She and Ham walked quietly past the solemn group—workers being sent out to the docks, men off to work one of the outer mills alongside the river or lake, lesser noblemen wishing to travel. All had to have a good reason to leave the city; the Lord Ruler strictly controlled travel inside his realm.

Poor things, Vin thought as she passed a ragged band of children carrying pails and brushes—probably on duty to climb the wall and scrub mist-grown lichen off the parapets. Ahead, up near the gates, an official cursed and shoved a man out of the line. The skaa worker fell hard, but eventually picked himself back up and shuffled to the end of the line. It was likely that if he wasn't let out of the city, he wouldn't be able to do his day's work—and no work meant no food tokens for his family.

Vin followed Ham past the gates, heading down a street parallel to the city wall, at the end of which Vin could see a large building complex. Vin had never studied the Garrison headquarters before; most crewmembers tended to stay a good distance away from it. However, as they approached, she was impressed by its defensive appearance. Large spikes were mounted on the wall that ran around the entire complex. The buildings within were bulky and fortified. Soldiers stood at the gates, eyeing passersby with hostility.

Vin paused. "Ham, how are we going to get in *there*?"

"Don't worry," he said, stopping beside her. "I'm known to the Garrison. Besides, it's not as bad as it looks—the Garrison members just put on an intimidating face. As you can imagine, they aren't very well liked. Most of the soldiers in there are skaa—men who have, in exchange for a better life, sold out to the Lord Ruler. Whenever there are skaa riots in a city, the local garrison is usually hit pretty hard by malcontents. Hence the fortifications."

"So . . . you know these men?"

Ham nodded. "I'm not like Breeze or Kell, Vin—I can't put on faces and pretend. I'm just who I am. Those soldiers don't know I'm a Misting, but they know I work in the underground. I've known many of these guys for years; they've consistently tried to recruit me. They generally have better luck getting people like me, who are already outside mainstream society, to join their ranks."

"But, you're going to betray them," Vin said quietly, pulling Ham to the side of the road.

"Betray?" he asked. "No, it won't be a betrayal. Those men are mercenaries, Vin. They've been hired to fight, and they'll attack friends—even relatives—in a riot or rebellion. Soldiers learn to understand these kinds of things. We may be friends, but when it comes to fighting, none of us would hesitate to kill the others."

Vin nodded slowly. It seemed . . . harsh. *But, that's what life is. Harsh. That part of Reen's teaching wasn't a lie.*

"Poor lads," Ham said, looking at the Garrison. "We could have used men like them. Before I left for the caves, I managed to recruit the few that I thought would be receptive. The rest . . . well, they picked their path. Like me, they're just trying to give their kids a better life—the difference is, they're willing to work for *him* in order to do it."

Ham turned back to her. "All right, you wanted some tips on burning pewter?"

Vin nodded eagerly.

"The soldiers usually let me spar with them," Ham said. "You can watch me fight—burn bronze to see when I'm using Allomancy. The first, most important thing you'll learn about Pewterarming is when to use your metal. I've noticed that young Allomancers tend to always flare their pewter, thinking that the stronger they are, the better. However, you don't always want to hit as hard as you can with each blow.

"Strength is a big part of fighting, but it's not the only part. If you always hit your hardest, you'll tire faster and you'll give your opponent information about your limitations. A smart man hits his hardest at the *end* of a battle, when his opponent is weakest. And, in an extended battle—like a war—the smart soldier is the one who survives the longest. He'll be the man who paces himself."

Vin nodded. "But, don't you tire slower when you're using Allomancy?"

"Yes," Ham said. "In fact, a man with enough pewter can keep fighting at near-peak efficiency for hours. But pewter dragging like that takes practice, and you'll run out of metals eventually. When you do, the fatigue could kill you.

"Anyway, what I'm trying to explain is that it's usually best to vary your pewter burning. If you use more strength than you need, you could knock yourself off balance. Also, I've seen Thugs who rely on their pewter so much that they disregard training and practice. Pewter enhances your physical abilities, but not your innate skill. If you don't know how to use a weapon—or if you aren't practiced at thinking quickly in a fight—you'll lose no matter how strong you are.

"I'll have to be extra careful with the Garrison, since I don't want them to know I'm an Allomancer. You'll be surprised at how often that's important. Watch how I use pewter. I won't just flare it for strength—if I stumble, I'll burn it to give me an instant sense of balance. When I dodge, I might burn it to help me duck out of the way a little faster. There are dozens of little tricks you can do if you know when to give yourself a boost."

Vin nodded.

"Okay," Ham said. "Let's go, then. I'll tell the garrisoners that you're the daughter of a relative. You look young enough for your age that they won't even think twice. Watch me fight, and we'll talk afterward."

Vin nodded again, and the two of them approached the Garrison. Ham waved to one of the guards. "Hey, Bevidon. I've got the day off. Is Sertes around?"

"He's here, Ham," Bevidon said. "But I don't know that this is the best day for sparring. . . ."

Ham raised an eyebrow. "Oh?"

Bevidon shared a glance with one of the other soldiers. "Go fetch the captain," he said to the man.

A few moments later, a busy-looking soldier approached from a side building, waving as soon as he saw Ham. His uniform bore a few extra stripes of color and a few gold-colored bits of metal on the shoulder.

"Ham," the newcomer said, stepping through the gate.

"Sertes," Ham said with a smile, clasping hands with the man. "Captain now, eh?"

"Happened last month," Sertes said with a nod. He paused, then eyed Vin.

"She's my niece," Ham said. "Good lass."

Sertes nodded. "Could we speak alone for a moment, Ham?"

Ham shrugged and let himself get pulled to a more secluded place beside the complex gates. Vin's Allomancy let her make out what they were saying. *What did I ever do without tin?*

"Look, Ham," Sertes said. "You won't be able to come spar for a while. The Garrison is going to be . . . occupied."

"Occupied?" Ham asked. "How?"

"I can't say," Sertes said. "But . . . well, we could really use a soldier like you right now."

"Fighting?"

"Yeah."

"Must be something serious if it's taking the attention of the entire Garrison."

Sertes grew quiet for a moment, and then he spoke again in a hushed tone—so quiet that Vin had to strain to hear. "A rebellion," Sertes whispered, "right here in the Central Dominance. We just got word. An army of skaa rebels appeared and attacked the Holstep Garrison to the north."

Vin felt a sudden chill.

"*What?*" Ham said.

"They must have come from the caves up there," the soldier said. "Last word was that the Holstep fortifications are holding—but Ham, they're only a thousand men strong. They need reinforcements desperately, and the koloss will never get there in time. The Valtroux Garrison sent five thousand soldiers, but we're not going to leave it to them. This is apparently a very big force of rebels, and the Lord Ruler gave us permission to go help."

Ham nodded.

"So, what about it?" Sertes asked. "Real fighting, Ham. Real battle pay. We could really use a man of your skill—I'll make you an officer right off, give you your own squad."

"I . . . I'll have to think about it," Ham said. He wasn't good at hiding his emotions, and his surprise sounded suspicious to Vin. Sertes, however, didn't appear to notice.

"Don't take too long," Sertes said. "We plan to march out in two hours."

"I'll do it," Ham said, sounding stunned. "Let me go drop off my niece and get some things. I'll be back before you leave."

"Good man," Sertes said, and Vin could see him clap Ham on the shoulder.

Our army is exposed, Vin thought in horror. *They're not ready! They were supposed to take Luthadel quietly, quickly—not face the Garrison straight out.*

Those men are going to get massacred! What happened?

No man dies by my hand or command except that I wish there had been another way. Still, I kill them. Sometimes, I wish that I weren't such a cursed realist.

25

KELSIER TOSSED ANOTHER WATER JUG into his pack. "Breeze, make a list of all the hideouts where you and I recruited. Go warn them that the Ministry might soon have prisoners who could give them away."

Breeze nodded, for once refraining from making any witty remarks. Behind him, apprentices scrambled through Clubs's shop, gathering and preparing the supplies that Kelsier had ordered.

"Dox, this shop should be secure unless they capture Yeden. Keep all three of Clubs's Tineyes on watch. If there's trouble, head for the bolt-lair."

Dockson nodded in acknowledgment as he hurriedly gave orders to the apprentices. One had already left, bearing a warning to Renoux. Kelsier thought that the mansion would be safe—only that one group of barges had left from Fellise, and its men had thought that Renoux wasn't in on the plan. Renoux wouldn't pull out unless absolutely necessary; his disappearance would require removing both himself and Valette from their carefully prepared positions.

Kelsier stuffed a handful of rations into his pack, then swung it onto his back.

"What about me, Kell?" Ham asked.

"You're going back to the Garrison, like you promised. That was clever thinking—we need an informant in there."

Ham frowned apprehensively.

"I don't have time to deal with your nerves right now,

Ham," Kelsier said. "You don't have to scam, just be yourself and listen."

"I won't turn against the Garrison if I go with them," he said. "I'll listen, but I'm not going to attack men who think I'm their ally."

"Fine," Kelsier said curtly. "But I sincerely hope you can find a way not to kill any of our soldiers, either. Sazed!"

"Yes, Master Kelsier?"

"How much speed do you have stored up?"

Sazed flushed slightly, glancing at the numerous people scurrying around. "Perhaps two, three hours. It is a very difficult attribute to collect."

"Not long enough," Kelsier said. "I'll go alone. Dox is in charge until I get back."

Kelsier spun, then paused. Vin stood behind him in the same trousers, cap, and shirt she had worn to the Garrison. She had a pack like his slung over her shoulder, and she looked up at him defiantly.

"This is going to be a difficult trip, Vin," he said. "You've never done anything like this before."

"That's fine."

Kelsier nodded. He pulled his trunk out from beneath the table, then opened it and poured Vin a small pouch of pewter beads. She accepted it without comment.

"Swallow five of those beads."

"*Five?*"

"For now," Kelsier said. "If you need to take some more, call to me so we can stop running."

"Running?" the girl asked. "We're not taking a canal boat?"

Kelsier frowned. "Why would *we* need a boat?"

Vin glanced down at the pouch, then grabbed a cup of water and began to swallow beads.

"Make sure you have enough water in that pack," Kelsier said. "Take as much as you can carry." He left her, walking over to lay a hand on Dockson's shoulder. "It's about three hours before sunset. If we push hard, we can be there by noon tomorrow."

Dockson nodded. "That might be early enough."

Maybe, Kelsier thought. *The Valtroux Garrison is only three days' march from Holstep. Even riding all night, a messenger couldn't have gotten to Luthadel in under two days. By the time I get to the army . . .*

Dockson could obviously read the worry in Kelsier's eyes. "Either way, the army is useless to us now," he said.

"I know," Kelsier said. "This is just about saving those men's lives. I'll get word to you as soon as I can."

Dockson nodded.

Kelsier turned, flaring his pewter. His pack suddenly became as light as if it had been empty. "Burn your pewter, Vin. We're leaving."

She nodded, and Kelsier felt a pulsing come from her. "Flare it," he ordered, pulling two mistcloaks from his trunk and tossing one to her. He put on the other, then walked forward, throwing open the back door to the kitchen. The red sun was bright overhead. Frantic crewmembers paused for a moment, turning to watch as Kelsier and Vin left the building.

The girl hurried forward to walk at Kelsier's side. "Ham told me that I should learn to use pewter only when I need it—he said it's better to be subtle."

Kelsier turned to face the girl. "This is not a time for subtlety. Stay close to me, try to keep up, and make absolutely certain you don't run out of pewter."

Vin nodded, suddenly looking a bit apprehensive.

"All right," Kelsier said, taking a deep breath. "Let's go."

Kelsier took off down the alleyway in a superhuman dash. Vin jumped into motion, following him out of the alley and onto the street. Pewter was a blazing fire within her. Flared as it was, she would probably go through all five beads in barely an hour.

The street was busy with skaa workers and noble carriages. Kelsier ignored the traffic, bolting out into the very center of the street, maintaining his ridiculous speed. Vin followed, growing increasingly worried about what she had gotten herself into.

I can't let him go alone, she thought. Of course, the last time she'd forced Kelsier to take her with him, she'd ended up half dead in a sickbed for a month.

Kelsier wove between carriages, brushing past pedestrians, charging down the street as if it were meant only for him. Vin followed as best as she could, the ground a blur beneath her feet, people passing too quickly to see their faces. Some of them called out after her, their voices annoyed. A couple of these, however, choked off immediately, falling silent.

The cloaks, Vin thought. *That's why we're wearing them—that's why we always wear them. Noblemen who see the mistcloaks will know to stay out of our way.*

Kelsier turned, running directly toward the northern city gates. Vin followed. Kelsier didn't slow as he approached the gates, and the lines of people began to point. Checkpoint guards turned with surprised faces.

Kelsier jumped.

One of the armored guards crumpled to the ground with a cry, smashed down by Kelsier's Allomantic weight as the crewleader passed overhead. Vin took a breath, dropped a coin to give herself a bit of lift, and jumped. She easily cleared a second guard, who looked up with surprise as his companion squirmed on the ground.

Vin Pushed against the soldier's armor, throwing herself higher into the air. The man staggered, but stayed on his feet—Vin was nowhere near as heavy as Kelsier.

She shot over the wall, hearing cries of surprise from the soldiers on top of it. She could only hope that nobody recognized her. It wasn't likely. Though her cap flew free as she soared through the air, those who were familiar with Valette the courtgoing lady would probably never connect her to a Mistborn in dirty trousers.

Vin's cloak whipped angrily in the passing air. Kelsier completed his arc before her and began to descend, and Vin soon followed. It felt very strange to use Allomancy in the sunlight. Unnatural, even. Vin made the mistake of looking down as she fell. Instead of comfortable swirling mists, she saw the ground far below.

So high! Vin thought with horror. Fortunately, she wasn't too disoriented to Push against the coin Kelsier had used to land. She slowed her descent to a manageable level before thumping against the ashen earth.

Kelsier immediately took off down the highway. Vin followed him, ignoring merchants and travelers. Now that they were out of the city, she had thought Kelsier might slow down. He didn't. He sped up.

And, suddenly, she understood. Kelsier didn't intend to walk, or even jog, to the caves.

He planned to dash all the way there.

It was a two-week trip by canal. How long would it take them? They were moving fast, horribly fast. Slower than a galloping horse, certainly, but surely a horse couldn't maintain such a gallop for very long.

Vin didn't feel fatigue as she ran. She relied on the pewter, only passing a little of the strain onto her body. She could barely feel her footsteps hitting the ground beneath her, and with such a large reserve of pewter, she felt that she could maintain the speed for a decent length of time.

She caught up to Kelsier, falling into place beside him. "This is easier than I thought it would be."

"Pewter enhances your balance," Kelsier said. "Otherwise you'd be tripping over yourself right now."

"What do you think we'll find? At the caves, I mean."

Kelsier shook his head. "No use talking. Save your strength."

"But, I'm not feeling weary at all!"

"We'll see what you say in sixteen hours," Kelsier said, speeding up even more as they turned off the highway, running onto the wide towpath beside the Luth-Davn Canal.

Sixteen hours!

Vin fell behind Kelsier slightly, giving herself plenty of space to run. Kelsier increased their speed until they were going at a maddening pace. He was right: In any other context, she would have quickly missed her step on the uneven road. Yet, with pewter and tin guiding her, she managed to stay on her feet—though doing so required increasing attention as the evening grew dark and the mists came out.

Occasionally, Kelsier threw down a coin and launched himself from one hilltop to another. However, he mostly kept them running at an even pace, sticking to the canal. Hours passed, and Vin began to feel the fatigue that he had implied would come. She maintained her speed, but she could feel something underneath it—a resistance within, a longing to stop and rest. Despite pewter's power, her body was running out of strength.

She made certain to never let her pewter run low. She feared that if it ever went out, the fatigue would come upon her so powerfully that she wouldn't be able to get started again. Kelsier also ordered her to drink a ridiculous amount of water, though she wasn't that thirsty.

The night grew dark and silent, no travelers daring to brave the mists. They passed canal boats and barges tied up for the night, as well as the occasional camp of canalmen, their tents huddled closely against the mists. Twice they saw mistwraiths on the road, the first one giving Vin a terrible start. Kelsier just passed it by—completely ignoring the terrible, translucent remnants of the people and animals who had been ingested, their bones now forming the mistwraith's own skeleton.

Still he kept running. Time became a blur, and the running came to dominate all that Vin was and did. Moving demanded so much attention that she could barely even focus on Kelsier ahead of her in the mists. She kept putting one foot ahead of the other, her body remaining strong—yet, at the same time, feeling terribly exhausted. Every step, quick though it was, became a chore. She began to yearn for rest.

Kelsier didn't give it to her. He kept running, forcing her on, maintaining the incredible speed. Vin's world became a timeless thing of forced pain and burgeoning enervation. They slowed occasionally to drink water or swallow more pewter beads—but she never stopped running. It was like . . . like she *couldn't* stop. Vin let the exhaustion overwhelm her mind. Flared pewter was everything. She was nothing else.

Light surprised her. The sun began to rise, the mists vanishing. But Kelsier didn't let the illumination stop them. How could he? They had to run. They had to just . . . had . . . to . . . keep . . . running. . . .

I'm going to die.

It wasn't the first time the thought had occurred to Vin

during the run. In fact, the idea kept circling in her mind, picking at her brain like a carrion bird. She kept moving. Running.

I hate running, she thought. *That's why I've always lived in a city, not out on the countryside. So I wouldn't have to run.*

Something within her knew that the thought didn't make any kind of sense. However, lucidity was not currently one of her virtues.

I hate Kelsier too. He just keeps on going. How long has it been since the sun rose? Minutes? Hours? Weeks? Years? I swear, I don't think—

Kelsier slowed to a stop on the road ahead of her.

Vin was so stunned that she nearly collided with him. She stumbled, slowing herself maladroitly, as if she had forgotten how to do anything other than run. She stopped, then stared down at her feet, dumbfounded.

This is wrong, she thought. *I can't just stand here. I have to be moving.*

She felt herself begin to move again, but Kelsier grabbed her. She struggled in his grip, resisting weakly.

Rest, something within her said. *Relax. You've forgotten what that is, but it's so nice. . . .*

"Vin!" Kelsier said. "Don't extinguish your pewter. Keep burning it or you'll fall unconscious!"

Vin shook her head, disoriented, trying to make out his words.

"Tin!" he said. "Flare it. Now!"

She did so. Her head blazed with a sudden headache that she had almost forgotten, and she had to close her eyes against the blinding sunlight. Her legs ached, and her feet felt even worse. The sudden wash of senses restored her sanity, however, and she blinked, looking up at Kelsier.

"Better?" he asked.

She nodded.

"You've just done something incredibly unfair to your body," Kelsier said. "It should have shut down hours ago, but you have pewter to make it keep going. You'll recover—you'll even get better at pushing yourself like this—but right now you just have to keep burning the pewter and stay awake. We can sleep later."

Vin nodded again. "Why . . ." Her voice croaked as she spoke. "Why did we stop?"

"Listen."

She did. She heard . . . voices. Yelling.

She looked up at him. "A battle?"

Kelsier nodded. "The city of Holstep is about an hour more to the north, but I think we've found what we came for. Come on."

He released her, dropping a coin and jumping over the canal. Vin followed, following him as he rushed up a nearby hill. Kelsier crested it, peeking over the top. Then he stood up, staring at something to the east. Vin crested the hill, and easily saw the battle—such as it was—in the distance. A shift in the wind brought scents to her nose.

Blood. The valley beyond was speckled with corpses. Men still fought on the far side of the valley—a small, ragged group in unmatched clothing was surrounded by a much larger, uniformed army.

"We're too late," Kelsier said. "Our men must have finished off the Holstep Garrison, then tried to march back to the caves. But Valtroux City is only a few days away, and its garrison is five thousand strong. Those soldiers got here before we did."

Squinting, using tin despite the light, Vin could see that he was right. The larger army wore imperial uniforms, and if the line of corpses was any indication, it had ambushed the skaa soldiers as it passed. Their army didn't have a chance. As she watched, the skaa began to throw up their hands, but the soldiers just kept on killing them. Some of the remaining peasants fought desperately, but they were falling almost as quickly.

"It's a slaughter," Kelsier said angrily. "The Valtroux Garrison must have orders to wipe out the entire group." He stepped forward.

"Kelsier!" Vin said, grabbing his arm. "What are you doing?"

He turned back to her. "There are still men down there. My men."

"What are you going to do—attack an entire army by yourself? For what purpose? Your rebels don't have Allomancy—they won't be able to run away on swift feet and escape. You can't stop an entire army, Kelsier."

He shook himself free of her grip; she didn't have the strength to hold on. She stumbled, falling to the rough black dirt, throwing up a puff of ash. Kelsier began to stalk down the hill toward the battlefield.

Vin climbed to her knees. "Kelsier," she said, shaking quietly with fatigue. "We aren't invincible, remember?"

He paused.

"*You're* not invincible," she whispered. "You can't stop them all. You can't save those men."

Kelsier stood quietly, his fists clenched. Then, slowly, he bowed his head. In the distance, the massacre continued, though there weren't many rebels left.

"The caves," Vin whispered. "Our force would have left men behind, right? Maybe they can tell us why the army exposed itself. Maybe you can save the ones who stayed behind. The Lord Ruler's men will certainly search out the army's headquarters—if they aren't trying already."

Kelsier nodded. "All right. Let's go."

Kelsier dropped down into the cavern. He had to flare tin to see anything in the deep darkness, lit only by a bit of reflected sunlight from far above. Vin's scraping in the crack above sounded thunderous to his overenhanced ears. In the cavern itself . . . nothing. No sound, no light.

So she was wrong, Kelsier thought. *No one stayed behind.*

Kelsier breathed out slowly, trying to find an outlet for his frustration and anger. He'd abandoned the men on the battlefield. He shook his head, ignoring what logic told him at the moment. His anger was still too fresh.

Vin dropped to the ground beside him, her figure no more than a shadow to his straining eyes.

"Empty," he declared, his voice echoing hollowly in the cavern. "You were wrong."

"No," Vin whispered. "There."

Suddenly, she was off, scrambling across the floor with a catlike litheness. Kelsier called after her in the darkness, gritted his teeth, then followed her by sound down one of the corridors.

"Vin, get back here! There's nothing—"

Kelsier paused. He could just barely make out a flicker of light ahead of him in the corridor. *Bloody hell! How did she see it from so far away?*

He could still hear Vin ahead of him. Kelsier made his way more carefully, checking his metal reserves, worried about a trap left by Ministry agents. As he drew nearer to the light, a voice called out ahead. "Who's there? Say the password!"

Kelsier continued walking, the light growing bright enough for him to see a spear-holding figure backlit in the corridor ahead. Vin waited in the darkness, crouching. She looked up questioningly as Kelsier passed. She seemed to have gotten over the drain of the pewter drag, for the moment. When they finally stopped to rest, however, she'd feel it.

"I can hear you!" the guard said anxiously. His voice sounded slightly familiar. "Identify yourself."

Captain Demoux, Kelsier realized. *One of ours. It's not a trap.*

"Say the password!" Demoux commanded.

"I need no password," Kelsier said, stepping into the light.

Demoux lowered his spear. "Lord Kelsier? You've come . . . does that mean the army succeeded?"

Kelsier ignored the question. "Why aren't you guarding the entrance back there?"

"We . . . thought it would be more defensible to retreat to the inner complex, my lord. There aren't a lot of us left."

Kelsier glanced back toward the entrance corridor. *How long until the Lord Ruler's men find a captive willing to talk? Vin was right after all—we need to get these men to safety.*

Vin stood and approached, studying the young soldier with those quiet eyes of hers. "How many of you are there?"

"About two thousand," Demoux said. "We . . . were wrong, my lord. I'm sorry."

Kelsier looked back at him. "Wrong?"

"We thought that General Yeden was acting rashly," Demoux said, blushing in shame. "We stayed behind. We . . . thought we were being loyal to you, rather than him. But we should have gone with the rest of the army."

"The army is dead," Kelsier said curtly. "Gather your men, Demoux. We need to leave *now*."

That night, sitting on a tree stump with the mists gathering around him, Kelsier finally forced himself to confront the day's events.

He sat with his hands clasped before him, listening to the last, faint sounds of the army's men bedding down. Fortunately, someone had thought to prepare the group for quick departure. Each man had a bedroll, a weapon, and enough food for two weeks. As soon as Kelsier discovered who had been so foresighted, he intended to give the man a hefty promotion.

Not that there was much to command anymore. The remaining two thousand men included a depressingly large number of soldiers who were past or before their prime—men wise enough to see that Yeden's plan had been insane, or men young enough to be frightened.

Kelsier shook his head. *So many dead.* They'd gathered nearly seven thousand troops before this fiasco, but now most of them lay dead. Yeden had apparently decided to "test" the army by striking at night against the Holstep Garrison. What had led him to such a foolish decision?

Me, Kelsier thought. *This is my fault.* He'd promised them supernatural aid. He'd set himself up, had made Yeden a part of the crew, and had talked so casually about doing the impossible. Was it any wonder that Yeden had thought he could attack the Final Empire head on, considering the confidence Kelsier had given him? Was it any wonder the soldiers would go with the man, considering the promises Kelsier had made?

Now men were dead, and Kelsier was responsible. Death wasn't new to him. Neither was failure—not anymore. But, he couldn't get over the twisting in his gut. True, the men had died fighting the Final Empire, which was as good a death as any skaa could hope for—however, the fact that they'd likely died expecting some sort of divine protection from Kelsier . . . that was disturbing.

You knew this would be hard, he told himself. *You understood the burden you were taking upon yourself.*

But, what right had he? Even members of his own crew—Ham, Breeze, and the others—assumed that the Final Empire was invincible. They followed because of their faith in Kelsier, and because he had couched his plans in the form of a thieving job. Well, now that job's patron was dead; a scout sent to check the battlefield had, for better or worse, been able to confirm Yeden's death. The soldiers had put his head on a spear beside the road, along with several of Ham's officers.

The job was dead. They had failed. The army was gone. There would be no rebellion, no seizing of the city.

Footsteps approached. Kelsier looked up, wondering if he even had the strength to stand. Vin lay curled up beside his stump, asleep on the hard ground, only her mistcloak for a cushion. Their extended pewter drag had taken a lot out of the girl, and she had collapsed virtually the moment Kelsier had called a halt for the night. He wished he could do the same. However, he was far more experienced with pewter dragging than she was. His body would give out eventually, but he could keep going for a bit longer.

A figure appeared from the mists, hobbling in Kelsier's direction. The man was old, older than any that Kelsier had recruited. He must have been part of the rebellion from earlier—one of the skaa who had been living in the caves before Kelsier hijacked them.

The man chose a large stone beside Kelsier's stump, sitting with a sigh. It was amazing that one so old had even been able to keep up. Kelsier had moved the group at a fast pace, seeking to distance them as much as possible from the cave complex.

"The men will sleep fitfully," the old man said. "They aren't accustomed to being out in the mists."

"They don't have much choice," Kelsier said.

The old man shook his head. "I suppose they don't." He sat for a moment, aged eyes unreadable. "You don't recognize me, do you?"

Kelsier paused, then shook his head. "I'm sorry. Did I recruit you?"

"After a fashion. I was one of the skaa at Lord Tresting's plantation."

Kelsier opened his mouth slightly in surprise, finally recognizing a slight familiarity to the man's bald head and tired, yet somehow strong, posture. "The old man I sat with that night. Your name was . . ."

"Mennis. After you killed Tresting, we retreated up to the caves, where the rebels there took us in. A lot of the others left eventually, off to find other plantations to join. Some of us stayed."

Kelsier nodded. "You're behind this, aren't you?" he said, gesturing toward the camp. "The preparations?"

Mennis shrugged. "Some of us can't fight, so we do other things."

Kelsier leaned forward. "What happened, Mennis? Why did Yeden do this?"

Mennis just shook his head. "Though most expect young men to be fools, I've noticed that just a little bit of age can make a man far more foolish than he was as a child. Yeden . . . well, he was the type who was too easily impressed—both by you and by the reputation you left for him. Some of his generals thought it might be a good idea to give the men some practical battle experience, and they figured a night raid on the Holstep Garrison would be a clever move. Apparently, it was more difficult than they assumed."

Kelsier shook his head. "Even if they'd been successful, exposing the army would have made it useless to us."

"They believed in you," Mennis said quietly. "They thought that they couldn't fail."

Kelsier sighed, resting his head back, staring up into the shifting mists. He slowly let his breath exhale, its air mingling with the currents overhead.

"So, what becomes of us?" Mennis asked.

"We'll split you up," Kelsier said, "get you back into Luthadel in small groups, lose you among the skaa population."

Mennis nodded. He seemed tired—exhausted—yet he didn't retire. Kelsier could understand that feeling.

"Do you remember our conversation back on Tresting's plantation?" Mennis asked.

"A bit," Kelsier said. "You tried to dissuade me from making trouble."

"But it didn't stop you."

"Troublemaking is just about the only thing I'm good at,

Mennis. Do you resent what I did there, what I forced you to become?"

Mennis paused, then nodded. "But, in a way, I'm thankful for that resentment. I believed that my life was over—I awoke each day expecting that I wouldn't have the strength to rise. But . . . well, I found purpose again in the caves. For that, I'm grateful."

"Even after what I did to the army?"

Mennis snorted. "Don't think quite so highly of yourself, young man. Those soldiers got *themselves* killed. You might have been their motivation, but you didn't make the choice for them.

"Regardless, this isn't the first skaa rebellion to get slaughtered. Not by far. In a way, you've accomplished a lot—you gathered an army of considerable size, and then you armed and trained it beyond what anyone had a right to expect. Things went a little more quickly than you anticipated, but you should be proud of yourself."

"Proud?" Kelsier asked, standing to work off some of his agitation. "This army was supposed to help overthrow the Final Empire, not get itself killed fighting a meaningless battle in a valley weeks outside of Luthadel."

"Overthrow the . . ." Mennis looked up, frowning. "You really expected to do something like that?"

"Of course," Kelsier said. "Why else would I gather an army like this?"

"To resist," Mennis said. "To fight. That's why those lads came to the caves. It wasn't a matter of winning or losing, it was a matter of doing something—anything—to struggle against the Lord Ruler."

Kelsier turned, frowning. "You expected the army to lose from the beginning?"

"What other end was there?" Mennis asked. He stood, shaking his head. "Some may have begun to dream otherwise, lad, but the Lord Ruler can't be defeated. Once, I gave you some advice—I told you to be careful which battles you chose to fight. Well, I've realized that this battle *was* worth fighting.

"Now, let me give you another piece of advice, Kelsier, Survivor of Hathsin. Know when to quit. You've done well, better than any would have expected. Those skaa of yours killed an entire garrison's worth of soldiers before they were caught and destroyed. This is the greatest victory the skaa have known in decades, perhaps centuries. Now it's time to walk away."

With that, the old man nodded his head in respect, then began to shuffle back toward the center of the camp.

Kelsier stood, dumbfounded. *The greatest victory the skaa have known in decades . . .*

That was what he fought against. Not just the Lord Ruler, not just the nobility. He fought against a thousand years of conditioning, a thousand years of life in a society that would label the deaths of five thousand men as a "great victory." Life was so hopeless for the skaa that they'd been reduced to finding comfort in expected defeats.

"That wasn't a victory, Mennis," Kelsier whispered. "I'll *show* you a victory."

He forced himself to smile—not out of pleasure, and not out of satisfaction. He smiled despite the grief he felt at the deaths of his men; he smiled because that was what he did. That was how he proved to the Lord Ruler—and to himself—that he wasn't beaten.

No, he wasn't going to walk away. He wasn't finished yet. Not by far.

THE END OF PART THREE

PART FOUR

DANCERS IN A SEA OF MIST

I am growing so very tired.

26

VIN LAY IN HER BED at Clubs's shop, feeling her head throb.

Fortunately, the headache was growing weaker. She could still remember waking up on that first horrible morning; the pain had been so strong she'd barely been able to think, let alone move. She didn't know how Kelsier had kept going, leading the remnants of their army to a safe location.

That had been over two weeks ago. Fifteen full days, and her head *still* hurt. Kelsier said it was good for her. He claimed that she needed to practice "pewter dragging," training her body to function beyond what it thought possible. Despite what he said, however, she doubted something that hurt so much could possibly be "good" for her.

Of course, it might well be a useful skill to have. She could acknowledge this, now that her head wasn't pounding quite so much. She and Kelsier had been able to run to the battlefield in under a single day. The return trip had taken two weeks.

Vin rose, stretching tiredly. They'd been back for less than a day, in fact. Kelsier had probably stayed up half the night explaining events to the other crewmembers. Vin, however, had been happy to go straight to bed. The nights spent sleeping on the hard earth had reminded her that a comfortable bed was a luxury she'd started to take for granted.

She yawned, rubbed her temples again, then threw on a robe and made her way to the bathroom. She was pleased to see that Clubs's apprentices had remembered to draw her a bath. She locked the door, disrobed, and settled into the warm, lightly scented bathwater. Had she ever really found those scents obnoxious? The smell would make her less inconspicuous, true, but that seemed a slim price for ridding herself of the dirt and grime she'd picked up while traveling.

She still found longer hair an annoyance, however. She washed it, combing out the tangles and knots, wondering how the court women could stand hair that went all the way down their backs. How long must they spend combing and primping beneath a servant's care? Vin's hair hadn't even reached her shoulders yet, and she was already loath to let it get longer. It would fly about and whip her face when she jumped, not to mention provide her foes with something to grab on to.

Once finished bathing, she returned to her room, dressed in something practical, and made her way downstairs. Apprentices bustled in the workroom and housekeepers worked upstairs, but the kitchen was quiet. Clubs, Dockson, Ham, and Breeze sat at the morning meal. They looked up as Vin entered.

"What?" Vin asked grumpily, pausing in the doorway. The bath had soothed her headache somewhat, but it still pulsed slightly in the back of her head.

The four men exchanged glances. Ham spoke first. "We were just discussing the status of the plan, now that both our employer and our army are gone."

Breeze raised an eyebrow. "Status? That's an interesting way of putting it, Hammond. I would have said 'unfeasibility' instead."

Clubs grunted his assent, and the four turned to her, apparently waiting to see her reaction.

Why do they care so much what I think? she thought, walking into the room and taking a chair.

"You want something to eat?" Dockson said, rising. "Clubs's housekeepers fixed some baywraps for us to—"

"Ale," Vin said.

Dockson paused. "It's not even noon."

"Ale. Now. Please." She leaned forward, folding her arms on the table and resting her head on them.

Ham had the nerve to chuckle. "Pewter drag?"

Vin nodded.

"It'll pass," he said.

"If I don't die first," Vin grumbled.

Ham chuckled again, but the levity seemed forced. Dox handed her a mug, then sat, glancing at the others. "So, Vin. What *do* you think?"

"I don't know," she said with a sigh. "The army was pretty much the center of everything, right? Breeze, Ham, and Yeden spent all their time recruiting; Dockson and Renoux worked on supplies. Now that the soldiers are gone . . . well, that only leaves Marsh's work with the Ministry and Kell's attacks on the nobility—and neither are things he needs us for. The crew is redundant."

The room fell silent.

"She has a depressingly blunt way of putting it," Dockson said.

"Pewter drag will do that to you," Ham noted.

"When did *you* get back, anyway?" Vin asked.

"Last night, after you were asleep," Ham said. "The Garrison sent us part-time soldiers back early, so they wouldn't have to pay us."

"They're still out there, then?" Dockson asked.

Ham nodded. "Hunting down the rest of our army. The Luthadel Garrison relieved the Valtroux troops, who were actually pretty beat up from the fighting. The majority of the Luthadel troops should be out for a long while yet, searching for rebels—apparently, several very large groups broke off of our main army and fled before the battle started."

The conversation lulled into another period of silence. Vin sipped at her ale, drinking it more out of spite than any belief that it would make her feel better. A few minutes later, footsteps sounded on the stairs.

Kelsier swept into the kitchen. "Good morning, all," he

said with customary cheerfulness. "Baywraps again, I see. Clubs, you really need to hire more imaginative housemaids." Despite the comment, he grabbed a cylindrical baywrap and took a large bite, then smiled pleasantly as he poured himself something to drink.

The crew remained quiet. The men exchanged glances. Kelsier remained standing, leaning back against the cupboard as he ate.

"Kell, we need to talk," Dockson finally said. "The army is gone."

"Yes," Kelsier said between bites. "I noticed."

"The job is dead, Kelsier," Breeze said. "It was a good try, but we failed."

Kelsier paused. He frowned, lowering his baywrap. "Failed? What makes you say that?"

"The army is gone, Kell," Ham said.

"The army was only one piece of our plans. We've had a setback, true—but we're hardly finished."

"Oh, for the Lord's sake, man!" Breeze said. "How can you stand there so cheerfully? Our men are *dead*. Don't you even care?"

"I care, Breeze," Kelsier said in a solemn voice. "But what is done is done. We need to move on."

"Exactly!" Breeze said. "Move on from this insane 'job' of yours. It's time to quit. I know you don't like that, but it's the simple truth!"

Kelsier set his plate on the counter. "Don't Soothe me, Breeze. *Never* Soothe me."

Breeze paused, mouth open slightly. "Fine," he finally said. "I won't use Allomancy; I'll just use truth. Do you know what I think? I think you never intended to grab that atium.

"You've been using us. You promised us wealth so we'd join you, but you never had any intention of making us rich. This is all about your ego—it's about becoming the most famous crewleader that ever lived. *That's* why you're spreading all these rumors, doing all this recruitment. You've known wealth—now you want to become a legend."

Breeze fell quiet, eyes hard. Kelsier stood with his arms

folded, regarding the crew. Several glanced aside, shamed eyes proving that they had considered what Breeze was saying. Vin was one of those. The silence persisted, all of them waiting for a rebuttal.

Footsteps sounded on the stairs again, and Spook burst into the kitchen. "Willing the care and upping to see! A gathering, in the fountain square!"

Kelsier didn't look surprised by the boy's announcement.

"A gathering in the fountain square?" Ham said slowly. "That means . . ."

"Come on," Kelsier said, standing up straight. "We're going to watch."

"I'd rather not do this, Kell," Ham said. "I avoid these things for a reason."

Kelsier ignored him. He walked at the head of the crew, who all—even Breeze—wore mundane skaa clothing and cloaks. A light ashfall had begun, and careless flakes floated down from the sky, like leaves dropped from some unseen tree.

Large clusters of skaa clogged the street, most of them workers from factories or mills. Vin knew of only one reason why the workers would be released and sent to gather in the city's central square.

Executions.

She'd never gone to them before. Supposedly, all the men in the city—skaa or noble—were required to attend execution ceremonies, but thieving crews knew how to remain hidden. Bells rang in the distance, announcing the event, and obligators watched at the sides of the streets. They would go into mills, forges, and random houses searching for those who disobeyed the call, meting out death as a punishment. Gathering this many people was an enormous undertaking—but, in a way, doing things like this simply worked to prove how powerful the Lord Ruler was.

The streets grew even more crowded as Vin's crew approached the fountain square. Building roofs were packed, and people filled the streets, pressing forward. *There's no way they'll all fit.* Luthadel wasn't like most other cities; its population was enormous. Even with only the men in attendance, there was no way everyone would have a view of the executions.

Yet, they came anyway. Partially because they were required, partially because they wouldn't have to work while they watched, and partially—Vin suspected—because they had the same morbid curiosity that all men possessed.

As the crowds grew thicker, Kelsier, Dockson, and Ham began to shove the crew a path through the onlookers. Some of the skaa gave the crew looks of resentment, though many were just dull-eyed and compliant. Some appeared surprised, even excited, when they saw Kelsier, though his scars were not showing. These people moved aside eagerly.

Eventually, the crew reached the outer row of buildings surrounding the square. Kelsier picked one, nodding toward it, and Dockson moved forward. A man at the doorway tried to bar his entrance, but Dox pointed toward the roof, then hefted his coinpouch suggestively. A few minutes later, the crew had the entire rooftop to themselves.

"Smoke us please, Clubs," Kelsier said quietly.

The gnarled craftsman nodded, making the crew invisible to Allomantic bronze senses. Vin walked over and crouched beside the roof's lip, hands on the short stone railing as she scanned the square down below. "So many people . . ."

"You've lived in cities all your life, Vin," Ham said, standing next to her. "Surely you've seen crowds before."

"Yes, but . . ." How could she explain? The shifting, overpacked mass was unlike anything she'd seen. It was expansive, almost endless, its trails filling every street leading away from the central square. The skaa were packed so closely, she wondered how they even had room to breathe.

The noblemen were at the center of the square, separated from the skaa by soldiers. They were close to the central fountain patio, which stood about five feet above the rest of the square. Someone had constructed seating for the nobility, and they lounged, as if they were visiting some show or horse race. Many had servants holding up parasols against the ash, but it was falling lightly enough that some just ignored it.

Standing beside the noblemen were the obligators—regular ones in gray, Inquisitors in black. Vin shivered. There were eight Inquisitors, their lanky forms standing a head above the obligators. But, it wasn't just height that separated the dark creatures from their cousins. There was an air, a distinctive posture, about the Steel Inquisitors.

Vin turned, studying the regular obligators instead. Most of them held themselves proudly in their administrative robes—the higher their position, the finer the robes. Vin squinted, burning tin, and recognized a moderately familiar face.

"There," she said, pointing. "That one's my father."

Kelsier perked up. "Where?"

"At the front of the obligators," Vin said. "The shorter one with the golden robe-scarf."

Kelsier fell silent. "*That's* your father?" he finally asked.

"Who?" Dockson asked, squinting. "I can't make out their faces."

"Tevidian," Kelsier said.

"The *lord prelan?*" Dockson asked with shock.

"What?" Vin asked. "Who's that?"

Breeze chuckled. "The lord prelan is the leader of the Ministry, my dear. He's the most important of the Lord Ruler's obligators—technically, he's even higher ranked than the Inquisitors."

Vin sat, dumbfounded.

"The lord prelan," Dockson mumbled, shaking his head. "This just keeps getting better."

"Look!" Spook suddenly said, pointing.

The crowd of skaa began to shuffle. Vin had assumed that they were too packed to move, but apparently she was wrong. The people began to pull back, making a large corridor leading to the central platform.

What could make them—

Then she felt it. The oppressive numbness, like a massive blanket pressing down, choking away her air, stealing her will. She immediately burned copper. Yet, like before, she swore that she could feel the Lord Ruler's Soothing despite the metal. She sensed him coming closer, trying to make her lose all will, all desire, all strength of emotion.

"He's coming," Spook whispered, crouching down beside her.

A black carriage drawn by a pair of massive white stallions appeared down a side street. It rolled down the corridor of skaa, moving with a sense of . . . inevitability. Vin saw several people get clipped by its passing, and suspected that if a man were to fall into the carriage's path, the vehicle wouldn't even slow as it crushed him to death.

The skaa sagged a bit more as the Lord Ruler arrived, a visible ripple washing across the crowd, their postures drooping as they felt his powerful Soothing. The background roar of whispers and chatting dampened, an unreal silence falling over the enormous square.

"He's so *powerful*," Breeze said. "Even at my best, I can only Soothe a couple hundred men. There have to be tens of thousands of people here!"

Spook looked over the rim of the rooftop. "It makes me want to fall. To just let go . . ."

Then, he paused. He shook his head, as if waking up. Vin frowned. Something felt different. Tentatively, she extinguished her copper, and realized that she could no longer feel the Lord Ruler's Soothing. The feeling of awful depression—of soullessness and emptiness—had strangely disappeared. Spook looked up, and the rest of the crewmembers stood just a little straighter.

Vin glanced around. The skaa below looked unchanged. Yet, her friends—

Her eyes found Kelsier. The crewleader stood straight-backed, staring resolutely at the approaching carriage, a look of concentration on his face.

He's Rioting our emotions, Vin realized. *He's counteracting the Lord Ruler's power.* It was obviously a struggle for Kelsier to protect even their small group.

Breeze is right, Vin thought. *How can we fight something like this? The Lord Ruler is Soothing a hundred thousand people at once!*

But, Kelsier fought on. Just in case, Vin turned on her copper. Then she burned zinc and reached out to help Kelsier, Rioting the emotions of those around her. It felt like she was Pulling against some massive, immobile wall. Yet, it must have helped, for Kelsier relaxed slightly, shooting her a grateful look.

"Look," Dockson said, probably unaware of the unseen battle that occurred around him. "The prisoner carts." He pointed toward a set of ten large, bar-lined carts traveling down the corridor behind the Lord Ruler.

"Do you recognize anyone in them?" Ham said, leaning forward.

"I'm not of the seeing," Spook said, looking uncomfortable. "Uncle, you really the burn, right?"

"Yes, my copper is on," Clubs said testily. "You're safe. We're far enough away from the Lord Ruler that it wouldn't matter anyway—that plaza is enormous."

Spook nodded, then obviously began burning tin. A moment later, he shook his head. "Notting of the recognizing anyone."

"You weren't there for a lot of the recruiting, though, Spook," Ham said, squinting.

"True," Spook replied. Though his accent remained, he was obviously making an effort to speak normally.

Kelsier stepped up to the ledge, holding a hand up to shade his eyes. "I can see the prisoners. No, I don't recognize any of the faces. They aren't captive soldiers."

"Who, then?" Ham asked.

"Mostly women and children, it appears," Kelsier said.

"The families of the soldiers?" Ham asked, horrified.

Kelsier shook his head. "I doubt it. They wouldn't have taken the time to identify dead skaa."

Ham frowned, looking confused.

"Random people, Hammond," Breeze said with a quiet sigh. "Examples—casual executions made in order to punish the skaa for harboring rebels."

"No, not even that," Kelsier said. "I doubt the Lord Ruler even knows, or cares, that most of those men were recruited from Luthadel. He probably just assumes that it was another countryside rebellion. This . . . this is just a way of reminding everyone who is in control."

The Lord Ruler's carriage rolled up a platform onto the central patio. The ominous vehicle pulled to a stop in the exact center of the square, but the Lord Ruler himself remained inside.

The prisoner carts pulled to a stop, and a group of obligators and soldiers began to unload them. Black ash continued to fall as the first group of prisoners—most struggling only weakly—were dragged up onto the raised central platform. An Inquisitor directed the work, gesturing for prisoners to be gathered beside each of the platform's four bowl-like fountains.

Four prisoners were forced to their knees—one beside each running fountain—and four Inquisitors raised obsidian axes. Four axes fell, and four heads were sheared free. The bodies, still held by soldiers, were allowed to spurt their last lifeblood into the fountain basins.

The fountains began to glisten red as they sprayed into the air. The soldiers tossed the bodies aside, then brought four more people forward.

Spook looked away sickly. "Why . . . why doesn't Kelsier do something? To saving them, I mean?"

"Don't be foolish," Vin said. "There are *eight* Inquisitors down there—not to mention the Lord Ruler himself. Kelsier would be an idiot to try something."

Though I wouldn't be surprised if he considered it, she thought, remembering when Kelsier had been ready to rush down and take on an entire army by himself. She glanced to the side. Kelsier looked like he was forcibly holding himself back—white-knuckled hands gripping the chimney beside him—to keep himself from rushing down to stop the executions.

Spook stumbled over to another part of the rooftop where he could retch without spilling bile onto the people below. Ham groaned slightly, and even Clubs looked saddened. Dockson watched solemnly, as if witnessing the deaths were some sort of vigil. Breeze just shook his head.

Kelsier, however . . . Kelsier was angry. His face red, his muscles tense, his eyes ablaze.

Four more deaths, one of them a child.

"This," Kelsier said, angrily waving his hand toward the central square. "*This* is our enemy. There is no quarter here, no walking away. This is no simple job, to be thrown aside when we encounter a few unexpected twists."

Four more deaths.

"Look at them!" Kelsier demanded, pointing at the bleachers full of nobility. Most of them appeared bored—and a few even seemed to be enjoying themselves, turning and joking with one another as the beheadings continued.

"I know you question me," Kelsier said, turning to the crew. "You think that I've been too hard on the nobility, think that I relish killing them too much. But, can you honestly see those men laughing and tell me that they don't *deserve* to die by my blade? I only bring them justice."

Four more deaths.

Vin searched the bleachers with urgent, tin-enhanced eyes. She found Elend sitting amid a group of younger men. None of them were laughing, and they weren't the only ones. True, many of the nobility made light of the experience, but there were some small minority who looked horrified.

Kelsier continued. "Breeze, you asked about the atium. I'll be honest. It was never my main goal—I gathered this crew because I wanted to change things. We'll grab the atium—we'll need it to support a new government—but this job isn't about making me, or any of you, wealthy.

"Yeden is dead. He was our excuse—a way that we could do something good while still pretending to just be thieves. Now that he's gone, you can give up, if you want. Quit. But, that won't change anything. The struggle will go on. Men will still die. You'll just be ignoring it."

Four more deaths.

"It's time to stop the charade," Kelsier said, staring at them each in turn. "If we're going to do this now, we have to be upfront and honest with ourselves. We have to admit that it isn't about money. It's about stopping *that*." He pointed at the courtyard with its red fountains—a visible sign of death for the thousands of skaa too far away to even tell what was happening.

"I intend to continue my fight," Kelsier said quietly. "I realize that some of you question my leadership. You think I've been building myself up too much with the skaa. You whisper that I'm making myself into another Lord Ruler—you think that my ego is more important to me than overthrowing the empire."

He paused, and Vin saw guilt in the eyes of Dockson and the others. Spook rejoined the group, still looking a bit sick.

Four more deaths.

"You're wrong," Kelsier said quietly. "You have to trust me. You gave me your confidence when we began this plan, despite how dangerous things seemed. I still need that confidence! No matter how things appear, no matter how terrible the odds, we have to keep fighting!"

Four more deaths.

The crew slowly turned toward Kelsier. Resisting the Lord Ruler's Pushing on their emotions didn't seem like half as much a struggle for Kelsier anymore, though Vin had let her zinc lapse.

Maybe . . . maybe he can *do it,* Vin thought, despite herself. If there was ever a man who could defeat the Lord Ruler, it would be Kelsier.

"I didn't choose you men because of your competence," Kelsier said, "though you are certainly skilled. I chose each of you specifically because I knew you to be men of conscience. Ham, Breeze, Dox, Clubs . . . you are men with reputations for honesty, even charity. I knew that if I were going to succeed at this plan, I would need men who actually *cared.*

"No, Breeze, this isn't about boxings or about glory. This is about war—a war we have been fighting for a thousand years, a war I intend to end. You may go, if you wish. You know I'll let any of you out—no questions asked, no repercussions exacted—if you wish to go.

"However," he said, eyes growing hard, "if you stay, you have to promise to stop questioning my authority. You can voice concerns about the job itself, but there will be no more whispered conferences about my leadership. If you stay, you follow me. Understood?"

One by one, he locked eyes with the crewmembers. Each one gave him a nod.

"I don't think we ever really questioned you, Kell," Dockson said. "We just . . . we're worried, and I think rightly so. The army was a big part of our plans."

Kelsier nodded to the north, toward the main city gates. "What do you see up in the distance, Dox?"

"The city gates?"

"And what is different about them recently?"

Dockson shrugged. "Nothing unusual. They're a bit understaffed, but—"

"Why?" Kelsier interjected. "Why are they understaffed?"

Dockson paused. "Because the Garrison is gone?"

"Exactly," Kelsier said. "Ham says that the Garrison could be out chasing remnants of our army for months, and only about ten percent of its men stayed behind. That makes sense—stopping rebels is the sort of thing the Garrison was created to do. Luthadel might be exposed, but no one ever attacks Luthadel. No one ever has."

A quiet understanding passed between the members of the crew.

"Part one of our plan to take the city has been accomplished," Kelsier said. "We got the Garrison out of Luthadel. It cost us far more than we expected—far more than it should have. I wish to the Forgotten Gods that those boys hadn't died. Unfortunately, we can't change that now—we can only use the opening they gave us.

"The plan is still in motion—the main peacekeeping force in the city is gone. If a house war starts in earnest, the Lord Ruler will have a difficult time stopping it. Assuming he wants to. For some reason, he tends to step back and let the nobility fight each other every hundred years or so. Perhaps he finds that letting them at each other's throats keeps them away from his own."

"But, what if the Garrison comes back?" Ham asked.

"If I'm right," Kelsier said, "the Lord Ruler will let them chase stragglers from our army for several months, giving the nobility a chance to blow off a little steam. Except, he's going to get a lot more than he expected. When that house war starts, we're going to use the chaos to seize the palace."

"With what army, my dear man?" Breeze said.

"We still have some troops left," Kelsier said. "Plus, we

have time to recruit more. We'll have to be careful—we can't use the caves, so we'll have to hide our troops in the city. That will probably mean smaller numbers. However, that won't be an issue—you see, that garrison is going to return eventually."

The members of the group shared a look as the executions proceeded below. Vin sat quietly, trying to decide what Kelsier meant by that statement.

"Exactly, Kell," Ham said slowly. "The Garrison will return, and we won't have a big enough army to fight them."

"But we *will* have the Lord Ruler's treasury," Kelsier said, smiling. "What is it you always say about those Garrisoners, Ham?"

The Thug paused, then smiled too. "That they're mercenaries."

"We seize the Lord Ruler's money," Kelsier said, "and it means we get his army too. This can still work, gentlemen. We can *make* it work."

The crew seemed to grow more confident. Vin, however, turned her eyes back toward the square. The fountains ran so red that they seemed completely filled with blood. Over it all, the Lord Ruler watched from within his jet-black carriage. The windows were open, and—with tin—Vin could just barely see a silhouetted figure sitting within.

That's our real foe, she thought. *Not the missing garrison, not the Inquisitors with their axes. That man. The one from the logbook.*

We'll have to find a way to defeat him, otherwise everything else we do will be pointless.

I think I've finally discovered why Rashek resents me so very much. He does not believe that an outsider such as myself—a foreigner—could possibly be the Hero of Ages. He believes that I have somehow tricked the philosophers, that I wear the piercings of the Hero unjustly.

According to Rashek, only a Terrisman of pure blood should have been chosen as the Hero. Oddly, I find myself even more determined because of his hatred. I must prove to him that I can perform this task.

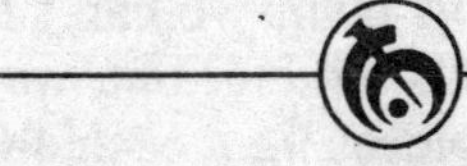

27

IT WAS A SUBDUED GROUP that returned to Clubs's shop that evening. The executions had stretched for hours. There had been no denunciations, no explanations by the Ministry or the Lord Ruler—just execution, after execution, after execution. Once the captives were gone, the Lord Ruler and his obligators had ridden away, leaving a pile of corpses on the platform and bloodied water running in the fountains.

As Kelsier's crew returned to the kitchen, Vin realized that her headache no longer bothered her. Her pain now seemed . . . insignificant. The baywraps remained on the table, thoughtfully covered by one of the house maids. No one reached for them.

"All right," Kelsier said, taking his customary place leaning against the cupboard. "Let's plan this out. How should we proceed?"

Dockson recovered a stack of papers from the side of the room as he walked over to seat himself. "With the Garrison gone, our main focus becomes the nobility."

"Indeed," Breeze said. "If we truly intend to seize the treasury with only a few thousand soldiers, then we're certainly going to need something to distract the palace guard and keep the nobility from taking the city away from us. The house war, therefore, becomes of paramount importance."

Kelsier nodded. "My thoughts exactly."

"But, what happens when the house war is over?" Vin said. "Some houses will come out on top, and then we'll have to deal with them."

Kelsier shook his head. "I don't intend for the house war to ever end, Vin—or, at least, not for a long while. The Lord Ruler makes dictates, and the Ministry polices his followers, but the nobility are the ones who actually force the skaa to work. So, if we bring down enough noble houses, the government may just collapse on its own. We can't fight the entire Final Empire as a whole—it's too big. But, we might be able to shatter it, then make the pieces fight each other."

"We need to put financial strain on the Great Houses," Dockson said, flipping through his papers. "The aristocracy is primarily a financial institution, and lack of funds will bring *any* house down."

"Breeze, we might need to use some of your aliases," Kelsier said. "So far, I've really been the only one in the crew working on the house war—but if we're going to make this city snap before the Garrison returns, we'll need to step up our efforts."

Breeze sighed. "Very well. We'll just have to be very careful to make certain no one accidentally recognizes me as someone I shouldn't be. I can't go to parties or functions—but I can probably do solitary house visits."

"Same for you, Dox," Kelsier said.

"I figured as much," Dockson said.

"It will be dangerous for both of you," Kelsier said. "But speed will be essential. Vin will remain our main spy—and we'll probably want her to start spreading some bad information. Anything to make the nobility uncertain."

Ham nodded. "We should probably focus our attentions on the top, then."

"Indeed," Breeze said. "If we can make the most powerful houses look vulnerable, then their enemies will be quick to strike. Only after the powerful houses are gone will people realize that *they* were the ones really supporting the economy."

The room fell quiet for a second, then several heads turned toward Vin.

"What?" she asked.

"They're talking about House Venture, Vin," Dockson said. "It's the most powerful of the Great Houses."

Breeze nodded. "If Venture falls, the entire Final Empire would feel the tremors."

Vin sat quietly for a moment. "They're not all bad people," she finally said.

"Perhaps," Kelsier said. "But Lord Straff Venture certainly is, and his family sits at the very head of the Final Empire. House Venture needs to go—and you already have an in with one of its most important members."

I thought you wanted me to stay away *from Elend,* she thought with annoyance.

"Just keep your ears open, child," Breeze said. "See if you can get the lad to talk about his house's finances. Find us a bit of leverage, and we'll do the rest."

Just like the games Elend hates so much. However, the executions were still fresh in her mind. That sort of thing had to be stopped. Besides—even Elend said he didn't like his father, or his house, very much. Maybe . . . maybe she could find something. "I'll see what I can do," she said.

A knock came at the front door, answered by one of the apprentices. A few moments later, Sazed—clad in a skaa cloak to hide his features—entered the kitchen.

Kelsier checked the clock. "You're early, Saze."

"I try to make it a habit, Master Kelsier," the Terrisman replied.

Dockson raised an eyebrow. "That's a habit someone else could afford to pick up."

Kelsier snorted. "If you're always on time, it implies that you never have anything better you should be doing. Saze, how are the men?"

"As good as can be expected, Master Kelsier," Sazed replied. "But they can't hide in the Renoux warehouses forever."

"I know," Kelsier said. "Dox, Ham, I'll need you to work on this problem. There are two thousand men left from our army; I want you to get them into Luthadel."

Dockson nodded thoughtfully. "We'll find a way."

"You want us to keep training them?" Ham asked.

Kelsier nodded.

"Then we'll have to hide them in squads," he said. "We don't have the resources to train men individually. Say . . . a couple hundred men per team? Hidden in slums near one another?"

"Make sure none of the teams know about the others," Dockson said. "Or even that we still intend to strike at the palace. With that many men in town, there's a chance some of them will eventually get taken by the obligators for one reason or another."

Kelsier nodded. "Tell each group that it's the only one that didn't get disbanded, and that it's being retained just in case it's needed at some point in the future."

"You also said that recruitment needed to be continued," Ham said.

Kelsier nodded. "I'd like at least twice as many troops before we try and pull this off."

"That's going to be tough," Ham said, "considering our army's failure."

"What failure?" Kelsier asked. "Tell them the truth—that our army successfully neutralized the Garrison."

"Though most of them died doing it," Ham said.

"We can gloss over that part," Breeze said. "The people will be angry at the executions—that should make them more willing to listen to us."

"Gathering more troops is going to be your main task over the next few months, Ham," Kelsier said.

"That's not much time," Ham said. "But, I'll see what I can do."

"Good," Kelsier said. "Saze, did the note come?"

"It did, Master Kelsier," Sazed said, pulling a letter from beneath his cloak and handing it to Kelsier.

"And what would that be?" Breeze asked curiously.

"A message from Marsh," Kelsier said, opening the letter and scanning its contents. "He's in the city, and he has news."

"What news?" Ham asked.

"He doesn't say," Kelsier said, grabbing a baywrap. "But he gave instructions on where to meet him tonight." He walked over, picking up a regular skaa cloak. "I'm going to go scout the location before it gets dark. Coming, Vin?"

She nodded, standing.

"The rest of you keep working on the plan," Kelsier said. "In two months' time, I want this city to be so tense that when it finally breaks, even the Lord Ruler won't be able to hold it together."

"There's something you're not telling us, isn't there?" Vin said, looking away from the window, turning toward Kelsier. "A part of the plan."

Kelsier glanced over at her in the darkness. Marsh's chosen meeting place was an abandoned building within the Twists, one of the most impoverished skaa slums. Kelsier had located a second abandoned building across from the one they would meet in, and he and Vin waited on the top floor, watching the street for signs of Marsh.

"Why do you ask me that?" Kelsier finally said.

"Because of the Lord Ruler," Vin said, picking at the rotting wood of her windowsill. "I felt his power today. I don't think the others could sense it, not like a Mistborn can. But I know you must have." She looked up again, meeting Kelsier's eyes. "You're still planning to get him out of the city before we try to take the palace, right?"

"Don't worry about the Lord Ruler," Kelsier said. "The Eleventh Metal will take care of him."

Vin frowned. Outside, the sun was setting in a fiery blaze of frustration. The mists would come soon, and supposedly Marsh would arrive a short time later.

The Eleventh Metal, she thought, remembering the skepticism with which the other crewmembers regarded it. "Is it real?" Vin asked.

"The Eleventh Metal? Of course it is—I showed it to you, remember?"

"That's not what I mean," she said. "Are the legends real? Are you lying?"

Kelsier turned toward her, frowning slightly. Then he smirked. "You're a very blunt girl, Vin."

"I know."

Kelsier's smile deepened. "The answer is no. I'm not lying. The legends are real, though it took some time for me to find them."

"And that bit of metal you showed us really is the Eleventh Metal?"

"I think so," Kelsier said.

"But you don't know how to use it."

Kelsier paused, then shook his head. "No. I don't."

"That's not very comforting."

Kelsier shrugged, turning to look out the window. "Even if I don't discover the secret in time, I doubt the Lord Ruler will be as big a problem as you think. He's a powerful Allomancer, but he doesn't know everything—if he did, we'd be dead right now. He's not omnipotent, either—if he were, he wouldn't have needed to execute all of those skaa to try and frighten the city into submission.

"I don't know what he is—but I think he's more like a man than he is a god. The words in that logbook . . . they're the words of a regular person. His real power comes from his armies and his wealth. If we remove them, he won't be able to do anything to stop his empire from collapsing."

Vin frowned. "He might not be a god, but . . . he's something, Kelsier. Something different. Today, when he was in the square, I could feel his touch on my emotions even when I was burning copper."

"That's not possible, Vin," Kelsier said with a shake of his head. "If it were, Inquisitors would be able to sense Allomancy even when there was a Smoker nearby. If that were the case, don't you think they'd hunt down all of the skaa Mistings and kill them?"

Vin shrugged.

"You know the Lord Ruler is strong," Kelsier said, "and you feel like you *should* still be able to sense him. So you do."

Maybe he's right, she thought, picking off another bit of the windowsill. *He's been an Allomancer for far longer than I have, after all.*

But . . . I felt something, didn't I? And the Inquisitor that nearly killed me—somehow, he found me in the darkness and rain. He must have sensed something.

She let the matter drop, however. "The Eleventh Metal. Couldn't we just try it and see what it does?"

"It's not that simple," Kelsier said. "You remember how I told you never to burn a metal that wasn't one of the ten?"

Vin nodded.

"Burning another metal can be deadly," Kelsier said. "Even getting the wrong mixture in an alloy metal can make you sick. If I'm wrong about the Eleventh Metal . . ."

"It will kill you," Vin said quietly.

Kelsier nodded.

So, you're not quite as certain as you pretend, she decided. *Otherwise, you'd have tried it by now.*

"That's what you want to find in the logbook," Vin said. "A clue about how to use the Eleventh Metal."

Kelsier nodded. "I'm afraid we weren't very lucky in that respect. So far, the logbook hasn't even mentioned Allomancy."

"Though it does talk about Feruchemy," Vin said.

Kelsier eyed her as he stood by his window, one shoulder leaning against the wall. "So Sazed told you about that?"

Vin glanced down. "I . . . kind of forced him to."

Kelsier chuckled. "I wonder what I've unleashed upon the world by teaching you Allomancy. Of course, my trainer said the same thing about me."

"He was right to worry."

"Of course he was."

Vin smiled. Outside, the sunlight was nearly gone, and diaphanous patches of mist were beginning to form in the air. They hung like ghosts, slowly growing larger, extending their influence as night approached.

"Sazed didn't have time to tell me much about Feruchemy," Vin said carefully. "What kind of things can it do?" She waited in trepidation, assuming that Kelsier would see through her lie.

"Feruchemy is completely internal," Kelsier said in an offhand voice. "It can provide some of the same things we get from pewter and tin—strength, endurance, eyesight—but each attribute has to be stored separately. It can enhance a lot of other things too—things that Allomancy can't do. Memory, physical speed, clarity of thought . . . even some strange things, like physical weight or physical age, can be altered by Feruchemy."

"So, it's more powerful than Allomancy?" Vin said.

Kelsier shrugged. "Feruchemy doesn't have any external powers—it can't Push and Pull emotions, nor can it Steelpush or Ironpull. And, the biggest limitation to Feruchemy is that you have to store up all of its abilities by drawing them from your own body.

"Want to be twice as strong for a time? Well, you have to spend several hours being weak to store up the strength. If you want to store up the ability to heal quickly, you have to spend a great deal of time feeling sick. In Allomancy, the metals themselves are our fuel—we can generally keep going as long as we have enough metal to burn. In Feruchemy, the metals are just storage devices—your own body is the real fuel."

"So, you just steal someone else's storage metals, right?" Vin said.

Kelsier shook his head. "Doesn't work—Feruchemists can only access metal stores they themselves created."

"Oh."

Kelsier nodded. "So, no. I wouldn't say that Feruchemy is more powerful than Allomancy. They both have advantages and limitations. For instance, an Allomancer can only flare a metal so high, and so his maximum strength is bounded. Feruchemists don't have that kind of limitation; if a Feruchemist had enough strength stored up to be twice as strong as normal for an hour, he could choose instead to be *three* times as strong for a shorter period of time—or even four, five, or six times as strong for even shorter periods."

Vin frowned. "That sounds like a pretty big advantage."

"True," Kelsier said, reaching inside of his cloak and pulling out a vial containing several beads of atium. "But we have *this*. It doesn't matter if a Feruchemist is as strong as five men or as strong as fifty men—if I know what he's going to do next, I'll beat him."

Vin nodded.

"Here," Kelsier said, unstoppering the vial and pulling out one of the beads. He took out another vial, this one filled with the normal alcohol solution, and dropped the bead in it. "Take one of these. You might need it."

"Tonight?" Vin asked, accepting the vial.

Kelsier nodded.

"But, it's just Marsh."

"It might be," he said. "Then again, maybe the obligators caught him and forced him to write that letter. Maybe they're following him, or maybe they've since captured him and have tortured him to find out about the meeting. Marsh is in a very dangerous place—think about trying to do the same thing you're doing at those balls, except exchange all the noblemen for obligators and Inquisitors."

Vin shivered. "I guess you have a point," she said, tucking away the bead of atium. "You know, something must be wrong with me—I barely even stop to think how much this stuff is worth anymore."

Kelsier didn't respond immediately. "I have trouble forgetting how much it's worth," he said quietly.

"I . . ." Vin trailed off, glancing down at his hands. He usually wore long-sleeved shirts and gloves now; his reputation was making it dangerous for his identifying scars to be visible in public. Vin knew they were there, however. Like thousands of tiny white scratches, layered one over the other.

"Anyway," Kelsier said, "you're right about the logbook—I had hoped that it would mention the Eleventh Metal. But, Allomancy isn't even mentioned in reference to Feruchemy. The two powers are similar in many respects; you'd think that he would compare them."

"Maybe he worried that someone would read the book, and didn't want to give away that he was an Allomancer."

Kelsier nodded. "Maybe. It's also possible that he hadn't Snapped yet. Whatever happened in those Terris Mountains changed him from hero to tyrant; maybe it also awakened his powers. We won't know, I guess, until Saze finishes his translation."

"Is he close?"

Kelsier nodded. "Just a bit left—the important bit, hopefully. I feel a little frustrated with the text so far. The Lord Ruler hasn't even told us what he is supposed to accomplish in those mountains! He claims that he's doing something to protect the entire world, but that might just be his ego coming through."

He didn't seem very egotistical in the text to me, Vin thought. *Kind of the opposite, actually.*

"Regardless," Kelsier said, "we'll know more once the last few sections are translated."

It was growing dark outside, and Vin had to turn up her tin to see properly. The street outside her window grew visible, adopting the strange mixture of shadow and luminance that was the result of tin-enhanced vision. She knew it was dark, logically. Yet, she could still see. Not as she did in regular light—everything was muted—but it was sight nonetheless.

Kelsier checked his pocket watch.

"How long?" Vin asked.

"Another half hour," Kelsier said. "Assuming he's on time—and I doubt he will be. He *is* my brother, after all."

Vin nodded, shifting so that she leaned with arms crossed across the broken windowsill. Though it was a very small thing, she felt a comfort in having the atium Kelsier had given her.

She paused. Thinking of atium reminded her of something important. Something she'd been bothered by on several occasions. "You never taught me the ninth metal!" she accused, turning.

Kelsier shrugged. "I told you that it wasn't very important."

"Still. What is it? Some alloy of atium, I assume?"

Kelsier shook his head. "No, the last two metals don't follow the same pattern as the basic eight. The ninth metal is gold."

"Gold?" Vin asked. "That's it? I could have tried it a long time ago on my own!"

Kelsier chuckled. "Assuming you wanted to. Burning gold is a somewhat. . . . uncomfortable experience."

Vin narrowed her eyes, then turned to look back out the window. *We'll see,* she thought.

"You're going to try it anyway, aren't you?" Kelsier said, smiling.

Vin didn't respond.

Kelsier sighed, reaching into his sash and pulling out a golden boxing and a file. "You should probably get one of these," he said, holding up the file. "However, if you collect a metal yourself, burn just a tiny bit first to make certain that it's pure or alloyed correctly."

"If it isn't?" Vin asked.

"You'll know," Kelsier promised, beginning to file away at the coin. "Remember that headache you had from pewter dragging?"

"Yes?"

"Bad metal is worse," Kelsier said. "Far worse. Buy your metals when you can—in every city, you'll find a small group of merchants who provide powdered metals to Allomancers. Those merchants have a vested interest in making certain that all of their metals are pure—a grumpy Mistborn with a headache isn't exactly the kind of slighted customer one wants to deal with." Kelsier finished filing, then collected a few flakes of gold on a small square of cloth. He stuck one on his finger, then swallowed it.

"This is good," he said, handing her the cloth. "Go ahead—just remember, burning thc ninth mctal is a strangc experience."

Vin nodded, suddenly feeling a bit apprehensive. *You'll never know if you don't try it for yourself,* she thought, then dumped the dustlike flakes into her mouth. She washed them down with a bit of water from her flask.

A new metal reserve appeared within her—unfamiliar and different from the nine she knew. She looked up at Kelsier, took a breath, and burned gold.

She was in two places at once. She could see herself, and she could see herself.

One of her was a strange woman, changed and transformed from the girl she had always been. That girl had been careful and cautious—a girl who would never burn an unfamiliar metal based solely on the word of one man. This woman was foolish; she had forgotten many of the things that had let her survive so long. She drank from cups prepared by others. She fraternized with strangers. She didn't keep track of the people around her. She was still far more careful than most people, but she had lost so much.

The other her was something she had always secretly loathed. A child, really. Thin to the point of scrawniness, she was lonely, hateful, and untrusting. She loved no one, and no one loved her. She always told herself, quietly, that she didn't care. Was there something worth living for? There had to be. Life couldn't be as pathetic as it seemed. Yet, it had to be. There wasn't anything else.

Vin was both. She stood in two places, moving both bodies, being both girl and woman. She reached out with hesitant, uncertain hands—one each—and touched herself on the faces, one each.

Vin gasped, and it was gone. She felt a sudden rush of emotions, a sense of worthlessness and confusion. There were no chairs in the room, so she simply squatted to the ground, sitting with her back to the wall, knees pulled up, arms wrapped around them.

Kelsier walked over, squatting down to lay a hand on her shoulder. "It's all right."

"What was that?" she whispered.

"Gold and atium are complements, like the other metal pairs," Kelsier said. "Atium lets you see, marginally, into the future. Gold works in a similar way, but it lets you see into the past. Or, at least, it gives you a glimpse of another version of yourself, had things been different in the past."

Vin shivered. The experience of being both people at once, of seeing herself twice over, had been disturbingly eerie. Her body still shook, and her mind didn't feel . . . right anymore.

Fortunately, the sensation seemed to be fading. "Remind me to listen to you in the future," she said. "Or, at least, when you talk about Allomancy."

Kelsier chuckled. "I tried to put it out of your mind for as long as possible. But, you had to try it sometime. You'll get over it."

Vin nodded. "It's . . . almost gone already. But, it wasn't just a vision, Kelsier. It was *real*. I could touch her, the other me."

"It may feel that way," Kelsier said. "But she wasn't here—I couldn't see her, at least. It's an hallucination."

"Atium visions aren't just hallucinations," Vin said. "The shadows really do show what people will do."

"True," Kelsier said. "I don't know. Gold is strange, Vin. I don't think anybody understands it. My trainer, Gemmel, said that a gold shadow was a person who didn't exist—but could have. A person you might have become, had you not made certain choices. Of course, Gemmel was a bit screwy, so I'm not sure how much I'd believe of what he said."

Vin nodded. However, it was unlikely that she'd find out more about gold anytime soon. She didn't intend to ever burn it again, if she could help it. She continued to sit, letting her emotions recover for a while, and Kelsier moved back over by the window. Eventually, he perked up.

"He's here?" Vin asked, crawling to her feet.

Kelsier nodded. "You want to stay here and rest some more?"

Vin shook her head.

"All right, then," he said, placing his pocket watch, file, and other metals on the windowsill. "Let's go."

They didn't go out the window—Kelsier wanted to maintain a low profile, though this section of the Twists was so deserted that Vin wasn't sure why he bothered. They left the building via a set of untrustworthy stairs, then crossed the street in silence.

The building Marsh had chosen was even more run-down than the one Vin and Kelsier had been sitting in. The front door was gone, though Vin could see remnants of it in the splintered refuse on the floor. The room inside smelled of dust and soot, and she had to stifle a sneeze.

A figure standing on the far side of the room spun at the sound. "Kell?"

"It's me," Kelsier said. "And Vin."

As Vin drew closer, she could see Marsh squinting in the darkness. It was odd to watch him, feeling like she was in plain sight, yet knowing that to him she and Kelsier were nothing more than shadows. The far wall of the building had collapsed, and mist floated freely in the room, nearly as dense as it was outside.

"You have Ministry tattoos!" Vin said, staring at Marsh.

"Of course," Marsh said, his voice as stern as ever. "I had them put on before I met up with the caravan. I had to have them to play the part of an acolyte."

They weren't extensive—he was playing a low-ranked obligator—but the pattern was unmistakable. Dark lines, rimming the eyes, running outward like crawling cracks of lightning. There was one, single line—much thicker, and in bright red, running down the side of his face. Vin recognized the pattern: These were the lines of an obligator who belonged to the Canton of Inquisition. Marsh hadn't just infiltrated the Ministry, he'd chosen the most dangerous section of it to infiltrate.

"But, you'll always have them," Vin said. "They're so distinctive—everywhere you go, you'll be known as either an obligator or a fraud."

"That was part of the price he paid to infiltrate the Ministry, Vin," Kelsier said quietly.

"It doesn't matter," Marsh said. "I didn't have much of a life before this anyway. Look, can we hurry? I'm expected to be somewhere soon. Obligators lead busy lives, and I only have a few minutes' leeway."

"All right," Kelsier said. "I assume your infiltration went well, then?"

"It went fine," Marsh said tersely. "Too well, actually—I think I might have distinguished myself from the group. I assumed that I would be at a disadvantage, since I didn't have the same five years of training that the other acolytes did. I made certain to answer questions as thoroughly as possible, and to perform my duties with precision. However, I apparently know more about the Ministry than even some of its members do. I'm certainly more competent than this batch of newcomers, and the prelans have noticed that."

Kelsier chuckled. "You always were an overachiever."

Marsh snorted quietly. "Anyway, my knowledge—not to mention my skill as a Seeker—has already earned me an outstanding reputation. I'm not sure how closely I want the prelans paying attention to me; that background we devised begins to sound a bit flimsy when an Inquisitor is grilling you."

Vin frowned. "You told them that you're a Misting?"

"Of course I did," Marsh said. "The Ministry—particularly the Canton of Inquisition—recruits noblemen Seekers diligently. The fact that I'm one is enough to keep them from asking too many questions about my background. They're happy enough to have me, despite the fact that I'm a fair bit older than most acolytes."

"Besides," Kelsier said, "he needed to tell them he was a Misting so that he could get into the more secretive Ministry sects. Most of the higher-ranking obligators are Mistings of one sort or another. They tend to favor their own kind."

"With good reason," Marsh said, speaking quickly. "Kell, the Ministry is far more competent than we assumed."

"What do you mean?"

"They make use of their Mistings," Marsh said. "*Good* use of them. They have bases throughout the city—Soothing stations, as they call them. Each one contains a couple of Ministry Soothers whose only duty is to extend a dampening influence around them, calming and depressing the emotions of everyone in the area."

Kelsier hissed quietly. "How many?"

"Dozens," Marsh said. "Concentrated in skaa sections of the city. They know that the skaa are beaten, but they want to make sure things stay that way."

"Bloody hell!" Kelsier said. "I always thought that the skaa inside Luthadel seemed more beaten down than others. No wonder we had so much trouble recruiting. The people's emotions are under a constant Soothing!"

Marsh nodded. "The Ministry Soothers are good, Kell—*very* good. Even better than Breeze. All they do is Soothe all day, every day. And, since they're not trying to get you to do anything specific—instead just keeping you from extreme emotional ranges—they're very hard to notice.

"Each team has a Smoker to keep them hidden, as well as a Seeker to watch for passing Allomancers. I'll bet this is where the Inquisitors get a lot of their leads—most of our people are smart enough not to burn when they know that there's an obligator in the area, but they're more lax in the slums."

"Can you get us a list of the stations?" Kelsier asked. "We need to know where those Seekers are, Marsh."

Marsh nodded. "I'll try. I'm on my way to a station right now—they always do personnel changes at night, to maintain their secret. The upper ranks have taken an interest in me, and they're letting me visit some stations to become familiar with their work. I'll see if I can get a list for you."

Kelsier nodded in the darkness.

"Just . . . don't be stupid with the information, all right?" Marsh said. "We have to be careful, Kell. The Ministry has kept these stations secret for quite some time. Now that we know about them, we have a serious advantage. Don't waste it."

"I won't," Kelsier promised. "What about the Inquisitors? Did you find anything out about them?"

Marsh stood quietly for a moment. "They're . . . strange, Kell. I don't know. They seem to have all of the Allomantic powers, so I assume that they were once Mistborn. I can't find out much else about them—though I do know that they age."

"Really?" Kelsier said with interest. "So, they're not immortal?"

"No," Marsh said. "The obligators say that Inquisitors change occasionally. The creatures are very long-lived, but they do eventually die of old age. New ones must be recruited from noblemen ranks. They're people, Kell—they've just been . . . changed."

Kelsier nodded. "If they can die of old age, then there's probably other ways to kill them too."

"That's what I think," Marsh said. "I'll see what I can find, but don't get your hopes up. The Inquisitors don't have many dealings with normal obligators—there's political tension between the two groups. The lord prelan leads the church, but the Inquisitors think that they should be in charge."

"Interesting," Kelsier said slowly. Vin could practically hear his mind working on the new information.

"Anyway, I should go," Marsh said. "I had to jog all the way here, and I'm going to be late getting to my appointment anyway."

Kelsier nodded, and Marsh began to move away, picking his way over the rubble in his dark obligator's robe.

"Marsh," Kelsier said as Marsh reached the doorway.

Marsh turned.

"Thank you," Kelsier said. "I can only guess how dangerous this is."

"I'm not doing this for you, Kell," Marsh said. "But . . . I appreciate the sentiment. I'll try and send you another missive once I have more information."

"Be careful," Kelsier said.

Marsh vanished out into the misty night. Kelsier stood in the fallen room for a few minutes, staring after his brother.

He wasn't lying about that either, Vin thought. *He really* does *care for Marsh.*

"Let's go," Kelsier said. "We should get you back to Mansion Renoux—House Lekal is throwing another party in a few days, and you'll need to be there."

Sometimes, my companions claim that I worry and question too much. However, while I may wonder about my stature as the hero, there is one thing that I have never questioned: the ultimate good of our quest.

The Deepness must be destroyed. I have seen it, and I have felt it. This name we give it is too weak a word, I think. Yes, it is deep and unfathomable, but it is also terrible. Many do not realize that it is sentient, but I have sensed its mind, such that it is, the few times I have confronted it directly.

It is a thing of destruction, madness, and corruption. It would destroy this world not out of spite or out of animosity, but simply because that is what it does.

28

KEEP LEKAL'S BALLROOM WAS SHAPED like the inside of a pyramid. The dance floor was set on a waist-high platform at the very center of the room, and the dining tables sat on four similar platforms surrounding it. Servants scuttled through the trenches running between the platforms, delivering food to the dining aristocrats.

Four tiers of balconies ran along the inside perimeter of the pyramidal room, each one a little closer to the point at the top, each one extending just a little bit more over the dance floor. Though the main room was well lit, the balconies themselves were shadowed by their overhangs. The design was intended to allow proper viewing of the keep's most distinctive artistic feature—the small stained-glass windows that lined each balcony.

Lekal noblemen bragged that while other keeps had larger windows, Keep Lekal had the most detailed ones. Vin had to admit that they were impressive. She'd seen so many stained-glass windows over the last few months that she was beginning to take them for granted. Keep Lekal's windows, however, put most of them to shame. Each of these was an extravagant, detailed marvel of resplendent color. Exotic animals pranced, distant landscapes enticed, and portraits of famous noblemen sat proudly.

There were also, of course, the requisite pictures dedicated to the Ascension. Vin could recognize these more easily now, and she was surprised to see references to things she had read in the logbook. The hills of emerald green. The steep mountains, with faint wavelike lines coming from the tips. A deep, dark lake. And . . . blackness. The Deepness. A chaotic thing of destruction.

He defeated it, Vin thought. *But . . . what was it?* Perhaps the end of the logbook would reveal more.

Vin shook her head, leaving the alcove—and its black window—behind. She strolled along the second balcony, wearing a pure white gown—an outfit she would never have been able to even imagine during her life as a skaa. Ash and soot had been too much a part of her life, and she didn't think she'd even had a concept of what a pristine white looked like. That knowledge made the dress even more wondrous to her. She hoped she would never lose that—the sense within herself of how life had been before. It made her appreciate what she had so much more than the real nobility seemed to.

She continued along the balcony, seeking her prey. Glittering colors shone from backlit windows, sparkling light across the floor. Most of the windows glowed inside small viewing alcoves along the balcony, and so the balcony before her was interspersed with pockets of dark and color. Vin didn't stop to study any more of the windows; she'd done quite a bit of that during her first balls at Keep Lekal. This night she had business to attend to.

She found her quarry halfway down the east balcony walkway. Lady Kliss was speaking with a group of people, so Vin paused, pretending to study a window. Kliss's group soon broke up—one could generally only take so much of Kliss at a time. The short woman began to walk along the balcony toward Vin.

When she drew close, Vin turned, as if in surprise. "Why, Lady Kliss! I haven't seen you all evening."

Kliss turned eagerly, obviously excited by the prospect of another person with whom to gossip. "Lady Valette!" she said, waddling forward. "You missed Lord Cabe's ball last week! Not due to a relapse of your earlier malady, I hope?"

"No," Vin said. "I spent that evening dining with my uncle."

"Oh," Kliss said, disappointed. A relapse would have made a better story. "Well, that's good."

"I hear you have some interesting news about Lady Tren-Pedri Delouse," Vin said carefully. "I myself have heard some interesting things lately." She eyed Kliss, implying that she'd be willing to trade tidbits.

"Oh, that!" Kliss said eagerly. "Well, *I* heard that Tren-Pedri isn't at all interested in a union with House Aime, though her father is implying that there will be a wedding soon. You know how the Aime sons are, though. Why, Fedren is an *absolute* buffoon."

Inwardly, Vin rolled her eyes. Kliss just kept on talking, not even noticing that Vin had something she herself wanted to share. *Using subtlety on this woman is about as effective as trying to sell bathwater perfumes to a plantation skaa.*

"That *is* interesting," Vin said, interrupting Kliss. "Perhaps Tren-Pedri's hesitance comes because of House Aime's connection to House Hasting."

Kliss paused. "Why would that be?"

"Well, we all know what House Hasting is planning."

"We do?" Kliss asked.

Vin pretended to look embarrassed. "Oh. Perhaps that isn't known yet. Please, Lady Kliss, forget that I said anything."

"Forget?" Kliss said. "Why, it's already forgotten. But, come now, you can't just stop. What do you mean?"

"I shouldn't say," Vin said. "It's just something I overheard my uncle talking about."

"Your uncle?" Kliss asked, growing more eager. "What did he say? You know that you can trust me."

"Well . . ." Vin said. "He said that House Hasting was relocating a lot of resources back to its plantations in the Southern Dominance. My uncle was quite happy—Hasting has withdrawn from some of its contracts, and my uncle was hoping to get them instead."

"Relocating . . ." Kliss said. "Why, they wouldn't do that unless they were planning to withdraw from the city. . . ."

"Could you blame them?" Vin asked quietly. "I mean, who wants to risk what happened to House Tekiel?"

"Who indeed . . ." Kliss said. She was practically shaking with eagerness to go share the news.

"Anyway, please, this is obviously only hearsay," Vin said. "You probably shouldn't tell anyone about it."

"Of course," Kliss said. "Um . . . excuse me. I need to go refresh myself."

"Of course," Vin said, watching the woman zip away toward the balcony stairs.

Vin smiled. House Hasting was making no such preparations, of course; Hasting was one of the strongest families in the city, and wouldn't likely withdraw. However, Dockson was back at the shop forging documents which, when delivered to the right places, would imply that Hasting was planning to do what Vin had said.

If all went well, the entire city would soon expect a Hasting withdrawal. Their allies would plan for it, and might even begin to withdraw themselves. People seeking to buy weapons would instead look to other places, fearing that Hasting wouldn't be able to make good on contracts once it left. When Hasting *didn't* withdraw, it would make them look indecisive. Their allies gone, their income weakened, they could very well be the next house to fall.

House Hasting, however, was one of the easy ones to work against. It had a reputation for extreme subterfuge, and people would believe that it was planning a secret retreat. In addition, Hasting was a strong mercantile house—meaning it depended a great deal upon its contracts to survive. A house with such an obvious, dominating source of income also had an obvious weakness. Lord Hasting had worked hard to increase his house's influence over the last few decades, and in doing so he had extended his house's resources to their limits.

Other houses were far more stable. Vin sighed, turning and strolling down the walkway, eyeing the massive clock set between the balconies on the other side of the chamber.

Venture would not fall easily. It remained powerful through the sheer force of fortune; though it participated in some contracts, it didn't rely on them like other houses. Venture was rich enough, and powerful enough, that even mercantile disaster would only jostle it.

In a way, Venture's stability was a good thing—for Vin, at least. The house had no obvious weaknesses, so maybe the crew wouldn't be too disappointed when she couldn't discover any way to bring it down. After all, they didn't *absolutely* need to destroy House Venture; doing so would simply make the plan go more smoothly.

Whatever happened, Vin had to make sure that Venture didn't suffer the same fate as House Tekiel. Their reputation destroyed, their finances unhinged, the Tekiel had tried to pull out of the city—and this final show of weakness had been too much. Some of Tekiel's nobility had been assassinated before they left; the rest had been found in the burned-out ruins of their canal boats, apparently hit by bandits. Vin, however, knew of no thieving band who would dare slaughter so many noblemen.

Kelsier still hadn't been able to discover which house was behind the murders, but the Luthadel nobility didn't seem to care who the culprit was. House Tekiel had allowed itself to grow weak, and nothing was more embarrassing to the aristocracy than a Great House that couldn't maintain itself. Kelsier had been right: Though polite groups met at balls, the nobility were more than willing to stab each other square in the chest if it benefited them.

Kind of like thieving crews, she thought. *The nobility really aren't that different from the people I grew up around.*

The atmosphere was only made more dangerous by its polite niceties. Underneath that front were plots, assassinations, and—perhaps most importantly—Mistborn. It was no accident that all of the balls she had attended recently had displayed great numbers of guards, both wearing armor and not. The parties now served the additional purpose of warning and showing strength.

Elend is safe, she told herself. *Despite what he thinks of his family, they've done a good job of maintaining their place in the Luthadel hierarchy. He's the heir—they'll protect him from assassins.*

She wished those assertions sounded just a bit more convincing. She knew that Shan Elariel was planning something. House Venture might be safe, but Elend himself was a little bit . . . oblivious sometimes. If Shan did something against him personally, it might or might not be a major blow against House Venture—but it would certainly be a major blow against Vin.

"Lady Valette Renoux," a voice said. "I do believe that you're late."

Vin turned to see Elend lounging in an alcove to her left. She smiled, glancing down at the clock, noticing that it was indeed a few minutes past the time when she had promised to meet him. "I must be picking up bad habits from some friends of mine," she said, stepping into the alcove.

"Now, see, I didn't say it was a *bad* thing," Elend said, smiling. "Why, I'd say that it is a lady's courtly duty to be a bit dilatory. It does gentlemen good to be forced to wait upon a woman's whims—or, so my mother was always fond of telling me."

"It sounds like she was a wise woman," Vin said. The alcove was just large enough for two people standing sideways. She stood across from him, the balcony overhang a short distance to her left, a marvelous lavender window to her right, their feet nearly touching.

"Oh, I don't know about that," Elend said. "She married my father, after all."

"Thereby joining the most powerful house in the Final Empire. You can't do much better than that—though, I suppose she could have tried to marry the Lord Ruler. Last I knew, though, he wasn't in the market for a wife."

"Pity," Elend said. "Maybe he'd look a little less depressed if there were a woman in his life."

"I guess that would depend on the woman." Vin glanced to the side as a small group of courtgoers strolled past. "You know, this isn't exactly the most private location. People are giving us odd looks."

"You're the one who stepped in here with me," Elend pointed out.

"Yes, well, I wasn't thinking about the gossip we might start."

"Let it start," Elend said standing up straight.

"Because it will make your father angry?"

Elend shook his head. "I don't care about that anymore, Valette." Elend took a step forward, bringing them even closer together. Vin could feel his breath. He stood there for a moment before speaking. "I think I'm going to kiss you."

Vin shivered slightly. "I don't think you want to do that, Elend."

"Why?"

"How much do you really know about me?"

"Not as much as I'd like to," he said.

"Not as much as you need to, either," Vin said, looking up into his eyes.

"So tell me," he said.

"I can't. Not right now."

Elend stood for a moment, then nodded slightly and pulled away. He walked out onto the balcony walkway. "So, shall we go for a stroll, then?"

"Yes," Vin said, relieved—yet just a bit disappointed as well.

"It's for the best," Elend said. "That alcove has absolutely *terrible* reading light."

"Don't you dare," Vin said, eyeing the book in his pocket as she joined him on the walkway. "Read when you're with someone else, not me."

"But that's how our relationship began!"

"And that's how it could end too," Vin said, taking his arm.

Elend smiled. They weren't the only couple walking the balcony, and down below, other pairs spun slowly to the faint music.

It seems so peaceful. Yet, just a few days ago, many of these people stood and watched idly as women and children were beheaded.

She felt Elend's arm, his warmth beside her. Kelsier said that he smiled so much because he felt he needed to take what joy he could in the world—to relish the moments of happiness that seemed so infrequent in the Final Empire. Strolling for a time beside Elend, Vin thought she was beginning to understand how Kelsier felt.

"Valette . . ." Elend said slowly.

"What?"

"I want you to leave Luthadel," he said.

"*What?*"

He paused, turning to look at her. "I've thought about this a lot. You may not realize it, but the city is becoming dangerous. Very dangerous."

"I know."

"Then you know that a small house without allies has no place in the Central Dominance right now," Elend said. "Your uncle was brave to come here and try to establish himself, but he chose the wrong time. I . . . I think things are going to get out of hand here very soon. When that happens, I can't guarantee your safety."

"My uncle knows what he's doing, Elend."

"This is *different*, Valette," Elend said. "Entire houses are falling. The Tekiel family wasn't slaughtered by bandits—that was the work of House Hasting. Those won't be the last deaths we see before this is through."

Vin paused, thinking of Shan again. "But . . . you're safe, right? House Venture—it's not like the others. It's stable."

Elend shook his head. "We're even more vulnerable than the rest, Valette."

"But, your fortune is large," Vin said. "You don't depend on contracts."

"They may not be visible," Elend said quietly, "but they're there, Valette. We put on a good show, and the others assume that we have more than we do. However, with the Lord Ruler's house taxings . . . well, the only way we maintain so much power in this city is through income. Secret income."

Vin frowned, and Elend leaned closer, speaking almost in a whisper. "My family mines the Lord Ruler's atium, Valette," he said. "That's where our wealth comes from. In a way, our stability depends almost completely on the Lord Ruler's whims. He doesn't like to bother collecting the atium himself, but he gets *very* perturbed if the delivery schedule is disrupted."

Find out more! instinct told her. *This is the secret; this is what Kelsier needs.* "Oh, Elend," Vin whispered. "You shouldn't be telling me this."

"Why not?" he said. "I trust you. Look, you need to understand how dangerous things are. The atium supply has been having some troubles lately. Ever since. . . . well, something happened a few years ago. Ever since then, things have been different. My father can't meet the Lord Ruler's quotas, and last time that happened . . ."

"What?"

"Well," Elend said, looking troubled. "Let's just say that things could soon grow very bad for the Ventures. The Lord Ruler depends on that atium, Valette—it's one of the prime ways he controls the nobility. A house without atium is a house that can't defend itself from Mistborn. By keeping a large reserve, the Lord Ruler controls the market, making himself extremely wealthy. He funds his armies by making atium scarce, then selling extra bits for lavish amounts. If you knew more about the economics of Allomancy, this would probably make a lot more sense to you."

Oh, trust me. I understand more than you think. And now I know far more than I should.

Elend paused, smiling pleasantly as an obligator strolled along the balcony walkway beside them. The obligator looked them over as he passed, eyes thoughtful within their web of tattoos.

Elend turned back to her as soon as the obligator had passed. "I want you to leave," he repeated. "People know that I've paid attention to you. Hopefully, they'll assume it was just to spite my father, but they could still try to use you. The Great Houses wouldn't have any qualms about crushing your entire family just to get at me and my father. You have to go."

"I'll . . . think about it," Vin said.

"There isn't much time left for thinking," Elend warned. "I want you to leave before you get too involved with what is going on in this city."

I'm already involved so much more than you think. "I said I'd think about it," she said. "Look, Elend, I think you should be more worried about yourself. I think Shan Elariel is going to try something to strike against you."

"Shan?" Elend said with amusement. "She's harmless."

"I don't think she is, Elend. You need to be more careful."

He laughed. "Look at us . . . each one trying to convince the other how dreadfully dire the situation is, each one bull-headedly refusing to listen to the other."

Vin paused, then smiled.

Elend sighed. "You're not going to listen to me, are you? Is there anything I can do to make you leave?"

"Not right now," she said quietly. "Look, Elend, can't we just enjoy the time we have together? If things continue as they are, we might not have many more opportunities like this for a while."

He paused, then finally nodded. She could see he was still troubled, but he did turn back to their walk, letting her gently take his arm again as they strolled. They walked together for a time, silent until something drew Vin's attention. She removed her hands from his arm, instead reaching down to take his hand in her own.

He glanced at her, frowning in confusion as she tapped the ring on his finger. "It really is metal," she said, a bit surprised, despite what she'd been told.

Elend nodded. "Pure gold."

"Don't you worry about . . ."

"Allomancers?" Elend asked. He shrugged. "I don't know—they're not the sort of thing that I've ever had to deal with. You don't wear metal, out on the plantations?"

Vin shook her head, tapping one of the barrettes in her hair. "Painted wood," she said.

Elend nodded. "Probably wise," he said. "But, well, the longer you stay in Luthadel, the more you'll realize that little we do here is done in the name of wisdom. The Lord Ruler wears metal rings—and so, therefore, does the nobility. Some philosophers think that's all part of His plan. The Lord Ruler wears metal because he knows that the nobility will mimic him, and therefore give his Inquisitors power over them."

"Do you agree?" Vin asked, taking his arm again as they walked. "With the philosophers, I mean?"

Elend shook his head. "No," he said in a quieter voice. "The Lord Ruler . . . he's just arrogant. I've read of warriors, long ago, who would run into battle without armor on, supposedly to prove how brave and strong they were. That's how this is, I think—though admittedly on a far more subtle level. He wears metal to flaunt his power, to show how unfrightened—how unthreatened—he is by anything we could do to him."

Well, Vin thought, *he's willing to call the Lord Ruler arrogant. Perhaps I can get him to admit a little more. . . .*

Elend paused, glancing over at the clock. "I'm afraid I don't have a whole lot of time tonight, Valette."

"That's right," Vin said. "You'll need to go off and meet with your friends." She glanced at him, trying to gauge his reaction.

He didn't seem very surprised. He simply raised an eyebrow in her direction. "Indeed, I will. You're very observant."

"It doesn't take much observing," Vin said. "Anytime we're at Keeps Hasting, Venture, Lekal, or Elariel, you run off with the same people."

"My drinking friends," Elend said with a smile. "An unlikely group in today's political climate, but one that helps annoy my father."

"What do you do at these meetings?" Vin asked.

"We talk philosophy, mostly," Elend said. "We're kind of a stuffy lot—which isn't too surprising, I guess, if you know any of us. We talk about the government, about politics . . . about the Lord Ruler."

"What about him?"

"Well, we don't like some of the things he's done with the Final Empire."

"So you *do* want to overthrow him!" Vin said.

Elend gave her a strange look. "Overthrow him? What gave you that idea, Valette? He's the Lord Ruler—he's God. We can't do anything about him being in charge." He looked away as they continued to walk. "No, my friends and I, we just . . . wish the Final Empire could be a little different. We can't change things now, but maybe someday—assuming we all survive the next year or so—we'll be in positions to influence the Lord Ruler."

"To do what?"

"Well, take those executions a few days ago," Elend said. "I don't see that they did any good. The skaa rebelled. In reprisal, the Ministry executed a few hundred random people. What is that going to do besides make the populace even *more* angry? So, next time the rebellion will be bigger. Does that mean that the Lord Ruler will order more people beheaded? How long can that continue before there just aren't any skaa left?"

Vin walked thoughtfully. "And what would you do, Elend Venture?" she finally said. "If you were in charge."

"I don't know," Elend confessed. "I've read a lot of books—some that I'm not supposed to—and I haven't found any easy answers. I'm pretty certain, however, that beheading people won't solve anything. The Lord Ruler has been around for a long time—you'd think that he'd have found a better way. But, anyway, we'll have to continue this later. . . ." He slowed, turning to look at her.

"Time already?" she asked.

Elend nodded. "I promised I'd meet them, and they kind of look to me. I suppose I could tell them I'll be late. . . ."

Vin shook her head. "Go drink with your friends. I'll be fine—I have a few more people I need to talk to anyway." She did need to get back to work; Breeze and Dockson had spent hours planning and preparing the lies that she was supposed to spread, and they would be waiting for her report back at Clubs's shop after the party.

Elend smiled. "Maybe I shouldn't worry about you so much. Who knows—considering all of your political maneuvering, maybe House Renoux will soon be the power in town, and I'll just be a lowly beggar."

Vin smiled, and he bowed—winking at her—then was off

toward the stairs. Vin walked slowly over to the balcony railing, looking down at the people dancing and dining below.

So he's not a revolutionary, she thought. *Kelsier was right again. I wonder if he ever gets tired of that.*

But still, she couldn't feel too disappointed with Elend. Not everyone was so insane that they'd think to overthrow their god-emperor. The mere fact that Elend was willing to think for himself set him apart from the rest; he was a good man, one who deserved a woman who was worthy of his trust.

Unfortunately, he had Vin.

So House Venture secretly mines the Lord Ruler's atium, she thought. *They must be the ones who administer the Pits of Hathsin.*

It was a frighteningly precarious position for a house to be in—their finances depended directly on pleasing the Lord Ruler. Elend thought that he was being careful, but Vin was worried. He wasn't taking Shan Elariel seriously enough—of that, Vin was certain. She turned, walking intently from the balcony and down to the main floor.

She found Shan's table easily; the woman always sat with a large group of attendant noblewomen, presiding like a lord over his plantation. Vin paused. She'd never approached Shan directly. Someone, however, needed to protect Elend; he was obviously too foolish to do it himself.

Vin strode forward. Shan's Terrisman studied Vin as she approached. He was so different from Sazed—he didn't have the same . . . spirit. This man maintained a flat expression, like some creature carved of stone. A few of the ladies shot disapproving glances toward Vin, but most of them—Shan included—ignored her.

Vin stood awkwardly beside the table, waiting for a lull in the conversation. There was none. Finally, she just took a few steps closer to Shan.

"Lady Shan?" she asked.

Shan turned with an icy glare. "I didn't send for you, country girl."

"Yes, but I've found some books like you—"

"I no longer require your services," Shan said, turning

away. "I can deal with Elend Venture on my own. Now, be a good little twit and stop bothering me."

Vin stood, stunned. "But, your plan—"

"I *said* that you are *no longer needed.* You think I was harsh on you before, girl? That was when you were on my good side. Try annoying me now."

Vin wilted reflexively before the woman's demeaning gaze. She seemed . . . disgusted. Angry, even. Jealous?

She must have figured it out, Vin thought. *She finally realized out that I'm not just playing with Elend. She knows that I care for him, and doesn't trust me to keep her secrets.*

Vin backed away from the table. Apparently, she would have to use other methods to discover Shan's plans.

Despite what he often said, Elend Venture did not consider himself to be a rude man. He was more of a . . . verbal philosopher. He liked to test and turn conversation to see how people would react. Like the great thinkers of old, he pushed boundaries and experimented with unconventional methods.

Of course, he thought, holding his cup of brandy up before his eyes, inspecting it musingly, *most of those old philosophers were eventually executed for treason.* Not exactly the most successful role models.

His evening political conversation with his group was finished, and he had retired with several friends to Keep Lekal's gentlemen's lounge, a small chamber adjacent to the ballroom. It was furnished in deep green colors, and the chairs were comfortable; it would have been a nice place to read, had he been in a slightly better mood. Jastes sat across from him, puffing contentedly on his pipe. It was good to see the young Lekal looking so calm. These last few weeks had been difficult for him.

House war, Elend thought. *What terrible timing. Why now? Things were going so well. . . .*

Telden returned with a refilled drink a few moments later.

"You know," Jastes said, gesturing with his pipe, "any one of the servants in here would have brought you a new drink."

"I felt like stretching my legs," Telden said, settling into the third chair.

"And you flirted with no less than three women on your way back," Jastes said. "I counted."

Telden smiled, sipping his drink. The large man never just "sat"—he lounged. Telden could look relaxed and comfortable no matter what the situation, his sharp suits and well-styled hair enviably handsome.

Maybe I should pay just a little more attention to things like that, Elend thought to himself. *Valette suffers my hair the way it is, but would she like it better if I had it styled?*

Elend often intended to make his way to a stylist or tailor, but other things tended to steal his attention. He'd get lost in his studies or spend too long reading, then find himself late for his appointments. Again.

"Elend is quiet this evening," Telden noticed. Though other groups of gentlemen sat in the dim lounge, the chairs were spread out enough to allow for private conversations.

"He's been like that a lot, lately," Jastes said.

"Ah, yes," Telden said, frowning slightly.

Elend knew them well enough to take the hint. "Now, see, why must people be like this? If you have something to say, why not simply say it?"

"Politics, my friend," Jastes said. "We are—if you haven't noticed—noblemen."

Elend rolled his eyes.

"All right, I'll say it," Jastes replied, running his hand through his hair—a nervous habit that Elend was sure contributed somewhat to the young man's growing baldness. "You've been spending a lot of time with that Renoux girl, Elend."

"There is a simple explanation for that," Elend said. "You see, I happen to like her."

"Not good, Elend," Telden said with a shake of his head. "Not good."

"Why?" Elend asked. "You seem pleased enough to ignore class variances yourself, Telden. I've seen you flirt with half the serving girls in the room."

"I'm not heir to my house," Telden said.

"And," Jastes said, "these girls are trustworthy. My family hired these women—we know their houses, their backgrounds, and their allegiances."

Elend frowned. "What are you implying?"

"Something's strange about that girl, Elend," Jastes said. He'd gone back to his normal nervous self, his pipe sitting unnoticed in its holder on the table.

Telden nodded. "She got too close to you too quickly, Elend. She wants something."

"Like what?" Elend asked, growing annoyed.

"Elend, Elend," Jastes said. "You can't just avoid the game by saying you don't want to play. It'll find you. Renoux moved into town just as house tensions began to rise, and he brought with him an unknown scion—a girl who immediately began to woo the most important and available young man in Luthadel. Doesn't that seem odd to you?"

"Actually," Elend noted, "I approached her first—if only because she had stolen my reading spot."

"But, you have to admit that it's suspicious how quickly she latched on to you," Telden said. "If you're going to dabble with romance, Elend, you need to learn one thing: You can play with women if you want, but don't let yourself get too close to them. That's where the trouble starts."

Elend shook his head. "Valette is different."

The other two shared a look, then Telden shrugged, turning back to his drink. Jastes, however, sighed, then stood and stretched. "Anyway, I should probably be going."

"One more drink," Telden said.

Jastes shook his head, running a hand through his hair. "You know how my parents are on ball nights—if I don't go out and bid farewell to at least *some* of the guests, I'll be nagged about it for weeks."

The younger man wished them good night, walking back toward the main ballroom. Telden sipped his drink, eyeing Elend.

"I'm not thinking about her," Elend said testily.

"What, then?"

"The meeting tonight," Elend said. "I'm not sure if I like how it went."

"Bah," the large man said with a wave of his hand. "You're getting as bad as Jastes. What happened to the man who attended these meetings just to relax and enjoy time with his friends?"

"He's worried," Elend said. "Some of his friends might end up in charge of their houses sooner than he expected, and he's worried that none of us are ready."

Telden snorted. "Don't be so melodramatic," he said, smiling and winking to the serving girl who came to clear away his empty cups. "I have a feeling that this is all just going to blow over. In a few months, we'll look back and wonder what all the fretting was about."

Kale Tekiel won't look back, Elend thought.

The conversation waned, however, and Telden eventually excused himself. Elend sat for a while longer, opening *The Dictates of Society* for another read, but he had trouble concentrating. He turned the cup of brandy in his fingers, but didn't drink much.

I wonder if Valette's out yet. . . . He'd tried to find her once his meeting was over, but apparently she'd been in a private gathering of her own.

That girl, he thought lazily, *is far too interested in politics for her own good.* Perhaps he was just jealous—only a few months in court, and she already seemed to be more competent than he was. She was so fearless, so bold, so . . . interesting. She didn't fit any of the courtly stereotypes he'd been taught to expect.

Could Jastes be right? he wondered. *She certainly is different from other women, and she did imply there were things about her I didn't know.*

Elend pushed the thought out of his mind. Valette was different, true—but she was also innocent, in a way. Eager, full of wonder and spunk.

He worried about her; she obviously didn't know how dangerous Luthadel could be. There was so much more to politics in the city than simple parties and petty intrigues. What would happen if someone decided to send a Mistborn to deal with her and her uncle? Renoux was poorly connected, and none of the court's members would blink twice at a few assassinations in Fellise. Did Valette's uncle know how to take the proper precautions? Did he even worry about Allomancers?

Elend sighed. He'd just have to make certain that Valette left the area. That was the only option.

By the time his carriage reached Keep Venture, Elend had decided that he'd drunk too much. He made his way up to his rooms, looking forward to his bed and pillows.

The hallway to his bedroom, however, passed by his father's study. The door was open, and light still spilled out despite the late hour. Elend tried to walk quietly on the carpeted floor, but he'd never really been all that stealthy.

"Elend?" his father's voice called from the study. "Come in here."

Elend sighed quietly. Lord Straff Venture didn't miss much. He was a Tineye—his senses were so keen that he'd probably heard Elend's carriage approaching outside. *If I don't deal with him now, he'll just send the servants to pester me until I come down to speak with him. . . .*

Elend turned and walked into the study. His father sat in his chair, speaking quietly with TenSoon—the Venture Kandra. Elend still wasn't used to the creature's most recent body, which had once belonged to a servant in the Hasting household. Elend shivered as it noticed him. It bowed, then quietly retreated from the room.

Elend leaned against the doorframe. Straff's chair sat in front of several shelves of books—not a single one of which, Elend was confident, his father had ever read. The room was lit by two lamps, their hoods mostly closed to allow out only a bit of light.

"You attended the ball tonight," Straff said. "What did you learn?"

Elend reached up, rubbing his forehead. "That I have a tendency to drink far too much brandy."

Straff was not amused by the comment. He was the perfect imperial nobleman—tall, firm-shouldered, always dressed in a tailored vest and suit. "You met with that . . . woman again?" he asked.

"Valette? Hum, yes. Not for as long as I would have liked, though."

"I forbade you from spending time with her."

"Yes," Elend said. "I remember."

Straff's expression darkened. He stood, walking over to the desk. "Oh, Elend," he said. "When are you going to get over this childish temperament you have? Do you think I don't realize that you act foolishly simply to spite me?"

"Actually, I got over my 'childish temperament' some time ago, Father—it just seems that my natural inclinations work even better to annoy you. I wish I had known that earlier; I could have saved a great deal of effort in my younger years."

His father snorted, then held up a letter. "I dictated this to Staxles a short time ago. It is an acceptance of a lunch appointment with Lord Tegas tomorrow afternoon. If a house war *does* come, I want to make certain we are in a position to destroy the Hastings as quickly as possible, and Tegas could be a strong ally. He has a daughter. I'd like you to dine with her at the luncheon."

"I'll consider it," Elend said, tapping his head. "I'm not sure what kind of state I'll be in tomorrow morning. Too much brandy, remember?"

"You'll be there, Elend. This is not a request."

Elend paused. A part of him wanted to snap back at his father, to make a stand—not because he cared about where he dined, but because of something far more important.

Hasting is the second-most-powerful house in the city. If we made an allegiance with them, together we could keep Luthadel from chaos. We could stop the house war, not enflame it.

That's what his books had done to him—they had changed him from rebellious fop into would-be philosopher. Unfortunately, he'd been a fool for so long. Was it any wonder that Straff hadn't noticed the change in his son? Elend himself was only starting to realize it.

Straff continued to glare at him, and Elend looked away. "I'll think about it," he said.

Straff waved his hand dismissively, turning.

Trying to salvage something of his pride, Elend continued. "You probably don't even have to worry about the Hastings—it seems that they're making preparations to bolt the city."

"*What?*" Straff asked. "Where did you hear that?"

"At the ball," Elend said lightly.

"I thought you said you didn't learn anything important."

"Now, see, I never said anything of the sort. I just didn't feel like sharing with you."

Lord Venture frowned. "I don't know why I even care—anything you learn is bound to be worthless. I tried to train you in politics, boy. I really did. But now . . . well, I hope I live to see you dead, because this house is in for dire times if you ever take control."

"I know more than you think, Father."

Straff laughed, walking back to sit in his chair. "I doubt that, boy. Why, you can't even bed a woman properly—the last, and only, time I know about you trying it, *I* had to take you to the brothel myself."

Elend flushed. *Careful,* he told himself. *He's bringing that up on purpose. He knows how much it bothers you.*

"Get to bed, boy," Straff said with a wave of his hand. "You look terrible."

Elend stood for a moment, then finally ducked out into the hallway, sighing quietly to himself.

That's the difference between you and them, Elend, he thought. *Those philosophers you read—they were revolutionaries. They were willing to risk execution. You can't even stand up to your father.*

He walked tiredly up to his rooms—where, oddly, he found a servant waiting for him.

Elend frowned. "Yes?"

"Lord Elend, you have a guest," the man said.

"At this hour?"

"It's Lord Jastes Lekal, my lord."

Elend cocked his head slightly. *What in the Lord Ruler's name . . . ?* "He's waiting in the sitting room, I assume?"

"Yes, my lord," the servant said.

Elend turned regretfully away from his chambers, walking back down the hallway. He found Jastes waiting impatiently.

"Jastes?" Elend said tiredly, walking into the sitting room. "I hope you have something *very* important to tell me."

Jastes shuffled uncomfortably for a moment, looking even more nervous than normal.

"What?" Elend demanded, his patience waning.

"It's about the girl."

"Valette?" Elend asked. "You came here to discuss Valette? *Now?*"

"You should trust your friends more," Jastes said.

Elend snorted. "Trust *your* knowledge of women? No offense, Jastes, but I think not."

"I had her followed, Elend," Jastes blurted out.

Elend paused. "What?"

"I had her carriage followed. Or, at least, I had someone watch for it at the city gates. She wasn't in it when it left the city."

"What do you mean?" Elend asked, his frown deepening.

"She wasn't *in the carriage,* Elend," Jastes repeated. "While her Terrisman was producing papers for the guards, my man snuck up and peeked through the carriage window, and there was nobody inside.

"The carriage must have dropped her off somewhere in town. She's a spy from one of the other houses—they're trying to get at your father through you. They created the perfect woman to attract you—dark-haired, a bit mysterious, and outside of the regular political structure. They made her lowborn enough that it would be a scandal for you to be interested in her, then set her on you."

"Jastes, this is ridicu—"

"Elend," Jastes interrupted. "Tell me one more time: How did you meet her the first time?"

Elend paused. "She was standing on the balcony."

"In your reading spot," Jastes said. "Everyone knows that's where you usually go. Coincidence?"

Elend closed his eyes. *Not Valette. She* can't *be part of all this.* But, immediately, another thought occurred to him. *I told her about the atium! How could I be so stupid?*

It couldn't be true. He wouldn't believe that he had been duped so easily. But . . . could he risk it? He was a bad son, true, but he was no traitor to the house. He didn't want to see Venture fall; he wanted to lead it someday, so that perhaps he'd be able to change things.

He bid Jastes farewell, then walked back to his rooms with a distracted step. He felt too tired to think about house politics. However, when he finally got into bed, he found that he couldn't sleep.

Eventually, he rose, sending for a servant.

"Tell my father I want to make a trade," Elend explained to the man. "I'll go to his luncheon tomorrow, just as he wants." Elend paused, standing in his evening robe by his bedroom door.

"In exchange," he finally said, "tell him I want to borrow a couple of spies so that they can follow someone for me."

The others all think I should have had Kwaan executed for betraying me. To tell the truth, I'd probably kill him this moment if I knew where he'd gone. At the time, however, I just couldn't do it.

The man had become like a father to me. To this day, I don't know why he suddenly decided that I wasn't the Hero. Why did he turn against me, denouncing me to the entire Conclave of Worldbringers?

Would he rather that the Deepness win? Surely, even if I'm not the right one—as Kwaan now claims—my presence at the Well of Ascension couldn't possibly be worse than what will happen if the Deepness continues to destroy the land.

29

IT'S ALMOST OVER, VIN READ.

> We can see the cavern from our camp. It will take a few more hours of hiking to reach it, but I know that it is the right place. I can feel it somehow, feel it up there . . . pulsing, in my mind.
>
> It's so cold. I swear that the rocks themselves are made of ice, and the snow is deep enough in places that we have to dig

our way through. The wind blows all the time. I fear for Fedik—he hasn't been quite the same since the creature made of mist attacked him, and I worry that he will wander off a cliffside or slip through one of the many icy rifts in the ground.

The Terrismen, however, are a wonder. It is fortunate that we brought them, for no regular packmen would have survived the trip. The Terrismen don't seem to mind the cold—something about their strange metabolisms gives them a supernatural ability to resist the elements. Perhaps they have "saved up" heat from their bodies for later use?

They won't talk about their powers, however—and I am sure that Rashek is to blame. The other packmen look to him for leadership, though I don't think he has complete control over them. Before he was stabbed, Fedik feared that the Terrismen would abandon us up here in the ice. I don't think that will happen, however. I am here by providence of Terris prophecies—these men will not disobey their own religion simply because one of their number has taken a dislike to me.

I did finally confront Rashek. He did not want to speak to me, of course, but I forced him. Unleashed, he spoke at great length regarding his hatred of Khlennium and my people. He thinks that we have turned his people into little more than slaves. He thinks that Terrismen deserve far more—he keeps saying that his people should be "dominant" because of their supernatural powers.

I fear his words, for I see some truth in them. Yesterday, one of the packmen lifted a boulder of enormous size, then tossed it out of our way with an almost casual throw. I have not seen such a feat of strength in all my days.

These Terrismen could be very dangerous, I think. Perhaps we have treated them unfairly. However, men like Rashek must be contained—he irrationally believes that all people outside of Terris have oppressed him. He is such a young man to be so angry.

It is so cold. When this is finished, I think I should like to live where it is warm all year. Braches has told of such places, islands to the south where great mountains create fire.

What will it be like, when this is all over? I will be just a regular man again. An unimportant man. It sounds nice—more desirable, even, than a warm sun and a windless sky. I am so tired of being the Hero of Ages, tired of entering cities to find either armed hostility or fanatic adoration. I am tired of being loved and hated for what a bunch of old men say I will eventually do.

I want to be forgotten. Obscurity. Yes, that would be nice.

If men read these words, let them know that power is a heavy burden. Seek not to be bound by its chains. The Terris prophecies say that I will have the power to save the world. They hint, however, that I will have the power to destroy it as well.

I will have the ability to fulfill any wish of my heart. "He will take upon himself authority that no mortal should hold." Yet, the philosophers warned me that if I am self-serving with the power, my selfishness will taint it.

Is this a burden that any man should bear? Is this a temptation any man could resist? I feel strong now, but what will happen when I touch that power? I will save the world, certainly—but will I try to take it as well?

Such are my fears as I scribble with an ice-crusted pen on the eve before the world is reborn. Rashek watches. Hating me. The cavern lies above. Pulsing. My fingers quiver. Not from the cold.

Tomorrow, it will end.

Vin eagerly turned the page. The back page of the booklet, however, was empty. She turned it over, rereading the last few lines. Where was the next entry?

Sazed must not have finished the last part yet. She stood, sighing as she stretched. She'd finished the entire newest portion of the logbook in one sitting, a feat that surprised even her. The gardens of Mansion Renoux extended before her, the cultured pathways, broad-limbed trees, and quiet stream creating her favorite reading spot. The sun was low in the sky, and it was beginning to get chilly.

She wound her way up the path toward the mansion. Despite the chill evening, she could barely imagine a place like the one the Lord Ruler described. She had seen snow on some distant peaks, but she had rarely seen it fall—and even then it was usually just an icy slush. To experience that much snow day after day, to be in danger of having it fall upon you in great crushing avalanches . . .

A part of her wished that she could visit such places, no matter how dangerous. Though the logbook didn't describe the Lord Ruler's entire journey, some of the marvels it did include—the ice fields to the north, the great black lake, and the Terris waterfalls—sounded amazing.

If only he'd put in more detail about what things look like! she thought with annoyance. The Lord Ruler spent far too much time worrying. Though, admittedly, she was beginning to feel an odd sort of . . . familiarity with him through his words. She found it hard to associate the person in her mind with the dark creature that had caused so much death. What had occurred at the Well of Ascension? What could have changed him so drastically? She had to know.

She reached the mansion and went searching for Sazed. She was back to wearing dresses—it felt odd to be seen in trousers by anyone but the crewmembers. She smiled at Lord Renoux's interior steward as she passed, eagerly climbing the main entryway stairs and seeking out the library.

Sazed wasn't inside. His small desk sat empty, the lamp extinguished, the inkwell empty. Vin frowned in annoyance.

Wherever he is, he'd better be working on the translation!

She went back down the stairs, asking after Sazed, and a maid directed her to the main kitchen. Vin frowned, making her way down the back hallway. *Getting himself a snack, perhaps?*

She found Sazed standing amongst a small group of servants, pointing toward a list on the table and speaking in a low voice. He didn't notice Vin as she entered.

"Sazed?" Vin asked, interrupting him.

He turned. "Yes, Mistress Valette?" he asked, bowing slightly.

"What are you doing?"

"I am seeing to Lord Renoux's food stores, Mistress. Though I have been assigned to assist you, I am still his steward, and have duties to attend to when I am not otherwise occupied."

"Are you going to get back to the translation soon?"

Sazed cocked his head. "Translation, Mistress? It is finished."

"Where's the last part, then?"

"I gave it to you," Sazed said.

"No, you didn't," she said. "This part ends the night before they go into the cavern."

"That is the end, Mistress. That is as far as the logbook went."

"*What?*" she said. "But . . ."

Sazed glanced at the other servants. "We should speak of these things in private, I think." He gave them a few more instructions, pointing at the list, then nodded for Vin to join him as he made his way out the back kitchen exit and into the side gardens.

Vin stood dumbfounded for a moment, then hurried out to join him. "It can't end like that, Saze. We don't know what happened!"

"We can surmise, I think," Sazed said, walking down the garden path. The eastern gardens weren't as lavish as the ones Vin frequented, and were instead made up of smooth brown grass and the occasional shrub.

"Surmise what?" Vin asked.

"Well, the Lord Ruler must have done what was necessary to save the world, for we are still here."

"I suppose," Vin said. "But then he took the power for himself. That must have been what happened—he couldn't resist the temptation to use the power selfishly. But, why isn't there another entry? Why wouldn't he speak further of his accomplishments?"

"Perhaps the power changed him too much," Sazed said. "Or, maybe he simply didn't feel a need to record any more. He had accomplished his goal, and had become immortal as a side benefit. Keeping a journal for one's posterity becomes somewhat redundant when one is going to live forever, I think."

"That's just . . ." Vin ground her teeth in frustration. "It's a very unsatisfying end to a story, Sazed."

He smiled in amusement. "Be careful, Mistress—become too fond of reading, and you may just turn into a scholar."

Vin shook her head. "Not if all the books I read are going to end like this one!"

"If it is of any comfort," Sazed said, "you are not the only one who is disappointed by the logbook's contents. It didn't contain much that Master Kelsier could use—certainly, there was nothing about the Eleventh Metal. I feel somewhat guilty, since I am the one who benefited most from the book."

"But, there wasn't very much about the Terris religion either."

"Not much," Sazed agreed. "But, truly and regretfully, 'not much' is far more than we knew previously. I am only worried that I will not have an opportunity to pass this information on. I have sent a translated copy of the logbook to a location where my brethren and sister Keepers will know to check—it would be a pity if this new knowledge were to die with me."

"It won't," Vin said.

"Oh? Has my lady suddenly become an optimist?"

"Has my Terrisman suddenly become a smart-mouth?" Vin retorted.

"He always has been, I think," Sazed said with a slight smile. "It is one of the things that made him a poor steward—at least, in the eyes of most of his masters."

"Then they must have been fools," Vin said honestly.

"So I was inclined to think, Mistress," Sazed replied. "We should return to the mansion—we should not be seen out in the gardens when the mists arrive, I think."

"I'm just going to go back out into them."

"There are many of the grounds staff that do not know you are Mistborn, Mistress," Sazed said. "It would be a good secret to keep, I think."

"I know," Vin said, turning. "Let's go back then."

"A wise plan."

They walked for a few moments, enjoying the eastern garden's subtle beauty. The grasses were kept carefully trimmed, and they had been arranged in pleasant tiers, the occasional shrubbery giving accent. The southern garden was far more spectacular, with its brook, trees, and exotic plants. But the eastern garden had its own peace—the serenity of simplicity.

"Sazed?" Vin said in a quiet voice.

"Yes, Mistress?"

"It's all going to change, isn't it?"

"What specifically do you mean?"

"Everything," Vin said. "Even if we aren't all dead in a year, the crewmembers will be off working on other projects. Ham will probably be back with his family, Dox and Kelsier will be planning some new escapade, Clubs will be renting his shop to another crew. . . . Even these gardens that we've spent so much money on—they'll belong to someone else."

Sazed nodded. "What you say is likely. Though, if things go well, perhaps the skaa rebellion will be ruling Luthadel by this time next year."

"Maybe," Vin said. "But even still . . . things will change."

"That is the nature of all life, Mistress," Sazed said. "The world must change."

"I know," Vin said with a sigh. "I just wish . . . Well, I actually *like* my life now, Sazed. I like spending time with the crew, and I like training with Kelsier. I love going to balls with Elend on the weekends, love walking in these gardens with you. I don't want these things to change. I don't want my life to go back to the way it was a year ago."

"It doesn't have to, Mistress," Sazed said. "It could change for the better."

"It won't," Vin said quietly. "It's starting already—Kelsier has hinted that my training is almost finished. When I practice in the future, I'll have to do it alone.

"As for Elend, he doesn't even know that I'm skaa—and it's my job to try and destroy his family. Even if House Venture doesn't fall by my hand, others will bring it down—I know Shan Elariel is planning something, and I haven't been able to discover anything about her schemes.

"That's only the beginning, though. We face the Final Empire. We'll probably fail—to be honest, I don't see how things could possibly turn out otherwise. We'll fight, we'll do some good, but we won't change much—and those of us who survive will spend the rest of our lives running from the Inquisitors. Everything's going to change, Sazed, and I can't stop it."

Sazed smiled fondly. "Then, Mistress," he said quietly, "simply enjoy what you have. The future will surprise you, I think."

"Maybe," Vin said, unconvinced.

"Ah, you just need to have hope, Mistress. Perhaps you've earned a little bit of good fortune. There were a group of people before the Ascension known as the Astalsi. They claimed that each person was born with a certain finite amount of ill luck. And so, when an unfortunate event happened, they thought themselves blessed—thereafter, their lives could only get better."

Vin raised an eyebrow. "Sounds a bit simpleminded to me."

"I do not believe so," Sazed said. "Why, the Astalsi were rather advanced—they mixed religion with science quite profoundly. They thought that different colors were indications of different kinds of fortune, and were quite detailed in their descriptions of light and color. Why, it's from them that we get some of our best ideas as to what things might have looked like before the Ascension. They had a scale of colors, and used it to describe the sky of the deepest blue and various plants in their shades of green.

"Regardless, I find their philosophies regarding luck and fortune enlightened. To them, a poor life was only a sign of fortune to come. It might be a good fit for you, Mistress; you could benefit from the knowledge that your luck cannot always be bad."

"I don't know," Vin said skeptically. "I mean, if your bad luck were limited, wouldn't your *good* luck be limited too? Every time something good happened, I'd be worried about using it all up."

"Hum," Sazed said. "I suppose that depends on your viewpoint, Mistress."

"How can you be so optimistic?" Vin asked. "You and Kelsier both."

"I don't know, Mistress," Sazed said. "Perhaps our lives have been easier than yours. Or, perhaps we are simply more foolish."

Vin fell silent. They walked for a short time longer, weaving their way back toward the building, but not rushing the walk. "Sazed," she finally said. "When you saved me, that night in the rain, you used Feruchemy, didn't you?"

Sazed nodded. "Indeed. The Inquisitor was very focused on you, and I was able to sneak up behind him, then hit him with a stone. I had grown many times stronger than a regular man, and my blow threw him into the wall, breaking several of his bones, I suspect."

"Is that it?" Vin asked.

"You sound disappointed, Mistress," Sazed noted, smiling. "You expected something more spectacular, I suppose?"

Vin nodded. "It's just . . . you've been so quiet about Feruchemy. That makes it seem more mystical, I guess."

Sazed sighed. "There is really little to hide from you, Mistress. The truly unique power of Feruchemy—the ability to store and recover memories—you must surely have already guessed. The rest of the powers are not different, really, from the powers granted to you by pewter and tin. A few of them are a little more odd—making a Feruchemist heavier, or changing his age—but they offer little martial application."

"Age?" Vin said, perking up. "You could make yourself younger?"

"Not really, Mistress," Sazed said. "Remember, a Feruchemist must draw his powers from his own body. He could, for instance, spend a few weeks with his body aged to the point that it felt and looked ten years older than he really was. Then, he could withdraw that age to make himself seem ten years younger for an equal amount of time. However, in Feruchemy, there must be a balance."

Vin thought about that for a moment. "Does the metal you use matter?" she asked. "Like in Allomancy?"

"Most certainly," Sazed said. "The metal determines what can be stored."

Vin nodded and continued to walk, thinking over what he'd said. "Sazed, can I have a bit of your metal?" she finally asked.

"My metal, Mistress?"

"Something you've used as a Feruchemical store," Vin said. "I want to try burning it—maybe that will let me use some of its power."

Sazed frowned curiously.

"Has anyone ever tried it before?"

"I'm sure someone must have," Sazed said. "But, I honestly can't think of a specific example. Perhaps if I were to go search my memory copperminds . . ."

"Why not just let me try it now?" Vin asked. "Do you have something made from one of the basic metals? Something you haven't stored anything too valuable in?"

Sazed paused, then reached up to one of his oversized earlobes and undid an earring much like the one Vin wore. He handed the earring's tiny backing, used to hold the earring in place, to Vin. "It is pure pewter, Mistress. I have stored a moderate amount of strength in it."

Vin nodded, swallowing the tiny stud. She felt at her Allomantic reserve, but the stud's metal didn't seem to do anything different. She tentatively burned pewter.

"Anything?" Sazed asked.

Vin shook her head. "No, I don't . . ." She trailed off. There *was* something there, something different.

"What is it, Mistress?" Sazed asked, uncharacteristic eagerness sounding in his voice.

"I . . . can feel the power, Saze. It's faint—far beyond my grasp—but I swear that there's another reserve within me, one that only appears when I'm burning your metal."

Sazed frowned. "It's faint, you say? Like . . . you can see a shadow of the reserve, but can't access the power itself?"

Vin nodded. "How do you know?"

"That's what it feels like when you try to use another Feruchemist's metals, Mistress," Sazed said, sighing. "I should have suspected this would be the result. You cannot access the power because it does not belong to you."

"Oh," Vin said.

"Do not be too disappointed, Mistress. If Allomancers could steal strength from my people, it would already be known. It was a clever thought, however." He turned, pointing toward the mansion. "The carriage has already arrived. We are late for the meeting, I think."

Vin nodded, and they hurried their pace toward the mansion.

Funny, Kelsier thought to himself as he slipped across the darkened courtyard before Mansion Renoux. *I have to sneak into my own house, as if I were attacking some nobleman's keep.*

There was no avoiding it, however—not with his reputation. Kelsier the thief had been distinctive enough; Kelsier the rebellion instigator and skaa spiritual leader was even more infamous. That didn't, of course, keep him from spreading his nightly chaos—he just had to be more careful. More and more families were pulling out of the city, and the powerful houses were growing increasingly paranoid. In a way, that made manipulating them easier—but sneaking around their keeps was getting very dangerous.

In comparison, Mansion Renoux was virtually unprotected. There were guards, of course, but no Mistings. Renoux had to keep a low profile; too many Allomancers would make him stand out. Kelsier kept to the shadows, carefully making his way around to the east side of the building. Then he Pushed off a coin and guided himself up onto Renoux's own balcony.

Kelsier landed lightly, then peeked through the glass balcony doors. The drapes were shut, but he could pick out Dockson, Vin, Sazed, Ham, and Breeze standing around Renoux's desk. Renoux himself sat in the far corner of the room, staying out of the proceedings. His contract included playing the part of Lord Renoux, but he didn't wish to be involved in the plan anymore than he had to.

Kelsier shook his head. *It would be far too easy for an assassin to get in here. I'll have to make sure that Vin continues to sleep at Clubs' shop.* He wasn't worried about Renoux; the kandra's nature was such that he didn't need to fear an assassin's blade.

Kelsier tapped lightly on the door, and Dockson strolled over, pulling it open.

"And he makes his stunning entry!" Kelsier announced, sweeping into the room, throwing back his mistcloak.

Dockson snorted, shutting the doors. "You're truly a wonder to behold, Kell. Particularly the soot stains on your knees."

"I had to do some crawling tonight," Kelsier said, waving an indifferent hand. "There's an unused drainage ditch that passes right under Keep Lekal's defensive wall. You'd think they'd get that patched up."

"I doubt they need worry," Breeze said from beside the desk. "Most of you Mistborn are probably too proud to crawl. I'm surprised you were willing to do so yourself."

"Too proud to crawl?" Kelsier said. "Nonsense! Why, I'd say that we Mistborn are too proud *not* to be humble enough to go crawling about—in a dignified manner, of course."

Dockson frowned, approaching the desk. "Kell, that didn't make any sense."

"We Mistborn need not make sense," Kelsier said haughtily. "What's this?"

"From your brother," Dockson said, pointing at a large map laid across the desk. "It arrived this afternoon in the hollow of a broken table leg that the Canton of Orthodoxy hired Clubs to repair."

"Interesting," Kelsier said, scanning the map. "It's a list of the Soothing stations, I assume?"

"Indeed," Breeze said. "It's quite the discovery—I've never seen such a detailed, carefully drawn map of the city. Why, it not only shows every one of the thirty-four Soothing stations, but also locations of Inquisitor activity, as well as places that the different Cantons are concerned about. I haven't had the opportunity to associate much with your brother, but I must say that the man is obviously a genius!"

"It's almost hard to believe he's related to Kell, eh?" Dockson said with a smile. He had a notepad before him, and was in the process of making a list of all the Soothing stations.

Kelsier snorted. "Marsh might be the genius, but I'm the handsome one. What are these numbers?"

"Inquisitor raids and dates," Ham said. "You'll notice that Vin's crewhouse is listed."

Kelsier nodded. "How in the world did Marsh manage to steal a map like this?"

"He didn't," Dockson said as he wrote. "There was a note with the map. Apparently, high prelans *gave* it to him—

they've been very impressed with Marsh, and wanted him to look over the city and recommend locations for new Soothing stations. It seems that the Ministry is a bit worried about the house war, and they want to send out some extra Soothers to try and keep things under control."

"We're supposed to send the map back inside the repaired table leg," Sazed said. "Once we are done this evening, I shall endeavor to copy it in as short a time as possible."

And memorize it as well, thereby making it part of every Keeper's record, Kelsier thought. *The day when you'll stop memorizing and start teaching is coming soon, Saze. I hope your people are ready.*

Kelsier turned, studying the map. It was as impressive as Breeze had said. Indeed, Marsh must have taken an extremely great risk in sending it away. Perhaps a foolhardy risk, even—but the information it contained . . .

We'll have to get this back quickly, Kelsier thought. *Tomorrow morning, if possible.*

"What is this?" Vin asked quietly, leaning across the large map and pointing. She wore a noblewoman's dress—a pretty one-piece garment that was only slightly less ornate than a ball gown.

Kelsier smiled. He could remember a time when Vin had looked frighteningly awkward in a dress, but she seemed to have taken an increasing liking to them. She still didn't move *quite* like a noble-born lady. She was graceful—but it was the dexterous grace of a predator, not the deliberate grace of a courtly lady. Still, the gowns seemed to fit Vin now—in a way that had nothing at all to do with tailoring.

Ah, Mare, Kelsier thought. *You always wanted a daughter you could teach to walk the line between noblewoman and thief.* They would have liked each other; they both had a hidden streak of unconventionality. Perhaps if his wife were still alive, she could have taught Vin things about pretending to be a noblewoman that even Sazed didn't know.

Of course, if Mare were still alive, I wouldn't be doing any of this. I wouldn't dare.

"Look!" Vin said. "One of these Inquisitor dates is new—it's marked as yesterday!"

Dockson shot a glance at Kelsier.

We would have had to tell her eventually anyway. . . . "That was Theron's crew," Kelsier said. "An Inquisitor hit them yesterday evening."

Vin paled.

"Should I recognize that name?" Ham asked.

"Theron's crew was part of the team that was trying to dupe the Ministry with Camon," Vin said. "This means . . . they probably still have my trail."

The Inquisitor recognized her that night when we infiltrated the palace. He wanted to know who her father was. It's fortunate that those inhuman things make the nobility uncomfortable—otherwise, we'd have to worry about sending her to balls.

"Theron's crew," Vin said. "Was . . . it like last time?"

Dockson nodded. "No survivors."

There was an uncomfortable silence, and Vin looked visibly sick.

Poor kid, Kelsier thought. There was little they could do but move on, though. "All right. How are we going to use this map?"

"It has some Ministry notes on house defenses," Ham said. "Those will be useful."

"There doesn't appear to be any pattern in the Inquisitor hits, however," Breeze said. "They probably just go where the information leads them."

"We'll want to refrain from being too active near Soothing stations," Dox said, lowering his pen. "Fortunately, Clubs's shop isn't close to any specific station—most of them are in the slums."

"We need to do more than just avoid the stations," Kelsier said. "We need to be ready to take them out."

Breeze frowned. "If we do, we risk playing our hand recklessly."

"But think of the damage it would do," Kelsier said. "Marsh said there were at least three Soothers and a Seeker at *every* one of these stations. That's a hundred and thirty Ministry Mistings—they must have recruited across the entire Central Dominance to gather those kinds of numbers. If we were to take them all out at once . . ."

"We'd never be able to kill that many ourselves," Dockson said.

"We could if we used the rest of our army," Ham said. "We've got them stashed throughout the slums."

"I have a better idea," Kelsier said. "We can hire other thieving crews. If we had ten crews, each assigned to take out three stations, we could clear the city of Ministry Soothers and Seekers in barely a few hours."

"We'd have to discuss timing, though," Dockson said. "Breeze is right—killing that many obligators in one evening means making a major commitment. It won't take the Inquisitors long to retaliate."

Kelsier nodded. *You're right, Dox. Timing will be vital.* "Would you look into it? Find some appropriate crews, but wait until we decide on a time before giving them the locations of the Soothing stations."

Dockson nodded.

"Good," Kelsier said. "Speaking of our soldiers, Ham, how are things going with them?"

"Better than I expected, actually," Ham said. "They went through training in the caves, and so they're fairly competent. And, they consider themselves the more 'faithful' segment of the army, since they didn't follow Yeden to battle against your will."

Breeze snorted. "That's a convenient way of looking past the fact that they lost three-fourths of their army in a tactical blunder."

"They're good men, Breeze," Ham said firmly. "And so were those who died. Don't speak ill of them. Regardless, I worry about hiding the army as we are—it won't be too long before one of the teams gets discovered."

"That's why none of them know where to find the others," Kelsier said.

"I do want to mention something about the men," Breeze

said, seating himself in one of Renoux's desk chairs. "I see the importance of sending Hammond to train the soldiers—but honestly, what is the reason for forcing Dockson and myself to go and visit them?"

"The men need to know who their leaders are," Kelsier said. "If Ham were to become indisposed, someone else will need to take command."

"Why not you?" Breeze asked.

"Just bear with me," Kelsier said, smiling. "It's for the best."

Breeze rolled his eyes. "Bear with you. We seem to do an awful lot of that. . . ."

"Anyway," Kelsier said. "Vin, what news from the nobility? Have you discovered anything useful about House Venture?"

She paused. "No."

"But the ball next week will be at Keep Venture, right?" Dockson asked.

Vin nodded.

Kelsier eyed the girl. *Would she even tell us if she knew?* She met his eyes, and he couldn't read a thing in them. *Blasted girl's far too experienced a liar.*

"All right," he said to her. "Keep looking."

"I will," she said.

Despite his fatigue, Kelsier found sleep elusive that night. Unfortunately, he couldn't go out and roam the hallways—only certain servants knew he was at the mansion, and he needed to keep a low profile, now that his reputation was building.

His reputation. He sighed as he leaned against the balcony railing, watching the mists. In a way, the things he did worried even him. The others didn't question him out loud, as per his request, but he could tell that they were still bothered by his growing fame.

It's the best way. I may not need all of this . . . but, if I do, I'm going to be glad I went to the trouble.

A soft knock came at his door. He turned, curious, as Sazed peeked his head into the room.

"I apologize, Master Kelsier," Sazed said. "But a guard came to me and said he could see you up on your balcony. He was worried that you'd give yourself away."

Kelsier sighed, but backed away from the balcony, pulling the doors closed and shutting the drapes. "I'm not meant for anonymity, Saze. For a thief, I'm really not all that good at hiding."

Sazed smiled and began to withdraw.

"Sazed?" Kelsier asked, causing the Terrisman to pause. "I can't sleep—do you have a new proposal for me?"

Sazed smiled deeply, walking into the room. "Of course, Master Kelsier. Lately, I've been thinking that you should hear about the Truths of the Bennet. They fit you quite well, I think. The Bennet were a highly developed people who lived on the southern islands. They were brave seafarers and brilliant cartographers; some of the maps the Final Empire still uses were developed by Bennet explorers.

"Their religion was designed to be practiced aboard ships that were away at sea for months at a time. The captain was also their minister, and no man was allowed to command unless he had received theological training."

"Probably weren't very many mutinies."

Sazed smiled. "It was a good religion, Master Kelsier. It focused on discovery and knowledge—to these people, the making of maps was a reverent duty. They believed that once all of the world was known, understood, and catalogued, men would finally find peace and harmony. Many religions teach such ideals, but few actually managed to practice them as well as the Bennet."

Kelsier frowned, leaning back against the wall beside the balcony drapes. "Peace and harmony," he said slowly. "I'm not really looking for either right now, Saze."

"Ah," Sazed said.

Kelsier looked up, staring at the ceiling. "Could you . . . tell me about the Valla again?"

"Of course," Sazed said, pulling a chair over from beside Kelsier's desk and seating himself. "What specifically would you like to know?"

Kelsier shook his head. "I'm not sure," he said. "I'm sorry, Saze. I'm in a strange mood tonight."

"You are always in a strange mood, I think," Sazed said with a slight smile. "However, you choose an interesting sect to ask after. The Valla lasted longer into the Lord Ruler's dominion than any other religion."

"That's why I ask," Kelsier said. "I . . . need to understand what kept them going for so long, Saze. What made them keep fighting?"

"They were the most determined, I think."

"But they didn't have any leaders," Kelsier said. "The Lord Ruler had slaughtered the entire Vallan religious council as part of his first conquest."

"Oh, they had leaders, Master Kelsier," Sazed said. "Dead ones, true, but leaders nonetheless."

"Some men would say that their devotion didn't make sense," Kelsier said. "The loss of the Vallan leaders should have broken the people, not made them more determined to keep going."

Sazed shook his head. "Men are more resilient than that, I think. Our belief is often strongest when it should be weakest. That is the nature of hope."

Kelsier nodded.

"Did you want further instruction on the Valla?"

"No. Thanks, Saze. I just needed to be reminded that there were people who fought even when things looked hopeless."

Sazed nodded, rising. "I think I understand, Master Kelsier. Good evening, then."

Kelsier nodded distractedly, letting the Terrisman withdraw.

Most of the Terrismen are not as bad as Rashek. However, I can see that they believe him, to an extent. These are simple men, not philosophers or scholars, and they don't understand that their own prophecies say the Hero of Ages will be an outsider. They only see what Rashek points out—that they are an ostensibly superior people, and should be "dominant" rather than subservient.

Before such passion and hatred, even good men can be deceived.

30

IT TOOK RETURNING TO THE Venture ballroom to remind Vin what true majesty was.

She'd visited so many keeps that she had begun to grow desensitized to the splendor. There was something special about Keep Venture, however—something that the other keeps strived for, but never quite achieved. It was as if Venture were the parent, and the others were well-taught children. All of the keeps were beautiful, but there was no denying which one was the finest.

The enormous Venture hall, lined by a row of massive pillars on each side, seemed even more grand than usual. Vin couldn't quite decide why. She thought about it as she waited for a servant to take her shawl. The normal limelights shone outside the stained-glass windows, spraying the room with shards of light. The tables were immaculate beneath their pillared overhang. The lord's table, set on the small balcony at the very end of the hallway, looked as regal as ever.

It's almost . . . too perfect, Vin thought, frowning to herself. Everything seemed slightly exaggerated. The tablecloths were even whiter, and pressed even flatter, than usual. The servants' uniforms seemed particularly sharp. Instead of regular soldiers at the doors, hazekillers stood looking intentionally impressive, distinguished by their wooden shields and lack of armor. All together, the room made it seem as if even the regular Venture perfection had been heightened.

"Something's wrong, Sazed," she whispered as a servant moved off to prepare her table.

"What do you mean, Mistress?" the tall steward asked, standing behind her and to the side.

"There are too many people here," Vin said, realizing one of the things that was bothering her. Ball attendance had been tapering off during the last few months. Yet, it seemed like everyone had returned for the Venture event. And they all wore their finest.

"Something's going on," Vin said quietly. "Something we don't know about."

"Yes . . ." Sazed said quietly. "I sense it too. Perhaps I should go to the stewards' dinner early."

"Good idea," Vin said. "I think I might just skip the meal this evening. We're a bit late, and it looks like people have already started chatting."

Sazed smiled.

"What?"

"I remember a time when you would *never* skip a meal, Mistress."

Vin snorted. "Just be glad I never tried to stuff my pockets with food from one of these balls—trust me, I was tempted. Now, get going."

Sazed nodded and moved off toward the stewards' dinner. Vin scanned the chatting groups. *No sign of Shan, thankfully,* she thought. Unfortunately, Kliss was nowhere to be seen either, so Vin had to choose someone else to go to for gossip. She strolled forward, smiling at Lord Idren Seeris, a cousin to House Elariel and a man she had danced with on several occasions. He acknowledged her with a stiff nod, and she joined his group.

Vin smiled at the other members of the group—three women and one other lord. She knew them all at least passingly, and had danced with Lord Yestal. However, this evening all four of them gave her cold looks.

"I haven't been to Keep Venture in a while," Vin said, falling into her persona as a country girl. "I'd forgotten how majestic it is!"

"Indeed," said one of the ladies. "Excuse me—I'm going to go get something to drink."

"I'll go with you," one of the other ladies added, both of them leaving the group.

Vin watched them go, frowning.

"Ah," Yestal said. "Our meal has arrived. Coming, Triss?"

"Of course," the final lady said, joining Yestal as they walked away.

Idren adjusted his spectacles, shooting Vin a halfhearted look of apology, then withdrew. Vin stood, dumbfounded. She hadn't received such an obviously cold reception since her first few balls.

What's going on? she thought with increasing trepidation. *Is this Shan's work? Could she turn an entire room full of people against me?*

No, that didn't feel right. It would have required too much effort. In addition, the oddity wasn't just around her. All of the groups of noblemen were . . . different this evening.

Vin tried a second group, with an even worse result. As soon as she joined, the members pointedly ignored her. Vin felt so out of place that she withdrew, fleeing to get herself a cup of wine. As she walked, she noticed that the first group—the one with Yestal and Idren—had re-formed with exactly the same members.

Vin paused, standing just inside the shade of the eastern overhang and scanning the crowd. There were very few people dancing, and she recognized them all as established couples. There also seemed to be very little mingling between groups or tables. While the ballroom was filled, it seemed most of the attendees were distinctly trying to ignore everyone else.

I need to get a better view of this, she thought, walking to the stairwell. A short climb later, she came out on the long, corridorlike balcony set into the wall above the dance floor, its familiar blue lanterns giving the stonework a soft, melancholy hue.

Vin paused. Elend's cubbyhole sat between the rightmost column and the wall, well lit by a single lantern. He almost always spent Venture balls reading there; he didn't like the pomp and ceremony that came from hosting a party.

The cubbyhole was empty. She approached the railing, then craned out to look toward the far end of the grand hallway. The host's table sat on an overhang at the same level as the balconies, and she was shocked to see Elend sitting there dining with his father.

What? she thought incredulously. Never once, during the half-dozen balls she'd attended at Keep Venture, had she seen Elend sit with his family.

Down below, she caught sight of a familiar, colorful-robed figure moving through the crowd. She waved toward Sazed, but he had obviously already seen her. As she waited for him, Vin thought she faintly heard a familiar voice coming from the other end of the balcony. She turned and checked, noticing a short figure she'd missed before. Kliss was speaking with a small group of minor lords.

So that's where Kliss went, Vin thought. *Maybe* she'll *talk to me.* Vin stood, waiting for either Kliss to finish her conversation or Sazed to arrive.

Sazed came first, leaving the stairwell, breathing heavily. "Mistress," he said in a low voice, joining her by the railing.

"Tell me you discovered something, Sazed. This ball feels . . . creepy. Everyone's so solemn and cold. It's almost like we're at a funeral, not a party."

"It is an apt metaphor, my lady," Sazed said quietly. "We have missed an important announcement. House Hasting said it is not going to hold its regular ball this week."

Vin frowned. "So? Houses have canceled balls before."

"House Elariel canceled as well. Normally, Tekiel would come next—but that house is defunct. House Shunah has already announced that it won't be holding any more balls."

"What are you saying?"

"It appears, Mistress, that this will be the last ball for a time . . . perhaps a very long time."

Vin glanced down at the hall's magnificent windows, which stood above the independent—almost hostile—groups of people.

"*That's* what's going on," she said. "They're finalizing alliances. Everyone is standing with their strongest friends and supporters. They know this is the last ball, and so they all came to put in an appearance, but they know they've no time left for politicking."

"It seems that way, Mistress."

"They're all going on the defensive," Vin said. "Retreating behind their walls, so to speak. That's why no one wants to talk to me—we made Renoux too neutral a force. I don't have a faction, and it's a bad time to be gambling on random political elements."

"Master Kelsier needs to know this information, Mistress," Sazed said. "He planned on pretending to be an informant again tonight. If he's ignorant of this situation, it could seriously damage his credibility. We should leave."

"No," Vin said, turning toward Sazed. "I can't go—not when everyone else is staying. They all thought it was important to come and be seen at this last ball, and so I shouldn't leave until they start to."

Sazed nodded. "Very well."

"You go, Sazed. Hire a carriage and go tell Kell what we've learned. I'll stay for a little longer, then leave when it won't make House Renoux look weak."

Sazed paused. "I . . . don't know, Mistress."

Vin rolled her eyes. "I appreciate the help you've given me, but you don't need to keep holding my hand. Plenty of people come to these balls without their stewards to watch after them."

Sazed sighed. "Very well, Mistress. I shall return, however, after I have located Master Kelsier."

Vin nodded, bidding him farewell, and he retreated down the stone stairwell. Vin leaned against the balcony in Elend's spot, watching until Sazed appeared below and disappeared toward the front gates.

Now what? Even if I can find someone to talk to, there's really no point in spreading rumors now.

She felt a feeling of dread. Who would have thought that she would come to enjoy noble frivolity so much? The experience was tainted by her knowledge of what many noblemen were capable of, but even still, there had been a . . . dreamlike joy to the entire experience.

Would she ever attend balls like these again? What would happen to Valette the noblewoman? Would she have to put away her dresses and makeup, and return to simply being Vin the street thief? There probably wouldn't be room for things like grand balls in Kelsier's new kingdom, and that might not be a bad thing—what right did she have to dance while other skaa starved? Yet . . . it seemed like the world would be missing something beautiful without the keeps and dancers, the dresses and the festivities.

She sighed, leaning back from the railing, glancing down at her own dress. It was of a deep shimmering blue, with white circular designs sewn around the base of the skirt. It was sleeveless, but the blue silk gloves she wore ran all the way past her elbows.

Once she would have found the outfit frustratingly bulky. Now, however, she found it beautifying. She liked how it was designed to make her look full through the chest, yet accentuated her thin upper torso. She liked how it flared at the waist, slowly fanning out into a wide bell that rustled as she walked.

She'd miss it—she'd miss it all. But, Sazed was right. She couldn't stop the progression of time, she could only enjoy the moment.

I'm not *going to let him sit up there at the high table all evening and ignore me,* she decided.

Vin turned and walked along the balcony, nodding to Kliss as she passed. The balcony ended in a corridor that turned, and—as Vin had correctly guessed—led out onto the ledge that held the host's table.

She stood inside the corridor for a moment, looking out. Lords and ladies sat in regal outfits, basking in the privilege of being invited up to sit with Lord Straff Venture. Vin waited, trying to get Elend's attention, and finally one of the guests noticed her, then nudged Elend. He turned with surprise, saw Vin, then flushed slightly.

She waved briefly, and he stood, excusing himself. Vin ducked back into the stone corridor a bit so they could speak more privately.

"Elend!" she said as he walked into the corridor. "You're sitting with your father!"

He nodded. "This ball has turned into something of a special event, Valette, and my father was fairly insistent that I obey protocol."

"When are we going to have time to talk?"

Elend paused. "I'm not sure that we will."

Vin frowned. He seemed . . . reserved. His usual, slightly worn and wrinkled suit had been replaced by a sharp, well-fitted one. His hair was even combed.

"Elend?" she said, stepping forward.

He raised a hand, warding her back. "Things have changed, Valette."

No, she thought. *This can't change, not yet!* "Things? What 'things'? Elend, what are you talking about?"

"I am heir to House Venture," he said. "And dangerous times are coming. House Hasting lost an entire convoy this afternoon, and that's only the beginning. Within the month, the keeps will openly be at war. These aren't things I can ignore, Valette. It's time I stopped being a liability to my family."

"That's fine," Vin said. "That doesn't mean—"

"Valette," Elend interrupted. "You are a liability too. A very big one. I won't lie and claim that I never cared for you—I did, and I still do. However, I knew from the start—as you did—that this could never be anything more than a passing dalliance. The truth is, my house needs me—and it's more important than you are."

Vin paled. "But . . ."

He turned to go back to dinner.

"Elend," she said quietly, "please don't turn away from me."

He paused, then looked back at her. "I know the truth, Valette. I know how you've lied about who you are. I don't care, really—I'm not angry, or even disappointed. The truth is, I expected it. You're just . . . playing the game. Like we all are." He paused, then shook his head and turned away from her. "Like I am."

"Elend?" she said, reaching for him.

"Don't make me embarrass you in public, Valette."

Vin paused, feeling numb. And then, she was too angry to be numb—too angry, too frustrated . . . and too terrified.

"Don't leave," she whispered. "Don't you leave me too."

"I'm sorry," he said. "But I have to go meet with my friends. It was . . . fun."

And he left.

Vin stood in the darkened corridor. She felt herself shiver

quietly, and she turned to stumble back out onto the main balcony. To the side, she could see Elend bid good evening to his family, then head through a back corridor toward the keep's living section.

He can't do this to me. Not Elend. Not now . . .

However, a voice from within—a voice she had nearly forgotten—began to speak. *Of course he left you,* Reen whispered. *Of course he abandoned you. Everyone will betray you, Vin. What did I teach you?*

No! she thought. *It's just the political tension. Once this is over, I'll be able to convince him to come back. . . .*

I never came back for you, Reen whispered. *He won't either.* The voice felt so real—it was almost like she could hear him beside her.

Vin leaned up against the balcony railing, using the iron grating for strength, holding herself up. She wouldn't let him destroy her. A life on the streets hadn't been able to break her; she wouldn't let a self-important nobleman do so. She just kept telling herself that.

But, why did this hurt so much more than starvation—so much more than one of Camon's beatings?

"Well, Valette Renoux," a voice said from behind.

"Kliss," Vin said. "I'm . . . not in the mood to talk right now."

"Ah," Kliss said. "So Elend Venture finally spurned you. Don't worry, child—he'll get what he deserves shortly."

Vin turned, frowning at the odd tone in Kliss's voice. The woman didn't seem like herself. She seemed too . . . controlled.

"Deliver a message to your uncle for me, will you dear?" Kliss asked lightly. "Tell him that a man such as himself—without house alliances—might have a difficult time gathering intelligence in the upcoming months. If he needs a good source of information, tell him to send for me. I know lots of interesting things."

"You're an informant!" Vin said, pushing aside her pain for the moment. "But, you're . . ."

"A foolish gossip?" the short woman asked. "Why, yes I am. It's fascinating, the kinds of things you can learn when you're known as the court gossip. People come to you to spread obvious lies—such as the things you told me about

House Hasting last week. Why would you want me to spread such untruths? Could House Renoux be making a bid for the weapons market during the house war? Indeed—could Renoux be *behind* the recent attack on the Hasting barges?"

Kliss's eyes twinkled. "Tell your uncle that I can be made to keep quiet about what I know—for a small fee."

"You've been duping me all along. . . ." Vin said numbly.

"Of course, dear," Kliss said, patting Vin's arm. "That's what we do here at court. You'll learn eventually—if you survive. Now, be a good child and deliver my message, all right?"

Kliss turned, her squat, gaudy dress suddenly seeming a brilliant costume to Vin.

"Wait!" Vin said. "What was that you said about Elend earlier? He's going to get what he deserves?"

"Hum?" Kliss said, turning. "Why . . . that's right. You've been asking after Shan Elariel's plans, haven't you?"

Shan? Vin thought with rising concern. "What is she planning?"

"Now *that*, my dear, is an expensive secret indeed. I could tell you . . . but then, what would I have in return? A woman of an unimportant house like myself needs to find sustenance somewhere. . . ."

Vin pulled off her sapphire necklace, the only piece of jewelry she was wearing. "Here. Take it."

Kliss accepted the necklace with a thoughtful expression. "Hum, yes, very nice indeed."

"What do you know?" Vin snapped.

"Young Elend is going to be one of the first Venture casualties in the house war, I'm afraid," Kliss said, stuffing the necklace into a sleeve pocket. "It's unfortunate—he really does seem like a nice boy. Too nice, probably."

"When?" Vin demanded. "Where? How?"

"So many questions, but only one necklace," Kliss said idly.

"It's all I have right now!" Vin said truthfully. Her coin pouch contained only bronze clips for Steelpushing.

"But it's a *very* valuable secret, as I've said," Kliss continued. "By telling you, my own life would be—"

That's it! Vin thought furiously. *Stupid aristocratic games!*

Vin burned zinc and brass, hitting Kliss with a powerful

blast of emotional Allomancy. She Soothed away all of the woman's feelings but fear, then took hold of that fear and yanked on it with a firm tug.

"Tell me!" Vin growled.

Kliss gasped, wobbling and nearly falling to the ground. "An Allomancer! No *wonder* Renoux brought such a distant cousin with him to Luthadel!"

"Speak!" Vin said, taking a step forward.

"You're too late to help him," Kliss said. "I'd never sell a secret like this if it had a chance of turning on me!"

"Tell me!"

"He'll be assassinated by Elariel Allomancers this evening," Kliss whispered. "He might be dead already—it was supposed to happen as soon as he withdrew from the lord's table. But if you want revenge, you'll have to look toward Lord Straff Venture too."

"Elend's father?" Vin asked with surprise.

"Of course, foolish child," Kliss said. "Lord Venture would love nothing more than an excuse to give the house title to his nephew instead. All Venture had to do was withdraw a few of his soldiers from the rooftop around young Elend's room to let in the Elariel assassins. And, since the assassination will occur during one of Elend's little philosophy meetings, Lord Venture will be able to rid himself of a Hasting and a Lekal too!"

Vin spun. *I have to do something!*

"Of course," Kliss said with a chuckle, standing up. "Lord Venture is in for a surprise himself. I've heard that your Elend has some very . . . choice books in his possession. Young Venture should be much more careful about the things he tells his women, I think."

Vin turned back to the smiling Kliss. The woman winked at her. "I'll keep your Allomancy a secret, child. Just make certain I get payment by tomorrow afternoon. A lady must buy food—and as you can see, I need a lot of it.

"As for House Venture . . . well, I'd distance myself from them, if I were you. Shan's assassins are going to make *quite* the disturbance tonight. I wouldn't be surprised if half the court ended up in the boy's room to see what the ruckus was about. When the court sees those books Elend has . . . well, let's just say that the obligators are going to become very interested in House Venture for a time. Too bad Elend will already be dead—we haven't had an open execution of a nobleman in quite some time!"

Elend's room, Vin thought desperately. *That's where they must be!* She turned, holding the sides of her dress and rustling frantically down the balcony walkway toward the corridor she had left moments before.

"Where are you going?" Kliss asked with surprise.

"I have to stop this!" Vin said.

Kliss laughed. "I already told you that you're too late. Venture is a very old keep, and the back passages leading to the lords' quarters are quite the maze. If you don't know your way, you'll end up lost for hours."

Vin glanced around, feeling helpless.

"Besides, child," Kliss added, turning to walk away. "Didn't the boy just spurn you? What do you owe him?"

Vin paused.

She's right. What do *I owe him?*

The answer came immediately. *I love him.*

With that thought came strength. Vin rushed forward despite Kliss's laughter. She had to try. She entered the corridor and moved into the back passageways. However, Kliss's words soon proved true: The dark stone passageways were narrow and unadorned. She'd never find her way in time.

The roof, she thought. *Elend's rooms will have an outside balcony. I need a window!*

She dashed down a passage, kicking off her shoes and pulling off her stockings, then running as best she could in the dress. She searched frantically for a window big enough to fit through. She burst out into a larger corridor, empty save for flickering torches.

A massive lavender rose window stood on the far side of the room.

Good enough, Vin thought. With a flare of steel, she threw herself into the air, Pushing against a massive iron door behind her. She flew forward for a moment, then Pushed powerfully against the rose window's iron bindings.

She lurched to a stop in the air, Pushing both backward and forward at the same time. She strained, hanging in the empty corridor, flaring her pewter to keep from being crushed. The rose window was enormous, but it was mostly glass. How strong could it be?

Very strong. Vin groaned beneath the strain. She heard a snap behind her, and the door began to twist in its mountings.

You . . . must . . . give! she thought angrily, flaring her steel. Chips of stone fell around the window.

Then, with a *crack* of sound, the rose window burst free from the stone wall. It fell backward into the dark night, and Vin shot out behind it.

Cool mist enveloped her. She Pulled slightly against the door inside the room, keeping herself from going out too far, then Pushed mightily against the falling window. The enormous dark-glassed window tumbled beneath her, churning the mists as Vin shot away from it. Straight up, toward the roof.

The window crashed to the ground just as Vin flew up over the edge of the rooftop, her dress fluttering madly in the wind. She landed on the bronze-plated roof with a thump, falling to a crouch. The metal was cool beneath her toes and fingers.

Tin flared, illuminating the night. She could see nothing out of the ordinary.

She burned bronze, using it as Marsh had taught her, searching for signs of Allomancy. There weren't any—the assassins had a Smoker with them.

I can't search the entire building! Vin thought, desperately, flaring her bronze. *Where are they?*

Then, oddly, she thought she sensed something. An Allomantic pulse in the night. Faint. Hidden. But enough.

Vin rose to dash across the rooftop, trusting her instincts. As she ran, she flared pewter and grabbed her dress near the neck, then ripped the garment down the front with a single yank. She pulled her coin pouch and metal vials from a hidden pocket, and then—still running—she ripped the dress, petticoats, and attached leggings free, tossing it all aside. Her corset and gloves went next. Underneath, she wore a thin, sleeveless white shift and a pair of white shorts.

She dashed frantically. *I can't be too late,* she thought. *Please. I can't.*

Figures resolved in the mists ahead. They stood beside an angled rooftop skylight; Vin had passed several similar ones as she ran. One of the figures pointed toward the skylight, a weapon glittering in its hand.

Vin cried out, Pushing herself off the bronze roof in an arcing jump. She landed in the very center of the surprised group of people, then thrust her coin pouch upward, ripping it in two.

Coins sprayed into the air, reflecting light from the window below. As the glistening shower of metal fell around Vin, she *Pushed.*

Coins zipped away from her like a swarm of insects, each one leaving a trail in the mist. Figures cried out as coins hit flesh, and several of the dark forms dropped.

Several did not. Some of the coins snapped away, Pushed aside by invisible Allomantic hands. Four people remained standing: Two of them wore mistcloaks; one of them was familiar.

Shan Elariel. Vin didn't need to see the cloak to understand; there was only one reason a woman as important as Shan would come on an assassination like this. She was a Mistborn.

"*You?*" Shan asked in shock. She wore a black outfit of trousers and shirt, her dark hair pulled back, her mistcloak worn almost stylishly.

Two Mistborn, Vin thought. *Not good.* She scrambled away, ducking as one of the assassins swung a dueling cane at her.

Vin slid across the rooftop, then Pulled herself to a brief halt, spinning with one hand resting against the cold bronze. She reached out and Pulled against the few coins that hadn't escaped out into the night, yanking them back into her hand.

"Kill her!" Shan snapped. The two men Vin had felled lay groaning on the rooftop. They weren't dead; in fact, one was climbing unsteadily to his feet.

Thugs, Vin thought. *The other two are probably Coinshots.*

As if to prove her right, one of the men tried to Push away

Vin's vial of metals. Fortunately, there weren't enough metals in the vial to give him a very good anchor, and she kept hold of it easily.

Shan turned her attention back to the skylight.

No you don't! Vin thought, dashing forward again.

The Coinshot cried out as she approached. Vin flipped a coin and shot it at him. He, of course, Pushed back—but Vin anchored herself against the bronze roof and flared Steel, Pushing with a firm effort.

The man's own Steelpush—transmitted from the coin, to Vin, to the roof—launched him out into the air. He cried out, shooting off into the darkness. He was only a Misting, and couldn't Pull himself back to the rooftop.

The other Coinshot tried to spray Vin with coins, but she deflected them with ease. Unfortunately, he wasn't as foolish as his companion, and he released the coins soon after Pushing them. However, it was obvious that he couldn't hit her. Why did he keep—

The other Mistborn! Vin thought, ducking to a roll as a figure leaped from the dark mists, glass knives flashing in the air.

Vin just barely got out of the way, flaring pewter to give herself balance. She came to her feet beside the wounded Thug, who stood on obviously weak legs. With another flare of pewter, Vin slammed her shoulder into the man's chest, shoving him to the side.

The man stumbled maladroitly, still holding his bleeding side. Then he tripped and fell right into the skylight. The fine, tinted glass shattered as he fell, and Vin's tin-enhanced ears could hear cries of surprise from below, followed by a crash as the Thug hit the ground.

Vin looked up, smiling evilly at the stunned Shan. Behind her, the second Mistborn—a man—swore quietly.

"You . . . You . . ." Shan sputtered, her eyes flaring dangerously with anger in the night.

Take the warning, Elend, Vin thought, *and escape. It's time for me to go.*

She couldn't face two Mistborn at once—she couldn't even beat Kelsier most nights. Flaring Steel, Vin launched herself backward. Shan took a step forward and—looking determined—Pushed herself after Vin. The second Mistborn joined her.

Bloody hell! Vin thought, spinning in the air and Pulling herself to the rooftop's edge near where she had broken the rose window. Below, figures scrambled about, lanterns brightening the mists. Lord Venture probably thought that the fuss meant his son was dead. He was in for a surprise.

Vin launched herself into the air again, jumping out into the misty void. She could hear the two Mistborn land behind her, then push off as well.

This isn't good, Vin thought with trepidation as she hurled through the misty air currents. She didn't have any coins left, nor did she have daggers—and she faced two trained Mistborn.

She burned iron, searching frantically for an anchor in the night. A line of blue, moving slowly, appeared beneath her to the right.

Vin yanked on the line, changing her trajectory. She shot downward, the Venture grounds wall appearing as a dark shadow beneath her. Her anchor was the breastplate of an unfortunate guard, who lay atop the wall, holding frantically to a tooth in the battlements to keep himself from being pulled up toward Vin.

Vin slammed feet-first into the man, then spun in the misty air, flipping to land on the cool stone. The guard collapsed to the stone, then cried out, desperately grabbing his stone anchor as another Allomantic force Pulled against him.

Sorry, friend, Vin thought, kicking the man's hand free from the battlement tooth. He immediately snapped upward, yanked into the air as if pulled by a powerful tether.

The sound of bodies colliding sounded from the darkness above, and Vin saw a pair of forms drop limply to the Venture courtyard. Vin smiled, dashing along the wall. *I sure hope that was Shan.*

Vin jumped up, landing atop the gatehouse. Near the keep, people were scattering, climbing in carriages to flee.

And so the house war starts, Vin thought. *Didn't think I'd be the one to officially begin it.*

A figure plummeted toward her from the mists above. Vin cried out, flaring pewter and jumping to the side. Shan landed dexterously—mistcloak tassels billowing—atop the gatehouse. She had both daggers out, and her eyes burned with anger.

Vin jumped to the side, rolling off the gatehouse and landing on the walltop below. A pair of guards jumped back in alarm, surprised to see a half-naked girl fall into their midst. Shan dropped to the wall behind them, then Pushed, throwing one of the guards in Vin's direction.

The man cried out as Vin Pushed against his breastplate as well—but he was far heavier than she, and she was thrown backward. She Pulled on the guard to slow herself, and the man crashed down to the walltop. Vin landed lithely beside him, then grabbed his staff as it rolled free from his hand.

Shan attacked in a flash of spinning daggers, and Vin was forced to jump backward again. *She's so good!* Vin thought with anxiety. Vin herself had barely trained with daggers; now she wished she'd asked Kelsier for a little more practice. She swung the staff, but she'd never used one of the weapons before, and her attack was laughable.

Shan slashed, and Vin felt a flare of pain in her cheek as she dodged. She dropped the staff in shock, reaching up to her face and feeling blood. She stumbled back, seeing the smile on Shan's face.

And then Vin remembered the vial. The one she still carried—the one Kelsier had given her.

Atium.

She didn't bother to grab it from the place she had tucked it at her waist. She burned steel, Pushing it out into the air in front of her. Then, she immediately burned iron and yanked on the bead of atium. The vial shattered, the bead heading back toward Vin. She caught it in her mouth, swallowing the lump and forcing it down.

Shan paused. Then, before Vin could do anything, she downed a vial of her own.

Of course she has atium!

But, how much did she have? Kelsier hadn't given Vin much—only enough for about thirty seconds. Shan jumped forward, smiling, her long black hair flaring in the air. Vin gritted her teeth. She didn't have much choice.

She burned atium. Immediately, Shan's form shot forth dozens of phantom atium shadows. It was a Mistborn standoff: The first one who ran out of atium would be vulnerable. You couldn't escape an opponent who knew exactly what you were going to do.

Vin scrambled backward, keeping an eye on Shan. The noblewoman stalked forward, her phantoms forming an insane bubble of translucent motion around her. She seemed calm. Secure.

She has plenty of atium, Vin thought, feeling her own storage burn away. *I need to get away.*

A shadowy length of wood suddenly shot through Vin's chest. She ducked to the side just as the real arrow—apparently made with no arrowhead—passed through the air where she had been standing. She glanced toward the gatehouse, where several soldiers were raising bows.

She cursed, glancing to the side, into the mists. As she did so, she caught a smile from Shan.

She's just waiting for my atium to burn out. She wants me to run—she knows she can chase me down.

There was only one other option: attack.

Shan frowned in surprise as Vin dashed forward, phantom arrows snapping against the stones just before their real counterparts arrived. Vin dodged between two arrows—her atium-enhanced mind knowing exactly how to move—passing so close that she could feel the missiles in the air to either side of her.

Shan swung her daggers, and Vin twisted to the side, dodging one slice and blocking the other with her forearm, earning a deep gash. Her own blood flew in the air as she spun—each droplet tossing out a translucent atium image—and flared pewter, punching Shan square in the stomach.

Shan grunted in pain, bending slightly, but she didn't fall.

Atium's almost gone, Vin thought desperately. *Only a few seconds left.*

So, she extinguished her atium early, exposing herself.

Shan smiled wickedly, coming up from her crouch, right-hand dagger swinging confidently. She assumed that Vin had run out of atium—and therefore assumed that she was exposed. Vulnerable.

At that moment, Vin burned her last bit of atium. Shan paused just briefly in confusion, giving Vin an opening as a phantom arrow streaked through the mists overhead.

Vin caught the real arrow as it followed—the grainy wood burning her fingers—then rammed it down into Shan's chest. The shaft snapped in Vin's hand, leaving about an inch protruding from Shan's body. The woman stumbled backward, staying on her feet.

Damn pewter, Vin thought, ripping a sword from a sheath beside the unconscious soldier at her feet. She jumped forward, gritting her teeth in determination, and Shan—still dazed—raised a hand to Push against the sword.

Vin let the weapon go—it was just a distraction—as she slammed the second half of the broken arrow into Shan's chest just beside its counterpart.

This time, Shan dropped. She tried to rise, but one of the shafts must have done some serious damage to her heart, for her face paled. She struggled for a moment, then fell lifeless to the stones.

Vin stood, breathing deeply as she wiped the blood from her cheek—only to realize that her bloody arm was just making her face worse. Behind her, the soldiers called out, nocking more arrows.

Vin glanced back toward the keep, bidding farewell to Elend, then Pushed herself out into the night.

Other men worry whether or not they will be remembered. I have no such fears; even disregarding the Terris prophecies, I have brought such chaos, conflict, and hope to this world that there is little chance that I will be forgotten.

I worry about what they will say of me. Historians can make what they wish of the past. In a thousand years' time, will I be remembered as the man who protected mankind from a powerful evil? Or, will I be remembered as a tyrant who arrogantly tried to make himself a legend?

31

"I DON'T KNOW," KELSIER SAID, smiling as he shrugged. "Breeze would make a pretty good Minister of Sanitation."

The group chuckled, though Breeze just rolled his eyes. "Honestly, I don't see why *I* consistently prove to be the target of you people's humor. Why must you choose the only dignified person in this crew as the butt of your mockery?"

"Because, my dear man," Ham said, imitating Breeze's accent, "you are, by far, the best butt we have."

"Oh, please," Breeze said as Spook nearly collapsed to the floor with laughter. "This is just getting juvenile. The teenage boy was the only one who found *that* comment amusing, Hammond."

"I'm a soldier," Ham said, raising his cup. "Your witty verbal attacks have no effect on me, for I'm far too dense to understand them."

Kelsier chuckled, leaning back against the cupboard. One problem with working at night was that he missed the evening gatherings in Clubs's kitchen. Breeze and Ham continued their general banter. Dox sat at the end of the table, going over ledgers and reports, while Spook sat by Ham eagerly, trying his best to take part in the conversation. Clubs sat in his corner, overseeing, occasionally smiling, and generally enjoying his ability to give the best scowls in the room.

"I should be leaving, Master Kelsier," Sazed said, checking the wall clock. "Mistress Vin should be about ready to leave."

Kelsier nodded. "I should get going myself. I still have to—"

The outside kitchen door slammed open. Vin stood silhouetted by the dark mist, wearing nothing but her dressing undergarments—a flimsy white shirt and shorts. Both were sprayed with blood.

"Vin!" Ham exclaimed, standing.

Her cheek bore a long, thin gash, and she had a bandage tied on one forearm. "I'm fine," she said wearily.

"What happened to your dress?" Dockson immediately demanded.

"You mean this?" Vin asked apologetically, holding up a ripped, soot-stained blue mass of cloth. "It . . . got in the way. Sorry, Dox."

"Lord Ruler, girl!" Breeze said. "Forget the dress—what happened to *you!*"

Vin shook her head, shutting the door. Spook blushed furiously at her outfit, and Sazed immediately moved over, checking the wound on her cheek.

"I think I did something bad," Vin said. "I . . . kind of killed Shan Elariel."

"You did *what*?" Kelsier asked as Sazed tisked quietly, leaving the small cheek cut alone as he undid the bandage on her arm.

Vin flinched slightly at Sazed's ministrations. "She was Mistborn. We fought. I won."

You killed a fully-trained Mistborn? Kelsier thought with shock. *You've practiced for barely eight months!*

"Master Hammond," Sazed requested, "would you fetch my healer's bag?"

Ham nodded, rising.

"You might want to grab her something to wear too," Kelsier suggested. "I think poor Spook's about to have a heart attack."

"What's wrong with this?" Vin asked, nodding toward her clothing. "It's not that much more revealing than some of the thief's clothing I've worn."

"Those are undergarments, Vin," Dockson said.

"So?"

"It's the principle of the matter," Dockson said. "Young ladies do not run around in their undergarments, no matter how much those undergarments may resemble regular clothing."

Vin shrugged, sitting as Sazed held a bandage to her arm. She seemed . . . exhausted. And not just from the fighting. *What else happened at that party?*

"Where did you fight the Elariel woman?" Kelsier asked.

"Outside Keep Venture," Vin said, looking down. "I . . . think some of the guards spotted me. Some of the nobles might have too, I'm not certain."

"That's going to be trouble," Dockson said, sighing. "Of course, that cheek wound is going to be pretty obvious, even with makeup. Honestly, you Allomancers . . . Don't you ever worry about what you're going to look like the day *after* you get into one of these fights?"

"I was kind of focused on staying alive, Dox," Vin said.

"He's just complaining because he's worried about you," Kelsier said as Ham returned with the bag. "That's what he does."

"Both wounds will require immediate stitching, Mistress," Sazed said. "The one on your arm hit the bone, I think."

Vin nodded, and Sazed rubbed her arm with a numbing agent, then began to work. She bore it without much visible discomfort—though she obviously had her pewter flared.

She looks so exhausted, Kelsier thought. She was such a frail-looking thing, mostly just arms and legs. Hammond put a cloak around her shoulders, but she appeared too tired to care.

And I brought her into this.

Of course, she should know better than to get herself into this kind of trouble. Eventually, Sazed finished his efficient sewing, then tied a new bandage around the arm wound. He moved onto the cheek.

"Why would you fight a Mistborn?" Kelsier asked sternly. "You should have run. Didn't you learn anything from your battle with the Inquisitors?"

"I couldn't get away without turning my back on her," Vin said. "Besides, she had more atium than me. If I hadn't attacked, she would have chased me down. I had to strike while we were equally matched."

"But how did you get into this in the first place?" Kelsier demanded. "Did she attack you?"

Vin glanced down at her feet. "I attacked first."

"Why?" Kelsier asked.

Vin sat for a moment, Sazed working on her cheek. "She was going to kill Elend," she finally said.

Kelsier exhaled in exasperation. "Elend Venture? You risked your life—risked the plan, and our lives—for that fool of a boy?"

Vin looked up, glaring at him. "Yes."

"What is wrong with you, girl?" Kelsier asked. "Elend Venture isn't worth this."

She stood angrily, Sazed backing away, the cloak falling the floor. "He's a good man!"

"He's a nobleman!"

"*So are you!*" Vin snapped. She waved a frustrated arm toward the kitchen and the crew. "What do you think *this* is, Kelsier? The life of a skaa? What do any of you know about skaa? Aristocratic suits, stalking your enemies in the night, full meals and nightcaps around the table with your friends? That's not the life of a skaa!"

She took a step forward, glaring at Kelsier. He blinked in surprise at the outburst.

"What do you know about them, Kelsier?" she asked. "When's the last time you slept in an alley, shivering in the cold rain, listening to the beggar next to you cough with a sickness you knew would kill him? When's the last time you had to lay awake at night, terrified that one of the men in your crew would try to rape you? Have you ever knelt, starving, wishing you had the courage to knife the crewmember beside you just so you could take his crust of bread? Have you ever cowered before your brother as he beat you, all the time feeling thankful because at least you *had someone who paid attention to you?*"

She fell silent, puffing slightly, the crewmembers staring at her.

"Don't talk to me about noblemen," Vin said. "And don't say things about people you don't know. You're no skaa—you're just noblemen without titles."

She turned, stalking from the room. Kelsier watched her go, shocked, hearing her footsteps on the stairs. He stood, dumbfounded, feeling a surprising flush of ashamed guilt.

And, for once, found himself without anything to say.

Vin didn't go to her room. She climbed to the roof, where the mists curled in the quiet, unlit night. She sat down in the corner, the rough stone lip of the flat rooftop against her nearly bare back, wood beneath her.

She was cold, but she didn't care. Her arm hurt a bit, but it was mostly numb. She didn't feel nearly numb enough herself.

She crossed her arms, huddling down, watching the mists. She didn't know what to think, let alone what to feel. She shouldn't have exploded at Kelsier, but everything that had happened . . . the fight, Elend's betrayal . . . it just left her feeling frustrated. She needed to be angry at *someone*.

You should just be angry at yourself, Reen's voice whispered. *You're the one who let them get close. Now they're all just going to leave you.*

She couldn't make it stop hurting. She could only sit and shiver as the tears fell, wondering how everything had collapsed so quickly.

The trapdoor to the rooftop opened with a quiet creak, and Kelsier's head appeared.

Oh, Lord Ruler! I don't want to face him now. She tried to wipe away her tears, but she only succeeded in aggravating the freshly stitched wound on her cheek.

Kelsier closed the trapdoor behind him, then stood, so tall and proud, staring up at the mists. *He didn't deserve the things I said. None of them did.*

"Watching the mists is comforting, isn't it?" Kelsier asked.

Vin nodded.

"What is it I once told you? The mists protect you, they give you power . . . they hide you. . . ."

He looked down, then he walked over and crouched before her, holding out a cloak. "There are some things you can't hide from, Vin. I know—I've tried."

She accepted the cloak, then wrapped it around her shoulders.

"What happened tonight?" he asked. "What *really* happened?"

"Elend told me that he didn't want to be with me anymore."

"Ah," Kelsier said, moving over to sit beside her. "Was this before or after you killed his former fiancée?"

"Before," Vin said.

"And you still protected him?"

Vin nodded, sniffling quietly. "I know. I'm an idiot."

"No more than the rest of us," Kelsier said with a sigh. He looked up into the mists. "I loved Mare too, even after she betrayed me. Nothing could change how I felt."

"And that's why it hurts so much," Vin said, remembering what Kelsier had said before. *I think I finally understand.*

"You don't stop loving someone just because they hurt you," he said. "It would certainly make things easier if you did."

She started to sniffle again, and he put a fatherly arm around her. She pulled close, trying to use his warmth to push away the pain.

"I loved him, Kelsier," she whispered.

"Elend? I know."

"No, not Elend," Vin said. "Reen. He beat me over, and over, and over. He swore at me, he yelled at me, he told me he'd betray me. Every day, I thought about how much I hated him.

"And I loved him. I still do. It hurts so much to think that he's gone, even though he always told me he would leave."

"Oh, child," Kelsier said, pulling her close. "I'm sorry."

"Everyone leaves me," she whispered. "I can barely remember my mother. She tried to kill me, you know. She heard voices, in her head, and they made her kill my baby sister. She was probably going to kill me next, but Reen stopped her.

"Either way, she left me. After that, I clung to Reen. He left too. I love Elend, but he doesn't want me anymore." She looked up at Kelsier. "When are you going to go? When will you leave me?"

Kelsier looked sorrowful. "I . . . Vin, I don't know. This job, the plan . . ."

She searched his eyes, looking for the secrets therein. *What are you hiding from me, Kelsier? Something that dangerous?* She wiped her eyes again, pulling away from him, feeling foolish.

He looked down, shaking his head. "Look, now you got

blood all over my nice, dirty, pretend informant's clothing."

Vin smiled. "At least some of it is noble blood. I got Shan pretty good."

Kelsier chuckled. "You're probably right about me, you know. I don't give the nobility much of a chance, do I?"

Vin flushed. "Kelsier, I shouldn't have said those things. You're good people, and this plan of yours . . . well, I realize what you're trying to do for the skaa."

"No, Vin," Kelsier said, shaking his head. "What you said was true. We're not really skaa."

"But, that's good," Vin said. "If you were regular skaa, you wouldn't have the experience or courage to plan something like this."

"They might lack experience," Kelsier said. "But not courage. Our army lost, true, but they were willing—with minimal training—to charge a superior force. No, the skaa don't lack courage. Just opportunity."

"Then it's your position as half skaa, half nobleman that has given *you* opportunity, Kelsier. And you've chosen to use that opportunity to help your skaa half. That makes you worthy of being a skaa if anything does."

Kelsier smiled. "Worthy to be a skaa. I like the sound of that. Regardless, perhaps I need to spend a little less time worrying about which noblemen to kill, and a little more time worrying about which peasants to help."

Vin nodded, pulling the cloak close as she stared up into the mists. *They protect us. . . . give us power . . . hide us. . . .*

She hadn't felt like she needed to hide in a long time. But now, after the things she'd said below, she almost wished that she could just blow away like a wisp of mist.

I need to tell him. It could mean the plan's success or failure. She took a deep breath. "House Venture has a weakness, Kelsier."

He perked up. "It does?"

Vin nodded. "Atium. They make certain the metal is harvested and delivered—it's the source of their wealth."

Kelsier paused for a moment. "Of course! That's how they can pay the taxes, that's why they're so powerful. . . . He *would* need someone to handle things for him. . . ."

"Kelsier?" Vin asked.

He looked back at her.

"Don't . . . do anything unless you have to, all right?"

Kelsier frowned. "I . . . don't know that I can promise anything, Vin. I'll try and think of another way, but as things stand now, Venture has to fall."

"I understand."

"I'm glad you told me, though."

She nodded. *And now I've betrayed him too.* There was a peace in knowing, however, that she hadn't done it out of spite. Kelsier was right: House Venture was a power that needed to be toppled. Oddly, her mention of the house seemed to bother Kelsier more than it did her. He sat, staring into the mists, strangely melancholy. He reached down, absently scratching his arm.

The scars, Vin thought. *It isn't House Venture he's thinking about—it's the Pits. Her.* "Kelsier?" she said.

"Yes?" His eyes still looking a bit . . . absent as he watched the mists.

"I don't think that Mare betrayed you."

He smiled. "I'm glad you think that way."

"No, I really mean it," Vin said. "The Inquisitors were waiting for you when you got to the center of the palace, right?"

Kelsier nodded.

"They were waiting for us too."

Kelsier shook his head. "You and I fought some guards, made some noise. When Mare and I went in, we were quiet. We'd planned for a year—we were stealthy, secretive, and very careful. Someone set a trap for us."

"Mare was an Allomancer, right?" Vin asked. "They could have just sensed you coming."

Kelsier shook his head. "We had a Smoker with us. Redd was his name—the Inquisitors killed him straight off. I've wondered if he was the traitor, but that just doesn't work. Redd didn't even know about the infiltration until that night, when we went and got him. Only Mare knew enough—dates, times, objectives—to have betrayed us. Besides, there's the Lord Ruler's comment. You didn't see him, Vin. Smiling as he thanked Mare. There was . . . honesty in his eyes. They say the Lord Ruler doesn't lie. Why would he need to?"

Vin sat quietly for a moment, considering what he'd said. "Kelsier," she said slowly, "I think that Inquisitors can sense our Allomancy even when we're burning copper."

"Impossible."

"I did it tonight. I punctured Shan's coppercloud to locate her and the other assassins. That's how I got to Elend in time."

Kelsier frowned. "You've got to be mistaken."

"It happened before too," Vin said. "I can feel the Lord Ruler's touch on my emotions, even when I'm burning copper. And I swear that when I was hiding from that Inquisitor who was hunting me, he found me when he shouldn't have been able to. Kelsier, what if it's possible? What if hiding yourself by Smoking isn't just a simple matter of whether or not your copper is on? What if it just depends on how strong you are?"

Kelsier sat thoughtfully. "It could be possible, I suppose."

"Then Mare wouldn't have had to betray you!" Vin said eagerly. "Inquisitors are extremely powerful. The ones who were waiting for you, maybe they just felt you burning metals! They knew that an Allomancer was trying to sneak into the palace. Then, the Lord Ruler thanked her because she was the one who gave you away! She was the Allomancer, burning tin, that led them to you."

Kelsier's face took on a troubled expression. He turned, sitting himself so he was directly in front of her. "Do it now, then. Tell me what metal I'm burning."

Vin closed her eyes, flaring bronze, listening . . . feeling, as Marsh had taught her. She remembered her solitary trainings, time spent focusing on the waves Breeze, Ham, or Spook gave off for her. She tried to pick out the fuzzing rhythm of Allomancy. Tried to . . .

For a moment, she thought she felt something. Something very strange—a slow pulsing, like a distant drum, unlike any Allomantic rhythm she'd felt before. But it wasn't coming from Kelsier. It was distant . . . far away. She focused harder, trying to pick out the direction it was coming from.

But suddenly, as she focused harder, something else drew her attention. A more familiar rhythm, coming from Kelsier. It was faint, difficult to feel over the pulsing of her own heartbeat. It was a bold beat, and quick.

She opened her eyes. "Pewter! You're burning pewter."

Kelsier blinked in surprise. "Impossible," he whispered. "Again!"

She closed her eyes. "Tin," she said after a moment. "Now steel—you changed as soon as I spoke."

"Bloody hell!"

"I was right," Vin said eagerly. "You *can* feel Allomantic pulses through copper! They're quiet, but I guess you just have to focus hard enough to—"

"Vin," Kelsier interrupted. "Don't you think Allomancers have tried this before? You don't think that after a thousand years' time, someone would have noticed that you could pierce a coppercloud? *I've* even tried it. I focused for hours on my Master, trying to sense something through his coppercloud."

"But . . ." Vin said. "But why . . . ?"

"It must have to do with strength, like you said. Inquisitors can Push and Pull harder than any regular Mistborn—perhaps they're so strong that they can overwhelm someone else's metal."

"But, Kelsier," Vin said quietly. "I'm not an Inquisitor."

"But you're strong," he said. "Stronger than you have any right to be. You killed a full Mistborn tonight!"

"By luck," Vin said, face flushing. "I just tricked her."

"Allomancy is nothing *but* tricks, Vin. No, there's something special about you. I noticed it on that first day, when you shrugged off my attempts to Push and Pull your emotions."

She flushed. "It can't be that, Kelsier. Maybe I've just practiced with bronze more than you. . . . I don't know, I just . . ."

"Vin," Kelsier said, "you're still too self-effacing. You're good at this—that much is obvious. If that's why you can see through copperclouds . . . well, I don't know. But learn to take a little pride in yourself, kid! If there's anything I can teach you, it's how to be self-confident."

Vin smiled.

"Come on," he said, standing and holding out a hand to help her up. "Sazed is going to fret all night if you don't let him finish stitching that cheek wound, and Ham's dying to hear about your battle. Good job leaving Shan's body back at Keep Venture, by the way—when House Elariel hears that she was found dead on Venture property . . ."

Vin allowed him to pull her up, but she glanced toward the trapdoor apprehensively. "I . . . don't know if I want to go down yet, Kelsier. How can I face them?"

Kelsier laughed. "Oh, don't worry. If you didn't say some stupid things every once in a while, you certainly wouldn't fit in with *this* group. Come on."

Vin hesitated, then let him lead her back down to the warmth of the kitchen.

"Elend, how can you read at times like this?" Jastes asked.

Elend looked up from his book. "It calms me."

Jastes raised an eyebrow. The young Lekal sat impatiently in the coach, tapping his fingers on the armrest. The window shades were drawn, partially to hide the light of Elend's reading lantern, partially to keep out the mists. Though Elend would never admit it, the swirling fog made him just a bit nervous. Noblemen weren't supposed to be afraid of such things, but that didn't change the fact that the deep, caliginous mist was just plain creepy.

"Your father is going to be livid when you get back," Jastes noted, still tapping the armrest.

Elend shrugged, though this comment did make him a little bit nervous. Not because of his father, but because of what had happened this night. Some Allomancers had, apparently, been spying on Elend's meeting with his friends. What information had they gathered? Did they know about the books he'd read?

Fortunately, one of them had tripped, falling through Elend's skylight. After that, it had been confusion and chaos—soldiers and ballgoers running about in a semi-panic. Elend's first thought had been for the books—the dangerous ones, the ones that if the obligators found he possessed, could get him into serious trouble.

So, in the confusion, he'd dumped them all in a bag and followed Jastes down to the palace side exit. Grabbing a carriage and sneaking out of the palace grounds had been an extreme move, perhaps, but it had been ridiculously easy. With the number of carriages fleeing the Venture grounds, not a single person had paused to notice that Elend himself was in the carriage with Jastes.

It's probably all died down by now, Elend told himself. *People will realize that House Venture wasn't trying to attack them, and that there wasn't really any danger. Just some spies who got careless.*

He should have returned by now. However, his convenient absence from the palace gave him a perfect excuse to check on another group of spies. And this time, Elend himself had sent them.

A sudden knock on the door made Jastes jump, and Elend closed his book, then opened the carriage door. Felt, one of the House Venture chief spies, climbed into the carriage, nodding his hawkish, mustached face respectfully to Elend, then Jastes.

"Well?" Jastes asked.

Felt sat down with the keen litheness of his kind. "The building is ostensibly a woodcrafter's shop, m'lord. One of my men has heard of the place—it's run by one Master Cladent, a skaa carpenter of no small skill."

Elend frowned. "Why did Valette's steward come here?"

"We think that the shop is a front, m'lord," Felt said. "We've been observing it ever since the steward led us here, as you ordered. However, we've had to be very careful—there are several watchnests hidden on its roof and top floors."

Elend frowned. "An odd precaution for a simple craftsman's shop, I should think."

Felt nodded. "That's not the half of it, m'lord. We managed to sneak one of our best men up to the building itself—we don't think he was spotted—but he had a remarkably difficult time hearing what's going on inside. The windows are sealed and stuffed to keep in sound."

Another odd precaution, Elend thought. "What do you think it means?" he asked Felt.

"It's got to be an underground hideout, m'lord," Felt said. "And a good one. If we hadn't been watching carefully, and been certain what to look for, we would never have noticed the signs. My guess is that the men inside—even the Terrisman—are members of a skaa thieving crew. A very well-funded and skilled one."

"A skaa thieving crew?" Jastes asked. "And Lady Valette too?"

"Likely, m'lord," Felt said.

Elend paused. "A . . . skaa thieving crew . . ." he said, stunned. *Why would they send one of their members to balls? To perform a scam of some sort, perhaps?*

"M'lord?" Felt asked. "Do you want us to break in? I've got enough men to take their entire crew."

"No," Elend said. "Call your men back, and tell no one of what you've seen this night."

"Yes, m'lord," Felt said, climbing out of the coach.

"Lord Ruler!" Jastes said as the carriage door closed. "No wonder she didn't seem like a regular noblewoman. It wasn't her rural upbringing—she's just a thief!"

Elend nodded, thoughtful, not certain what to think.

"You owe me an apology," Jastes said. "I was right about her, eh?"

"Perhaps," Elend said. "But . . . in a way, you were wrong about her too. She wasn't trying to spy on me—she was just trying to rob me."

"So?"

"I . . . need to think about this," Elend said, reaching out and knocking for the carriage to start moving. He sat back as the coach began to roll back toward Keep Venture.

Valette wasn't the person that she'd said she was. However, he'd already prepared himself for that news. Not only had Jastes's words about her made him suspicious, Valette herself hadn't denied Elend's accusations earlier in the night. It was obvious; she had been lying to him. Playing a part.

He should have been furious. He realized this, logically, and a piece of him did ache of betrayal. But, oddly, the primary emotion he felt was one of . . . relief.

"What?" Jastes asked, studying Elend with a frown.

Elend shook his head. "You've had me worrying over this for days, Jastes. I felt so sick that I could barely function—all because I thought that Valette was a traitor."

"But she *is*. Elend, she's probably trying to scam you!"

"Yes," Elend said, "but at least she probably isn't a spy for another house. In the face of all the intrigue, politics, and backbiting that has been going on lately, something as simple as a robbery feels slightly refreshing."

"But . . ."

"It's only money, Jastes."

"Money is kind of important to some of us, Elend."

"Not as important as Valette. That poor girl . . . all this time, she must have been worrying about the scam she would have to pull on me!"

Jastes sat for a moment, then he finally shook his head. "Elend, only *you* would be relieved to find out that someone was trying to steal from you. Need I remind you that the girl has been lying this entire time? You might have grown attached to her, but I doubt her own feelings are genuine."

"You may be right," Elend admitted. "But . . . I don't know, Jastes. I feel like I *know* this girl. Her emotions . . . they just seem too real, too honest, to be false."

"Doubtful," Jastes said.

Elend shook his head. "We don't have enough information to judge her yet. Felt thinks she's a thief, but there have to be other reasons a group like that would send someone to balls. Maybe she's just an informant. Or, maybe she is a thief—but not one who ever intended to rob me. She spent an awful lot of time mixing with the other nobility—why would she do that if I was her target? In fact, she spent relatively *little* time with me, and she never plied me for gifts."

He paused—imagining his meeting Valette as a pleasant accident, an event that had thrown a terrible twist into both of their lives. He smiled, then shook his head. "No, Jastes. There's more here than we're seeing. Something about her still doesn't make sense."

"I . . . suppose, El," Jastes said, frowning.

Elend sat upright, a sudden thought occurring to him—a

thought that made his speculations about Valette's motivation seem far less important. "Jastes," he said. "She's skaa!"

"And?"

"And she fooled me—fooled us both. She acted the part of an aristocrat almost perfectly."

"An inexperienced aristocrat, perhaps."

"I had a real skaa thief with me!" Elend said. "Think of the questions I could have asked her."

"Questions? What kind of questions?"

"Questions about being skaa," Elend said. "That's not the point. Jastes, she *fooled* us. If we can't tell the difference between a skaa and a noblewoman, that means that the skaa can't be very different from us. And, if they're not that different from us, what right do we have treating them as we do?"

Jastes shrugged. "Elend, I don't think you're looking at this in perspective. We're in the middle of a house war."

Elend nodded distractedly. *I was so hard on her this evening. Too hard?*

He had wanted her to believe, totally and completely, that he didn't want anything more to do with her. Part of that had been genuine, for his own worries had convinced him that she couldn't be trusted. And she couldn't be, not at the moment. Either way, he'd wanted her to leave the city. He'd thought that the best thing to do was break off the relationship until the house war was through.

But, assuming she's really not a noblewoman, then there's no reason for her to leave.

"Elend?" Jastes asked. "Are you even paying attention to me?"

Elend looked up. "I think I did something wrong tonight. I wanted to get Valette out of Luthadel. But, now I think I hurt her for no reason."

"Bloody hell, Elend!" Jastes said. "Allomancers were listening to our conference this night. Do you realize what could have happened? What if they'd decided to kill us, rather than just spy on us?"

"Ah, yes, you're right," Elend said with a distracted nod. "It's best if Valette leaves anyway. Anyone close to me will be in danger during the days to come."

Jastes paused, his annoyance deepening, then he finally laughed. "You're hopeless."

"I try my best," Elend said. "But, seriously, there's no use worrying. The spies gave themselves away, and likely got chased off—or even captured—in the chaos. We now know some of the secrets that Valette is hiding, so we're ahead there too. It's been a very productive night!"

"That's an optimistic way of looking at it, I guess. . . ."

"Once again, I try my best." Even still, he would feel more comfortable when they got back to Keep Venture. Perhaps it had been foolhardy to sneak away from the palace before hearing the details of what had happened, but Elend hadn't exactly been thinking carefully at the time. Besides, he'd had the previously arranged meeting with Felt to attend, and the chaos had made a perfect opportunity to slip away.

The carriage slowly pulled up to the Venture gates. "You should go," Elend said, slipping out of the carriage door. "Take the books."

Jastes nodded, grabbing the sack, then bidding Elend farewell as he shut the carriage door. Elend waited as the carriage rolled back away from the gates, then he turned and walked the rest of the way to the keep, the surprised gate guards letting him pass with ease.

The grounds were still ablaze with light. Guards were already waiting for him at the front of the keep, and a group of them rushed out into the mists to meet him. And surround him.

"My lord, your father—"

"Yes," Elend interrupted, sighing. "I assume I'm to be taken to him immediately?"

"Yes, my lord."

"Lead on, then, Captain."

They entered through the lord's entrance on the side of the building. Lord Straff Venture stood in his study, speaking with a group of guard officers. Elend could tell from the pale faces that they had received a firm scolding, perhaps even threats of beatings. They were noblemen, so Venture couldn't execute them, but he was very fond of the more brutal disciplinary forms.

Lord Venture dismissed the soldiers with a sharp gesture, then turned to Elend with hostile eyes. Elend frowned, watching the soldiers go. Everything all seemed a little too . . . tense.

"Well?" Lord Venture demanded.

"Well what?"

"Where have you been?"

"Oh, I left," Elend said offhandedly.

Lord Venture sighed. "Fine. Endanger yourself if you wish, boy. In a way, it's too bad that Mistborn *didn't* catch you—they could have saved me a great deal of frustration."

"Mistborn?" Elend asked, frowning. "What Mistborn?"

"The one that was planning to assassinate you," Lord Venture snapped.

Elend blinked in startlement. "So . . . it wasn't just a spying team?"

"Oh, no," Venture said, smiling somewhat wickedly. "An entire assassination team, sent here after you and your friends."

Lord Ruler! Elend thought, realizing how foolish he had been to go out alone. *I didn't expect the house war to get so dangerous so quickly! At least, not for me . . .*

"How do we know it was a Mistborn?" Elend asked, gathering his wits.

"Our guards managed to kill her," Straff said. "As she was fleeing."

Elend frowned. "A full Mistborn? Killed by common soldiers?"

"Archers," Lord Venture said. "Apparently, they took her by surprise."

"And the man who fell through my skylight?" Elend asked.

"Dead," Lord Venture said. "Broken neck."

Elend frowned. *That man was still alive when we fled. What are you hiding, Father?* "The Mistborn. Anyone I know?"

"I'd say so," Lord Venture said, settling into his desk chair, not looking up. "It was Shan Elariel."

Elend froze in shock. *Shan?* he thought, dumbfounded. They'd been engaged, and she'd never even mentioned that she was an Allomancer. That probably meant . . .

She'd been a plant all along. Perhaps House Elariel had planned to have Elend killed once an Elariel grandson was born to the house title.

You're right, Jastes. I can't avoid politics by ignoring it. I've been a part of it all for much longer than I assumed.

His father was obviously pleased with himself. A high-profile member of House Elariel was dead on Venture grounds after trying to assassinate Elend. . . . With such a triumph, Lord Venture would be insufferable for days.

Elend sighed. "Did we capture any of the assassins alive, then?"

Straff shook his head. "One fell to the courtyard as he was trying to flee. He got away—he might have been Mistborn too. We found one man dead on the roof, but we aren't sure if there were others in the team or not." He paused.

"What?" Elend asked, reading the slight confusion in his father's eyes.

"Nothing," Straff said, waving a dismissive hand. "Some of the guards claim there was a third Mistborn, fighting the other two, but I doubt the reports—it wasn't one of ours."

Elend paused. *A third Mistborn, fighting the other two . . .* "Maybe someone found out about the assassination and tried to stop it."

Lord Venture snorted. "Why would someone else's Mistborn try to protect *you*?"

"Maybe they just wanted to stop an innocent man from being murdered."

Lord Venture shook his head, laughing. "You are an idiot, boy. You understand that, right?"

Elend flushed, then turned away. It didn't appear that Lord Venture wanted anything more, so Elend left. He couldn't go back to his rooms, not with the broken window and the guards, so he made his way to a guest bedroom, calling for a set of hazekillers to watch outside his door and balcony—just in case.

He prepared for bed, thinking about the conversation. His father was probably right about the third Mistborn. That just wasn't the way things worked.

But . . . that's the way it should be. The way it could be, maybe.

There were so many things Elend wished he could do. But, his father was healthy, and young for a lord of his power. It would be decades before Elend assumed the house title, assuming he even survived that long. He wished he could go to Valette, talk to her, explain his frustrations. She'd understand what he was thinking; for some reason, she always seemed to understand him better than others.

And, she's skaa! He couldn't get over the thought. He had so many questions, so many things he wanted to find out from her.

Later, he thought as he climbed into bed. *For now, focus on keeping the house together.* His words to Valette in that area hadn't been false—he needed to make certain his family survived the house war.

After that . . . well, perhaps they could find a way to work around the lies and the scams.

Though many Terrismen express a resentment of Khlennium, there is also envy. I have heard the packmen speak in wonder of the Khlenni cathedrals, with their amazing stained-glass windows and broad halls. They also seem very fond of our fashion—back in the cities, I saw that many young Terrismen had traded in their furs and skins for well-tailored gentlemen's suits.

32

TWO STREETS OVER FROM CLUBS'S shop, there was a building of unusual height compared with those surrounding it. It was some kind of tenement, Vin thought—a place to pack skaa families. She'd never been inside of it, however.

She dropped a coin, then shot herself up along the side of the six-story building. She landed lightly on the rooftop, causing a figure crouching in the darkness to jump in surprise.

"It's just me," Vin whispered, sneaking quietly across the sloped roof.

Spook smiled at her in the night. As the crew's best Tineye, he usually got the most important watches. Recently, those were the ones during the early evening. That was the time when conflict among the Great Houses was most likely to turn to outright fighting.

"Are they still going at it?" Vin asked quietly, flaring her tin, scanning the city. A bright haze shone in the distance, giving the mists a strange luminescence.

Spook nodded, pointing toward the light. "Keep Hasting. Elariel soldiers with the attacking tonight."

Vin nodded. Keep Hasting's destruction had been expected for some time—it had suffered a half-dozen raids from different houses during the last week. Allies withdrawing, finances wrecked, it was only a matter of time before it fell.

Oddly, none of the houses attacked during the daytime. There was a feigned air of secrecy about the war, as if the aristocracy acknowledged the Lord Ruler's dominance, and didn't want to upset him by resorting to daylight warfare. It was all handled at night, beneath a cloak of mists.

"Wasing the *want* of this," Spook said.

Vin paused. "Uh, Spook. Could you try to speak . . . normal?"

Spook nodded toward a distant, dark structure in the distance. "The Lord Ruler. Liking he wants the fighting."

Vin nodded. *Kelsier was right. There hasn't been much of an outcry from the Ministry or the palace regarding the house war, and the Garrison is taking its time getting back to Luthadel. The Lord Ruler expected the house war—and intends to let it run its course. Like a wildfire, left to blaze and renew a field.*

Except this time, as one fire died, another would start—Kelsier's attack on the city.

Assuming Marsh can find out how to stop the Steel Inquisitors. Assuming we can take the palace. And, of course, assuming Kelsier can find a way to deal with the Lord Ruler . . .

Vin shook her head. She didn't want to think poorly of Kelsier, but she just didn't see how it was all going to happen. The Garrison wasn't back yet, but reports said it was close, perhaps only a week or two out. Some noble houses were falling, but there didn't seem to be the air of general chaos that Kelsier had wanted. The Final Empire was strained, but she doubted that it would crack.

However, maybe that wasn't the point. The crew had done an amazing job of instigating a house war; three entire Great Houses were no more, and the rest were seriously weakened. It would take decades for the aristocracy to recover from their own squabbling.

We've done an amazing job, Vin decided. *Even if we don't attack the palace—or if that attack fails—we'll have accomplished something wonderful.*

With Marsh's intelligence about the Ministry and Sazed's translation of the logbook, the rebellion would have new and useful information for future resistance. It wasn't what Kelsier had hoped for; it wasn't a complete toppling of the Final Empire. However, it was a major victory—one that the skaa could look to for years as a source of courage.

And, with a start of surprise, Vin realized that she felt proud to have been part of it. Perhaps, in the future, she could help start a real rebellion—one in a place where the skaa weren't quite so beaten down.

If such a place exists . . . Vin was beginning to understand that it wasn't just Luthadel and its Soothing stations that made skaa subservient. It was *everything*—the obligators, the constant work in field and mill, the mind-set encouraged by a thousand years of oppression. There was a reason why skaa rebellions were always so small. The people knew—or thought they knew—that there was no fighting against the Final Empire.

Even Vin—who'd assumed herself a "liberated" thief—had believed the same. It had taken Kelsier's insane, over-the-top plan to convince her otherwise. Perhaps that was why he'd set such lofty goals for the crew—he'd known that only something this challenging would make them realize, in a strange way, that they *could* resist.

Spook glanced at her. Her presence still made him uncomfortable.

"Spook," Vin said, "you know that Elend broke off his relationship with me."

Spook nodded, perking up slightly.

"But," Vin said regretfully, "I still love him. I'm sorry, Spook. But it's true."

He looked down, deflating.

"It's not you," Vin said. "Really, it isn't. It's just that . . . well, you can't help who you love. Trust me, there are some people I really would rather *not* have loved. They didn't deserve it."

Spook nodded. "I understand."

"Can I still keep the handkerchief?"

He shrugged.

"Thank you," she said. "It does mean a lot to me."

He looked up, staring out into the mists. "I'm notting a fool. I . . . knew it wasing not to happen. I see things, Vin. I see lots of things."

She laid a comforting hand on his shoulder. *I see things. . . .* An appropriate statement, for a Tineye like him.

"You've been an Allomancer for a long time?" she asked.

Spook nodded. "Wasing the Snap when I was five. Barely even remember it."

"And since then you've been practicing with tin?"

"Mostly," he said. "Wasing a good thing for me. Letting me see, letting me hear, letting me feel."

"Any tips you can pass on?" Vin asked hopefully.

He paused thoughtfully, sitting by the edge of the slanted rooftop, one foot dangling over the side. "Tin burning . . . Notting about the seeing. Wasing about the *not seeing.*"

Vin frowned. "What do you mean?"

"When burning," he said, "everything comes. Lots of everything. Distractions here, there. Iffing the power of wants, *ignoring* the distractions of both."

If you want to be good at burning tin, she thought, translating as best she could, *learn to deal with distraction. It isn't about what you see—it's about what you can ignore.*

"Interesting," Vin said thoughtfully.

Spook nodded. "When looking, seeing the mist and seeing the houses and feeling the wood and hearing the rats below. Choose one, and don't get distracted."

"Good advice," Vin said.

Spook nodded as a sound thumped behind them. They both

jumped and ducked down, and Kelsier chuckled as he walked across the rooftop. "We really have to find a better way of warning people that we're coming up. Every time I visit a spynest, I worry that I'm going to startle someone off the rooftop."

Vin stood, dusting off her clothing. She wore mistcloak, shirt, and trousers; it had been days since she'd worn a dress. She only put in token appearances at Mansion Renoux. Kelsier was too worried about assassins to let her stay there for long.

At least we bought Kliss's silence, Vin thought, annoyed at the expense. "It's time?" she asked.

Kelsier nodded. "Nearly so, at least. I want to stop somewhere on the way."

Vin nodded. For their second meeting, Marsh had chosen a location that he was supposedly scouting for the Ministry. It was a perfect opportunity to meet, since Marsh had an excuse to be in the building all night, ostensibly Seeking for any Allomantic activity nearby. He would have a Soother with him for a good deal of the time, but there would be an opening near the middle of the night when Marsh figured he would have a good hour alone. Not much time if he had to sneak out and back, but plenty of time for a pair of stealthy Mistborn to pay him a quick visit.

They bid farewell to Spook and Pushed off into the night. However, they didn't travel the rooftops for long before Kelsier led them down onto the street, landing and walking to conserve strength and metals.

It's kind of odd, Vin thought, remembering her first night practicing Allomancy with Kelsier. *I don't even think of the empty streets as creepy anymore.*

The cobblestones were slick from mistwater, and the deserted street eventually disappeared into the distant haze. It was dark, silent, and lonely; even the war hadn't changed very much. Soldier groups, when they attacked, went in clumps, striking quickly and trying to overrun the defenses of an enemy house.

Yet, despite the emptiness of the nighttime city, Vin felt comfortable in it. The mists were with her.

"Vin," Kelsier said as they walked. "I want to thank you."

She turned to him, a tall, proud figure in a majestic mistcloak. "Thank me? Why?"

"For the things you said about Mare. I've been thinking a lot about that day . . . about her. I don't know if your ability to see through copperclouds explains everything, but . . . well, given the choice, I'd rather believe that Mare *didn't* betray me."

Vin nodded, smiling.

He shook his head ruefully. "It sounds foolish, doesn't it? As if . . . all these years, I've just been waiting for a reason to give in to self-delusion."

"I don't know," Vin said. "Once, maybe I would have thought you a fool, but . . . well, that's kind of what trust is, isn't it? A willful self-delusion? You have to shut out that voice that whispers about betrayal, and just hope that your friends aren't going to hurt you."

Kelsier chuckled. "I don't think you're helping the argument any, Vin."

She shrugged. "Makes sense to me. Distrust is really the same thing—only on the other side. I can see how a person, given the choice between two assumptions, would choose to trust."

"But not you?" Kelsier asked.

Vin shrugged again. "I don't know anymore."

Kelsier hesitated. "This . . . Elend of yours. There's a chance that he was just trying to scare you into leaving the city, right? Perhaps he said those things for your own good."

"Maybe," Vin said. "But, there was something different about him . . . about the way he looked at me. He knew I was lying to him, but I don't think he realized that I was skaa. He probably thought I was a spy from one of the other houses. Either way, he seemed honest in his desire to be rid of me."

"Maybe you thought that because you were already convinced that he was going to leave you."

"I . . ." Vin trailed off, glancing down at the slick, ashen street as they walked. "I don't know—and it's your fault, you know. I used to understand everything. Now it's all confused."

"Yes, we've messed you up right properly," Kelsier said with a smile.

"You don't seem bothered by the fact."

"Nope," Kelsier said. "Not a bit. Ah, here we are."

He stopped beside a large, wide building—probably another skaa tenement. It was dark inside; skaa couldn't afford lamp oil, and they would have put out the building's central hearth after preparing the evening meal.

"This?" Vin asked uncertainly.

Kelsier nodded, walking up to tap lightly on the door. To Vin's surprise, it opened hesitantly, a wiry skaa face peeking out into the mists.

"Lord Kelsier!" the man said quietly.

"I told you I'd visit," Kelsier said, smiling. "Tonight seemed like a good time."

"Come in, come in," the man said, pulling the door open. He stepped back, careful not to let any of the mist touch him as Kelsier and Vin entered.

Vin had been in skaa tenements before, but never before had they seemed so . . . depressing. The smell of smoke and unwashed bodies was almost overpowering, and she had to extinguish her tin to keep from gagging. The wan light of a small coal stove showed a crowd of people packed together, sleeping on the floor. They kept the room swept of ash, but there was only so much they could do—black stains still covered clothing, walls, and faces. There were few furnishings, not to mention far too few blankets to go around.

I used to live like this, Vin thought with horror. *The crew lairs were just as packed—sometimes more so. This . . . was my life.*

People roused as they saw that they had a visitor. Kelsier had his sleeves rolled up, Vin noticed, and the scars on his arms were visible even by emberlight. They stood out starkly, running lengthwise up from his wrist past his elbows, crisscrossing and overlapping.

The whispers began immediately.

"The Survivor . . ."

"He's here!"

"Kelsier, the Lord of the Mists . . ."

That's a new one, Vin thought with a raised eyebrow. She stayed back as Kelsier smiled, stepping forward to meet the skaa. The people gathered around him with quiet excitement, reaching out to touch his arms and cloak. Others just stood and stared, watching him with reverence.

"I come to spread hope," Kelsier said to them quietly. "House Hasting fell tonight."

There were murmurs of surprise and awe.

"I know many of you worked in the Hasting smithies and steel mills," Kelsier said. "And, honestly, I cannot say what this means for you. But it is a victory for all of us. For a time, at least, your men won't die before the forges or beneath the whips of Hasting taskmasters."

There were murmurs through the small crowd, and one voice finally spoke the concern loud enough for Vin to hear. "House Hasting is gone? Who will feed us?"

So frightened, Vin thought. *I was never like* that . . . *was I?*

"I'll send you another shipment of food," Kelsier promised. "Enough to last you for a while, at least."

"You've done so much for us," another man said.

"Nonsense," Kelsier said. "If you wish to repay me, then stand up just a little straighter. Be a little less afraid. They *can* be beaten."

"By men like you, Lord Kelsier," a woman whispered. "But not by us."

"You'd be surprised," Kelsier said as the crowd began to make way for parents bringing their children forward. It seemed like everyone in the room wanted their sons to meet Kelsier personally. Vin watched with mixed feelings. The crew still had reservations regarding Kelsier's rising fame with the skaa, though they kept their word and remained silent.

He really does seem to care for them, Vin thought, watching Kelsier pick up a small child. *I don't think it's just a show. This is how he is—he loves people, loves the skaa. But . . . it's more like the love of a parent for a child than it is like the love of a man for his equals.*

Was that so wrong? He was, after all, a kind of father to the skaa. He was the noble lord they always *should* have had. Still, Vin couldn't help feeling uncomfortable as she watched the faintly illuminated, dirty faces of those skaa families, their eyes worshipful and reverent.

Kelsier eventually bid the group farewell, telling them he had an appointment. Vin and he left the cramped room, stepping out into blessedly fresh air. Kelsier remained quiet as they traveled toward Marsh's new Soothing station, though he did walk with a bit more of a spring in his step.

Eventually, Vin had to say something. "You visit them often?"

Kelsier nodded. "At least a couple of houses a night. It breaks up the monotony of my other work."

Killing noblemen and spreading false rumors, Vin thought. *Yes, visiting the skaa would be a nice break.*

The meeting place was only a few streets away. Kelsier paused in a doorway as they approached, squinting in the dark night. Finally, he pointed at a window, just faintly lit. "Marsh said he'd leave a light burning if the other obligators were gone."

"Window or stairs?" Vin asked.

"Stairs," Kelsier said. "The door should be unlocked, and the Ministry owns the entire building. It will be empty."

Kelsier was right on both counts. The building didn't smell musty enough to be abandoned, but the bottom few floors were obviously unused. Vin and he quickly climbed up the stairwell.

"Marsh should be able to tell us the Ministry reaction to the House War," Kelsier said as they reached the top floor. Lanternlight flickered through the door at the top, and he pushed it open, still speaking. "Hopefully, that Garrison won't get back too quickly. The damage is mostly done, but I'd like the war to go on for—"

He froze in the doorway, blocking Vin's view.

She flared pewter and tin immediately, falling to a crouch, listening for attackers. There was nothing. Just silence.

"No . . ." Kelsier whispered.

Then Vin saw the trickle of dark red liquid seeping around the side of Kelsier's foot. It pooled slightly, then began to drip down the first step.

Oh, Lord Ruler . . .

Kelsier stumbled into the room. Vin followed, but she knew what she'd see. The corpse lay near the center of the chamber, flayed and dismembered, the head completely crushed. It was barely recognizable as human. The walls were sprayed red.

Could one body really produce this much blood? It was just like before, in the basement of Camon's lair—only with a single victim.

"Inquisitor," Vin whispered.

Kelsier, heedless of the gore, stumbled to his knees beside Marsh's corpse. He raised a hand as if to touch the skinless body, but remained frozen there, stunned.

"Kelsier," Vin said urgently. "This was recent—the Inquisitor could still be near."

He didn't move.

"Kelsier!" Vin snapped.

Kelsier shook, looking around. His eyes met hers, and lucidity returned. He stumbled to his feet.

"Window," Vin said, rushing across the room. She paused, however, when she saw something sitting on a small desk beside the wall. A wooden table leg, tucked half-hidden beneath a blank sheet of paper. Vin snatched it as Kelsier reached the window.

He turned back, looking over the room one last time, then jumped out into the night.

Farewell, Marsh, Vin thought regretfully, following.

"'I think that the Inquisitors suspect me,'" Dockson read. The paper—a single sheet recovered from inside the table leg—was clean and white, free from the blood that stained Kelsier's knees and the bottom of Vin's cloak.

Dockson continued, reading as he sat at Clubs's kitchen table. "'I've been asking too many questions, and I know they sent at least one message to the corrupt obligator who supposedly trained me as an acolyte. I thought to seek out the secrets that the rebellion has always needed to know. How does the Ministry recruit Mistborn to be Inquisitors? Why are Inquisitors more powerful than regular Allomancers? What, if any, are their weaknesses?

"'Unfortunately, I've learned next to nothing about the Inquisitors—though the politicking within the regular Ministry ranks continues to amaze me. It's like the regular obligators don't even care about the world outside, except for the prestige they earn by being the most clever or successful in applying the Lord Ruler's dictates.

" 'The Inquisitors, however, are different. They are far more loyal to the Lord Ruler than the regular obligators—and this is, perhaps, part of the dissension between the two groups.

" 'Regardless, I feel that I am close. They *do* have a secret, Kelsier. A weakness. I'm sure of it. The other obligators whisper of it, though none of them know it.

" 'I fear that I've prodded too much. The Inquisitors tail me, watch me, ask after me. So, I prepare this note. Perhaps my caution is unnecessary.

" 'Perhaps not.' "

Dockson looked up. "That's . . . all it says."

Kelsier stood at the far side of the kitchen, back to the cupboard, reclining in his usual position. But . . . there was no levity in his posture this time. He stood with arms folded, head slightly bowed. His disbelieving grief appeared to have vanished, replaced with another emotion—one Vin had sometimes seen smoldering darkly behind his eyes. Usually when he spoke of the nobility.

She shivered despite herself. Standing as he was, she was suddenly aware of his clothing—dark gray mistcloak, long-sleeved black shirt, charcoal trousers. In the night, the clothing was simply camouflage. In the lit room, however, the black colors made him look menacing.

He stood up straight, and the room grew tense.

"Tell Renoux to pull out," Kelsier said softly, his voice like iron. "He can use the planned exit story—that of a 'retreat' back to his family lands because of the house war—but I want him gone by tomorrow. Send a Thug and a Tineye with him as protection, but tell him to abandon his canal boats one day out of the city, then return to us."

Dockson paused, then glanced at Vin and the others. "Okay . . ."

"Marsh knew everything, Dox," Kelsier said. "They broke him before they killed him—that's how Inquisitors work."

He let the words hang. Vin felt a chill. The lair was compromised.

"To the backup lair, then?" Dockson asked. "Only you and I knew its location."

Kelsier nodded firmly. "I want everyone out of this shop, apprentices included, in fifteen minutes. I'll meet you at the backup lair in two days."

Dockson looked up at Kelsier, frowning. "Two days? Kell, what are you planning?"

Kelsier strode over to the door. He threw it open, letting in the mist, then glanced back at the crew with eyes as hard as any Inquisitor's spikes.

"They hit me where it couldn't have hurt worse. I'm going to do likewise."

Walin pushed himself in the darkness, feeling his way through the cramped caverns, forcing his body through cracks nearly too small. He continued downward, searching with his fingers, ignoring his numerous scrapes and cuts.

Must keep going, must keep going . . . His remaining sanity told him that this was his last day. It had been six days since his last success. If he failed a seventh time, he would die.

Must keep going.

He couldn't see; he was too far beneath the surface to catch even a reflected glimpse of sunlight. But, even without light, he could find his way. There were only two directions: up and down. Movements to the side were unimportant, easily disregarded. He couldn't get lost as long as he kept moving down.

All the while, he quested with his fingers, seeking the telltale roughness of budding crystal. He couldn't return this time, not until he'd been successful, not until . . .

Must keep going.

His hands brushed something soft and cold as he moved. A corpse, stuck rotting between two rocks. Walin moved on. Bodies weren't uncommon in the tight caverns; some of the corpses were fresh, most were simply bones. Often, Walin wondered if the dead ones weren't really the lucky ones.

Must keep going.

There wasn't really "time" in the caverns. Usually, he returned above to sleep—though the surface held taskmasters with whips, they also had food. It was meager, barely enough to keep him alive, but it was better than the starvation that would come from staying below too long.

Must keep—

He froze. He lay with his torso pinched in a tight rift in the rock, and had been in the process of wiggling his way through. However, his fingers—always searching, even when he was barely conscious—had been feeling the walls. And they'd found something.

His hand quivered with anticipation as he felt the crystal buds. Yes, yes, that was them. They grew in a wide, circular pattern on the wall; they were small at the edges, but got gradually bigger near the center. At the direct middle of the circular pattern, the crystals curved inward, following a pocketlike hollow in the wall. Here, the crystals grew long, each one having a jagged, sharp edge. Like teeth lining the maw of a stone beast.

Taking a breath, praying to the Lord Ruler, Walin rammed his hand into the fist-sized, circular opening. The crystals ripped his arm, tearing long, shallow gashes in his skin. He ignored the pain, forcing his arm in further, up to his elbow, searching with his fingers for . . .

There! His fingers found a small rock at the center of the pocket—a rock formed by the mysterious drippings of the crystals. A Hathsin geode.

He grasped it eagerly, pulling it out, ripping his arm again as he withdrew it from the crystal-lined hole. He cradled the small rock sphere, breathing heavily with joy.

Another seven days. He would live another seven days.

Before hunger and fatigue could weaken him further, Walin began the laborious climb back upward. He squeezed through crevasses, climbed up juttings in walls. Sometimes he had to move to the right or left until the ceiling opened up, but it always did. There were really only two directions: up and down.

He kept a wary ear out for others. He had seen climbers killed before, slain by younger, stronger men who hoped to steal a geode. Fortunately, he met nobody. It was good. He was an older man—old enough to know that he never should have tried to steal food from his plantation lord.

Perhaps he had earned his punishment. Perhaps he deserved to die in the Pits of Hathsin.

But I won't die today, he thought, finally smelling sweet, fresh air. It was night above. He didn't care. The mists didn't bother him anymore—even beatings didn't bother him much anymore. He was just too tired to care.

Walin began to climb out of the crack—one of dozens in the small, flat valley known as the Pits of Hathsin. Then he froze.

A man stood above him in the night. He was dressed in a large cloak that appeared to have been shredded to strips. The man looked at Walin, quiet and powerful in his black clothing. Then he reached down.

Walin cringed. The man, however, grabbed Walin's hand and pulled him out of the crack.

"Go!" the man said quietly in the swirling mists. "Most of the guards are dead. Gather as many prisoners as you can, and escape this place. You have a geode?"

Walin cringed again, pulling his hand toward his chest.

"Good," the stranger said. "Break it open. You'll find a nugget of metal inside—it is very valuable. Sell it to the underground in whatever city you eventually find yourself; you should earn enough to live on for years. Go quickly! I don't know how long you have until an alarm is raised."

Walin stumbled back, confused. "Who . . . who are you?"

"I am what *you* will soon be," the stranger said, stepping up to the rift. The ribbons of his enveloping black cloak billowed around him, mixing with the mists as he turned toward Walin. "I am a survivor."

Kelsier looked down, studying the dark scar in the rock, listening as the prisoner scrambled away in the distance.

"And so I return," Kelsier whispered. His scars burned, and memories returned. Memories of months spent squeezing through cracks, of ripping his arms on crystalline knives, of seeking each day to find a geode . . . just one, so that he could live on.

Could he really go back down into those cramped, quiet

depths? Could he enter the darkness again? Kelsier held up his arms, looking at the scars, still white and stark on his arms.

Yes. For her dreams, he could.

He stepped over to the rift and forced himself to climb down inside of it. Then he burned tin. Immediately, he heard a cracking sound from below.

Tin illuminated the rift beneath him. Though the crack widened, it also branched, sending out twisting rifts in all directions. Part cavern, part crack, part tunnel. He could already see his first crystalline atium-hole—or what was left of it. The long, silvery crystals were fractured and broken.

Using Allomancy near atium crystals caused them to shatter. That was why the Lord Ruler had to use slaves, and not Allomancers, to collect his atium for him.

Now the real test, Kelsier thought, squeezing down further into the crack. He burned iron, and immediately he saw several blue lines pointing downward, toward atium-holes. Though the holes themselves probably didn't have an atium geode in them, the crystals themselves gave off faint blue lines. They contained residual amounts of atium.

Kelsier focused on one of the blue lines and Pulled lightly. His tin enhanced ears heard something shatter in the crack beneath him.

Kelsier smiled.

Nearly three years before, standing over the bloody corpses of the taskmasters who had beaten Mare to death, he had first noticed that he could use iron to sense where crystal pockets were. He'd barely understood his Allomantic powers at the time, but even then, a plan had begun to form in his mind. A plan for vengeance.

That plan had evolved, growing to encompass so much more than he'd originally intended. However, one of its key parts had remained sequestered away in a corner of his mind. He could find the crystal pockets. He could shatter them, using Allomancy.

And they were the only means of producing atium in the entire Final Empire.

You tried to destroy me, Pits of Hathsin, he thought, climbing down further into the rift. *It's time to return the favor.*

We are close now. Oddly, this high in the mountains, we seem to finally be free from the oppressive touch of the Deepness. It has been quite a while since I knew what that was like.

The lake that Fedik discovered is below us now—I can see it from the ledge. It looks even more eerie from up here, with its glassy—almost metallic—sheen. I almost wish I had let him take a sample of its waters.

Perhaps his interest was what angered the mist creature that follows us. Perhaps . . . that was why it decided to attack him, stabbing him with its invisible knife.

Strangely, the attack comforted me. At least I know that since another has seen it. That means I'm not mad.

33

"SO . . . THAT'S IT?" VIN ASKED. "For the plan, I mean."

Ham shrugged. "If the Inquisitors broke Marsh, that means they know everything. Or, at least, they know enough. They'll know that we plan to strike the palace, and that we're going to use the house war as a cover. We'll never get the Lord Ruler out of the city now, and we'll certainly never get him to send the palace guard into the city. It doesn't look good, Vin."

Vin sat quietly, digesting the information. Ham sat cross-legged on the dirty floor, leaning against the bricks of the far wall. The backup lair was a dank cellar with only three rooms, and the air smelled of dirt and ash. Clubs's apprentices took up one room to themselves, though Dockson had sent away all of the other servants before coming to the safe house.

Breeze stood by the far wall. He occasionally shot uncomfortable looks at the dirty floor and dusty stools, but then decided to remain standing. Vin didn't see why he bothered—it was going to be impossible to keep his suits clean while living in what was, essentially, a pit in the ground.

Breeze wasn't the only one taking their self-imposed captivity resentfully; Vin had heard several of the apprentices grumble that they'd almost rather have been taken by the Ministry. Yet, during their two days in the cellar, everyone had stayed in the safe house except when absolutely necessary. They understood the danger: Marsh could have given the Inquisitors descriptions and aliases for each crewmember.

Breeze shook his head. "Perhaps, gentlemen, it is time to pack up this operation. We tried hard, and considering the fact that our original plan—gathering the army—ended up so dreadfully, I'd say that we've done quite a marvelous job."

Dockson sighed. "Well, we certainly can't live off of saved funds for much longer—especially if Kell keeps giving our money away to the skaa." He sat beside the table that was the room's only piece of furniture, his most important ledgers, notes, and contracts organized into neat piles before him. He had been remarkably efficient at gathering every bit of paper that could have incriminated the crew or given further information about their plan.

Breeze nodded. "I, for one, am looking forward to a change. This has all been fun, delightful, and all of those other fulfilling emotions, but working with Kelsier can be a bit draining."

Vin frowned. "You're not going to stay on his crew?"

"It depends on his next job," Breeze said. "We aren't like other crews you've known—we work as we please, not because we are told to. It pays for us to be very discerning in the jobs we take. The rewards are great, but so are the risks."

Ham smiled, resting with his arms behind his head, completely unconcerned about the dirt. "It kind of makes you wonder how we ended up on this particular job, eh? Very high risk, very little reward."

"None, actually," Breeze noted. "We'll never get that atium now. Kelsier's words about altruism and working to help the skaa were all well and good, but I was always hoping that we'd still get to take a swipe at that treasury."

"True," Dockson said, looking up from his notes. "But, was it worth it anyway? The work we did—the things we accomplished?"

Breeze and Ham paused, then they both nodded.

"And that's why we stayed," Dockson said. "Kell said it himself—he picked us because he knew we would try something a little different to accomplish a worthwhile goal. You're good men—even you, Breeze. Stop scowling at me."

Vin smiled at the familiar banter. There was a sense of mourning regarding Marsh, but these were men who knew how to move on despite their losses. In that way, they really were like skaa, after all.

"A house war," Ham said idly, smiling to himself. "How many noblemen dead, do you think?"

"Hundreds, at least," Dockson said without looking up. "All killed by their own greedy noble hands."

"I'll admit that I had my doubts about this entire fiasco," Breeze said. "But the interruption in trade this will cause, not to mention the disorder in the government . . . well, you're right, Dockson. It was worth it."

"Indeed!" Ham said, mimicking Breeze's stuffy voice.

I'm going to miss them, Vin thought regretfully. *Maybe Kelsier will take me with him on his next job.*

The stairs rattled, and Vin moved reflexively back into the shadows. The splintery door opened, and a familiar, black-clothed form strode in. He carried his mistcloak over his arm, and his face looked incredibly wearied.

"Kelsier!" Vin said, stepping forward.

"Hello, all," he said in a tired voice.

I know that tiredness, Vin thought. *Pewter drag. Where has he been?*

"You're late, Kell," Dockson said, still not looking up from his ledgers.

"I strive for nothing if not consistency," Kelsier said, dropping his mistcloak on the floor, stretching, then sitting down. "Where are Clubs and Spook?"

"Clubs is sleeping in the back room," Dockson said. "Spook went with Renoux. We figured you'd want him to have our best Tineye to keep a watch."

"Good idea," Kelsier said, letting out a deep sigh and closing his eyes as he leaned against the wall.

"My dear man," Breeze said, "you look terrible."

"It's not as bad as it looks—I took it easy coming back, even stopped to sleep for a few hours on the way."

"Yes, but where *were* you?" Ham asked pointedly. "We've been worried sick that you were out doing something . . . well, stupid."

"Actually," Breeze noted, "we took it for granted that you were doing something stupid. We've just been wondering *how* stupid this particular event would turn out to be. So, what is it? Did you assassinate the lord prelan? Slaughter dozens of noblemen? Steal the cloak off the Lord Ruler's own back?"

"I destroyed the Pits of Hathsin," Kelsier said quietly.

The room fell into a stunned silence.

"You know," Breeze finally said, "you'd think that by now we'd have learned not to underestimate him."

"Destroyed them?" Ham asked. "How do you destroy the Pits of Hathsin? They're just a bunch of cracks in the ground!"

"Well, I didn't actually destroy the pits themselves," Kelsier explained. "I just shattered the crystals that produce atium geodes."

"All of them?" Dockson asked, dumbstruck.

"All of them that I could find," Kelsier said. "And that was several hundred pockets' worth. It was actually a lot easier to get around down there, now that I have Allomancy."

"Crystals?" Vin asked, confused.

"Atium crystals, Vin," Dockson said. "They produce the geodes—I don't think anyone actually knows how—that have atium beads at the center."

Kelsier nodded. "The crystals are why the Lord Ruler can't just send down Allomancers to Pull out the atium geodes. Using Allomancy near the crystals makes them shatter—and it takes centuries for them to grow back."

"Centuries during which they won't produce atium," Dockson added.

"And so you . . ." Vin trailed off.

"I pretty much ended atium production in the Final Empire for the next three hundred years or so."

Elend. House Venture. They're in charge of the Pits. How will the Lord Ruler react when he finds out about this?

"You madman," Breeze said quietly, eyes open wide.

"Atium is the foundation of the imperial economy—controlling it is one of the main ways that the Lord Ruler maintains his hold over the nobility. We may not get to his reserves, but this will eventually have the same effect. You blessed lunatic . . . you blessed *genius*!"

Kelsier smiled wryly. "I appreciate both compliments. Have the Inquisitors moved against Clubs's shop yet?"

"Not that our watchmen have seen," Dockson said.

"Good," Kelsier said. "Maybe they didn't get Marsh to break. At the very least, maybe they don't realize that their Soothing stations were compromised. Now, if you don't mind, I'm going to sleep. We have a lot of planning to do tomorrow."

The group paused.

"Planning?" Dox finally asked. "Kell . . . we were kind of thinking that we should pull out. We caused a house war, and you just took out the imperial economy. With our cover—and our plan—compromised . . . Well, you can't honestly expect us to do anything more, right?"

Kelsier smiled, staggering to his feet and moving into the back room. "We'll talk tomorrow."

"What do you think he's planning, Sazed?" Vin asked, sitting on a stool beside the cellar's hearth as the Terrisman prepared the afternoon meal. Kelsier had slept through the night, and had yet to rise this afternoon.

"I really have no idea, Mistress," Sazed replied, sipping the stew. "Though, this moment—with the city so unbalanced—does seem like the perfect opportunity to move against the Final Empire."

Vin sat thoughtfully. "I suppose we could still seize the palace—that's what Kell always wanted to do. But, if the Lord Ruler has been warned, the others don't see that happening. Plus, it doesn't seem like we have enough soldiers to do much in the city. Ham and Breeze never finished their recruiting."

Sazed shrugged.

"Maybe Kelsier plans to do something about the Lord Ruler," Vin mused.

"Perhaps."

"Sazed?" Vin said slowly. "You collect legends, right?"

"As a Keeper I collect many things," Sazed said. "Stories, legends, religions. When I was young, another Keeper recited all of his knowledge to me so that I could store it, and then add to it."

"Have you ever heard about this 'Eleventh Metal' legend that Kelsier talks about?"

Sazed paused. "No, Mistress. That legend was new to me when I heard of it from Master Kelsier."

"But he swears that it's true," Vin said. "And I . . . believe him, for some reason."

"It is very possible that there are legends I haven't heard of," Sazed said. "If the Keepers knew everything, then why would we need to keep searching?"

Vin nodded, still a bit uncertain.

Sazed continued to stir the soup. He seemed so . . . dignified, even while performing such a menial task. He stood in his steward's robes, unconcerned with how simple a service he was performing, easily taking over for the servants the crew had dismissed.

Quick footsteps sounded on the stairs, and Vin perked up, sliding off her stool.

"Mistress?" Sazed asked.

"Someone on the stairs," Vin said, moving to the doorway.

One of the apprentices—Vin thought his name was Tase—burst into the main room. Now that Lestibournes was gone, Tase had become the crew's main lookout.

"People are gathering in the square," Tase said, gesturing toward the stairs.

"What's this?" Dockson said, entering from the other room.

"People in the fountain square, Master Dockson," the boy said. "Word on the street is that the obligators are planning more executions."

Retribution for the Pits, Vin thought. *That didn't take long.*

Dockson's expression darkened. "Go wake Kell."

"I intend to watch them," Kelsier said, walking through the room, dressed in simple skaa clothing and cloak.

Vin's stomach twisted. *Again?*

"You all may do as you wish," Kelsier said. He looked much better after his extended rest—his exhaustion was gone, replaced with the characteristic strength Vin had come to expect from him.

"The executions are probably a reaction to what I did at the Pits," Kelsier continued. "I'm going to watch those people's deaths—because indirectly, I caused them."

"It's not your fault, Kell," Dockson said.

"It's all of our faults," Kelsier said bluntly. "That doesn't make what we do wrong—however, if it weren't for us, these people wouldn't have to die. I, for one, think that the least we can do for these people is bear witness to their passing."

He pulled open the door, climbing the steps. Slowly, the rest of the crew followed him—though Clubs, Sazed, and the apprentices remained with the safe house.

Vin climbed the musty-aired steps, eventually joining the others on a grimy street in the middle of a skaa slum. Ash fell from the sky, floating in lazily flakes. Kelsier was already walking down the street, and the rest of them—Breeze, Ham, Dockson, and Vin—quickly moved to catch up with him.

The safe house wasn't far from the fountain square. Kelsier, however, paused a few streets away from their destination. Dull-eyed skaa continued walking around them, jostling the crew. Bells rang in the distance.

"Kell?" Dockson asked.

Kelsier cocked his head. "Vin, you hear that?"

She closed her eyes, then flared her tin. *Focus,* she thought. *Like Spook said. Cut through the shuffling feet and murmuring voices. Hear over the doors shutting and the people breathing. Listen. . . .*

"Horses," she said, dampening her tin and opening her eyes. "And carriages."

"Carts," Kelsier said, turning toward the side of the street. "The prisoner carts. They're coming this way."

He looked up at the buildings around him, then grabbed hold of a raingutter and began to shimmy up a wall. Breeze rolled his eyes, nudging Dockson and nodding toward the front of the building, but Vin and Ham—with pewter—easily followed Kelsier up to the roof.

"There," Kell said, pointing at a street a short ways away. Vin could just barely make out a row of barred prison carts rolling toward the square.

Dockson and Breeze entered the slanted rooftop through a window. Kelsier remained where he was, standing by the roof's lip, staring out at the prison carts.

"Kell," Ham said warily. "What are you thinking?"

"We're still a short distance from the square," he said slowly. "And the Inquisitors aren't riding with the prisoners—they'll come down from the palace, like last time. There can't be more than a hundred soldiers guarding those people."

"A hundred men are plenty, Kell," Ham said.

Kelsier didn't seem to hear the words. He took another step forward, approaching up onto the roof's edge. "I can stop this. . . . I can save them."

Vin stepped up beside him. "Kell, there might not be many guards with the prisoners, but the fountain square is only a few blocks away. It's packed with soldiers, not to mention the Inquisitors!"

Ham, unexpectedly, didn't back her up. He turned, glancing at Dockson and Breeze. Dox paused, then shrugged.

"Are you all crazy?" Vin demanded.

"Wait a moment," Breeze said, squinting. "I'm no Tineye, but don't some of those prisoners look a bit too well dressed?"

Kelsier froze, then he cursed. Without warning, he jumped off the rooftop, dropping to the street below.

"Kell!" Vin said. "What—" Then she paused, looking up in the red sunlight, watching the slowly approaching procession of carts. Through tin-enhanced eyes, she thought that she recognized someone sitting near the front of one of the carts.

Spook.

"Kelsier, what's going on!" Vin demanded, dashing down the street behind him.

He slowed just a bit. "I saw Renoux and Spook in that first

cart. The Ministry must have hit Renoux's canal procession—the people in those cages are the servants, staff, and guards we hired to work at the mansion."

The canal procession . . . Vin thought. *The Ministry must know that Renoux was a fake. Marsh broke after all.*

Behind them, Ham appeared out of the building and onto the street. Breeze and Dockson were slower in coming.

"We have to work quickly!" Kelsier said, picking up his pace again.

"Kell!" Vin said, grabbing his arm. "Kelsier, you can't save them. They're too well guarded, and it's daylight in the middle of the city. You'll just get yourself killed!"

He paused, halting in the street, turning in Vin's grasp. He looked into her eyes, disappointed. "You don't understand what this is all about, do you, Vin? You never did. I let you stop me once before, on the hillside by the battlefield. Not this time. This time I can do something."

"But . . ."

He shook his arm free. "You still have some things to learn about friendship, Vin. I hope someday you realize what they are."

Then he took off, charging in the direction of the carts. Ham barreled past Vin, heading in a different direction, pushing his way through skaa on their way to the square.

Vin stood stupidly for a few moments, standing in the falling ash as Dockson caught up to her.

"It's insanity," she mumbled. "We can't do this, Dox. We're not invincible."

Dockson snorted. "We're not helpless either."

Breeze puffed up behind them, pointing toward a side street. "There. We need to get me to a place where I can see the soldiers."

Vin let them tow her along, suddenly feeling shame mix with her worry.

Kelsier . . .

Kelsier tossed away a pair of empty vials, their contents ingested. The vials sparkled in the air beside him, falling to shatter against the cobblestones. He ducked through one final alleyway, bursting out onto an eerily empty thoroughfare.

The prisoner carts rolled toward him, entering a small courtyard square formed by the intersection of two streets. Each rectangular vehicle was lined with bars; each one was packed with people who were now distinctly familiar. Servants, soldiers, housekeepers—some were rebels, many were just regular people. None of them deserved death.

Too many skaa have died already, he thought, flaring his metals. *Hundreds. Thousands. Hundreds of thousands.*

Not today. No more.

He dropped a coin and jumped, Pushing himself through the air in a wide arc. Soldiers looked up, pointing. Kelsier landed directly in their center.

There was a quiet moment as the soldiers turned in surprise. Kelsier crouched amid them, bits of ash falling from the sky.

Then he Pushed.

He flared steel with a yell, standing and Pushing outward. The burst of Allomantic power hurled soldiers away by their breastplates, tossing a dozen men into the air, sending them crashing into companions and walls.

Men screamed. Kelsier spun, Pushing against a group of soldiers and sending himself flying toward a prison cart. He smashed into it, flaring his steel and grabbing the metal door with his hands.

Prisoners huddled back in surprise. Kelsier ripped the door free with a burst of pewter-enhanced power, then tossed it toward a group of approaching soldiers.

"Go!" he told the prisoners, jumping down and landing lightly in the street. He spun.

And came face-to-face with a tall figure wearing a brown robe. Kelsier paused, stepping back as the tall form reached up, lowering his hood, revealing a pair of eyes impaled by spikes.

The Inquisitor smiled, and Kelsier heard footsteps approaching down side alleyways. Dozens. Hundreds.

"Damnation!" Breeze swore as soldiers flooded the square.

Dockson pulled Breeze into an alley. Vin followed them in,

crouching in the shadows, listening to soldiers yelling in the crossroads outside.

"What?" she demanded.

"Inquisitor!" Breeze said, pointing toward a robed figure standing before Kelsier.

"*What?*" Dockson said, standing.

It's a trap, Vin realized with horror. Soldiers began to pile into the square, appearing from hidden side streets. *Kelsier, get out of there!*

Kelsier Pushed off a fallen guard, throwing himself backward in a flip over one of the prison carts. He landed in a crouch, eyeing the new squads of soldiers. Many of them carried staves and wore no armor. Hazekillers.

The Inquisitor Pushed himself through the ash-filled air, landing with a thump in front of Kelsier. The creature smiled.

It's the same man. The Inquisitor from before.

"Where's the girl?" the creature said quietly.

Kelsier ignored the question. "Why only one of you?" he demanded.

The creature's smile deepened. "I won the draw."

Kelsier flared pewter, dashing to the side as the Inquisitor pulled out a pair of obsidian axes. The square was quickly becoming clogged with soldiers. From inside the carts he could hear people crying out.

"Kelsier! Lord Kelsier! Please!"

Kelsier cursed quietly as the Inquisitor bore down on him. He reached out, Pulling against one of the still full carts and yanking himself into the air over a group of soldiers. He landed, then dashed to the cart, intending to free its occupants. As he arrived, however, the cart shook. Kelsier glanced up just in time to see a steel-eyed monster grinning down at him from atop the vehicle.

Kelsier Pushed himself backward, feeling the wind of an axehead swing beside his head. He landed smoothly, but immediately had to jump to the side as a group of soldiers attacked. As he landed, he reached out—Pulling against one of the carts to anchor himself—and Pulled against the fallen iron door he had thrown before. The barred door lurched into the air and crashed through the squad of soldiers.

The Inquisitor attacked from behind, but Kelsier jumped away. The still tumbling door careened across the cobblestones in front of him, and as he passed over it, Kelsier Pushed, sending himself streaking into the air.

Vin was right, Kelsier thought with frustration. Below, the Inquisitor watched him, trailing him with unnatural eyes. *I shouldn't have done this.* Below, a group of soldiers rounded up the skaa that he had freed.

I should run—try to lose the Inquisitor. I've done it before.

But . . . he couldn't. He wouldn't, not this time. He had compromised too many times before. Even if it cost him everything else, he *had* to free those prisoners.

And then, as he began to fall, he saw a group of men charging the crossroads. They bore weapons, but no uniforms. At their head ran a familiar form.

Ham! So that's where you went.

"What is it?" Vin asked anxiously, craning to see into the square. Above, Kelsier's form plunged back toward the fight, dark cloak trailing behind him.

"It's one of our soldier units!" Dockson said. "Ham must have fetched them."

"How many?"

"We kept them in patches of a couple hundred."

"So they'll be outnumbered."

Dockson nodded.

Vin stood. "I'm going out."

"No, you're not," Dockson said firmly, grabbing her cloak and pulling her back. "I don't want a repeat of what happened to you last time you faced one of those monsters."

"But . . ."

"Kell will be just fine," Dockson said. "He'll just try to stall long enough for Ham to free the prisoners, then he'll run. Watch."

Vin stepped back.

To her side, Breeze was mumbling to himself. "Yes, you're afraid. Let's focus on that. Soothe everything else away. Leave you terrified. That's an Inquisitor and a Mistborn fighting—you don't want to interfere with *that*. . . ."

Vin glanced back toward the square, where she saw a soldier drop his staff and flee. *There are other ways to fight,* she realized, kneeling beside Breeze. "How can I help?"

Kelsier ducked back from the Inquisitor again as Ham's unit crashed into the imperial soldiers and began cutting its way toward the prisoner carts. The attack diverted the attention of the regular soldiers, who appeared all too happy to leave Kelsier and the Inquisitor to their solitary battle.

To the side, Kelsier could see skaa beginning to clog the streets around the small courtyard, the fighting drawing the attention of those waiting up above at the fountain square. Kelsier could see other squads of imperial soldiers trying to push their way toward the fight, but the thousands of skaa crowding the streets seriously slowed their progress.

The Inquisitor swung, and Kelsier dodged. The creature was obviously growing frustrated. To the side, a small group of Ham's men reached one of the prisoner carts and broke open its lock, freeing the prisoners. The rest of Ham's men kept the imperial soldiers busy as the prisoners fled.

Kelsier smiled, eyeing the annoyed Inquisitor. The creature growled quietly.

"Valette!" a voice screamed.

Kelsier turned in shock. A well-dressed nobleman was pushing his way through the soldiers toward the center of the fighting. He carried a dueling cane and was protected by two beleaguered bodyguards, but he mostly avoided harm by virtue of neither side being certain of wanting to strike down a man of obvious noble blood.

"Valette!" Elend Venture yelled again. He turned to one of the soldiers. "Who told you to raid House Renoux's convoy! Who authorized this!"

Great, Kelsier thought, keeping a wary eye on the Inquisitor. The creature regarded Kelsier with a twisted, hateful expression.

You just go right on hating me, Kelsier thought. *I only have to hang on long enough for Ham to free the prisoners. Then, I can lead you away.*

The Inquisitor reached out and casually beheaded a fleeing servant as she ran by.

"No!" Kelsier yelled as the corpse fell at the Inquisitor's feet. The creature grabbed another victim and raised its axe.

"All right!" Kelsier said, striding forward, pulling a pair of vials from his sash. "All right. You want to fight me? Come on!"

The creature smiled, pushing the captured woman aside and striding toward Kelsier.

Kelsier flicked the corks off and downed both vials at once, then tossed them aside. Metals flared in his chest, burning alongside his rage. His brother, dead. His wife, dead. Family, friends, and heroes. All dead.

You push me to seek revenge? he thought. *Well, you shall have it!*

Kelsier paused a few feet in front of the Inquisitor. Fists clinched, he flared his steel in a massive Push. Around him, people were thrown back by their metal as they were hit by the awesome, invisible wave of power. The square—packed with imperial soldiers, prisoners, and rebels—opened up in a small pocket around Kelsier and the Inquisitor.

"Let's do it, then," Kelsier said.

I never wanted to be feared.

If I regret one thing, it is the fear I have caused. Fear is the tool of tyrants. Unfortunately, when the fate of the world is in question, you use whatever tools are available.

34

DEAD AND DYING MEN COLLAPSED to the cobblestones. Skaa crowded the roads. Prisoners cried out, calling his name. Heat from a smoky sun burned the streets.

And ash fell from the sky.

Kelsier dashed forward, flaring pewter and whipping out his daggers. He burned atium, as did the Inquisitor—and they both probably had enough to last for an extended fight.

Kelsier slashed twice in the hot air, striking at the Inquisitor, his arms a blur. The creature dodged amid an insane vortex of atium-shadows, then swung an axe.

Kelsier jumped, pewter lending his leap inhuman height, and passed just over the swinging weapon. He reached out and Pushed against a group of fighting soldiers behind him, throwing himself forward. He planted both feet in the Inquisitor's face and kicked off, flipping backward in the air.

The Inquisitor stumbled. As Kelsier fell, he Pulled on a soldier, yanking himself backward. The soldier was pulled off his feet by the force of the Ironpull, and he began to streak toward Kelsier. Both men flew in the air.

Kelsier flared iron, Pulling against a patch of soldiers to his right while still Pulling against the single soldier. The result was a pivot. Kelsier flew to the side, and the soldier—held as if by tether to Kelsier's body—swung in a wide arc like a ball on a chain.

The unfortunate soldier crashed into the stumbling Inquisitor, smashing them both into the bars of an empty prison cart.

The soldier toppled, unconscious, to the ground. The Inquisitor bounced off the iron cage, falling to its hands and knees. A line of blood ran down the creature's face, across its eye tattoos, but it looked up, smiling. It didn't seem the least bit dizzy as it stood.

Kelsier landed, cursing quietly to himself.

With an incredible burst of speed, the Inquisitor grabbed the empty, boxlike prison cell by a pair of bars, then ripped the entire thing free of the cartwheels.

Bloody hell!

The creature spun and hurled the massive iron cage at Kelsier, who stood only a few feet away. There was no time to dodge. A building stood right behind him; if he Pushed himself back, he'd be crushed.

The cage crashed toward him, and he jumped, using a Steelpush to guide his body through the open doorway of the spinning cage. He twisted within the cell, Pushing outward in all directions, holding himself in the metal cage's exact center as it smashed into the wall, then bounced free.

The cage rolled, then began to skid across the ground. Kelsier let himself drop, landing on the underside of the roof as the cage slowly slid to a halt. Through the bars, he could see the Inquisitor watching him amid a sea of fighting soldiers, its body surrounded by a twisting, dashing, moving cloud of atium-images. The Inquisitor nodded its head to Kelsier in a slight sign of respect.

Kelsier Pushed out with a yell, flaring pewter to keep from crushing himself. The cage exploded, the metal top flipping into the air, the bars ripping free and bursting outward. Kelsier Pulled the bars behind him and Pushed the ones in front of him, sending a stream of metal shooting toward the Inquisitor.

The creature raised a hand, expertly dividing the large missiles. Kelsier, however, followed the bars with his own body—shooting himself toward the Inquisitor with a Steelpush. The Inquisitor Pulled himself to the side, using an unfortunate soldier as an anchor. The man cried out as he was wrenched away from his duel—but he choked off as the Inquisitor jumped, Pushing against the soldier and crushing the man to the ground.

The Inquisitor shot into the air. Kelsier slowed himself with a Push against a group of soldiers, tracking the Inquisitor. Behind him, the top of the cage crashed back to the ground, throwing up chips of stone. Kelsier blasted against it and hurled himself upward, after the Inquisitor.

Flakes of ash streaked past him. Ahead, the Inquisitor turned, Pulling against something below. The creature switched directions immediately, instead hurling toward Kelsier.

Head-on collision. Bad idea for the guy without spikes in his head. Kelsier frantically Pulled against a soldier, lurching downward as the Inquisitor passed diagonally overhead.

Kelsier flared pewter, then crashed into the soldier he had Pulled up toward him. The two of them spun in midair. Fortunately, the soldier wasn't one of Ham's.

"Sorry, friend," Kelsier said conversationally, Pushing himself to the side.

The soldier shot away, eventually smashing into the side of a building as Kelsier used him to soar over the battlefield. Below, Ham's main squad had finally reached the last prison cart. Unfortunately, several more groups of imperial soldiers had pushed their way through the gawking skaa crowds. One of them was a large team of archers—armed with obsidian-tipped arrows.

Kelsier cursed, letting himself fall. The archers set up, obviously preparing to fire straight into the fighting crowd. They would kill some of their own soldiers, but the brunt of their attack would be borne by the fleeing prisoners.

Kelsier dropped to the cobblestones. He reached to the side, Pulling against some discarded bars from the cage he had destroyed. They flew toward him.

The archers drew. But he could see their atium-shadows.

Kelsier released the bars and Pushed himself to the side just slightly, allowing the bars to fly between the archers and the fleeing prisoners.

The archers fired.

Kelsier grabbed the bars, flaring both steel and iron, Pushing against one tip of each bar and Pulling against the opposite tip. The bars lurched in the air, immediately beginning to spin like furious, lunatic windmills. Most of the flying arrows were sprayed to the side by the spinning rods of iron.

The bars clanged to the ground amid the scattered, discarded arrows. The archers stood, stupefied, as Kelsier jumped to the side again, then Pulled lightly on the bars, flipping them up into the air in front of him. He Pushed, sending the bars crashing toward the archers. He turned away as men screamed and died, his eyes seeking his true foe.

Where is that creature hiding?

He looked into a scene of chaos. Men fought, ran, fled, and died—each one bearing a prophetic atium-shadow to Kelsier's eyes. In this case, however, the shadows effectively doubled the number of people moving on the battlefield, and only served to increase the sense of confusion.

More and more soldiers were arriving. Many of Ham's men were down, most of the rest were retreating—fortunately, they could simply discard their armor and blend into the skaa crowds. Kelsier was more worried about that last prisoner cart—the one with Renoux and Spook in it. The trajectory at which Ham's group had entered the battle had required them to move up the line of carts, back to front. Trying to get to Renoux first would have required passing by the five other carts, leaving their people still trapped.

Ham obviously didn't intend to leave until Spook and Renoux were free. And, where Ham fought, the rebel soldiers held. There was a reason Pewterarms were also called Thugs: there was no subtlety to their fighting, no clever Ironpulls or Steelpushes. Ham simply attacked with raw strength and speed, throwing enemy soldiers out of his way, laying waste to their ranks, leading his squad of fifty men toward the final prison cart. As they reached it, Ham stepped back to fight off a group of enemy soldiers as one of his men broke the cart's lock.

Kelsier smiled with pride, eyes still searching for the Inquisitor. His men were few, but the enemy soldiers seemed visibly unsettled by the skaa rebels' determination. Kelsier's men fought with passion—despite their other, numerous hindrances, they still had this one advantage.

This is what happens when you finally convince them to

fight. This is what hides within them all. It's just so hard to release. . . .

Renoux exited the cart, then stepped to the side, watching as his servants rushed free from their cage. Suddenly, a well-dressed figure burst from the melee, grabbing Renoux by the front of his suit.

"Where's Valette?" Elend Venture demanded, his desperate voice carrying to Kelsier's tin-enhanced ears. "Which cage was she in?"

Kid, you're really starting to annoy me, Kelsier thought, Pushing himself a path through the soldiers as he ran toward the cart.

The Inquisitor appeared, leaping out from behind a pile of soldiers. It landed on top of the cage, shaking the entire structure, an obsidian axe grasped in each clawlike hand. The creature met Kelsier's eyes and smiled, then dropped from the top of the cage and buried an axe in Renoux's back.

The kandra jerked, eyes opening wide. The Inquisitor turned toward Elend next. Kelsier wasn't certain if the creature recognized the boy. Perhaps the Inquisitor thought Elend to be a member of Renoux's family. Perhaps it didn't care.

Kelsier paused for just a moment.

The Inquisitor raised his axe to strike.

She loves him.

Kelsier flared steel within, stoking it, raging it until his chest burned like the Ashmounts themselves. He blasted against the soldiers behind him—throwing dozens of them backward—and streaked toward the Inquisitor. He crashed into the creature as it began to swing.

The discarded axe clicked against the stones a few feet away. Kelsier gripped the Inquisitor by its neck as the two hit the ground; then he began to squeeze with pewter-enhanced muscles. The Inquisitor reached up, grabbing Kelsier's hands, desperately trying to force them apart.

Marsh was right, Kelsier thought through the chaos. *It fears for its life. It* can *be killed.*

The Inquisitor gasped raggedly, the metal spikeheads protruding from its eyes just inches from Kelsier's face. To his side Kelsier saw Elend Venture stumble back.

"The girl is fine!" Kelsier said through gritted teeth. "She wasn't on the Renoux barges. Go!"

Elend paused uncertainly; then one of his bodyguards finally appeared. The boy let himself get dragged away.

Can't believe I just saved a nobleman, Kelsier thought, struggling to choke the Inquisitor. *You'd better appreciate this, girl.*

Slowly, with straining muscles, the Inquisitor forced Kelsier's hands apart. The creature began to smile again.

They're so strong!

The Inquisitor pushed Kelsier back, then Pulled against a soldier, yanking itself in a skidding motion across the cobblestones. The Inquisitor hit a corpse and flipped backward, up to its feet. Its neck was red from Kelsier's grip, bits of flesh torn by his fingernails, but it smiled still.

Kelsier Pushed against a soldier, flipping himself up as well. To his side, he saw Renoux leaning against the cart. Kelsier caught the kandra's eyes and nodded slightly.

Renoux dropped to the ground with a sigh, axe in his back.

"Kelsier!" Ham yelled over the crowd.

"Go!" Kelsier told him. "Renoux is dead."

Ham glanced at Renoux's body, then nodded. He turned to his men, calling orders.

"Survivor," a rasping voice said.

Kelsier spun. The Inquisitor strode forward, stepping with pewter's lithe power, surrounded by a haze of atium-shadows.

"Survivor of Hathsin," it said. "You promised me a fight. Must I kill more skaa?"

Kelsier flared his metals. "I never said we were done." Then, he smiled. He was worried, he was pained, but he was also exhilarated. All of his life, there had been a piece of him that had wished to stand and fight.

He'd always wanted to see if he could take an Inquisitor.

Vin stood, trying desperately to see over the crowd.

"What?" Dockson asked.

"I thought I saw Elend!"

"Here? That sounds a bit ridiculous, don't you think?"

Vin flushed. *Probably.* "Regardless, I'm going to try and get a better view." She grabbed the side of the alleyway.

"Be careful," Dox said. "If that Inquisitor sees you . . ."

Vin nodded, scrambling up the bricks. Once she got high enough, she scanned the intersection for familiar figures. Dockson was right: Elend was nowhere to be seen. One of the carts—the one off of which the Inquisitor had ripped the cage—lay on its side. Horses stomped about, hedged in by the fighting and the skaa crowds.

"What do you see?" Dox called up.

"Renoux is down!" Vin said, squinting and burning tin. "Looks like an axe in his back."

"That may or may not be fatal for him," Dockson said cryptically. "I don't know a lot about kandra."

Kandra?

"What about the prisoners?" Dox called.

"They're all free," Vin said. "The cages are empty. Dox, there are a *lot* of skaa out there!" It looked like the entire population from the fountain square had crowded down to the small intersection. The area was in a small depression, and Vin could see thousands of skaa packing the streets sloping upward in all directions.

"Ham's free!" Vin said. "I don't see him—alive or dead—anywhere! Spook's gone too."

"And Kell?" Dockson asked urgently.

Vin paused. "He's still fighting the Inquisitor."

Kelsier flared his pewter, punching the Inquisitor, careful to avoid the flat disks of metal sticking out the front of its eyes. The creature stumbled, and Kelsier buried his fist in its stomach. The Inquisitor growled and slapped Kelsier across the face, throwing him down with one blow.

Kelsier shook his head. *What does it take to kill this thing?* he thought, Pushing himself up to his feet, backing away.

The Inquisitor strode forward. Some of the soldiers were trying to search the crowd for Ham and his men, but many just stood still. A fight between two powerful Allomancers was something whispered about, but never seen. Soldier and peasant stood dumbfounded, watching the battle with awe.

He's stronger than I am, Kelsier acknowledged, watching the Inquisitor warily. *But strength isn't everything.*

Kelsier reached out, grabbing smaller metal sources and Pulling them away from their owners—metal caps, fine steel swords, coin pouches, daggers. He threw them at the Inquisitor—carefully manipulating Steelpushes and Ironpulls—and kept his atium burning so that each item he controlled would have a fanning multitude of atium-images in the Inquisitor's eyes.

The Inquisitor cursed quietly as it deflected the swarming bits of metal. Kelsier, however, just used the Inquisitor's own Pushes against it, Pulling each item back, whipping them around at the creature. The Inquisitor blasted outward, Pushing against all the items at once, and Kelsier let them go. As soon as the Inquisitor stopped Pushing, however, Kelsier Pulled his weapons back.

The imperial soldiers formed a ring, watching warily. Kelsier used them, Pushing against breastplates, lurching himself back and forth in the air. The quick changes in position let him move constantly, disorienting the Inquisitor, allowing him to Push his different flying pieces of metal where he wanted them.

"Keep an eye on my belt buckle," Dockson asked, wobbling slightly as he clung to the bricks beside Vin. "If I fall off, give me a Pull to slow the fall, eh?"

Vin nodded, but she wasn't paying much attention to Dox. She was watching Kelsier. "He's incredible!"

Kelsier lurched back and forth in the air, his feet never touching the ground. Bits of metal buzzed around him, responding to his Pushes and Pulls. He controlled them with such skill, one would have thought they were living things. The Inquisitor slapped them away with a fury, but was obviously having trouble keeping track of them all.

I underestimated Kelsier, Vin thought. *I assumed that he was less skilled than the Mistings because he'd spread himself too thin. But that wasn't it at all. This.* This *is his specialty—Pushing and Pulling with expert control.*

And iron and steel are the metals he personally trained me in. Maybe he understood all along.

Kelsier spun and flew amid a maelstrom of metal. Every time something hit the ground, he flicked it back up. The items always flew in straight lines, but he kept moving, Pushing himself around, keeping them in the air, periodically shooting them at the Inquisitor.

The creature spun, confused. It tried to Push itself upward, but Kelsier shot several larger pieces of metal over the creature's head, and it had to Push against them, throwing off its jump.

An iron bar hit the Inquisitor in the face.

The creature stumbled, blood marring the tattoos on the side of its face. A steel helmet struck it in the side, tossing it backward.

Kelsier began to shoot pieces of metal quickly, feeling his rage and anger mount. "Were you the one who killed Marsh?" he yelled, not bothering to listen for an answer. "Were you there when I was condemned, years ago?"

The Inquisitor raised a warding hand, Pushing away the next swarm of metals. It limped backward, putting its back against the overturned wooden cart.

Kelsier heard the creature growl, and a sudden Push of strength washed through the crowd, toppling soldiers, causing Kelsier's metal weapons to shoot away.

Kelsier let them go. He dashed forward, rushing the disoriented Inquisitor, scooping up a loose cobblestone.

The creature turned toward him, and Kelsier yelled, swinging the cobblestone, his strength fueled almost more by rage than by pewter.

He hit the Inquisitor square in the eyes. The creature's head snapped back, smacking against the bottom of the overturned cart. Kelsier struck again, yelling, repeatedly smashing his cobblestone into the creature's face.

The Inquisitor howled in pain, reaching clawlike hands for Kelsier, moving as if to jump forward. Then it suddenly jerked to a stop, its head stuck against the cart's wood. The spike tips that jutted from the back of its skull had been pounded into the wood by Kelsier's attack.

Kelsier smiled as the creature screamed in rage, struggling to pull its head free from the wood. Kelsier turned to the side, seeking an item he had seen on the ground a few moments before. He kicked over a corpse, snatching the obsidian axe off the ground, its rough-chipped blade glittering in the red sunlight.

"I'm glad you talked me into this," he said quietly. Then he swung with a two-handed blow, slamming the axehead through the Inquisitor's neck and into the wood behind.

The Inquisitor's body slumped to the cobblestones. The head remained where it was, staring out with its eerie, tattooed, unnatural gaze—pinned to the wood by its own spikes.

Kelsier turned to face the crowd, suddenly feeling incredibly wearied. His body ached from dozens of bruises and cuts, and he didn't even know when his cloak had ripped free. He faced the soldiers defiantly, however, his scarred arms plainly visible.

"The Survivor of Hathsin!" one whispered.

"He killed an Inquisitor. . . ." said another.

And then the chanting began. The skaa in the surrounding streets began to scream his name. The soldiers looked around, realizing with horror that they were surrounded. The peasants began to press in, and Kelsier could feel their anger and hope.

Maybe this doesn't have to go the way I assumed, Kelsier thought triumphantly. *Maybe I don't have—*

Then it hit. Like a cloud moving before the sun, like a sudden storm on a quiet night, like a pair of fingers snuffing a candle. An oppressive hand stifled the budding skaa emotions. The people cringed, and their cries died out. The fire Kelsier had built within them was too new.

So close . . . he thought.

Up ahead, a single, black carriage crested the hill and began to move down from the fountain square.

The Lord Ruler had arrived.

Vin nearly lost her grip as the wave of depression hit her. She flared her copper, but—as always—she could still slightly feel the Lord Ruler's oppressive hand.

"Lord Ruler!" Dockson said, though Vin couldn't tell if it was a curse or an observation. Skaa that had been packed in to view the fight somehow managed to make room for the dark carriage. It rolled down a corridor of people toward the corpse-littered square.

Soldiers pulled back, and Kelsier stepped away from the fallen cart, moving out to face the oncoming carriage.

"What is he doing?" Vin asked, turning toward Dockson, who had propped himself up on a small outcropping. "Why doesn't he run? This is no Inquisitor—this isn't something to fight!"

"This is it, Vin," Dockson said, awed. "This is what he's been waiting for. A chance to face the Lord Ruler—a chance to prove those legends of his."

Vin turned back toward the square. The carriage rolled to a stop.

"But . . ." she said quietly. "The Eleventh Metal. Did he bring it?"

"He must have."

Kelsier always said that the Lord Ruler was his *task,* Vin thought. *He let the rest of us work on the nobility, the Garrison, and the Ministry. But this . . . Kelsier always planned to do this himself.*

The Lord Ruler stepped from his carriage, and Vin leaned forward, burning tin. He looked like . . .

A man.

He was dressed in a black and white uniform somewhat like a nobleman's suit, but far more exaggerated. The coat reached all the way to his feet, and trailed behind him as he walked. His vest wasn't colored, but a pure black, though it was accented with brilliant white markings. As Vin had heard, his fingers glittered with rings, the symbol of his power.

I'm so much stronger than you, the rings proclaimed, *that it doesn't matter if I wear metal.*

Handsome, with jet black hair and pale skin, the Lord Ruler was tall, thin, and confident. And he was young—younger than Vin would have expected, even younger than Kelsier. He strode across the square, avoiding corpses, his soldiers pulling back and forcing the skaa away.

Suddenly, a small group of figures burst through the line of soldiers. They wore the mismatched armor of rebels, and the man leading them looked just a bit familiar. He was one of Ham's Thugs.

"For my wife!" the Thug said, holding up a spear and charging.

"For Lord Kelsier!" yelled the other four.

Oh no . . . Vin thought.

The Lord Ruler, however, ignored the men. The lead rebel bellowed in defiance, then rammed his spear through the Lord Ruler's chest.

The Lord Ruler just continued to walk, passing the soldier, spear sticking all the way through his body.

The rebel paused, then grabbed a spear from one of his friends and drove this one through the Lord Ruler's back. Again, the Lord Ruler ignored the men—as if they, and their weapons, were completely beneath his contempt.

The lead rebel stumbled back, then spun as his friends began to scream under an Inquisitor's axe. He joined them shortly, and the Inquisitor stood above the corpses for a moment, hacking gleefully.

The Lord Ruler continued forward, two spears sticking—as if unnoticed—from his body. Kelsier stood waiting. He looked ragged in his ripped skaa clothing. Yet, he was proud. He didn't bend or bow beneath the weight of the Lord Ruler's Soothing.

The Lord Ruler stopped a few feet away, one of the spears nearly touching Kelsier's chest. Black ash fell lightly around the two men, bits of it curling and blowing in the faint wind. The square fell horribly silent—even the Inquisitor stopped his gruesome work. Vin leaned forward, clinging precariously to the rough brickwork.

Do something, Kelsier! Use the metal!

The Lord Ruler glanced at the Inquisitor that Kelsier had killed. "Those are very hard to replace." His accented voice carried easily to Vin's tin-enhanced ears.

Even from a distance, she could see Kelsier smile.

"I killed you, once," the Lord Ruler said, turning back to Kelsier.

"You tried," Kelsier replied, his voice loud and firm, carrying across the square. "But you can't kill me, Lord Tyrant. I represent that thing you've *never* been able to kill, no matter how hard you try. I am hope."

The Lord Ruler snorted in disdain. He raised a casual arm, then backhanded Kelsier with a blow so powerful that Vin could hear the crack resound through the square.

Kelsier lurched and spun, spraying blood as he fell.

"*NO!*" Vin screamed.

The Lord Ruler ripped one of the spears from his own body, then slammed it down through Kelsier's chest. "Let the executions begin," he said, turning toward his carriage and ripping out the second spear, then tossing it aside.

Chaos followed. Prompted by the Inquisitor, the soldiers turned and attacked the crowd. Other Inquisitors appeared from the square above, riding black horses, ebony axes glistening in the afternoon light.

Vin ignored it all. "Kelsier!" she screamed. His body lay where it had fallen, spear jutting from his chest, scarlet blood pooling around him.

No. No. NO! She jumped from the building, Pushing against some people and throwing herself over the massacre. She landed in the center of the oddly empty square—Lord Ruler gone, Inquisitors busy killing skaa. She scrambled to Kelsier's side.

There was almost nothing remaining of the left side of his face. The right side, however . . . it still smiled faintly, single dead eye staring up into the red-black sky. Bits of ash fell lightly on his face.

"Kelsier, no . . ." Vin said, tears streaming down her face. She prodded his body, feeling for a pulse. There was none.

"You said you couldn't be killed!" she cried. "What of your plans? What of the Eleventh Metal? What of *me*?"

He didn't move. Vin had trouble seeing through the tears. *It's impossible. He always said we aren't invincible . . . but that meant me. Not him. Not Kelsier. He* was *invincible.*

He should have been.

Someone grabbed her and she squirmed, crying out.

"Time to go, kid," Ham said. He paused, looking at Kelsier, assuring for himself that the crewleader was dead.

Then he towed her away. Vin continued to struggle weakly, but she was growing numb. In the back of her mind, she heard Reen's voicc.

See. I told you he would leave you. I warned you.

I promised you. . . .

THE END OF PART FOUR

PART FIVE

BELIEVERS IN A FORGOTTEN WORLD

I know what will happen if I make the wrong choice. I must be strong; I must not take the power for myself.

For I have seen what will happen if I do.

35

TO WORK WITH ME, KELSIER had said, *I only ask that you promise one thing—to trust me.*

Vin hung in the mist, immobile. It flowed around her like a quiet stream. Above, ahead, to the sides, and beneath. Mist all around her.

Trust me, Vin, he'd said. *You trusted me enough to jump off the wall, and I caught you. You're going to have to trust me this time too.*

I'll catch you.

I'll catch you. . . .

It was as if she were nowhere. Among, and *of*, the mist. How she envied it. It didn't think. Didn't worry.

Didn't hurt.

I trusted you, Kelsier, she thought. *I actually did—but you let me fall. You promised that your crews had no betrayals. What of this? What of your betrayal?*

She hung, her tin extinguished to let her better see the mists. They were slightly wet, cool upon her skin. Like the tears of a dead man.

Why does it matter, anymore? she thought, staring upward. *Why does anything matter? What was it you said to me,*

Kelsier? That I never really understood? That I still needed to learn about friendship? What about you? You didn't even fight him.

He stood there again, in her mind. The Lord Ruler struck him down with a disdainful blow. The Survivor had died like any other man.

Is this why you were so hesitant to promise that you wouldn't abandon me?

She wished she could just . . . go. Float away. Become mist. She'd once wished for freedom—and then had assumed she'd found it. She'd been wrong. This wasn't freedom, this grief, this hole within her.

It was the same as before, when Reen had abandoned her. What was the difference? At least Reen had been honest. He'd always promised that he would leave. Kelsier had led her along, telling her to trust and to love, but Reen had always been the truthful one.

"I don't want to do this anymore," she whispered to the mists. "Can't you just take me?"

The mists gave no answer. They continued to spin playfully, uncaring. Always changing—yet somehow, always the same.

"Mistress?" called an uncertain voice from below. "Mistress, is that you up there?"

Vin sighed, burning tin, then extinguishing steel and letting herself drop. Her mistcloak fluttered as she fell through the mists; she landed quietly on the rooftop above their safe house. Sazed stood a short distance away, beside the steel ladder that the lookouts had been using to get atop the building.

"Yes, Saze?" she asked tiredly, reaching out to Pull up the three coins she'd been using as anchors to stabilize her like the legs of a tripod. One of them was twisted and bent—the same coin she and Kelsier had gotten into a Pushing match over so many months ago.

"I'm sorry, Mistress," Sazed said. "I simply wondered where you had gone."

She shrugged.

"It is a strangely quiet night, I think," Sazed said.

"A mournful night." Hundreds of skaa had been massacred

following Kelsier's death, and hundreds more had been trampled during the rush to escape.

"I wonder if his death even meant anything," she said quietly. "We probably saved a lot fewer than were killed."

"Slain by evil men, Mistress."

"Ham often asks if there even *is* such a thing as 'evil.' "

"Master Hammond likes to ask questions," Sazed said, "but even he doesn't question the answers. There are evil men . . . just as there are good men."

Vin shook her head. "I was wrong about Kelsier. He wasn't a good man—he was just a liar. He never had a plan for defeating the Lord Ruler."

"Perhaps," Sazed said. "Or, perhaps he never had an opportunity to fulfill that plan. Perhaps we just don't understand the plan."

"You sound like you still believe in him." Vin turned and walked to the edge of the flat-topped roof, staring out over the quiet, shadowy city.

"I do, Mistress," Sazed said.

"How? How can you?"

Sazed shook his head, walking over to stand beside her. "Belief isn't simply a thing for fair times and bright days, I think. What is belief—what is faith—if you don't continue in it after failure?"

Vin frowned.

"Anyone can believe in someone, or something, that always succeeds, Mistress. But failure . . . ah, now, that is hard to believe in, certainly and truly. Difficult enough to have value, I think."

Vin shook her head. "Kelsier doesn't deserve it."

"You don't mean that, Mistress," Sazed said calmly. "You're angry because of what happened. You hurt."

"Oh, I mean it," Vin said, feeling a tear on her cheek. "He doesn't deserve our belief. He never did."

"The skaa think differently—their legends about him are growing quickly. I shall have to return here soon and collect them."

Vin frowned. "You would gather stories about Kelsier?"

"Of course," Sazed said. "I collect all religions."

Vin snorted. "This is no religion we're talking about, Sazed. This is Kelsier."

"I disagree. He is certainly a religious figure to the skaa."

"But, we *knew* him," Vin said. "He was no prophet or god. He was just a man."

"So many of them are, I think," Sazed said quietly.

Vin just shook her head. They stood there for a moment, watching the night. "What of the others?" she finally asked.

"They are discussing what to do next," Sazed said. "I believe it has been decided that they will leave Luthadel separately and seek refuge in other towns."

"And . . . you?"

"I must travel north—to my homeland, to the place of the Keepers—so that I can share the knowledge that I possess. I must tell my brethren and sisters of the logbook—especially the words regarding our ancestor, the man named Rashek. There is much to learn in this story, I think."

He paused, then glanced at her. "This is not a journey I can take with another, Mistress. The places of the Keepers must remain secret, even from you."

Of course, Vin thought. *Of course he'd go too.*

"I will return," he promised.

Sure you will. Just like all of the others have.

The crew had made her feel needed for a time, but she'd always known it would end. It was time to go back to the streets. Time to be alone again.

"Mistress . . ." Sazed said slowly. "Do you hear that?"

She shrugged. But . . . there was something. Voices. Vin frowned, walking to the other side of the building. They grew louder, becoming easily distinct even without tin. She peered over the side of the rooftop.

A group of skaa men, perhaps ten in number, stood in the street below. *A thieving crew?* Vin wondered as Sazed joined her. The group's numbers were swelling as more skaa timidly left their dwellings.

"Come," said a skaa man who stood at the front of the group. "Fear not the mist! Didn't the Survivor name himself Lord of the Mists? Did he not say that we have nothing to fear from them? Indeed, they will protect us, give us safety. Give us power, even!"

As more and more skaa left their homes without obvious repercussion, the group began to swell even further.

"Go get the others," Vin said.

"Good idea," Sazed said, moving quickly to the ladder.

"Your friends, your children, your fathers, your mothers, wives, and lovers," the skaa man said, lighting a lantern and holding it up. "They lie dead in the street not a half hour from here. The Lord Ruler doesn't even have the decency to clean up his slaughter!"

The crowd began to mutter in agreement.

"Even when the cleaning occurs," the man said, "will it be the Lord Ruler's hands that dig the graves? No! It will be our hands. Lord Kelsier spoke of this."

"Lord Kelsier!" several men agreed. The group was getting large now, being joined by women and youths.

Clanking on the ladder announced Ham's arrival. He was joined shortly by Sazed, then Breeze, Dockson, Spook, and even Clubs.

"Lord Kelsier!" proclaimed the man below. Others lit torches, brightening the mists. "Lord Kelsier fought for us today! He slew an immortal Inquisitor!"

The crowd grumbled in assent.

"But then he died!" someone yelled.

Silence.

"And what did we do to help him?" the leader asked. "Many of us were there—thousands of us. Did we help? No! We waited and watched, even as he fought for us. We stood dumbly and let him fall. We watched him die!

"Or did we? What did the Survivor say—that the Lord Ruler could never really kill him? Kelsier is the Lord of the Mists! Is he not with us now?"

Vin turned to the others. Ham was watching carefully, but Breeze just shrugged. "The man's obviously insane. A religious nut."

"I tell you, friends!" screamed the man below. The crowd was still growing, more and more torches being lit. "I tell you the truth! *Lord Kelsier appeared to me this very night!* He said that he would always be with us. Will we let him down again?"

"No!" came the reply.

Breeze shook his head. "I didn't think they had it in them. Too bad it's such a small—"

"What's that?" Dox asked.

Vin turned, frowning. There was a pocket of light in the distance. Like . . . torches, lit in the mists. Another one appeared to the east, near a skaa slum. A third appeared. Then a fourth. In a matter of moments, it seemed like the entire city was glowing.

"You insane genius . . ." Dockson whispered.

"What?" Clubs asked, frowning.

"We missed it," Dox said. "The atium, the army, the nobility . . . that wasn't the job Kelsier was planning. *This* was his job! Our crew was never supposed to topple the Final Empire—we were too small. An entire city's population, however . . ."

"You're saying he did this on purpose?" Breeze asked.

"He always asked me the same question," Sazed said from behind. "He always asked what gave religions so much power. Each time, I answered him the same. . . ." Sazed looked at them, cocking his head. "I told him that it was because their believers had something they felt passionate about. Something . . . or someone."

"But, why not tell us?" Breeze asked.

"Because he knew," Dox said quietly. "He knew something we would never agree to. He knew that he would have to die."

Breeze shook his head. "I don't buy it. Why even bother with us, then? He could have done this on his own."

Why even bother . . . "Dox," Vin said, turning. "Where's that warehouse Kelsier rented, the one where he held his informant meetings?"

Dockson paused. "Not far away, actually. Two streets down. He said he wanted it to be near the bolt-lair. . . ."

"Show me!" Vin said, scrambling over the side of the building. The gathered skaa continued to yell, each cry louder than the one before. The entire street blazed with light, flickering torches turning the mist into a brilliant haze.

Dockson led her down the street, the rest of the crew trailing behind. The warehouse was a large, run-down structure squatting disconsolately in the slum's industrial section. Vin walked up to it, then flared pewter and smashed off the lock.

The door slowly swung open. Dockson held up a lantern, and its light revealed sparkling piles of metal. Weapons. Swords, axes, staves, and helmets glittered in the light—an incredible silvery hoard.

The crew stared at the room in wonder.

"*This* is the reason," Vin said quietly. "He needed the Renoux front to buy weapons in such numbers. He knew his rebellion would need these if they were going to succeed in taking the city."

"Why gather an army, then?" Ham said. "Was it just a front too?"

"I guess," Vin said.

"Wrong," a voice said, echoing through the cavernous warehouse. "There was so much more to it than that."

The crew jumped, and Vin flared her metals . . . until she recognized the voice. "Renoux?"

Dockson held his lantern higher. "Show yourself, creature."

A figure moved in the far back of the warehouse, staying to shadow. However, when it spoke, its voice was unmistakable. "He needed the army to provide a core of trained men for the rebellion. That part of his plan was . . . hampered by events. That was only one bit of why he needed you, however. The noble houses needed to fall to leave a void in the political structure. The Garrison needed to leave the town so that the skaa wouldn't be slaughtered."

"He planned this all from the start," Ham said with wonder. "Kelsier knew that the skaa wouldn't rise up. They'd been beaten down for so long, trained to think that the Lord Ruler owned both their bodies and their souls. He understood that they would never rebel . . . not unless he gave them a *new* god."

"Yes," Renoux said, stepping forward. The light glittered off his face, and Vin gasped in surprise.

"Kelsier!" she screamed.

Ham grabbed her shoulder. "Careful, child. It's not him."

The creature looked at her. It wore Kelsier's face, but the eyes . . . they were different. The face didn't bear Kelsier's characteristic smile. It seemed hollow. Dead.

"I apologize," it said. "This was to be my part in the plan, and is the reason Kelsier originally contracted with me. I was to take his bones once he was dead, then appear to his followers to give them faith and strength."

"What are you?" Vin asked with horror.

Renoux-Kelsier looked at her, and then his face shimmered, becoming transparent. She could see his bones through the gelatinous skin. It reminded her of . . .

"*A mistwraith.*"

"A kandra," the creature said, its skin losing its transparency. "A mistwraith that has . . . grown up, you might say."

Vin turned away in revulsion, remembering the creatures she had seen in the mist. Scavengers, Kelsier had said . . . creatures that digested the bodies of the dead, stealing their skeletons and images. *The legends are even more true than I thought.*

"You were part of this plan too," the kandra said. "All of you. You ask why he needed a crew? He needed men of virtue, men who could learn to worry more for the people than for coin. He put you before armies and crowds, letting you practice leadership. He was using you . . . but he was also training you."

The creature looked to Dockson, Breeze, then Ham. "Bureaucrat, politician, general. For a new nation to be born, it will need men of your individual talents." The kandra nodded to a large sheet of paper affixed to a table a short distance away. "That is for you to follow. I have other business to be about."

It turned as if to leave, then paused beside Vin, turning toward her with its disturbingly Kelsier-like face. Yet, the creature itself wasn't like Renoux or Kelsier. It seemed passionless.

The kandra held up a small pouch. "He asked me to give you this." It dropped the pouch into her hand, then continued on, the crew giving it a wide berth as it left the warehouse.

Breeze started toward the table first, but Ham and Dockson beat him to it. Vin looked down at the bag. She was . . . afraid to see what it contained. She hurried forward, joining the crew.

The sheet was a map of the city, apparently copied from the one Marsh had sent. Written at the top were some words.

My friends, you have a lot of work to do, and you must do it quickly. You must organize and distribute the weapons in this warehouse, then you must do the same in two others like it located in the other slums. There are horses in a side room for ease of travel.

Once you distribute the weapons, you must secure the city gates and subdue the remaining members of the Garrison. Breeze, your team will do this—march on the Garrison first, so that you can take the gates in peace.

There are four Great Houses that retain a strong military presence in the city. I have marked them on the map. Ham, your team will deal with these. We don't want an armed force other than our own inside the city.

Dockson, remain behind while the initial strikes happen. More and more skaa will come to the warehouses once word gets out. Breeze and Ham's armies will include the troops we have trained, as well as augmentations—I hope—from the skaa gathering in the streets. You will need to make certain that the regular skaa get their weapons, so that Clubs can lead the assault on the palace itself.

The Soothing stations should already be gone—Renoux delivered the proper order to our assassin teams before he came to get you to bring you here. If you have time, send some of Ham's Thugs to check out those stations. Breeze, your own Soothers will be needed amongst the skaa to encourage them to bravery.

I think that's everything. It was a fun job, wasn't it? When you remember me, please remember that. Remember to smile. Now, move quickly.

May you rule in wisdom.

The map had the city divided, with the various divisions labeled with various crewmembers' names. Vin noticed that she, along with Sazed, were left out.

"I'll go back to that group we left by our house," Clubs said in a grumbling voice. "Bring them here to get weapons." He began to hobble away.

"Clubs?" Ham said, turning. "No offense, but . . . why did he include you as an army leader? What do you know of warfare?"

Clubs snorted, then lifted up his trouser leg, showing the long, twisting scar that ran up the side of his calf and thigh—obviously the source of his limp. "Where do you think I got this?" he said, then began to move away.

Ham turned back with wonder. "I don't believe this is happening."

Breeze shook his head. "And I assumed that *I* knew something about manipulating people. This . . . this is amazing. The economy is on the verge of collapsing, and the nobility that survive will soon be at open warfare on the countryside. Kell showed us how to kill Inquisitors—we'll just need to pull down the others and behead them. As for the Lord Ruler . . ."

Eyes turned on Vin. She looked down at the pouch in her hand, and pulled it open. A smaller sack, obviously filled with atium beads, fell into her hand. It was followed by a small bar of metal wrapped in a sheet of paper. The Eleventh Metal.

Vin unwrapped the paper.

Vin, it read. *Your original duty tonight was going to be to assassinate the high noblemen remaining in the city. But, well, you convinced me that maybe they should live.*

I could never figure out how this blasted metal was supposed to work. It's safe to burn—it won't kill you—but it doesn't appear to do anything useful. If you're reading this, then I failed to figure out how to use it when I faced the Lord Ruler. I don't think it matters. The people needed something to believe in, and this was the only way to give it to them.

Please don't be angry at me for abandoning you. I was given an extension on life. I should have died in Mare's place years ago. I was ready for this.

The others will need you. You're their Mistborn now—you'll have to protect them in the months to come. The nobility will send assassins against our fledgling kingdom's rulers.

Farewell. I'll tell Mare about you. She always wanted a daughter.

"What does it say, Vin?" Ham asked.

"It . . . says that he doesn't know how the Eleventh Metal works. He's sorry—he wasn't certain how to defeat the Lord Ruler."

"We've got an entire city full of people to fight him," Dox

said. "I seriously doubt he can kill us all—if we can't destroy him, we'll just tie him up and toss him in a dungeon."

The others nodded.

"All right!" Dockson said. "Breeze and Ham, you need to get to those other warehouses and begin giving out weapons. Spook, go fetch the apprentices—we'll need them to run messages. Let's go!"

Everyone scattered. Soon, the skaa they had seen earlier burst into the warehouse, holding their torches high, looking in awe at the wealth of weaponry. Dockson worked efficiently, ordering some of the newcomers to be distributors, sending others to go gather their friends and family. Men began to gear up, gathering weapons. Everyone was busy except for Vin.

She looked up at Sazed, who smiled at her. "Sometimes we just have to wait long enough, Mistress," he said. "Then we find out why exactly it was that we kept believing. There is a saying that Master Kelsier was fond of."

"There's always another secret," Vin whispered. "But Saze, everyone has something to do except me. I was originally supposed to go assassinate noblemen, but Kell doesn't want me to do that anymore."

"They have to be neutralized," Sazed said, "but not necessarily murdered. Perhaps your place was simply to show Kelsier that fact?"

Vin shook her head. "No. I have to do more, Saze." She gripped the empty pouch, frustrated. Something crinkled inside of it.

She looked down, opening the pouch and noticing a piece of paper that she hadn't seen before. She pulled it out and unfolded it delicately. It was the drawing that Kelsier had shown her—the picture of a flower. Mare had always kept it with her, dreaming of a future where the sun wasn't red, where plants were green. . . .

Vin looked up.

Bureaucrat, politician, soldier . . . there's something else that every kingdom needs.

A good assassin.

She turned, pulling out a vial of metal and drinking its contents, using the liquid to wash down a couple beads of atium.

She walked over to the pile of weapons, picking up a small bundle of arrows. They had stone heads. She began breaking the heads off, leaving about a half inch of wood attached to them, discarding the fletched shafts.

"Mistress?" Sazed asked with concern.

Vin walked past him, searching through the armaments. She found what she wanted in a shirtlike piece of armor, constructed from large rings of interlocking metal. She pried a handful of these free with a dagger and pewter-enhanced fingers.

"Mistress, what are you doing?"

Vin walked over to a trunk beside the table, within which she had seen a large collection of powdered metals. She filled her pouch with several handfuls of pewter dust.

"I'm worried about the Lord Ruler," she said, taking a file from the box and scraping off a few flakes of the Eleventh Metal. She paused—eyeing the unfamiliar, silvery metal—then swallowed the flakes with a gulp from her flask. She put a couple more flakes in one of her backup metal vials.

"Surely the rebellion can deal with him," Sazed said. "He is not so strong without all of his servants, I think."

"You're wrong," Vin said, rising and walking toward the door. "He's strong, Saze. Kelsier couldn't feel him, not like I can. He didn't know."

"Where are you going?" Sazed asked behind her.

Vin paused in the doorway, turning, mist curling around her. "Inside the palace complex, there is a chamber protected by soldiers and Inquisitors. Kelsier tried to get into it twice." She turned back toward the dark mists. "Tonight, I'm going to find out what's inside of it."

I have decided that I am thankful for Rashek's hatred. It does me well to remember that there are those who abhor me. My place is not to seek popularity or love; my place is to ensure mankind's survival.

36

VIN WALKED QUIETLY TOWARD KREDIK Shaw. The sky behind her burned, the mists reflecting and diffusing the light of a thousand torches. It was like a radiant dome over the city.

The light was yellow, the color Kelsier had always said the sun should be.

Four nervous guards waited at the same palace doorway that she and Kelsier had attacked before. They watched her approach. Vin stepped slowly, quietly, on the mist-wetted stones, her mistcloak rustling solemnly.

One of the guards lowered a spear at her, and Vin stopped right in front of him.

"I know you," she said quietly. "You endured the mills, the mines, and the forges. You knew that someday they would kill you, and leave your families to starve. So, you went to the Lord Ruler—guilty but determined—and joined his guards."

The four men glanced at each other, confused.

"The light behind me comes from a massive skaa rebellion," she said. "The entire city is rising up against the Lord Ruler. I don't blame you men for your choices, but a time of change is coming. Those rebels could use your training and your knowledge. Go to them—they gather in the Square of the Survivor."

"The . . . Square of the Survivor?" a soldier asked.

"The place where the Survivor of Hathsin was killed earlier today."

The four men exchanged looks, uncertain.

Vin Rioted their emotions slightly. "You don't have to live with the guilt anymore."

Finally, one of the men stepped forward and ripped the symbol off his uniform, then strode determinedly into the night. The other three paused, then followed—leaving Vin with an open entrance to the palace.

Vin walked down the corridor, eventually passing the same guard chamber as before. She strode inside—stepping past a group of chatting guards without hurting any of them—and entered the hallway beyond. Behind her, the guards shook off their surprise and called out in alarm. They burst into the corridor, but Vin jumped and Pushed against the lantern brackets, hurling herself down the hallway.

The men's voices grew distant; even running, they wouldn't be able to keep up with her. She reached the end of the corridor, then let herself drop lightly to the ground, enveloping cloak falling around her body. She continued her resolute, unhurried pace. There was no reason to run. They'd be waiting for her anyway.

She passed through the archway, stepping into the dome-roofed central chamber. Silver murals lined the walls, braziers burned in the corners, the floor was an ebony marble.

And two Inquisitors stood blocking her path.

Vin strode quietly through the room, approaching the building-within-a-building that was her goal.

"We search all this time," said an Inquisitor in his grinding voice. "And you come to us. A second time."

Vin stopped, standing about twenty feet in front of the pair. They loomed, each of them nearly two feet taller than she, smiling and confident.

Vin burned atium, then whipped her hands from beneath her cloak, tossing a double handful of arrowheads into the air. She flared steel, Pushing powerfully against the rings of metal wrapped loosely around the arrowheads' broken hafts. The missiles shot forward, ripping across the room. The lead Inquisitor chuckled, raising a hand and Pushing disdainfully against the missiles.

His Push ripped the unattached rings free from the hafts, shooting the bits of metal backward. The arrowheads themselves, however, continued forward—no longer Pushed from behind, but still carried by a deadly momentum.

The Inquisitor opened his mouth in surprise as two dozen arrowheads struck him. Several punched completely through his flesh, continuing on to snap against the stone wall behind him. Several others struck his companion in the legs.

The lead Inquisitor jerked, spasming as he collapsed. The other growled, staying on his feet, but wobbling a bit on the weakened leg. Vin dashed forward, flaring her pewter. The remaining Inquisitor moved to block her, but she reached inside her cloak and threw out a large handful of pewter dust.

The Inquisitor stopped, confused. To his "eyes" he would see nothing but a mess of blue lines—each one leading to a speck of metal. With so many sources of metal concentrated in one place, the lines would be virtually blinding.

The Inquisitor spun, angry, as Vin dashed past him. He Pushed against the dust, blowing it away, but as he did so, Vin whipped out a glass dagger and flipped it toward him. In the confusing mess of blue lines and atium shadows, he missed noticing the dagger, and it took him square in the thigh. He fell, cursing in a crackly voice.

Good thing that worked, Vin thought, leaping over the groaning body of the first Inquisitor. *Wasn't sure about those eyes of theirs.*

She threw her weight against the door, flaring pewter and tossing up another handful of dust to keep the remaining Inquisitor from targeting any metals on her body. She didn't turn back to fight the two further—not with the trouble one of the creatures had given Kelsier. Her goal this infiltration wasn't to kill, but to gather information, then run.

Vin burst into the building-within-a-building, nearly tripping on a rug made from some exotic fur. She frowned, scanning the chamber urgently, searching for whatever the Lord Ruler hid inside of it.

It has to be here, she thought desperately. *The clue to defeating him—the way to win this battle.* She was counting on the Inquisitors being distracted by their wounds long enough for her to search out the Lord Ruler's secret and escape.

The room had only one exit—the entrance she'd come

through—and a hearth burned in the center of the chamber. The walls were decorated with odd trappings; furs hung from most places, the pelts dyed in strange patterns. There were a few old paintings, their colors faded, their canvases yellowed.

Vin searched quickly, urgently, looking for anything that could prove to be a weapon against the Lord Ruler. Unfortunately, she saw nothing useful; the room felt foreign, but unremarkable. In fact, it had a comfortable hominess, like a study or den. It was packed full of strange objects and decorations—like the horns of some foreign beast and a strange pair of shoes with very wide, flat bottoms. It was the room of a pack rat, a place to keep memories of the past.

She jumped as something moved near the center of the room. A pivoting chair stood by the hearth, and it spun slowly, revealing the wizened old man who sat in it. Bald, with liver-spotted skin, he appeared to be in his seventies. He wore rich, dark clothing, and he frowned angrily at Vin.

That's it, Vin thought. *I've failed—there's nothing here. Time to get out.*

Just as she was spinning to dash away, however, rough hands grabbed her from behind. She cursed, struggling as she glanced down at the Inquisitor's bloodied leg. Even with pewter, he shouldn't have been able to walk on it. She tried to twist away, but the Inquisitor had her in a powerful grasp.

"What is this?" the old man demanded, standing.

"I'm sorry, Lord Ruler," the Inquisitor said deferentially.

Lord Ruler! But . . . I saw him. He was a young *man.*

"Kill her," the old man said, waving his hand.

"My lord," the Inquisitor said. "This child is . . . of special interest. Might I keep her for a time?"

"What special interest?" the Lord Ruler said, sighing as he sat again.

"We wish to petition you, Lord Ruler," said the Inquisitor. "Regarding the Canton of Orthodoxy."

"This again?" the Lord Ruler said wearily.

"Please, my lord," said the Inquisitor. Vin continued to struggle, flaring her pewter. The Inquisitor pinned her arms to her sides, however, and her backward kicking did very little good. *He's so strong!* she thought with frustration.

And then, she remembered it. The Eleventh Metal, its power sitting within her, forming an unfamiliar reserve. She looked up, glaring at the old man. *This had better work.* She burned the Eleventh Metal.

Nothing happened.

Vin struggled in frustration, her heart sinking. And then she saw him. Another man, standing right beside the Lord Ruler. Where had he come from? She hadn't seen him enter.

He had a full beard and wore a thick, woolen outfit with a fur-lined cloak. It wasn't rich clothing, but it was well constructed. He stood quietly, seeming . . . content. He smiled happily.

Vin cocked her head. There was something familiar about the man. His features looked very similar to those of the man who had killed Kelsier. However, this man was older and . . . more alive.

Vin turned to the side. There was another unfamiliar man beside her, a young nobleman. He was a merchant, from the looks of his suit—and a very wealthy one at that.

What is going on?

The Eleventh Metal burned out. Both newcomers vanished like ghosts.

"Very well," said the elderly Lord Ruler, sighing. "I agree to your request. We will meet in several hours' time—Tevidian has already requested a gathering to discuss matters outside the palace."

"Ah," said the second Inquisitor. "Yes . . . it will be good for him to be there. Good indeed."

Vin continued to squirm as the Inquisitor pushed her to the ground, then lifted his hand, gripping something she couldn't see. He swung, and pain flashed through her head.

Despite her pewter, all went black.

Elend found his father in the north entryway—a smaller, less daunting entrance to Keep Venture, though only when compared with the majestic grand hall.

"What's going on?" Elend demanded, pulling on his suit coat, his hair disheveled from sleep. Lord Venture stood with his guard captains and canalmasters. Soldiers and servants scattered through the white-and-brown hallway, rushing about with an air of apprehensive fright.

Lord Venture ignored Elend's question, calling for a messenger to ride for the east river docks.

"Father, what's happening?" Elend repeated.

"Skaa rebellion," Lord Venture snapped.

What? Elend thought as Lord Venture waved for another group of soldiers to approach. *Impossible.* A skaa rebellion in Luthadel itself . . . it was unthinkable. They didn't have the disposition to try such a bold move, they were just . . .

Valette is skaa, he thought. *You have to stop thinking like other noblemen, Elend. You have to open your eyes.*

The Garrison was gone, off to slaughter a different group of rebels. The skaa had been forced to watch those gruesome executions weeks ago, not to mention the slaughter that had come this day. They had been stressed to the point of breaking.

Temadre predicted this, Elend realized. *So did half a dozen other political theorists. They said that the Final Empire couldn't last forever. God at its head or not, the people would someday rise up. . . . It's finally happening. I'm living through it!*

And . . . I'm on the wrong side.

"Why the canalmasters?" Elend asked.

"We're leaving the city," Lord Venture said tersely.

"Abandon the keep?" Elend asked. "Where's the honor in that?"

Lord Venture snorted. "This isn't about bravery, boy. It's about survival. Those skaa are attacking the main gates, slaughtering the remnants of the Garrison. I have no intention of waiting until they come for noble heads."

"But . . ."

Lord Venture shook his head. "We were leaving anyway. Something . . . happened at the Pits a few days ago. The Lord Ruler isn't going to be happy when he discovers it." He stepped back, waving over his lead narrowboat captain.

Skaa rebellion, Elend thought, still a little numb. *What was it that Temadre warned in his writings? That, when a real re-*

bellion finally came, the skaa would slaughter wantonly . . . that every nobleman's life would be forfeit.

He predicted that the rebellion would die out quickly, but that it would leave piles of corpses in its wake. Thousands of deaths. Tens of thousands.

"Well, boy?" Lord Venture demanded. "Go and organize your things."

"I'm not going," Elend surprised himself by saying.

Lord Venture frowned. "What?"

Elend looked up. "I'm not going, Father."

"Oh, you're going," Lord Venture said, eyeing Elend with one of his glares.

Elend looked into those eyes—eyes that were angry not because they cared for Elend's safety, but because Elend dared defy them. And, strangely, Elend didn't feel the least bit cowed. *Someone has to stop this. The rebellion could do some good, but only if the skaa don't insist on slaughtering their allies. And, that's what the nobility should be—their allies against the Lord Ruler. He's our enemy too.*

"Father, I'm serious," Elend said. "I'm going to stay."

"Bloody hell, boy! Must you insist on mocking me?"

"This isn't about balls or luncheons, father. It's about something more important."

Lord Venture paused. "No flippant comments? No buffoonery?"

Elend shook his head.

Suddenly, Lord Venture smiled. "Stay then, boy. That's a good idea. Someone should maintain our presence here while I go rally our forces. Yes . . . a very good idea."

Elend paused, frowning slightly at the smile in his father's eyes. *The atium—Father is setting me up to fall in his place! And . . . even if the Lord Ruler doesn't kill me, Father assumes I'll die in the rebellion. Either way, he's rid of me.*

I'm really not very good at this, am I?

Lord Venture laughed to himself, turning.

"At least leave me some soldiers," Elend said.

"You can have most of them," Lord Venture said. "It will be hard enough to get one boat out in this mess. Good luck, boy. Say hello to the Lord Ruler in my absence." He laughed again, moving toward his stallion, which was saddled and readied outside.

Elend stood in the hall, and suddenly he was the focus of attention. Nervous guards and servants, realizing that they'd been abandoned, turned to Elend with desperate eyes.

I'm . . . in charge, Elend thought with shock. *Now what?* Outside, he could see the mists flaring with the light of burning fires. Several of the guards were yelling about an approaching mob of skaa.

Elend walked to the open doorway, staring out into the chaos. The hall grew quiet behind him, terrified people realizing the extent of their danger.

Elend stood for a long moment. Then he spun. "Captain!" he said. "Gather your forces and the remaining servants—don't leave anyone behind—then march to Keep Lekal."

"Keep . . . Lekal, my lord?"

"It's more defensible," Elend said. "Plus, both of us have too few soldiers—separated, we'll be destroyed. Together, we might be able to stand. We'll offer our men to the Lekal in exchange for protecting our people."

"But . . . my lord," the soldier said. "The Lekal are your enemies."

Elend nodded. "Yes, but someone needs to make the first overture. Now, get moving!"

The man saluted, then rushed into motion.

"Oh, and Captain?" Elend said.

The soldier paused.

"Pick out five of your best soldiers to be my honor guard. I'll be leaving you in charge—those five and I have another mission."

"My lord?" the captain asked with confusion. "What mission?"

Elend turned back toward the mists. "We're going to go turn ourselves in."

Vin awoke to wetness. She coughed, then groaned, feeling a sharp pain in the back of her skull. She opened dizzy eyes—

blinking away the water that had been thrown on her—and immediately burned pewter and tin, bringing herself completely awake.

A pair of rough hands hoisted her into the air. She coughed as the Inquisitor shoved something into her mouth.

"Swallow," he ordered, twisting her arm.

Vin cried out, trying without success to resist the pain. Eventually, she gave in and swallowed the bit of metal.

"Now burn it," the Inquisitor ordered, twisting harder.

Vin resisted nonetheless, sensing the unfamiliar metal reserve within her. The Inquisitor could be trying to get her to burn a useless metal, one that would make her sick—or, worse, kill her.

But, there are easier ways to kill a captive, she thought in agony. Her arm hurt so much that it felt like it would twist free. Finally, Vin relented, burning the metal.

Immediately, all of her other metal reserves vanished.

"Good," the Inquisitor said, dropping her to the ground. The stones were wet, pooled with a bucketful of water. The Inquisitor turned, leaving the cell and slamming its barred door; then he disappeared through a doorway on the other side of the room.

Vin crawled to her knees, massaging her arm, trying to sort out what was going on. *My metals!* She searched desperately inside, but she found nothing. She couldn't feel any metals, not even the one she had ingested moments before.

What was it? A twelfth metal? Perhaps Allomancy wasn't as limited as Kelsier and the others had always assured her.

She took a few deep breaths, climbing to her knees, calming herself. There was something . . . Pushing against her. The Lord Ruler's presence. She could feel it, though it wasn't as powerful as it had been earlier, when he had killed Kelsier. Still, she didn't have copper to burn—she had no way to hide from the Lord Ruler's powerful, almost omnipotent, hand. She felt depression twisting her, telling her to just lie down, to give up. . . .

No! she thought. *I have to get out. I have to stay strong!*

She forced herself to stand and inspect her surroundings. Her prison was more like a cage than a cell. It had bars running along three of the four sides, and it contained no furniture—not even a sleeping mat. There were two other cell-cages in the room, one to either side of her.

She had been stripped, they had only left her with her undergarments. The move was probably to make certain that she didn't have any hidden metals. She glanced around the room. It was long and thin, and had stark stone walls. A stool sat in one corner, but the room was otherwise empty.

If I could find just a bit of metal . . .

She began to search. Instinctively, she tried to burn iron, expecting the blue lines to appear—but, of course, she had no iron to burn. She shook her head at the foolish move, but it was simply a sign of how much she'd come to rely on her Allomancy. She felt . . . blinded. She couldn't burn tin to listen for voices. She couldn't burn pewter to strengthen her against the pain of her hurting arm and head. She couldn't burn bronze to search for nearby Allomancers.

Nothing. She had nothing.

You functioned without Allomancy before, she told herself sternly. *You can do it now.*

Even so, she searched the bare floor of her cell, hoping for the chance existence of a discarded pin or nail. She found nothing, so she turned her attention to the bars. However, she couldn't think of a way to get off even a flake of the iron.

So much metal here, she thought with frustration. *And I can't use any of it!*

She sat back on the ground, huddling up against the stone wall, shivering quietly in her damp clothing. It was still dark outside; the room's window casually allowed in a few trails of mist. What had happened with the rebellion? What about her friends? She thought that the mists outside looked a bit brighter than usual. Torchlight in the night? Without tin, her senses were too weak to tell.

What was I thinking? she thought with despair. *Did I presume to succeed where Kelsier had failed? He knew that the Eleventh Metal was useless.*

It had done something, true—but it certainly hadn't killed the Lord Ruler. She sat, thinking, trying to figure out what had happened. There had been an odd familiarity about the things the Eleventh Metal had shown her. Not because of the way the visions had appeared, but because of the way Vin had felt when burning the metal.

Gold. The moment when I burned the Eleventh Metal felt like that time when Kelsier had me burn gold.

Could it be that the Eleventh Metal wasn't really "eleventh" at all? Gold and atium had always seemed oddly paired to Vin. All of the other metals came in pairs that were similar—a base metal, then its alloy, each doing opposite things. Iron Pulled, steel Pushed. Zinc Pulled, brass Pushed. It made sense. All except for atium and gold.

What if the Eleventh Metal was really an alloy of atium or of gold? *It would mean . . . that gold and atium* aren't *paired. They do two different things. Similar, but different. They're like . . .*

Like the other metals, which were grouped into larger bases of four. There were the physical metals: iron, steel, tin, and pewter. The mental metals: bronze, copper, zinc, and brass. And . . . there were the time-affecting metals: gold and its alloy, and atium and its alloy.

That means there's another metal. One that hasn't been discovered—probably because atium and gold are too valuable to forge into different alloys.

But, what good was the knowledge? Her "Eleventh Metal" was probably just a paired opposite of gold—the metal Kelsier had told her was the most useless of them all. Gold had shown Vin herself—or, at least, a different version of her that had felt real enough to touch. But, it had simply been a vision of what she could have become, had the past been different.

The Eleventh Metal had done something similar: Instead of showing Vin's own past, it had shown her similar images from other people. And that told her . . . nothing. What difference did it make what the Lord Ruler *could* have been? It was the current man, the tyrant that ruled the Final Empire, that she had to defeat.

A figure appeared in the doorway—an Inquisitor dressed in a black robe, the hood up. His face was shadowed, but his spike-heads jutted from the front of the cowl.

"It is time," he said. Another Inquisitor waited in the doorway as the first creature pulled out a set of keys and moved to open Vin's door.

Vin tensed. The door clicked, and she sprang to her feet, scrambling forward.

Have I always been this slow without pewter? she thought with horror. The Inquisitor snatched her arm as she passed, his motions unconcerned, almost casual—and she could see why. His hands moved supernaturally quickly, making her seem even more sluggish by comparison.

The Inquisitor pulled her up, twisting her and easily holding her. He smiled with an evil grin, his face pocked with scars. Scars that looked like . . .

Arrowhead wounds, she thought with shock. *But . . . healed already? How can it be?*

She struggled, but her weak, pewterless body was no match for the Inquisitor's strength. The creature carried her toward the doorway, and the second Inquisitor stepped back, regarding her with spikes that peeked out from beneath its cowl. Though the Inquisitor who carried her was smiling, this second one had a flat line of a mouth.

Vin spat at the second Inquisitor as she passed, her spittle smacking it right on one of its spike-heads. Her captor carried her out of the chamber and through a narrow hallway. She cried out for help, knowing that her screams—in the middle of Kredik Shaw itself—would be useless. At least she succeeded in annoying the Inquisitor, for he twisted her arm.

"Quiet," he said as she grunted in pain.

Vin fell silent, instead focusing on their location. They were probably in one of the lower sections of the palace; the hallways were too long to be in a tower or spire. The decorations were lavish, but the rooms looked . . . unused. The carpets were pristine, the furniture unmarked by scuff or scratch. She had the feeling that the murals were rarely seen, even by those who often passed through the chambers.

Eventually, the Inquisitors entered a stairwell and began to climb. *One of the spires,* she thought.

With each climbing step, Vin could feel the Lord Ruler getting closer. His mere presence dampened her emotions, stealing her willpower, making her numb to everything but lonely depression. She sagged in the Inquisitor's grip, no longer struggling. It took all of her energy to simply resist the Lord Ruler's pressure on her soul.

After a short time in the tunnel-like stairwell, the Inquisitors carried her out into a large, circular room. And, despite the power of the Lord Ruler's Soothing, despite her visits to noble keeps, Vin took just a brief moment to stare at her surroundings. They were majestic like none she'd ever seen.

The room was shaped like a massive, stocky cylinder. The wall—there was only one, running in a wide circle—was made entirely of glass. Lit by fires from behind, the room glowed with spectral light. The glass was colored, though it didn't depict any specific scene. Instead, it seemed crafted from a single sheet, the colors blown and melded together in long, thin trails. Like . . .

Like mist, she thought with wonder. *Colorful streams of mist, running in a circle around the entire room.*

The Lord Ruler sat in an elevated throne in the very center of the room. He wasn't the old Lord Ruler—this was the younger version, the handsome man who had killed Kelsier.

Some kind of impostor? No, I can feel him—just as I could feel the one before. They're the same man. Can he change how he looks, then? Appearing young when he wishes to put forth a pretty face?

A small group of gray-robed, eye-tattooed obligators stood conversing on the far side of the room. Seven Inquisitors stood waiting, like a row of shadows with iron eyes. That made nine of them in all, counting the two that had escorted Vin. Her scar-faced captor delivered her to one of the others, who held her with a similarly inescapable grip.

"Let us be on with this," said the Lord Ruler.

A regular obligator stepped forward, bowing. With a chill, she realized that she recognized him.

Lord Prelan Tevidian, she thought, eyeing the thin balding man. *My . . . father.*

"My lord," Tevidian said, "forgive me, but I do not understand. We have already discussed this matter!"

"The Inquisitors say they have more to add," the Lord Ruler said in a tired voice.

Tevidian eyed Vin, frowning in confusion. *He doesn't know who I am,* she thought. *He never knew he was a father.*

"My lord," Tevidian said, turning away from her. "Look outside your window! Do we not have better things to discuss? The entire *city* is in rebellion! Skaa torches light up the night, and they dare go out into the mists. They blaspheme in riots, attacking the keeps of the nobility!"

"Let them," the Lord Ruler said in an uncaring voice. He seemed so . . . worn. He sat strongly on his throne, but there was still a weariness to his posture and his voice.

"But my lord!" Tevidian said. "The Great Houses are falling!"

The Lord Ruler waved a dismissive hand. "It is good for them to get purged every century or so. It fosters instability, keeps the aristocracy from growing too confident. Usually, I let them kill each other in one of their foolish wars, but these riots will work."

"And . . . if the skaa come to the palace?"

"Then I will deal with them," the Lord Ruler said softly. "You will not question this further."

"Yes, my lord," Tevidian said, bowing and backing away.

"Now," the Lord Ruler said, turning to the Inquisitors. "What is it you wished to present?"

The scarred Inquisitor stepped forward. "Lord Ruler, we wish to petition that leadership of your Ministry be taken from these . . . men and granted to the Inquisitors instead."

"We have discussed this," the Lord Ruler said. "You and your brothers are needed for more important tasks. You are too valuable to waste on simple administration."

"But," the Inquisitor said, "by allowing common men to rule your Ministry, you have unwittingly allowed corruption and vice to enter the very heart of your holy palace!"

"Idle claims!" Tevidian spat. "You say such things often, Kar, but you never offer any proof."

Kar turned slowly, his eerie smile lit by the twisting, colored windowlight. Vin shivered. That smile was nearly as unsettling as the Lord Ruler's Soothing.

"Proof?" Kar asked. "Why, tell me, *Lord Prelan*. Do you recognize that girl?"

"Bah, of course not!" Tevidian said with a wave of his hand. "What does a skaa girl have to do with the government of the Ministry?"

"Everything," Kar said, turning to Vin. "Oh, yes . . . everything. Tell the Lord Ruler who your father is, child."

Vin tried to squirm, but the Lord Ruler's Allomancy was so oppressive, the Inquisitor's hands were so strong. "I don't know," she managed to say through gritted teeth.

The Lord Ruler perked up slightly, turning toward her, leaning forward.

"You cannot lie to the Lord Ruler, child," Kar said in a quiet, rasping voice. "He has lived for centuries, and has learned to use Allomancy like no mortal man. He can see things in the way your heart beats, and can read your emotions in your eyes. He can sense the moment when you lie. He knows . . . oh, yes. He knows."

"I never knew my father," Vin said stubbornly. If the Inquisitor wanted to know something, then keeping it a secret seemed like a good idea. "I'm just a street urchin."

"A Mistborn street urchin?" Kar asked. "Why, that's interesting. Isn't it, Tevidian?"

The lord prelan paused, his frown deepening. The Lord Ruler stood slowly, walking down the steps of his dais toward Vin.

"Yes, my lord," Kar said. "You felt her Allomancy earlier. You know that she is a full Mistborn—an amazingly powerful one. Yet, she claims to have grown up on the street. What noble house would have abandoned such a child? Why, for her to have such strength, she must be of an extremely pure line. At least . . . *one* of her parents must have been from a very pure line."

"What are you implying?" Tevidian demanded, paling.

The Lord Ruler ignored them both. He strode through the streaming colors of the reflective floor, then stopped right in front of Vin.

So close, she thought. His Soothing was so strong that she couldn't even feel terror—all she felt was the deep, overpowering, *horrible* sorrow.

The Lord Ruler reached out with delicate hands, taking her by the cheeks, tilting her face up to look into his eyes. "Who is your father, girl?" he asked quietly.

"I . . ." Despair twisted inside of her. Grief, pain, a desire to die.

The Lord Ruler held her face close to his own, looking into her eyes. In that moment, she knew the truth. She could see a piece of him; she could sense his power. His . . . godlike power.

He wasn't worried about the skaa rebellion. Why would he have to worry? If he wished, he could slaughter every person in the city by himself. Vin knew it to be the truth. It might take him time, but he could kill forever, tirelessly. He need fear no rebellion.

He'd never needed to. Kelsier had made a terrible, terrible mistake.

"Your father, child," the Lord Ruler prompted, his demand like a physical weight upon her soul.

Vin spoke despite herself. "My . . . brother told me that my father was that man over there. The lord prelan." Tears rolled down her cheeks, though when the Lord Ruler turned from her, she couldn't quite remember why she had been crying.

"It's a lie, my lord!" Tevidian said, backing away. "What does she know? She's just a silly child."

"Tell me truthfully, Tevidian," the Lord Ruler said, walking slowly toward the obligator. "Have you ever bedded a skaa woman?"

The obligator paused. "I followed the law! Each time, I had them slain afterward."

"You . . . lie," the Lord Ruler said, as if surprised. "You're uncertain."

Tevidian was visibly shaking. "I . . . I think I got them all, my lord. There . . . there was one I may have been too lax with. I didn't know she was skaa at first. The soldier I sent to kill her was too lenient, and he let her go. But I found her, eventually."

"Tell me," the Lord Ruler said. "Did this woman bear any children?"

The room fell silent.

"Yes, my lord," the high prelan said.

The Lord Ruler closed his eyes, sighing. He turned back

toward his throne. "He is yours," he said to the Inquisitors.

Immediately, six Inquisitors dashed across the room, howling in joy, pulling obsidian knives from sheaths beneath their robes. Tevidian raised his arms, crying out as the Inquisitors fell on him, exulting in their brutality. Blood flew as they plunged their daggers over and over again into the dying man. The other obligators backed away, looking on in horror.

Kar remained behind, smiling as he watched the massacre, as did the Inquisitor who was Vin's captor. One other Inquisitor remained back as well, though Vin didn't know why.

"Your point is proven, Kar," the Lord Ruler said, sitting wearily on his throne. "It seems that I have trusted too much in the . . . obedience of mankind. I did not make a mistake. I have never made a mistake. However, it is time for a change. Gather the high prelans and bring them here—rouse them from their beds, if need be. They will witness as I grant the Canton of Inquisition command and authority over the Ministry."

Kar's smile deepened.

"The half-breed child will be destroyed."

"Of course, my lord," Kar said. "Though . . . there are some questions I wish to ask her first. She was part of a team of skaa Mistings. If she can help us locate the others . . ."

"Very well," the Lord Ruler said. "That is your duty, after all."

Is there anything more beautiful than the sun? I often watch it rise, for my restless sleep usually awakens me before dawn.

Each time I see its calm yellow light peeking above the horizon, I grow a little more determined, a little more hopeful. In a way, it is the thing that has kept me going all this time.

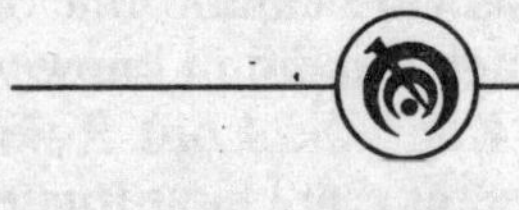

37

KELSIER, YOU CURSED LUNATIC, Dockson thought, scribbling notes on the table map, *why do you always just saunter away, leaving me to handle your messes?* However, he knew his frustration wasn't real—it was simply a way of keeping himself from focusing on Kell's death. It worked.

Kelsier's part in the plan—the vision, the charismatic leadership—was finished. Now it was Dockson's turn. He took Kelsier's original strategy and modified it. He was careful to keep the chaos at a manageable level, rationing the best equipment to the men who seemed the most stable. He sent contingents to capture points of interest—food and water deposits—before general rioting could steal them.

In short, he did what he always did: He made Kelsier's dreams become reality.

A disturbance came from the front of the room, and Dockson looked up as a messenger rushed in. The man immediately sought out Dockson at the center of the warehouse.

"What news?" Dockson asked as the man approached.

The messenger shook his head. He was a young man, in an imperial uniform, though he had removed the jacket to make himself look less obtrusive. "I'm sorry, sir," the man said quietly. "None of the guards have seen her come out, and . . . well, one claimed he saw her being carried toward the palace dungeons."

"Can you get her out?" Dockson asked.

The soldier—Goradel—paled. Until just a short time before, Goradel had been one of the Lord Ruler's own men. In truth, Dockson wasn't even certain how much he trusted the man. Yet, the soldier—as a former palace guardsman—could get into places that other skaa could not. His former allies didn't know he'd switched sides.

Assuming he really has switched sides, Dockson thought. But . . . well, things were moving too quickly now for self-doubt. Dockson had decided to use this man. He'd have to trust his initial instincts.

"Well?" Dockson repeated.

Goradel shook his head. "There was an *Inquisitor* holding her captive, sir. I couldn't free her—I wouldn't have the authority. I don't . . . I . . ."

Dockson sighed. *Damn fool girl!* he thought. *She should have had better sense than this. Kelsier must have rubbed off on her.*

He waved the soldier away, then looked up as Hammond walked in, a large sword with a broken hilt resting on his shoulder.

"It's done," Ham said. "Keep Elariel just fell. Looks like Lekal is still holding, however."

Dockson nodded. "We'll need your men at the palace soon." *The sooner we break in there, the better chance we have of saving Vin.* However, his instincts told him that they'd be too late to help her. The main forces would take hours to gather and organize; he wanted to attack the palace with all of their armies in tandem. The truth was he just couldn't afford to spare men on a rescue operation at the moment. Kelsier would probably have gone after her, but Dockson wouldn't let himself do something that brash.

As he always said—*someone* on the crew needed to be realistic. The palace was not a place to attack without substantial preparation; Vin's failure proved that much. She'd just have to look after herself for the moment.

"I'll get my men ready," Ham said, nodding as he tossed his sword aside. "I'm going to need a new sword, though."

Dockson sighed. "You Thugs. Always breaking things. Go see what you can find, then."

Ham moved off.

"If you see Sazed," Dockson called, "tell him that . . ."

Dockson paused, his attention drawn by a group of skaa rebels who marched into the room, pulling a bound prisoner with a cloth sack on his head.

"What is this?" Dockson demanded.

One of the rebels elbowed his captive. "I think he's someone important, m'lord. Came to us unarmed, asked to be brought to you. Promised us gold if we did it."

Dockson raised an eyebrow. The grunt pulled off the hood, revealing Elend Venture.

Dockson blinked in surprise. "You?"

Elend looked around. He was apprehensive, obviously, but held himself well, all things considered. "Have we met?"

"Not exactly," Dockson said. *Blast. I don't have time for captives right now.* Still, the son of the Ventures . . . Dockson was going to need leverage with the powerful nobility when the fighting was over.

"I've come to offer you a truce," Elend Venture said.

". . . excuse me?" Dockson asked.

"House Venture will not resist you," Elend said. "And I can probably talk the rest of the nobility into listening as well. They're frightened—there's no need to slaughter them."

Dockson snorted. "I can't exactly leave hostile armed forces in the city."

"If you destroy the nobility, you won't be able to hold on for very long," Elend said. "We control the economy—the empire will collapse without us."

"That is kind of the point of this all," Dockson said. "Look, I don't have time—"

"You *must* hear me out," Elend Venture said desperately. "If you start your rebellion with chaos and bloodshed, you'll lose it. I've studied these things; I know what I'm talking about! When the momentum of your initial conflict runs out, the people will start looking for other things to destroy. They'll turn on themselves. *You must keep control of your armies.*"

Dockson paused. Elend Venture was supposed to be a fool and a fop, but now he just seemed . . . earnest.

"I'll help you," Elend said. "Leave the noblemen's keeps

alone and focus your efforts on the Ministry and the Lord Ruler—they're your real enemies."

"Look," Dockson said, "I'll pull our armies away from Keep Venture. There's probably no need to fight them now that—"

"I sent my soldiers to Keep Lekal," Elend said. "Pull your men away from *all* the nobility. They're not going to attack your flanks—they'll just hole up in their mansions and worry."

He's probably right about that. "We'll consider . . ." Dockson trailed off, noticing that Elend wasn't paying attention to him anymore. *Blasted hard man to have a conversation with.*

Elend was staring at Hammond, who had returned with a new sword. Elend frowned, then his eyes opened wide. "I know you! You were the one who rescued Lord Renoux's servants from the executions!"

Elend turned back to Dockson, suddenly eager. "Do you know Valette, then? She'll tell you to listen to me."

Dockson shared a look with Ham.

"What?" Elend asked.

"Vin . . ." Dockson said. "Valette . . . she went into the palace a few hours back. I'm sorry, lad. She's probably in the Lord Ruler's dungeons right now—assuming she's even still alive."

Kar tossed Vin back into her cell. She hit the ground hard and rolled, her loose undershirt twisting around her, her head knocking against the cell's back wall.

The Inquisitor smiled, slamming the door. "Thank you very much," he said through the bars. "You just helped us achieve something that has been a long time in coming."

Vin glared up at him, the effects of the Lord Ruler's Soothing weaker now.

"It is unfortunate that Bendal isn't here," Kar said. "He chased your brother for years, swearing that Tevidian had fathered a skaa half-breed. Poor Bendal . . . If only the Lord Ruler had left the Survivor to us, so that we could have had revenge."

He looked over at her, shaking his spike-eyed head. "Ah,

well. He was vindicated in the end. The rest of us believed your brother, but Bendal . . . even then he wasn't convinced—and he found you in the end."

"My brother?" Vin said, scrambling to her feet. "He sold me out?"

"Sold you out?" Kar said. "He died promising us that you had starved to death years ago! He screamed it night and day beneath the hands of Ministry torturers. It is very hard to hold out against the pains of an Inquisitor's torture . . . something you shall soon discover." He smiled. "But, first, let me show you something."

A group of guards dragged a naked, bound figure into the room. Bruised and bleeding, the man stumbled to the stone floor as they pushed him into the cell beside Vin's.

"*Sazed?*" Vin cried, rushing to the bars.

The Terrisman lay groggily as the soldiers tied his hands and feet to a small metal ring set into the stone floor. He had been beaten so severely that he barely seemed conscious, and he was completely naked. Vin turned away from his nudity, but not before she saw the place between his legs—a simple, empty scar where his manhood should have been.

All Terrisman stewards are eunuchs, he had told her. That wound wasn't new—but the bruises, cuts, and scrapes were fresh.

"We found him sneaking into the palace after you," Kar said. "Apparently, he feared for your safety."

"What have you done to him?" she asked quietly.

"Oh, very little . . . so far," Kar said. "Now, you may wonder why I spoke to you of your brother. Perhaps you think me a fool for admitting that your brother's mind snapped before we drew out his secret. But, you see, I am not so much a fool that I will not admit a mistake. We should have drawn out your brother's torture . . . made him suffer longer. That was an error indeed."

He smiled wickedly, nodding to Sazed. "We won't make that mistake again, child. No—this time, we're going to try a different tactic. We're going to let you watch us torture the Terrisman. We're going to be very careful, making certain his pain is lasting, and quite vibrant. When you tell us what we want to know, we'll stop."

Vin shivered in horror. "No . . . please . . ."

"Oh, yes," Kar said. "Why don't you take some time to think about what we're going to do to him? The Lord Ruler has commanded my presence—I need to go and receive formal leadership of the Ministry. We'll begin when I return."

He turned, black robe sweeping the ground. The guards followed, likely taking positions in the guard chamber just outside the room.

"Oh, Sazed," Vin said, sinking to her knees beside the bars of her cage.

"Now, Mistress," Sazed said in a surprisingly lucid voice. "What did we tell you about running around in your undergarments? Why, if Master Dockson were here, he would scold you for certain."

Vin looked up, shocked. Sazed was smiling at her.

"Sazed!" she said quietly, glancing in the direction the guards had gone. "You're awake?"

"Very awake," he said. His calm, strong voice was a stark contrast to his bruised body.

"I'm sorry, Sazed," she said. "Why did you follow me? You should have stayed back and let me be stupid on my own!"

He turned a bruised head toward her, one eye swollen, but the other looking into her eyes. "Mistress," he said solemnly, "I vowed to Master Kelsier that I would see to your safety. The oath of a Terrisman is not something given lightly."

"But . . . you should have known you'd be captured," she said, looking down in shame.

"Of course I knew, Mistress," he said. "Why, how else was I going to get them to bring me to you?"

Vin looked up. "Bring you . . . to me?"

"Yes, Mistress. There is one thing that the Ministry and my own people have in common, I think. They both underestimate the things that we can accomplish."

He closed his eyes. And then, his body changed. It seemed to . . . deflate, the muscles growing weak and scrawny, the flesh hanging loosely on his bones.

"Sazed!" Vin cried out, pushing herself against the bars, trying to reach him.

"It is all right, Mistress," he said in a faint, frighteningly weak voice. "I just need a moment to . . . gather my strength."

Gather my strength. Vin paused, lowering her hand, watching Sazed for a few minutes. *Could it be . . .*

He looked so weak—as if his strength, his very muscles, were being drawn away. And perhaps . . . stored somewhere?

Sazed's eyes snapped open. His body returned to normal; then his muscles continued to grow, becoming large and powerful, growing bigger, even, than Ham's.

Sazed smiled at her from a head sitting atop a beefy, muscular neck; then he easily snapped his bindings. He stood, a massive, inhumanly muscular man—so different from the lanky, quiet scholar she had known.

The Lord Ruler spoke of their strength in his logbook, she thought with wonder. *He said the man Rashek lifted a boulder by himself and threw it out of their way.*

"But, they took all of your jewelry!" Vin said. "Where did you hide the metal?"

Sazed smiled, grabbing the bars separating their cages. "I took a hint from you, Mistress. I swallowed it." With that, he ripped the bars free.

She ran into the cage, embracing him. "Thank you."

"Of course," he said, gently pushing her aside, then slamming a massive palm against the door to his cell, breaking the lock, sending the door crashing open.

"Quickly now, Mistress," Sazed said. "We must get you to safety."

The two guards who had thrown Sazed into the chamber appeared in the doorway a second later. They froze, staring up at the massive beast who stood in place of the weak man they had beaten.

Sazed jumped forward, holding one of the bars from Vin's cage. His Feruchemy, however, had obviously given him strength only, no speed. He stepped with a lumbering gait, and the guards dashed away, crying for help.

"Come now, Mistress," Sazed said, tossing aside the bar. "My strength will not last long—the metal I swallowed wasn't large enough to hold much of a Feruchemical charge."

Even as he spoke, he began to shrink. Vin moved past him, scrambling out of the room. The guard chamber beyond was quite small, set with only a pair of chairs. Beneath one, however, she found a cloak rolled around one of the guards' evening meals. Vin shook the cloak free, tossing it to Sazed.

"Thank you, Mistress," he said.

She nodded, moving to the doorway and peeking out. The larger room outside was empty, and had two hallways leading off of it—one going right, one extending into the distance across from her. The wall to her left was lined with wooden trunks, and the center of the room held a large table. Vin shivered as she saw the dried blood and the set of sharp instruments lying in a row on the table's side.

This is where we'll both end up if we don't move quickly, she thought, waving Sazed forward.

She froze mid-step as a group of soldiers appeared in the far hallway, led by one of the guards from before. Vin cursed quietly—she would have heard them earlier if she'd had tin.

Vin glanced backward. Sazed was hobbling through the guard chamber. His Feruchemical strength was gone, and the soldiers had obviously beaten him soundly before tossing him into the cell. He could barely walk.

"Go, Mistress!" he said, waving her forward. "Run!"

You still have some things to learn about friendship, Vin, Kelsier's voice whispered in her mind. *I hope someday you realize what they are. . . .*

I can't leave him. I won't.

Vin dashed toward the soldiers. She swiped a pair of torturing knives from the table, their bright, polished steel glistening between her fingers. She jumped atop the table, then leapt off of it toward the oncoming soldiers.

She had no Allomancy, but she flew true anyway, her months of practice helping despite her lack of metals. She slammed a knife into a surprised soldier's neck as she fell. She hit the ground harder than she had expected, but managed to scramble away from a second soldier, who cursed and swung at her.

The sword clanged against the stone behind her. Vin spun, slashing another soldier across the thighs. He stumbled back in pain.

Too many, she thought. There were at least two dozen of them. She tried to jump for a third soldier, but another man swung his quarterstaff, slamming the weapon into Vin's side.

She grunted in pain, dropping her knife as she was thrown to the side. No pewter strengthened her against the fall, and she hit the hard stones with a crack, rolling to a dazed stop beside the wall.

She struggled, unsuccessfully, to rise. To her side, she could barely make out Sazed collapsing as his body grew suddenly weak. He was trying to store up strength again. He wouldn't have enough time. The soldiers would be on him soon.

At least I tried, she thought as she heard another group of soldiers charging down the rightmost hallway. *At least I didn't abandon him. I think . . . think that's what Kelsier meant.*

"Valette!" a familiar voice cried.

Vin looked up with shock as Elend and six soldiers burst into the room. Elend wore a nobleman's suit, a little ill-fitting, and carried a dueling cane.

"Elend?" Vin asked, dumbfounded.

"Are you all right?" he said with concern, stepping toward her. Then he noticed the Ministry soldiers. They seemed a bit confused to be confronted by a nobleman, but they still had superior numbers.

"I'm taking the girl with me!" Elend said. His words were brave, but he was obviously no soldier. He carried only a nobleman's dueling cane as a weapon, and he wore no armor. Five of the men with him wore Venture red—men from Elend's keep. One, however—the one who had been leading them as they charged into the room—wore a palace guard's uniform. Vin realized that she recognized him just vaguely. His uniform jacket was missing the symbol on its shoulder. *The man from before,* she thought, stupefied. *The one I convinced to change sides . . .*

The lead Ministry soldier apparently made his decision. He waved curtly, ignoring Elend's command, and the soldiers began to edge around the room, moving to surround Elend's band.

"Valette, you have to go!" Elend said urgently, raising his dueling cane.

"Come, Mistress," Sazed said, reaching her side, moving to lift her to her feet.

"We can't abandon them!" Vin said.

"We have to."

"But you came for me. We have to do the same for Elend!"

Sazed shook his head. "That was different, child. I knew I had a chance to save you. You cannot help here—there is beauty in compassion, but one must learn wisdom too."

She allowed herself to be pulled to her feet, Elend's soldiers obediently moving to block off the Ministry soldiers. Elend stood at their front, obviously determined to fight.

There has to be another way! Vin thought with despair. *There has to . . .*

And then she saw it sitting discarded in one of the trunks along the wall. A familiar strip of gray cloth, one single tassel, hanging over the trunk's side.

She pulled free of Sazed as the Ministry soldiers attacked. Elend cried out behind her, and weapons rang.

Vin threw the top pieces of cloth—her trousers and shirt—out of the trunk. And there, at the bottom, lay her mistcloak. She closed her eyes and reached into the side cloak pocket.

Her fingers found a single glass vial, cork still in place.

She pulled the vial out, spinning toward the battle. The Ministry soldiers had retreated slightly. Two of their members lay wounded on the floor—but three of Elend's men were down. The small size of the room had, fortunately, kept Elend's men from being surrounded at first.

Elend stood sweating, a cut in his arm, his dueling cane cracked and splintered. He grabbed the sword from the man he had felled, holding the weapon in unpracticed hands, staring down a much larger force.

"I was wrong about that one, Mistress," Sazed said softly. "I . . . apologize."

Vin smiled. Then she flipped the cork free from her vial and downed the metals in one gulp.

Wells of power exploded within her. Fires blazed, metals raging, and strength returned to her weakened, tired body like a dawning sun. Pains became trivial, dizziness disappeared, the room became brighter, the stones more *real* beneath her toes.

The soldiers attacked again, and Elend raised his sword in a determined, but unhopeful, posture. He seemed utterly shocked when Vin flew through the air over his head.

She landed amid the soldiers, blasting outward with a Steelpush. The soldiers on either side of her smashed into the walls. One man swung a quarterstaff at her, and she slapped it away with a disdainful hand, then smashed a fist into his face, spinning his head back with a crack.

She caught the quarterstaff as it fell, spinning, slamming it into the head of the soldier attacking Elend. The staff exploded, and she let it drop with the corpse. The soldiers at the back began to yell, turning and dashing away as she Pushed two more groups of men into the walls. The final soldier left in the room turned, surprised, as Vin Pulled his metal cap to her hands. She Pushed it back at him, smashing it into his chest and anchoring herself from behind. The soldier flew down the hallway toward his fleeing companions, crashing into them.

Vin breathed out in excitement, standing with tense muscles amidst the groaning men. *I can . . . see how Kelsier would get addicted to this.*

"Valette?" Elend asked, stupefied.

Vin jumped up, grabbing him in a joyful embrace, hanging onto him tightly and burying her face into his shoulder. "You came back," she whispered. "You came back, you came back, you came back. . . ."

"Um, yes. And . . . I see that you're a Mistborn. That's rather interesting. You know, it's generally common courtesy to tell one's friends about things like that."

"Sorry," she mumbled, still holding on to him.

"Well, yes," he said, sounding very distracted. "Um, Valette? What happened to your clothes?"

"They're on the floor over there," she said, looking up at him. "Elend, how did you find me?"

"Your friend, one Master Dockson, told me that you'd been captured in the palace. And well, this fine gentleman here—Captain Goradel, I believe his name is—happens to be a palace soldier, and he knew the way here. With his help—and as a nobleman of some rank—I was able to get into the building without much problem, and then we heard screaming down this hallway. . . . And, um, yes. Valette? Do you think you could go put your clothes on? This is . . . kind of distracting."

She smiled up at him. "You found me."

"For all the good it did," he said wryly. "It doesn't look like you needed our help very much. . . ."

"That doesn't matter," she said. "You came back. No one's ever come back before."

Elend looked down at her, frowning slightly.

Sazed approached, carrying Vin's clothing and cloak. "Mistress, we need to leave."

Elend nodded. "It's not safe anywhere in the city. The skaa are rebelling!" He paused, looking at her. "But, uh, you probably already know that."

Vin nodded, finally letting go of him. "I helped start it. But, you're right about the danger. Go with Sazed—he's known by many of the rebel leaders. They won't hurt you as long as he vouches for you."

Elend and Sazed both frowned as Vin pulled on her trousers. In the pocket, she found her mother's earring. She put it back on.

"Go with Sazed?" Elend asked. "But, what about you?"

Vin pulled on her loose overshirt. Then she glanced upward . . . sensing through the stone, feeling *him* up above. He was there. Too powerful. Now, having faced him directly, she was certain of his strength. The skaa rebellion was doomed as long as he lived.

"I have another task, Elend," she said, taking the mistcloak from Sazed.

"You think you can defeat him, Mistress?" Sazed said.

"I have to try," she said. "The Eleventh Metal worked, Saze. I saw . . . something. Kelsier was convinced it would provide the secret."

"But . . . the Lord Ruler, Mistress . . ."

"Kelsier died to start this rebellion," Vin said firmly. "I have to see that it succeeds. This is *my* part, Sazed. Kelsier didn't know what it was, but I do. I have to stop the Lord Ruler."

"The Lord Ruler?" Elend asked with shock. "No, Valette. He's immortal!"

Vin reached over, grabbing Elend's head and pulling him down to kiss her. "Elend, your family delivered the atium to the Lord Ruler. Do you know where he keeps it?"

"Yes," he said with confusion. "He keeps the beads in a treasury building just east of here. But—"

"You *have* to get that atium, Elend. The new government is going to need that wealth—and power—if it's going to keep from getting conquered by the first nobleman who can raise an army."

"No, Valette," Elend said shaking his head. "I have to get you to safety."

She smiled at him, then turned to Sazed. The Terrisman nodded to her.

"Not going to tell me not to go?" she asked.

"No," he said quietly. "I fear that you are right, Mistress. If the Lord Ruler is not defeated . . . well, I will not stop you. I will bid you, however, good luck. I will come to help you once I see young Venture to safety."

Vin nodded, smiled at the apprehensive Elend, then looked up. Toward the dark force waiting above, pulsing with a tired depression.

She burned copper, pushing aside the Lord Ruler's Soothing.

"Valette . . ." Elend said quietly.

She turned back to him. "Don't worry," she said. "I think I know how to kill him."

Such are my fears as I scribble with an ice-crusted pen on the eve before the world is reborn. Rashek watches. Hating me. The cavern lies above. Pulsing. My fingers quiver. Not from the cold.

Tomorrow it will end.

38

VIN PUSHED HERSELF THROUGH THE air above Kredik Shaw. Spires and towers rose around her like the shadowed tines of some phantom monster lurking below. Dark, straight, and ominous, for some reason they made her think of Kelsier, lying dead in the street, an obsidian-tipped spear jutting from his chest.

The mists spun and swirled as she blew through them. They were still thick, but tin let her see a faint glistening on the horizon. Morning was near.

Below her, a greater light was building. Vin caught hold of a thin spire, letting her momentum spin her around the slick metal, giving her a sweeping view of the area. Thousands of torches burned in the night, mixing and merging like luminescent insects. They were organized in great waves, converging on the palace.

The palace guard doesn't have a chance against such a force, she thought. *But, by fighting its way into the palace, the skaa army will seal its own doom.*

She turned to the side, the mist-wetted spire cold beneath her fingers. The last time she had jumped through the spires of Kredik Shaw, she had been bleeding and semiconscious. Sazed had arrived to save her, but he wouldn't be able to help this time.

A short distance away, she could see the throne tower. It wasn't difficult to spot; a ring of blazing bonfires illuminated its outside, lighting its single stained-glass window to those inside. She could feel Him inside. She waited for a few moments, hoping, perhaps, that she might be able to attack after the Inquisitors had left the room.

Kelsier believed that the Eleventh Metal was the key, she thought.

She had one idea. It would work. It had to.

"As of this moment," the Lord Ruler proclaimed in a loud voice, "the Canton of Inquisition is granted organizational dominance of the Ministry. Inquiries once addressed to Tevidian should now go to Kar."

The throne room fell silent, the collection of high-ranking obligators dumbfounded by the night's events. The Lord Ruler waved a hand, indicating that the meeting was finished.

Finally! Kar thought. He raised his head, his eye-spikes throbbing as always, bringing him pain—but, this evening it was the pain of joy. The Inquisitors had been waiting for two centuries, carefully politicking, subtly encouraging corruption and dissension among the regular obligators. And finally it had worked. The Inquisitors would no longer bow before the dictates of inferior men.

He turned and smiled toward the group of Ministry priests, knowing full well the discomfort the gaze of an Inquisitor could cause. He couldn't see anymore, not as he once had, but he had been given something better. A command of Allomancy so subtle, so detailed, that he could make out the world around him with startling accuracy.

Almost everything had metal in it—water, stone, glass . . . even human bodies. These metals were too diffuse to be affected by Allomancy—indeed, most Allomancers couldn't even sense them.

With his Inquisitor's eyes, however, Kar could see the iron-lines of these things—the blue threads were fine, nearly invisible, but they outlined the world for him. The obligators before him were a shuffling mass of blues, their emotions—discomfort, anger, and fear—showing in their postures. Discomfort, anger, and fear . . . so sweet, all three. Kar's smile widened, despite his fatigue.

He had been awake for too long. Living as an Inquisitor drained the body, and he had to rest often. His brethren were already shuffling from the room, heading toward their rest chambers, which lay intentionally close to the throne room. They would sleep immediately; with the executions earlier in the day and the excitement of the night, they would be extremely fatigued.

Kar, however, stayed behind as both Inquisitors and obligators left. Soon, only he and the Lord Ruler remained, standing in a room lit by five massive braziers. The external bonfires slowly went out, extinguished by servants, leaving the glass panorama dark and black.

"You finally have what you want," the Lord Ruler said quietly. "Perhaps now I can have peace in this matter."

"Yes, Lord Ruler," Kar said, bowing. "I think that . . ."

A strange sound snapped in the air—a soft click. Kar looked up, frowning as a small disk of metal bounced across the floor, eventually rolling to a stop against his foot. He picked up the coin, then looked up at the massive window, noting the small hole broken through it.

What?

Dozens more coins zipped through the window, scattering it with holes. Metallic clinks and tinkling glass rang in the air. Kar stepped back in surprise.

The entire southern section of the window shattered, blasting inward, the glass weakened by coins to the point that a soaring body could break through.

Shards of colorful glass spun in the air, spraying before a small figure clad in a fluttering mistcloak and carrying a pair of glittering black daggers. The girl landed in a crouch, skidding a short distance on the bits of glass, mist billowing through the opening behind her. It curled forward, drawn by her Allomancy, swirling around her body. She crouched for just a moment in the mists, as if she were some herald of the night itself.

Then she sprang forward, dashing directly toward the Lord Ruler.

Vin burned the Eleventh Metal. The Lord Ruler's past-self appeared as it had before, forming as if out of mist to stand on the dais beside the throne.

Vin ignored the Inquisitor. The creature, fortunately, reacted slowly—she was halfway up the dais steps before it thought to chase her. The Lord Ruler, however, sat quietly, watching her with a barely interested expression.

Two spears through the chest didn't even bother him, Vin thought as she leapt the last bit of distance up to the top of the dais. *He has nothing to fear from my daggers.*

Which was why she didn't intend to attack him with them. Instead, she raised her weapons and plunged directly toward the past-self's heart.

Her daggers hit—and passed right through the man, as if he weren't there. Vin stumbled forward, skidding directly through the image, nearly slipping off the dais.

She spun, slicing at the image again. Again, her daggers passed through it harmlessly. It didn't even waver or distort.

My gold image, she thought in frustration, *I was able to touch that. Why can't I touch this?*

It obviously didn't work the same way. The shadow stood still, completely oblivious of her attacks. She'd thought that maybe, if she killed the past version of the Lord Ruler, his current form would die as well. Unfortunately, the past-self appeared to be just as insubstantial as an atium shadow.

She had failed.

Kar crashed into her, his powerful Inquisitor's grip grabbing her at the shoulders, his momentum carrying her off the dais. They tumbled down the back steps.

Vin grunted, flaring pewter. *I'm not the same powerless girl you held prisoner just a short time ago, Kar,* she thought with determination, kicking him upward as they hit the ground behind the throne.

The Inquisitor grunted, her kick tossing him into the air and ripping his grip free of her shoulders. Her mistcloak came off in his hands, but she flipped to her feet and scrambled away.

"*Inquisitors!*" the Lord Ruler bellowed, standing. "*Come to me!*"

Vin cried out, the powerful voice striking pain in her tin-enhanced ears.

I have to get out of here, she thought, stumbling. *I'll need to come up with a different way to kill him. . . .*

Kar tackled her again from behind. This time he got his arms wrapped completely around her, and he squeezed. Vin cried out in pain, flaring her pewter, pushing back, but Kar forced her to her feet. He dexterously wrapped one arm around her throat while pinning her own arms behind her back with his other. She fought angrily, squirming and struggling, but his grip was tight. She tried throwing them both back with a sudden Steelpush against a doorlatch, but the anchor was too weak, and Kar barely stumbled. His grip held.

The Lord Ruler chuckled as he sat back down on his throne. "You'll have little success against Kar, child. He was a soldier, many years ago. He knows how to hold a person so that they can't break his grip, no matter how strong they may be."

Vin continued to struggle, gasping for breath. The Lord Ruler's words proved true, however. She tried ramming her head back against Kar's, but he was ready for this. She could hear him in her ear, his quick breathing almost . . . passionate as he choked her. In the reflection on the window, she could see the door behind them open. Another Inquisitor strode into the room, his spikes gleaming in the distorted reflection, his dark robe ruffling.

That's it, she thought in a surreal moment, watching the mists on the ground before her, creeping through the shattered window wall, flowing across the floor. Oddly, they didn't curl around her as they usually did—as if something were pushing them away. To Vin, it seemed a final testament to her defeat.

I'm sorry, Kelsier. I've failed you.

The second Inquisitor stepped up beside his companion. Then, he reached out and grabbed something at Kar's back. There was a ripping sound.

Vin dropped immediately to the ground, gasping for breath. She rolled, pewter allowing her to recover quickly.

Kar stood above her, teetering. Then, he toppled limply to the side, sprawling to the ground. The second Inquisitor stood behind him, holding what appeared to be a large metal spike—just like the ones in the Inquisitor's eyes.

Vin glanced toward Kar's immobile body. The back of his robe had been ripped, exposing a bloody hole right between the shoulder blades. A hole big enough for a metal spike. Kar's scarred face was pale. Lifeless.

Another spike! Vin thought with wonder. *The other Inquisitor pulled it out of Kar's back, and he died. That's the secret!*

"What?" the Lord Ruler bellowed, standing, the sudden motion tossing his throne backwards. The stone chair toppled down the steps, chipping and cracking the marble. "Betrayal! From one of my own!"

The new Inquisitor dashed toward the Lord Ruler. As he ran, his robe cowl fell back, giving Vin a view of his bald head. There was something familiar about the newcomer's face despite the spike-heads coming out the front—and the gruesome spike-tips jutting from the back—of his skull. Despite the bald head and the unfamiliar clothing, the man looked a little like Kelsier.

No, she realized. *Not Kelsier.*

Marsh!

Marsh took the dais steps in twos, moving with an Inquisitor's supernatural speed. Vin struggled to her feet, shrugging off the effects of her near-choking. Her surprise, however, was more difficult to dismiss. Marsh was alive.

Marsh was an Inquisitor.

The Inquisitors weren't investigating him because they suspected him. They intended to recruit him! And now he looked like he intended to fight the Lord Ruler. *I've got to help! Perhaps . . . perhaps he knows the secret to killing the Lord Ruler. He figured out how to kill Inquisitors, after all!*

Marsh reached the top of the dais.

"Inquisitors!" the Lord Ruler yelled. "Come to—"

The Lord Ruler froze, noticing something sitting just outside the door. A small group of steel spikes, just like the one Marsh had pulled from Kar's back, lay piled on the floor. There looked to be about seven of them.

Marsh smiled, the expression looking eerily like one of Kelsier's smirks. Vin reached the bottom of the dais and

Pushed herself off a coin, throwing herself up toward the top of the platform.

The awesome, full power of the Lord Ruler's fury hit her halfway up. The depression, the anger-fueled asphyxiation of her soul, pushed through her copper, hitting her like a physical force. She flared copper, gasping slightly, but wasn't completely able to push the Lord Ruler off of her emotions.

Marsh stumbled slightly, and the Lord Ruler swung a backhand much like the one that had killed Kelsier. Fortunately, Marsh recovered in time to duck. He spun around the Lord Ruler, reaching up to grab the back of the emperor's black, robelike suit. Marsh yanked, ripping the cloth open along the back seam.

Marsh froze, his spike-eyed expression unreadable. The Lord Ruler spun, slamming his elbow into Marsh's stomach, throwing the Inquisitor across the room. As the Lord Ruler turned, Vin could see what Marsh had seen.

Nothing. A normal, if muscular, back. Unlike the Inquisitors, the Lord Ruler didn't have a spike driven through his spine.

Oh, Marsh . . . Vin thought with a sinking depression. It had been a clever idea, far more clever than Vin's foolish attempt with the Eleventh Metal—however, it had proven equally faulty.

Marsh finally hit the ground, his head cracking, then slid across the floor until he ran into the far wall. He lay slumped against the massive window, immobile.

"Marsh!" she cried, jumping and Pushing herself toward him. However, as she flew, the Lord raised his hand absently.

Vin felt a powerful . . . *something* crash into her. It felt like a Steelpush, slamming against the metals inside her stomach—but of course it couldn't have been that. Kelsier had promised that no Allomancer could affect metals that were inside of someone's body.

But he had also said that no Allomancer could affect the emotions of a person who was burning copper.

Discarded coins shot away from the Lord Ruler, streaking across the floor. The doors wrenched free from their mountings, shattering and breaking away from the room. Incredibly, bits of colored glass even quivered and slid away from the dais.

And Vin was tossed to the side, the metals in her stomach threatening to rip free from her body. She slammed to the ground, the blow knocking her nearly unconscious. She lay in a daze, addled, confused, able to think of only one thing.

Such power . . .

Clicks sounded as the Lord Ruler walked down his dais. He moved quietly, ripping off his torn suit coat and shirt, leaving himself bare from the waist up save for the jewelry sparkling on his fingers and wrists. Several thin bracelets, she noticed, pierced the skin of his upper arms.

Clever, she thought, struggling to her feet. *Keeps them from being Pushed or Pulled.*

The Lord Ruler shook his head regretfully, his steps kicking up trails in the cool mist that poured across the floor from the broken window. He looked so strong, his torso erupting with muscles, his face handsome. She could feel the power of his Allomancy snapping at her emotions, barely held back by her copper.

"What did you think, child?" the Lord Ruler asked quietly. "To defeat me? Am I some common Inquisitor, my powers endowed fabrications?"

Vin flared pewter. She then turned and dashed away—intending to grab Marsh's body and break through the glass at the other side of the room.

But then, *he* was there, moving with a speed as if to make the fury of a tornado's winds seem sluggish. Even within a full pewter flare, Vin couldn't outrun him. He almost seemed casual as he reached out, grabbing her shoulder and yanking her backward.

He flung her like a doll, tossing her toward one of the room's massive support pillars. Vin quested desperately for an anchor, but he had blown all of the metal out of the room. Except . . .

She Pulled on one of the Lord Ruler's own bracelets, ones that didn't pierce his skin. He immediately whipped his arm upward, throwing off her Pull, making her spin maladroitly in the air. He slammed her with another of his powerful Pushes, blasting her backward. Metals in her stomach wrenched, glass quivered, and her mother's earring ripped free of her ear.

She tried to spin and hit feet-first, but she crashed into a stone pillar at a terrible speed, and pewter failed her. She heard a sickening snap, and a spear of pain shot up her right leg.

She collapsed to the ground. She didn't have the will to look, but the agony from her torso told her that her leg jutted from beneath her body, broken at an awkward angle.

The Lord Ruler shook his head. No, Vin realîzed, he didn't worry about wearing jewelry. Considering his abilities and strength, a man would have to be foolish—as Vin had been—to try and use the Lord Ruler's jewelry as an anchor. It had only let him control her jumps.

He stepped forward, feet clicking against broken glass. "You think this is the first time someone has tried to kill me, child? I've survived burnings and beheadings. I've been stabbed and sliced, crushed and dismembered. I was even flayed once, near the beginning."

He turned toward Marsh, shaking his head. Strangely, Vin's earlier impression of the Lord Ruler returned. He looked . . . tired. Exhausted, even. Not his body—it was still muscular. It was just his . . . air. She tried to climb to her feet, using the stone pillar for stability.

"I am God," he said.

So different from the humble man in the logbook.

"*God* cannot be killed," he said. "*God* cannot be overthrown. Your rebellion—you think I haven't seen its like before? You think I haven't destroyed entire armies on my own? What will it take before you people stop questioning? How many centuries must I prove myself before you *idiot* skaa see the truth? How many of you must I kill!"

Vin cried out as she twisted her leg the wrong way. She flared pewter, but tears came to her eyes anyway. She was running out of metals. Her pewter would be gone soon, and there was no way she would be able to remain conscious without it. She slumped against the pillar, the Lord Ruler's Allomancy pressing against her. The pain in her leg throbbed.

He's just too strong, she thought with despair. *He's right. He is God. What were we thinking?*

"How dare you?" the Lord Ruler asked, picking up Marsh's limp body with a bejeweled hand. Marsh groaned slightly, trying to lift his head.

"How dare you?" the Lord Ruler demanded again. "After what I gave you? I made you superior to regular men! I made you dominant!"

Vin's head snapped up. Through the haze of pain and hopelessness, something triggered a memory inside of her.

He keeps saying . . . he keeps saying that his people should be dominant. . . .

She reached within, feeling her last little bit of Eleventh Metal reserve. She burned it, looking through tearstained eyes as the Lord Ruler held Marsh in a one-handed grip.

The Lord Ruler's past self appeared next to him. A man in a fur cloak and heavy boots, a man with a full beard and strong muscles. Not an aristocrat or a tyrant. Not a hero, or even a warrior. A man dressed for life in the cold mountains. A herdsman.

Or, perhaps, a packman.

"Rashek," Vin whispered.

The Lord Ruler spun toward her in startlement.

"Rashek," Vin said again. "That's your name, isn't it? You aren't the man who wrote the logbook. You're not the hero that was sent to protect the people . . . you're his servant. The packman who hated him."

She paused for a moment. "You . . . you killed him," she whispered. "That's what happened that night! That's why the logbook stopped so suddenly! You killed the hero and took his place. You went into the cavern in his stead, and you claimed the power for yourself. But . . . instead of saving the world, you took control of it."

"You know nothing!" he bellowed, still holding Marsh's limp body in one hand. "You know nothing of that!"

"You hated him," Vin said. "You thought that a Terrisman should have been the hero. You couldn't stand the fact that he—a man from the country that had oppressed yours—was fulfilling your own legends."

The Lord Ruler lifted a hand, and Vin suddenly felt an impossible weight press against her. Allomancy, Pushing the metals in her stomach and in her body, threatening to crush her back against the pillar. She cried out, flaring her last bit of pewter, struggling to remain conscious. Mists curled around her, creeping through the broken window and across the floor.

Outside, through the broken window, she could hear something ringing faintly in the air. It sounded like . . . like cheering. Yells of joy, thousands in chorus. It sounded almost like they were cheering her on.

What does it matter? she thought. *I know the Lord Ruler's secret, but what does it tell me? That he was a packman? A servant? A Terrisman?*

A Feruchemist.

She looked through dazed eyes, and again saw the pair of bracelets glittering on the Lord Ruler's upper arms. Bracelets made of metal, bracelets that pierced his skin in places. So . . . so that they couldn't be affected by Allomancy. Why do that? He supposedly wore metal as a sign of bravado. He wasn't worried about people Pulling or Pushing against his metals.

Or, that was what he claimed. But, what if all the other metals he wore—the rings, the bracelets, the fashion that had made its way to the nobility—were simply a distraction?

A distraction to keep people from focusing on this one pair of bracers, twisting around the upper arms. *Could it really be that easy?* she thought as the Lord Ruler's weight threatened to crush her.

Her pewter was nearly gone. She could barely think. Yet, she burned iron. The Lord Ruler could pierce copperclouds. She could too. They were the same, somehow. If he could affect metals inside of a person's body, then she could as well.

She flared the iron. Blue lines appeared pointing to the Lord Ruler's rings and bracelets—all of them but the ones on his upper arms, piercing his skin.

Vin stoked her iron, concentrating, Pushing it as hard as she could. She kept her pewter flared, struggling to keep from being crushed, and she knew somehow that she was no longer breathing. The force pushing against her was too strong. She couldn't get her chest to go up and down.

Mist spun around her, dancing because of her Allomancy. She was dying. She knew it. She could barely even feel the pain anymore. She was being crushed. Suffocated.

She drew upon the mists.

Two new lines appeared. She screamed, *Pulling* with a strength she had never known before. She flared her iron higher and higher, the Lord Ruler's own Push giving her the leverage she needed to Pull against his bracelets. Anger, desperation, and agony mixed within her, and the Pull became her only focus.

Her pewter ran out.

He killed Kelsier!

The bracelets ripped free. The Lord Ruler cried out in pain, a faint, distant sound to Vin's ears. The weight suddenly released her, and she dropped to the floor, gasping, her vision swimming. The bloody bracelets hit the ground, released from her grip, skidding across the marble to land before her. She looked up, using tin to clear her vision.

The Lord Ruler stood where he had been before, his eyes widening with terror, his arms bloodied. He dropped Marsh to the ground, rushing toward her and the mangled bracelets. However, with her last bit of strength—pewter gone—Vin Pushed on the bracelets, shooting them past the Lord Ruler. He spun in horror, watching the bracelets fly out the broken wall-window.

In the distance, the sun broke the horizon. The bracelets dropped in front of its red light, sparkling for a moment before plunging down into the city.

"*No!*" the Lord Ruler screamed, stepping toward the window.

His muscles grew limp, deflating as Sazed's had. He turned back toward Vin, angry, but his face was no longer that of a young man. He was middle-aged, his youthful features matured.

He stepped toward the window. His hair grayed, and wrinkles formed around his eyes like tiny webs.

His next step was feeble. He began to shake with the burden of old age, his back stooping, his skin sagging, his hair growing limp.

Then, he collapsed to the floor.

Vin leaned back, her mind fuzzing from the pain. She lay there for . . . a time. She couldn't think.

"Mistress!" a voice said. And then, Sazed was at her side, his brow wet with sweat. He reached over and poured something down her throat, and she swallowed.

Her body knew what to do. She reflexively flared pewter, strengthening her body. She flared tin, and the sudden increase of sensitivity shocked her awake. She gasped, looking up at Sazed's concerned face.

"Careful, Mistress," he said, inspecting her leg. "The bone is fractured, though it appears only in one place."

"Marsh," she said, exhausted. "See to Marsh."

"Marsh?" Sazed asked. Then he saw the Inquisitor stirring slightly on the floor a distance away.

"By the Forgotten Gods!" Sazed said, moving to Marsh's side.

Marsh groaned, sitting up. He cradled his stomach with one arm. "What . . . is that . . . ?"

Vin glanced at the withered form on the ground a short distance away. "It's him. The Lord Ruler. He's dead."

Sazed frowned curiously, standing. He wore a brown robe, and had brought a simple wooden spear with him. Vin shook her head at the thought of such a pitiful weapon facing the creature that had nearly killed her and Marsh.

Of course. In a way, we were all just as useless. We should be dead, not the Lord Ruler.

I pulled his bracelets off. Why? Why can I do things like he can?

Why am I different?

"Mistress . . ." Sazed said slowly. "He is not dead, I think. He's . . . still alive."

"What?" Vin asked, frowning. She could barely think at the moment. There would be time to sort out her questions later. Sazed was right—the aged figure wasn't dead. Actually, it was moving pitifully on the floor, crawling toward the broken window. Toward where his bracelets had gone.

Marsh stumbled to his feet, waving away Sazed's ministrations. "I will heal quickly. See to the girl."

"Help me up," Vin said.

"Mistress . . ." Sazed said disapprovingly.

"Please, Sazed."

He sighed, handing her the wooden spear. "Here, lean on this." She took it, and he helped her to her feet.

Vin leaned on the shaft, hobbling with Marsh and Sazed toward the Lord Ruler. The crawling figure reached the edge of the room, overlooking the city through the shattered window.

Vin's footsteps crackled on broken glass. People cheered again below, though she couldn't see them, nor see what they were cheering about.

"Listen," Sazed said. "Listen, he who would have been our god. Do you hear them cheering? Those cheers aren't for you—this people never cheered for you. They have found a new leader this evening, a new pride."

"My . . . obligators . . ." the Lord Ruler whispered.

"Your obligators will forget you," Marsh said. "I will see to that. The other Inquisitors are dead, slain by my own hand. Yet, the gathered prelans saw you transfer power to the Canton of Inquisition. I am the only Inquisitor left in Luthadel. *I* rule your church now."

"No . . ." the Lord Ruler whispered.

Marsh, Vin, and Sazed stopped in a ragged group, looking down at the old man. In the morning light below, Vin could see a massive collection of people standing before a large podium, holding up their weapons in a sign of respect.

The Lord Ruler cast his eyes down at the crowd, and the final realization of his failure seemed to hit him. He looked back up at the ring of people who had defeated him.

"You don't understand," he wheezed. "You don't know what I do for mankind. I *was* your god, even if you couldn't see it. By killing me, you have doomed yourselves. . . ."

Vin glanced at Marsh and Sazed. Slowly, each of them nodded. The Lord Ruler had begun coughing, and he seemed to be aging even further.

Vin leaned on Sazed, her teeth gritted against the pain of her broken leg. "I bring you a message from a friend of ours," she said quietly. "He wanted you to know that he's not dead. He can't be killed.

"He is hope."

Then she raised the spear and rammed it directly into the Lord Ruler's heart.

Oddly, on occasion, I sense a peacefulness within. You would think that after all I have seen—after all I have suffered—my soul would be a twisted jumble of stress, confusion, and melancholy. Often, it's just that.

But then, there is the peace.

I feel it sometimes, as I do now, staring out over the frozen cliffs and glass mountains in the still of morning, watching a sunrise that is so majestic that I know that none shall ever be its match.

If there are prophecies, if there is a Hero of Ages, then my mind whispers that there must be something directing my path. Something is watching; something cares. These peaceful whispers tell me a truth I wish very much to believe.

If I fail, another shall come to finish my work.

EPILOGUE

"THE ONLY THING I CAN conclude, Master Marsh," Sazed said, "is that the Lord Ruler was both a Feruchemist *and* an Allomancer."

Vin frowned, sitting atop an empty building near the edge of a skaa slum. Her broken leg—carefully splinted by Sazed—hung over the edge of the rooftop, dangling in the air.

She'd slept most of the day—as, apparently, had Marsh, who stood beside her. Sazed had carried a message to the rest of the crew, telling them of Vin's survival. Apparently, there had been no major casualties among the others—for which Vin was glad. She hadn't gone to them yet, however. Sazed had told them that she needed to rest, and they were busy setting up Elend's new government.

"A Feruchemist and an Allomancer," Marsh said speculatively. He had recovered quickly indeed—though Vin still bore bruises, fractures, and cuts from the fight, he seemed to have already healed his broken ribs. He leaned down, resting one arm on his knee, staring out over the city with spikes instead of eyes.

How does he even see? Vin wondered.

"Yes, Master Marsh," Sazed explained. "You see, youth is one of the things that a Feruchemist can store. It's a fairly useless process—in order to store up the ability to feel and look a year younger, you would have to spend part of your life feeling and looking one year older. Often, Keepers use the ability as a disguise, changing ages to fool others and hide. Beyond this, however, no one has ever seen much use for the ability.

"However, if the Feruchemist were *also* an Allomancer, he might be able to burn his own metal storages, releasing the energy within them tenfold. Mistress Vin tried to burn some of my metals earlier, but couldn't access the power. However, if you were able to make up the Feruchemical storages yourself, then burn them for the extra power . . ."

Marsh frowned. "I don't follow you, Sazed."

"I apologize," Sazed said. "This is, perhaps, a thing that is difficult to understand without a background in both Allomantic and Feruchemical theory. Let me see if I can explain it better. What is the main difference between Allomancy and Feruchemy?"

"Allomancy draws its power from metals," Marsh said. "Feruchemy draws its powers from the person's own body."

"Exactly," Sazed said. "So, what the Lord Ruler did—I presume—was *combine* these two abilities. He used one of the attributes only available to Feruchemy—that of changing his age—but fueled it with *Allomancy* instead. By burning a Feruchemical storage that he himself had made, he effectively made a new Allomantic metal for himself—one that made him younger when he burned it. If my guess is correct, he would have gained a limitless supply of youth, since he was drawing most of his power from the metal itself, rather than his own body. All he would have to do was spend the occasional bit of time aged to give himself Feruchemical storages to burn and stay young."

"So," Marsh said, "just burning those storages would make him even younger than when he started?"

"He would have had to place that excess youth inside of another Feruchemical storage, I think," Sazed explained. "You see, Allomancy is quite spectacular—its powers generally come in bursts and flares. The Lord Ruler wouldn't have wanted all of that youth at once, so he'd have stored it inside of a piece of metal which he could slowly drain, keeping himself young."

"The bracelets?"

"Yes, Master Marsh. However, Feruchemy gives decreasing returns—it takes more than the proportionate amount of strength, for instance, to make yourself four times as strong as a regular man, as opposed to simply twice as strong. In the Lord Ruler's case, this meant that he had to spend more and more youth to keep from aging. When Mistress Vin stole the bracelets, he aged incredibly quickly because his body was trying to stretch back to where it should have been."

Vin sat in the cool evening wind, staring out toward Keep Venture. It was bright with light; not even a single day had passed, and Elend was already meeting with skaa and noblemen leaders, drafting a code of laws for his new nation.

Vin sat quietly, fingering her earring. She'd found it in the throne room, had put it back in her torn ear as it began to heal. She wasn't certain why she kept it. Perhaps because it was a link to Reen, and the mother who had tried to kill her. Or, perhaps, simply because it was a reminder of things she shouldn't have been able to do.

There was much to learn, still, about Allomancy. For a thousand years, the nobility had simply trusted what the Inquisitors and Lord Ruler told them. What secrets had they shadowed, what metals had they hidden?

"The Lord Ruler," she finally said. "He . . . just used a trick to be immortal, then. That means he wasn't ever really a god, right? He was just lucky. Anyone who was both a Feruchemist and an Allomancer could have done what he did."

"It appears that way, Mistress," Sazed said. "Perhaps that

was why he feared Keepers so much. He hunted and killed Feruchemists, for he knew that the skill was hereditary—just as Allomancy is. If the Terris lines ever mixed with those of the imperial nobility, the result could very well have been a child who could challenge him."

"Hence the breeding programs," Marsh said.

Sazed nodded. "He needed to make absolutely sure that the Terrismen weren't allowed to mix with the regular populace, lest they pass on latent Feruchemical abilities."

Marsh shook his head. "His own people. He did such horrible things to them just to keep hold of his power."

"But," Vin said, frowning, "if the Lord Ruler's powers came from a mixture of Feruchemy and Allomancy, what happened at the Well of Ascension? What was the power that the man who wrote the logbook—whoever he was—was supposed to find?"

"I don't know, Mistress," Sazed said quietly.

"Your explanation doesn't answer everything," Vin said, shaking her head. She hadn't spoken of her own strange abilities, but she had spoken of what the Lord Ruler had done in the throne room. "He was so *powerful*, Sazed. I could feel his Allomancy. He was able to Push on metals inside my body! Perhaps he could enhance his Feruchemy by burning the storages, but how did he get so strong at Allomancy?"

Sazed sighed. "I fear that the only person who could have answered these questions died this morning."

Vin paused. The Lord Ruler had held secrets about the Terris religion that Sazed's people had been searching for centuries to find. "I'm sorry. Maybe I shouldn't have killed him."

Sazed shook his head. "His own aging would have killed him soon anyway, Mistress. What you did was right. This way, I can record that the Lord Ruler was struck down by one of the skaa he had oppressed."

Vin flushed. "Record?"

"Of course. I am still a Keeper, Mistress. I must pass these things on—history, events, and truths."

"You won't . . . say too much about me, will you?" For some reason the idea of other people telling stories about her made her uncomfortable.

"I wouldn't worry too much, Mistress," Sazed said with a

smile. "My brethren and I will be very busy, I think. We have so much to restore, so much to tell the world. . . . I doubt details about you need to be passed on with any urgent timing. I will record what happened, but I will keep it to myself for a while, if you wish."

"Thank you," Vin said, nodding.

"That power that the Lord Ruler found in the cave," Marsh said speculatively, "perhaps it was just Allomancy. You said that there is no record of any Allomancers before the Ascension."

"It is indeed a possibility, Master Marsh," Sazed said. "There are very few legends about the origins of Allomancy, and nearly all of them agree that Allomancers first 'appeared with the mists.'"

Vin frowned. She'd always assumed that the title "Mistborn" had come about because Allomancers tended to do their work at night. She'd never considered that there might be a stronger connection.

Mist reacts to Allomancy. It swirls when an Allomancer uses his abilities nearby. And . . . what did I feel at the end? It was like I drew something from *the mists.*

Whatever she'd done, she hadn't been able to replicate it.

Marsh sighed and stood. He had been awake only a few hours, but he already seemed tired. His head hung slightly, as if the weight of the spikes were pulling it down.

"Does that . . . hurt, Marsh?" she asked. "The spikes, I mean?"

He paused. "Yes. All eleven of them . . . throb. The pain reacts to my emotions somehow."

"Eleven?" Vin asked with shock.

Marsh nodded. "Two in the head, eight in the chest, one in the back to seal them together. That's the only way to kill an Inquisitor—you have to separate the top spikes from the bottom ones. Kell did it through a beheading, but it's easier to just pull out the middle spike."

"We thought you were dead," Vin said. "When we found the body and the blood at the Soothing station . . ."

Marsh nodded. "I was going to send word of my survival, but they watched me fairly closely that first day. I didn't expect Kell to make his move so quickly."

"None of us did, Master Marsh," Sazed said. "None of us expected it at all."

"He actually did it, didn't he?" Marsh said, shaking his head in wonder. "That bastard. There are two things I'll never forgive him for. The first is for stealing my dream of overthrowing the Final Empire, then actually succeeding at it."

Vin paused. "And the second?"

Marsh turned spike-heads toward her. "Getting himself killed to do it."

"If I may ask, Master Marsh," Sazed said. "Who *was* that corpse that Mistress Vin and Master Kelsier discovered at the Soothing station?"

Marsh looked back over the city. "There were several corpses, actually. The process to create a new Inquisitor is . . . messy. I'd rather not speak about it."

"Of course," Sazed said, bowing his head.

"*You*, however," Marsh said, "could tell me about this creature that Kelsier used to imitate Lord Renoux."

"The kandra?" Sazed said. "I fear even the Keepers know little of them. They are related to mistwraiths—perhaps even the same creatures, just older. Because of their reputation, they generally prefer to remain unseen—though some of the noble houses hire them on occasion."

Vin frowned. "So . . . why didn't Kell just have this kandra impersonate him and die in his stead?"

"Ah," Sazed said. "You see, Mistress, for a kandra to impersonate someone, they first must devour that person's flesh and absorb their bones. Kandra are like mistwraiths—they have no skeletons of their own."

Vin shivered. "Oh."

"He is back, you know," Marsh said. "The creature is no longer using my brother's body—he has another one—but he came looking for you, Vin."

"Me?" Vin asked.

Marsh nodded. "He said something about Kelsier transferring his contract to you before he died. I believe the beast sees you as its master, now."

Vin shivered. *That . . . thing ate Kelsier's body.* "I don't want it around," she said. "I'll send it away."

"Do not be quite so hasty, Mistress," Sazed said. "Kandra are expensive servants—you must pay them in atium. If Kelsier bought an extended contract for one, it would be foolish to waste its services. A kandra might prove a very useful ally in the months to come."

Vin shook her head. "I don't care. I don't want that thing around. Not after what it did."

The trio fell silent. Finally, Marsh stood, sighing. "Anyway, if you will excuse me, I should go make an appearance at the keep—the new king wants me to represent the Ministry in his negotiations."

Vin frowned. "I don't see why the Ministry deserves any say in things."

"The obligators are still quite powerful, Mistress," Sazed said. "And, they are the most efficient and well-trained bureaucratic force in the Final Empire. His majesty would be wise to try and bring them to his side, and recognizing Master Marsh may help achieve this."

Marsh shrugged. "Of course, assuming I can establish control over the Canton of Orthodoxy, the Ministry should . . . change during the next few years. I'll move slowly and carefully, but by the time I'm done, the obligators won't even realize what they've lost. Those other Inquisitors could present a problem, though."

Vin nodded. "How many are there outside of Luthadel?"

"I don't know," Marsh said. "I wasn't a member of the order for very long before I destroyed it. However, the Final Empire was a big place. Many speak of there being around twenty Inquisitors in the empire, but I never was able to pin anyone down on a hard number."

Vin nodded as Marsh left. However, the Inquisitors—while dangerous—worried her far less now that she knew their secret. She was more concerned about something else.

You don't know what I do for mankind. I was your god, even if you couldn't see it. By killing me, you have doomed yourselves. . . .

The Lord Ruler's final words. At the time, she thought he'd been referring to the Final Empire as the thing he did "for mankind." However, she wasn't so certain anymore. There had been . . . fear in his eyes when he'd spoken those words, not pride.

"Saze?" she said. "What was the Deepness? The thing that the Hero from the logbook was supposed to defeat?"

"I wish that we knew, Mistress," Sazed said.

"But, it didn't come, right?"

"Apparently not," Sazed said. "The legends agree that had the Deepness not been stopped, the very world would have been destroyed. Of course, perhaps these stories have been exaggerated. Maybe the danger of the 'Deepness' was really just the Lord Ruler himself—perhaps the Hero's fight was simply one of conscience. He had to choose to dominate the world or to let it be free."

That didn't sound right to Vin. There was more. She remembered that fear in the Lord Ruler's eyes. Terror.

He said "do," not "did." "What I do *for mankind." That implies that he was still doing it, whatever it was.*

You have doomed yourselves. . . .

She shivered in the evening air. The sun was setting, making it even easier to see the illuminated Keep Venture—Elend's choice of headquarters for the moment, though he might still move to Kredik Shaw. He hadn't decided yet.

"You should go to him, Mistress," Sazed said. "He needs to see that you are well."

Vin didn't reply immediately. She stared out over the city, watching the bright keep in the darkening sky. "Were you there, Sazed?" she asked. "Did you hear his speech?"

"Yes, Mistress," he said. "Once we discovered that there was no atium in that treasury, Lord Venture insisted that we go seek help for you. I was inclined to agree with him—neither of us were warriors, and I was still without my Feruchemical storages."

No atium, Vin thought. *After all of this, we haven't found a speck of it. What did the Lord Ruler do with it all? Or . . . did someone else get to it first?*

"When Master Elend and I found the army," Sazed continued, "its rebels were slaughtering the palace soldiers. Some of them tried to surrender, but our soldiers weren't letting them. It was a . . . disturbing scene, Mistress. Your Elend . . .

he didn't like what he saw. When he stood up there before the skaa, I thought that they would simply kill him too."

Sazed paused, cocking his head slightly. "But . . . the things he said, Mistress . . . his dreams of a new government, his condemnation of bloodshed and chaos . . . Well, Mistress, I fear that I cannot repeat it. I wish I'd had my metalminds, so that I could have memorized his exact words."

He sighed, shaking his head. "Regardless, I believe that Master Breeze was very influential in helping calm that riot. Once one group started listening to Master Elend, the others did too, and from there . . . well, it is a good thing that a nobleman ended up as king, I think. Master Elend brings some legitimacy to our bid for control, and I think that we will see more support from the nobility and the merchants with him at our head."

Vin smiled. "Kell would be angry with us, you know. He did all this work, and we just turned around and put a nobleman on the throne."

Sazed shook his head. "Ah, but there is something more important to consider, I think. We didn't just put a nobleman on the throne—we put a *good man* on the throne."

"A good man . . ." Vin said. "Yes. I've known a few of those, now."

Vin knelt in the mists atop Keep Venture. Her splinted leg made it harder to move around at night, but most of the effort she used was Allomantic. She just had to make certain that her landings were particularly soft.

Night had come, and the mists surrounded her. Protecting her, hiding her, giving her power . . .

Elend Venture sat at a desk below, beneath a skylight that still hadn't been patched from the time Vin had thrown a body through it. He didn't notice her crouching above. Who would? Who saw a Mistborn in her element? She was, in a way, like one of the shadow images created by the Eleventh Metal. Incorporeal. Really just something that *could* have been.

Could have been . . .

The events of the last day were difficult enough to sort

through; Vin hadn't even tried to make sense of her emotions, which were a far bigger mess. She hadn't gone to Elend yet. She hadn't been able to.

She looked down at him, sitting in the lanternlight, reading at his desk and making scribbled notes in his little book. His meetings earlier had apparently gone well—everyone seemed willing to accept him as king. Marsh whispered that there were politics behind the support, however. The nobility saw Elend as a puppet they could control, and factions were already appearing amongst the skaa leadership.

Still, Elend finally had an opportunity to draft the law code he'd been dreaming of. He could try to create the perfect nation, try to apply the philosophies he had studied for so long. There would be bumps, and Vin suspected that he would ultimately have to settle for something far more realistic than his idealistic dream. That didn't really matter. He would make a good king.

Of course, compared with the Lord Ruler, a pile of soot would make a good king. . . .

She wanted to go to Elend, to drop down into the warm room, but . . . something kept her back. She'd been through too many recent twists in her fortune, too many emotional strains—both Allomantic and non-Allomantic. She wasn't certain what she wanted anymore; she wasn't certain if she were Vin or Valette, or even which of them she wished that she were.

She felt cold in the mists, in the quiet darkness. The mist empowered, protected, and hid . . . even when she didn't really want it to do any of the three.

I can't do this. That person who would be with him, that's not me. That was an illusion, a dream. I am that child who grew up in the shadows, the girl who should be alone. I don't deserve this.

I don't deserve him.

It was over. As she had anticipated, everything was changing. In truth, she'd never really made a very good noblewoman. It was time for her to go back to being what she was good at. A thing of shadows, not of parties and balls.

It was time to go.

She turned to leave, ignoring her tears, frustrated with herself. She left him, her shoulders slumped as she hobbled across the metallic roof and disappeared into the mist.

But then . . .

He died promising us that you had starved to death years ago.

With all the chaos, she'd nearly forgotten the Inquisitor's words about Reen. Now, however, the memory made her pause. Mists passed her, curling, coaxing.

Reen hadn't abandoned her. He'd been captured by the Inquisitors who had been looking for Vin, the unlawful child of their enemy. They'd tortured him.

And he had died protecting her.

Reen didn't betray me. He always promised that he would, but in the end, he didn't. He had been far from a perfect brother, but he had loved her nonetheless.

A whispered voice came from the back of her mind, speaking in Reen's voice. *Go back.*

Before she could convince herself otherwise, she dashed limpingly back to the broken skylight and dropped a coin to the floor below.

Elend turned curiously, looking at the coin, cocking his head. Vin dropped down a second later, Pushing herself up to slow the fall, landing only on her good leg.

"Elend Venture," she said, standing up. "There is something I've been meaning to tell you for some time." She paused, blinking away her tears. "You read too much. Especially in the presence of ladies."

He smiled, throwing back his chair and grabbing her in a firm embrace. Vin closed her eyes, simply feeling the warmth of being held.

And realized that was all she had ever really wanted.

ARS ARCANUM

Find extensive author's annotations of every chapter of this book, along with deleted scenes and expanded world information, at www.brandonsanderson.com.

ALLOMANCY QUICK-REFERENCE CHART

METAL	EFFECT	MISTING TITLE
Iron	Pulls on Nearby Metals	Lurcher
Steel	**Pushes on Nearby Metals**	**Coinshot**
Tin	Enhances Senses	Tineye
Pewter	**Enhances Physical Abilities**	**Pewterarm, Thug**
Brass	Soothes Emotions	Soother
Zinc	**Riots Emotions**	**Rioter**
Copper	Hides Allomancy	Smoker
Bronze	**Reveals Allomancy**	**Seeker**

(Note: External metals have been italicized. Pushing metals have been bolded.)

ALLOMANCY ALPHABETICAL REFERENCE

BRASS (EXTERNAL MENTAL PULLING METAL) A person burning brass can Soothe another person's emotions, dampening them and making particular emotions less powerful. A careful Allomancer can Soothe away all emotions but a single one, essentially making a person feel exactly as they wish. Brass, however, does not let that Allomancer read minds or even emotions. A Misting who burns brass is known as a Soother.

BRONZE (INTERNAL MENTAL PUSHING METAL) A person burning bronze can sense when people nearby are using Allomancy. Allomancers burning metals nearby will give off "Allomantic pulses"—something like drumbeats that are audible only to a person burning bronze. A Misting who can burn bronze is known as a Seeker.

COINSHOT A Misting who can burn steel.

COPPER (INTERNAL MENTAL PULLING METAL) A person burning copper gives off an invisible cloud that protects anyone inside of it from the senses of a Seeker. While within one of these "copperclouds," an Allomancer can burn any metal they wish, and not worry that someone will sense their Allomantic pulses by burning bronze. As a side effect, the person burning copper is themselves immune to any form of emotional Allomancy (Soothing or Rioting). A Misting who can burn copper is known as a Smoker.

LURCHER A Misting who can burn iron.

PEWTER (INTERNAL PHYSICAL PUSHING METAL) A person burning pewter enhances the physical attributes of their body. They become stronger, more durable, and more dexterous. Pewter also enhances the body's sense of balance and ability to recover from wounds. Mistings who can burn pewter are known as both Pewterarms and Thugs.

PEWTERARM A Misting who can burn pewter.

IRON (EXTERNAL PHYSICAL PULLING METAL) A person burning iron can see translucent blue lines pointing to nearby sources of metal. The size and brightness of the line depends on the size and proximity of the metal source. All types of metal are shown, not just sources of iron. The Allomancer can then mentally yank on one of these lines to Pull that source of metal toward them.

A Misting who can burn iron is known as a Lurcher.

RIOTER A Misting who can burn zinc.

SEEKER A Misting who can burn bronze.

SMOKER A Misting who can burn copper.

SOOTHER A Misting who can burn brass.

STEEL (EXTERNAL PHYSICAL PUSHING METAL) A person burning iron can see translucent blue lines pointing to nearby sources of metal. The size and brightness of the line depends on the size and proximity of the metal source. All types of metal are shown, not just sources of steel. The Allomancer can then mentally Push on one of these lines to send that source of metal away from them. A Misting who can burn steel is known as a Coinshot.

TIN (INTERNAL PHYSICAL PULLING METAL) A person burning tin gains enhanced senses. They can see farther and smell better, and their sense of touch becomes far more acute. This has the side effect of letting them pierce the mists, allowing them to see much farther at night than even their enhanced senses should have let them. A Misting who can burn tin is known as a Tineye.

TINEYE A Misting who can burn tin.

THUG A Misting who can burn pewter.

ZINC (EXTERNAL MENTAL PUSHING METAL) A person burning zinc can Riot another person's emotions, enflaming them and making particular emotions more powerful. It does not let one read minds or even emotions. A Misting who burns zinc is known as a Rioter.

Please turn the page for a sneak preview of . . .

THE WELL OF ASCENSION Mistborn Book Two

. . . the next book in the MISTBORN series

Coming soon from Gollancz.

I write these words in steel, for anything not set in metal cannot be trusted.

THE ARMY CREPT LIKE A dark stain across the horizon.

King Elend Venture stood motionless upon the Luthadel city wall, looking out at he enemy troops. Around him, ash fell from the sky in fat, lazy flakes. It wasn't the burnt white ash that one saw in dead coals; this was a deeper, harsher black ash. The Ashmounts has been particularly active lately.

Elend felt the ash dust his face and clothing, but he ignored it. In the distance, the bloody red sub was close to setting. It backlit the army which had come to take Elend's kingdom back from him.

'How many?' Elend asked quietly.

'Fifty thousand, we think,' Ham said, leaning against the parapet, beefy arms folded on the stone. Like everything in the city, the wall had been stained black by countless years of ash-falls.

'Fifty thousand soldiers . . .' Elend said, trailing off. Despite heavy recruitment, Elend barely had twenty-thousand men under his command –

and they were peasants with under a year of training. Maintaining even that small number was straining his resources. If they'd been able to find the Lord Ruler's atium, perhaps things would be different. As it was, Elend's rule was in serious danger of economic disaster.

'I don't know El,' Ham said quietly. 'Kelsier was always the one with the vision.'

'But you helped him plan,' Elend said. 'You and the others, you were his crew. You were the ones who came up with a strategy for overthrowing his empire, then made it happen.'

Ham fell silent, and Elend felt as if he knew what the man was thinking. *Kelsier was central to it all. He was the one who organised, the one who took all of the wild brainstorming and turned it into a viable operation. He was the leader: the genius.*

And he'd died a year before, on the very same day that the people – as part of his secret plan – had risen up in fury to overthrow their god emperor. Elend had taken the throne in the ensuing chaos. Now it was looking more and more like he would lose everything that Kelsier and his crew had worked so hard to accomplish. Lose it to a tyrant who might be even worse than the Lord Ruler. A petty, devious bully in 'noble' form. The man who had marched his army on Luthadel.

Elend's own father, Straff Venture.

'Any chance you can . . . talk him out of attacking?' Ham asked.

'Maybe,' Elend said hesitantly. 'Assuming the Assembly doesn't just surrender the city.'

'They close?'

'I don't know, honestly, I worry that they are. That army has frightened them, Ham.' *And with good reason*, he thought. 'Anyway, I have a proposal for the meeting in two days. I'll try to talk them out of doing anything rash. Dockson got back today, right?'

Ham nodded. 'Just before the army's advance.'

'I think we should call a meeting of the crew,' Elend said. 'See if we can come up with a way out of this.'

'We'll still be pretty shorthanded,' Ham said, rubbing his chin. 'Spook isn't supposed to be back for another week, and the Lord Ruler only knows where Breeze went. We haven't had a message from him in months.'

Elend sighed, shaking his head. 'I can't think of anything else, Ham.' He turned, staring out over the ashen landscape again. The army was lighting campfires as the sun set. Soon, the mists would appear.

I need to get back to the palace and work on that proposal, Elend thought.

'Where'd Vin run off to?' Ham asked, turning back to Elend.

Elend paused. 'You know,' he said, 'I'm not sure.'

Vin landed softly on the damp cobblestones, watching as the mists began to form around her. They puffed into existence as darkness fell, growing like tangles of translucent vines, twisting and wrapping around one another.

The great city of Luthadel was still. Even now – a year after the Lord Ruler's death and the rise of Elend's new free government, the common people stayed in their homes at night. They feared the mists, a tradition that went far deeper than the Lord Ruler's laws.

Vin slipped forward quietly, senses alert. Inside herself, as always, she burned tin and pewter. Tin enhanced her senses, making it easier for her to see the night. Pewter made her body stronger, made her lighter on her feet. These, along with copper – which had the power to hide her use of Allomancy from others who were burning bronze – were metals that she left on almost all the time.

Some called her paranoid. She thought herself prepared. Either way, the habit had saved her life on numerous occasions.

She approached a quiet street corner and paused, peeking out. She'd never really understood *how* she burned metals – she could remember doing it as long as she'd been alive, using Allomancy instinctively even before she was formally trained by Kelsier. It didn't really matter to her. She wasn't like Elend; she didn't need a logical explanation for everything. For Vin, it was enough that when she wallowed bits of metal, she was able to draw on their power.

Power she appreciated, for she well knew what it was like to lack it. Even now, she was not what one would likely envision as a warrior. Slight of frame and barely five feet tall, with dark hair and pale skin, she knew she had an almost frail look about her. She no longer displayed the underfed look she had during her childhood on the streets, but she certainly wasn't someone any man would find intimidating.

She liked that. It gave her an edge – and she needed every edge she could get.

She also liked the night. During the day,

Luthadel was cramped and confining despite its size. But at night the mists fell like a deep cloud. They dampened, softened, shaded. Massive keeps became shadowed mountains, and crowded mountains, and crowded tenements melted together like a chandler's rejected wares.

Vin crouched beside her building, still watching the intersection. Carefully, she reached within herself and burned steel – one of the other metals she'd swallowed earlier. Immediately, a group of translucent blue lines sprung up around her. Visible only to her eyes, the lines all pointed from her chest to nearby sources of metal – all metals, no matter what type. The thickness of the lines was proportionate to the size of the metal pieces they met. Some pointed to bronze door latches, others to crude iron nails holding boards together,

She waited silently. None of the lines moved. Burning steel was an easy way to tell if someone was moving nearby. If they were wearing bits of metal, they would trail telltale moving lines of blue. Of course, that wasn't the main purpose of steel. Vin reached her hand carefully into her belt pouch and pulled out one of the many coins that sat within, muffled by cloth batting. Like all other bits of metal, this coin had a blue line extending from its centre to Vin's chest.

She flipped the coin into the air, then mentally grabbed its line and – burning steel – Pushed on the coin. The bit of metal shot into the air, arcing through the mists, forced away by the Push. It plinked to the ground in the middle of the street.

The mists continued to spin. They were thick and mysterious, even to Vin. More dense than a simple fog and more constant than any normal weather pattern, they churned and flowed, making rivulets around her. Her eyes could pierce them – tin made her sight more keen. The night seemed lighter to her, the mists less thick. Yet, they were still there.

A shadow moved in the city square, responding to her coin – which she had Pushed out into the square as a signal. Vin crept forward and recognised OreSeur the kandra. He wore a different body than he had a year ago, during the days when he had acted the part of Lord Rendoux. Yet, this balding, nondescript body had now become just as familiar to Vin.

OreSeur met up with her. 'Did you find what you were looking for, Mistress?' he asked, tone respectful – yet somehow a little hostile. As always.

Vin shook her head, glancing around in the darkness. 'Maybe I was wrong,' she said. 'Maybe I *wasn't* being followed.' The acknowledgment made her a bit sad. She'd been looking forward to sparring with the Watcher again tonight. She still didn't even know who he was; the first night, she'd mistaken him for an assassin. And, maybe he was. Yet, he seemed to display very little interest in Elend – and a whole lot of interest in Vin.

'We should go back to the wall.' Vin decided, standing up. 'Elend will be wondering where I went.'

OreSeur nodded. At that moment, a burst of coins shot through the mists, spraying towards Vin.

Brandon Sanderson was born in Nebraska in 1975. Since then he has written the Mistborn series, amongst others, become a *New York Times* bestselling author and been hailed as the natural successor to Robert Jordan. He lives in Utah.

http://www.brandonsanderson.com/